JASMINE NIGHTS

JULIA GREGSON

First published in Great Britain in 2012 by Orion Books,
an imprint of The Orion Publishing Group Ltd
Orion House, 5 Upper Saint Martin's Lane
London WC2H 9EA

An Hachette UK Company

1 3 5 7 9 10 8 6 4 2

A CIP catalogue record for this book is
available from the British Library.

ISBN (Hardback) 978 1 4091 0809 2
ISBN (Export Trade Paperback) 978 1 4091 0810 8

Typeset at The Spartan Press Ltd,
Lymington, Hants

Printed and bound in Great Britain by
Clays Ltd, St Ives plc

The Orion Publishing Group's policy is to use papers that
are natural, renewable and recyclable products and made from wood
grown in sustainable forests. The logging and manufacturing
processes are expected to conform to the environmental
regulations of the country of origin.

www.orionbooks.co.uk

For Barry and Vicki

Acknowledgements

My thanks to all at Orion, especially my editor Kate Mills, and to Clare Alexander my gold standard agent.

I needed a lot of expert advice while writing this book and many people gave generously of their time and knowledge. Any mistakes are entirely mine.

I am hugely indebted to John Rodenbeck for his editing skills and fascinating emails on Egypt and the Middle East. To Tom Brosnahan and John Dyson for showing me around Turkey and sharing their knowledge of the country.

Sema Moritz and, Vanessa Dodd, Leda Glyptis and Virginia Danielson helped me greatly with information about singing Özgü Ötünç was my guide in Istanbul.

Anthony Rowell for his amusing and invaluable help. Historian, Dillip Sarkar, for his vast knowledge of aircraft, squadrons and Battle of Britain pilots.

For lending a precious family diary, my thanks to Sheila Must.

Grateful thanks to: Cordelia Slater, Brian Shakespeare, Jerome Kass, Pam Enderby; to Owen Sheers, Michael Haag, Peter Sommer, Ibrahim Abd Elmedguid; to Phyllis Chappell for her knowledge of the Bay area in Cardiff during the war and her book *A Tiger Bay Childhood*; to Tara Maginnis for make-up in the forties.

For reading early drafts and general hand holding, thanks to my sister Caroline, Delia, Sadie, Annie Powell, and all the shedettes and the entire Gregson clan.

If I've forgotten to thank anyone who helped in the early days my apologies.

Finally, there aren't words enough to thank Richard who has been my champion through thick and thin and my dearest travelling companion.

There are days we live
as if death were nowhere
in the background; from joy
to joy, from wing to wing,
from blossom to blossom to
impossible blossom, to sweet impossible blossom.

'From Blossoms' by Li-Young Lee

Chapter 1

QUEEN VICTORIA HOSPITAL, EAST GRINSTEAD, 1942

It was only a song. That was what he thought when she'd put her hat on and gone, leaving the faint smell of fresh apples behind. Nothing but a song; a pretty girl.

But the very least he could say about the best thing to have happened to him in a long time was that she'd stopped him having the dreams.

In the first, he was at the end of a parachute with about three and a half miles between the soles of his feet and the Suffolk countryside. He was screaming because he couldn't land. He was rushing through the air, a light, insubstantial thing, like thistledown or a dead moth. The bright green grass, so familiar and so dear, swooped towards him, only to jerk away again. Sometimes a woman stood and gaped at him, waving as he floated down, and then was gone on a gust of wind.

In the second dream, he was in his Spitfire again. Jacko's aircraft was alongside him. At first it felt good up there in the cold, clear sunlight, but then, in a moment of nauseous panic, he felt his eyelids had been sewn together, and he could not see.

He told no one. He was one of the lucky ones – about to go home after four months here. There were plenty worse off than him in this place of dark corridors and stifled screams. Every day he heard the rumble of ambulances with new burns victims, picked up from shattered aircraft up and down the east coast.

The ward, an overspill from the hospital, was housed in a long, narrow hut with twenty beds on either side of it, and in the middle a pot-bellied stove, a table and a piano with two brass candlesticks arranged festively on top.

The ward smelled of soiled dressings, of bedpans, of dying and living flesh: old men's smells, although most of the fighter pilots in here were in their early twenties. Stourton, at the end of the ward, who had been flying Hurricanes from North Weald, had been a blind man for two weeks now. His girlfriend came in every day to teach him Braille. Squeak Townsend, the red-faced boy in the next bed with the hearty, unconvincing laugh, was a fighter pilot who'd broken his spine when his parachute had failed, and who'd confessed to Dom a few days ago that he was too windy to ever want to fly again.

Dom knew he was lucky. He'd been flying a Spitfire at 20,000 feet over a patchwork of fields when his cockpit was transformed into a blowtorch by the explosion of the petrol tank that sat in front of his instrument panel. His hands and face were burned – typical fighter-pilot injuries, the surgeon said – and in the excruciating moments between the flames and the ground, he'd opened the plane's canopy, fumbled for the bright green tag that opened his parachute, swooned through space for what felt like an eternity, and finally landed, babbling and screaming, on top of a farmer's haystack on the Suffolk coast.

Last week, Dr Kilverton, the jaunty new plastic surgeon who now travelled from hospital to hospital, had come to the Queen Victoria and examined the burn on the right side of his face.

'Beautiful.' Kilverton's bloodshot eye had peered through a microscope at the point where the new skin graft taken from Dom's buttock had been patchworked over his burns. 'That'll take about six or seven weeks to heal; then you should be fully operational. Good skin,' he added. 'Mediterranean?'

'My mother,' Dom explained through clenched teeth. Kilverton was peeling off old skin at the time, probing the graft. 'French.'

'Your father?'

Dom wanted him to shut up. It was easier to go inside the pain and not do the cocktail-party stuff.

'British.'

'Where did you learn to fly? Tilt your head this way, please.' The snub nose loomed towards him.

'Cambridge. The University Air Squadron.'

'Ah, my father was there too; sounded like jolly good fun.'

'Yes.'

Kilverton talked some more about corpuscles and muscle tone and youth still being on his side; he'd repeated how lucky Dom was. 'Soon have your old face and your old smile back,' as if a smile was a plastered-on thing.

While he was listening, Dom had that nightmare sensation again of floating above himself, of seeing kind faces below and not being able to reach them. Since the accident, a new person had taken up residence inside the old face, and the old smile. A put-together self who smoked and ate, who joked and was still capable of cynical wisecracks, but who felt essentially dead. Last week, encouraged by the doctors to take his first spin on his motorbike, he'd sat on a grass verge outside the Mucky Duck, on what was supposed to be a red-letter day, and looked at his hand around the beer glass as if it belonged to someone else.

During his first weeks in hospital, now a blur of drips and ambulance rides and acid baths, his sole aim in life had been to not let the side down by blubbing or screaming. Blind at first, he'd managed to quip, 'Are you pretty?' to the nurse who'd sat with him in the ambulance that took him away from the smouldering haystack.

Later, in the wards, he made a bargain with himself: he would not deny the physical pain, which was constant, searing, and so bad at times it was almost funny, but emotionally he would own up to nothing. If anyone asked him how he was, he was fine.

It was only in the relative quiet of the night, in the lucid moments when he emerged from the morphine haze, that he thought about the nature of pain. What was it for? How was one to deal with it? Why had he been saved and the others were gone?

And only months later, when his hands had sufficiently healed, had he started to write in the diary his mother had sent him. Reams of stuff about Jacko and Cowbridge, both killed that day. A letter to Jacko's fiancée, Jill, not sent. Letters to his own parents, ditto, warning them that when he was better, he was determined to fly again.

And then the girl.

When she walked into the ward that night, what struck him most was how young she looked: young and spirited and hopeful. From his bed, he drank in every detail of her.

She was wearing a red polka-dot dress, nipped in at the waist, and a black hat with an absurd little veil that was too old for her and made her look a little like a four-year-old who had raided her mother's dressing-up box. She couldn't have been more than twenty-two.

He saw a roll of glossy dark hair under her hat. Generous lips, large brown eyes.

She stood next to the piano, close to the trolley that held dressings and rolled bandages. Half imp, half angel. She was smiling as if this was where she wanted to be. A real professional, he thought, trying to keep a cynical distance. A pro.

She explained in her lightly accented voice – Welsh? Italian? Hard to say – that her name was Saba Tarcan, and that she was a last-minute replacement for a torch singer called Janice Sophia. She hoped they wouldn't be disappointed, and then threw a bold look in Dom's direction – or so he imagined – as if to say *you won't be.*

A fat man in khaki uniform, her accompanist, sat down heavily at the piano, began to play. She listened, swaying slightly; a look of calm settled on her face as she sang about deep purple nights, and flickering stars, and a girl breathing a boy's name whilst she sighed.

He'd tried every trick in his book to keep her at arm's length, but the song came out of the darkness like a wild thing, and her voice was so husky, so sad, and it had been such a long time since he'd desired a woman that the relief was overwhelming. *Through the mist of a memory you wander back to me.* So much to conceal now: his fear of being ugly, his shame that he was alive with the others gone. And then he'd felt a wild desire to laugh, for 'Deep Purple' was perhaps not the most tactful of songs to sing: many of the men in the ward had purple faces, Gentian violet being the thing they painted over the burns victims, after they'd been bathed in tannic acid.

Halfway through the song, she'd looked startled, as if realising her mistake, but she'd kept on singing, and said nothing by way of apology at the end of it. He approved of that: the last thing any of them needed was sympathy and special songs.

When she'd finished, Dom saw that beads of perspiration had formed on her upper lip and rings of sweat around the arms of her dress. The ward was kept stiflingly hot.

When she sang 'I'm in the Mood for Love', Curtis, ignorant bastard, called out: 'Well, you know where to look, my lovely.'

Dom frowned. *Saba Tarcan*: he said the name to himself.

'Two more songs,' said Staff Nurse Morrison, tapping her watch. 'And then it's night-night time.'

And he was relieved – it was too much. Like eating a ten-course meal after starving for a year.

But Saba Tarcan paid no attention to the big fat nurse, and this he approved of too. She took off her hat and laid it on the piano, as if to say *I shall stay until I've finished.* She pushed back a tendril of hair from her flushed cheek, talked briefly to the pianist, and took Dom to the edge of what was bearable as she began to sing 'They Didn't Believe Me'. The song Annabel had loved, singing it softly to him as they walked one night hand in hand beside the Cam, in the days when he felt he had everything: flying, Cambridge, her, other girls too. As the tears dashed through the purple dye, he turned his head away, furious and ashamed.

Annabel was considered a catch: a tall, pale, ethereal girl with long, curly fair hair, a sweet smile, and clever parents: her father a High Court judge, her mother a don. She'd come to see him religiously at first, forehead gleaming in the stifling ward, reading to him with nervous glances around her at some of the other freaks.

'I can't do this, Dom, I'm not strong enough,' she'd said after two weeks. 'It's not you.' She'd swallowed.

'I'm starting to dread it.' She'd glanced at the boy in the bed beside him. The side of his face, grafted with his own skin to his chest, looked like a badly made elephant's trunk.

'So sorry,' she'd whispered softly, shortly before she left. Her round blue eyes had filled with tears. 'Can we stay friends?'

Not the first woman to have bolted out of this terrifying ward, not the last. 'Amazing how potent cheap music is': the kind of thing he might have said once to excuse the tears. His Noël Coward imitation had been rather admired at Cambridge. It wasn't even Annabel so much; it was everything lost, even the foolishly innocent things – perhaps particularly them.

His set, the self-proclaimed 'it' boys of their year, had spent days spragged out on sofas, smoking and drinking cheap sherry, elaborately bored and showing off wildly about Charlie Parker, or Pound, or Eliot – anything that amused them. How young they seemed, even at this distance. The first heady days away from home, the steady stream of good-looking undergraduate girls smuggled into their rooms, and they'd had their pick. He'd tried to be fair to Annabel, telling her after her tearful confession that he perfectly understood, didn't blame her in the slightest, in truth he'd always had the guilty sense that his ardour did not equal hers, that she was not, as people said, 'the one'. There'd been so many other girls around, and Cambridge felt like a time when the sun would never stop shining.

Smetheren, whose famously untidy room was opposite his on the quad, had been killed two months ago. Clancy, one of his best friends, also a flying fanatic and among the cleverest men he'd ever met, shot down over France a month before his twenty-second birthday. And Jacko, of course. All changed within a year, and the boy he'd been could never have imagined himself like this: in bed at 8.30 in his PJs, desperately trying not to cry in front of a pretty girl. It was nothing but notes. He bit the inside of his lip to gain control: notes and a few minor chords, some well-chosen words. Only a song.

A clink of bottles, a rumble of wheels. The night medicines were coming round on a trolley. They were stoking up the boiler in the middle of the room, dimming the lights.

'Last one,' she said.

She was wearing her ridiculous little veiled hat again. The pianist had put away his music, so she sang 'Smoke Gets in Your Eyes' unaccompanied, her voice strong and clear, her expression intent and focused.

And then she'd walked around the beds to say good night.

Good night to Williams, who had both legs in traction, and to poor blind Billy at the end of the ward, and to Farthingale, who was off to theatre tomorrow to have his eyelids sewn back on again. She didn't seem to mind them, or was that part of the training?

When she got to Dom, Curtis, the bloody idiot, called out: 'Go on, love! Give him a night-night kiss.' He'd turned his head away, but she'd leaned towards him, so close he could see the mound of her stomach under the red and white dress. He felt the tickle of her hair. She smelt young and fresh, like apples.

When she kissed his cheek, he'd said to protect himself, 'You wouldn't kiss that if you knew where it came from,' and she'd leaned down again and whispered in his ear, 'How do you know that, you silly bugger?'

He'd stayed awake for the next hour thinking about her, his heart in a sort of delighted suspension. Before he went to sleep, he imagined her on the back of his motorbike. It was a summer's day.

They were sitting on a grass verge outside a country inn. They were teasing each other, they were laughing. She was wearing a blue dress, and the sky was just a sky again, not something you fell from screaming.

Chapter 2

ST BRIAVELS, GLOUCESTERSHIRE

My dear Saba Tarcan: his first attempt at a fan letter, written from the Rockfield Convalescent home in Wiltshire, was lobbed into the waste-paper basket. It was far too formal and avuncular for that mocking little face. Her address he'd cajoled from one of the nurses who organised the entertainments and who'd promised once the letter was written to forward it to 'the relevant party'.

Dear Saba, I would like to tell you how splendidly I thought you sang the other night when I heard you at Queen Victoria's. Oh, worse! That sounded like some port-winey old stage-door Johnny. Oh fuck it! Damn! He hurled it in the basket. He'd waited six weeks before writing to her, to make sure he was fit to be seen and thinking that once he was home again and not a patient, the old confidence would return and the letter would flow mellifluously from his pen, but if anything, he felt even more bewildered by what he was trying to say, which made him angry – a girl had never made him feel like that before. A poem ran through his mind – one he'd thought about in connection with her.

'Thank you, whatever comes.' And then she turned
And, as the ray of sun on hanging flowers
Fades when the wind hath lifted them aside,
Went swiftly from me. Nay, whatever comes
One hour was sunlit and the most high gods
May not make boast of any better thing
Than to have watched that hour as it passed.

He'd copied it into his diary in hospital, certain he wouldn't send that either. Poetry made people suspicious when they didn't know you, and frankly, bollocks to the one-hour-being-lovely idea; he wanted to hear her sing again, nothing else.

'Coffee, Dom darling?' His mother's voice wafting from the kitchen; she sounded more French when she was nervous.

'I'm in the sitting room.' He glanced discreetly at his watch. Blast! He'd hoped to finish the letter first. 'Come and have it with me,' he said, trying with every ounce of his being not to sound like a person raging with frustration.

His mother was hovering. He'd felt her there all morning, trying to be unobtrusive. Thin as a wisp, elegant in her old tweed suit, in she bounded now with the tray, sat down on the edge of the piano stool and poured the coffee. 'Thank you, Misou,' he said, using his childhood name for her.

He took her hand. 'It's all right,' he wished she would stop looking so worried. 'Nothing hurts now. Look, hold it properly.' A surge of anger as he felt her tentative squeeze.

She bobbed her head shyly, not sure what to say. She'd been so proud of him once. Now his injuries seemed to have brought with them a feeling of shared shame – there was too much to say and to conceal.

During his months in hospital, he'd fantasised about being exactly where he was today, on this sofa, in this house in St Briavels, a tiny village on the borders of Wales and Gloucestershire. Sitting on the train that took him from Chepstow to Brockweir, he'd been determined to give his mother at least a few days of happiness to make up for the months of misery and worry she'd endured. No talk about flying again; no talk about friends, and maybe, in a couple of days' time over a glass of wine, an upbeat account of Annabel's departure.

A taxi had met him at the station. As they crossed a River Wye sparkling in the spring sunshine, a line of swans, stately and proud, were queening it across the water, and on the far side of the river a herd of Welsh ponies grazed, one with a sparrow sitting on its rump.

He asked the taxi driver to stop for a while. He said he wanted to look at the view, but in fact he was having difficulty breathing. The choking feeling, now familiar, came sudden as an animal leaping from the dark, and made his heart pound and the palms of his hands grow clammy. It would pass. He stubbed out his cigarette, and sat breathing as evenly as he could, trying to concentrate on only good things.

'Lovely,' he said at last when it was over. 'Beautiful sight.'

'Perfect morning to come home, sir,' said the driver, his eyes firmly ahead. 'Ready to move off?'

'Yep. Ready.'

As the car rose up the steep hill, he concentrated fiercely on the field of black Welsh cattle on his right, the scattered cottages bright with primroses and crocuses. He was going home.

A long rutted track led to the farm; from it he saw the Severn estuary gleaming like a conch shell in the distance, and when Woodlees Farm came into view, his eyes filled with helpless tears. This was the charming whitewashed house his parents had moved to twenty-five years ago, when his father had first become a surgeon. Low-ceilinged, undistinguished, apart from large south-facing windows, it stood on its own in the middle of windswept fields. The small wood behind it was where he'd played cowboys and Indians with his sister Freya when he was a boy. They'd raced their ponies here too, dashing along muddy tracks and over make-shift jumps. He'd been born behind the third window to the right upstairs.

The car crunched up the drive between the avenue of lime trees his mother, a passionate gardener, had planted in the days when she was a homesick girl missing her family in Provence. Sparkling with rain, glorious and green, unsullied by the dust of summer, they appeared like a vision. He'd grown to hate the severely clipped privet hedges surrounding the hospital lawns. Beyond the trees, new grass, new lambs in the field, a whole earth in its adolescence.

His mother ran down the drive when she heard the taxi. She stood under the lime trees and took his face in both her hands. 'My darling Dom,' she said. 'As good as new.'

As they walked back to the house arm in arm, dogs swirled around their legs and an old pony in the field craned nosily over the gate. She'd said, 'How was it at Rockfield?' All she knew about it was that this was the place the burns boys were sent to, to shoehorn them back into 'real life'.

'Surprisingly jolly,' he said. He told her about the lovely house near Cheltenham, loaned by some county lady, about the barrels of beer, the pretty nurses, the non-stop parties, the complaints from the neighbours, who said they'd expected convalescents, not larrikins. Hearing his mother's polite, anxious laugh, he'd fought the temptation to hang his head like a guilty boy; early that morning he'd been 10,000 feet above the Bristol Channel, zooming over the grazing sheep, the little patchwork fields, the schools, the church steeples, the whole sleeping world, and it had been bloody marvellous. Tiny Danielson, one of his last remaining friends from the squadron, had wangled a Tiger Moth kept in a hangar near Gloucester. Dom's hands had shaken as he'd buckled on the leather flying helmet for the first time in months, his heart thumping as he carefully taxied down the runway with its scattering of Nissen huts on either side, and then, as he'd lifted off into the clear blue yonder, he'd heard himself shout with joy.

Wonderful! Wonderful! Wonderful! He was flying again! He was flying again! In hospital, the idea that he might have to go back to a desk job had made him sweat with terror. He'd worried that he'd be windy, that his hands wouldn't be strong enough now, but he'd had no trouble with the controls, and the little aircraft felt as whippy as a sailing craft under his fingers. The air was stingingly cold, there was a bit of cumulus cloud to the left, and he felt suddenly as if a jumble of mismatched pieces inside him had come together again.

Hearing his shout of pleasure, Tiny had echoed it, and a few minutes later clapped him on the shoulder.

'Down now, I think, old chap – we don't want to get court-martialled.'

A noisy breakfast followed – toast, baked beans, brick-coloured tea – shared with Tiny and a pilot wearing a uniform so new that it still had the creases in it. Nobody asked him any questions about the hospital; no one made a fuss – economy of emotion was the unspoken rule here. In the mess, there was even a 'shooting a line' book that fined you for any morbid or self-congratulatory talk. And that was good, too. Four of his closest friends were dead now, five missing presumed dead, one captured behind enemy lines. He was five months shy of his twenty-third birthday.

'You'll notice a few changes.' His mother, light-footed and giddy with happiness, had almost danced up the drive. 'We've been planting carrots and onions where the roses were. You know, "dig for victory" and all zat. Oh, there's so much to show you.'

She took him straight up the stairs so he could put his suitcase in his old room. The bed looked inviting with its fresh linen sheets and plumped pillows. A bunch of lavender lay on the bedside table. He gazed briefly at the schoolboy photographs of him that she'd framed. The scholarship boy at Winchester, flannelled and smirking in his first cricket XI; and there a muddied oaf, legs planted, squinting at the camera, Jacko sitting beside him beaming. Jacko, who he'd persuaded to join up, who he'd teased for being windy, who he'd last seen clawing at his mask in a cauldron of flame, screaming as the plane spiralled down like a pointless piece of paper and disappeared into the sea.

He must go up to London and talk to Jilly, Jacko's fiancée, about him soon. He dreaded it; he needed it.

His mother touched his arm.

'Come downstairs,' she said quickly. 'Plenty of time to unpack later.'

A whiff of formaldehyde as they passed his father's study on the way down. On the leather desk, the same gruesome plastic model of a stomach and intestines that Dom had once terrified his sister with, by holding it up at her bedroom door, a green torch shining behind it; the same medical books arranged in alphabetical order.

'He'll be home after supper.' His mother's smile wavered for a second. 'He's been operating day and night.'

'Things any better?' slipped out. He'd meant to ask it casually over a drink later.

'Not really,' she said softly. 'He's never home – he works harder now if anything.'

In the tiled hall, near the front door, he glanced at his face in the mirror. His dark hair had grown again; his face looked pretty much the same.

Lucky bastard.

Selfish bastard. He could at least have answered Jilly's letter.

Lucky first of all to have been wearing the protective gloves all of them were supposed to put on when they flew, and he so often hadn't, preferring the feel of the joystick in his fingers. Lucky to have been picked up quickly by an ambulance crew and not burned to a crisp strapped into his cockpit. Luckiest of all to have been treated by Kilverton. Kilverton, who looked, with his stumpy hands and squat body, like a butcher, was a plastic surgeon of genius.

He owed his life to this man. He'd gone to him with his face and hands black and smelling of cooked meat – what they now called airman's burns, because they were so common. The determined and unsentimental Kilverton, a visiting surgeon, had placed him in a saline bath and later taken him into theatre, where he'd meticulously jigsawed tiny strips of skin taken from Dom's buttock to the burns on the side of his face. All you could see now was a row of pinpricks about an inch long and two inches above his left ear. His thick black hair had already covered them.

Last week Kilverton had called Dom into his chaotic consulting room and boasted freely about him to two awestruck young doctors.

'Look at this young man.' He turned on the Anglepoise lamp on his desk so they could all get a better look at him. Dom felt the gentleness of those fat fingers, the confidence they gave you. One of the other chaps in the ward had said it was like getting 'a pep pill up your arse'.

'I defy you to even know he's been burned – no keloid scars, the skin tone around the eyes is good.'

'So why was he so lucky?' one of the doctors asked, his own young skin green with fatigue under the lamp. They'd had five new serious cases in the day before, a bomber crew who'd bought it off the French coast.

'A combination of factors.' Kilverton's eyes swam over his half-glasses. 'A Mediterranean skin helps – all that olive oil. His mother's French, his father's English.'

Dom had smiled. 'A perfect mongrel.'

'The rest,' Kilverton continued, 'is pure chance. Some men just burn better than others.'

Dom had gone cold at this.

Thompson had died in East Grinstead, after being treated with tannic acid, a form of treatment Kilverton had said was barbaric and had fought to ban. Collins, poor bastard, burned alive in his cockpit on his first training run. He was nineteen years old.

The same flames, the surgeon had continued in his flat, almost expressionless voice, the same exposure to skin- and tissue-destroying heat, and yet some men became monsters, although he did not use that word; he'd said 'severely disabled' or some other slightly more tactful thing. Having the right skin was, he said, a freak of nature, like being double-jointed or having a cast-iron stomach.

To illustrate his point, he'd lifted a pot of dusty geraniums from the windowsill.

'It's like taking cuttings from this: some thrive, some die, and the bugger of it is we don't yet know exactly why. As for you . . .' he looked directly at Dom again, 'you can go home now. I'll see you in six weeks' time.'

Dom had pretended to be both interested and grateful, and of course he was, but sometimes at night he sweated at the thought of this luckiness. Why had he lived and others died? Privately, it obsessed him.

'Can I fly again?' It was all he wanted now. 'Can you sign me off?'

'I'll see you in six weeks.' Kilverton switched off his light. He was shrugging on his ancient mackintosh, standing near the door waiting to leap into another emergency.

'I want to fly again.' The obsession had grown and grown during the period of his convalescence.

'Look, lad.' Kilverton had glared at him from the door. 'Your father's a surgeon, isn't he? Why not give him and your poor bloody mother a break and let somebody else do the flying for a while? I'll see you in six weeks' time.'

'My hands are strong. I'm fit. Four weeks.'

'Bloody steamroller.' Kilverton hadn't bothered to look up. 'It'll be six months if you don't shut up.'

His mother always did three things at once: right now she was in the kitchen up the flagstone hallway, making bread to go with a special lunch she'd prepared for him. Its warm, yeasty smell filled the room. She was roasting lamb in the Aga. She'd darted into the room to ask if he'd like a whisky and soda before lunch, and now she was standing beside the gramophone wearing what he thought of as her musical face, as she lowered the needle.

Tender and evanescent as bubbles, the notes of Mozart's Piano Concerto No. 9 floated out and his throat contracted. Home again: music, roast lamb, the faint tang of mint from the kitchen, his mother humming and clattering pans. The cedar parquet floors smelling faintly of lavender where he and Freya had been occasionally allowed to ride their tricycles. The rug in front of the fireplace where they sat to dry their hair on Sunday nights.

He stretched his legs out and put his arms behind his head, and looked at the pictures his mother had hung above the fireplace.

There was a reproduction of Van Gogh's *Starry Night*, a Gwen John self-portrait.

He stood up and stared at them, as if by examining the pictures he could see her more clearly. How cleverly she'd arranged them – not too rigidly formal, but with a plan that pleased the eye.

She did everything well: cooking, dressing, gardening, entertaining and stitching. The sofa he sat on was covered, too covered for real comfort, in her tapestry cushions. He picked one up now, marvelling at the thousands and thousands of tiny, painstaking stitches that had measured out her afternoons, pinning unicorns and stilled butterflies to her canvas.

While the Mozart swept majestically on, he heard the faint pinpricks of a spring shower against the window. His mother had once dreamed of being a professional musician; as a child, Dom had loved lying in his bed with Liszt's Polonaises drifting up to his room like smoke, or the brisk rat-tat-tat of her little hands swashbuckling through her own rendition of the Ninth. But now her piano sat like some grand but disregarded relative in the corner of the room, almost entirely covered by family photographs. The gorgeous Steinway that had once been her life, that had almost bankrupted her father.

Dom's own father had put an end to it. Not intentionally, maybe. Two months after he'd married his clever young bride, he'd developed tinnitus and couldn't stand, so he said, any extra noises in his head. And then the children – Freya first, and two years later Dom – her husband's determined move up the career ladder, and lastly, in the cold winter of 1929, she'd developed chilblains and stopped for good. No more Saint-Saëns, or Scott Joplin to make guests laugh; no more duets even, for she had taught Dom as a little boy, and told him he would be very good if he stuck at it. What had once been a source of delight became a source of shame, a character flaw. Even as a child he was aware how it clouded her eyes when people turned to her and said: 'Didn't you once play the piano rather well?'

Dom examined silver-framed Freya, on the front of the piano. Freya – of the laughing eyes and the same thick black hair – was in the WAAF now, in London, working at Fighter Command, loving her life 'whizzing things around on maps', as she put it.

There he was, a ghost from another life, striking a jokey pose in a swimsuit on the beach at Salcombe. His cousins Jack and Peter, both in the army now, had their arms around him. They'd swum that night, and cooked sausages on the beach, and stayed out until the moon was a toenail in the sky. The beach was now littered with old bits of scrap metal, barbed wire and sandbags, the rusted hulks of guns. In another photo, his mother's favourite, he sat on the wing of the little Tiger Moth he'd learned to fly in, self-conscious in his first pilot's uniform, almost too young to shave.

The year he and Jacko had started to fly had been full of thousands of excitements: first set of flying clothes; Threadnall, their first instructor, roaring abuse: 'Don't pull back the control column like a barmaid pulling a pint, lad'; first solo flight; even the drama of writing your first will out when you were twenty-one years old. There was nothing the earth could offer him as exciting as this.

That first flight was when he'd cut the apron strings, and all the other ropes of convention and duty that bound him here, and thought to himself, *Free at last*, shockingly and shamefully free as he soared above the earth, terrified and elated, over churches and towns, schools and fields. *Free at last!*

As the music dropped slowly like beads of light in the room, bringing him to the edge of tears, he thought about Saba Tarcan again: her daft little hat, the curve of her belly in the red satin dress, her husky voice.

He did not believe in love at first sight. Not ever, not now. At Cambridge, where he'd broken more than his fair share of hearts and where, even at this distance, he now thought of himself as being a tiresome little shit, he'd had a whole spiel that he could produce about what a ridiculous concept it was. His reaction to Saba Tarcan felt more complex – he'd admired the way she'd carried herself in that noisy ward, neither apologising, nor simpering, nor asking for their approval. He remembered every detail: the fighter boys lying in a row, stripped of their toys and their dignity, some tricked up like elephants with their skin grafts, and the girl with only her songs, taking them beyond the world where you could define or set limits on things, or be in simple human terms a winner or a loser. What power that was.

'I've brought you some cheese straws.' His mother appeared with a tray. 'I saved up our cheese ration for them.'

'Misou, sit.' He patted the sofa beside him. 'Let's have a drink.'

She poured herself a small Dubonnet and soda, her lunchtime tipple, a beer for him.

'Well, how nice this is.' She crossed her impeccable legs at the ankle. 'Oh golly! Look at that.' A small piece of thread that had come loose on one of her cushions. She snapped it off between her small teeth.

'Misou, stop fussing and drink up. I think you and I should get roaring drunk together one night.'

She laughed politely; it would take her a while to thaw out. Him too – he felt brittle, dreamlike again.

'Have another.' She passed him the cheese straws. 'But don't spoil your appetite. Sorry.' The plate bumped his hand. 'Did that hurt?'

'No.' He took two cheese straws quickly. 'Nothing hurts now. These are delicious.'

She filled the small silence that followed by saying: 'I've been meaning to ask you, do you have any pills you should be taking, any special med—'

'Mother,' he said firmly. 'I'm all right now. It wasn't an illness. I'm as fit as a fiddle – in fact, I'd like to go for a spin on Pa's motorbike after lunch.'

'I don't think he'd mind – that sounds fun. He doesn't use it now.' He felt her flinch, but he would have to start breaking her in gently. 'It's in the stable. There should be enough petrol,' she added bravely.

'For a short spin, anyway.'

'So nothing hurts now?'

'No.' It was no good, he simply couldn't talk about it to her – not now, maybe never – this wrecking ball in the middle of his life that had come within a hair's breadth of taking pretty much everything: his youth, his friends, his career, his face.

'Well, all I can say,' she shot a darting look in his direction, 'is that you look marvellous, darling.'

Which didn't sit well with him either. His mother had always cared too much about how people looked. The reproach in her voice when she pointed out a nose that was too long or somebody who had a big stomach seemed to indicate that its owner was either careless or stupid. or both. Some of the boys in the ward had been so badly burned they were scarcely recognisable, but they were still human beings underneath it.

'Do I?' Impossible to keep the note of bitterness out of his voice. 'Well, all's well that ends well.'

And now he had hurt her and felt sorry. She'd moved to the other end of the sofa, he felt her bunched up and ready to fly.

'That music was wonderful,' he said. 'Thank you for putting it on. All we heard in hospital was a crackly wireless and a few concerts.'

'Any good?'

'Not bad, one or two of them.' *A singer?* He imagined her saying it, and then, with her sharp professional face on, *Was she any good?*

'I was thinking in hospital,' he said, 'that I'd like to play the piano again.'

'Are you sure?' She looked at him suspiciously, as if he might be mocking her.

'Yes.'

She took his hand in hers. 'Do you remember last time?' She was looking pleased. 'Such sweet little hands.' She waggled her own elegant fingers in a flash of diamonds. 'Like chipolatas. First Chopsticks,' she mimed his agricultural delivery, 'then Chopin. You know, you could have been very, very good,' she said, 'if you'd stuck at it.'

'Yes, yes,' he said. It was an old argument between them. 'I did Walter Gieseking a great good turn when I gave up.'

'And what about you nearly amputating these *sweet little hands*?' he teased. They'd had a corker of a row one day, when he'd been racing through 'Für Elise' as loudly as he could, loving the racket he was making. She'd ticked him off for not playing with more light and shade, and he'd roared: 'I'M A LOUD-PLAYING BOY AND I LIKE THINGS FAST.' And she – oh, how quick and ferocious her temper was in those days – had brought the lid down so sharply she'd missed his fingers by a whisper and blackened the edge of the nail on his little finger.

She covered her face with her hands. 'Why was I so angry?'

Because, he wanted to say, it mattered to you; because some things affected you beyond reason.

'I don't know,' he said gently, seeing her furious face again, under the lamplight, stabbing at her tapestry.

'Listen, you loud-talking boy,' she said. She stood up and walked towards the kitchen. 'Lunch is ready. Let's eat.'

'Yes, Mis, let's eat.' It seemed the safest thing to do.

*

When they faced each other over the kitchen table, there didn't seem quite enough of them to fill the room, but at least she hadn't asked him yet about Annabel, a relief, for she would be upset – she'd approved of Annabel's clothes, her thinness, her clever parents – and then she'd be fiercely indignant at anyone foolish enough to reject her son. He'd rehearsed a light-hearted account of the episode, in truth, he was almost relieved now that Annabel had gone: one less person to worry about when he flew again.

Misou poured him a glass of wine and filled a plate with the roast lamb mixed in with delicious home-grown onions and carrots and herbs. He ate ravenously, aware of her watching him and relaxing in his pleasure.

Over coffee he said, 'That was the best grub I've had for months, Ma, and by the way, I really would like to play the piano again.'

And then she shocked him by saying: 'You want to fly, don't you? That's what you really want to do.' She gave him a searching look; he could not tell whether she was pleading with him or simply asking for information.

He put his cup down. 'Don't you think we should talk about this later?' he asked gently.

She got up suddenly and went to the sink.

'Yes,' she said. 'Later.'

She ran the tap fiercely; he saw her drying-up cloth move towards her eyes. 'Not now,' she said several seconds later.

'I don't think I could stand it.'

Chapter 3

POMEROY STREET, CARDIFF, 1942

Dom's letter to Saba had arrived in the morning post. Reading it brought a flush of colour to her cheek. She remembered that boy, but not clearly.

She'd been so wound up before the concert, terrified that she would fail, or be overwhelmed by the patients, and later so tremendously happy when it had gone well.

But it did mean something – quite a lot, actually – that he had found the evening special too. She felt like dashing downstairs with the letter right away, forcing her family to read it – *See, what I do means something. Don't make me stop* – but since no one in the house was properly talking to her, she put it in the drawer beside her bedside table. There was too much going on in her head to answer it.

Her family were at war. Two weeks previously, a brown envelope had arrived for Saba with *On Her Majesty's Service* written on it, and all of them hated her as a result of it. Inside was a letter from ENSA, the Entertainments National Service Association. A man called John Merrett had asked her to attend an audition at the Drury Lane Theatre in London on 17 March at 11.30. She was to take her music and dancing shoes. Her expenses would be paid.

At that time she was living in the family's three-bedroomed terraced house in Pomeroy Street, down at the docks, between the canal and the river, a few streets away from Tiger Bay. It was here, in an upstairs room of this cramped and cosy house, that Saba had shot into the world twenty-three years ago. She was three weeks early, red-faced and bellowing. 'Little old leather-lungs right from the beginning,' her mother had once said proudly.

In peacetime she shared the house with her mother, Joyce, her little sister, Lou, and occasionally her father, Remzi, who was a ship's engineer and often away at sea. And of course there was good old Tansu, her Turkish grandma, who'd been living with them for the past twenty years.

Apart from Tan, asleep by the fire in the front room, she was alone in the house when the letter came. She tore the envelope open, read it in disbelief, and then got so excited she didn't know what to do with herself. She raced upstairs, crashed into her small bedroom, raised her arms in exultation, gave a silent scream, sat down in front of her kidney-shaped dressing table and saw her shocked white face gazing back at her from three mirrors.

Yah! Hallelujah! Saved! Mashallah! The wonderful thing had happened! She danced on her own on the bare floorboards, her body full of a savage joy. After months of performing in draughty factories and YMCAs for weary workers and troops, ENSA wanted her! In London! A place she'd never been before. Her first proper professional tour.

She couldn't wait to tell her mother, and paced all afternoon in an agony of suspense. Mum, who was working the day shift at Curran's factory, and who'd been on at her to get a job there too, usually got home about five thirty. When Saba heard the click of the front door, she bounded downstairs two at a time, flung her arms around her and blurted out the news.

Later, she realised that her timing was unusually off. Tea had to come before surprises. Her mother was highly strung, and, to say the least, unpredictable in her responses. Sometimes standing up for Saba, sometimes caving in, entirely depending on her husband's moods . . . Or perhaps Saba should have told Tansu first. Tan, who had a theatrical flair for these moments, would have put it better.

Her mother looked tired and plain in the ugly dungarees and turban she now wore for work. She took the letter from Saba's hand and read it without a word, her mouth a sullen little slit. She stomped into the front room and took her shoes off, and snapped: 'Why did you let the fire go out?' as if this was just an ordinary day.

The envelope was still in her hand as she looked straight at Saba and said, 'This is the last bloody straw,' almost as if she hated her.

'What?' Saba had shouted.

'And you're not bloody going.'

Saba had rushed into the kitchen and then out the back door where they kept the kindling. When she returned, her mother was still sitting poleaxed by the unlit fire. Tansu sat opposite her, mumbling away at herself in Turkish the way she did when she was agitated or afraid.

'Give me that.' Joyce snatched the paper and the kindling from Saba's hands. She scrumpled the paper, stabbed it with the poker they kept in a brass ship near the fire.

'You look tired, Mum.' Saba, who'd put a few lumps of coal on top of the wood, was trying diplomacy. 'I'll bring you in some tea, then you can read the letter again.'

'I don't want to read the bloody letter again,' her mother had shouted. 'And you're not going anywhere until we've asked your father.'

The flames roared as she put a match to the paper. Tansu, nervous and scampering, had gone to get the tea, while Joyce sat breathing heavily, bright spots of temper colour on her cheeks.

Saba then made things worse by telling her mother that she thought it was a wonderful opportunity for her, and that even Mr Chamberlain had said on the wireless that everyone should now do their bit for the war effort.

'I've done enough for the sodding war effort,' Joyce shouted. 'Your sister's gone and God knows when she'll be back. Your father's never here. I'm working all hours at Curran's. It's time you got a job there too.'

'I'm not talking about you, Mum!' Saba roared. 'I'm talking about me. You were the one who told me to dream big bloody dreams.'

'Oh for goodness' sake.' Her mother snatched off her turban and lashed on her pinafore. 'That was a joke. And anyway, Mr Chamberlain didn't mean you singing songs and waving your legs in the air.'

Saba stared at her mother in disbelief. Had she honestly and truly said that? The same Joyce who'd thundered roaring and laughing down the aisle with her at *Snow White* at the Gaiety when they'd asked for children on the stage. Who'd taken her to all those ballet lessons, squishing her plump feet into good toes, naughty toes. Who'd stayed up half the night, only three months ago, sewing the red dress for the hospital concert, and cried buckets when she'd heard her sing 'All Through the Night' only the week before.

'It wasn't a joke, Mum,' she shrieked, her dander well up now. 'Or if it was, you might have bloody let me in on it.' She was thinking of the harder stuff – the diets, the singing lessons, breaking two ribs when the trapeze they used for 'Showtime' had snapped.

'Yes it was. It was off a film, and we're not people in films.'

And then Tansu, usually her one hundred per cent friend and ally, had made that disapproving Turkish *tut tut tut* sound, the clicking of the tongue followed by a sharp intake of breath, that really got on Saba's nerves, and which loosely translated to *no, no, no, no.* Tansu said if she went to London, the bombs would fall on her head. Saba replied that bombs were falling on their bloody heads here. There had already been one in Pomeroy Street. Joyce said she would wash Saba's mouth out with soap if she swore at her gran again, then Joyce and Tansu stomped into the kitchen.

'Listen!' Saba followed them. 'I could go anywhere: to Cairo, or India, or France or somewhere.' As she said it, she saw herself silhouetted against a bright red sky, singing for the soldiers.

'Well you can forget about that, too.' Her mother slammed the potatoes into cold water and lit the gas, her hands fiery with chilblains. 'Your father will go mad. And for once, I don't blame him.'

Ah! So they had come to it at last: the real heart of the matter. Her father would go mad. Mum's emotional weathervane was always turned towards him and the storms that would come.

'I'm twenty-three years old.' Saba and her mother faced each other, breathing heavily. 'He can't tell me what to do any more.'

'Yes he can,' her mother yelled. 'He's your flaming father.'

She'd looked at her mother with contempt. 'Do you ever have a single thought of your own, Mum?' That was cruel: she knew the consequences of her mother sticking up for herself.

Her mother's head shot up as if she'd been struck.

'You haven't got a clue, have you?' she said at last. 'You're a stupid, selfish girl.'

'Clue about what, Mum?' Some devil kept Saba going.

'What it's like for your father on the ships. It's carnage in the shipping lanes – half the time they go around with their knees bent, expecting another bomb to drop on their heads.'

That brought them both to the edge of tears.

'I want to do something that makes sense to me – I don't want to just work in the factory. I can do something more.'

'Uggh,' was all her mother said.

That hurt too, and made it worse – her mother, her great supporter, talking as if she couldn't stand her at a moment that should have been so fine. She ran down the dark corridor where photos of her father's severe-looking Turkish ancestors gazed down on one side, and her mother's glum lot from the Welsh valleys on the other. Slamming the door behind her, she ran into the back yard. She sat down in the outside privy, sobbing.

She was nearly twenty-four years old and completely stuck. The year the war had started was the year in which she had had a whole wonderful life worked out – her first tour with The Simba Sisters around the south coast; singing lessons with a professional in Swansea; freedom, the chance to have the life she'd trained for and dreamed of for so long. Nothing to look forward to now except a factory job, or, if she was lucky, the odd amateur concert or radio recording.

'Saba.' A timid knock on the door. Tansu walked in wearing her floral pinny and her gumboots, even though it wasn't raining. She had her watering can in her hand. 'Saba,' she gave a jagged sigh, 'don't go ma house.' *Don't go ma house* was Tansu-speak for 'I love you, don't leave me.'

'I don't understand, Tansu,' she said. 'You've come to the concerts. You've seen me. You've said I was born to do this. I thought we were all in this together.'

Tansu pulled a dead leaf off the jasmine bush she'd planted in the back yard that had resolutely refused to thrive. 'Too many people leave this house,' she said. 'Your sister has gone to the valley.'

'She hasn't gone,' Saba protested. Lou, at eight the baby of the family, had been sent away to avoid the bombs to a nice family in the Rhondda Valley. She came home with her little suitcase on the bus most weekends.

'Your father at sea.'

'He wants to be there. It's his life.'

'You no ma pinish.' Another way of saying don't go.

'Tansu, I've dreamed about this for the whole of my life. I'll make money for us. I'll buy you a big house near Üsküdar.' The place Tan always mentioned when she talked about Turkey.

'No.' Tansu refused to meet her eye. She stood there, legs braced, eyes down, as old and unmovable as rock.

Saba looked over her head, at the darkening sky, the seagulls flying towards the docks. 'Please help me, Tan,' she said. They'd sung together once. Tan had taught her baby songs.

'I say nothing,' said Tansu. 'Talk to your father.'

Her father, Remzi, was an engineer on the Fyffes' ships that had once carried bananas and coal and rice all around the world. Dark-haired and with a permanent five o'clock shadow, he was handsome and energetic. As a child, he seemed to her a God-like figure who ruled the waves. The names of the ships he sailed on – *Copacabana*, *Takoradi*, *Matadi* – intoxicated her like poetry or a drug. On his visits home, she'd ride high and proud on his shoulders down Pomeroy Street and into the Bay, listening to other local men stop and say hello to him or ask him respectfully whether he could put in a good word for them and get them work.

And the big joke, not so funny now, was that it was her father who had first discovered she could sing. They'd been at the Christmas party in St William's church hall, and little old leather-lungs had stood on a chair and sung 'D'Ye Ken John Peel' and brought the house down. His face had bloomed with love and pride, and he'd encouraged her to sing at family parties: Turkish songs, Arabic songs, the French songs he'd learned from sailors.

Her 'Archontissa', performed with much wailing and fluttery arm movements, reduced strong Greeks to tears. He'd even taken her to talent contests – she remembered the choking sound he'd made when she won – and afterwards they'd walk home together high as kites and stop at the Pleeze café on Angelina Street for ice cream.

But then, aged about thirteen, she'd started to grow breasts. Little buds, nothing really, but the first soft wolf whistles down at the YMCA had been her swansong as far as he was concerned. His eyes had glowered at her from the front row.

'Men are animals.' He'd all but dragged her home down the street. 'For some men, one woman is like another.' His lips had twisted in disgust, as if she'd already fatally let him down. 'They will lie down with whoever is around.'

Horrified, embarrassed, she'd said nothing, not understanding that those whistles marked the beginning of her own dual life. When he was at sea, she did a few concerts – although there was hell to pay if he found out; apart from that, nothing but respectable events such as eisteddfods, and recitals down at the Methodist Hall, which frankly, as she often complained to Joyce, had become a deadly bore.

Her father had grown up on the outskirts of the village of Üvezli, not far from the Black Sea coast. She'd loved hearing him talk about it once. There were donkeys on the farm, plane trees, a pump, and chickens. On feast days, he told her, twenty people would sit down for lunch, and his mother would cook, roasted chickens and stuffed tomatoes and milk puddings with nuts in them. When he told her about these lovely things, his eyes filled with tears.

Once when she'd said, only half attending, 'Don't you miss it, Baba?' he'd turned his hooded eyes on her and said savagely,

'I think about my village every day. I remember every stone in our house, every tree in the orchard,' and she'd felt a darkness fall around them, and that she must never ask him about this place again.

Nowadays, with the ships he worked on carrying nothing but coal for the war, and his little girl disturbingly grown, her father seemed in a permanent sulk, and Saba was fed up with it. He hated Joyce working full time at Curran's, resented the fact that the three women seemed perfectly capable of running the house without him, and at home behaved like a permanent defensive guest. The way he sat brooding beside the fire in the front room reminded Saba of the new cock they had once introduced in the chicken house in the back yard, who'd sat frozen and alone on his perch amid a babble of companionable and clucking hens. She watched how Tan, who adored him, made hectic efforts to cheer him up. How she'd hover at mealtimes by his chair, ready to spring into the kitchen for any tasty morsel that took his fancy, and shake her head approvingly at almost everything he said, like a ventriloquist. She saw too how her mother, normally so confident and funny, changed into an entirely different person when he was home: the anxious, darting looks, the way her voice seemed to rise an octave, how she would often shoo Saba upstairs as if she was a nothing, to get his slippers, or some book he wanted. It broke her heart to see Tan and Mum working so hard; why couldn't he try harder too?

It was time to drop the bombshell. The ENSA letter had burned a hole in her pocket all week, and the pilot's letter had given her an extra boost of confidence. Her father's kitbag was in the front hall. He'd come home on Wednesday from Portsmouth, had a bath in the front room and retired since then in virtual silence to his shed out the back, only appearing for meals.

Her mother, pale at the row that must come, begged Saba not to show him the ENSA letter until the day before he went to sea again. 'He's already got the hump,' she said. 'Tell him now and he'll sulk for the whole ten days.'

'Why do you let him, Mum?' Saba blazed. 'It must be torture for you.'

She'd lost patience with the lot of them, and decided in a few hours' time to step into the lion's den. Saturday night was the time when custom dictated that the family gathered around the little plush-covered table in the front room, got the best china out and Joyce and Tan cooked favourite dishes. When Saba thought back to the best of these times, she remembered the fire crackling in the grate, glasses winking on the table, little dishes Tan used to make: hummus and Caucasian chicken – cold shredded chicken with walnuts. Her father even danced sometimes, clicking his fingers and showing his excellent teeth.

Maybe Tan was trying to lighten the dreadful atmosphere in the house by reviving these happier times. For two days now she'd been in and out of the kitchen. She'd gone to Jamal's, the Arab greengrocer on Angelina Street, and wheedled cracked wheat and preserved lemons from the owner. She'd saved up her meat ration for two weeks to make the little meatballs that Remzi loved. As she cooked, the wailing sounds of Umm Kulthum, the famous Egyptian singer, burst from the gramophone and majestic sorrows swept through the house – like a funeral cortège drawn by big black horses. Remzi had collected her records during his Mediterranean tours.

While Tan was cooking, Saba rehearsed the best words to use.

It's a perfectly respectable organisation, Baba, it's part of the army now. We'll be well protected . . .

There's even a uniform, it's not just a band of actors and singers . . .

They do so much good for the troops. It keeps everybody's spirits up . . .

It will give me a proper future in singing, I can learn from this . . .

She watched the clock all day, every bone in her body rigid with nervous tension. When six o'clock came, she took her place quietly at the table in the front room. A few moments later, her father walked in erect, unsmiling. He'd changed into the long dressing gown he wore at home, which made him look, with his short, well-trimmed beard and his dark hooded eyes, like an Old Testament prophet. Peeping out from underneath it were the English gentleman's brogues he wore, which Joyce cleaned every morning before she went to the factory.

During supper they discussed only safe topics: the weather, dreadful; the war, showing no sign of getting better; Mrs Orestes next door, everyone agreeing that sad as it was about her son Jim, killed in France a few months ago, it was time she pulled her socks up (Joyce said she hadn't been out of her dressing gown since, and still wouldn't answer the door, not even to take the cake she'd baked for her). When the plates had been emptied, her father thrilled them all by producing from the folds of his robe some toffees he'd bought in Amsterdam. Tan crept mouse-like to the kitchen to get his glass of sage tea. When Joyce left too, Saba took a deep breath and said to her father:

'Do you want me to give her a hand, or can we talk?'

'Sit down, Shooba,' he said, using his pet name for her. He pointed to a footstool near his chair.

She sat, careful not to block the heat of the fire from his legs. She could hear her own heart thumping as she sipped her water and tried to look calm.

'I haven't spoken to you properly for a long time,' he said in his deep voice.

True – she'd circled warily around him since he came home.

The sage tea arrived; Tan scuttled out again. He took a sip and she felt his hand rest softly on her head.

She handed him the letter. 'I'd like you to read this.'

'Is this for me?'

'Yes.' Thinking *no, it's for me.*

A deep line developed between his eyebrows as he read it, and when he had finished, he snatched at the paper and read it again.

'I don't understand this.' His expression darkened. 'How do these people know about you?'

'I don't know.' Her voice was wobbly. 'They must have heard me somewhere.'

Her father put his glass down. He shook his head in disgust. There was a long silence.

'You're lying to me,' he said at last. 'You've been out again, haven't you? You've been performing in public.'

He made it sound as if she'd been in a strip show. She felt like a cowering dog at his feet, so she stood up.

'Only a couple of times,' she said. 'At a hospital, and a church.'

He read the letter again, and then scratched his head furiously. Joyce, who must have been listening behind the door, appeared, a tea towel in her hand. She looked drawn.

'Have you seen this?' His voice a whip crack.

A look of complete panic crossed Joyce's face. They'd reached the end of something and it felt terrible.

'Yes.'

'What did you tell her?'

'Nothing.' It was rare to see her mother trembling, but she was. 'They must have seen her at the Methodist Hall,' she faltered.

'*Yaa, eşek!*' he yelled. The Turkish word for donkey. 'Don't tell me lies.'

The whoop of an air-raid siren stopped them all in their tracks for a moment, and then went away. They were used to false alarms in those days.

'You said she should have her voice trained,' her mother ventured bravely. 'She can't stay home for ever.'

'She's been ill,' her father shouted. Saba had had tonsillitis six months ago.

'No, she's not flipping well ill, and if you were at home more, you'd know that!' her mother shrieked.

He threw his tea against the wall, the glass shattered and they all shrieked, thinking it was a bomb.

'Don't you talk back to me!' Her father on his feet, hand raised.

'I'm sorry. I'm sorry.' Her mother's little spark of bravery went out; she was stammering again. She'd dropped her tea towel and was scrabbling under the table, picking up shards of glass with her bare hands, and when she crawled up from under the tablecloth, scarlet in the face, she turned the full force of her rage on Saba.

'You stupid girl,' she said, her mouth all twisted with rage. 'You have to do it your way, don't you?'

Later, Saba heard them going at it hammer and tongs through the thin partition wall that separated her bedroom from theirs. His voice rising as he told Joyce it was her fault, that Saba was spoilt and stupid; his thump, her rabbit-like squeal and thin wail; his footsteps going downstairs. He slammed the front door so hard the whole house trembled.

The next day, Saba took her leather suitcase down from the top of the wardrobe and laid it on the bed. At the bottom of it she placed her red tap shoes, then her polka-dot dress, stockings, wash bag. She put the khaki-coloured ENSA letter on top of the clothes, and was just folding the piece of paper with directions to the Drury Lane Theatre when she heard the sound of the front door click.

Apart from Tan, she was alone. Joyce was at the factory. She sat down on the floral eiderdown, every muscle straining as she listened to the squeak of his shoes on the stairs, the uneven sound of the cracked floorboard on the landing.

He came into her room carrying an instrument in his hand that they had often joked about when she was a child. It was a short whip with two leather lashes at the end of it. He'd told her once that his own father had thrashed him with it regularly. For her, it had only ever been a prop in a deliciously frightening childhood game they'd played together. Remzi, growling ferociously, would race around the back yard brandishing the thing, she squealing with delight as she got away.

But today he put the martinet down on the bed, on top of her sheet music. He looked at her with no expression in his eyes whatsoever.

'Daddy!' she said. 'No! Please don't do this.' As if she could save him from himself.

'I cannot let you go on disobeying me,' he said at last. 'Not in front of your mother, your grandmother. You bring shame on our house.'

'Shame on our house! Shame on our house!' It was like someone in a panto. Someone with a Sinbad beard, a cutlass. But the time when she could have joked with him about that had gone. As she moved away from him, the ENSA letter fell on the floor. He swooped on it and held it in his hand.

'You're not going,' he said. 'Bad enough that your mother has to work in a factory now.'

She looked at him and heard a kind of shrilling sound in her ears.

'I am going, Daddy,' she said. 'Because I'll never get another chance like this again.'

His eyes went black; he shook his head.

'No.'

If he hadn't torn up the letter then and there, everything might have stayed the same. But he tore it and scattered it like confetti over the lino, and then all hell let loose because that letter was living proof that something you wanted really badly to happen could happen.

And to be fair, she hit him first: a glancing blow on the arm, and then he rushed at her, groaning like an animal, smacking her hard around the head and shoulders with his fists. For a few breathless moments they roared and grunted, then Tansu rushed in shrieking like a banshee and throwing her apron over her head and shrieking, '*Durun! Yapmayin!*' Stop it, don't!

He left Saba sitting on the bed, trembling and bleeding from her nose. She felt horribly ashamed of both of them.

Her father had always been a strict, even a terrifying parent – your father runs a dictatorship not a democracy, her mother had told her once with a certain pride – but never, at least to her, a violent man. She'd thought him too intelligent for that. But on this day, she felt as if she'd never known him, or perhaps only experienced him in bits and pieces, and that this bit of him was pure evil.

'If you go,' his voice went all shuddery with rage, 'I never want to see your face again.'

'I feel the same,' she said quietly, 'so that's good.'

She wanted to hit him again, to spit on him. It was only later she collapsed in a flood of tears, but before she did, she wrote her first letter to Dominic Benson, an act of defiance that changed everything.

Dear Pilot Officer Benson,

I expect to be in London, at the Theatre Royal, Drury Lane, on 17 March for an audition at ENSA. Perhaps we could meet after that?

With best wishes,

Saba Tarcan

Chapter 4

Alone for the first time, and in London, when she swung her feet on to the cold lino and sat on the edge of her bed, her hands shook so much it was hard to do up her dress.

She'd been awake for most of the night in the nasty little bed and breakfast in Bow Street that ENSA had recommended. On top of the bedside table scarred with old cigarette burns, there was a Gideon Bible and an empty water carafe with a dead fly in it. She'd lain with her eyes open under a slim green damp-smelling eiderdown, listening for bombs and trying not to think about home, and Mum.

Her mother had taken an hour off work to walk her down to the railway station.

'When will you be back, then?' she'd asked, her face white as death under the green turban.

'I don't know, Mum – it depends. I may not get it.'

'You'll get it,' her mother said grimly. 'So what shall I tell Lou?'

'Tell her what you like.'

'It'll break her heart if you go.'

'Mum, be fair – you started this too.' Well, it was true: all the lessons, the dreaming, the fish and chips at the Pleeze as a treat when she'd won the singing competitions, and seeing Joyce so magically transported.

Inside the train station, they'd looked at each other like shipwrecked strangers.

'Well, bye then, Mum,' as the train drew in.

'Bye, love.' But at the very last minute, Saba had buried her face in her mother's shoulder and they'd held each other's shuddering bodies.

'Don't hate me, Mum,' she murmured.

'I don't hate you,' Joyce said, her face working violently.

'Good luck,' she said at last. The guards were slamming the doors. When Saba stepped inside, her mother turned and walked away. Her thin back, the green turban, her jaunty attempt at a wave at the mouth of the station had broken Saba's heart. She was a monster after all.

There was a gas heater in the bed and breakfast. The landlady had explained how to turn on its brass spigot and where to apply the match, but Saba had avoided it, frightened it would explode. Instead she wrapped herself in the eiderdown and tried to concentrate on the audition. She was convinced at this low point that it would be a disaster, and regretted making the date to meet the pilot after it. He'd got her letter, and written back that, by coincidence, he would be up in London that week staying at his sister's house, not far from the Theatre Royal. Perhaps they could either meet for tea or maybe a drink at the Cavour Club. His telephone number was Tate 678.

At around three thirty, someone had pulled a lavatory chain in the corridor outside. Saba sat up in bed and decided to phone him in the morning and cancel the appointment. The audition was enough worry for one day, and he'd probably thought her cheap to have accepted in the first place.

Before dawn, the rumbling of bombers going over London woke her again. Forty thousand people had died here in the Blitz, or near enough; that was one of Mum's last cheery messages for her. Shivering in the inky black of her room, she put the bedside light on, moved the Bible out of the way, took her diary from her suitcase and wrote LONDON on top of a new page.

I have either made the stupidest and worst decision of my life, or the best. Either way, I must write it down, I may need it (ha ha!) for my autobiography.

She gazed in disgust at the false bravado of the *ha, ha*, as if some other crass creature had written it.

Dear Baba, she wrote next. *Please try and forgive me for what . . .*

She scrumpled it, dropped it in the waste-paper basket. It was his fault too; she would not crawl and she would not be forgiven, she knew that now. It was the first plan she had ever made in her life without anybody else's permission, and she must stick to it even if the whole bloody thing ended in disaster.

Her breakfast of toast and powdered eggs was a solitary affair, eaten in a freezing front parlour with the gas fire unlit and only her new landlady's collection of pink and white china dolls for company. After it, she walked the two streets to the Theatre Royal in Drury Lane, amazed at the crush of vans and shouting people.

In a telephone box on the corner of the street, she dropped coins into the slot, put the cloth bag which held her dress over one arm, and phoned Dominic Benson's number.

'Hello?' A woman's voice – charming, amused.

'Look, this is Saba Tarcan speaking. I have a message for Pilot Officer Benson. Can you give it to him?'

'Of course.'

'I'm very sorry, we had a sort of arrangement to meet today, but I can't make it – I don't know where I'll be.'

'Ah.' The woman sounded disappointed.

'Can I ask who you are?'

'Yes, of course, it's Freya, his sister. I'll make sure he gets the message.'

'Thank you.' She was about to say she would phone later, but it was too late. The receiver clicked, the line went dead.

She stepped out into the street again, breathing rapidly. She was in such a state about the audition now, and the fact that she was in London by herself, it was all she could think about.

The first confusion was that the Theatre Royal, Drury Lane, was in fact in Catherine Street, so she got lost trying to find it. When she did see it, she was disappointed, what with the theatre looking so drab and workmanlike in its wartime uniform. There were no thrilling posters advertising musical stars or famous actors hanging about, no twinkling lights or liveried doormen, no scented and glamorous ladies in furs outside – only a large painted officey-looking sign saying that this was the headquarters of the Entertainments National Service Association, and inside, what looked like a rabbit warren of hastily erected offices, out of which the Corinthian columns soared like the bones of a once beautiful woman.

She walked upstairs and into the foyer, where a harassed-looking NCO sat at a desk with a clipboard and a list, and a pile of official-looking forms.

'I've come for the ENSA audition,' she told him. She hadn't expected to feel so nervous on her own, but then Mum was usually with her.

'Overseas or domestic?'

'I don't know.'

'Name?' He consulted his list.

'Saba Tarcan.' She felt almost sick with nerves and regretted the powdered egg earlier.

'You're an hour early,' he said, adding more kindly, 'Sit over there, love, if you want to.'

She sat on a spindly gilt chair, and gazed up at the gold ceiling, the one beautiful thing not covered by partitions and desks.

'Smashing, isn't it?' An old man in a green cardy and with a mop and bucket had been watching her. His peaked cap looked like the remains of a doorman's uniform. 'But nothing like it used to look.'

His name was Bob, he said. He'd been a doorman at this theatre for over ten years and loved the place. When a 500lb bomb had fallen through the roof during the Blitz the year before, he'd taken it hard.

'Wallop,' he said. 'Straight through the galleries and into the pit. The safety curtain looked like a crumpled hanky, the seats was sodden from the fire brigade. We've cleared it up a bit since then.'

He asked her the name of the show she was auditioning for; she said she didn't have a clue – she'd just been told to come at 11.30.

If he had to take a guess, he told her out of the corner of his mouth, she'd be replacing a singer called Elsa Valentine, but it was a shambles here at the moment, particularly since the new call-up. In one company alone over in France, seventy-five per cent of the performers, including the hind legs of a pantomime horse, were on the sick.

'So don't worry, love,' he added. 'They're really scraping the barrel now, they're that desperate.'

'Well there's tactful,' she said, and he winked at her.

'I'm joking, my darling,' he said. 'You're a little corker.'

She hated it when she blushed, but right there and then she got what her little sister called one of her red-hot pokers – she felt it creeping up her chest and neck until her whole face was on fire.

Next, forms to fill in, stating her name and business, which she did with a shaking hand. An hour later, as she followed Bob up some marbled steps and down a dark corridor, he flung out snippets of history. This, love, was the boardroom, where Sheridan had written *The School for Scandal.* And there, he opened heavy oak doors and pointed towards the darkened stage, was where Nell Gwyn, 'you know, the orange lady', had performed.

'Wardrobe' – he shouted towards a room full of whirling sewing machines, backcloths, wigs. 'And here,' he stopped and put his finger to his lips, 'is where a body was found.' He pointed into a dark room. 'The most famous one,' he added, his eyes very round. 'A real body,' he whispered, 'under the stage here, and his ghost haunts us to—'

His hat hit the floor before he could finish the sentence.

'Bad boy!' A gorgeous blonde appeared in a jangle of charm bracelets. She gave him a mock blow around the head, and kissed him on the cheek, and the air filled with the rich scent of roses and jasmine.

'Arleta Samson as I live and breathe.' The doorman lit up. 'No one told me you were coming.'

'Audition. They should know how fabulous I am by now, but apparently not.' She threw up her hands in surprise.

'Give me that, girl.' Bob couldn't stop smiling as he took a pink leather vanity case from her hands. 'So, where've you been, darling?'

'Palladium for two months, before that Brighton. And who is this poor girl you're trying to frighten to death?'

'Saba Tarcan.' A further jingling of charms as she shook her hand. 'I'm here for the audition, too.'

'Well, I'm happy to meet you.' Arleta's handshake was firm. 'I'll take you to the dressing room.'

And swept along in the wake of her rich perfume, the terrors of the night began to recede, because this was it! The famous theatre, the ghost, the glamorous blonde woman with her vamp walk and her swishing stockings, talking so casually about the Palladium as if everyone performed there, and soon, one way or the other, her future to be decided.

'Actually, Bob's right about the ghost,' Arleta said as they walked down a long corridor. 'Some young chap was murdered in, I dunno, when was it, love? Sixteen hundred and something. He was making whoopee with the director's wife. They found his body under the stage when they were doing the renovations, but his ghost only comes during the day, and only if the show is going to be a success, so we all like him.' Her cynical rich laugh thrilled Saba. She estimated Arleta to be at least thirty.

'Have you seen him today?' she asked.

'Not yet, love,' said Bob. 'But we will.'

*

The dressing room was part of a tangle of dim and dusty rooms behind the stage. When they got there, Arleta placed her vanity case in front of the mirror, switched on a circle of lights and stared intently at her reflection, running a finger along her eyebrow.

'How many are they seeing today?'

'Seven or eight,' said Bob.

'Are you quite sure, love?' Arleta sounded surprised. 'The last time there were about a hundred. We waited all day.'

Bob consulted a crumpled list. 'Yep. Two gels, three acrobats, the dancer, and it just says comedian here, don't know his name. Cup of tea, my darlings? They've got a kettle up in Wardrobe.'

'Little pet!' said Arleta. 'You read my mind.

'I don't get it.' She was still looking puzzled as the door shut behind Bob. 'They usually send out a minimum of fifteen to a show. But never mind, hey.' She sat down at a dressing table littered with dirty ashtrays and dried and decapitated roses from some ancient bouquet. 'They do love their little secrets, and it means I can hog the mirror before the others come. D'you mind?'

'Help yourself.' Saba hung her dress on a hook, wishing her mother were here to help with her make-up. In the old days Joyce would have been cracking jokes, smoking her Capstans; she'd loved all this before she'd seen how it would end.

'Right then.' Arleta took a deep breath and gazed intently at herself. 'Maximum dog today, I think,' she said in a faraway voice. 'I really, *really* want this.'

She opened up the pink vanity case – its many terraced shelves bulged with lipsticks, pansticks, glass bottles full of face cream, cotton wool, a variety of brushes, a little twig for fluffing up her hair, rollers for heightening it. At the bottom of the case, a blonde hairpiece lounged like a sleeping puppy.

She took out a stick of foundation and went into a light trance as she smoothed it over her high cheekbones with a little sponge. Apricot Surprise, she informed Saba, quite the best under lights. Next, a breath of Leichner's powdered rouge applied with a brush, a dab of highlighter under the eyebrows and on top of the cheekbones. Loose powder from a pink swansdown puff, and then 'Phzz' as she spat into caked mascara and widened her eyes against the mirror, stroking the blackness on to each lash. She parted her lips into a mirthless smile and drew around them in pencil, and then a smear of lipstick, Max Factor's Tru Colour. 'Expensive,' she told Saba in the same faraway voice, 'but worth it.' The generous hoop of red she left on a tissue looked like blood.

She pulled off her headband with a dramatic flourish, her hair falling in a mass of golden waves around her face. She began to hum as her fingers gently probed for tangles; a final haughty glance at herself in the mirror, and she caught the right side of her hair in her hands and fastened it with a gold barrette.

'Your hair is lovely.' Saba was finding it hard not to stare. Arleta was easily the most glamorous women she'd ever met, and there was nothing furtive about this performance.

'Oh you wouldn't say that if you'd seen me last year!' Arleta bared her teeth to check for lipstick on them. 'I was in a hair-dressing salon in Valetta – that's in Malta – and this woman gave me a perm, and when I woke the next morning, half my hair's on the pillow beside me having a lovely little sleep. I nearly had a fit.'

They were laughing when the door burst open. A fat old man in dinner suit, white gloves and large patent pumps jumped into the room.

'Do I recognise that bell-like sound?' He raised his painted eyebrows.

'Oh my Lord!' Arleta stood up and gave the old man a huge hug. 'Little thing! No one told me you'd be here.

'Now this,' she told Saba, 'is the famous Willie Wise. He was one of the Ugly Sisters in Brighton, and we've also been on the road together in Malta and North Africa, haven't we, my darling?

'And this gorgeous creature,' Arleta added, 'is Saba Tarcan. What are you, love? A soubrette?'

When Saba said she might be replacing a singer called Elsa Valentine, they both stared at her.

'Whoooooh!' said Arleta. 'Well, you must be good. Did I hear a rumour that she had a breakdown in Tunis?'

Saba felt a wiggle of fear in her stomach. 'Why?'

'Oh, I can't actually remember,' said Arleta. 'A lot do fall by the wayside. It's—'

'Now.' Willie put his hand up to stop the flow. 'Don't you dare put her off. I've been sent down here to tell you two to get your skates on and get down to the auditorium. You're on next.'

*

As they walked down a dark corridor that tilted towards the stage, a beautifully dressed blond man with a significant walk pushed in front of them.

'Yes, sweetie-puss, I'm back,' he said to the uniformed figure beside him. 'I honestly feel like a mole here after all that light, but needs must.' When his friend mumbled something sympathetic, the blond man pushed back his hair with a languid gesture. 'Oh she was an absolute horror,' he said. 'Complained about everything. Nothing like as talented as she thought she was.'

Arleta dug Saba in the ribs and mimicked the man's swishy walk for a few strides. When he opened the door into the auditorium, her heart started thumping. Oh Jesus, Mary and Joseph, this was it! The famous Theatre Royal stage; in a matter of minutes, triumph or humiliation to be decided. When her eyes had grown accustomed to the gloom, she saw that the stage, crudely boarded off for auditions, looked disappointingly small, far smaller than she'd imagined, and in a ghostly gloom without the front lights switched on. But never mind, she was here! Whatever comes, she told herself, I will remember this for the rest of my life. I'll have danced and sung on this stage, and that will mean something.

Her heart was thumping uncomfortably as she watched the blond man fold his coat fastidiously and put it on the seat behind him. He lit a cigarette and talked intensely to three uniformed men who sat in the stalls surrounded by rows and rows of empty seats, some of them still covered by dust sheets and bits of rubble from the bomb damage.

A pale girl in ballet shoes sat four rows behind them clutching a black bag on her lap. Beside her, silent and pensive-looking, the old comedian.

'Right now. Shall we crack on then?' A disembodied voice from the stalls. 'We've got a lot to cover today. The old man, Willie, you first. Come on!'

A stenographer with a clipboard sat down quietly beside the three men. The music struck up, whistles and trumpets and silly trombones. A few seconds later, old Willie ran out, fleet-footed in his patent-leather pumps, shouting, 'Well here we are then!'

Arleta clutched Saba's hand, digging her nails into the palm. 'He needs this so badly,' she whispered in the dark. 'His wife died a few months ago. Married thirty-four years. Heartbroken.'

Willie went down arthritically on one knee and sang 'Old Man

River' with silly wobbling lips. The silence from the auditorium was deafening – no laughter from the watching men, no applause. For his next trick he deadpanned what Arleta whispered was his speciality: a hopelessly garbled version of a nursery rhyme called 'Little Red Hoodingride and the Forty Thieves'.

Saba joined in with Arleta's rich laughter; Willie was really funny.

After his next joke, about utility knickers – 'One Yank and they're off' – a shadowy figure stood up behind the orchestra pit and said:

'Mr Wise, I take it you understand our blue-joke policy?'

'Sorry?' The old man walked towards the spotlight and stood there blinking nervously.

'If you get chosen, all scripts must be submitted to us for a signature. We're clear about the standards we want to live up to; we hope you are too.'

'All present and correct, sir.' Willie stood in a blue haze, smiling glassily. 'Appreciate the warning.' He clicked his heels and saluted, and it was hard to tell in that unstable light whether he was mocking or simply scared.

The pale girl rose. She had long limbs, very thin eyebrows and beautiful hands. She wafted towards the main spotlight and stood there smiling tensely.

'Janine De Vere. I'm from Sadler's Wells, you might remember.' The posh voice bore faint traces of Manchester.

'What have you got for us, Miss De Vere?' from the dark.

'My wide-ranging repertoire includes tap and Greek dancing. Ah'm very versatile.'

'Oh get you,' murmured Arleta.

'Well perhaps a small sample. We don't have long.'

Miss De Vere cleared her throat and faced the wings. She held a beseeching hand towards a woman in an army uniform and sensible shoes who put the needle down on the gramophone. Syrupy music rose and sobbed. Miss De Vere took a tweed coat off and in a sea-green tutu sprang into action with a series of leaps across the stage. With her long pale arms moving like seaweed as she twirled and jumped and with light patting sounds, she ran hither and yon with her hands shading her eyes as if she was desperately searching for someone. Her finale, a series of flawless cartwheels across the stage, covered her hands in dust. She sank into the splits and flung a triumphant look across the spotlights.

'Lovely. Thank you. Next.' The same neutral voice from the stalls.

'Saba Tarcan. On stage, please. Hurry! Quick.'

Dom, hidden in the upper circle of the theatre, sat up straight when he heard this. He trained his eyes on her like a pistol. He'd got her message, and ignored it because he wanted to hear her sing again. It was a kind of dare – for himself, if nothing else – to prove he could have her if he wanted to.

He'd sneaked in after slipping half a crown to the friendly doorman, who'd shaken his hand and said, 'We owe a lot to you boys in blue.' He'd kept her original letter to him in his wallet: *I expect to be in London, at the Theatre Royal, Drury Lane, on 17 March for an audition at ENSA.*

She walked down the aisle and on to the stage, childlike from the back in her red frock, he admired once again her fantastic posture, her refusal to scuttle. That kind of poise was a statement in itself. *Watch me*, it seemed to say, *I matter.*

He'd heard her laughing earlier – a full-throated laugh at the comedian. If she was feeling overawed by this, she certainly wasn't showing it.

She didn't see him at all. She stood in the weak spotlight, smiling at the dim figures in the stalls, thinking, *this is it, kid.* The accompanist took her music without smiling. She cleared her throat, and thought briefly about Caradoc Jones, her old music teacher from home. He'd given her lots of advice about opening her throat, and relaxing, and squeezing her bum on the high notes – 'I'll train you so well,' he'd told her, 'you won't have to worry about your diaphragm or your breath or whether you'll be able to hold a high note, it will all be there.' But what he'd talked about most, apart from developing technique, was being brave.

She'd gone to him first aged thirteen, pretty and shy, but keen on herself too, having easily won two of the talent competitions organised by the Riverside Youth Club. She'd warbled her way through 'O For the Wings of a Dove', thinking he'd be charmed as most people were.

And Caradoc, a famous opera singer before the booze got him, had not been in the slightest charmed. This fat, untidy man, with ash on his waistcoat, had listened for a bit and then asked:

'Do you know what all bad singers have in common?'

When she said no, he'd slammed down the piano lid and stood up.

'They do this . . .' He'd made a strangled sound like a drowning kitten. 'I want you to do this . . .' He'd bared his ancient yellow teeth, his tongue had reared in his huge mouth, and he'd let out a roar so magnificent it had sprayed her and his checked waistcoat with spittle.

He'd glared at her ferociously. 'For Christ's sake, girl, have the courage to make a great big bloody mistake,' and she heard her mother gasp: *Swearing! Children!* 'Nothing good will ever happen,' he said, 'unless you do.'

Now the pianist rippled out the first soft chords to 'God Bless the Child'. She went deep inside herself, blocking out the pale and exhausted faces of the ENSA officials and the bored-looking stenographer, and she sang. For a brief second she took in the vastness of the space around her, the ceiling painted in white and gold, where the bomb hadn't got it, the rows and rows of empty seats, the magic and glory of this famous theatre, and then she got lost in the song.

When it was over, she looked out into the auditorium. She saw no movement at all, except for Arleta, who stuck her thumbs up and clapped.

Dom sat and listened too, confused and frightened. When he'd heard her first, or so he'd reasoned with himself many times, he'd been at the lowest ebb of his life, and she'd smelled so good, and seemed so young, and he was vulnerable.

But there she was again, with everything to lose – or so it felt to him – in the middle of the stage, making his heart race because she seemed so brave, so pure suddenly in the way she'd gathered herself up and flung herself metaphorically speaking into the void, where those bored-sounding fuckers in khaki sat with their clipboards and pencils.

And sitting on his own in the dark, he felt a tremendous emptiness. How foolishly schoolboyish of him to have written to her – she was everybody's and nobody's – but once again she'd called up a raw part of him, a part that normally he went to great lengths to try and hide. And although he'd always known he didn't love Annabel, or not enough, he was shaken still by the loss of her, the blow to his pride as much as anything, the sense of everything being so changeable.

'Anything else for us, Miss Tarcan?' one of the men asked. She did 'Smoke Gets in Your Eyes', and hearing the stenographer give a little gasp, a sound she recognised, dared to hope that after all the many anxieties of the day, things were going well.

She sang her last song, 'Mazi', on her own and when she finished, faced them close to tears. Tan had taught her that song; she'd sung it with her father in the chicken shed.

One of the nameless men who were watching her stood up. He took out a handkerchief and wiped his head. He looked at her aslant, as if she was a piece of furniture he would shortly measure.

The pianist smiled for the first time that day.

'Right-ho, a break for lunch now,' was all he said. 'We'll see the Banana Brothers at three and Arleta after them. We'll meet at four for our final decision.'

'Flipping heck,' Arleta joked to Saba. They had paused on the island between two rows of busy traffic; they were on their way to lunch. 'Now I'm going to sound like something the cat's sicked up after you, so thank you very much. But actually' – she held out a protective arm as an army truck passed – 'I'm more in the novelty-dance line myself. I really just sing to fill in the gaps.'

The truck driver wolf-whistled; Arleta gave him a coy wave. 'Naughty,' she called out happily.

They ate lunch at Sid's, a workman's café with steamy windows, full of people in khaki. The set menu, a two-and-six special, featured strong tea in thick white china cups, a corned-beef patty made with greyish potatoes, tinned peas, and a custard slice for pudding. While they were eating, the three Banana Brothers arrived. Lean, athletic men whose age Saba guessed to be around forty.

'Well whoop de whoop,' said Arleta, who seemed to know everyone. 'Look who's here.' She kissed each one of them on both cheeks and did the introductions.

'This is Lev, and that's Alex.' The two men folded into graceful bows. 'This little titch,' she pointed towards a younger man whose hair was dyed an improbable black, 'is called Boguslaw.' He closed his eyes dramatically and let his lips nuzzle their hands. 'You won't remember that,' she added. 'You may call him Bog or Boggers, or Bog Brush.'

She explained to Saba that they'd all worked together before, too, in panto in Bristol. 'And they all behaved *appallingly*.' She narrowed her green eyes at them, like a lioness about to slap her cubs. The acrobats, squirming and smirking, seemed to love it.

Close up, Bog was handsome, with a chiselled jaw and the kind of shine and muscle definition most usually seen on a thoroughbred horse. He sat down next to Saba, tucking his napkin in when the waitress came. He asked for a piece of fruit cake but refused the corned-beef patty, because, he said, they were auditioning after lunch and he didn't like to do anything on a full tummy. He looked Saba straight in the eye as if he'd said something mightily suggestive.

Arleta was pouring tea for all of them from a stained enamel pot. 'I hope we all make it, and I hope it's Malta,' she added. 'I had a lovely time there last time.'

'Do you never know where you're going until they tell you?' Saba put down her knife. She was trying not to seem as shy as she felt.

'Never,' Arleta said. 'It's a complete lucky dip, that's what I like about it.'

When the boys had gone, Arleta, pouring more tea, gossiped in a thrilling whisper about the acrobats. They were from Poland originally, she said, and were a first-class act. Lev and Bog were real brothers. They had lost almost their entire family during the war, and sometimes they drank and got angry about it, so it was better not to talk too much about families unless they brought it up. Bog, the younger one, was a womaniser and had got two girls, to her certain knowledge, in the pudding club. He had been excused call-up because of his hammer toes, although how you could be an acrobat with hammer toes was a complete mystery to her, but they wouldn't mention hammer toes either, unless it came up naturally, which it almost never did in conversation. Ha ha ha. Arleta, digging into her custard slice, was in high spirits. She told Saba she'd been very, very low indeed before the audition, but this was just what she needed. 'It's the greatest fun on earth, ENSA,' she said. 'A real challenge.'

'Are you nervous?' Saba said.

'Not really.' Arleta winked. She took out her handkerchief and wiped the lipstick from her cup. 'I more or less know I'm in,' she said cockily.

'How?'

Arleta stuck her tongue into her cheek, closed her eyes and squinted at Saba.

'Let's just say I have friends in high places,' was all she would say.

Chapter 5

After all the auditions had ended, Dom hung around outside the stage door for nearly two hours, waiting for her. The doorman, sitting in a glass box, read his *Sporting Life* from cover to cover. Dom watched prop baskets and racks of clothes come and go, listening with a certain exasperation to snatches of conversation: 'I worked with Mabel years ago. She's a marvel, but puffed sleeves, imagine!' from a loud middle-aged woman with dyed hair, and 'I'd try the wig department, if I were you' from a mincing little type in a checked overcoat.

And then, she emerged from behind him, so buoyantly that she could have been walking on air. There were bright spots of red on her cheeks; she was smiling to herself. It was starting to rain, and the street was full of dun- or dark-coated people putting up umbrellas.

She looked straight at him as she stepped on to the pavement.

'It's Dominic,' he said. 'I've been waiting for you.'

'Waiting for me?' She looked confused and embarrassed, and then the penny dropped.

'Heavens,' she said. 'I'm not sure I would have recognised you out of your pyjamas. You're as good as new.'

The same thing his mother had said, and so untrue.

'Look, I'm sorry about today,' she added, colouring. 'It was all too much. It's my first time in London.'

'And my first time for being jilted.' He made it sound like a joke, but it was true. Almost.

'Well get you!' She was mocking him and smiling too, reminding him again of their hospital kiss.

'Must you dash? Can't I buy you a drink? A nice cup of cocoa maybe?' Oh, the habits of facetiousness did die hard, even when your heart was going like a bloody tom-tom. It's only a dare, he told himself. Calm down.

While she considered this, he noticed the feverish look in her eyes, as though she was floating above the earth and not aware of her surroundings.

'Well, all right then,' she said after a pause. 'I'm absolutely starving. I was so nervous before.' He touched her arm to warn her of a passing car that could have knocked her over, and she continued in the same dream-like voice, 'I can't believe it. Any of it. I honestly don't know what to *do* with myself.'

They had to walk. It was rush hour now, the buses were crammed. He said he would take her to Cavour's in the Strand. When it started to rain harder, he took off his greatcoat and draped it around her shoulders.

Halfway up Regent Street she sat down on a bench like a vagabond and took her right shoe off. Her new shoes had given her a blister. Her hair was wet and plastered around her face, which was triangle-shaped and high-cheekboned, and she suddenly looked so vulnerable, cocooned in his greatcoat and with London rushing around her, and her little foot now curved for his inspection, that he wanted to take it in his hand and kiss it better. He touched her instep lightly; she did not move away.

'Nasty,' he said. 'Amputation? Ambulance? What do you think?'

She swung her handbag at his head.

'Idiot! Twit!' A tomboy moment which delighted him. He'd never liked ladylike girls with their pearls, and handbags on their laps, and talk of horses and Mummy and parties, but where did her high spirits come from? She was so very excited, and seemed to give off a kind of electricity.

'Honestly, what a day!' she said to him. 'What a day,' she repeated. 'Such wonderful things!'

The waiter took their orders: half a bitter for him, a glass of lemonade for her, and whatever sandwiches the kitchen could rustle up. He asked for a seat as far away from the bar as possible so they could talk.

'Are you sure it shouldn't be champagne?' he said, making sure he sounded offhand.

'Well maybe,' she said quietly. 'I got the job. I'm going to be measured for my uniform tomorrow.'

She seemed to get an attack of nerves when she said that. She said she was going to be busy the whole of the next day, and that she was not actually normally in the habit of going out with strange men.

'I'm not a strange man. Don't forget,' he teased her to hide his dismay, 'we've kissed. Don't you remember? In hospital.'

She looked sweet when she went red like that, but he saw her legs move away from him under the table and worried he might have pushed it too far.

'So whereabouts in Wales do you live?'

The blush had receded and the pale honey of her cheeks returned. 'In Cardiff,' she told him. 'Pomeroy Street. Near the notorious Tiger Bay.' She was teasing him now.

'And your parents? Are they singers?'

'No.' She looked unhappy again. He thought that she had the most beautiful eyebrows he'd ever seen – dark wings over dark eyes.

'I'm not surprised you got the job,' he said, hoping to cheer her up. 'You were really quite good . . . that's what I came to tell you.'

'Quite good.' She shot him a look. 'You silver-tongued lizard. Anyway, you don't know that: you didn't even hear me.'

'I did. I bribed the doorman. I wanted to see you.' He had nothing to lose now.

She narrowed her eyes and looked at him, mock-suspicious. 'Why?'

'Because . . .' he took a sip of his drink, 'because . . .' He closed his eyes, thinking *hold it in, hold it in.* This was the last thing on earth that he wanted – to feel out of control again. 'Because you're OK.'

'Oh, very GI Joe,' she said.

'Tell me more about the job,' he asked. He wanted to hold her hand, for her to stay for a week or two so they could get to know each other better. 'Do you know where you're going, or when?'

'No.' She still had that coming-out-of-a-dream look, as if she couldn't quite believe what she was saying. 'And even if I did, we're not allowed to say. All I know is I've got to have all the injections: you know, cholera, and yellow fever and typhoid.'

She looked terrified when she said that. She was faking her air of calm. He recognised the signs all too well. His heart sank. So most likely the Middle East, where things were hotting up, or India, or Burma, which was bloody miles away.

'Shame, I was hoping it would be down the end of the pier at Southend so we could do this again.'

'Do what again?' All her dimples came out when she smiled at him like that.

'Well, talk, have a laugh.'

'Well . . .' She gave him a quizzical look and took a sip of her lemonade '. . . It's not, so we can't—'

He cut her off quickly. 'First time abroad?'

'Yes.'

'Parents know yet?'

'No.' She squeezed her eyes shut.

An uncle-ish part of him rose up when she said this. He wanted to scold her, to warn her of clear and present dangers ahead. Of men in remote places who would want to seduce her, of bad beds and frightening transport and bombs, and stinging insects.

'Will they mind?' He hoped they would.

'It's going to break their hearts,' she said. She grimaced into her lemonade. 'I thought I'd be able to go back and see them before we left – I promised my mum I would – and now it sounds like I won't, there's no time. That's horrible.' She squeezed her eyes shut. 'So let's talk about something else.'

The bar was starting to fill up. The barman was reciting his cocktails – Singapore Sling, White Lady, Naval Grog – to a group of army officers. Dom was staring at her across the table, his brain trying to accommodate, to understand. It was all such unfamiliar territory.

'I know what that feels like,' he said at last. 'I'm flying again; my mother doesn't know yet. I'm going home next week to tell her.'

'Why?' It was her turn to look shocked. 'Don't they let you stop once you've been shot down?'

'I don't want to stop.'

'Why not? Aren't you frightened now?'

'No.' That could never be admitted, not even to himself. 'I can't stop now. It feels like the thing I was born to do – if that doesn't sound fantastically corny.'

She was staring at him properly now.

'No, not corny,' she said. 'Hard.'

Her hands were resting on the table between them. A schoolgirl's hands, no rings, no nail varnish.

'Are you fit enough to go?'

'Yep.' He didn't like talking about it, not with a girl, particularly. It made him feel breathless, hunted. 'I'm fine now.'

'How do they know?'

'Had the X-ray, been spun in a chair. Fit for active service.'

She looked at him steadily. 'I liked that poem you sent me,' she said.

'Oh God, did I?' His turn to be embarrassed – he'd written it out, and when Misou came into the room, must have stuffed it into the envelope by mistake.

'*Whatever comes, one hour was sunlit*,' she said dreamily. 'Such a good thing to say. Sometimes one hour is enough.'

'Pound actually rewrote the poem later – he said two weeks was better.'

Her dimples appeared. 'Dom – I'm going!' Playfully, as if they were children and the game was tag.

'I know, so am I. So let me walk you home,' he said. 'I could help you pack, or sew on your uniform pips or something. I'm good at sewing.'

'No.' She put her hands over her face.

'A cup of coffee, then.' He had half a bottle of whisky in his greatcoat, just in case.

'I can't.' She touched his hand. 'I'm definitely going to take that job. I decided as soon as they asked me. I can't let anything stop me now.'

'I know.' He did too, understand. Unfortunately.

She laid the key to the B and B on the table. She'd produced it proudly for his inspection earlier, thought it was very trusting of her landlady considering this was London. He felt a pang looking at it. How easy it would have been to creep up the stairs together, and how blameless it would feel – all the old rules of courtship had been bent out of shape since the war began.

'Saba.'

'Yes.'

'When you're cleared for security, let me know where you are.'

She was about to answer when the waiter interrupted. He'd

returned to smile at them, to squint at the wings on Dom's uniform and ask what squadron he was with. The management would be honoured to offer him and his good lady a cocktail on the house. They were brave men and they deserved it. Dom, going through the usual nonchalant disclaimers, felt shamingly pleased to be in the spotlight in front of her and also glad not to have to say more about the medical, which had for reasons not explicable made him feel angry and defensive, like a small boy required to drop his trousers.

They ordered Singapore Slings. She wrinkled her nose as she drank it, like a kitten dipping a paw into water. She wasn't half the sophisticate she pretended to be.

When her glass was half emptied, her lit-up look returned like a flash of lightning. He wondered if she was thinking about her job again, and feeling at a sudden loss, he stood up, and on the pretext of hurrying the waiter along with their food, walked as casually as he could over to the bar.

He was standing there when a slight figure came out of the shadows, and stood in a puddle of light in front of him. It was Jilly, Jacko's fiancée. Later, it made perfect sense to him that she would come here to either torture or comfort herself, but on this night they gaped at each other like actors from different plays. She was wearing a blue dress, with the small RAF wings brooch Jacko had bought her pinned to the lapel. She was thinner.

He expected her to cut him, but instead she moved towards him and hugged him hard.

'Dom,' she said at last. She was gripping his hand so hard it hurt. 'Are you all right?'

'Not bad,' he muttered back. 'You?'

'Awful,' she said. She put her arms around his neck again. 'I tried to find you at the funeral.'

'You did?' He'd avoided her all day, couldn't cope. 'I had to go. I'm sorry I didn't speak to you then.'

He'd been throwing up in the bushes in a muddy field behind the graveyard, sure she must blame him for everything. Who else had talked Jacko into flying at Cambridge, and later, teased him in the mess the week before he was shot down? Good joke, Dom – one of your better ones.

Jacko, screaming behind the Perspex of his cockpit and in flames. The rictus of his almost smile before his aircraft went down.

'I missed you.'

'You did. I—'

'But I can't talk now.' When she grabbed both his forearms, he saw she was slightly tight, not that he blamed her. 'I'm with someone.'

A tall chap got up from the booth, she put her hand on Dom's face and said: 'Wonderful to see you, Dom, you look as good as new. Sorry to hear about Annabel, by the way – come and have a drink with us soon.' She was gabbling, her new man frowning, and protective, sliding an arm around her waist.

Dom stood there frozen for a while, and when he turned, Saba was gone. Jilly had kept her hand on his arm while they were talking. Saba must have seen it all. When he went back to their table, their half-drunk cocktails were still there, the waiter hovering unsure.

'Did you see the lady go?' Dom asked him.

'Yes, sir. She must have left this.' The waiter dived underneath the table and came up with a blue coat over his arm. Dom took it and ran out into the street.

It was completely dark outside the restaurant now. The streets still wet. He ran almost all the way back down to the Theatre Royal, worried about her on her own, desperate to return the coat, to say goodbye properly. No sign of her. The crowds of London rushed by him, splashing him, no lights, no stars, the statue of Eros at Piccadilly all covered now to protect it from bombs.

When he reached the theatre, the doorman he'd bribed earlier stood under a dripping tarpaulin.

'Evening, gov,' he said. 'Stinking day, innit? You can stop inside if you like.'

'I need to find Saba Tarcan,' he said. 'She was at the audition earlier. I have her coat.'

'I don't know her, sir. We have hundreds coming every day at the moment. Do you want to leave it here in case she comes back for it?'

'No. No. I have her home address.' He'd suddenly remembered. 'I'll post it.'

No time left for him to try and find her; his leave was over the next day – he'd be training again for the next few weeks.

'Any idea where the company is going next?' he asked casually, fumbling for another half a crown.

'No idea whatsoever, sir.' The doorman looked stolidly ahead at the crowds and the rain, at London preparing itself for another night of bombs. 'But I suppose if I had to take a wild guess, I'd stick my pin in Africa.'

Chapter 6

There was no time to go home and say goodbye. After the injections and three days of rehearsals, Saba was fitted for her ENSA uniform, which she thought was pretty hideous: khaki, rather like the ATS uniform, with a badge on its shoulder, three Aertex shirts to go with it, two terrible-looking brassieres and some huge khaki-coloured knickers.

When she asked Arleta where she thought they were going, Arleta said Aertex shirts meant somewhere hot, but apart from that, not a clue: it could be an aerodrome, a desert camp, Malta, Cairo. 'From now on, darling,' she said, 'consider yourself a little pawn in the big boys' war game – you won't know a thing until the last minute, and if you try and work it out, you'll go a little mad.'

So more waiting, endless cups of tea, and then, on the Thursday of the following week, Saba, Arleta and Janine were told to pack a light bag and to tell no one they were leaving. Their families would be informed when it was safe to do so.

They waited all afternoon and half the night for the ghostly-looking blacked-out bus to pull up outside the Theatre Royal. Props and wig baskets were loaded, and when they hopped aboard, Saba was surprised to find the interior of the bus half empty. Sitting next to the driver were two ENSA staff: a bossy, relentlessly smiling man, all moustaches and a leather swagger stick, who said his name was Captain Crowley, and that he was responsible for their safety and welfare. Beside him, a pale young soldier was reading a map by torchlight.

The acrobats sat at the back, Willie, the comedian, next to Arleta, Janine pale as death at the front, and Saba in the middle of the bus, her feet, unfamiliar in their clumpy new shoes, resting on her kitbag. When the outskirts of London had given way to the blackness of countryside, Crowley handed them each a cardboard box with two stale cheese sandwiches in it, a tiny bar of chocolate and a bottle of water. He warned them to make it last: it could be some time before they reached where they were going.

Their plane touched down at four in the morning on a narrow strip of tarmac on the edge of a desert, under a night sky dazzling with millions of the brightest stars she'd ever seen. 'North Africa,' Arleta whispered, shortly before they landed. 'I've just heard.'

It was heaven to feel fresh air again, even though it was surprisingly cold and stank of petrol fumes. They stood at the edge of the runway, the wind blowing small heaps of sand around their feet. A truck arrived, seemingly from nowhere, with two British army officers inside it. They had guns tucked into their holsters. They shouted at some men wearing what looked like long nightshirts and stained woollen hats who swarmed on to the plane, deftly unloading the portable stage, a generator, and, to Willie's shouted instructions – ''Ere, watch it! Mind that!' – his ukulele case.

They were held up for hours while the paperwork was sorted out, and it was already getting warm by the time they left in a cloud of dust. Saba, peering through the truck's canvas flaps, felt a shiver of wonder move up her spine, at the sight of the desert stretching out as far as the eye could see, now stained with the beginnings of a blood-red sunrise.

Arleta fell asleep, her head resting on her kitbag, her hair spilling on to Saba's knee.

'I'd get some shut-eye if I were you,' she'd advised earlier. 'If we're going south, it's miles and miles of bugger all – we could be driving for days.'

But Saba was too excited. She'd been sick three times on the aeroplane, and felt, as it rose above the clouds and lurched and swooped, so bad not saying goodbye to Mum and Tan, it was like an empty ache inside her, an actual physical pain as if she'd been kicked. But this! Well . . . already hope was starting to bloom inside her like the sunrise. This was living! What she'd come for. The greatest adventure of her life so far.

Their truck accelerated through an abandoned airfield, lined with rolls of barbed wire and the rusted hulks of old aircraft, and once again she could see desert on either side of the long, straight road. The sand was crinkled and dark like the sea at dusk, and there, flat and parched as an overcooked omelette. A large sand dune, as big as hills at home, and then a waterhole winking like a ruby in the dawn light. The phenomenal space of it – such a relief after the cramped aircraft – dwarfed everything; it made their noisy truck feel as temporary and insubstantial as a child's toy.

When she woke, they were passing through a small village with flat-roofed mud houses on either side of them. A man standing outside his hovel was feeding a donkey from a bundle of bright green leaves. A woman drawing water from a well stopped and shielded her eyes as they passed.

The sun was frazzling her eyes and sweat dripped down the inside of her blouse and stuck her back to the lorry seat, which was almost too hot to touch. Captain Crowley, changed into khaki shorts and displaying long white legs, was making some sort of announcement. She heard his jaw grind. The matey version of Captain Crowley had gone; he was back in the army now. Janine, who sat on his right, listened as alert as the star pupil in a deportment class; opposite her, old Willie, cradling his head, an exhausted bulldog as he lifted his eyes.

'It needn't concern you where we are at the moment,' Crowley barked. 'All you need to know is that we expect to arrive in Cairo at roughly thirteen hundred hours. You three girls will be staying at the digs which are on Ibrahim Pasha Street just behind our offices. You chaps,' he said to the men, 'have temporary digs at the YMCA.'

The men were too tired and too hot to make jokes about leaving them. Willie in particular looked green with fatigue. Earlier, Arleta had confided in a perfumey whisper that he'd had heart troubles towards the end of his run in *Puss in Boots*, but he didn't want anyone to know about them. She said he was a tough old bird and that Dr Footlights would see him through, or he'd snuff it on stage, which would probably be the best possible thing for him anyway.

'At around sixteen hundred hours,' Crowley continued, 'assuming we can organise the transport, we'll pick you up again, and you'll be taken to our HQ in the Kasr-el Nil Street. If we can't, get a gharry. At HQ you'll be briefed about security arrangements, rehearsals and concerts. I'm afraid it's not going to be exactly a picnic from now on, but at least we won't be flying for a while.' He gave Saba a hard look, as if to say: *Listen, girl with three sick bags, I hope you're up to this.*

Their driver shifted gears and slowed down; they'd reached a ramshackle collection of tents, a grim little town. Saba saw two British soldiers do a perfect double-take as Arleta, freshly lipsticked and combed, gave them a regal wave. The men's thin faces swam into focus and disappeared into a dusty wake.

'Those poor sods look done in.' Willie had joined them at the back of the truck.

'I'm not surprised,' Crowley said quietly. 'It's been a long, hard slog, and there's worse to come.'

They were covered in a fine white dust by the time they arrived in Cairo, and the light was so bright that Saba felt her eyeballs shrink back in their sockets.

Their digs were on the top floor of what had once been a hotel but was now converted into flats. It was a narrow, stained building with small rusted wrought-iron balconies that overlooked the street. 'A bit of a dump,' Janine was quick to remark, gazing up at it mistrustfully.

An old Egyptian man in a djellaba welcomed them inside with a broad smile. His name, he said in broken English, was Abel; if they wanted anything, he was their man. They followed his battered sandals and cracked heels up to the first floor, where he stopped outside a door labelled *Female Latrines*. Inside, he proudly showed them a dim little bathroom with an old-fashioned geyser and a cracked lavatory with a huge bottle of DiMP repellent resting on the lid.

On the next floor was their small two-bedroomed flat with cool tiled floors. The sitting room, furnished with dark old-fashioned furniture and faded lithographs of desert scenes, gave on to the small balcony with intricately carved shutters on either side which overlooked the street. A woman padded into the room with a glass bowl with three oranges and three bananas in it. Saba's mouth filled with saliva. She hadn't eaten a banana since the war began.

'*Shukran*,' she said to the woman. 'They look lovely.' Adding in Arabic, 'This is a very nice place.'

'Blimey,' said Arleta when the door had closed again. 'Where did you learn to speak wog?'

Janine, who'd sat down, ankles crossed, on the edge of a cane sofa, looked equally startled, as if Saba had committed a serious faux pas.

'I grew up near Tiger Bay,' Saba explained. 'There were two Arab families living in our street and one of them was my friend, and by the way, it's not wog, it's Arabic.'

'What was an Arab doing in your street?' Janine had a superior way of lowering her eyelids when she spoke.

'There were all sorts there.' Saba resented her already. 'Greek, Somali – our fathers went to sea together. Still do. My father's a ship's engineer.'

Janine thought about this. 'So he's an educated man?'

'Yes. He reads books and everything.' Stuck-up idiot, Saba was thinking. She had half a mind to boast about how much her father knew about astrology, how many languages he spoke, how his own father had been the headmaster of a school, but decided against it. This was already the most words they'd ever said to each other.

'Well, gosh,' Janine said softly, with a slight shake of her head. She rearranged her elegant limbs. 'It takes all sorts.' The slight northern nasal twang broke through her carefully pitched voice. They stared at each other for a while.

'So.' Arleta leapt to her feet suddenly. 'I am absolutely pooped. Which bed do you want, darlings? I can sleep anywhere, so you two can fight it out for the spare room.'

Well in that case, Janine said, would it be all right if she slept alone? The slightest thing woke her up, and sometimes she liked to read at night.

'Absolutely fine, darling,' Arleta grinned.

Stopping only to pick up a banana, Janine left the room bouncing on the balls of her feet, like a principal ballerina leaving the stage after tumultuous applause.

'Oh for Christ's sake!' said Arleta, when the door had closed behind her. 'What horse did she ride in on?'

'I think she was in the corps de ballet somewhere,' Saba whispered back. 'She's quite posh.'

'Oh.' Arleta went all bendy for a moment and fluttered her arms in a perfect arabesque. 'Sorry I spoke.

'So.' She pointed towards a piece of faded chintz hanging from a pole. 'Which side of this beautiful wardrobe do you want?'

Saba didn't care. Her legs still felt fuzzy from the plane and her head was buzzing. While Arleta unpacked, she lay down fully dressed on the bed, and listened to the babble of sound in the street outside, the honk of traffic, the clip-clop of horses' feet.

When she woke up, Arleta was sitting on the bed opposite her. She was staring intensely at a photograph and then she put it away and wiped her eyes. It felt like a private moment so Saba pretended to be asleep, but through half-closed eyes examined Arleta.

Her feet were bare, and she'd changed into a peach silk nightdress that emphasised her narrow waist, her perfect bottom shimmering in silk.

She unpacked a pair of pink feathered slippers, the two gym-mistressy shirts that were standard army issue, a delicate pair of silver sandals, a khaki hat, a vanity bag bulging with little bottles, a penknife, a blonde wig, a gorgeously boned corset with satin drawstrings. This weird variety of things reminding Saba of a cardboard doll she'd had as a child that came with clothes to hook on for a marvellous variety of lives: glamour puss, vamp, ice skater, horsewoman.

And now . . . ah! Horrible! She was undoing a cloth bag and had taken a small animal out. She turned and laughed when she heard Saba gasp.

'Don't worry, pet, it's not alive.' As she held a mink stole against her face, Saba caught a draught of some rich perfume. 'But isn't it heaven? A present from an admirer, and absolutely useless here,' she said, 'but I couldn't bear to leave the poor thing behind.' She spoke about it softly, sadly, as though it really was alive.

Saba wondered who had given it to her, and if he was the one who had made her cry; she didn't know her well enough to ask yet.

There was a faint tang of soap in the air when Saba went into the bathroom later in the afternoon. She took off all her clothes and washed herself from head to foot. She felt shockingly adrift and needed a job to do. Couldn't bear to think of home at all. Mum in the floral chair by the fire, how her face would look. Janine had been at the basin before her, laying out her flannel, her toothbrush, her jar of aspirins and her shampoo, so neatly she might have used a set square to do so. Saba changed into a clean uniform shirt, brushed her hair, and gazed at herself in amazement. Was this really her? On her own, in Cairo, and part of a professional company?

*

They were out in the street now, in the blinding light and an oven blast of heat. Arleta, like the old hand she was, flagged down a gharry and instructed the driver to take them to the ENSA offices.

Crowley had warned them earlier that every hour was rush hour in Cairo at the moment: in the last three months more than 30,000 Allied troops had arrived from Canada, the US, Australia. When Lev, the acrobat, had asked why, Crowley had rolled his eyes and said, 'Polish, do you spend your entire life hanging upside down on a flaming trapeze? There's a war on here; the Germans are coming.' He'd given his hostile smile, and when he'd turned away, Lev had thrust his two fingers violently in the air at him and murmured, 'Bastard.' With an ugly look on his face.

Unreal city. Peeping from behind the stained curtains of the horse-drawn carriage clip-clopping through the streets, Saba almost forgot to breathe she was so excited. There were shops bursting with silks and clothes and shoes, dark passages like the mouths of tombs hung with handbags and pots, piles of mouth-watering oranges and peaches. On the narrow pavements, khaki-clad soldiers jostled for room alongside women holding children, a man on a donkey with huge candelabra on his back.

At the crossroads, a policeman stopped them as a red Studebaker car passed, narrowly avoiding a camel airily depositing a load of dung. When they slowed down outside a restaurant called Ali Baba's, Arleta informed them that this was where the troops drank. 'Other ranks, you know,' she said in a posh voice.

A couple of soldiers who seemed to have been drinking all afternoon appeared from the restaurant and did mock staggers at the sight of them. The little one whistled at them like a bird and waggled his hips.

'Oh honestly!' Janine shrank behind the soiled canvas of their gharry, her face almost comically prissy. 'If it's going to be like this, I'd just as soon go home.'

'Where are you going, darl?' the tall soldier asked Saba in an Aussie accent. He had a long scar on his face and a hungry expression.

'We're performing artistes.' Arleta's hair was dazzling in the sunlight. 'You'll have to come to our concerts to find out.'

'Woo-hoo, get you.' She'd made them laugh. 'So where will you be?' the other one insisted. Both men were jogging alongside their gharry now, much to the amusement of the driver, who made a playful attempt to touch one with his whip.

'We haven't got a single clue yet,' Arleta said. 'Watch for the posters.'

'I'll come, love,' the taller man assured Arleta breathlessly, 'but not him. He's as mean as shit.' More gasps from Janine. 'He's got snakes in his purse.'

Their carriage shot off. Their delighted driver shouting, 'Very naughty boys!'

'For goodness' *sake*!' When Janine pulled her skirt down, Saba noticed that she bit her nails quite badly. 'Why on earth encourage them?'

When they arrived at the offices and the driver discovered they had no money, his cheerful expression turned into an incredulous snarl. Rolling his eyes and clawing at his mouth, he made it plain that they had now ruined his life. His horse would never eat again; neither would his wife and four children.

'I'm so sorry,' Saba explained in her pidgin Arabic. 'No piastres, but if you wait, I will get.'

An army officer, thin and red-headed, burst down the narrow stairs apologising profusely. He said his name was Captain Nigel Furness. His freckled hand pressed a bundle of notes into the waiting driver's palm.

'We were going to pick you up ourselves,' he explained with a weary, insincere smile, 'but we're desperately short of transport. Four groups of talent arrived all at once, so a bit of a shambles.'

Willie and the acrobats waited for them in a cramped office on the first floor. Beside them, two uniformed typists clattered away at their typewriters surrounded by teetering piles of manila folders, and baskets labelled *Props*. A large fan ground away in the corner.

Furness sat down underneath a wall chart with a large map of Africa on it studded with pins. The sight of that map made Saba feel almost weak with excitement. She was here! This was it! God knows where they'd be going from now on!

Arleta, who had a fabulous walk, stately and self-regarding and designed to show off her body, took her time entering the room.

'Any chance of a cup of tea or a biscuit?' she asked Furness as soon as they'd sat down. She smoothed her skirt over her knees and added huskily, 'I'm starving, darling.'

Saba heard one of the secretaries titter softly and Willie murmur, 'Oh good girl.'

'Less of the darling, thank you.' Furness fought down a smirk, but his pale skin had flushed. 'We're in the army now.'

'Oh heavens! Sorry!' Arleta wiggled on her chair like a naughty schoolgirl and gave him her deadpan look. 'I shan't be bad again.' She gave Saba a slight wink; Furness turned his back on them and got busy with his wall map. In a muffled voice he asked one of the secretaries to bring them all tea.

Tea arrived in thick china cups stained with old brew-ups, with a plate of Garibaldi biscuits and they all fell on it. When Janine, sitting with her legs at an elegant slant, said only tea for her thank you, no sugar and no biscuit, they looked at her in amazement.

'You haven't eaten all day,' said Arleta, forgetting the banana.

'I may have some little thing tonight,' Janine said faintly. 'I eat like a bird even at the best of times.'

Furness, looking at Arleta over the rim of his cup, said, 'You should go out and have lunch after this. Can't think on an empty stomach.' He smiled, shy as a schoolboy.

When Arleta whispered, 'You're an angel,' and looked deeply into his eyes, one of the typists, a plain woman with hockey-player calves, rolled her eyes, but Saba was fascinated. Her own mother had once accused her of being a born flirt and she had found the remark confusing – it seemed to her that if you liked someone you let them know. It was not a thing you decided to do – well not always. But with Arleta it was like watching a flirting champion in action; there was a hot teasing energy about her performance that felt like a game, and she didn't give a damn who saw her.

Furness stood up quickly. 'I think we'd better crack on.' He moved purposefully towards his wall chart. 'For obvious reasons,' he picked up a pointed stick, 'there's only so much we can or want to tell you about the current situation in Egypt and the Mediterranean, except to say in the most general terms that what happens here in the next few months could be, in strategic and political terms, absolutely vital to the outcome of this war.'

He stuck a piece of blank paper on his wall chart.

'So, potted history,' he continued. 'In the last three months, Allied troops have been pouring into Cairo from Canada, the US, Australia. Why have they come? Well, now France has fallen and large parts of the Mediterranean have been cut off, there aren't many places where our lot and the Commonwealth troops can engage the Germans.'

He drew a vast spider with legs on his sheet of paper. 'We're at the centre of this.' He pointed to the body of the creature he had drawn, then scrawled a rough approximation of Egypt, with Libya on one side and the Suez Canal on the other. 'Our boys are here to protect these areas.' He pointed towards Suez, and the oil fields in Iraq and Iran. 'Down here,' he indicated an empty space below his map, 'we have thousands of men in the desert. Some of them have been here since 1940, and they've had a pretty tough time of it. The heat, as you'll find out, is merciless, food and ammunition often in short supply. They're desperately in need of some light relief.'

Janine was chewing the inside of her lip; she was staring at the map. Arleta wound a strand of hair round her index finger.

'I'm telling you this,' all vestiges of public-school bonhomie had gone as Furness let his gaze travel from one face to the next, 'because some of the artistes who've been here recently have thought of Cairo as a kind of foxhole, or a rest cure. It's not, and it's important that you understand the gravity of the situation at this present point. As a matter of fact,' he lowered his voice, 'HQ were on the point of cancelling this tour, and it's still entirely possible that you may have to be evacuated at a moment's notice. I say this not to frighten you – we'll do everything we can to keep you safe – but to warn you.'

'Can't you even tell us where we're going?' Janine asked in a strained voice. 'No one's said a thing yet.'

'You'll be moving quite a bit in the next few weeks,' Furness said. 'You'll have to learn to be flexible about arrangements. At the moment,' he sighed heavily and mopped his brow with a handkerchief, 'I'm not sure whether you'll be in a Sunderland Flying Boat, a lorry or a hearse, and I'm not joking.'

Arleta and Saba laughed anyway; Janine's left foot was tapping the floor, her eyes were closed as if she was praying.

'I travelled in a pig lorry in Malta,' Arleta told them. 'The pong – indescribable. I had to wash my hair for days afterwards.' She lifted it in her hands and let it fall in shining waves around her shoulders.

'So, splendid, splendid.' Furness looked at her with relief. 'You know the score.' He glanced at his watch. 'Some forms for you to fill in.' He handed out seven buff-coloured cards. 'Don't bother with them now, do them over breakfast.'

'What's an N15?' asked Janine.

'If you're captured,' Furness said, 'it's to let the enemy know that you're now members of the British Armed Forces. Let's hope you don't need it.

'Couple more things: food – don't eat from local stalls, or drink water without boiling it. The rule with fresh food is: can you boil it or peel it? If not, forget it. Locals: never walk around on your own here, not around the camps and never, never in the native areas. Some of their men have the wrong idea about our women.' He cleared his throat. 'They think you're, how shall I put this . . . ?'

'Pushovers,' Arleta said helpfully. 'A man once offered two thousand sheep for me in West Africa. I probably should have taken it.'

'That sort of thing.' Furness's thin skin had flushed faintly again. He ripped his spider diagram from the chart and seemed anxious to be rid of them.

'So, what about pay?' Arleta prompted. 'Or did I miss that bit?'

'Ah. Sorry.' Furness unlocked his desk and handed each one of them a small manila envelope. 'Here's your first week's salary: ten pounds each in advance. From now on you'll be collecting it from the NAAFI. But by the looks of you, you could do with a good meal today. Also, while you're on tour you have officer status and are entitled to use the mess.'

On their way down the clattery stairs he told them they would start rehearsing the next day and do a couple of concerts before the end of the week. 'We're hoping Max Bagley will get here tonight,' he said. 'He's your tour director.' He hesitated for a moment. 'As long as you do what he says, I don't think you'll have any problems with him. He's certainly experienced. That's all for now. Dismissed.' Their brief conversation had ended.

Chapter 7

Dear Saba, he'd written to her,

> *I am so sorry about the other night. It must have looked very strange to you, but that girl was not a girlfriend, but someone who has recently lost a chap I flew with, a friend. When you are cleared for security, let me know where you are.*

He couldn't bring himself to go into more detail about Jacko; it felt cheap to use him as an excuse.

Jilly had kept her hand on his arm while they were talking. Saba had seen it all. When that other chap had left the table to claim her, Jilly had given Dom a guilty smile and he'd probably returned it. How strange that grief might look so like lust.

Dear Pilot Officer Benson, her mother had replied,

> *I wonder if you can help me? I happened to open, in error, the letter you sent to my daughter. She's gone away to . . .* the censor had cut a large hole here, *and we've not heard a word since. Have you? I wonder if, being in the services, you might find out more information for us. My husband and I are very worried about her.*
>
> *Yours sincerely,*
> *Joyce Tarcan*

He was stationed at Brize Norton when he got the letter, training young pilots, champing at the bit because it was so much quieter now than the Battle of Britain days, and when they weren't flying, the air in the mess was stale with boredom, endless games of cribbage, cigarette smoke. He'd gone as soon as he could get a day's leave, grateful for a semi-legitimate reason for doing so.

As the train entered the Severn Tunnel, Dom felt a denser

darkness outside him. He heard the hissing of steam as the brakes went on, and then the vague announcement from a sleepy guard that they might be here for quite a long time.

This was greeted by jeering and good-natured laughter from the other passengers in the stuffy carriage – delays were an inevitable part of life now. But Dom, sweating in his greatcoat, felt both feverish and furious with himself. Since the crash, he'd suffered from a form of claustrophobia, which he knew he had to fight if he was to fly in combat again. These attacks leapt at him with no warning, the first sign a crushing in the throat, a sense that his whole body had been transformed into a violently overworking pump that would explode if he didn't breathe properly, or run somewhere. He was dismayed that even a train stuck in a tunnel could affect him this way.

He sat breathing heavily with his head down, sweating, terrified, and when the feeling passed, as it usually did, he asked himself what he was doing on this wild goose chase anyhow. The girl had gone to North Africa, or so the doorman had hinted, she'd have no use for the blue overcoat which he'd placed in the luggage rack above his head. In the right-hand pocket of the coat, he'd found a delicate filigree gold charm shaped like the palm of a hand. He'd put it in the pocket of his greatcoat. It was new.

He touched the charm now. As a boy, he'd been obsessed by magic amulets, and he recognised this one as a Hamsa hand, which was supposed to ward off the evil eye, the envy of others, the kind of envy that could kill a person's dreams and wishes stone dead. The reason why peasant Egyptian mothers dirtied up the faces of their children, why English children were taught not to boast.

Cambridge and the RAF had trained him out of magic-thinking guff, but nevertheless his fingers had clutched the gold charm during his fear attack as if the tiny hand would help him. And when his heartbeat had slowed to normal, and the prickling sweat on his body had dried, he mocked himself: Dom, the great cynic, was on a train going nowhere – oh the potency, et cetera of cheap music.

A pretty WAAF sat opposite him, stockinged legs gracefully aslant, clumpy shoes carefully arranged. She unwrapped a packet of sandwiches and asked if he would care for one. When he said no thank you, she ate hers daintily, and, after wiping her mouth with a handkerchief, asked what squadron he was flying with now.

When he said none as yet, she began a tentative conversation about some friend of hers in 55 Squadron who was flying night fighters over France. Her eyes were questing: Are you enjoying this? Am I going too far? She had a heart-shaped face and auburn hair. Good legs, too. On another day, in another mood, he might have answered her properly. They might have had a drink together later that night, exchanged telephone numbers, gone at some point to bed. That was the way of it now: you took comfort where you could, and she looked like a nice girl, a good sport. He sensed her smile fading as he glanced at his newspaper again.

Half asleep, he heard another soldier talking to her. The scrape of matches as they lit up fresh cigarettes. The pleasant burr of the man's Gloucestershire accent was telling the girl that this same train had been chased only a few weeks ago by a German fighter plane, and how the engine driver had put his foot down to ninety miles an hour. She replied, pleasantly, 'Gosh, I hope that doesn't happen again today,' with a mildly discouraging conversation-closed thread running through her voice. Who could ever fathom the randomness of human desire? Why him, now feigning sleep behind his newspaper; why not her?

He was thinking of Saba's eyes now, dark brown or mid brown? They'd gazed at him like caged animals through the veil of that mad little hat; they'd glowed with life. And one of the songs she'd sung, about God blessing the child who'd got it's own, was a plea for independence, for life, for dignity, but not, now he came to think of it, for a man.

She was pretty, no doubt about it, but he'd had plenty of time in hospital to mistrust mere attractiveness in another human being. He thought about the girls who'd run screaming from the ward when they'd seen the new faces of their former loves. Annabel had at least exited with some degree of decorum, assuring him over and over again it wasn't him, it was what she'd termed vaguely, her pale blue eyes flickering as they did when she was being sincere, 'the whole situation'. A thought which led him to Peter, a close friend from Cambridge, a man with a passion for girls, T. S. Eliot and cars. It was Peter who had sat on a bridge near the Cam and read to him aloud from the *Four Quartets*: *Teach us to care and not to care* was the line Dom suddenly recalled.

A year before his aircraft had been shot down over France, Peter had bought himself a dazzlingly green Austin 10 for £8 from a local mechanic. He was amazed by his good luck and they'd driven like the clappers through the Oxfordshire countryside in it on one glorious day in summer. The car exploded after a week, and the last time Dom had seen Peter, he was sitting on the grass, its remnants spread around him.

'It's my fault,' Peter said. 'I was a fool. I was taken in by the colour like a girl with beautiful eyes.' After a short silence he'd added: 'It's a hopeless fucking machine.'

It was still dark in the tunnel. To give himself something to do, Dom read the mother's letter again by torchlight. When he'd first read it, he'd felt the sting of disappointment – so Saba had definitely and defiantly gone – and he'd been longing in his impatient way to put the thing to rest. But then he'd felt something like relief.

Because what did he know about the girl? Only that she sang, and that he admired her courage, and that for that one moment, when he had told her where his skin graft had come from, they'd both roared with laughter like young people again.

There were moments like that in life, he thought, that you couldn't really explain or understand but that had the perfect rightness of a billiard ball falling smoothly into a pocket, or of a mountain bend taken at high speed, but with a slowed-down perfection.

And the bird called, in response to the unheard music hidden in the shrubbery. Oh what a perfect bloody fool he had become. He blamed the war.

A light rain was falling over Cardiff Bay as he walked towards Pomeroy Street. It fell softly over a pearly sea where there was barely a line between water and sky, and blurred the edges of a row of houses above which the seagulls cried. It splattered on the tarpaulins protecting the vegetables outside a Middle Eastern grocer's shop on the edge of Loudon Square. This is where Saba lives, he thought.

He put up the collar of his greatcoat and checked his watch. He had a twenty-four-hour leave: three hours at the most between now and the return train.

A woman in a sari with a mackintosh over it smiled at him at the street corner. A boy went by on a bicycle: 'Where's your plane, mista?' he said.

At the corner of the next street, a house sliced in half by a bomb stood shamefully exposed, like a girl with her knickers down, or a shabby stage set with its faded rose wallpaper, and green cooker, and sooty rafters. A poor house, in a struggling poor street.

Saba's streets. 'The notorious Tiger Bay.' She'd warned and teased him with it.

Because she had a natural dignity and the stateless confidence of an artiste, he had not given much thought to her background, and was struggling now to hold those two images of her together in his mind. Annabel's parents had owned a lovely old Tudor house in Wiltshire with a moat with swans and ducks floating on it, as well as an apartment at Lincoln's Inn. His own mother had thoroughly approved of them, their cleverness, their impeccable furniture, their season ticket to Glyndebourne. She'd probably planned his wedding in their garden. He hadn't had the heart to tell her yet.

The front door of the house in Pomeroy Street had a brass knocker shaped like a lion's head. He took a deep breath and banged it.

An old lady appeared wearing a black dress and Wellington boots. Her eyes gleamed from the gloom of the hall – dark and inquisitive.

All the way here, walking down the sooty streets that led to the bay and to Pomeroy Street, he'd had a conversation with himself which had ended in an agreement. He was here simply to return the blue coat; if her mother wanted help, he would do what he could in a dignified way and then beat a discreet and hasty retreat. There must be no whiff of the stage-door Johnny about him; it was a simple act of kindness.

But the old lady's face lit up immediately when she saw him; she put her hand on his sleeve and became immensely animated.

'Quick, Joyce!' she shouted over her shoulder, as if he was the prodigal son. 'Come! Come quickly. The boy is here!'

A door at the end of the corridor burst open and a handsome woman, fortyish he guessed, came towards him. Her thick dark hair looked freshly waved and she was wearing lipstick. A woman who kept herself nicely, or who had dressed up especially for his visit.

She led him into the parlour on the right of the hall – a cosy room with a small fire burning in the grate. In the corner was a piano with a sheet of music on the stand. The old lady saw him glance at it and smiled encouragingly.

'I can play,' she boasted. 'Saba ma teach me. She like very much.'

'Tansu,' the younger woman said firmly, 'go and take your boots off. I'll make Mr Benson a cup of tea – or would you prefer coffee? We have both.'

'Coffee, please,' he said. 'If you have enough,' and then, embarrassed, 'I mean, with rationing and everything.'

'Turkish? English? My husband works on the ships, that's one thing we do have.'

'Turkish, please.' He'd never had it before, but why not? Everything was strange enough already.

'Oh, and I've called you Mister.' She gazed at him warily. 'And forgotten your rank.'

'Pilot officer,' he said. His rapid commission had never felt quite real to him anyway; it felt unearned, like being alive again.

He glanced quickly at the wall of books, and the gramophone, with a pile of records neatly stacked beside it. These were not what he thought of as normal working-class people.

Above the gramophone there was a framed photograph of a stout-looking woman in sunglasses standing proudly in front of the Sphinx.

'Umm Kulthum.' The old lady had returned. She was wearing a pair of floral carpet slippers, and looked at the photograph with a look of extreme adoration on her face. 'Very, very good.' She gestured towards the records and touched one or two gently. 'Beautiful,' she said softly.

While they waited for coffee, she brought him another photograph and put it down gently on his lap. It was Saba. She was standing in front of a band wearing a long dress of some satin shiny stuff; she had a flower in her hair and was smiling that reckless smile towards an audience of young men with short hair and boyish necks. Like sea anemones searching for light or food, they leaned towards her in the gloom of what looked like a large hangar. Knowing what terrible thoughts lurked inside them brought a moment of insecurity. This visit was ridiculous.

'Saba and the Spring Tones,' the old lady was proudly explaining to him. She held up two fingers. 'Second concert . . .' And she mimed boisterous clapping. Her carpet slippers did a little shuffling dance.

'Tansu.' Joyce came back with a tinkling tray. 'Take the poor man's coat, let him have his cup of coffee. Please.'

'Thinking of coats . . .' He handed her the bag at his feet. 'Saba left hers – we were having a drink together.'

'Ah, Lord.' The mother put down the tray and snatched the coat out of the bag. 'Goodness me, she's careless. Typical. Look . . . I don't want to be rude, but how long have you got?' She fixed her eyes on him. 'I'm on shift work. I've got less than an hour.'

'My train leaves at four,' he said. 'I'm flying tomorrow.' He said this to comfort himself, not to boast.

'And do you fly Spitfires or Hurricanes?' The polite hostess again, pouring his coffee from a small brass pot.

'Harvards at the moment,' he said. 'I'm at a retraining unit. I actually met your daughter in hospital. I had a bit of a prang over France. I'm all right now.'

'I can see that.' She smiled for the first time.

'She came to sing for us.'

'Yes, she did a bit of that before she left . . .' Her expression was thin-lipped and guarded again. She took a sip of her own coffee, and then put it down and sighed sharply.

The old lady had returned, this time with a bowl of chickpeas on a wooden plate.

'Please.' She pointed towards them. 'Eat. Come on.'

'Thank you, Mrs Tarcan.'

'Tansu,' she said firmly. She put her hand over her somewhat magnificent bosom. 'My name is Tansu.

'Oh!' She'd seen the blue coat, and her gnarled fingers touched the cloth tenderly, as if it was a holy relic.

'Tell me more about where you met Saba,' the mother said.

At the mention of her name, the grandmother let out a groan and fixed her anxious old eyes on Dom. Joyce fiddled with her cup; she hadn't taken a sip yet.

'I was in hospital. East Grinstead,' he said. 'She came to sing – she said she was a last-minute replacement.'

He looked at Joyce, who was sitting on the edge of her chair. *Go, go, go, said the bird.*

'I thought she was wonderful.' For a moment they looked straight at each other.

'Yes,' said Joyce. She shook her head and gave a deep sigh. 'And *selfish.*'

Her voice shuddered with suppressed fury.

'Selfish?'

'Yes.' She swallowed hard and put her cup down. 'We haven't had a night's sleep since she left.'

'Where is she?'

'That's the point, we don't know.'

The old lady had been following their conversation with her eyes, she let out an almost inaudible squeak and covered her face with her apron.

'Tansu, would you get cake. Get *cake* from the kitchen.' When she was gone Joyce said, 'She doesn't understand everything, but I don't want her to hear this. She cries herself to sleep every night.'

Dom saw she had blue circles under her eyes, the numb look of panic barely held in check.

'You have no idea where she is?'

'We had an aerogramme a week or so ago saying she was in Egypt. In Cairo and leaving soon. We were not to worry. Since then – nothing.'

He saw the effort it took to control herself, and felt for the first time in his life the desolation of those left behind. He hadn't allowed himself to think like this before – of his own mother, in her cold sitting room, stitching and waiting, or lying in the dark listening for the slow rumble overhead of a plane that might be his.

'A week isn't long,' he reminded her gently. 'The posts are terrible. Where is . . . is there . . . ?' He asked this delicately. You couldn't assume anything nowadays.

'Her father?'

'Yes.'

She directed his gaze towards the mantelpiece. The man in the photograph had a strong-jawed, handsome face, piercing dark eyes, thick black hair – he didn't look English.

'His name is Remzi,' she said. 'He's an engineer with Fyffes. He hasn't spoken to me since this happened.' She shuddered. 'He blames me for everything.'

The old lady had returned with the cake tin in one hand and a lute-like instrument in the other.

'This mine. Tambur.' She held the thing up proudly.

'Ah, a household of musicians,' he said politely.

'She doesn't play it; her husband did,' the mother said. 'But there's lots of music down here in the Bay – we actually had Hoagy Carmichael come here before the war broke out.'

The old lady put the cake down on the table. She held out a new photograph.

'My son,' she said. 'I have four sons: three finish.' Her face twisted. 'He no here now. When he—'

'Tan, leave it to me,' Joyce almost shouted. 'Please!'

'When she go,' the old lady ignored her, 'when she go,' she pointed towards Saba's photograph, 'he . . .' She picked up an imaginary stick and mimed a beating, then she shook her head violently. 'Very very bad,' she said.

In the short silence that fell, Joyce fiddled with the coffee cups.

'It's true,' she said at last. 'He's not a violent man, but he was furious with her when he found out she'd been performing. ENSA was the last blimmin' straw. But what could she do?' she asked him, her eyes naked. 'Singing's like breathing for her, she needed to do it, and all of us encouraged her at first – he was as proud as Punch himself. You've heard her.'

'I understand,' he said. 'I really do.'

The old woman's eyes fixed on them again, and then she leapt up and fumbled with the lid of the gramophone, as if she wanted to play them something.

'Not now, Tan,' Joyce said. 'I don't have time. I need to say this quickly.

'Look at me running on.' She smiled suddenly, 'I haven't a clue why you're here.'

'Well . . . really to . . .' He looked at the blue coat, ashamed of the flimsy lie already.

'But can you help, now you know the situation?' Her eyes brightened at the thought of it.

'Maybe, I don't know. Is there anything else you're worried about?'

'Well . . . it sounds a bit silly, but my husband thinks there's something fishy going on.'

'Why?'

'Well, normally, you have to be twenty-five to get into ENSA; she's twenty-three, and she was gone in a flash; normally, he says, they'd leave a few months for the jabs against yellow fever, the forms, and the other stuff. Where was the rush?'

'Maybe they just needed entertainers there fast – I think something like three and a half thousand Allied troops have moved to

North Africa to be with the Eighth Army.' His mind was racing furiously. The desert war was where the action was now.

'I don't even understand what we're doing in Africa,' she said mournfully. 'It seems such a long way away.'

'It is,' he said gently. He briefly thought of explaining its strategic importance, but this was not the time for a history lesson, and half his mind anyway was thinking about 89 Squadron's wing in North Africa. He'd been there once on a training run, two weeks waiting in the desert, mostly drinking bad gin by a wadi waiting for a fight.

'It's not impossible,' he said out loud. Flying through the vast emptiness of it, the huge blue skies, the closest he'd ever come to being a bird.

'Do you know anyone there?' she said.

'Not many – a few.' It felt wrong to raise her hopes. 'But to go back to what you were saying. Why does your husband think they want her there?'

'I don't know,' she said, her expression closed. 'You'd have to ask him. He could be exaggerating it all. He has terrible memories of Turkey and that part of the world. Lots of people disappeared from his village during the First World War. He was away at sea. He thinks his brothers were executed. Poor bugger.' She sighed heavily. 'No wonder he's frightened.'

'Does Saba know this?'

'No. She's his little ray of sunshine – or was. He wanted to keep her like that.'

'What was she like?' The question popped out. 'As a child, I mean.'

'Naughty, wonderful! My auntie once said, "I've never known a child light up a room like she does." Headstrong. We used to go up to the valleys to see my parents; they had this horse and cart, and she always wanted to take over the reins, even when she was four years old. "Give them to me, Mam! I can do it! You're not the boss of this horse and cart." When the horse ran away with us one day she loved it, said it was the best day of her life!'

She was a pretty woman when she laughed like that.

'She was mad keen on all kinds of singers: Billie Holiday, Dinah Shore, Helen Forrest. When we got her the record of "Deep Purple", she must have played the thing five million times, it drove us mad, and she'd be up there in her bedroom hour after hour, learning the phrasing.

'But careless.' She glared at the coat again. 'Half the time she's thinking of songs, so . . .' She looked up suddenly. 'Look, will you help if you can?'

'I don't know. She's probably fine. The posts are famously slow there – you'll probably get a letter as soon as I leave.'

'I'm torn,' Joyce said. 'She did sound happy, she's always happy when she's working, but she's much too gullible.'

'If I should find myself there,' he was thinking hard, 'what should I say to her? I can't just turn up a perfect stranger, or almost, and order her home.' The absurdity of this had suddenly struck him.

'No! No! No! Don't do that.' Joyce's face had suddenly lit up, and she'd shed ten years. 'It's a wonderful experience for her. Just go and see her. I don't know, tell her I do understand but . . . I just want to know she's safe.'

She glanced at the clock on the mantelpiece. It was four twenty.

'I've got to go,' she said.

'Me too.'

'If you like, we can walk down together.'

'Last question.' He felt he had to know. 'Do you open all her letters? I mean, the ones other people send to her.'

'Most of them.' She looked at him defiantly. 'I don't want her father to be any angrier than he is already, and nor would you if you knew him.'

'And has anyone else written to her?'

'Only young men like yourself.'

The stab of envy he felt was sharp and took him by surprise. He had no right to feel like that about her, but he did.

'You mean, men who've heard her sing?'

'Yes, and Paul, of course.'

'Paul?'

'Her fiancé, for a second,' Joyce said bitterly. 'Fine young man, training to be a schoolteacher, lovely family. He would have married her like a shot. She left him shortly before she went to London, got out of the car one night and ran off in a paddy. I still don't really know what happened, but he's broken-hearted. People like her are a bit like electricity, on a different wattage – they don't realise how badly they can hurt people.'

A warning, this, or a threat? He couldn't be sure.

But later, as they walked together down Pomeroy Street, he

found himself filled with a tremendous, impatient unexpected excitement.

He needed a new challenge – he wanted to fly and fight again for complicated reasons, not all of them to do with Jacko. Saba's presence would add to the adventure; provided he could approach it all in a light-hearted, cautious way, he was pretty sure he would not get his fingers burned.

Chapter 8

CAIRO

The girls had started to breakfast in the courtyard restaurant of the Minerva, a small hotel around the corner from their flat. It was a pretty spot, with jasmine and bougainvillea scrambling up its walls, and a small fountain in the middle splashing water with a gentle, silky sighing sound that was hypnotic. A couple of weeks after they'd arrived, Saba was sitting there on her own when a lanky Englishman sauntered over.

He introduced himself with a charming smile. 'My name's Dermot Cleeve. I do some of the Forces recordings for the BBC. I'm hoping to meet you all soon.' As if to reassure her this wasn't a pick-up.

He was young, good-looking, with his long aquiline nose and very intelligent blue eyes. She took off her sunglasses. They were the first pair she'd ever owned, and she was ridiculously pleased with them. She slid them into their pigskin sheath.

'The other girls have been held up,' she said, in fact by a fierce squabble over the bathroom. She toyed with the idea of lighting up a cigarette, another new habit, but was worried it would make her cough.

'Would it be a frightful bore if I joined you for coffee?' Cleeve asked. 'I'll shove off when the others come.'

'Of course not,' she answered. There was a small pause while he sat down and placed his panama hat carefully on the chair beside him.

Samir, her favourite waiter, bounced through the beaded curtain brandishing a silver platter above his head piled with fresh peaches, melons and bananas. He'd been delighted to find that Saba was half-Turkish, and already made a fuss of her.

'Your usual breakfast, madame?' he said. Every morning so far they'd indulged in real coffee and real eggs and real butter and eaten the small M*oza cavendishii* bananas, which they declared the best and tastiest in the world.

'I'll wait for the others,' she said, putting on her sunglasses and putting a cigarette in her holder. 'I can't believe the food here,' she told Cleeve. 'It makes me feel such a heel after rationing.'

'Oh, you mustn't feel like that.' He clicked his lighter and held the flame towards her. 'Enjoy it while you can; it'll be hard tack and bully beef once you get on the road. Do you know when you're leaving, by the way?'

'No, not yet.'

'It won't be long,' he said. When he stretched out his legs, the two small birds that had been tussling over a bread roll under the table flew away.

Samir fussed around them for a while, adjusting napkins and pouring coffee. When she asked him how he was that morning, he turned his radiant smile on her and said, '*Il-hamdu li-llah*,' and Cleeve smiled at her lazily, approving.

'What did he say?'

'*Il-hamdu li-llah* means God be thanked – it covers everything from "fine" to "I'm at death's door but mustn't grumble".'

'And do you always speak to waiters in their own language?'

'No,' she laughed. 'Only a few words. My father taught me – he's actually Turkish.' She stubbed out her cigarette: ugh! It would take a while to learn to like it.

Cleeve took two sugars and stirred them into his coffee.

'So you speak Turkish?' He pushed his floppy boy's hair out of the way and squinted at her through the sun, amused and curious.

'I can get by in it. We spoke it at home.'

The two sparrows were back again, pecking furiously at the bread.

'Cheeky blighters,' he grinned. 'They must be the fattest birds in Cairo – they probably have to rent that pitch.'

There was a small commotion at the door to the restaurant. Arleta had arrived, her uniform tightly belted, hair gleaming in the sunlight.

'Listen,' he rose quickly, 'I'm going to shove off and leave you to your friends. Bon appétit.

'Oh, I meant to ask you.' He picked up his hat, and turned. 'Where are you rehearsing?'

'At the old cinema in Mansour Street,' she told him. 'Today's our first proper rehearsal with Max Bagley.'

'Nervous?' His smile was quizzical.

'A little.'

'I might pop by later,' he said. 'I've known Bagley since Oxford. We've done a few programmes together.'

She hoped he'd add, 'You must come and sing on one,' but he didn't.

'Don't be frightened of Bagley, by the way,' were his last words. 'He has a terrifying reputation but he's actually a sheep in wolf's clothing, and very, very talented. You'll learn from him.'

'Nice,' Arleta said approvingly, watching Cleeve's elegant back disappear. 'What did he want?'

'He said he runs the Forces broadcasts here,' Saba said. 'D'you know him?'

'No, they change their producers all the time, but a bit dishy, I thought.'

'He was charming too,' said Saba. 'Very friendly. I'll be twenty stone if I go on like this,' she added, putting butter on her second hot roll. 'These are the best breakfasts I've ever had.'

'All right today?' Arleta took her hand and gazed at her kindly. When she'd caught Saba having a gasping, choking cry in the bathroom the night before, she'd put down her sponge bag and given her a huge hug.

'I'm fine,' Saba said. 'You know, it's just . . .' The homesickness had pounced on her like a wild animal; she hadn't expected it, still couldn't talk about it with complete confidence. That look on her mother's face as the train pulled out. Her last wave. She wished she hadn't made that mean remark before she left about Mam never standing up for herself . . . Who would in her shoes? And now, what if a bomb dropped on her? On Tan, on all of them?

Arleta patted her hand. 'It's like a kick in the guts sometimes – but you're doing fine, kiddo, and we'll be working soon.'

'I'll be better then.' Correct. Work was a powerful anaesthetic as well as everything else, but she was starting to well up again, and was hoping Arleta would stop talking now and eat breakfast. Samir had just swooped with more coffee and a fresh basket of buttery croissants.

'Ladies, please – more, more, more,' he said, anticipating their pleasure. 'You are too . . .' He brought his hands in to show disapproval at their tiny waists, and turned his mouth down.

'They do so love a pinger here,' Arleta said when he'd gone.

'And a pinger is?' Saba put on her sunglasses.

'The kind of fat lady who goes *ping!* when you do this.' Arleta poked her finger in Saba's side.

They were laughing when Janine arrived looking pale and almost transparently thin in this bright sunshine. As she sat down, a plane thundering overhead made their table shudder. She'd slept badly, thank you very much: too many flies, too much noise from the street. When Samir arrived with his fruit platter, she waved him away saying it would give her a gippy tummy – she'd have black tea and a piece of toast instead.

A mangy cat regarded her. It moved from its spot in the shade and rubbed its back against her legs.

'Don't touch it, don't talk to it.' Janine's eyes were trained on her tea. 'A friend of mine with Sadler's Wells had to have twenty-eight injections in her tummy after being bitten by a cat in West Africa. She's still not right. Shoo! Shoo! Away, you foul creature.' She aimed an elegant kick at the cat. Another friend, poor woman, she continued, wiping her mouth carefully with her napkin, had got lost in a jeep in the Western Desert. A sand storm. She and the rest of the company had run out of water and had to drink their, you know, natural fluids, until they were rescued on the point of death.

'Were you always such a cock-eyed optimist?' Arleta asked her when this was over, and Janine had called for more hot water and perhaps a slice of lemon.

'It won't be hot – the water,' she said when Samir had gone. 'They never get it right. I'm being a realist,' she continued. 'You heard what Captain Furness said, we shouldn't even be here, most of the companies have been evacuated. There's no point in being an ostrich.'

And Saba felt momentarily out of focus. There was another world out there, as close as the dark kitchen behind the beaded curtain, a world that might hurt them.

A dog appeared from the shade of a jasmine bush. It flopped down under their table and looked at her with its pale amber eyes. When she absent-mindedly patted its head, Janine almost shouted, '*Don't!* I said don't,' and then apologised. 'I'll be better when we start working,' she said. 'I'm more highly strung than I look, you know.'

Arleta sagged and rolled her eyes behind Janine's back, but Saba, for the first time, felt sorry for her. Sometimes it seemed realistic to be scared.

Their rehearsal studio at Mansour Street smelt strongly of Turkish cigarettes and faintly of urine. Once a cinema, none of the overhead fans worked and the poorly converted stage was rickety and inclined to give them splinters in their feet, but they were, as Furness impatiently explained to them, lucky to have it – there was a desperate shortage of accommodation in Cairo that month, with more and more troops flooding in.

Max Bagley, their musical director, a small, plump, carelessly dressed man in a cravat, was standing at the door looking livid when they arrived. Behind him, the straggling notes of a trumpet warming up, a burst of violin music.

'You're late.' He tapped the watch on his hairy wrist. 'I said ten thirty, not ten forty-five. Do that again and I'll dock your wages. I've got a band here ready to go.'

They'd been told via Arleta, who knew a friend who knew a friend, that before the war Bagley, a one-time organ scholar at Gonville and Caius, Cambridge, had been a rising star in London in the world of sophisticated revues and musical comedies. According to Arleta's friend, although he was a plain little man, half the women who worked with him ended up in love or in bed with him. Honest to the point of cruelty, his secret was to make you feel he had understood yours, and that he would do his level best to bring out the best in you, which, let's face it, not many men did, Arleta had concluded.

During their ticking-off, Janine flushed with rage. She travelled with two alarm clocks in case one malfunctioned and had wanted them to leave earlier, but Arleta had insisted there was masses of time, which there was until a car in front of them had broken down and the road ahead was blocked by shrieking men striking their foreheads.

When Arleta blustered, 'Darling, we're absolutely mortificato, we—' Bagley snapped, 'My name is Mr Bagley; I'll let you know when I want you to call me darling.'

'Oops,' said Arleta softly to Saba as they walked into their dressing room, 'crosspatch.' But Saba admired the way she didn't make a big fuss about it, or look too mortified herself. Arleta, she was beginning to understand, had a core of pure steel.

It was bone-meltingly hot. Saba's fingers slipped as she fumbled with the hooks and eyes on her black skirt and wrestled on her leotard and tap shoes. She pulled her hair tightly behind her head, and put on a slick of lipstick. Janine, panicked by being late, did something out of character and stood by the window bare-bottomed, saying 'Don't look' as she wrestled her pink tights on.

'Absolutely nobody is looking at your bottom,' Arleta said, running her tongue around scarlet lips.

'So, ready, girls?' she said when they were all dressed and standing by the door. 'Into the mouth of the dragon.'

They walked on to the stage where Bagley was talking to Willie and the Polish acrobats, also late, and a scruffy-looking six-piece band, The Joy Boys, who had been in Cairo for three months now. Willie was giving Arleta an elaborate eyes, mouth and chest salaam when Bagley said, 'That's enough of that, let's get cracking.'

He stood in front of them, sweating and fierce, and told them to regard themselves, at least for the next few weeks, as artistic sticking plaster and not really a fully fledged touring company. There were too few of them for that, and as they probably already knew, there was a distinct possibility all of them would soon have to be evacuated from Cairo. He warned them that this work was cumulatively exhausting, and if they went over the top too soon they'd be in trouble. A previous performer, he said, had got her knickers in such a twist about all the travelling and performing that she'd burst into an unscripted tirade at the end of a concert in Aswan which had crescendoed in 'This is all bollocks', before exiting stage left into the desert in full costume and make-up.

'Honestly,' murmured Janine, who hated swearing.

'That was Elsa Valentine,' Arleta whispered to Saba. 'Your predecessor.'

The show he'd been writing, Bagley continued, resting his leg athletically on a chair as he spoke, was provisionally called *On the Razzle*. The plan was that they would open it for one night at the Gezira Sporting Club in Cairo, and then take it out on the road to all the random desert spots and aircraft bases and hospitals that were on the itinerary, most of which they would never know the name of.

'How does that sound?' He suddenly smiled at all of them, an infectious boyish grin.

'Lovely, *Mr* Bagley sir,' Arleta said.

Saba felt Janine shudder beside her, and although she couldn't stand the woman, she felt some sympathy for her. Sometimes Arleta could seem a little overconfident, and the truth was that she was scared too.

From ten to one, they worked solidly on new routines, new songs, entrances and exits. First on came the acrobats, flinging themselves across the stage in soft thumps and complaining about the splinters.

Lev, the oldest, had the wiry body of a young boy, and Saba thought the saddest eyes she'd ever seen. He stopped suddenly at the end of a dazzling row of cartwheels and addressed Bagley over the footlights as if he'd only just thought of something.

'Are there any more solo acts coming? They said in London we are joining another company.'

'Well they may come and they may not,' was all Max would say about this. 'We may all be gone soon.'

The faint whiff of that rumour again, that Rommel's troops were advancing, that soon Cairo would have the same blackout restrictions and air-raid drills as London.

'But no war talk during rehearsals,' Bagley shouted to them. 'If I've only got you lot to work with, I've a mountain to climb.' He raised his arms, the sharp smell of his sweat filling Saba's nostrils.

Now Arleta was under one weak spotlight, her khakis tightly belted, a jaunty naval cap on her head.

'Right, ducky, off you go,' Max shouted.

She sang a mildly suggestive number called 'Naval Boys', much saucy grinning, flapping hands, and then, 'Let Yourself Go'.

'That's all fine,' Bagley jumped athletically on to the stage, 'but I'm thinking a kind of hornpipe flavour, a hip, hop, change, when you sing "the sea". He held Arleta's arm and pushed her towards the flats. 'Then a step ball change before you go *la la la.*' He sang the notes confidently. 'Otherwise, all moving in the right direction.'

Willie – paunch already soaked with sweat, a handkerchief knotted over his bald pate – sang '*As soon as I touched me seaweed, I knew it was going to be wet*', and rattled off a few gags in his deadpan style. He put on a fez and did a belly dance, his hand pointing like a unicorn's horn from his head.

'I'm off now,' he said at the end with a ghastly leer, 'to pop me weasel.'

Max said it would do for now, but when they got back from the tour they'd work up some new stuff together.

'Happy to oblige.' Willie sat down on a chair on the stage and stared gloomily at his feet.

'And let's not make the jokes any bluer,' Max added. 'The snake-charmer one might have had its day.'

'Blimey.' Willie's voice was weak and fluttery. 'I go much bluer than that.'

'Well don't,' warned Max. 'There are spies in ENSA who swoon like a bunch of virgins at anything even vaguely smutty,' he said. 'We can't afford to offend them.'

Willie had stopped listening.

'Are you all right, old man?'

'Never better,' Willie wheezed. 'How about you?' His breathing sounded laboured, there was a heat rash all over his face.

Saba's turn now. As she jumped on to the stage, the door at the back of the theatre opened in a flash of sunshine. The blond man who had talked to her at breakfast walked in and took a seat by himself at the back. He gave her a pleasant smile when she glanced at him and put his palms up as if to say *ignore me*, which she did. She was concentrating now, one hundred per cent, on trying to sing well and impress Max Bagley who stood next to her.

'So,' Bagley said narrowing his eyes, 'let me tell you what I want from you. Are you frightened of heights?'

'No.' She stared back at him.

For the important opening number, he said, he wanted her and Arleta to appear down a golden rope in the middle of the stage. He sketched this out with his plump hands. Saba would sing a song he'd written called 'The Sphinx is a Minx', Arleta and Janine would cavort around her. The lyrics to this song would be presented by Arleta, dressed as Cleopatra, as hieroglyphics drawn on ancient tablets; that way the soldiers could sing along.

'But I'm searching for a big song to end the show with,' he was staring at Saba and talking to himself, 'What I really need to do today is test you.'

'Test me?' She gave him a quizzical look.

'To know your vocal limits. Once you're out there singing two concerts, sometimes more, a day, it's going to really count.'

She could hear Janine making agreeing noises in the wings. She took a deep breath and looked back.

'Don't you think you should listen to me before you test me?'

He pinched his nose between his fingers. 'Fair comment. I don't *know* what I want from you yet. Look, you lot clear off now,' he said to Arleta and Janine who were waiting.

'Can't we stay?' said Janine. 'We all came in a taxi together.'

'Don't care. Do what you like.' His eyes were trained on Saba again. 'It's just that this may take a while. There's something I need to know I can get from this young lady.'

Saba felt her heart thump. The blond man at the back was sitting with his legs stretched out as if this was some kind of spectator sport.

The band was dismissed, apart from the pianist, Stanley Mare, an aggrieved-looking man with smoke-stained fingers, who lit another cigarette and left it smouldering in an ashtray on top of the piano.

'What do you want?' he asked.

'Not sure.' Bagley retreated inside his own circle of smoke; he was thinking hard.

Saba was conscious of the rest of the cast staring at her from the wings, an unpleasant current of excitement in the room. She was under pressure and they were enjoying it.

'Let's start with "Strange Fruit", Max said at last. 'Do you know it?'

'Yes, I know it, and the other side, "Fine and Mellow".' She'd played the record obsessively when it first came out, made Tan laugh by using the bottom of a milk bottle as her microphone pretending to be Billie Holiday.

'OK. Then go,' Max said softly. 'Start her off in D, Stan.'

Stanley rippled his hands softly over the opening bars. If he was confused at Bagley's choice of this dark song about lynchings and death, he didn't show it, and nor did Saba, who closed her eyes, relieved he'd chosen something she knew and determined to give it her all.

She sang her heart out, and when she'd finished she heard a smattering of applause from the rest of the company.

'Well that'll wipe the smile off their faces,' Willie said loudly. 'I thought we was supposed to be jolly.'

Max said nothing. He'd put a pair of dark glasses on and it was hard to see what he was thinking.

'It's not going to be in the show.' He'd heard what Willie said. 'I'm listening for . . .' He sighed heavily. 'Doesn't matter. Next song. How about "Over the Rainbow", but not like Judy does it.'

'I don't do it like Judy does it, I do it like I do it!' He was beginning to get her goat.

She was halfway through it, enjoying her own voice soaring, sad and flung like bright streamers against the sky, when he held his hand up.

'Stop! Stop! Stop!'

He took his dark glasses off and looked at her very coldly.

'It's early days, but let me try and explain what it is that I think I'm not getting from you.' He thought for a while.

'Are you familiar with that line of poetry – Coleridge, I think – that talks about how *I see, not feel* how beautiful the stars are. I want you to feel it more and sing it less. No need to be operatic.'

'I *am* feeling it.' She was stung to the quick by his words. She'd wanted to show everyone how good she was, not get a public dressing-down.

'So, let me put it another way,' he said in his soft, well-educated voice. 'You're just a shade too chirpy for my taste.' When Saba saw Janine close her eyes in agreement, she wanted to knock her sanctimonious block off. 'Feel it to the maximum, and then pull it back a little.'

She opened her mouth to start again, but he was looking at his watch.

'Damn, time's up – we'll have another run at it tomorrow.'

As the band was packing up their instruments to go, he turned to her and said unsmiling, 'Don't be discouraged – we'll find something for you to sing.' Which made her feel even worse. 'There are some songs,' he said, 'that have a natural flow more suitable for young girls. You'll see where the sentences are going,' as if she was some kind of halfwit.

She gazed at him numb and miserable, wishing that he would stop now. The blond man from the BBC had beaten a hasty retreat too. He probably thought she was rotten as well. Awful, awful day.

*

As she left the theatre, blinking in the sudden glare of the street outside, a truck full of GIs slowed down. The wolf-whistling sounded like an aviary of mad birds.

'Well they certainly appreciate you, and so did I,' said a soft voice behind her. Dermot Cleeve skipped a couple of paces to keep up with her. 'As a matter of fact,' he added, 'I thought you were rather good.'

'Thank you,' she said, not believing him. If she'd known him better, she might have explained that she hadn't minded Bagley's criticisms – or not that much. She liked clever people. She enjoyed hard things. The most painful part had been their airing in front of the smug and unbearably delighted Janine.

'So, can I tempt you with an ice cream in Groppi's?' Cleeve asked. 'It's not far from here.'

She said no, she was too het up, and besides, she'd heard vague rumours of a dress-fitting appointment later that day.

'Well, at least take my card.' He shook one out of an elegant little silver holder and put it in the palm of her hand. 'I'll be seeing you,' he sang softly, and then he tipped his hat, and to her relief disappeared into the crowd.

Chapter 9

That night, unable to sleep, and raw still from her strange and disappointing day, she wrote a letter to the one person who had once had the power to make everything feel better.

Dear Baba,

You may have heard this already from Mum, but I wanted to let you know that I have arrived in Cairo, and I am safe. Work is going not too badly. The other artistes in the company are very kind and we take good care of each other. We will be gone soon on tour, and I hope one day you might be proud of me. You can get a letter to me c/o the NAAFI. I hope you will write, but maybe you still find it hard to forgive me.

Love Saba

Next, after some debate with her internal censor she wrote to Dom, a protectively jaunty letter saying sorry she'd run away so quickly that night, but she had work to do and could see he'd met up with a friend, as she had herself later that night. She, by the way, was in Cairo now and hoped he was safe and had got the posting he wanted.

Childish of her to add the imaginary friend, but she had been surprised and deflated by what happened. He'd seemed so intense before, so lively, so happy to be with her. It had felt like a night of celebration whose jarring ending had . . . well, it didn't matter now.

A carefully casual conversation with Arleta about it had been unsatisfactory. All those fighter-pilot boys were the same, she said, immature and stuck-up – they thought they were God's gift to women.

*

Two weeks after she sent the letters, she stood at the NAAFI counter.

'Quite sure there's nothing for me?' she said to the soldier. He'd searched, twice, through the large blue canvas bag. 'I've been here ages now.'

'Quite sure, love.' The soldier's weary face was sympathetic. 'We've lost a few mail planes recently, and it's not called the Muddle East for nothing.'

He handed Arleta three letters with SWALK and ITALY plastered all over them in a splashy purple writing. Janine had two aerogrammes, which she snatched and took off like a dog with a bone.

They moved to a table behind a tattered rattan sunscreen. A thermometer strapped to a dusty palm tree registered 105 degrees. Arleta, pouring lemonade and tearing open her first letter, read it with little squeaks and moans, occasionally patting Saba's hand saying she was not to worry, she was sure to get heaps on the next plane.

But Saba felt ludicrously upset. She was abandoned, simple as that. Dom hadn't replied and she felt a fool for writing at all.

No letter from Mum, or her father either. Saba felt the sweat pour down the front of her blouse. The rehearsals had helped the homesickness quite a bit, but thoughts of her family played underneath her present life like a tune with the volume turned down low but always there. What if they all hated her now? Maybe her father destroyed her letters. He'd said he didn't want to see her again. What if she could never go home?

Hearing her sigh, Arleta gave her hand a squelchy squeeze.

'Thinking too much.' Arleta was frowning. 'What are you thinking?'

'That I'll go mad if we don't get on the road soon,' she replied without thinking. 'I really will.' Once they were out there, performing in hospitals, army camps, it would shock her out of this fear she carried around now like an extra skin, and why else would she be here unless she was the stupidest person in the world?

On their way back to their digs they bumped into Captain Furness walking in a self-important, head-down, arm-pumping sort of way towards the office, swagger stick under his arm.

'Splendid, splendid,' he said when he saw them. 'I've been looking for you lot.' He burrowed in his briefcase saying he had an invitation somewhere for them for an evening reception at Mena House Hotel on the following night. He added, 'If it's not cancelled, of course; at the moment, we're assessing the military situation day by day.'

'Has it changed?' Janine asked.

'We'll brief you on that when necessary,' he said. 'All you need to think about at the moment is getting ready for the party tonight – this kind of socialising is jolly important out here.'

'I'm starting to hate that patronising little prat,' Arleta said as she watched his stiff back disappear into the crowd. 'Won't tell us when we're touring, won't tell us what's happening with the war, and now he behaves as if a party was a form of water torture. The Mena House is divine – wait till you see it. Maximum dog, I'm thinking.'

Maximum dog in Arleta-speak meant posh frocks, full make-up, lashings of Shalimar, and her mannequin-on-castors walk.

'Don't worry, darling,' she added. 'We'll soon be suffering, enjoy it while you can.'

The next day Max Bagley pushed a letter under their door telling them to report to the props and wardrobe department on Sharia Maarouf and borrow clothes for the evening reception. They were to look as glam as possible.

'This is a fabulous opportunity for us.' Arleta snatched the note from Saba's hand. 'Because I happen to know the man who decides on all the talent at the Mena. His name is Zafer Ozan, he's an absolutely sweetie, and very, very rich, and if he likes you, your future is pretty much assured.'

'How do you know him?' Janine asked suspiciously.

'We had a steaming affair,' said Arleta, who would stop at nothing in her game of shocking Janine. 'He was heaven. We went to his tent in the desert. He smelled of sandalwood and was incredibly generous. He was the one who gave me a necklace,' she added to Saba.

'Oh honestly.' Janine closed her eyes. 'She's joking, you know,' she warned Saba. 'She doesn't mean it.'

*

Later that morning, a severely elegant woman called Madame Eloise met them at the door of the props department, a dim and shuttered building three blocks from the Nile.

Madame had once been a model for Lanvin, the famous Parisian designer. Her commanding height and the baked-in-the-oven perfection of her chignon was intimidating at first, but her smile was warm. She sped them through a room lined with racks of clothes and meticulously organised shelves covered in wigs and boxes. 'Oh, this is fun,' she said, 'three gorgeous girls. I must put my thinking cap on.'

At the end of the room she stood them next to a floor-length mirror, and went into a light trance.

'Dresses.' She tapped her teeth with her finger and regarded them impersonally. The blackboard beside her was covered with mysterious messages: 'Ten wigs, Tobruk, rolled scenery and portable generator Ismailia. Ten Tahitian skirts, base number 32. Five pink hats, "On Your Toes".'

And Saba, hearing the faint drone of an aeroplane moving overhead and seeing their three drab khaki reflections in the mirror merge and separate again, thought, this is a mad, mad world I'm in now. Three girls in hot pursuit of the perfect dress, at a time when Cairo, so the rumour mills went, was about to be bombed to smithereens or invaded by Rommel. Furness had promised them earlier they'd be gone soon from the city, with its neon lights and nightclubs and dress shops. Picked up from the fairy ring and dropped into the desert like brightly wrapped sweeties; the kind grown-ups hand out to frightened children to distract them from the dentist, or some other alarming operation. She stood in the clammy air and shivered.

'You.' Madame was looking at Saba. Her manicured finger tapped her teeth. 'Dark hair, olive skin,' she muttered. 'Got it!' She darted into the racks and produced a white garment bag. 'Something quite fantastic. This dress was made originally from the most divine sari fabric. I copied an old Schiaparelli design and it's . . .' She stopped modestly. 'Well, see for yourself.'

She whisked out the dress.

'Ooh!' They gasped like children. The dress fluttered like a butterfly in the breeze from the fan, its bodice inlaid with filaments of silver so fine they looked like gossamer thread; its long silk skirt so delicate that it shivered in the wind, and then they stood wincing as the aeroplane noise outside rose to an intolerable level.

'Not fair, not fair at all.' Arleta pretended to bat Saba about the head. 'I want it, and I'm older than her.'

'It's been on tour with *Scheherazade*.' Madame held it against Saba. 'I made it out of a shawl that belonged to a maharajah's daughter; that's real silver in the bodice by the way. What is your waist size?'

'Twenty-four inches.'

'Perfect, try it on. Wash your hands first, please.' She indicated a bowl and a piece of soap in the corner of the room.

Saba slipped out of her dusty uniform. She peeled the shirt from her back. A sluggish breeze came from the window tinged with the smell of petrol.

'There.' Madame squirted her quickly with a tasselled bottle of scent; the dress surged over her head. 'Stand here.' She was pulled in front of the mirror. 'Hold in there.' Madame lashed a delicate silver rope around her waist. 'Hair down.' She tucked Saba's hair behind her ears.

'Now look.' She scrambled through a glass-fronted cupboard with many drawers in it, and came out with a tiny diamanté brooch, that she pinned on to the bodice of the dress. 'No jewellery apart from that,' she ordered. 'The hair waved, the pin and the dress, *ça suffit*.'

'Oh Lord.' A band of gauzy sunlight fell diagonally across Saba and she stood in shock. The dress had changed her into a marvellous mythical creature and her eyes filled with tears because she'd just pictured her mother, who was poignantly susceptible to luxury, standing next to her gasping.

But then she remembered the slant-eyed, ciggie-smoking aspect of her mother, who might have ruined this outing altogether. They'd had a shocking bust-up once when Saba had refused to wear a hideous dress her mother had made on her sewing machine. Lots of swearing, lots of shouting, Saba storming off to bed, shaking the house with her slamming door, Mum shouting upstairs very sarky: 'Oh little Miss Know-it-all upset, is she? Oh dear! Dear! Dear!'

The dawning sense that quite a few of Mum's creations hadn't quite hit the mark had crept up over the last few years. That polka-dot dress, for instance, though conceived with dash, did have quite an uneven hem, and hasty bits of bias binding over the neckline. Things changed whether you wanted them to or not. Just as Mum changed like a weathervane whenever her father was around.

'Can I really wear this?' she asked Madame Eloise.

'Of course. But if you spoil it, you pay for it.' They were talking to each other's reflection, so it was hard to see if this was a joke or not. 'How much do they pay you now?'

'Ten pounds a week!' Saba still couldn't quite believe it. 'Four pounds for the chorus, it's a fixed salary for all the artistes. And you?' she asked back. 'Fair's fair.'

'None of your beeswax.' Madame made the gesture of a geisha hiding behind a fan. 'Not enough money to stay here if the war gets too hot, which I hear . . . Oh, never mind.' She pretended to smack her face. 'Concentrate on important things. A dress for you now, Arleta.'

Arleta, stripped to her peach underwear, was combing her hair luxuriously by the window, enjoying the play of sunlight on its gold and red tints. When Madame asked if she'd ever helped the colour along, Arleta said Coty's Tahitian Sunset had been used once or twice, but mostly God did all. She flicked it dramatically over her shoulder.

Madame said they were a riot and turned confidential. She also ran a service, she said, that tailored men's uniforms, and the men were every bit as vain as women; the way they carried on about fitting a trouser, or the exact positioning of scrambled egg on the shoulder of a senior officer, was a caution. She offered them coffee and a piece of halva and warned them to watch out for the serving men here, who were sex-starved and like wild animals. The stories she'd heard she would not repeat. She promised that when they got back from their tour, she would take them to a bazaar shop that sold the finest silks in Cairo. She asked them whether they had boyfriends here.

'We've been told not to go into the native quarter.' Janine interrupted her. She'd been sitting by the window, deep in thought, her hands folded in her lap.

'Oh pouf, boring!' said Madame. 'Go. It's exciting. You're in much more danger near the British barracks, and besides, I like the Egyptians, they are so funny, and so intelligent – I mean, please! They built the Pyramids, wonderful art, the first telescope, and we treat them like . . .' she turned her mouth down in comical disgust and waggled her hand, 'wogs, gyppos! So stupid!'

'Hmm.' Janine was not convinced.

'So you!' Madame looked at Arleta. 'For you, something sensational.' She returned with a dress coiled over her arm and covered in sequins the colour of old gold.

'Oh *ding dong*!' said Arleta when it was on. She stared at herself in the mirror and shimmied her hips. She kissed Madame and said she said she felt like a mermaid in it, and who would have thought you'd have to go to Cairo to find a decent dress. 'Would it be entirely impossible,' she asked winningly, 'for me to take it on tour when we leave? I'll look after it.'

Saba knew this was not true. Arleta stepped out of her dresses at night and left them where they lay on the floor, much to Janine's disgust. Janine said it only took an extra five minutes to put things back on their hangers.

Janine got a pale green chiffon dress with silver shoes, and a long rope of fake pearls, which Madame knotted dramatically at her waist.

'*Voilà*.' She lined them all up side by side in the mirror. 'Let me see you all together. Not there, there.' She changed the angle of Saba's brooch. 'Beautiful, beautiful girls,' she purred. 'One more thing.' She darted towards a velvet pincushion and pulled out three hatpins. 'In your handbags, just in case.'

'In case of what?' Saba said.

'Attack,' said Madame. 'I've told you already, the men are a long way from home, and some of them are very fresh. I don't think they mean to be,' she said, hearing Janine's squeak. 'It's just that out here, particularly in the desert, men get lonely – the kind of loneliness that nothing but a woman can drive away. Simple as that, and who can blame them.

'You're looking very shocked, dear.' She gave Janine's arm a little pat. 'But you're a dancer, you must know these things. There are certain professions that excite men more than others.

'Speaking of which,' she said quietly to Saba as Janine

disappeared behind the curtain, 'your taxi is waiting outside. You're running late.'

'Just for me?' she said, surprised.

'Just for you,' she answered. 'The message came from the ENSA headquarters, so it must be right – off you go.'

Chapter 10

An unmarked taxi picked her up outside the props department and sped her across town towards the recording studio for the British Forces Overseas. But then to her confusion the car veered from the main road, Sharia Port Said, bumped down a nondescript street and stopped outside a block of grey flats with washing hanging from their windows. When they arrived, the taxi driver handed her a typed note: *Go up to the third floor; you'll be picked up in an hour.*

Inside the ancient clanking lift, she looked around nervously at the filthy glass light on the ceiling half full of dead flies and sand, and at her own wavery reflection in a wall mirror. This didn't look like a recording studio.

Dermot Cleeve was standing on the landing of the third floor. He pulled back the wire door.

'Lovely,' he cupped her hand, 'what a treat. It's very sweet of you to come.' Today he was smartly dressed in a tropical suit and wearing a spotted bow tie. The fine blond hair that flopped over his eyes and his broad artless smile gave him the air of a bouncy schoolboy.

He led her into a small, dark flat that smelled faintly of fenugreek – a spice she recognised from Tan, who loved to cook with it, and whose dresses smelt of it.

'I hope you don't mind meeting here,' he said, 'rather than at the studio – it's easier to talk.'

She felt herself relaxing as she sat down on the edge of a sofa scattered at one end with records and sheet music. The untidy room, with its shelves crammed with books and tapes, its bottles of Gordon's gin, its gramophone, felt homely and familiar if not exactly what she'd expected.

The small kitchen at the end of the room had no door; while he bustled around making tea on a gas ring, he chatted as if they were old friends, first about tea which he said he drank too much of, but you could get some delicious blends out here if you knew where to look, and then about cooking. His *suffragi*, Badr, he said, did the cleaning and the errands, but got cross with him for wanting to do his own cooking, but he hated people bowing and scraping to him and it was easier, particularly with the hours they worked.

With her tea he brought out a plate of delicious cakes – 'You must try these,' he said, 'they're from Groppi's. The family is Swiss, and they make the most perfect macaroons and strudel I've ever tasted – absolutely divine.'

She was crunching away at a chocolate-flavoured macaroon when he said he thought Max Bagley had been far too harsh with her the other day. 'I thought you were marvellous, and your "Strange Fruit" raised the hairs on the back of my neck – as a matter of fact,' he jumped up to look in the mirror, 'one or two of them may still be up,' which made her laugh, not that it took much today; she felt keyed up and strangely excitable.

'It's such a powerful thing to be able to sing well.' He gazed at her with frank admiration. 'And a wonderful thing to see how the faces of serving men change when they listen to a decent song. It seems to soothe them, it makes them human again.

'You know one of the things the top brass don't get,' he stirred some sugar into his tea and took a delicate sip, 'is that men by and large fight for their sweethearts and for their mums, their children; none of that – excuse French – balls about freedom and democracy. And men need reminding of that, and that's what you do, and it's much, much more important than most people will ever understand.'

He was saying the perfect thing at the right time. The heat, the homesickness meant she'd had trouble sleeping for the last few nights, and in the darkest hours everything that had seemed so exciting about coming to North Africa had turned into everything that was shallow and dreadful about her. You're a wicked girl, the night-time goblins had told her: black with sin and ambition and a terrible daughter to boot. Your poor mother is crying at home, your father hates you. No wonder you get no letters.

More tea was poured. She tried not to scoff the macaroons; she was starving suddenly. He'd gone on to talk in the same admiring way about the absolutely splendid extra work that some female singers had undertaken.

'I can't name names of course, but they have been an absolutely vital part of the war work. They have tremendous power, more than they realise, because they're obviously able to travel around freely without it seeming suspicious, and also, of course, to make people forget themselves. Do you understand what I'm getting at?' He watched her carefully and then, in a curiously personal gesture, brushed crumbs off her cuff.

She wasn't sure, and if she did, it seemed presumptuous, even fanciful, to say so.

'If anything did come up like this,' his long fingers played with his pen, 'would you be game?'

'Game?' In Wales it meant something not quite nice, as in *on the game*.

He corrected himself quickly. 'Interested?'

'I might be, but I don't really know what you're asking me to do.'

'Let me give you a small example,' he said. 'Tonight, at this party at the Mena House, you'll be part of the main group, but you could, if you agreed to it, do a little job for us.'

'What sort of job?'

'An easy-peasy job,' he said, 'and you don't have to do it if you don't want to. You told me earlier that you speak some Turkish, and that was of interest because there is a man who will come to the party. His name is Zafer Ozan, and he is a Turk who also happens to be an influential figure in North Africa. Would you be prepared to sing him a song or two in Turkish?'

'Only that?'

'Only that.' He grinned at her. 'He loves European singers but he's a fierce patriot too so I think he'll love you, and of course if he does, it could lead to lots of work for you after the war.'

'Gosh,' she said, 'that sounds quite exciting.'

He uncapped his golden fountain pen, and made a few marks in a small notebook.

'But I don't understand, I thought I'd come here to do a wireless broadcast . . .' She glanced at a large tape machine on his sideboard.

'Oh definitely, I'm very keen for you to do that too. I've just started a Forces Favourites hour, it's gone down a treat with the men – we play some songs, let them record their own messages home, it's very, very moving. It's just that this new thing has come up, and honestly, I cannot stress enough that if you don't want to do it, that's fine too. I imagine though that you're someone who likes being busy,' he added pleasantly.

'We're all keen to start work,' she said, scooting up a bit on the sofa. 'We should get our itinerary this week.'

'I've seen it,' he said evenly. 'You're going to be flat out soon.' And then, more quietly, 'That's partly why I needed to see you now. Go on, have another.' He pushed the last two cakes towards her.

'No thanks,' she said. There was still a chance he might ask her to sing, and she couldn't do that stuffed with macaroons. 'So you've seen our itinerary? I thought it was all very hush-hush.'

'It is, although you've probably twigged already that nothing is very hush-hush out here – they say that gossip seems the only reliable source of news.

'Saba.' When he looked at her, his pale blue eyes were tired; they had thin veins of blood running through them and close up he was older than she'd first thought. 'I don't have much time,' he glanced around the room, 'and neither do you, so I'd better get on with it. As well as my broadcasting here, I do have a working relationship with another key part of the government that, from time to time, does more secret things. Do you know what I'm getting at?'

'I think so.' She felt a slither of alarm inside her, and a vagrant excitement, as if she'd suddenly been inducted into a grown-up, serious world.

He rubbed his nose. The skin on it was very pale and she could see a tracery of burst capillaries.

'So tonight.' He got up and adjusted the curtains, sat down again. 'This is a very small do, so don't look worried.' He patted her knee in a friendly-uncle sort of way. 'It should be fun, and we have no interest in throwing you in at the deep end; if you like, it's a little test, to see how much you want to do with us – you'll be perfectly safe. In fact, I'll be there, but you won't talk to me.

'There will be the usual mix of people – the few Brits who are left, some businessmen, some army officers, and some important locals who we want to do business with. They often ask the girls to these shindigs to pretty things up – no one will think it the slightest bit odd that you're there and they'll want you to sing.'

Cleeve was whispering now, the twinkly look in his eyes had disappeared and he was entirely focused and serious.

'This man, Ozan, is one of the richest men in the Middle East and, by the way, a very nice man, good fun. I don't know how much you understand about Turkish politics at the moment, but Istanbul is now strategically and politically one of the most important neutral cities in the world – both the Allies and the Axis forces are simply itching to get their hands on it, so any little crumb . . .'

'But—'

Cleeve clutched her hand quickly and let it go. 'Let me finish, I know what you're going to say. "Of what possible use can I be?" Here's the point. Ozan's passion and weakness is music. Before the war, he got all the great musicians to come here – Bessie Smith and Ella and Edith Piaf, and some wonderful singers from Greece you may not have heard of, and now the man's frustrated: there's an embargo on bringing foreign artistes here unless of course they're with ENSA, or the Yanks. When he hears you, I guarantee he'll be interested, he's a great talent-spotter.'

Saba licked her lips nervously. Oh how exciting it all sounded. And one in the eye to bloody old Bagley.

'After the war is over, he'll go back to doing what he enjoys most – organising tours all over the Mediterranean. It's a very lucrative market, and he'd be a helpful person to be friends with.'

'So?' she whispered.

'Well, they have a very good band at the Mena: an Egyptian band that knows how to play all the old standards. At some point in the evening, I'd like you to surprise him by singing one song in English, and another in Arabic or in Turkish, it doesn't matter which. Can you do that?'

'Yes, my gran and I were always singing them at home. But what then?'

'Nothing really, except if Mr Ozan asks you to sing at his club, which is what we're hoping for, simply send me a postcard here that says *The show went well.* I'll know what you mean. Don't sign your name. Here's my address.' He scribbled it on a piece of paper. 'Look at it now and memorise it. Is that clear?' He smiled at her encouragingly. 'Not too difficult, is it?'

'I thought you said you'd be there.'

'I will, but I don't want you to talk to me.' He threw back his floppy hair and twinkled at her again – the bad boy of the quad organising a midnight feast.

She looked at the address, scrumpled up the piece of paper and handed it back to him again.

'Am I supposed to eat this or something?' she whispered.

He grinned at her. 'Any more questions?'

'Does Arleta or Mr Bagley, or Captain Furness, or anyone else in the company know anything about this?'

'Max Bagley knows as much as he needs to know,' Cleeve said confusingly. 'But nobody else, so never discuss it with anyone. Regarding the girls, casually drop it into a conversation that you might be doing a couple of songs for me on the Middle East Forces Programme. It's transmitted over the Egyptian State Broadcasting. That leaves it open. Anything else?'

'Just one thing.' She gave him a frank look. 'When you say I'm to make friends with Mr Ozan, you do mean just a friend?' Because if he honestly thought she'd go any further, he had another think coming.

'Oh, you should see your eyes flashing,' he teased. 'Your mother would be proud of you. *I'm not that sort of girl*,' he mocked in a high falsetto.

'I repeat,' he said, 'all you have to do is sing a few songs and keep your ears open, and you may get the chance to do something that will make you feel proud of yourself for the rest of your life . . . but if you want to go away and think about it . . .' He opened his arms to release her.

'No, no, no, I want to do it,' she said. She had a fizzy, excited feeling in her veins. She'd already imagined telling her father about it one day, the softening of his craggy features, the look of pride in his eyes as she said: 'You see, Baba, I wasn't just singing, I was helping the British government.'

'Good.' Cleeve's long fingers squeezed her hand. 'You're on.'

Chapter 11

No one seemed to notice she'd been out when she got home, mostly because Arleta and Janine had had an enormous row, and Arleta was full of it.

'In the taxi going home,' she explained, 'I said it was complete balls what Madame Eloise said about women here needing hatpins in their handbags to preserve their modesty – half the WAACS and WAAFS I've met here and in London simply hurl themselves at anything in trousers.' And good for them too, Arleta continued, in full cry: war meant freedom for women and men – freedom from lies and hypocrisy. Cairo for young women was like being a child in a sweet shop – so much choice, so many lonely men around the girls called them meal tickets.

'Then she said, "Have you *quite* finished yet?" ' Arleta, who did a brilliant Janine, closed her eyes and wobbled her head. ' "Because personally speaking, I don't want freedom from convention at all, and I feel sorry for girls who do – men know when they're handling soiled goods." '

'Soiled goods,' Arleta snorted. 'What a twit. She's upstairs now with the burned feathers and the smelling salts. Much too good for this world.' She closed her mouth prissily.

Arleta asked Saba to take Janine's evening dress to her room – Arleta was going to have a bath and some shut-eye – she couldn't bear to look at the silly cow.

All these overwrought emotions gave Saba a sense of the fragility of this world they lived in. Bickering about frocks and men when outside the dusty window she could hear planes grumbling and tanks mingling with the sounds of a typical Cairo rush hour – the blasting of horns, the increasingly desperate shrieks from the man who sold fly whisks on the corner; the bubbling sound of passers-by beneath their window speaking in a dozen or so different languages.

Janine was asleep when she walked in, as still as a wax doll. She'd put a green satin eye mask over her eyes and stuffed her ears with cotton wool. On her chest of drawers there was a photograph of her parents in Guildford – a tensely smiling couple – next to her Pond's cream and her bottle of gut reviver. Her leather-covered alarm clock said it was five fifteen, three hours to go before the party.

Saba looked down at her. Poor Janine. Nobody had taken to her. Willie had told her earlier that Janine was older than she looked, thirty he reckoned, and had never married. The narrowness of her training, her strange obsessive personality seemed to have made her better at dancing than life, but she wasn't such a bad stick really – just hard to warm to. Gossiping about her yesterday, Willie had hinted she might still be a virgin, an ENSA first, he'd added.

Arleta was asleep, too, when Saba went back to their room: strangely innocent-looking with her blonde hair mussed and wafted by the fan, her soft lips parted, arms spread out as if she was saying yes to pretty much everything. It wasn't fair, thought Saba, looking down at her: Arleta was everything your mother had warned you never to be, the perfect mixture of damage and glamour, and men adored her for it. Women liked her too. Arleta, for all her outrageousness, was kind – it was only narrow-minded people like Janine who got her goat. And yet, people were complicated, never exactly one thing or the other, because earlier, and for the first time, Saba had seen that look of hurt and slight competitiveness in Arleta's eyes when Saba had mentioned she might be doing a wireless broadcast for Cleeve. Most performers couldn't help themselves like this. It was the chimp-house thing – when one chimp was handed an extra bunch of bananas, everyone was thrown.

When Arleta woke she switched off the fan and got out of bed wearing nothing but silk pyjama bottoms and a frothy bra – she'd thrown all her khaki underwear in the dustbin on their first night in Cairo, crooning, 'Nice knowing you.'

'Can I bags first bath?' Arleta said yawning. 'I must wash my hair.'

'Only a ten-turner,' warned Saba.

The turns referred to the egg timer that Janine had brought on tour with her to stop people hogging the bath. They were absolutely essential, she'd said.

Inside the bathroom, there was a cracked bowl underneath the sink with Janine's leotards soaking in it and the bottle of shampoo that she marked with a pencil like an old brigadier hoarding sherry. Saba heard Arleta turn on the taps from which the rust-coloured water trickled out at an agonisingly slow pace, and while she splashed and groaned, Saba moved restlessly around the room thinking about her strange conversation with Mr Cleeve, a conversation which had thrilled and frightened her.

Her borrowed dress was hanging in front of the wardrobe like a new life waiting to begin; the shadows were lengthening in the street outside, and her stomach was in knots. For that moment everything in her existence felt unstable.

To calm herself she ran through possible songs she might sing for Mr Ozan, moving her hips and humming the first bars of 'Mazi', one of her father's favourites. It was ages since she'd sung a song in Turkish and every time she sang it she felt a wave of sorrow and rage sweep over her. Not a word yet from her father, how mean of him, and what a loss for both of them who had once been so close. Singing the next verse for him straight from the heart, it seemed to her that the song had taken her over and was singing her – a strange effect she'd noticed before, particularly when she sang in Turkish. When it was over, she dashed her tears away. Damn you, Baba. You were the one who told me I could sing. Why should I stop?

When it was her turn to get in the bath, her mood flipped again and Dom stole into her mind. Seeing him with that other girl in Cavours had hurt her pride but she still thought about him. She wanted him to be here tonight, to see her in this wonderful dress, to take account of how much she had already changed and what a prize he had missed out on. Soaping her armpits, she ran a film of it in her mind. Dom on a terrace in a dinner jacket, rumpled hair, palm trees behind him, she walking towards him in the sunset, a woman now in her Schiaparelli dress, cigarettes and pearl holder, her smile slightly mysterious now because of the important war work.

'Saba!' Janine's tight voice through the keyhole. 'Could you please stop making that horrible noise, and also, you've had at least twenty turns in the bath,' followed by Arleta's bellow: 'Come in, boat number four – taxi in half an hour.'

*

Later, stepping into the street, even Janine was forced to admit it was the most perfect night for a party. The evening air was soft and warm, and as they drove past the bronze lions on the Khedive Ibrahim Bridge, the lights of the river barges made red and gold reflections on the surface of the Nile. In the distance against a lurid horizon, the sails of the feluccas fluttered like large moths.

A jeep crammed with hooting and whistling GIs drove by as they got into the taxi. They made obscene gestures at the girls. One man clawed at his mouth like a starving man.

'I absolutely hate that,' said Janine, regal in pale green and clasping her evening bag tight. 'It's so unnecessary.'

Now they passed through Cairo streets loud with rackety music, past a stretch of water with what appeared to be a dead donkey floating on top of it. A crowd of men in white djellabas were holding lanterns over it, the ropes to get it out.

'Oh golly!' Janine held her nose and winced. 'What a d*readful* pong.'

'Nah, lovely,' Arleta joked. 'It's Eau de Nile.'

Saba laughed out loud. This morning she'd felt so distraught, so wrong about everything; tonight the randomness of driving through Cairo's corkscrewed streets in a borrowed evening dress felt marvellous.

Clear of the city a brand-new life sped past her window – some large and luxurious houses surrounded by trees, an old man sitting by the road having a quiet smoke by a fire; a skinny horse waiting patiently to be unloaded, a group of street children jumping and laughing. Samir, whose wife cleaned their rooms in the mornings, had already told them how dreadful this year's crops had been, a disaster, great hardship for the villagers, and yet there was a feeling of almost enviable peace and ordinariness about these scenes. Of quiet worlds that would continue stubbornly despite the Desert War.

It took about forty minutes to get to Giza and the hotel. In a long drive lit with flaming torches Arleta turned and said with some ceremony:

'Girls, I want you to pay attention to me. Tonight is a blue-moon night – and you're to enjoy every minute of it.'

Janine, who had complained of car sickness on the way out, looked puzzled, but Saba understood and approved. Blue-moon nights were Arleta-speak for the choicest gigs you could ever possibly get, the magical nights that might only happen once or twice in a lifetime. It was important to recognise them, bask in them, and use them as nourishment for when you were back in some crummy digs in an English seaside town doing panto.

When the car set them down in front of a glowing building, a uniformed porter wearing a huge ornamental sword stepped forward and helped them out.

In front of her Saba saw the three ancient Pyramids of Giza, jutting out into a night sky that glittered with a thousand million stars. She was stunned by their beauty – in her mind pyramids belonged with unicorns and mermaids in some other mystical world; they were not the backdrops for a party.

Even Janine was impressed. 'Golly,' she said, her highest accolade. 'This is actually quite pretty.'

The hotel itself stood on the crest of a small hill against a cobalt-blue sky. Dozens of lanterns shifting in a slight breeze made the building seem to float against the sky like a skittish little pleasure craft, and lavish planting of jasmine bushes on the terraces made the air piercingly sweet.

'Ready, girls?' Arleta took both their arms. 'Down we go.'

Arleta had a fabulous red-carpet walk, both slouchy and stately, which she deployed to maximum effect on these occasions and which she and Saba sometimes practised for fun in their PJs in their digs. You blanked your eyes, lengthened your neck, stuck your hips out, and swung your bottom negligently as if you didn't give much of a damn about anything.

They were having fun with it now as they walked down the short flight of steps that led to the party. A dramatic pause on the first terrace, then the band struck up a jazzy tune, and a group of young men in dinner jackets froze at the sight of them like Pompeii statues. Captain Furness, wearing a regimental bum-freezer dinner jacket that showed a large and surprisingly girlish bottom for a military man, stepped out of the crowd, eager to claim them.

'Before you get lost,' he put a moist hand on Saba's arm, 'there are quite a few people I'd like you to meet,' and then, as if remembering Mr Manners, 'Girls, well done, you look jolly nice.'

Down to the lower terrace now where red-faced servants were adding sprigs of rosemary to an open fire on which two whole skinned lambs were roasting. On a long table beside the fire, a feast was laid out: wobbling terrines, jewel-coloured salads, a large turkey, a mountain of salmon and prawns. Saba, who had hardly eaten since breakfast, felt her mouth fill with saliva, and then the usual pang of guilt. So much food here, and so little at home, it did feel wicked sometimes.

'Look, look, look!' Arleta's hair had turned to liquid gold in the firelight. She was as excited as a child. She led Saba down another flight of steps to where a swimming pool framed by masses of tiny candles shimmered and shifted like a vast sapphire.

Saba began to search the roaring faces for the famous Mr Ozan. She'd imagined him to be old and fat and rich and Middle Eastern-looking, but saw no one who matched that description. The faces on the terrace were mainly pale and European.

'Girls, round me.' Furness, who seemed slightly plastered, wanted to introduce them to everyone.

'Jolly nice to have some new blood,' one of the English wives bellowed, an anxious red face gleaming in the lamplight. 'Lots of us have gone, you see.'

They were handed from group to group, smiled at, examined closely and asked more or less the same questions: had they come by sea or air? Were they singers or dancers? Gosh, what fun, how marvellous! What discipline! So necessary, one added, to have treats for the men. Now, did they play any instruments? Yes, Arleta extemporised gaily, she played the xylophone; her friend Saba, she'd given her a pinch here, was a dab hand at the Welsh harp. Some admired their frocks and asked for news of home. A couple said they felt guilty about rationing, but what could one do, no point in starving oneself. Another said that when she'd stepped off the ship in Durban with her banker husband a year or so ago, she'd been bowled over by two things: the stunning brightness of the light, and the food, but now she absolutely longed for grey skies, for rain, for home. It frightened her being separated from her children. Particularly at a time like this.

'Now, now, now!' her husband interrupted. 'You know the rules. No war talk on a night like this.' He bared his teeth at the girls. 'Enjoy it while the going's good, what?'

'You'll probably leave too soon,' the woman muttered before she was led away. Most of the wives and families of military personnel, had already gone to South Africa or Sudan, somewhere safer than here. Her sensible Home Counties face sweated in the flickering light. She pointed out the young, recently widowed wife of a naval officer who'd somehow slipped through the net and not been evacuated. Awfully brave. The woman was listening, polite and attentive, to an older man who was leaning towards her telling a story. She had a small glass of sherry in her hand.

The moon rose higher, lighting the tips of the Pyramids, more stars came out, dazzling the dark velvet of the sky. The girls were handed around and around like delicacies, until eventually the faces on the terrace grew indistinct, and the older officers said, Gosh! Was that really the time? and pressed sticky hot hands into theirs and said how lovely it had been to meet them, and they would be sure to come and see them in concert. But still no sign of Mr Ozan, and no sign of Mr Cleeve either. Saba didn't know whether to be disappointed or relieved.

When the old people had gone, the young men loosened their bow ties and took off their dinner jackets. A band started to play some sleepy jazz on a small dance floor fringed with palm trees near the swimming pool.

But no Mr Ozan. To fill in time, Saba danced with a gaunt young Scottish doctor, who apologised for stepping on her toes. He said he'd been out near Tripoli, operating for six days straight. 'It's pretty hairy out there, sorry I'm such a lousy dancer.' She was rescued by a group of rowdy Desert Air Force pilots who sank to their knees in front of her and declared undying love.

She was tempted to ask if they knew Dominic but felt she couldn't face being teased about him, or explain a relationship that basically didn't exist, and yet – what an idiot – she'd pictured him earlier on the terrace waiting for her, thinking how lovely she looked in her dress.

She was laughing in a hollow way at herself when suddenly she was aware of a dip in the laughter and the conversation; the band's tune abruptly ending. The partygoers were turned towards a portly man in a startling burgundy-coloured dinner jacket, making his stately way down the steps. He was patting arms, he was smiling graciously, and now a small wave at the band that had struck up 'For He's a Jolly Good Fellow'. As he walked towards the dance floor, Arleta appeared at Saba's side, a gold mermaid in the moonlight.

'One second, darling.' She smiled charmingly at the young doctor waiting for another dance. She drew Saba aside.

'Zafer Ozan,' she whispered, her eyes mocking and mirthful, 'the one I told you about. The stinking-rich one.'

Ozan had spotted them; he was looking at them both from across the dance floor.

'Don't you think,' Arleta blew him a kiss, 'he's rather attractive in a Bunter sort of a way?' She waved him over.

Saba stared at Ozan and looked away. She saw his teeth flash as he shook the hand of another guest. 'Everyone loves him,' Arleta said, her blonde hair tickling Saba's ear. She was wiggling her fingers at him discreetly like a shy little girl.

'You're a shocking flirt,' said Saba.

'I know,' said Arleta happily. 'And I can assure you he doesn't mind.'

As he walked towards them, Arleta said quickly, 'Darling, as a treat for him, I'm going to ask the band to play "Night and Day". Would you sing it? It's his signature tune.'

'Why don't you sing it?' Saba was thoroughly confused now: had Cleeve arranged for Arleta to sing too, or was this pure coincidence?

'Come off it, darling. I'm the dancer; you're the one with the voice. Even bloody old Janine says that.'

'She does?' Saba was amazed. 'She never told me.'

'Well of course she hasn't, silly – she's jelly bag. I am too, but I'm better at hiding it.' She play-pinched Saba on the arm. 'Hop up now before he meets you.'

Saba got on to the small stage. The little band with its piano and tenor saxophone and double bass apparently knew she was coming. They slipped into the music and when the pianist gave her a wink she joined them, nervous at first because of the strangeness of all this and then forgetting because in the end a song was a song and beyond things. She blotted them all out and closed her eyes and sang into the jasmine-scented night. Happiness flowed like golden honey through her veins. This was what she loved; what she was good at.

There was a roar of approval when the song was over. Ozan came to the edge of the stage, stood in front of her and just looked at her. His eyes dark, almost bruised-looking, the flames from the fire reflected in them.

'Do you know other songs?' he said. 'Sing one for me, please?'

And knowing this might be her only chance, she launched into a

Turkish song, 'Fikrimin Ince Gülü', a song her father had once sung and translated for her. *You are always in my heart like a delicate rose; you are in my heart like a happy nightingale.* The audience looked puzzled, but she saw Mr Ozan's eyes light up, and how the waiters bustling around him glanced at her in surprise. Next – oh how she was enjoying this suddenly, the night, the challenge of it – the band joined her in a verse of 'Ozkorini', a famous Arabic song that Umm Kulthum, the greatest Arabic singer of all, sang. *Ozkorini*, her father had once explained, meant think of me. Remember me. The waiters surged towards the stage thrilled and clapping, as Saba sang an extract from a song they recognised.

Saba felt nervous at first stepping in the footsteps of this goddess, but she gave the sobbing lyrics their full worth, and when she'd finished, cries of 'Allah!' and '*Ya Hayya!*' came out of the darkness, and her eyes filled with tears. For that moment her father, her hateful, lovable father, was powerfully with her, and yet he would have hated this.

Mr Ozan said nothing; he looked at her and shook his head.

'It's too noisy to talk here,' he said, gesturing towards the crowd. 'Tomorrow,' he shouted. 'I'll see you tomorrow.'

The band clapped him as he walked away, as if he was the true star of the evening, and then, almost immediately, Captain Furness, who must have been lurking in the undergrowth, jumped on to the stage.

'That was interesting. I didn't expect that,' he said into Saba's ear. Although his lips were smiling, his hand on her arm was tourniquet tight. He said he'd taken the liberty of ordering a taxi for them. He advised Arleta in his barking voice to put her shoes back on; there were scorpions that sometimes hid in the cracks of the pavements. Janine said that was quite right, a friend of hers had ended up in hospital with a very nasty bite. There was still no sign of Cleeve.

Chapter 12

By the time they got home, the stars were fading and the pale streaks of dawn breaking over the Nile, an interlude of peace before the insane muddle of daylight in Cairo began.

'Isn't this so often the best time of a party?' Arleta stretched out her legs. 'When you take the wampum off and put on your jammys, and stop showing off.'

It was four in the morning, and the air was like warm milk. Janine, after doing her fifty splashes, went straight to bed; Arleta and Saba were sitting on their balcony in their pyjamas under a cotton sheet.

Down in the alleyway, a donkey croaked; the man who sold fly whisks slept beside it on a raffia mat with a few rags over him.

When Arleta got up to make tea, Saba stayed where she was, her feet still throbbing from the dancing, the music pounding in her veins like a strong drug. She felt the relief a high diver might feel, or a mountain climber, when the scaring thing was done, but 'Night and Day' had sounded good, and she hadn't made a complete fool of herself with 'Ozkorini', even though she'd suddenly felt shockingly nervous before singing it.

'Bliss.' Arleta put a cup of tea and a biscuit in Saba's hand. 'Don't they call this *l'heure bleue*?' She'd tied her hair back in an old scarf and changed into a silk kimono. 'The time when it's not quite light and not quite dark,' she closed her eyes, 'when most people die or fall in love.

'Well you were a big success tonight,' she said in the same sleepy voice. 'The belle of the ball, or should I say the belly dancer of the balley. Ozan was very taken.'

'Where did you meet him?' Saba said. The moment the question was out of her mouth, she felt awkward; she didn't want to start spying on Arleta, but she was curious.

Arleta yawned. 'On my first tour with the Merrybelles; the rules were more relaxed so we were allowed to sing for a couple of nights at his nightclub in Alexandria, the Cheval D'Or. It was fun, and I thought he was very attractive and . . .' She lit a cigarette and flicked the match away. 'As I said, we were lovers for a while, but not for long. He'd just got married, I think for the third time.'

Her cigarette hadn't lit properly, she groped around for another light, and although Saba was shocked, she couldn't help thinking that Arleta was the least hypocritical woman she'd ever met. She liked, sex, she liked men, none of that mealy-mouthed talk about being led on, or letting the stars get in her eyes, no talk of being duped or dumped or feeling guilty. What a revelation!

'I knew it wouldn't last,' Arleta ruminated through a plume of smoke. 'But it was great fun. I'd just come out of an affair with a real Frigidaire Englishman and it was just what I needed. Also, let's be frank – he's the biggest booker of talent in the Middle East and I want to go on working when the war's over. He's a good contact for you, Saba.' Arleta had her professional voice on now. 'He loves English girls and he was very taken with all that headless horror stuff you did.' Her name for Eastern music.

'But tell me something, darling.' Arleta leapt in quickly. 'I've been meaning to ask you, have you ever been really in love?' She squeezed Saba's hand briefly. 'Don't look so shocked – it's usually the first thing women want to know about each other.'

'I'm not sure.'

'If you're, um, *not sure*, you definitely haven't been.'

'Ah, so, trick question.'

'Oh get on with it!' Arleta's voice came like a lazy slap across the night. 'Ugh! This tea is vile,' she said. 'That ghastly buffalo milk always tastes so funny. There's half a bottle of champers in the fridge, Willie put it there – it's a bit flat but better than tea. Come on, and don't be cross – I want to know everything about you. I bet you've had dozens of boyfriends.' A barefoot Arleta padded back with two glasses and a bottle in her hand. 'You're so pretty.'

'I was engaged, but only for a bit,' Saba explained. 'And that was because my dad approved of him, and thought I should marry him. His name was Paul Llewellyn. He was in the class above me at school. He was sweet and kind. He wrote poems for me, said we would marry one day. I don't know why I'm talking about him in the past tense. He's still alive, he's in the army, he wants to be a schoolteacher when the war's over. All his family are schoolteachers. He hated me being a singer.' She dipped her head, remembering the terrible row. 'He liked the eisteddfods and the singing competitions, but when he saw me performing in front of men, well he went bloody mad. My father hates it too.'

She seemed to be blurting things out suddenly, perhaps the champagne or the late hour.

Arleta tutted and took another sip. 'Not bad is it, there are still a few bubbles left – carry on.'

'Well, I was doing this show in a factory near Bristol. My first big show really. Lots of men there, but perfectly respectable. I went on stage and sang "Where or When" and a few of the men did, you know, the wolf whistles and whatever. But it was *so* exciting, Arleta, my first show, and a dressing room even, well just a little bit curtained off. Paul wanted to come. He sent me flowers, he tried to be happy for me, he'd even hired a car, but when we were driving home, he went absolutely silent, and when I asked him what was the matter, he suddenly shouted,' Saba put down her cup and did his voice, ' "*You*, you're the matter – you made a real spectacle of yourself tonight." He said he felt like a twerp sitting there on his own with nothing to do.'

'Oh Lordy, what a fibber he sounds. The truth was, he couldn't bear it, nor could your father.'

'Bear what?'

'You being the centre of attention. Normal male behaviour in my experience. So then what?'

'It's different with my father, Arl, it goes so deep with him it hurts, but anyway, this Paul, when he said that, I knew in a flash it wouldn't work. I can't stop doing this.' The pain seemed fresh for a moment. 'I know it's not what some men want, but I've got to do it. I told him to stop the car, and I got out.' And she had. They'd been a mile or so from home, and she'd run back past the canal, down to the docks, sobbing her heart out. Her mother had been waiting at the lit door, dying to hear how it had all gone, and one of the worst things about it all was showing up like that all tear-stained and with the new dress Mum had spent hours on, splattered with mud. It was like murdering two dreams at once. Her mother had listened, frozen-faced, then sent her to bed and she'd lain there awake most of the night, her heart filled with a feeling of dreary darkness, a foreboding she couldn't name.

'The next morning, I posted his engagement ring back. Paul said

I was being dramatic, but I knew it couldn't work. My family haven't forgiven me either. He was suitable and he was—'

'Oh Christ!' Arleta interrupted with some violence. '*Suitable.*'

Saba could still see his face all twisted and wet. She'd felt so bad and so bloody determined at the same time, but she wanted to stop her story now.

'Are you a virgin?' There was nothing prurient about Arleta's question; it was a straightforward enquiry.

'No.'

'I think it's very overrated,' Arleta said, taking a swig of her champagne.

Saba silently agreed with her. She had lost her virginity in Paul's bedroom in Cardiff. His parents were away for the weekend visiting relatives in Tonypandy. He'd turned down the sheets of his narrow boyhood bed and kept his pyjama bottoms on until the lights were out, and it had happened surrounded by his school pictures and hockey sticks, and afterwards she'd felt calmer and freer. It was something she'd worried about a great deal, and now she didn't have to. In the middle of that night, safely back in her own bed, she'd woken feeling a little wicked (God knows what her father would have said) but mostly happy, as if a great weight had been lifted from her mind.

'Unless of course,' Arleta stared thoughtfully into her glass, 'you get PWL.'

'PWL?'

'Pregnant without leave. It happened to a girl in the Merrybelles on my last tour, and she was sent back home immediately with no pay. The hypocrisy was appalling, the brass hats swooning away like virgins themselves when half the men here have the clap.'

'What about you?' Saba said. 'Are you in love?'

'Oh, plenty of time for that later.' Arleta's voice was a little slurred.

'No, play fair.' Saba took a sip of champagne. 'Off you go.'

'Well . . .' Arleta didn't seem to know where to begin. 'The answer is no,' she said after a pause, 'but there is someone – a submariner, Bill, in the navy. I have no idea at all where he is now. He bought me this.' She jangled her charm bracelet. 'He's got no money.

'I'm in a bit of a bind about it actually.' Arleta had gone unusually still. 'We got carried away on my last night in England, because he was terribly frightened about going away and getting killed, and now he thinks we're going to get married. I've been a bit of a coward with this one . . . He's very sweet, though,' she added with a wan smile. 'I'm no good at breaking things off . . . hopeless actually.'

'So, not the mink buyer?' The indiscreet question slipped out, but Arleta had surprised her. She'd imagined a string of rich admirers.

'No, no, no, no, no.' Saba heard the clink of her glass and another sip. 'Another admirer altogether – he's got pots of it. The thing about Bill is he made me laugh, or did, but so much has happened since then, I can hardly remember him.' She stopped suddenly and laid her head on Saba's shoulder.

'Isn't that awful? Awful but true.' She sighed. 'I'd better show you the love of my life.' She went into their bedroom, and came back with a small, creased plastic folder that she thrust into Saba's hand. Inside it was a polyphoto of a small boy with sleepy blue eyes and blond curls. He had Arleta's curved humorous mouth and was roaring with laughter. 'His name is George, he's three, and as far as ENSA knows, he doesn't exist.'

'Arlie!' Saba, shocked, took the photograph. 'You must miss him horribly.'

'I do, I do – can't bear to think about him actually.' Arleta took the photo and gazed at him deeply. 'He lives with my mum at the moment, in Kent. I'm saving all my money for him. Don't tell anyone, will you?

'Don't forget to have a baby, Sabs,' she offered suddenly. 'People are so busy telling you how much it hurts, and how hard and ghastly it is, that they forget to tell you how much fun it is too. I have such a laugh with George – he's so noisy and cheeky and opinionated, he's got the dirtiest laugh. I'll tell you more about him later if you like.' Her face was completely lit up. 'Not that I want to bore you,' she added hopefully.

'He's gorgeous, Arlie, and I want to hear all about him,' said Saba. She surprised herself by adding, 'You're lucky,' and meaning it. Normally speaking, she found people being soppy about their children boring, all that talk about its little fingers and funny little ways, but in this impermanent world, having a baby seemed a wonderful thing, an act of bravery in itself.

'Yes, I am lucky,' Arleta agreed. 'As long as I can keep a roof over that little varmint's head, I'll feel proud of myself, and so far, I have . . . because what I . . .' Her voice was drifting, and trailing; sleep was catching up on her at last. 'What I . . . one day . . .' but she'd already gone to sleep.

Janine woke them up at nine o'clock the next morning. She stood, feet in third position, the perfect arc of her eyebrows raised in the direction of their empty bottle, the overflowing ashtrays, their smudged mascara, and, worst sin of all, the fact that they'd slept in their make-up. She tapped her feet rhythmically until they opened their eyes.

'Sorry to be the bearer of bad tidings,' she said, although a small twitch seemed to have developed in her lip, 'but we're leaving for the desert tomorrow. Max Bagley came around earlier in an absolute fury because you were so late to bed. I hope I heard this wrong, but I think he said something about sending you both home. He'll be back in an hour.'

Chapter 13

'Ignore the stupid cow,' Arleta said when Janine, having dropped her bombshell, waddled off in her feet-splayed ballet-dancer way. 'There's one in every company – in the Merrybelles we called them the EMS – the Envy, Malice and Spites – and it's written all over her. It's probably because she wasn't asked to do one of her special dances last night.'

But Janine hadn't made the story up. At eleven thirty, a muffled male voice came through the door. 'Are you decent, girls?'

'Oh damn it to buggeration.' Arleta, who'd run out of Tahitian Sunset was standing in her silk kimono with half a bottle of peroxide on her head. 'Wait! Wait! Wait!' she shouted as the knocking grew louder.

She wrapped her hair in a turban and opened the door.

'Mr Bagley!' She switched her professional smile on. 'What a lovely treat, but why so early?'

His linen suit was rumpled; he looked as if he hadn't slept.

'Cut the flannel, Arleta,' he said, curtly. 'I'm furious with both of you, but no time to talk now. All Cairo concerts cancelled. I've been up most of the night making the new arrangements. We leave tomorrow.'

'Oh for God's sake!' Arleta tugged at her turban. 'Darling, do give me a second, I've absolutely got to wash this stuff off.'

'I haven't got a second.' Bagley's eyes were bulging, he was breathing like a train. 'I must dash round and tell the others.'

'Why are they moving us so fast?' Janine walked in – her face shining with cold cream.

'I think they think the Germans are coming. Yet again.' Bagley smiled unpleasantly.

'Well I've got my panic bag packed.' She shot the girls a triumphant look. 'You see, I knew this would happen.'

Janine's panic bag, as she was fond of telling them, held her emergency tutus, her pyjamas, her medical supplies, toothbrush, make-up and gut reviver. Arleta had tried to pull her leg when she'd first heard about the gut reviver. 'It's for tennis racquets, but it prolongs the life of my ballet shoes,' Janine had told her without the trace of a smile.

'Yes, I think panic bags are a good idea,' said Bagley quietly. 'Leave anything inessential at the ENSA offices. With any luck we'll be back soon, or so they tell me.'

'So you'll be travelling with us? Definitely?' Janine stared at him like a child about to be separated from its cuddly toy.

'Yep, I'll be there; Captain Furness will be pulling our strings from Cairo. Now, if you'll excuse me,' he turned on his heel, 'I've got a mass of things to do. Saba, put your shoes on and come with me. I need to have a word with you in private.

'She'll be back in about an hour and a half,' he informed the others. 'Pack up the flat while she's gone.'

'What in hell were you up to last night?' Bagley exploded as soon as they were alone in the car together. He was driving erratically, one hand on the wheel, the other clenched. 'Who asked *you* to get up and sing? Who asked you to sing in Arabic, for God's sake? For all I know, you could have been singing "Eskimo Nell". I really should send you home immediately, the *cheek* of you.' When he turned and looked at her, his face was so contorted with rage she thought he might strike her.

Saba was thunderstruck. She'd assumed Cleeve would warn him, but now, what to say in her defence?

She heard herself mumble, 'I'm sorry, it was only a bit of fun.'

'A bit of fun.' Bagley roared the engine and drove wildly for a while in and out of the traffic. 'Do you have any idea, Saba, how stupid that sounds? This could not be a more sensitive time.' He spat the words out one at a time.

'I know.'

'No you don't. No,' he gunned the engine again, 'of course you don't. You don't think because your head is up your . . . because you have an ostrich mentality. You don't see that the brass hats think of us most of the time as a bloody nuisance because we can't follow orders, or that last night, after you'd had your *bit of fun*, I got hauled over the coals by Captain Furness.'

'I'm sorry,' she said. 'I really am.' Inwardly raging at the unfairness of this.

'The other thing is' – he pulled the car over to the side of the road, almost knocking over an old man selling watermelon juice. He turned off the ignition and jerked on the brake – 'and perhaps more importantly, well at least to me – you *weren't very good*.'

Ouch, that hurt.

'The band seemed to like it.'

'Shut up,' he shouted. 'What the hell does it matter what the band likes? You probably thought you were marvellous, but you weren't. And that matters to me. My reputation is on the line.'

She could hear herself breathing shallowly; he was attacking her, and not for the first time.

Two days before, they'd had, at his request, a private session together, ostensibly to choose new songs, and it had not gone well. She'd sung, 'The Man That Got Away' for him without accompaniment, and halfway through, he'd held his hand up to stop her.

'No, no, no, no, that's hopeless,' he'd said at last. 'And I'm going to tell you exactly why – will you mind that?' He'd pulled her around so that she stood right in front of him.

'Of course not,' she said, feeling completely exposed.

He'd lit a cigarette, removed a piece of tobacco from his tongue, and looked at her again.

'You're a good-looking girl,' he said, exhaling smoke. 'Men find you attractive. You could stand up there and wiggle your shoulders and flash your smile and sing in tune – and there is no question that because your natural voice is good, you will, for most known purposes, thrill them to bits. But the problem for me is I'm not getting *you*. Not yet.'

'What do you mean, you're not getting me?' She wanted to smack him round the chops but was determined to remain calm. How dare he manhandle her like that?

'Don't get me wrong,' his kindness almost more upsetting. 'Your voice is warm in tone, and sometimes you're brave in your delivery – the image I get is of a child flinging herself off a rock into the sea, but at the moment, I only get that girl in flashes.' He sighed, ignoring the tears that had started their maddening descent. 'It's potent stuff when I get that: for example, yesterday, when you sang "Deep Purple", the hairs stood up on the back of my neck. But then you did "St Louis Blues" like some weary old black lady that's got to pick a bale of cotton before she goes to bed, and that's when I feel I'm getting Saba doing a pretty good imitation of Bessie Smith; you used all her intonations and phrasings, and why not, she's brilliant. But that's lazy stuff, and at some point you have to ask yourself: do I want to be a second-rate imitation of Bessie Smith, or Helen Forrest or whoever is your idol, or do I want to be me?'

Her anger died and she felt instantly shamed; what he said was partly true. She'd learned her jazz standards from the records of the people who sang them: breathed when they breathed, asked her accompanists to play the tunes as close to their arrangements as possible. Was it laziness or insecurity that had made her swallow their magic whole? She'd never really questioned this before; nor for that matter had anybody else.

And the most painful part was that although she didn't like Bagley, she held him in high esteem – they all did. The cast had nicknamed him BG for Boy Genius; and she'd seen in rehearsal the lightning speed with which he transcribed music into different keys, or picked up a harmony and sang with you. How he could make up lyrics on the spot. When he'd talked about finding her special songs to sing her spirits had soared, thinking she could learn from him, but now she saw she had desperately disappointed him in every way.

It took her a while to realise that he had been driving her around in a circle for the purposes of this rocket. Outside on the streets, she saw more soldiers and airmen than she had before, and it seemed to her that the sky was darker than usual although she could not be sure.

'Please don't send me home,' she said. 'I couldn't bear it now, not without doing a proper concert.' Going home now would feel like one of the biggest defeats of her life.

'I can't,' he said grimly. 'No replacement, but do that again and you'll be on that plane so fast you won't know what's hit you. Understand?'

He slipped his hand suddenly down her brassiere and squeezed her breast hard.

'*Understand?*'

'What are you doing?' She leapt away, her face scarlet.

'Nothing,' he said coldly. 'What did you think I was doing?'

'Something,' she said, glaring at him. 'Do that again, and I'll deck you one.'

He dipped his head and gave her a blank look, as if she was speaking some obscure foreign language.

'Oh dearie me!' he muttered. 'Don't we take ourself seriously.'

'Not really,' she spat out, 'but I don't like that.'

'Well, there is something else you might like to know,' he continued smoothly, as if absolutely nothing had taken place. 'A probably more important thing,' he said with a sarcastic smile. 'From now on, we'll be going to some very dangerous places. Last week one of the ENSA groups at a hospital camp near Alex was bombed very badly. A shocking do, blood and bodies everywhere. It hasn't been on the news yet, but you'll soon hear. So the party is well and truly over. Got that?'

'Got that. Why didn't you tell us?'

'Didn't want to frighten you. You can still go home if you want to.'

'I can't,' she said. 'I don't want to.'

'Well done,' he said. He was gazing at her intently, and then lifting her hand from the car seat, he kissed it and gave her a very strange look indeed.

'I'm sorry,' he said. 'Are we friends again?'

She said an almost inaudible yes without meaning it, feeling compromised and miserable and disliking his rather patronising smirk but not knowing what else to say. She was going to have to watch him now.

Next they drove to the ENSA offices at Sharia Kasr-el-Nil, Bagley told her to stay in the car while he dashed upstairs to talk to Furness about a portable stage.

A few moments later, an NCO clattered down the stairs with the car keys in his hand.

'Mr Bagley says they've had a message from radio ops. I'm to take you over to Port Said Street.'

Cleeve's address.

'Are you sure that's right?' She was terrified now of doing anything without Bagley's permission.

'It's written down here, miss.' The NCO showed her the official form. 'And then you're to go straight back to your quarters and pack – you're leaving Cairo at sixteen hundred hours tomorrow.'

*

'Relax, Saba,' Cleeve said, when she told him this. They were in a small, anonymous café two blocks from his apartment. It was empty apart from them. 'I know your itinerary, and we have time for coffee, ice cream and a chat. Cheer up, old bean,' he handed her one of the cones, 'it may never happen.'

'It almost did,' she said. 'Max Bagley heard me singing last night at the Mena House. He's livid – I thought you said you were going to tell him. Listen, I didn't order this, I don't want it, you eat it.'

He licked one of the glistening scoops.

'Yum, yum,' he said. 'You should try this mastika one – it has a kind of raisiny, liqueury flavour and is much better than the strawberry one. Quite sure I can't tempt you?'

When she didn't answer, he said, 'Saba. Listen. Bagley will be dealt with, and you were marvellous last night – you did so well.' He tapped his ice-cream spoon against her arm. 'Ozan's sure to book you.'

She gave him a watery smile. 'Really?'

'Really. I mean, my Arabic is not perfect, but you looked and sounded so right. The dress too: absolute perfection.'

'I like singing those songs,' she told him humbly. 'They remind me of home.' Battered after her horrible morning with Bagley, she was soaking up his compliments like a thirsty plant.

'I didn't see you there,' she said suddenly.

'I didn't want you to,' he said quietly. 'And I didn't expect Max to be there either – so sorry about that. Did you say anything to him?'

'You told me not to.'

'Good,' he said quietly. 'Next time we ask you to do something, we'll clear it with him, but don't forget, as far as he's concerned, I'm only the broadcast man.

'You're very special, young lady,' he added randomly.

She could see through the café window the NCO walking towards them.

'You'll be off to the Canal Zone soon, and then touring,' Cleeve said quickly – he'd seen him too. 'But I have a small job for you before you go.'

'How do you know where we're going? We haven't been told.'

'I know.' He licked a smear of ice cream from his lips; drained the rest of his coffee. 'I'll be in contact again, maybe in a week.'

'How?'

'I'll do a broadcast. Some of the troops in Ismailia have been badly neglected. It won't ruffle any feathers whatsoever.'

The NCO got out of the car and folded his arms.

'He's waiting for me,' Saba said.

'Before you go,' he said softly, 'one last question.'

'What?'

'Do you have a boyfriend?'

'No.'

'Good. Safer for everyone. If you get one, be careful what you write to him.'

'I will.' Her heart began to hammer in her chest, as if it knew something she didn't.

'And the best of British, out in the desert.' Cleeve's hand was moist with sweat as he shook hers. 'It will be an experience you will never forget.'

Willie was practising his fez routine in his room at the YMCA when he saw the first flutterings of charred black paper go past his window.

A drunken soldier had warned him, two nights before, in the Delta Bar, that the burning of official papers at the British Embassy would be the first sign that the Germans were coming. And so, it had come. He felt both calm and brave as he took off his fez, sat on the bed and put his shoes on. His first thought was for Arleta – he'd loved her for so long, and now he must get his fat old carcass across town and rescue her and the other girls.

It was hard to find a taxi, so he shuffled and wheezed the three blocks towards the girls' digs. He toiled his way up the dark and narrow staircase, bent double near the bathroom on the first floor to get his breath back.

Janine opened the door.

'Are you gels all right?' he gasped. Three buttons of his pyjama top had come undone, and the sweating mound of his stomach poked through.

'Fine,' Janine regarded him with some distaste, 'but desperately busy. We're all leaving tomorrow – Saba's on her way back now.'

He sat down heavily in a wicker chair.

'I know,' he said, 'but take a look at this.' He hauled himself out of the chair and opened their shutters. The air outside was smoky and full of charred bits of paper.

'Oh good God.' Janine's shoulders had collapsed. 'What on earth . . . ?' She started to cough delicately.

Arleta appeared from the bathroom, damp and delicious in a silk nightie.

'What's up?'

Willie led her by the hand to the window. The burned papers fluttered on down. Janine slammed the shutters. 'Don't let them see any light,' she said.

'What is it, pet?' When Arleta squeezed the old man's hand, his heart swelled with protective love for her.

'The situation is as follows.' Fear made Willie maddeningly slow and inarticulate. 'I was having this drink the other night with a squaddie I met . . . not the Grenadier but the other one . . . Do you know the place on . . . Oh damn, what is it? . . . Oh yes, Soliman Pasha Square. Anyway, I was having a beer with this fellow from . . . it was either the Royal Scots Guards or the—'

'Darling, could you put this in a slightly smaller nutshell?' Arleta tugging at her turban. 'We don't need to know every little thing.' When she stroked the back of his head he almost sank into her arms.

'Well,' Willie's old eyes were milky and unfocused, 'he said they was burning all the official papers at the Embassy; that all the other civilians left town last week and that it's a bloody disgrace they've left us here. The three other groups have gone to Alexandria.' The words at last came out in a spurt.

'Oh blast it to buggeration!' Arleta grabbed her turban and ran out of the room.

'She's taken it hard, love her,' said Willie as the door slammed. 'We can't just crack up at the first thing. Our job,' a sterner version of himself emerged out of the mists, 'is to keep calm and carry on.'

'She's had trouble with her hair dye,' said Janine. Muffled shouts from the bathroom from Arleta. 'The first lot didn't work.'

'Oh God.' Willie, who'd had a difficult wife, understood the significance of this. He hauled himself to his feet. 'I'll leave you ladies to it then.' He said he was going home to pack, had been told that they were to stay put until transport was organised. 'I don't care what it is at the moment,' he said with a wheezy laugh. 'A sidecar across the desert would do me fine at the moment.'

After he'd gone, Arleta appeared, her hair a pale green colour.

'Well it's a disaster,' she said. 'I can't imagine what I was thinking about, doing it twice.'

'The Germans coming, maybe.' Janine's voice was low and bitterly sarcastic. 'I wonder if that felt *slightly* more important than your hair.'

The shimmering silence in the room was like the still before an electrical storm, and then she added breezily, 'Even if it does fall out, which of course, *dear*, I very much hope it doesn't.'

Arleta had warned them in advance about her terrible temper. Janine's fake concern fell like a lit match on a well-laid fire.

'I'm sorry? What did you say?' Arleta's green eyes widened and narrowed. She appeared to be listening very intently.

'I said, I very much hope it doesn't fall out,' quavered Janine.

Arleta stepped forward, and pointed her index finger squarely at Janine's forehead. 'You,' she said, 'are a stupid, stupid cow, and I'm sick of your whining, and all that splashing in the bathroom, and your twirly bits,' she spun around on the floor, 'and I'm sick of the bloody Germans too: they stopped me having a wonderful run in Southend in *Puss in Boots*, they completely buggered up my run with the Follies at the Palladium. They're taking me away from Cairo, and they're about to make me blasted well bald.'

'I had a career too,' Janine screeched. 'I was learning ballet from the age of three, I practically bankrupted my family, I was about to join Sadler's Wells, and anyway, don't exaggerate, stupid woman yourself!' Her face was contorted with malice. 'It's only gone a bit green.'

When Saba burst into the room, their lips were furled, their colour high and Arleta was screaming. It was almost funny, except the palm of Arleta's hand was open and she was balancing herself on the balls of her feet as if about to give Janine a perfectly timed forehand drive to the head.

Saba stepped between them.

'Hey! Hey, hey, hey! Stop! Stop, stop! Calm down. Your hair is fine, stop it!'

'Don't you dare say stop it.' Janine's pale face was a map of bulging veins. 'The city is on fire, the Germans are coming.'

'The city isn't on fire,' said Saba. 'I've just driven through it, and I didn't see any Germans. I'm sure it's all right.' When she went to the window and opened the shutters, it was a bit of a shock to see the sky full of floating grey paper, the light beyond it coppery and shimmering.

They heard the boom, boom, boom of shoes on the stairs, stiffened in terror as the doorknob turned and sagged with relief as the door burst open. It was Bagley. He was agitated and had a piece of burned paper stuck to his forehead.

'Panic over, girls,' he said. 'No Germans. There was an explosion at the paper factory near the Muski that frightened everyone to death, but our orders are the same. The Embassy are very jumpy, things are on the move, they want us out as quickly as possible. The truck will pick you up tomorrow afternoon.

'And so, our work begins.' Bagley seemed to be relishing his own Richard the Third moment. He looked at Arleta and Janine, who were sitting as far away from each other as possible. 'The most important thing for us now is to work as a team.' He looked searchingly at each one of them. 'Pack your bags, girls, check your papers are in order, don't leave any portable props behind, and the best of British luck to all of you. Knock 'em dead.'

Chapter 14

Telling his mother he was going to North Africa was awful. He'd kept the secret for days feeling ghost-like and fraudulent in his boyhood home, as if he was a bad understudy pretending to be a son. What made it worse was she'd been so very happy and lit up at having her boy, not only home but at a loose end for once. She'd cooked all his favourite meals, they'd gone through the family albums together. One night she'd even consented to play the piano for him: Joplin and Liszt and a faltering Chopin etude that had wrung his heart and made her wince with frustration. 'I used to know this so well.'

She was standing in the hall when he told her. She was wearing her dog-walking coat. Bonny, their old Labrador, was on a lead. He said the good news first, that there was the possibility that he would soon be promoted to flying officer, and then she listened quietly and obediently to the rest – that he was about to join a wing of the Desert Air Force in North Africa. Their camp was in the desert midway between Cairo and Alexandria. An amalgamated squadron full of Aussies and South Africans and Brits. They'd mostly be flying escort to medium bombers and attacking enemy airfields.

'They're very short out there at the moment, Ma,' he told her. 'And I'll be learning to fly Kittyhawks. I've never done that before.' All true; there was never any point in lying to her: she was an intelligent woman, an avid newspaper reader. 'They're quite busy there too.' He saw her eyes widen. 'There's a push planned.'

She bent down and stroked Bonny's ears. 'I thought you might be off soon,' she said.

She'd heard his complaints in the last few months about how quiet things were at his new station, an Operational Training Unit at Aston Down. They did nothing but training runs there now and putting your life in the hands of a windy or reckless new pilot was hair-raising – every bit as dangerous as being in combat. That's what he said. It was partly true.

Bonny started to whine. Time for his walk, she said. He watched from the window as she headed briskly towards the woods. She was thinner than he remembered her – almost childlike in the gumboots she'd worn in case the weather changed.

She was gone longer than usual. Her eyes were red and swollen when she came back. She went upstairs to her bedroom and came out before supper with fresh lipstick on and in a pretty frock.

They met on the stairs.

'*Such* a lovely night,' she said, as if nothing had passed between them. 'I think we should eat on the terrace.' Much to the relief of the local farmers, who were haymaking, the rain that had threatened all day had not fallen. The sky above the Severn estuary had burst into a recklessly beautiful sunset.

'That sounds wonderful, Ma,' he said. 'Thank you,' as if she had magically procured the night.

'I can't say it yet,' he heard her throat click as she touched his face, 'but I am proud of you.' Her own father had died of a sudden heart-attack, aged thirty-six. 'I really am. It may take a little while to show it.'

'Nothing to be proud of,' he muttered, and meant it.

In the kitchen, he helped her mash the potatoes. She gave him a tray of cutlery and plates and told him to set the table on the terrace.

'For two or for three?' he asked out of habit, although he usually knew the answer.

'Well, set for him but don't expect him.' She stood in a cloud of steam checking the spinach.

It was warm out on the terrace, where she'd lit a candle. The air was full of the peanutty smell of cut grass. In the far field they could see the bobbing light of a tractor working its way up and down the field, anxious to get the hay in before the weather changed.

They were eating her wonderful game stew when they heard the sound of his father's little Austin spraying gravel in the drive. He'd put the bigger car, the Rover, up on blocks in the stable; it was too heavy on petrol.

'He knows your news,' his mother said quickly. 'I told him earlier, but please don't talk about it before we eat.' Her face haggard in the candlelight, working against tears.

His father stood for a moment under the porch light, gaunt in his dark hat and dark suit. There was a bulging briefcase in his hand.

'Honestly, *men*.' His mother stood up in a sudden fury. 'Why do they always come late?'

She went into the kitchen, leaving her own stew to go cold.

'So, old chap.' His father gave him an awkward pat on the shoulder. 'Off again, I hear. North Africa, is it?'

'Yes,' Dom said. 'I—'

'Frank, what have you been up to? Let's hear something about you for a change.' His mother came charging back with the plates; the air volatile around her. Her old dog jumped as she banged the tray down, and glanced anxiously at his mistress and then at Frank.

'I'm hungry, dear one,' his father said in a strained voice. 'So perhaps you'll allow me to take my hat off and eat first? I've been operating since nine o'clock this morning.'

His mother took a deep jagged breath; she sat on the edge of her chair, her meal untouched, her eyes staring. When Dom saw his father squeeze her hand under the table, he felt both relieved and guilty. The baton must be handed on. He'd taken on the role of her protector for too long, and there wasn't enough left of him now, but still it was sad to see tears held in check all day roll down her cheeks, and to see her brush them away like an angry little girl.

For dessert they had the stewed damsons she'd bottled the year before, followed by the real coffee his father had been given by a grateful patient. She'd gathered herself up again, and although it was a brittle performance, he admired the way she talked about the weather, about plums, about a lovely concert she'd heard on the radio, as if she hadn't a care in the world. His father sat silently, picking his teeth discreetly with a toothpick. At ten o'clock, looking half dead with tiredness, he retired to bed.

'He's a good man, you know,' she said when the light went on in the upstairs bathroom and they could hear the gurgling of water as he cleaned his teeth. 'It was his single-mindedness I most admired when we first met.' She lit a cigarette, and looked Dom squarely in the eyes. 'I can hardly blame him for that now, can I?'

The most she'd ever said to him about her marriage.

They watched the tractor's wavering light go down the track towards Simpson's farm next door and stayed at the table on the terrace and talked until their clothes were damp with dew and the light had all but faded from the day.

When the candle wavered and guttered, she pinched it between her fingers and it was then he felt the urge to confide in her. They hadn't done well on this score before, both of them performing some semblance of what the other wanted, but not really laughing or talking or letting their hair down.

'I have another reason for going to North Africa,' he told her shyly. 'Well . . . maybe. At least I hope I do. It's partly ridiculous.'

'Hang on.'

She went inside and got a rug. She huddled inside it listening intently.

'I've grown up an awful lot in the last two years, Ma,' he told her, making her smile: as if she didn't know! 'I think I was a conceited ass before. I took so much for granted, you, this,' he lifted his glass towards the house, dark now the light in the bathroom had gone out, 'Cambridge, my friends.' When he stopped suddenly, she grasped his hand.

'Tell me about it,' she said. 'If it would help. You must tell someone.'

'No! No, no.' He shook his head. 'I don't want to. I'm not talking about that.'

He felt the thumping in his heart, and wanted to stop already – why not accept the soul's loneliness and get on with it. Why bother the poor woman?

'Please, Dom. Sorry.' She touched his hand tentatively and then took hers away.

He downed his whisky.

'I'm talking about someone else . . . I . . . Look, it's not important.'

He was about to tell her about Saba's singing, but it suddenly felt ridiculous, because there was nothing now to tell – he would sound like a lovelorn loon.

'What happened to Annabel?' she said, in a brave spurt. 'I thought she was such a darling girl.' Her face was tense; she'd been steeling herself for this.

'Nothing.'

'But it can't have been nothing – she was mad about you.'

'I told you before, Mother – she didn't like the hospital, she said it was nothing personal. I don't blame her.'

'Well I do.' Her face tightened like a fist. 'I think it was perfectly bloody of her. Darling, sorry, I know you hate this, but you look so good again.' His poor mother, terrified of him, miserable and shrunken in the twilight, huddled in her rug. 'Couldn't you try again. Write to her or have her down for a few days?'

'No,' he said. 'Absolutely not.'

'Why not?'

'Because I don't want it.'

A silence fell between them, rigid and dark with unsaid things, and he wondered, as he had many times in hospital, how much honesty it was kind to burden your parents with.

'There was someone . . . a girl in hospital,' he blurted out. 'It will probably sound completely ridiculous . . . but I fell for her.' As soon as he started he regretted it.

'No!' She turned to him, her eyes shining. 'No! Not ridiculous at all.' She took a tremulous breath. 'Who was she?'

'She came to sing for us.'

'Any good?' His mother had her sharp professional face on.

'Yes.'

She gave him the strangest look.

'I'm happy for you,' she said at last, 'because I . . .' When she swallowed hard, he thought, I've never seen her cry before, how odd that today it should happen twice.

'Because I . . . think . . . I sort of know that . . . well I think that everyone should die knowing they've had one great passion.'

'Mother . . .' He wanted to stop her right there. She was jinxing him; stepping into his dream.

'It may sound silly and schoolgirlish, but I believe it. It gives you a tremendous confidence, a sense that you haven't been cheated even if it does go wrong, and you mustn't let anyone talk you out of it,' she added fiercely. 'If you get it wrong, at least it's your mistake.'

She'd squeezed his hand so hard, he'd felt some great secret iced up inside her, and hoped profoundly that she wouldn't tell him what it was. He knew her well enough to know she would regret it later.

'It's nothing yet,' he muttered to himself.

'Is she really good?' she asked again. 'As a singer, I mean.'

He smiled sardonically to himself at the sharpness of her tone. She liked people with a centre to them, and had treated one or two of the pretty girls he'd brought home before Annabel not exactly coldly, but with a certain drawing aside of skirts that had infuriated him at the time.

'She's very good,' he couldn't stop himself, 'It's so impressive.'

'Well now listen!' she warned. 'Don't get all foolish and romantic about her. If she's like that, her life will be as important as yours. You will have to understand this and it will be very, very hard for you. I'm afraid you're rather used to being the centre of attention yourself.'

'Oh thanks, Ma,' he mocked her. 'A fascinating bighead, is that it? Anyway, I like her passion. I'm not frightened of it.' It was too late now, an act of cruelty almost, to tell his mother about how badly that first and last date had ended.

And looking at her son, Alys Benson had a piercing sense of how much war had already taken from him: his youth, his two best friends. She told herself to remember him like this, tonight, his dark hair wet with dew, his eyes so bright.

'Anyway,' he helped himself to one of her cigarettes and lit it, 'North Africa is where everything's happening at the moment, and I'm,' he shook his head, 'I'm a fighter boy now.' He bunched his fists and struck a Tarzan pose – her silly schoolboy again. 'And we're not getting enough of it at the moment. I can't stay doing nothing for ever. It will drive me mad.'

'I can imagine,' she'd said, thinking, *I hate flying, I wish your father had never told you about it.*

And he thought, *No you can't.* Only another fighter pilot could know how shockingly addictive the whole thing was. It was the way he formed friendships with other men far deeper than anything he'd ever experienced before; the way he frightened himself, defined himself as a man. Could any woman possibly understand this? He had no way of knowing, although he'd thought about it recently in connection with Saba. He'd written one more letter to her but heard nothing back. With her, he would have to fly blind.

Chapter 15

As the morning progressed, Arleta's hair grew greener and her mood darkened until it was positively dangerous and it was imperative to get her to the hairdresser's before they left town.

Willie, desperate to help, had dashed over to Cicurel's, the so-called Harrods of Cairo, to see if they stocked Tahitian Sunset, or, failing that, any other cure for green hair, and drawn a blank with the smart French woman who ran their cosmetic department. He'd fared no better with the snooty, heavily powdered English girl behind the make-up counter at Chemla's, another fancy emporium, who told him in a fake Home Counties drawl it was madness to try and dye your own hair, particularly out here. In desperation he ran back to the barber's shop in the bazaar and came back with a pot of black goo that the proprietor highly recommended, and which Arleta looked at dubiously, particularly when she learned its source. When she snapped, 'He sounds like the same idiot that sold me this,' Willie slunk off to the corner like a dog that had been badly beaten but still longed to please.

Then Arleta had a brainwave. Why on earth hadn't she thought of it before?

Scrabbling through her knapsack, she said a friend of hers on the last Cairo tour with the Merrybelles had highly recommended a hairdressing shop on Sharia Kasr-el-Nil, not far from the office. Where in the hell was it? She thumbed through her address book; here it was: The Salon Vogue, number 37, proprietor Mitzie Duhring.

'Go with her,' Willie softly pleaded with Saba. 'I'd offer, but she'd bite my head off. You could have your own done there.'

Saba needed no persuading. She felt sorry for Arleta, who suddenly seemed so vulnerable, and besides, her own hair had grown remarkably in the heat and had had no attention since her last cut at Pam's of Pomeroy Street. Willie said there was plenty of time between now and leaving.

An hour and ten minutes later, they both sat wrapped in towels, sipping tea in a discreetly furnished, softly lit salon that felt like a private sitting room. The owner of the salon, a severely dressed, quietly spoken woman, more doctor than hairdresser, unwrapped Arleta's turban, and was closely examining the damage. She rubbed the hair between her fingers; as she held it for inspection under the light she murmured in a guttural voice, '*Gott in Himmel*, Good God! What have they done to you?'

Saba and Arleta glanced quickly at each other. She couldn't be . . . surely not – even in the topsy-turvy world of Cairo. But her name was Mitzie Duhring, which sounded pretty German. Saba's heart started to pound. If she told Cleeve about this so early in her employment, he might think her ridiculous, like an overeager schoolgirl on her first day at school pumping her hand in the air. But surely she should say something.

In a silence conspicuously lacking in the usual *going anywhere nice tonight?* and *where have you come from?* Mitzie ordered her assistant to wash Arleta's hair thoroughly four times. Next, she silently cut Saba's hair – her efficient, bony hands winking with diamonds, her face in partial shadow in the mirror.

Saba, pretending to read an old copy of *Vogue*, watched her carefully when it was safe to do so. She estimated that if she left the salon by four o'clock, there would be time to get a taxi to Cleeve's and be back at the flat to get her packing done.

Arleta, visibly relaxing in Madame Duhring's calmly professional hands, winked at Saba when she caught her eye. She was in the middle of telling Saba that Mitzie had just told her she could so easily have gone bald again, just like in Malta, when a small brass bell over the salon door jingled, and a stunning young Egyptian woman walked in – pale-complexioned, with almond-shaped eyes and dressed in high heels, silk stockings and a beautifully tailored blue silk suit. The two long braids that hung to her waist swung as she walked and so did her hips, giving the impression of a knowing and provocative schoolgirl.

The assistant, who was washing Arleta's hair, let out a gasp when she saw her. This was someone of importance. She excused herself, rinsed her hands and ushered the highly scented stranger to the chair beside Saba's.

Saba watched Mitzie's reflection in the glass. She heard her greet the woman, first in French then in English The braids were released, the thick black hair combed and discussed with the same muted seriousness with which Arleta's problems had been addressed. Five minutes later, the woman sat down again – her hair wet and wound in a turban. When Saba caught her eye in the mirror, the exotic stranger smiled at her.

'Do you mind if I smoke?' she asked. She took out a mother-of-pearl cigarette holder.

'Not one bit.' Saba pushed the ashtray towards her.

Saba's ears were on stalks as the assistant wound the woman's hair into an elaborate series of pin curls. Mitzie addressed the woman formally as Madame Hekmet. When she complimented her on how well her skin was looking, the woman dimpled prettily and said she had her own mother to thank for that. She had been very fussy with her ever since she was a child. Lots of fresh vegetables and fruit and nuts and seeds. 'And of course the dancing helps,' she added. 'It keeps me healthy.'

So Egyptian. A dancer. A successful one, judging by the impeccable handbag, the pale suede shoes. Saba wondered if she was a belly dancer – the ones Willie called gippy tummies.

Mitzie was combing out the woman's heavy cloud of hair now – it came almost to her waist.

'So, cut it all off?' Mitzie smiled at what was obviously an old joke between them.

'We'll keep it for now.' The woman's voice was husky and self-satisfied. 'I'm giving a party, for some of your people.'

Mitzie's scissors stopped snipping.

'Ah.' She raised her eyebrows and glanced quickly at Saba.

The dancer looked older in her turban and with her hair scraped back. She moved her finger along her eyebrow. 'So, I want something special.'

'One second.'

Mitzie walked over to Saba, and with an automatic smile, tested the dryness of her hair with a finger; she put her under a hairdryer, and flicked the switch.

Saba, inside its deafening hum, wondered if her own imagination was overheating. If this German-sounding person was really German, was she allowed to run a business here when the rest had gone? And if she was German, why had the dancer said *a party for some of your people*, so openly and in English. It made no sense.

Half an hour later, Mitzie turned off the hairdryer and again, without conversation, combed her out. Saba was delighted: Her hair fell in a brilliantly shiny, sophisticated Veronica Lake-ish swoop over her right eye. Mitzie definitely knew her stuff.

Arleta did a mock double-take and put her two thumbs in the air.

'How long are you going to be?' Saba mouthed, tapping her watch.

'One hour,' said Arleta. There was a tray of coffee beside her and some petits fours.

'I'm going back to pack.' Saba pointed towards the clock on the wall.

Arleta beckoned her over. 'What's the verdict?' She lifted the corner of her hairnet. 'Still a gremlin?'

Saba peeped under the hood. Arleta's new hair was a hot white-blonde – much blonder than she'd been before.

'Sensational,' she said. 'You're going to love it.'

'Listen.' Half an hour later, Saba was sitting on Cleeve's sofa. His lift had broken down; she was breathless from the stairs. 'I have no idea whether this is important or not, but I thought I should tell you anyway.'

She told him about the green hair, the Salon Vogue, the possibly German proprietor. 'At least I'm almost certain she was, although she spoke mostly in English.'

Cleeve sprawled and clasped his hands behind his head. He looked at her approvingly.

'Full marks,' he said, 'for picking up on that one. I know Mitzie well – everybody does – she's a fixture on the Cairo social scene.'

Saba flushed with embarrassment – she'd made a twit of herself thinking this was hot news.

'No, your instincts were spot on,' Cleeve said. 'And she is an interesting anomaly. Lady Lampson, the Ambassador's wife, is one of her clients, also, or so I've heard, Freya Stark the explorer when she's not off on some donkey somewhere, but her most famous client, and the one she owes her liberty to, is Queen Farida, the wife of the Egyptian king.'

Saba was totally confused – the wife of the English ambassador having her hair cut by a German? It made no sense at all.

'Here's the thing,' Cleeve said. 'The Embassy would love to see Frau Duhring interned with the rest of the Germans in Cairo, but they dare not come between a woman and her hair because Queen Farida adores her. Funny when you think of it, the fate of a nation resting on the queen's curls.'

'But is she a Nazi?' Saba felt a crawling up her spine.

'No, because she and her husband refused to join the Nazi party – they've been cast out by the German community, but her situation is precarious. Her husband has already been interned and Sir Miles Lampson, an awful twit, would love to send her away; he doesn't like the idea of a German national snooping on all that juicy hairdressing-salon gossip. But he can't afford to – we're desperately unpopular with the Egyptians at the moment, and this, silly as it may sound, could be the straw that breaks the camel's back. We simply can't afford to upset Farida – the King adores her, he's said to buy her a new jewel every month.

'Any other good nuggets while you were there?' he threw out casually while he was making tea.

'Well maybe . . . I don't know. Probably nothing.'

'Say it.'

'Well only this, there was another woman there, very beautiful, a dancer, Madame Hekmet they called her; she's giving a party for German people. It sounded as if she thought Mitzie knew who was going to be there, but I couldn't hear all of it – Mitzie put me under the dryer.'

'Hmm . . .' Cleeve drummed his fingers against his lip. 'Nothing else?'

'No.'

'Could be a hole in one, could be straight into the rough – you simply never know.'

She had no idea what he was talking about.

'Did she say where the party was?'

'No.'

'Almost certainly in Imbaba, where the Cairo houseboats are moored – it's near the Kit Kat Club where she probably dances. Anyway,' he added briskly, 'we can easily check that out.'

'How?'

'That's for me to know and you to find out.' He smiled at her playfully. 'Tea?'

'No thanks; I've got to run. We leave tomorrow. I'll get a rocket from Bagley if I'm late.'

The lift was working again, clanking and complaining, its filthy yellow ceiling light stacked with more dead flies.

'You're quite the girl, aren't you?' Cleeve remarked softly before he shut the cage door behind her. He peered through the bars at her and smiled. 'I had a feeling you'd be rather good at this, and if you are, we have something quite important coming up.'

He pressed the button and, as the lift cranked down, she saw his face, his knees, his desert boots disappearing and then heard only his echoing voice coming down the dark shaft, saying something valedictory like farewell, or good luck, or break a leg, and hearing this, she got a great rush of almost unbearable excitement thinking that at last her life was truly taking off. They were leaving. Tomorrow.

Chapter 16

There was a mad dash the next day to pack up the flat, and get their kit in order before their truck picked them up at 1600 hours. They were going, Furness had finally told them, to Abu Sueir, an airbase in the Canal Zone, about seventy-five miles north-east of Cairo.

Before they left, Saba wrote to her father.

Dear Baba,

We're leaving Cairo today to go on the road and start our proper work. I want you to know that if anything happens to me – which it won't! – I have done what I felt I was meant to do here, and that I am sorry that what has made me happy has hurt you so. I hope one day we will understand each other better. Where is your ship now? Please tell me, and please write. You can send a letter to me here at ENSA, Sharia Kasr-el-Nil. The posts are terribly slow but it would be good to hear from you.

Saba

There were other things she wanted to tell him, both trivial and large: how it had felt that night singing 'Mazi' in front of the Pyramids at the Mena House; how magical Cairo could be with its lurid sunsets, its feluccas sailing like giant moths down the Nile; the amazing shops – some far posher than any she'd seen in Cardiff; how awful too, with its heat and blare and noise and stinks – the drains and camel dung, the spices from the markets, the jasmine ropes sold at restaurants at night, the indefinable smell of dust. She wanted to say that she feared for him. (Janine, whose brother-in-law was in the merchant navy, had spelled out for her in grisly detail the carnage in the shipping lanes at home.) She wanted to say that she missed him, that she hated him too for being so childish. Such a muddle in her head about him, such a stupid waste of love.

Her sweaty fingers made the letters of the address run. Pomeroy

Street, Butetown, Cardiff felt like a million miles away from here. Searching for moisture in her dry mouth, she licked the edges of a yellow aerogramme and wondered if she'd ever see him again.

They left Cairo a few hours later in a battle-scarred bus and headed north-east to Abu Sueir. Bagley and some soldiers had gone ahead of them to set up the portable stage.

Saba sat by herself – in this heat a body next to you felt like a furnace, and there were enough empty seats for them to have a row each. Arleta and Janine – still no-speakies – were at opposite ends of the bus; the acrobats at the back; Willie, dead to the world, snored percussively under a copy of the NAAFI newspaper and Captain Furness sat tensely behind the driver, his swagger stick on the seat beside him, ham-like knees stretched out in the aisle.

She made a pillow of her khaki jacket – it was too hot to rest your head against the glass – and though she already felt car sick from the fumes, tried to tell herself the adventure was beginning. Outside the window there was precious little to see but miles and miles of crinkled sand, a few dead trees, a heap of animal bones.

She was half asleep when Willie staggered towards her and dropped some paper in her lap.

'For you, my love. They came from the NAAFI earlier but you was asleep.'

Two letters. For her! She woke up immediately. One was written in her mother's slapdash hand, and postmarked South Wales. The other's unfamiliar handwriting made her stomach clench. She turned it around in her hand and stuffed it in the canvas bag under her feet.

Dear Saba, her mother wrote,

Everyone is fine on Pomeroy Street, apart from Mrs Prentice who went to Swansea to see her sister two weeks ago and got bombed. I'm still working all the hours God sends at you know where. Tansu was a bit mopey for a while without you but now is part of a knitting group at the Sailors' Hall, which has cheered her up no end. Little Lou has started a new school in Ponty and she is happy there and still comes home at the weekends. Did you get her letter yet? Your father is away again, working for . . . a crudely cut hole from the censor's scissors here, *but I think he has written to you. I don't know what to say about that, so I*

will leave it to him, but if he hasn't written know that the posts are terrible and try not to worry too much, it may not mean anything.
Your loving Mam xoxo

Post script (it was Joyce's habit to always write this in full)

I got a pattern off an old copy of Woman's Friend, *and I've made you a dress out of cream parachute silk. (They had a sale of it in Howell's and the queues were round the block, I got there early.) I posted it with this letter.*

Mam. My mam. She held the letter to her cheek smiling and so glad to hear from her she could have wept.

She read it again – it hurt thinking about her mother standing like Switzerland now between Dad and her, also to picture her queuing for hours for parachute silk, her hopeful whirlings on the Singer sewing machine she was so proud of. The Schiaparelli of Pomeroy Street. Saba wished she'd make something beautiful for herself for a change. The dress had not arrived, and even if it had, she probably wouldn't want to wear it anyway, except out of sentiment or loyalty. How frightening it was how quickly things changed – even things you wanted to stay the same. All Saba wanted now was for them to stay alive, and for her mother to be happy while she was away – was that so terrible? Probably, she sighed, and looked out the window – she'd turned out to be a rotten daughter.

The other letter now. The buff-coloured envelope poked out from the bag. She put her nail under the flap and had it half open when Willie appeared.

'Mind if I join you for a bit?' He sat down heavily beside her. 'Sorry about the get-up,' he'd changed from his khakis into a dubious-looking green striped pyjama top, 'but I'm baking. You've lost your little friend, I see.' He pointed towards Arleta, who was fast asleep four seats ahead of them.

'Yes, well . . .' She showed him the letter. 'I've just got these, my first, and I think she thought . . .' She hoped he'd take the hint, but Willie was not famous for subtlety.

'I hear there was a right old dust-up earlier.' He pointed at Janine, sitting close to the driver, as upright as a startled ostrich, and drew so close that the hairs from his ears tickled Saba's chin.

'That stuck-up madame needs a bit of a seeing-to,' he said, 'if you know what I mean. One of the acrobats said he'd do it. Lev, I think. Lovely job.'

'Willie!' She sprang away. 'That's naughty.'

'It would help her dancing and all. I mean it. Arleta almost lost her hair.' Willie grabbed his own bald pate and looked anguished. 'I hear she nearly went mad.' He gave a wheezy laugh and looked back at Arleta. 'Very spirited, that one,' he said softly, and then he sighed.

'I hope they make up,' said Saba. 'It's so boring if no one's speaking.'

'Arleta's as good as gold,' Willie said. 'She'll get her out of it. It's bad for the company,' he added self-righteously, 'if people can't get along, we've got to stick together.' He mopped his damp face. 'None of us have a clue what's round the next corner now, do we, girl?'

'No we don't, Willie,' she said. Both of them stopped. The bus suddenly swerved to avoid a team of camels crossing the road. The men who led them looked up at them – their eyes expressionless, faces swathed against the dust. Behind them stretched miles and miles of sand shimmering and dissolving in a heat haze. 'We certainly don't. Thank you for pointing that out to me.'

When Willie went back to his seat, she pulled the buff-coloured envelope from her bag again. The heat inside the bus was now 120 degrees; her wet hand had dissolved part of her address.

. . . *ear* . . . *aba.* Damn it! The censor's vigilance meant the letter hung like a paper chain in her hands – she couldn't even work out the date. She put the flimsy aerogramme against the window and in daylight so bright her eyeballs flinched, made out part of a word at the top of the letter: *une* and then *42*. A hole above the date where the address might have been. His address, or her crazy thinking? All she knew was part of her had leapt into life like a flame when she'd seen the letter, and that now she was shocked at how disappointed she felt, and annoyed with herself too. Why would he write to her now?

Some food came round in a cardboard box: bully-beef sandwiches and warm water, a sickly-smelling banana turning black and wilting in its own skin. After it, to block out the heat, they tried to sleep again, and when she woke, the dust had cleared and she saw more sand stretching out to the horizon like a limitless sea. If you were not in a good state of mind, the scale of it could make everything look stunningly pointless; their little lorry a piece of thistledown blown by any random wind.

When Furness stood up to brief them on what to expect, dried saliva had caked in the corners of his mouth, and his face streamed with sweat. For the next ten days, he said, they would be whisked from place to place to perform at RAF camps, field units and hospitals in what he described vaguely as the Canal Zone; after that they'd be moving west to follow in the footsteps of the Eighth Army. Some of these camps would be secret, or too small even to have proper names. Sometimes, Arleta had whispered, they didn't even tell you where you were, especially if you were near enemy lines.

When Furness had stopped talking and gone back to his seat, Saba lay stretched out over two seats, feeling the juddering desert road beneath her, thinking about Dom and their exciting, painful evening together. It annoyed her to still think of him, but that evening, its disappointing ending, had got stuck in her mind like the pieces of a mismatched puzzle she needed to solve.

She thought about the gentleness of his hand holding her foot when she'd sat down with the blister from those blasted shoes. He'd rubbed her toes between his fingers, and even though she'd been embarrassed, hoping her feet weren't sweaty from the audition and the dancing, she'd honestly wanted to purr like a kitten because it was so sudden and shockingly intimate. The wet pavement; him kneeling, his brown eyes looking at her under a lock of dark hair, the light in them tender, that was what she thought of. It was so unexpected after their wisecracking, it had seemed to iron out all the sharp angles of the day, and she'd believed in it.

And the next bit ruined everything. She'd definitely seen him kiss that girl in the club. Their heads had stayed together for a long time, talking intensely like lovers do, and all of it had made her think her own instincts were hopelessly wrong, and it got her goat to think of how she had let him spoil what had been such a marvellous day.

Oh God, she woke enraged and breathing heavily and with a raging thirst, having already drunk her pint of chemical-tasting water. Sweat trickled down between her breasts as the bus was rocked down a rough bit of road. Opening her eyes, all she could see was flipping sand and a skinny goat, eating a thorn bush, that leapt away in terror at the sight of them.

'Please, I am sitting?' A pair of well-muscled thighs slid into the empty seat beside her. Boguslaw the acrobat.

Bog, Boggers, Bog Brush – he answered to all of them – brought nerve-racking news. While she'd been dreaming, the plans had changed: tonight, instead of the small first concert planned, they would perform for up to a thousand troops, RAF personnel and medics at a transit camp near Abu Sueir. The portable stage, the piano, the props and the costumes had gone ahead; they were setting up now.

'Please Gods, they don't expect a big company and a big show,' Bog grimaced. Max Bagley had made no secret of the fact that they were spectacularly under-rehearsed, and they'd all hoped for a day's rest first.

Saba hadn't seen Bog for the past few days. The acrobats had been billeted in another part of town, and Arleta – the girls' expert on the dark side of life – had whispered that the boys had been out on the razz.

'I'm not trying to shock you,' she'd said in her husky, thrilling voice, 'but the boys like to play, and there's this street they go to in Cairo called Wagh-al-Birkat that caters for all tastes: young girls, dogs, sheep, chickens. And I'll tell you a true story,' she added, her eyes green slits, 'early this year, a young naval officer was caught stark naked in the Shepheard Hotel. He was had up for indecent exposure and got off by quoting from the rulebook: "an officer is deemed to be in uniform if he is appropriately dressed for the port in which he is engaged". Ha, ha, ha, isn't that wonderful?'

Janine's beautifully plucked eyebrows shot up to her hairline. 'Well you see,' she'd said, 'I don't find that even remotely funny,' and up they'd shot again when Arleta said that she personally thought that the British army should do what the French and the Italians did and set up legal brothels for soldiers. They were young and lusty – it was inhuman to expect them to do without creature comforts for so long. At which point Janine had removed a damp flannel she kept in her handbag, and wiped her hands very deliberately.

'I am watching you earlier.' Boguslaw cosied up to Saba, his left leg so close she could feel the tickle of the hairs against her leg. 'Does your letter make you sad?' He gave a deep sigh.

'A little,' she said.

His leg moved closer.

'You're too pretty to be sad,' he said. 'Is a man?'

'Yes. No.'

'A strong man?' A biceps appeared like a giant cobra in his arm. 'Strong like this.'

'Very, very strong.' It was much too hot for flirting. When the bus slowed down, in an effort to divert him, she pointed to a fruit stand on the side of the road. A man, his donkey; a veiled wife sat passive beside a pile of dried beans, some sugar-beet stalks, some dates. The woman was swatting flies from a sleeping baby on her lap. Two other children played in the dirt beside them.

'Are you married, Bog?' she asked him – she'd teased him and taught him songs but they hadn't talked properly yet.

'Not now,' he said. 'I was.' She heard him inhale sharply. 'They're dead,' he said at last. He moved his leg away from her. 'Wife, daughter, mother, family . . . My family.' He took a deep breath. 'We all lived in Warsaw before the war. Mother, father, wife, children, us boys, circus.' He did the shadow of a cartwheel in his seat. 'Always working. Not good, not good. One day, we are away doing a show, and when we come home, the Germans have been.' He threw up his hands, a look of deep disgust on his face. 'My family is all gone.' He clicked his fingers. 'Now, I can't go home.

'I hate the fucking bastard Germans,' he said at last, 'and the fucking bastard Russians too. I can't forgive them.'

Saba clasped his hand, horrified at having asked her question so carelessly; Arleta had warned her the boys had a sad background.

'I'm sorry, Boguslaw,' she said. 'I should . . . I would never . . .'

'No, no, no, no. It's OK.' He stood above her, eyes shut. 'I wanted to tell you, it's not your fault.' He was sweating. 'I go and sit with my brothers now.'

They arrived at their destination late in the afternoon, so covered in dust they looked like porcelain figures. A harried subaltern marched them down a dusty track and showed them the female quarters – a four-man tent. Janine moaned softly when she saw it. The tent stank of DiMP and the camp beds were so close they touched. There were three rusty nails on a post to hang their costumes on; a cracked mirror on the wall would serve as their dressing room. Arleta took the mirror down immediately saying it was bad luck, and hung the framed four-leafed clover she carried with her on the nail.

In a small hut outside there was an Elsan and a roll of lavatory paper that had crisped up in the heat, and a jerrycan containing their water, which was severely rationed – one pint a day for drinking, one to wash in. When Arleta joked there'd be no face-splashing that night, Janine's lips thinned.

'Come on, love.' Arleta patted Janine softly on the arm. 'Let's get on. I'm no good at sulking.'

'I'm sorry too,' Janine said in a tight voice. Her eyes filled with tears. 'Sorry I came.' Her chin wobbled violently for a moment. She told them both in a violent rush that her fiancé had given her the push before she came on tour, and she was so upset she couldn't talk about it yet. She was sorry to have been such a pain. She'd hoped the tour would take her mind off it but she really wasn't strong enough for it yet.

'Oh love! Say no more!'

'No, no, no, don't.' She wasn't ready yet for Arleta's lavish sympathies, and physically backed away, one delicate hand in the air. She was incapable of a clumsy gesture, even two foot from an Elsan. 'But I did mean to say earlier,' she ventured timidly, 'your hair looks nice.'

Which it did – a dazzling white-blonde now, quite spectacular. The boys had all done double-takes and whistled when they'd seen it, which had cheered Arleta up no end.

'I expect we're all on edge a bit,' Janine said. 'It feels so terribly disorganised, I'm not used to that.' She looked down at the narrow camp beds, with their stained mosquito nets. 'We're supposed to check under them for snakes and scorpions,' she said, getting down on her hands and knees. 'It's all so sudden.' Her voice was shuddery as she straightened up. 'I'm never going to do this again,' she said.

An hour later, Max Bagley's voice, strained and disembodied, came through the canvas flap.

'One hour till showtime,' he said. 'If the piano goes flat, ignore it – it was damaged on the way here. Keep your shoes on,' he warned, his voice scarily monotone, 'the stage is very uneven and the floodlights near the front are still not working. No plummets into the audience, *s'il vous plaît*.'

'This will be a disaster,' Janine predicted when he had gone. She was lying under a sheet with an eye mask on. 'No proper piano, no costumes, no flaps.' The props truck had broken down earlier – it was touch and go whether they'd get the stage up in time. To block her out, Saba spat on her sponge – they were already low on water after a quick cup of tea – and began her make-up. Her scared-looking eyes swam into view in Arleta's mirror, and then her reflection wavered, turned yellow and went out.

'Blast it.' Arleta lit their acetylene lamp again – the generators were temporarily on the blink.

'Thirty minutes, ladies.' Bagley's voice again. 'The spots are working now.'

'Good.' Saba only half heard him. She was humming her songs in her head.

'Darling,' said Arleta, bobbed down beside her, back pearly with sweat. 'Be an angel and do up my top popper.' She looked very pale.

Saba clicked it into place.

'Thank you, sweetheart.' Arleta kissed her, a faint whiff of gin on her breath.

'All right?' Saba said.

'Terrified – thanks for asking,' said Arleta. Her first number was a Josephine Baker send-up and she was putting a plastic pineapple on her head. 'A real old attack of the collywobbles; I get it sometimes, especially at the beginning of a tour.'

'*Crepi il lupo!*' Saba said, squeezing her hand.

'Come again?'

'My old singing teacher used to say it before the curtain went up,' Saba explained. 'It's better than break a leg. First he'd say to me "*In bocca al lupo*", that's Italian for "in the wolf's mouth", then I'd say "*Crepi il lupo*", which means "the wolf dies".'

'Well my lupo is alive and bloody kicking, but I'll give it a whirl.' Arleta put her arms around Saba and said in a muffled voice. 'Thank you.'

'What for?'

'For being a wonderful friend.'

*

Half an hour later the call came.

'Ready, girls?'

'Ready.'

'Ready, Janine?'

'Hope so.' Janine was chalking her shoes.

Arleta stood up, pineapple securely fastened to her head with a double row of kirby grips. '*Crepi il lupo!*' She strode towards the desert stage and their first proper concert together.

The portable stage looked not bad considering. Its red lights pulsed like a swollen heart in the middle of the drab huts, the barbed wire and the rows of tents. Saba walked up the steps to the back of the stage. She peeped around the dusty curtain and saw rows and rows of soldiers waiting like patient children underneath a starlit sky. There were uniformed nurses from the base hospital in the aisles, their patients dark mounds on stretchers beside them.

The running order was written on a blackboard in the wings. She checked it again. The Banana Brothers first, then Willie, then her first two numbers. Her mouth and eyes felt gritty with sand, her heart beat faster. This was the high-board moment. Bagley was waiting on the other side of the stage to start the show. When he looked at her, she lifted her chin and stood straighter, blocking out everything he'd said about her shortcomings – she couldn't afford to think of that now; that way lay the sick bucket and the leaping wolf.

Bagley lifted his hand. 'Five minutes,' he mouthed. He smiled at her, moving with fluid grace between the portable generator and the lights and the curtains. Arleta came up beside her and linked arms. She did a little running dance on the spot.

Bagley's arm came down. The band struck up, Willie dashing on to the stage to some jolly farting and squeaking circus music, pretending with his butterfly net to catch the dancing insects in front of the spotlights. They were on.

'Ladies and Gentlemen, hold on to your hats because we're here, the marvellous, the incomparable Razzle-Dazzles, live from Cairo and Orpington. Tonight there are but eight of us . . . but good things come in small packages, so be prepared to be amaaaaazed!!!!'

Bog came first, in a blue spangled suit, leaping high into two amber-coloured pools of light. Roars and laughter from the audience as Willie, trying to follow him, did rickety handstands near the wings. Bog cartwheeled hectically, one two three four five times across the stage. Lev appeared and flung Bog into the air like a juggling ball. Hey!! And now a triumphant Bog tossed on top of a shouting human pyramid, beaming and quivering his legs and making anguished faces to show how brilliant they were. When he saw the girls in the wings he winked at them and they winked back.

'Bravo, Boggers,' Saba said. She blew him a kiss. 'Magnificato.'

Some of the stretcher cases were laughing now, their faces crimson-washed from the lights of the ambulances that would take them home. The able-bodied men sitting on uncomfortable tin seats were clapping wildly, the air thick with their blue cigarette smoke. Willie came back for a bit and rattled off a few gags, then Janine appeared, and he dashed after her with his butterfly net as she fluttered against the desert sky like a green moth, dashing hither and yon as if in frantic pursuit of another moth to mate with to the opening chorus from *Scheherazade*. The men looked wistful.

Saba, hearing the dying chords of violins, felt her own heart plucked hard. From where she stood, hidden by the curtain, she could see Janine waving and leaping as she flew off the stage, another person altogether. Her name was rubbed off the blackboard.

'*Ah nooooowa, the verrrra beautiful . . .*' Willie appeared in a huge baggy suit, clutching his throat and staggering. He glanced at her briefly in the wings to see if she was there, '. . . *the verrray alllarmingly charming, our own little desert song birdaa, Missa Saba Tarcaaaaan.*'

Arleta stood with her in the wings. She squeezed her hand, and gave her a push. 'Knock 'em dead, girl,' she whispered.

Saba felt a sluggish breeze as Bog and Lev lifted her through the red and yellow lights and placed her down in the centre of the stage. They jutted their arms towards her like stamens towards a flower. Bagley appeared behind a battered-looking piano – the spotlight on him illuminating a fresh cloud of dark insects. He raised his hand, played a few notes and they leapt together into 'Get Happy'.

You could see so much from the stage: the faces of the nut-brown men softening, a soldier, raised up from his stretcher, beaming and waving. She flung herself into the song, loving the syncopated rhythms that Bagley slyly threw in so as not to make it too ordinary and corny, and loving too her own wide-throated ending when she threw her head back into a cloud of stars and gave it all she could. By the end of the song she was steaming with heat, the audience roaring and stamping, and when she glanced at Bagley and saw him put his thumbs up, she felt a hot surge of triumph. Not so bad, hey?

When Bagley swung into a larky version of 'You Must Have Been a Beautiful Baby' the men moaned and hollered and stamped as she danced and sang about driving young girls mad. Bagley, in spite of a personal dislike of the saccharine, constantly reminded them to sing sweet.

'These men don't fight for democracy, freedom, or any of that guff. They fight for their mum or for their girl, and as far as they're concerned, you're it for the ten minutes you're on stage.'

The night air felt still and soft around Saba's face. Max had told her if things were going well to sing a third song, and they were, so she could relax now. She waited for the low rumble of a plane to pass high above the stars, and then felt a deep silence descend on the men as she told them she was going to sing her favourite song, 'All the Things You Are'.

Insects obscured Bagley now. He played the opening bars, and when she sang, part of her could hear she was too soft. Bagley had warned her that when she was singing outdoors in a large space she would have to learn to throw her voice differently. Also, technically, it was harder to hold a line in a slow song than in one of the perky little numbers she'd started with. But she loved this song so much, she stopped caring, and after a few tentative notes hit her stride, remembering to use her microphone, as Bagley had taught her, as the confidential friend you told your secrets to, and as she and the song joined up, she felt a deep and creamy kind of contentment move through her veins. It was almost a shock at the end of it to remember where she was, to look out and see tears sparkling like diamonds in some of the men's eyes. As she left the stage, the men roared and whistled and stamped.

'Oh you little lamb. Well done, darling.' Arleta, slick with sweat and scent, hugged her as she came off stage. 'Brilliant, brilliant girl! You were nervous and you did it.'

She added something else that Saba couldn't hear because the crowd were still clapping and shouting. She pointed towards the dark desert, the tin huts.

'Darling, do me a huge, huge favour,' she said. 'Go to our tent and get me some face powder. I'm sweating like a pig. Hurry! Hurry! Hurry! I'm on next.'

Still high as a kite from her performance, Saba took the torch and ran along the forty yards or so of dirt road that led to their tent. From a distance, the portable stage glowed like a huge lit-up butterfly wing and felt like the magnetic centre of the night. She could hear the boom of Willie's voice; he was on fire now:

'*Are you all alllllllll riggggghhhhhht?*' And the answer: '*Yyeeeeeesssssssss!*'

The desert night was bright with stars. When she got to the tent, there was a dim light shining inside the canvas, a dark silhouette. She pulled back the flap; Dom was sitting on a chair waiting for her. When she first saw him, she tripped on the guy rope and almost fell into his arms.

Chapter 17

As he stood up, a shock of dark hair fell over his eyes.

'You!' she said. 'How on earth . . . ?'

'I'll tell you later.' His smile was mischievous.

'Do you know Arleta?' Her mind was struggling with this; her heart bounding.

'I do now.'

'Oh God,' she suddenly remembered. 'She's on—'

'Don't bother,' he said. 'That was a put-up job – we're both guilty.'

'I've got to go back in a minute for my curtain call.'

'You must.' His lips had a beautiful curve to them. After months of telling herself he was out of bounds now, she was shocked by how much she wanted to kiss them.

'I've borrowed a jeep,' he said. 'Can I take you out for supper after the show?'

'Yes.' She was so relieved. 'But I must dash back.'

He said that he would wait here. He asked if she would get into trouble if she left the camp.

'No,' she said, although she wasn't sure.

She flew down the dusty path and onto the stage, into a shrill blast of whistles, beaming and waving and blowing kisses. Arleta was waiting in the wings when she came off.

'He's here,' she whispered.

'I know,' Arleta's hug enveloped her in greasepaint and Shalimar, 'and quite a dish if I may say so.'

'Can I leave the camp tonight without permission?'

'No one's said we can't.' Arleta's expression was perfectly bland. 'No curfew I know of yet. And honey bun, if I may say so, you've kept *him* under wraps.'

'He's a fighter pilot,' Saba whispered, pulling her finger across her throat. Arleta had warned her to avoid them like the plague.

They were conceited, she'd said, and unreliable, also a bad bet, because most of them didn't come back.

'Well, you old dark horse!' Arleta tugged a strand of her hair and gave her a kiss on her forehead. 'Don't say you haven't been warned.'

As they raced across the desert in a battered jeep, the risen moon was so bright it seemed to have turned the night into a photographic negative of day, and she was dazzled by it.

'What happened to you in London that night?' he said immediately. 'When I got back to our table, you were gone, and this was a heck of a long way to come to find you.'

'Oh, I had a ton of things to do.' She couldn't bear the thought of him knowing how much it had hurt; how foolish it had made her feel. 'I needed an early night, and you . . . you seemed to have your hands full.' She glanced up at him.

'It wasn't what you thought.' His voice was neutral, his eyes on the road. 'She was the girlfriend of a chap from our squadron. It was the first time I'd seen her since he died. The timing wasn't brilliant. I'm sorry about that.'

She stared at him, cringing at the memory of herself stomping out like a child, grateful he hadn't seen her, but there was another feeling too, of sweet release.

'I was in a bit of a state myself,' she said. 'There was too much going on.'

'Yes,' he said softly. 'Much too much.'

'Was he a friend? The chap who died, I mean.'

'Yep. We were at school together, and at university.'

'How old?'

'Twenty-two.'

He gunned the accelerator. The faint pinprick of the jeep's lights picked up nothing but sand and rock. Saba shivered and hugged herself – the vastness of the desert around them felt like a warning of how tiny they were and how quickly snuffed out.

'This feels like blind man's buff,' she said, thinking one may as well be brave; it could all be over for all of them in a flash. 'Where are we going?'

'My name,' he said, 'is Alish Barbour. I'm a white-slave trader. I've already lost the map.' She was relieved to see him smiling again.

He drove easily and fast, one hand draped over the wheel.

'I know a place we can eat in Ismailia – about a twenty-minute drive from here.'

The gleam of his white teeth in the moonlight as he turned and smiled at her.

'Hungry?' he said. He put his foot down on the accelerator.

'Starving.' Though she was too excited for real hunger. She could feel his heat beside her, a sense of heightened awareness that was almost unbearable. *Calm down, calm down*, she told herself.

'Where have you been?' she said, hoping to sound sensible. 'I mean before you came here.'

He said he'd been in Abu Sueir himself, a couple of weeks before she'd arrived. They'd been on a training exercise, on the new Kittyhawks, the fighter planes they'd be using from now on. Afterwards, they'd flown south to Luxor and spent a couple of days going up the Nile on an old steamer.

'You could have come with me,' he said with a swift glance in her direction.

'I could,' she said, 'but I was working.'

On the outskirts of Ismailia, rackety music burst from a street that smelled of roasted sweet potatoes, and charcoal and old drains. There was a café on the corner where a group of men sat in the glow of an acetylene light smoking and drinking and playing board games.

He drove down another narrow street and parked the jeep there. He held her hand as he led her down a crumbling pavement to the restaurant he knew called Chez Henri. He stopped outside a heavily carved wooden door with a grille above it. When the door opened it was on to a simply furnished candlelit room where no more than six or seven tables were covered in white cloths. On each table there was a jam jar with a spray of jasmine in it.

'Ismailia is a town full of prisoners now,' he told her, 'Germans, thousands of Italians, but fortunately not Henri – he escaped from Paris. He had a restaurant there before the war.'

'It's lovely.' She closed her eyes, terribly happy suddenly, and inhaled the room – its smell of roasting meat, of jasmine, of cigarette smoke.

Henri appeared between them, portly and suave in his long white apron and wreathed in smiles.

'Monsieur, madame, good evening!' If they'd been babies he

would have kissed them and pinched their cheeks. He led them to a table in the corner. He lit the wicks of two cork candles.

When the flames glowed, Saba saw this was not a proper restaurant at all, more like an ordinary sitting room with its simple furnishings and comfortable sofa and family pictures on the wall. Its door was open to the night; from the window of the shabby house opposite came the croak of a sleepy child, the silhouette of a woman staring down at them. The woman pulled behind the curtain when Saba looked up.

Henri brought a carafe of wine, and after her first sip she said to Dom, 'How did you get here? How did you find me?'

'Elementary, my dear Watson. I went to Cairo and asked the girl at the ENSA office where you were.' He smiled with the innocent confidence of a man women tell things to. 'And I sent you a letter.'

'This?' She took her purse out of her bag and showed him its tattered remains. 'I didn't know it was you.'

'Ah, well the mystery is solved. Did you hope it was?' He raised his eyes and looked at her.

She looked at the menu. They think they're God's gift to women, Arleta had warned her – girls literally lie down at their approach.

'Maybe. I'll let you know. I still don't understand,' she said. His hand on the menu was brown and beautiful. He had long fingers. 'What are you doing in North Africa?'

'Oh, that part was easy,' he said. 'They're very short of pilots and a friend of mine is with the Desert Air Force. He fixed it. We're based between Cairo and Alexandria.'

'Were you pleased – after what happened to you, I mean.' She felt his slight move away from her. He was looking towards the door.

'Yes.' He turned back with a polite social look. She had definitely strayed into enemy territory. 'I was pleased – it was becoming a bore in England. There are only so many games of chess you can play in the mess.'

And then a sudden shyness seemed to overtake them. Dom drew a pattern with his hand on the tablecloth and she, overwhelmed by the concert and the shock of seeing him, warned herself to slow down.

'Where are you staying tonight?'

'There are rooms upstairs,' Dom said. 'I'll stay here, after I've dropped you back of course.' He slid his eyes towards her.

'Of course,' she said demurely. His brown fingers were on the table playing with the salt pot. She could feel her own heart beating and took a quick breath.

Henri appeared again, followed by a plump child of about five wearing pyjamas. Henri put a menu on the table, some flat bread, and two water glasses. The little boy put down their side plates with the fastidious air of an altar boy placing a chalice and was rewarded by a noisy kiss from his father.

'What would you like to eat?' Henri smiled at them.

'She's starving,' Dom told him. 'What's good tonight?'

'I propose roast duck served with honey, lavender and thyme. It is delicious,' their host said simply. 'We have lamb cooked with preserved lemons, that's good too.'

They chose the lamb, and while they were waiting, Dom half filled Saba's glass and pushed it towards her. 'How long have we got?' he said. He looked young in that moment, anxious too.

'There's no rush,' she said. It was already too late and she didn't care.

He touched her lightly on the hand.

'I want to say something . . . you were so good tonight.'

'When?' She was confused.

'The concert.'

'You heard me?' She hadn't expected that.

'Yes.' His eyes had the large pupils of a child. There were tortoiseshell lights in them. He took her hand and this time kept it in his. 'Tell me something. What does it feel like?'

'What does what feel like?' She thought for a moment he meant being with him, and was trying to compose an answer.

'Singing like that?'

She let his hand go. No one had ever asked her this before.

'Well . . . I don't know . . . it's hard to explain. Panic at first, especially tonight. We were so late, and it was our first proper concert, and all those men waiting, and then one of those beetles almost flew into my mouth, and then the music sounded so strange, that piano was a bit flat, but then . . . I don't know. There was a moment when I was singing "All the Things You Are", when I . . . well, it's hard to describe how good it feels, it's like a wave that travels through you.'

She'd given up trying to make it sound hard; the truth was she'd loved almost every minute of it, the sense of being part of the war effort, of being allowed to do regularly what she'd practised for so long, of living way beyond her natural limits, of doing well at what she most wanted to do – it felt so good. Her entire body, her spine, the tips of her toes, her belly, her head, was still in the glow of it.

'A wave that you catch.'

'Yes.'

'Ooh, that does sound good.'

'You're teasing me.' She caught his wrists in her hands.

'No. I promise I'm not.' He was watching her closely.

'For that moment, you feel complete, as if there's nothing missing. Does that sound batty to you?

'No.' He took a sip of wine. 'It feels like flying.'

'Does it?'

'Yes, but carry on, you first.'

They gazed at each other almost warily.

'And all those men, crying out in the night for you,' he continued in a lighter tone. 'I could hear them from the tent. How does that feel?'

'That's not why I do it,' she said. The truth was that what she'd felt most earlier that night was not the thrill of being admired, but something more difficult to put into words without sounding too what her mum would call stuck on yourself – the pain of the men coming towards her, the pain of homesickness, of lost friends, of exhaustion and prolonged fright, changing as if by magic into delight and relief, and how that felt like turning water into wine, but of course you couldn't say that without sounding like a complete prat.

'You seemed very confident.'

She felt exposed, as if she had said it.

'It's all right.' His dark intelligent eyes gazed at her steadily. 'I thought . . .' he seemed to choose his words carefully, 'I thought you were tremendous . . . really.' He was about to say something else, but stopped.

Henri was back flourishing a tray above his head. He'd brought them a selection of doll-sized dishes he called *mizzi'at*, filled with spicy vegetables and hummus and some olives; the olives he said were smuggled out of France.

'Tell me the honest truth,' Dom said when they were alone

again. He drew closer to her across the table, his gaze intense. 'Is it the best thing in your life?'

'I don't know.' Had he read her blasphemous mind? 'I do,' she added. 'Love it, I mean.' She tore a piece of bread in half, and dipped it in oil. 'I don't know yet if it's the best thing in my life, but it's where I feel most myself.' She watched the expression in his eyes sharpen.

'What does that mean – most yourself? Do you think you have a self, I mean a proper self, not just a reflection of what other people want you to be?'

'I'm not sure.' She felt in dangerous territory again. 'But I have a lot to learn,' she heard herself apologising. 'Max Bagley, our musical director, thinks I get some songs wrong.'

'In what way?'

'He says I copy other people.' The admission was still painful. She put her head close to his and sang a line softly. 'When I sang it the other day, he said I was doing a Bessie Smith and trying to sound like some weary old black lady about to pick a bale of cotton, and I should sing it just like me.'

'If you do that again, I'll have to take that old cotton picker to bed,' he breathed in her hair. They looked at each other with surprise and burst out laughing.

'No, no, no,' she was alarmed by how excited she felt and could feel the blush spreading from the roots of her hair. 'This is serious! Talk to me!' But it felt good, so good to laugh with him. When he picked up her hand and kissed the palm of it, she didn't pull away.

'To return to Mr Bagwash, or whatever his name is.' Their hands were side by side on the table. 'Surely what he said is partly rot. How do you learn anything without listening, copying, practising? Sorry, it's definitely rubbish, ignore it altogether.'

He talked passionately and seriously to her then about Picasso, who'd pinched from everyone; about T. S. Eliot, who he'd studied at Cambridge, the steady building up of technique, the learning from other people, the final drawing together of all these influences to make a whole. Charlie Parker, he added, was laughed off the stage the first time he performed.

'Who he?'

'Ah! So I have a discovery for you. I'm going to buy you a record. He had to practise for hours before he dared to play in public again. It doesn't happen overnight, I'm sure it doesn't; don't let him stomp on your dream.'

When the roast lamb came it was sweet and tender, and after it Henri's boy, half asleep now, brought a home-made ice cream served in a glass and flavoured with rosewater, and then a bottle of sweet-tasting wine on the house.

'Have some of this.' Henri was smiling at them as if they delighted him. 'It's from Alexandria, it's called zabib.' He poured Saba half a glass. 'It's better than Beaumes de Venise.'

'This is delicious,' she said, and it was, sweet and flowery. 'I'll be drunk,' she told Dom.

'I'll look after you,' he said. 'I have to see you again.' He looked at her steadily. 'I have an important package for you.'

'A package?' She narrowed her eyes, mock suspicious. 'What's in it?'

'Ah, you'll have to wait.'

'Why?'

'Some things have to be earned.'

'Yes?'

'Yes. It's from your mother.'

'Liar.'

'You'll see – and I want a full apology when you do.'

Over coffee, Dom became serious again. He told her about his mother's career as a pianist, and how angry it had made his father. One of the abiding memories of his childhood had been watching her come home alone after a concert – her first – that his father had been too busy, or too disapproving, to attend. He remembered her smart suit, the taxi, and her leather case with the music in it. How lonely she'd seemed to him, letting herself into the house that had gone to bed. Not long after that she'd given up. He'd been too young at the time to understand why, but it was wrong, he felt, to have a passion like that and to shut it down.

'It's almost as if everybody in life has a river running through them, let's say like the Nile,' his eyes were flashing now as he expounded his thesis, 'a river that gives you your own particular life. You dam it up at your peril.'

'All that water pouring out your ears,' she teased him. But she liked him talking like this; he was by far and away the most interesting man she'd ever met.

'What about you?' she asked over a second glass of zabib.

Earlier, when the candle had flared and she'd seen the scar on the side of his face she'd remembered the hospital, the other young men with their skin grafts like elephant's trunks, their ruined faces. 'Are you flying a lot?'

'Yes.'

'Is it busy?'

'Honest truth?'

'Yes.'

'It is quite busy up there.' He shifted in his seat.

'Busier say than the Battle of Britain?' She narrowed her eyes. 'And none of that Boy Biggles landing like an angel's kiss stuff.'

'Well . . .' He lit a cigarette. 'It is quite hot,' he said softly. He didn't expand, except to say their aerodrome was out in the desert, not far from enemy lines. That he shared a tent with a chap called Barney, someone he knew from school, who had got him the transfer in the first place.

'But what do you do?'

He said they were flying missions, sometimes as escorts for bombers or supply trucks, and sometimes in direct combat. He looked at her, and was about to say something else when she interrupted him.

'Why did you come to Egypt? Did you have to?'

'Yes,' he said quietly. 'I had to. This awful girl stood me up in London.'

'Be serious. Why?'

Several expressions seemed to move across his face.

'It's complicated. I'll tell you some other time.'

'Tell me one,' she urged. While they'd been talking, the restaurant had emptied. The boy was curled on the sofa asleep with his thumb in his mouth; Henri, folding napkins, closing the shutters. Dom put a cork back on the bottle of zabib.

'All right then,' he said. 'Just one: flying. You know what you said earlier about feeling most yourself when you were singing. That's how I feel in a plane. Free.'

She pictured him spinning in space miles above earth, and felt sick. If she hadn't been to the hospital she would never have known what could so easily come next. There were other things to ask, but she was frightened she'd jinx him.

'So, both misfits,' she joked instead. 'No feet on the ground here.'

'Anti-gravity,' he said. 'Well, that's always a risk. Oh God!'

Henri was blowing the candles out. He put the bill on the table and shrugged regretfully. Their supper was over.

As he drove her home across the desert, she fell into that kind of dark and dreamless sleep that feels like falling into a pit. When she opened her eyes again, she could see his brown fingers on the wheel, the dark outline of his hair, his straight nose, and felt glad in a way to be going home. She longed for him in a way that frightened her: it was too much, it had happened too quickly, she would have to give it some sort of more serious attention later.

While she'd been sleeping, her body had scooted up against his as if to a magnet; her head was resting against his shoulder, and she could smell him again, the same woody smell, but this time mingled with the faint aroma of petrol and dust. When she moved herself back to a respectable distance, she opened her eyes wide and looked out at the stars. High above her, like a cluster of sapphires, was the brilliant blue of the Seven Sisters, and there, the cloudy Milky Way. Her father, who knew them like old friends, had taught her their names when she was a girl. Five minutes later she saw the faint glimmer of red-brick buildings, the tracer lights around the transit camp, leaking out into the night.

'Saba.' His voice came to her out of the dark. 'We're nearly back. I've been thinking. I have some leave at the end of the month. Do you know where you'll be?'

A convoy of British army lorries trundled past them – a long glow-worm drowning out her reply. In their taillights she saw a thorn bush, a mound of rocks. 'I can show you fear in a handful of dust': he'd said that earlier. The fact that he knew such poems, and about Charlie Parker and other things, was already part of his attraction for her: they were young, they could learn together. Over supper, he'd told her that he hoped to be a writer when the war was over, and to keep flying.

Half a mile from the transit camp, he stopped the jeep and turned to her. He took her hair in both hands and held it behind her neck as he kissed her.

'We could meet in Alexandria,' he said. 'Or Cairo.'

'Oh God,' she murmured into his hair, 'I don't know.'

'Don't be frightened,' he said.

'I'm not frightened,' she said, which wasn't true. 'I don't know where I'll be,' she gasped. Her whole body felt soft and yielding – it was terrifying to feel it leap towards him. 'That's what I meant. We never seem to know.'

Dom glanced at her and drew back.

'You can write to me. You can write to me and let me know.'

'It's not that . . .' She could hear her voice faltering. 'Of course I'll do that . . . but . . .' Thinking of Cleeve, his warnings about boyfriends.

'If there's someone else,' he moved away from her and looked in her eyes, 'tell me straight away. I shall have him killed, of course, but at least I'll know.'

'It's not that.' She felt overwhelmed by everything. The nearness of him, and all that lay ahead.

When he put his arm around her and kissed her again, she could feel him thinking; a slight chill of separation between them.

At the high wire fence on the outskirts of the camp, they stopped at the guard's hut. A soldier checked Dom's papers.

'Lovely concert, Miss Tarcan,' the soldier said, not bothering to check hers. 'Our first for over a year. Would it be cheeky to ask for your autograph here?'

She scribbled her signature on a torn piece of paper. The guard folded it carefully and put it in his top pocket.

'Will you be on tomorrow?' he asked.

'We don't have a clue yet,' she said. Everything was so up in the air. 'But they'll probably put a sign up near the NAAFI.'

The soldier thanked her again; he said he had only been married for three weeks when he came here, his first kiddy had been born while he was away. His wife was finding it hard. 'I hope she's still there when I get back,' he said in a jocular voice.

'Oh, hang about.' They were driving off when the guard called them back. 'Forgot to tell you: Captain Ball, dropped by to see if you were back. Something about a party at the officers' mess tonight. He seemed very keen for all you ENSA girls to go.' He twitched the corner of his eye, a modified wink, out of respect for Dom maybe.

Ludicrous to feel so immediately flustered, but she did. 'It's part of the job,' she told Dom with a shrug. 'The party.'

His expression didn't change. 'You don't have to explain yourself to me,' he said. 'I'm sure you've got lots of admirers.'

And then he left her, after a quick peck on the cheek, a ruffling of her hair that made her feel like a younger sister or something. He said he'd write, and then he floored the accelerator and sped away in a ball of dust.

Later, lying in her canvas bed, she went through every detail of the evening, raging at herself for the awkward way she had ended it. Her rushed goodbye, her evasive answer when he'd asked when they could meet again – it sounded so furtive, jarring. She didn't want to start by having secrets from him.

Chapter 18

He took off at dusk in the Spitfire he'd been asked to deliver to LG39, the squadron's temporary base in the desert. Before he left, he went through the usual instrument and safety checks: oil, air pressure, oxygen feed, parachute stowed securely under his seat. The petrol gauge registered almost full, easily enough for the one-hour hop.

It was growing dark as the plane lifted off. The dust storm that had grounded all planes earlier had cleared, leaving a shimmering coppery patina in the air. At 20,000 feet, flying down a corridor of cloud, he heard himself singing and then laughing. It was mad, it was crazy and impossible, but he was completely and utterly in love for the first time.

When he pictured her standing in her red dress in the pool of light singing 'All the Things You Are', he felt with alarm all the carefully suppressed emotions of the last year burst into life again like a desert landscape after rain. She'd felt like the magnetic centre of the night. Later, when she'd confided in him in the restaurant how much she had to learn, he'd felt like her protector already – there were too many old farts in life who couldn't wait to slap you down, and she didn't deserve it. She was too original, too free. He increased the engine speed, felt the little plane lift, flew above and then through a few cottony clouds and when he came out the other side he was still thinking of her. Saba, asleep in the jeep, curled up like a child, her flood of dark hair over his knee.

And then, in the middle of all this euphoria, as sudden as an engine cutting out, he located a new feeling for him in connection with a woman: she frightened him. He felt like someone who'd been given some strange, beautiful, semi-tamed animal with no idea yet of how to handle it. She was powerful. If emotions were weather, she could stir up a tornado.

He'd felt it the first night he'd met her at the hospital, and even more intensely this time. He'd almost stopped breathing when she walked on the stage for fear something would go wrong. She'd stood in the spotlight owning the night with a reckless bravado he found both touching and admirable. When she was singing, the men on either side of him had leaned towards her and exhaled a kind of group sigh. One or two of them had groaned softly, a few muttered obscenities. He understood it – of course he did: strip away all the bravado and the false cheer, and they were all lonely men stuck in the middle of nowhere, bored or scared shitless most of the time, hungry for wives or sweethearts. But it disturbed him already that they should think of her like that. In fact, face it, he was already having to wrestle with a feeling of deep dismay about her – a feeling that disturbed and weakened him. He was jealous.

He gunned the engine, glanced at the darkening sky beneath him and the few faint stars winking on his starboard side, and then at the wavering lights below. One of the many dangers of night flying was that it was possible to get distracted by random stars and mistake them for airport lights, the perfect metaphor, he suddenly thought, for falling for the wrong girl.

Half an hour from the landing ground, he stopped thinking of her altogether as he tapped the altimeter and glanced down again. This was a tricky little runway, lit only by feeble gas flares and deliberately concealed. Concentrate!

One of the many things he loved about flying was that it did stop you thinking in an everyday way. Up here, miles away from the hectic, scurrying earth, you became as alive as any wild animal to its moods and changes: what clouds were forming, the shape and texture of rain, the dips of valleys. That fluffy grey cloud that had just sailed by might, on another continent, hide a mountain wall that could kill you, or the wingtip of one of the Messerschmitt 109s that flew in regularly from nearby Sicily and Italy.

He was looking for them now as he descended. Before he'd flown east, three days ago, he'd been warned by his flight commander, Paul Rivers, that if he became tangled up in a 'show' on the way home, he was to get himself down as quickly as possible.

'The planes are more important than you mate,' he'd joked. 'We can't afford to lose any more, and besides, I want to go home now.' He'd stuck his finger in his mouth like a baby. 'I miss my mummy.'

Rivers, like Dom, had flown in the Battle of Britain. The plan was that as soon as Dom had got his bearings he would replace him.

On their brief tour of the airfield a few weeks ago, Rivers, his blunt, pug-nosed face covered in dots of calamine lotion from his desert sores, had told Dom that things had got pretty hot out here recently, and that he was bloody grateful that he was tour-expired. He'd had enough sand in his bloody underpants and his bloody coffee and his fucking ears to last him a lifetime. He also had a wife and a new baby waiting for him on his parents' property in Queensland.

'Yeh, it will be quite nice to see the little tyke,' he agreed with an unconvincing show of reluctance, which made Dom smile. For a brief moment he'd envied him his settled future and guaranteed life.

Rivers had told him over a disgusting cup of chlorine coffee that the Germans now outnumbered them by four to one. They were well supplied with bases in Greece and Sicily, had better and more numerous planes. Young pilots like Dom had flown in from all over the world to help the Allies with this final push. 'We reckon,' the Aussie had drawled, 'it's going to be like a second Battle of Britain here soon, only hotter and longer and harder.'

That was another thing Dom hadn't told her. Another major offensive, in five days? A month? Two months? The whole place seethed with rumours, no one ever really knew.

From the air the small runway looked as insignificant as a toenail. He steered down gently, and after he'd landed, reached under his seat and grabbed his kitbag. An hour or so later, as he walked towards his tent, a young man with the broad shoulders and easy lope of an athlete stood up and walked towards him smiling. 'Dom, you old bastard. Where've you been?'

Barney got a Stella beer for Dom from the sandpit where the ice had melted hours ago. He didn't have to ask. They'd been part of the same gang at school. Barney was the captain of the cricket team and about to get an England trial before the war bounced that one. It was Barney who helped him get the transfer to the Desert Air Force. They'd done their basic training together at Brize Norton what seemed like a lifetime ago.

On the day they'd both flown solo from Coggershill to Thame, a feeble hop in retrospect, they had gone out together and got royally plastered at their local pub, the Queen's Head. If either of them then had declared over a pint that they were fighting for England or for their fellow men, they would have died laughing. Flying was the thing. It still was, but different now. There was a new wariness, a hardness that Dom saw in Barney's eyes that he recognised in his own. They had both been shot down and hurt badly, they had both killed and wanted to kill again. Most of the pilots in the squadron were like this: fiercely competitive in a languid, don't-give-a-damn way. Parts of them frozen in shock. They had lost half their friends – Jacko the worst for both of them. They never talked about him except in a kind of distancing code.

They drank a couple of beers each outside their tent, and then Barney, not known for his sensitivity, glanced at Dom and said:

'You look different. You all right?'

Dom said never better.

Barney said he'd spent the morning flying with the air reconnaissance boys, having a snoop at the German aerodrome at Sidi Nisr, trying to locate exactly where their runways were. All their boys got home safe and sound. They'd spent the afternoon in Cairo, swimming at the Gezirah Club, had a meal and come home. That was the way of their confusing lives now: war in the morning and fun in the afternoon.

'So how was your trip, old cock?'

'Not bad. Rather fun actually.'

He couldn't tell Barney about Saba, not yet. He wanted to keep the shining feeling for a little while longer; couldn't bear the thought of the inevitable ribbing that would follow – 'An ENSA singer, oh for God's sake, we all fall in love with them.'

Their tent stank of curry and Barney's old socks. It was lit by a gas torch. It was boiling, boiling hot.

'Gotcha, little bastard.' Barney walloped a cockroach on the wall with his grimy pillow. 'Well, glad it was fun, because there's a rumour that all leave is going to be cancelled for the next ten days,' he said.

Dom slung his kitbag on the floor and sprawled on the camp bed, exhausted.

'They're sending us off to some deep desert place for extensive training. We had a briefing this morning from Davies. The rumour is that there's a push planned in the next ten days.'

'When will we hear?'

'Don't know; when they feel like telling us, as per.'

Barney said this in a humorous drawl, a look of concealed excitement in his eyes. Dom felt it too: a surge of pure adrenalin that stopped him sleeping for an hour or two even though his body was worn out. He was half waiting for the jangling telephone call that could wrench him and the rest of the squadron from their beds in the early hours of the night and have them sprinting towards the already shuddering planes. He was half listening to fragmented parts of 'All the Things You Are', playing underneath him now. It was new to him, this jumbled, jazzed-up feeling. It felt like falling off the edge of his known world.

When sleep finally came, he dreamt that he and Saba were lying in each other's arms on warm sand somewhere. A motorboat with sails like a felucca was chug-chug-chugging across a calm blue bay. She loved him; he could feel it like a transfusion of light in his veins. They were floating together in some warm and womb-like state. It was so simple.

He'd gone to sleep without undressing; his head was resting on his kitbag. The motorboat with sails, which was a Junkers Ju 88, rumbled above them and disappeared into cloud.

Chapter 19

The day after the concert, Saba was driven back to Ismailia and to a grimy apartment block where Dermot Cleeve was staying. They sat on rattan chairs drinking bottled lime juice in a dismal little room with cracks on the ceiling and a naked bulb overhead. Cleeve, his face pink and freshly shaven, wore new-looking linen trousers. Before he sat down, he folded a tea towel and placed it carefully on his chair with the air of a man decidedly not in his natural habitat. He said he'd being driving around all week trying to put together a programme for the troops. No more ENSA artistes were allowed into Cairo until the situation improved there, and the difficulties of getting actual shows to remote desert areas had become so great, he said, they were relying more and more on broadcasts.

'But enough dreary shop talk.' He stretched out his legs, and put his hands behind his head. 'Because I now know two or three things about last night. First that the concert went well, which is splendid, and also that you were out rather late,' he added playfully. 'May one ask who the lucky young man was?'

She felt a childish urge to say *none of your business.*

'He's a friend.'

'Quite a pretty friend, I hear,' he said archly. 'And if by chance he becomes more than a friend, may I warn you not to tell him about our conversations.'

She jumped. 'Did you follow us?'

He took a silver cigarette case out of his top pocket. 'May I?' He lit up and took a sip of his juice, looking disdainfully at the thick glass it came in.

'No. But you do remember what I said to you in Cairo?' he said in a low voice. 'Not a word to anyone, and get a pass next time, or ask permission. I can sometimes swing it if you want to ask me.'

'We're allowed out,' she whispered back. 'I haven't taken Holy

Orders and no one said we needed a pass to have a drink after the show.'

'Oh, fiery girl!' He pursed his lips. 'Of course you're allowed out, of course you are, you'd go mad without it, it's just that I have two exciting bits of news for you, and I'd prefer that you didn't get court-martialled before it happens.'

He'd found out that for the next two weeks the company would be travelling west, more or less in the footsteps of the Eighth Army. In early August they would join up with a large company, The Fearsome Follies, and then God and the British army willing, do one week in Alexandria at the Gaiety. A darling little theatre, although appalling acoustics. Did she know it?

She didn't.

Cleeve arranged the crease in his trousers and looked around him.

'If that happens, you'll do two shows with the company, and then we have another job for you – the one I mentioned.' He looked at her significantly. 'Quite important, actually, if it comes off. Zafer Ozan wants to book you for a short engagement at the Cheval D'Or in Alexandria for two nights in the middle of August.' She'd surely heard of that?

'Yes,' she said. Arleta had mentioned it.

'Well, it's an incredible honour. I can't remember another ENSA entertainer on tour ever being asked to do it.'

The club, he explained, was on a plum spot on the Corniche, close to the Cecil Hotel. Some wonderful artistes had played there before the war: Django Reinhardt, Maurice Chevalier, Tina Roje, Asmahan. Had she heard of Tina Roje? No, she hadn't heard of her either, but her heart was beating with excitement.

'Who do I have to get permission from?'

'No one,' he said softly. 'You can leave that to us. It's all arranged. But at some point, if things go as we hope, you'll be asked to go to a party at Ozan's house. He's a great party man, and he'll want to show you off. The house, I hear, is heaven, like something out of *One Thousand and One Nights*. He has some important friends coming for supper and you'll sing a couple of songs.'

'A couple of songs?' she asked. Her stomach was churning. 'Will anyone else be there? From the company, I mean.' They felt like family now.

'No, but Madame Eloise – the wardrobe woman from Cairo – is living there temporarily. I think she has, or had, a small shop near the Corniche. I've arranged for you to stay with some friends of hers. She's a delightful person. She knows Ozan, not well, but she'll look after you.'

'Does she know? About me, I mean.'

'No. Your cover story is that you've been given a couple of weeks' leave to do some broadcast work and that you've been asked to sing for Mr Ozan. I've told her how talented you are.' He gave her a quick sincere smile; he seemed as excited as she was.

'Thank you.' She hardly heard him. 'So I just have to sing at the club and this party?'

'That's all.' He drained his glass and put it down on the table. 'For the time being the party is the most important thing – some businessmen, politicians, relatives of the royal family, movers and shakers will be there. Your job is to throw your teeth around and sing.'

'Throw my teeth around?'

'Charm them, get to know them. Men love to boast to pretty girls. We're not asking you to be Mata Hari, but if anyone should drop information helpful to us . . . Asmahan, for example, is a gorgeous Syrian singer, rumoured to have liaisons with two high-ranking German officers. She may not be there, of course.'

'And that's all?'

'For the time being.' He started to put papers away in his brief-case. 'There might be another, much bigger job later. I don't want to talk about it now, so . . .' The quick bright smile was switched on again. 'Anything else you'd like to ask me before we wrap it up?'

'Yes. Couldn't Arleta come too? She's hard-working, she's loyal; wouldn't it seem more natural, particularly as she knows him?'

A shadow passed over his face, whether of irritation or im-patience she couldn't tell.

'We've been through this,' he reminded her. 'Arleta can't sing in Turkish, can she? That was the thing that melted Ozan's heart about you, actually,' he whispered roguishly. 'To be perfectly frank, I don't think she can sing at all.'

'I don't agree,' Saba said loyally – it pained her to understand what he meant. 'The men love her.'

'A little too much,' he replied tartly. 'A bit of a reputation, if you know what I mean.'

'For what?'

He gazed at her steadily.

'You must know by now.'

'I don't.'

'Don't look so cross – it's a fact of life that gorgeous girls like you get more offers, the same way as powerful men do. It doesn't mean they're depraved, just luckier; some can resist, some can't, but this . . .' his larky look disappeared, his voice dropped, 'is too important to take risks.'

He grimaced as a bomber flew low over their heads, drowning out his next sentence.

'I think it would be polite to reply to Ozan soon.' Some dusty birds flew in a cloud past the window. 'They're a kind of kite,' Cleeve said. 'Disgusting creatures, God knows what they're doing around here.

'Oh, and by the way, Madame Eloise has agreed to lend dresses again, and Bagley will rehearse your tunes. He was thrilled to hear about your possible booking at the Cheval D'Or. In the quaint little sphere we inhabit, this kind of thing doesn't happen very often.'

'Was he?' She felt a surge of triumph – maybe, not so bad after all? 'So, is everything arranged?'

'It has. Am I to assume your answer is yes?'

'Of course,' she said. One of the birds let out a jarring shriek at the very moment she was trying to look calm and collected. 'So, when will I see you again?'

'In August, in Alexandria, *inshallah*.'

He said goodbye to her with a courteous touch of his panama hat. He was going to spend the rest of his day, he said, recording a marvellous composer and oud player, Mohamed El Qasabgi, for posterity. That wasn't the kind of thing, he noted regretfully, one could play for the troops, who, of course, adored sentimental music, but it kept one sane.

Later, back at the camp, and walking towards her tent, she wondered if it was possible to die of excitement. Cleeve had insinuated that she was about to join some exclusive club, and that her singing could, just possibly, help change the way the war went. What a thought! She imagined her mother rolling around with laughter at it, her father apologising with tears in his eyes – yet who would not feel proud?

And Dom. He was close to Alexandria too. Her mind had locked on to this while Cleeve had been talking. She had to think of a way they could meet that would not be too dangerous for both of them.

She was deep in thought and almost at the tent when she saw another kite streaking across the sky with a stolen sausage link in its mouth.

And then the bothering bit crept into her mind again.

At the end of their meeting, Cleeve had warned her to keep her mouth shut about why she was in Alexandria, so what to tell Dom? She was not someone who enjoyed or was good at lying – her Mum had once pointed out that she always signalled a whopper on the way by putting her right hand over her right eye, like one of those *see no evil* monkeys. But she had given her word, and she would try.

Chapter 20

When Saba walked into the tent, Arleta was washing her blue silk nightdress in a canvas basin.

'Darling,' she wrapped Saba in a soapy embrace, 'where have you been, you wicked creature? I've been having kittens!'

'Not many kittens,' Saba teased, kissing the top of her head. After she'd said goodbye to Dom she'd gone back to the tent and found it empty. About three in the morning, Arleta's head had poked through the canvas flap and Saba had listened to the sparkling crackle of her hair being tended, her teeth being brushed, the delicate jasmine and rose puff of Guerlain's Shalimar – without which Arleta claimed she couldn't sleep a wink, silly as that sounded – the click of the torch going out, and finally the luxurious sigh that signalled that Arleta had had rather a good night of her own.

'So! Last night.' Arleta abandoned her laundry. 'What on earth was going on?'

'Well, the show seemed to go well.' Saba felt wary – the rule in the company was tell one tell all.

'Oh don't be ridiculous. The beautiful man, who was he?'

'Well . . . he came unexpectedly to see me.'

'I saw that, stupid.'

'And he's . . .' Saba closed her eyes. 'Look, I don't know, I don't know . . . oh.' Her happiness spilled out; it was very hard to keep things from Arleta, it felt like meanness. 'I met him before in London, and before that in hospital – and yes, he's a fighter pilot!' She curled her fingers into a pair of devil horns. 'And please don't tell me what you think about them, because I already know.' She tickled Arleta under the arm.

'If you have beans to spill,' Arleta's eyes were glowing, 'spill them now. It's only fair.'

Saba couldn't resist. As she sketched out briefly how Dom had come to the audition, how they'd walked the streets of London that evening, how he'd driven her across the desert last night, she felt a rising elation.

'I mean, he's just so beautiful, and we have such interesting conversations together already, and he makes me laugh and . . . oh bugger, in a way it feels so simple and uncomplicated, as if he's been there waiting . . . Does that sound daft?'

'Oh dear, oh dear, oh dear.' Arleta dried her hands properly and sat down on the bed. She pulled Saba into the camp chair beside it. 'She's got it bad. And, by the way, it's never simple and uncomplicated. Did you sleep together?'

'No, but last night, I wanted to so badly. I've never felt so . . .' she gazed around her wildly, 'completely out of control.'

'Gosh.' Even Arleta was impressed. She did a stage fall on to her camp bed and then sat up and hugged Saba. 'Oh little lamb,' she murmured into her hair. 'Do be careful. It's so exciting, but he *is* a fighter pilot, enough said, or should be.'

'But all of our lives are dangerous here,' Saba said passionately. 'And I know I'm definitely going to see him again.' Oh God, she thought, what a hopeless spy she was going to be; she'd already said more about him than Cleeve would probably approve of.

'Of course they are and of course you will.' Arleta patted her on the knee. 'Of course you will.'

She blew out air and jumped to her feet. She tied a piece of string across the tent and pegged out the blue silk nightdress and a pair of frothy matching knickers.

'And your night?' Saba poked her in the side.

Arleta narrowed her cat's eyes.

'Well . . . I was doing my bit for the Anglo-American alliance,' she said. 'I'll tell you all about him later.'

'Sounds interesting.'

'It was, and a little bit alarming too. I'm too tired to give it full throttle now, I'll tell you later.'

Lunch was bully-beef sandwiches and prunes. After it, Saba, Arleta, Janine, Willie and the acrobats were rounded up and put into what Willie called a wog wagon, a small converted lorry with scalding metal seats shaped like bedpans arranged one behind the other.

They were followed by another truck carrying rolled scenery, the stage, their kitbags, and Willie's fez, chicken feet and Hitler moustache, accompanied by Max Bagley, Captain Crowley and two soldiers with pistols in their holsters. The only information they'd been given was they were bound for a field hospital approximately fifty miles into the Western Desert.

The sun shrank their eyeballs as it swept across the cloudless sky, and the desert was so full of glassy mirages that it looked like a flat sea. The temperature rose to 125 degrees in the non-existent shade, and everyone in the lorry felt ratty and disinclined to talk.

After two hours' travelling they stopped at a settlement where the only visible signs of life were a scattering of flat-roofed houses and a rust-coloured watering hole by the side of the road. A house made of red mud was open to the street and a few wooden tables were scattered outside. A barefoot man served them flatbread, a tiny piece of white chewy cheese and hot, sweet mint tea which Willie told them in a cheerful whisper tasted like camel's pee. This annoyed Janine, who hated coarseness. 'Oh touchy, touchy,' he said as she removed herself to another table and fell asleep, her delicate head like a drooping flower in her hands.

Their host was refilling their glasses when shouts came from outside: some trouble with the chassis of their lorry, parts of which now hung down like sheep udders. Crowley, who liked to show off about all the countries he had served in, was shouting at two bewildered-looking men in oily robes in the language they had all started to imitate and call Lingo Bingo. 'Come on, you bastards, *jaldi jow*, chop, chop. Under lorry bang bang.'

'God, what a rude sod he is,' Arleta murmured. 'One day he's going to get himself shot.'

But the men smiled. They lay down under the lorry with their spanners while the cast rested. They had two performances ahead of them that night.

The acrobats took their bedrolls, did a bit of play wrestling and then fell asleep under a thorn tree beside the waterhole. Janine, who hated putting her fair skin in the sun, stayed inside the restaurant asleep at the table. Arleta and Saba lay under a juniper tree looking up at the patterned sky through its branches. Beside them, a donkey was lashed to another tree and hee hawed at the sight of them.

'Poor little thing.' When Saba offered it bread, it nibbled her hands with velvet lips and gazed at her with kindly eyes. 'Why do they treat their animals so badly here?' she asked Arleta. 'No water, no food, no shade.'

Arleta said that life was hard on these people too: on her last tour of Egypt, she'd seen men walking round and round and round in the blazing sun all day pushing a wheel just to get the water out of a well. 'They probably think that donkey has a whale of a time.'

'Well, I don't think so.' Saba jumped up. 'The poor little thing can hardly move its head. I don't think the owner would mind if I lengthened the rope.'

'I wouldn't interfere if I was you,' advised Arleta, but Saba ignored her. She jumped up, loosened the rope, patted the donkey's neck and gave it another piece of flatbread. 'There you are, dear little man.'

'You're a shocking softie,' Arleta said drowsily. 'You'll get yourself hurt one day, and you'll be crawling with fleas tonight.'

When Arleta fell asleep, Saba, watched with mild curiosity by the donkey, got a writing pad out of her kitbag. She shook the sand out of its creases.

Dear Dom, she wrote,

I'm going to Alex in August. Any chance we could meet there?

Now she must think of a safe way of getting the message to him – one that Cleeve would approve of.

Closing her eyes, she had an almost photographic image of Dom flying alone over the desert, with its tanks and hidden aerodromes and landmines.

She shook her head. He would live, she must believe he would, else there would be no peace from now on.

A fly woke Arleta up.

'Sod off.' She brushed it away. 'How long have I been asleep?'

'Twenty minutes.'

'*Yalla yalla*, girls.' Crowley was waving his swagger stick in their direction. He made a cone of his hands and bellowed, 'Truck fixed, get mobile in ten minutes. Don't leave anything behind. Got that, Willie boy?' he roared at Willie, who he treated like a halfwit. 'Ten minutes. Don't forget your hat.' Willie was dozing on the veranda; his knotted handkerchief had fallen into the dust.

'Sabs,' Arleta said quickly, 'before we get on the truck, I want to tell you something about last night. I wouldn't feel right without passing it on.'

It seemed that while Saba had been out with Dom, Arleta and Janine had gone to the officers' mess to have a drink with some of the bigger wigs on the base. These included an air commodore who had flown in from Tunisia, an army doctor with the worst case of desert sores that Arleta had ever seen and a padre who banged on a bit about Willie's rude jokes, so it was no contest at all really, she continued, when her eye lit on an American colonel: a full colonel, mind, and awfully handsome with blond, blond hair, broad shoulders, honey-coloured skin; a real Southern gentleman in spite of his striking good looks. Arleta's voice grew low and husky.

'And I do so like Americans.' When she threw back her hair, Saba saw a bruise on her neck. 'We had a lovely talk and then he smuggled me into his rooms and we made love. I think he thought all his Christmases and Thanksgivings had come at once.'

Arleta, as always, was strikingly unrepentant about such matters, and if she felt guilty about betraying her Bill, she showed little sign of it. Once, when Saba had asked about this, she'd said they had an arrangement – she'd said it in the French way, which made it sound more fun – he'd written to her saying she should take her pleasures where she might, because he was going to.

'Oh grow up, darling,' she had said to Saba's shocked face. 'There's a war on. I don't want him to live like a monk and he knows I'm not cut out for nun-dom or whatever you call it. This way is much more sensible.'

'Anyway,' she continued, 'shut up for a moment because this is what I want to tell you. Later, much later, when we were having a brandy and a cigarette, the lovely Wentworth Junior the Third – that was his name – told me something that he said he shouldn't have. He has some kind of intelligence job, and in his opinion the war here will be over very, very soon.' Arleta took a deep breath and shook her head vigorously.

'Over! Are you sure?' Saba was shocked to find herself a little disappointed.

'No, silly, course I'm not sure, nobody is, but here's the point: he said there is going to be the mother and father of all battles soon.'

'But they're always saying that.'

'He was convinced this was the one. He was actually shocked that we hadn't been sent home already.'

'Where will they be fighting?'

'Didn't say, wouldn't, but it's bound to be near the coastline, that's where all the Germans are, and the various supply lines; that's where they're bombing mostly.'

'Near Alexandria? Near Cairo?'

'Alexandria. He says it's an open secret among the men that the battle will happen in the next few weeks there. And if we're sent there, we should jump ship, it's just too dangerous.'

Arleta went on to say that she knew for a fact that they'd just moved another ENSA company, The Live Wires, out from Alex to Palestine. 'I actually worked with one of the girls in it – Beryl Knight, a dancer, awful frizzy hair but a very nice girl,' she added loyally.

'So, will we have to go soon?'

'No, this is the point. Wentworth's good buddy,' Arleta slipped into an unconvincing American twang, 'is Captain Furness. I swore to him this morning I wouldn't say anything, but apparently we're not going to be sent away – we'll be following the Eighth Army into the desert.'

'Heavens.'

They exchanged a strange look.

'Do you want to do that?' Saba asked.

'Girls, come on! *Jaldi jow.*' Captain Crowley, red-faced and shouting now.

'Do you mean keep going?'

'Yes.'

'I do. You?'

'Yes,' said Saba. 'I couldn't bear to go home now.'

Arleta just looked at her.

'We must be mad,' she said. She squeezed Saba's hand and they laughed shakily.

For the next leg of their journey, Bagley got on the bus with them and said they were going to have another rehearsal of the doo-wop song. He'd explained to them before that doo-wop was a kind of African music he'd heard in a club in Harlem before the war began. The song was called 'My Prayer', he said. He couldn't remember the exact lyrics but it was about the kind of sacred promises you make when you're in love.

'The chorus is fabulous, come on, Bog, you try it, and Arleta. The melody goes like this, *Umbadumba umbadumb ummmmbbbuumm.* You should see the negro men who sing this stuff – they beam, they strut, they shoot their cuffs.' He did a bit of portly strutting up the centre of the bus to demonstrate. 'So: you sing the line, Saba, and the rest of you do the *umbas.*

'What's so fascinating about this new kind of music,' Bagley continued, 'is that it has distinct echoes of the madrigal. *Now is the month of maying, when merry lads are playing,*' he sang in his clear, high voice. '*Fa la la la la la la* – you get it – *de wop de wahhhh,*' he ended in a black voice.

Beside him, Crowley sat rigid with alarm and embarrassment. He never knew where to look when they were messing around like this.

But Bagley was on fire, and so were the rest of them, magically transformed by a song which ended in a roar of laughter. Bagley told them to shut up now and save their voices for that night. Saba, who had slipped into the seat beside Willie, was shocked when she glanced at him to see two great tears running down his cheeks like marrowfat peas. She looked at him more closely – the whites of his eyes were red with crying; with his knotted hankie on his head again he looked like a sad fat baby.

'What's the matter, Willie, is it your ticker?' she whispered. When she put her hand in his, he gripped it hard. Usually he hated being asked about his health – he was terrified of being sent home – but this felt different.

He gave a small snort and a shuddering sigh.

'In a way,' he said at last, 'your fault – you'd better not sing that "My Prayer" to the troops; you'll have them in floods.'

'Willie, come on – there must be something else.'

He glanced around to check it was safe to talk.

'Tell me.' She squeezed his hand. 'I won't blab.'

He looked across at Arleta, who was fast asleep, her blonde hair spilling into the aisle.

'It is my ticker, but it's not in a medical way.' He swallowed noisily. 'It's her.' As he spoke, Arleta's tumbling waves shifted from side to side, picking up reflections from the sun.

'Arleta?'

'Yes.'

There was a long, fraught silence.

'D'you remember,' Willie said at the end of it, 'what a wonderful surprise it was seeing me at the auditions in London that day and how we'd worked together in Malta and Brighton? Well it's no coincidence. I've tried to get on every tour she's been on, but she's killing me, Saba.' As he said this, the faded irises of his eyes floated under their lids and another tear rolled down the side of his face.

Saba clutched his hand. He must have seen Arleta leave with her blond American the night before.

'But Willie, has she ever given you any reason to think . . . ?'

'Well, you tell me. She's always telling me I'm wonderful and she loves me and I'm the funniest man she's ever met. She's so beautiful . . .' he ended brokenly.

'Yes, but Willie . . .'

'I know, I know, we all go on like that in the business, and I'm the silliest old man that ever lived for thinking she really meant it.' He stopped suddenly. More tears rolling down his face, and a large *whoomph* into his handkerchief. 'Sorry, love, I'm not much fun, am I?'

'No, no, no, no, it's all right, Willie, but not being nosy or anything, I thought you had a wife and that she passed away a few months before we went on tour. That's what Arleta told me.'

'Well that's another can of worms,' he said. 'So to speak. Arleta puts a lovely slant on it, but the truth is, we were married for over thirty-four years, and I hardly knew her, and that was my fault too. I love all this,' he gestured around the dusty lorry, 'the touring, the performing, I can't seem to stop.' He added that he had two girls, now grown up, and he hardly knew a thing about them either.

'My dad's a bit like that,' Saba said.

'Performer?' he asked, picking up a bit. 'If he is, he should be very, very proud of you.'

'No, to both parts. He hates me doing this. We didn't even say goodbye.'

'Oh blimey – that's a bit serious, can't you make up?'

'Can't,' she said. 'He's at sea.'

'Well send a letter home,' he said. 'He must go home sometimes.'

'Umm, maybe.' She hated to talk about it – it felt so shameful.

To cheer them both up, Willie got a couple of melted peppermints from his pocket, which seemed to have a calming effect.

He said she was young enough to take a bit of advice from him, because, in his opinion, there was good and bad excitement in life, and the excitement of performing could turn around sometimes, and bite you on the you-know-what. It was too much, it was unwise, and it skewed other things in your life.

'I'll tell you a little story,' he said. 'One time I went home to our house in Crouch End – I'd been away for ages doing a wonderful panto in Blackpool and I was as high as a flaming kite and very taken with myself. But when I got home the missus was livid. I hadn't seen her for two months and I hadn't even remembered to tell her what time I was coming home, so she leaves a note on the doorstep saying "Baked beans and bread in the cupboard, I'm out."

'But she'd forgotten to leave the key under the mat, so I tried to climb through the cloakroom, and I'm so fat, I got wedged in the window, and looking at my house from this angle I thought, *I can't do this any more, it's too small and too cramped. I can't do it.* But you have to do it sometimes, don't you . . . you have to be ordinary and learn to like it.'

He was so het up he had to look out of the window where light was draining from the day and the desert sand was drenched in a brilliant geranium red.

'You all right now, love?' Willie asked. 'Arleta says you were homesick at first.'

'I'm getting a bit addicted myself, Willie,' she said, mesmerised by the sunset, and upset to have seen Willie crying, 'but I do miss home. It's the first time I've been further than Cardiff on my own, so a bit of a step.'

He patted her hand softly. 'I'm here if you ever need me – don't forget that, gel.'

'Thank you, Willie.'

'Two concerts tonight, then. A bit of shut-eye in order.'

'You all right now, Willie?' She gave him a quick kiss on the cheek.

'Course I am.' He tried to wink at her. 'That'll learn you to sing songs to silly old men.' He held his Adam's apple between his fingers, wobbled it and warbled: '*Because I love yoooouuuuuu.*'

When he extended the last note into a dog's trembling howl everyone in the bus burst out laughing, except Arleta who was still asleep and Crowley who was frowning over the maps again.

Chapter 21

Dom had never known that love could feel so like fear. But that night as he lay in his camp bed and conjured up her image, he recognised fear's physical sensations – the powdery limbs, the pounding heart. He pictured her glossy hair, the playful twist to her smile when she teased him. How in the restaurant, when they'd been talking, she'd fixed her big brown eyes on him and seemed to drink him in.

And now he saw her – it almost made him furious to do so – with that tiny band of performers racketing around desert outposts and transit camps and aerodromes, all of them sitting ducks for the Germans, who were circling closer and closer. There were land-mines in the desert – one of their aircrew had had his leg blown off the week before – and serious supply shortages already. What if a truck they were on broke down in the wrong place? There was always now the distinct possibility of a sudden air-raid attack by the Germans, and lately, the Italians.

Saba had told him a German Stuka had hit part of the stage before the ack-ack could get it during another ENSA group's performance near Suez. They'd got to the chorus of 'A Nightingale Sang in Berkeley Square' when *boooom!!!!* It had shot through part of a comedian's baggy trousers – she'd made a funny story out of it.

They'd kept on singing of course – well bully for them – but he didn't want her to have to take part in these kinds of heroics, and he was furious at the authorities for not sending them away to safety, although he would never have dared tell her that.

And so, on the borderlines of sleep, when you're free to think anything, he pleaded, *Send her home; let the troops do without music. She's too young for this.*

Six o'clock the next morning. A field telephone woke him. The usual instant boggle-eyed awakeness.

Paul Rivers wanted Dom and Barney to report to the crew room after breakfast. Four new pilots had arrived for retraining before the big push. They were to take them shadow flying that afternoon.

After breakfast, it was overcast and humid and they waited until the last possible moment to climb into the flight suits that made you sweat like a pig. Six of them made their way to the sand airstrip where the ground crew were preparing their aircraft.

The new boys were Scott, an awkwardly hearty Canadian whose hand squelched with sweat and made whoopee-cushion noises as it pumped Dom's, and his friend Cliff, a silent Midwesterner, whose massive, impassive face looked like a rock carving. Scott said he'd learned to fly as a crop duster in the States. The other two would join them after lunch.

They were waiting for take-off in a tin hut at the end of the runway when Scott said, 'So, what's the situation here, fellows? Do we have a snowball's chance in hell of winning this thing?'

'Well, on the whole, snowballs don't have much of a life expectancy out here,' Barney said pleasantly.

'Oh very English, pip-pip and all that.' The Canadian scowled and looked at Dom now. 'But what's the score?'

Not an unreasonable question.

'Well, the Hun have aerodromes now in Tunisia, in Libya, and scattered around the Western Desert, and they're moving east, or at least trying to. If they can capture Alexandria and Cairo we're stuffed, so the next bit is not to let them do that.'

When he stopped to spit some sand out of his mouth, Barney took over.

'The fighting here is not the old Battle of Britain man-against-man stuff,' he said. 'We're mostly covering bomber patrols, escorting tanks, protecting supply lines. We haven't had any major offensives yet, but that could change at a moment's notice.

'One of their main problems, ours too, is running out of water. You may have noticed,' he rubbed his bristling chin, 'it's not in plentiful supply here.' He screwed up his eyes against the sun and they followed his gaze towards the miles and miles and miles of desert behind him. He was getting irritable; it was time to fly and stop talking.

Dom felt it too, a craving to leave the ground.

Half an hour later, he climbed into the tight mouth of the Kittyhawk, put the parachute under his seat, plugged in the oxygen, turned it on full and then squeezed tubes to see if it was coming through. At the RT command of *all right, chaps, off we go*, they rose into the air.

The new pilots had been briefed about shadow shooting. Now Dom and Barney flew in formation together, elegant as Ginger and Fred and showing off to the new boys just a bit as they dipped and spun and glided across the desert, letting their shadows drop like giant ink spots.

It was boiling hot as usual inside the Perspex and tin universe of the aircraft, but already he could feel the fears of the night and the petty worries of the day recede. He was flying again.

'OK now, watch it now! Watch it! We're coming over,' Dom told the new boys through his radio transmission.

And then *boom! boom! boom! boom!* Each aircraft had been given three rounds of ammunition to unleash. Dom could hear Scott laughing, and the taciturn American whooping and hollering as he emptied his guns into their black shadows.

Once, such moments were the high points of Dom's life, the times when he forgot everything – lovers, parents, home – to play the most dangerous and exhilarating game devised by man or devil. He'd loved all of it then: the feeling of mastery, the freedom from petty earth, the danger, the fear, but now a smear of shame was mixed into the exhilaration. Nothing he could talk about yet, to anyone – not to his parents, not to his living friends, certainly not to a woman – but always there.

The first shadowings had come in the early days of the Battle of Britain. He'd gone up in a Spitfire, misread the altimeter, and the plane had plunged down at top speed towards the coast of Norfolk. The earth had come hurtling towards him. His stomach hit his brains. It was only at the last possible moment he'd managed to swerve and climb again.

That was the day when he'd sworn to himself that if he got down in one piece, he'd go straight to his flight commander and say he would never fly again. He'd passed out for a few moments after landing and woke tasting his own vomit in his crash helmet. But on his way back to the mess, walking on jelly legs and staggering under the weight of his parachute, he'd changed his mind again. He simply couldn't stop. It was what he needed to feel alive.

And then, much later and much worse, he'd persuaded Jacko to go up again even though he knew Jacko was struggling with the mathematics of flight. There was something about coordinating hand, eye, foot, maps, controls and the altimeter that didn't come naturally to him. He'd tried to tell Dom he was windy and Dom had teased him out of it, or tried – a moment of casual cruelty that would stay with him for the rest of his life.

What happened next was the rock under the sunny surface of things. But he mustn't dwell on it; they'd been warned about that. 'Be economic with emotion,' the wing commander had told them on day one at flying school. 'Look at the chap on your right, and now at the one on your left; soon one of them will be dead.'

He must forget his joke; forget Jacko's face on fire, the plane spinning towards the sea like a pointless toy.

His new priorities were clear: flying, fighting, and seeing Saba again.

Chapter 22

When Willie collapsed on stage, ten days later, it was Janine who saved his life. They were performing at a fuel depot close to an infantry camp near Burg el Arab; Arleta was pretending to be Josephine Baker dancing the famous banana dance that had enchanted *tout* Paris; Willie was the ravenous little boy eating her bananas while she leapt around blissfully unaware. It was very funny and Saba loved it. She was roaring with laughter in the wings when she saw Willie's eyes go blank and float up into his lids. She thought it was a stunt, until he crashed heavily to the floor and the curtain came hurriedly down.

He fell on a rusty nail in the wings that shot into a hand that instantly spurted blood. Janine whipped off her tights, twisted them into a makeshift tourniquet, and then ran on muscles of steel towards the much-derided panic bag for emergency iodine and bandages, all applied with ice-cool efficiency.

The cause of his initial faint was diagnosed as jaundice, possibly contracted from food from one of the fly-blown street stalls he insisted were far safer than the jellied-eel stands in London. He was now in a military hospital on the base looking yellow and uncertain, but still alive. Saba and Arleta had gone to see him every day, with Janine, who was shyly the heroine of the hour, until Arleta had herself gone yellow and come down with jaundice. The eight-piece combo that was supposed to arrive from Malta hadn't. Janine, who'd been offered a transfer to India, delayed her departure, and sometimes read to Willie in the afternoons. The last time Saba had arrived she'd been brushing his hair and blushed bright red at the sight of her.

'Do you want to do this?' Bagley asked when the official request came through for Saba to transfer to Alex and do a week of wireless broadcasts. 'With Willie and Arleta off, there's sod all to do here, and a couple of nights at the Cheval D'Or would be quite a feather in your cap.' His forehead had wrinkled as he'd read the order again. 'But I hear it's pretty hot there – I mean you could probably go home now if you pushed it. I'd certainly help you.'

She'd looked at him in amazement. Stop now! Was he completely mad?

But four days later, stepping off the plane in Alexandria, she felt a complicated mix of emotions: orphanish to be sure at leaving the company (both Willie and Arleta had cried; Bog had offered to marry her), excited about the possibility of performing at the Cheval D'Or, desperate to get some kind of safe message to Dom. If they were ever to have a chance of meeting, it would have to be here.

'Darling.' Madame Eloise stepped out of a sea of dun-coloured soldiers to meet her, looking like some cool and exotic flower in her white linen dress and pale primrose hat.

'Madame.' Saba tried to sidestep the little groaning kisses on both cheeks. She'd been sick again on the plane, and Madame smelled delicious – a tart fragrance like grapefruits and sweet roses.

'Oh don't bother with all that Madame business.' Madame's voice had a faint cockney twang Saba hadn't noticed before. 'That's for my shop customers. Call me Ellie.'

As they walked across the road, Ellie explained the fortunate coincidence that had led her here.

'I happened to be here on business,' she said, 'when Captain Furness, an old friend, asked me to step in. The other chaperone got stuck in Cairo, where all the wretched trains have stopped. So we're orphans together. Doing what, I'm not entirely sure.' She stopped smiling and frowned; it made her look older – Saba guessed at least forty.

'To be honest with you, Ellie,' Saba said, 'I haven't got a flipping clue either. I was whisked out of the desert this morning and told I'd get my orders when I arrived here.'

'Well, all to be revealed soon.' Ellie put up a parasol. 'I hope.'

A taxi took them down a desert road littered on both sides with wrecked tanks and burned-out jeeps, and when they turned towards the city Saba was shocked. Arleta, who'd once done a three-week tour here, had waxed eloquent about its fabulous beaches, and shops as good as London, and cosmopolitan street cafés, and perfect climate, but as they drove closer, Saba saw shattered pavements and charred houses, an old woman with a bandage around her head scavenging for food.

'This looks like a dangerous place to live,' she said. She found it hard to imagine that there would be a nightclub open here.

'Don't worry, pet.' Ellie patted her hand. 'We're staying in a staff house that belonged to a Colonel Patterson, in Ramleh, in the eastern part of town, away from all this. God it's bright outside.'

The black shadows of flowers moved across her face as she pulled the taxi's home-made blackout curtains.

'People are on edge here naturally after the flap,' she continued breezily, 'but life goes on, people are swimming again and partying, and most of them say the Germans will bypass Alexandria.'

'We've been living inside a bit of a bubble lately,' Saba said, thinking how easily this battered town could be circled by a line of German tanks, 'and travelling so much.' When she peered around the curtain she saw a group of men staring helplessly at a collapsed shop window in which a few stained dresses and cardboard boxes remained. 'It's hard to know who to trust.'

'Keep that closed.' Ellie jerked the fabric and made it dark again. She patted Saba's hand and crossed her legs with a sucking sound. 'I hear you girls have done heroic work in the desert, and if I may say so, you look absolutely done in,' she said. 'Look at you!' A circle of dust had formed around Saba's feet; the laces in her shoes were clogged with it. 'A bath first, I think, then a decent lunch. Tomorrow you've been asked out to lunch with Zafer Ozan which should be fun. Have you seen his house?'

'I met him once. He heard me sing in Cairo.'

'Oh well, glory, you are in for a treat. I hear it's stunning.'

'Are you coming?' Saba hoped she was.

Ellie hesitated. 'Not sure yet – let's wait and see.'

The charming villa they were staying in had iron grilles on its windows and blackout curtains inside. When the taxi stopped outside it, a *suffragi* took Saba's dusty kitbag from the back of the car and led them towards the house.

'The house is lovely and cool, you'll be happy to hear,' Ellie said. They had stepped into a tiled hall. Her heels clattered emptily into a sitting room smelling of furniture polish which looked like a dentist's waiting room with its half-empty bookshelves and old copies of *Country Life*. 'We keep all the shutters closed during the day, and use the fans at night.'

The Pattersons, it seemed, had gone for longer than a holiday. There were gaps on the wall where pictures had disappeared; the teak floor had a pale square in the middle of it where the rug had been. When a servant took Saba to the guest room on the first floor where she felt a dizzying wave of tiredness at the sight of the clean white sheets, the mosquito net, the soft-looking bed. All of the company were exhausted now and she hadn't had a decent night's sleep for what felt like a long time. In a saucer beside her bed, someone had lit a Moon Tiger – its green coils of insect repellent gently smouldering, dropping ash on the floor.

'Bath first, then bed.' Ellie padded into the room in her stockinged feet. She had a jar of violet-coloured bath salts in one hand, towels in the other. She followed Saba into the bathroom where the water was already flowing. She handed Saba a green silk kimono and said she must use it while she was here.

'You're very kind,' said Saba. Her limbs were aching for her first proper bath in a month.

'Not kind, happy to see you.' Ellie opened her mouth to say something else, but left it at that. 'Hop in,' she said. 'I'll see you at supper.'

The water was hot and smelled so good. Saba, scrubbing herself with soap, was astounded at how much dust and sand had stuck to her skin. The day before, they'd all been caught in a dust storm as they'd left the rehearsal tent. For ten minutes the sand had lashed and stung them; when they got back to their tents they laughed at each other – they were so coated in dust that Saba said they should be on a plinth at the Cairo museum. The pint of water they'd shared to wash it off had left them all with grit in their underwear, their teeth, their hair and made them feel irritable and out of sorts.

Sunlight bounced off the water. Bliss! A whole bath to herself without Janine's wretched egg-timer or her damp sighs behind the door. It was only when Saba was washing her hair with the shampoo thoughtfully provided that she felt a wiggle of loneliness. Arleta usually rinsed her hair for her, and helped her dry it in a way that made her feel like a cherished baby. Before she left, Arleta had hugged her tight; she'd pinched Saba's cheeks and said she wanted her back soon: they were family now. Even Janine had pecked her on the cheek.

When she'd gone to see Willie in hospital, he'd pretended to bawl his eyes out like a fat baby. Arleta said she didn't think he'd last long.

The water was almost cold when she woke. She heard the grumble of aeroplanes overhead, the gurgle of pipes from the kitchens below and, for a moment, had no idea where she was.

She dressed and went downstairs. 'Well, you had a good one,' Ellie said. She'd changed into a pair of pale grey silk lounging pyjamas and knotted a long rope of pearls around her neck. She was drinking a gin and tonic. She went over to the window and checked that the dark blue blackout curtains were fully drawn, and told Saba that after supper they would have some fun trying on clothes.

'Ozan throws a great party, or so I've heard.' She closed her eyes ecstatically. 'Marvellous music, rivers of Bollinger – wish I'd kept up with *my* singing lessons.'

'What did you do before the war?' Saba asked quickly. Ellie's hints made her uneasy – she still wasn't sure what she was doing here, or whether it was safe for her to go to the party. She wished Cleeve was around to brief her again.

'A long story.' Ellie took a sip of her gin. There was a taut perkiness about her tonight that Saba hadn't noticed before that made her wonder if she was more nervous than she was letting on. 'Which I'll nutshell: went to Paris when I was young, instantly fell in love with the city – an absolute *coup de foudre*. In those days, no interest in clothes whatsoever – lived in jodhpurs and twinsets – but one day, shopping in a local market, a man saw me, great gawky thing that I was. He asked me to be a house model for Jean Patou. They made me lose half a stone, taught me how to make up and then I did three of their collections.'

She stood up and walked in a haughty way towards the blackout curtain: 'Feather on the head, tail on the derriere, that's how they taught us to walk.'

'*Numéro un – une robe blanche*,' she imitated the gloomy voice of a vendeuse, and then *pring pring* she played an imaginary piano. '*Numéro deux – une robe noire*. Dead boring, but suppose it was a start. The main thing was, I lived independently for the first time. That was wonderful.'

*

They ate supper together in a sparsely furnished dining room, where the only light came from a fringed lamp on the sideboard.

Ellie had organised a local dish called kushari, a cumin-scented mix of lentils and onions and vegetables smothered in a spicy sauce. She apologised for serving peasant food. 'The Egyptians call it a messy mix,' she said, 'but I adore it, much better than ghastly tinned sausages and all that bully-beef rubbish.' They washed it down with a glass of French wine. Ellie said it was a present from a new boyfriend, a French-Egyptian wine merchant.

'He's Free French and I'm quite taken,' she said, her eyes lighting up. Saba was surprised; surely forty was too old for passion?

Saba ate heartily; she loved the food and said so. It reminded her of the dishes Tansu used to make. She told Ellie, a good listener, about Tan: how they used to lie in bed listening to music on the wireless together, how brave Tan had been arriving in Wales from Turkey with nothing but her suitcase. Ellie smiled at her as if she was her own child.

'I'm feeling quite nervous actually, Ellie,' Saba said when they were eating tiny pastries and drinking Turkish coffee. 'I've never sung at a proper nightclub before, or at a really posh party like Mr Ozan's. I don't know what songs they'll like even.'

Ellie leaned forward; she grabbed both of Saba's hands and held them between hers. She looked her intently in the eyes. 'They'll love you,' she said. 'Dermot Cleeve says you're a real find.'

Saba looked at her. So she did know Cleeve.

'I thought he might be here tonight,' said Saba. She was aware of how her voice bounced in the empty, rugless room. It almost felt as if they were on a stage.

'Don't worry,' said Ellie. 'Everything is falling into place. While you were in the bath I got a telephone call from Furness. You're to rehearse with a woman called Faiza Mushawar; her husband used to own the Café de Paris, not the real one of course, but the one on the Corniche. She is a fine singer herself, although more in that moany, waily Arab style than is to my taste – have you ever been to one of their concerts, darling? Well don't. Hideous. They go on for absolutely days. Anyway, anyway, I hear they have a first-class band there.' Her diamond ring flashed as she patted Saba's hand. 'A lovely change from singing in the desert. That must have been so depressing.'

'It's not,' Saba said. How to explain how shockingly alive it had made her feel, and proud too to be doing her bit. 'When do we start?' She wanted Ellie to say immediately so she could stop feeling nervous.

'The day after tomorrow at ten.'

The business part of their conversation seemed over, and now, as darkness deepened outside the house, Ellie babbled on amiably – about the dresses she'd brought, how she'd help with make-up if necessary. She'd done the models at Patou and still had her kit with all the old favourites in it. Tangee's Red Red was fabulous under lights. Saba tuned her out. She was thinking about her songs. 'Stormy Weather', her head nodded as she silently sang it; the doo-wop maybe for a bit of light relief; 'My Funny Valentine' definitely, she loved singing that. It would be a treat, she thought, not to sing the relentlessly chirpy songs ENSA insisted on even to men who looked half dead.

The tray of coffee cups rattled as the servant left the room. There was a distant boom, followed by the rat-tat-tat of anti-aircraft guns. The servant stopped and waited expectantly. Ellie listened hard, her eyes wide open, her nostrils flared.

'There's an air-raid shelter behind the courtyard,' she said, 'if we need it. Personally, I can't be bothered to run out at every single thing. It's nothing like as bad as London was, I can assure you.' The flame of her match caught her tense smile, and Saba felt fearful and dislocated again. In Cardiff, when the bombs were this close and she and Tan couldn't be fagged to go to the shelter, they'd lie under the table in the front room together. They'd hug each other and sing songs, the mountainous upholstered bulk of her gran as solid as a sofa or a building.

The anti-aircraft guns stopped; she heard the shrill sound of a rocket. To distract herself she picked up the photograph on the sideboard of the sensibly departed Pattersons, they stood in front of a large grey slab of a building next to a flag at what looked like a passing-out parade. Grey English sky above them. The colonel's pleasant long-jawed face bent towards a Mrs Patterson smiling rigidly at the camera.

'Amazing, isn't it.' Ellie took the photo from her. 'How scared some people get at the slightest thing. Ever since I've been in Egypt,' she stretched her feet and admired her toes, 'they've gone on about the big push. I'd have been gone eight or nine times if I believed them, and to what? Some awful little flat in London, where thousands and thousands of people have been killed already.'

'So, will you stay after the war?' Saba asked.

'If a certain someone wants me to,' Ellie said with a cat-that-got-the-cream smile, 'I'd definitely stay.' She added softly, 'I love it here, I really do.'

The bombing had stopped. The doors were double-locked; the servants dismissed. Saba took the plunge.

'Ellie,' she said, 'you know in Cairo you asked us about . . . you know . . . men friends?' She used the phrase shyly, but 'boyfriend' sounded wrong, too. 'Well there is someone I'd like to see while I'm here. He's in the Desert Air Force, and he has some leave coming up.'

'Does Dermot know about him?' Ellie asked pleasantly. She pushed a box of Turkish delight towards her. 'Have one – they're delish.'

'No.'

'Ummm.' Ellie put her sweet down on a saucer, her teeth marks clearly imprinted. 'Gosh.' Her thoughtful expression had changed. She leaned forward and clasped Saba's hand. 'So funny you asked me this,' she said quietly.

She got up and poured them both a small brandy even though Saba had not asked for one. She paced around for a bit with her drink in her hand taking small excited sips, and then she sat down.

'Saba,' she said. 'Listen.' She drained her glass and then explained in a low voice that her new boyfriend mentioned earlier, whose name was Tariq, was actually in Alexandria that week and she was absolutely longing to see him. Not that she had minded, of course, but she'd had to cancel a weekend away with him to be Saba's chaperone. He was a very passionate man, and they'd had rather a bust-up about this, but now, well maybe . . .

'Saba,' she added, in an urgent whisper, 'will you promise me not to breathe a word of this to Captain Furness or Dermot Cleeve or any of the ENSA gang for that matter. But I don't want to lose this man and I wasn't sure I'd have time to see him. He's off himself next week to Beirut.' She looked carefully at Saba. 'Tell me your friend's name again.'

'His name is Dom. Pilot Officer Dominic Benson.'

'Shall I see what I can do?'

Saba sank to her knees, and clasped her hands together in mock prayer. 'Please.'

Ellie chewed her bottom lip and stared thoughtfully at Saba.

'If I do this, you must keep schtum. People are frightful gossips here – it's very easy to lose your reputation, so the fewer people we tell the better,' by which Saba assumed she meant they would tell no one. Which was fine with her.

Chapter 23

The following day, a uniformed chauffeur drove up to the house in a Bugatti, the most beautiful car Saba had ever seen, with a blue china evil eye swinging from its front mirror.

The chauffer delivered a note on elaborately engraved paper requesting the pleasure of Miss Saba Tarcan's company at Mr Zafer Ozan's house near Montazah at one o'clock. He hoped that she would honour him by staying for lunch.

If Ellie was miffed at not being asked she hid her disappointment generously. After breakfast, she took Saba up to her bedroom and told her to take her pick from the row of beautiful and expensive dresses hanging like highly scented corpses in white cotton bags in her wardrobe. After some consideration, they chose an exquisitely simple blue silk that Ellie said she'd picked up in Paris, at a Christian Dior sample sale. She insisted Saba take the matching bag as well – a bright blue feathery thing that lay like a dead bird at the bottom of the wardrobe in a shoebox lined with tissue paper.

During these procedures, Ellie became electric with excitement. She insisted on a ladylike waspy corset, and a stole; she darted towards her jewellery case and produced a pair of pearl earrings, which she clipped on Saba's ears, murmuring *of course, of course* as if she had reached the end of some daunting religious crisis; she grabbed a brush and pulled it through Saba's hair, saying she had fabulous hair and should thank her lucky stars for it. Fat chance anyone had of finding a decent hairdresser in Alex at the moment.

Saba forgot to answer. She was thinking about her songs again and found Ellie's bright stream of chat distracting. She also disliked being prodded and poked like this. It made her feel like a doll.

'Gorgeous. Beautiful!' Ellie squinted at her in the mirror. 'Now.' She opened a glass bottle with a tassel on it, and dabbed Saba's wrist. 'It's called Joy and the occasional free bottle was one of the perks of working with Patou, and now of course I'm addicted to the ruddy stuff. If you like it, I can give you some.'

Saba sniffed her wrist and wrinkled her nose. Ellie's eyes had closed and her expression become stagily ecstatic. 'Let it settle,' she commanded. 'Every ounce of its essence is made with twenty-eight dozen roses and ten thousand six hundred jasmine flowers. Can you imagine!'

In the same reverent voice she said that after the stock market had crashed in America, Patou had made the perfume for women who could no longer afford his clothes. 'He called it the gift of memory,' she said. 'So sweet of him. It's supposed to be the most expensive scent in the world.'

Saba was beginning to find Ellie's world confusing. A present to cheer poor women up that was the most expensive scent in the world. It had cost the lives of twenty-eight dozen roses and ten thousand six hundred jasmine flowers; that seemed quite a high price to pay for some decent pong.

Later that morning, Ozan's extraordinary car stopped outside their house again and Saba felt as if she had taken up residence in another life, and not one she was sure she wanted. While she and Arleta had had some good laughs at the expense of the ENSA uniform, with its laughable knickers and khaki brassieres, it had given her a comforting sense of doing the right thing, of belonging. Now, standing in the dusty street outside the Pattersons' house – powdered, scented, silk-covered and with the bird bag – she felt like a made-up thing, a toy.

Her driver, a handsome Egyptian, was separated from her by a glass partition. As they moved off, she noticed him glance at her sharply through his rear-view mirror – a hard sexual stare after the earlier smiles and bows. In his own world, she imagined, few women would travel alone like this.

The mainly European suburb of Ramleh came with smart houses, green lawns, carefully tended borders and roads that led down to the beach that were tarmacked and well maintained. But then she saw opposite them in a scruffy native quarter a sandy street covered in the footprints of mules and donkeys, like a road breaching two centuries.

Out of town, their beautiful car purred past white-robed men riding bicycles or donkeys and, at one crossroad, a Bedouin family with camels tied nose to tail. To the left of them the Mediterranean dazzled like smashed pieces of blue glass; to the right was a wilderness of sand studded with the wrecks of jeeps and the occasional aeroplane.

A group of English soldiers, bare-chested and standing by a broken-down tank, shaded their eyes and goggled at the magnificent car as it drove past. When one of them blew her a kiss, the driver's eyes narrowed to murderous slits in the rear-view mirror.

'We are nearly there, madame.' He spoke for the first time. He put his foot down on the accelerator. She glanced in the direction he was looking at, at the bright sea and a ring of green vegetation where she imagined the house to be.

Over a supper the night before she'd asked Ellie what she knew about Mr Ozan, because she didn't really know a thing. Nerves had taken away her appetite and her rice and chicken fell like a stone in her stomach.

'Well that makes two of us.' Ellie had carried on eating. 'I know nothing, apart from what Tariq tells me.'

'What does he say?'

'Well, he only supplies him with wine, he's hardly a bosom friend.'

'And?'

'Well, all I really know is common knowledge: that the man owns lots of different businesses and nightclubs and that he's extraordinarily rich and well connected. I'd love to see his house.' Ellie tucked her feet up and grew conspiratorial in the lamplight. 'Apparently he has houses everywhere – Beirut, Istanbul, Cairo. Funny to think of a little Turkish man doing so well, although he may well be half Egyptian too, I'm not sure. Can I get you another drink, darling?'

Ellie had walked towards the sideboard and poured herself one. 'I can't wait to hear what you make of it all.' She sat down again and swirled her ice around with her finger. 'Tariq says that his parties are quite spectacular. He says Ozan has a rival in Cairo, another impresario, and the two of them are like children – always trying to outdo each other.'

Ozan, Ellie continued, was one of the biggest collectors of Islamic art in the world. She imagined that the most valuable stuff would be locked away at the moment, but even so . . . 'God, how I'd love to spend a day looking through it.'

Saba, seeing Ellie's body go slack with pleasure at the thought of this, remembered the conversation she and Dom had had that night about people and their passions; how they flowed through you like some secret river that you dammed at your peril. For Ellie, dresses, bits of china, jewellery; for Dom, flying; for his mother, her piano. Her passion for it had not died, he thought, but been diverted, unsuccessfully, into a search for some unattainable domestic perfection that was exhausting, ridiculous. For instance, if the tray of roast potatoes she was cooking weren't the right shade of brown, she would chuck the whole lot away and start again. Her photo albums were so rigorously maintained that the family were filed and labelled almost before the camera had been clicked.

Saba, thinking about her own mother's wonky efforts with the sewing machine, the box of unsorted photos under the bed near the potty, had felt an unexpected surge of gratitude for her. There was something sad and unsettling about the wrong kind of high standards.

She was deeply into this train of thought when the driver had to tap on the window between them. They had arrived at Mr Ozan's and he didn't want her to miss a moment of it.

In fact she was disappointed. From a distance, there seemed nothing special here – just a sprawling flat-roofed house with iron grilles over its windows. The windows, partly camouflaged by palm leaves, gave the house a sneaky eye-patched look.

An armed sentry waved them through iron gates and up an imposing avenue of trees with well-tended gardens on either side. There was a high wall around the garden with bunches of barbed wire on top of it. The driver's back was sweating now; he drove up a strip of gravel towards the front door, pulled aside the glass partition and said gruffly, 'We stop.'

A servant wearing a uniform of no recognisable country opened the door. He led her into a large marble hall which had a chokingly rich smell, somewhere between perfume and charcoal. It was only when she was standing inside the hall that Saba saw that the house was like biting into an expensive chocolate, and far more spectacular inside than out. In a magnificent reception room with a gold-leaf ceiling and marbled floors, gorgeous low velvet sofas were arranged, Arabic-style, around the edges of the room, and piled high with jewelled cushions. One wall was entirely covered by painted cabinets, lit with soft lights and stuffed with what looked to

Saba like all the treasures of the Orient: marbled eggs, masks, exquisitely inlaid boxes.

She was sitting on the edge of a sofa, trying not to goggle too obviously at all this, when another servant appeared to announce that Mr Ozan could see her now. He was waiting for her in the garden.

The servant led her towards a heavily carved door at the end of the marbled corridor. Before he opened it, he smiled at her, almost furtively, as if to say *don't miss this – it's special.* And it was. When he stepped aside, she stepped over the threshold and into a garden like a vision of Eden in an old-fashioned Bible print. In the foreground was a series of maze-like water channels that led to beds of roses and lilacs, and then to trees which filled the air with the scents of almond, cypress and Arabian jasmine.

In the middle of this vision, both artless-seeming and brilliantly contrived, the eye was drawn towards a huge and beautiful alabaster fountain carved with birds and fishes. The water flung so recklessly into the air seemed to laugh at the desert in the distance, at the huge blue sky above it and at the distant sea sparkling like an amethyst.

She sat down on a stone bench near the fountain. It was baking hot here after the dim coolness of the house. A noisy bird was singing extravagantly in the jasmine bush and, in the distance, she heard a telephone ringing, the scattering of feet, what seemed like a world away.

'Miss Tarcan.' Mr Ozan burst from the house, plump, bustling, beautifully groomed in his well-cut European suit and expensive shoes. He bounced down the path, hand extended, beaming at her like a favourite uncle. 'Great pleasure for me.' She caught a whiff of some pungent perfume as he shook her hand. 'I am very happy to see you again. But bad news for me too.' He glanced at his watch. 'Something unexpected has come up. I have to fly to Beirut this afternoon, but you are in my house now, I can explain some things to you – my hope is you will stay for lunch then I must go.' His smile was protective and warm.

At a table near the fountain, a tray had been laid out for them: tea served in little glasses, small dishes of dates and pastries.

Mr Ozan took a sip of tea. 'So, do you actually remember me?' He looked at her teasingly over the rim of his cup, his eyes so thickly lashed they looked as though they were ringed with kohl. 'We met before at the Mena House.'

'Of course,' she said.

'That's right.' He snorted with laughter at the memory. 'And you sang some Umm Kulthum. I thought that was very brave of you. She is our national treasure.'

'I didn't know that,' Saba grinned. 'I learned bits of it from my father. He's an engineer on ships. Lots of crew were Egyptian. I don't think I got all the words right. Did I?'

He shook his head fondly. 'Not all of them, but it was very charming,' he said. 'So I wanted to meet you. And now, here is the thing – forgive me for coming so quickly to the point, but my plane won't wait. I have some big parties coming up soon. Some important people: we make good food, we have dancers, singers, some of the best musicians we can find.' His eyes sparkled at the thought of it. 'And I would like you to sing for me. Would you do that? If it works well, I can prepare for you a proper booking at one of my clubs.'

She was flattered. How could she not be? Arleta had told her that Ozan, before the war, went to a famous nightclub called Le Grand Duc where he had talent-spotted great artistes – Ellie called it a rich man's hobby. But there was something else about him that stirred her on a deeper level – the sight of his dark eyes twinkling at her reminded her of her father. Not her recent furiously disapproving dad, but the baba from earlier days who'd chased her round the back yard laughing.

'I know some other Turkish songs,' she announced eagerly, for that moment the child who'd stood on the table singing. 'I'm half Turkish.'

His expression softened. 'Me too, with a bit of Greek and Egyptian thrown into the pot, but what part of you is Turkish?' he said gently.

Without thinking, she put her hand over her heart.

'This part.'

Mr Ozan burst out laughing, showing beautiful white teeth.

'I meant your mother or your father.' His English was excellent, but he had a way of adding a soft purr to the end of *motherrrr, fatherrrr*, just as her father did.

'My father.'

'And where does he hail from?'

She told him briefly about the farm, the plane trees, about his father the schoolteacher – surprised all over again at how little she knew – Ozan listened raptly. He closed his eyes as if in pain.

'Did they have to leave their farm?'

'Yes.'

'Do you know what happened?'

'No.' She felt tears come to her eyes. 'He didn't talk about it.'

'It's hard to leave your land.' He looked at her sadly. 'But we can talk more about this later. This is not forrr the idle chat.' Again he purred his r's like a cat.

She watched him crumble a sticky pastry between his fingers. He told her that he had been educated at a Jesuit school in Cairo, and also in London for one year. He said that although he was a successful businessman, 'I am in here,' he'd clutched his chest, 'a musician – but one, I am sad to say, who cannot play for toffees or sing.' What he'd most enjoyed before the war he told her, his eyes gleaming, was to go to a big city like Paris or London and listen to the best singers there. 'Everybody thinks that people in this part of the world only like the *aaaahhhhh*,' he twisted his wrists around and wailed like an Arab singer, 'but I have heard Piaf and Ella Fitzgerald, Sarah Vaughan, Jacques Brel, all of the great ones – I like them as much as Umm Kulthum.'

One of the pleasures of his life, he said, was to discover the good young singers. He mentioned a few names, none of them familiar to her, and talked tantalisingly of the tours he arranged for them across the Mediterranean in the nightclubs he owned: in Istanbul, in Cairo, Beirut and Alexandria. 'I have learned that all great singers need practice,' he said. 'Not just practice to sing, but practice to perform. And we make the perfect place to learn, for many of these people,' which he pronounced *bipple*.

'But now,' he gave an eloquent shrug, 'there is a big drought on talented artistes in Egypt, so when I heard you sing, it made me very happy. I saw something in you, something exciting. In our language we would call you a Mutriba, she is one who creates *tarab* – literally enchantment – with her songs.'

The blue silk dress had made her feel all cool and sophisticated, but now she could feel herself grinning.

'What kind of songs do you want me to sing at your parties?' She knew she would do it now. 'I need to practise.'

'I've been thinking about that.' He gave a powerful snort. 'We need tact. The parties will be in Beirut, where some of my clients dislike Western music very much indeed. They must be happy too. So two, maybe three Arabic songs. Can you do this?'

'I'll need to rehearse,' she said. 'I don't want to make a fool of myself.'

'I have arranged for Faiza to teach you at the club. She's old now, but she is still considered one of the best singers in Egypt. It will be interesting for you.'

'Count me in.' She put her hand out, he shook it.

'So, we have a deal,' he said. When his eyes lit up like that, she saw what a sweet child he must have been.

A bottle of Bollinger appeared in an ice bucket with two exquisite champagne flutes. She'd never drunk during the day before, but the occasion felt so odd and special she let him pour her a glass.

Ozan waved; a servant appeared at almost a jog trot, setting down on the table a mass of small alabaster dishes. When the lids were whisked away, she saw a dish of tiny birds no bigger than budgies covered in herbs and oranges; some rice covered in almonds. The servant danced around them placing pickles and small salads and olives and bread in a semicircle around them.

'It's a picnic today.' Mr Ozan tucked his napkin in. 'When you come to my party, I make a proper feast for you.'

He helped Saba to a portion of the baby quail, watching her fondly while she ate a dish so delicious it was all she could do to stop herself groaning with pleasure. It was overwhelming after the ghastly food in the desert.

Mr Ozan seemed a hearty eater, sucking his fingers and chewing noisily and picking up the small bones of the bird to crunch them. While he was thus engaged, his eyes went distant and blank, and he occasionally gave a small grunt of pleasure.

He was wiping his chin with a napkin when a servant brought a telephone to him. There was the rat-tat-tat of conversation and then Mr Ozan ripped his napkin out of his shirt and started to breathe heavily and sigh. Heavy footsteps in the hall, a dark-suited man stood at the door. When Ozan saw him he stopped talking and stood up.

'Forgive me.' He took her hand. 'This is unfortunate but the plane is already waiting, there is some mistake. I'll be in touch when I get back from Beirut. Sorry for the rush. Please be my guest and stay for as long as you like.' He bowed slightly and disappeared into the house.

A lovely woman appeared in the doorway almost as soon as he was gone. She smiled shyly at Saba. 'I am Mr Ozan's wife,' she said. 'My name is Leyla.'

Leyla was a classic Turkish beauty with high cheekbones, thick black eyebrows and shining hair which she wore loose. The sight of her, cool as a mountain stream in her green silk dress, made it almost impossible to believe in the harshness of the desert that surrounded them, or that Rommel's army might be as close as forty miles away.

'Zafer is very sorry he had to leave so quickly,' she said. Her English, like his, was excellent. 'If you will please wait here, the car comes in ten minutes,' she added. She bowed and left the garden, still smiling.

The champagne and the hypnotic sounds of the fountain made Saba feel drowsy, and she closed her eyes after Leyla had gone, happy to have a few moments' peace. Half in a dream, she heard more heavy boots walking across the marble floor. The soft voice of a woman, a door closing.

'Madame,' a servant stood at the door, waiting for her, 'the car is here.'

Reluctant to leave the enchanting garden, she followed him through the heavy doors and across the marble hall. She was almost out the front door when, damn! She remembered she'd left Ellie's blue-feathered bag on the sofa in the reception room.

'One moment, please,' she told the servant. 'I have left my . . .' She pointed towards the room which lay sombre and stately behind the carved door, its precious objects flashing and winking.

When the door opened a fraction wider she saw two men in grey uniforms sitting near the window. They were clean-shaven with very short hair. Their legs were sprawled in front of them as though they were at ease here. When the man closest to her stood up, she felt a jolting fear – she was looking into the eyes of a German officer. He was less than a foot away. He clicked his heels and bowed.

'*Das Mädchen ist schön*,' he said to his friend, who looked her up and down appreciatively.

Saba froze for a moment, and then smiled at them while her

brain slowly began to function. She mimed a handbag, and shrugged helplessly.

The younger man stood up. He had fine intelligent eyes. He dug under a cushion and held up the handbag by its delicately feathered strap. He handed it to her with a pleasant smile.

'*Shukran*,' she murmured.

'*Ellaleqa*.'

She returned his slight bow, turned and walked with her heart pounding towards the waiting car.

Chapter 24

'Mr Cleeve's here,' Ellie was standing at the door when Saba got home. She looked pale. She pointed upstairs towards the bedroom. 'He came suddenly on the Cairo train. He's having a little rest upstairs.' There was a warning note in her voice. 'Don't forget to keep schtum about our other arrangements,' she whispered, steering her into the sitting room. 'It could spoil everything and I have some rather good news for you.

'A big gin or a tiddler?' Ellie pushed her gently into a chair. She drew the blackout curtains and lit a small lamp. 'I'm going to have a big one – it's been quite a busy day, and I'm dying to hear,' she added in her more social voice, 'about yours – do tell all.'

Saba looked at her and made a rapid calculation. If Cleeve were here, it would be safer to tell him and no one else about the Germans. Ellie was still such a new friend.

Ellie took a sip of her gin. 'Saba, I'll say this quickly before he comes.' She lowered her voice and glanced towards the ceiling. 'Damn!' The sound of a chair moving across the floorboards. 'I'll have to tell you later – Dermot wants to talk over songs and recordings and things with you, so I'm going to make myself scarce.' She stood up. 'Can't wait to hear what the house was like,' she resumed in a brighter tone as Cleeve loped into the room carrying a briefcase in his hand.

'My goodness.' Cleeve put his head on one side in mock admiration and smiled at Saba. 'What a stunning frock. I can see Madame E has performed her usual magic.'

'Drink, Dermot?' Ellie said quickly. 'Then I'll go up and change for supper and leave you both to it.'

'Gin and it, sweetheart,' he said. 'Oh what heaven to be back in civilisation.' He sank into a chair. 'I sat on that bloody Cairo train for four hours,' he complained. 'They were loading all these cars for the big brass. One of the porters eventually switched on the wireless in one of them, so we could listen to some music, otherwise I would have been a mad person by now. Which reminds me.' He gulped some gin and opened his briefcase. 'Pressie for Saba,' he said. 'A Hoagy Carmichael recording. It was smuggled over from New York. Quite superb.'

The package sat in Saba's lap.

'Well open it,' he said, crinkling his eyes.

'Thank you,' she said woodenly – Ellie was hovering at the door. 'Perhaps later.'

'Darlings, I'm off,' said Ellie quickly. 'See you at dinner. I'm glad you like the dress, Dermot.' They could hear her scampering footsteps going upstairs.

'She doesn't know anything,' Dermot said when the door had closed. 'She's only your dresser, and I would have arranged to meet you somewhere else tonight, but it was impossible to arrange transport. Are you hungry?' he added in his conversational voice. 'I'm starving. I could call for something.'

'No,' she said. She pulled her chair so that it faced him and looked him squarely in the eye. 'I'm not hungry, and I don't want to talk about dresses, and I don't want to talk about Hoagy Carmichael. What I want to know is why you let me go to Zafer Ozan's house on my own when you knew what was going on there.'

'I don't know what you're talking about.'

'You must know,' Saba exploded. 'There were two German officers there.' She wanted to spit with fury. 'One of them was trying to speak to me. I could have been captured, I could have been raped. Why didn't anyone warn me?'

'Darling.' Cleeve was almost pleading with her. 'What a nasty fright, I'm so sorry about it. Hang on . . .' He stood up, placed his finger on his lips and put Hoagy Carmichael's 'Stardust' on the Pattersons' gramophone. 'I do so love this man,' he said mildly, lowering the needle. 'He knows the notes, he knows the melody, but best of all he knows how to make a tune swing. She thinks we're rehearsing,' he whispered.

'Now listen.' He leaned towards Saba. 'It's important you understand this: someone like Ozan doesn't see the Germans as the great bogymen that we do. Half the shopkeepers in Alexandria now have signs in German underneath their counters saying "*wilkommen*" in case it goes the other way. It's human nature, darling. Point the second,' there was a signet ring on his little finger, 'Ozan is Turkish, or most of him is. Turkey is neutral. He is an international businessman, he can ask who the hell he likes to his house. If you're a guest of his, you are perfectly safe.'

'You don't know that.'

'I do.'

'How?'

'I just do.' Cleeve took a long sip of gin and rattled the ice.

'Now listen, settle down and talk to me, because I'm leaving shortly – what did these Germans say to you?'

'I don't know – I don't speak the language.'

'So what did you say?'

'To whom?' She glared at him still.

'To the man who talked to you. The German.'

'Nothing, I answered him in Arabic.'

He blew out air.

'Good girl. Quick thinking. How well do you actually speak Arabic?'

'Hardly at all,' she said through gritted teeth, 'that's the point – only the few words a friend taught me at school. If that man had spoken the language he would have been on to me in a flash. I could have been killed or captured.'

'Darling, darling.' He held up his hand to stop her. 'I think we've gone right off into the realms of melodrama here. There are several things I need to explain to you.'

He steepled his hands under his chin. Pashas like Ozan, he said, were largely oblivious to the war; they ducked and dived, their lifeblood was business and they would sell to the highest bidder. 'And a lovely man, of course,' he added quickly. 'Passionate about music. But having said all that,' he opened his cigarette case and seemed to select his words as carefully as he did his cigarette, 'I'm somewhat surprised to hear that our German friends are so blatantly there at the moment. I'm going to have to discuss this with my superior. We need to work out a careful strategy.'

'Who is your superior?'

'I can't tell you that just yet.' A fly caught in the lampshade momentarily distracted him. He picked up a *Parade* magazine, rolled it, and whacked the insect dead. 'I'm not trying to be deliberately evasive, it's just that I need time to brief him on the situation. What did Ozan ask you to do?'

'If you tell me more about why I was there, I'll tell you about today.' This seemed her only bargaining chip.

He sighed and placed the dead fly in the ashtray.

'We have a strong suspicion that Ozan has changed the location of his party from Alexandria to either Beirut or Istanbul; it's important for us to know, as soon as possible, which place he decides on. If it's Istanbul we may have a little job for you to do there that could turn into rather an important job. I won't waste time by discussing it now.'

'And the parties are important because . . . ?' She was not going to let him off the hook now.

'Some of the key people in the Middle East go to them, and you might just pick up something of vital importance. The point is,' he leaned forward, his face sweating, 'his lot hold the keys to victory.'

'What lot?'

'The suppliers. Ozan – thanks to the parties and the nightclubs – has a large network of friends and business acquaintances, some of whom control the supplies of oil and now water, and without oil and water, we may as well all go home now.'

'Is there anything else?'

'My, what a terrier.' He looked at her in mock alarm. 'I wouldn't like to be interrogated by you.'

Patronising twit. She felt like thwacking him over the head.

'Radar,' he said simply.

'The British want to make use of Turkish airbases. Strategically, they are absolutely vital, and it so happens that Ozan's family own the land around one of them, about fourteen miles from Ankara. It would be helpful to know which way he's going to jump.'

She heard the drone of distant aircraft, and from upstairs the faint splashes of Ellie performing her evening toilette.

'Listen, Saba,' he said. He opened his arms as if he were freeing a bird. 'If you don't feel like doing any of this, you can go home now. Right back to England if you like.'

She sat in silence, a million conflicting thoughts going through her head. There was a kindly, understanding look in Cleeve's eyes when she looked up – the usual look of amused curiosity.

'I'll do it,' she said.

Chapter 25

As soon as the front door clicked behind him, Saba raced upstairs.

'Ellie,' she whispered urgently through the keyhole of her bedroom. 'He's gone. What did you want to tell me?'

'Come in and close the door behind you.

'Well now,' Ellie's kidney-shaped dressing table gave back three smug reflections of herself, 'I think you're going to be rather pleased with me. You see, I've found him.' She powdered her nose in a spirited way. 'Your Pilot Officer Benson.'

Saba sank to the floor beside her.

'Is this a joke?'

'No.' Ellie swivelled around and looked at her seriously. 'But it's a secret, and you've got to swear to keep it.'

Saba saw her own flushed face in the mirror.

'How did you find him?'

'I'd like to claim some great victory,' Ellie said. 'But I can't. I was having a drink this afternoon in Pastroudis, a group of pilots were there on leave, I asked if they knew him and of course they did. Easy-peasy.'

'And?' Saba's body was literally vibrating with excitement.

'They said they'd get a message to him, that, as far as they knew, he was in town. If all goes to plan, he'll be down at the Cheval D'Or tonight. Tariq's sending a taxi for us at around nine thirty, which just about gives you time to have a bath and get dressed.'

'Did you tell Mr Cleeve? He mustn't know.'

'Of course not, you twit.' Ellie stood up and smoothed her dress down. 'Listen, Saba,' she said, 'I am supposed to be your chaperone – but don't you ever get sick of the boys making all the rules?' She gave a little wink. 'But we don't have much time, so let's discuss this later,' she'd gone back to her chaperone voice, 'over a drink at the club. I'd have a bath now if I was you; it's been an awfully long day, and who knows what the night may bring?'

She stood up and opened her wardrobe door. While she rummaged, she told Saba that she'd meet Faiza Mushawar that night too – the singing teacher. Faiza, although as old as God, would be dressed up to the nines, probably even to the tens, that was the Egyptian way.

'What about this little number?' She put a black sequinned cocktail dress on the bed. 'Or this?' A green satin skirt was flung beside it.

'No,' said Saba. She was quite clear about this – if Dom was coming, she wanted to feel like herself.

She stood in her half-slip and looked at herself in the mirror. Her hair was below her shoulders now, and she was thinner than she had been; her arms had grown brown in the sun. When she tried to put on her favourite silver bracelet, her hands were trembling too much to do up its fiddly catch.

After some deliberation, she chose the red silk dress that she had worn that night in Ismailia. It was a bit creased but she loved it; it meant something to her now.

A taxi drew up outside the house; Ellie's boyfriend, Tariq, had arrived, a short, powerfully built man whose wire-rimmed glasses and impeccable clothes gave him a serious, even scholastic air. He'd brought a string of jasmine for Ellie, whom he was clearly mad about. 'Jasmine,' he explained, 'was the flower of love in Egypt.'

Earlier, Ellie had seemed anxious to explain to Saba that her boyfriend was not, as she put it, 'a typical native', but half French and half Egyptian; a civilised man of the world whose four passions in life were wine (he'd spent his childhood on a small vineyard near Bordeaux), music, women and Egyptology. He'd first come to this city in search of buried bones, but when archaeology had proved an expensive occupation, he'd financed it by importing fine wines, which he'd done with some success.

He seemed to bring out a more kittenish, excitable side of Ellie's nature. They bounded together towards the waiting car and jumped inside it as if they couldn't wait for the evening to begin, and soon the air was full of everybody's combined scents: sandalwood from Tariq's side, Joy on all Ellie's pulse points; even their driver with his brass box of ambergris and frankincense on his dashboard added to the rich and frankly overpowering air.

Tariq, sitting close to Ellie on the back seat, apologised for the scruffiness of the car and also for the brevity of the trip he was about to take them on. 'It would have been fun to show you Alexandria by night,' he said, 'but there's bad shortage of petrol here, so we must do it some other time.'

Saba, drawing aside a blackout curtain, saw a city half in hiding. Empty roads bathed in shrouded street lights; an empty tram sliding down potholed streets towards the sea, and, in dark cafés between burned-out buildings, the silhouettes of male figures drinking coffee or arak by candlelight. Tariq said, with a smile to hide the bitterness of his words, that the people of Alexandria had got nothing out of the war except inflation and darkness. 'You are seeing Alex in her widow's weeds,' he said protectively. 'The bombings have been horrible, but it will pass. She will recover.'

He told Saba that this city that he loved had been planned by Alexander the Great and laid out like a gigantic chessboard. It was called the pearl of the Mediterranean. Before the war, he said, there were taverns everywhere, and some of the smartest clothes shops in the Middle East.

'Here is for your antiques, some wonderful shops, very expensive some of them, and just as good as Paris; here,' he pointed towards the sea, 'for your fish markets. There for your banking. Up there in the alleyways,' he made a vague gesture out of the taxi window, 'is where all the bad girls live.'

'Of which there are plenty,' Ellie added.

Tariq wondered if it was possible to have a city that was really a city that didn't have the promise of something sinful there. Otherwise why would young men bother to leave home?

'Don't listen to him.' When Ellie covered Saba's ears, she heard the boom of laughter. 'He's wicked and depraved. She's a nice young girl,' she told him.

'My favourite streets,' Tariq explained, 'are down by the sea. Normally it has shops and cafés and peanut sellers and all kinds of fun, but the people are very nervous to be out too late after dark now.'

'I'm not.' Ellie's scented presence stirred beside her. Saba saw her squeeze Tariq's hand. She heard her breath quicken.

'I'm not either,' he said. 'Everywhere in the Middle East is dangerous now, so let me be in Alexandria with two beautiful women.'

'Flatterer!' Saba heard the huskiness in Ellie's voice, then the light sipping of kisses, like cats drinking milk, a rustling, a deep sigh. Tariq stopped talking for a while, and Saba, so close to them, felt both embarrassed and aroused and slightly shocked. Wasn't Ellie too old for this?

Ten minutes later, their taxi slowed down. Tariq came up for air and said they'd reached the Corniche; it was a shame that she couldn't see it in all its glory, on summer evenings glittering like an enormous necklace, and full of people, not just soldiers. Winding down her window, Saba caught the fresh smell of the sea and heard its slap.

A black horse clip-clopped beside her, making her start. The only light came from a small charcoal brazier underneath the carriage that moved like a ruby through the darkness. Behind its half-drawn curtains two figures embraced.

A small boy ran beside them, a tray around his neck.

'Big welcome for you, Mrs Queen.' He thrust a tray of cheap pens and bracelets through their moving window. 'English good.' Skinny little fingers covered in cheap rings made the 'V' sign. 'German no good. Churcheeel good. Hitler very bad boy. Please have a look.' He gazed at them winsomely, head on one side.

Tariq laughed, gave him a coin. 'The perfect diplomat meets the real world economy.'

'Very sensible too,' Ellie said. 'When you have absolutely no idea what side your bread is buttered on.

'Now, darling, can you see it?' Ellie gave Saba a sly pinch. 'It's over there. The club,' she whispered. She pointed towards a faint strip of light in the middle of a row of dark houses.

'I try never to look at the ships,' she said as they walked towards it. 'Too depressing. Men and their fucking wars.' Her curse word leapt out of the darkness, startling Saba. It seemed so out of character with Ellie's meticulous make-up, her reverence for Patou.

''Scuse the French.' Ellie gave her elbow a little wiggle. 'It slipped out. What I really meant was let's have as much fun as we can while we can. There's nothing wrong with that.'

A shiver of anticipation ran through Saba like electricity. Ellie was right: nothing wrong with that at all. The fear would come back soon enough.

A Nubian doorman smiled at her as she walked through the door of the club, his teeth lit blue by the painted-over lamps. She could hear the wail of a jazz trumpet, the clink of glasses, the solid blare of conversation just out of reach. She checked her watch. Nine thirty-five.

'He's coming at ten,' Ellie whispered. 'At least, he said he would.'

'Who?' It was childish to pretend she didn't know, but the thought of being stood up now was unbearable.

'Don't be daft.' Ellie play-pinched her. '*Him.*'

'Oh *him*. Well that would be nice.' As if he was just an ordinary man, and this an ordinary day, but some things felt too overwhelming to be shared. Particularly now, and maybe never with Ellie. She didn't know enough about her yet, or for that matter about him.

Tariq walked ahead of them, parting cigarette smoke with his hands like waves. Inside, there were many tables lit by tiny candles in glass jars. The tables were crammed with soldiers, some with girls on their laps. A babble of voices: French, Greek, Australian, American.

There was a bar in the corner. Beside it, a small stage where an overwrought Egyptian singer lassoing his microphone cord about him sobbed his way through 'Fools Rush In' in an accent so heavy it might have been another language. An old lady sat behind the stage, her face half lit by the spotlight. She watched the singer closely, with an expression of deep disdain.

'Faiza,' whispered Tariq.

Faiza wore a brilliant purple evening dress. Her hair was brightly hennaed, her lips a red slash. On her lap there was a splendid grey Persian cat, as impeccably groomed as its owner and wearing a jewelled lead. It watched the couples dancing cheek to cheek with a look of faintly nauseous contempt.

In the car coming over, Tariq had been keen to impress on Saba that Faiza was almost as famous as Umm Kulthum, a singer he worshipped. Like Umm, she was the daughter of a poor family, and when young, she'd disguised herself as a boy to sing. Faiza was, he said, a proper artist, not a common crooner: she sang verses from the Koran, her training had been long and arduous; she was also a great friend of Mr Ozan.

When the song had reached its last wail of agony, Faiza looked around her. When she saw them she beckoned them towards her with a regal wave.

'I know who you are,' she said to Saba. She stared at her intently – her huge black eyes were ringed with kohl, a little smudged in the heat – and then she shook her hand with a great rattle of bracelets. 'You, come upstairs. You go and dance,' she told Tariq and Ellie.

She took a kerosene lamp from the corner of the stage and made her imperious way through the packed club.

'I have apartments upstairs,' she said. 'We can talk there.'

The cat dashed in front of Saba as she followed the old woman up the steps. She felt the shiver of its fur on her calf. At the top of the stairs, Faiza put a key in the lock and opened the door, on to a candlelit room where there was a piano, and a number of comfortable-looking sofas, covered in silk cushions.

'This is where we have our proper parties now,' she said. 'Please, sit down. Something to drink?'

'No. No thank you.' There was a clock on the wall behind the old lady's head. It was already nine forty-five.

The cat purred like a little motor as Faiza moved her fingers up and down its spine.

'We don't have much time before I sing again,' she said, 'so I will start right away. Mr Ozan cannot be here tonight, but he tells me that you are a very good singer. The authorities have forbidden any of us to employ foreign singers for the past two years, and honestly, it's very, very boring for all of us.' She smiled warmly. 'We are artistes, we want to hear everything, see everything,' her bracelets jangled as she sketched out the world, 'so the curfew is one great big bloody bore. Sorry for the word.' They beamed at each other like people who shared a secret.

'And you want me to sing here?'

Faiza shrugged. A shrewd expression came into her face.

'Not impossible. We cannot make a living without new people,' she pronounced it *bipple* too, 'but now we must be more discreet.

'Before the war, my husband worked with Mr Ozan, we go everywhere to find the best people. We have here Argentinian dancers, French singers, Germans, Italians, such a wonderful place. Now . . .' The old girl's shrug was dismissive.

'And your husband?'

'Dead. A heart attack last year.' She scooped the cat up and held it against her breast.

Downstairs, Saba could hear the sound of the band playing Arab music: drums, violin, oud, tabla, their wild, bounding rhythms ripping through the night. Also, the sound of a plane, close enough for the rotations of its propellers to be heard quite distinctly.

Faiza stopped talking to listen too. As the plane passed, she shrugged eloquently, as if to say *who cares.*

'So,' she resumed, 'Mr Ozan wants me to teach you.' Her expression brightened.

'Do you mind?' Saba said. 'I know your own training took you ages.'

'No.' Faiza looked surprised. 'Of course not. I am very happy to try. Mr Ozan is a wonderful man. We make lovely parties for him whenever he wants them.'

'You see, I don't have very long here,' Saba explained. 'I'm with an ENSA company.' Faiza looked confused. 'We sing songs for soldiers in the desert. I'm in the army.'

'Our songs are not easy to learn.' The old lady had not understood her. 'They are very beautiful, but you will have to learn a new technique.' She pointed to her nose, her chest. 'We sing from here too.'

'I know one or two songs,' Saba said. 'My grandmother, she's Turkish, loves the old songs.'

She sang a snatch of 'Yah Mustapha'; the old lady laughed and sang along.

'Ya Allah!' she called out softly. 'I will teach you. Come tomorrow, here? Tea first, and then our first lesson.'

'I'd love that,' Saba said, and she meant it. 'Tariq says you're famous.' The old lady inclined her head modestly to one side, but did not deny it. 'I love learning new songs.'

'I'm old now, and my voice . . .' Faiza mimed herself being strangled. 'But we will have some fun. Come tomorrow at ten thirty here. Don't be late, I have a hair appointment at lunchtime.'

She glanced at the clock; Saba half rose. The time was ten to ten.

'Wait! Wait, wait.' Faiza took both of Saba's hands in hers. 'Come with me. I have something to show you.'

As they walked across the room, Saba felt tango rhythms vibrate through the soles of her feet. The hoarse cries, the clapping, the stamp of shoes. She followed the old woman into a small room lit by a kerosene light in its corner. There was a sequinned costume hung on a hook; a dressing table littered with make-up. And sitting on a chair near the window, there was Dom.

‘Saba.’ He stepped out of the darkness and put his arms around her.

‘Oh my God!’ Both of them were close to tears.

Faiza stood at the door. She was smiling.

‘I will leave you now,’ she said. ‘If you want me, I am singing downstairs.’

When the door closed, they kissed each other savagely, and then she cried with joy. She’d had no idea until then how frightened she’d been.

She stepped back and looked at him. It seemed that they had already gone beyond a place of self-control and she didn’t care.

He was wearing a scruffy khaki shirt and trousers. His hair needed cutting. His skin had turned a deep nut brown since she saw him last. He was beautiful. After a long, slow kiss, a kind of claiming, he pushed her away.

‘Let me look at you.’ He pulled her down on the sofa beside him. ‘What in hell are you doing here?’ He couldn’t stop smiling. ‘Do you understand this?’

‘You first,’ she said, playing for time. How much was it safe to tell him?

He ran his hands through her hair as he spoke.

‘Did you get my message, my letter I mean, I wrote it over a week ago?’

‘No. Did you get mine?’

‘No. I got a message from your friend Madame whatever-her-name-is; she said you’d be here tonight. That was all.’

They kissed again. These details were trivial. There was a war on, messages got lost all the time.

When they stopped, he put both arms around her and hugged her tight, and she felt his heart beating against her and happiness ran through her like a river, as if every cell in her body was saying thank you for the miracle of him – here, and alive.

He told her that for the past ten days they’d been out in the desert south of Alex training. He didn’t tell her what the training involved, or what it was for, only that it was over now, at least for the time being, and that the whole squadron had been given a week off because it had been pretty flat out and they wanted them rested. For the next month, all leave was cancelled.

He gathered her hair in his hands, smoothed it back from her face and looked her straight in the eyes.

'I can't believe this,' he said.

She stroked his face. 'Guess what?' she said. The tip of his finger was exploring her dimple. 'No, really, *guess what*? As far as I know, I'm here for at least a week, and pretty much on my own. I have to do some work, but we can see each other.'

'What work?' She saw a look of confusion in his eyes. 'I don't understand. Where are the others? Your friend Arleta? The acrobats?'

'They're not here.' She hated having to start like this. 'They'll probably come soon.' Her right hand was covering her eye. 'I'm going to do a couple of broadcasts. I didn't write to you because I didn't know I'd do them here, it was a very sudden thing.' Too much, she was talking too much.

He took her hand down from her face, turned it palm upwards and kissed it.

'Whom does it depend on?' he said. 'Your staying, I mean.'

'I honestly don't know.'

'You don't know!' Oh, not a good thing to say, more confusion. 'But it's bloody dangerous here, most people have been evacuated. I don't want you to get hurt.'

He was about to say something else when the music from downstairs reached a straggling halt, and then the woop-woop-woop of an air-raid siren broke through.

A muddle of voices out on the street below them now, the patter of feet on their way to the air-raid shelter. They decided to stay.

'At home, my gran wouldn't go to the shelters,' she told him, 'so I used to lie under the dining-room table with her. She's thirteen stone. I've still got the dents.' When he laughed, she felt his breath on her cheek. 'And afterwards, we'd lie in bed together listening to the wireless.'

'Well now I'm insane with jealousy.' He tightened his arms around her. 'Listen,' he said. 'There'll be no gran and no wireless in our bed.'

Our bed: he'd said it.

A wonderful laughter bubbled through them: the laughter of being young, of knowing something you'd longed for was happening.

Our bed. It would happen tonight, she knew it. She stood beside him at the window, shimmering with happiness. She loved how he just assumed it would. No holding back, no false coquetry; the wave had caught them and they would ride it.

When he pulled back half an inch of blackout curtain she saw his profile etched on the wall, clear and distinct like a silhouette – the straight nose, the tousled hair, the shadow of his arm around her. A wash of light moved over the bay and the dark blue sea, and then the rat-tat-tat of anti-aircraft guns. In the heartbeat of silence he pulled her closer, and then from downstairs she heard the music again, jolly and impertinent, two fingers to the war.

'Let's get out of here,' he said.

Chapter 26

There are rooms you know you won't forget; they are like songs that are part of you.

Number 12, Rue Lepsius was such a place: an old apartment building with an elaborate balcony, which overlooked the street. Walking towards it, she saw, by the light of the moon, animal heads – lions, dolphins, griffins – carved into its walls.

As they drove there, Dom explained that the Desert Air Force rented three rooms here for overnight stays in Alexandria. 'It's nothing special,' he told her, helping her out, 'but it's quiet, and as safe as anywhere. Are you all right?' he asked. 'Not frightened?'

'No.'

'I'll look after you.'

'Yes.'

The ground floor was deserted and dark.

'Here.' He clicked open a lighter and led her upstairs. On the first-floor landing he kissed her softly, and unlocked a door and led her by the hand into a whitewashed room with high ceilings. When he lit two candles; she saw a white bed in the middle of the room, a mosquito net draped around it. There was a washstand, a chest of drawers, a half-drawn curtain with a bath behind it. The sight of his clothes – desert boots, shirt, trousers – flung carelessly on a wicker chair alarmed and delighted her.

He put the candles into two red glass bowls attached to the wall by an iron sconce and closed the wooden shutters. The window glass behind the shutters was criss-crossed with strips of tape in case of bomb blasts. The breeze from an overhead fan ruffled her hair as she stepped out of her clothes. There were no words, no preliminaries. She got into bed and waited for him in the dark like a hungry young animal. The brown gleam of his chest was lit by the candlelight as he lay down beside her.

'Here.' He pulled her to him, and the kissing began again, and when he entered her swiftly all she could think was *thank God, thank God at last.* It was like riding the curve of a wave; nothing in her life had felt so absolutely right and unstoppable.

They laughed when it was over. A laugh of triumph and possession.

He lay gasping, one hand on her breast, one tanned leg over the sheets.

'At long bloody last,' he said, and they laughed again.

When she was a girl, she'd read other people's descriptions of falling in love: the tears, the madness, the irrational laughter, the melting, the raging, the burning, and she'd worried because she'd never felt even remotely like that. But when she woke the following morning, her first thought was: *It's happened. My first miracle.*

He was still asleep, lying on his back, one arm flung in an arc above his head. She looked at him, her body still singing from the night before: at the tuft of dark hair under his arm; at his lips which were soft and clearly carved; there was a small scar underneath them. She must ask him where he got it. He breathed out, his lips slightly parted, teeth white against tanned skin. There was a faint depression under his eyes where the skin was paler than the rest of his face, maybe where his flying goggles had been. His left ear was slightly bigger than his right ear, and below it, when she examined the miraculous skin graft, she saw that it was now almost imperceptible: that the scar which ran from the bottom of his left ear down to the hollow of his neck had faded but you could see, if you looked closely, the raised skin of the surgeon's neat stitches. Gazing at those stitches, thinking about the hospital, she heard her breath come jaggedly. How could she bear it if it happened again? She ran her hand down the side of his ribs. She stroked the curve of his hip bone, saw the point beneath the rumpled sheet where his suntan ended and his whiter skin began.

'Umm.' His eyelashes flickered as he stirred. 'Lovely,' he murmured, and went back to sleep again, and slept, and slept. He was exhausted, she could see that; they'd hardly slept a wink the night before, and before that, endless nights on call in the desert.

When he woke up, he looked at the clock and groaned.

'What a waste, come back to bed.' She was half dressed and about to leave a note.

'Can't,' she said, 'I'm busy.'

'I'm starving.' His voice was sleepy; his hair stood on end.

'You're dressed. Do you want breakfast? There's a hotel next door: eggs, coffee, falafel, omelette. I'll get up in a tick.'

'Told you, I can't.' She sat down beside him on the bed. 'I'm off to work.' She watched his expression change to one of confusion.

'To work?' He dropped her hand. 'I don't understand. Where? Why? You said there were no concerts here.'

She sat down on the wicker chair and put one hand over her eye.

'Down at the club. I'm learning new songs.'

'Can't that wait?'

'No. I'm supposed to be doing a broadcast soon.'

'Oh. So, will you come back? Can we have dinner tonight?' Their voices stilted now.

'Of course.' She got down on her hands and knees and buried her head into his chest. 'I'm sorry.'

She copied down the number from the telephone in the hall, so she could phone him as soon as she got there. She told him to promise not to move until she was back.

'I'm going to move.' He'd got out of bed like a fluid whip. 'I'm going to find you a taxi so you're safe; I'm going to pay the driver so he returns. Saba,' he looked at her, 'I don't want to sound like your Great-Uncle Sid, but I'm not sure you really understand how dangerous this city is at the moment.'

She said that she did, but she didn't, not really. She was becoming more and more aware of the innocent and isolated bubble that she had been moving in. To be sure, she'd seen the victims of this war, the haggard faces of the men, the hospital stretchers lying in the aisles, but they had been kept apart from any concrete news. And that morning, before Dom woke, the door of the wardrobe that held his clothes had swung open. She'd got up, gone towards it like a sleepwalker, and stared inside it, at his dusty kitbag stained with oil, at a streak of what looked like rust-coloured blood on his overalls.

She laid her head against his chest.

'Let me take you to the club.' He stroked her hair. 'Please. We can come back here afterwards.'

'No,' she said, ruffling his hair. 'I'm a big girl now.' The risk that Cleeve had missed the Cairo train, or that Ozan might appear, seemed too great. 'I'll only be a couple of hours. I'll rehearse then I'll come back in a taxi and you can take me to lunch.'

He smiled at her, thinking *damn, damn, damn!* A whole day eaten up – what a waste.

Please God, she thought, hearing her own voice assert all this so confidently, don't let there be any complications, or hold-ups, or extra events that nobody has bothered to tell me about. I don't think I could bear it now.

'Oh thank heavens! You're back, you're safe.' When Saba walked through the door of Colonel Patterson's house an hour later, Ellie sprang from her chair. She was in the living room, still dressed in evening dress; in the early-morning light her face looked gaunt, and there were dark circles under her eyes.

'I tried to find you last night, but I think the air raid confused everyone. It was bedlam, wasn't it? And I knew you were with your young man, so I assumed you were safe. I mean we both took a bit of a risk last night.' Her eyes anxious as the words tumbled out.

'I was safe.' Saba felt herself grinning, almost in spite of herself. 'I was fine.'

She declined the drink that Ellie offered, and the chance of breakfast; she was suddenly exhausted.

'So, a lovely time was had by all?' Ellie's sly look made it clear she was waiting for girlish confidences.

'Yes,' Saba said. 'A lovely time.' Even if she'd wanted to she couldn't describe how wonderful. Her body felt so light, her mind in a state of bliss.

Ellie's eyebrow shot up. She wanted more.

'A lovely time?'

'Yes.' Saba looked her straight in the eye. 'Thank you. Look, I'm sorry you had to wait up for me, I hope you're not too tired.' She heard Ellie sigh and saw her sag, at which point she might have asked about her evening with Tariq, but she knew already this was not on the conscientious-chaperone script Ellie was reading from.

'If you don't mind,' Saba said, 'I'll shoot up now, have a bath and change. Faiza's expecting me at ten thirty; she has a hair appointment at lunch, I can't be late.'

'Shall I pick you up then?' Ellie seemed to be testing the waters. *Is this too far? Is this?* It was clear she was longing to see Tariq again.

'There's really no need,' said Saba. 'I've made an arrangement to meet Dom for lunch. He only has five days here.'

'And do you have any leave owing to you?' Ellie was thinking hard.

'None of us have had a holiday since we came.'

'And so you're insisting on this – making your own arrangements at the club,' Ellie had her shrewd expression on again, 'because you want to be on top form for the wireless broadcasts and for Mr Ozan's party.' They were back on the script again.

'Exactly.'

'Well.' Ellie kicked her shoes off and walked around, her stockinged feet leaving pawprints on the floor. 'As long as we're discreet, I think both of us can be at ease for a few days, if you get my drift. You can stay here if you like. Both of you.' She'd dropped her voice to a whisper.

'Dom's got an apartment on Rue Lepsius,' Saba said. 'He'll look after me. It's quiet and private and close to the club. We're all trying to save petrol.' They exchanged another look.

'Yes – we're all trying to save petrol, but you must promise not to say a word of this to Cleeve. Do you know that he forgot to pay me for the last two weeks; I don't imagine he thinks I can live on air. If it wasn't for Tariq, I'd be destitute, honestly destitute; if he ever finds out, you're to tell him that.'

'Don't you get paid by the government like we do?'

'For some jobs, yes . . . it depends . . . it's complicated. Anyway, not a word to Cleeve, and if you see Tariq at this house, not a word about him either.' Ellie winked. 'He'll be off again soon.'

She gave Saba some bath salts and a fresh towel; she hugged her. She said she would make it her business to sit in on some of Saba's rehearsals at the club – this with an ostentatious protectiveness, as if it was now her sole aim in life. And by the way, it would be better not to say too much to Faiza about Dom – Egyptians were shocking gossips.

Saba, in the bath, puzzled again about Ellie. In some ways, her presence in the city was as mysterious as her own. And then she forgot her; she was in love and gloriously happy.

Chapter 27

Dom was waiting in the flat at Rue Lepsius when she got back from her rehearsal. She bounded upstairs and into their room, thrilled to see him and a little shy. She'd never lived with a man for consecutive days before and it made her feel as if they were playing house together.

He saw the flush of her cheeks, her dark hair swinging as she walked into the room, and thought: *I'm sunk*. He'd missed her all morning and resented every second she'd been away. He wrapped his arms around her and said he could make her some tea – he'd discovered a tiny kerosene stove behind the floral curtain in the corner of the room. When he asked her if she was hungry, she said she was starving and had eaten neither breakfast nor lunch that day.

'I'll take you to Dilawar's,' he said, happy to feel more in control of things again. 'It's the best café around here, and it's quiet.'

Hand in hand they went downstairs together, and out into the street and down a narrow alleyway with chairs on either side that spilled out from an almost hidden café where people were drinking tea and eating pastries as if the war had never come. The warm air was full of the scent of jasmine from an old vine planted against a trellis. There was a fountain. On the marble counter inside the café was a huge old Russian samovar.

He chose a seat behind a screen where they could not be seen. He said he didn't want to talk to anyone but her.

It was too early for dinner and too late for lunch, so they ordered cheese and flatbreads which came with doll-sized bowls of hummus and spicy vegetables. While they were waiting, he took both her hands in his, and kissed them softly.

'Did you miss me?' He put his fingertips inside her dimples. 'I love these things.'

'Didn't give you a thought,' when she was aching to kiss him. 'My day was really exciting.'

'Even more exciting than the night before?' His voice was husky. She felt a huge surge of sexual desire leap through her.

'Almost.'

He gave her a questioning look. 'Really?'

'Really.' She kissed the palm of his hand. 'Almost.'

In truth, it had been a wonderful day for her in every way: the memory of their lovemaking, in her body all day like a melody underneath the surface of things, had made a fascinating lesson with Faiza even better.

'Tell me what you did.' He leaned towards her. 'Tell me everything about you.'

'Why should I?'

'Because you want to.' When he narrowed his eyes like that, she felt another jolt of desire, and thought, *slow down, be careful, anything could happen in the next few weeks.*

She took a deep breath, 'Well . . . she's a funny old bird, but wonderful. You saw her last night, like a little Christmas pudding: huge earrings, great big sparkly dress, no, don't laugh, that's how she was, but today she was plainly dressed, quite strict – she's so passionate about what she does.'

I don't want you to be passionate about anything but me. The thought was so instinctive it shamed him.

He watched her eyes sparkling as she described how Faiza spoke fluent French, English, Arabic and Greek, and before the war had worked in Paris at the Le Gemy Club on the Champs-Elysées. She'd been booked by a man called Monsieur Leplée, who'd discovered Piaf on the street, and done her first recordings with her. Mr Leplée had been murdered. There was another bit to this story that Saba kept to herself even though it was interesting. Apparently – Faiza had told her this with much flashing of her kohled eyes and clutchings on the arm for emphasis – the rumour was that Piaf was a frequent performer for the German forces' social gatherings, but that she really worked for the Resistance.

'Do you believe this?' Saba had asked.

Faiza's shrug had been immense; everybody's at it, it seemed to imply. 'And then what?' Dom tucked a strand of hair behind her ear.

'Well, she started to sing for me, and it was wonderful. She sang this . . .' She put her mouth to his ear and sang a phrase of 'Ya Nar Fouadi', the song they'd been working on with much laughter and some difficulty that morning. 'But she's a jazz singer too, Ella Fitzgerald, Dinah Washington. She's brilliant, Dom, so alive. I can really learn from her.'

'What did she say? What did she say that was different?' He had stopped teasing; he was excited for her.

'She told me that when she was a girl she had a flawless voice, a gift from God that could span five octaves quite easily, and it was wonderful. Now, technically, she's diminished, she has to change the keys to make it easier.'

'How sad. To know you once did it so much better.' He wasn't jealous now, this was quite interesting.

'She wasn't sad – that was her point. She said that if you listen to your true voice you get better with age, but to find your true voice you have to really work to find the space inside you. Is this boring?'

'No, no, no.' He threaded his fingers through hers. 'Keep going, I like it.'

'She says her voice is better now because she's less keen to please everyone, because she's suffered more: her husband is dead, two of her children have died, one in a bombing only nine months ago. Even having a baby, she said, lowered her voice by an octave.

'Also, she is a follower of Sufism; she explained all this to me first, she said it was very important that I understood this about her because everybody has their song: it's like a message from God that speaks directly to them and that part of the singer's job is to find their song. Does that sound ridiculous?'

'No,' even though it was the kind of talk he would have scoffed at during his Cambridge days, 'not at all, but do you believe that? Here, come, eat.' He had made a sandwich for her with the flatbread while she talked.

'I do.' She held the bread in her hand, gazing directly at him. 'I never quite understand it, but there are songs which go through you like a rocket. They're frightening.'

'Ah, now that I do believe,' he said quietly.

'At home, I used to listen to Tansu singing her Turkish songs; she'd have a cigarette clamped between her teeth, and then she'd put it down on the hearth and sing her heart out. She was back home then, completely connected with who she was.'

'I used to feel that about my mother,' he told her. 'At home, her piano was right under my bedroom, I'd lie in bed as a child and listen to her. She was good, very good, and for a child it was comforting too – I could feel her back in her own natural element; the strength she got from it.'

'Did she really give up?'

'She gave up,' he said. 'She used to sing all the time when I was a child, but she stopped that too. For years I didn't understand why. When I asked her once she said that she never wanted to do anything that she was second rate at – that seems to me such a bad thing to say, cowardly and falsely grand. You have to be humble about these things, don't you, to be prepared to live in suspense, maybe for a long time. But go on, what else did this Faiza say?'

He found that he was riveted – he'd never had a girl like this; usually you had to get the talking over before the fun part began.

'So many things: how she had to fight to be a singer; how her family hated it – she had to dress as a boy at first. She also told me I must never worry about looking ugly when I sing.'

'Ugly! What a strange thing to say. How could you?' He looked at her in amazement. 'When you walked into the ward that night, you were like a vision. Maybe she got the word wrong.'

'No, no, no! That's not what she meant. Yes, of course I must dress up and look nice, but it was more like . . .' she squeezed up her face at the effort of getting the words right, 'I must learn to forget myself and be the song.'

'To forget yourself. That's quite a tall order.' He leaned across the table and took both of her hands in his. 'At least for me.'

'You're teasing me.'

'No. I was thinking how sweet you'd look in glasses.'

'You are teasing me and I don't care.' She mock-biffed him round the ears. 'I expect you think you're too clever for me.'

'No I don't.'

'Yes you do.'

And she was thinking how she didn't usually go on like this. With Paul, her last boyfriend, conversation had felt like some sort of heavy chore, like housework, or a lever that had to be planned for and manipulated and got jammed on certain topics with agonising silences in between.

'Let's talk about you,' she said when they'd settled down again. 'I mean, how long, seriously, do you think it would take me to really get to know you?'

'Ten minutes, fifteen maximum.' He poured her a glass of wine. 'You know what they say about the Brylcreem boys.'

'No,' she said, although Arleta had told her. Conceited, self-centred, God's gift, et cetera. 'Oh very cynical.' She pulled one of his ears.

'Well maybe, but there is a point to disguises,' he told her. 'Do you know that poem by Yeats called "The Mask"?'

'No.'

'A woman tells a man to *put off that mask of burning gold with emerald eyes*. She says she wants to find what's behind it, love or deceit; the man tells her it was the mask that *set your heart to beat, not what's behind*. I think your man has a point there.'

'I don't care about bloody old Yeats,' she told him. 'I want to know what happened to you.'

'What do you mean?' He blinked and looked away from her.

'The hospital. We haven't talked about it.'

'Oh, the hospital.' The smell of old meat was what he thought of when he thought of it, the smell of living and dying flesh, warm and sickly and sweet and cut with just enough Dettol to make it bearable; at other times he remembered Annabel's *It's not you, it's all this*, her regretful smile, a damp, sympathetic hand on his brow. Nothing he could joke about yet, nothing he could share.

'What a vision you were.' He pretended to be lost in a reverie: 'Red dress, dark hair. I wanted to take you to bed right there and then.'

'I'm not talking about that.' She put her hand over his mouth and said softly, 'What happened to you?'

'What happened?' She felt the soft rasp of his teeth against her fingers while he thought.

'I'll tell you one day,' he said at last. 'I do trust you.'

He felt he must tell her soon – he'd been on the verge of it several times – that he'd wanted to see her again so badly, he'd taken the train to Cardiff, had seen her house in Pomeroy Street. Something stopped him – pride maybe, or training, a sense that he might have trespassed on her secrets. Life wasn't a childish game of show and tell, and easy confidences that made everything better before bed. It felt too early to take the risk.

'I want you to trust you,' he said. 'Am I right to?'

'Yes.' She put her hand over her right eye. 'I think so.'

'You think so? Not know so?'

'Well . . .'

'You're looking very serious,' he said. 'What's the matter?'

'I don't know. Nothing. It's the war sometimes.'

'Well I can offer three possible cures,' he said. 'A, we could order an ice cream. B, drink another bottle of wine and sing some Arab songs. Or C, go back to the Rue Lepsius and make mad passionate love.'

'I feel greedy tonight,' she grinned at him, 'so, ice cream at Rue Lepsius.'

'And I feel greedy too,' he said. 'I want you to lie in my arms and sing to me.'

'Any special requests?'

'"Smoke Gets in Your Eyes".'

She often sang to him in bed during the four days that followed; the days she counted as the happiest of her life, the most exquisitely painful, the most complete. The sounds of the war, filtered through shuttered windows, the occasional groans from ships in the harbour, the droning planes above, the whooping of the air-raid sirens, all of it made life feel almost unbearably precious. They would snatch every bit of it, take nothing for granted. They would be lovers; have a future, however short.

They made a pact not to have any solemn war talks, but they knew what they were going back to now. Total amnesia no longer possible. But everything felt so clear here: in this room with its whitewashed walls, their rumpled bed with its mosquito net, the whirling fan above, the comforting clutter of domestic items behind the floral curtain – the kettle, the stove, their cups, the lapis-blue pen she'd bought him in the market. Their temporary room was home.

There were sudden starvations after they'd made love that could only be sated by running down to Dilawar's – their café now. At night, candles were lit in little glass jars and put deep inside the café where they would not draw any attention to themselves, and a group of old men with carved faces gathered in the dimmest recesses to smoke their narghiles or take falafel from Ismail, the owner's son, a handsome, smiling boy who was teased because he wore a gas mask to cook falafels in, to stop the fumes going up his nose.

When the falafel smoke had cleared, the scent of jasmine permeated the alleyway. The sturdy old vine grew and grew up the trellised walls. Ismail gathered its flowers after dark when the scent was more powerful; he sold them in long ropes which they took back to their room.

In the mornings they drank tea in bed together like sensible old Darby and Joan types. 'Here you are, Mrs Benson,' Dom said in an old man's whistle, doing a bandy walk to the bed to make her laugh. 'There's your cuppa.'

He ran around the corner to get fresh rolls from the baker. They were warm still when he brought them, and they would eat them in bed together, or if it was too hot, they'd sit side by side on the floor.

After breakfast Saba would wash and get dressed and on limbs that felt sunlit run to catch the tram down to the club. She and Faiza were making progress now: she had three Arabic songs she could sing with some fluency and Faiza had taught her how to ululate with her tongue vibrating behind her teeth; also the different ways she had to take her breath (more of a cat's sip than a bellows breath) to accommodate the new rhythms. When she came back to Dom she would sing them for him, sometimes standing up, sometimes lying with him chest to chest, cheek to cheek. He'd pull her towards him without a word.

'I like that "Ozkorini" best,' he told her.

'I only know a snatch of it,' she said.

Umm Kulthum had been sent away from Cairo now – both sides frightened she'd be used for propaganda purposes. Saba didn't tell him that. She told him instead that Ozkorini meant 'Think of me. Remember me.' Faiza had told her it was one of the few Arabic love songs addressed directly to a woman, most dealt with the pain of longing.

'What are they longing for?' she'd asked Faiza.

'For God,' came the simple reply. 'Or another country, or to be a happy again. Life is hard for many bipples here.' As she was saying this, it flashed through her mind that 'Ozkorini' was one of Ozan's favourite song too, and wished it wasn't. She wanted it to be her and Dom's song. She loved him. It was such a simple shock to know this. It wasn't just that he was so beautiful to her; there were other things more difficult to name: a particular sympathy they shared, as though they were tuned to the same frequency. The way they laughed at the same things, the way they'd listened to each other as though on tenterhooks as each laid out for the other the important events of their lives, and the trivial: she knew now, for instance, that he had once in a fit of rage thrown a lamp at his sister's head after she'd put his teddy down the lavatory; that he felt guilty about frightening his mother, and sorry for her too, feeling her loneliness and isolation; that he and his friends at school had once teased a boy because a girl had written a poem to him saying 'and I love your long white neck'; how it felt to go night flying for the first time: the terror and the magic of flying half blind beyond the earth's crust.

And that was about all he'd said to her so far about flying; some unspoken agreement had been reached that the subject would not be discussed. There was no wireless in their room, and they didn't want one. They had shut down the outside world for a few precious days. But every morning, as she made her way down the Rue Lepsius, down the Rue Massalla and towards the innocently glistening blue sea, she saw more sandbags stacked on half-ruined streets, more aeroplanes making marks on the clear blue sky.

One afternoon, while he was cheerfully splashing in the bath, she went to the cupboard, opened it as quietly as she could and took a closer look at his things. There was a pair of desert boots in the corner, the suede scuffed at the toes and covered in dust. In the toe of the left foot, she found a map of North Africa; in the right foot she felt the cold steel of a revolver. Underneath the boots, a pair of khaki overalls covered in dust and oil. They belonged to another world and made her stomach somersault.

'What are you doing?' His voice came from behind the curtain; the slap of water as he moved.

'Looking in the cupboard.'

'My stuff's normally in my locker,' he said, as if that would make them safer. 'I came here straight from the aerodrome.'

When he walked into the room again, there was a towel around his waist and his hair was wet. He looked so alive, she felt, for one moment, almost crazed with fear for him.

When he saw her face, he took her to bed without words and they made love. Later that night, over dinner at their café, he told her that she was easily the most interesting, the most wonderful girl he'd ever met, that when the war was over, he was going to learn to smoke a pipe and they'd buy a cottage with roses around it, and they were going to make lots of babies together, in between her doing concerts all over the world.

'There's ambitious,' she teased him in order to hide her intense pleasure. This was the first time he'd talked like this. 'So what are you going to be: a kept man?'

'I want to fly and write,' he said it quickly, 'but I can't think that far ahead.'

'Superstitious?'

'No. Maybe.'

The white bed, the purple sky, visible through the shutters before the blackout curtain was drawn. The ruddy glow of two candles before the last breath of day was blown on them. His miraculous brown body beside her in the mornings. His heat, his gaiety, his clever mind. She had not known you could have all this at once.

Four days, then three, and a terrible last day when everything that had seemed so wonderful went wrong. It began with a signal from the duty officer saying Dom was to report to Wadi Natrun. They would be flying again next week.

Chapter 28

On their last but one day, Ellie turned up unannounced at the club. She looked pale and out of sorts. She wore flat shoes and no jewellery, and had left the back of her hair unbrushed.

'Darling, listen,' she said. 'I have an urgent message for you. A man called Adrian McFarlane from ENSA has just phoned and left a message. He's staying at the Cecil Hotel. You won't say anything, will you, about our arrangement?' Her lip was trembling with nerves. 'They want you to take the train back to Cairo. Apparently the company are re-forming there. They've sent a ticket.'

Saba's heart sank. 'When?'

'I don't know yet. I may have to go with you.' Ellie looked glum. 'Promise not to say a word about Tariq?'

Saba promised. 'But what about Ozan's party?'

'He asked me to lend you a couple of evening dresses, so I assume it's still on. I thought I'd pack the blue dress, and that gold and silver sari dress that you wore at the Mena House. Does that sound right to you?'

'Well . . . but . . . they're yours . . . I can't just take them.' Her mind was racing. What about Dom, how to explain this to him.

'Don't worry about that. I won't be out of pocket.' Ellie seemed quite sure about this. 'Let's just do exactly what they say.'

'Is that all?' Saba said.

'All that I know. Don't forget,' she almost snapped, 'I'm just the wardrobe lady.'

Half an hour later, she came back with another new message. The man from ENSA wanted Saba to report to a recording studio on Mahmoud Street at seven p.m. the following night for a Forces' Favourites programme called *Alexandria Calling.*

'Well, you're a very popular girl,' Faiza beamed.

'Yes.' Her heart sank to her boots. The timing could not have been more terrible.

*

He thought it was a joke at first.

'A recording?' he said. 'On our last night? Surely you can change it?'

She went silent, then said she couldn't.

And looking at her he believed her, and thought: this will drive you mad – leave her now while you can.

'Well thanks for letting me know.' He heard the coldness in his own voice.

'I didn't know myself until a few hours ago.'

'Really?'

'Really.'

It was mid-afternoon. They were lying in bed in each other's arms at the time, sated and slick with sweat. He'd just run a bath. A moment or two before, they'd been joking about his socks, which she'd insisted on washing the day before and hung on a hanger. Watching her rinse them so inexpertly, he'd felt sadness close over him like dark water – a sense that they were trying to cram a future that might never come into a few short days. And this was the problem: everything seemed so heightened and raw.

He disengaged himself from her arms.

'Can't you change it?' How hard would it be? he asked himself indignantly.

'No.'

'That's ridiculous.' He leapt out of bed and faced her. 'It's a wireless programme. You'll be singing a *song*. It's not like opening night at La Scala blooming Milan.'

'Yes, a *song*.' She got up on her elbow and glared at him. 'Nothing but a bloody song, very unimportant. Candy floss. Let's cancel everything to suit Dom's arrangements.'

'My *arrangements*?' He scowled. Oh the things he could have frightened her with had he chosen to.

'Yes, your arrangements.'

They both had quick tempers, had already made each other laugh with cheerful warnings of the bad behaviour that would inevitably come. He confessed to kicking his mother once when he was six years old and she'd made him practise too long at the piano. She'd kicked him smartly back; Saba had inspected the scar on his knee and said he'd deserved it. Saba owned up to several dramatic exits from Pomeroy Street with a packed bag dating back to when she was a toddler.

Now he watched the bomb he'd ignited explode. She stormed around the room like a clockwork toy, telling him he was selfish and thoughtless and mean and overbearing too, and she was fed up to the back teeth with men telling her what to do. She stamped her foot and, after a few moments of this, collapsed into the bath behind the floral curtain in a flood of tears.

He'd run that bath for himself. His last bath before going back to the desert again; possibly his last bath ever. The sound of her thoughtless splashings had enraged him.

'Overbearing, me?' he bellowed through the curtain. 'That's a bit rich coming from you.'

'*I am not overbearing*,' she yelled.

And then, he could hardly believe the words were coming out of a mouth twisted with rage. 'I mean, I let you go off and sing for hundreds and thousands of men who don't even know you.'

'You. Let. Me. Go. Off!' The voice behind the curtain was low and incredulous. 'What a bloody cheek! You don't own me. You hardly even *know* me.'

'No, I don't, and thank God for that. Spoilt and self-centred,' he'd muttered. 'An idiot.'

'What did you say?'

'Nothing.'

He'd heard her gulp. She filled the bath with more water and thrashed around in it like a netted fish. Breathing heavily, he put on his shorts and sat down near the window with his head in his hands. After a few moments of savage self-pity his temper went out as quickly as a summer storm, but the splashing in the bath continued, and then low gasping sounds.

'Saba.' He felt stranded, and wanted a way back. He lit a cigarette.

'Sorry, can't hear,' she said. 'I'm too self-centred.'

'A very grown-up thing to say.' His voice softened.

And then he scribbled a note to her that read: *Ben bir eşeğim*, the Turkish for 'I am a donkey'. She'd written the phrase on a napkin a few days before, when he'd asked for instruction in curse words. He wrapped the note around a piece of Turkish delight – the kind she liked, pale pink and full of pistachio nuts. The kind she normally ate with a sensual, eye-rolling relish that made him laugh. He lowered it on a string over the curtain and into the bath.

The splashing stopped as she read the note. When he heard her chuckle, his eyes filled with tears of gratitude.

'Come here,' she said – the sweetest sound he'd ever heard.

When he drew back the curtain, he couldn't believe how cruel he had been, how selfish. She looked so young lying there, hair wet, eyes swollen with weeping. So beautiful too with her brown skin gleaming, her black hair shifting like seaweed in the water. He took a flannel and washed her face and her shoulders, her belly; he gathered her in his arms and they went to bed together, mingling their tears and telling each other they were stupid and sorry and had never meant to hurt one another and never would again.

The following day, while she was asleep in the crook of his arm, he lay tense and watchful as he listened to the unmistakable roar of a Spitfire engine moving overhead; for the first time, he recoiled from it.

When he opened the shutter, a flock of birds flew through the vaporous air the aircraft had left behind, and Alexandria, battered, abandoned, came into focus again, and he was frightened for it. Nobody could say with any certainty how much of it would remain next month, next week even. All the talk now was of one final push.

'Are there a lot of them?' She'd been watching him.

'A lot of what?' he said cautiously. He combed her hair with his fingers.

'Aeroplanes.'

'A few.' It was unusual, he thought, to see aircraft moving so flagrantly over the city, and wondered if some were being delivered to LG39. They were desperately short now.

'Are you worried?'

'No.' He hesitated, knowing what he said might stay with her for a long time. 'Please don't worry about me. I've had a wonderful time. I'm sorry I nearly spoilt it last night.' He got up, closed the shutter, and got back into bed with her.

'Saba, no!' He put his arms around her; she was howling, but without much sound, just deep breaths and swallows, a look of vivid distress in her eyes as she tried to control herself.

He dried her eyes on the corner of the sheet.

'This has been the best week of my life,' he said. He buried his face in her hair and they clung together as if it was their last moment on earth.

Their breakfast on the following day was curiously formal, as if part of them had already gone. They went to Dilawar's and ordered coffee and croissants which she toyed with and half ate. They arranged to meet between her rehearsal and what she now called 'the blasted broadcast'.

'I'm sure you'll enjoy it once you're there,' he said, diplomatic today. 'It'll cheer the troops up.'

'I hope so,' she said softly. 'I'll be back as soon as it's over.' She looked at her watch and said she'd better go.

Before she left, they said goodbye to Ismail together – the handsome youth often stared at them from behind the beaded curtain that separated the café from the kitchen. A hungry, unabashed stare. A few nights earlier, during a general conversation with him about the war and Egypt and his life, he'd told them he thought they were lucky. He could never afford to get married; he lived with his mother.

They'd glanced at each other shyly during this outburst, pleased that he thought they were husband and wife.

They shook his hand, gathered their things, and walked out into the blare and glare of the street. As Saba's tram moved off, Dom stood and waved at her from the street corner. He had no fixed plan yet for the rest of the morning – he'd hoped he would spend it with her. He felt sick with fear as he watched her go.

Chapter 29

As Saba wove in and out of the trinket sellers down by the Corniche, she was thinking of Dom in all his manifestations. There was the brown-skinned Dom whose body, both predatory and tender, claimed her at night, eyes gleaming in the candlelight; the silly schoolboy who sang to her from the bath and made her helpless with laughter; the kind and fatherly man who brought cups of tea in the morning and separated oranges fussily on the tray into neat segments; the clever one who challenged and mocked her, and who every now and then withdrew into an intense silence that frightened her; the ghost in their wardrobe who wore oil- and blood-stained overalls, who knew how to use a revolver – who refused to talk.

He still hadn't spoken about the day he was shot down, which made her wonder if other friends had been killed or if he'd made some irretrievable mistake that haunted him. Sometimes she wondered if he felt unmanned by her having seen him too vulnerable for masculine pride in hospital. She couldn't tell. When conversation strayed in this direction a shuttered look came to his face and she got nothing.

But last night, sitting opposite him at Dilawar's, their toes touching under the table, she'd thought, *you can't die. I love you too much*, as though intensity of thought could stop it, and then a strange sort of rage at him for frightening her so, and now a terrible hollowness inside her because he was leaving so soon, and so was she. But there was something else too, almost too confusing to contemplate, or was it simply self-protective, the almost automatic and balancing and surely wrong thought that their parting left her free to work again. Could all these separate parts of her ever be smoothly joined? She somehow doubted it. Even on a morning like this, it was comforting to slip, like an animal into some secret pond, into the half-light of the club and know that for the next two hours she would only think about her singing lesson with Faiza.

The chairs were up on the tables when she walked in, and the air was stale and cigarettey. From upstairs the muffled sound of tango music, the kind of staid European tango that Faiza liked, not the wild South American brand, next came Ella Fitzgerald. Faiza's taste in music was broad; you could say her soul was in the East but her head, and wherever it was a sense of style resided, in the West, and Ella was her favourite jazz artiste. She liked to gossip and tut about the singer's awful start in life – the brothels, the homes – as if they were close friends, and it was Faiza who had made Saba pay attention to her idol's musicality, her impeccable timing.

Faiza was jiggling around to 'A-Tisket, A-Tasket' as she opened the door, a pencil stuck behind her ear. During the day she wore a faded robe and large unfashionable specs and looked like anybody's auntie from Alexandria; it was at night that the garish frocks and hectic make-up, the brilliantly dyed hair (a wig as it happened) appeared.

Saba knew more now about Faiza's plans, which were ambitious. Before the war, and thanks to Ozan, she'd had a successful career singing on the Mediterranean circuit – in Italy, Greece, France and Istanbul. Now, having gone down well with the GI's and British audiences, her grand plan was an American tour. She might sing at the Apollo, or meet Ella Fitzgerald in person – Faiza lit up like a girl when she discussed all this, and although Saba privately felt that at fifty-five she had one foot in the grave, she had been helping Faiza with her English pronunciation, in return for help with the Arabic and Turkish songs.

After rehearsals they'd drunk tea and already talked of many things – music and food, poetry and men. Faiza admitted that her husband when young had beaten her. Like many Egyptian men he'd believed that virtuous maidens did not sing in public – it was neither proper nor respectable. It had caused her much pain for many years and a great split inside her. But in the end, she said, she'd been right to insist on doing what she knew she was put on this earth to do. Now, she didn't give a damn – sorry for the word – what other people thought or said about her. And eventually, she said with a shrug, and a cynical twinkle in her eye, she'd made enough money for husband and children to forgive her.

The other big love of Faiza's life was Mr Ozan's father, another rich businessman, who had discovered her, a rough-and-ready girl, singing at a Bedouin wedding. He'd heard something special right from the start, and later encouraged her to dress properly, to learn languages, to listen to artistes from all over the world. Thanks to him, she now had the kind of life she'd once only dreamed of: enough money to buy herself and her widowed mother a very nice house in a village near Alexandria, even a motor car.

Today, they were working on getting the words right for 'Ozkorini'. Umm Kulthum's recording of this song had swept the Arab world.

Faiza showed Saba, with many terrible and exaggerated grimaces, how she must learn to use the frontal bones of her face to sing this well. She needs nasality, Faiza calls it *ghunna*, also an intentional hoarseness (*bahha*) that is hard to do and indicative of huge emotions. 'Listen to how her voice cracks at the end of this song too. Faiza darts to the gramophone, young in her enthusiasm.

Umm is, in her estimation, a far greater singer than all the Piafs, the Fitzgeralds and the Washingtons rolled into one. She had already implied that Saba ran the risk of performing a kind of blasphemy when she sings her songs; that she would never in her lifetime learn the whole thing for herself. Even if her Arabic was good enough, English people did not listen to music in the same way. In Egypt it was like worship, like prayer. In old classical Arabic singing a performer would often repeat a single line over and over again, and by doing so rouse the audience to an almost orgasmic and ecstatic state. A single concert might go on for four to six hours. When Umm Kulthum sang her radio broadcasts, bakers stopped baking, bankers banking, mothers let their children lie on their laps. People flew in from all over the Arab world to hear her; both the Allies and the Axis had used her in their radio broadcasts. That was power. The kind of power that made demands on an audience.

This was not the first time Saba had heard this encomium, and today she desperately hoped Faiza would nutshell it. Downstairs, Faiza sat in a circle of light near the piano, Saba waiting for the nod of her head that said she could begin. They were working on the middle portion of 'Ozkorini', a song that had already stretched its tentacles deep inside her. When the music started and Saba began to sing, her voice was throbbing and raw with pain. She was begging Dom to stay alive.

'This is the best you have sung,' Faiza said when she stopped. 'You did it from here.' She made a circular swirling movement with both hands in the direction of her guts. 'You are nearly ready to sing her.'

The sound of clapping made them jump.

It was Ellie, in a white dress and the usual perfect coiffeur. Her shadow flew across the wall as she walked towards them.

'Sorry to burst in on you, Sabs,' she said, 'but I need a quick word. Marvellous music, by the way. You sound just like the real thing.'

Saba, still in the song and vulnerable, blinked towards her. She could hear Faiza's cat underneath the table, the sound of its rough tongue mixed with its purring.

Faiza's smile was lemony – she disliked being interrupted during rehearsals and being seen without full make-up by people who didn't know her well.

'Five minutes,' she said. 'I'm going upstairs to get dressed.'

'Saba, for God's sake, where have you been?' Ellie said when they were alone. A sweat shield had worked loose in the arm of her dress. She snatched it away and put it in her handbag.

'You know perfectly well where I've been.' Saba was fed up with this charade. She'd seen Tariq's suitcase at the Pattersons' house and knew he'd stayed there while she was away. 'You said the broadcast was tonight.'

'You really should have told me,' Ellie continued shamelessly. 'Anyway, a new man from ENSA phoned this morning; he wants to see you right away. He's staying at their offices on Karmuz Street. There's a taxi outside. The driver knows where it is; I've paid him and tipped him, so don't get stung again. When you've seen him, come straight back home to the Pattersons', and I mean it. No more running off. Honestly!'

But there were no ENSA offices on Karmuz Street, or if there were they'd been burned down long ago, along with the other miserable ruins. Instead, the driver drove fast down a nondescript road two hundred yards ahead and stopped next to a street stall that sold lurid, flyblown sweets threaded on to strings.

He gestured to her to get out; he led her across a crumbling pavement and banged on the front door of an apartment with a green grille outside it that was padlocked.

Several locks were clicked, Cleeve opened the door. He was

wearing glasses, had darkened his hair and was dressed in a shiny dark travelling salesman kind of suit.

'Sorry about the Charlie Chaplin get-up,' he said. His breath smelled of cigarettes and mints and something staler. 'I'm travelling incognito this time.'

He glanced quickly up and down the empty street.

'Upstairs,' he muttered. 'I've got some news.'

He took her to a scruffy room, with overflowing ashtrays and a stained mug of coffee on the table. His suitcase was on the floor, half unpacked.

'Sit down.' He pointed at a sagging sofa. 'Quite a bit to fill you in on. How are you, darling, by the way? You look marvellous.' He drew the blackout curtains; the lamp he switched on stained his face in a strange hallucinatory wash of green light.

'Thank you,' she said, thinking that sometimes too much happening in your life was worse than too little.

'Right.' Cleeve lit a cigarette and stretched his legs out. 'I'm catching the train back to Cairo tonight, so I don't have long, but let me bring you up to date.

'Ozan has definitely decided on Istanbul for his party – he has a house there on the Bosphorus – much safer and more fun. He wants you to go with him for the party and for a limited run at his club. We'd like you to do this if you can, and frankly, you'll be much safer there – perfectly natural for a half-Turkish girl to go home and sing in the country of her birth. Are you happy to do that?'

A crash of conflicting thoughts went through her head. The desire to be brave and do good things for her country, excitement at singing in a foreign place, the fear of putting the Mediterranean between her and Dom – although his leave, it was true, had been cancelled for the next month, the arrangement felt precarious.

'How long will I be away?'

Cleeve gave his charming, lopsided smile.

'No more than a week at the absolute most. Ozan has promised to pay you well, you'll be put up in a nice hotel, and we'll keep an eye on you from a distance.'

'Should he pay me? It doesn't feel right.'

'It's the safest way. If he doesn't, it will look suspicious.'

'What do I have to do?'

He looked at her in a friendly way. 'Again, the answer is maybe nothing, maybe a lot – we simply don't know yet.'

He spread a map on the table. 'At the moment, Istanbul is the most important neutral city in the world because it's roughly equidistant from Germany, Russia and the Western powers. The country has become very popular with German secret-service agents on large expense accounts, which is where our friend Ozan has cleaned up at his clubs. Some of these chaps are jokes, they're just keeping their heads down until the war is over, but there are other people there with vital information to share.

'There's a young man in Istanbul, a pilot who we believe could be of great interest to us; we hope you'll meet him – I'll brief you on this later.' Cleeve's foot had started to jiggle up and down. 'What we need is to collect any kind of intelligence we can about which way the Germans are going to jump. The British have been making plans to move in to German-occupied Greece. If this happens, they will want to make use of Turkish landing strips, which will mean Turkey cannot remain neutral for long.'

He stubbed his cigarette out, and fixed her with an intense look. 'Can you take all this in?'

'Yes, I can.' She held his gaze, certain she couldn't, but determined not to show him that.

He opened a pigskin notebook. 'Ozan looks after his performers well – you'll probably stay at the Pera Palace, which is charming, or the Büyük Londra. The usual run at the club is two weeks. If at any point you want to come back, or feel you have something you need to tell us, all you have to do is phone me in Cairo. My number is . . .' He started to scribble. 'Phone me and say: "Could you book me at the Gezirah next week?" I'll know what you mean. Otherwise, I'll be in Istanbul on the second of September. I'll be staying at an apartment on Istiklal Caddesi under the name of William McFarlane. I'll leave a note for you at the front desk of the hotel; I'll sign it from your cousin Bill. Got it?'

'Got it.'

He smiled at her, a fan again, his eyes glistening sincerely. 'D'you know, I think people are so wrong to imagine that showbiz types are fragile; we've found you marvellous to work with on the whole – fearless and patriotic. I suppose you excite people, they want to tell you things, or maybe for you to make them feel things they might not feel by themselves . . .' He tailed off almost sadly, as if he was talking to himself, and switched off the green lamp.

He looked at his watch. 'Got to go, sorry, I must always seem so pressed for time,' he said. This hadn't occurred to her – almost everyone you met now seemed either bored or madly rushed.

Before he left, he warned her that when she was in Istanbul she must not meet anyone she didn't know in a place outside of her hotel. He gave her an envelope with a wad of Turkish lira in it. The equivalent of £100, he told her. She must keep a careful note of what she spent, and if Mr Ozan wanted to pay her too, why not? She'd been working hard and he was as rich as Croesus, and a man like him enjoyed rewarding people.

And then, after some hesitation, he delved into his suitcase and brought out a small gun.

'You won't need this, but they're always useful.'

'I don't know how to use it,' she said.

'You don't need to,' he twinkled. 'It's like baby's first gun, all you have to do is point and shoot, exactly like a water pistol. The bullets go in here.'

She took the gun and held it in the palm of her hand; for the first time, she was afraid.

She asked him again what day she might be leaving. He said he didn't know yet. Mr Ozan would tell her. It would probably be at the end of the week.

'Don't look nervous,' he said. 'It should be fun.'

Chapter 30

While Saba was rehearsing, Dom wandered for a while, trying not to resent this other life that took her away from him. He already recognised that when she was performing she was quite startlingly someone else, someone he shared and was in awe of, someone not quite normal in the way she was able to seem so natural, so zestful and alive in front of thousands of strangers. What had felt precious about their last few days was that this faintly troubling double image of her had disappeared and their life together had become simple.

With two hours to fill, he walked down the Rue Fuad where he found a small jeweller's shop that sold exquisite enamel work. After careful deliberation he spotted, in its dim interior, what he hoped would be the perfect present for her: a blue enamel bracelet, carved in fine silver lines with the outlines of gods and goddesses, each one encased in its own delicate link.

The store owner was fat and expansive with one cloudy eye. He brought Dom a chair, patted his knee, and insisted they share a glass of mint tea, or maybe some Stella beer, together. He put the bracelet on some velvet and explained each symbol to him with the eagerness of a man introducing a bunch of old and much-loved pals to a new friend. This was Horus, he pointed towards the one-eyed god of protection, Osiris, god of resurrection and fertility, Isis with her magic spells, and ah, this – the man's fat finger caressed the slender waist of a goddess with a pair of silver horns growing out of her head – this was Hathor, goddess of many things: love and music and beauty. She also represented the vengeful eye of Ra, goddess of drunkenness and destruction. The man laughed uproariously.

Oh the joy of finding the perfect present at the right time for the person you loved. Dom – who'd never gone beyond chocolates and flowers before – was so happy. He asked the jeweller to engrave her name on the back, and then, in a flash of inspiration that pleased him, *Ozkorini*. Think of me.

When the present was engraved and wrapped inside a pretty box, smelling faintly of frangipani, he longed to give it to her immediately, but there was still time to kill before meeting her. He decided on a beer at the Officers' Club, which was within walking distance, but felt a strange reluctance to go there. Usually he was excited at the thought of joining the squadron again. But today would soon be tomorrow, and tomorrow would mean men and only men, apart from the odd ATS girl, sand, tents, reeking latrines buzzing with flies, the telephone hurling them from bed at all kinds of ungodly hours, and all the rest . . . the bone-jarring exhaustion, the cauterising of feeling and emotion. The dread of letting his flight down in some major way.

Thoughts leading, inevitably, to Jacko. The flash picture of his screaming face behind the Perspex of his Spitfire, before the flames ate him.

Stepping from the pavement's shade into stunning heat, he thought about the awful meal with Jacko's parents after the funeral – his mother's sudden wild look of *j'accuse* as she passed him the gravy, swiftly modified into a hostess's smile. Jacko would never have flown had he not met Dom, and she knew it.

'Sorry.' He'd bumped into an old lady who glared at him.

Pay attention. *Stop it!* There was a war on. What did he expect?

'Heil, Dom! Old fucker!' When he walked into the bar, the tall figure of Barney unfurled from a leather chair and walked towards him. He was so glad to see him, the height, the heft of him, he could almost have cried. People didn't tell you how exhausting new love could be, thought Dom, sitting down beside him. The fear it brought.

'Where have you been?'

'Can't talk!' He clutched his throat like an expiring man. 'Parched.'

Once, he thought, watching Barney slope off to get a beer, he would have made a funny story out of the row with Saba the night before – her spitting rage, his own stupidity – but the walls had shifted again.

In the middle of the night, at around three, he'd got up for a glass of water, and when he'd got back into bed, he'd lain propped up on his elbow and looked at her. And watching her like this – the candlelight flickering over her face as she'd slept, unguarded as a child – what he'd most felt was a humbling of himself. He loved her – he knew that now without a shadow of doubt. Her fierceness, her talent, her vitality. He wanted to be loyal to her, to keep her safe. His own sharp tongue, his quick temper, his impatience must be curbed. He must not hurt her.

'Sorry, old cock, they've run out of Beechers, they've only got Guinness.' Barney put the drinks down between them and grinned. 'God, I'm glad to see you.'

He took a long, noisy swig. Most of the wing, he said, when his glass was mostly froth, had opted to go to Cairo for their last leave, it was safer there. He'd been bored shitless, reduced to playing bridge with some brigadier and the matron from the local hospital.

He opened a second bottle and poured it. 'Cheers!' They touched glasses. 'Enjoy it while you can,' Barney told him. He'd been at LG39 the day before to see if there was any news; the signals had been coming and going like tart's knickers.

'I saw some planes flying over the harbour this morning,' Dom said. 'I wondered if they were for us.'

'Let's hope,' Barney said tersely. 'I was talking to a fitter the day before yesterday – quite a few of ours are kaput, something about sand bunging up their backsides.'

While they were talking, four Australian pilots strolled into the bar wearing new uniforms with ironed arm creases that showed how scruffy the rest of them looked in their dusty khakis. Drinks were bought, they sprawled in the leather chairs exchanging names, squadrons, brief biographies, all affecting a nonchalant indifference that none of them felt now. Theirs was a stick insect's reaction: camouflage, fear, prudence. More and more men were being drafted in now, according to one of the Aussie pilots; they'd heard the big one would come in less than ten days. The man sighed after this announcement as though telling them nothing more thrilling than a railway timetable.

This news went straight to Dom's brain like a drug of delight and confusion. Only an hour ago, sitting in the jeweller's shop, captivated by the goddess talk and with her present in his hand, he'd felt so changed, so pure, and yet this urge to fight, to fly, he felt he couldn't control it, any more than he could control wanting her, or his growing sense of wanting to be her protector.

He ate a horrible cheese sandwich, drank another beer. In some ways, yes, it was a definite relief after the exhausting heights of the last few days to be back, so to speak, at base camp and in the company of men – to be laughing about Buster Cartwright's hairy landing, so close to the hangar it had swept the turban off a nearby Indian fitter, or even listening to a long-winded account from one of the Aussies, a tall red-headed man with white eyebrows, about why he always attached his own car wing mirror to his own aircraft to give him an extra pair of eyes.

But halfway through his second beer, Dom thought with a rush of emotion about Saba in the bath: her body gleaming, the swirling mass of her hair underwater. She'd be singing now, focused and happy. In spite of her tears last night, she had a strong centre, and he was glad. She would need it.

A couple of beers later, he put the jewellery box in his top pocket and decided to go down to the Cheval D'Or and surprise her after her rehearsal. When Saba had warned him with a firmness that surprised him not to go there again without an invitation, he'd felt both amused and resentful. He wasn't used to a woman giving him orders. But today, their last together, was surely different. The important thing, he reasoned as he walked towards the Corniche, was not to spoil it all by getting too morbid or sad, for he had felt dangerously close to tears himself when she'd cried the night before, and that wouldn't do.

A swim, he thought, seeing the dazzling turquoise sea ahead of him. The perfect thing. They could go down to Stanley Beach, hire costumes from the club and drink afterwards at one of the beachside stalls; a taxi back to the flat would leave her time to wash and get dressed and get to wherever she was going to do the wireless bloody thing. Although he'd bent over backwards to make amends for his rant about the programme, the lizard-brain part of him was still thinking *damn and blast it.* Tonight, he wanted her for himself.

She must have gone straight to the recording, he thought. He had arranged himself casually against a lamp post across the road from the Cheval D'Or, waiting for the door to open. Either that, or it had been an exceptionally long rehearsal. In the harsh sunlight of early afternoon, the club with its faded awnings and dusty shutters looked spectacularly unglamorous. When he strained his ears to hear her singing, all he heard were the ordinary sounds of the Corniche, the clip-clopping of a few exhausted gharry horses, the faraway babble of foreign voices melting in the heat. Watching a pi-dog sitting in the gutter, absorbed in a fierce hunt for fleas, Dom's delight at the prospect of seeing her went away and he felt unpleasantly furtive – this was her territory and he was encroaching on it. He stood in the blistering sun and then grew disgusted – stick to the plan, he told himself, it was undignified to stay like this, skulking now behind sandbags like some sort of cut-price spy. Walk back to the Rue Lepsius and wait for her there. It would give him time to pack.

Walking back, the houses seemed to jump and blur. From now on, he warned himself, feeling sweat trickle down his back like an insect, he must close down his emotions. It was a near cert, when he got back, that he would be promoted to flight commander. Paul Rivers – exhausted now and longing to get home – had told him that, and now the lives of many men would depend on him; he couldn't afford to behave like a hysterical girl.

Also, Alexandria was now, officially, the most dangerous city in Egypt. The evidence was around him – the scared-looking people, the charred houses, the wild cats and dogs roaming the streets. True, a few diehards had refused to leave and were still swimming at Cleopatra Beach, or drinking Singapore Slings in deserted hotels, but it wasn't all that long ago that lines of panicky people had queued outside embassies and banks, desperate to leave. It had been madness to meet her here, with Rommel planning to take over the city any day now. He would advise her, more forcibly than ever, to leave.

Some street children swarmed towards him shouting, 'Any gum, chum?' in excruciating American accents, begging him to relieve them of cigarettes and 'first-quality whisks'.

'Meet my sister, mister,' said one with an unpleasant leer and the beginnings of a moustache on his top lip.

At the next street corner he watched a peasant farmer and his donkey pass, the beast piled high with bundles of sugar cane, the man shouting.

In their room on the Rue Lepsius, he sat for the first hour smoking, listening for the light skim of her tread running upstairs, the burst of song, but all he heard was a muddle of foreign voices from the street outside.

He started to pack his kit: his desert boots, his pistol, a couple of shirts; he took his socks down from the hanger where she'd left them. He smoked another cigarette, and when he got hungry, left her a note, dashing down the stairs to buy a foul-tasting falafel from a street vendor. It was then, standing in the street and seeing a large yolk-coloured sun beginning to set, that he started to panic. What if she hadn't gone to the recording studio? Or had been held up there and not able to contact him, or been caught by a stray hand grenade and was lost and bleeding in some dusty street somewhere; maybe their stupid row had upset her more than she'd admitted and she was punishing him by making him wait.

He walked around for hours trying to find her. First to the ENSA offices, where a note on the padlocked door said they had moved to Cairo, then to Dilawar's, empty except for the three old men who were regulars there.

He walked up shuttered alleyways, where blue lights shone eerily from wrought-iron lamp posts. As he walked, he wondered if jealousy had driven him a little mad. (For he was jealous, had been almost from the moment he'd first met her, without really understanding why.) And he thought about mirages. It was part of a pilot's training to understand how a mirage could conjure up lakes and rivers, whole mountains out of nothing but desert sands. A confusion of perspective, a longing for something that wasn't there. He'd seen her work the same kind of magic on the men she sang for – their tired faces lit up with hope and happiness; her songs the mirror that gave them back their life. God help him if he'd mistaken four days of blissful lovemaking for something solid and real.

He was certain now she was gone. At six o'clock, he ran wildly down the street in the direction of the club again. Someone must know where she was.

Late afternoon was fading as he ran into dusk: the sun setting over the harbour in a molten furnace of ochre and peach-coloured clouds that seemed to mock him. Fool, fool, fool for thinking you could contain her. When he got to the club, he stood gasping for breath on the pavement outside it. He banged on the locked door for five minutes and then he kicked it. An upstairs window opened; an old lady scowled down, he saw the pink of her scalp through wet hair.

'Where is she?' he shouted up. 'Where is Saba?'

She told him to wait, ran downstairs and after an interminable scraping of locks opened the door. It took him a few seconds to see that this was Faiza Mushawar minus make-up. In the yellow light of sunset, her skin looked jaundiced. The line of her eyebrows had been drawn artificially high with a wobbly brown pencil.

'What is it?' she said crossly. 'Who are you?'

'Dominic Benson,' he said. 'You must remember, I was here with Saba. We met in your room.'

She stared at him, her brown eyes bulging. 'No.' A green-eyed cat was trying to force its way around her. She blocked its way with a slippered foot. 'Many men come here.'

'Please,' he said. 'Where is she?'

He told her he had to leave in the morning, that he was going back to the desert, that he and Saba had arranged to meet for lunch, that he'd waited all afternoon for her. While he talked, she sucked in her mouth and shook her head.

'I don't know where she's gone.' She glanced over his shoulder. 'Another city, another concert. People don't stay long.' Her shrug indicating *what do you expect? She's a singer, there's a war on. Things happen for no meaning.*

'Do you have any idea when she is coming back?' he asked as gently as he could.

She shrugged again – 'She is working, is never sure' – it seemed to him her accent grew thicker by the moment. 'Ask British peoples, I don't know.' Soon he felt she would be denying even knowing her all.

'Can you tell me the names of the people she has been staying with in Alex?'

This had driven him mad all afternoon: Palmerston? Petersen? Mathieson? In all the excitement of meeting her again, he hadn't paid proper attention. The old lady's eyes rolled a little.

'No.'

Stop messing about, you bloody old fool, I know you speak English.

'Listen.' He heard his voice pleading, when he wanted to shout. The cat blinked at him, the red glow of sun reflected in its eyes.

'Mrs Mushawar, please help me. You taught her. She respected you. You must know.' In a matter of hours, the truck would come, it would take him back to the desert; he might never see her again. 'Please.'

Her skinny eyebrows rose. It seemed she might be on the verge of some sort of explanation or apology when she drew back and said, 'Sorry for this, but I don't know. She here this morning, very nice, she not here now.' She closed the door in his face.

He had come to the end of anything that could be called a plan. He spent the next few hours visiting the usual watering holes for the English, hoping by some miracle that she might be there. The Cecil bar was full of ATS girls. One or two of them crossed their legs and smiled hopefully as he walked in. Another said, if this Saba was still in Alex, she needed her head read. It was a deadly dump, give her Beirut any day.

It was dark by the time he got back to their room. From the harbour he heard the long, mournful blast of a foghorn. He sat on the chair, his head in his hands. He was meeting Barney outside the Officers' Club at seven o'clock the next morning. Barney had arranged a lift back to the aerodrome in a supply truck. He had to go, he wanted to. On the following day, the whole squadron would be briefed on what they jocularly called the big one. This would be their last leave for a long time; from now on the fighting would be fierce and relentless. He could die without saying goodbye to her.

He felt mad with frustration at wasting this precious time. He told himself to calm down. He shaved, he made the bed, and he put the rest of his stuff, his khaki drills, his map, and the socks she'd washed, into his kitbag. It was then he saw her note.

Gone away suddenly for more concerts. So sorry. I love you. I hope to be back soon.
Love Saba

He read it several times, unable to believe his eyes – so brief, so offhand. No address, no proper information, almost a brush-off. And she'd been back, he could see that now, her hairbrush and soap gone, clothes too, apart from her red dress, which she'd left in the cupboard. He took the dress from its hanger and lay on the bed with it. He inhaled its faint scent of roses and jasmine, and gave an anguished cry. He'd never imagined love could hurt this much – he felt winded, wounded, as if he'd been kicked hard in the stomach.

Chapter 31

As their plane roared through the night towards Istanbul, Saba had the nightmarish feeling of slippage, of things happening too fast and out of sequence. Ozan lay asleep three seats ahead of her, with his usual air of plump contentment, but she had not envisaged being on her own with him like this. Where was his wife? His entourage? What was Dom doing now? She hated the thought of hurting him like this.

She and Ellie had had a fierce row about it before she'd left Alexandria.

'I can't go without telling him,' she'd told Ellie. 'He's waiting for me – he's going back to his squadron tomorrow . . . I'm going to run down there straight away.'

Ellie had been doing what she called Hollywood packing – hurling clothes into an open suitcase, with none of her usual tissue-paper-and-folding malarkey. At the end of it, she opened her arms wide in a curiously wild gesture.

'There *is* no time,' she said. 'I know it's mad-making, but they're picking you up in twenty minutes, and your plane leaves tonight and there's not a damn thing I can do about it.' Her eyes looked nakedly red without their usual careful coating of mascara. 'I'm not happy about this either,' she said, 'because now I have no job, and nowhere to live. And I'm sick of other people making all the decisions . . . and Tariq's furious and I was hoping he'd propose this week, so it's all a real mess, isn't it?'

In the end, they'd compromised.

'Listen, darling,' Ellie had coaxed. 'Write him a letter – I'll take it down to him the minute you've gone, and then at least he'll know.'

Saba had gone blank with alarm – given Cleeve's warnings, what could be safely said? So in the end, a hopeless, scrappy, heartless-seeming note – her mind lurched with shame when she thought of him reading it. What would he think of her now?

*

'May I join you for one moment?' Mr Ozan, dressed superbly today in a pale suit and pearl-grey tie, had woken and decided to be sociable. He came swaying down the aisle and wedged himself beside her. His powerful, fat little body felt oppressively close – she was starting to feel airsick as well as everything else.

'Are you happy about our change of plan?' he roared over the engine noise. 'Have you been to Turkey before?' He half turned to gauge her reaction to what he obviously felt would be a great treat. 'You were telling me your father was born there.'

'They left when he was young,' she had to shout back. 'My father wanted to travel . . . *wanted to travel.*' She hoped he'd shut up now.

'And, remind me, what town . . . *what town* did he hail from?' He was relentless.

'A small village called Üvezli,' she said. 'They didn't talk about it much.'

'I know it, I think – it's on the way from Üsküdar to the Black Sea coast,' he said. 'A pretty place, we can show you when we get there. Don't look worried,' he added gaily, 'you are going to have the life of your time.' He corrected himself: 'The time of your life.'

The plane's engine had settled into an easy hum. Through the small windows she saw clouds, and miles and miles below, the desert quietly filling up with the pinks and golds of the setting sun.

'I forgot to ask,' Mr Ozan said. 'Your lessons with Faiza – did you like them?'

'Very much – I'd only sung a few Turkish baby songs before, but never in Arabic.'

Ozan shifted in his seat. He shook his head.

'You won't need those songs now – Arabic is the official language in Beirut and my friends there are very sensitive about it being the language of song. In Istanbul,' a proud curve came to his lips, 'people are more Western-looking. We don't care so much.'

She felt an odd mixture of relief and anticlimax – like a pupil who's worked hard only to find their exam has been cancelled at the last moment. He'd been so passionate about the songs before; now they sounded about as important as whether to have cheese straws or peanuts at his party.

'So is there a band in Istanbul?'

She warned herself, *keep your mouth shut.* She was here for a reason, with a job to do. She mustn't mess it up. If she didn't keep this firmly in mind, she would lose her centre and start to feel completely out of her depth; also, she would miss Dom more than was bearable.

'Yes, and they are first rate,' Ozan assured her. 'Every time any good new record has come out in Paris or in London, I have collected it for them, so they are bang up to the minute too.'

He grinned at her. 'I am excited, are you?' And in a way she was – a sick kind of excitement that seemed to have bunched every muscle in her body.

'And of course, the other thing is . . .' Ozan stared down at the now dark and crinkled sea beneath them, 'it will be nice to be away from this ghastly business for a while. Things are really hotting up. We are the lucky ones.'

Dom, waking the following morning, reached into an empty space beside him. A phone was ringing in the hall downstairs, half dressed, he sprinted down and got the usual mild electric shock as he grabbed it. His face in the mirror above it looked so fraught he hardly recognised himself.

'Oh good, still there.' A faint voice at last through the crackles. 'Well, it's Saba's friend, Madame Eloise, here. Damn, dreadful line, sorry.' More static, the faint hootings of her voice.

'Did you get the letter from Saba? Yes . . . good, she had to shoot off rather suddenly. But anyway . . . I understand you're off tomorrow, or is it today? Anyway . . . yes. No . . . sorry, what? Oh blast this . . .' The line cleared for a few seconds.

'She was in too much of a rush to give me any details – something about a party somewhere, or another concert – but she wants you to know she's safe and well and that she'll contact you as soon as she knows where she's going, if that doesn't sound too Alice in Wonderland. An address for her? No, sorry, no clue. I'm just the wardrobe lady. I think the best thing to do is to send letters to ENSA in Cairo; they'll . . . oh blast this awful line . . . they'll send them on. I didn't get the impression she'd be gone long. Goodbye then. Good luck! Sorry about this.'

Barney's lift had fallen through, so he thumbed a ride back to the aerodrome in a supply truck. He sat on his own in the back and gave himself a severe talking-to. A fighter pilot, Barney had told him once, only half facetiously, was good for three things: eating, flying and killing, and that was the way it had to be now. With things hotting up, he must simply close her down, seal her off like an engine that wouldn't function, otherwise, she would kill him.

When he got back, he played a game of football with the lads in the dust, and for several hours felt a consoling and enveloping blankness.

Next he had a beer with his flight commander, Rivers, who as expected, said he'd completed his two hundred hours' flying time, and was now tour-expired. His weary face, swollen with desert sores and pink circles of calamine, could not hide its relief.

'So, Dom, they want you to take over, at least for the time being, so whizzo,' he added flatly, 'tons of fun ahead.'

A feeling of something that might under other circumstances have been called pride in his accomplishment struggled through the humiliations of the day, like a bright fish in an ocean of grime. It was an honour, something solid and worth fighting for, something which under other circumstances he would have felt proud to tell her about.

It was Barney who handed Dom a warm Worthington's to celebrate, and Barney who later, during a game of chess, held a queen in his silvered hand and said, 'I've been meaning to ask: did you hear from that ENSA girl again?' wrecking his small moment of pleasure.

Dom forced a smile. 'Not a dicky bird.' They finished the game in silence. He hadn't meant to, but he'd told Barney a little about Saba after their meeting in Ismailia. He'd been high as a kite and unable to stop himself. Barney, who'd had a few, had immediately sung, 'I'm Dreaming of a White Mistress', and then had put his hand on Dom's arm and added with the solemnness of the half-cut. 'Now listen! Listen . . . listen, very important announcement to make, and I want you to listen very hard to me: everyone falls in love with those ENSA popsies, so be careful.' He'd made it sound so trivial, so ordinary, Dom was furious with himself for telling him.

When the light faded, about eight p.m., they packed the chessmen away in silence and went to bed. Barney was exhausted, Dom too. He lay down on the damp camp bed, pulled up his blanket and before he closed his eyes felt her absence with a physical ache like a kick in the guts. He was too hurt to feel angry, too old to cry, but he wanted to. She was gone, just like that, and he had no idea where.

There was a briefing on the following morning. An important one: Air Commodore Bingley, a rangy man with a headmaster's stoop, came from Advanced Air Headquarters to tell them the long wait was over. The training, the shadow fighting, the cross-country recces, the forced landings, the sitting in sweaty flying suits for take-offs cancelled at the last minute. They were on full squadron alert now.

Dom sat and listened in the middle of the dusty group of twenty-six young men. They lounged in their chairs in the boiling-hot dispersal hut without any visible display of interest or enthusiasm, but everyone's heart was pounding.

Bingley told them sharply to pay attention now. British Intelligence had discovered a fact of singular significance. On the night of 30 August, a full moon, General Rommel planned a surprise attack on the southern section of the Allied front near El Alamein. He would attack by night, and as far as they knew, through a gap between Munassib and Qaret El Huneunat, a place he believed was lightly held and lightly mined. If the attack succeeded it would open up the road to Alexandria, and then God knows what would happen. 'Our job, bluntly put, is to try and shatter the Luftwaffe in the next ten days.'

And Bingley, gazing at the young men, had a private moment of anguish as he said this, wondering who would be spared and who taken. He barked out that he sincerely hoped they'd all had their beauty sleep, because for the foreseeable future their job would be to fly as escorts to the Vickers Wellington bombers based at LG91. They would be on permanent call. All leave was cancelled for the foreseeable future, he added, and Dom, for complicated reasons, was relieved.

'Any questions?'

'How many days do you estimate it will take?'

'Hopefully it will be a short mission,' Bingley continued. 'A few days and then out, but this could be the big one.' His eye travelled up and down the lines of exhausted young men. 'If Rommel manages to break through our lines and occupy Egypt, he'll have the perfect launch pad for more attacks on the Mediterranean. If we stop him, I think we'll have a very good chance of ending this war.'

'Thank you, sir.' Dom got up after this short speech was over. 'We'll do our best.'

Walking back to the mess together, Bingley confided that he'd heard a worrying rumour that some of the new Kittyhawks had an operational fault – their oxygen refurb system opened without warning and sometimes choked with sand. Also that they only had ten serviceable Spitfires left, six of these on the battle line, and a couple of them definitely approaching retirement age.

When he asked Dom if he would be prepared to fly back with him the next day and pick up a repaired Spit, Dom said yes immediately. It would be something to do, something to take his mind off things.

Chapter 32

In Istanbul, another beautiful car throbbed away on the tarmac, waiting to carry them away. This one, Mr Ozan told her, was a 1934 Rolls Bentley, with an aluminium body, very rare, he said, his plump hand caressing its low, sleek sides. He suggested a brief tour of the city before they drove out to his summer house in Arnavutköy, which was some seven miles from the city and a lovely drive.

It was dusk, and as they drove towards the heart of the city, the Golden Horn was soaked in peach-coloured light. From the back seat of the Bentley, Saba saw ferry boats crinkling the waves, mosques, palaces, weird wooden buildings and felt as if she was part of some elaborate hallucination.

Passing through the Roman walls on the edge of the city, the potholed street made the car lurch from side to side for a few moments like a paper cup in the ocean. She stared out at two women sitting in a dim alleyway peeling vegetables, surrounded by scrawny cats; an old man selling sesame rings under a kerosene light.

Closer to the centre of the city, it surprised her how elegant and Westernised these Stamboulis looked: the women in their smart hats and silk stockings, the men in sober dark suits and white shirts. She'd imagined this place would be full of unsophisticated Tan-type people, but this was much posher than Cardiff. Ozan watched her reactions playfully. 'So what is your verdict on our town?' he said.

'It's beautiful,' she answered in a low voice, thinking *Stay calm, stay calm.* She had not prepared herself for the shock of being back in her father's world again. There were so many men here that had the same erect bearing, his dark intense eyes. When they looked at her, part of her shrivelled, as if he'd found her here and would shortly snatch her away.

They drove back towards the Bosphorus and left along the coast road. The moon was high and so bright it darted ahead of them through the trees, shedding light over branches and occasional gleams of water.

His summer house at Arnavutköy, Ozan said, was the relic of a life that was gone now. The year after Turkey had become a republic, in 1923, all members of the Ottoman Imperial Dynasty – the princes, the princesses, spouses, children – had been booted out. Many of his rich neighbours who were related to them had fled to Nice, to Egypt, to Beirut. A relative of his – he said with that proud little twitch of his mouth that came when he was boasting – had married into the Egyptian royal family; a few like him had been allowed to stay on and run successful businesses. She didn't know whether to believe him or not, but one thing was clear: he was a man who enjoyed an audience, and she for the time being was it.

She was woken by a gentle pat on her arm.

'We're here,' he said. 'My house.'

She looked out of the car window at one of the most beautiful houses she had ever seen. Bathed in silvery moonlight, it stood right at the water's edge, and was made of interlocking panels of exquisitely carved wood. High windows gave back the shifting patterns of the sea, and with its many dips and crevices and elaborate mouldings it had the look of a carved wooden puzzle or a magic ship in a child's fairy-tale book.

Ozan gave a deep sigh. He stepped out of the car and loosened his tie.

'Pretty, no?' The night air smelt of lemon trees and jasmine and the faint salty tang of the sea. He inhaled it with a satisfied snort. Such houses, he told her proudly, were called *yalis* by Stamboulis and were much prized because of their position right on the edge of the Bosphorus. Underneath his balcony – he pointed towards the water – his boats were moored.

He said she would sleep here for two nights and then move to a room at the Büyük Londra Hotel, close to the club where she would rehearse.

'But don't think about that tonight.' He'd seen her try to stifle a yawn with her hand. 'Tonight is for a good night's sleep – we have put you in one of the front rooms, where you can hear the waves.'

*

Leyla was waiting in the marbled hall to greet them. Her face lit up when she saw her husband, and although she didn't kiss him, the atmosphere between them was charged as she placed a gentle hand on his arm. The three young children who peeped out behind her skirts had Ozan's dark-rimmed eyes, and the beginnings of important noses. They beamed at Saba shyly and hugged their father.

'So, Miss Tarcan, this is a great pleasure for me to meet you again,' Leyla said, extending a cool hand. 'I hope you will be very happy with us here. My husband,' she said with a humorous look in his direction, 'says he is going to make you a star.'

It was Leyla who showed her around the gardens and the house on the following day. These were the moments Saba longed to share with her mother, so unpredictable in so many ways, but constant in her wistful, indignant love of luxury. 'Never!' she would have muttered, examining the glorious house that seemed to float this morning on calm waters. 'Oh for God's sake – look at that!' at the solid marble in its hall. Saba, absorbing this place, its sunlit rugs, its exquisite walls and windows open to the sea, hoped she could take some of it back – a small bone to comfort her mother's large hungers, but something.

What struck her later, as she followed her hostess down the sun-warmed paths, was the extreme neatness of the very rich, their attention to detail. The beautifully planted terraced gardens were a chessboard of sweetly scented herbs and shrubs; the small vineyard was laid out with mathematical precision; the immaculate stables where Ozan kept ponies for the children, and his own pure-bred Arabs with their pretty turned-up noses and long-lashed flirty eyes, had identically knotted ropes hanging outside each door, each one attached to scarlet halters on brass hooks.

As they left the stables, three peacocks picking their way through cypress trees made Saba jump when they squawked like a bunch of cats whose tails had been stamped on.

When Leyla laughed, it seemed to Saba to be their first natural moment together. Though faultlessly polite, in a hostessy way, Leyla had been more constrained today, so much so that Saba wondered if she longed to be alone with her husband, who, it seemed, was rarely in one place for longer than a few days; or maybe it was the thought of all the parties he had planned in the coming weeks, and she was tired of his habit of collecting people, which she alluded to very gently. 'We've had lots of singers staying here,' she told Saba. 'From all over the world,' she added – like Ozan, keen to emphasise their cosmopolitan credentials.

After lunch, Saba was told she could rest in her bedroom, which overlooked the Bosphorus and was large, light and airy. The high brass bed, covered in an exquisitely worked silk and gold bedspread, was placed so she could see the sea without moving from her pillows – it felt like being inside a sumptuous barge. Above the bed was a rose-tinted glass chandelier, and at the end of the room, all for her, a wonderful bathroom made of Carrera marble, with a shower and brass taps. Ozan had boasted at lunch that he'd employed a French architect 'of the highest quality' to modernise the house and install the plumbing, and that it was far more up to date than most of the now crumbling but still beautiful houses where the other grandees of the Ottoman Empire had once lived.

Lying half dazed in this room, propped up on her elbow and looking at the sea, Saba felt as if she'd wandered into the pages of *One Thousand and One Nights*. It was so far away from Pomeroy Street with its lino floor, and chenille bedspread, and Baba's suitcases stored above her one narrow wardrobe. For a brief moment a song felt like a magic carpet, one that could land you splat for sure, but also take you to places never dreamed of.

The only bad thing was Dom – her stomach was in knots about it.

She slept for two hours. When she woke, the moon was shedding its light on black water, in the distance, pinpricks of light from houses on the dark shoreline of Asia. She heard the splashing waves, and snatches of music from the ferries going back to the Galata Bridge. She was so far away from anything that could be considered normal that she felt she was dangling on a fine thread between dreams and nightmares. She thought of the stories Tan had told her once, of the bodies of murdered harem girls smuggled out to the Golden Horn and drowned. She thought about Dom and the miles and miles of sea that separated them now. He was flying again, in danger.

She almost couldn't bear to think of the house on Rue Lepsius now. On the morning she'd gone, she'd opened her eyes first and felt him beside her, awake. She'd felt his hand on the nape of her neck, his mouth on her hair. When she'd turned to face him, they'd looked at each other with wonder – a steady look, no jokes this time, no evasions. And then a long, slow kiss.

What must he think of her now?

On the next day, after a fine breakfast of fresh fruits, yoghurt, croissants, eggs and hot coffee, she was taken upstairs to Ozan's study for their first meeting. The large marble desk he sat at commanded a magnificent view of the sea. The smell of his sharp lemony aftershave filled the room.

'Sit down,' he said. In Alexandria, her impression had been of an ebullient, hospitable man: a back-slapper, a topper-up of drinks, a pincher of babies' cheeks. Now, with his black eyes magnified by a large pair of horn-rimmed glasses, he was all business and keen to get on.

He opened his diary. 'We are moving you today,' he said, not unkindly, but not waiting for her answer either. 'To a hotel in Beyoğlu, a lively part of Istanbul. In three days' time, we make a party at this house for business friends of mine and maybe some of their girlfriends.' He looked at her briefly. 'I'd like you to sing some songs for them. Cheerful things.

'After that, you will sing at the club called the Moulin Rouge, and after that maybe Ankara – I have some businesses there. I will check all the dates today.' He started to scribble in his diary with a gold pen.

So not the week *at the absolute most* that Cleeve had predicted. She had that uneasy feeling of slippage again, of being out of control.

'How many rehearsals?' she asked. She didn't care for him rapping out orders to her as if she was some sort of mechanical toy. 'I can't just sing cold for your friends. I want it to be good.'

'I know, I know.' His stern expression softened as if to convey he understood and respected that art had its own rules. 'There is no need for you to worry about that; the band, as you will see, is top class, so let me see . . .' He pursed his lips and consulted his diary again.

'Today you rehearse with them, but before that Leyla will take you shopping – she knows all the best shops in Beyoğlu. You can buy some dresses, I will pay.'

'I have dresses,' she said.

'I know,' he said. He removed his glasses and looked at her. A look that for the first time gleamed with possibilities. 'But you can have some more if you want,' he said softly. He adjusted his weight in his chair and carried on scribbling in his book. 'There will be lots of parties. I want you to look good.'

'I'm honestly fine, thank you,' she said, thinking *damn you, Mr Cleeve, you said this wouldn't happen.* 'I brought my own clothes.'

'Ahhh.' With his chair at a precarious angle, he leaned back and appraised her, like a man at an auction deciding what to bid. 'Are you one of those new women?' He gave a quizzical smile. 'What are they called, suffragettes?'

'They're not so new,' she said. 'We've all moved on a bit since then.' She smiled to show him no hard feelings. 'And by the way, you don't have to be a suffragette to want to wear your own things.'

He ignored this. 'Well, if you see anything you want, talk to Leyla, who will show you around. She is also a liberated woman,' he added. 'But happy here too.' He opened his arms to include the room, the view, the glittering cabinets. From the room downstairs came the gurgling sound of a child laughing, its scampering feet.

'I'm not surprised,' she said. 'It's beautiful.'

Again that strange proud curve of his lip – almost a smirk. 'And when the singing is over,' his paternal look had returned, 'it will be my great pleasure to take you to your family's village. It's not far from here – maybe you will find some of your people there.' When he said that, she had a vision of herself as a tree – a tree like one of the ancient cedars that grew around the *yali* – that might grow another root in the ground. It was oddly comforting, but seemed unlikely too.

'Thank you,' she said, 'I'd like that.'

Back in her room, she saw that a walnut-wood gramophone and wireless had been placed there – a monster of a thing with green lights shining from its control panel, and pleated material in its front. Beside it, Ozan had left a pile of the records he frequently alluded to that he'd collected from all over the world: Fats Waller, Duke Ellington, Billie and Ella, Dinah Washington. Two by Turkish singers Saba had never heard of. When she turned on the radio, she heard the crackling of static like flames, and then a burst of tango music.

She twiddled some more, her heart in her mouth, and at last an English voice saying, 'and this is Bela Bartok's Romanian Folk

Dances' bled into by the Arabic wailing. While she dressed, she kept the wireless tuned to the same station, hearing the sounds coming and going, and eventually, on the hour, the pips, and a calm Home Counties voice saying: 'This is the BBC coming to you from North Africa. Today the Desert Air Force and five infantry units engaged with the Luftwaffe sixty miles west of Alexandria, on the edge of the Western Desert. We have no news yet of casualties.'

She almost stopped breathing, terrified of missing a single word. But that was it: *We have no news yet of casualties.* Loss of life was a foregone conclusion.

When the caterwauling music swept on again, she switched it off and lay on the bed, and felt, for the first time in her life, a powerful dislike of herself and her work. Being a singer had once felt so simple, so pure, so natural to her; now it felt like a cannibal that might eat her heart out. For there must be consequences, she saw that now. They would split her apart and cause other people pain, and it was stupid of her not to have thought of this before.

To stop herself thinking, she switched on the wireless again. Turkish tango music again – bounding and impertinent with its swooping rhythms, its stops and starts. Ozan said there was a craze for it in Istanbul and she'd soon be singing some. She turned it up, went into the bathroom and took off all her clothes.

In the shower, she laid her head against the cool tiled wall and closed her eyes as the water flowed over her. The bugger of it is, she thought, that what I most need now is to work. I'm no good to anyone without it.

Leyla drove her to her first rehearsal later that day.

They were early. In the elegant lobby of the Pera Palace Hotel, they sat drinking coffee and eating feather-light macaroons while a uniformed chauffeur waited patiently on the pavement outside.

Leyla, dressed today in a severely cut Chanel suit and a row of double pearls, was greeted by the head waiter with bows and twinkling smiles.

In the middle of a bland conversation about clothes and all the wonderful tourist attractions Saba should see, Leyla blurted out, 'Do you like your life?' She dabbed the corner of her mouth with a napkin and waited with watchful eyes for the answer.

'My life?' Saba was startled. Their conversation in the car hadn't strayed much beyond the polite formalities. 'Well, yes. I do – at least I think so.'

'No problems within your family?'

'How do you mean?' Saba had already been conscious of Leyla's confusion about her, the darting looks as if she was a puzzle she was working on.

'Well . . . so . . . well . . . they don't mind you singing or anything like that?' Leyla took a black Sobranie from a pearl cigarette case. 'Or travelling alone. Here, have one of these, please!' She pushed the cigarettes towards her.

'No thanks.' She'd given it up because they made her cough. 'We live in Wales.' Saba made a quick decision not to tell Leyla about her father; she didn't know her well enough and it would make her feel too vulnerable. 'People like a bit of a sing-song there.'

'And we like it too.' Leyla's manicured hand patted hers reassuringly. 'It was only before Atatürk that women were silenced.' Atatürk, who'd died four years ago, was, she said, their leader and pro-democracy, the great moderniser of Turkey. Before him, women could only really sing and dance for each other, in the *hamam*, the Turkish baths, but at a stroke he had let them out of their cages – they could sing and dance in public after centuries of it being forbidden. What relief! What joy! Except that in some poorer villages, 'sorry for this – and no rudeness intended – but a singing girl is still a great disgrace. Some girls are beaten by their fathers if they do. In Anatolia there are whole villages still where only men are allowed to sing.'

'Goodness!' Saba felt the surge of a blush spread over her face. Her father seemed to have missed this revolution, but what Leyla had said explained so much.

'And how did you meet Mr Ozan?' she asked to break the awkward silence that followed.

'In London, before the war.' Leyla stretched out her legs and studied her impeccable shoes. 'Actually, I was studying to be a doctor.'

Saba tried not to look surprised.

'A doctor! How wonderful – do you do it now?'

'No – I never did.'

They glanced at each other warily.

'So, did you like London?' Saba asked after a while.

'No, forgive me. Not at all.' Leyla smiled and shook her head. 'I was very, very lonely, and I felt so sorry for the wife of the man I lived with. An English woman, a friend of my father's, but so busy all the time! Flowers, servants, cooking – no peace! And she was lonely too, I think, with no aunties at home, and her children at boarding school, her husband working all the time. I don't think she knew what to do with me.'

'So you must have been happy to meet Mr Ozan?'

'It was like a miracle. He was over there going to the theatre, the music, doing a hundred and one business things exactly like now.' She smiled fondly. 'I was at St Thomas's Hospital for my first year. The first person in my family to do something like that. My grandfather was very unhappy about it, he hardly ever spoke to me again, but my father was progressive.'

It made Saba feel queasy to remember that she should probably be paying close attention to these confidences: writing them down, pinning notes to her knickers. Part of her knew already she wasn't a natural spy.

'Zafer and I met at a party with some other Turkish people, friends of my family in London. We fell in love, we married the next year.' Leyla's voice had become somewhat mechanical. 'No, no thank you,' she snapped at a simpering waiter who had appeared with a new tray of pastries.

'Did you mind? Not finishing your studies, I mean.'

'Not at all.' Leyla said it so quickly Saba was frightened she'd overstepped the mark. They both drew in a breath and looked at their shoes.

'Well . . . sometimes . . . maybe . . . not so much.' Leyla laughed without rancour at her own contradictions. 'I did enjoy medicine but my parents were very pleased, he is a very good man, very successful too. I have my children, my family.' Her eyes were sparkling. 'Never a dull moment as you would say. Now please, a bit more coffee, or shall we look at the shops before your rehearsal? By the way,' she murmured while they were picking up their things, 'I don't think you should tell Mr Ozan I have talked to you of such things.'

The two of them exchanged a look.

'I don't think he would exactly mind,' Leyla shook the crumbs from her skirt, 'but we have never spoken of these things, and I hardly think of them – it's almost as if it never happened.'

*

After coffee, they went to the Londra hotel, where Felipe Ortiz, the bandleader, stood waiting for her beside an enormous potted palm tree near the front desk. Ortiz, a small, neat man with brilliantined slicked-back hair and a thin moustache, explained as they walked up the marble stairs that he was half Spanish and half Jewish, and had, like many Jews, fled to Istanbul two years ago. Before that he'd played all over Europe – France, Berlin, Italy, Spain. Hearing the sounds of a saxophone in an upstairs room, her steps quickened.

Felipe, though small in stature, was a man who gave off confidence like a lamp gives light. He told Saba they would rehearse for two hours each day in the morning. They had a lot to get through. The clientele at Ozan's parties and clubs were varied: Spanish, Jewish, Greeks, White Russians and the Free French. The Turks, who were tango mad, tended not to like the new jazz; the French adored it; the Germans were sentimental and loved oompah music and of course, and here Felipe had an unsuccessful stab at a cockney accent, 'blooming old "Lili Marleen"'. He gave Saba a stack of sheet music to study later, and then they briefly discussed tempos and keys, the songs they liked, and Saba sang a few songs a cappella for him.

A fat drummer with a bulging paunch and sleepy eyes shambled into the room. His name was Carlos. Saba was briefly introduced, the band tuned to an up-tempo version of 'I've Got You Under My Skin' and they were off.

When the song was ended, Felipe looked pleased – pretty good, his immaculate eyebrows indicated. Next came a jolly bouncing Turkish tango song called 'Mehtaph Bir Gecede', which Carlos said meant 'on a moonlit night'. Saba tried to follow it but couldn't. For her, the highlight came after a break, when Felipe, fiddling quietly with his guitar, resolved the notes into a jazz version of 'Stormy Weather'.

'You.' He looked at Saba, who sang along with him. Claude, the piano player, added a few soft touches.

And not for the first time, Saba was shocked at the sense of relief that singing brought to her. Nothing else would do sometimes. 'At the end of the song,' Felipe instructed the pianist, 'I think when she sings about it raining all the time, you must,' he put his finger to his lips, 'bring it up on the last bit.' He demonstrated on his own guitar – a silky progression of notes that gave Saba goose bumps. The band was good. Ozan was right about that. Felipe was pleased with her. For that moment, nothing else mattered.

After the rehearsal, they went down to the heavily ornate bar and drank Turkish tea in small glasses, and laughed at the two ancient parrots that sat in a cage in between the heavy drapes, like old and bitchy women muttering Turkish threats together. Felipe told her that when the war was over, the band hoped to tour again and would be looking for a vocalist. North Africa, Europe, maybe America; they'd had an offer from the Tropicana in Cuba where he'd played before the war, a magical time, he'd said with his sad, sweet smile. The names affected her like a drug. 'Mr Ozan is keen to help us,' he'd added. And now to complete the complications of the day, she felt herself shiver with excitement; she couldn't wait for the concerts to begin.

Chapter 33

He read the letter again, tore it in half, and burned both halves in his lighter flame.

Dear Dom, Arleta had written in her slapdash hand,

I hope you don't mind me calling you this. No, not a word have I heard from Saba either since she left us, so I've been worried too. I think she must have joined another tour, or gone away, maybe gone back to England. She was sent to Alex to do some wireless broadcasts. I wrote to her, she didn't reply to me, and our little lot has broken up anyway, because of illness, accidents, etc. I don't think she even knows that our poor old comedian, Willie, died suddenly on stage, poor love, which is how he'd have wished to go. I tried to contact Janine, a dancer on our tour, but she went off, I believe to India. It's hard to keep in touch at the mo as you yourself probably know.

Sorry can't be more helpful. If I do here from her I will definitely let her know. I miss her dreadfully, she was great fun and really talented. If you here from her, please do contact me.

All the best,
Arleta Samson

He'd taken a comfort he knew was both unpleasant and snobbish in the schoolgirl handwriting, the poor spelling. Performers were superficial, uneducated, unreliable and forgettable. He'd got himself lost like a man in a room of funfair mirrors. It would never have worked.

As a pilot he'd been trained to see that human beings had one big design fault in their brains. They saw fragments of reality and tried to build a whole world from them. When he, Barney and Jacko had sat down to learn the first rules of navigation, their instructor had roared five words at them – compass, deviation, magnetic, variation, true – and they'd bellowed back the mnemonic Cadbury's Dairy Milk very tasty. But the principle was sound: what seemed real could trick you. The mountain, hiding behind those gorgeous fluffy clouds you were flying into, could shatter you into a million pieces. That line of stars on your starboard side masquerading as the welcoming lights of a runway or dancing like native girls waving strings of white flowers. Never mistake what you wanted for what was there – as she so clearly wasn't.

And so, a casual face-saving letter back to Arleta:

Thanks for contacting me. Do let me know if you hear anything. For the foreseeable future I'll be moving around with the DAF so safest to send letters to me either to the NAAFI in Wadi Natrun, or to the Wellington Club in Cairo. Good luck with your tour.
Dominic Benson

And that was that.

Chapter 34

On 1 September, as Saba walked into the Büyük Londra's lobby, the desk clerk handed her an envelope with the sheet music to 'Night and Day' in it. Inside the front cover was a pencilled note:

> *Can we meet tomorrow at 43 Istiklal Caddesi. I'm directly opposite the French pastry shop on the first floor. Take the lift and turn right. I shall be there from 10.30 a.m. onwards.*
> *Cousin Bill*

And she was relieved. She had been brought here for a reason, and would be back in North Africa soon where she could explain things properly to Dom. For that morning, lying in the scented luxury of her hotel room, she'd stopped breathing when she heard the calm voice of the BBC man announcing: 'Today, there was more heavy bombing in the Western Desert where the Desert Air Force have been in action.'

The news as usual was deliberately vague, but her mind had raced to fill in the gaps. Dom could be anywhere now: desperate, suffering, and here she was in a room with a rose crystal chandelier above her bed, and Persian carpets, and thick white towels in her own bathroom. From the window she could see ferry boats crossing the Golden Horn, the mosques on the skyline behind it. She would drink fresh orange juice for breakfast with fresh coffee and buttery croissants, and all the time – no point in fibbing about it – excited in a queasy way about rehearsing with the new band.

Because the confusing thing was that if she could forget about the war, which of course she never could, and Dom, this had been, professionally speaking, one of the most interesting weeks of her life.

Felipe, notwithstanding the sleepy eyes, the spivvy moustache, the slightly drunken manner, was the most exciting musician she had ever sung with. He'd been discovered playing flamenco in a bar on the back streets of Barcelona, and could play just about anything – torch songs, jazz standards, sad old folk songs – with a sort of elegant insouciance which hid the precision and verve of his technique. The band worshipped him, longed to please him, and forgave his occasionally ferocious outbursts when they didn't live up to his demands. Before the war, he'd told her in his voice cracked and glazed by the constant little cigarillos he smoked, he'd moved to Germany and raised a family there. Ozan had first heard him at the Grand Duc in Paris, and later pulled the necessary strings to get him out of Paris before the Germans arrived – hence their mutual love affair.

And it had given Saba a surge of confidence, particularly after her rough ride with Bagley, to find that Felipe seemed pleased with her, almost to accept her as an equal; someone capable of learning and going far. No words to this effect had been exchanged, but she'd seen it in his eyes when they duetted together, and the more she felt it, the better she sang.

At their last rehearsal, he'd accompanied her on piano for 'Why Don't You Do Right?' and she'd had a very strange experience with him, a moment that probably only another musician would know or recognise. For four or five bars they'd slotted into a rhythm that was so perfect that it felt like sitting inside a faultlessly constructed puzzle, or like dancing together in perfect rhythm. Nothing you could fake or force, but Felipe, who was generally quite reserved, had closed his eyes and yelped with pleasure afterwards, and her blood had sung for hours. She was dying to try it again in concert that night.

After breakfast, she read Cleeve's note again, memorised the street number on Istiklal Caddesi, and then, feeling faintly absurd, taken a box of matches up to her room and burned the note over the lavatory. As she watched its charred remains swirl away, her mood improved, but the stomach churning did not go away. The thought of seeing Cleeve again had made her unexpectedly nervous, and then in less than nine hours from now – she counted out the hours on her wristwatch – she'd be at Ozan's house for the band's first performance together. Even Felipe seemed het up about this. Yesterday, after their last rehearsal, she'd seen a look of strain in his eyes as he'd warned them that Ozan, for all his easy-going ways, was a perfectionist; if the band did not please him, they'd be sent away. When he'd tried to smile, his mouth had twitched – apart from Istanbul and Ozan, Felipe had no home and no job now.

She spent the day wandering alone in and out of the narrow passages of Beyoğlu. She loved this old part of town: the dim alleyways where vegetables, tomatoes, aubergines, fat bunches of parsley were laid out as lovingly as flowers, the butchers' shops with sheep's heads in the window, their entrails neatly plaited beside them, the shop where preserved fruits lay like fat shining jewels in big glass jars.

She lingered for a while watching two old ladies prod potatoes and glare at apples with the same severe and forensic attention that Tan gave hers in the Cardiff market, and then moved on to Istiklal Caddesi, a wide thoroughfare filled with fashionably dressed people, where she hopped on to a tram. She got off at the wrong stop, walked for half a mile, then found it: Cleeve's temporary house – a narrow, ramshackle old Ottoman building with stained-glass windows between a shoe shop and an elegant French patisserie. She had no idea what she would tell him tomorrow, or what he wanted from her; this part of her life seemed precarious, unreal. I don't like being whatever it is I am to Cleeve, she thought suddenly. It doesn't suit me – I don't like shades of grey.

She ate lunch at one of the more modest establishments on the street, which served only *börek* – soft envelopes of pastry stuffed with either meat or cheese or vegetables – her father's favourite meal. She often saw faces like his now, in the streets, on trams – darkly handsome features with heavy beards that needed to be shaved twice a day. Yesterday she'd watched one man chasing his little boy in the street, and felt a sharp pang of regret. She and Baba had had good times once; the sing-songs, the secret trips to buy ice creams on Angelina Street, all ending with that groaning shameful tussle in the bedroom. Her slap – she'd hit him! – when he'd torn the ENSA letter, still so shocking even when she thought of it now, would not be forgiven, not in this lifetime, and not by her now. She was fed up to the back teeth of waiting for his approval, for letters from him that would not come. Sometimes it seemed you just had to stop yourself going down an old mousehole where there was no cheese.

Istanbul, whether she liked it or not, had brought him into sharp focus again, raising questions. Why had he left this beautiful place with its mosques and scented bazaars, its bright glimpses of blue seas and distant shores, for the cold grey streets of Cardiff, where once, no one spoke his language? Why had he never come back? What was the source of the simmering anger she'd felt in him that had driven her away?

Later, back in her hotel room, alone, a singer again, her father was banished. She stood in front of a mirror in the blue dress Ellie had loaned her, shaking with nerves at the thought of Ozan's party a matter of hours away now. This is horrible! she thought. Why put myself through this?

A kaleidoscope of thoughts flashed through her mind as she spread panstick over her cheeks and stretched her mouth for lipstick. Tonight would be a humiliating failure, she was sure of it now, under-rehearsed, embarrassing, a jumble of mismatched songs that would bewilder an audience whose tastes she had no clear idea of. Tonight would be a triumph, Ozan would love her, Paris and New York would follow. Dom would surprise her – he'd suddenly show up.

Later, in the back of the chauffeur-driven car Mr Ozan sent for her, her eyes were closed and she was entirely oblivious to the moon rising over the Golden Horn or the fishermen dropping their lines over shadowy bridges, to men going to the mosque to pray, the shoe cleaner outside the gates of the British Consulate packing his things to go home. She was tuned to her songs.

At Taksim Square, Felipe and the rest of the band got in. Smart dinner suits, fresh white shirts and lashings of brilliantine. Felipe kissed her hand and said she looked sensational. The car headed down the steep hill and then turned again, following the sea and the dying day. On the left-hand side of them were the dark shadowed woods, where Felipe told her there were wolves; on their right the gleam of the sea metallic as beaten copper in the dusk, the lights of ferry boats cutting through the waves.

Ozan's house at dusk was a marvellous sight; with light pouring out from every window, it seemed to float in the moonlit waters of the Bosphorus, ethereal and glittering like some outlandish ocean liner. Walking towards it, Saba heard the steady pump of tango music coming from inside.

Leyla – ravishing tonight in emeralds and pale green silk – stood at the door to greet them. Ozan, she said, had been roaring around the house all day overseeing everything, the food, the stage, the guest list. She rolled her big black eyes behind her husband's back – what a man! A monster!

She led them to a small room on the first floor where they could store their instruments, then down to a kitchen where five extra cooks and fourteen waiters had been drafted in to pluck quail and chop coriander and dill and pound walnuts and make up the dozens of delicious little mezes for the guests to nibble at.

The cooks made a big fuss of Saba as she poked her head around the door. They smiled and bowed and offered her little bits to taste, but she ate only a tiny bowl of rice and some kind of divine-tasting chicken stew. She was nervous again and very rarely ate before singing.

'Come! Come.' Leyla was excited too. She led Saba by the hand upstairs where they peeped around the door and saw a large handsome panelled room crammed with people talking and laughing. The light from dozens of small candles poured down like golden honey on silks and satins and long-necked women with diamonds around their throats. Through open windows a full moon shone over the dark sea.

Inside, food and much male laughter, the clink of glasses and piles of pink Sobranie cigarettes lying in crystal bowls for anyone to smoke. It was, thought Saba, the kind of party you dreamed about when you were young. Mum would have fainted at it.

'Who are they?' she whispered to Felipe.

'All kinds,' he whispered back, his moustache tickling her ear. 'Ozan's business friends, film people, writers and traders, embassy staff, journalists – nearly a hundred and fifty of them, or so Leyla says.'

Mr Ozan hove into view, portly and suave in a ruby-coloured velvet dinner jacket with braid around the cuffs, moving like a giant whale through the glowing room, eyes skimming the crowd, smiling, kissing, patting arms, pinching cheeks, accepting many compliments with a dignified and neutral dip of his head, as if to say *what did you expect?*

He'd given them strict instructions not to start to play until the guests had settled in and had time to chat and have a couple of drinks. And then, at nine o'clock precisely, he looked significantly in their direction, tapped his watch and the roar of the partygoers fell to an expectant hush. The curtain opened, a spotlight fell on the stage. 'Ready,' Felipe said quietly, checking them all. He raised his beautifully plucked eyebrows at Saba.

Deep breath, shoulders back. Crepi il lupo!

And they were off. Their first song, 'Zu Zu Gazoo', was a nonsense thing composed by Felipe as an icebreaker. Carlos set its rapid pulse, Felipe's hands raced over his guitar, Saba leapt in singing, scatting, dancing, losing herself in a feeling of almost ecstasy that didn't feel conscious until the song ended and she heard the audience roar and clap. Felipe's smile said *it's working.* All the small incremental moments of practice, of building technique, of making mistakes, of learning when to hold and when to let go had made the song feel effortless and the night magical, and Saba knew that if she was a billionaire, she could never, ever replace this feeling of satisfaction and delight.

Next, 'That Old Black Magic', with Felipe furling his lip now and doing his Satchmo imitation and doowapbababbing on the chorus. Then a beautiful Turkish song, 'Veda Bûsesi', 'the parting kiss', and finally 'J'ai Deux Amours'. It was pure fun and she loved it.

The candles burned down, leaving a hazy glow in the room; outside, the moon sank like a giant ripe peach in the sea, and the fishermen who had lingered in their boats outside to enjoy the music went home. Sounds of muffled laughter came from an upstairs room where Felipe had told her the narghiles and the lines of cocaine were laid out. He'd gone up there once or twice himself during their breaks. After midnight, the band, purring along now like some well-oiled engine, began to play all the schmoozy old favourites: 'Blue Moon', 'The Way You Look Tonight'.

And Saba, watching the dancers drawing closer, and stealing kisses, felt her moment of happiness change in a heartbeat to one of shocking anxiety. Every cell in her body longed to dance with him, to feel his soft shining hair, his cheek on hers.

Please God, keep him safe. Don't let him die.

' "These Foolish Things",' Felipe whispered. She loved this song. In an earlier rehearsal he'd shown her a way of holding back some of the notes by half a beat. 'Sometimes in order to make them cry you need to make them wait,' he'd said.

When the song ended, one or two of the dancers turned towards her entranced. They clapped their hands softly. She blew a kiss towards them from the palm of her hand.

'*Mashallah*!' Mr Ozan shouted as he clambered on to the stage. Felipe raised his thumbs and smiled at her.

'Miss Saba Tarcan, my half-Turkish songbird,' Mr Ozan said in a muffled voice in the microphone; the audience gave her a loud ovation, they whistled and clapped. For that moment, at least, she could do no wrong.

'Well golly, golly, golly. Tremendous!' Cleeve clapped his hands together softly when, on the following day, she told him about the party. 'Safely over the first fence. The band like you, Ozan is besotted, the rest should be a piece of cake.'

They were sitting in his flat – an anonymous room, scruffy like the Alexandria one; his unpacked suitcase in the corner, a half-eaten kebab on a table whose wonky leg was propped up with a faded copy of *Le Monde*.

'But I've interrupted you.' He leaned forward eagerly. 'Carry on. What happened next?'

They were drinking Turkish tea together out of mismatched glasses. Saba looked at her watch. Eleven o'clock.

'I can't stay long,' she warned him. 'As a treat, Mr Ozan wants to take Leyla and me for a drive. He's going to try and find the place where my family once lived.'

'Really.' Cleeve's smile was a quick grimace – he had no interest in this whatsoever. He pushed away the kebab wrapper. 'This place is a dump, sorry, I've only hired it for a couple of days – it's better we don't meet in hotels.'

'I wasn't even born then,' she said. 'It feels like I took no interest in them before I came here.'

'Isn't that true of most people?' He dropped two discarded pieces of meat into the wrapper, and threw it into the waste-paper basket. 'Your parents only really exist for you as your parents.' He lit a cigarette.

I know nothing about you either, Saba thought. Only the twinkly smile, the jokes, the matey conversations about music.

'So,' he said. 'The party.'

'It was the most glamorous party I've ever been to,' she said. 'I couldn't believe it.'

'Some of these people have made colossal profits from the war,' Cleeve said. 'Chiefly from sugar, salt, fuel. They've never had so much money, and they're not shy about spending it. What happened?'

'We played for about an hour,' Saba continued, 'and when we stopped, Mr Ozan asked me to dance with some of the men who had come. He seemed proud of the fact that I was Turkish, that I'd come home, kept telling them how much I loved Istanbul.'

'And do you?'

'Far more than I'd expected.'

'And did you mind? The dancing, I mean.'

She hesitated.

'I don't like Ozan telling me who to dance with – it makes me feel cheap – but that's hardly the point, is it?'

'Did you say anything?'

'No – in case I heard something.'

'Good girl, oh they'll give you a great big medal for this when you get back.'

Patronising prat.

'And some dolly mixtures?'

'Don't get cross, Saba, and please go on, this is all tremendous. Who did you dance with?'

'A man called Necdet, a Levantine tobacco trader; he speaks seven languages and he smelt of almonds. Yuri somebody or other, fat and jolly. He said that most of the ships going up and down the Bosphorus belong to him. A White Russian, Alexei something like Beloi was his surname – he's here to write a book on economics. He made a pass at me.'

'A serious one?'

'No. He told me Istanbul was stuffed to the gills with spies, all waiting to see which way the Turks jump. He made it sound like a joke.'

'Well, true up to a point. Anything else?'

'Yes. There were four German officers there. I danced with two of them. That felt horrible but I didn't show it.' She looked at him anxiously. 'I'm just used to thinking of them as people who drop bombs, who kill people . . . Anyway,' seeing his neutral expression, 'I wanted to spit in their eyes, but I smiled nicely, and they smiled nicely back. One was called Severin Mueller; he's something in the embassy but didn't say what. He only wanted to talk about the music.'

'Ah.' Cleeve's head jerked up. 'Now he is quite important to us – he's a new attaché from the embassy in Ankara. Why did you leave the best bit till last? Did you say anything to him?'

'Only a few words, but I was frightened – what if they realise I am English?'

He gave her his sincere look. 'There are lots of parties here, Saba, where the German big brass and the English are in the same room together. I'm not saying they're making beautiful love to each other, but they talk, exchange the odd frigid smile, that sort of thing. And also, when you're with Ozan you're as safe as houses. Anything else?'

'Nothing else. Some of the men got pretty drunk by the end of the evening. They asked me to sing "Lili Marleen". I'd rehearsed it with Felipe in German. But Dermot,' she was determined to tell him this and make him listen, 'lovely as it is here, I don't want to swan around indefinitely. When will I get back to North Africa?' She heard her voice rising and made an effort to control herself. 'Do you understand what I'm saying? If you have a definite job for me to do here I will do it as well as I can, but I'm not a spy, I'm a singer.'

He put his hands out and held her arms as though she had become briefly and unreasonably hysterical. 'Darling sweets!' he said. 'Saba my love.' He planted a paternal kiss on her forehead. 'Of course you're a singer. And of course we'll have you back soon, but there is something very important for you to do first, which is why I've asked you here today – to bring everything, hopefully, to a happy conclusion.'

He drew close enough for her to smell the faint tang of cigarettes on his breath.

'Right, ready. Now listen.'

Somewhere in the building the lift thunked and squealed.

He steepled his fingers together and looked at her.

'Saba my love, you are part of an operation that has been going on for months in Turkey. Felipe is a key part of it. While you were dancing with the Germans, Felipe was doing a little exploring in the guest bedrooms of Ozan's house.'

'Felipe?'

'Felipe is one of our key operatives here. Last night he was checking to see if Ozan's guests had been careless about what they left on their bedside tables.'

'Why didn't you tell me this before?'

'I'm telling you now. We had to see how well you worked first.'

She felt a kick of satisfaction and fear: so there was a reason for this.

'Does anyone else in the band know?'

'No one. Now,' Cleeve drew closer, his voice dropped, 'here's the next part. Listen very carefully.

'One year ago, a German fighter-pilot ace called Josef Jenke was shot down over the Black Sea. A pilot who happens to be on our payroll too. He was picked up by the Turkish police, brought to Istanbul for questioning, and in accordance with international law, he was not sent to prison but billeted in a small pension in Pera. He's been treated pretty cushily there – allowed out for much of the day on parole, fed nicely, even supplied with the odd girl.

'Over the months and weeks of his arrest Josef has become part of the German clan. There aren't all that many of them here and for obvious reasons they stick together. He is a charming fellow, handsome, brave, the ladies like him, and he often dines out discreetly on his fighter-pilot exploits – his longing to fly again and take another shot at Johnny Britisher, that sort of thing. The situation now is that he gets invited to most of the parties, and he has become very close to a man called Otto Engel, who is part of an organisation called the Ostministerium – the Ministry of the East. Their main activities as far as we can work out are black-marketeering and having a rollicking good time.

'Now here is the point.' Cleeve looked down, as if someone might be crouching under the scruffy table. 'Because Istanbul is now the most important neutral city in the world, we need urgently to speak to Jenke – he's done some brilliant work for us, but we think his days are numbered. We suspect that someone inside the Ostministerium has started to smell a rat. Certain enquiries have been made to his squadron; it's possible that any day now they will discover that he was a deserter. We need to get him out fast.'

Cleeve anticipated her question.

'Josef loves women and music. He's a regular guest at house parties held at a private house that the Germans use in Tarabya, which is close to their summer embassy. One of Ozan's cronies supplies music and alcohol and girls, but he very rarely goes there.

'These evenings are very informal; it's difficult to know exactly what night Jenke will be there, but he knows you are coming, he knows who you are. When you get there you will sing, and maybe dance with a few people, and at some point in the evening Jenke will ask if he can have his photo taken with you. If you pose with him it will seem like the most natural thing in the world, a fan photograph if you like, and then we can snip him off,' Cleeve scissored his nicotined fingers and smiled briefly, 'make him a false passport and get him out of the country as quickly as possible.'

'All in one night?'

'Felipe is confident it can be done in one night – two at the very most.'

'How will I know it's him?'

Cleeve took some sheet music from his briefcase. 'Jenke will flirt with you, and at some point he will walk up to the stage and you will hand him this, so he can sing a few bars with you. It's the sheet music to "My Funny Valentine". He rifled through the pages until he got to a paper clip and a loose page.

'The instructions he needs are all written here invisibly. All you need to do is to open the music at the right page – he's experienced, he knows what to do. He'll take it when he's ready. It shouldn't be too difficult; all the lights will be turned down low and everyone will be drinking.'

Saba watched a seagull take off from the windowsill, and dissolve into mist. She heard the lift clanking through the building, the wheeze of its door opening.

'I can do that.' Although she wasn't sure she could, she felt strong feelings stir in her.

'Do you love your country, Saba?' Cleeve said softly. He was watching her closely.

She went very still for a moment. Did she love it enough to put her own life up for grabs? She hadn't really thought about patriotism except to know that if there was a crowd bellowing 'There'll Always Be an England' or 'Jerusalem', her heart would be swelling, but with Germans dropping bombs on your green and pleasant land, this was hardly an unusual emotion.

'Yes,' she said at last. 'I do.'

'Good girl.' He patted her hand. 'Perhaps I should warn you that the parties at Tarabya occasionally get a little wild.' Cleeve sucked in his cheeks and looked at her waggishly. 'It's where the Germans go to let their hair down. But Felipe will be there to keep an eye on you, and of course none of them want to upset Ozan either, he's much too important to them.'

'And what then? I mean after this job. I don't want to stay indefinitely.'

'Absolutely not,' Cleeve was indignant. 'We don't want you hanging around either. As soon as Jenke has his photo and his papers, he'll be gone and you'll be on a courier plane back to Cairo. If you want to come back here after the war, I'm sure Ozan will give you work – so everybody wins.

'But listen, Saba,' his smile became a kindly frown, 'it has to be your decision – are you sure you can do this?'

She bowed her head. Her worst nightmare as a child had her dashing on to a stage in front of a huge audience only to discover she'd forgotten her lines, what play she was in and who she was. But to back out now was more or less impossible – it was too late, and her dander was up, and she had already climbed the steps and was on the high board with Felipe and the others looking down. She took a quick breath and looked at him.

'I'll do it,' she said.

Chapter 35

When Dom woke up, Barney's size-twelve foot was thumping him on the ear. Rain pattered down on his sleeping bag. He'd been dimly aware of it falling when he'd woken in the night, but now it poured with a steady soaking sound, seeping under the canvas flaps, making their clothes clammy and damp; there would be a sea of mud when they stepped outside.

He shone his torch on his watch – 4.30 – closed his eyes and tried to go back into the dream again, a feat he'd managed quite easily as a boy in cold prep school dormitories, but no more it seemed. In the dream, he'd given birth to twins. His heart burst with love for them – these babies with their Buddha-like tummies, and deep dimples, and wrists that looked as if they had rubber bands on them. He soaped their plump little arms, held his hands over their eyes to stop soap getting in them. He lifted them out of the bath and blew raspberries in their soft flesh; he powdered them and wrapped them in warm towels, and then he handed them to a woman who put them in pyjamas and jiggled them on her knee. When she tickled them with her hair, they made chortling sounds like the deep bubbling of a stream. When he'd propped them up on cushions in front of a fire, their clear blue eyes had looked back at him – entirely content. *We trust you*, they were telling him. *We're safe.*

Oh what a tit. He opened his eyes and sighing got up, lit a cigarette and smoked it under a dripping tarpaulin outside the tent. And gazing at the sea of mud around him, the grey skies, the rusty plates smeared with beans from last night's meal, he mocked the midnight dreamer.

Fat babies, fat chance. It was shameful, ridiculous how much he dreamed about her, or some version of her, of which you didn't have to be Freud to know that the twins were a part, and he was so staggeringly tired now; he simply couldn't afford to go on like this.

Since October, the round-the-clock bombing sorties had gone on with the regularity of seaside trains, and yesterday, flying between Sidi Barrani and LG101, dazed and hallucinatory, he had seen the desert as a huge piece of crinkled art paper on which his plane drew enormous lines back and forth, back and forth. When he saw he'd stopped working the controls and was simply gazing slack-jawed at this, he'd had to pinch himself and sing to get safely home.

They'd lost five Spitfires in the relentless raids of the last few weeks; two pilots, one fitter who'd crashed in a jeep in a dust storm. Today, weather permitting, he planned to fly down on his own to a temporary hangar, close to Marsa Matruh, to see if any of the old patched-up Spits being repaired there would be usable or whether they were death traps.

When Barney had heard about this plan, over supper last night, they'd fallen out about it, and gone to bed angry at each other, a thing he could never remember happening before – not at school, not at university, affable old Barney, normally speaking, was a golden retriever of a man – but tiredness, it seemed, made even the best of them chippy and humourless.

'Forget it, Dom,' Barney had advised flatly. 'It's our first afternoon off in weeks.' Barney had tried to tempt him with pleasant Cairo alternatives: some cold beers for once instead of the warm rubbish they were drinking now; Dorothy Lamour at the Sphinx – Barney waggled his hips, outlined huge bosoms with his hands. It could be their last day off for a long, long time.

All true.

'We need the Spits,' Dom said flatly.

Which was true too – every single aircraft was needed now, because Bingley's confident assertion that they would banish the Luftwaffe from Africa during the August raids had proved a pipe dream and now a new last push was planned. There had been no formal briefings yet, but the mess and the bars of Cairo were buzzing with rumours that the Allies were about to descend on North Africa in the biggest seaborne invasion the world had ever seen; that once the beaches and ports had been secured, the ground bases and airfields could be quickly established, and then tick, tick, tick, like a game of Chinese chequers, Italy would be open to invasion, the Allies would have dominance in the air, and the whole sodding thing would soon be over. Dom was in two minds as to how he felt about that. He wanted it over now, and dreaded it too.

How did one come down from this – this nerve-shredding life, this death. Life post-Africa. And life post-Saba, even though, as he often reminded himself, he hardly thought of her now.

When Dom didn't answer, Barney stopped his silly Dorothy dancing.

'You are not seriously thinking about it, are you?'

'Not thinking about it. I've said yes.'

There was a long, tense silence.

'You're a silly bugger, Dom,' Barney said at last. 'You're exhausted.'

'I'm not.' Though he hardly slept now – his body felt the shudder and vibration of an aircraft all the time.

Barney tried again, screwing his face up in the effort.

'I don't know if you remember this, Dom, but my father used to train a couple of racehorses, and he told me once that there was a very fine line between the horse who was a wonderfully brave jumper and the one that was an absolute fucking eejit. You've stepped over it.' Barney pronounced eejit in a jokey Irish way, to soften the words, but there was a flash of real fury in his eyes.

They'd looked at each other, breathing heavily.

'You of all people should know that,' Barney said next.

Barney had seen Jacko go down too; he'd taken Dom aside before take-off, and said, 'Tell him not to go – he's too windy.' He'd heard the fading screams as the plane twirled like a useless piece of charred paper until it hit the sea.

They never spoke of it.

'If you want to blame me for that,' said Dom, 'don't bother. I do a good job of it every single day.'

'Dom, that's mad.' It took Barney a moment to decode this, and now the expression on his face was one of sorrow and concern. 'He was a free agent – we all were.'

And Dom, looking down on Barney, whose enormous feet now dangled over the end of his camp bed, wished with all his heart he could subscribe to the free-agent idea too, but it was not possible and never would be.

'So, shutting up now.' Barney's face grew cold and dark. He reached for a cigarette. 'Fly the bloody thing.' When he looked like that, Dom saw how he'd aged. He seemed long-suffering, like quite another person.

'Great,' said Dom. 'Give my regards to Dorothy.'

*

Dom had a brief conversation with a nineteen-year-old mechanic inside a hangar when he got to Marsa Matruh. The boy's face was waxy green with fatigue, he'd worked all through the night to repair the Spit. They shared a quick meal from a random collection of half-empty tins. After the last mouthful of beans, Dom put on his damp flying suit, stuffed torch, map, parachute and revolver under the cockpit seat, and took off again as quickly as he could, hoping to be home before night fell.

Grey afternoon light, the desert a dun-coloured porridgy mass below him, a bank of cumulus cloud in the west where more rain threatened.

He was flying at 15,000 feet and making good progress, concentrating hard on the engine's noise, when he heard another sound, insignificant at first, like a fly swatter landing on cardboard. Glancing through the canopy, he saw from the corner of his eye the black shadow of an Me 109, and then heard the rat-tat-tat of more bullets before the plane sped away.

His first reaction was to swear, and then the weary everyday thought, *oh fucking hell, not again*, wondering how much he'd be hurt this time. In a heartbeat he heard his own voice, panicked, shouting *no, no, no*, then he was gagging, the wet of his vomit in the gas mask now, the cockpit full of choking cordite fumes and glycol that made his nose run and his eyes stream. Eight seconds, *eight seconds*, the words pounded in his ears – eight measly seconds in which to bale out, to tear off his oxygen mask, release straps, turn the plane upside down and get himself out.

He wrestled desperately with the controls for a moment, and then realised it was no good. He grabbed the parachute from under the seat, ripped open the canopy and flung himself into the air, crying out as the parachute bunched between his legs, refusing to open, and then the long swooning dive towards the tilting earth.

Chapter 36

They were driving towards the German party house for their first engagement when Felipe glanced at Saba almost coyly, and said, 'Were you surprised when Mr Cleeve told you about me?'

'Yes. I was, very,' she said. 'And relieved too. I haven't done this sort of thing before.'

'Don't be nervous, Saba.' He patted her hand, the long fingernails on his playing hand scratched her slightly. 'I don't think our pilot will come for a few days, and these men don't want to make trouble; they want to have a good time, to eat a lot of bratwurst, get a bit little drunk, forget about the war for one night. You have nothing to fear.'

She sat watching the light fade from the tops of the trees, hoping all this was true. Felipe's usually excellent English seemed a little more garbled during this explanation. His red satin shirt had a ring of sweat around armpits that smelled of ripe fruit.

She asked, 'Does Mr Ozan know all these people well?' When what she really wanted to ask was: do you trust him? Will he keep us safe?

Felipe glanced at her quickly.

'He knows everyone, all the politicians, most of the Germans. He is a very important man.'

'How do you become so important?'

'In Turkey, if you want to be very, very wealthy, I mean *really* wealthy, you make deals with politicians, it's just the way it is,' Felipe muttered. 'This war is a nice earner for many of them.'

'But—' Saba felt alarmed again, but Felipe cut her off.

'That's enough – he is a very good man. He is good to us, and we have our own other reasons for being here.'

The car slowed down to avoid an enormous pothole. 'Now, concentrate, please,' Felipe said. 'I want to run through the plan again. As far as they are concerned you are a Turkish girl singer, a friend of Ozan's, your folks came from a village near Üsküdar and you're new to my band. What is the name of the village of your father?'

'Üvezli.'

'Üvezli. We need to know if they ask. I don't think they will. Tonight will be a getting-to-know you night – is for the relax, the music, we have a good time.' Felipe gave a shaky smile. 'So, we will play two or three sets of music – you can leave all this to me – and when we're not playing, we will sit and eat and drink, you may be asked to dance and that is fine. When you are dancing, smile a lot and talk as little as possible – they'll expect you to be shy.'

Felipe pulled at his bow tie.

'It's hot tonight, isn't it?'

When he opened the car window, she felt the sticky scented air move over her face and was glad of it.

'Hot for autumn – in winter the winds come down from Russia they cut like a knife.'

The smell of his sweat and his cologne filled the car. He told her she was not to panic if he occasionally left the room where they would perform. Part of his work there was to make a detailed map of the house, and to check if any of the officers had been careless with the official papers they sometimes travelled with. During these breaks, he might be upstairs under the pretext of having a 'pee-pee' or a smoke. If she saw him take a girl upstairs, or having a pinch of naughty salt with the Germans, she mustn't be shocked. It was important for him to be one of the boys. He would never be gone long.

The faint pinpricks of light they were driving towards became a small village. The scent of roasting meat and spices filled their car and made Saba's mouth water – in the excitement of performing, she had forgotten to eat.

On the outskirts of the village, a group of old men were drinking coffee outside a café lit by a kerosene lamp; further on a family sat eating a meal together underneath a trellis heavy with jasmine and vines. The young woman had a baby on her lap. A toddler rested against the side of a young man and waited for its food; a donkey, munching a bundle of fresh green leaves, looked pleased with itself. A family at rest with the world and each other.

'They looked happy,' she said to Felipe. For that moment, it seemed like the most seductive thing in the word.

'Yes.' He gunned the accelerator.

And the sudden thought came to her that she knew not a thing about Felipe's private life. He was not a gabby man, and though they had talked about various things – music they liked, future plans, other musicians – their moments of real intimacy came when he accompanied her on his guitar.

'Do you like this kind of work, Felipe?' she asked. 'You know . . . the other work at the German house . . . not the music part.'

She still found it impossible to utter the word spying – it sounded preposterous, like a child's game of pretend, or maybe too frightening to say out loud.

'No.' His face glowed green in the dash lights. 'No! I don't like it too much, but I do it. Mr Cleeve says our man Jenke has important information – that's enough for me. We . . .'

His voice tailed off like a bag with the air punched out of it, then he said, 'I hate the bloody Nazis – I would like to strangle them all.'

The air between them seemed to thicken and become full of terrible things. After a silence he added, 'I had a wife before . . . in Berlin . . . her name was Rachel. A beautiful woman,' he said, 'Jewish. I had a daughter too – Naomi – as lovely as her mother, very musical. You remind me of her.'

'Please don't . . . if you . . . I'm so sorry.'

'No. No. It's all right. I should say these things before. I was on tour with the band, six months. Barcelona, France, Madrid. Good fun, well, you know. I came back to Berlin. Lots of presents.' He took both hands off the wheel to show how full his arms had been. 'Our apartment smashed, family gone.'

'I am so sorry, I . . .' She could have kicked herself for her stupid question. Felipe was another heartbroken stray like Bog and the acrobats. She seemed to be making a speciality of these innocent enquiries that detonated a bomb.

The car filled with cigarillo smoke.

'Don't say sorry.' He gave a great exhaling sigh. 'No, don't. Is necessary you know why I do this – I should have told you before. I had a bad choice to make after it happened: I could stay and be arrested myself – I'm half Jewish, you see – or I could come to Istanbul. I don't know if I've made the good choice, the only thing I know is that without this,' he turned and touched his guitar on the back seat, 'I would have killed myself.'

He started to hum, either to end the conversation, or maybe as an expression of some relief at having poured out even a tiny bit of his heart. By the time they arrived at the white house in Tarabya, he had his work face on again.

Felipe looked for a place to park, Saba gazed around her. The house was set in a clearing surrounded by a screen of pine trees and bounded by a high wooden fence. Beyond the fence were some nondescript cypress and Judas trees, scrub, a dirt road and no nosy neighbours, which was probably why the Germans had chosen it. Close enough, Cleeve had said, to their official summer residence to be convenient, but far enough away for it to function as a sort of unofficial officers' mess, where they could bring girls and have gambling parties and entertain local business people without too much bothersome protocol.

A couple of cars were there already – a Buick with German number plates on it and an Opal. Inside the high white windows the curtains were drawn, with a dim reddish light shining through them.

Felipe found a spot near a pair of iron gates. He pulled on the handbrake and checked the rear-view mirror.

'If anything goes wrong while we're here, I shall tell you to sing "Quizas, Quizas, Quizas". It's an old Spanish song, so no one will ask for it as a request; after that we quietly leave. Our excuse will be we have to get the night air, or go outside to smoke a cigarette. No panic, no shouting.'

He said he would always park the car as close to the gate as possible.

'I'm telling you this as a precaution; nothing bad will happen.'

His satin shirt was soaked through now – he put on his dinner jacket to cover it. He lifted his guitar from the back seat, he gathered up their sheet music. His calmness seemed genuine and she needed it because her mouth was dry as they crunched across the gravel for that first party. When she thought of Germans en bloc, she thought of bogeymen – torturers, rapists, assassins – and in spite of all Felipe's reassurances, she was very frightened.

Otto Engel opened the door, a thick-necked, smiling man in a wine-stained satin smoking jacket. Felipe had told her earlier that Engel, a member of the German Secret Service, was nicknamed Minister of Fun. He and his cronies took lots of bogus trips, had mistresses, and of course gave parties. The German Secret Service, unlike the British Secret Service, was not centralised, Felipe said, but made of many divisions, all of whom plotted and organised vendettas against each other.

Engel's florid face lit up when he saw them; he clapped his hands and gave one of those booming, empty laughs that wipe the smile off your face. Felipe, whose German was fluent too, introduced Saba with the air of a magician pulling something lovely out of a hat. He said it would be just him and her for the next few nights; the other band members had picked up a stomach bug. Engels closed his eyes, nuzzled Saba's hand with his lips, looked at Felipe approvingly as if to say *nice, well done.*

She stepped through the door remembering Ellie's *Feather on head, tail on bum. No panic.*

Otto was booming at her side and holding her arm as she walked through a low-ceilinged room blurry and blue with smoke. Twenty or so young men stood around laughing, talking, drinking. They looked taller than most of the young men she knew, some of the younger ones were extremely good-looking with their high cheekbones and strong, athletic bodies. The two or three young girls there were mostly bottle blondes in cheap-looking frocks and high heels. When Saba walked in, there was a dip in conversation, a low murmur of appreciation as the men smiled at her or made quick sly comments to each other.

A small stage had been rigged up for them in a bay window at the far end of the room, but Engel wanted to feed them first from a table in the kitchen groaning with cheeses and hunks of pâté, German sausages, booze. He was sweating in his eagerness.

'First we play.' Felipe was all winning smiles now; it was as if he'd never known a bad moment in his life. 'Later we drink.'

He straightened his bow tie and bounded towards the stage. 'Let's go, babeee.' He bared his teeth in the fake Satchmo grin that usually made her laugh.

Ten minutes later they leapt into 'Zu Zu Gazoo'. Saba felt tense to start, but after a while the galloping rhythms of Felipe's guitar claimed her. It felt good playing together like this – no drums, no piano, just them.

The two primitive spotlights that had been placed next to the stage shone too brightly. Before their next number, Felipe fiddled with them discreetly and made the stage more intimate by sitting them both in a circle of light surrounded by shadows. He smiled at Saba, a gentle conspiratorial smile that said *we can do this*, and began a silky version of 'Besame Mucho'. When he said something in German to the group of young men waiting silent around the beer keg, she knew he was saying this was a song about kissing written by a Mexican girl who'd never been kissed in her life. They suddenly roared their approval.

'*Besame, besame mucho* . . .' Saba sat on her stool loving the clever variations Felipe was playing. She narrowed her eyes, scanning the room. No monsters here, or none visible, just a crush of men, miles away from home, watching her with hopeful, hungry eyes. From here she felt like a large reflecting mirror that could control them and make them feel what she wanted them to feel – already one or two of them had their lips puckered up like children waiting for their night-night kiss.

One man in particular stood out. He was tall and blond with a sensitive suffering face, and she was aware of him watching her closely but discreetly. When she asked Felipe during the break if he was the pilot, Felipe said no. 'That man is called Severin – Severin Mueller. You danced with him at Ozan's party? He works for the embassy in Ankara.

'Jenke won't come tonight,' he added. He smiled suavely, half at the audience, half at her; he fiddled with his guitar. 'In five minutes I'm going to leave you and go upstairs – you stay here and sing.'

She did as she was told, but she was terrified. She sang two Turkish songs, and waggled her hips, aware that the tall blond man was slightly frowning at her as if to say *this is not my kind of music.* When she stopped singing he clapped quietly, and then in a gesture that seemed not to fit his anxious aesthetic face, he touched his lips with his long fingers and blew her a kiss.

They were an instant success – without much competition. The Germans loved them, begged them to come back. They needed, it seemed, some magic added to that anonymous house so far from home. But the two parties they went to there seemed so strange to Saba. Both times there were obscene amounts of food – bratwurst and smoked salmon and cheeses, hams and sausages; and booze too – crates of Bollinger under the kitchen table, schnapps, German beer. Cocaine upstairs. Women – daring secretaries from local embassies, lonely wives, heavily made-up blondes; White

Russians – pale girls with jutting cheekbones for whom the Germans seemed to have a particular weakness.

Her own drug was the joy of singing with Felipe, which made it almost disturbingly easy to forget where she was. As they raced through the woods on the way to the parties, he taught her new songs: songs by Brecht, songs by a Cuban composer, a lovely Spanish song called 'La Rosa y el Viento', the black version of 'The Choo Choo Train' that he'd learned in a club in Harlem. One night, he said: 'If you make a mistake in a song, don't forget every breath is a new beginning and a new chance.'

But the magic wasn't always reliable, and there were times when the room, with its mismatched furniture, flickering lamps and poor acoustics, felt like some hastily assembled approximation of home on a stage somewhere, and the eyes of the girls sitting on the men's knees looked glazed and peculiar, almost as if they distrusted her too, and the whole experience took on a nightmarish quality. Sometimes the men took the girls upstairs to snort cocaine or to make love in makeshift bedrooms where a red scarf was thrown over the bedside lamp to give instant atmosphere. On the nights when there were no girls, the men stood around a beer keg playing drinking games. And it was then that Saba almost pitied them: they looked like large lost children determined to have a midnight feast.

But what was good was that bit by bit, Felipe was managing to put a detailed map together, and the Germans, drugged by their music, seemed to suspect nothing. Gradually Saba began to get to know some of the principal players: Severin, the blond attaché from Ankara, and Finkel the Frog, as she and Felipe called Otto Engel, who stood too close to her, his protruding eyes working their way up and down her as he mentally undressed her.

When the other men flirted with her in a more respectful way, she replied with shrugs and helpless glances towards Felipe, her translator. They asked for requests. They often wanted their pictures taken with her, and she always agreed.

On the night it happened, Felipe parked the car for the first time outside the gates. He turned off the engine. 'Jenke will come here tonight,' he said softly. He pointed towards a gap between two cypress trees, 'There's a broken piece of the fence there, do you see it? That's the quickest way out, if we should ever need it, but it won't happen like that.' He shrugged. 'It never has. I'm telling you just in case.' And she believed him, because she wanted to.

'How do you know?'

'Cleeve. I met him yesterday.'

'Thank God for that.' She was growing impatient with the pilot and the parties. 'What took him so long?'

'I don't know.' Felipe's face was in shadow. 'All I know is they want Jenke urgently back in North Africa. Cleeve said something about enemy airfields.' The war, he said in a quick aside, was at boiling point over there.

She felt herself go cold. She couldn't bear to think of Dom.

'So, tonight. The passport. Let's go through the routine again.'

Felipe turned and picked up a songbook from the back seat of the car. One of the pages was held with a paper clip.

'His name as far as the Germans are concerned is Josef Jenke. He's a medium-sized man, muscular, brown hair. He'll be wearing a red waistcoat. He will request "My Funny Valentine". You will get the nod from me. All the documents he needs are on page fourteen of this book.' He placed it in her hands.

'After you've sung the song, slip the loose page from the book, but leave it on the music stand – he can collect it later when it's safe to do so. Don't hand it to him. Wait. After that, all you have to do is the nice smiley photo with him. He will take care of the rest. All very simple.'

Felipe smiled at her. He looked especially elegant tonight – the thin moustache trimmed, the carefully folded black handkerchief in the pocket of his cream dinner jacket. His skin shiny and freshly shaved.

'You look beautiful tonight.' When the words flew out of her, she was embarrassed.

'You ain't so bad yourself, kid,' he growled in his Satchmo voice. 'Gimme some skin.'

She leaned over and hugged him.

'I've had the best time singing with you,' she said, and his wounded eyes looked back at her.

'Yes,' he said softly and shook his head.

As usual, it was Otto who stepped out of the noisy crowd to greet them. He spoke to Felipe in German which Felipe translated into a mixture of pidgin English and Turkish. When Felipe admired his latest smoking jacket – a gaudy affair in blue silk – he preened for Saba and told Felipe it was one of a set he'd got a tailor at the Grand Bazaar to run up for him. He kissed the back of her hand, leaving a little of the froth from the beer he had been drinking. When he laughed and licked it off it gave her the creeps though she tried not to show it. Tonight, he told them, they were celebrating some good news from Berlin – his brother had had his first child, and everyone was to help themselves to what they wanted to drink – champagne, beer, schnapps, kanyak, he added, pointing towards the Turkish brandy, although he personally – a roar of laughter here – thought it tasted like horse piss.

'He says no offence to you, little lady.' Otto kissed her hand again and waggled his eyebrows. 'He's an idiot,' Felipe added softly, still smiling.

As the evening progressed, the roar of sound from the sitting room rose until it seemed to form a solid wall. At the end of the room, near the big bay window, a group of men stood around a wooden beer keg shouting, '*Stein, Stein, Stein,*' and then gulping down huge glasses of beer. Three young girls, drafted in from God knows where, sat on the sofa looking tense and expectant. Only one of them, with bare goose-pimpled legs and wearing a cheap thin frock, was laughing heartily as if she got the joke.

It was so hot that Saba could feel sweat coiling down her back like a snake. When Severin opened the shutters, a cool breeze flowed through the room. When Felipe started to play, it was Severin who shushed the drinkers and stared at Saba as if he could will her to begin. She'd noticed before he was hungry for music like a drug addict, in the way the others weren't. When she sang, she saw how his tense finely boned face relaxed – how he seemed to visibly exhale as if some secret crisis was over.

Felipe, who'd made it his business to drink with as many of the Germans as he could, had told her that Severin was lonely. He was only twenty-six years old and had a wife in Munich and a child born while he was away. He hadn't seen them for three years. He missed them. Felipe said this with no warmth – *bastard*, he may as well have added, *it serves you right.*

Saba didn't feel like that. In certain lights, Severin's ascetic face looked both innocent and lost and there was a quick, intuitive sympathy in his glance. It was confusing to know that if he hadn't been German she would definitely have talked to him, had fun with him; become, at the very least, friends.

Felipe was adjusting his guitar for the next song when there was a small commotion near the door where more guests had arrived. Otto was clapping them on the shoulder; laughing his braying laugh.

Felipe turned to her and breathed in her hair, 'The pilot is here – the one on the right. Keep singing.

'And for our next song,' he announced in German, 'a very hot Spanish love song.'

The drinking Germans gave a drunken *wooohhhhh*. Those who were dancing put their cheeks next to the Russian girls. Saba picked up the microphone.

She glanced at the pilot; they briefly locked eyes and then he looked away. He had a pleasant, nondescript face: medium height, short military hair, a genial air. He was standing next to Engel, who was already drunk; he was laughing at something Engel said.

He looked so relaxed, so happy to be here that she wondered for an instant whether there were people who got a positive kick out of spying – the way some people loved secrets. She knew now she wasn't one of them.

A Russian girl moved towards him. There were tufts of damp hair under her arms when she lifted them up. She wanted to dance. Saba sensed Felipe frowning beside her. A girl might complicate things.

Saba sang a Turkish song now – one Tan had taught her as a child. Out of the corner of her eye she was aware of Severin watching her impatiently. This kind of folk thing bored him stiff – his requests were always for jazz, or the new blues singers. As soon as she'd finished, he walked up to Felipe and spoke to him in German.

Felipe looked at Saba and smiled. He played the opening bars to Bessie Smith's 'Fine and Mellow' and she sang along, careful as always to add some Turkish-sounding English, which was never difficult – she simply imitated Tan. Felipe's supple guitar riffs were like calm waves breaking.

She glanced across the room again. The pilot had disappeared into the crowd; he was keeping his distance, biding his time.

She wanted Severin to leave now, to join the dancers to keep the coast clear, but he was sitting quietly near them watching her, watching Felipe, waiting for his next fix, and as usual the song seemed to affect him powerfully – she saw his young man's Adam's apple bob at the end of it as he turned away.

Otto appeared, waggling his finger, swaying his stout hips. He'd dropped a glob of sour cream on the lapel of his smoking jacket. He wanted them to play 'Lili Marleen' – a banned song now in Germany because it was so popular with the English, but he loved it and so did the other men.

She sang the words in German as Felipe had taught her and when she got to the bit about Lili's sweet face appearing in dreams, a cluster of men formed around the small stage. Every boy in the world had it seemed fallen for Lili – that husky-voiced tramp waiting under a streetlight outside the barracks. These men who, half an hour ago, had roared like hogs over their drinking games seemed so sad suddenly, as if they'd all been recently jilted.

'*Noch! Noch!*' Otto shouted in a kind of childish ecstasy before the song was even over, his scarlet face running with sweat.

Now the pilot was standing near the window. When she looked at him he shook his head slightly, and then joined in with the singing which had become hearty and jarring, like trays of crockery breaking.

Someone had opened the terrace doors to let the smoke out. Beyond them she saw the shadows of black trees against a dark blue sky. A few stars. The pilot, still singing, started to move towards her. His left hand was in his pocket; he looked comfortable in his skin. He had all the time in the world.

When the song was over, he smiled at Felipe. Did they by any chance know 'My Funny Valentine', an American song? He'd heard it in a nightclub in Berlin before the war.

He hummed the opening bars; Saba took a sip of water, her mouth was dry. Felipe's fingers trembled slightly as they worked their way through a pile of sheet music on the chair beside him.

'Do you know this?' he asked Saba. Two lines of sweat trickled down his face into his thin moustache. He pushed the song book towards her.

'I know it,' she said.

'Let's go,' said Felipe.

He picked up the tortoiseshell plectrum; he stroked his guitar.

The crotchets and quavers on page fourteen jumbled in front of her eyes.

She sang the sad sweet words about the beautiful unphotographable girl. She smiled at Felipe, a radiant smile as she put her hand on the page and worked it free.

The pilot was so relaxed she couldn't be sure he hadn't winked at her.

She watched Felipe's fingers, his eyes. She scanned the room. Severin was dancing with a blonde – she caught his brief agonised look over the girl's shoulder. Engel was telling a story.

When the song ended there was a smattering of applause.

The pilot stepped forward, one hand in his pocket, a cigarette in the other.

'*Nehmen Sie bitte fotographie mit dem Mädchen?*' he said to Felipe. He looked at Saba, and gave a slight bow. Felipe, who was often asked to do this now, took a Box Brownie out of his guitar case. The pilot put his arm around her and struck a swaggering pose. He took the loose page from the stand.

The camera clicked, the bulb flashed. '*Danke*,' said the pilot. He gave a proper wink now and she patted his arm. And watching him make his leisurely way through the partygoers, and leave through the side door with Engel, she felt relief surge through her like new blood. Why had she felt so nervous about this? It had been nothing in the end. The job was done, she could go home, the strangest period of her life was now officially over.

When the pilot disappeared into the fug of the crowd, Felipe turned to her and said softly, 'I need a smoke. You stay here. I'll be back in twenty minutes. I think your boy would like a dance.'

Marlene Dietrich was singing 'Falling in Love Again' on the gramophone when Severin stepped out of the shadows and gave a short bow. '*Möchten Sie Tanzen?*' he said. He clicked his heels, smiled his gentle smile and pulled her out of her chair.

It was too hot, and he was too close; she felt hemmed in by his intense gaze.

When the song ended, she pretended to be overcome by the heat, and excused herself with a fanning gesture. When he frowned, she pointed at her watch and held up five fingers, forcing herself to smile.

She had meant to go outside and sit in the cool for a while, but the door was blocked by shouting men, so she ran quickly up the short flight of uncarpeted wooden stairs to the bathroom on the right of the first landing.

Her face in the mirror looked pinched and tired. It was ten past twelve; she longed for home now, not the hotel room in Istanbul, but somewhere with Dom if he'd have her. She flushed the chain, stepped out on the landing, and looked up. There was a light on in the bedroom, and she saw with relief Felipe's patent-leather shoes gleaming, his trousered legs half visible in the door frame.

'Felipe,' she walked towards him, 'any chance we could leave soon? I'm fagged out.'

The door opened. Inside was a double bed covered with greatcoats. The bedside light, partly concealed by a silk scarf, cast a sludgy red glow over the room. One of Felipe's cigarillos was smouldering in an ashtray.

'Has our friend gone?' she asked softly.

'Yes,' he said. 'You did well.'

'You're a good boy to tidy up here,' she joshed him, he was about to reply when she saw the imperceptible shake of his head.

She saw it too now – a smudged face in the wardrobe mirror behind him. When it came into focus, she saw Severin at the door; he was holding a gun.

'So, you are here,' he said softly. 'My little Valentine. Your English has improved.

'Look at me,' he said to Felipe, who was breathing rapidly. 'Kneel down, and then empty your pockets. Put everything on the bed.'

'Don't hurt her.' Felipe's eyes had shrunk into his head. 'She knows nothing about this.'

'Empty your pockets, please.' Severin's voice was polite, even regretful.

A silk handkerchief was placed on the eiderdown, three tortoiseshell plectrums, a packet of cigarillos, a photograph of a woman holding a child's hand.

'And now the inside pocket. *Danke.* I don't enjoy this, you know,' he said in the same quiet voice. 'My wife is a musician also.'

A piece of paper with a diagram fluttered down; some numbers, figures, what looked like a list of names.

Severin groaned; Saba felt the gun prod her side.

'We're going to have to do something, you know,' he said to Felipe. 'I shall call the others up in a minute. I have no choice.'

'Don't hurt her.'

'I shall do what I have to do.'

The rumbling surge of boots sounded like rock falling off a cliff. She could not bear to look at Felipe, who was shaking and moaning. From downstairs, shouting, and Marlene still singing on the gramophone. For a few seconds the lights in the house were switched off and she heard the high-pitched scream of one of the girls, and then more shouting before several cars drove away in a wash of lights that swept over the room, and illuminated Felipe's mask-like face in the mirror. He must have known he was done for.

When the lights came on, two men were holding him, and there appeared to be an intense debate going on about what to do with Saba. In the end Severin stepped forward; he was calmer than Engel, who was practically gibbering with fear and panic.

Felipe, still immaculate in his dinner jacket, managed to smile at her before a man who she did not recognise came into the room. He put a gun to Felipe's temple and pulled the trigger. There was a look of mild surprise in Felipe's eyes before they went blank, and blood and bits of his brain began to splatter the floor.

She heard herself scream; in the moment of panic that followed, she stumbled into Severin's arms and shouted senselessly at him.

When she pushed him away, he fumbled through the coats and found a silk scarf, which he tied around her mouth, and then the world went black as a blindfold went on and a gun was pressed into her ribs.

The coppery smell of blood, and then the dull thump of boots going into Felipe's sides, and the swish of his coat as they dragged him out of the room. Downstairs she heard shouting, as if a furious argument was going on, what sounded like a tray of glasses breaking, and all the while Marlene, stuck in the groove of a record, singing and singing; obscenely and endlessly singing, as if she was trying to deliberately drive them mad.

She waited for them to come upstairs and get her, but the next thing she heard was the crunch of gravel, and the receding sounds of their footsteps, a car engine starting up with a roar and driving off fast.

She felt Severin's mouth against her ear. A hot jet of air into the darkness.

'You're with me,' he said, 'until they come back.'

Chapter 37

I'm blind, was her first thought when she woke up. There was a mattress under her, but she was hemmed in by total darkness. When she tried to touch herself to see what hurt, the bed she'd been tied to made a hollow rattling sound and she felt a stinging, burning sensation in her ankles and wrists, as if she'd been stung by a giant wasp.

Her numbed brain remembered running feet, doors slamming, the wash of car headlights leaping through the trees. She wiggled her feet as violently as she could without making any sound, but it was no good, they were tied tightly, and more awake now, she could feel her scalp, tight with terror. They'd be back soon; all she could do was lie and wait like a bound animal.

'Where is everyone?' she mumbled into her gag. It was deathly quiet in the rooms underneath with the partygoers gone. Her blindfold – a stocking? – smelled musty and faintly of cheese, and all she could hear was her own jagged breathing and the wind, and what sounded like the faint peepings of a far-off bird. She expected to die; it would now be obvious to all of them that she was Felipe's accomplice, and they would shoot her as they had shot him – the warm, meaty smell of his blood still filled her nostrils, the memory of that look of mild surprise in his eyes before they'd gone blank made her feel sick with disgust and sorrow for him. And if they shot her too, none of the people she had known and loved would have the slightest idea she was here.

If she squeezed her eyes very tight, the darkness whirled and the faint pinpricks of light that appeared made her think of Dom's description of night flying: how you could feel on the rim of the world up there. Dom would think she hadn't cared, or, maybe, gone to meet someone else. *I'm sorry, Dom*, she said to him, *I'm so sorry*.

She slept for maybe an hour or so – time felt slippery in the dark – and waking and feeling tears leaking down the side of her face, she gave herself a fierce talking-to. The blindfold would make her hysterical – it was happening already. Something must be done. She tried, for a while, to turn it into a cinema screen on which she could project any kind of film she liked. She was sitting with Dom having lunch in a restaurant with checked tablecloths overlooking the sea. After lunch, they walked down to a pebbly beach; they sat there talking and eating ice creams. They took a bicycle ride down an avenue of poplar trees leading to a country pub; they walked into her parents' house at Pomeroy Street. Tan was there cooking lunch, she could smell it, roast lamb and rice and spices, every one hugging and kissing her, even her father.

She was playing this game when she heard, from the room below, the high-pitched screech of what sounded like a singing kettle coming to the boil, the scuff of a chair, the faint chink of china being moved. Someone was there – she wasn't alone. She lay listening to her own heart pumping; a few moments later a man's footsteps ascended the stairs slowly step by step, and then the lift and release of the door opening.

'Who is it?' Her voice muffled by the gag.

No sound, just the door closing, and the creak of floorboards, and then the soft exhalation of a cushion as a body sat down on a chair, maybe two feet from the bed, the sound of a deep sigh.

'Please tell me.' She felt someone's breath rustling her face, her blindfold being adjusted by fingers that were neither rough nor gentle, and then the ropes that tied her to the bed being tightened too.

She smelled coffee being poured, then heard the clink of a cup and a gentle, well-bred slurp, a discreet swallow, a man's cough.

Whoever it was began to chew slowly on what smelled like rye bread, and something sharp and sweet like jam. His chewing was not noisy. He swallowed more coffee, and she felt herself intensely stared at. She heard the cup being put carefully back on the tray, and a shuffling towards the door where the tray was set down, and then footsteps coming back towards her. The darkness was shrilling behind her blindfold now; the footsteps were more decisive.

She gasped, feeling his bulk sit down on the bed beside her.

'Who are you?' she mumbled into the gag.

Some hair tickled her ear; the heat of coffee on his lips and its smell.

'Severin.' His voice was low and uncertain. 'Don't be frightened.'

One night when she was young, a family of bats had flown through an open window and into the house. She'd seen a tiny webbed hand around the attic door, and felt the same kind of crawling dread now as his hand stroked her hair.

'I will take this off,' he loosened the gag, 'but not if you scream.'

'I won't . . . but please . . .' she heard his stifled moan as his free hand gently kneaded the crown of her head, his fingers moving in circles, 'please don't, and take this off too.' She twitched her face around the blindfold. 'I can't see.'

Calm down, calm down, else you're a dead duck: an almost jocular voice inside her. His hand moved towards the nape of her neck, probing the muscles there.

'Please, talk to me.' No reply, nothing but a small shivery jet of air coming from his nostrils, as his hand moved down towards her belly. When the hand stopped, it seemed he was weighing up several possibilities at once, like a boy who has captured a bird and who is not sure whether he will hurt it or not.

'Severin,' she said. 'Please don't do this. I don't think you want to.'

He loosened the blindfold, and pushed it back into her hair. In the ruddy glow of the lamp, his chest looked hairless and smooth like a girl's. She heard the soft clink of his belt as it hit the floor. The smell of charred cloth from the scarf draped over the lamp gave her the mad thought that maybe the house would burn down first.

A line of fine blond hair went down from his navel to the top of the trousers he was now unzipping. His neck, too long for a man, gave him a startled giraffe look.

'They've gone now,' he said. 'I will look after you until they come back.' He bent down towards her. His eyes were red-rimmed – had he been crying? – and there was the strangest expression on his face, somewhere between compassion and menace.

'Sorry about all the mess in here and all the noise before,' he said mildly.

To stop herself screaming, she bit the inside of her lip.

His voice was soft. 'He was a good musician, your friend,' he said.

She squeezed her eyes tight shut to block out the sound of

Felipe's dying before they'd dragged him downstairs. The drip and slurp of his head emptying on the floor.

'Why have they left me here?'

'I told you, I will look after you until they come back.' He stopped suddenly and wrinkled his nose, as if smelling the blood for the first time.

He untied her roughly and pulled her to her feet, then snatched the blindfold off. She saw the brass bed, a sagging sofa with a rug over it, all soaked in the rust-coloured glow of the lamp. On the wall, above a chest of drawers, there were a couple of badly framed reproductions. Severin led her over to one in which a man in the foreground stood against a sea of mist with trees poking out of it. 'I like this one,' he said softly. 'I studied art history, you know, before I was in the army. It's called *A Wanderer in a Sea of Fog*, the artist is Friedrich,' he added in a mechanical lecturer's voice.

'A wanderer in a sea of fog.' His voice broke suddenly. 'I feel this at the moment, because I liked your friend, I admired him even, I didn't want it to happen like this.'

He was holding his belt in his hands, lip stuck out, his eyes innocent-looking and sad; for one confused moment she thought he would burst into tears.

When he kissed her, his breath stank of sausage and cigarettes.

'No, no, please, no.'

'This is pretty,' he said woodenly. His hand squeezed her breast. 'Your dress. It's pretty, I like it.' They both stared at the green silk, Felipe's blood splattered on its hem. She began to thrash and push him off.

'Don't, don't.' She crossed her hands over her breasts.

'I won't hurt you,' he said, his Adam's apple leaping in his throat. 'Just take your dress off, please, there is too much blood. Lie face down on the bed, and rest, all I want to do is to look at you.'

The zipper of her dress was on the right side. She pretended to struggle with it, her mind racing furiously.

'So you studied art history?' She forced herself to look directly at him. He was adjusting the silk scarf over the light, all fuss and long white fingers. 'Where, may I ask?'

'In Berlin – my college is a heap of bricks now.' He inhaled noisily. 'Take that off – I know the game you play.' His voice was rough and would take no more nonsense. He jerked the dress over her head. She was wearing silk stockings and a suspender belt.

'Lie down on the bed, take off your underclothes and brassiere.'

Her mind went a complete blank.

'I'm not surprised to hear you were an art student,' she said. She unhooked her suspender belt, still looking at him. 'You have a very sensitive face.' She could hear her heart thumping.

He looked surprised.

'All I want to do is look at you,' he said unsteadily.

'Like a model in a life class,' she said. 'One who would like to stay alive.'

'One who would like to stay alive,' he repeated. She could hear him thinking.

'So, if you are a model, let's say in a sculpture class, I must measure you to get the proportions right.'

She felt something hard go down her spine – a belt buckle? A gun? – and suppressed a scream.

'First, north and south.' The cold scratch of steel moving down her buttocks. 'You have a beautiful back,' he said. 'Then west and east' – his voice slurred and he pronounced it *wessa* and *eassa.* 'Whoops!' He stumbled against her. He was drunker than she'd thought. The smell of vodka combined with sausage as he belched. 'Begging your pardon.'

'Accepted. The others,' she said. 'When will they get back?'

'Not for a long time, shut up your mouth.' His voice was petulant, she had spoiled his game.

There was nothing playful now about his hand shovelling between her legs. She could feel her hysteria rising; soon she would spit or scream or strike him.

'Severin,' she forced her voice low, 'you're too good for this. For your own sake, don't do it.'

He was muttering in German, and then, 'Shut up. You don't know me.'

He turned her over abruptly, put the blindfold on again, and stuffed a pillow under her. 'Keep quiet.'

Her jaw went into a kind of rigor mortis as he climbed on top of her. For a few seconds he flung himself blindly against her, groaning and swearing, but then she felt the flop of him against her stomach like a rag doll.

'You can't do this because you're a good man,' she told him, unclenching her jaw. She felt her head bang against the brass bedstead. 'Your wife is a good person, you're a good person.'

'Don't talk about her!' he shouted. 'Don't say anything.'

His fingers jabbed inside her.

'That is me,' he shouted, 'and that is me, and that is me.'

It hurt, it felt horrible, and when it was over, even though she could feel his full weight on her, his fluid leaking down the back of her legs, she thought quickly: *It hasn't happened, it didn't. He didn't rape me.* Wishing she had her gun on her, so she could hurt him and hammer him, could shoot him dead.

His weight shifted; he grunted, an animal grunt of dismay, exasperation.

'I should have told the others about you,' he said, as if this was her fault and she disgusted him. 'They only know about Felipe. I should have told them.' He stood up abruptly and left the room, slamming the door behind him. She waited, her heart jumping out of her chest, listening for his footsteps on the stairs, but there was only silence. He was standing on the landing, or so she imagined, waiting to pounce again.

A second or so later, the door opened. He came over to the bed and jerked her roughly to her feet.

'Get up, put your clothes on and do your hair.'

Her legs buckled as her feet touched the bare boards. She dressed herself in a daze and patted her hair, bewildered by the sight of her face in the mirror. He led her barefoot around the patch of dark blood where Felipe's head had spilled, down the stairs into the hall near the kitchen.

When she yelled, he prodded her sharply in the back. 'Do that again,' he said in a low voice, 'and I will shoot you.'

In the kitchen, the wreckage of the party lay on a worn Formica table – a plate of half-eaten cheeses swimming in wine; smeared glasses; a pat of butter covered in ash and old cigarettes. He locked the door behind them.

He handed her a tea towel after she had been sick. *Stay calm*, she told herself, *you must stay calm.*

'They've taken your friend away.' Severin's face was pale and twitching. 'They wanted you to go with him, but I said I would question you first.'

His unimpressive performance in the bedroom had clearly rattled him. His gestures were muddled, jerky; he seemed to have trouble looking at her. He threw crockery and food into a half-full sink, shattering several glasses as he did so. He swooped down on her, and pulled her so roughly on to the table that her arms almost jerked out of their sockets. He picked up his gun; it was pointing towards her as he inched backwards groping in the direction of a portable gramophone that sat incongruously on the sideboard surrounded by dirty plates and glasses.

He had several tries at lowering the needle on to a record.

'Don't move, Turkish girl,' he said. 'Stay there and sing your songs.'

When the music came on, she was concentrating so hard that the room seemed to tilt wildly.

She felt filthy and defiled. She hurt. But she wanted to live – it felt like the most important thing on earth. The record was old – for the first few bars it crackled like forest flames. And then she heard the sprightly introduction to 'Mazi', the song with a tango beat that had once made Tan sigh and roll her eyes. *The past is a wound in my heart. My fate is darker than the colour of my hair.* Thank God she knew it.

'Sing it.'

Her mouth felt sore from the gag, but she sang the first verse as clearly and confidently as she could, amazed at the sounds that came out of her – truly, it was like another person singing. When she got to the first chorus, though, her confusion was evident, and she felt giddy with fear – in a couple of bars she'd come to the end of the words she knew.

The swooping violins dissolved into silence. He took the needle off, and looked at her, shaking his head. His skin was so white that she could see the blue bulge of the veins in his temples as he spoke.

'I am a translator, madame,' he said softly. 'My Turkish, I think, is better than yours.'

He poured himself a glass of brandy and drank it quickly. There was a kitchen clock behind his head; it was almost five o'clock. My last day, she thought; they'll know now for sure.

'Why didn't you tell them about me?' she said.

He put a piece of half-eaten salami into his mouth; he chewed it, still looking at her.

'I should have.'

'Felipe's dead,' she said. She still couldn't believe it.

'Yes.'

A stray piece of salami rind hung from his lips; his tongue made a slapping sound as it pulled it back.

'What was your game with him anyway?' he asked almost mildly. 'Were you sleeping together?'

'No – we've only just started to play together.'

'Why did you come out here with him alone?'

'That's what we were told to do.'

She looked at him blearily. It crossed her mind to tell him she'd been booked through Mr Ozan, about ENSA, but they seemed to have reached a point where she could only say simple things.

'What about the others, when will they be back?'

'I don't know.' He was drinking the dregs from several glasses. 'You were not very kind always, you wouldn't sing the songs I wanted,' he complained, pushing a heap of dirty plates aside.

'I'm sorry,' she answered with the wooden politeness of a waitress dealing with a tiresome customer. 'Which did you want? I could sing them now.'

He squeezed his eyes tight shut.

'Yes.' Some of his brandy had dribbled down his chin. 'Something nice for me, for once.'

He was staggering now and when he asked for two German songs, it occurred to her that he had confused her with somebody else. 'This is a lovely song,' she said quickly. She sang 'J'ai Deux Amours' without taking her eyes off him.

'More songs,' he said. He was sounding sleepy.

Behind him the hands of the clock slid to ten past five; it was possible the others would be back soon.

She sang 'The Raggle Taggle Gypsies', the songs coming randomly into her head now with no particular meaning to them. *Tonight she'll sleep on the cold dark earth,* her own voice as thin and scared as a runaway child.

'A draggle toggle is a funny word,' he said, his mouth lopsided. 'What does this mean?'

'I don't know exactly.' Her throat was sore now, she was giddy. 'A collection of things with no meaning.'

'All these songs, what do they mean?' He put his hand against the table to steady himself.

'I don't know. I don't know.' She shook her head.

He asked her then if she knew a song by Purcell called 'Dido's Lament', mumbled something about a sister.

She said she did not know it, so he sang it for her in German first. The melody was hauntingly sad, even though his voice was slurred.

'What do the words mean, Severin?'

She saw his lips quiver.

'In English it goes '*Remember me, remember me, but ah! forget my fate*'. They sang it for my sister.'

'Your sister?' He was shaking.

'She was a musician too, she was on her way to college; one of your bombers got her.'

He started to cry; his blond hair poked through his fingers. He shuddered and groaned, and shook his head vigorously as if in violent dispute with himself. Then he looked up at her, shrugged, and they exchanged the strangest look – somewhere between wild hilarity and sorrow.

'I have a wife also in Germany,' he told her. They were sitting opposite each other now, the wrecked party between them. 'We are childhood sweethearts. I miss her . . . I want to go home.

'It was my wife who sang this at my sister's funeral; she was at college with my sister. She would be horrified . . .' His face convulsed. 'They took me to concerts, they . . .' His eyes looked shrunken and red.

He reached out for his glass again; her hand stopped him.

'Listen,' she said, 'if one of the others had stayed behind, it could have been much, much worse for me. I know that. I'm sure of it.'

He gave her a foggy look.

'I nearly did a bad thing. I was so close.' He held his thumb and index figure together. '*This* close.'

She felt the sting of sick rise in her throat just at the thought of it.

'I wanted to,' he mumbled, his head on the table again.

She touched him on the crown of his hair.

'Listen. Do me one favour – just one! Drive me somewhere, anywhere. I won't say it was you.'

He looked at her for the longest few seconds of her life, and then at the clock with a start.

'Oh my God! My God! *Dummkopf! Dummkopf!*' He banged his hand to his forehead. 'Where are the keys? The keys.' He pulled a drawer out of the kitchen dresser so violently that it fell on the floor. When he found them, he grabbed her hand and flung her out the door.

*

Dawn had come in a wash of dull grey light as they made their way towards the car. He made her sit beside him in the front, and placed his revolver between them, and then he abruptly changed his mind and tied her up again and made her lie in a foetal position in the boot, which stank of petrol. A canvas bag of tools dug into her cheek. He drove off in a skid of tyres, and then it was like being a passenger on the worst fairground ride you could possibly imagine, as he drove on and on, faster and faster down the curving road, the car veering from side to side, the canvas tool bag bumping her face.

She was going to die now, she was sure of it, thinking of his pale sweating face, the brandy he'd sunk in greedy gulps before they'd left.

She tried to think of some prayers from school: 'Oh my God, I am sorry and beg pardon for my sins . . . forgive me, forgive me my trespasses. I'm sorry . . .' And then a cracking, tearing sound like a giant forest fire, a dull thunk as her head hit the spare wheel, a shriek of tyres, and then the car left the road, and tumbled over and over and over again until it stopped.

Chapter 38

It was Barney's father Dom first thought of when he found himself face down in the sand and rigid with shock. So good old Barney's pa was right, he reflected, absent-mindedly picking bits of glass out of his wrist – one more effing overconfident eejit had bitten the dust. He turned over and lay for a while on his back, taking in with an expression of almost dopey wonderment the array of brightly coloured lights jumping behind the shroud of his parachute.

He tried to work out how badly hurt he was this time. He wiggled his feet, he could feel them; he blinked, he could see. He mentally drew a line down his spine, no pain there, and he could feel earth beneath him – good, that was good – but then he smelled the strong stink of burning fuel, the taste of it in his mouth, and pulling back the parachute silk, he saw his aircraft on fire. And apart from one wing that had been flung clear, it was well on its way to a heap of pointless ash. He swore and would have gone on swearing but it hurt his ribcage. Crawling on hands and knees, too weak to disentangle himself from his parachute's run lines, he dragged himself towards the wing and lay down underneath it.

It had happened again, a strange, disconnected, jaunty voice inside him observed – only this time worse: he was in the middle of what looked like endless fucking miles of desert, stretched out dreadfully all around him. He had no map – that had fried in the flames – no cheerful English ambulance staff arriving on the scene, no nurses waiting for him in hospital; he was completely and utterly alone, quite possibly behind enemy lines.

And joy! it had been raining here too, just as it had rained for the last two weeks at the base at LG39, almost without cease. The sand his face was pressed against was a gritty mash, and at this time of year, when night fell, the temperature would dip to near freezing.

The pain, when he tried to sit up, was excruciating. 'Don't! Don't, don't,' he gasped, as if taking instruction from someone else. Maybe a couple of ribs smashed . . . maybe worse. He opened his eyes and lifted his head an inch or two; the desert, sodden and glistening after a recent shower, looked more like the sea. There was no chance, he estimated, that anyone would come and look for him tonight, if ever. Losing planes was a fact of life here, not an emergency; there were too many other things going on. Horrible to die in a place you didn't even know the name of was his last despairing thought before he went to sleep; and without her.

A shower of rain woke him just before dawn. He opened his eyes and looked up in confusion at the parachute silk that had blown over his face like a caul. He tore it off quickly, roaring in pain. He must not do that again. The fingers of his right hand were blistered, but at least he could see now. Above him a few stars pricked through a dense black sky, and around him nothing but sand. There were wild animals in the desert, he knew that, foxes and hyenas, but here nothing but the faint rustling of wind and the sound of his own breath. He was completely and entirely alone.

He observed for a while the shape of his hands. When he lifted them to his nose they smelled of oil. He wished there was something practical he could do with them – open a map efficiently, wrap them around a gun, switch on a torch, something solid that would help get his brain working again.

He'd picked up the enemy plane at a landing ground close to Sidi Abd al-Rahman, about twenty-three miles east of Marsa Matruh – that much he remembered. If his map and compass hadn't become kindling, he could work out exactly where he'd been shot down, but anyway, Marsa Matruh was one hundred and fourteen miles west of Alexandria. The desert between here and Alex was jam-packed with landmines, left from what had been German artillery outposts, and some POW camps. It was also an area the Allies had attacked almost continuously. If the Germans didn't get him, his lot would.

He lay back. Enough . . . enough thinking . . . even this much had brought on a great urge to rest, to fall into a dream-like state where pleasant, nebulous thoughts and images drifted through his brain – thoughts of Saba and songs and Woodlees Farm, a barking dog in a meadow full of buttercups, the river at

Brockweir. And while he slept, it rained, not heavily, and the parachute silk settled like a second skin on his ribs.

When he woke, hot and shivering, several hours later, he lay squinting at a sky whose dull grey made it impossible to work out the time. 'Nothing has changed,' he said out loud, surprised to hear how weak his voice was. A few moments later, he froze. He could hear the distant drone of planes in the sky somewhere far above the blank wall of cloud. They had come for him after all.

Chapter 39

'Saba.' Cleeve was there when she opened her eyes. 'Thank God!' he said. He began to cry.

His face was all nostrils and wide eyes, he was telling her the trees had broken her fall, telling her she was lucky, lucky, lucky, and she mustn't be frightened now. She was safe, and sound. He'd come to pick her up when Felipe was so late.

'Felipe!' She started towards him in panic.

'Later,' he said, 'I'll tell you later – let's get you out of here first.'

Everything was too fast. Having to sit up, having to try and walk up the muddy slope towards the road on legs that felt weak as pipe cleaners. Cleeve rolled up his trousers, his ankles white and skinny; his linen suit got covered in her blood as he pushed her up the hill, bundled her into the back of the car and drove her at top speed back to Istanbul. She sat behind him, forehead on the window, gazing slackly at treetops whizzing by. There was pain in her head and it spread through her body like an oil slick. She slept, and when she woke she was sitting with Cleeve in a bright white room, where an English doctor said she'd been a very lucky girl, and where she was sick. They shone a sharp light in her eye; this won't hurt, the doctor said. He gave her an injection in the arm; she slept.

When she woke in the aircraft, it was like sloshing around in the guts of some large and noisy whale. The pain in her head felt worse. There was someone sitting beside her who had a white skirt on and who smelled of Dettol. When they wiped her head with a cool flannel it was nice.

A clunk, and then a softness as she was lifted into bed. Lovely, lovely sleep at last, and strange flickering underwater journeys inside her head that had music in them. She was not unhappy.

Oh skylark, I don't know if you can find these things
But my heart is riding on your wings
So if you see them—

She was flying on a song when the nurse came.

'Saba.'

'No.'

'Saba, Miss Tarcan. Come on now, *come on*.'

'No, no, no, safe here.' Someone patted her face, but she wanted to stay on the ocean bed swimming in a golden patch of water.

Squeaking sound. Shoes. No, no, no! I don't want to come up. Nice here. Like driftwood, like bones.

Time . . . goes . . . Ouch! Her head hit a big rock and she slept again. A flicker of white light, a spider in front of her, ouch, ouch, ouch, it hurts to open your eyes.

'Saba.' *Go away, go away.* The patting continues. 'Saba, Saba, it's me . . . it's me.'

When she opened her eyes, Arleta was sitting on the bed next to her. Saba was sick all over her and went back to sleep.

Arleta came again the next day. There was a bunch of wilted roses in her hand. She was crying.

'Saba, thank God, thank God. What happened to you?'

Saba touched the swathe of crêpe bandages around her head; her hand felt wooden and separate.

'Someone hit me on the head.'

'Well that's a statement of the bleeding obvious,' Arleta said. They began to giggle weakly.

'Where am I?'

'You're in hospital, darling – the Anglo-American. You've been sleeping like a champion.'

Arleta smelled beautiful; roses and lemons said the bells of St Clement's. She was dressed in a brilliantly blue frock; her hair was so dazzling it hurt to look at it. It was like electric sparks coming out of her. When Saba put her hand out, Arleta's kisses left bright red wings all over it.

'Don't talk. I'm not supposed to be here; they'll kick me out.' Arleta started blowing her nose. 'Oh dear, this is so wonderful. I thought we'd . . . I was so worried . . . Oh I'm such a fool.'

Squeak of shoes on linoleum, a loud voice – o*w!* – said cross things that she was too tired to listen to, and then *visiting hours* in an explosion of sound that made her head shrink. *No, don't go, help me,* but when she woke up she was alone again, and swimming through a long, shadowy stretch of water. Her heart felt waterlogged, her spine, her neck, her head ached in a dull, persistent way and the shadows frightened her. She kept swimming, trying to break through into the sunlit shallows where the bright fishes were, but the shadow got thicker and thicker, it was endless.

In the middle of the night, when most of Cairo was asleep, and everyone seemed to have gone, a moth rattling inside the shade of her bedside light woke her. She sat up, confused by the spartan room with its hard polished surfaces. In the corner of her room there was a child's wooden wheelchair, with a knitted elephant inside it.

She looked around her.

'Where's Dom?' she asked, her heart racing with fear.

She pulled a red cord above her bed.

'Where's Dom?' she said to the nurse when she came in.

'I don't know who you mean, dear, I was *asleep*.' The night nurse gave her a beady look. Her hair was on end, her apron untied. 'It's three o'clock in the flipping morning.'

The nurse, seeing her wild expression, got her a drink of water, and made her take two pink pills that she said would help her sleep. 'You've had a very nasty bang on the head, dear.' The nurse had recovered her professional self. 'You're bound to feel upset.'

She held the pills in her mouth, and spat them out when the nurse was gone. She had to wake up, to pay attention now. Where was Dom? A sudden premonition that she would not see him again made sweat prickle all over her. He'd died without her, or at least the certainty of her. She'd thrown away the most precious gift of her life, and she was dirty now too, thanks to her greedy determination to do and have everything. She understood her father's look of utter revulsion for her. She deserved to die.

Crying made the blood pound in her temples like a sledgehammer; the migraine that followed brought a kind of perverse comfort – she was being punished, and rightly so. Now she remembered that while she was unconscious, a conversation had turned on and off in her head like a faulty light, a question needing an answer. She was lying in water, somewhere beautifully calm and comfortable, waiting for waves to settle over her, but something else – she'd experienced it as a sharp jab, as if she was pond life being stirred by a bullying boy – kept trying to rouse her, to call her back. *I was a fool*, she thought before she went to sleep. *I should have let myself die.*

The next day, Pam – the nice nurse – put her sensible English head round the door.

'A nice fresh eggie for breakfast? We got them from the market yesterday. Eggie and soldiers. You haven't had anything to eat for a long time.'

'How long have I been here?'

'A week – no, hang on.' She consulted a chart at the end of the bed. 'Goodness! Ten days already – you *have* been poorly.'

Pam put a cool hand on Saba's head. 'I'll take your temperature later.' She straightened the sheet with a snap. 'And I'll do you a blanket bath, love. You've got a visitor today.' She plumped one of the pillows which had fallen on the floor.

'Dom?' she said softly, but the nurse didn't hear. Felipe, she'd remembered, was dead. Cleeve had told her that, and she couldn't stop thinking about the gurgling sounds he'd made just after they'd shot him, the sound of water stuck in a drain, his eyes so gentle, so surprised. She remembered the tall German, the clunk of his belt, his breath smelling of sausages, his fingers. She'd sung for him like a wind-up doll, let him hug her. How could she? *How could she?* It made her want to vomit just to think of him.

'Yes, your ENSA friend has come every single day since you were admitted.' Pam removed the dead moth from inside the lampshade. 'Isn't she gorgeous! Not like you, disgusting thing.' She dropped the moth in the waste-paper basket. 'And so nice with it – she gave us all your choccies and flowers and she was so upset about you. The acrobats came too, and Captain Furness. It was quite good fun really, although you weren't the best company, if I may say so.'

'Arleta,' she said weakly. 'When can I see her?'

'You've seen her! Silly billy. You spoke to her yesterday and the day before that.'

'How long have I been here?'

'Ten days, you've just asked me that. Oh, we are a dozy girl today.'

When Pam closed the doors on the shiny world outside, Saba slept again. She and Mum were at home, it was summer and her legs were bare; a warm breeze came through the kitchen window. Tan was cooking up something spicy in the kitchen, and they were laughing because Mum was playing the chicken song on the piano, and Baba was there too, warbling the chorus, vibrating his throat with his fingers: '*keep that chickie a peck peck innnnnnnnchick chock chicken I do*'. And his laugh was so deep and happy, and she was happy too. '*Akşam yemeğiniz hazir*,' Tan called from the kitchen. 'Get it while it's hot.'

When she woke up, Arleta was sitting at the end of her bed, not blurred around the edges, but real time and in focus. She'd brought a tiny paper fan, and a packet of humbugs from the NAAFI.

'Hooray.' She put her hands gently around Saba's face. 'You're back. You've had a rotten time.' When they embraced, Saba could hear the grinding sound inside Arleta's jaw as she fought to control herself.

When Arleta released her, Saba said: 'Dom. Have you seen him?'

Arleta glanced at her, and then towards the window.

'No,' she said, 'I don't really know him.' She sounded genuinely surprised.

Saba watched her with fierce concentration. Arleta was never a very good actress, but she seemed to be telling the truth.

'Do you want me to try and find him?'

'Yes.' Saba grabbed Arleta's hand so hard the whites of her knuckles showed. 'Flight Lieutenant Dominic Benson, Desert Air Force. Wadi Natrun is where the transit camp is . . . he might be anywhere.'

It felt like bad luck to even say his name.

'Sweetheart, darling, please, please, please don't cry. I promise I'll look for him tomorrow. It'll be all right.'

But it wouldn't be all right. That was what Saba felt now: that there were no more safety nets, just as there hadn't been for Felipe and his wife and daughter, for Bog and his family and for all the other hundreds and thousands of people whose luck had run out. Why had she thought special old her would be exempt from punishment?

'What's happened to you, my darling?' Arleta dipped a hanky in the glass of water. She wiped Saba's face, which was flushed and feverish again. 'Try and tell me.'

She pulled her chair closer to the bed.

Saba told her as much of it as she could bear – about Turkey, and the parties, and Felipe, then she remembered and clapped her hand over her mouth.

'Oh bugger. I'm not supposed to say any of this. It's a secret.'

'Don't worry, my pet.' Arleta calmly patted her hand. 'My lips are sealed, and you've got concussion, and I've done a little bit in that line myself, though nothing as dramatic, and the main thing is you're safe. But tell me – this German chap you sang for, it must have been *terrifying*.'

'It was.' Oh, the relief of holding Arleta's hand and talking: like pricking a boil and seeing poison spurt out.

'His name was Severin. He made me stand on a table and sing for him – it was the most bloody awful feeling, like being a chimpanzee in nappies.'

Arleta started to splutter. 'Oh you are a one, you still make me laugh. Not the having to sing, but the chimpanzee bit.' She wanted this to be a funny story.

'He loved music,' Saba continued. 'Can I have some water, please?'

'Love, you're trembling.' Arleta tightened her grip.

Saba's voice had become wooden. 'He loved the music, that's what he said. He blamed me.'

'Saba, I've lost you – blamed you for what?'

'For making him do things.'

Stale stockings came back to her, unwashed silk stockings tied tightly around her mouth; the smell of vodka and sausages too.

'Oh my God, my God!' Arleta was appalled. 'What happened?'

'I had to stand on the table and sing for him. It was so creepy.' Saba couldn't bear to tell her the whole story – not yet. Maybe never.

'Just that?'

'He started to cry and tell me how much he loved his wife.'

Arleta's eyes were wide open. 'Talk about being saved in the nick of.'

'And then he sang a song to me in English – it's called "Dido's Lament".'

'Never heard of it – sounds a hoot.'

'He drove off the road and into a tree . . . they found me by the side of the road . . . I don't remember . . . I think he's dead . . . I don't know for sure.'

After a pause she continued.

'I've gone mad, Arleta. There was this lovely Turkish family Felipe and I saw on the way to the party. I keep having this dream of driving into their house and killing them, but we didn't, did we? Did anyone say anything about that?'

'No, love, no, that's not likely.' Arleta put her arms around her and held her tight. 'It's normal to have these peculiar thoughts when you've had a shock, but they're not real.'

'I thought Severin was better than the others because he liked music so much. Can you think of anything more stupid? I hate the fact that I sang for him. It makes me feel so cheap,' she added with a soft wail.

'Now that is a pile of steaming whatnot,' Arleta said severely. 'You were singing for your sodding life.'

'If Dom was dead, you would tell me, wouldn't you?' Saba clutched her arm. 'I've got the most awful feeling. Have the nurses told you?'

'No, love.' Arleta had tears in her eyes. 'Not a thing. But listen,' she said quickly. Matron had just opened the door; she was tapping her watch significantly. 'I'm going to make you a promise. Tomorrow I shall go out. I will scour Cairo for this young man of yours – if he's in town, I'll find him and bring him here.' Her confidence was frightening, wonderful. 'Is that a deal?'

'It's a deal.' They hugged each other hard.

Chapter 40

Barney was sitting in a dark corner of the Windsor Club in Soliman Pasha Street when Arleta entered the men-only bar like a force-ten gale. She click-clacked towards him in a tight green dress, fair hair swinging. 'Ha,' she'd spotted his uniform, 'the very man I wanted to see.'

The air filled with her rich perfume as she sat down. She crossed her stockinged legs with a swish, and placed them at a fetching angle.

'I've just seen your friends at Shepheard's,' she said. 'They said you'd be here.'

'Why are you looking for me?' Barney was unshaven. There were two smeared glasses on the table beside him.

'A friend of mine is looking for Dominic Benson.'

'Wass name?'

'Saba Tarcan,' Arleta was beaming, 'and I have some wonderful news – she's alive. She's convalescing in the Anglo-American.'

Barney looked up from his drink mumbling a string of words, two of which he'd never said in front of a woman before.

Arleta leapt up, eyes blazing. 'I beg your pardon.'

'A see you on Tuesday, I said – wass matter with that?'

'Don't you dare say that to me. I'll smack your silly head in.'

'Sorry,' he reached for a packet of Camels, 'but I'm not a great fan of your friend.' He shook his head and turned away.

'Dom's gone,' he said after a while. 'He's missing, presumed dead.'

'Oh for Christ's sake.' Arleta sat down beside him. 'Not another.' She took several deep breaths. 'What happened?'

'I don't know . . . Look . . . I'm sorry, but I can't . . .'

He couldn't speak: first Jacko, now Dom. The blackest ten days of his life so far.

'What happened?'

'Not sure . . .' he said at last. 'He went off to collect a plane . . . too tired . . . exhausted . . . they'll probably give him a posthumous DFC . . . so, bully for him.' He toasted Dom bleakly with an empty glass.

'Barney, you're plastered,' said Arleta. 'I'm going to get you some coffee, and then we're going to talk, and then I want you to go to bed.'

He was in no fit state to leer. It made him look sweet and a bit dopey.

'Sit there like a good boy,' said Arleta. 'I'll be back.'

She returned with two cups and a plate of sandwiches.

'Come on, eat up,' she said, 'and have a big cup of coffee. Don't spill it now. Sit up, pay attention. There.'

He drank half a cup, and when he slopped some on his saucer, he gave her a guilty look.

'I shouldn't have sworn at you,' he said. 'It's such a mess, though.'

Arleta squeezed his hand. 'Don't worry, don't worry,' she murmured. 'It's a horrible mess, and he was your friend, and that poor girl . . .' With a thunk, his head collapsed on the table and she stroked his hair.

'Poor girl.' His head jerked up sharply. 'No, I don't hate many people, but I hate her. She ditched him cold in Alexandria. He was so torn up.'

'Now stop that right now.' Arleta put her hand over his mouth. 'Finish your coffee, I'll pay the bill.' Her face had paled. 'We could go to the Gezirah Club and walk in the gardens. You need to keep moving.'

In the park, when he broke down, she lent him a perfumed silk hanky to dry his eyes.

'I haven't talked about him . . . not yet,' he said with a whoop of sorrow. 'You see, I've known him for such a long time and I liked him so much, he was . . . we were at school together, he was one of my best friends . . . we . . . and so many good people gone now, you know, people who would have been doctors, and lawyers, teachers, had children. Oh for God's sake . . . sorry about this.'

He straightened his back, widened his eyes, gave a gasping sigh – determined not to let the side down. It was one of the saddest things she'd ever seen.

'You don't have to stop,' she murmured. 'You must miss him like mad.'

'I do,' he gave a strange groaning laugh, 'I do . . . it's as if there's a huge gap in the squadron now. He was such good fun – the men and the officers liked him too. I'm sorry, I'm talking too much.'

'Barney, for God's sake come here.' She pressed his head against her bosom. 'Come here,' she murmured, 'and don't be an idiot. Of course you want to talk about it. I would too if I were you. I have to ask you one thing myself. What did he say about Saba? She was mad about him, by the way.'

'I didn't actually speak to him about it.' His look was furtive and far away. 'Oh damn it, what does it matter now anyway. I read his diary. They gave me his things.'

'Tell me more.' She gave him an encouraging squeeze. 'I would have done the same thing by the way.'

A green and red parrot flew down from a tamarind tree. It landed on the grass beside them and screeched.

'Hope he didn't see that.' Barney disengaged himself from her arms; his dopey spaniel look had returned. 'That bird, I mean.'

'Oh stop that.' Arleta fluffed her hair out. 'Sit down for a moment.' She pointed to a bench under the tree.

'I've met Dom,' she said. 'He came to a show we were doing, a show near Fayid. He'd come to see Saba. He was very determined – and very attractive too, I thought.'

'I wouldn't know about that,' Barney almost smiled, 'but girls certainly thought so – it was his bad luck to bump into your friend.'

'Shut up! Right now.' Arleta's eyes had narrowed into mean green slits. 'I'll tell you about it later.'

'A fat lot of good it will do him now.'

'Tell me about Dom.' She looked him in the eye. 'Have you known him for long?'

'Since prep school,' Barney cleared his throat, 'and then at Cambridge we joined the squadron together. It was fun; Dom was a brilliant pilot – my father, who was an amateur jockey, says it has to do with the same things: nerve, and feel; quick reactions. Dom adored it, it was like a drug, for me too. He talked us all into joining up – when things went badly wrong, it cut him up terribly.'

He gave her a wild look. 'I still can't believe it.'

'Do you know what happened? Only say if you want to.' She stroked his thumb.

'I don't know anything. He went to pick up a Spitfire, he didn't come back. That's all I know. I was in Cairo that day. When I got back I saw them rubbing his name off the blackboard, I was furious. It was too early. I've seen men strolling back into camp ages after you've written them off – bad things don't always happen. But that was two weeks ago, and I'm trying to . . . just . . . I don't know what.' Barney ran out of words.

They stood up and walked again, down an avenue of large date palms that flung spiky shadows on the path. An English nanny, nasal, bored, called to two small children – 'Rose, Nigel, play nicely else we'll go straight home – I shan't tell you again.'

Arleta stopped. She looked at her watch and groaned.

'Blast.' She put a hand on his arm. 'Oh, sugar. Barney, I've got to go – we have a performance at eight – an outdoor number for the troops in the Ezbekiya Garden. Come if you like – we could have some supper afterwards. I want to hear as much as I can before I see her tomorrow morning.'

He looked momentarily stunned, like a man whose electricity supply had been abruptly cut off.

'Priorities straight – get the hair done.' His attempt at a joke was not a success.

'Well yes, I do need to do all that, as it happens.' She gave him a level look. 'I don't suppose you'd fly without a helmet on.'

'Tough lady.'

'Nope,' she smiled at him, 'not really. Just a person doing a job, and if you want my advice, you'll go back to the club, have a zizz and a shave and meet me later at Londees – you've had a tough day.'

'Right ho, nanny.'

When she said she would probably be late, he said that would be fine, he would wait for her.

Later that night, as Arleta scissored her way across the terrace at Londees, every man in the room turned to look at her, except Barney, who was reading intently from the menu, embarrassed, it seemed, to have been caught out earlier in his emotional underwear.

'Supper's on me, darling,' she said as she sat down, 'because I asked you, and because I got paid today.' She ordered lavishly and ate heartily – fried fish, fresh vegetables, a bottle of wine – and while Barney picked at his food, she talked brightly about the director of their show, a man called Bagley, who was back in town again and a bit of a bully. How he expected West End magic with two acrobats – one had done his tendon in – no comedian, no Saba, and three new recruits, shattered after a tour in India, was beyond imagining. When Bagley had called them all into the dressing room afterwards and given them a real rollicking, she'd wanted to bite his eye.

'I'm sorry,' Barney said politely, 'bite his eye – that sounds a bit extreme.'

'Sorry, love,' she said, 'an old Cockney form of endearment.' He laughed for the first time since Dom had died.

Over coffee and liqueurs on a candlelit terrace overlooking the Nile, the mood softened and grew more intimate. 'I'm so sorry I swore at you earlier,' Barney said again. 'I've never done that before . . . and it was horribly rude . . . It's no excuse, but I'd just finished writing to Dom's mother. I used to spend summer holidays with them.'

'You've said sorry already.' She touched his hand gently. 'You can stop now. What on earth did you say?'

'Well, I know them pretty well, so the usual guff,' Barney's voice wobbled, 'about how proud she should be, and how ghastly this bloody mess was, but what a good time he'd had out here until . . . well . . . It's true, you know . . . he said they'd been the best days of his life.'

Rain had begun to fall on the Nile, dimpling the surface of the water, blurring and fading the coloured lights on the pleasure boats. On the far shore, a peasant family lay like sardines under a tarpaulin.

'What's she like?' he said suddenly. 'I mean really like. I'm not trying to be rude, but it's awfully hard to tell with people like you.'

'What do you mean?' Arleta was laughing.

'Well, don't take this wrongly, but it's part of your job to get people to fall for you. You're the dream girls, but not really real, sort of like those pictures of country cottages with hollyhocks round the door and stuff that people buy to put on the walls of their flats when they live in London.'

Arleta was silent, just looking at him, and then she shook her head. 'You are such a twerp, Barney,' she said at last. 'Saba's lovely

– she's my friend. And she's exciting because she's good at something – *really* good.'

'Well . . .' His mouth turned down, he was not convinced.

'And it's not as much fun as you might think, the dream girl thing – men can feel very let down when they see how ordinary you are without your war paint on.'

Barney grunted.

'Mind you, it took me a while to forgive her for being so good.' Arleta stirred her coffee. 'Not that she would have known.'

'Really?'

'If I'm honest, I was jealous of her when we first met. Well, you know, or you probably don't, but when you're a dancer or a singer, people tell you all the time that talent is seventy per cent hard work, thirty per cent talent, all that stuff, and it's true, up to a point, until it's so obviously a lot of old cobblers. Because here was this girl, this *thing*, this funny little thing from *Wales* – awful clothes, no real experience, certainly no West End experience, but with this terrific voice. Well, more than the voice, a real sparkle about her – what's that word? Caramba? Charmisma? Anyway, the *it* thing. Everybody recognises it when they see it, and of course, she was younger than me. I'm thirty-two, you know – one foot in the grave in showbiz terms.'

'Conceited too, I expect.' Barney gave another deep sigh and put his elbows on the table.

'No,' Arleta took a swig of wine, 'not particularly – no more than most of us – anyway, I got over it. She's a good one, and we've had so many laughs on tour and I hate feeling jealous, it's not me at all – I don't know why men always think women are such bitches to each other, it's mostly not true you know – it's the girls who support you.'

'What a saint. Strange she jilted my friend without so much as a by your leave.'

'Now listen.' Arleta gave him her tigress look. 'And shut up. I've had enough of that, so stop it.' There was a long pause.

'Barney,' Arleta lit a cigarette, 'can you keep a secret? I'm serious now.'

'Yes.'

So she told him, in a low voice, as much as she could safely say about Saba's sudden departure from Alexandria and the Turkish assignment.

'She was warned not to tell your friend Dom. She was protecting him.'

'Protecting him?' Barney was looking at her aslant, as if he didn't believe a word of this.

'Look, I honestly don't give a big rat's arse whether you believe me or not.' Arleta's eyes were flashing. 'It just happens to be true.'

He stared at her, horrified, fascinated. He had no idea how to handle a woman like this.

'Don't bite my eye,' he said softly. 'This is quite unexpected, that's all. Now please don't take this wrongly again, but it's just I never think of women doing work . . . I mean like this . . . so . . . Oh Lord . . . give me a second . . . let me think about this.' Barney sat with his head in his hands. He shook it several times. 'It's possible I've been an idiot,' he said at last. 'And if I have, I'm sorry. I don't think I've ever hated anyone as much, I may have got it wrong. How did you find out?'

'I don't think she would have 'fessed up at all except she was badly concussed,' said Arleta, 'and she's still in quite a state and covered in bruises; she thinks it was a car crash, but there's more to it than that, I think. And the one thing she goes on and on about is seeing Dom.'

Arleta's eyes filled with tears.

'Oh God, I'm going to have to tell her tomorrow, aren't I? That'll be fun.'

Chapter 41

The new nurse said her name was Enid; she whipped back the curtains on grey sky, grey rooftops, a glum-looking pigeon sitting on a chimneypot. Rain was good, said Enid: those gyppo farmers, poor blighters, were absolutely desperate for it after the summer droughts. She left a cup of tepid tea on Saba's bedside table and said she would be back shortly.

'Personally speaking . . .' Enid returned with a carafe of cloudy red water in her hand; she couldn't wait to go back home now. Sick of the flies, sick of the heat in summer, murder it had been, this one; sick of not enough leave and now sick of the rain. You never expected to be cold in Egypt, did you, but it was horrible out and the houses never seemed to have enough heating, they weren't set up for cold, were they?

Enid snapped the coverlet taut and twinkled at her. 'But you're going to have a nice day anyway – your friend Arleta is coming to see you with a young man.'

Saba stopped breathing for a moment. 'Who?'

'Heavens. Hang on.' The nurse put her finger under the rim of her starched hat and scratched.

'Let me think . . . a Pilot Officer somebody or other . . . I'm not sure but I think his name was Barney.'

Fear shot through her veins like electricity. Dom's friend. He was coming to tell her something, and it would not be good.

'Thank you, Nurse,' she said politely.

When Enid closed the frosted-glass door behind her, Saba lay perfectly still with her eyes closed. She'd lost him.

The door opened again. 'Brekkie!' Enid walking towards her with her nursey smile on.

'I'm not hungry,' Saba said. 'You have it.' She had seen Enid wolfing down leftovers in the ward late at night.

'Oh don't be so silly.' The nurse put the tray down. 'I won't eat it. And you'll never get better if you eat like a bird.'

Saba smiled blankly, not hearing a word. When the door closed again, she got up and hobbled to a basin in the corner of the room and stared at her reflection in the mirror. There was a large crêpe bandage around her head; both her eyes were still swollen like bad plums, with yellow and purple bruises extending from the lower lids to halfway down her cheekbones. On her way back to bed, the room swung so violently that she had to cling on to the child's wicker wheelchair in the corner of the ward. When its wheels slid across the floor she nearly fell.

Back in bed again, she looked at the clock on the wall. Nine o'clock. Usual visiting hours were between eleven and twelve. Soon the frosted-glass door that stood between the ward and everything else would open.

She wished her mother was here – someone to wait with, someone who knew her well enough not to talk. She'd thought a lot about her recently, what it must have felt like with a husband at sea for most of her married life, the terror of waiting, the memory of her mother's face frozen in concentration listening to the shipping forecast on the wireless every night, and then – *click!* – forecast over, jolly or angry depending on the mood, Mum again: shouting, cracking jokes, cooking, finding socks, always knowing she was one knock on the door away from disaster. Her cheerfulness felt heroic to Saba now; one more thing taken for granted.

Shortly before lunch, she heard the clickety-clack of high-heeled shoes coming down the corridor – quite different from the cautious squeak of the nurses' crêpe soles. The shoes stopped outside her door.

'Darling?' Arleta's voice muffled through the frosted glass. 'Are you decent?'

The handle half turned. When the door opened, Saba sat up in bed white-faced.

'Yes. Say it quickly,' she said when she saw Arleta's face. 'I know what you're going to say.' The dark silhouette of a man outside the glass door.

'I'm sorry,' said Arleta. She kicked off her heels, got on to the bed and they held each other tight.

'Oh love,' she said softly. 'This is brutal.'

A flash of pain went like forked lightning through her head when Arleta said it. She sobbed without sound for a while. He'd gone; she knew it. Enid, hovering sympathetically, handed her a sick bowl in case she needed it, a warm flannel and one of her own mints to suck.

A uniformed man walked in – a big red-faced blank to Saba, a noise, standing over the bed.

'Do you want me to leave?' he said immediately. 'I could come back later.'

She nodded her head. She wanted to hide like a sick animal and howl. The roar of sound in her head was almost unbearable. The nurse said she could have a pill soon, a phenobarbital, if she wanted to sleep.

'It's nothing personal.' Her words bounced off the walls. 'Thank you for coming.'

The man twisted his hat in his hands. He touched her arm.

'I'm sorry,' he said before he left. He put a package on her bedside table and said something about Dom's locker, but she wasn't listening properly.

When Arleta left, a new nurse came in. She said how chilly it was getting now that the nights were drawing in; she left two painkillers for Saba's head, which was full of forked lightning again. 'Night-night, then, love.' The nurse drew the curtains; she switched off the overhead lights and closed the frosted door.

She'd been longing for everyone to leave, but now that she was alone, the night seemed to stretch out all around her like a dark sea in which she might easily drown.

She woke after midnight, parched from crying, and reached for the water carafe. When she turned on the light, her hand touched the parcel the tall man had left for her. She sat up in bed and opened it clumsily. Inside the wrappings there was a box filled with tissue paper, and in it a blue enamel bracelet with the outlines of Egyptian gods and goddesses carved in silver. She turned it in her hand and saw engraved on its back *Ozkorini.*

Think of me.

It was beautiful. It must have cost him every last penny of his pay packet. Tucked inside the box was a card engraved with the address of a jeweller in Alexandria.

She was throwing away the wrapping paper when she found the remains of a letter written on a torn and crumpled bit of paper.

Adjusting the lamp, she saw that it wasn't a proper letter, more like a draft with words crossed out, in two spots so violently that the pen had pierced the paper. A letter written in high emotion, something he'd never meant to send.

The words floated senselessly in front of her eyes like cinders. She smoothed the paper out, pieced the torn bits together and still couldn't take them in, until one sentence leapt out: *Maybe in the end, life is shoddier than songs.*

Her hands trembled as she pieced together the two bits of paper with numbers on them: August 2nd. 1942.

She moaned softly. So, no escape from it now – he'd bought the bracelet, his first proper present for her, full of hope and excitement; and died bewildered and disappointed, maybe even hating her. She would not forgive herself for this.

Chapter 42

After she left hospital, Saba moved in with Arleta, who had found a sublet on Antikhana Street. The flat with its pentagon-shaped rooms and round windows gave the charming illusion of living on the top deck of an ocean liner, and it was cheap too.

Arleta insisted on paying Saba's half-share of the rent, and even cooked for her from her eccentric and limited repertoire: Mess number one was rice, beans and meat, boiled on a small gas ring in the kitchen. Mess number two was rice, beans, fish and whatever fresh vegetables were available. Sometimes there was a salad with a dash of gin added to the dressing. And Arleta was a firm believer in daily treats too – a bringer of buns and cream cakes from Groppi's, the buyer of a lurid lime-green nightie with tassels on it from the souk with a twist of pistachio halva tucked inside it.

But best of all, Arleta was furiously busy for most of the day, with rehearsals, hair appointments, dates, parties (Cairo was crammed that month with young officers back from the desert with plenty of pay to spend), and for Saba it was easier to be alone when she felt such wretched company. There were whole days now when she felt so awful she could hardly be bothered to get out of her nightdress, when grief felt like a kind of flu of the soul which made quite ordinary activities such as eating and walking insurmountable. At other times, her feelings were so extreme it was as if someone had poured petrol on her and set her alight.

Grief had also rendered her dithery and weak and incapable of making a decision: sometimes the thought of leaving Cairo without knowing what had happened to Dom felt like an appalling act of betrayal; at other times, it felt pointless to stay and she longed for home.

On the day before she left hospital she'd been struck by another blow. Enid had waddled in with her nice nursey smile on, and placed an airmail letter on her bed saying that this would cheer her up anyway, which was unintentionally comical in its way. It was from her father, who knew nothing of her accident. He wrote:

Dear Saba,

It is with great pain and after much suffering that I send this to you, but your mother tells me that I cannot carry on not *answering your letters. You have caused a great rift in our family and brought shame to all of us by disrespecting my wishes and going away. It is an insult to my honour, and one I cannot find it in my heart to forgive you for. Now it would be better, for your mother and me if you stay with your choice and don't come home. You have made your decision, and I have made mine. You are no longer a daughter to me. I am at sea at the moment, moving between . . . and . . . so I have not told your mother yet, but I will inform her of my decision when I get home. It would be better for us all if you did not see your mother and grandmother either.*

I am sorry it is like this.

Followed by his careful signature: *Remzi Tarcan.*

Her first reaction after reading this was one of boiling rage. *Hypocrite, liar, jailer. Why could you choose a travelling life and not me?* She'd been part of the war effort too. She knew now what a difference they had made to the men's morale: this was not flannel, it was true, and how dare he make it sound so trivial, so wrong. When the anger wore off, she wanted to bury her head in her mother's lap and say, 'Forgive me.' Her mother, she knew, would be in turmoil about this: longing to write, not daring to, in case it got her into a fight with her husband, who was perfectly capable of using his fists on her when he was roused.

And so it was that all the happiness about singing, and Dom, and travelling, and even the thought of home and Pomeroy Street, the simple marvel of being alive, now felt not wrong exactly, but like a form of extreme naivety that deserved punishment. How could she not have seen the world's traps; nor felt the cruelty and randomness of war; nor seen that people were almost never who you thought they were? The hard truth was she'd broken up her family by coming here.

During the long days of convalescence in the flat, lonely and cut adrift from work, she began to hate the talents that had led her here. She'd gone around in this stupid bubble of self-regard and now the bubble had burst and she deserved everything she'd got.

After a few days' rest, she went to see Furness at the ENSA office at the Kasr-el-Nil to ask about a flight home to England. She'd more or less decided, when the war was over, to go back to Wales and get a sensible job, in an office, or perhaps as a nanny to some family. There was a peculiar atmosphere about this meeting – Furness had given her a sort of deaf smile before he'd said he was sorry to hear she'd been unwell. He'd fiddled irritably during their interview with the files on his desk as if he couldn't wait for her to leave. He'd do what he could, he said at last, with a shuddering sigh, but there were now vast numbers of ENSA entertainers stuck here with no exit visas, plus the flipping king was coming out for a royal visit soon – so anything else she'd like him to do for her?

And then Cleeve turned up. Cleeve who was usually so careful about meeting in anonymous places. Their first meeting since he'd lifted her out of the smashed car beside the road to Istanbul.

He strolled into her apartment, a civilised man again in his nice-looking raincoat and trilby. She was trying to light a fire with green wood, and the apartment was choking with smoke.

'Good God, Saba,' he said, batting the fumes away with his hand. 'What on earth are you trying to do – commit suttee?'

'What are you talking about?' She stared at him; she'd forgotten to lock the door and was thrown to see him in the middle of her sitting room.

'You know, those Hindu widows who throw themselves on the burning pyre.'

He'd looked mortified.

'Oh God, how tactless! I came to say I was sorry to hear about your chap. Not a good start. Sorry.'

'How did you hear?' She was staring at him.

'Well, you know – all part of the job? Look, can we go out for a cup of tea or something? I shouldn't really be here.'

In the coffee shop he changed places twice and fiddled with his spoon. 'Saba,' he said, 'I'm sorry it's taken me so long to come and see you – I was desperately upset about what happened in Turkey, but it wasn't safe for me to hang around.'

She saw a new look in his eye, a crumpled look of hurt and what may or may not have been intense concern; who knew who to trust now? He cleared his throat.

'Where did you find me?' she said. 'In Turkey, I mean.'

'Under a tree, in a ditch. The car was burning beside you, you were jolly lucky.'

He held his top teeth over his lower lip, which had begun to tremble. She looked away.

'It was horrid, Saba. I feel guilty about what happened. Ten minutes later and I don't like to think.'

'Well don't.' She couldn't stand the thought of him being emotional, or talking about Felipe – not yet.

'What happened to Jenke?' she asked him. 'I'd at least like to know that. He had the documents. Did he get away?'

'Yes.'

She waited for more.

'Is that it? Just yes, nothing else?' She could hear her voice rising.

'No.'

'Was it useful – his information?'

'I think so.'

Cleeve lit a cigarette and gave a little gasp.

'I think it was all right,' he said faintly. He leaned over and took her hand and looked her in the eye in a way she found unnerving.

'Saba,' he said, 'are you really all right? I've been so very worried about you.'

She felt his fingers close around her hand and hoped he would take them away soon.

'I'm not sure we should have sent you there.'

'It wasn't your fault,' she said. 'It was mine. I wanted to travel, I loved the singing – everybody has their Achilles heel, I found mine.'

'You still have bruises.' When he pointed in a hangdog way towards her forehead, she clenched her fists under the table – his sympathy was almost unbearable.

'Listen,' she said. 'I want to go home, you can help me with that. When I asked Captain Furness last week, he would hardly talk to me. He also didn't ask a thing about the accident, he couldn't wait to get rid of me.' Her voice throbbed with rage. 'Doesn't that strike you as odd that I—'

'No, it doesn't, Saba,' he interrupted her, 'because this could ruin his career: the ENSA set-up is incredibly fragile: the brass hats resent the fact that they take up time and trucks and things, they think of performers as badly behaved children, so when things go belly-up, both sides rush to bury it.'

'Dermot,' she'd been steeling herself for this ever since they'd sat down, 'there's one thing I really do need to ask you. My friend . . . the pilot . . . he's missing presumed dead. Is there any chance . . .'

'No.' Cleeve pulled away from her. 'None whatsoever . . . sorry, but absolutely none.' His eyes were focused on a tatty poster hanging on the wall above her head, it showed a woman floating down the Nile and drinking Ovaltine. 'Don't you think it's always better to tell the truth?'

'Surely someone can help me look – Jenke or someone?'

'No. Sorry, Saba . . . let's be clear right away. This work doesn't come with a quid pro quo. I shouldn't be here now.' He fiddled with his raincoat belt.

'Well, give Jenke my regards when you see him,' she said, standing up.

'I don't think I will see him again,' he said softly. 'That's how it is here – ships passing in the night, although sometimes the consonant could easily be changed.'

The following day, Max Bagley dropped by, so happy to be back in Cairo, he said, he could have cried. He'd been in the punishment zone, Ismailia, this summer directing a company that made their lot look like models of sanity. Half the dancers had gone down with foot rot because it was so hot; one of the comedians had turned out to have epilepsy.

He took her to Groppi's, ordered macaroons and ice cream, and after some small talk, and a sprinkling of compliments, he looked at her with his bright, calculating eyes.

'The shows I mentioned. We've got some absolute corkers coming up. No chance of you coming back, I suppose?'

His smile was as sweet and innocent as the ice cream that ringed his mouth, but she'd acquired, almost overnight it seemed, the habit of suspicion.

'No chance, Max, I'm afraid. I'm waiting to go home.'

'So I hear.' He pushed a macaroon towards her. 'Try one of these, they're divine.'

'No thanks, I've just had breakfast.' A lie but she couldn't stand another lecture about eating up.

'Well let me tickle your fancy with this, Super Sabs,' he said, through a mouthful of crumbs. 'Thing is, I've written a musical.' Pause for a look of thrilling intensity. 'It's easily the best thing I've ever done. I'll be casting after Christmas, should you change your mind.'

'Thanks, Max,' she said quietly, 'but I won't change my mind. It's nice of you to think of me.'

'Saba, may I say one thing?' He propped his chin in his hands and looked deeply into her eyes. 'I know I was a bit sharp with you during rehearsals. I've got a nasty tongue sometimes because I want everything to be perfect, but I only do it with people I respect, and what I should have made perfectly clear to you is that you were . . . are,' he corrected himself, 'good, very good. I think you have a great future ahead of you. End of apology. More grovel to follow if necessary.' He touched his forehead, mouth and chest in a mock-salaam.

There was no glow of pleasure when he said this. It all sounded like flannel to her.

'Sorry, Max,' she said. 'I'm not trying to be a prima donna.'

He wiped his mouth with a napkin and stared at her.

'It's like being an athlete, Sabs, you can't let the muscles go slack.'

'I know that.'

'It's not just the talent fairy waving her little wand.'

'Gosh. Really?' She pushed the crumbs into a little pile with her finger, and looked at him.

'Did that sound patronising?'

'Only a bit, Max, but thanks for trying.'

As he drained his cup in one draught, she felt the click of his charm being switched off. She knew by now how Max's mind worked: the wheels would already be churning inside his brain about who to cast as her replacement; and later there would probably be a satisfying bitch to whoever was at hand about how that Saba Tarcan wasn't as good as she thought she was – how he'd put his finger on her unique flaws the moment he'd seen her – for there was a fire of ego inside Max Bagley that needed to be stoked more or less constantly.

'What happened to Janine?' she asked him while he was searching for his hat.

'She went to India and then, or so I gather, was sent home.' He gave her a beady look. 'Couldn't cope at all.' There was a pause. 'She was an awful drip, wasn't she?' he added. 'Lovely line, but no sense of humour whatsoever.'

'When I thought about her later,' she said, 'I mean after I left the company, I felt sorry for her. She told me once she'd been having ballet lessons since she was three years old, that every scrap of the family money went on her. She didn't have a childhood, and now she won't have a proper career because just when everything was starting to open up for her, the war came – she's sure she'll be past her prime when it's over; dancers are unlucky like that.'

'Well the war's ballsed up a lot of lives.' Max wasn't the slightest bit interested. 'So I can't feel very boo-hoo about that.'

He did at least insist on walking her home; it had started to drizzle and the sky was thunderously grey.

'Funny, isn't it, being in a company?' he said as they picked their way over broken pavements. 'One moment you're all madly cosy – you know all about each other's love affairs, the state of their bowels, what they like to eat for breakfast, their weaknesses, their breaking points – and the next, *pouff!* Gone. When you're in a show, it seems like the most important thing in the world.' His voice trailed off wearily.

'What will you do when the war's over, Max?'

'Dunno. Another job maybe,' he said grimly. 'Go on tour again.' She was shocked by how worn-out he sounded.

'Why not go home for a while and have a proper holiday?' He'd talked about a place in London.

'To my bedsit in Muswell Hill,' he said in the same flat voice. 'If it's still standing. Whizzoo! What fun.'

Boggers next, en route to a job in India. The usual leotard replaced by a shiny ill-fitting suit made, he told her proudly, by a tailor in the souk. He stood in the middle of the room discreetly tensing and flexing various muscles and made a stumbling speech he'd obviously prepared beforehand. He told Saba that she was a very nice and beautiful lady, and that when the war was over they should move to Brazil and form a double act there. If she wanted it very much they could get married.

She stumbled through a speech of her own: so kind of him, wonderful opportunity, but going home, etc., and she was tremendously grateful when Arleta suddenly arrived with enough energy left over from a two-hour rehearsal to admire the suit, which had obviously been bought for the occasion, and pinch his cheeks, and ask him to share mess number one with them. Saba watched her in awe.

When he left, Arleta collapsed on to the sofa like a rag doll and said:

'God, I feel *dire.* I'm practically certain I'm getting a cold or flu or something, which is why I have a huge, *huge* boon to beg of you.'

She rolled on to the floor, clasped her hands together in prayer, and begged Saba to help her out the following night at a small concert to be held at a supply depot near Suez.

'Get up, you silly woman!' Saba didn't feel like joking, much less performing. 'What do you have in mind?'

She knew she wasn't ready for work. But Arleta was persuasive. Only a couple of duets, she said. It would be fun. Good old Dr Footlights would get her through.

But he hadn't. She'd done it for Arleta, who, red-nosed and even croakier than the day before, was thrilled to have her back. At the depot, Arleta did a very grown-up version of 'Christopher Robin is Saying His Prayers' (*Wasn't it fun in the bath tonight? The cold's so cold, and the hot's so hot*), and they'd sung a couple of duets together, light-hearted things: 'Makin' Whoopee', done with two prams, then a spoof on 'Cheek to Cheek', when they pretended to be GI Janes whose cheeks got stuck together by chewing gum. Arleta, radiantly restored to health, had chewed up the scenery a bit with some extravagant shimmying at the end of the choruses, but the men seemed to love it and they left the stage to a shrill blast of wolf whistles.

And Saba, looking down from the stage at the sea of khaki men with their lonely, eager faces, made an unhappy discovery: you didn't need heart or soul to make an audience cheer and clap – at a pinch, another part of you would take over like a well-schooled circus pony.

After the interval, Arleta, who was about to do her solo, ran from the stage into the wings clutching her throat dramatically and pretending to strangle herself.

'I can't. *Can't.*' Her voice cracked into a faint whisper. 'Voice completely gone.'

Well, maybe it was a trick, and maybe it wasn't, but there was nothing for it but for Saba, unrehearsed and unprepared, to take over. She was doing fine, until a boy in the front row asked for 'Smoke Gets in Your Eyes'. The last time she'd sung it, they'd been in bed together, in the Rue Lepsius room, her face against his chest, his hand combing her hair.

Halfway through the song, she felt a wave of blackest misery sweep over her; her throat seemed to close down. The boy who'd requested the song – a skinny kid, with a new short back and sides – looked baffled as she left the stage early, the band still playing an echo of the chorus.

She ran down the steps that led from the stage towards the scruffy tented village, the Nissen huts, the row of rubbish bins. There were no stars that night, just black cloud, and miles of mud and barbed wire. Arleta found her in a gangway between two rows of tents, sitting in the mud sobbing her guts out.

'I'm so sorry, darling,' Arleta said, sitting down beside her. 'I got it wrong. I think it's time you went home.'

Chapter 43

For several days Dom slipped in and out of consciousness. His wet hair was plastered over his forehead, his lips had turned blue, parts of his parachute were still wrapped around him like a grotesque half-hatched pupa with a human head.

A desert lark was singing its strange *choo eee cha cha wooeee* song on a leafless tree nearby. The pile of ashes that had been the plane was now a soggy mess with a few bits of wire poking out, and smashed pieces of glass.

From time to time a boy, like a figure in a dream, appeared, shimmering and unreliable, sometimes with goats around him. A skinny boy with a look of horrified disgust on his face who muttered at him and occasionally screamed, who feinted and retreated and seemed to want to kill him. This time, breathing heavily, the boy tied his donkey to the tree. He stared at Dom. He inched towards him, his heart pumping wildly, snatched the scattered objects around him, the compass, the razor, the bottled tablets from his escape kit, stuffed them in his pocket, and was about to ride off again when he heard Dom sigh.

When Dom woke, hot and shivering, several hours later, he lay squinting at a sky whose dull grey made it impossible to work out the time. 'Nothing has changed,' he said out loud, shocked at how feeble his voice sounded. A few moments later, he froze hearing the distant drone of planes in the sky somewhere far above the blank wall of cloud. They would see him soon; they would get him. As a boy, he'd listened one night breathless with horror as his grandfather, fuelled by several whiskies too many, recalled his time as a prisoner of war – captured in a ditch before Ypres – the chicken-cage beds, the claustrophobia, the beatings, the sense of utter degraded helplessness. Being captured was one of his worst nightmares.

His muscles were taut as violin strings as he listened. The white sky had changed, and he saw, sliding out from behind what were black blobs of reflected cloud, four planes flying in formation above him – 5,000, 7,000 feet? It was hard to tell from here. Four 109s, swastikas painted like large insects underneath them. The sound faded, grew louder. Then, above the German planes, he heard the unmistakable roar of Spitfires and stopped breathing as he pictured himself stretched out like a human target on the sand. Jesus Christ Almighty. Now what?

Face down he lay, listening with his whole body for his own death, and then he heard the sounds of the planes flying away, followed by his own lungs creaking and retching as he coughed.

After they'd gone a wave of pure exhilaration swept through him. He was alive! He was alive. He rolled over on his side, gritted his teeth, took several deep breaths, and yelling, stood up. He was standing, squinting and swaying, watching the dissolving and loosening of solid reality, when he saw the boy again, this time on a donkey coming towards him from some way off. There was a man with him.

The man looked at him for a long time, scratching his armpit. He lifted the aircraft wing and he and the boy stared at him together – a pale, half-dead *agnabi* who had dropped from the sky. Dom started to cry, feeling the stag beetles crawling over him. Two vultures flew above him in a speculative way, and around him the desert stretched out, implacable, vast. It didn't care. When the sun came out it would roast the flesh off his bones, or if it rained, there were no trees for shelter. He would die within days, if these two people didn't kill him.

He was still raving as they bundled up the parachute and tied it to the donkey. Telling them to leave him, telling them he wanted to die. They threw him sideways across the beast's bony back, his flying boots dragging in the mud. They took him back to their temporary home – four ramshackle tents whose guy ropes were covered in tattered bits of cloth. In front of the tents there was a hobbled camel, and a small donkey, now honking furiously at its mother's return. A skinny dog, its tail at a crazy pipe-cleaner angle, barked at them.

Dom had stopped his noise. He ached all over now, he longed for nothing more than to lie down. They took him to the largest of the tents and unrolled a thin mattress for him behind a curtain. He lay all night in this windowless corner, breathing in the fumes of a tallow candle, and camel dung, and the goat's hair the tent was made of. His lungs squeaked, his face burned. While he slept, three toddlers came to the mouth of the tent, barefoot and in grimy pyjamas, picking their noses, laughing nervously. From time to time a man's curious face appeared around the door and stared at him without expression. He called his wife in to look at Dom. They did not know if he was German or English, and it did not particularly matter because an *agnabi* was an *agnabi* and their war had ruined the land, the cotton crops, the price of fuel, and made their lives even harder than they already were. As soon as he was well, he would go.

The boy's mother, Abida, who was only twenty-eight and soft-hearted, felt differently. Her last job of the day was to check on the goats, to put fava beans on to cook for tomorrow's breakfast, and lastly to pull down the various bits of sacking that made their dwelling relatively watertight. Before she went to bed, she went out into the vast star-studded night, crept round to the side of the tent where he lay and, raising a candle over his face, sneaked another look at him. He was soaked with sweat, coughing and muttering. He was a handsome boy, and he was dying. It was the will of Allah, but it was sad.

Chapter 44

One Wednesday morning she was in the sitting room at Antikhana Street when Mr Ozan walked in. He was plumply poured into a beautiful dark suit and held an enormous bunch of lilies in his hand. She jumped.

'Saba, my dear.' His voice was stern, his eyes full of concern. 'You are a woman alone, please lock your door in future.'

He sat down and looked around him. Arleta, who had the occasional attack of neatness – Tiggywinkles, she called them – had draped the sofa with some silk throws and put a bowl of Turkish delight on the table to try and tempt Saba, who was still too thin.

'Nice, very nice,' he said approvingly. 'I've only just heard about your accident.' Her hand went instinctively to her head. 'What can I do?'

'You've only just heard?' Hard not to sound sceptical.

'Yes!' Ozan sounded angry. 'I was travelling, and when I came back you'd gone and nobody knew where.'

His eyes looked capable of murder as he asked for details, reminding her of her father during similar interrogations. Who was at the house that night? Who was driving her? Who did she blame most?

'That's all I remember,' she lied. If she told him about Severin, she would have to think about it again, and male outrage would follow, and the thought of that exhausted her – she no longer cared.

'I would kill him if I knew.' Ozan's dark eyes flashed. 'The German house is boarded up now, and I've heard that Engel was sent back to Germany to go on trial there. The ambassador knew nothing about the party house, and was furious about it; some of them were even selling drugs from there. They stole the drugs from military hospitals. They were very bad men.'

For a moment she thought he was going to cry. 'I had no idea they were such bad men, Saba. You should not have been there – for this, I can never forgive myself.'

'You heard about Felipe?' Her eyes filled with tears.

'They shot him. I heard that. Yes. This was a terrible tragedy. I was very fond of him. I should never have taken you to Istanbul,' he said mournfully.

'No,' she told him. 'It was my fault too. I'd heard all about your clubs. I must take some of the blame.'

'If your father was here, he would blame me, and me only, but . . .' Mr Ozan gave a shrug so big he seemed to be trying to turn himself inside out. 'I wanted new singers, I thought you were good. I was excited.'

'I don't think my father would care any more,' she said. Wearily she told him about the letter. 'He doesn't want to see me again,' she added, 'he hates all this.'

Ozan kneaded his forehead between his fingers, he made the clucking sound Tan made when she was upset.

'Well,' he said at last, 'you saw his village.' As if this explained everything. 'There was nothing there for you,' he said, staring at her. 'Was there?'

'No.'

She felt a pinch of pain just thinking about it. They'd gone to Üvezli on a perfect autumn day – hard bright sunshine, the bluest sky imaginable – but Ozan was right: not much there, apart from a few whitewashed houses, a mosque, a primary school, a sleepy café beside a square, with cats snoozing under the tables. They'd taken flowers, presents, all the rich promise of Ozan's wealth and Saba's youth and beauty. The stage set for a beautiful reunion, except no one came: no cries of joy from ancient relatives, and no stirring of memories in the half-dozen houses they'd called at. Just a few old men sitting on wooden chairs in the dusty street, each one shaking his head. Closed as oysters. They either hadn't understood or hadn't wanted to, or they'd come too late.

On their way back home, Ozan had explained in a low, apologetic voice, as if he were personally responsible, that many of the people here were descendants of the Turkish Muslims from the Caucasus who'd fled from the approaching Russian armies during the Ottoman war with Russia in 1877. Others were driven out in 1920, first rounded up by the British and French who had occupied the area around Istanbul, then shot for joining the irregular Turkish nationalist forces. They were naturally suspicious of strangers. As her father had been, all his life. She saw this clearly now.

Later that day, Ozan, obviously still smarting, had urged her to write a letter to her father: *At least he'll know you tried to find him; he'll know you cared*, she'd tried, but found it impossible to finish. There were too many barriers between them now, and she felt something else too, something the war had taught her: that she had no God-given right to secrets he didn't want to tell.

Mr Ozan was kneading his forehead again, trying to find some sliver of hope here.

'There is one thing I would say about your father's decision,' he said at last. 'It will set you free as an artiste – just as Faiza had to be set free, and Umm Kulthum. It is hard for people like you to serve two masters.'

She said nothing, because that part of her felt so dead now and because the word artiste seemed falsely grand in connection with her. Hearing him sigh again, she passed the box of Turkish delight.

'Who gave you this?' He stopped her arm and looked at her bracelet.

'A friend. An English pilot.'

He examined it closely. 'It's beautiful. These two,' he touched the tiny engraved figures with the familiarity of old friends, 'are Bastet and Hathor, they are both the goddesses of music and other things. This one,' he moved his fingers to the right, 'is Nut, she is for the sky and the heavens. They call Bastet the Lady with the Red Clothes; do you know why?'

Because she could not talk, she took the bracelet off and handed it to him. While he was squinting at the inscription, she mopped her eyes hurriedly on the hem of her skirt.

'Ozkorini,' he said. 'How does an Englishman know these things?'

'Because . . .' he waited for her patiently, 'he was with me in Alexandria when I learned the songs. He was interested in such things.'

'He was a good man.'

'Yes . . . He died while I was in Istanbul.'

She was training herself to say this now, it cut out speculation and false hope, and having to listen to stories about other people who'd walked into camp months after they'd been shot down.

Mr Ozan closed his eyes. A muscle twitched in his jaw.

'I am sorry for this.'

'I should have expected it,' she said. 'So many of them have gone.'

'But these are such young men. How old was yours?' There was a stillness about Mr Ozan, as if he had all the time in the world to listen.

'Twenty-three.' She heard her own voice, watery and choked with regret. Without a word he handed her a beautifully monogrammed handkerchief.

'Saba, listen to me,' his voice was gentle, 'this is an awful thing for you, but you will meet someone else, *inshallah*.'

'I don't think so.'

'Many men will love you because of who you are. They'll want to marry you.'

'The thing is,' she said, 'I let him down.'

'What happened?' His voice was gentle, so like her father's when he'd been kind.

She said more than she meant to: about the burns hospital, about Alexandria. He listened, calm and attentive.

'Who knows,' he said softly when she was finished. 'He may still come back – not always do bad things happen.'

'No,' she said, 'I thought that for a while, I don't now. So many have gone.'

Every breath is a new beginning and a new chance. Felipe's words. Not true. Not for him.

She suddenly felt exhausted by Ozan – his crinkled forehead, his big kind eyes, the large spotlight of his attention on her. She hoped he would leave soon.

'Would it help to find out how he died?'

'No . . . not necessarily . . . I don't know. Anyway, we've tried.'

He consulted the gold watch nestling in his hairy wrist.

'I'm flying back to Istanbul tonight,' he wiped his chin, 'so forgive me, but I must ask you one more thing before I go. When the war in Egypt is over, which *inshallah* it will be soon, I make a big party for everyone: for Egyptians, for Turkish people, for the English, for everyone in Alexandria and Cairo. Faiza will come, and I'll get the best dancers, acrobats, jugglers. I want you to sing.' He looked at her expectantly; this was supposed to be a great treat.

She stood up and walked to the window. Outside, the sky was grey again, the day drawing in; soon it would be Christmas.

'That's kind of you, Mr Ozan, but I'm going home soon – at least I hope I am.'

'Will your government fly you home?'

'Yes.' She watched two dark birds flying above the wet rooftops and towards the sea. 'As soon as they can.'

'But there's still plenty of work here for artistes. I've never seen Cairo so full – your people, our people, Americans, lots of people under thirty wanting to have fun again.'

'I know, but I don't want to sing again.'

Mr Ozan's jaw dropped. 'You are a singer. You can't stop.'

'I can.'

He thumped his fist softly on the table. His voice rose.

'If you stop singing, you will hurt the best part of yourself.'

'I don't think my father would agree with you about that.'

'Well, sorry for the word, but the man is a twit. Not all men think as he does – not even all Turkish men. The world moves on. Listen.' He leapt to his feet, gesticulating wildly, and for once his impeccable English let him down. 'Think of other bipples,' he said passionately. 'When you have a gift like you have a gift, it's the honey you lay down – not just for yourself but for your children's happiness also.'

'Well that's a nice idea,' she said. Beads of sweat had broken out on his forehead. 'It's just that I don't believe it any more.' Severin's face flashed into her mind like a bilious dream.

'You are saying no?' Ozan clapped his hand to his temples, incredulous, heartbroken. 'This concert will be tremendous – fireworks and horses, singers – like nothing these cities have ever seen.'

'I'm saying no,' she said. 'I can't do it any more.'

Chapter 45

For the first four days he lay in a torpor in the corner of the tent, wheezing and coughing and sleeping, then sleeping again. Sometimes the boy, or an older man with spongy red gums and two teeth, came and held a rough cup to his lips with some bitter brackish medicine in it that made him splutter. Twice a day the boy fed him some floury-tasting grain, occasionally with vegetables in it. From time to time he was aware of the dull pitter-patter of rain falling, or the screech of a bird, or, from another part of the house, male voices laughing and the rattle of some game they were playing. Once, an aeroplane flew so low over the tent it almost took the roof off, but he wasn't frightened, he simply noted it in a kind of dim anaesthetised way, as if it was happening to someone else and in another place.

When he woke up properly, with a thumping headache and a tight chest, the boy was sitting at the end of his bed. He looked about twelve, had a wild mop of black curls, and a pallid complexion as if he might have suffered from malaria, or bilharzia. The boy smiled at him shyly; he touched his fingers to his mouth as if to ask if he was hungry. Dom nodded his head, bewildered and disoriented. When the boy skedaddled on his skinny legs out of the room to get food, Dom took stock of the desperate poverty of his surroundings. The greasy pile of quilts he lay on didn't look as if they'd been washed for years let alone weeks. On a makeshift shelf at the back of the tent there were small amounts of grain, and dried food in sacks that spoke of frugal housekeeping and small rations.

The boy returned with an older man who wore a faded djellaba and whose flapping sandals were tied with string. He came over to the bed and patted Dom's arm, beaming with joy, as if his recovery had presented them with a tremendous gift.

'Karim,' he said, pointing to himself. 'Ibrahim.' The boy beamed.

'My name is Dom,' he told them. He had never felt so far away from the person who had that name, or more vulnerable. When Ibrahim handed him an earthenware bowl, he was surprised to find he needed help to feed himself. The boy held the spoon to his lips and dribbled in a thin lentil soup, opening his own mouth as he did so like a mother bird feeding her young.

When he had finished eating, Dom fell back on the pillows, rummaging around in his brain for the word for thank you. Instead he held up his fingers and asked in English: 'How long have I been here?' When the boy held up four fingers he was amazed, and then the boy counted out five more and made a joke of it, counting out more. Dom closed his eyes, overwhelmed. He might have been here for weeks for all he knew.

When he woke in the night, scratching himself and very cold, he thought about what a burden he must have been to this poor family, who could barely afford to feed themselves, and how lightly they carried it. He already felt ashamed of the man he'd been who'd first come to North Africa – God, was it less than a year ago – who'd looked at people like these from the air, and seen only toy-like figures moving their animals around. They'd given up their land for foreign soldiers to fight in and he'd barely spared them a thought.

As a child, Egypt had been a vital part of his imagination and his games, the link formed during a bad bout of measles when his mother read to him every day from a book that obsessed him about the archaeologist Howard Carter. When his mother got to the part where Carter had walked down out of the sunlight one day in the Valley of Kings, taken a piece of clay out of a wall and *whoosh!* – the smell of spices, the feeling of hot air – found himself staring into Tutankhamen's chamber. Dom had jammed himself against her side, hardly daring to breathe.

He'd loved the drama and the anguish of the archaeologist's long and fruitless-seeming search. How, only a week before he found the treasures, an exhausted, heartbroken Carter had made the decision to go back to England, and live more sensible dreams. How he'd stumbled on a step that led to Tut's chamber and, looking up, seen the entrance. How he'd walked a couple more steps, found the seal covering the entrance of the tomb, and, breaking it and holding his candle up, seen huge gold couches, jewels, priceless treasures. How the friend waiting outside had asked, 'Have you found anything?'

and Carter, scarcely able to breathe, had said, 'Yes. Wonderful things.'

When he'd recovered from measles, Dom spent months scouring the countryside around Woodlees Farm, turning over damp leaves, going through wood piles, looking for his own buried treasure.

But war had a way of making things squalid. The dun-coloured phrasebook handed to serving officers on arrival contained mostly warnings about washing hands, boiling water, guarding wallets, and staying away from local prostitutes, and nothing to do with Egypt's extraordinary past, or for that matter the humbling hospitality of its people. Today, when the boy had fed him the last spoonful of lentil soup, he had placed his hand over his worn winter jumper and said, '*Sahtayn*,' which he knew from his phrasebook meant 'two healths to you'.

Later, Karim, the boy's father, came back carrying a battered wooden board. He threw some counters down on the quilt and became tremendously animated trying to explain to Dom the rules of a game, which Dom had never played and failed to understand. It seemed to be some distant relative of draughts, but he couldn't make out the rules, and both of them eventually smiled at each other, embarrassed by their mutual incomprehension.

To break the silence, Dom mimed writing, and paper, praying that this family was not illiterate.

Karim sprang up and fetched an old notebook from behind a jar of rice, which had a pencil and a string attached. Dom drew a picture of an aircraft, and then the sea – when lost in North Africa, the first rule of navigation was a simple one: turn north until you hit the coast. He pointed to himself, and then the sea, and looked enquiringly at Karim.

His chest still felt tight and wheezy, but he couldn't stay for much longer; he could see already how carefully this family eked out its supplies of rice and lentils and corn. He handed his map to Karim – who looked completely bewildered by it. At last he pointed to a spot that Dom estimated would be about forty miles south of Marsa. Dom then drew a train, wondering if one stopped near here. Karim shook his head, and looked confused. He held up four stained fingers, then drew a crude donkey on the page. Four days, or at least that was what Dom thought he'd said.

Karim padded out again, slip-slopping in his broken sandals, and Dom lay scratching himself vigorously. There were bed bugs – though he was used to them by now; mobile dandruff they called them in the squadron, and they didn't bother him unduly. Much more troubling was the thought of now what? He seemed to have reached some frightening state of spiritual and mental emptiness and the idea of going back to the squadron made him feel weak with exhaustion and a peculiar kind of sorrow he could not put his finger on. The curious life the pilots led here – the frantic drinking, the parties in Alex and Cairo then back to the desert for the killing, the bombing raids – had already created a kind of unhappy split in him that was widening.

Meeting Saba had healed the split. She'd made him feel so lucky, so sure, so rescued from the self he was becoming, even though she was not, in conventional terms, what his mother would call 'marriage material'. It wasn't just her lovely dimples, or her singing, or the way they both shouted with laughter at the same things; she had returned him to something essential in himself – her own passion and self-belief connecting him to the boy he'd been, the boy who'd dreamed of a long and arduous journey towards buried treasure. When he'd confessed to her his plan of one day being able to write as well as fly, that night in the restaurant in Ismailia – a dream he hadn't dared to confess even to Barney – she hadn't looked sceptical, or amazed, or made him feel pretentious; she'd gone out and bought him a pen and notebook. That was how it happened in her world: you did it and you did it until you got it right.

When Ibrahim came bouncing back later that day, he was followed by two toddlers with black curious eyes and runny noses. The boy pulled a long sad face, that mocked Dom's serious expression. He'd brought the board game back with him, and was prepared to try again with the dim *agnabi*. And this time Dom concentrated, wondering if this game was a distant relative of Senet, the board game played by ancient Egyptians, charting their journey towards a longed-for afterlife. An elaborately carved version of this game had been found inside Tutankhamen's tomb.

The boy was babbling passionately now, his dark curls bobbing as he spoke. He placed a bundle of grimy counters in Dom's hand and, pointing to the dark squares, grimaced and rolled his eyes to indicate the terrible disasters that would befall him should one of his counters land there. The pale squares were plainly the good-luck ones, and the boy's expression became secretive and calm as he reached them. Because he was enjoying himself, Dom did too. A clear case of cheating was overlooked at one point, when the boy skimmed one of his counters over a bad-luck square, his face crafty, only to move it swiftly back, perhaps frightened of antagonising the gods. And afterwards, Dom, thinking he would teach him snakes and ladders, drew out a board on the piece of paper. The boy leaned eagerly towards him, his face bright with anticipation. When the lead in the pencil crumbled beyond repair, the boy gasped with disappointment. There wasn't another.

They sat in silence for a while contemplating this disaster, and then a strange look came over the boy's face. He put his hands to his lips to shush Dom, looked towards the door, and then rushed out.

He returned flushed and breathless ten minutes or so later. He shut the door carefully, sat down on the bed, and drew out of his pocket a stained piece of rag. Inside it were Dom's watch – the glass on its face smashed – his small compass in its leather case, and the pen that Saba had bought him. In the other rag he'd wrapped the three small bottles of tablets: the benzedrine amphetamine, the salt tablets, the water purification tablets – all standard issue in pilot's escape kits. The boy lined them up carefully on the dirt floor.

With a carefully neutral expression, he watched Dom seize the pen and hold it, thrilled to have it in his hands again. When he set the pen down, the boy watched him anxiously as he slipped his index finger between two narrow pieces of leather in the lid of his compass case, and felt for the twenty Egyptian pound notes, all pilots were given in case of emergency. They were still there.

He didn't care about the watch. The pen was the most important thing. And the money – the relief he felt at being able to reward the family was overwhelming. He wondered when the right time would be to give it to them, and before he went to sleep that afternoon, tucked it under his pillow.

Daylight was fading into blood-red dusk when he heard the rackety cries of the goats returning, the hollow jangle of their bells. When the boy's father appeared in his room, Dom drew a picture of the sea on the notepad and pointed vigorously towards himself.

The boy looked sad, but Karim looked pleased, and even more so when Dom peeled off some of the notes and gave them to him, banging his hand on his heart to show how grateful he was. He owed them his life, and with their help there was a good chance – landmines and bombs not withstanding – that he could get to wherever home was now.

Chapter 46

The next time Mr Ozan came back, the chauffeur kept the car engine running while he ran up her stairs.

'Now listen.' His shrewd black eyes glared at her around the door. 'I've been thinking of our talk the other day, and I am going to make you an offer which you may think is cruel. But I am a businessman. I have a show to put on and I want you in it. If you agree, I will help you look for him, and if he is dead,' there was no sugar coating this time, 'you will know.' He glared at her again.

She stared at him. It was seven forty-five in the morning. She was still in her nightdress, which made her feel furious – her instinctive covering of her breasts when what she most wanted was to perform some violent retaliatory act of her own like screaming or striking him violently around the face. His bargain stood for everything she had begun to loathe about show business – its tin-pot values, its selfishness, its determination that the show must go on, no matter what the cost to other people.

'This sounds like blackmail to me,' she said.

'It is,' he said, discreetly ogling her. 'I shall come back tomorrow and you can give me your answer.'

'Don't bother, and don't come back,' she screamed at him like a wild animal. 'They've been looking for him, you stupid man. He's dead, and I'm going home now. My ticket came through last week.'

The door slammed, he was gone. She threw on a raincoat and walked down towards the Nile, sobbing with fury. Gharries, cars, donkey carts swept by her, splattering her stockings with rain. Crossing roads, dodging traffic, ignoring wolf whistles from a passing army truck, her mind flipped back and forth: Ozan was a bully – as bad as the rest of them. What he offered was sleazy and underhand, a song for a life, or a song for death confirmed.

The stone lions on the Khedive Ibrahim Bridge shone with rain as she passed them; fishermen hung over its sides shrouded in tarpaulins or old newspapers, the Nile flowing beneath them, sluggish and grey in the rain, the twinkling fairy lights on the barges dead as fish eyes. *By the waters of Babylon, there we sat down, yea we wept* she'd sung these words, set to music by William Walton, with Caradoc once. Her teacher flaming with passion, with something akin to a sorrowful joy, as he told her to feel it, feel it feel it to the nth degree and then rein it back. Looking down at the water, she thought about their first days here. The laughs with Arleta as they'd hurtled in a taxi on their way to that blue-moon night at the Mena House. The rowdy sing-songs on the way home; peaceful breakfasts in the courtyard of the Minerva; her first sunglasses, left God knows where and never replaced; the concerts. The richest period of her life so far, in spite of all the hardships. Now she saw nothing but sadness in the expressions of the gaunt old men who sat by their braziers selling trinkets, the bored young soldiers prowling through the waterlogged souks looking for cheap souvenirs to take home. *Yea, wept, wept! And hanged our harps upon the willow.* The words flew back disjointedly.

I want to die now. The thought was so familiar it no longer shocked her.

She was walking across the bridge with no specific destination in mind when she heard the pattering of feet behind her.

'Saba, stop!' Arleta shouted. Her hair lay in wet strands around her face. 'Where are you going?'

'I'm all right – honestly, leave me, I'm fine.'

She felt a sort of dispassionate sorrow for Arleta – grief was so boring too.

'Balls,' said Arleta, seeing her face. 'Let's get in a taxi and go home.'

They were soaked by the time they got back to Antikhana Street. Arleta made some Camp coffee and they wrapped their wet hair in turbans and sat in their dressing gowns in front of a single-bar electric fire.

'Saba.' Arleta leaned over and took her hand. 'This is no good, you know. You've got to talk to me. You frightened me to death.'

She tried to fob Arleta off at first with vague talk about feeling low and wanting to go home.

'Is that all, Sabs?'

'No.' She fiddled with the cups for a while. 'I've decided not to sing again.'

'Oh stop that! You know you don't mean it.'

'I do.'

'What?' Arleta sounded genuinely shocked.

'I've been thinking for a while, it's not worth it.'

'Not worth what?'

'Well you know, those few rapturous moments.' Saba closed her eyes. 'It's caused so much pain to the people around me.'

'I must warn you, Saba, that you are making no sense to me.' Arleta's eyes were slitty and mean.

'And you see, I had this all straight in my mind, that I'd go home, do something else with my life, something – I don't know, teaching or being a librarian or a secretary – that doesn't make you feel guilty, or vain, or stupid, and now Mr Ozan has made me this offer.'

Which she tried to explain even though Arleta's eyes looked lethal, and she was tugging her own hair.

'And you see, now he's left me with no choice,' Saba said on a rising note. 'I've got to do it: one concert in Alexandria, one in Cairo, and I can't tell you how much I dread it.'

'I don't think it will be that hard once you start.' Arleta's eyes were open and friendly again, her voice coaxing. 'If I'm around, we could do our duet.'

'And Ozan does know everyone,' Arleta said. 'If anyone can find Dom, he can.'

'Yes,' she said, thinking, I wish people would stop pretending now.

'And if you do do it,' Arleta was quite lit up now, 'I have one suggestion to make – don't get cross – that we track down Madame Eloise again, and that you start eating, that you get out of those blasted pyjamas, and we go straight forth to the hairdresser's, because no one wants a girl who is dull with stringy hair.'

And Saba smiled for the first time that day.

'You're an idiot,' she said. 'And I love you.'

'Don't go all soppy on me.'

'Don't worry, I won't.'

*

They sat talking by the fire for the next hour, Arleta, who had a performance that night at the open-air cinema, winding her hair into pin curls. 'Sabs,' she said, neatly skewering one with a grip, 'since we are having a nose-to-nose, I have one more thing to confess and you mustn't be angry with me.'

Saba looked at her.

'Don't hate me,' Arleta said, 'but I've got a new boyfriend.'

'Why should I hate you? Listen, Arlie, just because of Dom doesn't mean I—'

'No, listen, shut up, it's Barney – Dom's friend.'

There was a beat of silence while the news sank in.

'Dom's friend. When?' Saba felt a kind of swirling unreality.

'While you were in hospital.' Arleta put down her toast. 'We met and we talked, and suddenly we were sleeping together.'

'Oh, come off it Arl, what do you mean, you were suddenly sleeping together – that's such a stupid expression.' Saba was properly angry now. 'You don't just *suddenly* sleep with people, like flies who collide in the air, so just say it out loud – we were making love.'

'All right – we were making love.' Arleta's cat eyes narrowed as she considered this. 'Although I wouldn't call it that.'

'So what would you call it?'

'A mercy fuck, if you'll excuse my French. He was in a complete state about Dom, and I was so worried about you.'

'Oh. So you slept with him because you were worried about me? How very kind.'

'Partly, yes. Look, no excuses but I was in a state myself. I thought you were going to die.' Arleta's eyes filled with tears. 'And I'm quite fond of you really,' she said.

And this was so obviously true now that Saba, trembling with rage, forced herself to calm down. She didn't know Barney, she didn't own him – her response was unbalanced, like everything else in her life.

'Oh Arlie, I'm sorry.' She gave her a brief hug. 'I'm so mean at the moment, I don't know what to do with myself. Do you love him?'

'I could do, but it won't do me much good. He's a mess. Anyway, don't you remember, I'm spoken for, and there's the small matter of my little boy.' She took the picture out of her pocket; her face crumpled at the sight of his blond curls, his sweet face.

'Ghastly little varmint,' she said.

'Maybe you should tell Barney – wouldn't he be pleased?'

'I don't think so.' It was Arleta's turn to sound bleak. 'Men don't usually find other men's children a great aphrodisiac.'

'But if he loves you . . .' She couldn't help it, she felt a deep dismay at this – it seemed so unfair. 'He might. It would be nice to have a family after the war.'

'No. Lovely thought,' Arleta was quite decisive, 'but let's keep our feet on the ground: the man isn't thinking of me as wife material; practically every friend that he has ever had has died and I am like a sucky blanket for him, and that's fine. I'm ten years older than him, and he's in so much shock about your fellow, he can hardly think straight. There was another one too, called Jacko. Did Dom talk about him?'

'No.'

'They were all at school together?'

'Yes.'

They both looked towards the window. A muezzin was calling out the evening prayers. The sky had flushed with the dying sun, and turned the tips of the houses opposite into rose coloured castles.

'Barney said he was shot down, and that Dom blamed himself for it, and that he shouldn't.'

'Bit late for that. Poor Dom.'

'Poor everyone,' said Arleta. 'War is so bloody awful – I don't know why men like it so much.' She gave a huge sigh and put her hair net on.

'Tell me something else,' Saba said. 'Does Barney know about me?'

'A little, I think.'

'He must hate me. Dom must have told him how I left.'

Arleta's silence said it all.

'It was tricky,' she said at last. 'I told him what I could about your Turkish adventure. I'm not sure he believed me. Come on, love.' Arleta stood up abruptly, her face full of a sadness Saba had never seen before. She put the photo of her little boy into her vanity case. 'Let's switch dem lights off and get you to bed.'

*

When Saba woke, around two in the morning, it was pitch black outside their window and she was thinking about Arleta's fiancé Bill, a man Arleta rarely mentioned now. She wondered if Bill was dead already, or comforting himself with someone else, or back home in pieces with his mum, and for those few moments she saw war as a vast fracturing mirror shattering all their lives.

Chapter 47

When he left the tent for the last time, the woman who had been cooking his beans and his flatbread appeared quickly in the mouth of the tent as a pair of liquid, curious brown eyes that stared, blinked, and, in response to her husband's sharp bark, hurriedly disappeared.

Karim and the boy helped Dom on to a donkey laden with saddlebags. Today Karim was wearing a pair of broken-down sandals patched from what looked like old car tyre; Ibrahim, who led the donkey, had a definite air of swagger about him. He was wearing his best clothes: a spotless, perfectly ironed djellaba, on his head a long scarf wound over and around a woollen cap.

Karim waved his hands at the horizon indicating that this would be a long journey; Dom thought he heard him say Marsa Matruh, but could not be sure; the way the locals pronounced their words was so different, and the long discussion that had followed made him cough.

It was a bright, cold day. For the first hour he saw nothing but the desert stretching around him and the occasional blighted tree. He could feel the boy at his side, casting anxious, furtive looks in his direction. They were friends now – Dom had found a piece of paper in his pocket and made him paper aeroplanes, and after the first shy overtures, the boy had brought his board back and they'd made up all kinds of games on it together.

After nearly four hours' walk, the dust road became tarmac and he saw the dusty sign ahead of him. It was Marsa and quicker than he'd anticipated. There was a railway station there. He was back in civilisation again – or some approximation of it.

He pointed to it, put his thumbs up, tried to smile, but what he felt most was a profound sadness and shame. On his way here, he'd seen through their eyes the destruction of the land all around: the charred jeeps abandoned by the roadside, the shattered pavements, the aircraft, looking like a broken pterodactyl, half-buried in sand.

The boy seemed excited at the adventure of going into town, but Karim, after looking around him, gave Dom the strangest look, a wry shrug, as if to say *What can you do? This is life and life only*. And Dom thought again of his own elation when he'd dropped bombs on a fuel dump not far from here; the time when the Karims and Ibrahims of this world were tiny toys on the ground. They owed him nothing.

The railway station was on the edge of the town. As they drew closer, Ibrahim's frail shoulders began to droop, and his eyes grew frightened. It was clear he hadn't been this far before.

When they reached the ticket office, Dom got down from the donkey. There were British and Australian soldiers walking on the pavements, some of them watching him, and he was beginning to feel self-conscious in the djellaba they'd given him to travel in. The boy was grinning and jiggling around in the dust; Karim touched him lightly on the arm.

And though he was already half-back in his world again, what Dom most wanted looking at them for the last time was to kneel at their feet and thank them over and over again for their incredible kindness.

'Here.' He pulled out the leather compass case. The beautiful old-fashioned compass with its scratched leather case and faded mauve velvet lining had once belonged to his father. There were still fourteen Egyptian pounds inside its lid. He peeled off four pounds for himself and handed the rest to Karim – at least they would have a decent meal here and buy some provisions, and perhaps a bundle of alfalfa for the donkey who stood patiently by.

'This,' he said to Ibrahim, 'is for you.' He handed him the compass and the case. The boy looked completely stunned. He bit his lip as he stared at it, then he looked at his father who was smiling. 'For you.' Dom closed the boy's fingers over his gift. '*Sukran.*' He held his own hand over his heart, and when they had turned watched the small boy, the man, the donkey get smaller and smaller until they'd dissolved in dust and heat. That was it. They'd said goodbye. Dom was saved; it didn't feel like it.

*

Inside the station, he bought a one-way ticket to Alex, a two-hour journey from Marsa. Alex was the last place on earth that Dom wanted to be without Saba, but he had no choice. He didn't have enough money to get to Cairo, and he would be close to the squadron there.

When he arrived, he found a cheap hotel near the Rue Nebi Daniel called the Waterloo. It looked like a dive from the outside, but the bedrooms were clean and quiet, and it was cheap and perfect for his purpose, which was sleep, which he did for close to thirteen hours. When he woke up, he gazed in bewilderment at a long flypaper, covered in dead insects, hanging from the ceiling; at the rough walls. He was out of time and out of place and the dust-covered robe that lay on the floor seemed to belong to someone else.

He was staggeringly tired. The early starts, the late nights, the shock of being shot down, the chest infection which had left him wheezing and weak, had caught up with him. His back still ached from the donkey ride, and he felt light-headed and unreal as he walked out into the street near his hotel. Two doors down, in a dim little shop whirring with sewing machines, a tailor sold him a pair of Western trousers and a white shirt. His flying boots he transformed into black shoes by ripping off the detachable sheep-skin on the calf – grateful now for the clever bod at the MOD who'd come up with this idea of inconspicuous shoes for men on the run. Next door to the tailor was a Greek barber who shaved him with a cut-throat razor, heating the water in a little brazier next to his chair, and touching his face afterwards with a cologne that smelled of sandalwood.

The clothes, the shave gave him a sense of being in slightly clearer focus. After two cups of coffee he returned to his hotel and phoned the squadron to tell them he was back.

'That's good news, sir,' the voice at the end of the phone said with no notable surprise or emotion. When he was told that Barney was in Suez, training, and Rivers had gone, he felt relieved rather than sorry. He couldn't face them yet. Too bloody feeble was how he put it to himself, furious at his weakness.

He was about to hang up when another, more authoritative voice came on the line. A hearty, rushed voice, saying he was Dom's replacement, Tom Philips.

'Wonderful news you're back,' the voice boomed. 'I expect . . .'

The line filled with static, so he couldn't hear the rest, but it sounded effusive. And then in a roar, 'Do you need medical treatment? I repeat. Do. You. Need. Medical treatment? Over.'

Dom said no. After the burns hospital he couldn't stand the thought of being incarcerated again.

'I'd like to take a week's leave,' he shouted back. 'I've got reasonable digs here.' He gave his new address, received in another staticky roar.

Some version of the message must have got through. Two days later, the squadron's padre came to see him, a whispery, sympathetic man with bad breath. He'd had a wretched bout of pneumonia himself last year, he confided in an eggy blast. He advised Dom not to overdo it. He'd had a word with the CO before coming to see him, he added, and with Tom Philips. They both thought Dom should take a couple of weeks' leave. There had been a nasty outbreak of influenza at Wadi Natrun and several landing grounds, and it was pretty quiet here anyway now that the Germans had retreated to Tunis.

The padre brought a care package with him: some clean clothes, a month's back pay and a copy of the *Bugle*, a forces newspaper that advertised local goings-on. Then he broke the wary silence that followed with what sounded like a warmed-up sermon.

'I think Alexandria has something to teach all of us about resilience,' he said. 'Nothing but invasions since Alexander came in 332 BC. First him, then the Romans, then . . . well, I've forgotten who next, but now look at 'em. Back on their feet again. New buildings going up already, roads being built, concerts, music, marvellous. I brought you this in case you want some distraction.'

He pointed towards a line of advertisements in the *Bugle*'s entertainments section.

Dom skimmed his eyes down the page, desperate for the old bore to bugger off.

And saw her name.

Saba Tarcan.

The other names – Faiza Mushawar, Bagley, Arleta, Asmahan – scrambled in front of his eyes.

What a thing, he told himself, too shocked to feel angry. What a thing! She'd been here all along. Not posted, or gone home, or any of the other excuses he'd made for her. Here in Egypt all along, working and almost certainly with a new man.

He smiled and shook the padre's hand.

'Very good of you to come. Goodbye.'

When he was gone, Dom needed to walk. On the steps of the hotel, he turned right towards the tram station, watching people flowing in and out of it, from gloom to brilliant winter sunshine.

Not so bad, not so bad. He was testing himself like a man trying to walk on a badly broken leg. A train would carry him away soon – away from Alexandria, away from North Africa. He'd go back to England and start another kind of life.

He turned away from the station and walked down towards the sea. The padre was right, he noted pleasantly to himself, Alex was showing signs of speedy recovery. Although the blackout was still officially in place, some of the blue paint that had covered the streetlights had been scrubbed off. A team of gardeners were planting seedlings in the municipal gardens, workmen were banging their hammers again, restoring the charred buildings. He could fight it too – all the dying and the dead friends, the false hopes, the bogus emotions. He would not fall into the trap of useless nostalgia. When it was over, it was over.

At the corner of Rue Fuad a legless boy stretched out a hand to him.

'Long live Mrs Queen and the Royal Dukes of England.'

Dom dropped a coin into his cup, and walked on.

If it did hurt, he had only himself to blame. After his desert prang, he'd come undone for a while, he could see that now. Lying in bed in Karim's tent, he'd wanted to think his life out clearly, but all that time her songs had played underneath his conscious mind – like a bridge from one thought to the next, a way of talking, deeper than words. And he'd kept the songs playing because he knew he could not keep going without her.

Back there, with the desert stretching all around him, the vast sky above, he'd seen something so clearly. That all human beings were lonely and separated creatures who needed each other, as he'd needed her – whether a mirage or real hadn't seemed to matter.

At night, before he went to sleep, he'd focused the whole thing in his mind like a series of scenes in a film – Saba lying in the bath singing 'Louisville Lou' to him; the sight of her inexpertly washing his socks and putting them on hangers; the sudden breathless joy of catching her eye across a room and seeing her face light up. Oh, and it had gone on – dreams about the twins again, a cottage in the country, friends round a table for dinner, the whole thing played forward, not backwards, so they could have a future together.

Complete balls. He must stop that now. In the real world, mirages could kill you, they could eat up a life.

A light rain began to fall. He turned his collar up and, fixing his eyes on the sea, set off at a brisk pace, thinking he must build up his strength and go back to the squadron soon, but inside he was like a man stumbling from bog to bog, because everywhere reminded him of her. There was the shop where he'd bought the blue bracelet from the fat jeweller with the glass eye who'd told him about the goddesses, and there the café where they'd drunk wine one night, where the old man had played an oud and then, as a special treat for her, a record by Asmahan, and she'd listened, enchanted. And there was the corner of the street where they'd hugged each other before she'd disappeared into the crowd, as it turned out for ever. And around the next corner, the house on Rue Lepsius where he'd sobbed uncontrollably on the night she left – a memory that made him wince with shame. It must not happen again.

Take it! he told himself. *Take it, take it, take it!* The hour had passed.

Chapter 48

When Mr Ozan got permission to hold his gala concert in the grounds of the Montazah Palace, he let out a bellow of delight like a young bull let loose in a field of cows. The Royal Summer Palace with its fairy-tale turrets and towers, its panoramic views of the Mediterranean and its fabulous Turko-Florentine-style gardens, was the perfect setting for what was to be the concert of the year – no, the decade. Tickets would be free – this was his present to Alexandria. Interviewed by the *Egyptian Gazette*, Ozan's black eyes had filled with tears when he quoted the old Arabian proverb: '"If you have much, give of your wealth, if you have little, give of your heart." I am giving of both,' he'd said, omitting to add that the concert would also be the perfect knockout blow against Ya'qub Halabi, the Cairo impresario with whom he competed fiercely.

Preparations began immediately: Luc Lefevre, a well-known Parisian artist, designed a superb art-nouveau-style poster, with the Pharos lighthouse beaming out again, and the caption: *Dance Alexandria Dance.*

A Cairo tent-maker made an elaborate outdoor stage designed to look like the interior of an exotic Bedouin tent; sewing machines whirred in the souks to fill it with sumptuous embroidered drapes and cushions, and in the Attarine souk, three glass-blowers worked around the clock to make over two thousand specially designed glass lights to be filled with candles and hung like fireflies from the trees.

For the party afterwards, crates of Haut-Brion 1924 and Fonseca 1912, and raki and cognac were ordered for the guests. Madame Eloise, who was promoted to chief costume designer, hired in five extra seamstresses, and became grandly French again and prone to soliloquies about Patou.

And in the streets, the souks and the coffee shops of Manshiya and Karmuz people talked of little else: after three years of being bombed, and often hungry and afraid, Alexandria was ready for a party.

I can do this, Dom thought on the day of the concert: I can go back to the squadron – or to Cairo for the few days' leave still owing. That morning, wandering through the Palace Gardens, he'd watched a team of excitable workmen slotting together the steel struts that formed the frame of the tented stage. Yards of embroidered fabrics were flung to hide the ugly skeleton underneath, then long skeins of coloured lights were threaded in and out of the trees, and bit by bit an empty patch of grass was filled by a magical and illusory world, a patch which, he reminded himself, would be empty again when they took it all down.

No self-pity, he thought, walking back to his hotel. *No looking back.* This was her world and he was well out of it, and he thoroughly disliked himself like this – desiring and undesired, indecisive. He wanted his old self back. In the distance he could still hear music playing, and the boom and retreat of a voice testing a microphone: '*Wahd, athnan, thlathh, rb'h, khmsh . . .*' Thanks to Ibrahim, he could count up to twenty fluently now.

And hearing the music, his mind changed again: he could do this, he could stay – but why go through it? another part of him argued. What he most needed now was to get back to the squadron, to fly again, to talk to what friends remained, to bed down again in his own reality. A different kind of longing, but just as fierce in its way.

When he went to the railway station to check on train times to Cairo, a smiling ticket clerk told him not to bother to book. Who in their right mind, his wry expression signalled, would want to leave Alex on a night like this?

When twilight fell, he stood on his own at the edge of a jostling and excited crowd, wanting to die of misery.

At the last possible moment, he'd stepped off the train. He wanted to hear her sing one more time; it felt like a vital necessity. The sensible side of him had tried to fashion this into a rational decision. Why not? The clerk was right, it was an historical event; he could go as a disinterested observer, not speak to her, not make his presence known, be simply one of the anonymous crowd already flowing like a river towards the trams and the gharries that would take them to the Palace Gardens.

He knew where she was staying. Earlier that afternoon, he'd followed her in a taxi from the gardens to the small smart private hotel on the Corniche. She'd come up in the world, he noted wryly, remembering her humorous description of that grim little London bed and breakfast before her first audition.

It would have been fun to share these things with her. Now it felt squalid following her, like a private detective, and he'd disliked himself exceedingly for doing so. With his collar up, and camouflaged by a crowd in a holiday mood, he'd watched her leave the hotel, half an hour later, cross the road and sit down by herself on a bench overlooking the bay. She was wearing a dark crimson coat, a velvet hat. She'd looked small sitting against the vast sweep of the sky. She'd shielded her eyes with her hand and looked out to the sea, which was choppy. *You shouldn't be here on your own. It's still dangerous in Alexandria*, he'd told her. *All of us think we lead charmed lives but we don't.*

And then, in a flood of bitterness: *If you'd really wanted to find me*, *it would have been so easy: you could have phoned the squadron, left a proper letter, left a message with one of your friends.*

He'd almost crossed the road. He might have tapped her on the shoulder and said lightly: 'What a coincidence – fancy meeting you here again.' Banter might have followed, shrieks of embarrassed laughter. It would not seem at all extraordinary him being in Alex on a night like tonight. He would tell her he was here with the squadron, tell the heart-wrenching tale of being shot down again and rescued in the desert, show her what dangerous and important things took place in the real world.

He took a deep breath, put his toe over the kerb and pulled it back again. He imagined her polite double-take, the look of panic in her eyes – *damn, trapped* – a muddled explanation, insincere concern for him – theatricals were good at that. *Darling sweetie pie, what happened? Gosh, so thin! Poor little pet!* et cetera. Except, of course, she'd never really been like that, and what he'd liked about her at first was how straight she'd seemed, which made the trap all the more cleverly disguised.

This was all going through his head when a new agony presented itself. A youngish man – twenty-five, thirty? Hard to tell from this distance – had approached her from the western end of the Corniche. A blond, long-legged fellow, walking towards her – a civilian arty type by the looks of his pale linen suit and lolloping gait. She turned and looked at him – Dom was almost certain she smiled. He'd sat down on the bench beside her. They talked intently, heads together, a stream of words for what felt like a long, long time. A lovers' quarrel? An insistent fan? A new admirer pressing his suit? Impossible to tell. The only thing he must get into his big fat head now was that there would always be men, and they would want to get close to her.

The man stood up; a small boy, a Corniche hawker, approached them, head winningly on one side, offering souvenirs. She shook her head. The man bowed at her slightly, raised his hat. He walked off briskly in the direction he'd come from.

Alone again, she'd stood up and looked towards the sea, and then turned her back to it. He'd winced as he watched her fling herself into the busy traffic to cross the road. He'd hidden in a dark alleyway beside the hotel as she climbed its stairs and closed the big brass doors behind her.

She's gone, he'd told himself trembling. Nothing to do with me now.

One or two of the local newspapers had questioned the wisdom of having an outdoor concert in Alex in the middle of winter, and in truth, before the war, and the blackout, had properly ended, but Ozan's confident prediction that the gods would smile on them was correct (oh, how Ya'qub Halabi would gnash his teeth!) because on the night he'd planned, 17 January, the sun set in a molten lava flow of pinks, golds and oranges, followed by a calm, cold night and a sky full of stars.

By the time it grew dark, the streets were jammed with people making their way down the Corniche, by tram, donkey, gharry and taxi to the Palace Gardens.

The stones surrounding the statues of Muhammad Ali Pasha were taken down, garlands of flowers left in their place. By eight o'clock, the air in the Palace Gardens was full of the smells of roasting meat and fried chickpeas. Sleepy black-eyed children were hoisted on to their parents' shoulders and given sweets and dates to eat. Old grandpas in djellabas were propped up by their young. Crowds of English and New Zealanders, Indian soldiers, a Scottish piper with his bagpipes were there, and the ATS girls, nurses bussed in from local field and military hospitals. And whatever hard feelings (and there were many) remained between the British, the Egyptians, the Jews, the Greeks, the Arabs who were there, they were put off for this one night. Tonight the whole city was breathing a collective sigh of relief: with luck and a fair wind it looked like they'd come through. Tonight was for singing and dancing.

Ten minutes before the curtain went up, the jugglers who'd wandered through the crowd stopped juggling and the lutists who'd been singing the old Arabic songs put away their instruments, and a rapt silence fell over the crowd.

Ozan, working on the principle of nothing succeeds like excess, had gone magnificently overboard, and when the curtain slowly rose on the stage, it appeared to open a fantastic jewellery box. When dancers rose up from the cushions, and the stage began to pulsate with colour and glitter and noise, the crowd gasped and groaned with delight. This was living; this was what they'd come for. An orchestra of twenty-five hand-picked musicians playing ouds and lutes and violins burst into a frenzy of notes. The crowd yelled, some of the women made strange wild sounds with their tongues.

At the back of the stage, the spotlight suddenly fell on a large mother-of-pearl Aladdin's chest, and there were drum rolls and the shimmering of tambourines as Ozan stepped out. He was wearing one of the beautiful dinner suits his Parisian tailor had made before the war, and a purple cummerbund. He bounded towards the front of the stage, held his hands up to quell the madly cheering crowd, issued a torrent of Arabic words which made them cheer and clap and wave their flags, and then he roared out into the night:

'Dance, Alexandria, dance, Hitler has no chance.'

Longing to leave, rooted to the spot, Dom waited for her. There was no programme, or none that he had been able to understand, and he had stayed away from the groups of European people. He sat through the fireworks, the acrobats, the incomprehensible Arabic comedian who had the audience howling with laughter;

Faiza Mushawar, exuding a kind of haughty self-confidence; Arleta, singing and wiggling and making the Tommies hoot and yell.

When Saba came on stage after the first interval, he almost stopped breathing. She was wearing a new red dress, her hair was loose. In spite of all the nonsense that had gone on between them, his guts twisted for her. The crowd seemed enormous and she looked so small. There were only three Europeans in her backing group: a pianist, a guitarist and a double bassist.

The crowd hushed as they began to tune up. She turned and smiled at the pianist, gave him a nod of her head. He felt the surprise of the crowd around him as she sang what sounded like an Arabic song, but he couldn't be sure. He was so hurt, and helplessly admiring too. She seemed so foreign, so focused, so sure of herself and the night. Around him the fairy lights shivered in the dark trees which swayed and sighed, and the crowd moved with them, the guitarist threw soft notes at her, the pianist looked quietly ecstatic and so did she. What could I possibly have added to that? he thought.

When the song was done, it took a while for the whooping and clapping to die down, and then the guitarist noodled away on his guitar and the lights around the stage faded to a more intimate glow. She sat down on a stool near the piano, and announced matter-of-factly that her next song would be 'Smoke Gets in Your Eyes'.

Their song. The song she'd sung for him.

As she held the microphone and told her secrets, he felt a sick fury spread through his body. How could you? A million stupid songs to sing, and you chose this one.

She seemed to be breathing the song and yet he could hear every word.

When it was over, she looked up, her face like a holy painting in its sadness. A triumph of training and technique and controlled emotion, no running out of air, no false notes – nothing for him, everything for the cheering crowd.

He took a step back. This night would soon be over, he told himself; by this time next year, they would all have packed up their tents and gone home.

He sat under a tree with his head in his hands. Oh Christ! he thought, clenching his teeth tight. *Don't you dare.*

*

The moon had risen to its furthest height now over the Palace Gardens. It cast its glow over the trees, and the turreted fairy-tale towers at the back of the stage. When the show was over, the principal characters bounded on to the stage again and took their bows like performers in a pantomime. First the Egyptian band, waving and cheering, the local acrobats doing five handstands and a twist apiece, followed by Boguslaw and Lev, Max Bagley clasping his hands in triumph above his head like a prize fighter, Arleta Samson walking her fabulous walk, touching her crimson nails to her mouth and sending out passionate kisses, three Arab horses in scarlet bridles trotting, the fire-eaters, Faiza Mushawar, regal and with a small but distinct distance separating her from the Europeans; Saba, changed into a silver dress, smiling and waving and having the time of her life, graciously accepting the elaborate salaams of the clowns.

And lastly Ozan, hands held out in modest protest at the roar of love and appreciation that greeted him. After what Dom presumed was the Egyptian national anthem and 'God Save the Queen', three dozen white doves of peace were released from the bamboo cages they'd been kept in backstage all day. The flustered birds rose in the darkening air, hovered in lights that tinted them red and green, circled and flew towards the sea.

Dom glanced towards the man who had released the birds and saw him smiling broadly; he didn't give a damn whether they came back or not. Their point was theatrical effect, their usefulness over; that was the way it was in show business it seemed. One showy gesture and they were gone.

Chapter 49

The pavements of the Corniche were crowded after the performance, so she took a gharry, pleading with the driver to go as fast as he could. The horse kept shying, frightened by the commotion, and when they got close to the Cecil Hotel, where Cleeve had requested one last meeting, they were held up by drunken soldiers dancing a conga line.

Cleeve had told her to meet him in the cocktail bar, to the right of the hotel's reception area and lifts. Since everyone would still be leaving the concert, it would be quiet and he had some news for her. No need for disguises now, he said, they would simply appear as a couple having a few drinks together.

It seemed to her, as she walked into the hotel with its subdued gleam of well-polished brass, its marble floors and copious flower arrangements, that Cleeve was back in his natural habitat again. In the candlelit bar, beyond the lobby, an elegant negro in a dinner jacket was noodling away at a piano underneath a potted palm tree. She could hear the clink of glasses, the murmur of well-bred voices, and there was Cleeve himself, partly concealed behind a leather banquette, elegant, long-legged, languid, the kind of well-dressed Englishman who contrived to look as if he didn't give a hoot about his clothes, quietly taking it all in.

But that first impression of ease and sophistication didn't last. When he saw her, he leapt to his feet and switched on a quick bright smile – like a gauche boy on his first date – and she saw, above the faultless linen of his shirt, a dried-up trickle of blood where he had shaved too closely. There'd been no time to change after the concert, so she arrived in the same beautiful silver dress she'd taken the curtain call in, her shoulders covered in a fine floating silk stole.

'Saba,' he said. 'You look wonderful. Gosh, you've grown up.'

The fulsome compliment threw her; his smile, lopsided, sentimental, raised alarm bells. Was he drunk?

'I'm sorry I'm late, and I can't stay long.' She slid into the banquette beside him. 'Ozan's giving a cast party – he's asked all the local bigwigs and I can't let him down.'

'Of course, of course . . . it's just that I was passing through Alexandria, and I couldn't . . . I felt it was my last . . .' He abandoned this and blathered helplessly, 'Look, before I say a word, Saba . . . I mean I've got to . . . well I'll just say it: what an absolutely fantastic night this must have been for you. I've heard you before but this . . . you were extraordinary – I shan't forget it ever, that's all. There, I've said it. Sort of.'

'Thank you.' It was hard to see him so lit up when she felt so empty.

'Darling, are you all right . . . what's wrong with me . . . a drink?' His hand went up for the waiter. 'It must be jolly tiring.' He'd never called her darling before; the word hung awkwardly between them.

'Waiter,' he said. 'Champagne, hors d'oeuvres, a menu for mademoiselle.'

'I can't stay to eat,' she repeated. 'Did you say you had some news for me?'

'I did. But surely time for a small bite – there's a terrific new chef here.'

'Dermot, honestly, I can't,' she said more firmly. 'It's a working night for me.'

'So, all right, sorry, crack on,' a note of truculence in his voice. 'Here's my news.'

He looked around him, checking the other drinkers were well out of earshot, his face wavering through the candlelight.

'Jenke is back in London and has been debriefed. I can't be absolutely specific with you for security reasons, but his information, not just from Turkey but from North Africa too, has been absolutely vital . . . and you' – he gave her his important finger-on-the-pulse look – 'I'm here to tell you that your part in the operation has been noted at the very highest levels. How do you feel about that?'

A slight swelling of piano music from behind the palm tree; their waiter appeared flapping a napkin on her lap. She waited until he left.

'How do I feel about what?'

'About being . . . I don't know . . . how should one put it . . . is heroine too much of an exaggeration?'

'Nothing,' she said finally, 'I feel nothing.'

'Really?' He took a sip of his drink, gave her a quizzical look. 'Why not?'

'I don't know.' Because the price was too high, because I wasn't particularly brave, more a child drawn into adult games I didn't understand, because the whole thing finally felt sleazy; because it cost me Dom – all flashing through her head.

He shook his head slightly, with the air of a schoolmaster regretting the wasted talents of a bright pupil.

'Well,' he said huffily. 'I obviously can't tell you what to think, but I would have thought it was an honour.'

'Tell me something.' She spoke before the thought had formed in her brain. 'Was it really worth it? Or is it something people who get caught up in this sort of thing need to feel – particularly when other people die?'

'I don't understand the question.'

'You should do, or at least ask it.'

He drained his drink.

'Steady, Saba,' he warned her, and gave her the most peculiar look – canny and spiteful and affronted. 'No, seriously, steady the buffs, because I have some other news to pass on to you – and you might say something you'll regret.'

She took a deep breath and stared at her glass. Calm down, Saba, it's not his fault what happened.

'Really?'

He lowered his voice – the pianist had stopped playing.

'Really.'

'What news?'

He took a deep breath and called the waiter over.

'Another whisky for me, please, and for mademoiselle?'

She put her hand over her champagne flute.

'No, Dermot, please – just order for yourself. I have to go soon.'

'I think you'll want to stay for this, Saba.'

He leaned towards her and licked his lips.

'They've found him,' he whispered. 'Your man – he's in Alex.'

'What man?' He looked so serious she thought for one mad moment he meant Severin Mueller. 'Who?'

'Your pilot.'

'My pilot?' Nothing in his expression suggested good news. 'Jenke?'

'No, not Jenke,' he said at last. 'Dominic Benson. He's staying at the Waterloo. It's a small private hotel near the railway station. He's been there for nearly a fortnight.'

'Is this a joke?' She felt a tremendous numbness, as if all the feeling parts of her were closing down. 'How do you know?'

'Because I've been looking for him. Ozan asked me to.'

'But you said you couldn't or wouldn't.'

He pushed the ice around in his whisky with his finger.

'I was told to say that. We didn't want you derailed before the concert, but for God's sake, Saba, don't tell anyone I told you that.'

'Is this true?'

He nodded his head and sighed.

'Saw him in the street yesterday. He saw me talking to you. And so, Saba,' he drained his drink and stubbed his cigarette out, 'as the good fairy says in the panto: my job here is ended. News of honours and boyfriend in one evening. Or perhaps I'm more the Widow Twankey in this enterprise. Anyway, if it goes wrong, you know where to find me. I'm going back to England shortly.'

He stood up, still smiling, and when he tried to put his overcoat on missed the arm. He looked in an owlish, deliberate way at his wristwatch.

'Crikey! *Tempus fugit.* I expect you'll want to dash off now. I can't give you a lift, I'm afraid, I'm wanted in another part of town. Here's the address. Tell him from me he's a lucky man.'

As he scribbled down words on a piece of paper, the news began to percolate through her brain and into her blood and down her spine to her nerve endings.

'Dermot,' she smiled at him radiantly, 'is it true?'

He held two fingers up. 'Scout's honour.'

'Really true?'

'Yep.'

She stared at him.

'Thank you, from the bottom of my heart.' She would forgive him, had already, for delaying the news until after the concert. It wasn't as if Ozan hadn't warned her what his priorities were.

'And if it all goes wrong,' he put some soiled notes on the table for the waiter, and tucked a piece of paper in her hand, 'give your old Uncle Dermot a ring.' He picked up his hat. 'It's my sister's address in England – shouldn't really give it to you, but what the hell. I doubt you'll use it.'

Alive! As she stepped out into the street again and looked at the address, she didn't know whether to laugh or scream or cry. Dom was alive! and in Alexandria. All around her the streets pulsated with crowds and street musicians, dancing, singing, shouting. A bonfire burned in one of the city gardens, its sparks flying into the night. No possible chance of a taxi now. She dashed up the street, propelled by a starry elation, and terror too. What if she'd missed her chance? Or he had another girl now and didn't want to see her.

When she stopped near the statue of Muhammad Ali Pasha, her chest was heaving.

Hotel Waterloo, she read from the note Cleeve had thrust into her hand. *Off Rue Nebi Daniel, near railway station.*

After half an hour of frantic searching, she found the hotel in a dilapidated street, wedged between a barber's shop and a Syrian bakery.

Inside the deserted lobby, the night porter was reading the evening paper.

'Where is he?' she said when she had caught her breath. 'Dominic Benson. He's staying here.'

The man looked at her in amazement. A goddess in a silver dress, her sandals filled with dirt and litter, and then he recognised her.

'Madame, madame?' His eyes lit up. 'Your singing was very good. Write your name, *merci*.' He thrust a piece of paper at her. 'Special for me.'

She wrote her name wildly.

'Help me,' she said. 'Please help me. I'm looking for someone.'

'Who?' He was confused.

'Dominic Benson. He's a guest here.'

He opened a drawer under the desk, and pulling out a dusty ledger, took an agonising time locating the page, the day.

'No, madame,' he shook his head regretfully, 'no here. Not now. Tonight . . .' he mimed the carrying of suitcases, 'he's gone to Cairo.'

'When, when?' She grabbed his wrist, pointed at his watch. 'When train?'

He shrugged. 'One hour.' He shrugged again. 'Two hours, maybe. Train special for concert. Sorry.'

The city's main railway station, the Misr, was roughly a mile away from her. She took a taxi, abandoned it when it got stuck in traffic, ran flat out towards the station, her feet sinking into rubbish and horse manure, broken pavements, stones.

When she got to the station, a line of carriage horses stood in a row outside it munching grain from hoods that made them look like prisoners about to be executed. Gasping for air, she ran in and out of them, into a station heaving with people. Searching the crowd for European faces she saw a group of Scottish soldiers standing near the ticket desk.

'Cairo train,' she blurted out.

'Don't break a leg, love,' a kilted soldier warned her. 'The train's gone, it's just left . . . Hang on . . . hang on.' He swayed around, looking at her. 'Were ye not at the—'

'Where? Where?' she shouted.

'Platform two,' they replied in unison.

She ran towards it, past bundles of sleeping beggars, and drunken partygoers, young lovers, soldiers, a peasant farmer carrying his bed on his back, and saw the backside of the train steaming down a long track into a tangle of wires and shattered suburbs, and then on to nowhere.

She stood on the platform in her beautiful wrecked silver dress, her white stole floating wildly in the updraught.

'Stop the bloody train!' she shouted in a Welsh roar designed to carry from valley to valley. '*Stop it! Stop it! Stop it!* Right now!' She tripped and almost fell as she pounded down the platform after it. The train kept going, out of the gloom of the station and into the night, until at the very last minute a porter standing outside the final carriage saw her: a screaming houri in a white robe leaping through smoke.

He shrieked over and over again, dashed inside, pulled the red emergency cord. The train came to a creaking halt.

Under normal circumstances, it might have been a punishable offence, but the mood in the city that night was defiantly playful. People hung from the windows laughing, cheering as she jumped on to a train still wheezing and protesting at its reversal. She ran down cramped corridors calling his name, and through the glass carriage doors peered at strangers: men in tarbooshes and bowler hats and turbans; families tucking down for the night; a group of soldiers who waved and cheered at her.

When she found him, he was sitting by the window in the last carriage but one. She wasn't even sure it was him at first. He looked older, thinner. Before he turned and saw her there, she saw him sigh.

'Dom.' She walked up to him and touched his face. She could hear the grumble of the engine about to start again. The guards shouting. 'Get off the train.'

'Saba.' When he looked at her, there was nothing but pain and confusion in his eyes. 'What's this? What's going on?'

'For God's sake, Dom, get off the train – it's moving.' She felt it throbbing underneath her feet.

'No,' he said. 'Not like this.'

She stood on the seat, stretched above him, tore down his case and threw it through the window on to the platform.

'I can explain, Dom,' she shouted, as the platform moved away. '*Get off the train!*'

Three soldiers leaned from their carriages as they stepped from the train, and stared goggle-eyed at the girl on the platform in the sensational dress having a humdinger of a row with her boyfriend.

'There's no point,' Dom yelled over the noise of the engine. 'Because it's not a stupid game for me.'

'Dom, please,' she said. 'Shut up and walk with me.'

It was too noisy to talk in the station. They stomped off down the street and towards his hotel, she still holding his suitcase.

On the corner of the street, he stopped.

'Saba, listen,' he said, his eyes very black under the street lamp. 'I've made up my mind, I don't want it like this . . . it's not possible. I waited for you, it nearly killed me. Where for Christ's sake did you go? Honest answer for once.'

'Fine.' She slammed his suitcase down. 'Honest answer. I went to a party.'

'A party?'

They looked at each other in hysterical disbelief.

'Oh for pity's sake,' he said. 'Well everything's perfectly clear now. Thank you for at least being straight with me.'

'Dom.' The strap of her sandal had loosened and she had to hobble to keep up with him. 'The party was in Turkey.'

'Oh fine.' He set his jaw and stepped up the pace. 'Fantastic. Terrific. The party was in Turkey. I feel much better already.'

'Listen, you blasted nitwit,' she yelled. They were passing a back-street bar where some young naval officers were drinking. 'Take me back to your room,' she shouted, 'and I'll tell you what happened.'

'*Woo-hoo*,' came from the direction of the naval boys, who were spilling on to the pavement, and from one: 'I wouldn't turn that one down, mate!'

'Fuck off,' Dom shouted.

Back at the Waterloo Hotel, they walked up the dimly lit stairs like sleepwalkers. A new receptionist, half asleep at the desk, gave them a new key, a new room, no questions asked. Upstairs, Dom switched on a tasselled bedside light. There was only one wooden chair, next to a sink, so they sat side by side on the bed.

'Saba, listen to me,' he said. He took hold of both her wrists in his hands and looked into her eyes very seriously. 'We're here because it's a quiet place to talk, but before you say a word, I saw you with a man earlier – if you're otherwise engaged, don't bother making up a story, because you see, at the risk of sounding dramatic, or a little bit theatrical myself, I don't want to go through this again, and I'm not going to.'

'Dom.' The simple miracle of him being there was starting to break through.

'Don't.' He stood up and walked to the chair, that was as far away from her as possible.

So she told him what she could about Istanbul and Ozan, Cleeve.

He listened with no change of expression, and then:

'Saba, are you serious?' he said. 'Did they give you a toupee and false glasses?'

'Deadly serious.' She put her hand over his mouth. 'There's more.'

She told him about the German parties, but not about Severin. She couldn't, not yet, perhaps never.

'I had an accident. A car accident.' He sat beside her on the bed now. She drew back her hair and showed him the scar. 'They were taking me away from the house.'

'Oh God.' He touched her for the first time, a light touch on the temple.

'Why didn't you trust me – tell me where you were going? I could have kept it secret.'

'I couldn't.' Her face looked pinched in the lamplight. 'I was told to avoid boyfriends because, if you were arrested, or captured, it might have been dangerous for you.'

'What else happened?' He searched her face intently. 'Something else did, I feel it.'

'A lot . . . I'll tell you later . . . some good things too. Cleeve told me tonight that Jenke's information had made a difference, but he wouldn't be more specific. Even telling me where you were broke all the rules.'

'You'll probably end up with more medals than me.'

'Probably.'

He saw the flash of her white teeth, her dimples.

'Incredible,' he murmured gathering her in his arms. 'Unbelievable. Ridiculous. You on the train,' he started to laugh, 'and before that . . . I went to the concert . . . it was torture listening to you.'

He wiped tears from her face with his handerchief.

'What happened to you?' she said at last. 'You're not well.'

'I had a prang,' he said. 'I'll tell you later. I don't want to talk about it now.'

And because the peace was new and precarious, she let him get away with this.

'We thought you were dead,' she said. 'Barney gave me a letter from you; he found it in your locker. Didn't he tell you?'

'I haven't seen Barney – he's been away. I've hardly seen anyone since I was picked up, but what letter? Oh for heaven's sake, no.' It had suddenly dawned on him. 'That stupid letter. I was so angry . . . I didn't mean to send it.'

'I got this too.' She held up her wrist and showed it to him.

'The bracelet. Do you wear it?'

'All the time.'

He leaned down and kissed her then. He touched her face there, and there; he held her hair in his hands. He led her over to the wooden chair near the sink, and washed the dirt off her feet, grumbling at the state they were in.

'Thank you, Nursey,' she said. He soaped them and dried them, kissed them gently toe by toe. When he was done, she stood up and he unhooked her dress and they got into the bed together, and she held him close and gave him the sweetest kiss of his life, and then they wept unashamedly. 'I thought you were dead,' she sobbed. 'And I wanted to die with you.' And he believed her because she was a truthful person; some part of him had known that from the beginning.

Chapter 50

Spring came in a rush of flowers – mallow and poppies, purple and white anemones, coltsfoot, marigolds and celandine. She picked handfuls of them from the back garden of the house Ozan had lent them at Muntazah Beach.

By Ozan's standards the house was no more than a hut, but they were delighted by its long verandas, its sunny whitewashed rooms, and the small garden at the back, where acacia and jasmine were blooming, and oranges, tangerines and lemons burst from the trees. The house was private, and apart from a honking donkey tethered nearby and some morning birds, it was quiet – a rare luxury after living in camps and communal tents.

In the mornings, Yusuf, one of Ozan's servants, arrived on a bicycle with a basket full of wine and fresh bread, cheeses and whatever fish had been netted that day. In a sunny kitchen with blue and white tiles, Saba tried, with mixed success, to learn how to cook.

But for the first two days, they lay in their whitewashed bedroom in each other's arms and slept like exhausted animals, laughing when they were awake at what a waste of time this was. Then came the long, lazy days of making love and swimming, of sunbathing and eating barefoot meals by candlelight on their veranda, which overlooked the sea.

'Look,' she said one night, gazing up into the night sky. 'That's Berenice's Hair.' She pointed out a line of stars just above the dark. 'No idea who Berenice was,' she added. 'My dad showed me them. In a book.'

'She was the wife of a Macedonian king,' he told her. 'When the king went to war, she made a pact with Aphrodite, the goddess of love, that if she cut off her hair he would be protected. She took her hair to the temple, but it disappeared. A court astronomer claimed he'd found it again, as a new constellation, which was tactful otherwise all hell would have broken loose.'

'How do you know these things?'

'From flying and general brilliance.' He was still peering at the stars, light years away himself for that moment.

She liked him knowing things. It comforted her.

He'd been reading Cavafy's poems to her. He'd discovered the poet had once lived in the Rue Lepsius, four doors down from them.

There's no ship for you, there's no road.
Now that you've wasted your life here, in this small corner,
You've destroyed it everywhere in the world.

'That was how I felt,' Dom told her. 'When you left and I couldn't find you. It was the worst feeling in the world.'

Sometimes you are happy without knowing it, and sometimes you are happy and completely aware of it – its preciousness, its fleetingness.

And there were times when the almost mystical perfection of these days frightened Saba – everything felt right, nothing was lacking. It was so unlike the rest of life, with its uncertainties, its suffering and boredom, and all the other tragedies, large and small, she had witnessed. She wanted to make it last for ever, but was old enough now to know this was impossible. The world was changing and would change again. Dom was waiting to hear about his next posting – the Desert Air Force had mostly packed up its tents and gone home, its pilots flown to other squadrons in Sicily or Burma. Saba was rehearsing for Ozan's next extravaganza in Cairo, and singing for what troops remained in Suez or Cairo. Out in the desert all the bric-a-brac of war – the hangars, temporary runways, fuel depots – were disappearing under heaps of sand.

Halfway through their time at Muntazah, Arleta came to stay. She arrived with Saba's mail, two packets of Turkish delight with pistachio nuts in it, a bottle of gin and a toy camel, found in a souvenir shop, with bulging crimson eyes that glowed horrifyingly when you plugged it in.

She handed Saba a letter written in her mother's round schoolgirl hand.

Saba took it into the bedroom, locked the door behind her. Her hands were shaking as she opened it, thinking it brought news of her father's death – something she dreamed of regularly, always with a shocking feeling of loss.

But here was good news: little sister Lou was back from the valleys, cheeky as ever, doing well in her exams, a proper little grown-up girl. Tan, fit as a flea and with a new friend, another Turkish lady who lived in their street. And in the last paragraph, her mother sounded an unusual note of treason.

Don't you dare not come to Pomeroy Street when you get back to Blighty, because this will always be your home, no matter what your father says. He has just signed on for another tour with Fyffes and is away even more than he used to be, so we'll have plenty of time, and to be honest with you, Saba love, I'm glad you've made your decision. You have your own life to lead and I have mine, and I should have left him years ago – he's always wanted things his way and I'm fed up to the back teeth with it.

This was a shock.

Up until now she'd seen her mother in a number of confusing, contradictory guises – good sport, loyal peacemaker, theatrical cheerleader, food maker – but that small snarl of underdog rage in the last sentence made her wonder if she'd ever truly known her at all, and the thought that the war might have changed Mum too was upsetting. She talked it over with Arleta during one of their long, lazy morning swims towards a raft, moored a hundred yards or so from the beach.

She told her how Mum – a woman who once wouldn't leave the house unless hair and make-up were band-box fresh – had happily gone off for her daily shifts at Curran's factory in her dreadful overalls and turban, and how she'd told Saba it was a lot more fun than being in the house all day, particularly if your husband was at sea.

'Fair comment.' Arleta took this calmly. 'It would drive me mad being home all day – and you. *Boring.*'

Arleta, who was trying not to get her hair wet, had the look of a startled Afghan hound being forced to swim for the first time.

'I mean, look at all this,' she panted. She waved her hand at the wide horizon. 'We got it through work, and we'll miss it, won't we?'

Saba looked around her: at the dazzling blue sea, the cloudless sky, the shore with its fine white sand, the house on the cliff where she and Dom had been so happy.

'Do we have to leave?' A pointless question.

'Don't be a prat,' said her friend. 'England will be horrible, but it's our kind of horrible.'

They'd reached the raft. Arleta, trimmer than ever after weeks of dancing, sprang from the water like a glamorous Aphrodite; she shook her hair out and flopped down beside Saba, then lifted each leg in the air, profoundly pleased by what she saw.

They lay for a while, side by side, arms touching, soaking up the sun, and then Arleta asked:

'Have you thought about the India tour yet?' She slid her eyes towards her.

Saba sighed – this was tricky. They'd both been offered a three-week ENSA tour in India, but she hadn't yet found the moment to mention it to Dom.

'I honestly can't decide at the moment; it depends on Dom's posting too, and other things.'

'Saba.' Arleta sat up and looked at her very seriously. 'Can I say something, and don't misunderstand me.'

'If you like.' Saba sensed a warning she didn't want.

'Well, it's just this . . . not saying that you and Dom don't seem blissfully happy together – you do, and not saying he doesn't adore you and that you're not mad about him, and that it's not all very romantic.' Arleta clutched her bosom and swirled her eyes. 'Just . . . don't give him everything; keep something for yourself.'

'I know that, Arleta,' she said, even though she was struggling with it. At this moment, all she wanted was to have his babies, to learn to cook, to carry on feeling this honeyed contentment day after day after day. 'One of the best things about being in ENSA has been doing what I was trained to do, and it's been tremendous – I really do know that.'

Arleta's eyebrow was still raised. 'When you thought he was dead,' she persisted, 'you stopped singing, or at least you wanted to, and take it from your Auntie Arl, no man is worth that.'

There was a thread of unhappiness in Arleta's voice. It wasn't the first time Saba had noticed it since she'd arrived.

'Arl, don't say a word if you don't want to, but what happened to Barney? You've hardly mentioned him.'

Arleta's voice sounded hazy. 'Barney?' she said. 'Oh, finished.

Completely. I meant to tell you. It's fine, darling, honestly – you don't have to say anything. He's going back to England and I knew it would happen. I didn't want to tell you in front of Dom in case I said bitter and twisted things and Dom felt forced to defend him.'

'So good, not upset then?' Saba trod cautiously – Arleta loathed people feeling sorry for her.

'Not at all,' Arleta said firmly. 'I knew it would happen. It did. End of story, and besides, I need to see my little boy again and to at least try and stop messing around for a few years, but oh God, I shall miss it here too – it's been heavenly.' She sang *heavenly* like an opera singer.

'What will you miss most, Arlie: the scorpions? The dead dog under the stage in Suez? Sand in your knickers? Sharing a canvas sink with Janine?'

'Ha, ha, ha – hard to tell, smartypants. Well, all that too. Let's not get too sentimental.'

They were quiet for a while. Arleta sighed deeply.

'I'll miss you,' she said, the way she came out with things sometimes, simple and clean.

'You've been a good friend.'

They were silent for a moment, and then Arleta stood up and muttered, 'Last swim, to hell with it.' She flung herself into the air and wildly bicycling her legs, broke the surface of the water with a splash. With her wet hair plastered around her face, she looked ten years younger.

'Oh God, that's wonderful,' she spluttered. 'That's the way to have a proper swim,' and they headed side by side towards the shore.

Arleta left the next day on the back of Dom's motorbike – he'd offered to drop her at the train station in Alexandria. They were standing on the doorstep when she appeared, a film star today in dark glasses, hair swathed in chiffon. She turned to Saba.

'Give me a hug, you mad little creature.' She put her arms around her, and enveloped her in Shalimar. Tears poured down her face. She brushed them away and got on the bike with a chorus girl's high kick. Shortly before she disappeared in a cloud of dust, she kissed her fingers, flung them passionately towards Saba shouting, '*Crepi il lupo*,' a dramatic gesture that almost derailed the motorbike.

And Saba, standing in the dust listening to the fading roar of the motorbike, wondered if she would see her again. Arleta had said it might not be for ages, maybe for never – that was how it was in show business.

When Dom got back at lunchtime he was covered in dust. He was carrying a package in one hand and an envelope in the other.

Saba was in the kitchen inexpertly hacking up some bread, and trying to remember how long Mum had done her hard-boiled eggs for. One of the many pleasures of this time was feeding him – the laying out of cheese and ripe tomatoes, early melons and bread on a plate filled her with a tender protectiveness never felt before.

She stood at the window smiling. She heard the motorbike cut out. He came into the kitchen and kissed the back of her neck.

'My girl.' He put his arms around her. 'My beautiful girl. Are you sad?'

'A bit.' But glad too that it was just them again.

He slid his hand around her waist and inhaled her hair.

'Come and have a drink with me. I've got a surprise.'

He led her to the veranda. They sat down together on a wicker chair. He handed her the envelope, watching her closely while she opened it.

Two tickets.

She read them, put her hand over her mouth and gasped.

'A cruise up the Nile. Oh Dom! How fantastic!' She squealed and jumped into his lap.

'The timing,' he said excitedly, 'is perfect. The AOC has given us a fortnight's leave, and who knows when we'll have to leave Egypt now, and I thought, what the hell, I'll go ahead and book it. It's a beautiful old-fashioned boat, the *Philae*, and we can call in on all those old pharaohs in their pyramids, they're all opening again now the war's over. We can go to the Valley of the Kings.' His eyes gleamed with excitement.

'Hang on, hang on, Dom.' She examined the tickets more closely. She'd stopped listening.

'The first week, that should be fine shouldn't it?'

'No, Dom,' she said with a sinking feeling. 'No. I absolutely can't. No chance. It leaves on the twenty-third of March – the week of Ozan's Cairo concert.'

'Oh *fuck*.' He made no attempt to hide his disappointment.

'Didn't you remember that? And do you mind not swearing in front of me like that,' even though she didn't mind all that much.

'No,' he said flatly, although she had told him. 'No, I didn't remember. So, is it always going to be like this?' he said. There was a steely note in his voice she hadn't heard before.

'Like what?'

'Like this.'

'Probably,' thinking *blast it, you* should *have remembered – it's important to me.*

She slammed down her glass, stood up and glared at him.

'Dammit, Saba, don't look at me like that.'

'Look at you like what?' she bellowed. 'I'm not looking like anything.'

And so on until they were shouting so loudly that the donkey in the next door field started honking with alarm.

He flung open the veranda gate and went down to the beach, and sat down with his head in his hands, childishly crushed. He'd pictured the whole thing on the way home – the boat drifting up the Nile; waking up in her arms; seeing feluccas and little villages, and then the wonderful drama of the Valley of the Kings, with her by his side. He'd waited for so long.

After a few moments of intense self-pity, he stood up and, walking to the edge of the sea, chose a flat stone and hurled it, making it hop four times across the water before it sank.

So would it always be like this? He chucked another stone as hard as he could – the compromises, the confusions, the sense that her plans might be just as important as his. Because if it was, he couldn't stand it. Thank God there was still time to back out – no binding promises had been made.

She watched him from the veranda, skimming stone after stone into the sea, and then she went into the bedroom and lay down.

She wept, furious at first, and then in sorrowful confusion. *I love him but do I really want this?* The tears, the resentments, the appeasing, the yelling. *I'd simply turn into another version of my mother.*

She was lying face down on their bed when he walked in. She'd closed the shutters and soaked the pillow.

'I can't do it,' she said in a muffled voice, 'not like this.'

He put his hand on her back.

'I know.'

He got into bed, put his face against hers.

'Saba,' he said. 'It would kill me to lose you now.'

'I went through this with my father,' she said, 'feeling wrong all the time – as if my work was a disgrace.'

'I never want you to feel like that.'

Oh, the sweetness of feeling his hand on her hair, the relief of knowing he loved her still and that they could talk like this without the world crashing in.

'I'm sorry I ruined your surprise.' She kissed his chest. 'It was such a lovely idea . . . and I do want to do it. But I can't let the company down.'

He was gently unbuttoning her dress; she was smiling at him, but as she lay in his arms afterwards, she felt for the first time the rub of trying to jigsaw two lives together. A premonition that it would not be easy, that it could take a lifetime.

That night they ate supper together on the veranda at a moment in the day when the sun was leaving and the moon rising and the two halves of the water in the bay were silver and gold. It was, they agreed politely, beautiful but she saw it rather than felt it because the row had shaken them both, and Saba felt precariously close to tears as she passed him food and wine and there was a tiptoeing quality to their conversation that was new to them.

At the end of a long silence she said, 'Dom, tell me what you're thinking. You look sad.'

He took both of her hands in his.

'I was thinking about flying.' He looked sheepish.

'Flying! Where to?' She wanted to laugh suddenly. 'Away from me?'

'No! No – it's just that . . . well,' he fiddled with his fork, and looked at her, 'I was thinking that when you learn to fly, the taking-off part is the easy bit – it's the landing that's tricky.' He raised the fork in the air. 'It's not like a car, it's more like a one-wheel bicycle – you have to balance the thing longitudinally and latitudinally, and after it's gone up, you have to learn how to gently come down . . .' He looked at her thoughtfully, 'I don't want to mess it up.'

'I know.' She swallowed hard.

In the silence that followed, she heard the rusty cry of the donkey again. He was fed with a bundle of grass every night around eight.

She took a deep breath and held Dom's hand. 'Will you solemnly promise me two things?' she said.

'This sounds serious.'

'It is.' She said it quickly. 'I want you to promise that you won't ask me to marry you – not yet.'

She almost laughed – he looked so surprised, or was it relieved?

He looked at her for a long time. 'How strange. I'd sort of worked my way round on the beach this afternoon to going down on one satined knee quite soon.'

'I said not yet.' She was grinning broadly at him. 'I want to feel free for a little while longer – maybe for the first time in my life.'

What she'd been thinking that afternoon came out in a rush.

'I want to work. I don't want to feel guilty about it. I've had years of that with my dad, and I've had enough. But I don't want to lose you either.'

She could feel him thinking.

'Wedlock,' he said at last. 'It's such an attractive word, don't you think? It fills one with confidence. The lock bit particularly.'

'I'm not joking, Dom.' Or was she, now she'd said it out loud? Part of her longed to leap into his arms and forget entirely about being her.

But he was. The old bad habits resurfacing, because this was a new way of thinking for him. It would take some getting used to, and he wasn't sure yet whether he'd been turned down or not.

Around midnight the sea was black, apart from a strip of gauzy moonlight that ran from the shoreline to the horizon lighting up the raft.

'I think we should stop talking now and go for a swim,' he said.

'Are you mad?' She was relieved to see him smile again. 'It's probably freezing.'

'We're British,' he told her, striding towards the waves. 'We're bred for it. Take your clothes off, woman, and jump in.'

When they'd stripped, he flung her over his shoulder and ran towards the sea, and when he dropped her in, she squealed in fright, both pretended and real, because it wasn't as cold as she thought it would be, and because she liked feeling his arms around her. The comforting maleness of him.

Side by side they swam up the hazy corridor of light, the sea inky black around them, and when they got closer to the raft, they could see in the distance the smudge of the horizon and a boat with one dark sail.

Dom was a strong swimmer and had to slow himself down to stay with her.

She was thinking about the North Sea, and how cold it would feel at night; about her father, who might or might not be sailing there.

Nothing will be the same, she thought; going back to England will be like stepping through a door into the complete unknown.

'I would like to take another run at my proposal,' he said. 'I stuffed it up last time.' They were sitting on the raft together, their feet dangling in the sea. 'If I don't, I'll kick myself for the rest of my life. So here goes.'

His face looked pearly in the moonlight, and she could see the sharp planes of his cheekbones. You hardly saw his scars at all now except in bright light.

'I had a moment of truth in the desert; I saw it so clearly – my dream version of you and your reality – and I saw that I needed you both. And if having you means the odd bloody great row, or a bit of saucepan-throwing, who cares? At least I'll be with someone I adore and admire, and who can sing in the bath.'

'Oh God.' She put her hand over his mouth. 'Stop it. I shouted so much earlier – aren't you terrified?'

'Terrified.' He put his hand around her shoulder and pulled her towards him. 'You're a brute. And I am going to be a very unhappy, henpecked husband.'

'Let's swim,' she said. It was too much – too confusing, too wonderful.

'Wait, wait, wait, impatient woman – I haven't finished yet. What I mean is some arrangement that won't involve . . . I don't know, confetti and matching cutlery, but will take in babies, and perhaps an aircraft for me, and you singing. Is that completely impossible?'

'Probably.' She kissed him full on the mouth. 'It sounds awfully good to me.'

The sea was a fraction colder as they dived in – it took their breath away. When they had caught their breath and were swimming side by side, they sang loudly and childishly, '*A life on the ocean wave . . .*' By the time they got to the sandbank, they were planning a new trip up the Nile together, and Dom told her something interesting, something she didn't know before. He told her how Howard Carter, after years of frustration and false hope, had shone his torch inside Tutankhamen's burial chamber and seen the wall of solid gold, the strange animal statues.

Wonderful things. She tasted the words as they swam side by side towards the indistinct shore. To be young, to be alive, to have a future together; the promise of her own life, still hidden. From here she could see a faint straggling light coming from their bedroom window, could feel the water growing warm, then cold, shadowy and clear again, the tug of invisible currents against her skin.

Scientific Foundations of Paediatrics

Edited by

JOHN A. DAVIS

M.B., B.S., M.Sc., F.R.C.P.

Professor of Paediatrics and Child Health, University of Manchester; Honorary Consultant Paediatrician, United Manchester Hospitals and Royal Manchester Children's Hospital; Chairman, Academic Board, British Paediatric Association

and

JOHN DOBBING

B.Sc., M.B., B.S., M.R.C.Path.

Senior Lecturer, Department of Child Health, University of Manchester; Honorary Consultant, United Manchester Hospitals; Member of the Academic Board, British Paediatric Association

LONDON

WILLIAM HEINEMANN MEDICAL BOOKS LTD

First published 1974

ISBN 0 433 07190 7

Text set in 10/11 pt. Monotype Times New Roman, printed by letterpress, and bound in Great Britain at The Pitman Press, Bath

To

R. A. McCance

Ronald Mac Keith

Mary Sheridan

Donald Winnicott

all of them James Spence medallists of the British Paediatric Association who, in their several ways have been responsible for reminding British paediatricians that their primary concern should be with growth and development and its relationship to medical practice.

PREFACE

In compiling this account of the Scientific Foundations of Paediatrics, we have tried not to duplicate the excellent textbooks of clinical paediatrics which already exist, especially in respect of those many aspects of paediatrics which it shares with the rest of medicine. However, we have long felt the need for a book dealing with what we regard as the essential distinguishing characteristic of the medicine of childhood: its concern with growth and development. The extensive literature on this subject has hitherto been scattered in a variety of books and journals and, as far as we are aware, not presented in a single volume directed to studies of paediatric medicine.

This book is about growth and development as a background to paediatric practice; it is intended for those who have chosen paediatrics as a career in medicine. We had hoped to treat its essential theme more or less comprehensively, dealing in detail with some topics of especial clinical rather than theoretical importance; but inevitably some subjects have been better or worse covered than others, mainly because of the difficulty of finding willing contributors with the right qualifications for undertaking reviews of the kind we were looking for. To our sorrow and loss, two authors died before the completion of their manuscripts, while others failed to meet the publisher's deadline leaving no option but to leave out sections that we had hoped to include and felt to be important. Some authors provided us with monographs rather than chapters but of such scope and quality that we decided that it would be wrong to ask for them to be reduced; others, often because their subjects have not yet been studied in depth or breadth, were only able to give us relatively brief accounts of topics which obviously require more study and may be given more extended treatment in possible future editions. For the resultant omissions, inadequacies and lack of balance we take responsibility and apologize; but we feel nevertheless that our book does provide a source of information hitherto not available to our anticipated readership and important for those now entering paediatric practice and research. It may be that we shall one day have the opportunity of making a second attempt, for which the present first edition will serve as an invaluable foundation. For this reason we appeal now to our colleagues, our critics and our readers to write to us with any constructive suggestions how we may further improve a volume intended as a scientific background for the postgraduate study of clinical paediatrics. We would particularly like to hear from those who might be prepared to contribute future chapters.

Finally, we wish to thank the many people who have already helped us: our contributors for their industry, patience and tolerance of our editing and our importunities: our secretarial helpers, and particularly Mrs. Irene Warrington, for their immense labour on our behalf; colleagues who have provided helpful comments on or translations of some of the manuscripts submitted: the librarians of our Medical School Library who have helped in checking references; Miss Jean Sands for undertaking the daunting task of compiling an index; and our publishers, especially Mr. Richard Emery for his patient co-operation.

John A. Davis
John Dobbing

LIST OF CONTRIBUTORS

M. C. Adinolfi, M.D., Ph.D.
Senior Lecturer, Paediatric Research Unit, Guy's Hospital, London, England.

R. H. Anderson, B.Sc., M.D.
Lecturer in Anatomy, University of Manchester; Honorary Lecturer in Child Health, University of Liverpool, Liverpool, England.

G. T. Ashley, B.Sc., M.D.
Late Reader Elect, Department of Anatomy, University of Manchester, Manchester, England.

P. Barkhan, M.D., Ph.D., M.R.C.Path.
Consultant Haematologist, Guy's Hospital; Honorary Lecturer in Haematology and Medicine, Guy's Hospital Medical School, London, England.

A. J. Barson, M.D., D.C.H.
Senior Lecturer in the Department of Pathology, University of Manchester; Consultant Paediatric Pathologist, United Manchester Hospitals, Manchester, England.

P. J. Black, M.A., M.B., B.Chir.
Senior Registrar, Department of Haematology, Guy's Hospital, London, England.

D. Betty Byers Brown, M.S.C.T.
Lecturer in Speech Pathology and Therapy, University of Manchester, Manchester, England.

C. O. Carter, M.A., D.M., F.R.C.P.
Director, MRC Clinical Genetics Unit; Honorary Consultant Geneticist, The Hospital for Sick Children, Great Ormond Street, London, England.

K. W. Cross, M.B., D.Sc., F.R.C.P.
Professor of Physiology, The London Hospital Medical College, London, England.

Madeleine E. V. Davis
Housewife and Mother of 5 children; Voluntary Worker with the Probation and After-Care Service (Home Office), Alderley Edge, Cheshire, England.

John A. Davis, M.B., B.S., M.Sc., F.R.C.P.
Professor of Paediatrics and Child Health, University of Manchester; Honorary Consultant Paediatrician, United Manchester Hospitals and Royal Manchester Children's Hospital, Manchester, England; Chairman, Academic Board, British Paediatric Association.

John Dobbing, B.Sc., M.B., B.S., M.R.C.Path. Senior Lecturer, Department of Child Health, University of Manchester; Honorary Consultant, United Manchester Hospitals, Manchester, England; Member of the Academic Board, British Paediatric Association.

Constance C. Forsyth, M.D., F.R.C.P.
Senior Lecturer, Department of Child Health, University of Dundee, Dundee, Scotland.

Shelagh E. Gill, B.Sc., M.Sc., Ph.D., M.P.S.
Research Assistant in Departments of Pharmacology and Child Health, University of Manchester, Manchester, England.

S. Godfrey, M.D., Ph.D., M.R.C.P.
Senior Lecturer, and Consultant Paediatrician, Department of Child Health, Hammersmith Hospital, London, England.

R. B. Harcourt, M.B., B.Chir., F.R.C.S., D.O.
Consultant Ophthalmic Surgeon, United Leeds Hospitals and Leeds Regional Hospital Board; Clinical Lecturer in Ophthalmology and in Paediatric Ophthalmology, University of Leeds, Leeds, England.

R. Harris, B.Sc., M.D., M.R.C.P., M.R.C.Path.
Reader in Medical Genetics, University of Manchester; Hon. Consultant Physician, United Manchester Hospitals, Manchester, England.

Alison A. Hislop, B.Sc., Ph.D.
Lecturer, Department of Experimental Pathology, Cardiothoracic Institute, University of London, London, England.

A. Holzel, M.D., F.R.C.P., D.C.H.
Professor of Child Health, University of Manchester, Honorary Consultant Paediatrician, Booth Hall Children's Hospital, the Royal Manchester Children's Hospital, and the Manchester Royal Eye Hospital, Manchester, England.

I. B. Houston, M.D., M.R.C.P., D.C.H.
Senior Lecturer in Child Health, University of Manchester; Consultant Paediatrician, United Manchester Hospitals, Royal Manchester Children's Hospital, and Booth Hall Children's Hospital, Manchester, England.

David Hull, B.Sc., M.R.C.P., D.C.H.
Professor of Child Health, University of Nottingham, Nottingham, England.

Wellington Hung, M.D., F.A.A.P., F.A.C.P.
Professor of Child Health and Development, George Washington University School of Medicine; Endocrinologist, Children's Hospital of the District of Columbia; Chief, Section of Endocrinology, Research Foundation of the Children's Hospital of the District of Columbia; Lecturer in Pediatrics, Georgetown University; Consultant and Lecturer in Pediatrics, Howard University; Consultant in Pediatrics, Washington Hospital Centre and Providence Hospital, Washington, D.C.; Consultant in Pediatrics, DeWitt Army Hospital, Fort Belvoir, Virginia; Consultant in Pediatrics, Holy Cross Hospital of Silver Spring, Silver Spring, Maryland.

J. E. J. John, B.Sc.
Senior Lecturer in Audiology, University of Manchester, Manchester, England.

A. Jolleys, M.D., F.R.C.S.
Consultant Paediatric Surgeon, Royal Manchester Children's Hospital and Booth Hall Hospital for Children; Honorary Lecturer, Department of Child Health, University of Manchester, Manchester, England.

M. Masud R. Khan, B.A., M.A.
Editor, International Psychoanalytic Library; Director of Freud Copyrights; Co-redacteur étranger, *Nouvelle Revue de Psychoanalyse*; Visiting Professor, Deutschen Akademie fur Psychoanalyse in Berlin; Associate Editor, *International Journal of Psychoanalysis*; Hon. Librarian and Archivist, Institute of Psychoanalysis, London, England.

G. H. Lathe, M.D.C.M., Ph.D.
Professor of Chemical Pathology, University of Leeds, Leeds, England.

Ian Leck, M.B., Ph.D., F.F.C.M.
Reader in Social and Preventive Medicine, University of Manchester; Honorary Consultant in Social Medicine, Medical Director of the Regional Cancer Epidemiology Unit, Manchester Regional Hospital Board, Manchester, England.

Ronald J. Lemire, M.D.
Associate Professor of Pediatrics, University of Washington, School of Medicine, Seattle, Washington.

Jennifer M. H. Loggie, M.B., B.Ch.
Associate Professor of Pediatrics and Pharmacology, University of Cincinnati, College of Medicine, Cincinnati, Ohio.

D. de la C. MacCarthy, M.D., F.R.C.P., D.C.H.
Consultant Paediatrician, Stoke Mandeville Hospital, and Amersham Hospital; Honorary Consultant Paediatrician, Institute of Child Psychology, London, England.

H. B. Marsden, M.B., F.R.C.Path., D.C.H., D.Path.
Consultant Pathologist to the Royal Manchester and Booth Hall Children's Hospitals; Honorary Lecturer, University of Manchester, Manchester, England.

W. A. Marshall, B.Sc., M.B., Ph.D., F.I.Biol.
Reader in Child Health and Growth, Department of Growth and Development, Institute of Child Health, London, England.

F. L. Mastaglia, M.D., M.R.A.C.P., M.R.C.P.
Senior Lecturer in Neurology, Department of Medicine, University of Western Australia.

Frances H. McLean, R.N., B.S.N.
Nurse-Administrator, Neonatal Unit, Royal Victoria Hospital, Montreal, Canada.

V. Miller, M.B., Ch.B., D.C.H., M.R.C.P.
Consultant Paediatrician with special interest in Gastroenterology, Booth Hall Children's Hospital, Manchester, England.

J. N. Mills, M.A., B.Ch., D.M., M.D.
Brackenbury Professor of Physiology, University of Manchester, Manchester, England.

R. D. G. Milner, M.A., Ph.D., M.D., M.R.C.P.
Senior Lecturer, Department of Child Health, University of Manchester; Honorary Consultant, United Manchester Hospitals, Manchester, England.

E. J. Moynahan, F.R.C.P.
Physician in Charge, Dermatological Department, The Hospital for Sick Children, Great Ormond Street; Physician in Charge, Dermatological Department, Guy's Hospital, London; Lecturer in Paediatric Dermatology, Institute of Dermatology, University of London, London, England.

Niels C. R. Räihä, M.D.
Associate Professor of Pediatrics, Department of Obstetrics and Gynecology, University Hospital, Helsinki, Finland.

O. H. Oetliker, P.D., Dr. Med.
Head, Division of Pediatric Nephrology, University Children's Hospital, Bern, Switzerland.

H. L. Owrid, M.A., Ph.D.
Senior Lecturer in Audiology, University of Manchester, Manchester, England.

W. W. Payne, M.B., B.S., F.R.C.P.
Chemical Pathologist, Hospital for Sick Children, Great Ormond Street, London; Honorary Senior Lecturer in Chemical Pathology, Hammersmith Hospital, London, England.

Lynne Reid, M.D., F.R.C.P., F.R.A.C.P., F.R.C.Path.
Professor of Experimental Pathology, Cardiothoracic Institute, University of London, London, England.

P. Royer, M.D.
Professor de Pédiatrie, Directeur de l'Unité de Recherche sur les maladies du métabolisme chez l'enfant (INSERM) Hôpital des Enfants Malades, Paris, France.

F. J. Schulte, M.D.
Professor of Pediatrics; Co-Chairman, Department of Pediatrics; Chairman, Department of Neuropediatrics, University of Göttingen, Göttingen, Germany.

V. Schwarz, B.Sc., Ph.D.
Reader in Chemical Pathology, Departments of Medical Biochemistry and Child Health, University of Manchester, Manchester, England.

C. G. Scorer, M.A., M.D., F.R.C.S.
Consultant Surgeon, Hillingdon Hospital, Middlesex, England.

Elliot A. Shinebourne, M.D., M.R.C.P.
Consultant Paediatric Cardiologist, Brompton Hospital, National Heart and Chest Hospitals, London; Honorary Lecturer, Cardiothoracic Institute, University of London, London, England.

J. M. Tanner, M.D., D.Sc., F.R.C.P., F.R.C.Psych.
Professor of Child Health and Growth, Department of Growth and Development, Institute of Child Health, London, England.

David C. Taylor, M.A., M.D., M.R.C.Psych., D.P.M.
Consultant in Developmental Medicine, The Park Hospital for Children, Oxford; Clinical Tutor in Psychiatry, University of Oxford, Oxford, England.

I. G. Taylor, M.D., M.R.C.P., D.P.H., F.C.S.I.
Ellis Llwyd Jones Professor of Audiology and Education of the Deaf, University of Manchester, Manchester, England.

Walter M. Teller, M.D.
Professor of Paediatrics and Paediatric Endocrinology;

Head, Department of Paediatrics, University of Ulm, Ulm, Germany.

B. C. L. TOUWEN, M.D.
Senior scientific co-worker in Child Neurology, Department of Developmental Neurology, State University, Groningen, The Netherlands.

J. TRUETA, M.D., F.R.C.S., F.A.C.S.
Nuffield Professor Emeritus of Orthopaedic Surgery, University of Oxford, Oxford, England.

E. P. TURNER, M.Sc., D.D.S., L.D.S.
Reader in Oral Pathology, University of Manchester; Honorary Consultant Dental Surgeon, United Manchester Hospitals, Manchester, England.

R. H. USHER, M.D.
Associate Professor, Pediatrics, Obstetrics and Gynecology, McGill University, Montreal; Director of Newborn Nurseries, Royal Victoria Hospital and Jewish General Hospital, Montreal, Canada.

H. K. A. VISSER, M.D.
Professor of Paediatrics, Erasmus University, Academic Hospital/Sophia Children's Hospital and Neonatal Unit, Rotterdam, The Netherlands.

ELSIE M. WIDDOWSON, D.Sc.
Head of Infant Nutrition Research Division, Dunn Nutritional Laboratory, Cambridge, England.

B. FRASER WILLIAMS, M.B., Ch.B., M.R.C.Path.
Consultant Microbiologist, The Royal Manchester Children's Hospital, Booth Hall Children's Hospital, and Monsall Hospital, Manchester; Honorary Lecturer in Bacteriology, University of Manchester, Manchester, England; Honorary Consultant Bacteriologist, Public Health Laboratory Service.

INGLE WRIGHT, M.R.C.S., L.R.C.P., D.C.P., M.R.C.Path., Ph.D.
Senior Lecturer in Otolaryngology, University of Manchester, Manchester, England.

SECTION I

NATURE AND NURTURE

SECTION II

CLIMACTERICS

SECTION III

GROWTH AND DEVELOPMENT OF SYSTEMS

SECTION IV

SPECIAL TOPICS

SECTION I

NATURE AND NUTURE

SECTION I

1. GENETICS

C. O. CARTER

NORMAL INHERITANCE

Introduction

A child starts life as a zygote formed by the fusion of two gametes, a sperm provided by the father and an ovum by the mother. The nucleus of the zygote formed by the union of the nuclei of sperm and ovum contains the genetic programme which, interacting with the environment, will control the child's future development as an embryo, as a fetus, as an infant, as a child, as an adolescent and through into old age. The overall strength of the genetic control of development is profound and extends into details of, for example, facial features, as may be seen in the strong facial resemblance of monozygotic twins separated at birth and raised apart. The control extends throughout life as exemplified by genetic diseases of late onset, for example, Huntington's chorea, and in the resemblance of monozygotic twins in age at death and cause of death.

Chromosomes

The genetic programme is contained in the 46 "chromosomes," comprising 23 pairs, one member of each pair coming from the father through the sperm and one from the mother through the ovum. The two members of each and every pair are homologous in the female, where sex determination is by the presence of two X chromosomes. In the male, however, the sex-determining pair (the X and Y) are not alike. The Y chromosome is much smaller and at present is not known to carry any genetic information other than that which causes virilization.

The 22 pairs other than the sex chromosome pair are called "autosomes." The human chromosomes in a male are illustrated in Figure 1. They are best seen at the metaphase stage of somatic cell division, when the individual chromosomes are already split into two daughter chromatids joined only at the chromomere. The chromomere is a convenient point by which to divide the chromosome into two arms, a long and a short arm. The chromosomes other than the sex chromosome pair, collectively called the autosomes, are numbered in descending order of size from 1 to 22. The chromosomes are also classified into 7 groups A to G.[8] The A to G groups are easily recognized. Distinction within a group has until recently not always been possible, though facilitated by autoradiography. In the last few years, however, new methods of preparation and staining have become available which reveal bands along the length of the chromosome and make their individual identification relatively easy. This new technique has shown that the smallest chromosome is that which is present in triplicate in Down's syndrome. This therefore should be called chromosome 22, but it is intended to continue to call it 21 and give the label 22 to the other member of the G group.

Chromosomes 1–3 (Group A) are large with approximately median centromeres which are readily distinguished from each other. Chromosomes 4 and 5 (Group B) are large with submedian centromeres; 4 is a little the larger. Chromosomes 6–12 (Group C) are medium-sized chromosomes with submedian centromeres. The X-chromosome also falls morphologically into this group. Chromosomes 13–15 (Group D) are medium-sized chromosomes with nearly terminal centromeres (acrocentric); chromosomes

13 and 14 frequently, and 15 occasionally, have "satellites" on the ends of the short arms. Chromosomes 16–18 (Group E) are rather short with approximately submedian centromeres. Chromosomes 19 and 20 are short with approximately median centromeres. Chromosomes 21 and 22 (Group G) are very short with nearly terminal centromeres and the Y-chromosome is also included in this group. Both 21 and 22 have satellites at the end of the short arms.

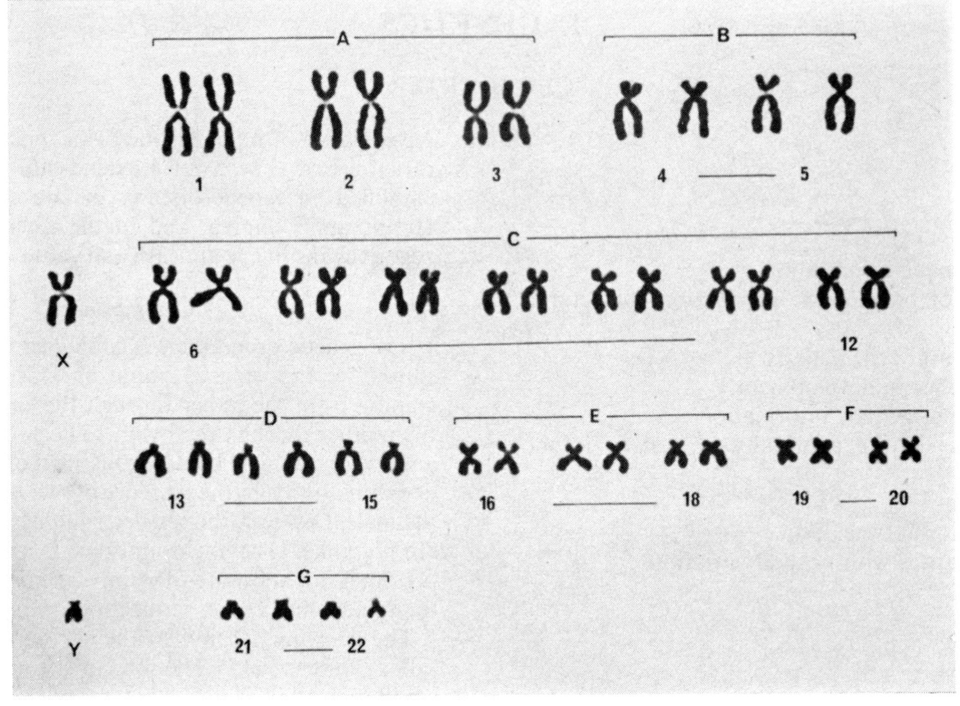

FIG. 1. Human chromosomes—normal male.

In somatic growth by repeated cell division, each cell division is accompanied by a division of each chromosome such that each daughter cell receives a complete set of chromosomes. Every cell in the body then contains a complete set of chromosomes identical with those present in the original zygote.

There is no clear indication of extra-chromosomal inheritance, for example cytoplasmic inheritance, in man.

The Coding of Genetic Information

The coding of genetic information in the chromosomes depends on their structure. The backbone of the chromosomes is a continuous double strand of deoxyribonucleic acid (DNA) twisted in the form of a helix.[28] The continuous backbone of each strand is made up of a sugar–phosphate–sugar–phosphate–sugar chain. Attached to each sugar is a base. There are four bases concerned—adenine and guanine (purines), and cytosine and thymine (pyrimidines). The two sugar–phosphate–sugar chains are linked by these bases. This is illustrated in Fig. 2. The special relationships are such that each base link must be between a purine and pyrimidine such that adenine is always linked to thymine and guanine to cytosine. The first linkage involves three hydrogen bonds and the second two hydrogen bonds. The helical structure of the molecule is illustrated in Fig. 3.

```
           Sugar — Guanine — Cytosine — Sugar
Phosphate{                                   }Phosphate
           Sugar — Adenine — Thymine  — Sugar
Phosphate{                                   }Phosphate
           Sugar — Cytosine — Guanine — Sugar
Phosphate{                                   }Phosphate
           Sugar — Guanine — Cytosine — Sugar
Phosphate{                                   }Phosphate
           Sugar — Thymine — Adenine  — Sugar
Phosphate{                                   }Phosphate
           Sugar — Cytosine — Guanine — Sugar
```

FIG. 2. Chemical composition of double strand of DNA.

In cell division the simultaneous division of each chromosome is brought about by uncoiling of the two strands of DNA by the separating of the linked bases. The two single chains then reconstitute themselves as a double helix by attaching to themselves sugar-phosphate base units to form a complementary DNA strain. The forced relationship of the complementary bases ensures that the two newly formed double chains are identical with those of the original chromosome. This mechanism was confirmed by growing bacteria in heavy nitrogen until all the nitrogen in the DNA was of the heavy form, and then returning the bacteria to a medium containing normal nitrogen.[22] Thereafter, it was found that with each cell division the DNA content of heavy nitrogen in each bacterium was halved.

The coding of genetic information depends on the sequence of bases along the strands of DNA. The length of DNA in a chromosome which behaves as a functional unit is called a "gene," or more precisely a cistron. The position of a gene on a chromosome is called a "gene-locus." The function of most genes is to produce a polypeptide which may combine with other polypeptides to produce biologically active proteins such as enzymes. The basic relationship is that one nucleotide with a triplet of bases codes for one aminoacid. However, since there are only 20 aminoacids commonly found in biological proteins and 4^3 or 64 different combinations of base triplets may be made from the 4 possible bases, adenine, guanine, cytosine and thymine, it is inevitable that there can be more than one base which can code for a particular aminoacid.

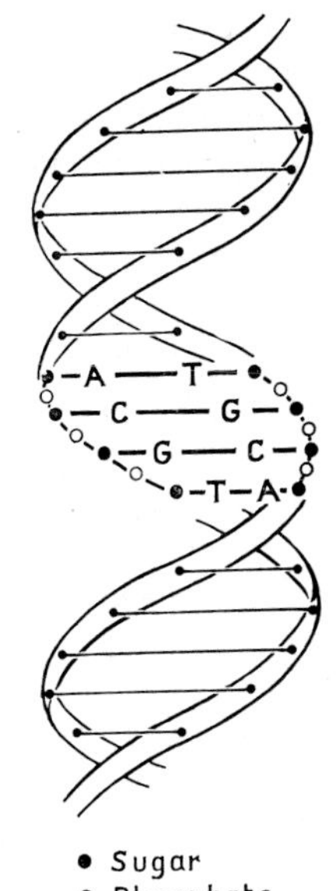

FIG. 3. Structure of DNA molecule.

Genetic Control of Polypeptide Production—Structural Genes

The actual formation of polypeptides by the activity of genes demands some intermediary steps. The DNA is fixed in the chromosomes within the nucleus. Polypeptides are produced outside the nucleus in the cytoplasm at structures known as ribosomes. The first stage is the production by the gene of a complementary copy of itself, a short strand only the length of the gene, which is called messenger RNA, or m-RNA. This strand is detached and is then capable of diffusing out of the nucleus into the cytoplasm and so is capable of reaching the ribosomes. The sequence of bases in the m-RNA strand will be complementary to that in the gene (a difference is that the thymine of DNA is replaced by uracil in the m-RNA). No change in "language" is involved and so the process is called "transcription." When the m-RNA strand is in the cytoplasm, several ribosomes thread themselves along the m-RNA and, as they do so, the m-RNA attracts to itself from the cytoplasm small molecules, which are a complex of a single aminoacid and a small unit of RNA (called transfer RNA, or t-RNA). The aminoacids pulled in in this way join up to form peptides, releasing the t-RNA molecules. The usual complementary relationship of m-RNA base and t-RNA base applies. The attachment of t-RNA and aminoacid depends on the "coding" of base-triplets and aminoacid. The sequence of aminoacids in the newly forming peptide therefore depends on the sequence of triplet bases in the m-RNA which in turn depended on the sequence of bases in the gene. Thus, if the original triplet of bases in the gene was AAA (adenine–adenine–adenine), the triplet in the m-RNA will be UUU (uracil–uracil–uracil), and that in the t-RNA aminoacid complex will be again AAA and the aminoacid pulled into the peptide will be phenylalanine. If the next triplet in the gene is GGA, then the complementary triplet in the m-RNA will be CCU and the aminoacid pulled in and attached to phenylalanine will be proline. A succession of aminoacids is joined up in this way until the end of the m-RNA is reached. This is illustrated in Fig. 4, where a short peptide chain of phenylalanine, proline and alanine is already formed and lysine will be the next to be incorporated. A single piece of m-RNA, after producing several molecules of polypeptide, will disintegrate. However, further m-RNA will be produced by the gene and polypeptide will continue to be formed so long as the gene is active.

The details of the code were determined *in vitro* using systems comprising aminoacids, amino-acyl-RNA synthetase, t-RNAs, ribosomes, ATP and other necessary factors. Adding to this certain synthetic m-RNA composed only of uracil it was found that a peptide containing only phenylalanine was formed and so UUU must code for phenylalanine. Further, it was found possible to make synthetic trinucleotides (RNA's only three bases long) which behaved as a small section of m-RNA and caused aminoacids to be attached to the ribosomes by their t-RNA's. By adding radioactively labelled aminoacids to the system, it was possible to see which was caused to be attached by each trinucleotide. The code is usually given for messenger RNA and the completed table is shown in Fig. 5.[10,23] The

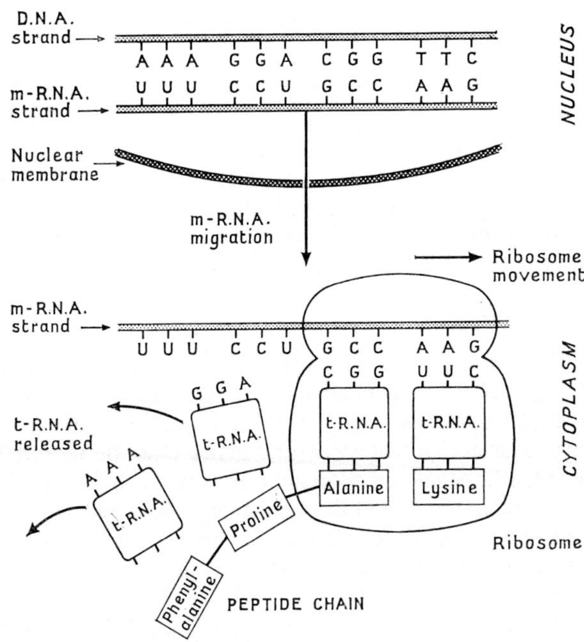

FIG. 4. Transcription of genetic code and translation into peptide chain at the ribosome.

triplets UAA, UAG and UGA do not code for any amino-acids. They probably code for ending of polypeptide chain synthesis. AUG, in addition to coding for methionine, can code for the start of polypeptide chain synthesis. It will be seen that the code is degenerate, only methionine and tryptophan having a unique coding. It is usually not important which of the two purines or which of the two pyrimidines is in the third position. It is also apparent that the less

1st base	2nd base: U	C	A	G	3rd base
U	Phenylalanine	Serine	Tyrosine	Cysteine	U
	Phenylalanine	Serine	Tyrosine	Cysteine	C
	Leucine	Serine	?	?	A
	Leucine	Serine	?	Tryptophan	G
C	Leucine	Proline	Histidine	Arginine	U
	Leucine	Proline	Histidine	Arginine	C
	Leucine	Proline	Glutamine	Arginine	A
	Leucine	Proline	Glutamine	Arginine	G
A	Isoleucine	Threonine	Asparagine	Serine	U
	Isoleucine	Threonine	Asparagine	Serine	C
	Isoleucine	Threonine	Lysine	Arginine	A
	Methionine	Threonine	Lysine	Arginine	G
G	Valine	Alanine	Aspartic acid	Glycine	U
	Valine	Alanine	Aspartic acid	Glycine	C
	Valine	Alanine	Glutamic acid	Glycine	A
	Valine	Alanine	Glutamic acid	Glycine	G

FIG. 5. The genetic code showing the probable codings for 20 aminoacids.

soluble aminoacids tend to occur in the upper left of the table and the more soluble in the lower right. This will minimize the effect of mutation by base substitution, since such substitution will often either not change the aminoacid coded or substitute an aminoacid of similar structure.

These details of the way in which structural genes code for polypeptides were worked out by studies of the bacterium Escherichia Coli; but there is good reason to suppose that the details are similar for all living organisms.

Control of Structural Gene Activity

All genes are present in every cell in the body; but tissues vary greatly in their chemical activity, and during embryology the same tissue may show changes in chemical activity. The activity of structural genes must be modifiable during embryonic development and tissue differentiation. Some understanding of the mechanisms have been achieved for bacteria, but little is known for higher organisms.

In E. Coli two types of controller genes have been demonstrated—operator and regulator genes.[17] In bacteria with a single ring chromosome, it is common to find that a series of structural genes, which produce enzymes catalyzing successive stages in a biochemical process, are located in line along the chromosome. At one end of the series is an operator gene, which controls the activity of the whole series. The operator gene itself is under the control of a regulator gene usually situated some distance away on the ring chromosome. This regulator gene when active produces a protein which represses the activity of the operator gene. Various external influences may block the activity of the repressor substance and so switch on the operator gene and the structural genes it controls. The principle is illustrated in Fig. 6. Normally in E. Coli little beta-galactosidase is produced, but if lactose is added this blocks the activity of the repressor substance and beta-galactosidase is rapidly synthesized. At the same time, an adjacent structural gene starts to produce thiogalactoside transacetylase, whose function is unknown, and another starts to produce permease which is necessary for the transport of beta-galactosides into the cell. A contrasting form of control is illustrated by tryptophan synthesis in E. Coli. This synthesis is brought about by a series of enzymes produced by a linked series of genes, probably under the control of an operator gene. In the absence of tryptophan, the synthesis proceeds actively. If, however, tryptophan is added to the medium the production of the enzymes stops. In the case of beta-galactosidase, enzyme activity is, logically enough, induced when required. In the case of the synthesis of

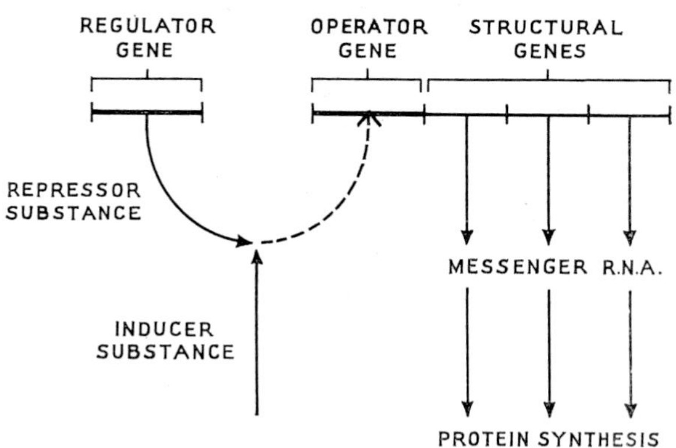

FIG. 6. The action of operator and regulator genes.

tryptophan enzyme activity is normally active, but repressed when not required.

The Control of Genes in Development

The elucidation of the mechanisms of the control of gene activity in tissue differentiation is the key to embryology, yet little is known about it. In vertebrates there is no indication that chromosomes or parts of chromosomes are lost in embryonic development; nor is there evidence for irreversible inactivation of genes. On the contrary, from experiments in amphibians, in which nuclei-free differentiated cells from the gut are transplanted into enucleated ova and induce normal development of the egg, it would appear that even differentiated nuclei retain all their genetic potential.[3] In the fruit fly the changing patterns of activity of specific regions can be studied in the giant chromosomes (formed by the close alignment of replicated chromosomes) present in certain tissues. When a gene is active, and can be shown by autoradiography to be producing much RNA, the corresponding region of the chromsome swells up to produce "chromosome puffs." These come and go according to the activity of the gene.

The Transmission of Genetic Information

In somatic cell division (mitosis) chromosome division accompanies cell division and each daughter cell therefore receives a complete set of chromosome pairs and a complete set of genes. The process is illustrated diagrammatically in Fig. 7. In germ cell formation, however, there are two cell divisions accompanying one division of the chromosomes. At the first, a reduction division of the oocyte or spermatocyte, although the chromosomes split into two chromatids

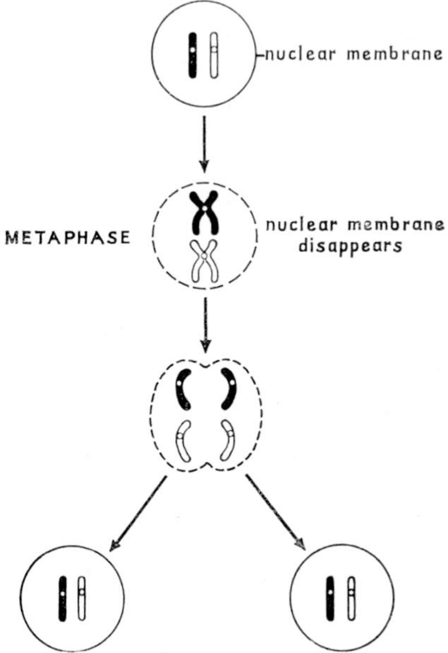

FIG. 7. Mitosis: the behaviour of one pair of chromosomes.

before the cell division only one member of each chromosome pair passes into a daughter cell. The other member of the pair passes into the other daughter cell. Each daughter cell then contains 23 split but unpaired chromosomes. At the second mitotic division of germ-cell formation, the split halves of each chromosome separate and pair into the daughter cells, which therefore again contain 23 unpaired chromosomes. The spermatocyte thus divides into 4 sperms. In ovum formation, one daughter cell at the first division receives little cytoplasm, forms a polar body and degenerates, and again one daughter cell at the second division forms a polar body, so that an oocyte produces an ovum containing most of the original cytoplasm of the oocyte. The process is illustrated diagrammatically for sperm cell function in Fig. 8.

The segregation of chromosome pairs at meiosis is a random process and occurs independently for each chromosome pair. There are therefore, as a result of segregation, an enormous number of different chromosomal combinations(2^{23}) that a parent can transmit to a particular child, and potentially an enormous variety (2^{46}) of genetically different children that may be born to a particular parental couple. The variety is in fact even greater since the two members of a chromosome pair may exchange material. This occurs as a result of breakage of two adjacent chromatids and their cross-union. These cross-unions are seen as an attachment of the two homologous chromosomes called a "chiasma" and there are usually several chiasmata to be seen, implying several "cross-overs." In Fig. 8, just one cross-over is depicted. Normally the exchange is symmetrical so the two resulting new chromatids each have a full complement of genes.

Because of meiotic segregation the chance that a child will inherit a particular gene possessed by one parent, rather than the corresponding gene on the other member of a chromosome pair is 1 in 2. One parent and child have half

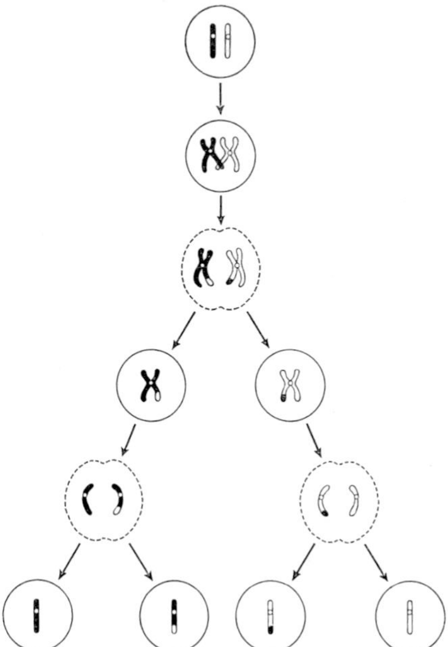

FIG. 8. Meiosis, showing one cross-over: the behaviour of one pair of chromosomes.

their genes in common. The chance that a pair of sibs will inherit the same gene from one parent is also 1 in 2. A pair of sibs on average have half their genes in common but may have somewhat more or somewhat less. Grandfather and grandchild will have a quarter of their genes in common. Uncle and nephew or uncle and niece on average will have a quarter of their genes in common, but may have more or less. First cousins will have on average an eighth of their genes in common.

Linkage

Genes on one chromosome will tend to be transmitted together, and are said to be "linked." Such linkages, however, may be broken by crossing-over. The closer two gene-loci are on a chromosome the less likely they are to be separated by a cross-over. Estimates of the cross-over frequency between genes are therefore a measure of the distance apart of the gene-loci. In experimental animals the linkage groups may be established, the cross-over frequency estimated and the linkage group correlated with individual genes by observing the genetic effects of chromosomal deletions. In man some half-dozen linkage groups are known and at least two have been reliably allocated to individual chromosomes, but the only approach to a map is for the X-chromosome, where the study of linkage is much facilitated by the relationship with sex.[25] Two groups of gene loci are now known on the X-chromosome, which are some distance apart. One is based on the X-linked blood group gene locus Xg and the other on the two loci for common forms of colour-blindness—deutan and protan. The map as so far established is illustrated in Fig. 9. In the first group, the approximate distances in cross-over units are indicated, with the locus for Xg at one end and that for X-linked ichthyosis nearest, next that for ocular albinism and furthest that for angiokeratoma. In the second group, the blood group locus Xm is closely linked to those for deutan, protan, glucose-6-phosphate dehydrogenase

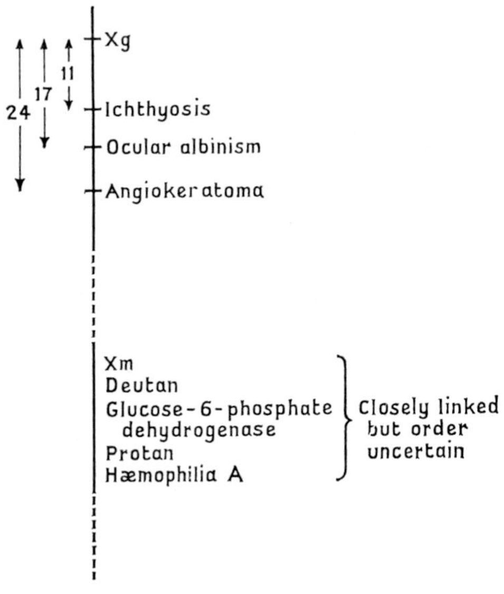

FIG. 9. Tentative map of the human X chromosome. (After Sanger and Race).[25]

deficiency and haemophilia A (Factor VIII deficiency). The order and distances within this group are not known.

Mutation—Breaks in the Continuity of Genetic Information

On the whole the copying process, at the dissociation of a chromosome into the two daughter chromatids and the reconstitution of these into two chromosomes, is remarkably accurate both in somatic cell division and in germ-cell formation. Occasionally, however, errors occur. These are known to be of a number of different types. A few are probably small chromosome deletions, a few are small chromosome duplications, and others are small inversions. (This type of mutation is discussed in Chapter 2.) The majority, however, are known to be single basic substitutions in just one triplet of bases in a single gene, which itself may be over 100 bases long. The best evidence for this in man comes from the detailed "finger-printing" of human haemoglobin variants. Most of these are found to involve just one aminoacid change in either the α or the β peptide chain of the globin molecule. Thus, in sickle-cell haemoglobin (haemoglobin S), that found in patients with sickle-cell anaemia, lysine is substituted for glutamic acid in the sixth position of the β-chain. In haemoglobin C, lysine is substituted for glutamic acid at the same site. Reference to the coding table (Fig. 4) showed that the change in haemoglobin S would be produced by a change of adenine to uracil as the second base of the triplet in the messenger RNA code (or of thymine to adenine in the DNA of the gene). The change in haemoglobin C would be produced by a change of guanine to adenine in the first base. In either case, a change of just one base is involved; whereas haemoglobin C could not have come from haemoglobin S without a change in two bases. Some further examples for abnormal haemoglobin are illustrated in Fig. 10[9], and some 40 such changes are known.

The clinical effect of such substitutions will be very varied. Some base substitutions, particularly in the third base, will produce no aminoacid substitution. Some aminoacid substitutions will not appreciably alter function, while others will have varying effects up to and including a complete loss of function. Some will result in only a part of the peptide being formed and some in the formation of a protein which is highly unstable. Where the peptide product of a gene forms part of an enzyme and the altered gene product results in a loss of efficiency, it is usual to find that the "heterozygote" (those with one mutant gene and one normal gene) have about 50 per cent of normal enzyme activity, due to the peptide produced by the normal gene. Such heterozygotes usually show no clinical abnormality.

chain affected	amino acid position in chain	amino acid in wild type	amin acid in mutant	possible RNA codon change
α	16	Lys	Asp	AA_G^A GA_C^U
α	30	Glu	Gln	GA_G^A CA_G^A
α	57	Gly	Asp	GG_C^U GA_C^U
α	58	His	Tyr	CA_C^U UA_C^U
α	68	Asn	Lys	AA_G^A AA_C^U
β	6	Glu	Val	GA_G^A GU_G^A
β	6	Glu	Lys	GA_G^A AA_G^A
β	7	Glu	Gly	GA_G^A GG^A_G
β	26	Glu	Lys	GA_G^A AA_G^A
β	63	His	Tyr	CA_C^U UA_C^U
β	63	His	Arg	CA_C^U CG_C^U
β	67	Val	Glu	GU_G^A GA_G^A
β	125	Glu	Gin	GA_G^A CA_G^A

FIG. 10. Amino acid changes in human haemoglobin. In all, except the first, it will be seen that the aminoacid change can be accounted for by a single base change in the nucleic acid.

However, "homozygotes" for the mutant gene, that is those with mutant genes on both members of the chromosome pair, have little or no enzyme activity and are clinically affected. This is the case, for example, with phenylketonuria, galactosaemia and many other inborn errors of metabolism. In other instances, even the heterozygote for the mutant gene is clinically seriously affected. Though the detailed mechanisms are usually not known here, it is plausible to suppose that in many, for example skeletal disorders such as classical achondroplasia, the peptide product of the gene is required for the formation of a protein involved in cell or tissue structure.[19]

Induced Mutation

It is perhaps an error to look for the cause of most gene mutation. Rather it is remarkable that the process of DNA replication is on the whole so accurate. Nevertheless, experimental methods are known of increasing the rate of mutation. Ionizing radiation, X-rays and alpha, beta and gamma radiation are mutagenic, causing both gene mutation and chromosomal damage leading to deletions, inversions and translocations. This is not surprising as these radiations are known to break chemical bonds. The dose of ionizing radiation in mammals which would double the mutation rate is probably of the order of 100 rads and the natural background radiation is of the order of 3 rads over 30 years.[21] A dose given over many years is less mutagenic than one given rapidly and so it is unlikely that this radiation accounts for more than about 3 per cent of mutation. Diagnostic radiology may at present be contributing a dose about equivalent to the natural radiation. Ultraviolet light is also mutagenic in bacteria but is relatively non-penetrant and little reaches the gonads in man. The mechanism here is better understood since it is known that this form of radiation causes adjacent pyrimidine bases, particularly thymine, to cross-link.

Chemical mutagens are of two classes. One class has a direct action on DNA, for example on DNA virus particles or bacterial transforming DNA. The other class acts only on replicating DNA. An example of the first class is nitrous oxide which deaminates the bases in DNA. Adenine is deaminated to hypoxanthine, which in the next replication behaves as if it were guanine and pairs with cytosine rather than thymine, so that an adenine–thymine base pair is replaced by guanine–cytosine. The large class of alkylating agents, which include nitrogen mustard, appear to alkylate the 7 position of guanine. This then has only a labile linkage to the deoxyribose residue and so tends to be released from DNA. The resulting gap may be repaired by any of the four bases. The class of chemicals, which are mutagenic only on DNA replication, mostly have structures closely resembling one of the four natural bases and are capable of entering DNA in place of the natural base and therefore cause errors in replication. Chemical mutagens have been important in giving information about the structure of DNA. They are not known to be of practical importance in clinical medicine. It is obviously important, however, that new chemicals, particularly those used in food production, should be monitored for their potential effect in causing mutagenesis.

The Genetics of Normal Variation

From the discussion on the nature of gene mutation it will be appreciated that many such mutations will have little effect on fitness. Those that have a major deleterious effect will tend to be kept at a low frequency in the population because of their elimination by natural selection, and this is discussed below in relation to disorders due to mutant genes of large effect. Those rare mutations that give a substantial natural selective advantage will tend in time to become the common gene at that particular gene locus. For mutations of little effect, the balance of selective advantage or disadvantage may be equivocal. The mutant gene may have advantages in some environments and not in others. Or the heterozygote may have an advantage over either the homozygote for the mutant gene or the homozygote for the normal gene. It is not difficult to imagine in general terms that the heterozygote with two somewhat different forms of a gene product may be tolerant of a wider range of environmental stress. A well-established example of heterozygote advantage is the greater resistance to malignant tertian malaria of the heterozygous carrier of the gene for haemoglobin S (who has some 40 per cent of sickle-cell haemoglobin) than the normal individual with only haemoglobin A_1 and A_2.[1] The homozygote for the S-gene, however, at least in West Africa, usually dies from anaemia.

Not surprisingly, therefore, it is being found that, whereever it is possible to examine fairly directly the products of genes at a particular gene locus, there is in a substantial proportion of cases not just one normal gene at the locus, but several alternative forms of the gene. Where two or more are present with a frequency of at least 1 per cent, the situation is called "genetic polymorphism." Such genetic polymorphism was first demonstrated at the gene locus for the genes determining the ABO blood groups; and then for a succession of other gene loci at which genes were concerned with red-cell antigens, MNS locus, the Rhesus locus, the Kell locus and others. More recent examples have come from gene loci at which genes produce red-cell enzymes. For example, the acid phosphatase in red cells occurs in 5 common electrophoretically distinguishable patterns, which are attributable to 3 alleles at one gene locus, giving 6 possible heterozygous and homozygous combinations.[13] Each genotype shows some variation in phenotypic expression (probably due to the modifying action of genes at other gene loci). Overall, however, the variation approximates to a "Normal" (or Gaussian) distribution.

Both red-cell antigens and enzymes are direct, or nearly direct, products of structural genes. Further, sensitive methods, immunology in one case and electrophoresis in the other, are available for their recognition. In most instances of variation for a measurable character, such as stature, or total finger-print ridge count, or systolic pressure, or intelligence test score, the observed character is some distance away from the primary action of the individual genes. It is likely that there is an interaction of the primary products of many genes in the development of the character. If there is polymorphism at several of the gene loci involved, then it is likely that the variation in the population for the character will be continuous and on a suitable scale will be distributed approximately Normally. If, in addition, the expression of at least some of the genes concerned is modified by environmental factors, then the latter will give further variation in the population for the character being studied.

Conversely, wherever the variation for a character in a population is continuous and the distribution of measurements for the character has a Normal or near Normal distribution, it is reasonable to suppose that its development depends on the interaction of many factors. These factors will usually be both genetic and environmental, but if it can be shown (for example by twin studies) that most of the population variance is due to genetic variation then the genetic variation is likely to depend on polymorphism at several, perhaps many, gene loci.

The way in which polymorphism at several gene loci will tend to build up to a normal distribution, assuming there is no dominance, is shown in Fig. 11. The distribution with polygenic inheritance is not much disturbed by dominance provided that this is not consistently in the same direction.

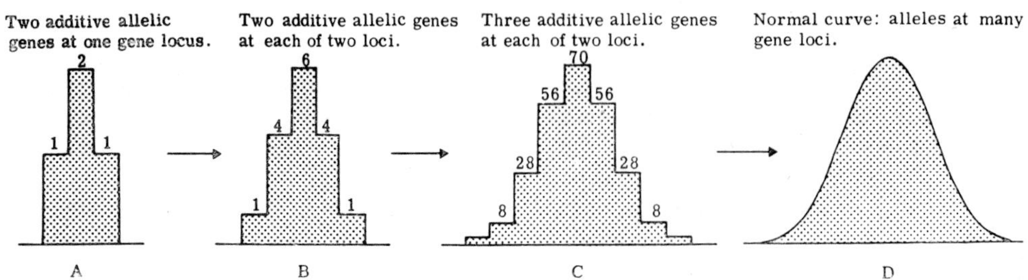

FIG. 11. To show how additive polygenic inheritance tends to give a normal distribution.

Familial Resemblances with Normal Variation

(a) Where the Products of the Genes are Identifiable. The resemblances of relatives are simply deducible (from the behaviour of chromosomes in germ-cell formation) for polymorphisms where the product of each allele may be indentified, provided that the relative frequencies of the alleles in the particular population are known. In the case of the ABO blood groups the presence of the A-antigen and the presence of the B-antigen may be detected since anti-A and anti-B sera are available. The presence of the O-antigen must be inferred from the family blood groups (or the probability of its presence estimated when this cannot be so inferred) since no anti-O serum is available. Thus, where a group AB father is married to a Group O mother, the father's genotype is known to be AB and the mother's OO, children have an equal probability of being Group A (genotype AO) or B (BO). If father is Group A and mother is Group B and they already have one Group O child, then it may be inferred that the father's genotype is AO and mother's BO; so any further children have an equal probability of being Group A (AO), Group B (BO), Group AB (AB) and Group O (OO). If a Group O mother has a Group A child, then it may be inferred that the father must have one gene for A. If mother is Group O and father's group is not known, then the children have a probability of being Group A (AO), Group B (BO) and Group O (OO), equal to that of the relative frequencies of the genes for A, B and O antigens in the population. In southern England these are 0·27, 0·06 and 0·67 respectively. These proportions may be calculated from the proportions for Group A, O, B and AB, which are about 45, 44, 8 and 3 per cent respectively in southern England.

In the case of the Xg blood group locus, only one antibody to a single antigen called Xg^a is available and so sera are scored Xg(a+) and Xg(a−). The Xg(a−) women must be homozygous for Xg and her sons must be Xg(a−) irrespective of her husband's group. Her daughters will be Xg(a−) or Xg(a+) according to whether the husband is Xg(a−) or Xg(a+). If the husband's group is not known, then the probability of the daughter being Xg(a+) or Xg(a−) will be that of the relative frequencies of the two genes which in England is 0·62 and 0·38.

(b) Where the Products of Individual Genes are not Identifiable but only their Summed Effects. Where inheritance is polygenic—that is, due to allelism at several gene loci—but there is no significant variation in the population from environmental variation, it is possible to make predictions of the mean score of relatives of particular degree from the theoretical correlations between relatives. An individual relative may vary on either side of this mean according to the lottery of chromosome segregation.

Total finger-print ridge count provides a good example. For each of the 10 fingers, it is possible to count the ridges between the centre of the pattern and the "triradius" at the edge of the pattern. This is illustrated in Fig. 12. These counts are added for all the fingers to give the total count. This may vary from 0 to over 300. The distribution in British males is shown in Fig. 13. The patterns are laid down early in foetal life and do not change thereafter. It is simple to get good prints from whole families. Since monozygotic twins have all their genes in common, the theoretical correlation for such twins is 1·00. Since men and women do not choose their spouses by their ridge count, the theoretical correlation between husband and wife should be 0·00. Since one parent transmits half his or her genes for ridge count to a child, and the other parent's genes will be representative of those of the general population, the theoretical correlation between parent and child, assuming that there is no dominance and the effects of the genes are additive, is 0·50. This implies that if the parent differs from the population mean by a count of x, where $\bar{x}$ is the population mean, the children will have counts scattered round a score of $\bar{x} + x/2$. Since sibs, whether brother and

FIG. 12. Examples of the three basic types of finger print pattern.

brother, brother and sister, or sister and sister, have on average half their genes in common, the theoretical correlation between sibs is 0·50. Similarly, the theoretical correlation for dizygotic twins is 0·50. Where the score of both parents is known the scores of their children should be scattered round the mean of the two parents, with a mean the same as the mid-parental value, since all the children's genes must come from the parents. The regression of child

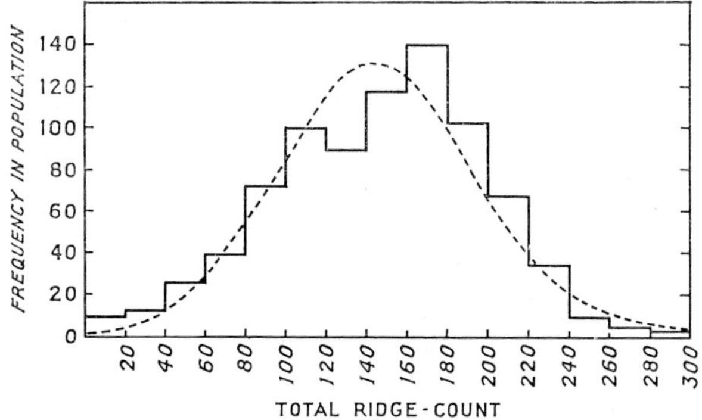

FIG. 13. Distribution of total finger print ridge count in 825 British males. After Holts.[15]

on mid-parent is 1·00. In contrast only half the parental genes are represented in a child, the other half (that is, those which were not transmitted to the child) will be representative of those in the general population, and so the regression of child on mid-parent is 0·50. It follows that the theoretical correlation of child and mid-parent is $\sqrt{(1 \times 0{\cdot}5)}$, i.e. 0·71. The observed correlations for fingerprint ridge counts in two large series[15,16] are shown in Table. 1. The theoretical

TABLE 1

CORRELATION BETWEEN RELATIVES FOR FINGER-PRINT RIDGE COUNTS

Relatives	*Observed Correlation*	*Theoretical Correlation*
Husband-wife	0·05 ± 0·07	0·00
Monozygotic twins	0·95 ± 0·07	1·00
Dizygotic twins	0·49 ± 0·08	0·50
Sib-sib	0·50 ± 0·04	0·50
Parent-child	0·48 ± 0·03	0·50
Midparent-child	0·66 ± 0·03	0·71

correlations for other relatives also depend on the number of genes in common. Thus the correlation for grandfather and grandchild, or uncle and nephew, or half-sibs, will be 0·25, and between first cousins, or great-uncle and great-nephew, will be 0·125.

Heritability

The variation in ABO groups is entirely genetically determined: there are no known environmental factors which influence the expressions of the genes concerned. It is also possible to estimate approximately the degree to which the variation for quantitative characters such as ridge count, stature or intelligence-test score is due to genetic variation.[11] The variation in the population is conveniently measured as the "variance" which is defined as the sum of the scores of the deviations of the individual values from the population mean. For multifactorially determined characters the total-population-variance (V_T) may be regarded as made of the variance due to genetic variation (V_G) plus the variation to environmental factors (V_E) and an interaction factor (V_{GE}). The latter component is difficult to handle and does not appear to be important in the analysis of most human variation. It will be omitted in the further discussion. The variance due to genetic variation (V_G) may be split into two elements: the variation due to the "additive" genetic variation (V_{Ga}) and the variation due to "dominance" (V_{Gd}). The latter is a measure of the degree to which the effect on development of the character of two alleles, A and a, on the hetrozygote Aa, is not half-way between that of the two homozygotes AA and aa. This component may also conveniently, though with oversimplification, be regarded as including also the variation that is due to the relationship of the effects of two genes, A and B, at different gene loci not being additive. The environmental variance (V_E) may usefully be divided into that which is due to the environmental variation that one may get within families (V_{Ew}) and that which one may get between families (V_{Eb}). Since the latter type of variation will tend to raise the correlation between members of a family, it is often called "common family environment" (V_{Ec}). The partition of the total variance for the population may then be written:

$$V_T = V_{Ga} + V_{Gd} + V_{Ec} + V_{Ew}$$

Heritability in the wider sense of the term is given by $(V_{Ga} + V_{Gd})/V_T$. However the dominance component is not a source of resemblance between parent and child and the term "heritability" (h^2) is usually used in the narrower sense of V_{Ga}/V_T.

The variation between relatives is less than the total population variation because of shared genes and shared common family environment and it is this "co-variance" of relative, divided by total population variance which gives the correlation between relatives. For example since there are no genetic sources of variation between the two members of an MZ pair the correlation of MZ pairs (rMZ) is a measure $(V_{Ga} + V_{Gd} + V_{Ed})/V_T$. Where V_{Ec} is unimportant then rMZ is itself a measure of heritability in the wider sense, and where V_{Gd} is also unimportant rMZ (0·95 for ridge count) is a measure of h^2. There is little reason to suppose that either dominance or the early intrauterine environment are important for total ridge count so the h^2 for this character is about 95 per cent. The possible influence of common post-natal environment in raising the MZ twin correlation may be eliminated by estimating the correlation for MZ twins reared apart from infancy. The correlation for finger-print ridge count will be the same in MZ twins reared apart as those reared together. For stature the MZ correlation is little reduced for twins apart and remains about 0·90. For I.Q. score, one series from England showed no alteration in the correlation where MZ twins were reared apart.[26] It remained at about 0·80, the figure for the MZ twins reared together, implying a heritability in the broad sense of about 80 per cent. Another series from England and one from the United States showed a reduced correlation to about 0·70 in MZ twins reared apart.

The effect of common environment for MZ twins reared together may also be eliminated (on the assumption that the common environment is as alike for MZ as DZ twins) by the comparison of MZ and DZ twins. The correlation for DZ twins (rDZ) if there is no correlation between spouses is $(\frac{1}{2}V_{Ga} + \frac{1}{4}V_{Gd} + V_{Ec})/V_T$. It follows that, by subtraction, one may eliminate V_{Ec} and $2(rMZ - rDZ) = V_A + 1\frac{1}{2}V_{Gd}$. If V_{Gd} is small, then $2(rMZ - rDZ)$ is a measure of h^2 and for the ridge-count data this method gives an estimate of 92 per cent. This method is less satisfactory when there is a genetic correlation between spouses. This cannot raise the MZ correlation but can raise the DZ correlation. Unless a correction is made for this, the twin correlation difference will underestimate the heritability. For example, correlations for I.Q. for MZ twins are of the order of 0·8 and for DZ about 0·5. Without a correction for the genetic correlation of spouses, this gives a heritability estimate of about 60 per cent, but with such a correction a heritability of about 80 per cent. It is noteworthy that a high correlation of both MZ and DZ twins indicates a low heritability. This has been found, for example, in scores on the Vineland Social Maturity Scale.[16]

Further estimates of heritability may be obtained from parent–child and sib–sib correlations. Dominance does not enter the parent–child correlations. Accordingly, the regression of child on mid-parent correlation overestimates h^2 only by the component of common family environment. For total ridge count this regression is about 0·92, implying, if V_{Ec} is small, a heritability of 92 per cent. The correlation of parent and one child is given $(\frac{1}{2}V_{Ga} + V_{Ec})/V_T$ and so the observed correlation of 0·48 for finger-print ridge count implies, if V_{Ec} is small, a heritability of 96 per cent. The like sib–sib correlation, and the DZ correlation, is given by $(\frac{1}{2}V_{Ga} + \frac{1}{4}V_{Gd} + V_{Ec})/V_T$ and so the observed correlation of 0·50 implies, if V_{Gd} and V_{Ec} are small, an h^2 of close to 100 per cent. No correction for genetic correlation between spouses need be made for estimates of heritability for the child on mid-parent; but without such correction, estimates based on child and one parent and sib–sib correlations will be over-estimates.

It is important to note that estimates of heritability apply to the particular population studied and need not apply to other populations. The high heritability of finger-print ridge count would probably apply to any human population. An estimate of heritability for I.Q. obtained for a group of London school children might well be higher than that for populations with less uniformity in living standards, for example school children in Bombay. It is also important to note that heritability estimates apply essentially to populations and not individuals. A heritability of 80 per cent for I.Q. score does not mean, as is sometimes believed, that an individual child's I.Q. is 80 per cent genetically determined and 20 per cent environmentally determined. It does, however, have predictive value. If a group of parents have mid-parents I.Q. of 140, that is 40 above the population mean, the mean I.Q. of their children is likely to be of the order of 100 + (0·8 × 40), that is 132, and may be raised closer to the mid-parental level by common family environment.

GENETICS IN THE AETIOLOGY OF DISEASE

Introduction

There is probably some genetic component in the development of almost all disease processes; but the extent of this component varies. There is a continuous spectrum from diseases almost entirely determined by an individual's genetic constitution at conception, through those in which both genetic and environmental factors make a substantial contribution, to those almost entirely determined by environmental experiences. This gradation is seen with each of the three main types of genetic predisposition to disease, chromosome anomalies, mutant genes of large effect, and polygenic predisposition (depending on numerous genes of individual small effect).

In the case of chromosome anomalies the development of Down's syndrome, due to trisomy 21, is perhaps little affected by environmental factors, though the variation in severity of the condition may be in some part environmentally determined. In the case of the XYY syndrome, however, there is evidence that the likelihood of the patient developing strong antisocial characteristics is much influenced by his home background. Similarly in the case of most disorders due to mutant genes of large effect, the environment has little influence on whether the child has or does not have the basic disorder, for example achondroplasia or Huntington's chorea. However, medical or surgical measures may be available to modify the course of the disease, for example dietary treatment of phenylketonuria or surgical treatment for multiple polyposis of the colon. Some such mutant gene-determined conditions, however, may cause little clinical disorder except in special environmental circumstances. For example, the form of glucose-6-phosphate dehydrogenase deficiency common in Negroes may cause little or no trouble except when the patients take certain drugs, such as primaquine. Similarly, the South African form of porphyria may cause little clinical upset unless barbiturates are take. In contrast, where the genetic predisposition is polygenic, there will very often be a substantial environmental component in development of the disorder.

A rough guide to the heritability of a particular disease is given by twin studies. The twin method depends on finding "index patients" who are twin-born and then comparing the proportion of MZ and DZ co-twins who also have the disease. The comparison is often best made with DZ twins of the same sex as the index patient. The interpretation of results may be summarized as follows:

1. If MZ co-twins are no more often affected than are DZ twins, it is probable that the genetic variation is of little importance in determining who does or does not develop the disease. For example, for twins reared together, the attack rate for measles is over 90 per cent for co-twins whether MZ or DZ or not.
2. If the MZ twins are almost always affected, but the like-sex DZ co-twins are substantially less often affected,

it is probable the disease is very largely determined by genetic factors. For example, only two or three examples are known where a MZ co-twin of a patient with Down's syndrome did not also have Down's syndrome. These few instances may be attributed to non-disjunction in an early somatic cell division, perhaps restoring a trisomy 21-cell line to a normal one.

3. If the MZ co-twins are by no means almost always also affected, but are so affected substantially more often than are the like-sex DZ co-twins, then it is very probable that both genetic factors and environmental experiences are important in the causation of the disease. Some illustrative findings for common disease in the National Danish Twin Study[14] are illustrated in Table 2. In the table, each concordant pair is counted only once, though where both twins were "index patients" in the sense that they were independently ascertained, each concordant pair will provide two affected co-twins. The method of collection was such that often both twins will have been index patients.

TABLE 2

FINDINGS IN THE NATIONAL DANISH TWIN STUDY[14]

Disease	*Concordance* Monozygotic Twins	Dizygotic Twins Like Sex
Manic-depressive psychosis	10/15	2/23
Schizophrenia	4/9	4/33
Arterial hypertension*	20/80	10/106
Coronary occlusion†‡	22/84	22/159
Cerebral apoplexy‡	22/98	16/148
Tuberculosis*	50/135	42/267
Rheumatic fever	30/148	12/226
Rheumatoid arthritis	16/47	2/71
Bronchial asthma*	30/64	24/101

* Differences significant at the 1/100 level.
† Updated to 1969 (M. Hauge, personal communication).
‡ Differences significant at the 1/20 level.

Chromosome Anomalies

These will be considered in the next chapter on cytogenetics. They are present in a high proportion of zygotes, probably more than 4 per cent. The majority result in spontaneous abortion and are the cause of perhaps as many as 60 per cent of spontaneous first trimester miscarriages. Chromosome anomalies that will seriously affect health occur in about 1 in 200 children surviving till term. The most common are: Down's syndrome, which affects about 1 live-born in 700; Klinefelter's syndrome, affecting about 1 in 800 live-born males; the XYY syndrome affecting about 1 in 700 live-born males; and the XXX syndrome affecting about 1 in 1,000 live-born girls.

Conditions Due to Mutant Genes of Large Effect

The total birth frequency of conditions due to mutant genes of large effect is not accurately known, but may be as much as 1 in 100. Their contribution to miscarriages is not known. The severity ranges from those which are incompatible with more than a few minutes survival, for example homozygous achondroplasia, to those which cause disability only in old age, for example some of the more mildly affected patients with dystrophia myotonica.

The Family Patterns given by Mutant Genes of Large Effect

It is convenient to divide diseases due to mutant genes of large effect into dominant, recessive and X-linked. The term "dominant" and "recessive" are used in genetics operationally. While a dominant condition is one in which the patient is heterozygous for the mutant gene, it is well recognized that the homozygote if ever encountered is likely to be more severely affected. The homozygote for the mutant gene for achondroplasia dies perinatally and is as severely affected as a thanatophoric dwarf. It is also recognized that while in recessive conditions the patient is homozygous for the mutant gene, sufficiently sensitive tests if available will detect abnormality in the heterozygote. However, some conditions are truly intermediate in the sense that heterozygotes and homozygotes may present as patients, but the homozygotes are more severely affected. A good example of this is thalassaemia where the homozygote with "thalassaemia major" usually dies in childhood unless very well treated, while the heterozygote is fully viable, but may have a significant degree of anaemia.

The terms recessive and dominant are also applied to X-linked conditions according to whether the heterozygous carrier girl or woman may present as a patient. However, because of the inactivation of one X-chromosome, the tissues of heterozygous women are mosaics with some cells of the chromosome with the normal gene active and the others with the chromosome with the mutant gene active.[18] At the cellular level the latter cells are affected and so occasionally some clinical manifestation in the heterozygous woman is to be expected for all X-linked conditions, especially in those women in whom the proportion of affected cells happens to be high.

Dominant Conditions: The characteristic family pattern given by dominant conditions is that the first patient in the family is a sporadic case with unaffected parents and unaffected brothers and sisters. This patient is affected as a result of a fresh mutation. If he survives, on average 1 in 2 of his offsprings are affected according to whether he transmits the mutant gene or the normal gene, and thereafter the 1-in-2 risk applies to children of affected members of the family. This is illustrated in Fig. 14. The number of generations affected depends in part on the lottery of the 1-in-2 risk and in part on the "fitness" of the affected individuals, using fitness in the sense of the likelihood of the patient replacing himself and his wife with 2 children who will reach adult life. Where fitness is low, for example in Apert's type of acrocephalosyndactyly, almost all cases are sporadic and only a few instances are known of patients having children. With tuberose sclerosis some 80 per cent of patients occur sporadically. These sporadic cases are as much genetically determined as those in which one or other parent is affected, but they are affected as a result of fresh gene mutation in one or other of the germ-cells formed by the parents. In contrast, since the onset of Huntington's chorea is usually in the fifth decade, many parents reproduce and some pedigrees with individuals affected over many generations are known. More often

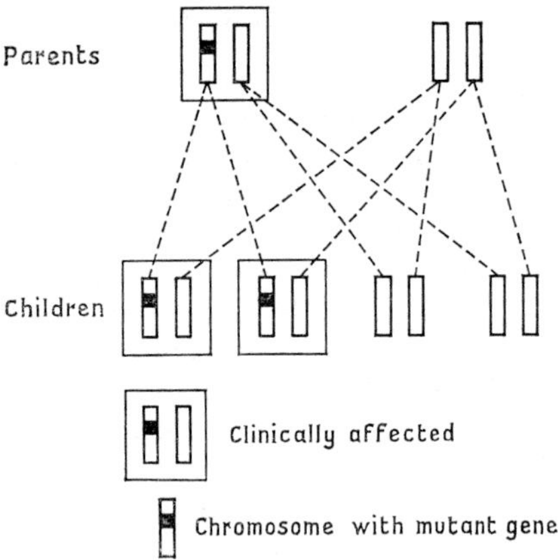

FIG. 14. Inheritance of an autosomal dominant condition.

than not, a patient has an affected parent. Where fitness is precisely 0·5 and the population is just about replacing itself, about half the patients will be born to normal parents, about a quarter will have an affected parent but no affected grandparent, and the remaining quarter will have an affected grandparent and perhaps earlier ascendants affected. A pedigree of dominant multiple epiphyseal dysplasia is shown in Fig. 15.

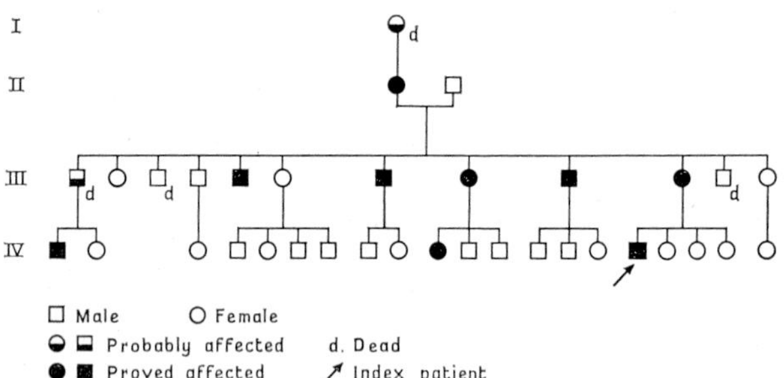

FIG. 15. Multiple epiphyseal dysplasia: a dominant pedigree

Many dominant conditions show remarkable variation in the severity of manifestation of the disorder, and a few are incompletely dominant in that some heterozygotes show no clinical manifestation at all. They may, however, be detected by special biochemical tests, for example increased protoporphyrin in the faeces of an individual heterozygous for porphyria variegata.

Recessive Conditions: The characteristic family pattern given by recessive conditions is that it is not uncommon for brothers and sisters of index patients to be affected, but it is rare for anybody else in the family to be affected. The 1-in-4 risk to sibs is illustrated in Fig. 16. The relatives with the next highest risk after the 1-in-4 risk to sibs are double first cousins with a 1-in-16 risk, but few patients have double first cousins. Where sibships are usually small, the 1-in-4 risk means that many index patients are sporadic cases. Where a patient has only one sib, this patient will be unaffected 3 times out of 4. The proportion of children affected in sibships will be more than 1 in 4 because the family does not come to notice unless it contains at least one affected member. Somewhat elaborate methods have been devised to correct for this. In practice, the best method is to define accurately the index patient (a family may contain 2 index patients if both were independently ascertained) and then count the proportion affected among the sibs of the index patient. Where a family has more than one index patient this family is included once for each index patient.

For example, with two-child families born to two heterozygous carrier parents and complete ascertainment of all patients in a population, on average 1 in 16 will have 2 children affected, 6 in 16 one child affected, 9 in 16 no child

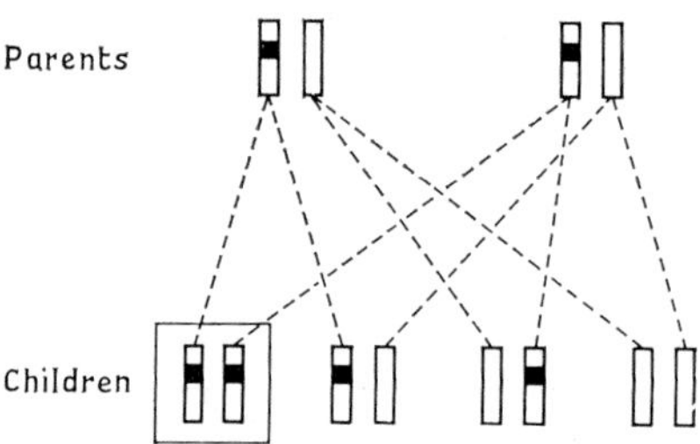

FIG. 16. Inheritance of an autosomal recessive condition.

affected. With complete ascertainment, each patient will be an index patient. So the family with both affected will contribute 2 affected children, the families with one affected child will contribute 6 normal children, the families with only unaffected children will not be ascertained. This will give overall 2 in 8, the theoretical 1 in 4, affected. If, however, the likelihood of ascertainment is low and proportional to the number of affected children in the family, then families with two affected children would be ascertained twice as often as those with one affected child, but only one child would be an index case in each family with 2 affected. So once again 1 in 4 of the sibs of index patients would be found affected. In populations with extensive genetic counselling, such that many parents who have had an affected child decide not to risk having more children, there will be few second affected children in the family and almost all patients will appear as sporadic cases. In these circumstances, only the few affected children born after the index patient provide a useful estimate of the risk to sibs.

A second feature of pedigrees of recessive conditions is that the parents are not uncommonly cousins. The rarer the condition, the higher the proportion of cousin marriage among the parents. The reason for this is that if a man who carries a gene for a recessive condition marries an unrelated wife, the chance that she carries the same gene is approximately twice the gene frequency, for example 1 in 100 in the case of a condition with a birth frequency of 1 in 40,000. Whereas a wife who is a first cousin would have, because of the relationship, a 1-in-8 probability of carrying the same gene. However, the frequency of cousin marriage in most of Europe and North America is now very low,

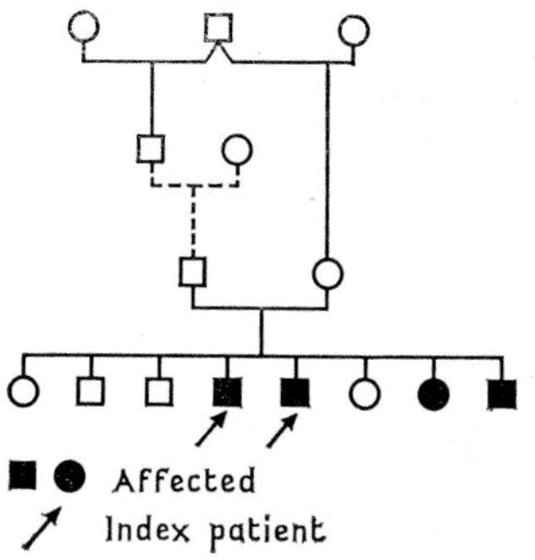

Affected
Index patient

FIG. 17. Morquio's disease: an autosomal recessive condition, showing consanguinity.

to a small parish on the north-east coast of the country at the start of the 18th century.

X-linked Conditions: The family patterns of conditions due to mutant genes on the X-chromosome are characterized especially by the 1-in-2 risk of the disorder in the sons of heterozygous women and the 1-in-2 risk of daughters of such women being heterozygotes. This is illustrated in Fig. 19. Males who possess the mutant gene on their single X-chromosome will be clinically affected. Heterozygous females will in most instances be clinically unaffected, since on average half their cells will contain the X-chromosome carrying the normal allele on the active chromosome. Occasionally women, who by chance have a high proportion of cells with the X-chromosome carrying the mutant gene on the active chromosome, will show some clinical disorder though they will seldom be as severely affected as male patients. There are a few

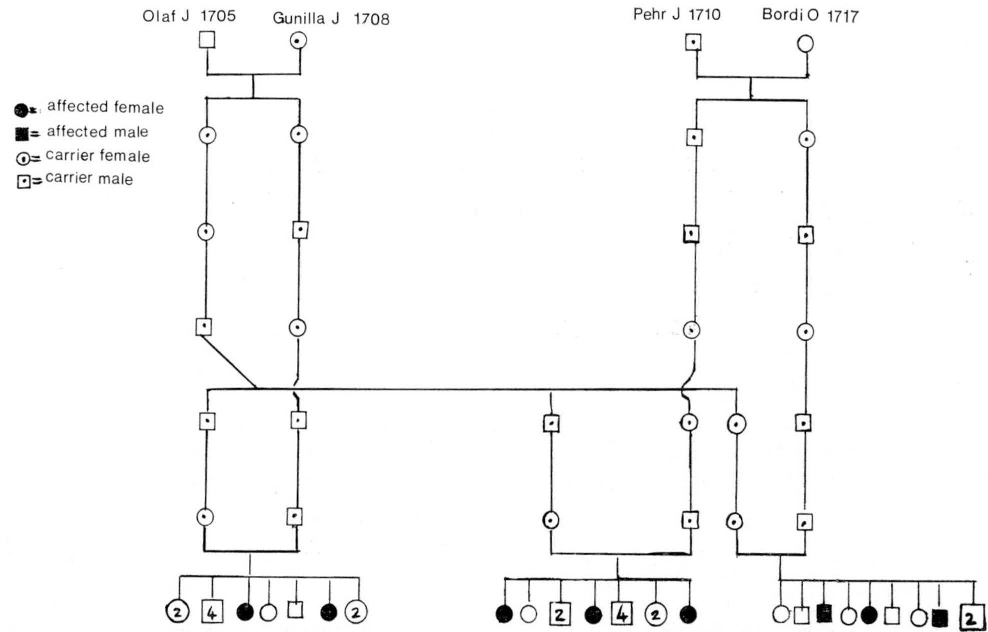

FIG. 18. Part of Sjögren and Larsson's pedigree[27] of mental defect with spastic limbs and scaly red skin.

probably only 1 to 2 per 1,000 marriages in Britain, so that even a twelvefold increase in the cousin-marriage rate among parents with a recessive condition will not be readily apparent in a series of less than about 100 index patients.

A pedigree of Morquio's disease is shown in Fig. 17. The consanguinity of the parents was not known until an enquiry was made following the recognition of the recessive condition in their children. In countries with excellent parish records, for example Sweden and Switzerland, or in religious isolates such as the Amish in the United States, it is often possible to discover remote parental consanguinity not known to the parents. An example of this for the recessive syndrome including mental retardation, spasticity and ichthyosis congenita[27] is shown in Fig. 18. The three illustrated Swedish sibships with index patients both had parental consanguinity and common ancestry traced back

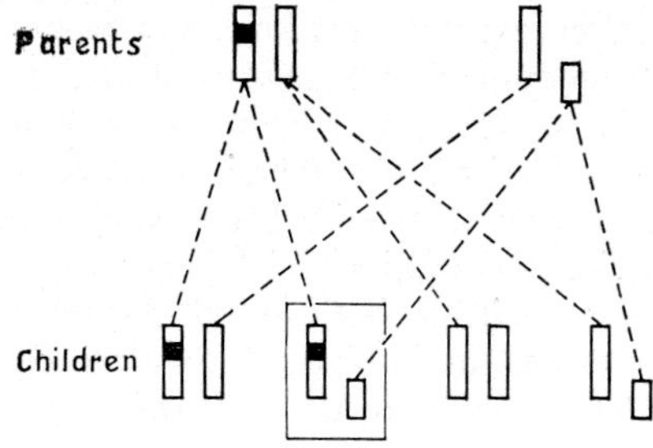

FIG. 19. Inheritance of an X-linked recessive condition.

conditions where some clinical expression of the disorder in heterozygous women is usual, an example is the X-linked phyophosphataemic type of vitamin D-resistant rickets. There are at least two conditions, the oro-facio-digital syndrome and incontinentia pigmenti, where the effect of the mutant gene on development is so severe that affected males are seldom born alive and the majority of patients are heterozygous females.

Where affected males are able to have children all their sons will be unaffected, since the affected male transmits his Y-chromosome to his son. This feature is useful in distinguishing X-linked from sex-linked dominant inheritance. All his daughters will be heterozygotes since they will receive his single X-chromosome which contains the mutant gene. In the unlikely event of such an affected male marrying a heterozygous female, half the sons will be patients, depending entirely on which X-chromosome the mother transmits, and half the daughters will be homozygotes and half heterozygotes, again depending on which X-chromosome the mother transmits. A homozygous woman is not likely to be more severely affected than an affected male once the inactivation of the second X-chromosome has occurred in the third week after conception. A few examples are known of homozygotes for classical haemophilia. All the sons of such homozygous women will be affected and all her daughters will be heterozygous carriers. However, in a number of instances where an apparent female has been found to be a patient with an X-linked condition which is not usually manifest in heterozygotes it has been found that the patient has an XO genotype (as in Turner's syndrome) or an XY genotype (as in testicular feminization).

An example of an X-linked pedigree is provided by the descendants of Queen Victoria who was heterozygous for classical haemophilia (Factor VIII deficiency) and part of the pedigree is shown in Fig. 20. One of her sons was affected and at least two of her daughters were heterozygotes. The affected son survived till the age of 33. He had a son who was inevitably unaffected and a daughter who was inevitably a heterozygote. She in turn had an affected son.

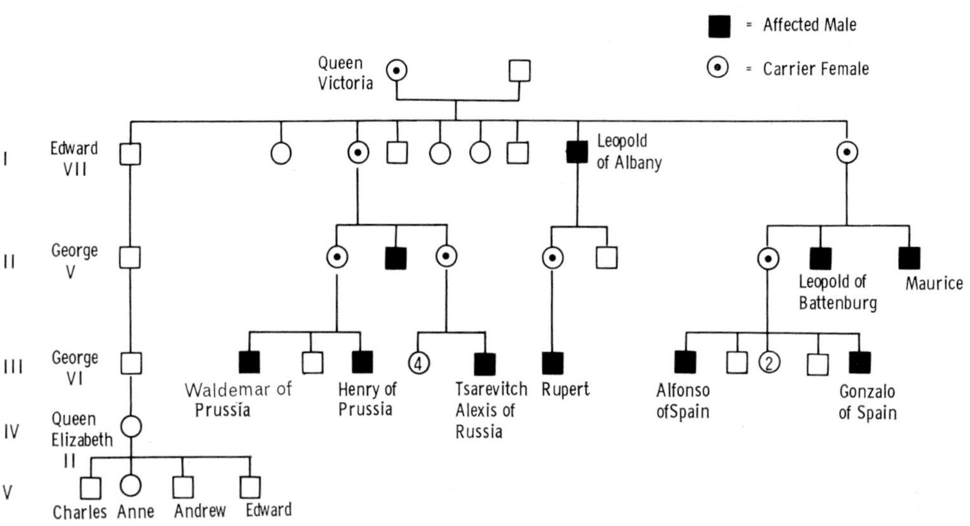

FIG. 20. Haemophilia—Queen Victoria's offspring,

It is to be expected, particularly where affected males do not reproduce, that a substantial proportion of cases will appear sporadically. Assuming equal mutation rates in sperm and ovum formation, about one-third of affected males will be affected as a result of fresh mutation in the ovum and neither his brothers nor his mother's brothers are at risk. In addition, in about a third of cases, the mother will be a heterozygote as a result of fresh mutation and so will not have affected brothers or uncles, but may have another affected son. In about another third of cases the grandmother at least, and perhaps one or more of her maternal ascendants, will be heterozygotes and the patient's mother's brothers and perhaps his mother's mother's brothers were at risk. When a test for the heterozygote is available it is often possible to detect in which generation the mutation occurred. In Fig. 21 are illustrated three pedigrees of Duchenne muscular dystrophy. In family A the

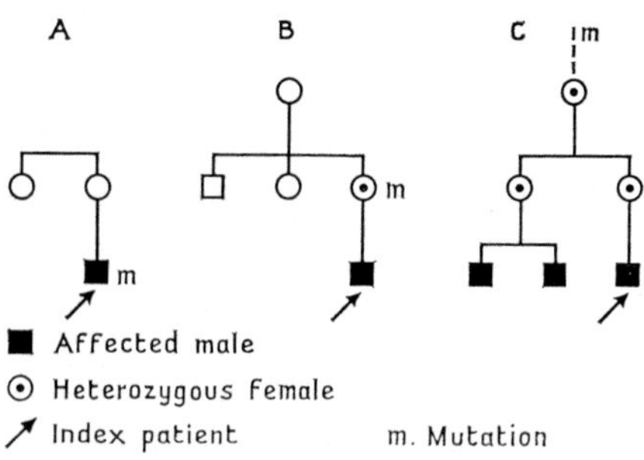

FIG. 21. X-linked severe (Duchenne) type of muscular dystrophy, showing when mutation occurred.

patient was affected as a result of a fresh mutation. In family B the mother was affected as a result of a fresh mutation, in family C the mutation had occurred at least as far back as the mother's mother.

Y-linked Inheritance: No Y-linked diseases are yet known. The characteristic family pattern would be that the first patient in the family would be a male born to normal parents as a result of fresh mutation and thereafter all the male descendants would be affected. It has been claimed but not fully confirmed that the condition of "hairy ears," common in India, in which there are hairs along the rim of the pinna, is Y-linked.

The Population Genetics of Conditions Due to Mutant Genes of Large Effect

With conditions due to mutant genes of large effect the birth frequency depends on: (a) the mutation rate, and (b) the biological fitness of those who possess the gene. Here biological fitness is used in the sense of relative fitness, that is the likelihood that the individual will have as many children as the average member of the population. Thus, where the average family size is 2·1 children and achondroplastics average, say, 0·21 children, the biological fitness of achondroplastics is 0·1. Where patients invariably die before reproductive age, their fitness is zero. Where they have a normal or near-normal expectation of life but are sterile, as with Klinefelter's syndrome or the testicular feminization syndrome, then fitness is also zero. With recessive and X-linked conditions in addition to the fitness of patients the fitness of heterozygotes also enters the equation, if this fitness of heterozygotes differs from 1·0.

Dominant: The relationship between mutation and selection is most straightforward with dominant conditions. If one calls the mutation rate, defined as the proportion of germ cells containing a fresh mutation at a particular gene locus, "m," and calls the mutation rate in sperm m_1, and that in ova m_2, then the proportion of zygotes affected by a fresh mutation at that particular gene locus will be $m_1 + m_2$. If m_1 equals m_2, then the proportion of zygotes freshly heterozygous for a mutant gene at that locus is $2m$. If fitness is zero (it is almost zero, for example, in the case of acrocephalosyndactyly of Apert type), then $2m$ will be the birth frequency of the condition and conversely half the birth frequency is a measure of the mutation rate. Where fitness is not zero, then in addition to patients born to normal parents and affected as a result of fresh mutation, there will be patients who have a parent, but no grandparent affected, and also patients who have a parent and a grandparent and perhaps earlier ascendants affected. The lower the fitness, the fewer generations the mutant gene is likely to persist. It is only very mild conditions, such as Dupuytren's contracture or conditions which usually have an onset in middle age, such as Huntington's chorea, which are likely to persist for several generations. The total birth frequency of individuals affected with dominant conditions is given by the expression $2m/1-f$, where f is the average fitness of patients. With a dominant condition such as classical achondroplasia, fitness about 0·1, the total birth frequency will be $2{\cdot}2m$ and only 1 patient in 10 will have an affected parent. Where a condition has a fitness about 0·5, as is probably the case with untreated multiple polyposis of the colon, the total birth frequency will be $4m$. In a stationary population (that is, one with family size at replacement level) about half the patients will be affected as a result of fresh mutation, about a quarter will have a parent, but no grandparent affected, about an eighth will have a parent and grandparent but no great-grandparent affected, and in the remaining eighth the condition will be present in 4 or more generations. At a birth frequency of $4m$ in a stationary population there

Alleles on the other chromosome	Alleles on one chromosome: *A* 1–p	*a* p
A 1–p	*AA* $(1-p)^2$	*Aa* p(1–p)
a p	*Aa* p(1–p)	*aa* p^2

FIG. 22. Relation between gene and genotype frequencies.

is a balance between the genes lost in each generation, since of these $4m$, only half replace themselves and $2m$ fresh cases occur as a result of fresh mutation. The mean persistence of each mutant gene in a stationary population is 2 generations. In a population which has such a high birth rate that it is doubling its numbers in each generation, a mutant gene with a fitness of a half will tend to persist indefinitely, but the birth frequency will remain $4m$.

Recessive: With recessive conditions in the simplest situation where heterozygous fitness is 1·0, that is, the same as that of normal individuals, and there is no change in the proportion of marriages which are consanguineous from generation to generation, the birth frequency is given by the expression $m/(1-f)$. The factor of 2 present in the expression for dominants has disappeared because with the failure to reproduce of each homozygous patient, 2 mutant genes are lost and not 1 as is the case with dominant conditions. However, the persistence of each mutant gene is very much greater than with dominants. When the mutation first occurs it will almost invariably be paired with a normal gene and the first zygote to receive the mutant gene will be a heterozygote. Married to an individual with 2 normal genes the heterozygote will have heterozygous and normal children in equal proportion. In this way the mutant gene is likely to be transmitted for many generations in heterozygotes causing no clinical abnormality. If the heterozygote fitness is 1·0 it will not be subject to negative selection until two heterozygotes marry. In a population in equilibrium, with marriage at random, the relation between the gene frequency, the proportion of homozygotes for the mutant gene (i.e. the birth frequency of patients with the recessive condition), the heterozygotes and the homozygotes for the normal gene is (using "*A*" for the normal gene, "*a*" for the mutant gene and "p" for the frequency of gene "*a*") is shown in Fig. 22. The proportions are for *aa*, *Aa* and *AA* respectively, p^2, $2p(1-p)$ and $2(1-p)^2$. Thus, with a recessive condition with birth frequency, p^2, of 40,000, it follows that with random mating p is 1 in 200 and so the proportion of the population who are heterozygous carriers is $2 \times 199/200^2$, that is a little less than 1 in 100. The proportion of mutant genes in heterozygotes to those in homozygotes is $2p(1-p)$ to $2p^2$ (each homozygote has 2 mutant genes), which, where p is 1/200, is 199 to 1. This means that even where the fitness of homozygotes is zero each mutant gene will survive in a large, stationary, randomly mating population for nearly 200 generations, that is 5,000 to 6,000 years.

With recessives, however, the simple relationships between birth frequency, fitness and the mutation rate may be upset in two ways. The first is by change in the rate of cousin marriage and of other forms of inbreeding. The effect of inbreeding is simply to bring heterozygotes together in marriage more often than would occur with random mating, and so to decrease somewhat the proportion of heterozygotes in the population necessary to produce sufficient loss of genes through homozygotes to balance the mutation rate. Changes in the amount of inbreeding will temporarily disturb the balance between mutation rate, fitness and birth-frequency of homozygotes. An increase in inbreeding, as when a small group of migrants comes to a new country and then marry only among themselves, will give a true increase in the birth-frequency of homozygotes, and so of patients, above the equilibrium level. The resultant increased loss of genes will gradually restore the birth frequency of patients to the original level. Conversely, a decrease in the amount of inbreeding, such as that which has occurred all over Europe, would temporarily reduce the birth-frequency of recessive conditions below the equilibrium level. The equilibrium is likely to be restored unless counter measures are taken, such as are discussed below.

MAINTENANCE OF 1% FREQUENCY OF SICKLE-CELL ANAEMIA BY $12\frac{1}{2}$% HETEROZYGOTE ADVANTAGE

Genotypes	Genotype frequencies of parents	Fitness	Gemete frequencies	Genotype frequencies of children
Normal homozygotes (AA)	0·81	80/81	0·8A	0·81
Heterozygotes (AS)	0·18	10/9	{0·1A, 0·1S}	0·18
Mutant homozygotes (SS)	0·01	0	0	0·01

FIG. 23. Maintenance of 1 per cent frequency of sickle-cell anaemia by 120 per cent heterozygote advantage.

A more important factor in disturbing the simple relationship between birth-frequency, fitness and the mutation rate for recessive conditions is that the fitness of heterozygotes may not be 1·0. Where it is less than 1·0, the mutant genes in heterozygotes are subject to negative selection and the birth-frequency of heterozygotes will be determined by the expression $2m/1-f$ which was given for dominants. Even if "f" is only slightly reduced, say to 0·95, this would mean that homozygotes are very rarely seen. Their frequency would only be 1 in 4 million births, where "m" was 1 in 40,000. Some recessive conditions in man do appear to be very rare and the explanation may be some selection against the heterozygote. Conversely, where the fitness of the heterozygote is greater than 1·0, the effect will be to maintain the frequency of the mutant gene in the population at a relatively high level in spite of a much reduced fitness of homozygotes. The size of the selective advantage of the heterozygote for sickle-cell anaemia in areas of high prevalence of malignant tertian malaria, required to maintain the birth-frequency of homozygotes at 1 in 100, is about $12\frac{1}{2}$ per cent over the homozygous normal. This is shown in Fig. 23. The nature of the selective advantage has recently been demonstrated to be that when the erythrocyte of the carrier, which contains about 40 per cent of sickle-cell haemoglobin, is parasitized, the effect is to reduce oxygen tension, deform the cell and lead to its destruction by the reticulo-endothelial system. The parasite is destroyed before it can complete its intra-erythrocytic stage of development. Where there is heterozygote advantage, the mutation rate plays little part in maintaining the birth-frequency of patients with recessive conditions.

Other recessive conditions which have birth-frequencies in local populations sufficiently high to imply heterozygote advantage are β-thalassaemia in countries bordering the Mediterranean, in the Near East and across to south-east Asia, cystic fibrosis all over northern and central Europe, phenylketonuria in Ireland, infantile Tay-Sach's disease and familial dysautonomia in Askenazi Jews, and familial Mediterranean fever in North Africa.

X-linked Conditions: The frequency of X-linked conditions among male births, provided that the fitness of heterozygous carrier women is 1·0, and the mutation rate is the same in sperms and ova, is given by the expression $3m/(1-f)$. The birth-frequency in males is "$3m$" when the fitness of affected males is zero. This is made up of "m" boys affected as a result of fresh mutation in ovum formation by their mothers, and "$2m$" affected because their mothers are heterozygotes. At this level there is balance between mutation and selection. The "m" mutant genes in boys affected as a result of fresh mutation are replaced by fresh mutations in males in each generation. The loss of "$2m$" mutant genes in boys born to heterozygous carrier mothers is replaced by "$2m$" mutant genes in girls who are made carriers by fresh mutation. Where the fitness of affected boys is 0·5, the balance is struck when the frequency in male births is "$6m$".

Multifactorially Determined Conditions

Conditions due to chromosomal anomalies are not uncommon since non-disjunction appears to be a common event. But there are a limited number of disorders determined in this way. Over 1,000 different conditions due to mutant genes of large effect are known; but if at all serious, they tend to be individually rare for reasons explained above. There is evidence from twin and family studies that many relatively common conditions, for example the common congenital malformations, such as neural tube malformations and congenital heart malformations, and some common diseases of adult life, such as duodenal ulcer and schizophrenia, are in considerable part genetically determined, but that neither chromosome anomalies nor mutant genes of large effect are involved. The family patterns shown by such disorders indicate that they are threshold phenomena—that underlying them is a continuously variable "liability," analogous to that for stature, or I.Q. or fingerprint ridge count, and that those affected are individuals who deviate from the population mean beyond a threshold.[6,11] With some disorders, it is apparent that the clinician has consciously drawn an arbitrary threshold. Thus hypertension is defined arbitrarily as a blood pressure above a limit drawn in relation to the patient's age and sex. The threshold of "mental handicap" corresponds approximately to an I.Q. about 2 standard deviations below the population mean of 100, at an I.Q. level on most standard tests of about 70. While "severe mental handicap," with an I.Q. below 50, is in considerable part due to pathological conditions, such as Down's syndrome or maldevelopment of the brain, most cases of mental handicap with an I.Q. level between 50 and 70 may be regarded as part of the normal variation of I.Q. and the threshold of 70 is an arbitrary one. With most disorders and diseases, however, there is a real threshold between normality and abnormality. A child either has cleft lip or it has not got cleft lip, though there are minimal degrees of lip scarring without any actual cleft which grade into normality. The concept of a normally distributed liability with a threshold is illustrated in Fig. 24.

The liability will be made up of two components: a genetic component, which is likely to be polygenic—that is, dependant on genetic variation at several gene loci—and an environmental component which again may well be composed of numerous factors of small effect. The liability may be assumed to be normal on an appropriate scale. Then,

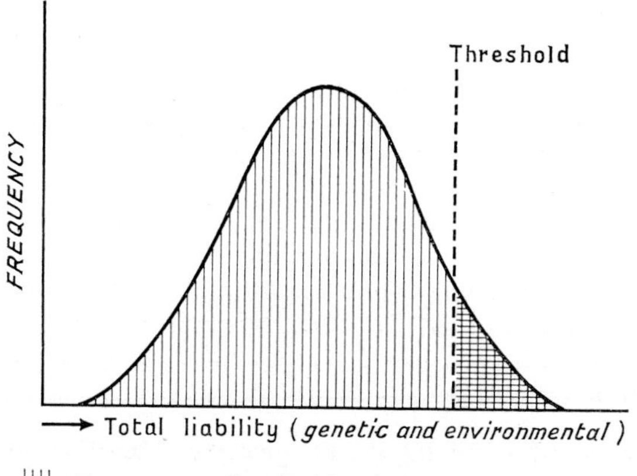

FIG. 24. Falconer's model of polygenic inheritance.[12]

knowing the birth frequency of the condition in the particular population, it is possible to work out the family patterns that would be given by the threshold model, from the mathematical properties of the normal curve and the expected correlations between relatives. The principles are illustrated in Fig. 25, and the necessary tables have been compiled.[11] For example, in Fig. 25 the threshold is such that the average deviation of those affected from the population mean is x units. Then, if first-degree relatives have a correlation of 0·5 with the index patients, their distribution will be about a point $x/2$ units from the population mean. The distribution of these relatives will not be quite normal, but no great error is introduced by assuming that it is and the proportion of first-degree relatives beyond the threshold may be calculated. If third-degree relatives have a correlation of 0·125 with the index patients then their distribution will be about a point $x/8$ units from the population mean, and again the proportion beyond the threshold may be

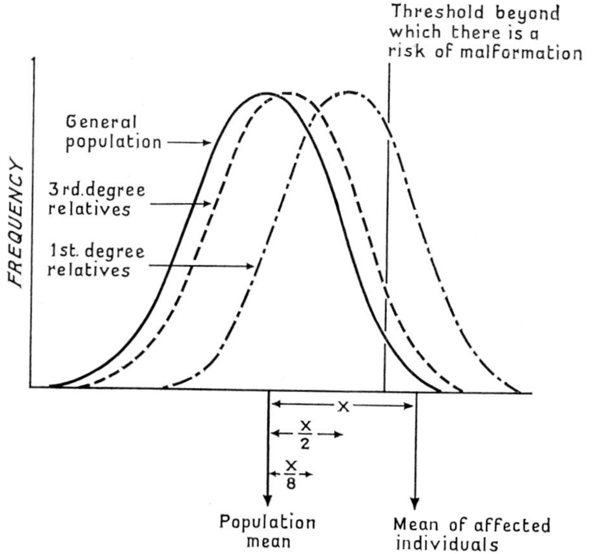

FIG. 25. Model for polygenic inheritance of harelip.

calculated. For example, if the birth-frequency of the condition is 1 in 1,000 and the correlation for first-degree relatives is 0·5, for second degree 0·25 and for third degree 0·125, as one would expect if inheritance was simply polygenic, there was no assortative marriage, and heritability was 100 per cent, then the proportion of first-degree relatives beyond the threshold and so affected may be calculated to be 8·0 per cent, second degree 1·2 per cent, and third degree 0·4 per cent. This is a family pattern quite distinct from that given by mutant genes of large effect but one that is found for several congenital malformations, except that the correlations are rather less than 0·5, 0·25 and 0·125, implying that heritability is less than 100 per cent.

This type of family pattern differs from that given by even modified recessive inheritance in that the proportion of children affected is as high as the proportion of sibs affected, and differs from even much modified dominant inheritance in that the reduction in the proportion of relatives affected falls off by more than 50 per cent with each step from first to second to third-degree relatives. X-linked inheritance would not be considered unless there were a preponderance of one sex affected, but is excluded by frequent instances of affected fathers having affected sons. Where the birth-frequency of a condition is about 1 per cent, as with schizophrenia as defined by European psychiatrists (American psychiatrists use the term to cover a wider range of illness), the proportion of first-, second-, and third-degree relatives affected assuming correlations of 0·5, 0·25 and 0·125 with index patients, is 16 per cent, 5 per cent and 1·7 per cent respectively. The distinction between modified dominant inheritance and polygenic inheritance is now more difficult, though the reduction with each further step away in relationship is still by two-thirds rather than a half. However, if the birth-frequency is as high as 4 per cent the reduction is similar with dominant and polygenic inheritance.

An example of a condition with a birth-frequency of 1 in 1,000, which gives a family pattern strongly suggestive of multifactorial determination with a threshold, is uncomplicated cleft lip with or without lateral cleft palate.[4] The malformation also occurs as part of syndromes with their own form of genetic determination (for example, D trisomy and van de Woude's syndrome) and in family analysis these must be excluded. The mid-line cleft palate malformation is also genetically and embryologically distinct from uncomplicated mid-line cleft palate without cleft lip. No large consecutive studies of twins are available but the proportion of MZ co-twins affected is about 40 per cent and of DZ about 5 per cent. This in itself indicates a substantial genetic determination but a heritability well below 100 per cent. The proportion of relatives affected in a London series where the birth frequency is about 1 in 1,000 (0·1 per cent) is shown in Table 3. It will be seen that the pattern is very much that

TABLE 3

THE PROPORTIONS AFFECTED OF RELATIVES OF PATIENTS WITH CLEFT LIP (± CLEFT PALATE)[4]

	Sibs	*Children*	*Aunts, Uncles, Nephews, Nieces*	*First-Cousins*
Index patients, 291	3·2 (25/774)	3·0 (17/565)	0·6 (22/3525)	0·2 (7/3518)

Birth frequency 0·1 per cent

which would be given by multifactorial aetiology with a threshold but that the proportion affected of first-, second- and third-degree relatives are less than would be given by the theoretical correlation of 0·5, 0·25 and 0·125 with the index patients. The proportion of these relatives affected in the London series indicates correlations of about 0·35, 0·19 and 0·085, suggesting a heritability of about 70 per cent for each type of relative. It should be noted that the estimate will be an overestimate since it will include the contribution of common family environment. Common family environment will be least, and so the overestimate least, for cousins. Further, the similarity of the risk to DZ co-twins and sibs suggests that the immediate intrauterine environment is not of great importance and the similarity of the risk to sibs and children also suggests that persistent features of the intrauterine environment provided by the mother are not important. Similar studies in Copenhagen and Utah in the U.S.A. have given essentially similar findings but have indicated rather a higher degree of heritability. The reason is, that the London series was deliberately based on survivors who had had the opportunity to have children and so excluded a higher proportion of the more severely affected patients some of whom will have died in childhood. The proportion of MZ co-twins also affected, 40 per cent, is also compatible with a heritability of about 70 per cent.

This type of inheritance will show certain further features which are not given by mutant genes of large effect. One is, that the risk to relatives will be higher when the index patient has a more severe degree of the malformation, in so far as the more severe degree of malformation represents a more extreme deviation beyond the threshold. For example, the risk to sibs after an index patient with bilateral cleft lip and palate is about 6 per cent, and after a unilateral cleft lip is only about 2 per cent. Similarly, the risk of recurrence of Hirschsprung's disease is greater the longer the length of the aganglionic segment of bowel.[2] Another feature is that where there is a markedly higher birth-frequency in one sex than another, provided that the genetic mechanisms are basically the same in the two sexes, the risk to first-degree relatives will be greater where the index patient belongs to the sex less often affected.[7] An example is pyloric stenosis with a male to female sex ratio of 5 to 1. The proportion affected among the children of girl patients is 19 per cent for sons and 7 per cent for daughters, while that for the children of male patients is 5 per cent for sons and 2·5 per cent for daughters. Another feature is that the risk to relatives will be increased where the index patient already has one relative affected. With recessive inheritance it is immaterial whether two parents had had 1, 2 or 3 affected children the risk remains 1 in 4 and all parents at risk (unless one or other parent is a homozygote) have the same 1-in-4 risk for their children. With polygenic inheritance, however, the risks will vary from one couple to another, according to where their own mid-parental level of the genetic component in liability lies, and the presence of two affected individuals will often indicate a high-risk family.

When the genetic predisposition to develop a disease has been shown to be polygenic, an attempt should be made to identify the individual gene loci involved. In the case of duodenal ulcer, for example, it has been shown that genetic variation at two gene loci, that for the ABO blood groups and that for secretor status, contribute to the liability to develop the disorder. Together, however, they account for only about 3 per cent of the resemblance of sibs for the condition.[24]

Factors Determining the Frequency of Multifactorially Determined Disease

The high frequency of some multifactorially determined disease in the face of high mortality or substantially reduced fertility is not easily explained. Changes in the intensity of the environmental component may occur fairly rapidly and substantially alter the frequency. The high rate of early death from ischaemic heart-disease in developed countries may plausibly be attributed to an intensification of environmental factors such as over-eating, lack of exercise, and smoking. But many multifactorially determined conditions appear to have a high birth-frequency in many different environments. For example, though the British birth-frequency of nearly 5 per 1,000 of the neural tube malformations is exceptional, they have a frequency of over 1 per

1,000 in most parts of the world. One possible explanation is a form of heterozygote advantage, whereby both extremes of the distribution are relatively unfit, and deaths from neural-tube malformations are balanced by some reduced fitness at the other end of the polygenically determined scale.

Genetic Counselling

Genetic counselling consists in giving information to parents on any special genetic risks to children that may exist in the particular family because of some genetic condition already present in a member of the family, together with information which would put the risk into perspective. The decision on what action to take in the light of the information given rests with the parents. The objectives of counselling are: firstly, to provide the information to parents; secondly, to draw the attention of their medical advisers to any special risk to future children so that diagnosis may be made early and any treatment that is available started promptly; thirdly, to prevent an increase following successful new treatments and ultimately to substantially reduce the birth-frequency of children born genetically predisposed to severe handicap. This last objective is discussed in the final section of this chapter.

Accurate assessment of genetic risks depends essentially on a precise diagnosis and on a good family history with verification from hospital or other records of diseases present in other members of the family. Occasionally, the family history itself will clearly indicate the mode of inheritance of the condition, particularly where this is typical of straightforward dominant, recessive or X-linked inheritance. But in these days of small families, such guidance from the family history is exceptional and reliance must usually be placed on a precise diagnosis and knowledge from previous formal genetic studies of the mode of inheritance of the condition present. Precise diagnosis is of special importance in genetic counselling since many conditions that clinically appear to be unitary prove on genetic analysis to consist of different entities which may be inherited in different ways. In the case of gargoylism it was first noted that though inheritance was apparently autosomal recessive there was an excess of male patients. Then some characteristic X-linked pedigrees were noted. Then some of the clinical features which help to distinguish the autosomal recessive Hurler's form from the X-linked Hunter's form were recognized. Now, six genetically distinct variants of mucopolysaccharidosis are recognized.[19] In the same way, dominant, recessive and X-linked forms of spondyloepiphyseal dysplasia are now recognized and the muscular dystrophies are defined primarily in terms of their mode of inheritance.

In practice, risks tend to fall into three categories: those in which the risk of disorder in a child born to the couple is no more than the risk for any birth taken at random; those in which there is a high risk of recurrence—a high risk may be arbitrarily defined as 1 in 10 or worse; those in which there is a moderate risk of recurrence, that is, better than 1 in 10 and in practice usually better than 1 in 20, but much more than the random risk.

Random risks apply when the child has a handicap due to some environmental agent which is not likely to occur in any later pregnancy. A good example is a child with rubella embryopathy or one with thalidomide embryopathy. It is important to recognize that random or near-random risks also apply with a number of genetically determined conditions where the genetic anomaly was present at conception, but due to a fresh mutation in germ-cell formation was not present in either parent. This applies with the majority of instances of births affected by chromosome anomalies. For example, after the birth of a child with regular trisomy 21 (Down's syndrome) the recurrence risk, where parents have normal chromosomes, is increased over the random risk at young maternal ages, but is still only of the order of 1 per cent. After the birth of a child with a straightforward dominant condition, such as classical achondroplasia, the risk of recurrence may be a little increased over the random risk because of the possibility that the mutation may have occurred a few divisions back in the germ-cell line, causing a small segment of a gonad to mutate; but no undoubted example of two children with classical achondroplasia born to normal parents has been reported. Many dominant conditions are much more variable in their manifestation than achondroplasia and here it is important to examine both parents carefully to make sure that neither of them carry the gene.

High-risk Situations

The great majority of conditions which may give a high risk of recurrence are due to mutant genes of large effect. Only in a small minority of conditions due to chromosomal anomalies and in a minority of multifactorial conditions is there a high risk. The chromosomal anomalies carrying a high risk are structural anomalies, especially translocations, where one or other parent has a balanced translocation and there is a risk of an unbalanced anomaly (see Chapter 2). Regular trisomy 21 (Down's syndrome) carries a high risk to the offspring of female patients, but because of the severe mental handicap they seldom reproduce. Women with the XO genotype and men with the XXY genotype are sterile, and women with the XXX genotype and men with the XYY genotype usually have normal children.

With dominant conditions the high risk, 1 in 2 for a fully dominant condition, is for the children of patients. There are no difficulties for fully dominant conditions of early onset. Difficulties arise where a heterozygote may have no clinical manifestation. An example of this possibility is retinoblastoma. Probably, almost all instances of bilateral retinoblastoma are dominant, but occasional instances are known where a patient has transmitted to a grandchild through an unaffected child. It is therefore not certain that an unaffected person does not carry the gene and so normal parents of a sporadic case cannot be told that there is little risk of recurrence in later children. No special tests are helpful with retinoblastoma, but with other such conditions, special tests may help to detect the clinically unaffected heterozygote. An example is tests for increased protoporphyrin in the stools of clinically unaffected heterozygotes for the gene for variegate porphyria and tests for increased red-cell fragility in heterozygotes for the gene for acholuric jaundice. With dominant conditions which are often of late onset such as Huntington's chorea or the adult form of dystrophia myotonica, it is often not possible to determine whether a young adult, a child of a patient, is or is not a carrier and here it is only possible to give the overall risk of 1 in 4 to such a child derived from the half-chance that he or she is himself a carrier and the half-chance that if so he or she will transmit to a particular child. As the enquirer grows older and does not develop the disease, the probability that he is a carrier steadily decreases according to the life table of age of onset of the disease.

With recessive conditions the essential genetic risk is the 1-in-4 risk to later sibs of the first apparently sporadic patient born to normal parents, a complete contrast to the low risk to later sibs of the first sporadic case of a dominant condition. Again in contrast to the situation with dominants, there is little risk to the offspring of a patient with a recessive condition. Such a patient cannot have an affected child unless he or she has happened to marry a heterozygote for the mutant gene involved. Consanguineous marriage excepted, the risk of this is just the gene frequency. For example, the frequency of the gene for phenylketonuria over much of Britain and the United States is about 1 in 120. Even with relatively common recessive conditions such as cystic fibrosis in Britain, the gene frequency is only between 1 in 40 and 1 in 45 and so this is the expected proportion affected among the offspring of survivors. The risk to nephews and nieces of patients is one-third of the risk to children. Genetic counselling for recessive conditions becomes more precise once tests for carriers become available. It is then possible to test these genetically at risk and, if need be, their prospective spouses.

With X-linked conditions the important risk is the 1-in-2 risk to the sons of carrier women. The problem is then to determine the likelihood that a woman is a carrier. A woman is almost certainly a heterozygote if she has an affected son and any other male relative affected. Thus, a woman with two sons, a son and a brother or a son and a mother's brother affected is almost certainly a carrier. The daughter of an affected man is certainly a carrier. A woman with an affected son, but no other male relative affected may or may not be a carrier. She will not be a heterozygote if her son is affected as a result of a fresh mutation. The odds that such a woman is a carrier may, assuming equal mutation rates in men and women, be estimated from the number of her unaffected sons and brothers. Again, genetic counselling is made more precise if special tests are available for the carrier state. Fortunately, because of the random inactivation of one X-chromosome, it is often possible to find a relatively simple clinical test for the carrier state even though the precise biochemical error is not known. Thus, creatine kinase levels in serum provide useful information in the majority of young women genetically at risk of being carriers of the gene for X-linked muscular dystrophy. The relative probability of being or not being a carrier from the clinical test may be combined with the genetic risk to give a total probability that the woman is or is not a carrier.

Moderate Risk Situations

Where a condition is multifactorially determined the recurrence risk is usually below 1 in 10 and often below 1 in 20 but nevertheless is many times more than the random risk. For example, the 4 per cent risk to the later sibs of a patient with the cleft lip (±cleft palate) malformation, where neither parent is affected, in Caucasian populations is 40 times the birth frequency in the general population. Recurrence risks of this kind are determined by larger-scale family studies of patients drawn from the same population as the enquirers. The risks are essentially empirical and represent an average risk. In the particular family in question they may be higher or lower than the average, but there is usually no way of knowing this and so the average risk is the best guide. However, it is found that the recurrence risk may vary with the sex of the index patient as in pyloric stenosis.[7] It is usually increased if the patient already has one near-relative affected. It may be increased after more severely affected patients as with Hirschsprung's disease.

The Future Control of the Birth-frequency of Genetically Determined Disease

Future reduction in the birth frequency of chromosomal disorders is likely to come mostly from the offer of prenatal screening to those parents who would wish for a termination of the pregnancy if the fetus were found to have a major chromosomal anomaly. There are no immediate prospects of controlling the frequency of chromosomal nondisjunction. Only a minority of patients with chromosomal anomalies are born to parents of whom one or other has a balanced chromosomal anomaly. Prenatal screening, initially of the relatively high-risk mothers who are over 35 years of age, is therefore the only procedure likely to be effective in reducing the birth-frequency of such disorders.

In the case of conditions due to mutant genes of large effect, prenatal detection will only be practicable where the specific risk to the fetus is known. However, genetic counselling supplemented by prenatal diagnosis where this is possible is capable of bringing about a substantial reduction in the birth-frequency of such conditions. If all patients with dominant conditions were informed of the 1-in-2 risk to their offspring and all decided to have no children, the only patients would be those affected by fresh mutation. The birth-frequency would be just twice the mutation rate. For many less serious dominant conditions such strict family limitation is neither necessary nor desirable. However, even with those of moderate severity, once methods of prenatal diagnosis become available, either by biochemical tests or linkage, most parents are likely to make use of the procedure to have only unaffected children. With recessive conditions, it is theoretically possible to prevent the birth of almost all patients. Simple genetic counselling will reduce the birth frequency of serious recessive disorders by about one-sixth if parents who have had one affected child are told of the 1-in-4 risk and all decide to have no more children, or, with the aid of amniocentesis, no more affected children. However, where individual recessive conditions are especially common in particular populations and heterozygote detection is possible, the birth-frequency of affected children may be substantially reduced by ascertaining and informing all heterozygotes, so that they do not unwittingly marry each other. Prenatal screening may make it possible to avoid the birth of a homozygote in those instances where heterozygotes do choose to marry. With serious X-linked recessive conditions, about a third of patients are affected as a result of fresh mutations which are not likely to be preventable. However, many of the two-thirds of patients born to heterozygous carrier mothers will be preventable by genetic counselling once carrier detection is possible. Further, once predetermination of sex becomes possible, surviving patients with X-linked conditions, such as haemophilia, will be able to plan to rear only male children who, since they will have received the patient's Y-chromosome, will be unaffected and will not transmit the mutant gene involved.

With multifactorially determined conditions, a reduction in birth-frequency is most likely to come by protecting fetuses, known to be genetically at risk, from the additional environmental triggers which finally determine the clinical abnormality.

REFERENCES

1. Allison, A. C. (1954), "Protection Afforded by Sickle-cell Trait against Subtertian Malarial Infection," *Brit. med. J.*, **i**, 290–294.
2. Bodian, M. and Carter, C. O. (1963), "A Family Study of Hirschsprung's Disease," *Ann. Hum. Genet.*, **26**, 261–271.
3. Briggs, R. and King, T. J. (1959), "Nucleocytoplasmic Interactions in Eggs and Embryos," in *The Cell*, Vol. 1, p. 537 (J. Brachet and A. E. Mirsky, Eds.). New York: Academic Press.
4. Carter, C. O. (1965), "The Inheritance of Common Congenital Malformations," in *Progress in Medical Genetics*, Vol. IV, Ch. 3 (A. G. Steinberg and A. G. Bearn, Eds.). London: Heinemann Medical Books.
5. Carter, C. O. (1969), *An ABC of Medical Genetics*, p. 2. London: *Lancet*.
6. Carter, C. O. (1969), "The Genetics of Common Diseases," *Brit. med. Bull.*, **25**, 52–57.
7. Carter, C. O. and Evans, K. A. (1969), "Inheritance of Congenital Pyloric Stenosis," *J. med. Genet.*, **6**, 233–239.
8. Chicago Conference (1966), "Standardisation in Human Cytogenetics," *Birth Defects: Original Article Series*, **2**, No. 2.
9. Cove, D. J. (1971), *Genetics*, p. 152. London: Cambridge University Press.
10. Crick, F. H. C. (1966), "The Genetic Code," part III. *Scient. Am.*, 55–60.
11. Falconer, D. S. (1960), *Introduction to Quantitative Genetics*. Edinburgh and London: Oliver and Boyd.
12. Falconer, D. S. (1965), "The Inheritance of Liability to Certain Diseases, Estimated from the Incidence Among Relatives," *Ann. Hum. Genet.*, **29**, 51–76.
13. Harris, H. (1969), "Enzyme and Protein Polymorphism," *Brit. med. Bull.*, **25**, 5–13.
14. Harvald, B. and Hauge, M. (1965), in *Genetics and the Epidemiology of Chronic Diseases* (J. V. Neel, M. W. Shaw and W. J. Schull, Eds.). Public Health Service Publications, No. 1163, Washington, D.C.
15. Holt, S. (1961), "Quantitative Genetics of Fingerprint Patterns," *Brit. med. Bull.*, **17**, 247–250.
16. Huntley, R. M. C. (1966), "Heritability of Intelligence," in *Genetic and Environmental Factors in Human Ability*, p. 201 (J. E. Meade and A. S. Parkes, Eds.). Edinburgh: Oliver and Boyd.
17. Jacob, F. and Monod, J. (1961), "Genetic Regulatory Mechanisms in the Synthesis of Proteins," *J. Molec. Biol.*, **3**, 318–356.
18. Lyon, M. F. (1961), "Gene Action in the X-chromosome of the Mouse (Mus Musculus L.)," *Nature*, **190**, 372–373.
19. McKusick, V. A. (1966), *Heritable Disorders of Connective Tissue*, p. 17. St. Louis: The C.V. Mosby Co.
20. McKusick, V. A. (1966), *Heritable Disorders of Connective Tissue*, Chap. 9. St. Louis: The C. V. Mosby Co..
21. Medical Research Council (1960), *The Hazards to Man of Nuclear and Other Radiations*. H.M.S.O.
22. Meselson, M. and Stahl, F. W. (1958), "The Replication of DNA in Escherichia Coli," *Proc. nat. Acad. Sci.* (*Wash.*), **44**, 671–682.
23. Nirenberg, M. W. (1963), "The Genetic Code," *Sci. Amer.*, **208**, 80–94.
24. Roberts, J. A. F. (1955), *Genetics and the Epidemiology of Chronic Diseases*, p. 77 (J. V. Neel, M. W. Shaw and W. J. Schull, Eds.). Public Health Service Publications, No. 1163, Washington, D.C.
25. Sanger, R. and Race, R. R. (1970), *Modern Trends in Human Genetics* (A. E. H. Emery, Ed.). London: Butterworths.
26. Shields, J. (1962), *Monozygotic Twins, Brought Up Apart and Brought Up Together*. London: Oxford University Press.
27. Sjogren, T. and Larsson, T. (1957), "Oligophrenia in Combination with Congenital Ichthyosis and Spastic Disorders. A Clinical and Genetic Study," *Acta Psychiat. Neurol. Scand.*, **32** (Suppl. 113).
28. Watson, J. D. and Crick, F. H. C. (1953), "The Structure of DNA," *Cold Spr. Harb. Symp. quant. Biol.*, **18**, 123–131.

2. CHROMOSOMES IN DEVELOPMENT

R. HARRIS

CONGENITAL MALFORMATIONS

In medically advanced countries there has been a dramatic fall in infant and childhood mortality during the last century. For example, in Britain between 1841 to 1900 about 150 infants per thousand live births died in the first year of life, while the comparable figure for 1968 was 18 per thousand. This 8-fold improvement is largely attributable to the control of epidemic disease by the provision of proper sanitation and water supply, by improved nutrition and more recently by the introduction of effective chemotherapy and antibiotics. As a direct consequence of this change in infant and child mortality, abnormalities of prenatal development and congenital malformations are now among the most important causes of postnatal mortality. Some also argue that increasing environmental pollution associated with industrialization may have led to an absolute increase in congenital malformations attributable to teratogens.

AETIOLOGY AND FREQUENCY OF CONGENITAL DEFECTS

The true frequency of birth defects is unknown and estimates vary widely according to the population sampled. For example, hospital returns usually include greater frequencies of birth defects when compared with vital statistics collected outside hospital. Defects, including serious ones, are not always apparent at birth and become evident only during the first year or so of life. It is also extremely difficult to define precisely what is meant by a congenital malformation since some observers include only major malformations whilst others include any macroscopic maldevelopment present at birth. In spite of these difficulties, there is general agreement that 1 per cent to 3 per cent of live-born infants have significant birth defects requiring medical attention.

Birth defects have many causes, although in at least half the aetiology is obscure and the interaction of several genes and environmental factors are postulated. In about one-tenth, exposure to viral or other known teratogens is recorded during gestation and in perhaps one-fifth the family history and the clinical manifestations of the malformation make it clear that Mendelian dominant or recessive inheritance is involved. Among new-born children with malformations approximately 1 in 10 (approximately 0·3 per cent of all new-born) has recognizable chromosomal anomalies. However, 0·5 per cent to 2 per cent of *all* newborn infants investigated in various surveys have recognizable chromosomal anomalies and it is re-emphasized that the frequencies obtained depend upon the methods used for sampling and the criteria of clinical and chromosomal "normality."

CHROMOSOME SYNDROMES IN THE NEW-BORN

Down's Syndrome (Mongolism—47 G21+)

About 1 infant in 700 has Down's syndrome (Fig. 1) and will be mentally and physically retarded. These children are

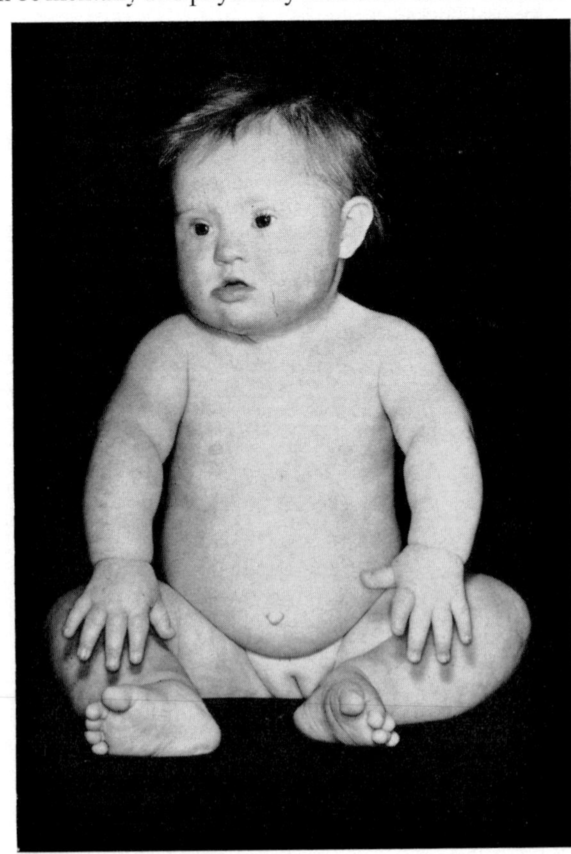

FIG. 1. Infant with Down's syndrome (mongolism).

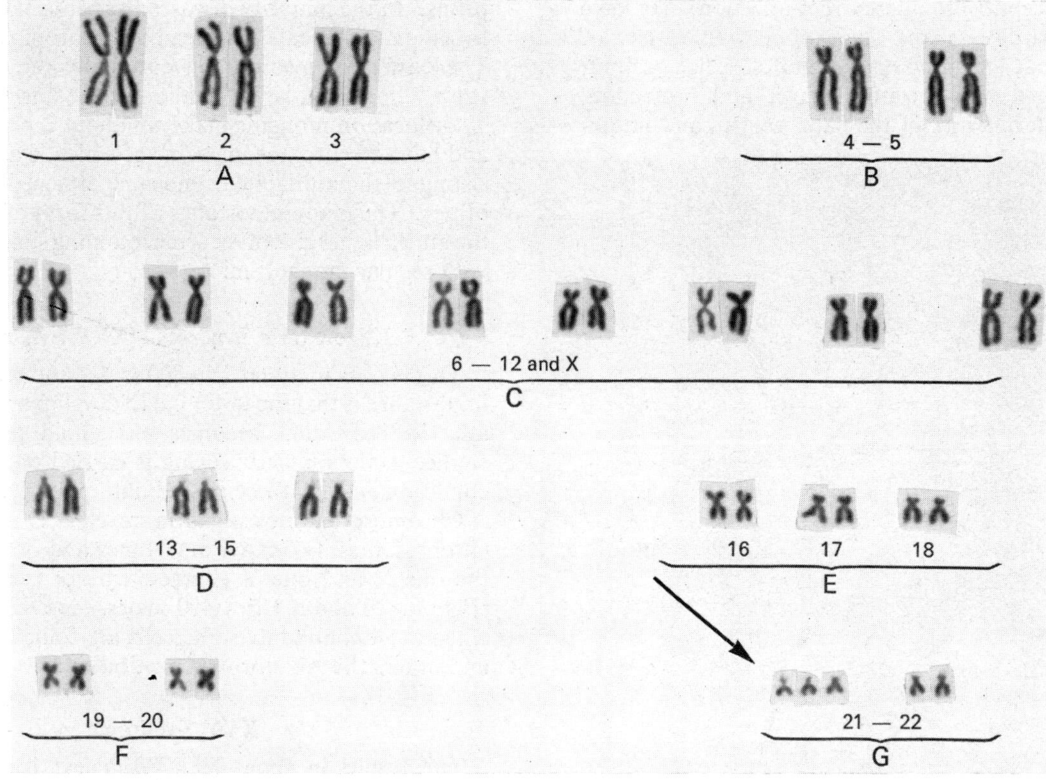

FIG. 2. Karyotype of child with "regular mongolism" (47G21+) showing the extra small acrocentric chromosome—conventionally known as number 21. The identification of individual chromosomes by Giemsa and fluorescent banding has confirmed that the arrangement of chromosomes in karyotypes is to some extent arbitrary.

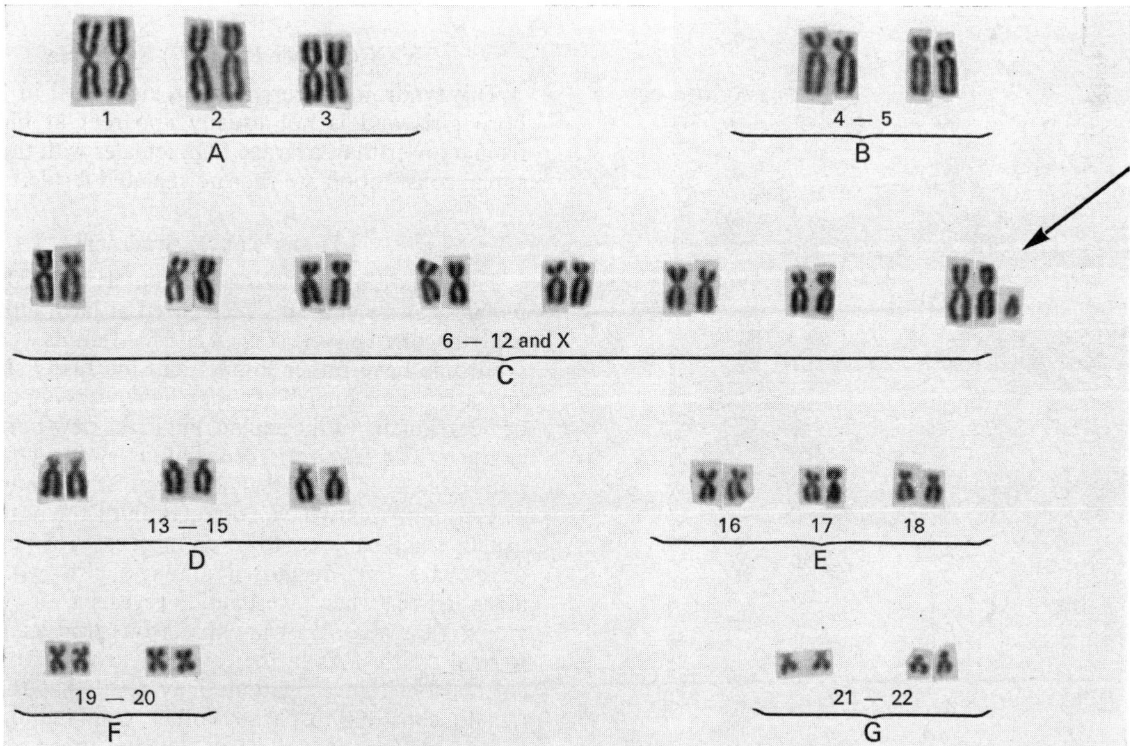

FIG. 3. Karyotype of individual with Klinefelter's syndrome (47 XXY) showing extra sex chromosome.

abnormally susceptible to intercurrent infection, may have congenital heart-disease and some of a wide variety of "minor" stigmata including epicanthic folds, flat occiput, small low-bridged nose, relatively large and protruding tongue and abnormalities of the palm creases and finger-prints. In the majority of cases (97 per cent) chromosomal investigation reveals 47 instead of 46 chromosomes (Fig. 2). The extra chromosome, conventionally known as chromosome number 21, is the smallest of the normal human set. Translocation mongols make up about 3 per cent of cases and have 46 chromosomes one of which is abnormal, consisting of the mongol chromosome attached to one of the others. The main importance of this form of mongolism is the much higher risk of recurrence among siblings compared with regular mongolism.

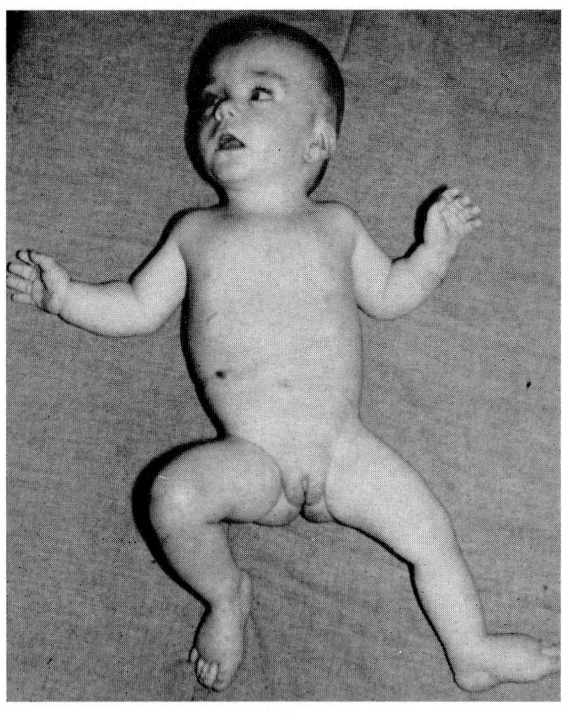

(a)

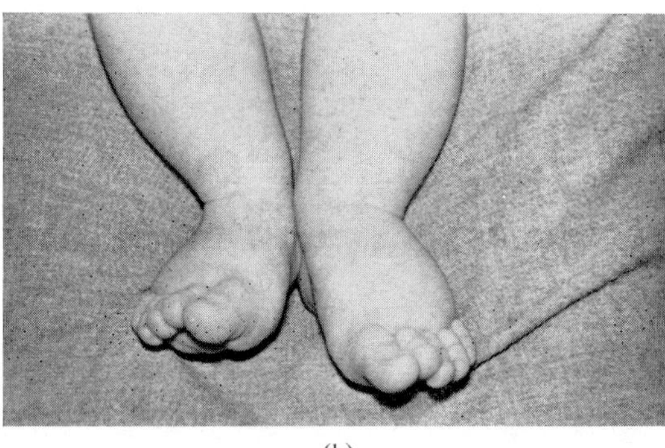

(b)

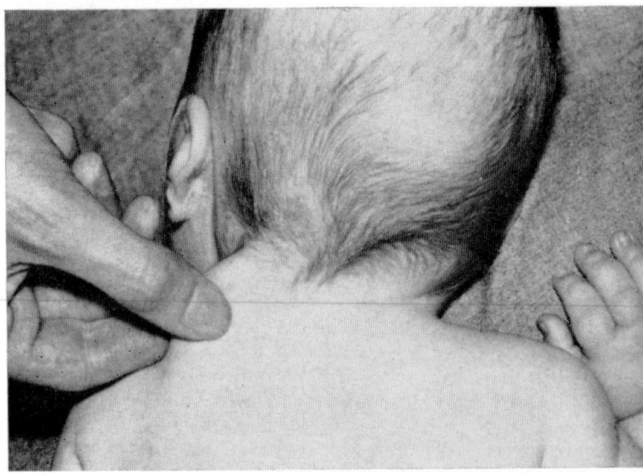

(c)

Fig. 4. Infant with Turner's syndrome (a) showing oedema of the feet (b) and loose skin of the neck (c).

Klinefelter's Syndrome (XXY Syndrome)

This occurs in about 1 in 800 males and its chief clinical importance is that the testes fail to develop properly and the affected individual becomes eunuchoid and is usually sterile. Unless nuclear sexing is carried out at birth, this condition is likely to be missed until puberty.

Chromosomal investigation reveals 47 instead of 46 chromosomes, two X-chromosomes and one Y instead of the one X and one Y characteristic of the normal male (Fig. 3). In about 1 in 1,400 males, mosaicism is detected when most commonly some cells are found to have XXY and others the XY normal constitution.

XYY Syndrome

This occurs in about 1 in 700 males; but so far as we know, produces no abnormality in the new-born and is therefore unlikely to be detected unless chromosome studies are carried out fortuitously. The full significance of this syndrome is not yet clear, and although some males with this constitution become unusually tall the evidence is unconvincing that they usually become criminals.

XXX ("Super Female") Syndrome

This syndrome occurs in approximately 1 in 1,000 new-born girls and is not usually apparent at birth. Apart from a lower-than-average I.Q., females with this chromosomal constitution are near normal and fertile.

Turner's (XO) Syndrome

This condition occurring in about 1 in 2,500 new-born females can be clinically recognized at birth although it is probably often missed (Figs. 4 and 5). Infants with Turner's syndrome have rather low-set and unusually shaped ears and a low hair line. They may have webbing of the neck or occasionally of the axillae, but in the new-born the most characteristic feature is oedematous swelling particularly noticeable over the dorsal surfaces of the hands and feet. These infants may have co-arctation of the aorta and are usually small babies. However, most cases of Turner's syndrome are first diagnosed amongst girls with primary amenorrhoea when investigation reveals a very short individual (less than 5 ft.) with fibrous streaks instead of normal ovaries. As in the case of Klinefelter's syndrome, chromosomal investigations may reval that the girl is a female constitution. Many other combinations of cell types have been described in this and other sex-chromosome mosaics.

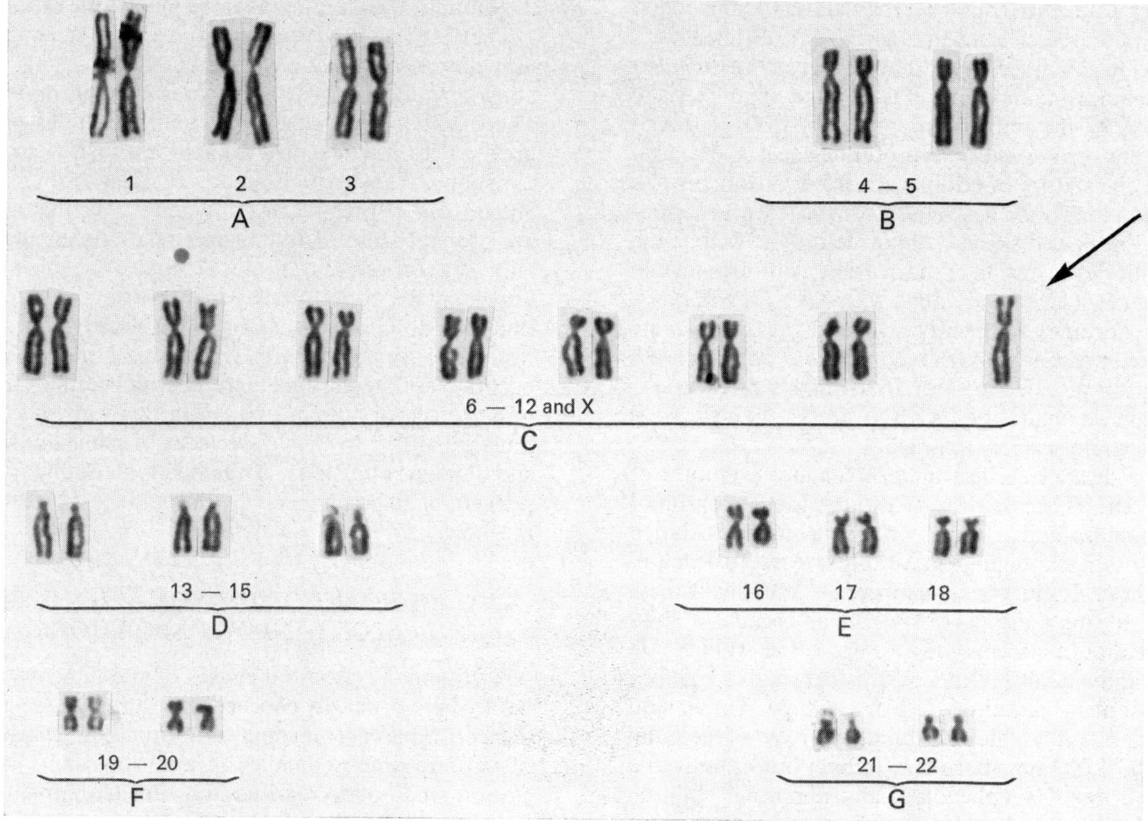

Fig. 5. Karyotype of child with Turner's syndrome (45 XO).

Trisomy 18 (Edwards' Syndrome)

This occurs in about 1 in 3,000 or 4,000 new-born infants. Affected children are severely retarded and usually have a clenched hand with overlapping of the fingers. The feet may have the characteristic rocker-bottom shape. Rather more girls than boys appear to be affected. The majority have an extra chromosome, number 18.

Trisomy 13+ (Patau's Syndrome)

This condition is relatively rare, occurring in less than 1 in 7,000 infants. Severe defects of mid-face, eye and forebrain may be the consequence of a single defect of the precordal mesoderm at about 3 weeks gestation. Infants with Patau's syndrome usually have microcephaly, cleft lip with or without cleft palate, congenital heart lesions and many other defects. Although not all infants with these clinical manifestations have demonstrable chromosomal abnormalities, characteristically an extra chromosome, number 13, is found.

Miscellaneous Conditions

A wide variety of other chromosomal abnormalities have been described in congenitally abnormal infants. For example, the loss ("partial deletion") of the short arm of chromosome number 5 is associated with the "Cri-du-chat" syndrome. In addition to a cat-like mewing cry, these infants have mental deficiency, microcephaly and a variety of other congenital abnormalities. Children with other "syndromes" have on some occasions, but not others, been found to have chromosomal anomalies. New developments, allowing the recognition of individual chromosomes and of structural rearrangements by fluorescence and Giesma banding will probably allow the identification of many new chromosomal syndromes.

For fuller descriptions of human malformation syndromes (whether chromosomal in origin or not) *see* Smith (1970) and Valentine (1969).

POSTNATAL DEVELOPMENT OF CHILDREN WITH CHROMOSOMAL ANOMALIES

The majority of chromosomal anomalies lead to serious defects of development and this is especially true of those involving autosomal chromosomes. Thus, most infants with Trisomy 13 or Trisomy 18 die in the first year of life and the survivors have major physical and mental handicaps. The average life-expectancy for children with mongolism is greatly reduced although the introduction of antibiotics has allowed many more mongols to survive into adolescence or adult life. The combination of mental retardation and multiple physical defects indicates the profound and generalized nature of the abnormalities of development in children with autosomal anomalies.

In contrast sex chromosome anomalies have relatively little effect on development during infancy. The XXX syndrome is associated with a virtually normal phenotype and the XYY syndrome is not thought to be associated with obvious developmental anomalies although some of these children may be eunuchoid or may develop anti-social tendencies and excessive height. The XXY (Klinefelter's syndrome), on the other hand, is almost always associated with eunuchoidism and infertility with a characteristic degeneration of the seminiferous tubules. XO (Turner's syndrome) has perhaps the most profound effect on development since the stature of adults with this syndrome is less than 5 ft. and they often have characteristic features including webbed neck and skeletal abnormalities as well as the characteristic degeneration of the ovaries. Although formal I.Q. testing of children and adults with XXY, XYY, XXX and XO syndromes frequently shows slight-to-moderate reduction compared with the population norm, severe retardation is unusual. However, individuals with rarer sex-chromosome anomalies (48 XXXX, 48 XXXY, etc.) are often much more severely retarded.

As was indicated earlier, there are many examples of congenital defects occurring with a wide variety of chromosomal anomalies and it might be erroneously concluded that chromosomal anomalies inevitably give rise to developmental defects. It must be remembered that many of these chromosomal anomalies were sought for because a child had congenital malformations. Population studies on unselected individuals reveal a surprisingly high frequency of chromosomal "variations." For example, Turner and Wald carried out a "double blind" survey of hospital deliveries of 1,000 new-born live infants in Pennsylvania U.S.A., and found 47 phenotypically abnormal children but only 14 of them had chromosomal anomalies. Nineteen normal-appearing neonates had chromosomal aberrations. As might be expected, babies with clinical abnormalities had defined chromosomal syndromes (mongolism, 18 Trisomy, cri-du-chat syndrome, intersex states including among others Turner's syndrome). In contrast, amongst the normal-appearing children sex-chromosome aberrations predominated (XXX, XXY, XYY and XO/normal mosaics).

Observations on new-born infants therefore indicates that autosomal anomalies are more or less catastrophic, while sex-chromosome anomalies and a variety of morphological "variations" of chromosome structure may have relatively little effect on viability and development if one excludes later reproductive and intellectual impairment. However, the new-born infant has already demonstrated his viability in a very real way, since gestation is a period of ruthless selection when almost half of all conceptions are lost, giving a mortality higher in Britain than at any time until the eighth decade of life.

THE FREQUENCY OF SPONTANEOUS ABORTIONS

In Britain a fetus becomes legally viable after 28 weeks of pregnancy, although premature infants younger than this have survived. In practice 20 to 22 weeks of pregnancy is a better guide to viability and the term abortion, whether spontaneous or induced, should perhaps be restricted to the termination of pregnancy before 20–22 weeks. Incidentally, this is more consistent with the change in attitude of the mother to her baby since once fetal movements are felt by the mother, the child tends to become "one of the family."

The frequency with which abortions occur in hospital data differs from that collected outside hospitals and many abortions occurring at home are probably not recorded. There is, however, general agreement that 15 per cent of pregnancies in women of all ages are lost as spontaneous abortions. This figure is greater in older mothers and over 30 per cent of pregnancies in women over the age of forty are probably lost. These figures relate to the incidence of clinical abortions and, to this estimate, one must add those unrecognized conceptions which are so grossly abnormal that they do not implant or are lost shortly after implantation. The frequency with which this unrecognizable loss occurs is unknown, but there is evidence that 30 per cent of all fertilized human ova fail in this way and this figure must be added to the 15 per cent of clinically recognized spontaneous abortions. Thus, the remarkable figure of 45 per cent of all pregnancies are probably lost before the fetus is viable.

CHROMOSOME ANOMALIES AND SPONTANEOUS ABORTIONS

Of the many potential causes of spontaneous abortions we are here primarily concerned with those associated with demonstrable chromosomal abnormalities. Our knowledge of chromosome anomalies in abortions must be derived from a study of recognized abortions comprising at most only one-third of the total loss. Unfortunately, observations made in this way, are open to considerable bias for the following reasons: The material is obtained in hospitals and contains a deficiency of early conceptuses. It is known that the earlier a conception is lost the more likely it is to be chromosomally abnormal (*see below*). There is also a natural tendency for fetuses with visible malformations to be referred for chromosomal investigation. Thus, the frequency and type of chromosomal abnormalities found in pre-viable conceptions must be interpreted with great caution and must be related to data collected from "random" abortions carried out for "social" reasons.

It is hardly surprising that rather different results have been obtained in various studies. Based on his own observations in Canada and on a survey of the literature, Carr has calculated that 36 per cent of spontaneous abortions are chromosomally abnormal, although the earlier an abortion occurs the more likely it is to be chromosomally abnormal. Carr found the following frequencies of chromosomally abnormal abortions: 40 per cent up to 13 weeks, 25 per cent between 13 and 17 weeks, 3·5 per cent after 17 weeks, and 3·2 per cent in abortions induced therapeutically. It must be emphasized, however, that the figure for therapeutic abortions may not be properly corrected for gestational age.

TYPES OF CHROMOSOMAL ABNORMALITIES FOUND IN ABORTIONS

Of all chromosomal abnormalities associated with spontaneous abortion, 45 per cent involve one extra chromosome (trisomy). In 25 per cent, polyploidy occurs, in four out of five cases of polyploidy triploidy occurs (69 chromosomes per cell) and in one-fifth of cases tetraploidy (92 chromosomes per cell). In 20 per cent of spontaneous abortions with chromosomal abnormalities, there is a missing sex chromosome (45, XO). The remaining 10 per cent are made up of monosomies (45 chromosomes) involving autosomal chromosomes and situations where although 46 chromosomes are present visible structural abnormalities can be detected. Table 1 compares the frequency of the different

TABLE 1

INCIDENCE AND LETHALITY OF CHROMOSOMAL ABERRATIONS

A. *Chromosomal Aberrations in Spontaneous Abortions*		
Autosomal trisomies	45%	36% of all spontaneous abortions
Polyploidy	25%	
Turner's syndrome	20%	
XXY, XYY, XXX	Nil	
Others, including autosomal monosomies	10%	
B. *Chromosomal Aberrations in the Newborn*		
Autosomal trisomies		
Mongolism	0·14%	(1/700)
Edwards' syndrome	0·028%	(1/3,500)
Patau's syndrome	0.014%	(1/7,000)
Polyploidy	Virtually nil	
Turner's syndrome	0·04%	(1/2,500 females)
Klinfelter's syndrome	0·125%	(1/800 males)
XYY	0·14%	(1/700 males)
XXX	0·1%	(1/1,000 females)
C. *Prenatal lethality of Chromosomal Aberrations*		
Sex chromosomes		
XO	97%	
Others	Very low	
Autosomal trisomies	85%	
Polyploidy	100%	
Autosomal monosomies	100%	
Overall	90%	

types of chromosomal aberrations which are found in spontaneous abortions and in the new-born.

EFFECTS OF CHROMOSOMAL ABNORMALITIES IN PRENATAL DEVELOPMENT

The following general conclusions may be made about the effects on prenatal development of the various chromosomal anomalies. Firstly, the commonest abnormalities seen in the new-born (mongolism XXY, XYY and XXX) are either rare or do not occur at all in the series of spontaneous abortions that have been studied. In contrast the chromosomal constitution 45 XO found in 20 per cent of spontaneous abortions is found in only 1 in 2,500 new-born females and it has been calculated that 90 per cent of conceptions with this constitution are lost before birth. Similarly, virtually 100 per cent of polyploids and 85 per cent of autosomal trisomies (with the exception of mongolism) die before birth. Trisomy 13 (Edwards' syndrome) and Trisomy 18 (Patau's syndrome) are particularly interesting since, together with mongolism, they represent the only autosomal trisomies which may permit survival to term. In contrast, autosomal trisomies involving chromosomes of groups A, B, C and F and chromosomes 14 and 15 of the D group and 16 and 17 of the E group occur less frequently in spontaneous abortions than they would by chance and are not found at all in the new-born. This suggests that these trisomies are lethal in the pre- and immediately post-implantation period. This is also probably true of all monosomies (45 chromosomes) with the exception of the XO constitution.

In summary, some chromosomal aberrations involving extra chromosomes, especially when the extra chromosome is a sex chromosome, are compatible with survival to term although in the case of the autosomal trisomies there is a heavy prenatal mortality and reduced postnatal viability. Other trisomies, monosomies, with the exception of XO and polyploidy are almost invariably lethal prenatally.

THE MECHANISM OF CHROMOSOME ANOMALIES

Most chromosomal syndromes detectable at birth are associated with aneuploidy where the modal number of chromosomes is reduced to 45 (monosomy) or increased to 47 (trisomy). Turner's syndrome is the only example of monosomy in the live-born, while mongolism and the sex-chromosome anomalies XXY, XYY and XXX are examples of trisomies. Most cases of aneuploidy affecting all cell lines probably arise during meiotic division when the chromosomes of a homologous pair fail to separate and consequently move into the same gamete. Such non-disjunction results in daughter cells one of which has only 22 chromosomes whereas the other daughter-cell has 24. Fertilization of these daughter cells by a gamete bearing the normal haploid set of 23 chromosomes will result in zygotes with monosomy (45 chromosomes) or trisomy (47 chromosomes). "Anaphase lag" describes the accident by which a chromosome is lost, failing to enter either of the daughter cells. Fertilization of such a gamete will always lead to monosomy. Very little is known about the derangements of cell division which lead to non-disjunction although the increased frequency with which mongol children are born to older women results from a greater likelihood of non-disjunction with increasing maternal age.

Triploidy can arise by a failure of the second polar body to separate resulting in an ovum with 46 chromosomes followed by fertilization by a normal sperm carrying 23 chromosomes resulting in a zygote with 69 chromosomes. Alternatively, a normal ovum may be fertilized by two sperms or by an abnormal sperm with a double set of chromosomes. Tetraploidy, which is rarer, probably results from a failure of the cytoplasm of the zygote to divide following normal nuclear division. Why polyploidy should occur is unknown.

WHY ARE CHROMOSOMAL ANOMALIES USUALLY SO DISASTROUS IN DEVELOPMENT?

Some chromosome anomalies are not disastrous in development and those involving the sex chromosomes are good examples. Since normal males always have a single X-chromosome and normal females always lack a Y-chromosome, the human organism must have some resiliance to variation in sex chromosome numbers. This may be because human sex chromosomes carry relatively few genes apart from those concerned with sexual development. However, this cannot be the only reason because many genetic loci, unconnected with sex, are known to occur on the X-chromosome (for example, some of those concerned with normal muscle function and normal blood-clotting revealed by the pathological states of X-linked muscular dystrophy and haemophilia). Turner's syndrome (XO) is unusual amongst sex-chromosome anomalies since the prenatal mortality associated with this anomaly is high (97 per cent), and it is suspected that most of the survivors are mosaics with sufficient cells of the XX constitution to permit normal development.

In contrast, chromosome anomalies involving autosomes are much more catastrophic and it is not immediately obvious why *extra* chromosomal material such as occurs in the trisomies and in polyploidy, should interfere with development to such a profound extent. However, loss of chromosomal material, such as is seen in monosomies, might well be expected to be more serious since many deleterious recessive genes may be thereby revealed.

Although there are considerable difficulties in distinguishing, in material from abortuses, the individual members of the D, E and G groups of chromosomes, chromosomes 13, 18 and 21 can be identified by autoradiography because in contrast to the other members of their groups their DNA replicates relatively late in mitosis. In addition, all three chromosomes stain more heavily in the Giemsa banding technique than the other members of their groups suggesting that these chromosomes contain a great deal of repetitive DNA. These observations are thought by some cytogeneticists to be consistent with a relatively unimportant role for chromosomes 13, 18 and 21 in the early stages of development perhaps because they mainly carry genes which are important in later development and postnatal life.

It is known that the normal process of cell division may be disturbed by chromosomal abnormalities, especially in meiosis where chromosomes must pair exactly with their homologues. Structural rearrangements, translocations, deletions, etc., interfere with this exact pairing process. Recent work with mammalian cells in tissue culture suggests that chromosomal damage induced by radiation or chemicals, results in grossly inefficient cell division and failure of damaged cells to establish colonies. However, chromosomal changes seen in established cultures of malignant cells are apparently associated with escape from growth control showing that some anomalies may be actually advantageous at least in the abnormal conditions of tissue culture. Evidence is accumulating that the arrangement of genetic loci along the length of the chromosome and the spatial relationship of different chromosomes to each other is of paramount importance in the normal processes of cell division and differentiation. Perhaps the majority of incidents leading to abnormalities of chromosomal number or structure disrupt the essential intra- and inter-chromosomal organization and lead to abortion of fetal development.

CONCLUSIONS

It is likely that nearly one-half of all pre-viable conceptions are lost although only about 15 per cent of pregnancies terminate in clinically recognized spontaneous abortions. Possibly 36 per cent of all spontaneous abortions are chromosomally abnormal and the earlier abortion occurs the more likely is this to be the case. Some chromosome abnormalities lead inevitably to prenatal death but others may permit survival to term and beyond. At present, about 10 per cent of new-born infants with malformations have recognizable chromosomal abnormalities but new chromosomal banding techniques will probably lead to the identification of many new "chromosome syndromes."

FURTHER READING

Carr, D. H. (1971), "Chromosomes and Abortion", in *Advances in Human Genetics*, pp. 201–257 (H. Harris and K. Hirschhorn, Eds.). New York, London: Plenum Press.

Editorial (1971), "Revolutionary Cytogenetics", *New Engl. J. Med.*, **285,** 1,482.

Ferguson-Smith, M. E., Ferguson-Smith, M. A., Nevin, N. C. and Stone, M. (1971), "Chromosome Analysis before Birth and its Value in Genetic Counselling", *Brit. med. J.*, **4,** 69–74.

Polani, P. E. (1970), "The Incidence of Chromosomal Malformations", *Proc. roy. Soc. Med.*, **63,** 50–52.

Saxén, L. and Rapola, J. (1969) "Congenital Defects", in *Developmental Biology Series* (J. D. Ebert, Ed.). New York: Holt, Rinehart and Winston, Inc.

Smith, D. W. (1970), *Recognizable Patterns of Human Malformation, Genetic, Embryologic and Clinical Aspects.* Volume VII in the series "Major Problems in Clinical Pediatrics" (A. J. Schaffer, Ed.). Philadelphia: W. B. Saunders Co.

Turner, J. H. and Wald, N. (1970), "Chromosome Patterns in a General Neonatal Population", in *Human Population Cytogenetics*, pp. 154–158 (P. A. Jacobs, W. H. Price and P. Law, Eds.). University of Edinburgh Pfizer Medical Monographs 5. Edinburgh: University Press.

Valentine, G. H. (1969), *The Chromosome Disorders. An Introduction for Clinicians*, 2nd edition. London: William Heinemann Medical Books Ltd.

Infants at Risk: An Historical and International Comparison, Office of Health Economics. London (1964).

3. THE INFLUENCE OF SEXUAL DIFFERENTIATION ON GROWTH DEVELOPMENT AND DISEASE

DAVID C. TAYLOR

"Can two walk together except they be agreed?"
"Will a lion roar in the forest when he hath no prey?" (*Amos, Chapter 3: 3 and 4*)

INTRODUCTION

Progress in understanding the mechanisms of sexual differentiation in man has been rapid in the last decade. In the light of new knowledge it seems that these mechanisms, and those by which sexual dimorphism is achieved and maintained, exert a widespread influence on the biology of the two sexes. The profound inequality of the sexes as reflected in the representation of disease has been known for a long time. But as so often happens, when a biological explanation for these differences is not immediately apparent, they have been attributed to a variety of factors, most frequently to social factors. There is, in current popular comment, a confusion between social equality, in the sense of justice, and biological sameness.* Rarely, even in informed writing, are the sex differences not immediately related to the process of sexual reproduction, regarded as being necessary consequences and fundamental aspects of sex-differentiating mechanisms. But there is evidence to support this and even to suggest that these biological inequalities might be part of the mechanism which regulates sexual reproduction and sexual selection. Some of the issues will become clearer if we also consider why sex exists at all.

FITNESS AND MECHANISMS OF REPRODUCTION

Fitness

Before discussing the issues of sexual reproduction, it is necessary to comment on a concept which underlies so much biological thinking about reproduction and selection: that is fitness. Fitness, in the biological sense, means the likelihood of surviving in future generations. Degrees of fitness, imply the extent to which a gene, or group of genes, or trait, or ethnic group, or species will increase in frequency in future generations as compared with other genes, traits, or groups. Fitness can therefore only be ascribed from observation. It is not a measurable characteristic of an individual organism. It cannot be predicted in an absolute sense, though it is possible to state that certain circumstances are likely to preclude or limit fitness. Thus it can be argued that mechanisms which are widely represented are "better than" or "advantageous over," those which are extinct or which exist only in more primitive forms, or which persist in forms that are not very numerous. Consider an analogy from modern technology; the motor-car "evolves" under similar pressures. At the moment, it might be considered "fit." Certain forms of motor-car are, however, already extinct, others are becoming rare, and we must define these forms as unfit.*

Asexual Reproduction

Asexual reproduction is unsatisfactory for a variety of reasons which were explained by Fisher (*see* Cavalli-Sforza and Bodmer, 1971). The spread of advantageous mutations would be extremely slow, and the individual in which an advantageous change took place might leave no progeny. Asexual reproduction favours genetic stability.

* Perhaps in a male-dominated society there are few, who are in a position to do so, who would care to contrast the biological inferiority of men with their tradition of maintaining dominance. Indeed, it has been suggested that unconscious recognition of this inferiority is the source of man's wish to dominate woman.

Evolution implies instability, variability, and the maximization of the number of viable changes available for selection. We can expect therefore by definition, that more evolved forms will reflect these characteristics.

Sexual Reproduction

The essence of sexual reproduction is the pooling and sharing of genetic information. There is really no need for a system more complex than one giving a chance for random recombination of gametes in a suitable environment. There is in nature an abundance of methods whereby sexual reproduction is achieved. Yet bisexuality seems to be preferred

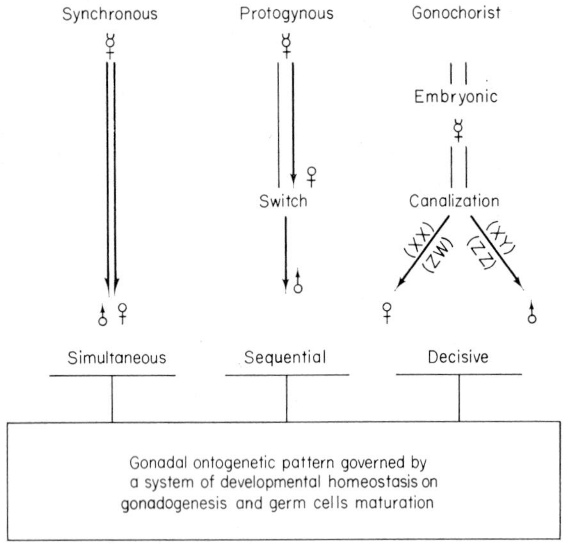

FIG. 1. Patterns of sexuality in relation with ontogeny of the gonad. (From Chan, S.T.H. (1970) *Phil, Trans. Roy. Soc. Lond.* B. **259**, 59–71)

over polysexuality, and in mammals, with few exceptions, there is a single type of sexual differentiation, mating, and recombination. It is worth considering some of the alternative methods of sexual reproduction which exist, even in vertebrates, before concentrating more fully on that of man. This should emphasize that the form of reproduction we take for granted as obvious and stable is not the only mechanism available. It will, then, be worth considering why it should be that the sexual differentiating and sexual reproductive system of man has been "successful."

The figure (Fig. 1) is taken from Chan (1970). He portrays firstly synchronous hermaphroditism, in which both gametes develop and mature in parallel in one organism. In this case self-fertilization remains possible and may be one reason for this mechanism being regarded as the most primitive. In the hypothetical case, there is no reason for separation of sex chromosomes from autosomes in this type of organism. Secondly, there are hermaphrodites which reverse their sex in the course of their development. There are only two alternatives in bisexuals. Some are "female" first and then become "male" (protogynous), others are "male" first (protandrous). The importance of this knowledge is that it is difficult to define such a creature (Monopterus, for example) as "really male," or "really female," except in a functional sense and then only at a particular point in its development. As we shall see, the developmental point of view, which it is necessary to adopt in this case, could prove helpful in understanding the dilemmas of definition in the sex differentiation of man. Further, whilst some genetic mechanism must be postulated for determining sex and possibly (but not necessarily) regulating the sex change, it would be unwise to ascribe too concrete a relationship between a given genetic make-up and sex since this either has changed or will change during development.

In gonochorists (like man) the pattern of gonadal development and differentiation is "decisive," by definition. This suggests, and is intended to suggest, that *either* development is totally female *or* totally male, rather than that an emphasis is placed in one or other direction. At this point in evolution a genetic or chromosomal system, which is separate from the autosomes and which exerts this emphasis or bias, has to be introduced.

* Hitherto, most of the evolutionary concepts derived from thinking upon Darwinian lines have been anthropocentric, in essence asking the question—"How did we get to be so clever?" and have depended upon the concept of fitness outlined above. They are no longer entirely satisfactory today except in so far as maintaining fitness might require the ingenuity to limit the total size of the human population of the world.

SEX DIFFERENTIATION

It was thought at one time that the genetics of sex differentiation in man was managed by a balance of factors which were tipped in one or other direction. The X chromosome was regarded as necessary to female differentiation but the Y chromosome was responsible only for activating the maturation of sperm. It is now known that as a general rule one sex is homogametic, having two identical sex chromosomes, and the other is heterogametic having unlike sex chromosomes. In the absence of the "odd" chromosome, differentiation proceeds in the direction of the morphology of the sex with like chromosomes. In man, the female is homogametic (XX) and the presence of the Y chromosome is necessary, and prepotent, in determining the male development. In birds and certain other species the female is heterogametic (ZW) and individuals lacking W are males. Perhaps these two systems reflect the two available evolutions of protogynous and protandrous hermaphroditism respectively.

The course of sexual differentiation will thus begin to be determined by the sex chromosomal make-up of the zygote. This in turn would have been decided by the gametes which fused. The sperm may contain either an X or a Y chromosome. Either should be equally likely. The zygote should be equally likely to be male or female and the primary sex ratio (the sex ratio of zygotes) should be 100:100.

SEXUAL DIMORPHISM

Sexual reproduction means genetic diversity and individual uniqueness. Sexual reproduction does not necessarily demand that the sexes be recognizably different in phenotype. The process of sexual differentiation brings these changes about. The extent, and precise nature, of the differences between the sexes will have been subject to evolutionary selection. It is a feature of increasingly evolved forms that selection or choice is increasingly exercised in the manner of these genetic recombinations. Against a general background of features which make individuals look either "male" or "female," so as to be available for selection for mating, are a number of checks against random mating. The human is able to exercise very precise choices about who will share the progeny. Selection is possible for physical features, behaviour, attitudes, kindred, social background, and the likely stability of the relationship with the mating partner. Today it is possible to decide separately about mating partner(s) and sexual partner(s). However, man shares with the Gibbons the unusual good fortune of a female partner who is usually sexually receptive (instead of being available only at oestrus) and who is probably a permanent partner. It seems likely that mutually satisfying behaviours, including sexual behaviours, tend to maintain the partnership during the prolonged period of helplessness of the offspring, which characterizes man. The relationship thus developed may survive the needs of the children and persist in mutual interdependence.

The importance of sexual behaviour in man and the significance of his reproductive cycle were the themes of the psychoanalytic movement. Freud believed that the final proof of his premises would come from biology rather than from clinical psychiatry. As the mechanisms underlying man's sexual behaviour are beginning to be unravelled, it seems even more likely that they occupy a central place in his biology. Probably it is "reproduction" rather than sexuality which is the central issue. Man's continuation of his biological self depends uniquely on his ability to reproduce. Many of man's miseries stem from the problems of sustaining the necessaries for his reproduction. Most mystics wisely eschew it.

SEX CHROMOSOMES AND THEIR CONSEQUENCES

Sexual differentiation in man is achieved through the activity of the X- and the Y-chromosomes. The XY make-up of a zygote can be construed as "male" and XX as "female" though, as we shall see, much depends upon the definition of these terms.

Even at this stage of development, the X-chromosome might be regarded as sexually neutral since it is more the presence or absence of the Y-chromosome that will determine whether or not the fetal gonad becomes a testis, which is the next phase in the differentiating mechanism.

But in achieving differentiation in this way, certain differences between the sexes will be introduced other than those directly concerned with sexual reproduction. At the chromosomal level the differences are the existence of more than one X in females and the presence of the Y-chromosome in males. What are the consequences of this?

THE Y-CHROMOSOME AND ITS MESSAGE

If it could be shown that there were important gene loci on the Y-chromosome which were in any way homologous with those on the X-chromosome: or if it could be demonstrated cytogenetically that there was pairing and crossing-over at meiosis, some of the problems of apparent inequality of genetic material might be solved. As it is, there appear to be no gene loci on the Y-chromosome except those related to hairy ears in generation after generation of males in certain Indian and Egyptian families.[15] Any system of crossing-over would have to be incredibly selective, otherwise the purpose of separating-off chromosomes involved in the differentiation of two sexes from the rest of the autosomes would be destroyed. However, without cross-over with the X, genes on the Y-chromosome would be the prerogative of males alone and no female could ever possess the characteristics due to such genes. Moreover, the genotype 45XO is probably the most commonly occurring sex chromosome aneuploidy and the phenotype is sufficiently like that of a normal female for a number to avoid detection clinically until they present with primary amenorrhoea. It is known, however, that the "male" syndrome is available in the "female" genome provided it is elicited by suitable hormonal manipulation, a fact attested to in part by the naturally occurring female pseudophermaphroditism caused by adrenal tumours in genetic females.

In effect except for a later, more specific, role in spermiogenesis, the presence of the Y-chromosome appears only to be necessary (though prepotent) to determining the development of the fetal testis from the indifferent gonad about the 7th week of intrauterine life. Thereafter, male characteristics seem to be determined through the action of hormonal mediators upon a variety of tissues. Mittwoch has shown, from the point of view of a geneticist, that it is not necessary to postulate genes on the Y-chromosome which are male-determining. The mechanism responsible for differentiating the indifferent gonad into a testis prior to its otherwise becoming an ovary might, in her opinion, lie in differential growth rates.[35]

> "Owing to the difference in size between the X- and the Y-chromosome in man, the amount of DNA per cell in females is nearly 2 per cent more than in males (Chicago Conference 1966). If one assumes that the time taken for DNA synthesis is proportional the amount of DNA, DNA synthesis would be a slightly slower process in females and, other things being equal, the rate of cell proliferation would be slower in females than in males. This would be in accordance with the smaller size of women, but it could not account for sex differentiation. For this, a positive role of the Y-chromosome is required. I suggest that at a given stage in the development of the embryo the Y-chromosome may boost the already slightly increased growth rate of male embryos possibly increasing the number of mitoses in the developing gonads. This might cause the gonads to develop into testes which will then produce hormones and these, in turn, will control the subsequent male development in the embryo."

According to her evidence, testes grow faster than ovaries. And in a recent paper[36] she draws the parallel between the cell growth retardation due to slower DNA synthesis in trisomies (such as mongolism) and that due to sex-chromosome dimorphism where there could be a slight increase in the cell growth rate of XY as compared with XX cells.

The growth rate of the male fetus exceeds that of the female, but the process is governed by the rate of deceleration of growth so that this, if achieved first in females, would lead to their being smaller at birth. Ounsted and Ounsted (1970) and Ounsted (1972) have reviewed the subject of Y-chromosome antigenicity in pregnancy and have produced data to support the suggestion that superior male growth is mediated via the Y-chromosome message. Several authors have used the concept of Y-chromosome antigenicity to explain a variety of data, but previously there has been no unifying hypothesis. Kirby *et al.* (1967) and Kirby (1970) suggested that blastocysts genetically dissimilar from the mother were favoured at implantation. This is consistent with certain variations in the sex ratios from theoretical equality which we will consider in detail later. Ounsted (1972) also reviewed other aspects of the antigenetic problem in pregnancy especially that suggesting an association between male births and toxaemia of pregnancy, and that relating the sex of the child to the type of onset of schizophrenia in pregnancy. Turning to growth rate, the Ounsteds predicted that in twin births of known zygocity the order of size of mean birth-weight would be as follows:

1. Boys in dizygous all-male sibships.
2. Boys in mixed sibships
3. Girls in mixed sibships
4. Boys in monozygous sibships
5. Girls in dizygous all-female sibships
6. Girls in monozygous sibships

Using the suggestion of Taylor and Ounsted (1971), they suggested a unifying hypothesis. The presence of the Y-chromosome produces greater antigenic dissimilarity between the mother and fetus. This enhances fetal growth rate, not only of male fetuses but of female co-twins as well, so that girls in mixed sibships will be larger than girls in dizygous all-female sibships. It has been difficult to understand how this "antigenic dissimilarity" is created by a chromosome so devoid of gene loci. However, this particular aspect of the problem was discussed by Ounsted and Taylor (1972) when considering another problem and it deserves a digression here.

While working on certain immunological problems, Eichwald and Silmser (1955) inbred mice to a point where genetic differences between members of a strain were negligible. Skin could then be grafted without rejection between these animals. But although grafts took readily from male to male, and from female to female, and from female to male, grafts from male to female were rejected. From later more complex experiments by other authors it was concluded that "antigenic Y substance" could contaminate the progeny whose parents had been grafted. It was proposed that "Histoincompatability" genes exist on the Y-chromosome. Ounsted and Taylor (1972) thought that incompatability might arise because the Y-chromosome of the male donor evoked information from autosomes which was not manifest in the female recipient although she carried their potential.

Thus antigenicity effects in pregnancy due to male conceptus can be similarly regarded. In the process of eliciting the male syndrome from the autosomes of the developing fetus more information of a potentially antigenic nature is elicited. Though this may be advantageous in terms of the sex ratio and growth rates, it might be disadvantageous in respect of the effects of maternal toxaemia and other problems due to the larger size of the male fetus.

The activity of the Y-chromosome in evoking, regulating, and maintaining maleness was considered in detail by Ounsted and Taylor (1972). The full consequences of maleness are rather alarming and deserving of study. Childs (1965) suggested a mortality difference during the life span from 15 to 35 per cent of females. "Such a figure is surprising, even alarming and urges study partly in the interests of otherwise doomed males but also for the insight into mechanisms of disease. . . ." Consider the evidence accumulated by The National Child Development Study,[13] at almost every stage the males are disadvantaged as compared with females. This was evident in our own area of special interest, epileptology. It seemed that the attack rate was different between the sexes and that this difference had consequential effects upon outcome. The peak attack rate in females came before (chronologically younger) that in males. Reviewing evidence drawn from a wide variety of disorders, this difference seemed practically universal and seems to suggest that the sexes developed at different rates.[53] This is confirmed by a variety of psychological evidence.[23] The differences in pace of development lead to secondary differentiation as a result of pace. Consider the analogy of two identical motor-cars proceeding up the same highway. The speed of the two cars is such that one exceeds the other marginally. Distance will appear between the cars and will gradually increase so that the experiences enjoyed on the journey will begin to be different. Thus, Ounsted and Taylor proposed:

1. That the differential ontogenesis of the two sexes depends wholly on the Y-chromosome.
2. The Y-chromosome transmits no significant information specific to itself.
3. Transcription of expressed genomic information in males occurs at a slower ontogenetic pace.
4. The operation of the Y-chromosome is to allow more genomic information to be transcribed.

If the mechanism of the Y-chromosome is to regulate the *pace* of development, as might an anticatalyst, in order to achieve sexual differentiation, then there will be repercussions from this apparent throughout development and revealed in many systems. They will all be of medical significance.

X-CHROMOSOMES AND THEIR ROLE

The X-chromosome is unlike the Y in its morphology and also in respect of the amount of gene loci known to exist upon it. Indeed, it is one chromosome in which the gene loci are likely to be mapped and about 7 of its 70 known gene loci have been placed in relation to each other.[3,46] Although the XX constitution signifies the genetic female, none of the genes so far determined relate to failures of development of particular facets of female morphology. But it seems likely that a double dose of a gene located on the short arm of the X-chromosome is necessary to support functional ovaries. Castrated male and ovariectomized rats develop adequate female morphology as do humans of XO constitution. They fail to develop secondary sexual characteristics which are dependent upon the activity of functional ovaries. An interesting point of view about the role of genes in female differentiation was expressed by Beatty (1970).

> '. . . just as mankind is human because of the total gene complex and we do not go looking for specific genes causing humanness, it might also be that a woman is female because of her total gene complex and not because of a few specific genes causing femaleness."

Thus, at present it seems that although sex determination is ascribed to the activity of sex chromosomes, there is a variety of evidence to suggest that neither male nor female differentiation is mediated through specific genes placed upon these chromosomes. Rather, the process of differentiation may be entirely set in train by different growth rates, though a mechanism to support the gonad to allow reproduction seems necessary.

The presence of an additional X in females would lead to gene imbalance. A variety of mechanisms have been proposed by which the effective dose of X-chromosome could be reduced in females to equal that of males. The most likely story seems to be that of Lyon (1961, 1970), who proposed that all except one X-chromosome in each cell are rendered inactive. The inactivation takes place early in embryonic development, affects either the maternal or paternal X-chromosome (or the extra X-chromosome) in each cell and all further X-chromosomes derived from the cell stem from the same line. Females therefore are a mosaic compound of cells derived from randomly "Lyonized" X-chromosomes.

In some ways, the X-chromosome can be regarded as an autosome of which one is active in each somatic cell in either sex. No karyotype not containing one X-chromosome at least has ever been recognized. The second X-chromosome can probably be regarded as inactive in most somatic cells and so genetic imbalance does not arise. Only in the gonads themselves does X inactivation not occur: perhaps this is the special way in which the double dose of X (or an active Y) maintains the integrity of the gonad.

The result of this inactivation, however, is only a partial restoration of a fair balance since females have a choice of two X-chromosomes available rather than two per cell. For the genetic errors of omission on a faulty X-chromosome inherited from one parent the other X, active in other somatic cells, can "cover up." Special tests are necessary to detect the female carriers of these X-linked disorders which can be lethal to males or at least totally inhibit fitness. Some such tests are available, for X-linked muscular dystrophy and X-linked mucopolysaccharidosis (Hunter's) for example.

The consequences of a two-allele system were worked out by Childs in a simple model.

TABLE 2

GENOTYPES OF THE TWO SEXES WITH GENE FREQUENCIES IF THE LOCUS IS IN THE X-CHROMOSOME AND THERE ARE TWO ALLELES IN THE POPULATION, EACH WITH A FREQUENCY OF 0·5

Sex	*Genotypes*		
Female	AA	Aa	aa
Frequencies	0·25	0·5	0·25
Male	A	—	a
Frequencies	0·5		0·5

(From B. Childs (1965), *Pediatrics*, **35**, 5, 798–812.)

The table shows that there are three possible genotypes for females as opposed to two for males. What this means in effect, is that the females have greater flexibility. If (A) is deleterious, more females will be affected because of the group (Aa): but it could also be compensated for by (a). In that case, only (AA) will be deleterious and there are less of these for females than there will be for males. But the same holds true for certain advantageous changes. We have seen that the inequality of the representation of these diseases between the sexes is an inevitable consequence of the system of sexual differentiation which has evolved in man.

ERRORS OF THE DIFFERENTIATING PROCESS

Sex Chromosome Aneuploidy

One consequence of the sex-chromosome mechanism seen in disease states occurs through failures in cell division in parental gonads. The gamete then bears the incorrect chromosome complement into the zygote. Thirteen different combinations of sex chromosomes have been described so far.

TABLE 3

HUMAN SEX-CHROMOSOME ANEUPLOIDIES

Male Phenotype	*Female Phenotype*
46 XY	45, XO
47, XYY	
48, XYYY	
47, XXY	46, XX
48, XXYY	
48, XXXY	47, XXX
49, XXXYY	
49, XXXXY	48, XXXX
	49, XXXXX

(From C. E. Ford (1970), *J. Biosoc. Sci.* Suppl. 2, 7–30.)

Yet the individuals with these aneuploidies are not strikingly abnormal in their phenotype. Female morphology emerges in the absence of the Y-chromosome whether the contribution of the X-chromosome is represented once or five times over.

These facts themselves suggest that the X-chromosome Lyonization mechanism is a very powerful inactivator since similar aneuploidies in the autosomes would have extremely serious effects. They also suggest that the Y-chromosome is inactive or else carries no significant genetic information other than that about the pace of development.

But there are features of the aneuploidies which are worth thinking about for what they might suggest about the differentiating process and its mechanism.

Turner's Syndrome

Turner's syndrome is associated with karyotypes other than 45 XO but this karyotype is always associated with this syndrome. The phenotype should be recognizable at birth. The mean birth weight is 2,900 grams,[48] areas of transient congenital lymphoedema occur, and the skin tends to be loose. The thorax is broad, the maxilla narrow, the hair line low, the nails are narrow and hyperconvex, and the skin frequently shows pigmented naevi. There is no adolescent growth spurt and secondary sexual characteristics usually fail to appear.

On psychological testing, patients with Turner's syndrome show reduced ability in performance tasks though their verbal abilities might be quite good.

Multiple X-Syndromes

Though triple-X women are unremarkable, more numerous replications of the X-chromosome have been associated with degrees of mental handicap and relatively trivial somatic defects.

XYY Syndrome

Welch (1969) argued that a similarity exists between patients with the XYY karyotype and recidivists. There are problems of selection bias: but tall stature and psychological immaturity are probably reasonable, reliable, traits of persons with this syndrome. The contrast with XO is marked.

XXY Syndrome

Klinefelter's syndrome is of some historical importance since it reflects the fashion of interpretation over the years as genetic information has become available. Originally the diagnosis was clinical, based on testicular atrophy, eunuchoidism, azoospermia, gynaecomastia, and some degree of mental handicap was fairly common. The presence of the extra X was described by Jacobs and Strong (1959) but this had been suggested by the sex-chomatin pattern which seemed to be female. Now the diagnosis rests on examination of the karyotype. Patients with this syndrome are slightly taller than average.

Observations on the relationship between stature and genotype were made by Tanner *et al.* (1959) who postulated genes on the Y-chromosome which regulated growth. Although the relationship between stature and the presence of the Y-chromosome is quite clear, there is no need to postulate the existence of such specific genes. Some form of dosage effect does, however, seem possible. People with XYY constitution seem taller than XY males and certain families with extra-large Y-chromosomes resemble the XYY's in some ways.

TABLE 4

SEX CHROMOSOMES AND STATURE

	"N"	*Mean Height, cm.*
45, XO	128	141·8
46, XX	Women	162·0
47, XXX	30	163·07
46, XX	Few males	165·7
46, XY	Men	174·7
47, XXY	118	175·69
48, XXYY	22	180·52
47, XYY	19	182·95
46, XY	—	Tall

Table 4 shows the relationship which exists between sex chromosomes and stature. It is consistent with the idea that the Y-chromosome promotes developmental delay and allows the increased growth.

True Hermaphroditism

Polani (1970) produced some striking evidence about the lateralization of the gonad in true hermaphrodites.

TABLE 5

GONADS IN RELATION TO SIDE AND SEX-CHROMOSOME COMPLEMENTS IN 132 LATERAL OR UNILATERAL TRUE HERMAPHRODITES

	Type of Gonad	*Right*	*Left*
46, XX and chromatin positive	Ovary	28	43
	Testis or Ovotestis	56	41
	Testis	25	14
46, XY and chromatin negative	Ovary or Ovotestis	*a* 23	34

(From P. Polani (1970), *Phil. Trans. Roy. Soc. Lond.*, **B.259**, 187–204.)

About 50 per cent of left gonads are ovaries as compared with 20 per cent of right gonads. The situation is more or less reversed for testes. The right gonad becomes a testis more easily than the left. Polani points out that in birds the right gonad generally involutes and becomes non-functional as an ovary.

The significance of these powerful lateralization effects is considerable because similar arguments applied to differential cerebral organization between sexes (*see later*) tend to have a hollow ring about them. If there is a lateralization bias by sex for the gonad which can be proved by existing techniques, why not for the brain even though it is far more difficult to prove?

ENDOCRINE PROCESSES

Sex Differentiation and its Failures

The developing fetus is sexually bipotential but not equipotential. At every stage, maleness has to be actively imposed by the mechanism which is relevant and active at each stage of ontogeny. After differentiation the fetal gonad forms hormones which are responsible for further differentiation of testis, genital tract, and the hypothalamus. Castration of developing male rats leads to failure to differentiate further as males.[26] Similarly, pregnant female rats treated with antiandrogens (cyproterone acetate) produced progeny that looked female although some parts of the internal genitalia, notably the gonads, remained male.[39] In these animals the mammary glands and the brain centres become fully feminized and the condition of the animal is comparable with the clinical picture of testicular feminization in man.

Testicular Feminization

The existence of this condition (about 1 per 100,000 of the population) is of some practical, much theoretical, and great conceptual significance. The practical significance is that these persons, of female habitus, but with absent sex hair and only rudimentary Wolffian or Mullerian derivatives, have testes either intra-abdominally or inguinally which can become malignant.

The theoretical importance is that it clarifies the role played by androgens in producing the male sex syndrome. Since the sexual orientation is absolutely feminine, social adjustment excellent, and attitudes to child-rearing normal, it can be assumed that most of the psychological aspects as well as the morphological aspects of the female sex syndrome are available in the genome without a specific internal system being necessary to promote them.

Conceptually, it prompts a developmental and sensible reply to the question, what is the sex of this person? Conventionally, we regard sex as a genetic characteristic which remains unchanged throughout postnatal life. But sex is usually a statement which is ascribed at any given moment on the best information available at that time, together with a series of conventional and statistical probabilities based on what is apparent. The person with the testicular feminization syndrome is genetically male, anatomically partly female, psychologically largely female, socially entirely female, but biologically neuter. We will return later to the concept of maleness and femaleness seeking a more complete definition.

Since it can be understood that the male sex syndrome must be promoted from the neutral (female) condition then we can expect more variety in maleness than in femaleness in any of the senses of those terms as used above, and more sex/gender problems in males than in females.

Adrenogenital Syndromes

Adrenogenital syndromes occur in genetic males and females. The masculinization of females is apparent at birth and the condition is treatable. But recently Money (1971) has published the I.Q. scores of 70 subjects with the adrenogenital syndrome. There is a bias to increased intelligence. Similarly, he found that 10 genetic females, masculinized to varying degrees by progestin given to their mothers during pregnancy, all had I.Q. scores above 100 of whom 6 had scores above 130. This work supports earlier findings by Dalton (1968).

Specific and General Hormonal Effects

The specific effect of androgens on sexual differentiation is the once-for-all effect upon the developing hypothalamus. This influence must be exerted within certain critical limits of time. In man the "sexing" of the brain takes place between 60 and 120 days of intrauterine life.[20] The male pattern of behaviour is characterized by a lack of cycling in sexual activities and an active rather than a passive sex role.

But androgens exert a more general anabolic influence and in the brain this affects neural and glial growth, cell size, cell numbers, and brain weight. Male/female differences are lost if the males are castrated in embryo.[25]

Certain potential pharmacological effects from the hormonal differences which characterize the sexes were cited by Broverman *et al.* (1968). They suggest that the hormonal background could influence the balance between sympathetic and parasympathetic activation with females more displaced towards sympathetic activation.

SOMATIC PROCESSES

Most diseases show some degree of sexual bias. Two extreme and opposed points of view can be taken to explaining sex limitation. One is that the male chooses to undertake foolish and unnecessary practices by virtue of which he risks losing his life. The other is that all the variation in mortality and morbidity between the sexes is another aspect of the sex-differentiating mechanism: in a broad sense, part of being a male. The former argument however, tends to be interjected, ontogenetically, after the age of reason to explain phenomena which have existed prior to birth. Although we do not know what the primary sex-ratio is, there is no doubt that the late abortions and still births over-represent males. Perinatal mortality is greater for males. More males die very young of infectious diseases. Yet males are bigger at birth, grow bigger hearts and lungs, and are generally more adapted for strenuous work. They seem fitter. How can the apparent paradox be resolved?

First, the values of our society dignify male attributes so that muscularity and athleticism might be quite wrongly regarded as representing good health. There is more construction than one to the concept of "being fit" and the survival of men over a long life span is one in which they compare poorly with females in most western societies. There are interesting exceptions to this, as we shall see.

Consider again the mechanism of sex-differentiation. Males are seen to be overdeveloped females. They have taken their development relatively more slowly, seemingly because they have more steps to fulfil. The genome, that is all the potential information available in all the genes on all the chromosomes, is not translated in full into the phenotype. There are very good disease models by which to show this, for example Huntington's Chorea. The gene may not express in itself in the natural life-span of some individuals. To what extent did they *have* Huntington's Chorea?

Through the Y-chromosome evoking a male sex-syndrome, the male is "exploring" his genome more than a female would. We might expect to find the male with certain advantages and disadvantages.

Indeed, we have considered[43] the possible evolutionary value of this mechanism. If the genome is explored more in the male than in the female, this is a device for experimentation which carries less risk of disaster to the species, since males are, in evolutionary terms, the more expendable during a period of population growth.

to problems of growth alone. Cravioto (1970) has shown how growth problems repercuss upon intellectual ability. He sees a spiral effect occurring so that ignorance, infection, and malnutrition lead to the production of people who are only capable of dealing with their problems in suboptimal ways. They rear their own children unsuitably and so the "social structure," the "culture" is perpetuated; but it is mediated by biological processes.

Grey Walter originally pointed out that times of rapid change in a developing organism were times of special

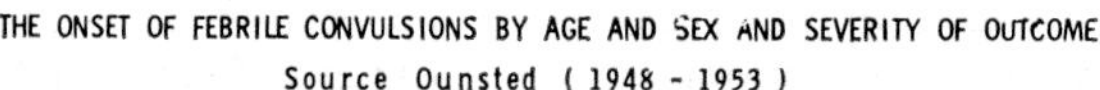

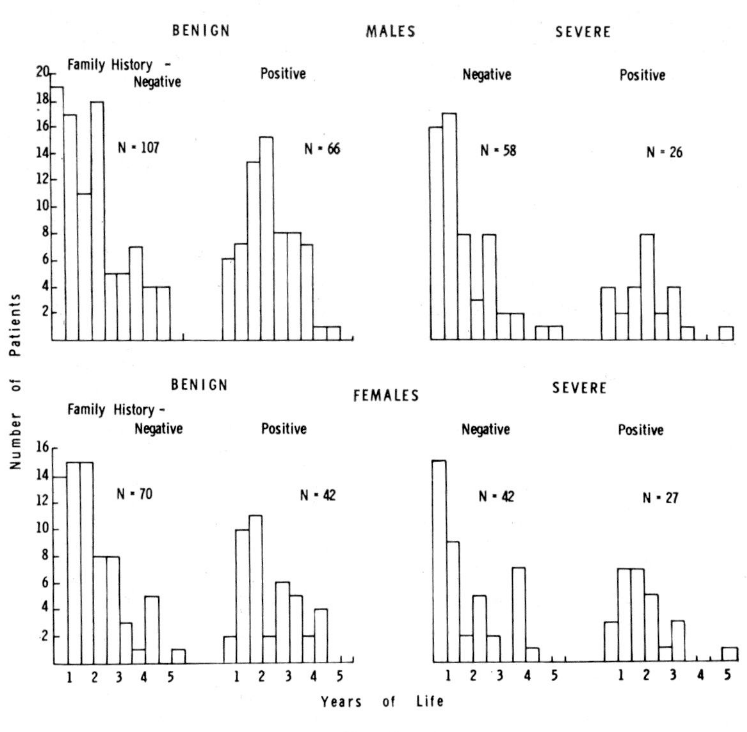

FIG. 2

Because males are deflected by Y-chromosome function into maleness, because they need to continue reinforcing this throughout life, they tend also to be relatively more seriously affected by adverse environmental circumstances. By the same token, if girls are found who have been seriously affected by circumstances, they will have needed worse circumstances. The principle as far as it concerns growth is called homeorrhesis.

For example, a study was made in Heliconia in Columbia[49] into marasmus and kwashiorkor. In that region, all children were malnourished to some degree. The effect of this was generally to retard skeletal growth and maturation. But females made catch-up growth in adolescence, whereas males did not. This reduced the sex dimorphism for body size. Males needed to achieve not just some growth, but the extra amount of growth typical (or possible) for males. When the stress becomes sufficient to produce marasmus or kwashiorkor, the females could not take their more modest growth spurt either.

But the significance of these sex differences is not confined

risk of things going wrong. The quicker the changes are made (step function changes), the less are the chances of anything coincidentally interfering with them. But should it do so, the faster the changes, the more drastic the results. Comparative surveys of the development of males and females show that females develop more rapidly than males in many important ways. More rapid development, for example in the immune system,[134] in the activity of certain enzyme systems, will give the female advantage in respect of any stresses which require to be met be deployment of these systems. However, the development of the female more rapidly than the male exposes her to more severe effects, but less frequently. A particular example that has been comprehensively examined[31,52] is that of convulsions associated with fever.

Figure 2 shows a multiple histogram of 438 children who have a convulsion triggered by fever, located by family history, and by severity of outcome, in each case by the age at which the original seizure occurred.

Consider first the different pattern of onset between the

four histograms, FH negative, and the four FH positive. In each instance, the age of onset histogram for FH negative is exponential in type with one major step-like change, but the FH positive histograms all rise to a peak and then decline. There are at least two factors operating; a general decline risk, but a later period of special risk in those with positive FH. This decays with the general risk. Then the peak in FH positive and the step-like decline in FH negative group are differently located between the sexes. In every case, they come 6–12 months earlier in the females.

In this study, relatively more females than males later suffered serious chronic epilepsy, although more males than females were affected originally.

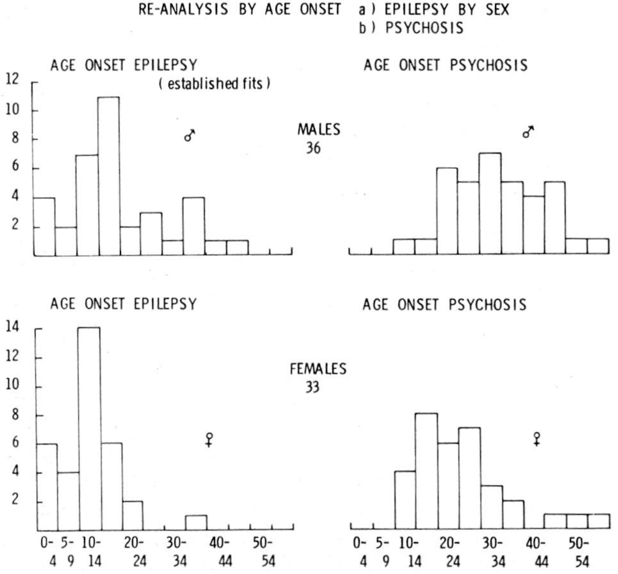

Fig. 3
(From Taylor, D. C. (1971). *Psychological Medicine*, **1**, 247)

Another example from the seizure disorders comes from a reanalysis of epileptic patients with chronic psychoses.[47,51] Females are disproportionately over-represented. The figure (Fig. 3) shows that they have their peak of onset of epilepsy in the quinquenium before the peak is reached in the males. Similarly, they become psychotic sooner than the males. Epilepsy later associated with psychosis starts disproportionately often during the years of puberty.

Figure 4 shows a comparison of the age of onset of epilepsy in the psychotic patients, as compared with other serious cases of temporal-lobe epilepsy without psychosis.

The pubertal growth spurt is itself the best example of a developmental step taken first by females. But it is reflected in the age of onset of bone cancers in young people (Fig. 5).

Interestingly, the females even lead the males into the phase of skeletal involution and height shrinkage[33,40] If females start this process before the males, then, much later in life, they will suffer relatively more than males from the more advanced forms of bone demineralization. Similarly, the apocrine glands of females involute ahead of those of males.[38] From what he calls the depressingly long list of diseases to which the male is more prone, Childs[8] notes the exception of auto-immune diseases. Systemic Lupus Erythmatosus, for example, is moverall six times ore common in girls. But this information requires a caveat. Examine

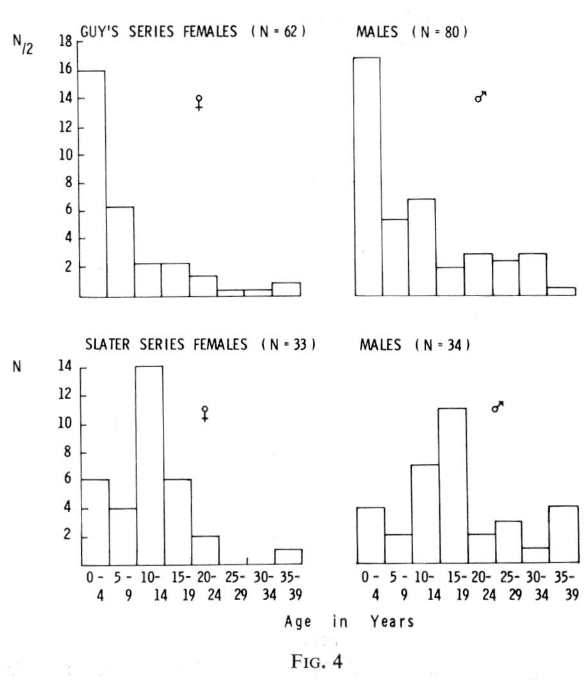

Fig. 4
(From Taylor, D. C. (1971). *Psychological Medicine*, **1**, 247)

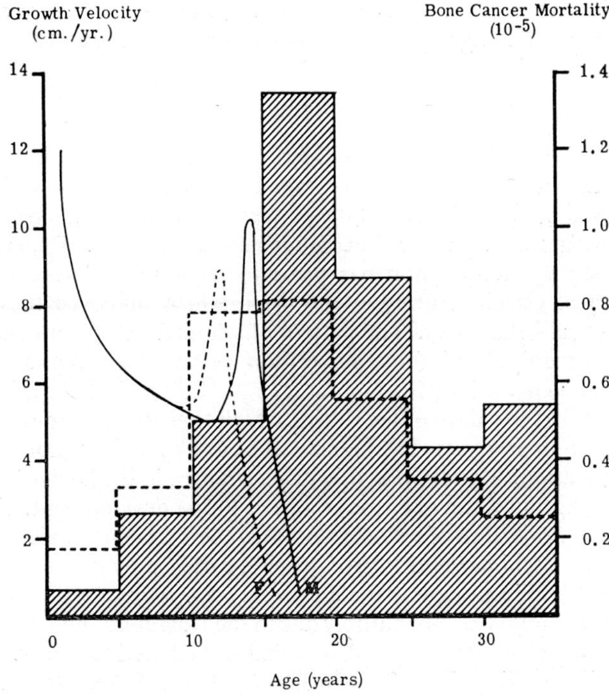

Fig. 5. Modal ages of onset of bone cancer in males and females. (From Hems, G. (1970). *Brit. J. Bone Cancer*, **24**, 208)

Fig. 6. Prior to the age of 10 years, no males were affected in these two large series. Then for a decade, 1 in 10 cases was male. Later, by the 7th decade, were a correction made

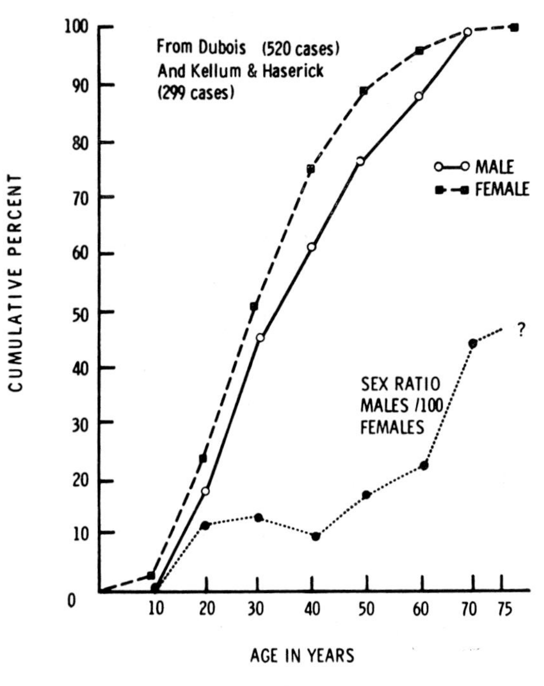

FIG. 6

(From Taylor, D. C., Ounsted, C. (1972) Gender Differences: Their Ontogeny and Significance)

for the fact that there are twice as many women alive as men at that age, the proportions would be nearly equal!

NERVOUS-SYSTEM PROCESSES

Male and female brains differ. "Females" show a cyclical pattern of sexual activity called oestrous, or menstrual cycling. Females also show patterns of behaviour at coitus often called passive, but better called receptive. Experimental manipulation has proved that hormones directly affect certain centres in the brain which influence these sexual behaviours. The pattern of sexual development can be manipulated fully but within certain time limits in ontogeny. Thus, for laboratory rats, this period occupies the first few days of life during which time its development is comparable to the human fetus at about four months gestation. For each, at this stage, changes in the hormonal background can alter the course of future development. A single injection of testosterone into a newly-born female rat causes an increased rate of growth, earlier puberty, loss of "cycling" and a loss of female sexual behaviour. The growth rate changes are not entirely due to the "anabolic" effects of male hormones but are also probably mediated centrally.

It would be important to know whether deliberate manipulation of the hormonal system *in utero* could bias the form of intelligence in the unborn child. But there are no reports so far which suggest that genetic females, exposed to masculinizing hormones, have had significantly increased spatial ability so as to shift them towards the "male" sort of intellectual style.

By this, I refer to the tendency of females to excel in tests of verbal ability and precise motor skills, and the male to excel in spatial tasks and in creativity and reasoning. At present, these are contentious areas. However, recent major reviews[5,23] lend considerable support not only to bias in the skills between the sexes, but also bias between the activities of the cerebral hemispheres underlying the relevant skills.

There is some evidence accruing which suggests a morphological basis for the predominance of the left hemisphere in acquiring the lateralized speech centre.[5] The evidence refers to greater specific gravity of the left hemisphere, a larger planum temporale on the left side (speech area), and includes Landsell's reanalysis of the data of Connel (*see* above review for references) which suggests a greater degree of myelination in the relevant brain area on the left in four-year-old girls, and on the right in boys of similar age. The material available was, however, small. Buffery and Gray concluded that the human brain had an innate and usually left-sided neural mechanism for speech. Its function was accelerated in females. A more bilateral, though predominantly right-sided representation for non-verbal function was established in the male brain. This might possibly result from the less emphasis on acquiring speech early.

There is no doubt that females do indeed begin to speak earlier, and at every stage their executive speech abilities are superior to those of men. Males, however, tend to be more creative with language, i.e. poetry, and in manipulating and relating verbal concepts.[23]But there is evidence of female bias towards increased auditory sensitivity from the earliest stages. At 14 weeks Watson (1969) found auditory reinforcers better for females and visual ones better for males in a task of visual fixation.

There are differences in mothering between the sexes, but these might as easily be due to the type of signals used by the infants as due to preformed maternal attitudes to children of one or other sex. Girl neonates are more smily and more passive. Males make more movement.

The beginnings of interest in things rather than in people can be seen in the nursery school. Males tend to explore objects more and to find more novel uses for them. Females help each other, especially younger girls, and they are more sedentary. C. Hutt (1972) regards the female as biologically biased towards a nurturant role. She is stable, reliable, consistent. Her skills and her language are executive, for actually *doing* it, even though the male may be more skillful at conceptualizing.

Even so, most reviews tend not to discuss the secondary effects of sex differences upon the psychology of people of that sex. If language comes readily to young girls, then it will surely immediately begin to reinforce itself. Males meanwhile makeshift with their infantile semaphore. In agonistic encounters, it cannot be without effect that boys are stronger than girls. Those exploratory drives by which the male extends himself are the drives which lead male children to casualty departments so much more frequently than females. The problems of delayed speech are translated later to problems with reading and referral to child guidance, either on these grounds, or else on a combination of exploratory exuberance and reading retardation. The sex ratio of referrals to child guidance is 200 males per 100 females. The sex ratio in language disorders, including autism, is over 400:100.

Baldwin (1968) provides reliable figures from referrals to child and adolescent services in Scotland.

Figure 7 shows the rate of referral per thousand by age. From 15 years on there are more girls than boys referred whereas prior to that there were substantially more boys. In Fig. 8 the rates of males and females are compared, but a crude diagnostic categorization is included. The excess rates of referral for females after the age of 15 is largely due to "neurosis." Male behaviour disorders (social deviance) decline. Davie *et al.* (1972) provide a similar picture based on their national study.

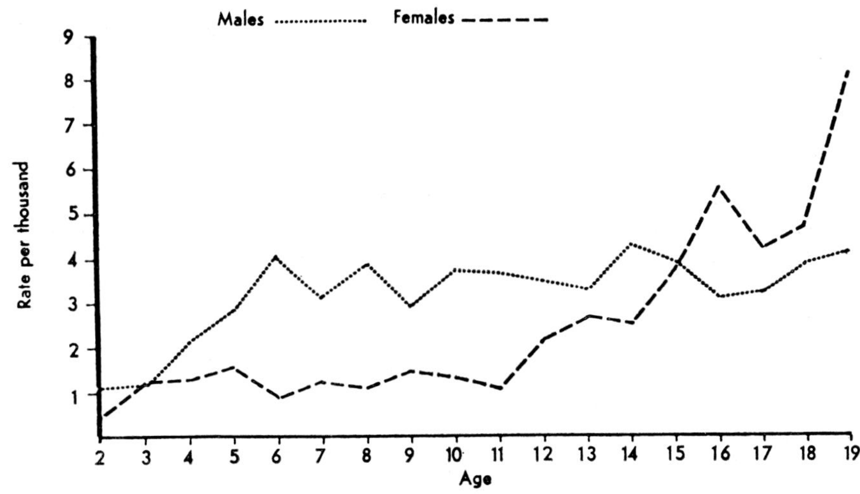

FIG. 7. Children and adolescents from North-East Scotland. First referrals to psychiatric services in 1965 and 1966. Mean annual sex and age specific rates per thousand. (From Baldwin, J. A. (1968). *Acta Psychiatrica Scandinavica.*

But later in life these differences in personality traits, in styles of approach to the world, might be among the determinants of the sorts of mild psychiatric illness seen in general practice. Complaints to the doctor by mothers about health matters are of relevance to paediatricians because it so often happens that the complainant, rather than child, is out of sorts. In a sophisticated study of psychiatric illness in general practice, Cooper (1972) found that women outnumbered men by three to one, a ratio he regards as typical for chronic neurosis in general practice. But cases were matched with controls in this study and in Fig. 9, which compares the mean clinical scores of reported symptoms, it is clear that female controls score quite differently from male controls. Women are thus both more prone to these disorders and more sensitive of their minor adumbrations, However, granted "psychiatric illness" the symptom scores vary little between the sexes (except that males would be that much worse than their controls than are females).

SEX AND GENDER

Gender Identity

Some people are unclear as to which sex they belong From the diversity of steps in the processes which regulate sexual dimorphism it is clear that this could happen for a variety of reasons. Certain medical clinics have established a reputation for helping such people and the experience gained from them has contributed significantly to knowledge. But the experiences which have been gained from the study of abnormal psychology and abnormal anatomy and physiology have, at times, been expanded rashly into general theories of sexual development. Diamond (1965) challenged what was then the strongest theoretical position; that of Money and the Hampsons (*see* Mensh, 1972). These authors believed that at birth the human was psychosexually undifferentiated to such a degree that up to 27 months of life it was possible to reassign the sex ascribed thereto and recast the individual in a different sex role. As more time was spent in rehearsing a gender role, it became more and more difficult to reverse it even though it might have been, on more "objective" evidence (chromosomes, internal anatomy) the wrong one. It was construed that since ascribed sex was so potent a factor in determining to which sex someone felt they belonged, then ascription and rehearsal, the social factors of themselves, were prepotent in determining the outcome. But the issue was a confused one because of a lack of clarity in thinking about "sex" on the one hand and "gender identity" on the other. Gender identity is a perception, either of the self or of others, which is normally consistent with all the other components of the sex syndrome, but which might be detached and inconsistent. Often, but by no means always, there are understandable anatomical and/or physiological reasons for this, but transexuals, who feel trapped inside a body of inappropriate anatomical sex and who actively seek sex-change

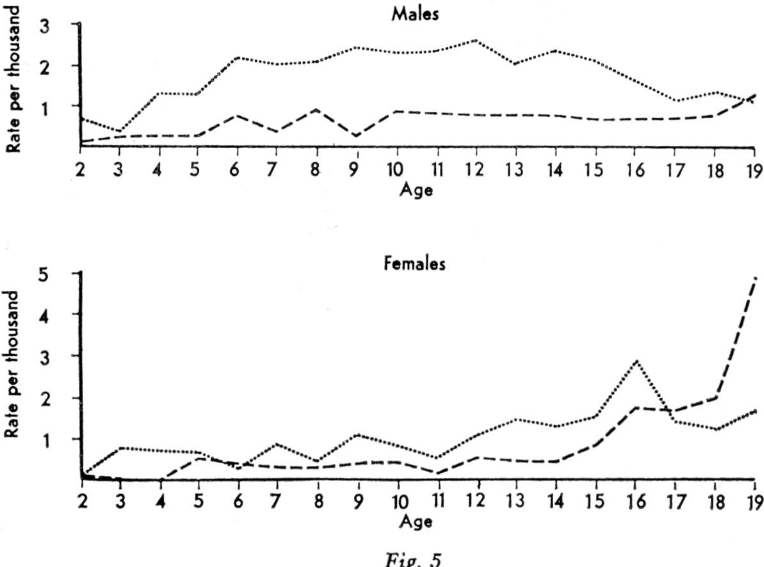

Fig. 5

FIG. 8. Children and adolescents from North-East Scotland. First referrals to psychiatric services in 1965 and 1966. Diagnosed behaviour disorders and neuroses mean annual sex and age specific rates per thousand. (From Baldwin, J. A. (1968). *Acta Psychiatrica Scandinavica*)

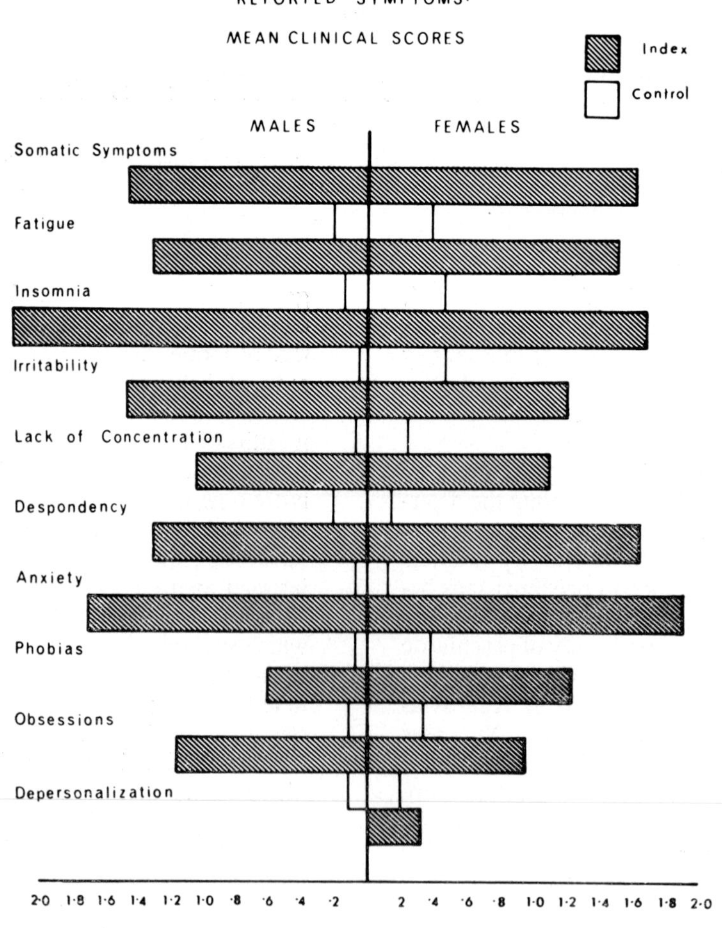

FIG. 9

(From Cooper, B., 1972. *Proc. roy. Soc. Med.* **65**, 509, 512)

surgery (mostly from male to female) usually suffer no known defect in the function of their somatic sex.

We have to accept that gender identity, the way an individual feels about their sex ascription, is an important part of the sex syndrome. Its disturbance might be understandable or might be derived from abnormal psychological processes leading to the denial of an identity consistent with the somatic self. The real significance of this denial cannot be understood until a definition of "sex" is agreed.

Maleness and Femaleness

Sex can be regarded as "ascribed" or "achieved." Ascribed sex is that which the available evidence leads us to assume of a person. It may be deliberately misleading (transvestism) or it may be more or less congruent with each other part of the emergent sex syndrome. Thus, the general terms "male" and "female," although usually applied to persons whose entire sex syndrome is perfectly congruent, can create difficulties. There must be *some* irrefutable definition. We have proposed[43] that the female is "she who bears live-born children" and the male is, "he who impregnated her." But their young must be reared to an age when they can themselves reproduce. Potentiality in either regard is inadequate. Whether a mating dyad is sterile by choice or mischance, the dyad is unfit and neither partner achieves their sex of ascription.

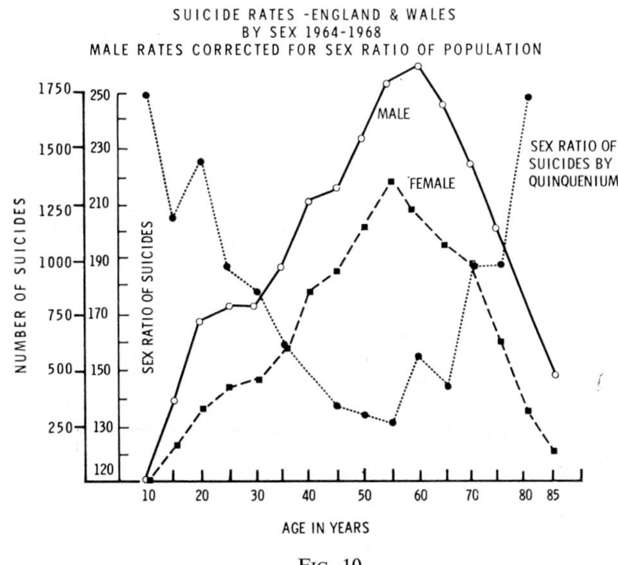

FIG. 10

The advantage of these definitions will be very obvious in the practical situation of dealing with children with ambiguous genitalia since the physician will be able to consider how much of either gender syndrome an individual might sustain.

The definitions also form a basis for considering reproductive failure and its potential psychological effects. The Vulnerable Child,[18] Hyperpaedophilia,[41] and The Battered Baby Syndrome[21] are each rooted in aspects of the failure of self-realization which reproductive failure implies.

Regarding the full gender syndrome as emerging and later collapsing after active reproduction rather than being set for all time by the chance of fertilization, allows a developmental approach to the various sex differentiations. Certain male/female differences will be more or less apparent at different stages in ontogeny.

An example comes from suicide statistics,[53] The figure (Fig. 10) shows that the overall sex ratio of 135:100 is actually only apparent for the period of maximal risk. On either side of this period, suicide is a behaviour strongly biased

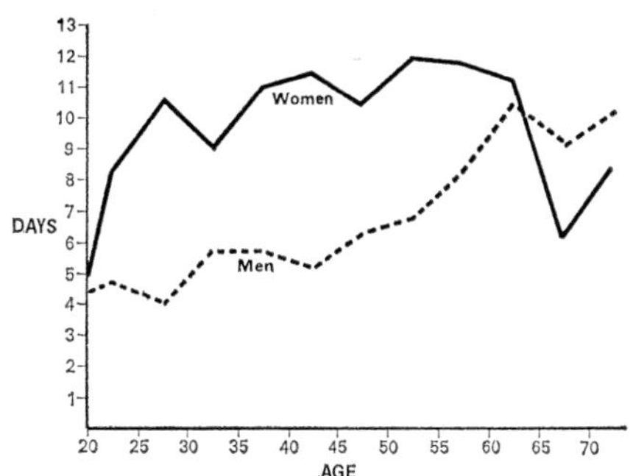

FIG. 11. Average number of days certified sick leave per person per year by age in Civil Service non-industrial staff in the years 1967–69. (From Thomson, D. (1972.) *Proc. roy. Soc. Med.* **65,** 572–577)

towards males. It seems that at the time of maximal risk, some other factor takes over which is independent of sex.

Thomson (1972) examined sickness absence in the Civil Service. Figure 11 shows that the average number of days of certified sick-leave is about two and a-half times as much in women as men between the ages of 25 and 29. But, whereas the number of days off work for men is a function of age, for women it is not and from 55 onwards the number of days off falls. There is, of course, a vast variety of factors operating: but one thing is clear, there is little similarity between "illness" statistics and the death-rate (*see* Fig. 12).

SEX RATIOS

From what is known of the genetic mechanisms determining sex the expected proportion of males and females should be equal. Moreover, an equal number of males and females has been considered (by Fisher, for example) to be likely to occur through evolutionary selection.

However, some of the sex ratios, at conception (Primary) at birth (Secondary) at reproductive age (Tertiary) are not in fact equal. Figure 12 shows that in this country at the present time equal numbers do not appear until age 45–50. This is because the secondary sex ratio is 105:100 approximately, and because the death-rate for young males is greater than females.

After the age of 45, the death-rate for males as compared to females is such that by the age of 70 there are twice as many women as men surviving. A comparison with the Dutch population is included in the figure. The tendency in Holland is the same but serious differences might be due to World War II, to the social structure, etc.

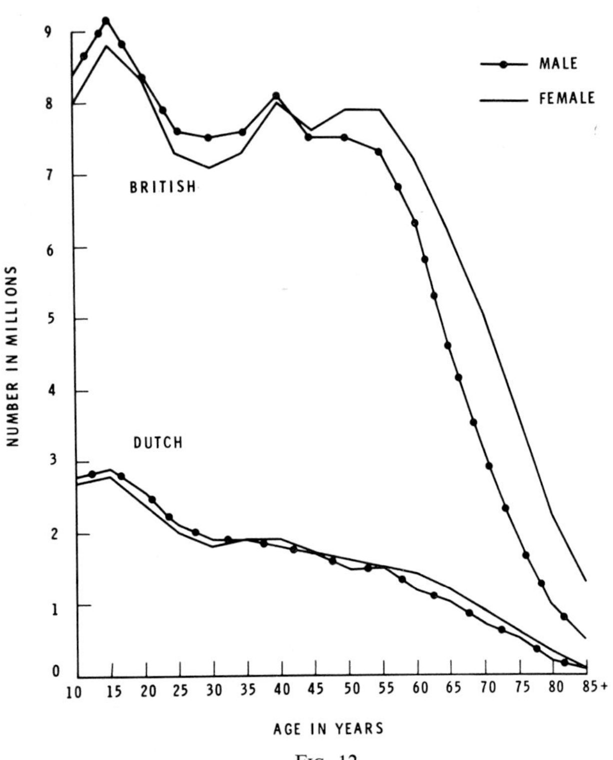

FIG. 12

Primary Sex Ratio

The sex ratio of zygotes is not known in man. But it has been thought to favour males excessively. More recently, these views have been disputed but the alternative is that very many female zygotes must be wasted very early on. The reasons are that throughout the periods of pregnancy where accurate sexing is possible, more males than females have been wasted yet still the secondary sex-ratio is higher for males.[44]

Secondary Sex Ratio

One hundred and five males per 100 females born is a typical figure in Western Europe and the U.S.A. This secondary sex-ratio is influenced independently by birth order, race, and social class.[54] Social-class effects seem to be the greatest, though the mechanism by which these operate are not fully explained. Some studies in exceptionally privileged families have revealed sex ratios at birth of over 110:100.

The biological explanation of these effects is by no means worked out but they do imply that quite sharp changes in population structure could result from changes in socioeconomic fortunes. This is an example of one way in which circumstances which are regarded as "social effects" and others seen as "biological effects" become intimately tied together.

Tertiary Sex Ratio

The sex ratio at the time of reproduction is of considerable interest when considering the process of sexual selection. In the area of the Oxford Regional Hospital Board two-thirds of all maternities occur between 20 and 30 years. The mean age at maternity is 26 years. The sex ratio in England and Wales at this age is 103:100. Granted that this is reflected in the population available for marriage, then females have some choice of partner and males compete.

But from age 45 onwards, the proportion of males declines and females are thereafter increasingly in excess. Here is another situation where a social problem (an excess of lonely widows insufficiently integrated in the social structure) arises in relation to a biological effect, to differential mortality. Quite apart from such problems, this will influence the social structure of groups and the type of influence which the aged exert on the young, which will be principally mediated by females.

Yet where the mores are quite different from our own, then the biological effects are quite different. Among the Old Order Amish—a genetic isolate inbred for over 200 years—the mean number of children per marriage is vastly increased so that the age structure of the population is the reverse of that seen in Table 6.[11]

TABLE 6

DISTRIBUTION OF THE HOLMES COUNTY AMISH POPULATION BY AGE AND SEX IN DECEMBER, 1964

Age in Years	*Males*		*Female*		*Total*	
	No.	%	No.	%	No.	%
0–4	747	7·68	710	7·30	1,457	14·98
5–9	676	6·95	662	6·81	1,338	13·76
10–14	588	6·05	625	6·43	1,213	12·48
15–19	498	5·12	531	5·46	1,029	10·58
20–24	438	4·50	396	4·07	834	8·57
25–29	339	3·49	327	3·36	666	6·85
30–34	219	2·25	273	2·81	492	5·06
35–39	201	2·07	242	2·49	443	4·56
40–44	193	1·98	203	2·09	396	4·07
45–49	167	1·72	171	1·76	338	3·48
50–54	147	1·51	178	1·83	325	3·34
55–59	143	1·47	138	1·42	281	2·89
60–64	136	1·40	104	1·07	240	2·47
65–69	87	0·89	81	0·83	168	1·72
70–74	79	0·81	61	0·63	140	1·44
75–79	55	0·57	46	0·47	101	1·04
80–84	37	0·38	21	0·22	58	0·60
85–89	14	0·14	4	0·04	18	0·18
90–94	5	0·05	3	0·03	8	0·08
95–99	1	0·01	0	0·00	1	0·01
Unknown	84	0·86	94	0·97	178	1·83
Total	4,854	49·90	4,870	50·09	9,724	99·99

(From H. E. Cross and V. A. McKusick (1970), *Social Biology*, **17**, 2, 83.)

CONCLUSION

In this chapter, I have described something of the mechanism of sexual differentiation in man. The mechanism is genetically very simple but a vast array of differences both gross and subtle are set in train by it. The simple genetic system, of which we have a glimpse, implies that rarely if ever can any genetic message be regarded as having an unique effect—there are large numbers of consequential effects which are of no less significance for being remote in time or place of operation. These effects are not side effects or subsidiary issues, they are part of the whole. Man develops as a whole organism, inescapably interactive with his social environment. The study of phenomena from the developmental viewpoint saves paediatricians from the belief that it is possible to divide up the individual—brain from body—mind from brain—body from society—and make operations upon any one of these without producing consequences upon others, for all that so very very often we might wish to do so.

ACKNOWLEDGEMENT

Much of this work was undertaken whilst the author was Senior Medical Research Officer with the Human Development Research Unit. The Human Developmental Research Unit is supported by grants from the Department of Education and Science, the Wolfson Foundation and the Department of Employment and Productivity.

REFERENCES

1. Baldwin, J. A. (1968), "Psychiatric Illness From Birth to Maturity; An Epidemiological Study," *Acta Psychiatrica Scandinavica*, **44**, 313–333.
2. Beatty, R. A. (1970), "Genetic Basis for the Determination of Sex," *Phil. Trans. Roy. Soc. Lond. B.*, **259**, 3–14.
3. Berg, K. (1967), "Practical Possibilities of Mapping the Human X Chromosome as Given by Available Markers," *Bull. European Soc. Hum. Genetics*, **1**, 46–57.
4. Broverman, D. M., Klaiber, E. L., Kobayashi, Y. and Vogel, W. (1968), "Roles of Activation and Inhibition in Sex Differences in Cognitive Abilities," *Psychol. Rev.*, **75**, 23–50.
5. Buffery, A. and Gray, J. (1972), "Sex Differences in the Development of Spatial and Linguistic Skills," in *Gender Differences: Their Ontogeny and Significance*, pp. 123–158 (C. Ounsted and D. C. Taylor, Eds.). London: Churchill Livingstone.
6. Cavalli-Sforza, L. L. and Bodmer, W. F. (1971), *The Genetics of Human Populations.* San Francisco: W. H. Freeman & Co.
7. Chan, S. T. H. (1970), "Natural Sex Reversal in Vertebrates," *Phil. Trans. Roy. Soc. Lond. B.*, **259**, 59–72.
8. Childs, B. (1965), "Genetic Origin of Some Sex Differences Among Human Beings," *Pediatrics*, **35**, 798–812.
9. Cooper, B. (1972), "Clinical and Social Aspects of Chronic Neurosis," *Proc. Roy Soc. Med.*, **65**, 509–512.
10. Cravioto, J. (1970),"Neuro-Integrative Development of School-Age Children," in *The Post-Natal Development of Phenotype*, pp. 57–70 (S. Kazda and V. H. Denenberg, Eds.). London: Butterworths.
11. Cross, H. E. and McKusick, V. A. (1970), "Amish Demography," *Social Biology*, **17**, 83–101.
12. Dalton, K. (1968), "Antenatal Progesterone and Intelligence," *Brit. J. Psychiat.*, **114**, 1377–1382.
13. Davie, R., Butler, N. and Goldstein, H. (1972), *From Birth to Seven.* A Report of the National Child Development Study. London: Longman.
14. Diamond, M. (1965), "A Critical Evaluation of the Ontogeny of Human Sexual Behaviour," *Quart. Rev. Biol.*, 147–175.
15. Dronamraju, K. R. (1965), "The Function of the Y Chromosome in Man, Animals and Plants," *Advan. Genet.*, **13**, 227–310.
16. Eichwald, E. and Silmser, C. (1955), "Skin," *Transplantation Bulletin*, **2**, 148–149.
17. Ford, C. E. (1970), "Cytogenetics and Sex Determination," *J. biosoc. Sci. Suppl.*, **2**, 7–30.
18. Green, M. and Solnit, A. J. (1964), "Reaction to the Threatened Loss of a Child: A Vulnerable Child Syndrome," *Pediatrics*, **34**, 58–66.
19. Grey Walter, W. (1956), in *Discussions in Child Development.* Third Meeting of the World Health Organization Study Group on the Psychobiological Development of the Child. Geneva 1955, p. 192 (J. M. Tanner and B. Inhelder, Eds.). London: Tavistock.
20. Harris, G. W. (1971), "Coordination of the Reproductive Processes" in Biosocial Aspects of Human Fertility, Suppl. 3, *J. Biosocial Science*, **5.**
21. Helfer, R. E. and Kempe, C. H. (1968), *The Battered Child.* Chicago and London: Univ. Chicago Press.
22. Hems, G. (1970), "Aetiology of Bone Cancer and Some Other Cancers in the Young," *Brit. J. Cancer*, **24**, 208–214.
23. Hutt, C. (1972), "Neuroendocrinological, Behavioural and Intellectual Aspects of Sexual Differentiation in Human Development," in *Gender Differences: Their Ontogeny and Significance*, pp. 73–122 (C. Ounsted and D. C. Taylor, Eds.). London: Churchill Livingstone.
24. Jacobs, P. A. and Strong, J. A. (1959), "A Case of Human Intersexuality Having a Possible XXY Sex-Determining Mechanism," *Nature, Lond.*, **183**, 302–303.
25. Jacobson, M. (1970), *Developmental Neurobiology* (James D. Ebert, Ed.), New York: Holt, Rinehart and Winston Inc.
26. Jost, A. (1970), "Hormonal Factors in the Sex Differentiation of the Mammalian Foetus," *Phil. Trans. Roy. Soc. Lond. B.*, **259**, 119–132
27. Kirby, D. R. S. (1970), "The Egg and Immunology," *Proc. Roy. Soc. Med.*, **63**, 59–61.
28. Kirby, D. R. S., McWhirter, K. G., Teitelbaum, M. S. and Darlington, C. D. (1967), "A Possible Immunological Influence on Sex Ratio," *Lancet*, **ii**, 139–140.
29. Lyon, M. F. (1961), "Gene Action in the X-Chromosomes of the Mouse," *Nature*, **190**, 372–373.
30. Lyon, M. F. (1970), "Genetic Activity of Sex Chromosomes in Somatic Cells of Mammals," *Phil. Trans. Roy. Soc. London B.*, **259**, 41–52.
31. Lennox, M. (1949), "Febrile Convulsions in Childhood: Their Relationship to Adult Epilepsy" *J. Pediat.*, **35**, 427–435.
32. Mensh, I. N. (1972), "Personal and Social Environmental Influences in the Development of Gender Identity," in *Gender Differences: Their Ontogeny and Significance*, pp. 41–56 (C. Ounsted and D. C. Taylor, Eds.). London: Churchill Livingstone.
33. Miall, W. E., Ashcroft, M. T., Lovell, H. G. and Moore, F. (1967), "A Longitudinal Study of the Decline of Adult Height with Age in Two Welsh Communities," *Hum. Biol.*, **39**, 445–454.
34. Michaels, R. H. and Rogers, K, D. (1971), "A Sex Difference in Immunologic Responsiveness," *Pediatrics*, **47**, 120–123.
35. Mittwoch, U. (1970), "How does the Y Chromosome Affect Gonadal Differentiation?", *Phil. Trans. Roy. Soc. Lond. B.*, **259**, 113–118.
36. Mittwoch, U. (1972), "Hypothesis: Mongolism and Sex. A Common Problem of Cell Proliferation," *J. Med. Genet.*, **9**, 92–95.
37. Money, J. W. (1971), "Pre-Natal Hormones and Intelligence: A Possible Relationship," *Impact of Science on Society*, **XXI**, 285–290.
38. Montagna, M. (1956), "Ageing of the Axillary Apocrine Sweat Glands in the Human Female," in *Ciba Foundation Colloquia on Ageing*, Vol. 2, pp. 188–201. (G. Wolstenholme and E. Millar, Eds.). London: Churchill.
39. Neumann, F., Elgar, W. and Steinbeck, H. (1970), "Anti-androgens and Reproductive Development," *Phil Trans. Roy. Soc. Lond. B.*, **259**, 179–186.
40. Nordin, B. E. C. (1971), "Clinical Significance and Pathogenesis of Osteoporosis," *Brit. med. J.*, **i**, 571–576.
41. Ounsted, C. (1955), "The Hyperkinetic Syndrome in Epileptic Children," *Lancet*, **ii**, 303–311.

42. Ounsted, C. and Ounsted, M. (1970), "Effect of Y Chromosome on Fetal Growth-Rate," *Lancet*, **ii**, 857–858.
43. Ounsted, C. and Taylor, D. C. (1972), "The Y Chromosome Message: A Point of View," in *Gender Differences: Their Ontogeny and Significance*, pp. 241–262 (C. Ounsted and D. C. Taylor, Eds.). London: Churchill Livingstone.
44. Ounsted, M. (1972), "Gender and Intrauterine Growth. With a note on the use of the sex of the proband as a research tool," in *Gender Differences: Their Ontogeny and Significance*, pp. 177–202 (C. Ounsted and D. C. Taylor, Eds.). London: Churchill Livingstone.
45. Polani, P. E. (1970), "Hormonal and Clinical Aspects of Hermaphroditism and the Testicular Feminising Syndrome in Man," *Phil. Trans. Roy. Soc. Lond. B.*, **259**, 187–206.
46. Sanger, R. and Race, R. R. (1970), "Towards Mapping the X Chromosome," in *Modern Trends in Human Genetics*, Vol. 1, pp. 241–266 (A. E. H. Emery, Ed.). London: Butterworths.
47. Slater, E., Beard, A. W. and Glithero, E. (1963), "The Schizophrenia-Like Psychoses of Epilepsy," *Brit. J. Psychiat.*, **1–9**, 95–150.
48. Smith, D. W. (1970), "Recognisable Patterns of Human Malformation. Genetic Embryologic and Clinical Aspects," *Major Problems in Clinical Pediatrics*, Vol. VII. Philadelphia, London and Toronto: W. B. Saunders Co.
49. Stini, W. A. (1969), "Nutritional Stress and Growth: Sex Difference in Adaptive Response," *Am. J. Phys. Anthrop.*, **31**, 417–426.
50. Tanner, J. M., Prader, A., Habich, A. and Ferguson-Smith, M. A. (1959), "Genes on the Y Chromosome Influencing Rate of Maturation in Man. Skeletal Age Studies in Children with Klienfelter's (XXY) and Turner's (XO) Syndromes," *Lancet*, **ii**, 141–144.
51. Taylor, D. C. (1971), "Ontogenesis of Chronic Epileptic Psychoses: A Reanalysis," *Psychological Medicine*, **1**, 247–253.
52. Taylor, D. C. and Ounsted, C. (1971), "Biological Mechanisms Influencing the Outcome of Seizures in Response to Fever," *Epilepsia*, **12**, 33–45.
53. Taylor, D. C. and Ounsted, C. (1972), "The Nature of Gender Differences Explored Through Ontogenetic Analyses of Sex Ratio in Disease," in *Gender Differences: Their Ontogeny and Significance*, pp. 215–240. (C. Ounsted and D. C. Taylor, Eds.). London: Churchill Livingstone.
54. Teitelbaum, M. S. (1970), "Factors Affecting the Sex Ratio in Large Populations," *J. biosoc. Sci. Suppl.*, **2**, 61–71.
55. Thomson, D. (1972), "Sickness Absence in the Civil Service," *Proc. Roy. Soc. Med.*, **65**, 572–577.
56. Watson, T. S. (1969), "Operant Conditioning of Visual Fixation in Infants Under Visual and Auditory Reinforcement," *Developmental Psychology*, **1**, 508–516.
57. Welch, J. P. (1969), "The XYY Syndrome—A Genetic Determinant of Behaviour," in *Birth Defects*, Original Article Series, **5**, 10–15.

4. NUTRITION

ELSIE M. WIDDOWSON

NUTRITION OF THE FETUS

From its earliest beginnings the new organism must be nourished, and the embryo or fetus is fed in three different ways between the time the ovum is fertilized and the baby is born. First there is the stage when the blastocyst is free and unattached in the uterus, which lasts for a variable number of days in different species. During this time it absorbs nutrients through its outer layer, the trophoblast, from the secretions of the uterine glands, the so-called 'uterine milk'. This must vary in composition from one species to another; in the mare it has been reported to contain 18 per cent protein, 0·006 per cent fat, 0·14 per cent calcium and 0·2 per cent phosphorus.

After the blastocyst has become implanted in the uterine epithelium, but before the placental circulation has been established, a sinusoidal space, the syncitium, is formed between the fetal and maternal tissues, and the blood and degenerating cells within it provide the nutrients for the developing organism until the placenta has developed and the placental circulation is ready to take over, which, in man, has occurred by the third month. Once the placental circulation has been established all the nutrients required by the fetus reach it through its umbilical blood vessels. At the end of the third month of gestation the human fetus weighs only 30 g. or so. Almost all its growth in size, therefore, and hence the transfer of most of the material in its body at term, takes place during the last 6 months. Towards the end of gestation the fetus lays down in its body 500 mg. nitrogen, over 300 mg. of calcium and about 200 mg. of phosphorus each day.

At one time the placenta was thought of as a semi-permeable membrane between maternal and fetal blood, and it was believed that what was transferred to the fetus was an ultrafiltrate of maternal plasma. It was then realized that the concept was far too naive, for many of the nutrients being transmitted to the fetus are at a higher concentration in fetal than in maternal plasma, although some are at a lower one.

It seems likely that gases and water diffuse freely across the placenta, but we still do not know exactly how the other materials are transmitted. It is often said that active transport is involved; this must be so, but Hytten and Leitch (1964) have also emphasized the importance of the different parts of the placenta in the transport. The gradient is not directly from maternal to fetal blood, but from maternal blood to the syncitiotrophoblast, the maternal part of the placenta, where concentration may go on, and proteins, enzymes, nucleic acids and hormones may be synthesized. Further conversions and syntheses go on in the cytotrophoblast, the fetal part of the placenta, and we have no idea at present about the gradients within the different parts of the placenta, or between the fetal side of the placenta and the fetal blood.

Carbohydrate reaches the fetus as glucose, and the fetus synthesizes its own glycogen. The serum of the fetal lamb and of other ungulates has high concentrations of fructose, and this has been shown to be formed from glucose in the maternal plasma by the placenta[19]. Here, therefore, is a clear example of the placenta altering a nutrient during its passage through it. The fructose disappears from the plasma of the lamb within a few days after birth, and what its function is is still unknown.

The concentration of glycogen in the liver and skeletal muscles of the human fetus increases during the latter part of gestation[30], just as it does in the tissues of other species[29].

TABLE 1

CONCENTRATION OF CARBOHYDRATE (G. PER 100 G.) IN FETAL HEART, LIVER AND SKELETAL MUSCLE (SHELLEY, 1964)

Maturity weeks	*Heart*	*Liver*	*Muscle*
31	0·76	0·98	1·63
40	1·01	3·92	2·67

Table 1 shows Shelley's (1964) mean values for the concentration of carbohydrate at two stages of development. The whole body of the human fetus probably has about 9 g. of carbohydrate at 33 weeks gestation and 34 g. at term.

During the early stages of gestation the developing organism lays down no fat apart from the essential lipids and phospholipids in the nervous system and cell walls. Some species, for example the mouse, rat, cat, dog and pig, are born before the deposition of white fat begins, and in the human fetus there is only about 0·5 per cent of fat in the body until the middle of gestation, but then white fat begins to be laid down, and the percentage in the body rises to about 3·5 by the time the fetus is 28 weeks, 7–8 per cent at 34 weeks and 16 per cent at term. The fetus lays down 14 g. or so of fat a day during the last month *in utero*.

All evidence goes to show that fatty acid synthesis is well in evidence in the fetus during the last part of gestation, but the rate of fatty acid oxidation is very low. This fits in with the high carbohydrate "diet", but the problem still remains as to whether any significant amount of fatty acids is transported across the placenta or not. At one time it was believed that only the essential ones were transported from mother to fetus, but more recent evidence suggests that this may not be entirely true[16].

Apart from the γ globulins, which are in a special position, nitrogen is transferred to the fetus primarily as amino acids. It was demonstrated as long ago as 1913 that the concentration of free amino acids is higher in fetal than in maternal blood[35], and this has been confirmed many times since[7,24]. It seems that the l-isomer passes to the fetus more readily than the d-isomer[25], which suggests that an active process is responsible for their transport. The concentration gradient from maternal and fetal plasma is not the same for all amino acids, which indicates that they are not taken up by the fetal body in the same proportions that they occur in plasma. This is confirmed by the work of Southgate (1971), who measured the incorporation of the separate amino acids into the body of the fetal rat.

Räihä (1958) showed that dehydroascorbic acid rapidly crosses the placenta whereas ascorbic acid does not, and he suggested that vitamin C reaches the fetus as dehydroascorbic acid and that this is then reduced by the fetus to the laevo form. Thiamine passes easily through the placental barrier, and the same is true of folate and vitamin B_{12}[2]. Vitamin A has been found in varying amounts in the liver of the human fetus[23,39]. The concentration of vitamin A, and more strikingly of carotenoids, is lower in the fetal than the maternal blood[22]. These authors also found that the administration of large doses of vitamin A or carotene to the mother during the last part of pregnancy produced no increase in their concentrations in the blood of the fetus. Just how vitamin A is transferred to the fetus, and what controls the transfer is not completely clear. We also know very little about the transport of vitamin D, and in view of the new work on the high activity of its metabolite, 1–25 dihydroxy-cholecalciferol[21], the vitamin D metabolism of the fetus becomes a particularly interesting problem for study. Does the fetal kidney make its own 1–25 dihydroxy-cholecalciferol from the precursor, the 25-hydroxy compound, or is it transported across the placenta as an active metabolite rather than as Vitamin D?

We have more quantitative information about the rate of movement of inorganic substances across the placenta than we have about the organic, because the use of isotopic tracers has enabled direct measurements to be made. For example, it was shown that at term 500–1000 times as much sodium reaches the human fetus as it requires for growth[8,12], and almost all of it returns to the mother's circulation. Calcium and phosphorus are not supplied in such generous amounts, at any rate in small laboratory animals. Studies in which ^{45}Ca and ^{33}P were injected into pregnant rabbits and rats showed that the quantities of calcium and phosphorus reaching the fetuses were only just enough to meet their requirements, particularly if the litter was a large one[35,38]. Fetal guinea pigs and rats near term incorporate into their bodies amounts of calcium and phosphorus equal to the whole of the calcium and inorganic phosphorus in their mother's plasma every hour. The human fetus grows more slowly than the rat and guinea pig, and it is smaller in proportion to the size of the mother than the litters of these two species. It has been calculated that the human fetus requires 5 per cent of the total calcium in the plasma of the mother and 10 per cent of the phosphorus every hour during the last 3 months of gestation.

TABLE 2

COMPOSITION OF FETAL AND MATERNAL PLASMA

	Fetus		Mother at term
	Immature	*Full term*	
Na mequiv./l.	140	140	140
Cl mequiv./l.	105	105	105
K mequiv./l.	10·0	6·8	5·0
Ca mg./100 ml.	9·0	11·0	10·0
P mg./100 ml.	14·9	5·8	4·0
Mg mg./100 ml.	2·8	2·5	2·0
Fe μg./100 ml.	40	160	60
Cu μg./100 ml.	200	50	250
Zn μg./100 ml.	300	125	70

Table 2 compares the inorganic composition of fetal and maternal plasma in man. Potassium, phosphorus, calcium and magnesium are at a higher concentration in fetal plasma. The same is true of iron and zinc, but not of copper. The problem as to how iron, copper and zinc cross the placenta is a particularly interesting one. They are all wholly or mainly attached to specific proteins in the plasma. Up to the 6th month of gestation the concentration of iron in fetal plasma is low, but it rises, so that at term the fetal plasma has nearly three times as high a concentration as the maternal[34]. The concentration of copper falls, not rises, during gestation, and fetal plasma has much less copper than maternal. It seems that the difference between mother and fetus is due to the higher concentration of the copper–protein enzyme caeruloplasmin in the mother's plasma, and the concentration of copper not in this form is approximately the same on both sides of the placenta[28]. Presumably it is only the non-caeruloplasmin fraction that passes over to the fetus.

The plasma of the immature fetus has a high concentration of zinc[3,4]. Babies born prematurely have a higher concentration than those born at full term, but even at term the concentration of zinc is higher in fetal than in maternal plasma. All the zinc in the plasma is attached to protein, and how it is transmitted to the fetus is still an unsolved problem.

THEORETICAL ASPECTS OF NUTRITION AFTER BIRTH

Energy Requirements after Birth

At all ages a supply of food is needed first and foremost to provide energy for all the vital processes of the body, both at the organ and cellular level, and after birth to maintain the body temperature sufficiently high to enable these processes to continue at an optimal rate. The amount of energy that has to be expended in order to maintain the body temperature at the normal level is greater at lower than at higher temperatures, and the environmental temperature at which the oxygen consumption and metabolic rate is at its lowest, that is at its basal level, is described as the critical temperature or thermoneutral zone. In the first 24 hours after birth this temperature is 34–36°C, and falls to 30–32°C by 7–10 days of age. Table 3 shows the basal oxygen consumption

TABLE 3

BASAL OXYGEN CONSUMPTION AND ENERGY EXPENDITURE OF FULL TERM BABIES DURING FIRST YEAR (HILL, 1964)

Age	*Oxygen consumption* ml. O_2/Kg. min.	*Energy expenditure* kcal/Kg. 24 h.
0–6 hours	4·8	33·0
18–36 hours	6·6	45·5
6–10 days	7·0	48·3
10 days to 1 year	7·0	48·3

and energy expenditure of full term babies from birth to 1 year, expressed per Kg. of body weight. The values rise between birth and 7–10 days without any important change in body weight, which has the effect of enabling the baby to withstand a lower environmental temperature without having to increase its heat production in order to stay in thermal balance. From about 1 week up to 1 year the basal oxygen consumption remains at about 7 ml./Kg. per min, which is equivalent to 48 kcal/Kg. per 24 hours. At environmental temperatures below the critical one the energy expenditure and oxygen consumptions are higher, and the increase is roughly proportional to the decrease in environmental temperature. The amount of the increase varies from baby to baby, but a naked baby with a metabolic rate of 2 kcal/Kg. hr at 32° may well double this to 4 kcal/Kg. hr if the environmental temperature is lowered to 28°. Part of this increase is probably due to movements of the baby in the less comfortable surroundings, part to shivering and "thermal muscular tone", and part to biochemical processes in muscle and other organs—the non-shivering thermogenesis.

Crying increases the metabolic rate, sometimes to 3 or 4 times the sleeping level, so a baby that cries a great deal will expend more energy than one which spends nearly all its time sleeping or lying quietly in its cot.

The other requirement for energy is for growth. Table 4 shows the calorific value of the increments in protein and fat in the body of the full term baby as it grows from 3·5 Kg. at birth to 10·5 Kg. at one year. The values are only approximate, but they do show how little calorific material is added to each kilogram of body after the age of 4 months or so. In addition to the calorific value of the fat and protein actually laid down in the body, energy must be expended on the anabolic process—the so-called energy cost of growth. We do not know how many calories this is likely to be. Ashworth (1969) and Brooke and Ashworth (1972) working

TABLE 4

ENERGY VALUE OF INCREMENTS IN PROTEIN AND FAT IN BODY OF BABY BETWEEN BIRTH AND 1 YEAR

Age	*Energy value of increments in protein and fat* Total kcal.	kcal./day	kcal./Kg. day
Between 0 and 2 months	9100	149	33
Between 2 and 4 months	6920	113	18
Between 4 and 6 months	3580	59	7
Between 6 and 8 months	2350	39	4
Between 8 and 10 months	2500	41	4
Between 10 and 12 months	1850	31	3

in Jamaica, have shown that children recovering from severe undernutrition and gaining weight rapidly have a considerably greater rise in oxygen consumption after each meal and the value stays high longer than in the same children after they have returned to their normal weight. She suggests that children grow in spurts, a little after each meal, and the rise in oxygen consumption is a reflection of the energy cost of growth. No parallel studies have been made of young babies over the first months while they are gaining weight at a rapid rate.

Table 5 gives some idea of how a baby's energy is expended. It is only during the first two months that as much as a third of the energy intake is accounted for by increments of protein and fat in the body. From 4 months onwards the value is less than 10 per cent.

TABLE 5

INTAKE AND EXPENDITURE OF ENERGY
kcal./Kg. 24 h.

Age months	*Intake*	*Expenditure* *Basal metabolism*	*Increment in body*	*Remainder, for thermogenesis, activity and energy cost of growth*
0–2	126	48	33	45
2–3	116	48	18	50
3–4	106	48	18	40
4–5f	100	48	7	45
5–12	100	48	4	48

It is energy expenditure that regulates energy intake, and babies have to adjust their intakes to their changing metabolic requirements. Because they are becoming heavier they need more and more food, but less and less of it per unit of body weight. The percentage of the total energy value of the food used for growth is high initially but it falls as the baby becomes larger and the rate of incremental growth slows down. This is a far more complicated situation than the one facing the adult, and yet infants seem to be able to take the right amount of food for their requirements from the time they are born, even though these requirements are changing all the time.

Fomon and his co-workers[15] measured the voluntary food intake of 82 infants fed ad lib. Milk was the only source of energy and it provided 67 kcal per 100 ml. Besides showing the variation in volume of milk taken by the children per Kg. body weight, the results of this investigation demonstrated how the food, and therefore calorie intake per Kg. body weight, decreased with age. Most children took more than 180 ml. of milk per Kg., providing 120 kcal/Kg. during the first two months, but few of them accepted this amount after 3 months.

During the last weeks of gestation the male fetus grows faster than the female, and it is well known that, when large numbers are considered, boys weigh more than girls at birth. They continue to gain weight faster after birth and Fomon, Filer, Thomas, Rogers and Proksch (1969) have shown that they have bigger appetites and take more milk in order to do so.

The quantity of food a baby will consume voluntarily is determined by bulk as well as by energy needs, and calorie intakes therefore depend to some extent on the composition of the food and its calorific value per 100 ml. This was demonstrated by Fomon *et al.* (1969), who gave one group of full term infants a relatively dilute formula, and another a more concentrated one. Those given the dilute formula took larger volumes, but not enough to compensate for the difference in calorific value so that the total energy intake was significantly less than that of infants receiving the more concentrated feeding. The babies having the dilute formula gained weight more slowly than those having the one that was more concentrated.

Protein Requirements

The full term baby has about 380 g. of protein in its body[37], and it will put on approximately the same amount during the time it is doubling its birth weight, for there is probably little change in the percentage of protein in the body during this time. Any increase in the concentration of protein in the lean body tissue is offset by an increase in the percentage of fat. If we suppose that the baby weighs 3·5 Kg. at birth, and takes 20 weeks to double this weight, then it is laying down protein at an average rate of 2·7 g. a day (Table 6). In addition to the protein required for growth the baby, like the adult, must have protein for maintenance, to make good the losses of urea and other substances that are produced as a result of protein catabolism and excreted in the urine. The magnitude of this is related to the basal metabolism, and in older children and adults the relationship is reckoned to be 2 mg. N for every basal kilocalorie. It is believed to be about the same for infants after the immediate neonatal period. Just after birth it is considerably lower. If the value of 48 kcal/Kg. 24 h. is taken for basal energy expenditure of the baby over the first 20 weeks, then the nitrogen required for maintenance comes to $2 \times 48 = 96$ mg. N/Kg. day, which is equivalent to 0·6 g. protein/Kg. day. For a mean body weight of 5·25 Kg. (while the baby grows from 3·5 to 7·0 Kg.), the calculated requirement of protein for maintenance is 3·15 g. per day. To this must be added 2·7 g. of protein a day required for growth, giving 5·85 g. a day. A provision must be made for inefficiency of utilization, that is, losses in the faeces, and for losses through the skin. The allowance generally made is 30 per cent, so that the mean protein requirement of the full term baby while it is doubling

TABLE 6

PROTEIN REQUIREMENTS DURING THE FIRST 20 WEEKS AFTER BIRTH WHILE THE BABY DOUBLES ITS BIRTH WEIGHT

Protein for Growth

Total protein in body of baby weighing 3·5 Kg.	380 g.
Total protein in body when weight is doubled	760 g.
Total protein laid down in new body tissue	380 g.
Mean amount of protein laid down per day	2·7 g.

Protein for Maintenance

Energy expenditure on basal metabolism 48 kcal./Kg. day
Minimum daily loss of N in urine due to protein catabolism is 2 mg. N/kcal.
N required for maintenance = 2 × 48 = 96 mg. N/Kg. day
= 600 mg. protein/Kg. day
Mean weight of baby growing from 3·5 to 7·0 Kg. = 5·25 Kg.
Mean protein requirement for maintenance = 0·6 × 5·25 = 3·15 g./day

Total Protein Requirement

For growth and maintenance = 2·7 + 3·15 = 5·85 g./day
Add 30 per cent for provision for inefficiency of utilization (losses in faeces, skin etc.) 5·85 × 100/70 = 8·4 g./day or 1·6 g./Kg. day

its birth weight is 8·4 g./day or 1·6 g./Kg. day. The latest figure that a FAO/WHO Committee on Protein Requirements has suggested for the protein requirement of infants is in fact 1·6 g./Kg. day.

Protein Intakes

The intake of protein depends upon the kind of milk the baby receives. Human milk contains about 1·2 per cent protein, full cream cow's milk 3·3 per cent. Modified cow's milk formulae contain amounts in between these two values. The energy value of human and cow's milk is not very different, so if the baby feeds for energy, which we know it does, then it will get 3 times as much protein if it is fed on full cream cow's milk as it will if it is breast fed. Table 7 shows that if it takes 2½ oz. milk/lb. body weight

TABLE 7

Protein Intakes

Assume baby takes 2½ oz. milk per lb. body weight per day, which is equivalent to 156 ml./Kg. body weight per day.

Human milk 1·2 per cent protein
Cow's milk 3·3 per cent protein

Intake of protein from human milk = 1·87 g./Kg. day
Intake of protein from full cream cow's milk = 5·15 g./Kg. day

day, which is equivalent to 156 ml./Kg. day, then from human milk it will obtain 1·87 g. protein/Kg. day which is more, but not much more, than the calculated requirement of 1·6 g./Kg. If the baby has full cream cow's milk then its protein intake will be 5·15 g./Kg. day. It will retain a little more protein in its body on this higher intake, but it cannot possibly retain the large amounts that the results of some metabolic balance studies have suggested. Much of the absorbed amino acids from cow's milk protein will be catabolized to urea in the liver and this will have to be excreted by the kidneys if the blood urea is not to rise. This is over and above the urea from basal protein catabolism. In the period soon after birth renal function has not matured sufficiently to enable the baby to excrete all the additional urea, and the blood urea inevitably rises. It has been shown that the concentration of urea in the young infant is directly related to the protein intake. Table 8

TABLE 8

NITROGEN BALANCES OF BABIES 6–8 DAYS OLD

	Breast milk	*Cow's milk formula*
N intake mg./Kg. 24 h.	397	598
N in faeces mg./Kg. 24 h.	67	73
N in urine mg/Kg. 24h	115	227
N absorbed mg/Kg. 24h	330	525
N retained mg/Kg. 24h	213	340
Blood urea mg/100 ml	17.5	37.9

illustrates this. It shows the nitrogen intakes, excretions and retentions of babies one week old fed on breast milk or a cow's milk formula made from full cream cow's milk with added lactose[31]. The breast fed babies were taking in 400 mg. nitrogen/Kg. day; they absorbed about 80 per cent of this, and they retained over 50 per cent for the purposes of growth. They excreted in the urine about 30 per cent of the amount taken in the food, which was well within the capacity of the function of their kidneys, and the blood urea was very low. In spite of this, if the urea clearances of these one week old breast fed babies are calculated they appear very low by adult standards, as babies' clearances always do, but this is no indication that their kidneys are incapable of doing the work required of them if they are fed on mother's milk. When we consider that by the seventh day the full term breast fed baby is dealing with more protein per kilogram body weight than an adult who is having 100 g. of protein a day, and his blood urea is low, we realise the vital importance of the stabilizing effect of growth. The babies having the cow's milk preparation containing added lactose had a higher nitrogen intake than the breast fed babies, though not as high as it would have been had no carbohydrate been added. They absorbed more, and excreted twice as much in the urine, but this was not sufficient to keep the blood urea low, and their blood urea concentration was 20 mg./100 ml. higher than that of the breast fed babies. This difference in blood urea would account for 70 mg. of the retained nitrogen, so the amount retained for purposes of growth by the babies fed on the cow's milk preparation was 340 — 70 = 270 mg./Kg. day as compared with 213 mg./Kg. day for those that were breast fed. Mother's milk is just right for the integration of growth and renal function in each species, and it is no stranger that cow's milk should more than saturate a baby's growth requirements for nitrogen than that human milk should not support the growth requirements of the fast growing rat.

The young of some species, for example the pig and the calf, absorb γ globulins as intact protein molecules through the intestine during a limited period of hours or days after birth. The human baby does not obtain antibodies from the colostrum in this way, and it was assumed until recently that the antibodies in colostrum were of no benefit to the baby. However, Bullen, Rogers and Leigh (1972) have shown that human milk, and particularly human colostrum, contains comparatively large amounts of the iron binding protein lactoferrin. This has a powerful inhibitory effect on E. Coli in the intestine, and hence babies receiving colostrum and breast milk are less likely to develop gastroenteritis due to E. Coli infection than those having cow's milk preparations, which do not contain the antibodies and lysozome associated with lactoferrin.

Intakes and Absorptions of Fat

Mature human milk has a slightly higher percentage of fat, 4·5 per cent as compared with whole cow's milk (3·7 per cent), but the amount of fat in breast milk is known to vary considerably from the beginning to the end of the feed. It has been known for many years that babies do not absorb the fat of cow's milk as well as that of human milk[18] and this has been attributed to the difference in fatty acid composition. Table 9 shows the fatty acid composition of the fat of human colostrum and transitional and mature human milk, and of mature cow's milk. Palmitic and oleic acids are quantitatively the most important fatty acids in both milks, together making up about 60 per cent of the total. There is a larger proportion of long chain saturated fatty acids, notably stearic acid, in cow's milk fat, and a smaller proportion of the essential unsaturated acid, linoleic.

TABLE 9

FATTY ACIDS AS PERCENT OF TOTAL FAT IN HUMAN AND COW'S MILK

	Human milk Colostrum 1–5 *days*	Transitional 6–10 *days*	*Mature*	*Cow's milk*
C 8: 0 Caprylic	0·4	0·3	0·3	1·2
C10: 0 Capric	2·2	1·8	1·7	2·6
C12: 0 Lauric	1·8	5·6	5·8	2·2
C14: 0 Myristic	3·8	9·4	8·6	10·5
C16: 0 Palmitic	26·0	23·6	22·6	26·3
C18: 0 Stearic	8·8	7·8	7·7	13·2
C16: 1 Hexadecenoic	2·4	3·2	2·9	3·1
C18: 1 Oleic	36·6	34·6	36·4	32·2
C18: 2 Linoleic	6·8	7·1	8·3	1·6
C18: 3 Linolenic	0·3	—	0·4	<1·0

In the stomach the fats in the food are converted to a coarse emulsion with the aid of the phospholipids, and some free fatty acids are liberated, though they are not absorbed. In the stomach of the young rat a lipase breaks down the lipoproteins in the milk. We do not know whether this is also true of the breast fed human infant, but infants fed on evaporated or dried cow's milk preparations would not have the benefit of a milk lipase. Newborn babies have a low activity of pancreatic lipase, and also comparatively small amounts of bile salts in their intestines[10]. These are necessary for the formation of micelles, the tiny droplets containing fatty acids and the β monoglycerides, which pass through the microvilli into the cells of the upper jejunum. At every point, therefore young babies are handicapped in their digestion and absorption of fat, and the surprising thing is that they are able to absorb the large amounts that they do. The amount of fat taken by a young baby per kilogram of body weight corresponds to about 350 g. a day for a 70 kilogram man. Long chain unsaturated fatty acids are hydrolysed more readily by pancreatic lipase than saturated acids of the same chain length, and this is probably one reason why young babies are able to absorb the fat of human milk more readily than that of cow's milk.

The so-called medium chain fatty acids, C8-C10, are taken up by the mucosal cell without being hydrolysed, so the young baby is able to absorb these well in spite of the limited amounts of bile salts and lipase in its intestine.

Table 10 shows the mean intakes absorptions and faecal excretions of fat by four groups of full-term babies 1 week old. Ten were fed on human milk from the breast, which was transitional milk at this age, ten on lyophilized mature human milk and ten on a dried cow's milk preparation with added lactose[36]. Some results of Fomon (1967) for five babies having evaporated cow's milk are also shown. The difference between human and cow's milk is clear. There is no essential difference between the dried and evaporated cow's milk. The fat of the mature human milk, which had been freeze-dried, reconstituted, homogenized and pasteurized by heating, was not absorbed as well as the fat of transitional milk taken from the breast. Whether it was due to the slight difference in composition between transitional and mature human milk fat, or to the loss of milk lipase in the lyophilized milk or to some alteration in the nature of the fat brought about by processing we do not know, but it makes one wonder whether babies would absorb the fat of cow's milk better if it were not processed but taken direct from the cow.

TABLE 10

INTAKES, ABSORPTIONS AND FAECAL EXCRETIONS OF FAT BY BABIES HAVING HUMAN MILK AND COW'S MILK PREPARATIONS (g./Kg. day)

Food	*Intake*	*Excretion*	*Absorption*	*Absorption as % intake*
Human milk				
From the breast	4·91	0·38	4·53	92
Lyophilized, reconstituted and heated	4·54	0·83	3·71	82
Cow's milk with added carbohydrate				
Dried	4·18	1·55	2·63	63
Evaporated (Fomon, 1967)	4·14	1·62	2·52	61

The fatty acid composition of the fat is not the only thing that determines how much fat will be absorbed. The amount of fat given to the baby is also important. For both breast milk and cow's milk the more milk and hence the more fat taken in the more was found to be excreted in the faeces[33]. The relation between intake and excretion was exponential in type, so that there came a level for each milk above which very little further fat was absorbed. For cow's milk the critical intake at 1 week seems to be about 12 g. a day, for breast milk it is considerably higher.

There is yet another characteristic of fat that determines how much of it will be absorbed at any given level of intake, the triglyceride structure[11]. Pancreatic lipase hydrolyses fatty acids in the 1 and 3 position, but not in the 2 position, so what is absorbed by the intestine are free fatty acids originally attached in the 1 and 3 position and 2-monoglycerides. Table 11 shows the percentage of total palmitic and

TABLE 11

PERCENTAGE OF PALMITIC AND STEARIC ACID IN THE 2-POSITION IN THE TRIGLYCERIDES OF MILK FAT AND LARD

	Palmitic acid C16:0	*Stearic acid* C18:0
Human milk	74	8
Cow's milk	39	17
Lard	84	8

```
CH2———OOC.R1
 |
CH————OOC.R2
 |
CH2———OOC.R3
```

stearic acids esterified in the 2 position in human milk, cow's milk and lard. Palmitic acid, which is quantitatively by far the most important long chain saturated fatty acid in milk fat, is much better absorbed by rats as 2-monopalmitin than it is as the free fatty acid. In human milk fat 74 per cent of the palmitic acid is esterified in the 2 position, but in cow's milk only 39 per cent, and this may be another reason why babies absorb more of the fat of human milk than they do of cow's milk fat. Lard has even more of its palmitic acid esterified in the 2 position than human milk fat, and Filer, Mattson and Fomon (1969) have used this fact to make an interesting experiment. They fed one group of babies on a milk preparation in which the milk fat was replaced by lard, and another group of babies a similar milk preparation in which the milk fat was replaced with lard which had previously been heated with sodium methoxide, which has the effect of "randomizing" the triglyceride structure of the fat so that now only 33 per cent of the palmitic acid instead of 84 per cent is esterified in the 2 position. Table 12 shows that the babies absorbed the fat of untreated lard as well as they did the fat of human milk. The "randomization" of the triglyceride structure of the lard prevented so much of the fat being absorbed, and it is clear that the triglyceride structure of the fat in the milk, particularly the position in which palmitic acid is esterified, is important in determining how much fat young babies are able to absorb.

To overcome the poor absorption of cow's milk fat by young babies commercial firms in the United States and

TABLE 12

EFFECT OF TRIGLYCERIDE STRUCTURE OF THE FAT ON ITS ABSORPTION AND FAECAL EXCRETION (G./KG. DAY)
(Filer, Mattson and Fomon, 1969)

	Intake	*Excretion*	*Absorption*	*Absorption as % intake*
Lard	6·37	0·30	6·07	95
Randomized lard	6·33	1·79	4·54	72

some European countries have developed preparations which contain no butter fat, but have a mixture of animal and vegetable fats so designed that the fatty acid composition resembles that of the fat of human milk. The policy in other countries, notably Holland, has been to use a single oil of plant origin containing far more of the unsaturated fatty acids, particularly linoleic acid, than human milk, but which has been shown to be well absorbed by babies. Linoleic acid which is present in much smaller amounts in the fat of cow's milk than in that of human milk, is sometimes supplied in quite large amounts in these so called "filled" milks.

The Digestion of Carbohydrate

The carbohydrate peculiar to milk is lactose, and human milk has a particularly high percentage, 6·5–7 per cent as compared with 4·5–5 per cent in cow's milk. When lactose reaches the brush border of the small intestine it is split by lactase into galactose and glucose, which are then absorbed through the intestine against a concentration gradient. Babies can also absorb sucrose readily, for there is sucrase activity in the intestine from birth. They can also deal with partial hydrolysis products of starch, called loosely dextrimaltose, and it has been reported that quite young babies can digest cooked starch, for they have the maltase activity necessary for breaking it down. In the normal baby, therefore, the kind of carbohydrate is not so important as the quantity, for if more disaccharide is given than can be hydrolysed it passes on to the colon and exerts an osmotic load which leads to the passage of frequent loose stools. Lactase deficiency presents special problems which will not be dealt with here.

Calcium and Phosphorus

Table 13 shows the total amounts of these two elements in the body of a full term baby at birth[37]. We do not know how much calcium and phosphorus there should be in the body of an older baby, but these amounts must be added to the body while the weight is being doubled if the concentration in the body does not change. Assuming as before that doubling of the birth weight takes 20 weeks, then the baby would have to retain 0·2 g. of calcium and 0·115 g. of phosphorus a day to maintain the concentration in its body of these two elements that it had at birth. Per unit of body weight these values are 38 and 22 mg./Kg. day for calcium and phosphorus respectively.

Table 13 also gives an idea of the intake of calcium and phosphorus from human and cow's milk over the same period of time. For both elements the intake from human

TABLE 13

REQUIREMENTS AND INTAKES OF CALCIUM AND PHOSPHORUS

	Ca	*P*
Requirement		
Total amount in body of baby weighing 3·5 Kg. (g.)	28	16
Total amount in body when weight is doubled (g.)	56	32
Gain in 20 weeks (g.)	28	16
Gain per day (g.)	0,20	0·115
Gain/Kg. day (g.)	0·038	0·022
Intake		
Concentration in human milk mg./100 ml.	33	15
Concentration in cow's milk mg./100 ml.	125	96
Intake from human milk g./day	0·27	0·12
Intake from cow's milk g./day	1·03	0·79
Intake from human milk g./Kg. day	0·051	0·023
lIntake from cow's milk g./Kg. day	0·196	0·150

milk provides just about enough if the whole of the calcium and phosphorus in the milk is absorbed and retained. Table 14 shows that 1-week old breast fed babies were in fact taking 24 mg. phosphorus per Kg. day. Of this they absorbed 22 mg. and retained virtually all of it, for their urine contained only traces. The intake from the cow's milk preparation was much higher. The absorption was 96 mg./Kg. day which was far more than the babies needed. They excreted 40 mg./Kg. day in the urine, and retained 56 mg., which was considerably more than their calculated requirement of 22 mg./Kg. day.

Calcium presents more of a problem because it is not nearly so readily absorbed from the intestine as phosphorus. Table 15 shows the intakes, faecal excretions and absorptions of calcium by babies having the four kinds of milk described in Table 10. The intakes from the human milks corresponded closely with the calculated intake of 51 mg./Kg. day, which was a little above the calculated requirement of 38 mg. Absorption was not quite so good from the treated as from the fresh breast milk, but from neither milk was the absorption up to the calculated requirement. The babies did no better on cow's milk, although their intakes were much higher. One wonders how they manage to maintain the degree of calcification of their bones, let alone increase it. Fomon (1967) has measured the retentions of calcium by babies up to 6 months of age, and his results show consistent retentions of only 20–30 mg./Kg. day from breast milk. Absorption from cow's milk formulae improved as the babies grew older and was about 60 mg./Kg. day between 3 and 6 months. Little wonder, then, that the degree of calcification of the cortex of the long bones, as measured by the calcium: nitrogen ratio, falls between birth and 6 months of age[9]. This happens in other species too, rabbits and kittens for example, while they are living on mother's milk. It should probably be regarded as physiological, and due to the fact that the bones are growing so rapidly that calcification does not keep pace with the formation of new matrix.

We know that the kind and amount of fat in the food has an important influence on the absorption of calcium. Faecal excretions of fat and calcium are positively correlated, with a value of about 30 mg. calcium per gram of fat. Anything we can do, therefore, to improve the absorption of fat will at the same time improve the absorption of calcium.

TABLE 14

INTAKES, ABSORPTIONS AND EXCRETIONS OF PHOSPHORUS BY BABIES HAVING HUMAN MILK AND A COW'S MILK PREPARATION (mg./Kg. day)

Food	*Intake*	*Excretion*		*Absorption*	*Retention*	*Absorption as % intake*
		Faeces	*Urine*			
Human milk						
From the breast	23·6	2·0	0·5	21·6	21·1	91
Cow's milk with added carbohydrate						
Dried	126	30	40	96	56	76

TABLE 15

INTAKES, ABSORPTIONS AND FAECAL EXCRETIONS OF CALCIUM BY BABIES HAVING HUMAN MILK AND COW'S MILK (mg./Kg. day)

Food	*Intake*	*Faecal excretion*	*Absorption*	*Absorption as % intake*
Human milk				
From the breast	43·7	21·5	22·2	51
Lyophilized, reconstituted and heated	52·4	32·2	20·2	39
Cow's milk with added carbohydrate				
Dried	163	136	27	17
Evaporated (Fomon, 1967)	137	160	−23	0

Fat does not interfere with the absorption of phosphorus, so the situation sometimes arises, particularly when large amounts of cow's milk are fed, when the amount of phosphorus absorbed far exceeds the amount of calcium. Newborn babies, particularly premature babies, have a low renal clearance for phosphate, and if they absorb more phosphorus from the food than they can utilize for growth and their kidneys can excrete, then the serum phosphorus will rise, and the serum calcium will fall. This may give rise to hypocalcaemic tetany, and cases which were probably due to this cause have been reported.

Magnesium

Table 16 sets out the calculated requirements and intakes for magnesium. Intake from human milk exceeds requirement for growth by 4–5 times, and from cow's milk by more than 20 times. More than 50 per cent of the magnesium in the food is absorbed and it seems unlikely therefore that healthy babies will be short of magnesium.

TABLE 16

REQUIREMENTS AND INTAKES OF MAGNESIUM

Requirement	
Total amount in body of baby weighing 3·5 Kg. (g.)	0·76
Total amount in body when weight is doubled g.	1·52
Gain in 20 weeks	0·76
Gain per day mg.	5·4
Gain per Kg. day mg.	1·03
Intake	
Concentration in human milk mg./100 ml.	3
Concentration in cow's milk mg./100 ml.	14
Intake from human milk mg./day	24·5
Intake from cow's milk mg./day	113
Intake from human milk mg./Kg. day	4·7
Intake from cow's milk mg./Kg. day	21·5

Sodium and Potassium

There are probably small changes in the concentrations of sodium, potassium and chloride in the body during the 20 weeks after birth, but their magnitude is not known and the values in Table 17 for the requirements of these two elements do not take these into account. This makes no difference to the conclusions. Both milks contain an ample sufficiency of the three electrolytes, and the danger is not a deficiency but an excess. If dried cow's milk preparations are made up more concentrated than the manufacturer's instructions, and the baby has a raised body temperature for some reason and is sweating there may be insufficient water available for the kidneys to excrete all the sodium that has been absorbed.

TABLE 17

REQUIREMENTS AND INTAKES OF SODIUM AND POTASSIUM

	Na	K	Cl
Requirement			
Total amount in body of baby weighing 3·5 Kg. mequiv.	243	150	160
Total amount in body when weight is doubled mequiv.	486	300	320
Gain in 20 weeks mequiv.	243	150	160
Gain per day mequiv.	1·73	1·07	1·14
Gain per Kg. day mequiv.	0·33	0·20	0·22
Intake			
Concentration in human milk mequiv./100 ml.	0·65	1·33	1·80
Concentration in cow's milk mequiv./100 ml.	2·16	4·10	2·75
Intake from human milk mequiv./day	5·15	10·8	14·8
Intake from cow's milk mequiv./day	17·9	33·8	22·6
Intake from human milk mequiv./Kg. day	0·98	2·05	2·80
Intake from cow's milk mequiv./Kg. day	3·44	6·40	4·30

Iron

The low concentration of iron in milk, and its inadequacy to provide for the needs of the growing baby if the concentration in the body and the haemoglobin level are to be maintained, were realized many years ago. Table 18 sets out the problem. The full term baby has a little over 300 mg. of iron in its body at birth, and if it is to maintain the concentration over 20 weeks while it is doubling its birth weight it needs to retain 2·3 mg. per day. Its intake from human milk only amounts to about 0·33 mg. and from cow's milk 0·74 mg. a day, and it will certainly not absorb the whole of its intake, however low the haemoglobin falls. A low concentration of iron in milk is not peculiar to man and the cow. It is true of the milk of all species, and young animals like the puppy, kitten and rat that are helpless at birth and have no access to food other than mother's milk all show considerable fall in haemoglobin concentration during the first days or weeks after birth. One wonders whether this, like the fall in the degree of calcification of the bones, should not be regarded as physiological rather than pathological. Be that as it may, it is customary to give babies additional iron, and manufacturers of many dried infant foods add iron to their preparations. Even National Dried milk, which did not contain supplementary iron until 1970, then had it added.

TABLE 18

"REQUIREMENTS" AND INTAKES OF IRON

"Requirement"	
Total Fe in body of baby weighing 3·5 Kg.	320 mg.
Requirement for growth in 20 weeks if concentration in body is to be maintained	320 mg.
Gain per day	2·3 mg.
Intake per day without Fe supplement	
Human milk	0·33 mg.
Cow's milk	0·74 mg.
Intake per day from formulae containing added Fe	
National Dried Milk	6·2
Ostermilk 1	7·8
Ostermilk 2	11·3
Cow and Gate 1 and 2	4·1
SMA	7·0

Table 19 shows the concentration of iron in a number of infant foods both per ounce of dry powder and per 100 ml. milk made up 16 oz. to 5¼ pints as recommended by the manufacturers. The average intakes per Kg./day from

TABLE 19

IRON IN INFANT FOODS

	Per ounce dry powder mg.	*Per 100 ml. milk made up 16 oz. to 5¼ pints i.e. ½ oz. to 100 ml. mg.*
Human milk	—	0·04
Cow's milk	—	0·09
National dried milk	1·5	0·75
Ostermilk 1	1·9	0·95
Ostermilk 2	2·75	1·38
Cow and Gate 1	1·0	0·5
Cow and Gate 2	1·0	0·5
SMA	1·7	0·85

these milks are also shown. All are well above the calculated "requirement" of 2–3 mg. day, and on the milk containing the least, the baby would be able to maintain the concentration in its body if it absorbed half its intake. Whether the addition of iron to infant formulae has saturated any lactoferrin the dried milk may have contained so that it is no longer effective against E. Coli is not known.

Copper and Zinc

The liver at term contains astonishingly large amounts of copper. The concentration is more than 10 times as high as in adult liver, and the total amount of copper in the liver of the full term baby is about 1½ times the amount in the liver of an adult. In fact liver copper accounts for at least half the copper in the whole body[37]. This copper is in the mitochondria as a specific copper-protein complex, which seems to be a storage compound, not an enzyme[26]. Values for the concentration of copper in milk vary considerably, but all agree that it is very low, and that cow's milk contains less than human milk. The baby would need considerably more than the amounts provided by either milk to maintain the concentration in its body and liver while it is doubling its birth weight, even if most of the copper in the milk were absorbed. It is probable that copper is absorbed more efficiently from human than from cow's milk because of the known interaction between copper and zinc. Human milk contains enough zinc for the growing baby while it is doubling its birth weight and cow's milk 6 times as much. The zinc: copper ratio in human milk is about 4, that in cow's milk is considerably higher. An excess of zinc is known to depress the absorption of copper, and copper deficiencies have been reported in premature babies and older infants who are recovering from malnutrition while growing very rapidly and being fed on cow's milk. The Codex Alimentarius Commission has recommended the addition of copper to infant formulae, but in fact very few such formulae contain added copper at the present time. We know that the store of copper in the liver at birth is drawn upon during the first months afterwards while the baby is living on milk. There is ample sufficiency of it to provide for the needs of the rest of the body during this time and it is a matter of opinion whether it is necessary to provide extra copper by mouth to the full term well nourished baby. Premature babies, and older infants recovering from malnutrition in whom copper deficiency has been reported, do not have the benefit of the store of copper in the liver that the full term newborn baby has.

Vitamins

Table 20 sets out the amounts of the various vitamins in 100 ml. of mature human and cow's milks and the recommended intakes of these vitamins by infants up to 1 year of age. For all except vitamin D one litre of either milk would provide approximately these amounts.

TABLE 20

VITAMINS IN MATURE HUMAN AND COW'S MILK

	Human milk per 100 ml.	*Cow's milk per 100 ml.*	*Recommended intake up to 1 year*
Thiamine mg.	0·02	0·04	0·3
Riboflavine mg.	0·03	0·15	0·4
Nicotinic acid equivalents mg.	0·49	0·88	5
Ascorbic acid mg.	3·5	1·5	15
Vitamin A Retinol equivalents μg.	51	38	450
Vitamin D Cholecalciferol μg.	0·025	0·025	10

The requirement for vitamin D by mouth depends on the exposure to sunlight, and sunlight can provide sufficient for all the needs of the body. However, in Northern latitudes, particularly in winter, it is considered advisable to provide supplementary vitamin D, and most proprietary infant foods contain additional amounts. The dried milks on sale in Britain contain 6·25–8·75 μg. cholecalciferol per 100 g. powder, which corresponds to about 1 μg. cholecalciferol per 100 ml. of milk diluted according to the manufacturer's instructions.

REQUIREMENTS OF THE PREMATURE BABY

The nutritional requirements of the premature baby and how best to meet these requirements presents a new problem to paediatricians. Let us take as an example a baby born at 28 weeks gestation weighing 1·1 Kg. From analyses of the bodies of fetuses and full term still born babies we know the approximate amounts of the various constituents likely to be in the body of the premature baby when it is born, and in the body of a baby weighing 3·5 Kg. and born after a gestation of 40 weeks (Table 21). The gain between 28 and 40 weeks, represents the amount of the various substances laid down in the body of the fetus during the last 12 weeks of gestation. These are the amounts the premature baby

TABLE 21

COMPOSITION OF BODY OF PREMATURE BABY WEIGHING 1·1 Kg. (28 WEEKS) AND 2 Kg. (33 WEEKS) AND OF FULL TERM BABY WEIGHING 3·5 Kg.

Total amount in body	N g.	Ca g.	P g.	Mg g.	Fe mg.	Cu mg.	Zn mg.
28 weeks 1·1 Kg.	17	7	4	0·24	74	3·8	18
33 weeks 2·0 Kg.	37	15	8	0·46	160	8·0	35
40 weeks 3·5 Kg.	66	28	16	0·76	320	13·7	53
Gain 28–40 weeks	49	21	12	0·52	246	9·9	35
Gain 33–40 weeks	29	13	8	0·30	160	5·7	18

must absorb from its food through the intestine and retain in its body by the time it reaches a weight of 3·5 Kg. if it is to have the same bodily make-up as a full term baby. Table 22 shows the total intakes of the various constituents by premature babies growing from 1·1 Kg. to 3·5 Kg. assuming that they take 200 ml. milk/Kg. day. Values are given for human milk and cow's milk. Calculations have been made on the basis of the baby taking 12 and 16 weeks to reach a weight of 3·5 Kg. If these values are compared with those for the total increment in the body *in utero* it is evident that human milk does not provide enough calcium, phosphorus, copper or zinc and only a fraction of the iron that the baby needs. Cow's milk provides more of all constituents, but what has been said about problems in absorption of minerals by full term infants applies with much more force to premature ones, and it seems unlikely that any milk at present on the market would provide the small premature baby with all its needs.

Table 23 shows similar calculations for the premature baby born at 33 weeks gestation weighing 2 Kg. while it grows to 3·5 Kg., assuming it takes 7 weeks to do so. Again intakes from human milk are inadequate for all constituents except nitrogen and magnesium, and for zinc unless 100 per cent of it is absorbed. Again cow's milk appears more adequate, but absorption of all nutrients will be poorer from cow's milk, and it is doubtful whether even babies born weighing 2 Kg. will absorb and retain enough calcium, iron and copper for their requirements.

TABLE 22

REQUIREMENT AND INTAKE OF NUTRIENTS BY PREMATURE BABIES GROWING FROM 1·1 to 3·5 KG. (Assuming mean intake of 200 ml. milk per Kg. day)

	N g.	Ca g.	P g.	Mg g.	Fe mg.	Cu mg.	Zn mg.
Amount laid down in body during growth from 1·1 to 3·5 Kg. *in utero*	49	21	12	0·52	246	9·9	35
Total intake from human milk in 12 weeks	74	13	6	1·5	15	6·2	25
in 16 weeks	97	17	8	2·1	21	8·2	34
Total intake from cow's milk in 12 weeks	200	48	37	4.7	35	8·0	154
in 16 weeks	268	64	50	6·2	46	10·3	205

TABLE 23

REQUIREMENT AND INTAKE OF NUTRIENTS BY PREMATURE BABIES GROWING from 2 to 3·5 Kg.

	N g.	Ca g.	P g.	Mg g.	Fe mg.	Cu mg.	Zn mg.
Amount laid down in body during growth from 2·0 to 3·5 Kg. *in utero*	29	13	8	0·3	160	5·7	18
Total intake from human milk in 7 weeks	51	9	4	1·1	11	4·4	18
Total intake from cow's milk in 7 weeks	141	34	26	3·3	24	5·4	108

REFERENCES

1. Ashworth, A. (1969), "Metabolic Rates During Recovery from Protein-calorie Malnutrition; the Need for a New Concept of Specific Dynamic Action," *Nature*, (*Lond.*), **223,** 407–409.
2. Baker, H., Ziffer, H., Pasher, I. and Sobotka, H. (1958), "A Comparison of Maternal and Foetal Folic Acid and Vitamin B_{12} at Parturition," *Brit. med. J.*, **1,** 978–979.
3. Berfenstam, R. (1949), "Studies on Carbonic Anhydrase in Premature Infants," *Acta paediat. Stockh.*, **37,** Suppl. 77.
4. Berfenstam, R. (1952), "Studies on Blood Zinc," *Acta paediat. Stockh.*, **41,** Suppl. 87.
5. Brooke, O. G. and Ashworth, A. (1972), "The Influence of Malnutrition on the Postprandial Metabolic Rate and Respiratory Quotient," *Brit. J. Nutr.*, **27,** 407–415.
6. Bullen, J. J., Rogers, H. J. and Leigh, L. (1972), "Iron-binding Proteins in Milk and Resistance to Escherichia Coli Infection in Infants," *Brit. med. J.*, **1,** 69–75.
7. Christensen, H. N. and Streicher, J. A. (1948), "Association Between Rapid Growth and Elevated Cell Concentrations of Amino Acids. I. In Fetal Tissues," *J. biol. Chem.*, **175,** 95–100.
8. Cox, L. W. and Chalmers, T. A. (1953), "The Transfer of Sodium Across the Human Placenta Determined by Na^{24} Tracer Methods," *J. Obstet. Gynaec. Brit. Commonw.*, **60,** 203–213.
9. Dickerson, J. W. T. (1962), "Changes in the Composition of the Human Femur During Growth," *Biochem. J.*, **82,** 56–61.
10. Droese, W. (1964), "Besonderheiten der Resorption und ihrer Störunger im Kindesalter," *Klin. Ernährungslehre.*, **13,** 55–70.
11. Filer, L. J., Mattson, F. H. and Fomon, S. J. (1969), "Triglyceride Configuration and Fat Absorption in the Human Infant," *J. Nutr.*, **99,** 293–298.
12. Flexner, L. B., Cowie, D. B., Hellman, L. M., Wilde, W. S. and Vosburgh, G. J. (1948), "The Permeability of the Human Placenta to Sodium in Normal and Abnormal Pregnancies and the Supply of Sodium to the Human Fetus as Determined with Radio-active Sodium," *Amer. J. Obstet. Gynec.*, **55,** 469–480.
13. Fomon, S. J. (1967), *Infant Nutrition.* Philadelphia and London: W. B. Saunders Co.
14. Fomon, S. J., Filer, L. J., Thomas, L. N., Rogers, R. R. and Proksch, A. M. (1969), "Relationship Between Formula Concentration and Rate of Growth of Normal Infants," *J. Nutr.*, **98,** 241–254.
15. Fomon, S. J., Owen, G. M. and Thomas, L. N. (1964), "Milk or Formula Volume Ingested by Infants Fed *ad libitum*," *Amer. J. Dis. Child.*, **108,** 601–604.
16. Hahn, P. (1972), "Lipid Metabolism and Nutrition in the Prenatal and Postnatal Periods," in *Nutrition and Development*, pp. 99–134 (M. Winick, Ed.). New York: John Wiley and Sons.
17. Hill, J. R. (1964), "The Development of Thermal Stability in the Newborn Baby," in *The Adaptation of the Newborn Infant to Extra-uterine Life*, pp. 223–228 (J. H. P. Jonxis, H. K. A. Visser and J. A. Troelstra, Eds.). Leiden: H. E. Stenfert Kroese N.V.
18. Holt, L. E., Tidwell, H. C., Kirk, C. M., Cross, D. M. and Neale, S. (1935), "Studies in Fat Metabolism. I. Fat Absorption in Normal Infants," *J. Pediat.*, **6,** 427–489.
19. Huggett, A. St. G. (1961), Carbohydrate Metabolism in the Placenta and Foetus," *Brit. med. Bull.*, **17,** 122–12.
20. Hytten, F. E. and Leitch, I. (1964), *The Physiology of Human Pregnancy*. Oxford: Blackwell.
21. Kodicek, E. (1972), "Recent Advances in Vitamin D Metabolism. *Clinics Endocr. Metab.*, **1,** 305–323.
22. Lewis, J. M., Bodansky, O., Lillienfeld, M. C. C. and Schneider, H. (1947), "Supplements of Vitamin A and of Carotene During Pregnancy," *Amer. J. Dis. Child.*, **73,** 143–150.
23. Lewis, J. M., Bodansky, O. and Shapiro, L. M. (1943), "Regulation of Level of Vitamin A in Blood of Newborn Infants," *Amer. J. Dis. Child.*, **66,** 503–510.
24. Lindblad, B. S. (1971), "The Plasma Aminogram in 'Small for Dates' Newborn Infants," in *Metabolic Processes in the Foetus and Newborn Infant*, pp. 111–126 (J. H. P. Jonxis, H. K. A. Visser and V. J. A. Troelstra, Eds.). Leiden: H. E. Stenfert Kroese N.V.
25. Page, E. W., Glendening, M. B., Margolis, A. and Harper, H. A. (1957), "Transfer of D- and L-histidine Across the Human Placenta," *Amer. J. Obstet. Gynec.*, **73,** 589–597.
26. Porter, H. (1966), "The Tissue Copper Proteins: Cerebrocuprein, Erythrocuprein, Hepatocuprein, and Neonatal Hepatic Mitochondrocuprein," in *The Biochemistry of Copper*, pp. 159–174 (J. Peisach, P. Aisen and W. E. Blumberg, Eds.). New York: Academic Press.
27. Räihä, N. (1958), "On the Placental Transfer of Vitamin C. An Experimental Study on Guinea Pigs and Human Subjects," *Acta physiol. scand.*, **45,** suppl. 155.
28. Scheinberg, I. H., Cook, C. D. and Murphy, J. A. (1954), "The Concentration of Copper and Ceruloplasmin in Maternal and Infant Plasma at Delivery," *J. clin. Invest.*, **33,** 963.
29. Shelley, H. J. (1961), "Glycogen Reserves and Their Changes at Birth and in Anoxia," *Brit. med. Bull.*, **17,** 137–143.
30. Shelley, H. J. (1964), "Carbohydrate Reserves in the Newborn Infant," *Brit. med. J.*, **1,** 273–275.
31. Slater, J. (1961), "Retentions of Nitrogen and Minerals by Babies 1 Week Old," *Brit. J. Nutr.*, **15,** 83–97.
32. Southgate, D. A. T. (1971), "The Accumulation of Amino Acids in the Products of Conception of the Rat and in the Young Animal after Birth," *Biol. Neonate*, **19,** 272–292.
33. Southgate, D. A. T., Widdowson, E. M., Smits, B. J., Cooke, W. T., Walker, C. H. M. and Mathers, N. P. (1969), "Absorp-' tion and Excretion of Calcium and Fat by Young Infants,' *Lancet*, **i,** 487–489.
34. Vahlquist, B. C. (1941), "Das Serumeisen, eine pädiatrisch-klinische und experimentelle Studie," *Acta paediat., Stockh.*, **28,** suppl. 5.
35. Wasserman, R. H., Comar, C. L., Nold, M. M. and Lengemann, F. W. (1957), "Placental Transfer of Calcium and Strontium in the Rat and Rabbit," *Amer. J. Physiol.*, **189,** 91–97.
36. Widdowson, E. M. (1970), "The Effect of the Amount and Kind of Fat in the Diet of Young Infants on their Absorption of Calcium, Magnesium and Phosphorus," in Collett Nutrition Symposia, pp. 104–116. Oslo: P.M. Bye og Snorre.
37. Widdowson, E. M. and Spray, C. M. (1951), "Chemical Development *in utero*," *Arch. Dis. Childh.*, **26,** 205–214.
38. Wilde, W. S., Cowie, D. B. and Flexner, L. B. (1946), "Permeability of the Placenta of the Guinea Pig to Inorganic Phosphate and its Relation to Fetal Growth," *Amer. J. Physiol.*, **147,** 360–369.
39. Wolff, L. K. (1932), "On the Quantity of Vitamin A Present in the Human Liver," *Lancet*, **223,** 617–620.

5. EFFECTS OF EMOTIONAL DISTURBANCE AND DEPRIVATION (MATERNAL REJECTION) ON SOMATIC GROWTH

DERMOD MacCARTHY

"Like so many people who have been traumatized in the early phase of infancy, he (Descartes) had special rituals of eating and a very cautious diet. Now he had to attend interminable court dinners and he deferentially gulped the six courses of meat which he abhorred."

Karl Stern*

The nature of deprivation

The clinical picture

Hormonal influence on growth

Nutrition and growth

Undereating as a cause of growth failure

Age of onset of growth failure

Growth failure in the higher percentile ranges

Adaptation to smallness

Indigestion

Conclusions as to the mechanism of growth failure

Character disorder in the mother

THE NATURE OF DEPRIVATION

A child may be emotionally disturbed or deprived of care and affection, or maltreated, or generally made unhappy; and yet because of intermittency of these stresses and a tendency in all children to be resilient and to exploit their natural drives in play, aggressivity and activity, their somatic growth may not be affected. When it is affected, we may be sure that a continuous, deep psychological stress is present and moreover that this has been present for a considerable time. The stress is that of being rejected by the mother. In this chapter, it is chiefly the concept of maternal rejection that is understood by the less specific terms in the title, "Emotional Disturbance and Deprivation."

"Deprivation" must not be confused with "Separation". In the latter, there is much emotional expression due to the previous existence of love and attachment, which is then broken. In Deprivation, there is nothing. Feeling has gone and attachments do not exist, except on a very superficial level and of a kind which are not worth the child's preserving. However, separation easily becomes deprivation, unless the parental ties are kept alive with special care and skill and the child receives some maternal warmth and stimulation till reunited. It has been emphasized[13] that much of the harm attributed to Separation is due to the privation inherent in failure to provide such substitute parenting, and also that harm caused by maternal "deprivation in the home" may be relieved by removing the child and providing such substitute parenting. Although this may be true, everyone who works with children in hospitals, or in any setting in which children are cared for other than at home, knows that mothering good enough or continuous enough to prevent such harm is hard to come by. Few are the children who do not feel, even under the best conditions, the initial void caused by the broken ties or, in the case of privation in the home, by the non-existence of such ties. They feel wounded by being rejected, regardless of whether such rejection is imputed by the child or a fact.

In the days when physical care of infants and young children was all that we were concerned about, many of them suffered from deprivation. It was three decades ago[2] that such harm was recognized and the condition which came to be known later as "Hospitalism" and its somatic effects were described. The condition, variously known as "emotional deprivation," "deprivation in the home," "intrafamilial hospitalism," "psycho-social dwarfism" or "maternal rejection and stunting of growth"[20] which is probably as old as the history of man, has also been increasingly recognized.

There are now many new ways of studying the somatic effects of these emotional disturbances, but what is the cause, especially of the growth failure, still remains confused.

THE CLINICAL PICTURE

The signs of good or bad mothering in the first year of life will now be discussed:

A child's health and vigour closely reflects the amount of care and devotion which he is getting. With good mothering, the skin is glowing and gives out warmth and is without blemishes; the muscles are surprisingly strong, the baby notices a lot and responds to all he sees and hears by movement in further pursuit of the object. There is a great deal of spontaneous movement and spontaneous noise. A child given poor mothering has a pale, dull skin, which is cold or dappled; he is flabby; he moves far less. Though he may be alert to his surroundings and follows things with his eyes, he tends not to move his head and body correspondingly, giving a curious appearance of physical apathy, although mentally alert. This has been described as "radar gaze." Such a child will probably be growing at a slower rate and have a poorer weight for length than the well mothered infant.

The most severe manifestation of maternal rejection of an infant is her failure to feed him. Figure 1 shows a six months old infant admitted as a case of "gastroenteritis," who was suffering from nothing else but acute food shortage

* Karl Stern referring to Descartes at the court of Queen Christina, p. 98 *The Flight from Woman*, George Allen & Unwin Ltd., London, 1966.

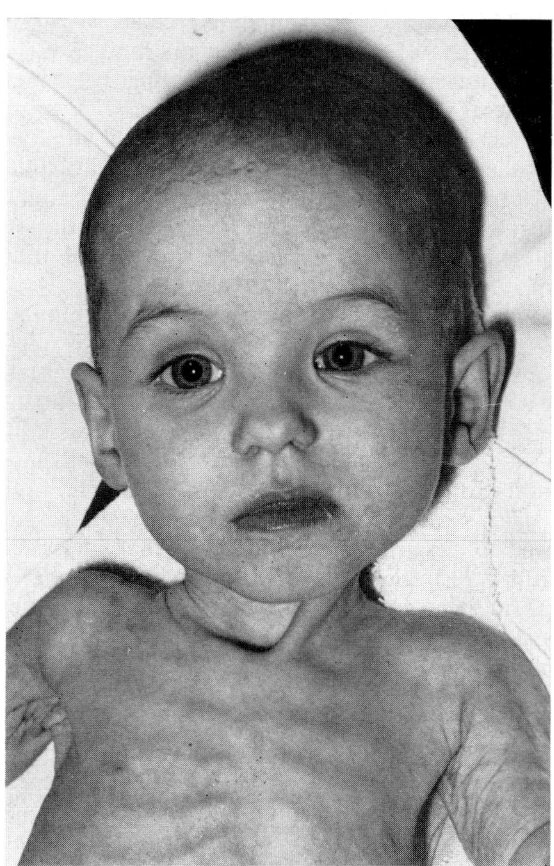

FIG. 1. This baby simply lacked food.

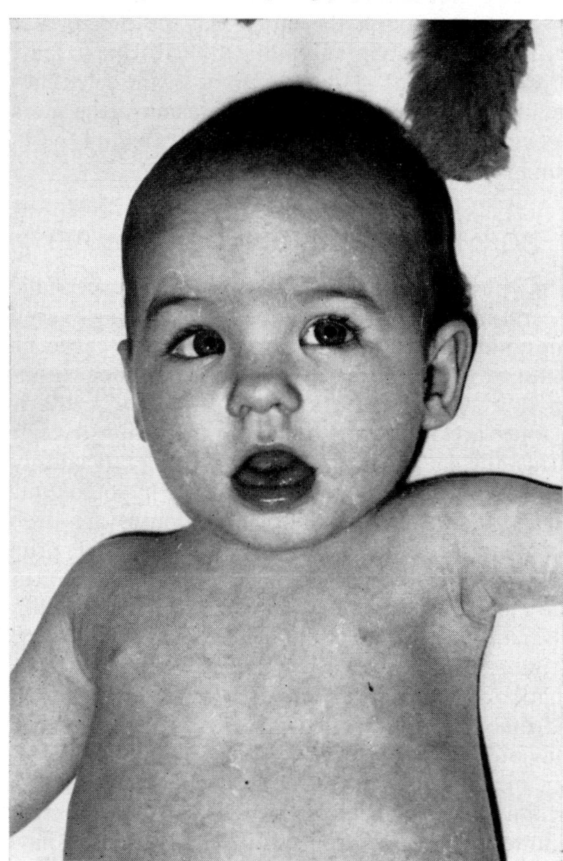

FIG. 2. Same baby after 3 weeks on normal feeds.

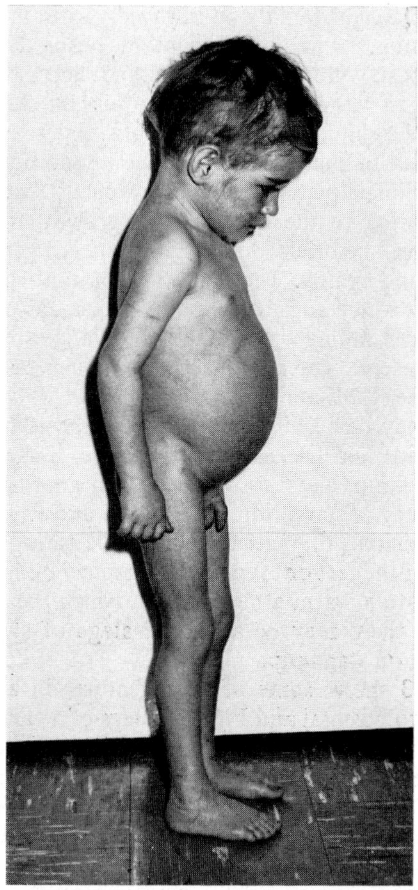

FIG. 3. Age 3 years 9 months. Height 88·5 cm. (34¾ inches). Mean height age 2 years 3 months. Distended abdomen, hair thinning out, many bruises. With acknowledgements to Dr. D. H. Garrow.

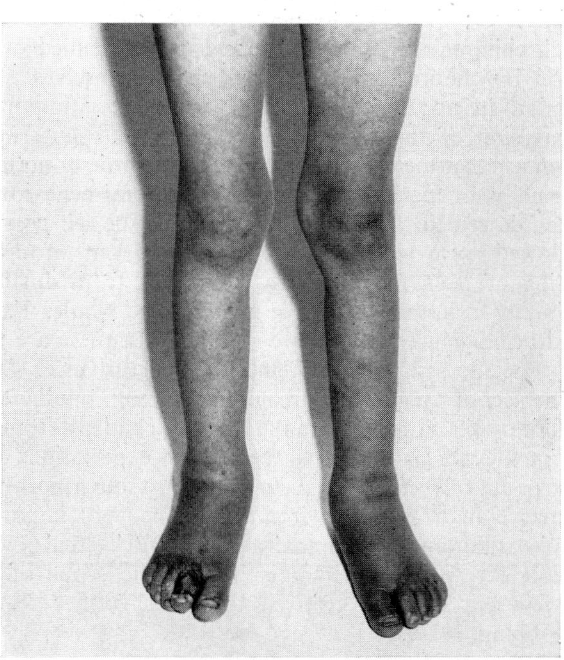

FIG. 4. Acrocyanosis of legs and feet. Both feet oedematous. Early gangrene right second toe.

and gained weight rapidly on full feeds, without diarrhoea and vomiting, from the moment of hospital admission onwards as shown in Fig. 2. To return such a baby to the same mother, without very careful inquiry into her relationship with the child, could be disastrous.

The effect of maternal rejection on somatic growth is part of a clinical picture which shows many features; and before coming to the question of growth, these other features[20] will be briefly described. There is a general air of dejection and apathy. The skin is pale or mottled and tends to be cold, which suggests hypothyroidism, as does also a thinning and falling out of the hair. Patches of alopecia may be present. The abdomen is sometimes enlarged and coeliac type stools are reported.

There may be a quite striking acrocyanosis or pinkness of the hands and feet as in pink disease, if they are very cold and damp, as is also described in anorexia nervosa and in states of starvation. The hands and feet may have minor abrasions, tiny pitted ulcers or ulcerating chilblains. Oedema of the feet or even of the legs may be seen. When brought into a warm atmosphere in which the circulation improves, there may be an initial stage of swelling and acute pain on standing.

Figure 3 shows some of these features in a child just admitted to hospital and Fig. 4 the legs of a child who was several times admitted to hospital in this condition in winter. States of starvation, or the semi-starvation of anorexia nervosa, include such features as lowered body temperature, oedema, loss of drive; and if we add to these, as may well have been the case with this child in Fig. 4, infection and some minor trauma, we have the conditions in which gangrene may easily be precipitated.

The symptoms and behaviour pattern which go along with the somatic effects are important to note, for the failure to thrive in part stems from them. They are catatonia or flexibilitas cerea, which appears to be a symptom of the extraordinary state of passivity and apathy in which the child lives; inability to play, inertia, and solitariness. Such children are easy victims and can be bullied or sat upon by children much younger than themselves. Perversion in appetite and feeding are a very important expression of their emotional disturbance. Quite apart from whether the child is said to be eating little or nothing, normally, or more than others, freakish oral behaviour is often described. For instance, there may be self gorging, followed by vomiting, scavenging food out of doors, eating of pet's food or grass or scraps from dustbins, drinking from the lavatory or gulping food whole. Faecal and urinary incontinence are common but these are very non-specific symptoms of emotional disturbance. Signs of neglect or rough usage are not uncommon[9] but there are seldom severe injuries as in the battered child syndrome.

Intelligence is likely to be below expectations and personality development disturbed[5,6,26] though both may improve in a better environment. The very important subject of brain growth impairment and intellectual poverty secondary to malnutrition is beyond the scope of this review but may be referred to under further reading (Dobbing, 1973).

The want of affection and attachment between mother and child is betrayed by the indifference shown when the two are separated and again when the mother visits the child in hospital. The normal fretting behaviour of the 1–3-year old child in hospital is not seen.

The fact of rejection, unless conscious and admitted by the mother, can only be ascertained by psychiatric inquiry, but it can often be assumed on the basis of the physical findings and very often with the help of the mother's own childhood history. (*See below*, "Character Disorder in the Mother").

When removed from the damaging relationship into an atmosphere which is sympathetic, stimulating, accepting and peopled with friendly adults and children, these patients rapidly lose the aspects described and after a time begin to show typical, so called, "deprived child behaviour," such as shallowly and indiscriminately attaching themselves to mother or father figures or nurses, attention-getting and petty stealing: also gluttonous feeding, gorging if allowed to get at cupboards unobserved, aggressiveness, tantrums, frustration, intolerance and occasional aggressive faecal smearing and bed stripping. At the same time, the clinical picture, so suggestive of malabsorption states, endocrine deficiencies or other organic diseases changes almost in a few days to that of a healthy, happy, well nourished child.

The dwarfism which is the main subject of discussion in this chapter, is often striking, most of the children being well below the third percentile for height. The weight is below that expected for the height, though exceptionally it is appropriate and the child appears well nourished. The condition is not that of starvation, nor of kwashiorkor nor of marasmus, though the latter may be precipitated by acute infection in an infant failing to thrive due to maternal deprivation (Fig. 5). However, some of the scientific data on starvation, kwashiorkor and marasmus, (the literature is enormous) can be drawn upon in discussing the mechanism of the dwarfism in this syndrome.

HORMONAL INFLUENCE ON GROWTH

The phylogenetically old brain (rhinencephalic or "visceral brain") is concerned with correlating every form of internal and external perception (smell, taste, mouth sensations, visceral, sexual, visual and auditory sensations) with the emotions. Neural connections with the hypothalamus are numerous and easy to demonstrate.[21] By contrast the neopallium has comparatively little autonomic representation and connections with the hypothalamus are difficult to find. Our emotional responses are probably still dominated by this relatively crude and primitive rhinencephalic system. While the neopallium "knows" it is the rhinencephalon that "feels";[21] and although such anatomical explanations may be an over-simplification, it is interesting to note how frequently people with psychosomatic disorders and children with the deprivation syndrome display oral and visceral symptoms and primitive behaviour. The anatomical approach has moreover led after much research to the localization of the specific hormone-releasing centres in the hypothalamus on which the anterior pituitary depends. Many clinicians have felt

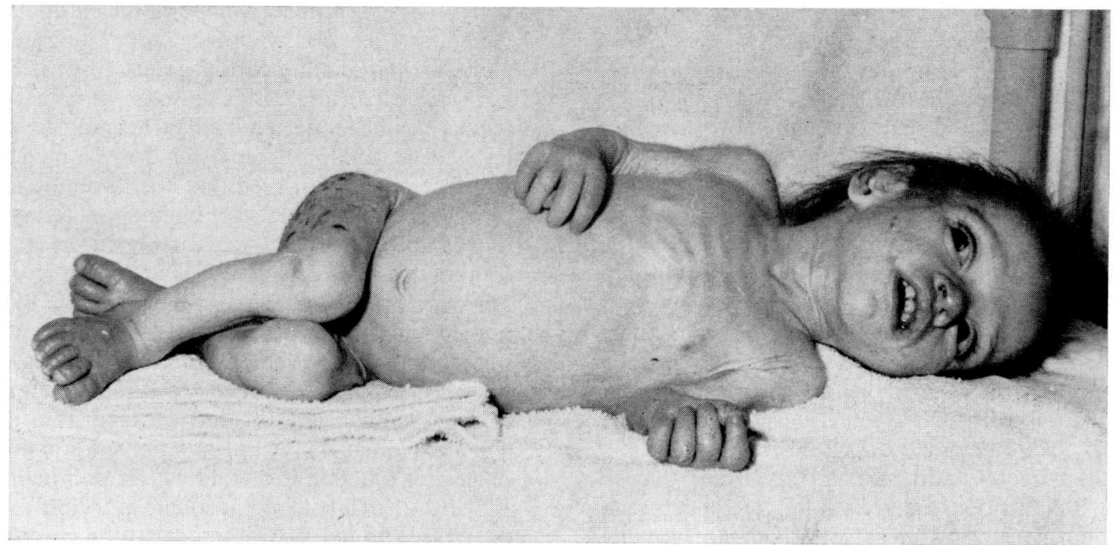

FIG. 5. Failure to thrive precipitated into marasmus by a mild chest infection.

that depressed states in childhood affect growth rates (i.e. in height as well as weight) to an extent that cannot be accounted for entirely by diminished intake of food.[14] This is particularly so in infants to whom adequate amounts of protein and calories have been given in no uncertain fashion and yet present with failure to thrive.[2] Patton and Gardner (1962) who redescribed the maternal deprivation syndrome[23] and discussed its aetiology on the basis of 6 very thoroughly studied children, favoured a theory of emotional influence on the hypothalamus with secondary hormonal insufficiencies as the main cause of the dwarfism. Later endocrinological studies by others have given a good deal of support to this view though the reports have been conflicting. Growth hormone has of course been the one factor to which all workers have chiefly looked for an explanation of the picture.

In one study,[25] 13 children, very carefully selected as typical of the deprivation syndrome, underwent a period of intensive endocrinological study in hospital, then a stay of several months in a good environment away from home, then a repeat of the endocrine studies in hospital Metapyrone responses were low at the start of investigations and in all but one case were still impaired on repetition after a growth period of a few months. However, inadequate dosage and duration of the exhibition of metapyrone is suggested by another author as accounting for this apparent pituitary insufficiency.[18] Growth hormone secretion as measured by insulin hypoglycaemic response was also absent or very low in 6 out of 8 cases tested. On retesting after a period of growth, all 6 children with deficient growth hormone responses were found to respond normally. PBI figures were normal at the start (except for one, unaccountably high) and on return. These workers considered their findings to have demonstrated a diminished release of growth hormone, which was reversible, i.e. functional hypopituitarism. Seven of their 13 children, who were said to have voracious appetites, were not underweight for height (an observation difficult to reconcile with the theory that the dwarfism is due only to undernutrition) and caloric deficiency was therefore assumed not to have been the cause of their dwarfism. These voracious appetites have been seen in settings away from the home and a history of gluttonous feeding at home is therefore to be believed though it may be only spasmodic. The credibility of dietary histories given by the mother has however been seriously shaken as will be discussed under the heading "Nutrition and Dwarfism."

Another study[28] also records deviations in 14 out of 21 cases similarly suggestive of impairment of pituitary function. The responses to hypoglycaemic stress, fasting GH levels, PBI and metapyrone tests were however nearer to those of the normal child than those of the child with true hypopituitary dwarfism.

Deficient growth hormone release after insulin-induced hypoglycaemia was found in 5 out of 7 children with so called "psychosocial dwarfism";[18] however, these patients were able to produce growth hormone at other times and perhaps in response to other stimuli, as shown by their raised fasting levels on admission to hospital. They also had subnormal cortisol responses to the hypoglycaemia stress, though base-line levels were normal and metapyrone responses were also normal. In only one patient was there an associated thyroid deficiency (PBI 2·0) suggesting a true hypopituitarism. The child was severely undernourished and the PBI level rose as this improved. Plasma T4 was in the low normal range in the majority of patients tested. The authors speculate that food deprivation may have caused both the growth failure and the endocrine abnormalities; arguing that malnutrition evoked pituitary hyperfunction which later progressed to hypofunction as a result of hypothalamic exhaustion and insensitivity; for others[16] have found that an elevated fasting level of human growth hormone appears to alter the responsiveness to stimulation tests and have suggested that this is due to exhaustion of the releasing centre or of the pituitary. This is postulated in cases of anorexia nervosa showing unresponsiveness to hypoglycaemia.[22] No other evidence of pituitary insufficiency was found in the "psychosocial" dwarfs except symptomatic insulin sensitivity reactions in three of them, which is suggestive.

The authors[18] considered that they had shown conclusively, in testing a wide variety of cases of growth retardation and controls, that the only children whose growth hormone response to insulin-induced hypoglycaemia was at a diagnostically low level were the true pituitary dwarfs.

In a study of 12 children who had "dwarfism without apparent physical cause" others also[1] have been unable to find evidence for growth hormone deficiency, nor any other hormonal disturbance. The tests used were insulin hypoglycaemia for growth hormone and metapyrone and ACTH stimulation tests for the integrity of the pituitary/adrenal axis.

Looking at it another way it could be argued that if children with malnutrition and growth failure are deficient in growth hormone, treatment with human growth hormone should produce some measurable effects. One generally accepted index of the action of growth hormone on protein metabolism that can be easily measured is a fall in urinary nitrogen on replacement therapy. This has been studied in West Indian children suffering from kwashiorkor and marasmus,[12] in whom, a dose of 0·2 mg /kg./day given in the second week of dietary restoration produced no significant effect on the urinary nitrogen, nor on the free fatty acid mobilization when given in larger doses just before food intake was increased.

The authors consider that, although the adequacy of the dose may be questioned, 0·2 mg./kg./day would probably have been enough to produce a striking fall in urinary nitrogen (i.e. a striking retention of nitrogen) had the condition been really comparable to 'primary hypopituitarism, for in that condition children do respond by dramatic falls in nitrogen excretion on such doses. In the interpretation of the results of growth hormone tests, the following variations of normal response have to be taken into account: (a) fasting levels are higher in infants and young children than in those over 3 years; (b) a high fasting level appears to alter responsiveness to stimulation; (c) responsiveness to hypoglycaemia is less in children than in adults; (d) exercise before the test may falsify the result; (e) stress may act as a stimulation and the tests may be stressful *per se;* (f) different and contradictory responses may be obtained in the same child to different provocative tests; (g) the same child may respond differently to the same test on different occasions. To say that reports on growth hormone levels in children should be taken with a pinch of salt would do great injustice to the elaborate and careful researches that have been carried out in children, but the variations enumerated help one to maintain a balanced view when considering the overall results: indeed authors themselves have had to discuss their results at greater length on account of them.

If growth hormone secretion is not deficient in so-called deprivation dwarfism, how then is it acting? It is perhaps defending the child against hypoglycaemia, mobilizing free fatty acids for energy and diminishing glyconeogenesis and hence conserving protein stores from breakdown. If there is any surplus protein available, the hormone should be stimulating its cellular uptake, promoting cellular multiplication, particularly cartilagenous growth. In kwashiorkor one of the earliest signs of onset if height is measured regularly is a decline in growth, yet fasting growth hormone levels in plasma have been found to be increased,[24] from which it may be inferred that the hormone is playing no more than a defensive role, building materials having run out; and the growth failure is truly due to lack of protein. In anorexia nervosa likewise high fasting levels of growth hormone have been found[22] but response to insulin was poor, possibly due to diminished pituitary reserves or releasing factor depletion. In cystic fibrosis raised levels have been found[11] and here growth materials are certainly in short supply, due to food wastage from the intestine. Thus growth hormone appears to have a highly important protective function in a child who is starving or near to it. In the no-man's-land of "adequate nutrition" as opposed to plenty, we do not know quite what the hormone is doing; for one adaptation to limited food supply is by becoming small and keeping small, and many enzymes and hormone changes are answerable for this.

NUTRITION AND GROWTH

It is sometimes difficult for medical scientists to believe that a process so homeostatic as somatic growth can be influenced by emotional disturbance, but this is without doubt the case, as many reports now show, and is reversible by removing or mitigating the underlying psychological stress. The mechanism of the growth failure is not clear. The question of hormonal insufficiency, in particular of growth hormone, has been considered and a complete explanation is not to be found here. Other possibilities are insufficient food, the wrong food and indigestion. Faulty assimilation has not been demonstrated in any case on hospital investigation, though a coeliac picture with gassy abdomen and bulky stools occurs as mentioned above in the overall clinical picture.

Several writers in recent years have inclined to the view that the dwarfism is the result of insufficient food intake. It is difficult to begin to think about this without knowing what is enough food for an infant or young child, and in particular, what is enough protein. Between conditions of moderate surplus both of protein and calories and conditions of extreme shortage of both of these (or of protein in the presence of adequate calories) there is a wide margin of uncertainty due to the extraordinary adaptability of the body in coping with scarcity of materials. Once growth has ceased in adulthood, the supply of essential proteins for maintenance of health need only be very small. The organs with a fast turnover of essential proteins such as the liver, the marrow, gut and pancreas, can draw upon a general "pool" of nitrogen reserves in the body,[30] and, at times of extreme shortage, protein can be mobilized from structures of the organism less essential to life. The same, of course, applies to children when growth is still going on, but cellular multiplication is likely to be slowed up and growth may come to a standstill. Limitation of cell numbers over a critical period may have something to do with failur to achieve full catch-up growth after a period of arrest. By contrast, short periods of severe malnutrition do not appear to preclude the attainment of normal height, weight and build in later childhood.

The bodily proportions of children with deprivation dwarfism remain infantile (Fig. 6). A 5-year-old still looks like a toddler because his legs are short. The child in Fig. 7 on the other hand, though much under weight from cystic fibrosis, has normal leg length, probably because her failure to thrive did not become serious till she was past 3 years. Long periods of growth arrest are likely to be reflected in leg length. And it has even been shown[19] that leg length can be correlated with expenditure on food. Such periods of arrest are shown in Figs. 8 and 9. The accompanying weight records of these children (Figs. 10 and 11) show incidentally that the period of growth arrest was always associated with episodes of serious weight loss while living at home.

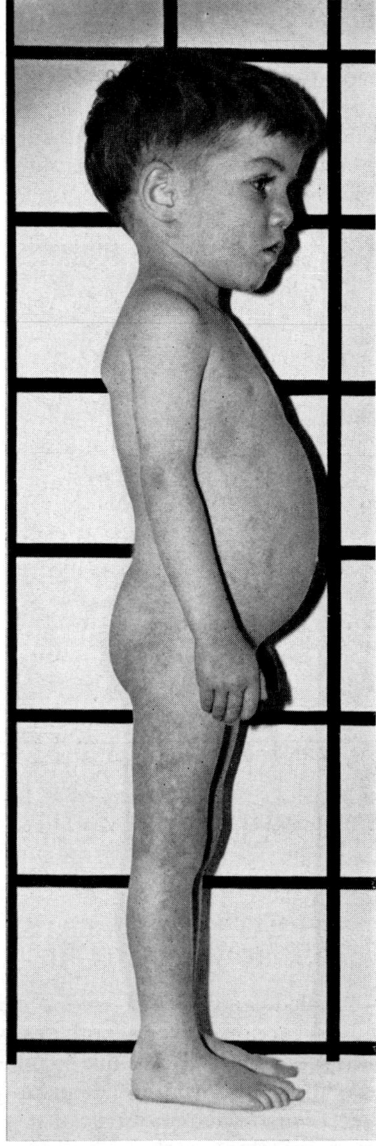

FIG. 6. Age 5 years 1 month. Height 89 cm. (35 inches). Mean height age 2 years 4 months. Enlarged abdomen, short legs, normal sized head, "infantile" bodily proportions.

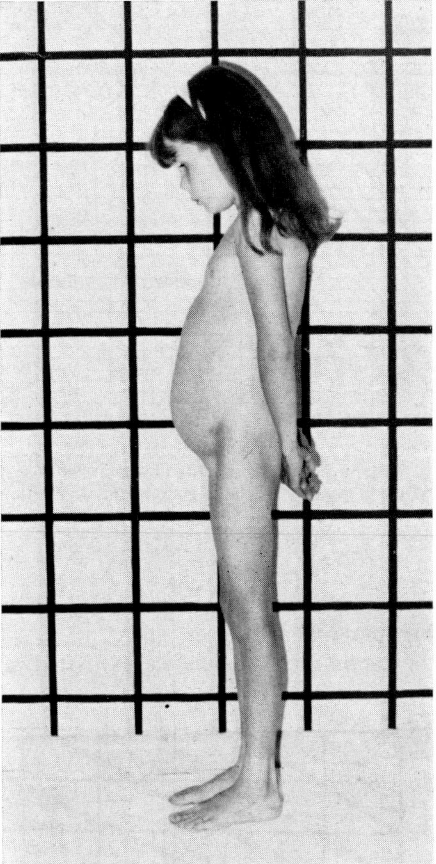

FIG. 7. Cystic fibrosis. Age 8 years 6 months. Mean height age 6 years 6 months. Normal leg length.

The crucial factor in childhood nutrition is the velocity of growth at the time of food shortage. The rate of somatic growth is never again so high as in fetal life; and although it is in fact slowing from fertilization onwards and is still falling steeply from birth onwards the rate is nonetheless very fast for the first three years and particularly in the first year of life.[15] This then is the most vulnerable period for a child to be short of food (Fig. 12). Thereafter the

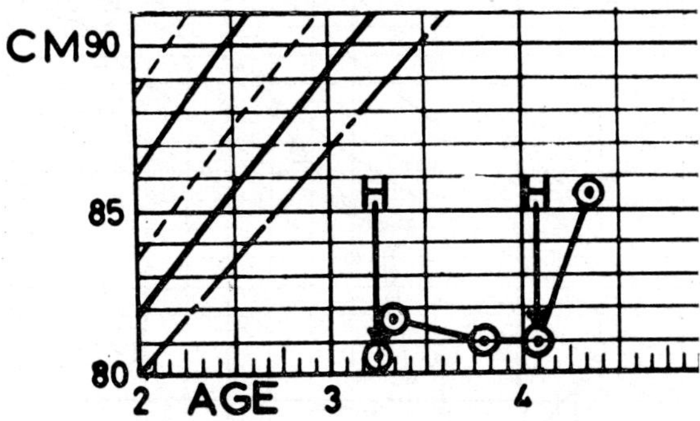

FIG. 8. Growth virtually at a standstill for 11 months. Good growth spurt when kept in hospital (H) for one month and four months.

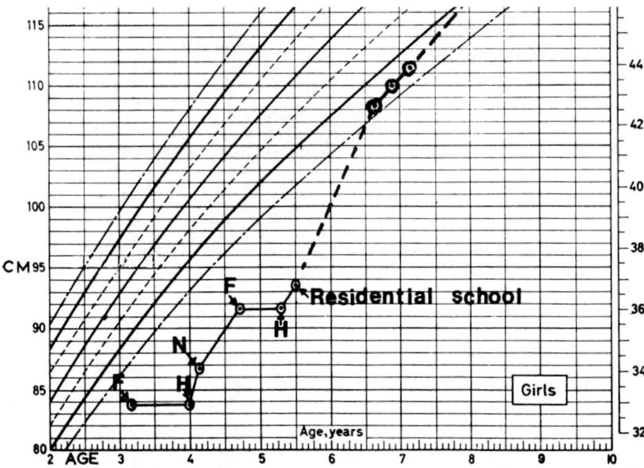

Fig. 9. Pattern of alternating growth and arrest of growth. F return to family. H admission to hospital. N discharge to residential nursery. After discharge to residential school—catch-up growth is seen.

growth rate is much slower until puberty, and slower than in any other mammalian species.

It can be established in some cases that dwarfism has

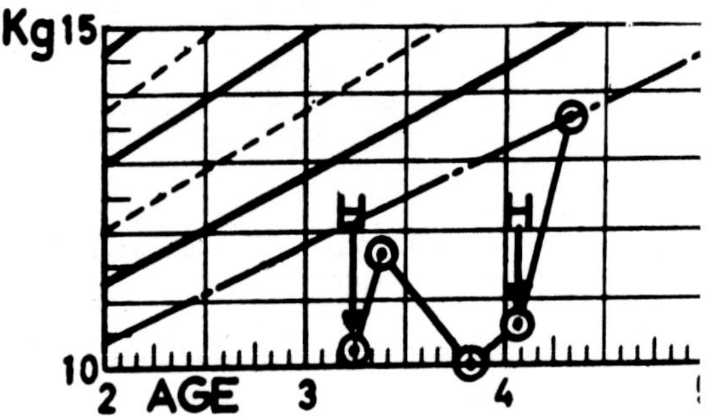

FIG. 10. Weight gained in hospital and lost at home between two admissions. H.

resulted from emotional privation or rejection by the mother, causing a serious degree of under-feeding at this period. In other cases this is a matter of conjecture or appears definitely not to be so; for some children, though

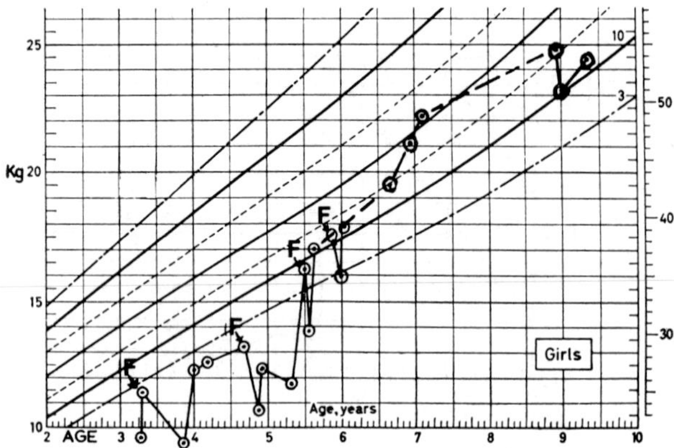

FIG. 11. Severe weight loss every time child returned to her family (F).

dwarfed, have a fair covering of fat and a reasonable weight relative to their height; and it is difficult to believe that they are not getting the small amount of protein necessary for growth, e.g. 12·7 g./day aged 1–3 years (WHO). Nutrition experts have for many years tended to play for safety in their recommendations for children's needs but as time elapses and more data become available, the figures for optimal and minimal protein requirements have tended to come down.[30,31,35,36] It must be remembered, however, that unless the overall calorie intake is adequate the protein may be used for calories and the needs for growth will not be met. The protein sparing effect of carbohydrate and fat has been demonstrated in animals and in man.

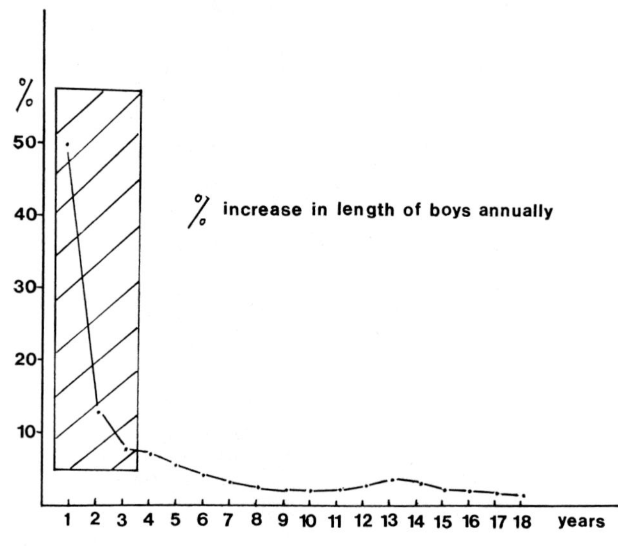

FIG. 12.

(From Hubble D.V. (1957) Br Med J (i) 601).

UNDEREATING AS A CAUSE OF GROWTH FAILURE

In a very detailed study of 13 emotionally deprived infants aged 3–24 months[33] two hypotheses were tested: firstly, that the failure to thrive was due to under-nutrition only; and secondly, that given an adequate food intake, mothering and stimulation are not crucial to thriving and growth. Thirteen infants went through an initial period of study in which they were placed in a windowless room and received basic physical care only. This somewhat ruthless treatment was justified by the authors as being merely a continuation of the depriving conditions they were already accustomed to. They were fed without being taken up and were not talked to or smiled at except by visiting parents. Each infant was fed to a schedule of 140 cal./kg. of ideal weight for length. And to each was accorded an arbitrary rate of weight gain on admission, which was that of the 50th percentile level for the infant's age. Nine of the infants made twofold to sevenfold increases in rate of weight gain during 2 weeks of this treatment. They ate well and did not show any outward signs of being affected by the depriving conditions that went with it. Six of these infants, while keeping their calorie intake at 140/kg./24 hrs., were then "subjected to a high level of mothering and sensory stimulation in the form of fondling, social contact and physical handling." The result was that two maintained the same rate of weight gain, while two increased their rate still further. Two showed virtually no change in weight throughout this test period, nor in the previous 2 weeks of deprivation plus high calories. They were aged 11 months and 15 months and gave a history of persistent anorexia and forced feeding by the parents. All of the 13 children were seen again 2 weeks after discharge and all had reverted to their original very slow rate of gain.

The study continued as follows. Four of the original 13 babies, who were aged 6–12 months, had food brought to them in their own home by a professional worker. The feeds provided an adequate calorie intake. The mothers were told that this was a further attempt to solve the puzzle of why their babies did not thrive. The professional worker merely observed the meal being given and took away anything that was refused, for measurement.

Three newly referred deprived children, aged 11–23 months, whose mothers were unaware of the diagnosis, were added to the cohort. They had not been through the two in-patient studies. In this group, the meals taken to the home were replicas of what the mothers said their children were eating. The professional worker looked on but gave no advice or comment. The mothers were told that the recording of the composition of the food taken was important for the study of the failure to grow. Excellent weight gains were seen in all children during the 2-week period of this experiment. Two weeks later after the observer was withdrawn and meals were no longer sent in, the original 4 babies in the cohort had all dropped back to their previous very slow rate of gain. One of the newly referred children had continued to gain spectacularly, the other two were not traced.

The author's comments on these findings are very important:

"The home feeding program embarked upon as an investigative tool unexpectedly had some therapeutic value. The relationship between the improved weight gain and being fed an adequate diet by the mother was so unequivocal that two of the three mothers whose infants were not hospitalized spontaneously verbalized, after the home feeding program, that they were now aware that they previously underfed the infant and were resolved to correct this. They volunteered that they had slept through meals, permitted the infant to sleep through meals, at times had given them a cookie instead of a meal etc. Each had previously claimed a consistently adequate intake and had attributed the growth retardation to constitutional factors."

In the situation described another factor may have been contributing to the benefits. The mother could feel herself taken care of by the observer who so kindly brought the food, i.e. the mother herself was having a bit of mothering. (*See below*, "Character Disorder in the Mother.")

There must have been something wrong with these babies' reactions as they would normally have made their hunger known by yelling for more. This indeed was said to be so with some of the babies, but their mothers are reported to have withheld more food because they were "afraid it would make him sick" or because they were told by a neighbour that "babies can be overfed." There is a false ring about such statements, however, as the withholding of food by mothers from babies who are crying out for it is most unnatural behaviour and savours very strongly of rejection. The infant in Fig. 1 is an example. The mothers of these children certainly had distorted ideas about feeding, compounded of ignorance, wrong advice, misinterpretation of advice, disgust with eating and probably phobias, fetishes and other unconscious reasons. We do not know whether these underfed babies cried out for food or not. In general it can be said that children with this syndrome show great apathy, dejection and nonreactivity which suggests that they probably have a passive acceptance of being half starved.

The conclusions that one can draw, then, from this interesting experiment would seem to be these:

(i) The children would eat well and thrive when fed by anyone else but the mother and regardless of whether the atmosphere was depriving or stimulating, cold or warm. It was the elimination of the mother that was important.

(ii) The mothers knew what their children ought to be eating and would ensure that the right amount was taken provided the food was brought to the house and there was an onlooker during the meal. Left to themselves, they neglected to feed the child and, it is conceivable, ignored cries of hunger.

(iii) The statements of the mothers of rejected children as to poor intake of the child may be fabricated and are not to be relied on.

(iv) Measurement of length was considered unreliable because of the shortness of the experimental periods, but where weight gain is rapid, growth may be expected to follow. The children were in an age period of high velocity of growth and therefore the authors' claim that "growth failure from maternal deprivation is secondary to undereating only" is supported by these few examples.

Another study[1] has made penetrating inquiries, based on paediatric, psychiatric and social teamwork to discover the truth about food intake of dwarfs in Bristol of the kind this chapter deals with. Their exhaustive clinical, biochemical and endocrine tests on all the children satisfactorily ruled out the operation of pathological causes in the stunting of growth and by inference they also point to underfeeding as the cause. Further pursuit of the children's background and food inventories[26] showed that "the calorie content of the diet as calculated from these inventories is on the average 57·2 per cent of that given by the accepted authorities as normal for a child of like age, and 63·4 per cent of the normal for a child of like height (for 36 cases)."

The work of Talbot, N. B., Sobel, E. H., Burke, B. S., Lindeman, E. and Kaufman, S. B. (1947)[27] which foreshadowed most of what is now known about these children must not be omitted from a review of this kind; for one thing they appear to have been the first to point to "chronic grief" as one of the causes of dwarfism. In studying over 100 dwarfs of all kinds, they were left with a residue without definite organic cause, who numbered 28 boys and 23 girls, aged 2½–15 years. "Generally speaking the nutritional histories of these children," these authors said, "indicated clearly that they were difficult feeding problems and had been so for the major portion of their lives, in many cases, since infancy."

Talbot *et al.* accepted on the evidence of other studies[3] that a child can be in positive nitrogen balance and therefore able to grow on as little as 0·7 gm. protein/kg. body weight/day. On this basis, the widely accepted figure of 2 gm./kg. seemed to them well in excess of the minimum requirements. Where they were able to obtain nutritional data of protein intake of their patients (admittedly an unreliable process as we have seen), the figures were lower than the average recommended at that time by the National Research Council for their ages. But when viewed in relation to their actual body weight, the protein intake was reasonable, ranging from 1·5–3·6 gm./kg body weight, average 2·2 gm. They also established by nitrogen balance studies that protein requirements for growth of an individual child, whatever those may be, may become inadequate if the total calorie intake is insufficient for energy needs, the protein being used for calories and no longer available for somatic growth. They showed that a 6-year-old, thin, dwarfed girl could gain weight on 48 gm. protein (8 gm. nitrogen) per day if her food supplied about 90 calories/kg./day. She lost weight on the same nitrogen intake when the calories were reduced to about 73/kg./day. But she gained weight again on half the previous nitrogen intake (25 gm. protein or 1·9 gm./kg.) when the total calories were raised once more to 90/kg./day.

Talbot *et al.* postulated that a child having once become undersized continues with a basically reduced protein and calorie requirement and that pituitary function having become adaptively reduced, he fails to respond with normal function when the diet improves. Some children, therefore, remain small though apparently well-nourished. Having no potent pituitary hormone, he treated a number of his dwarfed patients with the anabolic hormone testosterone and found that both the well-nourished and the thin ones were capable of good growth and over many months. Could it have acted incidentally as an appetite improver? Lastly, he revealed by psychiatric and social studies that the background of these children could be grossly abnormal and listed the following features: in 21 thin dwarfs—rejection 34 per cent, poverty 14 per cent, mental deficiency inpatient 19 per cent, "chronic grief" 14 per cent, maternal delinquencies and breakdown 14 per cent, no abnormality 5 per cent. And in 7 well-nourished dwarfs: no abnormality in 3, but maternal delinquency or breakdown in 3 and rejection in 1. Here were 4 children with disturbed maternal relationships who were dwarfed, but who nonetheless appeared well nourished. This strongly suggested that consumption of food in terms of calories was not the whole answer to the cause of the dwarfism, and led to the pursuit of hypothalamic and pituitary studies by others in later years, as described above.

AGE OF ONSET OF GROWTH FAILURE

Associated with maternal attitudes, inadequate mothering and family disturbances as a whole, is the question of the time of onset of growth arrest or decline. Many of these children who come under medical supervision because of short stature have been hospital patients in infancy or earlier years, usually with so-called gastro-enteritis or a semi-marasmic condition precipitated by an infection. The case notes may give some clues as to when the baby was at one stage well nourished, and the weight after correction of dehydration will be recorded; but we shall be lucky if the length or height have been recorded, so often is the opportunity of diagnosing the deprivation syndrome missed in such cases and one of feeding mismanagement made instead. However, study of many records[26] has shown poor gains from birth in 20 per cent with failure of a good start in the first few days of life in all of these. In 40 per cent, the decline began at 5–9 months with the changeover to solid foods, a process which at the present day is often smoothed in from birth onwards with elimination of any weaning crisis. In 30 per cent, the slowing began after 9 months, the latest onset being over 3 years. The change from being fed to self-feeding has sometimes appeared critical. In 10 per cent, it was not possible to time the onset.

GROWTH FAILURE IN THE HIGHER PERCENTILE RANGES

Children with heights above the arbitrary "3rd percentile" have been studied in the Newcastle-upon-Tyne survey.[4] "Inadequate appetite" was discovered in 5 per cent of boys and 15 per cent of girls in a 12-year-old population and was associated with significantly smaller heights and weights at ages 3, 5 and 9 years, but these children were not classed by the author as dwarfed. This was associated with early and persistent difficulties of mother-child relationship and frequently with neurotic difficulties in the mother. The word neurotic used in this context covered a very wide description in which the following characteristics of the mother occur, (a) regarded as unduly reliant upon grandparents, (b) regarded as suffering from mental illness or instability, (c) reported themselves as unhappy in childhood. These definitions also fit into the overall description of "character disorder" which is the predominant type of disturbance among mothers whose children are stunted in growth to a severe degree and rejected.[8] (*See below*, "Character Disorder in the Mother.")

ADAPTATION TO SMALLNESS

Waterlow (1968)[32] has spoken of smallness being sometimes a useful adaptation and discusses the complex ways in which the body can deal with protein to preserve health when it is in short supply.

Children with stunting of growth at three years or older, whose mothers have a character disorder, generally with accompanying social and marital problems, are likely to have had insufficient food in terms of total calories throughout this period. They present as dwarfed children. They always have other physical signs and symptoms of a characteristic pattern which are pathognomonic of the syndrome of maternal rejection. They seldom present a picture of starvation and usually have enough on their bones to suggest that they ought to be growing. For this reason, their retarded growth is difficult to explain absolutely in terms of not eating enough food.

INDIGESTION

Unpleasant emotions, anger, hatred, grief and depression affect both appetite and digestion. How continuously and at what age such effects could be operating to the extent of impairing nutrition is uncertain, but two studies of the subject stand out in the literature. The first is that in which an infant had been given an artificial oesophageal fistula in the neck on account of stenosis, through which she was fed by an indwelling tube.[7] The tube also enabled samples of gastric juice to be taken under various conditions. The child became deprived because the mother had a horror of the tube and was afraid to move her and would not nurse her. At 15 months the child was in a state of "depression-withdrawal." During 5 months of hospital care, though becoming socially responsive and outgoing to many, she easily switched into her depression-withdrawal state at the approach of strangers or "bad" people. Gastric juice samples showed repeatedly over a period of 5 months that total hydrochloric acid secretion was consistently related to the total behaviour response of the child. When she was outgoing, playful or aggressive, acid secretion rose; when confronted with "bad" people or in her depression-withdrawal reaction it fell or ceased.

The second example of the effect of disturbing emotions on appetite and digestion was afforded by a study of children in two German orphanages just after World War II.[34] A dietary supplement which was expected to produce faster weight gains was introduced in one orphanage (b) using the other (a) as control. Contrary to expectation, it was the control group who gained weight and grew a little faster during the experimental period of 6 months. Afterwards, it was discovered that the Matrons of the two orphanages had swapped over at about the time of the start of the dietary supplement. The Matron of (b) had been kindly, the Matron of (a) who now came to the experimental group was harsh and harrangued the children at meal times. This could well have caused some achlorhydria and also anorexia, though it is hardly to be expected that the children would have been allowed to leave anything on their plate. One may speculate therefore that through "indigestion," the dietary supplement was wasted. This report, which deserves detailed study, is one of the best-documented demonstrations that nutritional intake need be no guide to growth performance, and that non-nutritional "emotional" factors can be overriding. The occurrence of pot bellies and coeliac type stools in the syndrome of deprivation does suggest that indigestion is at any rate an additional factor in the failure to thrive.

CONCLUSIONS AS TO THE MECHANISM OF THE GROWTH FAILURE

Hormonal dysfunction appears to be minimal and although hypothalamic insensitivity to stress, perhaps due to exhaustion of releasing centres, has been demonstrated in some cases, pituitary performance appears much nearer to normal than to that of primary hypopituitary dwarfs. If there is an explanation, it is probably more in terms of nutrition than of endocrine disturbance or an "emotional hypophysectomy" and it could be stated as follows: mechanisms of adaptation of the organism, which are in fact of immense complexity, can ensure that the body having once become undersized (from shortage of food) tends to remain small by an adjustment of normal enzyme and hormone action, with a modified internal protein turnover and considerable conservation of nitrogen, so that health is preserved on a reduced food intake, but at the cost of slowing of growth. The slowing is most conspicuous if this adaptation has to take place in the first 3 years of life. For the cause of the reduced food intake, we must look to the nature of rejection and the relationship between mother and child in these cases. With relief from the stresses of rejection, interest in food returns, appetite revives and may indeed become prodigious, the mechanism of adaptation is no longer required, growth does then take place and continues at a rate faster than normal, sometimes till catch up growth is complete, sometimes to a level somewhat short of this (Fig. 9).

CHARACTER DISORDER IN THE MOTHER

The mothers of children with non-organic dwarfism have severe personal problems; yet they may be succeeding reasonably well with all their children except one, whom they reject. The rejection may have existed from the moment of conception. If not, then the mother's failure to respond to her baby may go back to the first few days, the first hours or even the first moment of seeing the newborn baby—a moment of truth for all parents, in which there are no defences against the impressions that reach the eye or ear and which may take instant and permanent root in the mind. Feelings of rejection at such a moment may be ineradicable.

The child may also at any times become a scapegoat in the mother's eyes because he reminds her of what she regards as bad or to be rejected in herself, or in her husband, or in the father of the child who is not her husband. Further reasons for hostility may be the child's responding better to the husband than to her, his mothering of the child becoming better than hers.

Mothers with character disorders have disturbed early histories, and have often been rejected or ill-treated by their own mothers. They have an intense need to be taken care of. They have literal concrete thinking patterns and poor capacity for abstraction or of looking into the future. A verbal approach is not useful in trying to help them. They feel criticized. Psychoneurotic mothers on the other hand are easier to help because they have insight.[8]

Penetrating psychological exploration of a few mothers

with children showing non-organic failure to thrive[20] has shown in all of them the expression of profound emotional and physical deprivation apparently extending back through their own early childhood. Also inability to perform on a level commensurate with their intelligence and "a self concept which is that of an extremely damaged and deprived individual, unworthy of the attention of others, seeking the support and approval of significant adult figures in their lives." They tend to fuse together sexuality and aggression and are concerned about the status of themselves in the eyes of their own parents, harking back to their childhood again. Contributions of the husbands of these women to family life were minimal.

On the other hand let it be said of the fathers of these children that, in the experience of the author of this chapter, they certainly do have, unlike their wives, a capacity for concern and have even wept at the removal of the child into foster care when this has been necessary.

There remains one difficult question to answer. Why are not all the children of such a mother failing to thrive? Why is it only one, or sometimes two in a family? It would seem that a special vulnerability of the child enters into the picture. A rejecting attitude is somehow evoked in her towards this child and because of her character she cannot rectify it. If the child is removed, she may even make a scapegoat of another. Other children may be tough enough to develop and thrive in spite of it; this one is psychologically more wounded and somatic effects appear.

But the mania for explanation from which we all suffer should not distract our gaze from the two outstanding facts; the mother has a psychological problem and the child is affected by it. If this is tackled in the right way, the child will improve without the necessity for any treatment whether dietary, hormonal or of other kinds. The characteristic symptoms, behaviour and clinical signs with which these children are presented to the doctor have now been described as fully as any classical disease and they point with certainty to the need for initiating an inquiry into the social background and psychiatric history of the mother.

The essence of the problem is rejection. It may be unconscious and not admitted, though glaringly obvious. It may also be quite conscious, confessed and regretted. It may be subtle and prolonged, but who can be a more faithful reflector of subtle feelings or lack of feelings than a child? Or the rejection may be imputed by the child, when in fact it is due to circumstances. But the mother, or perhaps mother-figure taking her place, is unable to compensate for these circumstances because of her own problems. She cannot warm this child's heart; so from the child's point of view it comes to the same thing. The term rejection is objectionable if loosely used, for as Anna Freud has, with much wisdom said "No child is wholly loved."[10] However, the diagnostic term "maternal rejection and stunting of growth" seems to the author of this review to be the most apt because it indicates the point at which we should try to act. It is also the point at which looking back into the mother's own childhood action might have prevented the perpetuation of a syndrome.

ACKNOWLEDGEMENTS

I wish to acknowledge the help of Dr. Edith M. Booth, Consultant Child Psychiatrist to the Buckinghamshire County Council, Dr. C. Bagg, Consultant Psychiatrist, St. John's Hospital, Aylesbury and Dr. Mary Lindsay, Consultant Child Psychiatrist, Aylesbury Child Guidance Clinic in the study of a number of cases of the syndrome and also Professor Renata Gaddini di Benedetti and Professor Sir Douglas Hubble for encouraging me to believe in the psychosomatic basis of the Failure to Thrive.

REFERENCES

1. Apley, J., Davies, J., Russell Davis, D. and Silk, B. (1971), "Dwarfism Without Apparent Cause." *Proc. roy. Soc. Med.* **64,** 135–138.
2. Bakwin, H. (1942), "Loneliness in Infants," *Amer. J. Dis. Child.*, **63,** 30–40.
3. Bartlett, W. M. (1926), "Protein Requirements as Determined in Diabetic Children," *Amer. J. Dis. Child.*, **32,** 641–654.
4. Brandon, S. (1970), "Epidemiological Study of Eating Disturbances," *J. Psychosomatic Res.*, **14,** 253–257.
5. Cravioto, J. and Delicardie, E. R. (1966), "Nutrition, Growth and Neurointegrative Development," *Supplement to Pediatrics*, **38,** 319–372.
6. Clarke, A. D. B. (1972), "Commentary on Koluchova's 'Severe Deprivation in Twins: A Case Study'." *J. of Child Psych. and Psychiatry*, **13,** 103–106.
7. Engel, G. L., Reichsman, F. and Segal, H. L. (1956), "A Study of an Infant with a Gastric Fistula," *Psychosom. Med.*, **18,** 374–398.
8. Fischoff, J., Whitton, C. F. and Pettit, M. G. (1971), "Psychiatric Study of Mothers of Infants with Growth Failure Secondary to Maternal Deprivation," *J. Paediat.*, **79,** 209–215.
9. Fontana, U. J., Donovan, D. and Wong, R. J. (1963), "The 'Maltreatment Syndrome' in Children," *New Eng. J. Med.*, **269,** 1389–1394.
10. Freud, Anna (1954), "An Inquiry into the Concept of the Rejecting Mother," *Psychoanal. Study Child.*, **9,** 9–74.
11. Green, O. C., Fefferman, R. and Nair, S. (1967), "Plasma Growth Hormone Levels in Children with Cystic Fibrosis and Short Stature: Unresponsiveness to Hypoglycaemia," *J. Clin., Endocr.*, **27,** 1059–1061.
12. Hadden, D. R. and Rutishanser, I. H. E. (1967), "Effect of Human Growth Hormone in Kwashiorkor and Marasmus," *Arch. Dis. Childh.*, **42,** 29–33.
13. Howells, J. G. (1969), *Modern Perspectives in Child Psychiatry*, Chap. 9. Oliver and Boyd.
14. Hubble, D. V. (1965), *Recent Advances in Paediatrics*, Chap. "Disorders of Growth," p. 203, (D. Gairdner, Ed.). London: Churchill.
15. Hubble, D. V. (1957), "Hormonal Influence on Growth," *Brit. med. J.*, **i,** 601–607.
16. Kaplan, S. L., Abrams, C. A. L. and Bell, J. J. (1968), "Changes in Serum Level of Growth Hormone Following Hypoglycaemia in 134 Children with Growth Retardation," *Paediat. Res.*, **2,** 43–63.
17. Kreiger, I. (1970), "Growth Failure and Congenital Heart Disease: Energy and Nitrogen Balance in Infants," *Amer. J. Dis. Child.*, **120,** 497–502.
18. Kreiger, I. and Mellinger, R. C. (1971), "Pituitary Function in the Deprivation Syndrome," *J. Pediat.* **79,** 216–225.
19. Leitch, I. (1951), "Growth and Health," *Brit. J. Nutr.*, **5,** 142–151.
20. MacCarthy, D. and Booth, E. M. (1970). "Parental Rejection and Stunting of Growth," *J. Psychosomatic Res.*, **14,** 259–265.
21. MaClean, P. D. (1949), "Psychosomatic Disease and the Visceral Brain," *Psychsom. Med.*, **11,** 338–353.
22. Marks, V., Howarth, N. and Greenwood, F. C. (1965), "Plasma Growth Hormone Levels in Chronic Starvation in Man," *Nature*, **208,** 686–687.

23. Patton, R. G. and Gardner, L. I. (1962), "Influence of Family Environment on Growth: the Syndrome of 'Maternal Deprivation'." *Pediatrics*, **30**, 957–962.
24. Pimstone, B. L., Wittmann, W., Hansen, J. D. L. and Murray, P. (1966), "Growth Hormone and Kwashiorkor. Role of Protein in Growth Hormone Homeostasis," *Lancet*, **ii**, 779–780.
25. Powell, G. F., Brasel, J. A. and Blizzard, R. M. (1967), "Emotional Deprivation and Growth Retardation Simulating Idiopathic Hypopituitarism," *New. Engl. J. Med.*, **276**, 1271–1283.
26. Russel Davis, D. (1971), "Physical and Mental Stunting," Paper read at International Congress of Paediatrics, Vienna 29.8.71.
27. Talbot, N. B., Sobel, E. H., Burke, B. S., Lindeman, E. and Kaufman, S. B. (1947), "Dwarfism in Healthy Children: Its Possible Relation to Emotional, Nutritional and Endocrine Disturbances," *New. Engl. J. Med.*, **263**, 783–793.
28. Thompson, R. G., Parra, A., Schultz, R. B. and Blizzard, R.M. (1969), "Endocrine Evaluation in Patients with Psychosocial Dwarfism," *Amer. Fed. Clin. Res.*, **17**, 592 (Abstract).
29. Togut, M. R., Allen, J. E. and Lelchuck, L. (1969), 'A Psychological Exploration of the Nonorganic Failure to Thrive Syndrome," *Dev. Med. Ch. Neurol.*, **11**, 601–607.
30. Waterlow, J. C. (1957), "Human Protein Requirements and Their Fulfilment in Practice," *Proceedings of a Conference in Princetown, United States* (1955), p. 48, J. C. Waterlow and J. M. L. Stephen, F.A.O. and W.H.O., Eds.). New York: Josiah Macey Jr., Foundation.
31. Ibid p. 132.
32. Waterlow, J. C. (1968), "Observations on the Mechanism of Adaptation to Low Protein Intake," Charles West Lecture delivered in London, October 3rd, *Lancet*, **ii**, 1091–1097.
33. Whitton C. F., Pettit, M. G. and Fischoff, J. (1969), "Evidence that Growth Failure from Maternal Deprivation is Secondary to Undereating," *J. Amer. med. Ass.*, **209**, 1675–1682.
34. Widdowson, E. M. (1951), "Mental Contentment and Physical Growth," *Lancet*, **i**, 1316–1318.
35. World Health Organization Technical Report Series No. 301 (1965), "Protein Requirements," p. 5 and p. 23. Report of a Joint F.A.O./W.H.O. Expert Group, Geneva.
36. Ibid p. 51.

FURTHER READING

McCance and Widdowson (1968), *Calorie Deficiencies and Protein Deficiencies*. London: J. & A. Churchill Ltd.

Rutter, M. (1972), *Maternal Deprivation Reassessed*. Penguin Books.

Dobbing, J. and Smart, J. L., "Early Undernutrition, Brain Development and Behaviour," in *Ethology and Development*, Clinics in Developmental Medicine No. 47. London: Heinemann.

SECTION II

CLIMACTERICS

6. NORMAL FETAL GROWTH AND THE SIGNIFICANCE OF FETAL GROWTH RETARDATION

ROBERT H. USHER and FRANCES H. McLEAN

Normal fetal growth

Measurement of normal fetal growth
Growth velocity
Incremental growth rate
Extrauterine "fetal" growth after premature birth

Fetal Growth retardation

Pathogenesis of fetal growth retardation
Characteristics of growth retarded infants at birth
Perinatal mortality and fetal growth retardation
Cause of death with fetal growth retardation
Clinical aspects of chronic fetal deprivation

Increased understanding of the causes of perinatal death and brain damage has led to the recognition that fetal growth retardation plays an important role. Idiopathic growth failure during intrauterine life is often associated with evidences of malnutrition and hypoxia, indicating a state of chronic fetal deprivation. Such fetuses have a high risk of fetal death, perinatal asphyxia, and hypoglycemia. They show an increased incidence of malformations.

In this chapter, normal fetal growth will be described and the significance of fetal growth retardation assessed. Diagnostic criteria for fetal growth retardation and the clinical management of affected pregnancies are discussed.

NORMAL FETAL GROWTH

Measurement of Normal Fetal Growth

During the third trimester the normal fetus, given optimal intrauterine conditions, grows at the maximum rate it is capable of achieving. Assuming that measurements of infants delivered at different gestational ages are representative of the fetuses who remain *in utero*, grids of normal fetal growth can be constructed from the infants delivering at each gestational age. As intrauterine growth is affected by socioeconomic and nutritional factors, as well as by family size, smoking patterns, altitude, and perhaps race and heredity, it is best to utilize growth grids developed from the same type of population to which one is applying them. In general, populations with the same average birthweight (about 3,400 g. for most developed countries) have comparable fetal growth patterns.

In Fig. 1 are growth grids constructed from measurements (Table 1) of birthweight, crown-heel length, head and chest circumference developed from a sea-level Canadian Caucasian population of mixed national origins and socioeconomic background.[14] They were obtained from 300 carefully-selected infants including only those from mothers with known last normal menstrual periods, where the clinical assessment of the infant at

TABLE 1

SMOOTHED CURVE MEASUREMENT DATA AGAINST GESTATIONAL AGE[14]

Gestation (Weeks)	*Birth Weight (Gm.)*			*Crown-heel Length (cm.)*			*Head Circumference (cm.)*			*Chest Circumference (cm.)*		
	−2 *S.D.*	*Mean*	+2 *S.D.*	−2 *S.D.*	*Mean*	+2 *S.D.*	−2 *S.D.*	*Mean*	+2 *S.D.*	−2 *S.D.*	*Mean*	+2 *S.D.*
25	650	850	1,050	31·6	34·6	37·6	20·7	23·2	25·7	16·9	19·8	22·7
26	703	933	1,163	32·6	35·6	38·6	21·4	24·0	26·6	17·3	20·2	23·1
27	746	1,016	1,286	33·5	36·6	39·7	22·1	24·8	27·5	17·9	20·8	23·7
28	813	1,113	1,413	34·5	37·6	40·7	22·9	25·6	28·3	18·4	21·3	24·2
29	898	1,228	1,558	35·6	38·8	42·0	23·9	26·6	29·3	19·1	22·1	25·1
30	1,023	1,373	1,723	36·6	39·9	43·2	24·8	27·6	30·4	20·0	23·0	26·0
31	1,140	1,540	1,940	37·8	41·1	44·4	25·9	28·7	31·5	20·9	24·0	27·1
32	1,277	1,727	2,177	39·0	42·4	45·8	26·8	29·6	32·4	22·0	25·1	28·2
33	1,400	1,900	2,400	40·3	43·7	47·1	27·7	30·5	33·3	23·2	26·3	29·4
34	1,553	2,113	2,673	41·5	45·0	48·5	28·7	31·4	34·1	24·5	27·6	30·7
35	1,717	2,347	2,977	42·7	46·2	49·7	29·6	32·2	34·8	25·5	28·7	31·9
36	1,889	2,589	3,289	43·8	47·4	51·0	30·5	33·0	35·5	26·6	29·8	33·0
37	2,118	2,868	3,618	45·0	48·6	52·2	31·4	33·8	36·2	27·6	30·9	34·2
38	2,333	3,133	3,933	46·1	49·8	53·5	32·0	34·3	36·6	28·9	32·2	35·5
39	2,500	3,360	4,220	47·0	50·7	54·4	32·6	34·8	37·0	29·6	32·9	36·2
40	2,560	3,480	4,400	47·4	51·2	55·0	33·0	35·1	37·2	30·0	33·4	36·8
41	2,617	3,567	4,517	47·9	51·7	55·5	33·2	35·2	37·2	30·2	33·6	37·0
42	2,553	3,513	4,473	47·7	51·5	55·3	33·2	35·1	37·0	30·1	33·5	36·9
43	2,446	3,416	4,386	47·5	51·3	55·1	33·2	35·0	36·8	29·7	33·2	36·7
44+	2,414	3,384	4,354	47·2	51·0	54·8	32·8	34·6	36·4	29·5	33·0	36·5

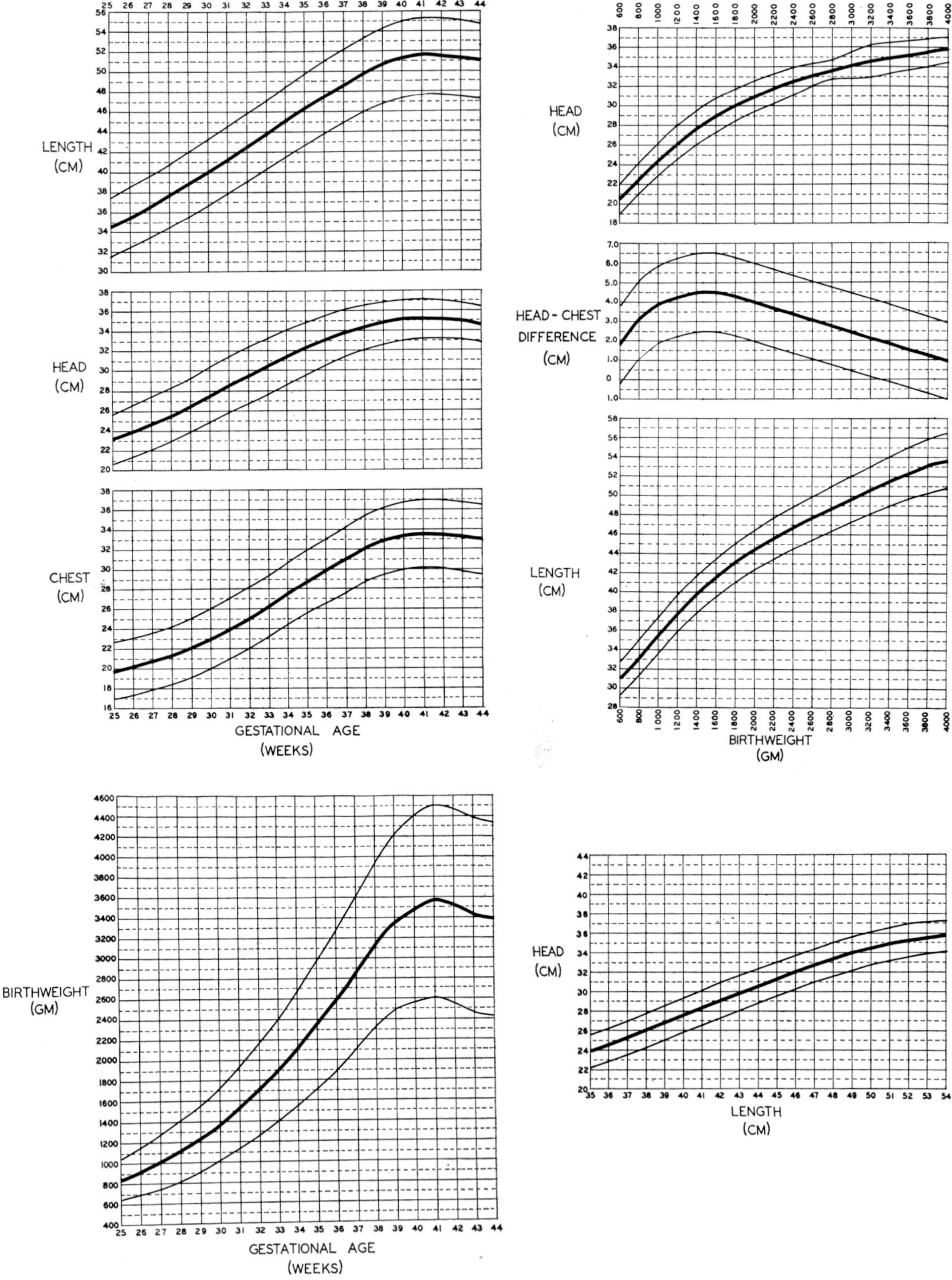

FIG. 1. Smoothed curve values for the mean ±2 standard deviations of measurements of birthweight, crown-heel length, head and chest circumference made on 300 infants of known gestational age.[14]

birth concurred with the known post-menstrual gestational age. The curves represent combined data from male and female infants. Infants with major congenital anomalies, erythroblastosis, fetal growth retardation and infants of diabetic mothers were excluded.

In absolute terms, the fetus grows at an accelerating rate until approximately 38 weeks from the onset of the last normal menstrual period. Fetal growth rate declines from 38–40 weeks and weight loss apparently occurs for fetuses remaining *in utero* more than 41 or 42 weeks. Since, however, the incidence of fetal soft tissue wasting does not increase post-term,[10] and since fetal size seems to be one factor in timing of onset of labour, the decelerating growth rate after 38 weeks may be more apparent than real. Fetuses heavier than average may deliver slightly before term, and those lighter than average slightly after term, producing the apparently flattened fetal growth curve after 38 weeks.

Growth Velocity

Fetal growth velocity increases from about 5 g./day at 16 weeks, to 10 g./day at 21 weeks,[11] 20 g./day at 29 weeks, and reaches a peak of more than 35 g./day by 37 weeks.

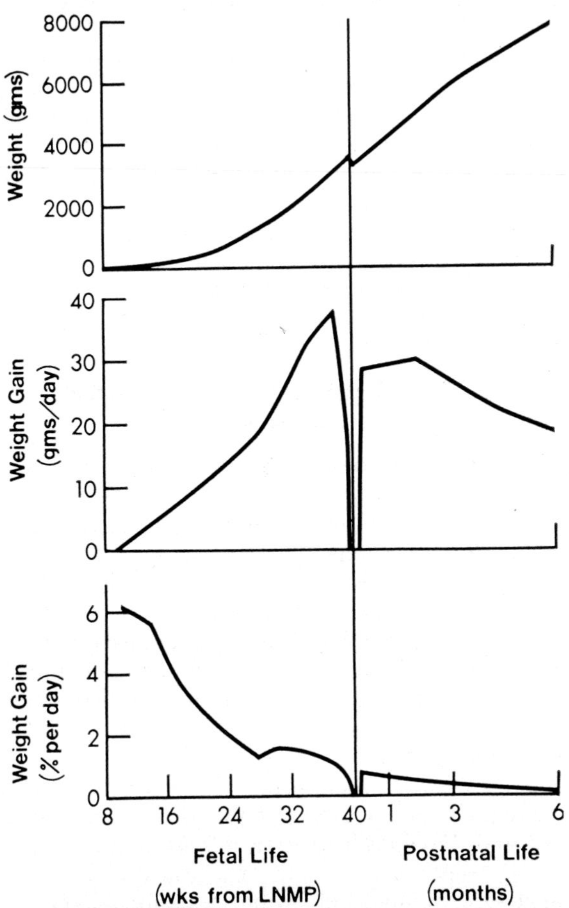

FIG. 2. Smoothed curve values for fetal and postnatal growth of absolute weight in grams, growth velocity in grams per day and incremental growth rate by per cent increase in body weight per day between 8 weeks fetal life and 6 months postnatal life.[3,11,14]

Postnatally, after feedings have become adequately established at about a week of age, the absolute growth rate is 30–35 g./day, and subsequently reduces to 30 g./day by 2 months, 20 g./day by 6 months, and 10–15 g./day by 9 months of age[3] (Fig. 2).

Incremental Growth Rate

When growth rate is expressed incrementally, as a proportionate increase in body weight, a different pattern emerges. The fetus 12 weeks from the last normal menstrual period is growing at an increment of 6 per cent increase in body weight per day. This growth increment reduces rapidly to 2·5 per cent/day by 20 weeks, and 1·2 per cent/day by 26 weeks fetal age. After this the decelerating fetal growth increment changes course, accelerating to a peak of 1·6 per cent/day by 29–32 weeks. There is then a slow decrease to 1·3 per cent/day by 38 weeks.

During the post-natal period, after 1 week of age, incremental growth proceeds at a slower rate of 0·8 per cent/day, and continues to decleerate so that the 6-month-old infant grows at a rate of only 0·25 per cent/day (Fig. 2).

In other words, fetal and early infantile incremental growth expressed as a proportional increase in body weight per day, is a gradually decelerating process from the earliest measureable stages of fetal life until 6 months of post-natal life, with the exception of a phase between 26 and 32 post-menstrual weeks of fetal life when incremental growth accelerates.

Extrauterine "Fetal" Growth After Premature Birth

If it can be considered that, at least until 38 weeks of gestational age, nutritional supply *in utero* is adequate, then the growth rate observed is the maximum growth potential of which the fetus is capable. Infants born prematurely can only be considered to be receiving adequate nutrition after birth when their growth attains a rate characteristic of the fetus who remains *in utero*. Until recent years this growth rate was considered unattainable, especially for the smallest premature infants, for the first several weeks of life. It is now possible using modern nutritional methods to achieve intrauterine growth rates after the first week of life even in the smallest premature infants.

Figure 3 shows the growth rate of two 900–1,000 g. premature infants, one treated in 1958 using dilute formula without parenteral nutrition, and the second in 1972 using concentrated milk preparations and intravenous nutritional supplements such that adequate calories and protein were provided from the first day of life. Each is representative of the premature infants cared for in the nursery at that time. Until concentrated milk feedings and intravenous supplementary nutrition were employed, the smallest premature infants commonly lost 15–25 per cent of their birthweight over the first few days of life and did not regain this weight for 3–4 weeks. They were, therefore, severely growth retarded before they were capable of taking adequate nutrition, and they seldom made up this growth deficit.

The introduction of more vigorous nutritional methods in recent years has resulted in post-natal weight loss being limited to 5–10 per cent and birthweight being regained by 1 week. Whereas infants of 28 weeks and 1,000 g. formerly stayed in hospital 3–4 months to reach 2,500 g., and were then markedly growth retarded, modern methods usually allow discharge in 2 months, with their 2,500 gram-weight appropriate for their gestational age. The long-term effects of this nutritional improvement on brain development may be important.[18]

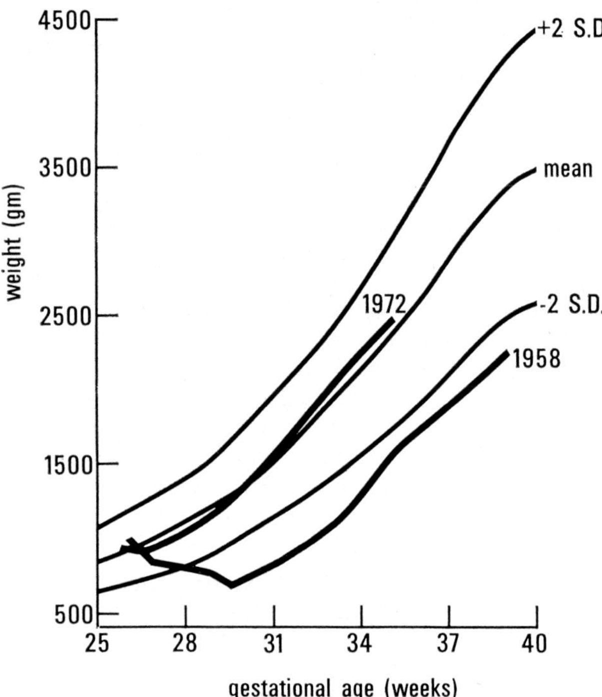

FIG. 3. Individual postnatal weight gains of two premature infants using different nutritional methods compared with expected intrauterine growth rate.

FETAL GROWTH RETARDATION

Pathogenesis of Fetal Growth Retardation

Fetuses who do not grow at normal rates during their intrauterine life should be considered, as their infant counterparts are considered, to have "failed to thrive." The simple fact of small size of a rapidly-growing organism is too often an indication of pathology, or of a poor prognostic significance, to be disregarded as a "normal variant" without careful search for intrinsic pathology or extrinsic cause of the small size. Unless there is some pathological or genetic condition within the fetus to account for this slow fetal growth rate, its cause must be considered to be intrauterine fetal deprivation of calories, oxygen, or other essential requirements for adequate fetal growth. Since very few abnormally small fetuses for gestational age can be shown to have chromosomal, genetic, infectious, or other causes of their small size, most such infants are considered to have been victims of "fetal malnutrition," "placental insufficiency," "chronic fetal distress," or at least of "intrauterine growth retardation."

The common associated finding of soft tissue wasting in infants who are born underweight-for-date, and the decreased skin thickness and thigh circumference even of those who are not clinically wasted, suggest that a state of malnutrition usually accompanies idiopathic intrauterine growth retardation. The lack of carbohydrate reserves and the resultant hypoglycemia often present in such infants, as well as their increased stillbirth, fetal distress, and asphyxia rates, all support the contention that idiopathic fetal growth retardation should be considered as a pathological condition caused by insufficient nutrition and oxygenation of the fetus. This pathological state resulting in the combination of fetal growth retardation, malnutrition, and asphyxia, will be referred to throughout the remainder of this chapter as "chronic fetal deprivation."

It is evident that the cause of chronic fetal deprivation is multifactorial. Toxemia of pregnancy (if severe), single umbilical artery, twinning, severe maternal starvation, and massive infarctions of the placenta provide obvious causes of fetal deprivation for a minority of cases observed.

In the vast majority, however, there are no evident causes, either intrinsic or extrinsic to the fetus, and it is among this large group of infants that certain interesting features are noted. The incidence and degree of cigarette smoking in the mothers is striking, the mothers' pre-pregnant weights (but not heights) are below normal, and the obstetrical history indicates that previous infants delivered to the same mother were usually also growth retarded. Socioeconomic and racial factors play a less important role. The increased incidence in primipara as well as in grand multipara is striking.[10]

Characteristics of Growth Retarded Infants at Birth

Infants at birth who have suffered fetal growth retardation, whether or not they appear clinically wasted, have been found to be smaller in all dimensions than normally-grown infants of similar gestational age. In fact, the anthropometric studies have shown the body length and head circumference of growth retarded full-term infants to be the same as those of similar weight premature infants.[7] Measurements of body proportions do not therefore provide a useful diagnostic tool in the distinction of growth retarded versus premature infants of the same low birth-weight.

Figure 4 shows measurements of crown-heel length and head circumference of 30 growth retarded but not clinically wasted and 31 clinically-wasted infants compared to the mean ± 2 standard deviations of measurements made on normally-grown infants of various gestational ages.

Both head circumference and length are markedly decreased when compared to infants of the same gestational age, but similar to (premature) infants of the same birth-weight. Similar findings have been reported in a larger study by Vandenberg and Yerulshalmy.[16] It is therefore to be expected, as shown in Figs. 5 and 6, that the ratios of weight-to-length or of weight-to-head circumference of infants with fetal growth retardation are similar to those of infants of normal weight for gestational age.

Growth-retarded infants, whether or not they appear clinically wasted, have decreased subcutaneous tissue, as shown by measurement of double skin thickness (Fig. 7), not only when compared with like-gestation controls, but even when compared with more premature infants of the same birthweight.

Epiphyseal ossification of the knee has been shown to

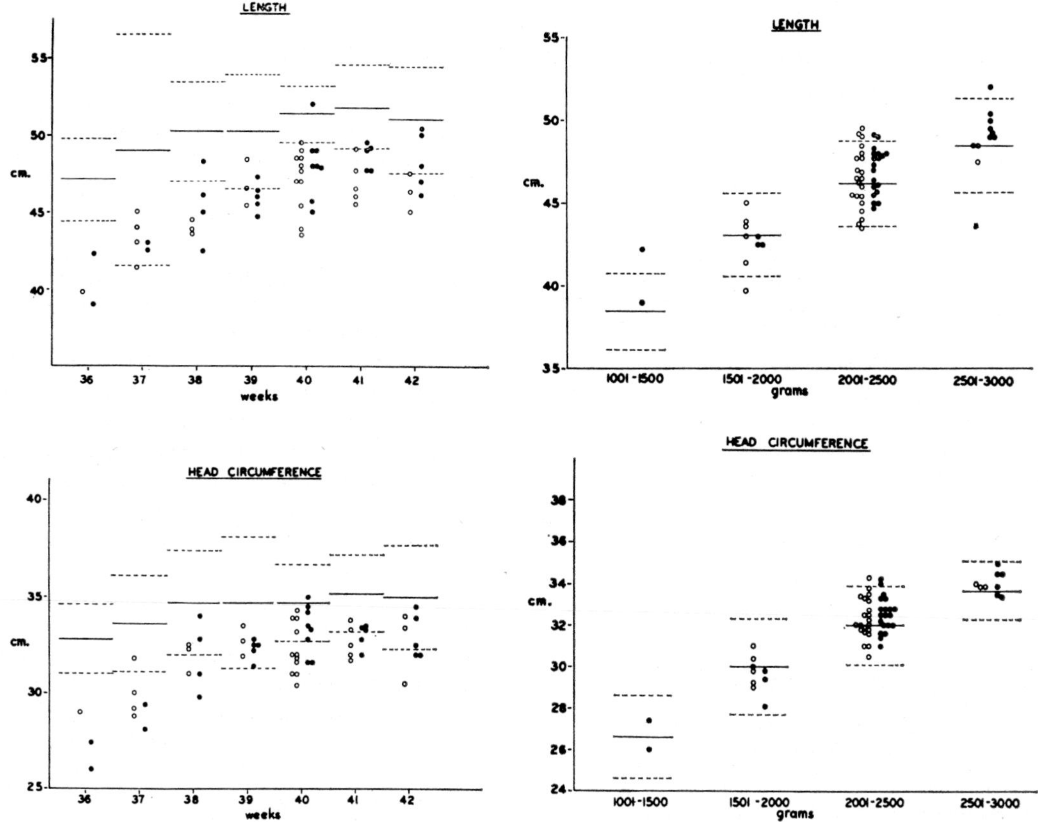

FIG. 4. Measurements of crown-heel length and head circumference of 30 growth retarded but not clinically wasted (○) and 31 growth retarded and clinically wasted infants (●) compared to normal values. Solid lines represent normal mean values; broken lines above and below denote 2 standard deviations from the mean. Reprinted from Biol. Neonate 1970.[7]

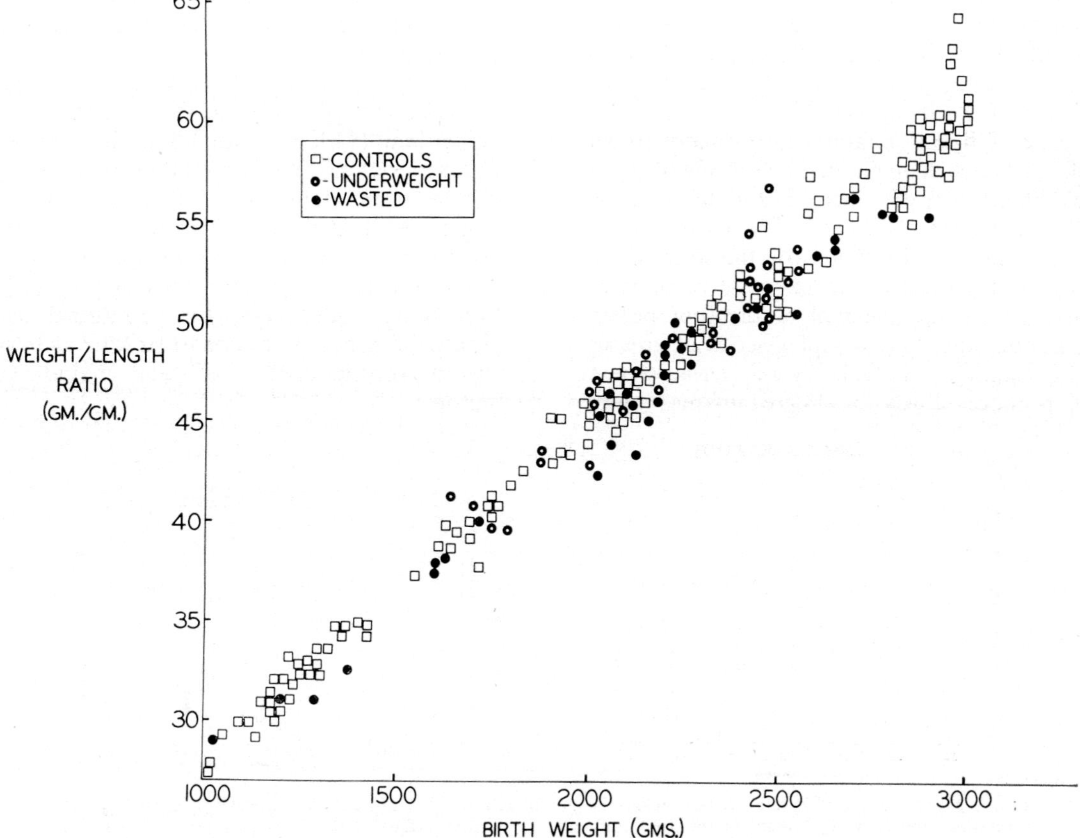

FIG. 5. Weight-length ratio of 35 growth retarded infants who were both underweight for gestational age and clinically wasted (●), 31 infants who were underweight but not clinically wasted (○), and 144 control infants who were appropriate weight for gestational age (□), plotted against birthweight. Reprinted from Pediat. Clin. North Am., 1966.[13]

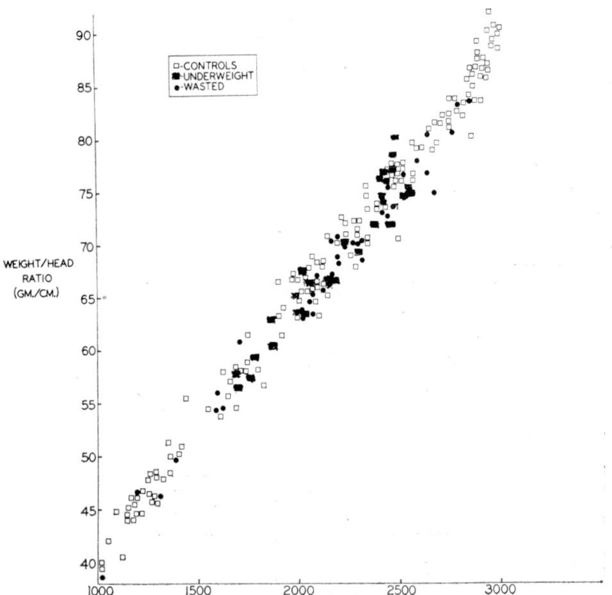

FIG. 6. Weight-head circumference ratio of 35 growth retarded infants who were both underweight for gestational age and clinically wasted (●), 31 infants who were underweight but not clinically wasted (■), and 142 control infants who were appropriate weight for gestational age (□), plotted against birthweight. Reprinted from Pediat. Clin. North Am., 1966.[13]

be delayed in fetuses suffering intrauterine growth retardation. In normally-grown fetuses, the distal femoral ephiphyses calcifies by a gestational age of 36 weeks and the proximal tibial epiphyses by 38 weeks. Growth-retarded fetuses usually show lack of calcification of epiphyses until 38–40 weeks or later.[9]

Growth-retarded full-term infants and normally-grown premature infants can be distinguished by specific physical features which differentiate with increasing gestational age but are unaffected by growth rate.[13] The most reliable of these characteristics are the creases on the soles of the feet which progress down the sole from one or two creases running transversely across the ball of the foot before 36 weeks gestational age, to a complex series of creases over the entire length of the sole by full term. These creases develop more slowly in Negro infants.[1] The texture of the hair on the head changes from a fuzzy or wooly texture at 36 weeks to single silky strands at term. The cartilage in the ear develops during the last weeks of pregnancy, so that by 40 weeks the ear stands out from the head with distinct ridges of cartilage. In male infants, the testes gradually descend after 36 weeks from the lower inguinal canal into the scrotum and the scrotum gradually becomes larger, more pendulous, and covered with rugae. The breast nodule, which is not palpable before 33 weeks gestational age, is 3 mm. or less at 36 weeks, and increases to an average of 7 mm. by 40 weeks. Infants underweight for gestational age may have retarded breast development so that although large breast nodules always indicate full term, small nodules may indicate either prematurity or intrauterine growth retardation.

Since more than 90 per cent of growth-retarded fetuses deliver at or near full term, their gestational age can usually be corroborated by the demonstration of simple physical features of full maturity. Features of a full-term infant associated with a low birthweight are sufficient to establish the diagnosis of fetal growth retardation in most instances. Neurological signs have also been shown to be good indicators of maturity in healthy newborn infants.[2]

At autopsy, growth of some organs is found to be more markedly affected by intrauterine growth retardation than others. Liver and thymus are smaller in fetuses and infants with marked intrauterine growth retardation. These organs are lighter in weight than those of similar weight normally-grown fetuses. The brain appears to be relatively spared, being slightly heavier than normally-grown fetuses of the same weight although still markedly underweight for gestational age.[6]

Comparison of brain weight to liver weight at autopsy provides a rough index of fetal growth retardation. The upper limit (94th percentile) brain-to-liver ratio was found in a series of 133 perinatal autopsies of appropriate weight for gestation infants to be 5·0/1 prior to 32 weeks, decreasing to 3·5/1 at term. This limit was exceeded in 12/25 (48 per cent) of growth-retarded infants who died. Average brain-to-liver weight ratios were slightly higher in infants who were underweight for gestational age (Table 2). These differences were not so striking as to provide clear-cut diagnostic criteria of fetal malnutrition, even at autopsy.

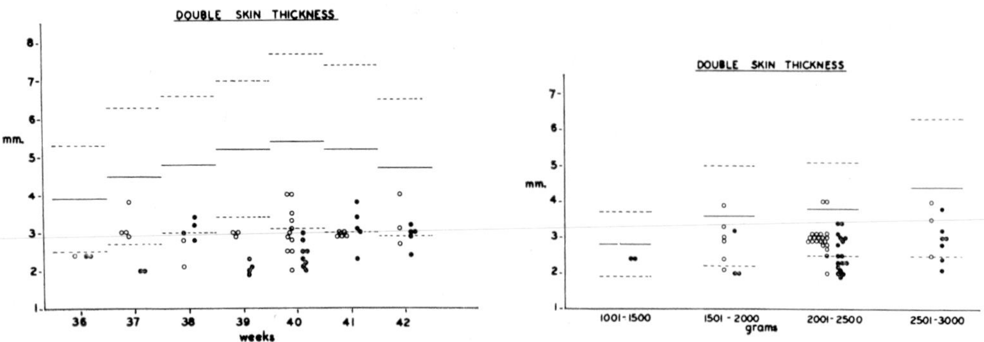

FIG. 7. Measurements of double skin thickness of 30 growth-retarded but not clinically wasted (○) and 31 growth retarded and clinically wasted infants (●) compared to normal values. Solid lines represent normal mean values; broken lines above and below denote 2 standard deviations from the mean. Reprinted from Biol. Neonate 1970.[7]

TABLE 2

BRAIN WEIGHT AND LIVER WEIGHT WITH FETAL GROWTH RETARDATION [INFANTS OF 35 WEEKS' GESTATION AND OVER] (MEAN VALUES)

	Number	*Body Weight*	*Brain Weight*	*Liver Weight*	*Brain/Liver Ratio*
	Not Growth Retarded				
Neonatal deaths	31	3,059	365·7	123·0	2·97
Stillbirths	27	3,480	405·7	163·8	2·48
	Fetal Growth Retardation				
Neonatal deaths	18	2,157 (−29·5%)	302·2 (−17·4%)	80·2 (−34·8%)	3·77
Stillbirths	8	2,240 (−35·6%)	299·8 (−26·2%)	99·3 (−39·4%)	3·02

The autopsy is more valuable in ascertaining gestational age by renal differentiation. The subcapsular nephrogenic zone of glomeruli in the process of formation is usually clearly identifiable until 34 weeks, and not present after 36 weeks of gestation (Table 3). This provides firm evidence

TABLE 3

NEPHROGENIC ZONE AND GESTATIONAL AGE

Gestational Age (Completed Weeks)	*Present*	*Borderline*	*Absent*
Less than 33	20	0	0
33–34	4	1	2
35–36	1	2	7
More than 36	0	1	19

to distinguish which low birthweight perinatal deaths are premature, and which are underweight full-term infants.

Perinatal Mortality and Fetal Growth Retardation

The risk of perinatal death rises incrementally with progressive degrees of fetal growth retardation. In order to assess this risk quantitatively, 44,256 consecutive over-500 gram births at the Royal Victoria Hospital, Montreal, were analysed for a 14-year period ending in 1971.

Birthweight was related to gestational age at time of birth in livebirths, and at time of fetal death in stillbirths. Fetal growth rate was assessed in terms of standard deviations from the mean, according to the fetal growth curves described above, developed from the same hospital population.[14] A sample of 6,109 consecutive births over 500 g. was used to determine the distribution of all births by fetal growth rate in three gestational categories: less than 34 weeks, 34–36 weeks and 37–43 completed weeks. For perinatal deaths, fetal growth rate distribution was determined from all of the deaths of known gestational age. Extrapolations of these samples (which included 14 per cent of all births, 79 per cent of all deaths) were then made to provide mortality rates according to fetal growth rate at each gestational interval for the whole population of 44,256 births and 952 perinatal deaths (Figs. 8, 9, 10).

The population analysed was with few exceptions Caucasian, received antenatal care from the first trimester,

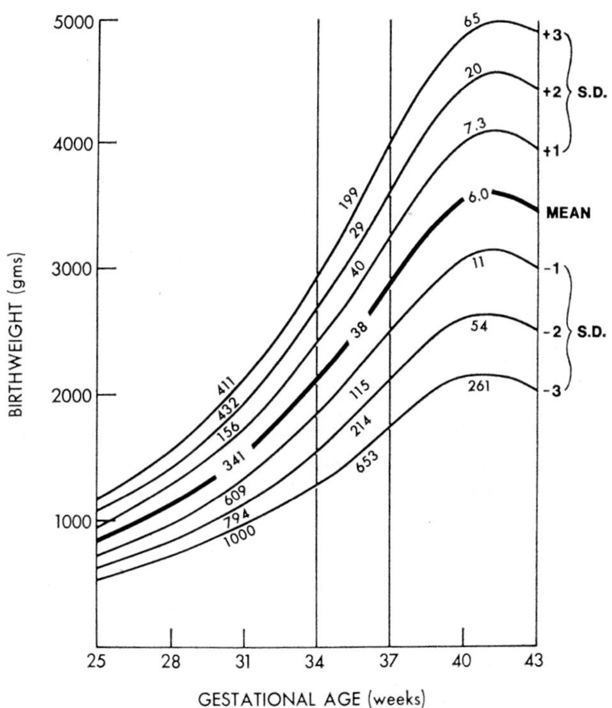

FIG. 8. Perinatal mortality rates per 1,000 births over 500 g. for infants with different growth rates assessed in terms of standard deviation from the mean of normal values of birthweight for gestational age in three gestational categories.

and was provided neonatal evaluation and care by the same team of neonatologists. Gestational age was calculated from the onset of the last normal menstrual period and was always accepted as valid unless clinical signs of gestational age were grossly disparate. Premature induction for fetal growth retardation was introduced during the last half of the period, and contributed to a somewhat lower mortality associated with the condition than would otherwise have been obtained.[17]

Perinatal mortality was 15·9/1,000 for infants within

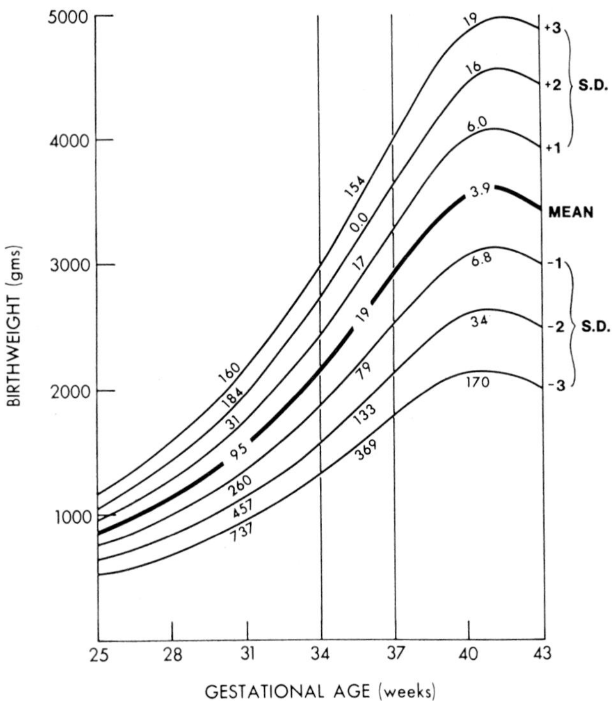

FIG. 9. Stillbirth rates per 1,000 births over 500 g. for infants with different growth rates assessed in terms of standard deviations from the mean of normal values of birthweight for gestational age in three gestational categories.

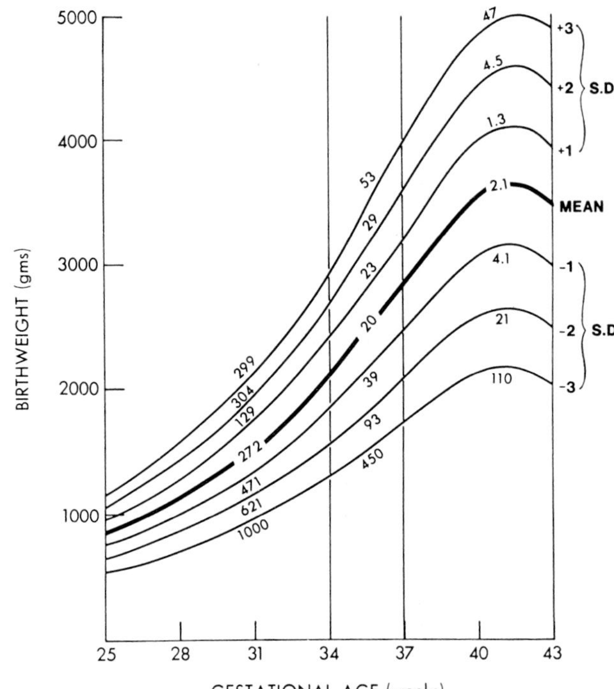

FIG. 10. Neonatal mortality rates per 1,000 livebirths over 500 g. for infants with different growth rates assessed in terms of standard deviations from the mean of normal values of birthweight for gestational age in three gestational categories.

2 standard deviations of mean weight for their gestational age, and 189/1,000 for those more than 2 standard deviations underweight for date, including the total over 500-gram population (Table 4).

Considering only those who reached 37 weeks gestation alive, perinatal mortality thereafter was 6·0/1,000 for those within 1 standard deviation of mean weight for date, 11/1,000 for those 1–2 standard deviations underweight, 54/1,000 for those 2–3 standard deviations underweight, and 261/1,000 for those more than 3 standard deviations underweight (Fig. 8). This increase in mortality risk after 37 weeks gestation was as great for stillbirths (3·9 to 170/1,000 in Fig. 9) as for neonatal deaths (2·1 to 110/1,000 in Fig. 10).

Cause of Death with Fetal Growth Retardation

Following each perinatal death, a clinical-pathological conference was held and a primary cause of death was assigned taking obstetrical, neonatal, and in 95 per cent of cases autopsy findings, into consideration. The 952 perinatal deaths are analysed by primary cause, expressed as cause-specific death rates per 1,000 births over 500 g., in Table 4.

The 15·9 perinatal deaths per 1,000 births of infants whose fetal growth rate was within 2 standard deviations of the mean was comprised of 2·1 due to anomalies, 3·7 due to asphyxia caused by recognized obstetrical complications, 2·9 due to respiratory distress syndrome, and 2·5 from all other specific causes. This left 4·7 deaths/1,000 as otherwise unexplained perinatal deaths of obscure cause.

Infants who were growth retarded at birth (more than 2 standard deviations below mean weight for date) had a perinatal mortality rate of 189·3/1,000 comprised of 45·8 due to anomalies, 17·7 due to asphyxia of known obstetrical cause, 6·2 from respiratory distress syndrome,

TABLE 4

PERINATAL DEATHS BY CAUSE AND FETAL GROWTH RATE PER 1,000 BIRTHS OVER 500 GRAMS

		Anomalies						*Asphyxia*					*e*					
Fetal Growth	*Number Births*	*Anen-cephaly*	*Other C.N.S.*	*Cardiac*	*Renal*	*Other*	*Total Anomalies*	*Abruptio*	*Labor & Delivery*	*Cord Causes*	*Other*	*Total Asphyxia*	*R.D.S.*	*Infec-tion*	*Erythro-blastosis*	*Other*	*Obscure Cause*	*Total*
2 S.D. or more above mean	874	0	1·4	1·4	0	4·0	6·8	3·1	8·7	4·5	1·6	17·9	14·6	3·0	24·6	6·1	3·1	76·1
Within 2 S.D. of mean	42,254	0·1	0·4	0·8	0·1	0·7	2·1	1·3	0·8	1·4	0·2	3·7	2·9	1·1	0·5	0·9	4·7	15·9
2 S.D. or more below mean	1,128	19·2	2·4	4·7	3·1	16·4	45·8	13·2	3·3	1·2	0	17·7	6·2	7·4	1·1	4·7	106·4	189·3
TOTAL	44,256	0·6	0·5	0·9	0·1	1·2	3·3	1·7	1·0	1·4	0·2	4·3	3·3	1·3	0·1	1·1	7·2	20·6

13·2 from all other specific causes, and 106·4/1000 unexplained deaths of obscure cause.

From Table 5 it can be seen that 24 per cent of perinatal deaths of growth-retarded infants are due to anomalies, 9 per cent to known causes of asphyxia, and 11 per cent to all other specific causes of perinatal death. This leaves 56 per cent of the mortality due to obscure cause.

TABLE 5

CAUSES OF PERINATAL DEATH OF 214 GROWTH-RETARDED* INFANTS

Cause of Death	%
Anomalies:	
—Anencephaly	10·1
—Other Anomalies	14·0
Asphyxia of Known Cause:	
—Abruptio Placenta	7·0
—Other Asphyctic Causes	2·4
Respiratory Distress Syndrome	3·3
Infection	3·9
Erythroblastosis	0·6
Other Specific Causes	2·5
Unexplained or Obscure Cause	56·2
TOTAL	100·0

* 2 standard deviations or more underweight for date, of infants with birthweight over 500 g.

Lethal anomalies occurred 22 times as frequently in growth-retarded as in normal infants, with almost one-half of this increase due to anencephaly (Table 4). Anencephalic infants would be expected to be 15 per cent underweight for date because of the missing cranial contents, but 22 of 28 growth-retarded cases were in fact more than 37 per cent (3 standard deviations) under mean weight for date. This indicates that severe overall growth retardation exists in anencephaly.

At the present time it remains uncertain as to whether fetal growth retardation is a consequence or a cause of congenital malformations. If fetal growth retardation is primary, the implication must be that intrauterine deprivation ultimately leading to fetal growth retardation has its origin, at least in some instances, in the first trimester of pregnancy when it can affect organogenesis.

All specific causes of perinatal death other than anomalies, when considered as a group, killed 4 times as many growth-retarded as normally-grown infants (Table 4). Although numbers were small there was suggestive evidence that deaths due to abruptio placenta and intrauterine infection were particularly frequent in growth-retarded infants. The association with abruptio placentae may imply that under conditions where chronic fetal deprivation occurs *in utero*, the placenta is less firmly attached and tends to separate prematurely.

The most clinically significant deaths of growth-retarded infants were those of obscure cause, which may be considered to have resulted from chronic fetal deprivation. In many cases these took place as unexplained fetal deaths prior to labour of apparently normal fetuses in apparently healthy mothers. Another large group of deaths of obscure cause were those dying of peripartum asphyxia, either from fetal distress during labour, from severe birth asphyxia, or from meconium aspiration; all without obstetrical complications or fetal disorders which could have accounted for asphyxia. A small number of deaths listed here from obscure cause were due to classical hypoglycemia associated with fetal malnutrition, as well as a few instances of unexplained neonatal deaths of very small infants.

Deaths of "obscure cause" occurred 22 times more frequently in growth-retarded than in normally-grown infants. They accounted for 59 per cent of the increased mortality risk in growth-retarded infants. It seems highly probable that they are due to a combination of chronic intrauterine malnutrition and hypoxemia of uncertain origin. These would account for the growth retardation, soft tissue wasting, fetal deaths and birth asphyxia found in such cases.

Clinical Aspects of Chronic Fetal Deprivation

Fetuses who are growth retarded are at risk of dying or becoming brain damaged[4] from chronic nutritional deprivation and asphyxia. The cause of their intrauterine state of deprivation is usually unknown, but they can be diagnosed during pregnancy as growth-retarded infants in jeopardy. If they have reached a stage of development compatible with viability, selective premature delivery can prevent death or permanent brain damage.

In Table 6 the 89 growth-retarded fetuses dying after 29 weeks of gestation of obscure cause (presumably of fetal deprivation) are tabulated by gestational age at time of fetal death (or of livebirth for the neonatal deaths). Thirty-one other fetuses dying of obscure cause at or before 29 weeks gestation are not included in this analysis because they all weighed less than 1,000 g. at birth and were so premature at time of death that salvage by premature delivery would have been most unlikely.

Table 6 indicates that recognition of fetal growth retardation at 40 weeks would only allow salvage of up to 14 per cent of fatal cases. Earlier recognition by 38 weeks might save 36 per cent, by 36 weeks 58 per cent and by 34 weeks up to 70 per cent of post-29-week fetuses dying of chronic fetal deprivation. Seldom is premature delivery attempted for salvage from fetal deprivation before 34 weeks gestation, because of the uncertainties involved in diagnosis and assessment of severity of this condition.

When evaluating a pregnancy with suspected fetal growth retardation, it is possible by clinical means, radiologically, and most accurately by means of ultrasound, to estimate the fetal size. From this estimate, the fetus may be estimated to be underweight by 1, 2, 3 or more standard deviations for its gestational age as calculated from the onset of the last normal menstrual period. Gestational assessment can be corroborated by amniocentesis, X-ray, and review of findings during pregnancy. A decision to risk a premature induction will depend on the relative risks of premature birth if delivered early, against those of chronic fetal deprivation if the pregnancy is allowed to continue.

The risks of premature delivery, primarily that of

TABLE 6

GESTATIONAL AGE* OF DEATHS FROM CHRONIC FETAL DEPRIVATION†

Gestational Age (Completed Weeks)	*Stillbirths Number*	*Neonatal Deaths Number*	*Perinatal Deaths Number*	*Perinatal Deaths Cumulative Per Cent*
42+	0	1	1	1
40–41	7	5	12	14
38–39	14	5	19	36
36–37	18	2	20	58
34–35	8	2	10	70
32–33	11	0	11	82
30–31	12	4	16	100
TOTAL	70	19	89	

* Gestational age at time of fetal death *in utero*, or of livebirth

† Infants with birthweight 2 S.D. or more underweight for date, dying of obscure cause after 29 weeks of gestation

respiratory distress syndrome, have been analysed previously from the same hospital's population.[15] For vaginal deliveries they amount to 8 per cent at 32 weeks, 2 per cent at 34 weeks, and 0·3 per cent at 36 weeks. Cesarean section at the same gestational ages carries higher risks, of 23 per cent, 18 per cent and 6 per cent respectively.

The risk of perinatal death from chronic fetal deprivation is assessed in Table 7 for the present population of births, including only those pregnancies where the fetus remained alive until 33 weeks gestation. Perinatal death from obscure cause in the non-growth retarded population was only 2·5/1,000 for infants not more than 1 standard deviation underweight, and 5·3/1,000 for those 1–2 standard deviations underweight. Perinatal mortality from obscure cause (chronic fetal deprivation) among growth-retarded infants rose to 28·5/1,000 at 2–3 standard deviations, 150/1,000 at 3–4 standard deviations, and 400/1,000 at more than 4 standard deviations underweight for date. Each standard deviation is approximately 12 per cent of mean weight.

It would therefore seem advisable, when fetal size appears to be more than 2 standard deviations (or 25 per cent) underweight for date, to deliver the infant prematurely between 36 and 38 weeks of gestation, depending on other signs indicative of fetal jeopardy. Fetuses appearing to be 3–4 standard deviations (or 37–50 per cent) underweight should be induced about 34 weeks, and those rare cases more than 4 standard deviations (50 per cent) underweight perhaps even earlier. Although such infants will be very small because of their combined prematurity and fetal growth retardation, their outlook is better when removed from a hostile intrauterine environment than if they were left longer *in utero*.

Chronic fetal deprivation in this series accounted for 12 per cent of all perinatal deaths, killing 2·7/1,000 births. As mentioned earlier, the use of selective early delivery during the latter part of the period reviewed, means that these figures probably under-estimate the spontaneous losses from this process.

It seems advisable, in order to prevent death or brain damage from chronic fetal deprivation, to diagnose affected cases early, follow them closely for signs of progressive growth retardation or clinical deterioration, and deliver them early if such signs present. Gestational age must be calculated accurately, if possible from a menstrual history obtained early in pregnancy. Abnormal length or irregularity of menstrual cycle and usage of oral contraceptives until the last cycle before conception occurred, should be ascertained to prevent calculation errors. Clinical corroboration of the calculated gestational age is obtained when an early pregnancy pelvic examination demonstrates an appropriate uterine size for duration of pregnancy, and when subjective symptoms of pregnancy,

TABLE 7

PERINATAL DEATHS AFTER 33 WEEKS AND DEGREE OF FETAL GROWTH RETARDATION

Degree of Fetal Growth Retardation	*Number of Fetuses Alive at 33 Weeks*	*Perinatal Deaths*			
		Total		*Of Obscure Cause*	
		Number	0/1000	*Number*	0/1000
Not Growth Retarded*	35,443	289	8·2	88	2·5
>1 S.D. to 2 S.D. Below Mean	7,341	103	14·0	39	5·3
>2 S.D. to 3 S.D. Below Mean	843	57	67·6	24	28·5
>3 S.D. to 4 S.D. Below Mean	160	46	287·5	24	150·0
>4 S.D. Below Mean	35	21	600·0	14	400·0

* Birthweight within 1 S.D. of the mean or heavier

fetal movements and first auscultation of the fetal heart on serial prenatal examinations coincide with the appropriate gestational ages calculated from the last normal menstrual period. Laboratory aids in confirming gestational age include amniotic fluid fat cells and creatinine, bilirubin and lecithin concentrations measured after amniocentesis. An early ultrasonic measurement of fetal head size prior to 24 weeks of gestation when proportionate head growth is very rapid and growth retardation has usually not yet become pronounced also provides a valuable confirmation of gestational age.[12] X-rays of fetal bone age are useful if positive but absence of development of epiphyseal centres may be due either to fetal growth retardation or to prematurity *per se*.[9]

Decreased fetal growth rate is usually suspected from repeated clinical evaluations of uterine size which show a relatively small uterine size for the duration of gestation. This clinical estimation is made more accurate when abdominal circumference or symphysis-to-fundus height are actually measured by tapemeasure or calipers on serial visits. Maternal weight gain is a less reliable guide as dieting during pregnancy or diuretics may mimic fetal growth retardation in producing reduced maternal weight gain, and the contrary problem exists when fluid retention or overeating results in maternal excess weight gain even in the presence of fetal growth retardation.

Ultrasound measurements of transverse diameter of the skull provide the most accurate method of assessing fetal size *in utero*. As was indicated earlier, fetal head size relates closely to body weight of the fetus, and not necessarily to gestational age.[7] If the skull diameter, and by extrapolation the body weight, is lower than expected for gestational age, and especially if serial ultrasound measurements at weekly intervals show little or no growth in head size, fetal growth retardation should be considered likely. Abdominal X-rays of the mother provide another, less accurate, estimate of fetal size *in utero*.

Once fetal growth retardation is suspected, the degree to which the fetus is compromised by intrauterine deprivation can be roughly estimated by either maternal urinary estriol excretion rate,[5] or by an oxytocin-type fetal stress test.[8] In our experience, 24-hr. collections of urinary estriols, as a measure of the integrity of both fetal adrenal and placental function, have more closely reflected the fetal state than spot plasma estriol measurements. To be useful, urinary estriols should be obtained every day or two (which may be done at home as well as in hospital), as they sometimes decrease only 2–3 days before fetal death; and they should be accompanied by urinary creatinine measurements to demonstrate the completeness of the 24 hr. urine specimen. Laboratory services should be available for this procedure every day of the week. Oxytocin stress tests have been introduced more recently into the assessment methods of fetal condition, and seem useful to assess which fetus has decreased oxygen reserve, by eliciting fetal bradycardia even with mild uterine contractions.

Diagnosis of fetal growth retardation or compromised fetal state prior to 34 weeks gestation is rarely an indication for early delivery. At this stage bedrest may help to increase uterine blood flow, as well as certain pharmacologic agents which are being tried (e.g. isoxsuprine) in an attempt to improve fetal nutrition and oxygenation. If persistent fetal growth retardation is evident, labour is usually induced at 36–38 weeks. When fetal growth retardation is severe, or estriol excretion and oxytocin stress tests indicate a compromised fetal state, earlier induction may be performed.

Fetuses with chronic intrauterine deprivation tolerate labour contractions poorly. In such patients, the progress of labour whether spontaneous or induced, should be monitored with exceeding care, and Cesarean section performed readily for even mild manifestations of fetal distress. Expert resuscitative assistance should be available at delivery whenever a growth-retarded fetus is delivered.

With the approach to management outlined here, it is possible to diagnose most growth-retarded fetuses 4–6 weeks before term and deliver them appropriately early, thus avoiding having small-for-date infants delivering undiagnosed at term. Death and severe asphyxia from chronic fetal deprivation after 34 weeks gestation can be almost eliminated, along with an equivalent reduction in long-term neurological sequelae.

The neonatal care of the infant suffering from chronic fetal deprivation is by comparison direct and simple. Asphyxia and meconium aspiration are treated appropriately. Hypoglycemia may either be watched for and treated as it develops, or preferably treated prophylactically. Using prophylactic glucose intravenously from birth until 24–48 hr. of age in all infants below the third percentile of weight for date, it is possible to avoid hypoglycemia and its sequelae.

Fetal growth retardation caused by chronic fetal deprivation provides a clinical problem which the developmental biologist, obstetrician, and neonatologist must combine to comprehend and eventually prevent. Research in this area may also bring about a greater understanding of the closely-associated problem of malformations. Even in our present state of ignorance about etiology, much can be done by alert clinicians to diagnose the chronically-deprived fetus and intervene before permanent brain damage or death ensues.

REFERENCES

1. Damoulaki-Sfakianaki, E., Robertson, A. and Cordero, L. (1972), "Skin Creases on the Sole of the Foot as a Physical Index of Maturity: Comparison Between Caucasian and Negro Infants," *Pediatrics*, **50**, 483.
2. Dubowitz, L. M. S., Dubowitz, V. and Goldberg, C. (1970), "Clinical Assessment of Gestational Age in the Newborn Infant," *J. Pediat.*, **77**, 1.
3. Falkner, Frank (1962), "Some Physical Growth Standards for White North American Children," *Pediatrics*, **29**, 467.
4. Fitzhardinge, P. M. and Stevens, E. M. (1972), "The Small-for-date Infant. II Neurological and Intellectual Sequelae," *Pediatrics*, **50**, 50.
5. Greene, John W. and Touchstone, Joseph C. (1963), "Urinary Estriol as an Index of Placental Function," *Amer. J. Obstet. Gynecol.*, **85**, 1.
6. Gruenwald, Peter (1963), "Chronic Fetal Distress and Placental Insufficiency," *Biol. Neonat.*, **5**, 215.

7. McLean, F. and Usher, R. (1970), "Measurements of Liveborn Fetal Malnutrition Infants Compared with Similar Gestation and with Similar Birth Weight Normal Controls," *Biol. Neonate*, **16**, 215.
8. Ray, M., Freeman, R., Pine, S. and Hesselgesser, R. (1972), "Clinical Experience with the Oxytocin Challenge Test," *Amer. J. Obstet. Gynecol.*, **114**, 1.
9. Scott, K. E. and Usher, R. H. (1964), "Epiphyseal Development in Fetal Malnutrition Syndrome," *New Engl., J. Med.*, **270**, 822.
10. Scott, Kenneth E. and Usher, Robert (1966), "Fetal Malnutrition: Its Incidence, Causes and Effects," *Amer. J. Obstet. Gynecol.*, **94**, 951.
11. Streeter, G. L. (1920), "Weight, Sitting Height, Head Size, Foot Length and Menstrual Age of the Human Embryo," *Contrib. Embryol.*, **11**, 143.
12. Thompson, H. E., Holmes, J. H., Gottesfeld, K. R. and Taylor, E. S. (1965), "Fetal Development as Determined by Ultrasonic Pulse Echo Techniques," *Amer. J. Obstet. Gynecol.*, **92**, 44.
13. Usher, Robert, Mclean, Frances and Scott, Kenneth E. (1966), "Judgment of Fetal Age II. Clinical Significance of Gestational Age and an Objective Method for its Assessment," *Pediat. Clin. N. Amer.*, **13**, 835.
14. Usher, Robert and McLean, Frances (1969), "Intrauterine Growth of Liveborn Caucasian Infants at Sea Level: Standards Obtained from Measurements in 7 Dimensions of Infants Born Between 25 and 44 Weeks of Gestation," *J. Pediat.*, **74**, 901.
15. Usher, Robert H., Allen, Alexander C. and McLean, Frances H. (1971), "Risk of Respiratory Distress Syndrome Related to Gestational Age, Route of Delivery, and Maternal Diabetes,' *Amer. J. Obstet. Gynecol.*, **111**, 826.
16. Vanden Berg, B. J. and Yerushalmy, J. (1966), "The Relationship of the Rate of Intrauterine Growth of Infants of Low Birthweight and Mortality, Morbidity, and Congenital Anomalies," *J. Pediat.*, **69**, 531.
17. Usher, Robert H. (1971), "Clinical Implications of Perinatal Mortality Statistics," *Clin. Obstet. Gynecol.*, **14**, 885.
18. Winick, Myron and Rosso, Pedro (1969), "The Effect of Severe Early Malnutrition on Cellular Growth of Human Brain," *Pediat. Res.*, **3**, 181.

7. CARDIO-RESPIRATORY EVENTS AT BIRTH

K. W. CROSS

Introduction

The lungs at birth

Development of ideas on lung surfactant

Cardiovascular and pulmonary adjustments at birth

Respiratory distress in the newborn

Resiscitation of the asphyxiated infant

Asphyxia

The onset of breathing after delivery is undoubtedly one of the most important events of any individual's life, and yet it is ill-understood. Looking at it as a respiratory physiologist, there are great problems. Thus the fetus is in an environment in which the arterial blood supply to the brain may have a PO_2 of about 30 mm. Hg., a Pco_2 of about 50 mm., and a pH of 7·2. These are values which in a conscious and reactive adult would cause quite remarkable hyperventilation. In the fetus, however, although there are small respiratory movements, it remains largely quiescent. It is generally supposed that the tremendous sensory bombardment of the central nervous system which arises because of the infant losing weightlessness, losing complete thermal insulation, and undergoing the postural gymnastics of birth causes activation of the reticular system and a new "setting" of the respiratory centres. These are large and vague concepts which will take an enormous amount of analysis to substantiate or reject.

It is not proposed to pursue these matters further in this chapter, but one would refer readers to Dawes' monograph.[6] Purves and Biscoe[22] have suggested that a change in the sympathetic activity of the nerve supplying the carotid chemoreceptors may change the sensitivity of these receptors to PO_2. If this is correct, then we should have to regard carotid chemoreceptors as being under central nervous control in the same way that muscle spindles are controlled centrally via the gamma efferent nerves.

Before turning to the main subjects in this chapter, it is perhaps worth alerting paediatricians to recent changes in our views on respiratory movements *in utero*. Barcroft[1] reported that there was an inhibition of the respiratory response to tactile and proprioceptive stimulation after about 60 days gestation in the sheep. This quiesence of respiratory activity *in utero* was widely accepted and, unless the stimulus is very severe, one rarely sees respiratory movements of the warmed exteriorized oxygenated fetal lamb. Dawes, Fox, Leduc, Liggins and Richards[7] have shown that there are rapid irregular breathing movements in lambs in the latter half of pregnancy. These may be inhibited for two to three days after operation and are therefore best seen in chronic preparations. The movements shift little fluid and are associated with rapid-eye-movement sleep. That these respiratory movements are not a quirk confined to the fetal lamb is shown by the fact that Boddy and Robinson[3] have recorded chest activity in the human fetus by the use of ultrasound.

One aspect of respiratory activity in the newborn is shown by the work of Johnson, Robinson and Salisbury,[16] who showed that fetal lambs would make respiratory movements when the cord was clamped and they were delivered into warm saline, but that there was very prolonged or even lethal apnoea if water, glucose or milk was introduced into the upper air passages. It is becoming apparent from their work that this inhibition arises from taste receptors in the entrance to the larynx. This may provide an explanation for the dangers associated with feeding in the premature infant, and makes it possible that some apnoeic spells are reflex responses to the regurgitation of food.

THE LUNGS AT BIRTH

Another aspect of fetal/neonatal respiratory physiology has been investigated by Strang and his coworkers. They have re-emphasized that the fetal lung is not collapsed in the sense that alveolar walls are in apposition, but is partially distended with fluid. The disappearance of fluid requires an explanation, and while some of the fluid which comes from the nose and mouth during vaginal delivery may arise from the lungs, it is certain that the squeeze of the birth canal could not remove all that is present in the lungs. Humphreys, Normand, Reynolds and Strang[15] have shown that in the fetal lamb considerable volumes of fluid are normally drained into the lung lymphatics and after the onset of ventilation, the lymph flow increases threefold or more.

In this chapter, it is proposed to discuss some aspects of the existence of lung surfactant and the induction of lung surfactant. Secondly, I propose to examine the changes in the fetal circulation at birth and some of the applied physiology of these changes.

DEVELOPMENT OF IDEAS ON LUNG SURFACTANT

(*See also* chapter by Godfrey, noting particularly Fig. 1.)

There are two important stages in the development of our ideas and knowledge of surfactant. The first arose from the observations of Pattle[21] that fluid squeezed from the lung contained many tiny bubbles which were persistent. It was the persistence of these bubbles which surprised him for he knew that fluids, such as beer, if left standing over the lunch hour would become totally bubble-free. He recognized that the persistence of the bubbles indicated that lung fluid must have a remarkably low surface tension for Laplace's law states that the Pressure (P) inside a bubble is directly proportional to twice the Tension (T) in the wall (a function of surface tension) and is inversely proportional to the radius (r) of the bubble—$P = 2T/r$. Thus when r is very small, the pressure will become large, hence the gases in the bubble will dissolve and the bubble itself will disappear at an increasing speed as the bubble gets smaller. The bubble does not burst, of course, because the envelope is providing the pressure. The persistence of these bubbles demanded a surface tension in lung extract which was orders of magnitude lower than the surface tension of plasma which is 50 dynes/cm.

Investigation showed that the surface-tension-lowering agent (surfactant) was a phospholipid which had the further property of diminishing its surface tension even more as the area it covered diminished. Thus, an alveolus which may be regarded as a bubble does not tend to collapse and discharge itself into a next-door alveolus as it becomes smaller in expiration. The behaviour of alveoli without surfactant can best be illustrated by attempting to blow up two toy balloons on a Y tube. One balloon (A) will always expand first, and if the air from the expanded balloon A is expressed into the unexpanded ballon (B), then all the air will pass to B when A is smaller than B. No amount of juggling leaves the two balloons equally expanded. This knowledge of surfactant applied to the lung, explained the existence of alveoli of different sizes—a problem which had been recognized by very few physiologists and largely ignored. A great deal of work has established that surfactant is not present in the very immature lung, that it is much diminished in babies with respiratory distress, and that it could be diminished by breathing 100 per cent oxygen. It has been claimed[10] that the prognosis for the respiratory performance of a premature human fetus can be determined by measuring the ratio of the lecithin of sphyngomyelin in the amniotic fluid which has been obtained either by amniocentesis or at birth. Bhagwanani, Fahmy and Turnbull[2] have recently made excellent predictions by the measurement of lecithin alone—levels above 3·5 mgm./100 ml. being associated with good lung function.

The second major development with respect to surfactant has been a by-product of research into the onset or parturition. Liggins, Kennedy and Holm[1] showed that coagulation of 70 per cent or more of the fetal lamb anterior pituitary resulted in prolonged gestation. Fetal adrenalectomy had a similar effect. Conversely, intra-peritoneal injection of ACTH into the fetus induced premature labour, but for our present purpose it is only important to note that the prematurely-born fetus had a lung which: (a) could be expanded, and (b) remained functional after birth at an age when this would not normally be possible. Liggins and his colleagues have found further that ACTH, cortisol, or, most effectively, dexamethosone induced the early production of surfactant and hence a stable lung. Preliminary reports from Liggins and his colleagues in Auckland suggest that maternal administration of dexamethosone may prevent Hyaline Membrane Disease if the drug can be given to the mother early enough and for long enough before premature delivery occurs.

In Hyaline Membrane Disease where surfactant is definitely diminished and hence there is a great tendency for the lungs to collapse, Tooley and his colleagues[13] have shown that continuous positive airway pressure aids greatly in the treatment of distressed infants. Other workers have achieved success in the artificial ventilation of these infants by allowing only a very short period for expiration. This presumably achieves the same result by maintaining an end expiratory pressure which is positive.

CARDIO-VASCULAR ADJUSTMENTS AT BIRTH

Anatomical events which must take place after birth if a normal adult circulation is to be achieved are illustrated in the accompanying diagram from Dawes.[6] They are:

1. Closure of the umbilical vessels.
2. Closure of the foramen ovale.
3. Closure of the ductus arteriosus.
4. Relaxation of the pulmonary vascular resistance.

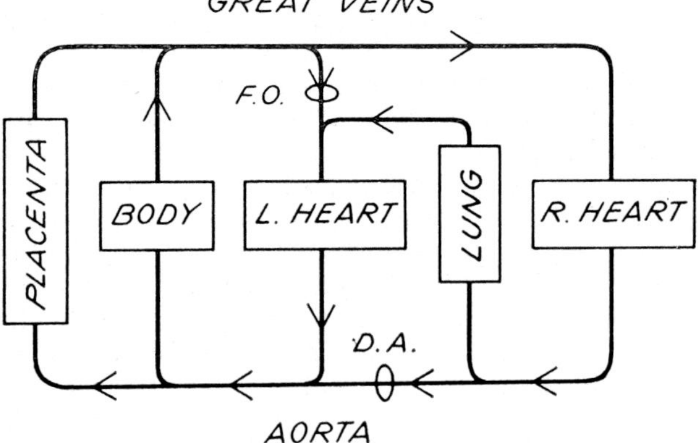

FIG. 1. Plan of the fetal circulation, to show that the two sides of the heart pump blood from the great veins to the aorta in parallel by way of the foramen ovale (F.O.) and ductus arteriosus (D.A.). (Redrawn from Born, Dawes, Mott and Widdicombe, 1954.[6]

The umbilical vessels can be considered separately. It should be appreciated that mammals have reproduced themselves for millions of years without the help of midwives, and in nature the cord constricts as a consequence—most commonly—of trauma. Certain species have an umbilical sphincter, but in general tearing, chewing, twisting and crushing all produce effective mechanical stimuli which cause the vessels to constrict. It is the less traumatic scalpel or scissors which may provide an inadequate stimulus and hence a bleeding cord. Modern obstetrics will, however, very properly continue and hence the treatment of the cord will be left in their hands.

The physiological closure of the foramen ovale and of the ductus arteriosus are closely related to the increase of blood-flow through the lungs consequent upon the relaxation of pulmonary vascular resistance. This itself is a direct consequence of ventilation of the lungs with air. Figure 2, which is from a classic paper of Dawes, Mott, Widdicombe and Wyatt, has, with hind sight, a great deal of the most important information about pulmonary vascular resistance and the causes and consequences of its changing at birth. We see that before ventilating the lungs with air, the pulmonary arterial pressure exceeds systemic pressure and hence there is a right-to-left shunt through the ductus arteriosus. At this time, the flow through the left pulmonary artery is very small and the left atrial pressure is low. The low flow through the pulmonary artery is a consequence of the high pulmonary vascular resistance.

Ventilation of the lungs with air alters this picture dramatically. There is a five-fold increase in pulmonary blood flow which occurs in spite of the consequent fall in pulmonary blood pressure. This fall in pulmonary blood pressure is somewhat buffered by a reversal of the pulmonary/systemic pressure relationship, and hence a large left-to-right ductus shunt. Cutting-off the placental bed by tying the cord raises the systemic and hence the pulmonary pressure only slightly. The extent of the ductus shunt can be judged by the effect of temporary occlusion of the ductus. We see that this raises the systemic pressure and lowers the

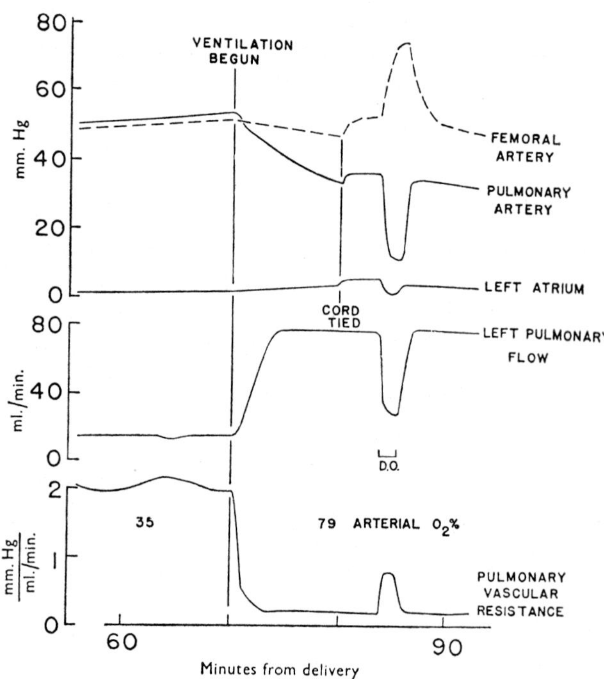

FIG. 2. Changes in the circulation with the onset of ventilation. The fetus of the sheep had been exteriorized, but the umbilical circulation had been maintained and the fetus kept warm. Seventy minutes after delivery, surgery had been completed, pressure and flow meters inserted and base line measurements made. See text for prolonged discussion.

pulmonary pressure (and flow) very markedly. One consequence of occluding the ductus which does not seem explicable is the increase in pulmonary vascular resistance when the ductus is occluded. Is it that $\frac{\text{pressure across the lungs}}{\text{flow}}$ is not a complete expression of resistance, or is it that the pulmonary vasculature is showing an unexpected reaction to the fall of pressure?

Lastly in this important diagram, note the rise in left atrial pressure with increasing pulmonary flow (and the fall of left atrial pressure with occlusion of the ductus). The valve of the foramen ovale is a simple flap and its patency or closure is dependent on the relative pressures in the two atria.

It is important to note, although not explicit in this diagram, that these effects are obtained in their most complete form when the lungs are *expanded* and *ventilated* with air or oxygen, i.e. not only is the PO_2 raised, but the Pco_2 is lowered. It is also important to note that these effects are largely direct effects on the pulmonary vasculature as they can be obtained in isolated perfused fetal lungs.

So far the active ventilation has enormously increased the pulmonary blood flow and has as a consequence inaugurated functional closure of the valve of the foramen ovale. The open ductus at this point is augmenting blood flow through the lungs and it has been shown[8] that this extra blood flow is associated with a higher systemic PO_2 than occurs when the ductus is occluded and some of the left ventricular output is no longer recirculated through the lung.

The normal closure of the ductus arteriosus is also a secondary effect of effective pulmonary ventilation with air. This seems to be brought about by the direct effect of raised PO_2 on the muscle of the ductus, for in an isolated heart-ductus-artificial lung preparation[5] the ductus can be shown to constrict as the PO_2 is raised and to relax as the PO_2 is lowered. The constriction is associated with a murmur caused by the turbulent flow of the blood. This can be readily heard in the lamb and has been detected by skilled observers in the human baby. Severe asphyxia in the whole animal will also cause constriction of the ductus in the lamb. This is thought to be due to the release of pressor amines from the adrenal medulla—a system which is particularly well-developed in the lamb. These results in the intact or semi-intact animal are confirmed by the finding that isolated spirals of ductus muscle respond as expected to PO_2 and administration of adrenaline or noradrenaline.[17]

It must be stressed that there is still a strange anomaly here when we consider the behaviour of the arterial smooth muscle of the newborn. Increasing levels of oxygen cause relaxation of the pulmonary arterioles whereas the same gas changing in the same direction causes contraction of the smooth muscle of the ductus.

Does the lamb provide a good model of cardio-pulmonary behaviour for the human subject? The answer appears to be that it is an excellent model, although the time course of events in the human is probably slower, particularly in the premature infant. In both species the changes that have been described are at first all reversible and the commonest cause of reversal is hypoxia.

RESPIRATORY DISTRESS IN THE NEWBORN

Two important aspects of applied physiology are worth mentioning. Firstly, with respiratory distress in the newborn, a vicious circle is readily established. The collapsing lung fails adequately to oxygenate the pulmonary venous blood. Pulmonary blood pressure rises and the falling flow may lower the left atrial pressure and hence the foramen ovale can open when right atrial pressure exceeds left atrial pressure. Next, the now relaxing ductus arteriosus may allow a reversal of flow from the pulmonary artery to the aorta. There are many records of the preductal aortic blood having a higher PO_2 than the blood in the descending aorta. This has important implications, both in the dangers of oxygen therapy and for that matter, the dangers of not giving oxygen. The infant with respiratory distress demands a most sophisticated appreciation of the changes and reversals of change which can occur with hypoxic episodes.

RESUSCITATION OF THE ASPHYXIATED INFANT

The other important application of knowledge of the fetal circulation is concerned with the resuscitation of the asphyxiated infant. This is a subject which has aroused many emotionally-charged discussions—partly because participation in a successful resuscitation, or what seems to be a successful resuscitation, is one of the most dramatic events that can be witnessed in the whole field of medicine. Much of the folklore that has accumulated around the subject of infant resuscitation arises from the fact that no one who sees an asphyxiated baby for the first time can make an accurate diagnosis on the inadequate data which will be available. Two babies may both have a slow pulse, a poor colour, no tone and no response to noxious stimuli, and yet one, if left alone, will spontaneously take its first breath, and the other, if left alone, will die. Any treatment applied to the first baby will appear to be effective and will reinforce the therapist's faith in the treatment which he uses. Only genuinely effective treatment will resuscitate the baby that is "beyond its last gasp". As a correct diagnosis cannot be made, then the logic of the situation seems to demand that effective treatment should always be given. The evidence is that artificial ventilation of the lung with air or with oxygen is by far the most effective treatment available. If the baby has completed its respiratory gasping *in utero*, it will be delivered with a slow heart rate and a falling blood pressure. The pulmonary blood flow will be a mere trickle for all the conditions are correct to produce maximal pulmonary vaso constriction.

ASPHYXIA

It seems worth recounting a little of the experimental data on neonatal asphyxia which has been obtained in the laboratory. This has given rise to a nomenclature which is valuable in our discussion of the asphyxiated baby. Much of this work has been done on the fetal rabbit which has been delivered (without anaesthesia to itself or its mother) directly into saline at body temperature. This work has been referred to as "irrelevant experiments on drowned rabbits", but the analogy between this situation and that of the baby whose umbilical cord is acutely obstructed *in utero* does not seem to be too far-fetched—unless we are to refer to such asphyxiated babies as "drowned babies". The pattern of behaviour in the fetal or neonatal rabbit is very characteristic. After some initial gasping, there is a period of apnoea (primary apnoea) which may last several minutes (usually about two). Gasping starts again and continues until asphysixia has been total for about twenty minutes. In rabbits, but not necessarily in other species, an acceleration of gasping heralds *the last gasp* (terminal or secondary apnoea).

In other species, the time course is quite different and in naturally-occurring asphyxia, the onset is not normally so catastrophic, but the phenomenon of primary and terminal apnoea is common to all species and the phrase "the last gasp" has real meaning and defines a real situation. The fetus or newborn animal differs from the adult of its own species by showing a prolonged resistance to asphyxia. The basis of this probably lies in the ability of the nervous system

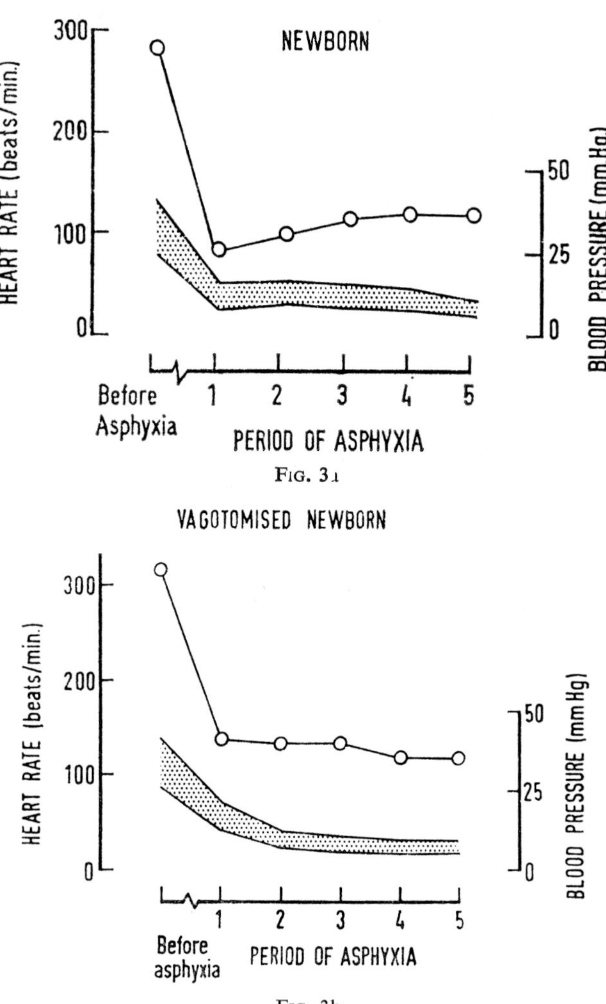

FIG. 3a

FIG. 3b

FIGS. 3a and 3b. Heart rate and blood pressure in newborn rabbits who were allowed to breathe nitrogen after the initial observations. Note the more precipitate fall in heart rate in the unvagotomized animals, but also note that the heart rate and blood pressure are indistinguishable in the two groups at the end of the fifth period of asphyxia—about twenty minutes. No reflex activity whatsoever can be demonstrated at this time. (Figs. 6 and 7 from reference 11).

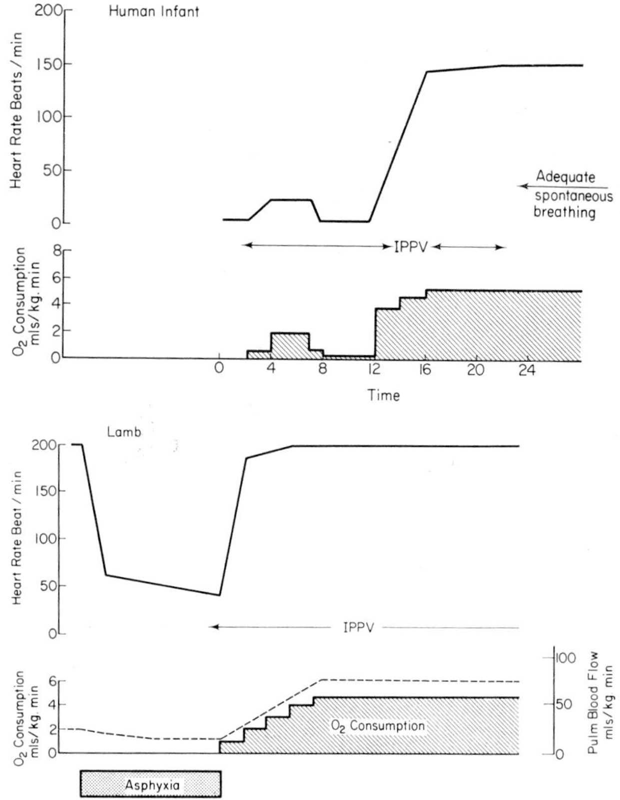

FIG. 4. Highly diagrammatic representation of heart rate and oxygen consumption during resuscitation by Intermittent Positive Pressure Ventilation (IPPV) in human infant and in lamb (the pulmonary blood flow is also illustrated in the lamb to indicate the very close correlation between oxygen consumption and pulmonary flow during recovery from asphyxia). The infant was being resuscitated after vaginal delivery when shoulder dystocia had caused severe asphyxia. The lamb was experimentally asphyxiated by cord clamping after insertion of appropriate measuring devices. The interruption of IPPV in the infant was for suction and clearing the tracheal tube. The infant also needed three periods of cardiac massage. (Data of Fig. 5, reference 14; and Figs. 4 and 5, reference 4).

to survive conditions which would cause irreparable damage or death in the adult, but more importantly for our present purpose, the difference resides in the cardio-vascular system. The heart continues to beat (often regularly) with a miniscule blood pressure for long periods after all gasping activity has ceased. There is an excellent correlation in different species between survival time and the initial concentration of cardiac glycogen. and when cardiac glycogen is varied experimentally, this correlation is sustained.[20,23]

The cardiac behaviour is worth careful study in asphyxia because it provides the best guide to the efficacy of treatment in cases beyond the last gasp. With acute cord clamping or with administration of nitrogen, there is a precipitate fall in the heart rate which then recovers a little. In fact, the heart rate is often slower immediately after the insult than at the end of the gasping period. This initial slowing is partly vagal in origin for vagotomized animals show a slower initial fall in heart rate. At the last gasp, however, the heart-rates of vagotomized and non-vagotomized animals are identical. This is part of the important evidence which tells us that we are dealing with a physiologically denervated heart when resuscitation is essential (Figs. 3a and 3b).

If, after the last gasp, artificial ventilation is given with air or oxygen, then recovery in all species studied is heralded by initial increase in the heart rate. This has not been formally investigated, but it seems reasonable to assume that this reaction is caused by a small amount of oxygen-richer blood reaching the heart itself through the coronary arteries. The cardiac acceleration is soon accompanied by an increase in the blood pressure and gasping occurs only after these two aspects of the circulation are restored towards normality. See, for example, Fig. 69 of Dawes' monograph.[6] If the heart does not accelerate or if cardiac irregularity occurs, cardiac massage is frequently effective in initiating the events just described.

The evidence for the behaviour of the overall circulation is largely from the rabbit, while the lamb has been the experimental animal of choice for more-detailed studies. There is every reason to believe that the cardio-respiratory behaviour of these species in asphyxia is a good general model for the human newborn, although the time relationships are different. One correlation which gives one great confidence is that when one resuscitates the severely asphyxiated lamb, the uptake of oxygen is slow at first and the evidence seems to be that this is limited by the poor pulmonary blood flow determined by the slow release of severe pulmonary vasoconstriction.[4] A similar limitation of oxygen uptake is seen in the resuscitation of the severely asphyxiated human infant. Figure 4 shows a diagrammatic comparison in the two species.

A final point which should be made is that analeptic drugs have nothing to offer in the treatment of the infant asphyxiated beyond the last gasp and are even likely to hinder recovery. These drugs cause gasping and rapid recovery if given during primary asphyxia in the experimental animal. If they are given during terminal asphyxia, they do not cause gasping but do cause considerable deterioration of the blood pressure which represents the last hope of recovery of the animal.[12]

REFERENCES

1. Barcroft, J. (1946), *Researches on Prenatal Life*, Oxford: Blackwell Scientific Publications.
2. Bhagwanani, S. G., Fahmy, D. and Turnbull, A. C. (1972), "Prediction of Neonatal Respiratory Distress by Estimation of Amniotic-Fluid Lecithin", *Lancet*, **i**, 159–162
3. Boddy, K. and Robinson, J. S. (1971), "External Method for Detection of Fetal Breathing *in utero*", *Lancet*, **ii**, 1231–1233.
4. Bolton, D. P. G., Cross, K. W., Eitzman, D. V. and Kelly, J. (1969), "The Oxygen Uptake and Pulmonary Blood Flow During Resuscitation from Asphyxia in Foetal and Adult Sheep", *J. Physiol.*, **205**, 417–434.
5. Born, G. V. R., Dawes, G. S., Mott, J. C. and Rennick, B. R. (1956), "The Constriction of the Ductus Arteriosus caused by Oxygen and Asphyxia in Newborn Lambs", *J. Physiol.*, **132**, 304–342.
6. Dawes, G. S. (1968), *Foetal and Neonatal Physiology.* Chicago: Year Book Medical Publishers Inc.
7. Dawes, G. S., Fox, H. E., Leduc, B. M., Liggins, G. C. and Richards, R. T. (1972), "Respiratory Movements and Rapid Eye Movement Sleep in the Foetal Lamb", *J. Physiol.*, **220**, 119–143.
8. Dawes, G. S., Mott, J. C. and Widdicombe, J. G. (1955), "The Patency of the Ductus Arteriosus in Newborn Lambs and its Physiological Consequences", *J. Physiol.*, **128**, 361–383.
9. Dawes, G. S., Mott, J. C., Widdicombe, J. G. and Wyatt, D. G. (1953), "Changes in the Lungs of the New-born Lamb", *J. Physiol.*, **121**, 141–162.
10. Gluck, L., Kulovich, M. V., Borer, R. C., Brenner, P. H., Anderson, G. C. and Spellacy, W. N. (1971), "Diagnosis of the Respiratory Distress Syndrome by Amniocentesis", *Amer. J. Obstet. Gynec.*, **109**, 440–445.
11. Godfrey, S. (1968), "Respiratory and Cardiovascular Changes During Asphyxia and Resuscitation of Foetal and Newborn Rabbits", *Quart. J. exp. Physiol.*, **53**, 97–118.
12. Godfrey, S., Bolton, D. P. G. and Cross, K. W. (1970), "Respiratory Stimulants in Treatment of Perinatal Asphyxia", *Brit. Med. J.*, **1**, 475–477.
13. Gregory, G. A., Kitterman, J. A., Phibbs, R. H., Tooley, W. H. and Hamilton, W. K. (1971), "Treatment of the Idiopathic Respiratory Distress Syndrome with Continuous Positive Airway Pressure", *New Engl. J. Med.*, **284**, 1333–1340.
14. Hey, E. and Kelly, J. (1968), "Gaseous Exchange During Endotracheal Ventilation for Asphyxia at Birth", *J. Obstet. Gynaec. Brit. Commonw.*, **75**, 414–424.
15. Humphreys, P. W., Normand, I. C. S., Reynolds, E. O. R. and Strang, L. B. (1967), "Pulmonary Lymph Flow and the Uptake of Liquid from the Lungs of the Lamb at the Start of Breathing", *J. Physiol.*, **193**, 1–29.
16. Johnson, P., Robinson, J. S. and Salisbury, D. (1972/73), "Some Factors Affecting the Onset and Control of Respiration in the Neonate", *Barcroft Centenary Symposium on Foetal and Neonatal Physiology. London:* Cambridge University Press. In press.
17. Kovalcik, V. (1963), "The Response of the Ductus Arteriosus to Oxygen and Anoxia", *J. Physiol.*, **169**, 185–197.
18. Liggins, G. C. (1969), "The Foetal Role in the Initiation of Parturition in the Ewe", *Foetal Autonomy*, 218–231. London: J. &. A. Churchill Ltd.
19. Liggins, G. C., Kennedy, P. C. and Holm, L. W. (1967), "Failure of Initiation of Parturition after Electrocoagulation of the Pituitary of the Fetal Lamb", *Amer. J. Obstet. Gynec.*, **98**, 1080–1086.
20. Mott, J. C. (1961), "The Ability of Young Mammals to Withstand Total Oxygen Lack", *Brit. Med. Bull.*, **17**, 144–148.
21. Pattle, R. E. (1955), "Properties, Function and Origin of the Alveolar Lining Layer", *Nature*, **175**, 1125–1126.
22. Purves, M. J. and Biscoe, J. T. (1966), "Development of Chemoreceptor Activity", *Brit. Med. Bull.*, **22**, 56–60.
23. Shelley, H. J. (1961), "Glycogen Reserves and their Changes at Birth and in Anoxia", *Brit. Med. Bull.*, **17**, 137–143.

8. BIOCHEMICAL ADAPTATIONS AT BIRTH

W. W. PAYNE

Neonatal acidosis
Energy metabolism
Blood glucose
Lactic acid
Flat metabolism
Enzymes
Urea
Phosphorus
Sodium, fluid balance and osmolarity
Potassium
Plasma protein
Packed cell volume
Calcium and magnesium
Serum magnesium

At birth the fetus has to rearrange its circulation and henceforward to fend for itself for sources of energy.

NEONATAL ACIDOSIS

The process of birth entails a period during which gaseous exchange via the placenta ceases when gaseous exchange via the lungs is not fully operational. Anaerobic processes such as the breakdown of glucose to lactic acid will supply the necessary energy for a time but this entails the production of fixed acid which reduces the blood pH. The

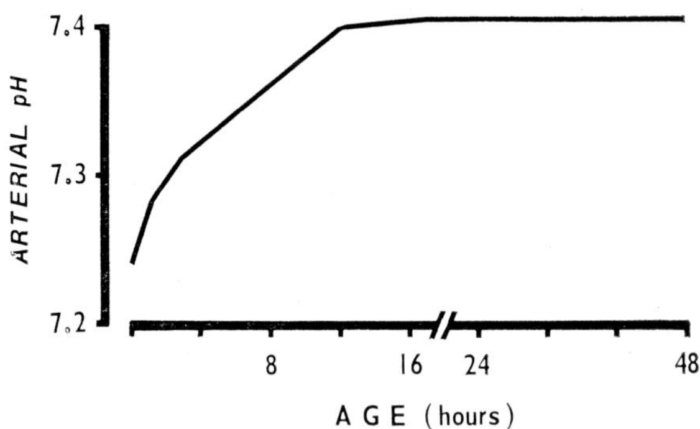

FIG. 1. Mean values of arterial blood pH of 13 normal infants of birthweight 1500–2500 g.

buffering systems of the body will be able to cope with this excess of hydrogen ions if it is not too big but it is inevitable that most babies are born with some degree of acidosis. Where pathological conditions are present, such as maternal eclampsia, sampling the fetal blood has shown that acidosis is present before birth and these infants will be born with a higher degree of acidosis.

With the establishment of good gaseous exchange and adequate circulation through the lungs the excess lactic acid will be rapidly oxidized in the liver and the pH returns to normal.

It will be seen that even severe acidaemia is usually quickly dealt with (Fig. 1) but the final attainment of the normal is slower. In some cases the return of lactic acid levels to normal may be delayed for two or more days;[15] in such cases a variable degree of abnormality in the mother or in the birth was present (Fig. 2).

Besides the use of buffer systems the body responds to acidosis by exchanging intracellular potassium for extracellular hydrogen ions. This in effect utilizes the high

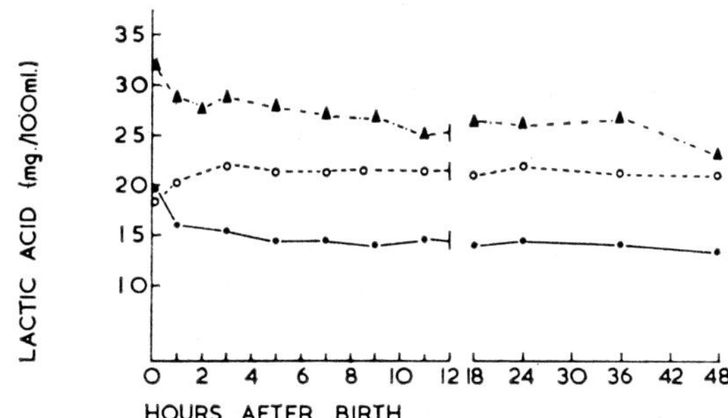

FIG. 2. Mean values of lactic acid in:—
·——·——· normal infants
o - - - o infants delivered by stressful procedures.
▲ - - - ▲ infants surviving respiratory distress syndrome.

protein content of the intracellular fluid as a buffer. Correcting the pH to normal reverses this change. The transfer of potassium to extracellular fluid accounts for the increase in plasma potassium (*see* Fig. 9) in the early minutes of life, with its rapid return to lower levels when gaseous exchange is established.

Another change caused by acidaemia is the breakdown of intracellular phosphoric esters (acid soluble phosphorus) which liberates phosphorus and the organic radicles.[9] This causes a rise in the extracellular phosphorus concentration.

ENERGY METABOLISM

The need of the newborn for energy can be met by utilization of food stores (glycogen and fat) if adequate oxygen is available. Since in infants the brain uses about 50 per cent of the total body consumption of oxygen there is a special need for carbohydrates and/or acetone bodies[2] or possibly aminoacids; the brain will not use fat. As the infant's intake of food in the first two days is low the necessary carbohydrate has to be supplied mainly from glycogen stores which are usually only adequate for about twelve hours. Carbohydrate can also be produced from other food stores: for example, the glycerol of fat can be converted to glucose in the liver. Persson *et al.*[16] have studied the arteriovenous difference of the cerebral circulation; they found that carbohydrate, acetoacetic acid and β-hydroxybutyric acid were taken up but not free fatty acid, lactic or pyruvic acids, or glycerol. The rate of usage of the acetone bodies increased with the rise in their blood levels. They also found that the acetone bodies after a night fast were higher in "infants" under six years than in older children.

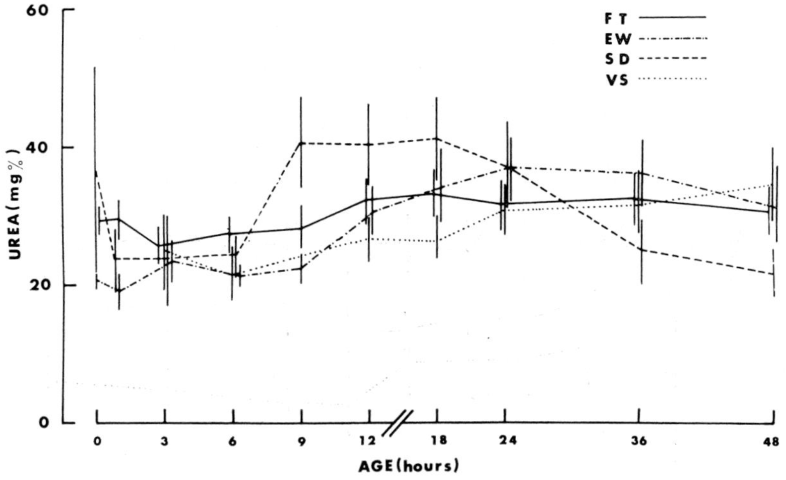

FIG. 3. Mean blood urea values in healthy infants.
FT = full term over 2500 g.
EW = under 2500 g. but of expected weight for gestational age.
SD = infants with birth weight less than 25th percentile for gestational age.
VS = infants with birth weight under 1500 g.
Vertical lines = Standard error of the mean.

Since at birth the available carbohydrate stored as glycogen is only enough for about twelve hours the energy supplies for the brain have to be supplemented by the acetone bodies. The rapid rise of the blood fats in the first twelve hours will give rise to an increase in the blood level of this substrate.

If starvation is too prolonged tissue protein will have to be utilized. In consequence urea may be produced at a faster rate than can be excreted by the infant's kidneys and a rise in blood urea will occur (Fig. 3). Also as cell proteins are used up intracellular potassium will be liberated. This is more marked in stressed infants, e.g. those with respiratory distress syndrome or infections. It will be seen that the rise in urea coincides in time with a rise in potassium and glucose (Fig. 4).

Thus the need of the organism for energy leads to the use of protein from sources such as muscle and shows how important it is to give the immature and stressed infants readily available food such as glucose. The energy needed to keep the body warm must be minimized by reducing loss of heat and by keeping the external environment at the optimum temperature.

BLOOD GLUCOSE

The need of the brain for glucose presents a problem, especially as regards the immature or small-for-dates infant. His store of glycogen is insufficient to maintain an adequate glucose level until enough exogenous carbohydrate is taken in through the alimentary tract. In the full term normal infant the blood sugar falls to levels which in the child or adult would produce hypoglycaemic symptoms, and this is more marked the less well the baby. Figure 5 shows the mean blood sugar values for full term, immature, small-for-dates and very small infants. It shows a progressive

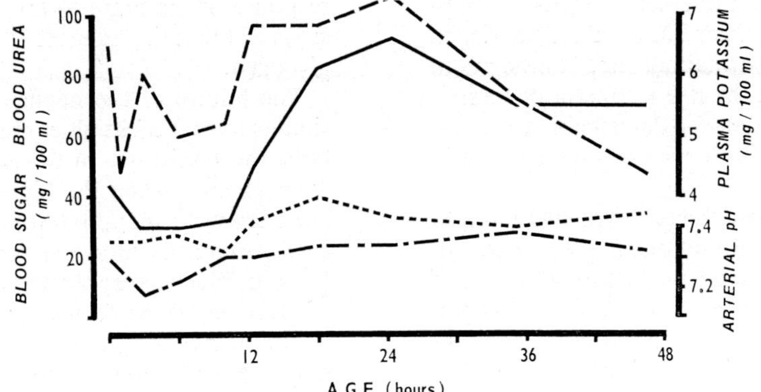

FIG. 4. Mean values of
Blood pH
Plasma potassium
Blood urea
Blood glucose
in seven very small infants (birth weight under 1500 g.) who recovered from respiratory distress syndrome.

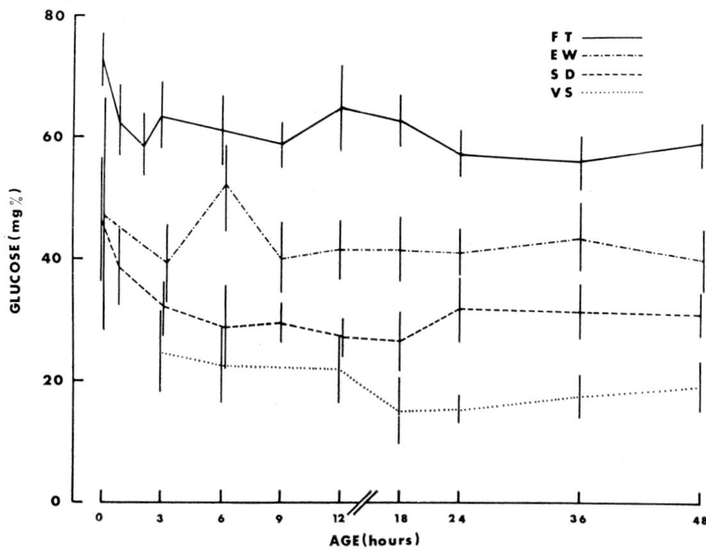

FIG. 5. Mean blood sugar values with standard error of the mean in the same four groups as in Fig. 3.

lowering of the glucose level with a lowering of the birth weight and immaturity.

It is generally accepted that a blood glucose level of 20 mgm. or less per 100 ml. is potentially dangerous and liable to cause symptoms. If the low blood sugar is uncorrected, brain damage can occur. However, in many infants the blood sugar falls below 20 mgm. without symp′ toms occurring and no apparent brain damage results. It seems that an early (up to 12 hours) fall of the blood sugar has less ill effect than later low values. This suggests that the early fall of blood sugar seen in all infants can be dealt with by calling on food stores or by use of alternatives such as lactic acid or acetone bodies by the brain, but later on these more readily available food stores are used up and the only available source of carbohydrate is from body protein (gluconeogenesis) with a small contribution from the glycerol of fats.

Cortisone stimulates gluconeogenesis and in some stressed cases is found to be increased. Harris (unpublished) has shown that in small-for-dates babies the rise in free fatty acids is less than in normal full-time babies, but in anoxic small-for-dates babies the rise in free fatty acids is greater. In hypoglycaemic small-for-dates babies, the rise of free fatty acids was less in those with symptoms than in those without.

The danger of long continued severe hypoglycaemia to the brain in the very underweight infants is very great. In our own study[25] of the blood sugar in the first 48 hours of life every infant whose birth weight was under 1500 gm. at some time had a value of 20 mgm. per cent or less. In most infants this low level was of only a few hours duration and with early feeding a more satisfactory level was subsequently maintained. Whenever it was not, steps were taken to increase the blood sugar; glucagon or hydrocortisol injections being tried before a final recourse to intravenous dextrose. In these circumstances care must be taken to avoid a fall in the blood sugar due to the infused glucose causing an increase in insulin secretion and in consequence prolonged hypoglycaemia. Gradual reduction of the rate of infusion should help reduce this hypersecretion of insulin.

Blood sugar levels can be related to the availability of stored glycogen. This is found in the liver and muscles, both voluntary and cardiac. In fatal cases of the respiratory distress syndrome the amount of glycogen in the liver is very low.[18] The final failure of the heart is not due to exhaustion of the cardiac glycogen[11], but to low pH inhibiting enzymatic processes or to a rise in plasma potassium. The liver is probably the only organ which will liberate important amounts of glucose in response to a fall in glucose levels: glucose is not liberated by voluntary or cardiac muscle in response to low blood sugar levels, nor in response to adrenalin or glucagon. Muscular exercise, however, liberates much lactic acid which can be converted to glycogen by the liver. Thus it may be a despairing response of the brain to low blood sugar to cause convulsions so liberating glucose-forming lactic acid from muscle glycogen.

The failure of the neonate to establish a glucose level similar to that of an older child is due to its different metabolic mechanisms. In the adult liver, glycogen is formed from glucose when the blood sugar level is raised above normal level (about 100 mgm. per 100 ml.) and the converse occurs as blood sugar falls below about 90 mgm. glucose. Such a response would be of no use for the storing of glycogen in the fetal liver. With a fetal blood sugar of 70–100 mgm. the point at which the glycogen is formed must be much lower and the point at which glucose is formed from glycogen must be still lower. That this is so has been shown by Walker[20] in a study of the enzyme systems of the fetal liver. The level of the blood sugar in infants cannot be regulated as in the adult. The level of blood sugar needed to stimulate insulin excretion in the neonate is probably also lower; and studies of the response of infants to intravenous glucose shows that increased insulin excretion occurs at much lower blood sugar levels than in an adult.[17]

LACTIC ACID

Lactic acid in the cord blood is nearly always high. This is caused by two factors:— the rise of maternal blood lactic acid during labour, and the period of anoxia the majority of infants experience at birth. Lactic acid has been shown to be able to cross the placenta with equal facility in either direction. As soon as the infant's blood is adequately oxygenated the lastic acid level falls. In a group of infants born abnormally (Caesarian section, forceps delivery, or with maternal pre-eclampsia) this fall in the lactic acid level does not occur and there may even be a further rise. There was no evidence of respiratory failure, and no difference between those infants with peripheral cyanosis and those with normal colour.[15] It is possible that some areas of the body have inadequate blood flow but there is no evidence to support this and at present no satisfactory explanation of this persistently raised lactic acid level is known.

There is a small group of infants who suffer from persistent and often fatal lactic acid acidosis. There is yet no adequate explanation for this abnormality. It may resemble the situation in adults who are found to have high lactic acid levels in excess of the normal lactic acid—pyruvic acid ratio[10] and again the only acceptable explanation is a failure of capillary circulation in some areas. There is a marked rise in lactic acid in shock with a similar failure of capillary circulation.

FAT METABOLISM

In the neonate the needs of the body for energy and growth vary from organ to organ and the proportion of cardiac output circulating to any organ is some index of its needs. Almost half of the cardiac output goes to the head and as the brain is not able to use fat the whole of its energy needs must be supplied by carbohydrates or ketone bodies. Since the carbohydrate stores at birth are much smaller than the fat stores the needs of the rest of the body will have to be met mainly by fat (*see* chapter Hull). Apart from that required for body function and growth, energy is also needed soon after birth for thermoregulation and this is economically provided by brown fat. Brown fat differs from depot fat in having a much greater blood supply and in being able to oxidize fatty acids *in situ*, thus producing heat. This warms the blood which is then re-circulated to the body. An increase of several degrees in skin temperature over areas of brown fat can be detected. Since the brown fat organ only consumes fatty acids, the glycerol moiety escapes into the blood and can be changed in the liver into much needed carbohydrate. The brown fat organ can be stimulated by adrenalin secreted by the suprarenal as a response to cooling of the skin, but for this adequate oxygen supplies are essential and if the blood oxygen is low, theinfant is unable to maintain its optimal temperature.

Fat is carried in the blood as free fatty acid, chlycomicrons and lipo-proteins. The utilization of free fatty acid, which has a biological half life of 2 to 3 minutes, varies with its blood level; and thus the blood level is an index of the rate of its use. The utilization of the other blood fat elements is in general less affected by their blood level. Studies of the utilization of free fatty acid and glucose by a perfused beating heart have shown that the heart muscle uses free fatty acid in preference to glucose, thereby economizing in the use of carbohydrate.

The level of fats in cord blood is very low as would be expected since while in the uterus the fetus is building up fat stores and not oxidizing fats. Soon after birth the blood fat level starts to rise and by 12 hours it has doubled with the most marked rise in the free fatty acids. A change in total body metabolism is shown by a change in the Respiratory Quotient which at birth is about one; within a few hours it rapidly falls to nearly 0·7, suggesting a predominant use of fat. This fall is greater in the under-weight infant presumably owing to carbohydrates being less available.

ENZYMES

Some enzymes are present in adequate amounts at birth; others are present in small amounts and need to increase in activity. This entails protein synthesis and there is ample evidence of increased protein production in the neonatal liver. So great is the demand for nitrogen that the blood urea falls in the first few hours of life[1] and, as shown by balance experiments[23] little appears in the urine in the first 24 hours. Unless new aminoacids are absorbed from the gut, the need for essential aminoacids for synthesis will require the breakdown of existing protein within a few hours to obtain them. This will cause the blood urea to rise again (Fig. 3). The stimulus to increased enzyme production may be the accumulation of substrate or the changes in the environment caused by birth. Some enzymes increase after birth irrespective of the maturity of the infant at birth (*see* chapter Raiha).

Many of the enzymes associated with degradation of aminoacids are of low activity at birth but reach adult levels within a few days. Thus the urine passed in the first few days of life has an abnormal aminoacid pattern especially in respect of tyrosine, phenylalanine and tryptophan.

UREA

Urea is an end product of nitrogen metabolism. In the neonate nitrogen is in great demand for growth purposes and for enzyme production and, in the rapidly growing neonate almost all the nitrogen intake is utilized for growth and urea production is very small. In the human neonate the balance studies of Wilkinson *et al.*[23] show that in its 2–3 day period of weight loss the nitrogen balance is negative, but when weight becomes stationary in the next 3–4 days the nitrogen balance is positive.

PHOSPHORUS

The level of the inorganic blood phosphorus in the cord blood is rather variable and depends both on the maternal

TABLE 1

	Cord Blood mg. P/100 ml.	*Capillary Blood* *24 hr* mg. P/100 ml.	*72 hr*
Inorganic blood phosphorus	4·7	4·22	4·75
Acid soluble organic phosphorus in red cells	43·6	40·35	41·3
Number of cases	74	108	60

Phosphorus in unselected cases in a general hospital Maternity Unit.

level and on the development of the fetus. Thus a small group[14] of entirely normal full-term infants whose birth was equally normal gave a mean value of 5·65 mg. per 100 ml.[1] Premature infants of expected weight for gestational age gave a mean of 4·1 mg.[4] An unselected group of 74 cord

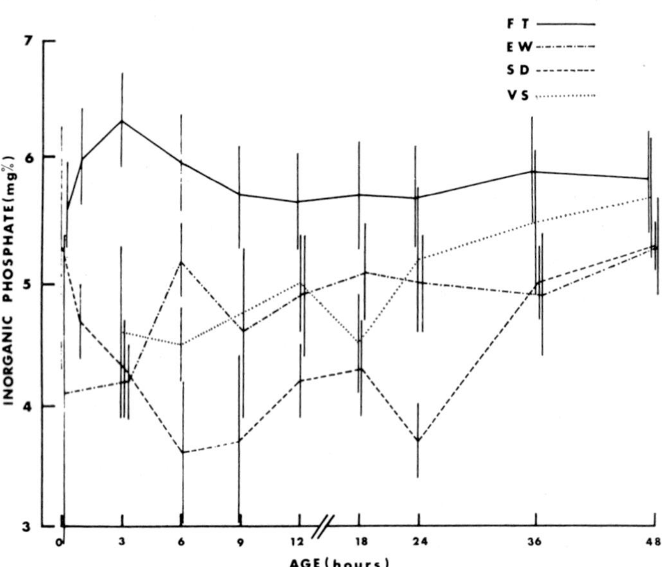

FIG. 6. Mean values of whole blood inorganic phosphorus in the same four groups of healthy infants as in Fig. 3.

bloods from a general obstetric unit gave a mean of 4·7 mg. (Payne unpublished observations).

Watney *et al.*[21] in an unselective consecutive series in a Midland maternity hospital found the overall cord blood phosphorus to be 5·98 mg per 100 ml. During the gestational period the maternal inorganic phosphate was low—about 3 mg. per 100 ml., but six weeks after the birth of the child the mean value had risen to 3·8 mg. Dividing their cases according to the 6th day serum calcium level of the baby they found that the mothers of babies with lower calcium levels also had lower phosphorus levels.

In the 14 normal infants the mean blood phosphorus rose to 6·35 mg. at 3 hours and fell to 5·71 mg. per 100 ml. blood at 24 hours. In the 74 unselected cases at 24 hours the mean phosphorus was 4·22 mg. per 100 ml. blood. In the earlier study at a London maternity hospital of cases where the labour had not been normal the mean phosphorus level was higher than in the normals and remained raised for the 48 hours of the study.[15]

In a later unpublished study the blood phosphorus was found to be lower in infants needing special care and levels under 3 mg. per 100 ml. blood were frequently found.

Such low levels also occurred during the succeeding 48 hours in all groups. They were sometimes associated with low total acid soluble phosphate but could not be related to any clinical manifestation nor to birth weight nor maturity.

In the second unselected group the acid soluble organic phosphorus was estimated. This fraction of the blood phosphorus is entirely in the red cells. The total acid soluble phosphorus in the whole blood was estimated and from the packed cell volume of the red cells the cell content of acid soluble phosphorus was calculated in cord blood and in capillary blood (heel) at 24 and 72 hours. The results are given in Tables I, II and III. There are no great differences between the levels at birth, 24 and 72 hours, but there is a small fall in the acid soluble phosphorus in the red cells at 24 hours. Despite this fall the total phosphorus of the blood is higher at 24 hours but this is due to the increase in the packed cell volume. The differences between the 24 and 72 hour values are not significant however but the difference between cord blood and 24 hour blood is significant.

The acid soluble organic phosphates are a mixture of various phosphoric esters in varying proportions depending on the cell type. In red cells the preponderant phosphoric

TABLE 2

Effect of Breast Milk and Half Cream Cow's Milk	*Breast Fed* *3rd day* mg. P/100 ml.	*10th day*	*Cow's Milk* *3rd day* mg. P/100 ml.	*10th day*
Inorganic blood phosphorus	4·79	4·53	4·97	4·93
Acid soluble organic phosphorus in red cells	46·5	52·8	49·2	54·0
Number of cases	44		57	

Phosphorus in normal cases in a small Maternity Hospital.

TABLE 3

	Day 3 Normal weight	Day 3 S.D.	Day 3 Prem.	Day 7 Normal weight	Day 7 S.D.	Day 7 Prem.
	mg. P/100 ml.			mg. P/100 ml.		
Inorganic blood phosphorus	3·3	3·1	3·42	4·04	3·86	4·2
Acid soluble organic phosphorus in red cells	36·0	39·0	39·1	40·9	41·8	39·3
Number of cases	6	11	11	5	9	11

Phosphorus in cases in a Special Care Baby Unit.
S.D. = weight less than 25th percentile for gestational age.
Prem. = weight under 2,500 g. but expected weight for gestational age.

ester is 2·3 diphosphoglyceric acid which combines with haemoglobin and causes the dissociation curve of O_2 to shift to the left.[14] Adenosine triphosphate (ATP) is present in all live cells. In muscle phosphocreatine is highest but glycerol phosphate and glucose phosphate are also present. In anoxic brain cells these compounds break down to liberate phosphoric acid, ATP being the last to do so. In acidosis a similar breakdown occurs.

SODIUM, FLUID BALANCE AND OSMOLARITY

The sodium level in the cord blood at birth is approximately equal to the mean maternal level but in the next 3–6 hours the plasma sodium level falls in most full-term babies (Fig. 7). In premature and small-for-dates infants however this fall occurs much less often. After 6 hours or so the sodium level rises to above the level at birth, the height of the rise depending on the amount of water given. The fall in our series was not due to loss of sodium in the urine since very little sodium was excreted in the first 12 hours and the subsequent rise occurred without any sodium being given. It may be due to transfer of sodium between extracellular and intracellular fluid.

As soon as the infant starts breathing he loses water in the expired air and soon also by insensible or even obvious sweating. The loss of weight which occurs in the first few days of life is nearly all due to water loss, that due to oxidation of carbohydrate, fat and sometimes protein accounting for only 10–15 per cent of the total. Various estimations of the amount of insensible water loss have been made but environmental factors such as temperature and humidity inevitably play a big part. A figure of 1 gram per kilogram per hour, of which 50 per cent is lost by the lungs, has been given by O'Brien *et al.*[13] This would give a daily loss of 2·4 per cent of the initial bodyweight. The mean loss of weight at the end of the third day of life is 7·22 per cent but this figure includes some feeding of the infant and also the weight of urine and stools passed.

Murdock in an as yet unpublished report has studied the water: solids balance in the first four days of life in two groups of infants, one group premature but of expected weight, the other group underweight for their gestational age. In both groups early feeding was given and over the four days the total solids balance was unchanged, but the water balance was negative. The total weight change was almost exactly equal to the water balance change. Urine volume in the first 24 hours was very small and the osmolarity of the urine was greater than that of the serum, though on and after the second day more urine was passed with an osmolarity less than that of the serum. By the

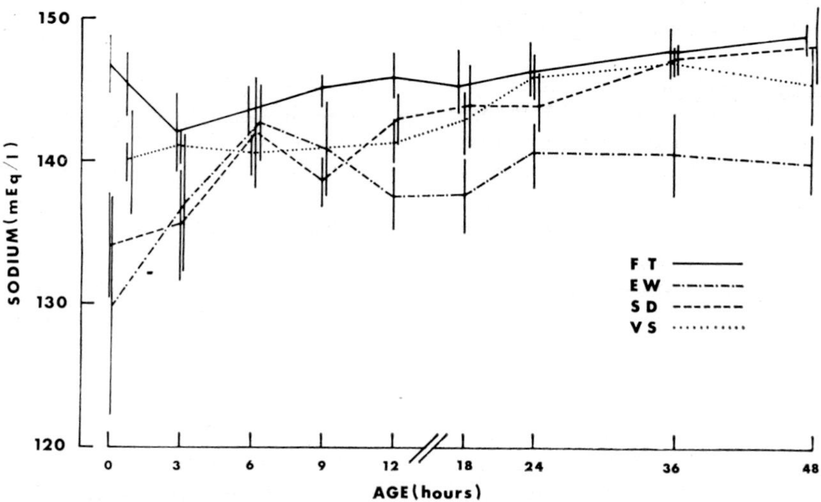

FIG. 7. Mean values of plasma sodium with standard error of the mean in the same groups of healthy infants as in Figure 3.

third day fluid intake balanced water loss and the babies began to gain weight. The serum osmolarity showed no correlation with the overall water balance and the rise of osmolarity on 3rd–5th days described by Davis *et al.*[3] and Dormandy and Begum[5] did not occur. These changes were probably due to inadequate fluid intake. Feldman and Drumond[6] report no regular change, and unpublished observations of Thearle and Chamberlain also show no significant changes during the first week.

In terms of sodium balance there is a slight positive balance by the end of the third day[23] so that an increase in the sodium concentration in the body fluids is inevitable. Friis-Hansen[7] has shown that the loss of water is spread evenly between extracellular and intracellular fluids during the early weeks of life. In this way the body cells become

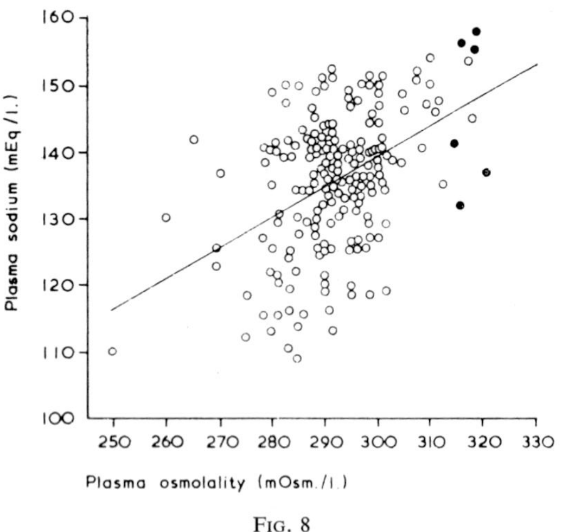

FIG. 8

smaller and more concentrated, but the osmotic gradient between the cellular contents and the extracellular fluid is unaltered. Although sodium salts represent the major factor in determining the osmotic pressure and there is an overall relation between them, the individual variations are considerable. Thus, in Figure 8 at an osmolarity of 290 micromols the sodium content of the plasma may vary from 110 meg. to 150 meg.

The deleterious effect of high sodium levels, especially in the brain, are well documented but it is more likely that the damage is related to the rise in osmotic pressure. In a study reported by Davis *et al.*[3] it was found that in dehydration fever occurring in the first week of life every case had a raised osmotic pressure but in only 3 of the 6 cases was the sodium level raised. Dormandy *et al.*[5] have pointed out that in the first days of life when growth is not occurring there is a catabolic metabolism in which large molecules are broken down to small ones. As the osmotic pressure depends on the number of molecules and not on their size it is probable that in the catabolic phase there would be an increase in the number of small organic molecules such as glucose, aminoacids and urea, and he attributes the increase in osmotic pressure to this. When growth starts an anabolic phase of metabolism starts in which small molecules are converted to one large molecule—which would account for the discrepancy between sodium and osmolarity. In our studies we were not able to estimate the osmotic pressure but during the anabolic phase of the first 48 hours we estimated the sodium, glucose, aminoacids, urea and lactic acid but did not find any rise except a small one in the urea quite inadequate to account for the rise of the osmotic pressure recorded by Davis *et al.*[3] and by Dormandy and Begum.[5]

The breakdown of large molecules such as glycogen fat and protein which occurs to supply energy is balanced by the rapid oxidation of small molecules; but it is possible that in those cases where the osmotic pressure rose more than the sodium, the rate of oxidation was slow or the the breakdown much greater, and in such cases blood examination might show an increase in the various metabolites of the plasma. In some unpublished observations by Thearle and Chamberlain in which sodium, potassium, sugar, urea and protein were estimated in the same plasma as the osmolarity, there was a good agreement between the calculated and observed osmolarity, but only minimal daily variations were found during the first week of life. All the subjects had been adequately fed water and milk. In our studies in one infant with extreme metabolic disturbance the sugars, lactic acid and urea alone represented 56 milliosmols; and despite a fall in the sodium to 130 m.eq., the osmolarity of the plasma would have been over 315 milliosmols, a value at which symptoms occur. Similar calculations in some fatal cases of the respiratory distress syndrome indicate a considerable rise in the osmolarity from metabolites.

POTASSIUM

As already discussed, potassium leaves the cells of the body to go into the acid extracellular fluid, returning into cells when the acidity is corrected (Fig. 9). Potassium also leaves a cell when some of its contents are used to obtain energy. When a cell dies the whole of the intracellular inorganic contents are liberated into the extracellular fluid. The level of potassium in the neonate is therefore liable to changes and may reach quite high levels for some or all of the above reasons. The effect of changes of the potassium level are most marked in muscle and in particular in the electrical activity of the heart. Too high a potassium level can cause cardiac failure and in the more mature organism levels of over 8 or 9 m.eq. can be dangerous. In the neonate the effect of the potassium level is less marked and values of 10 m.eq. sometimes cause no changes in the E.C.G., indeed such levels can be well tolerated and do not need specific treatment. As mentioned earlier the inorganic contents of a cell may be liberated into the extracellular fluid, and phosphorus levels in particular will show variations which parallel those of potassium.

PLASMA PROTEIN

The total plasma proteins in the neonate are about 6 g per 100 ml. which is less than the mean adult value. In a group of full-term normal infants who were not fed for 48 hours[1] the value rose to 7 g per 100 ml. This was probably due to water loss, as a similar rise in sodium also occurred. In infants over 1500 g body weight the value in premature babies was 5·6 g per 100 ml., and in small-for-dates babies it was 5·7 g per 100 ml. while in the very small group under 1500 g it was 5·1. The albumen content showed very little variation, the values being 3·8, 3·6 and 3·7 g per 100 ml. respectively, but the gobulin values were 1·7 g per 100 ml. in the babies of expected weight for dates but low gestational age, 2·0 g per 100 ml. in the small-for-dates (but of greater gestational age) and 1·3 g per 100 ml. in the very small.[4]

That such low values of plasma proteins do not give rise to oedema may be due to the lower capillary pressure which arises from the lower blood pressure of the infant. The variation in the globulin with gestational age is due to the lower level of immune globulins in the premature infant.

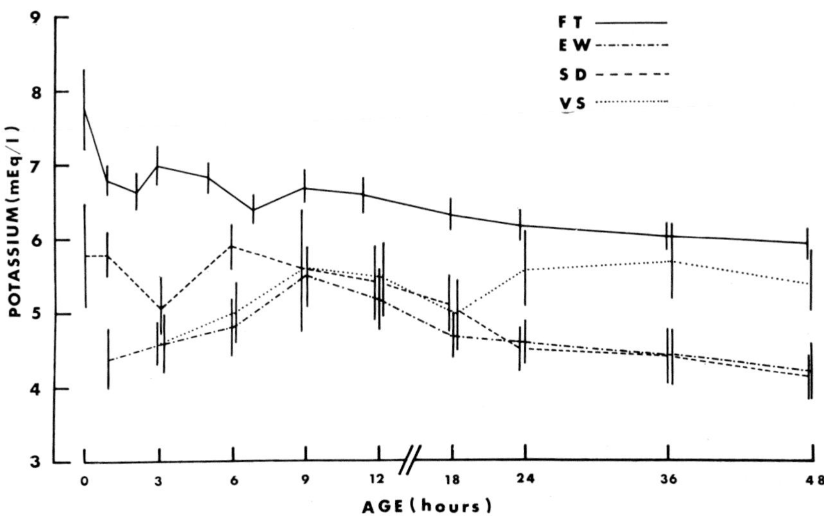

FIG. 9. Plasma potassium—mean values with standard error of the mean in the four groups as in Fig. 3.

PACKED CELL VOLUME

The packed cell volume (P.C.V.) in the cord blood was 54 per cent with a range of 43 to 62 per cent, but the capillary P.C.V. would be higher owing to the smaller calibre of the vessels. Duplicate readings taken 5–10 minutes after birth showed a mean increase of 9 per cent compared with the cord blood. During the next few hours the P.C.V. increased slowly falling after the peak value (mean value 70 per cent) to read 50 per cent at the end of the second day. These high packed cell volumes must have had a slowing effect on the circulation as a high viscosity increases the resistance to flow.

The rise in the first hours is due[8] to the opening up of the capillary bed of the lungs. The flow of particles and fluid through a tube gives rise to a layering of the contents, the particles tending to be more centrally placed while the wall is lined with fluid. The entrapment of plasma by the capillary walls of the lung would reduce the available plasma and thus cause a rise in the P.C.V.

CALCIUM AND MAGNESIUM

The calcium in the cord blood was a little higher than the maternal serum calcium but after birth the baby's serum calcium steadily fell, reaching a mean low value of 7·7 mg per 100 ml. between 24 and 48 hours. The lowest value recorded in a group of symptomless normal infants was 5·9 mg. per 100 ml. at 48 hours[1] (Fig. 10). These infants were not fed milk until 48 hours old. Comparison with premature infants who were fed milk from 12 hours showed that their values were somewhat higher, but the lowest values occurred in the very small infants and other observers report lower calcium levels in the smaller infants.[25]

Homeostasis of calcium is controlled in the adult by parathormone and calcitonin stimulating the osteocytes to liberate or retain bone calcium, by absorption from the gut, and by renal excretion. In the infant bone structure is more primitive; the osteocytes are less active; and the control of the serum calcium resembles that of the adult rat whose bone is also primitive in structure.[19] In the rat and infant human the calcium level is maintained by the same three factors—intake of calcium, deposition of calcium in bone, and excretion of calcium in the urine. With no calcium intake and uncalcified osteoid tissue taking up calcium and even though very little calcium appears in the urine, the serum calcium falls. As soon as an adequate calcium intake is obtained the serum calcium rises. Occasionally the serum calcium falls so low that symptoms occur (infantile tetany). The symptoms are due to a fall in ionic calcium and the level of ionic calcium partly depends on the pH, being higher in acidosis. Thus ammonium chloride by mouth, which causes an acidosis, has been used to treat infantile tetany in addition to administration of calcium, orally or intravenously, or of parathormone.

A little later at 6th–8th day of life a second fall in serum calcium may occur. This is more common in infants fed cow's milk preparations and usually occurs in well developed infants who are putting on weight. The reason for this second fall of calcium is not clear. It has been postulated that if too much phosphorus is absorbed the solubility constant calcium and phosphorus is raised above its limit and calcium phosphate ($CaHPO_4$) is deposited as insoluble material. This can certainly occur since in hypercalcaemia if intravenous phosphates are given the calcium level falls and in some cases pathological deposits of calcium have been found. But it is unlikely to be the cause in infancy since if the correct solubility factor for the calcium and phosphorus of serum is taken it is not found to be exceeded since much calcium and some phosphorus are not in ionic solution in the plasma. There is much variability from baby to baby in the relation between calcium and phosphorus in the serum and some infants have high phosphate values and normal calcium levels.

Dormandy and Begum[5] have reported some unexpected results in studying the response of infants to oral feeds. They found that in infants calcium in solution caused a rise in serum calcium while glucose caused a fall. However, when pure water was given, in some infants the calcium rose, while in others it fell or did not change. When they considered the osmolarity of the serum they found that in all cases in which the serum calcium rose the initial osmolarity was over 319 milliosmols. No observations on the osmolarity of the plasma in infantile tetany have been published.

SERUM MAGNESIUM

This varies in a manner closely linked with calcium. The normal value is about 1·8 to 2·2 mg. per 100 ml. As with

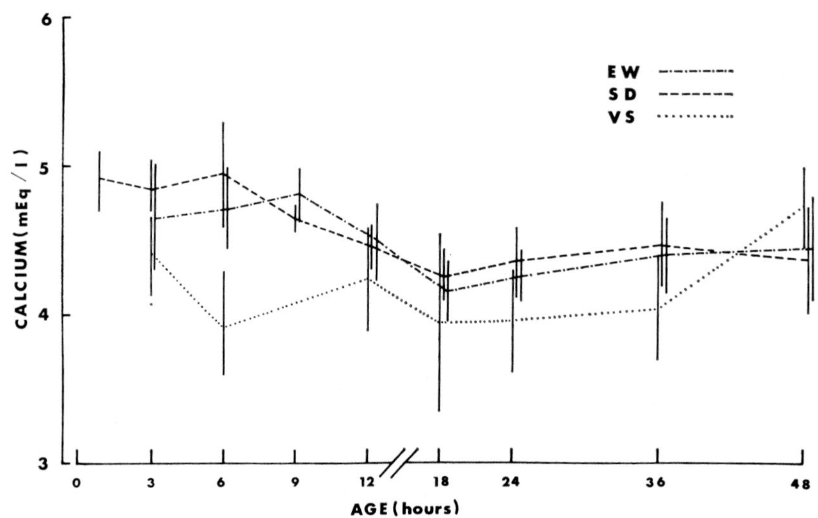

FIG. 10. Mean plasma calcium with standard error of the mean in three of the four groups of Fig. 3.

Balance experiments on various diets[24] show that more calcium is retained with breast feeding than with some cow's milk formulae. The controlling factor is the actual calcium absorption. Widdowson *et al.*[22] have shown that the faecal calcium is related to the faecal fat—in particular to palmitic and stearic acid content. Phosphorus is well absorbed. In the neonate the urinary calcium and phosphate excretion is very low and can be neglected.

Once the calcium is absorbed it will be utilised for bone formation if enough free phosphate is available.

Nichols and Rogers[12] have shown that calcification of bone appears to be brought about by bone cells lying between extracellular fluid and the protein matrix of bone. These cells take up calcium in large amounts and are influenced by parathormone, their calcium content falling with parathyroidectomy and increasing after parathormone. If PO_4 is increased in the extracellular fluid efflux of calcium from bone stops and influx of calcium increases; the calcium of the fluid bathing them is thus lowered. This would seem to be the experimental counterpart of the state of affairs in some infants whose plasma phosphate rises more rapidly than the plasma calcium. To avoid low calcium the calcium intake should be increased.

calcium, in the very small infants under 1500 g birthweight the level is lower, being 1·6 mg per 100 ml. at its lowest at 24 hours and rising to 1·8 mg. per 100 ml. at 48 hours.

The relation between calcium and magnesium can be shown in the uncommon condition of hypomagnesiaemia. Here the serum calcium is low but no treatment will increase the serum calcium until serum magnesium is brought to normal level. The reason for this linkage of calcium and magnesium is not known. The cause of the low level of magnesium in some cases was due to maternal factors, the mother being also hypomagnesic; in others to an abnormality of absorption, very little magnesium being absorbed; and in a single case neither factor was present.

REFERENCES

1. Acharya, P. T. and Payne, W. W. (1965), "Blood Chemistry of Normal Full-term Infants in the First 48 hr. of Life," *Arch. Dis. Childh.*, **40**, 430–435.
2. Cahill, G. F., Jr. (1970), "Starvation in Man," *New Engl. J. Med.*, **282**, 668–675.
3. Davis, J. A., Harvey, D. R. and Stevens, J. F. (1966), "Osmolality as a Measure of Dehydration in the Neonatal Period," *Arch. Dis. Childh.*, **41**, 448–450.

4. Davis, J. A., Payne, W. W., Stevens, J. and Yu, J. (1969), "Some Metabolic Aspects of the Ill Premature Infant with the Respiratory Distress Syndrome," *Helv. paediat. Acta*, **24**, 609–632.
5. Dormandy, T. L. and Begum, R. (1969), "The Plasma Calcium and Plasma Magnesium Response to Standard Metabolic Loads in Infants," in *Mineral Metabolism in Paediatrics*, pp. 31–50 (D. Barltrop and W. L. Burland eds.). Oxford: Blackwell.
6. Feldman, W. F. and Drumond, K. N. (1969), "Serum and Urine Osmolality in Normal Full-term Infants," *Canad. med. Ass. J.*, **101**, 595.
7. Friis-Hansen, B. (1957), "Changes in Body Water Compartments During Growth," *Acta paediat. Stockh.*, suppl. 110, **46**, 1–68.
8. Gairdner, D., Marks, J., Roscoe, J. D. and Brettell, R. O. (1959), "The Fluid Shift from the Vascular Compartment Immediately After Birth," *Arch. Dis. Childh.*, **33**, 489–498.
9. Guest, G. M. (1953), "Relationship of Potassium and Inorganic Phosphorus to Organic Acid Soluble Phosphates in Erythrocytes; Metabolic Effects of Acidosis," *J.—Lancet*, **373**, 188–189.
10. Huckabee, W. E. (1959), "Relationships of Pyruvate and Lactate During Anaerobic Metabolism. III. Effect of Breathing Low-oxygen Gases," *J. clin. Invest.*, **37**, 264–271.
11. Klionsky, B. (1968), "Role of Hyperkalaemia in Experimental Fetal Asphyxia," *Arch. Dis. Childh.*, **43**, 747.
12. Nichols, G., Jr. and Rogers, P. (1971), "Mechanisms for the Transfer of Calcium Into and Out of the Skeleton," *Pediatrics*, **47**, 211–228.
13. O'Brien, D., Hansen, J. D. L. and Smith, C. A. (1954), "Effect of Supersaturated Atmospheres on Insensible Water Loss in the Newborn Infant," *Pediatrics*, **13**, 126–132.
14. Orzalesi, M. M. and Hay, W. W. (1971), "The Regulation of Oxygen Affinity of Fetal Blood. I. *In Vitro* Experiments and Results in Normal Infants," *Pediatrics*, **48**, 857–864.
15. Payne, W. W. and Acharya, P. T. (1965), "The Effect of Abnormal Birth on Blood Chemistry During the First 48 hr. of Life," *Arch. Dis. Childh.*, **40**, 436–441. *M*
16. Persson, B., Settergren, G. and Dahlquist, G. (1972), "Cerebral Arterio-venous Difference of Acetoacetate and D-β-hydroxybutyrate in Children," *Acta paediat. Stockh.*, **61**, 273–278.
17. Schiff, D. (1968), *Ph. D. Thesis*. University of London.
18. Shelley, H. J. (1964), "Carbohydrate Reserves in the Newborn Infant," *Brit. med. J.*, **i**, 273–275.
19. Steendijk, R. (1969), "Bone and Calcium Homeostasis in the Fetus and Young Infant," in *Mineral Metabolism in Paediatrics*, pp. 51–52 (D. Barltrop and W. L. Burland, eds.). London: Blackwell.
20. Walker, D. G. (1962), "The Development of Hepatic Hexokinases After Birth," *Biochem. J.*, **84**, 118P–119P.
21. Watney, P. J. M., Chance, G. W., Scott, P. and Thompson, J. M. (1971), "Maternal Factors in Neonatal Hypocalcaemia: A Study in Three Ethnic Groups," *Brit. med. J.*, **ii**, 432–436.
22. Widdowson, E. M., McCance, R. A., Harrison, G. E. and Sutton, A. (1963), "Effect of Giving Phosphate Supplements to Breast-fed Babies on Absorption and Excretion of Calcium, Strontium, Magnesium and Phosphorus," *Lancet*, **ii**, 1250–1251.
23. Wilkinson, A. W., Stevens, L. H. and Hughes, E. A. (1962), "Metabolic Changes in the Newborn"' *Lancet*, **i**, 983–987.
24. Williams, M. L., Rose, C. S., Morrow, G., Sloan, S. E. and Barness, L. A. (1970), "Calcium and Fat Absorption in Neonatal Period," *Amer. J. clin. Nutr.*, **23**, 1322-1330.
25. Yu, J., Payne, W. W., Ifekwunigwe, A. and Stevens, J. (1965), "Biochemical Status of Healthy Premature Infants in the First 48 hr. of Life," *Arch. Dis. Childh.*, **40**, 516–525.

9. PERINATAL DEVELOPMENT OF SOME ENZYMES OF AMINO ACID METABOLISM IN THE LIVER

NIELS C.R. RÄIHÄ

INTRODUCTION

Development and differentiation is the translation of genetic information of the egg, embodied in its DNA, to form the living breathing organism. The main problem in this process lies in the regulation of protein synthesis which is the basis for the orderly differentiation of specific cells. How are some DNA segments made to call out their information at certain critical periods and others suppressed? Now that considerable information has accumulated concerning mechanisms of protein synthesis and regulation of enzymic activity it should soon be possible to interpret developmental events in molecular terms. The conceptual and practical application of the new biochemical knowledge to problems of mammalian differentiation is only beginning, and although it might seem difficult to extrapolate this knowledge to clinical medicine, it is from here that the understanding of human growth and development will evolve.

The process of development may be considered to begin with the fertilization of the ovum and the biochemistry of the early mammalian embryo is a field of research which recently has shown much progress.[9] During the latter part of intrauterine life the fetus increases its capacity to perform many of the biochemical and physiological functions which are typical for the differentiated tissues and cells. Many of the processes of maturation occur around birth and continue for sometime thereafter.

The liver plays an important role in the metabolic homeostasis of the mammalian organism and the biochemical development and differentiation of this organ has been one of the most extensively studied during recent years.[64,22] The main concern is the mechanism underlying the transformation of the quantitative and qualitative pattern of enzymes of fetal liver to adult liver. This process of enzymic differentiation involves both positive changes such as the appearance or sudden rise in the amount of some enzymes, and negative changes, such as the decrease in the amount of other enzymes. The liver of the newborn mammal must rapidly adapt to meet the metabolic demands which extrauterine life exerts on it. The content of this chapter will deal only with the development of a few of these many functions of the liver, namely amino acid biosynthesis and nitrogen excretion. The metabolic development of the human fetus and neonate and the clinical implications of this development will be especially stressed. The obvious difficulties in the past in obtaining suitable human material have meant that most of the available data in the literature on enzyme development have been obtained from studies performed on laboratory animals. These data cannot always be applied to human development due to great species differences in the speed and manner of maturation, and in the different stages of maturity reached at birth by different species.

Regulation of Enzyme Synthesis in the Liver

Change in activity of an enzyme can be due to an activation of a pre-existing enzyme protein or to a change in the rate of its synthesis or degradation. It is well established that the synthesis of many enzyme proteins, especially in the liver, is regulated by hormones. This effect is fairly specific since large changes in the rate of synthesis of specific enzyme proteins can be detected under conditions where total protein synthesis is not affected.

The inducible enzyme tyrosine α-ketoglutarate transaminase (TTA) in the liver is one of the most extensively studied enzymes during the perinatal period in rat, and thus it seems pertinent to review some of the data known about the regulation of the activity of this enzyme. TTA has uniformly very low activity in fetal livers of all species studied and increases rapidly within hours after birth.[46] Greengard and Dewey[23] have suggested that postnatal hypoglycemia stimulates glucagon release, which then acts through cyclic AMP by increasing liver TTA activity. Their finding that postnatal administration of glucose decreases the normal increase in TTA activity is in agreement with this hypothesis. Thus, glucagon released as a result of the postnatal hypoglycemia and acting though cyclic AMP may be responsible in all mammalian species for the accumulation of TTA. The failure of adrenalectomized newborn rats to undergo the normal postnatal increase in TTA activity, the induction of TTA synthesis by the administration of hydrocortisone to these animals[63] and further the observation by Franz and Knox[14] that administration of hydrocortisone to newborn rats did not elevate TTA activity until after the postnatal increase had occurred, suggest that glucocorticoids apparently also participate in the postnatal increase of TTA activity. Thus, TTA can be induced *in vivo* by hydrocortisone administration only in postnatal rats.[63,21,69] Other inducing agents such as glucagon, adrenaline and cyclic AMP act *in vivo* by elevating liver TTA activity in fetal animals,[20] but a definite developmental trend in the competence to react to these agents has been found. Greengard[21] recently presented a scheme (Fig. 1) indicating the development of the competence of the fetal rat liver to respond to glucagon and cyclic AMP *in vivo*. Her results demonstrate that the competence of liver to synthesize TTA under the influence of cyclic AMP is present 4 days before birth, but glucagon alone does not induce TTA at this developmental stage. During the next fetal days the capacity develops to raise the concentration of cyclic AMP on exposure to glucagon and noradrenaline, and thus the TTA activity can be evoked by these hormones as well as by cyclic AMP.

The development of the competence for the regulation of TTA activity does not stop at birth. Soon after birth while the enzyme is still responsive to glucagon it becomes inducible also by hydrocortisone. Throughout postnatal life administration of cortisone can induce a four- to five-fold increase in the amount of liver TTA within a few hours. After the age of two weeks in the rat glucagon has substantially no effect on TTA activity. Thus, the newly born

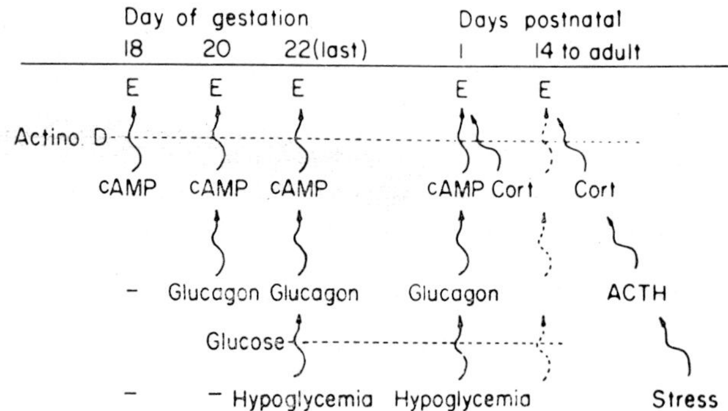

FIG. 1. The development of the competence for regulating the level of TTA in the perinatal rat. E = enzyme; cAMP = cyclic AMP; Actino = actinomycin D; Cort. = glucocorticoids. Greengard (8).

rat begins to synthesize TTA presumably due to the hypoglycemic stimulation on secretion of glucagon (or noradrenaline), which causes an increase in the cellular content of cyclic AMP, which in turn initiates the synthesis of the enzyme. Although glucocorticoid does not trigger this induction of TTA at birth, its presence may be important for the operation of the normal postnatal trigger mechanism. During adult life corticosterone becomes the main hormonal regulator of TTA activity.

Studies *in vitro* on rat liver explants in culture[69,70] have shown that term fetal liver can be stimulated to increase synthesis of TTA by glucagon, insulin and cyclic AMP, and that hydrocortisone is an effective inducer of TTA in cultures of liver from 17-day fetuses. Our own studies have demonstrated that fetal rat liver maintained in organ culture is not competent to respond to hydrocortisone by increasing the TTA activity before day 13–14 of gestation, although glucagon and cyclic AMP produce a stimulus at this age.[58] Thus, it seems evident from the available data that the competence to react by increased TTA activity in response to corticosteroids appears in fetal liver maintained in culture at an earlier developmental stage than *in vivo*. These findings are also in agreement with the hypothesis presented by Kenney *et al.*[32] that the induction of TTA activity by hydrocortisone is produced by a mechanism different from that of glucagon and adrenaline. Studies on TTA induction in cultures of hepatoma cells[31] are consistent with the hypothesis that steroid hormones act by promoting specific transcription, resulting in an increase in the *m*RNA which codes for the enzyme induced. The other hormones which can be thought of acting via increased cellular levels of cyclic AMP, glucagon and epinephrine, act by a mechanism distinct from that initiated by corticosteroids. Thus, it has been suggested that regulation of translation may be involved in the action of nonsteroid hormonal regulators of enzyme synthesis.[31]

Human fetal liver TTA activity is also low and a post-natal increase can be observed as in the other mammals studied. Liver explants in culture from a 28-week-old human fetus can be stimulated to increased TTA synthesis after the addition of the synthetic glucocorticoid triamcinolone to the medium. This induction of TTA by corticosteroid hormone cannot be observed in explants in culture from younger human fetuses.[58]

DEVELOPMENT OF SOME ENZYMES INVOLVED IN THE FORMATION "NON-ESSENTIAL" AMINO ACID

The "Non-essential" Amino Acids

The non-essential amino acids by definition, are those which can be formed within the mammalian organism. These are the following: *Alanine* which is formed by transamination of pyruvate (glucose) with glutamate, *arginine*

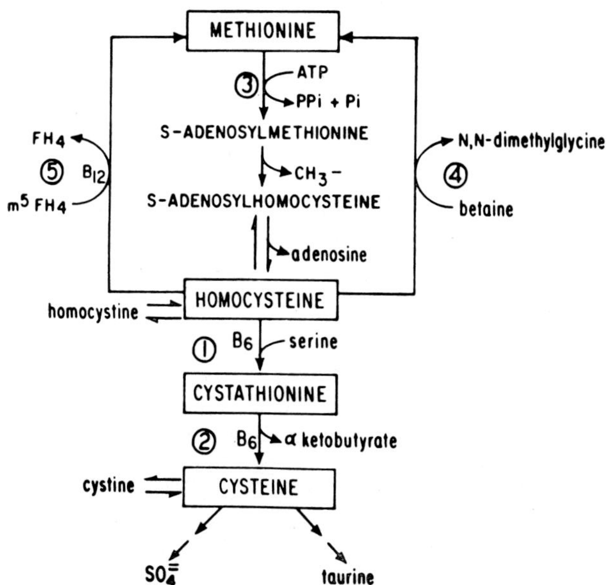

FIG. 2. The transsulfuration pathway.
1. Cystathionine synthase 2. Cystathionase 3. Methionine-activating enzyme 4. Betain-homocysteine methyltransferase 5. N^5-methyltetrahydrofolate-homocysteine methyltransferase.

by the reactions of urea biosynthesis (Fig. 5), *aspartate* by transamination of oxalacetate (from glucose) with glutamate, *cyst(e)ine* via the transsulfuration pathway from methionine (Fig. 2), *glutamate* by reductive amination of α-ketoglutarate (from glucose), *glycine* by the removal of the hydroxymethyl group from serine, *proline* from glutamate via glutamate semialdehyde and pyrroline carboxylate, *serine* by transamination of hydroxypyruvate or phosphohydroxypyruvate (from glucose) with alanine or glutamate and *tyrosine* from phenylalanine by hydroxylation. Thus, theoretically all the non-essential amino acids except cyst(e)ine and tyrosine can be made in the organism by feeding sufficient ammonium salts together with glucose to provide the carbon skeleton. The development of the pathways for cyst(e)ine and tyrosine biosynthesis will therefore be discussed in detail. Clinical and biochemical studies have provided evidence which suggest that these amino acids may be essential for the immature human infant.[67,65] The development of the oxidative metabolism of tyrosine will also be discussed due to its important clinical relevance and further arginine biosynthesis via the urea cycle will be dealt with.

Development of the Transsulfuration Pathway: Cyst(e)ine Biosynthesis

The majority of the amino acids essential for the rapid growth of the fetus are readily transported through the placenta from the maternal blood,[71] although the biosynthetic pathways for the production of certain amino acids may not be fully developed in the fetus.

After birth the supply of amino acids through the placenta ends and any amino acid which cannot be synthesized must be supplied in the nutrition of the animal.

In the adult mammal and also in the human, most of the ingested methionine is converted to cyst(e)ine,[61] a non-essential amino acid, via the transsulfuration pathway (Fig. 2).

In many mammals including the human, the concentration of amino acids is much higher in the fetal blood than in the maternal. An exception to this is cystine which shows a lower concentration in the guinea pig, monkey and human fetal blood as compared to the maternal blood.[71,16,20]

It has recently been shown[67] that the last enzyme in the transsulfuration pathway, cystathionase, is completely absent in the human fetal liver and brain in the presence of considerable activity of the other enzymes of this pathway: methionine-activating enzyme and cystathionine synthase. The appearance of cystathionase activity in human liver seems to be a post-natal phenomenon (Table 1). In premature infants who die soon after birth the cystathionase in the liver is absent. It appears slowly after the first week of life. In the full-term infant the activity is also very low at the moment of birth, and values of one-half to two-thirds of normal activity at 5–6 days of age have been found. The time of appearance of full activity in the human infant is not known, but it appears to be late in low birth weight infants.[67]

The activity of cystathionase in the liver of fetal rats at 18–20 days of gestation is not absent but considerably lower than that of the mother, and the liver of fetal mouse shows similar activities of cystathionase to those in the rat. The liver of the fetal guinea pig has levels of cystathionase close to adult values near term, but no activity at an early stage of gestation. In the rabbit no cystathionase activity

TABLE 1

ENZYMES OF TRANSSULFURATION AND CONCENTRATION OF CYSTAFLUONINE IN DEVELOPING HUMAN LIVER

Gestation	*Birth Weight (grams)*	*Time of death (hours)*	*Methionine-Activating Enzyme**	*Cystathionine Synthase**	*Cystathionase*	*Cystathionine Concentration (μmoles/100 g.)*
Fetus			26 ± 3	21 ± 4	0	14 ± 2
Premature	830	11	29	3	0	14
Premature	1,000	8	13	22	0	16
Premature	1,060	14	36	31	0	20
Premature	1,260	3	29	18	0	7
"Small-for-dates"	1,500	96	17	21	49	4
Full term	3,450	7	10	32	9	32
Full term	4,250	72	15	25	85	2
Full term	2,730	96	18	138	66	4
Mature Controls (9)			86 ± 16	98 ± 19	126 ± 12	0

* Enzymatic activities expressed as nanomoles product formed/mg. soluble protein/hr. ± standard error.

could be found at 15 days of gestation and only very low activity could be measured at 25 days (31-day gestation). The liver of the fetal Rhesus monkey has no activity at a late stage of gestation (152–159 days) but the fetal baboon has cystathionase activity present at the end of gestation. Thus, considerable species variations occur in the development of cystathionase activity in the liver and the Rhesus monkey and the rabbit seem to be closest to the human with regard to the perinatal development of cystathionase activity.[17]

The concentration of cystathionine, the substrate for cystathionase which is present in low concentration in normal adult human liver, was found to be high in fetal liver, as well as in newborn infants with low cystathionase activities. In older infants who showed increasing cystathionase activity, the cystathionine concentration was low (Table 1). These findings concerning the concentrations of cystathionine in human fetal liver are in agreement with the enzymatic results showing the absence of cystathionase.[67]

The human placenta cannot perform the transsulfuration function for the fetus, since the enzymatic mechanism is also absent.[67] Thus, cyst(e)ine may be an essential amino acid until sometime after birth, and the human fetus is entirely dependent upon the mother for its supply of cyst(e)ine for protein synthesis.

When transfer of amino acids into human fetuses with intact placental circulation was studied by infusion of the amino acid to be investigated into the maternal circulation the following was found: methionine accumulated in the fetal plasma against a three-fold concentration gradient; and leucine which is transported by the same carrier system as methionine in most tissues, behaved similarly. Cystine which is lower in the fetal plasma showed a slow increase after the infusion and was always lower than the maternal concentration. Ornithine which in most tissues is transported like cystine showed a similar rapid transplacental transport as methionine and leucine. Thus, cyst(e)ine was not transferred across the human placenta against a concentration gradient by active transport but probably by simple facilitated diffusion.[16]

Cyst(e)ine is a potent inhibitor of the methionine activating enzyme, the first step in the transsulfuration pathway converting methionine to S-adenosylmethionine.[16] Preliminary studies[16] have pointed out that the inability of the human fetus to synthesize cyst(e)ine might be a way of conserving homocysteine which in turn is used in the transmethylation of 5-methyltetrahydrofolate to tetrahydrofolate which reacts with serine to form 5,10-methylenetetrahydrofolate a precursor of the DNA-specific nucleotide thymidylate. Thus, the low fetal concentration of cyst(e)ine and the slow transfer across the placenta may be an adaptation to a more rapid growth and DNA synthesis during intrauterine life.

Clinical Implications

The fact that cystathionase is absent from the fetus and that all three transsulfuration pathway enzymes are absent from the placenta suggests that the fetus is entirely dependent upon the mother for its supply of cyst(e)ine. This has obvious implications concerning fetal growth and development in cases where the mother is malnourished.

Cystathionase activity does not appear especially in the premature infants before sometime after birth and thus, during this period cyst(e)ine is an essential amino acid. In light of current interest in the effects of nutritional factors on brain development during early periods of growth and development (see chapter Dobbing), the question of nutritional requirements for cyst(e)ine and perhaps other amino acids as well, becomes very important. These observations have raised the question of cyst(e)ine supplementation in the diet of low birth weight infants and in poorly nourished mothers.[17]

Human milk is known to be relatively low in protein (1·1 per cent), high in cystine and low in methionine, whereas cow's milk contains more protein (3·6 per cent), but is low in cystine and high in methionine.[2] A controversy has existed in clinical pediatrics for some time concerning the optimal amount of protein that should be fed to premature infants.[12] Gordon *et al.*[18] have shown that when premature infants were fed cow's milk formula they gained weight faster than those fed human milk. These diets were isocaloric but they were not controlled for mineral content and thus the infants fed on the cow's milk formula probably retained more water due to the higher mineral content. Later Davidson *et al.*, using only cow's milk formulae with controlled mineral contents concluded that a protein intake of about 4 g./kg./day was better than about 2 g./kg./day as far as weight gain was concerned.[13]

Our studies concerning the inability of premature infants to synthesize cyst(e)ine raise the possibility that infants fed a cow's milk formula with a high protein content retain more nitrogen and grow faster than infants fed a cow's milk formula containing a lower concentration of protein,[65] close to that found in human milk, because the amount of cystine rather than the total protein content may be the limiting factor for protein synthesis and growth. Thus, in order to grow well a premature infant with a slow maturation of cystathionase activity in the liver should need a milk formula with a quality of protein the same as human milk containing relatively high levels of cystine. This is also true for intravenous feeding of newborn infants. It has been observed that the plasma methionine concentrations are high and cystine low after the administration of caseine hydrolysates to low birth weight infants.[66]

The enzymatic findings are also relevant to the neonatal screening for metabolic diseases. The absence of cystathionase provides an enzymatic explanation for the high frequency of cystathionuria in premature infants and for the high methionine levels in the blood of infants fed high protein diets.[44,35] These results also point out the importance of understanding the normal developmental course of a particular enzyme in the human before diagnosis of a genetic enzyme deficiency can be made.

Development of Phenylalanine Hydroxylase and Tyrosine Synthesis

In adult mammalian liver tyrosine is formed by a complex enzyme system which converts the essential amino acid phenylalanine to tyrosine. This system consists of several enzymes and cofactors and the final reaction forming tyrosine requires the enzyme phenylalanine hydroxylase and a tetrahydropterin cofactor. Either the naturally occurring compound tetrahydrobiopterin or the synthetic analog 6,7-dimethyltetrahydropterin can function as cofactor. In the presence of catalytic concentrations of the pterin cofactor the hydroxylation of phenylalanine is also dependent on a tetrahydropterin regenerating system such as dihydropteridine reductase and NADPH[28] (Fig. 3).

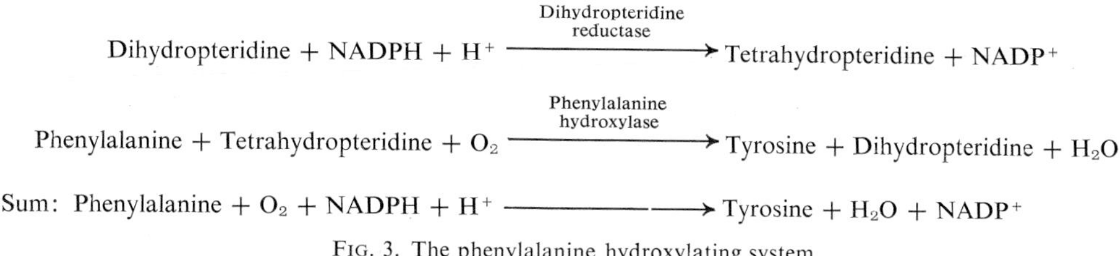

FIG. 3. The phenylalanine hydroxylating system.

For many years it was thought that the phenylalanine hydroxylase belonged to that group of mammalian liver enzymes that were essentially inactive or absent at birth.[33] These findings have been interpreted to mean that the enzyme defect in the newborn animal is the same as that found in the genetic disease phenylketonuria in which the cofactor and dihydropteridine reductase are present and phenylalanine hydroxylase is missing.[27] Elevated blood levels of phenylalanine in some newborn infants have been regarded as transient phenylketonuria of the newborn.

In 1965 is was shown, however, by Brenneman and Kaufman that in the rat phenylalanine hydroxylase was not inactive at birth.[8] They found that when supplemented by dihydropteridine reductase and the pterin cofactor the hydroxylase activity in newborn rat liver was equal to that of the adult. The levels of cofactor and dihydropterine reductase were however relatively low in newborn rat liver. In fetal rat liver phenylalanine hydroxylase is not present until about one day before term, when a rapid increase in activity occurs so that adult activity is reached at about 6 hours of age.[15] Marked species differences seem to exist in the development of phenylalanine hydroxylase activity. Thus, in the guinea pig considerable hydroxylase activity appears already much before term.[15]

Three reports concerning phenylalanine hydroxylase activity during human development appear in the literature. Kenney and Kretchmer[30] report the absence of the enzyme in one premature infant studied at necropsy, Ryan and Orr[55] reported that immature human fetuses were able to form tyrosine in the liver when ^{14}C-phenylalanine was infused into the umbilical vein after death, and during the course of our own studies Friedman and Kaufman[15] reported the presence of phenylalanine hydroxylase activity in the liver of one 23-week old human fetus. Studies in our laboratory[55] have shown that phenylalanine hydroxylase activity is present in human fetal liver after the 8th week of gestation, and activities similar to those found in adult livers are reached around the 13th fetal week (Table 2). Tyrosine was also formed when isolated human fetal livers were perfused with phenylalanine.

Clinical Implications

Clinical studies on the ability of the newborn infant to form tyrosine are somewhat conflicting. Thus, some

TABLE 2

DEVELOPMENT OF PHENYLALANINE HYDROXYLASE ACTIVITY IN HUMAN LIVER

ADULT *Age*	*Sex*	*Tyrosine formed µmoles/g. protein/h.*
22 years	female	130
42 years	female	136
54 years	male	154
72 years	male	140
78 years	female	93
FETAL *Gestation*	*Length*	
7 weeks	2·0 cm. C-R	0
8 weeks	5·0 cm. C-R	100
10 weeks	5·5 cm. C-R	74
12 weeks	7·0 cm. C-R	83
13 weeks	9·0 cm. C-R	172
13 weeks	10·0 cm. C-R	73, 110
14 weeks	11·5 cm. C-R	100
15 weeks	12·0 cm. C-R	100
16 weeks	13·0 cm. C-R	100, 135
18 weeks	16·0 cm. C-R	190
18 weeks	16·0 cm. C-R	60
19 weeks	17·0 cm. C-R	85
21 weeks	20·0 cm. C-R	67, 78
22 weeks	21·0 cm. C-R	86, 144
NEWBORN *Age*	*Weight*	
1½ days	780 g.	86 (1½ h.)
3 days	1,780 g.	73 (1 h.)
1 day	2,250 g.	30 (3 h.)
6 days	2,600 g.	54 (1 h.)
1 day	2,950 g.	90 (1 h.)

The numbers in parenthesis indicate the time in hours after death at which the liver samples were excised.

studies have reported elevated blood levels of phenylalanine in many premature and in some full term infants,[39,25,48] and decreased tolerance of phenylalanine loads in the normal newborn have been reported by Bremer and Neumann.[6] The elevated blood phenylalanine concentrations found especially in low birth weight infants have generally been attributed to a transient low activity of phenylalanine hydroxylase and thus paralleled with phenylketonuria.

On the other hand Levine *et al.*[40] have demonstrated that after administration of phenylalanine there is an increased urinary excretion of tyrosine in both premature and full-term newborn infants and Menkes and Avery[48] found normal phenylalanine tolerance tests in premature infants. Light *et al.*[45] observed moderate elevation of serum phenylalanine concentrations associated with a marked elevation of serum tyrosine in 25 per cent of low birth weight infants. Both serum phenylalanine and tyrosine levels returned to normal when 100 mg. daily of ascorbic acid was administered. Distinction from patients with phenylketonuria was possible by the recognition of the elevated tyrosine levels and by the response to administered ascorbic acid.

Our own studies indicate that phenylalanine hydroxylase is present in the liver from a very early stage of human development. The hyperphenylalaninemia observed in many premature infants for some time after birth should thus not be paralleled with a transient form of phenylketonuria (i.e. phenylalanine hydroxylase deficiency), but could rather be caused by excessive protein feeding or to a relative deficiency of the pteridine cofactor or the dihydropteridine reductase. In the newborn rat the pterin cofactor and the dihydropteridine reductase have been found to be low.[8] Snyderman[65] has been able to obtain data which indicate that tyrosine is a dietary requirement for the majority of premature infants, and that certain full-term infants also require it. This requirement persists for some months after birth. The results are based on studies on weight gain and nitrogen retention in infants fed on a 2 g. protein per kg. cow's milk formula with and without tyrosine supplementation. These results suggest that the phenylalanine hydroxylating system might be deficient in some premature infants although the enzyme phenylalanine hydroxylase is present.

DEVELOPMENT OF THE TYROSINE OXIDIZING SYSTEM

Tyrosine metabolism (Fig. 4) in the liver begins with a transamination with α-ketoglutarate, catalyzed by the

Phenylalanine
↓ (1)
Tyrosine
↓ (2)
p-Hydroxyphenylacetic Acid (6) ← *p*-Hydroxyphenylpyruvic Acid (5) → *p*-Hydroxyphenyllactic Acid
↓ (3)
Homogentisic Acid
↓ (4)
Fumarylacetoacetic Acid

The six steps are catalysed by the following enzymes:

(1) Phenylalanine hydroxylase.
(2) Tyrosine transaminase.
(3) *p*-Hydroxyphenylpyruvic acid oxidase.
(4) Homogentisic acid oxidase.
(5) *p*-Hydroxyphenylpyruvic acid dehydrogenase.
(6) *p*-Hydroxyphenylpyruvic acid decarboxylase.

FIG. 4. Metabolic pathway of tyrosine oxidation.

specific transaminase, tyrosine-α-ketoglutarate transaminase (TTA). The resultant *p*-hydroxyphenylpyruvate (*p*HPP) is then oxidized by an oxidase which contains ferrous iron. *p*HPP-oxidase activity is markedly inhibited by administration of tyrosine[34] and by its substrate *p*HPP.[72] This inhibition is reversible and can be restored by 2,6-dichlorophenolindophenol and ascorbic acid *in vitro* as well as *in vivo*.[34,72,73] Homogentisate is then attacked by another oxidase and an isomerase converts the formed maleoylacetoacetate to fumaroylacetoacetate which is then hydrolysed to yield fumarate and acetoacetate.

The collection of enzymes essential for the oxidation of tyrosine has been called the tyrosine oxidizing system. This tyrosine oxidizing activity of livers from fetal rats and premature infants has been reported to be very low.[38]

The development of TTA has been discussed earlier in this chapter and it is evident that this first enzyme in the oxidative pathway of tyrosine has very low activity in fetal livers of all mammals studied. Kretchmer[36] reported TTA activity of about 10 per cent of adult values in premature infants at necropsy. In our studies the TTA activity in human fetal livers at 14–24 weeks of gestation was approximately twice that activity found in fetal rat livers, and in a 1,000 g. premature infant who died at 12 hours of age the TTA activity wqs about twice that found in the fetuses.[58] Thus, a postnatal increase takes place as in the rat.

Goswami and Knox[19] demonstrated that in rat and guinea pig fetal liver the basal *p*HPP-oxidase activity is markedly lower than in adult animals. According to these authors the basal level of the enzyme (without activation) represents the available activity *in vivo*, since low levels of this fraction was correlated with the excretion of *p*HPP in the tyrosine fed adult guinea pig.

After birth the enzyme activity rose to adult levels gradually in the rat and more rapidly (within 1 day) in the guinea pig. The low fetal enzyme activities could be elevated several fold to 60–80 per cent of adult activity by preincubating the enzyme *in vitro* with 2,6-dichlorophenolindophenol and glutathione.[19] Thus, in fetal animals the enzyme *p*HPP-oxidase is partly in an inactive form.

Kretchmer and coworkers[37] have reported low activity of *p*HPP-oxidase in the liver of premature infants. The activity could be activated *in vitro* by the addition ot ascorbic acid.[36] These data indicate that also in the liver of the human premature infant the *p*HPP-oxidase is present in an inhibited form which can be activated.

Clinical Implications

The classic studies by Levine, Gordon and Marples[41,42,43] demonstrated a defect in tyrosine metabolism in premature infants on a rather high protein, low ascorbic acid intake. These infants showed an increased urinary output ot tyrosine and its metabolites and in most cases the blood tyrosine levels were above those seen in normal adult subjects.[48,45] Serum tyrosine levels were also high in some full-term infants.[4,3] The tyrosinemia was proportional to the protein intake of the infant and the defect was corrected when vitamin C was administered.[43] The biochemical basis for this transient defect in tyrosine metabolism in newborn infants is complex as discussed above, and may be due to several causes. One of these may be delayed development of TTA or *p*HPP-oxidase, together with its susceptibility to inactivation by its substrate and by tyrosine during increased protein load. It may also be caused by a deficiency of ascorbic acid. The tyrosinemia and tyrosinuria correlate well with the gestational age, and hence the serum tyrosine level after a protein load has been suggested as a useful biochemical assessment of gestational age in low-birth weight infants.[60]

The pattern of urinary tyrosine and phenolic acids in tyrosinemic patients is very similar to that in low-birth weight infants with transitory hypertyrosinemia. These infants, however, have no cirrhosis or renal tubular defects and their response to phenylalanine loads after the first weeks of life is normal compared with that of patients with hereditary tyrosinemia.[5]

No clinical abnormalities have been observed in low birth weight infants with transitory hypertyrosinemia at the time when the plasma tyrosine level is elevated.[3] Menkes and coworkers[49] were unable to find a significant difference at two years of age in the neurologic status of infants whose blood tyrosine levels were elevated during the neonatal period as compared to those with lower tyrosine levels. Similar negative results have been reported by others at the age of 22 and 43 months.[53]

In a recent follow-up study, however, Menkes and coworkers[50] report the first evidence that tyrosinemia in low birth weight infants at the age of 7–8 years may have permanent deleterious effects on intellectual functions in the area of visual perception. These authors suggest the possibility that the high protein formula feeding to low birth weight infants which has been in vogue during the past decade could be one of the causative factors responsible for the increased number of children with "minimal brain damage".

DEVELOPMENT OF UREA SYNTHESIZING ENZYMES IN MAMMALIAN LIVER

In the mammal excess nitrogen is excreted in the form of urea which is formed in the liver. There are five enzymes involved in the biochemical conversion of ammonia and CO_2 to urea (Fig. 5).

The first two enzymes, carbamylphosphate synthetase and ornithine transcarbomylase are mitochondrial. The other three enzymes, argininosuccinate synthetase or condensing enzyme, the argininosuccinase or cleavage enzyme and the arginase are found in the soluble portion of the cell.[24] The arginine synthetase system, composed of the condensing argininosuccinate synthetase and the cleaving argininosuccinase, catalyses the synthesis of arginine from citrulline.[59] In urea biosynthesis the arginine synthetase system contains the rate-limiting step, namely arginosuccinate synthetase.[11,57]

The development of the nitrogen excreting mechanism in the mammal can be compared to the evolutionary adaption for nitrogen excretion, where animals living in an aqueous environment excrete most of their nitrogen or ammonia into the water;[52] but in the progress towards terrestrial living, ammonia cannot be excreted as effectively and has to be detoxified by the formation of urea. A well known example of this is the tadpole which changes from ammonia excretion to urea production during metamorphosis.[10]

In the rat the urea producing capacity of the liver starts just prior to birth and increases rapidly after birth,[54] with a parallel increase in activity of all the five urea producing enzymes.[57] The observations that puromycin—an inhibitor of protein synthesis—inhibits the postnatal rise of the arginine synthetase system is compatible with the concept that the rise in the urea synthesizing capacity

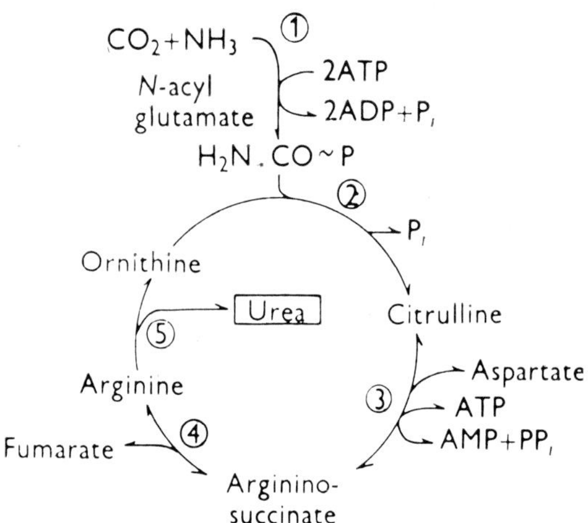

FIG. 5. The urea cycle.

around birth in the rat is due to the formation of new enzyme protein.[57]

Adrenalectomy at the moment of birth causes an inability of the newborn rat to undergo the normal postnatal increase in the arginine synthetase activity and this can be prevented by injections of corticosteroid.[57] Schwartz[62] has also found that corticosteroid administration during the perinatal period increases the activity of the arginine synthetase system within 24 hours after the steroid was given. The administration of glucagon which increases arginine synthetase system activity in adult rats was without effect in newborn rats but at five days of age a moderate rise could be observed. No stimulation could be elicited in fetuses after either corticosteroid of glucagon administration *in utero*.[62] The lack of stimulation *in utero* by steroid or glucagon suggests that either the liver is incapable of responding at this stage of development or that some suppressive phenomenon is present *in utero*. The first of these possibilities is unlikely, since both steroid and glucagon increases the activity of the arginine synthetase system *in vitro* when added to incubated fetal liver explants.[62] Thus, the hormonal regulation around birth of the urea synthesizing system resembles in many ways that of tyrosine transaminase.

In the developing pig on the other hand Kennan and Cohen[29] found all the urea cycle enzymes present at significant concentration in the liver of the youngest fetus studied at the 28th day of a 112–116-day gestation. These authors have discussed this marked difference between the rat and the pig in relation to the differences in the placental membranes and the maturation of the excretory organs in the two animals. The pig has an epitheliochorial placenta with several layers of membranes in comparison to the haemochorial relatively simple placenta of the rat. Thus the pig would be expected to have a lower rate of placental exchange and need a more efficient mechanism for detoxication of nitrogenous excretory products during fetal life. There is also an early appearance of the mesonephric kidney in the pig, and an increasing concentration of urea in the allantoic vesicle during the functional period of this kidney.[47]

The developmental pattern of the urea synthesizing enzymes in human liver is also different from that found in the rat.[56] The arginine synthesizing system is present with considerable activity already at an early stage of fetal development. The same is true for the other enzymes of the urea cycle.[56] Slices of human fetal liver are also able to produce urea when incubated under optimal conditions.[56] Again in the human, in contrast to the rat, mesonephric glomeruli have been noted at an early stage of development.[7] It has been suggested that there is a relationship in animals between the ability to synthesize urea and the degree of kidney development, thus in the placental mammals the urea synthesizing ability apparently starts when the embryonic glomelular kidney has developed.

CONCLUSION

The perinatal period in the mammal is characterized by intensive growth combined with functional development of individual organs. Specific proteins are synthesized at a rapid rate during critical periods of cellular proliferation in order to achieve the orderly completion of maturity and function of different parts of the organism. The availability of amino acids as building blocks for this protein synthesis is of crucial importance in order to achieve optimal results. The development of the brain is of special concern in the light of the current findings which show a permanent retardation caused by nutritional deprivation (*see* chapter Dobbing). Due to enzymic immaturity of the liver some amino acids cannot be synthesized and may be essential for the human fetus and neonate for some time after birth. Others are not metabolized and their concentration may reach high levels in infants fed diets rich in protein. This may also cause brain damage and mental retardation.

Our knowledge of the biochemical development of the human fetus and neonate and specially of the factors which regulate this development is still insufficient and needs further research. Based on the foregoing discussion concerning the nutritional implications of immature chemical development in the fetus and newborn infant it is suggested that nutritional management of the low birth weight infant should, in the future to a greater extent than before, take into consideration the specific needs and disabilities of the developing organism governed by its biochemical state of development. In this way we might promote an optimal intellectual development.

In this chapter the development of many important functions of the liver such as: carbohydrate and fat metabolism, detoxification, etc., have not been touched upon, but the reader is referred to recent good review papers on these subjects.[1,51,26]

Acknowledgement

Experimental work by the author presented in this article was supported by the Association for the Aid of Crippled Children, the Lalor Foundation and the Sigrid Juselius Stiftelse.

REFERENCES

1. Adam, P. (1971), "Control of Glucose Metabolism in the Human Fetus and Newborn Infant, in *Advances in Metabolic Disorders*, Vol. 5, pp. 183–275 (R. Levine and R. Luft, Eds.). New York: Academic Press.
2. Armstrong, M. D. and Yates, K. N. (1963), "Free Amino Acids in Milk," *Proc. Soc. exp. Biol. Med.*, **113**, 680–683.
3. Avery, M. E., Glow, C. L., Mnekes, J. H., Ramos, A., Scriver, C. R., Stern, L. and Wasserman, B. P. (1967), "Transient Tyrosinemia in the Newborn: Dietary and Clinical Aspects," *Pediatrics*, **39**, 378–384.
4. Bloxam, H. R., Day, M. G., Gibbs, N. K. and Woolf, L. I. (1960), "An Inborn Defect in the Metabolism of Tyrosine in Infants on a Normal Diet," *Biochem. J.*, **77**, 320–326.
5. Bodegard, G., Gentz, J., Lindblad, B., Lindstedt, S. and Zetterström, R. (1969), "Hereditary Tyrosinemia. III On the Differential Diagnosis and the Lack of Effect of Early Dietary Treatment," *Acta paediat. scand.*, **58**, 37–48.
6. Bremer, H. J. and Neumann, W. (1966), "Phenylalanin-Toleranz bei Frühgeborenan, reifen Neugeborenen, Säulingen und Erwachsenen," *Klin. Wschr.*, **44**, 1076–1081.
7. Bremer, J. L. (1916), "The Interrelation of the Mesonephros, Kidney and Placenta in Different Classes of Animals," *Amer. J. Anat.*, **19**, 179–182.
8. Brenneman, A. R. and Kaufman, S. (1965), "Characteristics of the Hepatic Phenylalanine Hydroxylation System in Newborn Rats," *J. biol. Chem.*, **240**, 3617–3622.
9. Brinster, R. L. (1971), "Biochemistry of the Early Mammalian Embryo," in *The Biochemistry of Development*, pp. 161–174 (P. F. Benson, Ed.). London: Heinemann.
10. Brown, G. W., Brown, W. R. and Cohen, P. P. (1959), "Comparative Biochemistry of Urea Synthesis. II. Levels of Urea Cycle Enzymes in Metamorphosing Rana Catesbeiana Tadpoles," *J. Biol. Chem.*, **234**, 1775–1780.
11. Brown, G. W. and Cohen, P. P. (1960), "Comparative Biochemistry of Urea Synthesis. III. Activities of Urea Cycle Enzymes in Various Higher and Lower Vertebrates," *Biochem. J.*, **75**, 82–91.
12. Cox, W. M. and Filer, L. J. (1969), "Protein Intake for Low Birth Weight Infants," *J. Pediat.*, **74**, 1016–1020.
13. Davidson, M., Levine, S. J., Bauer, C. H. and Dann, M. (1967), "Feeding Studies in Low Birth Weight Infants. I. Relationships of Dietary Protein, Fat and Electrolyte to Rates of Weight Gain, Clinical Course and Serum Chemical Concentrations," *J. Pediat.*, **70**, 695–713.
14. Franz, J. M. and Knox, W. E. (1967), "The Effect of Development snd Hydrocortisone on Tryptophan Oxygenase, Formamidase and Tyrosine Aminotransferase in the Livers of Young Rats," *Biochemistry*, **6**, 3464–3471.
15. Friedeman, P. A. and Kaufman, S. (1971), "A Study of the Development of Phenylalanine Hydroxylase in Fetuses of Several Mammalian Species," *Arch. Biochem. Biophys.*, **146**, 321–326.
16. Gaull, G. E., Räihä, N. C. R., Saarikoski, S. and Sturman, J. A. (1972), "Transfer of Methionine and Cyst(e)ine Across the Human Placenta and the Role of Cyst(e)ine in Fetal Growth," *Pediat. Res.*, **6**, 336/76.
17. Gaull, G., Räihä, N. C. R. and Sturman, J. A. (1972), "Develop ment of Mammalian Sulfur Metabolism: Absence of Cysta thionase in Human Fetal Tissues," *Pediat. Res.*, **6**, 538.
18. Gordon, H. H., Levine, S. J. and McNamara, H. (1947), "Feeding of Premature Infants. A Comparison of Human and Cow's Milk," *Amer. J. Dis. Child.*, **73**, 442–452.
19. Goswami, M. N. and Knox, W. E. (1961), "Developmental Changes of *p*-hydroxyphenylpyruvate-oxidase Activity in Mammalian Liver," *Biochem. Biophys. Acta*, **50**, 35–40.
20. Greengard, O. (1969), "Enzymic Differentiation in Mammalian Liver," *Science*, **163**, 891–895.
21. Greengard, O. (1969), "The Hormonal Regulation of Enzymes in Prenatal and Postnatal Rat Liver. Effects of Adenosine 3′5′-(cyclic)-monophosphate," *Biochem. J.*, **115**, 19–24.
22. Greengard, O. (1970), "The Developmental Formation of Enzymes in Rat Liver," in *Biochemical Actions of Hormones*, Vol. I, pp. 53–87 (G. Litwack, Ed.). New York: Academic Press.
23. Greengard, O. and Dewey, H. K. (1967), "Initiation by Glucagon of the Premature Development of Tyrosine Aminotransferase, Serine Dehydratase and Glucose-6-phosphatase in Fetal Rat Liver," *J. Biol. Chem.*, **242**, 2986–2991.
24. Grisolia, S. and Cohen, P. P. (1953), "Catalytic Role of Glutamate Derivatives in Citrulline Biosynthesis," *J. Biol. Chem.*, **204**, 753–757.
25. Hsia, D. Y-Y., Litwack, M., O'Flynn, M. and Jakovicic, S. (1962), "Serum Phenulalanine and Tyrosine Levels in the Newborn Infant," *New Eng. J. Med.*, **267**, 1067–1070.
26. Hsia, D. Y-Y. and Porto, S. (1970), "Detoxification Mechanisms of the Liver," in *Physiology of the Perinatal Period*, pp. 625–639 (U. Stawe, Ed.). New York: Appleton-Century-Crofts.
27. Kaufman, S. (1958), "Phenylalanine Hydroxylation Cofactor in Phenylketonuria," *Science*, **128**, 1506–1507.
28. Kaufman, S. (1971), "The Phenylalanine Hydroxylating System from Mammalian Liver," *Advances in Enzymology*, **35**, 245–319.
29. Kennan, A. L. and Cohen, P. P. (1969), "Biochemical Studies of the Developing Mammalian Fetus," *Develop. Biol.*, **1**, 511–525.
30. Kenney, F. T. and Kretchmer, N. (1959), "Hepatic Metabolism of Phenylalanine During Development," *J. Clin. Invest.*, **38**, 2189–2196.
31. Kenney, F. T. and Reel, J. R. (1971), "Hormonal Regulation of Enzyme Synthesis: Transcriptional or Translational Control?" in *Hormones in Development*, pp. 161–167 (M. Hamburger and E. J. W. Barrington, Eds.). New York: Appleton-Century-Crofts.
32. Kenney, F. T., Reel, J. R., Hager, C. B. and Wittliff, J. L. (1968), "Hormonal Induction and Repression," in *Regulatory Mechanism for Protein Synthesis in Mammalian Cells*, pp. 119–142 (A. San Pietro, M. R. Lamborg and F. T. Kenney, Eds.). New York: Academic Press.
33. Kenney, F. T., Reem, G. H. and Kretchmer, N. (1958), "Development of Phenylalanine Hydroxylase in Mammalian Liver," *Science*, **127**, 86.
34. Knox, W. E. and Goswami, M. N. D. (1960), "The Mechanism of *p*-hydroxyphenylpyruvate Accumulation in Guinea Pigs Fed Tyrosine," *J. Biol. Chem.*, **235**, 2662–2666.
35. Komrower, G. M. and Robins, A. J. (1969), "Plasma Amino Acid Disturbance in Infancy. I. Hypermethioninaemia and Transient Tyrosinaemia," *Arch. Dis. Childh.*, **44**, 416–421.
36. Kretchmer, N. (1959), "Enzymatic Patterns During Development. An Approach to a Biochemical Definition of Immaturity," *Pediatrics*, **23**, 606–617.
37. Kretchmer, N., Levine, S. Z. and McNamara, H. (1957), "The *in vitro* Metabolism of Tyrosine and its Intermediates in the Liver of the Premature Infant," *Amer. J. Dis. Child.*, **93**, 19–20.

38. Kretchmer, N., Levine, S. Z., McNamara, H. and Barnett, H. L. (1956), "Certain Aspects of Tyrosine Metabolism in the Young. I. The Development of the Tyrosine Oxidizing System in Human Liver," *J. Clin. Invest.*, **35**, 236–244.
39. La Du, B. N., Howell, R. R., Michael, P. J. and Sober, E. K. (1963), "A Quantitative Micromethod for the Determination of Phenylalanine and Tyrosine in Blood and its Application to the Diagnosis of Phenylketonuria in Infants," *Pediatrics*, **31**, 39–46
40. Levine, S. Z., Dann, M. and Marples, E. (1943), "A Defect in the Metabolism of Tyrosine and Phenylalanine in Premature Infants. III. Demonstration of the Irreversible Conversion of Phenylalanine to Tyrosine in the Human Organism," *J. Clin. Invest.*, **22**, 551–562.
41. Levine, S. Z., Marples, E. and Gordon, H. H. (1939), "A Defect in the Metabolism of Aromatic Amino Acids in Premature Infants: The Role of Vitamin C," *Science*, **90**, 620–621.
42. Levine, S. Z., Marples, E. and Gordon, H. H. (1941), "A Defect in the Metabolism of Tyrosine and Phenylalanine in Premature Infants. I. Identification and Assay of Intermediary Products," *J. Clin. Invest.*, **20**, 199–207.
43. Levine, S. Z., Marples, E. and Gordon, H. H. (1941), "A Defect in the Metabolism of Tyrosine and Phenylalanine in Premature Infants. II. Spontaneous Occurrence and Eradication by Vitamin C," *J. Clin. Invest.*, **20**, 209–213.
44. Levy, H. L., Shih, V. E., Madigan, P. M., Karolkewicz, V., Carr, J. R., Lum, A., Richards, A. A., Crawford, J. D. and MacCready, R. A. (1969), "Hypermethioninemia with Other Hyperaminoacidemias. Studies in Infants on High Protein Diets," *Amer. J. Dis. Child.*, **117**, 96–103.
45. Light, I. J., Berry, H. K. and Sutherland, J. M. (1966), "Amino-acidemia of Prematurity," *Amer. J. Dis. Child.*, **112**, 229–236.
46. Litwack, G. and Nemeth, A. M. (1965), "Development of Liver Tyrosine Aminotransferase Acitivity in the Rabbit, Guinea Pig and Chicken," *Arch. Biochem. Biophys.*, **109**, 316–320.
47. McCance, R. A. and Dickerson, J. W. T. (1957), "The Composition and Origin of the Fetal Fluids of the Pig," *J. embryol. exp. Morphol.*, **5**, 43–48.
48. Menkes, J. H. and Avery, M. E. (1963), "The Metabolism of Phenylalanine and Tyrosine in the Premature Infant," *Bull. Johns Hopk. Hosp.*, **113**, 301–319.
49. Menkes, J. H., Chernick, V. and Ringel, B. (1966), "Effect of Elevated Blood Tyrosine and Subsequent Intellectual Development of Premature Infants," *J. Pediat.*, **69**, 583–588.
50. Menkes, J. H., Welcher, D. W., Levi, H. S., Dallas, J. and Gretsky, N. E. (1972), "Relationship of Elevated Blood Tyrosine to the Ultimate Intellectual Performance of Premature Infants," *Pediatrics*, **49**, 218–224.
51. Myant, N. B. (1971), "Developmental Aspects of Lipid Metabolism," in *The Biochemistry of Development*, pp. 96–140 (P. F. Benson, Ed.). London: Heinemann.
52. Needham, N. J. T. M. (1942), *Biochemistry of Morphogenesis*. London: Cambridge University Press.
53. Partington, M. W., Delahaye, D. J., Masotti, R. E., Read, J. H. and Roberts, B. (1968), "Neonatal Tyrosinemia: A Follow-up Study," *Arch. Dis. Childh.*, **43**, 195–199.
54. Räihä, N. C. R. (1971), "Development of Arginine and Ornithine Metabolism in the Mammal," in *The Biochemistry of Development*, pp. 141–160 (P. W. Benson, Ed.). London: Heinemann.
55. Räihä, N. C. R. (1972), "Phenylalanine Hydroxylase in Human Liver During Development," *Pediat. Res.* In press.
56. Räihä, N. C. R. and Suihkonen, J. (1968), "Development of Urea Synthesizing Enzymes in Human Liver," *Acta paediat. scand.*, **57**, 121–124.
57. Räihä, N. C. R. and Suihkonen, J. (1968), "Factors Influencing the Development of Urea Synthesizing Enzymes in Rat Liver," *Biochem., J.*, **107**, 793–797.
58. Räihä, N. C. R., Schwartz, A. L. and Lindroos, M. C. (1971), "Induction of Tyrosine-α-ketoglutarate Transaminase in Fetal Rat and Fetal Human Liver in Organ Culture," *Pediat. Res.*, **5**, 70–76.
59. Ratner, S. (1955), "Enzymatic Synthesis of Arginine (Condensing and Splitting Enzymes)," in *Methods in Enzymology*, Vol. 2, pp. 356–367 (S. P. Colowick and N. O. Kaplan, Eds.). New York: Academic Press.
60. Rizzardini, M. and Abeliuk, P. (1971), "Tyrosinemia and Tyrosinuria in Low-birth-weight Infants: A New Criterion to Assess Maturity at Birth," *Amer. J. Dis. Child.*, **121**, 182–185.
61. Rose, W. C. and Wixom, R. L. (1955), "Amino Acid Requirements of Man. XIII. Sparing Effect of Cystine on Methionine Requirement," *J. biol. Chem.*, **216**, 763–773.
62. Schwartz, A. L. (1972), "Influence of Glucagon, 6-N,2′-O-dibutyryladenosine 3′:5′-cyclic Monophosphate and Triamcinolone on the Arginine Synthetase System in Perinatal Rat Liver," *Biochem. J.*, **126**, 89–98.
63. Sereni, F., Kenney, F. T. and Kretchmer, N. (1959), "Factors Influencing the Development of Tyrosine-α-ketoglutarate Transaminase Activity in Rat Liver," *J. Biol. Chem.*, **234**, 609–612.
64. Sereni, F. and Principi, N. (1965), "The Development of Enzyme Systems," *Pediat. Clin. N. Amer.*, **12**, 515–534.
65. Synderman, S. E. (1971), "The Protein and Amino Acid Requirements of the Premature Infant," in *Metabolic Processes in the Fetus and Newborn Infant*, pp. 128–143 (J. H. P. Jonxis, H. K. A. Visser and J. A. Troelstra, Eds.). Leiden: Stenfert Kroese.
66. Stegnik, L. D. and Baker, G. L. (1971), "Infusion of Protein Hydrolysates in the Newborn Infant: Plasma Amino Acid Concentrations," *J. Pediat.*, **78**, 595–602.
67. Sturman, J., Gaull, G. and Räihä, N. C. R. (1970), "Absence of Cystathionase in Human Fetal Liver; is Cystine Essential?" *Science*, **169**, 74–76.
68. Sturman, J. A., Niemann, W. H. and Gaull, G. E. (1971), "Maternal-foetal Relationship of Methionine and Cystine in the Pregnant Rhesus Monkey," *Biochem. J.*, **125**, 78.
69. Wicks, W. D. (1968), "Induction of Tyrosine-α-ketoglutarate Transaminase in Fetal Rat Liver," *J. biol. Chem.*, **243**, 900–906.
70. Wicks, W. D. (1969), "Induction of Hepatic Enzymes by Adenosine 3′5′-monophosphate in Organ Culture," *J. biol. Chem.*, **244**, 3941–3950.
71. Young, M. (1971), "Placental Transfer of Amino Acids," in *Metabolic Processes in the Fetus and Newborn Infant*, pp. 97–110 (J. H. P. Jonxis, H. K. A. Visser and J. A. Troelstra, Eds.). Leiden: Stenfert Kroese.
72. Zannoni, V. G. and La Du, B. N. (1960), "Studies on the Defect in Tyrosine Metabolism in Scorbutic Guinea Pigs," *J. biol. Chem.*, **235**, 165–168.
73. Zannoni, V. G. (1962), "The Tyrosine Oxidation System of Liver. V. The Ability of Various Quinoses to Reactivate Inhibited *p*-hydroxyphenylpyruvic Acid Oxidase," *J. biol. Chem.*, **237**, 1172–1176.

10. NEWBORN JAUNDICE: BILE PIGMENT METABOLISM IN THE FETUS AND NEWBORN INFANT

G. H. LATHE

INTRODUCTION

Studies of the newborn reveal the extraordinary character of the transitional period. By comparison with the affluent fetal condition and the relatively steady state of the second two weeks, the transition of the first few minutes, hours and days after birth involves extreme biochemical hazards—anoxia, acidosis, hypoglycaemia and accumulation of a poisonous substance which shows up by the coincidence of its colour. Many are still content to call this potentially toxic state "physiological jaundice," possibly on the questionable assumption that all must be good in the best of all possible worlds. Newborn jaundice has been partly clarified by detailed biochemical study and in turn the clinical problems have contributed much to our biochemical knowledge. Newborn jaundice still remains a stimulus and challenge to paediatricians and biochemists.

Although many features were elaborated 15–20 years ago and are outlined in reviews of that time[100] our knowledge of some aspects has been greatly extended since then and others are seen in quite a new way. The following account will emphasize these more recent developments and will be limited to unconjugated hyperbilirubinaemia, largely because it is still not yet possible to discuss cholestatic jaundice in biochemical terms.[101]

PATTERN OF NEWBORN JAUNDICE

Jaundice appears in about half of newborn infants and can be very pronounced. It therefore attracted the attention of nineteenth-century clinicians and at the turn of the century systematic studies were made, using the tools and concepts of the day. It was generally held that increased haemolysis caused the jaundice. This was suggested by the high haematocrit at birth which usually falls thereafter and by the occurrence of extreme jaundice in known haemolytic disease. Plasma bilirubin concentrations of 60 mg./100 ml., or more, used to occur in untreated haemolytic disease of the newborn. Modern methods of estimating red-cell degradation in the normal newborn indicate that the rate is not very much greater than in the adult. Studies based on ^{51}chromium-labelled red blood cells suggest an increased turnover of about 30 per cent[184] and recent measurements of carbon monoxide generation[123] suggest that in the newborn infant haemoglobin breaks down at twice the adult rate. The "early labelled peak" of bilirubin, from non-haemoglobin haemoproteins and from degradation of red cells in the bone-marrow before release, is also somewhat increased in the newborn.[183]

Haemolytic conditions in the newborn infant depend largely on inherited features, such as blood groups (Rh, ABO, Duffy, S, etc.) and enzyme defects (congenital spherocytosis, pyruvate kinase, glucose-6-phosphate dehydrogenase), but environmental factors (in glucose-6-phosphate dehydrogenase deficiency naphthalene from christening clothes which have been kept in moth balls may lead to haemolysis) and therapeutic agents (excess vitamin K analogues) may contribute. All of these have been implicated as causes of gross hyperbilirubinaemia and kernicterus. One suspects that in developing countries many causes remain undefined.

In 1941 Davidson, Merrit and Weech[46] made a thorough study of jaundice in 106 newborn infants in an American hospital. Although the methods available to them would not meet modern standards, and it was before the discovery of Rh-isoimmunization, the pattern they defined by daily measurement of plasma bilirubin (Fig. 1) has been generally confirmed. Weech[188] reviewed the subject in 1947 and observed, "attempts to demonstrate a relationship between amount of haemoglobin destroyed and intensity of bilirubinaemia have ended in failure." He directed attention to "maturity" and this emphasis was greatly increased when hyperbilirubinaemia was noted to be more extreme in premature infants,[77] and in infants free of haemolytic disease was correlated with length of gestation and birth weight (Fig. 2). This is borne out by many studies,[117] for example the control group of small infants in the study by Trolle[179] which is shown in Fig. 21. Among 286 infants of 1–2·5 kg., 50 per cent had a hyperbilirubinaemia of 11 mg./100 ml. or more, while only 20 per cent of infants over 2·5 kg. exceeded this level. Although the correlation of birth weight with subsequent hyperbilirubinaemia is indisputable, variation between infants is very marked (Fig. 2), making hazardous the prediction of the clinical course of individual infants.

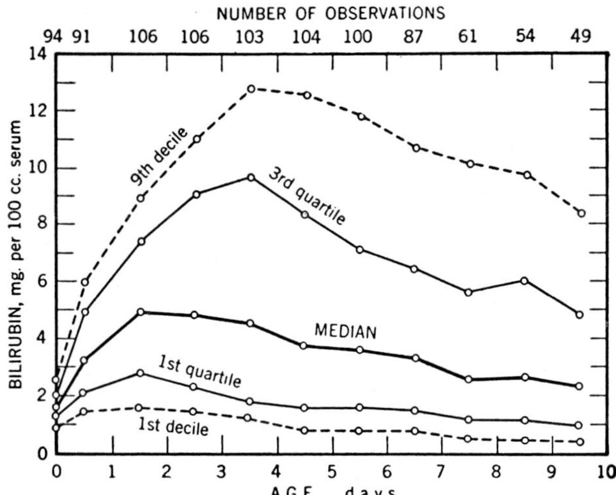

FIG. 1. Serum bilirubin concentrations in newborn infants.[46]

Large systematic studies have been limited to the Caucasian populations of Europe and North America. However, in Hong Kong[200] and Singapore[32] hyperbilirubinaemia is more common and extreme among Chinese, Indian and

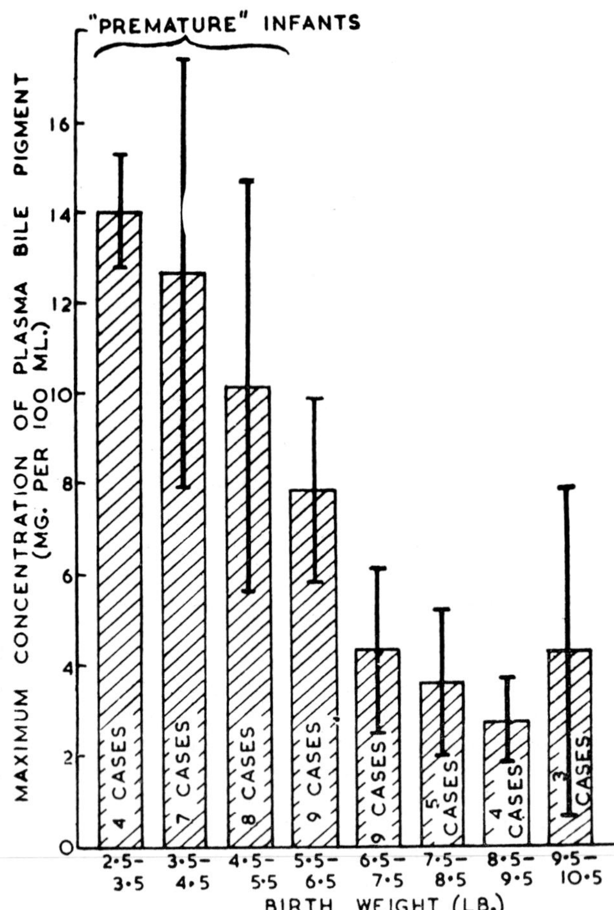

FIG. 2. Maximum plasma bilirubin concentration of infants (without Rh haemolytic disease) arranged by birth weight (without Rh haemolytic disease) arranged by birth weight.[20] The mean and S.D. is given for each group.

Malay infants. There is clearly a great need for studies, in Asia, Africa, South America and the Indian subcontinent, of environmental and constitutional factors affecting liver function (and red-cell survival) in the newborn.

HAEM SYNTHESIS AND DEGRADATION IN THE ADULT

The need to describe immaturity in biochemical terms led to a re-examination of bile pigment metabolism. Advances made in the past two decades have been reviewed[98,107,164] and will be summarized here before discussing the unusual features of the newborn infant.

Most of our knowledge of the biochemical basis of haem turnover concerns haemoglobin as it is the predominant haemoprotein of the body. Many other haemoproteins have the same prosthetic group, namely, iron protoporphyrin (in the ferro form this is referred to as haem). Some haemoproteins, notably those of liver, have a rapid turnover, measured in hours, and they may contribute to the

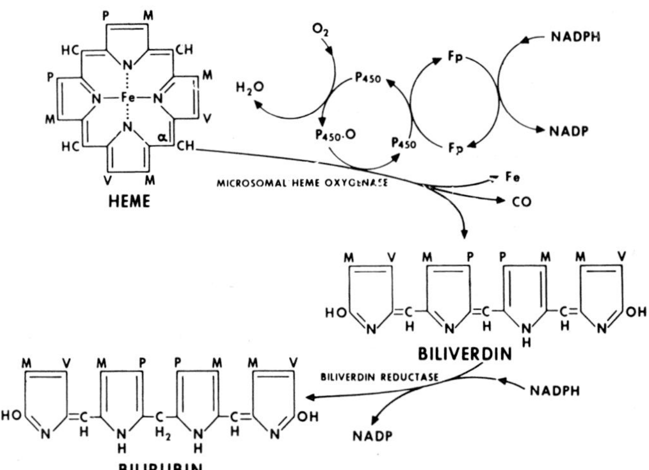

FIG. 3. Metabolic pathway of haem degradation to bilirubin as established by Tenhunen, Marver and Schmid.[164]

production of bilirubin, the main degradation product of haem. Once formed, bilirubin is rapidly dealt with by the adult mammal. A small dose given intravenously to a rat begins to appear in the bile in seconds and 50 per cent is excreted within 20 min. In contrast, administration of haemoglobin or sensitized erythrocytes produces a rise of bilirubin in bile after about 30 min. and most is excreted within 3 hours. Some of the biochemical steps involved in this delay have now been elucidated.

Tenhunen, Marver and Schmid[173] described an enzyme (haem oxygenase) present in liver, spleen, kidney, bone marrow and in macrophages of lung and peritoneal cavity which opens the macro-ring of haem (Fig. 3) to yield biliverdin, which in turn is reduced to bilirubin by a widely distributed enzyme, biliverdin reductase. The initial cleavage of haem yields carbon monoxide which can be used to monitor the rate of haemoglobin or haem breakdown.[123] The activity of the biliverdin reductase of all tissues studied greatly exceeds that of the haem oxygenase which therefore controls the rate of production of bilirubin from haem.

Additional cellular and biochemical factors are undoubtedly involved in the removal of haem from haemoglobin but little is known of them.[98] Haem oxygenase is substrate-inducible.[145,146] The injection of haemoglobin may increase the enzyme of spleen 2–7-fold. It is also increased by hormones like noradrenalin and glucagon whose action is mediated by cyclic AMP.[12]

Under physiological conditions bilirubin is very insoluble. Thus, bilirubin, formed in the reticuloendothelial system, passes to the liver in combination with plasma albumin (Fig. 4) which has a very high affinity for it (*see* p. 110). The

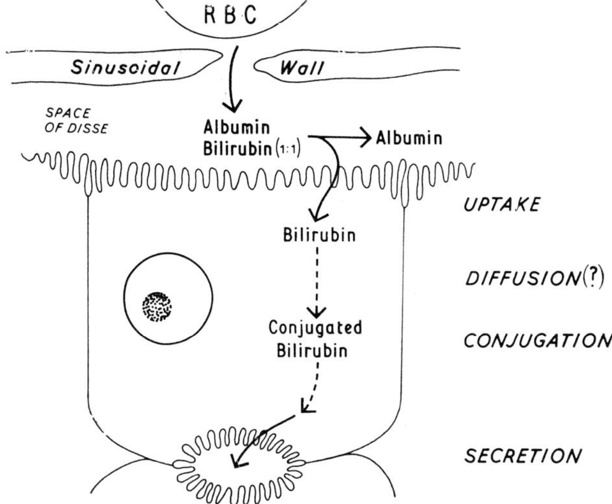

FIG. 4. Stages in the disposal of bilirubin by the liver cell.[98]

liver cells are bathed in an albumin-rich fluid since the sinusoids of liver have large pores. There are at least three phases of liver activity: uptake, conjugation and secretion of the conjugates. In the process of uptake, it seems unlikely that albumin passes into the liver with bilirubin. There is probably a relatively specific uptake mechanism for bilirubin, as shown by selective inhibition.[70,71] Within the liver bilirubin is probably bound to a protein, ligandin, which has an affinity for many anionic substances[108,116] (*see* p. 108).

The major change to bilirubin in the liver is its conversion from a fat-soluble to a water-soluble substance by conjugation with sugar residues. Until recently it was accepted that the main product was bilirubin diglucuronide (Fig. 5), but Kuenzle[94] was unable to find any bilirubin diglucuronide in human bile and considered that the main sugar residues attached to bilirubin were disaccharides containing glucuronic acids. Heirwegh, Van Hees, Leroy, Van Roy and Jansen,[75] using a more direct technique, found that the diglucuronide predominated but there were also other conjugates, which were increased in bile from post-obstruction patients. This field is under very active investigation. "Conjugated bilirubin" will be used here as a generic name for the main products of liver action on bilirubin, without assumptions as to the nature of the sugar residues.

Bilirubin diglucuronide is formed in the endoplasmic reticulum of the liver by an insoluble enzyme(s), glucuronyl transferase, which derives the glucuronic acid group from the sugar nucleotide, uridine diphosphate glucuronic acid (UDPGA) (Fig. 5). This nucleotide is generated in the cell sap by a (NAD-dependent) dehydrogenase which acts on uridine diphosphate glucose (UDPG), an important intermediate of carbohydrate metabolism which is the precursor of glycogen. Thus conjugation may be limited by the availability of glucose residues.

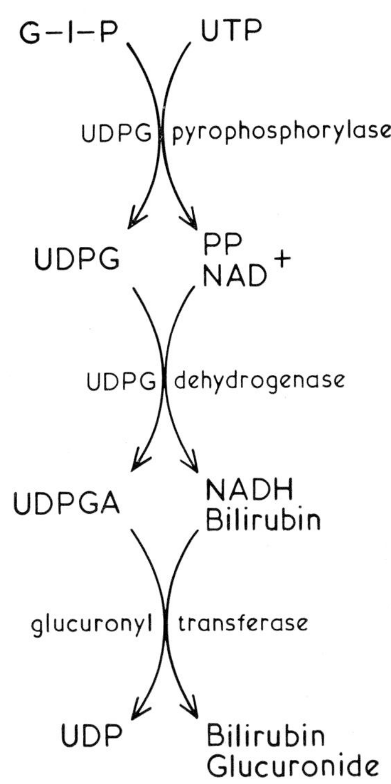

FIG. 5. Metabolic pathways in biosynthesis of bilirubin glucuronide.[98]

Normally all, or nearly all, of the bilirubin in plasma is unconjugated.[182] This suggests that conjugated bilirubin is passed rapidly from the endoplasmic reticulum, where it is formed, to the canalicular wall through which it is secreted, or that it is walled off in some way which prevents escape into the plasma. Although it is a common clinical observation that this transport process is frequently limited (or that escape becomes possible), there is little definitive information at a molecular level about the mechanism of cholestatic jaundice.

PERINATAL DEVELOPMENT OF LIVER

Haem Oxygenase

There is no information yet regarding haem oxygenase in newborn human liver, but the enzyme is present in fetal rat liver at twice the adult concentration.[176] It doubles again during the first few days of life and falls to the adult value after weaning (Fig. 6). In contrast, fetal spleen has half as much enzyme as the adult, and the enzyme increases after weaning. Since haem oxygenase is substrate- and hormone-inducible, it may be asked whether metabolic factors or the rate of haemoglobin breakdown has the greater influence on the amount of enzyme and perhaps on the rate at which bilirubin is generated. Three days fasting at the end of gestation doubled the enzyme in the maternal-rat liver but

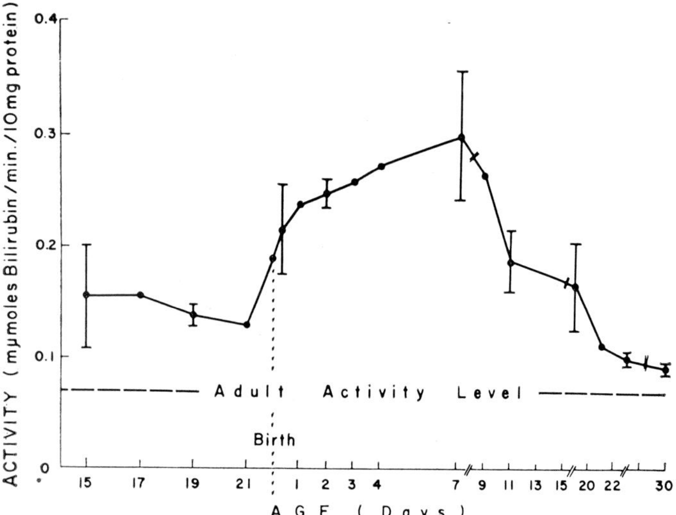

FIG. 6. Development of hepatic haem oxygenase in fetal and young rats.[176]

increased that of the fetuses by only 20 per cent. If newborns were fasted, the hepatic enzyme doubled.[12] Unfortunately, we do not know whether fasting increases bilirubin production from a pre-existing haem pool, though this may contribute to the bilirubin load in the newborn.

Ligandin

The idea that uptake of bilirubin by the liver might be effected by a liver protein which has a greater affinity, or capacity, for bilirubin than has plasma albumin, was greatly strengthened when two groups[33,108] found that in liver sap, of all mammals which had been studied, bilirubin was bound to large molecules which differed from albumin. Levi, Gatmaitan and Arias[108] fractionated liver cell sap by gel filtration and showed that two proteins "Y" and "Z" could bind bilirubin and other anionic substances like the diagnostic agents, bromosulphthalein (BSP) and indocyanine green, but not bile salts. "Y" protein was found to have the higher affinity for bilirubin. It was soon realized that this protein was being studied in other laboratories concerned with the cytoplasmic binding of liver carcinogens and of polar metabolites of corticosteroids. The three groups have subsequently agreed on the name "ligandin."[116] It is a basic protein of intermediate size and accounts for 4 per cent of the protein of rat liver sap.[54] Bilirubin, added either in trace or large amounts, intravenously or to a liver homogenate, becomes attached to ligandin and is found with protein "Z" only if very large amounts of bilirubin are used. There are experimental difficulties in showing that ligandin is the agent mediating uptake of bilirubin by liver cells since at present the location of bilirubin can be studied only in broken cell preparations.

Three pieces of evidence about ligandin support a functional role (not necessarily of uptake). Rat liver has seven times as much ligandin as other tissues.[54] Secondly, it has been suggested that the capacity of liver to take up, chemically alter and secrete a wide range of lipid-soluble, endogenous and exogenous, substances may have been evolved to meet the problems of transition from marine to land existence. Ligandin may play a part in this as it occurs only in land animals[110] and in amphibia it appears during metamorphosis.

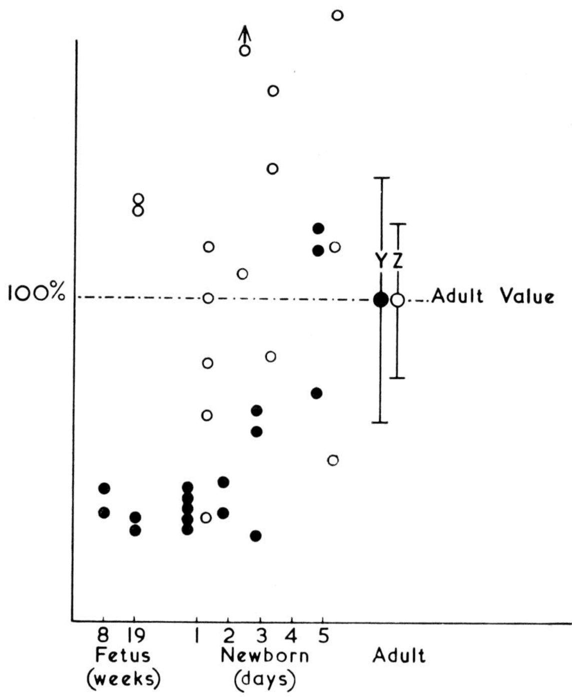

FIG. 7. Development of hepatic ligandin (Y protein) and Z protein in *M. mulatta*. Redrawn from[109].

Thirdly, in *M. mulatta* (Fig. 7) there is a several-fold increase of ligandin during the first few days of life[109] (while the amount of protein "Z," although variable, is relatively constant during the fetal and neonatal period). The possibility that liver uptake is deficient in the jaundiced newborn infant, due to a ligandin deficiency, has been considered.[66,109] It is consistent with this that administration of phenobarbitone, which increases BSP clearance in adult rats and ameliorates hyperbilirubinaemia in newborn infants (*see* p. 117) also enhances the amount of liver ligandin. Possibly it is more complicated, as a number of agents which interfere with the clearance of plasma bilirubin (flavaspidic acid, bunamiodyl, iodipamide) compete with bilirubin for "Z" protein but not for ligandin.

Bilirubin Glucuronyl Transferase

When it was demonstrated that secretion of bilirubin could only take place if it were first conjugated, the possibility was considered that a defect in the conjugating system might be the explanation of newborn hyperbilirubinaemia. Conjugation can be examined *in vivo* by administering a substance like N-acetyl-*p*-aminophenol[11] or salicylamide[170] which are excreted in the urine as glucuronides but there probably are several transferases of different specificities. The conjugation of bilirubin can be tested *in vitro* with either liver-slices or homogenates. With the latter it is necessary to add excess of the glucuronyl donor, UDPGA (Fig. 5), since it is not generated by broken cell preparations. When UDPGA is added only one function is being studied, that of the enzyme bilirubin glucuronyl transferase. Early studies showed reduced bilirubin conjugation in the newborn rat[65] and low *o*-aminophenol (OAP) conjugation in the guinea pig.[34]

There are very few studies of human infants. The livers of three premature infants were tested with bilirubin immediately after death by Lathe and Walker,[102] and Dutton[51] examined 2 fetuses of 3–4 months gestation (using OAP). Lucey and Villee[120] studied 11 fetuses of 3–6 months (using *p*-nitrophenol). Gartner and Arias[58] studied one 5-month fetus (using OAP). N-Methylumbelliferone has also been used as substrate for liver biopsies of newborn infants.[49] Microsomes have been studied with *p*-nitrophenol.[133] All the results showed very low values for conjugation as compared with adult animals.

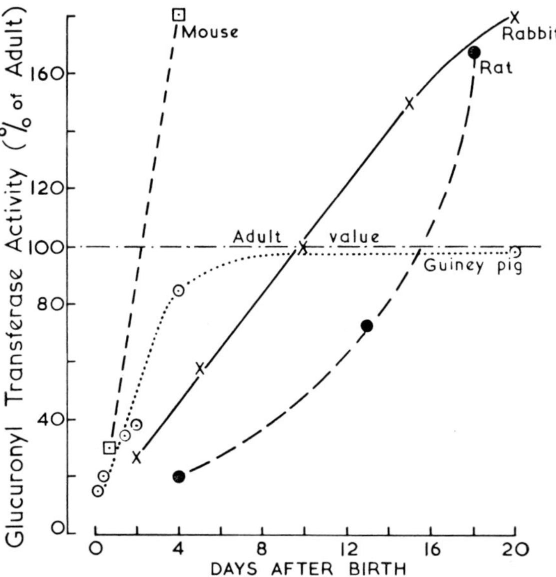

FIG. 8. Development of bilirubin glucuronyl transferase in young animals.[98]

The recent demonstration that detergents[24,68] greatly increase the apparent activity of bilirubin glucuronyl transferase has necessitated a re-examination of the early work with laboratory animals. The very low activity in the fetus and newborn rat has been confirmed.[69] Figure 8 shows available data on the rate of development of the enzyme in newborn animals using bilirubin as a substrate. Other substrates may show a different developmental pattern[69] since there are other glucuronyl transferases.

Reports on *M. mulatta*[62,63] state that during the first 36 hours after birth the conjugating ability is approximately 5 per cent of the adult value which is reached by the 4th day. Thus there is a remarkably similar pattern of development in several species. The dog appears to be an exception.[17,107]

When bilirubin was injected into the dog fetus *in utero*, most of it was conjugated and excreted in the bile and by birth the conjugating activity of the liver was "near" that of the adult. In the monkey, only 10 per cent of injected bilirubin

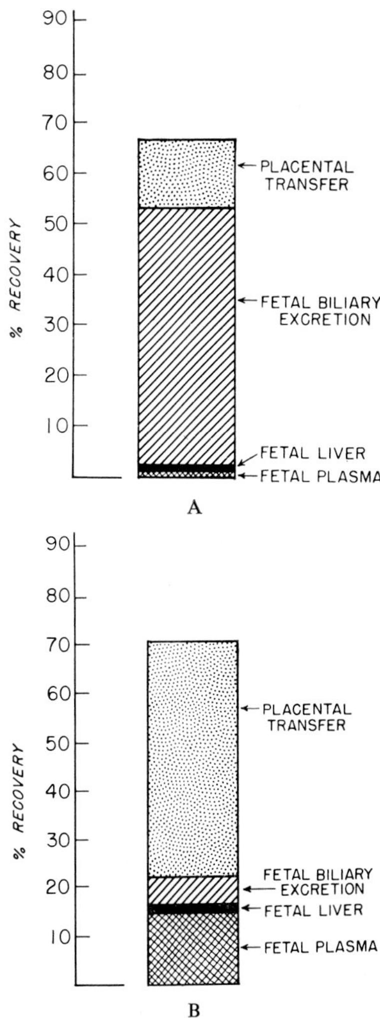

FIG. 9. Disposal of a small dose of labelled bilirubin given to intrauterine fetus of (A) dog and (B) *M. mulatta*.[17]

reached the bile, the placenta being the main route of disposal (Figs. 9A and B).

Most laboratory animals do not have appreciable hyperbilirubinaemia during the newborn period. The newborn Rhesus monkey (Fig. 10) has an elevated, but falling, bilirubin for several days.[63,109]

UDP-Glucuronic Acid Production

Glucuronyl transferase has two substrates, bilirubin and UDPGA; either or both could be rate limiting. The cytoplasmic enzyme UDPG dehydrogenase, which produces UDPGA has been examined less fully than glucuronyl transferase, except in the guinea pig[34] where its development is very similar to that of glucuronyl transferase (studied with OAP) (Fig. 11). A 30-fold increase in UDPGA concentration and a 100-fold increase in its turnover have been noted between the fetal and the adult states in the guinea pig.[57] In the newborn rat the molar rate of conjugation of OAP by liver slices is much higher than that of bilirubin. On the basis of this it has been argued, incorrectly,[102] that

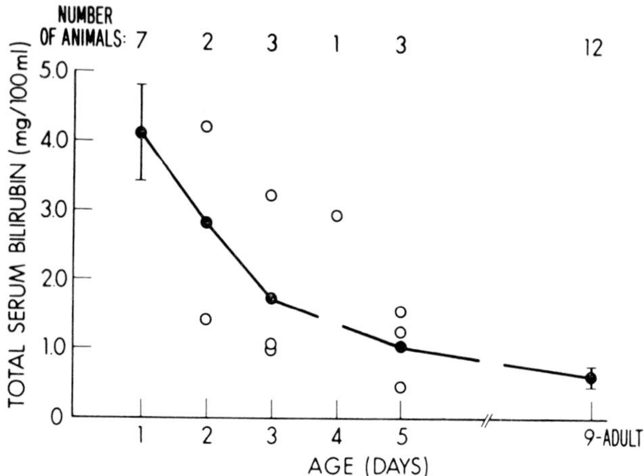

FIG. 10. Hyperbilirubinaemia of newborn *M. mulatta*.[109]

UDPGA is not rate-limiting for bilirubin conjugation. A distinction must be made between rate-limiting and *the* rate-limiting factor. Where there are two substrates for an enzyme both may be rate-limiting. Many biological systems do not have one rate-limiting factor.

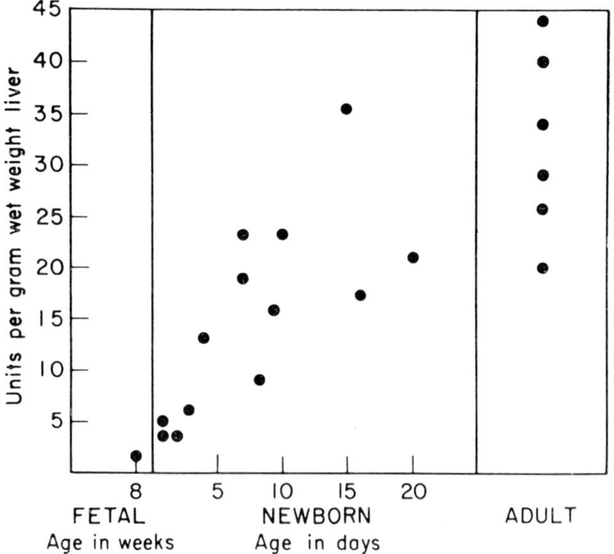

FIG. 11. Development of UDPG dehydrogenase in guinea pig.[34]

There is little evidence regarding the availability of UDPGA in the human fetus and infant. In human fetuses at 3–4 months gestation the UDPGA concentration was about 10 per cent of that in the adult mouse liver.[51] In fetal liver the UDPG dehydrogenase has been reported not to be as low, relatively, as was the glucuronyl transferase (*p*-nitrophenol).[120]

Whether or not a substrate is rate-limiting depends on its concentration relative to the Km of the enzyme (the substrate concentration at which the enzyme has half maximum activity). The Km for glucuronyl transferase (acceptor: bilirubin) has been variously recorded as 0·46–1·66 mmol./l.[194] In rat liver, the concentration of UDPGA has been reported to be 0·28 and 0·4,[194,195] and thus it would limit the rate of reaction. This low concentration may also potentiate steroid inhibitors (p. 112). The relation between UDPG, UDPGA and other sugar nucleotides has been reviewed.[98] The availability of carbohydrate may affect the UDPGA concentration as UDPG is an important branch point in metabolism (Fig. 12). A relation between hypoglycaemia

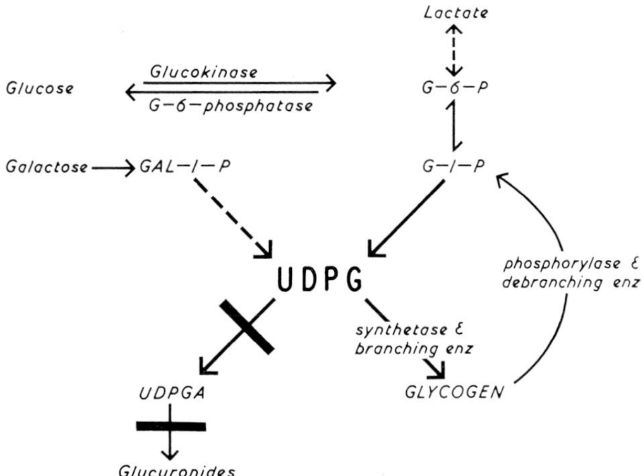

FIG. 12. Metabolic pathways involving UDPG. The "blocks" of UDPGA and glucuronide formation in the fetus are shown by bars.[99]

and hyperbilirubinaemia would be expected[99] from the position of UDPG in the metabolic pathway.

Underfeeding or starvation may increase bilirubin in two additional ways. Haem oxygenase is enhanced 2–3-fold in starved adult and newborn animals and the production of bilirubin may be increased.[12] Secondly, it has been found that the development of glucuronyl transferase is retarded by food withdrawal from newborn rabbits.[55a] Food deprivation has been noted to raise the plasma bilirubin, as high as 3-fold, in patients with Gilbert's disease[53a] who have about half the normal amount of glucuronyl transferase, and in Gunn rats, which have no glucuronal transferase for bilirubin, plasma bilirubin may double.[14a] The mechanism has not been defined in either case. An association between hypoglycaemia and hyperbilirubinaemia in the newborn infant has been observed.[200]

Secretion of Conjugated Bilirubin

The idea that conjugation was rate-limiting in the newborn infant arose from the observation that there was negligible conjugated pigment in newborn plasma and was supported by the direct determination of conjugating capacity. That newborn animals had a lower capacity to secrete conjugated bilirubin than had adult animals was first shown in the guinea pig fetus and newborn.[160,161] After cannulating the bile duct the excretion of injected conjugated pigment or bile was measured. A more detailed comparison of uptake, conjugation and secretory capacity of the newborn guinea pig under maximum bilirubin load[59] has shown that the capacity to excrete conjugated bilirubin was 10 per cent of the adult, per unit weight at birth, doubled during the first 2 days and then gradually rose to the adult value at 25 days. Bilirubin glucuronyl transferase (with optimum UDPGA) reach an adult value at day 2. In spite of this, during the maturation period there was no striking increase in the proportion of direct pigment in serum after infusion of bilirubin. In the adult, maximum conjugating capacity was 8·3 μg./100 g. body wt./min. compared with excretory capacity of 14 μg. Although glucuronyl transferase capacity developed more rapidly it is doubtful whether the rate of conjugation *in vivo* exceeds excretion.

Comparable figures have been established in the adult monkey infused with bilirubin.[61] The mean rate of conjugation was 30μg./100 g. body wt./min. compared with maximum excretion of 17–24μg. The monkey's greater relative capacity to conjugate, may be the reason why, following bilirubin injection, the monkey liver had 2–10 times the hepatic concentration of conjugated pigment compared with the guinea pig. The monkey liver had more conjugated than free pigment, suggesting that in this species secretion is limited. Studies in the newborn monkey are in progress.[63] Although the fetal monkey liver at term has a very limited capacity to conjugate and excrete bilirubin, it secretes bile salts efficiently.[104]

Not infrequently, severe haemolytic disease of the newborn is associated with marked conjugated hyperbilirubinaemia, which may appear suddenly or be present at birth.[101] It is called "inspissated bile syndrome," probably in error, and is an intriguing mystery. Possibly it represents a failure to synchronize development of glucuronyl transferase with that of the transport system.

INHIBITION OF GLUCURONYL TRANSFERASE AND BREAST-MILK JAUNDICE

It has been suggested that the activity of glucuronyl transferase may be lowered by endogenous inhibitors. The concept of inhibitors originated in the observation that the serum of pregnant women and of cord blood reduced the conjugation of bilirubin by rat-liver slices[103] (Fig. 13). Serum of cord blood was slightly less inhibitory than that of the mother. The inhibitory property disappeared about 10 days after birth. A number of steroids, for instance 3α, 20α-pregnanediol (of the 5β series) and its glucuronide, were inhibitory, some at concentrations as low at 1μmol./1. Inhibitors could not be the main explanation for the very low activity in neonatal liver homogenates since adult liver which was added to neonatal liver was not inhibited.

It was concluded that maternal steroids were not the primary cause of newborn jaundice because they had much less effect on broken cell preparations in which the glucuronyl transferase defect of the newborn infant was demonstrable. Further, there was no correlation between the inhibitory activity of newborn serum and the degree of hyperbilirubinaemia. The possibility remained, however, that inhibition was a contributory factor. "Transient

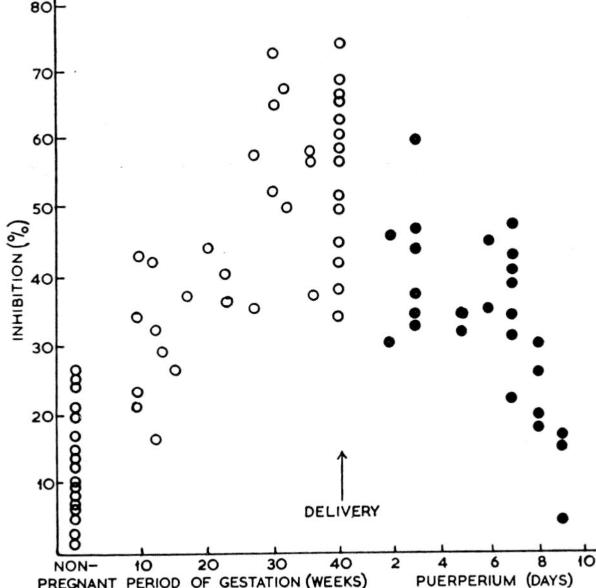

FIG. 13. Development of the inhibitory property of human female serum during pregnancy.[103] The serum was tested on rat liver slices in a system forming bilirubin glucuronide.

familial hyperbilirubinaemia" in which the maternal plasma was very inhibitory has been described in eight families.[9]

Prolonged hyperbilirubinaemia has been described in breast-fed infants of 1–6 weeks[134] (Fig. 14). If cows' milk was substituted, the serum pigment fell. Arias, Gartner, Seifter and Furman[7] noted that the breast milk inhibited a number of glucuronide-forming systems *in vitro* and isolated an unusual steroid, the 20β-isomer of pregnanediol, from the milk. It inhibited glucuronide formation (with various substrates) by livers of rats, guinea pigs and the

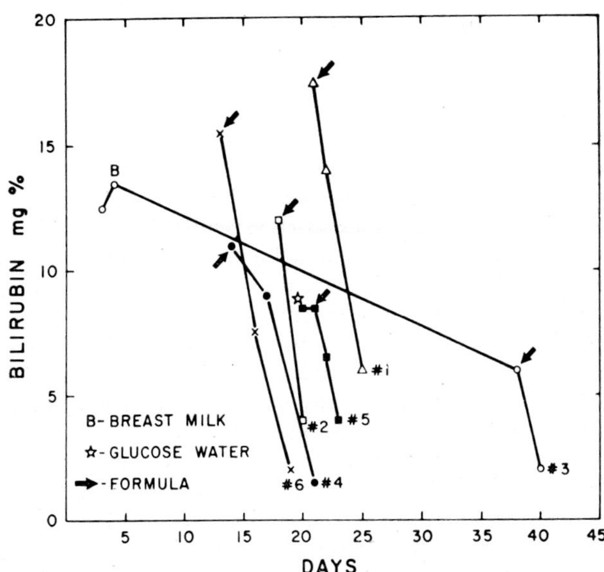

FIG. 14. Plasma bilirubin concentration in infants with breast milk jaundice.[134] The arrows indicate the time at which breast milk was withdrawn and a formula substituted.

human. Administration of 20β-diol to newborn infants increased their plasma bilirubin in one report[5] though this has been questioned.[153] Administration of progesterone, pregnanediol, androstenedione and dehydroepiandrosterone has not produced strong evidence of increased plasma bilirubin.[156,157,158]

The clinical condition, breast-milk jaundice, has been reported from a number of centres, and infants on breast milk have higher mean plasma bilirubin than those on cows' milk.[10,155] Adlard and Lathe[3] reviewed the subject and there have been four more reports of the 20β-diol in human milk since then.[91,115,159,168] The 20β-diol has also been observed in the urine of mothers with icterogenic milk.[154] Adlard and Lathe doubted that this steroid was the cause of the jaundice because of the small amounts present in milk

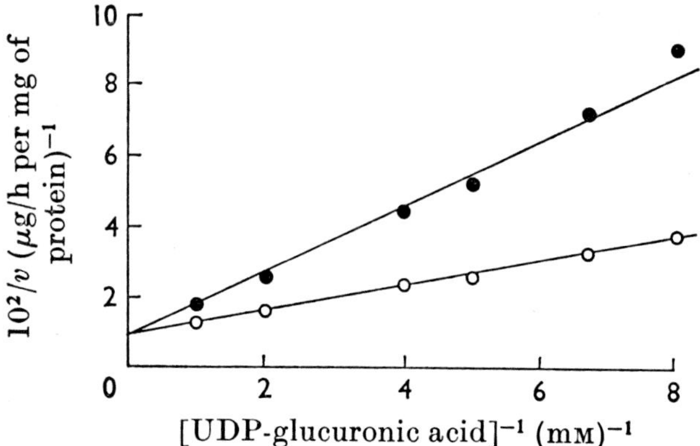

FIG. 15. Double-reciprocal plot of the bilirubin glucuronyl transferase activity of solubilized rat liver microsomes in the presence (●) and absence (○) of oestrone sulphate (0·15 mmol/l). The inhibition is "apparently competitive" with UDPGA.[2]

and because the pregnanediols are inactive with liver slices and homogenates of *M. mulatta* and of man.[3] There are also a number of differences between the inhibitory effects of breast milk and those of pregnandiol. Hargreaves[72] has suggested that the *in vitro* inhibition may be due to fatty acids. Moreover, not all inhibitory milks produce jaundice. Although the 20β-diol has been reported from five laboratories others have not found it.[73,153] Other steroids, especially those of 5α structure (which are not inhibitory) occur in milk.[159] Further work is required to explain the function of milk steroids and their relation, if any, to breast-milk jaundice. The primary cause of breast-milk jaundice probably remains to be defined.

Inhibition by steroids *in vitro* shows a number of unexpected features in addition to the variation between species. Inhibitors are not necessarily substrates for conjugation, and substrates for conjugation are not all inhibitory with rat-liver slices, for example testosterone and cortisol. Oestrogens inhibit rat and human liver at concentrations of 5×10^{-5} mol./l. An unusual finding[2] was that oestrogens behaved, kinetically, like competitive inhibitors of UDPGA, the second substrate (Fig. 15). As oestrogens have little structural similarity to sugar nucleotide, it was concluded that the steroid was altering the conformation of the enzyme, allosterically.

It follows from the kinetics that the inhibition by oestrogens will be greater the smaller the concentration of UDPGA. The generation of UDPGA is probably limited in the newborn (p. 110). (This feature would be missed in tests with homogenates of newborn liver as large amounts of UDPGA are added.) Thus, three features may combine to limit conjugation—little transferase, large amounts of steroid in the fetal body fluids and reduced UDPGA which enhances the inhibitory properties.

Recently it has been reported[197] that at day 5 or later jaundice is much more common (more than 50 per cent) among breast-fed infants of women who have taken contraceptive steroids than among breast-fed infants of those who have not (25 per cent). A similar association between a plasma bilirubin above 15 mg./100 ml. and the taking of contraceptive pills by the mother has also been noted (among breast feeders). Among artificially fed infants, the incidence of jaundice is not related to previous consumption of contraceptive pills by the mother. Further, an earlier survey shows that there was no association between breast-feeding and jaundice in 1960, before contraceptive steroids were widely used.[196] An association between hyperbilirubinaemia and oestrogens has been reported in infants whose mothers received oestradiol benzoate intramuscularly on the day before delivery.[90] From the third day, these children had a significantly higher mean plasma bilirubin than had controls. Coincidentally, all children in this study were breast fed.

ENTEROHEPATIC CIRCULATION OF BILIRUBIN

A number of fat-soluble substances undergo an enterohepatic circulation. It has been argued that the biological advantage in the conjugation of bilirubin may be to prevent this recirculation by converting bilirubin to a large polar molecule which will not be reabsorbed. It has been shown in the rat[105] and man[106] that bilirubin is appreciably absorbed while conjugated pigment is not. Much of the pigment in the gut[95] and stools[29] of the newborn infants is unconjugated, presumably from the action of intestinal or bacterial β-glucuronidase. There is thus potentially an enterohepatic circulation. Attempts have been made to interrupt recirculation by giving a bilirubin-binding agent orally. Cholestyramine[165] was ineffective but charcoal[181] lowered plasma bilirubin appreciably. Poland and Odell[147] reported that agarose, a component of agar, has a high affinity for bilirubin and can be used to lower bilirubin in the newborn (p. 118).

BILIRUBIN-ALBUMIN INTERACTION AND COMPETITION

Bilirubin interacts with albumin in a number of ways. Under highly artificial conditions, one molecule of human plasma albumin can combine with 30 or more molecules of bilirubin.[128] At the highest plasma bilirubin concentrations occurring *in vivo*, 70 mg./100 ml., albumin binds 2 moles of pigment but normally only 1 albumin molecule in 60 has pigment attached. Early studies[142] showed that bilirubin could be dialysed away from albumin as long as there were more than 2 molecules bound, which was interpreted as a looser binding of the 3rd pigment molecule. A sensitive method of determining unbound bilirubin[28] shows that the 1st binding site has an affinity about 300 times that of the 2nd site.[80] From the dissociation constant of the 1st site ($K = 7 \times 10^{-9}$), the concentration of free bilirubin can be calculated by a rearrangement of the usual dissociation equation.

$$[\text{free bilirubin}] = \frac{K[\text{albumin-bilirubin}]}{[\text{albumin}]}$$

At normal bilirubin concentrations the molecules of the albumin-bilirubin complex are in equilibrium with an exceedingly low concentration of unbound bilirubin—in the nmol./l. range. This has been confirmed by direct determination.

The concentration of free bilirubin would be expected to determine the extent of any biochemical effects. It is sometimes argued on qualitative grounds that these effects would not be produced until the 1st site is saturated (for 4·1 per cent plasma albumin this would be 35 mg./100 ml. bilirubin, which is well above the 20 mg. level at which the risk of kernicterus becomes appreciable). Considered quantitatively, however, the above equation indicates that there is no abrupt change in free bilirubin concentration as the total pigment concentration rises. The concentration of free bilirubin doubles when the total bilirubin rises from 15–20 mg./100 ml., quadruples by 25 mg./100 ml. and increases 8-fold by 30 mg./100 ml.

Determination of the free bilirubin concentration in plasma of newborn infants, with concentrations of total bilirubin of 6–17 mg./100 ml., reveals much higher concentrations of free bilirubin than the above equation would suggest.[82] This might result from (1) a lower affinity of newborn albumin (which is not supported by determination on cord sera), or (2) competition, or displacement from the first bilirubin binding site.

The possibility that bilirubin may be displaced from albumin by exogenous or endogenous substances has been widely considered since it was noted that kernicterus occurred with a low plasma bilirubin in premature infants on a therapeutic regime of water-soluble sulphonamide (sulphisoxazole, Gantrisin). This drug can displace bilirubin from albumin[85] as was shown in the Gunn rat (Fig. 16), a strain with constantly elevated plasma bilirubin due to an inability to conjugate it. This displacement phenomenon may be more marked in the rat since the affinity of rat albumin for bilirubin is lower than that of human albumin but displacement by sulphisoxazole has been confirmed with human albumin *in vitro*.

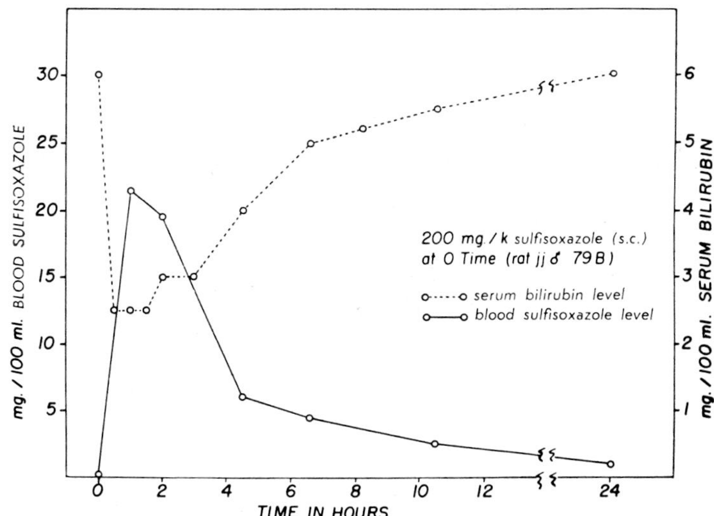

FIG. 16. Displacement of bilirubin from plasma albumin by sulphisoxazole in a hyperbilirubinaemic Gunn rat. The sulphisoxazole was given subcutaneously at 0 time.[85]

As non-esterified fatty acids are also bound to albumin, competition with bilirubin has been examined. The first four molecules of fatty acid to be taken-up by albumin do not compete with the first binding site for bilirubin but the fifth molecule does so.[83]

Plasma-free fatty acid does not usually reach this concentration, but it may do so during intravenous feeding with fat preparations. In one experiment administration of a lipid mixture led to a 5-fold increase in concentration of free bilirubin.[202] Excessive free fatty acid might also arise from activation of clearing factor by heparin. The reason for the excessive amounts of free bilirubin in some newborn plasmas under other conditions is not known. Estimation of the degree of saturation of the first site has been attempted as a means of predicting the hazards of kernicterus (p. 114).

BILIRUBIN TOXICITY

In vitro studies have shown that bilirubin is a powerful biochemical agent. It inhibits the oxygen consumption of brain brie at millimolar concentrations. It enhances oxygen consumption of liver mitochondria at 20 μmol./l. and inhibits at greater concentrations.[131] Brain mitochondria do not show this stimulation but are 50 per cent inhibited at 3 μmol./l. Bilirubin completely uncouples oxidative phosphorylation at 88 μmol./l., reduces the respiratory control index of mitochondria at lower concentrations, causes them to swell[43,131] and inhibits NAD-dependent electron transport.[43] Bilirubin also increases acetate oxidation[174] and the synthesis of haem,[96] DNA[174] and protein.[43] There have been few studies of individual enzymes but bilirubin has been observed to inhibit alcohol dehydrogenase.[56]

Mitochondria take up bilirubin from media probably because of interaction with mitochondrial lipid.[132] Albumin will compete with mitchondria and the protective action of albumin has been demonstrated in mitochondrial suspensions[96,131] and cultures of fibroblasts[111] and L-929 cells.[43] Hydrocortisone protected cells against cell death.[190]

Odell[135] showed that the amount of bilirubin bound by mitochondria *in vitro* is enhanced by acidosis (pH 7·0 and 6·5). The measurements were made at bilirubin-albumin ratios above 1 when competition with the second bilirubin-binding site would be involved. The mechanism by which acidosis increased mitochondrial bilirubin may be complex. The isoelectric point of albumin is 4·7 and as this is approached the negative charge becomes less and presumably also its affinity for anions. Studies of the amino acids in the region of the bilirubin-binding site[81] may provide more precise information about the changes with acidity. Alteration of the charge on bilirubin may also occur. Its pK is considered to be 7·95[143] so the carboxyl groups are predominantly associated at pH 7·4. However, there is evidence of conformational change with pH.

Mustafa and King[132] consider that lipophilicity may be the property on which electron transport, oxidative phosphorylation and other effects depend. As lipids are important constituents of membranes, and hydrocortisone stabilizes some of these, this aspect merits further examination.

In spite of the considerable information on the action of bilirubin the mechanism of damage to neurons is not clear. *In vivo* studies of ATP showed a reduction in the brain of kernicteric rats,[163] but not in liver.[43] Mitochondria prepared from the brains of newborn guinea pigs which had been injected with bilirubin did not show the uncoupling which occurs *in vitro*.[47]

KERNICTERUS

Hyperbilirubinaemia, whether due to prematurity, haemolytic diseases of the newborn or inherited transferase deficiency (Crigler-Najjar syndrome) is occasionally associated with pigmentation of the brain stem and cerebellar nuclei, called kernicterus.[100] Basal ganglia, cerebellum, hippocampus and the eighth nerve nuclei are more frequently affected. Affected infants show neurological disturbances referable to these structures (Fig. 17).

The relative importance of different causative factors remains controversial. The predisposition of the brain to anoxic damage led early workers to consider the pigmentation as secondary to anoxic damage. This view was not supported by the greatly increased incidence of kernicterus in infants with haemolytic disease in which anaemia had been corrected by simple transfusion. It has also been argued that the blood-brain barrier of the newborn was inadequately developed to exclude bile pigment from the brain. Evidence against this has been reviewed.[50]

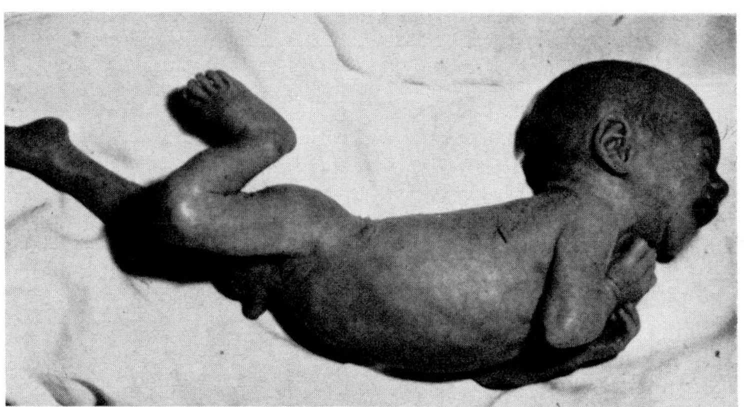

FIG. 17. Opisthotonus in a kernicteric premature infant.

The finding in 1953 that the predominant bile pigment of newborn sera was lipophilic and that of obstructive jaundice was water-soluble suggested that the two pigments might have different biochemical effects and that lipophilic bilirubin might be involved as a cause of kernicterus. This would also explain why kernicterus does not occur in the adult.

Attempts of early workers to produce kernicterus in animals were defeated by the extraordinary capacity of adult animals to secrete administered bilirubin into the bile. The use of newborn animals is technically difficult, but brain damage can be produced in the newborn guinea pigs.[47] Labelled bilirubin has been used to measure the movement of bilirubin into tissues, including the brain.[127] Acidosis, whether respiratory or following administration of HCl, increased the amount of labelled pigment in the brain of newborn guinea pigs, as also did salicylate.[48]

A technique for producing pigmentation of the brain in Gunn rats is based on the displacement of bilirubin from binding sites. Gunn rats, which lack glucuronyl transferase for bilirubin, have plasma bilirubin concentrations of 6–15 mg./100 ml. (rat serum albumin has a lower affinity, and perhaps capacity, than human albumin). Large amounts of bilirubin occur in the tissues and some of these animals develop brain damage and pigmentation. By giving sulphis-

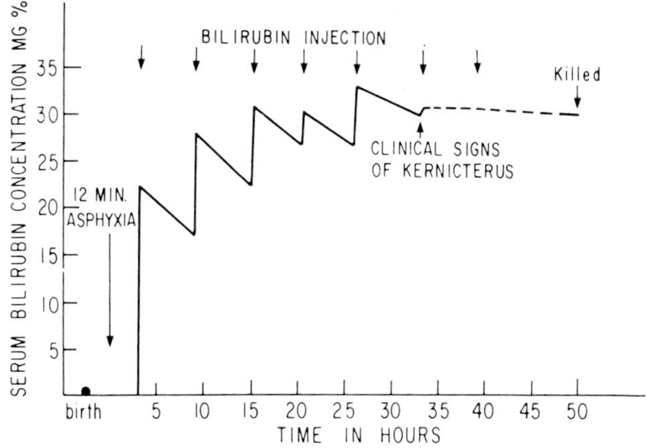

FIG. 18. Serum bilirubin of a newborn *M. mulatta* monkey receiving repeated injections of bilirubin.[119]

oxazole (Fig. 6) which competes for plasma albumin (and possibly tissue proteins) bilirubin is displaced from albumin and brain pigmentation consistently appears.[127,163]

The differences in brain structure and development are so great between species that only the most general conclusions can be applied from experimental rodents to human kernicterus. Studies on primates are essential, but even here Windle[193] has noted that the newborn Rhesus monkey is a little more advanced in its development than the human infant. In the newborn monkey hyperbilirubinaemia can be produced and maintained because of the low conjugating capacity of its liver. By repeated bilirubin injections, the plasma level has been kept at 30–50 mg./100 ml. for 1–2 days.[119] Slight lethargy occurred but not kernicterus. If the newborn monkeys were asphyxiated at birth, resuscitated and then hyperbilirubinaemia were produced (Fig. 18) the characteristic pathological lesions, hyper-irritability and the postural changes of kernicterus occurred (Fig. 19). Thus kernicterus was caused in the newborn Rhesus monkey only by a combination of factors. However, the species' differences have to be considered and it may be that the less-mature human brain is more vulnerable to bilirubin alone. Nevertheless, anoxia, acidosis and possibly hypoglycaemia, may increase the hazards of hyperbilirubinaemia. The striking difference in the incidence of kernicterus[129a] in a controlled trial of simple transfusion (32 per cent) and exchange transfusion (6 per cent), both of which would correct anaemia, suggests an important role for some factor other than anoxia, such as hyperbilirubinaemia. Acidosis and possibly hypoglycaemia may also increase the hazard of hyperbilirubinaemia.

For some years a plasma bilirubin concentration of 20 mg./100 ml.was considered to be marginally dangerous for newborn infants[100] and exchange transfusion was recommended before this value was reached. However, a number of studies have indicated that in premature infants kernicterus may develop at lower concentrations.[64,74] Some mature infants have survived plasma bilirubin concentrations in the 30's, apparently unscathed. Experience with the Crigler-Najjar syndrome suggests that a small group of affected patients may not show brain damage, or it may not appear for a long time (Schmid).[164]

MONITORING PLASMA BILIRUBIN

Determination of plasma bilirubin offers a number of difficulties because of the need to take small, heel-prick, specimens (which are frequently contaminated with haemoglobin), the light sensitivity of bilirubin, the lack of a stable bilirubin standard, and the need to determine conjugated bilirubin (to exclude cholestatic jaundice). Recently, an expert work party has made recommendations[22] which, if applied, should enable a far higher standard of analytical work to be available for care of the newborn infant. The method, based on that of Michaelsson,[129] can be adapted to 50 μl. of plasma. The experience of the Perinatal Laboratory at the Leeds Maternity Hospital is that, at a concentration of 20 mg./100 ml., the (between batch) analytical error (S.D. over a period of a month) is about 0·5 mg.

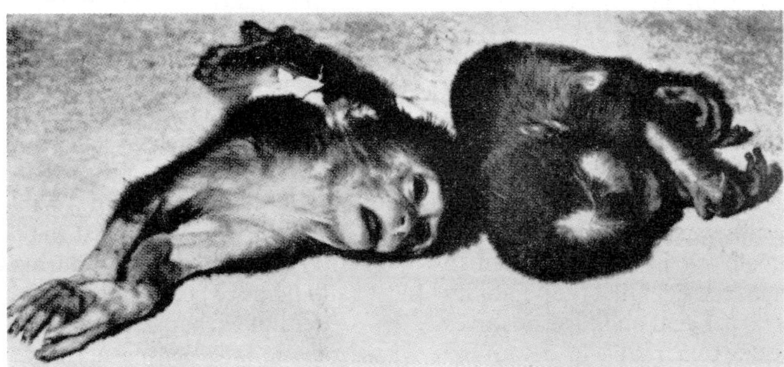

FIG. 19. A newborn *M. mulatta* monkey which was asphyxiated and then injected with bilirubin (see Fig. 18) is shown on the left with a normal control on the right.[119]

In predicting the need for exchange transfusion, it is a

great help to chart the plasma bilirubin against time (age). Three questions of interpretation frequently arise. Is a second analytical result different from a previous one? To provide 95 per cent confidence the two values must differ by more than 2·8 S.D., or 1·4 mg. Is a value significantly different from 20 mg./100 ml.? This requires a difference of 2 S.D. or 1 mg. How often should a second determination be made? This is a more complex question depending on the apparent rate of change. A second determination should not be made before the plasma concentration will have had time to move 2·8 S.D., or about 1·4 mg. (at 10–20 mg./100 ml.). There is a possibility, greater than 1 in 20, that a smaller change could be due to analytical error. It will be clear that clinicians can use the laboratory results scientifically only if laboratories determine the analytical error of their methods and make them known.

As the incidence of kernicterus is not closely correlated with plasma bilirubin, due among other things, to the fact that albumin-bound bilirubin is not toxic, attempts have been made to measure the extent to which the first binding site of plasma albumin is saturated or the concentration of free bilirubin, on which the biochemical effect will depend. Various methods have been used: capacity of plasma albumin to take up dyes,[148,172] change in absorption spectrum of bilirubin on addition of salicylate,[137] estimation of unbound bilirubin by gel filtration techniques[84,88,138,202] and by direct enzymatic determination of free bilirubin.[82] There appears to be only one comparative study[40] and it favours gel filtration. Experience in applying the results clinically is rather limited at the present time. Those who have used these methods, and who have published, tend to recommend them. Clearly they are promising and further study is indicated.

DETERMINATION OF BILE PIGMENTS IN LIQUOR AMNII

In 1953 Bevis suggested that the composition of liquor, obtained by transabdominal amniocentesis, could be used to monitor the extent of haemolytic disease *in utero*. At that time the use of exchange transfusion to tide the infant over the period of reduced liver capacity was not fully appreciated. However, once this was recognized, pigment studies in liquor became a mainstay in deciding when to terminate pregnancy. Clinicians consider that the reliability of the prediction is probably 90 per cent and false positives are about 5 per cent. This is quite remarkable in view of the technical problems of pigment determination and the biological variability of the disease process.

The most common method of measuring bile pigment is derived from that used by Bevis.[18] He measured the absorption spectrum of liquor and noted an increase at the peak of bilirubin absorption at 450 nm. A major difficulty, due to turbidity, was partly overcome by Liley[113] who suggested that a line corresponding to the absorption due to turbidity, be drawn on the semi-logarithmic plot of the absorption spectrum of liquor. In practice, a tangential line is drawn from the absorptive minimum, near 365 nm., to touch the curve at 550 nm. The difference at 450 nm., between this tangent and the actual absorption, gives $\Delta 450$ which is attributed to bile pigments. Additional interference may arise from haemoglobin and methaemalbumin, and calculations based on a few measurements, rather than a full scan, have been recommended.[55] As is common with empirical methods many variations have been proposed.[139]

The experimental error in the determination of $\Delta 450$ is large since it is based on differences between low values: the error may amount to 50 per cent at a $\Delta 450$ value of 0·05, equivalent to about 0·05 mg. bilirubin/100 ml. Methods for minimizing the errors have been given.[36] Moreover, various methods for removing turbidity, by centrifugation, by filtration through paper, membrane or Seitz filters, give somewhat different results, and all remove some of the bile pigment. This has led one clinician to council in despair "it is necessary for each centre to analyse sufficient numbers of samples and patients to be able to compile its own prediction tables."[53] The clinical significance assigned to $\Delta 450$ varies from one method to another and takes account of such factors as the normal fall in the value as term is approached. Reviews must be consulted for the indications requiring clinical action.[55,113,114,144]

Direct determinations of bile pigment would have great advantages. The concentration in liquor (0·05 mg./100 ml. is significant clinically) is too low to use the diazo reaction. Attempts have been made to overcome this by extracting liquor with chloroform and determining the pigment directly[27] or after concentration.[144] Chloroform extraction is likely to miss any conjugated bilirubin which may be present,[30] but this would not necessarily affect the reliability of predictions.

BIOCHEMICAL FEATURES OF EXCHANGE TRANSFUSION

Exchange transfusion was designed, originally, to replace an affected infant's vulnerable red-blood cells with others which would not be haemolysed. Later, repeated transfusions were used when hyperbilirubinaemia persisted, on the assumption that the haemolytic process had not been sufficiently reduced. These repeated transfusions proved effective and were recommended.[4] About the same time, an alternative function for the exchange was suggested by the observation[35,97] that the concentration of bile pigment in the plasma removed during exchange was higher than it should have been on the basis of the theoretical curve of the extent of exchange (Fig. 20). This meant that pigment was moving into the plasma from the tissues. The size of the pool of extra-vascular bile pigment has never been determined in haemolytic disease of the newborn. In the more chronic condition of hyperbilirubinaemia due to Crigler-Najjar syndrome it has been found to be 2–14 times larger than the calculated plasma pigment pool.[21,166] In the adult, there is an extra-vascular pool of albumin 1–2 times the size of the vascular pool.[192]

The efficiency of exchange transfusion, as a means of washing out bilirubin, can be improved by adding a bilirubin-binding agent, plasma albumin[41,136,180] which competes for the bilirubin held by tissue binding sites of lower affinity.

The plasma bilirubin, immediately after exchange, may

rise rapidly within an hour or two. This "rebound" phenomenon is probably due to equilibration with the tissue bilirubin, but it may be produced by haemolysis of the new cells due to their age or for other reasons.

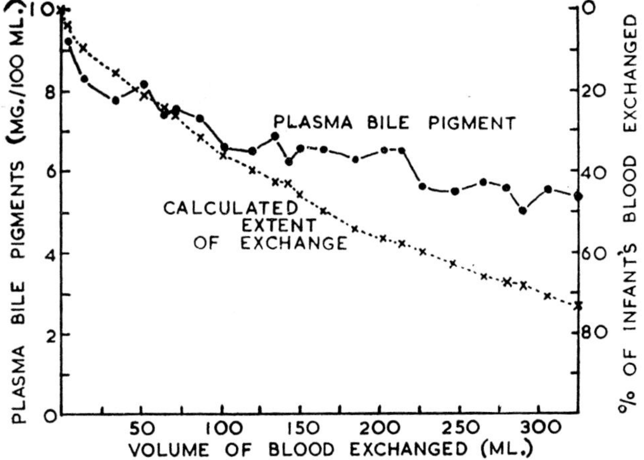

FIG. 20. Comparison of the fall in plasma bilirubin, during an exchange transfusion, with the calculated extent of the exchange, in a newborn infant with haemolytic disease.[97]

OTHER METHODS OF TREATING HYPERBILIRUBINAEMIA

Phototherapy

The well-known light-sensitivity of bilirubin was utilized clinically by Cremer, Perryman and Richards[44] who exposed infants to natural and artificial light and observed appreciably reductions in serum bilirubin. This method has been extensively used in some centres, especially in sunny climates, and a great reduction in the number of exchange transfusions in premature infants has been reported. Clinical and laboratory studies on phototherapy were brought together in 1970.[16] Lucey[118] reviewed five controlled trials of phototherapy involving over 500 premature infants. Among the controls, 44 per cent reached a serum bilirubin value of over 12 mg./100 ml. but only 8 per cent of the treated did so. Above 15 mg. the figures were 22 and 1·6 per cent. Lucey[118] reported the peak bilirubin values of 97 small infants which he had treated by phototherapy. The values were plotted on the same cumulative basis as Trolle[179] used for phenobarbitone-treated small infants and their untreated controls (Fig. 21). Lucey[118] found no deleterious effect on growth but noted more frequent loose green stools during irradiation. In a controlled study irradiated premature infants were re-examined at 31–64 weeks and found to be smaller, although growing faster, than the controls.[76] Two studies of the effect of irradiation on newborn Gunn rats gave conflicting results regarding retardation of growth,[14,86] but this has been partly explained as a light-induced diminution of lactation and suckling.[13]

Considerable attention has been given to determining whether the photodecomposition products of bilirubin are toxic. The nature of the products varies with the conditions of illumination. In alkaline and chloroform solutions biliverdin is one of the main products, but it is less important (or itself unstable) if a solution of bilirubin-albumin is irradiated.[140,141] The products give a Stokvis reaction[141,149] suggesting that dipyrroles are produced but the only product positively identified is a monopyrrole.[112] There is also evidence against biliverdin as an intermediate product.[121] It seems probable that there are several pathways of bilirubin degradation under different circumstances, all of which may be remote for the conditions in irradiated skin. Ostrow[141] cannulated the bile ducts of hyperbilirubinaemic Gunn rats and noted that during irradiation there was an immediate increase in the bilirubin degradation products in

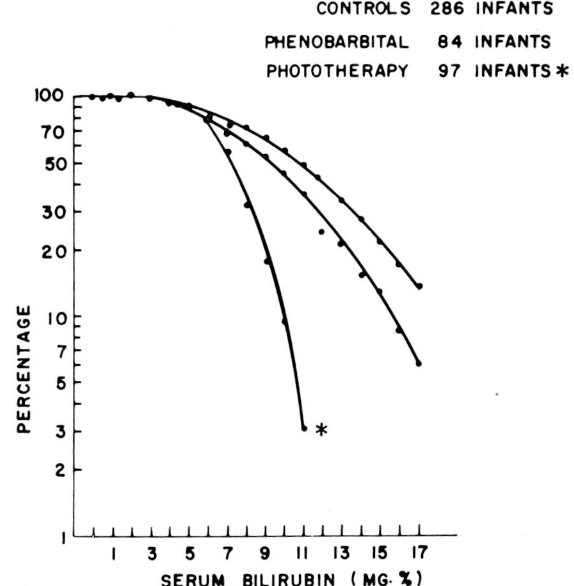

FIG. 21. Plot of the peak serum bilirubin of 3 groups of infants of low birth weight (less than 2·5 kg.). The ordinate gives the percentage of infants which had a serum bilirubin higher than the value indicated on the abscissa. The upper two curves are from Trolle's comparison of controls and phenobarbitone-treated infants[179] and the lowest is a group given phototherapy by Lucey (1970), from whom the figure is taken.[118]

the bile. These were water-soluble and mainly diazo-negative.

The toxicity of bilirubin photodegradation products have been examined in many systems. They do not uncouple oxidative phosphorylation of rat-liver mitochondria,[31] and do not increase acetate oxidation, or inhibit DNA synthesis.[174] In a variety of biological systems they are non-toxic: fibroblast cultures,[149] myelinating cerebellum cultures[169] and in newborn guinea pigs.[47] Irradiated newborn Gunn rats had much less damage to the Purkinje cells of the cerebellar vermis[86] than had untreated controls.

Behrman and Hsia[15] came to the conclusion that phototherapy should be reserved for infants with a demonstrated hyperbilirubinaemia of 10 mg./100 ml., or more and emphasized the need for further controlled studies.

Glucuronyl Transferase Induction

The treatment of newborn jaundice with phenobarbitone arose from the discovery that it was one of a wide variety of compounds which stimulate increased metabolism of drugs and of some endogenous substances.[42] Inducing agents increase liver weight, total protein and endoplasmic reticulum, especially the smooth reticulum which contains a number of drug-metabolizing enzymes. Many of the latter involve hydroxylating reactions mediated by NADPH-requiring oxidase systems in which cytochrome P-450 is the terminal electron acceptor (haem oxygenase belongs to this class). Under optimum stimulation, these enzymes may increase 10-fold. Glucuronyl transferase, which is also present in endoplasmic reticulum, seldom increases more than 2-fold in animals.

Phenobarbitone was first used as an inducing agent to treat inherited hyperbilirubinaemia of infants or adults. "Constitutional" hyperbilirubinaemia occurs in three varieties: (1) classical Crigler-Najjar syndrome, type I of Arias[6] (with plasma bilirubin of 17–40 mg./100 ml.); (2) type II of Arias[6] (with plasma bilirubin of 5–20 mg.), and (3) Gilbert's disease[150] (with plasma bilirubin of 1–3·3 mg.). Bilirubin glucuronyl transferase of the liver is essentially absent in the first type,[164] which has colourless bile. It is markedly deficient in the second and in Gilbert's disease is about 25 per cent of normal adult values.[23]

The plasma bilirubin can be reduced by administering phenobarbitone to patients with Arias type II hyperbilirubinaemia[45,92,199] and to patients with Gilbert's disease.[26] Although increase in glucuronyl transferase has been demonstrated in animals, and a variety of drugs increase the liver transferase in patients without jaundice,[19] there has been no clear demonstration that this increase is the mechanism by which plasma bilirubin can be lowered in Gilbert's disease and in Arias' type II. Phenobarbitone also increases bile flow and even has an effect on plasma bilirubin in cholestatic jaundice.[175,178] Alternative pathways of degradation or the secretory process itself may be activated.

The possibility that phenobarbitone might accelerate transferase development in the fetus and newborn has been explored in animal experiments with consistently positive results, it not striking increases. Thus, in rats daily administration during the last third of pregnancy led to a 2½-fold increase in liver transferase of the newborn, but this was still only 10 per cent of the adult value.[69] However, newborn mice of treated mothers had adult values.[39]

The administration of phenobarbitone to pregnant women lowered their plasma bilirubin and that of their newborn infants.[152] If treatment was delayed until birth, the effect was smaller. The most extensive trial has been carried out by Trolle[179] who found a marked reduction in the number of severely hyperbilirubinaemic infants, even with small infants (Fig. 21). This conclusion has been supported by a number of controlled trials,[38,87,122,126,185] one of which (Yaffe)[199] is shown in Fig. 22. Walker[186] in a retrospective study found no effect with small infants, but another retrospective study observed a decrease.[151] Chinese infants are particularly prone to hyperbilirubinaemia, even in the absence of Rh haemolytic disease, and the number of exchanges was reduced to a tenth by phenobarbitone treatment.[201]

The only observed disadvantage of phenobarbitone treatment has been lethargy,[93,199] but there are a number of possible dangers. Inducing agents increase some hydroxylating enzymes which are involved in normal metabolic processes, such as the production of bile salts, metabolism of vitamin D[67] and the conversion of steroid hormones like testosterone. Testosterone is essential in the fetus for the development of male secondary structures and in the male newborn rat for maturation of appropriate sexual attitudes. The effect of phenobarbitone requires much further study.

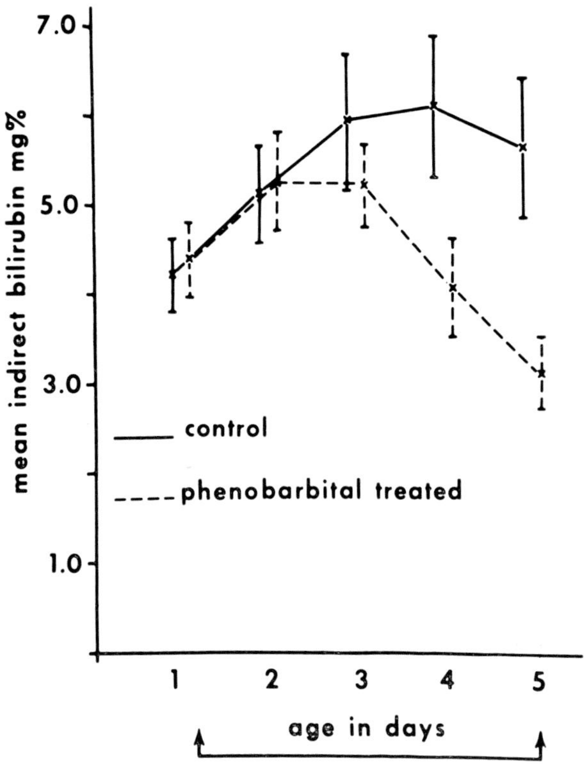

FIG. 22. Serum bilirubin concentrations in 20 normal newborn infants given phenobarbitone (8 mg./kg./day) after day 1, compared with 20 untreated controls.[198] Means and S.E.M.'s are given.

The time taken for the plasma bilirubin to fall, and the limited extent of the reduction, suggest that phenobarbitone on its own cannot be successfully applied to treatment of haemolytic disease, in which the plasma pigment commonly rises 5–10 mg./day. It is possible, however, that it may be useful in the treatment of premature infants, or in mild haemolytic disease, particularly if other inducing agents free of the disadvantages can be devised. For instance, the N-phenyl analogue of phenobarbital, phetharbital, is not a sedative but is an inducing agent.[78,79] Ethanol,[187] diethylnicotinamide,[52,167] and dicophane[177] are also effective.

Miscellaneous Methods

Poland and Odell[147] suggested that there was an appreciable enterohepatic circulation of bilirubin (p. 110). They gave agar by mouth to newborn infants to trap bilirubin in the gut. By day 3 there was a significant reduction in plasme bilirubin compared with the controls (Fig. 23). The stools, which must be of larger volume than in the untreated infants, were found to contain more pigment though this occurred so early as to suggest that the two groups might not be identical at the start.

Since the amount of UDPGA in the newborn liver is probably limiting for conjugation, attempts have been made to increase this by giving precursors—aspartic and orotic acids for uridine[89,124] and UDPG for UDPGA.[37]

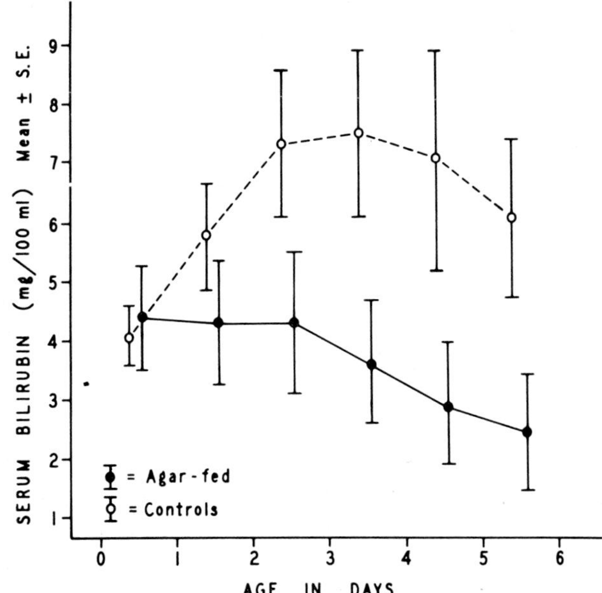

FIG. 23. Serum bilirubin concentration in 9 healthy, full-term, newborn infants given agar by mouth from the 1st day, compared with 10 untreated controls.[149] Means and S.E.M.'s are given. The differences are significant on day 3 and after.

Significantly reductions in plasma bilirubin were reported from each.

Recently it has been shown[60] that in hypophysectomized rats the secretion of bile, the capacity to conjugate OAP and to excrete conjugated bilirubin were defective. The *in vitro* conjugation of bilirubin was normal, however. Thyroxin or thyrotropic hormone restored the deficiencies. Thyroid treatment does not improve newborn jaundice.[130] Occasionally congenital hypothyroidism presents as prolonged unconjugated hyperbilirubinaemia.[189] This responds to thyroid.

ACKNOWLEDGEMENT

I am indebted to Miss S. Stewart and Miss S. Lathe for checking references and preparing the final manuscript.

I am indebted to Dr. M. F. G. Buchanan for Fig. 17.

REFERENCES

1. Ackerman, B. D., Dyer, G. Y. and Leydorf, M. M. (1970), "Hyperbilirubinemia and Kernicterus in Small Premature Infants," *Pediatrics, Springfield*, **45**, 918–925.
2. Adlard, B. P. F. and Lathe, G. H. (1970), "The Effect of Steroids and Nucleotides on Solubilized Bilirubin Uridine Diphosphate-Glucuronyl Transferase," *Biochem. J.*, **119**, 437–445.
3. Adlard, B. P. F. and Lathe, G. H. (1970), "Breast Milk Jaundice: Effect of 3α 20β-pregnanediol on Bilirubin Conjugation by Human Liver," *Arch. Dis. Childh.*, **45**, 186–189.
4. Allen, F. H. and Diamond, L. K. (1954), "Prevention of Kernicterus. Management of Erythroblastosis Fetalis According to Current Knowledge," *J. Amer. med. Ass.*, **155**, 1209–1213.
5. Arias, I. M. and Gartner, L. M. (1964), "Production of Unconjugated Hyperbilirubinemia in Full-term Newborn Infants Following Administration of Pregnane-3α, 20β-diol," *Nature, Lond.*, **203**, 1292–1293.
6. Arias, I. M., Gartner, L. M., Cohen, M., Ezzer, J. B. and Levi, A. J. (1969), "Chronic Nonhemolytic Unconjugated Hyperbilirubinemia with Glucuronyl Transferase Deficiency," *Amer. J. Med.*, **47**, 395–409.
7. Arias, I. M., Gartner, L. M., Seifter, S. and Furman, M. (1964), "Prolonged Neonatal Unconjugated Hyperbilirubinemia Associated with Breast Feeding and a Steroid, Pregnane-3 (alpha), 20 (beta)-diol, in Maternal Milk that Inhibits Glucuronide Formation *in vitro*," *J. clin. Invest.*, **43**, 2037–2047.
8. Arias, I. M. and London, I. M. (1957), "Bilirubin Glucuronide Formation *in vitro*; Demonstration of a Defect in Gilbert's Disease," *Science, N.Y.*, **126**, 563–564.
9. Arias, I. M., Wolfson, S. Lucey, J. F. and McKay, R. J., Jr. (1965), "Transient Familial Neonatal Hyperbilirubinemia," *J. clin. Invest.*, **44**, 1442–1450.
10. Arthur, L. J. H., Bevan, B. R. and Holton, J. B. (1966), "Neonatal Hyperbilirubinemia and Breast Feeding," *Develop. Med. Child Neurol.*, **8**, 279–284.
11. Axelrod, J., Schmid, R. and Hammaker, L. (1957), "A Biochemical Lesion in Congenital, Non-obstructive, Non-haemolytic Jaundice," *Nature, Lond.*, **180**, 1426–1427.
12. Bakken, A. F., Thaler, M. M. and Schmid, R. (1972), "Metabolic Regulation of Heme Catabolism and Bilirubin Production. I: Hormonal Control of Hepatic Heme Oxygenase Activity," *J. clin. Invest.*, **51**, 530–536.
13. Ballowitz L. (1971), "Effects of Blue and White Light on Infant (Gunn) Rats and on Lactating Mother Rats," *Biol. Neonate*, **19**, 409–425.
14. Ballowitz, L., Heller, R., Natzscha, J. and Ott, M. (1970), "The Effect of Blue Light on Infant Gunn Rats." In ref. 16, pp. 106–113.
14a. Barrett, P. V. D. (1971), "The Effect of Diet and Fasting on the Serum Bilirubin Concentration in the Rat," *Gastroenterology*, **60**, 572–576.
15. Behrman, R. E. and Hsia, D. Y. Y. (1970), "Summary of a Symposium on Phototherapy for Hyperbilirubinemia." In ref. 16, pp. 131–136.
16. Bergsma, D., Hsia, D. Y. Y. and Jackson, C. (1970), Editors of *Bilirubin Metabolism in the Newborn.* Baltimore: Williams and Wilkins.
17. Bernstein, R. B., Novy, M. J., Piasecki, G. J., Lester, R. and Jackson, B. T. (1969), "Bilirubin Metabolism in the Fetus Dog and Monkey," *J. clin. Invest.*, **48**, 1678–1688.
18. Bevis, D. C. A. (1956), "Blood Pigments in Haemolytic Disease of the Newborn," *J. Obstet. Gynaec. Brit. Commonw.*, **63**, 68–75.
19. Billing, B. H. and Black, M. (1971), "The Action of Drugs on Bilirubin Metabolism in Man," *Ann. N.Y. Acad. Sci.*, **179**, 403–410.
20. Billing, B. H., Cole, P. G. and Lathe, G. H. (1954), "Increased Plasma Bilirubin in Newborn Infants in Relation to Birth Weight," *Brit. med. J.*, **2**, 1263–1265.
21. Billing, B. H., Gray, C. H., Kulczycka, A., Manfield, P. and Nicholson, D. (1964), "The Metabolism of (^{14}C) Bilirubin in Congenital Non-haemolytic Hyperbilirubinemia," *Clin. Sci.*, **27**, 163–170.
22. Billing, B., Haslam, R. and Wold, N. (1971), "Bilirubin Standards and the Determination of Bilirubin by Manual and Technicon Autoanalyser Methods," *Ann. clin. Biochem.*, **8**, 21–30.
23. Black, M. and Billing, B. H. (1969), "Hepatic Bilirubin UDP-glucuronyl Transferase Activity in Liver Disease and Gilbert's Syndrome," *New Engl. J. Med.*, **280**, 1266–1271.

24. Black, M., Billing, B. H. and Heirwegh, K. P. M. (1970), "Determination of Bilirubin UDP-glucuronyltransferase Activity in Needle-biopsy Specimens of Human Liver," *Clinica chim. Acta*, **29**, 27–35.
25. Black, J. B., Pennington, G. W. and Warrell, D. W. (1969), "Clinical Application of a New Chemical Method for the Estimation of Bilirubin in Liquor Amnii," *J. Obstet. Gynaec. Brit. Commonw.*, **76**, 112–116.
26. Black, M. and Sherlock, S. (1970), "Treatment of Gilbert's Syndrome with Phenobarbitone," *Lancet*, **i**, 1359–1362.
27. Brazie, J. V, Bowes, W. A. and Ibbott, F. A. (1969), "An Improved Rapid Procedure for the Determination of Amniotic Fluid Bilirubin and its Use in the Prediction of the Course of Rh-sensitized Pregnancies," *Amer. J. Obstet. Gynec.*, **104**, 80–86.
28. Brodersen, R. and Bartels, P. (1969), "Enzymatic Oxidation of Bilirubin," *Eur. J. Biochem.*, **10**, 468–473.
29. Broderson, R. and Hermann, L. S. (1963), "Intestinal Reabsorption of Unconjugated Bilirubin. A Possible Contributing Factor in Neonatal Jaundice," *Lancet*, **i**, 1242.
30. Brodersen, R., Jacobsen, J., Hertz, H., Rebbe, H. and Sorensen, B. (1967), "Bilirubin Conjugation in the Human Fetus," *Scand. J. clin. Lab. Invest.*, **20**, 41–48.
31. Broughton, P. M. G., Rossiter, J. E. J. R., Warren, C. B. M., Goulis, G. and Lord, P. S. (1965), "Effect of Blue Light on Hyperbilirubinaemia," *Arch. Dis. Childh.*, **40**, 666–671.
32. Brown, W. R. and Boon, W. H. (1965), "Ethnic Group Differences in Plasma Bilirubin Levels of Full-term, Healthy, Singapore Newborns," *Pediatrics, Springfield*, **36**, 745–751.
33. Brown, W. R., Grodsky, G. M. and Carbone, J. V. (1964), "Intracellular Distribution of Tritiated Bilirubin During Hepatic Uptake and Excretion," *Amer. J. Physiol.*, **207**, 1237–1241.
34. Brown, A. K. and Zuelzer, W. W. (1958), "Studies on the Neonatal Development of the Glucuronide Conjugating System," *J. clin. Invest.*, **37**, 332–340.
35. Brown, A. K., Zuelzer, W. W. and Robinson, A. R. (1957), "Studies in Hyperbilirubinaemia II. Clearance of Bilirubin from Plasma and Extravascular Space in Newborn Infants During Exchange Transfusion," *Amer. J. Dis. Childh.*, **93**, 274–286.
36. Burnett, R. W. (1972), "Instrumental and Procedure Sources of Error in Determination of Bile Pigments in Amniotic Fluid," *Clin. Chem.*, **18**, 150–154.
37. Carreddu, P. and Marini, A. (1968), Stimulating Bilirubin Conjugation," *Lancet*, **i**, 982.
38. Carswell, F., Kerr, M. M. and Dunsmore, I. R. (1972), "Sequential Trial of Effect of Phenobarbitone or Serum Bilirubin of Preterm Infants," *Arch. Dis. Child.*, **47**, 621–625.
39. Catz, C. and Yaffe, S. J. (1968), "Barbiturate Enhancement of Bilirubin Conjugation and Excretion in Young and Adult Animals," *Pediat. Res.*, **2**, 361–370.
40. Chan, G., Schiff, D. and Stern, L. (1971), "Competitive Binding of Free Fatty Acids and Bilirubin to Albumin. Differences in HBABA Dye versus Sephadex G-25. Interpretation of Results," *Clin. Biochem.*, **4**, 208–214.
41. Comley, A. and Wood, B. (1968), "Albumin Administration in Exchange Transfusion for Hyperbilirubinaemia," *Arch. Dis. Childh.*, **43**, 151–154.
42. Conney, A. H. (1967), "Pharmacological Implications of Microsomal Enzyme Induction," *Pharmac. Rev.*, **19**, 317–366.
43. Cowger, M. L., Igo, R. P. and Labbe, R. F. (1965), "The Mechanism of Bilirubin Toxicity Studied with Purified Respiratory Enzyme and Tissue Culture Systems," *Biochemistry, N.Y.*, **4**, 2763–2770.
44. Cremer, R. J., Perryman, P. W. and Richards, D. H. (1958), "Influence of Light on the Hyperbilirubinaemia of Infants," *Lancet*, **i**, 1094–1097.
45. Crigler, J. F. and Gold, N. I. (1969), "Effect of Sodium Phenobarbital on Bilirubin Metabolism in an Infant with Congenital, Nonhemolytic, Unconjugated Hyperbilirubinemia and Kernicterus," *J. clin. Invest.*, **48**, 42–55.
46. Davidson, L. T., Merritt, K. K. and Weech, A. A. (1941), "Hyperbilirubinemia in the Newborn," *Amer. J. Dis. Child.*, **61**, 958–980.
47. Diamond, I. F. (1970), "Studies on the Neurotoxicity of Bilirubin and the Distribution of its Derivatives." In ref. 16, pp. 124–127.
48. Diamond, I. and Schmid, R. (1966), "Experimental Bilirubin Encephalopathy. The Mode of Entry of Bilirubin—^{14}C into the Central Nervous System," *J. clin. Invest.*, **45**, 678–689.
49. Di Toro, R., Lupi, L. and Ansanelli, V. (1968), "Glucuronation of the Liver in Premature Babies," *Nature, Lond.*, **219**, 265–267.
50. Dobbing, J. (1961), "The Blood-brain Barrier," *Physiol. Rev.*, **41**, 130–188.
51. Dutton, G. I. (1959), "Glycuronide Synthesis in Foetal Liver and Other Tissues," *Biochem. J.*, **71**, 141–148.
52. Ertel, I. J. and Newton, W. A. (1969), "Therapy in Congenital Hyperbilirubinemia: Phenobarbital and Diethylnicotinamide," *Pediatrics, Springfield*, **44**, 43–48.
53. Fairweather, D. V. I., Millar, M. D. and Whyley, G. A. (1972), "Factors Influencing the Spectrophotometric Evaluation of Liquor Amnii," *J. Obstet. Gynaec. Brit. Commonw.*, **79**, 433–440.
53a. Felsher, B. F. Rickard D. and Redeker A. G. (1970), "The Reciprocal Relation between Calorie Intake and the Degree of Hyperbilirubinemia in Gilbert's Syndrome," *New Engl. J. Med.*, **283**, 170–172.
54. Fleischner, G., Robbins, J. and Arias, I. M. (1972), "Immunological Studies of Y Protein. A Major Cytoplasmic Organic Anion-binding Protein in Rat Liver," *J. clin. Invest.*, **51**, 677–684.
55. Fleming, A. F. and Woolf, A. J. (1965), "A Spectrophotometric Method for the Quantitative Estimation of Bilirubin Liquor Amnii," *Clin. chim. Acta*, **12**, 67–74.
55a. Flint, M., Lathe, G. H. and Ricketts, T. R. (1963), "The Effect of Undernutrition and Other Factors on the Development of Glucuronyl Transferase Activity in the Newborn Rabbit," *Ann. N.Y. Acad. Sci.*, **111**, 295–301.
56. Flitman, R. and Worth, M. H. (1966), "Inhibition of Hepatic Alcohol Dehydrogenase by Bilirubin," *J. biol. Chem.*, **241**, 669–672.
57. Flodgaard, H. (1968), "UDPGA Turnover in Guinea-pig Liver During Perinatal Development," *Abstracts of Fifth FEBS Meeting*, p. 104. Praha: Csechoslovak Biochemical Society.
58. Gartner, L. M. and Arias, I. M. (1963), "Developmental Pattern of Glucuronide Formation in Rat and Guinea Pig Liver," *Amer. J. physiol.*, **205**, 663–666.
59. Gartner, L. M. and Arias, I. M. (1969), "The Transfer of Bilirubin from Blood to Bile in the Neonatal Guinea Pig," *Pediat. Res.*, **3**, 171–180.
60. Gartner, L. M. and Arias, I. M. (1972), "Hormonal Control of Hepatic Bilirubin Transport and Conjugation," *Amer. J. Physiol.*, **222**, 1091–1099.
61. Gartner, I. M., Lane, D. L. and Cornelius, C. E. (1971), "Bilirubin Transport by Liver in Adult Macaca mulatta," *Amer. J. Physiol.*, **220**, 1528–1535.
62. Gartner, L. M. and Lane, D. (1972), "Hepatic Metabolism and Transport of Bilirubin During Physiologic Jaundice in the Newborn Rhesus Monkey," *Pediat. Res.*, **5**, 413.
63. Gartner, L. M. and Lane, D. L. (1972), "The Physiology of Physiologic Hyperbilirubinemia of the Newborn," in *Proceedings of the Third International Conference on Medicine and Surgery in Primates*, Lyon, June 1972. In the press.
64. Gartner, L. M., Snyder, R. N., Chabon, R. S. and Bernstein, J. (1970), "Kernicterus: High Incidence in Premature Infants with Low Serum Bilirubin Concentrations," *Pediatrics, Springfield*, **45**, 906–917.
65. Grodsky, G. M. and Carbone, J. V. (1957), "The Synthesis of Bilirubin Glucuronide by Tissue Homogenates," *J. biol. Chem.*, **226**, 449–458.
66. Grodsky, G. M., Kolb, H. J., Fanska, R. E. and Nemechek, Cf (1970), "Effect of Age of Rat on Development of Hepatic Carriers for Bilirubin: a Possible Explanation for Physiologic

Jaundice and Hyperbilirubinemia in the Newborn," *Metabolism*, **19**, 246–252.

67. Hahn, J. J., Birge, S. J., Sharp, C. R. and Avioli, L. V. (1972), "Phenobarbital-induced Alterations in Vitamin D Metabolism," *J. clin. Invest.*, **51**, 741–748.
68. Halac, E. and Reff, A. (1967), "Studies on Bilirubin UDP-glycyronyl Transferase," *Biochim. biophys. Acta*, **139**, 328–343.
69. Halac, E. and Sicignano, C. (1969), "Re-evaluation of the Influence of Sex, Age, Pregnancy, and Phenobarbital on the Activity of UDP-glucuronyl Transferase in Rat Liver," *J. Lab., clin. Med.*, **73**, 677–685.
70. Hammaker, L. and Schmid, R. (1967), "Interference with Bile Pigment Uptake in the Liver by Flavaspidic Acid," *Gastroenterology*, **53**, 31–37.
71. Hargreaves, T. (1966), "The Effect of Male Fern Extract on Biliary Secretion," *Brit. J. Pharmac. Chemother*, **26**, 34–40.
72. Hargreaves, T. and Piper, R. F. (1971), "Breast Milk Jaundice. Effect of Inhibitory Breast Milk and 3α, 20β-pregnanediol on Glucuronyl Transferase," *Arch. Dis. Childh.*, **46**, 195–198.
73. Harkness, R. A. and Darling, J. A. B. (1971), "Steroid Levels in Milk," *Acta endocr. Copnh.*, Supp. **155**, 92.
74. Harris, R. C., Lucey, J. F. and MacLean, R. J. (1958), "Kermicterus in Premature Infants Associated with Low Concentrations of Bilirubin in the Plasma," *Pediatrics, Springfield*, **21**, 875–884.
75. Heirwegh, K. P. M., Van Hees, G. P., Leroy, P., Van Roy, F. P. and Jansen, F. H. (1970), "Heterogeneity of Bile Pigment Conjugates as Revealed by Chromatography of Their Ethyl Anthranilate Azopigments," *Biochem. J.*, **120**, 877–890.
76. Hodgman, J. (1970), "Effect of Phototherapy on Subsequent Growth and Development of the Premature Infant." In ref. 16, pp. 75–82.
77. Hsia, D. Y-Y, Allen, F. H., Diamond, L. K. and Gellis, S. S. (1953), "Serum Bilirubin Levels in the Newborn Infant," *J. Pediat.*, **42**, 277–285.
78. Hunter, J., Maxwell, J. D., Carrella, M., Stewart, D. A. and Williams, R. (1971), "Urinary D-glucaric Acid Excretion as a Test for Hepatic Enzyme Induction in Man," *Lancet*, **i**, 572–575.
79. Hunter, J., Thompson, R. P. H., Rake, M. O. and Williams, R. (1971), "Controlled Trial of Phetharbital, a Non-hypnotic Barbiturate, in Unconjugated Hyperbilirubinaemia," *Brit. med. J.*, **2**, 497–499.
80. Jacobsen, J. (1969), "Binding of Bilirubin to Human Serum Albumin—Determination of the Dissociation Constants," *FEBS Lett.*, **5**, 112–114.
81. Jacobsen, C. (1972), "Chemical Modification of the High-affinity Bilirubin Binding Site of Human Serum Albumin," *Eur. J. Biochem.*, **27**, 513–519.
82. Jacobsen, J. and Fedders, O. (1970), "Determination of Non-albumin-bound Bilirubin in Human Serum," *Scand, J. clin. Lab. Invest.*, **26**, 237–241.
83. Jacobsen, J., Thiessen, H. and Brodersen, R. (1972), "Effect on Fatty Acids on the Binding of Bilirubin to Albumin," *Biochem. J.*, **126**, 7P.
84. Jirsova, V., Jirsa, M., Heringora, A., Koldovsky, O. and Weirichova, J. (1967), "The Use and Possible Diagnostic Significance of Sephadex Gel Filtration of Serum of Icteric Newborn," *Biol. Neonatale*, **11**, 204–208.
85. Johnson, L. M., Sarmiento, F., Blanc, W. A. and Day, R. L. (1959), "Kernicterus in Rats with an Inherited Deficiency of Glucuronyl Transferase," *Amer. J. Dis. Childh.*, **97**, 591–608.
86. Johnson, L. and Schutta, H. S. (1970), "Quantitative Assessment of the Effect of Light Treatment in Infant Gunn Rats," in ref. 16, pp. 114–118.
87. Jouppila, P. and Suonio, S. (1970), "The Effect of Phenobarbital given to Toxaemic and Normal Parturients on the Serum Bilirubin Concentration of Newborn Infants," *Ann. clin. Res.*, **2**, 209–213.
88. Kapitulnik, J., Blondheim, S. H. and Kaufmann, N. A. (1972), "Sephadex Absorption of Bilirubin from Neonatal and Adult Serum," *Clin. Chem.*, **18**, 43–47.
89. Kintzel, H. W., Hinkel, G. K. and Schwarze, R. (1971), "The Decrease in the Serum Bilirubin Level in Premature Infants by Orotic Acid," *Acta. Paediat. Stockh.*, **60**, 1–5.
90. Koivisto, K., Ojala, A. and Jarvinen, P. A. (1970), "The Effect on Neonatal Bilirubin Levels of Oestrogen given to the Mother before Delivery," *Ann. clin. Res.*, **2**, 204–208.
91. Krauer-Mayer, B., Keller, M. and Hottinger, A. (1968), "Uber den frauenmilchinduzierten Icterus prologatus des Neugeborenen," *Helv. paed. Acta*, **23**, 68–76.
92. Kreek, M. J. and Sleisenger, M. H. (1968), "Reduction of Serum Unconjugated Bilirubin with Phenobarbitone in Adult Congenital Non-haemolytic Unconjugated Hyperbilirubinaemia," *Lancet*, **ii**, 73–77.
93. Kron, R. E., Stein, M. and Goddard, K. E. (1966), "Newborn Suckling Behaviour Affected by Obstetric Sedation," *Pediatrics*, **37**, 1012–1016.
94. Kuenzle, C. C. (1970), "Bilirubin Conjugates of Human Bile. The Excretion of Bilirubin as the Acyl Glycosides of Aldobiuronic Acid, Pseudoaldobiuronic Acid and Hexuronosylhexuronic Acid, with a Branched-chain Hexuronic Acid as one of the components of Hexuronosylhexuronide," *Biochem. J.*, **119**, 411–435.
95. Kunzer, W., Schenck, W. and Vahlenkamp, H. (1963), "Bilirubinadsorption aus Duodenalsaft durch Kohle," *Klin. Wschr.*, **41**, 1108.
96. Labbe, R. F., Zaske, M. R. and Aldrich, R. A. (1959), "Bilirubin Inhibition of Heme Biosynthesis," *Science, N.Y.*, **129**, 1741–1742.
97. Lathe, G. H. (1955), "Exchange Transfusion as a Means of Removing Bilirubin in Haemolytic Disease of the Newborn," *Brit. med. J.*, **1**, 192–196.
98. Lathe, G. H. (1972), "The Degradation of Haem by Mammals and its Excretion as Conjugated Bilirubin," *Essays in Biochemistry*, **8**, 107–148.
99. Lathe, G. H. (1972), "Liver Function in the Newborn," *Symposium of the Royal College of Physicians of Edinburgh* (R. F. Robertson, ed.). Edinburgh. pp. 7–22.
100. Lathe, G. H., Claireaux, A. E. and Norman, A. P. (1958), "Jaundice in the Newborn Infant. I: Non-obstructive Jaundice," in *Recent Advances in Paediatrics*, 2nd edition, pp. 87–124 (D. Gairdner, ed.). London: Churchill.
101. Lathe, G. H., Claireaux, A. E. and Norman, A. P. (1958), "Jaundice in the Newborn Infant. II: Obstruction and Allied Forms of Jaundice," in *Recent Advances in Paediatrics*, 2nd edition, pp. 125–144 (D. Gairdner, ed.). London: Churchill.
102. Lathe, G. H. and Walker, M. J. (1958). "The Synthesis of Bilirubin Glucuronide in Animal and Human Liver," *Biochem. J.*, **70**, 705–712.
103. Lathe, G. H. and Walker, M. W. (1958), "Inhibition of Bilirubin Conjugation in Rat Liver Slices by Human Pregnancy and Neonatal Serum and Steroids," *Quart. J. exp. Physiol.*, **43**, 257–265.
104. Lester, R., Jackson, B. T. and Smallwood, R. A. (1970), "Fetal Hepatic Function." In ref. 128, pp. 16–21.
105. Lester, R. and Schmid, R. (1963), "Intestinal Absorption of Bile Pigments. I: Enterohepatic Circulation of Bilirubin in Rat," *J. clin. Invest.*, **42**, 736–747.
106. Lester, R. and Schmid, R. (1963), "Intestinal Absorption of Bile Pigments. II: Bilirubin Absorption in Man," *New Engl. J. Med.*, **269**, 178–182.
107. Lester, R. and Troxler, R. F. (1969), "Progress in Gastroenterology. Recent Advances in Bile Pigment Metabolism," *Gastroenterology*, **56**, 143–169.
108. Levi, A. J., Gatmaitan, Z. and Arias, I. M. (1969), "Two Hepatic Cytoplasmic Protein Fractions, Y and Z, and their Possible Role in the Hepatic Uptake of Bilirubin, Sulfobromophthalein, and other Anions," *J. clin. Invest.*, **48**, 2156–2167.
109. Levi, A. J., Gatmaitan, Z. and Arias, I. M. (1970), "Deficiency of Hepatic Organic Anion-binding Protein, Impaired Organic Uptake by Liver and 'Physiologic' Jaundice in Newborn Monkeys," *New Engl. J. Med.*, **283**, 1136–1139.
110. Levine, R. I., Reyes, H., Levi, A. J., Gatmaitan, Z. and Arias, I. M. (1971), "Phylogenetic Study of Organic Anion Transfer

from Plasma into the Liver," *Nature New Biology, Lond.*, **231,** 277–279.

111. Lie, S. O. and Bratlid, D. (1970), "The Protective Effect of Albumin on Bilirubin Toxicity on Human Fibroblasts," *Scand. J. clin. Lab. Invest.*, **26,** 37–41.
112. Lightner, D A. and Quistad, G. B. (1972), "Bilirubin-imide Products of Photo-oxidation," *Nature New Biol., Lond.*, **236,** 203–205.
113. Liley, A. W. (1961), "Liquor Amnii Analysis in the Management of the Pregnancy Complicated by Rhesus Sensitization," *Amer. J. Obstet. Gynec.*, **82,** 1359–1370.
114. Liley, A. W. (1968), "Diagnosis and Treatment of Erythroblastosis in the Foetus," *Adv. Pediat.*, **15,** 29–63.
115. Linhart, J. and Starka, J. (1969), "Steroid Jaundice in a Newborn Boy," *Cslka. Pediat.*, **24,** 1110–1112.
116. Litwak, G., Ketterer, B. and Arias, I. M. (1971), "Ligandin: a Hepatic Protein which Binds Steroids, Bilirubin, Carcinogens and a Number of Exogenous Organic Anions," *Nature, Lond.*, **234,** 366–467.
117. Lucey, J. F. (1960), "Hyperbilirubinaemia of Prematurity," *Pediatrics, Springfield*, **25,** 690–710.
118. Lucey, J. F. (1970). In ref. 16, pp. 63–70.
119. Lucey, J. F., Hibbard, E., Behrman, R. E., Esquivel de Gallardo, F. O. and Windle, W. F. (1964), "Kernicterus in Asphyxiated Newborn Rhesus Monkeys," *Expl. Neurol.*, **9,** 43–58.
120. Lucey, L. F. and Villee, C. A. (1962), "Observations on Human Fetal Hepatic UDPG Dehydrogenase and Glucuronyl Transferase Activity." Communication No. 537, *Abstracts of Papers, X International Congress of Pediatrics, Lisbon.*
121. McDonagh, A. F. (1972), "Evidence for Singled Oxygen Quenching by Biliverdin 1X-α Dimethyl Ester and its Relevance to Bilirubin Photo-oxidation," *Biochem. biophys. Res. Commun.*, **48,** 408–415.
122. McMullin, G. P., Hayes, M. F. and Arora, S. C. (1970), "Phenobarbitone in Rhesus Haemolytic Disease. A Controlled Trial," *Lancet*, **ii,** 949–952.
123. Maisels, M. J., Pathak, A., Nelson, N. M., Nathan, D. G. and Smith, C. A. (1971), "Endogenous Production of Carbon Monoxide in Normal and Erythroblastotic Newborn Infants," *J. clin. Invest.*, **50,** 1–8.
124. Matsuda, I. and Shirahata, T. (1966), "Effects of Aspartic Acid and Orotic Acid upon Serum Bilirubin Level in Newborn Infants," *Tokuhu J. exp. Med.*, **90,** 133–136.
126. Maurer, M. H., Wolff, J. A., Finster, M., Poppers, P. J., Pantuck, E., Kuntzman, R. and Conney, A. H. (1969), "Reduction in Concentration of Total Serum-bilirubin in Offspring of Women Treated with Phenobarbitone During Pregnancy," *Lancet*, **ii,** 122–124.
127. Menken, M., Barrett, P. V. D., Swarm, R. L. and Berlin, N. I. (1966), "Kernicterus. Development of an Experimental Model Using Bilirubin 14-C," *Archs. Neurol. Psychiat., Chicago*, **15,** 68–73.
128. Meuwissen, J. A. T. P. and Heirwegh, K. P. M. (1970), "Transfer of Adsorbed Bilirubin to Specific Binding Proteins," *Biochem. J.*, **120,** 19P.
129. Michaelsson, M., Nosslin, B. and Sjolin, S. (1965), "Plasma Bilirubin Determination in the Newborn Infant," *Pediatrics, Springfield*, **35,** 925–931.
129a. Mollison, P. L. and Walker, W. (1952), "Controlled Trials of the Treatment of Haemolytic Disease of the Newborn," *Lancet*, **i,** 429–433.
130. Morrow, G., Bongiovanni, A. M., Bomberger, J. H. A. and Boggs, T. R. (1966), "The Effect of Triiodothyronine on Neonatal Hyperbilirubinaemia," *J. Pediat.*, **68,** 413–417.
131. Mustafa, M. G., Cowger, M. L. and King, T. E. (1969), "Effects of Bilirubin on Mitochondrial Reactions," *J. biol. Chem.*, **244,** 6403–6414.
132. Mustafa, M. G. and King, T. E. (1970), "Binding of Bilirubin with Lipid. A Possible Mechanism of its Toxic Reactions in Mitochondria," *J. biol. Chem.*, **245,** 1084–1089.
133. Neubaur, J. and Hollman, S. (1966), "The Glucuronyltransferase Activity in the Liver of Human Fetuses and Premature Infants," *Klin. Wschr.*, **44,** 723–724.
134. Newman, A. J. and Gross, S. (1963), "Hyperbilirubinaemia in Breast-fed Infants," *Pediatrics, Springfield*, **32,** 995–1001.
135. Odell, G. B. (1970), "The Distribution and Toxicity of Bilirubin," *Pediatrics, Springfield*, **46,** 16–24.
136. Odell, G. B., Cohen, S. N. and Gordes, E. H. (1962), "Administration of Albumin in the Management of Hyperbilirubinaemia by Exchange Transfusion," *Pediatrics, Springfield*, **30,** 613–621.
137. Odell, G. B., Cohen, S. N. and Kelly, P. C. (1969), "Studies in Kernicterus. II: The Determination of the Saturation of Serum Albumin with Bilirubin," *J. Pediat.*, **74,** 214–230.
138. Odievre, M., Pinon, F., Schirar, M., Luzeau, R. and Sauvageot, M. (1970), "The Fraction of Unconjugated Bilirubin not Bound to Albumin in the Course of Hyperbilirubinaemia of the Newborn," *Arch. franc. Pediat.*, **27,** 225–235.
139. Ojala, A. (1971), "Studies on Bilirubin in Amniotic Fluid," *Acta Obstet. gynec.* scand., **50,** Suppl. 10.
140. Ostrow, J. D. (1972), "Mechanisms of Bilirubin Photodegradation," *Seminars in Haematology*, **9,** 113–125.
141. Ostrow, J. D. and Branham, R. V. (1970), "Photodecay of Bilirubin *in vitro* and in the Jaundiced (Gunn) Rat." In ref. 16, pp. 93–99.
142. Ostrow, J. D. and Schmid, R. (1963), "The Protein Binding of C^{14} Bilirubin in Human and Murine Serum," *J. clin. Invest.*, **42,** 1286–1299.
143. Overbeek, J. Th. G., Vink, C. L. J. and Deenstra, H. (1955), "The Solubility of Bilirubin," *Rec. Trav, chim. Pays-Bas Belg.*, **74,** 81–84.
144. Pennington, G. W. and Hall, R. (1966), "Method for the Determination of Small Amounts of Bilirubin in Liquor Amnii and Other Body Fluids," *J. clin. Path.*, **19,** 90–91.
145. Pimstone, N. R., Engel, P., Tenhunen, R., Seitz, P. T., Marver, H. S. and Schmid, R. (1971), "Inducible Heme Oxygenase in the Kidney: A Model for the Homeostatic Control of Haemoglobin Catabolism," *J. clin. Invest.*, **50,** 2042–2050.
146. Pimstone, N. R., Tenhunen, R., Seitz, P. T., Marver, H. S. and Schmid, R. (1971), "The Enzymatic Degradation of Hemoglobin to Bile Pigments by Macrophages," *J. exp. Med.*, **133,** 1264–1281.
147. Poland, R. L. and Odell, G. B. (1971), "Physiologic Jaundice: The Enterohepatic Circulation of Bilirubin," *New Engl. J. Med.*, **284,** 1–6.
148. Porter, E. G. and Waters, W. J. (1966), "A Rapid Micro Method for Measuring the Reserve Albumin Binding Capacity in Serum from Newborn Infants with Hyperbilirubinemia," *J. Lab. clin. Med.*, **67,** 660–668.
149. Porto, S. O. (1970), "*In vitro* and *in vivo* Studies on the Effect of Phototherapy upon Bilirubin." In ref. 16, pp. 83–89.
150. Powell, L. W., Hemingway, E., Billing, B. H. and Sherlock, S. (1967), "Idiopathic Unconjugated Hyperbilirubinemia (Gilbert's Syndrome)," *New Engl. J. Med.*, **277,** 1108–1112.
151. Powell, J., Waterhouse, J., Culley, P. and Wood, B. (1969), "Effect of Phenobarbitone and Pre-eclamptic Toxaemia on Neonatal Jaundice," *Lancet*, **ii,** 802.
152. Ramboer, C., Thompson, R. P. H. and Williams, R. (1969), "Controlled Trials of Phenobarbitone Therapy in Neonatal Jaundice," *Lancet*, **i,** 966–968.
153. Ramos, A., Silverberg, M. and Stern, L. (1966), "Pregnanediols and Neonatal Hyperbilirubinemia," *Amer. J. Dis. Child.*, **11,** 353–356.
154. Rosenfeld, R. S., Arias, I. M., Gartner, L. M., Hellinan, L. and Gallagher, T. F. (1967), "Studies of Urinary Pregnane-3α, 20β-diol during Pregnancy, Post Partum, Lactation and Progesterone Ingestion," *J. clin. Endocr. Metab.*, **27,** 1705–1710.
155. Sas, M., Gellen, J. and Viski, S. (1969), "Steroid Excretion and Serum Bilirubin Levels in Newborn Infants Receiving Human Milk or an Artificial Diet," *Zentbl. Gynakol.*, **91,** 1296–1302.
156. Sas, M. and Herczeg, J. (1970), "Serum Bilirubin Level and Steroid Excretion following Progesterone Load in Newborn Infants," *Acta Paediat., Budapest*, **11,** 35–40.
157. Sas, M. and Herczeg, J. (1970), "Serum Bilirubin and Steroid Excretion in Newborns after Oral Administration of 3α, 20α and 3α, 20β Pregnanediol," *Arch. Gynakol.*, **209,** 58–70.

158. Sas, M. and Herczeg, J. (1970), "The Relation of Steroid Excretion and the Serum Bilirubin in Newborns after C_{19}-steroid Administration," *Arch. Gynakol.*, **209**, 50–57.
159. Sas, M., Viski, S. and Gellen, J. (1969), "Steroid Content of Human Milk," *Arch. Gynakol.*, **207**, 452–459.
160. Schenker, S., Dawber, N. H. and Schmid, R. (1964), "Bilirubin Metabolism in the Fetus," *J. clin. Invest.*, **43**, 32–39.
161. Schenker, S. and Schmid, R. (1964), "Excretion of C^{14}-bilirubin in Newborn Guinea Pigs," *Proc. Soc. exp. Biol. Med.*, **115**, 446–448.
162. Schenker, S., McCandless, D. W. and Wittgenstein, E. (1966), "Studies *in vivo* of the Effect of Unconjugated Bilirubin on Hepatic Phosphorylation and Respiration," *Gut*, **7**, 409–414.
163. Schenker, S., McCandless, D. W., Zollman, P. E. and Wittgenstein, E. (1966), "Studies of Cellular Toxicity of Unconjugated Bilirubin in Kernicteric Brain," *J. clin. Invest.*, **45**, 1213–1220.
164. Schmid, R. (1972), "Hyperbilirubinemia," in *The Metabolic Basis of Inherited Disease*, pp. 1141–1178 (J. B. Stanbury and D. S. Fredrickson, eds.). New York: McGraw-Hill.
165. Schmid, R., Forbes, A., Rosenthal, I. M. and Lester, R. (1963), "Lack of Effect of Cholestyramine Resin on Hyperbilirubinaemia of Premature Infants," *Lancet*, **ii**, 938–939.
166. Schmid, R. and Haymaker, L. (1963), "Metabolism and Disposition of C^{14}-bilirubin in Congenital Non-hemolytic Jaundice," *J. clin. Invest.*, **42**, 1720–2734.
167. Sereni, F., Perletti, L. and Marini, A. (1967), "Influence of Diethylnicotinamide on the Concentration of Serum Bilirubin of Newborn Infants," *Pediatrics, Springfield*, **40**, 446–449.
168. Severi, F., Rondini, G., Zaverio, S. and Vegni, M. (1970), "Prolonged Neonatal Hyperbilirubinaemia and Pregnane-3(alpha), 20(beta)-diol in Maternal Milk," *Helv. paed. Acta*, **5**, 517–521.
169. Silberberg, D., Johnson, L., Schutta, H. and Ritter, L. (1970), "Photodegradation Products of Bilirubin Studied in Myelinating Cerebellum Cultures." In ref. 16, pp. 119–123.
170. Stern, L., Khanna, N. N., Levy, G. and Taffe, J. J. (1970), "Effect of Phenobarbital on Hyperbilirubinemia and Glucuronide Formation in Newborns," *Amer. J. Dis. Childh.*, **120**, 26–31.
171. Stiehl, A., Thaler, M. and Admirand, W. H. (1972), "Effects of Phenobarbital on Bile-salts and Bilirubin in Cholestatic States," *New Engl. J. Med.*, **286**, 858–861.
172. Svenningsen, N. W., Dahlquist, A. and Lindquist, B. (1970), "HBABA—Index in Neonatal Icterus," *Acta paediat., Stockh.*, **60**, 105–108.
173. Tenhunen, R., Marver, H. S. and Schmid, R. (1969), "Microsomal Heme Oxygenase. Characterization of the Enzyme", *J. biol. Chem.*, **244**, 6388–6394.
174. Thaler, M. (1970), "Toxic Effects of Bilirubin and its Photodecomposition Products," in ref. 128, pp. 128–130.
175. Thaler, M. M. (1972), "Effect of phenobarbital on Hepatic Transport and Excretion of ^{131}I-Rose Bengal in Children with Cholestasis," *Pediat. Res.*, **6**, 100–110.
176. Thaler, M. M., Gemes, D. L. and Bakken, A. F. (1972), "Enzymatic Conversion of Heme to Bilirubin in Normal and Starved Fetuses and Newborn Rats," *Pediat. Res.*, **6**, 197–201.
177. Thompson, R. P. H., Stathers, G. M., Pilcher, C. W. T., McLean, A. E. M., Tobinson, J. and Williams, R. (1969), "Treatment of Unconjugated Jaundice with Dicophane," *Lancet*, **ii**, 4–6.
178. Thompson, R. P. H. and Williams, R. (1967), "Treatment of Chronic Intrahepatic Cholestasis with Phenobarbitone," *Lancet*, **ii**, 646–648.
179. Trolle, D. (1968), "Decrease of Total Serum-bilirubin Concentration in Newborn Infants after Phenobarbitone Treatment," *Lancet*, **ii**, 705–708.
180. Tsao, Y. C. and Yu, U. Y. H. (1972), "Albumin in Management of Neonatal Hyperbilirubinaemia," *Archs. Dis. Childh.*, **47**, 250–256.
181. Ulstrom, R. A. and Eisenklam, E. (1964), "The Enterohepatic Shunting of Bilirubin in the Newborn Infant. Use of Oral Activated Charcoal to Reduce Normal Serum Bilirubin Values," *J. Pediat.*, **65**, 27–37.
182. Van Roy, F. P., Meuwissen, J. A. T. P., De Meuter, F. and Heirwegh, K. P. M. (1971), "Determination of Bilirubin in Liver Homogenates and Serum with Diazotised *p*-iodoaniline," *Clin. chim. Acta*, **31**, 109–118.
183. Vest, M. F. (1967), "Studies on Haemoglobin Breakdown and Incorporation of (^{15}N) Glycine into Haem and Bile Pigment in the Newborn," in *Bilirubin Metabolism*, pp. 47–53, edited by Bouchier, I. A. D. and Billing, B. H. Oxford: Blackwell.
184. Vest, M. and Grieder, H. (1961), "Erythrocyte Survival in the Newborn Infant as Measured by Chromium^{51} and its Relation to the Postnatal Serum Bilirubin Level," *J. Pediat.*, **59**, 194–199.
185. Vest, M., Signer, E., Weisser, K. and Olafsson, A. (1970), "A Double Blind Study of the Effect of Phenobarbitone on Neonatal Hyperbilirubinaemia and Frequency of Exchange transfusion," *Acta Paediat., Stockh.*, **59**, 681–684.
186. Walker, W., Hughes, M. I. and Barton, M. (1969), "Barbiturate and Hyperbilirubinaemia of Prematurity," *Lancet*, **i**, 548–551.
187. Waltman, R., Bonura, F., Nigrin, G. and Pipal, C. (1969), "Ethanol in Prevention of Hyperbilirubinaemia in the Newborn," *Lancet*, **ii**, 1265–1267.
188. Weech, A. A. (1947), "The Genesis of Physiologic Hyperbilirubinaemia," *Adv. Pediat.*, **2**, 346–366.
189. Weldon, A. P. and Danks, D. M. (1972), "Congenital Hypothyroidism and Neonatal Jaundice," *Archs. Dis. Childh.*, **47**, 469–471.
190. Wennberg, R. P. and Rasmussen, L. F. (1971), "Pharmacological Modification of Bilirubin Toxicity in Tissue Culture," *Paed. Res.*, **5**, 420.
191. Whitfield, C. R., Neely, R. A. and Telford, M. E. (1968), "Amniotic Fluid Analysis in Rhesus Iso-immunization," *J. Obstet. Gynaec. Brit. Commonw.*, **75**, 121–127.
192. Wilkinson, P. and Mendenhall, C. L. (1963), "Serum Albumin Turnover in Normal Subjects and Patients with Cirrhosis Measured by ^{131}I-Labelled Human Albumin," *Clin. Sci.*, **25**, 281–292.
193. Windle, W. F. (1963), "Neuropathology of Certain Forms of Mental Retardation," *Science, N.Y.*, **140**, 1186–1189.
194. Wong, K. P. (1971), "Bilirubin Glucuronyltransferase. Specific Assay and Kinetic Studies, *Biochem. J.*, **125**, 27–35.
195. Wong, K. P. (1971), "Formation of Bilirubin Glucoside," *Biochem. J.*, **125**, 929–934.
196. Wong, Y. K., Culley, P. E. and Wood, B. S. B. (1972), "Jaundice in the Breast-fed Neonate and Maternal Oral Contraceptive Pills," *Communication to the Neonatal Society*, Sheffield, May 1972.
197. Wong, Y. K. and Wood, B. S. B. (1971), "Breast-milk Jaundice and Oral Contraceptives," *Brit. med. J.*, **4**, 403–404.
198. Yaffe, S. J., Catz, C. S., Stern, L. and Levy, G. (1970), "The Use of Phenobarbital in Neonatal Jaundice," In ref. 16, pp. 37–45.
199. Yaffe, S. J., Levy, G., Matsuzawa, T. and Baliah, T. (1966), "Enhancement of Glucuronide Conjugating Capacity in a Hyperbilirubinemic Infant due to Apparent Enzyme Induction by Phenobarbital," *New Engl. J. Med.*, **275**, 1461–1465.
200. Yeung, C. Y. (1972), "Blood Sugar Changes in Neonatal Hyperbilirubinaemia and Phenobarbitone Therapy," *Archs. Dis. Childh.*, **47**, 246–249.
201. Yeung, C. Y. and Field, C. E. (1969), "Phenobarbitone Therapy in Neonatal Hyperbilirubinaemia," *Lancet*, **ii**, 135–139.
202. Zamet, P. and Chunga, F. (1971), "Separation by Gel Filtration and Microdetermination of Unbound Bilirubin. II: Study of Sera in Icteric Newborn Infants," *Acta paediat. Stockh.*, **60**, 33–38.
203. Zetterstrom, R. and Ernster, L. (1956), "Bilirubin an Uncoupler of Oxidative Phosphorylation in Isolation Mitochondria," *Nature, Lond.*, **178**, 1335–1337.

11. PUBERTY

W. A. MARSHALL and J. M. TANNER

INTRODUCTION

There is no satisfactory and generally accepted definition of puberty; most authors simply use the term to designate the period during which an individual changes from a child to a man or woman and acquires the ability to reproduce.

We prefer to use the physical changes themselves as the basis of our definition and therefore, in this chapter, "puberty" will refer to those morphological and physiological changes which are associated with the conversion of the gonads from their infantile to their adult state, and which further result in the physical capacity to conceive and successfully rear young.

Thus puberty is a conglomeration of changes rather than an epoch in the life of the individual. The changes do, of course, occupy a number of years in each child's life but the length of this period varies greatly from one individual to another, as does the age at which it begins. The sequence in which the changes occur also varies, except when one event is the essential precursor of a following one. We therefore begin by considering the changes themselves: firstly in each organ or system; then in the body as a whole, noting where sequences of change are variable and where they are constant between individuals. We then discuss the relationship between the neuroendocrine phenomena which accompany puberty and the factors which may influence its course and timing.

The changes which constitute puberty may be classified as follows:

(1) Acceleration and then deceleration of skeletal growth (the adolescent growth spurt).

(2) Altered body composition as a result of skeletal and muscular growth together with changes of the quantity and distribution of fat.

(3) Development of the circulatory and respiratory systems, leading, particularly in boys, to increased strength and endurance.

(4) The development of the gonads, reproductive organs and secondary sex characters.

(5) A combination of factors, not yet fully understood, which modulates the activity of those nervous and endocrine elements which initiate and co-ordinate all these changes.

The above list is not, of course, chronological. Changes in the different systems are largely concurrent, although there must be some development under headings 4 and 5 before the other events can occur. However, we shall discuss the events in the order set forth, coming last to the endocrine and other factors which initiate and sustain them.

THE ADOLESCENT GROWTH SPURT

Figure 1 shows the height at different ages of a boy and a girl who had the mean birth length, always grew at the mean speed for the population, reached their maximum adolescent growth rate (peak height velocity or PHV) at the mean age, and finally reached the mean adult stature.[80] Very few individuals actually approximate all these conditions, and certainly measurements made on a single

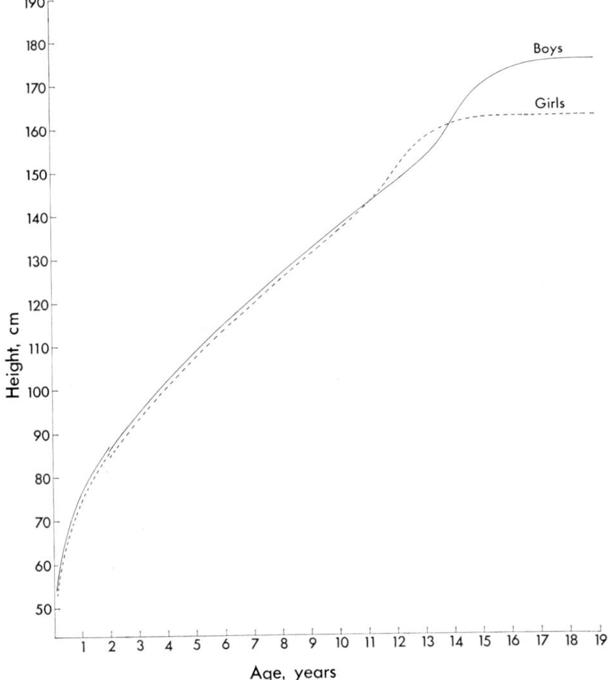

FIG. 1. Height at different ages of boys and girls of mean birth length, who grew at the mean rate and experienced the adolescent growth spurt at the mean age for their sex. Each finally reached the mean adult stature.[80] (Reproduced by permission of authors and editor of *Archives of Disease in Childhood.*)

subject throughout childhood would lead to curves which are less regular than these. Nevertheless the figure shows the general relationship of height for age in the two sexes. The steep part of the curve (in early teenage) is the adolescent growth spurt, which occurs on the average some 2 years earlier in girls than boys. Figure 2 shows the height velocity, or speed of growth, of these 2 children at different ages. The adolescent spurt is in evidence as a sharp increase in velocity. Once the velocity has reached its maximum it immediately begins to decrease again, so that the time of peak height velocity is clearly defined and is a useful landmark in the growth process.

In a series of 49 healthy boys of the Harpenden Growth Study the actual value of peak height velocity averaged 10·3 cm./year with a standard deviation of 1·54 cm./year. These boys were measured every 3 months by a single skilled observer. The peak velocity of 41 girls in the same study averaged 9·0 cm./year with a standard deviation of 1·03 cm./year. These values are obtained from a smoothed curve drawn by eye through the observations on each subject. The velocity over the whole year centred on the peak, that is including the 6 months before it and 6 months after it, averaged 9·5 cm./year for boys and 8·4 cm./year for

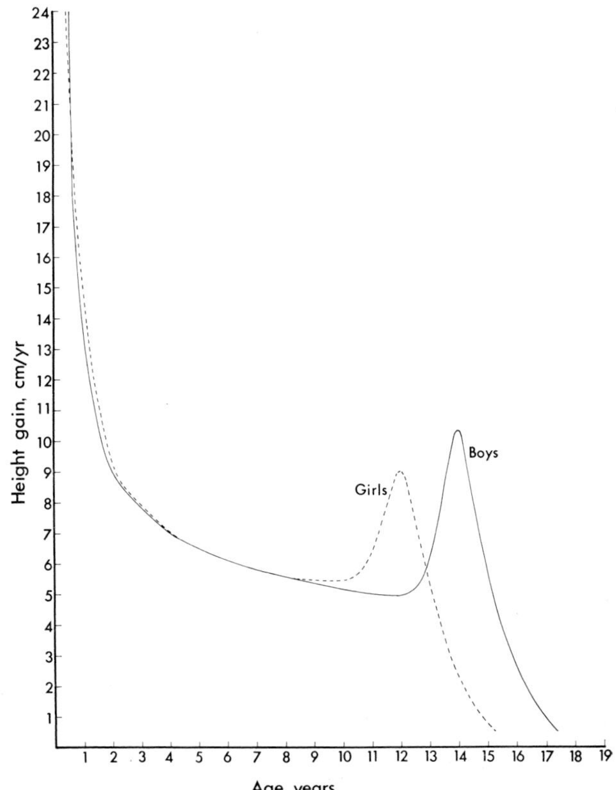

FIG. 2. Speed of growth in cm./yr. at different ages of the boys and girls whose statures are shown in Fig. 1.[80] (Reproduced by permission of author and editor, *Archives of Disease in Childhood.*)

girls, whereas the mean growth rate immediately before the spurt begins is in the region of 5 cm./year for both sexes. Thus for a year or more during adolescence the velocity of growth is nearly doubled. During the year which includes the moment of peak height velocity a boy usually gains between 7 and 12 cm. in stature and a girl between 6 and 11 cm. Children who have their peak at an early age usually reach a higher maximum growth velocity than those who have it late. The correlation of peak height velocity and the age at which it occurs is about −0·45.

The mean age of reaching peak height velocity in the girls studied by Marshall and Tanner[49] was 12·14 ± 0·14 years with a standard deviation of 0·88 years. In boys the mean was 14·06 ± 0·14 years with an SD of 0·92 years.[50]

MATHEMATICAL DESCRIPTION OF SPURT

Several authors have attempted to obtain a mathematical description of growth in stature and other dimensions during adolescence by fitting curves to repeated measurements of individuals. Such repeated measurements constitute "longitudinal" data as distinct from "cross-sectional" data obtained by measuring a number of different individuals at each age. The models most commonly used have been the Gompertz and logistic functions both of which give sigmoid curves. Their relative merits can only be assessed by testing the accuracy with which they will fit the actual measurements of individuals.

The equation of the Gompertz curve can be written

$$Y = P + Ke^{-ea-bt}$$

where Y = dependent variable, e.g. stature
t = independent variable, e.g. age
P = lower asymptote, in this case stature at the beginning of the adolescent growth spurt
K = total increase in Y, i.e. height gained during the adolescent growth spurt
a = constant of integration; depending on the position of the origin
b = rate constant (1/age). According to Deming[19] it may be thought of as the individual's constant inherent rate of maturation through the adolescent growth cycle.

The equation of the logistic curve can be written

$$Y = P + \frac{K}{1 + e^{a-bt}}$$

where the symbols have the same meanings as above. By differentiation of either the Gompertz or logistic curves fitted to a child's measurements, a growth velocity curve can be obtained. With the logistic model this is symmetrical while with the Gompertz model it is not (*see* Fig. 3).

Deming[19] gives a detailed account of the Gompertz function in the analysis of the growth process. She fitted curves to the stature observed at intervals during the adolescent growth cycle of 48 individual boys and girls and found significant sex differences in the value of the constants K and b and in the level of the lower and upper asymptotes of the curve. The first derivative, or growth velocity curves, showed sex differences in the timing of the adolescent growth spurt similar to those found by other methods.

Marubini *et al.*[51] fitted both Gompertz and logistic functions to 3-monthly measurements of height, sitting height, leg length and biacromial diameter in 23 boys and 18 girls. The fit of the curves was equally good for boys and girls, and rather better for sitting height, leg length and biacromial diameter than for stature. Residuals, i.e. discrepancies between actual measurements and the fitted curves, were of the same order of magnitude as measuring error. In most cases the logistic curve appeared to be a slightly better fit than the Gompertz and was recommended as the best equation fitting skeletal growth data at adolescence.

SPURT IN OTHER SKELETAL DIMENSIONS

The growth of nearly all skeletal dimensions accelerates to some extent at adolescence but the increase in growth rate is not uniform throughout the body and most of the adolescent spurt in stature is due to growth of the trunk rather than the legs.

Also, the spurt does not occur at the same time in all parts of the body. This variation is the result of "maturity gradients" which are a fundamental feature of the growth process and are manifested in the early embryo by the greater development of its cranial than its caudal end. At birth, the head is much nearer to its adult size than the remainder of the body and constitutes about a fifth of the child's total length while the legs are delayed in their maturation and are therefore small at birth. Throughout childhood, however, there is apparently a reverse gradient within the limbs themselves so that the hands and feet are more mature, and hence relatively large in relation to the lower leg and forearm, while these distal segments are in

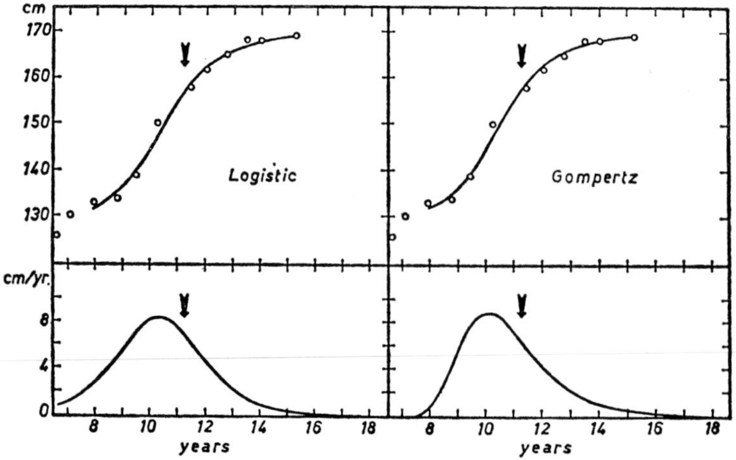

FIG. 3. Adolescent cycle of growth in length of a girl, fitted by means of the Gompertz function (right) and the Logistic function (left). The arrow indicates menarche. Above: distance curve, Below: velocity curve.[51] (Reproduced by permission of author and Wayne State University Press.)

turn more advanced than the proximal segment of the limbs.

At adolescence, leg length appears to be the first dimension to reach its peak growth velocity but the gradient within the limb is still apparent. The foot has its rather small acceleration about 6 months before the calf and thigh, while the calf, in turn, accelerates a little earlier than the thigh. Foot length is probably the first of all dimensions below the head to stop growing. Some adolescents, particularly girls, become concerned because they have large feet at a time when they know that they are still growing. However, the foot is usually near its final size at this time.

In the arm, there is a similar gradient to that seen in the leg, according to Maresh,[46] with the forearm having its peak velocity about 6 months ahead of the upper arm.

The trunk reaches its maximum growth rate about 6 months after the legs, so that stature, which is the sum of these components, lies between the two in the timing of its spurt. Since the spurt in sitting height or trunk length, is greater than that of the legs, the ratio of trunk length to leg length increases. The hips and shoulders reach their maximum growth rate at approximately the same time as sitting height.

The growth of the head is nearly completed in early childhood, but nevertheless, there is a significant acceleration of growth in both head length and head breadth in boys at adolescence although the actual growth rate is very small.[71] One longitudinal study of skull radiographs showed that the lengths of the frontal and parietal arcs increased only by 1 or 2 per cent after age 12 but the thickness of the bones and scalp tissues increased by some 15 per cent with a spurt at adolescence.[64,96,97] These observations are not entirely supported by another radiographic longitudinal study of head width from age 9–14 years[73] which showed that in both sexes, growth was due mainly to increase in the thickness of soft tissue and the width of the cranial cavity, with very little increase in thickness of bone. Girls showed more increase in soft tissue growth while boys showed more growth in the width of the cranial cavity.

Bjork[6] in a radiographic study of 243 boys at age 12 and subsequently again at 20, showed that the forward growth of the forehead at adolescence could be accounted for by the development of the brow ridges and frontal sinuses. However, the middle and posterior cranial fossae do enlarge to some extent. The cranial base posterior to the sella turcica is lowered[100] and also increases in length.[24]

The growth of most facial measurements accelerates to reach a peak velocity a few months after the stature peak.[54] The greatest spurt is in the mandible where 25 per cent of the total growth in height of the ramus is completed between the ages of 12 and 20 years compared to the 6–7 per cent of growth in the cranial base remaining to be completed in this period. In a mixed longitudinal radiographic study, Savara and Tracy[68] showed that increments during adolescence were greatest for mandibular length and least for bigonial width. Ramus height followed a similar pattern to length. Thus at adolescence, particularly in boys, the jaw becomes considerably longer in relation to the front part of the face, somewhat more projecting, and thicker. However, the growth of the chin is not completed until after puberty, as further apposition of bone at the mandibular symphysis usually occurs between 16 and 23 years of age. Though these changes are much less marked in girls, there is a definite adolescent acceleration of mandibular growth.[83] The growth of the mandible is accompanied by accelerated forward growth of the maxilla directly above the upper incisor teeth so that the prognathism of both jaws is increased, though the increase in the lower jaw is greater. However, the literature on maxillary growth is difficult to interpret as different authors have employed different techniques and in one of the most recent studies[67] less acceleration was found in maxillary length than in some measures of height and width.

In most boys the point of the nose is brought forward and downwards relative to the rest of the face by accelerated growth of bone and soft tissue but this change is not detectable in all children.

Growth in length of the pharynx is accelerated so that the hyoid bone which, before puberty, was level with the mandible becomes relatively much lower. There is less change in the anterior-posterior diameter of the pharynx.[39]

HEART, LUNG AND VISCERAL GROWTH

Radiographic measurements of the transverse diameter of the heart show a clear adolescent spurt.[7,44,45] Though Maresh found the spurt less marked in girls than in boys, Simon *et al.*[72] in a longitudinal study of chest radiographs noted that the heart diameter had a spurt of about equal magnitude in both sexes. The age at peak velocity for both heart diameter and lung width coincides with the age for peak height velocity. The peak for lung length however occurs about 6 months later than that for lung width. The growth spurt in the lungs is of similar magnitude in both sexes but the actual mean lung width of girls does not exceed that of boys even at the peak of the girls' spurt when all other measurements, except those of the head and feet, are greater in girls.

The limited evidence that is available suggests that there is some adolescent spurt in the growth of all the abdominal viscera including the liver, kidneys, pancreas and non-lymphatic portion of the spleen.

LYMPHATIC TISSUES

The only apparent exceptions to the general acceleration of growth at puberty are the lymphatic tissues, the thymus and the subcutaneous fat. Autopsy data from children who died within 48 hr. of an accident show that the weight of the thymus increases from birth up to a maximum in the 11–15 age range then decreases.[11,28,29] A study of the width of the thymus shadow on tomographic X-rays makes it clear that the involution takes place at the time of the adolescent spurt.[84] The maximum size of the thymus was observed at age 12 in girls and at 14 in boys with a decrease occurring the following year, but the data were cross-sectional with a relatively small number of children at each age. Probably the maximum value for the lymphatic parenchyma occurs a little earlier as a small proportion of the gland is composed of connective tissue whose absolute weight continues to increase through puberty. The lymphatic tissue in other organs such as the spleen, intestine, appendix and mesenteric lymph nodes regresses at the same time.[69] In a series of 300 cases of death within 10 hr. of an injury, the lymphatic tissue of the appendix decreased in amount from the 1–10 year age group to the 11–20 age group whereas the remainder of the appendix tissue showed a distinct increase with indications of an adolescent spurt.[33] In the spleen the absolute amount of lymphatic tissue increased slightly between these two decades but not nearly as much as did other tissues, so that the percentage of the total that was lymphatic dropped from 10·8–7·7.[34] Scammon's spleen data show an actual decrease in splenic lymphatic tissue at adolescence.

SEX DIFFERENTIATION

Puberty results in the further development of sex differences in body shape, though many are already present long before. Some, like the difference in the external genitalia, develop during fetal life, while others, such as the greater relative length and breadth of the forearm of the male when compared with the length of the whole arm or the whole body, develop continuously throughout childhood and adolescence by sustained differential growth rates. The most noticeable of the sex differences primarily developed at puberty are the greater stature of the male and his broader shoulders as compared with the woman's wider hips. Boys and girls are almost the same height up to the time that girls begin their pubertal acceleration of growth. Boys have a greater adolescent spurt in height and also have two more years of pre-adolescent growth than girls; thus when their spurt starts they are on an average about 10 cm. taller than the girls were at the beginning of their spurt. The longer period of pre-adolescent growth is also largely responsible for men's legs being longer than women's in relation to their body length, as immediately before adolescence the legs grow relatively faster than the trunk.

The origin of the sex difference in the relationship between shoulder and hip widths is illustrated by Fig. 4. In relation to their stature, girls have a large adolescent spurt in hip width which increases as much as that of boys, although the girls' spurt in other dimensions is considerably less. Shoulder width increases much more in boys than in girls. These differences arise because cartilages in the hip joint area of the pelvis are specialized to multiply in response to oestrogens, and cartilage cells in the shoulder region are specialized to respond to androgens such as testosterone. Girls at birth already have a wider pelvic outlet than boys. The basis for the adaptation for child-bearing is therefore present at an early age. The changes at puberty are more concerned with widening the pelvic inlet and broadening the hips.

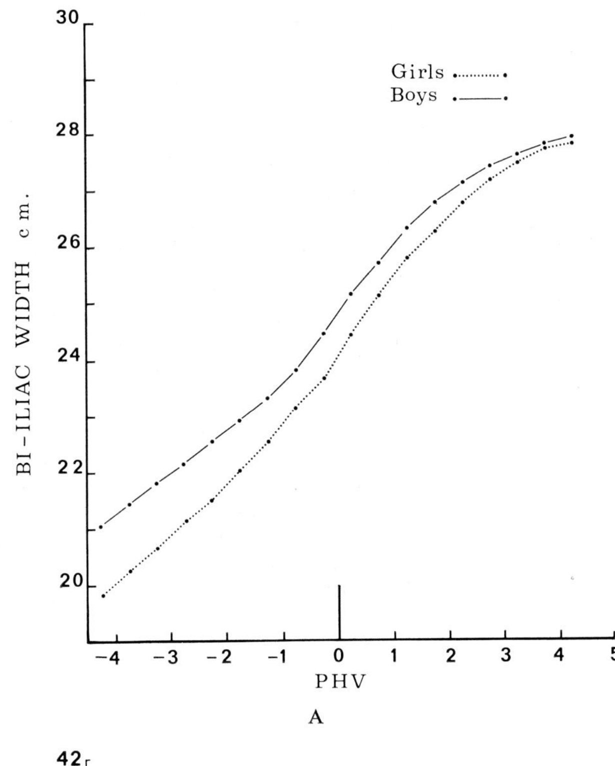

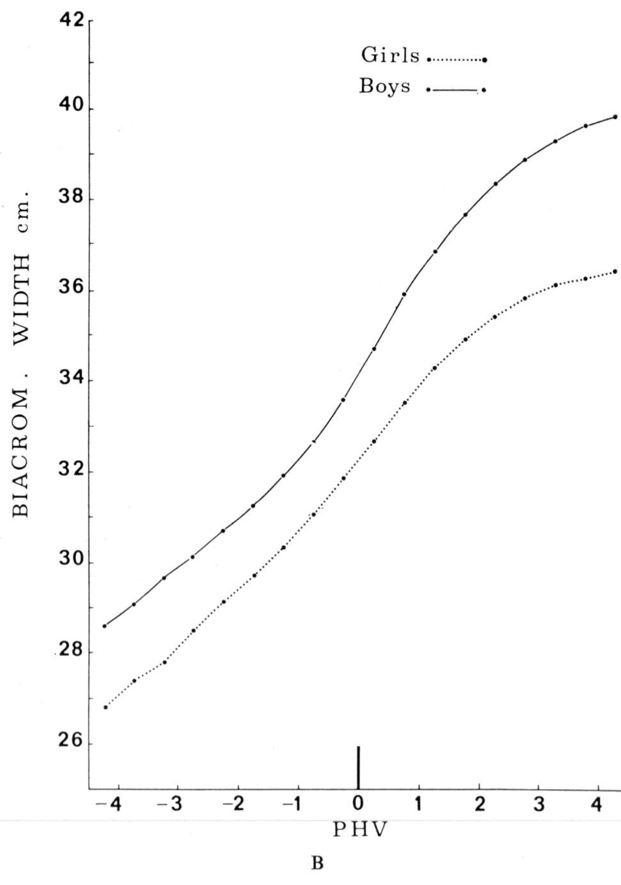

FIG. 4. Growth in width of (a) hips and (b) shoulders in girls and boys. In order to eliminate the difference in age at which the adolescent spurt occurs in the two sexes, the measurements have been plotted against a scale of years before and after peak height velocity (PHV).[47] (Reproduced by permission of Harper & Row, Publishers, Inc.)

BODY COMPOSITION

Tanner[76] has reported measurements of the width of bone, muscle and fat as shown in radiographs of the limbs. Figure 5 shows the results of such measurements in 28 boys

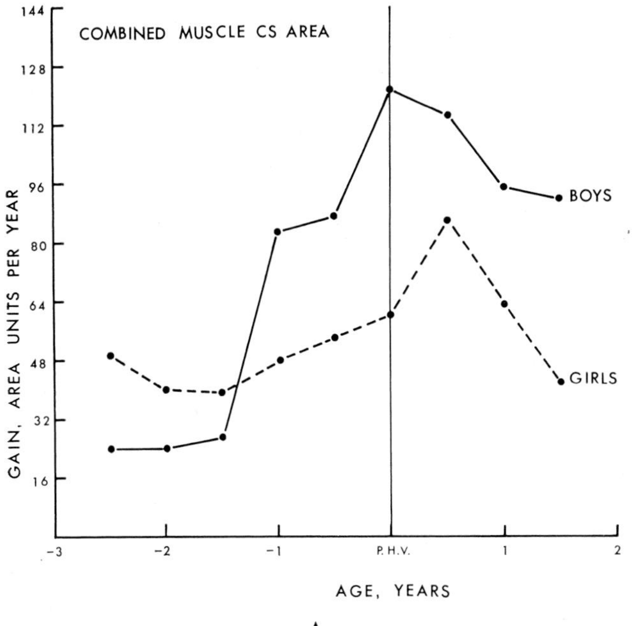

A

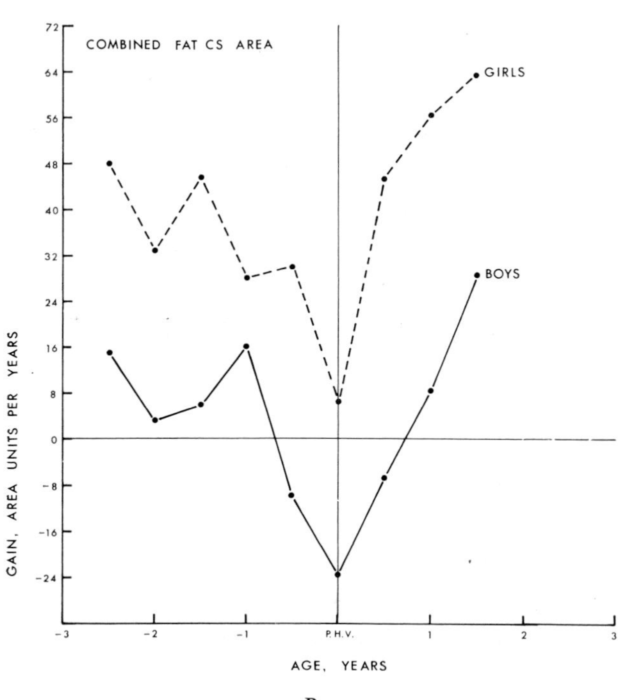

B

FIG. 5. Mean rate of increase in cross-sectional area of (a) muscle and (b) fat. Measurements from calf, arm and thigh combined.[76] (Reproduced by permission of Pergamon Press, Ltd.)

and 21 girls taken at intervals during puberty. In each limb the widths of bone, muscle and fat were measured at the same level and then the cross-sectional area of each tissue at this level was calculated on the assumption that the limb was circular.

The data plotted represent a summation of the measurements of the calf, thigh and upper arm with values of thigh halved before being added in. The average measurements for the group were calculated in relation to a time scale in which the zero point was the moment of peak height velocity for each child. Thus, instead of age, the x-axis shows years before and after peak height velocity. This method of plotting allows us to observe the changes of body composition during puberty in the whole group.[73] If the measurements had been plotted against chronological age the relationship between these changes and puberty would have been obscured because different individuals, at any given age, would have been at different stages of the adolescent growth spurt.

The rate of growth of limb muscle reaches its maximum in boys at approximately the time of peak height velocity. The changes in subcutaneous fat are almost exactly opposite to those in muscle. Most children put on fat steadily from the age of about 8 years until adolescence but the rate of increase in the thickness of subcutaneous fat slows down as growth of the skeleton and muscles accelerates. The rate of fat gain reaches its minimum at about the same time as the growth rate in bone and muscle reaches its maximum. As Fig. 5 shows, the minimum rate of fat gain in boys has a negative value. In other words, the typical boy actually loses fat and becomes thinner at adolescence. In contrast, the average girl continues to get fatter although she does so more slowly during the adolescent growth spurt than either before or after. The accumulation of fat does not slow down as much on the trunk as on the limbs.[75]

As it is believed that the amount of DNA in cell nuclei is constant, the DNA content per gram of muscle may be taken as a measure of the number of cells per gram. If, in addition, it is assumed that the creatinine excretion per day reflects the muscle mass of the individual under appropriately controlled circumstances, the number of cells per gram of muscle may be multiplied by the muscle mass to give a figure which reflects the cell population of the entire musculature. Also, if the protein content per gram of muscle is known and the number of cells per gram is known, an index of cell size can be obtained from the protein/DNA ratio. Cheek[16] has used these methods to study muscle growth in children using biopsies taken from gluteal musculature. Contrary to what is taught on the basis of older animal studies, he found a steady increase in cell number from birth onwards. In girls, the rate of increase was more or less constant until maturity, whereas in boys there was an acceleration starting at about age 11. By the age of 16 or 17 years, that is after sexual maturity, boys had about one-third more muscle cells than girls. In girls after the age of about $10\frac{1}{2}$ years there was little, if any, further increase.

Changes in body composition during puberty have also been studied by the determination of body density, which can be calculated on the basis of Archimedes' principle if the subjects are weighed under water.[31,56] Body density of boys increases more than that of girls, reflecting the greater gain of muscle and decrease in the relative amount of fat in boys. Other measurements which reflect the amount of muscle in the body, e.g. total body potassium estimated by ^{40}K measurement, also increase more in boys than girls.[13,14]

STRENGTH AND ENDURANCE

The pubertal increase in muscle size in boys is accompanied by an increase in strength which may be reinforced by biochemical changes which increase the force of contraction exerted by a given amount of muscle.[53] At the same time the heart and lungs become bigger, not only in absolute terms but also in relation to the rest of the body. The systolic blood pressure rises and the resting heart rate becomes slower, while a considerable rise in the haemoglobin concentration gives the blood a great capacity for carrying oxygen. The chemical products of exercise such as lactic acid are neutralized more efficiently. These changes result in a marked increase not only of muscular strength but in the ability to endure hard physical effort over a long period of time. There is no truth in the popular belief that boys "outgrow their strength" at puberty. However, the greatest increase in strength may not occur for a year or so after the maximum rate of growth in height and not until sexual development is more or less complete. There may therefore be a period in some boys' lives when they look "grown up" but have not yet attained their adult strength and stamina. Though they may not be as strong as they look, they are certainly much stronger than they were when puberty began.

A boy who undergoes the adolescent growth spurt and the pubertal increase in strength at an early age becomes during this time not only bigger than his fellows but also very much stronger. This may give him considerable advantage in some sports and other activities for which physical prowess is an asset, but these advantages will be lost when those boys who mature later experience their spurts in both size and strength. Late maturing boys sometimes need reassurance to the effect that they will eventually be big and strong like the others.

At the same time the early maturer should sometimes be warned that his physical prowess may be only temporary and that he will not always be bigger and stronger than his peers.

THE REPRODUCTIVE ORGANS AND SECONDARY SEX CHARACTERS—MALES

The Testes

The size of the testes can be studied by comparing them with standards of known volume. The most convenient standard is the "Prader Orchidometer" which is a series of plastic models (rotation ellipsoids of known volume) which are mounted on a string in order of increasing size. The models are numbered according to their volume in ml. Testes of sizes 1 and 2, and sometimes 3, on this scale are found in prepubertal boys but a greater size usually indicates that puberty has begun. The size of the adult testis usually varies between 12 and 25 ml. when measured by this technique, and its mean weight is in the region of 20 g.

Nearly all this growth occurs during puberty. Figure 6 shows the variation in testis size at different ages according to Prader *et al.*[58] Alternative standards are shown in Fig. 7 which is based on data from van Wieringen *et al.*[87]

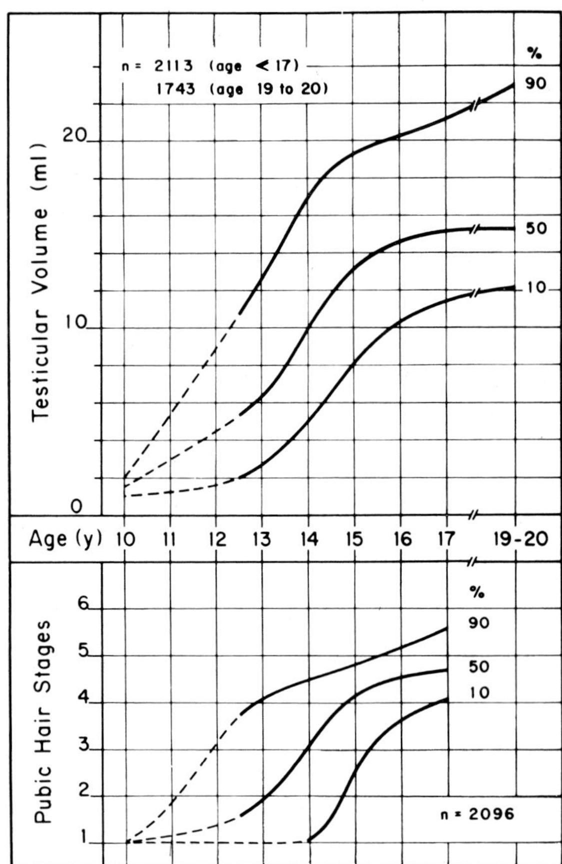

FIG. 6. 10th, 50th and 90th centiles of testis volume at different ages, as measured by palpation and comparison with models.[58] (Reproduced by kind permission of Professor A. Prader.)

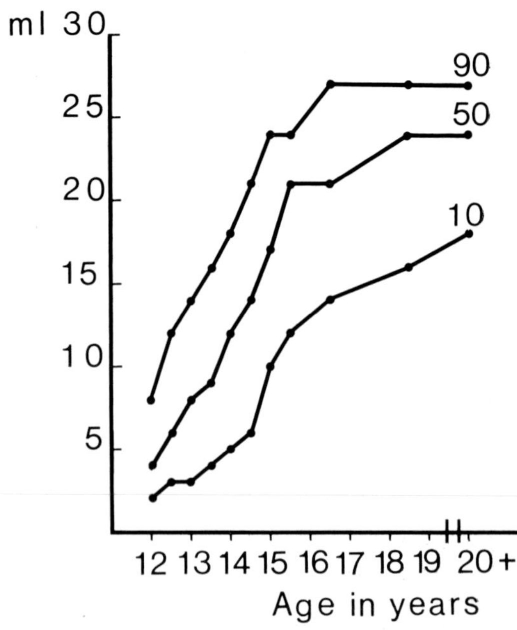

FIG. 7. 10th, 50th and 90th centiles of testis volume as measured by visual comparison with models. Based on data from Wieringen, *et al.*[87]

These data were obtained by using an orchidometer similar to, but not identical with, that of Prader. The values at each age are higher than those reported by Prader *et al.*[58] Shonfield and Beebe,[70] and Dooren *et al.*[21] These last three groups of workers measured the testis by palpation and tactile comparison with the models, whereas van Wieringen *et al.*[87] visually compared the testis (with the scrotum held tightly) with the models. The palpation technique is more widely used than the visual one but there is no evidence as to which is more reliable.

In the prepubertal testis the interstitial tissue has a loose appearance and there are no Leydig cells. The seminiferous tubules are cord-like structures having a diameter between 50 and 80 μ. In early childhood the tubules grow slowly and there is a gradual increase in spermatogonia although the Sertoli cells remain undifferentiated. The first signs of a lumen usually appear in the tubules round about the age of 6 years but the lumen does not become distinct until puberty.

At puberty, Leydig cells, differentiated from the interstitial mesenchyme, produce increasing quantities of androgens, and possibly oestrogen. There is considerable increase in size and tortuosity of the tubules. A thin tunica propria containing elastic fibres develops; Sertoli cells differentiate and the basally situated spermatogonia divide. This is the beginning of the changes in the germinal epithelium which lead gradually to spermatogenesis. The exact chronological relationship between the differentiation of the Leydig cells and the onset of maturation in the seminiferous tubules is not known. The evidence which is available suggests that the Leydig cells appear more or less at the same time as mitotic activity in the germinal epithelium. By the time the Leydig cells are fully differentiated histologically, meiotic activity leading to the development of spermatids and spermatozoa has already begun. Hence the Leydig cells seem to secrete androgens before they are fully differentiated (*see also* below). When the testis is mature, about two-thirds of the tubule consists of germinal epithelium while the remainder is made up of sertoli cells.

The Accessory Sex Organs

The epididymis, seminal vesicles and prostate grow very little before puberty, when a rapid increase in size accompanies the development of function (Fig. 8).

Development of External Genitalia—Penis and scrotum

The development of the genitalia can be conveniently divided for descriptive purposes into five stages, as shown in Fig. 9.[75]

Stage 1—is the pre-adolescent stage and persists from birth until the pubertal development of the testes has begun. The general appearance of the testes, scrotum and penis changes very little during this period although there is some overall increase in size.

Stage 2—is shown by enlargement of the testes and scrotum with some reddening and change in texture of the scrotal skin. The attainment of this stage is usually the first external evidence that puberty has begun.

Stage 3—The penis has increased in length and to a lesser extent in breadth. There has been further growth of the testes and scrotum.

Stage 4—The length and breadth of the penis have increased further and the glans has developed. Testes and scrotum are further enlarged with the darkening of the scrotal skin.

Stage 5—The genitalia are adult in size and shape.

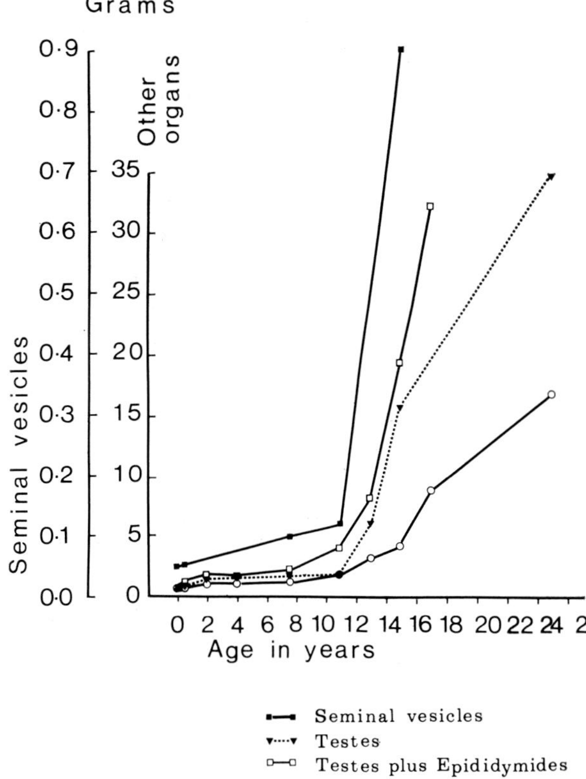

FIG. 8. Mean weights of male reproductive organs at various ages. Based on data from Boyd.[12]

There is a wide variation in the age at which boys arrive at each stage of genital development as shown in Fig. 10 which is based on data reported by Marshall and Tanner[50] and by van Wieringen *et al.*[87] The studies were concerned with boys of European origin. Enlargement of the genitalia may begin at any time after the 9th birthday but a boy who shows no development by the age of 14 is not necessarily abnormal. Some boys experience perfectly normal sexual development although their genitalia have remained infantile until after their 15th birthday. The earliest maturers have fully developed genitalia before they are 13 but some boys do not complete their development until they are 18 or more.

Pubic Hair

The development of pubic hair may also be described in five stages.

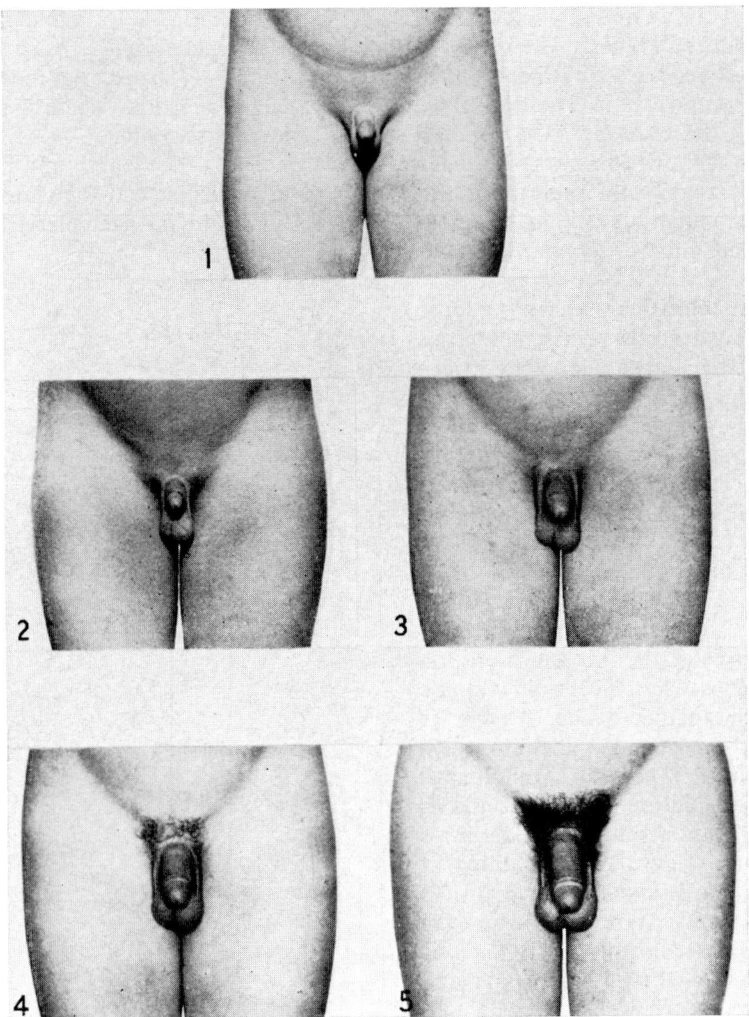

FIG. 9. Standards for genital maturity ratings in boys.[75] (Reproduced by permission of Blackwell Scientific Publications, Ltd.)

Stage 1—The prepubertal stage in which there is no true pubic hair although there may be a fine vellus over the pubes, similar to that over the abdominal wall.

Stage 2—There is sparse growth of long straight, or only slightly curled, and lightly pigmented hair chiefly at the base of the penis.

Stage 3—The hair spreads sparsely over the junction of the pubes and is considerably darker, coarser and more curled.

Stage 4—The hair is now adult in character but covers an area considerably smaller than in most adults. There is no spread to the medial surface of the thighs.

Stage 5—Hair is distributed in an inverse triangle as in the adult female. It has spread to the medial surface of the thighs but not up the linea alba or elsewhere above the base of the inverse triangle. In most men the pubic hair spreads beyond the pattern described as Stage 5 and some authors have used the term Stage 6 to indicate the spread of hair higher on the abdominal wall. However, as this full adult hair distribution is seldom reached before the mid-twenties, it need not be regarded as a stage of pubertal development. The variation in age at which each stage of pubic hair is reached is shown together with the genital stages in Fig. 10.

Axillary and Facial Hair

We are not aware of any reliable data on the variation in age at which axillary and facial hair appear. However, axillary hair is not usually seen until the development of the genitalia is well advanced and on the average about 2 years after the first pubic hair; but this interval is very variable and sometimes the axillary hair may appear first.

Facial hair usually begins to grow at about the same time as the axillary hair. Usually the first thing to happen is an increase in length and pigmentation of the hairs at the corner of the upper lip. This change then spreads medially to complete the moustache. The upper part of the cheek and the region just below the lower lip in the mid-line are the next sites at which hair appears, followed by the sides and lower border of the chin. According to Tanner[75] it is unusual for hair to grow on the chin before the development of both genitalia and pubic hair is complete.

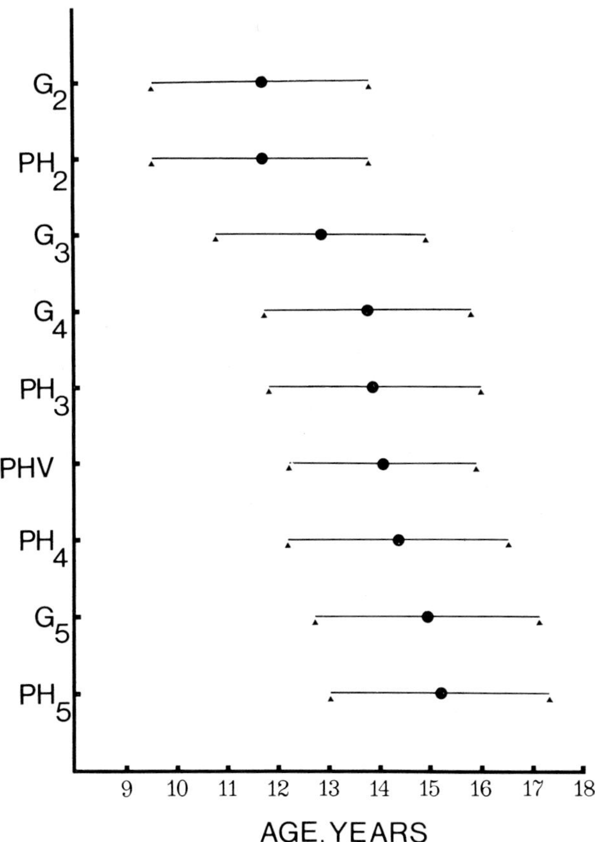

FIG. 10. Age on reaching each stage of puberty in boys. Genitalia (G), pubic hair (PH) peak height velocity (PHV). The centre of each symbol represents the mean and the length of the symbol is equivalent to two standard deviations on either side of the mean. (Based on data from Marshall and Tanner[50] and van Wieringen, *et al.*[87]

The Breast

An increase in the diameter of the areola is a normal event of male puberty and is permanent. Sometimes there is enlargement of underlying breast tissue to an extent which may cause discomfort or embarrassment. This enlargement usually regresses in about a year but occasionally it may persist or even increase. Rarely the breasts become large enough to cause a real psychological or social difficulty so that surgical treatment may be desirable.

Variation in Duration of Stages

The normal variation in the time which boys take to pass through some of the changes of puberty has been studied by Marshall and Tanner.[50] This time can be expressed as the difference between the age at which a boy reached one stage of genital or pubic hair development and the age at which he reached a later stage. Table 1 shows the mean values of the differences between the ages at which the genitalia reached the various stages of development. The 2·5 and 97·5 centiles are also shown. Table 2 gives the corresponding means and centiles for the stages of pubic hair development. The "interval" between two consecutive stages is the time for which the boy remains in the earlier stage, e.g. the interval G2–G3 is the difference between the age at which the boy's genitalia first attained the appearance that we described as Stage 2 and the age at which they first attained the appearance that we described as Stage 3. The interval is thus the period of time for which the genitalia remained in Stage 2. The interval G2–G5 represents the whole period of pubertal development of the external genitalia. In these data the interval PH2–PH5 is much shorter than the interval G2–G5 but the former is probably underestimated because the observations were made on serial photographs which probably did not reveal the first appearance of pubic hair. It is particularly noteworthy that the interval G2–G5 in some boys is less than the interval G2–G3 in others. The time spent in Stage G2 may be anything up to $2\frac{1}{2}$ years while, on the other hand, some boys may go through their complete genital development in a shorter time than this. Others may take 5 or more years to complete the process of genital change, regardless of the age at which it began.

TABLE 1

CENTILES OF DIFFERENCE (IN YEARS) BETWEEN AGE ON REACHING ONE STAGE OF GENITAL DEVELOPMENT AND AGE ON REACHING A LATER STAGE

Stages	*Time in years (centiles)*		
	2·5	50	97·5
G2–G3	0·4	1·1	2·2
G3–G4	0·2	0·8	1·6
G4–G5	0·4	1·0	1·9
G2–G5	1·9	3·1	4·7

(Based on data from Marshall and Tanner)[50]

Relationship Between Pubertal Changes in Different Structures

Marshall and Tanner's[50] data showed that boys were not always in the same stage of genital development when they reached a given stage of pubic hair development. Peak height velocity also was reached at different stages of

TABLE 2

CENTILES OF DIFFERENCE (IN YEARS) BETWEEN AGE ON REACHING ONE STAGE OF PUBIC HAIR GROWTH AND AGE ON REACHING A LATER STAGE

Stages	*Time in years (centiles)*		
	2·5	50	97·5
PH2–PH3	0·1	0·4	0·9
PH3–PH4	0·3	0·4	0·5
PH4–PH5	0·2	0·7	1·4
PH2–PH5	0·8	1·6	2·7

(Based on data from Marshall and Tanner)[50]

TABLE 3

PERCENTAGE OF BOYS IN EACH STAGE OF GENITAL DEVELOPMENT WHEN THEY REACHED EACH STAGE OF PUBIC HAIR DEVELOPMENT

Pubic hair stage	2	3	4	5
No. of boys seen entering PH stage	115	115	104	104
% in genitalia stage 1	1	0	0	0
2	13	4	0	0
3	45	17	6	0
4	41	75	65	10
5	0	4	29	90

(From Marshall and Tanner.[50] Reproduced by permission of Editor and *Archives of Disease in Childhood*)

genital and pubic hair maturity in different boys. Table 3 shows the percentage of boys who were in each stage of genital development when they were first seen in each successive pubic hair stage. Of the 115 boys seen on reaching pubic hair Stage 2, only 1 was in genital Stage 1 while 13 per cent were in genital Stage 2. The great majority were in genital Stages 3 or 4. Thus it is very unusual for boys to experience any growth of pubic hair before there are visible changes in the external genitalia and it is quite normal for there to be no pubic hair growth before the genitalia have reached Stage 4. None of the boys in this study reached peak height velocity before their genitalia were in Stage 3 and very few did so before they were in genital Stage 2. Twenty per cent of the boys had still not reached peak height velocity when their genitalia reached the adult stage. The percentage of boys who were in each stage of pubic hair development when they attained peak height velocity is shown in Table 4.

TABLE 4

PERCENTAGE OF BOYS IN EACH STAGE OF GENITAL DEVELOPMENT ON REACHING PEAK HEIGHT VELOCITY

Genital stage	1	2	3	4	5	N
% boys at PHV	0	0	5	74	21	60

(Data from Marshall and Tanner)[50]

Van Wieringen *et al.*[87] have shown that testis volumes also vary greatly amongst boys in any one stage of either pubic hair or genital development.

THE REPRODUCTIVE ORGANS AND SECONDARY SEX CHARACTERS—FEMALES

In the perinatal period, the pelvic reproductive organs and the breasts are subject to the influence of maternal hormones, but their effects soon disappear, and there is little change in the reproductive organs until the child herself begins to secrete significant quantities of oestrogen. The growth of the reproductive system is not completed until after menarche.

The Ovaries

The ovaries of the newborn lie at the pelvic rim. Each one measures approximately 1·5 × 0·3 × 0·25 cm. and weighs approximately 0·3 gm. The germinal epithelium consists mainly of cuboidal cells and the cortex mainly of primordial follicles, in groups which are separated by strands of connective tissue. Each primordial follicle contains one primordial oocyte ringed by a layer of small indifferent cells. The follicles furthest from the surface epithelium are largest. The medulla is composed of loose fibrous connective tissue, blood vessels and nerves.

When puberty approaches there is an increase in the number of large follicles in various stages of development. These follicles may grow to a considerable size before they regress but there is no ovulation. The ovaries, uterine tubes and uterus sink lower in the expanding pelvic cavity so that by the time of menarche they are in their adult position. The uterine tubes become straighter and larger in diameter. More complex folds develop in the tubal mucosa and the tubal epithelium develops ciliated cells for the first time.

During the period of approximately 2 years preceding menarche the ovaries become much larger and, a year before menarche, each ovary is said to weigh between 3 and 4 gm. There is increased follicular growth and an increase in the number of follicles that grow to a large size; however, most of these follicles still regress. There is usually a number of anovulatory periods preceding the first ovulatory cycle. The average weight of an ovary at the time of the first period is approximately 6 gm.

There has been much discussion as to whether oogenesis is a continuous process during reproductive life or whether the ova which reach maturity in adult life are derived from germ cells which were present at birth. The general consensus of opinion at present is that the oocytes which mature during the reproductive years are drawn from those already present at birth.

The Vagina

At birth the vagina is approximately 4 cm. in length. The mucosa is hypertrophied as a result of stimulation by maternal hormones and is folded into high ridges. The superficial layer consists of 30–40 layers or cells and accounts for most of the thickness of the mucosa. Its cells are large and irregularly shaped. There is little cornification and glycogen is present in large quantities. The hypertrophic changes in the newborn are more marked than those seen at any other time of life except during pregnancy. Vaginal smears taken of newborn infants are cytologically very similar to those of post-menarcheal girls.

During childhood the length of the vagina increases by only 0·5–1 cm. The lower one-third is fixed and inelastic because of the rigidity of the musculo-fascial components of the pelvic floor. The upper two-thirds, however, is more distensible. Histologically, the immature vaginal epithelium is similar to that over the external cervix, with a well-defined basal layer and intermediate zone and little or no superficial layer. There is no cornification. Vaginal smears during this period are made up of small round cells with darkly staining cytoplasm and large nuclei typical of the parabasal layer of the epithelium.

The cytological changes of the vaginal epithelium are usually the first clear indication of puberty and normally occur before there is any development of breasts or pubic hair. Smears taken in late childhood show fewer small cells typical of the basal layer than those taken in early childhood. The intermediate cells are more numerous and are larger with medium size nuclei; their cytoplasm stains less darkly. As oestrogen stimulation increases the number of superficial cells in the smear becomes greater until an adult type smear is eventually obtained. Usually 5–15 per cent of the cells in a vaginal smear are from the superficial layer before there are other signs of sexual development and before the mucosa of the vulva or distal half of the vagina shows visible signs of oestrogenic stimulation.

Lengthening of the vagina usually begins before the secondary sex characters appear and continues until menarche or a little later. By the time the vagina shows a clearly defined oestrogen response its length has increased to between 7 and 8·5 cm., and at menarche, it is usually between 10·5 and 11·5 cm. long.

During the premenarcheal period the vulva and vaginal mucosa become softer and thicker. The hymen also becomes thicker and its orifice increases in diameter to about 1 cm. The vestibular (Bartholin's) glands become active. The superficial cell layer of the vaginal epithelium is thickened and the cells contain glycogen. A vaginal smear consists largely of adult type superficial cells, some of which are cornified. The upper vagina is more distensible but deep cornices have not yet been formed.

pH of Vaginal Contents

At birth the pH of the vaginal contents ranges between 5·5 and 7·0. Within 24 hr. lacto-bacilli appear in the vaginal flora and lactic acid formed by these organisms lowers the pH to between 5 and 4. The reaction remains acid for a few days and then, as oestrogen stimulation is withdrawn, it becomes first neutral and then alkaline. In early childhood there is little vaginal fluid and the pH ranges from between 5·5 and 7·5. In the year or so preceding menarche the amount of fluid greatly increases and its reaction becomes acid again.

Uterus

The uterus of the newborn is usually between 2·5 and 3·5 cm. long and weighs between 2 and 4 gm. At this time it is larger than it will be again until the child is 5 or 6 years of age. The cervix comprises two-thirds of the whole organ at birth but shrinks rapidly in the post-natal period. The external os is not distinctly formed.

The myometrium is thick and the endometrium, measuring from 0·2 to 0·4 mm. in depth, consists of a sparse scattering of stromal cells with a surface layer of low cuboidal epithelium. In some infants the uterine glands are quite well developed. Ober and Bernstein[55] state that 68 per cent of 169 newborn infants had uteri with endometria in the proliferative phase. Twenty-seven per cent showed some degree of secretory activity and progestational changes were found in 5 per cent. However, these changes subside rapidly and the endometrium is in a resting or quiescent state from soon after birth until shortly before menarche.

At the age of 6 months the uterus is about 20 per cent smaller than it was at birth. Most of this post-natal regression involves the cervix. The corpus is reduced only slightly in size.

By about the 5th year the uterus has regained approximately its neonatal size and slow growth continues after this. It is not until the premenarcheal period that rapid growth gives a size and shape somewhat similar to that found in the adult. During childhood, the uterus lies with its long axis in the craniocaudal plane and there is no uterine flexion.

The corpus increases only slightly in size during the first few years of childhood, and at the age of 5 years is still less than 1 cm. in diameter. But by about the 10th birthday, its length may equal that of the cervix. The growth of the corpus, at this stage, is due primarily to myometrial proliferation, rather than to endometrial development, which begins to occur only a short time before menarche. Earlier the surface of the uterine cavity is covered by a single layer of low cuboidal cells with small darkly staining nuclei and dense cytoplasm, and there is no evidence of secretory activity.

In the cervix the effects of maternal hormonal stimulation usually disappear within 3 weeks after birth. The endocervical canal becomes narrower and the mucosal epithelium consists of a single layer of low cuboidal cells. The squamous epithelium covering the external cervix also becomes thinner during the 2 or 3 weeks after birth. The endocervical mucosa remains essentially unchanged during childhood. During the immediate premenarcheal period the cervix develops its adult shape and increases considerably in size. The cervical canal becomes larger and the cervical glands become active. At this time the cervix is still rather long in relation to the corpus.

The secretion of the cervical epithelium becomes copious and mucoid shortly before menarche. Its clarity and tendency to form threads, together with the formation of fern-like crystals when dried in thin preparations, are indices of oestrogen stimulation. Such changes are typical of the mid-portion of the ovarian cycle in older girls and adults.

It is interesting that at adolescence the corpus of the uterus grows in response to oestrogen while it does not do so in late foetal life when most of the growth is in the cervix. Whatever the reason for this, adolescent growth is in the corpus rather than the cervix so that the two portions of the uterus are approximately of equal length by the time of menarche.

The uterine tubes have no function before ovulation begins and little is known about their motility or secretion in premenarcheal children. Tubal movements increase in amplitude and become more frequent as the oestrogen level rises during the preovulatory phase of the ovarian cycle. After ovulation the tubal movements gradually become less but secretory activity is greater during the ovulatory and post-ovulatory phases of the cycle.

Vulva

At birth the vulval region is a rounded prominence divided by the genito-urinary cleft. The genital or labio-scrotal swellings which formed the vestibule of the foetus are still present and are the precursors of the labia majora. They are large in the newborn but flatten out after a few weeks. The labia majora do not develop as distinct structures until late childhood.

The labia minora are relatively larger and thicker at birth and for several weeks afterwards than they will be in later life. The clitoris is also much larger in comparison to other vulval structures than it will be later, while the hymen is an inverted cone protruding outward into the vestibule. It is quite thick at birth and becomes thinner when the stimulus of maternal hormones is withdrawn. Its central opening is usually about 0·5 cm. in diameter.

A week or so after birth, as the effect of maternal hormones disappears, the vulval tissues develop the appearance which then changes little for about 7 years. The genital swellings and the labia minora are flatter. The clitoris does not grow in proportion to the other vulval structures and therefore appears smaller. The normal vulval and vaginal mucosa during early childhood is thin and usually has a somewhat glazed appearance. The hymen is thin and flat. Gradual deposition of fat thickens the mons pubis and increases the size of the labia majora. The surfaces of the labia begin to develop fine wrinkles which become more marked during the immediate premenarcheal period. The clitoris increases slightly in size while the urethral hillock becomes more prominent. The hymen gradually becomes thicker with a larger central orifice.

Breasts

Neonatal engorgement of one or both mammary glands at birth is not uncommon in either sex. There may also be a secretion of so-called "Witch's Milk." This engorgement soon subsides and for descriptive purposes the further development of the breasts may be divided into five stages based on their superficial appearance:[75]

Stage 1—is the infantile state which persists from the time that the effects of maternal oestrogen have regressed until the changes of puberty begin.

Stage 2—the "bud" stage. The breast and papilla are elevated as a small mound and there is an increase in the diameter of the areola. This appearance is the first indication of pubertal change in the breast.

Stage 3—the breast and areola are further enlarged to create an appearance rather like the small adult breast with a continuous rounded contour.

Stage 4—the areola and papilla enlarge further to form a secondary mound projecting above the contour of the remainder of the breast.

Stage 5—is the typical adult breast with smoothed rounded contour, the secondary mound present in Stage 4 having disappeared.

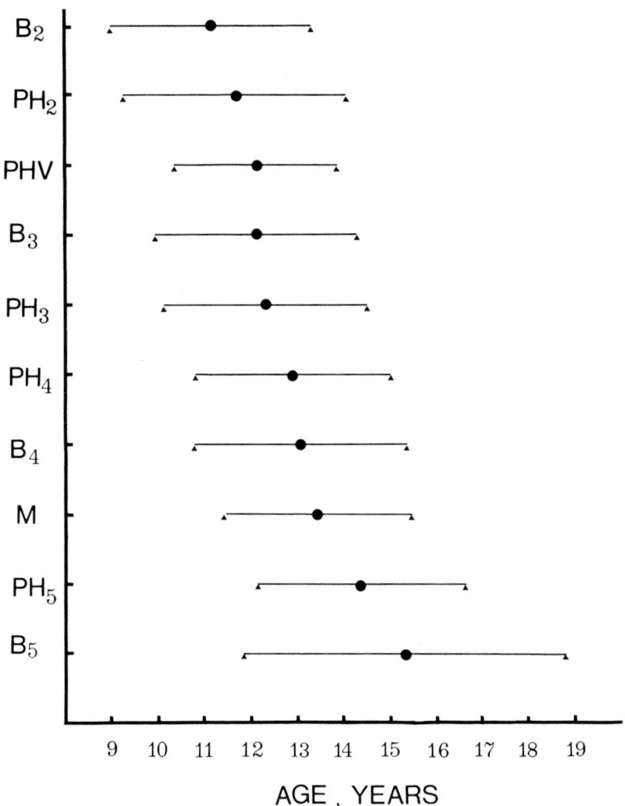

FIG. 11. Age on reaching each stage of puberty in girls. Breasts (B), pubic hair (PH), peak height velocity (PHV), menarche (M). The centre of each symbol represents the mean and the length of the symbol is equivalent to two standard deviations on either side of the mean. (Based on data from Marshall and Tanner.)[49]

In some girls Stage 5 is apparently never reached and Stage 4 persists until the first pregnancy or even beyond. A few girls never show Stage 4, passing directly from Stage 3 to 5. Figure 11 shows the range of ages at which each stage of breast development is reached in British girls according to Marshall and Tanner.[49] The data are in good agreement with those of other authors who have studied comparable populations.

The first sign of breast development may occur at any age from about 8 onwards in normal girls and it is unusual for breast development not to have begun by the age of 13 years. However, there are some 5 per cent of girls in whom breast development begins outside the limits indicated in Fig. 11. In some girls the breasts are fully mature before the 12th birthday but in others maturity is not reached until the age of 19 or even later.

Pubic Hair

The descriptive stages for pubic hair growth in girls are essentially the same as those for boys with the exception that the first appearance of hair (Stage 2) is usually on the labia although, sometimes, it is on the mons pubis. Marshall and Tanner's data on the age at reaching each pubic hair stage is shown in Fig. 11 but their values for Stage 2 are probably too high as their photographic technique does not reveal the first appearance of pubic hair. Van Wieringen *et al.*[87] give a 50th centile age of 11·3 years for the appearance of pubic hair Stage 2, with the 10th and 90th centiles lying at 9·5 and 13·0 years respectively. These figures were based on direct inspection of the child and were probably more accurate than those of Marshall and Tanner. The range of ages over which pubic hair growth may begin is very similar to that for the beginning of breast development, although in the individual girl, pubic hair growth and breast development do not necessarily begin at the same time (*see* below). The adult distribution of hair is usually attained between the ages of 12 and 17 approximately.

Menarche

Menarche occurs near the end of the sequence of pubertal changes. In the U.K., the average age of occurrence is 13·0 years with an S.D. of approximately 1 year. Thus 95 per cent of the population have menarche between their 11th and 15th birthday at the present time. Differences between populations are discussed below.

Cutaneous Glands

The apocrine glands of the axilla and vulva begin to function at about the same time as pubic and axillary hair appear. The sebaceous glands and merocrine sweat glands of the general body skin also become more active.

Variations in Duration of Stages

Table 5 indicates the mean lengths of the intervals between the ages at which girls reached various stages of puberty and also the variation in these intervals, e.g. the interval between the earliest time at which a girl's breasts can be described as being in Stage 2 to the earliest time at which they can be described as Stage 3 is on the average 0·9 years but some girls will go through this part of their development in about 0·2 years while others may take over a year. The whole process of breast development from the appearance of Stage 2 to the attainment of Stage 5 takes on the average 4 years but is also very variable. There are comparable variations between girls in the rate at which pubic hair develops.

Interrelationship Between Events

It is commonly believed that there is a close relationship between the development of the breasts and that of the pubic hair, but this is not strictly true. Although most girls have some breast development before their pubic hair appears, some reach breast Stage 4 before there is any growth of hair. On the other hand, there is an appreciable number of girls in whom pubic hair is the first indication that puberty

TABLE 5

CENTILES OF DIFFERENCE (IN YEARS) BETWEEN AGE ON REACHING ONE STAGE OF DEVELOPMENT AND AGE ON REACHING A LATER STAGE

Stages	*Time in years (centiles)*		
	95	50	5
B2–B3	1·0	0·9	0·2
B3–B4	2·2	0·9	0·1
B4–B5	6·8	2·0	0·1
B2–B4	3·6	1·8	0·7
B3–B5	7·5	3·1	0·9
B2–B5	9·0	4·0	1·5
PH2–PH3	1·3	0·6	0·2
PH3–PH4	0·9	0·5	0·2
PH4–PH5	2·4	1·3	0·6
PH2–PH4	2·0	1·1	0·5
PH3–PH5	3·8	1·8	0·9
PH2–PH5	3·1	2·5	1·4

(Based on data from Marshall and Tanner)[50]

has begun. It may even reach Stage 3 or 4 before the breasts begin to develop.

Axillary hair does not usually appear until the breasts are in Stage 3 or 4 but again there are a few perfectly normal girls in whom the growth of axillary hair may precede the breast development.

In the great majority, menarche occurs in breast Stage 4. It is very unusual for a girl to menstruate before her breasts have reached Stage 3, although 25 per cent of girls do so while actually in this stage. There are even about 10 per cent of girls who do not menstruate until the breasts have reached Stage 5.

There are no data which enable us to define the maximum interval which may be allowed after the attainment of Stage 5 before it can be assumed that menarche will not occur, but the assessment of skeletal age (*see* below) is useful in these circumstances. If the bone age is in excess of 14·5 "years" there is a high probability of primary amenorrhoea but if the bone age is less than this there is reasonable hope that menarche will occur.

In girls, the adolescent growth spurt usually begins early in puberty but its relationship to the development of the breasts is by no means constant. Approximately 30 or 40 per cent of girls reach their maximum rate of growth in height (PHV) while they are still in breast Stage 2 and thereafter growth decelerates steadily. Thus when we see a girl whose breasts are just beginning to develop we cannot assume that the great increase in stature which results from the adolescent growth spurt is still to come, because she may already have experienced the greater part of this spurt. In this respect, there is a striking difference between girls and boys for the boy's spurt occurs rather late in puberty and we can say with considerable confidence that a boy whose genitalia are beginning to develop has the whole of the adolescent spurt still before him. The majority of girls reach peak height velocity when they are in breast Stage 3 but there are about 10 per cent who do not do so until they are in breast Stage 4. There is a remarkably close relationship between menarche and the adolescent growth spurt. There is no record of any normal girl having begun to menstruate before she has passed peak height velocity. We can therefore confidently reassure the tall girl who has reached menarche that her growth is now slowing down and that she will not continue to grow at the same speed as she did during the previous year or so.

In view of the variability of the relationships between the androgen controlled events (e.g. pubic hair growth) and those which are oestrogen controlled (e.g. breast development) it is unlikely that a common central mechanism is responsible for initiating both these phenomena. On the other hand, the fact that they do vary to some extent independently might provide a basis for investigating the relative importance of androgen and oestrogen in those processes whose underlying mechanism is less clear, e.g. the adolescent growth spurt and menarche. This problem is discussed more fully below.

SEX DIFFERENCES IN AGE AT PUBERTY

The adolescent growth spurt occurs at an earlier age, on the average, in girls than in boys and there is about 2 years difference in the mean ages at which they reach peak height velocity. The average 12-year-old girl is at or near her maximum growth rate whereas most boys of this age are still growing at a preadolescent rate. There is therefore an overall tendency for girls to become bigger than boys at about this age but this does not, of course, imply that all girls are bigger than all boys. There are many early maturing boys who will experience the adolescent growth spurt before late maturing girls. Girls who are rather tall, but not excessively so, sometimes become alarmed at this stage because they realize that they are becoming taller in relation to boys of the same age. However, in most cases, they are reflecting the normal sex difference in growth at this age and there is no cause for alarm.

It is however, not true that the secondary sex characters develop at a much earlier age in girls than in boys. The boys' genitalia begin to develop at approximately the same age as the breasts in girls and complete sexual maturity is reached at approximately the same average age in both sexes. However, from the social point of view puberty does appear to be earlier in girls because their early growth spurt tends to make them bigger and the development of their breasts is obvious even when they are fully clothed. In boys, on the other hand, the early development of the genitalia is not obvious when clothed and the changes which are readily apparent, e.g. the growth spurt, the breaking of the voice and the development of facial hair, do not occur until the genitalia are approaching maturity.

RELATION BETWEEN PUBERTY AND MATURATION OF THE SKELETON

At puberty there is a close relationship between the maturity of the skeleton and the percentage of a child's ultimate height that has been reached. This relationship is used in the prediction of adult height. It is often assumed that the changes of puberty are equally closely related to skeletal maturation but recent studies show that this is not true except in the case of menarche and pubic hair growth (i.e. the attainment of Stage PH3). Using data from the Harpenden mixed longitudinal growth study, Marshall[48] found that the beginning and completion of breast development in girls were just as variable in relation to skeletal age as they were in relation to chronological age. However, most girls begin to menstruate between skeletal ages 13 and 14 years and any girl who has not menstruated by skeletal age 14·5 is sufficiently unusual for an abnormality to be suspected. However, neither the skeletal nor the chronological age at the beginning of breast development may be used to predict the chronological age at menarche.

The fact that only an androgen-controlled event, pubic hair growth, is related to skeletal maturation in the same way as menarche suggests that androgens may be involved in the initiation of menstruation. This possibility is further supported by the close relationship between menarche and the adolescent growth spurt.

Similarly in boys, the skeletal age at which genital development begins is just as variable as the chronological age. Therefore, a boy's skeletal age does not help us to predict when his puberty may begin. The variation in skeletal age at peak height velocity is slightly less than the chronological age but the reduction in variance is not sufficiently great to be of practical value.

ENDOCRINOLOGY OF PUBERTY

The fact that the changes of puberty are so variable in relation to both chronological age and skeletal maturation has an important implication for research into the mechanisms underlying the pubertal changes. It is clearly wrong to regard puberty as a single phenomenon, and to study, for example, the changing blood or urine content of hormones at the beginning of puberty by defining the "beginning of puberty" as *either* the first sign of breast development or pubic hair growth. Endocrine or other factors must be investigated in relation to either breast or pubic hair development independently, or to any other single pubertal event. Unfortunately much of the existing endocrine literature does not make this simple distinction.

Indeed our understanding of the evidently complex series of hormonal changes underlying the events of puberty is still fragmentary. Only very recently have reliable methods for estimating blood and urine levels of pituitary and gonadal hormones become available, and secretion rates are still for the most part unobtainable. Some hormones, such as growth hormone and LH, are not secreted at a constant rate during the day but only episodically in response to some internal rhythm or external stimulus. This pulsatile nature of hormone release is an added problem, making continuous blood sampling during the whole 24-hr. cycle necessary to obtain integrated secretion rates. Thus the study of normal subjects is inevitably limited. And since as usual in studying the physiology of growth, it is changes with time that we want to know about rather than status at a given time, we need to make longitudinal studies. Very few such studies of hormonal change at adolescence have been done or are in progress.

Certain things, however, are becoming clear. The adrenal and thyroid glands, as well as the testes and ovaries, show an adolescent growth spurt in weight. The anterior pituitary also has a spurt, which is much greater in girls than boys. Before puberty there is little if any sex difference in pituitary weight or sella turcica volume; after puberty girls are bigger in both respects due to a greater increase in acidophil cells, presumably those that secrete prolactin. However, it is wrong to argue from the size of a gland, or even from its content of a hormone, to the amount of hormone it is secreting or releasing. The amount of growth hormone, for example, in the human pituitary is amazingly high, amounting to 1 per cent of the wet weight of the gland. A good burst of secretion resulting in high blood values for 1 hr. would reduce this amount by only 1 or 2 per cent, which is undetectable.[77]

We should also be somewhat wary in interpreting the chemical assays of hormone levels. Radioimmunoassay, the standard method for pituitary hormones, measures only a short sequence of 5 or 6 amino-acids in the peptide (out of a total sequence of 1 or 200). At least in principle, therefore, it is possible for an assay to measure the "wrong" sequence, that is a fragment which is without biological activity. Also the immunological structure of gonadotrophic hormones changes as they are metabolized in the body so that antigenic sites may be lost, or, indeed, uncovered. One has to consider the perhaps remote possibility that some age changes in radioimmunoassayable hormone are artefacts of the method, the changes being of molecular structure rather than amount of biologically active fragment.

With these provisos, however, we will look, first at studies of the levels of gonadotrophins and gonadal steroids and then at the inter-relation between the two.

Gonadotrophins

Both FSH and LH have been shown by radioimmunoassay to be present in blood and urine from birth (and probably before) onwards. The bioassay methods previously used were insufficiently sensitive to detect small amounts or to distinguish clearly between FSH and LH, as recent radioimmunoassay methods do.

The timing of the hormonal events of puberty has best been characterized in the mixed longitudinal study of Faiman and Winter,[22] in which blood was taken once a year for 4 years from 56 normal boys aged 6–14 on entry and once a year for 3 years from 58 girls aged 6–16 on entry. Such a study, in which the whole age range is covered by a series of interlocking short-term longitudinal sections needs special statistical handling to produce mean trends unbiassed by subjects entering and leaving it.[76,78]

Faiman and Winter[22] used these methods to produce the results shown in Figs. 12 and 13.

In Fig. 12 the mean values for FSH, LH and testosterone are plotted against chronological age, while in Fig. 13 the more critical plot against stage of puberty is given. The criteria for the stages unfortunately mix genital and pubic

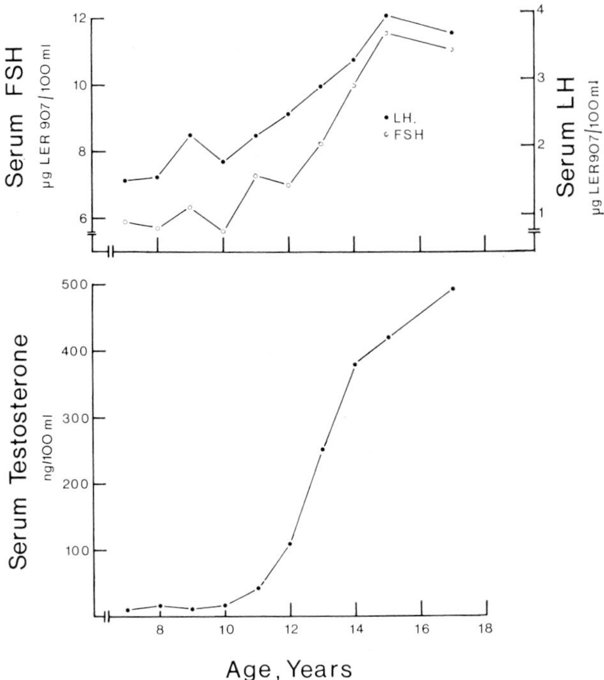

FIG. 12. Blood levels of LH, FSH and testosterone in 56 healthy boys studied semi-longitudinally throughout puberty. (Rederawn from Faiman and Winter).[22]

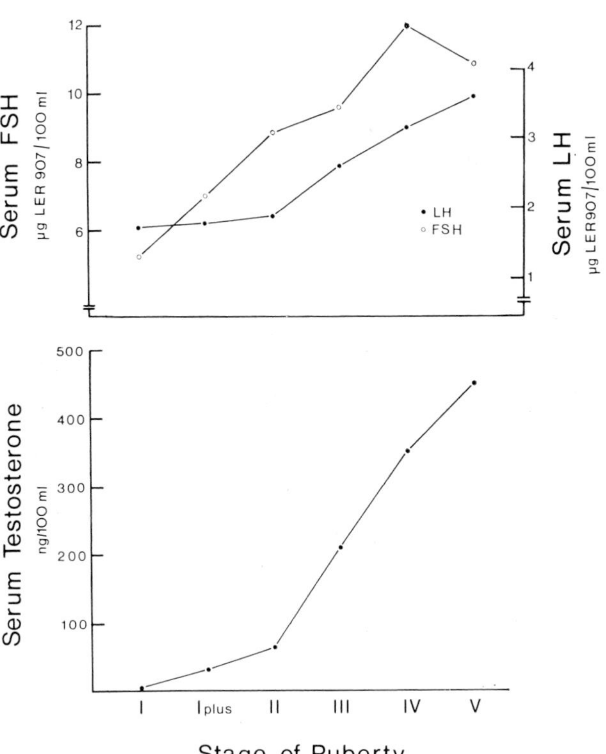

FIG. 13. Blood levels of LH, FSH and testosterone in 56 healthy boys studied semi-longitudinally, plotted against stage of puberty. Stage 1 plus represents boys who one year later had entered stage 2. (Redrawn from Faiman and Winter.)[22]

hair development, combining (in an illegitimate way, *see* above) the five stages for each described above. Stage 1 Plus refers to boys who were 1 year only before entry to Stage 2 while Stage 1 describes boys who were 2 years or more before entry to Stage 2.

Figure 13 brings out the time relations better than Fig. 12. FSH rises first, increasing by 50 per cent from Stages 1–2, during which time neither LH nor testosterone change significantly. FSH continues to rise, and reaches the adult male value a little before all the morphological changes of puberty are complete. LH, on the other hand, begins its rise only after Stage 2 has been reached, and continues to

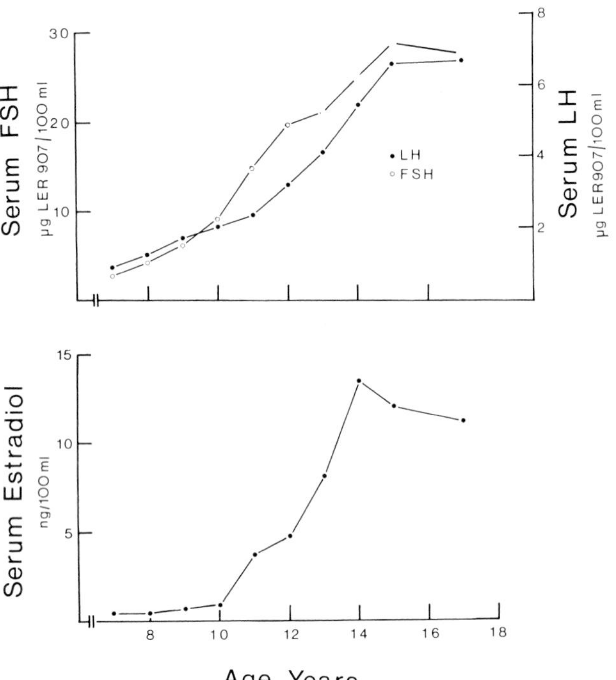

FIG. 14. Blood levels of LH, FSH and oestradiol in 58 healthy girls studied semi-longitudinally throughout puberty. (Redrawn from Faiman and Winter.)[22]

rise from Stage 4–5. Testosterone has an exactly comparable curve. The more restricted cross-sectional data are mostly in agreement with these results.[2,3,15,37,60,61,86,95]

Finkelstein *et al.*[23] have recorded plasma LH levels every 20 min. throughout 24 hr. in a number of children and adolescents. When LH first began to rise it did so in bursts released during sleep. Later in puberty bursts occurred during wakefulness also but the sleep bursts remained predominant (giving a sleep mean value of 13·3 mI.U./ml. compared with a wakefulness mean value of 9·6 mI.U./ml., 2nd IRPHMG). When puberty was completed the sleep and waking values became equal. The release of LH occurred during non-REM sleep, and was inhibited in REM sleep.

In girls the increases of FSH and LH are similar in timing to those of boys. Figure 14, also taken from Faiman and Winter,[22] shows the mixed longitudinal data plotted against chronological age. FSH rises first and LH later. Neither FSH nor LH showed any rise in the 6–10 group, though FSH was high in the first year after birth. Cross-sectional data are mostly confirmatory.[36,37,43,74,94]

Urinary Output of Gonadotrophins per 24 hr. has been studied by a number of investigators, though only cross-sectional results have so far been published. The urinary output may be expected to integrate the fluctuations of blood level and may therefore better represent the 24 hr. production rate. In the blood, increases in the rate may be made either by increasing the amplitude or the frequency of the pulses of release; in the urine, providing renal clearance is not much dependent on blood level, amplitude and frequency changes are integrated.

As in the case of serum, FSH values rise in early puberty, and reach maximum levels by Stage 3 or 4. Means for each stage for boys were 2·2, 4·4, 7·1, 7·8, 6·9 I.U./24 hr. (International Reference Preparation HMG 2) in the studies of Raiti *et al.*[60] and Baghdassarian *et al.*[3] The LH rise, in contrast, was mainly from Stage 3 onwards, with means of 2·6, 8·6, 12·7, 23·0 and 31·1 I.U./24 hr.; quantitatively the increase of LH excretion (about 12 times from childhood to adulthood) is much greater than that of FSH (about 4 times); in serum the increases are about 3 times for LH and 2 times for FSH. At each stage of puberty there is great variability between individuals, with standard deviations of the order of 50 per cent of the mean.

Gonadal Hormones

Data on plasma testosterone in boys are in good agreement in showing the sharp rise illustrated in Figs. 12 and 13.[2,22,25,86] The longitudinal data indicate that the rise is slight until Stage 2 has been reached, and then continues at a high rate until Stage 5 when mean values of between 400–500 ng./100 ml. are reported. The rise continues beyond this point, and young adult males have mean levels of 600–700 ng./100 ml. (Stage 5 is complete as a rule before moustache and beard have grown much, and axillary hair may still be incompletely developed.)

Plasma testosterone apparently rises in girls as well as in boys, though of course to a much smaller extent. Faiman and Winter[22] found mean levels of about 20 ng./100 ml. prepubertally (which is comparable with the level in prepubertal males), rising to about 40 ng./100 ml. in early puberty with Stage 2 or 3 pubic hair, and 50 ng./100 ml. in post-menarcheal girls. Such a level would only characterize Stage 2 boys and presumably could not sustain the adult growth of pubic hair in males; perhaps, however, females are more sensitive. Testosterone production rate in adult men is said to be of the order of 7 mg./24 hr. compared with that in women of 0·3 mg./24 hr.[32] Testosterone in women is believed largely to come from peripheral conversion of androstenedione, secreted by the ovary and/or the adrenal.

Plasma Oestradiol Levels in girls rise in the manner shown in Fig. 14. Newborns have a high value for a few days (100–300 pg./ml.[5,66] Levels rise in girls at puberty, reaching about 30 pg./ml. at breast Stages 2 and 3 and adult levels (ranging from 10–200 pg./ml.) by the time of menarche or soon after.[22,36]

Boys have a rise in plasma oestradiol in early puberty to an average of 33 pg./ml. which is the same as in adult males.

It is not known for certain where the male oestradiol is produced; it is likely to be the adrenal.

Plasma Oestrone, which is produced, it is believed, exclusively by the adrenal and not the ovary, has the same range of values as oestradiol in both sexes from age 1–6. However, from 7–10, according to Saez and Movera[66] the mean rises to 36 pg./ml., also in both sexes, this being at an age before any similar rise in oestradiol has occurred. These findings appear to provide real evidence of the existence of an adrenal increase in hormone production in the so-called "mid-growth" years, before puberty.

Adrenal Androgens

In Blood. The main "androgens" secreted by the adrenals are dehydroepiandrosterone, dehydroepiandrosterone sulfate, and 11-β-hydroxyandrostenedione, with smaller quantities of androstenedione. All these have been found in the adrenal vein blood of adult men and women. In mixed venous blood the main substances found are dehydroepiandrosterone sulfate and androsterone sulfate.

In children very little of either substance is detectable in mixed blood before about age 7, but from then on a steady rise appears to occur, leading to levels just before puberty of about a third of the young adult value.[52,65]

After this possible "mid-growth" increase a sharp rise presumably occurs at puberty though no longitudinal values, nor even values based on puberty stages or bone age, are yet available. Boon *et al.*[10] report figures for the age range 9–20 years, which show a negligible sex difference in dehydroepiandrosterone sulfate level, but a level of androsterone sulfate in older males which is about double that in females. Neither the blood level[65] nor the excretion[98] of dehydroepiandrosterone sulfate is increased by injection of human chorionic gonadotrophin in prepubertal children; whereas the plasma level of dehydroepiandrosterone is said to be increased.

In the adult the highest levels are found in the twenties, followed by a decrease with age, so that by 60 or 70, on the average, the immediately prepubertal level is reached. In young adults the production rate of dehydroepiandrosterone plus its sulfate is variously estimated as between 10 and 50 mg./24 hr.; that is equal to or greater than the average cortisol production rate, so that we must assume that the adrenal androgens have a clearly important function at and after puberty.

Adrenal Corticosteroid secretion does not show any particular change at puberty. Cortisol production rate rises, but only in proportion to the increase in body size.[38] The same is true of the amount of cortisol metabolites found in urine. This is in sharp distinction to the adolescent rise of adrenal androgen metabolites in urine, represented by 11-deoxy-17-ketosteroids, as opposed to 11-oxy-17-ketosteroids which are cortisol and corticosterone products (*see* Fig. 15).

"Adrenarche Hormone"

It is clear that at puberty the adrenal rapidly increases its production of androgenic hormones, just as do the testes. This adrenal component of puberty is sometimes referred to as "adrenarche", an inaccurate term if taken literally, since corticosteroids and aldosterone are secreted through the whole of childhood just as in the adult.

What causes this increase in adrenal androgens is far from clear. An increase of ACTH secretion cannot alone account for it, because ACTH always causes a greater increase in corticoids than in androgens in children and adults alike. Either there is some pituitary hormone other than ACTH involved—we might call it "adrenarche hormone"—or else something modifies the adrenal response to ACTH.

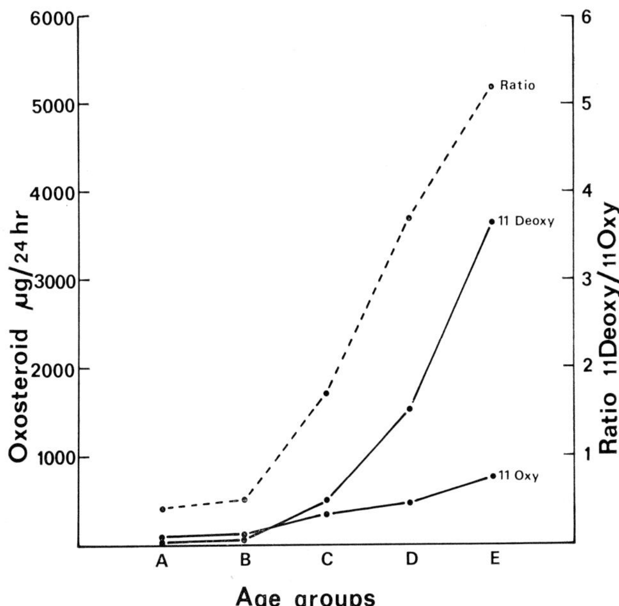

FIG. 15. Changes in 11-deoxy-17-ketosteroid and 11-oxy-17-ketosteroid excretion with age. A—infants (14): B—preadolescent children (13): C—children in early adolescence (10): E—adults. Cross-sectional data, sexes combined. (Based on data from Teller.)[181]

Thyroid Hormone

Serum TSH, measured by radioimmunoassay, rises during puberty in both sexes, from a prepubertal value of about 17 μU./ml. to a peak of about 22 μU./ml. and then declines to the adult value of 15 μU./ml.[26] A relative increase occurs during puberty in basal metabolic rate; that is to say, there is a temporary stop put to the decline which continues from birth to adulthood.[75] Presumably, this relatively small increase in activity of the thyroid follows an increased peripheral utilization of hormone as growth takes place.

Growth Hormone

Since growth hormone is secreted only intermittently, the difficulties in determining whether changes occur at adolescence are formidable, and have not yet been entirely overcome. Blizzard and his colleagues [8,40] used a small suction pump strapped on the back which extracted blood continuously at 1 ml./hr. through an indwelling arm catheter and stored it over a whole 24 hr. period. Thus integrated 24 hr. blood levels were obtained. In young adult males this value averaged 1·8 ng./ml. with an SD of 1·0 ng./ml.; in adult premenopausal females 3·0 ng./ml., and post-menopausal females 1·5 ng./ml. In 17 boys aged 7–16 the average value was 5·6 ng./ml. but there was no obvious relationship with age or stage of puberty or testosterone blood level. Ten girls aged 8–13 averaged 4·9 ng./ml., again without obvious relation to age or puberty. On present evidence therefore 24 hr. blood values are higher in children than adults, but probably do not rise during puberty. Production rates, calculated using limited data on elimination of radioactive HGH, worked out at 0·9 mg./m.²/24 hr. in children and adolescents compared with 0·35 mg./m.²/24 hr. in adult males.

Pineal

In some mammals the pineal gland produces a substance which inhibits the development of the gonads. The production of this substance is apparently increased by darkness and reduced by light. Through this mechanism the pineal clearly plays a part in the action of different environments on the gonadal development of rodents. However, there is, at present, no clear evidence that the pineal has any role in human sexual development, although the possibility has not been excluded.

RELATION OF ENDOCRINE TO MORPHOLOGICAL EVENTS

We must now try to relate these hormonal changes to the morphological ones.

Adolescent Growth Spurt

The adolescent growth spurt in size is produced by the joint actions of growth hormone, adrenal androgens and testosterone, but the exact role each plays is still not clear. Both testosterone and growth hormone are certainly necessary for the normal male growth spurt to occur.[59] We have followed the growth of 2 male patients, lacking all pituitary function due to operated craniopharyngiomas. They continued for several years on thyroxine, cortisone, vasopressin and growth hormone and then at bone ages of 13·5 "years" and 13·1 "years" were given 250 mg. of testosterone oenanthate i.m. every 2 weeks. At the same time growth hormone was stopped for the first 3 months, added for the second 3 months, left off for the third and added for the fourth quarter. Both patients had a greater velocity when on growth hormone in addition to testosterone. The average quarterly values for the 2 patients were: on testosterone alone 4·4 cm./year; on testosterone plus growth hormone 8·4 cm./year; on testosterone alone 3·1 cm./year; on testosterone plus growth hormone 8·2 cm./year. Patients lacking both hormones and treated only with testosterone throughout puberty have a spurt of 5 or 6 cm./year instead of the normal 9 cm./year.[79] Thus it would seem that testosterone and growth hormone are responsible for roughly half each of the spurt. The most satisfactory hypothesis at present is that in normal puberty growth hormone continues to be secreted at about the childhood rate and is responsible for a continuation of the pre-adolescent velocity of 4 cm./year or so and that testosterone and adrenal androgens superimpose on this a spurt rising to an extra 5 cm./year at peak.

In girls, it is presumably the adrenal androgens which are responsible for the extra spurt velocity, though there is no certain evidence of this.

Muscle and Fat Changes

The increase in muscle and in width of bone cortex at adolescence is presumably caused by adrenal androgens in both sexes, with testicular testosterone being responsible for the much greater increase in the male. The loss of fat, particularly in the limbs, may be similarly caused.

Pubic, Axillary and Facial Hair

The differential growth of hair at pubes, axillae and face seems most easily explained on the basis of locally differing thresholds to stimulation, coupled perhaps with a predilection of hair follicles at each site for either testicular or adrenal androgen. Presumably these local differences depend on the tissues' ability to metabolize the hormone to the intracellularly active forms; in the case of testosterone, for example, on the presence of a 5α-reductase to convert it to dihydrotestosterone. Probably the concentrations of such enzymes have their own particular courses of maturation, time-dependent in a way we do not yet understand. Large doses of testosterone given to boys whose testes fail to develop at puberty cause a rapid growth of pubic hair and penis, but have little effect on the facial hair follicles. Zachmann and Prader[99] have suggested that the testosterone induced development of secondary sex characters may be growth-hormone dependent, but this is not in accord with our clinical experience.

Closure of Epiphyses

In the absence of puberty, the bone age in both girls and boys sticks at about 13 "years." The last stages of maturation are sex-hormone dependent.

The Initiation of Puberty

The manner in which puberty is initiated has been the subject of much research recently. The signal to start the train of events is given by the brain, not the pituitary. This much has been clear ever since the classic experiments of Harris and Jacobsohn,[30] showing that the pituitary of a newborn rat successfully grafted in place of an adult pituitary at once begins to function in an adult manner and does not have to wait until its normal time of maturation has been passed. It is the hypothalamus (or higher parts of the brain) which has to mature before puberty begins.

It is established in rats that removal of the gonads during

infancy causes a rise in gonadotrophins and that this can be prevented in the female by giving doses of oestrogen much below the level which causes sexual maturation. Accordingly, Donovan and van der Werff ten Bosch[20] suggested that at birth the hypothalamus is inhibited from producing gonadotrophin releaser by small amounts of sex hormones secreted by the infantile gonads. A feed-back circuit is established with both gonadotrophins and sex hormones at low levels. At puberty, it is supposed that a change occurs in sensitivity of the hypothalamic receptor cells such that the small amounts of sex hormones no longer are sufficient to inhibit them. Gonadotrophin-releasing hormones are thus secreted, FSH and LH rise and cause in turn the level of sex hormones to rise. This continues until the same feedback circuit is re-established, but now at a higher level of gonadotrophins and sex hormones. The latter are now high enough to stimulate the growth of the secondary sex characters and support mating behaviour.

children were only about one-third of the level in adults. Thus the increase in both groups was to about 3 times basal. However, one cannot tell from this "acute" experiment what the situation might be after a month, say, of LHRH injections (*see* below).

Another possibility proposed for positive feed-back is more drastic. In the adult menstrual cycle an increase of oestrogen does not inhibit gonadotrophin release; on the contrary it stimulates it. To get from the pubescent girl, then, to the post-menarcheal woman seems to require a change in the hypothalamic response to peripheral oestrogen, a flip from negative to positive feed-back. Such a change is said to occur in Rhesus about a year after menarche. Nothing is known about its occurrence in the human or how the mechanism might work.

A second point that is clearly established is that the prepubertal testes will respond to injections of human chorionic gonadotrophin (HCG), which closely resembles LH

TABLE 6

PLASMA TESTOSTERONE VALUES (ng./100 ml. ± SEM) BEFORE AND AFTER 3 CONSECUTIVE DAYS OF 2,000 I.U. HCG/day[93]

No.	*Pubertal stage*	*Before stimulation*	*After 1 dose*	*After 3 doses*
8	I	18 ± 4	61 ± 16	173 ± 27
17	III	95 ± 27	427 ± 131	607 ± 106
16	V (Age 20/21)	534 ± 36	1,333 ± 150	1,391 ± 93

This is a very attractive hypothesis, especially in the notion of a single feed-back system operating at two levels. Evidence that a similar mechanism operates in man is rapidly accumulating, though it seems likely that this is not the only mechanism involved. Prepubertal children with multiple pituitary hormone deficiency have blood levels of LH and FSH which are only some 50 per cent of normal prepubertal values, as expected.[2] Castration in man before puberty, represented chiefly by gonadal dysgenesis in females and the rarer developmental anorchia in males, leads to FSH and LH levels well above the normal range in the prepubertal years.[57,91] It is not yet certain that the suppressors from the gonads are testosterone and oestrogen, since to demonstrate that their levels in castrates are still lower than the normal prepubertal ones is very difficult with present methods; however, Saez and Movera[66] report exactly this finding for oestradiol in gonadal dysgenesis. Adrenal as well as gonadal suppressors may be involved.

Winter and Faiman's data on castrates show that from about 11 years onwards both FSH and LH levels were above those seen before this age, suggesting that the normal changes "may involve not only a reduction in gonadal negative feed-back but also a direct stimulus to gonadotrophin production." This may be an increased sensitivity to luteinizing hormone releasing hormone (LHRH). Illig *et al.*[35] found that the blood levels of LH following a single intravenous injection of synthetic LHRH in prepubertal

in its action, by secreting testosterone. A single injection of HCG produces only a very modest response,[98] but continuous treatment for 2 weeks or more is said to result in blood testosterone levels in the range of unstimulated adults.[25,65] Winter, Tarasaka and Faiman[93] made a detailed study on 68 young males without endocrine disorder, giving 2,000 I.U. HCG for 3 consecutive days. Under this regime the values partly abstracted in Table 6 were obtained.

In young adults a single dose raised the blood level to an amount (1,333 ng./100 ml.) indistinguishable statistically from the level (1,391 ng./100 ml.) produced by 3 doses. But in prepubertal children this was far from the case, the values being 61 and 173 ng./100 ml. Evidently it takes a good deal of stimulation before the Leydig cells will respond maximally to HCG, because they have first to synthesize their own structural protein (since before puberty they are virtually invisible[4] and to induce, presumably, the enzymes for particular steroidogenic pathways. Whether, even given time, HCG can produce Leydig cells in prepubertal boys which are capable of responding to produce adult blood levels is not certainly known. In the bull and the rat androstenedione, (or androstandiol respectively) are secreted before puberty in preference to testosterone, both at rest and in response to HCG stimulation. Thus in these species, at least, the pathway to testosterone production seems to need something other than LH to mature it; and

TABLE 7

AGE OF MENARCHE IN RECENT YEARS

(All estimates by probits or logits unless indicated; recalculated from authors' data if necessary)

Country		*Year*	*Mean age and SE*	*Reference*
Norway	Oslo	1970	13·2	106
Finland	All	1969	13·2 ± 0·02	118
Denmark	Copenhagen	1964	13·2 ± 0·2	101
Holland	All	1965	13·4	143
Belgium	Brabant	1965 ca	13·0	117
Switzerland	Basle	1956	13·5 ± 0·10	115
England	London	1959	13·1 ± 0·02	131
	Bristol	1956	13·2 ± 0·02	146
	London	1966	13·0 ± 0·02	135
Scotland	Edinburgh	1952	13·4	129
France	All	1950	13·5 ± 0·01	102
Italy	Cararra	1968	12·6 ± 0·04	125
	Naples, rural	1969	12·5 ± 0·02	109
Hungary	All	1959	13·2 ± 0·02	104
	Budapest	1959	12·8 ± 0·08	137
	Szeged	1966	12·7 ± 0·19	113
	W. Hungary	1965	13·1 ± 0·01	112
	Kosice	1968	12·8 ± 0·03	140
Poland	Warsaw	1965	13·0 ± 0·04	127
	Wroclaw	1966	13·2 ± 0·03	126
	Rural	1967	14·0 ± 0·02	120
Yugoslavia	Zemun	1963	14·3 ± 0·06	148
Rumania	3 towns	1963	13·5 ± 0·06	110
	3 rural areas	1963	14·6 ± 0·07	110
U.S.S.R.	Moscow	1965	13·0†	141
	Tbilisi	1962	13·2†	141
	2 Provincial towns	1960–2	13·7†	141
	Rural area	1958	14·3†	141
	Buriat Rep. villages	1957	15·0†	141
Israel	Tel-Aviv	1959	13·2 ± 0·02	134
	Jerusalem	1958	13·9	133
Iraq	Baghdad, well-off	1969	13·6 ± 0·06	132
	poorly-off	1969	14·0 ± 0·05	132
Turkey	Istanbul, rich	1965	12·4 ± 0·15	128
	average	1965	12·9 ± 0·11	128
	poor	1965	13·2 ± 0·10	128
	All	1965	12·8 ± 0·06	128
Iran	North, Rasht	1963	13·3 ± 0·18	142
India	Madras, urban	1960	12·8 ± 0·14	123
	Madras, rural		14·2 ± 0·13	123
	Kerala, urban		13·2 ± 0·17	123
	Kerala, rural		14·4 ± 0·14	123
	Lucknow	1967	14·5 ± 0·17	119
Burma/Assam	Town, well-nourished	1957	13·2 ± 0·08	114
Ceylon	Colombo	1950	12·8 ± 0·07	144, 145
	Rural		14·4 ± 0·16	144, 145
Singapore	Rich	1968	12·4 ± 0·09	103
	Average		12·7 ± 0·09	103
	Poor		13·0 ± 0·04	103
Hong Kong	Rich	1962	12·5 ± 0·18	122
(Chinese)	Average		12·8 ± 0·20	122
	Poor		13·3 ± 0·19	122
New Guinea	Bundi, highlands	1967	18·0 ± 0·19	124
	Kaipit, lowlands		15·6 ± 0·25	124
Australia	Melbourne	1957	13·2	138

TABLE 7 (*continued*)

Country		*Year*	*Mean age and SE*	*Reference*
U.S.A.	All (Nursing Students)	1964	12·6* ± 0·02	147
Cuba	Negro	1963	12·4 ± 0·07	121
	White		12·4 ± 0·03	121
	Mulatto		12·6 ± 0·06	121
Mexico	Xochimilco	1966	12·8 ± 0·18	111
Guatemala	Well-off Spanish	1963	13·3 ± 0·40	130
	Maya, villages		15·1 ± 0·25	130
Chile	Santiago (middle-class)	1970	12·6 ± 0·12	149
Senegal	Dakar	1970	14·6‡ ± 0·08	105
Nigeria	Ibo (Well-off)	1960	14·1 ± 0·16	136
Uganda	Kampala, Buganda (Well-off)	1960	13·4 ± 0·16	107
Egypt	Nubians	1966	15·2 ± 0·30	139
Rwanda, E. Africa	Tutsi	1958	16·5 ± 0·16	116
	Hutu		17·1 ± 0·30	116
S. Africa	Bantu, Transkei			
	Not poor	1958	15·0 ± 0·03	108
	Poor		15·4 ± 0·04	108

* Recollected-age data.
† Obtained by graphical probits only.
‡ Recalculated by estimated probit.

it has been suggested that this might be FSH. A similar suggestion has been made for man; but species differences in reproductive physiology are so marked that one should be very wary about arguing from one animal to another.

As for the basic change in the sensitivity (and perhaps even the "sigh") of the hypothalamic receptors, it remains quite unexplained. It may itself be a consequence of change in afferent input, though from where is not known.

GENETIC AND ENVIRONMENTAL INFLUENCES ON PUBERTY

The changes of puberty are dependent upon a complex interaction of genetic and environmental factors. The importance of inheritance was shown by Tisser and Perrier[82] who found that, in France, the mean difference in menarcheal age for identical twins was 2 months whilst that between non-identical twin sisters was 8 months. Also, it is a common clinical experience that children with late puberty have a history of similarly late maturity in one or both parents. Although a relationship between parents and children in age at puberty is widely accepted, attempts to document it have generally not been satisfactory owing to the problems created by the secular trend (*see* below) and succeeding generations living in different social conditions. When the members of a population live in a reasonably uniform environment which provides the basic essentials for good nutrition and health, the variability in menarcheal age is due mainly to genetic differences.

Table 7 shows that members of different populations have menarche at widely differing ages. The estimation of the age at menarche in a population is subject to errors which vary with the method by which the data are collected and analysed. Three methods have been used by different authors.

The Cross-sectional Retrospective Method

This was used in nearly all the older surveys. Each subject is seen on only one occasion and is asked the age at which she began to menstruate. Clearly the recollected age will be inaccurate in many cases while some girls, particularly those who were much earlier or later than their friends, may give deliberately false answers. The result will also be biased if the sample includes many girls who have not yet begun to menstruate. This point was illustrated by Wilson and Sutherland[89] who showed that the difference in recalled age in two samples was due to inclusion of more premenarcheal girls in the sample giving the lower mean value. Further bias extends from the usual practice of stating ones age as that at the preceding birthday. In a large sample the mean is thereby underestimated by 0·5 years but with smaller samples the bias is less consistent.

The Longitudinal Method

The same subjects are seen repeatedly and asked on each occasion if they have begun to menstruate. If the interval between visits is short, the exact date can usually be determined. This is the most accurate method of determining the age at menarche in individuals, but, owing to the financial and administrative difficulties involved, it has not yet been possible to study sufficiently large or representative samples to reflect the situation in whole populations.

The Status Quo Method

This method requires from each subject only her exact age and a statement as to whether or not she has begun to menstruate. This leads to a record of the percentage of "yes" answers at each age. To this percentage distribution a probit or logit transformation is applied and then the mean and variance can be estimated. This method gives no information about the age at menarche in individuals but is the best method of estimating the mean and variance for the population, provided the sample is sufficiently large and a wide enough range of ages is included. All the estimates in Table 7 except those specifically noted were obtained by the status quo method.

There remains the problem of distinguishing between the results of genetic and environmental factors. The influence of the environment on age at menarche has been demonstrated by many authors. In many countries the environmental differences between socio-economic groups have a clear effect. In the Netherlands, de Wijn[88] found a mean menarcheal age of 13·8 years in girls whose fathers' were in the lower and middle social classes while the daughters of those in the higher classes gave a figure of 13·5. In Britain, a social class difference is no longer obvious. Wider variations in some other populations may reflect greater differences in the economic conditions of the social classes. For example, in North-east Slovenia, the mean menarcheal ages of girls of good, medium and poor social standing were 13·3, 13·7 and 14·2 years.[41]

Menarche tends to be later in rural than in urban communities and at higher than lower altitudes.[85]

Both number of siblings and birth order are reflected in the age at menarche. Roberts and Dann[63] found a delay of 0·17 years per sibling; but for a family of given size, the girls who were born later had earlier menarche by about 0·19 years per birth rank.

Each of the above influences on age at menarche is probably a combination of several factors of which nutrition is generally believed to be the most important. However, except in severe undernutrition there is no clear evidence in support of this view. Even in near starvation the effects of the undernutrition itself are difficult to separate from other environmental conditions which accompany it.

Table 7 gives several examples of menarche occurring at different ages in members of different races, but it is difficult to distinguish between the effect of race and that of the differences in nutrition, culture and climate. There is some evidence that the potential may be different in different races. Cuban girls have the earliest recorded menarche. Chinese girls in Hong Kong also have a very early menarche and even those who are very poor begin to menstruate as early as Europeans in much better economic circumstances.[42] East Europeans seem to mature earlier than West Europeans, especially when economic circumstances are matched. Americans, if comfortably off, are slightly ahead of West Europeans. Well-off Africans are not much later than Europeans although poorly-off Africans (e.g. South African Bantu) are. The Bundi of the New Guinea Highlands constitute the only group in which menarche nowadays is as late as it was in the countryside in Europe a century ago.

It has long been thought that the age of menarche is influenced by climate but the evidence has been unsatisfactory as the effects of climate were always confounded with other factors such as race. Roberts[62] used data from thirty-nine samples studied by the "status quo" method to compare the effects of climate within racial group. His sample included 21 European (Caucosoid series), 5 Eastern Asian (East Mongoloid), 6 from India and neighbouring territories in South Asia and 7 from Africa (Negroid). Multiple co-variance analyses showed that, within races, the regression of menarcheal age on mean temperature was significant ($r = -0{\cdot}40$). The regression of menarcheal age on mean temperature, and year of investigation combined was also significant ($r = +0{\cdot}522$). When these effects were taken into account there remained highly significant differences between the adjusted means for the racial groups.

The Trend Towards Earlier Puberty

During the last 100 years or so children have been maturing progressively earlier in Europe, North America and some other parts of the world. The best evidence for this is given by the age of menarche at various times in the past, as compared with the present day. Confirmation comes from the data on children's heights and weights which show them to have been getting taller and heavier at any given age. This increase in size need not in itself simply imply that the adolescent spurt is occurring earlier, since it could mean only that these children will become bigger adults. However, this does not appear to be the case. Adults have been getting larger also but not to the same extent as children. The increase in children's size is chiefly due to the fact that at any given age they are now nearer to their adult size than they used to be. The maximum height in men is now reached at 17 or 18 years whereas some 50 years ago it was not reached until the age of about 26.

The data on menarche at different times over the past 100 years or so are, of course, variable in their reliability. But when several countries are studied as shown in Fig. 16 they are remarkably consistent in showing a decrease in the age of menarche with the passage of time. Menarche in Europe has apparently been getting earlier during the past 100 years by between 3 and 4 months each decade. The trend in height and weight at the age of puberty is in good agreement with this as 12-year-old children, 30 or 40 years ago, were about the size of 11 year olds today.

There is evidence that the trend towards earlier maturation is continuing in many countries although presumably it will not go on indefinitely, and there are indications that it may be stopping in Britain.[18] We do not know when the trend began. Clearly the lines in Fig. 16 cannot be extrapolated backwards. There is no clear evidence as to the cause of the trend although it is generally assumed that better infant nutrition particularly an increase in the protein content of the infant's diet, is the main factor.

If nutrition is the main cause then one might have expected that the trend towards earlier puberty and greater size in childhood would have been less in better off children than in the poor, on the grounds that in most industrialized countries the conditions of the poor have altered to a greater extent than those of the rich during the last 100 years. The trend in menarcheal age in England has been somewhat less in the well-off than in the poor, but the difference is not so great for height or weight and the changing menarche differential may simply be because both rich and poor are

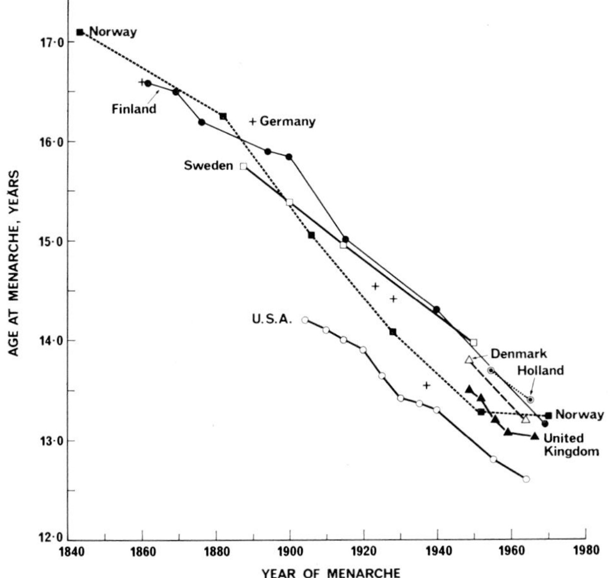

FIG. 16. Secular trend in age at menarche 1830–1960. Values are plotted at year in which the average menarche took place, i.e. in 'recollected-age'' data in average menarche of 40 year olds interrogated in 1900 was 15 years, this is plotted at 1875. This places old data on same age scale as modern probit data. Where age of interrogation is not recorded an estimated amount has been corrected where necessary (i.e. "13 year olds" centred at 13·5, not 13, as in some older literature). (Redrawn, with additions, from Tanner.)[75]

now beginning to reach the limit of the genetic potential. The latest English and Scottish data show no significant differences at age of menarche between girls whose fathers are in different occupational groups which reflect, at least approximately, differences in their family income. In Hong Kong the data show a difference of 9 months between rich and poor, presumably because the poor are much worse off than the poor in England. Perhaps one of the most convincing arguments for nutritional causes is the example of the Laps who had practically the same age of menarche, $16\frac{1}{2}$ years, from 1780–1930 while maintaining their pastoral nomadic way of life. During the same period the neighbouring Norwegians being settled farmers became 2 years earlier in their age at menarche.

ADOLESCENT STERILITY

There are several recorded instances of conception occurring before menarche. This means that the endometrium may go through a complete cycle prior to the first menstrual period. In most girls, however, ovulation does not occur before menarche and there is no progesterone to create a secretory endometrium. Usually, an ovulatory ovarian cycle does not occur until there have been a number of menstrual periods. Corner and Csapo[17] have shown that the mechanisms that are necessary for uterine contractility do not develop until late in childhood, correlated with the premenarcheal rise in oestrogen level.

Gorer[27] states that the Himalayan Lepthas people believe that puberty in the female is the result of sexual intercourse and it is therefore necessary for girls to have intercourse if they are to develop. The girls are betrothed and occasionally married from about the age of 8 years and boys from the age of 12. From this time intercourse may take place regularly. In spite of the fact that contraceptives are completely unknown and there is no cultural necessity for the practice of abortion, pregnancy rarely occurs before the 22nd year. Gorer states that menarche occurs in this population round about the age of 13 years and the first seminal emission in boys at the age of about 15. There is however a high overall rate of adult sterility in this population. The whole subject of adolescent sterility is reviewed by Ashley Montague.[1]

SUMMARY

We may summarize by saying that puberty is a group of partially concurrent changes which include maturation of the gonads and the development of full reproductive capacity. The reproductive organs and secondary sex characters grow; the adolescent growth spurt occurs; ability to sustain prolonged physical effort increases, especially in boys, and there are changes in body composition.

During the adolescent growth spurt, growth in height accelerates to reach a maximum velocity at an average age of about 14 years in boys and 12 in girls. Some girls reach this maximum very early in relation to their sexual development, but it is unusual for a boy to do so before his genitalia are well developed. The first external evidence of puberty (which may be breast, genital or pubic hair development) appears at approximately the same average age in both sexes, but both boys and girls vary by as much as 5 years in the age at which they reach any given stage of sexual development.

There is no close relationship between the different manifestations of puberty. For example, some girls have pubic hair before their breasts begin to develop, while others have none until their breasts are nearly mature. Though skeletal age is closely linked to age at menarche, it is not linked to breast development at all, and only slightly to the development of pubic hair. In the U.K. menarche usually occurs between skeletal ages 13 and 14 years and any girl who has not menstruated by skeletal age 14·5 years is sufficiently unusual for an abnormality to be suspected.

Because changes of puberty are so variable in relation to each other, as well as to skeletal and chronological age, it is clearly wrong to regard puberty as a single phenomenon. The influence of endocrine or other factors on, for example, breast development, pubic hair growth or menarche should therefore be studied independently.

Gonadal development is initiated by changes in the central nervous system. The sensitivity of the hypothalamus to the inhibiting feedback of circulating gonadal hormones becomes reduced. This allows the amount of gonadotrophin in the circulation to increase, FSH first and LH later, causing an increase of gonadal steroids to a level sufficient to stimulate secondary sex character growth, before the feedback is again established at a new level. The situation is probably somewhat more complex than this, since in late puberty oestrogen appears to stimulate, rather than inhibit gonadotrophin release.

The adrenals secrete increasing amounts of androgen from the age of about 7 onwards but the cause of this increase in unknown.

Both growth hormone and androgen appear to be necessary to sustain a normal adolescent growth spurt. The greater spurt in boys than in girls is probably due to testosterone.

The age at which puberty occurs in an individual depends upon interaction between his inherited developmental pattern and the many environmental factors which act continuously upon him.

REFERENCES

1. Ashley-Montague, M. F. (1957), *The Reproductive Development of the Female*. New York: Julian Press.
2. August, G. P., Grumbach, M. M. and Kaplan, S. L. (1972), "Hormonal Changes in Puberty: III. Correlation of Plasma Testosterone, LH, FSH, Testicular Size and Bone Age with Male Pubertal Development," *J. clin. Endocr. Metab.*, **34,** 319–326.
3. Baghdassarian, A., Guyda, H., Johanson, A., Migeon, C. J. and Blizzard, R. M. (1970), "Urinary Excretion of Radioimmunoassayable Luteinizing Hormone (LH) in Normal Male Children and Adults, According to Age and Stage of Sexual Development," *J. clin. Endocr. Metab.*, **31,** 428–435.
4. de la Balze, F. A., Mancini, R. A., Arrillaga, F., Andrada, J. A., Vilar, O., Gurtman, A. I. and Davidson, O. W. (1960), "Puberal Maturation of the Normal Human Testis: A Histological Study," *J. clin. Endocr. Metab.*, **20,** 266–285.
5. Bidlingmaier, F. and Knorr, D. (1973), "Plasma Estrogens in Childhood and Adolescence," *Proc. European Soc. Paed. Endoctrinol. Acta Paed. Scand.*, **62,** 86.
6. Björk, A. (1955), "Cranial Base Development. A Follow-up X-ray Study of the Individual Variation in Growth Occurring Between the Ages of 12 and 20 years and its Relation to Brain Case and Face Development," *Amer. J. Orthodont.*, **41,** 198–225.
7. Bliss, C. I. and Young, M. S. (1950), "An Analysis of Heart Measurements of Growing Boys," *Hum. Biol.*, **22,** 271–280.
8. Blizzard, R. M. (1973), Paper given at the Conference on Puberty Mechanisms, Washington, D.C. In press.
9. Blizzard, R. M., Johanson, A., Guyda, H., Raiti, S., Baghdassarian, A. and Migeon, C. (1970), "Recent Developments in the Study of Gonadotrophin Secretion in Adolescence," in *Adolescent Endocrinology* (F. Heald and W. Hung, Eds.). Appleton-Century-Crofts.
10. Boon, D. A., Keenan, R. E., Slaunwhite, W. R. and Aceto, T. (1972), "Conjugated and Unconjugated Plasma Androgens in Normal Children," *Pediat. Res.*, **6,** 111–118.
11. Boyd, E. (1936), "Weight of the Thymus and its Component Parts and Number of Hassall Corpuscles in Health and Disease," *Amer. J. Dis. Child.*, **51,** 313–335.
12. Boyd, E. (1952), *An Introduction to Human Biology for First Year Medical Students*. Denver: Child Research Council.
13. Brozek, J. (1965), "Changement avec l'âge et variation sexuelles du corps chez l'enfant et chez l'adolescent," *Biotypologie*, **26,** 98–144.
14. Brozek, J. (1966), "Age Changes and Sex Differences During Childhood and Adolescence," *J. Ind. Anthrop. Soc. Cal.*, **1** 27–61.
15. Burr, I. M., Sizonenko, P. C., Kaplan, S. L. and Grumbach, M. M. (1970), "Hormonal Changes in Puberty. I. Correlation of Serum Luteinizing Hormone and Follicle Stimulating Hormone with Stages of Puberty, Testicular Size and Bone Age in Normal Boys," *Pediat. Res.*, **4,** 25–35.
16. Cheek, D. B. (1968), *Human Growth*. Philadelphia: Lea and Febiger.
17. Corner, G. and Csapo, A. (1953), "Action of Ovarian Hormones on Uterine Muscle," *Brit. med. J.*, **1,** 687–693.
18. Dann, T. C. (1973), "The end of the trend," *Proc. Soc. Study Hum. Biol.*, November 1972.
19. Deming, J. (1957), "Application of the Gompertz Curve to the Observed Pattern of Growth in Length of 48 Individual Boys and Girls During the Adolescent Cycle of Growth," *Hum. Biol.*, **29,** 83–122.
20. Donovan, B. T. and van der Werff ten Bosch, J. J. (1965), *Physiology of Puberty*. London: Edward Arnold and Co.
21. Dooren, L. J., van Geldern, H. H. and Hamming, H. D. (1963), "Testis Volume and Pubic Hair in Boys 10–15 Years of Age," *Ned. T. Geneesk.*, **107,** 1519–1522.
22. Faiman, C. and Winter, J. S. D. (1973), "Gonadotrophins and Sex Hormone Patterns in Pubescence: Clinical data," *Proc. Paed. Endocrin. Acta Paed. Scand.*, **62,** 92.
23. Finkelstein, J. W., Boyar, R. M., Roffwang, H. and Hellman, L. (1973), "Synchronisation of Luteinizing Hormone Secretion with Sleep at the Initiation of Puberty," *Proc. Europ. Soc. Paed. Endocrin. Acta Paed. Scand.* **62,** 92.
24. Ford, E. H. R. (1958), "Growth of the Human Cranial Base," *Amer. J. Orthodont.*, **44,** 498–506.
25. Frasier, S. D., Gafford, F. and Horton, R. (1969), "Plasma Androgens in Childhood and Adolescence," *J. clin. Endocr. Metab.*, **29,** 1404–1408.
26. Goldstein-Golaire, J. and Delange, F. (1971), "Serum Thyrotrophin Level During Growth in Man," *Europ. J. Clin. Invest.*, **1,** 405–407.
27. Gorer, G. (1938), *Himalayan Village*. London: Michael Joseph.
28. Hammar, J. A. (1906), "Über Gewicht, Involution und Persistenz der Thymus in Postfötalleben des Menschen," *Arch. Anat. Entw. Gesch.*, suppl. to vol. for 1906, 91 pp.
29. Hammar, J. A. (1926), "Die Menschenthymus in Gesundheit und Krankheit Teil I. Das normale Organ," *Z. mikr.-anat. Forsch.*, suppl. to vol. 6, 570 pp.
30. Harris, G. W. and Jacobsohn, D. (1952), "Functional Grafts of the Anterior Pituitary Gland," *Proc. roy. Soc. B.*, **139,** 263–276.
31. Heald, S. P., Hunt, E. E., Schwarz, R., Cook, C. D., Elliott, O. and Vajdan, B. (1963), "Measures of Body Fat and Hydration in Adolescent Boys," *Pediatrics*, **31,** 226–239.
32. Horton, R. and Tait, J. F. (1966), "Androstendione Production and Interconversion Rates Measured in Peripheral Blood and Studies on the Possible Sites of Conversion to Testosterone. *J. clin. Invest.*, **45,** 301–313.
33. Hwang, J. M. S. and Krumbhaar, E. B. (1940), "The Amount of Lymphoid Tissue of the Human Appendix and its Weight at Different Age Periods," *Amer. J. med. Sci.*, **199,** 75–83.
34. Hwang, J. M. S., Lipincott, S. W. and Krumbhaar, E. B. (1938), "The Amount of Splenic Lymphatic Tissue at Different Ages," *Amer. J. Path.*, **14,** 809–819.
35. Illig, R., Bambach, M., Pluznik, S. and Prader, A. (1972), "Studies on the Pituitary Responsiveness to Synthetic Luteinizing Hormone-releasing Hormone (LH–RH) in Children," *Proc. Europ. Soc. Paed. Endoc. Acta paed. Scand.*, **62,** 93.
36. Jenner, R. M., Kelch, R. P., Kaplan, S. I. and Grumbach, M. M. (1972), "Hormonal Changes in Puberty: IV. Plasma

Estradiol, LH and FSH in Prepubertal Children, Pubertal Females and in Precocious Puberty, Premature Thelarche, Hypogonadism, and a Child with a Feminizing Ovarian Tumor," *J. clin. Endocr. Metab.*, **34**, 521–530.

37. Johanson, A. J., Guyda, H., Light, C., Migeon, C. J. and Blizzard, R. M. (1969), "Serum Luteinizing Hormone by Radioimmunoassay in Normal Children," *J. Pediat.*, **74,** 416–424.
38. Kenny, F. M., Gaucagco, G. P., Heald, F. P. and Hung, W. (1966), "Cortisol Production Rate in Adolescent Males in Different Stages of Sexual Maturation," *J. clin. Endocr. Metab.*, **26,** 1232–1236.
39. King, E. W. (1952), "A Roentgenographic Study of Pharyngeal Growth," *Angle Orthodont.*, **22,** 23–37.
40. Kowarski, A., Thompson, R. G., Migeon, C. J. and Blizzard, R. M. (1971), "Determination of Integrated Plasma Concentrations and True Secretion Rates of Human Growth Hormone," *J. clin. Endocr. Metab.*, **32,** 356–360.
41. Kralj-Cercek, L. (1956), "The Influence of Food, Body Build and Social Origin on the Age at Menarche," *Hum. Biol.*, **28,** 398–406.
42. Lee, M. M., Chang, K. S. and Chan, M. M. (1963), "Sexual Maturation of Chinese Girls in Hong Kong," *Pediatrics*, **32,** 389–398.
43. Lee, P. A., Midgley, A. R., Jr. and Jaffe, R. B. (1970), "Regulation of Human Gonadotrophins. VI. Serum Follicle Stimulating and Luteinizing Hormone Determinations in Children," *J. clin. Endocr. Metab.*, **31,** 248–253.
44. Lincoln, E. M. and Spillman, R. (1928), "Studies on the Hearts of Children. II. Roentgen-ray Studies," *Amer. J. Dis. Child.*, **35,** 791–810.
45. Maresh, M. M. (1948), "Growth of the Heart Related to Bodily Growth During Childhood and Adolescence," *Pediatrics*, **2,** 382–404.
46. Maresh, M. M. (1955), "Linear Growth of Long Bones of Extremities from Infancy Through Adolescence," *Amer. J. Dis. Child.*, **89,** 725–742.
47. Marshall, W. A. (1970), "Physical Growth and Development," in *Brennemann's Practice of Pediatrics* (V. C. Kelley, Ed.). University of Washington: Harper and Row.
48. Marshall, W. A. (1973), "Interrelations and Independence of Maturation in Different Systems," *Ann. Hum. Biol.* In press.
49. Marshall, W. A. and Tanner, J. M. (1969), "Variation in the Pattern of Pubertal Changes in Girls," *Arch. Dis. Childh.*, **44,** 291–303.
50. Marshall, W. A. and Tanner, J. M. (1970), "Variation in the Pattern of Pubertal Changes in Boys," *Arch. Dis. Childh.*, **45,** 13–23.
51. Marubini, E., Resele, L. F. and Barghini, G. (1971), "A Comparative Fitting of the Gompertz and Logistic Functions to Longitudinal Height Data During Adolescence in Girls," *Hum. Biol.*, **43,** 237–252.
52. Migeon, C. J., Keller, A. R., Lawrence, B. and Shephard, T. H. (1957), "Dehydroepiandrosterone and Androsterone Levels in Human Plasma. Effect of Age and Sex: Day to Day and Diurnal Variations," *J. clin. Endocr. Metab.*, **17,** 1051–1062.
53. Morris, C. B. (1948), "The Measurement of the Strength of Muscle Relative to the Cross-section," *Res. Quart. Amer. Ass. Hlth.*, **19,** 295–303.
54. Nanda, R. S. (1955), "The Rates of Growth of Several Facial Components Measured from Serial Cephalometric Roentgenograms," *Amer. J. Orthodont.*, **41,** 658–673.
55. Ober, W. and Bernstein, J. (1955), "Observations on the Endometrium and Ovary in the Newborn," *Pediatrics*, **16,** 445–460.
56. Parizkova, J. (1961), "Age Trends in Fat in Normal and Obese Subjects," *J. appl. Physiol.*, **16,** 173–174.
57. Penny, R., Guyda, H., Baghdassarian, A., Johanson, A. and Blizzard, R. M. (1970), "Correlation of Serum Follicular Stimulating Hormone (FSH) and Luteinizing Hormone (LH) as Measured by Radioimmunoassay in Disorders of Sexual Development," *J. clin. Invest.*, **49,** 1847–1852.
58. Prader, A., Hafliger, H., Kind, H. P. and Zachmann, M. (1972), "Testicular Volume—Cross-sectional and Longitudinal Results," *Proc. XIth meeting of Growth Teams*, London, 1972. International Children's Centre.
59. Prader, A., Illig, R., Szeky, J. and Wagner, H. (1964), "The Effect of Human Growth Hormone in Hypopituitary Dwarfism," *Arch. Dis. Childh.*, **39,** 535–544.
60. Raiti, S., Johanson, A., Light, C., Migeon, C. J. and Blizzard, R. M. (1969), "Measurement of Immunologically Reactive Follicle Stimulating Hormone in Serum of Normal Male Children and Adults," *Metabolism*, **18,** 234–240.
61. Raiti, S., Light, C. and Blizzard, R. M. (1969), "Urinary Follicle Stimulating Hormone Excretion in Boys and Adult Males as Measured by Radioimmunoassay," *J. clin. Endocr. Metab.*, **29,** 884–890.
62. Roberts, D. F. (1969), "Race, Genetics and Growth," *J. Biosoc. Sci.*, suppl. 1, 43.
63. Roberts, D. F. and Dann, T. C. (1967), "Influences on Menarcheal Age in Girls in a Welsh College," *Brit. J. Prev. Soc. Med.*, **21,** 170–171.
64. Roche, A. F. (1953), "Increase in Cranial Thickness During Growth," *Hum. Biol.*, **25,** 81–92.
65. Saez, J. M. and Bertrand, J. (1968), "Studies on Testicular Function in Children. Plasma Concentrations of Testosterone, Dehydroepiandrosterone and its Sulfate Before and After Stimulation with Human Chorionic Gonadotrophin," *Steroids*, **12,** 749–761.
66. Saez, J. M. and Movera, A. M. (1973), "Plasma Oestrogens Before Puberty in Humans," *Proc. Europ. Soc. Paed. Endocr. Acta Paed. Scand.*, **62,** 84.
67. Savara, B. S. and Singh, I. J. (1968), "Norms of Size and Annual Increments of Seven Anatomical Measures of the Maxillae in Boys from 3 to 16 Years of Age," *Angle Orthodont.*, **38,** 104–120.
68. Savara, B. S. and Tracy, W. E. (1967), "Norms of Size and Annual Increments for Five Anatomical Measures of the Mandible in Boys from 3 to 16 Years of Age," *Arch. Oral Biol.*, **12,** 469–486.
69. Scammon, R. E. (1930), "The Measurement of the Body in Childhood," in *The Measurement of Man*, J. A. Harris, C. M. Jackson, D. G. Paterson and R. E. Scammon, Eds.). University of Minnesota Press.
70. Schonfield, W. A. and Beebe, G. W. (1942), "Normal Growth and Variation in the Male Genitalia from Birth to Maturity," *J. Urol.*, **48,** 759–777.
71. Shuttleworth, F. K. (1939), "The Physical and Mental Growth of Girls and Boys Aged 6 to 19 in Relation to Age at Maximum Growth," *Monogr. Soc. Res. Child Dev.*, **4,** No. 3.
72. Simon, G., Reid, L., Tanner, J. M., Goldstein, H. and Benjamin, B. (1972), "Growth of Radiologically Determined Heart Diameter, Lung Width, Lung Length from 5–19 Years with Standards for Clinical Use," *Arch. Dis. Childh.*, **47,** 373–381.
73. Singh, I. J., Savara, B. S. and Newman, M. T. (1967), "Growth of the Skeletal and Non-skeletal Components of Head Width from 9–14 Years of Age," *Hum. Biol.*, **39,** 182–191.
74. Sizonenko, P. C., Burr, I. M., Kaplan, S. L. and Grumbach, M. (1970), "Hormonal Changes in Puberty. II. Correlation of Serum Luteinizing Hormone and Follicle Stimulating Hormone with Stages of Puberty and Bone Age in Normal Girls," *Pediat. Res.*, **4,** 36–45.
75. Tanner, J. M. (1962), *Growth at Adolescence*, 2nd edition, 325 pp. Oxford: Blackwell Sci. Publ. and Springfield: Thomas.
76. Tanner, J. M. (1965), "Radiographic Studies of Body Composition," in *Body Composition*, Symposia of the Society for the Study of Human Biology, Vol. 7, p. 211 (J. Brozek, Ed.). Oxford: Pergamon.
77. Tanner, J. M. (1972), "Human Growth Hormone," *Nature*, **237,** 431–437.
78. Tanner, J. M. and Gupta, D. (1968), "A Longitudinal Study of the Excretion of Individual Steroids in Children from 8 to 12 Years," *J. Endocr.*, **4,** 139–156.
79. Tanner, J. M., Whitehouse, R. H., Hughes, P. C. R. and Vince, F. P. (1971), "The Effect of Growth Hormone Treatment for 1–7 Years on Growth of 100 Children, with Growth Hormone Deficiency, Low Birthweight, Inherited Smallness, Turner's

Syndrome and Other Complaints," *Arch. Dis. Childh.*, **46,** 745–782.

80. Tanner, J. M., Whitehouse, R. H. and Takaishi, M. (1966), "Standards from Birth to Maturity for Height, Weight, Height Velocity, and Weight Velocity; British Children, 1965," *Arch. Dis. Childh.*, **41,** 454, 613–635.
81. Teller, W. M. (1967), "Die Ausscheidung von C_{19} und C_{21} steroiden im Harn unter normalen und pathologischen bedingungen der Entwicklung und reifung," *Zeitschrift Experimentelle Med.*, **142,** 222–296.
82. Tisserand-Perrier, M. (1953), "Etudes comparatives de certains processus de croissance chez les jumeaux," *J. Génét. Hum.*, **2,** 87–102.
83. Tracy, W. E. and Savara, B. S. (1966), "Norms of Size and Annual Increments of Five Anatomical Measures of the Mandible in Girls from 3–16 Years of Age," *Arch. Oral Biol.*, **11,** 587–598.
84. Turpin, R., Chassagne, P. and Lefebevre, J. (1939), "La megalothymie prépubertaire. Etude plainigraphique du thymus au cours de la croissance," *Ann. Endocr.*, **1,** 358–378.
85. Valšik, J. A., Stukovsky, R. and Bernatova, L. (1963), "Quelques facteurs géographiques et sociaux ayant une influence sur l'âge de la puberté," *Biotypologie*, **24,** 109–123.
86. Wieland, R. G., Chen, J. C., Zorn, E. M. and Hallberg, M. C. (1971), "Correlation of Growth, Pubertal Staging, Growth Hormone, Gonadotrophins and Testosterone Levels During the pubertal Growth Spurt in Males," *J. Pediat.*, **79,** 999–1001.
87. van Wieringen, J. C., Wafelbakker, F., Verbrugge, H. P. and de Haas, J. H. (1968), *Groediagrammen nederland* 1965. Groningen: Wolterns-Noordhoff. n.v.
88. de Wijn, J. F. (1966), "Estimation of Age at Menarche in a Population," in *Somatic Growth of the Child*, p. 16. (J. J. van der Werff ten Bosch and A. Haak, Eds.). Leiden: Stenfert-Kroese.
89. Wilson, D. C. and Sutherland, I. (1949), "The Age at Menarche," *Brit. med. J.*, **2,** 130–132.
90. Winter, J. S. D. and Faiman, C. (1972a), "Pituitary-gonadal Relations in Male Children and Adolescents," *Pediat. Res.*, **6,** 126–135.
91. Winter, J. S. D. and Faiman, C. (1972b), "Serum Gonadotropin Concentrations in Agonadal Children and Adults," *J. clin. Endocr. Metab.*, **35,** 561–564.
92. Winter, J. S. D., Reyes, F. and Faiman, C. (1972), "Testosterone and Estradiol Concentrations in Human Fetal Gonads and Adrenals," *Proc. Int. Endoc. Congr. Abstr.* 192, Washington, D.C.
93. Winter, J. S. D., Tarasaka, S. and Faiman, C. (1972), "The Hormonal Response to HCG Stimulation in Male Children and Adolescents," *J. clin. Endocr. Metab.*, **34,** 348–353.
94. Yen, S. S. C. and Vicic, W. J. (1969), "Serum Follicle Stimulating Hormone Levels in Puberty," *Amer. J. Obstet. Gynec.*, **105,** 134–137.
95. Yen, S. S. C., Vicic, W. J. and Kearchner, D. V. (1969), "Gonadotropin Levels in Puberty. Serum Luteinizing Hormone," *J. clin. Endocr. Metab.*, **291** 382–385.
96. Young, R. W. (1957), "Post-natal Growth of the Frontal and Parietal Bones in White Males," *Amer. J. phys. Anthrop. N.S.*, **15,** 367–386.
97. Young, R. W. (1959), "Age Changes in the Thickness of the Scalp in White Males," *Hum. Biol.*, **31,** 74–79.
98. Zachmann, M. (1972), "The Evaluation of Testicular Endocrine Function Before and in Puberty," *Acta endocr.*, **70,** suppl. 164.
99. Zachmann, M. and Prader, A. (1970), "Anabolic and Androgenic Effect of Testosterone in Sexually Immature Boys and its Dependency on growth Hormone," *J. clin. Endocr. Metab.*, **30,** 85–93.
100. Zuckerman, S. (1955), "Age Changes in the Basicranial Axis of the Human Skull," *Amer. J. phys. Anthrop. N.S.*, **13,** 521–539.
101. Andersen, E. (1968), *Skeletal Maturation of Danish School Children, in Relation to Height, Sexual Development and Social Conditions.* Universitats forlaget, Aarhus, 1968.
102. Aubenque, M. (1964), "Note documentaire sur la puberté et la taille des filles," *Biotypologie*, **25,** 136–146.
103. Aw, E. and Tye, C. Y. (1970), "Age of Menarche of a Group of Singapore Girls," *Hum. Biol.*, **42,** 329–335.
104. Bottyan, O., Dezsö, C. Y., Eiben, O., Farkas, G. Y., Rajkai, T., Thoma, A. and Veli, G. Y. (1963), "Age at Menarche in Hungarian Girls," *Ann. Hist.-Nat. Mus. Nat. Hung. Pars Anthropol.*, **55,** 561–571.
105. Bouthreuil, E., Niang, I., Michaut, E. and Darr, V. (1972), "Etude préliminaire de la puberté de la fille à Dakar," *Ann. Pediat.*, **19,** 685–690.
106. Brundtland, G. H. and Walløe, L. (1972), "Menarcheal Age in Norway," *Nature*, **241,** 478–479.
107. Burgess, A. P. and Burgess, H. J. L. (1964), "The Growth Pattern of East African Schoolgirls," *Hum. Biol.*, **36,** 177–193.
108. Burrell, R. J. W., Healy, M. J. R. and Tanner, J. M. (1961), "Age at Menarche in South African Bantu Girls Living in the Transkei Reserve," *Hum. Biol.*, **33,** 250–261.
109. Carfagna, M., Figurelli, E., Matarese, G. and Matarese, S. (1972), "Menarcheal Age of Schoolgirls in the District of Naples, Italy, in 1969–70," *Hum. Biol.*, **44,** 117–126.
110. Cristescu, M., Bulai-Stirbu, M. and Feodorovici, C. (1964), "L'influence des facteurs géographiques et sociaux sur le développement des enfants," *Ann. Roumain d'Anthrop.*, **1,** 65–80.
111. Diaz de Mathman, C., Rico, V. M. L. and Galvan, R. R. (1968), "Crecimiento y desarrallo en adolescentes femeninos 2) edad de la menarquia," *Bol. med. Hosp. infant.* (Mex.), **25,** 787–794.
112. Eiben, O. G. (1972), "Genetische und demographische Faktoren und Menarchealter," *Anthrop. Auz.* **33,** 205–212.
113. Farkas, G. (1969), "Untersuchungsergebnisse an Knaben und Mädchen aus Szeged (Südungarn) unter besonderer Berücksichtigung der Reifsmerkmale," *Wissensch. Zeitschr. Humboldt Univ. Berlin Math-Nat.*, **18,** 931–940.
114. Foll, C. V. (1961), "The Age at Menarche in Assam and Burma," *Arch. Dis. Childh.*, **36,** 302–304.
115. Heimendinger, J. (1964), "Die ergebnisse von Körpermessungen am 5000 Basler kindern von 2–18 Jahren," *Helv. Paed. Acta*, **19,** suppl. 13.
116. Hiernaux, J. (1965), "La croissance des écoliers Rwandais," *Proc. Acad. Sci. Outre-Mer, Brussels*, **16,** no. 2.
117. Jeurissen, A. (1969), "L'âge au moment des premières règles et son évolution en Belgique au cours des quarante dernières années," *Acta paediat. belg.*, **23,** 319–330.
118. Kantero, R. L. and Widholm, O. (1971), "II. The Age of Menarche in Finnish Girls in 1969," *Acta obstet. et gynec. scand.*, suppl. 14, 7.
119. Koshi, E. P., Brasad, B. G. and Bhushan, V. (1971), "A Study of the Menstrual Pattern of School Girls in an Urban Area," *Indian J. med. Res.*, **58,** 1647–1652.
120. Laska-Mierzejewska, T. (1970a), "Effect of Ecological and Socio-economic Factors on the Age at Menarche, Body Height and Weight of Rural Girls in Poland," *Hum. Biol.*, **42,** 284–292.
121. Laska-Mierzejewska, T. (1970b), "Morphological and Developmental Difference Between Negro and White Cuban Youths," *Hum. Biol.*, **42,** 581–597.
122. Lee, M. M. C., Chang, K. S. F. and Chan, M. M. C. (1963), "Sexual Maturation of Chinese Girls in Hong Kong," *Pediatrics*, **42,** 389–398.
123. Madhavan, S. (1965), "Age of Menarche of South Indian Girls Belonging to the States of Madras and Kerala," *Indian J. med. Res.*, **53,** 669–673.
124. Malcolm, L. A. (1969), "Growth and Development of the Kaipit Children of the Markham Valley, New Guinea," *Amer. J. phys. Anthrop.*, **31,** 39–51.
125. Marubini, E. and Barghini, G. (1969), "Richerche sull'età media di comparsa della pubertà nella popolazione scolare femminile di Cararra," *Minerva pediat.*, **21,** 281–285.
126. Milicer, H. (1968), "Age at Menarche of Girls in Wroclaw, Poland in 1966," *Hum. Biol.*, **40,** 249–259.
127. Milicer, H. and Szczotka, F. (1966), "The Age at Menarche in Warsaw Girls in 1965," *Hum. Biol.*, **38,** 199–203.
128. Neyzi, O., Yalcindag, A. and Alp, H. (1970), "Skeletal Maturation of the Normal Turkish Child in the Preadolescent and Adolescent Years," *Proc. of Xth Reunion of Growth Study Teams of International Children's Centre*, Davos, 1970.

129. Provis, H. S. and Ellis, R. W. B. (1955), "An Anthropometric Study of Edinburgh Schoolchildren. Part I, Methods, Data and Assessment of Maturity," *Arch. Dis. Childh.*, **30**, 328–337.

130. Sabharwal, K. P., Morales, S. and Mendez, J. (1966), "Body Measurements and Creatinine Excretion Among Upper and Lower Socio-economic Groups of Girls in Guatamala," *Hum. Biol.*, **38**, 131–140.

131. Scott, J. A. (1961), "Report on the Heights and Weights (and Other Measurements) of School Pupils in the County of London in 1959," London County Council.

132. Shakir, A. (1971), "The Age at Menarche in Girls Attending Schools in Baghdad," *Hum. Biol.*, **43**, 265–270.

133. Shiloh, A. (1960), "A Study of Menarche Among Jerusalem School Girls," *J. Israel Med. Assoc.*, **54**, 305–307.

134. Shiloh, A. and Goldberg, R. (1965), "A Study of the Menarche Among Tel Aviv School Girls," *J. Israel Med. Assoc.*, **68**, 161–163.

135. Tanner, J. M. and Carter, B. S. (1974), "The Age of Menarche in London Schoolgirls, 1966," *Ann. Hum. Biol.* In press.

136. Tanner, J. M. and O'Keefe, B. (1962), "Age at Menarche in Nigerian Schoolgirls, with a Note on their Heights and Weights from Age Twelve to Nineteen," *Hum. Biol.*, **34**, 187–196.

137. Thoma, A. (1960), "Age at Menarche, Acceleration and Heritability," *Acta biologica Acad. Sci. Hungaria*, **11**, 241–254.

138. Towns, J., Johnson, J. M. and Roche, A. F. (1966), "The Age of Menarche in Melbourne Schoolgirls," *Austr. Paed. J.*, **2**, 67–69.

139. Valsik, J. A., Strouhal, E., Hussien, F. H. and El-Nofely, A. (1970), "Biology of Man in Egyptian Nubia," *Mat. Prace Antropologicze*, **78**, 93–98.

140. Valsik, J. A., Stukowsky, R. and Paruk, A. (1972), "Die Geschlectsreife der Mädchen von Kascau (Kosice)," *Acta fac. rev. mat. Univ. Comen Anthropol.*, **20**, 149–160.

141. Vlastovsky, V. G. (1966), "The Secular Trend in the Growth and Development of Children and Young Persons in the Soviet Union," *Hum. Biol.*, **38**, 219–230.

142. Wadsworth, G. R. and Eurani, A. R. (1970), "Heights and Weights of Adolescent Girls in a City in Northern Iran," *J. trop. Med.* (*Hyg.*), **73**, 172–173.

143. van Wieringen, J. C., Wafelbakker, F., Verbrugge, H. P. and de Haas, J. H. (1971), *Growth Diagrams* 1965, *Nederlands*, Netherlands Inst. Prevent. Medicine, 68 pp.

144. Wilson, D. C. and Sutherland, I. (1950), "Age at Menarche," *Brit. med. J.*, **2**, 862–866.

145. Wilson, D. C. and Sutherland, I. (1953), "The Age of the Menarche in the Tropics," *Brit. med. J.*, **2**, 607–608.

146. Wofinden, R. C. and Smallwood, A. L. (1958), "School Health Service," Annual Report of the Principal School Medical Officer to City and County of Bristol Education Committee, Bristol.

147. Zacharias, L., Wurtman, R. J. and Schatzoff, M. (1970), "Sexual Maturation in Contemporary American Girls," *Amer. J. Obstet. Gynec.*, **108**, 833–846.

148. Zivanovic, S. and Adasevic-Frolov, V., (1964), "Prilog proncavanju fizicko-pubertetnog razvoja ucenica osnovnih skola u Zemenu," *Rev. Soc. Anthrop. Yougoslave*, **1**, 75–79.

149. Rona, R. and Pereiva, G. (1973), "Genetic Factors that Influence Age of Menarche in Girls in Santiago, Chile," *Human Biology*, **45**, in press.

SECTION III

GROWTH AND DEVELOPMENT OF SYSTEMS

12. CHANGES IN BODY PROPORTIONS AND COMPOSITION DURING GROWTH

ELSIE M. WIDDOWSON

Growth, although such a commonplace affair, is a highly complex process, but at the same time it takes place in a completely orderly fashion. The word growth means different things to different people. To parents it implies the increase in height and weight of their child. To the embryologist and anatomist it involves differentiation and change of shape, to the physiologist the development of function, and to the biochemist the assembly and interaction of all the organic and inorganic components of the body. It is the purpose of this chapter to describe briefly some of the actions and interactions that go on from the time the human ovum is fertilized to the achievement of the size and stature of the full grown man or woman.

GROWTH AND COMPOSITION OF THE FETUS

The initial division of the fertilized ovum is not preceded by any increase in its size, and this is true also for a few further divisions, so that each cell becomes progressively smaller, and there is no increase in total size. By the time the blastocyst has become implanted in the wall of the uterus, however, about the 9th day after fertilization, synthesis of proteins from the amino acids, and the water and inorganic substances that reach it, begin to enlarge the cells before they divide. There is an alteration, too, in the timing of the divisions. The first few occur almost simultaneously, but after a few days cell division becomes staggered so that only a few cells are dividing at the same time.

The immature organism is characterized by the large percentage of extracellular fluid within it. When the ovum is fertilized, however, and for the first few generations of division, the new organism is entirely cellular, so there must come a time in early development when extracellular fluid becomes part of it. It seems likely that this happens at the time of implantation, for at this stage fluid passes from the uterine cavity through the outer cells, which act as a dialysing membrane, into the intercellular spaces between the centrally placed inner cell mass and the outer cells. This is probably an essential step, before growth of cells becomes possible, because nutrients can only reach a cell through the extracellular fluid. In the early embryo the material between the cells is amorphous, but later viscous substances are synthesized within it, particularly hyaluronic acid and chondroitin sulphate, which make it gel-like and able to hold a large amount of water.

There is an upper limit to the size a cell can attain. This is partly because as it grows its volume increases with the cube of the radius but its surface area with the square. The volume determines its biochemical activity, but the materials necessary for this activity must pass in through the surface membrane. Further, as the cell increases in size the ratio between cytoplasm and nucleus increases, and there is again an upper limit to the amount of cytoplasm that the nucleus can control.

In the first two or three weeks of human development inside the uterus growth takes place entirely by cell division, without any increase in the average size of the cell. Differentiation, however, soon begins and as the organs and tissues appear, each develops its own characteristic kind of cells, its own relation between cells and intercellular material, and its own contribution to the weight of the organism as a whole. With differentiation comes a slowing down of cell division and as this occurs the average size of the cells begins to increase. This is accompanied by a progressive increase in the proportion of the organ occupied by cells and a decrease in the percentage of extracellular fluid. This process goes on after birth as well as before. Each organ has its own pattern of chemical development which will be described in more detail later in this chapter.

At the same time as these changes are taking place in the cellular organs there are changes going on in the organs arising from connective tissue—the skeleton, the skin, and the adipose tissue. Towards the end of the first month of fetal life the primitive connective tissue cells in the region of the skeleton become more closely packed. Then they lay down a matrix between them—the developing cartilage—with collagen and chondroitin sulphate making up 80 per cent of the solid matter. During the second month of fetal life this cartilaginous framework begins to ossify, and this involves the deposition of bone mineral in it. Before this time there is very little calcium in the fetal body, but from the 8th week onwards the amount increases more and more rapidly as the bones grow in size and their degree of calcification increases. The growth of the skeleton is important in determining the size and shape of the body.

In the early stages of gestation the developing organism lays down no fat apart from the essential lipids in the nervous system and phospholipids in the cell walls. For the first half of gestation the fetus has no more than 0·5 per cent of fat, but then white fat begins to be deposited in connective tissue cells under the skin and in the omenta. Brown adipose tissue accumulates round the neck and between the scapulae. By 28 weeks the fetus has about 3·5 per cent of fat in its body, at 34 weeks 7·5 per cent and a full-term baby weighing 3·5 kg. has about 16 per cent.

One of the characteristics of mammalian development is a fall in the percentage of water in the fat-free body tissue. The smallest human fetuses that have been analysed weighed less than a gram, and they contained 93–95 per cent water so they were more "dilute" than normal adult plasma. The percentage of water falls to about 88 per cent by the time the fetus weighs 200 g. and continues to fall until at term water accounts for 82 per cent of the fat-free weight. The value for the adult is 72 per cent, so the baby still has quite a long way to go before it reaches mature chemical composition. When fat is being deposited rapidly in the body the percentage of water in the whole body shows a corresponding fall, and this accounts for some of the fall in the percentage of water during the last part of gestation. On a whole body basis the average baby has about 69 per cent of water in its body at the time of a full-term birth.

Table 1 shows the amounts of water, fat, nitrogen and minerals per kilogram of whole body or fat-free body tissue of the human fetus while it grows from 30 g. at about 13 weeks gestation to 3,500 g. at term. The cellular constituents, nitrogen and potassium, rise and chloride falls in parallel with the changing relationships of the intra- and extracellular fluid. Sodium falls much less than chloride because, although in early fetal development nearly all the sodium in the body is in the extracellular fluid, from the seventh month of gestation onwards the fall in extracellular sodium is just about counter-balanced by the increase in the amount of sodium being deposited in the skeleton.

The youngest fetuses that have been analysed contained about 1 g. calcium per kg. The concentration increases rapidly at first and then more slowly to term, when the value is about 10 g./kg. fat-free body tissue. This is to be compared with 22 g./kg. fat-free tissue in the adult. The concentration of phosphorus also increases during fetal life and at term the value is about half that in the adult. The calcium in the body is confined almost entirely to the skeleton, but phosphorus is the main anion of cells as well as being an important constituent of bone. It is generally agreed that ossification of the cartilagenous model of the skeleton starts at about the eighth week of gestation. Before this time there is probably less calcium than phosphorus, but no analyses have been made. At about 13 weeks the amounts of calcium and phosphorus are approximately equal, but as the fetus grows the skeleton becomes more and more highly calcified, so that the proportion of calcium in the body increases more rapidly than that of phosphorus. The Ca/P ratio at term is between 1·7 and 1·8. In the full term baby 98 per cent of the calcium, about 80 per cent of the phosphorus and 60 per cent of the magnesium in the body are in the bones.

While the composition of the body per unit weight is changing the body itself is growing, and the increments of nitrogen and minerals at each stage of development are partly the result of changing chemical composition and partly of increasing size. In some instances one, and in some the other is more important. Table 2 shows the total amounts of water, fat, nitrogen and minerals in the body at the same stages of development as those given in Table 1. Increase in size accounts for most of the increment of nitrogen and potassium, but alteration in composition requires more calcium and phosphorus than growth in size.

TABLE 1

CHEMICAL COMPOSITION OF THE BODY OF THE DEVELOPING FETUS

Body Weight (g.)	*Approx. Fetal Age* (*Weeks*)	*Per Kg. Whole Body*		*Per Kg. Fat-free Body Tisues*										
		Water (g.)	*Fat* (g.)	*Water* (g.)	N (g.)	Ca (g.)	P (g.)	Mg (g.)	Na (meq.)	K (meq.)	Cl (meq.)	Fe (mg.)	Cu (mg.)	Zn (mg.)
30	13	900	5	906	10	3·0	2·0	0·10	20	40	81	—	—	—
100	15	890	5	894	10	3·0	2·0	0·10	100	40	70	50	—	—
200	17	885	5	889	14	4·0	3·0	0·15	100	40	70	50	3·5	18
500	23	880	6	885	14	4·4	3·0	0·20	100	44	66	56	3·5	18
1,000	26	860	10	869	14	6·1	3·4	0·22	90	44	66	65	3·5	18
1,500	31	847	23	867	17	6·8	3·8	0·24	85	44	66	68	3·8	18
2,000	33	810	50	853	20	7·9	4·3	0·24	85	44	63	84	4·2	18
2,500	35	776	74	838	21	9·0	4·8	0·25	85	48	56	95	4·3	18
3,000	38	727	120	826	21	9·5	5·3	0·27	90	49	55	95	4·5	18
3,500	40	686	160	816	21	10·2	5·8	0·27	95	51	54	95	4·8	18

GROWTH AND COMPOSITION AFTER BIRTH

There is virtually no direct analytical evidence about the changes in chemical composition of the whole body of the child after birth. A variety of indirect methods have been applied to living children of different ages. Some measure the fat, others measure a constituent of the lean body tissue, in particular water or potassium.

Determination of body fat

The density if body fat is less than that of other components of the body and therefore the greater the amount

TABLE 2

TOTAL AMOUNTS OF WATER, FAT, NITROGEN AND MINERALS IN THE BODY OF THE DEVELOPING FETUS[36]

Body Weight (g.)	*Approx. Fetal Age* (*Weeks*)	*Water* (g.)	*Fat* (g.)	N (g.)	Ca (g.)	P (g.)	Mg (g.)	Na (meq.)	K (meq.)	Cl (meq.)	Fe (mg.)	Cu (mg.)	Zn (mg.)
30	13	27	0·2	0·4	0·09	0·09	0·003	3·6	1·4	2·4	—	—	—
100	15	89	0·5	1·0	0·3	0·2	0·01	9·0	2·6	7·0	5·1	—	—
200	17	177	1·0	2·8	0·7	0·6	0·03	20	7·9	14	10·0	0·7	2·6
500	23	440	3·0	7·0	2·2	1·5	0·10	49	22	33	28	2·4	9·4
1,000	26	860	10·0	14·0	6·0	3·4	0·22	90	41	66	64	3·5	16·0
1,500	31	1,270	35	25·0	10·0	5·6	0·35	125	60	96	100	5·6	25·0
2,000	33	1,620	100	37·0	15·0	8·2	0·46	160	84	120	160	8·0	35·0
2,500	35	1,940	185	49·0	20·0	11·0	0·58	200	110	130	220	10·0	43·0
3,000	38	2,180	360	55·0	25·0	14·0	0·70	240	130	150	260	12·0	50·0
3,500	40	2,400	560	62·0	30·0	17·0	0·78	280	150	160	280	14·0	53·0

of fat the lower will be the density of the whole body. The density of the body, as of any other object, is the weight in air divided by the volume. The volume of the body is determined from the volume, or weight of water it displaces, and this is measured as the difference between the weight in air and the weight completely submerged in water. The weight under water is measured by suspending the subject from a spring balance in a tank of water while sitting or lying in a frame of known weight and density. The weight recorded must be corrected for residual air in the lungs. For this the subject breathes out as much air as he can from his lungs before he is immersed, and as soon as he surfaces afterwards he breathes from a bag containing oxygen, and the dilution of the oxygen with N_2 and CO_2 is determined. The formula generally used for calculating fat from density is that of Siri.[34] $\% \text{ fat} = \left(\frac{4{\cdot}95}{\text{density}} - 4{\cdot}5\right)$. This method has serious limitations. It can only be applied to co-operative subjects who are not frightened by submersion, which in practice usually means that they are good swimmers. It is therefore useless for young children, but has been applied to older ones. Durnin and Rahaman[10] studied 48 adolescent boys and 38 adolescent girls in this way and found mean densities of 1·0625 and 1·0445, corresponding to mean percentages of body fat of 15·9 and 24·0 for boys and girls respectively.

An anthropological approach to the determination of body fat has been to measure the skinfold thickness with standard calipers at a number of specified sites. Many types of caliper have been designed in different countries, the ones most usually used in Britain are the Harpenden Skinfold Calipers (British Indicators Ltd., St. Albans, Herts.). Durnin and Rahaman[10] devised regression equations to calculate body fat from skinfold measurements at 4 sites—over the biceps and triceps, just below the scapula and just above the iliac crest. The regression equations predicted body density (Y) from the log of the sum of the four skinfold measurements measured in mm. (X).

$$\text{Adolescent boys } Y = 1{\cdot}533 - 0.0643\, X$$
$$\text{Adolescent girls } Y = 1{\cdot}1369 - 0{\cdot}0598\, X$$

Others have used different equations to relate skinfold thickness to body density in younger children.[4,15,24,31]

Fat can also be calculated as the difference between lean body mass and total body weight. Cheek, Mellits and Elliott[7] give linear regression equations relating height and weight on the one hand and the total body water, measured by the volume of distribution of D_2O, on the other. Table 3

TABLE 3

PERCENTAGE OF FAT IN THE BODIES OF BOYS AND GIRLS (PERCENTILE)

Age (*years*)	*Boys*			*Girls*		
	10*th*	50*th*	90*th*	10*th*	50*th*	90*th*
5	8·8	12·5	16·0	8·3	15·3	24·4
6	9·0	12·7	16·6	8·5	14·0	20·4
7	10·4	14·0	18·3	9·5	14·0	20·3
8	11·7	16·1	21·4	9·6	14·7	21·6
9	12·0	16·9	23·0	10·0	15·4	23·6
10	11·6	17·6	22·8	10·0	16·0	23·8
11	10·4	16·9	22·2	11·7	18·8	25·8
12	8·5	14·9	20·7	13·3	19·5	25·9
13	6·9	12·6	20·0	15·6	22·0	27·5
14	5·8	11·4	17·9	17·5	23·1	28·6
15	6·8	11·4	18·1	18·3	23·3	28·9
16	5·8	11·8	18·3	19·6	23·8	28·7
17	—	12·3	—	—	24·6	

shows values obtained by Rauh and Schumsky[33] for the percentage of fat in the bodies of 4,158 boys and 4,280 girls, between the ages of 5 and 17 years, calculated according to this equation. Tenth, 50th and 90th percentiles are shown at each age. In the boys there was an increase in the percentage of fat between 5 and 10 years, and this was followed by a decrease to 17 years. In the girls the percentage did not change appreciably between 5 and 10 years, but then it rose so that from 13 years onwards the girls had twice as high a percentage of fat in their bodies as the boys. These 50th percentile figures for boys, and for girls over 11 are close to Pařisková's mean values calculated from densitometric measurements. For girls 8–11 years she obtained values of about 20%.

We have less information on the amount of fat in the bodies of younger children.

The mean is about 16 per cent. Fomon[12] has set out some values for the composition of the "male reference infant" during the first year after birth; he suggests that at 2 months the percentage of fat is 22, and from 3–12 months the percentage of fat remains at about 24.

If these two sets of values are comparable there must be a fall in the percentage of fat in the body over the next 4 years, but this seems reasonable and indeed any measurements that have been made confirm that this is so.

MEASUREMENT OF LEAN BODY MASS AND ITS COMPONENT PARTS

Total body water

Various solutes have been used for the determination of total body water by dilution techniques—antipyrene, urea, alcohol, and tritium and deuterium oxides. Fig. 1 shows the values obtained by Edelman, Haley, Schloerb, Sheldon, Friis-Hansen, Stoll and Moore[11] for the percentage of water in the bodies of children between 2 days and 8½ years. Deuterium oxide was used for the dilution studies. The range of values obtained by the same investigators in 34 normal men 17–34 years of age is also shown in the Figure. The fall in the proportion of water which takes place during gestation (Table 1) continues for the first month or so of postnatal life, but by the time the child weighs 7–8 kg. its body appears to have reached the water—solid relationships characteristic of the adult. Similar results were obtained by Friis-Hansen,[17] Owen, Jensen and Fomon[30] and Hanna.[21] Owen, Filer, Maresh and Fomon[29] have added the information that there is a sex difference in the percentage of water in the body by 4–7 months of age. From this age onwards boys have more water than girls.

Extracellular and intracellular water

Figure 2 shows the changes in the proportion of extracellular fluid in the human body during growth, as measured by the volume of distribution of thiosulphate.[17] Extracellular fluid accounts for approximately 45 per cent of the weight of the full-term baby, or 65 per cent of the body water. The proportion falls steeply during the first two months after birth, to 30 per cent of the body weight at 4–5 kg. The fall in the percentage of extracellular fluid is greater than the fall in total body water because there is a simultaneous rise in intracellular water. The proportion of extracellular water continues to fall for much longer than does total water and it is still well above the adult value of 16 per cent at a weight of 25–30 kg. Friis-Hansen's[17] values for the percentage of intracellular fluid, calculated as the difference between the deuterium oxide and thiosulphate spaces, showed an increase from 35 per cent of the body weight at birth to 47 per cent at 7–16 years.

The amount of K in the body measured by scintillation counting of gamma ray emission of ^{40}K

The whole body counter consists of a chamber shielded usually by 4–8 inches of steel against environmental or background radiation. The gamma rays emitted by the body are detected by scintillators. There are of two types—the sodium iodide crystal detector and the liquid or plastic scintillation detector. The main advantage of the first is its high energy resolution and of the second that it costs less. Descriptions of the apparatus and method have been given by Anderson[1] and Miller, Remenchik and Kessler.[25] A small whole body counter for use with young children was devised and used by Garrow.[18]

This method of analysing the living body has been applied to large numbers of children.[6,13,14,16,27,28] During the first 6 months there is a fall in the concentration of potassium in the body due to the increasing percentage of fat, but this is followed by a rise.[23] From the age of 5 years upwards boys of a given weight have more potassium in their bodies than girls. This is attributed to the larger amount of muscle in the boys and the larger amount of fat in the girls.

Values for the amount of potassium in the body have been used to calculate the lean body mass. The validity of this depends upon a constant concentration of potassium in the lean body mass, but this is open to question, and it is generally agreed that the variation in potassium is greater than the variation in the percentage of water. The concentration of potassium in the lean body mass depends upon the extracellular-intracellular relationships within the body, and also in the contributions of the organs and tissues, each with its own particular composition, to the total body weight. The concentration of potassium in adult skeletal muscle for example is between 90 and 100, and in the skin between 20 and 25 meq./kg.,[41] but the value varies from one muscle and one part of the skin to another. The values for the internal organs resemble those for muscle, and for the skeleton those for the skin. Variations in the relative proportions of the three major tissues, muscles, skin and skeleton, clearly alter the concentration of potassium in the lean body mass, quite apart from the fact that in young children there is a larger proportion of extracellular fluid in the lean body mass than in older children and adults. Garrow, Fletcher and Halliday[19] give values for potassium per kg. of fat-free body weight, which rises from 51 meq./kg. at birth to 58 at 1 year, 65 at 4 years and 72 in the adult. It is wiser not to assume a constant relationship between K and lean body mass, but to consider the values for body K as an end in themselves.

CHEMICAL DEVELOPMENT OF THE MAJOR ORGANS

The body is made up of many different organs and tissues and the composition of the whole body depends upon the composition and relative weight of all its component parts. Both of these change with age. Table 4 shows the contribution of some of the organs and tissues to the human body at three different stages of development—the 20 weeks fetus, the full-term baby and the adult. Some, for example skeletal muscle, increase as a percentage of body weight. Others, like the brain, decrease. The composition of all organs and tissues changes with age, but they all change at different rates, and chemical development of the body as a whole is a complicated process, made up as it is

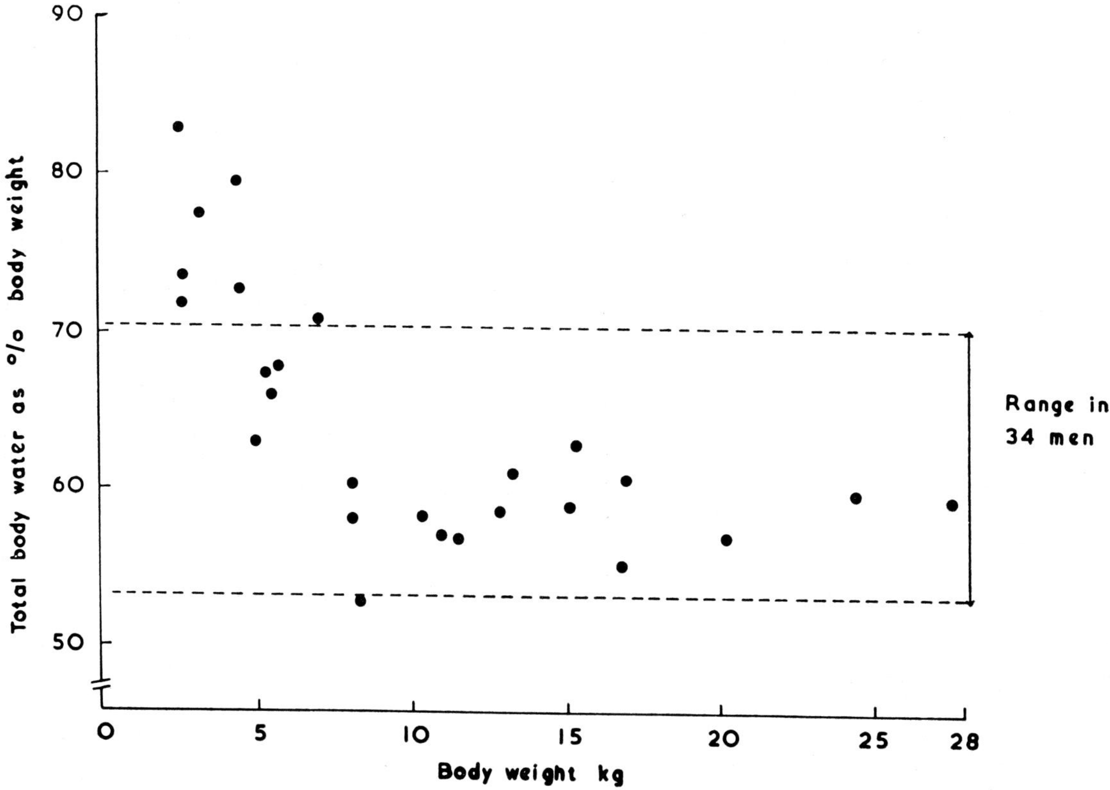

FIG. 1. Effect of postnatal development on the percentage of total water in the human body as measured by deuterium oxide dilution.[41]

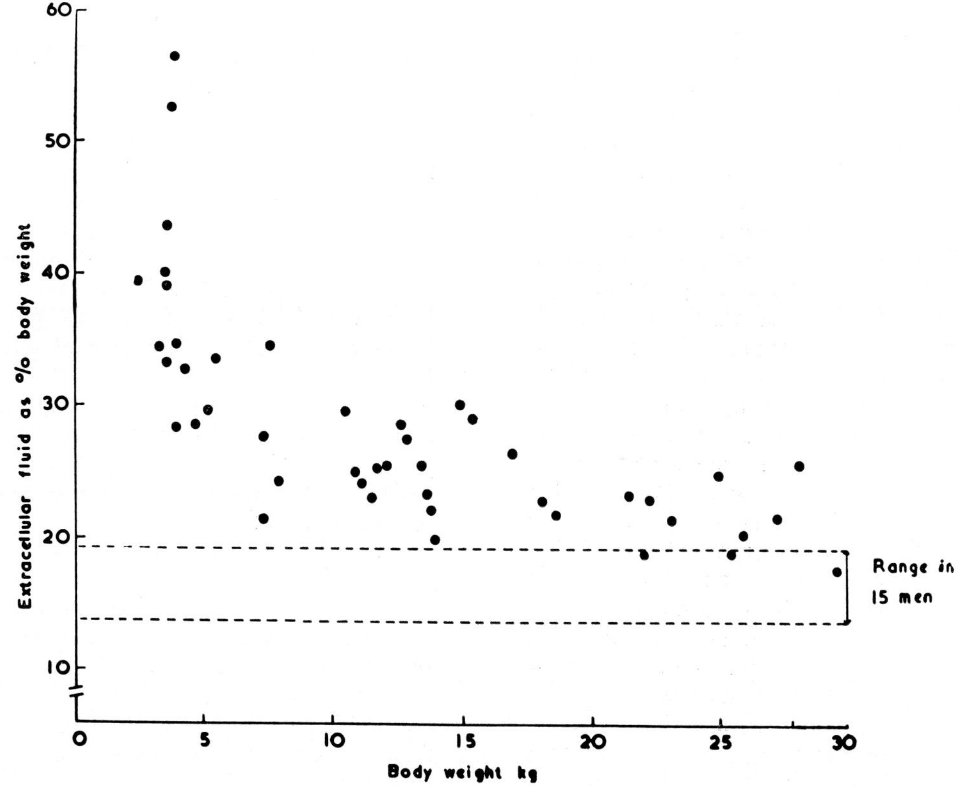

FIG. 2. Effect of postnatal development on the percentage of extracellular fluid in the human body.[41]

TABLE 4

CONTRIBUTION OF ORGANS AND TISSUES TO BODY WEIGHT AT VARIOUS AGES (% BODY WEIGHT)

	Fetus 20–24 *weeks*	*Full term newborn*	*Adult*
Skeletal muscle	25·0	25·0	40·0
Skin	13·0	4·0	6·0
Skeleton	22·0	18·0	14·0
Heart	0·6	0·5	0·4
Liver	4·0	5·0	2·0
Kidneys	0·7	1·0	0·5
Brain	13·0	12·0	2·0

of the changing weights and compositions of all its component parts. Those that make most difference to the composition of the whole body are the large organs, muscle, skin, skeleton and adipose tissue, and of the organs liver and brain. The first five of these will be considered here. The composition of the brain forms the subject of a separate account.[9]

Skeletal muscle

From the point of view of the composition of the body skeletal muscle is quantitatively the most important soft tissue; it accounts for 25 per cent of the weight of the full-term baby and 40 per cent of the weight of a man. Its composition, moreover, changes more during the latter part of fetal, and during post natal life, than that of many other soft tissues. The fundamental change that takes place in muscle, as in other tissues, during development is increase first in number, and then in the size of the cells or fibres. Muscle fibres originate from myoblasts, which are long narrow cells with many nuclei. These fuse to form myotubes with centrally situated nuclei which are large in proportion to the diameter of the cell. The spaces between the myotubes are filled with the ground substance of the extracellular phase, which has fibroblasts and fine reticulin fibres within it. These myotubes, become arranged in bundles. There is little growth at first in the diameter of the fibres and the nuclei are still relatively large, although they have now migrated to the periphery of the fibres and they lie immediately under the sarcolemma. As the fibres grow in length and diameter the extracellular fluid comes to form a smaller and smaller percentage of the muscle mass, falling from 67 per cent at 14 weeks gestation to 35 per cent at term, and 18 per cent in the adult. At the same time the percentages of protein and of intracellular cation potassium increase. Table 5 sets out some information about the chemical composition of the skeletal muscle at various ages, which illustrates these points. In no respect has skeletal muscle reached its mature chemical composition at the time of a full-term birth. The extracellular proteins form the sheaths round the muscle fibres, the bundles of fibres, and whole muscles, and, broadly speaking the percentage of extracellular proteins, collagen and elastin, increase when the fibres are increasing in number, and decrease when they are increasing in size.

TABLE 5

COMPOSITION OF SKELETAL MUSCLE (PER 100 g.)[36,41]

Constituent	*Fetus*		*Baby*		*Adult*
	13–14 *weeks*	20–22 *weeks*	*Full term newborn*	4–7 *months*	
Water (g.)	91	89	80	79	79·0
Protein (g.)	6·2	8·0	12·6	16·7	17·4
DNA (mg.)	490	347	130	93	74
Protein (mg.) / DNA (mg.)	12·7	23·0	96·5	180	235
Extracellular protein (g.)	0·4	1·0	2·2	2·6	0·8
Na (meq.)	10·1	9·1	6·0	5·0	3·6
K (meq.)	5·6	5·8	5·8	9·0	9·2
Cl (meq.)	7·6	6·6	4·3	3·6	2·2
P (mg.)	113	124	205	205	182
Mg (mg.)	14·0	13·0	18·0	24·0	20·0
Ca (mg.)	11·0	14·0	8·0	6·0	5·0

The percentage of intracellular proteins increases throughout.

The idea was first put forward at the end of the last century that the full number of muscle fibres found in adult sartorius muscle was already present in the fetus of 5 months gestation.[22] Montgomery[26] put the age a little later when full fibre number is attained—at or soon after full-term birth—but it seems that the number of fibres does not increase once differentation is complete.[20] Subsequent growth is believed to be due entirely to hypertrophy of existing fibres. The total number of fibres that a particular muscle receives is determined genetically, but the size of the fibres is determined by the environmental conditions to which the muscle is subjected. It was also believed for a long time that once the myoblasts had fused to form myotubes there was no further mitosis or increase in number of nuclei in a muscle fibre, so that the number in the myotube determined the number of nuclei in the fibre right on into adult life. Those concerned with the structure of muscle have been puzzled, however, as to how the comparatively few nuclei that exist in mammalian fetal muscle are sufficient for the bulk of muscle in the adult, and it is now certain that there is an increase in the sarcolemmal nuclei throughout muscle growth in man. This has been confirmed by both histological and biochemical techniques, the latter based on the amount of DNA in the muscles. At first it was thought that the number of nuclei increased by mitotic division within the fibres, but it has more recently been shown that the increase in number of nuclei is due to the incorporation of nucleated satellite cells into the muscle fibre.

Cheek[6] has used DNA as an index of muscle development in man. He obviously could not obtain weights of individual muscles of living children, so he determined the concentration of DNA in biopsy samples of gluteal muscles, assumed that this was representative of all the muscles of the body and calculated from this value the amount of DNA in the whole muscle mass. He estimated the muscle mass from the creatinine excretion, using a figure of 1 g. of creatinine excreted in 24 hr. as equivalent to 20 kg. of muscle. His results on 33 boys and 19 girls suggested that there was an increase in the number of muscle nuclei right through human childhood, and that in the boy there is a "spurt" in the rate of increase of nuclei at the time of puberty, so that between 10 and 16 years the number of nuclei doubles. There is a 14-fold increase in the number of muscle nuclei during growth after birth. In the girl there is also an increase, but a smaller one. Cheek used the ratio mg. protein: mg. DNA as a measure of the relationship between the cytoplasm and nucleus, and showed that in the girl this value reached a stable level at 10½ years whereas the value for boys was still increasing at 16 years. More recently Widdowson, Crabb and Milner[39] have analysed gastrocnemius muscles of 56 human fetuses of various ages to term for protein and DNA. Figure 3 shows the combined results of Widdowson et al. and of Cheek for the protein: DNA ratio of human skeletal muscle in the 6 months before and the 6 months after full-term. In spite of the fact that the gastrocnemius muscle was studied before birth and the gluteal muscle after, the values fit in with each other, and suggest that the rapid rise in the ratio during the last 10 weeks of intrauterine life continued at a similar rapid rate during the 6 months after birth.

Table 6

COMPOSITION OF SKIN[40]

Constituents	Fetus		Baby		Adult
	13–14 weeks	*20–22 weeks*	*Full term newborn*	*4–7 months*	
Water (g.)	92	90	83	68	69
Total N. (g.)	1·2	1·2	2·3	5·5	5·3
Callagen N. (g.)	—	0·2	1·7	3·9	4·6
Na (meq.)	—	12·0	8·7	6·5	7·9
K (meq.)	2·4	3·6	4·5	4.4	2·4
Cl (meq.)	9·1	9·6	6·7	7.2	7·1
P (mg.)	130	87	98	108	43
Mg (mg.)	—	4·6	5·6	8·9	3·7
Ca (mg.)	8·8	12·2	20·0	22.8	19·0

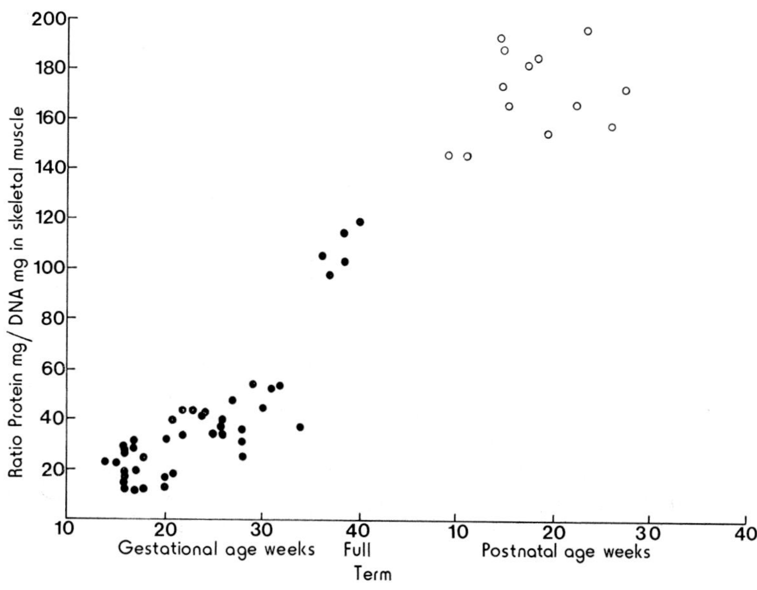

Fig. 3. Ratio $\frac{\text{Protein}}{\text{DNA}}$ in skeletal muscle before and after birth.
● Widdowson, Crabb & Milner, 1972;[39] ○ Cheek, 1968.[6]

The skin

The skin of the fetus is remarkably thin, but it remains healthy even though it is submerged in an isotonic solution, mainly of sodium chloride, the amniotic fluid. Only after birth does it begin to thicken and lay down much collagen.

Table 6 shows some values for the composition of human skin taken from the abdomen or thigh at various ages[40]. The percentage of water falls during development of skin, as it does in skeletal muscle. This is due to an increase in the percentage of protein, which is mainly being deposited as collagen in the corium. The skin of the immature fetus contains 90 per cent of water. A small amount of this is cellular but most is bound by the mucopolysaccharides and non-fibrous proteins of the extracellular phase, and this gives the skin an oedematous appearance. At 3 months gestation the concentration of glycosaminoglycans was found to be 20 times the adult value; at 5½ months it was 5 times and at full-term twice the adult level.[3] The amount of collagen in skin at this age is small and in fact there are no mature collagen fibres at 20 weeks gestation, but a fine interlacing network of reticulin fibres in which the cells are embedded.

The skin of the newborn baby contains fewer cells, loosely scattered in the corium, but mature glands are present and the epidermis has also matured. The glands and epidermis together probably contribute to the increase in the concentration of potassium during the latter part of gestation. At full term the corium is loosely packed with collagen fibres. The skin at term makes up 4 per cent of the body weight.

The thickness of the skin increases during postnatal growth, and there is a big increase in the percentage of collagen. Although the surface area is much smaller in relation to body weight in adult man than in the newborn baby, his skin contributes more, about 6 per cent, to his body weight.

At all ages over two thirds of the water in human skin is accounted for by extracellular fluid. The distribution of this water changes with development, for the proportion of it associated with collagen fibres increases along with the increase in collagen, whereas the proportion of interstitial water falls. The percentage of the total water inside the cells rises to a maximum at the time of birth, and falls to a lower level afterwards.

The skeleton

Bone is a specialized form of connective tissue and it contains cells and a matrix consisting of the same kind of substances, mucopolysaccharides, collagen fibres, and extracellular water as those of the connective tissue of skin, but differs from skin in its characteristic hardness, due to the deposition of crystals of bone mineral within the matrix. As ossification takes place the percentage of water in the bone falls. The matrix of the future skeleton is differentiated during the first month of foetal life, and in the second month bone formation begins. A few bones, such as the clavicle and vault of the skull, ossify directly in the connective tissue, or are ossified in membrane. In most bones, however, collagen is laid down in the connective tissue to form cartilage and this forms a template on which the bone mineral is deposited. The cartilaginous model continues to grow by deposition of more cartilage on its surface and this quickly becomes ossified, but the formation of matrix must of necessity always be a little ahead of the deposition of bone mineral until growth of the bone ceases. Then ossification catches up with the formation of matrix, and a constant relation between mineral and matrix is reached. When a bone is growing very rapidly calcification does not quite keep pace with increase in size of the matrix, and this is no doubt why the degree of calcification of the human femur falls during the first 6 months after birth.[8] A similar fall occurs in the long bones of other species around the time of birth.[35]

Although the relation between bone matrix and mineral varies from time to time during development, the relation between calcium and phosphorus is remarkably constant. The $\frac{\text{Ca}}{\text{P}}$ ratio of the cortext of the femur, for example, remains at 2·2 — 2·3 from 15 weeks gestation to adulthood. Bone also contains appreciable amounts of magnesium and sodium, both of which are believed to be adsorbed on the surfaces of the crystals of bone mineral, and some sodium is also in the extracellular fluid of the bone and in the hydration layer. How these two elements vary with age in human bone does not seem to have been investigated, but by analogy with other mammals it seems likely that Mg/Ca ratio falls as the size of the crystals increases during growth. On the whole the Na/Ca ratio seems to rise.

The adipose organ

The percentage of fat in the body of an adult can vary from about 4 to 70. There is probably not such a wide range in the full-term baby, but even here values as low as 11 per cent and as high as 28 per cent have been reported.[42] The premature baby has much less that a full-term one—some 42 g. when it is born weighing 1·2 kg., 165 g. when it weighs 2·2 kg. and 560 g. when it weighs 3·5 kg.

The fat of the body is contained in connective tissue cells, but it is believed that these are a specific kind of cells which have a particular distribution in the body in the subcutaneous tissues and round the internal organs. The fat deposits in the body are chiefly a way of storing energy, and at any stage they can come and go according to the nutritional status of the individual.

The adipose tissue of a young baby is different from that of the adult. At birth fat accounts for only 45 per cent of adipose tissue, water 46 per cent and protein most of the remainder. By six months the percentage of fat has risen to 60 and the water fallen to 27.[2] The fat cells at birth are small and separated by watery connective tissue. DNA gives no measure of the number of cells in adipose tissue because a large proportion of the nuclei are in the connective tissue between the cells. There are two methods for counting cells in adipose tissue. One is to remove the collagen in the connective tissue with collagenase, fix the fat in the cells with osmium tetroxide, suspend the little balls of fat in glycerol and count them electronically in a Coulter Counter. The other is to cut frozen sections of the tissue and measure the area of the cells or count them in a field of known dimensions under the microscope. In both the cell has to contain some fat to be counted, and empty cells are not recorded. The fat in the tissue is determined chemically on another portion and the amount of lipid per cell is taken as a measure of mean size.

Brook[5] has estimated the number of cells with fat in the bodies of 64 children of average weight and of 52 that were obese. He used the Coulter Counter for counting the cells in a portion of adipose tissue obtained at operation or by aspiration biopsy, and calculated the total amount of fat in the body from skinfold measurements using the formula of Durnin and Rahaman[10] for children over 12 years, and a formula suggested by himself[4] for the younger ones. His results are shown in Fig. 4. There seems to be about a threefold increase in the number of cells with fat in the first year after birth, and a fivefold increase between 1 and 13 years. Brook made the further point that there was no clear difference between the sexes in the number of cells, so girls must owe their greater adiposity to having each cell more generously filled with fat. Children who had become obese during their first year had more cells with fat than those of average weight, but this was not true of those who became fat later, although the amount of fat in the body was similar in the two obese groups.

The Liver

At birth the liver is relatively very large (Table 4). One reason for this is that before birth it functions as a blood-forming organ. It is a unique organ in many ways—it

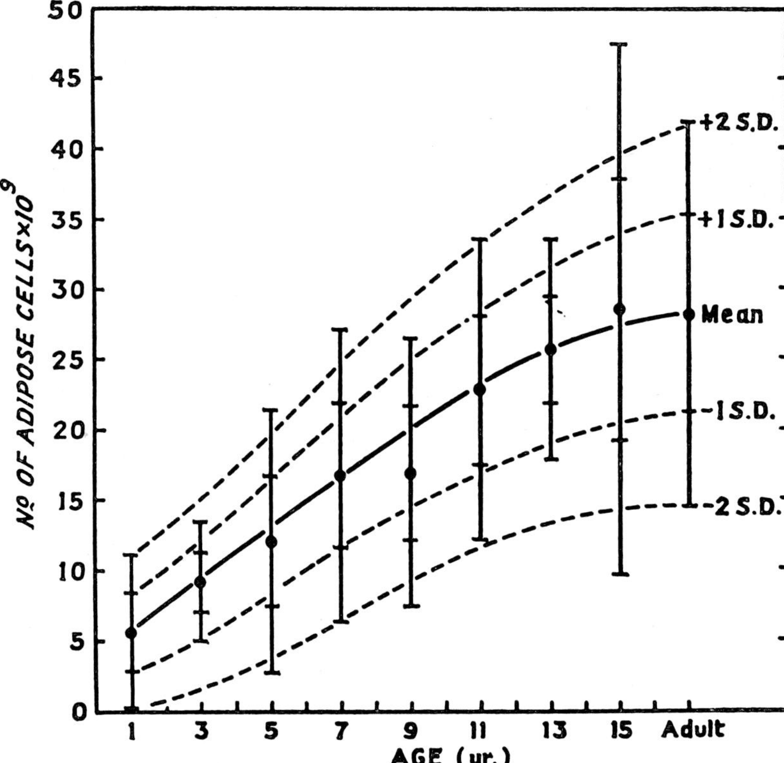

FIG. 4. Increase during growth, in total number of cells containing fat.[5]

stores glycogen and fat, and iron, copper and other trace elements, and it has remarkable powers of regeneration. Further, it changes more in size and chemical composition in response to alterations in diet than most of the other organs.

Table 7 shows some values for the composition of the human liver at four stages of development. The percentage of water falls and that of protein rises. Fat and carbohydrate contribute only small amounts to the weight of the liver at all ages. The concentration of DNA was found to be 4 times as high in the livers of 13–24 week fetuses as in the mature organ, but there was a big increase in the total amount of DNA in the organ. Even at term the total DNA was only 13 per cent of the adult value. Some of the DNA in the fetal liver was undoubtedly in the haemopoetic tissue, and there is no way of telling how much. The ratio Protein/DNA, which is generally considered to give some measure of the relation between cytoplasm and nucleus, did not begin to increase until after 22 weeks gestation, but by term it was more than twice as high as in the immature fetus, and in the liver of the adult the value had doubled again. Polyploidy is known to occur in hepatocytes at all ages, but there is evidence that the amount of cytoplasm in hepatocytes is proportional to the ploidy in the cell, so the Protein/DNA ratio may still be a valid index of changes in mean cell size.

One of the functions of the liver is to act as a storage organ for iron and other metals. More iron crosses the placenta than the fetus requires for growth and, although there is considerable variation from one fetus to another, the concentration of storage iron in the fetal liver is generally high. It falls to a minimum at about 2 years and then rises again. Iron is stored in the liver as haemosiderin and

TABLE 7

COMPOSITION OF LIVER[38,39,41]

	Fetus		*Baby*	
	13–14 *weeks*	20–22 *weeks*	*Full term newborn*	*Adult*
Weight of liver (g.)	1·3	13·6	130	1,210
Total in liver (mg.)	13·4	129	570	3,150
Composition per 100 *g.*				
Water (g.)	83	81	79	75
Fat (g.)	3·9	3·2	2·5	3·8
Carbohydrate (g.)	1·0	2·1	2·6	1·1
Protein (g.)	12·0	12·3	13·0	14·6
DNA (mg.)	1,030	950	438	260
Protein (mg.) / DNA (mg.)	11·7	12·9	29·7	56·0
Na (meq.)	—	5·5	6·0	4·3
K (meq.)	8·2	9·3	5·9	7·5
Cl (meq.)	6·2	5·7	5·6	3·8
P (mg.)	256	272	175	266
Mg (mg.)	—	18·0	13·0	18·0
Ca (mg.)	—	4·6	6·0	5·6
Cu (mg.)	—	6·3	7·6	0·5
Zn (mg.)	—	27·0	11·3	6·6
Mn (mg.)	—	0·12	0·15	0·8
Cr (μg.)	—	6·4	5·0	4·5
Co (μg.)	—	13·0	10·3	12·2

ferritin. The former is a colloidal ferric hydroxide-phosphate, the latter a globulin to which iron as ferric hydroxide phosphate is bound on the surface.

The high concentration of copper in the fetal liver is remarkable, for even at 20 weeks gestation the value was more than 10 times as high as in the adult.[38] In fact the liver at full-term had nearly $1\frac{1}{2}$ times as much copper as the adult organ. Porter[32] has shown that much of the copper in fetal liver is in the mitochondria as a copper-protein complex which he called "neonatal hepatic mitochondrocuprein." This complex is peculiar to the fetus and contains 10 times as much copper as any other known copper protein. It begins to disappear soon after birth and the copper set free is presumably used for the other tissues of the growing body.

The concentration of zinc was higher in the livers of the immature fetuses than in those of the baby at term, and in the adult the value was lower still. Most of the zinc in the liver is bound to proteins, some of it as metalloenzymes. It is at its highest concentration in the cytoplasm. Manganese is primarily in the mitochondria and nuclei of the liver cells, and it is also bound to protein. The fetal liver does not appear to "store" manganese as it does copper, and to a lesser extent iron and zinc, and the concentration of manganese in milk is very low. While the liver contributes to the needs of the newborn for copper after birth, and milk provides the infant with its zinc, how the baby gets enough manganese is puzzling, particularly in view of the fact that it is in negative manganese balance for a time after birth.[37] The bones of adult rabbits and fetal pigs have been shown to have a higher concentration of manganese than other tissues, and it may be that the bones constitute the fetal "store." There seems to be no accumulation of chromium or cobalt in the liver before birth.

REFERENCES

1. Anderson, E. C. (1968), "Organic Scintillation Detectors and Their Use in the Study of Body Composition," in *Body Composition in Animals and Man*, pp. 266–290. Washington D.C.: National Academy of Sciences, Publication No. 1598.
2. Baker, G. L. (1969), "Human Adipose Tissue Composition and Age," *Amer. J. clin. Nutr.*, **22,** 829–835.
3. Brean, M., Weinstein, H. G., Johnson, R. L., Veis, A. and Marshall, T. (1970), "Acidic Glycosaminoglycans in Human Skin During Fetal Development and in Adult Life," *Biochim. biophys. Acta*, **201,** 54–60.
4. Brook, C. G. D. (1971), "Determination of Body Composition of Children from Skinfold Measurements," *Arch. Dis. Childh.*, **46,** 182–184.
5. Brook, C. G. D. (1972), "Evidence for a Sensitive Period in Adipose-cell Replication in Man," *Lancet*, **ii,** 624–627.
6. Cheek, D. B. (1968), *Human Growth.* Philadelphia: Lea & Febiger.
7. Cheek, D. B., Mellits, D. and Elliott, D. (1966), "Body Water, Height and Weight During Growth in Normal Children," *Amer. J. Dis. Child.*, **112,** 312–317.
8. Dickerson, J. W. T. (1962), "Changes in the Composition of the Human Femur During Growth," *Biochem. J.*, **82,** 56–61.
9. Dobbing, J. and Sands, J. (1973), "The quantitative Growth and Development of the Human Brain," *Arch. Dis. Childh.* In press and *see* Chapter Dobbing.
10. Durnin, J. V. G. A. and Rahaman, M. M. (1967), "The Assessment of the Amount of Fat in the Human Body from Measurements of Skinfold Thickness," *Brit. J. Nutr.*, **21,** 681–689.
11. Edelman, I. S., Haley, H. B., Schloerb, P. R., Sheldon, D. B., Friis-Hansen, B. J., Stoll, G. and Moore, F. D. (1952), "Further Observations on Total Body Water. 1. Normal Values Throughout the Life Span," *Surg. Gynec. Obstet.*, **95,** 1–12.
12. Fomon, S. J. (1967), *Infant Nutrition.* Philadelphia: W. B. Saunders Co.
13. Forbes, G. B. (1964), "Growth of Lean Body Mass During Childhood and Adolescence," *J. Pediat.*, **64,** 822–827.
14. Forbes, G. B. (1965), "Toward a New Dimension in Human Growth," *Pediatrics*, **36,** 825–835.
15. Forbes, G. B. and Amirhakimi, G. H. (1970), "Skinfold Thickness and body Fat in Children," *Hum. Biol.*, **42,** 401–418.
16. Forbes, G. B. and Hursh, J. B. (1963), "Age and Sex Trends in Lean Body Mass Calculated from ^{40}K Measurements: With a Note on the Theoretical Basis for the Procedure," *Ann. N.Y. Acad. Sci.*, **110,** 255–263.
17. Friis-Hansen, B. (1957), "Changes in Body Water Compartments During Growth," *Acta paediat. Stockh.*, suppl. 46, **110.**
18. Garrow, J. S. (1965), "The Use and Calibration of a Small Whole Body Counter for the Measurement of Total Body K in Malnourished Infants," *W. Indian med. J.*, **14,** 73–81.
19. Garrow, J. S., Fletcher, H. and Halliday, D. (1965), "Body Composition in Severe Infantile Malnutrition," *J. clin. Invest.*, **44,** 417–425.
20. Goldspink, G. (1970), "Morphological Adaption Due to Growth and Activity," in *The Physiology and Biochemistry of Muscle as a Food*, pp. 521–536 (E. J. Briskey, R. G. Cassens and B. B. Marsh, Eds.). Madison: University of Wisconsin Press.
21. Hanna, F. M. (1963), "Changes in Body Composition of Normal Infants in Relation to Diet," *Ann. N.Y. Acad. Sci.*, **110,** 840–848.
22. MacCallum, J. B. (1898), "On the Histogenesis of Striated Muscle Fibers and the Growth of the Human Sartorius Muscle," *Bull. Johns Hopk. Hosp.*, **9,** 208–215.
23. Maresh, M. and Groome, D. (1966), "Potassium-40: Serial Determinations in Infants," *Pediatrics*, **38,** 642–646.
24. Michael, E. D., Jr. and Katch, F. I. (1968), "Prediction of Body Density from Skinfold and Girth Measurements of 17-year-old Boys," *J. appl. Physiol.*, **25,** 747–750.
25. Miller, C. E., Remenchik, A. P. and Kessler, W. V. (1968), "Precision of Assay of Whole-body Potassium in Man," in *Body Composition in Animals and Man*, pp. 350–383. Washington D.C.: National Academy of Sciences, Publication No. 1598.
26. Montgomery, R. D. (1962), "Growth of Human Striated Muscle," *Nature*, **195,** 194–195.
27. Novak, L. P., Hamamoto, K., Orvis, A. L. and Burke, E. C. (1970), "Total Body Potassium in Infants. Determination of Whole-body Counting of Radioactive Potassium (^{40}K)," *Amer. J. Dis. Child.*, **119,** 419–423.
28. Oberhausen, E., Burmeister, W. and Huycke, E. J. (1965), "Das Wachstum des Kalium bestandes im Menschen genessen mit dem Ganz Korperzahler," *Ann. paediat.*, **205,** 381–400.
29. Owen, G. M., Filer, L. J., Jr., Maresh, M. and Fomon, S. J. (1968), "Body Composition of the Infant. Part II. Sex-related Difference in Body Composition in Infancy," in *Human Development*, p. 246 (F. Falkner, Ed.). Philadelphia: W. B. Saunders Co.
30. Owen, G. M., Jensen, R. L. and Fomon, S. J. (1962), "Sex-related Difference in Total Body Water and Exchangeable Chloride During Infancy," *J.Pediat.*, **60,** 858–868.
31. Pařizková, J. (1961), "Total Body Fat and Skinfold Thickness in Children," *Metabolism*, **10,** 794–807.
32. Porter, H. (1966), "The Tissue Copper Proteins: Cerebrocuprein, Erythrocuprein, Hepatocuprein, and Neonatal Hepatic Mitochondrocuprein," in *The Biochemistry of Copper*, pp. 159–712 (J. Peisach, P. Aisen and W. E. Blumberg, Eds.). New York: Academic Press.
33. Rauh, J. L. and Schumsky, D. A. (1968), "Lean and Non-lean Body Mass Estimates in Urban School Children," in *Human*

Growth, pp. 242–252 (D. B. Cheek, Ed.). Philadelphia: Lea & Febiger.

34. Siri, W. E. (1956), "The Gross Composition of the Body," in *Advances in Biological and Medical Physics. IV* (J.H. Lawrence, and C. A. Tobias, Eds.). New York: Academic Press.
35. Weidmann, S. M. and Rogers, H. J. (1958), "Studies on Skeletal Tissues. 5. The Influence of Age upon the degree of Calcification and the Incorporation of ^{32}P in Bone," *Biochem. J.*, **69,** 338–343.
36. Widdowson, E. M. (1968), "Growth and Composition of the Fetus and Newborn," in *Biology of Gestation Vol.* 2, pp. 1–49, (N. S. Assali, Ed.). New York: Academic Press.
37. Widdowson, E. M. (1969), "Trace Elements in Human Development," in *Mineral Meatabolism in Paediatrics*, pp. 85–98 (D. Barltrop and W. L. Burland, Eds.). Oxford: Blackwell.
38. Widdowson, E. M., Chan, H., Harrison, G. E. and Milner, R. D. G. (1972), "Accumulation of Cu, Zn, Mn, Cr and Co in the Human Liver Before Birth," *Biol. Neonat.* **20,** 360–367.
39. Widdowson, E. M., Crabb, D. E. and Milner, R. D. G. (1972), "Cellular Development of Some Human Organs Before Birth," *Arch. Dis. Childh.*, **47,** 652–655.
40. Widdowson, E. M. and Dickerson, J. W. T. (1960), "The Effect of Growth and Function on the Chemical Composition of the Soft Tissues," *Biochem. J.*, **77,** 30–43.
41. Widdowson, E. M. and Dickerson, J. W. T. (1964), "The Chemical Composition of the Body," in *Mineral Metabolism Vol. 2A*, pp. 1–246 (C. L. Comar and F. Bronner, Eds.). New York: Academic Press.
42. Widdowson, E. M. and Spray, C. M. (1951), "Chemical Development *In Utero*," *Arch. Dis. Childh.*, **26,** 205–214.

13A. GROWTH AND DEVELOPMENT OF THE CARDIOVASCULAR SYSTEM: (a) Anatomical Development

R. H. ANDERSON and G. T. ASHLEY

INTRODUCTION

That ontogenetic cardiac development is a complicated procedure is indicated by the many congenital malformations documented in textbooks of Paediatric Cardiology.[16,18,24,58] Each of these malformations results from one or more defective processes in growth of the heart tube. Much has already been written concerning embryogenesis of cardiac defects, but learned authorities continue to disagree on several important matters. That such disagreement should exist is hardly surprising, since interpretation of development involves retrospective study of four dimensional procedures. Each different theory is invariably based on careful reconstructive investigations, and it would be imprudent to attempt to resolve any controversies on the basis of the limited embryonic material we have at our disposal. However, it is equally clear that for any theory of development to be correct, it must also explain the results of maldevelopment, or arrested development, which appear as cardiac anomalies. We are therefore fortunate in having access to the extensive collection of congenital heart defects at the Royal Liverpool Children's Hospital. Consequently we have attempted to interpret controversial theories in the light of both embryological and pathological studies, and to illustrate the accepted theories of development using original diagrams based more on definitive structures than on actual appearances during ontogenetic development of the heart.

In our description, we have considered the growth of the cardiovascular system (and more particularly the heart tube) in stages, and have then immediately discussed the more important maldevelopments referable to each stage. We would stress that all these stages are occurring simultaneously. We have purposely avoided the description of timing of growth changes by the use of crown–rump fetal measurements, or other estimations of fetal maturity. Instead we have grouped this material together as Table 1. Those interested in further information on this particular aspect of embryology are referred to the detailed investigations of Streeter.[42]

EARLY DEVELOPMENT OF THE CARDIOVASCULAR SYSTEM

Our understanding of the early development of the cardiac tube and its associated vessels owes much to the careful studies performed at the Carnegie Institute by Davis[9] and Streeter[42], and for a detailed account the reader is referred to these works. Since it is essential for placental animals rapidly to establish a circulatory system, erythrocytes are amongst the first cells to be differentiated. They appear during the third week when the embryo is still a piriform disc, and are established as blood islands in the yolk sac, body stalk, chorionic villi and within the embryonic disc itself (Fig. 1). The endothelial cells surrounding the blood islands coalesce into channels which form the earliest blood vessels. Those in the yolk sac join up to form the vitelline system, whilst the body stalk and chorionic islands produce the umbilical and placental circulation. The blood islands in the embryonic area itself form both arterial and venous channels, which make contact in the region anterior to the prochordal plate.

This is the cardiogenic area and it is related to the portion of lateral plate mesoderm destined to become the pericardial cavity (Fig. 2A). Two channels are formed in this area which coalesce to form a single endothelial heart tube. Subsequent to this the entire head end of the embryonic disc becomes involved in head fold formation. This folding, which tucks in part of the endoderm of the yolk sac to form the fore-gut, carries the endothelial heart tube ventral to the recently formed gut, but dorsal to the pericardial cavity. Subsequently the block of tissue originally at the head end of the embryo becomes fused with the body stalk to form the septum transversum (Fig. 2). The endothelial heart tube now invaginates the pericardial cavity from its dorsal aspect and acquires its myo-epicardial mantle (Fig. 3). In future development the original endothelial tube remains as endocardium, whilst the myocardium, specialized tissue, fibrous tissue and epicardium are all derivatives of the myo-epicardium. As this process is continuing the heart tube also establishes connections with the blood-channels referred to above. At the head end the tube becomes connected with medially situated arterial channels running the length of the embryo alongside the notochord and neural tube. In their course from the heart tube these channels have to pass around the developing pharynx and the channel around the gut is the first aortic arch. The venous channels formed in the body stalk and yolk sac establish connections with the tail end of the heart tube, and in doing so pass medially through the septum transversum, whilst the lateral channels of the

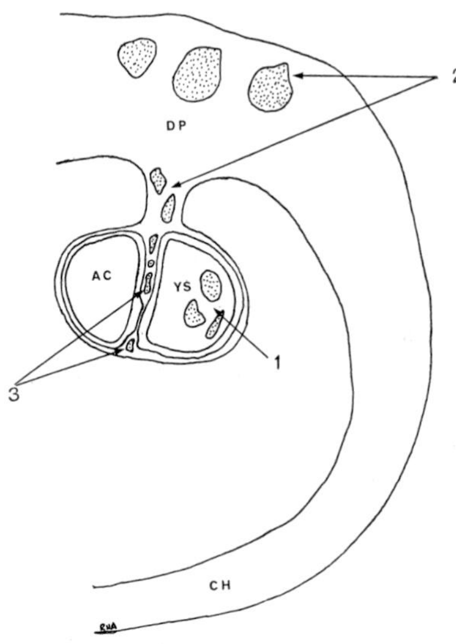

FIG. 1. Diagram to show the positions of the developing blood islands in the bilaminar disc embryo. They are present (1) in the yolk sac (YS) (2) in the connecting stalk and developing placenta (DP) and (3) in the bilaminar disc. AC—amniotic cavity. CH—chorion.

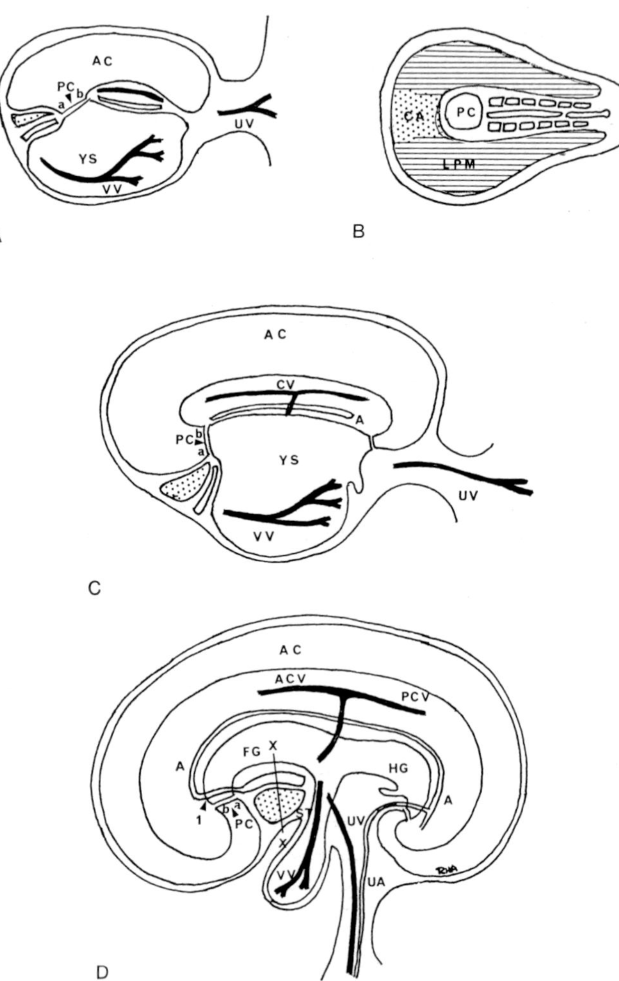

FIG. 2. Diagrams to show the positions of the cardiogenic area (CA) and the cardinal (AVC, PCV), umbilical (UV) and vitelline (VV) veins before (A, B) during (C) and after (D) head fold formation. Figs. 2a,c and d are in the sagittal plane of the embryo. Fig. 2b is a plan view of 2a. The ends of the prochordal plate (PC) are labelled a and b. In the plan view it can be seen that the cardiogenic area is the anterior extent of the lateral plate mesoderm (LPM) and is anterior to the prochordal plate before head fold formation. After fold formation the veins come into contact with the original head end of the heart tube, whilst the aortae (A) pass round the pharynx to reach the original tail end of the tube (1). FG—foregut, HG—hindgut. UA—unbilical artery X–X is the plane through which Fig. 3 is taken. The abbreviations given above will also be used in subsequent legends.

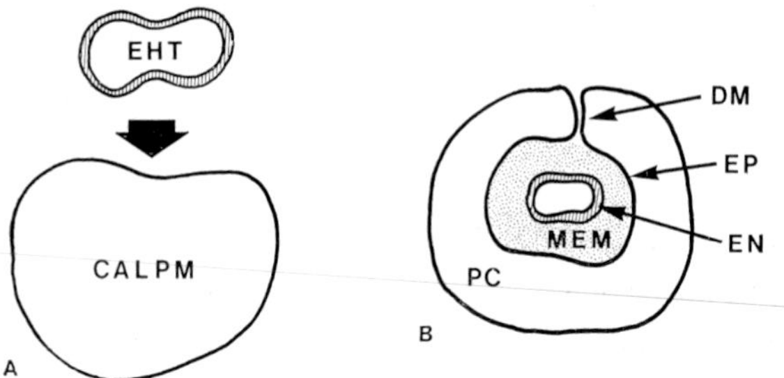

FIG. 3. Diagrams drawn in cross-section to show the invagination of the mesoderm by the endothelial heart tube (shown as already fused from its two primary components). EHT endocardial heart tube. CALPM—Cardiogenic area of lateral place mesoderm. EP—epicardium MEM—myoepicardial mantle. EN—endocardium. DM—dorsal mesocardium. PC—Pericardial cavity.

embryonic area, the cardinal veins, also pass through the septum transversum to join the lateral aspect of the heart tube (Fig. 2). Thus at the close of the third week a single heart tube is formed with established connections to both arterial and venous systems. The arterial end of the heart tube is at first connected round the pharynx with the dorsal aortae in the substance of the first branchial arch. The dorsal aortae are originally present as separate vessels throughout the embryo, but they subsequently fuse to form a single channel between the fourth thoracic and fourth lumbar segments. Caudally they are again present as two vessels, and the paired umbilical arteries arise in this region to carry blood to the placenta (Fig. 2).

As the six branchial arches develop in the region of the fore gut, aortic arches are formed in each pair of branchial arches which connect the arterial chamber of the heart tube (truncus arteriosus) with the dorsal aortae. Although aortic arches are formed in all six branchial arches (Fig. 4), the full complement is never seen at any one time, since some degenerate before the others appear. The major arteries of the thorax, head and neck are formed from the persisting portions of the aortic arches; the third and fourth arches forming the common carotids and the definitive aortic arch, and the sixth aortic arches persisting as the pulmonary arteries and ductus arteriosus (Fig. 4). Branches of the aorta are formed in relationship to the gut, the intermediate cells mass and the body wall. Three unpaired vessels are formed in relation to the gut and they supply the fore-, mid- and hind-gut respectively. In adult life they persist as the coeliac axis and superior and inferior mesenteric vessels. The intermediate cell mass arteries are paired vessels supplying the kidneys, suprarenals and gonads. The parietal vessels are segmental structures, and thus during development a pair is formed in each segment. Of particular importance are the seventh cervical and fifth lumbar pairs since these become the axial arteries of the upper and lower limbs respectively.

Following formation of the head fold the sinus venosus receives the vitelline, umbilical and cardinal veins on each side, opening into the right and left sinus horns. The cardinal veins consist of anterior and posterior channels draining either end of the embryo, and these fuse to join a common channel, the common cardinal vein. This is the most lateral of the structures entering the sinus horn. The terminations of all these veins together with the sinus horns are enclosed within the substance of the septum trans-

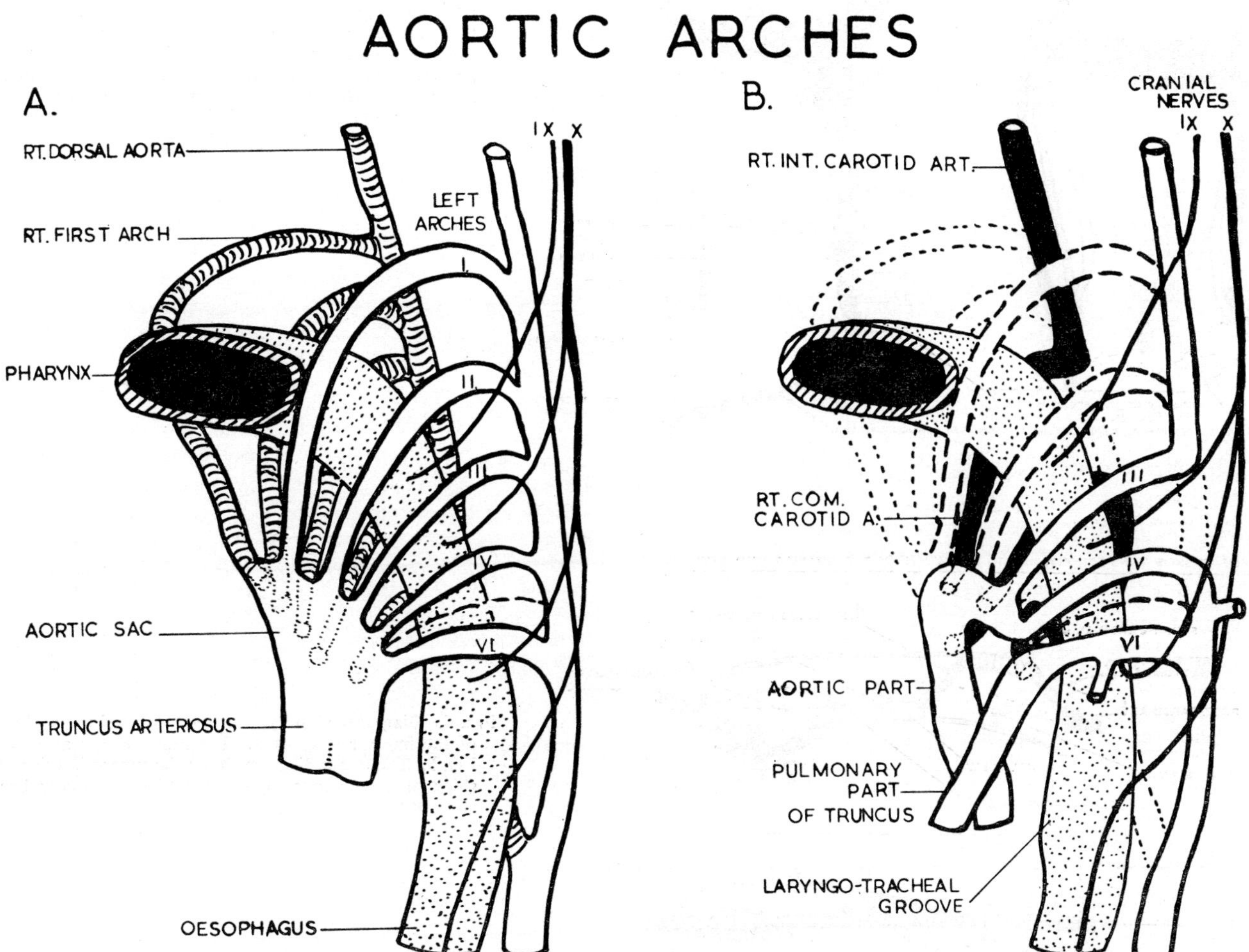

Fig. 4. Diagrammatic representations of the aortic arch systems. A. shows an idealized situation with all six arches present (the fifth arch is always rudimentary) passing round the pharynx from the truncus to make contact with the dorsal aortae, which in turn fuse into a single vessel. B. is an idealized diagram to show which arches degenerate and which persist to form definitive arterial channels.

versum. Further systems of veins develop within the embryo, lying ventral and dorsal to the cardinal system. These are the supra- and sub-cardinal complexes. Anastomoses develop between all the cardinal systems to produce a complicated series of longitudinal venous channels. Two transverse anastomoses between right and left cardinal systems are of particular importance. These are formed in the cervical and pelvic regions and have the effect of diverting blood from the left to the right side of the body. This produces enlargement of right sided venous structures and regression of the left sided veins. The anastomosis in the cervical region forms the brachiocephalic veins and the pelvic anastomosis forms the commencement of the inferior vena cava, but above this point segments of both supra- and sub-cardinal complexes are incorporated in the formation of the vein which terminates by draining through the right vitelline vein to the sinus horn (Figs. 5 and 6).

Whilst these changes have been occurring in the cardinal system, the anlagen of the liver has been laid down as cords of hepatic cells in the septum transversum. As a result of vigorous hepatic growth the trunks of the vitelline and umbilical veins are broken up into multiple intercommunicating vascular sinusoids (Fig. 7).

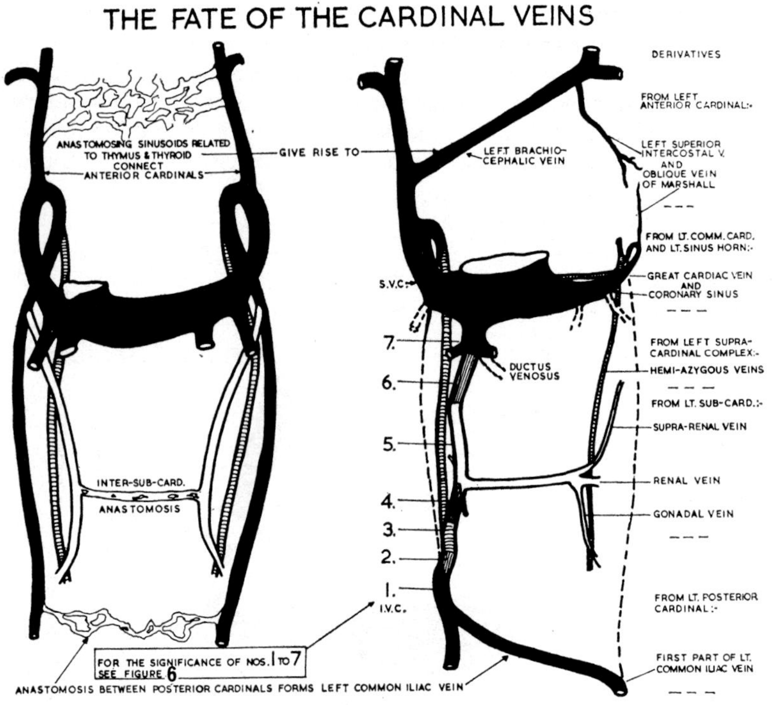

FIG. 5. Diagrams to show the fate of the cardinal veins. The left hand figure shows the common cardinal vein entering the sinus venosus as the most lateral of three channels on each side. Also shown are supra-cardinal veins (cross hatched) and the sub-cardinals (plain vessels). The right hand diagram shows the definitive veins formed from those embryonic primorida. The numbers relative to the inferior vena cava are explained in greater detail in Fig. 6.

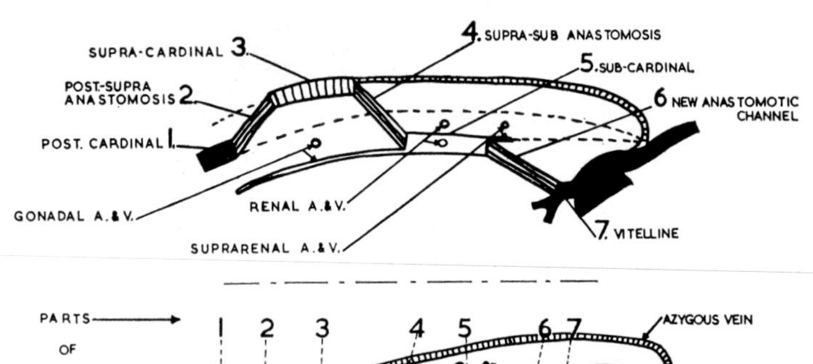

FIG. 6. Diagrams showing the derivation of the various parts of the inferior vena cava. The numbers are also shown on Fig. 5. The upper diagram shows the supero-inferior relationships of the various segments, which eventually become a straight tube (lower diagram).

Subsequently the following changes occur. The right umbilical veins and the proximal part of the left vitelline vein degenerate. An anastomotic channel is then developed from liver sinusoids which connects the persisting left umbilical vein to the right vitelline veins as it enters the sinus horn. This channel is the ductus venosus (Fig. 8). The terminal portion of the right vitelline vein also becomes the termination of the inferior vena cava (Fig. 6). The segments of vitelline veins related to the fore-gut also undergo anastomoses to form the portal vein and the stem of the superior mesenteric vein (Fig. 8).

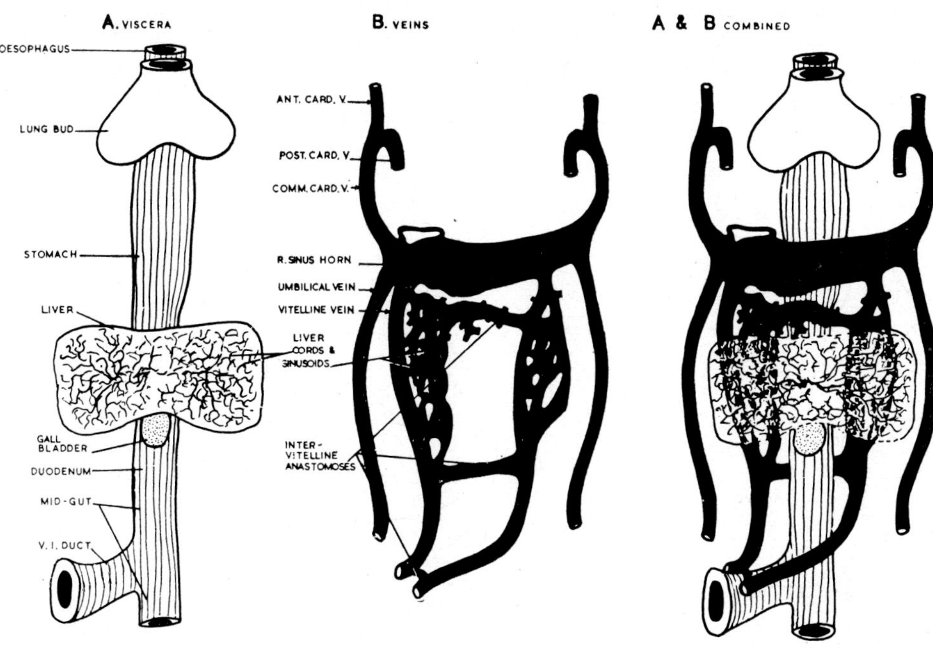

FIG. 7. Composite diagrams showing the relationships between the tributaries of the sinus venosus and the developing liver. The left hand diagram shows the foregut derivatives, the centre diagram shows the venous structures. The right hand diagram is a superimposition of the first two diagrams.

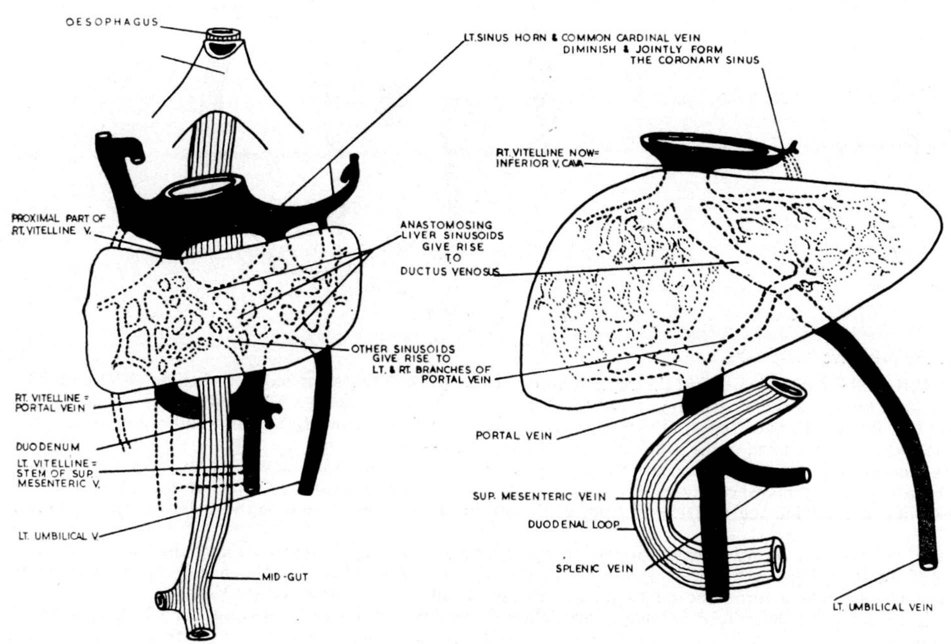

FIG. 8. These diagrams show the fate of the venous structures seen in Fig. 7. The left hand diagram is an earlier stage to that depicted in the right hand figure.

FURTHER DEVELOPMENT OF THE HEART TUBE

Normal Development

As the endothelial heart tubes sink into the primitive pericardial cavity and acquire their myo-epicardial mantle, they fuse to form a single tube. The studies of de Vries and Saunders[13] show that evidence of the duality of the cardiac tube persists for some time during subsequent development, but it is simpler to describe changes as though they were occurring in a single tube. As the heart tube is formed within the pericardial cavity it is firmly anchored at both its ends. Caudally, at the venous end, the two sinus horns are deeply embedded within the substance of the septum transversum. At the rostral, arterial, end the aortic arches anchor the heart tube to the developing pharynx and fore-gut (Fig. 9A). Each sinus horn at this stage receives vitelline, umbilical and common cardinal veins, and communicates with the sinus venosus. The sinus itself passes from the septum transversum to open into the expanded primitive atrial chamber of the heart tube, and the opening is guarded by the right and left venous valves. Rostrally the atrial chamber opens through a constricted canal into the primitive ventricular chamber, the canal being the atrioventricular canal. When traced further rostrally two further dilatations are found in the heart tube, and these are the bulbus cordis and truncus arteriosus. The bulbus is separated from the ventricle by endothelial ridges named by Davis[9] as the right and left bulboventricular ridges. The truncus gives rise to the aortic arches which are developing at this time around the pharynx (Fig. 9A).

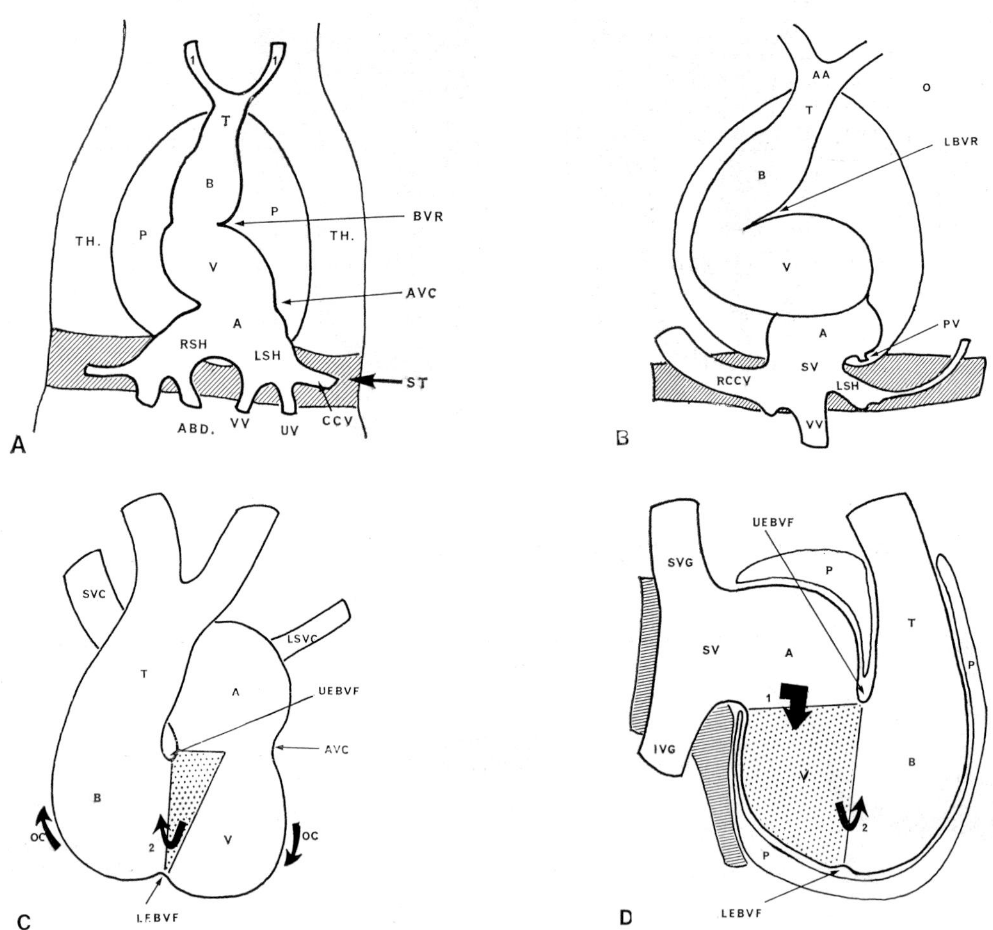

FIG. 9. Diagrams showing growth and flexion of the primitive heart tube.

A. Straight tube stage with the sinus horns (RSH, LSH) embedded within the septum transversum (ST). Each horn receives vitelline (VV), umbilical (UV) and common cardinal (CCV) veins. The septum separates the developing thorax (TH) from the abdominal cavity (ABD). Rostrally the heart tube exhibits the dilatations of the atrial (A) ventricular (V), bulbar (B) and truncal (T) chambers. The atrioventricular canal (AVC) and bulboventricular ridges (BVR) are also evident. The first aortic arches (1) anchor the head end of the heart tube to the pharynx. P—Pericardium.

B. The atrium has become mobilized and has incorporated the sinus venosus into its walls. The right sinus horn receives now only the common cardinal and vitelline veins whilst the left sinus horn is greatly diminished in size. The pulmonary vein (PV) has appeared as a new diverticulum in the left side of the atrial chamber. The atrioventricular flexion has carried the ventricle in front of the atrium, and at the same time the bulboventricular flexion is commencing.

C. At this stage the bulboventricular loop is fully formed and shows a flexion of 180° in the frontal plane (2). The upper edge of the bulboventricular foramen (UEBVF) bisects the shorter inner curve of the loop, the lower edge (LEBVF) bisects the much longer outer curve. The shaded area represents the posterior wall of the primitive ventricular chamber which possibly forms the inflow portion of the definitive right ventricle (See Fig. 12).

D. This diagram is a right sided view of the saggital section of the heart tube following completion of the flexion processes. The ventricle is beneath the fully mobilized atrial chamber, showing 90° of flexion in the sagittal plane (1). The portion of ventricle possibly incorporated into, the right ventricle is again shaded.

At the stage described the heart is a straight tube contained within the pericardial cavity. Subsequent growth is concerned with retraction of the sinus venosus from the septum transversum into the atrial chamber and increase in length of the bulbo-ventricular limbs of the tube. As the sinus is absorbed from the septum the atrium becomes a more obvious chamber. During the previous growth period anastomoses formed at the head and tail ends of the embryo have diverted the bulk of the venous blood into the right handed venous channels. The effect of this diversion is that the right sinus horn increases in size whilst the left horn decreases. Thus when the sinus venosus is absorbed into the atrium it is absorbed as a right sided structure, and the right and left venous valves are found in the right side of the chamber (Fig. 10). The changes in the venous system are such that only three channels now open within the venous valves, the right common cardinal and vitelline veins and the left sinus horn. In adult life these structures persist as the superior and inferior cavae and the coronary sinus. During the incorporation of these structures into the atrium a new outgrowth has appeared in the left sided portion of the atrial chamber. This is the primitive pulmonary vein. There is controversy as to whether this structure originally grows from within the sinus or from the atrial chamber itself. Earlier investigators[6] believed it to be of sinus origin, but the exact studies of Los[33] and Van Praagh and Corsini[53] have shown that the original outgrowth is from the primitive atrium, and examination of the embryos in our collection endorses their view (Fig. 11).

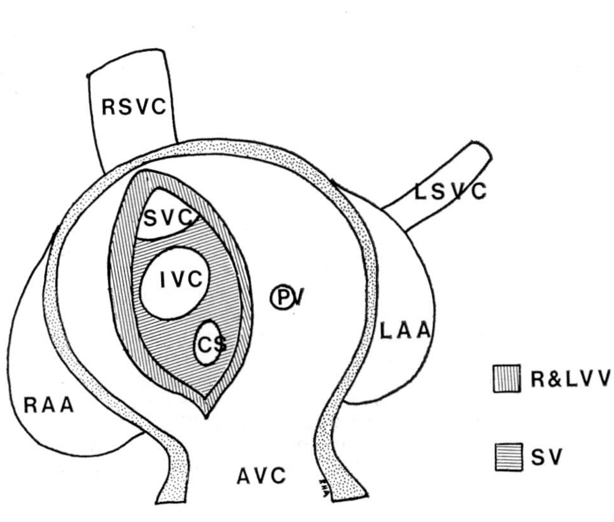

FIG. 10. Diagrammatic frontal view of the atrial chamber following mobilization and incorporation of the sinus venosus (SV). The openings of the superior and inferior venae cavae (SVC, IVC) together with the coronary sinus (Left sinus horn) lie within the right and left venous valves (R & LVV). The pulmonary vein opens into the left side of the chamber. Also seen are the right and left atrial appendages (R & LAA) which continue growing and pass to either side of the truncus as it ascends in front of the atrium.

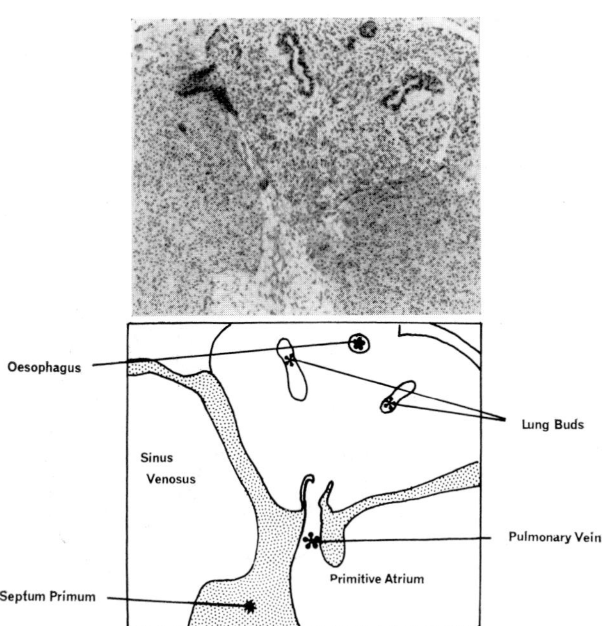

FIG. 11. Section of the developing pulmonary vein from an 8 mm. crown-rump length human embryo. The lower diagram shows the structures present.

As the atrial chamber is mobilized within the pericardial cavity, the increase in length of the heart tube necessitates bending in order that it may be accommodated within the cavity. This bending occurs in two positions. The first flexion takes place between the atrial and ventricular chambers. This bend is through a right angle and occurs in the sagittal plane (Fig. 9D). The second flexion occurs within the bulboventricular limbs of the tube, and the bulboventricular ridges form the hinge. This bend takes place in the frontal plane, and is through 180° so that the truncus continues to convey arterial blood towards the head (Fig. 9B,C). A further effect of the bending is to produce two curvatures in the bulboventricular loop, a long outer curve and a much shorter inner curvature.

At this stage the bending produced in the bulboventricular limb of the heart tube means that the atrioventricular canal is to the left of and posterior to the bulboventricular foramen (Figs. 12, 13). Thus all atrial blood passes through the foramen to reach the truncus. Rightward migration of the atrioventricular canal relative to the bulbotruncal junction is therefore necessary to produce a heart tube approximating to its definitive shape. The migratory process is also involved in the production of the muscular interventricular septum, and the mechanics of migration are a source of much controversy. The leftward hinge of migration is the left bulboventricular ridge, and authorities agree that this structure forms the anterior portion of the interventricular septum, which lies between the left ventricle, of primitive ventricular origin, and the infundibulum, of bulbar origin (Fig. 13). The disagreement concerns the formation of the right ventricle and the posterior interventricular septum. Pernkopf and Wirtinger[40] and Goerttler[17] defined the descending limb of the loop as the pro-ampulla and the ascending limb as meta-ampulla and bulbus. They considered that the meta-ampulla was absorbed into the pro-ampulla in such a way that pro-ampulla (primitive ventricle) gave rise to the inflow portions of both ventricles, whilst the meta-ampulla (bulbus) contributed to the inflow portion of the right ventricle. The bulbus formed the outflow tracts of both ventricles (Fig. 14B). Thus the posterior septum was an intraventricular structure and was distinct from the anterior bulboventricular septum. In contrast, Streeter[42] and de Vries and Saunders[13] showed that the trabeculated pouch of the right ventricle was a derivative of the bulbus, whilst that of the left ventricle was a primitive ventricular structure (Figs. 12, 13). They considered that the interventricular septum was the ridge (bulboventricular) between them, and therefore postulated that the right ventricle was of purely bulbar origin. The atrioventricular and bulboventricular canals were considered as primary heart tube, and were distinct from the trabeculated pouches (Fig. 12). Migration of the extremities of the primary heart tube relative to each other was also connected with septation of the atrioventricular canal, and occurred in such a way that the right hand portion of the atrioventricular canal contacted the bulbus with the right bulboventricular ridge becoming the posterior interventricular septum. Thus according to de Vries and Saunders[13] the entire interventricular septum remained a bulboventricular structure (Fig. 14C). This controversy is most relevant to the embryogenesis of single ventricle (*vide infra*) but is still unresolved. Although the study of de Vries and Saunders[13] was based on reconstructed embryonic hearts, their illustrations of the process of migration of the canal, so vital to their concept, are somewhat uninformative. In our opinion further study of embryos from the developmental stages of atrioventricular canal migration are necessary to elucidate this important facet of growth of the heart.

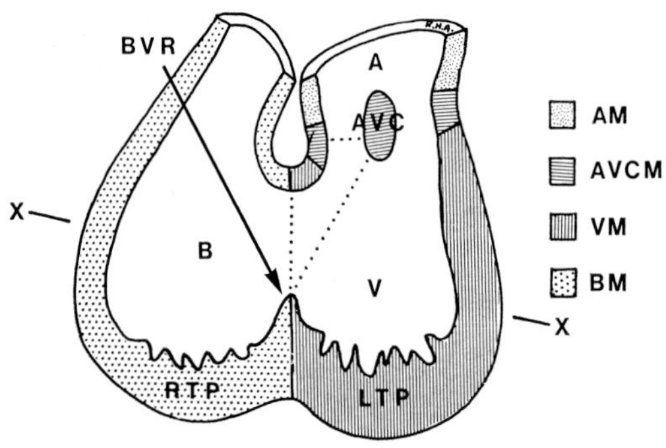

Fig. 12. Diagrammatic frontal section of the bulboventricular loop showing the constituents of its walls. AM—atrial musculature AVCM-atrioventricular canal musculature; VM—ventricular musculature; BM—bulbar musculature. The right trabeculated ventricular pouch (RTP) develops in the bulbus and the left pouch (LTP) develops in the primitive ventricle; the two are separated by the bulboventricular ridge (BVR). The area within the dotted triangle may constitute a sleeve of primitive ventricular musculature which is incorporated into the right ventricle. X–X represents the plane of section of Fig. 13.

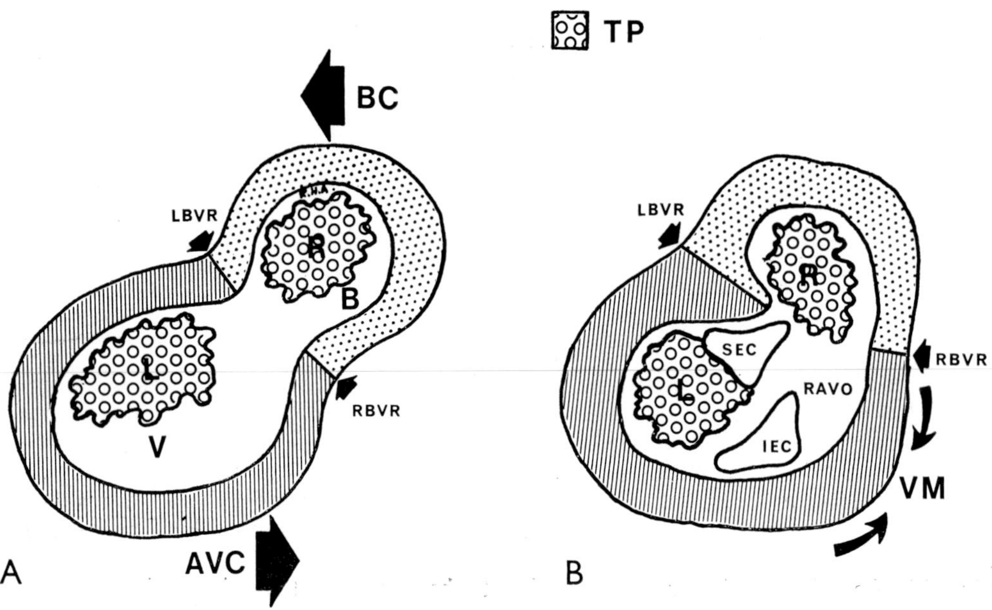

Fig. 13. Transverse sections of the bulboventricular loop in the level of X–X in Fig. 12 (A) shows the position before migration of the AV canal. The channel between the bulboventricular ridges is the bulboventricular foramen. The pouches are seen in plan view as though the distal segment of the loop was viewed from above. Migration occurs by the canal shifting to the right (AVC →) but at the same time the bulbus shifts to the left (← BC). (B) shows a similar section after migration. It will be noted that the left bulboventricular ridge is now an interventricular structure whilst a portion of the ventricle is incorporated into the right ventricle posterior to the right ridge (↶ VM ↷). See also Figs. 10 and 12). Cross hatched areas as indicated by key to Fig. 12. TP—Trabeculated pouches.

Whichever method is correct, the end result of migration is that the bulbus comes to lie anterior to the atrioventricular canal. One effect of this migration is that the inner curve of the bulboventricular loop has become a groove which bisects the developing heart in the frontal plane (Fig. 15). At the base of this groove the atrial musculature is reflected into the bulbus with the intervention of a small segment of ventricular musculature. The groove can therefore be termed the bulboatrioventricular ledge, or ridge, and it is important to appreciate that it is a well formed component of the heart at this stage of development. Its left hand margin overlies the anterior portion of the interventricular septum, whilst its right hand margin forms the basis of the crista supraventricularis of the right ventricle. Before complete septation of the heart tube can occur it is necessary for the posterior portion of the distal bulbus to migrate posteriorly in relation to the atrioventricular canal so that it overlies the anterior extent of the primitive ventricular chamber. By necessity this involves a change in orientation of the bulboventricular foramen. It will be appreciated that this structure is bounded by the bulboatrioventricular ledge superiorly, and by the left bulboventricular ridge and interventricular septum inferiorly and to the left (Fig. 16A). The so-called dextral border is dependant upon which concept of right ventricular growth is adopted, but is relatively unimportant (Fig. 16). Following the right–left migration of the atrioventricular canal and bulbus the superior and inferior rims of the foramen are in the same vertical plane (Fig. 16B), and constitute the primary interventricular foramen. The process of posterior migration of the bulbus incorporates the bulbo-atrioventricular ledge into the septating atrioventricular canal, and means that the superior rim of the bulboventricular foramen

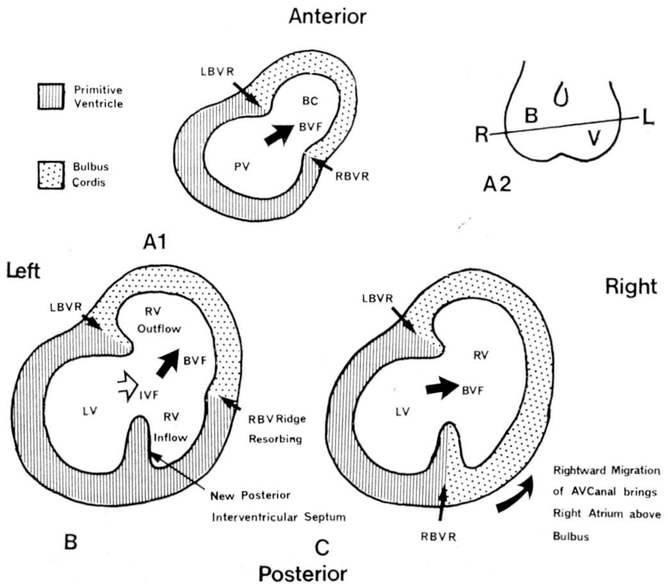

FIG. 14 Diagrams to show the two theories of formation of the inflow tract of the right ventricle. A1 and A2 show the position before migration of the AV canal. All subsequent diagrams use the same orientation of specimens. It is as though the distal segment of the heart is viewed from above. (B) shows the theory of Goerrtler[17] and Pernkopf and Wirtinger.[40] The bulbus forms only the infundibulum and the posterior septum is a new intraventricular structure. (C). shows the theory of de Vries and Saunders.[13] The bulbus is considered to form the entire right ventricle, and the entire septum is a bulboventricular structure.

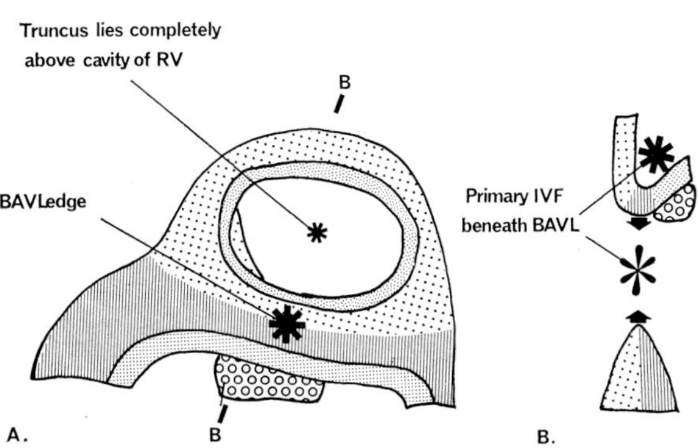

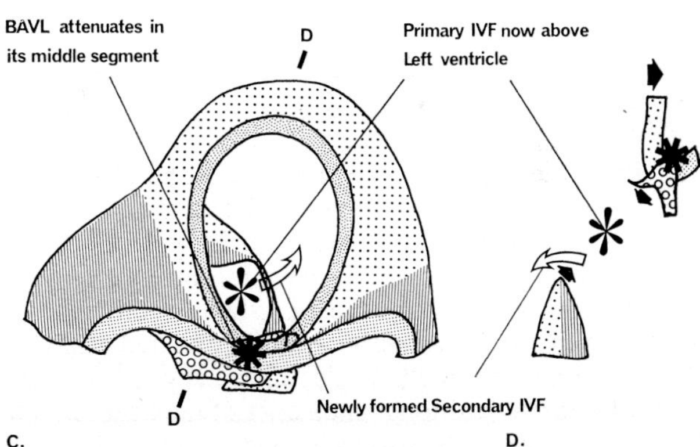

FIG. 16. Diagrams illustrating the attenuation of the bulbo-atrioventricular ledge during posterior migration of the bulbus. (A) is before migration and (B) is a sagittal section in the plane B–B. (C) and (D) are similar diagrams after migration. Note how the primary interventricular foramen becomes re-orientated as the outflow tract of the aorta.

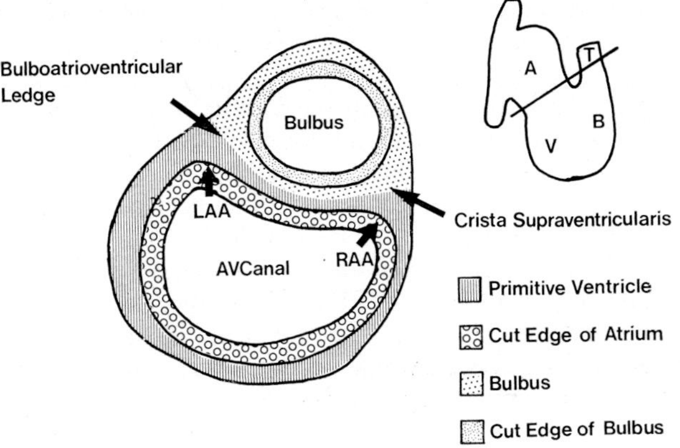

FIG. 15. Diagrammatic representation to show the heart tube after migration of the loop components. The position of the bulbo-atrioventricular ledge is shown, its right margin forming the basis of the crista supraventricularis of the right ventricle.

moves posteriorly relative to the inferior rim. The primary interventricular foramen therefore becomes orientated in an oblique plane overlying the anterior segment of the primitive ventricle, and forms the outflow tract of the primitive ventricle (Fig. 16C,D). This process is considered further in relation to septation of the bulboventricular loop, which, together with septation of the atrial chamber and atrioventricular canal, is considered separately below. Before that consideration will be given to congenital anomalies which can be directly related to maldevelopment during the primary heart tube stage of growth.

Positional Anomalies of the Heart

The normal position of the heart is in the left hemithorax, and is associated with normal position of the other thoraco-abdominal viscera (Fig. 17A). This normal situation results from the persistence of right sided venous channels at the expense of left sided primordia and is termed the situs solitus position. In association with solitus atrial chambers, it has been shown that the bulboventricular loop usually folds to the right so that the right ventricle is formed on the right hand side of the body. This is termed a D-bulboventricular loop and is spoken of as the concordant loop for the solitus individual.

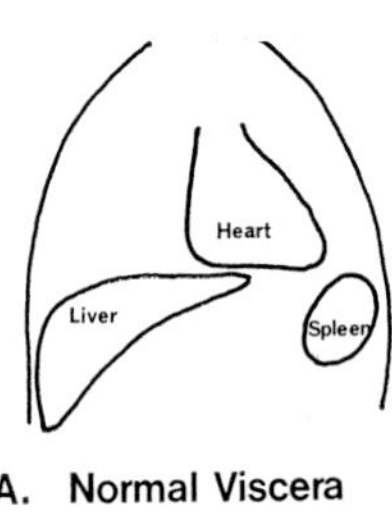

A. Normal Viscera

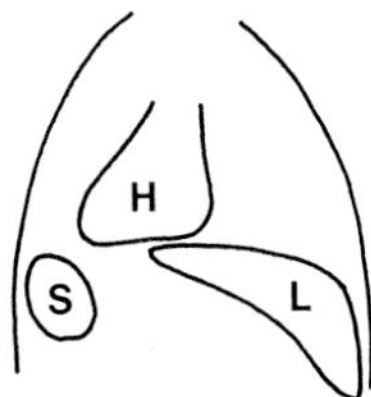
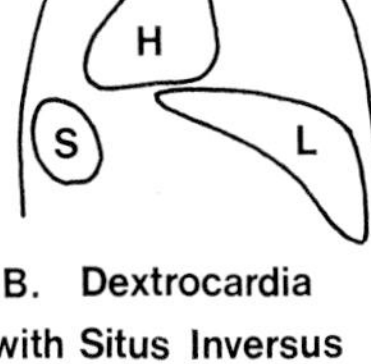

B. Dextrocardia with Situs Inversus

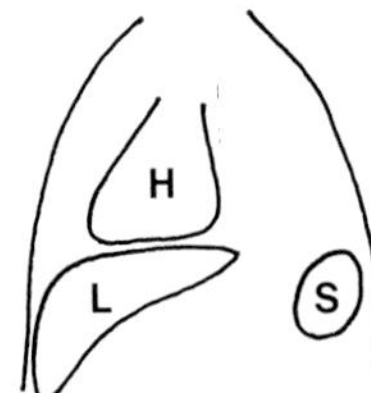

C. Isolated Dextrocardia

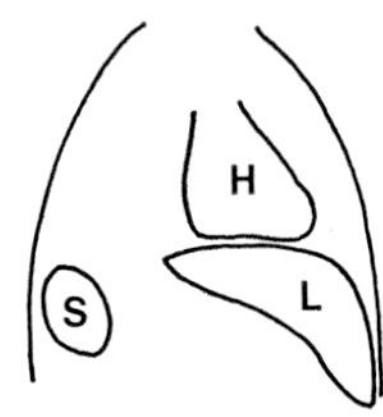

D. Laevocardia

FIG. 17. Diagrams showing the nomenclature commonly used to describe abnormal positions of the thoraco-abdominal viscera.

If, during development, left sided venous primordia develop at the expense of the normal right sided structures, then mirror inversion of the thoraco-abdominal viscera results. Thus the heart develops in the right chest, and the liver becomes a left sided structure. As the atrial chambers invariably develop in one unit with the viscera, the venous atrium becomes a left sided structure, and the position is described as situs inversus (Fig. 17B). In the majority of inversus individuals the bulboventricular loop also folds sinistrally to produce the L-bulboventricular loop, concordant with the inversus position. Since the great arteries are usually developed in inverse but normally related positions, the heart is inverted but otherwise normal in this positional anomaly. The situation is referred to as dextrocardia with situs inversus.

Unfortunately positional anomalies of the heart are not all as simple as the above example. The heart can be situated in the right hemithorax in the solitus individual, the atrial chambers will therefore be in the solitus position, and hence abnormality cannot be related to reversal in development of venous primordia. The position of the heart in this situation is often referred to as isolated dextrocardia, but is better described as dextrocardia with situs solitus (Fig. 17C). The comparable position in the inversus position has the heart in the left chest and is referred to as laevocardia.[43] This term is also ambiguous because the normal heart is in a position of laevocardia, so the abnormal situation is best described as laevocardia with situs inversus (Fig. 17D).

It is clear that usage of the terms dextrocardia or laevocardia gives no indication as to the internal arrangement of the cardiac chambers. In the types described above the atrial chambers have been in normal and inverted positions. Description of the visceroatrial situs indicates the position of the atrial chambers and is an improved terminology, but this usage still conveys no information regarding the arrangement of the ventricles or great vessels. Various nomenclatures have been devised to incorporate this information in the descriptive term, but the results include such phrases as "mixed laevocardia," which are not immediately understandable.[59] In an attempt to circumvent these difficulties Van Praagh and his associates[49] suggested that the positional anomaly should be stated first. Thereafter, the positions of each segment of the primary heart tube should be catalogued according to the possibilities available in embryonic development (Fig. 18). Thus the atrial chambers would be solitus or inversus, D- or L-bulboventricular loops would be present and the great vessels would be transposed or non-transposed. This excellent system is simple and readily understandable, does not use ambiguous terms, and can be used to describe any heart in a manner comprehensible to all.

However, the positional anomalies are further complicated by the documentation of abnormally positioned hearts in association with abnormalities of the spleen.[18] Thus a syndrome is documented in which absence of the spleen is associated with double "right sided" organs. The heart possesses two right atrial chambers, both lungs are trilobed, and multiple intracardiac anomalies are also to be expected. In association with multiple spleens, a further syndrome is described in which the organs exhibit twin "left-handed" characteristics. Thus both lungs are bi-lobed, and although the atrial chambers each receive superior venae cavae, the internal architecture is reminiscent of twin left atria. These two syndromes increase the embryologic possibilities in the classification of atrial chambers suggested by Van Praagh *et al.*[49] and should be included in any documentation.

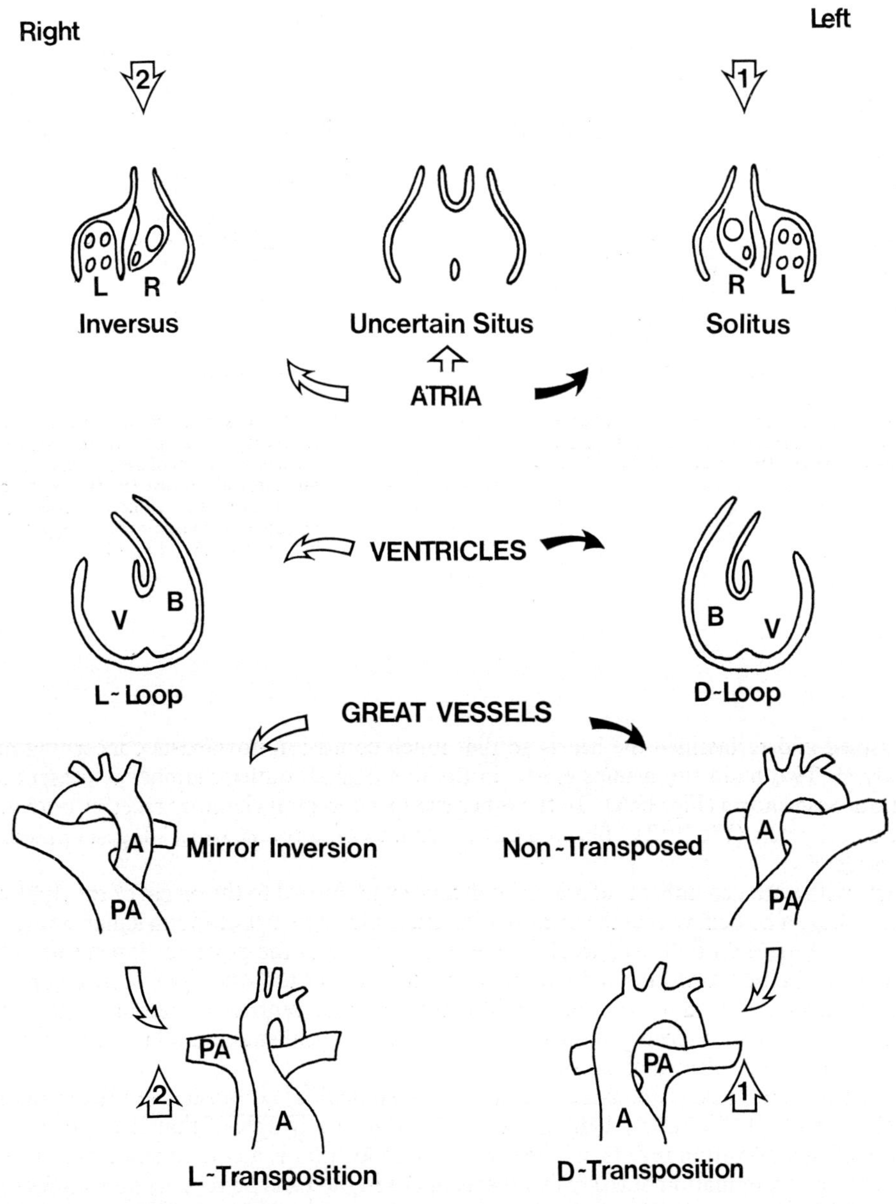

FIG. 18. Diagrams illustrating the nomenclature positions that may be adopted by the segments of the primitive heart tube. Based on Van Praagh, Van Praagh, Vlad and Keith.[49]

Primitive State of the Bulboventricular Loop

Several congenital anomalies are due to arrested development at the primitive heart tube stage, following bending but prior to septation. The most primitive of these conditions is exceedingly rare and there is failure of septation in atrium, ventricle and truncus. The syndrome is known as cor biloculare, and review of several cases is given in Hudson's work.[18] He points out that atresia of tricuspid or mitral valves produces a heart very similar to cor biloculare, and of the cases we have personally studied, all showed evidence of a rudimentary chamber on close examination, and were due to such atrioventricular valve stenosis. Most of the true bilocular hearts are associated with either the asplenic or polysplenic syndromes.

Much more common hearts, although still rare in absolute terms, are the specimens in which the atrial chamber is septated but bulboventricular septation is incomplete. These cases were first described as cor triloculare biatriale, but subsequent investigators have classified and reclassified the hearts so that much confusion now exists concerning nomenclature and subdivision of the anomaly.[32] Two main sub groups exist: in the one a small outlet chamber is present anteriorly which gives rise invariably to the transposed aorta (Fig. 19A). In the other group a common chamber receives both atrioventricular orifices and gives rise to both great vessels (Fig. 19B). Because of the arguments, a recent work suggests that all the hearts should be termed primitive ventricles.[32]

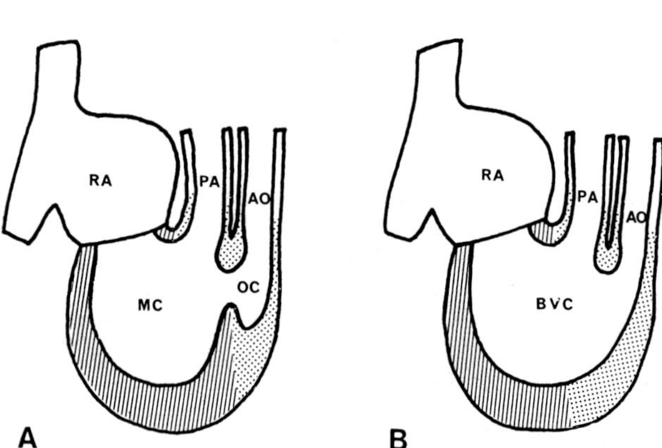

FIG. 19. Sagittal sections illustrating the two frequent varieties of single ventricle. (A) shows the single ventricle with outlet chamber[32] whilst (B) illustrates the "common" ventricle.[32]

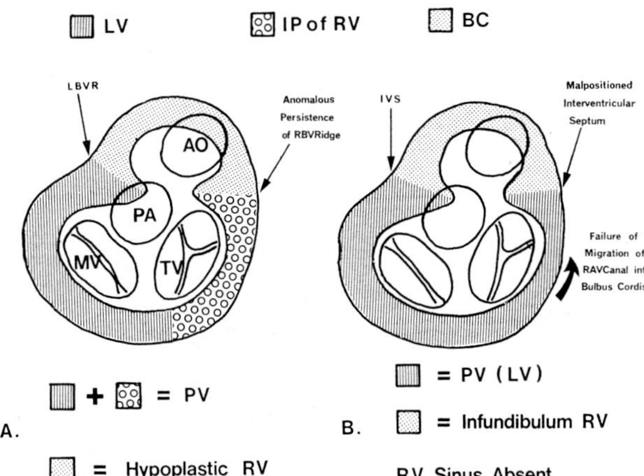

FIG. 20. Diagrams to illustrate the two possible modes of formation of "single" ventricle with outlet chamber. (A) depicts the theory of Lev, Liberthson, Kirkpatrick, Eckner and Arcilla[32] whilst (B) shows the concept espoused by de la Cruz and Miller.[11] These concepts have great import with regard to the origin of the right ventricular inflow tract. (See Fig. 14).

The primitive ventricle with outlet chamber is of great significance with regard to the origin of the right ventricle, and warrants separate consideration. Those who believe that the primitive ventricle gives rise to both ventricular sinuses interpret the anomaly as representing persistence of the right bulboventricular ridge and absence of the posterior interventricular septum (Fig. 20A). Others who consider that the bulbus forms the right ventricle contend either that the right ventricular sinus is absent[50] or that the atrioventricular canal has failed to migrate rightwards so that the interventricular septum is malpositioned (Fig. 20B).[11] Anderson *et al.* have considered these concepts in the light of both histological studies and previous embryological reports and are unable on present evidence to decide which is correct.[2]

More evidence relative to this matter may come from a study of hearts with juxtaposition of the auricular appendages. Lack of migration is a possible cause of the outlet chamber heart. It is generally agreed that juxtaposition is due to incomplete migration. In a D loop left juxtaposition results, whereas right juxtaposition is a consequence of failure of migration in an L loop and is hence much rarer. Examination of the relevant specimens in the Liverpool collection shows that the hearts are quite different in morphology to primitive ventricles, but further study is necessary before any firm conclusion can be reached regarding the embryogenesis of primitive ventricles.

FURTHER GROWTH AND SEPTATION OF THE ATRIAL CHAMBERS

After the development of the anastamoses in the venous system, the sinus venosus opens into the right half of the primitive atrial chamber and the sinuatrial junction is marked by the right and left venous valves. These valves fuse in front of the superior cava to form a spur in the atrial roof, the septum spurium, whilst inferiorly they are in contact with the atrioventricular canal. Within the valves open the superior and inferior venae cavae and the coronary sinus. The valves contact each other between the three vessels as the two limbic bands (Fig. 21A). The superior band subsequently becomes the tubercle of Lower between superior and inferior cavae, whilst the lower band forms part of the sinus septum between inferior cava and coronary sinus (Fig. 22A). The right venous valve is more extensive than the left, and forms flap valves which guard the inferior canal and coronary sinus openings, the Eustachian and Thebesian valves respectively (Figs. 21, 22).

The first sign of septation of the atrial chamber is the appearance of a sagittal crest in the atrial roof to the left of the septum spurium (Fig. 21A and B). This is the septum primum, which together with the left venous valve, grows from the left margin of the sinus venosus.

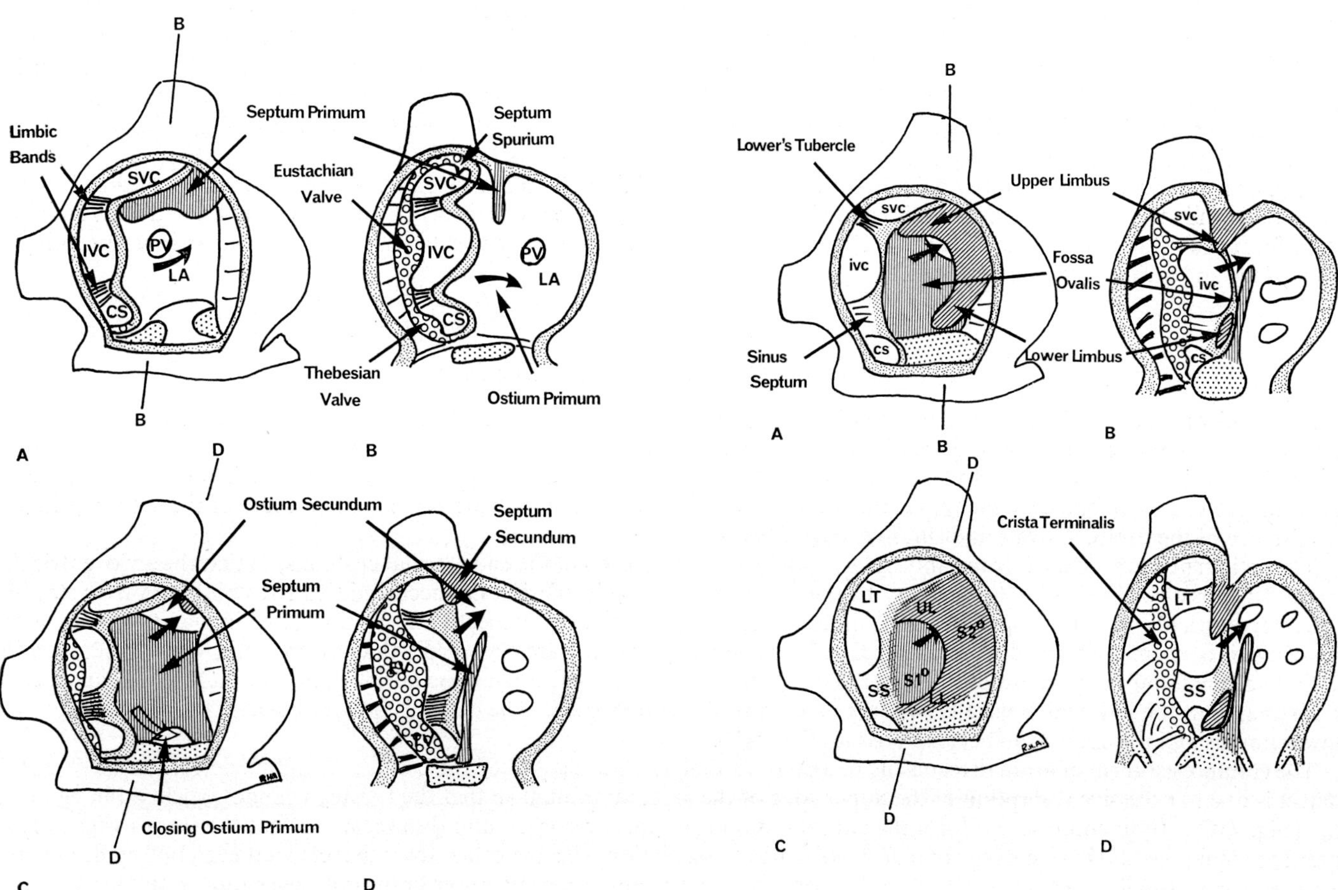

FIGS. 21, 22. Various stages of septation of the atrial chambers. (21A) and (C) and (22A) and (C) show the atria as viewed from the right side, (B) and (D) are frontal sections in the depicted planes on (A) and (C).

||||||||||| Septum Primum ▨ Septum secundum OOOO Right venous valve :::::: Left venous valve

:::::::: Endocardial cushion tissue

The septum advances distally across the atrial chamber towards the atrioventricular canal, with anterior and posterior limbs leading (Fig. 21A). At the same time swellings of the endocardial tissue appear in the superior and inferior margins of the atrioventricular canal. As the septum nears the cushions the anterior limb meets the superior cushion, and the posterior limb meets the inferior cushion. All then fuse so that the ostium primum, originally present between limbs and cushions, becomes obliterated (Figs. 21, 22). Simultaneously with closure of the ostium primum, the septum primum breaks down in the roof of the atrium anterior to the superior cava so forming the ostium secundum (Fig. 21C and D).

Subsequent to formation of the ostium secundum the interatrial fold in the anterior portion of the atrial roof becomes reduplicated to form the limbus fossae ovalis, or septum secundum. According to some authorities,[38] the septum grows posteriorly with superior and inferior limbs. The superior limb forms the upper limbus and fuses with the left venous valve. The inferior limb grows extensively to form the lower limbus, and fuses with endocardial cushion tissue to contribute to the formation of the sinus septum where it fuses with the inferior limbic band. However, according to Los,[34] the fold is only formed superiorly as a reduplication of atrial wall which is overlapped by the free upper margin of the septum primum on its left side. The interatrial communication between limbus and septum primum is the foramen ovale which persists during foetal life as part of the foetal circulation, and usually closes in early neonatal life.

In the definitive atrium the actual interatrial septum is the small area consisting of limbus and fossa ovalis, floored by septum primum. The majority of the chamber is rough walled and represents the primitive atrium. The crista terminalis is probably a derivative of the right venous valve, together with the valves of the inferior cava and coronary sinus.

At the stage at which the septum primum grows from the interatrial fold, the pulmonary vein becomes visible as an evagination outwards from the common atrium. There is some divergence of opinion regarding the origin. Earlier investigators considered that it grew out from the sinus chamber.[6] Van Praagh and Corsini[53] considered it was a mid line structure forming beneath the septum primum but did not indicate its exact origin. Los,[33] in a careful study, showed that it appeared on the left side of the primitive atrial chamber (Fig. 11). Whichever portion it does grow from the vein starts as a blind capillary which grows posteriorly to contact the developing lung buds. It bifurcates several times during this growth, and the first two dichotomies are incorporated to form a common venous channel which forms the only opening into the left atrial chamber. During this growth period the vein, particularly its right branches, is intimately related to the sinus venosus, and lies between the superior cava and the regressing left superior cava. As the veins grow into the lung buds they contact the developing pulmonary venous plexuses. Again there is some disagreement as to whether the venous plexus is derived from the fore-gut splanchnic venous plexus, or from direct growth of the pulmonary venous outgrowth.[5,41] Be that as it may, once contact is established between lungs buds and atrium, the pulmonary veins constituting the common stem are reabsorbed into the chamber, and in its definitive state form the greater part of the left atrial chamber with the four pulmonary venal ostia, the primitive atrium remaining as appendage and atrioventricular vestibule.

Anomalous Growth of the Atrial Chambers

Since lack of space precludes consideration of anomalous growth of all atrial structures, such as the sinus venosus derivatives, only the more important malformations will be described.

The interested reader is referred to Hudson's excellent review[18] for description of the rarer anomalies. The commonest defects of atrial growth are referable to incomplete septation. Three groups are described: incomplete closure of the ostium primum, persistence of the foramen ovale and sinus venosus defects.

The ostium primum defect is invariably linked with incomplete fusion of the endocardial cushions, so that the atrioventricular canal defect is also classified in this group. In the canal type no cushion fusion has occurred and two common valves straddle the interventricular septum (Fig. 23A). The limbs of septum primum usually meet both cushions, and in many such hearts the fossa ovalis is normally formed. Various types of atrioventricular canal are classified, which decrease in severity between the complete canal and the pure ostium primum defect.[7] In the primum defect itself the cushions are normally fused apart from a small area to the left, which usually produces a cleft in the mitral valve. The defect is present beneath the normally formed lower limbus and the endocardial cushion tissue (Fig. 23B).

The commonest form of atrial defect is the persistent foramen ovale, also called the ostium secundum defect. In all cases this defect is due to excessive resorption of the upper edge of the septum primum so that the foramen cannot be closed in neonatal life (Fig. 23C). In its more severe form the entire septum primum is resorbed and disappears so that the fossa ovalis is completely patent (Fig. 23D). This type of defect can exist in association with the other atrial defects, and even in "single atrium" a bar of tissue usually stretches across the chamber, probably representing the lower limbus of the septum secundum.

The rarest group of atrial defects is the sinus venosus defect. The wall of the sinus beneath the superior cava is defective, and the right pulmonary veins always drain into the right atrium through the defect. This defect underlines the embryologic connection between the right pulmonary veins and the sinus venosus, since the right pulmonary fold is a normal constituent of the interatrial septum on its left side.

The main defect occurring in the left atrial chamber is anomalous incorporation or drainage of the pulmonary veins. The entire common venous chamber may fail to be absorbed into the left atrium, and persist as a separate chamber which opens into the primitive left atrium through the stenosed common pulmonary vein. Originally believed to represent malincorporation of the veins,[15] the condition is termed cor triatriatum. Recently the morphology and embryogenosis have been thoroughly studied by Van Praagh and Corsini,[53] who conclude that the condition is due to entrapment of the common pulmonary vein within the absorbing sinus venosus.

Anomalous pulmonary veins can drain into almost any adjacent venous channel within the thorax, but most commonly drain to the sinus venosus and its major tributaries. This fact is strong evidence for their origin from the splanchnic fore-gut venous plexus, and emphasizes once again the connection between pulmonary veins and sinus venosus. The condition is reviewed extensively by Hudson.[18]

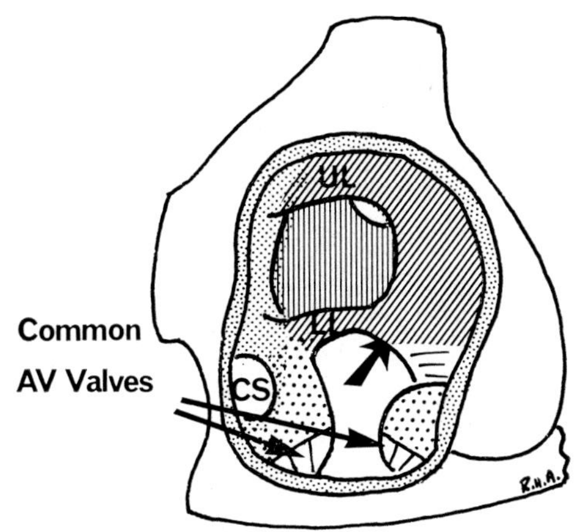

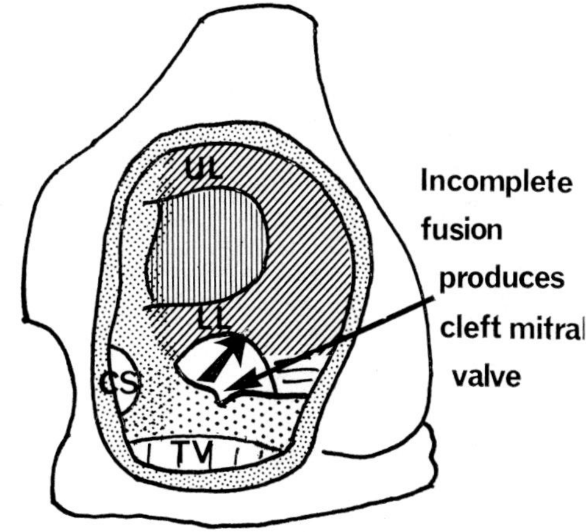

A. Atrioventricular Canal

B. Ostium Primum Defect

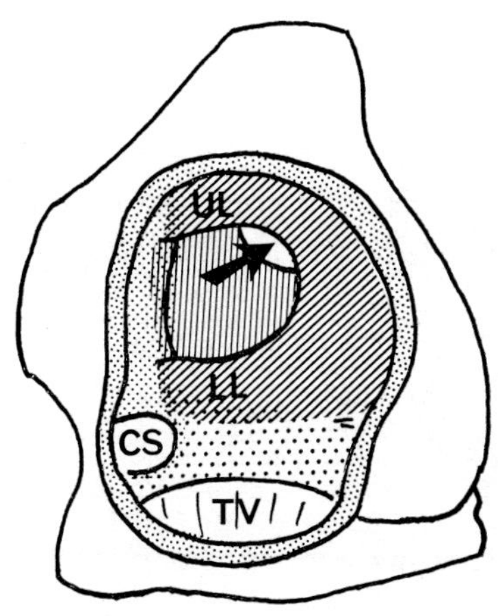

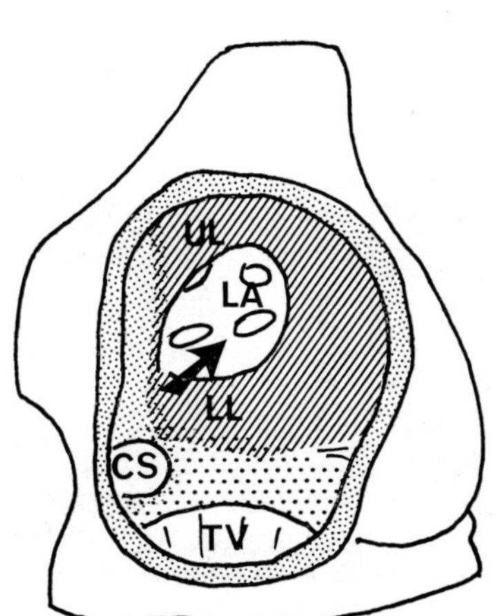

C. Persistent Foramen Ovale

D Patent Fossa Ovalis

FIG. 23. These diagrams illustrate the defects resulting from atrial malseptation.

||||||||||| Septum Primum ▨▨▨ Septum secundum OOOO Right venous valve

⁚⁚⁚⁚ Left venous valve ::::: Endocardial cushion tissue

FURTHER GROWTH AND SEPTATION OF THE BULBOVENTRICULAR LOOP

We have already described how bending and migration of the segments of the bulboventricular loop are responsible for producing two ventricles and the intervening muscular septum. For the remainder of this section we shall presume that the posterior septum is a result of septation of the primitive ventricle, although as we have indicated, this concept may not be correct. We have also shown previously that the posterior portion of the bulbus migrates into the atrioventricular canal region to bring the aortic root above the left ventricle (Figs. 15, 16). However, we have not indicated the involvement in this process of the cushion tissue derived from the endothelial lining of the primary heart tube.

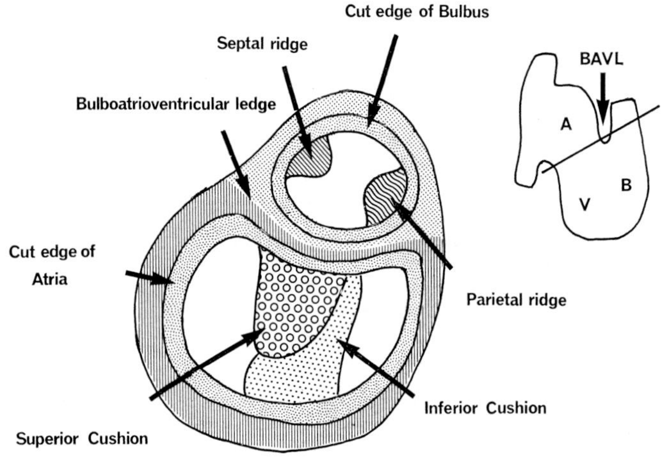

FIG. 24. Diagram of the heart tube after migration of its components showing the positions of the cushion musculature. See Fig. 14 for orientation of specimen.

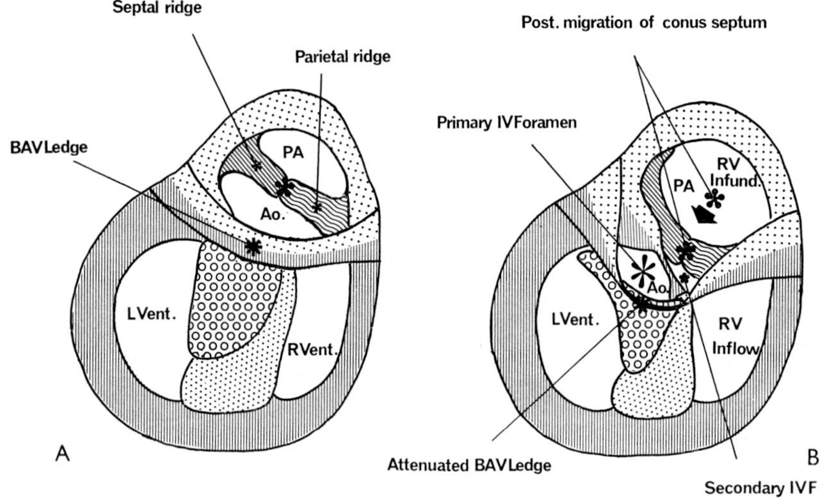

FIG. 25. Diagrams showing the bulboventricular ledge before (A), and after (B), backward migration of the bulbus. Attenuation of the ledge brings the primary IV foramen above the primitive ventricle. At the same time the newly fused conal ridges also move posteriorly to block off the anterior segment of the newly formed secondary foramen. Compare with Fig. 16. Shading as in Fig. 24.

Cushions are formed in relation to both the atrioventricular canal and bulbotruncus simultaneously with the bending processes already described. We referred briefly to the atrioventricular cushions during the description of atrial septation. Although generally described as rounded cushions which grow at the superior and inferior margins of the canal, the reconstructions of Los[34] have shown that the two cushions differ considerably from each other in shape and form. Thus the superior cushion is triangular in shape and after their fusion, overlies the prismatic elongated, lower cushion. After fusion, both cushions are relations of the left AV orifice but only the inferior cushion bounds the right orifice (Fig. 24). Simultaneously with the growth of these cushions, elongated swellings are formed within the distal bulbus and truncus. At present we are concerned only with the proximal ends of these ridges which encroach upon the bulbar cavity. Growth of the distal parts of these ridges will be considered subsequently in the section devoted to the truncus. The proximal ends grow from the dextrodorsal and sinistroventral aspects of the bulbus, and are named as such by Van Mierop *et al.*[46] Los[34] refers to the swellings as parietal and septal ridges respectively, and we shall conform to his nomenclature (Fig. 24). As the two ridges fuse they form the lower end of the septum between the developing great arteries and can therefore be termed the conus septum. At this stage the truncus still completely overrides the bulbar cavity and the interventricular foramen is therefore a ventriculobulbar structure (Fig. 25A). With posterior migration of the truncobulbar junction into the AV canal, as already described (Figs. 15, 16), the bulboatrioventricular ledge becomes absorbed into the fused endocardial cushions, in particular the superior cushion (Figs. 15, 16). This process has many important consequences. Firstly the middle portion of the ledge becomes attenuated (Fig. 25B). This area eventually becomes fibrous in the definitive heart as the fibrous trigones, and results in the aorta arising directly from fibrous tissue in its posterior quadrant rather than from bulbar musculature as in its other quadrants and as with the pulmonary artery. It also produces the fibrous continuity present in the normal heart between the aortic and mitral valves (Fig. 26). In addition the attenuation of the ledge and cushions results in part of the fibrous aortic root separating the aortic lumen from the right atrial chamber (Fig. 27).

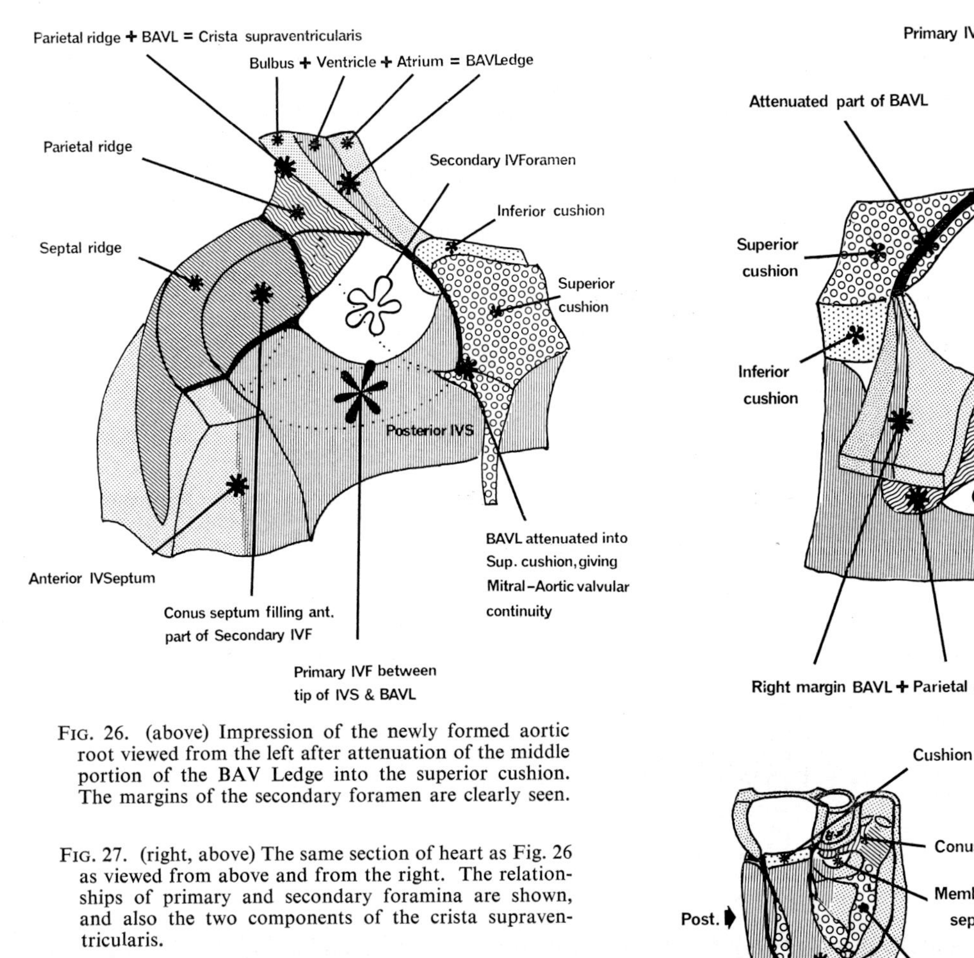

FIG. 26. (above) Impression of the newly formed aortic root viewed from the left after attenuation of the middle portion of the BAV Ledge into the superior cushion. The margins of the secondary foramen are clearly seen.

FIG. 27. (right, above) The same section of heart as Fig. 26 as viewed from above and from the right. The relationships of primary and secondary foramina are shown, and also the two components of the crista supraventricularis.

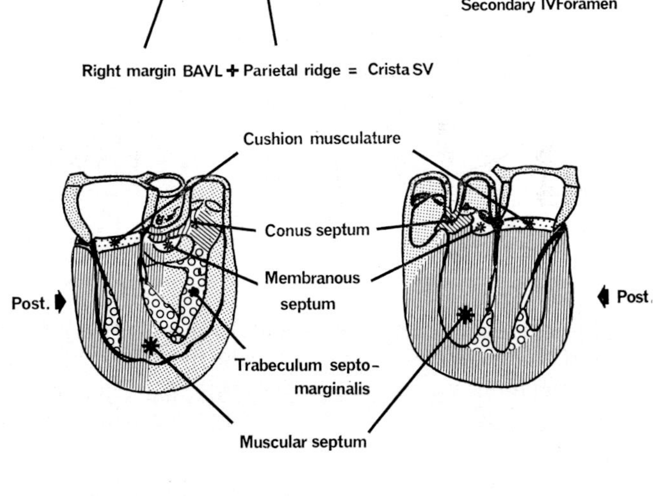

FIG. 28. (right, below) The definitive ventricular septum viewed from right and left sides showing the embryologic origin of its components.

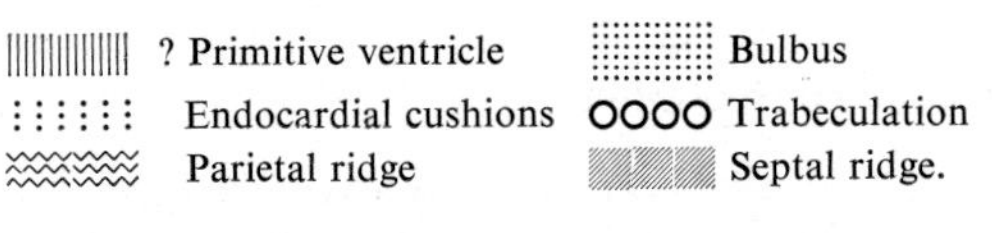

The second consequence of bulbar migration is that the primary interventricular foramen, between the tip of the muscular septum and the BAV Ledge, becomes reorientated in oblique plane as the opening to the aortic root (Figs. 15, 16, 24–28). This process also produces the secondary interventricular foramen which is in the right wall of the primary foramen, between it and the bulbus. Thirdly, the migratory process carries the conus septum posteriorly. This has the immediate effect of closing off the antero-superior portion of the secondary foramen, since the septal ridge of the septum fuses with the anterior interventricular septum (Figs. 26, 27). After migration has occurred the parietal ridge then arches laterally from the interventricular septum across the roof of the right ventricle, lying beneath the right margin of the bulboatrioventricular ledge (Figs. 26, 27). These two components together form the crista supraventricularis, normally found between the tricuspid and pulmonary valves. Thus the remaining secondary foramen is bounded antero-superiorly by the conus septum, inferiorly by the tip of the muscular septum and posteriorly by the endocardial cushions. This is the area which is filled by growth from the inferior cushion,[34] and thus becomes the membranous part of the interventricular septum (Fig. 28).

Whilst differing from the classical account of closure of the interventricular foramen,[37] this concept seems to us to fit in best with the concept of posterior migration which is essential to carry the aorta above the left ventricle.[46] It also accounts for the normal appearance of the heart, and as will emerge, it affords a simple explanation for malformations occurring during bulboventricular growth. In particular it emphasizes that the secondary interventricular foramen when closed becomes the membranous septum, whilst the primary foramen persists as the ostium to the aorta. This point, shown most clearly in the work of Van Mierop *et al.*,[46] is surprisingly not referred to in some otherwise authoritative reviews.[38]

Following completion of the interventricular septum the atrioventricular valves are formed within the newly partitioned right and left ventricles. The attached margins are formed from the endocardial cushions together with lateral cushions (Fig. 29). Both Van Mierop *et al.*[46] and Los[34] suggest that the parietal ridge, having arched above the right ventricle, comes into contact with the tricuspid orifice and forms part of the valvular tissue. However, study of malformed hearts casts doubts on this concept. Rather paradoxically Los's reconstructions show that whilst the tricuspid valve is derived from only two cushions, the mitral valve has three cushion components. The cusps, chordae and papillary muscles are formed by trabeculation and undermining of the ventricular surfaces (Fig. 29). Van Mierop *et al.*[46] believe that such trabeculation is also responsible for producing the trabeculum septomarginalis and moderator band of the right ventricle. Others consider that these structures represent the downward extension of the septal ridge into the ventricular cavity, and some suggest that septal and parietal ridges fuse towards the apex, thus forming a muscular band between the right ventricular inflow and the infundibular portions.[35]

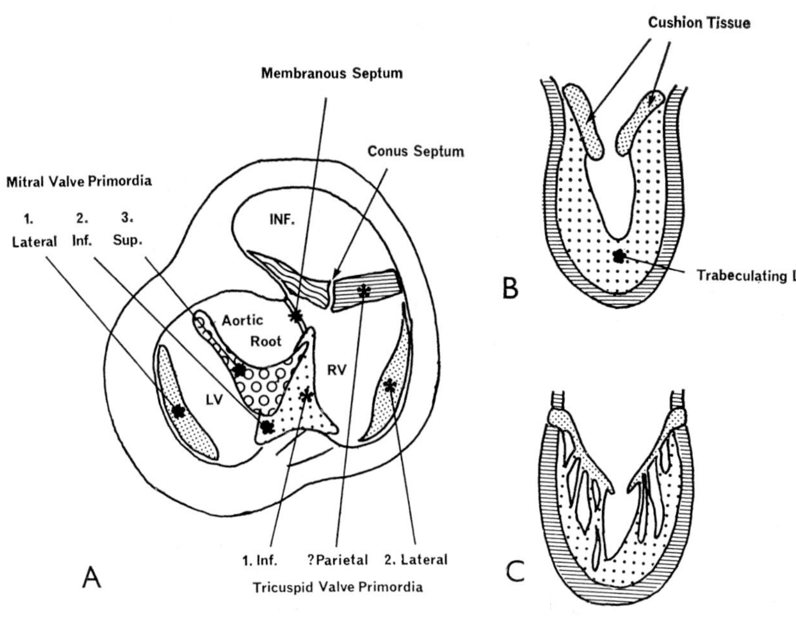

FIG. 29. Diagrams showing the components of the atrioventricular valves. (A) cushions contributing to the valves. It is possible that the lateral cushion of the tricuspid valve may be formed from the parietal ridge (34, 46). (B) and (C) show stages in the formation of the valvular tension apparatus from the trabeculating myocardial layer (based on Walmsley, T.—Quain's Anatomy 4 III p. 59, 1929).

In a normal heart there are marked differences between the trabecular pattern in the right and left ventricles. This provides a means of chamber differentiation since the right trabeculations are coarse, whilst the left are exceedingly fine. It is claimed that such trabeculation is a result of embryologic determination,[50] but study of malformed hearts suggests that pressure and flow characteristics in the chambers may modify the original trabecular pattern present.

Abnormalities of Bulboventricular Growth and Septation

As in the atria, the commonest malformations represent defective closure or formation of the interventricular septum. As explained above, the septum is formed in part from the endocardial cushions, and in part from the membranous, muscular and conal septa. Defects of the cushions of necessity produce valvular defects, and are classified together with ostium primum defects of the interatrial septum as atrioventricular canals (*see* p. 178). Defects in any of the other segments can present as isolated malformations. The commonest type is produced by failure of closure of the secondary interventricular foramen and is termed a membranous defect (Fig. 30A). Less common are the defects in the muscular septum, often multiple, which represent excessive septal trabeculation (Fig. 30B). Rarest are the defects in the conus septum, also termed supracristal, since they are above the crista supraventricularis.

Ventricular septal defect is a common feature of other bulboventricular malformations. This is hardly surprising as it will be appreciated that normal closure of the septum is dependant upon normal growth and migration of several loop components. The major abnormalities involving defective bulboventricular growth are Fallot's tetralogy, various types of double outlet right ventricle, and transposition of the great vessels. It may be thought that these abnormalities represent different morphogenetic faults. Van Mierop *et al.*[47] correlated the first two as faulty transfer of the posterior great artery, but considered that transposition was quite different, and represented faulty formation of the truncal ridges. They therefore postulated that Fallot's tetralogy was due to faulty incorporation of the aorta into the superior cushion, but that incorporation was sufficient to ensure mitral aortic continuity. The tetralogy is, of course, represented by dextroposition of the aorta, VSD, pulmonary stenosis and right ventricular hypertrophy. They thought that a double outlet right ventricle represented persistence of the embryonic stage of the loop in which both great vessels arose above the bulbus, and in which they were separated from the atrioventricular canal bythe bulboatrioventricular ledge. However, they considered that the anatomy of transpositions was no different from that of normal hearts, except that the great vessels were reversed, with the aorta slightly more to the right than the position of the pulmonary artery. This concept of transposition, dependent upon straight fusion of truncal ridges, had already been generally accepted, but it did not appeal to Van Praagh and his associates. They showed in a series of persuasive reviews that the bulk of

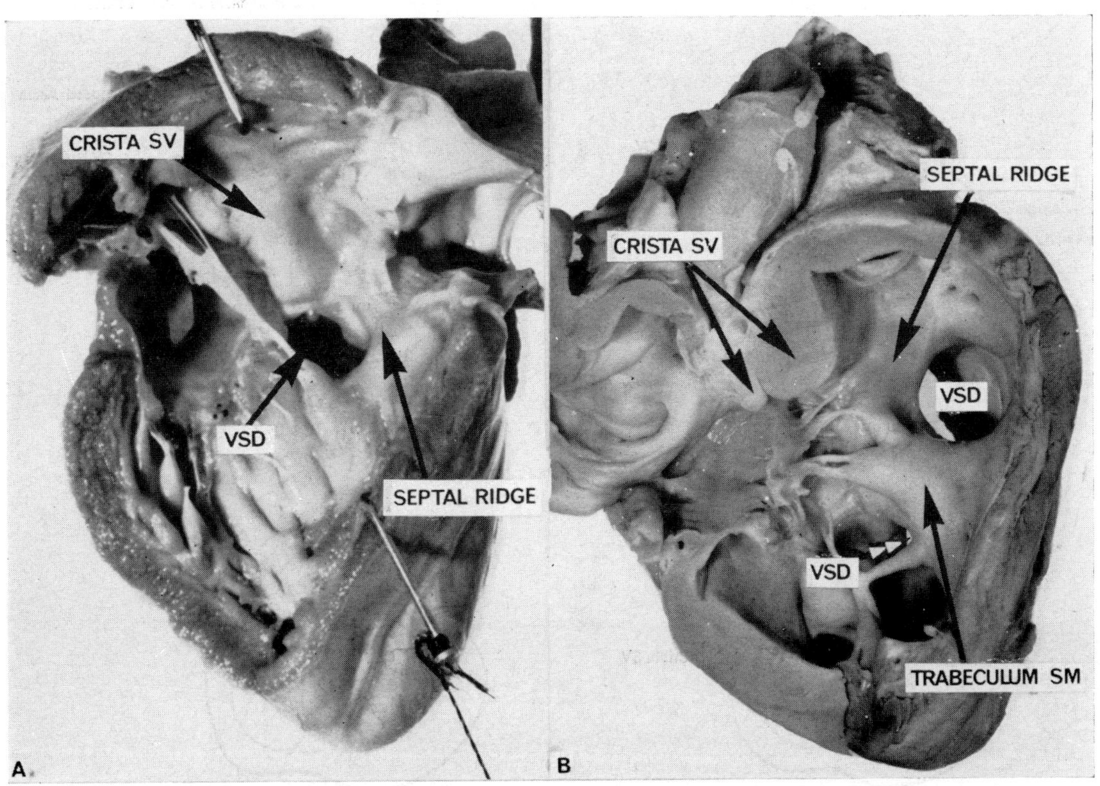

FIG. 30. Photographs of heart specimens showing (A) membranous and (B) two muscular defects. It is possible that (B) represents absence of the anterior bulboventricular septum, and that the defects continuous but are bridged by the trabeculum septomarginalis. The conducting tissue in this heart was intimately related to the lower defect.[28] Note also the large crista made up of two distinct components.

evidence made the truncal ridge hypothesis of transpositions untenable.[51,54,55] They concluded that transpositions were the result of a bulboventricular anomaly, and that all such anomalies were explainable on their new hypothesis of differential conal growth.

This hypothesis postulates that in the development of the normal heart the pulmonary artery originates in a posterior position. During growth it expands and develops a muscular conus. The aorta, however, does not grow and retains its posterior position and its fibrous conus. Fallot's tetralogy is therefore explainable on the basis of hypoplastic growth of the pulmonary conus, as this one factor could produce all four features of the classical tetrad.[54] Double outlet right ventricle is explained by equal growth of both conuses.[51] According to them transposition is due to expansile growth of the sub-aortic conus, with lack of growth of the pulmonary conus.[55] The major point in favour of this hypothesis is that it explains all forms of transposition,[24] whereas Van Mierop *et al.* only accepted the presence of classically complete and classically corrected transposition.[48]

In collaboration with colleagues in Liverpool we have studied over two hundred hearts with bulboventricular malformations. These investigations are of great relevance to this problem. We agree with Van Mierop *et al.* regarding the morphogenesis of Fallot's tetralogy and double outlet right ventricle. However, we believe that our findings demonstrate a further link between the two, and between them and transpositions. Thus we believe that in Fallot's tetralogy the parietal ridge is attached further towards the anterior aspect of the infundibulum having migrated through 30–45° from the normal position. This has the effect of increasing the width of the crista, and prevents complete backwards migration of the bulbus and closure of the VSD (Fig. 31B). It also forces the conus septum to encroach upon the lumen of the pulmonary artery, and excessive growth of this septum produces the infundibular stenosis. In a double outlet right ventricle the parietal ridge has migrated even further, indeed through a right angle, and is completely divorced from the bulboatrioventricular ledge which persists as the crista (Fig. 31C). The conus septum is therefore in the sagittal plane, and prevents any backward migration of the bulbus, which retains its embryonic relationship with the canal as the persistent bulboatrioventricular ledge. The septal ridge fuses with the ventricular septum, but in

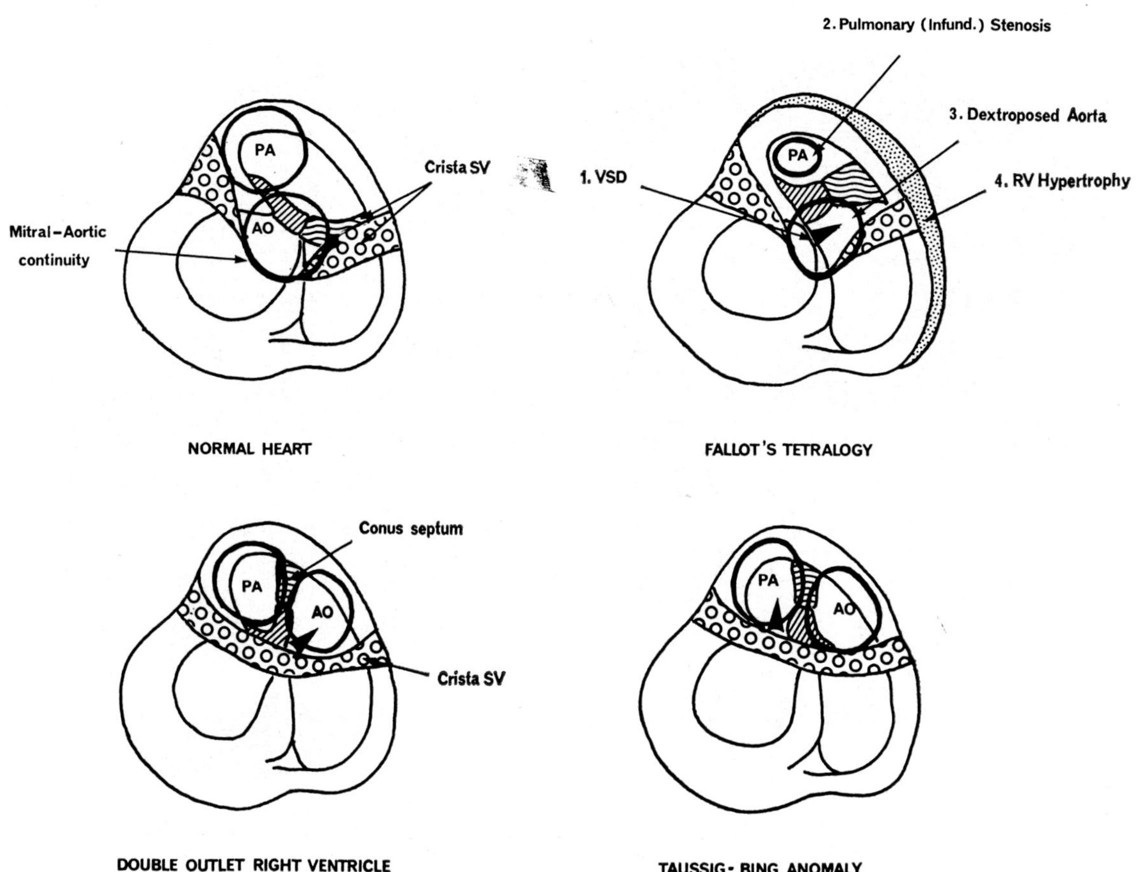

Figs. 31, 32. Diagrams showing how the major bulboventricular anomalies can be explained on the basis of malposition of the conus septum and persistence of the bulboatrioventricular ledge. Based on a study of 200 specimens in the pathologic collection of the Royal Liverpool Children's Hospital.[4]

○○○ BAV Ledge   ▨▨▨ Septal ridge   ≋≋≋ Parietal ridge.

the absence of migration it blocks part of the primary, and not the secondary, bulboventricular foramen. If the septal ridge fuses with the left side of the anterior septum then the persisting defect lies beneath the aorta, and the typical double outlet right ventricle results (Fig. 31C). If, however, it becomes fused to the right side of the foramen, the remaining defect is beneath the pulmonary artery, and the malformation is known as the Taussig-Bing anomaly[44] (Fig. 31D).

Finally, although the above findings are in accord with the concept of Van Mierop *et al.*,[47] our morphologic findings regarding transposition are in close agreement with those of Van Praagh *et al.*[51,54] In addition, we have noted that the ventricular septum is completely in the sagittal plane in transpositions (Fig. 32A). We concede that such findings are not due to straight fusion of the truncal ridges. However, we are unable to accept the concept of differential conal growth. This concept supposes that the pulmonary conus is originally posterior, illustrated by them at the straight tube stage. Actually if any straight tube is bent in the manner of the heart tube, the component originally lying posteriorly automatically becomes anterior in the bulbar area.[60] Moreover, reconstructions show that the infundibulum is normally produced in an anterior position, with the aorta lying posteriorly[34,46] We therefore believe that growth is not necessary to produce an anterior pulmonary artery. In transpositions we also believe that the conal ridges are positioned exactly as in the Taussig-Bing anomaly. However, the sub-pulmonary defect is enlarged to such an extent that the conus septum fuses completely with the ventricular septum, producing a sagitally orientated

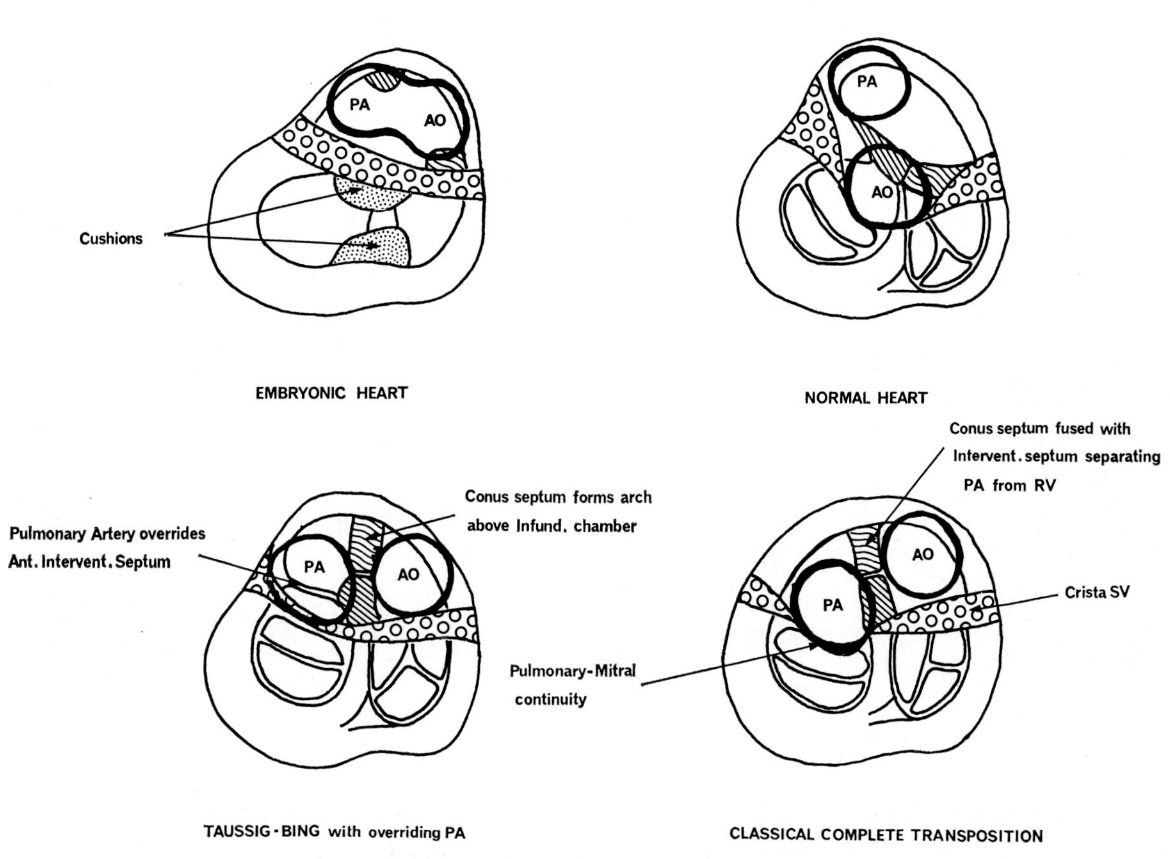

FIG. 32.

septum. The bulboatrioventricular ledge can then become attenuated on the left side to allow pulmonary-mitral valve continuity (Fig. 32B), and the pulmonary artery arises completely from the left ventricle. The aorta retains its embryonic position above the right ventricle. Thus, in our opinion, all major bulboventricular anomalies represent incorrect orientation of the conus ridges, and are explained on the basis of persistence of embryonic characteristics.

Anomalous growth within the ventricles can also produce valvular anomalies. If the endocardial and lateral cushions fail to separate correctly then either atresia or less commonly stenosis of the valves occurs. The anomaly is usually accompanied by hypoplasia of the underlying ventricular chamber. A further valvular deformity peculiar to the tricuspid valve is produced by lack of undermining of the septal or posterior cusp. The cusp therefore becomes firmly adherent to the ventricular wall and the condition is known as Ebstein's anomaly.

DEVELOPMENT OF THE TRUNCUS AND AORTIC ARCHES

From the bulbotruncal junction, the truncus extends cranially in front of the atrial chamber, lying between the atrial appendages, until it becomes the aortic sac. From this sac the aortic arches are developed and grow round the fore-gut. As already described, the first three arches do not persist, whilst the fifth arch is rudimentary. Thus, after folding of the tube, only the fourth and sixth arches originate from the aortic sac (Fig. 33). Mention has already been made of the endothelial cushions which appear within the lumen of the truncus, and extend cranio-caudally between the bulbar cavity and the aortic sac. The relations of the proximal ends to the bulbus have already been described in some detail. Van Mierop *et al.* consider that the bulbar swellings are in fact distinct from the truncal ridges, but the reconstructions of Los[34] show that the two form a continuous primordiuum. Both workers, however, agree regarding the disposition of the ridges within the truncus.

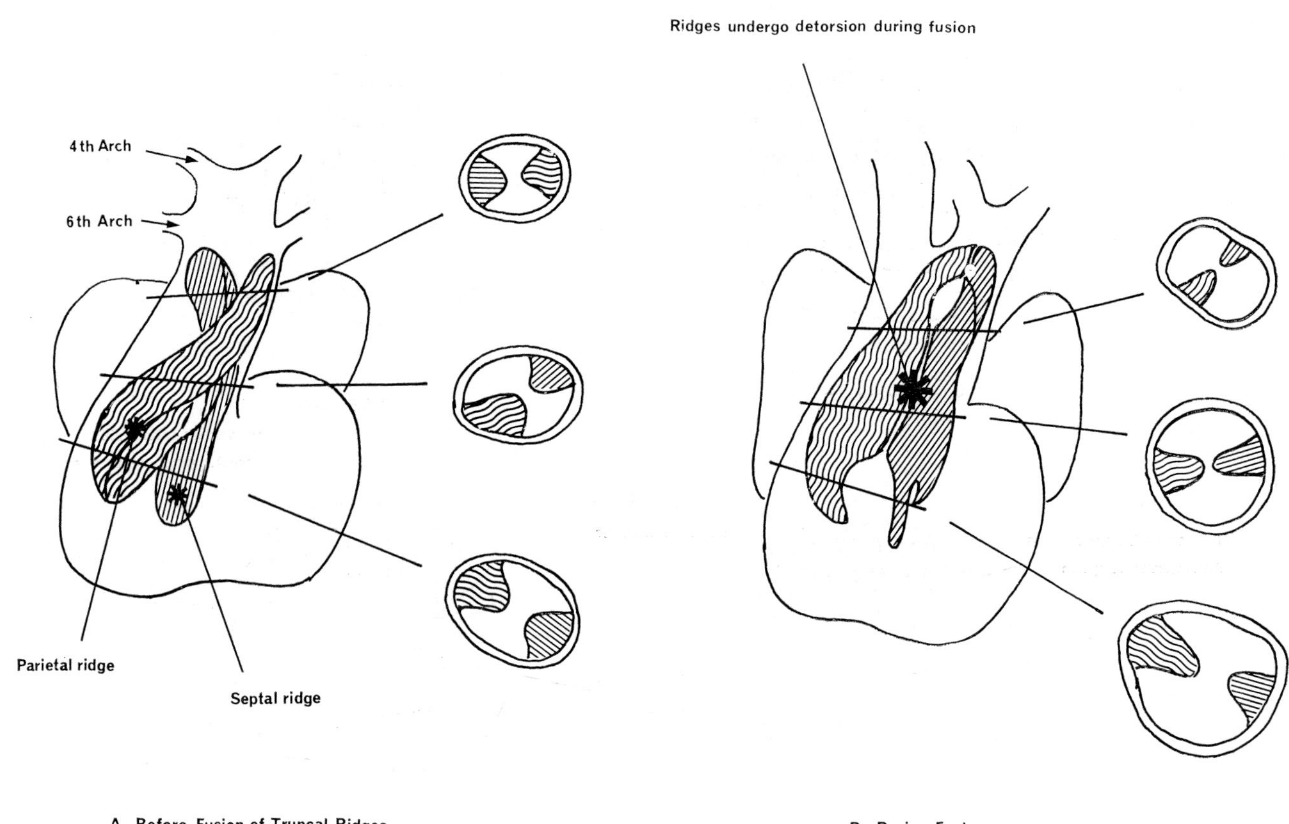

FIG. 33. Diagrams showing the mode of fusion of the cushions septating the distal bulbus and proximal truncus. Based on the reconstructions of Los, J. A.[34]

The ridge attached to the anterior interventricular septum, the sinistroventral[46] ridge or septal[34] ridge, runs distally to cross behind the lumen of the truncus, and ends proximal to the right sixth arch artery. The dextro-dorsal,[46] or parietal,[34] ridge runs in a similar direction, but crosses the front of the truncal lumen, and ends proximal to the left sixth arch artery (Fig. 33). According to Los,[34] as the two ridges gradually fuse to divide the truncus into the aorta and pulmonary artery, there is an associated posterior growth of the proximal aortic sac and sixth arch arteries. This has the effect of displacing the origin of the fourth arch arteries in an anterior and rightward direction. As growth proceeds the two ridges fuse at their opposing edges, so that the anterior cavity of the truncus becomes connected to the expanded sixth arch portion of the sac, whilst the posterior channel becomes continuous with the arteriorly deviated fourth arch arteries. The division of the aortic sac portion is accomplished by ingrowth of a wedge of extracardiac mesenchyme between the two arches. This aortico-pulmonary septum fuses with the distal end of the truncal septum. Los therefore believes that the ridges undergo detorsion as they fuse, rather than the torsion which is generally accepted as producing the helicoidal truncus septum (Fig. 33). In Los's opinion, this torsion is the result of the asymmetric growth of the aortic sac components. Regarding the growth of the truncal ridges the interpretations of Van Mierop *et al.*[46] are in agreement with those of Los,[34] but Van Mierop *et al.* do not comment on the septal detorsion noted by Los.

Originally all the aortic arches are connected with the dorsal aorta on both sides (Fig. 4A) but only the left fourth arch persists as the definitive aortic arch (Fig. 4B). During foetal life the connection between the sixth arch and the aorta persists as the ductus arteriosus.

According to Van Mierop and his colleagues[46] the semi-lunar valves are formed at the junction of conal and truncal ridges. They believe that the cuspidal primordia appear as paired tubercles on the distal faces of the truncus swellings. The third primordium appears on the aortic and pulmonary walls between the fused truncal swellings. These are termed the intercalated valve swellings.[27] The valves and sinuses are subsequently formed by excavation of the swellings and truncal wall in a proximal direction.

Maldevelopment of the Truncus

Should the truncal swellings fail to fuse in whole or in part then the various forms of persistent truncus arteriosus arise. Thus a single artery emerges from the heart, guarded by a single semilunar valve. Although this valve ought to possess four cusps, two from the truncus ridges and two from the intercalated swellings, normally the valve in truncus cases is tricuspid. In such

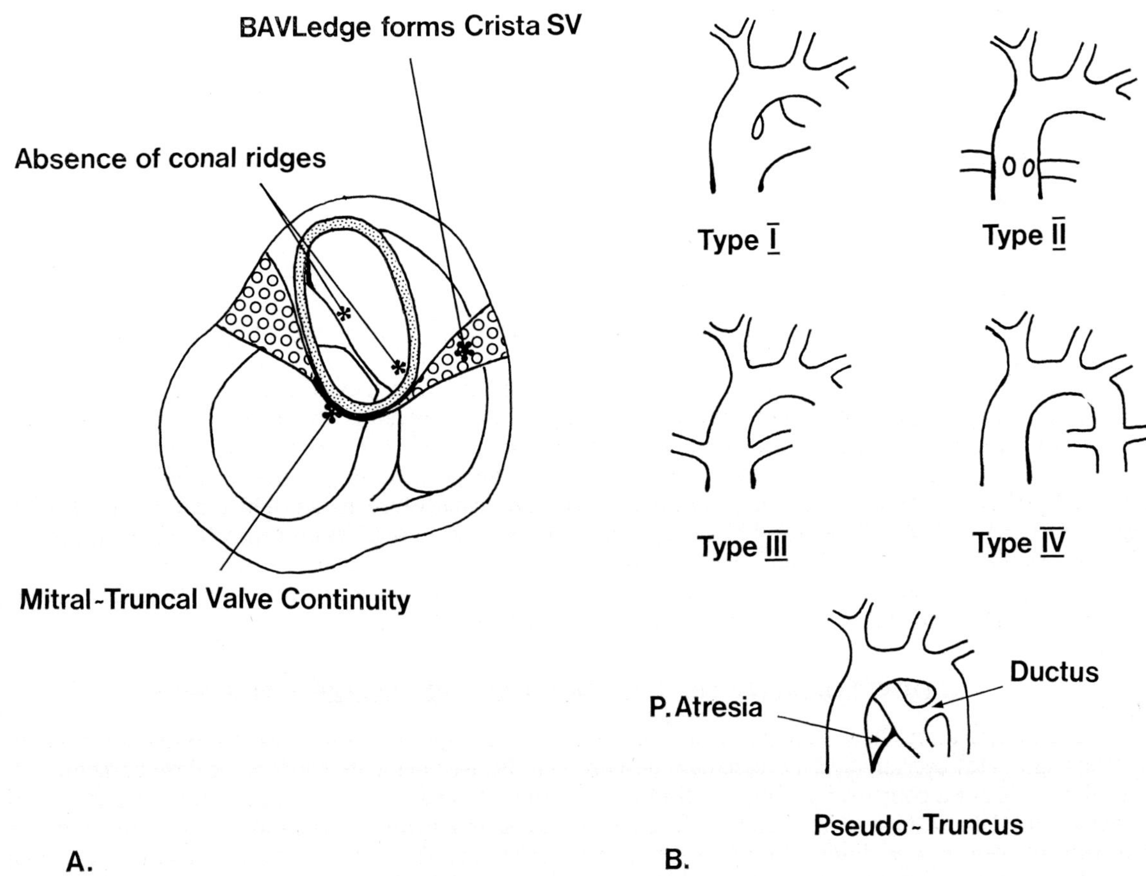

FIG. 34. (A) Plan view of the truncus deformity. (B) Classification of truncus defects. Based on Wilkinson and Acerete's[59] modification of the work of Collett and Edwards.[9]

hearts the posterior part of the truncus is usually absorbed into the atrioventricular cushions so that mitral semilunar fibrous continuity is present, but in the absence of the conus septum the right margin of the primary interventricular foramen persists as a wide defect beneath the truncal cavity.

The manner in which the great arteries arise from the truncus has been used to subdivide the anomalies into classes,[8] but in all true truncus deformities the pulmonary arteries arise from the common trunk. When they arise from the ductus arteriosus a pseudo-truncus is present, and usually indicates the presence of pulmonary atresia (Fig. 34).

In other cases the truncus may be septated in its proximal segment so that two valves are present. A wide defect is present distally between the aorta and pulmonary artery. This type of anomaly is termed an aortico-pulmonary window and represents incomplete development and fusion of the extracardiac aortico-pulmonary mesenchyme with the truncus septum.

A commoner defect of the truncal area is persistence of the ductus arteriosus. This structure in the fetus allows right ventricular blood to reach the aorta without traversing the pulmonary circulation, and normally it closes rapidly in the neonatal period. Associated with the remoulding of these vessels which occurs at birth is the anomaly of coarctation of the aorta. During fetal life the segment of arch between the left subclavian artery and the ductus is narrowed since it carries little blood, and is termed the isthmus. Following normal closure of the ductus, the isthmus gradually enlarges until it is the same diameter as the rest of the aorta. If the narrowing persists, it produces coarctation of the aorta (Fig. 35). Two types are described; the infantile form in which the ductus remains patent, and the adult type which presumably develops after normal ductal closure due to deficient growth of the isthmus compared with the remainder of the aorta. This allows the typical collateral channels of coarctation to develop and enables life to be maintained.

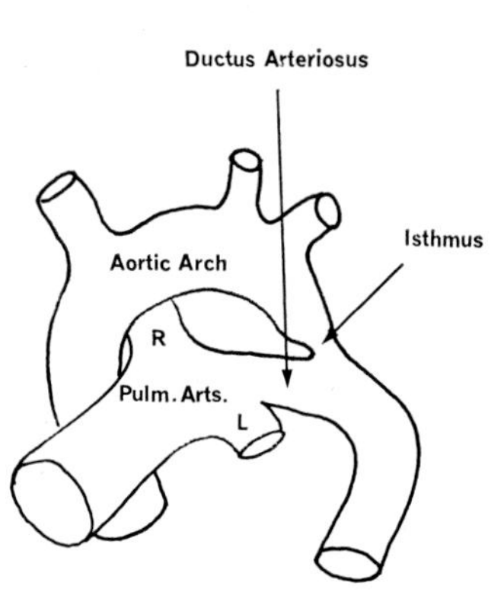

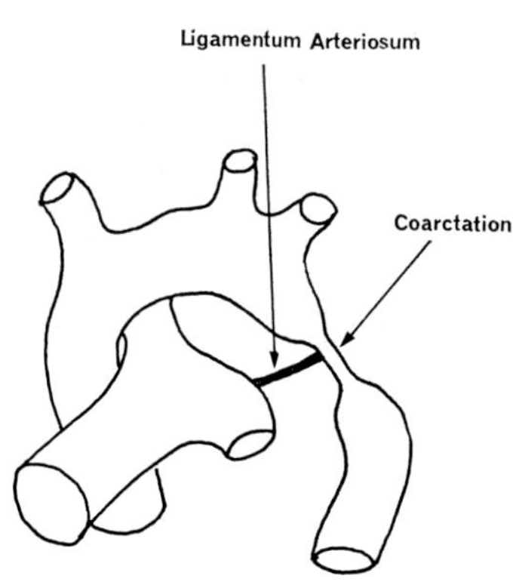

FIG. 35. Diagrams showing (A) the normally narrowed aortic isthmus during fetal circulation and (B) the common situation of the stenosed segment in adult-type coarctation.

Deformities of the semilunar valve primordia produce, as with the atrioventricular valves, either stenosis or atresia depending on the severity of the maldevelopment.

Many authorities consider that transposition of the great arteries is due to a truncal malformation. They postulate that the truncal ridges fuse in straight rather than helicoidal fashion, and consequently the anterior infundibulum of the right ventricle becomes attached to the anterior fourth arch part of the aortic sac.[12,30,48] Two main arguments contravene this hypothesis. Firstly, if the straight ridge theory is correct then the heart in transposition should have normal conal morphologies;[48] it does not. Secondly, the reconstructions of Los[34] show that the ridges normally fuse in a straight and not in a helicoidal fashion. For these reasons we agree with Van Praagh and his associates that another hypothesis is necessary to explain the morphogenesis of transpositions. As we have explained above we do not accept their differential conal growth hypothesis, and in its place we propose the concept of malposition of the conus septum,[4] with associated incorporation of the pulmonary artery from its normal embryonic position (above the bulbus) into the left ventricle (Figs. 32, 33).

DEVELOPMENT OF THE CARDIAC SPECIALIZED TISSUE

Many studies and investigations have been performed on the cardiac conducting tissue since it was first adequately described about eighty years ago. However, many aspects remain obscure, not the least being its ontogenetic development.

The sinuatrial node is not a controversial object. It develops from sinus venosus tissue at the anterolateral junction of the superior vena cava and the primitive atrial chamber. There is some disagreement as to the time at which the nodal cells can be differentiated from adjacent myocardium. We have examined a specimen at about the age of closure of the ventricular septum in which the node was distinguishable. At a stage shortly after this the nodal cells can be distinguished by their histochemical reaction, but histological differentiation is still minimal (Fig. 36).

The mode of connection between the nodal cells and the atrial myocardium is disputed. Some have described cellular tracts originating from the sinuatrial node which can be traced to the atrioventricular node. The criterion of differentiation of these tracts was the presence of larger atrial cells at points along the course of these reputed tracts.[20] Others have pointed out that such large cells are common throughout the atrial tissues, and after careful study were unable to confirm these findings.[45] Yet others deny the presence of histologically specific cells, but consider the tracts to exist as separate entities since direct fibre to fibre nodal contact is mediated through their substance.[36] James,[22] who originally described the tracts, summed up evidence for and against them and concluded that although rapidly conducting atrial pathways were definitely present, they were not composed exclusively of special conducting cell types as in the ventricular system. After careful studies of the atrial tissues in foetuses and neonates we can find no evidence that the internodal myocardium is in any way histologically or histochemically specialized. Furthermore, although the shortest internodal route is through the anterior limbus of the fossa ovalis, this tissue is of primitive atrial origin. Both on ontogenetic and architectural grounds it seems to us more reasonable to propose that the main nodal input occurs through the sinus septum and crista terminalis, both of primitive sinus venosus origin (Fig. 37).

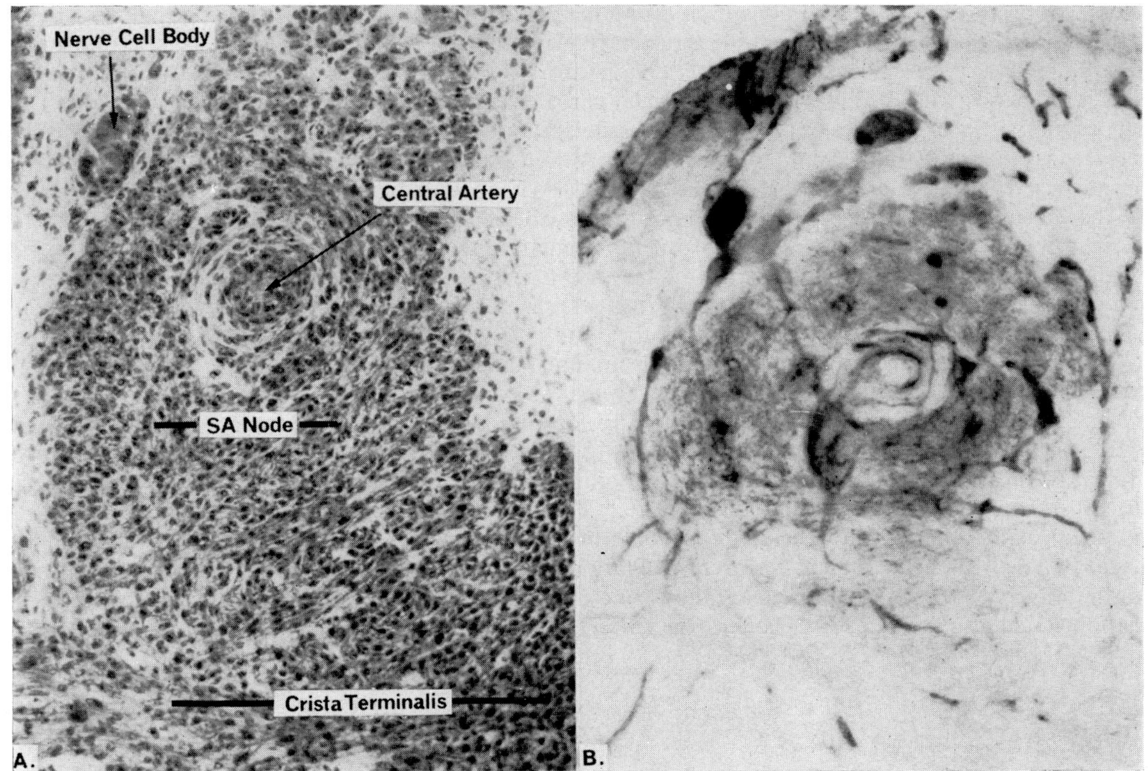

Fig. 36. Sections from the SA node of a 46 mm. crown rump length human fetus. (A) is a section showing routine histology. The node is poorly differentiated. (B) shows the cholinesterase-positive nature of the nodal tissue. Section processed using Gomori's technique with acetylthiocholine iodide as substrate. No inhibitors employed.

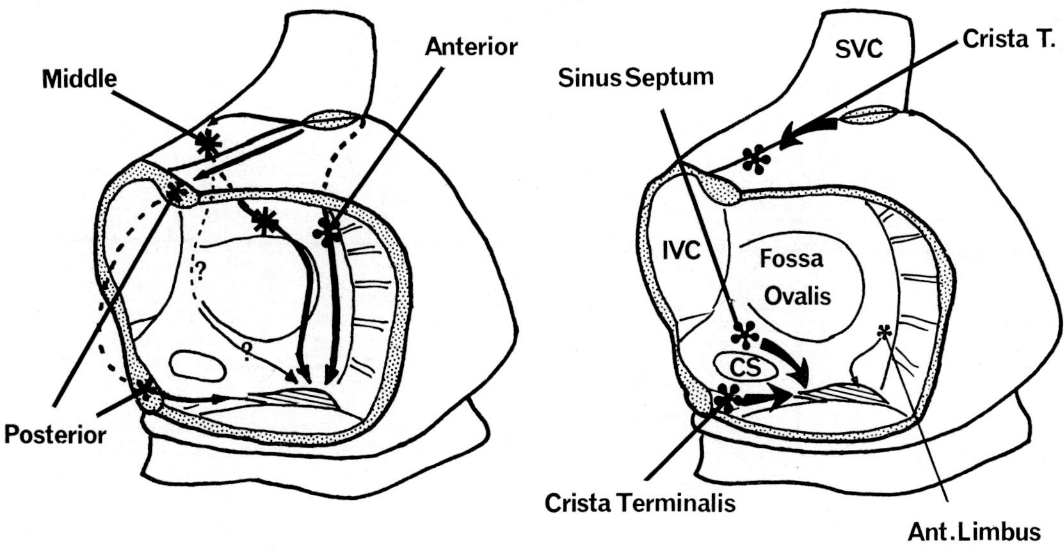

Fig. 37. (A) shows the postulated position of the internodal tracts described by James.[20] It is not clear from his diagram if the middle tract passes anteriorly or posteriorly in relation to the fossa ovalis, (B) shows the morphologic findings of our studies. No evidence is found for histologically distinct tracts. The main morphologic nodal inputs based on cellular orientation are from the crista terminalis and the sinus septum. The anterior fibres mostly overlie the main nodal tract. (See Figs. 38 and 39).

The development of the atrioventricular node itself is another controversial topic. Some contend that it is of left sinus horn origin.[39] Others believe that it is derived from the atrioventricular canal.[25] Examination of early embryos leaves little doubt that the primordium of the node is a continuum of cells with the atrioventricular bundle, developing astride the muscular septum, which extends into the posterior wall of the atrioventricular canal beneath the inferior cushion. This tissue layer then extends into the right and left atrial extremities of the AV canal tissue[1,34] (Fig. 38). Subsequently the definitive node is developed by further specialized layers being stratified onto the lower tract. Although these are likely to be derived partly from the endocardial cushions, various valve remnants and atrial septal tissues, it is also conceivable that they may be partially formed by anterior migration of the left sinus horn (Fig. 39). When the node is finally defined it lies distinctly anterior to the coronary sinus and is close to the right fibrous trigone. However most of the fibres entering the node are derived from the posterior right and left atrial walls, and only tenuous connections exist with anterior septal fibres. In the definitive heart there is also evidence that the extension of the nodal continuum into the tricuspid ring persists as an annulus of specialized cells,[1] and in an anterolateral position these cells are expanded into a second node-like structure as originally described by Kent[26] (Fig. 40). Although usually separated from the ventricular myocardium by the fibrous annulus, in several specimens we have studied this ring tissue is in direct ventricular contact and is expanded at such points.

Some have suggested that the atrioventricular bundle is formed by migration from the node,[56] it is now generally accepted that the ventricular specialized tissue is formed *in situ*,[1,23] probably as a result of separate migration from the myoepicardial mantle.[10] In early embryonic hearts the migration of specialized cells occupies the entire bulboventricular subendocardium, and is continuous with atrioventricular canal musculature.[1] However, after migration and septation of the bulboventricular components, the proximal bundle branches are found only in the ventricular outflow tracts, and they communicate via the atrioventricular bundle with the developing atrioventricular node (Fig. 40). Possibly the conducting tissues retain their embryonic position within the heart, and the ventricular inflow tracts may grow excessively in relation to the static specialized tissue.[34] This explanation would also account for the anterior position of the atrioventricular node (Fig. 40).

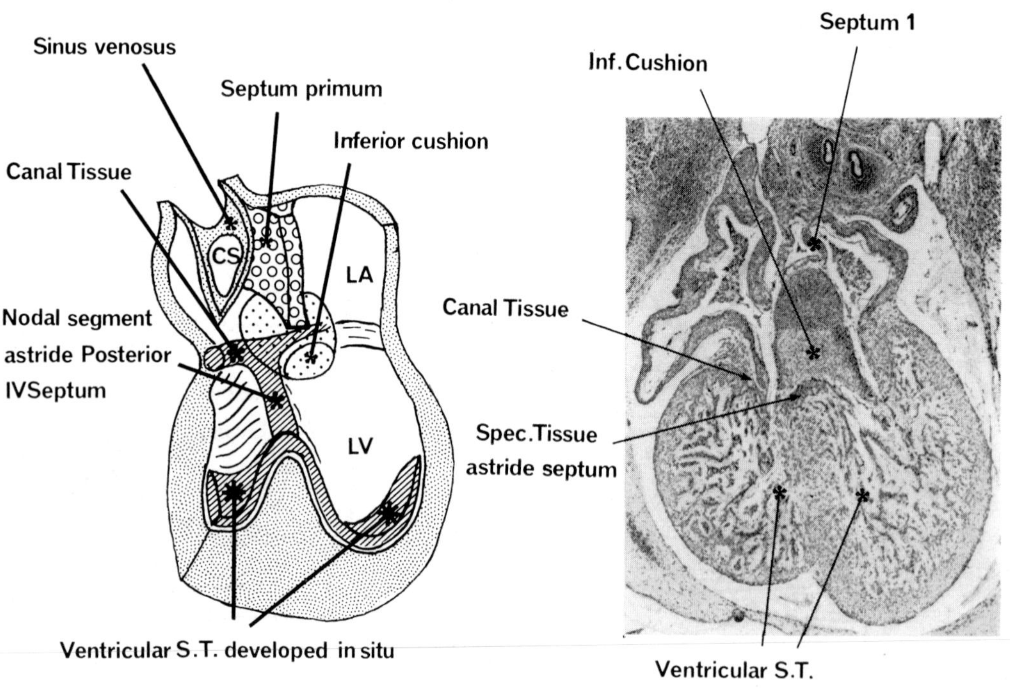

FIG. 38. (A) Diagram showing the position of specialized tissue astride the qosterior interventricular septum, and its connections with the atrioventricular canal musculature and sub-endocardial ventricular specialized tissue.

(B) Frontal section of a series from which the plan shown in (A) was constructed (11 mm. crown-rump length human embryo).

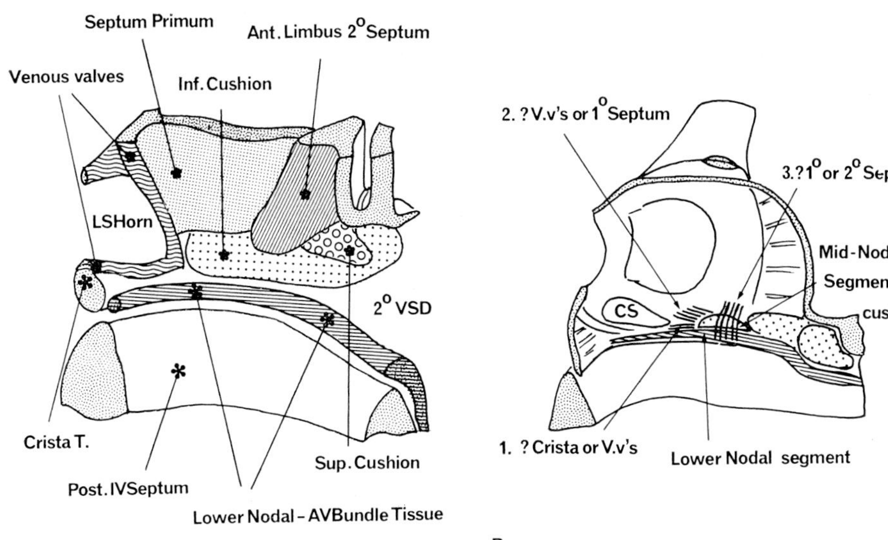

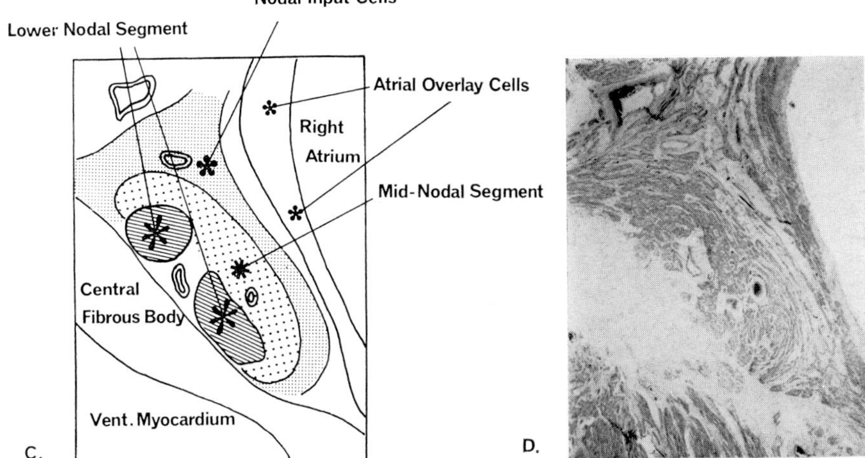

FIG. 39. (A) Diagram showing the components taking part in atrial septation which may contribute to the definitive atrioventricular node. They are laid down upon the tissue illustrated in Fig. 38.

(B) The nodal inputs which are composed of specialized tissue and their possible embryologic origin. In our experience these are the only segments of internodal musculature to exhibit specialized features.

(C) Diagram of the infantile atrioventricular node showing the possible embryologic origins of its three segments (1).

(D) Section through infantile node in frontal plane from which (C) was constructed. Stained with the trichrome technique.

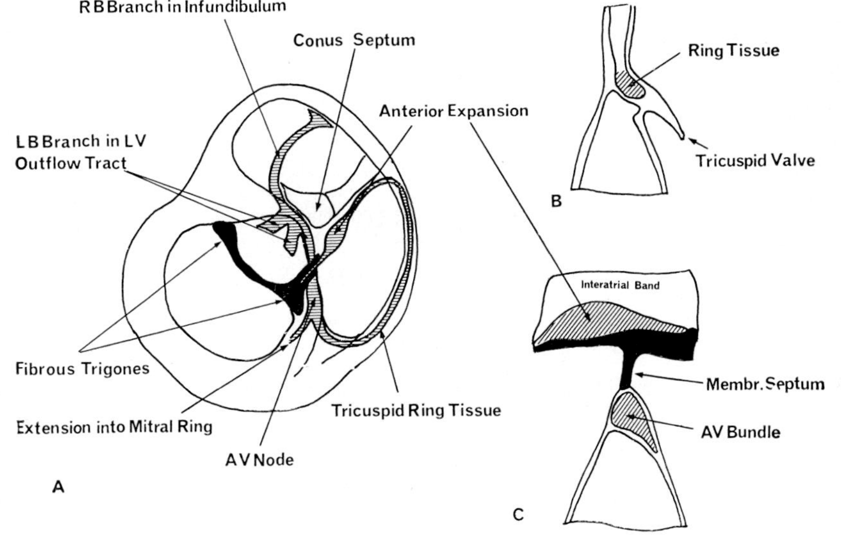

FIG. 40. (A) Diagram showing how the original atrioventricular canal musculature persists as a ring of specialized tissue related to the tricuspid orifice, and its expansion into a second node-like structure (1).

(B) Frontal section through the lateral part of the ring.

(C) Frontal section through the antero lateral expansion, showing that is separated from the AV bundle by only the fibrous annulus and the conal septal musculature.

Relationship Between Specialized Tissue and Cardiac Anomalies

As increasing numbers of patients with grossly deformed hearts become amenable to cardiac surgery, it becomes vital for the surgeon to know the precise location of cardiac specialized tissues. Such tissue has been extensively studied in the commoner anomalies,[18,31] but detailed studies are not available for all malformations. Knowledge of the ontogenetic development of these tissues enables their position to be predicted with some accuracy. Thus we have been able to prepare certain basic rules (Table 2).

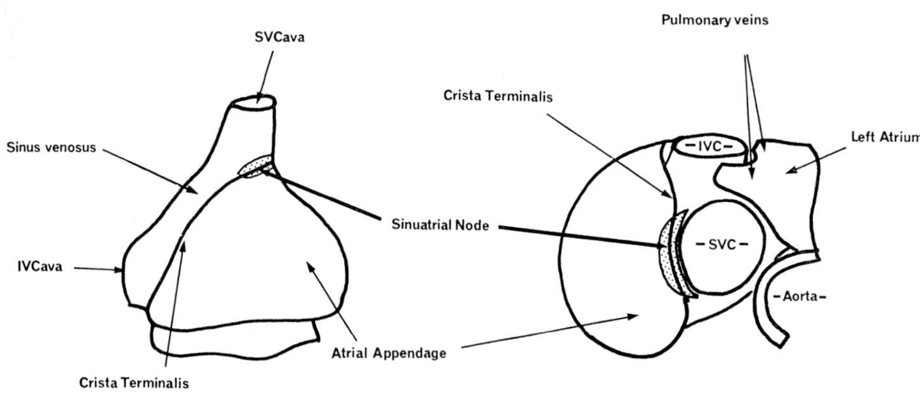

Fig. 41. Diagrams showing the position of the sinuatrial node (A) from the right side and (B) from above.

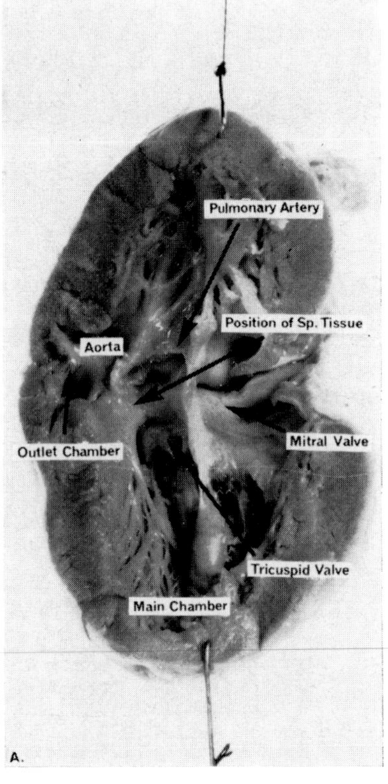

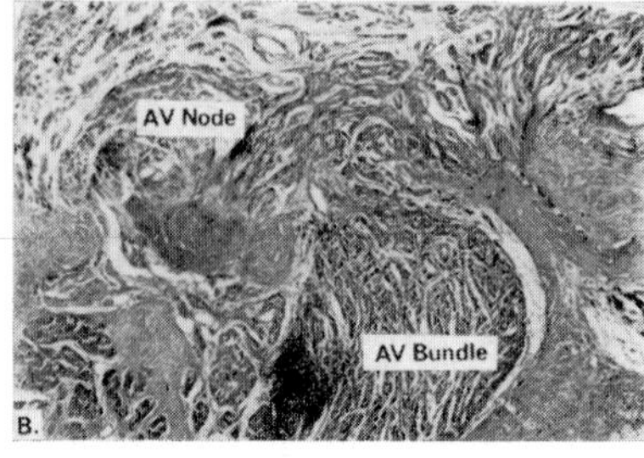

A B

Fig. 42. Photograph of a "single" ventricle with outlet chamber, with (B) the connecting atrioventricular specialized tissue. The node is formed from the antero-lateral expansion of ring tissue shown in Fig. 40.[2]

The sinuatrial node is always related to the superior vena cava and is located at the apex of the crista terminalis[19] (Fig. 41). It should be remembered that in hearts with persistent left superior venae cavae opening to the left atrium sinuatrial nodes may be related to each superior cava. In view of the physiologic evidence concerning internodal tracts it is probably wise to avoid incisions or sutures involving the interatrial septum, particularly the limbus fossae ovale, sinus septum and crista terminalis.

The atrioventricular node is usually developed in the venous atrium, although it has been described in the arterial atrium in a case of classically corrected transposition.[30] We have observed that both the normal node and the antero-lateral expansion of the ring tissue can effect atrioventricular connections. Since normal development is dependent upon normal formation of the posterior interventricular septum, an abnormally situated node may be expected in patients in whom the septum is absent or misplaced. The commonest malformation exhibiting this feature is "single" ventricle with outlet chamber, and the anterior node was uniformly identified in a series of fifteen such hearts[2] (Fig. 42). The other situation where such unusual connections may exist is classically corrected transposition, where the sinistral twist of the loop takes the outflow tracts away from the posterior septum.[57] When the posterior septum is partly formed, as in atrioventricular canals, the atrioventricular node is displaced posteriorly and the bundle runs an elongated course along the septum (Fig. 43A).

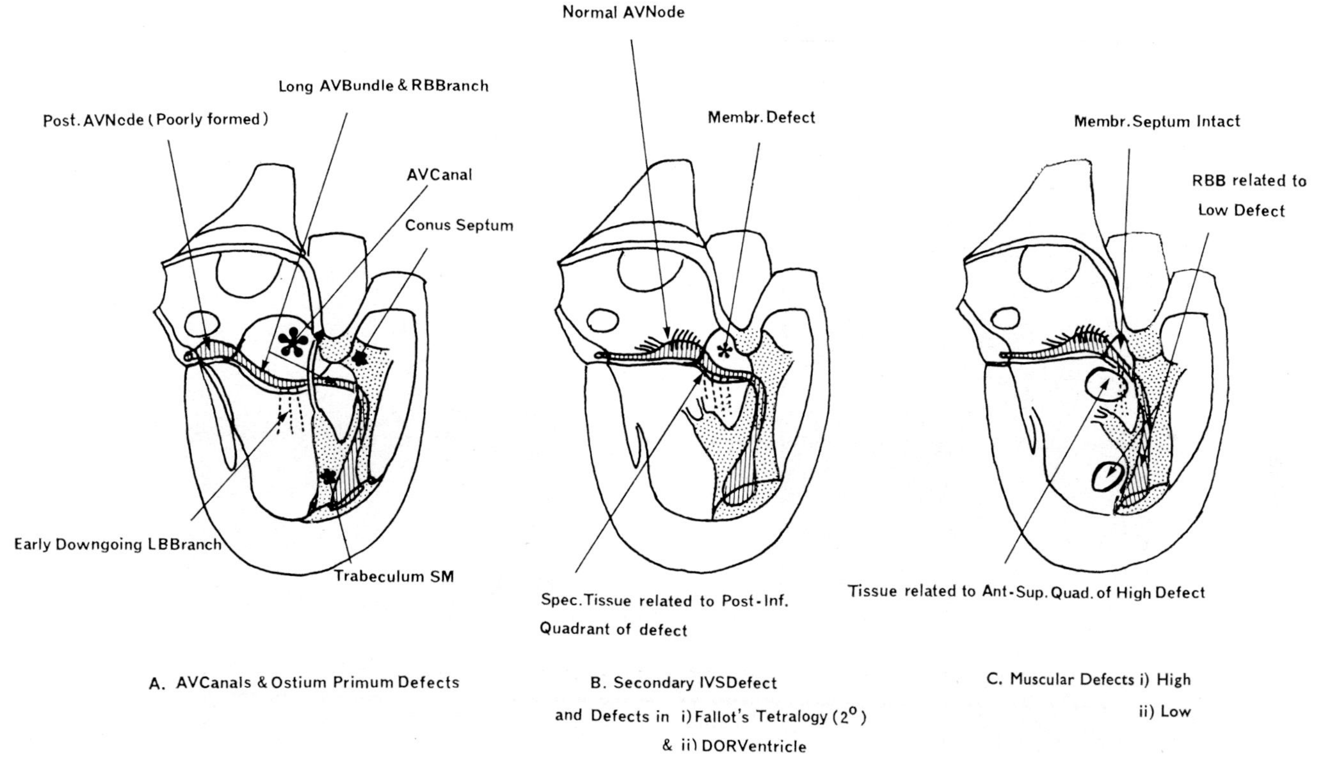

Fig. 43. Diagrams showing the position of specialized tissue in congenital malformations. These positions can be deduced from knowledge of the morphogenesis of the anomalies.

Since the bundle develops along the crest of the muscular ventricular septum, and the branches are in the ventricular outflow tracts, the specialized tissue is always related to primary or secondary interventricular septal defects. These defects are present in double outlet right ventricle, Fallot's tetralogy and isolated membranous defects. The tissue is always present in the postero-inferior quadrants of such defects (Fig. 43C). We have recently observed that in some transpositions the conducting tissue may not be related to the defect at all, but this finding requires further investigation. We have, however, established the importance of differentiating between membranous and high muscular defects. In the latter, the septal crest is above the defect, and therefore the tissue is related to its anterosuperior quadrants. If the situation is not recognized then traumatic heart block can follow surgical repair (Figs. 43C, 44).[28]

The development of the cardiac conducting tissue is of great significance with regard to ventricular pre-excitation.[13] Usually this arrhythmia implies presence of an accessory atrioventricular connection, which may be intra- or extra-nodal. It will be appreciated that the presently described morphological findings offer many opportunities for accessory pathways. The existence of ring tissue provides the potential for specialized tissue bridges to be formed at any point round the tricuspid orifice in the presence of defects in the fibrous annulus. This is particularly likely to occur posteriorly beneath the coronary sinus, and anteriorly in the position of the anterior node. In addition stratified formation of the atrioventricular node makes it feasible for separate conducting pathways to exist within the node, a possibility which has been established in the rabbit heart using electrophysiological techniques.[3]

The conducting tissue may also be of major significance in explaining sudden unexpected death in infancy (cot or crib death). It has been suggested that the atrioventricular bundle is in the process of active resorbtion and moulding in all neonatal hearts.[21] This enables several conducting pathways to exist, and promotes the possibility for pre-excitation which in turn can produce paroxysmal tachycardia and death. This possibility of this arrangement is further strengthened by findings in one of our "crib death" hearts. In this specimen a definite accessory connection was identified in an anterior position, and conducting tissue abnormalities were found in two further hearts studied.

Clearly many further studies are required before the exact disposition and workings of the cardiac specialized tissues are elucidated.

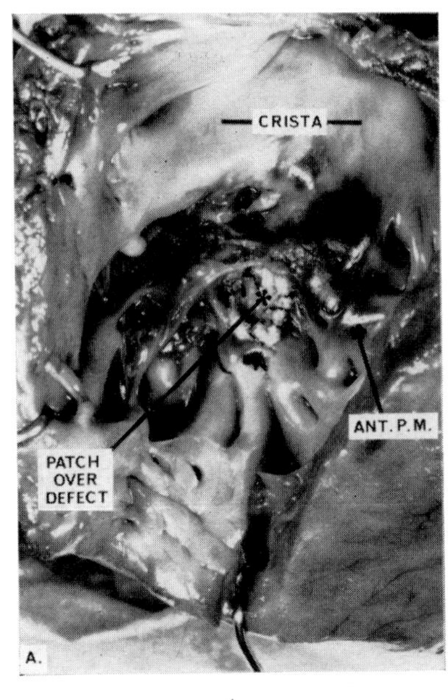

A

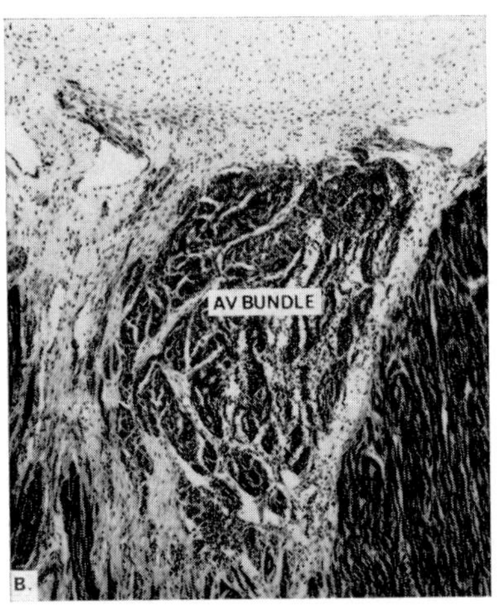

B

FIG. 44. Photograph of a ventricular septal defect after surgical repair. Although it appeared to the surgeon as a membranous defect, the hole was in the muscular septum. Suturing at the antero superior margin of the defect produced haemorrhage in the AV bundle (Fig. 44B) and subsequent fatal heart block.[28]

ACKNOWLEDGEMENTS

It will be clear from reading this account that we have drawn freely from work performed by one of us (R.H.A.) in collaboration with colleagues at Liverpool. Many of the concepts presently expressed have been elucidated following discussions with these colleagues, and they have kindly allowed us to incorporate results from as yet unpublished studies. We therefore would like to acknowledge their assistance, in particular Drs. J. Wilkinson, R. Arnold, M. K. Thapar, R. S. Jones and J. Bouton.

In addition we would like to thank colleagues who have assisted during preparation of the manuscript: Professor G. A. G. Mitchell of the University of Manchester, Drs. A. E. Becker and J. Los of the University of Amsterdam, and Dr. E. Shinebourne of the Brompton Hospital.

Histological material was prepared by Mrs. A. Smith, and photographic material by Messrs. P. Howarth, K. Walters and R. Wylie.

Finally we would like to thank Susan Laycock and Susan Tomlinson for typing this manuscript at extremely short notice.

TABLE 1

CHANGES IN THE HEART TUBE DURING DEVELOPMENT RELATED TO EACH OTHER AND TO THE AGE OF THE FETUS. BASED ON THE STUDIES OF STREETER[42] AND DE VRIES AND SAUNDERS[13]

Horizon	*No. of Somites C-R Length*	*Post-ovulation Age (days)*	*General Features*	*Atrial Chambers*	*Ventricles*	*Great Vessels*
	1 somite	16	Anterior cardiogenic plate	—	—	—
	4 somites	18	Rotation of head fold Paired cardiogenic folds	—	Bulbus and ventricle separated by grooves	
	6–8 somites	20	Formation of bulboventricular loop	Venous channels in septum transversum	Bulbus and ventricle separated Heart tubes fused	Truncus
	8–12 somites	22	Continuing growth of bulboventricular loop	Right side of atrial chamber enlarging	AV canal formed to left	Arterial arches appeared
XI	14–20 somites	24	Cardiac contraction commences	Sinus venosus elaborating	Trabeculated pouches formed	2nd arch developed
XII	26 somites	26	BV loop fully formed	AV junction ventral to L. atrium	Trab. pouches well formed	3rd arch forming
XIII	30 somites	28	Cushion tissue appearing	Truncus lies between atria	AV migration beginning	1st and 2nd regress 4th arch forming
XIV	4–6 mm.	30	Endocardial cushions dividing AV canal	Septum primum appearing	AV canal Septating	Aortic sac leads to 3rd, 4th and 6th arches
XV	6–9 mm.	32	Post. migration of bulbus Attenuation of BAVL	Common pulm. vein grown from L. atrium	Muscular septum prominent	Truncus ridges well formed Aortic pulm. septum appears
XVI	9–12 mm.	34	Aorta and pulm. arches distinct	Septum primum approaching AV cushions	Cushions increasing in size around 2° IVF	Truncus ridges fusing
XVII	12–15 mm.	36	Right to left AV canals now separated	Ostium primum closed Ostium secundum formed	Membranous septum forming	Semilunar valves appearing
XVIII	15–18 mm.	38	Approximates definitive appearance	Septum secundum appearing	2° IVF closed	Aorta and PA in contact solely with appropriate ventricle
	20 mm. → 40 mm.	6–8 weeks	Further changes mostly confined to atrial chambers	Absorption of venous valves Growth of septum secundum Incorp. of pulm. veins	—	—

TABLE 2

DEVELOPMENT OF CARDIAC SPECIALIZED TISSUE

<table>
<tr><th colspan="3">Tissue</th><th>Origin</th><th>Landmarks</th><th>Significance to Congenital Anomalies</th></tr>
<tr><td colspan="3">Sinuatrial node</td><td>Sinus venosus</td><td>Junction of SVC, sinus venosus and atrial appendage</td><td>(a) Avoid suturing or incisions of nodal area during atrial surgery.
(b) Two nodes may be present in presence two superior venae cavae (Asplenia syndrome).</td></tr>
<tr><td rowspan="5">ATRIOVENTRICULAR NODE</td><td colspan="2">1. Lower nodal segment</td><td>AV canal musculature and tissue astride posterior IV septum</td><td>IV septum posterior to interventricular foramen</td><td>(a) May not contact ventricular tissue in absence or misplacement of posterior septum ("single" ventricle and classical corrected transposition).
(b) Displaced posteriorly in endocardial cushion defects.</td></tr>
<tr><td colspan="2">2. Mid nodal segment</td><td>? Septum primum
? Endocardial cushions</td><td>Distal IA septum overlying R. side of central fibrous body</td><td>Hypoplastic in endocardial cushion defects.</td></tr>
<tr><td rowspan="3">3. INPUT SEGMENTS</td><td>1. Crista terminalis</td><td>Right venous valve</td><td>Tissue beneath coronary sinus</td><td>Impinges on ring specialized tissue. Common site of accessory AV connections.</td></tr>
<tr><td>2. Sinus septum</td><td>Left venous valve and septum primum</td><td>Tissue between coronary sinus and IV cava</td><td>(a) Main morphologic input.
(b) Avoid suturing in area.</td></tr>
<tr><td>3. Anterior limbus of Fossa ovalis</td><td>Septum primum and septum secundum</td><td>Anterior limbus</td><td>(a) Deficient in endocardial cushion defects.
(b) Main input according to James[20,23]</td></tr>
<tr><td colspan="3">Atrioventricular bundle</td><td>Tissue astride posterior IV septum</td><td>Post-inferior quadrant of primary inter-ventricular foramen</td><td>(a) Forms one unit with lower nodal segment.
(b) May fail to contact ventricular tissue producing heart block.
(c) Elongated bundle in endo-cardial cushion defects.</td></tr>
<tr><td colspan="3">Bifurcation and bundle branches</td><td>Subendocardial ventricular specialized tissue</td><td>Formed astride muscular septum at junction of posterior and anterior segments</td><td>(a) Related to postero, inferior quadrants of primary and secondary interventricular defects, e.g. membranous defect, Fallot's tetralogy, DORV, truncus anomalies.
(b) Related to antero superior quadrants of muscular defects close to AV ring.</td></tr>
<tr><td colspan="3">Atrioventricular ring specialized tissue</td><td>AV canal musculature</td><td>Occupies distal segment of R. atrial musculature</td><td>May form accessory atrioventricular connections at any point round tricuspid orifice.</td></tr>
<tr><td colspan="3">Anterior expansion of AV ring tissue</td><td>AV canal musculature</td><td>R. margin BAV ledge</td><td>In absence or misplacement of posterior septum ("single" ventricle or classical corrected transposition) may form sole atrioventricular connection.</td></tr>
</table>

REFERENCES

1. Anderson, R. H. and Taylor, I. M. (1972), "Development of Atrioventricular Specialized Tissue in Human Heart," *Brit. Heart J.*, **34,** 1205–1214.
2. Anderson, R. H., Arnold, R., Thapar, M. K., Jones, R. S. and Hamilton, D. I. (1973), "Analysis of the Specialized Conducting Tissue in Hearts with an Apparently Single Ventricular Chamber," *Amer. J. Cardiol.* Submitted for publication.
3. Anderson, R. H., Janse, M. J., van Capelle, F. J. L., Billette, J., Durrer, D. and Becker, A. E. (1973), "A Combined Morphologic and Electrophysiologic Study of the Rabbit Atrioventricular Node," *Circulation Res.* Submitted for publication.
4. Anderson, R. H., Wilkinson, J. L., Arnold, R. and Jones, R. S. (1973), "The Morphogenesis of Transposition of the Great Vessels." In preparation.
5. Auer, J. (1948), "The Development of the Human Pulmonary Vein and its Major Variations," *Anat. Rec.*, **101,** 581–594.
6. Brody, H. (1942), "Drainage of Pulmonary Vein into Right Side of the Heart," *Arch. Path.*, **33,** 221–240.
7. Campbell, M. and Missen, G. A. K. (1957), "Endocardial Cushion Defects Common Atrioventricular Canal and Ostium Primum," *Brit. Heart J.*, 403–418.
8. Collett, R. W. and Edwards, J. E. (1949), "Persistant Truncus Arteriosus. A Classification According to Anatomic Types," *Surg. Clin. N. Amer.*, **29,** 1245–1270.
9. Davis, C. L. (1924), "The Cardiac Jelly of the Chick Embryo," *Anat. Rec.*, **27,** 201–202.
10. DeHaan, R. L. (1961), "Differentiation of the Atrioventricular Conducting System of the Heart," *Circulation*, **24,** 458–470.
11. De La Cruz, M. V. and Miller, B. L. (1968), "Double Inlet Left Ventricle," *Circulation*, **37,** 249–262.
12. De La Cruz, M. V. and Da Rocha, J. P. (1956), "An Ontogenetic Theory for the Explanation of Congenital Malformations Involving the Truncus and Conus," *Amer. Heart J.*, **51,** 782–805.
13. De Vries, P. A. and Saunders, J. B. C. M. (1962), "Development of the Ventricles and Spiral Outflow Tract in the Human Heart," *Contr. Embryol.*, **37,** 89–114.
14. Durrer, D., Schuilenberg, R. M. and Wellens, H. J. J. (1970), "Pre-excitation Revisited," *Amer. J. Cardiol.*, **25,** 690–697.
15. Edwards, J. E., Du Shane, J. W., Alcott, D. L. and Burchell, H. B. (1951), "Thoracic Anomalies III. Atresia of the Common Pulmonary Vein, the Pulmonary Veins Draining Wholly into the Superior Vena Cava (Case 3). IV. Stenosis of the Common Pulmonary Vein (Cor Triatriatum) (Case 4). *Arch. Path.*, **51,** 454–460.
16. Gasul, B. M., Arcilla, R. A. and Lev, M. (1966), *Heart Disease in Children, Diagnosis and Treatment*. London: Pitman Medical.
17. Goerttler, K. (1963), "Entwicklungsgeschichte des Herzens," in *Das Herz des Menschen*, Vol. 1, p. 21 (W. Bargmann and W. Doer, Eds.). Stuttgart. Georg: Thieme Verlag. Cited by Lev.[32]
18. Hudson, R. E. B. (1965). *Cardiovascular Pathology*, pp. 1645–2097. London: Arnold.
19. Hudson, R. E. B. (1967), "Surgical Pathology of the Conducting System of the Heart," *Brit. Heart J.*, **29,** 646–670.
20. James, T. N. (1963), "The Connecting Pathways Between the Sinus Node and the AV Node and Between the Right and Left Atrium in the Human Hearts," *Amer. Heart J.*, **66,** 498–508.
21. James, T. N. (1968), "Sudden Death in Babies: New Observations in the Heart," *Amer. J. Cardiol.*, **22,** 479–506.
22. James, T. N. (1970), "Cardiac Conduction System: Fetal and Post-natal Development," *Amer. J. Cardiol.*, **25,** 213–226.
23. James, T. N. and Sherf, J. (1971), "Specialized Tissues and Preferential Conduction in the Atria of the Heart," *Amer. J. Cardiol.*, **28,** 414–427.
24. Keith, J. D., Rowe, R. D. and Vlad, P. (1966), *Heart Disease in Infancy and Childhood.* New York: Macmillan.
25. Keith, A. and Mackenzie, I. (1910), "Recent Researches on the Anatomy of the Heart," *Lancet*, **i,** 101–103.
26. Kent, A. F. S. (1893), "Researches on the Structure and Function of the Mammalian Heart," *J. Physiol.*, **14,** 233–254.
27. Kramer, T. C. (1942), "The Positioning of the Truncus and Conus and the Formation of the Membranous Portion of the Interventricular Septum in the Human Heart," *Amer. J. Anat.*, **71,** 343–370.
28. Latham, R. A. and Anderson, R. H. (1972), "Anatomical Variations in Atrioventricular Conduction System with Reference to Ventricular Septal Defects," *Brit. Heart J.*, **34,** 185–190.
29. Lev, M. and Saphir, O. (1945), "A Theory of Transposition of the Arterial Trunks Based on the Phylogenetic and Ontogenetic Development of the Heart," *Arch. Path.*, **39,** 172–183.
30. Lev, M., Licata, R. H. and May, R. C. (1963), "The Conduction System in Mixed Levocardia with Ventricular Inversion (Corrected Transposition)," *Circulation*, **28,** 232–237.
31. Lev, M. (1968), "Conduction System in Congenital Heart Disease," *Amer. J. Cardiol.*, **21,** 619–627.
32. Lev, M., Liberthson, R. R., Kirkpatrick, J. R., Eckner, F. A. O. and Arcilla, R. A. (1969), "Single (Primitive) Ventricle," *Circulation*, **39,** 577–591.
33. Los, J. A. (1958), "De embryonale ontwikkeling van de venae pulmonales en de sinus coronarius bij de mens," Thesis, Leiden.
34. Los, J. A. (1969), "Embryology," in *Paediatric Cardiology*, pp. 1–28 (by Watson). London: H. Lloyd-Luke.
35. Lubkiewicz, K. (1968), "Observations on Crista Supraventricularis in Congential Anomalies of the Heart," Thesis, University of Liverpool.
36. Meredith, J. and Titus, J. L. (1968), "The Anatomic Atrial Connections Between Sinus and AV Node," *Circulation*, **37,** 566–579.
37. Odgers, P. N. B. (1938), "The Development of the Pars Membranacea Septi in the Human Heart," *J. Anat.*, **72,** 247–259.
38. Patten, B. M. (1953), "The Circulatory System," in *Human Embryology*, pp. 537–573. New York: Blakiston.
39. Patten, B. M. (1956). "The Development of the Sinoventricular Conduction System," *Univ. Mich. med. Bull.*, **22,** 1–56.
40. Pernkopf, E. and Wirtinger, Q. (1933), "Die transposition der herzostein-ein versuch der erklarung dieser erscheinung," *Z. ges. Anat.*, **100,** 563–711. Cited from Lev, M.[32]
41. Smith, J. C. (1951), "Anomalous Pulmonary Veins," *Amer. Heart J.*, **41,** 561–567.
42. Streeter, G. L. (1942, 1945, 1948), "Developmental Horizons in Human Embryos," *Contr. Embryol.*, **30,** 211–245; **31,** 27–63; **32,** 133–203.
43. Taussig, H. B. (1947). *Congenital Malformations of the Heart.* New York: Commonwealth Fund.
44. Taussig, H. B. and Bing, R. J. (1949). "Complete Transposition of Aorta and Levoposition of Pulmonary Artery," *Amer. Heart J.*, **37,** 551–559.
45. Truex, R. C. (1966), "Anatomical Considerations of the Human Atrioventricular Junction," in *Mechanisms of Therapy of Cardiac Arrhythmias*, pp. 333–340 (L. S. Dreifus and W. Likoff, Eds.). New York: Grune and Stratton.
46. Van Mierop, L. H. S., Alley, R. D., Kausel, H. W. and Stranahan, A. (1963), "Pathogenesis of Transposition Complexes. 1. Embryology of the Ventricles and Great Arteries," *Amer. J. Cardiol.*, **12,** 216–225.
47. Van Mierop, L. H. S. and Wiglesworth, F. W. (1963), "Pathogenesis of Transposition Complexes. II. Anomalies Due to Faulty Transfer of the Posterior Great Artery," *Amer. J. Cardiol.*, **12,** 226–232.
48. Van Mierop, L. H. S. and Wiglesworth, F. W. (1963), "Pathogenesis of Transposition Complexes III. True Transposition of the Great Vessels, "*Amer. J. Cardiol.*, **12,** 233–239.
49. Van Praagh, R., Van Praagh, S., Vlad, P. and Keith, J. D. (1964), "Anatomic Types of Congenital Dextrocardia. Diagnostic and Embryologic Implications," *Amer. J. Cardiol.*, **13,** 510–532.
50. Van Praagh, R., Van Praagh, S. and Swan, H. J. C. (1964), "Anatomic Types of Single or Common Ventricle in Man. Morphologic and Geometric Aspects of 60 Necropsied Cases," *Amer. J. Cardiol.*, **13,** 367–386.
51. Van Praagh, R. and Van Praagh, S. (1966), "Isolated Ventricular

Inversion. A Consideration of the Morphogenesis, Definition and Diagnosis of Non-transposed and Transposed Great Arteries," *Amer. J. Cardiol.*, **17**, 395–406.
52. Van Praagh, R. and Corsini, I. (1969), "Cor Triatriatum: Pathologic Anatomy and a Consideration of Morphogenesis Based on 13 Postmortem Cases and a Study of Normal Development of the Pulmonary Vein and Atrial Septum in 83 Human Embryos," *Amer. Heart J.*, **78**, 379–405.
53. Van Praagh, R. (1968), "What is the Taussig–Bing Malformation," *Circulation*, **38**, 445–449.
54. Van Praagh, R., Van Praagh, S., Nebasar, R. A., Muster, A. J., Sinha, S. N. and Paul, M. H. (1970), "Tetralogy of Fallot: Underdevelopment of the Pulmonary Infundibulum and its *Sequelae*," *Amer. J. Cardiol.*, **26**, 25033.
55. Van Praagh, R., Perez–Trevino, C., Lopez–Cuellar, M., Baker, F. W., Zuberbuhler, J. R., Quero, M., Perez, V. M., Moreno, F. and Van Praagh, S. (1971), "Transposition of the Great Arteries with Posterior Aorta, Anterior Pulmonary Artery, Subpulmonary Conus and Fibrous Continuity Between Aortic and Atrioventricular Valves," *Amer. J. Cardiol.*, **28**, 621–631.
56. Walls, E. W. (1947), "The Development of the Specialized Conducting Tissue of the Human Heart," *J. Anat.*, **81**, 93–110.
57. Walmsley, T. (1930), "Transposition of the Ventricles and the Arterial Stems," *J. Anat.*, **65**, 528–540.
58. Watson, H. (1968). *Paediatric Cardiology*. London: Lloyd–Luke.
59. Wilkinson, J. L. and Acerete, F. (1973), "Pitfalls in Terminology of Congenital Heart Disease," *Brit. Heart J.* In press.
60. Wilkinson, J. L. (1973). Personal communication.

13B. GROWTH AND DEVELOPMENT OF THE CARDIOVASCULAR SYSTEM

Functional Development

ELLIOT A. SHINEBOURNE

Profound changes in the circulation take place at birth with the transference of gas exchange from the placenta to the lungs, dramatic alterations in systemic and pulmonary vascular resistance, and the closure of the ductus arteriosus, foramen ovale and ductus venosus. Throughout intra-uterine and extra-uterine life, normal physiological changes influence manifestations of heart disease and at no time is this more so than at birth. Knowledge of these events is crucial to understanding the pathophysiology and clinical manifestations of congenital heart disease, for the concept that congenital cardiac defects are fixed anatomic entities with fixed haemodynamic disturbances is outmoded.

FUNCTIONAL ORGANIZATION OF THE FETAL CIRCULATION

The fetal circulation is shown diagramatically in Fig. 1. Information on the course of the fetal circulation is based largely on experimental work in fetal lambs. The distribution of cardiac output is thought to be similar in man with the exception of cerebral blood flow which is presumed to be a higher proportion of the combined ventricular output.

It is perhaps appropriate to consider the difficulties in studying the fetal circulation as it is only recently that quantitative studies have been performed on intact unanaesthetized fetuses maintained *in utero*. In the exteriorized fetal goat Huggett[41] found a higher oxygen content in carotid arterial blood than in blood from the descending aorta. The reasons for this were elucidated in cineangiographic studies[5,6] which showed the differential streaming of inferior vena caval blood through the foramen ovale, while the superior vena caval return passed preferentially through the tricuspid valve to the right ventricle. Dawes, Mott and Widdicombe,[23] also working with exteriorized animals, made estimates of the relative blood flow through the great vessels, foramen ovale and ductus arteriosus of the fetal lamb based on multiple measurements of oxygen content in blood samples from eight different sites in the circulation. Subsequently, flow through the pulmonary artery, ascending aorta, ductus arteriosus and umbilical vein was measured using electromagnetic flow meters,[4,21] but as the workers involved pointed out, exteriorization of the fetus, anaesthesia and manipulation of vessels may alter flow patterns.

This problem was overcome by Rudolph and Heymann[79] who cannulated fetal vessels through a small uterine incision and then exteriorized the catheters through the ewe's flank. Over the subsequent weeks, the cannulae were used to inject radioactive microspheres into the undisturbed fetus. The spheres, which were distributed in proportion to blood flow, were trapped in the capillary circulation. At a later date individual organs were separated and their radioactivity counted. By relating this measurement to the radioactivity of blood withdrawn at a steady

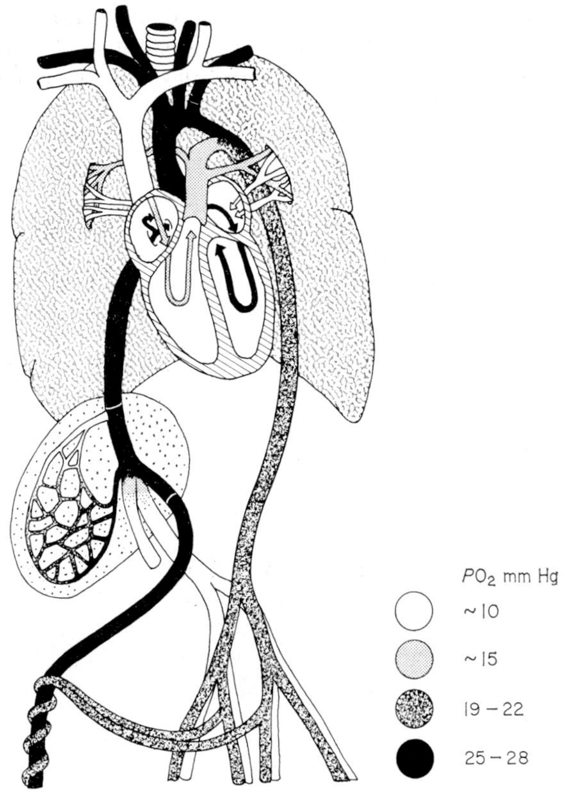

FIG. 1. Diagram of fetal circulation. See text for description. Shading code indicates PO_2 of blood.

rate during microsphere injection, it was possible to measure flow to individual organs and thus the distribution of cardiac output in a fetus maintained in its natural physiological environment.

Umbilical venous blood returning from the placenta is relatively well oxygenated with a PO_2 of 30 mm. Hg.[35,61] Between 40–60 per cent of the umbilical venous return bypasses the hepatic capillary circulation via the ductus venosus connecting the left branch of the portal vein to the hepatic vein at its junction with the inferior vena cava. In the fetus, the left atrium extends dorsally and inferiorly so that inferior vena caval blood can enter the left atrium directly.[5,6] Blood returning to the heart from the inferior vena cava divides into two streams at the crista dividens, (Fig. 2) so that about 60 per cent passes directly through the foramen ovale to the left atrium. The remainder passes into the right atrium where it mixes with less saturated blood (PO_2—18 mm. Hg.) returning from the head and neck via the superior vena cava and with coronary sinus blood.

Of blood returning to the heart from the superior vena cava not more than 3 per cent passes across the foramen ovale to the left atrium, the majority passing through the tricuspid valve to the right ventricle and pulmonary artery. Since the inferior vena cava receives the umbilical venous return, blood entering the left atrium and left ventricle has a higher PO_2 than that in the right ventricle. Blood ejected by the left ventricle passes through the aortic valve to the ascending aorta where it is distributed to the coronary arteries, cerebral circulation, head, neck and upper extremities. Of the right ventricular blood entering the main pulmonary artery, less than 10 per cent reaches the lungs, the remainder passing through the ductus arteriosus to the descending aorta.

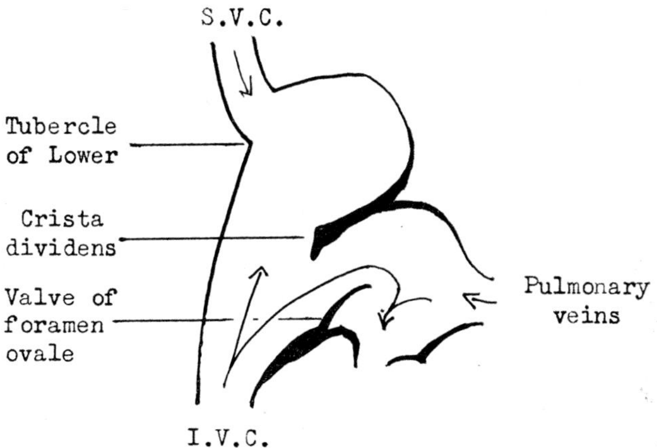

FIG. 2. Diagram to show inferior vena caval blood passing directly through foramen ovale to left atrium.

The design of the circulation in the fetus ensures that arterial blood with the highest O_2 content passes to the heart and brain and that more desaturated blood passes to the placenta and lower body. The PO_2 of ascending aortic blood is 25–28 mm. Hg. whereas that in the descending aorta is 19–22 mm. Hg. corresponding to O_2 saturations of around 60 and 38 per cent respectively.

The fetal ductus arteriosus is a large vessel that allows equilization of pressures in the aorta and pulmonary artery. As a consequence blood flow to the lungs and to the systemic vessels is dependant on local vascular resistance. The placenta which normally has a very low resistance receives 40–50 per cent of the combined output of the two ventricles whereas the lungs, which *in utero* have a high resistance, receive less than 10 per cent. This also explains why about 70 per cent of the combined cardiac output returns to the heart via the inferior vena cava and 20 per cent via the superior vena cava. The other 10 per cent of the total venous return to the heart is derived from pulmonary venous, bronchial, thebesian and coronary sinus return.

During the latter half of gestation, the total cardiac output increases in proportion to fetal weight as does umbilical blood flow.[80] As a proportion of total output, however, placental flow falls in late gestation. This implies that placental resistance has risen, that the relative vascular resistance of the rest of the fetus has fallen, or that both factors operate. In contrast to what happens in the adult where increased circulatory demands are met by increasing cardiac output, in the fetus higher demands for oxygen and nutrients at different phases of growth are met by a redistribution of flow. Examples of this in the lamb are the increase in pulmonary flow at about 120 days (term = 150 days) corresponding to the development of significant amounts of surfactant[40] and possibly the increase in flow to the gut at around 110 days gestation. In both these situations the increase in flow is fairly abrupt and would appear to be due to local vasodilatation perhaps dependent on local metabolites. In contrast, the gradual increase in cerebral blood flow occuring throughout gestation could be explained by enlargement of the vascular bed from production of new capillary networks.

INFLUENCE OF THE FETAL CIRCULATION ON THE HEART AND GREAT VESSELS OF THE NEONATE

There is an intimate relationship between the course of the circulation through the heart, patterns of flow in the major blood vessels of the fetus, and the anatomy of the great vessels at birth. In the newborn human infant the angiographic appearances of the aorta, pulmonary arteries and (when patent) ductus arteriosus reflect the distribution and pattern of flow in the fetus. *In utero* each ventricle ejects about 50 per cent of the combined cardiac output against the same vascular resistance. There is no reason why the ventricles should differ in thickness and the two sides of the fetal heart are similar.[33,88] The left ventricle ejects 50 per cent of the cardiac output into the ascending aorta which is a relatively wide vessel. As successive vessels are given off, the cross sectional area of the aorta diminishes, the arch being narrower than the ascending aorta and the isthmus (between the left subclavian and ductus arteriosus) narrower still.[81] In clinical practice the normal narrowing of the aortic isthmus must not be mistaken for a "hypoplastic segment" of the aorta (Fig. 3). The right ventricle ejects the remaining 50 per cent of the cardiac output and so the proximal pulmonary artery is approximately the same width as and has similar histological characteristics to the ascending aorta.[34] *In utero* not more than 10 per cent of the combined output goes to the lungs and therefore the right and left pulmonary arteries are small. The ductus arteriosus is a wide channel that *in utero* acts as the continuation of the main pulmonary artery connecting the latter to the descending aorta—a pattern well demonstrated in infants with a patent ductus arteriosus (Fig. 4). When the ductus arteriosus closes, its previous importance as the channel which carried the major part of the right ventricular output may be reflected by the size of the ductal diverticulum in some normal neonatal pulmonary arteriograms (Fig. 5). The presence of a 5–8 mm. Hg. pressure gradient between the main and peripheral pulmonary arteries in young human infants up to the age of 4 months also reflects the disparity between pulmonary flow in the fetus and newborn, for the right and left pulmonary arteries unaccustomed to a high flow arise at an acute angle from the main pulmonary trunk and are of disproportionately small size compared to those of a 1 year old.[17]

CARDIAC OUTPUT IN THE FETUS AND NEWBORN

The term "cardiac output" has different connotations in the fetus than in the animal enjoying extrauterine life. Because of the widely patent ductus arteriosus and other shunts, the pulmonary and systemic circuits are not in series as in post-natal life. Systemic cardiac output in adults equates with left ventricular output. In the fetus umbilical flow represents approximately half the combined ventricular output and will be used for comparison.

The most important single fact about cardiac output in the fetus and newborn is that it is greater per Kg. body weight than in the adult.[19] In the sheep, measurements of umbilical flow range from 140–180 mls./Kg./min.[23] in anaesthetized fetuses near term to 240 mls./Kg./min. in unanaesthetized fetuses *in utero*.[80] In the first 10 days following delivery the output rises to 450 mls./Kg./min.,[89] falling to 325 mls./Kg./min. between 20–60 days[16] and to 115–120 mls./Kg./min. in the adult.[62] Human infants similarly have resting cardiac outputs (180–240 mls./Kg./min.) 2–3 times adult values.[2]

In the fetus the low resistance placental circuit is thought to facilitate a high cardiac output. The higher cardiac output in the newborn may reflect a higher oxygen consumption (metabolic rate) (up to 7 mls./Kg./min. at 10 days) than in the adult ($\approx$3·9 mls./Kg./min.). This is probably related to temperature homeostasis[19] as small animals have a greater surface area in relation to body mass than large animals and therefore lose heat more readily.

BLOOD PRESSURE IN THE FETUS, NEWBORN AND CHILD

The low resistance placental circuit accounts for the low fetal arterial pressure despite its high cardiac output. In a variety of experimental animals arterial pressure rises gradually during gestation,[18] for instance in lambs the mean arterial pressure is 30 mm. Hg. at 90 days rising to 60 mm. Hg. at term (150 days). The rise in pressure with gestational age depends on complex alterations in the resistance of each organ but most probably is dominated by the increase in placental vascular resistance with maturation. The systolic blood pressure in newborn infants is around 70–90 mm. Hg., the arterial figure depending largely on the amount of the placental transfusion.[2] Between the ages of 1 and 5 years the average systolic pressure rises to about 100 mm. Hg. and between 5 and 15 years it gradually reaches 120 mm. Hg. with possible transient increments around puberty.[63] The normal ranges of pressure are shown in Table 1.[32]

Factors influencing the blood pressure both in intra- and extra-uterine life are complex. They include functional development of the sympathetic and parasympathetic

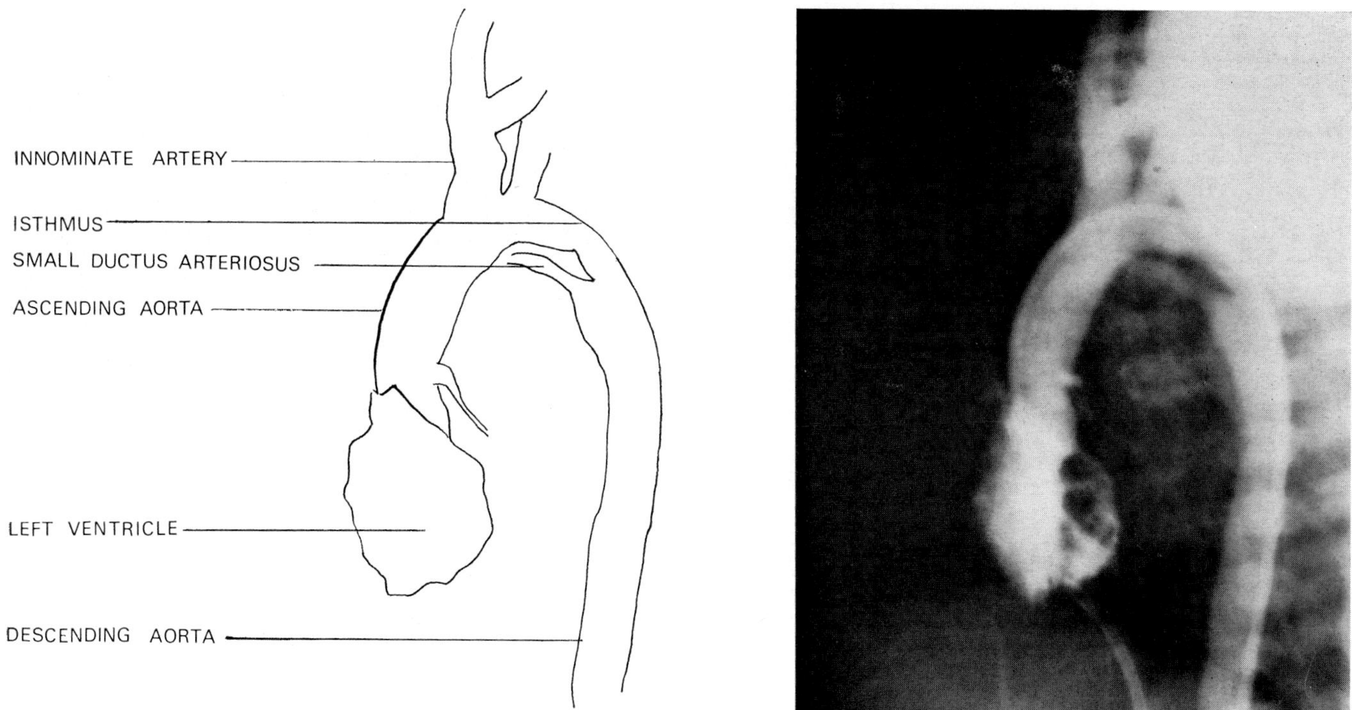

FIG. 3. Normal newborn aorta with small patent ductus arteriosus demonstrating apparent isthmal narrowing.

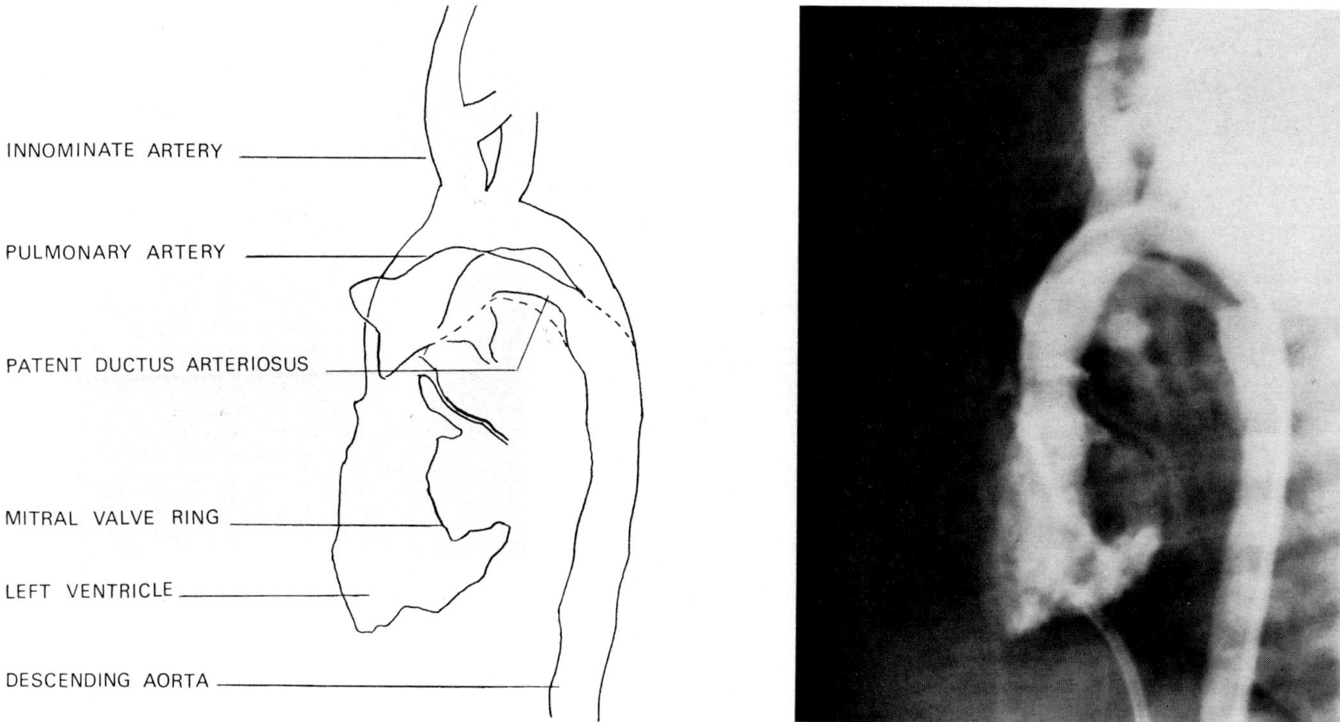

FIG. 4. Left ventricular angiogram in a neonate with patent ductus arteriosus. Retrograde filling of the main pulmonary artery back to the pulmonary valve occurs through the patent ductus. Compared with the fetus the ductus is partially constricted but the interrupted lines outline the (assumed) anatomy in the fetus.

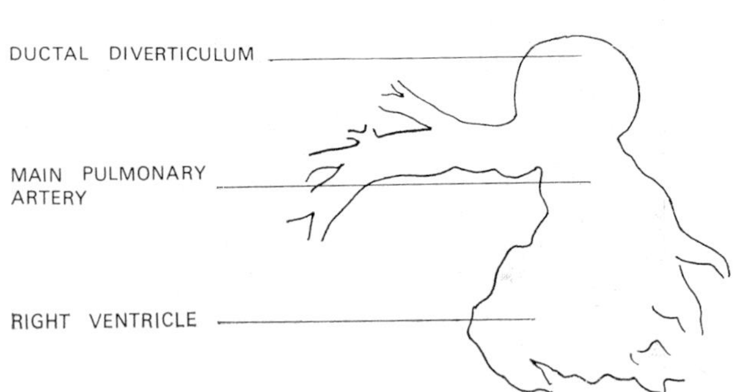

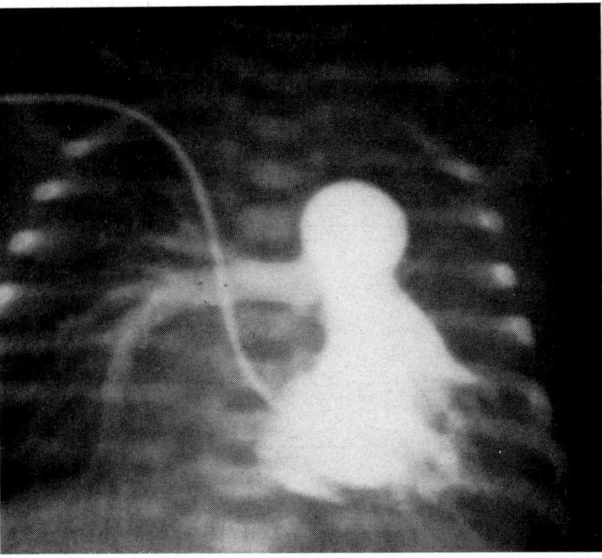

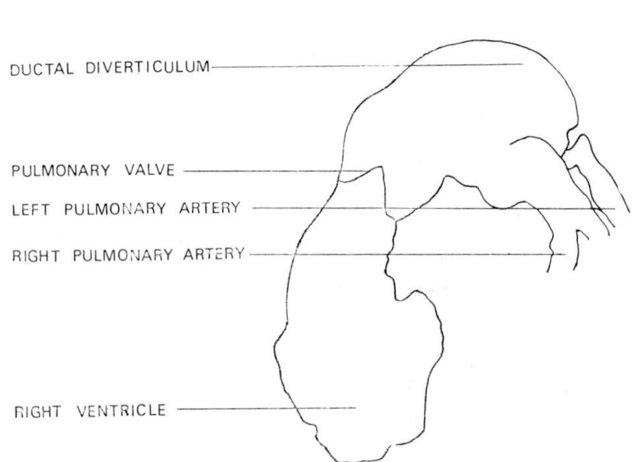

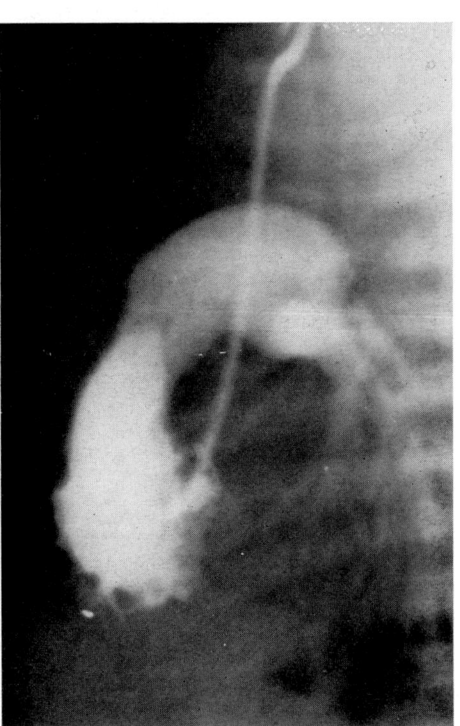

FIG. 5. Right ventricular angiogram in a neonate. The prominent ductal diverticulum is normal and reflects the fetal flow pattern.

nervous systems, the development of cardiovascular reflex activity, and alterations in the number, total cross-sectional area, length and degree of smooth muscle development of the principal resistive vessels.

TABLE 1

NORMAL BLOOD PRESSURES[63]
(Auscultation)

Ages	*Mean Systolic* ± 2 *S.D.*	*Mean Diastolic* ± 2 *S.D.*
Newborn	80 ± 16	46 ± 16
6 mos.—1 year	89 ± 29	60 ± 10*
1 year	96 ± 30	66 ± 25*
2 years	99 ± 25	64 ± 25*
3 years	100 ± 25	67 ± 23*
4 years	99 ± 20	65 ± 20*
5–6 years	94 ± 14	55 ± 9
6–7 years	100 ± 15	56 ± 8
7–8 years	102 ± 15	56 ± 8
8–9 years	105 ± 16	57 ± 9
9–10 years	107 ± 16	57 ± 9
10–11 years	111 ± 17	58 ± 10
11–12 years	113 ± 18	59 ± 10
12–13 years	115 ± 19	59 ± 10
13–14 years	118 ± 19	60 ± 10

* In this study the point of muffling was taken as the diastolic pressure.

FUNCTIONAL DEVELOPMENT OF PULMONARY CIRCULATION

At birth there is a dramatic increase in blood flow to the lungs with corresponding alterations in pulmonary arterial pressure and pulmonary vascular resistance. The control of the pulmonary circulation and its functional development are central to understanding cardiovascular events at birth, both in normal infants and in those with congenital heart disease.

In the fetus the pulmonary artery pressure is marginally higher than that in the descending aorta.[24] As a result of the extremely high pulmonary vascular resistance in the fetus, pulmonary blood flow is low, more than 90 per cent of the right ventricular output being diverted away from the lungs via the ductus arteriosus. Why is the pulmonary resistance so high? Although tortuosity and kinking of small pulmonary vessels has been suggested[76] a more probable explanation is the low PO_2 to which the small muscular pulmonary arterioles are exposed *in utero*. Changes in gas composition of blood perfusing unventilated fetal lung or of the gas mixture used for ventilation[12,15] produce large alterations in pulmonary vascular resistance. Gaseous expansion alone also causes pulmonary vasodilatation irrespective of changes in arterial blood gases[12,52] although the effects of ventilation with air or oxygen enriched mixtures are far greater than those of nitrogen.[24] Changes in alveolar PO_2 without gaseous distension of the lungs, and without appreciable changes in arterial PO_2 also result in pulmonary vasodilatation in the mature fetal lamb—as is shown by the response to expanding the lungs with dextran-saline solution of high O_2 content.[52] Whether arterial or alveolar Pco_2 influence the fetal or newborn pulmonary vascular resistance remains debatable. Cassin *et al.*[12] found in their experiments with mature fetal lambs that over the range of PO_2 16–34 and Pco_2 25–42 mm. Hg. either a 10 mm. Hg. rise in PO_2 or a 10 mm. Hg. fall in Pco_2 caused the same degree of pulmonary vasodilatation while Rudolph and Yuan[83] working with newborn calves found no relation between Pco_2 and pulmonary vascular resistance. All workers however, appear to agree that a fall in pH causes pulmonary vasoconstriction in the newborn. Reflecting the high pressure and vasoconstrictor tone in the fetus there is progressive increase in the ratio of the area of media to the area of intima in small pulmonary arteries of under 50 μ., i.e. a progressive increase in smooth muscle in the wall of these vessels.[64] In the second half of gestation the relative amounts of smooth muscle increase rapidly or extend further along the length of individual vessels[37] (*see* Chapter 10a). Thus in premature babies at birth the muscle in the walls of the small pulmonary ateries is underveloped, a factor that may be of importance in the manifestations of certain types of congenital heart disease.

At birth, all the factors mentioned previously operate to lower pulmonary vascular resistance and increase pulmonary blood flow. With the first breath, the introduction of air into the alveoli produces a gas-fluid interface. Surface forces tending to collapse alveoli may exert some distending force on the small vessels in the interalveolar spaces by holding them open.[59,77] In addition there is a rapid rise in alveolar PO_2 but at first sight it is not apparent how changes in alveolar gases should influence the precapillary pulmonary vessels which constitute the major site of pulmonary vascular resistance. Using a rapid freezing technique, however, Staub[90] showed that oxygen could diffuse from alveoli directly into the small pulmonary arteries so influencing them in this way.

Another fascinating question is why oxygen causes dilatation of pulmonary vessels while it causes all other vascular smooth muscle (including the ductus arteriosus) to constrict. Lloyd[58] suggested this was related to a substance produced by lung parenchyma, for isolated carotid and pulmonary artery strips suspended in a bath fail to constrict in response to hypoxia, though both vessels constrict when surrounded by a cuff of lung tissue. Bradykinin is a potent vasodilator of fetal pulmonary blood vessels[11] and may play an important part in events at birth.[60] Left atrial blood samples showed a fall in levels of kininogen, a bradykinin precursor when fetal lambs were ventilated with oxygen but not with nitrogen, suggesting that bradykinin is formed in the lungs.[36] Similarly, when the fetal PO_2 was raised by placing the ewe in a hyperbaric oxygen chamber, there was enhanced bradykinin formation.

The reactivity of the pulmonary vasculature decreases with age and shows marked species differences. The small pulmonary vessels of newborn animals have thick muscular walls and the pulmonary artery pressure is at systemic levels. In the newborn infant, following ductal closure, pulmonary arterial pressure falls to adult levels in about 2 weeks,[50] the major change taking place in the first 2–3 days. The initial fall is due to release of pulmonary vasoconstrictor tone with later thinning of the medial muscle layer in the vessel wall.[65] Newborn puppies[71] show a similar pattern to man but calves even at sea level may take 4–5 weeks before their pulmonary artery pressure reaches adult levels.[75] Small pulmonary vessels in these animals have extremely thick muscular walls and this is also thought to account for the greater reactivity of the newborn calf to a fall in PO_2 or pH.[83] Similarly, the pulmonary vasculature of the newborn human infant reacts more briskly (pulmonary artery pressure rises) to falls in alveolar or arterial PO_2 than does that of an older child or adult.[28,50,78]

After the first 2–3 weeks of life, mean pulmonary arterial pressure in man remains constant at around 15 (±5) mm. Hg., systolic pressure varying from 15–30 mm. Hg. and diastolic pressure from 5–10 mm. Hg. With growth, more blood passes through the lungs but the pressure drop across them remains constant. In the lungs the ratio of pressure drop (mm. Hg.) to flow (litres/min.) is loosely termed resistance (PVR). If flow is normalized for body surface area and expressed as cardiac index, i.e. litres. $min.^{-1}$ sq. $m.^{-1}$, pulmonary vascular resistance (PVR) remains constant from the age of 1 month to late adulthood. (If resistance is expressed simply as litres. $min.^{-1}$ mm. $Hg.^{-1}$ resistance is higher in the first year of life). As PVR remains constant with age, although the pulmonary vessels increase in length, either resistance vessels must dilate or the number of vessels must increase.[38] As the vessels still retain some capacity for dilatation, the former is unlikely and it has recently been shown[37] (Ch. 13A) that the number of small pulmonary arteries (acinar vessels) increase markedly during postnatal growth. Should this normal proliferation of vessels not occur then pulmonary hypertension would be expected.

APPLIED PHYSIOLOGY OF THE PULMONARY CIRCULATION AFTER BIRTH

The rate of fall of PVR is delayed in two situations; in the presence of hypoxia and in congenital cardiac abnormalities characterized by large communications between the systemic and pulmonary circulations.

Infants who are hypoxic from lung disease, or who exhibit persistent hypoventilation from cerebral causes for prolonged periods after birth show a slower rate of fall of PVR.[66] Similarly infants born at high altitude show a delayed fall of PVR compared to those born at sea level and have more muscle in the walls of small pulmonary arteries.[3] The higher pulmonary pressures and PVR may persist into adult life[70,86] and the retention of smooth muscle in the media of the pulmonary vessels is associated with enhanced responsiveness to vasoactive stimuli.[31]

Certain types of congenital heart disease such as patent ductus arteriosus, ventricular septal defect and truncus arteriosus are characterized by a high pressure shunt from the systemic to the pulmonary circuit.

The group of conditions shown in Table 2 have widely differing anatomy but in all of them the amount of blood shunted from left to right depends on the relationship of pulmonary to systemic vascular resistance; they have *dependent* shunts.[77]

TABLE 2

DEPENDENT SHUNTS

Ventricular septal defect Patent ductus arteriousus	±	Transposition of great vessels
Truncus arteriousus		
Aorto-pulmonary window		
Double outlet right ventricle Common ventricle		Without pulmonary stenosis
Transposition of great vessels + Tricuspid atresia		

Clinically patients with a large VSD or widely patent ductus arteriosus might be expected to go into cardiac failure in the first week of life but this is unusual and symptoms of left ventricular failure seldom occur before 4–12 weeks.[39] The explanation is a delay in fall of pulmonary vascular resistance accompanied by persistence of the fetal amount of muscle in the media.[93] Why subjection of the pulmonary artery to systemic pressures should cause a delayed fall in PVR is not known. The delayed fall in pulmonary vascular resistance limits the left to right shunt in term babies accounting for the time of onset of symptoms. In premature babies with a dependent shunt, however, cardiac failure may appear in the first week, presumably because the muscle in the media in these patients is relatively poorly developed at birth and a high PVR cannot be maintained in the face of systemic pressures.

Paradoxically the hypoxia and acidosis of respiratory infections may limit the magnitude of dependent left to right shunts and prevent heart failure. In the same way a higher PVR at altitude limits dependent left to right shunts and infants with ventricular septal defects in Denver at the moderate altitude of 5,280 ft. have lower pulmonary blood flows and a lower incidence of heart failure than infants with similar defects at sea level.[92]

The concept of dependent versus obligatory shunting[77] rationalises the approach to management of left to right shunt situations in congenital heart disease; and although not strictly pertinent to development of normal cardiovascular function, its importance in understanding the physiology of these conditions merits further comment. In obligatory shunt situations (Table 3) the anatomy is such that left to right shunting occurs irrespective of the relationship between pulmonary and systemic resistance. Such a shunt is that between the left ventricle and right

TABLE 3

OBLIGATORY SHUNTS

LV → RA (Common in endocardial cushion defect)
Gerbode defect
Sinus of Valsalva → RA fistula
Origin of RPA or LPA from aorta
(Hemitruncus)
Absence of RPA or LPA (Agenesis of lung)

atrium in defects of the atrioventricular portion of the ventricular septum. As the pressure in the left ventricle is always higher than that in the right atrium left to right shunting will occur irrespective of PVR. A similar situation is found in large congenital systemic arteriovenous fistulae, (i.e. hepatic or aneurysms of the great vein of Galen), sinus of Valsalva to right atrial fistulae, and in many endocardial cushion defects, (common atrio-ventricular canal defect, ostium primum atrial septal defect). The latter have various combinations of atrial and ventricular septal defects and abnormalities of both atrioventricular valves, in particular a cleft mitral valve. From examination of the anatomy alone, reconstruction of the physiological disturbance may not be possible; some will have predominantly dependent shunts from left to right ventricle, whereas others will shunt from left ventricle to right atrium through the cleft mitral valve and atrial septal defect, (an obligatory shunt).In terms of management, pulmonary arterial banding to raise the resistance against which the right ventricle ejects blood, would be an appropriate (if not necessarily *the* most appropriate) form of management for dependent shunts, whereas banding an obligatory shunt could prove disastrous by increasing right ventricular work without diminishing the left to right shunt.

PULMONARY VASCULAR RESERVE AS A FUNCTION OF AGE

No increase in resting pulmonary artery pressure occurs in adults who have had one lung removed although right ventricular pressure increases excessively on exercise, since PVR does not fall normally with increased flow.[10] In adult animals 60–80 per cent[26] of the lungs must be removed for pulmonary arterial pressure and resistance to rise, whereas pneumonectomy in young animals causes a definite rise in resting PA pressure.[72,82] Possibly the greater proportion of muscle in the thicker walls of the pulmonary vessels in young animals prevents the dilatation seen in equivalent adult vessels. In patients with one absent pulmonary artery or one arising from the aorta[38] (sometimes called hemitruncus), all the cardiac output has to pass through the normally attached pulmonary artery, (obligatory shunt), a situation similar haemodynamically to that after unilateral pneumonectomy. Many of these patients develop pulmonary hypertension,[13,73] again reflecting inability of the newborn pulmonary vascular bed to accommodate an increased flow by adjusting its resistance.

DEVELOPMENT OF AUTONOMIC CONTROL OF THE CIRCULATION

Autonomic control of the circulation requires a functional nerve supply to the heart and blood vessels with an intact reflex arc. The effector organs, namely myocardial and smooth muscle cells, must have the capacity to respond to the neurohumoral transmitter which in turn must be synthesized and produced in adequate amounts.

Histochemical techniques have shown that sympathetic innervation to rabbit[30] and rat heart develops largely in the post-natal period. The newborn guinea-pig is remarkably mature and has a nerve supply similar to the adult. Lambs[53] and man have a well developed cardiac sympathetic innervation at birth although not as extensive as in the adult, and there is considerable post-natal development. Parasympathetic innervation as evidenced by positive staining for cholinesterase is found much earlier in many species[68] in whom the pattern of innervation is also similar.

Nerve endings are found first in the right atrium and then in left atrium, right ventricle and left ventricle. From the histochemical findings it would seem that reflex control of the heart is dominated by the parasympathetic nervous system up to or until some time after birth. Physiological studies on isolated organs, exteriorized fetuses and intact lambs *in utero* support this view.

The fetal heart can respond to both sympathetic and parasympathetic neurohumoral transmitters remarkably early, heart rate increasing with beta sympathetic stimulation as early as 4 days in the chick[51] and 5 days in the rabbit. Studies in intact fetal lambs *in utero* have shown no change in responsiveness of the heart to sympathetic or parasympathetic agonists during the second half of gestation although there are marked changes in resting vasomotor tone during this time.[91] In chronically catheterized fetal lambs, (youngest 85 days) atropine increases heart rate, indicating resting parasympathetic tone. The effect is small in fetuses under 100 days (0·66 gestation), increases dramatically up to 120 days, but shows no further change until term, late gestation fetuses behaving similarly to newborn lambs. Alpha sympathetic activity shows a similar chronological development but the pattern of response to beta sympathetic blockade with propranolol is different. Little reduction in heart rate is produced before 120 days (0·8 gestation) but then the response increases up to term. The reduction in heart rate is greater in newborn lambs and in fact resting beta sympathetic tone increases in the neonatal period. Whether the changes are entirely related to sympathetic tone is uncertain as circulating catecholamines may influence the response. Nonetheless, both histochemical and physiological studies on the normal fetus maintained *in utero* show that the parasympathetic nervous system plays a dominant role in cardiac regulation. It is perhaps not too fanciful to suggest that should its activity go unchecked—for instance in the profound bradycardia produced by intra-uterine hypoxaemia—the effect of unopposed parasympathetic activity *per se* may be harmful, and in that case selective parasympathetic blockade might be useful therapeutically.

DEVELOPMENT OF REFLEX CONTROL OF THE CIRCULATION

It has been known since 1945[7] that the acute bradycardia resulting from intravenous injection of adrenaline into fetal lambs can be abolished by cutting the vagi and that reflex bradycardia follows baroreceptor stimulation. Baroreflex activity has been demonstrated in exteriorized fetuses[9,22] and recently a quantitative assessment has been made in intact fetuses *in utero*. Using a chronically implanted inflatable balloon catheter in the descending aorta for rapid elevation of blood pressure, the responsiveness of the baroreflex arc was assessed in fetuses from 90 days (0·6 gestation) to term.[85] Reflex activity could be elicited in all fetuses but a significant response was not always produced. The proportion of positive responses and the magnitude of the response increased throughout gestation to term. There was, however, considerable daily variability in baroreflex sensitivity, due at least in part to alteration in central nervous system function.

Both spontaneous changes in EEG activity associated with rapid eye movement sleep[20] and direct hypothalamic stimulation of the fetal brain[94] profoundly influence heart rate and blood pressure and would be expected to influence baroreflex sensitivity. Whether cardiovascular reflex activity has functional importance *in utero* is not known but what is apparent is that at birth autonomic and reflex control of cardiovascular function is well established and that little significant change occurs in subsequent extra-uterine life.

DEVELOPMENT OF CONDUCTING TISSUE*

The early embryonic chick heart exhibits automaticity, conductivity and contractility in a co-ordinated manner before definitive appearance of specialized conducting tissue, and it is probable that the human heart behaves similarly. Automaticity is dependant on spontaneous diastolic depolorization and is shown by most fetal myocardial cells.[14] This does not necessarily imply pacemaker activity which depends, amongst other things, on the amount of contractile protein within the cell.

In man the sinus node is readily discernible by the 6th week of gestational life.[8] The cells from which both sino-atrial and atrio-ventricular nodes are formed originate in the sinus venosus. In early development the small dark cells are all similar and are thought to be specialized *ab origine*.[49] Lieberman[54] favours the hypothesis that adult cardiac conducting tissue represents remnants of embryonic myocardium and that underlying the basic function of specialized conducting tissue is the extent of coupling between contiguous cells.

In the mature heart the area corresponding to the sinus venosus includes the ostea of the two venae cavae, the coronary sinus, most of the atrial septum, and the Eustachian ridge. This curved elliptical area is bounded at either end by the two nodes which develop from paired primordial pacemaking sites.[69] In the mature heart three conducting pathways connect the SA and AV nodes (including Bachmann's bundle) and one connects the left atrium with the SA node.[43] They correspond to the residuum of the sinus venosus—a fact which is not surprising phylogenetically, since in turtles and frogs the sinus venosus, which persists in the adult consists entirely of electrophysiologically specialized cells.[46] The conduction speed is higher in these internodal pathways than in working myocardium, but less than in the His bundle and its branches. In both dog and rabbit, preferential conduction from the SA and AV nodes has been demonstrated.[95]

The SA node is the dominant pacemaker in adults having a faster intrinsic rate, optimal distribution routes for pacemaking signals to pass to the atria and ventricles and an abundant autonomic innervation. There is also a disproportionally large central artery about which the sinus node is organized in a dense collagen framework. So prominent is this artery that in the adult the node resembles an enormous adventitia around it.[7] The artery is present in the young fetus but its size increases during childhood and adolescence.

Most of the cells in the fetal sinus node are similar to those in the adult and comprise two distinct cell groups.[49] The P cells form grape-like clusters and tend to be centrally located around the artery. They contain a few randomly distributed mitochondria and myofibrils with a scanty sarcoplasmic reticulum. Transitional cells are slender, elongated cells that form the small nodal fibres seen with the light microscope. They are found throughout the node but are the dominant cells in the outer half; a few fibres normally extend from the periphery of the node to the right atrial myocardium. The P cells connect only with each other or with transitional cells whereas the latter form the exclusive junction between SA node internodal and inter-atrial pathways. At birth the two cell types are readily distinguishable and further differentiation takes place within the first years of life.

There are fewer P cells in the adult than in the fetus or newborn, and the adult contains more transitional cells with much inter-weaving. Other features distinguishing the mature SA node from that of the fetus, in addition to the prominent central artery, are a highly developed collagen framework and a more extensive autonomic innervation. There is very little collagen in the fetal sinus node,[43] and after birth the collagen content increases until adult life, although the rate of increase and amount of collagen vary between individuals. The collagen connects the artery to the basement membrane and nodal cells and is perhaps a factor determining stability of the sinus pacemaker.

James[49] has suggested that the consistent location of the central artery and proximity of the artery's origin to the aorta makes this peri-arterial node an ideal sensing device for monitoring central aortic pressure. Changes in nodal arterial pulse wave alter the sinus pacemaking rate. One reason for the faster, less-stable heart rate of the fetus and newborn than adult may be lack of organization of the immature SA node—in particular the size and position of the artery the lack of a collagen framework and the incomplete autonomic innervation.

Sudden death in infancy or childhood may be associated with an abnormal thickening or obliteration of the central artery.[29,45,47] This would support the concept that the pulse in the central artery is transmitted to the SA node in

* "Controversy reigns over the embryonic origin of the SA and A-V nodes and on their cellular architecture. P cells are not recognized by all workers nor are the presence of preferential interatrial conduction pathways. Chapter 13A by Dr. R. Anderson gives a persuasive alternative viewpoint of the anatomy and development of the specialized conducting tissue which, as indicated by him, is in agreement with recent electrophysiological studies." E.A.S.

a way that modulates or even serves to synchronize otherwise random pacemaker activity; however there is no nodal artery in the rabbit and undoubtedly cells of the developing sinus node are capable of pacemaker activity independent of a functional relationship to the artery. Nonetheless, it is probable that in the mature node the anatomic organization of pacemaker cells, collagen and artery allow the node to function as a biologic servo-mechanism.

There are two main theories concerning the embryological origin of the A-V node, His bundle and its branches. One is that the His bundle grows forward from the original A-V node, and the other is that the His bundle and its branches originate *in situ* in ventricular tissue and then join up with the A-V node. The latter theory better explains the occurrence of some types of congenital heart block.

Certain lines of evidence suggest that the A-V node migrates inwards from its epi-cardial location as the dorsal endocardial cushion invaginates during atrio-ventricular valve formation. Thus the nutrient artery of the human A-V node originates from a vessel which makes a deep "U" turn beneath the posterior inter-ventricular vein near its junction with the coronary sinus, suggesting that as the dorsal cushion moves inwards, it carries its vessels with it.

In fetal and infant hearts the presence of shreds of A-V nodal tissue all along margins of the central fibrous body, including the crest of the inter-ventricular septum, also favours migration of the A-V node from an epi-cardial origin. These shreds of tissue are absorbed during post-natal development and are rare in adults. Congenital heart block or heart block developing within the first few months of life is sometimes due to mesotheliomas separating the A-V node from the His bundle. These tumours are derived from primitive cell rests presumably incorporated in the myocardium during A-V nodal migration.

In contrast, evidence in the chick heart where there is a delay in A-V impulse transmission before the left sinus horn migrates inwards, strongly suggests that the A-V node is derived from the embryonic atrio-ventricular ring.[55]

In the A-V node the principle cell is the transitional cell, there is less collagen than in the SA node and no central artery. Purkinje cells are found at its margins especially in the region between A-V node and right atrium. The His bundle and its branches consist almost exclusively of Purkinje cells and various features suggest a different embryologic origin than the node, namely:

1. Mesotheliomas, when present, are proximal to or within the A-V node, not distal.
2. Intra-cellular potentials are different in the node and His bundle.
3. In all cases of congenital heart block there is a gap between the A-V node and main His bundle, but both are present.
4. In a case of sino-atrio and atrio-ventricular block in a dog, A-V and SA nodal cells were absent but the His system was present.[48]

In man the recent use of intra-cardiac His bundle electrocardiograms[84] has shown in normal subjects that there is a delay in conduction between nodal depolorization, (N wave) and the His bundle spike, (H wave). If the His bundle and its branches grew out from the node, this electrical delay would be surprising. Furthermore, in many cases of congenital heart block the site of block has been demonstrated by His bundle electrocardiography to be between the node and bundle although even in the mature heart there is no sharp anatomical demarcation between the two structures.

Throughout fetal and post-natal development there is an interplay between collagen formation and the conduction system cells with considerable re-moulding of the His bundle and A-V node. Morphogenesis in all systems includes cell death, and focal degeneration in such critically important structures as the A-V node and His bundle may have grave consequences.[45] Development of heart block *in utero* or post-natally and some cases of sudden death in infants may reflect a derangement of this process.

The duration of the apparent refractory period of the A-V node differs in young and in adult animals. In newborn puppies, pigs and goats the refractory period of the A-V node is apparently shorter than that of the ventricular myocardium.[74] In the adult the longer refractory period allows the node to act as a filter preventing atrial ectopic beats from being conducted to the ventricle at a time when it is only partially repolarized. Should an atrial ectopic be conducted in this vulnerable period ventricular fibrillation may result. In the younger animals this is the case and suitably timed electrical stimuli to the atrium can initiate ventricular fibrillation.[74] Spontaneous atrial ectopics occur and possibly their timing may be such as to cause ventricular fibrillation and death *in utero* or infancy.

THE NORMAL ELECTROCARDIOGRAM FROM INFANCY TO ADOLESCENCE

The electrocardiogram shows great variability in childhood and in particular the amplitude of the QRS complex differs widely in normal children of the same age. Nonetheless a knowledge of normal standards is essential for proper interpretation of the ECG and without the use of voltage criteria, evidence of ventricular hypertrophy will be missed. Before presenting the excellent data assembled by Liebman[57] based on the work of Namin and Miller[67] and Alimurung, Joseph, Nadas and Massel[1] certain problems involved are mentioned.

Inscription of the ECG depends on the frequency response of the recorder. Direct writing recorders differ in their performance [25] and all produce inferior recordings to photographic recorders. Ziegler's[96] monograph which is often used as a reference source concerns information derived from an oscilloscope and is not strictly appropriate to current clinical practice.

In evaluating biological data information is normally presented as a mean and standard deviation but this assumes a normal Gaussian distribution. Normal electrocardiographic data shows a large amount of skew and therefore the data is best presented as the mean with 5th and 95th percentiles.[57]

Normal Values

Heart Rate

(Table 4.) The rate is less at birth than at one month after which there is gradual slowing. The high rates achieved by normal infants are not always appreciated.

TABLE 4

Age	Heart Rate (beats/min.)				
	Min.	5%	*Mean*	95%	*Max.*
0–24 hr.	85	94	119	145	145
1–7 days	100	100	133	175	175
8–30 days	115	115	163	190	190
1–3 months	115	124	154	190	205
3–6 months	115	111	140	179	205
6–12 months	115	112	140	177	175
1–3 years	100	98	126	163	190
3–5 years	55	65	98	132	145
5–8 years	70	70	96	115	145
8–12 years	55	55	79	107	115
12–16 years	55	55	75	102	115

P Wave

The P wave reflects atrial depolarization and shows surprisingly little variation with age. Mean voltage in lead II is between 0·15 and 0·18 mV. with a 95th percentile of 0·20 mV., amplitudes over 0·25 mV. usually being considered abnormal. Both right and left atrial enlargement may increase amplitude in lead II but the latter normally prolongs the P wave in addition. P wave duration (Table 5) increases with age and may reach 0·10 sec. in adolescents. This shorter duration in neonates makes the P wave appear peaked.

TABLE 5

Age	P–Wave Duration (sec.)				
	Min.	5%	*Mean*	95%	*Max.*
0–24 hr.	0·040	0·040	0·051	0·065	0·075
1–7 days	0·035	0·038	0·046	0·061	0·065
8–30 days	0·040	0·040	0·048	0·057	0·065
1–3 months	0·040	0·040	0·046	0·058	0·065
3–6 months	0·040	0·040	0·049	0·065	0·065
6–12 months	0·040	0·046	0·058	0·068	0·075
1–3 years	0·045	0·053	0·065	0·082	0·085
3–5 years	0·040	0·051	0·069	0·087	0·095
5–8 years	0·050	0·059	0·070	0·084	0·095
8–12 years	0.050	0·061	0·075	0·092	0·105
12–16 years	0·060	0·064	0·081	0·095	0·105

PR Interval

This also increases with age, (Table 6) as does *QRS duration* (Table 7). At all ages prolongation of the QRS complex above 0·10 sec. is considered abnormal.

TABLE 6

Age	PR Interval (sec.)				
	Min.	5%	*Mean*	95%	*Max.*
0–24 hr.	0·07	0·07	0·10	0·12	0·13
1–7 days	0·05	0·07	0·09	0·12	0·13
8–30 days	0·07	0·07	0·09	0·11	0·13
1–3 months	0·07	0·07	0·10	0·13	0·17
3–6 months	0·07	0·07	0·10	0·13	0·13
6–12 months	0·07	0·08	0·10	0·13	0·15
1–3 years	0·07	0·08	0·11	0·15	0·17
3–5 years	0·09	0·09	0·12	0·15	0·17
5–8 years	0·09	0·10	0·13	0·16	0·19
8–12 years	0·09	0·10	0·14	0·17	0·27
12–16 years	0·09	0·11	0·14	0·16	0·21

TABLE 7

Age	QRS Duration (sec.)				
	Min.	5%	*Mean*	95%	*Max.*
0–24 hr.	0·05	0·05	0·065	0·084	0·09
1–7 days	0·04	0·04	0·056	0·079	0·08
8–30 days	0·04	0·04	0·057	0·073	0·08
1–3 months	0·05	0·05	0·062	0·080	0·08
3–6 months	0·06	0·06	0·068	0·080	0·08
6–12 months	0·05	0·05	0·065	0·080	0·08
1–3 years	0·05	0·05	0·064	0·080	0·08
3–5 years	0·06	0·06	0·072	0·084	0·09
5–8 years	0·05	0·05	0·067	0·080	0·08
8–12 years	0·05	0·05	0·073	0·084	0·09
12–16 years	0·04	0·04	0·068	0·080	0·10

QRS Complex

The amplitudes for R and S waves in V_4R, V_1, V_2, V_4, V_5, and V_6 are shown for direct writing recorders in Tables 8–13. (1 cm. = 10 mV.) Recording of V_4R is mandatory for adequate interpretation of the scalar ECG in childhood.

Q Wave

Deep Q waves over the left chest leads may reflect septal hypertrophy although their interpretation must always be made in conjuction with the rest of the ECG. 95th percentiles for selected leads are shown in Table 14.

TABLE 8 AMPLITUDE LEAD V_4R (mm)

Age	*R Wave*					*S Wave*				
	Min.	5%	*Mean*	95%	*Max.*	*Min.*	5%	*Mean*	95%	*Max.*
30 hr.	3·5	4·0	8·6	14·2	15·0	0·0	0·2	3·8	13·0	12·0
1 month	3·0	3·3	6·3	8·5	12·0	0·0	0·8	1·8	4·6	9·0
2–3 months	0·5	1·1	5·1	10·1	15·0	0·0	0·0	3·4	9·3	15·0
4–5 months	2·0	2·4	5·2	7·5	9·0	1·0	0·3	3·5	6·7	9·0
6–8 months	2·0	1·3	4·4	7·1	7·0	0·0	0·2	3·9	11·7	10·0
9 months–2 years	1·0	0·2	4·0	6·6	8·0	0·0	0·8	4·9	8·1	10·5
2–5 years	1·0	1·6	3·4	7·4	8·0	1·0	1·2	4·8	9·5	12·0
6–13 years	0·2	0·6	2·5	5·7	7·0	0·5	0·9	5·8	12·5	20·0

TABLE 9 AMPLITUDE LEAD V_1 (mm)

Age	*R Wave*					*S Wave*				
	Min.	5%	*Mean*	95%	*Max.*	*Min.*	5%	*Mean*	95%	*Max.*
30 hr.	5·0	4·3	11·9	21·0	30·0	0·0	1·1	9·7	19·1	26·0
1 month	4·0	3·3	11·1	18·7	20·0	0·0	0·0	6·1	15·0	15·0
2–3 months	2·0	4·5	11·2	18·0	20·0	0·5	0·5	7·5	17·1	22·0
4–5 months	3·0	4·5	11·2	17·4	21·0	1·0	1·0	8·6	16·8	17·0
6–8 months	3·0	3·2	11·4	21·2	21·0	1·5	1·5	10·7	25·7	30·0
9 months–2 years	0·5	2·5	9·7	15·6	26·0	0·2	2·0	8·5	17·2	25·0
2–5 years	0·5	2·1	7·5	13·9	20·0	1·0	2·1	10·9	21·6	25·0
6–13 years	0·5	1·1	5·3	10·7	20·0	1·0	3·8	12·6	22·3	36·0

TABLE 10 AMPLITUDE LEAD V_2 (mm)

Age	*R Wave*					*S Wave*				
	Min.	5%	*Mean*	95%	*Max.*	*Min.*	5%	*Mean*	95%	*Max.*
30 hr.	—	—	—	—	—	—	—	—	—	—
1 month	—	—	—	—	—	—	—	—	—	—
2–3 months	—	—	—	—	—	—	—	—	—	—
4–5 months	—	—	—	—	—	—	—	—	—	—
6–8 months	—	—	—	—	—	—	—	—	—	—
9 months–2 years	3·0	5·9	15·3	25·2	30·0	0·3	5·0	14·2	25·5	28·0
2–5 years	3·5	4·2	12·5	20·8	25·0	4·0	5·4	17·3	29·7	33·0
6–13 years	2·0	3·7	9·7	15·9	21·5	6·0	8·6	19·5	29·8	35·0

TABLE 11 AMPLITUDE LEAD V_4 (mm)

Age	R Wave					S Wave				
	Min.	5%	*Mean*	95%	*Max.*	*Min.*	5%	*Mean*	95%	*Max.*
30 hr.	—	—	—	—	—	—	—	—	—	—
1 month	—	—	—	—	—	—	—	—	—	—
2–3 months	—	—	—	—	—	—	—	—	—	—
4–5 months	—	—	—	—	—	—	—	—	—	—
6–8 months	—	—	—	—	—	—	—	—	—	—
9 months–2 years	6·0	8·7	17·9	28·3	30	2·0	3·1	11·4	19·9	25·0
2–5 years	5·0	7·6	18·3	30·7	37	1·0	3·3	11·0	18·1	34·0
6–13 years	3·0	8·9	18·4	—	37	0·3	2·1	10·7	21·4	24·0

TABLE 12 AMPLITUDE LEAD V_5 (mm)

Age	R Wave					S Wave				
	Min.	5%	*Mean*	95%	*Max.*	*Min.*	5%	*Mean*	95%	*Max.*
30 hr.	2·0	3·1	9.4	16·6	20·0	0·5	2·4	9·5	18·5	22·0
1 month	3·8	3·8	15·0	24·2	30·0	0·0	2·8	8·3	16·3	20·0
2–3 months	6·0	9·5	20·7	26·2	32·0	1·0	1·2	7·9	14·4	28·0
4–5 months	10·0	10·0	20·8	28·8	34·0	2·0	2·6	8·9	16·0	16·0
6–8 months	12·0	12·0	20·1	29·0	38·0	1·5	1·5	7·9	19·6	25·0
9 months–2 years	4·0	7·3	17·4	28·4	34·0	0·0	0·6	5·4	10·5	18·0
2–5 years	7·0	9·4	21·5	33·3	40·0	0·0	0·6	4·3	8·9	13·8
6–13 years	5·0	12·4	22·0	33·0	46·0	0·0	0·0	4·0	9·2	17·0

TABLE 13 AMPLITUDE LEAD V_6 (mm)

Age	R Wave					S Wave				
	Min.	5%	*Mean*	95%	*Max.*	*Min.*	5%	*Mean*	95%	*Max.*
30 hr.	1·5	1·5	5·4	11·3	15·0	0·2	1·0	5·6	13·8	20·0
1 month	1·0	1·0	10·8	16·2	22·0	0·0	0·0	4·8	9·5	18·0
2–3 months	5·0	5·4	12·8	20·8	25·0	0·0	0·1	4·2	9·1	15·0
4–5 months	4·0	4·4	13·9	22·4	26·0	0·0	0·0	3·5	8·0	12·0
6–8 months	6·0	6·0	13·0	22·0	28·0	0·2	0·2	2·5	4·4	8·0
9 months–2 years	2·5	5·7	12·1	20·0	30·0	0·0	0·3	2·3	5·2	10·0
2–5 years	4·0	6·4	14·4	22·1	28·0	0·0	0·0	1·5	3·7	7·0
6–13 years	4·5	7·7	15·7	23·3	33·0	0·0	0·0	1·4	4·1	8·0

TABLE 14 95th PERCENTILES
Q WAVE (mm)

	aVF	V_5	V_6
0–9 months	3·5	3·0	2·3
10–24 months	3·5	4·0	2·5
2–5 years	1·7	4·2	2·8
Over 5 years	1·8	2·3	2·3

QRS Axis

(Table 15.) The mean frontal plane axis is way over to the right at birth moving considerably leftward in the first month with a further gradual change throughout life.

TABLE 15 MEAN FRONTAL PLANE AXES
QRS AND T WAVES

Age	*QRS Axis (Frontal Plane)*					*T Axis (Frontal Plane)*				
	Min.	5%	*Mean*	95%	*Max.*	*Min.*	5%	*Mean*	95%	*Max.*
0–24 hr.	60	60	135	180	180	−20	0	70	140	180
1–7 days	60	80	125	160	180	−40	−40	25	80	100
8–30 days	0	60	110	160	180	−20	0	35	60	120
1–3 months	20	40	80	120	120	0	0	35	60	80
3–6 months	40	20	65	80	100	0	20	35	60	60
6–12 months	20	0	65	100	120	−40	0	—	—	—
1–3 years	0	20	55	100	100	−20	0	30	80	80
3–5 years	0	40	60	80	80	−20	0	30	60	60
5–8 years	−20	40	65	100	100	−40	0	30	60	60
8–12 years	0	20	65	80	120	−40	0	30	60	60
12–16 years	−20	20	65	80	100	−40	0	35	60	60

T Wave

(Table 15.) At birth T waves are upright in all the chest leads but within hours they become isoelectric or inverted over the left chest. At this time (within the first 12 hrs.) T waves over the right chest are strongly positive. They remain upright for 2 or 3 days but by 7 days the T wave is inverted in V_4R, V_1 and across to V_4. From then on the T waves stay inverted over the right chest and upright over the left chest until sometime in adolescence when over the right chest they again become upright. Failure of T waves to become inverted in V_4R and V_1 by 7 days may be the earliest ECG evidence of right ventricular hypertrophy.

A detailed explanation of the normal ECG and its genesis is not appropriate in this review but some correlation of electrocardiographic and haemodynamic changes during development may be useful.

Compared with the adult the newborn has right ventricular dominance. At 30 weeks gestation the left ventricle is thicker than the right with an average ratio of 1·15:1, from 32–34 weeks they are the same thickness and by 36 weeks the RV/LV weight ratio is 1·3:1, the same as in the newborn.[64] In the first few days after birth there are major haemodynamic changes which, however, have not been shown to effect the QRS complex of the ECG.[56] There is in fact no real reason why they should, since the total ventricular mass is not changing during this time. The profound T wave changes seen in the 1st week[42] do not appear directly to correlate with haemodynamic events since the major circulatory adaptations to extra-uterine life have already occurred by the 3rd day.

The largest change in LV/RV weight ratio takes place during the 1st month and by 6 months the ratio is 2:1 as against 2·5:1 in the adult.[27] R to S ratios in the chest leads roughly correspond to changes in relative ventricular mass. Three useful terms introduced for describing these changes[1] are:

1. Adult R/S progression—S>R in the right chest leads, R>S in the left chest leads.
2. Partial reversal of R/S progression—R>S in both right and left chest leads.
3. Complete reversal of (adult) R/S progression—R>S in right chest leads, S>R in left chest leads.

The newborn has complete or partial reversion but never the adult R/S progression. By 1 month complete reversal is never seen in the normal, but adult R/S progression is common and by 18 months usual.

REFERENCES

1. Alimurung, M. M., Joseph, L. G., Nadas, A. S. and Massell, B. F. (1951), "The Unipolar Precordial and Extremity Electrocardiogram in Normal Infants and Children," *Circulation*, **4**, 420–429.
2. Arcilla, R. A., Oh, W., Wallgren, G., Hanson, J. S., Gessner, I. H. and Lind, J. (1967), "Quantitative Studies of the Human Neonatal Circulation. II. Haemodynamic Findings in Early and Late Clamping of the Umbilical Cord," *Acta pediat. scand.* (Suppl.), **179**, 23–42.

3. Arias-Stella, J. and Saldãna, M. (1962), "The Muscular Pulmonary Arteries in People Native to High Altitude," *Med. Thorac.*, **19**, 484–493.
4. Assali, N. S. and Morris, J. A. (1964), "Maternal and Fetal Circulations and Their Interrelationships," *Obstet. and Gynaec. Surg.*, **19**, 923–948.
5. Barclay, A. E., Franklin, K. J. and Prichard, M. M. L. (1944), *The Foetal Circulation and Cardiovascular System and the Changes That They Undergo at Birth*. Oxford: Blackwell Scientific Publications.
6. Barcroft, J. (1946), *Researches on Prenatal Life*. Oxford: Blackwell Scientific Publications.
7. Barcroft, J. and Barron, D. H. (1945), "Blood Pressure and Pulse Rate in the Foetal Sheep," *J. exp. Biol.*, **22**, 63–74.
8. Boyd, J. D. (1965), "Development of the heart," in *Handbook of Physiology* (*Circulation III*), pp. 2511–2543. Washington D.C.: American Physiological Society.
9. Brinkman, C. R. III, Ladner, C., Weston, P. and Assali, N. S. (1969), "Baroreceptor Function in the Fetal Lamb," *Amer. J. Physiol.*, **217**, 1346–1351.
10. Burrows, B., Harrison, R. W., Adams, W. E., Humphreys, E. M., Long, E. T. and Reimann, A. F. (1960), "The Postpneumonectomy State," *Amer. J. Med.*, **28**, 281–297.
11. Campbell, A. G. M., Dawes, G. S., Fishman, A. P., Hyman, A. I. and Perks, A. M. (1968),"The Release of a Bradykinin-like Pulmonary Vasodilator Substance in Foetal and Newborn Lambs," *J. Physiol.*, **195**, 83–96.
12. Cassin, S., Dawes, G. S., Mott, J. C., Ross, B. B. and Strang, L. B. (1964), "The Vascular Resistance of the Foetal and Newly Ventilated Lung of the Lamb," *J. Physiol.*, **171**, 61–79.
13. Caudill, D. R., Helmsworth, J. A., Daoud, G. and Kaplan, S. (1969), "Anomalous Origin of Left Pulmonary Artery from Ascending Aorta," *J. Thorac. Cardiovasc. Surg.*, **57**, 493–506.
14. Coltart, D. J., Spilker, B. A. and Meldrum, S. J. (1971), "An Electrophysiological Study of Human Foetal Cardiac Muscle," *Experientia*, **27**, 797–799.
15. Cook, C. D., Drinker, P. A., Jacobson, H. N., Levison, M. and Strang, L. B. (1963), "Control of Pulmonary Blood Flow in the Foetal and Newly Born Lamb," *J. Physiol.*, **169**, 10–29
16. Cross, K. W., Dawes, G. S. and Mott, J. C. (1959), "Anoxia, Oxygen Consumption and Cardiac Output in Newborn Lambs and Adult Sheep," *J. Physiol.*, **146**, 316–343.
17. Danilowicz, D., Rudolph, A. M. and Hoffman, J. I. E. (1965), "Vascular Resistance in the Large Pulmonary Arteries in Infancy," *Circulation*, suppl. II, **32**, 74.
18. Dawes, G. S. (1968), *Foetal and Neonatal Physiology*. Chicago Year Book Medical Publishers.
19. Dawes, G. S. (1968), "Sudden Death in Babies: Physiology of the Fetus and Newborn," *Amer. J. Cardiol.*, **22**, 469–478.
20. Dawes, G. S., Fox, H. E., Leduc, B. M., Liggins, G. C. and Richards, R. T. (1972), "Respiratory Movements and Rapid Eye Movement Sleep in the Foetal Lamb," *J. Physiol.*, **220**, 119–143.
21. Dawes, G. S. and Mott, J. C. (1964), "Changes in O_2 Distribution and Consumption in Fetal Lambs with Variations in Umbilical Blood Flow," *J. Physiol.*, **170**, 524–540.
22. Dawes, G. S., Mott, J. C. and Rennick, B. R. (1956), "Some Effects of Adrenaline, Noradrenaline and Acetylcholine on the Foetal Circulation in the Lamb," *J. Physiol.*, **134**, 139–148.
23. Dawes, G. S., Mott, J. C. and Widdicombe, J. G. (1954), "The Foetal Circulation in the Lamb," *J. Physiol.*, **126**, 563–587.
24. Dawes, G. S., Mott, J. C., Widdicombe, J. G. and Wyatt, D. G. (1953), "Changes in the Lungs of the Newborn Lamb," *J. Physiol.*, **121**, 141–162.
25. Dower, G. E., Moore, A. D., Ziegler, W. G. and Osborne, J. A. (1963), "On QRS Amplitude and Other Errors Produced by Direct-writing Electrocardiographs," *Amer. Heart J.*, **65**, 307–321.
26. Downing, S. E., Pursel, S. E., Vidone, R. A., Brandt, H. M. and Liebow, A. A. (1962), "Studies on Pulmonary Hypertension with Special Reference to Pressure Flow Relationships in Chronically Distended and Undistended Lobes," *Medicina Thoracalis*, **19**, 268–282.
27. Emery, J. L. and Mithal, A. (1961), "Weights of Cardiac Ventricles At and After Birth," *Brit. Heart J.*, **23**, 313–316.
28. Emmanouilides, G. C., Moss, A. J., Duffie, E. R., Jr. and Adams, F. H. (1964), "Pulmonary Arterial Pressure Changes in Human Newborn Infants from Birth to 3 Days of Age," *J. Pediat.*, **65**, 327–333.
29. Fraser, G. R., Froggatt, P. and James, T. N. (1964), "Congenital Deafness Associated with Electrocardiographic Abnormalities, Fainting Attacks and Sudden Death. A Recessive Syndrome," *Quart. J. Med.*, **33**, 361–385.
30. Friedman, W. F., Pool, P. E., Jacobowitz, D., Seagren, S. C. and Braunwald, E. (1968), "Sympathetic Innervation of the Developing Rabbit Heart. Biochemical and Histochemical Comparisons of Fetal, Neonatal, and Adult Myocardium," *Circulation Res.*, **23**, 25–32.
31. Grover, R. F., Vogel, J. H. K., Averill, K. H. and Blount, S. G. (1963), "Pulmonary Hypertension. Individual and Species Variation Relative to Vascular Reactivity," *Amer. Heart J.*, **66**, 1–3.
32. Haggerty, R. J., Maroney, M. W. and Nadas, A. S. (1956), "Essential Hypertension in Infancy and Childhood; Differential Diagnosis and Therapy," *Amer. J. Dis. Child.*, **92**, 535–549
33. Harvey, W. (1628), *Exercitatio anatomica de motu cordis et sanguinis in animalibus*. Francofurti: Fitzeri.
34. Heath, D., Du Shane, J. W., Wood, E. H. and Edwards, J. E. (1959), "The Structure of the Pulmonary Trunk at Different Ages and in Cases of Pulmonary Hypertension and Pulmonary Stenosis," *J. Path. Bact.*, **77**, 443–456.
35. Heymann, M. A. and Rudolph, A. M. (1966), "Physiological Observations of the Normal Fetus *In Utero*," *J. Pediat.*, **69**, 967–978.
36. Heymann, M.A., Rudolph, A. M., Nies, A. S. and Melmon, K. L. (1969), "Bradykinin Production Associated with Oxygenation of the Fetal Lamb," *Circulation Res.*, **25**, 521–534.
37. Hislop, A. A. (1971), "The Fetal and Childhood Development of the Pulmonary Circulation and its Disturbance in Certain Types of Congenital Heart Disease," Ph.D. Thesis, University of London.
38. Hoffman, J. I. E. (1972), *Diagnosis and Treatment of Pulmonary Vascular Disease*. In press.
39. Hoffman, J. I. E. and Rudolph, A. M. (1965), "The Natural History of Ventricular Septal Defects in Infancy," *Amer. J. Cardiol.*, **16**, 634–653.
40. Howatt, W. F., Avery, M. E., Humphreys, P. W., Normand, I. C. S., Reid, L. and Strang, L. B. (1965), "Factors Affecting Pulmonary Surface Properties in the Foetal Lamb," *Clin. Sci.*, **29**, 238–248.
41. Huggett, A., St. G. (1927), "Foetal Blood-gas Tensions and Gas Transfusion Through the Placenta of the Goat," *J. Physiol.*, **62**, 373–384.
42. Hait, G. and Gasul, B. M. (1963), "The Evolution and Significance of T Wave Changes in the Normal Newborn During the First Seven Days of Life," *Amer. J. Cardiol.*, **12**, 494–504.
43. James, T. N. (1963), "The Connecting Pathways Between the Sinus Node and the AV Node and Between the Right and the Left Atrium in the Human Heart," *Amer Heart J.*, **66**, 498–508
44. James, T. N. (1967), "Pulse and Impulse in the Sinus Node," *Henry Ford Hosp. Med. Bull.*, **15**, 275–299.
45. James, T. N. (1968), "Sudden Death in Babies: New Observations in the Heart," *Amer. J. Cardiol.*, **22**, 479–506.
46. James, T. N. (1970), "Cardiac Conduction System; Fetal and Postnatal Development," *Amer. J. Cardiol.*, **25**, 213–226.
47. James, T. N., Froggatt, P. and Marshall, T. K. (1965), "Sudden Death in Young Athletes," *Ann. intern. Med.*, **63**, 402–410.
48. James, T. N. and Konde, W. N. (1969), "A Clinicopathologic Study of Heart Block in a Dog, with Remarks Pertinent to the Embryology of the Cardiac Conduction System," *Amer. J. Cardiol.*, **24**, 59–71.
49. James, T. N., Sherf, L., Fine, G. and Morales, A. R. (1966), "Comparative Ultrastructure of the Sinus Node in Man and Dog." *Circulation*, **34**, 139–163.

50. James, L. S. and Rowe, R. D. (1957), "The Pattern of Response of Pulmonary and Systemic Arterial Pressures in Newborn and Older Infants to Short Periods of Hypoxia," *J. Pediat.*, **51**, 5–11.
51. Jones, D. S. (1958), "Effects of Acetylcholine and Adrenaline on the Experimentally Uninnervated Heart of the Chick Embryo," *Anat. Rec.*, **130**, 253–260.
52. Lauer, R. M., Evans, J. A., Aoki, M. and Kittle, C. F. (1965), "Factors Controlling Pulmonary Vascular Resistance in Fetal Lambs," *J. Pediat.*, **67**, 568–577.
53. Lebowitz, E. A., Novick, J. S. and Rudolph, A. M. (1972), "Efferent Sympathetic Development in the Fetal Lamb Heart," *Circulation*, suppl. II, **44**, 51.
54. Lieberman, M. (1970), "Physiologic Development of Impulse Conduction in Embryonic Cardiac Tissue," *Amer. J. Cardiol.*, **25**, 279–284.
55. Lieberman, M. and de Carvalho, A. P. (1965), "The Electrophysiological Organisation of the Embryonic Chick Heart," *J. gen. Physiol.*, **49**, 365–375.
56. Liebman, J. (1966), "The Normal Electrocardiogram in Newborns and Infants. (A Critical Review), in *Electrocardiography in Infants and Children*, (D. E. Cassels, and R. F. Ziegler, Eds.). New York: Grune and Stratton, Inc.
57. Liebman, J. (1968), "Electrocardiography," in *Heart Disease in Infants, Children and Adolescents*, pp. 183–231 (A. J. Moss and F. H. Adams, Eds.). Baltimore: Williams and Wilkins Co.
58. Lloyd, T. C. (1968), "Hypoxic Pulmonary Vasoconstriction: Role of Perivascular Tissue," *J. appl. Physiol.*, **25**, 560–565.
59. Macklin, C. C. (1946), "Evidences of Increase in the Capacity of the Pulmonary Arteries and Veins of Dogs, Cats and Rabbits During Inflation of the Freshly Excised Lung," *Rev. Canad. Biol.*, **5**, 199–232.
60. Melmon, K. L., Cline, M. J., Hughes, T. and Nies, A. S. (1968), "Kinins: Possible Mediation of Neonatal Circulatory Changes in Man," *J. clin. Invest.*, **47**, 1295–1302.
61. Meschia, G., Cotter, J. R., Breathnach, C. S. and Barron, D. H. (1965), "The Hemoglobin, Oxygen, Carbon dioxide and Hydrogen Ion Concentrations in the Umbilical Bloods of Sheep and Goats as Samples via Indwelling Plastic Catheters," *Quart. J. exp. Physiol.*, **50**, 185–195.
62. Metcalfe, J. and Parer, J. T. (1966), "Cardiovascular Changes During Pregnancy in Ewes," *Amer. J. Physiol.*, **210**, 821–825.
63. Nadas, A. S. and Fyler, D. C. (1972), *Pediatric Cardiology*, 3rd edition, p. 665. Philadelphia: W. B. Saunders Co.
64. Naeye, R. L. (1961), "Arterial Changes During the Perinatal Period," *Arch. Path.*, **71**, 121–128.
65. Naeye, R. L. (1966), "Development of Systemic and Pulmonary Arteries from Birth Through Early Childhood," *Biol. Neonat. (Basel)*, **10**, 8–16.
66. Naeye, R. L. and Letts, H. W. (1962), "The Effects of Prolonged Neonatal Hypoxemia on the Pulmonary Vascular Bed and Heart," *Pediatrics*, **30**, 902–908.
67. Namin, E. P. and Miller, R. A. (1966), "The Normal Electrocardiogram and Vectorcardiogram," in *Electrocardiography in Infants and Children* (D. E. Cassels and R. F. Ziegler, Eds.). New York: Grune and Stratton, Inc.
68. Navaratnam V. (1967), "The Ontogenesis of Cholinesterase Activity Within the Heart and Cardiac Ganglia in Man, Rat, Rabbit and Guinea-pig," *J. Anat.*, **99**, 459–467.
69. Patten, B. M. (1956), "The Development of the Sinoventricular Conduction System," *Univ. Mich. med. Bull.*, **22**, 1–21.
70. Penãloza, D., Sime, F., Banchero, N., Gamboa, R., Cruz, J. and Marticorena, E. (1963), "Pulmonary Hypertension in Healthy Men Born and Living at High Altitudes," *Amer. J. Cardiol.*, **11**, 150–157.
71. Phillips, C. E., Jr., DeWeese, J. A., Manning, J. A. and Mahoney, E. B. (1960), "Maturation of Small Pulmonary Arteries in Puppies," *Circulation Res.*, **8**, 1268–1273.
72. Pool, P. E., Averill, K. H. and Vogel, J. H. K. (1962), "Effect of Ligation of Left Pulmonary Artery at Birth on Maturation of Pulmonary Vascular Bed," *Medicina Thoracalis*, **19**, 362–369.
73. Pool, P. E., Vogel, J. H. K. and Blount, S. G., Jr. (1962), "Congenital Unilateral Absence of a Pulmonary Artery. The Importance of Blood Flow in Pulmonary Hypertension," *Amer. J. Cardiol.*, **10**, 706–732.
74. Preston, J. B., McFadden, S. and Moe, G. K. (1959), Atrioventricular Transmission in Young Mammals," *Amer. J. Physiol.*, **197**, 236–240.
75. Reeves, J. T. and Leathers, J. E. (1964), "Circulatory Changes Following Birth of the Calf and the Effect of Hypoxia," *Circulation Res.* **15**, 343–354.
76. Reynolds, S. R. M. (1956), "Fetal and Neonatal Pulmonary Vasculature in Guinea-pig in Relation to Hemodynamic Changes at Birth," *Amer. J. Anat.*, **98**, 97–123.
77. Rudolph, A. M. (1970), "The Changes in the Circulation After Birth. Their Importance in Congenital Heart Disease." *Circulation*, **41**, 343–359.
78. Rudolph, A. M., Auld, P. A. M., Golinko, R. J. and Paul, M. H. (1961), "Pulmonary Vascular Adjustments in the Neonatal Period," *Pediatrics*, **28**, 28–34.
79. Rudolph, A. M. and Heymann, M. A. (1967), "The Circulation of the Fetus *In Utero;* Methods for Studying Distribution of Blood Flow, Cardiac Output and Organ Blood Flow," *Circulation Res.*, **21**, 163–184.
80. Rudolph, A. M. and Heymann, M. A. (1970), "Circulatory Changes During Growth in the Fetal Lamb," *Circulation Res.*, **26**, 289–299.
81. Rudolph, A. M., Heymann, M. A. and Spitznas, U. (1972), "Hemodynamic Considerations in the Development of Narrowing of the Aorta," *Amer. J. Cardiol.*, **30**, 514–525.
82. Rudolph, A. M., Neuhauser, E. D. B., Golinko, R. J. and Auld, P. A. M. (1961), "Effects of Pneumonectomy on Pulmonary Circulation in Adult and Young Animals," *Circulation Res.*, **9**, 856–861.
83. Rudolph, A. M. and Yuan, S. (1966), "Response of the Pulmonary Vasculature to Hypoxia and H^+ Ion Concentration Changes," *J. clin. Invest.*, **45**, 399–411.
84. Scherlag, B. J., Lau, S. H., Halfant, R. H., Berkowitz, W. D., Stein, E. and Damato, A. N. (1969), "Catheter Technique for Recording His Bundle Activity in Man," *Circulation*, **39**, 13–18.
85. Shinebourne, E. A., Vapaavuori, E. K., Williams, R. L., Heymann, M. A. and Rudolph, A. M. (1972), "Development of Baroreflex Activity in Unanesthetised Fetal and Neonatal Lambs," *Circulation Res.*, **31**, 710–718.
86. Sime, F., Banchero, N., Penãloza, D., Gamboa, R., Cruz, J. and Marticorena, E. (1963), "Pulmonary Hypertension in Children Born and Living at High Altitudes," *Amer. J. Cardiol.*, **11**, 143–149.
87. Söderström, N. (1948), "Myocardial Infarction and Mural Thrombosis in the Atria of the Heart," *Acta med. scand.*, suppl. 217.
88. Spigelius, A. (1626), *De formatu foetu.* Patavy: Jo. Bap. de Martinis et Liviu Pasquatu.
89. Stahlman, M., Gray, J., Young, W. C. and Shepard, F. M. (1967), "Cardiovascular Response of the Neonatal Lamb to Hypoxia and Hypercapnia," *Amer. J. Physiol.*, **213**, 899–904.
90. Staub, N. C. (1963), "Site of Action of Hypoxia on the Pulmonary Vasculature" (Abstr.), *Fed. Proc.*, **22**, 453.
91. Vapaavuori, E. K., Shinebourne, E. A., Williams, R. L., Heymann, M. A. and Rudolph, A. M. (1972), *Biol. Neonat.* in press.
92. Vogel, J. H. K., McNamara, D. G. and Blount, S. G., Jr. (1967), "Role of Hypoxia in Determining Pulmonary Vascular Resistance in Infants with Ventricular Septal Defects," *Amer. J. Cardiol.*, **20**, 346–349.
93. Wagenvoort, C. A. (1962), "The Pulmonary Arteries in Infants with Ventricular Septal Defect," *Med. Thorac.*, **19**, 354–361.
94. Williams, R. L., Hoff, R., Heymann, M. A. and Rudolph, A. M. (1972), "Cardiovascular Effects of Hypothalamic Stimulation in the Chronic Fetal Lamb Preparation," *Circulation*, suppl. II, **46**, 5.
95. Yamada, K. M., Hariba, Y. and Sakaida, M. (1965), "Origination and Transmission of Impulse in the Right Auricle," *Jap. Heart J.*, **6**, 71–97.
96. Ziegler, R. F. (1951), *Electrocardiographic Studies in Normal Infants and Children.* Illinois: Charles C. Thomas Publisher, Springfield.

14A. GROWTH AND DEVELOPMENT OF THE RESPIRATORY SYSTEM—ANATOMICAL DEVELOPMENT

ALISON HISLOP AND LYNNE REID

INTRODUCTION

The lung at birth is not a miniature version of the adult lung since the structures within the lung differ in the rate at which they multiply and in their time pattern of differentiation. Even though it has to function efficiently soon after birth, the lung does not fulfil its postnatal function during intra-uterine development; it follows that the pattern of lung structure is genetically determined and not dependent upon the functional demands of the growing fetus.

The essential structures within the lung are the airways carrying gases to the respiratory or alveolar surface which contains blood vessels covered by a special epithelium. Airways, blood vessels and alveoli each have their peculiar pattern of growth; airways grow predominantly antenatally, whereas the alveoli grow post-natally, each being followed by the arteries of the region. This means that while lung development can be assessed overall by size and weight the pattern of growth and differentiation of each of these structures must be separately followed.

While anatomical and embryological studies have in the past been mainly descriptive, quantitative methods are today being increasingly used to analyse and describe structure and growth. For this reason, the pattern of lung growth has been summarized in the following three Laws of Lung Development. These resemble any other scientific law in that they summarize a state of affairs from which it may be possible to predict the effect of environmental variation.

(I) The bronchial tree is developed by the 16th week of intra-uterine life.

(II) Alveoli develop after birth, increasing in number until the age of eight years and in size until growth of the chest wall finishes with adulthood.

(III) The pre-acinar vessels (arteries and veins) follow the development of the airways, the intra-acinar that of the alveoli. Muscularization of the intra-acinar arteries does not keep pace with the appearance of new arteries.

Additional Laws could be formulated to cover vein structure, lymphatics, nerves etc., but the above three suffice to summarize the general pattern of growth.

Prediction is important in interpreting developmental anomalies and lung disease. By regarding the Laws as embodying a time-table it is possible to assess the stage in development at which certain anomalies have appeared and to predict those structures which will be most susceptible to disease at certain ages. With these Laws in mind, a precise comparison between normal and diseased lung is possible.

In this chapter lung growth, both normal and anomalous, has been considered in four separate stages of development:

(i) The first few weeks of gestation.
(ii) From five weeks gestation to birth.
(iii) The perinatal period.
(iv) Childhood and adolescence.

In addition, some features of normal lung structures related to function have been considered separately.

The Lung Units

The main topographical and functional units that will be referred to are described below.

The *segment* may be regarded as the topographic unit, since disease can be localized by reference to segments, and as the surgical unit, since a segment can be removed along the intersegmental boundaries. In the intersegmental plane the veins lie, receiving tributaries from adjacent segments, and dissection in this plane interrupts neither a large artery nor an airway. Lymphatic channels also pass across segmental boundaries. The segment, however, is not demarcated by a connective tissue sheath and collateral ventilation and collateral circulation occur across segmental and, of course, acinar boundaries.

The respiratory unit is the *acinus*, which represents lung supplied by the terminal bronchiolus. The acinus is not demarcated by connective tissue septa although part of its periphery may be; it is like a "grape" hanging on a stalk except that the "grapes" interdigitate like a three-dimensional jig-saw puzzle. This doubtless increases the surface area relative to the volume of such a unit and thereby increases the area available for collateral ventilation.

Along any airway, a small group of three to eight such acini are grouped to form a *lobule*. The acinus and the lobule are the last units to appear before birth and it is within these that remodelling of the lung occurs in the post-natal period.

EMBRYONIC PERIOD*

(the first five weeks after ovulation)†

Organ Development

In the first three weeks, the fetal membranes are established and the germ layers laid down in the embryonic disc. In the fourth to eighth weeks the main organs, including the lungs, appear.

In the fourth week of gestation, a ventral diverticulum lined by epithelium of endodermal origin arises from the foregut of the embryo. From this endoderm arises the lining epithelium of the whole respiratory system, including airways and alveoli. As the epithelium pushes out from the pharyngeal floor it is invested by the mesenchyme of the splanchnic mesoderm from the ventral surface of the foregut. Around the bronchial tree this condenses and differentiates into cartilage, muscle and connective tissue: it is from the mesenchyme also that the pulmonary blood vessels and lymphatics develop.

With growth the groove between the lengthening oesophagus and respiratory diverticulum deepens and they eventually separate. This remodelling occurs because of different rates of growth of epithelial cells and because of necrosis of some cells—a phenomenon that has been described in some detail for the duodenum.[127] The diverticulum divides dichotomously, each branch representing a future lung which divides progressively into the mesenchyme to form the bronchial tree.

Experimental Studies

Rudnick[124] has shown that transplants of lung buds from chick embryos will develop *in vitro*. The later the stage at which the transplant is removed the greater will be the ultimate differentiation, but budding and ramification of the bronchial tree will not occur in grafts of, as yet, unbranched

* The names for the stages of development are those given by the Commission on Embryological Terminology, in: *Nomina Embryologica*, Leningrad, 1970, edited by Arey, L. B. and Mossman, H. W. Federation of American Societies for Experimental Biology (F.A.S.E.B.), Bethesda, Maryland.

† In the present description for ages up to 7 weeks, age from ovulation has been used unless otherwise stated. Later it is not usually specified in the literature whether age is based on gestation or the last menstrual period: at this stage, the difference is not as critical as earlier. Streeter's assessment based on the rhesus monkey has been followed (1948), although several recent studies suggest that this underestimates age determined from crown–rump length.[130]

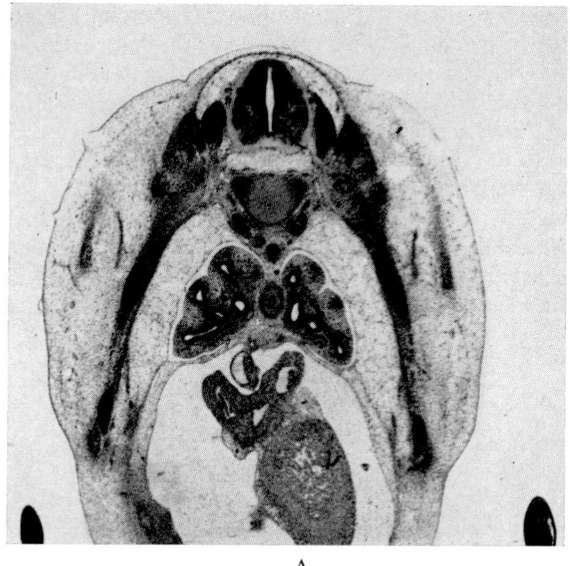
A

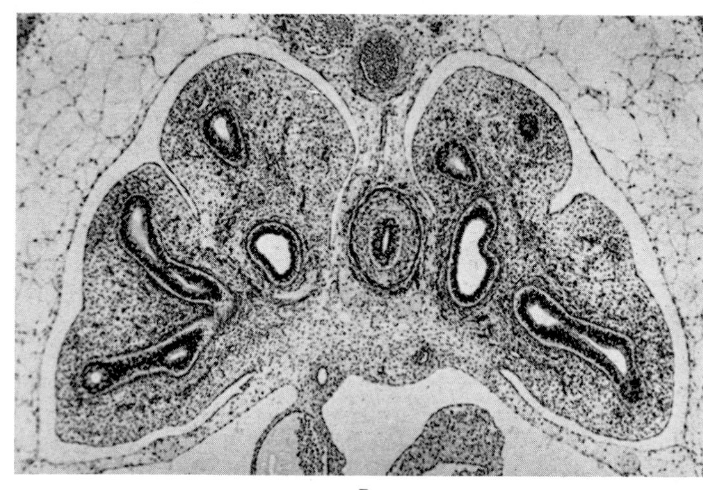
B

FIG. 1. Photomicrographs of transverse section through thorax of a 15 mm. human embyro.

1A—whole embryo. (×12) The lungs lie in the pleural cavity dorsal to the pericardium and heart and ventral to the notochord. The trachea lies between the two lungs: their outline shows small fissural depressions indicating segments.

1B—magnification of lungs from 1A. Segmental airways lined by columnar epithelium branch into the msesnchyme: the pleural cavity can be seen between lung and body wall. (×26)

lung bud if the mesoderm has been removed before transplantation. In the mouse lung, Alescio and Cassini[3] have demonstrated that the fate of mesenchyme is determined at an early stage, that of the trachea having different potential from that of the branching bronchi. By transplanting mesenchyme from the bronchial region to the tracheal, it was possible to induce growth of an extra branch: the tracheal epithelium is evidently not fully determined and still capable of being affected by overlying mesenchyme. Where mesenchyme had been removed this epithelio-mesenchymal interaction was lacking so that no further growth of bronchi occurred.

Growth and development would seem to depend upon glycolysis, the large stores of glycogen found in lung cells serving as a source of energy.[135] The terminal buds are richest in glycogen at the time when new cells are formed in the epithelium, glycogen disappearing as they mature.

Trachea and Large Bronchi

In the 4 mm. embryo (4-week) the endodermal lung buds are symmetrical and represent the two main bronchi. By the 8 mm. stage (5-week) the lobar bronchi to each lung are present. The airways continue to branch within the mesothelium and at 13·4 mm. (6-week) all subsegmental bronchi are present and segments can be identified by small fissural depressions on the outside of the lung, which disappear later in development (Fig. 1).[151]

The Main Pulmonary Artery

In the 4 mm. embryo (4-week) the aortic sac of the heart leads cranially into the primitive ventral aorta. In turn, the first to sixth pairs of aortic arch arteries appear from the ventral aorta or aortic sac and terminate dorsally in the dorsal aorta of the corresponding side. At no time are they all present. The six arches appear at about the 5 mm. stage (32-day) of development (Fig. 2) and soon give off branches descending to the vascular plexus surrounding the lung buds which have just appeared. In embryos of 10 mm. (37-day) the aortic sac is divided so that only blood from the right ventricle flows to the sixth arch and the lungs (Figs. 3). At this age the right sixth arch is becoming thinner, the left developing into the main pulmonary artery.

During this time the lung bud is also supplied by paired segmental branches arising from the dorsal aorta cranial to the coeliac arteries. During normal development these communications are lost and bronchial arteries develop from the aorta much later, between the 9th and 12th week.[15] Persistence of the early arteries from the dorsal aorta gives rise to one type of anomalous systemic supply to the lung.

By the 18 mm. stage (50-day) the adult pattern of blood supply to the lung is complete—the right sixth arch artery has disappeared and the left arch gives rise to the main as well as the left and right pulmonary artery, the last two coming closer together at their origin (Fig. 4). Now their only connection with the dorsal aorta is through the ductus arteriosus.

With subsequent growth in length of the embryo, the vessels and heart and lungs all progress caudally. Any vessels caudal to the arches will be carried down even further in a caudal direction so that any communication that persists between the dorsal aorta and lung may migrate below the diaphragm.

The Main Pulmonary Veins

Before the pulmonary vein is linked up with the heart, at 28–30 days, the veins drain to the systemic system, the systemic and pulmonary veins deriving from the same plexus. In the human embryo of 2–7 mm. (4–5-week) there are caudal and cranial evaginations of the left side of the sinu-atrial region of the heart. The cranial one gives rise to the stem of the pulmonary vein which, at this time, is connected with the splanchnic plexus around the oesophagus and trachea. The caudal type normally disappears as the sinus venosus is remodelled.[6] In the human adult there are still some connections between oesophageal veins and pulmonary veins at the lung roots.[28]

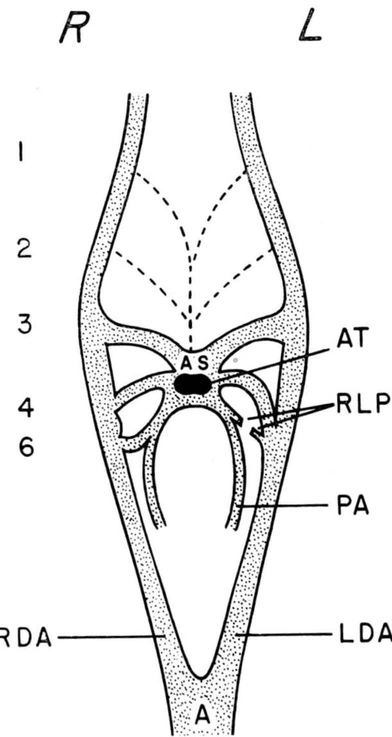

FIG. 2. Diagram of the branchial arch arteries connecting the ventral aortic sac (AS) with the right dorsal aorta (RDA) and left (LDA) in a 5 mm. embryo redrawn after Congdon.[35] The first and second arches have retrogressed, the third and fourth are complete. On the left the dorsal and ventral sprouts of the sixth (pulmonary) arch have nearly met (RLP) and on the right side the arch is complete. From the ventral sprouts plexiform vessels (PA) pass to the lung bud. A—aorta, AT—aortic trunk opening.

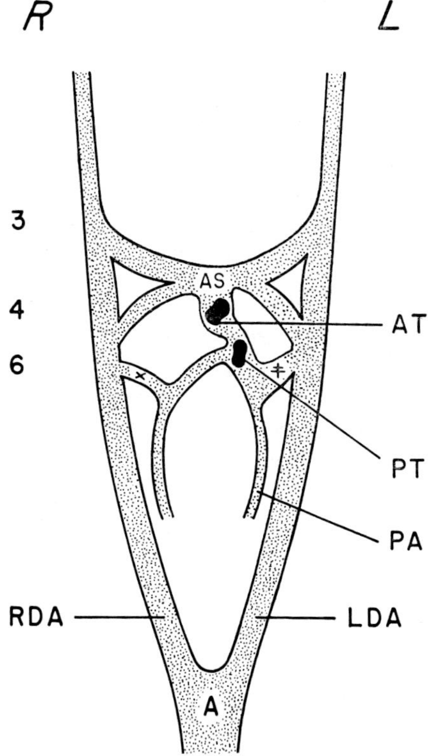

FIG. 3. Diagram of the branchial arch arteries in an 11 mm. embryo redrawn after Congdon.[35] The opening from the aortic sac (AS) is now double, the aortic trunk (AT) leads to the third and fourth arches and the pulmonary trunk (PT) to the sixth. The left fourth arch is increasing in size more than the right. The left sixth arch (ǂ) is increasing in size considerably while the dorsal part of the right sixth arch is disappearing (×). The right dorsal aorta (RDA) between the fourth arch and its junction with the left dorsal aorta (LDA) disappears and blood can only flow to the main dorsal aorta (A) via the fourth and sixth arches on the left. PA—pulmonary artery, A—aorta.

Pleura and Diaphragm

At about the fourth week the lungs bulge into the two primitive pleural canal-like cavities which, at this time, form part of the primitive body cavity, communicating with the future single peritoneal cavity and the large single anterior pericardial cavity (Fig. 5). In cross-section the pleural cavities are slit-like, the lungs growing backward and downward behind the heart.

As the heart descends in the body, the septum transversum, found anteriorly between the pericardium and peritoneum, is folded to form the pericardio-pleural membrane. The pleural cavity expands towards the body wall and a second membrane, the pleuro-peritoneal, which lies caudodorsal to the lung and is attached laterally to the body wall, appears between the pleural and peritoneal cavity, thus also separating the pericardial from the peritoneal cavity (Fig. 6).[52] This pleuro-peritoneal membrane enlarges with the cavity and is pushed caudally, eventually fusing with the

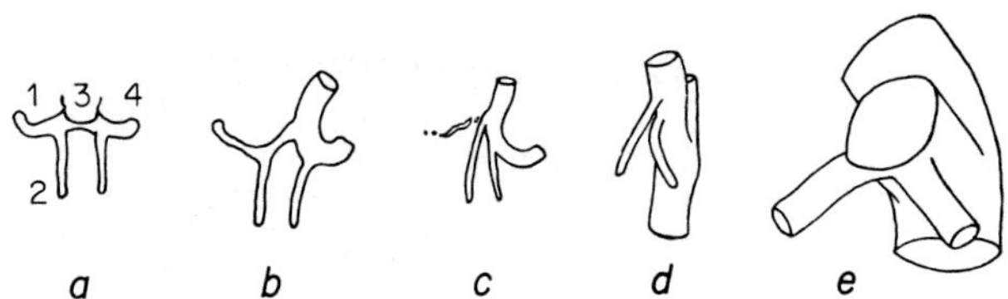

FIG. 4. Development of the pulmonary artery and ductus arteriosus redrawn after Congdon.[35] There is degeneration of the distal or dorsal part of the right arch (b and c) while the proximal or ventral part is incorporated into the right pulmonary artery. The dorsal part of the left sixth arch (4) becomes larger and remains in connection with the dorsal aorta to form the ductus arteriosus (d and e). The right and left pulmonary artery approach each other (d) and together join the main pulmonary trunk which is made up mainly of the ventral part of the left sixth arch.

(a) 7 mm. embryo, (b) 11 mm., (c) 13 mm., (d) 18 mm., (e) 43 mm. 1. right pulmonary arch, 2. right pulmonary artery, 3. communication with aortic sac.

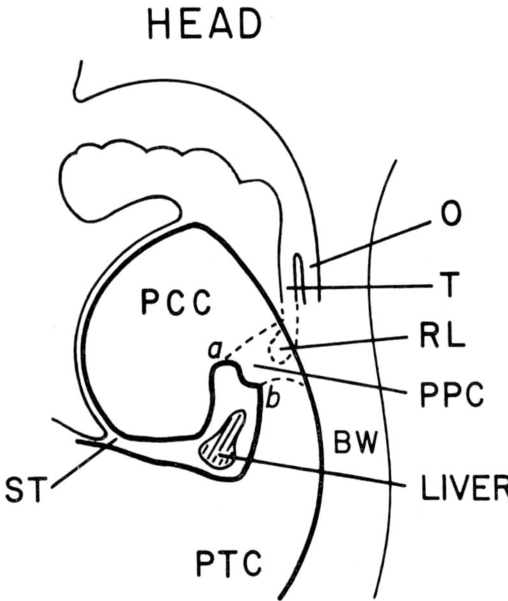

FIG. 5. Midline section of the pericardial region in a 7 mm. embryo redrawn from Hamilton, Boyd and Mossman.[52] Dotted lines show features in the right side of the body. The right pericardio-peritoneal canal (PPC) connects the pericardial (PCC) and the peritoneal cavities (PTC) and the right lung (RL) grows into this. A fold forming the pericardio-pleural membrane (a) is formed from the dorsal margin of the septum transversum (ST). As the pleural cavity enlarges the pleura-peritoneal membrane (b) forms and is also attached to the septum transversum. BW—body wall, T—trachea, O—oesophagus.

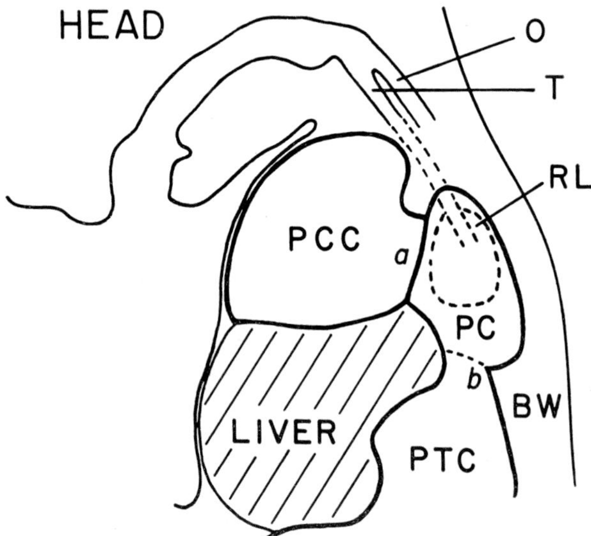

FIG. 6. Midline section of the pericardial region in a 16 mm. embryo, redrawn from Hamilton, Boyd and Mossman.[52] Dotted lines show structures in the right-hand side of the body. The pericardial cavity (PCC) is now separated from the pleural cavity (PC) by the completed pericardio-pleural membrane (a). The pleural cavity which is expanding into the body wall (BW) still communicates with the peritoneal cavity (PTC) at the medial area of the pleuro-peritoneal membrane (b) which now forms a distinct shelf between septum transversum and body wall. The liver has enlarged and bulged into the peritoneal cavity. RL—right lung, T—trachea, O—oesophagus.

lower part of the mesentery of the oesophagus. And so, in the 20 mm. embryo the diaphragm is complete. Since the phrenic nerve includes fibres from the third, fourth and fifth cervical somites, it is assumed that the diaphragm includes muscle from these somites also and that muscle and nerve grew into the diaphragm when it lay at the appropriate level and before its descent. The pleural cavities increase in size, shift around to the lateral side of the heart, and come to lie ventral to the pericardial cavity.

The "downward movement" of cervical structures probably arises mainly from the relatively faster growth of the dorsal than the ventral torso leading in fact to an "upward movement" of the spine over the structures lying anterior to it. It is this "overgrowth" that is responsible for the forward flexion of the head during fetal development.[106]

At no time during development do the lungs entirely fill the pleural space;[151] if the closure of the pleuro-peritoneal cavity is delayed the viscera may enter the pleural cavity and compress the lung. (*See* page 106 *et seq*.).

Congenital Anomalies Developing in the First Five Weeks After Ovulation

In an anencephalic fetus there may be no pleural space or lung although the fetus has developed well into the latter half of gestation, underlining how inessential are the lungs to fetal viability. Evidently, mesodermal dysplasia must have occurred early in development.

Agenesis or absence of a lung presumably develops as early as the fourth week of gestation when the division into two main airways should occur. One airway may fail to develop at all; a small nubbin of lung tissue around a simple tube may represent one lung.[125] It is tempting to suggest that the endodermal diverticulum has not established normal connection with a mesodermal cap. The varying degrees of hypoplasia of a lung, even when differentiation has proceeded normally, may represent a relative reduction in the amount of mesenchyme. Experimentally, lung agenesis can be produced in rats by Vitamin A deficiency in the mother.[153] While this is unlikely to be the only cause in the human, the possibility of inadequate local concentration or utilization of Vitamin A cannot be excluded.

Polycystic lung, particularly when associated with a polycystic condition of other organs such as breast or kidney, also suggests a widespread dysplasia of mesoderm or of the mechanisms of interaction between mesoderm and endoderm.[108]

Atresia of a bronchus has increasingly been recognized in recent years. It seems to affect particularly the bronchus to one or two segments in the upper lobe. While the bronchus lacks any tracheal communication centrally, distally it branches normally and collateral ventilation serves to keep the lobe aerated although not enough to allow of normal alveolar multiplication and growth: there is hypoplasia but it is associated with emphysema, i.e. large air spaces within the alveolar region.[120]

The airways occlusion could occur at about the fifth week of intra-uterine life when segmental airways appear. Such damage may have occurred, however, much later by interference with the blood supply of the bronchus, although no evidence of abnormal blood supply has been found in human bronchial atresia. Louw and Barnard[93] tied a branch of the mesenteric artery in the gut of the puppy at Caesarean operation nine days before term. The puppies then developed to term and spontaneous delivery. Atresia of the gut was found with no fibrous remnant between the two blind ends.

Inflammation in the fetal lung seems to differ from that in the adult. Dense fibrous sheets may sometimes be associated with congenital anomalies but, more often, the scarring and distortion with fibrosis associated with adult disease is lacking.

Localized adhesion between the chest wall and the underlying lung is often associated with an anomalous systemic artery penetrating the lung at a level well away from the hilum. In such a case, it is tempting to regard the change as the result of antenatal inflammation. In the present state of our understanding, it might well be useful to regard congenital anomalies as of two types—those that represent an intrinsic abnormality of the biochemical organizer system and those that arise from an inflammation such as occurs after infection.

FROM FIVE WEEKS' GESTATION TO BIRTH

Stages of Intrauterine Development

Between the gestation age of five weeks and birth three stages are recognized in lung growth and differentiation (Fig. 7). The first—the *pseudo-glandular* period—continues until the 16th week of gestation and during this phase the pre-acinar branching pattern of airways and vessels is established: respiration is not possible since the airways, although always hollow, are blind-ending tubules completely lined by epithelium, cuboidal at the periphery and, nearer the hilum, stratified. In section, the lung resembles an acinar gland.

The second or *canalicular* stage lasts from the fourth to the sixth month. It is at this time that vascularization of the mesenchyme rapidly increases and that the respiratory portion of the lung becomes delineated. In the last generations of tubules, small blood vessels grow under the cuboidal epithelium, thinning it, so that with the light microscope it is no longer possible to recognize a continuous epithelial lining. At the same time new branches are formed, all having the thinned epithelium. It was once doubted that at this time the lung was lined with a continuous epithelial layer but the increased resolution of the electron microscope has confirmed its presence. This means that throughout the whole of its development, and in the adult, the alveolus is lined by a continuous epithelial lining. At the end of the canalicular period respiration is possible.

The last three months of gestation are known as the *terminal sac* or *alveolar* period. During this time there is further differentiation of the respiratory region with additional respiratory bronchioli developing as well as saccules with flattened epithelium. Just before birth primitive alveoli can be detected in the wall of the saccules although true alveoli do not develop until after birth. It is during this period that surfactant can first be detected.

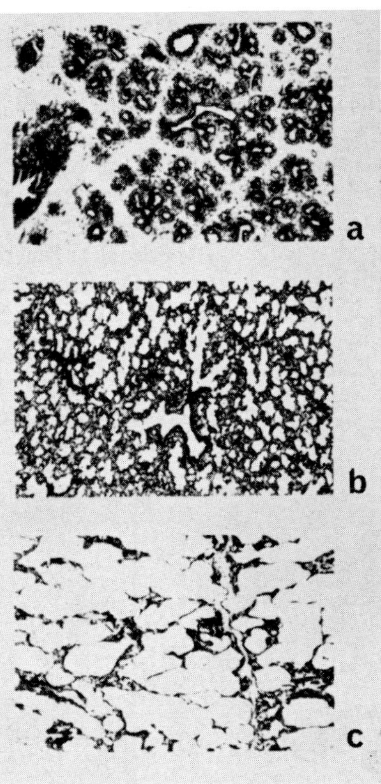

FIG. 7' Microscopic appearance of the three stages of fetal lung development. (a) Glandular: 5th–6th week. (b) Canalicular: 16th–24th week. (c) Alveolar: 24th week–Term. (Reproduced by permission of Lloyd-Luke (Medical Books) Ltd.[113]

These three phases have been recognized by all previous workers but opinions have differed as to their duration as seen in Table 1. Loosli and Potter's[91] scheme has the advantage of simplicity. The overlap included in Boyden's[18] suggests that epithelium at the end of a given airway thins as soon as its branching is complete. This would mean that differentiation is irregular throughout the lung; such regional variation is rarely seen. Boyden (personal communication) considers that the difference in alveolar size seen in the uninflated lung reflects irregularity in maturation. Boyden's term "terminal sac period" would seem best to describe the air spaces at this last period and the term "alveolar" could then be confined to the post-natal period.

TABLE 1

PREVIOUS DESCRIPTIONS OF STAGES OF INTRA-UTERINE LUNG DEVELOPMENT

Dubreuil, Lacoste and Raymond[42]	*Loosli and Potter*[92]	*Boyden*[18]
Glandular Up to 6 months	Glandular 5 weeks–4 months	Pseudo-glandular 5–17 weeks
Canalicular 7 months–birth	Canalicular 4–6 months	Canalicular 13–25 weeks
Alveolar After birth	Alveolar 6 months–birth	Terminal-sac period 24 weeks–birth

Airways

Branching

In the fetus of five weeks the lobar bronchi are already present and, by the sixth week, branches to the level of, and including, all segmental bronchi can be recognized. Between 10 and 14 weeks' gestation, there is a spurt within the segments of branching of airways into the mesenchyme and during this period (Fig. 8) 70 per cent of generations along an axial pathway arise. The airways within the longer segments of the lung continue to divide until the 16th week of gestation, at which time the number of airway generations arising from axial pathways in each segment varies from between 15 to 26,[22] the same range between segments as seen in the adult.[55] Thus, all pre-acinar airway branching is complete by the end of the glandular phase; and while there may be a drop in the number of pre-acinar generations between this time and birth, due to alveolization of one, or at most two, distal airways, there is never an increase in the number.

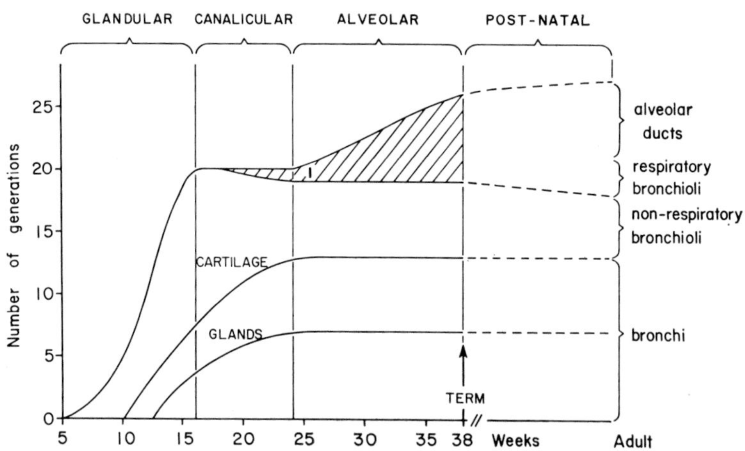

FIG. 8. Diagrammatic representation of the development of the bronchial tree. Lobar bronchi appear at the sixth week of gestation and by 16 weeks all non-respiratory airways are present. Most respiratory ones appear between 16 weeks and birth, some appear in infancy. Cartilage and glands appear later and their extension is complete by 24 weeks' gestation.

Cartilage

The first differentiation to cartilage occurs in the mesenchymal cells in the trachea in the fourth week of gestation when pre-cartilage appears.[7] At the end of the seventh week, distinct rings of cartilage are discernible along the trachea and by the 10th week in the main bronchi; but within the segmental airways it is only at the 12th week that cartilage appears, that is about six weeks after the airway appears. Cartilage is then found further towards the periphery but at no time extends to the end of the airway branches. Additional cartilage appears after bronchial branching is complete, new foci appearing until the 25th week of gestation when the plates have reached the adult levels (Fig. 8). The number of generations of airways free of cartilage varies widely along different pathways, any number between 3 and 9 being without cartilage support.[22] At term, however, the more distal plates are still immature and staining like pre-cartilage: even the proximal plates mature only in later fetal life.

New cartilage appears first centrally and appearance and differentiation proceed distally—this pattern is seen in the muscle and connective tissue of the airway walls and in the epithelium which also differentiate centrifugally. In the adult the respiratory epithelium is pseudo-stratified, ciliated, or columnar. After 10 weeks' gestation the tracheal epithelium is multi-layered with some ciliated cells; but along the main bronchi it gradually thins to a single layer of cylindrical cells and then, more peripherally, to cuboidal ones. By 13 weeks cilia can be detected to the end of the bronchial tree present at that time and at term they are found as far as the terminal bronchiolus.[23]

Goblet Cells

Goblet cells develop somewhat later than cartilage, appearing first in the layer of columnar cells in the trachea and large bronchi at 13 weeks. Up to birth and even later, the bronchial lumen is corrugated, and it is in the crypts that goblet cells first appear. These stain with Alcian blue—that is, they synthesize acid glycoprotein. As well as distended goblet cells there are narrow cells containing granules of neutral glycoprotein which tend to disappear as the fetus gets older and perhaps are precursors of the acid glycoprotein-secreting goblet cells. With age, the goblet cells extend peripherally; but during fetal life they are not found beyond the last plate of cartilage where, even in the normal adult, they are sparse. The goblet and precursor cells represent one in four of the superficial epithelial cells, the precursor cells being few in number.[111]

Mucous Glands

Mucous glands show the cranial-to-caudal pattern of appearance seen in cartilage. They first appear in the trachea after 12 weeks' gestation, which is later than cartilage. With age, glands extend to the periphery, appearing in bronchi at 13 weeks; but before birth they are not found as far as the last plate of cartilage.[23] They are more common cranially than caudally until the 17th week of gestation. By 28 weeks, seven-eighths of the potential adult number of glands have appeared.

The first sign of a developing gland is an accumulation of basal cells in a sharply defined cluster internal to the epithelial basement membrane but causing it to bulge. These cells multiply to form a solid bud penetrating into the sub-epithelial layers; a lumen then appears converting the solid cord into a primitive tubular gland with a duct opening on to the surface; from this duct, further budding gives rise to a gland with a simple acinar structure. By the 24th week acini are present in the proximal glands while distally only tubules are seen. At birth each gland is small but it occupies a relatively large part of the bronchial wall because the latter is so thin. During childhood the glands increase in size and complexity, but no new glands are formed. The glands grow relatively more slowly than the bronchial wall, so that between 6 and 12 months of post-natal age they are in the same proportion as in the adult[51] when expressed as the gland-wall ratio.[112] All the acinar secreting cells are mucous until the 26th week, when both mucous and serous cells can first be distinguished, though only proximally.

Once the lumen is formed in the gland, both neutral and acid glycoprotein can be identified histochemically within the cells. In the tracheal glands at 14 weeks' gestation there is active production of mucus. During fetal life no sialic acid can be identified within the epithelial cells, the acidic mucin being sulphated. Tracheal fluid in the fetus is more acid (pH 6·5) than amniotic fluid or serum. Within a few days of birth some sialic acid can be identified and this increases gradually with age.[83] The significance of this chemical shift is not clear, but in the adult viscosity of secretion is known to be related to its sialic-acid content.[115] It may be that the absence of this group before birth is associated with reduced viscosity.

Alveoli

First Appearance

Alveolar development does not begin until airway development is complete. During the canalicular stage from four to six months there is transformation of the last airway generation to form a respiratory bronchiolus with, probably, multiplication to give at least one additional respiratory airway generation. This forms the respiratory bronchiolar region distal to the last conducting airway. Capillaries multiply so that this region is highly vascularized and the epithelial lining becomes irregular in thickness because it is thinned at the points where it lies over a capillary. The spaces lined by the flat epithelium represent shallow primitive alveoli which can be recognized arising from respiratory bronchioli. The lung at this time loses its glandular appearance, the respiratory airways ending in a cluster of large, thin-walled saccules which are separated from each other by a loose connective tissue matrix and lined by flattened epithelium (Fig. 9).[14,92] It is at this stage that respiration can be supported.

During the terminal sac or alveolar period further generations of saccules appear with indentations in their walls that increase the surface area and represent primitive alveoli. There is also increase in the length of the respiratory bronchiolar generations with thin-walled alveoli increasing in number (Fig. 9). Counting these and the saccules as "alveoli", 8 per cent of the total adult number of alveoli may be said to be present at birth.[43] Boyden emphasises that at birth these are unlike the alveoli of the adult.[14]

Alveolar Epithelial Lining

Until the advent of the electron microscope, it was thought that the capillaries were in direct communication with the air spaces, but it is now known that all alveoli are lined by continuous flattened epithelial cells of endodermal origin. In the adult the alveolar lining layer has two types of cell—the Type I and Type II pneumonocytes.[29] The Type I cell covers the major part of the alveolar surface and contributes to the blood/gas barrier. The cytoplasm extends away from the nucleus over a large area; the cell can be compared to a fried egg with the nucleus as the yolk. The Type II pneumonocyte is taller, cuboidal, with a brush border and has characteristic osmiophilic inclusions probably linked to the production of surfactant (Fig. 10).[78,128] These two types of cell first become discernible in the sixth month of human gestation.[30] The most detailed study of development, both morphologically and with respect to surfactant, has been made in the rabbit, in which the age of gestation can be accurately determined.

Electron Microscopic Aspects. Three stages of development similar to those of the human can be recognized in the rabbit: the pseudo-glandular stage to the 24th day, the canalicular to the 27th, and the alveolar phase from then until term which is at 31 days.[78] In the pseudo-glandular phase, tubules lined by columnar cells that contain large amounts of glycogen are surrounded by loose mesenchymal cells (Fig. 11). The cells of the more proximal tubules remain columnar while in the distal tubules, representing the future alveolar region, the epithelium is flat (Fig. 12). By 24 days many capillaries have come close to the "alveolar" epithelium and by the 27th day they seem to be stretching the epithelium which now appears very thin and would not be detected by the light microscope (Fig. 13). At this time also both types of pneumonocyte can be identified for the first time. The capillaries covered by the thin epithelium seem to bulge into the alveolar space. The blood/gas barrier over such capillaries is the same as in the adult, though elsewhere the alveolar walls are thicker due to an increase in connective tissue.[88]

Surfactant

The surface tension of the alveolar lining is less than that of water vapour, evidently because a surface tension reducing substance—now commonly called surfactant—is present in the lining layer. Pattle[107] recognized it because of the stability of the bubbles in the froth of pulmonary oedema fluid, and Mead, Whittenberger and Radford[95] deduced its presence from their study of the "work done" during breathing. The substance seems to be a phospholipid —a lecithin derivative—whose function is discussed in

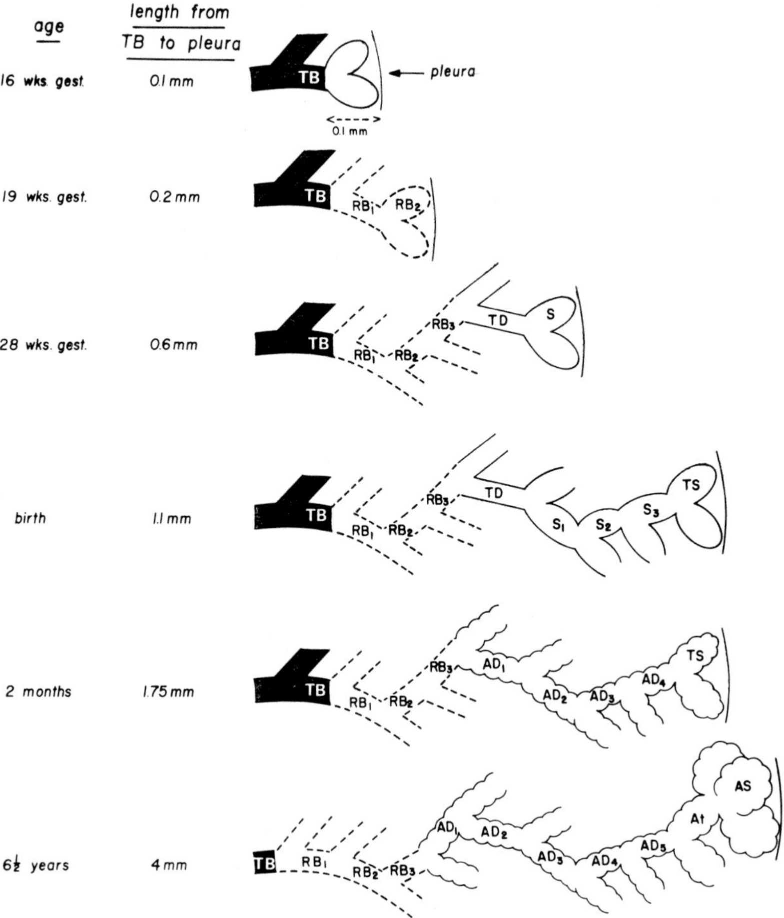

FIG. 9. Diagram illustrating schematically the growth of the acinus. A subpleural one is illustrated.

(i) at 16 weeks' gestation the airways end in a tubule close to the pleura; TB—terminal bronchiolus.

(ii) by 19 weeks' gestation the epithelium in the last generation of the airways has thinned and now forms the first respiratory bronchiolus (RB): branching has led to a second generation respiratory bronchiolus.

(iii) by 28 weeks' gestation further branching has given rise to a total of three generations of respiratory bronchioli and one generation of transitional ducts (TD) (12), each of the latter giving rise to a pair of primitive saccules (S).

(iv) by birth the number of generations of saccules has increased to three; these end in terminal saccules (TS). No true alveoli are present at this time although a few indentations representing future alveoli have appeared just before birth.

(v) by two months alveoli have developed in the walls of the respiratory bronchioli, transitional ducts and saccules, which transforms these last two into alveolar ducts (AD). Alveoli also open into the terminal saccules.

(vi) by six years several changes have occurred. Remodelling of respiratory bronchioli and alveolar ducts may be in one of four ways—(a) along some pathways a bronchiolus may be transformed into an extra generation of respiratory bronchioli by centripetal alveolization; (b) distal respiratory bronchioli may be transformed into alveolar ducts; (c) further branching of another one or two alveolar duct generations may occur, or (d) there may be no change.

Certainty for some of the above is not possible because of variation between acini and cases. At the distal end, however, the terminal sac has probably transformed into the adult atrium (At),[101] a short, wide passage lined by alveoli. This has given rise to a number of alveolar sacs (AS), formed by budding rather than branching and each lined by alveoli.

This pattern is similar to that seen in the adult; there is probably little further development save increase in size.

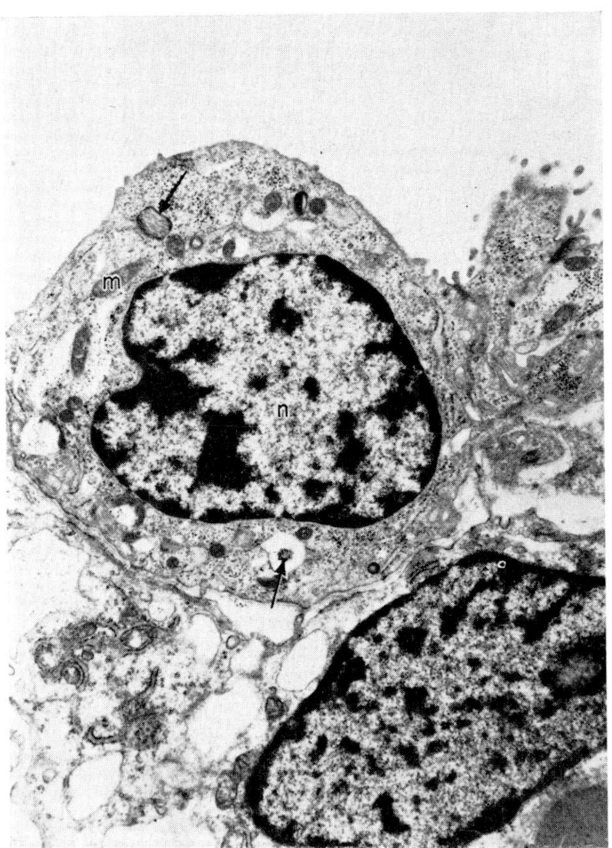

FIG. 10. Electron micrograph of a Type II pneumonocyte of a 28-day fetal rabbit, with osmiophilic inclusions at arrows, mitochondria (mi) and nucleus (n). (×7,500) (Reproduced by permission of *British Journal of Diseases of the Chest*.[98])

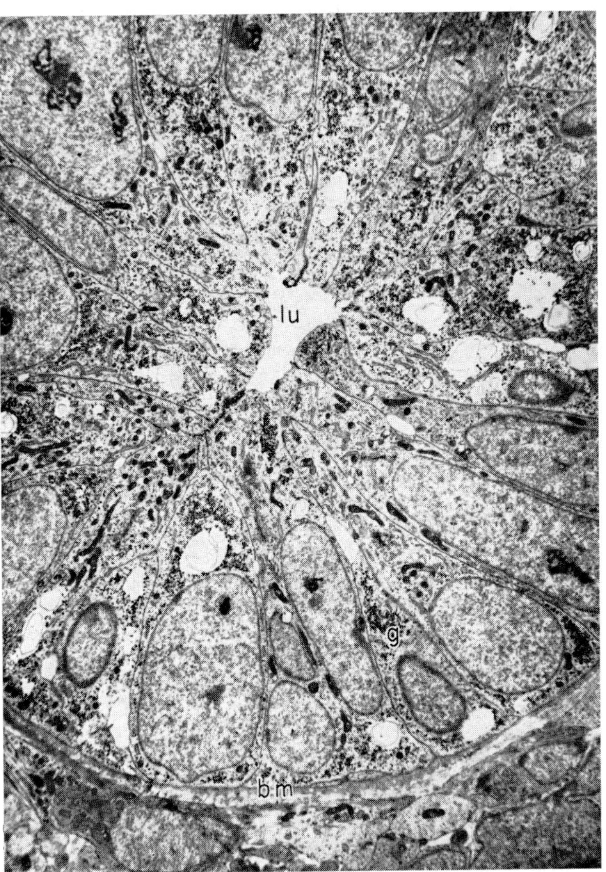

FIG. 11. Glandular stage of fetal rabbit—the distal end of a bronchial tubule. Columnar epithelium cells on a basement membrane (bm) are found around a lumen (lu). Fine black granules represent glycogen (g). (×2,800) (Reproduced by permission of *Le Poumon et le Coeur*.[117])

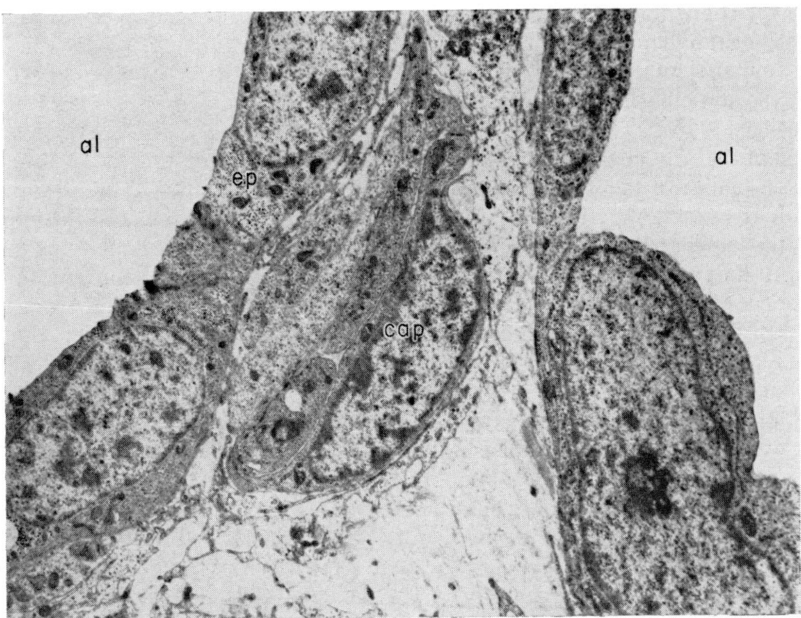

FIG. 12. Canalicular phase of fetal rabbit—an alveolar wall between two alveoli (al). The epithelium (ep) has become thinned by an underlying capillary (cap) whose lumen shows as a slit at arrow. (×4,200)
(Reproduced by permission of *Le Poumon et le Coeur*.[117])

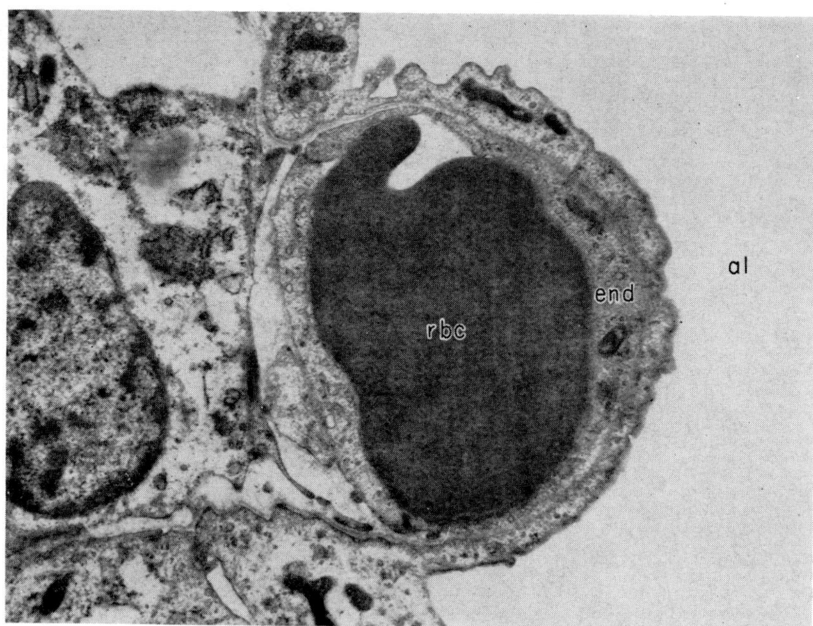

FIG. 13. Alveolar epithelium of rabbit at birth. A capillary lined by endothelium (end) and containing a red blood corpuscle (rbc) has thinned the epithelium and is bulging into the alveolar lumen (al). (×10,700)

Chapter 14B (Godfrey). This system is particularly important at birth when fluid in the lungs is replaced by air.

While intensive study of this substance in the last decade has added greatly to our understanding, many of the key questions can still not be answered with certainty. For example, an alveolar lining layer of phospholipid cannot be consistently and satisfactorily stained, which has led to the the suggesting that the "lining" is really a modification of the cell membrane of the alveolar pneumonocytes.

While the weight of the evidence favours the lamellated osmiophilic bodies of the Type II pneumonocyte as the site of synthesis of surfactant, metabolic studies have not charted the synthetic pathways and some authors still suggest that it is the Clara cell, the non-ciliated cell in the small bronchiolus, that is responsible.

The following gives some of the circumstantial evidence linking osmiophilic inclusion bodies of the Type II pneumonocyte to the production of surfactant activity.

In the fetal rabbit lung, the lamellated bodies appear at the same time as surfactant activity can first be demonstrated.[72,117] In most other species normal surface activity in the fetal lung corresponds well with the appearance of Type II cell inclusion bodies and also with the age at which the fetus can first live a separate life (Table 2.)[98]

In lambs, a dense osmiophilic alveolar lining layer can only be identified in lungs with inclusion bodies.[78]

Exposure of guinea-pigs to 15 per cent carbon dioxide increases pulmonary surface tension and reduces the number of lamellated bodies. Return to a normal atmosphere reverses both changes.[129]

Bilateral cervical vagotomy increases pulmonary surface tension and reduces the number of lamellated bodies.[81]

Type II pneumonocytes have been seen with lamellated bodies which appear to be discharging into the alveolar space. This could be ingestion which has been shown after introduction of thorotrast into alveoli.[36] In fact, little is taken up by either type of pneumonocyte, most being ingested by macrophages. Moreover, the lamellated bodies are too regular in shape to be ingested bodies.

TABLE 2

THE RELATION OF LENGTH OF GESTATION TO THE APPEARANCE OF SURFACTANT

Species	*Gestation* (days)	*Day at which surfactant detected and fetus viable*	*Time of gestation without surfactant* %
Human	280	160	59
Sheep	148	120	81
Rabbit	31	27	87
Rat	21	19	90
Mouse	20	18	80

Chloroform/methanol (a lipid solvent) extraction removes lamellated bodies from the Type II pneumonocyte but not the granules in the non-ciliated cell of the bronchioli.[5]

In fetal rabbit, 9-fluoroprednisolone, a corticosteroid, given at 24 days, accelerated the appearance of surfactant and lamellated bodies: the non-ciliated cell was unaffected.[149]

Using tritiated palmitate Askin and Kuhn,[5] with electron microscopy and autoradiography, found the majority of grains over Type II pneumonocytes with less over non-ciliated cells, indicating a faster lipid turnover in the Type II pneumonocyte.

The origin of the lamellated bodies is not yet established but several mechanisms have been suggested. Kisch[79] reported that they were transformed mitochondria, Sorokin[136]

that they arose from the multivesicular bodies which themselves originate in the Golgi apparatus. Transition forms between the multivesicular and lamellated bodies have been seen frequently in the authors' Department.

Amniotic Fluid

The amniotic fluid at term is diluted with urine which is present in small amounts from the fourth month of gestation. The lung also contributes fluid during fetal life, the lymph flow being much greater than in the adult sheep.[9] The osmotic pressure and protein content of tracheal effluent was similar to amniotic fluid, but a lower pH and lower CO_2 level[2] was reported in the tracheal than in the amniotic fluid. Surfactant has been demonstrated in amniotic fluid from 30 weeks' gestation onward, having first appeared in homogenized lung tissue at 20 weeks.[34]

Pulmonary Arteries

At all ages from 12 weeks' gestation on, the pulmonary arteries have recently been studied after injection with a radio-opaque medium.[61,64] The injection is made at the same temperature and at a high pressure, so that despite age differences all arteries have been treated in the same way and, for quantitative studies, can be regarded as comparable. This method ensures that all arteries are fully distended down to a diameter of 15 μm. and some at a diameter of 10 μm. but no medium passes through the capillary bed. Similarity of conditions is more important for quantitative measurements than injection the arteries at a pressure measured during life, which itself may be inaccurate or misleading.

Quantitative analysis has been used both with respect to the branching pattern—the number of generations and side branches has been counted—and to artery structure—muscle wall thickness and artery diameter have been measured and related to wall structure. In this way the normal is precisely defined and serves for comparison with any abnormal case.

Overall Pattern

Since the injection medium is radio-opaque the overall pattern of arterial branching can be studied on arteriograms. At 14 weeks' gestation, as seen in Fig. 14, the main axial pathways within a segment can be seen as well as the side branches, although at this time they are very small relative to lung size. By 20 weeks the lung has increased in size and more arterial branches can be seen (Fig. 15). The pattern of branching at this age is essentially the same as that seen in the adult but there is no background haze. In both the child and the adult the main pathways are obscured by a haze made up of the small vessels of the peripheral lung. At 38 weeks, the left lung (Fig. 16) has further increased in size, the number of small peripheral vessels is slightly increased producing some haze, although the arterial branching pattern is similar to that at 20 weeks. Variation can be seen between cases, due probably to genetic control since family similarities are seen.[65]

Measurements of the arteries on the arteriograms show that the vessels at the hilum grow faster than those at the periphery, so that the gradient of diameter against length increases with age. The hilar arteries increase in diameter

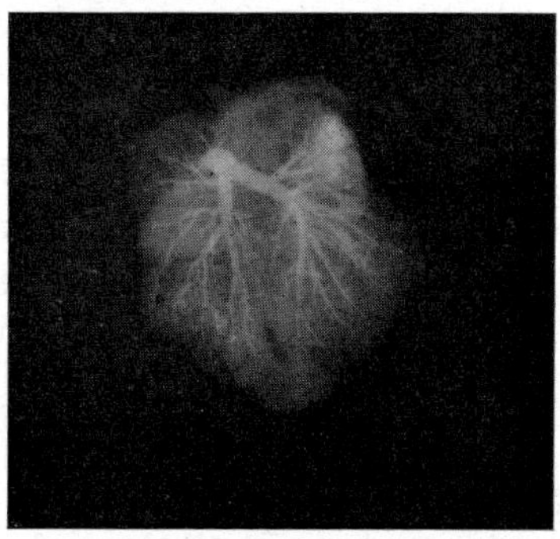

FIG. 14. Arteriogram of fetal lung of 14 weeks' gestation. Arteries filled with a barium-gelatine solution. Main pathways are present but small. (×1)

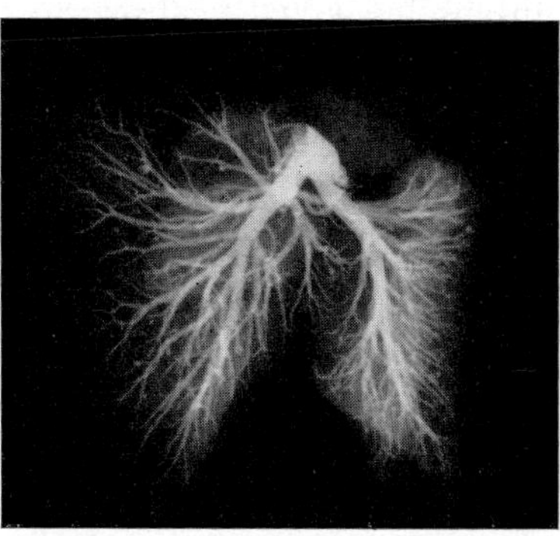

FIG. 15. Arteriogram of fetal lung of 20 weeks' gestation prepared as Fig. 14. The branching pattern is complete but there is no background haze. (×1)

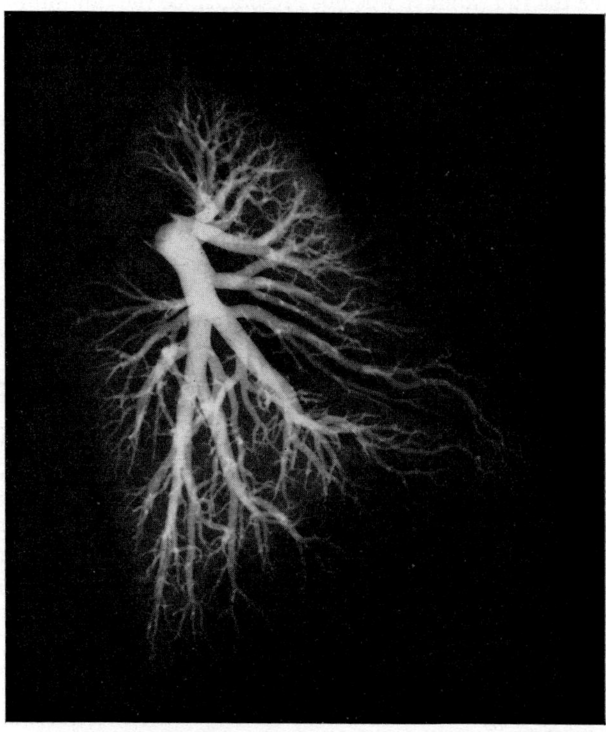

FIG. 16. Arteriogram of the left lung of a fetus of 38 weeks' gestation prepared as Fig. 14. The branching pattern is similar to that in Fig. 15 with a slight background haze (×1)

at the same rate as the arteries increase in length, and both increase faster than lung volume.

Branching Pattern

With serial reconstruction the branching pattern of the arteries can be traced precisely. In the adult, the main pulmonary arteries run alongside the airways and give rise to an arterial branch, known as a "conventional" artery, accompanying each airway branch. In addition, numerous branches arise from the axial artery and pass directly into adjacent respiratory tissue to supply the capillary bed, perhaps after branching several times.[45] These "supernumerary" arteries, as they are called, supply a respiratory unit "by the back door" as it were, and provide a collateral circulation analogous to collateral ventilation. The supernumerary arteries are more numerous at the periphery than centrally, both absolutely and relatively to conventional arteries. The ratio between supernumerary and conventional arteries over the whole pre-acinar length is 2·5–3·4 :1. The supernumerary arteries make up between 20 and 45 per cent of the total cross-sectional area of side branches and hence, in any given region, may be considered to carry a significant part of the blood flow.

During fetal life the arteries branch into the mesenchyme alongside the distal branching airways. Reconstruction has shown that the large number of arteries, both conventional and supernumerary, seen in the pre-acinar region in the adult lung does not grow in response to the demand of the growing lung but appears during ante-natal development at the same time as the airways, while there is still little blood flow. The types of artery were found to be in the same proportion in a 12-week fetus as in the adult—although at this age the full number was not present, since the full number of airways had not developed.

By the end of the fourth month of gestation the full complement of all pre-acinar vessels is present in every segment. Fig. 17 shows the branching pattern of the airway and axial artery to the posterior basal segment of the left lung in a 19-week fetus. To the level of the terminal bronchiolus there are 25 bronchial branches, a figure within the normal adult range. Accompanying these are 21 conventional arteries and 58 supernumerary arteries—a pattern essentially the same as that in the adult. Changes in the pre-acinar region up to birth and to adulthood are changes of size only. The ratio of supernumerary to conventional arteries remains relatively constant throughout fetal life, though there is individual variation.

During later fetal life there is arterial branching within the respiratory region of the lung as arteries develop that accompany respiratory bronchioli and, later, saccules. Within the acinus both conventional and supernumerary arteries can be identified; during childhood, however, there is yet considerable arterial branching to come. During fetal development the number of arteries per unit area of lung increases with increasing fetal age.

Arterial Wall Structure

In young fetuses the components of the arterial walls are immature. In the fetus of 12 weeks the elastic laminae are fine and do not stain satisfactorily. With increasing age the elastic laminae become thicker, more regular and further apart and stain appropriately. The muscle cells also, though morphologically identifiable in the young fetus, do not show the staining characteristics of mature muscle cells until

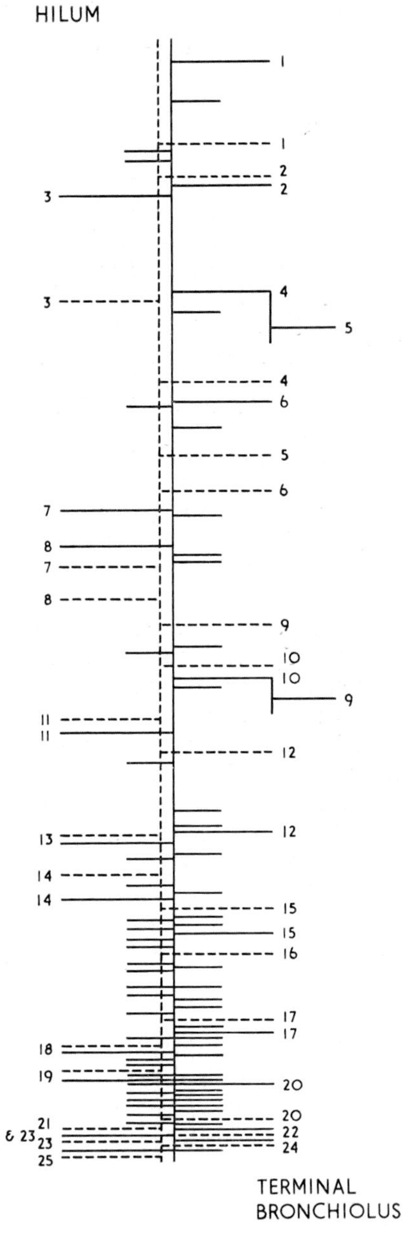

FIG. 17. Diagram representing the branching pattern of axial airway and artery to the posterior basal segment of the left lung in a fetus of 19 weeks' gestation. From lobar hilum to terminal bronchiolus there are 25 airway generations, accompanied by 21 conventional arteries, with, in addition, 58 supernumerary arteries.

23 weeks' gestation. Electron microscopy of the intrapulmonary vessels of a 14-week fetus has shown cells with some of the characterististics of muscle cells but not fully developed in comparison with the adult smooth muscle cell. The cell seen in Fig. 18 is identified as a muscle cell since it

has a basement membrane and includes myofibrils: its electron density is greater than that of surrounding cells and it contains a large amount of glycogen. It has not yet developed all the characteristics seen in the muscle cell in Fig. 19 which was taken from a small vessel in a normal adult lung.

During fetal life the main pulmonary artery has a wall structure similar to that of the aorta—that is, of an elastic artery. Its media is made up of numerous elastic laminae—more than seven between the internal and external elastic laminae—and with muscle cells between. At all ages the same wall structure is found in the largest intrapulmonary arteries. More peripherally a "transitional" structure is seen where between four and seven elastic laminae lie between the internal and external. This structure gives way to the muscular where there are fewer than four elastic laminae. The elastic fibres gradually reduce peripherally until eventually in small arteries there are only internal and external elastic laminae with muscle cells between.

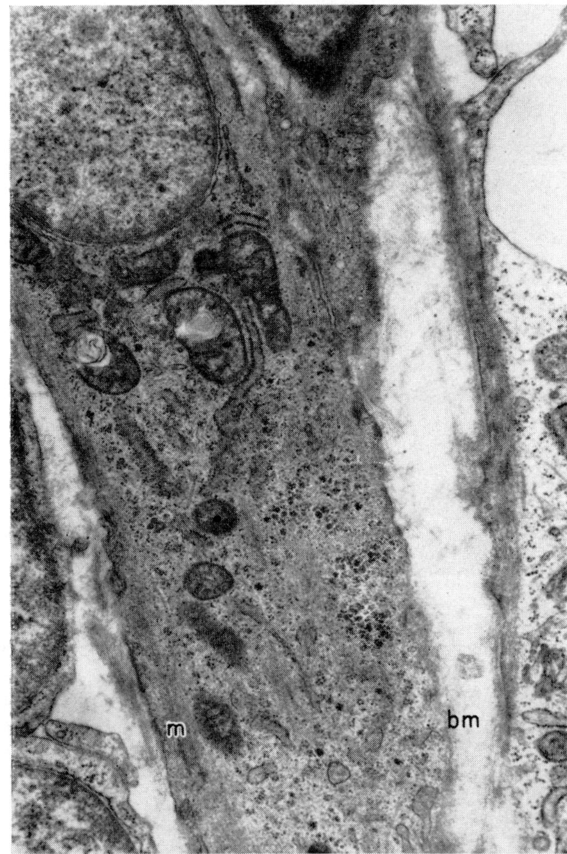

FIG. 18. Electron micrograph from the lung of a fetus of 14 weeks' gestation showing an immature muscle cell from the wall of a small blood vessel. The cell has dense cytoplasm, a basement membrane (bm) and myofibrils (m). (×15,000)

Along any pathway the wholly muscular wall gets thinner and eventually muscle is incomplete and present only in a spiral. In cross-section the spiral of muscle appears as a crescent and vessels with such a wall can be termed "partially muscular" (Fig. 20).[44,114] Further to the periphery the muscle disappears completely to leave a non-muscular wall with a single elastic lamina outside the endothelium.

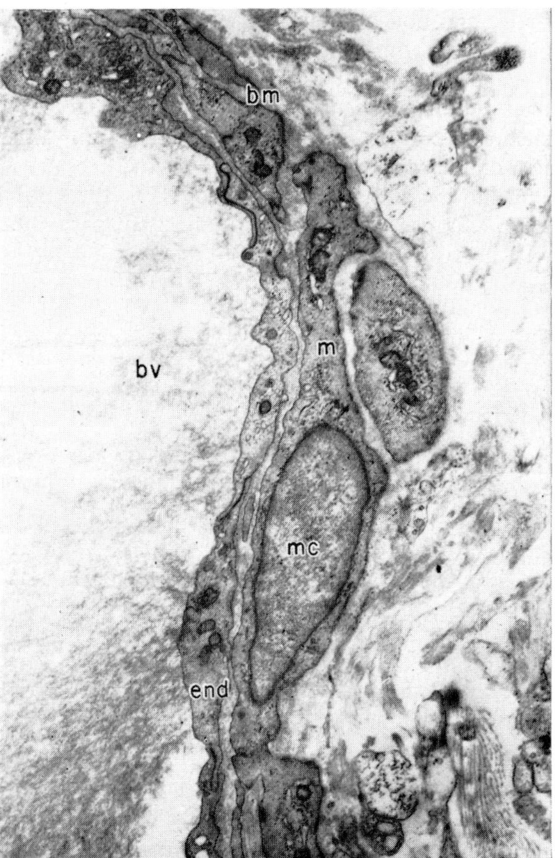

FIG. 19. Electron micrograph from normal adult lung showing a small blood vessel (bv) with endothelial cells (end) and mature muscle cells (mc) with characteristic basement membrane (bm) and myofilaments (m). (×7,500)

In the adult the structure of an arterial wall varies with its size. Elastic arteries are found to a diameter of 3,000 μm. which, along an axial pathway, is to about the seventh generation. Peripheral to this are found muscular arteries (transitional are here included with the muscular) down to a diameter of 30 μm. at alveolar level (Fig. 21). Partially

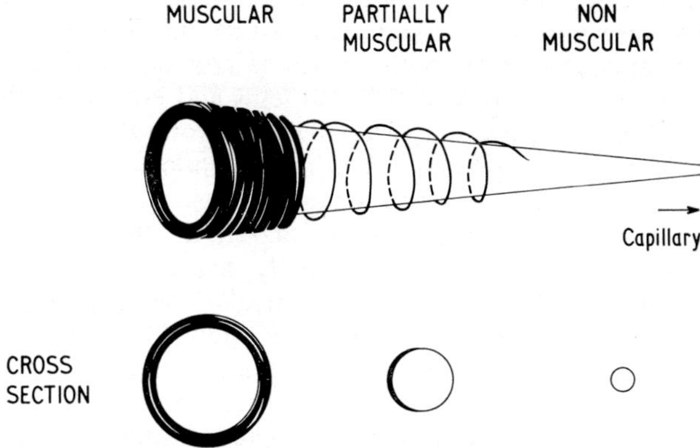

FIG. 20. Diagram representing the structure of a pulmonary artery at its distal end. The complete muscle coat gives way to a spiral of muscle before it completely disappears leaving a "non-muscular" artery. In cross-section vessels within the spiral region have a crescent of muscle and are termed "partially muscular".

muscular and non-muscular vessels may be found up to a diameter of 150 μm., these being still at alveolar level.

In the fetus, with age, there is a gradual extension of the elastic structure to the periphery until, by 19 weeks, it has reached the seventh generation, though at this time the arterial diameter at this level is only 760 μm. From 19 weeks of fetal life the elastic structure extends to the same level within the lung as in the adult, if judged by airway branch. At this diameter, partially muscular vessels appear and their percentage in the arterial population increases until for arteries of 87 μm. in diameter they comprise 63 per cent. They then decrease in number and the last are found at 37 μm. Non-muscular arteries are not seen above a diameter of 125 μm. and form 100 per cent of the arterial population of 35 μm. diameter. The curves in Fig. 22, illustrating the population count, are similar at all fetal ages and in the adult. This assessment of muscle distribution is by size but, because of the difference in lung size in fetus and adult, muscular arteries are found within the acinus in the adult but not in the fetus.[64]

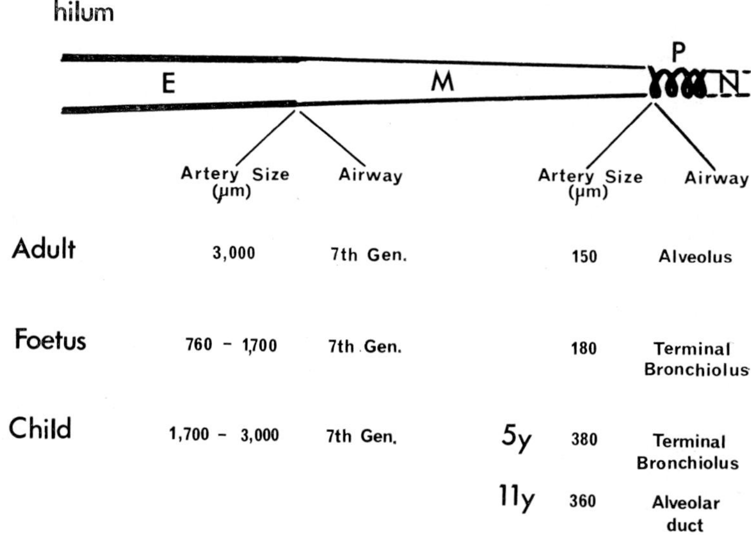

FIG. 21. Diagrammatic representation of an axial pathway showing changes in arterial wall structure related to diameter and airway branching.

As the arteries increase in size the lower limit of size for an elastic structure increases. It seems that the elastic structure is determined by the artery's position within the lung.

The diameter of the most proximal muscular arteries depends upon the size reached by the last elastic artery structure and increases with age, but the peripheral limit of muscular artery size is the same throughout fetal life as in the adult. At all fetal ages partially muscular and non-muscular arteries are also found in the same size ranges as in the adult. But though the diameter of these vessels is the same, their position within the lung is different. The change from muscular to partially muscular and non-muscular structure is more proximal in the fetus and even at birth there is no muscle within arterial walls beyond the level of the terminal bronchiolus. During childhood there is a change in muscular distribution (*see below*).

The relative size and position of arteries showing the transition from muscular to partially muscular and non-muscular structure is of interest, particularly with reference to hypersensitive pulmonary disease. Since the change in structure occurs at a different diameter along different pathways, an overall idea of the extent of muscle requires a count of a "population" of arteries. The diameter and structure of all small arteries in a given area of lung is recorded and, within a given size range, the percentage of each structural type of vessel is calculated. Fig. 22 shows the results of such a population count in a normal lung at birth. Above a diameter of 150 μm. all arteries are muscular in structure.

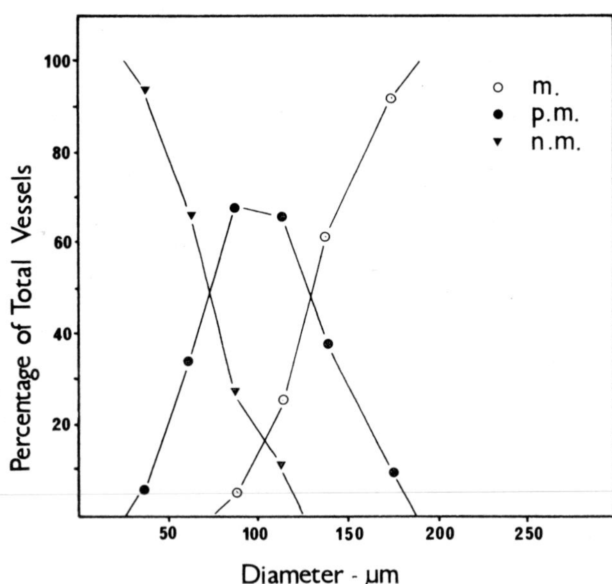

FIG. 22. Diagram illustrating "population" distribution curves of arteries at birth. In each size range the percentage of vessels with a given structure is shown. m—muscular, p.m.—partially muscular, n.m. non-muscular.

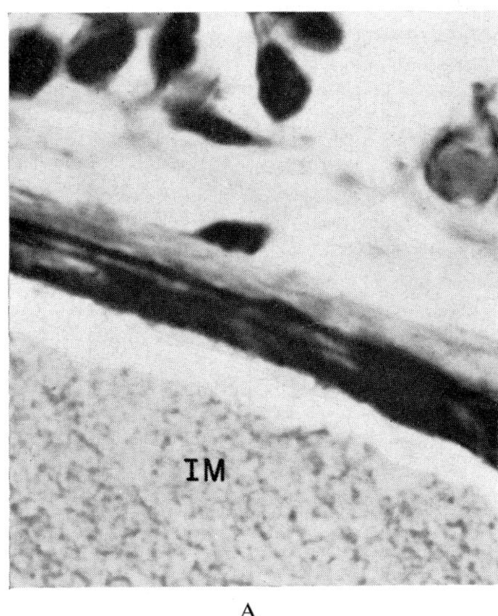

A

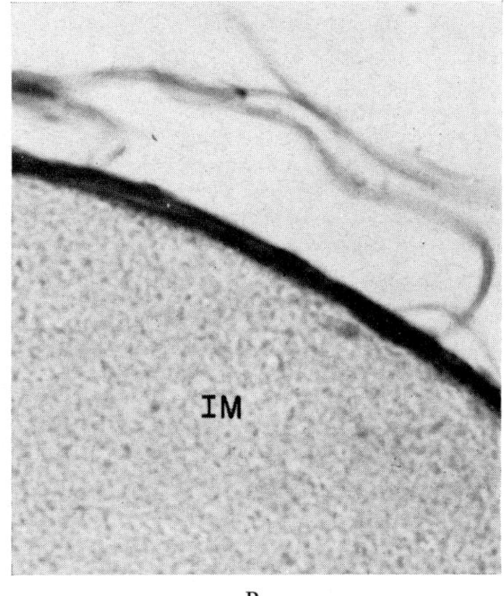

B

Fig. 23. Micrographs of the walls of arteries of 200 μm. external diameter distended by injection medium (IM). (Elastic-van Gieson). (×1,500)
A—birth, wall thickness 5 μm., B—10-year old, wall thickness 2·5 μm.

In the fetus the arteries are more muscular than in the adult in that the wall thickness is higher relative to the external diameter; the wall of a given-sized artery is, in the fetus, double that in the adult (Fig. 23). Fig. 24 shows the percentage wall thickness (that is, twice the wall thickness divided by the external diameter and multiplied by 100) for arteries in fetuses of 12, 19, 28 and 38 weeks' gestation. At all fetal ages, the percentage wall thickness is higher than the adult value of 1–2 per cent. The high figures at 12 weeks probably reflect the immature muscle. Between the other fetal ages difference in wall thickness is not significant. In the smaller arteries the wall thickness is particularly high.

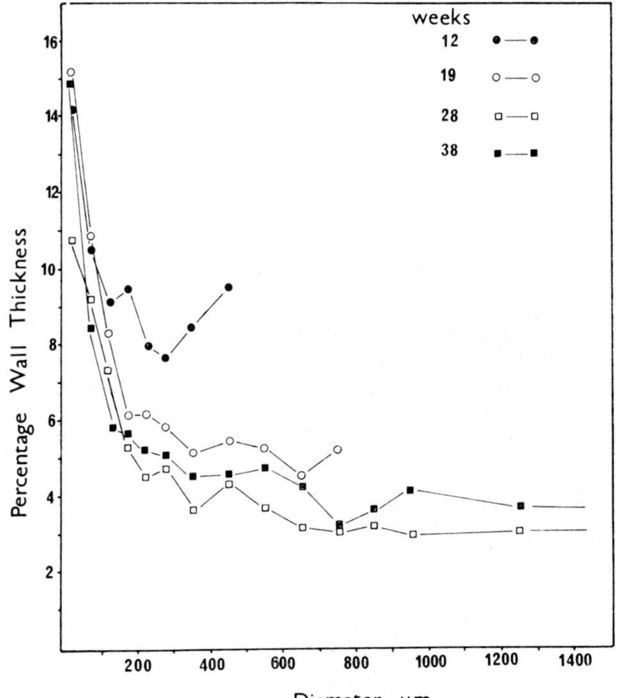

Fig. 24. Mean percentage wall thickness related to external diameter for pulmonary arteries from fetuses of 12, 19, 28 and 38 weeks' gestation. At 12 and 19 weeks vessels larger than those shown are not found.

Pulmonary Veins

Judged by the number of tributaries proximal to the level of the terminal bronchiolus, the pulmonary veins, like the arteries, are fully developed by the fifth month of gestation. The veins have a drainage pattern similar to the branching pattern of the arteries (Fig. 25) in that two types of tributary can be identified. Into each axial vein "conventional" tributaries drain, equivalent in number to the airways and "conventional" artery branches to that segment. In addition, there are a number of extra veins—"supernumerary veins", which are more numerous than the supernumerary arteries but, on average, smaller in diameter.[66] Of the supernumerary veins two types have been identified entering the main veins at right-angles. The first type (Type I) drains the lung tissue immediately surrounding the axial vein and only occasionally receives tributaries. These have no collagen sheath and pass directly through the sheath of the main vein to its lumen (Fig. 26). The Type II supernumerary veins are larger than the Type I, having travelled a greater distance from their capillary bed of origin. They vary in size according to the number of tributaries that they have received. At their junction with an axial vein they have a thin collagenous sheath continuous with that of the axial vein (Fig. 26). During development, the conventional and supernumerary veins appear together progressively from hilum to the periphery and maintain the same ratio throughout fetal life, childhood and in the adult.

During fetal life, the veins carry little blood and are free of muscle. It is not until 28 weeks' gestation that a muscle fibre is occasionally seen in the wall and it is only at term

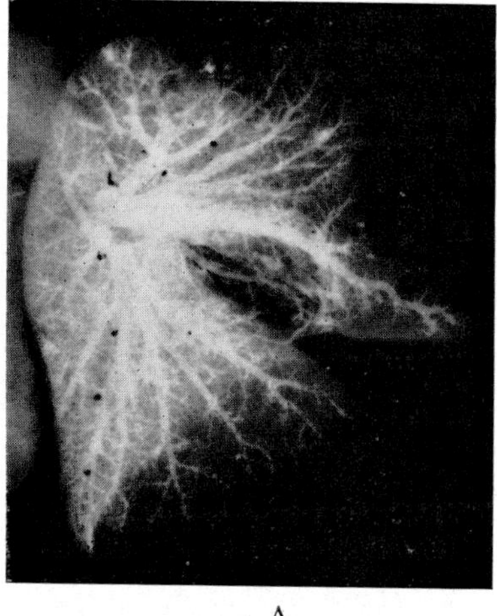
A

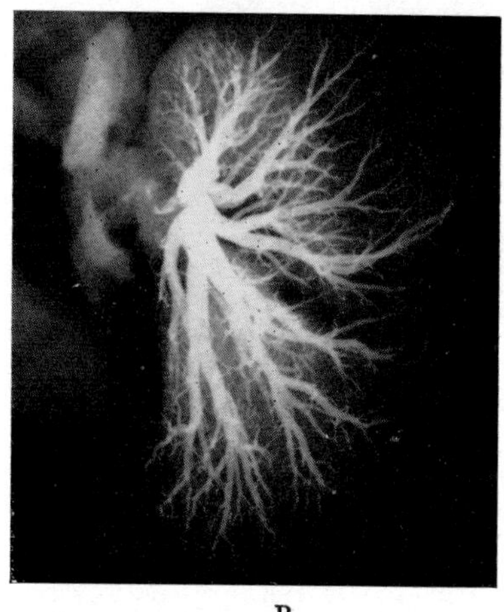
B

FIG. 25. (A) Venogram. (B) Arteriogram of left lung in cases of 28 weeks' gestation. In the venogram the side branches are nearly at a right angle and the background haze is greater. (×1)

that a continuous muscle layer is present. At this time, wall thickness, both absolutely and expressed as a percentage of the external diameter, is low. The thinnest vein wall is much thinner than the thinnest artery wall, suggesting that the muscle cells in the vein wall are different from those of the artery. Muscle extends into veins of 80 μm. size, similar to that to which muscle extends in the arteries.

Bronchial Arteries

In the human fetus bronchial arteries, as present in the adult, appear only between the ninth and twelfth week of gestation. They are variable outgrowths from the descending aorta. Boyden,[15] in a 12-week fetus, has described three to the left and one to the right lung. They are a secondary system implanted relatively late into the lung and supply the walls of the bronchial tree and large pulmonary vessels. In a 41 mm. (9-week) fetus the bronchial artery to the trachea and left main bronchus is present, being the first to appear.[16] At 83 mm. (12-week) the other bronchial arteries are present. Boyden believes that the proximity and maturing of the lung tissue close to the aorta induces capillary outgrowth from the aorta. The bronchial arteries grow along the airway as the cartilage plates form. The more peripheral regions of the lungs are supplied at this time only by the pulmonary arteries. With age, the bronchial arteries increase in size and number and, by birth, are found as far as bronchioli.

In the normal, earlier embryonic connections between the dorsal aorta and the lungs are lost. They may persist as anomalous pulmonary arteries of systemic origin, either having remained within the thorax or having been drawn

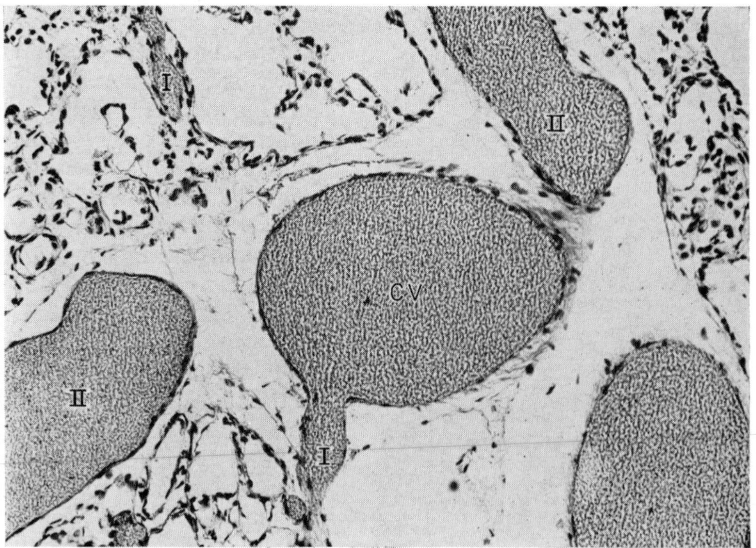

FIG. 26. Photomicrograph of "supernumerary" veins from a fetus of 28 weeks' gestation. Type I pass immediately from alveolar wall to the central vein (cv.): Type II are enclosed in their own connective tissue sheath. (Haematoxylin-eosin: ×156)

down to below the diaphragm by the caudal movement of such vessels as the coeliac artery.

Pulmonary Artery—Bronchial Artery Anastomoses

During a study of normal fetal lungs with pulmonary artery injection, it was found that though bronchial arteries were present, none was filled by the injection medium. There was evidently no connection between the pulmonary and bronchial artery systems greater than 15 μm. diameter, although communication by smaller vessels cannot be excluded.

By three days after birth the same technique gave cross-filling from the pulmonary to the bronchial system. In the early months of life only the proximal bronchial arteries were filled, but after 10 months filling occurred to the level of bronchioli. No large anastomoses were identified. Robertson,[122] using a microangiographic technique combined with serial reconstruction, demonstrated a small number of bronchopulmonary anastomoses, ranging in size from 35–100 μm., in 16 per cent of fetuses of all ages. He also identified bronchial arteries supplying pulmonary parenchyma and pulmonary arteries supplying bronchial walls. These vessels were of similar size to the anastomoses, but by 10 weeks of post-natal age were all obliterated by fibrin and muscle. As these decreased in number, more an astomoses developed: these were present in all cases older than one month and increased with age. Wagenvoort and Wagenvoort[147] found similar results and concluded that anastomoses were more important in the perinatal period than in the adult. They are available as an extra blood supply in cases of congenital heart disease.

Arterio-venous Anastomoses

In spite of claims to the contrary,[145] our own experience suggests that the pulmonary and bronchial artery systems communicate with the veins only through the capillary bed.

The Lung at 28 Weeks' Gestation

At 28 weeks' gestation—the generally accepted age for viability of the human fetus—the pre-acinar pattern of airways, arteries and veins is complete and their structure is as at birth although their size is smaller. At this age the alveolar region must be adequate for gas transfer. The blood/gas barrier is thin; capillary vessels are easily identified within the alveolar wall; Type I and Type II pneumonocytes are present; and within the Type II cells the distinctive lamellated bodies are seen. The presence of surfactant can be detected in tracheal fluid.

Congenital Anomalies Developing Between Five Weeks and Birth

Since the development of the pre-acinar airways and blood vessels is complete half-way through fetal life, disease or mechanical interference at this stage will have an irrevocable effect. Later in fetal development the multiplication and differentiation of alveoli is affected but, since these continue to multiply during childhood, some adjustment may occur. From the pattern of normal lung development that has been described above, the time of onset of a given abnormality can be assessed.

Growth abnormalities during fetal life can be conveniently considered to be of three types: hypoplasia, hyperplasia and dysplasia. In any specimen not all systems may show the same type of abnormality.

Hypoplasia

Underdevelopment of the lung may be manifested by too small a lung as judged by size or weight, perhaps associated with a reduction in the number of branches or units of some of the structures. Thus, to analyse the degree of hypoplasia a count of the number of airways, alveoli, arteries and veins may be necessary.

The lungs in children with congenital diaphragmatic hernia offer an example of under-development affecting the various lung structures differently. The lungs are reduced in size and in weight, the ipsilateral lung usually considerably more than the contralateral. Lobation is usually normal; but whereas the contralateral lung looks normal in shape, the ipsilateral is usually very distorted, and the segmental airway pattern may also be disturbed, suggesting interference as early as the fifth or sixth week of intra-uterine life.

Microscopic examination reveals that while there has been differentiation to the alveolar stage, the number of bronchial branches arising from an axial pathway is greatly diminished, sometimes to less than half. The two lungs may be affected equally in this respect or the smaller lung may show a greater reduction. Total alveolar number is greatly reduced but if the number of alveoli lying distal to the terminal bronchiolus is counted by the radial acinar count of Emery and Mithal[47] only minor reductions may be shown, which suggests that the number of alveoli within an acinus is less affected than the total number of alveoli or airways. The effect on alveolar size may vary: the alveoli are usually reduced in size, but in one case the largest alveoli were seen in the most hypoplastic lobe as judged by its small size, suggesting that it is not a reaction to reduction in space available.[80]

After surgical correction, the anaesthetist can usually inflate the ipsilateral lung but only to fill one-third to one-half of the hemithorax. The radiographic appearance gradually returns to normal, perhaps some four months later. While it is not possible to be certain that the findings in the cases that survive are the same as might be present in the fatal cases, it would seem likely that they are. This failure of the lungs immediately to distend and fill the chest suggests that they were compressed for perhaps months before birth. If this is so, such lungs offer a vicarious experiment for the study of hypoplasia.

Respiratory function tests on children whose hernia was repaired in the perinatal period would give an idea of the compensation that has occurred. Preliminary studies on a series of such children have shown that in all cases the lung volumes were normal (Dr. Mary Ellen Wohl, Children's Hospital, Boston, Mass., personal communication). Bronchographic demonstration of reduction in bronchial branching would be the best evidence of the presence of antenatal bronchial hypoplasia. The result of other function studies would also be of interest; for example, airway resistance might show a deviation from normal because the number of airway branches is reduced.

Because of the time taken by the organs to migrate back to the abdominal cavity from the umbilical region, it is likely that the herniation occurs early rather than later. Recent studies by Boyden[19] have explained why most diaphragmatic hernias occur on the left rather than the right side although the liver lies on both. It would seem that, in addition to the pleuroperitoneal openings lateral to the liver, an extension of the peritoneal cavity lies medial to the stomach which offers the most direct route from the umbilicus to the pleural space.

Hypoplasia of the lung due to encroachment on the thoracic space by abdominal organs may occur in other conditions. For instance, the large spleen and liver found in antenatal haemolytic conditions are sometimes associated with lungs of small size and inadequate function. Whether airway and alveolar number is reduced in these cases is currently being studied.

In a series of 50 cases with renal agenesis Potter[108] found that the lungs are always less than half their normal weight and consist principally of tubular structures similar to those found in the early fetal lung. These fail to become vascularized and consequently the alveoli are primitive or absent.

There would seem to be a connection between lung and kidney growth. It is at about 40 days, the time at which the main and lobar bronchi are invested by mesoderm, that the mesonephric duct establishes communication with the cloaca. This is essential for normal development of the kidney since only then can the ureteric duct grow out from the cloaca and establish communication with the blastema.[10]

Hyperplasia

No example of excessive airway number has ever been described and in only two conditions has an excessive number of alveoli been reported. Polyalveolar lobe is described below as one of the causes of childhood lobar emphysema (*vide infra*).[62] In the only case of agenesis in which the solitary lung has been analysed quantitatively, its volume was increased, airway number was reduced, but the alveolar number was higher than normal, being appropriate for two normal lungs at its age of three months.[125]

Dysplasia

Three examples of dysplasia will be described here:

(i) Unilateral small lung (or hypoplasia) with abnormal vascular communications.
(ii) "Sequestrated segment of the lung."
(iii) Simple cysts.

While the last is the simplest type, it probably develops latest and so the above order is preferred.

(i) Unilateral Small Lung (or "Hypoplasia"). In unilateral hypoplasia of a lung with normal anatomical arrangements as described earlier, the failure can be regarded as one of degree not of kind—the lung grew normally but insufficiently. On the other hand, there is a condition sometimes described as "hypoplasia" which is here considered to be dysplasia since the disturbance is greater because associated vascular and structural anomalies.

A wide range of changes may be seen but the pulmonary artery supply is either absent or greatly reduced, venous drainage abnormal and lung structure abnormal. The pleural cavity may be obliterated entirely or in part and muscle overgrowth may present tumour-like formation.[69] Such a combination of anomalies probably began in the first weeks of intra-uterine development.

(ii) Sequestrated Segment. This is a more localized manifestation of the above but because the condition is so characteristic, and commonly calls for surgical resection, it should be considered separately. The use of the word "sequestrated" is a cause of confusion, since it may refer to sequestration from the normal pulmonary artery supply or from the normal bronchial tree. Some authors only use the term if an abnormal systemic artery is present: this usage gives rise to least confusion. To understand the condition, it is necessary to consider several related anomalies. As far as can be determined, a lobe may be normal with respect to its airway and alveolar region and yet part of it be supplied by a systemic artery. Or, a cyst or cystic region may occur and yet be supplied by the pulmonary artery: thus, in a reconstruction of a fetus, Boyden[11] found a cyst but without any associated anomalous artery.

But a cystic part of a lung often receives a systemic artery supply. This is common in the lower lobes, particularly in the postero-medial and the right side. The common association of these anomalous regions with a systemic artery arising from the aorta, either above or below the diaphragm, suggests that this abnormality develops before the early systemic arterial connections to the lung normally disappear.

In the intralobar type of sequestrated segment, the abnormal region lies within the normal pleural covering of the lobe or is only separated by a partial fissure. In the extralobar type, an extra mass of tissue, resembling lung, lies within its own pleural covering. It has been suggested that the abnormal artery is the "cause" of the anomaly, but because of the range of combinations described above this seems unlikely. Rather, it would seem that there is some disturbance of the "organizer" system within the growing endoderm/mesoderm and that anomalies of respiratory and vascular tissue result secondary to this. When a systemic artery penetrates the lung well away from the hilum and through an adhesion between the parietal and visceral pleura, the possibility of intrapulmonary inflammation must be considered as the cause.

At the stage at which the airways are represented by blind tubules, the region of maximum growth and differentiation is at the end of each airway where cell division is fastest and "organizer" activity can be regarded as at its maximum. The nature and arrangement of the zones of activity at this site are not known but many developmental anomalies can be explained if it is imagined that an extra or autonomous centre of "growth" develops just distal to the normal epithelium. This centre is provided with the appropriate genetic information for multiplication and differentiation into airways and alveoli. In a so-called sequestrated segment examples of both structures are normally present. A similar mechanism is involved in the development of a cyst.

(iii) Cysts and Cystic Deformation. A "cyst" should strictly be taken as a closed space roughly spherical in shape and filled with air or fluid. A whole lobe may be represented by one or more cysts or the deformity may replace part of a lobe or a segment. The simplest example is often shown by a small fluid-filled cyst immediately under the pleura and surrounded by normal lung. The closed space lined with airway epithelium probably develops during the pseudo-glandular phase before the epithelium of terminal airways is modified in the development of alveoli during the canalicular phase. Probably the position of the cyst within the branching pattern of the airways indicates the time in development at which it occurred. Cysts may give rise to symptoms by pressure on large airways causing wheezing or by the check-valve effect whereby lung distal to the block increases in volume.

Childhood Lobar Emphysema

One of the common diseases affecting the young child is childhood lobar emphysema. Recently, the pathological basis of lobar emphysema presenting in the perinatal period or infancy has been shown to be varied: it is not always associated with changes in cartilage and perhaps is never caused by them.

Shortness of breath is the presenting sign, with displacement of the mediastinal structures evident in the radiograph because of an over-inflated and hypertransradiant lung region. It may be emphasized here that, because of rapid lung growth after birth, comparison must be made both with the findings to be expected in the newborn lung and also in a lung of the same age. The following patterns of lung growth were identified:

(i) Normal. In one case, all the lobe was normal save that the alveoli were abnormally large—by definition, this lobe showed emphysema. The hilum had rotated through 180°, the reason for which was not apparent. The lung did not deflate after this was corrected. The rotation may have resulted from an "accident" soon after birth but could also have arisen from some antenatal cause that we would not detect.[63]

(ii) Hypoplasia. In several other cases, numerical under-development of airways indicated that the disturbance represented some intrinsic failure of the lung that must have been manifest before the 16th week of intra-uterine life, when airway growth is complete.[59,113] The total number of alveoli was reduced below the normal at birth but the number within an acinus was relatively less affected than the total. The alveoli were increased in size. Artery number was appropriate to airway number but artery size was reduced. These cases have been seen with radiographic evidence of increased transradiancy but without any increase in volume of the affected lung region—an important diagnostic feature.

(iii) "Polyalveolar" or Hyperplastic Lobe. In one example of this striking anomaly, a lobe showed normal airway and blood-vessel number and normal artery size but throughout the three apical segments of the left upper lobe a five-fold increase in alveolar number. This represents a "giantism" within each individual acinus. In this condition, the airways and blood vessels evidently grow normally throughout intra-uterine life but, in its later part, alveolar multiplication was excessive. Whether the primary anomaly is within the epithelium or mesenchyme is not clear. This condition is not necessarily associated with emphysema but this was seen to have developed in two other cases of polyalveolar lobe.[62]

(iv) Atresia. Atresia of a bronchus has been considered on page 218 since the segmental bronchi appear just before the fifth week of intra-uterine development. The hypertransradiancy seen in the radiograph of these cases represents over-inflation of the abnormal segments. These are ventilated by collateral ventilation, a phenomenon that tends to maintain a lobe at inspiratory volumes. Severe emphysema may develop and the condition present soon after birth or the emphysema may develop more slowly and arise from failure of alveoli to multiply as well as from their over-inflation. These cases may present later, either in childhood or adulthood.

Increasingly, subacute cases of lobar emphysema are being seen that do not need surgical intervention, although the diagnosis is made from transradiancy in the lung fields (Drew, personal communication). These cases perhaps are due to hypoplasia since symptoms of compression are less severe. Some of the types of lobar emphysema in childhood are summarized in Table 3.

TABLE 3

CHILDHOOD LOBAR EMPHYSEMA

Type	*Airways No.*	*Alveoli*	
		No.	*Size*
Polyalveolar lobe	N	↑	N or ↑
Overinflation	N	N*	↑
Hypoplastic emphysema	↓	↓	↑
Atresia of bronchus	N	N*	↑

N = normal, ↑ = increased; ↓ = decreased

* After birth, alveolar multiplication is so rapid that this type may come to have too few alveoli for age if postnatal multiplication is impaired.

Abnormalities in the Blood Vessels

The pattern and structure of the pre-acinar vessels seem to be strongly influenced by genetic control rather than functional demand. This is also exemplified by the polyalveolar lobe in which five times as many alveoli as is normal may develop before birth but the pre-acinar pulmonary artery system is normal. This emphasizes the relative dissociation between function and development in the prenatal lung. On the other hand, on occasion—as when no pulmonary artery is present—systemic arteries may increase presumably "on demand".

The Lung in Congenital Heart Disease

After birth adjustment and development of the pulmonary circulation are dependent on normal haemodynamic relations being quickly established. Their disturbance can be most dramatically followed in cases of congenital heart disease. In some cases, at least, it would appear that disturbance was antenatal so that, although it is in the peri- and post-natal period that adjustments mainly occur, all are considered together here.

Occasionally, associated abnormalities of the airways are present but it is the number and structure of blood vessels that are most likely to be affected in congenital heart disease. Changes may represent separate congenital abnormalities in lung vessels or arise indirectly from the effects of abnormal flow or pressure on pulmonary blood vessels. In any study it is important to establish whether the vessels were abnormal before birth since this indicates abnormal growth rather than the functional changes that will mainly arise after birth.

The effect of the disturbed blood flow and pressure found in the lungs in congenital heart disease have been the subject of many investigations both functional, by catheter and radiographic studies in life, and by examination of artery structure in the specimens.

Recently, a study using precise methods of quantitative analysis has been made on a small series of infants and children with congenital heart disease of two types[61]—those with tetralogy of Fallot having a low flow of blood through the lungs and those with ventricular septal defect having a potentially high pulmonary blood flow. The results were complex, particularly in the latter group; and while it would be inappropriate to present them in detail here, certain generalizations can be made from the results which illustrate the way our understanding can be expected to increase from the use of quantitative methods.

Evidence that the pulmonary arteries were congenitally abnormal was seen in one case only two weeks old and with a ventricular septal defect. Since the arteries were more muscular and, more important, smaller than is normal at birth, it seems likely that antenatal development was abnormal. Since the youngest case with tetralogy of Fallot was over a year old, it was not possible to say here whether the lungs had been abnormal before birth—the arteries were larger than would be expected at birth but small for age.

In all cases in both groups, it appeared that the pre-acinar branching pattern of arteries, veins and airways was normal; that is, intra-uterine multiplication had been normal although the size of the vessels had been affected by the abnormal haemodynamic pattern. In cases with a low flow of blood through the pulmonary vessels, a reduction in size for age was seen of both the pulmonary arteries and pulmonary veins and, where flow had increased, an increase in size of the vessels. This applied irrespective of the cardiac lesion.

All cases also showed a change in the wall thickness of arteries—increase in all save in one case of ventricular septal defect in which there had been a decrease. This increase was seen whether there had been an increase or decrease in either flow or pressure. An increase in wall thickness in the arteries was accompanied by "arterialization" of the veins; that is an increase in both muscle and elastic laminae.

The intra-acinar region develops mainly after birth and its development is therefore affected by abnormal haemodynamic states. The vessels in this region were affected both in number and structure. In cases of tetralogy of Fallot, all of whom had a low pulmonary artery flow and pressure, there had been an increase in the number of arteries and veins in the acinar region and, at the same time a reduction in the number of alveoli. In the cases with ventricular septal defect there was a reduction in the number of arteries and veins in the acinar region, apparently due to lack of development of new vessels after birth. The structure of the intra-acinar arteries was also affected and in a similar way as the pre-acinar; that is, there was increase in muscularity in all, manifested by an increase in wall thickness and in some also by an extension of muscle into small vessels.

It seems then that the pre-acinar vessels that develop both in structure and number before birth, being genetically determined, only respond to abnormal function by change in size and structure. On the other hand, intra-acinar vessels, developing mainly after birth, are influenced both in number, size and structure by flow and pressure within them. Although the adaptation in the intra-acinar vessels might be expected to "protect" the veins, the changes in the veins resembled those in the pre-acinar arteries.

It is also significant that despite the difference in age ($1\frac{1}{4}$–8 years) in the cases with tetralogy of Fallot, the pathological changes seen in the lung were consistent, as were the clinical features and catheter studies. By contrast, in the cases with ventricular septal defect, although all were in the same age group (2 weeks–4 months), the changes varied, which points to the complexity of the haemodynamic changes in this clinical group and to the wide variation in effect on structure that these may have, as well as the speed with which, at this age, structural changes can occur.

PERINATAL PERIOD

During fetal life there is little blood flow to the lungs—perhaps 12 per cent of cardiac output—since most of the flow from the right ventricle passes through the patent ductus arteriosus to the aorta and on to the umbilicus. Due to the high resistance in the pulmonary circulation, the fetal lungs contain very little blood at any time. At birth, with the onset of breathing, flow to the lungs increases. The change to air breathing causes rapid adjustments in the functioning of the lung, but the anatomical changes take longer.

Removal of Lung Fluid

At birth the lungs of the fetus are full of liquid which has to be removed and replaced by air. In the mature fetal lamb, the liquid in the lung represents 10–20 ml./kg. of body weight, a volume similar to that of the functional residual capacity of gas after the onset of breathing.[139]

Since liquid in the lung differs from the amniotic fluid

both in total osmolality and in its protein, urea and bicarbonate concentrations, fluid would seem to be produced, or at least modified, within the lung.

At birth this fluid is removed from the alveoli into the interstitial tissue and thence via the lymphatic channels to the systemic veins. At the onset of breathing in a mature lamb a rapid rise in the flow of lymph is seen which later falls to pre-natal and adult levels. In an immature fetal lamb there is not such a rapid or marked rise in the rate of lymph flow on breathing and it may be that if the alveolar surface tension remains high as a result of lack of surfactant, liquid is drawn back on deflation into the alveolus from the interstitial tissue.[139]

Airways

The airways are fully mature in their structure and branching pattern at birth and there are no major changes either in the number of generations or in structure, but soon after birth some changes occur in the peripheral generations. Boyden and Tompsett[20] have found that by the age of two months the respiratory bronchioli have developed true alveoli in their walls and have grown in length (Figs. 27 and 28). At the same time, the peripheral saccules are being converted to alveolar ducts by development of alveoli in their walls (Fig. 9). Alveoli opening from the terminal saccule are also deepening. The respiratory unit may therefore increase its surface area without further branching. It is possible that during early childhood an additional terminal bronchiolus is transformed by centripetal alveolization into a respiratory bronchiolus. Within the acinus, branching may occur distally, but probably only up to 18 months of age, to give further alveolar ducts (Fig. 9). There may or may not be conversion of respiratory bronchioli into alveolar ducts.

Other perinatal changes in the airways concern the nature of the mucus being produced. During fetal life a large amount of sulphated acid mucin is produced but relatively little with a sialic acid. After birth the percentage of mucous cells producing sulphated mucin drops rapidly,[83] and by about 3–6 months sialic acid sensitive to sialidase appears. The reason for this is not clear but, in sputum, viscosity of secretion seems to increase with rise in sialic acid level.[115] It could be that the bronchial secretions at birth are less viscid than later.

Alveoli

With the onset of breathing, the surface active phospholipids which had been stored in the alveolar cells of the fetus are rapidly discharged into the alveolar space. Examination of rabbit lungs has revealed that in the inflated area of a lung the Type II cells (*see* Fig. 10) now contain vacuoles instead of the dense inclusion bodies of the fetus.[78]

Conflicting opinions have been expressed as to the thickness of the blood/gas barrier in the newborn. Electron microscopic measurement of the blood/gas barrier—that is, of endothelium, interstitial space and epithelium—reveals that it is similar to the adult (0·4μm.).[88] The alveolar wall may appear thicker overall because of an increase in connective tissue, perhaps because of the incomplete expansion of the lung, the tortuosity of its capillaries and perhaps their paucity compared with the older lung. This is accentuated by the focal distribution of connective tissue within the wall.

At birth the alveoli are only shallow indentations in the walls of saccules and respiratory bronchioli.[12] In fact, Boyden regards the saccules as the terminal units of the airways and the site of gas exchange at birth. An increase in the number of alveoli occurs in the first month after birth;

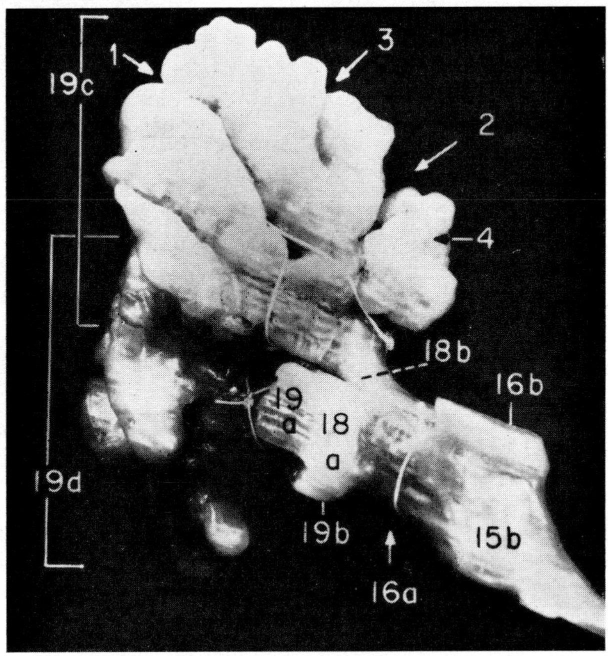

FIG. 27. Wax model of a terminal cluster in a 2-day infant. 15b is the terminal bronchiolus which gives rise to respiratory bronchioli (16) and smooth transitional ducts (18) before the terminal saccules (19c and d). (×45)

a few large alveoli appear on proximal bronchioli and, at the same time there is deepening of the alveoli of the saccules and terminal saccules. By the end of the second month the alveoli of the saccules have become still larger and, with this, there is lengthening of the saccules which are transformed to alveolar ducts. Respiratory bronchioli also develop more alveoli. No new acini are formed.

The primitive alveoli of late fetal life and at term are of different structure from those seen in the adult. Elastic fibres, in bundles, are confined to the edge of the alveolar opening, the main expanse of the alveolar walls containing no elastic tissue (Figs. 29 and 30). As the alveoli grow in size the elastic tissue increases, but even at five years is only at the alveolar mouth, and at 12 years still not well developed (Fig. 31). By 18 years there are elastic fibre bundles extending in a branching pattern throughout the alveolar walls (Fig. 32). The lack of elastic in the walls of the alveoli may facilitate expansion during the post-natal development.[92] There is, of course, elastic tissue in arteries, pleura and airways as early as the third month of intra-uterine life. Emery[46] suggests, as did Short,[131] that as peripheral alveoli grow in size the pull of the elastic bundles in their walls causes a segmentation of the wall and formation of new alveoli.

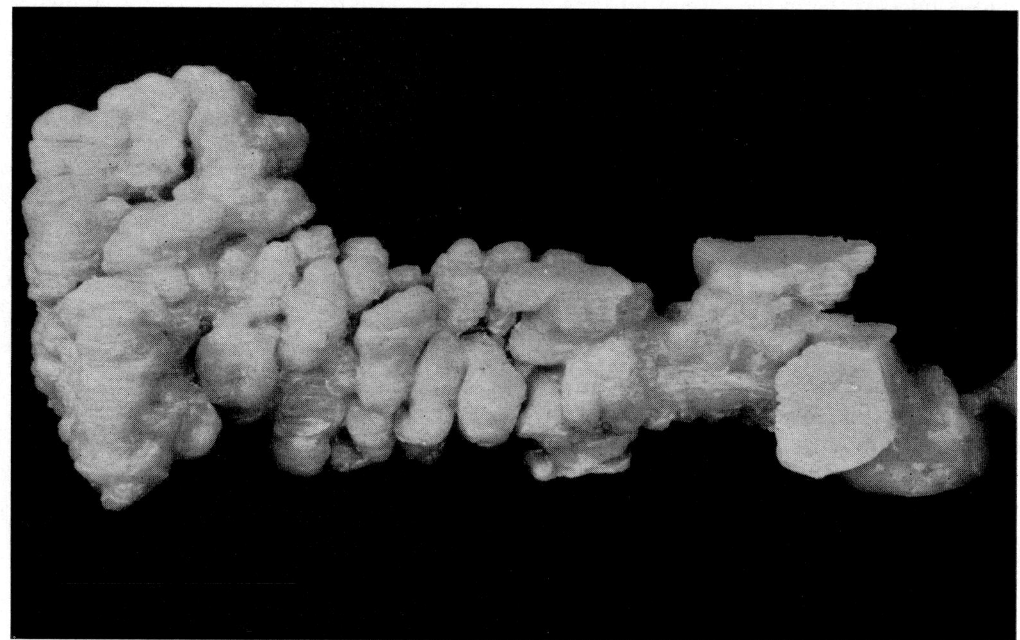

FIG. 28. Reconstruction of lung periphery of a 2-month old infant (born wax-plate method). The terminal cluster of alveolar saccules has changed relatively little from two days but these are now separated from the terminal bronchiolus by airways into which numerous alveoli open. (×50) (Figs. 27 and 28 Reproduced by permission of *Acta Anatomica.*[20])

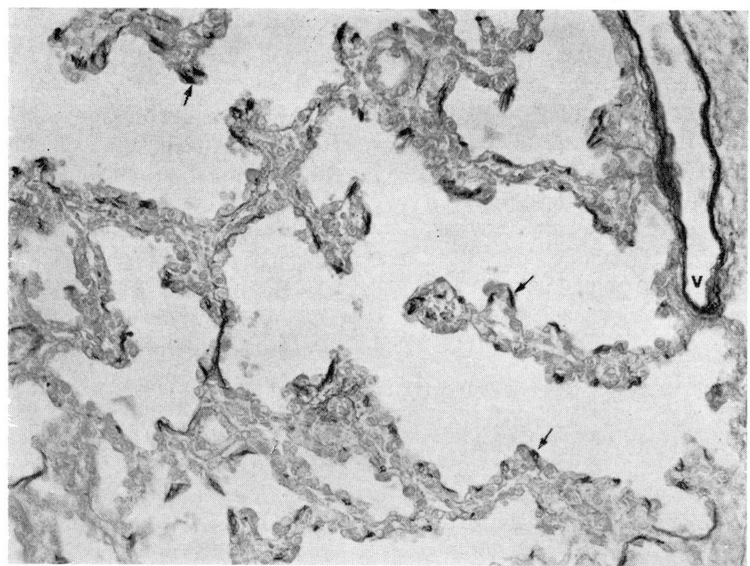

FIG. 29. Photomicrograph of a lung inflated with fixative from a fetus of 26 weeks' gestation that lived 8 days. There are large thick-walled spaces with elastic fibre bundles (arrows) on each side of the air space. Elastic fibres in the wall of a blood vessel (v) also stain deeply (Orcein stain: ×223). (Figs. 29–32 Reproduced by permission of *American Review of Respiratory Diseases.*[92])

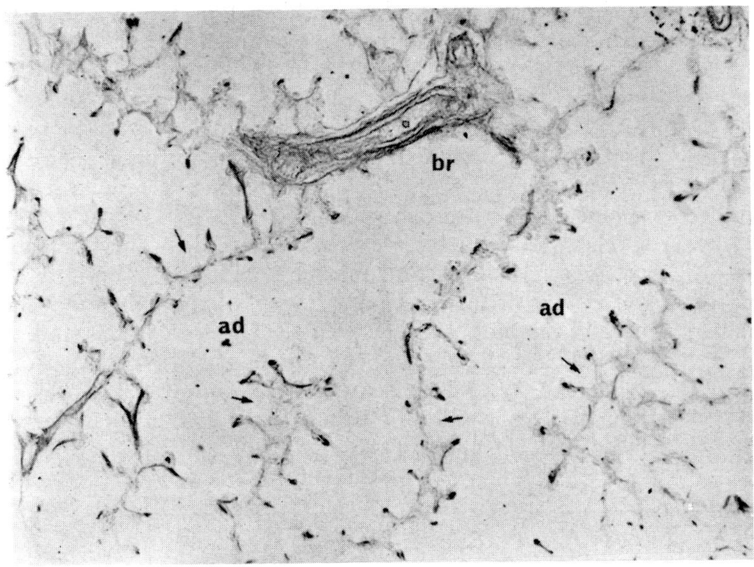

FIG. 30. Photomicrograph of an inflated lung of a stillborn infant of 38 weeks' gestation. A terminal bronchiolus (br) with accompanying arteriole (a). Alveolar ducts (ad) show small alveoli (arrows) with deeply staining elastic fibres at the tips of the alveolar walls. (Orcein stain: ×133)

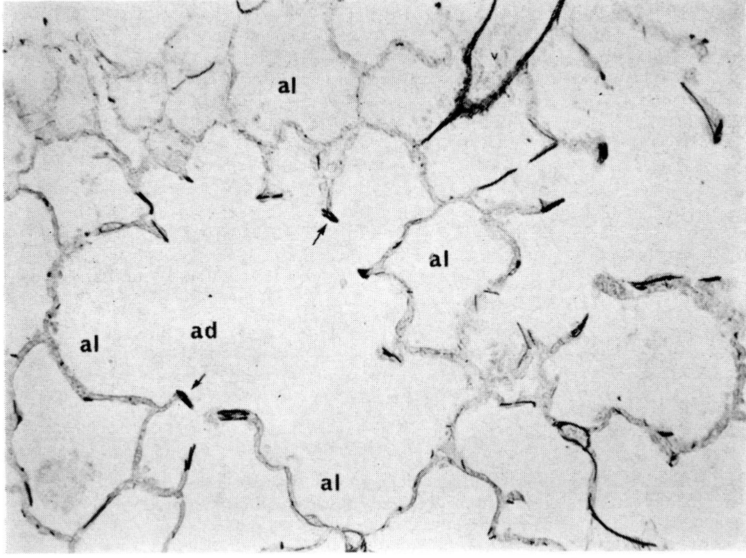

FIG. 31. Photomicrograph of an inflated lung of a child aged 12 years. Cross-section of an alveolar duct (ad) with alveoli opening into it (al). Deeply staining elastic fibres in walls of blood vessel (v) and at mouths of alveoli (arrows). (Orcein stain: ×120)

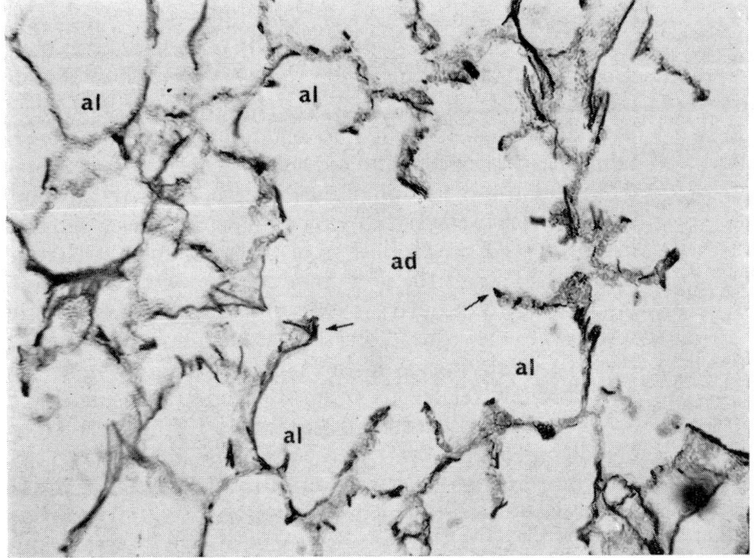

FIG. 32. Photomicrograph of inflated lung of young adult (18 years). Cross-section of alveolar duct and alveoli. Note increasing amount of elastic fibres in alveolar walls compared with those in the 12 year old shown in Fig. 31. (Orcein stain: ×123)

Pulmonary Artery

Closure of Ductus Arteriosus

In the fetus the ductus arteriosus has the structure of a muscular systemic artery with a thick media of circular smooth muscle, a thin intima and a fibrous adventitia.[53] The ductus closes functionally by constriction soon after birth. In the last three months of gestation, muscular elevations called endothelial cushions protrude into the ductus lumen and in the newborn a thin cover of fibrous tissue is seen over these. Closure of the lumen is by organization of intra-luminal thrombus by fibrous tissue growing from these intimal mounds. Eventually, after about two months, the ductus is transformed into a cord of tough, avascular fibrous tissue in which traces of muscle and elastic may be found—the ligamentum arteriosum.

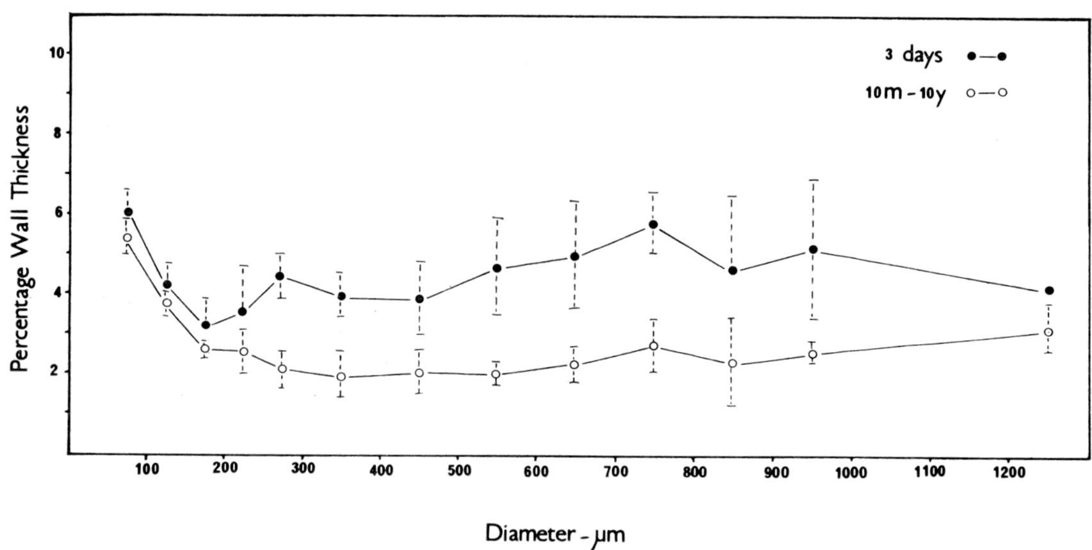

FIG. 33. Arterial wall thickness related to external diameter in a 3-day old infant and in children aged 10 months to 10 years. The mean and standard deviation for each size range is shown. In the 3-day old the arteries over 200 μm show the fetal pattern of wall thickness, while those less than 200 μm. show the childhood and adult state.

Pulmonary Artery Structure

During gestation, the pulmonary trunk is exposed to systemic pressures and not surprisingly shows similar structural features to the aorta. The walls of both are of similar thickness and both contains parallel elastic fibrils which, in the pulmonary trunk, are less regular. The drop in pulmonary artery pressure at birth does not immediately affect the structure of the pulmonary artery but, by six months, the elastic tissue has fragmented although still showing the parallel arrangement. By the end of the second year the adult pattern of fragmented slender elastic fibrils of irregular shape is seen.[58]

During fetal life the intra-pulmonary artery walls are thick but during the first few months after birth thin rapidly to adult levels. This thinning begins with birth and does not depend upon gestational age.[85] According to Naeye,[102] thinning is due to a drop in the number of muscle cells, not to a reduction in their size. Wagenvoort, Neufeld and Edwards[148] demonstrated a sudden drop in wall thickness during the first two weeks after birth, followed by a slower reduction over 18 months. Our quantitative analysis suggests that the early changes are due to dilatation of the small vessels, the later to a change in the rate of growth. Dilatation was also demonstrated by Parmentier[105] who showed that, at birth, even high pressures would not fill capillaries but, after birth, gradual relaxation of the "arteriolar fetal sphincter" allowed easier filling.

The precise measurements made possible by injecting the arteries, measuring wall thickness and expressing it as a percentage of the external diameter[62] have shown that in a child of three days the wall thickness of vessels under 200 μm. has already dropped to adult levels while that of the larger vessels is still at the high level of fetal life (Fig. 33).[68] There would seem to have been an immediate drop in the wall thickness of the small vessels, doubtless due to relaxation of the muscle cells with dilatation. This rapid drop is probably related to the fall in pulmonary artery pressure to adult levels by 11 days.[123] In a child of four months, the adult wall thickness had almost been reached in arteries of all sizes and in a child of 10 months had certainly been reached. The reduction in the large vessels is due to relative reduction of muscle cells, either by atrophy, as in the hilar vessels, or by increase in vessel size with lag in muscle cell production as in the mid-lung vessels (*see* Table 4). These structural changes to growth pattern and modification take place over some months, probably in response to the reduced pressure in the pulmonary arteries: the structural changes in the small vessels are immediate and probably related to an initial drop in pressure which arises from dilation of small arteries. In 1953 Dawes, Mott, Widdicombe and Wyatt[40] noted that in lambs, after birth, flow increased as the result of a drop in resistance in the pulmonary arteries which was associated with expansion whether by air, oxygen or nitrogen. Changes in gas tensions

TABLE 4

CHANGES IN PULMONARY ARTERIES DURING THE FIRST YEAR OF LIFE

	Small vessels <250 μ	*Medium vessels* >250 μm	*Hilar vessels*
At birth	Dilatation with decrease in wall thickness	—	—
Early months	Increase in external diameter: lag in muscle development	Increase in external diameter: lag in muscle development	Increase in external diameter: atrophy of muscle cells
After 4 months	Development of muscle to maintain adult percentage wall thickness		

produce dilation of blood vessels by affecting muscle cells, particularly those of the peripheral vessels closest to the alveolar air.

Adams[1] concluded that flow was under neuro-humoral control since drugs can cause vasodilatation in the fetal lung. Asphyxia always causes vasoconstriction and it is likely that the increase in alveolar oxygen tensions at birth causes the change in resistance. A possible mediator of this change is bradykinin. Melmon, Cline, Hughes and Nies[96] found that, in lambs, bradykinin constricted the umbilical vessels and ductus arteriosus but produced dilatation of the pulmonary vasculature. In the human, they found that bradykinin was at a higher level in the cord blood of newborn infants than in the adult and that an inactive kinin precursor and a kinin-releasing enzyme are also present in the blood. A decrease in body temperature, a release of neonatal granulocytes (found in increasing numbers before birth) and the changes in oxygen tension found in the newborn each leads to the release of kinin, perhaps the cause of dilatation of pulmonary vessels. The argyrophil or Kultschitsky cell of the airway epithelium was suggested by Lauweryns and Peuskens[87] as the possible site for the production of kinins.

Right Ventricle of Heart

The changes in the pulmonary arteries are accompanied by reduction in the weight of the right ventricle relative to the left. During fetal life the right, though never heavier than the left ventricle, is similar to it in weight[67] as determined by the method of Fulton, Hutchinson and Jones.[49] After birth the weight of the right ventricle drops relative to the left, so that the adult ratio is reached at least by ten months.[38] Keen[76] found that the right ventricle actually lost weight after birth and that it was a year before its birth weight was regained. Recavarren and Arias-Stella,[109] by their method, considered that the adult ratio was reached after four months. These changes correspond in time with the drop in wall thickness in the large pulmonary arteries rather than with the fall in pressure within them.

Pulmonary Veins

There is little structural change in the veins during the perinatal period. The pre-acinar venous draining pattern is complete by 16 weeks' gestation and the intra-acinar venous pattern develops after birth, together with new alveoli and their corresponding arteries. There is no change in the type of structure of the vein wall or in the thickness of muscle coat between birth and adulthood despite the increase in blood-flow through the veins.

Bronchial Arteries

In the latter part of fetal life the bronchial artery develops a thick muscular media with a distinct internal elastic lamina and a thin or incomplete external elastic lamina. During fetal life the lung is relatively immobile and longitudinal muscle does not develop.[57] After birth, systemic pressure in bronchial arteries and their rhythmic movement due to expansion and deflation of the lung in respiration are associated, by $7\frac{1}{2}$ months, with development of longitudinal muscle in the intima.[97] The extrapulmonary part of the bronchial artery has no longitudinal muscle.

Disease in the Perinatal Period

Idiopathic respiratory distress syndrome of the newborn —hyaline membrane disease—is one of the common causes of death in the perinatal period. It occurs particularly in babies born prematurely but is also common in abnormal babies such as those born to diabetic mothers, although perhaps born late and usually heavier than normal. It appears within a few hours of birth, when breathing becomes difficult and there is retraction of the intercostal and subcostal spaces. At autopsy the lungs are always poorly expanded with atelectasis a striking feature, and if the child has survived at least a few hours the alveoli are lined by the hyaline membrane that gives the disease one of its names. This clear eosinophilic membrane contains fibrin and probably represents a high-protein oedema fluid. Reduction in surfactant activity is also a striking feature. The surface tension of the lung is high and the lamellar bodies of the Type II pneumonocytes reduced in number.[50] Although this reduction may explain difficulty in breathing and inadequate expansion of the lungs, it is not clear whether it is the primary disturbance and arises from immaturity of the lung[121] or asphyxia, or whether surfactant levels are inadequate for other reasons such as the vasoconstriction that is also present.[31] The latter may be the primary change and a response, perhaps exaggerated, to hypoxia or to stress: for instance, this syndrome develops in the piglet after injection of epinephrine and in the newborn the level of adrenergic activity may be increased by stress. It has recently been shown that administration of steroids to the ewe before delivery protects a prematurely born lamb from developing the condition[41] and the preliminary results of a trial suggest that such steroid treatment also protects in the human[89], by stimulating faster maturation of the surfactant system. Maternal administration of heroin (Avery, personal communication) and thyroid hormone[110] have also been shown to hasten maturation.

Study of the lungs in fatal cases of respiratory distress of the newborn is made difficult by the fact that the child has usually been treated by high oxygen administration either at high concentration or pressure or both. High partial pressures of oxygen in inspired air are associated with damage to the alveolar walls; it seems that first the capillary epithelium is affected, then the alveolar epithelium.[26,100] Capillary permeability is increased and alveolar oedema develops. Such changes may resolve completely but absorption of intra-alveolar content may be associated with organization, and fibrosis of the alveolar wall may then develop.[50] There is evidence that multiplication of alveoli does not start until two months or so after birth but the effect of such lesions or their residue at the time of most active alveolar multiplication is not known.

The pulmonary circulation is under autonomic control and, after birth, important functional changes occur relatively quickly. It is surprising how rarely an improper balance of stimuli develops; this may happen when the pulmonary circulation seems tardy in dilating under the raised oxygen levels at birth. Several cases have been reported where vaso-dilation with a drop in resistance seemed to be achieved only when breathing an oxygen-enriched atmosphere.[25] Even this effect may be short-lived so that death ensues because of vasoconstriction that cannot be corrected. Because of the distribution of muscle in the pulmonary artery, the vasoconstriction affects the pre-acinar level so that the arteries are effectively reducing blood flow at a level well proximal to the alveolar region.

Various types of dysplasia at birth have been described such as alveolar wall thickening. This is very difficult to interpret as it may represent a premature lung or may be a true increase in connective tissue.

The Wilson-Mikity syndrome[152] is one condition developing at birth in which the radiograph shows a characteristic and striking appearance. The child is not usually premature and the shortness of breath is associated with a radiographic appearance suggesting soap bubbles through the lung. The condition is not necessarily fatal and the child often "grows out" of it. In cases where it has been possible to examine the lungs, no structural abnormality could be identified, but only alternating regions of relative over- and under-inflation. This suggests imbalance in inflation so that some parts expanded at the expense of neighbouring lung, which would be explained if maturation of the surfactant system were irregular.

Interstitial emphysema and pneumothorax may develop spontaneously, perhaps because of an airway block by mucus or meconium, or during treatment with a respirator.

CHILDHOOD AND ADOLESCENCE

Overall Lung Growth

Recently, on a unique series of 162 clinical radiographs, the overall growth of the lung in childhood has been assessed by measurement. Because the series were contacts of tuberculosis patients, annual radiographs had been taken; most cases were followed from 5 or 6 years to age 15 and some to age 20.[133]

Centile standards for heart diameter, lung width, lung "length" and lung "area" have been produced as well as mean velocity curves. Compared with other organs the lungs are unusual in several ways.

Fig. 34 shows the centiles for heart diameter, lung width and lung length. At six years the boys are, on average,

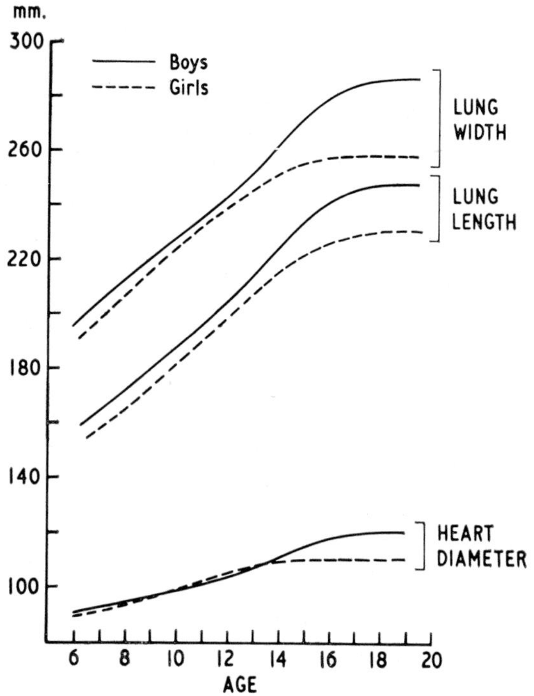

FIG. 34. Mean size change, with age, in lung length, lung width and heart diameter for boys and girls. (Reproduced by permission of *Archives of Disease in Childhood*.[133])

slightly bigger in all dimensions than the girls. By the end of growth, reached on average at 16 years in girls and 18 years in boys, there is a wider difference between them for each dimension. The adolescent spurt seen in all individuals is not marked because the "centiles" are mean figures and individuals differ in the age of this growth spurt. The heart diameter shows the usual pattern seen in muscular and skeletal growth—the boys start larger but the girls start their adolescent spurt earlier and so overtake the boys who later, during their spurt, overtake the girls and finish with a larger final diameter.

The lung measurements are unusual in that the girls never exceed the boys in lung length or width at any age. Only head measurements and foot length show a similar pattern.

The ages at peak velocity of growth for lung width and heart diameter coincide with that for height, the peak velocity for lung length occurring six months later. It is somewhat unusual that the peak velocity for lung length and width is similar in boys and girls, peak velocity of growth usually being greater in boys than girls.[142]

At age six the heart diameter is about 80 per cent of its

adult value while lung length and width are only 66 and 62 per cent respectively, suggesting their later growth development.

Airways

A lung model was described by Weibel[150] from measurements of selected airways in casts of normal adult lungs. Muir felt the need to know the dimensions of the airways in a series of child lungs of different ages.[70] As a practical approach to this formidable task, a single axial pathway has been traced from hilum to periphery in each of a series. The length of the axial artery was measured and

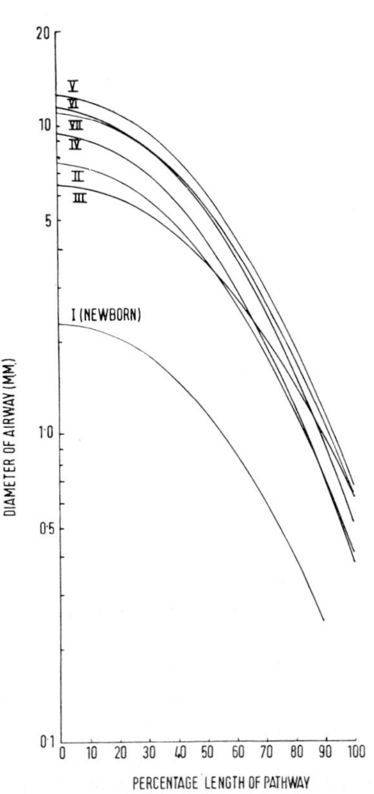

Fig. 35. Computed curves showing the diameter of the airways along axial pathways. At each age the length of the pathway is taken as 100 units. Each curve is based on grouped data. 1—newborn, 2—mean age 19 months, 3—mean age 4 years 4 months, 4—mean age 9 years 6 months, 5—adult lungs, lower lobes, 6—adult lungs, upper and middle lobes, 7—mean adult data.[150]

its diameter at the point of origin of each side branch, and the distance between branches. Since the number of generations measured in the terminal bronchiolus varied between cases, the whole of each pathway was taken to represent 100 units and any position along the airway was expressed as a percentage of the whole path length. The curve relating diameter to distance from the hilum was remarkably similar in shape at all ages and could be described by the same mathematical formula (Fig. 35). The curves were similar in the child and adult, suggesting that the airways of the newborn lung are the adult in miniature and that the pathways increase in size in uniform manner. Though the airways are smaller they are no more effective at stopping the penetration of airborne particles: on the other hand, aerosol penetration to alveoli is similar in the child and adult. The symmetrical growth means that the same aerosol size is appropriate to the child as to the adult and the newborn alveoli enjoy the same "protection" from inhaled particles as the adult.

Alveoli

During childhood there is rapid multiplication of alveoli. These can be studied either by the reconstruction of a single acinus, as Boyden has done for example,[12] or by random sampling and quantitative analysis to count the total number.

Reconstruction of the acinus would seem to indicate that increase in number of alveoli during childhood is mainly due to development of alveolar sacs at the periphery and new alveoli along alveolar ducts. The terminal saccule produces, probably by budding, a number of alveolar sacs (1–4) each containing many alveoli (Fig. 9). The terminal saccule takes on the appearance of the atrium seen in the adult.[101] Before the fourth year numerous alveoli of a new type appear, called by Boyden[13] the ductular alveoli, since they arise as outgrowths of bronchiolar diverticula. These become the "special alveoli" of the adult.[54] By the seventh year,[84] pores of Lambert appear, facilitating collateral ventilation. Neither these pores nor the ductular alveoli transform a terminal bronchiolus into a respiratory bronchiolus.[17]

Quantitative analysis has shown that the area of the air/tissue interface increased with age from 2·8 m.^{2} at birth to 32 m.^{2} at 8 years and 75 m.^{2} in the adult.[43] This shows a linear relationship to the increase in body surface area.

Davies and Reid[38] found similar increase in alveolar number during childhood to Dunnill,[43] i.e. from 24 million at birth to 300 million at 8 years (*see* Fig. 36). They also showed that alveolar size changes during growth. During the first three years of life the increase in lung size is mainly due to alveolar multiplication, there being little change in alveolar size. Then alveoli increase in size as well as number until the age of eight, after which it is only size that increases until the chest wall stops growing. From the age of four months the alveolar outline also increases in complexity, which adds to the increase in surface area.

Pulmonary Arteries

Arterial Number

During childhood, as new alveolar ducts and alveoli appear and enlarge there is growth by branching of new arteries within the acinus. Conventional arteries accompanying new airways appear up to 18 months of age. Supernumerary arteries appear up to eight years, becoming relatively more numerous with age, and supply alveoli directly. During early childhood there is also an increase in the number of supernumerary arteries in the intra-lobular and preacinar region, presumably to supply the increasing number of alveoli within the acinus (Figs. 37 and 38). As the alveoli increase in size, further branching at capillary level probably occurs; this can be demonstrated by counting the number of arteries per unit area of lung.[68]

With age, existing arteries increase in size. Measurement of diameter and length of the pre-acinar arteries has been made on arteriograms and the pattern of growth determined. A similar pattern emerged from microscopic measurement on the intra-acinar arteries. The length of the axial pathways increased with age, more rapidly during fetal life and the first 18 postnatal months of age than later. This is possibly similar to the more rapid growth in height for the first two years of life as seen by Tanner.[143] Diameter change in arteries showed a similar curvi-linear relationship to age (Fig. 39). On the other hand, the relationship was linear between artery diameter and length and also age and lung volume. The cube of the arterial diameter and length showed a linear relationship with age and lung volume: it is the "volume" of the artery that is related directly to the volume of lung.

In the pre-acinar region before birth and also in the intra-acinar region after birth, the proximal vessels increase in size more than the distal. This increase is probably related to the growth and multiplication of new vessels at the periphery and, up to 18 months of age, causes an increase in gradient from hilum to periphery. There would seem to be a change in the pattern of growth after 18 months of age, the multiplication of both arteries and alveoli becoming slower.

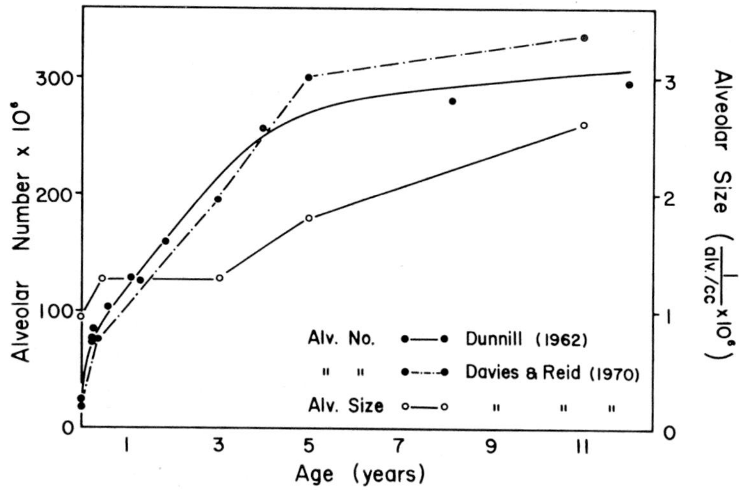

FIG. 36. The increase in number and size of alveoli with age using quantitative analysis. The curve of Dunnill's figures for number is fitted from his figures. The figures for number and size from Davies and Reid[38] are shown. Those for number fit well with Dunnell's curve.

The multiplication of vessels has been studied by serial reconstruction and also be estimating the number and distribution by size of vessels in a given area of alveolar region of lung. From four months to four years of age there is a marked increase in the number of arteries in a unit area in all size ranges up to 200 μm. This corresponds with the rapid increase in number of alveoli at this time. After five years the concentration of arteries reduces; this is probably related to the increase in size of alveoli since the ratio between arteries and alveoli remains the same throughout childhood. The distribution by size of these small vessels changes during childhood; several ages are shown in Fig. 40. At all ages there is a drop in the number of arteries falling within the larger ranges. In the fetus and infant, populations are very similar to each other, but with age there is a drop in the percentage of small arteries and a corresponding rise in the number of arteries over 100 μm. in diameter. This is particularly seen in the examples given of children aged 5 and 10 years. During the period when the number of arteries and alveoli increases, the size range remains constant but during the later phase of increase in alveolar size, vessel size also increases, despite the fact that the vessel number is still increasing.

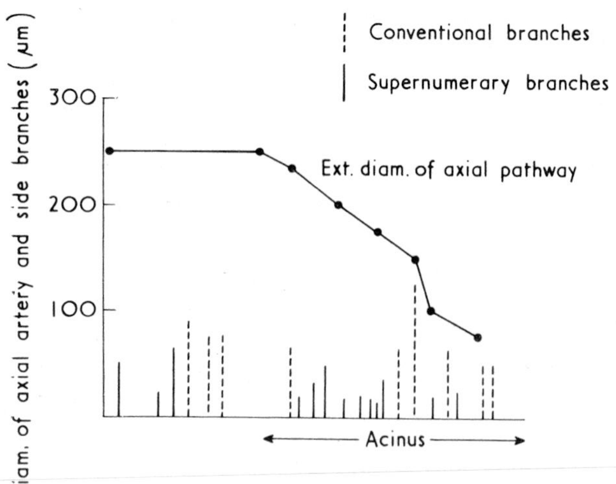

FIG. 37. Branching pattern of the arteries within an acinus and in its immediate pre-acinar region at birth. The diameter of the axial pathway and of conventional and supernumerary vessels is shown. Length of pathway traced is 2·17 mm. There are few supernumerary arteries in comparison with Fig. 38.

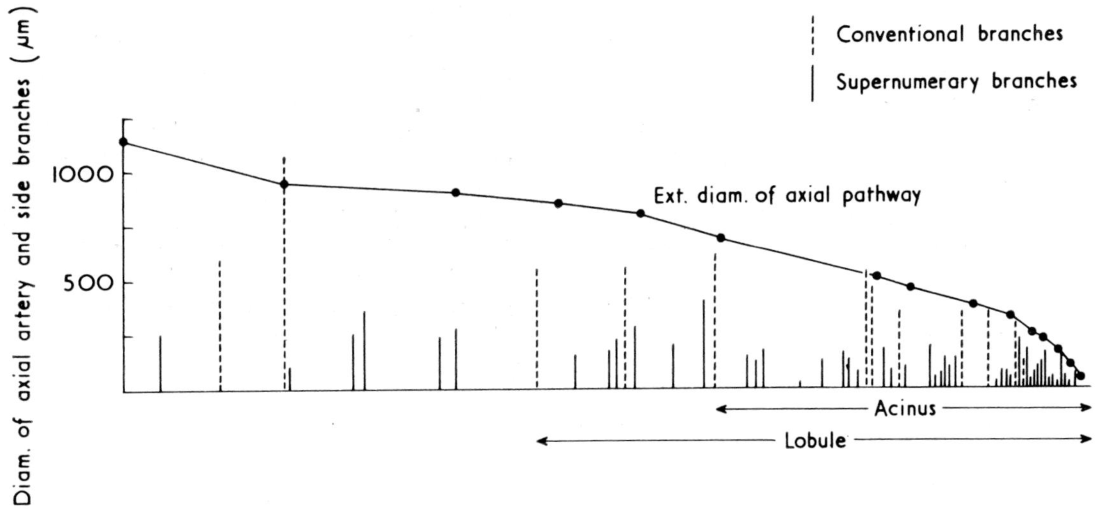

FIG. 38. Reconstruction of the arterial branching pattern within a lobule and its immediate pre-lobular region from a lung of a 5-year old child. The external diameter of the axial pathway and of the conventional and supernumerary arteries is shown. The length of the pathway traced is 1·26 cm. Increase in the number of supernumerary arteries is great; in the conventional small (cf. Fig. 37).

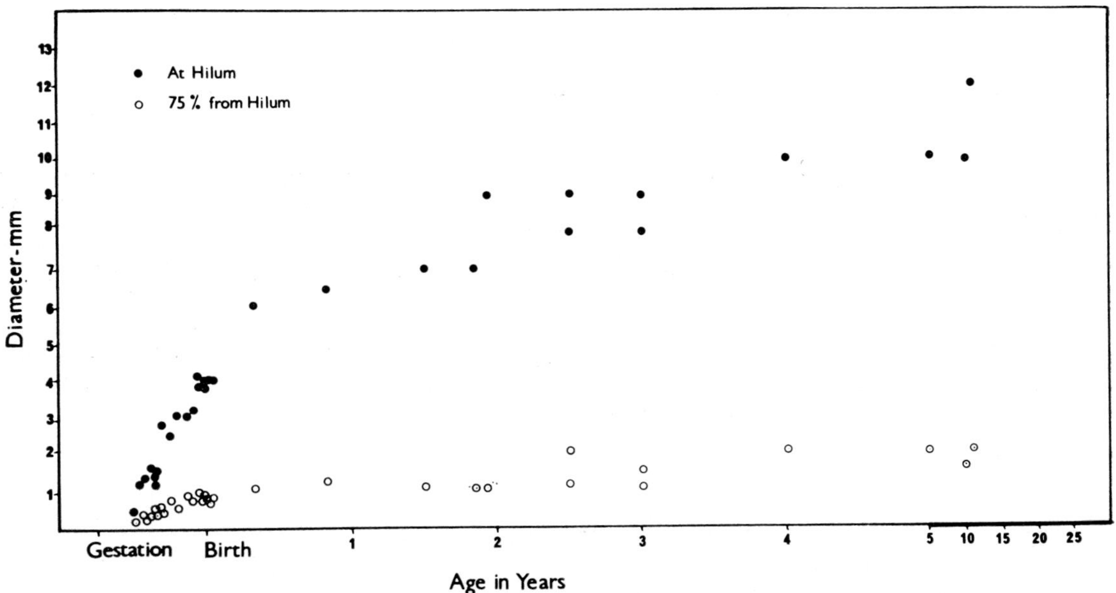

FIG. 39. Artery lumen diameter measured on arteriograms for the lower lobe during fetal life and childhood, at the hilum and at a point 75 per cent from the hilum to the periphery.

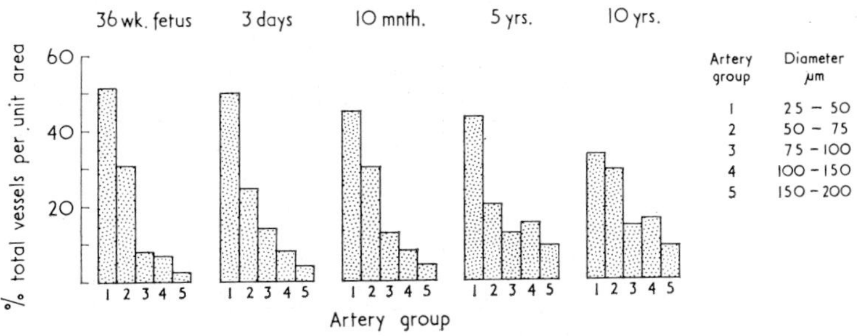

FIG. 40. The percentage of arteries in each size range from 25–200 μm. in a unit area of lung tissue of the alveolar region. With age there is a relative increase in the number of larger arteries.

Arterial Structure

During childhood, arterial structure shows important changes. By 4–10 months the percentage wall thickness of the arteries as related to external diameter has fallen to adult levels and this is maintained throughout childhood (Fig. 33). The distribution of elastic and transitional arteries, as judged by the branching pattern of accompanying airways, remains the same throughout childhood, though the diameter range for each structural type of artery increases with age.

It is the distribution of the small muscular, partially muscular and non-muscular vessels that shows the most striking change during childhood. In the fetus the distribution of those vessels as judged by size is the same as in the adult but the position of these vessels in the lung is different. During childhood it would be expected that as new arteries appear at the periphery and increase in size, muscle would appear in their wall with a gradual extension of muscle to the peripheral generations, but this is not the case. During childhood, from 4 months until the age of 11 years at least, the wholly muscular artery structure is not seen in such small vessels as in the adult, and partially muscular and non-muscular arteries appear first at a larger diameter than in the adult[38,68] (*see* Fig. 41). Studying the

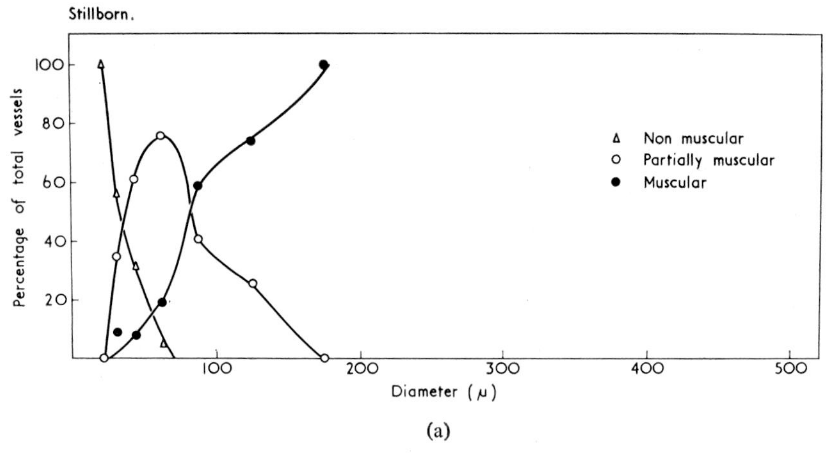

(a)

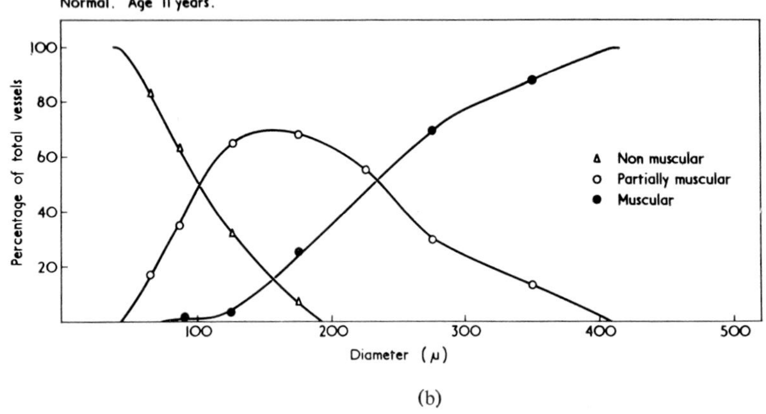

(b)

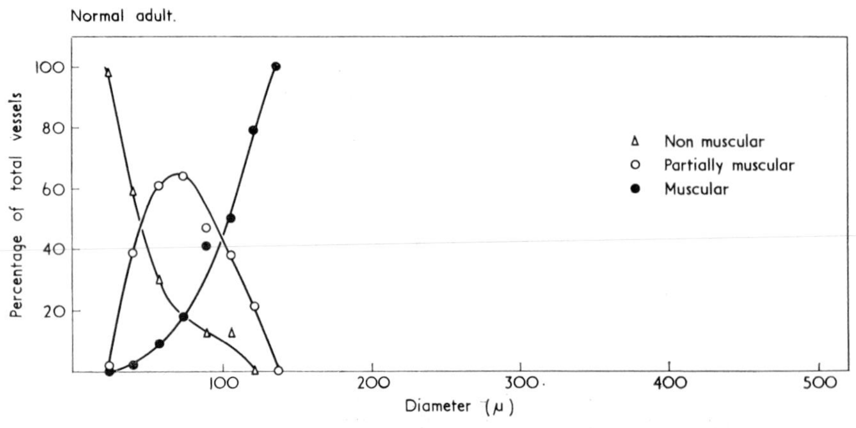

c)

FIG. 41. Population counts in (a) a stillborn, (b) a normal child aged 11 years, and (c) a normal adult. The pattern for the stillborn and adult are very similar but in all children from 18 months, at least up to 11 years, there is a change in the distribution of muscle. A partially muscular and non-muscular structure appear at a greater external diameter, that is the small arteries are less muscular than in the adult. (Reproduced by permission of *Thorax*.[38])

population of small arteries, the partially muscular and non-muscular arteries make up a much greater percentage of the total in the child than in either the fetus or adult.

This apparent "regression" of muscle is not due to atrophy, as can be established by reference to position of an artery in the lung. At birth, muscle extends to the terminal bronchiolus; during childhood there is a gradual but steady extension along the arteries towards the periphery of the acinus (Fig. 42). The apparent decrease in muscle in the small arteries is due to an increase in size of these vessels without the appearance of muscle in their wall. This time-lag in muscle growth occurs later than that causing the wall-thinning and continues at least until 5 years and probably to 10 years. During childhood, therefore, there is less muscle

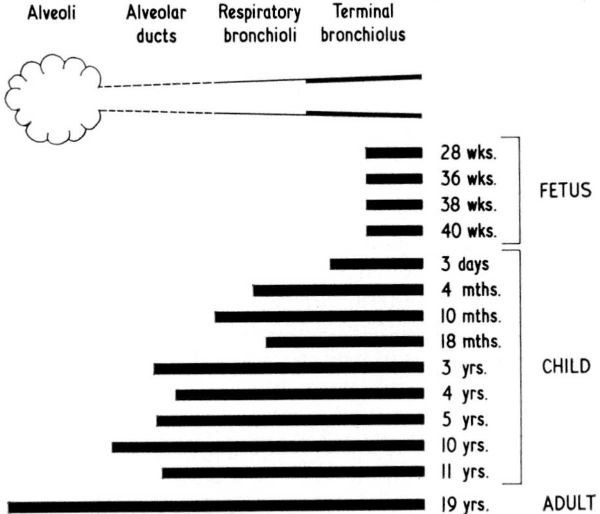

FIG. 42. Diagram illustrating the extension of muscle in the walls of arteries within the acinus. The end of the muscular region is shown by the black lines. There is no muscle within the acinus in the fetus. With age there is a gradual extension into the acinar region but even at 11 years muscular arteries are not present in the alveolar wall as they are in the adult.

in the acinar arteries than in the adult. There is gradual extension of the muscle to the periphery as more peripheral arteries become larger. However, even at eleven years, muscular arteries are only found as far to the periphery as the alveolar ducts and not to within the alveolar wall.[68] Staub[137] used frozen sections of cat lung to show that, during breathing of 100 per cent oxygen, gas transfer occurred in vessels up to 200 μm. external diameter. These vessels had muscular walls. During air breathing, oxygen transfer did not occur in vessels over 100 μm. diameter—probably the level of the largest non-muscular artery. Children with more non-muscular vessels may be at an advantage as compared with the acult in normal or low oxygen tensions.

It would seem that the small muscular arteries are those that react to hypoxia by vasoconstriction.[8] Using casts of the arterial system in the alveolar wall of rabbit lungs Burton[27] has shown that hypoxia causes vasoconstriction of muscle in vessels and Kato and Staub,[75] using rapid-frozen sections, arrived at a similar conclusion. Constriction takes place initially at this level and it may be that the stimulus to constriction in the more proximal artery is conducted from muscle cell to muscle cell.[60] It may be that in the child there is less reaction to hypoxia as there are fewer muscle cells in direct contact with alveoli for the initial reaction.

Pulmonary Veins

During childhood the veins increase in size in a similar way to the arteries, with the increase more rapid during early infancy. At the same time, and related to alveolar growth, there is an increase in the number of peripheral veins. The number of veins in a unit area of lung tissue is greater than the number of arteries, possibly because of a relatively greater flow through veins as a result of the contribution from the bronchial circulation.

Throughout childhood there is little or no change in the distribution of muscle in the vein walls. The percentage wall-thickness of the veins remains low and the muscle extends into vessels of the same size. As veins increase in size there is evidently an extension of muscle towards the periphery. The small amount of muscle is probably related to the low pressure in the system; it has been shown that reversal of pulmonary flow in dogs will lead to medial hypertrophy[134] and cases with mitral stenosis and anomalous pulmonary venous drainage also have medial hypertrophy of veins.[126]

Period of Adolescence

At adolescence there is a growth spurt in the total size of the lung as seen in clinical radiographs, which must be related to sudden increase in lung volume. Since the alveolar number is complete, increase in the size of the alveoli must occur until the adult size is reached. At the same time, there is some increase in the complexity of the alveolar outline so that the surface area increases considerably. Between 12 and 18 years there is an increase in the elastic fibres in the alveolar wall; they eventually branch through the alveolar walls rather than appearing only at the mouths (Fig. 32). This is the adult state.

There are no changes other than of size in the proximal airways and pulmonary vessels. In the acinar region the pulmonary arterial circulation is increasing in muscularity, with muscle extending into smaller vessels and therefor to the periphery of the acinus so that, by 19 years, muscular arteries are found within alveolar walls. As the alveoli increase in size, the number of small arteries in a unit area of lung decreases and their size increases, but the capillary bed enlarges and the area of the air-tissue interphase increases with age, more than doubling between eight years and the adulthood.[43]

Acquired Disease of Childhood

Disease acquired during childhood will affect mainly alveolar number and size and associated blood vessels. Although the airways may be obliterated or dilated, their complement is already complete.

Collapse

If a lobe or lung become airless the distal bronchi and bronchioli, like the alveoli, collapse and their walls come to be in apposition. This means that only the large bronchi with abundant cartilage in their wall, making up the first five or so generations along an axial pathway, stay patent.[56] The volume of the lobe and its long diameter are both greatly reduced. If this occurs during childhood the lobe will be small and will grow little, so that in the adult a lobe that collapsed during childhood will be very much smaller than one that has collapsed when growth was complete.

The bronchogram of such a lobe shows very incomplete filling, the airways that have filled usually having an irregular outline because they are no longer subject to normal stretch. The apparent airways occlusion is functional and therefore reversible. Such a collapsed lobe has been seen to expand many years later and to appear relatively normal in a radiograph, but how satisfactory gas exchange will be in such a lobe is not known.

With lapse of time the lobe can no longer be inflated and if infection supervenes it may quite quickly cause organic block of airways. Infection usually affects the distal end of the patent airway so that ulceration followed by healing will be associated with obliteration of the lumen.

Collapse even if without infection is thus one cause of bronchiectasis. Infection on its own may also cause bronciectasis. If it arises from endobronchial embolus, as after tonsilectomy, an endobronchial abscess may form with the ulcerative process affecting a large airway and extending beyond it. Healing may be associated with formation of a cystic space in communication centrally with the trachea, but with the airways beyond the abscess cavity cut off. Bronchitis obliterans is the best synonym for bronchiectasis,[32] emphasizing as it does the important functional disturbance of obliteration of airway lumen rather than the less disturbing one of change in size. If *all* airways in a lobe or lung are blocked or obliterated the lobe will become airless, but collateral ventilation may serve to maintain aeration even when many of its airways are blocked, either mechanically or structurally.

Although the pattern of increase in airway size shown by the studies of Hislop and her colleagues[70] emphasizes the similarity in form of the bronchial tree at all ages, in the small lung the small airways are smaller, being in the newborn about a quarter of the adult diameter. This means that blockage of the lumen occurs more easily whether by bronchial secretion, pus or mucus or tissue fluid—or by oedema of the wall. It is doubtless for reasons such as this that bronchiolitis in the small lung of a baby or child is more serious than in the adult.

MacLeod's Syndrome

The same pattern of behaviour may be seen if the damage affects mainly the small airways or bronchioli—bronchiolitis obliterans. There is really no anatomical point to distinguish the two, but the level of the airway affected modifies the bronchographic appearances.

Unilateral hypertransradiancy was described by Macleod[94] in a series of nine adults. The main radiographic feature of unilateral hypertransradiancy was combined with a small or normal-sized lung, a small artery, expiratory swing of the mediastinum to the contralateral side and no collapse of any part of the lung. The bronchogram in all the early cases published was usually described as normal, virtually normal or not normal but with no gross bronchiectasis. In fact, a bronchogram used as a respiratory function test to assess the ability of airways to conduct to the periphery, is never normal in this condition. Occasionally, one part of the lung may show normal filling, presumably a region important in maintaining collateral ventilation. Usually there is evidence of peripheral bronchiolar disease.

In the resected specimens that have become available,[119] the findings are of a lung normal or small in size for age, panacinar emphysema, bizarre distribution of soot through the affected lung, a hilar artery only slightly reduced in size (less so than the radiograph or agiogram suggests) and a hypoplastic intrapulmonary circulation. Most important of all is the patchy but widespread distribution of bronchiolar fibrosis, stenosis and obliteration. The number of alveoli is reduced since the lung is hypoplastic and the alveoli enlarged. Most patients offer a history of severe childhood infection.

It would seem that this condition is caused by infection affecting mainly the small airways before lung growth is complete. While obliterative lesions are widespread, enough airways must remain to provide collateral ventilation for the whole lung, the regions with the dust indicating direct ventilation, the fluffy pink parts those indirectly ventilated. Growth is in part a work hypertrophy and the work of the lung is represented by the ventilatory movements of inspiration and expiration. It is the alternate movements of ventilation that are mainly concerned with minute blood flow to the lung: it is during the expiratory phase that the capillary blood flow is greatest. In Macleod's syndrome ventilation is reduced to the affected lobe which is held mainly in the inspiratory position; thus "work" and blood flow are reduced.

The emphysema—that is, the large alveolar spaces—arise from failure of alveoli to multiply and their increase in distensibility due to low blood flow: it is an example of hypoplastic emphysema. The airway wall may share in this hypoplasia but any collapse of proximal airways reflects the more peripheral obstruction to the lumen and not inherent flabbiness of the walls.

In the original account Macleod[94] excluded any case with evidence of tuberculosis, but this he would now regard as unnecessary since the changes may be brought about by any infection. Change of this type may affect a lung, a lobe, a segment or a subsegment.

This condition has been dealt with at some length because it illustrates several principles important to an analysis of the effect on the child lung of acquired disease.

Bronchitis or bronchiolitis obliterans each affect ventilation and blood flow although it will be the concentration of these lesions within a given region that will determine the final effect. With the increasing control of childhood lung infections, including tuberculosis, it had been expected that this syndrome would no longer be seen, but it would seem that viral infections, still common in childhood,[71] are causing this syndrome (Prof. S. D. M. Court and Dr. P. S. Gardner, personal communication). The changes in Macleod's disease are not always confined to one lung. In a series that we studied[113] there was evidence of damage in the contralateral lung in about one-third of cases. Clearly, if both lungs are severely affected by bronchiolitis it is incompatible with life, as may be seen in cystic fibrosis, in which the bronchiolar lesions may be present and, additionally, hypersecretion of mucus, an important mechanical cause for airways obstruction.

Asthma

The adult lung at death, even after many incidents of status asthmaticus, may show no emphysema. So it would seem that intermittent or even chronic airways obstruction does not produce emphysema in the grown lung. It is much harder to gauge the hazard during the period of growth. Certainly it can be said that usually there is no evidence of any deleterious effect; the child may reach adulthood with a normal radiograph while respiratory function tests show no impairment. Occasionally, however, the thoracic configuration is abnormal or hypertransradiancy is seen at the lung base.

Measurements have recently been made on the radiographs of a series of children with asthma and the results related to the centiles of lung growth recently established by Simon *et al.*[133] This revealed that for the most disabled group of children there was evidence of increase in lung length even when maximum clinical improvement had been obtained, suggesting that, in these children, resting lung volumes were larger after persistent and serious asthma.[132]

Kyphoscoliosis

Infective damage and asthma may be regarded as examples of obstructive disease; scoliosis also interferes with lung growth but mainly through restriction. Kyphoscoliosis has an effect on the lungs after birth similar to that which congenital diaphragmatic hernia produces before birth. The lung shape is distorted, its volume smaller, alveolar number is reduced and is sometimes associated with decrease, sometimes with increase, in alveolar size. These changes affect each lung and its lobes unevenly. The number of airways is not affected since airways are present before birth.

The lung that lies in the concavity of the scoliotic curve is usually better seen on the radiograph and therefore it looks larger than the other and yet it is the lung spread over the convexity that is the larger and probably more vital to respiration. It is important to take this into account in deciding whether to operate for spinal correction or cosmetic reasons.

The blood vessel growth in the children with scoliosis may also be reduced: muscle is usually found in smaller arteries than is normal for age and is further to the lung periphery than is normal. Right ventricular hypertrophy is found only when airway obstruction is also present and then there is hypertrophy of the arterial muscle coat as well.[39]

In the light of recent knowledge of lung growth, it would seem important that the spinal curve be straightened as early as possible so that lung growth may be as nearly normal as possible. Straightening by splint or plaster, during the years before definitive surgical correction is contemplated, would seem desirable.

Hypoplasia because of restriction of available space is, perhaps, not a surprising finding but atrophy was not expected. A severe degree of atrophy may affect the lung compressed between the apex of the curve and the chest wall; in this region, in one case, the axial segmental arteries came to lie immediately under the pleura. In another, a young man, the lung volume and the total alveolar number were less than those of a child of three months although the attack of poliomyelitis that caused the scoliosis did not occur until he was five years old and presumably up to this time development had been normal.[39]

Arterio-venous Fistulae

Most of the intra-acinar blood vessels appear for the first time during childhood. In several of the cases of scoliosis, those associated with other evidence of mesodermal hypoplasia, there were more blood vessels than is normal suggesting some inherent defect in vessel multiplication. The lung vessels in multiple arterio-venous fistulae must also develop after birth. Arterio venous-fistulae on some occasions represent an opening-up of the capillary bed between normally placed proximal arteries and veins; in adjacent lung numerous dilated vessels are commonly seen.[116] Whether these represent an inherent defect in arterial multiplication or a functional response to local increase in flow is not clear.

Recently we have seen a case of a child of eight years (patient of Dr. R. G. Bonham-Carter) whose small intra-acinar blood vessels were too numerous and included too high a proportion of large ones. It is probably important to accept that disturbance of blood vessel multiplication may occur as a primary disturbance during childhood.

ADDITIONAL ANATOMICAL GROWTH

Total Lung Growth

The overall growth of the lung can be assessed either by weight, volume or linear dimensions. Emery and Mithal[48] have prepared comprehensive tables of lung weight related to age, crown-rump length and total body weight, based on examination of a large series of fetal, newborn and child lungs. Tanimura, Nelson, Hollingsworth and Shepard[141] related lung weight to total body weight in fetuses up to 500 gm. in weight.

The figures for lung length from a small series of fetal and child lungs, inflated and fixed in our Department, are given in Fig. 43. The prenatal growth curve is logarithmic and the data can be closely fitted to the curve

$$y = (0{\cdot}0873)t^{1{\cdot}235}$$

where y is lung length in cm., t is gestation age in weeks. This equation for rather more than 90 per cent of the variation in lung length: it will be seen from Fig. 43b, however, that for the greater part of this time the increase is practically linear.

The postnatal growth curve for lung length is of the same form but with different parameter—viz.:

$$y = 7{\cdot}0 + (2{\cdot}803)t^{0{\cdot}316}$$

where t is age measured in months from birth; or alternatively

$$y = 7{\cdot}0 + (1{\cdot}764)t^{0{\cdot}316}$$

if t is measured in weeks from birth. This equation fits best with the growth rate and also achieves the smoothest

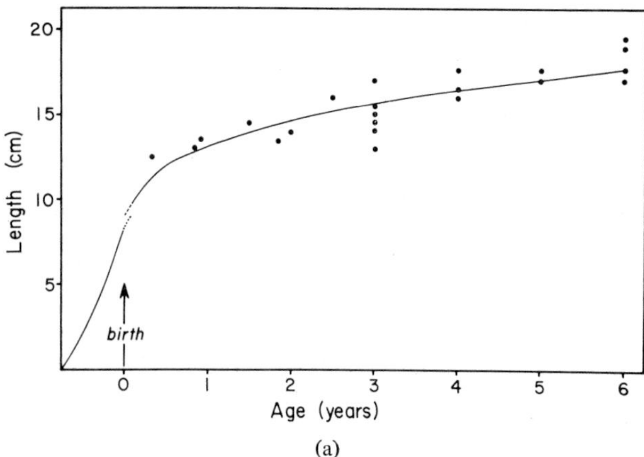

(a)

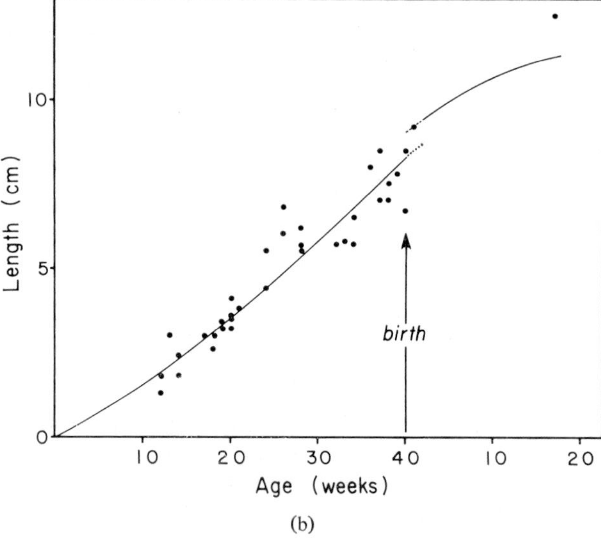

(b)

FIG. 43. Diagrams illustrating total lung growth. Fixed lung length as measured on an arteriogram is shown related to age (a) fetal life and up to 6 years, (b) ante- and peri-natal period in more detail.

junction with the prenatal curve albeit not an exact one since the rate of growth after birth is slowed. At birth the level increases by about 1 cm.; presumably this represents the effect of inflation with air at birth.

While the measurements of lung length and lung volume show the trend for increase in size with age, their numbers are not sufficient to serve as a standard for normal growth. A larger series of fetal and child lungs is required to produce a standard curve for these features which may be of more value to pathologist and physiologist in assessing lung normality than weight since this may vary with oedema.

Connective Tissue Septa

The bronchi and blood vessels of the lung are ensheathed by connective tissue and, in some places, connective tissue septa arise from the pleura and pass, roughly at right-angles to it, into the lung. These appear to the naked eye as white lines and resemble fascial places elsewhere in the body: serial section shows that nowhere is a unit of the lung isolated from its neighbour. It is only a lobe, and a lobe completely surrounded by pleura, that can be regarded as an end unit.

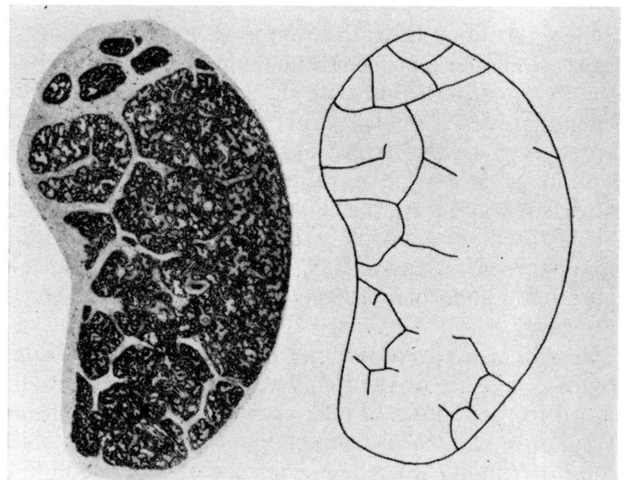

FIG. 44. Horizontal section of the apex of the right upper lobe, with diagram, of a 24-week fetus: septa are in the adult position being few over the lateral aspect of the lobe. (Reproduced by permission of *Thorax*.[118])

Septa are confined to the sub-pleural region and found particularly at the margins and sharp edges of the lung—the anterior edges of the upper lobes and lingula and middle lobes, the costo-diaphragmatic rim, the postero-medial margin. The costal or flat aspects of the lobe are relatively free. Where the edges sharply angle, the septa dipping in from both surfaces almost meet.

As the alveolar region develops, connective tissue septa appear within the mesenchyme. Septa are more obvious in the fetal and newborn than in the adult lung and first appear between the 18th and 20th week of gestation and are in the same number and pattern as in the adult but are proportionately smaller (Fig. 44).[118]

Collateral Ventilation

The incompleteness of the septa in man is essential to "collateral air drift" or "collateral ventilation", the term used by van Allen and Jung[4] to describe the phenomenon whereby air can drift from one alveolus to another, one acinus to another, lobule to lobule and segment to segment. It will be relatively impeded in those parts of the lung where there is considerable sub-division of respiratory tissue by connective tissue.

This phenomenon has long been of importance to the pathologist but is only recently being studied by the physiologist. The significance of air drift in normal healthy lung is not known. That it operates in disease can be shown in pathological specimens in which lung is well aerated although the supplying airways may be obliterated. Thus, even if alveoli appear normal, it does not follow that the supplying airway is normal. The protective effect of collateral ventilation is clear in that it makes it possible for airways and alveoli to be independent of each other. It facilitates equalization of gas pressures so that collapse or over-inflation may each, to some extent, be prevented.

Anatomical Basis of Collateral Ventilation

The relative importance of the various anatomical routes by which collateral ventilation may occur cannot be fully assessed but the following may contribute:

(i) The Accessory Bronchiole-alveolar Communications of Lambert.[84] These are small channels up to 30μm diameter which pass between the lumen of terminal or pre-terminal bronchioli to immediately adjacent alveoli. They are lined by a continuous layer of epithelium. They are not present in the human lung at the age of four, but have been identified at the age of eight.[13]

(ii) Interacinar "Pore".[17] An accessory communication as (i) has been identified between a small airway and alveoli of an adjacent acinus which was not supplied by the same airway.

(iii) "Pores" of Kohn.[82] Through these gaps within the alveolar wall one alveolar space is in direct continuity with its neighbour.

(iv) "Double Diffusion." Since diffusion occurs so rapidly across the blood/gas barrier the possibility cannot be excluded that diffusion may be responsible—equalization from an alveolus supplied by one airway with an adjacent one supplied by another airway.

Nerves Within the Lung

In the adult human, the tissues of the airways are well-endowed with motor and sensory nerves and something is known of their function and distribution: nerves are present within the epithelium in man[33,138] and in the rat from ultra-structural features both sensory and motor fibres have been found.[74b] Within the alveolar region, although the presence of nerves can be predicted from physiological[104] studies, even their presence within the alveolar walls deep within the acinus has not been established in man, although recently, by use of the electron microscope, it has in rat[99] and mouse.[74a]

The alveolar walls lying against connective tissue whether in pleura or around sheaths of large vessels and airways, may share the innervation of these structures. The manner and age at which these nerves develop have not been established.

The Diaphragm

The muscle of the diaphragm increases in area and weight with age but little detailed study has been made of the way in which the muscle mass or fibre size changes. In the adult it would seem that the weight of the diaphragm and also the mean fibre-size varies according to the weight rather than to the age of the subject.

In children the mean fibre size is smaller than in the adult and in two cases studied, of 3 and 10 years of age, the weight of the diaphragm had increased directly with age (Noah, personal communication).

Lymphatics

In the human lung, lymphatics are numerous around airways, arteries and veins and also in the pleura and interlobular septa. Valves are numerous in all lymphatics and flow is from the pleural to the deep lymphatics and thence to the hilum. Small lymph nodes are found throughout the lung.[146]

The lymphatic channels appear in the 26 mm. embryo (60-day) in the hilar region and are present throughout the lung by 70 days.[144] In the newborn the lymphatic system surrounds bronchi, pulmonary arteries and veins and can be traced distally to the alveolar ducts.

The pleural lymphatics are relatively larger and more numerous in the fetal and newborn than in the adult lung (Trapnell, personal communication). Lymph flow during the first few hours after birth is at its highest; but two days later it is lower than in the mature fetal lamb although higher than in the adult.[73] An immature lung of a lamb is not able to remove liquid so quickly as a mature lamb lung—this may be related to the lack of surface tension properties.[139] Most of the fluid in the lung at birth leaves through the lymphatics. Lymph channels can be clearly seen in the connective tissue in human lungs of 20 weeks' gestation.[46] Small aggregates of cells, about half of them of the lymphocytic series, can be seen from 15 weeks' gestation. By birth or immediately afterwards lymph nodes seem to be established in the adult positions and childhood growth is an enlargement of these structures.

Congenital Pulmonary Lymphangiectasis

Congenital pulmonary lymphangiectasis is one cause of early cyanosis and death in the newborn. The cut surface of the lung shows a series of "cysts" which lie in the lung's connective tissue framework and, by Laurence's[86] reconstruction, have been shown to represent dilated and intercommunicating lymphatic spaces. It would seem likely that these communicate with the main hilar ducts, but this has not been proved. The pleural surface shows the cobblestone pattern of dilated lymphatics which may be filled with fluid although after sectioning they are often empty. Associated developmental anomalies are often found and the respiratory tissue between the cysts has been regarded as immature. Of the cardiac malformations sometimes found, a high proportion would impede pulmonary venous flow and might induce increased lymphatic flow *in utero*. The age at which these changes develop is not clear. The lymphatics have probably reached the pleura during the pseudoglandular phase when they are particularly obvious. In about half the cases the anomaly is a solitary one (Laurence, personal communication).

The cystic form may represent a primary overgrowth of endothelium or some disturbance of the relation between endothelium and surrounding mesoderm.

An example of what is possibly a localized form of this condition in the middle lobe has been described.[37] A young adult was troubled by coughing-up casts of the bronchi of this lobe. As well as the dilated lymphatics the lobe was hypoplastic, with a normal number of airways but too few alveoli.

CONTROL OF LUNG GROWTH

Because of the exciting results from the experimental work on organogenesis, a couple of decades ago it might have been predicted that we would now be able to identify the chemical substances responsible in each organ for induction, differentiation and growth. We are far from being able to do this but studies of congenital anomalies, if regarded as vicarious experiments, make it possible to suggest a relationship between various factors such as space available for growth and endocrine balance. It is necessary also to analyse the effect of the development of airways, arteries and alveoli on each other, for the maturity of one structure may be essential to the normal development of another.

The Effect of Mechanical Factors on Lung Growth

Reduction of space available for development leads to lungs that are small in volume and in weight. These are not a miniature version of a normal lung of the same age for different structures respond independently. For example, restriction of space before birth will reduce the number of bronchial branches that have developed. Speaking generally, artery number is usually proportional to airway number. Alveolar differentiation occurs without the normal complement of airways or arteries present. Whether this implies that a different chemical "trigger" is concerned with airway and alveolar development is not clear. Alveolar number is harder to relate to space available; it would seem that restriction of available space entails a restriction in total alveolar number but if this is related to a reduced bronchial number, the number of alveoli in an acinus is less reduced than the number of alveoli in the lung as a whole. In a small hypoplastic lung, at birth, alveoli may be too few and are usually reduced or increased in size, suggesting that the number formed is independent of size. Postnatal impairment of growth as in scoliosis may give rise to too few alveoli, either too big or too small.[39]

In one condition, it has been shown that there is, at birth, a great excess of alveoli in an otherwise normal lobe and yet the size and the number of arterial branches, in the pre-acinar region certainly, were appropriate to the age of the lung and the normal airways present. This pointed to the pre-acinar arterial supply not being affected by the state of alveolar development.

Hormonal Control of Growth

The recent studies of Brody and his colleagues[21] have analysed the effect in rats of the implantation of a tumour-producing growth hormone and of the parenteral administration of the hormone. They showed that even in the adult animal, the hormone increased the weight of the lung beyond that of control animals, to a greater extent than could be explained by the increase in body weight. The lung elastic properties seemed normal; alveolar size, but not alveolar number, had increased. Estimations of DNA and RNA indicated that the effect was brought about by cell hypertrophy.

The effect of growth hormone after pneumonectomy was also followed.[24] At no time was an increase in lung units demonstrated—that is, alveolar number did not increase. After pneumonectomy the increase in lung size seemed to arise from cell hyperplasia as well as hypertrophy. Administration of additional growth hormone led to greater increase in lung volume but not in weight. Growth hormone would seem to be necessary even for the "physiological" response to resection in the rat, since after hypophysectomy and pneumonectomy the residual lung did not show an increase in total lung capacity. In similar studies on young rats, again no increase in alveolar number was demonstrated but weight and volume increased, particularly during the first month after resection, mainly due to cell hyperplasia.

Klionsky and Wigglesworth[77] administered two chemicals to pregnant rats to produce an animal "model" of fetal hypoplasia. One drug—cycloheximide—reduces protein, the other—hydroxyurea—DNA synthesis. Each drug was given at two stages of pregnancy. Inhibition of DNA synthesis caused reduction in organ cell population, inhibition of protein synthesis caused reduction in overall weight. The liver and brain were the two organs mainly studied, because of its small size the lung was unsatisfactory for study (Wigglesworth, personal communication).

It has been shown in the human that maternal German measles during pregnancy may be associated with an abnormally low cell number in the newborn.[103]

Lung Regeneration

Animal studies show that resection of one lobe leads to increase in volume and weight of the residual lung tissue that has expanded to fill the thoracic space, although this is not necessarily associated with increase in alveolar number. In one report it was claimed that resection in a young animal had led to increase in alveolar number in the residual lung[90] but the methods used were not as precise as those currently available and so these results cannot be regarded as conclusive. No quantitative analysis has been made of the behaviour of blood vessels in these experiments.

Quantitative analysis of an enlarged lung to which increased space had been available because of hypoplasia of the contralateral lung (*see* page 107) suggests that even during the first nine months after birth when alveolar multiplication is greatest, alveolar number does not increase beyond normal although compensatory emphysema was present.[59] It may be that a rate above the maximum cannot be achieved; but if the child had lived multiplication may have continued for longer, ultimately leading to a higher total.

It would seem from the above and from the studies of

Brody that hypertrophy of lung—that is, increase in weight and volume—occurs without increase in alveolar number; but since an abnormally high number has been reported in two conditions—agenesis of lung and polyalveolar lobe—it cannot be concluded that this could not occur.

On the available evidence, it is not possible to suggest at what age resection should be carried out to achieve the best functional results in the residual lung.

ACKNOWLEDGEMENTS

We should like to thank Professor E. A. Boyden (Department of Biological Structure, University of Washington) for much interesting discussion, Professor B. Benjamin (Director of Statistical Studies, Civil Service College) for his statistical advice, and Professor C. G. Loosli (Department of Medicine, University of Southern California) for sending us Figs. 29–32. We would also like to thank Dr. A. J. Palfrey (Department of Anatomy, St. Thomas' Hospital) who allowed us to study human fetal serial sections and Mr. J. Fenton who took the micrographs for Fig. 1. We are grateful to Mr. K. Moreman (Director of Department of Photography, Royal Marsden Hospital) for the remaining photomicrographs, and to Miss B. Meyrick and Mr. P. Jeffery for the electron micrographs. The original diagrams were drawn by Miss G. Leballeur and the late Miss J. Waldron. Miss J. Scott-Elliott and the staff of the Photographic Department, Royal Marsden Hospital, produced the prints.

REFERENCES

1. Adams, F. H. (1966), "Functional Development of the Fetal Lung," *J. Pediat.*, **68,** 794–801.
2. Adams, F. H., Moss, A. J. and Fagan, L. (1963) "The Tracheal Fluid in the Fetal Lamb," *Biol. Neonat.*, **5,** 151–158.
3. Alescio T. and Cassini, A. (1962), "Induction *in vitro* of Tracheal Buds by Pulmonary Mesenchyme Grafted on Tracheal Epithelium," *J. exp. Zool.*, **150,** 83–94.
4. van Allen, C. M. and Jung, T. S. (1931), "Postoperative Atelectasis and Collateral Respiration," *J. thorac. Surg* , **1,** 3–14.
5. Askin, F. O. and Kuhn, C. (1971), "The Cellular Origin of Pulmonary Surfactant," *Lab. Invest.*, **25,** 260–268.
6. Aüer, J. (1948), "The Development of the Human Pulmonary Vein and its Major Variations," *Anat. Rec.*, **101,** 581–594.
7. Bargmann, W. (1956), *Histologie und Mikroscopische Anatomie des Menschen*, 2nd edition. Stuttgart: Georg Thieme.
8. Bergofsky, E. H., Haas, F. and Porcelli, R. (1968), "Determination of the Sensitive Vascular Sites from which Hypoxia and Hypercapnia Elicit Rises in Pulmonary Arterial Pressure," *Fed. Proc.*, **27,** 1420–1425.
9. Boston, R. W., Humphreys, P. W., Reynolds, E. O. and Strang, L. B. (1965), "Lymph-flow and Clearance of Liquid from the Lungs of Foetal Lamb," *Lancet*, **2,** 473–474.
10. Boyden, E. A. (1924), "An Experimental Study of the Development of the Avian Cloaca, with Special Reference to a Mechanical Factor in the Growth of the Allantois," *J. exp. Zool.*, **40,** 437–472.
11. Boyden, E. A. (1958), "Bronchogenic Cysts and the Theory of Intralobar Sequestration: New Embryologic Data," *J. thorac. Surg.*, **35,** 604–616.
12. Boyden, E. A. (1965), "The Terminal Air Sacs and Their Blood Supply in a 37-day Infant Lung," *Amer. J. Anat.*, **116,** 413–428.
13. Boyden, E. A. (1967), "Notes on the Development of the Lung in Infancy and Early Childhood," *Amer. J. Anat.*, **121,** 749–762.
14. Boyden, E. A. (1969), "The pattern of Terminal Air Spaces in a Premature Infant of 30–32 weeks that Lived 19¼ hours," *Amer. J. Anat.*, **126,** 31–40.
15. Boyden, E. A. (1970a), "The Developing Bronchial Arteries in a Fetus of the Twelfth Week," *Amer. J. Anat.*, **129,** 357–368.
16. Boyden, E. A. (1970b), "The Time Lag in the Development of Bronchial Arteries," *Anat. Rec.*, **166,** 611–614.
17. Boyden, E. A. (1971), "The Structure of the Pulmonary Acinus in a Child of Six Years and Eight Months," *Amer. J. Anat.*, **132,** 275–300.
18. Boyden, E. A. (1972a), "Development of the Human Lung," In *Brennermann's Practice of Pediatrics*, Vol. IV, Chap. 64. Hagerstown: Harper & Row.
19. Boyden, E. A. (1972b), "The Structure of Compressed Lungs in Congenital Diaphragmatic Hernia," *Amer. J. Anat.*, **134,** 497–508.
20. Boyden, E. A. and Tompsett, D. H. (1965), "The Changing Patterns in the Developing Lungs of Infants," *Acta anat.*, **61,** 164–192.
21. Brody, J. S. and Buhain, W. J. (1972), "Hormone-induced Growth of the Adult Lung," *Amer. J. Physiol.* In press.
22. Bucher, U. and Reid, L. (1961a), "Development of the Intrasegmental Bronchial Tree: the Pattern of Branching and Development of Cartilage at Various Stages of Intra-uterine Life," *Thorax*, **16,** 207–218.
23. Bucher, U. and Reid, L. (1961b), "Development of the Mucus-secreting Elements in Human Lung," *Thorax*, **16,** 219–225.
24. Buhain, W. J. and Brody, J. S. (1972), "Effect of Growth Hormone on Post-pneumonectomy. Lung Regeneration," *Amer. Rev. resp. Dis.*, **105,** 1003–1004
25. Burnell, R. H., Joseph, M. C. and Lees, M. H. (1972), "Progressive Pulmonary Hypertension in Newborn Infants," *Amer. J. Dis. Child.*, **123,** 167–170.
26. Burri, P. H. and Weibel, E. F. (1971), "Morphometric Estimation of Pulmonary Diffusion Capacity. II: Effect of PO_2 on the Growing Lung," *Resp. Physiol.*, **11,** 247–264.
27. Burton, A. C. (1959), "The Relation Between Pressure and Flow in the Pulmonary Bed," in *Pulmonary Circulation*, pp. 26–33 (W. R. Adams and I. Vieth, eds.). New York: Grune & Stratton.
28. Butler, H. (1952), "Some Derivatives of the Foregut Venous Plexus of the Albino Rat, with Reference to Man," *J. Anat. (Lond.)*, **86,** 95–101.
29. Campiche, M. (1960), "Les inclusions lamellaires des cellules alvéolaires dans le poumon du raton. Relations entre l'ultrastructure et la fixation," *J. Ultrastruct. Res.*, **3,** 302–312.
30. Campiche, M., Gautier, A., Hernandez, E. I. and Reymond, A. (1963), "An Electron Microscope Study of the Fetal Development of Human Lung," *Pediatrics*, **32,** 976–994.
31. Chu, J., Clements, J. A., Cotton, E. K., Klaus, M. H., Sweet, A. Y. and Tooley, W. H. (1967) "Neonatal Pulmonary Ischaemia. 1: Clinical and Physiological Studies," *Pediatrics*, **40,** 709–782.
32. Churchill, E. D. (1952), *Obliterative Bronchitis and Bronchiectasis* (*The Alex-Simpson Smith Lecture*). London: Institute of Child Health.
33. CIBA Symposium (1970), *Breathing, Hering-Breuer Centenary Symposium* (Ruth Porter, Ed.). London: Churchill.
34. Clements, J., Platzker, A., Tierney, D., Hobel, C., Creasy, R., Margolis, A., Thibeault, D., Tooley, W. and Oh, W. (1972), "Assessment of the Risk of the Respiratory Distress Syndrome by a Rapid Test for Surfactant in Amniotic Fluid," *New Engl. J. Med.*, **286,** 1077–1081.
35. Congdon, E. D. (1922), "Transformation of the Aortic Arch System During the Development of the Human Embryo," *Contr. Embryol. Carneg. Instn.*, **14,** 47–112.
36. Corrin, B. (1970), "Phagocytic Potential of Pulmonary Alveolar Epithelium with Particular Reference to Surfactant Metabolism." *Thorax*, **25,** 110–115.
37. Davies, G. M. (1967), "Lymph-casts of the Bronchi," *Brit. J. Dis. Chest.*, **61,** 45–49.
38. Davies, G. M. and Reid, L. (1970), "Growth of the Alveoli and Pulmonary Arteries in Childhood," *Thorax*, **25,** 669–681.

39. Davies, G. M. and Reid, L. (1971), "Effect of Scoliosis on Growth of Alveoli and Pulmonary Arteries and on Right Ventricle," *Arch. Dis. Childh.*, **46,** 623–632.
40. Dawes, G. S., Mott, J. C., Widdicombe, J. G. and Wyatt, D. G. (1953). "Changes in the Lungs of the Newborn Lamb," *J. Physiol. (Lond.)*, **121,** 141–162.
41. De Lemos, R. A., Shermata, D. W., Knelson, J. H., Kotas, R. and Amery, M. E. (1970), "Acceleration of Appearance of Pulmonary Surfactant in the Fetal Lamb by Administration of Cortico-Steroid," *Amer. Rev. resp. Dis.*, **102**, 459–461.
42. Dubreuil, G., Lacoste, A. and Raymond, R. (1936), "Observations sur le développement du poumon humain," *Bull. Histol. Techn. physiol.*, **13,** 235–245.
43. Dunnill, M. S. (1962), "Postnatal Growth of the lung," *Thorax*, **17,** 329–333.
44. Elliott, F. M. (1964), *The Pulmonary Artery System in Normal and Diseased Lungs—Structure in relation to Pattern of Branching*. Ph.D. Thesis, University of London.
45. Elliott, F. W. and Reid, L. (1965), "Some New Facts about the Pulmonary Artery and its Branching Pattern," *Clin. Radiol.*, **16,** 193–198.
46. Emery, J. L. (1969), "Connective Tissue and Lymphatics," in *The Anatomy of the Developing Lung*, pp. 49–74 (J. L. Emery, ed.). London: Heinemann.
47. Emery, J. L. and Mithal, A. (1960), "The Number of Alveoli in the Terminal Respiratory Unit of Man During Late Intrauterine Life and Childhood," *Arch. Dis. Childh.*, **35,** 544–547.
48. Emery, J. L. and Mithal, A. (1969), "The Weight of the Lungs," in *The Anatomy of the Developing Lung*, pp. 203–209 (J. L. Emery, ed.). London: Heinemann.
49. Fulton, R. M., Hutchinson, E. C. and Jones, A. M. (1952), "Ventricular Weight in Cardiac Hypertrophy," *Brit. Heart J.*, **14,** 413–421.
50. Gandy, G., Jacobson, W. and Gairdner, D. (1970), "Hyaline Membrane Disease—I," *Arch. Dis. Childh.*, **45,** 289–310.
51. de Haller, R. (1969), "Development of Mucus-secreting Elements," in *The Anatomy of the Developing Lung*, pp. 94–115 (J. L. Emery, ed.). London: Heinemann.
52. Hamilton, W. J., Boyd, J. D. and Mossman, H. W. (1956), *Human Embryology*, 3rd edition. Cambridge: Heffer & Sons.
53. Harris, P. and Heath, D. (1962), *The Human Pulmonary Circulation*. Edinburgh: Livingstone.
54. von Hayek, H. (1960), *The Human Lung*. English translation by V. E. Krahl. New York: Hafner Publishing Co.
55. Hayward, J. and Reid, L. (1952a), "Observations on the Anatomy of the Intrasegmental Bronchial Tree," *Thorax*, **7,** 89–97.
56. Hayward, J. and Reid, L. (1952b), "The Cartilage of the Intra-Pulmonary Bronchi in Normal Lungs, in Bronchiectasis, and in Massive Collapse," *Thorax*, **7,** 98–110.
57. Heath, D. (1963), "Longitudinal Muscle in Pulmonary Arteries," *J. Path. Bact.*, **85,** 407–412.
58. Heath, D. (1969), "Pulmonary Vasculature in Postnatal Life and Pulmonary Haemodynamics," in *The Anatomy of the Developing Lung*, pp. 147–170 (J. L. Emery, ed.). London: Heinemann.
59. Henderson, R., Hislop, A. and Reid, L. (1971), "New Pathological Findings in Emphysema of Childhood. 3: Unilateral Congenital Emphysema with Hypoplasia, and Compensatory Emphysema of Contralateral Lobe," *Thorax*, **26,** 195–205.
60. Hilton, S. M. (1959), "A Peripheral Arterial Conducting Mechanism Underlying Dilatation of the Femoral Artery and Concerned in Functional Vasodilatation in Skeletal Muscle," *J. Physiol. (Lond.)*, **149,** 93–111.
61. Hislop, A. (1971), *The Fetal and Childhood Development of the Pulmonary Circulation and its Disturbance in Certain Types of Congenital Heart Disease*. Ph.D., London University.
62. Hislop, A. and Reid, L. (1970), "New Pathological Findings in Emphysema of Childhood. 1: Polyalveolar Lobe with Emphysema," *Thorax*, **25,** 682–690.
63. Hislop, A. and Reid, L. (1971), "New Pathological Findings in Emphysema of Childhood. 2: Overinflation of a Normal Lobe," *Thorax*, **26,** 190–194.
64. Hislop, A. and Reid, L. (1972a), "Intrapulmonary Arterial Development During Fetal Life—Branching Pattern and Structure," *J. Anat.* **113,** 35–48.
65. Hislop, A. and Reid, L. (1973c), "The Similarity of the Pulmonary Artery Branching System in Siblings," *Forensic Science*. In press.
66. Hislop, A. and Reid, L. (1973a), "Development of the Intrapulmonary Veins in Man—Branching Pattern and Structure," *Thorax*. In press.
67. Hislop, A. and Reid, L. (1972b), "Weight of the Left and Right Ventricle of the Heart During Fetal Life," *J. Clin. Path.*, **25,** 534–536.
68. Hislop, A. and Reid, L. (1973b), "Intrapulmonary Arterial Development During Childhood—Branching Pattern and Structure," *Thorax*. In press.
69. Hislop, A., Sanderson, M. and Reid, L. (1972), "Unilateral Congenital Dysplasia of Lung Associated with Vascular Anomalies," *Thorax*. In press.
70. Hislop, A., Muir, D. C. F., Jacobson, M., Simon, G. and Reid, L. (1972), "Postnatal Growth and Function of the Pre-Acinar Airways," *Thorax*, **27,** 265–274.
71. Horn, M. and Gregg, I. (1972), "Proceedings of 15th Aspen Conference," *Amer. Rev. resp. Dis.* In press.
72. Humphreys, P. W. and Strang, L. B. (1967), "Effects of Gestation and Prenatal Asphyxia on Pulmonary Surface Properties of the Foetal Rabbit," *J. Physiol. (Lond.)*, **192,** 53–62.
73. Humphreys, P. W., Norman, K. S., Reynolds, E. O. R. and Strang, L. B. (1967), "Pulmonary Lymph flow and the Uptake of Liquid from the Lungs of the Lamb at the Start of Breathing," *J. Physiol. (Lond.)*, **193,** 1–29.
74a. Hung, K. S., Hertweck, M. S. and Loosli, C. G. (1972), "Electron Microscopical Evidence for Innervation of Pneumonocyte in Mouse Lung," *Amer. Rev. resp. Dis.*, **105,** 1008–1009.
74b. Jeffery, P. and Reid, L. (1973), "Intra-epithelial Nerves in Normal Rat Airways—a Quantitative Electron Microscopic Study," *J. Anat.* In press.
75. Kato, M. and Staub, N. C. (1966), "Response of Small Pulmonary Arterioles to Unilobular Hypoxia and Hypercapnia," *Circulat. Res.*, **19,** 426–440.
76. Keen, E. N. (1955), "The Postnatal Development of Human Cardiac Ventricles," *J. Anat. (Lond.)*, **89,** 484–502.
77. Klionsky, B. and Wigglesworth, J. S. (1970), "Production of Experimental Models of Foetal Growth Retardation by Inhibition of DNA or Protein Synthesis," *Brit. J. exp. Path.*, **51,** 361–371.
78. Kikkawa, Y., Motoyama, E. K. and Gluck, L. (1968), "Study of the Lungs of Fetal and Newborn Rabbits," *Amer. J. Path.*, **52,** 177–209.
79. Kisch, B. (1955), "Electron Microscopic Investigations of the Lungs; Capillaries and Specific Cells," *Exp. Med. Surg.*, **13,** 101–117.
80. Kitagawa, M., Hislop, A., Boyden, E. A. and Reid, L. (1971), "Lung Hypoplasia in Congenital Diaphragmatic Hernia. A Quantitative Study of Airway, Artery and Alveolar Development," *Brit. J. Surg.*, **58,** 342–346.
81. Klaus, M., Reiss, O. K., Tooley, W. H., Piel, C. and Clements, J. A. (1962), "Alveolar Epithelium Cell Mitochondria as Source of the Surface Active Lung Lining," *Science*, **137,** 750–751.
82. Kohn, H. M. (1893), "Zur Histologie der indererenden fibrösen Pneumonie," *Münch. med. Wschr.*, **40,** 42–43.
83. Lamb, D. and Reid, L. (1972), "Acidic Glycoproteins Produced by the Mucous Cells of the Bronchial Submucosal Glands in the Fetus and Child: a Histochemical and Autoradiographic Study," *Brit. J. Dis. Chest.* **66,** 248–253.
84. Lambert H. W. (1955), "Accessory Bronchiole-alveolar Communications," *J. Path. Bact.*, **70,** 311–314.
85. Larroche, J. C., Nodot, A. and Minkowski, A. (1959), "Développement des artères et artérioles pulmonaires de la période foetale a la période néonatale," *Biol. Neonat. (Basel)*, **1,** 37–60.
86. Laurence, K. M. (1959), "Congenital Pulmonary Lymphanigectasis," *J. clin. Path.*, **12,** 62–69.

87. Lauweryns, J. M. and Peuskens, J. C. (1969), "Argyrophil (Kinin and Amine-Producing?) Cells in Human Infant Airway Epithelium," *Life Sci.*, **8,** 577–585.
88. Lauweryns, J. M. and Rosan, R. L. (1971), "The Unit Lobule: a Revised Concept of the Neonatal Lung," in *Proc. 2nd Europ. Congr. Perinatal Medicine*, pp. 259–263, London 1970. Basel: Karger.
89. Liggins, G. C. and Howie, R. N. (1972), "A Controlled Trial of Glucocorticoid Treatment for Prevention of Respiratory Distress Syndrome in Premature Infants," *Pediatrics*, **50,** 515–525.
90. Longacre, J. T. and Johansmann, R. (1940), "An Experimental Study of the Fate of the Remaining Lung Following Total Pneumonectomy," *J. thorac. Surg.*, **10,** 131–149.
91. Loosli, C. G. and Potter, E. L. (1951), "The Prenatal Development of the Human Lung," *Anat. Rec.*, **109,** 320–321.
92. Loosli, C. G. and Potter, E. L. (1959), "Pre- and Postnatal Development of the Respiratory Portion of the Human Lung," *Amer. Rev. resp. Dis.*, **80,** 5–23.
93. Louw, J. H. and Barnard, C. N. (1955), "Congenital Intestinal Atresia, Observations on its Origin," *Lancet*, **ii,** 1065.
94. Macleod, W. M. (1954), "Abnormal Transradiancy of One Lung," *Thorax*, **9,** 147–153.
95. Mead, J., Whittenberger, J. L. and Radford, E. P., Jr. (1957), "Surface Tension as a Factor in Pulmonary Volume Pressure Hysteresis," *J. appl. Physiol.*, **10,** 191–196.
96. Melmon, K. L., Cline, H. J., Hughes, T. and Nies, A. S. (1968), "Kinins: Possible Mediators of Neonatal Circulatory Changes in Man," *J. clin. Invest.*, **47,** 1295–1302.
97. Merkel, H. (1942), "Über verschluszfahige Bronchialarterien," *Virchow's Arch. path. Anat.*, **308,** 303–321.
98. Meyrick, B. and Reid, L. (1970), "The Alveolar Wall," *Brit. J. Dis. Chest.*, **64,** 121–140.
99. Meyrick, B. and Reid, L. (1971), "Nerves in Rat Intra-acinar Alveoli: an Electron Microscopic Study," *Resp. physiol.*, **11** 367–377.
100. Meyrick, B., Miller, J. and Reid, L. (1972), "The Effect of ANTU and Abnormal Oxygen Tension on the Alveolar Epithelial Cell., *Brit. J. exp. Path.*, **53,** 343–358.
101. Miller, W. J. (1947), *The Lung*, 2nd edition. Springfield: Thomas.
102. Naeye, R. L. (1966), "Development of Systemic and Pulmonary Arteries from Birth through Early Childhood," *Biol. Neonat. (Basel)*, **10,** 8–16.
103. Naeye, R. L. and Blanc, W. (1965), "Pathogenesis of Congenital Rubella," *J. Amer. Med. Ass.*, **194,** 1277–1283.
104. Paintal, A. S. (1970), "The Mechanics of Excitation of Type J Receptors, and the J Reflex," in *Breathing. Hering-Breuer Centenary Symposium*, pp. 59–76. CIBA Foundation. London: Churchill.
105. Parmentier, R. (1962), "L'aération, néonatale du poumon. Contribution expérimentale et anatomo-clinique," *Rev. belge Path.*, **29,** 123–244.
106. Patten, B. M. (1953), *Humam Embryology*, 2nd edition. New York: McGraw-Hill.
107. Pattle, R. E. (1955), "Properties, Function and Origin of the Alveolar Lining Layer," *Nature (Lond.)*, **175,** 1125–1126.
108. Potter, E. (1965), "Bilateral Absence of Ureters and Kidneys: a Report of 50 Cases," *Obstet. Gynec.*, **25,** 3–12.
109. Recavarren, S. and Arias-Stella, J. (1964), "Growth and Development of the Ventricular Myocradium from Birth to Adult Life," *Brit. Heart J.*, **26,** 186–192.
110. Redding, R. A., Douglas, W. H. J. and Stein, M. (1971), "Thyroid Hormone Influence upon Lung Surfactant Metabolism," *Science*, **175**, 994–996.
111. Reid, L. (1958), "Chronic Bronchitis and Hypersecretion of Mucus," *Lect. Sci. Basis Med.*, **8,** 235–255.
112. Reid, L. (1960), "Measurement of the Bronchial Mucous Gland Layer: a Diagnostic Yardstick in Chronic Bronchitis," *Thorax*, **15,** 132–141.
113. Reid, L. (1967), *The Pathology of Emphysema*. London: Lloyd-Luke (Medical Books) Ltd.
114. Reid, L. (1968), "Structural and Functional Reappraisal of the Pulmonary Artery System," in *The Scientific Basis of Medicine Annual Reviews*, pp. 289–307. London: The Athlone Press.
115. Reid, L. (1970), "Chronic Bronchitis—a Report on Mucus Research", *Proc. roy. Instn. G. B.*, **43,** 438–463.
116. Reid, L. and Hayward, J. (1949), "Cavernous Pulmonary Teliangiectasis," *Thorax*, **4,** 137–146.
117. Reid, L. and Meyrick, B. (1969), "Étude au microscope électronique due poumon foetale de lapin", *Poumon et le Coeur*, **25,** 201–206.
118. Reid, L. and Rubino, M. (1959), "The Connective Tissue Septa in the Foetal Human Lung," *Thorax*, **14,** 3–13.
119. Reid, L. and Simon, G. (1962), "Unilateral Lung Transradiancy," *Thorax*, **17,** 230–239.
120. Reid, L. and Simon, G. (1964), "The Role of Alveolar Hypoplasia in some Types of Emphysema," *Brit. J. Dis. Chest*, **58,** 158–168.
121. Reynolds, E. O., Jacobson, N., Motoyama, E. K., Kikkawa, Y., Craig, J. M., Orzalesi, M. and Cook, C. D. (1965), "The Effect of Immaturity and Prenatal Asphyxia on the Lung, and Pulmonary Function of Newborn Lambs: the Experimental Production of Respiratory Distress," *Pediatrics*, **35,** 382–392.
122. Robertson, B. (1967), "The Normal Intrapulmonary Arterial pattern of the Human Late Fetal and Neonatal Lung," *Acta paed. scand.*, **56,** 249–264.
123. Rowe, R. D. and James, L. S. (1957), "The Normal Pulmonary Arterial Pressure During the First Year of Life," *J. Pediat.*, **51,** 1–4.
124. Rudnick, D. (1933), "Developmental Capacities of the Chick Lung in Chorioallantoic Grafts," *J. exp. Zool.*, **66,** 125–154.
125. Ryland, D. and Reid, L. (1971), "Pulmonary Aplasia—a Quantitative Analysis of the Development of the Single Lung," *Thorax*, **26,** 602–609.
126. Samuelson, A., Becker, A. E. and Wagenvoort, C. A. (1970), "A Morphometric Study of Pulmonary Veins in Normal Infants and Infants with Congenital Heart Disease," *Arch. Path.*, **90,** 112–116.
127. Saunders, J. W. (1966), "Death in Embryonic Systems: Death of Cells in the Usual Accompaniment of Embryonic Growth and Differentiation," *Science*, **154,** 604–612.
128. Scarpelli, E. M. (1968), *The Surfactant System of the Lung*. Philadelphia: Lea and Febiger.
129. Schaefer, K. E., Avery, M. E. and Bensch K. (1964), "Time Course of Changes in Surface Tension and Morphology of Alveolar Epithelial Cells in CO_2 Induced Hyaline Membrane Disease," *J. clin. Invest.*, **43,** 2080–2093.
130. Shepard, T. J. (1969), "Growth and Development of the Human Embryo and Fetus," in *Endocrine and Genetic Diseases of Childhood*, Chap. 1 (L. I. Gardner, ed.). Philadelphia: Saunders.
131. Short, R. D. H. (1950), "Alveolar Epithelium in Relation to Growth of the Lung," *Phil. Trans. B.*, **235,** 35–86.
132. Simon, G., Connolly, N., Littlejohns, D. W. and McAllen, M. (1972), "Radiological Abnormalities in Children with Asthma and Their Relation to the Clinical Findings and Some Respiratory Function Tests," *Thorax*. In press.
133. Simon, G., Reid, L., Tanner, J. M., Goldstein, H. and Benjamin, B. (1972), "Growth of Radiologically Determined Heart Diameter, Lung Width and Lung Length from 5–19 years with Standards for Clinical Use," *Arch. Dis. Childh.*, **47,** 373–382.
134. Smiley, R. H., Jaques, W. E. and Campbell, G. S. (1966), "Pulmonary Vascular Change in Lung Lobes with Reversed Pulmonary Blood Flow," *Surgery*, **59,** 529–533.
135. Sorokin, S. (1965), "Recent Work on Developing Lungs," in *Organogenesis*, pp. 467–491 (R. L. de Haar and H. Ursprung, eds.). New York: Holt.
136. Sorokin S. (1967) "A Morphologic and Cytochemical Study on the Great Alveolar Cell," *J. Histochem. Cytochem.*, **14,** 884–897.
137. Staub, N. C. (1961), "Gas Exchange Vessels in the Cat Lung," *Fed. Proc.*, **20,** 107.
138. Spencer, H. and Leof, D. (1964), "The Innervation of the Human Lung," *J. Anat. (Lond.)*, **98,** 599–609.
139. Strang, L. B. (1967), "Uptake of Liquid from the Lungs at the

Start of Breathing," in *Development of the Lung*, pp. 348–375. (A. V. S. de Reuck and R. Porter, eds.). CIBA Symposium. London: Churchill.

140. Streeter, G. L. (1948), "Developmental Horizons in Human Embryos: Description of Age Groups XV, XVI, XVII and XVIII, being the Third Issue of a Survey of the Carnegie Collection," *Contr. Embryol. Carneg. Instn.*, **32,** 133–203.
141. Tanimura, T., Nelson, T., Hollingsworth, E. R. and Shepard, T. H. (1971), "Weight Standards for Organs from Early Human Fetuses," *Anat. Rec.*, **171,** 227–236.
142. Tanner, J. M. (1962), *Growth at Adolescence*, 2nd edition. Oxford: Blackwell.
143. Tanner, J. M. (1968), *Education and Physical Growth*. London: University of London Press.
144. Tobin, C. E. (1957), "Human Pulmonic Lymphatics; An Anatomic Study," *Anat. Rec.*, **127,** 611–633.
145. Tobin, C. E. (1966), "Arteriovenous Shunts in the Peripheral Pulmonary Circulation in the Human Lung," *Thorax*, **21,** 197–204.
146. Trapnell, D. H. (1964), "Recognition and Incidence of Intrapulmonary Lymph Nodes," *Thorax*, **19,** 44–50.
147. Wagenvoort, C. A. and Wagenvoort, N. (1967), "Arterial Anastomoses Bronchopulmonary Arteries and Pulmobronchial Arteries in Perinatal Lungs," *Lab. Invest.*, **16,** 13–24.
148. Wagenvoort, C. A., Neufeld, H. N. and Edwards, J. E. (1961), "The Structure of the Pulmonary Arterial Tree in Fetal and Early Antenatal Life," *Lab. Invest.*, **10,** 751–671.
149. Wang, N. S., Kotas, R. V., Avery, M. E. and Thurlbeck, W. M. (1971), "Accelerated Appearance of Osmiophilic Bodies in Fetal Lungs Following Steroid Injections," *J. appl. Physiol.*, **30,** 362–365.
150. Weibel, E. (1963), *Morphometry of the Human Lung*. Berlin: Springer-Verlag.
151. Wells, L. J. and Boyden, E. A. (1954), "The Development of the Bronchopulmonary Segments in Human Embryos of Horizons XVII to XIX," *Amer. J. Anat.*, **95,** 163–201.
152. Wilson, H. G. and Mikity, V. G. (1960), "A New Form of Respiratory Disease in Premature Infants," *Amer. J. Dis. Child.*, **99,** 489–499.
153. Wilson, J. G. and Warkany, J. (1949), "Aortic Arch and Cardiac Anomalies in the Offspring of Vitamin A Deficient Rats," *Amer. J. Anat.*, **85,** 113–155.

14B. GROWTH AND DEVELOPMENT OF THE RESPIRATORY SYSTEM

Functional Development

SIMON GODFREY

Man begins his existence as an aquatic parasite living in a stable, friendly environment. Quite suddenly he is ejected into the air and must thereafter rapidly adapt his physiology to that of a terrestrial mammal. This involves a drastic redirecting of his regional blood flow and the calling into service of his lungs which have so far been semi-collapsed, fluid filled sacks. From this time on, the function of the respiratory system has to keep pace with the growth of the body which increases its weight some 23 fold and its O_2 consumption some 10 fold. The maximum performance during severe exercise in an adult athlete may well require a 300 fold increase in ventilation and a 240 fold increase in oxygen uptake compared with that of the resting newborn infant. It should be clear from these figures that good development of pulmonary function is essential throughout childhood.

The Scope of Respiratory Function

Respiratory physiology can be conveniently divided into several interrelated subjects. Essentially there are four processes to be considered.

(a) The lungs as gas pumps

In order to enable gas to be exchanged, the lungs must form an effective pump for transporting gas to and from the alveoli. Such a pump has certain characteristics such as volume, stiffness and resistance which determine its efficiency and the effort needed to make it work.

(b) Gas exchange in the lungs

It is obviously essential that the gas ventilating the lungs should come into contact with the blood perfusing them so that O_2 and CO_2 can be exchanged. The process is complicated in mammals because the pump is of the bellows type and this means that some of the inspired gas remains in the conducting airways and is wasted. Moreover, some of the alveoli may get more than their fair share of ventilation and others may have proportionately too much blood flow. This process of ventilation-perfusion imbalance can render respiration inefficient. Alveolar O_2 has to diffuse through several different tissues until it finally reaches the haemoglobin molecules in the red blood cells and this diffusion process must also be considered.

(c) Gas transport in the blood

Respiratory physiology does not end with gas transfer in the lungs and it is important to consider how O_2 and CO_2 are carried in the blood and how the acid-base balance of the body is regulated. The transport of O_2 depends on the quantity and quality of the haemoglobin as well as on the CO_2 tension (P_{CO_2}) and pH of the blood. CO_2 transport depends upon the buffering capacity of haemoglobin and other proteins as well as on the level of O_2 saturation. It is not always realised that the lungs are the chief portal of excretion of acid by the body in the form of CO_2 and that the minute to minute regulation of pH is part of respiratory function. Gas exchange in the tissues is also a concern of respiration but relatively little is known about it and it is rarely disturbed even in disease.

(d) Control of breathing

The complex functioning of the mechanical and chemical aspects of respiration would be impossible without an adequate regulatory system. This is provided by a series of interlinked chemical and mechanical reflexes which aim to maintain the blood gases and pH within reasonable limits while utilising the lungs, diaphragm and chest wall in the most economical fashion. This control system must undergo an amazing reorganisation at birth when, in the space of a few seconds, it totally changes its setting. Thus blood gas tensions which are known to stimulate the newborn infant to vigorous respiration have no effect on the full term fetus. Apart from this sudden change at birth, the control system must adapt throughout childhood to the continuously changing mechanical properties of the respiratory system and the metabolic needs of the body.

For reasons which will become apparent, it is convenient to consider these aspects of respiratory physiology at three distinct phases of development. In the fetus, the chief problem is that of living "up a mountain in a cloud of CO_2" i.e. the problem of hypoxia and hypercapnia. In the newborn, the chief problem is the sudden transition from the fetal state. During the rest of childhood, the problem is essentially one of ordered growth to keep pace with the needs of the body.

Respiratory Function During Fetal Life

During fetal life all the functions of the lungs for gas exchange and acid-base balance are served by the placenta and the reader is referred to the monograph of Dawes[34] for a fuller consideration of these aspects of placental function. It is interesting to note however, that the placenta does not function simply like the gills of a fish, but the ventilation-perfusion relationships of the lungs to be considered later have their counterpart in the matching of fetal and maternal blood. The net result of placental gas exchange is such that the fetal O_2 tension (PO_2) remains reasonably constant and more or less independent of the maternal level.[21] It is against this background that one must observe the development of the lungs which must prepare them to be able to take over full respiratory function by about 65 per cent of the way through the normal gestation period in man.

(a) Mechanical function in fetal life

The growth and development of lung structure during fetal life is considered in Chapter 14A. The total complement of airways and blood vessels are developed by the 16th week of gestation in man but few alveoli are present even at term. The terminal airways however, are fully capable of acting as gas exchanging areas. Perhaps the most important structural event, because of its functional implications, is the appearance of osmophilic lamellated bodies in the Type II alveolar lining cells at about the 24th week of gestation. These granules almost certainly represent the precursor of surfactant—the lipoprotein complex which has the property of lowering the surface tension in the fluid film which lines the alveoli once the lungs are aerated ([72]; see Chapter 14A).

During fetal life the lungs are fluid-filled and there is no gas fluid interface. However, although the respiratory muscles can and do contract vigorously from an early stage of gestation[6,85] they cannot move much fluid in and out because of the large frictional forces. Such movements are not important for gas exchange but are an essential rehearsal for post-natal life. There has been considerable discussion on whether such movements were more apparent in early gestation than later and indeed whether they occurred at all in the normal state or were merely produced by asphyxia in animal experiments. Some recent studies in pregnant sheep and women using ultra-sound have now shown that respiratory movements are a normal feature throughout fetal life.[12,35]

The development of surfactant precursors in the alveolar lining cells has its counterpart in the mechanical properties of the fetal lungs. Before about 28 to 32 weeks of gestation the lungs are unable to retain gas within them after inflation and they collapse completely.[82] This is because the pressure within a bubble required to prevent its collapse due to surface tension is inversely proportional to its radius. The radii of the terminal lung units ("alveoli") are very small and therefore the collapsing forces are correspondingly high. Moreover, as the lungs deflate, the radii are further reduced and the collapsing forces are correspondingly increased. The stability of the lungs after about the 28th week of gestation in man is due to the presence of surfactant which has two very important properties. In the first place it is a surface tension-lowering agent. In the second place, surfactant has the interesting property of increasing its activity as its surface area is reduced. The presence of surfactant therefore lowers the surface tension so that gas can be retained in the lungs. It also stabilises them because, as the surface area of the film enlarges during inspiration, the surface tension tends to rise, while as the surface area decreases during expiration the surface tension tends to fall.

The changes in surface activity in the developing lungs of the lamb are illustrated in Fig. 1 taken from the work of Reynolds and Strang.[82] The upper loops relate the volume of gas in the lungs to the pressure applied at the mouth during inflation and deflation and the lower loops relate the surface tension of lung extracts to the surface area of the film during expansion and compression. The left hand pair of

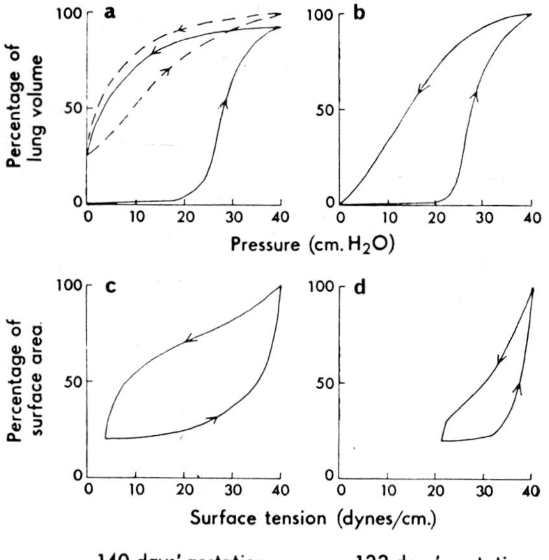

FIG. 1. Loops constructed by plotting lung volume against the pressure required to cause stepwise inflation and deflation of mature (a) and immature (b) fetal lamb lungs. The line represents the first breath and the dotted line in (a) represents subsequent breaths. Both loops are identical in (b). Similar loops for the relation between surface tension and the area of a film of lung extract are shown below for mature (c) and immature (d) fetal lambs. From Reynolds and Strange.[82]

loops refer to a mature fetal lamb and the right hand loops to an immature (non-viable) fetal lamb. The initial inflation of the lungs of the mature animal required a large pressure because they were collapsed and fluid filled at the start, but during deflation the lungs remained much more inflated and subsequent inflations required very little pressure. In the immature animal a similar initial inflating pressure was required, but on deflation the lungs collapsed completely and each subsequent inflation required the same high pressure as the first. These differences are reflected in the behaviour of the lung extracts which show that the surface tension was much lower in the sample from the mature animal especially at low surface areas during shrinkage. The difference in behaviour of the lungs and the extracts is due to the presence of much larger quantities of surfactant in the mature fetus.

Although surfactant can be detected in lung extracts from human fetuses as early as the 23rd week, the quantity increases greatly towards term. This is one of the important reasons for the older fetus having a greater chance of surviving in air. However complete organogenesis may be, the factor which seems to determine viability is the quantity (and probably the quality) of surfactant which is present. Deficiency of surfactant gives rise to the respiratory distress syndrome with the appearance of hyaline membranes. Avery and Mead[4] measured surface tensions in lung extract from infants, children and adults dying from various causes and found the mean value for adults, children and infants with a birth weight of 1200 g or more to be approximately 7·2 dynes/cm. Infants of birth weight lower than 1200 g had a mean surface tension of 26 dynes/cm and infants with hyaline membrane disease weighing between 1,260 and 3,300 g had a mean surface tension of 30 dynes/cm. The high incidence of the respiratory distress syndrome in premature infants is presumably due to their low initial concentrations of surfactant but the deciding factor which determines whether a particular premature infant develops the syndrome is probably asphyxial damage before or during birth.

Recently, there has been increasing interest in the detection of surfactant in amniotic fluid, where it has presumably been derived from the lungs. Bogwanani, Fahmy and Turnbull[11] estimated lecithin levels in amniotic fluid aspirated at various stages of gestation in women. They found that levels below 3·5 mg/100 ml immediately before delivery were very likely to be associated with the respiratory distress syndrome in the infant. Serial sampling showed little change in lecithin level before 30 weeks gestation and then a rapid rise, except in those infants who subsequently developed respiratory distress.

The mechanical aspects of pulmonary function during fetal life are thus concerned with the training of the respiratory muscles and the preparation of the lungs for inflation with air by the development of surfactant.

(b) Gas transfer in the fetal lung

Unlike other aspects of pulmonary physiology, almost nothing is known of the way in which the gas transfer capacity of the lungs develops. The structural basis of gas transfer lies in the development of the "alveolar capillary membrane" which consists of a double layer of cells separated by a basement membrane (see Chapter 14A). The development of terminal airways, a few alveoli and their accompanying small blood vessels is completed early on in gestation so that one would expect diffusion to be possible across the membrane. The only information available is about the composition of the fluid which fills the lungs in fetal life. It has been found that this does not have the same composition as the blood in the pulmonary capillaries or the amniotic fluid.[1] The $P\text{CO}_2$ is intermediate between that in blood and amniotic fluid while the pH is lower than in both. There are other differences in electrolyte and solute concentrations which suggest that the lung fluid is actually elaborated in the lungs and is not in simple equilibrium with blood, lymph or amniotic fluid. This does not of course mean that diffusion cannot occur across the foetal alveolar-capillary membrane but merely that it is only one of the factors contributing to lung fluid composition.

(c) Gas transport in fetal life

In contrast to the scanty knowledge of gas transfer in the fetus, there is a great deal of information available about the transport of gases in the fetal blood. Before birth the data is predominantly from animal work but this is one of the many areas in which there is relatively little species variation and the results can therefore be extrapolated to the human fetus.

Carbon dioxide tension (Pco_2) is known to fall in maternal arterial blood throughout pregnancy from about 35·5 mmHg at the 10th week to about 28 mmHg at term.[63] There is a small rise in maternal arterial oxygen tension (PO_2) but it remains in the region of 90 mmHg. The maternal pH in healthy women remains about 7·47 and the lower values given for animals are probably due to the experimental situation. In the healthy fetal monkey, umbilical venous Pco_2 is about 15 mmHg higher than in the maternal artery while the PO_2 is about 80 mmHg lower.[10] The fetal pH is about 0·12 units lower than that of the mother. The fetal Pco_2 closely follows that of the mother,[34] but the fetal PO_2 does not vary to anything like the same extent as that of the mother. Thus Behrman *et al.*[10] raised the maternal PO_2 by 150 mmHg but that of the fetus only rose by 8 mmHg. Conversely, a considerable fall in maternal PO_2 will have relatively little effect on the fetus which is thus protected against sudden fluctuations in PO_2. These maternal-fetal blood gas differences are also reflected in the differences across the placenta from afferent vessel (maternal artery or umbilical artery) to efferent vessel (maternal vein or umbilical vein). The maternal transplacental Pco_2 difference is about 10 mmHg and that of the fetus is about 5 mmHg, but the maternal PO_2 difference is about 70 mmHg while that of the fetus is only some 7 mmHg. These tension differences for O_2 and CO_2 can best be understood from a study of their dissociation curves in the fetus and mother since that for CO_2 is almost linear and the same in both bloods, while that for O_2 is sigmoid and different in fetal and maternal blood.

In order that the fetus should be able to carry an adequate amount of O_2 around the body in the presence of a relatively low PO_2, there is a difference in the O_2 dissociation curve and an increase in the haemoglobin concentration to some 16–18 g/100 ml. The haemoglobin during fetal life is predominantly of the foetal haemoglobin (HbF) type; towards the latter part of gestation some adult type haemoglobin (HbA) is made and by term only some 68 per cent of the haemoglobin is HbF.[9] Total replacement of HbF by HbA does not occur until some 3 months after birth.

Fetal blood has a greater affinity for O_2 than adult blood in almost all species studied, including fish, amphibians and birds. Man is no exception and the extent of the alteration in the O_2 dissociation curve was well documented by Darling, Smith, Asmussen and Cohen.[33] The results of their studies is shown in Fig. 2. One method of expressing the position of the dissociation curve is to measure the PO_2 at which the blood is 50 per cent saturated—the P_{50}. Most observers agree that the maternal P_{50} is about 28 mmHg while that of the fetus at term is about 23 mmHg, i.e. the fetal blood is half saturated at a lower PO_2 than maternal blood. The P_{50} in the pregnant woman is actually slightly higher than in the non-pregnant women and men (26 mmHg).

The cause of the difference in O_2 affinity between fetal and maternal blood was ascribed for many years to the presence of HbF. However, this rather cosy idea was rudely shattered by the work of Allen, Wyman and Smith[2] who found that solutions of HbF and HbA had identical P_{50} values after dialysis. They suggested that the differences in fetal and maternal dissociation curves was not due to the nature of the Hb itself, but rather to the surrounding medium. Recent work has very largely clarified the situation with the discovery that the substance 2-3-diphosphoglycerate (2-3-DPG) has the property of lowering the O_2 affinity of the haemoglobin molecule and can be eluted from blood haemolysates by dialysis. In a very elegant study Bauer *et al.* (1969) prepared haemolysates and dialysates of human fetal and adult blood to which they added 2-3-DPG. Their results are summarised in Table 1, which shows that haemolysis alone

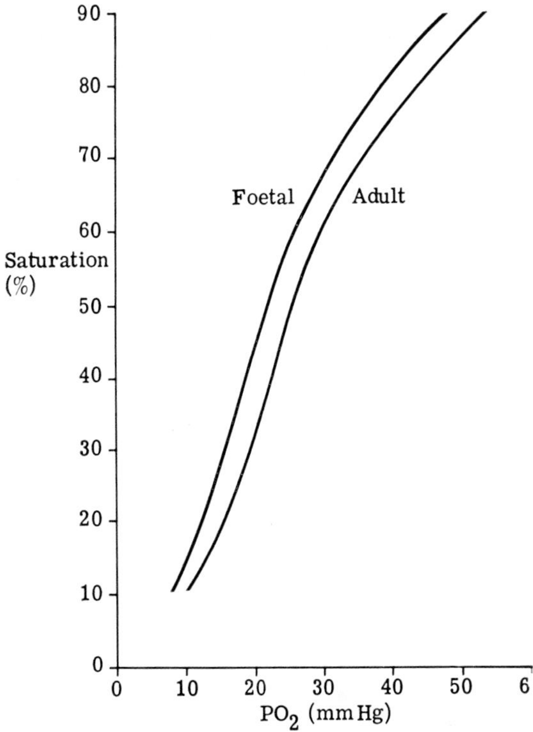

FIG. 2. Oxygen dissociation curves for fetal and adult blood. From Darling *et al.*[33]

somewhat increased the O_2 affinity of all types of blood, but dialysis removed 2-3-DPG and increased the O_2 affinity further to exactly the same level in fetal and maternal blood. The addition of equal amounts of 2-3-DPG to these dialysates virtually restored the O_2 affinities to those which existed in whole blood. Together with the finding that the absolute levels of 2-3-DPG are rather higher in fetal blood than adult blood, this suggests that the fetal haemoglobin is actually rather less sensitive to its depressing effect on O_2 affinity. In some ways then we have now come full circle to the conclusion that it really is the HbF molecule which is important because of its insensitivity to 2-3-DPG.

The increased O_2 affinity of fetal blood means that much more O_2 can be loaded on to the Hb molecules in the placenta at the relatively low PO_2 tension which exists there. This loading process is aided by the Bohr effect which shifts the whole O_2 dissociation curve to the left (more affinity) when CO_2 is unloaded into the placenta. However, the relative acidosis of fetal umbilical venous blood and alkalosis of maternal arterial blood (see above) actually tends to reduce the differences in O_2 affinity between them because of this

TABLE 1

	Controls	Pregnant Women	Infants at Birth
Haemoglobin (g./100 ml.)	15·1 ±1·2	12·8 ±1·0	16·1 ±1·0
2·3 DPG (μ moles/g. Hb.)	17·8 ±4·0	19·7 ±4.6	24·2 ±5·1
P50 (mm. Hg.)			
Whole Blood	26·1 ±0·6	30·5 ±0·9	22·9 ±2·5
Haemolysed Blood	24·3 ±0·6	26·4 ±1·0	22·8 ±2·7
Haemolysed and Dialysed Blood	19·1 ±0·9	19·7 ±1·3	19·7 ±0·9
Haemolysed, Dialysed and 30 μ moles 2·3 DPG added per gm. Hb.	28·8 ±0·6	29·4 ±1·5	22·4 ±1·4

Values for haemoglobin, 2·3 DPG concentration and the PO_2 for 50 per cent saturation in control blood from adults of both sexes, from pregnant women and from infants at delivery. Results from the study by Bauer *et al.*[9]

same Bohr effect, though a calculation of the reduction shows it to be very small. It might be thought that the great O_2 affinity of fetal blood would hinder the release of O_2 in the fetal tissues, but the simultaneous uptake of CO_2 shifts the dissociation curve to the right (less affinity) and the steepness of the curve as well as the very low tissue PO_2 (about 15 mmHg) ensures adequate O_2 delivery. The steepness of the fetal O_2 dissociation curve and its position are advantageous for normal fetal gas exchange but mean that the fetus is in danger of severe O_2 deprivation if the PO_2 falls due to premature separation of the placenta or other mechanisms causing birth asphyxia. No amount of O_2 given to the mother can help this problem, but even a modest increase of PO_2 as a result of other resuscitative measures will be very useful.

(d) Control of breathing in the fetus

During fetal life, the mechanical and chemical aspects of breathing are so perfected that by 24–26 weeks of gestation the fetus could certainly breathe if it were born. The interesting question is why does it not do so, since the level of hypoxia and hypercapnia in which it lives would be enough to make the same infant breathe furiously after birth? For some time it has been considered that the centres controlling breathing went through a period of relative insensitivity during the latter part of gestation.[6,7] More recently Purves and Biscoe[79] found little increase in activity in the sinus nerve coming from the carotid body of a fetal lamb exposed to low PO_2. It is thus possible that the reason why the fetus does not begin to breathe *in utero* is that the chemoreceptors are set at a lower level.

In contrast to this comparative inactivity of the chemoreceptors *in utero*, the infant responds very vigorously to asphyxial stimuli at birth. The mechanism of the onset of respiration is almost certainly multifactorial and chemical changes are but one aspect. The changes which occur at birth are discussed more fully in Chapter 7. In the present context it is worth noting that the setting of the chemoreceptors appears to change quite suddenly at birth. The new sensitivity to stimuli and the interaction between O_2 and CO_2 was very clearly demonstrated by Pagtakhan, Faridy

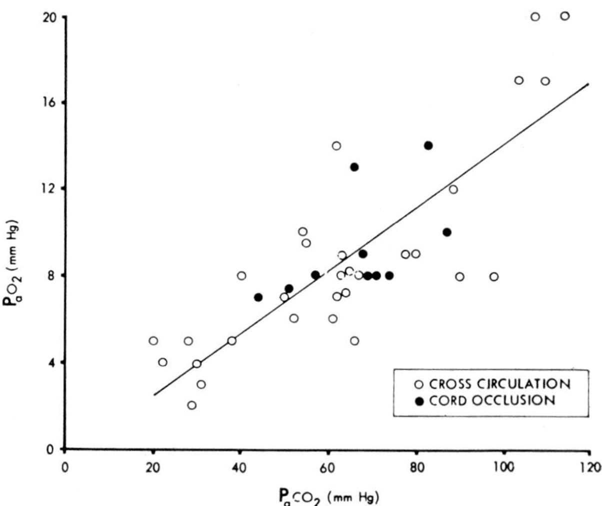

FIG. 3. Oxygen and carbon dioxide tensions at the onset of respiration in cord clamping and cross-perfusion experiments in fetal lambs. By contrast, the normal fetal PCO_2 would be about 50 mm Hg and the PO_2 would be about 15 mm Hg. This point lies well above the line and would not therefore be expected to initiate respiration. From Pagtakhan *et al.*[71]

and Chernik[71] who conducted cross-perfusion experiments in fetal lambs. They showed that placental occlusion did not initiate respiration if the fetal blood gases were maintained at the normal (fetal) level, but that hypoxia, hypercapnia, or various combinations of these stimuli could cause the animal to start breathing (Fig. 3). The sudden change in chemosensitivity at birth may be explained by the increase in sympathetic activity which occurs when the cord is clamped.[79] Such an increase could affect the blood flow through the carotid bodies and hence alter their setting.

Because of practical difficulties, very little is known of the development of the mechanical reflexes controlling breathing during fetal life. However, fetal and newborn rabbits behave in almost identical fashions when asphyxiated in terms of their respiratory and circulatory responses.[43,44] It would be interesting to record from the vagus in a fetal animal maintained apnoeic by cross-perfusion during inflation of the lungs with saline.

Respiratory Function in the Newborn

At birth the function of the placenta ceases and gas exchange begins through the lungs. This involves great alterations in the flow of gas and blood through the lungs and in the closure of various fetal vascular channels. These changes are described much more fully in Chapter 7 and we can now consider the function of the respiratory system in the first few hours and days after birth. In fact a considerable amount of information is available about neonatal respiratory physiology, not only because it is interesting to compare the newborn with the fetus, but also because the newborn infant can be induced to put up with measurements which no toddler would tolerate.

(a) **Mechanical function in the newborn**

Before the first breath the lungs are filled with fluid and this has to be replaced by air. The exact mechanism of this process is not certain, but some fluid is undoubtedly extruded from the mouth as can be seen from the radiographs of Karlberg[53] and of Lind, Stern and Wegelius.[61] The rest is probably absorbed into pulmonary lymphatics (see below). The physiological changes accompanying the first breath in man have been recorded in a remarkable series of observations by Karlberg, Koch and their colleagues using a face mask and an oesophageal cannula.[54] They found that the first breath was some 30–40 ml in size and it required a negative intrathoracic pressure of up to −40 to −100 cm H_2O to produce it.[55] This pressure is some 14 times that required to produce breaths of a similar size later on. It is required for the initial opening of the terminal airways (*see* Fig. 1) and also because the lungs are relatively stiff, i.e. their compliance (volume change for unit pressure change) is relatively low. Over the next few hours there is an increase in compliance from about 1·5 ml/cmH_2O to about 6 ml/cmH_2O and a tidal volume of 20–30 ml is established for which pressures of only some −5 cmH_2O are needed. At the same time the resistance to flow of gas through the airways also decreases from about 90 cmH_2O/1/sec in the first minute to about 25 cmH_2O/1/sec by the end of the first day.[56]

The very striking changes in mechanical properties of the lungs during the first few hours of life could be explained on the basis of either a true change in the properties of the tissues, or on the basis of a change in resting lung volume (thoracic gas volume, T.G.V.). This will be understood by considering the patient who has had a pneumonectomy. The remaining lung has not changed its compliance, but an intrathoracic pressure of −5 cmH_2O would only produce half the previous volume change, and the apparent compliance has fallen to half. In a study of 10 normal infants at various ages between 2 hours and 13 days, Auld, Nelson, Cherry, Rudolph and Smith[3] actually measured T.G.V. by the application of Boyles's law in a whole body plethysmograph.[40] They found very little change in T.G.V. (approximately 90 ml) after the first breath over the period studied and it seems that the increase in compliance and fall in resistance must be due to a true change in mechanical properties of the lungs. In fact, both changes could be explained by a continuing absorption of fluid from the lungs because most change occurs in the first 24 hours when the flow of lymph from the lungs is still very high.[13] A summary of the changes in the first 24 hours based on the work described above, is given in Fig. 4.

We can now consider the more extensive data on the mechanical behaviour of the lungs in the first few weeks of life. Since the infant is growing rapidly at this time, it is

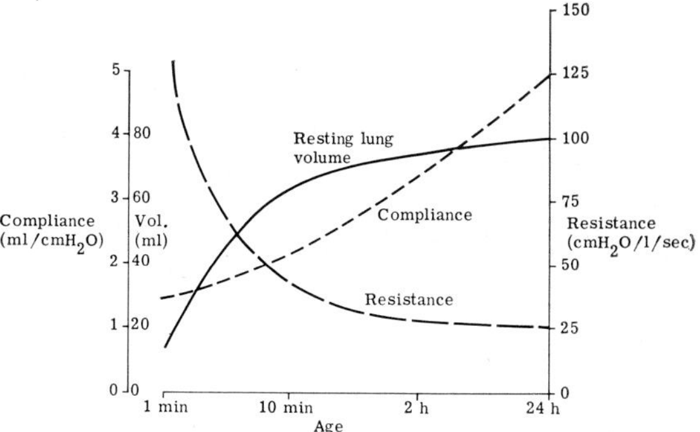

FIG. 4. Changes in the mechanical properties of the lungs expressed on a logarithmic scale during the first day of life. The source references for this and similar composite figures are given in the text.

necessary to take size into acount. One may note at this point that certain methods of expressing size have become traditional, e.g. "per Kg", "per cm" or "per m²", but not all methods are necessarily meaningful in this context, because unless the graph of the dependent variable (e.g. lung volume) against the independent variable (e.g. surface area) is linear and actually passes through zero, the ratio of dependent to independent (volume to area) will change with size.

The most important advance in the study of lung mechanics in the newborn was the development by Cross[24] of the whole body infant plethysmograph. This consists of a small chamber in which the infant lies breathing air from outside the box. A seal is placed around the whole face or around just the nose and mouth so that changes in lung volume as the infant breathes are reflected in changes in pressure within the box. Cross[24] studied 26 normal newborn infants in the first 13 days of life and Cross and Oppe[26] studied a further 30 premature infants (mean weight 1·97 Kg). The results of these two studies have been combined in Fig. 5 to show the

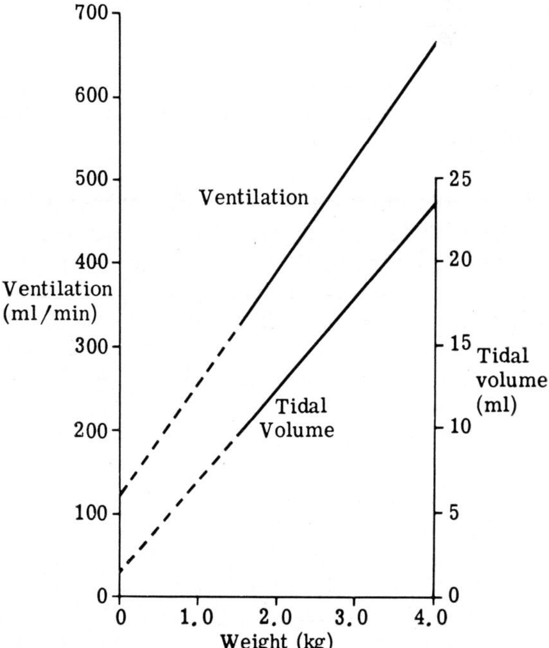

FIG. 5. Relationship between minute ventilation, tidal volume and weight in newborn infants.

relationship between tidal volume (volume of one breath), minute ventilation (total volume breathed per minute) and body weight. This graph shows that the tidal volume of the average 3 Kg infant is about 19 ml and its minute ventilation is about 530 ml/min and hence its frequency of breathing is about 28 breaths/min. Although there is a small intercept on the vertical axis, tidal volume may reasonably be predicted (in ml) as 6 times body weight (in Kg). These values have been amply confirmed by more recent studies, a selection of which are given in Table 2.

TABLE 2

Tidal Volume (ml.)	
Cook *et al.*[22]	16·0
Strang[86]	18·0
Doershuk and Matthews[38]	25·0
Koch[59]	16·6
Minute Ventilation (ml./min.)	
Cook *et al.*[22]	601
Nelson *et al.*[68]	605
Strang[86]	750
Koch[59]	632
Resting Lung Volume (ml.)	
Auld *et al.*[3]	85
Chu *et al.*[18]	115
Doershuk and Matthews[38]	90
Howlett[51a]	142
Pulmonary Compliance (ml./cm. H_2O)	
Cook *et al.*[22]	5·2
Chu *et al.*[18]	6·2
Polgar and String[75]	6·0
Howlett[51a]	8·8
Total Pulmonary Resistance including Nose (cm. H_2O/1/sec.)	
Cook *et al.*[22]	29·0
Swyer[89]	26·0
Polgar and String[75]	34·0
Howlett[51a]	20·6

Average values for pulmonary mechanics in newborn infants. Those studied by Howlett[51a] were rather older than the others but her results agree with the rest in relation to size.

Resting lung volume in the newborn infant has been measured either with the plethysmographic technique mentioned earlier, or else by the dilution of inert gases. The former method is more reliable and gives highly reproduceable results if performed carefully. The results of one such study on 24 normal infants carried out by Dr. Geraldine Howlett in the author's department are shown in Fig. 6. The small intercept on the volume axis means that resting lung volume (in ml) can be predicted as 35·5 times the body weight (in Kg) over the range studied. This compares well with the other studies in Table 2. Attempts have been made to calculate the total lung capacity of the newborn infant by stimulating him to cry and adding the volume of a cry, the crying vital capacity,[88] to the resting lung volume. Such calculations can only give approximate results, but they suggest that the total lung capacity of the newborn infant is about 63 ml/kg.[3]

The compliance of the lungs can be measured by dividing the tidal volume by the change in trans-pulmonary pressure

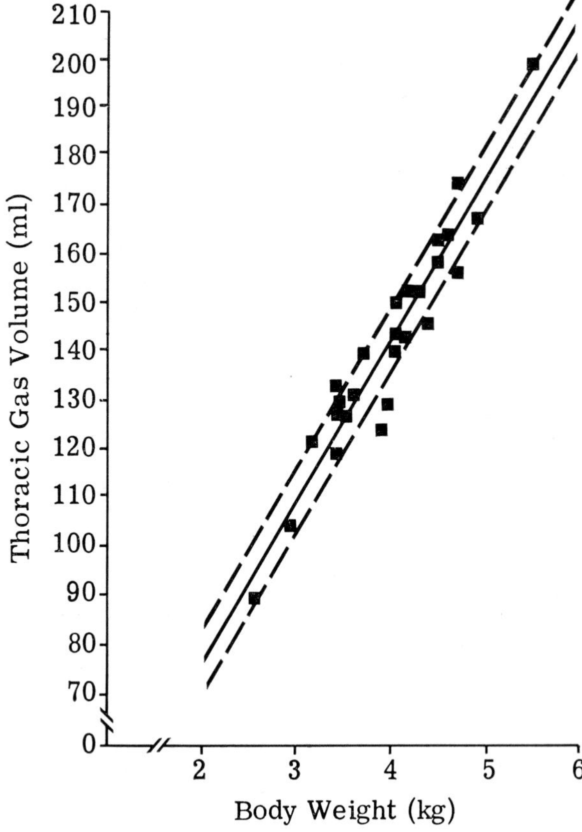

FIG. 6. Relationship between thoracic gas volume (resting lung volume or functional residual capacity) and weight in a group of newborn infants. From Howlett.[51a]

when there is no gas flowing, i.e. the difference in transpulmonary pressure between the end of inspiration and the end of expiration. The transpulmonary pressure is conveniently measured between a balloon in the oesophagus and atmospheric pressure at the mouth. As mentioned above, there is a close relationship between compliance and lung volume and the relationship for the infants studied by Dr. Howlett is shown in Fig. 7. The absolute value for the pulmonary

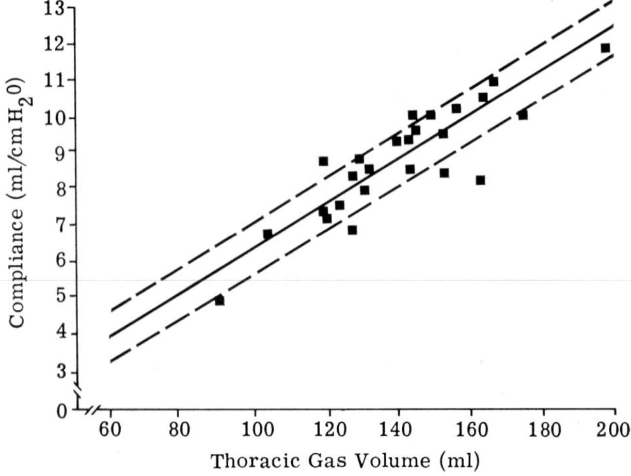

FIG. 7. Relationship between compliance of the lungs and thoracic gas volume in a group of newborn infants.[51a]

compliance of the newborn infant is about 6 ml/cmH_2O (Table 2) and the specific compliance (compliance/T.G.V.) from the data shown in Fig. 7 is 0·062 ml/cmH_2O/ml. The specific compliance of an adult is about 0·08 ml/cmH_2O/ml. The chest wall, too, is an elastic structure with a compliance which can be measured by relating change in chest volume to oesophageal pressure during artificial ventilation in the paralysed subject. Such measurements by Nightingale and Richards[69] suggest that the compliance of the lungs together with the chest wall in parallel is about 5 ml/cmH_2O in the newborn infant, and hence the compliance of the chest wall alone must be 30 ml/cmH_2O or 5 times that of the lungs alone, because

$$\frac{1}{\text{total compliance}} = \frac{1}{\text{lung compliance}} + \frac{1}{\text{wall compliance}}$$

Thus if the lungs and chest wall increase their volume by 30 ml, the total elastic pressure change will be 6 cmH_2O. Now, the lungs alone require 5 cmH_2O to expand 30 ml, hence only 1 cmH_2O is required to expand the chest wall by 30 ml, and the compliance of the chest wall is therefore 30 ml/cmH_2O. It would seem therefore that the chest wall of the newborn infant is a highly compliant structure and is relatively much more compliant than in the adult in whom pulmonary and chest wall compliance are about the same.[23]

Resistance is driving force divided by flow rate, whether for water, electricity or gas. In the lung the driving pressure is related to the flow rate of gas from the airway. The site of pressure recording determines which resistance is measured, i.e. if alveolar pressure is related to flow then the airway resistance is measured, but if oesophageal pressure is related to flow then pulmonary resistance is measured. The two measurements differ by the inclusion of the resistance to movement of lung tissue in the latter term. In the newborn one must also consider whether the infant is breathing normally through the nose or through the mouth because the nasal resistance is very high at this age. Since newborn infants are obligatory nose breathers, and since pulmonary resistance is easier to measure than airway resistance, most studies have measured the total pulmonary plus nasal resistance ("total resistance" from here on). It must be admitted that measurements of resistance in the newborn show considerable variation from series to series (Table 2) and even within series by the same groups. The average value for total resistance in the newborn taken from the studies given in Table 2 is 27·4 cmH_2O/1/sec. Polgar and Kong[73] estimated the nasal resistance of 5 normal newborn infants and found to be 12·1 cmH_2O/1/sec, but the absolute value would depend on the condition of the airway at the time of measurement. Even so, this suggests that nasal resistance is 44 per cent of the total resistance in the newborn.

Airway resistance can be measured by relating alveolar pressure to flow in a whole body plethysmograph.[41] A recent study by Doershuk and Matthews[38] on 51 newborn infants gave a value of 19·2 cmH_2O/1/sec for total airway resistance (including the nose), which suggests that the resistance of the lung tissue in the newborn infant is 8·3 cmH_2O/1/sec or 30 per cent of the total resistance. Polgar and String[75] found a similar value for tissue resistance. For comparison, the total pulmonary resistance of the adult is about 4·9 cmH_2O/1/sec and airway resistance about 1·2 cmH_2O/1/sec. Nasal resistance is about 49 per cent of the total and tissue resistance is about 24 per cent of the total and are therefore proportionately similar in the newborn and adult. Pulmonary resistance falls as lung volume increases because the airways also increase in diameter. It can be shown that the reciprocal of resistance, conductance, should increase in direct proportion to lung volume, and the ratio of conductance to resting lung volume is termed the specific conductance. Unfortunately, this calculation is rendered less valuable by the variation in measured resistance and by the fact that the conductance-volume graph rarely passes through zero (*see* comments above). For what it is worth, the specific conductance of the newborn infant is approximately 0·36 cmH_2O^{-1}.sec^{-1} (from the results of Dr. Howlett and calculated from the normal values for resistance and volume given above); the specific conductance of the adult is approximately 0·25 cmH_2O^{-1}.sec^{-1}.

The work of breathing can be calculated from the area of a pressure-volume loop for a breath or from formulae based on the measured compliance and resistance. Such calculations for the newborn infant suggest that the work per breath is 38 gm.cm and the work per minute is 1380 gm.cm.[22] About 75 per cent of this work is done against elastic forces and the rest against resistive forces. The work of breathing represents only some 1 per cent of the basal metabolic rate in both infants and adults.

(b) **Gas exchange in the newborn**

Having dealt with the mechanics of getting gas in and out of the lungs, we will now consider the exchange of O_2 and CO_2 between alveolar gas and pulmonary capillary blood.

Oxygen consumption can be measured quite easily in the newborn period using either open circuit or closed circuit methods, and the normal value is about 7 ml/min/Kg body weight.[29,32] The average newborn infant therefore has an O_2 consumption of some 22 ml/min, which is about twice that of the adult on a weight basis. In the newborn it is essential to control ambient temperature when measuring O_2 uptake, because the response of the infant to cold is to increase the metabolism of brown fat to produce heat.[36] This increased metabolism is naturally reflected in an increased O_2 uptake, which begins when the ambient temperature falls below a certain level termed the "critical temperature". This critical temperature falls from about 36°C at birth to 32°C at the end of the first week of life.[50] The value of 7 ml/min/Kg given above refers to measurements made in a thermoneutral environment above the critical temperature.

Carbon dioxide output keeps pace with O_2 consumption and the ratio between them is the respiratory quotient of the metabolizing tissues under steady state conditions. It is generally agreed that the RQ is rather low in the immediate post-natal period,[29] and this probably reflects the metabolism of stores of brown fat. The RQ is about 0·7 on the first day of life and rises to 0·8 by the end of the first week.[57] For the normal exchange of CO_2 between tissue, blood and lung, the enzyme carbonic anhydrase is very important. It catalyses the hydration and dehydration of carbonic acid and speeds up this relatively slow process by several times. However, the exchange of CO_2 can still occur when the enzyme is inhibited by acetazolamide which is used therapeutically to treat glaucoma and it is not surprising therefore that the foetus and newborn, who have very low levels of carbonic anhydrase seem to have no problem. Maren[64] reviewed the information available on carbonic anhydrase and noted that it is first detectable in the fetus about 75 per cent through gestation and is only about 10 per cent of the adult level at birth in the mouse. The human infant has about 17 per cent of the adult level and premature infants may have no detectable activity. The level rises rapidly to adult values by 7 weeks of age in the mouse and at a similar rate in the monkey.

The object of pulmonary ventilation is to effect gas exchange, and provided that there is no undue wasted ventilation (*see* below), minute ventilation should be determined by

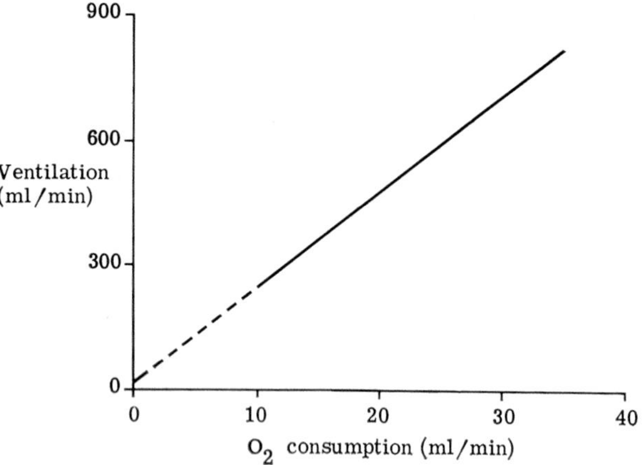

FIG. 8. Relationship between resting minute ventilation and oxygen consumption in the newborn. From Cross[31]

the metabolic rate. Cross (1961) collected data relating minute ventilation to O_2 uptake in premature and full term newborn infants and found a good correlation between them (Fig. 8). The line passes close to the origin so that one may conclude that 23·5 ml ventilation are required per ml O_2 taken up. A more recent estimate by Koch[57] gave a rather higher value of 28 ml/ml and the adult value would be about 32 ml/ml. From these figures it would seem that the newborn infant is somewhat more efficient in extracting O_2 from the environment.

The uptake of O_2 into the blood is a complex process involving transport across the alveolar-capillary membrane, itself a complex structure, transport through the plasma, and passage across the red cell wall and through the red cell stroma to the haemoglobin molecule. The total transfer process is sometimes loosely called "diffusion" but this is only a small part of the story. A measure of the ability to transfer a gas, the transfer factor (TL_{CO}), can be measured most easily for carbon monoxide which is handled very like O_2. Agreement is not very close about the value of TL_{CO} in the newborn but it has been reported as lying between 5 and 8 ml/min/mmHg/m^2.[67] The more recent estimation by Koch[57] gave a value of 10·1 ml/min/mmHg/m^2, which is equivalent to 2·2 ml/min/mmHg for the average newborn and is virtually the same as the adult TL_{CO} in relation to surface area.

The process of gas transfer also requires the good matching of gas and blood in the alveoli, known as the ventilation/perfusion balance or in conventional repiratory symbols, the V/Q. Unless V/Q is normal, some areas of lung may receive too much gas in relation to blood so that some ventilation is wasted and contributes to an enlarged dead space. Likewise, other areas of lung may receive too little gas in relation to blood and the blood may not be fully saturated. This blood passes on into the systemic circulation and can be considered as a right to left shunt or "venous admixture". There is also a small right to left shunt through extrapulmonary vessels, e.g. in the heart, but this amounts to no more than some 5 per cent of the systemic blood flow in the adult. It is generally agreed that the dead space of the newborn infant is between 2 and 3 ml/Kg,[87,57] with an average of 2·2 ml/Kg,[67] which is comparable with that of adults.[80] The absolute dead space for a new born infant is therefore about 7 ml, and since his resting tidal volume is about 20 ml, 35 per cent of each breath is wasted. The adult figure is approximately 30 per cent. Right to left shunting of blood in the newborn is increased above adult levels due to both V/Q problems in the lungs and some flow through persisting fetal vascular channels. The flow through the foramen ovale and especially the ductus arteriosus can increase considerably if the infant becomes hypoxic because reflex pulmonary vasoconstriction develops. This may create a vicious circle in such conditions as the neonatal respiratory distress syndrome.[19] In fact, the right to left shunt of the normal infant is about 24 per cent in the first hour and falls to about 10 per cent for the rest of the first week.[58] It falls to the normal adult level as fetal channels close and is reflected in the rising arterial O_2 tension during the first week of life (*see* below). It is a common but undesirable practice to calculate the right to left shunt from the O_2 tensions of inspired gas and arterial blood. This takes no account of variations in alveolar O_2 tension due to changes in P_{CO_2}, or to variations in total systemic blood flow.

(c) Gas transport in the newborn

Since the mechanical and gas transfer capabilities of the newborn lungs are proportionally similar to those of the adult, it should come as no surprise that the arterial blood gases and pH are also similar. A very detailed study of blood gases in the first week of life was carried out by Koch and Wendel[59] in which they obtained their first blood samples from the umbilical artery before the first breath. The results of their study have been plotted in Fig. 9. It can be seen that the relative hypoxia of the fetus is largely corrected by 5 min, the hypercapnia by 20 min and the acidosis by 24 hours. The PO_2 continues to rise to about 75 mmHg by 5 hours and then shows little change over the next week. The P_{CO_2} actually falls for the first day or two, reaching a low point of 33 mmHg and then slowly rises to 36 mmHg by the end of the week. There is a rise of pH throughout the first week towards normal. The initial acidosis is partly metabolic in origin and elevated blood lactate levels were noted by Koch and Wendel.[59]

Some caution is necessary when interpreting blood gas results in the newborn because umbilical arterial blood is "downstream" from the ductus arteriosus and will be contaminated by any hypoxic blood which has been shunted right to left. In a study on oxygen therapy in the newborn, Roberton, Gupta, Dahlenburg and Tizard[83] recorded radial to umbilical arterial differences greater than 10 mmHg in 6 out of 21 infants. However, they concluded that if the umbilical PO_2 was kept in the range of 60–90 mmHg, it was most unlikely that the retinal PO_2 would exceed 160 mmHg and retrolental fibroplasia would not occur. There is no doubt that sampling from the temporal artery or right radial artery, both of which take origin "upstream" from the ductus arteriosus is a safer procedure, but only if considerable care and skill is exercised in obtaining the samples.

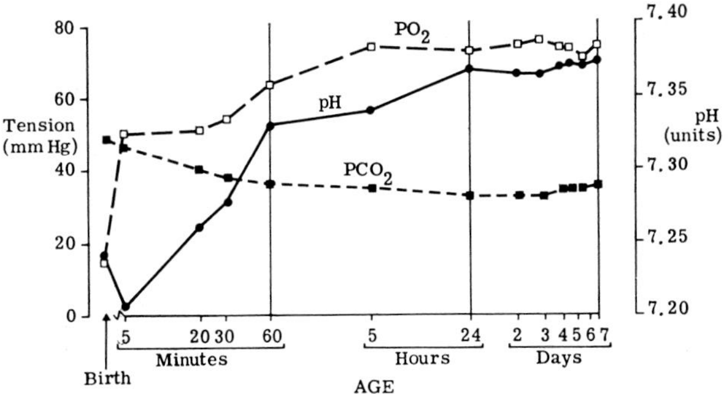

FIG. 9. Mean blood gases during the first week of life expressed on a logarithmic scale. From the data of Koch and Wendel[59]

Although the newborn is somewhat hypoxic by adult standards, even by the end of the first week of life, it must be recalled that his O_2 dissociation curve is shifted to the left and therefore his arterial O_2 saturation is 81 per cent at 5 min, 92 per cent at 1 hour and 97 per cent by the end of the first day of life. If one also considers the higher haemoglobin in the newborn, the actual volume of O_2 transported in the arterial blood is proportionately higher than in the adult. The advantages of the position of the O_2 dissociation curve do not remain for very long. At birth the infant has only about 60–70 per cent of fetal haemoglobin and this is completely replaced with adult haemoglobin by 3 months. Very few studies have been made of the effect of this change to adult haemoglobin on the dissociation curve, but in two infants Darling *et al.*[33] noted that the PO_2 for 50 per cent saturation rose progressively over the first month. Morse, Cassels and Holder[66] commented that the O_2 dissociation curve had reached the adult position by 1 to 2 months of age. It seems highly likely that the curve shifts its position in direct relation to the falling proportion of fetal haemoglobin and for practical purposes, it will have reached the adult position by the end of the first month of life.

(d) **Control of breathing in the newborn**

The events of birth radically alter the mechanical and chemical status of the respiratory system and it is therefore worth considering how well the control system is adjusted to the new circumstances. After all, the data given so far shows that the infant has passed from an apnoeic state immediately before birth with a PO_2 of 15 mmHg and a Pco_2 of 49 mmHg, to established respiration with a PO_2 of 50 mmHg and a Pco_2 of 46 mmHg in the space of 5 minutes.

The chief chemical factors controlling respiration in the adult are PO_2, Pco_2 and pH. It is known that PO_2 acts mainly through the peripheral chemoreceptors in the carotid and aortic bodies, while Pco_2 and pH act on the central chemoreceptors lying just deep to the ventro-lateral surface of the medulla.[65] Animal experiments have shown that cutting the sinus nerve abolishes the response to O_2 inhalation in the newborn lamb,[76,77] but does not affect the response to CO_2[78] and the reflex mechanisms are therefore presumably similar in newborn and adults.

The newborn human infant increases his ventilation when CO_2 is added to the inspired air.[28] This response has been

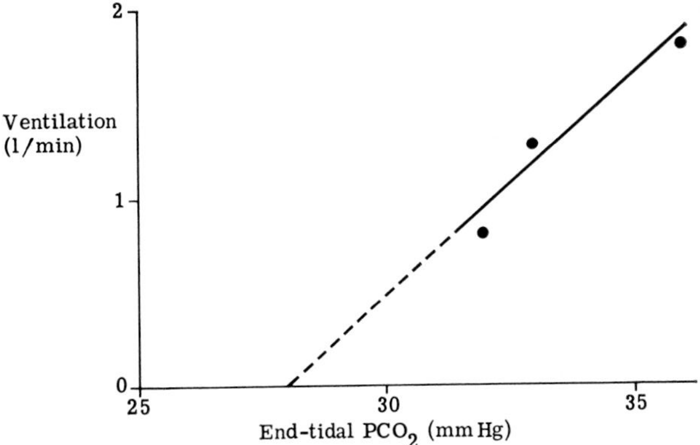

FIG. 10. Ventilatory response to inhaled CO_2 in the newborn infant redrawn from Way *et al.*[92]

quantitated in terms of the increase in ventilation per mmHg rise in end-tidal Pco_2 and the result of one such series of studies by Way, Costly and Way[92] is shown in Fig. 10. The slope of this CO_2 response curve is 0·26 l/min/mmHg and the intercept on the Pco_2 axis at which ventilation would (theoretically) fall to zero is 28 mmHg. The slope in normal adults is 2–4 l/min/mmHg and the intercept is 40–50 mmHg.[81,46] It is unreasonable to expect an infant to attain the same ventilation as an adult and one may obtain a better comparison of sensitivity by correcting the slopes for ventilatory capacity, e.g. by dividing ventilation by the resting ventilation. This would give the slope for both infants and adults a value of approximately 40 per cent resting ventilation/min/mmHg. The low value for the intercept in the newborn is difficult to interpret, but may in part reflect the relatively lower arterial Pco_2. An exactly similar conclusion was reached by Purves[78] about CO_2 sensitivity in the newborn lamb.

Oxygen has an interesting effect on the newborn. Giving high concentrations in the inspired gas depresses respiration,[27] and giving low concentrations stimulates it.[25] But unlike the effect of CO_2, the effect of hypoxia is only transient in the immediate post natal period. The stimulation passes off after about 2 minutes, despite the continuing hypoxia. This transient response becomes longer in duration as the days go by, and has developed into a fully sustained response by about the tenth day of life (Fig. 11[14]). There is no obvious advantage to the infant of this transient effect and it is not seen in newborn lambs. The quantitation of the effect of hypoxia is made difficult because the response is hyperbolic and not linear. This can be seen by studying the effect of various levels of O_2 on the slope of the CO_2 response curve.[62] The results of such an experiment carried out in newborn lambs by Purves[78] are shown in Fig. 12. Hypoxia increased the slope of the ventilatory response to

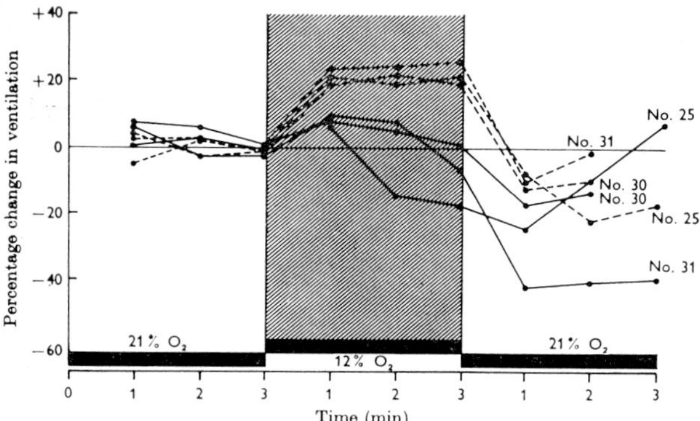

FIG. 11. Ventilatory response to hypoxia in 3 newborn human infants at 3 days (solid lines) and 10 days (interrupted lines). From Brady Ceruti.[14]

CO_2 and the increase in slope was related to PO_2 in an hyperbolic manner. This pattern is identical with that seen in adult man. The converse effect, namely potentiation of the effect of hypoxia by concomitant hypercapnia was demonstrated in the newborn human infant by Brady and Dunn,[15] but the response to hypoxia was still transient in infants under 10 days old.

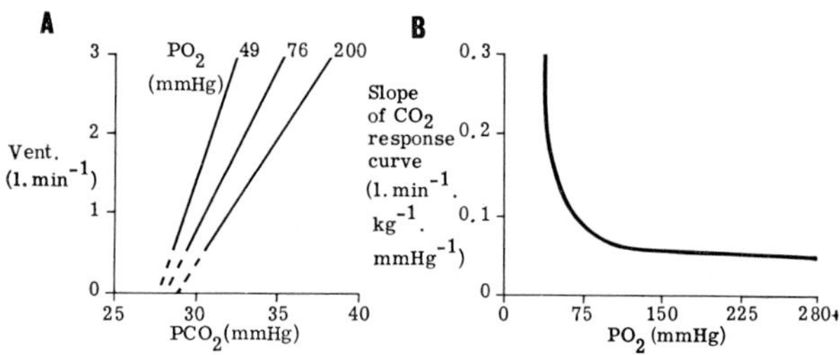

FIG. 12. (a) The effect of different levels of PO_2 indicated by the numbers, on the slope of the ventilatory response to CO_2 in the newborn lamb. (b) Slope of the CO_2 response curve plotted against the PO_2 at which the curve was performed. Redrawn from Purves[78]

The chemoreceptors are clearly effective in the newborn and clearly ineffective in the fetus at term, but how this change-over occurs is by no means certain. In the case of the response to O_2, there is some evidence that it may be related to the blood flow through the carotid bodies. This is under the control of the sympathetic nervous system and there is an increase in sympathetic activity at birth.[79]

The mechanical control of breathing is also well developed in the newborn infant. Inflation of the lungs causes apnoea through the Hering–Breuer inflation reflex and the duration of apnoea is related to the volume of the inflation.[30] In animals, deflation of the lungs results in tachypnoea but the human infant is rather upset by this manoeuvre. Sometimes, inflation of the lungs of the newborn results in an inspiratory gasp before the apnoea, which has been likened to the paradoxical response described in adults by Head.[49] It has been seen in both human infants and newborn animals (Fig. 13). This reflex is particularly prominent in the newborn and tends to fade out later on. It is most easily elicited when the

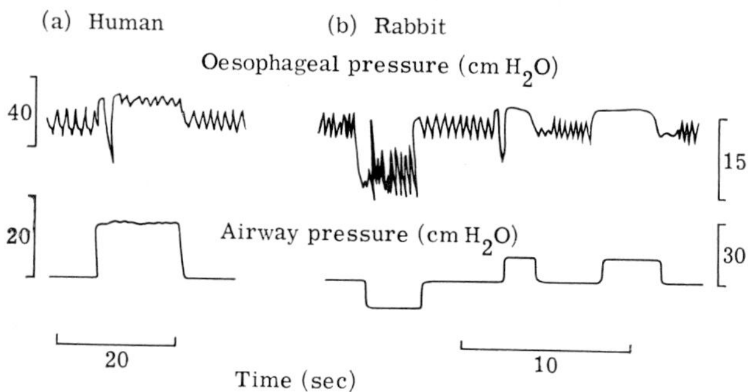

FIG. 13 (a). Respiratory reflexes in the newborn human infant redrawn from Cross.[31] (b) Respiratory reflexes in the newborn rabbit redrawn from Godfrey[44]

The oesophegeal pressure reflects respiratory movements. In both cases apnoea following lung inflation is due to the Hering-Breuer inflation reflex and the inspiratory gasp (downward deflection of oesophageal pressure record) on some inflations is the paradoxical response of Head. The rabbit record also shows a deflation reflex.

lungs are unstable and tending to collapse[44] and it is probably closely related to the spontaneous sighs which all animals, especially the newborn, take from time to time. Although it has been suggested that this reflex is important for the initiation of respiration, Godfrey[44] has shown that it is quite possible for the fetal or newborn rabbit to initiate respiration after all pulmonary reflexes have been abolished by vagotomy or asphyxia.

Growth of Respiratory Function Throughout Childhood

Having now considered the development of respiratory function in the fetus and newborn, it remains to trace its subsequent growth throughout childhood. In many respects the most complicated phase has already been dealt with, because further development is essentially a process of keeping pace with body size, the overall adult pattern having been established within the first two weeks of life. However, the greatest clinical use of pulmonary function investigation in childhood is made in the period about to be considered, and it is therefore worth detailing the changes from infancy to adulthood. The chief problem in presenting this information is the discontinuity in much of the data. There are ample results for infants and for children over 5 years of age, but very little for toddler age group because of the difficulty in obtaining co-operation. Despite this there have been some bridging studies and it is also possible to predict with considerable certainty what changes must have occurred in the very young child. In this account sex differences are ignored because they are largely insignificant below puberty and it is intended to indicate trends, not to produce tables or graphs of "normal values". The reader who requires such information is referred to the excellent monograph by Polgar and Promadhat.[74]

(a) **Mechanical function throughout childhood**

The total lung capacity of the newborn infant is about 150 ml while that of the 16 year old is about 5100 ml. This 34-fold increase in size is reflected in all other aspects of pulmonary mechanics such as the vital capacity, residual volume and volume of gas in the lungs at the end of a normal expiration. The way in which these volumes increase is shown in Fig. 14. Height has been used to indicate size because this is a simple and reliable index. The linear scale means that the lines are curved. Some published reports use a logarithmic scale which straightens out the lines, but it is much more difficult to read the axis in this case. As a rough guide to age, the heights for the 50th percentile of the ages

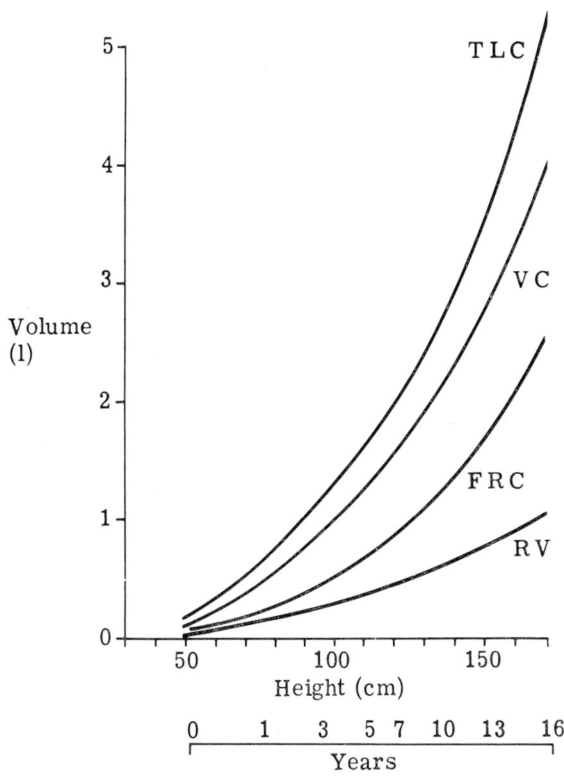

FIG. 14. Relationship between lung volumes and height throughout childhood. TLC = total lung capacity; VC = vital capacity; FRC = functional residual capacity (resting lung volume); RV = residual volume (See text for sources and further explanation).

shown are also indicated. A rough guide to age is also included, based on the 50th percentile for height. The only parameter for which the data is really continuous is functional residual capacity (resting lung volume) because the results of Doershuk, Downs, Matthews and Lough,[39] extend up to children of 5 years of age. The other results for infants were taken from Auld *et al.*[3] and Sutherland and Ratcliff,[88] while the results for older children were taken from the averaged graphs of Polgar and Promadhet.[74] All the curved lines for older children fall smoothly through the points for infants and parallel and curve for resting lung volume which was constructed from continuous data for all ages. This graph shows that the ratio of residual volume to total lung capacity is approximately 22 per cent throughout childhood.

The curved relationship between the various lung volumes and size is seen throughout the animal kingdom, where the usual reference is body weight. Tenney and Remmers[90] noted that the total lung capacity (TLC) of adults of different species was related to their weight (Wt) by the formula

$$TLC \propto Wt^{1\cdot02}$$

Using the data from Fig. 14 and converting height to weight with percentile charts, the equation for children of different sizes is

$$TLC \propto Wt^{1\cdot16}$$

The similarity of growth pattern, whether in the young of any one species or by comparison of adults of different species, suggests that lung size is adjusted to metabolic needs. In fact, Bartlett[8] showed that young rats reared in

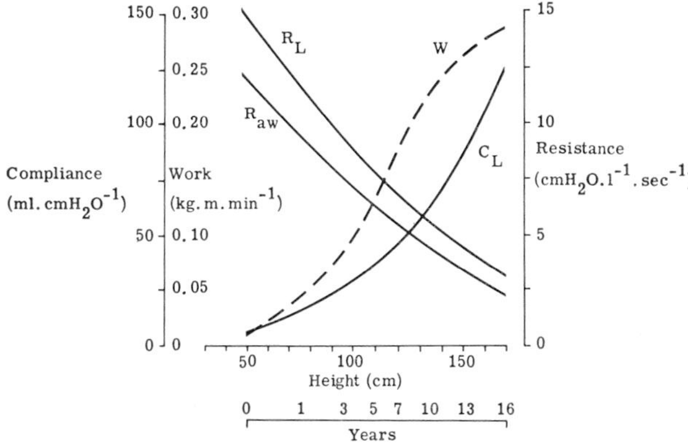

FIG. 15. Relationship between lung mechanics and height throughout childhood. R_L = pulmonary resistance excluding the nose; R_{aw} = airway resistance excluding the nose; C_L = lung compliance; W = work of breathing.

high O_2 concentrations may actually have retarded lung growth, but it is not certain whether this is due to O_2 toxicity or to true adaptation.

As the lungs grow there is a rapid multiplication in alveoli until about 8 years of age and then there is an increase in size of both alveoli and airways (*see* Chapter 14A). This growth is reflected in alterations in the elastic and flow resistive properties of the lungs. There is a large increase in compliance and fall in resistance as the child grows (Fig. 15). The increase in compliance essentially follows the increase in size of the lungs (Fig. 16) so that the specific compliance (compliance/resting lung volume) remains between about 0·05 and 0·06 ml/cmH_2O/ml throughout childhood. The compliance and volume data for these graphs was taken from Krieger,[60] Kemel, Weng, Featherby, Jackman and Levinson,[52] and other sources already given. The fall in resistance with growth occurs because the increase in airway diameter more than offsets the increase in airway length. Resistance can be partitioned into various compartments and comparisons are complicated by the fact that measurement on infants are almost invariably made during nose breathing, while measurements on older children and adults are made during mouth breathing. The lines in Fig. 15 were calculated by subtracting realistic estimates of nasal resistance from the infant data and show the pulmonary resistance and airway resistance in relation to height. The data was taken from the sources already listed and Engstrom, Karlberg and Swarts.[42] The difference between the two resistance lines in Fig. 15 represents the resistance of the lung tissues. The value for infants of 5·5 $cmH_2O/l/sec$ is somewhat lower than that found by Polgar and String,[75] but the value of about 2·0 $cmH_2O/l/sec$ in older children is very similar to that found by Bachofen and Duc.[5]

The reciprocal of resistance, conductance, has been found to rise in proportion to increasing lung volume in infants and toddlers[39] and older children,[52] and their combined results are shown in Fig. 16. The dashed line shows the actual value found by Doershuk *et al.*[39] for their nose breathing infants and suitable values of nasal resistance were subtracted to obtain the lower part of the solid conductance line. This intersects with the upper part of the solid line for older children at a resting lung volume of 1·01. The specific airway conductance (conductance/resting lung volume) for the older children is 0·39 $cmH_2O^{-1}.sec^{-1}$ but it cannot really be calculated for the lower part of the line since the graph does not pass through zero. Fig. 16 suggests that the rate of increase in conductance with lung volume (slope of the line) is lower for the infants and young children than for the older ones. This is interesting in the light of the pathological studies of Hogg, Williams, Richardson, Macklem and Thurlbeck,[51] who found that the conductance of the small airways was low in children under 5 years and rose rapidly in older children. The resistance of the larger airways changed little throughout childhood. The inflection in the conductance-volume line of Fig. 16 occurs at about 8 years of age and almost certainly is the physiological equivalent of the pathological studies of Hogg *et al.*[51] and the other changes described in Chapter 14A.

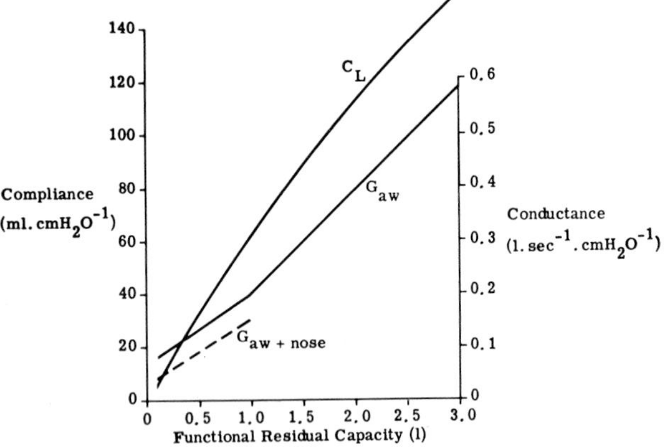

FIG. 16. Lung compliance (C_L) and airway conductance = 1/resistance (G_{aw}) in relationship to resting lung volume throughout childhood. The dotted line gives the relationship for the conductance of the airways including the nose in infants and children up to 5 years of age.

The metabolic needs of the growing child and the changes which occur in lung mechanics are reflected in the tidal volume, frequency of breathing and minute volume (Fig. 17). The lines are curved in relation to height as they were for the other parameters. The data for frequency was continuous for all ages and when expressed in terms of weight, yields the relationship

$$f \propto Wt^{-0 \cdot 29}$$

This is very similar to the relationship given by Tenney and Bartlett[91] for adult animals of different sizes. While the increasing minute ventilation reflects the increasing metabolic rate and dead space (*see* below), the tidal volume and frequency changes reflect lung mechanics and the ratio of tidal volume to total lung capacity remains at about 12 per cent throughout childhood. In fact, it is probable that the frequency and tidal volume are so chosen that the work of breathing, or possibly the force needed to breathe, are minimised. The work of breathing may be calculated from the measured tidal volume, frequency, resistance and com-

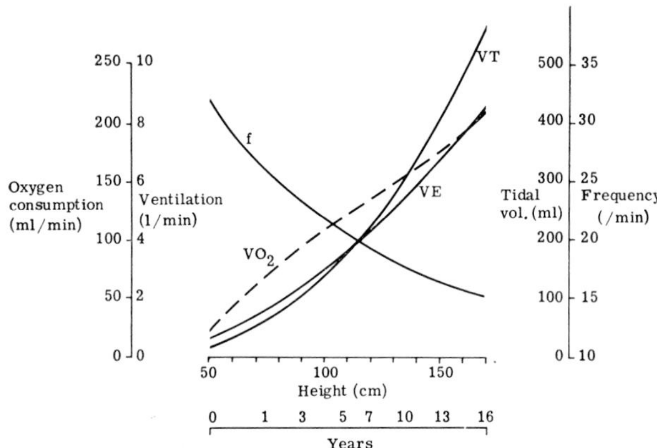

FIG. 17. Relationship between minute ventilation (VE), tidal volume (VT), frequency of breathing (f) and oxygen uptake (VO_2) with height throughout childhood.

pliance using the formula developed by Otis, Fenn and Rahn[70] and values for children in relation to height has been included as the dotted line in Fig. 15. They were calculated from the data in Figs. 15 and 17. As noted before the work of breathing represents no more than about 1 per cent of the basal metabolic rate at all ages.

In older children it is usual to assess the overall mechanical properties of the lungs by measuring the maximum ventilation which the child can sustain (usually for 15 sec.) and extrapolating this on to a maximum voluntary minute ventilation (MVV). Other indices of lung function which are related to airways resistance are the peak expiratory flow rate and the forced expired volume in the first second after a maximum inspiration (FEV_1). The average values for these parameters in relation to height, taken from several series, are shown in Fig. 18. Although the FEV_1–height relationship is curved and the others are linear, the differences in shape are small and the MVV is between 34 and 37 times the forced expired volume in 1 sec. It is interesting that a very similar relationship is found in adults,[20] and in children suffering obstructive lung diseases such as asthma or cystic fibrosis (personal observations).

(b) **Gas exchange throughout childhood**

The increase in resting ventilation which occurs throughout childhood closely follows the increase in oxygen

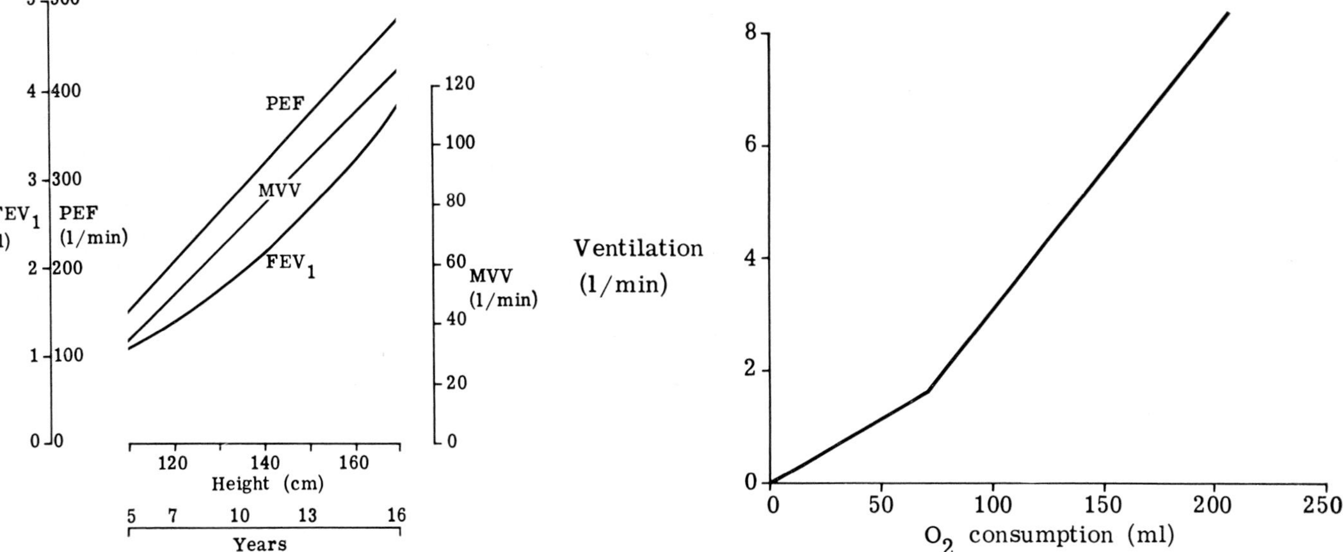

FIG. 18. Relationship between peak expiratory flow rate (PEF), maximum voluntary ventilation (MVV) and forced expired volume in 1 second (FEV_1) with height in children.

FIG. 19. Relationship of resting minute ventilation to oxygen uptake throughout childhood. The discontinuity of slope occurs about 1 year of age.

consumption (Fig. 17), but there is a discontinuity in the ventilation–O_2 consumption relationship at about 1 year of age (Fig. 19). The data for this line was obtained from the studies of Hill and Rahimtulla[50] and the collected data on ventilation from Fig. 17. This inflection accounts for the differences noted earlier in the ventilatory equivalent for oxygen (ventilation/O_2 uptake) and the value of 24 ml/ml for an infant calculated from Fig. 19 agrees with Cross,[31] while the ratio obviously increases with age. There is no obvious explanation for this change of slope. A reasonable approximation of the expected ventilation is given by 36 times the oxygen uptake at all ages. CO_2 production appears to follow the increase in O_2 consumption so that, after the first few days of life, the respiratory quotient remains fairly constant.

The transfer of gases between the lungs and the blood must increase with growth and it is not surprising to find that the transfer factor for carbon monoxide (TL_{CO}) increases with height in much the same way as the other parameters mentioned (Fig. 20). The graph was obtained by drawing a smooth curve through the data of DeMuth and Howatt[37] and extending it down to meet the infant data of Koch.[57] This line exactly parallels the increase in total lung capacity. By measuring the transfer factor at different levels of oxygenation (which alters the affinity of haemoglobin for carbon monoxide) it is possible to calculate the volume of blood in the pulmonary capillaries (Vc) and also the transfer factor for the alveolar-capillary membrane (Dm). Bucci, Cook and Barrie[16] undertook such studies on a group of subjects including children aged between 7 and 18 years. They found that Dm was between 2 and 2·5 times as large as the overall TL_{CO} which means that the membrane transfers gas more easily than the other tissues through which it has to pass. The values they found for Vc are shown in Fig. 20, but the results only cover a small age range and do not extend to infancy. In dogs from 2·5–27·0 Kg there is good evidence on functional and structural grounds to believe that Vc increases linearly with increasing weight.[84]

The process of gas transfer, as discussed earlier, involves the matching of ventilation and perfusion as well as diffusion.

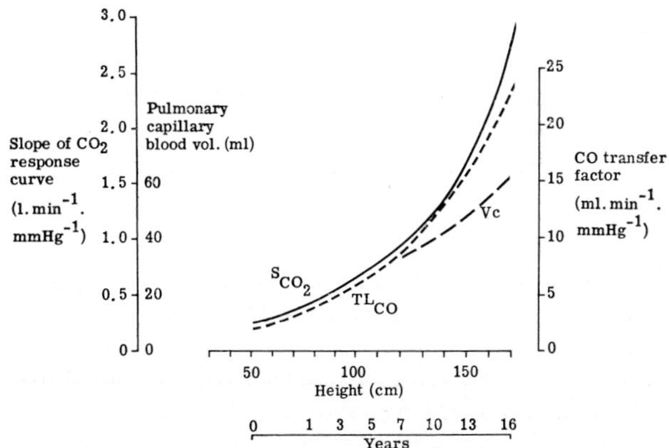

FIG. 20. Slope of CO_2 response curve (SCO_2), transfer factor for CO (TL_{CO}) and pulmonary capillary blood volume Vc, in relation to height in children.

The wasted ventilation in the physiological dead space has been measured in infants, children and adults and there is general agreement with the relationship found by Radford[80] that

$$\text{Dead Space (ml)} = 2{\cdot}2 \times \text{Weight (Kg)}.$$

This result has been confirmed by Godfrey and Davies[45] and by Weng, Lager, Featherby and Levison[93] for children over a wide size range and agrees with the conclusions of Tenney and Bartlett[91] based on comparative animal studies. Venous admixture due to low ventilation-perfusion ratios is very small in the normal child and does not amount to more than 3–5 per cent of the total cardiac output (personal observations).

(c) Gas transport throughout childhood

It has been noted earlier that the oxygen dissociation curve assumes the adult position by the end of the first month of life. Although Morse *et al.*[66] described the curve as lying rather to the right of the adult position during childhood, the difference was very small. The actual carrying capacity for O_2 also depends on the haemoglobin concentration, which is about 18 g/100 ml on the first day of life, falls to about 10·5 g/100 ml during the first three months and then rises slowly to about 14–15 g/100 ml by puberty. These alterations in carrying capacity have little significance under normal conditions because of the very great reserves of the cardio-respiratory system above normal requirements.

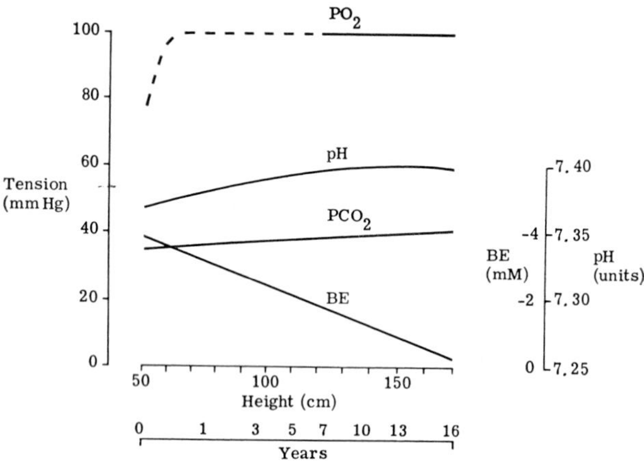

FIG. 21. Blood gases and calculated base excess (BE) throughout childhood.

The level of blood gases and pH are also established early on in life and change little after infancy. Reliable data on children is very hard to come by because of the very proper reluctance of investigators to sample arterial blood in normal children. Such data as are available have been summarised in Fig. 21 and includes some values obtained by Dr. M. R. H. Taylor from arterialised ear lobe blood using the techniques of Godfrey, Wozniak, Courtnay Evans and Samuels.[47] These results suggest that pH rises slowly from the infant figures of 7.37 to the adolescent value of 7·4, while at the same time P_{CO_2} also rises from about 35 mmHg to 40 mmHg. This rise of pH and P_{CO_2} together means that the buffer base of the blood must also increase and calculations from the data given by Cassells and Morse[17] suggest that the bicarbonate rises from 19 mm at the age of 2 years to 24 mm by 16 years. Arterial PO_2 is about 75 mmHg at the end of the first week of life and the earliest observations in children (5 years old in the author's studies) show that the PO_2 is at or above adult levels of 95 mmHg.

(d) Control of breathing throughout childhood

There is very little information about the control of breathing throughout childhood, not so much because of lack of acceptable techniques, but more because the natural inquisitiveness of children makes them poor subjects for such studies. Despite this problem, some studies have been carried out using simple rebreathing procedures[46,81] to measure CO_2 sensitivity and O_2 sensitivity in older children. The results of one such study in a 15 year old girl are shown in Fig. 22. Unpublished work by Silverman and Godfrey showed that the slope of the ventilation-P_{CO_2} response curve increased throughout childhood in a similar curved fashion to other parameters of pulmonary function. The actual slope of the CO_2 response curve increased from 0·8 l/min/mmHg at 5–6 years of age to 3·0 l/min/mmHg which is well within the normal adult range at about 16 years. The change in slope is entirely explicable in terms of the mechanical

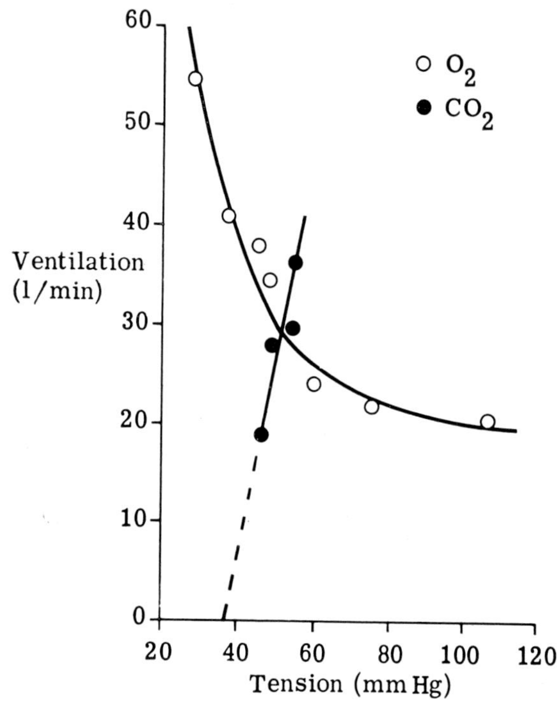

FIG. 22. Ventilatory response to CO_2 at constant high PO_2 and ventilatory response to hypoxia at constant normal PCO_2 in a 15-year-old girl.

properties of the respiratory system, since the slope of the curve represents approximately 2 per cent of the maximum voluntary ventilation per mmHg P_{CO_2} rise at all ages. There is thus no evidence to suggest that sensitivity to CO_2 alters with age. Unfortunately there is insufficient data to make any conclusions about O_2 sensitivity, but the pattern shown in Fig. 22 is identical to that seen in the adult.[46] Although mechanical reflexes controlling breathing can be elicited in the conscious newborn baby, they cannot be reliably demonstrated in conscious adults and have not been investigated in children. They can be produced in anaesthetised adults[48] and it is likely therefore that their activity is suppressed as cerebral cortical activity increases.

CONCLUSION

The growth and development of respiratory physiology is a logical process. The initial phase of life in utero is largely one of preparation for immediate function at birth so that there is a smooth transition to the new mechanical and chemical situation. Subsequent growth keeps pace with the bodily needs of the growing child. It should be noted that the respiratory system virtually reaches its full functional capacity in proportion to size within minutes or even seconds of birth, a feat not matched by any other system.

REFERENCES

1. Adamson, T. M., Boyd, R. D. H. Platt, H. S. and Strang, L. B. (1969), "Composition of Alveolar Liquid in the Foetal Lamb," *J. Physiol.*, **2–4**, 159–168.
2. Allen, D. W., Wyman, J. and Smith, C. A. (1953), "The Oxygen Equilibrium of Fetal and Adult Human Hemoglobin," *J. biol. Chem.*, **203**, 81–87.
3. Auld, P. A. M., Nelson, N. M., Cherry, R. B., Rudolph, A. J. and Smith, C. A. (1963), "Measurement of Thoracic Gas Volume in the Newborn Infant," *J. clin. Invest.*, **42**, 476–483.
4. Avery, M. E. and Mead, J. (1959), "Surface Properties in Relation to Atelactasis and Hyaline Membrane Disease," *Amer. J. Dis. Child,*. **97**, 517–523.
5. Bachofen, H. and Duc, G. (1968), "Lung Tissue Resistance in Healthy Children," *Paediat. Res.*, **2**, 119–124.
6. Barcraft, J. (1946), *Researches on Prenatal Life*, Oxford: Blackwell Scientific Publications.
7. Barcroft, J. and Karvonen, M. J. (1948), "The Action of Carbon Dioxide and Cyanide on Foetal Respiration Movements; The Development of Chemoreflex Function in Sheep," *J. Physiol.*, **107**, 153–161.
8. Bartlett, D. (1970), "Postnatal Growth of the Mammalian Lung: Influence of Low and High Oxygen Tension," *Resp. Physiol.*, **9**, 58–64.
9. Bauer, C., Ludwig, M., Ludwig, I. and Bartels, H. (1969), Factors Governing the Oxygen Affinity of Human Adult and Foetal Blood," *Resp. Physiol.*, **7**, 271–277.
10. Behrman, R. E., Peterson, E. N. and Lannoy, C. W. de (1969), "The supply of O_2 to the Primate Fetus with Two Different O_2 Tensions and Anesthetics," *Resp. Physiol.*, **6**, 271–283.
11. Bhagwanani, S. G., Fahmy, D. and Turnbull, A. C. (1972), "Prediction of Neonatal Respiratory Distress by Estimation of Amniotic Fluid Lecithin," *Lancet*, **1**, 159–162.
12. Boddy, K. and Robinson, J. S. (1971), "External Method for Detection of Fetal Breathing in Utero," *Lancet*, **2**, 1231–1233.
13. Boston, R. W., Humphreys, P. W., Reynolds, E. O. R. and Strang, L. B. (1965), "Lymph-flow and Clearance of Liquid From the Lungs of the Foetal Lamb," *Lancet*, **2**, 473–474.
14. Brady, J. P. and Ceruti, E. (1966), "Chemoreceptor Reflexes in the New-born Infant: Effects of Varying Degree of Hypoxia on Heart Rate and Ventilation in a Warm Environment," *J. Physiol.*, **184**, 631–645.
15. Brady, J. and Dunn, P. M. (1970), "Chemoreceptor Reflexes in the Newborn Infant. Effect of CO_2 on the Ventilatory Response to Hypoxia," *Pediatrics*, **45**, 206–215.
16. Bucci, G., Cook, C. D. and Barrie, H. (1961), "Studies of Respiratory Physiology in Children. V. Total Lung Diffusion, Diffusing Capacity of Pulmonary Membrane, and Pulmonary Capillary Blood Volume in Normal Subjects from 7 to 40 years of Age," *J. Pediat.*, **58**, 820–828.
17. Cassells, D. E. and Morse, M. (1962), *Cardiopulmonary Data for Children and Young Adults*, Springfield, Illinois: C. Thomas.
18. Chu, J. S., Dawson, P., Klaus, M. and Sweet, A. Y. (1964), "Lung Compliance and Lung Volume Measured Concurrently in Normal Full-term and Premature Infants," *Pediatrics*, **34**, 525–532.
19. Chu, J., Clements, J. A., Cotton, E., Klaus, M. H., Sweet, A. H., Thomas, M. A. and Tooley, W. H. (1965), "The Pulmonary Hypoperfusion Syndrome," *Pediatrics*, **35**, 733–742.
20. Clark, T. J. H., Freedman, S., Campbell, E. J. M. and Winn, R. R. (1969), "The Ventilatory Capacity of Patients with Chronic Airways Obstruction," *Clin. Sci.*, **36**, 307–316.
21. Comline, R. S., Silver, I. A. and Silver, M. (1965), "Factors Responsible for the Stimulation of the Adrenal Medulla During Asphyxia in the Foetal Lamb," *J. Physiol.*, **178**, 211–238.
22. Cook, C. D., Sutherland, J. M., Segal, S., Cherry, R. B., Mead, J., McIlroy, M. B. and Smith, C. A. (1957), "Studies of Respiratory Physiology in the Newborn Infant III. Measurement of Mechanics of Respiration," *J. clin. Invest.*, **36**, 440–448.
23. Cotes, J. E. (1968), *Lung Function*. Oxford: Blackwell Scientific Productions.
24. Cross, K. W. (1949), "The Respiratory Rate and Ventilation in the Newborn Baby," *J. Physiol.*, **109**, 459–474.
25. Cross, K. W. and Warner, P. (1951), "The Effect of Inhalation of High and Low Oxygen Concentrations on the Respiration of the Newborn Infant," *J. Physiol.*, **114**, 283–295.
26. Cross, K. W. and Oppe, T. E. (1952), "The Respiratory Rate and Volume in the Premature Infant," *J. Physiol.*, **116**, 168–174.
27. Cross, K. W. and Malcolm, J. L. (1952), "Evidence of Carotid Body and Sinus Activity in Newborn Foetal Animals," *J. Physiol.*, **118**, 10p.
28. Cross, K. W., Hooper, J. M. D. and Oppe, T. E. (1953), "The Effect of Inhalation of Carbon Dioxide in Air on the Respiration of the Full-term and Premature Infant," *J. Physiol.*, **122**, 264–273.
29. Cross, K. W., Tizard, J. P. M. and Trythall, D. A. H. (1957), "The Gaseous Metabolism of the Newborn Infant," *Acta paediat.*, **46**, 265–285.
30. Cross, K. W., Klaus, M., Tooley, W. H. and Weisser, K. (1960), "The Response of the New-born Baby to Inflation of the Lungs," *J. Physiol.*, **151**, 551–565.
31. Cross, K. W. (1961), "Respiration in the New-born Baby," *Brit. med. Bull.*, **17**, 160–163.
32. Cross, K. W., Flynn, D. M. and Hill, J. (1966), "Oxygen Consumption in Normal Newborn Infants During Moderate Hypoxia in Warm and Cool Environments," *Pediatrics*, **37**, 565–576.
33. Darling, R. C., Smith, C. A., Asmussen, E. and Cohen, F. M. (1941), "Some Properties of Human Fetal and Maternal Blood," *J. clin. Invest.*, **20**, 739–747.
34. Dawes, G. S. (1968), *Foetal and Neonatal Physiology*. Chicago: Year Book Medical Publishers Inc.
35. Dawes, G. S., Fox, H. E., Leduc, B. M., Liggins, G. C. and Richards, R. Y. (1970), "Respiratory Movements and Paradoxical Sleep in the Foetal Lamb," *J. Physiol.*, **210**, 47p.
36. Dawkins, M. J. R. and Hull, D. (1964), "Brown Adipose Tissue and the Response of Newborn Rabbits to Cold," *J. Physiol.*, **172**, 216–238.
37. DeMuth, G. R. and Howatt, W. F. (1965), "III Pulmonary Diffusion," *Pediatrics*, **35**, suppl. 185–193.
38. Doershuk, C. F. and Matthews, L. W. (1969), "Airway Resistance and Lung Volume in the Newborn Infant," *Pediat. Res.*, **3**, 128–134.
39. Doershuk, C. F., Downs, T. D., Matthews, L. W. and Lough, M. D. (1970), "A Method for Ventilatory Measurements in Subjects 1 Month–5 Years of Age: Normal Results and Observations in Disease," *Pediat. Res.*, **4**, 165–174.
40. DuBois, A. B., Botelho, S. Y., Bedell, H. N., Marshall, R. and Comroe, J. H., Jr. (1956), "A Rapid Piethysmograph Method for Measuring Thoracic Gas Volume: A Comparison with a Nitrogen Washout Method for Measuring Functional Residual Capacity in Normal Subjects," *J. clin. Invest.*, **35**, 322–326.
41. DuBois, A. B., Botelho, S. Y. and Comroe, J. H. (1956), "A New Method for Measuring Airway Resistance in Man Using a Body Plethysmograph: Values in Normal Subjects and in Patients with Respiratory Disease," *J. clin. Invest.*, **35**, 327–335.
42. Engstrom, I., Karlberg, P. and Swarts, C. L. (1962), "Respiratory Studies in Children. 9. Relationships. Between Mechanical Properties of the Lungs, Lung Volumes and Ventilatory Capacity in Healthy Children 7 to 15 Years of Age," *Acta paediat.*, **51**, 68–80.
43. Godfrey, S. (1966), "An Analysis of Factors Important in the Resuscitation of Asphyxiated Foetal and New-born Rabbits," Ph.D. Thesis, University of London.

44. Godfrey, S. (1968), "Respiratory and Cardiovascular Changes During Asphyxia and Resuscitation of Foetal and Newborn Rabbits," *Quart. J. exp. Physiol.*, **53,** 97–118.
45. Godfrey, S. and Davies, C. T. M. (1970), "Estimates of Arterial $P\text{CO}_2$ and Their Effect on the Calculated Values of Cardiac Output and Dead Space on Exercise," *Clin. Sci.*, **39,** 529–537.
46. Godfrey, S., Edwards, R. H. T., Copeland, G. M. and Cross, P. L. (1971a), "Chemosensitivity in Normal Subjects, Athletes and Patients with Chronic Airways Obstruction," *J. appl. Physiol.*, **30,** 193–199.
47. Godfrey, S., Wozniak, E. R., Courtnay Evans, R. J. and Samuels, C. S. (1971b), "Ear Lobe Blood Samples for Blood Gas, Analysis at Rest and During Exercise," *Brit. J. Dis. Chest*, **65** 58–64.
48. Guz, A., Noble, M. I. M., Trenchard, D., Smith, A. J. and Makey, A. R. (1966). "The Hering–Brewer Inflation Reflex in Man: Studies of Unilateral Lung Inflation and Vagus Nerve Block," *Resp. Physiol.*, **1,** 382–389.
49. Head, H. (1889), "On the Regulation of Respiration," *J. Physiol.* **10,** 1–70.
50. Hill, J. R. and Rahimtulla, K. A. (1965), "Heat Balance and the Metabolic Rate of New-born Babies in Relation to Environmental Temperature; and the Effect of Age and Weight on Basal Metabolic Rate," *J. Physiol.*, **180,** 239–265.
51. Hogg, J. C., Williams, J., Richardson, J. B., Maclem, P. T. and Thurlbeck, W. M. (1970), "Age as a Factor in the Distribution of Lower-airway Conductance and in the Pathalogic Anatomy of Obstructive Lung Disease," *New Engl. J. Med.*, **282,** 1283–1287.
51a. Howlett, G. (1972), "A Study of Lung Mechanisms in Normal Infants and Infants with Congenital Heart Disease," *Arch. Dis. Childh.* In press.
52. Kamel, M., Weng, T-R., Featherby, E. A., Jackman, W. S. and Levison, H. (1969), "Relationship of Mechanics of Ventilation to Lung Volumes in Children and Young Adults," *Scand. J. Res. Dis.*, **50,** 125–134.
53. Karlberg, P. (1960), "The Adaptive Changes in the Immediate Postnatal Period with Particular Reference to Respiration," *J. Pediat.*, **56,** 585–604.
54. Karlberg, P., Cherry, R. B., Escardo, F. and Koch, G. (1960), "Respiratory Studies in Newborn Infants," *Acta paediat.*, **49,** 345–357.
55. Karlberg, P., Cherry, R. B., Escardo, F. E. and Koch, G. (1962), "Respiratory Studies in Newborn Infants II. (Pulmonary Ventilation and Mechanics of Breathing in the First Minutes of Life, Including the Onset of Respiration)," *Acta paediat.*, **51,** 121–136.
56. Karlberg, P. and Koch, G. (1962), "Respiratory Studies in Newborn Infants III. (Development of Mechanics of Breathing During the First Week of Life. A Longitudinal Study)," *Acta paediat.*, **135,** suppl., 121–129.
57. Koch, G. (1968a), "Alveolar Ventilation, Diffusing Capacity and the A–a PO_2 Difference in the Newborn Infant," *Resp. Physiol.*, **4,** 168–192.
58. Koch, G. (1968b), "Venous Admixture Due to True Anatomic Shunt in the Newborn Infant During the First Week of Life," *Pädiat. Pädol.*, **4,** 211–224.
59. Koch, G. and Wendel, H. (1968), "Adjustment of Arterial Blood Gases and Acid Base Balance in the Normal Newborn Infant During the First Week of Life," *Biol. Neonat.*, **12,** 136–161.
60. Krieger, I. (1966), "Thoracic Gas Volume in Infancy," *Amer. J. Dis. Child.*, **111,** 393–399.
61. Lind, J., Stern, L. and Wegelius, C. (1964), *Human Foetal and Neonatal Circulation*. Springfield, Illinois: Charles C. Thomas.
62. Lloyd, B. B., Jukes, M. G. M. and Cunningham, D. J. C. (1958), "The Relation Between Alveolar Oxygen Pressure and the Respiratory Response to Carbon Dioxide in Man," *Quart. J. exp. Physiol.*, **43,** 214–227.
63. Lucius, H., Gahlenbeck, H., Kleine, H. O., Fabel, H. and Bartels, H. (1970), "Respiratory Functions, Buffer System and Electrolyte Concentrations of Blood During Human Pregnancy," *Resp. Physiol.*, **9,** 311–317.
64. Maren, T. H. (1967), "Carbonic Anhydrase: Chemistry, Physiology and Inhibition," *Physiol. Rev.*, **47,** 595–781.
65. Mitchell, R. A., Loeshcke, H. H., Severinghaus, J. W., Richardson, B. W. and Massion, W. H. (1963), "Regions of Respiratory Chemosensitivity on the Surface of the Medulla," *Ann. N.Y. Acad. Sci.*, **109,** 661–681.
66. Morse, M., Cassels, D. E. and Holder, M. (1950), "The Position of the Oxygen Dissociation Curve of the Blood of Normal Children and Adults," *J. clin. Invest.*, **29,** 1091–1097.
67. Nelson, N. M. (1966). "Neonatal Pulmonary Function," *Pediat. Clin. N. Amer.*, **13,** 769–799.
68. Nelson, N. M., Prod'hom, L. S., Cherry, R. B., Lipsitz, P. J. and Smith, C. A. (1962), "Pulmonary Function in the Newborn Infant. 2-Perfusion-Estimation by Analysis of Arterial-alveolar Carbon Dioxide Difference," *Pediatrics*, **30,** 975–989.
69. Nightingale, D. A. and Richards, C. C. (1965), "Volume Pressure Relations of the Respiratory System of Curarised Infants," *Anesthesiology*, **26,** 710–714.
70. Otis, A. B., Fenn, W. and Rahn, H. (1950), "Mechanics of Breathing in Man," *J. appl. Physiol.*, **2,** 592–607.
71. Pagtakhan, R. D., Faridy, E. E. and Chernik, V. (1971), "Interaction Between Arterial PO_2 and $P\text{CO}_2$ in the Initiation of Respiration of Fetal Sheep," *J. appl. Physiol.*, **30,** 382–387.
72. Pattle, R. E. (1963), "The Lining Layer of the Lung Alveoli," *Brit. med. Bull.*, **19,** 41–44.
73. Polgar, G. and Konig, G. P. (1965), "The Nasal Resistance of Newborn Infants," *J. Pediat.*, **67,** 557–567.
74. Polgar, G. and Promadhat, V. (1971), *Pulmonary Function Testing in Children*. Philadelphia: W. B. Saunders Company.
76. Polgar, G. and String, T. (1966), "The Viscous Resistance of the Lung Tissues in Newborn Infants," *J. Pediat.*, **69,** 787–792.
76. Purves, M. J. (1966a), "Respiratory and Circulatory Effects of Breathing 100 per cent Oxygen in the Newborn Lamb Before and After Denervation of the Carotid Chemoreceptors," *J. Physiol.*, **185,** 42–59.
77. Purves, M. J. (1966b), "The Effect of Hypoxia in the New-born Lamb Before and After Denervation of the Carotid Chemoreceptors," *J. Physiol.*, **185,** 60–77.
78. Purves, M. J. (1966c), "The Respiratory Response of the Newborn Lamb to Inhaled CO_2 With and Without Accompanying Hypoxia," *J. Physiol.*, **185,** 78–94.
79. Purves, M. J. and Biscoe, T. J. (1966), "Development of Chemoreceptor Activity," *Brit. med. Bull.*, **22,** 56–60.
80. Radford, E. P. (1954), "Ventilation Standards for Use in Artificial Respiration," *J. appl. Physiol.*, **7,** 451–460.
81. Read, D. J. C. (1967), "A Clinical Method for Assessing the Ventilatory Response to Carbon Dioxide," *Aust. Ann. Med.*, **16,** 20–32.
82. Reynolds, E. O. R. and Strang, B. (1966), "Alveolar Surface Properties of the Lung in the New-born," *Brit. med. Bull.*, **22,** 79–83.
83. Roberton, N. R. C., Gupta, J. M., Dahlenburg, G. W. and Tizard, J. P. M. (1968), "Oxygen Therapy in the Newborn," *Lancet*, **1,** 1323–1329.
84. Siegwart, B., Gehr, P., Gil, J. and Weibel, E. R. (1971), "Morphometric Estimation of Pulmonary Diffusing Capacity. IV. The Normal Dog Lung," *Resp. Physiol.*, **13,** 141–159.
85. Snyder, F. F. and Rosenfeld, M. (1937), "Direct Observation of Intra-uterine Respiratory Movements of the Fetus and the Role of Carbon Dioxide and Oxygen in Their Regulation," *Amer. J. Physiol.*, **119,** 153–166.
86. Strang, L. B. (1961), "Alveolar Gas and Anatomical Deadspace Measurements in Normal Newborn Infants," *Clin. Sci.*, **21,** 107–114.
87. Strang, L. B. and McGrath, M. W. (1962), "Alveolar Ventilation in Normal Newborn Infants Studied by Air Wash-in after Oxygen Breathing," *Clin. Sci.*, **23,** 129–139.
88. Sutherland, J. M. and Ratcliff, J. W. (1961), "Crying Vital Capacity," *Amer. J. Dis. Child.*, **101,** 93–100.
89. Swyer, P. R. and Wright, J. J. (1960), "Ventilation and Ventilatory Mechanics in the Newborn," *J. Pediat.*, **56,** 612–621.
90. Tenney, S. M. and Remmers, J. E. (1963), "Comparative

Quantitative Morphology of the Mammalian Lung: Diffusing Area," *Nature*, **197**, 54–56.

91. Tenney, S. M. and Bartlett, D. (1967), "Comparative Quantitative Morphology of the Mammalian Lung: Trachea," *Resp. Physiol.*, **3**, 130–135.
92. Way, W. L., Costley, E. C. and Way, E. L. (1965), "Respiratory Sensitivity of the Newborn Infant to Meperidine and Morphine," *Clin. Pharmacol. Ther.*, **6**, 454–461.
93. Weng, T. R., Langer, H. M., Featherby, E. A. and Levison, H. (1970), "Arterial Blood Gas Tensions and Acid-base Balance in Symptomatic and Asymptomatic Asthma in Childhood," *Amer. Rev. resp. Dis.*, **101**, 274–282.

15. THE GROWTH AND DEVELOPMENT OF THE CARDIO-PULMONARY RESPONSES TO EXERCISE

S. GODFREY

In other sections of this book the reader can find information about the growth and development of various individual systems of the body—respiratory, cardiovascular, neuromuscular, metabolic and endocrine. In this chapter, the way in which all these systems are co-ordinated during exercise will be considered, and especially the way in which the response of the child changes as growth occurs. It is not intended to present an authoritative account of exercise physiology, a number of which are cited in the references, but more to discuss the practical aspects of adaptation during physical maturation.

PHYSIOLOGICAL CHANGES NECESSITATED BY EXERCISE

During physical exercise, a very fit adult can increase his horizontal velocity to 36 km./hr. (22·5 miles/hr.) for a short time and to 24 km./hr. (15 miles/hr.) for a longer period. During such severe exercise his oxygen intake may increase to 5 l./min. or 20 times the resting value. In fact, running is probably not the most strenuous type of exercise since cross-country skiers have been reported to reach oxygen intakes in excess of 6 l./min.[40] Accompanying this increase in oxygen uptake is a comparable increase in cardiac output—as high as 36 l./min. or more, or 7 times the resting value[14]—so that the net O_2 transport to the metabolizing muscles is increased almost 150 times. Despite this increase, it is impossible to meet all the metabolic demands aerobically during strenuous exercise and energy can only be provided by anaerobic glycolysis with the production of lactic acid. The rise of lactate is not linearly related to work since submaximal exercise up to about two-thirds of maximum working capacity can be performed with little increase. Lactate rises very steeply as maximum work is approached and actually reaches its highest levels 2 or 3 minutes after stopping very strenuous exercise.

In adults, the increased cardiac output is achieved by an initial increase in stroke volume on beginning exercise, and subsequently by a rise in heart rate with constant stroke volume.[39] More oxygen is extracted from the blood so that the arterio-venous O_2 content difference widens. This means that mixed venous (pulmonary arterial) PO_2 is lower and a larger gradient exists between alveolar gas and capillary blood so that O_2 is taken up more rapidly into the blood in the lungs. In order to maintain alveolar PO_2 and, of course, to remove the large volumes of CO_2 produced by the tissues, alveolar ventilation is increased. This is achieved by an increase in respiratory frequency and tidal volume (VT) up to about 50 per cent of the vital capacity[3,29] after which tidal volume remains relatively fixed and frequency increases alone. Gas exchange is normally so efficient that it is unusual for there to be much change in arterial PO_2 or $P\text{CO}_2$ during exercise. At very high levels, there is lactic acidosis which may cause the arterial pH to fall considerably, and this additional stimulus to breathing may result in a small fall in $P\text{CO}_2$.[15,36]

The reasons why a subject eventually reaches breaking point on exercise has never been clearly established. In fact, a number of integrated functions appear to fail more or less simultaneously. Thus with a fixed stroke volume, cardiac output is limited by the maximum heart rate which can be achieved. At the same time, the rate of transfer of O_2 in the lung may become critical and also the work of breathing may increase to a point where little or no extra benefit is gained from an increase in ventilation. The ultimate factor deciding differences in the breaking point of exercise between otherwise similar individuals is undoubtedly psychological—the ability to withstand a variety of noxious stimuli. It is this as much as anything which distinguishes the successful athlete.[11] The question of fitness and training is very important in adults since there are such large differences in performance due to cultural factors. The so-called developed societies are notoriously unfit due to lack of exercise and over-eating. Children, on the other hand, habitually take more exercise than their elders and can generally be considered a comparatively homogenous and fit group. This is an important point because it suggests that the responses of children to exercise should be more uniform and hence that the sick child should stand out more clearly with exercise tests.[19,20]

As the child develops from infancy to adulthood, so the absolute amount of work of which he is capable increases and the way in which he works must change due to alteration in the size of organs. Relatively speaking, the work involved in taking a full feed during infancy is probably the same as that involved in running 1,500 m. as an adult. This question of relative work will recur throughout this account.

From what will be discussed later, it appears that the child maintains quite similar levels of gas exchange, blood gases and cardiac output to adults for equal rates of working. This suggests that certain biological norms are established very early on. It also presents problems in terms of the mechanics of gas exchange and circulation since a 5-year-old child will have a vital capacity of one-fifth that of an adult and a stroke volume of about one-quarter. One would therefore acticipate that children would exercise with tachypnoea and tachycardia relative to the adult. As the dimensions of the lungs and heart increase, so the need for tachypnoea and tachycardia will diminish. Throughout the growing period, therefore, there must be a continuous closely integrated, alteration in the mechanics of ventilation and circulation.

THE MEASUREMENT OF EXERCISE PERFORMANCE IN CHILDREN

Before going on to consider the physiology of exercise in growing children, it is worth considering the ways in which exercise performance can be measured in this age-group.

Below the age of 5 years it is unusual to get a child to co-operate with exercise tests, though the author has had occasional successes with younger children. Part of the problem is that very young children find it difficult to cycle on an ergometer and to keep up a fairly constant speed. Moreover, there is the practical problem that their legs may be too short to reach the pedals or the length of the crank may be too long. Some of these difficulties can be solved by using a treadmill, though this presents complications of its own.

From the age of 5 years and upwards, there is abundant data in the literature on exercise performance in children. Most of this concerns simple measurements of ventilation, gas exchange and heart-rate at submaximal and maximal levels of exercise Children will readily accept all the standard physiological procedures for such tests, and often co-operate better than adults. The details of the performance of exercise tests is beyond the scope of this chapter, but the reader is referred to monographs.[3,4,22] One simple practical point should be made, however. Most respiratory circuits for studying exercise include a tap and a one-way valve system. The dead space of such a combination made from standard adult apparatus will usually be about 100–150 ml. Now this is about equal to the physiological dead space of an adult, but is some three times that of a 5-year-old. This would impose a most unphysiological load on the child and so any circuit used for children should have minimal dead space. Even if the resistance were rather higher, this would not matter so much with the lower ventilation and higher internal resistance of the child.

Many exercise studies in adults involve sampling arterial

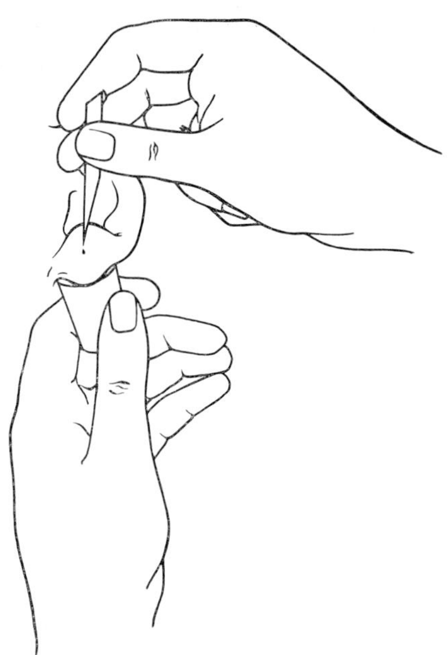

FIG. 1. Technique of puncturing ear lobe before collecting blood. (From[27]).

blood, either to measure gas tensions or to calculate cardiac output. Even if it were ethical, percutaneous arterial cannulation in young children is virtually impossible and direct needle arterial puncture is not practical during exercise. In most countries it is unacceptable to perform non-diagnostic arterial catheterization on normal children. The only studies of arterial blood during exercise in children have been in boys of 11 years and above reported from Sweden.[15,16] However, it has frequently been shown that arterialized capillary blood can approximate closely to true arterial blood. This capillary technique has been used during exercise by taking blood from the warmed finger pulp in children.[34] This is somewhat painful and rather frightening to most children. For this reason a technique was developed for taking arterialized ear-lobe capillary blood during exercise in children.[27] This procedure involves vasodilating the ear lobe with thurfyl nicotinate, puncturing with a sharp scalped blade (Fig. 1) and collecting the blood in the cup of a cut-off intravenous cannula (Fig. 2). When the cup is full, the blood is allowed to run into the capillary tube and is then stored on ice and analysed as soon as

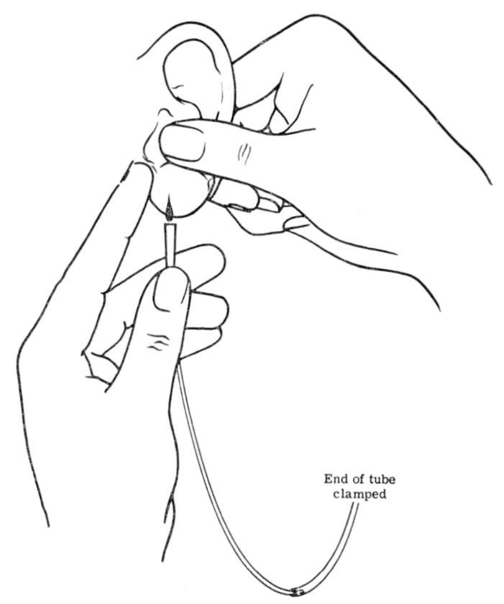

FIG. 2. Collection of ear lobe blood sample. The end of the tube is clamped by the observer's teeth until the cup is full of blood. (From[27])

possible. The correlation of $P\text{CO}_2$, PO_2 and pH with simultaneous arterial values was excellent in adults.

The reason why previous studies in children have not included measurements of cardiac output or stroke volume is that the standard procedures for these measurements involve catheterization of systemic and pulmonary arteries. There are, however, alternative methods for measuring cardiac output which do not involve blood sampling and the nitrous-oxide method was actually used in children over 45 years ago.[18] In general, inert-gas methods are difficult to perform for both subject and observer and are not readily applicable to young children.

The oldest method for measuring cardiac output in man is actually the so-called Indirect (CO_2) Fick method in which the lungs are used as tonometers to equilibrate alveolar gas with the blood in the pulmonary capillaries. Many different versions of this technique have been used in adults[6,10,31,35,37] but the most satisfactory for both adults and children is the plateau rebreathing procedure.[26] The child rebreathes a mixture of CO_2 in O_2 for 10 sec. (Fig. 3). During the first 4–5 sec., mixing occurs between the gas in the bag, the lungs, and the mixed venous blood in the pulmonary capillaries where it has arrived from the pulmonary artery. During the 6th to 10th sec. there is equilibrium between all three gas phases so that a plateau of CO_2 cencentration is recorded. After 10 sec., recirculation of CO_2 enriched blood breaks the plateau.

This Indirect (CO_2) Fick method has proved to be highly reproducible[42] and very suitable for either healthy or sick children.[20] In children with normal lungs, it is not even necessary to measure arterialized capillary $P\text{CO}_2$ since the dead space can be assumed to be normal and the PCO_2 calculated by the Bohr equation from the measured tidal volume and mixed expired gas $P\text{CO}_2$. If the lungs are abnormal, capillary blood must be used. In fact, there is quite a tolerance for error in the $P\text{CO}_2$ since the veno-arterial difference becomes large on exercise and small errors will have little effect on the calculated cardiac output.[21]

THE GROWTH OF MAXIMUM EXERCISE PERFORMANCE

One of the most basic tests of physical fitness is the standardized assessment of the maximum rate of working (power output) that a subject can achieve. Clearly the maximum power will depend on the preceding amount of work undertaken and the duration for which the subject is expected to maintain each submaximal power output on the way up to maximum. A simple, informative and standardized method for such a study in children consists of having the child cycle on an ergometer and increasing the load on the machine by a fixed increment every minute until the child is unable to continue any longer. Such a test is not a steady-state test, but because of the rapid adaptation of children to changing loads, it has proved to be very satisfactory for studying submaximal and maximal exercise. Indeed in the study of Davies, Barnes and Godfrey,[9] 92 per cent of children worked to within one increment of that at

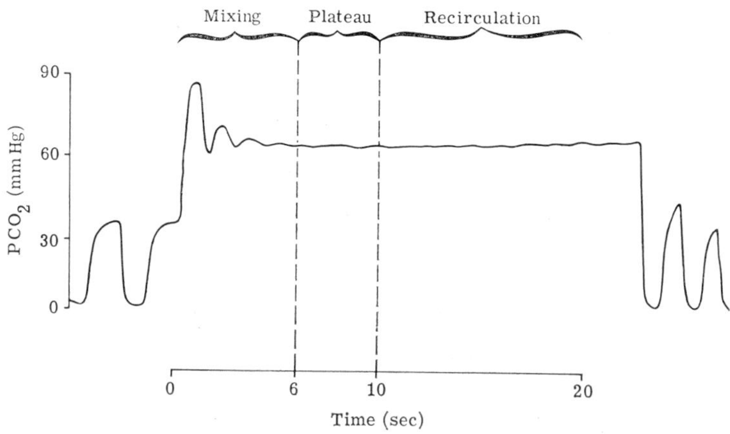

FIG. 3. Typical trace from a rapid CO_2 analyser sampling at the mouth during rebreathing showing the three phases obtained.

which they achieved their maximum aerobic power (*see below*).

With children of different sizes, it is important to grade the increment of work so that all children work for a similar total time. The author has found it convenient to use 10 W. increments for children under 125 cm. tall, 15 W. increments for children of 125 to 150 cm. and 20 W. increments for children over 150 W.[22] The results of this type of simple progressive exercise test for a group of 113 boys and girls between the ages of 5 and 15 years is shown in Fig. 4. Boys

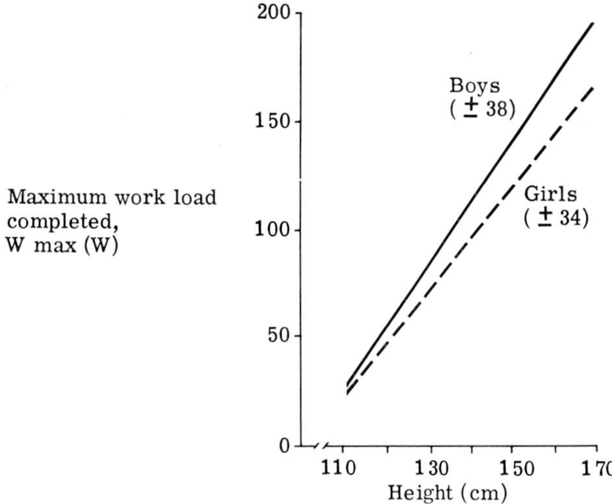

FIG. 4. The relationship between maximum power output and size. The figures in brackets in this and subsequent illustrations give ± 2 SE of the estimate of y about the regression line which is close to the 95 per cent confidence limits. (Modified from[23])

generally achieved higher power output (W. max.) than girls, especially in the larger children.

As a subject works progressively harder, so oxygen uptake increases until a plateau value is reached after which further increments of work are not accompanied by an increase in oxygen uptake. This level of oxygen uptake is called the maximum oxygen uptake ($\dot{V}O_2$ max) and the corresponding power output is the maximum aerobic power. The extra work is being performed entirely anaerobically and lactate is rising rapidly. Such work can thus only be continued for a short time. A typical example of this test in two subjects is shown in Fig. 5.

Many studies have been carried out to measure $\dot{V}O_2$ max. and other parameters of maximal exercise in children, including the very extensive studies of Robinson[38] and Astrand[3] as well as those of the author. All these studies came to essentially similar conclusions. As expected, $\dot{V}O_2$ max. increases with age in both boys and girls (Fig. 6) from about 1·0 l./min. at the age of 5 years to some 3·0–4·0 l./min. at puberty. There is little sex difference in the younger children, but as puberty is approached the performance of girls falls below that of boys when $\dot{V}O_2$ max. is considered simply in absolute terms. In order to compare the relative aerobic power at different ages, it has been customary to express the $\dot{V}O_2$ max. per kg. body weight (Fig. 7). On this basis, it can be seen that relative aerobic power also increases with age

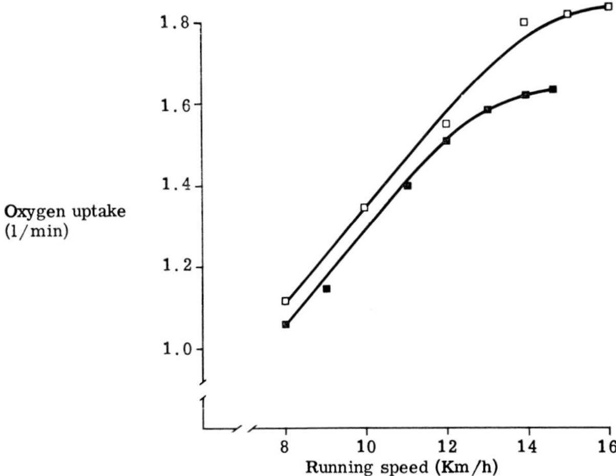

FIG. 5. The plateau in O_2 uptake in two subjects on reaching maximum aerobic power. (Redrawn from[3])

from about 45 ml./kg. at 5 years to around 50 ml./kg. in teenage boys. The peak level of 55–60 ml./kg. is reached in the early twenties and thereafter there is a steady decline to 25–30 ml./kg. in old age,[33] Even when corrected for weight, teenage girls still apparently achieve lower $\dot{V}O_2$ max. than teenage boys.

The use of any simple anthropometric basis for comparisons may not be valid, especially for bicycle ergometer exercise in which the body weight is supported and only the leg muscles are used. In the study of Davies *et al.*,[9] an estimate was made of the volume of muscle in the children's legs by measuring total limb volume using water displacement and subtracting values for fat and bone content. When $\dot{V}O_2$ max. was related to leg-muscle volume a constant relationship was found throughout childhood and adult life, and even more important, the sex difference disappeared

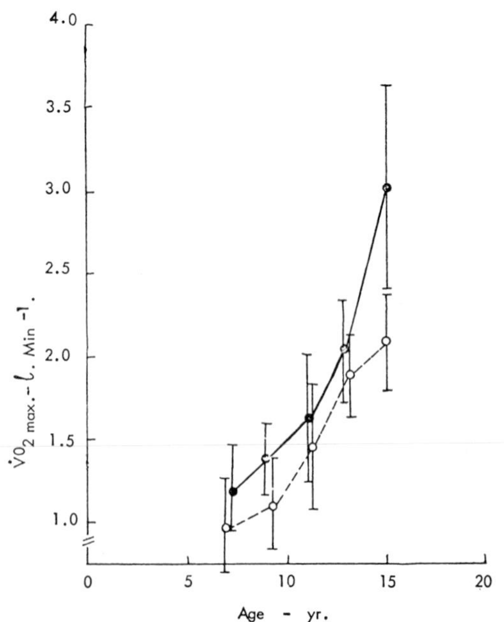

FIG. 6. Maximum O_2 uptake (± 1 SD) in relation to age and sex. (From[9])

(Fig. 8). Thus, it is possible that the increase in $\dot{V}O_2$ max. is a simple function of the quantity of muscle available for work, although other factors such as heart size and total body haemoglobin are also undoubtedly important.[3]

While there may be a four-fold increase in absolute $\dot{V}O_2$ max. during childhood there is a very small if any change in maximal heart rate. Like $\dot{V}O_2$, heart rate also reaches a

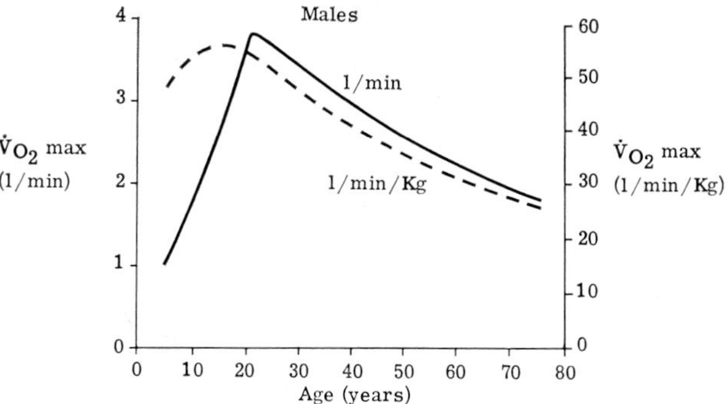

FIG. 7. Relation between absolute maximum O_2 uptake and maximum O_2 uptake per Kg body weight with age. (Redrawn from[33])

plateau at high levels of work but is about 200 per min. irrespective of age or sex. In fact, the maximal heart rate (H.R. max.) is between about 200 and 210 up to puberty with the highest values between 10 and 12 years of age.[3,38] It slowly declines thereafter. It is quite common for children to exceed 200 beats/min. during strenuous exercise, and a

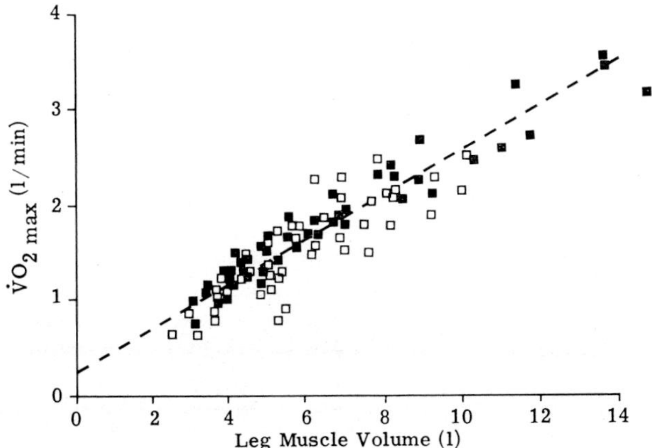

FIG. 8. Maximum O_2 uptake in relation to leg muscle volume (LV) in boys (closed symbols) and girls (open symbols). (From[9])

heart rate much below 195 must call the subject's co-operation into question during a maximal effort test. Providing there is no other factor limiting exercise, such as lung or neuromuscular disease, a child who stops exercise with a lower heart rate is probably not trying hard enough. This is also likely to be the cause of the rather lower H.R. max. in the youngest children. The maximum heart rate obtained falls steadily from the peak value in childhood to about 160 beats/min. by the age of 70.[38]

The minute ventilation at maximum work increases with age, as the absolute level of maximum work increases. When expressed as ventilation per litre of O_2 consumed at maximum work, the younger children tend to ventilate rather more—about 40 l./min./l. $\dot{V}O_2$ at the age of 5, falling to 32 l./min. $\dot{V}O_2$ at 16 (Fig. 9). Girls generally have rather higher maximum ventilations than boys of the same age.

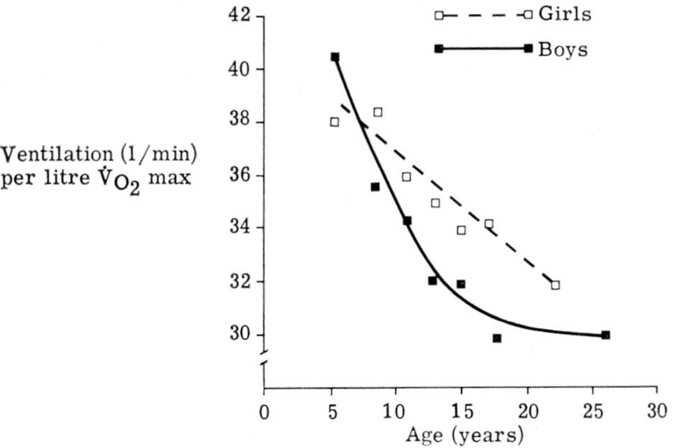

FIG. 9. Relation between maximum exercise ventilation expressed per litre of maximum O_2 uptake and age. Smaller children hyperventilate when standardized for O_2 uptake. (Redrawn from[3])

As will be seen later, children also tend to over-ventilate at sub-maximal levels compared with adults but it is not clear why this should occur unless they are more sensitive to the stimuli which occur during work.

It is also worth considering the maximum ventilation on exercise in relation to the maximum ventilation of which the

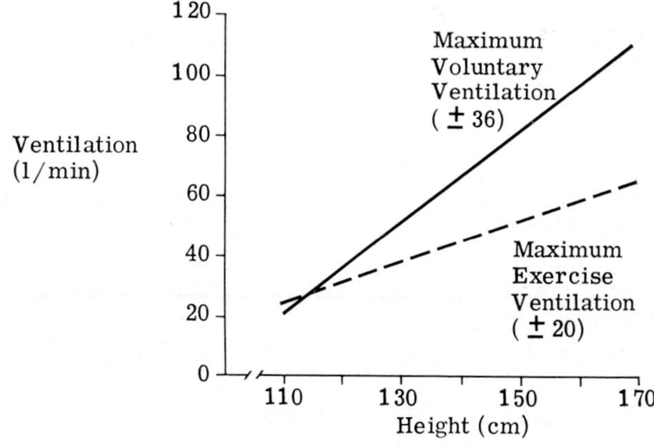

FIG. 10. Relation between maximum exercise ventilation, maximum voluntary ventilation and height.

child is capable, i.e. the maximum voluntary ventilation (M.V.V.—*see* Chapter 30). When this comparison is made, it is seen that most children do not reach their ventilatory capacity on exercise (Fig. 10) though, as might be anticipated from the above discussion, younger children with lower M.V.V. values use a greater proportion on maximum exercise.

Coincident with the growth of lung volume with size, the resting tidal volume (V.T.), increases and respiratory frequency falls (Chapter 30). The same applies to the V.T. and frequency on maximal exercise. Thus, maximal frequency falls from about 70 per min. at the age of 5 to 50 per min. at 17.[3] This is not to say that a 17-year-old could not breathe faster than 50 times per min., but that he elects to use the slower rate to achieve his maximum exercise ventilation, presumably because it is mechanically more efficient. This point may be seen in the study of children with cystic fibrosis by Godfrey and Mearns,[25] where the patients with lung disease could often achieve a maximum exercise ventilation higher than their measured maximum voluntary ventilation, presumably again by breathing in a more economical fashion. As maximum frequency falls, maximum tidal volume increases in absolute terms, but it usually remains about 45 per cent of the child's vital capacity. While maximum frequency is not normally reached until the highest work load, maximum exercise tidal volume is often reached at submaximal levels, the further increase in minute ventilation being due to the continuing increase of respiratory frequency.

One of the criteria that maximum aerobic power has been achieved is that blood lactate should be very high. Astrand[3] found that the lactate shortly after stopping maximal exercise actually rose with age from around 6·6 mM/l for 5-year-old children to 12·1 mM/l for adults. The most likely explanation he offered was that the circulation of the younger subjects adapts more rapidly at the onset of maximum exercise. In the study by the author and his colleague,[9] maximum lactate showed a smaller age-effect being mostly between 8 and 10 mM/l. There were no systematic sex differences.

The only reliable measurements of cardiac output and stroke volume on maximum exercise in children are those for Swedish boys aged 11–14 years using the dye dilution technique.[15,16] Their results are discussed more fully later, but they basically showed that the maximum cardiac output was what one would have predicted from the maximum oxygen uptake on the basis of the submaximal cardiac output/oxygen uptake relationship. These cardiac output values were a little less than one would expect from young adults. Maximum stroke volume was 67 ml. for 11- to 13-year-old boys and 87 ml. for 13- to 14-year-old boys. These values were no greater than these children would have achieved at sub-maximal work (*see* later). This emphasizes that maximal exercise performance is limited from the circulatory point of view by the maximum heart rate.

These workers noted that the maximum arterio-venous O_2 content difference found in their children was 145 ml./l. This is less than the 181 ml./l. which can be achieved by adults[12] and less than can be achieved by children with congenital heart block.[41] The reason for this difference is not clear.

Thus it seems that maximum exercise performance increases in an orderly fashion with growth provided the right criteria are used for comparison. Maximum aerobic power is probably related to muscle mass, at least for cycling. The only differences between children and adults after allowing for size appears to be a tendency to hyperventilate in the younger age-groups and to achieve maximum exercise with lower blood-lactate levels.

THE GROWTH OF SUBMAXIMAL EXERCISE PERFORMANCE

Although maximal exercise performance in children has been much studied in the past, it is also important to consider exercise at lower levels of work. In fact, children (and adults) rarely sustain maximal exercise for any significant period of time and most of their exercise is performed at submaximal levels. Moreover, the notion that the $\dot{V}O_2$ max. is a reliable index of fitness, is not entirely true since the correlation between $\dot{V}O_2$ and athletic performance is generally rather poor.[7]

Although different aspects of submaximal exercise physiology in children have been published, most series have been either small, restricted to narrow age-groups, or unsatisfactory in some way, such as using standard levels of exercise irrespective of size. Moreover, very little has been published about the circulatory response to exercise in children. This prompted the author and his colleagues to study a large group of children aged 5–16 years during exercise on a bicycle ergometer and a treadmill. Each child was studied at approximately one-third and two-thirds of his or her measured W. max. Many of the results in this section are taken from these steady-state studies.[1,23]

The Metabolic Cost of Exercise

As work increases, so the oxygen consumption must increase. By including data from children of different sizes working at different rates, it is possible to study the growth of the oxygen cost of work (Fig. 11). There is little scatter

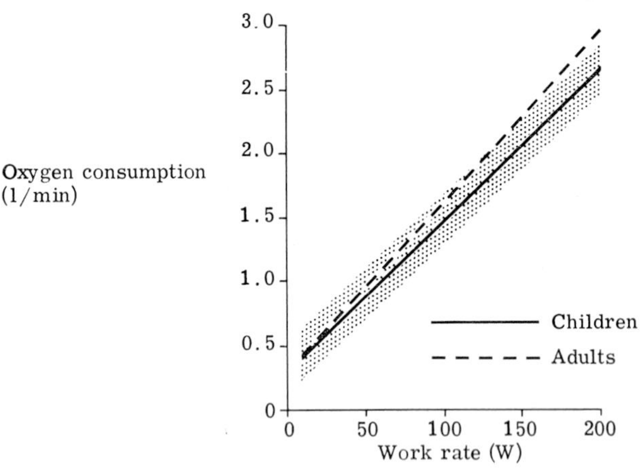

Fig. 11. The oxygen cost of work. The mean line for children (± 2 SEY) was taken from.[23] The adult line was taken from studies by E. Zeidifard in the same laboratory.

of points about the regression line showing that neither size nor sex had much influence on the oxygen uptake for any given work load although the line lay a little below that for adults. Although resting O_2 uptake is clearly size-related (Chapter 14B), this basal uptake forms so small a percentage of the total once a significant amount of work is being performed, that the size effect is no longer important. Using the relationship in Fig. 11, it is possible to calculate the mechanical efficiency of exercise in children. The mechanical equivalent of combustion carbohydrate and fat with a given amount of O_2 is known and this can be compared with the work being done on the ergometer. The mechanical efficiency of the children is 25 per cent and that of the adults is 21·6 per cent, which is close to the figure of 23 per cent found by Astrand.[3] This apparently greater efficiency of children may just reflect a lesser amount of fat to be carried.

Along with the increasing O_2 uptake, CO_2 production also increases, but the resting ratio of CO_2 and O_2 (respiratory exchange ratio, R) alters progressively. The resting value is difficult to measure in children because they rarely remain in a truly basal state, but it is approximately 0·85. At one-third of maximum working capacity (W. max.) this ratio has risen to 0·96 and by two-thirds of W. max. it is 1·07, i.e. more CO_2 is being produced than O_2 consumed. The cause of this change in R is partly that a higher proportion of fat being metabolized during exercise, but mainly due to lactate production at the higher work load liberating CO_2 from bicarbonate. At one-third W. max., blood lactate was 2·4 mM./l. and at two-thirds W. max. it was 5·1 mM/1.[23] These are similar to levels in adults at corresponding fractions of their W. max.

Ventilation and Blood Gases in Exercise

Submaximal ventilation seems to be closely related to oxygen consumption, and from what has been said above, it is no surprise that growth has little effect on exercise ventilation. The relationship between ventilation and oxygen uptake for children and adults are shown in Fig. 12.

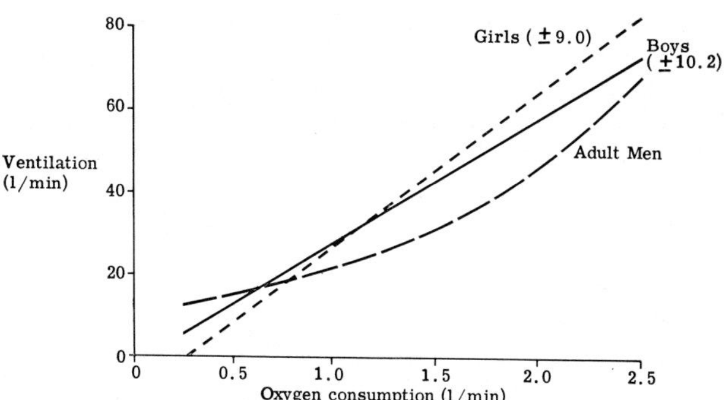

FIG. 12. Submaximal ventilation in relation to O_2 uptake in children[23] and adults.[28]

In fact, there is a little tendency for children to overventilate compared with adults, and this is seen more clearly by looking at their arterial $P\text{CO}_2$ which is inversely proportional to alveolar ventilation. It is difficult to obtain reliable estimates of arterial blood gases at rest in normal children (*see* Chapter 14B.), but such data as exists suggests that arterial $P\text{CO}_2$ is about 38–40 mm. Hg. in the age-range under consideration. At one-third W. max. arterial $P\text{CO}_2$ was 37·4 mm. Hg. in boys and 35·8 in girls, while at two-thirds W. max. it was 35·0 in boys and 33·9 in girls. There was no significant size-effect on the $P\text{CO}_2$ over the age range of 5–16 years. These data show that children, especially girls, tend to have alveolar hyperventilation on exercise relative to adults who normally keep their arterial $P\text{CO}_2$ about 40 mm. Hg.[36] This pattern of ventilation reflects what was seen earlier at maximal levels of work. However, the effect of this increased alveolar ventilation is rather small when looking at total minute ventilation (alveolar plus deadspace ventilation) and differences between children and adults are reduced.

The dead space (wasted) ventilation, V.D., of children on exercise has not previously been measured and as intimated

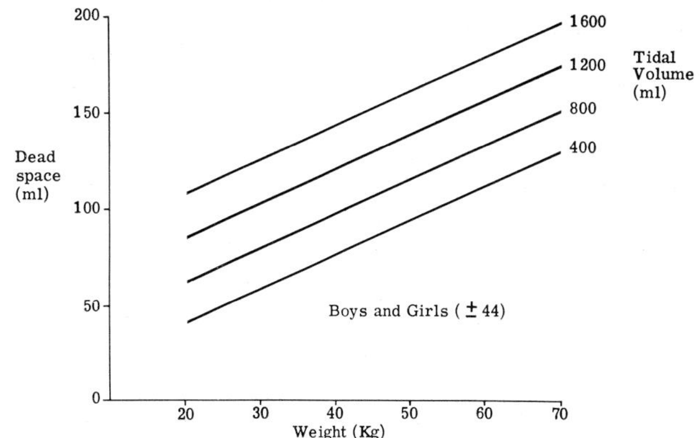

FIG. 13. Relation between physiological dead space, weight and tidal volume in children. (From[23])

earlier, the fact that it may be much smaller than in adults has largely been ignored. Using arterialized ear-lobe blood or end-tidal $P\text{CO}_2$ the relationship between V.D., tidal volume and weight shown in Fig. 13 was obtained. These data mean that the resting V.D. of a 20 kg. (5-year-old) child is 45 ml. and for a 60 kg. (15-year-old) child it is 115 ml. The V.D. increases by 5 ml. for every 100 ml. increase in

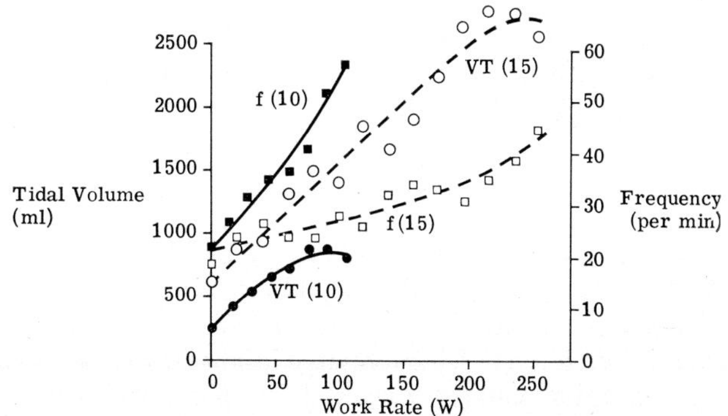

FIG. 14. Tidal volume (VT) and respiratory frequency (f) during progressive bicycle exercise in a 10-year-old and a 15-year-old boy. The size effect on VT and f can be seen as well as the levelling off of VT (at approximately 45 per cent of each individual's vital capacity).

tidal volume above the resting value. A very similar increment in V.D. with increasing V.T. was found in adults by Amussen and Nielsen[2] and this also fits the lower limit of increment found by Jones, McHardy, Naimark and Campbell.[32]

As with maximal exercise, so at submaximal levels, tidal volume (V.T.) increases with size and respiratory frequency falls at any given level of work. Typical results in two children aged 10 and 15 years are shown in Fig. 14. The plateau of V.T. before W. max. was reached can be seen. The V.T. at this stage represented 42 per cent of the vital capacity of the younger boy and 53 per cent of that of the older.

The changes in Pco_2 on exercise have been described above. There is virtually no change in Po_2 but pH tends to fall to about 7·35 at two-thirds W. max. and even lower at higher levels.[15] The calculated right-to-left shunt or venous admixture, i.e. the proportion of arterial blood which could have come directly from the right side of the heart, actually falls from about 5 per cent at rest to 2–3 per cent on exercise. These figures do not differ from those in adults.

Circulatory Changes on Submaximal Exercise

The simplest measurement and the one about which there is no disagreement is heart rate. At any given level of submaximal work, the rate is lower the larger the subject (Fig. 15). For children of any one size, the heart-rate increases linearly with work and the heart-rate of girls at any given submaximal level is 5–10 beats/min. higher than that of boys. Because of the fan-like nature of the heart-rate—$\dot{V}O_2$—height relationship, some information is lost by grouping children in relatively large height ranges. A useful approximation can be achieved by plotting heart-rate against height and log $\dot{V}O_2$ using multiple linear regression (Fig. 16).

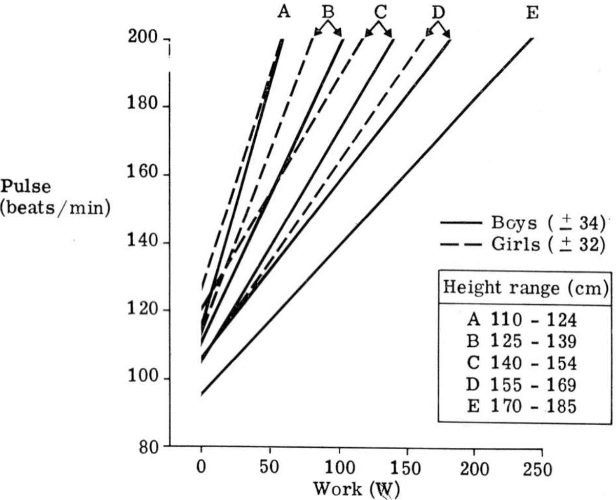

FIG. 15. Heart rate in relation to work and size during progressive bicycle exercise. (Modified from[23])

For reasons given earlier, virtually nothing was known about the cardiac output of children on exercise until quite recently. In fact, the earliest attempt to measure cardiac output ($\dot{Q}$) in children was probably by Galle[18] using the nitrous-oxide method. He made 22 resting studies in 4 subjects and 9 exercise studies in 2 subjects who were all 12-year-old boys. The mean values of $\dot{Q}$ in relation to $\dot{V}O_2$ which he found were in line with the best recent data, and he concluded that there was no difference between children and adults. In a very careful study using direct methods in conscious dogs, Barger, Richards, Metcalfe, and Gunther[5] measured $\dot{Q}$ on running at quite high levels of $\dot{V}O_2$ with animals weighing up to 26·5 kg. This would correspond in size to a 6-year-old child. They thought that $\dot{Q}$ was similar to that for adult man but the standards for man which they used were rather on the low side. The results of these two studies together with more recent studies in children are illustrated later on.

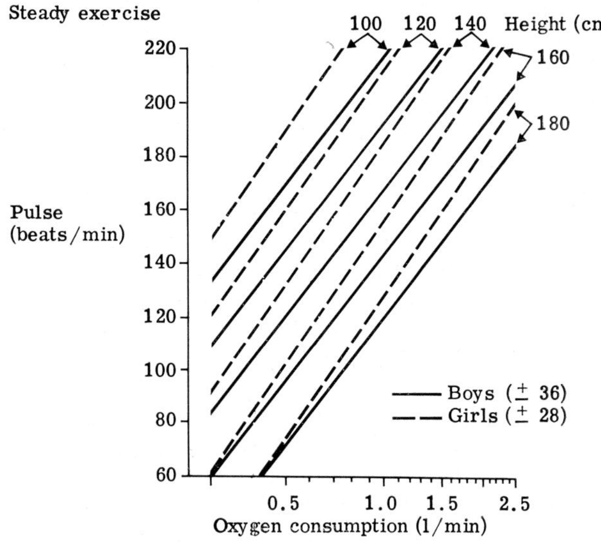

FIG. 16. Heart rate in relation to O_2 uptake and height during steady state exercise using a logarithmic axis. (Modified from[23])

The development of the Indirect (CO_2) Fick method by the Hammersmith Hospital Group[30,31] led to a study being performed to measure $\dot{Q}$ in 40 boys aged 9½–14½ years.[17] They also found $\dot{Q}$ values similar to adults studied in the same laboratory. They applied a correction factor to mixed venous Pco_2 which tends to give high values for $\dot{Q}$.[24] However, this was an important study because it showed that the CO_2 method could be used effectively in children. In two studies carried out in the author's department, this method was applied to a much wider age-range of normal children, extending down to 5-year-olds. The results for the ergometer study are shown in Fig. 17. There was a

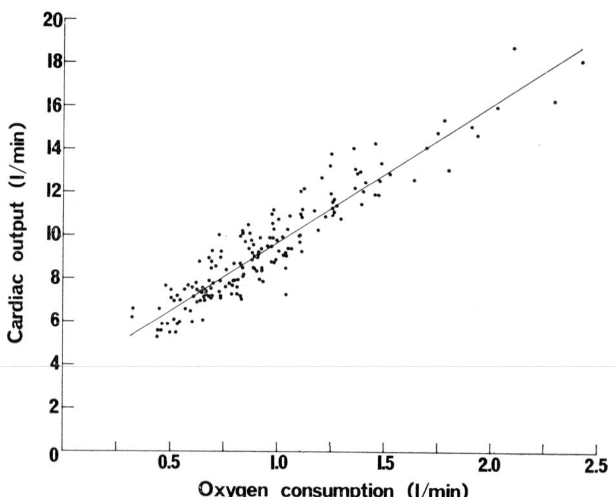

FIG. 17. Individual values of cardiac output and O_2 uptake during bicycle ergometer exercise in boys and girls aged 5–15 years. The regression line for all the points is shown and has the formula—Cardiac output (l./min.) = 6·3 × O_2 uptake + 3·3 ± 0·9 (SEY) (l./min.)

relatively small scatter of points about the regression line and no important sex difference. As in adults, $\dot{Q}$ was a little lower on running compared with cycling. The smallest children had values for $\dot{Q}$ about 1 l./min. lower than the largest children at the same oxygen uptake. Compared to adults, these studies showed that children had slightly lower $\dot{Q}$ values which depended on their size. An exactly similar conclusion was reached by Eriksson *et al.*[15] and Eriksson and Koch[16] in the only direct study of cardiac output in boys ages 11–14 years.

The results for various studies on cardiac output in children, adults and dogs at submaximal levels have been summarized in Fig. 18. The mean adult regression lines for dye

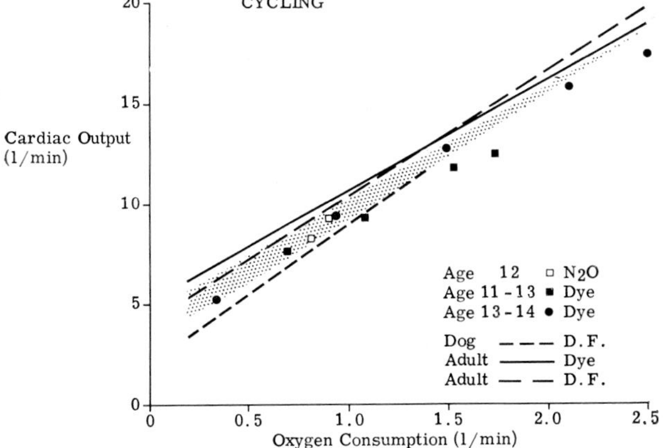

FIG. 18. Relationship between cardiac output and O_2 uptake in different studies by the methods shown, together with the shaded area indicating the range found for children using the CO_2 method and allowing for size. Godfrey, Davies *et al.*[23] The 12-year-old children were studied by Galle,[18] the 11–13-year-olds by Eriksson and Koch,[16] the 13–14-year-olds by Eriksson *et al.*[15] and the dogs by Barger *et al.*[5] The adult lines were constructed from data in the literature collected by E. Zeidifard.

dilution and direct Fick methods were obtained from the literature by E. Zeidifard (personal communication). It can be seen that children tend to fall a little below the adult lines. The dogs of Barger *et al.*[5] clearly fell on the same line as children of a similar size.

Taking the data on heart-rate and $\dot{Q}$ together, it is obvious that the exercise stroke volume must increase with size for any given level of work (Fig. 19). Girls have a relative tachycardia and hence a smaller stroke volume. In the individual child there is an increase of stroke volume of some 30 per cent from rest to upright exercise, but little further change with increasing work. $\dot{Q}$ and stroke volume are both larger in supine exercise in adults, but there is no data on normal children in this position.

Thus, at submaximal levels of work, O_2 uptake, minute ventilation, cardiac output and blood gases are largely unaffected by size, but tidal volume and stroke volume increase with size, and respiratory frequency and heart-rate decrease with size for any given level of work. Sex differences are small, with girls tending to hyperventilate more than boys and to have rather smaller stroke volumes.

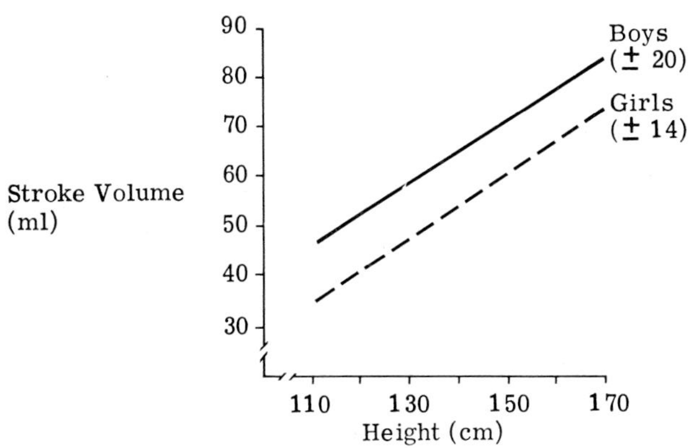

FIG. 19. Stroke volume on exercise in relation to size. (Modified from[23])

PHYSICAL TRAINING IN CHILDREN

Reliable studies of the effect of physical training in children are rare, mainly because of the technical problems involved in conducting repeated studies and ensuring adherence to the training programme. Two Swedish studies on 11-year-old boys[13] and 11- to 13-year-old boys[16] made observations before and after 4–6 months intensive physical training. In both studies, the $\dot{V}O_2$ max. rose after training by some 14 per cent, which is more than would occur due to growth, and indeed there was no significant rise in a control group of untrained children. In the study by Ekblom[13] continuation of training for 26 months resulted in a rise of $\dot{V}O_2$ max. of 55 per cent while the increase in the untrained control group due to growth was only 37 per cent. The rise in $\dot{V}O_2$ max. is accompanied by a rise in stroke volume and maximum cardiac output, though maximum heart-rate does not change. The larger stroke volume means that the heart-rate is relatively slower at all levels of work. All these changes in children are very similar to those seen in adults after training, and probably reverse just as quickly if training is halted. It should be emphasized that quite severe and frequent training is needed to alter $\dot{V}O_2$ max. in children (who are generally fit compared to adults) and this does not occur as a result of routine physical education in schools, even when this is quite strenuous.[8]

CONCLUSION

The growth and development of the response to exercise in childhood is an orderly process whereby adaptations occur to preserve inborn patterns in the face of the changing size of organs. Mechanical efficiency, exercise ventilation and cardiac output are only marginally affected by growth and overall power is a function of available muscle. The smaller heart and lungs of the child necessitate tachycardia and tachypnoea to preserve cardiac output and alveolar ventilation.

REFERENCES

1. Anderson, S. D. and Godfrey, S. (1971), "Cardio-respiratory Response to Treadmill Exercise in Normal Children," *Clin. Sci.*, **40**, 433–442.

2. Asmussen, E. and Nielsen, M. (1956), "Physiological Dead Space and Alveolar Gas Pressures at Rest and During Muscular Exercise," *Acta physiol. scand.*, **38**, 1–21.
3. Astrand, P-O. (1952), *Experimental Studies of Physical Working Capacity in Relation to Sex and Age*. Copenhagen: Ejnar Munksgaard.
4. Astrand, P–O. and Rodahl, K. (1970), *Textbook of Work Physiology*. New York: McGraw Hill.
5. Barger, A. C., Richards, V., Metcalfe, J. and Gunther, B. (1956), "Regulation of the Circulation During Exercise. Cardiac Output (Direct Fick) and Metabolic Adjustments in the Normal Dog." *Amer. J. Physiol.*, **184**, 613–623.
6. Collier, C. R. (1956), "Determination of Mixed Venous CO_2 Tensions by Rebreathing," *J. appl. Physiol.*, **9**, 25–29.
7. Cumming, G. R. (1972), "Correlation of Bone Age and Calf Muscle with Heart Volume, Aerobic and Anaerobic Power and Athletic Performance in 12- to 16-year-old Boys and Girls," Paper read at 4th International Symposium on Paediatric Work Physiology, Wingate, Israel.
8. Cumming, G. R., Goulding, D. and Baggley, G. (1969), "Failure of School Physical Education to Improve Cardiorespiratory Fitness," *Canad. med. Ass. J.*, **101**, 69–73.
9. Davies, C. T. M., Barnes, C. and Godfrey, S. (1972), "Body Composition and Maximal Exercise Performance in Children," *Hum. Biol.* **44**, 195–214.
10. Defares, J. G. (1958), "Determination of $P\bar{v}CO_2$ from the Exponential CO_2 Rise During Rebreathing," *J. appl. Physiol.*, **13**, 159–164.
11. Edwards, R. H. T., Jones, N. L., Oppenheimer, E. A., Hughes, R. L. and Knill-Jones, R. P. (1969), "Interrelation of Responses During Progressive Exercise in Trained and Untrained Subjects," *Quart. J. exp. Physiol.*, **54**, 394–403.
12. Ekblom, B. (1969a), "Effects of Physical Training on Oxygen Transport System in Man," *Acta physiol. scand.*, suppl. 328.
13. Ekblom, B. (1969b), "Effect of Physical Training in Adolescent Boys," *J. appl. Physiol.*, **27**, 350–355.
14. Ekblom, B. and Hermansen, L. (1968), "Cardiac Output in Athletes," *J. appl. Physiol.*, **25**, 619–625.
15. Eriksson, B. O., Grimby, G. and Saltin, B. (1971), "Cardiac Output and Arterial Blood Gases During Exercise in Pubertal Boys," *J. appl. Physiol.*, **31**, 348–352.
16. Eriksson, B. O. and Koch, G. (1972), "Effect of Physical Training on Haemodynamic Response During Submaximal and Maximal Exercise in 11- to 13-year-old Boys," *Acta physiol. scand.* In press.
17. Gadhoke, S. and Jones N. L. (1969), "The Responses to Exercise in Boys Aged 9 to 15," *Clin. Sci.*, **37**, 789–801.
18. Galle, P. (1926), "The Oxygen Consumption Per Litre of Blood in Children," *Skand. Arch. Physiol.*, **47**, 174–187.
19. Godfrey, S. (1970a), "The Diagnosis of Physical Fitness in Suspected Heart or Lung Disease by Means of Exercise Tests," *Lancet*, **ii**, 973–976.
20. Godfrey, S. (1970b), "The Physiological Response to Exercise in Children with Lung or Heart Disease," *Arch. Dis. Childh.*, **45**, 534–538.
21. Godfrey, S. and Davies, C. T. M. (1970), "Estimates of Arterial PCO_2 and Their Effect on the Calculated Values of Cardiac Output and Dead Space on Exercise," *Clin. Sci.*, **39**, 529–537.
22. Godfrey, S. (1972), "The Study of the Physiological Responses to Exercise of Children," M.D. Thesis, University of London.
23. Godfrey, S., Davies, C. T. M., Wozniak, E. and Barnes, C. A. (1971), "Cardio-respiratory Response to Exercise in Normal Children," *Clin. Sci.*, **40**, 419–431.
24. Godfrey, S., Katzenelson, R. and Wolf, E. (1972), "Gas to Blood PCO_2 Differences During Rebreathing in Children and Adults," *Resp. Physiol.*, **13**, 274–282.
25. Godfrey, S. and Mearns, M. (1971), "Pulmonary Function and the Response to Exercise in Cystic Fibrosis," *Arch. Dis. Childh.*, **46**, 144–151.
26. Godfrey, S. and Wolf, E. (1972), "An Evaluation of Rebreathing Methods for Measuring Mixed Venous PCO_2 During Exercise," *Clin. Sci.*, **42** 345–353.
27. Godfrey, S., Wozniak, E. R., Courtnay Evans, R. J. and Samuels, C. S. (1971), "Ear Lobe Blood Samples for Blood Gas Analysis at Rest and During Exercise," *Brit. J. Dis. Chest.*, **65**, 58–64.
28. Grimby, G. (1969), "Respiration in Exercise," *Med. Sci. Sports*, **1**, 9–14.
29. Hey, E. N., Lloyd, B. B., Cunningham, D. J. C., Jukes, M. G. M. and Bolton, D. P. G. (1966), "Effects of Various Respiratory Stimuli on the Depth and Frequency of Breathing in Man," *Resp. Physiol.*, **1**, 193–205.
30. Higgs, B. E., Clode, M., McHardy, G. J. R., Jones, N. L. and Campbell, E. J. M. (1967), "Changes in Ventilation, Gas Exchange and Circulation During Exercise in Norman Subjects," *Clin. Sci.*, **32**, 329–337.
31. Jones, N. L., Campbell, E. J. M., McHardy, G. J. R., Higgs, B. E. and Clode, M. (1967), "The Estimation of Carbon Dioxide Pressure of Mixed Venous Blood During Exercise." *Clin., Sci.*, **32**, 311–327.
32. Jones, N. L., McHardy, G. J. R., Naimark, A. and Campbell, E. J. M. (1966), "Physiological Dead Space and Alveolar-arterial Gas Pressure Differences During Exercise," *Clin. Sci.*, **31**, 19–29.
33. Knutgen, H. G. (1969), "Physical Working Capacity and Physical Performance," *Med. Sci. Sports*, **1**, 1–8.
34. Koch, G. (1965), "Comparisons of Carbon Dioxide Tension, pH and Standard Bicarbonate in Capillary Blood and in Arterial Blood," *Scand. J. clin. Lab. Invest.*, **17**, 223–229.
35. Lowy, A. and Schrotter, H. von (1905), "Untersuchungan uber die blutcirculation beim Menschen," *Z. exp. Path. Ther.*, **1**, 197–310.
36. Matell, G. (1963), "Time-courses of Changes in Ventilation and Arterial Gas Tensions in Man Induced by Moderate Exercise," *Acta physiol. scand.*, **58**, suppl. 206.
37. Plesch, J. (1909), "Hamodynamische Studien," *Z. exp. Path. Ther.*, **6**, 380–618.
38. Robinson, S. (1938), "Experimental Studies of Physical Fitness in Relation to Age," *Arbeitsphysiologie*, **10**, 251–323.
39. Rowell, L. B. (1969), "Circulation," *Med. Sci. Sports*, **1**, 15–22.
40. Saltin, B. and Astrand, P. O. (1967), "Maximum Oxygen Uptake in Athletes," *J. appl. Physiol.*, **23**, 353–358.
41. Taylor, M. R. H. and Godfrey, S. (1972), "Exercise Studies in Congenital Heart Block," *Brit. Heart J.*, **34**, 930–935.
42. Zeidifard, E., Silverman, M. and Godfrey, S. (1972), "Reproductibility of the Indirect (CO_2) Fick Method for the Calculation of Cardiac Output," *J. appl. Physiol.*, **33**, 141–143.

16. GROWTH AND DEVELOPMENT OF ENDODERMAL STRUCTURES

V. MILLER AND A. HOLZEL

NORMAL EMBRYOLOGY OF THE GASTROINTESTINAL TRACT

The entodermal tissue which will make up the future intestine is differentiated in the twelve-day blastocyst.[21] The mesoderm round this tissue becomes separated into somatic and splanchnic mesoderm. The splanchnic mesoderm and entoderm constitute the splanchonpleure, thus giving a primitive two-layered gut wall. The entoderm lining will differentiate into epithelium and glandular tissue, while the mesoderm will differentiate into the smooth muscle of the intestine and connective tissue.

At this stage of blastocyst formation, infoldings of the embryonic margins occur so that the embryonic and extra-embryonic germ layers are clearly defined. Rapid forward growth occurs in the cephalic region, producing a distinct tube-like structure—the forgut—from which arise the pharynx, thyroid, parathyroid, thymus, respiratory tract, oesophagus, stomach, upper duodenum liver and pancreas.[29] The hind gut is formed in a similar manner and gives rise to the large bowel from the splenic fixture to the upper anal canal. The midgut remains as an incomplete tube in communication with the yolk sac and will form the portion of intestines from the second part of the duodenum to the splenic flexure of the colon.

The ends of the forgut and hind gut fuse with the ectodermal layer and dimples occur which mark off the area of the stomodeum, and the proctodeum respectively. This occurs at about the 21st day. The head region is well formed at this time. The stomodeum is bounded laterally by two maxillary and two mandibular processes. Superiorly there is a nasofrontal process, which is subdivided into medial and lateral process which surrounds the olfactory pit. The maxillary processes grow forward and fuse, giving rise to the anterior nares, and upper jaw. Mandibular processes fuse to give rise to the lower jaw. The floor of the stomodeum perforates at the end of 4 weeks, and from the stomodeum arises the mucosa of the lips, cheeks, hard palate, anterior two-thirds of tongue including taste buds, dental lamina and enamel.

Behind the oral forgut the tube becomes flattered to give the pharynx. From the pharyngeal entoderm arises the mucosa of the pharynx, the submandibular and sublingual salivary gland, together with the posterior third of the tongue and soft palate.

Caudal to the pharynx, the tube again narrows to give a short area which will give the oesophagus, growth of this occurs later. At the lower end a dilatation appears at 4 weeks as the rudiment of the stomach.

At 4–5 weeks the intestine is growing faster than the body cavity and a loop of gut comes to lie in the yolk stalk. The apex of the loop connects with the yolk sac. The part of the gut cephaled to the connection with the yolk sac will give the lower duodenum, jejunum and upper ileum. It clearly grows faster than the caudal region which gives the terminal 2–3 ft. of ileum together with the large bowel. Remnants of the connection remain as a Meckle's diverticulum. As the gut loop grows it twists in an anticlockwise direction (as viewed from the front) to bring the caudal portion cephalad and ventral. The intestine returns to the abdominal cavity at 10 weeks and gives the characteristic coiling. Distal to the yolk sac connection, a dilatation occurs to give the caecum, the distal end of which remains narrow as the vermiform appendix. During its early development the large bowel is of a narrower diameter than the small bowel. Normal configuration occurs at about 20 weeks.

The gut wall can be divided into four regions.

(a) Mucosa, consisting of epithelium, tunica propria and muscularis mucosa.

(b) Submucosa, consisting of supportive tissue and lymphatic tissue.

(c) Tunica muscularis, which includes inner circular and outer longitudinal smooth muscle (striated in upper oesophagus).

(d) Serosa, consisting of the connective tissue coat.

Gastric pits are seen at 11 weeks and can be shown to secrete pepsin at 16 weeks. The oesophageal epithelium appears as simple epithelium at 6 weeks, changes to columnar epithelium at 10 weeks and then changes to stratified epithelium at 7 months. The large bowel has villi initially. In the small bowel villi are seen at 7 weeks, crypts and glands appear at 12 weeks and digestive enzymes at 3 months (*vide infra*).

The parotid, sublingual and submandibular salivary glands, together with salivary epithelium of the mucus membrane arise from the oral mucosa (stomodeal entoderm). The primordial mass pushes into mesenchyme and then branches. The submandibular and parotids glands appear at 6–8 weeks, while the sublingual gland appears at 7 months.

The pancreas arises from two outgrowths of the foregut. The ventral outgrowth is in close approximation to the common bile duct and develops into the head of pancreas. The dorsal outgrowth gives the tail of the pancreas. A third diverticulum of the foregut gives rise to the liver.

In the cloacal region of the hind gut, an invagination occurs, which becomes the alantois and forms into the urinary bladder. The posterior part of the cloaca gives rise to the rectum. It is closed by the cloacal membrane—the proctodeum—which should break down at 9 weeks.

Embryonic Anomalies

Having considered the normal anatomical development of the gut, the anomalies arising from maldevelopment become readily understood.

(1) Oesophageal atresia and tracheo—oesophageal fistula will result from failure of the respiratory tract to completely separate from the foregut at about 4 or 5 weeks.

(2) Intestinal atresia and stenosis are the commonest causes of obstruction seen in the neonate. One-third of these obstructions appear in the duodenal area, while the others are seen in the small intestine and rectum. The aetiology has been attributed to failure of the gut lumen to recanalize following the normal period of hyperplasia of the entoderm. More recently, experimental evidence has suggested that vascular disturbance during organogenesis is the likely cause, either resulting from volvulus or thrombosis.

(3) Rectal atresia may be in the form of a membrane due to failure of the proctodeal membrane to perforate at 2–3 months. Alternatively, a blind pouch may be present due to faulty development of the cloacal uro-rectal septum.

(4) Peritoneal bands result from faulty rotation or fixation of the gut and is most commonly seen at the duodeno-jejunal junction.

(5) Duplications and diverticulae may be in the form of blind sacs or may communicate with the intestinal lumen. The mucosa may be ectopic, gastric epithelium often being found. Complications may be due to pressure, haemorrhage, perforation, bacterial overgrowth and obstruction. The only common diverticulum is Meckle's which is due to persistence of the vitello intestinal duct. It lies on the antemesenteric border and is found in 1–2 per cent in people showing a sex ratio of male: female 3:1. In 75 per cent of cases the mucosa will be histologically that of the ileum, but 25 per cent of cases will have gastric mucosa.

(6) Umbilical fistulae, polyps and sinuses result from portions of the vitello intestinal duct failing to occlude.

(7) Hirschsprung's disease is due to failure of Meissner's and Auerbach's plexus to develop. This defect is most commonly seen in the recto-sigmoid region.

MOTILITY OF THE ALIMENTARY TRACT

A major function of the alimentary tract besides secretion, digestion and absorption, is motility. This entails the movement of its contents throughout the whole length of the system submitting them on the way to an astonishingly complex array of physical and chemical processes until the waste products are excreted at the caudal end. The main principle underlying this mechanism is the creation of pressure gradients in adjoining sections of the apparatus.

Swallowing, the first act in the transport of food, is initiated by movements of the tongue. The tongue brings a bolus into the midline between its anterior part and the hard palate, the jaw shuts, the soft palate elevates and the anterior part of the tongue closes the anterior portion of the mouth. As the bolus moves towards the oropharynx, the nasopharynx is shut off by the elevation of the soft palate and constriction of the palatopharyngeal muscles. The larynx rises, there is firm closure of the glottis, and the additus laryngi is covered by the epiglottis, which is partly pushed into position by the bolus moving into the oropharynx. Swallowing or deglutition is a reflex act started by stimulation of a large number of receptors in mouth and pharynx. The different impulses are conveyed by the glossopharyngeal nerve and the superior laryngeal branch of the vagus. The reflex is facilitated by higher centres in the medulla. The medullary system is located in the reticular formation, the nucleus solitarius, the Vth, VIIth, XIIth nuclei and the nucleus ambiguus. The efferent impulses reach five muscle groups which contract concurrently in a strictly orderly fashion. This generates high pressure and propels the bolus through the pharyngo-oesophageal sphincter.

In the human fetus swallowing can apparently first be elicited about the 12th week. The primitive condition of neural development at that stage suggests that swallowing does not require control by prosencephalic structures. By the 23rd week the human fetus can swallow amniotic fluid at the rate of 5 ml./kg./hr. and continues to do so until birth. At term this amounts to almost 500 ml./day, approximately half the volume of amniotic fluid.[3]

In normal adults swallowing occurs roughly 600 times/day, 350 times during waking hours, 200 times whilst eating and 50 times during sleep. No corresponding data are available for the different younger age-groups.

DYSPHAGIA

In view of the complex central and peripheral organization of the act of deglutition it is not surprising that dysphagia is not a rare disorder of the neonatal period. Gross anatomical defects can easily interfere with the structures involved, such as anomalies of the tongue, the palate, pharynx, and postnasal space and the larynx.

However, neuromuscular incoordination of the soft palate, the pharynx and the upper oesophagus are more difficult to recognize and interpret. Delayed maturation of the neuromuscular apparatus has been put forward as a likely explanation of the swallowing difficulties in premature and mentally deficient infants. It has also been regarded as a possible cause in newborns without any pathological findings in the central nervous system. Some of these babies have been studied by cineradiography which demonstrated lack of coordination in the contraction of the pharyngeal muscles, soft palate and tongue. It resulted in faulty clearing of the laryngeal aditus and aspiration in the trachea. In such instances, feeding by naso-oesophageal or nasogastric tube seems the only means by which serious aspiration pneumonias can be avoided. The period of tube-feeding may vary from several weeks to several months. Recovery is mostly complete.

Damage to the CNS antepartum, during delivery or shortly after birth probably account for the dysphagia seen in infants with cerebral palsy, with abnormalities of the cranial nerve nuclei, bulbar and suprabulbar palsies and the Moebius syndrome. Myasthenia gravis in the newborn period has been associated with deglutition difficulties. A number of clinically delineated syndromes are known to present in early life with swallowing disorders. They have been accepted as part of the Day–Riley syndrome or dysautonomia, the Cornelia de Lange and Prader–Willis syndromes.[14]

Toxic or inflammatory conditions in the newborn such as tetanus, diphtheria, poliomyelitis are fortunately very rare causes of severe dysphagia. Extensive moniliasis invading pharyngeal and oesophageal mucosa has been known not only to cause dysphagia but also to lead to aspiration pneumonias.

The recent finding of cow's milk antibodies in an unduly high proportion of mentally retarded children with temporary impaired deglutition including Down's syndrome patients may be due to repeated aspiration of small quantities of cow's milk into the trachea and bronchial system. Sensitization may thus occur in individuals, who are not genetically predisposed, since the bronchial mucosa lacks in proteolytic enzymes that break down the sensitizing polypeptides into non-allergenic oligopeptides. The role of the cow's milk antibodies actually producing allergic disease in these patients has not yet been clarified.

Motility is probably the main function of the oesophagus, as it hardly participates in secretion, digestion or absorption. Its structure is in that sense functional. The upper part of the muscular wall consists of striated muscle arranged in longitudinal fibre bundles surrounding a layer of circular fibre bundles. Between the muscle layers and the stratified squamous epithelium on the luminal surface is a thick submucous elastic and collagenous network. The substantial muscularis mucosae produces folds in the mucosa which practically obliterate the lumen. When swallowing takes place the mucosal folds are smoothed as the bolus passes through that part of the oesophagus. Transition between striated muscle above and smooth muscle below occurs in the middle third. Although there is no muscular structure which forms an anatomical sphincter at the lower end of the oesophagus, it behaves physiologically like a sphincter separating it from the stomach.[5]

The motor innervation of the upper, striated part of the oesophagus and the pharynx is not autonomic in character, it is provided by portions of the glossopharyngeal and vagus nerves. They contain efferent fibres to motor end plates and sensory fibres. The smooth muscles section of the oesophagus receives its nerve supply from the vagus. It is autonomous. The preganglionic fibres end in synapses with ganglion cells to form the myenteric plexus. The postganglionic fibres arising from the plexus innervate the smooth muscle cells. Both types of fibres are cholinergic. Sympathetic innervation is also present.

Monometric studies of intraluminal oesophageal pressure in the adult have contributed a great deal to the understanding of some phenomena relating to the movement of oesophageal and gastric content. There is ample evidence that reduction of pressure in the lower oesophageal sphincter may allow reflux of gastric content into the oesophagus. The mechanisms controlling adult oesophageal function however are incomplete at birth and in the early months of life. Whilst in an adult during the act of swallowing the pressure in the pharynx rises abruptly, the elevation only lasts a very short time, less than half a second. It leads to the opening of the pharyngo-oesophageal sphincter by the contraction of the muscles raising the cricoid cartilage. After the bolus has passed, the sphincter closes firmly and peristaltic wares begin in the upper end of the oesophagus. In the young infant the superior laryngeal sphincter is not firmly closed and peristalsis does not occur in the lower oesophagus. Contrary to the adult, there is also no abdominal oesophagus and the lower oesophageal sphincter does not close between swallows. An accessory closing mechanism is provided by the crural fibres of the diaphragm.

The absence of secondary oesophageal peristalsis in the young infant and the weakness of the oesophagopharyngeal sphincter allows frequently small amounts of gastric content to flow out of the mouth. A process which has variously been described as "possetting" "spitting" or "regurgitation." In the healthy thriving infant this is of little significance. Some babies regurgitate appreciable quantities of gastric fluid that appear relatively clear except for a small content of mucus. The reason for it is by no means clear as available studies have failed to provide a satisfactory explanation.

Onset of possetting in infants who present signs of ill health is to be regarded as an additional warning of the child's serious condition.

Chalasia—Oesophageal reflux is due to the failure to achieve the normal pressure gradient between lower oesophageal sphincter and cardia during the first 6–9 months of life. The clinical manifestations may be indistinguishable from those of a hiatus hernia. Persistent vomiting, failure to thrive, haematemesis and anaemia. The diagnosis rests on the results of the radiological examination. A barium meal will show the reflux and may also indicate signs of oesophagitis.

ACHALASIA OF THE OESOPHAGUS

Absence of the myenteric plexus in the lower part of the oesophagus has been accepted as the pathology underlying the condition in which the lower oesophageal sphincter fails to relax. Parasympathomimetic drugs lead to vigorous and prolonged contractions. It is possible that the sensitized muscle fibres are overreaching to the naturally produced acetylcholine.

Failure of the gastro-oesophageal sphincter to allow the normal passage of food, results in stagnation of oesophageal content, vomiting, and may be aspiration pneumonia. Chalasia is the more likely situation at the lower oesophageal sphincter. Achalasia is a very rare condition in the young child, but may be encountered in adolescents and adults.

Radiological examination clarifies the diagnosis.

Therapeutically thickening the feeds and placing the infant in a specially designed seat are usually successful measures. The upright position can be maintained for many weeks until recovery. The prognosis is essentially good.

Vomiting is the ejection of gastric content from the mouth and is preceded by retching. With the onset of retching the gastro-oesophageal sphincter and the oesophagus relax. Raised intraabdominal pressure with the contraction of the distal region of the stomach forces gastric content into the relaxed fundus, oesophagus, pharynx and out of the mouth. Throughout retching and vomiting all motor activity of the oesophagus ceases. It is accompanied by a sequence of closure of the nasal and respiratory passages. Violent vomiting in small infants may overcome the closure of the nasopharynx and food content appear at the nostrils causing nasal irritation and reflex coughing. In certain circumstances the first retching motion is so forceful that gastric content is expelled from the mouth and over some distance, "projectile vomiting." It is characteristic in pyloric stenosis, at the onset of acute infections and may also occur in cow's milk allergy. Not infrequently it accompanies the presence of a hiatus hernia. Symptoms begin within the first few weeks of life, regurgitation may alternate with vomiting. It often takes place at night. The vomitus on the bedlinen may contain altered blood. Respiratory difficulties often result from the inhalation of gastric content. Vomiting is a very common physical sign in childhood illnesses and its significance must be interpreted with regard to its persistence and content of bile, blood, faeces, and its association with other physical manifestations, such as diarrhoea. It is an important factor in disturbing the water and electrolyte balance of the young child, since it not only leads directly to loss of body fluids but prevents oral fluid intake.

Belching or gaseous reflux is the transport of gas from the stomach or the oesophagus to the mouth during inspiration by relaxation of the gastro-oesophageal and of the oesophago-pharyngeal sphincters. In adults who can easily belch this is voluntarily produced by an increase in intra-abdominal and intrathoracic pressure.

A small amount of air is swallowed with the food by all babies under six months. Excessively this can occur in breast-fed infants when the flow of milk is inadequate or in bottle-fed babies when the hole in the teat is too small. This may lead to overdistention of the stomach. Occasionally belching may be accompanied by regurgitation of small amount of food. Traditionally it is recommended to hold every baby upright over one shoulder after the feed and pat him gently over the back until he belches to the great relief of the majority of mothers and nurses.

Aerophagia in older children is a rare behavioural disorder which can lead not only to gastric but also to marked upper abdominal distension. A plain X-ray film of the abdomen will reveal the diagnosis. The condition can simulate serious organic disturbances by reducing appetite and food intake, causing malnutrition.

GASTRIC MOTILITY

The longitudinal and circular muscles of the stomach wall are continuous sheets and thus act as a unit. The reflexes that control gastric motility are initiated in visceral and somatic receptors. The most important visceral receptors are situated in the upper intestine. They respond to the presence of osmotically active substances and all the important constituents of gastric chyme, to physical contact and pressure on the mucosa and to stretch of the muscle. Somatic and visceral pain receptors set off reflexes that inhibit gastro intestinal motility. Emotional responses may initiate excitation or inhibition.

The visceral afferent fibres involved are in the vagus and in the sympathetic nerves. Vagal afferents are mainly concerned with normal regulation reflexes. The sympathetic afferents convey impulses due to noxious stimuli.

The efferent paths comprise motor and inhibitory fibres in both the vagal and sympathetic system. The fibres causing contraction of the stomach muscle whether vagal or sympathetic are cholinergic, sympathetic inhibitory fibres are adrenergic.

The empty stomach is relaxed and small. As it fills the corpus or central position is the largest, it adapts readily to changes of volume of contents, mixes and propels them.

The fundus acts as a reservoir capable of variations in size. The antrum and pylorus act as a functional unit which contract in a coordinated pattern.

Three kinds of movement occur in the full stomach: peristaltic waves, systolic contraction of the terminal antrum and diminution in size of fundus and corpus. A peristaltic wave begins as a pacemaker in the longitudinal muscle high on the greater curvature and moves over the longitudinal muscle of corpus, antrum and pylorus. The frequency of the waves is approximately 3 per minute. The longitudinal contraction precedes that of the circular muscle. When the excitation has spread to it the latter contracts with variable intensity.

The peristaltic wave moves as a circular band about 2 cm wide over the body and the antrum. The terminal antrum and the pylorus contract more forcefully but simultaneously. This is the systolic contraction which pumps the content through the pyloric canal into the duodenum. When the pressure in the terminal antrum rises and the pylorus abruptly closes part of the content in the terminal antrum is squirted back into the proximal antrum where it is mixed further with the digestive juices. Gastric emptying can be slowed by acids, triglycerides and salts of fatty acids with chains of 12–18 carbon atoms.

SLOW WAVES

The relationship of slow waves to motility has now been established.[4]

It is generally agreed that *intestinal slow waves* are generated by the longitudinal muscle layer and spread electrotonically to the underlying circular layer where they regulate the phasic changes in excitability associated with rhythmic contractions. The electrotonic spread occurs via interconnecting muscle bridges between the layers. *Gastric slow waves* are known to occur regularly in the antral musculature of the stomach and are probably absent from the cardia and fundus. Antral motility is characteristically peristaltic and probably myogenic rather than neurogenic in origin. Antral slow waves play a role in the coordination of the activity of the gastro-duodenal junction during gastric emptying. They propagate across the gastro-duodenal junction along the longitudinal muscle bundles which pass from antrum to duodenum.[2]

Hormonal Control of Gastric Motility

Gastrin liberated from the pyloric glandular mucosa stimulates antral motility and at the same time it increases the pressure in the lower oesophageal sphincter. Enterogastrone a hormone released from the duodenum after acidification has an inhibitory effect on gastric motility and reduces the pressure in the lower oesophageal sphincter. Secretin and Pancreozymin too inhibit gastrin-stimulated motility. Hypoglycaemia increases motility via a central nervous mechanism. Forceful peristaltic waves of the gastric wall are easily seen on physical examination in infants suffering from *hypertrophic pyloric stenosis*. They are part of the triad of cardinal clinical signs of the condition. The other two are projectile vomiting and a palpable tumour 2 cm to the right of the umbilicus. Radiological examination is regarded as diagnostic. Because of the narrowing of the pyloric canal only traces of barium enter it and form the so-called "string" or "wedge" sign. Characteristic is also the delay in the pylorus opening time. Normally barium will leave through the pylorus into the duodenum within 3–4 min. after entering into the stomach. In hypertrophic stenosis it may take 20–30 min. before the string sign appears.

However, visible gastric peristalsis is not limited to this condition it can be observed in some instances of cow's milk allergy, the adreno-genital syndrome in the male and in infants with hiatus hernia. The gastric peristalsis can be enhanced by the administration of a feed or by letting the infant suck at a comforter.

It may also be evident in babies with partial obstruction in the first part of the duodenum. As this is likely to be due to a congenital malformation. The clinical manifestations will become evident shortly after birth.

MOTILITY OF THE SMALL INTESTINE

The most important motion of the small intestine is segmentation, controlled by a basic electrical rhythm originating in the longitudinal muscles. It mixes the chyme with the digestive juices and exposes it to the absorptive properties of the small intestinal mucosa. The contents are further propelled by short peristaltic waves. Peristalsis is a local reflex of the smooth muscle layers, and their intrinsic plexuses.

The duodenal bulb i.e. the first part of the duodenum is a sensitive receptor area responding to qualities of the chyme entering it from the stomach. Osmotic receptors aid equilibration and centralization. Contraction of the muscularis mucosae determine the folding of the mucosa throughout the gut. They occur in response to local stimuli; or to stimulation of the sympathetic nerves.

The ileocaecal sphincter separating the terminal ileum from the colon has a higher resting pressure than that of the adjoining part of the caecum. It is kept closed, partly by a myenteric reflex. Mechanical stimulation of the caecal mucosa or distension of the viscous causes the pressure in the sphincter to rise and delays the passage of chyme. The sphincter has a valve like action which normally prevents the caecal content to spill over into the ileum.

The hormone gastrin causes sphincter pressure to fall and

gastric emptying is accompanied by an increase in ileal peristaltic activity. Eating is therefore followed by emptying of the ileum through the ileocaecal sphincter. This effect has been termed the gastro-ileal reflex.

It is probable that a very active gastro-ileal reflex in young infants accounts for the observation that feeding is often followed by the voiding of faeces.

The Large Intestine—The Colon

The length of the whole of the large bowel from the ileocaecal valve to the anus has been estimated in the newborn to be 40–66 cm., at the age of 5 years approximately 100 cm. and in the adult 120–160 cm. The caecum in the newborn is wider than long and changes its proportions only after the age of 2 years.

The longitudinal muscle of the colon is arranged in three bands, taeniae coli. The circular muscle, by its contraction produces the haustra, which are pouch-like subdivisions, variable in size and position. The ileo-caecal sphincter forms the proximal and the internal anal sphincter the distal end. Both myenteric and submucosal plexuses are present throughout the colon. Extrinsic parasympathetic innervation is derived from the preganglionic fibres of the vagus and supplies the ascending and part of the transverse colon. The rest of the large bowel receives its innervation from the pelvic nerves arising mainly from the sacral segments of the spinal cord. The preganglionic parasympathetic fibres synapse with ganglion cells in the myenteric plexures. Pre- as well as postganglionic fibres are cholinergic. The postganglionic sympathetic fibres end on blood vessels, where they are vasoconstrictor or in the myenteric plexuses.

The contents of the caecum, of the ascending and transverse colon are kneaded and turned over by churning movements which are not propulsive. The contents are slowly dried by absorption of water until they are firm but not hard. They are then slowly moved toward the rectum by serial or systolic segmental contractions, mass propulsion and peristalsis. After feeding transport is increased and the descending colon and rectum are frequently filled after a meal. Faeces which arrive in the rectum, distend it and evoke the defaecation reflex via the nervous centre in the sacral segments of the spinal cord.

Defaecation is not necessarily a reflex response to the fullness of the rectum, at least the urge to it can be precipitated by increased tension in the rectal wall. If the act of defaecation is not inhibited by higher centres it involves coordination of voluntary and involuntary muscle function. In the young infant until he has learned to exercise voluntary control, it is a reflex process.

If defaecation is inhibited by bringing higher nervous system centres into play, the rectum relaxes, faeces are returned to the upper part of the descending colon, the tension in the rectal wall relaxes and the defaecation is postponed.

TYPES OF COLONIC MOVEMENT

(1) **Haustral shuttling:** results from annular contractions in the transverse and descending colon in which liquid or semiliquid haustral content is moved randomly into adjoining haustral sacs. This action produces a forceful mixing of the chyme and since it is non-propulsive allows water absorption to proceed.

(2) **Segmental propulsion** moves the haustral content caudally, step by step.

(3) **Systolic multihaustral propulsion** involves the caudal movement of larger quantities of colonic content by simultaneous contraction of several adjacent haustral sacs.

(4) **Peristalsis** accounts for the directional movement of the faecal mass at the rate of 1–2 cm/min. Muscular relaxation precedes the wave of contraction. Peristaltic movements take place only in a limited number of individuals and only at certain times. *Segmental* propulsion is the most common type of movement in the adult particularly after meals and propels the colonic content at a net rate of 5 cm./hr. Colonic motility is strongly influenced by ileal outflow, and this as already stated, by feeding.

(5) **Mass propulsion** may start as a series of multihaustral movements or as peristalsis. It may originate in the caecum or in the transverse colon.

Meconium designates the contents of the whole of the intestine before birth. The quantity voided after birth amounts to 60–200 g. It consists of epithelia desquamated from the mucosa of the alimentary tract, from the skin and lipoid substances, bile, pancreatic, and intestinal secretion, lanugo hair and the residue of swallowed amniotic fluid.

On analysis meconium contains little fat, hardly any protein, mucopolysaccharides with blood group specificity and soluble mineral substances after incineration.

Meconium is usually passed in the first twelve hours but its passage can be delayed up to 48 hr. or on rare occasions even up to 72 hr. After 24 hr. steps should be taken to exclude any possible cause of obstruction even if the child's general condition does not suggest any serious underlying disorder. The absence of epithelial cells in the meconium may be of significance in the diagnosis of intestinal obstruction in the newborn. The presence of meconium in the amniotic fluid at birth raises the possibility of intrauterine asphyxia. The aspiration of large amounts of amniotic fluid containing meconium can produce serious lung disease in the newborn.

THE MECONIUM PLUG SYNDROME

A variety of reasons have been advanced to explain an uncommon form of low intestinal obstruction in the newborn. Inspissated meconium of rubbery consistency or sometimes stringy with mucus at the distal end of the plug, may resist the normal forces of propulsion. The syndrome is not associated with cystic fibrosis of the pancreas but there may be an absence of trypsin or chymotrypsin. It may have primarily been due to a reduced colonic motility which allowed excessive water absorption and inspissation of intestinal content, or it may be the initial phase of Hirschsprung's disease. The clinical manifestations of obstruction develop within 24 hours: abdominal distension, bile stained vomiting, dehydration, visible peristalsis. Radiological examination is of considerable help in establishing the diagnosis and may also have a therapeutic effect.

MECONIUM ILEUS

Meconium ileus is a complication of cystic fibrosis of the pancreas but may well be its first manifestation. It is found in about ten per cent of patients with the disease. The inspissation of the meconium occurs well before birth. Its consistency is putty-like and it lacks the black-green pigment. A high content of albumen probably as a result of absent proteolytic enzymes, secretion of an abnormally viscous intestinal mucus, reduced water secretion from the pancreas and biliary system may well contribute to the rubbery consistency of the meconium. Intestinal reabsorption could add an additional factor responsible for its dessication. The clinical features are those of intestinal obstruction. Radiological examination is often diagnostic, the intestinal content presenting a granular appearance. This is due to penetration of large numbers of tiny air-bubbles following the churning and kneading action of the obstructed gut. Local ischaemic changes can lead to perforation, atresia or volvulus.

Meconium entering the peritoneal cavity after perforation will precipitate a peritonitis, with calcium deposition. Cystic fibrosis is not the only cause of meconium peritonitis. It can occur in ileal atresia, or following rupture of an ischaemic gut wall without known aetiology. The treatment is surgical.

CONGENITAL MEGACOLON—HIRSCHSPRUNG'S DISEASE

This can be regarded as one of nature's more subtle experiments. It demonstrates the situation that arises when ganglion cells of the myenteric plexus are absent in a segment of the large intestine. Nerve fibres in that area are abundant. They are probably the terminal branches of preganglionic cholinergic parasympathetic fibres. The absence of postganglionic fibres causes the smooth muscle to be abnormally sensitive to acetylcholine liberated by the preganglionic fibres. When these fibres are activated as in the defaecation reflex, spasm of the segment occurs with failure of the faeces to pass through the constricted area, which lacks coordinated movement with the rest of the gut. Although the segment may contract rhythmically, its contractions are not propulsive. As a result it comes to enormous dilatation and hypertrophy of the colon proximal to the constriction. Faeces accumulate in large quantities. This may lead to stercoral ulceration—perforation and peritonitis. Short segment aganglionosis accounts for more than 70 per cent of cases. Most instances of Hirschsprung's disease are seen within the first week of life. The newborn fails to pass meconium—there follow abdominal distension, bilious vomiting and refusal to feed. Occasionally enemata or digital examination may lead to improvement. The remission can last for weeks or months. More difficult to understand is the fact that in some patients the clinical manifestation of the disorder remain unimpressive during early life and the full picture emerges only in later childhood.[3]

FUNCTIONAL MORPHOLOGY OF INTESTINAL TRACT

The internal surface of the small bowel is thrown into folds, the valvulae conniventes, which increases the internal surface by a factor of 3. The surface is further folded into smaller projections, the villi, which add a factor of 8 to the internal area. The villi are covered with epithelium, on the luminal surface of which, is the brush border, or microvilli, increasing the surface area 14–39 times. The overall effect of this folding is therefore an increase of the internal area by about 600 times compared with the outside area.

At a functional level, the absorptive unit is the villus and crypt. The villus height is normally about 3 times the crypt depth, but in some conditions, e.g. coeliac disease, the situation is reversed, due to rapid cell division in the crypt.

The crypt is the site of production of epithelial cells, with mitosis occurring in the lower crypt.[24] In this area cells have central nuclei with free ribosomes but few mitochondria. Cell division does not occur in the upper third of the crypt, where undifferentiated cells with a short brush border are found. Differentiation occurs as the cells leave the crypt and move up the villi. Three secretory cells are found in the crypt: Paneth cells containing large droplets whose function is unknown, Goblet cells producing mucus and Argentaffin cells producing 5-hydroxytryptamine.

The villus is lined with differentiated cells which are replaced every 48–72 hr., from the cells moving up from the crypts.[9] The method of migration is unknown, but animal studies have demonstrated that the epithelium rests on a moving sheet of fibroblasts and may thus be carried upwards. There is little information about normal rate of cell turnover in children. Adult rats have a faster rate of cell turnover than suckling rats. The converse is true of pigs. Studies on live born anencephalics suggest that cell production is slower than in normal adults, due to decreased rate of proliferation and migration. In the villus cells, mitochondria are larger and more numerous than in crypt-cells suggesting a more active metabolic state. The brush border is longer and enzymes increase in activity as cells move up the villi.

The surface of the microvilli are covered by a lipoprotein trilaminar membrane, the plasma membrane, from which project knobs of 60 Å size. The microvilli which are 1 μ long by 0·1 μ in diameter contain protein strands, microtubules, which pass down to the terminal web. The plasma membrane is covered with a polysaccharide enteric coat or glyocalyx, which appears to be excreted from the cell. Sugars are converted to polysaccharide in the region of the golgi apparatus and then pass to the cell surface. The enteric coat is subject to rapid turnover, and may either have a protective function or may provide a micro environment for digestion and absorption. It was thought that this PAS reacting layer represented mucus, but its close proximity to the plasma membrane has led to the current concept. The brush border is now known to be the major area of production of many digestive enzymes and the site of digestion of many nutrients.[17] The following table lists these enzymes which have been located in the brush border:

TABLE 1

Brush Border Enzymes[17]

Disaccharides—maltase
—isomaltase
—lactase
—sucrase
—palatinase
—trehalase

Alkaline phosphatase
ATP ase
Magnesium ATP ase
Copper ATP ase
Aminopeptidase
Cholesterol ester hydrolase
? Folate deconjugase
Dipeptidases

There is some evidence that disaccharidases are located on the outer plasma membrane, possibly in the terminal knobs or in the glyocalyx. It is further suggested that groups of adjacent cells produce a preponderance of a particular enzyme thus giving an enzyme excreting mosaic.

The embryo gut is known to be capable of producing enzymes.[5] Maltase, sucrase, isomaltase, palatinase, trehalase have all been detected in the three month fetal gut and reach normal amounts by 5–6 months gestation. Lactase does not reach normal levels till term, although it can be induced by lactose containing feeds in premature infants. Active transport of glucose has been demonstrated in the 8–10 week fetal gut. Selective amino acid absorption has been detected in the gut of a 12 week fetus. Several dipeptidases are present at 10 weeks gestation. It may be that some amniotic fluid solutes are metabolized by these enzymes or that the fluid is acting as an enzyme inducer. Alkaline phosphatase is present by 8–11 weeks gestation but is still below adult levels at 23 weeks gestation.

Factors Influencing Functional Morphology

Villus atrophy is seen in malnutrition, particularly protein malnutrition, due to a decrease in cell turnover. The atrophy leads to a decrease in absorptive and digestive surface thus aggravating the malnutrition.

Some enzymes are influenced by diet. Thus, experimentally a low sucrose low maltose diet will reduce the level of appropriate mucosal enzymes. After 3–5 days of normal diet the enzyme levels are re-induced (i.e. the time taken for a new generation of cells to form). The question of the induction of lactase is under active consideration.[10] Its inducibility in premature babies has been referred to. It has been long known that lactase levels fall in rats, pigs and cows after weaning. This has now been shown in man, but there is a racial variation. Thus it is absent in a large percentage of North American negroe adults and also in the Bantu from whom they descended. It is absent, past weaning, in a high proportion of Eskimos, Australian aboriginies, South American Indians, Thais, Japanese and Chinese. The widespread incidence of low lactase activity is most probably genetically determined, and the norm for the human race. The Caucasian with a high level of lactase activity during adult life appears to be the exception. Two theories have been advanced to explain the situation. The first suggests that natural selection favoured the individual with high lactose absorption in areas of abundant milk supply but dearth of other foodstuffs.[7] The second claims a specific advantage for the adult with undiminished lactose activity. It relates to lactose enhanced calcium absorption in an environment with low ultraviolet irradiation and low dietary supply of Vitamin D.[26]

Atrophic changes have been demonstrated in severe iron deficiency. In vitamin B_{12} deficiency the epithelial cells are larger and have larger nuclei, but the mitotic index is reduced.

Gluten induced enteropathy (coeliac disease) is associated with very marked increase in cell turnover as demonstrated by the mitotic index and by DNA turnover studies. The cause of the adverse effect of gluten is still unknown. There are two current theories. The first one implicates a lack of a peptidase, which results in a build up of toxic products of gluten.[9] Certainly peptidase deficiencies have been demonstrated, but they are reversible after treatment and are probably secondary. The second theory suggests an immunological defect.[16] Variable alternations in immunoglobulins are seen but some of these are reversible and again probably reflect the result of gluten sensitivity, rather than the cause. The detection of gluten antibodies has given varied and generally unhelpful results. Gluten withdrawal will reverse the clinical picture and, in children, restore the mucosa to normal. It is now recognized that the diet must be continued for life. A secondary gluten intolerance is also recognized. In this the patient develops a temporary gluten intolerance following some other disease. Tolerance develops after a short period of gluten withdrawal, provided the underlying primary condition is reversed.

Degrees of villus atrophy have also been described in chronic infection, e.g. salmonellosis, giardiasis, tuberculosis and ankylostomiasis. Minor villus changes are described following specific and non specific gastroenteritis, when associated secondary disaccharide intolerance may cause problems during re-introduction of oral feeds. In our experience this is best carried out utilizing a low lactose formula as the initial milk feed.

Various skin diseases have now been associated with abnormal villus patterns. These include dermatitis herpetiformis and Rosacea.

Minor histological changes have also been noted in a miscellaneous group of disorders including ulcerative colitis, regional enteritis, and following antibiotic therapy, particularly neomycin. Specific histological changes are seen in intestinal lymphangiectasis, α-β-lipoproteinaemia, amyloidosis, and Whipple's disease.

CARBOHYDRATE DIGESTION

In the neonate 50 per cent of ingested calories are provided by lactose in milk. After the neonatal period, 60 per cent of dietary carbohydrate is starch, 30 per cent is sucrose and 10 per cent lactose.

Starch occurs in two forms: Amylose consists of straight chains of glucose molecules joined by oxygen and linkages at 1–4 carbon points 25–200 molecules long. Amylopectin makes up about 80 per cent of ingested starch and consists of glucose joined at 1–4 points but with 1–6 branched chains (Fig. 1). Salivary and pancreatic amylase can split

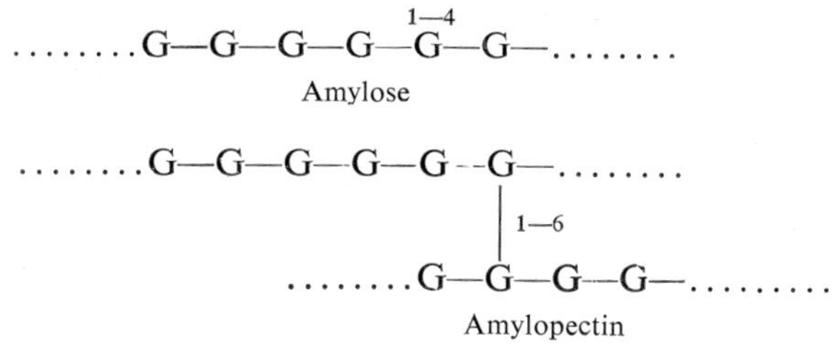

........G—G—G—G—G—G—........ (1—4)

Amylose

........G—G—G—G—G—G—........
(1—6)
........G—G—G—G—.........

Amylopectin

FIG. 1.

internal linkages to give maltose, maltotriose and limit dextrine but do not readily split to glucose. Pancreatic amylase reaches adult levels by 4 months of age. It probably acts intraluminally, but there is some evidence of mucosal binding.

The hydrolysed oligosaccharides produced by amylase action on starch, together with ingested disaccharides are digested by mucosal enzymes in the brush border where specific disaccharidases exist.[22] Thus

$$\text{SUCROSE} \xrightarrow[\text{Sucrase}]{} \text{FRUCTOSE} + \text{GLUCOSE}$$

$$\text{LACTOSE} \xrightarrow[\text{Lactase}]{} \text{GALACTOSE} + \text{GLUCOSE}$$

$$\text{MALTOSE} \xrightarrow[\text{Maltase}]{} \text{GLUCOSE} + \text{GLUCOSE}$$

$$\text{LIMIT DEXTRINE} \xrightarrow[\text{Isomaltase}]{} \text{GLUCOSE}$$

FIG. 2.

Differences have been found in single types of disaccharidase so that 4–5 maltases, 1–2 sucrases, 1–2 lactases are described, but this is of no clinical significance. As mentioned earlier, the disaccharidases are found in very early fetal life. The enzyme activity is greatest 10 cm. from Ligament of Treitz to upper ileum.[15] As a result of these intraluminal and brush border enzymes, dietary carbohydrate is finally broken down to give 80 per cent glucose, 15 per cent fructose and 5 per cent galactose.

It is thought that glucose binds to a specific macromolecule, probably a protein, on the outer side of the brush border, to be carried across and released as free glucose within the cell cytoplasm and then to diffuse to the capillary bed. Such a binding protein has been shown in bacteria to be associated with transport of sulphate ions, galactose, leucine, argenine, phenylanine, histadine, valine, isoleucine and glutamine.

The entry of glucose to the cell after being bound, depends on a mechanism mediated by a sodium pump, which appears to increase the affinity for glucose to the carrier and also effects transport velocity. The mechanism probably depends on sodium ATPase. Potassium has a reverse action on the cellular side of the plasma membrane. The same mechanism probably works for galactose, and means that glucose and galactose can move against a concentration gradient. Fructose, which cannot enter cells against a concentration gradient, has been said to be absorbed passively. Recent work suggests that it is carrier mediated and may involve an active process. Hydrolysed sugars are absorbed more rapidly than free monosaccharides probably due to their release close to their binding site. There appears to be an inter-relationship between the rate of hydrolysis and transport, so that sucrose and maltose are hydrolysed at just a slightly faster rate than the resulting monosaccharides are absorbed. This suggests that the concentration of glucose and galactose produced, limits the rate of breakdown of disaccharides to prevent wasteful hydrolysis occurring. Hydrolysis of lactose is slower and this is the rate-limiting factor in the absorption of hydrolysed products.

Disorders of Carbohydrate Absorption

In some conditions, the microscopic appearance of the intestinal mucosa is normal, but function is abnormal. This is the case in the primary disaccharidase deficiency disorders. Poor absorption is associated with osmotic diarrhoea which is further aggravated by fermentation. Associated intestinal hurry may lead to steatorrhoea.

Lactase deficiency results in the passage of profuse, watery stools following the introduction of milk feeds. The stool pH is low due to the presence of lactic acid. Lactose may be detected in the stool by testing for reducing sugars, e.g. Clinitest, or by sugar chromatography. It is important to test the fluid part of the stool or misleading results will be obtained. The diagnosis is confirmed by finding abnormally low lactase levels in small intestinal mucosal biopsies having normal histological appearances.

Sucrase-isomaltase deficiency is described as a primary condition. Vomiting and loose stools are noted following the introduction of starch to the diet. Diarrhoea increases with sucrose ingestion, due to its greater osmotic effect. Provocative tests with sucrose and starch may be used, but definitive diagnosis rests on small intestinal mucosal enzyme estimation.

The rarity of pure maltase deficiency is due to the fact that 4–5 different maltases exist which appear to be genetically different. It is therefore unlikely for all of these to be depleted as a primary disorder.

Primary monosaccharide disorders are recognized. The best documented is glucose-galactose intolerance, which is thought to result from a faulty transport mechanism. Although the levels of disaccharidases are normal in these patients, they are unable to tolerate disaccharides and can only utilize fructose as their source of sugar.

It is clear that secondary disaccharide intolerance may be expected to follow any condition which leads to significant villus atrophy.

PROTEIN DIGESTION

In the adult, more than 90 per cent of the protein which is ingested undergoes digestion and absorption. Stool nitrogen is mainly of endogenous origin and represents the breakdown products of enzymes, mucus and desquamated epithelium.

Gastric protease, pepsin, is capable of breaking protein down to large peptide molecules. However, this function is relatively unimportant in protein digestion, since most of digestion occurs in the small intestine, where two groups of proteases exist.

The endopeptidases, which include trypsin, chymotrypsin and elastase, act on interior peptide bonds, i.e.—CO—NH— links. The exopeptidases, such as carboxypeptidase act on the terminal COOH bonds. The proteases are produced in the acinar cells of the pancreas as inactive precursors. These precursors are secreted into the duodenal lumen where activation of trypsinogen is catalysed by enterokinase, an enzyme probably produced by the duodenal mucosa. After the hydrolysis of trypsinogen to trypsin begins, the trypsin acts autocatalytically to break down more trypsinogen. The trypsin then acts on the other peptidase precursors as shown below (Fig. 3) As each peptidase acts

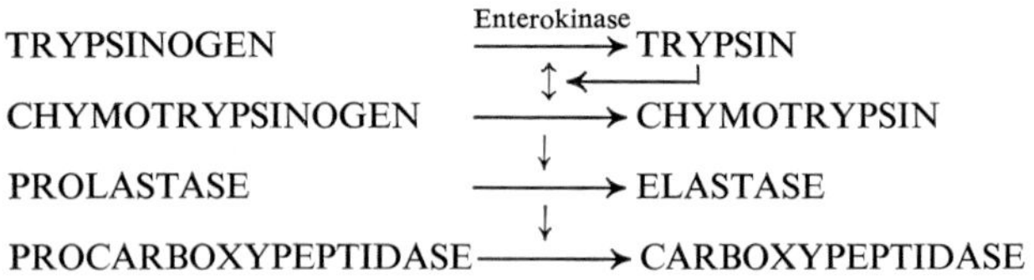

TRYPSINOGEN —(Enterokinase)→ TRYPSIN
↕ ←
CHYMOTRYPSINOGEN ——→ CHYMOTRYPSIN
↓
PROLASTASE ——→ ELASTASE
↓
PROCARBOXYPEPTIDASE ——→ CARBOXYPEPTIDASE

FIG. 3.

on a specific link, digestion of protein occurs in a stepwise fashion as shown below (Fig. 4).

70 per cent of protein will be hydrolysed to small peptides and 30 per cent to basic and neutral amino acids.

There is controversy whether most of protein digestion occurs intraluminally or at the brush border. Evidence exists that binding of protease to the brush border occurs. Brush border and intracellular di- and tri-peptidases appear to exist and are capable of hydrolysing small peptides. The importance of cellular digestion is supported by the finding that the absorption of amino acids is faster after ingestion of a mixture of peptides than after ingestion of a mixture of amino acids. Some peptides appear capable of entering the cell unchanged, e.g. some neutral peptides together with peptides containing proline and hydroxyproline. Most of these will be hydrolysed by intracellular enzymes, but 10 per cent will leave the cell unchanged.

Neutral amino acids are absorbed rapidly from the jejunum by a sodium mediated pump mechanism. There is relative competition between amino acids, so that methionine is absorbed faster than isoleucine. There are decreasing rates of absorption from leucine to valine, to phenylalanine, to tryptophan down to threonine. The different absorption rates may be due to variation in the affinity of amino acids to the transport mechanism. The dibasic amino acids and cystine are absorbed by a sodium pump mechanism at a rate of about 10 per cent that of neutral amino acids. They can also be absorbed without the pump. Proline and hydroxyproline may have to utilize a sodium mediated absorptive mechanism, but can be absorbed without. Glucose and galactose may inhibit the transport rates of neutral amino acids and therefore either have a common carrier or a common source of carrier energy.

As mentioned earlier, several dipeptidases have been detected in very early foetal life and selective amino acid absorption has been detected in the small foetus. Some neonatal animals are able to absorb intact protein for several weeks by pinocytosis. This may provide an important source of γ globulin for these animals. A recent study which compared serum immunoglobulins in breast fed babies with bottle-fed babies at five days has shown a significantly raised IgG, IgA and IgM levels in the breast fed group, suggesting that pinocytosis is of importance in the human neonate and adding support to the view that maternally secreted immunoglobulins can reach the baby via colostrum.

Disorders of Protein Digestion

Disorders of pancreatic exocrine function, such as cystic fibrosis, pancreatitis and pancreatic hypoplasia are associated with protein malabsorption.

In coeliac disease there is a degree of protein malabsorption, which follows from the marked reduction in the

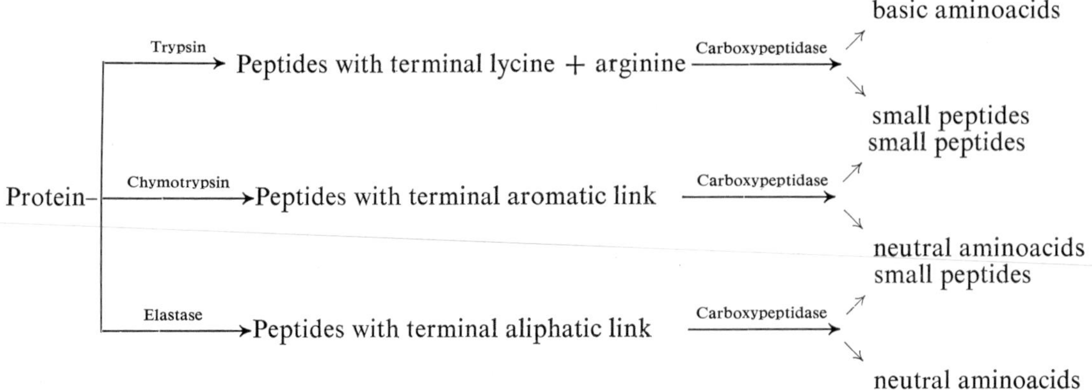

FIG. 4.

absorptive surface area and associated loss of intracellular peptidases. There is clear evidence that the mucosal cell turnover is increased, resulting in loss of cellular protein into the gut lumen. A protein losing enteropathy may be present, which will further aggravate the protein balance of the body.

It is now realized that the intestinal tract plays a part in the catabolism of plasma protein. Hypoproteinaemia will result if catabolism exceeds production, as seen in protein losing enteropathy. Protein losing enteropathy may be associated with several groups of disorders, such as:

(a) disorders of mucosal integrity, e.g. gastroenteritis, shigella dysentry, regional enteritis, ulcerative colitis, coeliac disease, tropical sprue and giardiasis;
(b) disorders of lymphatic flow, e.g. lymphangiectasia;
(c) generalized disease, dysgammaglobulinaemia, nephrotic syndrome and amyloidosis.

No primary pathological state has been clearly related to mucosal peptidase deficiency, although secondary peptidase deficiency is seen in coeliac disease. The peptidases reappear as the coeliac disease is treated.

Trypsinogen deficiency is now recognized as a rare cause of protein malabsorption. Cases of enterokinase deficiency have also been described and, no doubt, further protease deficiency states will be emerge in time.

Disorders of amino acid transport are well described and are more appropriately dealt with elsewhere. However, it should be noted that, in Hartnup disease, the transport of neutral amino acids across the gut is faulty in a similar way to the renal defect. The same is true in cystinuria, which is associated with defective transport of dibasic amino acids and cystine.

DIGESTION AND ABSORPTION OF FAT

Most of the dietary fat is in the form of long chain triglycerides of twelve to eighteen carbon links. These triglycerides are hydrolysed by pancreatic lipase in the duodenum and jejunum prior to absorption taking place. The products of hydrolysis are monoglycerides and fatty acids which are insoluble in water.

Bile salts are required in order to render the hydrolysed fat into a soluble form. When bile salts reach a critical concentration in the gut lumen, they aggregate to give macromolecular collections called micelles. Water insoluble substances such as monoglycerides and fatty acids, may be incorporated within the micelles and in this way become soluble. It is thought that cholesterol and fat soluble vitamins are rendered into a soluble form in a similar way. The micelles are about 4–40 Å in size and can therefore come into close contact with the plasma membrane of the microvillus. It is suggested that, as the micelle reaches the plasma membrane, the micelle is disrupted and the hydrolysed fats cross into the cell, while the bile salts pass to the terminal ileum where they are absorbed.

Re-esterification of the fatty acids takes place within the mucosal cell. The reconstituted triglyceride is coated with cholesterol and phospholipid to give a lipoprotein fraction, the chylomicron. In this form the triglyceride enters the lymphatics.

Medium chain triglycerides have less than ten carbon links and may be obtained in pure form by distillation of vegetable oils. They are absorbed differently from long chain triglycerides and because of this, have been utilized in the dietary management of diseases associated with deficiencies of lipase and bile salts; where the absorptive surface of the gut is reduced and in disorders of lymphatic drainage. Medium chain triglycerides do not require lipase for hydrolysis, are readily dispersed in water in the absence of bile salts, and rapidly enter the epithelial cell of the intestinal mucosa. Re-esterification and chylomicron formation does not occur. Medium chain triglycerides pass out of the cells to enter the portal vein and not the lymphatics.

Fat soluble vitamins are transported to the villus within the micelle. Vitamin A appears to undergo partial hydrolysis and, within the cell, is re-esterified. Vitamins D E and K appear to enter the cell unchanged. There is little evidence as to how early the infant may absorb fat soluble vitamins, but evidence is accumulating to suggest that premature infants may become deficient in Vitamin E.

Disturbance of Fat Absorption

Disorders which result in disturbed fat absorption include those associated with defective intraluminal lipolysis, defective intramucosal metabolism, and disorders of lymphatic transport.

Disorders of pancreatic function such as cystic fibrosis, pancreatitis and pancreatic exocrine deficiency with neutropenia, will be associated with steatorrhoea, due to the deficiency of lipase and defective alkalination of the intraluminal contents. Defective concentration of bile salts will prevent micelle production. This situation is seen in cirrhosis where there is impaired production of bile salts, and in biliary atresia where bile salts fail to reach the intestinal lumen. Disturbances of the bile salt pool, which results from resection of the ilium or following bacterial overgrowth in the small bowel will also lead to disordered micelle production. Bacterial overgrowth results in deconjugation of bile salts.

Intramucosal metabolism will be impaired if the absorptive area of the gut is reduced, as occurs with major resection of the small bowel, or with inflammatory disorders such as regional enteritis, or with disorders leading to villus atrophy. In all of these situations micelles have a reduced surface at which to present themselves and obviously, as the mucosal cell mass is reduced, re-esterification is impaired. In alipoproteinaemia, defective chylomicron formation occurs and fat accumulates in the mucosal cells. Hyperchylomicronaemia, Fredrickson's Type I hyperlipidaemia, is associated with a defective lipoprotein lipase clearing system.

Intestinal lymphangiectasia leads to leakage from the lymphatics so that lymphatic transport is impaired.

WATER AND ELECTROLYTE ABSORPTION

The rate and direction of movement of water and electrolytes across the intestinal mucosal cell depends on cell permeability and the presence of active transport systems in the cell membrane.[8]

Water, together with some electrolytes, pass into the cell through pores in the plasma membrane. This movement is regulated by electrochemical and osmotic forces. Glucose and other electrolytes cross the cell membrane via a carrier-mediated mechanism which can function against a concentration gradient. There is some interdependence between the passive and carrier-mediated transport mechanisms. Thus, after glucose is actively carried into the cell cytoplasm, the osmotic pressure within the cell will increase. This will induce a flow of water into the cell via the pores. As this happens, small solutes such as sodium will be carried into the cell. Hence, the major force for the movement of sodium is the active absorption of non-electrolytes such as sugars and amino acids.

Sodium transport is also influenced by the actively mediated transport of hydrogen and bicarbonate ions. Bicarbonate absorption and hydrogen excretion facilitate sodium transport by altering ionic gradients in favour of sodium. The plasma membrane pore size is smaller in the large bowel than in the small bowel. This is associated with an increase in active absorption of sodium in the large bowel.

Potassium transport appears to be passive, but it is not clear whether the potassium passes through pores or utilizes a carrier-mediated mechanism.

The diet will influence water and salt transport by altering osmotic gradients in the intestine. This effect will be determined by the rate of digestion and by the concentration of non-absorbed solutes. By the time food reaches the ligament of Trietz, dilution has occurred so that the osmolality in the intestinal lumen is equal to that of plasma and remains so in the ileum. It follows that, as sugars and amino acids are absorbed high up in the small bowel, osmolality low down depends on the concentration of electrolytes in the intestine and the rate of water absorption from the lumen. Fermentation of carbohydrate by bacteria in the intestine may increase intraluminal osmolality within the bowel. It has been estimated that, in adults, the colon absorbs on the average, 500 cc of water, 71 mEq of sodium, 34 mEq of chloride and excretes 4 mEq of potassium per twenty four hours. It has also been estimated that at this rate of absorption, the colon is functioning at 20 per cent of its capacity.

Evidence suggests that all of the transport mechanisms described exist in the young fetus.

Little is known regarding the functional ability of the infant intestine to handle minerals and vitamins, but there is little to suggest that the infant is at any disadvantage in this respect.

Pathogenesis of Diarrhoea

There has been much speculation regarding the pathogenesis of diarrhoea.[20] Diarrhoea is associated with disturbances of transport across cells which may result from decreased intestinal mucosal permeability. The intraluminal contents may have increased osmotic activity due to bacterial fermentation of carbohydrate. Intestinal motility is increased.

For a given amount of stool water, the sodium loss has been shown to vary in different diseases. There is no evidence of aldosterone control. The osmolality of stool water is in the region of $[(Na)^+ + (K)^+]2$. If there is carbohydrate malabsorption and bacterial fermentation, the osmolality will increase due to the sugars produced. This explains the non-specific benefit of giving antibiotics in fermentative diarrhoea. In infantile diarrhoea the osmolality of stool water may be low due to failure of the jejunum to absorb water. This may be related to mucosal damage or relative small mucosal pore size. If the sum of $(Na^+ + K^+) - Cl^-$ of stool is greater than the level of the plasma bicarbonate, the patient must be losing bicarbonate in the stool with resulting systemic acidosis. If the sum is less than the bicarbonate hydrogen ions are being lost and metabolic alkalosis occurs. This calculation is of more value than direct stool reading of pH or bicarbonate estimations which will be influenced by bacteria.

IMMUNOLOGY OF THE GASTROINTESTINAL TRACT

The gastrointestinal tract is rich in immunologically competent tissue, which may be thought of as having a central and peripheral component.[19,24,27]

The central lymphoid tissue consists of lympho-epitheleal derivatives of the gut such as the thymus, aggregated lymphoid tissue, e.g. Peyers patches and, in birds, the bursa of Fabricius. The central lymphoid tissue does not participate directly in immune responses, but does exert a profound influence over immune reactions in two ways.

Firstly, cellular immunity, i.e. delayed hypersensitivity reactions, depend on the competence of the central lymphoid tissue. Impaired cellular immunity is thus seen after thymectomy, which results in involution of the deep cortical areas of lymph nodes. Thymic hypoplasia results in similar changes.

The second area of influence of the central lymphoid tissue is on humoral, i.e. antibody immunity. This depends on plasma cell turnover which, in birds, is controlled by the bursa of Fabricius, an outgrowth of the cloaca. There is speculation as to which part of the gut may act in controlling humoral immunity in the human. The early prominence and later involution of the tonsils have been regarded as evidence that they could act as a regulating centre, but proof is scanty. Experimental evidence supports the appendix and Peyers patches as regulating areas but proof is incomplete. Studies in patients with defective humoral immunity, agammaglobulinaemia, does not offer an answer.

The gut functions as part of the peripheral lymphatic system by responding to antigenic stimulation by the production of coproantibodies and serum antibodies. These are produced locally by plasma cells situated in the lamina propria at all levels along the gut, and appear in the neonate three to four weeks after colonization of the gut by bacteria.

Immunofluorescent studies indicate that, in normal gut, 80 per cent of the immunoglobulin present is IgA, 12 per cent is IgM and 8 per cent is IgG. IgD and IgE containing cells have been demonstrated. Evidence suggests that serum transudation is only important in the catabolism of immunoglobulins, and that the immunoglobulins present are locally produced. Thus IgA is found in greater quantities in the gut than in serum, and is of a greater molecular weight due to a locally produced glycoprotein "secretory piece" which appears to protect the IgA from digestive enzymes. Perfusion studies indicate that secretory IgA contributes to the serum IgA by passing from the subepithelial pool to the lymphatics and portal venous system. The route of transport of IgA into the gut lumen is still incompletely understood.

The mode of action of IgA is not clearly understood. It is able to agglutinate bacteria and can fix complement. It may make bacteria easier to phagocytose and it has been suggested that it acts as an antitoxin and interferes with bacterial growth. An interesting suggestion, with some experimental evidence, is that IgA may mask antigenic sites. Thus commensal organisms are coated with IgA. The pathogens, being uncoated, are left to stimulate bacteriocidal IgG and IgM. Failure of IgA to mask food antigens may lead to food antibody production. The absence of IgA in neonates may explain why they readily form IgG and IgM antibodies to ingested bovine albumin, particularly as whole protein can cross the mucosa at this time (*vide infra*).

Much less is known about the cellular immune reactions of the gut as a peripheral lymphatic organ. Enormous numbers of lymphocytes are known to reach the epithelium daily, and evidence exists that the large lymphocytes reaching the lamina propria give rise to the plasma cells. Apart from this little is known of their function.

In the human, transplacental transfer of IgG occurs, but IgA is absent in the serum and saliva of the new born baby. Mechonium contains IgG but no IgA except in infants with cystic fibrosis, a fact which has suggested a method of screening for cystic fibrosis.

Human colostrum is rich in immunoglobulins, particularly IgAi These are not destroyed during transit through the gut, and the levels of IgA in the serum are higher in breast fed than bottle fed infants. Although breast fed babies are said to be less prone to enteric infections than bottle fed infants, it is not certain how important maternally secreted immunoglobulins are to the infantile gastrointestinal tract.

Immunological Disturbances of the Gastrointestinal Tract

In the malabsorptive states, there may be a loss of protein from the gut. This may result from: (a) failure to absorb ingested protein, (b) protein exudation through a damaged mucosa, and (c) rapid turnover of mucosal cells. In this situation, a hypercatabolic state, probably induced by the liver, exists in which, in an attempt to synthesize essential protein, other proteins are broken down. Albumin synthesis may be increased by 100 per cent, but even this may not compensate for intestinal loss, leading to a fall in serum albumin. As this fall continues, IgG may be sacrificed to release amino acids with a resulting fall in IgG levels. Because the half life of IgA and IgM is much shorter than that of IgG they are not so obviously affected.

Combined cellular and humoral deficiency leads to intractable diarrhoea, malabsorption and death. Malabsorption is seen in about 40 per cent of children with agammaglobulinaemia. Although infusions of plasma are said to be helpful in managing the malabsorption seen in this condition, the γ globulin which they receive, is unhelpful as it only contains IgG.

In dysgammaglobulinaemia, in which there are deficiencies of IgA and IgM, diarrhoea is common. Isolated IgA deficiency is said to exist in 1:500 of the population, but only 10 per cent of such people have symptoms due to the compensatory effect of IgM. Primary IgM deficiency has been described as giving rise to malabsorption.

In conditions having an immune basis, the number of immunologically competent cells are increased.

Coeliac Disease

Although gluten and some of its derivatives are known to be responsible for the clinical picture of coeliac disease, the basic aetiological cause of coeliac disease is still unknown. Two theories are popular.

The first suggests an inborn peptidase deficiency. Although peptidase deficiencies have been demonstrated in untreated patients, recovery of the enzyme level after treatment suggests that deficiency is a secondary phenomenon.

The second theory points to immunological defects. Serum antibodies to gluten may be found in some patients with coeliac disease, but are also found in normal people but clinical correlation is poor. Serum IgA and IgG is said to be raised while IgM is lowered in coeliac disease; the IgM returning to normal after treatment. However, the level of locally produced IgM is raised in coeliac disease. There is some evidence that local deficiency of IgA production in response to gluten may be an important factor in coeliac disease, but this requires further study. Ultra microscopic studies on the jejunal subepithelial connective tissue of patients with coeliac disease after single doses of gluten, demonstrate changes suggesting that an antigen antibody complex has been found. Conditions of lymphoreticular dysfunction, such as lymphoma, reticulosis, hypogammaglobulinaemia, are associated with coeliac disease, thus suggesting a loss of immuno surveillance.

Milk Allergy

Many conditions which are thought to have an immunological basis have been linked with milk allergy because of the presence of milk precipitating antibodies. However, milk antibodies are seen in normal infants.

Studies have been carried out to determine the normal immune responses of infants to ingestion of cow's milk. The ease with which the neonate produces antibodies to milk has been referred to earlier. Indeed antibodies may be detected within eight days of commencing milk feeds. The peak levels of antibodies are found between the 3–15 months and then decline. In a recent study, using immuno-diffusion and haemaglutination techniques, antibodies were first detected at one month; IgG antibodies reaching a peak at three months; IgA antibodies a peak at seven months; IgM antibodies showing a slow non-consistent rise. The low levels of antibodies detected at one year may be explained by (1) decreased permeability of the gut, (2) reduction of milk ingested, and (3) immune unresponsiveness.

In breast fed infants, the development of cow's milk antibodies relates inversely with the delay before introducing cow's milk to the diet.

Infants with diarrhoea, vomiting, occult intestinal bleeding, hypoalbuminaemia, hypogammaglobulinaemia, eosinophilia, eczema, rhinorrhoea and wheezing have been described, in whom a clear link with milk ingestion has been demonstrated. This association is based on the effect of milk challenge after a period of milk free diet, on the presence of serum and coproantibodies and on skin testing. However, these tests correlate poorly with clinical symptoms. Tests of complement activation such as B1C and immunoelectrophoresis have been shown to be of value in the diagnosis of milk allergy. In a group of patients with positive prick tests to milk, B1C levels fall in all the patients after milk challenge.[21] Alteration of complement was found in all those with gastrointestinal symptoms.

Measurement of IgE has been suggested as a screening test. In one series 7 out of 26 suspected cases showed abnormal IgE. Further work is currently being carried out on this.

Ulcerative Colitis

The aetiology of this condition is unknown. No pathogenic organism has been found. It has been shown that colonic epithelial cells from germ free rats contain antigenic similarities with the lipopolysaccharide of E. coli 014. This suggests the possibility of bacteria acting as auto-antigens to human colonic mucosa. By using human colonic extracts from the foetus or stillborn infant, precipitating and haemaglutinating antibodies have been found in the serum of children with ulcerative colitis. The serum of patients with colitis has been shown to react with colonic epithelial cells. Whether these humoral antibodies are of primary or secondary importance is open to question. The possibility of a delayed hypersensitivity reaction being implicated is suggested by the observation that leucocytes from patients with ulcerative colitis are cytotoxic for foetal colon cells in tissue culture.

Intestinal Lymphangiectasis

This condition is associated with hypogammaglobulinaemia and lymphopenia. Serum immunoglobulins are depressed due to loss of protein into the lumen of the gut. It is thought to represent a delayed hypersensitivity reaction.

Lymphoid Nodular Hyperplasia

This condition is usually associated with giardiasis. It has been associated with a variety of combinations of immunoglobulin deficiencies, e.g. deficiencies of:

(1) IgA and IgM.
(2) IgG and IgA and IgM.
(3) Isolated IgA but with poor quality IgM.

It appears that cellular hypertrophy occurs to compensate for deficiency of IgA.

INTESTINAL MICROFLORA

Germ free animals differ from normal animals in several respects. They have a reduced intestinal surface area. The migration of cells from the crypt to the villus takes twice as long. The mucosa is more regular and there may be a decrease in mucosal enzyme levels. In addition, there is decreased motility of the intestine and an increased production of mucus.

Increasing knowledge of normal and abnormal intestinal microflora has resulted from the introduction of selective culture media and improved anaerobic methods of culture.[13] The organisms most frequently encountered are obligatory anaerobes such as bacteroides and anaerobic lactobacilli. In optimum conditions bacteria divide every 30 minutes, but in the gut 0·5–5 divisions per day occur.

The stomach, duodenum, jejunum and upper ileum normally contain sparse microflora, consisting mainly of gram positive streptococci, diphtheroids, anaerobic lactobacilli and fungi, which are derived from the oral pharynx. The concentration of these organisms seldom exceed 10^3–10^4. In the distal ileum, gram negative coliforms and anaerobic bacteroides are found in levels of about 10^5–10^8. The colon shows a marked increase in organisms particularly anaerobes which outnumber aerobic organisms by 1,000–10,000:1 with total numbers in the region of 10^9. The normal stool contains in the region of 10^{11} organisms per gm. of faeces.

Although much is now known about the relative numbers and types of bacteria in the intraluminal fluid, evidence suggests that significant differences exist in the bacteria found in the intraluminal fluid, surface mucus and cellular homogenates from the gut wall. Much remains to be known about the site of metabolic activity of bacteria, but these findings would suggest that the mere presence of bacteria is not enough to ascribe functional significance to them. The bacteria are situated in a complex environment, with new bacteria being added via the mouth and nasopharynx, the available nutrients altering at different levels of the gut in type and concentration and the effect of motility all affecting bacterial concentration. Indeed, the effect of motility and dilution are probably the two main factors responsible for the low levels of bacteria seen in the stomach and upper intestine. In addition, the gastric acid is thought to be protective and bile also has an antimicrobial action. It is not until the terminal ileum is reached that the bacteria find themselves in a stable environment for bacterial multiplication.

Intestinal bacteria influence the metabolism of the intestine, either by their effect on the absorptive or motility function of the intestine or secondarily due to their absorption and metabolism of substances in the gut lumen. The metabolic effects of bacteria will depend on their concentration and species. Thus all strains of Streptococcus faecalis deconjugate bile salts, as can some strains of Bacteroides but Enterococci cannot. Bacterial action in breaking down substances may have a direct advantage to the host, e.g. the breakdown of cellulose in ruminants. They might produce excess vitamins which can be used by the host, e.g. vitamin K. Bacteria may play an important role in detoxification of ingested materials, since they are capable of breaking down a wide variety of organic materials. Indeed, some bacteria seem to co-operate with each other in breaking down complex molecules by acting on different chemical links. The action of one species may alter pH or ionic concentration in favour of another group. Bacteria may play a role in inducing mucosal enzyme activity and thus influencing digestion. The metabolic byproducts of bacteria may cause an osmotic effect, which will influence intestinal secretion rate and will also alter gut motility. Secretory IgA production is stimulated.

Bacterial Overgrowth

Many conditions are known to produce an increase in the bacterial flora of the gut.[12,14] Strictures, diverticulae, blind loops and disorders of motility associated with stasis, will result in bacterial overgrowth. In adults with achlorhydria, the jejunal bacterial count may increase by 100 per cent. In tropical sprue the response to antibiotics has suggested that a contaminated bowel syndrome leading to malabsorption of B_{12} and fat may be present. One recent study showed contaminated small bowel in 60 per cent of undernourished patients and in 100 per cent of patients with tropical sprue. In acute diarrhoeal illness in children due to cholera, salmonella, shigella and E. coli, the concentration of organisms may be high, e.g. 10^7–10^9 while a marked fall in commensal anaerobes to 10^5–10^6 may occur. Some of the organisms seen in diarrhoea may not be pathogenic but opportunistic, growing rapidly as anaerobes die off.

In the normal situation, where large numbers of bacteria are found in the ileum and colon, they can exert little metabolic effect since the major part of digestion has already occurred. However, in conditions leading to bacterial overgrowth in abnormal sites, profound effects may be observed.

The toxic effects of bacterial contamination include:

(a) Toxin release. Although bacterial toxin production in the gut is regarded as less important than earlier in the century, when colonic lavage was regarded as a useful treatment for many symptoms, it still plays a role in our concept of hepatic encephalopathy. Furthermore, in cholera and E. coli infections, there appears to be a filterable substance which leads to abnormal secretion of salt and water. A new interest in endotoxins is likely to emerge with the development of new techniques for identifying endotoxin release.

(b) Bacillary dysentry is associated with direct penetration of epithelium, with resulting ulceration.

(c) Salmonella is said to cause direct local injury with alteration in fluid transport in the ileum.

(d) Binding of ingested vitamin B_{12} can occur in stagnant loops.

(e) Disturbances of carbohydrate digestion may result from fermentation and disordered water transport.

(f) Fat digestion will be impeded by deconjugation of bile salts by enterococci or bacteroides, leading to defective micelle formation and direct toxic action of bile acids.

(g) Bacteria may lead to direct breakdown of protein, which is indicated by a raised indican level in the urine.

Changes in morphology occur during bacterial invasion probably due to an effect on the lamina propria. These changes consist of reduction of cell volume with alteration to a cuboidal form, loss of microvilli and mitochondria, nuclear swelling, infranuclear vacuolation, atrophy due to lytic changes of villus cells and lamina propria and exudative and inflammatory changes in the lamina propria. The crypt epithelium is less affected during bacterial invasion possibly due to increased amounts of IgA in the crypts.

These differences of gut anatomy and physiology between germ free, normal and states of bacterial overgrowth suggests that the gut has to adapt to cope with the bacterial flora, and that this adaptation is lost in disease.

Effect of Antibiotics

There is relatively little work done on the effect of antibiotics on gut flora. Although it is relatively easy to show that known pathogens disappear from the stool after administration of an antibiotic, little is known about the effect on normal flora and about the redistribution of bacteria after antibiotics. The antibiotic may be influenced by the gut flora, thus bacterial hydrolysis of the antibiotic may release the active molecule. In the case of chloramphenicol, the excretory glucuronide formed in the liver is hydrolysed by gut bacteria, enters the enterohepatic circulation and may be responsible for the toxic effects. The antibiotic may have direct toxic effects on the intestine, e.g. Tetracycline reduces protein metabolism and Neomycin causes morphological changes associated with malabsorption of fat.

EFFECT OF RESECTION OF GUT

One problem which has been receiving a lot of attention is the effect of gut resection.[1,28,29,30] The average length of the jejunum and ileum varies between observers as shown in the table.

TABLE 2

Length of jejunum and ileum at term

Benson	248 cms.
Potts	305 cms.
Wilkinson	200–250 cms.

Reiquam measured 389 intestines and found no relationship with weight or age of the child, but did find that the length was approximately 4–6 times the crown to heel length.

In order to deal with the problems following major gut resections in children, it is important to know how much of the gut is left and also which part. This is demonstrated in a review of 50 infants in whom resection had been undertaken for volvulus or atresia. All had less than 75 cms. of small bowel remaining, excluding the duodenum which was intact. There were no survivors in five patients with less than 15 cms. of small bowel. Seven out of fourteen survived with 15–38 cms. provided the ileo-caecal valve was intact, while all eight died who had less than 40 cms. of gut with no ileo-caecal valve. There was one death in twenty infants who had 38·75 cms. of gut remaining.

Part of the problem is whether there is adequate bowel remaining for absorption to take place. There is evidence that some functional adaptation can take place, thus the ileum can take over some functions of the jejunum, but the converse does not appear to happen. Thus, removal of the distal ileum is associated with failure to absorb vitamin B_{12}, and bile salts are unable to re-enter the enterohepatic cycle. Gastric hypersecretion follows distal small bowel resection possibly due to a loss of a humoral inhibitor.

In the case of the large bowel, a patient has been described where 7 cms. of terminal ileum, the whole of the caecum and colon to the terminal part of the pelvic colon, was removed for neonatal gangrene with no ill effects, and near normal growth up to the age of 9 years. It has been suggested that the diarrhoea following such surgery might be due to failure to re-absorb sodium and that salt reduction orally might prevent fluid loss.

The question as to whether gut hypertrophy occurs is still unsettled. Several reports suggesting mucosal hypertrophy after resection have appeared but other reports refute the possibility.

Another factor in the outcome of major resection is the presence of the ileo-caecal valve. This is said to protect the small bowel from retrograde soiling from the colon. The problems following loss of the ileo-caecal valve have been illustrated in the series of 50 resections mentioned earlier. It is, however, noteworthy that loss of the ileo-caecal valve and most of the colon as mentioned above was not associated with clinically apparent small bowel contamination.

REFERENCES

1. Benson, C. D., Lloyd, J. R. and Krabbenhoft, K. L. (1967), "The Surgical and Metabolic Aspects of Massive Small Bowel Resection with Newborn," *J. Pediat. Surg.*, **2,** 227–240.
2. Bortoff, A. (1972), "Digestion: Motility," *Ann. Rev. Physiol.*, **34,** 261–290.
3. Davenport, H. W. (1971), *Physiology of the Digestive Tract.* Chicago: Year Book Med. Publishers.
4. Doty, R. W. (1968), "Neural Organization of Deglutition," in *Motility, 1861–1902* (C. F. Code, Ed.); "Alimentary Canal IV," in *Handbook of Physiology.* Washington D.C.: American Physiology Society.
5. Driscoll, S. G. and Hsia, D. Y. (1958), "Development of Enzyme Systems During Early Infancy," *Pediatrics*, **22,** 811–813.
6. Edwards, D. A. W. (1971), "The Oesophagus," *Gut*, **12,** 948–956.
7. Flatz, G. and Rotthawe, H. W. (1973), Lactose Nutrition and Natural Selection. *Lancet*, **ii,** 76–77.
8. Fordtran, J. S. (1967), "Salt and Water Transport," *Fed. Proc.*, **26,** 1405–1414.
9. Frazer, A. C. (1968), "Pathogenesis: Gluten-induced Enteropathy," in *Malabsorption Syndromes*, pp. 71–88. London: Heinemann.
10. Friedman, N. B. (1945), "Cellular Dynamics in the Intestinal Mucosa," *J. exp. Med.*, **81,** 553–559.
11. Gilat, T., Russo, S., Gelman-Malchi, E. and Aldor, T. A. M. (1972), "Lactose in Man, A Nonadaptable Enzyme," *Gastroenterology*, **62,** 1125–1127.
12. Goldstein, F. (1971), "Mechanism of Malabsorption and Malnutrition in the Blind Loop Syndrome," *Gastroenterology*, **61,** 780–784.
13. Gorbach, S. L. (1971), "Intestinal Mucus Flora," *Gastroenterology*, **60,** 1110–1129.
14. Gracey, M. (1971), "Intestinal Absorption in the Contaminated Small Bowel Syndrome," *Gut*, **12,** 403–410.
15. Gray, G. M. (1970), "Carbohydrate Digestion and Absorption," *Gastroenterology*, **58,** 96–107.
16. Hobbs, J. R., Hopner, G. W., Douglas, A. P., Crabbe, P. A. and Johonsson, S. G. O. (1969), "Immunological Mystery of Coeliac Disease," *Lancet*, **ii,** 649–650.
17. Holmes, R. (1971), "The Intestinal Brush Border," *Gut*, **12,** 668–677.
18. Illingworth, R. S. (1969), "Sucking and Swallowing Difficulties in Infancy. Diagnostic Problem of Dysphagia," *Arch. Dis. Childh.*, **44,** 655–665.
19. Jones, E. A. (1972), "Immunoglobulins and the Gut," *Gut*, **13,** 825–835.
20. Low-Beer, T. S. and Read, A. E. (1971), "Diarrhoea Mechanism and Treatment," *Gut*, **12,** 1021–1036.
21. Matthews, T. S. and Soothill, J. F. (1970), "Complement Activation After Cows Milk Feeding in Children with Cow's Milk Allergy," *Lancet*, **ii,** 893–895.
22. Patten, B. M. (1964), "The Face and Oral Region," in *Foundations of Embryology*, pp. 422–433. New York, London, Toronto: McGraw-Hill.
23. Semenza, G. (1968), "Digestion and Absorption of Sugar," *Mod. Probl. Paediat.*, **11,** 32–47.
24. Shearman, D. J. C., Parkin, D. M. and McClelland, D. B. (1972), "The Demonstration and Function of Antibodies in the Gastrointestinal Tract," *Gut*, **13,** 483–499.
25. Shiner, M. (1968), "Dynamic Morphology of the Normal and Abnormal Small Intestinal Mucosa of Man," *Mod. Probl. Paediat.*, **11,** 32–47.
26. Simoons, F. J. (1970), Primary Adult Lactose Intolerance and the Milking Habit. A Problem in Biologic and Cultural Interrelations. *Amer. J. digest. Dis.*, **15,** 695–710.
27. Watson, D. W. (1969), "Immune Responses and the Gut," *Gastroenterology*, **56,** 944–965.
28. Weinstein, L. D., Shoemaker, C. P., Hersh, T. and Wright, H. K. (1969), "Enhanced Intestinal Absorptions After Small Bowel Resection in Man," *Arch. Surg.*, **99,** 560–562.
29. Wilkinson, A. W. (1967), "Some Effects of Extensive Resection in Childhood," *Mod. Probl. Paediat.*, **11,** 191–208.
30. Wilkinson, A. W. and McCance, R. A. (1973), "Clinical and Experimental Results of Removing the Large Intestine Soon After Birth," *Arch. Dis. Childh.*, **48,** 121–126.
31. Willis, R. A. (1962), in *Borderland of Embryology and Pathology*, pp. 186–191. London: Butterworth.

17. THE GROWTH AND DEVELOPMENT OF THE KIDNEYS

I. B. HOUSTON AND O. OETLIKER

ANATOMICAL DEVELOPMENT OF THE KIDNEY

The final excretory organ of the human fetus derives from the metanephros, itself the third such organ to develop, although it is not known whether the earlier pronephros and mesonephros are functional in the human being as they are in some animals. About the fifth week of intrauterine life the ureteric bud appears as an outgrowth of the mesonephric duct and becomes embedded in the nephrogenic mesenchyme. The duct divides into smaller branches around which mesenchyme collects to give rise to lobulation of the fetal kidney—an appearance which may persist as an innocent abnormality in extrauterine life. As the ureteric branches extend peripherally the mesenchyme condenses into oval masses which then assume an "S" shape and gradually differentiate into glomeruli and tubules which connect with the branches of the ureteric duct.[31,56] The oldest and most mature nephrons therefore, lie furthest from the kidney's surface and indeed those lying near the renal pelvis begin to involute and disappear even before birth. This "Congenital glomerulosclerosis" continues to a diminishing degree for 2–3 years after birth and must be born in mind when interpreting renal biopsy specimens from infants and young children.[21]

As the deeper nephrons involute the more superficial ones appear and mature until the total complement of nephrons is achieved at about 36 weeks of gestational age. At birth however, there is still a good deal of histological immaturity evident and considerable heterogeneity in the extent of maturation of individual nephrons (Fig. 1). Not only do the glomeruli appear hypercellular with cuboidal epithelium and scanty vascularization but the tubules are short and underdeveloped. Indeed, it has been shown that relative to the mature nephron, tubular volume is even more deficient than the surface area of the glomeruli.[19]

As cellular differentiation proceeds the kidneys migrate from their caudal position and, rotating as they do so, come to lie in their final positions in the loins. The reniform shape of the kidneys result from their position on the posterior abdominal wall and failure of this migration (ectopia of the kidney) or fusion of the kidneys which interferes with this ascent, usually leads to an abnormally shaped kidney.

Thus at birth, there is still appreciable immaturity of the anatomy of the kidneys. This helps to explain some of the observed functional changes in the infant's kidneys and is probably an important factor in the gradual functional maturation which proceeds to completion in the first year or two of life. However, shortly after birth it is clear that quite profound functional alterations occur at a rate which is too fast to be related to anatomical or histological changes.

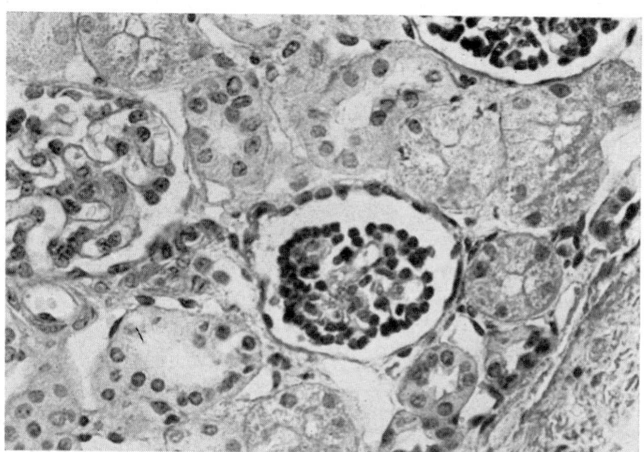

FIG. 1. At the upper left is seen the renal capsule and near to it a hypovascular immature glomerulus with a rosette of cells with dark-staining nuclei. Deeper in the kidney on the right is seen a mature glomerulus.

After the first two years of life most measurements of renal function seem to increase in magnitude at a rate which parallels growth in kidney size. For instance, glomerular filtration when corrected for a standard size (body surface area being the usual source of comparison) remains constant after the age of about 18 months. It is commonplace to correct such measurements to the "average" normal adult surface area of 1·73 m.^{2} (in Europe and America) or 1·5 m.^{2} (in Japan). However, correction for size is just as logical in adults as in children and rather than taking the awkward and rather arbitrary "average" adult surface area many workers now prefer to correct to an equally arbitrary but easier 1·0 m^2.

Care must be exercised in the wholesale application of size-corrections to any aspect of renal function or malfunction. It seems reasonable to apply it where sheer size or numbers of nephrons is physiologically the dominant factor; it may be less relevant to do so where there is very wide physiological variation in a function even for the same size of kidney. This objection could be taken to apply to some descriptions of renal tubular function and to such pathological variables as white cell excretion and proteinuria. While these functions are related to size[29] this may be a relatively insignificant variable by comparison with other influences and although size-correction is widely used in this chapter it should be interpreted with these reservations in mind.

FUNCTIONAL DEVELOPMENT OF THE KIDNEY

Intrauterine Function

After allowing for size discrepancies there is evidence in the piglet that the pre-natal blood flow to the kidneys, both in absolute terms and as a proportion of the total cardiac output is much less than that of the mature pig.[23] To some degree this may be due to the relatively poor vascularization already noted but the rapid increase which has been shown to occur after birth is largely due to a diminution of renal vascular resistance. In turn this suggests that ill-understood mechanisms may be reducing renal vascular flow in-utero (in the pig) perhaps by arteriolar vasoconstriction.

By contrast it is now becoming clear, more especially in the lamb where Alexander's work is noteworthy,[1] that despite a low renal blood flow the rate of output of urine is appreciable and that this is achieved by a considerable reduction in renal tubular reabsorption of sodium. Thus the lamb near term has a relatively low glomerular filtration rate but instead of reabsorbing perhaps 99·7 per cent and thus excreting 0·3 per cent of the filtered salt and water he rejects a good deal more, and so produces large volumes of urine with a low sodium concentration but representing a high total sodium output per unit of time. It is postulated that the high urine output is largely responsible for maintenance of the volume of the amniotic fluid in later pregnancy. This aspect of tubular behaviour could be regarded as evidence of histological immaturity—which microscopically is present in abundance but again the changes which occur after birth seem too rapid for this to be the only, or even the principal explanation. In the calf, lamb and piglet the hypertonicity of the renal papillae gradually increase with increasing gestational age[53]; in the first two of these species a medullary-cortical sodium gradient may be established before birth but is always much less than that observed post-natally and in the mature animal. As sodium accumulation is one of the means whereby the papillary osmolality is increased and as this transport of sodium (without water) is a function of Henle's loop, this is further evidence for the decreased tubular reabsorption of sodium already mentioned. Whether this is the result of functional depression or a consequence of morphological immaturity is uncertain; it seems likely that both play a part. Certainly the number of Henle's loops descending into the papilla and their lengths increase with increasing age.[18]

In view of the frequent occurrence of neonatal hypocalcaemia in the human some interest is attached to the ability of the renal tubule to handle phosphate and calcium. Again in lambs it is clear[2,50] that the fetal lamb can respond to hypocalcaemia by secreting parathormone and that the renal tubules respond in a quantitatively very similar way to that of older animals by inhibiting phosphate reabsorption and causing phosphaturia. The fetal lamb's urine is poor in phosphate but again this seems to be a perfectly normal physiological response to the suppression of parathyroid activity induced by persistent hypercalcaemia.

As will be seen and for obvious reasons, virtually all the precise information about intrauterine renal function is based on animal experimentation. In human beings such data as are available are compatible with the thesis that the human kidney, in utero is behaving much like that of the lamb. The human amniotic fluid, which in the later stages of pregnancy, is believed to be largely derived from fetal urine becomes more and more dilute with higher levels of creatinine and urea as gestation increases.[3,33] The maintenance at full-term of an osmolality gradient from maternal plasma to amniotic fluid of 27 mosmol/kg despite the rapid passage of water through the fetal membranes tending to eliminate this difference, bespeaks a considerable and regular outpouring of hypotonic fluid, presumably fetal urine, into the amniotic cavity. At birth the first urine produced by the infant, often within minutes of birth is largely the product of intrauterine function and McCance[34,37] has shown it to be dilute and low in phosphate just like the fetal lamb or piglet.[35] Again, like the lamb, fetal plasma at birth has a higher level of serum calcium than does maternal plasma[24,49] and by suppressing fetal parathyroid activity this may well account for the low urinary phosphate concentration. Clearly these human observations are susceptible of many other explanations but they are consonant with the observations derived from animal experimentation. Together they suggest that, despite a poor blood supply, the kidney in utero is producing a large volume of urine. Far from being a functionless organ sequestred from the bulk of its blood supply by some teleological insight on the part of the fetus it is performing a vital function in maintaining amniotic fluid volume. The squashed face, skeletal deformity and pulmonary hypoplasia which accompany Potters' Syndrome (Fig. 2) are testimony to the results of a lack of amniotic fluid consequent upon the renal agenesis therewith associated.[46] In the uterus the fetus is continually haemodialysed by the placenta and the maintenance of the "millieu intérieur" is not a role of the kidney: this is a function for which it becomes responsible only after birth.

Post-Natal Transition

Prenatally the kidney seems geared to the production of large quantities of urine at whatever cost in losses of water and salt—ample replacements are available via the placenta from maternal sources. Once the umbilical cord is severed the kidney must bear the brunt of the efforts to adjust fluid and electrolyte losses to balance the much reduced supply. The fetus emerges from the primeval water-rich swamp of the uterus to the extrauterine desert where fluid and electrolyte conservation become vital for its very existence. Although the cardiorespiratory changes at birth are clearly the most immediately vital, renal adaptation is no less important in the next few days.

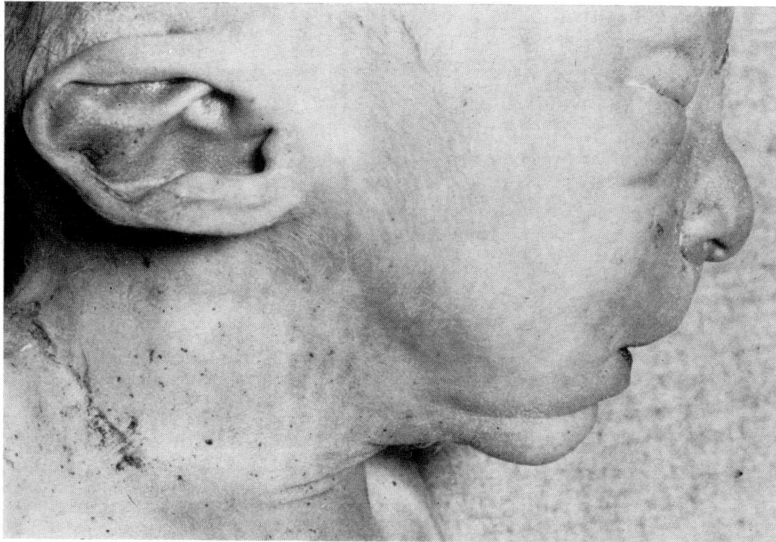

FIG. 2. Potter's facies. Note the squashed appearance of face and ears presumably a consequence of the lack of amniotic fluid associated with the renal agenesis.

Figure 3 shows characteristic examples of the changes in urinary sodium excretion which regularly occur in the first week of life. Whatever their gestational age or weight at birth all babies exhibit the same pattern of change, a relatively low rate of tubular sodium reabsorption and high urine flow rate in the first few hours of life falling

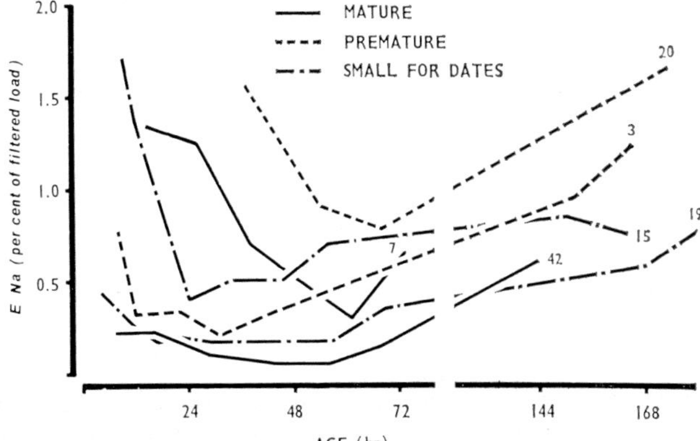

FIG. 3. Examples of sequential changes in fractional sodium excretion in individual infants. The pattern of change is remarkably similar, falling soon after birth and recovering toward the end of a week, but the level at which this occurs is very variable.

rapidly in the next few hours and days to rise again at the end of the first week of life. There is some suggestion that the degree of tubular sodium rejection may be greater among the babies born early but this is not significantly different from full-term babies in the small numbers so far studied. On average, in the first 12 hours of life, babies excreted about 1 per cent of their filtered load of sodium—an adult's kidney behaving similarly would excrete in 24 hours about 15 g. of sodium chloride! The precise level of this natriuresis is however very variable and one of the factors responsible for this variation is probably the volume of blood returned from the placenta to the baby soon after birth: the placento-fetal blood transfusion. Indirect evidence suggests that the larger this transfusion the greater the inhibition of sodium reabsorption and the larger the resulting natriuresis.

Glomerular filtration seems to follow a similar but less

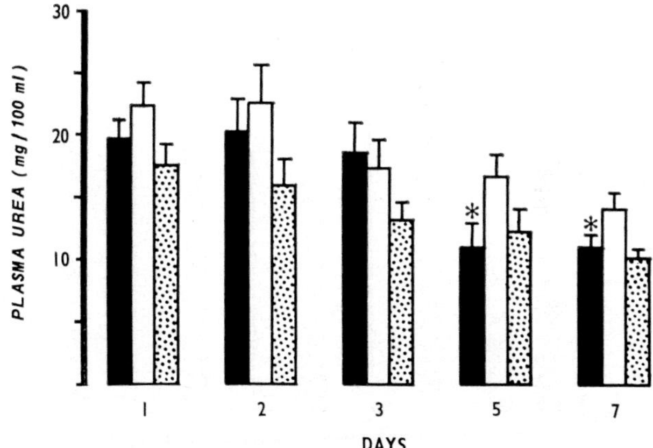

FIG. 4. Changes in plasma urea levels. Solid columns represent mature babies, hollow columns babies born early and stippled columns, babies small for dates. There are no significant differences between them. One standard deviation is shown at the top of each column except where starred when the mean and range are shown because small numbers were involved.

pronounced pattern with higher values just after birth and at the end of a week than in between. Despite this impairment of glomerular filtration, plasma creatinine and urea levels are higher at birth and fall steadily over the first week (Figs. 4 and 5). This must represent the clearing of a pool of these substances built up in utero either by accumulation from the maternal circulation or by failure of passage through the placenta in the reverse direction.[58] After birth the metabolic supply of these substances is clearly less than that in utero which allows the plasma concentration to fall despite the decreased filtration rate.

Patterns of change in plasma osmolality have been subject to wide variations in the literature[11,18] but where liberal supplies of a low solute milk are given from a few hours after birth plasma osmolality is, on average, constant over the first week (Fig. 6). Some reports have suggested that

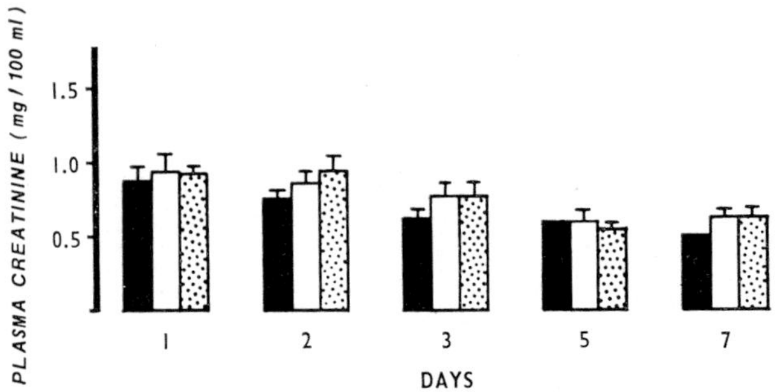

FIG. 5. Changes in plasma creatinine levels. Key as for Fig. 4.

osmolality rises at this time, others that it falls and the best explanation for these discrepancies lies in the different feeding regimens employed in different units. Given that the range of response available to the newborn kidney is limited, it is possible to give so much solute that the concentrating capacity is exceeded and there is net retention of solute with increasing osmolality. Over-dilute feeds, or

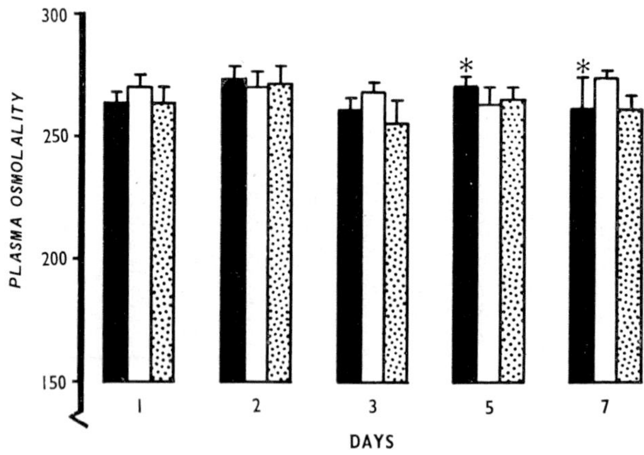

FIG. 6. Changes in plasma osmolality. Key as for Fig. 4.

5 per cent glucose in water could have the opposite effect if the volumes administered exceeded the kidneys limited capacity to excrete excess water. Just as delayed feeding with its consequences of enhanced weight loss and dehydration, jaundice and hypoglycaemia, has now been largely abandoned, the more recent advocation of high protein very concentrated feeds for premature babies seems unphysiological and potentially harmful.

It is of interest that at birth the cord blood of the human infant has calcium levels slightly higher than those of the mother,[24,49] a situation paralleling that found in the fetal lamb. This level falls after birth and in artificially fed babies is consistently lower than normal by the end of the first week.[45] This fall is accompanied by an increase of serum inorganic phosphorus levels and urinary inorganic phosphorus excretion of a quite remarkable degree (Fig. 7) (but not when the babies are breast fed[36]). Whereas the older child may reabsorb 80–90 per cent of the filtered load of phosphorus the week-old baby artificially fed may reabsorb none of it. Indeed in some babies at the end of the first week there is clear evidence of tubular *secretion* of phosphorus with a total excretion of phosphorus which exceeds the filtered load. Thus the hyperphosphataemia occurs despite heavy phosphaturia and is presumably due to the large dietary intake of phosphorus from feeds based

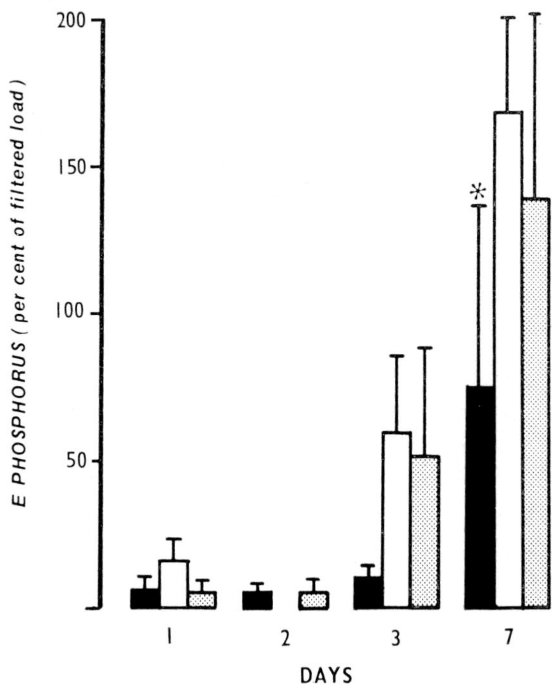

FIG. 7. Mean changes in fractional phosphorus excretion. Key as for Fig. 4. Note that the very high phosphorus excretion on day 7 can only be accomplished by tubular secretion of phosphate.

on Cow's milk. The pronounced phosphaturia also suggests appreciable hormonal stimulation of the renal tubules—probably by parathormone, though an effect by calcitonin cannot be excluded. Though the evidence is thus far very incomplete it suggests that the neonatal hypocalcaemia from which newborn babies suffer may not be the result of parathormone deficiency but a consequence of the large intake of dietary phosphorus initiated soon after birth.

With regard to renal acid-base homeostasis in the first week or two of life, there is evidence that the urine pH is inappropriately high for the degree of acidaemia often exhibited by newborn babies.[13] In slightly older infants this "physiological" acidaemia has been attributed to variations in renal tubular bicarbonate reabsorption,[15] perhaps itself related to the avidity with which sodium is reabsorbed[26,42] rather than an anatomical or physiological incapacity to secrete sufficient hydrogen ion to produce the gradient required to lower urinar pH. Whether such mechanisms are responsible in the first week of life is currently uncertain but it is tempting to suppose this may be so. As mentioned earlier, there is in the first 24 hrs. of life, a rather low rate of tubular sodium reabsorption, a situation which might be expected to lead to a greater degree of sodium and bicarbonate loss in the urine with a higher urine pH than would be appropriate for the observed acidaemia.

In summary therefore, there are quite remarkable changes occurring very rapidly in the first few days of life which seem likely to have their origins in a perfectly physiological response by the kidney to the new roles thrust upon it by its extra-uterine environment. Anatomical changes probably play a very slight part in this adaptation but become much more important in the later stage of renal maturation.

Renal Maturation in Infancy

It is clear that despite allowing for the growth of the kidney, for instance by correcting data to a standard surface area, the infant's kidney behaves as though it were smaller than it actually is. This discrepancy has been explained as due to "immaturity". For some aspects of renal function the data is more complete than others and measurements of glomerular filtration are perhaps best documented.

Glomerular Filtration

Over 30 years ago Barnett (1940)[5] made the observation that glomerular filtration rate is disproportionately low in the newborn baby and that it gradually increases with age.[6] In the first month of life the mean GFR is about 1/4th to 1/3rd of that expected for size rising to $\frac{1}{2}$ between 3 and 6 months of age, $\frac{3}{4}$ between 6 and 12 months of age and to 100 per cent of the figure expected for size about the middle of the second year of life.[51,57] It has been noted already that at birth many glomeruli are immature, some quite obviously non-functional and virtually avascular clumps of mesenchyme and others potentially functional but with cuboidal epithelial cells seeming to offer an appreciable barrier to filtration. Indeed there is evidence that the porosity of the glomerular filter is reduced, as judged by the clearance of dextran molecules of differing sizes[4] and micro-dissection measurements of individual glomeruli show their surface areas to be smaller in infancy.[19] However, histological maturation proceeds at a relatively slow pace as compared with the physiological changes and additional reasons must be sought.

Blood pressure is lower in infancy and rises rapidly at first and then much more gradually throughout childhood; this potential increase in perfusion pressure might be expected to increase glomerular filtration. However, though this may play a part, the magnitude and timing of the changes does not correspond with the variations in GFR. Renal blood flow and hence GFR are of course dependent not only upon arterial pressure but also upon renal vascular resistance. It has been shown that, in newborn piglets, both total cardiac output and the proportion of it which passes to the kidneys rapidly increase in the first few weeks after birth, evidence that there is a relatively greater decrease in vascular resistance in the kidneys than elsewhere.[23] In guinea pigs the effective perfusion pressure (glomerular capillary pressure — intratubular and plasma colloid osmotic pressures) has actually been measured by micropuncture techniques and shown to rise by a factor of 2·5 during the first 7 weeks of life.[52] In this last species it has been calculated that the maturational changes in GFR could be accounted for as a sum of these pressure changes, the increasing porosity of the glomerular membrane and the increasing surface area available for filtration as glomeruli differentiate morphologically. In man the data are clearly much less decisive but are, so far, consonant with the view that a similar combination of factors may be responsible.

Tubular Function

The newborn baby appears ill-equipped to excrete excessive loads of sodium and when fed a saline solution may become oedematous. Exactly why this occurs remains uncertain although the saline loads administered in some experiments have been very large as compared with the baby's size.[12] However, there remains a possibility that the "escape mechanism" which leads to natriuresis despite salt overload in older individuals is in some way defective.

In this respect it is interesting that techniques have recently been developed to study the distribution of blood within the kidney in various physiological and pathological circumstances.[9] Using this technique of "washing out" a radio-active gas it has been shown that in puppies up to 4 months old, a greater proportion of the renal blood flow goes to the juxta medullary nephrons than to the cortical ones. Other studies suggest that in states leading to a need for renal sodium conservation (*e.g.* dehydration) renal blood flow shifts to a predominantly juxta medullary one,[38] in salineloading where increased renal sodium excretion occurs more blood goes to the cortex. Thus, leaving aside the reasons for this distribution of blood in infancy it does equip the newborn baby to conserve sodium, its dominant need; it may also make it more difficult to excrete salt when excessive dietary loads are given.

It is known that the extraction of para-aminohippuric acid (P.A.H.) by the mature kidney is 85–100 per cent of that reaching it in the arterial blood. That is to say almost all P.A.H. in the plasma is removed by one passage through the kidney and the clearance of P.A.H. approximates to the renal plasma flow. In infancy however, P.A.H. extraction by one passage through the kidney can be as low as 50 per cent[8] showing that tubular secretion of this substance is limited. The maximal rates of tubular secretion of P.A.H. and reabsorption of glucose are also known to be reduced in infancy.[55] The "physiological acidaemia" of infancy has already been mentioned and is largely due to a diminished renal tubular threshold for bicarbonate. This threshold however, is altered according to the state of sodium, potassium and chloride depletion of the body and it is possible that the observed lower threshold for bicarbonate and consequent lower blood bicarbonate and pH levels of infancy is a secondary reflection of altered renal tubular handling of these ions.[39]

Morphologically there are adequate explanations for these differences in that tubular length and volume are much reduced as compared with their adult size. Moreover there is suggestive evidence that morphologically the tubules are even less mature than the glomeruli for the ratio of glomerular surface area to proximal tubular volume is 27·8 in the full term infant, 13·4 at 3 months of age and 3·1 in the adult.[19] However, the observations previously mentioned when discussing adaptive changes in the first hours and days after birth show that wide variations in tubular function are feasible even then. It remains to be seen whether the physiological evidence of tubular immaturity is solely a reflection of the morphology or partly related to entirely appropriate renal responses to physiological alterations elsewhere in the infant.

Acid-base Homeostasis

Blood pH is dependent on the relative concentrations of bicarbonate ions and carbonic acid (or dissolved CO_2) as defined by the Henderson-Hasselbach equation:

$$pH = pK + \log \frac{[HCO_3]}{[H_2CO_3]}$$

in turn the bicarbonate buffer system is a reversible chemical reaction:

$$H^+ + HCO_3^- \rightleftharpoons H_2CO_3 \rightleftharpoons CO_2 + H_2O$$

Thus in terms of the production of acidaemia, HCO_3^- losses are quantitatively of equal significance to retention of H^+ ion. Because of this, renal hydrogen ion excretion is often expressed as "net hydrogen ion excretion": the total of urinary excretion of free and buffered hydrogen ion in the urine — urinary bicarbonate.

Some 85 per cent of the filtered load of bicarbonate is ordinarily reabsorbed in the proximal tubule by a process involving the secretion of hydrogen ion into the tubular lumen. This combines with bicarbonate ion in the tubular fluid to yield carbonic acid; under the influence of carbonic anhydrase this is dehydrated to CO_2 which diffuses into the tubular cell to be reconstituted into bicarbonate and passed on into the plasma. On the usual human mixed diet all the remaining bicarbonate is reabsorbed in the distal tubule; the final urine has a low pH and is completely bicarbonate

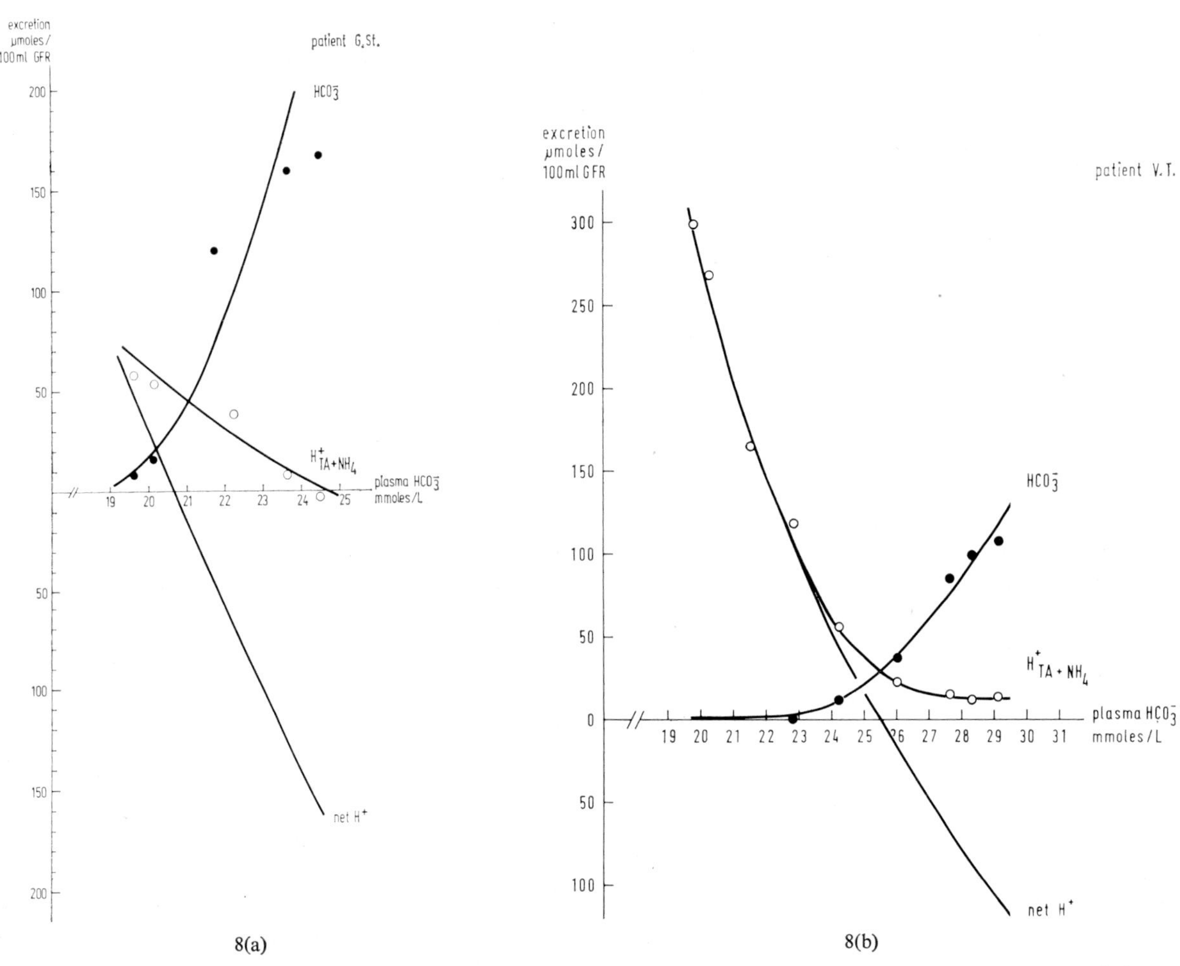

FIG. 8. Renal bicarbonate threshold in infancy. On the left patient G.St. was a week-old infant with a bicarbonate threshold of 19·5 m. moles/L as opposed to the 12-year-old patient V.T. on the right whose threshold is 23·5 m. moles/L. Alternatively the points at which H^+ ion and HCO_3^- ion excretion intersect are at plasma HCO_3 concentrations of 21 and 25·5 m. moles/L respectively—not the threshold but another representation of the level of HCO_3 reabsorption. (Partially from Oetliker, O., Chattas, A. S. and Schultz, S. M. (1971), "Characterization of Renal Contribution to Acid-Base Balance in the Pediatric Age Group", *Helv. Paediat. Acta*, **26,** 523–534, by permission.)

free. In the distal tubule a considerable hydrogen ion gradient is created by tubular secretion and this free ion is titrated against two main buffer systems:

$$HPO_4^{=} + H^+ = H_2PO_4^-$$

and

$$NH_3 + H^+ = NH_4^+$$

Although tests of the kidney's capacity to excrete acid often centre upon the ability to produce "titratable acid" (largely buffered phosphate) and ammonium it should be borne in mind that the quantity of hydrogen ion secreted to reabsorb bicarbonate is at least 20 times that excreted in the urine. Thus a failure of bicarbonate reabsorption in the proximal tubule can be of equal importance to a distal tubular failure to create a hydrogen ion gradient with which to titrate phosphate and ammonia buffers.

The infant commonly exhibits a lower blood pH and bicarbonate than the older child[36] and there is evidence that this is due to a reduction in the tubular reabsorption of bicarbonate, often expressed as a lower renal bicarbonate threshold.[16,54] A comparable but different expression of the decreased bicarbonate threshold in infancy can be obtained by measuring bicarbonate and hydrogen ion excretion simultaneously. When a double plot of these is made (Fig. 8) the point of intersection of these two lines describes a certain plasma bicarbonate level which is lower in infancy than later childhood.[40] This relative diminution in bicarbonate reabsorption leads to a urinary bicarbonate leak, lower levels of plasma bicarbonate (and hence lower blood pH). However, the lowering of plasma bicarbonate levels lowers the total of filtered bicarbonate and the tubules are then able to cope with the reduced load; the urine becomes bicarbonate-free and a new steady state is achieved at the expense of, by adult terms, a degree of acidaemia. In the puppy a similar process occurs and plasma bicarbonate can be increased by increasing the avidity with which the tubules reabsorb sodium (and bicarbonate alongside it).[39] Thus sodium depletion (and hypokalaemia[43]) tend to correct acidaemia when aldosterone secretion is normal, a phenomenon also observed in various pathological types of renal tubular acidosis resulting from a similar mechanism of renal tubular acidosis resulting from a similar mechanism.[30,41] When aldosterone secretion is deficient, as in congenital adrenal hyperplasia, it can be demonstrated that increasing the avidity of sodium reabsorption by the administration of fludrocortisone will also increase renal bicarbonate threshold[44] (Fig. 9). It seems likely therefore, that some at least, of the apparent renal tubular immaturity in this respect may be a secondary consequence of extra-renal changes, to which the kidney is responding in a comparatively "mature" fashion.

When an individual is rendered acidaemic by an oral load of ammonium chloride the urine pH falls within 3–4 hours to a minimum value, while titratable acid and ammonium excretion rise to plateau at a maximum rate at the same time. If this test is applied to children of three years old and over the results (corrected for size) are very similar to those of adults while the younger infant tends to produce a net

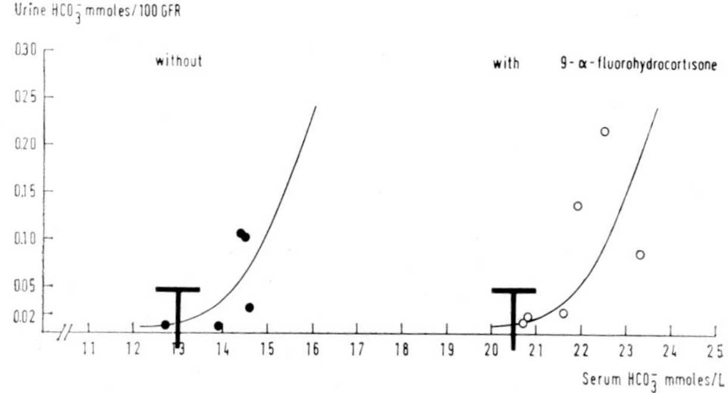

FIG. 9. Bicarbonate threshold and mineralocorticoid effect. The threshold (T) is increased by fludrocortisone administration. (From Oetliker, O. and Zurbrügg, R. P. (1970), "Renal Tubular Acidosis in Salt Losing Syndrome of Congenital Adrenal Hyperplasia," *J. Clin. Endocr. Metab.*, **31**, 447–450, by permission.)

hydrogen ion excretion of the same order but with greater titratable acid and lesser ammonia excretion[16,51] (Table 1). In this context some thought must be given to the infant's phosphorus intake, which is much higher in artificially fed babies than in those receiving human milk. The urinary excretion of phosphate and therefore the maximal levels of titratable acid excretion in the young breast fed baby are smaller either than those of older children or other infants fed on Cow's milk formulae.[20,25] This contrasts with the figures quoted in Table 1 derived from largely artificially fed babies on a much higher phosphorus intake whose titratable acid excretion is greater than that of older children. Of some interest too, is the observation[15] that growth retarded children of idiopathic and probably heterogeneous types exhibit a minor degree of acidaemia and also a diminution of hydrogen ion excretion when stressed with ammonium chloride. Whether the small stature of these children is related to this phenomenon, or as seems more likely, is a consequence of being small, remains uncertain. However, acidaemia seems capable of retarding growth both in experimental studies and in man and correction of the fault may lead to catch-up growth.[40]

TABLE 1

	Infants up to Age 12 Months	*Children 3–15 Years Old*
Urine pH	≤ 5·0	≤ 5·5
Titratable acid μEq./min./1·73 m.^{2}	62 (43–111)	52 (33–71)
Ammonium μEq./min./1·73 m.^{2}	57 (42–79)	73 (46–100)

Urine Concentration and Water Excretion

Conventional tests of renal concentrating capacity by fluid restriction and vasopression injection reveal that ordinarily the infant's kidney can only concentrate urine to a maximum of about 700–800 mosmol/kg whereas the adult and older child can achieve 1200–1400 mosmol/kg.[7,14]

However, it is now clear that this defect is not a reflection of renal immaturity in any morphological sense but a consequence of the lower level of production and excretion of urea by the growing baby (see below).[14] If the baby is placed on a high protein diet or given oral urea it is capable of producing urine almost as concentrated as that of an adult. This observation is explained because the hyper-osmolality of the renal papilla necessary to produce a concentrated urine is due both to interstitial sodium chloride and to urea: if little urea is available to the tubules then however mature they may be, a satisfactorily large osmotic gradient in the renal papilla cannot be produced. This phenomenon also explains the observation that more concentrated urine is produced when the usual quantity of milk powder is made up with half the usual amount of water and fed to the baby than when milk feeds are withheld entirely: the former regime permits protein intake and urea formation the latter severely restricts it. However, even on a high protein intake there is some persistent slight deficiency in renal concentrating capacity in the baby which improves with age and presumably this lesser defect is a true reflection of the morphological differences of fewer and shorter loops of Henle in the developing nephron.

In absolute terms the infant is as capable of diluting its urine (to a minimum of about 50 mosmol/kg) as the older child.[14] The rate of excretion of a water load is none-the-less diminished by adult standards; an oral water load is eventually all excreted but over a longer period.[34] This phenomenon could be secondary to other renal tubular changes or even to extra-renal influences, it does not seem to be due to a maturational defect in that segment of the nephron which lowers tubular fluid osmolality and dilutes the urine.

GROWTH AND THE KIDNEY

At birth the G.F.R. of the human kidney has about 1/4th to 1/3rd the efficiency expected if allowance is made for the baby's size. An adult whose renal function was thus reduced would inevitably exhibit some of the clinical and biochemical features of renal failure, particularly an increase in blood urea level. That a baby does not do so is a consequence largely of rapid somatic growth and emphasizes that somatic stability at this age is due to a dynamic interplay of nutrition, growth and renal function.[34]

The precise dietary requirements for human infants remain a matter of some debate but a reasonable estimate for protein requirements in the first months of infancy is about 3–4 g./kg./day—perhaps treble the needs of an adult. Most of this large intake is used for growth and the deposition of new tissue, any excess nitrogen is used metabolically in various ways and ultimately excreted as urea. As a result of the baby's growth urea production is kept to a minimum and the inefficient kidney can keep the blood urea "normal" because it is able to excrete this smaller amount. It follows that an increase in blood urea level in the baby may arise from true renal failure (as in older individuals), from any disease halting growth while permitting continued absorption of food, or because dietary protein intake exceeds even the large quantity usually needed (Fig. 10).

On the one hand this makes blood urea measurements difficult to interpret in babies and on the other implies that biochemical (and possibly clinical) abnormalities may be produced by excessive zeal in the use of high-protein feeds. It is perhaps well not to overemphasize the deleterious effects of high protein feeds themselves. It is doubtful if a modest increase in blood urea and the solute diuresis it induces are of clinical importance except in extreme circumstances; there is even some evidence that high-protein feeds enhance the rate of renal maturation.[17] However, it seems unlikely that such a state of affairs is usual or normal in nature when human infants are fed on human milk of lower protein content than most cow's milk based feeds. In our

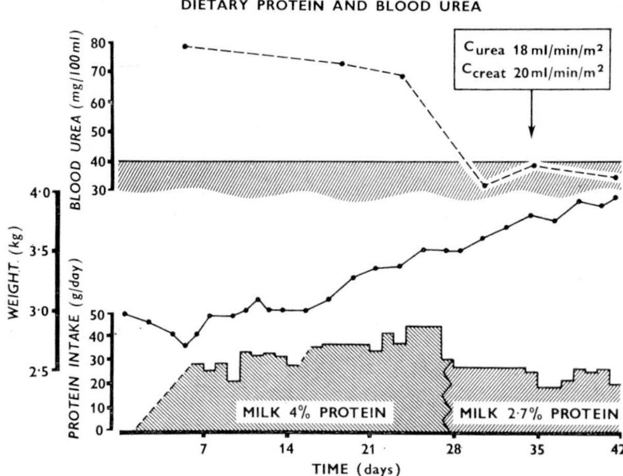

FIG. 10. Dietary protein and blood urea. A baby recovering from gastroenteritis and liberally fed on a high protein milk maintained a high blood urea which returned to normal when fed a lower protein formula of the same caloric value. Weight increase was not affected by the change in feed. Making allowance for renal immaturity, urea and creatinine clearances were normal for the baby's age.

present state of imperfect nutritional knowledge our most reliable (though not infallible) guide may be an imitation of the best naturally-occurring nutritional state possible: at least this thesis has the scientific merit of having withstood the experiment of evolutionary survival. The general unease expressed in relation to the protein content of infant food-stuffs has a counterpart when the other solutes of milk, especially sodium and potassium chloride are considered. Many parents have a belief that if milk is good for babies then "richer", "stronger", more concentrated milk may be even better. Such overconcentrated feeds have been recommended for feeding premature babies. While the growing, healthy baby may have sufficient renal compensatory capacity to cope with such a high solute-low solvent load it may well be disastrous for a poorly and perhaps dehydrated baby or for one with poor renal function. If a baby is given milk of a solute concentration higher than the maximum his kidneys can achieve, then of necessity he loses more water to excrete the solute than he obtains by mouth: he becomes dehydrated. He is in the same position as a shipwrecked sailor who takes to drinking hypertonic sea-water, a well known lethal occupation. Failure to consider the separate needs for water as well as nutrition can lead to serious aggravation of dehydration or dangerous deterioration in the function of kidneys which may be only moderately malfunctional at the start. Nutrition, growth and renal function are intricately intertwined in infancy, it is hard to assess one without precise knowledge of the others.

Growth of the Kidney

Much remains to be learned of the growth and development of the kidney both morphologically and physiologically. It has been shown that the growth of renal length and cross-sectional area can be related to age or height[27] (Fig. 11). A disease such as chronic pyelonephritis which

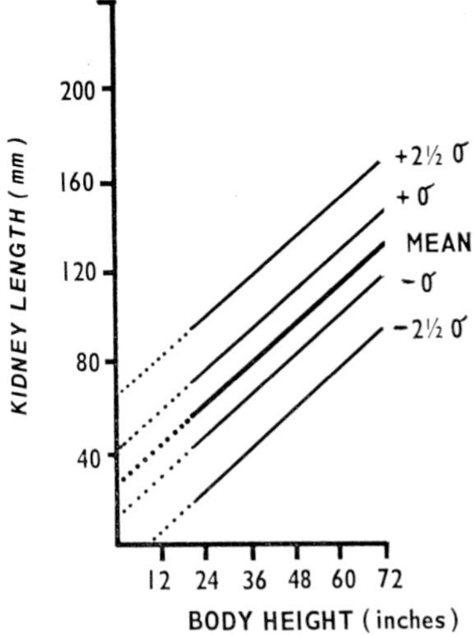

FIG. 11. Kidney length and body weight. Data derived from measurements of kidney size during intravenous pyelography. (From Hodson, C. J., Drewe, J. A., Karn, M. N. and King, A. (1962), "Renal Size in Normal Children. A Radiographic Study During Life," *Arch. Dis. Childh.*, **37**, 616–622, by permission.)

causes renal scarring may interfere with normal renal growth and such a finding has a rather sombre prognosis. The capacity for renal growth does not cease in adult life, though it may diminish.[32,47] Should one kidney be removed or destroyed the remaining kidney, if normal, will hypertrophy. The majority of this growth will occur within 6 weeks of a unilateral nephrectomy and virtually all within 3–6 months.

The Kidney and Growth

Somatic growth and the kidney are closely intertwined in numerous ways. It has already been suggested that being small in stature may in some unknown way, influence some parameters of renal function: for instance the maximal rate of excretion of ammonium in response to an acidaemia induced by ammonium chloride.[15] Growth hormone is known to be necessary to permit renal hypertrophy after nephrectomy and the acute administration of growth hormone has been shown transiently to increase renal blood flow and glomerular filtration rate.[10,22]

Conversely, a seriously malfunctioning kidney is regularly associated with growth retardation where the disease occurs in a child. Growth failure is relative not absolute.[28] Most children with chronic renal failure contrive to grow but at a rate well below the third percentile for their chronological age so that the discrepancy in size between them and their peers gets progressively wider as their age increases. The precise reasons for this growth retardation are unknown but certainly there is no shortage of growth hormone. To some extent sheer malnutrition may be responsible, for although long term haemodialysis will not itself stimulate growth, there have been reports that enhancement of the dietary caloric intake together with haemodialysis will do so.[28] Even then, the best that can usually be

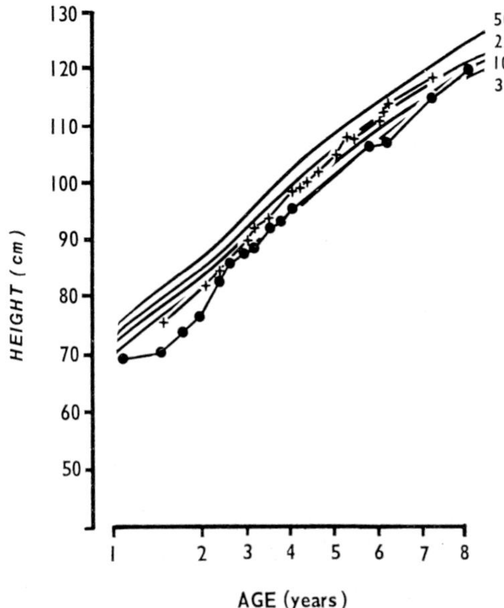

FIG. 12. Catch-up growth in treated renal tubular acidosis. Note how growth rate increases when acidaemia is corrected by sodium bicarbonate (or equivalent) therapy. (Modified from Nash, M. A., Torrado, A. D., Greifer, I., Spitzer, A. and Edelmann, C. M., Jr. (1972), "Renal Tubular Acidosis in Infants and Children," *J. Pediat.*, **80**, 738–748.)

achieved is to increase growth rate until it runs parallel to normal at a lower level, there is no catch-up growth. The influence of renal transplantation is still uncertain for experience is slender, but there is some evidence that the quality of growth may be better after this procedure than after haemodialysis alone.

Among patients with renal disease some of the most spectacularly growth-retarded are children with cystine-storage disease, a disorder causing multiple renal tubular malfunction but a fall in glomerular filtration rate rather later than most progressive types of renal disease. Such children exhibit growth failure at a very early stage of their disease when glomerular function may be quite well preserved. However they are usually markedly acidaemic because of massive losses of bicarbonate by the malfunctioning tubules.[42,48] Occasionally, and unrelated to cystine storage, such a form of "proximal" renal tubular acidosis may be the only malfunction and the patients present with acidaemia and growth failure but otherwise well preserved renal function. Animal experimentation suggests that growth retardation may be caused by acidaemia alone[48,49] and when small children with primary proximal renal tubular acidosis are treated with adequate doses of sodium bicarbonate or sodium citrate, they exhibit catch-up growth (Fig. 12). Thus acidaemia itself is sometimes the particular failure of homeostasis that interferes with growth—but in chronic renal failure correction of acidaemia is not alone sufficient to restore growth and additional factors are clearly involved.

REFERENCES

1. Alexander, D. P. and Nixon, D. A. (1961), "The Foetal Kidney", *Brit. Med. Bull.*, **17,** 112–117.
2. Alexander, D. P. and Nixon, D. A. (1969), "Effect of Parathyroid Extract in Foetal Sheep," *Biol. Neonat.*, **14,** 117–130.
3. Annotation (1972), "Assessment of Gestational Age from Amniotic Fluid," *Lancet*, **i,** 132–133.
4. Arturson, G., Groth, T. and Grotte, G. (1971), "Human Glomerular Membrane Porosity and Filtration Pressure: Dextran Clearance Data Analyzed by Theoretical Models," *Clin. Sci.*, **40,** 137–158.
5. Barnett, H. L. (1940), "Renal Physiology in Infants and Children. 1. Method for Estimation of Glomerular Filtration Rate," *Proc. Soc. exp. Biol. Med.*, **44,** 654–658.
6. Barnett, H. L., Hare, K., McNamara, H. and Hare, R. (1948), "Measurement of Glomerular Filtration Rate in Premature Infants," *J. clin. Invest.*, **27,** 691–699.
7. Barnett, H. L. and Vesterdal, J. (1953), "The Physiological and Clinical Significance of Immaturity of Kidney Function in Young Infants," *J. Pediat.*, **42,** 99–119.
8. Calcagno, P. L. and Rubin, M. I. (1963), "Renal Extraction of Para-aminohippurate in Infants and Children," *J. clin. Invest.*, **42,** 1632–1639.
9. Carriere, S., Thorburn, G. D., O'Morchoe, C. C. C. and Barger, A. C. (1966), "Intrarenal Distribution of Blood Flow in Dogs During Haemorrhagic Hypotension," *Circ. Res.*, **19,** 167–179.
10. Corvilain, J., Abramow, M. and Bergans, A. (1962), "Some Effects of Human Growth Hormone on Renal Haemodynamics and on Tubular Phosphate Transport in Man," *J. clin. Invest.*, **41,** 1230–1235.
11. Davis, J. A., Harvey, D. R. and Stevens, J. F. (1966), "Osmolality as a Measure of Dehydration in the Neonatal Period," *Arch. Dis. Childh.*, **41,** 448–450.
12. Dean, R. F. A. and McCance, R. A. (1949), "The Renal Responses of Infants and Adults to the Administration of Hypertonic Solutions of Sodium Chloride and Urea," *J. Physiol.*, **109,** 81–97.
13. Edelmann, C. M., Jr. (1967), "Maturation of the Neonatal Kidney," *Proc. 3rd Int. Congr. Nephrol.*, pp. 1–12. Basel: S. Karger.
14. Edelmann, C. M., Barnett, H. L. and Troupkou, V. (1960), "Renal Concentrating Mechanisms in Newborn Infants: Effect of Dietary Protein and Water Content, Role of Urea and Responsiveness to Antidiuretic Hormone," *J. clin. Invest.*, **39,** 1062–1069.
15. Edelmann, C. M., Jr., Houston, I. B., Rodriguez-Soriano, J., Boichis, H. and Stark, H. (1968), "Renal Excretion of Hydrogen Ion in Children with Idiopathic Growth Retardation," *J. Pediat.*, **72,** 443–451.
16. Edelmann, C. M., Jr., Rodriguez-Soriano, J., Biochis, H., Gruskin, A. B. and Acosta, M. (1967), "Renal Bicarbonate Reabsorption and Hydrogen Ion Excretion in Normal Infants," *J. clin. Invest.*, **46,** 1309–1317.
17. Edelmann, C. M., Jr., Wolfish, N. M. (1968), "Dietary Influence on Renal Maturation in Premature Infants," *Pediat. Res.*, **2,** 421–422.
18. Feldman, W., Drummond, K. N. (1969), "Serum and Urine Osmolality in Normal Full-term Infants," *Canad. Med. Ass. J.*, **101,** 595–596.
19. Fetterman, G. H., Shuplock, N. A., Phillipp, F. J. and Gregg, H. S. (1965), "The Growth and Maturation of Human Glomeruli and Proximal Convolutions from Term to Adulthood," *Pediatrics*, **35,** 601–619.
20. Fomon, S. J., Harris, D. M. and Jensen, R. L. (1959), "Acidification of the Urine by Infants Fed Human Milk and Whole Cow's Milk," *Pediatrics*, **23,** 113–120.
21. Friedli, B. (1966), "Le glomérule hyalin du nouveau-né," *Biol. Neonat.*, **10,** 359–372.
22. Gershberg, H. and Gasch, J. (1956), "Effect of Growth Hormone on Sulphate Tm, Urea Clearance and Fasting Blood Glucose," *Proc. Soc. exp. Biol. Med.*, **91,** 46–49.
23. Gruskin, A. B., Edelmann, C. M., Jr. and Yuan, S. (1970), "Maturational Changes in Renal Blood Flow in Piglets," *Pediat. Res.*, **4,** 7–13.
24. Hallman, N. and Salmi, I. (1953), "On Plasma Calcium in Cord Blood and in the Newborn," *Acta Paediat.* (*Uppsala*), **42,** 126–129.
25. Hatemi, N. and McCance, R. A. (1961), "Renal Aspects of Acid Base Control in the Newly Born: III. Response to Acidifying Drugs," *Acta Paediat. Scand.*, **50,** 603–616.
26. Hebert, C. S., Martinez-Maldonado, M., Eknoyan, G. and Suki, W. N. (1972), "Relation of Bicarbonate to Sodium Reabsorption in Dog Kidney," *Amer. J. Physiol.*, **222,** 1014–1020.
27. Hodson, C. J., Drewe, J. A., Karn, M. N. and King, A. (1962), "Renal Size in Normal Children. A Radiographic Study During Life," *Arch. Dis. Childh.*, **37,** 616–622.
28. Holliday, M. A., Potter, D. E. and Dobrin, R. S. (1971), "Treatment of Renal Failure in Children," *Pediat. Clin. N. Amer.*, **18,** 613–624.
29. Houston, I. B. (1965), "Urinary White Cell Excretion in Childhood," *Arch. Dis. Childh.*, **40,** 313–316.
30. Houston, I. B., Boichis, H. and Edelmann, C. M. (1968), "Fanconi Syndrome with Renal Sodium Wasting and Metabolic Alkalosis," *Amer. J. Med.*, **44,** 638–646.
31. Kissane, J. M. (1966), "Development of the Kidney," in *Pathology of the Kidney*, pp. 43–61. (R. H. Heptinstall, Ed.). Boston: Little, Brown & Co.
32. Krakower, C. A. and Heino, H. E. (1947), "Relationship of Growth and Nutrition to Cardiorenal Changes Induced in Birds by a High Salt Intake," *Arch. Path.*, **44,** 143–162.
33. Lind, T., Billewicz, W. Z. and Cheyne, G. A. (1971), "Composition of Amniotic Fluid and Maternal Blood Through Pregnancy," *J. Obstet. Gynaec. Brit. Cwlth.*, **78,** 505–512.
34. McCance, R. A. (1959), "The Maintenance of Stability in the Newly Born," *Arch. Dis. Childh.*, **34,** 361–370, 459–470.
35. McCance, R. A. and Stanier, M. W. (1960), "The Function of the Metanephros of Foetal Rabbits and Pigs," *J. Physiol.*, **151,** 479–483.
36. McCance, R. A. and von Finck, M. A. (1947), "The Titratable Acidity, pH, Ammonia and Phosphates in the Urines of Very Young Infants," *Arch. Dis. Childh.*, **22,** 200–209.
37. McCance, R. A. and Widdowson, E. M. (1961), "Mineral Metabolism of the Foetus and Newborn," *Brit. Med. Bull.*, **17,** 132–136.
38. Moffat, D. B. (1968), "Medullary Flow During Hydropenia," *Nephron*, **5,** 1–6.
39. Moore, E. S., Fine, B. P., Satrasook, S. S., Vergel, Z. M., Edelmann, C. M., Jr., Rodriguez-Soriano, J., Boichis, H., Gruskin, A. B. and Acosta, M. (1967), "Renal Bicarbonate Reabsorption and Hydrogen Ion Excretion in Normal Infants," *J. clin. Invest*, **46,** 1309–1317.
40. Nash, M. A., Torrado, A. D., Greifer, I., Spitzer, A. and Edelmann, C. M., Jr. (1972), "Renal Tubular Acidosis in Infants and Children," *J. Pediat.*, **80,** 738–748.
41. Oetliker, O., Chattas, A. J. and Schultz, S. M. (1971), "Characterisation of Renal Contribution to Acid Base Balance in the Pediatric Age Group," *Helv. paediat. Acta*, **26,** 523–534.
42. Oetliker, O. and Rossi, E. (1969), "The Influence of Extra-cellular

Fluid Volume on the Renal Bicarbonate Threshold. A Study of Two Children with Lowe's Syndrome," *Pediat. Res.*, **3**, 140–148.
43. Oetliker, O., Schultz, S., Schütt, B., Donath, A. and Rossi, E. (1971), "Hypokalaemia, a Factor Influencing Renal Bicarbonate Reabsorption: Continued Studies on the Regulatory Mechanisms Governing Renal Handling of Acid-Base in Children," *Pediat. Res.*, **5**, 618–625.
44. Oetliker, O. and Zurbrügg, R. P. (1970), "Renal Tubular Acidosis in Salt-Losing Syndrome of Congenital Adrenal Hyperplasia," *J. Clin. Endocrin. Metab.*, **31**, 447–450.
45. Oppe, T. E. and Redstone, D. (1968), "Calcium and Phosphorus Levels in Healthy Newborn Infants Given Various Types of Milk," *Lancet*, **i**, 1045–1048.
46. Potter, E. L. (1946), "Bilateral Renal Agenesis," *J. Pediat.*, **29**, 68–76.
47. Raynaud, C., Schoutens, A. and Royer, P. (1968), "Intérêt de la mesure du taux de la fixation renale du Hg dans l'étude de l'hypertrophie renale compensatrice chez l'homme," *Nephron*, **5**, 300–313.
48. Rodriguez-Soriano, J., Boichis, H. and Edelmann, C. M., Jr. (1967), "Bicarbonate Reabsorption and Hydrogen Ion Excretion in Children with Renal Tubular Acidosis," *J. Pediat.*, **71**, 802–813.
49. Smith, C. A. (1959), "The Physiology of the Newborn Infant," pp. 291–319. Oxford: Blackwell Scientific Publications.
50. Smith, F. G., Jr., Tinglof, B. O., Meuli, J. and Borden, M. (1969), "Fetal Response to Parathyroid Hormone in Sheep," *J. appl. Physiol.*, **27**, 276–279.
51. Spitzer, A. (1972), "The Kidneys and Urinary Tract: Physiology and Functional Development of the Kidney," in *Pediatrics* (H. L. Barnett and A. H. Einhorn, Eds.), pp. 1453–1459. New York: Appleton-Century-Crofts.
52. Spitzer, A. and Edelmann, C. M., Jr. (1971), "Maturational Changes in Pressure Gradients for Glomerular Filtration," *Amer. J. Physiol.*, **221**, 1431–1435.
53. Stanier, M. W. (1971), "The Renal Cortico-medullary Gradient in Foetal and Early Post-natal Life," *Proc. 2nd int. Symp. Pediat. Nephrol.*, pp. 43–44. Paris: Sandoz Editions.
54. Sulyok, E. and Heim, T. (1971), "Assessment of Maximal Urinary Acidification in Premature Infants," *Biol. Neonat.*, **19**, 200–210.
55. Tudvad, F. (1949), "Sugar Reabsorption in Prematures and Full-term Babies," *Scand. J. clin. lab. Invest.*, **1**, 281–283.
56. Vernier, R. L. and Birch-Anderson, A. (1962), "Studies of the Human Fetal Kidney. I. Development of the Glomerulus," *J. Pediat.*, **60**, 754–768.
57. West, J. R., Smith, H. W. and Chasis, H. (1948), "Glomerular Filtration Rate, Effective Renal Blood Flow and Maximal Tubular Excretory Capacity in Infancy," *J. Pediat.*, **32**, 10–18.
58. Zweymüller, E., Widdowson, E. M. and McCance, R. A. (1959), "The Passage of Urea and Creatinine Across the Placenta of the Pig," *J. Embryol. exp. Morph.*, **7**, 202–209.

FURTHER READING

Edelmann, C. M., Jr. (1967), "Maturation of the Neonatal Kidney," in *Proc. 3rd int. Congr. Neprol.*, Vol. 3, pp. 1–12 (E. L. Becker, Ed.). Basel: Karger.

Edelmann, C. M., Jr. (1970), "Glomerulo-tubular Balance in the Developing Kidney," in *Proc. 4th int. Congr. Nephrol.*, Vol. 1, pp. 22–28 (N. Alwall, F. Berglund and B. Josephson, Eds.). Basel: Karger.

Pitts, R. F. (1968), *Physiology of the Kidney and Body Fluids*. Chicago: Year Book Medical Publishers Inc.

Symposium in Pediatric Nephrology (1971), Edited by C. M. Edelmann, Jr., in *Pediat. Clin. N. Amer.*, **18**, 347–682.

18. THE BLOOD AND BONE MARROW DURING GROWTH AND DEVELOPMENT

P. J. BLACK AND P. BARKHAN

The Site of Haemopoiesis

Haemopoiesis in the Fetus

The haemopoietic cells are derived from the embryonic connective tissue, the mesenchyme, and first appear in the extra-embryonic mesoderm of the yolk-sac. In humans the first **mesoblastic** period of haemopoiesis commences at

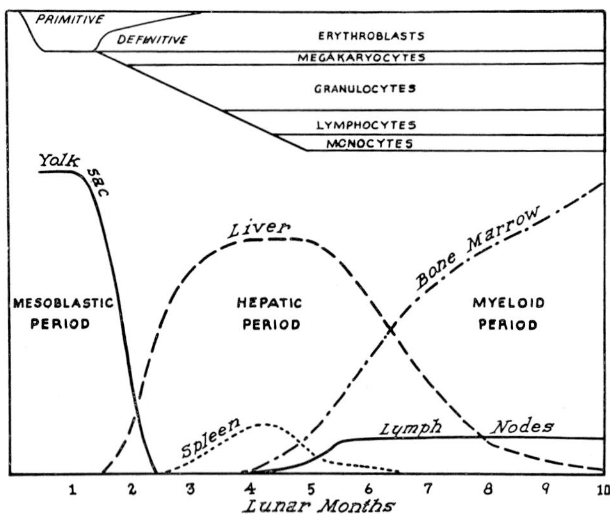

FIG. 1. The stages of haemopoiesis in the embryo and fetus, showing the contribution of the main centres of haemopoiesis and the approximate time at which the different types of cells make their appearance (from Wintrobe, M. M. (1967): *Clinical Haematology*, Lea and Febiger, Philadelphia).

16–19 days gestation with the appearance of solid rounded masses of proliferating mesodermal cells on the ventral aspect of the yolk-sac, projecting into the chorionic cavity.[57] The peripheral cells of these masses become the endothelium of the first blood vessels and the central cells become the first blood cells or haemocytoblasts.[22] These isolated vessels containing free cells constitute the blood islands and are generally confined to the yolk-sac mesoderm although in human embryos isolated foci of haemopoiesis are sometimes seen throughout the extra-embryonic mesoblastic tissue.

Blood vessels also arise from mesodermal cells in the chorion and in the embryo itself and these blood vessels link up with the vessels of the blood islands in the yolk-sac to form the complete circulation at three weeks' gestation.[57] Until the circulation is established haemopoiesis is confined to the blood islands and vessels of the yolk-sac, but thereafter new blood cells are formed throughout the circulation by omitotic division of the blood cells already present. During this initial period of haemopoiesis haemoglobin-containing cells are the predominant cells formed. These cells belong to the primitive generation of erythroblasts and morphologically resemble the megaloblasts of pernicious anaemia. By the sixth week of gestation, this intravascular mesoblastic phase of haemopoiesis begins to decline and has virtually disappeared after twelve weeks (Fig. 1).

The **hepatic** period of haemopoiesis begins about the fifth week of gestation and the liver is the chief organ of blood formation from the third to the sixth month of fetal life.[165] Thereafter, its haemopoietic activity declines until, at birth, blood formation has been almost completely taken over by the bone marrow. Haemopoiesis in the liver is almost exclusively erythropoietic[150] and is of the definitive normoblastic generation that is characteristic of the late antenatal and the whole postnatal period. Erythropoiesis in the liver is essentially extra-vascular. Megakaryocytes are also present but granulocyte precursors are virtually completely absent.

Haemopoiesis is also seen in the spleen (mainly erythropoietic) and in the thymus though it has been suggested that the spleen may be mainly a site of destruction of primitive generation erythroblasts, rather than of production of new haemopoietic cells.[134]

The final **myeloid** period of haemopoiesis in the bone marrow begins during the fourth to fifth fetal months. Initially, the bone marrow is mainly concerned with granulocyte formation, whilst the liver has an almost exclusively erythropoietic function. Megakaryocytes are present in both liver and bone marrow. Studies with cells found in the bone marrow and blood that will form colonies of haemopoietic cells in spleen and bone marrow when injected into lethally irradiated animals, have shown that in the mouse the type of haemopoiesis in any tissue is closely dependent upon the local micro-environment. This is not due to selective homing of precommitted progenitor cells to a particular tissue but rather to unknown local factors that selectively induce uncommitted stem cells to develop in a particular direction into erythropoietic, granulopoietic, megakaryocytic or lymphocytic cell lines.[105] Though care must be exercised in translating findings in animals to human situations, it seems likely that similar factors induce exclusively erythropoiesis in the liver and initially mainly granulopoiesis in the marrow. As liver erythropoiesis diminishes, the bone marrow takes over all haemopoietic activity, and during the last three months of gestation the bone marrow is the chief site of all blood-cell formation. Marrow cellularity becomes maximal at about the thirtieth week of cestation although the volume of marrow continues to ingrease until term along with the fetal weight. During this period, the marrow represents about 1·4 per cent of the body weight.[72]

The Marrow after Birth

At birth, blood-cell formation takes place almost exclusively in the bone marrow though there is still slight residual haemopoiesis in the liver and spleen. During the first few weeks of post-natal life, hepatic haemopoiesis may be re-activated by anaemia or by non-haematological diseases such as viral infections. During the first three or four years of life almost all the bones of the body contain active haemopoietic marrow with little difference in cellularity. Regression of haemopoiesis has been seen to commence in the terminal digits before term and the marrow of the toes is virtually completely fatty by the age of one year.[45] This regression in haemopoiesis is accelerated at the time of birth though the mechanism of this change is not known. The reserve of unutilized marrow space during the first few years of life is very limited and the infant responds to demands for increased haemopoiesis either by reducing the time of cell maturation or by an outward expansion of the total marrow mass. An increase in marrow volume may be seen readily in patients with severe congenital haemolytic anaemias in the form of expansion of the cranial diploic space which shows as the "hair-on-end" appearance of the calvarium on X-ray.

After the first few years of life the marrow content of the distal skeleton gradually decreases. The change from red haemopoietic to yellow fatty marrow occurs first in the hands and feet, and then in the forearm and leg. Shortly before puberty, a patch of yellow marrow appears in the distal ends of the long bones and gradually extends proximally until the age of twenty, when yellow marrow occupies the whole of the long bones with the exception of the upper end of the humerus and femur. Even in those bones that retain active haemopoiesis, the cellularity of the marrow gradually decreases with age until approximately half the available space is occupied by fat cells.

The Haemopoietic Stem Cell

For many decades one of the main controversies of haematology has centred round the recognition, origin and functional capacity of haemopoietic stem cells, i.e., whether the different cell lines of the blood develop from a common multipotential stem cell or separately from different stem cells. From mainly morphological observations a wide variety of explanations for the derivation of the different haemopoietic cells has been put forward. The issue has become much clearer in the last decade as a result of experimental work using living-cell systems, e.g., *in vitro* culture of spleen cells for their capacity to form colonies of haemopoietic cells, and the use of lethally irradiated animals for studying the haemopoietic potential of cells transplanted from bone marrow, liver, spleen, thymus and lymph nodes.[109]

The evidence from this experimental work now strongly favours the presence of multipotential stem cells that originate in the yolk-sac and migrate into the embryo to colonize the liver, spleen and bone marrow and also the lymph-nodes and thymus.

Mouse embryos cultured intact *in vitro* develop normally with the appearance of erythropoiesis within both the yolk-sac and the embryo itself. When embryos are cultured in the absence of the yolk-sac the blood remains totally acellular although the vascular system develops normally. On the other hand, isolated yolk-sacs cultured separately develop the normal primitive generation erythropoietic cells. That the influence of the yolk-sac is not purely humoral has been shown by the culture of the separated embryo and yolk-sac in the same system but divided by a millipore filter: again, erythropoiesis developed normally in the yolk-sac but the embryonic blood remained acellular.[109] Cells derived from the yolk-sac of eleven-day-old mouse embryos, when injected into lethally irradiated adult mice, are able to produce extensive repopulation of not only the bone marrow and spleen but also of the recipient thymus and lymphoid organs showing that the yolk-sac contains lymphocyte precursors even though lymphoid development has not yet taken place in the eleven-day-old mouse embryo.[109]

Multipotential stem cells are also present in the bone marrow and in smaller numbers in the circulating blood of adult mice.[105] Single-stem cells may cause repopulation of both myeloid and lymphoid tissues of lethally irradiated recipients. These stem cells appear to be ultimately responsible for the maintenance and renewal of granulopoietic, erythropoietic and megakaryocytic cell lines, of cells serving both cell-mediated and humoral immunity, of monocytes and tissue macrophages and perhaps even fibroblasts. These stem cells have not yet been identified morphologically though they ought to be recognizable since they are present in both blood and marrow. Their relationship to the haemocytoblast, the first recognizable haemopoietic cell in the blood islands of the yolk-sac, is not certain. They have been defined as primitive haemopoietic cells capable of extensive self-replication and endowed with a capacity for multiple differentiation.[105]

ERYTHROPOIESIS

Erythropoiesis in the Fetus

Red-cell precursors, erythroblasts, are the first morphologically recognizable haemopoietic cells to appear in the fetus in the blood islands of the yolk-sac. In all of the common laboratory mammals and in man there are two distinct generations of erythroblasts: the primitive and the definitive. Both generations derive from haemocytoblasts, developing through parallel and morphologically distinct lines of cells.[22] The second, definitive, generation develops separately directly from haemocytoblasts rather than by maturation of the preceding primitive generation. In mammals these two generations overlap, in time and space, the primitive generation developing in the first mesoblastic period and the definitive generation during the second hepatic period.

Primitive Erythropoiesis

The primitive erythroblasts first appear in the blood islands of the yolk-sac, and were called megaloblasts by

Ehrlich in 1880 because of their close resemblance to the erythropoietic precursors found in pernicious anaemia. Most of these cells do not develop into mature erythrocytes but retain their nuclei. They enter the embryonic circulation when it is established at 3 weeks gestation and there continue to multiply.[57] With increasing age, the proportion of early and intermediate primitive erythroblasts falls and that of late forms increases. Multiplication of the primitive erythroblasts has ceased at 10 weeks though they may persist in the circulation up to 12 weeks.[57] Though there is a close morphological resemblance between the primitive generation erythroblasts and the megaloblasts of vitamin B_{12} or folate deficiency, it is doubtful whether deficiency of these vitamins is the cause of the fetal megaloblasts. Attempts in animals to alter their morphology by injection of folic acid, liver or gastric juice have not been successful.[33]

Definitive Erythropoiesis

The replacement of primitive erythroblasts by the definitive generation begins at about the 6th week in the human fetus.[57] The definitive normoblastic erythropoiesis appears primarily in the liver but the separation of primitive and definitive generations is incomplete: at 8–9 weeks, definitive erythroblasts may be seen in the yolk-sac whilst megaloblastic cells resembling the primitive erythroblasts may be seen in the liver. At about 8 weeks, the definitive generation constitutes about 30 per cent of the cells in the blood and this figure rises to over 80 per cent at 10 weeks. Definitive erythroblasts are also present in the spleen and bone marrow and the marrow becomes the main site of haemopoiesis after the 26th week of fetal life.

The Control of Erythropoiesis

The hormone erythropoietin, a glycoprotein, is an important regulator of red-cell production in the adult.[58] It appears to be derived from an inert plasma precursor that is converted into active erythropoietin by a factor that is produced by the kidney and is called the renal erythropoietic factor or erythrogenin. In man, and most experimental animals, erythrogenin-like activity may also be found in other organs but the kidney is the main site of production. The chief action of erythropoietin is probably on a progenitor cell that is already committed to red-cell production. Erythropoietin induces differentiation of this progenitor cell into the morphologically recognizable red-cell precursors and also accelerates the subsequent divisional steps.

Though it is clear that erythropoietin is one of the main regulators of erythropoiesis in the adult animal, including man, it is not clear that it has the same importance during intra-uterine development. In the rat, bilateral nephrectomy produces complete cessation of red-cell production in the adult animal but has little effect on fetal erythropoiesis.[92] Neonatal rats produce very little erythropoietin in response to hypoxia and the adult type of response is not achieved until the thirtieth day of life.[93] In mice, suppression of maternal production of erythropoietin by hypertransfusion does not affect fetal erythropoiesis so that transplacental transfer of erythropoietin cannot be important in the maintenance of fetal erythropoiesis.[76]

In man, in contrast with these findings in experimental animals, erythropoietin is present in the plasma of the neonate at birth[95] and the fetus can react to hypoxia by increased erythropoietin production from the thirty-second week of gestation.[48] Elevated levels of erythropoietin have also been found in the cord blood and amniotic fluid of infants with haemolytic disease and anaemia.[47] It is possible that this discrepancy between the findings in man and in the rat can be explained by the fact that the rat at birth is in transition from hepatic to myeloid erythropoiesis and hence may be analogous to human erythropoiesis at about the fifth month of gestation rather than at term.

Erythropoietin disappears from the plasma of normal full-term infants after the first day of life and does not reappear until the third month. Its reappearance coincides with the resumption of marrow erythropoietic activity at this time.[95] (*See also* section on marrow changes in the early post-natal period, p. 309.)

Red Cell Values in Utero

In the early human embryo the red cell count (RCC), haemoglobin concentration (Hb), and packed cell volume (PCV) are very low whilst the red cells are very large and most of them are nucleated.[149,153,166] At 10 weeks, the red-cell count ranges from 1–1·5 × 10^6/μl., the haemoglobin level from 6·0–9·0 g./100 ml. and the PCV is approximately 25 per cent.

Between the 10th and 25th weeks the RCC, Hb and PCV increase rapidly and by the 25th week the haemoglobin level approximates to that of the adult, reaching about 14 g./100 ml. and remaining fairly steady at this level until the last few weeks of fetal life when it increases again to the mean of 16·8 g./100 ml. in cord blood. The red-cell count also rises rapidly during this period, approaching 3·5 × 10^6/μl. at the 25th week. The red-cell count continues to rise slowly until term, but this increase is matched by a steady decline in the mean cell volume (MCV) between the 25th and 26th weeks so that the haemoglobin concentration does not rise proportionately (Fig. 2).

Initially, the red cells are almost all nucleated and their MCV is almost three times that of the adult red cell. Both the nucleated red-cell count and the MCV fall rapidly between the 10th and 25th weeks along with the reticulocyte count which falls from 80 per cent at the 10th week to 10 per cent at the 25th week. These changes continue rather more slowly during the last trimester but are still incomplete at term, so that the red-cell values of the neonate differ considerably from those of the adult and a small number of nucleated red cells is still present (500–1,000/μl.).

During intra-uterine life the rate of red-cell production is much greater than in the adult for not only is the red-cell concentration increasing but the total blood volume is also expanding rapidly. The red-cell population, therefore, throughout fetal life and at birth is a relatively young one and this may account, at least in part, for the macrocytosis, the reticulocytosis and the persistence of small numbers of nucleated red cells until birth.

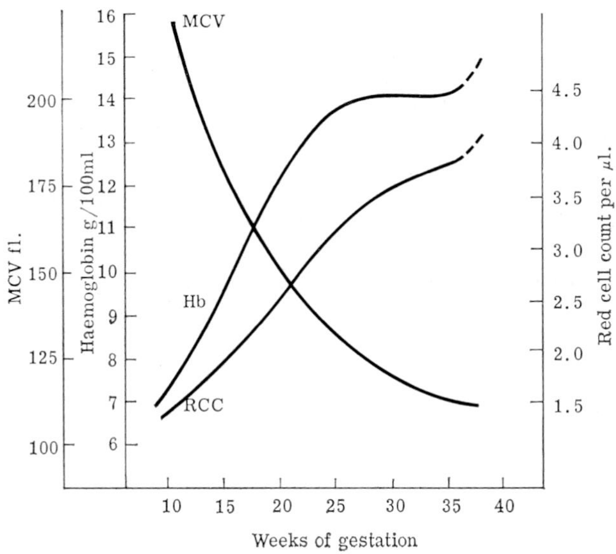

FIG. 2. Haemoglobin concentration, red cell count and red cell size in the human fetus. RCC = red cell count, Hb = haemoglobin concentration, MCV = mean cell volume.

The Haemoglobin and Red Cell Values at Birth

The Haemoglobin Concentration. From the 25th to the 36th week of fetal life the haemoglobin concentration appears to be relatively constant at about 14·0–14·5 g./100 ml., but values for the cord blood of full-term infants at birth are higher and vary more widely. Values from 11·2–26·6 g./100 ml. have been reported, but about 95 per cent of haemoglobin values fall between 13·7 and 20·2 g./100 ml. and it seems reasonable to take 13·5 g./100 ml. as the lower limit of the normal range.[122]

The mean haemoglobin concentration of cord blood is 16·8 g./100 ml. There appears to be a genuine increase in haemoglobin concentration over the last 2–4 weeks of fetal life, with an increase of about 1·3 g /100 ml. taking place place between the 38th and 40th weeks.[122,133]

The reported values for the red-cell count and the PCV vary like the haemoglobin values: mean values reported for the RCC vary from 4·6–5·3 million/μl. and mean values for the PCV from 51·3–56·0 per cent.[122]

The Red Cells. The red cells of the newborn infant differ strikingly from the red cells of adults in their osmotic and mechanical fragility, in their size and in their life span. They differ from adult cells also in their haemoglobin composition, metabolic activity, membrane composition and oxygen affinity. There are two main explanations for these differences.[173] Firstly, the red cells at birth are relatively young, and having been made during a period of intense erythropoiesis they may have missed a divisional step in the normal maturation process. For this reason, the red cells have many of the characteristics of young cells produced at any time of marked reticulocytosis. Secondly, some enzyme systems and some membrane components are not fully developed at birth, while the presence of fetal haemoglobin and its decreased reaction with 2,3-diphosphoglycerate increases the oxygen affinity of the red cells of the neonate.

Red Cell Size. Though the MCV has fallen considerably during the course of fetal development, the red cells of the newborn are still much larger than those of a normal adult. Reported values vary between 104 fl., and 118 fl., as compared with adult values of 75–100 fl.[97,100,158] The mean corpuscular haemoglobin (MCH) is increased proportionately, 33·5–41·4 pg. (27–32 pg. in adults), and thus the mean corpuscular haemoglobin concentration (MCHC) is very similar to that of the adult, varying from 30–35 per cent.

Reticulocyte Count. Polychromasia, a reticulocytosis and the presence of nucleated red cells in the cord blood are evidence of the intense erythropoiesis taking place until the time of birth. The reticulocyte count in the cord blood of full-term infants is about 5 ± 2 per cent and the normoblasts number 500–1,000/μl., both being more numerous in the blood of premature infants.[122]

Red Cell Life Span. In theory, since the mean cell age of the red cells of the neonate is less than that of the red cells of the adult a longer survival of neonatal red cells might be expected, but most studies have shown a shortened red-cell survival.

Some doubt has been cast on red-cell survival studies using cord red cells labelled with ^{51}chromium which binds predominantly to the beta chain of adult haemoglobin. Since cord red cells contain mainly haemoglobin F that has no beta chains, it is possible that they bind the chromium less firmly than adult cells. Excessive elution of the chromium from the cord red cells would give results suggesting an erroneously short red-cell survival. However, results using cells labelled with ^{51}chromium have been amply confirmed by other studies using different methods: the rate of disappearance of fetal red cells transfused into an adult using the agglutination technique of Ashby, the Kleihauer technique, fetal red cells labelled with radio-iron incorporated into haemoglobin or tagged with diisopropylfluorophosphate labelled with ^{32}phosphorus (DF^{32}P).[122] The accummulated data shows that the mean life span of red cells produced during the last 60 days of fetal life is between 45 and 70 days.[24]

Red Cell Fragility. The mean osmotic fragility of red cells from cord blood is not significantly different from that of adult red cells, but the range of osmotic fragility is greater in the neonate.[138] The majority of the red cells in the neonate are slightly more resistant to osmotic lysis but there is also a population of more fragile cells. These more fragile cells disappear from the circulation during the first few days of life and during this period the mean osmotic fragility becomes less than that of normal adult cells. The transition to the adult pattern of osmotic fragility occurs fairly rapidly and is normally complete within four weeks,[94] though it has been shown that more resistant cells are present throughout childhood.

Osmotic fragility does not correlate with the concentration of haemoglobin F. It has been suggested that the more resistant population represent cells that have skipped one cell division during maturation thus reaching the circulation with a higher surface to volume ratio, whilst the more fragile population reflects one or more of the several metabolic deficiencies of neonatal red cells.

The development of the antigenic components of the red-cell membrane, the metabolism of the red cell and of the haemoglobins is discussed later.

Red Cell Values in Infancy and Childhood

The First Two Weeks. During the first few hours after birth the haemoglobin concentration of the infant's blood rises by about 15–20 per cent over that of the cord blood.[52,161] This increase is mainly due to the transfer of blood from the placenta to the infant before the umbilical cord is clamped. The umbilical arteries constrict after delivery but the umbilical veins remain dilated so that blood can flow in the direction of gravity. An infant held beneath the level of the placenta will gain blood from the placenta, whilst an infant held above may lose blood into the placenta. At delivery the placenta contains about 125 ml. of blood or 33 per cent of the total blood volume.[169] If blood is allowed to drain from the placenta into the infant as completely as possible before the cord is clamped, the infant may receive a transfusion of up to 100 ml. of blood from the placenta. The transfusion is complete within three minutes of delivery and no further transfer of blood takes place if clamping the cord is delayed longer.[154,169]

The blood volumes of infants whose cords have been clamped late has been measured as 93 ml./kg. at 5 min. after birth, compared with a blood volume of 70 ml./kg. in infants whose cords have been clamped within 5 sec. of delivery.[169] The difference in red-cell volume is even more striking: 48 ml./kg. in the later-clamped group compared with only 31 ml./kg. in the early clamped group. Within the first four hours of post-natal life fluid is lost from the blood, and the plasma volume may contract by 24 per cent.[52,154] It seems likely that this is a direct compensation for the increase in blood volume associated with the placental transfusion: the larger the placental transfusion, the greater is the plasma loss so that the difference in whole blood volume between late-clamped and early-clamped infants is greatly reduced within four hours of birth although the difference in red-cell volume remains. However, other workers have concluded that the loss of plasma from the circulation is not related to placental blood transfer and takes place regardless of the volume of the placental transfusion, but their conclusions are not decisive.[52] The loss of plasma produces haemoconcentration which is shown as an increase in haemoglobin concentration and haematocrit, though the total red-cell volume is unaltered.[154] At four hours of age the mean haemoglobin concentration of capillary blood is between 19 and 21 g./100 ml. with a haematocrit of 60–66 per cent.

After this initial increase, the haemoglobin concentration begins to fall but it remains high during the first week of life and does not fall below that of the cord blood until sometime between the first and third week of life (Fig. 3).

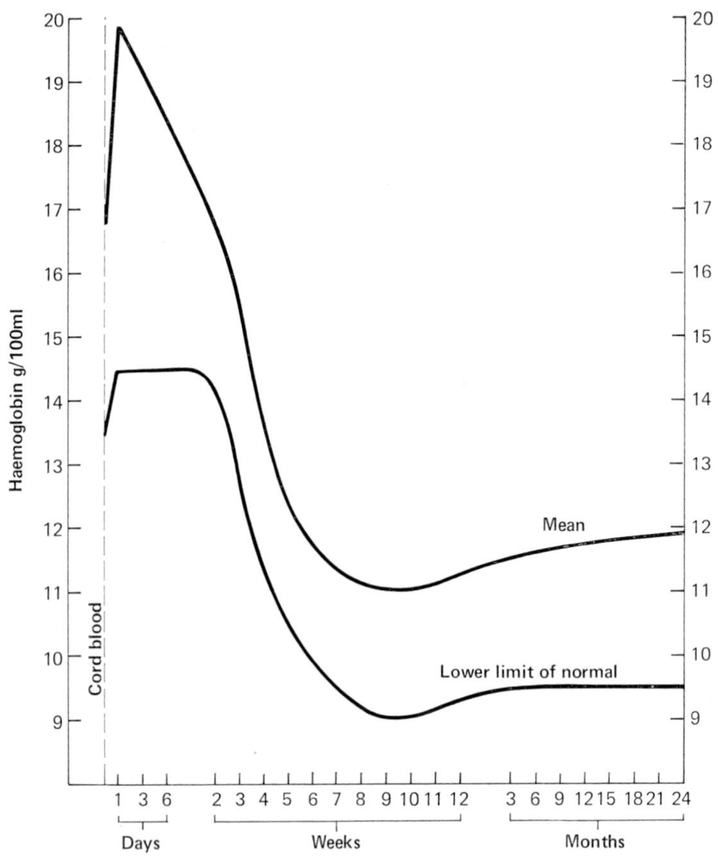

FIG. 3. The haemoglobin concentration during the first two years of life.[29,100,122,165]

The precise haemoglobin level depends not only on the time of sampling and the size of the placental transfusion but also on the site from which the sample is taken. The values in both arterial and capillary blood differ significantly from that in venous blood during the first week of life. Those for arterial blood are usually 0·5 g./100 ml. higher than those for venous blood whilst values for capillary blood, obtained by heel prick, may be up to 6 g. higher. A mean of 20·3 g./100 ml. for capillary blood haemoglobin during the first hour of life compared with 16·7 g./100 ml. for venous blood has been reported in one study.[113] It is believed that stasis of blood in the peripheral vessels with resultant loss of plasma is the cause of the high capillary haemoglobin. Clearly, the site of sampling should be the same for sequential studies of haemoglobin level and it is important to know the site of sampling for the diagnosis of neonatal anaemia.[108] A capillary haemoglobin of 14·5g./100 ml. and a venous haemoglobin of 13·0 g./100 ml. have been suggested as the lower limits of normal during the first week of life.[122]

It is well known that fetal red cells may enter the maternal circulation during birth. In 1 per cent of pregnancies this loss may be quite considerable and may be up to 100ml.[36] Feto-maternal transfusion of this type may explain some of the low haemoglobin values found in samples from apparently normal infants. Occasionally, the transfusion may occur from the mother to the fetus, resulting in abnormally high haemoglobin in the neonate.[7]

Changes in haematocrit follow the same trend as the haemoglobin level. There is an abrupt increase during the first hours of life followed by a slow decline, so that values at the end of the first week are similar to those of cord blood. The haematocrit increases from a mean of 53 per cent in cord blood[65] to a mean of 63 per cent in capillary samples during the first day of life.[55]

TABLE 1

NORMAL HAEMATOLOGICAL VALUES DURING THE FIRST TWELVE WEEKS OF LIFE

Hb = haemoglobin concentration
RBC = red cell count (electronic counting)
PCV = packed cell volume
MCV = mean cell volume
MCHC = mean corpuscular haemoglobin concentration
RETIC = reticulocyte count

From Matoth, Y. *et al.* (1971). *Acta Paediatrica Stockholm*, **60**, 317–23.

Age	*Number of cases*	Hb g./100 ml. ± SD	RBC × $10^6/\mu l$. ± SD	PCV% ± SD	MCV fl. ± SD	MCHC % ± SD	RETIC % ± SD
Days							
1	19	19·0 ± 2·2	5·14 ± 0·7	61 ± 7·4	119 ± 9·4	31·6 ± 1·9	3·2 ± 1·4
2	19	19·0 ± 1·9	5·15 ± 0·9	60 ± 6·4	115 ± 7·0	31·6 ± 1·4	3·2 ± 1·3
3	19	18·7 ± 3·4	5·11 ± 0·7	62 ± 9·3	116 ± 5·3	31·1 ± 2·8	2·8 ± 1·7
4	10	18·6 ± 2·1	5·00 ± 0·6	57 ± 8·1	114 ± 7·5	32·6 ± 1·5	1·8 ± 1·1
5	12	17·6 ± 1·1	4·97 ± 0·4	57 ± 7·3	114 ± 8·9	30·9 ± 2·2	1·2 ± 0·2
6	15	17·4 ± 2·2	5·00 ± 0·7	54 ± 7·2	113 ± 10·0	32·2 ± 1·6	0·6 ± 0·2
7	12	17·9 ± 2·5	4·86 ± 0·6	56 ± 9·4	118 ± 11·2	32·0 ± 1·6	0·5 ± 0·4
Weeks							
1–2	32	17·3 ± 2·3	4·80 ± 0·8	54 ± 8·3	112 ± 19·0	32·1 ± 2·9	0·5 ± 0·3
2–3	11	15·6 ± 2·6	4·20 ± 0·6	46 ± 7·3	111 ± 8·2	33·9 ± 1·9	0·8 ± 0·6
3–4	17	14·2 ± 2·1	4·00 ± 0·6	43 ± 5·7	105 ± 7·5	33·5 ± 1·6	0·6 ± 0·3
4–5	15	12·7 ± 1·6	3·60 ± 0·4	36 ± 4·8	101 ± 8·1	34·9 ± 1·6	0·9 ± 0·8
5–6	10	11·9 ± 1·5	3·55 ± 0·2	36 ± 6·2	102 ± 10·2	34·1 ± 2·9	1·0 ± 0·7
6–7	10	12·0 ± 1·5	3·40 ± 0·4	36 ± 4·8	105 ± 12·0	33·8 ± 2·3	1·2 ± 0·7
7–8	17	11·1 ± 1·1	3·40 ± 0·4	33 ± 3·7	100 ± 13·0	33·7 ± 2·6	1·5 ± 0·7
8–9	13	10·7 ± 0·9	3·40 ± 0·5	31 ± 2·5	93 ± 12·0	34·1 ± 2·2	1·8 ± 1·0
9–10	12	11·2 ± 0·9	3·60 ± 0·3	32 ± 2·7	91 ± 9·3	34·3 ± 2·9	1·2 ± 0·6
10–11	11	11·4 ± 0·9	3·70 ± 0·4	34 ± 2·1	91 ± 7·7	33·2 ± 2·4	1·2 ± 0·7
11–12	13	11·3 ± 0·9	3·70 ± 0·3	33 ± 3·3	88 ± 7·9	34·8 ± 2·2	0·7 ± 0·3

Table 1 gives the normal red-cell values during the first twelve weeks of life, obtained during a recent survey using an electronic cell counter.

The "Physiological Anaemia" of Infancy. After birth there is an immediate decrease in the erythropoietic activity of the bone marrow. The proportion of red-cell precursors in the bone marrow is halved by the end of the first week of life and this is reflected in a change in the myeloid/erythroid ratio from near unity at birth to about 3:1 at 2 weeks.[81] The drop in erythropoietic activity starts at birth in both the full-term and the premature infant. It is associated with the disappearance of erythropoietin from the plasma.[95]

The decrease in erythropoiesis is reflected in the peripheral blood by the rapid disappearance of the normoblasts present at birth and by a fall in the reticulocyte count. At birth, the full-term infant has 500–1,000 nucleated red cells/μl. After twelve hours, this number has been halved and it is unusual to see nucleated red cells in the peripheral blood after the fourth day of life. The elevated reticulocyte count of about 5 per cent found in cord blood persists for the first three days of life and then falls below 1 per cent by the seventh day of life.[122]

The decrease in erythropoiesis persists for the first four to six weeks of life. During this period erythropoiesis does not stop completely, for the reticulocyte count remains between 0·5 and 1·0 per cent and the haemoglobin level does not fall as much as it would in the complete absence of red-cell production.[100] After the fifth week, erythropoietin reappears in the plasma and there is a steady increase in erythropoietic activity of the bone marrow. By twelve weeks of age the number of red cell precursors in the bone marrow has returned to the level found in the newborn.[81] As erythropoiesis recovers the peripheral blood reticulocyte count gradually rises to about 2 per cent at the ninth week and then returns to 1 per cent by the twelfth week.[100]

The reduction in erythropoietic activity during this period is reflected by a fall in the haemoglobin concentration between the second and ninth weeks of life (Fig. 3). This fall is accentuated by the shorter life span of the neonatal red cells, by the fall in the mean cell volume (MCV) of the red cells and by the increase in total blood volume associated with the growth of the infant. The red-cell count drops steadily to reach its lowest point in the seventh week, remains unchanged during the following three weeks and then begins to increase slightly. The blood haemoglobin concentration continues to fall after the red-cell count has reached its lowest point because the MCV is continuing to drop. There is some disagreement concerning the time at which the lowest haemoglobin concentration is reached, reports varying between two months and one year. Provided that iron deficiency does not occur the lowest point of about 11·0 g./100 ml. on capillary blood is reached during the ninth week and the haemoglobin concentration then begins to rise again slightly (Fig. 3). The haematocrit falls to a mean of 31 per cent during the ninth week and then also begins to rise slightly.[100]

The MCV falls after birth and mean figures of 88 and 94·5 fl. have been reported at three months of age.[100,107] In the absence of iron deficiency it attains the normal adult range of 75–100 fl. by one year.[107] The mean corpuscular haemoglobin concentration (MCHC) remains very constant throughout infancy and childhood: though reported figures vary considerably, the range corresponds to the normal adult range of 32–36 per cent.[107] However, now that blood-counts are often done on electronic cell counters, the MCHC is no longer a useful guide to iron deficiency: the more useful indices are the MCV and MCH.[20,46,114]

From the third month until the end of the second year of life the haemoglobin concentration is fairly stable.[29] The mean value for capillary or venous blood remains between 11·5 and 12·0 g./100 ml. with a tendency to rise. Slight falls have been reported after the sixth month and again in the second half of the second year and it is possible that these can be eliminated by the prophylactic administration of iron. It has been suggested that 9·5 g./100 ml. is a realistic figure for the lower limit of normal during the period of three months to two years.[29]

The Haemoglobin Concentration in Childhood. After the second year of life there is a gradual increase in the haemoglobin concentration (Fig. 4), haematocrit and red-cell count. Until puberty there is no difference between these values for boys and girls. At puberty the values in both sexes are almost equal to those found in adult women with a mean haemoglobin concentration of 14·0 g./100 ml. and a lower limit of normal of 11·5 g./100 ml.[112,160] From this time changes in the blood of girls are slight, but the value for boys continues to increase to reach the levels for adult males at about eighteen years old: mean haemoglobin concentration 15·5 g./100 ml. and lower limit of normal 13·5 g./100 ml. in those living at sea-level.

The Development of the Components of the Red Cell

I. Red Cell Metabolism

The mature red cell is strictly limited in its range of metabolic activity: it has no nucleus, no mitochondria or ribosomes, no protein synthesis, no citric-acid cycle and no oxidative phosphorylation. It derives all its energy from the breakdown of glucose to pyruvate or lactate, mainly by anaerobic glycolysis and to a lesser extent by oxidation. In normal adult cells, approximately 90 per cent of the glucose is metabolized anaerobically through the glycolytic pathway and about 10 per cent by oxidation through the pentose phosphate pathway. These two pathways produce five key intermediate substances, namely, adenosine triphosphate (ATP), reduced nicotinamide-adenine dinucleotide ($NADH_2$), reduced nicotinamide-adenine dinucleotide phosphate ($NADPH_2$), reduced glutathione (GSH) and 2,3-diphosphoglycerate (2,3-DPG). ATP is the energy source of the cell, 2,3-DPG is essential for normal haemoglobin-oxygen dissociation, and the other three compounds confer reducing potential that is essential to protect haemoglobin, enzymes and the cell membrane against oxidation.

The Glycolytic Pathway. In this process one mole of glucose is metabolized to two moles of lactate or pyruvate (Fig. 5). Two moles of ATP are degraded to adenosine diphosphate (ADP) during the conversion of glucose to 1,3-diphosphoglycerate but four moles of ATP are produced during the further conversion of 1,3-diphosphoglycerate to pyruvate, resulting in a possible net gain of two ATP moles per mole of glucose utilized.

Reduced nicotinamide-adenine dinucleotide is also generated provided that the metabolism of glucose proceeds no further than pyruvate. If pyruvate is converted to lactate, then the $NADH_2$ generated earlier in the process of glucolysis is reoxidized to NAD with no net gain of $NADH_2$.

2,3-diphosphoglycerate (2,3-DPG) is also produced by the glycolytic pathway from 1,3-diphosphoglycerate by the action of the enzyme diphosphoglycerate mutase; 2,3-DPG is the phosphate that is present in greatest concentration in the red cell and is essential for normal haemoglobin-oxygen dissociation. During *in vitro* incubation the red cells of the neonate do not synthesize this compound as rapidly as do those of normal adults, so that a more rapid fall in concentration results.[60] The activity of the diphosphoglycerate

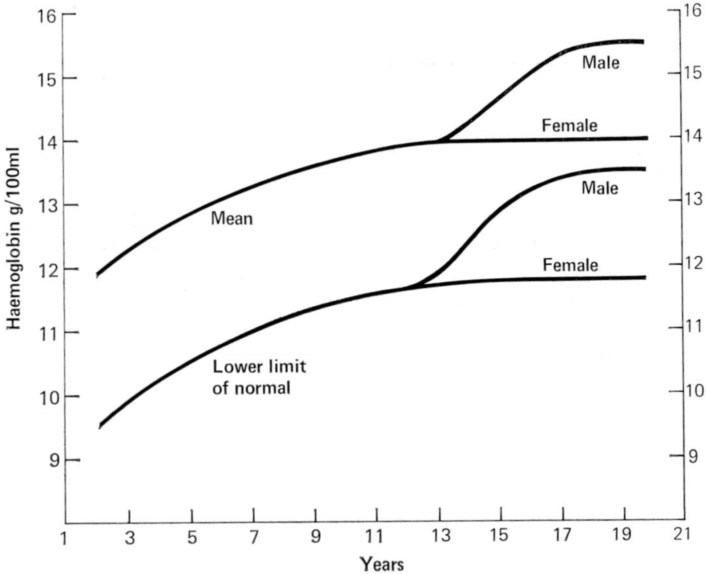

FIG. 4. The haemoglobin concentration during childhood.[29,65,107,112,122,123,165]

mutase is normal in neonatal cells[120] and the reason for and significance of the decreased synthesis of 2,3-DPG is unknown. The role of 2,3-DPG in the neonatal red cell is discussed more fully later.

The red-cell population of the neonate is a relatively young one and therefore red-cell metabolism differs from that of the normal adult. The rate of glucose consumption is therefore greater in the red cells of the neonate and the levels of most of the enzymes of the glycolytic pathway are increased as they are in any young red-cell population (Table 2). The activity of phosphoglycerate kinase and enolase appears to be disproportionately elevated,[118] whilst

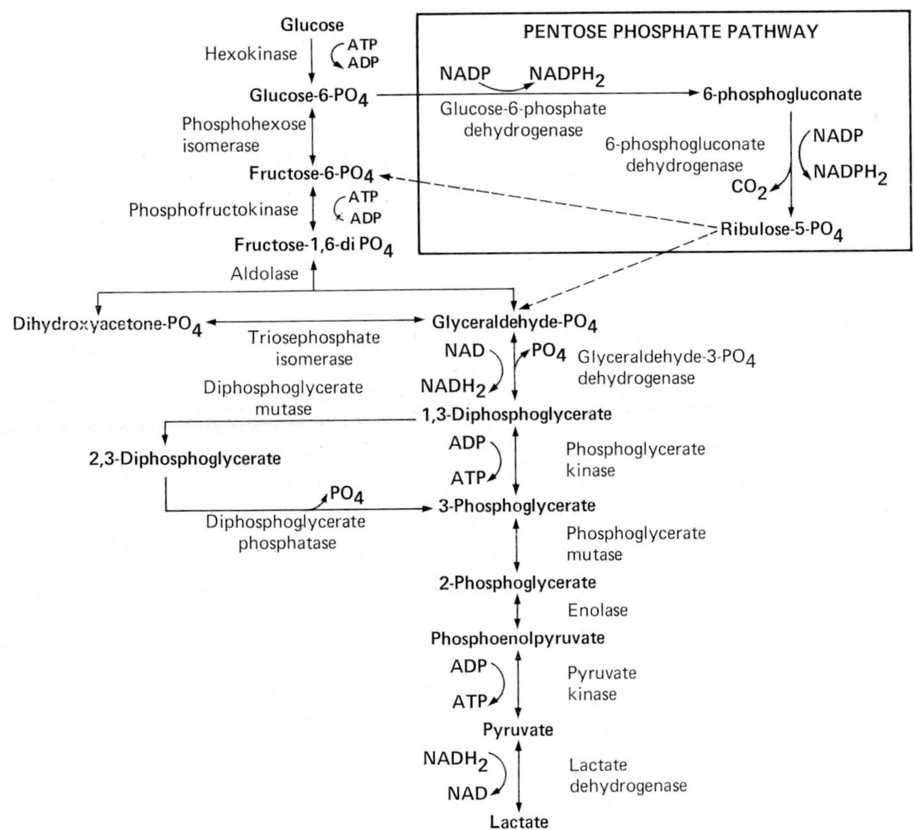

FIG. 5. Red cell glucose metabolism.

phosphofructokinase is unique among the enzymes of the glycolytic and pentose phosphate pathways in being decreased in activity in neonatal red cells.[63] The iso-enzyme patterns of hexokinase[70] and lactate dehydrogenase[163] of neonatal cells differ from those of adult cells.

Levels of adenosine triphosphate (ATP) are significantly higher in the red cells of the neonate than in the red cells of the adult and are even higher in the red cells of premature infants.[63] However, the ATP levels are not well maintained during *in vitro* incubation, unlike those of adult cells.[121] Possibly as a result of these alterations in energy metabolism neonatal red cells lose potassium at an increased rate both during incubation at 37°C and on storage at 4°C.[173]

TABLE 2

CHANGES IN THE GLYCOLYTIC PATHWAY IN THE RED CELLS OF THE NEWBORN INFANT

Enzymes that are increased in any young red cells including neonatal red cells

Hexokinase
Phosphohexose isomerase
Aldolase
Pyruvate kinase
Lactic dehydrogenase

Enzymes that are disproportionately elevated in neonatal red cells

Phosphoglycerate kinase
Enolase

Enzyme that is reduced in neonatal red cells

Phosphofructokinase

Enzymes that have characteristic iso-enzyme patterns in neonatal red cells

Hexokinase
Lactic dehydrogenase

The Pentose Phosphate Pathway. The pentose phosphate pathway is the main alternative pathway for metabolism of

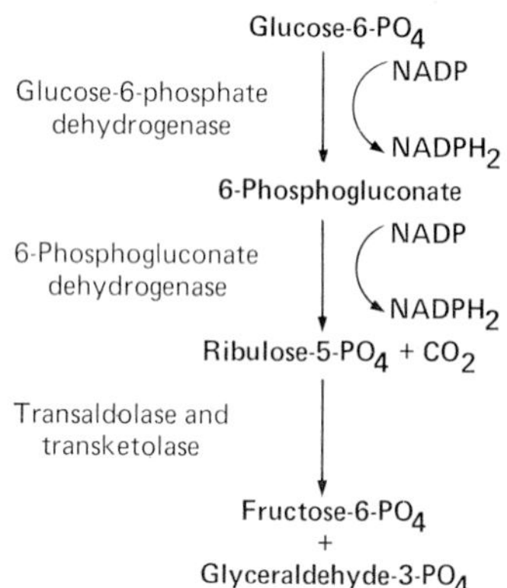

FIG. 6. The pentose phosphate pathway.

glucose in the red cell (Fig. 6). By this pathway, glucose-6-phosphate undergoes oxidative decarboxylation, with the consumption of oxygen and the production of carbon dioxide.

The most important role of the pentose phosphate pathway is in the production of $NADPH_2$, which acts as a hydrogen donor in several reactions that are important in the protection of both haemoglobin and red-cell enzymes from oxidative denaturation. The two main enzymes of the pentose phosphate pathway, glucose-6-phosphate dehydrogenase and 6-phosphogluconic dehydrogenase, are both increased in activity in neonatal red cells as in other young red cells.[62] $NADPH_2$ generation in the neonate is similar to that in the adult.

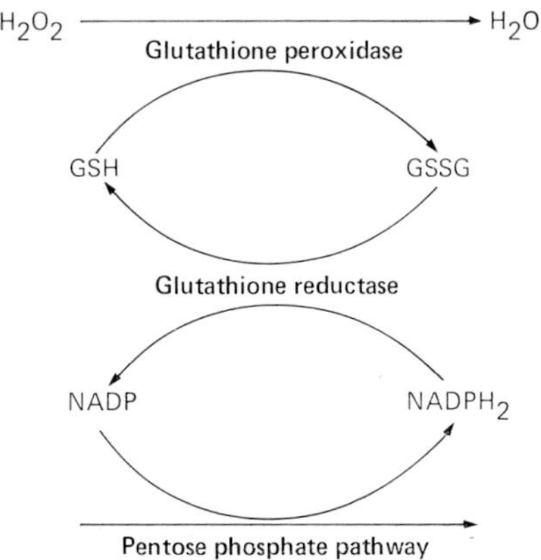

FIG. 7. Glutathione metabolism.

$NADPH_2$ serves as a hydrogen donor in the reduction of glutathione mediated by the enzyme glutathione reductase (Fig. 7). In the reduced form, glutathione contains a free sulfydryl group and this appears to play a central part in red-cell metabolism. It maintains the stability of sulfydryl-containing enzymes and protects free sulfydryl groups in the red-cell membrane, thus protecting haemoglobin from oxidative degradation. It also serves as the substrate for glutathione peroxidase, the enzyme principally responsible for detoxification of the hydrogen peroxide that is slowly generated within the red-cell. Glutathione reductase activity is increased[102] and the level of reduced glutathione is equal to or greater than that found in the adult (Table 3).[172] However, the level of glutathione peroxidase is lower than that of the adult[162] and this relative deficiency appears to render the cell more susceptible to the damaging effects of hydrogen peroxide, particularly when the generation of hydrogen peroxide is accelerated by the exposure of the

TABLE 3

CHANGES IN THE PENTOSE PHOSPHATE PATHWAY IN THE RED CELLS OF THE NEWBORN INFANT

Enzymes increased in activity

Glucose-6-phosphate dehydrogenase
6-phosphogluconate dehydrogenase
Glutathione reductase

Enzyme decreased in activity

Glutathione peroxidase

Other changes

Increased levels of reduced glutathione
Increased glutathione instability
Reduced levels of vitamin E in premature infants

red cell to the "oxidant" action of large doses of synthetic water-soluble vitamin-K analogues. Glutathione is relatively unstable in the neonate and levels fall more rapidly during the first 48 hours of life if the cells are exposed to "oxidant" drugs,[146] e.g., sulphonamides, aspirin and phenacetin.

Red cells are more vulnerable to exposure to hydrogen peroxide when they are deficient in vitamin E (tocopherol). The precise role of vitamin E in protecting the red cell from peroxidative damage is unknown, but a mild haemolytic anaemia occurs during the second month of life in premature infants deficient in vitamen E.[119] The ability to absorb vitamin E is related to gestational age and premature infants are not only relatively deficient of vitamin E but are unable to absorb oral doses fully.[104] Oral administration of iron also appears to reduce vitamin-E absorption in the premature infant.[103]

Methaemoglobin Reduction. About 1 per cent of haemoglobin is oxidized to methaemoglobin each day. Normally this is rapidly reduced to haemoglobin again by a methaemoglobin reductase that requires $NADH_2$ as co-factor. Methaemoglobin levels are significantly higher in the blood of full-term neonates than in the blood of adults and are even higher in the blood of premature infants.[86] This difference may persist for weeks. Newborn infants are also more likely to develop methaemoglobinaemia after exposure to oxidizing compounds such as nitrites.[173] This increased susceptibility to methaemoglobinaemia is probably mainly due to a decreased capacity to reduce methaemoglobin. Levels of $NADH_2$-dependent methaemoglobin reductase are very low in neonatal red cells and tend to be even lower in infants of low birth weight.[14] Enzyme levels reach adult values after two months of age.

Red cells also contain an $NADPH_2$-dependent methaemoglobin reductase but this enzyme is of lesser importance. The level of this enzyme in neonatal red cells approximates that of adults.[135]

Other Non-glycolytic Enzymes. Carbonic anhydrase, catalase, cholinesterase, and adenylate kinase are all present in reduced amounts in neonatal red cells.[122] These deficiencies do not appear to have any functional importance.

II. Red Cell Antigens

The development of the antigenic components of the red-cell membrane is important in the pathogenesis of haemolytic disease of the newborn. If an antigen does not develop at all or only weakly during intra-uterine life, then it is unlikely that maternal immunization will take place and if immunization does take place the clinical effects will be mild. The stimulation of maternal antibody formation against a fetal antigen will depend not only on the development of the antigen during intra-uterine life, but also upon its antigenicity, and the frequency of the presence of antigen in the fetus and its simultaneous absence in the mother. Even if maternal antibodies do develop they will only cause fetal disease if they are of IgG (7S) type that can cross the placental barrier. IgM (19S) and IgA (7S) antibodies cannot cross the placenta from the maternal to the fetal circulation and therefore do not cause fetal disease.

Antigens of the Blood Group Systems. *The Rhesus System.* Antigens of the Rhesus system are fully developed early in fetal life[35] and readily induce the formation of IgG maternal antibodies following even a minute feto-maternal haemorrhage. The Rh (D) antigen is the most potent Rhesus antigen and in Caucasians is the most important cause of haemolytic disease of the newborn. Maternal immunization against other antigens of the Rhesus complex, either alone or in combination with anti-D, may occur and may cause haemolytic disease, e.g., anti-D + C, anti-E, and anti-c; other antibodies, anti-D + E, anti-C and anti-e, are very rare.

In Caucasian population, about 83 per cent are Rh (D) positive and 17 per cent are Rh (D) negative. Of those who are positive, about 43 per cent are homozygous and 57 per cent are heterozygous. All children of homozygous fathers are Rh (D) positive but of those with heterozygous fathers half are positive and half negative.

In 10 per cent of pregnancies the mother is Rh (D) negative and the fetus Rh (D) positive but haemolytic disease of the newborn due to Rhesus antibodies occurs in only 0·5–0·75 per cent of pregnancies. During a first pregnancy, it is extremely unusual to find Rhesus antibodies in the mother's serum though they may be found if she has previously received a transfusion with Rh (D) positive blood. Most often sensitization, i.e. primary immunization without overt antibody formation, takes place during a previous pregnancy and then in a subsequent pregnancy with an Rh (D) positive fetus a secondary immune response occurs with the production of circulating anti-D antibodies which cause haemolytic disease in the fetus.

The ABO System. The antigens of the ABO system also develop early in fetal life and have been demonstrated in fetuses as early as 37 days gestation. However, during intra-uterine life the immunological reactivity of these antigens remains low and does not increase until after birth. Fetal red cells that are genetically of group A differ qualitatively from adult group A cells in that they lack the A_1 antigen and also other antigens of the A spectrum.[37] Fetal red cells of the A_1 genotype react as A_2 and those of the A_2 genotype react in a similar fashion to the adult A_x phenotype, that is, the cells react with the anti-A of group O serum but not that of group B serum.[38] Post-natally, the reactivity of the A antigen increases rapidly during the first two years and reaches adult strength between the second and fourth year.[38]

ABO incompatibility between mother and fetus is common but clinical haemolytic disease is relatively unusual, compared to disease due to Rhesus incompatibility. There are several explanations for this relative infrequency of ABO haemolytic disease. Firstly, the naturally occurring antibody, anti-A and anti-B, is an IgM and therefore does not cross the placenta. Secondly, even in those group O mothers who develop an immune anti-A or anti-B of the IgG type, the low reactivity of the corresponding fetal antigen produces relatively mild disease. Finally, maternal antibodies may be neutralized by soluble A and B substances in the plasma of the fetus.

Among early abortions the frequency of ABO incompatibility is significantly higher than expected. This observation suggests that ABO maternal incompatibility may be a factor in causing early abortion.[147]

ABO incompatibility between mother and fetus gives some protection against Rhesus immunization probably because the incompatible fetal cells will be cleared from the maternal circulation before they come into contact with the antibody forming cells in the mother. This protection is not complete, perhaps because fetal cells with weak A and B antigens may survive longer in an incompatible recipient than adult cells with full-strength A and B antigens.

The H antigen follows a similar pattern of development to that of the A and B antigens.[64] It is weak during fetal life when measured by anti-H in human sera though easily detected when measured with anti-H from the seeds of Ulex europaeus.[130]

The P System. The antigen P_1, like A_1, is usually not fully developed at birth and may not reach adult status for 7 years or more. Surprisingly, the P_1 antigen appears more potent in younger than in older fetuses.[75] Individuals of the very rare p phenotype always have a complex antibody, anti-P + anti-P_1 + anti-p^k in their serum and, like ABO incompatibility, this complex antibody is also associated with a high incidence of early abortion.[130]

The MNSs System. This system develops early in fetal life and is fully developed at birth; indeed M and S may be stronger in cord blood than in adult blood. Anti-M is almost always an IgM antibody and only rarely have cases of haemolytic disease of the newborn been reported associated with a 7S antibody that was presumably IgG. Anti-S and anti-s are IgG antibodies but are seldom encountered in clinical practice and rarely cause problems.

The Xg System. Though XgA has been detected as early as 12 weeks' gestation, it is very weakly developed during intra-uterine life and maternal immunization has not been recorded.[152] It is usually detectable at birth, though difficulty may be encountered in grouping the occasional cord sample. It is the only known red-cell antigen linked to the X-chromosome.

The Lewis System. The two Lewis groups are Le^a and Le^b. They are present as soluble blood group substances in serum and saliva at birth, but are absent from the red cells. The red cells of all fetuses and cord samples give the reaction Le (a−b−). The Le^a antigen first appears soon after birth and over 80 per cent of children are Le(a+) by three months. Le^b is not an allele of Le^a but rather the product of an interaction between the Le^a gene and the H gene which produces the precursor substance of the A and B antigens. Le^b develops slowly and the adult frequency of 70 per cent Le (b+) is not reached until about six years of age. As cells become Le (b+) the frequency of the Le (a+) falls to its adult level of 20 per cent.[79]

The Ii System. The red cells of almost all adults react strongly with anti-I antibody but very weakly with anti-i. The red cells of the neonate have the reverse reactivity, reacting strongly with anti-i and very weakly with anti-I. Commencing shortly after birth the anti-i reaction weakens, while the anti-I reaction strengthens, until at about 19 months of age the normal adult Ii status is established.[98]

In certain haematological disorders the strength of the i antigen may be increased, e.g. thalassaemia, chronic haemolysis, acute leukaemia, congenital dyshaemopoietic anaemias and aplastic anaemia. Experimentally, repeated venesections also cause an increase in i antigen strength.[68] However, in these conditions the I-antigen reactivity does not alter.

The Kell System. The antigen k occurs in adult frequency and strength in fetuses from the ninth week, while K has been found in adult strength in fetuses from 14 and 16 weeks.[152] Anti-K is a rare but potent cause of haemolytic disease of the newborn.

The Lutheran System. The two antigens of the Lutheran system are Lu^a and Lu^b. Lu^a has been detected in a fetus of 12 weeks' gestation and, in the homozygote, is present in adult strength and in cord blood. In the heterozygote, it is only weakly expressed at birth and increases in strength until the age of 15.[61] Lu^b is poorly developed in fetal life and is weak in cord blood.[152]

Isohaemogglutinins in the Fetus and the Neonate. Naturally occurring agglutinins (isohaemagglutinins) against the A and B antigens of red cells can be detected in low titre in the serum of 50–60 per cent of full-term infants. The main production of these haemagglutinins takes place at 3–6 months after birth and their titre reaches the adult range at 18–24 months.[54] They are antibodies, usually of the IgM class, and are assumed to be of fetal origin since IgM antibodies do not cross the placenta.[148] However, IgG isohaemagglutinins may also be found in cord serum and these have probably been transferred from the maternal circulation: they are found in ABO haemolytic disease and represent immune antibodies produced by the mother.

It has been suggested that isohaemagglutinin production is due to exposure to antigens structurally similar to blood-group A and B antigens and which occur normally in food and in the intestinal flora. Another suggestion is that both blood-group antigens and isohaemagglutinins are genetically determined and that the development of the agglutinins does not require exposure to exogenous antigens.

III. The Development of the Human Haemoglobins

Haemoglobin is an iron-containing protein. The molecular weight of all human haemoglobins is approximately 64,500 and they are made up of four polypeptide chains each of which is linked to a heme unit (containing a single iron atom). Each haemoglobin molecule consists of two pairs of polypeptide chains and the members of each pair are identical in structure. The three-dimensional structure of all the normal haemoglobins is very similar but the sequence of aminoacids of the different peptide chains varies considerably. The peptide chains are conventionally designated $\alpha, \beta, \gamma, \delta, \varepsilon$ and ζ (zeta). Each of the normal human haemoglobins (with the exception of Gower I and Portland I—*see below*) contains a pair of α-chains associated with a pair of another type. The structures of the normal human haemoglobins are summarized in Table 4.

The Embryonic Haemoglobins. The embryonic haemoglobins Gower I and Gower II are the first haemoglobins to appear in development, being found in the blood of embryos of less than 12 weeks' gestation (Fig. 8).[73] Haemoglobin Gower I is a tetramer of ε-chains (ε_4) and is the only normal haemoglobin that has 4 identical chains. Haemoglobin Gower II consists of 2 α-chains and two ε-chains ($\alpha_2\ \varepsilon_2$).

The bloods of embryos and small fetuses before 11 weeks' gestation contains 10–15 per cent of another haemoglobin designated haemoglobin Portland I. This also contains 2 pairs of globin chains: 1 pair of normal γ-chains and 1 pair of non-α-chains that have been designated ζ-chains,

TABLE 4

THE NORMAL HUMAN HAEMOGLOBINS

Haemoglobin A	$\alpha_2\ \beta_2$
Haemoglobin A_2	$\alpha_2\ \delta_2$
Haemoglobin F	$\alpha_2\ \gamma_2$
Haemoglobin Gower II	$\alpha_2\ \varepsilon_2$
Haemoglobin Gower I	ε_4
Haemoglobin Portland I	$\zeta_2\ \gamma_2$

and is therefore written as $\gamma_2\ \zeta_2$. The quantity of this haemoglobin decreases with the growth of the fetus and it has virtually disappeared after the 8th week of gestation,[124] though trace amounts have been found in normal cord blood.[67] It is thought that the ζ-chains are the product of a separate normal genetic locus.

Fetal Haemoglobin. The main haemoglobin of intra-uterine life is fetal haemoglobin or haemoglobin F (Fig. 8).

Huehns and Shooter

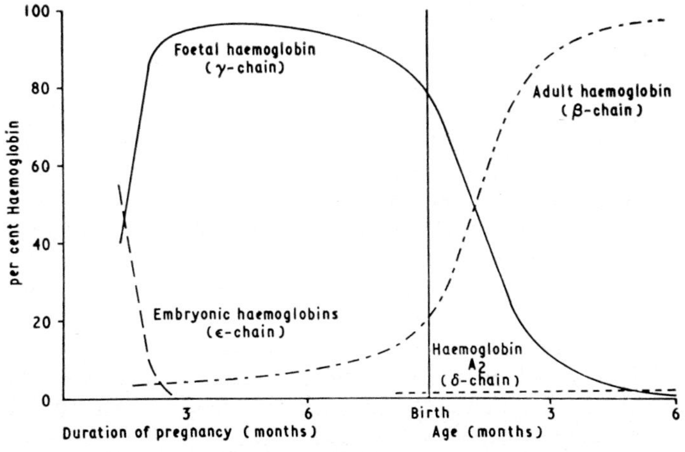

FIG. 8. The development changes in human haemoglobin, from Huehns, E. R. and Shooter, E. M. (1965), *Journal of Medical Genetics*, **21**, 48–90.

The molecule contains 2 α-chains and 2 γ-chains ($\alpha_2\ \gamma_2$). In most published work, the proportion of haemoglobin F (Hb F) is quoted as 90–95 per cent until about 36 weeks of gestation, but the actual percentage may be higher since the one-minute alkali denaturation technique used to measure Hb-F tends to underestimate at these high levels.[78] At about the 36th week of gestation γ-chain production begins to give way to β-chain production and the amount of Hb-F begins to fall but it is still the predominant haemoglobin at birth.

The proportion of Hb-F in the cord blood of full-term infants varies between 77 and 92 per cent (mean 85 per cent) when measured by column chromatography; with the one-minute alkali denaturation technique, the range is wider (47–95 per cent).[8] The remaining haemoglobin is Hb-A. Though Hb-F is the major haemoglobin at birth, the synthesis of γ-chains is already declining fast: of the haemoglobin being synthesized at the time of birth only 50–65 per cent is Hb-F, and this has declined to approximately 5 per cent by three months of age.[53] The fall in the amount of Hb-F lags behind the fall in the synthesis of γ-chains because the red cell continues to circulate for 3–4 months. The fall is gradual during the last 4 weeks of intra-uterine life and the first few weeks of post-natal life. Then, as bone-marrow activity recovers following the transient post-natal depression, synthesis of β-chains increases and accelerates the fall in the amount of the Hb-F. By 4 months, Hb-F comprises 10–15 per cent of the total and then gradually declines to adult level, though these may not be reached until puberty.[19] The majority of the Hb-F values are below 2 per cent by the end of the first year. During the second year of life, a mean value of about 1·8 per cent has been reported, with nearly a quarter of the values over 3 per cent and occasional values over 5 per cent. In children 5–9 years old, the mean value has been found to be about 0·7 per cent with the vast majority of values below 2·0 per cent but up to 3·0 per cent in a few children. In adults, 95 per cent of the values are less than 1 per cent (mean 0·5 per cent).

Adult Haemoglobin. Some adult haemoglobin (Hb-A; $\alpha_2\ \beta_2$) can be detected as early as 11 weeks of gestation, but β-chain synthesis remains at a very low level until about 36 weeks.[124] Hb-A concentration then starts to increase and has a reciprocal relationship with that of Hb-F. After 4 years, the haemoglobin of normal individuals consists almost entirely of Hb-A (97–98 per cent) with the minor component haemoglobin A_2 ($\alpha_2\ \delta_2$) accounting for 2–3 per cent. δ-chain production starts shortly before birth, but at term Hb-A_2 is barely detectable, constituting less than 1 per cent of the total haemoglobin, and rising to the adult level of 2–3 per cent by the age of 6 months.

Since α-chains are common to both Hb-F and Hb-A, failure of the synthesis or abnormalities of the α-chain may be clinically apparent both before and after birth. In the homozygous form of α-thalassaemia, in which there is total failure of α-chain production, only γ-chains are produced: all the haemoglobin consists of γ-chain tetramers, called haemoglobin Barts (γ_4). Infants with this condition are stillborn or die shortly after premature birth at gestational ages ranging from 28–38 weeks, with the clinical picture of hydrops fetalis. On the other hand, β-chain and thus haemoglobin-A production does not become predominant until after the second month of post-natal life. For this reason, abnormalities of structure or failure of production of β-chains do not become clinically apparent until after the first few months of life: infants with sickle-cell disease or those with β-thalassaemia major are clinically normal at birth and the diagnosis is usually not made until the latter half of the first year or the second year of life. However, Haemoglobin S and other abnormal haemoglobins such as C can be detected electrophoretically in cord blood in small amounts, and infants destined to develop thalassaemia major may show a complete absence of Hb-A at birth.

Hb-F synthesis continues after birth in hereditary haemolytic anaemias such as sickle-cell anaemia, hereditary spherocytosis and, particularly, in β-thalassaemia.[16] In hereditary persistance of fetal haemoglobin and also in the chromosomal anomaly D trisomy[164] its persistence is genetically determined. Hb-F synthesis may also be reactivated in aplastic anaemia and leukaemia, particularly in juvenile chronic myeloid leukaemia.[16] Small elevations have also been seen in maternal blood in the second trimester of pregnancy.[126]

The Switch Mechanism in Haemoglobin Production. During the course of development, α-chains combine in turn with ε-chains to produce Hb-Gower II, with γ-chains to produce Hb-F, and finally with β-chains to produce Hb-A and with δ-chains to produce Hb-A_2. This sequence takes place with remarkable smoothness and with little excess of any chain at any stage. As yet very little is known of the mechanism by which the switch from one form of globin chain production to that of another takes place. This could be a matter of considerable practical clinical importance since the clinical manifestations of sickle-cell disease and β-thalassaemia major only occurs after the change from γ-chain to β-chain production. If this switch could be completely or even partially prevented these diseases would be largely overcome, since Hb-F functions as well as Hb-A and in appropriate amounts tends to reduce the sickling of cells containing Hb-S.

The switch from Hb-F to Hb-A production is related to gestational age and is not affected by the time of birth whether premature or at term. In some mammals the type of haemoglobin produced is related to the site of production: in the mouse, the embryonic haemoglobin is produced exclusively by the erythropoietic cells of the yolk-sac while those in the liver, spleen and bone marrow all produce adult haemoglobin.[12] This is not the case in man in whom Hb-F and Hb-A are both produced in the liver and in the bone marrow.[151] Indeed, both Hb-F and Hb-A are produced within single cells.[49]

Hormonal influences may play an important part in certain situations. Increased levels of Hb-F have been found in some patients with thyrotoxicosis. In the bull frog, Rana catesbiana, the tadpole and the adult frog have different haemoglobins and the tadpole may be induced to produce the adult type of haemoglobin by the administration of thyroxine.[110,111] Both adult sheep and adult goats produce a different type of α-chain following acute blood loss. Plasma from sheep rendered anaemic by bleeding induces the same change in α-chain production when transfused into non-anaemic sheep, demonstrating that a plasma factor, perhaps related to erythropoietin, is involved.[51]

There is no definite evidence for the involvement of a hormone in the switch from fetal to adult haemoglobin in man. In particular it seems very unlikely that erythropoietin itself is involved. A proportion of normal women produce small amounts of fetal haemoglobin in early pregnancy and it is possible that the stimulus is a hormonal agent produced by the placenta and perhaps identical with chorionic gonadotrophin. Elevated levels of Hb-F are also found in the presence of a hydatidiform mole and these return to normal after removal of the mole.[26] However, the levels of Hb-F found in normal pregnancy or a mole pregnancy are relatively low, i.e. about 3–4 per cent, and it is doubtful whether chorionic gonadotrophins are important in the switch mechanism or whether they would be of any use in the treatment of sickle-cell anaemia or β-thalassaemia major.

The Genetics of the Haemoglobins. There is now strong evidence from family studies that the production of the different globin chains is determined by separate structural genes. From studies of the pattern of inheritance of abnormal haemoglobins, it is probable that the α and β-genes are located on separate non-homologous chromosomes. In contrast, there is evidence that the β and δ genes are closely linked on the same chromosome. It now appears that, at least in certain strains of mice, the locus for the γ-chain is also closely linked with the β locus. The findings in hereditary persistence of fetal haemoglobin in humans also suggest that the β, δ and γ loci are closely linked on the same chromosome.[136]

Until recently it has been assumed that each of the human haemoglobin chains is produced by a single pair of structural genes. However, it is known that certain globin chains of animals are produced by multiple non-allelic genes, e.g. the α-chain of goat haemoglobin,[74] and it now appears that there is duplication of the structural gene for the γ-chain of man.[137] The γ-chains produced by each of the two non-allelic genes are not quite identical in structure: at position 136 in the amino acid sequence one chain contains the amino-acid glycine while the other contains alanine. These two forms of Hb-F are both present during intra-uterine life in all individuals of all populations examined. As the entire population cannot consist of heterozygotes, these two forms cannot be the product of allelic genes at a single structural locus. That these two forms of Hb-F are the products of separate structural loci rather than the result of an ambiguity of translation of a single locus has been conclusively demonstrated by studies of the fetal haemoglobins of infants heterozygous for an abnormal haemoglobin F. In every case the abnormal haemoglobin contained either glycine or alanine and never both.

The two Hb-F loci do not work with equal efficiency. In cord blood the ratio of glycine-containing Hb-F to alanine-containing Hb-F is approximately 3:1. After birth, as the post-natally synthesized Hb-F becomes a significant fraction of the total Hb-F, the ratio gradually reverses so that in the child after six months of age and in the adult the ratio is approximately 2:3. This suggests that the mechanism suppressing production influences each of the two γ genes to a quantitatively different degree.[136]

Family studies make it certain that the structural genes for the β and δ-chains are not duplicated but uncertainty still remains over the α gene. With abnormalities of the β-chain, the amount of the mutant haemoglobin approaches 50 per cent of the total haemoglobin whereas with abnormalities of the α-chain the mutant haemoglobin amounts to 25 per cent or less of the total haemoglobin. Where identical mutations of both β and α-chains are known the ratio between the concentrations of the two is consistently 2:1. It has been postulated that this discrepancy could be explained by duplication of the α gene, so that a mutation on one site would affect only 25 per cent of the α-chain production.[89] This has been supported by the findings in two individuals, of a Hungarian family, who are both heterozygous for two α-chain variants.[25] In addition to the two variants, both individuals have approximately 50 per cent normal adult haemoglobin. This could be explained by duplication of the α-chain locus on each homologous chromosome: this gives rise to four α-chain genetic loci, any of which may be occupied by a mutant gene. Further examination of this family has suggested that the α-chain loci are not closely linked and may segregate independently. Some α-chain variants constitute more than 25 per cent of the total haemoglobin and it is possible that these variants are linked with a gene for α-thalassaemia.[50] Evidence from another family conflicts with the concept of the α gene duplication and it is possible that some populations have single loci while others have multiple loci.[4]

Duplication of the α-chain gene can also explain the wide clinical spectrum of α-thalassaemia. The possession of one affected gene would give the "silent" α-thalassaemia trait, while two affected genes would give the 'classical' α-thalassaemia trait. Haemoglobin H disease would be caused by the possession of three affected genes, while four would give the lethal hydrops fetalis with only haemoglobin Barts in the cord blood.

The Oxygen Affinity of Haemoglobin. It has long been known that fetal blood has a greater affinity for oxygen than has normal adult blood. The partial pressure of oxygen at which fetal blood releases 50 per cent of the oxygen that it carries is some 6–8 mm. Hg. lower than that of normal adult blood. This means that fetal blood releases less oxygen to the tissues at a given capillary partial pressure of oxygen than does adult blood but, conversely, this difference in oxygen affinity facilitates the transfer of oxygen from maternal to fetal blood across the placenta.

Though intact fetal cells possess a higher oxygen affinity than do intact adult cells, the oxygen affinities of pure solutions of Hb-F and Hb-A are identical.[5] Clearly, a second cellular component is also involved in determining the oxygen affinity of haemoglobin in intact red cells. This component is 2,3-diphosphoglycerate (2,3-DPG), which is the organic phosphate found in greatest concentration in human red cells.

2,3-DPG binds reversibly to normal adult haemoglobin (Hb-A), 1 mole of 2,3-DPG combining with 1 mole of deoxygenated Hb-A. Due to the changes in conformation that occur in the haemoglobin molecule during oxygenation, 2,3-DPG cannot combine with the oxygenated form of Hb-A. Though they do not combine with haemoglobin at the same site, oxygen and 2,3-DPG are in competition for Hb-A and the affinity of Hb-A for oxygen is inversely related to the intra-cellular concentration of 2,3-DPG.[18] As the concentration of 2,3-DPG increases, so the oxygen affinity of Hb-A decreases and more of the oxygen carried is released to the tissues under physiological conditions. Varying the intra-cellular concentration of 2,3-DPG, and thus the oxygen affinity of the blood, is a normal mechanism by which adjustment is made for changes in the oxygen content of the arterial blood and the tissue requirements for oxygen.

When an individual moves from sea-level to an altitude of 15,000 ft. the concentration of 2,3-DPG increases over a period of 24–36 hr., thus decreasing the oxygen affinity of haemoglobin.[90] This permits a greater proportion of the oxygen load to be released to the tissues, compensating for the decreased arterial oxygen saturation due to the lower partial pressure of oxygen at high altitudes. This process is rapidly reversed on returning to sea-level. A similar increase in 2,3-DPG concentration takes place in response to the decreased arterial oxygen saturation found in cyanotic congenital heart disease and in chronic lung disease, in response to the decreased oxygen-carrying capacity of the blood in chronic anaemias, and in response to the increased demand for oxygen by the tissues in thyrotoxicosis.[120]

Fetal haemoglobin (Hb-F) is unable to bind 2,3-DPG to the same degree as does adult haemoglobin and this seems to be the main reason why the blood of the fetus and neonate has a higher oxygen affinity than does the blood of the adult.[15] 2,3-DPG is acidic and binds to the basic groups of the amino acids exposed within the central cavity of the haemoglobin molecule: one of the main binding sites is probably the imidazole nitrogen of the histidine in position 143 (H21 in the helical notation) of the β-chain.[120] In the β-chain of HB-F, this basic amino acid histidine is replaced by the neutral amino acid serine which is unable to contribute to the binding of 2,3-DPG, and thus Hb-F has a lower affinity for 2,3-DPG and consequently a higher affinity for oxygen. 2,3-DPG is also bound at other sites within the central cavity of the haemoglobin molecule and these sites are present in both β and γ-chains so that though the effect of 2,3-DPG on oxygen affinity is reduced in Hb-F, it is not entirely abolished.[120]

At term, the oxygen affinity of the blood of the full-term normal neonate is greater than that of the normal adult. During the first week of post-natal life the oxygen affinity decreases rapidly and then continues to fall more gradually until 4–6 months of age, when the affinity of the infant's blood is similar to that of the adult. At 8–11 months of age, the oxygen affinity of the blood of many infants is actually less than that of normal adults.[120] During the first week of life the concentration of 2,3-DPG in the red cell rises sharply and this largely accounts for the initial decrease in oxygen affinity. Subsequently, the oxygen affinity falls as the level of Hb-F falls and that of Hb-A rises. However, the change in oxygen affinity of the red cells of a normal infant is correlated directly with the product of the concentration of the Hb-F and of 2,3-DPG, and not with either alone.

2,3-DPG is also important in blood transfusion. Blood which is normally stored in acid-citrate-dextrose (ACD) at 4°C develops a progressive increase in its oxygen affinity, and this is maximal at about 7 days. This increase is closely related to the fall in the concentration of red cell 2,3-DPG that occurs in stored blood.[27] Red cells that have been depleted of 2,3-DPG during storage, regenerate this compound following transfusion but several days may elapse before normal levels are reached.[155] The increase in oxygen affinity produced by small transfusions into relatively healthy individuals is probably not important but massive transfusions of stored blood may produce a marked shift in oxygen affinity that might conceivably have undesirable side-effects.[143]

Nutritional Requirements for Haemopoiesis

Iron

The fetus receives its iron from the maternal circulation via the placenta. Iron transport across the placenta is unidirectional from the mother to the fetus and can take place against a steep concentration gradient: at term the serum iron concentration in cord blood, mean about 160 μg./100 ml., is nearly twice that in maternal blood, mean 90 μg./100/ml.[122] The fetus gains most of its iron during the last 3 months of intra-uterine life, during the same period that it gains most of its weight and haemoglobin. The increase in total iron content is directly proportional to the increase in weight. Premature infants miss this late increase in total body iron and are particularly liable to develop iron deficiency during infancy. Severe maternal iron deficiency may also reduce placental iron transfer and cause iron-deficiency anaemia in infants at about 1 year of age.[142] Iron deficiency anaemia is less common in first-born children than later children and it is probable that repeated pregnancies produce depletion of maternal iron so that there is less available for subsequent children.[65]

At birth, the iron content of the neonate is approximately 75 mg./kg. of body weight, or about 250 mg. for a 3·5 kg. infant.[80] However, there is a wide variation in total iron in full-term infants, 150–370 mg., which depends on the birth weight, the haemoglobin concentration of the blood and the size of the transfusion of blood from the placenta at birth.[28] Iron in haemoglobin accounts for about 60 per cent of the total iron at birth, the remainder being mainly in myoglobin, and storage iron is relatively limited.

During the first 2 months of life the haemoglobin concentration falls, due mainly to the relative decrease in erythropoiesis and to a lesser extent to the shortened red-cell life span, and the excess iron is taken up in the tissue stores. By 2 months of age, only 40 per cent of the total body iron is present as haemoglobin iron and the quantity of storage iron is greatly increased. After the first 2 months of life when erythropoiesis increases this storage iron is very important because iron intake during the early neonatal period is very low: both human and bovine milk contain relatively very little iron, about 0·75 mg. per litre. About 70 per cent of haemoglobin iron at the age of 1 year and about 4 per cent at 2 years is still of maternal origin.[140]

Iron deficiency is still the commonest cause of anaemia in childhood, occurring most frequently between the ages of 6 months and 3 years. Inadequate diet and small iron stores at birth are the usual causes of iron deficiency. The iron requirements of the infant are about 0·5 mg. of iron daily during the first 6 months of life, 0·9 mg. daily during the second 6 months and 0·5 mg. daily during the second year,[139] but these requirements are barely supplied by the average intake in the United Kingdom. Like adults, infants absorb about 10 per cent of their daily intake of food iron, though a greater percentage is absorbed during the first year of life.[59] To meet iron needs, a daily intake of 8–10 mg. is required by the end of the first year of life, but it has been estimated that the average daily intake of iron in the United Kingdom is 8·0 mg. daily from 8–12 months of age and only 7·2 mg. daily in the second year of life.[106] Many infants receive less than this: 41 per cent of children aged 9–12 months and 63 per cent of those in the second year of life had an intake of 5 mg. daily or less.[106]

Vitamin B_{12}

The mean serum vitamin B_{12} concentration in cord blood is about 450 pg./ml. The concentration in maternal blood falls progressively during pregnancy and, at term, that in the cord blood is about twice that in the maternal blood.[122] The vitamin B_{12} content of the fetal liver increases steadily during normal pregnancy, reaching 20–25 μg. at term.[11]

Both human and bovine milk contain significant quantities of vitamin B_{12}: bovine 0·32–1·24 μg./100 ml., human 0·11 μg./100 ml. Intrinsic factor production by the stomach is already adequate at birth for normal vitamin B_{12} absorption.

Vitamin B_{12} deficiency is often associated with infertility, but occasionally pregnancy occurs in patients with untreated pernicious anaemia or nutritional vitamin B_{12} deficiency. The infants of these mothers have low hepatic stores of vitamin B_{12} at birth and the maternal milk contains very little vitamin B_{12}.[11,77,87] These infants may develop a megaloblastic anaemia during the first year of life due to vitamin B_{12} deficiency.

Folic Acid

Both serum folate and red-cell folate concentration are higher in cord blood from normal full-term infants than in maternal blood. Mean values of 598 ng./ml. for red-cell folate and 24·5 ng./ml. for serum folate have been reported.[156] The cord serum folate concentration is thus 3–4 times that of maternal blood. There is a significant correlation between maternal serum folate and cord serum folate concentrations and also between the corresponding red-cell folate concentrations, higher maternal values being associated with greater values in cord blood.[88] Cord blood concentrations are also greater in infants whose mothers have received folic-acid supplements during pregnancy. During the first 6 weeks of life, there is a rapid fall in both red-cell and serum folate levels and these are halved by the age of 3 months.[99,156]

The infant's requirements for folate have been estimated to be the order of 20–50μg./day. This is about 4–10 times adult requirements, weight for weight, due to the rapid rate of growth.[99,144] Fresh milk, both human and bovine, contains about 50 μg. of folate per litre (Table 5). However, heating, and particularly prolonged boiling, destroys folate: boiling for 5 sec. may reduce the folate content of fresh bovine milk by as much as 50 per cent. Ascorbic acid, which helps preserve folid acid from oxidation, is also destroyed by boiling. Processed milk, particularly if boiled after reconstitution, contains even less folate: 36 μg./l. unboiled and 15 μg/l. after boiling for 5 min. Artificially fed infants receive far less folate than breast-fed infants, and breast-fed infants have significantly higher whole-blood folate levels.[33,69]

TABLE 5

THE FOLATE CONTENT OF MILK (μg./l). FROM CHANARIN, I. (1969). THE MEGALOBLASTIC ANAEMIAS. BLACKWELL SCIENTIFIC PUBLICATIONS, OXFORD AND EDINBURGH

Human	52 (31–81)
Cow's	
fresh, unboiled	55 (37–72)
fresh, boiled (5 sec.)	30 (22–35)
fresh, boiled (5 min.)	31 (24–42)
pasteurised	54 (43–70)
pasteurised, boiled (5 min.)	10 (5–15)
Powdered milk	
unboiled	36 (31–48)
boiled (5 min.)	15 (10–21)
Goat's milk	6 (2–11)

In premature infants, values for cord blood are comparable with those of normal full-term infants, but after birth the fall in both serum and red-cell folate concentration is both more rapid and more marked. The steepest falls occur in the smallest babies and the lowest levels are reached between 4 and 8 weeks when serum folate levels are usually less than 6 ng./ml.[69,132,157] Premature infants probably have relatively poor folate stores at birth and the folate content of the milk usually used for premature infants is even lower than that of the full-cream milk given to full-term infants. For these reasons, folic-acid deficiency and megaloblastic anaemia are liable to develop in premature infants during the first 2 or 3 months of life.

An adequate intake of protein, pyridoxine and vitamin C is also required for normal haemopoiesis.

THE DEVELOPMENT OF LEUCOPOIESIS

Myelopoiesis in Utero

Haemopoiesis in the liver of the human fetus is almost exclusively erythropoietic and during the hepatic phase of haemopoiesis there are very few granulocytes in the peripheral blood.

Granulocytes first appear in the peripheral blood after the 10th week of gestation and increase in numbers very slowly during the second trimester, reaching 1,000/μl. at about the 25th week.[127,149] Mature granulocytes and their precursors (promyelocytes, myelocytes and metamyelocytes) are present in roughly equal proportions until the 20th week of gestation, but thereafter the majority of the cells are mature. Very few white-cell counts have been done on blood from fetuses between the 25th week of gestation and term but presumably the granulocyte count rises during the third trimester to reach the mean count of 8,000/μl. at term.

The granulocyte count in fetuses between the 16th and 25th weeks of gestation has been found to be higher in those that have been delivered by the vaginal route than in those that have been delivered by abdominal hysterotomy.[127] The mean granulocyte count in the vaginal group was about 2,000/μl. and in the abdominal group about 500/μl.

Eosinophils are present after the 12th week of gestation and number 100–200/μl. between the 20th week of gestation and term.

Lymphopoiesis

Lymphopoiesis begins in the lymph glands and thymus during the 3rd month of gestation and mature lymphocytes are found in the blood after the 10th week. The lymphocyte count increases rapidly after the 10th week of gestation to reach a mean level of about 5,000/μl. (range 2,000-10,000/μl.) at the 20th week. During the 3rd trimester, the lymphocyte count drops slightly and the mean at term is about 3,000/μl. The count is not affected by the method of delivery.[127]

Monocytes

Monocytes may be found in the blood as early as the 8th week of gestation. Between the 10th week and term, the monocyte count varies widely (range 0–1,000/μl.) and there is no consistent trend with fetal age.

The White Cell Count in Infancy and Childhood

The total white-cell count of cord blood has a wide normal range, 10,000–25,000/μl.,[40] with a mean of about 13,000/μl. During the first 24 hr. of post-natal life the total count increases to a mean of 20,000–22,000/μl.[83] It has been suggested that this increase is due to the haemoconcentration that takes place during the first few hours after birth; but the increase affects only the granulocyte count, without an equivalent rise in the lymphocyte count, and is more probably due to mobilization of granulocytes from the marginal pool distributed along the walls of blood vessels.

On the 2nd and 3rd days of life, the total white count drops to reach its lowest point on the 4th day and then rises to a mean of 12,000/μl. at the end of the first week.[122] After the first week, the mean white-cell count falls gradually to reach the adult level at or shortly after puberty. At the same time, the normal range gradually contracts from 5,000–21,000/μl. at 1 week to the normal adult range of 4,000–11,000/μl. after puberty (Table 6).[40]

TABLE 6

THE VARIATION WITH AGE OF THE TOTAL WHITE CELL COUNT. FROM DACIE, J. V. AND LEWIS, S. M. (1968). PRACTICAL HAEMATOLOGY. J. AND A. CHURCHILL LTD., LONDON

Normal total white cell counts	
Infants (full-term, at birth)	10,000–25,000 per μl.
Infants (1 year)	6,000–18,000 per μl.
Childhood (4–7 years)	6,000–15,000 per μl.
Childhood (8–12 years)	4,500–13,500 per μl.
Adults	4,000–11,000 per μl.

Most reports of the differential white-cell count during infancy and childhood give the figures in percentage and the

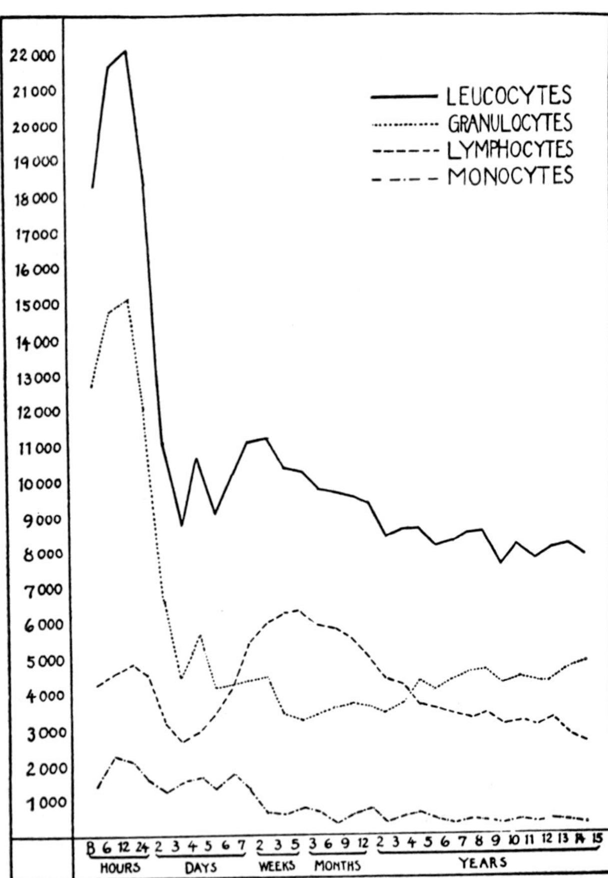

FIG. 9. The average values for total white cell count, neutrophils, lymphocytes and monocytes from birth to 15 years of age. From Kato, K. (1935), "Leucocytes in infancy and childhood," *Journal of Pediatrics*, **7**, 7–15.

absolute figures are not well documented. Figure 9 shows the trend with age of the total and differential white-cell counts[83] and Table 7 gives some of the published ranges for different ages.[6,40,116,117,168]

The Granulocyte Count. At birth the predominant white cell in the peripheral blood is the *neutrophil granulocyte*, which numbers 4,000–18,000/μl. This predominance is accentuated by the increase in the neutrophil count that occurs during the first 24 hr. During the first week of life, the neutrophils show a "shift to the left," with up to 50 per cent band forms. Metamyelocytes number up to 2,000/μl. practically disappear by the end of the first week. Small numbers of myelocytes, 100 750/μl., and occasional promyelocytes are also present during the first 72 hr.[16]

After the first 24 hr. the neutrophil count falls abruptly and sometime between the 4th and 7th day neutrophils become less numerous than the lymphocytes. The neutrophil count remains lower than the lymphocyte count until about the fourth year. After the fourth year, the neutrophil count has the normal adult range, 1,500/7,500/μl.

The Lymphocyte Count in cord blood is 2,000–10,000/μl. with a mean of about 5,000/μl. The lymphocyte count falls gradually from birth to reach its lowest point on the 3rd or 4th day. It then increases to become the predominant white cell (about 60 per cent of the total white-cell count) by the 4th to 6th month. This value is maintained until about the 4th year, when the neutrophil again becomes the predominant cell.

The Monocyte Count in cord blood is 200–1,600/μl. It is higher at 12 hr. of life and then gradually falls until the 3rd day of life. There is a further rise up to the 7th day of life. Between the 2nd and 3rd weeks, the monocyte count is 200–2,500/μl. (mean about 900/μl.). After this the count gradually falls and the normal adult values of 100–800/μl. are reached after 4 years.

The Eosinophil Count. The normal range for cord blood has been reported as 0–800/μl. with a mean of 230/μl. It is very variable during the first week of life and may reach 2,500/μl. The count remains high during infancy when compared to the normal adult range of 40–440/μl. It has been reported as 0–800/μl. between the 4th and 7th years and as 0–600/μl. between the 8th and 14th years.[116,117]

Premature babies have very low eosinophil counts in cord blood at birth. A steady rise is seen after the first week of life with a mean count of just over 1,000/μl. by the end of the first month. In premature infants whose progress is unsatisfactory, and who later die, the eosinophil count remains very low.[30]

The Basophil Count in cord blood is low and the count does not differ significantly from normal adult values, 0–100/μl., throughout infancy and childhood.

TABLE 7

THE DIFFERENTIAL WHITE CELL COUNT DURING INFANCY AND CHILDHOOD (per μl.)

Age	*Neutrophils*	*Lymphocytes*	*Monocytes*	*Eosinophils*	*Basophils*	*Reference*
Birth	6,000–26,000	2,000–11,000	400–3,100	20– 850	0–640	Altman & Dittmer[6]
96 hours	1,300– 6,900	2,200– 7,100	300–2,100	200–1,900		Xanthou[168]
7 days	1,500–10,000	2,000–17,000	300–2,700	70–1,100	0–250	Altman & Dittmer[6]
14 days	1,100– 9,500	2,000–17,000	200–2,400	70–1,000	0–230	Altman & Dittmer[6]
4 weeks	1,000– 9,000	2,500–16,500	150–2,000	70– 900	0–200	Altman & Dittmer[6]
6 months	1,000– 8,500	4,000–13,500	100–1,300	70– 750	0–200	Altman & Dittmer[6]
12 months	1,500– 8,500	4,000–10,500	50–1,100	50– 700	0–200	Altman & Dittmer[6]
4–7 years	1,500– 7,500	1,500– 8,500	0– 800	0– 800	0–200	Osgood *et al.*[117]
8–14 years	1,500– 6,500	1,500– 6,500	0– 800	0– 600	0–200	Osgood *et al.*[116]
Adult	2,500– 7,500	1,500– 3,500	200– 800	40– 440	0–100	Dacie & Lewis[40]

THE DEVELOPMENT OF HAEMOSTASIS

The Haemostatic Mechanism

Figure 10 illustrates the sequence of events in the formation of a haemostatic plug at the site of an injury to a blood vessel. There are three main components to the haemostatic response: the blood vessels, the platelets, and the coagulation factors in the plasma.[141]

The vessels assist haemostasis in two ways: they constrict at the site of injury and the sub-endothelial layers exposed by the injury provide the activating surface and tissue substance that initiate platelet reactions and coagulation.

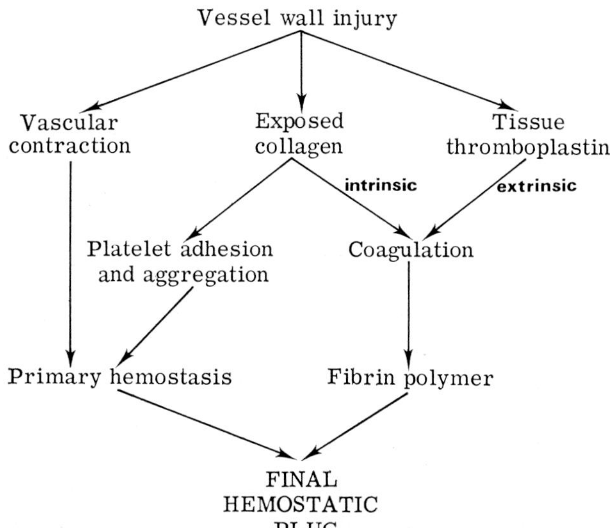

FIG. 10. A simplified outline of the haemostatic mechanism.

The platelets are indispensable both for the normal integrity of the vascular endothelium and for the repair of injured vessels. Platelets adhere to collagen and the basement membrane exposed in the sub-endothelial layers of the wall of the injured vessels. Adhesion to collagen causes the release of a number of substances from the platelets, including adenosine diphosphate (ADP) and 5-hydroxytryptamine. The most important of these substances is ADP that causes the platelets to aggregate and thus form a platelet plug round the end of the severed blood vessel. During the process of aggregation a phospholipid-protein complex (platelet factor 3), which is essential for the intrinsic pathway of blood coagulation, is made available in the surface of the platelets. Initially, the aggregation is reversible and the platelet clump is unstable. Irreversible aggregation with further release of platelet constituents is caused by thrombin produced by the plasma coagulation system.

Vascular constriction, together with the formation of a platelet plug, produces the initial or primary haemostasis. A simple and reliable screening test of primary haemostasis is the bleeding time performed by Ivy's technique. This is abnormal in thrombocytopenia, in disorders of platelet function, and in the presence of abnormal capillary fragility. Platelet function is assessed by measurement of adhesion to a standard glass surface, of aggregation in the presence of ADP, of clot retraction and assay of the availability of platelet factor 3. A heparin-neutralizing factor is present in platelets (platelet factor 4): this is released when platelets aggregate and can be used as a measure of platelet function.[170]

Coagulation. A simplified diagram of the coagulation reaction is shown in Fig. 11. Coagulation results in the formation of polymers of insoluble fibrin that are formed in

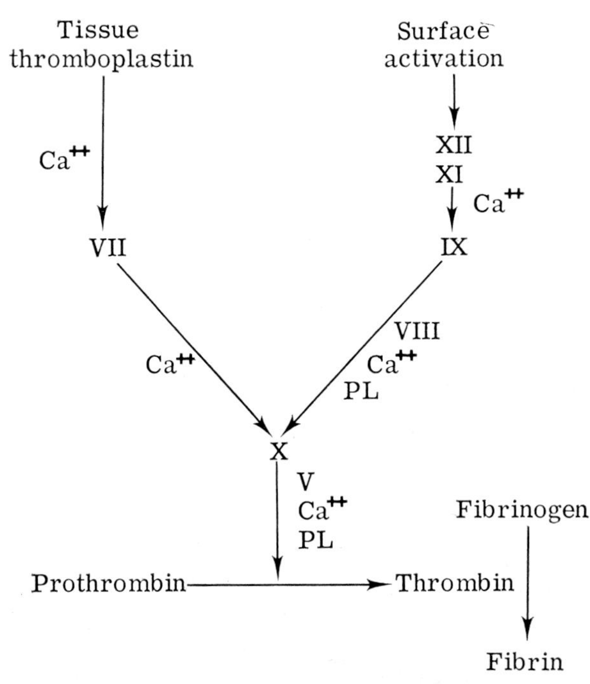

FIG. 11. A simplified outline of coagulation. Ca^{++} = calcium ions, PL = phospholipid derived from platelets in the intrinsic mechanism and from damaged tissues in the extrinsic mechanism.

and around the platelet plug to produce the stable haemostatic plug. Coagulation may take place either by the intrinsic pathway, initiated by contact with the sub-endothelial surfaces exposed by vascular injury, or by the extrinsic pathway that is initiated by thromboplastic substances from damaged tissues. In the intrinsic pathway of coagulation, plasma factors become activated in sequence. Three complexes form, each of which initiates the formation of the next complex in the sequence and leads finally to the activation of prothrombin. When plasma comes into contact with a suitable surface, such as the collagen of a damaged vessel wall, the contact factors XII and XI are converted to their active forms and together form the first complex. This complex, in the presence of calcium ions, activates factor IX (Christmas factor) which then combines with factor VIII (anti-haemophilic globulin), calcium ions and a phospholipid to form the second complex: the phospholipid in this complex is platelet factor 3 (PF-3). The second complex activates factor X which, in turn, forms a further complex with factor V, calcium ions and platelet factor 3.

This third complex changes prothrombin to thrombin, which then converts soluble fibrinogen to insoluble fibrin.

In the extrinsic system tissue thromboplastins, which are lipoproteins whose precise chemical structure is unknown, activate factor VII in the presence of calcium ions. The activated factor VII then converts factor X to its active form. From this point, the extrinsic and intrinsic pathways are identical. Phospholipid for the extrinsic pathway comes from tissue thromboplastin rather than from platelet factor 3.

The pre-activation of both factor V and factor VIII by thrombin is probably necessary for their participation in coagulation. In the absence of such activation coagulation is rather slow, but once small quantities of thrombin are formed factors V and VIII are activated and there is a rapid acceleration of the whole process. Thus, the coagulation reaction is autocatalytic.

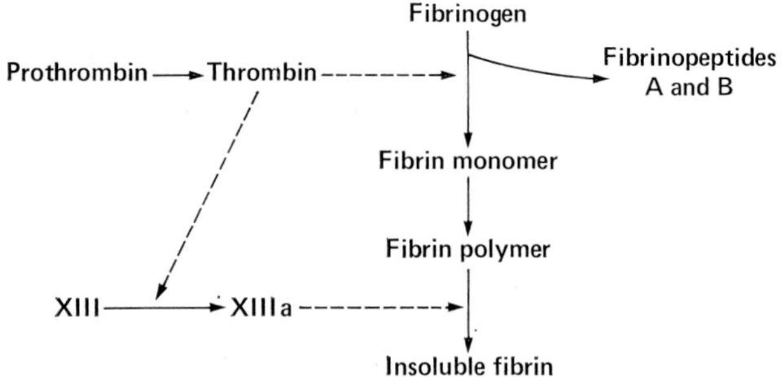

FIG. 12. The formation of fibrin.

The *in vivo* inter-relationship of the extrinsic and intrinsic pathways is not certain, but it seems that both are required for normal haemostasis. The role of factor XII *in vivo* is not clear since marked deficiency does not result in a clinical bleeding disorder. Recently, evidence has been presented that platelets provide a substance, distinct from PF-3, which in the presence of collagen activates factor XI directly.[159] This substance functions in the complete absence of factor XII and may help to explain the absence of a bleeding tendency in patients with congenital factor XII deficiency.

The final stages of fibrin formation are shown in more detail in Fig. 12. Thrombin splits off two pairs of peptides from fibrinogen to leave the fibrin monomer, which polymerizes spontaneously to form the insoluble fibrin polymers. The polymers are stabilized by covalent cross-linkage by factor XIII, which is a glutaminase, in the presence of calcium ions. Factor XIII also requires pre-activation by thrombin. Lack of factor XIII produces a haemorrhagic disorder.

In addition to the coagulation factors involved in fibrin formation, it is probable that there are plasma inhibitors for each stage in the coagulation mechanism. Of these, the antithrombins are well recognized but the others have received less study. Both natural and pathological inhibitors may play important roles in haemostasis and thrombosis.

All the coagulation factors are produced by the liver except for factors VIII and XIII whose site of origin is unknown. It seems likely that factor VIII is produced in the reticulo-endothelial system. Factors II (prothrombin), VII, IX and X require vitamin K for their production.

The intrinsic pathway of the coagulation system is tested by the whole-blood clotting time, the partial thromboplastin time (PTT) or kaolin cephalin time (KCT), and the thromboplastin generation test. These are screening tests and will detect deficiencies of factors XII, XI, IX, VIII, X, V, prothrombin and fibrinogen and all will be influenced by inhibitors of coagulation. The whole-blood clotting time is relatively insensitive and will only detect gross coagulation defects. The KCT is more sensitive but may be normal in the presence of mild deficiencies of clotting factors, e.g. in mild haemophilia where the diagnosis must be established by factor VIII assay. All the factors may be assayed separately and, with the exception of fibrinogen, are reported as percentages. The average normal adult value is designated 100 per cent and the normal range is from 50–200 per cent.

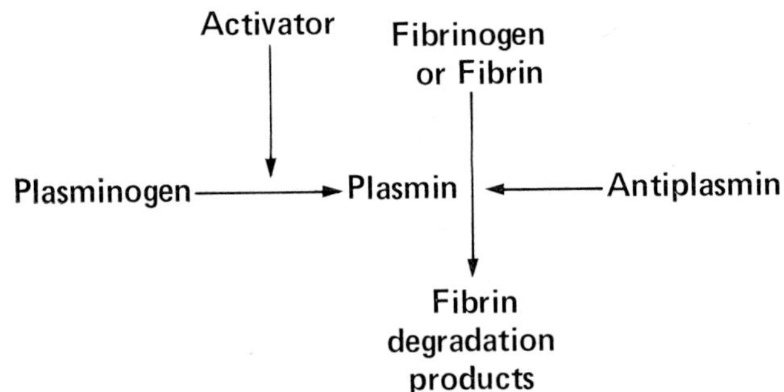

FIG. 13. The fibrinolytic mechanism.

The extrinsic coagulation pathway is tested by the prothrombin time which is sensitive to deficiencies of factors VII, X, V, prothrombin and fibrinogen and to coagulation inhibitors such as heparin. It may also be normal in the presence of mild deficiencies. Thrombotest is a variant of the prothrombin time and is sensitive to the vitamin K-dependent factors: it is also affected by inhibitors.

The thrombin time measures the thrombin-fibrinogen reaction. It is prolonged in the presence of heparin or the degradation products of fibrin, in severe deficiency of fibrinogen and in the presence of abnormal fibrinogen molecules which occur as congenital variants. It may also be prolonged by abnormal proteins such as may be found in myeloma and by excess bilirubin glucuronide.[85] The normal plasma concentration of fibrinogen in adults is 150–400 mg./100 ml. Deficiency of factor XIII is detected by the solubility of the fibrin clot in 5-molar urea in which normal clots are insoluble.

Fibrinolysis. The main reactions in the fibrinolytic system are illustrated in Fig. 13. Plasma contains a pro-enzyme, plasminogen, that may be converted to the active proteolytic enzyme, plasmin, by a variety of activators. Some activators act directly on plasminogen, while others act indirectly and require the presence of a pro-activator. The best established direct activator is urokinase, present in human urine, but others are released by tissue injury. Indirect activators are released from various tissues, particularly vein walls, and are also obtained from various bacteria, such as streptococci from which streptokinase is obtained.

Plasmin splits both fibrin and fibrinogen into smaller degradation products (FDP). The larger FDP may interfere with the thrombin fibrinogen reaction and prolong the thrombin time. Plasmin also splits other plasma proteins, such as factors V and VIII, converting them into inactive products.

Like the coagulation system, the fibrinolytic system is counterbalanced by inhibitors at each stage. Normal blood contains inhibitors both against the plasmin activators and also against plasmin itself.

The level of activators may be measured by the lysis time of dilute whole blood-clots or of clots formed from the euglobulin precipitate of plasma, or by measuring lysis of unheated fibrin on plates. Plasmin may be assayed directly by its proteolytic activity against casein or purified fibrinogen, or by its activity on heated fibrin plates. Plasminogen is assayed as plasmin after activation by streptokinase.

Haemostasis in the Embryo and Fetus

Both haemostatic and fibrinolytic activity commence in the fetus at about 11 weeks of gestation when platelets and clotting and fibrinolytic factors appear in the peripheral blood.[21] In fetuses younger than 11 weeks the blood is completely incoagulable. After the 11th week, individual coagulation factors develop at varying rates and not all have reached adult values at term.

Clotting factors are globulins of high molecular weight (up to 1,200,000). As they do not cross the placenta clotting factor activities in the fetus and neonate reflect fetal synthesis and thus haemophilia and congenital afibrinogenaemia may be diagnosed on plasma from cord blood.[31,128,129]

Platelets. Megakaryocytes may be found in the yolk sac of the embryo at 5–6 weeks of gestation and are present in the liver during the hepatic period of haemopoiesis. They are present in the bone marrow after the 3rd month of gestation. Platelets are found in the peripheral blood by the 11th week of gestation and by the 30th week megakaryocytic activity in the bone marrow and the platelet count are both similar to those of the adult.[82]

Coagulation. Prior to the 11th week of gestation the blood of the fetus does not clot.[171] After the 11th week, the ability to clot develops rapidly and the whole-blood clotting time is comparable to or even shorter than that in adults. The vitamin K-dependent factors, as measured by the thrombotest, also appears at about the 11th week of gestation and gradually increases to perinatal values when the thrombotest is 40–70 per cent. Factor V activity approximates to adult levels by 12–15 weeks of gestation and fibrinogen is being synthesized by the liver as early as the 5th week of gestation.

Fibrinolysis. Fibrinolytic activity is also detectable at about 11 weeks of gestation and increases in activity throughout pregnancy.[21,44]

Haemostasis at Birth

The platelet count and the levels of factors V and VIII have attained normal adult values but platelet function differs and levels of the contact factors (XII and XI) and the vitamin K-dependent factors (II, VII, IX and X) are still low. These deficiencies are accentuated in premature babies who are particularly prone to haemorrhage.[21]

Primary Haemostasis. Capillary fragility is normal in the full-term neonate and the bleeding time is the same as in the adult. In premature babies capillary fragility is increased and the bleeding time is prolonged roughly in proportion to the degree of prematurity.[21]

It is not certain whether the increased fragility and prolonged bleeding time in premature infants are due to vascular abnormalities or to immaturity of platelet function. Platelet counts are essentially the same as those in adults for both full-term and premature infants. Counts tend to be near the lower limit of the normal range of 150,000–400,000/μl. in the premature infants; but counts less than 100,000/μl. should be considered abnormal in even the smallest premature infant, provided that satisfactory specimens are obtained.[3,9]

Neonatal platelets show some qualitative differences when compared to adult platelets.[21] Platelet aggregation is reduced with both adenosine diphosphate and collagen. Clot retraction is poor and platelet factor 3 availability is diminished. The impairment in platelet aggregation may be due to drugs taken by the mother. Acetyl-salicylic acid taken during pregnancy may impair aggregation of the platelets of both mother and infant. The impairment is greater and longer-lasting in the infant's platelets.[39] Despite the lowered reactivity of neonatal platelets, the bleeding time is similar to that of normal adults and there is no associated bleeding tendency.

Coagulation. The coagulation parameters in newborn infants are summarized in Table 8. The whole-blood clotting time is normal or even accelerated in full-term infants though it may be prolonged in premature infants. The prothrombin time (PT) may be normal or slightly prolonged in full-term infants and the kaolin cephalin time (KCT) is prolonged. The prolongation of the PT and KCT reflect the deficiencies of the contact factors and of the vitamin K-dependent factors and they are even more prolonged in premature infants.[21]

The contact factors (XI and XII) are both moderately low in the plasma of full-term infants and the concentration of factor IX is lower in premature infants. Factor XII takes one or two weeks to reach normal adult levels after birth but factor XI may not reach normal adult values for one to two months. A third contact factor, the Fletcher factor, has been described and found to be low in the plasma of newborn infants.[66]

The clotting factors, II (prothrombin), VII, IX and X, that require vitamin K for their manufacture, are all reduced in the plasma of full-term infants at birth as compared to their concentration in adult plasma.[13,21] Their concentration is even lower in the plasma of premature infants. This low level of the vitamin K-dependent factors is the main cause of the prolonged KCT and PT of the neonate

TABLE 8

THE CONCENTRATIONS OF COAGULATION FACTORS, AND THE PLATELET COUNT, IN THE BLOOD OF FULL-TERM AND PREMATURE INFANTS COMPARED WITH THE VALUES FOR NORMAL ADULT BLOOD. PER CENT = PER CENT OF THE AVERAGE NORMAL ADULT LEVEL

	Premature newborn infant	*Full-term newborn infant*	*Normal adult values*
Screening tests (sec.)			
KCT	70–145	45–70	35–45
PT	12–21	13–20	12–14
TT	11–17	10–16	10–12
Contact factors (%)			
XII	?	25–70	50–200
XI	5–20	15–70	50–200
Vitamin K dependent factors (%)			
II	20–80	25–65	50–200
VII	20–45	20–70	50–200
IX	10–25	20–60	50–200
X	10–45	20–55	50–200
Other factors (%)			
V	50–85	50–200	50–200
VIII	20–80	50–200	50–200
XIII	100	100	80–140
Fibrinogen (mg./100 ml.)	120–300	120–300	150–400
Platelet count (*per* μl.)	100,000–350,000	120,000–400,000	150,000–400,000

and probably accounts for the haemorrhagic tendency of the premature infant.

Factors V and VIII are both present in normal concentration in the cord plasma of full-term infants but may be slightly reduced in the plasma of premature infants. Factor XIII (fibrin stabilizing factor) attains normal adult values before term and is normal in the cord plasma of both premature and full-term infants.

Throughout the perinatal period fibrinogen levels are in the normal adult range or slightly lower but the thrombin time is usually slightly prolonged.[131] In the absence of reduced levels of fibrinogen, the prolonged thrombin time must be due either to the presence of antagonists of the thrombin–fibrinogen reaction or to a less reactive fibrinogen molecule. The existence of a fetal fibrinogen analagous to fetal haemoglobin has been postulated and there is evidence for its existence from finger-printing of the peptides obtained by tryptic digestion of purified fibrinogen.[167] It is probable that different reactivity of fetal fibrinogen accounts for the prolonged thrombin time.

Fibrinolytic System. Spontaneous fibrinolytic activity is increased in cord blood, despite the fact that plasminogen levels are low. The explanation for this paradoxical finding is that cord blood contains increased levels of plasminogen activators, demonstrable by lysis of unheated fibrin on plates and by a shortened euglobulin clot lysis time. Levels of both plasmin inhibitors and activator inhibitors are high but these must be more than offset by the increased level of activators.[17,44,96]

Fibrinolytic activity decreases rapidly during the first hours of life and the level of plasminogen also falls.

FDP may be found in low titre in a small proportion of serum samples from normal cord blood in the absence of any other evidence of disturbed haemostasis. The amount of FDP does not correlate with the prolonged thrombin time.[34]

Haemostasis in Infancy

Townsend in 1894 described the syndrome of haemorrhagic disease of the newborn which occurs in the first week of life and is characterized by generalized bleeding and a favourable outcome in those living beyond the first days of life. His cases probably included a variety of bleeding disorders, but the term "haemorrhagic disease of the newborn" is now confined to those cases of neonatal haemorrhage due to a severe deficiency of the vitamin K-dependent factors.[2]

The concentrations of the vitamin K-dependent factors, II (prothrombin), VII, IX and X, in the cord blood of normal full-term infants are lower than those in normal adults, and values of 20–60 per cent of the average adult values are usual (Table 8).[21] However, the prothrombin time in the cord blood plasma of normal newborns is usually similar to that in adults probably because the concentrations of factor II, VII and X do not fall below 20 per cent. Following birth, they may fall even further to reach their minimum on the 2nd or 3rd day of post-natal life.[2] The levels of individual factors may fall below 10 per cent of the average normal adult value, and may reach zero. At these low levels the prothrombin time is grossly prolonged. After the 3rd day of post-natal life, the prothrombin time returns to the adult value perhaps due to vitamin K intake in the diet, and the concentration of the vitamin K-dependent factors rises to reach 40–70 per cent of the adult values at the 8th day.

The neonatal drop in these clotting factors appears to be

due solely to a deficiency of vitamin K since the drop can be completely prevented by a small parenteral dose of vitamin K given at the time of birth. An injection of as little as 25 μg. of vitamin K_1 is completely effective.[2]

Dietary factors are important in the development of the deficiency. Cow's milk contains 60 μg. of vitamin K activity per litre whilst human milk contains only 15 μg./l.[41] Prolongation of the prothrombin time and clinical bleeding develops only in those infants who are given human milk.[84,145] Early feeding also has a beneficial effect: the prothrombin time is grossly prolonged in 11 per cent of infants not fed until 36 hr., but in only 2 per cent of those fed at 8 hr. after birth.

It is not clear why vitamin K deficiency develops so rapidly in the neonatal period; at no other time of life does deprivation of vitamin K produce such a rapid disturbance of coagulation. It has been suggested that the lack of intestinal flora may be responsible; however, it is doubtful whether the water-insoluble vitamin K formed by bacterial synthesis in the large intestine is available to the host at all.[43] In animals, coprophagy is necessary for the bacterial vitamin K to be made available to the host.[71] An increase in prothrombin concentration has been shown in infants in whom menadione has been instilled into the colon, but this form of vitamin K is moderately water-soluble in contrast to the water-insoluble vitamin K produced by intestinal bacteria.[1]

Though vitamin K deficiency appears to be an important cause of the low neonatal levels of factors II, VII, IX and X, it is not the only one. Even in infants given prophylactic vitamin K, adult levels are not reached for 2–12 months and it is probable that the neonatal liver is incapable of optimal synthesis of these factors. The premature infant has even lower levels of the vitamin K-dependent factors at birth and the response to vitamin K is less predictable than in the full-term infant.[122]

REFERENCES

1. Aballi, A. J., Howard, C. E. and Triplett, R. F. (1966), "Absorption of Vitamin K from the Colon in the Newborn Infant," *J. Pediat.*, **68**, 305–308.
2. Aballi, A. J. and de Lamerens, S. (1962), "Coagulation Changes in the Neonatal Period and in Early Infancy," *Pediat. Clins. N. Amer.*, **9**, 785–817.
3. Aballi, A. J., Puapondh, Y. and Desposito, F. (1968), "Platelet Counts in Thriving Premature Infants," *Pediatrics*, **42**, 685–689.
4. Abramson, R. K., Rucknagel, D. L., Shreffler, D. C. and Saave, J. J. (1970), "Homozygous Hb J Tongariki: Evidence for Only One α-chain Structural Locus in Melanesians," *Science*, **169**, 194–196.
5. Allen, D. W., Wyman, J., Jr. and Smith, C. A. (1953), "The Oxygen Equilibrium of Fetal and Adult Human Hemoglobin," *J. biol. Chem.*, **203**, 81–87.
6. Altman, P. L. and Dittmer, D. S. (1961), "Blood and other body fluids," Federation of American Societies for Experimental Biology, Washington, D.C.
7. Andrews, B. F. and Thompson, J. W. (1962), "Materno-fetal Transfusion. A Common Phenomenon?," *Pediatrics*, **29**, 500–501.
8. Andrews, B. F. and Willet, G. P. (1965), "Fetal Hemoglobin Concentration in the Newborn," *Amer. J. Obstet. Gynec.*, **91**, 85–88.
9. Appleyard, W. J. and Brinton, A. (1971), "Venous Platelet Counts in Low Birth Weight Infants," *Biol. Neonate*, **17**, 30–34.
10. Baker, H., Ziffer, H., Pasher, I. and Sobotka, H. (1958), "A Comparison of Maternal and Foetal Folic Acid and Vitamin B_{12} at Parturition," *Brit. med. J.*, **1**, 978–979.
11. Baker, S. J., Jacob, E., Rajan, K. T. and Swaminathan, S. P. (1962), "Vitamin B_{12} Deficiency in Pregnancy and the Puerperium," *Brit. Med. J.*, **1**, 1658–1661.
12. Barker, J. E. (1968), "Development of the Mouse Haemopoietic System: I. Types of Hemoglobin Produced in Embryonic Yolk Sac and Liver," *Dev. Biol.*, **18**, 14–29.
13. Barkhan, P. (1957), "Christmas-factor Activity of Cord Blood," *Brit. J. Haemat.*, **3**, 215–219.
14. Bartos, H. R. and Desforges, J. F. (1966), "Erythrocyte DPNH Dependent Diaphorase Levels in Infants," *Pediatrics*, **37**, 991–993
15. Bauer, C., Ludwig, I. and Ludwig, M. (1968), "Different Effects of 2,3-diphosphoglycerate and Adenosine Triphosphate on Oxygen Affinity of Adult and Fetal Human Haemoglobin," *Life Sci.*, **7**, 1339.
16. Beavan, G. H., Ellis, M. J. and White, J. C. (1960), "Studies on Human Foetal Haemoglobin: II. Fotal Haemoglobin Levels in Healthy Children and Adults in Certain Haematological Disorders," *Brit. J. Haemat.*, **6**, 201–222.
17. Beller, F. K., Douglas, G. W. and Epstein, M. D. (1966), "The Fibrinolytic Enzyme System in the Newborn," *Amer. J. Obstet. Gynec.*, **96**, 977–984.
18. Benesch, R., Benesch, R. E. and Yu, C. I. (1968), "Reciprocal Binding of Oxygen and Diphosphoglycerate by Human Haemoglobin," *Proc. nat. Acad. Sci. U.S.A.*, **59**, 526–532.
19. Betke, H. (1960), "Fetal Hemoglobin in Health and Disease," *The Proceedings of the VIIIth International Congress of Haematology*, pp. 1033–1040. Tokyo: Pan Pacific Press.
20. Black, P. J. (1971), "Epitaph for the MCHC," *Brit. Med. J.*, **4**, 492–493.
21. Bleyer, W. A., Hakami, N. and Shepard, T. H. (1971), "The Development of Hemostasis in the Human Fetus and Newborn Infant," *J. Pediat.*, **79**, 838–853.
22. Bloom, W. and Bartelmez, G. W. (1940), "Hematopoiesis in Young Human Embryos," *Amer. J. Anat.*, **67**, 21–44.
23. Boger, W. P., Bayne, G. M., Wright, L. D., and Beck, G. D. (1957), "Differential Serum Vitamin B_{12} Concentrations in Mothers and Infants," *New Engl. J. Med.*, **256**, 1085–1087.
24. Bratteby, L. E., Garby, L. and Wadman, B. (1968), "Studies on Erythrokinetics in Infancy," *Acta paediat., Stokh.*, **57**, 305–310.
25. Brimhall, B., Hollán, S., Jones, R. T., Koler, R. D., Stocklen, Z. and Szelényi, J. G. (1970), "Multiple α-chain Loci for Human Haemoglobin," *Clin. Res.*, **18**, 184.
26. Bromberg, Y. M., Salzberger, M. and Abrahamov, A. (1957), "Alkali Resistant Type of Hemoglobin in Women with Molar Pregnancy," *Blood*, **12**, 1122–1124.
27. Bunn, H. F., May, M. H., Kochalaty, W. F. and Shields, C. E. (1969), "Hemoglobin Function in Stored Blood," *J. clin. Invest.*, **48**, 311–321.
28. Burman, D. (1971), "Iron Requirements in Infancy," *Brit. J. Haemat.*, **20**, 243–247.
29. Burman, D. (1972), "Haemoglobin Levels in Normal Infants Aged 3–24 Months, and the Effect of Iron," *Arch. Dis. Childh.*, **47**, 261–271.
30. Burrel, J. M. (1952), "A Comparative Study of the Circulating Eosinophil Level in Babies: I. Premature Infants," *Arch. Dis. Childh.*, **27**, 337–340.
31. Cade, J. F., Hirsh, J. and Martin, M. (1969), "Placental Barrier to Coagulation Factors: Its Relevance to the Coagulation Defect at Birth and to Haemorrhage in the Newborn," *Brit. Med. J.*, **1**, 281–283.
32. Capp, G. L., Rigas, D. A. and Jones, R. T. (1970), "Evidence for a New Haemoglobin Chain (ζ-chain)," *Nature*, **228**, 278–280.
33. Chanarin, I. (1969), *The Megaloblastic Amaemias.* Oxford and Edinburgh: Blackwell Scientific Publications.

34. Chessels, J. M. (1971), "The Significancents, Fibin Degradation Products in the Blood of Normal Infa" for *Biol. Neonat.* **17,** 219–226.
35. Chown, B. (1955), "On a Search for Rhesus Antibodies in Very Young Foetuses," *Arch. Dis. Childh.*, **30,** 232–233.
36. Cohen, F., Zuelzer, W. W., Gustafsen, D. C. and Evans, M. M. (1964), "Mechanisms of Isoimmunization: I. The Transplacental Passage of Fetal Erythrocytes in Homospecific Pregnancies," *Blood*, **23,** 621–646.
37. Constantoulakis, M. and Kay, H. E. M. (1962), "A and B Antigens of the Human Foetal Erythrocyte," *Brit. J. Haemat.*, **8,** 57–63.
38. Constantoulakis, M., Kay, H. E. M., Giles, C. M. and Parkin, D. M. (1963), "Observations on the A_2 Gene and H Antigen in Foetal Life," *Brit. J. Haemat.*, **9,** 63–67.
39. Corby, D. G. and Schulman, I. (1971), "The Effects of Antenatal Drug Administration on Aggregation of Platelets of Newborn Infants," *J. Pediat.*, **79,** 307–313.
40. Dacie, J. V. and Lewis, S. M. (1968), *Practical Haematology.* London: Churchill Ltd.
41. Dam, H., Glavind, J., Larsen, H. and Plum, P. (1942), "Investigations into the Cause of Physiological Hypoprothrombinaemia in Newborn Children," *Acta med. scand.*, **112,** 210.
42. Danon, Y., Kleimann, A. and Danon, D. (1970), "The Osmotic Fragility and Density Distribution of Erythrocytes in the Newborn," *Acta Haemat.*, **43,** 242–247.
43. Deutsch, E. (1966), "Vitamin K in Medical Practice: Adults," *Vitam. and Horm.*, **24,** 655–680.
44. Ekelund, H., Hedner, U. and Nilsson, I. M. (1970), "Fibrinolysis in Newborns," *Acta paediat. Stokh.*, **59,** 33–43.
45. Emery, J. L. and Follett, G. F. (1964), "Regression of Bone-marrow Haemopoiesis from the Terminal Digits in the Foetus and Infant," *Brit. J. Haemat.*, **10,** 485–489.
46. England, J. M., Walford, D. M. and Waters, D. A. W. (1972), "Re-assessment of the Reliability of Haematocrit," *Brit. J. Haemat.*, **23,** 247–256.
47. Finne, P. H. (1964), "Erythopoietin Levels in the Amniotic Fluid, Particularly in Rh-immunized Pregnancies," *Acta paediat. Stokh.*, **53,** 269–281.
48. Finne, P. H. (1968), "Erythropoietin Production in Fetal Hypoxia and in Anemic Uremic Patients," *Ann. N.Y. Acad. Sci.*, **149,** 497–503.
49. Fraser, I. D. and Raper, A. B. (1962), "Observations on the Change from Foetal to Adult Erythropoiesis," *Arch. Dis. Childh.*, **37,** 289–296.
50. French, E. A. and Lehmann, H. (1971), "Is Haemoglobin Gα Philadelphia Linked to α-thalassaemia?" *Acta Haemat.*, **46,** 149–156.
51. Gabuzda, T. G., Schuman, M. A., Silver, R. K. and Lewis, H. B. (1969), "The Control of Hemoglobin Phenotype in Calves and Sheep," *Ann. N.Y. Acad. Sci.*, **165,** 347–352.
52. Gairdner, D., Marks, J., Roscoe, J. D. and Brettell, R. O. (1958), "The Fluid Shift from the Vascular Compartment Immediately After Birth," *Arch. Dis. Childh.*, **33,** 489–498.
53. Garby, L., Sjölin, S. and Vuille, J.-C. (1962), "Studies of Erythrokinetics in Infancy: II. The Relative Rate of Synthesis of Haemoglobin F and Haemoglobin A During the First Months of Life," *Acta paediat. Stockh.*, **51,** 245–254.
54. Gartner, O. T., Gilbert, R., McDermott, M., Benovitz, S. and Wolf, A. M. (1967), "Anti-A and Anti-B Antibodies in Children," *J. Amer. med. Ass.*, **210,** 206–207.
55. Gatti, R. A. (1967), "Hematocrit Values of Capillary Blood in the Newborn Infant," *J. Pediat.*, **70,** 117–119.
56. Giblett, E. R. and Crookston, M. C. (1964), "Agglutinability of Red Cells by Anti-i in Patients with Thalassaemia Major and Other Haematological Disorders," *Nature*, **201,** 1138–1139.
57. Gilmour, J. R. (1941), "Normal Haemopoiesis in Intra-uterine and Neonatal Life," *J. Path. Bact.*, **52,** 25–55.
58. Gordon, A. S. (1971), "The Current Status of Erythropoietin," *Brit. J. Haemat.*, **21,** 611–616.
59. Gorten, M. K., Hepner, R. and Workman, J. B. (1963), "Iron Metabolism in Premature Infants," *J. Pediat.*, **63,** 1063–1071.
60. Greenwalt, T. J. and Ayers, V. E. (1960), "Phosphate Partition in the Erythrocytes of Normal Newborn Infants and Infants with Erythroblastosis Fetalis," *Blood*, **15,** 698–705.
61. Greenwalt, T. J., Sasaki, T. T. and Steane, E. A. (1967), "The Lutheran Blood Groups: A Progress Report with Observations on the Development of the Antigens and Characteristics of the Antibodies," *Transfusion, Philad.*, **7,** 189–200.
62. Gross, R. T. and Hurwitz, R. E. (1958), "The Pentose Phosphate Pathway in Human Erythrocytes," *Pediatrics*, **22,** 453–460.
63. Gross, R. T., Schroeder, E. A. R. and Brounstein, S. A. (1963), "Energy Metabolism in the Erythrocytes of Premature Infants Compared to Full-term Newborn Infants and Adults," *Blood*, **21,** 755–763.
64. Grundbacher, F. J. (1964), "Changes in the Human A Antigen of Erythrocytes with the Individual's Age," *Nature*, **204,** 192–194.
65. Guest, G. M. and Brown, E. W. (1957), "Erythrocytes and Hamoglobin of the Blood in Infancy and Childhood," *Amer. J. Dis. Child.*, **93,** 486–509
66. Hathaway, W. E. and Alsever, J. (1970), "The Relationship of 'Fletcher Factor' to Factors XI and XII," *Brit. J. Haemat.*, **18,** 161–169.
67. Hecht, F., Jones, R. T. and Koler, R. D. (1968), "Newborn Infants with Hb Portland I. An Indicator of α-chain Deficiency," *Ann. hum. Genet.*, **31,** 215–218.
68. Hillman, R. S. and Giblett, E. R. (1965), "Red Cell Membrane Alteration Associated with 'Marrow Stress'." *J. clin. Invest.*, **44,** 1730–1736.
69. Hoffbrand, A. V. (1970), "Folate Deficiency in Premature Infants," *Arch. Dis. Childh.*, **45,** 441–444.
70. Holmes, E. W. J., Malone, J. I., Winegrad, A. I., Oski, F. A. and Cox, G. S. (1967), "Hexokinase Isoenzymes in Human Erythrocytes: Association of Type II with Fetal Hemoglobin," *Science*, **156,** 646–648.
71. Hötzel, D. and Barnes, R. H. (1966), "Contributions of the Intestinal Microflora to the Nutrition of the Host," *Vitams. and Horm.*, **24,** 115–171.
72. Hudson, G. (1965), "Bone-marrow Volume in the Human Fetus and Newborn," *Brit. J. Haemat.*, **11,** 446–452.
73. Huehns, E. R. and Shooter, E. M. (1965), "Human Haemoglobins," *J. Med. Genet.*, **2,** 48–90.
74. Huisman, T. J. H., Brandt, G. and Wilson, J. B. (1968), "The Structure of Goat Hemoglobins: II. Structural Studies of the α-chains of the Hemoglobins A and B," *J. biol. Chem.*, **243,** 3675–3686.
75. Ikin, E., Kay, H. E. M., Playfair, J. H. L. and Mourent, A. E. (1961), "P_1 Antigen in the Human Foetus," *Nature*, **192,** 883.
76. Jacobson, L. O., Marks, E. K. and Gaston, E. O. (1959), "Studies on Erythropoiesis: XII. The Effect of Transfusion-induced Polycythemia in the Mother on the Fetus," *Blood*, **14,** 644–653.
77. Jadhav, M., Webb, J. K. G., Vaishnava, S. and Baker, S. J. (1962), "Vitamin-B_{12} Deficiency in Indian Infants," *Lancet*, **ii,** 903–907.
78. Jonxis, J. H. P. (1965), "The Development of Hemoglobin," *Pediat. Clin. N. Amer.*, **12,** 535–550.
79. Jordal, K. (1956), "The Lewis Blood Groups in Children," *Acta path. microbiol. scand.*, **39,** 399–406.
80. Josephs, H. W. (1959), "The Iron of the Newborn Baby," *Acta paediat.*, **48,** 403–418.
81. Kalpaktsoglou, P. K. and Emery, J. L. (1965), "The Effect of Birth on the Haemopoietic Tissue of the Human Bone Marrow," *Brit. J. Haemat.*, **11,** 453–460.
82. Kalpaktsoglou, P. K. and Emery, J. L. (1965), "Human Bone Marrow During the Last Three Months of Intra-uterine Life," *Acta Haemat.*, **34,** 228–233.
83. Kato, K. (1935), "Leucocytes in Infancy and Childhood," *J. Pediat.*, **7,** 7–15.
84. Keenan, W. J., Jewett, T. and Glueck, H. I. (1971), "Role of Feeding and Vitamin K in Hypoprothrombinemia of the Newborn," *Amer. J. Dis. Child.*, **121,** 271–277.
85. Kopeć, M., Darocha, T., Niewiarowski, S. and Stachwska, J. (1961), "The Antithrombin Activity of Glucuronic Esters of Bilirubin," *J. clin. Path.*, **14,** 478–481.

86. Kravitz, H., Elegant, L. D., Kaiser, E. and Kagan, B. M. (1956), "Methemoglobin Values in Premature and Mature Infants and Children," *Amer. J. Dis. Child.*, **91**, 1–5.
87. Lampkin, B. C. and Mauer, A. M. (1967), "Congenital Pernicious Anaemia with Coexistent Transitory Intestinal Malabsorption of Vitamin B_{12}," *Blood*, **30**, 495–502.
88. Landon, M. J. and Oxley, A. (1971), "Relation Between Maternal and Infant Blood Folate Activities," *Arch. Dis. Childh.*, **46**, 810–814.
89. Lehmann, H. and Carrell, R. W. (1968), "Difference Betweeen α- and β-chain Mutants of Human Haemoglobin and Between α- and β-thalassaemia. Possible Duplication of the α-chain Gene," *Brit. med. J.*, **4**, 748–750.
90. Lenfant, C., Torrance, J., English, E., Finch, C. A., Reynafarje, C., Ramos, J. and Faura, J. (1968), "Effect of Altitude on Oxygen Binding by Hemoglobin and Organic Phosphate Levels," *J. clin. Invest.*, **47**, 2652–2656.
91. Lie-Injo, L. E., Hollander, M. R. and Fudenberg, H. H. (1967), "Carbonic Anhydrase and Fetal Hemoglobin in Thyrotoxicosis," *Blood*, **30**, 442–448.
92. Lucarelli, G., Howard, D. and Stohlman, F. (1964), "Regulation of Erythropoiesis. XV. Neonatal Erythropoiesis and the Effect of Nephrectomy," *J. clin. Invest.*, **43**, 2195–2203.
93. Lucarelli, G., Porcellini, A., Carnevali, C., Carmena, A. and Stohlman, F. (1968), "Fetal and Neonatal Erythropoiesis," *Ann. N.Y. Acad. Sci.*, **149**, 544–559.
94. Luzzatto, L., Esan, G. J. F. and Ogiemudia, S. E. (1970), "The Osmotic Fragility of Red Cells in Newborns and Infants," *Acta Haemat.*, **43**, 248–256.
95. Mann, D. L., Sites, M. L., Donati, R. M. and Gallagher, N. I. (1965), "Erythropoietic Stimulating Activity During the First Ninety Days of Life," *Proc. Soc. exp. Biol. Med.*, **118**, 212–214.
96. Markarian, M., Githens, J. H., Jackson, J. J., Bannon, A. E., Lindley, A., Rosenblut, E., Martorell, R. and Lubchenco, L. O. (1967), "Fibrinolytic Activity in Premature Infants," *Amer. J. Dis. Child.*, **113**, 312–321.
97. Marks, J., Gairdner, D. and Roscoe, J. D. (1955), "Blood Formation in Infancy: III. Cord Blood," *Arch. Dis. Childh.*, **30**, 117–120.
98. Marsh, W. L. (1961), "Anti-i: A Cold Antibody Defining the Ii Relationship in Human Red Cells," *Brit. J. Haemat.*, **7**, 200–209.
99. Matoth, Y., Pinkas, A., Zamir, R., Mooallem, F. and Grossowicz, N. (1964), "Studies on Folic Acid in Infancy: I. Blood Levels of Folic Acid and Folinic Acid in Healthy Infants," *Pediatrics*. **33**, 507–511.
100. Matoth, Y., Zaizov, R. and Varsano, I. (1971), "Postnatal Changes in Some Red Cell Parameters," *Acta paediat. Stokh.*, **60**, 317–323.
101. McCracken, G. H. and Eichenwald, H. F. (1971), "Leukocyte Function and Development of Opsonic and Complement Activity in the Neonate," *Amer. J. Dis. Child.*, **121**, 120–126.
102. McDonald, C. D. and Huisman, T. J. H. (1962), "A Comparative Study of Enzymic Activities in Normal Adult and Cord Blood Erythrocytes as Related to the Reduction of Methemoglobin," *Clinica. chim. Acta.*, **7**, 555–559.
103. Melhorn, D. K. and Gross, S. (1971), "Vitamin E-dependent Anemia in the Premature Infant: I. Effects of Large Doses of Medicinal Iron," *J. Pediat.*, **79**, 569–580.
104. Melhorn, D. K. and Gross, S. (1971), "Vitamin E-dependent Anemia in the Premature Infant: II. Relationship Between Gestational Age and Absorption of Vitamin E," *J. Pediat.*, **79**, 581–588.
105. Metcalf, D. and Moore, M. A. S. (1971), "Haemopoietic Cells," Vol. XXIV of *Frontiers of Biology*. Amsterdam: North-Holland Publishing Company.
106. Ministry of Health (1968), "Reports on Public Health and Medical Subjects, No. 118. A Pilot Survey of the Nutrition of Young Children in 1963," London: H.M.S.O.
107. Moe, P. J. (1965), "Normal Red Blood Picture During the First Three Years of Life," *Acta Pediat.*, **54**, 69–80.
108. Moe, P. J. (1967), "Umbilical Cord Blood and Capillary Blood in the Evaluation of Anemia in Erythroblastosis Fetalis," *Acta Pediat.*, **56**, 391–394.
109. Moore, M. A. S. and Metcalf, D. (1970), "Ontogeny of the Haemopoietic System: Yolk Sac Origin of *In Vivo* and *In vivo* Colony Forming Cells in the Developing Mouse Embryo," *Brit. J. Haemat.*, **18**, 279–296.
110. Moss, B. and Ingram, V. M. (1965), "The Repression and Induction by Thyroxin of Hemoglobin Synthesis During Amphibian Metamorphis," *Proc. nat. Acad. Sci.*, **54**, 967–974.
111. Moss, B. and Ingram, V. M. (1968), "Hemoglobin Synthesis During Amphibian Metamorphosis: II. Synthesis of Adult Hemoglobin Following Thyroxine Administration," *J. molec. Biol.*, **32**, 493–504.
112. Natvig, H., Vellar, O. D. and Andersen, J. (1967), 'Studies on Hemoglobin Values in Norway," *Acta med. Scand.*, **182**, 183–191.
113. Oettinger, L., Jr. and Mills, W. B. (1949), "Simultaneous Capillary and Venous Hemoglobin Determinations in Newborn Infant," *J. Pediat.*, **35**, 362.
114. Okuno, T. (1972), "Red Cell Size as Measured by the Coulter Model S," *J. clin. Path.*, **25**, 599–602.
115. Orzalesi, M. M. and Hay, W. W. (1971), "The Regulation of Oxygen Affinity of Fetal Blood," *Pediatrics.*, **48**, 857–864.
116. Osgood, E. E., Baker, R. L., Brownlee, I. E., Osgood, M. W., Ellis, D. M. and Cohen, W. (1939), "Total, Differential and Absolute Leukocyte Counts and Sedimentation Rates for Healthy Children. Standards for Children Eight to Fourteen Years of Age," *Amer. J. Dis. Child.*, **58**, 282–294.
117. Osgood, E. E., Baker, R. L., Brownlee, I. E., Osgood, M. W., Ellis, D. M. and Cohen, W. (1939), "Total, Differential and Absolute Leukocyte Counts and Sedimentation Rates of Children Four to Seven Years of Age," *Amer. J. Dis. Child.*, **58**, 61–70.
118. Oski, F. A. (1969), "Red Cell Metabolism in the Newborn Infant: V. Glycolytic Intermediates and Glycolytic Enzymes," Pediatrics, **44**, 84–91.
119. Oski, F. A. and Barness, L. A. (1967), "Vitamin E Deficiency: A previously Unrecognized Cause of Hemolytic Anemia in the Premature Infant," *J. Pediat.*, **70**, 211–220.
120. Oski, F. A. and Gottlieb, A. J. (1971), "The Interrelationship Between Red Blood Cell Metabolites, Hemoglobin, and the Oxygen-equilibrium Curve." in *Progress in Hematology*, Vol. VII, pp. 33–67 (E. B. Brown and C. V. Moore, eds.). London: William Heinemann Medical Books Ltd.
121. Oski, F. A. and Naiman, J. L. (1965), "Red Cell Metabolism in the Premature Infant: I. Adenosine Triphosphate Levels, Adenosine Triphosphate Stability and Glucose Consumption," *Pediatrics*, **36**, 104–112.
122. Oski, F. A. and Naiman, J. L. (1972), *Hematologic Problems in the Newborn*. Philadelphia: E. B. Saunders Co.
123. Owen, G. M., Nelson, C. E. and Garry, P. J. (1970), "Nutritional Status of Preschool Children: Hemoglobin, Hematocrit and Plasma Iron Values," *J. Pediat.*, **76**, 761–763.
124. Pataryas, H. A. and Stamatoyannopoulos, G. (1972), "Hemoglobins in Human Fetuses: Evidence for Adult Hemoglobin Production After the 11th Gestational Week," *Blood*, **39**, 688–696.
125. Pearson, H. A. and Vertrees, K. M. (1961), "Site of Binding of Chromium-51 to Haemoglobin," *Nature*, **189**, 1019–1020.
126. Pembrey, M. E. and Weatherall, D. J. (1971), "Maternal Synthesis of Haemoglobin F in Pregnancy," *Brit. J. Haemat.*, **21**, 355.
127. Playfair, J. H. L., Wolfendale, M. R. and Kay, H. E. M. (1963), "The Leucocytes of Peripheral Blood in the Human Foetus," *Brit. J. Haemat.*, **9**, 336–344.
128. Preston, A. E. (1964), "The Plasma Concentration of Factor VIII in the Normal Population: I. Mothers and Babies at Birth," *Brit. J. Haemat.*, **10**, 110–114.
129. Pritchard, R. W. and Vann, R. L. (1954), "Congenital Afibrinogenemia; Report of a Child Without Fibrinogen and Review of Literature," *Amer. J. Dis. Child.*, **88**, 703–710.
130. Race, R. R. and Sanger, R. (1968), *Blood Groups in Man*. Blackwell Scientific Publications.

131. Roberts, J. T., Gray, O. P. and Bloom, A. L. (1966), "An Abnormality of the Thrombin-fibrinogen Reaction in the Newborn," *Acta paediat. Stokh.*, **55,** 148–152.
132. Roberts, P. M., Arrowsmith, D. E., Rau, S. M. and Monk-Jones, M. E. (1969), "Folate Status of Premature Infants," *Arch. Dis. Childh.*, **44,** 637–642.
133. Rooth, G. and Sjöstedt, S. (1957), "Haemoglobin in Cord Blood in Normal and Prolonged Pregnancy," *Arch. Dis. Childh.*, **32,** 91–92.
134. Rosenberg, M. (1969), "Fetal Hematopoiesis—Case Report," *Blood*, **33,** 66–78.
135. Ross, J. D. and Desforges, J. F. (1959), "Reduction of Methemoglobin by Erythrocytes from Cord Blood," *Pediatrics*, **23,** 718–726.
136. Schroeder, W. A. and Huisman, T. H. J. (1970), "Nonallelic Structural Genes and Hemoglobin Synthesis," pp. 26–33, *XIII International Congress of Haematology, Plenary Sessions*. Munich: J. F. Lehmanns Verlag.
137. Schroeder, W. A., Huisman, T. H. J., Shelton, J. R., Shelton, J. B., Kleihauer, E. F., Dozy, A. M. and Robberson, B. (1968), "Evidence for Multiple Structural Genes for the γ-chain of Human Fetal Hemoglobin," *Proc. nat. Acad. Sci. U.S.A.*, **60,** 537–544.
138. Sjölin, S. (1954), "The Resistance of Red Cells *In Vitro*," *Acta Paediat.*, **43,** 390–392.
139. Sjölin, S. and Wranne, L. (1968), "Iron Requirements During Infancy and Childhood," in *Symposia of the Swedish Nutrition Foundation: VI. Occurrence, Causes and Prevention of Nutritional Anaemias* (G. Blix, ed.). Uppsala: Almquist and Wikesll.
140. Smith, C. A., Cherry, R. B., Maletskos, C. J., Gibson, J. G., Roby, C. C., Caton, W. L. and Reid, D. E. (1955), "Persistence and Utilization of Maternal Iron for Blood Formation During Infancy," *J. clin. Invest.*, **34,** 1391–1402.
141. Stormorken, H. and Owren, P. A. (1971), "Physiopathology of Hemostasis," *Semin. Hematol.*, **8,** 3–29.
142. Strauss, M. B. (1933), "Anemia of Infancy from Maternal Iron Deficiency in Pregnancy," *J. clin. Invest.*, **12,** 345–353.
143. Sugarman, H. F., Davidson, D. T., Vibul, S., Delivoria-Papadopoulos, M., Miller, L. D. and Oski, F. A. (1970), "The Basis of Defective Oxygen Delivery from Stored Blood," *Surg. Gynec. Obstet.*, **131,** 733–741.
144. Sullivan, L. W., Luhby, A. L. and Streiff, R. R. (1966), "Studies of the Daily Requirement for Folic Acid in Infants and the Etiology of Folate Deficiency in Goat's Milk Megaloblastic Anemia," *Amer. J. clin. Nutr.*, **18,** 311.
145. Sutherland, J. M., Glueck, H. I. and Gleser, G. (1967), "Haemorrhagic Disease of the Newborn: Breast Feeding as a Necessary Factor in Pathogenesis," *Amer. J. Dis. Child.*, **113,** 524–533.
146. Szeinberg, A., Ramot, B., Sheba, C., Adam, A., Halbrecht, I., Rikover, M., Wishnievsky, S. and Rabau, E. (1958), "Glutathione Metabolism in Cord and Newborn Infant Blood," *J. clin. Invest.*, **37,** 1436–1441.
147. Takano, K. and Miller, J. R. (1972), "ABO Incompatibility as a Cause of Spontaneous Abortion: Evidence from Abortuses," *J. med. Genet.*, **9,** 144–150.
148. Thomaidis, T., Agathopoulos, A. and Matsaniotis, N. (1969), "Natural Isohemagglutinin Production by the Fetus," *J. Pediat.*, **74,** 39–48.
149. Thomas, D. B. and Yoffey, J. M. (1962), "Human Foetal Haemopoeisis: I. The Cellular Composition of Foetal Blood," *Brit. J. Haemat.*, **8,** 290–295.
150. Thomas, D. B. and Yoffey, J. M. (1964), "Human Foetal Haematopoiesis: II. Hepatic Haematopoiesis in the Human Foetus," *Brit. J. Hamat.*, **10,** 193–197.
151. Thomas, E. D., Lochte, H. L., Greenhough, W. B. and Whales, M. (1960), "*In vitro* Synthesis of Foetal and Adult Haemoglobin in Foetal Haemopoietic Tissues," *Nature*, **185,** 396–397.
152. Toivanen, P. and Hirvonen, T. (1969), "Fetal Development of Red-cell Antigens K, k, Lu^a, Lu^b, Fy^a, Fy^b, Vel and Xg^a," *Scand. J. Haemat.*, **6,** 49–55.
153. Turnbull, E. P. N. and Walker, J. (1955), "Haemoglobin and Red Cells in the Human Foetus," *Arch. Dis. Childh.*, **30,** 102–110.
154. Usher, R., Shephard, M. and Lind, J. (1963), "The Blood Volume of the Newborn Infant and Placental Transfusion," *Acta paediat.*, **52,** 497–512.
155. Valeri, C. R. and Hirsch, N. M. (1969), "Restoration *In Vitro* of Erythrocyte Adenosine Triphosphate, 2,3-disphosphoglycerate, Potassium Ion, and Sodium Ion Concentrations. Following the Transfusion of Acid-citrate-dextrose-stored Human Red Blood Cells," *J. Lab. clin. Med.*, **73,** 722–733.
156. Vanier, T. M. and Tyas, J. F. (1966), "Folic Aci d Status in Normal Infants During the First Year of life," *Arch.* Dis. *Childh.*, **41,** 658–665.
157. Vanier, T. M. and Tyas, J. F. (1967), "Folic Acid Status in Premature Infants," *Arch. Dis. Childh.*, **42,** 57–61.
158. Walker, J. L. and Turnbull, E. P. N. (1953), "Haemoglobin and Red Cells in the Human Fetus and Their Relation to the Oxygen Content of the Blood in the Vessels of the Umbilical Cord," *Lancet*, **ii,** 312–318.
159. Welsh, P. N. (1972), "The Effects of Collagen and Kaolin on the Intrinsic coagulant Activity of Platelets," *Brit. J. Haemat.*, **22,** 393–405.
160. Walsh, R. J., Arnold, B. J., Lancaster, H. O., Coote, M. A. and Cotter, H. (1953), "A Study of Haemoglobin Values in New South Wales," Special Report No. 5 of the National Health and Medical Research Council, Canberra.
161. Wegelius, R. (1948), "On Changes in Peripheral Blood Picture of Newborn Infant Immediately After Birth," *Acta paediat. Stokh.*, **35,** 1–4.
162. Whaun, J. M. and Oski, F. A. (1970), "Relation of Red Blood Cell Glutathione Peroxidase to Neonatal Jaundice," *J. Pediat.*, **76,** 555–560.
163. Wiggert, B. O. and Villee C. A. (1964), "Multiple Molecular Forms of Malic and Lactic Dehydrogenase During Development," Biol. Chem., **239,** 444–448.
164. Wilson, M. G., Schroeder, W. A., Graves, D. A. and Kach, V. D. (1967), "Haemoglobin Variations in D-trisomy Syndrome," *New Engl. J. Med.*, **277,** 953.
165. Wintrobe, M. M. (1967), *Clinical hematology*. Philadelphia: Lea and Febinger.
166. Wintrobe, M. M. and Shumaker, H. B. (1936), "Erythrocyte Studies in the Mammalian Fetus and Newborn," *Amer. J. Anat.*, **58,** 313–328.
167. Witt, I., Muller, H. and Künzer, W. (1969), "Evidence for the Existence of Foetal Fibrinogen," *Thromb. Diath. Haemorrh.*, **22,** 101–109.
168. Xanthou, M. (1970), "Leucocyte Blood Picture in Healthy Full-term and Premature Babies During Neonatal Period," *Arch. Dis. Childh.*, **45,** 242–249.
169. Yao, A. C., Moinian, M. and Lind, J. (1969), "Distribution of Blood Between Infant and Placenta After Birth," *Lancet*, **ii,** 871–873.
170. Youssef, A. and Barkhan, P. (1968), "Release of Platelet Factor 4 by Adenosine Diphosphate and Other Platelet-aggregating Agents. *Brit. med. J.*, **1,** 746–747.
171. Zilliacus, H., Ottelin, A. M. and Mattsson, T. (1966), "Blood Clotting and Fibrinolysis in Human Foetuses," *Biol. Neonat.*, **10,** 108–112.
172. Zinkham, W. H. (1959), "An *In Vitro* Abnormality of Glutathione Metabolism in Erythrocytes from Normal Newborns: Mechanism and Clinical Significance," *Pediatrics*, **23,** 18–32.
173. Zipursky, A. (1965), "The Erythrocytes of the Newborn Infant," *Semin. Haematol.*, **2,** 167–203.

19. THE DEVELOPMENT OF LYMPHOID TISSUES AND IMMUNITY

M. ADINOLFI

The immunological system has two fundamental functions which appear to be under the control of two different but interacting lymphoid systems present in all vertebrates. The first is that of protecting the body against invading micro-organisms by the synthesis of specific serum antibodies; the second function, exerted by a cell-mediated mechanism of immunity, is responsible for the resistance to certain bacterial, mycotic and viral infections, and for the "surveillance" of aberrant cell differentiation in the individual itself.[27]

Other serum proteins, such as the components of complement, lysozyme and interferon, also play to a various degree prominent roles in the mechanism of immunological defence.

During the past decade a considerable amount of new information has been accumulated on the development of acquired immunity and it is now apparent that in man both humoral and cellular immunity are well developed before birth.[8] It has also been shown that there are considerable differences in the way the immune response matures in various species.[182] In mice and rats, for example, immune reactions are relatively immature even in the newborn. In the lamb, on the other hand, some degree of immunological competence is achieved early during fetal life.[171]

The purpose of this chapter is to review the evidence for the fetal synthesis of immunoglobulins, the various components of complement, lysozyme, and interferon, and for the development of cell-mediated immunity in man. Similar studies in other mammals will be briefly mentioned only when relevant to the human development of immunological competence.

ONTOGENY OF HUMORAL AND CELL-MEDIATED IMMUNITY

(a) Structure and Biological Properties of Human Immunoglobulins

Five different classes of immunoglobulins have been identified in man on the basis of the discrete physico-chemical properties and distinct antigenic specificities associated with the polypeptide chains forming these molecules.[44,43] In order of relative concentration in serum, these five classes are: γG, γA, γM, γD and γE globulins. By virtue of subtle antigenic differences, four subclasses of γG (γG1, γG2, γG3 and γG4), two subclasses of γA and two subclasses of γM have been recognized so far (Table 1).

A structural model of immunoglobulin molecules was proposed by Porter.[44] According to it, immunoglobulins consist of a basic unit comprising two pairs of polypeptide chains, named, according to their molecular weight, "heavy" and "light" chains. The unit of each immunoglobulin molecule is formed by two identical heavy and two identical light chains; the heavy chains (γ, α, μ, δ and ε) confer upon the molecule its class designation (γG, γA,

TABLE 1

SOME PROPERTIES OF FIVE CLASSES OF HUMAN IMMUNOGLOBULINS

Terminology	γG(IgG)	γA(IgA)	γM(IgM)	γD(IgD)	γE(IgE)
Serum concentration (1) mg./100 ml.	1158 ± 305	200 ± 61	99 ± 27	0·3 to 40	248 ng./ml.
Molecular weight	150,000	150,000 to 400,000	900,000	150,000	200,000
Coefficient of sedimentation	7S	7S, 11S	19S	7S	8S
Crosses the placenta?	Yes	No	No	No	No
Light chains	κ, λ	κ, λ	κ, λ	κ, λ	κ, λ
Heavy chains	γ	α	μ	δ	ε
Sub-classes known	4	2	2		
Molecular formula	$\gamma_2\kappa_2$ $\gamma_2\lambda_2$	$(\alpha_2\kappa_2)n$T $(\alpha_2\lambda_2)n$T	$(\mu_2\kappa_2)5$ $(\mu_2\lambda_2)5$	$\delta_2\kappa_2$ $\delta_2\lambda_2$	$\varepsilon_2\kappa_2$ $\varepsilon_2\lambda_2$
Antibody activity	Yes	Yes	Yes		Yes
Complement fixation	Yes	No	Yes		

(1) References quoted in the text.

γM, γD, γE); the light chains are in contrast common to all immunoglobulins and exist in two forms, κ and λ (Fig. 1).

The largest part of the circulating antibodies is formed by γG globulins with a molecular weight near 150,000 and a coefficient of sedimentation between 6·6S and 7S (Table 1). In normal sera the ratio between γG globulins associated with κ or λ chains is near 65 to 35.[120,62,193] The concentration in serum of the four subclasses of γG is shown in Table 2. Antigenic analysis and studies of peptide maps have shown that γ1, γ2 and γ3 chains are closely related, while γ4 shows the largest degree of differences.[81] There is evidence that γG types differ in their biological properties;

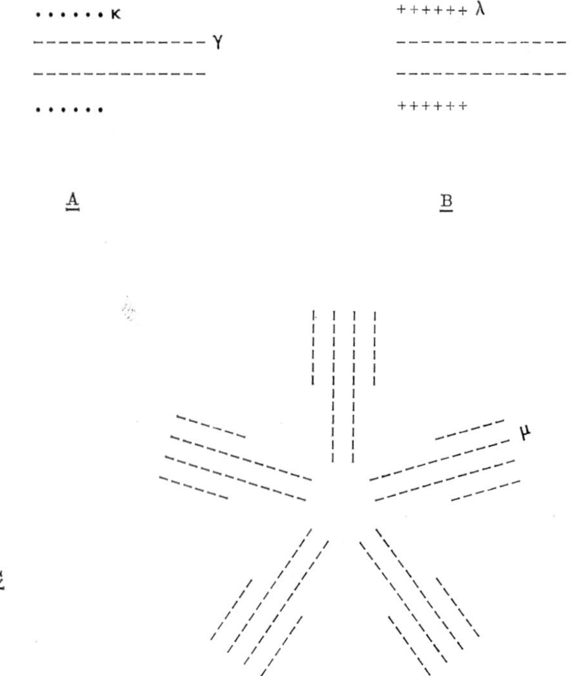

FIG. 1. γG molecules (A and B) are formed by two identica heavy chains (γ) and two light chains (κ or λ); γM molecules (C) are formed by five subunits each containing two heavy chains (μ) and two light chains common to all immunoglobulins.

for example with regard to skin attachment in heterologous species[192] and to their transfer through the human placenta.[91,213] Specific antibodies may be associated with predominantly one γG type; thus anti-A isoagglutinins and anti-tetanus are predominantly γG1, while antibodies to dextran, levan and techoic acid are mainly γG2.[220]

γA globulins constitute about 20 per cent of the total immunoglobulins in serum. Two major subclasses, γA1 and γA2, have been recognized. The basic structure of γA molecules comprises two heavy α chains and two light chains (κ or λ). The main component of serum γA has a sedimentation constant of approximately 7S but additional components ranging from 9S to 15S are present. Colostrum and parotid and bronchial secretions are rich in γA globulins. The sedimentation constant of γA in secretions is predominantly 11S and this exocrine γA is associated with an antigenically distinct fragment having a molecular weight of 60,000 (transport or T-piece) which links two four-chain units.[43,200] Antibodies against bacteria, viruses and blood group antigens associated with γA have been detected in serum and secretions.[10,111,160,199]

It is generally accepted that secretory γA antibodies present in colostrum, milk, saliva, intestinal and bronchial fluids serve to protect the mucosal surfaces from undesirable micro-organisms; however the mechanisms whereby this class of immunoglobulins exerts its protective function is still poorly understood. Several studies have been published which indicate that γA antibodies fail to lyse cells and bacteria in presence of complement (C),[10,93,100,206] but the question of the interaction of γA with components of complement remains still open, since secretory γA globulins have been shown to lyse bacteria in presence of C and lysozyme[7] and to have opsonizing activity in presence of C.[105]

About 8 per cent of the total immunoglobulins are γM. These molecules have a coefficient of sedimentation of 19S. Treatment of γM antibodies with mild reducing agents at neutral pH dissociates them into five sub-units; each sub-unit being formed by two heavy (μ) and two light chains (Fig. 1). The agglutination and precipitation activities of γM antibodies disappear following their dissociation by reducing agents,[11,85] although the sub-units retain their ability to combine with the antigens.[101,144] Several specific antibodies are associated with γM globulins and some of these, including anti-I cold agglutinins, anti-Lewis and anti-D isoagglutinins, antibodies to the O antigen of Salmonella, and the rheumatoid factors, are almost entirely confined to γM globulins.[11,73,131,220]

γD globulins are present in normal sera in a concentration between 2·3 and 40 mg./ml.[164] Their relationship to immunoglobulins has been firmly established on the basis of "structural" similarities with this group of proteins. In fact, γD molecules are formed by two heavy (δ) chains and two light chains which are similar to those present in other classes of immunoglobulins.

Studies of the nature of the skin-sensitizing antibodies and myeloma proteins have led to the identification of a new class of immunoglobulins, γE.[21,98,99,103] The concentration of γE globulin in serum of normal adults ranges between 66 and 1,830 ng./ml. (mean 248 ng./ml.) Levels are increased in about 50 per cent of patients with allergic diseases.[21] In studies of immediate-type hypersensitivity, the binding activity of γE globulins for an allergen in human sera correlates with the ability of these sera to sensitize passively human skin to that allergen. Most significantly, γE is able to inhibit completely passive skin sensitization by reaginic antibody (Prausnitz-Kustner reaction).[184]

The heterogeneity of immunoglobulins is also due to genetic, *allotypic*, differences in the primary structure of the heavy and light chains; the terms *allotypic* therefore designates those immunoglobulins which are controlled by allelic genes at one locus and are different in various groups of individuals within a species.[55,147]

The discovery of the Gm groups provided the first evidence of the inheritance of allotypic human γG globulins. In 1956, Grubb[82] noticed that human red cells (Rh+), sensitized with some incomplete antibodies (anti-Rh), were agglutinated by certain sera from patients with rheumatoid arthritis and that this agglutination was inhibited by approximately 60 per cent of normal sera. The ability of these sera, Gm (a+), to inhibit the agglutination was found to be inherited as an autosomal dominant trait. In 1959, Harboe[89] described an additional marker, Gm(b) and since then about thirty more Gm specificities have been discovered.[83,139] The Gm markers are all related to γG globulins. During the last few years, increasing attention has been paid to the distribution of the Gm markers between the various sub-classes of γG molecules and to their localization on different portions of γ chains. These studies have revealed that some Gm allotypic specificities are associated with one sub-class of γG globulin, while others, are expressed only in other sub-classes (Table 2). For example Gm(a), Gm(x) and Gm(f) are associated with γG1 globulins; Gm(b^1), Gm(b^3) and Gm(g) are associated with γG3 globulins and Gm(n) is associated with γG2.[83,110,121,139,]

TABLE 2

SUBCLASSES OF γG GLOBULINS AND Gm FACTORS (*)

Nomenclature	*Percentage Total γG*	*Type κ %*	*Type λ %*	*Gm Factors*
γG1	77	54·5	22·5	a, x, f, z
γG2	11	5·8	5·2	n
γG3	9	4·7	4·2	b, c, g
γG4	3	2·6	0·5	
		67·6	32·4	

(*) References quoted in the text.

Genetic studies of families and populations have shown that the Gm systems are inherited in certain fixed combinations and that each combination behaves as a unit of inheritance. There are good grounds for thinking that the structural genes controlling the various γG globulin heavy chains are closely linked. In fact, recombination of Gm specificities is seldom observed.[83,139]

Allotypic variants of α chains have now been discovered; and on the basis of family studies, it has been possible to establish that the structural genes controlling α polypeptide chains are linked to the structural genes controlling γ heavy chains.[112]

Allotypic variants of κ chains have also been demonstrated; they are referred to as Inv(1), Inv(2) and Inv(3). Inv antigens are inherited as autosomal co-dominant traits and the respective genes belong to one cistron.[83,139,163] Since the Inv antigens are associated with κ chains, they are present in all classes of immunoglobulins.

The genetic mechanism by which the synthesis of the various isotypic and allotypic immunoglobulins is controlled at cellular level is not yet known.

From studies of human myeloma proteins and the analysis of isolated antibodies, it appears that each immunoglobulin-producing cell synthesizes only one class or sub-class of immunoglobulins and that hybrid molecules are not formed *in vivo*. Studies using immunofluorescence have confirmed and extended these observations with the demonstration that single cells produce only one type of light and one type of heavy chain.[22,37,152] On the assumption that the synthesis at a particular polypeptide chain is controlled by a single gene, these observations suggest that only one structural gene controlling the light chains and one gene controlling the synthesis of the constant part of the heavy chains are active in each cell, the loci controlling the production of other isotypic molecules being inactive.

This restriction is extended to the products of allelic genes; in fact, clones of myeloma cells produce only one genetic type of immunoglobulin molecule in heterozygous individuals. Isolated human antibodies show similar restrictions[17] but this is by no means universal.

Recent studies suggest that such restrictions are probably limited to cells at a late stage of differentiation with respect to the regulation of heavy chain genes. Using tissue cultures of human haematopoietic origin, Takahashi and his colleagues[188b] have observed the co-existence of two different heavy chains in individual cells of five cell lines out of twenty-seven studied. The two categories of cells, one producing only one type of heavy chain and the second producing at least two heavy chains, seem to represent lymphoblasts at different stages of differentiation.

Since the product of only one allele at one locus is synthesized by a mature plasma cell that is genetically capable of producing several isotypic and allotypic immunoglobulins, it would appear that the genetic mechanisms controlling the formation of immunoglobulins are different from those controlling the synthesis of other proteins. For example, with haemoglobin, one reticulocyte synthesizes several different haemoglobins (e.g. HbA, HbA_2 and HbF), and, if a subject is heterozygous, each reticulocyte produces the products of both alleles.

Immunoglobulin synthesis constitutes the only known example of complete or partial inactivation of one or the other of a pair of autosomal allelic genes.

(b) Transfer of Immunoglobulins Through the Placenta

The levels of γG globulins in cord sera are similar or slightly higher than those observed in the corresponding maternal samples. The major part of γG molecules present in the newborn is derived from the maternal circulation; in fact, maternal γG antibodies against red cells, bacteria and viruses are readily detected in cord sera.[52,70,95,207a,216] At about the third month of gestation traces of γG globulins are already present in fetal sera so that even at this stage, fetal Rh(+) red cells may show a positive direct anti-γG globulin test due to the presence of maternal incomplete anti-Rh antibodies.[130] Furthermore, soon after the demonstration of the genetic polymorphism of γG globulins, it was observed that γG globulins present in newborn sera carried genetic markers (Gm) similar to those present in the maternal sera, irrespective of the genotype of the infants[83,84,115] (Table 3).

The published data on the Gm and Inv phenotypes in pairs of maternal and newborn sera show that these genetic markers are generally concordant. There are no recorded exceptions for Gm(x) and Gm(c) or Inv(1) and Inv(3). In a few instances Gm(a) and Gm(b) and Gm(e) were detected

TABLE 3

Gm(a) FACTOR IN MATERNAL SERUM AND IN SAMPLES OBTAINED FROM THE CORRESPONDING INFANT AT BIRTH AND AT 1 YEAR OF AGE

Serum	Gm Combination 1	2	3	4
Maternal	Gm(a+)	Gm(a+)	Gm(a−)	Gm(a−)
Infant at birth	Gm(a+)	Gm(a+)	Gm(a−)	Gm(a−)
Infant 1 year old	Gm(a−)	Gm(a+)	Gm(a+)	Gm(a−)

The maternal Gm factors present in the newborn serum are slowly replaced by the child's Gm molecules.

in maternal samples and yet were absent in the corresponding cord sera.[83]

The instances where the child contains Gm factors not present in the maternal serum are examples of fetal production of γG globulins as will be discussed later on.

Recently, selective transfer of γG subclasses through the human placenta has been observed.[213] Thus, while the concentrations of γG1, γG3 and γG4 are similar in maternal and cord samples, the mean level of γG2 globulins is lower in newborn sera than in maternal blood. However, the low concentration of γG2 in cord samples does not seem to affect the Gm grouping of this subclass of immunoglobulins; in fact in a group of twenty-nine pairs of samples, similar Gm(n) types were detected in newborn sera and the corresponding maternal blood.[124]

Investigations using papain fragments of rabbit γG labelled with ^{131}I, have, suggested that the chemical configuration essential for the transmission of γG to the fetus is located in the Fc fragment. This explains why diphtheria antitoxin prepared in the horse and treated with pepsin fails to cross the human placenta.[90]

The other four classes of immunoglobulins do not cross the human placenta; in fact maternal antibodies associated with γM and γA globulins are absent in cord sera and γD globulins have not been detected in newborn blood.[164] γE are present in normal cord sera, but since maternal reaginic antibodies do not cross the placenta and no correlation has been observed between the levels of γE in pairs of maternal and cord samples it appears this class of immunoglobulins can be produced during fetal life.[21]

(c) The Development of Lymphoid Tissues

At stages of fetal growth when the spleen and the lymph nodes are still poorly developed, the thymus appears to be an active lymphoid organ. In man, lymphopoiesis in the thymus has been observed in 35 mm.-long fetuses[76,86,87,107] (Fig. 2). The thymus, which develops from the ectoderm of the third branchial cleft, achieves its greatest size, in relation to body weight, at birth and thereafter declines.[88,106] Morphologically two major cell populations are present in the thymic tissues, the thymocytes, which resemble small lymphocytes, and the epithelial cell . In human fetuses about three months old, the thymic cortex is mostly composed of thymocytes, while the medulla contains the Hassall's corpuscles and more epithelial cells and blood cells than the cortex. Lymphopoiesis in the thymus, unlike lymphopoiesis elsewhere, is antigen-independent and very intense. In the fetus the proliferative activity of lymphoid cells is absent or low in all lymphoid tissues with the exception of the thymus.[126]

The origin of thymocytes during development is still controversial.[18,19,127,133,218] Recent studies by Moore,

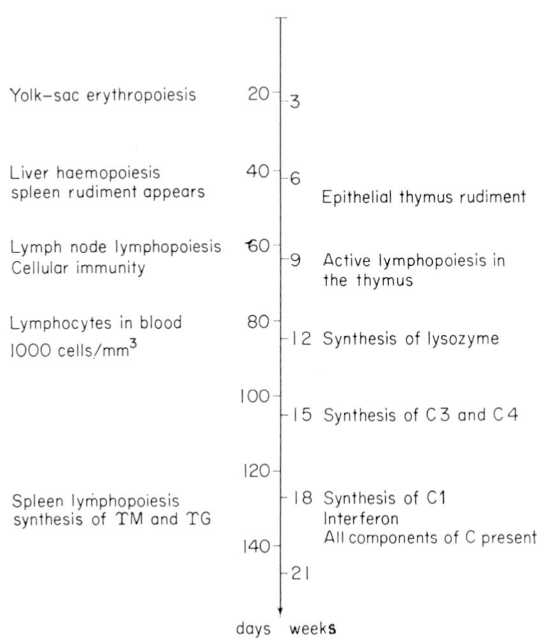

FIG. 2. Embryological events leading to the synthesis of immunoglobulins, components of lysozyme and interferon in man.

Owen and Metcalf[127,132,133] appear to confirm that thymocytes are derived from extrinsic cells which migrate into the primitive epithelial anlage at an early stage.[24,86,126,143] Using chromosome marker and histological techniques in combination with parabiosis and transplantation procedures, inflow of blood-derived stem cells into the chick embryo thymic rudiment was observed at any early stage of development. The primary source of stem cells was the area vasculosa of the yolk-sac.[133]

A similar process of cell migration, culminating in the development of the lymphoid system, has also been suggested in mice.[127,132] The embryological events leading to the dissemination of multi-potent cells to various target organs, and their differentiation at varying time during development, may be summarized as follows (Fig. 3): (1) the yolk sac is the primitive source of germ cells, erythroid and lymphoid cells in amniotes: (2) the yolk sac cells migrate to various organs and their differentiation into specific cell types results from interaction with inductive tissues; (3) release and relocation of cells permit new interactions between the new diversified cell types and result in the production of new stable cell lines capable of clonal proliferation.[19,127]

Interactions between the thymus derived cells (T cells) and the liver and bone marrow derived cells (B cells) is required for at least some of the immunological processes leading to antibody formation.[39,128,129,134,190]

Recently, Dwyer and MacKay[57] have observed that the thymuses of human fetuses between 20 and 22 weeks old contain antigen-binding thymocytes detectable after exposing the cells to radioiodine-labelled flagellin from *Salmonella adelaide* and *S. waycross*. The number of antigen-binding thymocytes was higher in fetal thymus than in postnatal and adult thymus. Cells with the ability to recognize self antigens have been demonstrated in the thymus of neonatal mice. This activity was found to increase sharply after birth, to decline within the first week of life and to be lost in adult animals.[97]

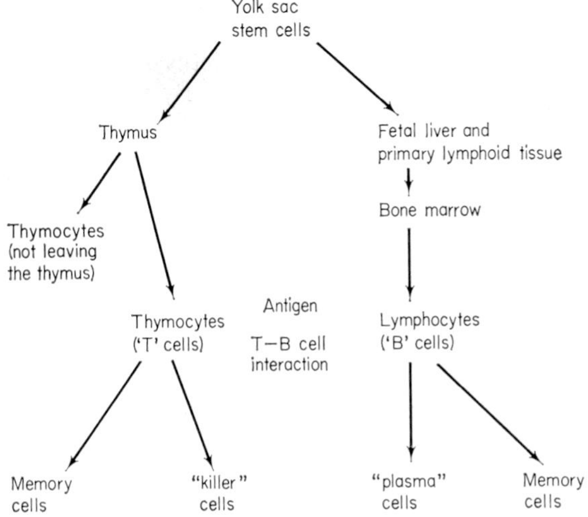

FIG. 3. Migration of yolk-sac cells and their differentiation into thymocytes (T) and bone marrow derived cells (B).

These findings suggest that the fetal thymus may plan an important role in the generation and the establishment of the diversity of antibody patterns, and that for a short time during immunological development, thymocytes are capable of recognizing both self and non-self antigens and therefore of inducing tolerance to self-antigens.

The first data on the development of lymph nodes in the human fetus can be traced back to 1881 when Chieritz[38] described the appearance of these tissues in fetuses about three months old; well developed lymph nodes were noticed by Ehrich[58] and Helleman[42] in fetuses at mid-gestation.

Gilmour,[76] in a detailed report on the development of erythropoietic tissue, observed small nodules showing active lymphopoiesis in the connective tissue of the neck of fetuses 25 and 28 mm. long. At this stage of gestation a few lymphocytes also appeared in the circulation. Definite lymph nodes were noticed in fetuses 48 mm. long, when lymphocytes were found inside the lymph vessels and in bone marrow. Lymphocyte counts near 1,000 cells/mm.^{3} have been observed in fetuses about 12 weeks old. The level of lymphocytes in fetal blood reaches values between 5,000 and 10,000 cells/mm.^{3} in fetuses about 24 weeks old.[155]

The spleen of early fetuses does not produce red cells or lymphocytes. Lymphopoiesis does not start until the fetus is about five months old.[76,165]

Other tissues appear to have lymphopoietic potentialities during life *in utero*. The presence of potential immunologically competent cells in fetal liver has been repeatedly demonstrated.[53,190,202,203]

The maturation of fetal liver cells is dependent upon intact thymic function. Fetal liver cells from mice have been shown to produce immunoglobulins when injected into sublethally irradiated recipients. The presence of the thymus is essential for the production of specific antibodies.[203] Fetal liver cells, cultured in combination with thymus for three days, have been shown to acquire immunological competence, as judged by the induction of splenomegaly on explants of neonatal spleen fragments. The same cells did not possess this capacity when cultured in the absence of thymic cells.

A high percentage of donor cells in bone marrow, spleen, thymus and lymph nodes has been observed in anaemic mice injected at birth with liver cells from normal fetal mice. It is of interest that, as judged by histochemical studies, granulopoiesis in the treated mice was completely taken over by the donor cells.[167]

The placenta is another tissue which should be considered as potentially immunocompetent. There is nothing in the morphology of the normal human placenta that would suggest that this tissue is capable of immunological function. Plasma cells have been observed only in placental tissue from women whose pregnancies were complicated by infections.

Direct attempts to demonstrate the synthesis of immunoglobulins by human placenta using *in vitro* cultures have been unsuccessful.[49a,208] However, Dancis *et al.*[49a] have observed that mouse placental cells, injected into thymectomized, newborn and irradiated adult mice, proliferate as haemopoietic and lymphopoietic cells.

(d) Synthesis of Immunoglobulins During Fetal Life

The concentration of γG globulins, estimated in infants bled at intervals soon after birth, appears to decrease during the first two months of life. For many years this phenomenon has been interpreted as evidence for the slow catabolism of maternal γG molecules which are not replaced by similar proteins produced by the infant.[52,77,80,145,175] However, as early as 1959 Trevorrow[201] showed that if the dilution of serum proteins, due to the expanding plasma volume, is taken into account, the amount of immunoglobulins during the first month of life is relatively constant. On the basis of these observations, Trevorrow stated that immunoglobulins are synthesized during life *in utero* in the course of normal pregnancies.

The apparent absence of plasma cells in the bone marrow and lymphatic tissue of human fetuses has also been used as evidence to argue that there is no synthesis of immunoglobulins during fetal life.[23,26] However, recent studies indicate that plasma cells are present in fetal tissue stained with methyl-green pyronin or studied using immunofluorescence techniques.[209]

The low frequency of plasma cells in normal human fetuses during the last third of gestation seems to be the result of the absence of environmental stimulation, rather than the cause of an inefficient antibody response. In fact, in pathological conditions the human fetus may respond to antigenic stimulation by the proliferation of plasma cells after the sixth month of gestation.

In 1904, Porcile observed plasma cells in the liver of two newborns with congenital syphilis. Subsequently, diffuse fibrosis accompanied by plasma cell infiltration has been observed also in lung, pancreas, spleen and heart of newborns with congenital syphilis. Plasma cells have also been detected in fetuses with toxoplasmosis.[159,173]

Following intrauterine infections, specific antibodies and high levels of γM globulins have been detected in cord sera. In congenital rubella, γM antibodies have been found in newborn sera.[14] In some congenital infections the presence of γM antibodies is associated with a relative deficiency of

TABLE 4

DATA SUPPORTING THE ANTENATAL SYNTHESIS OF IMMUNOGLOBULINS*

1. Presence in *normal cord sera* of γM antibodies not derived from the maternal circulation:
   (a) anti-λ chain determinants (frequent)
   (b) anti-I cold agglutinins (frequent)
   (c) anti-trypsinized human red cells (frequent)
   (d) anti-A and anti-B agglutinins (occasional)
   (e) antibodies against gram-negative bacteria and Listeria (occasional)
2. Presence in *normal cord sera* of γG variants absent in the mother and synthesized by the fetus under the control of paternal genes; evidence that the mother produces anti-bodies against Gm specificities synthesized by the fetus.
3. *In vitro* synthesis of γM and γG globulins using fetal spleen and lymph nodes.
4. Presence of antibodies against viruses and bacteria in *infants with congenital infections.*
5. Delayed type hypersensitivity in premature newborns.

* References are quoted in the text.

γG synthesis during early life.[183] Elevated levels of γM globulins have been detected in infants with cytomegalic inclusion disease, in whom specific antibody and virus were also detected,[117] in congenital infection with *Toxoplasma Gondii*[161] and in one or two cases of intrauterine herpes simplex infection.[169] The correlation between intrauterine infection and raised γM levels has been repeatedly confirmed.[15,186]

Antibodies associated with γM globulin have also been detected in normal newborns (Table 4). A high percentage of cord sera contain antibodies directed against antigenic determinants located on λ chains[60] and antibodies which cause reversible agglutination of trypsinized red cells.[124] Anti-I cold agglutinins, usually present in normal adult sera, have been found in newborn sera.[2] These antibodies, which are associated with γM globulins, are present in cord sera independently of their presence in the corresponding maternal blood. Recently, anti-A and anti-B agglutinins which could not have been derived from the maternal circulation have been detected in a percentage of cord sera;[36,195,198] γM antibodies against Listeria monocytogenes and gram negative bacteria have been occasionally detected in healthy neonates.[42,74]

Immunoglobulin molecules which behave as 7S proteins, as judged by gel filtration, but are antigenically related to γM globulins, have also been found in human cord sera.[149] It is of interest that 7S γM globulins have been observed in the lower vertebrates.[41]

The synthesis of γG during life *in utero* has been confirmed by detecting in cord sera γG molecules with genetic markers absent in the maternal serum. As mentioned previously, several allotypic variants of human γG globulins have been discovered in the past few years. If one of these variants absent in the maternal serum is found in the newborn circulation, the inference would be that this type of immunoglobulin is produced by the fetus under the control of a gene inherited from the father. By means of highly specific antisera against allotypic γG molecules, Gm specificities that were not present in maternal serum, have been detected in newborn samples.[121,122,211]

The demonstration that during normal pregnancy some mothers produce anti-Gm antibodies confirmed that the normal human fetus is capable of producing γG globulins with antigenic determinants inherited from the father. These molecules cross the placenta and induce the synthesis maternal anti-Gm.[72]

Antibodies directed against Gm or Inv factors have been detected in 4·1 per cent of pregnant women.[111b] Experimental work in rabbits and mice has shown that maternal antibodies against a specific genetic determinant of the fetal immunoglobulins may cross the placenta and inhibit the formation of that type of immunoglobulin in the offspring.[171] In an extensive investigation Thom and McKay[194] could not detect a relationship between the presence of anti-Gm and anti-Inv antibodies in pregnant women and the concentration of various subclasses of γG in their infants at the age of six months.

Information about the onset of the synthesis of γG and γM during fetal life has been obtained using *in vitro* cultures and immunoflorescence.[209]

The analysis by immunoelectrophoresis and autoradiography of the culture fluids from spleen tissue has shown that the human fetus is capable of producing γG and γM globulins after the twentieth week of gestation and that these proteins are synthesized mainly in the spleen. Immunoflorescent staining of the spleen tissue demonstrated that medium-sized and large lymphoid cells, as well as plasma cells, were positive for either γM or γG globulins. Peripheral blood was also shown to contain a small number of medium-size dlymphocytes reacting with anti-γM and anti-γG antibodies.

In contrast to the good evidence for the production of γG and γM during fetal life, γA has been shown to be present only in very low concentrations in the normal neonate.[93,215] However, high levels of γA have been detected in infants with congenital infections[187] and in infants previously transfused during life *in utero.*[46] γA globulins have also been found in sera from infants born in Nigeria during the wet season, when malaria, parasitic and viral infections are more frequent.[118]

In rare cases, the fetal γA globulins may cross the placenta and induce maternal synthesis of antibodies directed against antigenic determinants of these molecules that are not expressed in the mother.[212]

Using a quantitative complement fixation technique, γA globulins have been detected in parotid saliva of neonates in the absence of measurable γA in serum.[200] In healthy infants γA globulins were first detected in tears at the age of ten days.[119a]

As already mentioned, γD globulins are not present in cord sera and their synthesis starts some time after birth.

γE globulins are present in sera from normal newborns but in concentrations lower than those detected in adult subjects.[102,103,185] Due to the technical problems involved in extracting very low levels of γE, quantitation of this protein in cord sera is still not accurate. There is, however, clear evidence that the concentration of γE in cord serum is not correlated with its concentration in the relative maternal blood. This holds true also when levels of γE are compared between pairs of allergic mothers and their respective newborns. These results indicate that γE molecules are produced during life *in utero*. The level of γE increases slowly during the first year of life.[21]

(e) Synthesis of Antibodies During Perinatal Life, Following Natural or Intentional Stimulation

The development of the various classes of immunoglobulins during perinatal life and childhood is summarized in Fig. 4. The results of these studies[21,40,45,186,219] reveal a striking difference in the pattern of maturation of γM globulins as compared with the other classes of immunoglobulins. The level of γM, in fact, increases sharply during the first months of life in contrast to the slow rise of γA and γE.

Recent studies have shown that the level of γM is higher in women than in men.[16,30,114,217] The difference starts to be statistically significant after 7–9 years of age. The higher concentration of γM immunoglobulins, usually associated with "naturally" occurring antibodies in serum of healthy individuals, which has been observed in women rather than men, is consistent with the observation that women have a greater resistance to acute infectious diseases than men.[214,217]

Preliminary data have also been collected about the development of the subclasses of γG globulins. The estimation of the levels of Gm factors in sera collected from infants during the first year of life, suggests that Gm(b) factors are produced earlier than other Gm markers, such as Gm(a).[116,122] The final level of γG2 is reached later in life than the adult level of γG3. The sequential order of the development of at least three subclasses of γG globulins seems to be: γG3 → γG1 → γG2.

The early maturation of immunological competence in man is reflected in the production of specific antibodies during perinatal life.

The capacity of the very young infant to respond to antigenic stimulation has been repeatedly confirmed over a number of years.[50] Immunization before two months of neonatal life has been shown to be successful against various bacteria and viruses;[1,28,29,166] for instance, an adequate

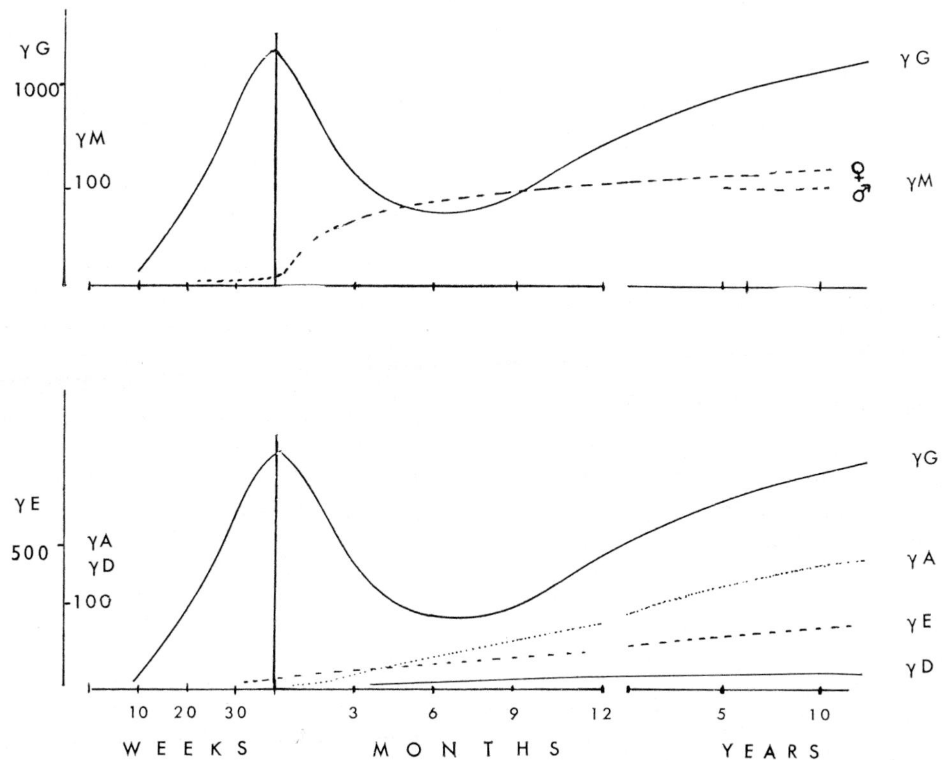

FIG. 4. The development of the various classes of immunoglobulins.

and prompt ability to form neutralizing antibodies against attenuated strain of polio viruses, at levels sufficient to control the infection, has been observed in a group of infants during their first month of life.[109] Neonatal infections with adenoviruses were also shown to induce an antibody response in most babies studied, although in this case the immune response was not as consistent as that observed following infections by enteroviruses.[59]

An extensive investigation of the immune response of infants to Salmonella antigens has been carried out by Smith and his associates.[176,178,179,180] Most infants, irrespective of maturity, were found to produce antibodies to H Salmonella antigens with titres comparable to those found in adults challenged with a similar antigenic stimulation. The first antibodies were associated with γM globulins. In contrast, antibodies against the somatic O antigens were not produced by the infants.

Similar results have been obtained using other bacterial antigens. Premature infants, injected within 48 hours of birth with typhoid-paratyphoid vaccine, produced γM antibodies against typhoid H and paratyphoid A and B antigens. Paratyphoid A and B antibodies predominantly associated with γG globulins occurred at an average age of 13 weeks.[65] It is of interest that high levels of typhoid antibodies were detected in spontaneous infections in the newborn by Neff and Schwartz.[141]

The synthesis of specific antibodies during perinatal life may be influenced by several factors, such as, for example, the presence of specific maternal antibodies in the newborn circulation. In fact the response of infants injected with poliomyelitis vaccine is often depressed by maternal γG antibodies.[29,150,151] A similar effect has been noticed in infants intentionally stimulated with Salmonella antigens[180] and pertussis, diphtheria or tetanus antigens.[113] It appears that whereas antibody synthesis may be depressed in the presence of high levels of maternal antibodies, it may be normal when the level of specific maternal antibodies is low.

Long-sustained antigenic stimulation of the fetus may also affect the synthesis of immunoglobulins during the first year. For instance, low levels of γG globulins have been observed during the first 12 months of life in infants with congenital rubella and high levels of γM globulins at birth. Some of these infants showed a high susceptibility to infection.[183]

(f) Ontogeny of Immunocompetence in other Mammals

The early maturation of immunological competence does not seem to be a characteristic limited exclusively to the human fetus. Synthesis of antibodies during life *in utero* has been observed in cow,[63] guinea pig,[196,204] sheep and monkey.[171,172,174] It should be noted, however, that immunological maturity is slowly attained by the mouse and the rabbit.

The studies of immunogenesis in fetal lambs have produced results which suggest that immunological competence to all antigens does not arise simultaneously. Rather, there is a step-wise maturation of the ability to respond to different antigens at various stages of development.[124,171] In fact, the intentional stimulation of fetal lambs with different antigens has shown that, at a time when the fetus is capable of producing antibodies against bacteriophage ΦX, other antigens, such as ferritin and egg albumin, are not immunogenic. Only later in gestation is immunological competence against these two antigens achieved.

The capacity to manifest cell-mediated reaction appears at about 120 days (gestation period: 150 days). According to Silverstein and his colleagues, the developmental sequence does not terminate at birth, but rather continues past this point. A remarkable precision in the development of antibody response to each antigen at a given stage of gestation was observed even when the antigens were introduced in a depot form with Freund's adjuvant. These data lend much evidence to the suggestion that the specific events of immunological maturation in the fetus are finely timed. Preliminary data suggest that a similar maturation sequence occurs in other species, with differences in the temporal order of antibody synthesis. In fetal Rhesus monkeys the ability to produce antibodies against sheep red cells in mid-gestation is similar to that observed in adult animals.

Another important point which emerges from the studies of Silverstein and his colleagues is that the immune response of the lamb is not impaired by the complete removal of its thymus at the end of the first third of gestation. Thymectomy at this time invariably results in a persistent state of relative lymphopenia in the neonate and in adult animals, and yet the normal sequence of immunological maturation is not altered.[171]

Another important observation has been that inbred strains of mice differ markedly in the rate at which the antibody response to a certain antigen develops in the immediate post-natal period.[153,154]

These findings in lamb and mouse suggest that genetic factors play a prominent role in promoting the normal maturation of specific immunological competence.

CELLULAR IMMUNITY IN THE HUMAN FETUS

The histocompatibility antigens of the HL–A system have been detected in the human fetus at an early stage of gestation[34,48] and are responsible for the stimulation of cytotoxic antibodies in a large proportion of pregnant women.[148,188,210]

Recent studies have shown that the lymphocytes collected from human fetuses at an early stage of gestation are already immunologically competent to respond to allogeneic stimuli, as judged by *in vitro* tests. In fact, fetal lymphocytes have been shown to be "stimulated" when mixed in culture with "foreign" HL–A antigens.[8,33,34]

Lymphocytes from newborns (umbilical cord blood) are excellent responders when confronted *in vitro* with allogeneic stimuli from unrelated individuals or from the father. In contrast, the response against HL-A antigens of the corresponding mother is usually low.

In contrast, it is of great interest that maternal lymphocytes, collected at delivery, are poor responders when tested against allogeneic stimuli from the related newborn or unrelated individuals. This reduced cellular immunity during pregnancy may play an important role in the protection of the fetus against the immunological attack by the mother.[33] The evidence that transplantation immunity in man develops at an early stage of gestation is in good agreement with the early ontogeny of cellular immunity observed in fetal lamb.[124,171] Cellular recognition by mouse lymphocytes *in vitro*, is instead delayed until a few days after birth at least as judged by experiments carried out in inbred animals.[13] Transplantation of allogeneic tissues in mice is therefore successfully achieved when performed during perinatal life; whereas the early maturation of cell-mediated immunity in man makes it difficult to transplant normal tissues into human newborns with inherited disorders using an approach similar to that used in certain experimental animals. The only successful transplants so far achieved are those attempted in children with thymus dependent immunological deficiencies.[207b]

of activation is very short and if during this period C4 does not react with the acceptor, it becomes inactive (C4i).[138] Once C4 is attached to the cell surface, it is retained even if the antibody molecules are removed.

The next step involves the uptake of C2. This component is heat labile, has a coefficient of sedimentation near 5·5S and the electrophoretic mobility of a β globulin. The concentration of C2 in normal sera is near 10 μg./ml.

Until recently the third component of complement (C3) was considered to be the terminal factor of the complement system. In the last few years it has been shown that C3 consists of at least six components.[136] At present, the term C3 is used to indicate that component of complement which reacts directly with EAC1a, 4, 2a. It has a coefficient of sedimentation near 9·5S. It is readily demonstrated by electrophoresis and the arc of prccipitation appears in the β-globulin (β1c) region. On ageing, C3 undergoes

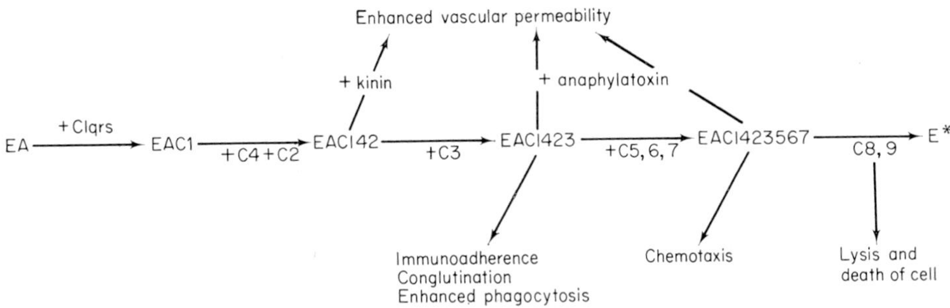

FIG. 5. The interaction of the components of complement.

degradation, and the resulting products have been termed β1A and α2D. β1A has a coefficient of sedimentation of 6·9S. α2D is electrophoretically faster than β1A and has a molecular weight near 75,000. β1C is present in human serum in a concentration near 1,200 μg./ml. The accumulated evidence indicates that C3 molecules are activated by the cell bound C4, 2a complex and that one C4, 2a complex, fixed on the cell surface, is capable of binding several hundred molecules of C3 to their receptor sites.[136]

C5 has been isolated and purified from human serum and, according to its electrophoretic mobility, was termed β1F.[141]

Components of complement similar to those present in human serum have been observed in all vertebrates studied, with the exception of the Cyclostomata.[75] Elasmobranchii, represented by the Lemon Shark and Nurse Shark, are the most primitive vertebrates possessing components of complement with serological properties similar to those present in higher vertebrates.[61]

ONTOGENY OF COMPLEMENT

(a) Properties of the Components of Complement

Extensive reviews of the physicochemical and biological characteristics of the various components of complement (C) have been published.[136,137] The present summary is only intended to help the reader with the complex terminology (Fig. 5).

A single molecule of γM antibody, in combination with the matching antigen localized on the cell surface is capable of binding one molecule of C1a; at least two molecules of γG antibody in close proximity being required for fixing C1a; it follows that the distribution of antigenic sites on the surface of the cell regulates the lytic activity of γG globulins.[25] The antibody absorbed on the cell activates C1 proesterase (C1s) in the presence of the other two C1 subunits (C1q and C1r).

C1q has a coefficient of sedimentation near 11S[135] and its electrophoretic mobility resembles that of γG globulins. The concentration of this component of complement in human sera ranges between 100 and 200 μg./ml.[136]

C4 was the first component of complement to be isolated and characterized physicochemically. On the basis of its electrophoretic mobility it was termed β1E globulin; its concentration in the serum of normal adults is near 430 μg./ml.

It has been suggested that C1a activates C4 molecules and that, following this activation, C4 reacts with some receptors localized on the cell surface and becomes bound. The state

(b) Synthesis of Complement During Fetal Life

There is good agreement that the mean level of total C in normal newborns is about half the value detected in maternal samples.[4,66,67] Using immunological techniques, C4 and C3 have been detected in serum of fetuses older than 15 weeks.[3,5,9]. In recent years, the introduction of the radial immunodiffusion technique for the quantitation of several components of C has made it possible to estimate the concentration of C3, C4 and C5 in fetal, premature and newborn sera (Table 5).[4,66] The results have shown that (a) C3 is present in measurable levels in all fetuses more than 15 weeks old; (b) C4 in all fetuses more than 18 weeks old; (c) the ratios of the mean values of C3, C4 and C5 in maternal and cord sera is near 2; (d) C1 is present in fetal sera and, at birth, its mean level is about half that observed in maternal blood; (e) the levels of C3, C4 and C5 increase during the first months of life and reach adult values at about 6 months.

Evidence for the synthesis of C3, C4 and C1 during life *in utero* has been obtained by means of the incorporation of labelled amino acids into these proteins, using *in vitro* cultures of fetal tissues.[4,6,46,197] Newly synthesized C3 and C4 have been detected in liver cell culture fluids of fetuses more than 14 weeks old. The small intestine and colon of a fetus 18 weeks old were found to be capable of producing, *in vitro*, haemolytically active C1.

TABLE 5

LEVELS OF C3 AND C4 (mg./ml.) IN MATERNAL AND CORD SERA

	C3			C4		
Sample	*No. Tested*	$\bar{x}$	S.D.	*No. Tested*	$\bar{x}$	S.D.
A. maternal	22	143·4	± 12·1	22	28·1	± 5·4
B. cord	22	54·4	± 11·8	22	16·1	± 6·9
Ratio A/B		2·6			1·7	

The fetal synthesis of human C3 has been confirmed by exploiting the allotypic differences of this protein in pairs of maternal and newborn samples. Out of twenty-five paired sera tested by Propp and Alper,[158] eight pairs showed different variants of C3. Most of the discrepancies involved the common allotypes F and S, but two involved a rare allotype $S_{0\cdot6}$. There was no evidence, within the limits of the technique employed, of placental transfer of C3.

The evidence of the early synthesis of the human components of C is in agreement with the preliminary observations on the development of C in other mammals. In 1930 Friedberger and Gurwitz[71] detected total complement activity in newborn guinea-pigs. Within the limits of the techniques available at that time, they were able to show that the "middle" and "end pieces" of complement were present in sera from fetuses obtained towards the end of the gestation period.

Total C activity has been detected after 123 days of gestation in fetal lamb[162] and after 115 days in the fetal goat.[4] However, C1 is already present in serum from sheep embryos 39 days old and by 2 days after birth the level of C reaches adult values.[47] Since in ungulates the placenta is an effective barrier to the transfer of maternal proteins, C1 is probably synthesized by lamb fetuses. It is of interest that neither thymectomy of the fetal lamb, nor antigenic stimulation leading to antibody formation, nor the homograft reaction are associated with an increased production of C1.

Total C activity has been detected in the fetal calf at the end of the first trimester of gestation and in fetal pigs at the 40th day of the 115–120-day-long gestation.[51] According to Day and his collaborators, pig colostrum contains large amounts of C1, C2 and C3, and the levels of these proteins are 30 times higher in suckling than in non-suckling piglets matched for age. However, components of C are present only in traces in human and sheep colostrum.

Data on the fetal synthesis of C5 in mice and the transfer of this component of C from the maternal to the fetal circulation have been obtained by using genetically deficient C5 mice.[188a] When homozygote C5 deficient females were mated with either heterozygote or homozygote "positive" males, C5 was shown to be synthesized in fetuses more than 11 days old. Using appropriate matings between positive and negative mice, maternal-fetal transfer of C5 could be excluded. Using specific antisera and precipitin tests, C3 was detected in fetuses 18 days old. In rabbits, C3 has been detected in sera from fetuses 24 days of age.[4]

ONTOGENY OF LYSOZYME AND INTERFERON

In recent years lysozyme (muramidase) has attracted new attention because of its differential diagnostic value in acute leukemias[104,142,146] and in certain renal disorders.[157] The enzyme is present in vertebrates as well as in some invertebrates, plants, bacteria and phages.[78] Some twenty closely related lysozymes are now known. These enzymes are all basic proteins with a molecular weight near 15,000. In man, the enzyme has been detected in plasma, saliva, tears, colostrum and milk.[7,35,68,69]

The amount of the enzyme in serum is correlated with the total leucocyte count. Senn *et al.*[168] using partially purified preparations of peripheral blood cells and exudate cells, demonstrated that normal human granulocytes contain approximately 7 μg. of lysozyme per million cells (values expressed using egg white lysozyme as a standard).

Investigations of lysozyme in sera from normal individuals between 15 and 70 years of age have shown that the levels of the enzyme are higher in men than in women and that the values increase with ageing.[64]

Until two years ago no information was available on the development of lysozyme in human fetuses and newborns. There were also no data about the ontogeny of this enzyme in other mammals.

In 1970 Glynn[78] and collaborators measured the levels of lysozyme in sera from 66 normal full-term newborns and their mothers and found that the mean concentrations of the enzyme, measured by the lysis of *Micrococcus lysodeikticus* were 9·5 μg./ml. in maternal sera and 13·6 μg./ml. in newborn samples. The difference of the two means was statistically significant ($P < 0{\cdot}001$). When the individual levels of lysozyme in pairs of maternal and newborn sera were compared, no correlation between the values was observed. In 14 cases the concentration of lysozyme in cord serum was at least twice that observed in the corresponding maternal serum.

The lack of correlation between the amount of lysozyme in pairs of maternal and newborn blood and the constant levels in sera collected during perinatal life both suggested synthesis of the enzyme during fetal life.

Direct evidence for the fetal synthesis of the enzyme has been obtained by showing intracellular activity of lysozyme in leucocytes collected from newborns (cord blood).[4]

Human interferon is also produced during life *in utero*; in fact *in vitro* synthesis of interferon has been induced in cells derived from fetuses more than 18 weeks old after their exposure to rubella viruses.[20,31,32,170] The amount of interferon produced *in vitro* per lymphocyte remains roughly constant and it is not correlated with the gestational age. The age-dependent differences in the interferon response expressed per unit of blood are therefore due to physiological changes in the lymphocyte counts.

Since indirect evidence suggests that interferon is one of the factors involved in the defence of the organism against virus infections, it is tempting to speculate on a causal connection between the fetal synthesis of interferon before and after the first trimester of gestation, and the changes in the susceptibility to virus infections of the human fetus at various stages of development.

REFERENCES

1. Adams, J. M., Kimball, A. C. and Adams, F. H. (1947), "Early Immunization Against Pertussis," *Amer. J. Dis. Child*, **74**, 10–18.
2. Adinolfi, M. (1965), "Anti-I Antibodies in Normal Human Newborn Infants," *Immunology*, **9**, 43–52.
3. Adinolfi, M. (1970), "Levels of Two Components of Complement (C′4 and C′3) in Human Fetal and Newborn Sera," *Dev. Med. Child Neurol.*, **12**, 306–308.
4. Adinolfi, M. (1972), "Ontogeny of Components of Complement and Lysozyme," in *Ontogeny of Acquired Immunity* (J. Knight, Associated Scient. Publishers). Ciba Foundation Symposium, pp. 65–81.
5. Adinolfi, M. and Gardner, B. (1967), "Synthesis of β_{1E} and β_{1C} Components of Complement in Human Foetuses," *Acta Paediat. scand.*, **56**, 450–454.
6. Adinolfi, M., Gardner, B. and Wood, C. B. S. (1968), "Ontogenesis of Two Components of Human Complement: β_{1E} and β_{1C-1A} Globulins," *Nature*, **219**, 189–191.
7. Adinolfi, M., Glynn, A. A., Lindsay, M. and Milne, C. M. (1966), "Serological Properties of γA Antibodies to Escherichia Coli Present in Human Colostrum," *Immunology*, **10**, 517–526.
8. Adinolfi, M. and Lessof, M. H. (1972), "Development of Humoral and Cellular Immunity in Man," *J. Med. Genetics*, **9**, 86–91.
9. Adinolfi, M., Martin, W. and Glynn, A. A. (1971), "Ontogenesis of Lysozyme in Man and Other Mammals," in *Protides of the Biological Fluids*, 18th Colloquium, Vol. 18, pp. 91–93 (H. Peeters, Ed.)
10. Adinolfi, M., Mollison, P. L., Polley, M. J. and Rose, J. M. (1966), "γA Blood Group Antibodies," *J. Exp. Med.*, **123**, 951–967.
11. Adinolfi, M., Polley, M. J., Hunter, D. A. and Mollison, P. L. (1962), "Classification of Blood Group Antibodies as β2M or Gamma Globulin" *Immunology*, **5**, 566–579.
12. Adinolfi, M. and Wood, C. B. S. (1969), "Ontogenesis of Immunolgobulins and Components of Complement in Man," in *Immunology and Development*, p. 27–61 (M. Adinolfi, Ed.) London: Spastics Int. Med. Pub.
13. Adler, W. H., Takiquchi, T., Marsh, B. and Smith, R. T. (1970), "Cellular Recognition by Mouse Lymphocytes *In Vitro*. II Specific Stimulation by Histocompatibility Antigens in Mixed Cell Culture," *J. Immunol.*, **105**, 984–1000.
14. Alford, C. A., Jr. (1965), "Studies on Antibody in Congenital Rubella Infection. I Physico-chemical and Immunologic Investigation of Rubella Neutralizing Antibody," *Amer. J. Dis. Child.*, **110**, 455–463.
15. Alford, C. A., Schaefer, J., Blankenship, W. J., Straumfjord, J. V. and Cassidy, G. (1967), "A Correlative Immunologic, Microbiologic and Clinical Approach to the Diagnosis of Acute and Chronic Infections in Newborn Infants," *New Engl. J. Med.*, **277**, 437–449.
16. Allansmith, M., McClellan, B. and Butterworth, M. (1969), "The Influence of Heredity and Environment on Human Immunoglobulin Levels," *J. Immunol.*, **102**, 1504–1510.
17. Allen, J. C., Kunkel, H. G. and Kabat, E. A. (1964), "Studies on Human Antibodies. II Distribution of Genetic Factors," *J. Exp. Med.*, **119**, 453–465.
18. Auerbach, R., (1967), "The Development of Immunocompetent Cells," in *Control Mechanisms in Developmental Processes* (M. Locke, Ed.). New York and London: Academic Press.
19. Auerbach, R. (1970), "Toward a Developmental Theory of Antibody Formation: The Germinal Theory of Immunity," in *Developmental Aspects of Antibody Formation and Structure*, pp. 23–33 (J. Sterzl and I. Riha, Eds.). New York and London: Academic Press.
20. Banatavla, J. E., Potter, J. E. and Best, J. M. (1971), "Interferon Response to Sendai and Rubella Viruses in Human Foetal Cultures, Leucocytes and Placenta Cultures," *J. gen. Virol.*, **13**, 193–201.
21. Bennich, H. and Johansson, S. G. O. (1971), "Structure and Function of Human Immunoglobulin E," *Advances in Immunology*, **13**, 1–55.
22. Bernier, G. M. and Cebra, J. J. (1965), "Frequency Distribution of α, β, κ and λ Polypeptide Chains in Human Lymphoid Tissues," *J. Immunol.*, **95**, 246–253.
23. Black, M. M. and Speer, F. D. (1959), "Lymph Node Reactivity. II. Fetal Lymph Nodes," *Blood*, **14**, 848–855.
24. Bloom, W. (1938), "Embryogenesis of Mammalian Blood," in *Handbook in Hematology*, (H. Downey, Ed.). New York: Hoeber.
25. Borsos, T. and Rapp, H. J. (1965), "Complement Fixation on Cell Surfaces by 19S and 7S Antibodies," *Science*, **150**, 505–506.
26. Bridges, R. A., Condie, R. M., Zak, S. J. and Good, R. A. (1959), "The Morphologic Basis of Antibody Formation Development During the Neonatal Period," *J. Lab. clin. Med.*, **53**, 331–357.
27. Burnet, F. M. (1969), *Cellular Immunology*. London: Cambridge University Press.
28. Butler, N. R., Benson, P. F., Wilson, B. D. R., Perkins, F. T., Ungar, J. and Beale, A. J. (1962), "Poliomyelitis Vaccine and Triple Antigen Efficacy Given Separately and Together," *Lancet* **i**, 834–836.
29. Butler, N. R., Benson, P. F., Urquart, J., Goffe, A. P., Knight, G. J. and Pollock, T. M. (1964), "Further Observations on Vaccination in Infancy with Oral Poliomyelitis Vaccine and Diphtheria Tetanus Pertussis Vaccine," *Brit. med. J.*, **ii**, 418–420.
30. Butterworth, M., McClellan, B. and Allansmith, M. (1967), "Influence of Sex on Immunoglobulin Levels," *Nature*, **214**, 1224–1225.
31. Cantell, K., Strandey, H., Saxen, L. and Meyer, B. (1968), "Interferon Response of Human Leukocytes During Interuterine and Postnatal Life," *J. Immunol.*, **100**, 1304–1309.
32. Carter, W. A., Hande, K. R., Essien, B., Prochownik, E. and Kaback, M. M. (1971), "Comparative Production of Interferon by Human Fetal, Neonatal and Maternal Cells,' *Infection and Immunity*, **3**, 671–677.
33. Ceppellini, R. (1972), "Old and New Facts and Speculations about Transplantation Antigens of Man," in *Progress in Immunology*. New York: Academic Press. In press.
34. Ceppellini, R., Bonnard, G. D., Coppu, F., Miggiano, V. C., Pospísil, M., Curtoni, E. S. and Pellegrino, M. (1971), "Mixed Leukocyte Cultures and HL-A Antigens. I. Reactivity of Young Foetuses, Newborns and Mothers at Delivery," *Transplantation Proc.*, **3**, 58–71.

35. Charlemagne, D. and Jollès, P. (1966), "Les lysozymes des leukocytes et du plasma d'origine humaine," *Nouvelle Rev. Franc. Hématol.*, **6**, 355–366.
36. Chattoraj, A., Gilbert, R. and Josephson, A. M. (1968), "Serological Demonstration of Fetal Production of Blood Group Isoantibodies," *Vox Sang.*, **14**, 289–291.
37. Chiappino, G. and Pernis, B. (1964), "Demonstration with Immunofluorescence of 19S Macroglobulins and 7S Gammaglobulins in Different Cells of the Human Spleen," *Pathol. et Microbiol. (Basel)*, **27**, 8–15.
38. Chievitz, J. H. (1881), "Zur Anatomie einiger Lymphdrusen im erwachsenen und fotalen Zustande," *Arch. Anat.*, **5**, 347–370.
39. Claman, H. N., Chaperon, E. A. and Triplett, R. F. (1966), "Immunocompetence of Transferred Thymus-marrow Cell Combinations," *J. Immunol.*, **97**, 828–832.
40. Claman, H. V. and Merrill, D. (1964), "Quantitative Measurement of Human Gamma-2 beta-2A and Beta-2H Serum Immunoglobulins," *J. Lab. Clin. Med.*, **64**, 685–693.
41. Clem, L. W. and Leslie, G. A. (1969), "Phylogeny of Immunoglobulin Structure and Function," in *Immunology and Development*, pp. 52–88 (M. Adinolfi, Ed.). Spastic Internat. Med. Publ.
42. Cohen, I. R. and Norins, L. C. (1968), "Antibodies of IgG, IgM and IgA Classes in Newborn and Adult Sera Reactive with Gram-negative Bacteria," *J. Clin. Invest.*, **47**, 1053–1062.
43. Cohen, S. (1971), "Structure and Biological Properties of Antibodies," in *Immunological Diseases*, pp. 39–65 (M. Samter, Ed.). Burton: Little, Brown Co.
44. Cohen, S. and Porter, R. R. (1964), "Structure and Biological Activity of Immunoglobulins," *Advances Immunol.*, **4**, 287–349.
45. Collins-Williams, C., Tkachyk, S. J., Toft, B. and Moscarello, M. (1967), "Quantitative Immunoglobulin Levels (IgG, IgA and IgM) in Children," *Int. Arch. Allergy*, **31**, 94–103.
46. Cotten, H. R., Gordon, J. M., Borsos, T. and Rapp, H. Y. (1968), "Synthesis of the First Component of Human Complement *In Vitro*," *J. Exp. Med.*, **128**, 595–604.
47. Cotten, H. R., Silverstein, A. M., Borsos, T. and Rapp, H. Y. (1968), "Ontogeny of the First Component of Sheep Complement," *Immunology*, **15**, 459–461.
48. Crome, P., Moffatt, B. and Adinolfi, M. (1971), "HL-A Antigens in Human Foetuses," in *Protides of the Biological Fluids*, 18th Colloquium, pp. 55–61 (H. Peeters, Ed.).
49a. Dancis, J., Braverman, N. and Lind, J. (1957), "Plasma Protein Synthesis in the Human Fetus and Placenta," *J. clin. Invest.*, **36**, 398–404.
49b. Dancis, J. Jansen, V., Gorstein, F. and Douglas, G W. (1968), "Hematopoietic Cells in Mouse Placenta," *Amer. J. Obstet. Gynec.*, **100**, 1110–1121.
50. Davies, P. A. (1971), "Bacterial Infection in the Fetus and Newborn," *Arch. Dis. Childh.*, **46**, 1–27.
51. Day, N. K. B., Pickering, R. J., Gervurz, H. and Good, R. A. (1969), "Ontogenetic Development of the Complement System," *Immunology*, **16**, 319–326.
52. De Muralt, G. (1962), "La maturation des immuno-globulines chez l'homme," *Vox Sang*, **7**, 513–525.
53. Doria, G., Goodman, J. W., Gengozian, N. and Congdon, C. C. (1962), "Immunological Study of Antibody-forming Cells in Mouse Radiation Chimeras," *J. Immunol.*, **88**, 20–30.
54. Dray, S. (1972), "Allotype Suppression," in *Ontogeny of Acquired Immunity* (J. Knight, Ed). Ciba Foundation Symposium. London: Associated Scient. Publishers. In press.
55. Dray, S., Dubiski, S., Kelus, A., Lennox, E. S. and Oudin, J. (1962), "A Notation for Allotype," *Nature*, **195**, 785–786.
56. Dubiski, A. and Swierszynska, Z. (1971), "Allotypic Suppression in Rabbits: Operational Characterization of the Target Cells," *Int. Arch. Allergy*, **40**, 1–18.
57. Dwyer, J. M. and MacKay, I. R. (1970), "Antigen-binding Lymphocytes in Human Fetal Thymus," *Lancet*, *'*, 1199–1202.
58. Ehrich, W. E. (1929), "Studies of the Lymphatic Tissue," *Amer. J. Anat*,. **43**, 385.
59. Eichenwald, H. F. and Kotsevalov, O. (1960), "Immunologic Responses of Premature and Full-term Infants to Infection with Certain Viruses," *Pediatrics*, **25**, 829–839.
60. Epstein, W. V. (1965), "Specificity of Macroglobulin Antibody Synthesized by the Normal Human Fetus," *Science*, **148**, 1591–1592.
61. Evans, E., Legler, D. W., Painter, B., Acton, R. T. and Attleberger, M. (1967)., "Complement Dependent Systems and the Phylogeny of Immunity," in *In Vitro: Differentiation and Defence Mechanisms in Lower Organisms*, Vol. III, pp. 146–153 (M. M. Sigel, Ed.).
62. Fahey, J. L. (1963), "Two Types of 6·6S γ-globulins, β2A Globulins and 18S γ1-macroglobulins in Normal Serum and γ-microglobulins in Normal Urine," *J. Immunol.*, **91**, 438–447.
63. Fennestad, K. L. and Borg-Petersen, C. (1962), "Antibody and Plasma Cells in Bovine Fetuses Infected with Leptospira Saxkoebing," *J. infect. Dis.*, **110**, 63–69.
64. Finch, S. C., Lamphere, J. P. and Jablon, S. (1964), "The Relationship of Serum Lysozyme to Leukocytes and Other Constitutional Factors," *Yale J. Biol. Med.*, **36**, 350–360.
65. Fink, C. W., Miller, W. E., Jr., Dorward, B. and Lospalluto, J. (1962), "The Formation of Macroglobulin Antibodies. II. Studies on Neonatal Infants and Older Children," *J. clin. Invest.*, **41**, 1422–1428.
66. Fireman, P., Zuchowski, D. A. and Taylor, P. M. (1969), "Development of Human Complement System," *J. Immunol.*, **103**, 25–31.
67. Fishel, C. W. and Pearlman, D. S. (1961), "Complement Components of Paired Mother-cord Sera," *Proc. Soc. exp. Biol. Med.*, **107** ,695–699.
68. Fleming, A. (1922), "On Remarkable Bacteriolytic Element Found in Tissues and Secretions," *Proc. roy. Soc. Lond. Series B*, **93**, 306–317.
69. Fleming, A. and Allison, V. D. (1922), "Observations on a Bacteriolytic Substance ('Lysozyme') Found in Secretions and Tissues," *Brit. J. exp. Path.* **13**, 256–260.
70. Freda, V. J. (1962), "Placental Transfer of Antibodies in Man," *Amer. J. Obstet. Gynec.*, **84**, 1756–1777.
71. Friedberger, E. and Gurwitz, J. (1930), "Weitere Beitrage zum immunologischen Verhalten des Normalserums. III Die Entstehung des Komplements," *Z. Immun. Forsch.*, **68**, 351–363.
72. Fudenberg, H. H. and Fudenberg, B. R. (1964), "Antibody to Hereditary Human Gamma-globulin (Gm) Factor Resulting from Maternal-fetal Incompatibility," *Science*, **145**, 170–171.
73. Fudenberg, H. H., Kunkel, H. G. and Franklin, E. C. (1959), "High Molecular Weight Antibodies," *Acta Haemat.*, **10**, 522.
74. Gardner, B. and Adinolfi, M. (1968), "Seriological and Physicochemical Characteristics of Antibodies Against *Listeria* Monocytogenes in Normal Human Sera," *Guy's Hosp. Rep.*, **117**, 19–30.
75. Gewurz, H., Finstad, J., Muschel, L. and Good, R. A. (1966), "Phylogenetic Enquiry into the Origins of Complement System," in *Phylogeny of Immunity*, p. 105 (R. T. Smith, P. A. Miescher and R. A. Good, Eds.). Gainesville: University Florida Press.
76. Gilmour, J. R. (1941), "Normal Haemopoiesis in Intra-uterine and Neonatal Life," *J. Path. Bact.*, **52**, 25–55.
77. Gitlin, D., Gross, P. A. M. and Janeway, C. A. (1959), "The Gamma Globulins and Their Clinical Significance. I Chemistry, Immunology and Metabolism," *New Engl. J. Med.*, **260**, 21–27.
78. Glynn, A. A. (1968), "Lysozyme: Antigen, Enzyme and Antibacterial Agent," in *Scientific Basis of Medicine*, pp. 31–52, Annual Reviews. Brit. Postgraduate Med. Fed. University of London: The Athlone Press.
79. Glynn, A. A., Martin, W. and Adinolfi, M. (1970), "Levels of Lysozyme in Human Foetuses and Newborns," *Nature*, **225**, 77–78.
80. Good, R. A. and Papermaster, B. W. (1964), "Ontogeny and Phylogeny of Adaptive Immunity," in *Advances in Immunology*, Vol. 4, pp. 1–96 (Dixon and Humphrey, Eds.). New York and London: Academic Press.

81. Grey, H. M. and Kunkel, H. G. (1967), "Heavy-chain Subclasses of Human Gamma-G-globulin: Peptide and Immunochemical Relationship," *Biochemistry*, **6**, 2326–2334.

82. Grubb, R. (1956), "Agglutination of Erythrocytes Coated with 'Incomplete' Anti-Rh by Certain Rheumatoid Arthritic Sera and Some Other Sera. The Existence of Human Serum Groups," *Acta path. microbiol. scand.*, **39**, 195–197.

83. Grubb, R. (1970), *The Genetic Markers of Human Immunoglobulins*. London: Chapman and Hall Ltd.

84. Grubb, R. and Laurell, A. B. (1956), "Hereditary Serological Human Serum Groups," *Acta path. microbiol. scand.*, **39**, 390–398.

85. Grubb, R. and Swahn, B. (1958), "Destruction of Some Agglutinins but Not of Others by Two Sulfhydryl Compounds," *Acta path. microbiol. scand.*, **43**, 305–309.

86. Hammar, J. A. (1905), "Zur Histogenese und Involution der Thymusdrüse," *Anat. Anz.*, **27**, 23 and 41.

87. Hammar, J. A. (1921), "The New Views as to the Morphology of the Thymus Gland and Their Bearing on the Problem of the Function of the Thymus," *Endocrinology*, **5**, 543 and 731.

88. Hammar, J. A. (1936), *Die normal-morphologische Thymusforschung im letzten Vierteljahrhundert*. Leipzig: Barth.

89. Harboe, M. (1959), "A New Hemagglutinating Substance in the Gm System, Anti Gmb," *Acta path. microbiol. scand.*, **47**, 191–198.

90. Hartley, P. (1951), "The Effect of Peptic Digestion on the Properties of Diphteria Antitoxin," *Proc. roy. Soc.*, **138**, 499–513.

91. Hay, F. C., Hull, M. G. R. and Torrigiani, G. (1971), "The Transfer of Human IgG Subclasses from Mother to Foetus," *Clin. exp. Immunol.*, **9**, 355–358.

92. Helleman, T. (1930), "Lymphgefässe, Lymphknötchen, and Lymphknoten," in *Handbuch der mikroscopischen Anatomie des Menschen*, Vol. 6/1, p. 233 (W. Von Mollendorff, Ed.). Berlin: Springer.

93. Heremans, J. F. (1960), "Les globulines seriques du systeme gamma. Leur nature et leur pathologie," *Masson et fie. Bruxelles; Arscia;* Paris.

94. Heremans, J. F. (1968), "Immunoglobulin Formation and Function in Different Tissues," in *Current Topics in Microbiology and Immunology*, Vol. 45, p. 131 (W. Arber *et al.*, Eds.). Berlin: Spring Verlag.

95. Hitzig, W. H. (1959), "Über die transplacentare Übertragung von Antikörper," *Schweiz. med. Wschr.*, **89**, 1249–1253.

96. Hobbs, J. R., Hughes, M. I. and Walker, W. (1968), "Immunoglobulin Levels in Infants After Intrauterine Transfusion," *Lancet*, **i**, 1400–1402.

97. Howe, M. J., Goldstein, A. L. and Battisto, J. R. (1970), "Isogeneic Lymphocyte Interaction: Recognition of Self Antigens by Cells of the Neonate Thymus," *Proc. nat. Acad. Sci.*, **67**, 613–619.

98. Ishizaka, K., Ishizaka, T. and Hornbrook, M. M. (1966), "Physico-chemical Properties of Reaginic Antibody. V. Correlation of Reaginic Activity with γE-globulin Antibody," *J. Immunol.*, **97**, 840–853.

99. Ishizaka, K., Ishizaka, T. and Terry, W. (1967), "Antigenic Structure of γE-globulin and Reaginic Antibody," *J. Immunol.*, **99**, 849–858.

100. Ishizaka, T., Ishizaka, K., Borsos, T. and Rapp, H. J. (1966), C′1 Fixation by Human Isoagglutinins: Fixation of C′ by γG and γM but not by γA Antibody," *J. Immunol.*, **97**, 716–726.

101. Jacot-Guillarmod, H. and Isliker, H. (1962), "Scission et réassociation der isoaglutinines traitées par des agents réducteurs des ponts disulfures. Préparation d'anticorps mixtes," *Vox Sang*, **7**, 674–695.

102. Johansson, S. G. O. (1968), "Serum IgND Levels in Healthy Children and Adults," *Int. Arch. Allergy*, **34**, 1–8.

103. Johansson, S. G. O. and Bennich, H. (1967), "Studies on a New Class of Human Immunoglobulin," in *Gamma Globulins*, pp. 193–197 (J. Killander, Ed.). Nobel Symposium 3 Interscience Publ.

104. Jollès, P., Sternberg, M. and Mathé, G. (1964), "Etude de la teneur en lysozyme du sérum chez des patients atteints de leucemies et hématosarcomes," *Proc. III Symp. Intern. sul Lisozima di Fleming*, pp. 14–20. Milan: Scuola Arti Grafiche O.S.F. Cesano Boscone.

105. Kaplan, M. E., Dalmasso, A. P. and Woodson, M. (1972), "Complement-dependent Opsonization of Incompatible Erythrocytes by Human Secretory IgA," *J. Immunol.*, **108**, 275–277.

106. Kay, H. E. M., Playfair, J. H. L., Wolfendale, M. and Hopper, P. K. (1962), "Development of the Thymus in the Human Foetus and its Relation to Immunological Potential," *Nature*, **196**, 238–240.

107. Knoll, W. (1932), "Die Blutbildung beim Embryo," in *Handbuch der allgemeinen Hämatologie*, p. 553. Edited by (H. Hirschfeld and A. Hittmair, Eds.). Berlin: Urhau and Schwarzenberg.

108. Kohler, P. F. and Muller-Eberhard, H. J. (1967), "Immunochemical Quantitation of Third, Fourth and Fifth Component: Concentrations in the Serum of Healthy Adults," *J. Immunol.*, **99**, 1211–1216.

109. Koprowski, H., Norton, T. W., Hummeler, K., Stokes, J., Hunt, A. D., Flack, A. and Jervis, G. A. (1956), "Immunization of Infants with Living Attenuated Poliomyelitis Virus," *J.A.M.A.*, **162**, 1281–1288.

110. Kunkel, H. G., Allen, J. C., Grey, H. M., Martensson, L. and Grubb, R. (1964), "A Relationship Between the H Chain Groups of 7S γ-globulin and the Gm System," *Nature*, **203**, 413–414.

111. Kunkel, H. G. and Rockey, J. H. (1963), "β2A and Other Immunoglobulins in Isolated Anti-A Antibodies," *Proc. Soc. exp. Biol. Med.*, **113**, 278–281.

112. Kunkel, H. G., Smith, W. K. and Natvig, J. B. (1971), "Human Antibodies to γA1 and γA2 Globulins: Detection of a γA2 Genetic Marker," in *Human Anti-human Gammaglobulins*, pp. 143–149 (R. Grubb and G. Samuelsson, Eds.). Pergamon Press.

113. Levi, M. I., Kravtov, F. E., Levova, T. M. and Fomenko, G. A. (1969), "The Ability of Maternal Antibody to Increase the Immune Response in Infants," *Immunology*, **16**, 145–148.

114. Lichtman, M. A., Vaughan, J. H. and Hamer, C. G. (1967), "The Distribution of Serum Immunoglobulins Anti-γG Globulins ('Rheumatoid Factors') and Antinuclear Antibodies in White and Negro Subjects in Evans County, Georgia," *Arthr. and Rheum.*, **10**, 204–215.

115. Linnet-Jepsen, P., Galatius-Jensen, F. and Hauge, M. (1958), "On the Inheritance of Gm Serum Group," *Acta genet.*, **8**, 164–196.

116. Lundevall, J. (1965), "The Development of Factor Gm(x) After Birth," *Scand. J. clin. Lab. Invest.*, **17**, 246–251.

117. McCracken, G. H. and Shinefield, H. R. (1965), "Immunoglobulin Concentrations in Newborn Infants with Congenital Cytomegalic Inclusion Disease," *Pediatrics*, **36**, 933–937.

118. McFarlane, H. and Udeozo, I. O. K. (1968), "Immunochemical Estimation of Some Proteins in Nigerian Paired Maternal and Foetal Blood," *Arch. Dis. Child.*, **43**, 42–46.

119a. McKay, E. and Thom, H. (1969), "Observations on Neonatal Tears," *J. Pediat.*, **75**, 1245–1256.

119b. McKay, E. and Thom, H. (1971), "Antibodies to Gamma Globulin in Pregnant Women. Incidence, Aetiology and Size," *J. Obstet. Gyneac. Brit. Commonw.*, **78**, 345–354.

120. Mannik, M. and Kunkel, H. G. (1963), "Two Major Types of 7S Normal γ-globulin," *J. exp. Med.*, **117**, 213–230.

121. Mårtensson, L. (1966), "Genes and Immunoglobulins," *Vox Sang*, **11**, 521–545.

122. Mårtensson, L. and Fudenberg, H. H. (1965), "Gm Genes and γG-globulin Synthesis in the Human Fetus," *J. Immunol.*, **94**, 514–520.

123. Mårtensson, L. and Kunkel, H. G. (1965), "Distribution Among the γ-globulin Molecules of Different Genetically Determined Antigenic Specificities in the Gm System," *J. exp. Med.*, **122**, 799–812.

124. Mellbye, O. J. (1966), "Reversible Agglutination of Trypsinized Red Cells by a γM Globulin Synthesized by the Human Foetus," *Scand. J. Haemat.*, **3**, 310–324.

125. Mellbye, O. J., Natvig, J. B. and Krarstein, B. (1971), "Presence of IgG Subclasses and C1q in Human Cord Sera," in *Protides of Biological Fluids*, Vol. 18, pp. 127–131 (H. Peeters, Ed.). Pergamon Press.
126. Metcalf, D. and Brumby, M. (1966), "The Role of the Thymus in the Ontogeny of the Immune System," *J. Cell Physiol.*, **67**, 149–168.
127. Metcalf, D. and Moore, M. A. S. (1971), *Haemopoietic Cells.* London: North Holland Publ. Co. Amsterdam.
128. Miller, J. (1971), "The Immunological Role of the Thymus," in *Immunological Diseases*, pp. 84–94 (M. Samter, Ed.). Boston: Little, Brown, and Co.
129. Mitchison, N. A. (1970), "Cell Co-operation in the Immune Response: The Hypothesis of an Antigen Presentation Mechanism," in *Immunopathology VIth International Symposium*, pp. 52–63 (Peter A. Miescher Ed.). Schwabe & Co.
130. Mollison, P. L. (1951), *Blood Transfusion in Clinical Medicine.* Oxford: Blackwell Scientific Pub. Ltd.
131. Mollison, P. L. (1967), *Blood Transfusion in Clinical Medicine.* Oxford: Blackwell Scientific Publications.
132. Moore, M. A. S. and Metcalf, D. (1970), "Ontogeny of the Haemopoietic System: Yolk Sac Origin of *In Vivo* and *In Vitro* Colony Forming Cells in the Developing Mouse Embryo," *Brit. J. Haem.*, **18**, 279–296.
133. Moore, M. A. S. and Owen, J. J. T. (1967), "Experimental Studies on the Development of the Thymus," *J. exp. Med.*, **126**, 715–726.
134. Mosier, D. E. (1967), "A Requirement of Two Cell Types For Antibody Formation *In Vitro*," *Science*, **158**, 1573–1575.
135. Müller-Eberhard, H. J. (1961), "Isolation and Description of Proteins Related to the Human Complement System," *Acta Soc. Med. Upsalien.*, **66**, 152–170.
136. Müller-Eberhard, H. J. (1968), "Chemistry and Reaction Mechanisms of Complement," in *Advances Immunol.*, **8**, 1–80.
137. Müller-Eberhard, H. J. (1969), "Complement," in *Ann. Rev. Biochem.*, pp. 289. Palo Alto. Annual Review Inc.
138. Müller-Eberhard, H. J., Dalmasso, A. P. and Calcott, M. A. (1966), "The Reaction Mechanism of β1C-globulin (C′3) in Immune Hemolysis," *J. exp. Med.*, **123**, 33–54.
139. Natvig, J. B. and Kunkel, H. G. (1968), "Genetic Markers of Human Immunoglobulins. The Gm and Inv System," in *Serum Groups*, Vol. 1, pp. 66–96 (K. G. Jensen and S. Killmann, Eds.). Copenhagen: Munksgaard.
140. Neff, F. C. and Schwartz, E. J. (1933), "Agglutinination Tests With Blood From a Newly Born Infant of a Typhoid Mother," *Quart. Bull. Univ. Kansas Med. Sch.*, **10.**
141. Nilsson, R. and Müller-Eberhard, H. J. (1965), "Isolation of β1F-globulin from Human Serum and its Characterization as the Fifth Component of Complement," *J. exp. Med.*, **122**, 277–298.
142. Noble, R. E. and Fudenberg, H. H. (1967), "Leukocyte Lysozyme Activity in Myelocytic Leukemia," *Blood*, **30**, 465–473.
143. Norris, E. H. (1938), "The Morphogenesis and Histogenesis of the Thymus Gland in Man," *Contr. Embryol. Carneg. Instn.* (Pub. 166), **27**, 191.
144. Onoue, K., Yagi, Y., Stelos, P. and Pressman, D. (1964), "Antigen-binding Activity of 6S Subunits of β2-macroglobulin Antibody," *Science*, **146**, 404, 405.
145. Orlandini, T. O., Sass-Kortsak, A. and Ebbs, J. H. (1955), "Serum Gamma Globulin Levels in Normal Infants," *Pediatrics*, **16**, 575–583.
146. Osserman, E. F. and Lawlor, D. P., (1966), "Serum and Urinary Lysozyme (Muramidase) in Monocytic and Monomyelocytic Leukemia," *J. exp. Med.*, **124**, 921–952.
147. Oudin, J. (1936), "L' 'allotypie' de certains antigènes protéidiques du serum," *C. R. Acad. Sci. (Paris)*, **242**, 2606–2608.
148. Payne, R. (1962), "The Development and Persistence of Leucoagglutinins in Parous Women," *Blood*, **19**, 411–424.
149. Perchalski, J. E., Clem, L. W. and Small, P. A. (1968), "7S Gamma M Immunoglobulins in Human Cord Serum," *Amer. J. med. Sci.*, **256**, 107–111.
150. Perkins, F. T., Yetts, R. and Gaisford, W. (1958), "Serological Response of Infants to Poliomyelitis Vaccine," *Brit. med. J.* **ii**, 68–71.
151. Perkins, F. T., Yetts, R. and Gaisford, W. (1959), "Response of Infants to a Third Dose of Poliomyelitis Vaccine Given 10–12 Months After Priminary Immunization," *Brit. med. J.* **i**, 680–682.
152. Pernis, B. (1967), "Relationships Between the Heterogeneity of Immunoglobulins and the Differentiation of Plasma Cells," in *Antibodies, Cold Spring Harbor Symposia on Quantitative Biology*, pp. 333–341.
153. Playfair, J. H. L. (1968a), "Strain Difference in the Immune Response of Mice. I. The Neonatal Response to Sheep Red Cells," *Immunology*, **15**, 35–50.
154. Playfair. J. H L. (1968b). Strain Differences in the Immune Responses of Mice. II. Responses by Neonatal Cells in Irradiated Adult Hosts," *Immunology*, **15**, 815–826.
155. Playfair, J. H., Wolfendale, M. R. and Kay, H. E. M. (1963), "The Leucocytes of Peripheral Blood in Human Foetus," *Brit. J. Haemat.*, **9**, 336–344.
156. Porcile, V. (1904), "Untersuchungen uber der Herkunft der Plasmazellen in der Leber," *Beitr. path. Anat.*, **36**, 375–381.
157. Prockop, D. J. and Davidson, W. D. (1964), "A Study of Urinary and Serum Lysozyme in Patients with Renal Disease," *New Engl. J. Med.*, **270**, 269–274.
158. Propp, R. P. and Alper, C. A. (1968), "C′3 Synthesis in the Human Fetus and Lack of Transplacental Passage," *Science*, **162**, 672–673.
159. Pund, E. R. and Von Haam, E. (1957), "Spirochetal and Veneral Disease, in *Pathology*, p. 264. (W. A. D. Anderson, Ed.). Missouri: Mosby, St. Louis.
160. Rawson, A. J. and Abelson, N. M. (1964), "Studies of Blood Group Antibodies. VI The Blood Group Iso-antibody Activity of γ1A," *J. Immunol.*, **93**, 192–198.
161. Remington, J. S. and Miller, M. J. (1966), "19S and 7S Anti-toxoplasma Antibodies in the Diagnosis of Acute Congenital and Acquired Toxoplasmosis," *Proc. Soc. exp. Biol. (N.Y.)*, **121**, 357–363.
162. Rice, C. E. and Silverstein, A. M. (1964), "Haemolytic Complement Activity of Sera of Foetal and Newborn Lambs," *Canad. J comp. Med.*, **28**, 34.
163. Ropartz, C., Lenoir, J. and Rivat, L. (1961), "A New Inheritable Property of Human Sera: The Inv Factor," *Nature*, **189**, 586.
164. Rowe, D. S. and Fahey, J. L. (1965), "New Class of Human Immunoglobulin: II Normal Serum IgD," *J. exp. Med.*, **121**, 185–199.
165. Rumpianesi, G. and Finotti, A. (1957), "Sulla composizione istologica della milza embrionale," *Arch Pat. Clin. Med.*, **34**, 343.
166. Sako, W. (1947), "Studies on Pertussis Immunization," *J. Pediat.* **30**, 29–40.
167. Seller, M. J. (1970), "Animal Models for Bone-marrow Transplantation," *Journal Med. Genetics*, **7**, 305–309.
168. Senn, H. J., Chu, B., O'Malley, J. and Holland, J. F. (1970), "Experimental and Clinical Studies on Muramidase (Lysozyme)," *Acta haemat.*, 65–77.
169. Sieber, O. F., Fulginiti, V. A., Brazie, J. and Umlauf, H. Y. (1966), "*In Utero* Infection of Fetus by Herpes Simplex Virus," *J. Pediat.*, **69**, 30–34.
170. Siewers, C. M. F., John, C. E. and Medearis, D. M. (1970), "Sensitivity of Human Cell Strain to Interferon," *Proc. Soc. exp. Biol. (N.Y.)*, **133**, 1178–1183.
171. Silverstein, A. M. (1972), "Immunological Maturation in the Foetus: Modulation of the Pathogenesis of Congenital Infectious Diseases," in *Ontogeny of Acquired Immunity.* Ciba Foundation Symposium. Associated Scient. Publ., pp. 17–25.
172. Silverstein, A. M. and Kraner, K. L. (1965), "Studies on the Ontogenesis of the Immune Response," in *Molecular and Cellular Basis of Antibody Formation*, pp. 341–350 (J. Sterzl *et al.*, Eds.). Prague: Publish. House of Czech. Acad. Scie.
173. Silverstein, A. M. and Lukes, R. J. (1962), "Fetal Response to Antigenic Stimulus. I Plasma-cellular and Lymphoid Reactions in the Human Fetus to Intrauterine Infection," *Lab. Invest.*, **11**, 918–932.

174. Silverstein, A. M. and Prendergast, R. A. (1970), "Lymphogenesis, Immunogenesis and the Generation of Immunologic Diversity," in *Developmental Aspects of Antibody Formation and Structure*, pp. 69–77 (J. Sterzl and I. Riha, Eds.). Academic Press.

175. Slater, R. J. and Sass-Kortsak, A. (1956), "The Turnover and Circulation of the Plasma Proteins in the Body," *Amer. J. Med. Sci.*, **231**, 669–693.

176. Smith, C. (1965), "Studies on the Thymus of the Mammal. XIV. Histology and Histochemistry of Embryonic and Early Postnatal Thumuses of C57 BL/6 and AKR Strain Mice," *Amer. J. Anat.*, **116**, 611–629.

177. Smith, R. T. (1960) "Response to Active Immunization of Human Infants During the Neonatal Period," in *Ciba Foundation Symposium on Cellular Aspects of Immunity*, pp. 348–368 (G. E. W. Wolstenholme and M. O'Connor. London: J. & A. Churchill.

178. Smith, R. T. (1961), "Immunological Tolerance of Non-living Antigens," *Adv. Immunology*, **1**, 67–129.

179. Smith, R. T. (1968), "Development of Fetal and Neonatal Immunological Function," in *Biology of Gestation*, Vol. II, pp. 321–354 (N. S. Assali, Ed.). Academic Press.

180. Smith, R. T., Eitzman, D. V., Catlin, M. E., Wirtz, E. O. and Miller, B. E. (1964), "The Development of the Immune Response. Characterization of the Response of the Human Infant and Adult to Immunization with Salmonella Vaccines," *Pediatrics*, **33**, 163–183.

181. Smith, R. T., James, J., Eitzman, D. V. and Miller, B. (1959). "Production of Type 19S γ-globulins Antibody by Neonatal Infants in Response to Typhoid Immunization," *Amer. J. Dis. Child.*, **98**, 644.

182. Solomon, J. B. (1971), "Foetal and Neonatal Immunology," *Frontiers of Biology* (A. Neuberger and E. L. Tatum, Eds.). London: North Holland Publishing Co. Amsterdam.

183. Soothill, J. F., Hayes, K. and Dudgeon, J. A. (1966), "The Immunoglobulins in Congenital Rubella," *Lancet*, **i**, 1385–1388.

184. Stanworth, D. R., Humphrey, J. H., Bennich, H. and Johansson, S. G. O. (1967), "Specific Inhibition of the Praunitz-Küstner Reaction by an Atypical Human Myeloma Protein," *Lancet*, **ii**, 330–332.

185. Stevenson, D. D., Orgel, H. A., Harburger, R. N. and Reid, R. T. (1971), "Development of IgE in Newborn Human Infants," *J. Allergy Clin. Immunol.*, **48**, 61–72.

186. Stiehm, E. R., Amnann, A. J. and Cherry, J. D. (1966), "Elevated Cord Macroglobulins in the Diagnosis of Intrauterine Infections," *New Engl. J. Med.*, **275**, 971–977.

187. Stiehm, E. R. and Fundenberg, H. H. (1966), "Serum Levels of Immune Globulins in Health and Disease: A Survey, *Pediatrics*, **37**, 715–727.

188a. Tachibana, D. K. and Rosenberg, L. T. (1966), "Fetal Synthesis of Hc[1], a Component of Mouse Complement," *J. Immunol.*, **97**, 213–215.

188b. Takahashi, M., Yagi, Y., Moore, G. E. and Pressman, D. (1969), "Pattern of Immunoglobulin Production in Individual Cells of Human Hematopoietic Origin in Established Culture," *J. Immunol.*, **102**, 1274–1283.

189. Taylor, R. B. (1965), "Pluripotential Stem Cells in Mouse Embryo Liver," *Brit. J. exp. Path.*, **46**, 376–383.

190. Taylor, R. B. (1969), "Cellular Co-operation in the Antibody Response of Mice to Two Serum Albumins: Specific Function of Thymus Cells," *Transpl. Rev.*, **1**, 114–149.

191. Terasaki, P. I., Mickey, M. R., Yamazaki, J. N. and Vredevoe, D. (1970), "Maternal-fetal Incompability. I Incidence of HL-A Antibodies and Possible Association wih Congenital Anomalies," *Transplantation*, **9**, 538–543.

192. Terry, W. D. (1965), "Skin-sensitizing Activity Related to γ-polypeptide Chain Characteristics of Human IgG," *J. Immunol.*, **95**, 1041–1047.

193. Terry, W. D., Fahey, J. L. and Steinberg, A. G. (1965), "Gm and Inv Factors in Subclasses of Human IgG," *J. exp. Med.*, **122**, 1087–1102.

194. Thom, H. and McKay, E. (1971), "Observations on Infants of Mothers with Antibodies to γ-globulin," *Biol. Neonat.*, **19**, 397–408.

195. Thomaidis, T., Fouskaris, G. and Matsaniotis, N. (1967), "Isohemagglutinin Activity in the First Day of Life," *Amer. J. Dis. Child.*, **113**, 654–657.

196. Thorbecke, G. J. (1964), "Development of Immune Globulin Formation in Fetal, Newborn and Immature Guinea Pigs," *Fed. Proc.*, **23**, 346.

197. Thorbecke, G. J., Hochwald, G. M., Van Furth, R., Müller-Eberhard, H. J. and Jacobsen, E. B. (1965), "Problems in Determining the Sites of Synthesis of Complement Reactions," in *Ciba Foundation Symposium on Complement*, pp. 99–114 (G. E. W. Wostenholme and J. Knight, London: J. & A. Churchill.

198. Toivanen, P., Rossi, T. and Hirvonen, T. (1969), "The Concentration of Gc Globulin and Transferrin in Human Fetal and Infant Sera," *Scand. J. Haemat.*, **6**, 113–118.

199. Tomasi, T. B. and Bienenstock, J. (1968), "Secretory Immunoglobulins," in *Adv. Immunology*, **9**, 2–96.

200. Tomasi, T. B., Jr., Tan, E. M., Solomon, A. and Prendergast, R. A. (1965), "Characteristics of an Immune System Common to Certain External Secretions," *J. exp. Med.*, **121**, 101–124.

201. Trevorrow, V. E. (1959), "Concentration of Gamma-globulin in the Serum of Infants During the First Three Months of Life," *Pediatrics*, **24**, 746–751.

202. Tyan, M. L. and Cole, L. J. (1963), "Mouse Fetal Liver and Thymus: Potential Sources of Immunologically Active Cells," *Transplantation*, **1**, 347–350.

203. Tyan, M. L., Cole, L. J. and Herzenberg, L. A. (1967), "Fetal Liver: A Source of Immunoglobulin Producing Cells in the Mouse," *Proc. Soc. exp. Biol. Med.*, **124**, 1161–1163.

204. Uhr, J. W. (1960), "Development of Delayed-type Hypersensitivity in Guinea Pig Embryos," *Nature*, **187**, 957.

205. Umiel, T., Globerson, A. and Auerbach, R. Cited by Auerbach, R. (1967), "The Development of Immunocompetent Cells," in *Control Mechanisms in Developmental Processes*, (M. Locke, Ed.). New York and London: Academic Press.

206. Vaerman, J. P. and Heremans, J. F. (1968), "Effect of Neuraminidase and Acidification on Complement-fixing Properties of Human IgA and IgG," *Int. Arch. Allergy* (*Basel*). **34**, 49–52.

207a. Vahlquist, B. (1958), "The Transfer of Antibodies from Mother to Offspring," *Advanc. Pediat.*, **10**, 305.

207b. Van Bekkum, D. W. (1972), "Treatment of Immune Deficiency with Bone Marrow Stem Cell Concentrates," in *Ontogeny of Acquired Immunity* (J. Knight, Ed.). Associated Scient. Publ. In press.

208. Van Furth, R. and Adinolfi, M. (1969), "*In Vitro* Synthesis of the Foetal α1-globulin in Man," *Nature*, **222**, 1297.

209. Van Furth, R., Schuit, H. R. E. and Hijmans, W. (1965), "The Immunological Development of the Human Fetus," *J. exp. Med.*, **122**, 1173–1188.

210. Van Rood, J. J., Van Leevwen, A. and Eernisse, H. J. (1959), "Leucocyte Antibodies in Sera of Pregnant Women," *Vox Sang*, **4**, 428–444.

211. Vierucci, A., Varone, D. and Ingiulla, A. (1964), "La sintesi delle immunoglobuline del tipo IgG (7S) nel periodo fetoneonatale studiata mediante l'impiego dei marcatori genetici Gm." *Rev. Clin. Paed.*, **74**, 505–510.

212. Vyas, G. N., Levin, A. S. and Fudenberg, H. H. (1970), "Intrauterine Isoimmunization Caused by Maternal IgA Crossing the Placenta," *Nature*, **225**, 275–276.

213. Wang, A. C., Faulk, W. P., Stuckey, M. A. and Fudenberg, H. H. (1970), "Chemical Differences of Adult, Fetal and Hypo-gamma-globulinemic IgG Immunoglobulins," *Immunochemistry*, **7**, 703–708.

214. Washburn, T. C., Medearis, D. N. and Child, B. (1965), "Sex Differences in Susceptibility to Infections," *Pediatrics*, **35**, 57–64.

215. West, C. D., Hong, R. and Holland, N. H. (1962), "Immunoglobulin Levels from the Newborn Period to Adulthood and in Immunoglobulin Deficiency States," *J. clin. Invest.*, **41**, 2054–2064.

216. Wiener, A. S. and Berlin, R. B. (1947), "Pérmeabilité du placenta humain aux iso-anticorps," *Rev. Hematol.*, **2**, 260.
217. Wood, C. B. S., Martin, W., Adinolfi, M. and Polani, P. E. (1970), "Levels of γM and γG Globulins in Women with XO Chromosomes," *Atti. Ass. Genet. Ital.*, **15**, 228–239.
218. Yoffrey, J. M. (1971), "The Stem Cell Problem in the Fetus," *Israel. J. Med. Sciences*, **7**, 825–831.
219. Yeung, C. Y. and Hobbs, J. R. (1968), "Serum-γG-globulin Levels in Normal Premature, Post Mature and Small-for-dates Newborn Babies," *Lancet*, **i**, 1167–1170.
220. Yount, W. J., Doner, M. M., Kunkel, H. G. and Kabat, E. A. (1968), "Studies on Human Antibodies: VI Selective Variations in Subgroup Composition and Genetic Markers," *J. exp. Med.*, **127**, 633–646.

20. THE GROWTH AND DEVELOPMENT OF THE SKELETAL MUSCLES

F. L. MASTAGLIA

I. INTRODUCTION

Striated muscle, the most ubiquitous and one of the most highly differentiated tissues in the body, is as unique in its mode of development as it is in its structure and function. The formation of the muscle fibre syncytium with its complex system of contractile proteins involves a series of cellular interactions and biosynthetic processes not encountered in the development of other tissues. Moreover, the close relationship between the muscle fibre and its nerve supply, its investing connective tissue sheath and tendinous attachments and the highly specialized sensory receptors, the muscle spindles and Golgi tendon organs, are anatomical features peculiar to muscle which add to the complexity of the developmental processes.

The application of specialized techniques to the study of developing muscle *in vivo* and in tissue culture over the past decade has led to considerable advances in knowledge in this field. Electron microscopy has elucidated the morphogenesis of the muscle fibre particularly of the contractile and sarcotubular systems and of the myoneural junctions. Tissue culture studies making use of electron microscopy and autoradiography have established beyond doubt that the multinucleate state of the muscle fibre results from fusion of mononucleated myoblasts rather than from division of nuclei already in the muscle cell. Histochemical and biochemical techniques have provided basic information on the time of appearance of certain key enzymic constituents of the developing muscle fibre and it has been found that differentiation of the main histochemical fibre types begins during intrauterine life soon after the muscle fibres acquire their nerve supply.

The possibility that certain human myopathies such as muscular dystrophy might be due to an abnormality of muscle development has acted as a strong stimulus to the study of myogenesis in man and in a variety of animal species. Although this concept of the pathogenesis of muscular dystrophy has not been particularly fruitful to date, it has nevertheless led to better understanding of the normal developmental processes in muscle. In addition, certain less common human muscle disorders have come to be regarded as being due to faulty development of the muscle fibre or of its nerve supply during intrauterine life.

II. HISTOGENESIS

A. The Primitive Mesoderm

The skeletal muscle of vertebrates is derived from the primitive mesoderm (*chordamesoderm*) which, in the human embryo, begins to bud off from the ectoblast in the vicinity of the primitive streak at about the 17th day of gestation.[14] The invaginated cells subsequently become organized into seven longitudinally-arranged bands. The median unpaired one forms the *notochord* which is flanked on either side by the *paraxial mesoderm*, the *intermediate cell mass* and the *lateral-plate mesoderm*. It is from the paraxial and lateral-plate mesoderm that muscle tissue is derived. The intermediate cell mass gives rise to the greater part of the urogenital system. The lateral plate is split by the coclom into an outer portion in contact with the ectoderm which will participate in the formation of the body wall (the *somatopleure*) and an anner portion in contact with the endoderm (the *splanchnopleure*).

By the end of the 3rd week of gestation the paraxial mesoderm begins to segment into bilaterally paired more-or-less cubical masses of cells, the *somites* (Fig. 1). The somites destined to form the musculature of the trunk appear first and somite formation subsequently extends along the whole length of the embryo so that by the end of the 4th week there are over twenty pairs of somites and by the end of the 5th week the full complement of thirty-eight somites has formed: 3 occipital, 8 cervical, 12 thoracic, 5 lumbar, 5 sacral and 5 coccygeal.[116] The somites are at first solid masses of cells resting against the neural tube and notochord. A cavity soon appears in each somite (Fig. 1) and in many animals is continuous with the coelom through the intermediate cell mass. The somites undergo rapid growth during the early weeks of embryonic life, the increase in volume being brought about by mitotic division of primitive mesodermal cells as well as by an increase in the size of individual cells.[79] The later somites grow at a faster rate than the early ones so that by the 4th–5th weeks the somites are all at about the same stage of development.[79] Cells from the medial wall and from a considerable portion of the cranial and caudal walls of the somite migrate medially to surround the neural tube and notochord as the *sclerotome* from which the vertebrae and their ligaments and the dura mater will develop. Cells from the lateral portion of the somite form the *dermatomes* which participate in the formation of the corium of the skin. The remaining portions of the lateral, dorsal and ventral walls of the somite constitute the *myotome* from which most of the striated muscle attached to the axial skeleton is derived. Each myotome forms a flat *muscle-plate* with a thin outer shell lying against the ectoderm and incurved dorsal and ventral margins and a medially-directed concavity or hilum. The main muscle mass is derived from the inner layers of the myotome. A dorsal extension of the muscle-plate comes to overly the neural tube and gives rise to the muscles of the back. A ventral extension into the somatopleure gives rise to some of the muscles of the lateral and anterior body wall.

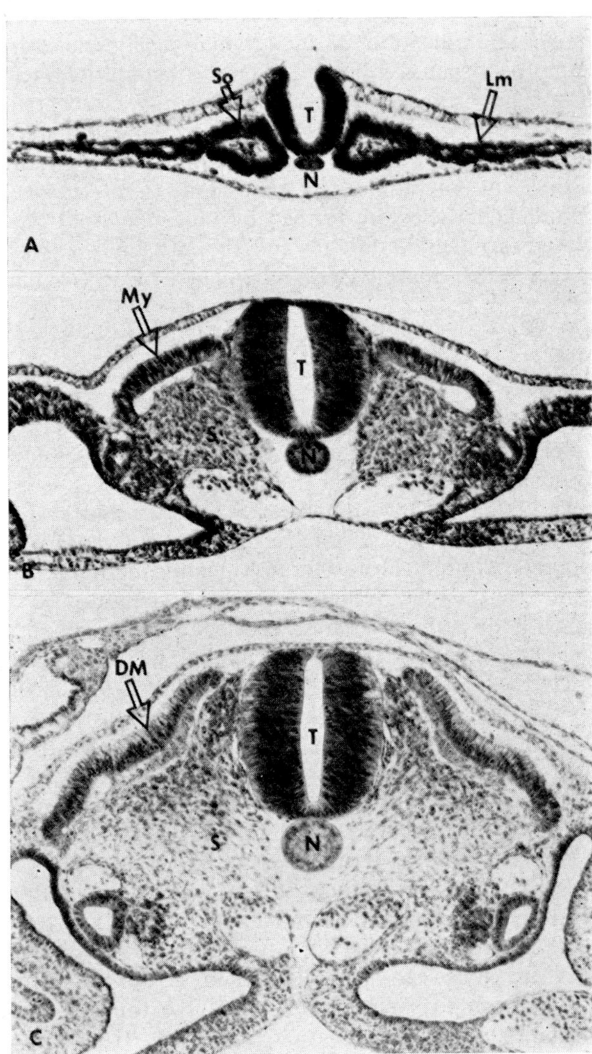

FIG. 1. Cross-sections of chick embryos at (A) 24 hr., (B) 48 hr., (C) 72 hr. At 24 hr. the neural tube (T) is still open and the notochord (N), cavitated somite (SO) and split lateral plate mesoderm (Lm) are seen. At 48 hr. the myotome (My) and sclerotome (S) are both seen. At 72 hr. the myotome (DM) has opened out and dermatomal cells are appearing on its outer surface and myogenic cells on its inner surface. (All ×110)

The primitive segmental arrangement of myotomes is

soon lost and individual skeletal muscles are formed by a process of fusion or splitting of muscle-plates or by re-orientation of muscle fibres or actual migration of muscles. In few muscles is the original cranio-caudal orientation of muscle fibres which exists in the myotomes retained. Most muscles are formed by fusion of components of several myotomes, each component retaining its segmental nerve supply, an indication of its original metameric origin. Examples of such composite muscles with a plurisegmental nerve supply are the rectus abdominis and sacrospinalis. The anterior strap muscles of the neck and the sterno-mastoid and trapezius are muscles formed by longitudinal splitting of myotomes. The oblique and transverse abdominal muscles are formed by tangential splitting of myotomes. The diaphragm and the latissimus dorsi are muscles which migrate during the course of development.

B. Trunk Musculature

The dorsal portion of each muscle-plate separates off and becomes continuous with the corresponding portion of neighbouring myotomes thus forming a longitudinal pre-muscle column which is innervated by the posterior primary rami of the spinal nerves. The muscles of the back of the neck and of the back of the trunk are formed from this column. The extent to which the myotomes contribute to the development of the musculature of the ventral body wall varies from species to species.[14] In the chick, the myotomes form the musculature of approximately the dorsal third of the body wall, the ventral half being formed from the lateral-plate mesoderm and the intervening part probably from both sources. In the human embryo, extensions from the ventral edges of the 8th cervical to the 2nd lumbar myotomes into the somatic mesoderm contribute to the development of the muscles of the ventrolateral thoracic and abdominal wall. The ventral portions of the lumbar myotomes and the upper sacral myotomes disappear in man. The third and fourth sacral myotomes persist and form the levator ani and coccygeus muscles. The diaphragm is derived almost entirely from the ventral portion of the fourth cervical myotomes.

C. Limb Musculature

The musculature of the limbs develops *in situ* from the mesoderm of the limb buds which is of somatopleuric origin. It is now accepted that the myotomes contribute little, if at all, to the development of the limb muscles in birds, amphibia and all tetrapods (including man).[14] The primitive limb musculature is originally laid down as ventral and dorsal sheets which are continuous with each other along the pre- and post-axial borders of the limb bud. The proximal muscles are the first to develop and there is subsequently a progressive proximo-distal differentiation, the muscles of the hand and foot being the last to differentiate. The muscles of the arm differentiate slightly earlier than those of the leg. In the developing arm most of the individual muscles are recognizable by the end of the 6th week but considerable re-arrangement subsequently occurs before the adult pattern is reached.[115] In the junctional regions between the limbs and trunk there appears to be an indefinite transition between muscles of myotomal origin and those which arise *in situ*. Many muscles of the shoulder and pelvic girdles are almost certainly of myotomal origin. On the other hand, muscles such as the latissimus dorsi and the pectoral muscles arise posteriorly in the arm and subsequently migrate to attach to the thoracic wall.

D. Musculature of the Head and Neck

The cranio-cervical muscles are derived from several separate sources. The pre- and post-vertebral muscles are formed from the cervical myotomes. The musculature of the tongue is derived from the occipital myotomes. Although in certain species such as elasmobranch fish cephalic myotomes which give rise to the orbital muscles are found, they have never been identified in the human embryo. In man, all the orbital muscles arise from a common pre-muscle mass which is first recognizable during the 5th week of gestation in close relationship to the optic vesicle (*see* chapter Harcourt). The muscles innervated by the trigeminal, facial, glossopharyngeal, vagus and accessory nerves are derived from the mesoderm of the branchial arches. The muscles of mastication arise from the mesoderm of the first arch. The muscles of the face, ear and scalp are formed from the mesoderm of the second arch. The muscles of the pharynx, palate and larynx are derived from the more caudal arches. The sternomastoid and trapezius muscles are derived at least in part from mesoderm related to the 6th branchial arch. They have, in the past, been considered to be formed entirely from branchial arch tissue.[116] However, a myotomal contribution seems likely at least in some mammals. The sternomastoid originates high up in the neck and subsequently extends posteriorly and ventrally to gain attachment to the clavicle and sternum during the 6th week of gestation. The trapezius migrates caudally from the neck to attach to the scapula and thoracic spine between the 4th and 7th weeks.[116]

III. CYTOGENESIS

A. The Origin of the Muscle Fibre

The origin of the multinucleated muscle fibre has been a matter of considerable controversy over the past 150 years. Schwann[157] concluded that it is formed by fusion of individual cells, a view which has now come to be accepted (the *multicellular theory*). On the other hand, Remak[150] first postulated an origin from a single cell (the *unicellular theory*) with repeated amitotic nuclear division and until recently this view has also had its protagonists (*see* [147,174]). Experimental *in vitro* studies of developing muscle have now established beyond doubt that undifferentiated uninucleate myogenic cells (*myoblasts*) undergo repeated mitotic division and subsequently fuse with each other to form syncytia. The nuclei of these multinucleated cells do not subsequently divide either mitotically or amitotically but their numbers are increased by the continued incorporation of myoblasts into the syncytium. The evidence, which is based largely on *in vitro* studies, may be summarized as follows:

(i) Mitotic division and fusion of myoblasts with each other and with multinucleated muscle cells (*myotubes*) can be observed in tissue cultures of fetal muscle using time-lapse cinematographic techniques.[20,29,154]

(ii) DNA synthesis can be demonstrated in the nuclei of uninucleate myoblasts by the uptake of tritiated thymidine but not in the nuclei of myotubes.[174]

(iii) Microspectrophotometric estimations of the DNA content of the nuclei of myotubes reveal only diploid nuclei and no tetraploid nuclei which would be expected if these nuclei were preparing to divide.[173]

(iv) Multinucleated muscle cells will form in myoblast cultures even when DNA synthesis is inhibited by nitrogen mustard.[109]

(v) The most direct and convincing evidence has come from the studies of Konigsberg[108] who has shown that single mononucleated myoblasts separated from chick embryo muscle explants by trypsinization may, under appropriate tissue culture conditions, undergo repeated mitotic division and form multinucleated syncytia.

B. The Myoblast

Terminology

In the past, the term myoblast has been used to refer to the primitive myogenic cells at a stage when they are indistinguishable from the mesenchymal cells destined to form the connective tissues.[66] With the advent of electron microscopy and the development of techniques for immunofluorescent labelling of muscle-specific proteins, the term myoblast has come to be applied only to those mononucleated cells showing morphological features which enable them to be distinguished from developing fibroblasts and which contain the muscle-specific proteins myosin and actin. The term premyoblast is used to refer to the primitive mesenchymal cells which have the capacity to develop into myoblasts but which do not themselves fuse or synthesize muscle-specific proteins[82,83] (Fig. 2).

Morphology

During the first few weeks of embryonic life the cell masses destined to form the myotomes consist of loosely-packed fusiform cells with undifferentiated cytoplasm. With further development myoblasts become recognizable by their elongated appearance and large heavily granulated nuclei (Fig. 3). Observations of fetal muscle cultures using the scanning electron microscope have shown that myoblasts are smooth and elongated and have a prominent nuclear bulge whereas fibroblasts are flattened and more branched[37] (Fig. 4). Both types of cell contain abundant ribonucleoprotein. In the myoblast, the ribosomal granules are dispersed throughout the cytoplasm and granular endoplasmic reticulum is sparse. In the fibroblast, the majority of ribosomes are present in the form of a well-developed granular endoplasmic reticulum, this being a feature of cells involved in the synthesis of extracellular proteins.[78] When myofilaments and cross-striated myofibrils make their appearance myoblasts are even more readily identified (Fig. 3).

Myoblast Division

The rapid increase in the volume of the somites which takes place during early embryonic life results principally from mitotic division of the primitive mesenchymal cells,

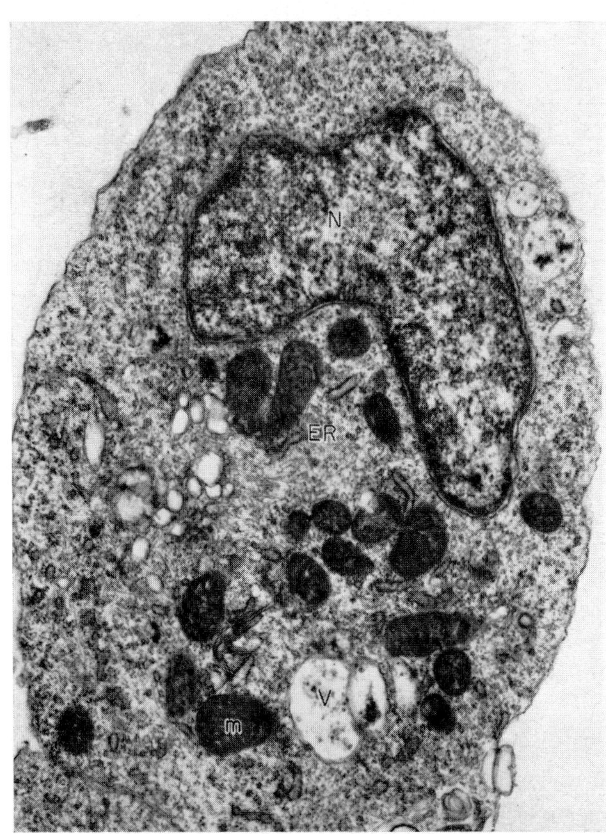

FIG. 2. Premyoblast from 18 hr. chick embryo muscle culture. The cytoplasm contains many ribosomal particles, granular endoplasmic reticulum (ER), mitochondria (m), membrane-bound vacuoles (v) and thin filaments in the central portion of the cell. N—nucleus. (× 16,200) (*By courtesy of Dr. J. M. Papadimitriou.*)

both myoblasts and fibroblasts. Most information on the mitotic activity of myoblasts has come from studies of developing chick muscle both *in vivo* and *in vitro*. Early studies of chick somites showed that cell proliferation occurs in spurts.[79] More recent studies of chick muscle[120] using the uptake of tritiated thymidine as an index of DNA synthesis have shown that there is an initial phase up to day 7 of incubation during which the majority of cells are proliferating. From day 7 onwards there is a transitional period during which there is a progressive decline in the number of dividing cells. By day 16 only small numbers of cells are proliferating. From day 9 to day 16 there is a corresponding increase in the duration of the presynthetic (G1) phase of the mitotic cycle, which precedes the phase of DNA duplication (S), from 4 to 9 hours while the duration of the synthetic (S), mitotic (M)

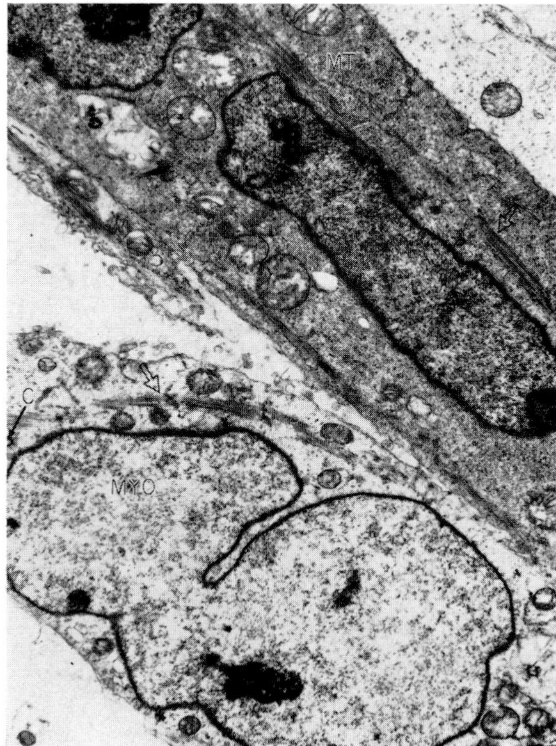

Fig. 3. Mononucleated myoblast (MYO) and multinucleated myotube (MT) in a 24 hr. culture of chick embryo muscle. Primitive myofibrils (arrows) are seen in both cells. The myoblast has a large nucleus with dispersed chromatin and a centriole (C). (×6,300) (*By courtesy of Dr. J. M. Papadimitriou.*)

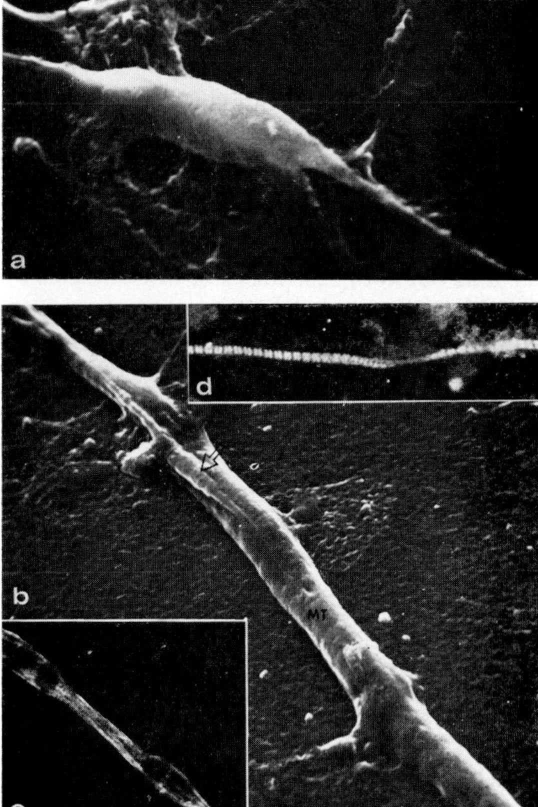

Fig. 4.(a) Scanning electronmicrograph of a chick myoblast in culture. Note the fusiform shape and central nuclear bulge. (×5,200) (*By courtesy of Dr. J. M. Papadimitriou.*) (b) Scanning electronmicrograph of a myotube (MT) from a culture of chick embryo muscle. A myoblast (arrow) is closely applied to the myotube. (×1,750) (*By courtesy of Dr. J. M. Papadimitriou.*) (c) and (d) Immunofluorescent staining of myotubes from cultures of human fetal (c) and chick embryo (d) muscle. Cross-striations are seen in (d) but not in (c). (Both ×320) (*By courtesy of Dr. R. L. Dawkins.*) (d) From.[37]

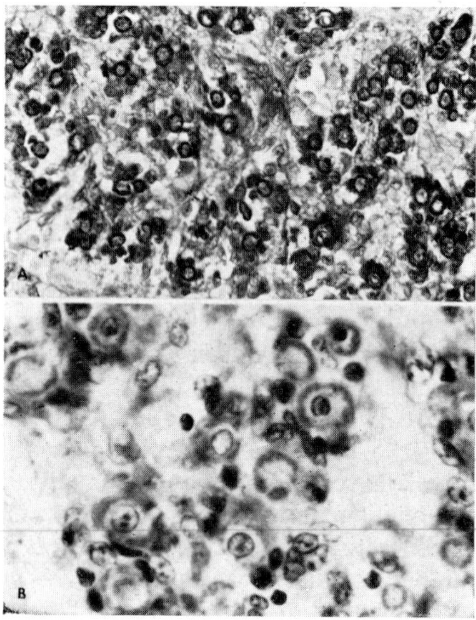

Fig. 5. Cross-sections of 10-day chick embryo muscle showing myotubes with peripheral rim of darkly-staining myofibrils and central cytoplasmic core and nuclei. Haematoxylin and eosin staining. ((a) ×600; (b) ×750)

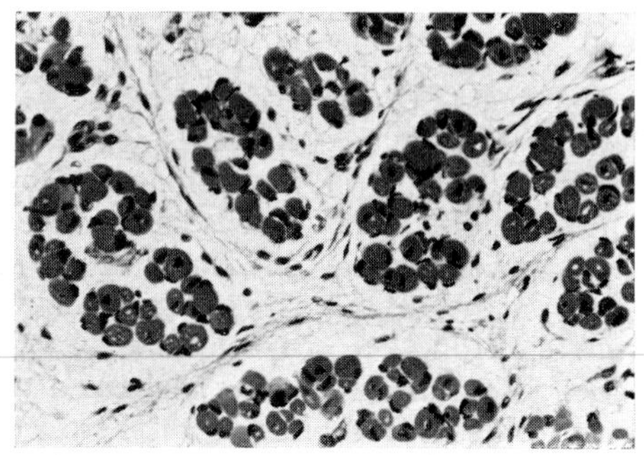

Fig. 6. Cross-section of a limb muscle of an 18-week human fetus showing fascicles of muscle fibres of varying size separated by loose connective tissue. Many fibres are still in the myotube stage. Haematoxylin and eosin. (×180)

and post-mitotic (G2) phases of the cell cycle remain constant. In the 17 day rat embryo the whole mitotic cycle has been estimated to occupy about 20 hours, mitosis itself lasting about $2\frac{1}{2}$ hours.[190] Tissue culture studies have shown that *in vitro* the events of myogenesis are accelerated. Thus the duration of the whole cell cycle in 2 day cultures of 10 day chick embryo muscle is about $9\frac{1}{2}$ hours and the duration of mitosis 0·8 hours.[12]

In vivo and *in vitro* studies of chick muscle using H^3-thymidine uptake as an index of DNA synthesis and binding of fluorescein-labelled antibody to myosin as a guide to myosin synthesis have shown that cell division and the synthesis of contractile proteins are mutually exclusive processes[174]. Thus, mononucleated myoblasts which are synthesizing DNA do not bind antimyosin. Conversely, mononucleated cells or multinucleated myotubes which bind antimyosin fail to incorporate H^3-thymidine. Similarly, cells arrested in metaphase by colchicine do not contain myosin or actin.[82] The conclusion from these observations is that at a critical point in the life cycle of the premyoblast sets of genes involved in cell multiplication, and pathways leading to DNA synthesis are repressed and sets of genes associated with the synthesis of muscle-specific proteins are derepressed. It has been postulated that after going through a number of mitotic cycles the premyoblast undergoes a "critical" or "quantal" mitosis which conditions it for this switch in cellular activities.[82] The premyoblast then starts to synthesize contractile proteins during the G1 phase and thereafter remains in G1 ("G1-arrest") losing its ability to undergo further mitotic division. This cell, now a myoblast, has withdrawn from the mitotic cycle and has engaged upon the synthesis of "luxury proteins".[82]

Myoblast Fusion

Direct evidence of myoblast fusion has come from cine-micrographic[20,29] and electron microscopic studies of embryonic muscle in tissue culture. Both light and electron microscopic studies have demonstrated fusion between mononucleated cells, between mononucleated cells and multinucleated myotubes, and between nascent multi-nucleated myotubes.[165]

The factors responsible for the initiation of cell fusion are not clearly understood. It is known from tissue culture studies that mere contact between cells does not necessarily trigger fusion. It seems certain that specific molecular configurations must exist on the surface of myoblasts and myotubes which are muscle-specific and which allow cellular recognition and subsequent membrane interactions. Thus, in mixed cultures of myoblasts, fibroblasts, chondroblasts and epithelial cells[137] fusion will only occur between myogenic cells. The properties of the cell surface are not species-specific and fusion may occur between myoblasts from different species.[188] These properties appear to be determined by the position of the cell in the mitotic cycle,[12] fusion only occurring during the G1 phase. In cultures of chick myoblasts a period of 5–8 hours elapses between the end of mitosis and fusion.[138] In the normal cell cycle DNA synthesis commences about 2 hours after the cell enters G1, so that the delay of 5 hours suggests that fusing cells have in fact withdrawn from the mitotic cycle. It has been postulated that the mitotic division prior to fusion is a critical one which conditions the cell for fusion by bringing about an abrupt shift from DNA synthesis to the synthesis of RNA required for fusion and the synthetic activity which follows.[137] Agents which act on the cell surface such as the antibiotic cytochalasin B interfere with myoblast fusion *in vitro*.[85] That the extracellular *milieu* is also of importance for fusion has been clearly shown by *in vitro* studies in which varying the pH or lowering the concentration of calcium ions in the culture medium prevents the formation of multinucleate cells.[82,162] These ionic variations may act by interferring with myoblast motility.

Fusion is a dynamic process as witnessed by time-lapse cinematography and may be complete within a period of 1 hour.[20] Visualization of the ultrastructural changes accompanying fusion has posed considerable problems as a high-resolution cinematographic technique is not available. Based upon the interpretation of static electron micrographs there has been considerable debate on the manner in which the adjoining plasma membranes of fusing cells coalesce. The recent study of chick muscle cultures by Shimada[165] has thrown a good deal of light on the matter. The plasma membranes of cells destined to fuse are closely applied to one another and are linked in places by localized thickenings of the cell membranes (*fasciae adherentes* or *tight junctions*). These focal adherences, which are similar to the desmosomes which join certain epithelial cells, have also been observed in developing rat muscle *in vivo*,[101] Small focal deficiencies or pores subsequently appear in the adjoining cell membranes which become continuous at the edges of the defect, thereby establishing a cytoplasmic bridge between the two cells. With further membrane breakdown remnants of the cell membranes are seen as small vesicles. Finally, even these remnants disappear and confluence of cytoplasm is established. Admixture of the cytoplasms of the two cells appears to be a relatively slow process and it is not uncommon still to be able to identify the adjoining cytoplasms on the basis of differing ribosomal concentrations in areas where the cell membranes have disappeared.[155]

C. The Myotube

The term myotube refers to the first recognizable multinucleate form of muscle fibre seen during embryonic development. Myotubes are thin tubular structures in which a peripheral rim of longitudinally-orientated cross-striated myofibrils surrounds a central core of cytoplasm which contains a variable number of large active nuclei arranged end-to-end and other cellular organelles such as mitochondria, Golgi apparatus, ribosomes and polyribosomes, endoplasmic reticulum and glycogen granules (Figs. 3–7). This distribution of myofibrils and other organelles accounts for the distinctive staining patterns of myotubes with routine stains and with specialized histochemical techniques which will be described in a later section.

In the human embryo the first generations of myotubes (*primary myotubes*) appear at about the 5th week and their numbers increase progressively thereafter.[58] With the continuous formation of myofibrils the central cytoplasmic core of the myotube is eventually lost and the nuclei migrate to take up their position at the periphery of the fibre. Few myotubes remain after the 20th week at which stage most fibres are packed with myofibrils and have peripheral nuclei.

There is still some uncertainty about the source of the later generations of myotubes. On the basis of light

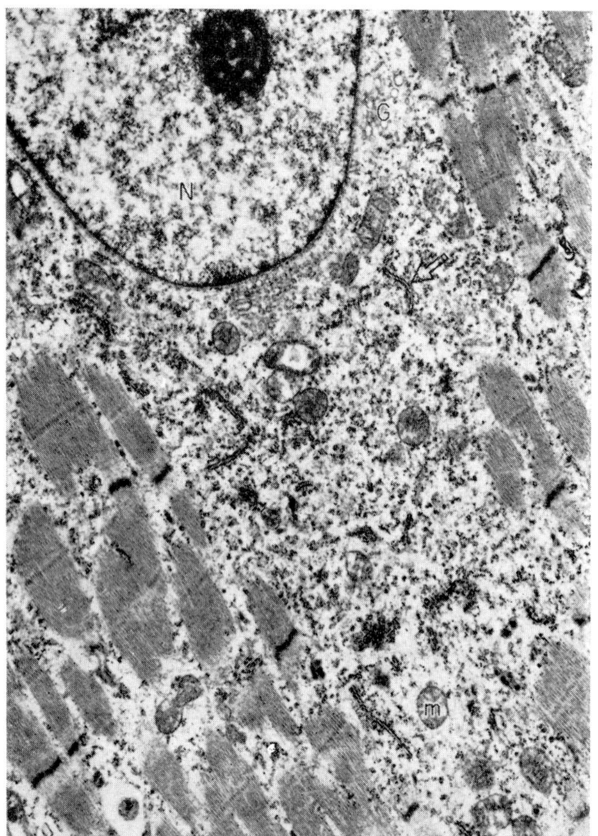

Fig. 7. Electronmicrograph of the central portion of a late myotube in regenerating mouse muscle. Well-developed myofibrils are present on either side of the nucleus (N). The perinuclear sarcoplasm contains many darkly-staining ribosomal particles, granular endoplasmic reticulum (arrow), Golgi apparatus (G) and mitochondria (m). (×13,100)

microscopic observations it was suggested that they are formed by a process of budding from or longitudinal splitting of existing muscle fibres.[35] The more accepted view based on electron microscopic observations is that secondary and subsequent generations of myotubes develop from a persisting population of mononucleated myoblasts which are found in close relationship to the primary myotubes.[101] These cells are closely applied to the early muscle fibres and at a later stage are seen to be enclosed by the basement membrane of the fibre (Fig. 8). Because of the presence of a well-developed granular endoplasmic reticulum they bear a close resemblance to fibroblasts.[90] The subsequent fate of these cells is uncertain. It is known that some of them go on to establish an

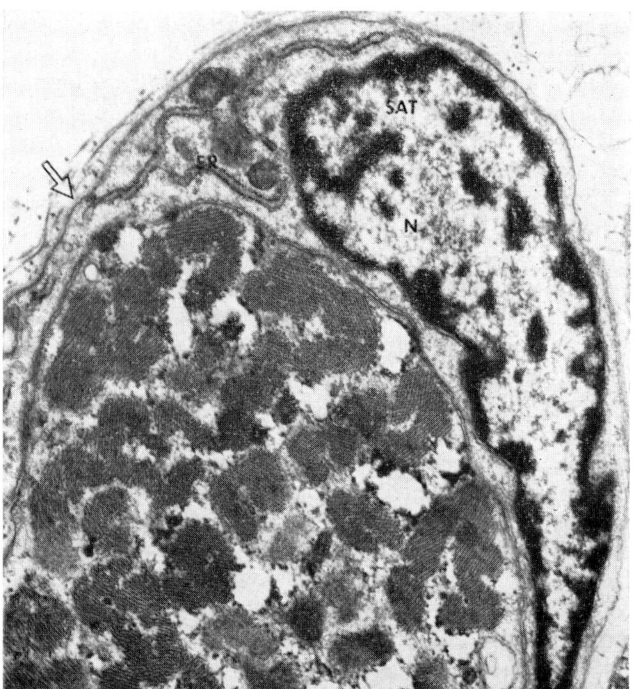

Fig. 8. Eighteen week human fetal muscle. A *satellite cell* (SAT) with a large nucleus (N) and prominent granular endoplasmic reticulum (ER) is closely-applied to a muscle fibre with well-developed myofibrils. A thin basement membrane is seen around the *satellite cell* in places (arrow). The vacuolation of the muscle fibre is a fixation artefact. (×13,100)

even closer relationship with the myotube by way of finger-like invaginations of the plasma membrane (Fig. 9; *see also* [101]) which may extend deeply to the vicinity of the nuclei of the myotube.[111] The nature of this relationship is at present speculative. It may represent a preliminary stage to fusion or alternatively it may be a temporary phase

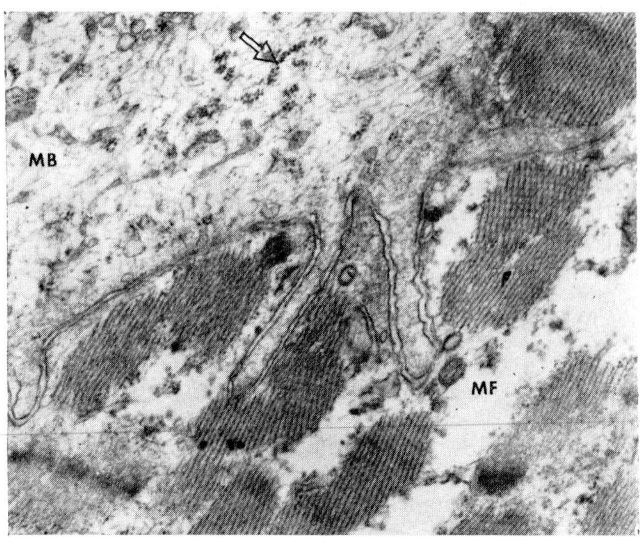

Fig. 9. Eighteen week human fetal muscle. Processes from a myoblast (MB) invaginate the plasma membrane of a muscle (MF) with mature myofibrils. The cytoplasm of the myoblast contains randomly-orientated thin filaments and polyribosomes (arrow). (×14,000)

through which the primary myotube in some way influences the subsequent differentiation of the less mature cells which then separate and go on to form a new generation of myotubes.

A proportion of the "*fibroblast-like*" cells associated with fetal muscle fibres are thought to remain in this situation as the *satellite cells* which are seen in muscle fibres in late human fetal[90] and early adult life[127] (Fig. 10). These cells therefore represent a population of post-mitotic mononucleated cells which are arrested in G1.

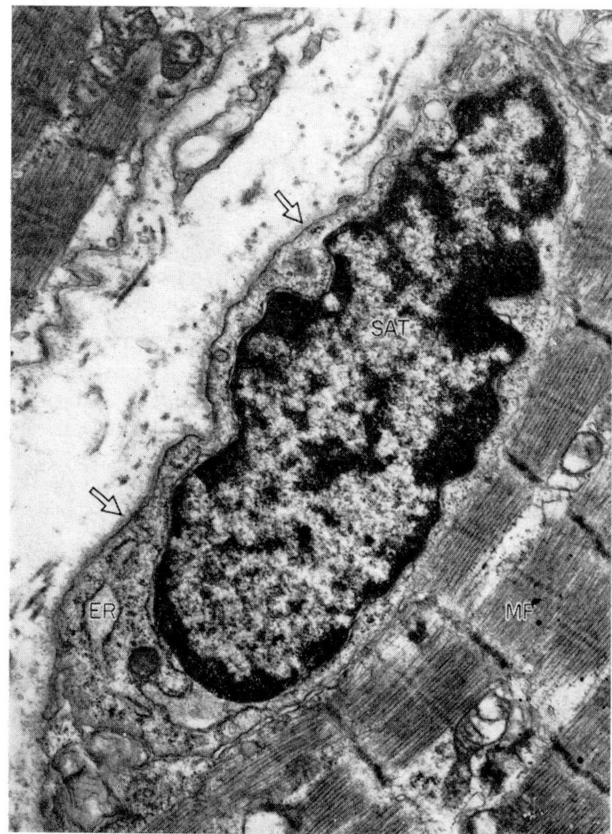

FIG. 10. Neonatal human muscle. A mononucleated *satellite cell* (SAT) with clumped nuclear chromatin and prominent granular endoplasmic reticulum (ER) is seen internal to the basement membrane (arrows) of a muscle fibre with mature myofibrils (MF). (×19,400)

They have presumably not undergone the "quantal" mitosis and do not fuse or synthesize contractile proteins.[82] As will be seen later, however, they may re-enter the mitotic cycle and are thought to participate in the postnatal growth of muscle fibres[161] and in the regeneration of adult muscle after injury.[159]

The development of successive generations of myotubes around primary myotubes is probably the way in which the fascicular pattern of skeletal muscle develops, each fascicle comprising fibres which have developed around a single or a few primary myotubes (Fig. 6). The presence of several generations of myotubes at different stages of growth accounts for the variability in the sizes of muscle fibres in developing muscles in late embryonic and fetal life (Fig. 6). It seems probable that the large "B fibres" described by Wohlfart[186] in human fetal muscle from the 4th month onwards merely represent the more developed generation of fibres derived from primary myotubes rather than a functionally distinct type of muscle fibre.

A detailed study of the development of the basement membrane of muscle fibres has yet to be carried out. During the early stages of myogenesis primitive muscle fibres do not have an identifiable basement membrane.[90] In the human fetus a basement membrane is present at 9 weeks (*see* [60]) but the actual time of appearance is not known, nor is it known which cells are responsible for the synthesis of the glycoproteins of the basement membrane. It may be that this is one of the functions of the mononucleated fibroblast-like cells which are found applied to developing muscle fibres. The prominent granular endoplasmi creticulum in these cells suggests that they could well be involved in the synthesis of such extracellular proteins.

In vitro studies of cultured fetal muscle have contributed significantly to our understanding of the mode of formation and cytological features of myotubes. Although the basic processes are the same as those which occur *in vivo*, the *in vitro* events differ in several respects. One major difference relates to the time-scale of events. Whereas the formation of multinucleate myotubes *in vivo* requires a period of several weeks, *in vitro*, myotubes with several hundred nuclei may form within 24 hours after the onset of fusion.[187] Other differences relate to the pattern of growth and the nuclear/cytoplasmic ratio. *In vitro*, lateral fusion of immature myotubes leads to an appearance of branching which is not seen *in vivo*. The nuclear/cytoplasmic ratio of myotubes *in vitro* is greater than *in vivo* and it seems likely that the accelerated synthesis of contractile proteins which occurs in myotubes *in vitro* is related to this relative hypernucleation.[137] *In vitro* studies have emphasized the importance of collagen in the elongation of myotubes.[76] Myotubes grown in suspension or in contact with glass or mica surfaces do not grow or elongate as they do when in contact with collagen.[82] It would appear, therefore, that the normal development of the muscle fibre is dependent upon the activities of surrounding non-myogenic mesenchymal cells as well as on the intrinsic processes occurring in the muscle cell.

D. Development of the Contractile Apparatus

The development of the contractile elements of the muscle fibre has been elucidated by studies utilizing analytical biochemical and immunological labelling techniques and particularly by electron microscopic examination of muscle developing *in vivo* and in tissue culture. As indicated previously, synthesis of the contractile proteins is initiated in the post-mitotic myoblast. Assembly of cross-striated myofibrils also begins in the myoblast[174] and continues after fusion and throughout the period of maturation of the fetal muscle fibres (Fig. 3). In some muscles striated myofibrils are well-developed in mononucleated myoblasts while in others they only appear after fusion to form myotubes. There is, therefore, no direct relationship between fusion and the initiation of contractile protein synthesis.[82]

The actin filaments ("*thin filaments*") appear to be the first component of the myofibril to be formed.[6,80,113,135] They are found randomly distributed throughout the cytoplasm of early muscle cells prior to the appearance of myosin filaments or Z-band material (Fig. 9). They are wavy in outline and measure approximately 60 Ångstrom units in diameter and about 1 micron in length. Each filament is composed of two tightly coiled strands which are made up of 50 Ångstrom spherical units of G-actin and which cross over one another at intervals of 350 Ångstroms.[6] Fetal actin filaments are morphologically indistinguishable from the thin filaments of mature muscle and there are no known differences in the primary structure of fetal and adult actin molecules. The actin filaments must be distinguished from other 50–100 Ångstrom filaments which are found in myoblasts and in many other kinds of cell. One hundred Ångstrom filaments which may exceed 2·6 micra in length and which do not have the solubility properties of actin have been found in presumptive myoblasts, fibroblasts and chondroblasts in chick embryos.[91] There is no good evidence to support the suggestion that these filaments are the precursors of the actin and myosin filaments.

The myosin filaments ("*thick filaments*") first appear at the periphery of the cell beneath the cell membrane.[62] The earliest aggregates of thick and thin filaments are also seen in this part of the cell and show the characteristic hexagonal pattern seen in the mature myofibril.[62] The myosin filaments measure approximately 160 Ångstroms in diameter in glutaraldehyde-fixed material and are about 1·5 micra in length. In contrast to the actin filaments, the myosin filaments are straight or only gently curved indicating that they are more rigid. They have tapered ends and regularly-spaced lateral projections along the shaft of the filament and are indistinguishable from the thick filaments of the A-band of adult muscle fibres. There do, however, appear to be certain enzymatic and immunochemical differences between fetal and adult myosin. It has been found that fetal myosin has a lower specific ATPase activity than myosin from adult muscle and that the activity of this enzyme increases as development proceeds.[143] Differences in amino acid composition and in low molecular weight components of myosin have also been found. In particular, 3-methyl histidine which is present in adult myosin has been found to be absent in fetal myosin.[143] Other studies have failed to find significant antigenic or chromatographic differences between fetal and adult myosin.[82]

The precursors of the Z-bands are amorphous aggregates of electron-dense material (Z-bodies) which lack the characteristic crystalline pattern of the adult Z-bands.[107] (Fig. 12 shows Z-bands and other structures in a mature muscle fibre.) Each Z-body appears to act as the initial focus for attachment of actin filaments which will subsequently occupy two adjacent sarcomeres.[103,125] Two to four Z-bodies coalesce to form a single Z-band. The Z-bands are at first wavy in outline but subsequently assume their straight well-defined appearance.[113] M-bands are not seen in early myofibrils but are well-formed by the time the myofibrils reach maturity.[62]

The contractile proteins are synthesized on specific polyribosome templates in the cytoplasm of the muscle cell. Polyribosomes are recognizable by electron microscopy as clusters or chains (Fig. 11) of particles of approximately 230 Ångstrom diameter joined together by a 10–15 Ångstrom strand of messenger-RNA (m-RNA).[141] The m-RNA acts as the "code" for the synthesis of the protein molecule and its length and molecular composition varies according to the protein for which it is coding. The amino acids to be incorporated into the protein molecule are carried to the ribosome attached to molecules of transfer-RNA. The usual concept of protein synthesis is that the ribosome moves along the m-RNA strand and that when the end of the strand is reached the polypeptide is complete and the ribosome disengages and is then either degraded by ribonuclease or attaches to another strand of m-RNA.[70] Recent electron microscopic observations have suggested that in the synthesis of myosin the ribosomes may in fact remain stationary and that the m-RNA moves along the row of ribosomes.[112]

Polyribosomes capable of synthesizing myosin, actin and tropomyosin (which is thought to be one of the constituents of thin filaments and Z-bands) have been isolated from embryonic chick muscle by sucrose gradient analysis.[80] The actin-synthesizing polysomes which consist of 15–25 individual ribosomes are the first to appear and can be isolated in large numbers from 10 day embryos. The myosin polysomes which consist of 50–60 ribosomes can be isolated from 14 day embryos. Tropomyosin is thought to be synthesized by polysomes containing 5–9 ribosomes which appear between days 14 and 18. Alpha and β-actinin, troponin and M-band protein-synthesizing polysomes have yet to be identified.

The myosin polysomes have also been identified by electron microscopy in developing myoblasts (Fig. 11) and at the periphery of developing A-bands or between the filaments of the A-bands in studies of developing[112] and regenerating muscle fibres (Fig. 11),[124] suggesting that, unlike the actin molecules, the myosin subunits are synthesized at the site of the developing myofibril. Apparent discrepancies between these electron microscopic observations which indicate that the myosin polysome consists of 20–30 ribosomes and the biochemical studies mentioned previously may be explained on the basis of a spiral arrangement of ribosomes about the developing myosin filament.

The factors responsible for the aggregation and accurate alignment of myofilaments into regularly-spaced sarcomeres are poorly understood. It is known that there is a natural affinity between actin filaments and the heavy meromyosin fraction of the myosin molecule,[81,89] and it seems reasonable to assume that the hexagonal pattern of thick and thin filaments in the myofibril is the direct result of this. It is likely that a similar affinity exists between actin filaments and Z-band proteins. Whether Z-body-actin filament complexing commences prior to actin-myosin complexing remains uncertain. In all probability they occur as simultaneous events.[62] Three transverse structures in the myofibril may be responsible for the orderly transverse alignment of the thick and thin filaments in the sarcomere. These are the Z-band, the M-band

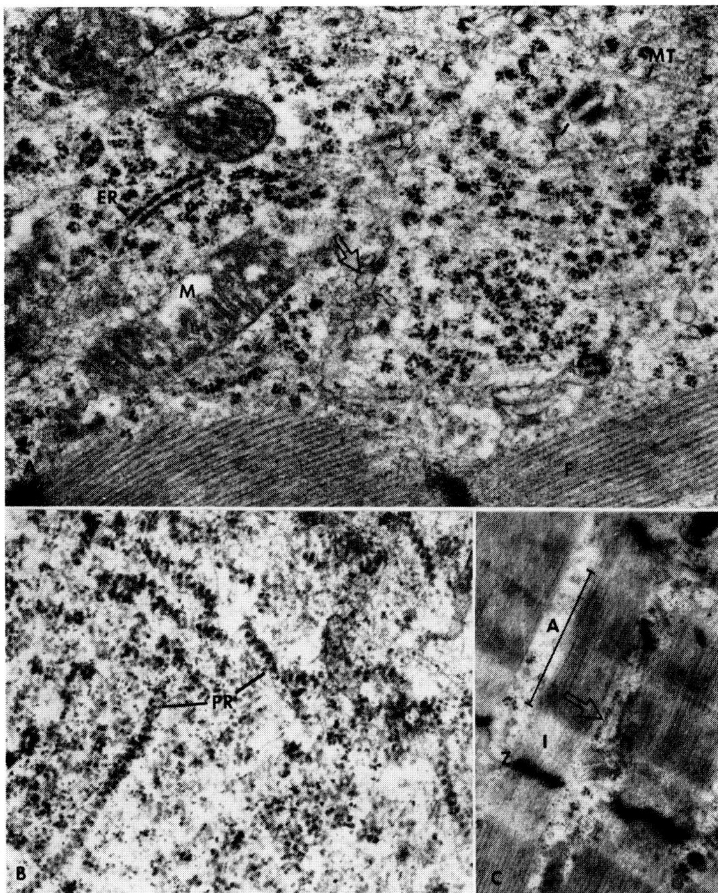

FIG. 11(a). Peripheral portion of a regenerating muscle fibre in grafted mouse muscle showing many densely-staining ribosomal clusters, granular endoplasmic reticulum (ER) microtubules (MT), developing elements of the sarcotubular system (arrow), mitochondria (M) and well-formed myofibrils (F). (×28,500). (b) Polyribosome chains (PR) in a chick embryo myoblast in culture. (×39,600). (c) Regenerating muscle fibre in a case of Duchenne muscular dystrophy showing polyribosome chains (arrow) at the edges of the A-bands (A) of two adjacent myofibrils. I—I-band; Z—Z-band. (×17,300)

cross-bridges between the thick filaments in the middle of the sarcomere and the cross-bridges between the thick and thin filaments where the A- and the I-bands overlap (Fig. 12).

The transverse alignment of myofibrils which exists in mature muscle fibres (Fig. 12) is not so clearly seen in fetal fibres (Fig. 13). Its development may be related to the formation of the tubular systems of the fibre.[6] The orientation initially of myofilaments and subsequently of primitive myofibrils in the longitudinal axis of myotubes may be related to cytoplasmic streaming and elongation of the myotube, processes for which the *microtubules* are thought to be responsible. These thin elongated tubular structures measure approximately 250 Ångstroms in outer diameter and are found in small numbers at the periphery of developing muscle fibres (Fig. 11). Exposure of myotubes to colchicine which interferes with microtubules prevents elongation and leads to the formation of rounded multinucleated myosacs. Although fibrillogenesis is not inhibited, the myofibrils are haphazardly-orientated. When the myosacs begin to elongate again, the longitudinal orientation of myofibrils is restored.[82] It has been suggested that the 100 Ångstrom filaments found in developing muscle cells may be part of a cytoskeletal supporting network around the myofibrils.[103] It is of interest that these filaments increase greatly in number in colchicine-exposed myotubes suggesting that they may also be a reservoir for microtubules.[82]

E. Development of the Tubular Systems

Striated muscle fibres possess two distinct interfibrillar membrane systems, the transverse tubular system (T-system) and the sarcoplasmic reticulum (SR), which are responsible for intracellular spread of the activation for contraction of the myofibrils. The development of these structures has been studied in embryonic chick muscle *in vitro* with the electron microscope. It has been found that both systems begin to develop at the early myotube stage when myofibril formation is already well-advanced.[55]

The membranes of the SR develop as multiple tubular projections from the granular endoplasmic reticulum.

These subsequently elongate and branch to form interconnected honeycomb structures which retain their continuity with the endoplasmic reticulum. The early SR-tubules have no clear relationship to the developing myofibrils. At a later stage tubules are found adjacent to the I- and Z-bands of the myofibrils and these subsequently form an interconnecting network which extends from sarcomere to sarcomere and from myofibril to myofibril.

FIG. 12. Two mature muscle fibres with well-aligned myofibrils. The A, I, Z and M-bands are labelled. The H-zone lies between the two arrow heads. NUC—nucleus. FB—endomysial fibroblast. (×9,600)

The T-system is formed by invagination of the cell membrane of the myotube, the earliest tubules being seen in the subsarcolemmal region. Continuity between the developing T-system and the exterior of the fibre has been demonstrated using ferritin as an electron-dense marker. The tubules subsequently extend deeply into the fibre and branching and network formation may occur. Simple contacts between T-system tubules and the SR are seen in early myotubes and consist merely of apposed membranes. More specialized connections are present in more advanced myotubes leading to the formation of the triads (Fig. 11) which are found alongside the I-bands or A–I junctions in adult muscle fibres. These structures consist of a central tubule derived from the T-system and a lateral sac on either side which is derived from the SR and which has a specialized zone of contact with the central tubule. This junctional area is the site across which excitation spreads from the T-tubule bringing about release of calcium ions from the lateral sacs which in turn activate the contractile system of the muscle fibre.

FIG. 13. Nineteen week human fetal muscle. Four thin muscle fibres with incompletely aligned myofibrils of varying size are seen. (×3,500)

IV. THE INNERVATION OF MUSCLE FIBRES

The establishment of neural contacts on developing muscle fibres represents a critical stage in muscle development. Whereas the early stages of myogenesis may proceed normally in the absence of a nerve supply,[75] intact neural connections enhance muscle development[145] and are important for the complete differentiation of muscle fibres. Many studies have shown that contacts between muscle fibres and nerve terminals exist from an early stage in myogenesis. In the human fetus primitive nerve branches ramify among the developing muscle cells during the 10th week and myoneural junctions begin to form during the 11th week of intrauterine life.[1,35,177] More recently, evidence of early motor end-plate formation has been found by electron microscopy in myotubes at the 10 week stage[60] and acetyl cholinesterase activity has been demonstrated histochemically as early as 8–9 weeks of intrauterine life.[121]

Electron microscopic studies of the intercostal muscles of rat embryos have elucidated the morphogenesis of the motor end-plate.[102] The earliest contacts between motor nerve terminals and myotubes in the rat are seen at day 16 of intrauterine life and are quite primitive, consisting merely of closely-apposed membranes with focal electron-opaque connecting zones. The relationship between these early contact zones and the motor end-plates which subsequently develop is uncertain. It has been suggested that they may, in fact, only be temporary contacts. Actual end-plate formation is first seen at 18 days when synaptic clefts begin to appear on large mytotubes and distinctive changes are seen in the post-synaptic muscle fibre membrane. Acetyl cholinesterase activity can also be demonstrated at this stage. These early motor end-plates are rudimentary and have few junctional folds. The neuromuscular junctions in the rat are still immature at the time of birth and mature end-plates with primary and secondary synaptic clefts are not seen until day 10 after birth. In man, the myoneural junctions are also not fully developed at birth and immature end-plates may be seen up to the age of 2 years.[27]

The changes occurring at the junctional zones on the muscle fibres (the *soleplate*) have been clarified with the electron microscope and certain misconceptions arising from earlier light microscope studies have been corrected. A local accumulation of sarcoplasm and of nuclei (*soleplate nuclei*) is seen in this region (Fig. 14) and, with the overlying nerve terminals (*telodendria*), are responsible for the "primitive eminence" originally recognized by light microscopy.[32] The soleplate sarcoplasm contains mitochondria, prominent granular endoplasmic reticulum and many ribosomes. The soleplate nuclei are characteristically large and rounded and have prominent nucleoli. These features all point to active protein synthesis in the soleplate region. In the past it was considered that the nuclei in this region are derived from existing nuclei in the muscle fibre which divide either mitotically[32] or amitotically.[189] This view is now no longer tenable as it is known that the nuclei of multinucleate muscle cells do not divide. It remains to be determined whether the soleplate nuclei represent existing myonuclei which are attracted to the junctional region as they are migrating to the periphery of the fibre, or whether primitive mononucleated cells are incorporated into the muscle fibre at the soleplate region.

It is now accepted that the changes occurring in the soleplate region develop as a result of contact with the nerve rather than anteceding this contact. The "trophic" influence of nerve on muscle is therefore apparent even at this early stage. The natural tendency for nerve fibres to form contacts on muscle fibres has been well-demonstrated by studies in which muscle and nerve cells have been grown together in tissue culture,[74,97] and is also known from *in vivo* observations of re-innervation of denervated muscle fibres by collateral sprouting of motor nerve axons.[4]

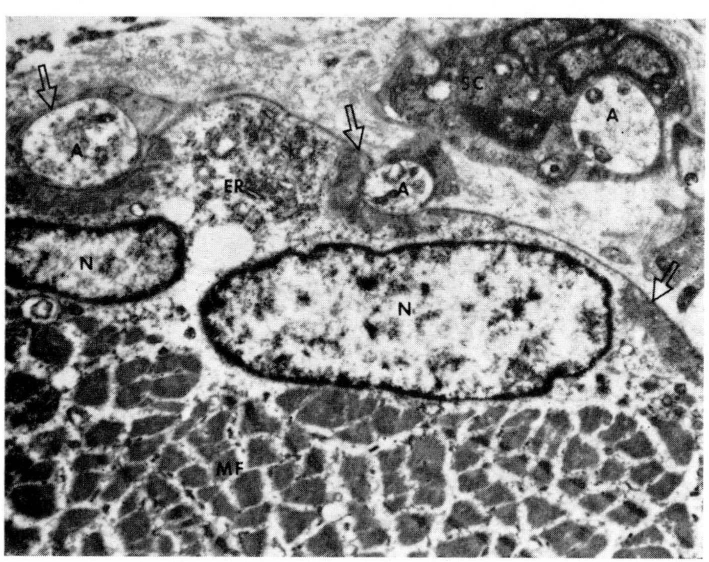

FIG. 14. Developing motor end-plates (arrows) on a regenerating muscle fibre (MF) in grafted mouse muscle. The characteristic thickening of the sarcolemma and early synaptic cleft formation are seen at the end-plate zone of the muscle fibre. N—soleplate nuclei; ER—granular endoplasmic reticulum; A—terminal nerve axons; SC—Schwann cell. (×3380)

It would be interesting to try to correlate the development of muscle innervation with current views on the anatomy of the motor unit based on electrophysiological data. Studies of limb muscles in the rat[49] and in the cat[128] have indicated that the muscle fibres belonging to a single motor unit are widely dispersed throughout the muscle never in groups of more than 4–6 fibres. Evidence that the same also applies in man has recently been presented.[185] It must be assumed, therefore, that the terminal branches of each motor nerve axon are distributed widely throughout the developing muscle with extensive overlapping of terminals from different motoneurones. The origin of the small subgroups of muscle fibres belonging to single motor units is accounted for by the observation in the fetal rat that the primary and later generations of myotubes, which together form small groups, are often innervated by axonal sprouts contained within the same Schwann cell and presumably derived from the same motor nerve axon.[102]

V. BIOCHEMICAL ASPECTS OF MUSCLE DEVELOPMENT

The main biochemical changes which occur during muscle development relate to the synthesis of the contractile proteins, the emergence of the enzyme systems concerned with energy production and utilization, and the evolution of the calcium-transporting system associated with the sarcoplasmic reticulum. The development of the contractile proteins has already been discussed and will not be considered any further. Histochemical studies of adult muscle in man and in other vertebrates have demonstrated the presence of different populations of muscle fibres with different enzymic constitutions which are intermingled in a mosaic pattern.[45,46] The most widely accepted classification of different fibre types is into two main groups: *Type I* fibres show a high concentration of oxidative enzymes such as succinic and lactic dehydrogenase which are concerned with aerobic metabolism. *Type II* fibres on the other hand show a high concentration of glycolytic enzymes such as phosphorylase and of myofibril-associated ATPase.[52] Fibres with enzyme activities intermediate between those of type I and type II fibres are also found in most muscles. The appearance of the more important enzymes and the development of the different fibre types will now be considered.

A. Enzymic Development

Myoblasts

Specific enzyme activities are low in mononucleated myoblasts. Histochemical staining for the oxidative enzymes succinic, lactic and nicotinamide adenine dinucleotide dehydrogenase shows low activities in comparison to multinucleate muscle fibres.[28] Phosphorylase, myofibrillar adenosine triphosphatase (ATPase) and creatine kinase cannot be demonstrated by present histochemical methods. Glyceraldehyde-3-phosphate dehydrogenase has been demonstrated by the more sensitive method of immunofluorescent staining.[50]

In vitro studies of dispersed rat myoblast cultures have shown that there is a steep rise in the production of creatine kinase, phosphorylase, and myokinase (adenylate kinase) after cell fusion commences.[163] In chick myoblast cultures creatine kinase levels only begin to rise after 24 hours in culture and enzyme production remains low if myoblast fusion is inhibited by lowering the calcium concentration in the culture medium (Fig. 15).[37] The initiation of enzyme synthesis is not, however, a direct consequence of cell fusion. Inhibition of RNA synthesis with actinomycin D a short time before the anticipated onset of fusion does not prevent the initial increase in enzyme activities which follows fusion suggesting that the messenger RNA coding for the synthesis of these enzymes is present in the myoblast prior to fusion.[163]

Early Myotubes

Multinucleated myotubes show a progressive increase in the activities of the oxidative enzymes during the first half of intrauterine life and, with minor variations, the activities of these enzymes remains uniform in the majority of fibres during this period. As shown in Fig. 16, activity is highest in the cytoplasmic core of the myotube between the nuclei indicating that the majority of mitochondria are

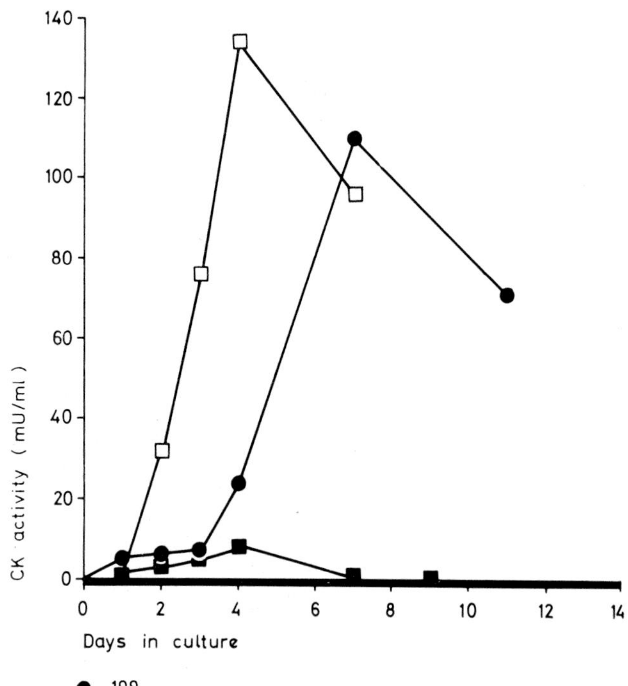

Fig. 15. Creatine kinase activity in cultures of chick embryo muscle grown in different media. With Medium 199 there is a lag phase before activity increases to a peak at 6–8-days. With Minimal Essential Medium the incremental phase is earlier and more rapid. With low calcium, high phosphate medium (MEM Suspension) enzyme activity does not rise above baseline levels. In the latter case the inhibition of creatine kinase synthesis correlates with a striking inhibition of myoblast fusion. (From Dawkins, Smith, Papadimitriou and Holt (1971) by courtesy of Dr. R. L. Dawkins.)

concentrated in this part of the fibre. In contrast, the activity of myofibrillar ATPase, as might be expected, is highest at the periphery of the myotube in relationship to the developing myofibrils (Fig. 16). The activity of this enzyme shows a steady rise over the major period of fibrillogenesis and remains more or less uniform in myotubes of equivalent sizes. Phosphorylase activity is first seen histochemically at about the 11th week in the human embryo and is distributed throughout the myotube surrounding the nuclei.[96] In the chick embryo[104] creatine kinase activity first appears at about day 15 of incubation and has a similar distribution to that of myofibrillar ATPase (Fig. 17a).

Fibre Type Differentiation

In the human embryo some variation in the uniform staining of myotubes may be seen as early as 10–11 weeks with the phosphorylase[96] and myofibrillar ATPase methods.[58] However, at this early stage fibres with high and low activities are not arranged in any definite pattern and the differences in intensity of reaction in different fibres may simply reflect differences in size and degree of maturation. For example, a large myotube with a greater number of peripheral myofibrils will appear to have a higher ATPase activity than a smaller myotube with fewer and less closely-packed myofibrils. Some workers have felt that the two major muscle fibre types develop as separate populations from an early stage in the human embryo.[58] However, the evidence for significant histochemical differences between fibres of an equivalent state of development at this early stage is far from compelling and a subdivision into two distinct histochemical fibre types cannot, in fact, be made with certainty until the 18th to the 20th weeks of gestation.[43] It seems likely that a common fibre type with active oxidative, glycolytic and myofibrillar enzyme systems is present up to this time and that different fibre types subsequently develop as a result of metabolic modifications in this common fibre type probably as a result of innervation.

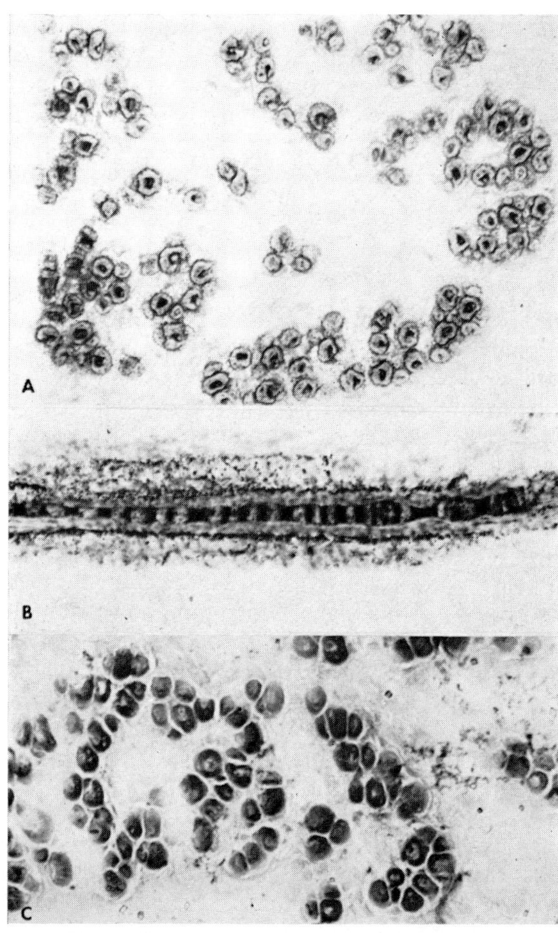

FIG. 16. Nineteen week human embryo. (a) and (b) show intense central staining for lactic dehydrogenase in myotubes, the myonuclei staining lightly. (c)—strong peripheral staining for myofibrillar ATPase. (×250, ×400, ×250)

From the 20th to the 26th weeks only a small proportion of fibres show the histochemical characteristics of type I fibres—viz. a high activity of oxidative enzymes and low activities of glycolytic enzymes (phosphorylase) and myofibrillar ATPase. The majority of fibres show a high activity of phosphorylase and ATPase and low oxidative enzyme activities and would therefore be classed as type II. The type I fibres, which constitute 10 per cent or less of muscle fibres at this stage, are usually the large fibres and are dispersed more-or-less evenly among the type II fibres. The Wohlfart B fibres described in early histological studies of human fetal muscle[186] correspond in size and distribution to these type I fibres.[43,57] After 26 weeks there is a progressive increase in numbers of type I fibres and from 30 weeks to term the muscle shows a chequerboard pattern similar to that of mature adult muscle with approximately equal numbers of type I and type II fibres.[43] It has not, as yet, been established whether the increase in numbers of type I fibres results from the conversion of some type II fibres to type I or from the *de novo* development of more type I fibres. The time of appearance of intermediate-type fibres has not been determined but probably occurs after birth.

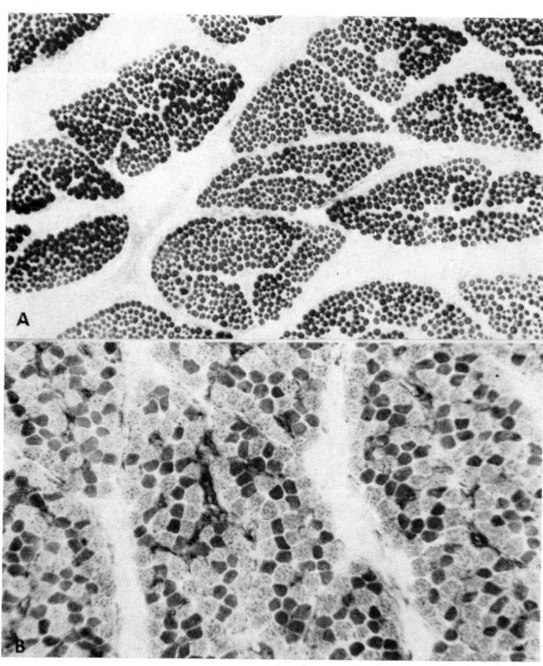

FIG. 17. Creatine kinase activity in chick embryo muscle. (a) Uniformly high activity in most fibres of the pectoralis muscle of a 20-day embryo (×100). (b) mosaic of fibres with high, low and intermediate activity in the gastrocnemius muscle of a 21-day embryo (×140). (From Khan, Holt, Papadimitriou and Kakulas (1971) by courtesy of Mr. M. Khan).

The histochemical differentiation of muscle has also been studied in a number of other species. In general, there appears to be a correlation between the degree of differentiation at birth and the degree of maturity and mobility of the animal at birth which in turn tends to correlate with the length of the gestational period. In the guinea pig, fibre type differentiation begins during the second half of pregnancy and is complete at birth.[43] In the hamster, muscle is also differentiated into two fibre types at the time of birth but further differentiation continues during the first months of life with the appearance of a third fibre type with high activity both of oxidative enzymes and of myofibrillar ATPase.[43,93] In the mouse and rat, fibre type differentiation has not taken place by the time of birth but is complete within the first few weeks of life.[43] In the newborn kitten differentiation is found in the forelimb muscles but not in muscles of the hind-limb.[134] By day 15 two fibre types and by day 40 three types have developed in the gastrocnemius which is a histochemically mixed muscle. On the other hand, the soleus, a red or slow-twitch muscle, remains of one fibre type (type I). Evidence of fibre type differentiation is found as early as day 14 of incubation in the chick embryo gastrocnemius by the creatine kinase technique and is complete before hatching (Fig. 17).[104] On the other hand, the pectoralis retains a uniform pattern of creatine kinase activity even after hatching (Fig. 17). Phosphorylase activity only appears after hatching.[30]

The Basis for Fibre Type Differentiation

A good deal of evidence has accumulated which suggests that the enzymic constitution and contractile properties of muscle fibres (i.e. whether they have a fast or a slow twitch) are determined by the *trophic* influence of the lower motor neurone. For instance, it has been found that in a mature muscle, all the muscle fibres belonging to a single motor unit, and therefore innervated by a single alpha motoneurone, are of the same histochemical type (type I, type II or intermediate).[49] Moreover, denervation of a muscle in the neonatal period interferes with its normal histochemical differentiation. Thus, in the guinea pig the normal transition of soleus from a "mixed" muscle to a predominantly type I muscle does not occur after neonatal sciatic neurectomy.[99] Perhaps the most compelling evidence to date has come from cross-innervation experiments which have shown that the histochemical and contractile characteristics of a muscle are not immutable and may be altered by changing the nerve supply to the muscle. When the nerves supplying the fast-twitch flexor muscles of the lower leg and the slow-twitch soleus muscle in the guinea pig are transposed, islands of type II fibres appear in the soleus which is normally almost exclusively a type I muscle, and islands of type I fibres appear in the flexor muscles.[47,99,156] Moreover, the speed of contraction of the soleus is increased and that of the flexor muscles slowed.[16,44,152]

Isoenzymes

The isozyme pattern of certain enzymes also appears to change during muscle development. The LDH-2, 3 and 4 isoenzymes of lactic dehydrogenase are predominant in human fetal muscle at 20 weeks and there is little variation in the isozyme pattern in different muscles at this time.[176] By full-term the LDH-5 isoenzyme is much more prominent and variations are found in the isozyme pattern in different muscles. In the case of creatine kinase only CK-1 is present at 8 weeks, CK-2 appears at the beginning of the 3rd month and CK-3 at the end of the 3rd month. CK-1 is the predominant form of the enzyme during fetal life whereas CK-2 and particularly CK-3 predominate postnatally.[100] The changes in isozyme patterns during fetal muscle development are also considered to be related to the process of innervation of the muscle.[176]

Sarcoplasmic Reticular ATPase

The specific ATPase activity of the sarcoplasmic reticulum which is considered to be related to the calcium-transporting role of the reticulum reaches its peak activity in the late fetal or early neonatal period. Peak activity develops earlier the more active the animal is at birth suggesting that the degree of use of the muscle directly influences the development of this enzyme system.[143]

B. Lipids during Development

The lipids of the muscle cell are present mainly in the sarcolemma and intracellularly in the membranes of the sarcoplasmic reticulum (SR) and transverse tubular system and in the mitochondria. The membranes of the sarcolemma, the SR and the mitochondria have distinctive lipid compositions.[144] The sarcolemma has the highest lipid/protein ratio and phospholipids account for about 50 per cent of the total lipids compared to 80 per cent of the total lipids in SR and mitochondria. The phospholipid fraction of sarcolemma has a 3- to 4-fold higher content of sphingomyelin and a 2-fold higher content of phosphatidylserine in comparison to the SR and mitochondria. The sarcolemma also differs from the SR and mitochondria in having a high content of cholesterol and free fatty acids.

Lipid analyses of human fetal muscle have shown a number of changes during development.[88] There is a progressive increase in choline plasmalogen which is complete within a few months of birth and a decrease in sphingomyelin which may continue into the second year of life. The development of the distinctive lipid patterns of the different cellular membranes has yet to be studied.

Histochemical studies of lipids in developing chick muscle[148] have shown an absence of stainable lipid in myoblasts. In myotubes a positive histochemical reaction for phospholipids, fatty acids, neutral fat and unsaturated lipids is obtained but not for cholesterol or cholesterol esters. With further differentiation the type I fibres acquire a higher content of neutral fat than the type II fibres.

C. Myoglobin

The haem-containing oxygen-combining protein myoglobin is dissolved in the sarcoplasm of muscle fibres giving them their red colour. Type I muscle fibres (*red* or *tonic*) which are capable of sustained contraction and which rely mainly on the Krebs cycle for energy are richer in myoglobin than the other fibre types.[130]

Studies of developing muscle *in vitro* have shown that, as in the case of the contractile proteins, myoglobin is not synthesized by replicating mononucleated cells and only appears in postmitotic myotubes.[83] The haem-containing pigment found in fetal muscle ("fetal myoglobin") has been shown to have properties which differ from those of adult myoglobin.[168] The fetal protein has a much more rapid electrophoretic mobility when studied as the metprotein. Conversion to the cyanmet form has little effect on the mobility of fetal myoglobin but markedly increases the mobility of the adult protein.[142] Adult myoglobin is first detected in small amounts at about term in the human fetus and increases during infancy.[168]

VI. IMMUNOLOGICAL DEVELOPMENT OF MUSCLE

Mature muscle possesses a number of apparently distinct antigenic determinants. Some, such as the contractile proteins are tissue-specific while others such as the histocompatibility antigens are species-specific but not tissue-specific.

A. Species-specific Surface Antigens

It is generally stated that skeletal muscle possesses a low concentration of histocompatibility antigens.[92] However, the demonstration of lymphocyte-mediated rejection of mature muscle transplants between allogeneic mice suggests that significant tissue-specific antigens do exist on the surface of adult muscle fibres.[126]

The presence of species-specific antigens on the surface of differentiating muscle cells has been demonstrated by immunofluorescent staining of monolayers of chick embryo muscle *in vitro*.[38] Such antigens are present on mononucleated myoblasts as well as on differentiated multinucleated muscle cells.

B. Tissue-specific Antigens

Tissue-specific antigens may be defined as those which react with antibodies produced by immunization with extracts of that tissue. In the case of muscle the most abundant tissue-specific antigens are associated with the contractile proteins. Others are sarcolemmal and subsarcolemmal.

Contractile Proteins

Antibodies to myosin and actin have been used to detect the onset of contractile protein synthesis in developing muscle and to localize these proteins in the cell. Antisera against myosin and actin react with extracts of amphibian and chick embryos as early as the late gastrula stage.[63] Myosin has subsequently been localized to the myotomes[84] and to the heart-forming areas in the chick embryo.[63] Actin may be detected at a somewhat earlier stage than myosin by precipitin reactions in the chick embryo.[136] The use of fluorescein-labelled antisera against myosin, actin and the meromyosin fractions of myosin demonstrates the presence of these proteins in mononucleated myoblasts and in myotubes.[84] Cross-striated myofibrils may be seen in elongated myoblasts using this technique but are best seen in myotubes (Fig. 4).

Non-myofibrillar Antigens

Tissue-specific antigens distinct from the contractile proteins are also known to exist in skeletal muscle as well as antigens which are common to skeletal, cardiac and smooth muscle.[98] Antigens common to rabbit skeletal and cardiac muscle can be localized to the sarcolemma and subsarcolemmal region by immunofluorescence with rabbit antisera to either heterologous heart or skeletal muscle.[48] Shared antigens also react with rabbit antisera to Freund's adjuvant emulsions of the cell walls of certain streptococci and with sera from some patients with rheumatic fever.[48] These non-myofibrillar antigens have yet to be studied in differentiating muscle.

Fibre-specific Antigens

It has been known for some time that there are antigenic differences between fibres in adult muscles.[56] Recently it has been found that immunization with certain components of muscle can induce antibodies which react specifically with one fibre type.[36,72] The use of such fibre type-specific antisera may therefore be of value in supplementing routine histochemical techniques. The evolution of these fibre-specific antigens during muscle development has yet to be studied.

VII. ELECTROPHYSIOLOGICAL CHANGES DURING MUSCLE DEVELOPMENT

Little is known of the electrical properties of developing skeletal muscle fibres or of the evolution of the distinctive properties of the muscle cell membrane. Most information has come from intracellular recordings from developing muscle cells in tissue culture.[33,61] Such studies have shown that myoblasts have a resting membrane potential of about −70 mV and behave in an electrically passive manner when depolarizing or hyperpolarizing pulses of current are passed into them.[74] Cells which are in contact are always electrically coupled. Myoblasts are sensitive to acetylcholine and when it is applied iontophoretically to the surface of the cell a long-lasting (15–30 secs.) hyperpolarization with a concomitant increase in membrane conductance is brought about. Fusion of myoblasts to form binucleate or multinucleate cells is accompanied by a fall in resting membrane potential to about −50 mV. Multinucleate cells may still show the slow hyperpolarizing response to acetylcholine but a dual response consisting of an initial fast depolarization followed by a slow hyperpolarization is more usual. Depolarizing stimuli produce little active response at this stage but hyperpolarization of the cell to about −150 mV with an abruptly terminated stimulus will elicit an action potential.

With further growth of myotubes the resting potentials increase[61,74] and action potentials which may be repetitive are evoked by depolarizing stimuli. Spontaneous action potentials arise in the most mature myotubes with a steady frequency of about 1 per second correlating with the observation that fairly mature multinucleate muscle cells contract spontaneously provided adequate culture conditions, particularly the calcium concentration, are maintained. The increasing membrane potential with maturation is thought to be due to changes in trans-membrane electrochemical gradients resulting from re-distribution of ions.

The electrophysiological changes associated with muscle fibre innervation have been studied in mixed cultures of muscle and spinal cord.[97] Recording from intracellular microelectrodes it has been possible to identify innervated fibres by the finding of end-plate potentials as well as evoked action potentials on stimulation of the spinal cord explant. Non-contractile myotubes with as few as three nuclei may show evidence of junctional transmission *in vitro*.[153] Innervated muscle fibres may also be recognized on the basis of their sensitivity to acetylcholine iontophoretically applied to the surface of the fibre. Prior to the formation of neuromuscular junctions muscle fibres are uniformly sensitive to acetylcholine and wherever it is applied on the surface of the cell a rapid depolarization results within 50 milliseconds. After innervation the acetylcholine-sensitive region of the fibre shrinks progressively and becomes confined to the end-plate zone.[41,74,97]

Studies in neonatal mice have shown that there is an increase in the membrane potential of muscle fibres during postnatal maturation.[73] The changes in membrane potential have been found to differ in fast and slow muscles. The mean resting membrane potential in the fast extensor digitorum longus muscle is lower than that in the slow soleus muscle in the first few weeks after birth but exceeds that in soleus by 4 months of age.[73]

VIII. FUNCTIONAL ASPECTS OF MUSCLE DEVELOPMENT

That immature muscle fibres possess intrinsic contractility unrelated to neural influences is well known from observations of spontaneous contraction in cultures of embryonic muscle.[132] This spontaneous activity of muscle *in vitro* is associated with a low threshold of electrical excitability and may be influenced by changes in the ionic composition of the culture medium and by a variety of pharmacological agents.[132] Whether such spontaneous contractility occurs at an equivalent state of differentiation *in vivo* is not known.

Although simple contacts between motor nerve terminals and muscle fibres exist from an early stage of embryogenesis, it is likely that effective neuromuscular transmission only occurs once motor end-plates are formed. This would be in keeping with the observation that consistent reflex movements are not elicited before the 12th gestational week in the human fetus[1] and fetal movements are not felt by the mother until the 4th month.

The skeletal muscles of most mammals are not functionally mature at birth. In the adult, the contractile properties of different limb muscles differ. Some, such as the flexor hallucis longus (FHL) and the extensor digitorum longus (EDL) have a fast contraction time while others, such as the soleus, contract much more slowly in response to a nerve stimulus. At birth, the limb muscles of most mammals are uniformly slow-contracting[10] and differentiation into fast and slow muscles only occurs during the early postnatal period.[26] The functional maturation of limb muscles has been studied mainly in the rat,[25] mouse[26] and cat.[17] In the rat and mouse the isometric twitch contraction times in the EDL and soleus are about the same at birth. Thereafter, the responses of both muscles speed up but that of EDL eventually becomes 2–3 times faster than that of soleus. The relaxation time in soleus is longer than in EDL even at birth and with further shortening of the relaxation time in EDL the difference becomes even greater. In the cat, the contraction and relaxation times of FHL are shorter than those of soleus at birth and the differences become progressively greater during the first few weeks of life due to speeding up of the FHL. These changes in the contractile properties of muscles after birth in the rat, mouse and cat parallel the histochemical maturation of the muscles which occur mainly in the postnatal period in these animals.[43,134] As mentioned previously, both processes appear to be neurally-determined.

IX. THE GROWTH OF SKELETAL MUSCLE

A. Mechanisms of Growth

The growth of the skeletal muscles results both from an increase in the number of muscle fibres and from an increase in size of individual fibres. The relative extent to which increase in numbers and increase in size of fibres contribute to postnatal muscle growth varies from species to species. Increase in fibre numbers is more characteristic of primates whereas in lower species such as the rat, increase in size of fibres plays a greater part.[21]

In man the greatest increase in fibre numbers occurs during fetal life. For example, there is a 20-fold increase in the number of fibres in the sartorius muscle from the third month of gestation to full-term.[118] The number of fibres continues to increase after birth and there is also a steady increase in the size of muscle fibres.[3] In the male, there is a 14-fold increase in the number of fibres from 2 months to 16 years of age with a rapid spurt at 2 years and a maximal rate of increase from 10 to 16 years during which time muscle fibre numbers double.[21] Muscle fibre size shows a steady linear increase from infancy through to adolescence and beyond in the male. In the female, the increase in fibre numbers occurs in a more linear fashion, the overall postnatal increase being about 10-fold. On the other hand, increase in muscle cell size is more rapid in the female after the age of 3½ years and reaches a plateau at 10½ years. The line for increase in muscle cell size in males crosses that for females at 14½ years, after which cell size goes on to exceed that in females.[21] Fibre counts in the superior rectus, biceps brachii and sartorius muscles in older individuals have shown that there is a steady increase in fibre numbers up to the middle of the 5th decade after which there is a steady decline.[2]

In the rat there is a rapid increase in fibre numbers in the first 2–3 weeks of life[22] but no increase thereafter.[51] In the marsupial quokka (Setonix brachyurus), there is a 30-fold increase in fibre numbers postnatally beginning at about day 15 of pouch life and increasing rapidly to day 100.[15] In sheep, all fibres are relatively small at birth and there is a steady but slow increase in diameter until about

60 days of postnatal life when a new population of small fibres appears. At about 100 days all fibres start to increase in diameter at a rapid rate.[94] In the mouse the number of muscle fibres does not increase after birth[68] and the increase in muscle bulk is due mainly to the growth of existing fibres.

The growth of muscle fibres postnatally and in the late fetal and early neonatal periods appears to be related to functional requirements. For example, in the human neonate the fibres of the diaphragm are twice the size of fibres in the intercostal and limb muscles presumably because respiration is the main form of muscular activity in the neonatal period. In older children, on the other hand, fibres in limb muscles are of about the same size as fibres in the diaphragm while extraocular muscle fibres are scarcely larger than at birth.[13] Hormonal influences are thought to be responsible for the different growth pattern of muscles in the two sexes.[21] Androgens may be responsible for the continued growth of muscle fibres after sexual maturation in the male and, with growth hormone, may also enhance multiplication of muscle nuclei. Oestrogens on the other hand, probably stimulate an increase in fibre size and at high levels restrict nuclear multiplication.[21]

B. Increase in Numbers of Muscle Fibres

There are three possible ways in which the increase in numbers of muscle fibres might come about:

(i) By the *de novo* formation of muscle fibres from undifferentiated mononucleated cells still remaining in the muscle.[31]

(ii) By budding from or longitudinal splitting of existing muscle fibres.[35]

(iii) By lengthening of short fibres which did not previously traverse the full length of the muscle so that there would be an apparent rather than a true increase in the number of fibres in a cross-section of the muscle.[129]

It is known from observations of serial cross-sections of developing muscles in the marsupial quokka that fibres extend the full length of the muscle.[15] It is unlikely, therefore, that the increase in fibre numbers is due simply to lengthening of short fibres. The suggestion that new fibres might be formed by budding from or splitting of existing differentiated muscle fibres was based on light microscopic observations[35] and has not been supported by electron microscope studies of fetal muscle.[90] Some support for the view that longitudinal fibre splitting may contribute to increases in fibre numbers has come from observations in the marsupial quokka in which it has been found that the cross-sectional area of individual muscle fibres decreases during the period that fibre numbers are rapidly increasing.[15] Fibre splitting is known to occur in adult rat muscle undergoing hypertrophy.[179] As mentioned previously, electron microscopic studies of fetal rat muscle have shown that new generations of muscle fibres appear to develop from undifferentiated mononucleated cells which are at first closely associated with primary myotubes and which presumably fuse to form new syncytia which subsequently separate from the primary myotube and continue to differentiate.[101]

C. Increase in Fibre Diameter and Cross-sectional Area

Studies in the mouse have shown that the postnatal increase in size of muscle fibres results principally from an increase in the numbers and sizes of myofibrils.[67] In the mouse biceps brachii the number of myofibrils in some fibres increases 16-fold during the postnatal growth period. Electron microscopic observations have shown that the numerical increase is brought about by longitudinal splitting of myofibrils once they attain a certain size. The distribution of myofibril sizes in postnatal mouse muscle fibres is a bimodal one and splitting myofibrils are about twice the size of non-splitting myofibrils suggesting that splitting occurs more or less down the middle of myofibrils. After splitting, the small myofibrils are again built up in size, presumably by the addition of newly-synthesized myofilaments circumferentially around sarcomeres, and may subsequently split again. It has been estimated that in the mouse the myofibrils of fibres which undergo the most extensive growth split four times during the animal's life time.[67] Splitting of myofibrils is also seen in human fetal muscle fibres (Fig. 13).

D. Increase in Length of Muscle Fibres

The mechanism of longitudinal growth of muscle fibres has been elucidated by studies in which markers were placed at intervals along the gracilis muscle in young mice.[106] The intervals between markers were found to remain constant over a period of time in spite of considerable increase in length of the whole muscle. It has been concluded therefore that muscle fibres increase in length by a process of appositional growth involving the addition of new sarcomeres at each end of the existing myofibrils.

E. Increase in Numbers of Myonuclei

The number of myonuclei in developing muscles increases steadily throughout the period of growth. In the human sartorius muscle there is a 10-fold increase after birth.[129] In the rat, up to 4-fold increases occur between the ages of 15 and 94 days.[51] Autoradiographic and electron microscopic studies in the growing rat have shown that the undifferentiated mononucleated *satellite cells* which are found in variable numbers internal to the basement membrane of muscle fibres, particularly in young animals,[127] are the probable source of additional muscle fibre nuclei.[5,159,119] These cells undergo mitotic division and one or both daughter nuclei may then be incorporated into the parent muscle fibre.[131] Nuclei already in the muscle fibre do not divide. Comparison of satellite cell numbers at birth and in the adult provide indirect evidence that these cells are incorporated into growing muscle fibres. Thus, while 32 per cent of muscle nuclei in the rat subclavius muscle belong to satellite cells at birth, the figure falls to 5 per cent in the adult muscle.[5] Satellite cell incorporation is also thought to occur in mature muscle fibres undergoing hypertrophy.[149] Autoradiographic studies of the mouse gracilis muscle have shown that the new nuclei appear mainly at the growing ends of muscle fibres.[106]

X. REGENERATION OF SKELETAL MUSCLE

The ability of mature muscle fibres to regenerate after injury is now well-established both after experimental lesions and as a sequel to segmental necrosis of muscle fibres in a variety of necrobiotic myopathies in man and in animals.[1] Regeneration of muscle is a unique process as it represents a form of repair to a syncytium which has usually only been partially damaged. The cytological events occurring during regeneration are fundamentally very closely related to the embryonic development of muscle and are therefore of relevance to this discussion.

Traditionally, two basic mechanisms of muscle regeneration are recognized. The first (*regeneration-in-continuity*) involves budding from the intact ends of a muscle fibre after a segment of the fibre has undergone necrosis and phagocytosis. This type of regeneration has been thought to occur when a muscle is divided or part of a muscle undergoes ischaemic necrosis[24] or some other form of focal injury,[158] but almost certainly plays only a minor role in the restitution of extensively damaged muscle fibres.[7,123] The second form of regeneration (*discontinuous* or *embryonal regeneration*) is of greater importance and is more closely analogous to embryonic myogenesis as it involves the appearance of undifferentiated mononucleated cells (*myoblasts*) which undergo mitotic divisions and subsequently fuse to form a new syncytium which replaces the damaged segment.[123] It is not unreasonable, as originally suggested by Volkmann[181], that both forms of regeneration should play a part in the reconstitution of the muscle fibre, the new syncytium eventually joining up with the small "buds" from the intact ends of the fibre. It is conceivable that repair of lesser injuries which do not interrupt the continuity of the muscle fibre may be effected without the intervention of new myogenic cells.

Despite suggestions of an origin from undifferentiated interstitial mesenchymal cells[114] or from circulating cells,[11] it is now generally accepted, mainly on the basis of autoradiographic studies, that myoblasts are derived from cells or nuclei already within the muscle fibre.[182] There is still considerable debate, however, as to whether they originate from the undifferentiated subsarcolemmal *satellite cells* of muscle fibres[127] or by a process of dedifferentiation of nuclei within the syncytium. Electron microscopic studies in the regenerating salamander limb[77] and in mice and rabbits[151] have shown that mononucleated cells do in fact separate off from injured muscle fibres by the formation of new cell membranes around a myonucleus and a portion of its surrounding sarcoplasm and that these cells subsequently redifferentiate. Significantly, *satellite cells* are not found in the mature muscle of these animals. It has been argued that because of the rarity of *satellite cells* in normal adult mammalian muscle they could not give rise to the large numbers of myoblasts which form during regeneration. The *satellite cell* theory, although an attractive one, is based essentially on circumstantial evidence such as the subsarcolemmal position of early myoblasts at the periphery of degenerating muscle fibres[123,159] and the impression that satellite cells are no longer seen once myoblasts begin to appear.[23] Although this matter is not yet settled, the evidence at present appears to be more in favour of the dedifferentiation concept. It could well be, however, that myoblasts are not derived from the same source in all species and that in those animals which do have significant numbers of satellite cells, such as the frog[127] and the bat,[23] these cells may differentiate into myoblasts.

Although the processes of myoblast division and fusion and the evolution of the contractile apparatus and tubular systems have not been as well-studied in regenerating muscle fibres as in embryonic muscle, observations to date have not revealed significant differences[125,146] (Figs. 7, 11, 18) and they will not therefore be considered further.

XI. DEVELOPMENT OF THE MUSCLE SPINDLE

The development of this complex stretch-sensitive receptor organ has been traced in the human fetus[34] and in the chicken.[39,177] In the human, the earliest stages of muscle spindle formation are seen at about the 11th week of intrauterine life when distinctive spiral nerve endings appear around a single or a small group of neighbouring myotubes which will eventually become the intrafusal muscle fibres. At about 12 weeks small collections of myoblasts appear around short segments of one or two of these myotubes and the incorporation of these cells into the fibre gives rise to the localized aggregate of nuclei which are a feature of the *nuclear bag* type of intrafusal muscle fibre. The bulge produced by these nuclei represents the future equatorial zone of the muscle spindle. The remaining muscle cells in the group retain the myotube form and will become the *nuclear chain* type of intrafusal muscle fibre. The first layer of the capsule of the muscle spindle forms at about the 12th week and consists of a single layer of connective tissue cells. At the 14th week, as a result of separation of the capsule from the developing intrafusal fibres, the *periaxial lymph space* appears. By the 14th week of fetal life the muscle spindle has acquired all its essential components and the main change thereafter is one of increasing dimensions. Further lamellae of connective tissue cells are laid down on the capsule, the lymph space widens and the intrafusal muscle fibres continue to grow in the same way as their extrafusal counterparts. Between the 24th to the 31st weeks the muscle spindle acquires its mature form (Fig. 20).

The nerve fibres supplying the muscle spindle are thinly myelinated at 14–15 weeks and by 24 weeks are thickly myelinated.[34] The major nerve of supply penetrates the capsule in the equatorial region and divides into a series of fine unmyelinated terminal branches while in the periaxial lymph space. These terminal ramifications form a network around the intrafusal muscle fibres. Two types of motor ending are found on intrafusal fibres. The *plate*

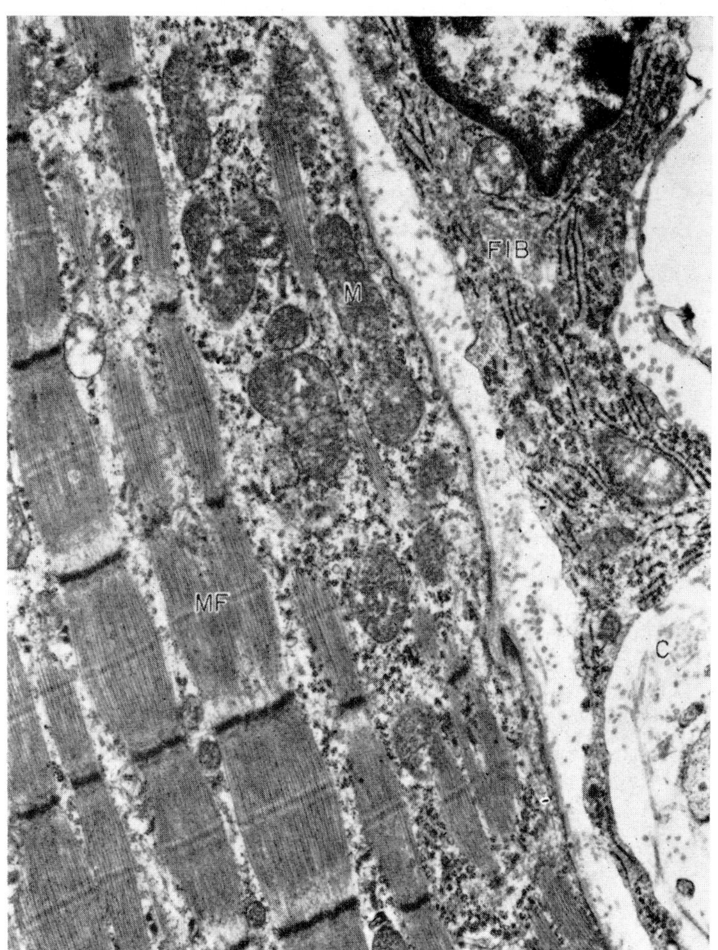

FIG. 18. Regenerating mouse muscle. Portion of a regenerating muscle fibre with well-formed myofibrils (MF), many ribosomal aggregates and large mitochondria (M), and an active endomysial fibroblast with prominent granular endoplasmic reticulum and surrounding collagen fibres (C). (×15,600)

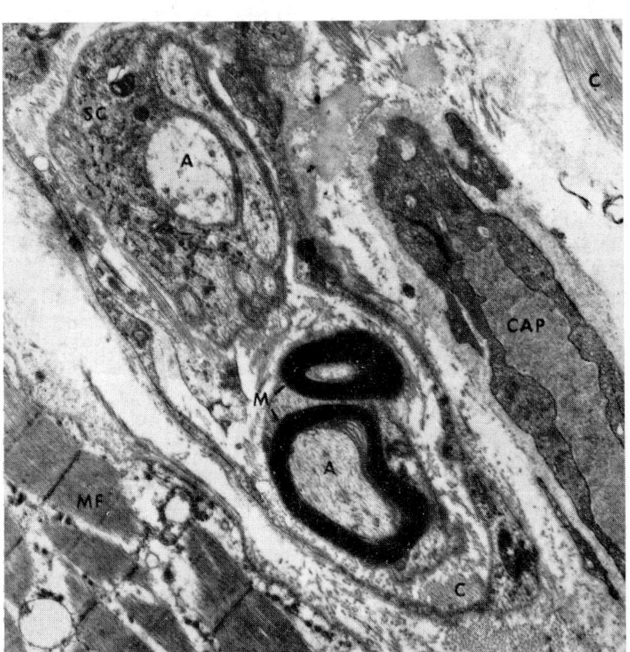

FIG. 19. Regenerating mouse muscle. Developing endomysial nerves and capillary (CAP). The lower nerve has a thin myelin sheath (M). SC—Schwann cell with enclosed unmyelinated axons (A). C—collagen. MF—muscle fibre. (×6,000)

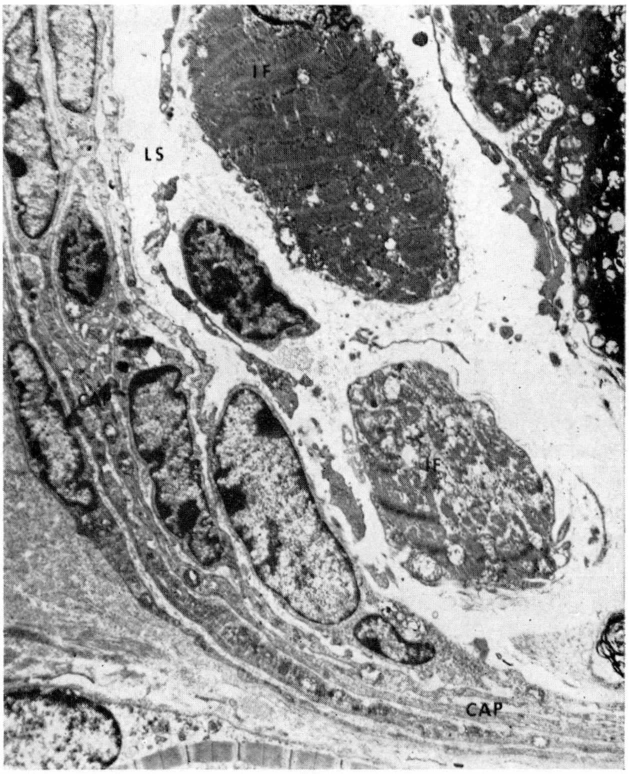

FIG. 20. Muscle spindle in regenerating mouse muscle. CAP—capsule. LS—lymph space. IF—intrafusal muscle fibres. (×2,560)

endings resemble the small round extrafusal motor end-plates while the *trail endings* are finer and more diffuse.[110] The plate endings develop on both types of intrafusal fibre but are found particularly on the portions of the nuclear bag fibres which extend outside the capsule. The trail endings are found mainly on nuclear chain fibres. The primary sensory ending (*annulo-spiral ending*) is coiled around the equatorial portion of the nuclear bag and nuclear chain fibres. The nerve ending is a flat structure which lies in a shallow trough on the surface of the muscle fibre. Whereas in the motor ending the basement membrane of the muscle fibre separates the plasma membrane of the muscle fibre from that of the nerve terminal, the sensory ending lies internal to the muscle fibre basement membrane and the two plasma membranes are therefore in direct contact.[110]

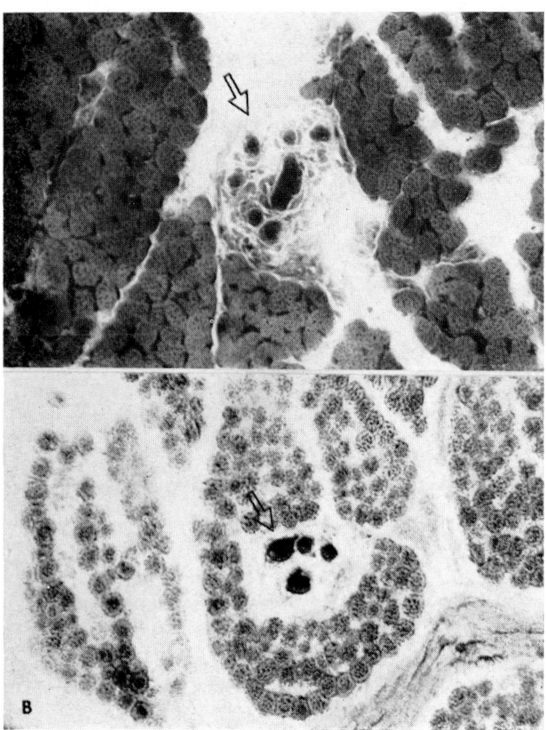

FIG. 21. Developing muscle spindles (arrows) in 20-day chick embryo leg muscle. (a) Haematoxylin and eosin (×210). (b) Succinic dehydrogenase. The intrafusal muscle fibres show a very intense reaction in comparison to the uniformly lesser reaction of the extrafusal fibres (×210.)

Histochemical studies in the chicken[39] have shown that in the early stages of spindle formation the equatorial zone is intensely positive for lipids, proteins, oxidative enzymes (Fig. 21) and cholinesterase. Glycogen and phosphorylase only appear at a later stage. By days 15–16 two histochemical fibre types are recognizable in the polar region and after day 17, a third type is also seen.

In mature spindles, all the intrafusal muscle fibres retain a level of oxidative enzyme activity which is greater than that of the extrafusal type I fibres.[133,172] In human muscle spindles the nuclear chain fibres also have a high activity of myofibrillar ATPase but have a low glycogen content and low phosphorylase activity. The nuclear bag fibres have a low glycogen content, low phosphorylase activity and a lower ATPase activity than the nuclear chain fibres. The nuclear bag fibres are not histochemically uniform and two subtypes can be recognized on the basis of ATPase activity. As in the case of the extrafusal muscle fibres, the intrinsic enzymic properties of the intrafusal muscle fibres are thought to be determined by their innervation. It is likely that the different metabolic types of intrafusal muscle fibre have their own contractile characteristics which are in turn of importance in determining the type of sensory discharge which they generate.

XII. DEVELOPMENT OF THE SUPPORTING TISSUES

A. Interstitial Connective Tissue

During the early weeks of embryonic life the primitive mesodermal cells destined to give rise to the connective tissue cannot be distinguished from the presumptive myoblastic cells. At the stage when the differentiation of myoblasts begins the connective tissue cells which are interspersed among them become recognizable by the presence of a well-developed granular endoplasmic reticulum and collagen fibrils begin to appear interstitially (Fig. 18). The developing connective tissue separates the early myotubes. Once subsequent generations of myotubes develop, small groups of muscle fibres are separated from each other by bands of connective tissue (Fig. 6 and 22). These bands which will subsequently become the *perimysium* which surrounds fascicles of muscle fibres are composed of sparse numbers of fibroblasts and developing small blood vessels lying in a loose collagenous stroma. Small numbers of histiocytic cells are also present and foci of haemopoietic tissue are not uncommon particularly in the more distal limb muscles.[1]

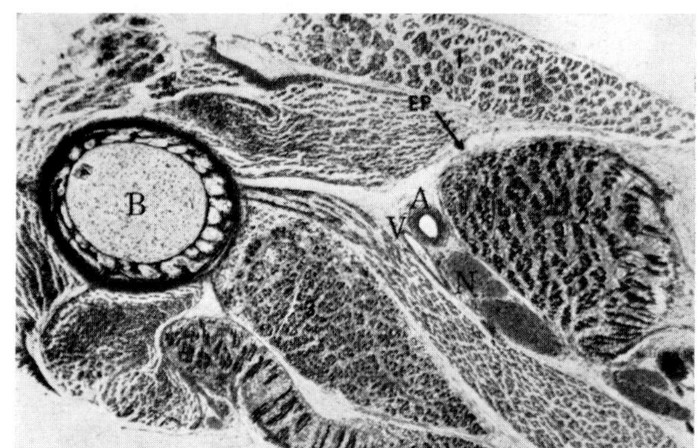

FIG. 22. Cross-section of the lower limb at the mid-thigh level in a 10-day chick embryo showing the developing bone (B) and individual muscles some of which run obliquely. In the muscles which are still at the myotube stage (1, 2, 3) the perimysial connective tissue is still prominent. EP—epimysium. The main artery, vein and nerve to the limb are also seen interstitially. (×2,440)

The *endomysium* does not assume its final form until late in fetal life. Prior to this, individual muscle fibres tend to be widely-spaced and are separated by loose connective tissue. The endomysial connective tissue consists of fine reticular fibrils which are closely applied to the muscle fibres but are separated from them by bundles of thicker collagenous fibres which spiral around the muscle fibre before ramifying and joining larger collagenous bundles in the endomysium and perimysium.[1] In the endomysium are found the capillary network which develops around muscle fibres and the terminal nerve filaments (Fig. 19). The elastic properties of the endomysium and perimysium are of considerable importance in that they allow for independent contraction of fascicles of muscle fibres or of individual muscle fibres within fascicles such as occurs during submaximal muscle contraction.

The *epimysium* which envelopes individual muscles, and the fascial sheaths which separate muscle compartments represent denser condensations of relatively acellular collagenous tissue.

B. Tendons and Musculotendinous Junctions

Tendons are composed of longitudinally orientated bundles of collagen fibres which are closely applied to rows of slender fibroblasts with little cytoplasm. Primary bundles which contain a small amount of elastic tissue as well as collagen become grouped into secondary bundles which are in turn surrounded by septa of loose connective tissue.[1] A fibrous sheath (the *vagina fibrosa*) subsequently forms around the whole tendon.

The nature of the myotendinous junction has been a matter of controversy and warrants further investigation. One school of thought has been that the terminal myofibrils of muscle fibres attach to the inner surface of the sarcolemma while the tendon fibrils attach to the outer surface. Others have contended that the myofibrils and tendon fibrils are continuous through pores in the sarcolemma at the ends of the fibre. Electron microscopy has clarified the situation and has shown a distinctive modification of the terminal sarcolemma (Fig. 23). A complex series of invaginations of the sarcolemma is seen at the end of the fibre and into these extend small bundles of parallel tendon fibrils. These penetrate to the depths of the primary and subsidiary invaginations and appear to join with the basement membrane lining these invaginations. Uniformly applied to the inner aspect of the muscle cell membrane is a continuous electron-dense zone of variable thickness which appears to represent the modified Z-bands of the terminal sarcomeres of the myofibrils. The filaments of the terminal I-bands appear to insert into this zone. It would seem likely that the invaginated tendon fibrils may gain a similar form of attachment to the outer surface of this modified terminal sarcolemma. Cholinesterase activity has been demonstrated histochemically in the region of developing myotendinous junctions in various species.[96,117] In the human fetus it is first seen between 10–14 weeks. This finding suggests that there may be some relationship between the formation of myotendinous junctions and the innervation of the muscle fibres. However, its precise significance is as yet unknown.

The formation and innervation of the *Golgi tendon organs* has been studied in a variety of species.[177] Innervation takes place at about the 12th week in the human fetus and a rich arborization of fine nerve endings forms around several adjacent tendinous bundles. The structure subsequently acquires a cylindrical capsule which is formed by condensation of fibroblasts and collagen. Progressive myelination of the nerves leaving the organ takes place from the 4th month onwards.[1]

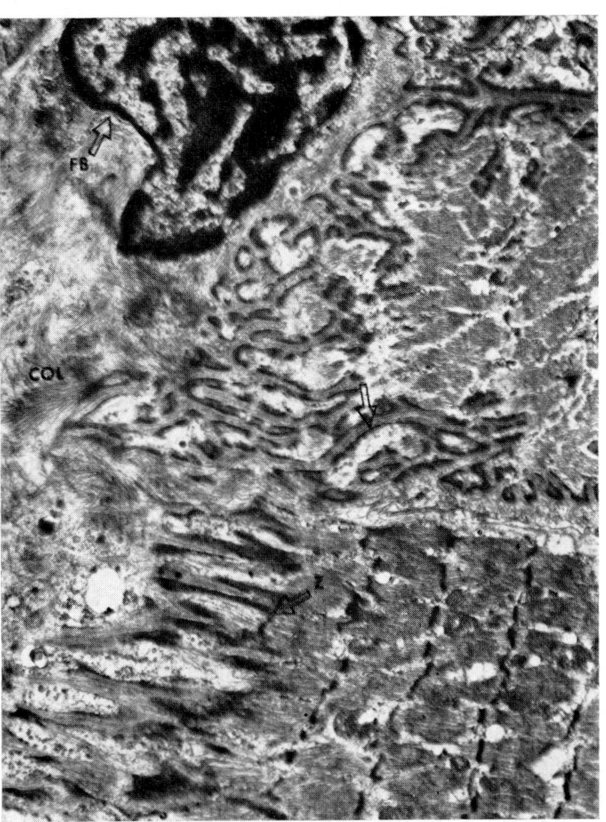

Fig. 23. Developing myotendinous junctions in two adjacent muscle fibres in regenerating mouse muscle. Bundles of collagen fibres (COL) extend deeply into crypts formed by invagination of the sarcolemma which is thickened and densely-staining (arrow). In the lower fibre the invaginations are less developed and the densely-staining portion of the sarcolemma appears to be continuous with the Z-bands of the terminal sarcomeres (Z). FB—fibroblast. (×4,570)

XIII. ABNORMALITIES OF MUSCLE DEVELOPMENT

Congenital disorders of the neuromuscular system are not uncommon and range from absence of single muscles to widespread involvement of most of the skeletal muscles of the body. Good summaries of these conditions are to be found in the monograph by Adams, Denny-Brown and Pearson[1] and in the paper by Dodge.[42] Although the clinical manifestations and the muscle pathology in these disorders are well-described, virtually nothing is known of their aetiology and pathogenesis. Our main reason for ignorance is the inaccessibility of the fetus to careful study during intrauterine life. Moreover, the interpretation of morphological findings in fetal tissues is difficult as the pathological changes in the developing neuromuscular system may not be comparable to those after maturation.[42] In some of these conditions hereditary factors appear to be responsible for the abnormality of muscle differentiation. On occasion there is also some anomaly of development in other organs as a clue to the period of intrauterine life during which the aetiological factor was active.

A. Congenital Absence of Muscles

Absence of one or more muscles is probably commoner than is generally recognized. Usually only a single muscle is absent on one side of the body or, at times, only portion of the muscle fails to develop. Occasionally the same muscle or muscles may be absent on both sides of the body. It has been stated that any muscle in the body may occasionally be absent.[1] The commoner examples are the sternocostal head of the pectoralis major, the palmaris longus, the trapezius, the serratus anterior and the quadratus femoris. The failure of these muscles to develop is usually of little consequence and the individual may not even be aware of the deficiency. Absence of the pectoralis major is occasionally associated with absence of the mammary gland or hypoplasia of the nipple, syndactylism, microdactyly, webbed fingers and scoliosis.

Some muscular deficiencies are of more serious significance. These include congenital absence of the diaphragm, which is usually associated with severe pulmonary atelectasis and pneumonia, and absence of the anterior abdominal wall which may be associated with severe gastro-intestinal and genito-urinary malformations. Moreover, occasional individuals with a congenitally absent muscle develop muscular dystrophy in later life. The commonest association is between congenital absence of the pectoralis muscle and the Landouzy-Déjérine facio-scapulo-humeral form of muscular dystrophy.

It remains uncertain whether these congenital deficiencies of skeletal muscles are due to a failure of the muscle itself to develop or to a pathological process affecting the muscle or its nerve supply during intrauterine life. The relationship between congenital muscle abnormalities and muscular dystrophy is also quite obscure.[42]

B. Congenital Disorders with Localized Weakness of Muscles

Under this heading are included cases of congenital ptosis which may on occasion be associated with iridoplegia or weakness of the extraocular muscles or may occasionally be the earliest manifestation of myotonic dystrophy or myasthenia gravis.[1] Another example, which may occur alone or in combination with lateral rectus palsies, is congenital facial diplegia (*Moebius syndrome*). In these cases the muscular weakness is generally considered to be secondary to an abnormality of the cranial nerve nuclei. In this category are also a number of cases of localized muscle weakness due to isolated congenital neuropathies or radiculopathies.

C. Congenital Contractures of Muscles

Examples of localized deformities due to fibrosis and shortening of muscles include congenital club-foot, torticollis and congenital elevation of the shoulder (*Sprengel's deformity*). In these cases ischaemia or some other form of local injury to the muscle in late fetal life or at birth are thought to be responsible for the contracture.

Also well known is the syndrome of *arthrogryposis multiplex congenita* due to contractures and deformities about several joints. A myopathic variety associated with so-called congenital muscular dystrophy and a neuropathic form associated with anterior horn cell disease have been distinguished.[9] However "myopathic" changes should be interpreted with caution since neurogenic involvement early in gestation, particularly when it is non-progressive, may lead to muscle changes indistinguishable from those seen in primary myopathy. In one such recent case with apparently myopathic histological features, electromyographic features in the muscles and impaired histochemical differentiation of fibre types, pointed to a neural rather than a primary muscle process.[86]

D. Congenital Muscular Hypotonia

A variety of metabolic, systemic and neuromuscular disorders may be responsible for widespread hypotonia and weakness in the neonatal period. This group of conditions has been well-reviewed by Tizard.[178] In those cases in which hypotonia is associated with systemic disease or mental retardation, and in the condition of benign congenital hypotonia[183] the skeletal muscles usually show no histological or histochemical abnormalities. In some severely retarded infants with hypotonia it has been claimed that histochemical maturation of muscles is incomplete.[59] In the following conditions distinctive pathological changes are found in the muscle fibres which may be due to an abnormality of development.

Centronuclear (Myotubular) "Myopathy"

In recent years a number of patients with hypotonia in infancy or non-progressive muscle weakness and wasting with involvement of the extraocular muscles during childhood have been found to have a large proportion of small muscle fibres with centrally-placed nuclei on muscle biopsy.[18,171] Because of the superficial resemblance of these fibres to fetal myotubes this condition was originally labelled "myotubular myopathy". Although in some cases the resemblance to myotubes is quite striking,[180] in several others the similarity has not been so close and the alternative label of centronuclear myopathy has been preferred.[164] In some cases, the abnormal fibres have been predominantly of one histochemical type (type I),[54,180] suggesting that the apparent failure of muscle fibre maturation may be neurogenically-determined due to an abnormality of the motor neurones.[54] The original designation of myopathy for these cases may therefore be incorrect. In several cases there has also been clinical or electro-encephalographic evidence of a cerebral abnormality.[105,164,171] Electron microscopic study of the abnormal muscle fibres has shown degenerative changes in the perinuclear region.[18]

Nemaline (Rod-body) Myopathy

In this condition, which may be familial, non-progressive weakness and hypotonia are present from birth or early infancy and are often associated with the skeletal changes of arachnodactyly.[87,166,170] Histological examination of the muscles reveals distinctive subsarcolemmal aggregates of small rod or thread-like structures which, with the electron microscope, are seen to originate from the Z-bands of myofibrils.[69] Similar involvement of intrafusal muscle fibres occurs[160] and may be responsible for the hypotonia and depression of the tendon stretch reflexes which is frequently seen in these cases. The precise biochemical composition of nemaline rods is still not known,[175] but an abnormal production of Z-band proteins seems to be involved. Histochemical studies have shown involvement of both major fibre types in some cases[64,160] whereas in others one fibre type has been predominantly affected,[69,166] again suggesting a possible neurogenic basis for this disorder.

It is now known that the formation of nemaline rods is not a specific pathological change confined to cases of this type but may also occur in adults with late-onset of progressive muscle weakness as well as in a variety of other situations, such as after tenotomy in the experimental animal.

Central Core Disease

This is a familial disorder which may be dominantly inherited or apparently sporadic and which presents with hypotonia from birth and mild non-progressive or slowly-progressive diffuse muscle weakness.[53,167] Histological examination of muscle shows a central core which is devoid of mitochondria and of oxidative enzymes and phosphorylase predominantly in type I fibres which are of normal size. The resemblance of these fibres to the target fibres which are characteristically found in denervating diseases has led to the suggestion that central core disease may also be due to an abnormality of neural influences during differentiation of the muscle fibres.[53]

E. The Development of Dystrophic Muscle

There have been a number of studies of the development of dystrophic muscle in tissue culture. Geiger and Garvin[65] concluded that muscle obtained from patients with Duchenne muscular dystrophy did not differentiate normally *in vitro*. More recent studies have shown that dystrophic myoblasts are often abnormal in shape, are slower to fuse than normal cells,[95] and contain excessive amounts of lipid and reduced succinic dehydrogenase activity.[71] Other workers have been unable to find significant differences in the growth pattern of normal and dystrophic human muscle.[169] Studies of dystrophic mouse myoblasts in culture have shown that they have fewer nucleoli[139] and a lower RNA content than normal cells.[154] Dystrophic chick myoblasts grow more rapidly than normal cells *in vitro* but show a growth pattern which differs from that of normal cells.[8] Although these findings suggest that the abnormality in dystrophic cells is manifest at an early stage of muscle development, their full significance remains to be determined. Careful electron microscopic, autoradiographic and biochemical studies are now needed to define more clearly the differences between normal and dystrophic muscle cells.

The early view that dystrophic muscle lacks the ability to regenerate[40] is now known to be incorrect. Regenerative changes are abundant in the early stages of Duchenne muscular dystrophy[122] even before the disease is clinically manifest.[140] Regeneration has also been shown to occur in response to experimental injury to dystrophic muscle.[184] Regenerating muscle fibres often show atypical features such as vacuolation and nuclear pyknosis, particularly in the later stages of the disease, and it has been suggested that regeneration may not proceed to completion.[122] However, in a recent histochemical and electron microscopic study of muscle fibres regenerating after a focal injury no significant differences could be demonstrated between normal and dystrophic subjects.[19] Although dystrophic muscle possesses the intrinsic capacity to regenerate, the disease is relentlessly progressive presumably because of continuing necrosis of muscle fibres.

ACKNOWLEDGEMENTS

The author gratefully acknowledges the help and constructive criticism provided by different members of the Department of Pathology of the University of Western Australia during the preparation of this work and the provision of facilities in that Department. Dr. R. L. Dawkins kindly read the manuscript, made many helpful suggestions and allowed Figures 4c and d and 15 to be reproduced. Dr. J. M. Papadimitriou kindly provided Figures 2, 3, 4a and b and 11b. Mr. M. Khan provided Figure 17. Professor B. A. Kakulas, editor of the *Proceedings of the II International Congress of Muscle Diseases, Perth, Australia,* 1972 kindly allowed Figures 4d, 15 and 17 to be reproduced. The author also thanks Mr. D. G. Gibb of the Department of Pathology and Dr. Packer of the Department of Zoology of the University of Western Australia for allowing him to prepare Figures 21 and 1 respectively from their slides.

Mr. H. Upenieks and Mr. R. Griffiths prepared the photographs. Mrs. M. Fletcher typed the manuscript.

REFERENCES

1. Adams, R. D., Denny-Brown, D. and Pearson, C. M. (1962), "Embryology and Histology of Skeletal Muscle," in *Diseases of Muscle, A Study in Pathology*, pp. 3–61. New York: Harper and Row.
2. Adams, R. D. and De Rueck, J. (1971), "Metrics of Muscle. *Proceedings of the II International Congress on Muscle Disease, Perth, Australia.* Amsterdam: Excerpta Medica. In Press.
3. Aherne, W., Ayyar, D. R., Clarke, P. A. and Walton, J. N. (1971), "Muscle Fibre Size in Normal Infants, Children and Adolescents. An Autopsy Study," *J. Neurol. Sci.*, **14,** 171–182.
4. Allbrook, D. B. and Aitken, J. T. (1951), "Reinnervation of Striated Muscle after Acute Ischaemia," *J. Anat.* (*Lond.*), **85,** 376–390.
5. Allbrook, D. B. and Hellmuth, A. E. (1971), "The Role of Satellite Cells in Postnatal Growth of Muscle," *II International Congress of Muscle Disease, Perth, Australia*, Excerpta Medica, International Congress Series, 237, p. 7 (Abs.).

6. Allen, E. R. and Pepe, F. (1965), "Ultrastructure of Developing Muscle Cells in the Chick Embryo," *Amer. J. Anat.*, **116,** 115–148.
7. Aloisi, M. (1969), "Patterns of Muscle Regeneration," in *Regeneration of Striated Muscle and Myogenesis*, pp. 180–193 (A. Mauro, S. A. Shafiq and A. T. Milhorat, Eds.). Amsterdam: Excerpta Medica.
8. Askanas, V., Shafiq, S. A. and Milhorat, A. T. (1971), "Normal and Dystrophic Chicken Muscle at Successive Stages in Tissue Culture," *Arch. Neurol.* (*Chic.*), **24,** 259–265.
9. Banker, B. Q., Victor, M. and Adams, R. D. (1957), "Arthrogryposis Multiplex Due to Congenital Muscular Dystrophy," *Brain*, **80,** 319–334.
10. Banu, G. (1922), *Recherches Physiologiques sur le Développement Neuromusculaire*. Paris.
11. Bateson, R. G., Woodrow, D. F. and Sloper, J. C. (1967), "Circulating Cells as a Source of Myoblasts in Regenerating Injured Mammalian Skeletal Muscle," *Nature* (*Lond.*), **213,** 1035–1036.
12. Bischoff, R. and Holtzer, H. (1969), "Mitosis and the Processes of Differentiation of Myogenic Cells *In Vitro*," *J. Cell Biol.*, **41,** 188–200.
13. Bowden, D. H. and Goyer, R. A. (1960), "The Size of Muscle Fibres in Infants and Children," *Arch. Path.*, **69,** 188–189.
14. Boyd, J. D. (1960), "Development of Striated Muscle," in *Muscle and Function of Muscle*, Vol. 1, pp. 63–85 (G. H. Bourne, Ed.). New York and London: Academic Press.
15. Bridge, D. T. and Allbrook, D. B. (1970), "The Growth of Skeletal Muscle in an Australian Marsupial (Setonix Brachyurus)," *J. Anat.* (*Lond.*), **106,** 285–295.
16. Buller, A. J., Eccles, J. C. and Eccles, R. M. (1960), "Interactions Between Motorneurones and Muscles in Respect of the Characteristic Speeds of Their Contraction," *J. Physiol.* (*Lond.*), **150,** 417–439.
17. Buller, A. J. and Lewis, D. M. (1965), "Further Observations on the Differentiation of Skeletal Muscles in the Kitten Hind Limb," *J. Physiol.*, **176,** 355–370.
18. Campbell, M. J., Rebeiz, J. J. and Walton, J. N. (1969), "Myotubular, Centronuclear or Peri-centronuclear Myopathy," *J. Neurol. Sci.*, **8,** 425–443.
19. Cancilla, P. A., Baloh, R., Kalyanaraman, K., Munsat, T. and Pearson, C. M. (1971), "Regeneration of Normal and Dystrophic Muscle After Injury. An Ultrastructural Study," in *Proceedings of the II International Congress on Muscle Diseases, Perth, Australia.* Amsterdam: Excerpta Medica. In press.
20. Capers, C. R. (1960), "Multinucleation of Skeletal Muscle *In Vitro*," *J. biophys. biochem. Cytol.*, **7,** 559–566.
21. Cheek, D. B. (1968), "Muscle Cell Growth in Normal Children," in *Human Growth, Body Composition, Cell Growth, Energy and Intelligence*, pp. 337–351. Philadelphia: Lea and Febiger.
22. Chiakulas, J. J. and Pauly, J. E. (1965), "A Study of Postnatal Growth of Skeletal Muscle in the Rat," *Anat. Rec.*, **152,** 55–62.
23. Church, J. C. T., Noronha, R. F. X. and Allbrook, D. B. (1966), "Satellite Cells and Skeletal Muscle Regeneration," *Brit. J. Surg.*, **53,** 638–642.
24. Clark, W. E. Le Gros (1946), "An Experimental Study of the Regeneration of Mammalian Striped Muscle," *J. Anat.* (*Lond.*), **80,** 24–36.
25. Close, R. (1964), "Dynamic Properties of Fast and Slow Skeletal Muscles of the Rat During Development," *J. Physiol.*, **173,** 74–95.
26. Close, R. (1967), "Dynamic Properties of Fast and Slow Skeletal Muscles of Mammals," in *Exploratory Concepts in Muscular Dystrophy and Related Disorders*, pp. 142–149 (A. T. Milhorat, Ed.). Amsterdam: Excerpta Medica.
27. Coërs, C. and Woolf, A. L. (1959), *The Innervation of Muscle. A Biopsy Study*. Oxford: Blackwell.
28. Cooper, W. G. and Konigsberg, I. R. (1959), "Succinic Dehydrogenase Activity of Myoblasts in Tissue Culture," *Anat. Rec.*, **133,** 368–9 (Abs.).
29. Cooper, W. G. and Konigsberg, I. R. (1961), "Dynamics of Myogenesis *In Vitro*," *Anat Rec.*, **140,** 195–205.
30. Cosmos, E. and Butler, J. (1967), "Differentiation of Fibre Types in Muscle of Normal and Dystrophic Chickens," in *Exploratory Concepts in Muscular Dystrophy and Related Disorders*, pp. 197–204 (A. T. Milhorat, Ed.), Amsterdam: Excerpta Medica, International Congress Series, No. 147.
31. Couteaux, R. (1941), cited by Boyd, J. D. (1960), in *Structure and Function of Muscle*, Vol. 1, pp. 63–85 (G. H. Bourne, Ed.). New York and London: Academic Press.
32. Couteaux, R. (1960), "Motor End-plate Structure," in *Structure and Function of Muscle*, Vol. 1, pp. 337–380 (G. H. Bourne, Ed.). New York and London: Academic Press.
33. Crain, S. M. (1965), "Muscle Tissues *In Vitro:* Electrophysiological Properties," in *Cells and Tissues in Culture*, Vol. 2, pp. 335–339, 344–347 (E. N. Willmer, Ed.). London: Academic Press.
34. Cuajunco, F. (1940), "Development of the Neuromuscular Spindle in Human Foetuses," Carnegie Inst. Wash. Publ. 518, *Contributions to Embryology*, **28/173,** 97–128.
35. Cuajunco, F. (1942), "Development of the Human Motor End Plate," Carnegie Inst. Wash. Publ. 541, *Contributions to Embryology*, **30,** 127–152.
36. Dawkins, R. L., Gibb, D. G. A. and Holt, P. G. (1971), "Demonstration of Immunological Differences Between Different Muscle Fibre Types," in *Proceedings of the II International Congress on Muscle Diseases, Perth, Australia* (B. A. Kakulas, Ed.). Amsterdam: Excerpta Medica. In press.
37. Dawkins, R. L., Smith, P. E., Papadimitriou, J. M. and Holt, P. G. (1971), "The Recognition and Quantitation of Myogenesis *In Vitro*; Immunofluorescence, Electron Microscopy and Creatine Kinase Activity," in *Proceedings of the II International Congress on Muscle Diseases, Perth, Australia* (B. A. Kakulas, Ed.). Amsterdam: Excerpta Medica. In press.
38. Dawkins, R. L. and Holborow, E. J. (1972), "Surface Antigens of Differentiated Muscle Cells in Monolayer Demonstrated by Immunofluorescence and Cytotoxicity," *J. Immunol. Meth.* In press.
39. De Anda, G. and Rebollo, M. A. (1968), "Histochemistry of the Neuromuscular Spindles in the Chicken During Development," *Acta Histochem.* (*Jena*), **31,** 287–295.
40. Denny-Brown, D. (1952), "The Nature of Muscular Diseases," *Canad. med. Ass. J.*, **67,** 1–6.
41. Diamond, J. and Miledi, R. (1962), "A Study of Foetal and New-born Rat Muscle Fibres," *J. Physiol.*, **162,** 393–408.
42. Dodge, P. R. (1961), "Congenital Neuromuscular Disorders," *Res. Publ. Ass. nerv. ment. Dis.*, **38,** 479–533.
43. Dubowitz, V. (1965), "Enzyme Histochemistry of Skeletal Muscle. Part I. Developing Animal Muscle. Part II. Developing Human Muscle," *J. Neurol. Neurosurg. Psychiat.*, **28,** 516–524.
44. Dubowitz, V. (1967), "Cross-innervated Mammalian Skeletal Muscle: Histochemical, Physiological and Biochemical Observations," *J. Physiol.* (*Lond.*), **193,** 481–496.
45. Dubowitz, V. and Pearse, A. G. E. (1960), "Reciprocal Relationship of Phosphorylase and Oxidative Enzymes in Skeletal Muscle," *Nature* (*Lond.*), **185,** 701–702.
46. Dubowitz, V. and Pearse, A. G. E. (1961), "Enzymic Activity of Normal and Dystrophic Human Muscle: A Histochemical Study," *J. Path. Bact.*, **81,** 365–378.
47. Dubowitz, V. and Newman, D. L. (1967), "Change in Enzyme Pattern After Cross-Innervation of Fast and Slow Skeletal Muscle," *Nature* (*Lond.*), **214,** 840–841.
48. Dumonde, D. C. (1966), "Tissue-specific Antigens," *Advances in Immunology*, **5,** 245–412.
49. Edström, L. and Kugelberg, E. (1968), "Histochemical Composition, Distribution of Fibres and Fatiguability of Single Motor Units," *J. Neurol. Neurosurg. Psychiat.*, **31,** 424–433.
50. Emmart, E. W., Kominz, D. R. and Miquel, J. (1963), "The Localisation and Distribution of Glyceraldehyde-3-phosphate Dehydrogenase in Myoblasts and Developing Muscle Fibres Growing in Culture," *J. Histochem. Cytochem.*, **11,** 207–217.
51. Enesco, M. and Puddy, D. (1964), "Increase in the Number of Nuclei and Weight in Skeletal Muscle of Rats of Various Ages," *Amer. J. Anat.*, **114,** 235–244.

52. Engel, W. K. (1962), "The Essentiality of Histo- and Cytochemical Studies of Skeletal Muscle in the Investigation of Neuromuscular Disease," *Neurology* (*Minneap.*), **12,** 778–794.
53. Engel, W. K. (1967), "A Critique of Congenital Myopathies and Other Disorders," in *Exploratory Concepts in Muscular Dystrophy and Related Disorders*, pp. 27–40 (A. T. Milhorat, Ed.). Amsterdam: Excerpta Medica.
54. Engel, W. K., Gold, G. N. and Karpati, G. (1968), "Type I Fiber Hypotrophy and Central Nuclei. A Rare Congenital Muscle Abnormality with a Possible Experimental Model," *Arch. Neurol.* (*Chic.*), **18,** 435–444.
55. Ezerman, E. B. and Ishikawa, H. (1967), "Differentiation of the Sarcoplasmic Reticulum and T System in Developing Chick Skeletal Muscle *In Vitro*, *J. Cell Biol.*, **35,** 405–420.
56. Feltkamp, T. W. and Feltkamp-Vroom, T. (1965), "Antibodies. Against Various Types of Skeletal Muscle Fibres," *Immunology*, **9,** 275–279.
57. Fenichel, G. M. (1963), "The B Fiber of Human Foetal Skeletal Muscle. A Study of Fibre Size Diameter," *Neurology* (*Minneap.*), **13,** 219–226.
58. Fenichel, G. M. (1966), "A Histochemical Study of Developing Human Skeletal Muscle," *Neurology* (*Minneap.*), **16,** 741–745.
59. Fenichel, G. M. (1967), "Abnormalities of Skeletal Muscle Maturation in Brain Damaged Children: A Histochemical Study," *Devel. Med. Child Neurol.*, **9,** 419–426.
60. Fidiańska, A. (1971), "Electron Miscroscopic Study of the Development of Human Foetal Muscle, Motor End-plate and Nerve· Preliminary Report," *Acta neuropath.* (*Berl.*), **17,** 234–247.
61. Fischbach, G. D., Nameroff, M. and Nelson, P. G. (1971), "Electrical Properties of Chick Skeletal Muscle Fibres Developing in Cell Culture," *J. Cell Physiol.*, **78,** 289–300.
62. Fischman, D. A. (1967), "An Electron Miscroscope Study of Myofibril Formation in Embryonic Chick Skeletal Muscle," *J. Cell Biol.*, **32,** 557–575.
63. Flickinger, R. A. (1962), "Embryological Development of Antigens," *Advances in Immunology*, **3,** 309–366.
64. Fulthorpe, J. J., Gardner-Medwin, D., Hudgson, P. and Walton, J. N. (1969), "Nemaline Myopathy. A Histological and Ultrastructural Study of Skeletal Muscle From a Case Presenting With Infantile Hypotonia," *Neurology* (*Minneap.*), **19,** 735–748.
65. Geiger, R. S. and Garvin, J. S. (1957), "Pattern of Regeneration of Muscle From Progressive Muscular Dystrophy Patients Cultivated *In Vitro* as Compared to Normal Human Skeletal Muscle," *J. Neuropath. Exp. Neurol.*, **16,** 532–543.
66. Godlewski, E. (1902), "Die Entwicklung des skelet- und Herzmuskelgewebes der Säugetiere," *Arch. mikr. Anat.*, **60,** 111–156.
67. Goldspink, G. (1970), "The Proliferation of Myofibrils During Muscle Fibre Growth," *J. Cell Sci.*, **6,** 593–604.
68. Goldspink, G. and Rowe, R. W. D. (1968), "The Growth and Development of Muscle Fibres in Normal and Dystrophic Mice," in *Research in Muscular Dystrophy*, pp. 116–131. London: Pitman Medical Publishing Co.
69. Gonatas, N. K., Shy, G. M. and Godfrey, E. H. (1966), "Nemaline Myopathy. The Origin of Nemaline Structures," *New Engl. J. Med.*, **274,** 535–539.
70. Goodman, H. M. and Rich, A. (1963), "Mechanisms of Polyribosome Action During Protein Synthesis," *Nature* (*Lond.*), **199,** 318–322.
71. Goyle, S., Virmani, V., Singh, B. and Susheela, A. K. (1971), "Cytochemical Studies on Cells Grown *In Vitro* From Explants of Normal and Dystrophic Human Skeletal Muscle, Subcutaneous Fat and Fascia," in *Proceedings of the II International Congress on Muscle Diseases, Perth, Australia.* Amsterdam: Excerpta Medica. In press.
72. Gröschel-Stewart, U. and Doniach, D. (1969), "Immunological Evidence for Human Myosin Isoenzymes," *Immunology*, **17,** 991–994.
73. Harris, J. B. and Luff, A. R. (1969), "Muscle Fibre Membrane Potentials in Fast and Slow Muscles of Developing Mice," *J. Physiol.*, **200,** 124–125.
74. Harris, A. J., Heinemann, S., Schubert, D. and Tarakis, H. (1971), "Trophic Interaction Between Cloned Tissue Culture Lines of Nerve and Muscle," *Nature* (*Lond.*), **231,** 296–301.
75. Harrison, R. G. (1904), "An Experimental Study of the Relation of the Nervous System to the Developing Musculature in the Embryo of the Frog," *Amer. J. Anat.*, **3,** 197–220.
76. Hauschka, S. and Konigsberg, I. R. (1966), "The Influence of Collagen on the Development of Muscle Clones," *Proc. nat. Acad. Sci.* (*Wash.*), **55,** 119–126.
77. Hay, E. D. (1959), "Electron Microscopic Observations of Muscle Dedifferentiation in Regenerating *Amblystoma* Limbs," *Devel. Biol.*, **1,** 555–585.
78. Hay, E. D. (1963), "The Fine Structure of Differentiating Muscle in the Salamander Tail," *Z. Zellforsch.*, **59,** 6–34.
79. Herrmann, H. (1952), "Studies of Muscle Development," *Ann. N.Y. Acad. Sci.*, **55,** 99–108.
80. Heywood, S. H. and Rich, A. (1968), "*In Vitro* Synthesis of Native Myosin, Actin and Tropomyosin from Embryonic Chick Polyribosomes," *Proc. nat. Acad. Sci.* (*Wash.*), **59,** 590–597.
81. Hitchcock, S. E. (1971), "Detection of Actin Filaments in Homogenerates of Developing Muscle Using Heavy Meromyosin," *Devel. Biol.*, **25,** 492–501.
82. Holtzer, H. (1970a), "Myogenesis," in *Cell Differentiation*, pp. 476–503 (O. Schjeide and J. de Vellis, Eds.). Van Nostrand Reinhold Co.
83. Holtzer, H. (1970b), "Proliferative and Quantal Cell Cycles in the Differentiation of Muscle, Cartilage and Red Blood Cells," in *Gene Expression in Somatic Cells*, pp. 69–88 (H. Padykula, Ed.). Academic Press.
84. Holtzer, H., Marshall, J. M., Jr. and Finck, H. (1957), "An Analysis of Myogenesis *In Vitro* Using Fluorescein-labelled Antimyosin," *J. Biophys. Biochem. Cytol.*, **3,** 705–723.
85. Holtzer, H. and Sanger, J. W· (1971), "Effects of 5-bromodeoxyuridine and Cytochalasin-B on Myogenesis," *II International Congress on Muscle Diseases, Perth, Australia*, Excerpta Medica, International Congress Series, 237, p. 8 (Abs.).
86. Hooshmand, H., Martinez, A. J. and Rosenblum, W. I. (1971), Arthrogryposis Multiplex Congenita. Simultaneous Involvement of Peripheral Nerve and Muscle," *Arch. Neurol.* (*Chic.*), **24,** 561–571.
87. Hudgson, P., Gardner-Medwin, D., Fulthorpe, J. J. and Walton, J. N. (1967), "Nemaline Myopathy," *Neurology* (*Minneap.*), **17,** 1125–1142.
88. Hughes, B. P. (1970), "Changes in Human Muscle Lipids With Development and in Disease," *Fifth Symposium on Current Research in Muscular Dystrophy and Related Diseases*, Muscular Dystrophy Group of Great Britain, London.
89. Huxley, H. E. (1963), "Electron Microscope Studies on the Structure of Natural and Synthetic Protein Filaments From Striated Muscle," *J. Mol. Biol.*, **7,** 281–308.
90. Ishikawa, H. (1966). "Electron Microscopic Observations of Satellite Cells With Special Reference to the Development of Mammalian Skeletal Muscles," *Zeitschrift fur Anatomie und Entwicklungsgeschichte*, **125,** 43–63.
91. Ishikawa, H., Bischoff, R. and Holtzer, H. (1968), "Mitosis and Intermediate-sized Filaments in Developing Skeletal Muscle," *J. Cell Biol.*, **38,** 538–558.
92. Ivanyi, P. (1970), "The Major Histocompatibility Antigens in Various Species," *Current Topics in Microbiology*, **53,** 1–90.
93. Johnson, M. and Pearse, A. G. E. (1971), "Differentiation of Fibre Types in Normal and Dystrophic Hamster Muscle," *J. Neurol. Sci.*, **12,** 459–472.
94. Joubert, D. M. (1955), "Growth of Muscle Fibres in the Foetal Sheep," *Nature* (*Lond.*), **175,** 936–937.
95. Kakulas, B. A., Papadimitriou, J. M., Knight, J. O. and Mastaglia, F. L. (1968), "Normal and Abnormal Human Muscle in Tissue Culture," *Proc. Aust. Ass. Neurol.*, **5,** 79–85.
96. Kamieniecka, Z. (1968), "The Stages of Development of Human Foetal Muscles With Reference to Some Muscular Diseases," *J.Neurol. Sci.*, **7,** 319–32 9.

97. Kano, M. and Shimada, Y. (1971), "Innervation and Acetylcholine Sensitivity of Skeletal Muscle Cells Differentiated *In Vitro* From Chick Embryo," *J. Cell Physiol.*, **78**, 233–242.
98. Kaplan, M. H. (1963), "Immunologic Relation of Streptococcal and Tissue Antigens. I. Properties of an Antigen in Certain Strains of Group A Streptococci Exhibiting an Immunologic Cross-reaction With Human Heart Tissue," *J. Immunol.*, **90**, 595–606.
99. Karpati, G. and Engel, W. K. (1967), "Neuronal Trophic Function. A New Aspect Demonstrated Histochemically in Developing Soleus Muscle," *Arch. Neurol.* (*Chic.*), **17**, 542–545.
100. Katsuki, S., Nagamine, M., Ishimatsu, M. and Goto, I. (1968), "Lactic Dehydrogenase and Creatine Phosphokinase Isozymes in Muscle From Neuromuscular Diseases," *Proc. Aust. Ass. Neurol.*, **5**, 73–77.
101. Kelly, A. M. and Zacks, S. I. (1969a), "The Histogenesis of Rat Intercostal Muscle," *J. Cell Biol.*, **42**, 135–153.
102. Kelly, A. M. and Zacks, S. I. (1969b), "The Fine Structure of Motor End Plate Morphogenesis," *J. Cell Biol.*, **42**, 154–169.
103. Kelly, D. E. (1969), "Myofibrillogenesis and Z-band Differentiation," *Anat. Rec.*, **163**, 403–425.
104. Khan, M. A., Holt, P. G., Papadimitriou, J. P. and Kakulas, B. A. (1971), "Histochemical and Biochemical Observations on Creatine Kinase Activity of Two Developing Skeletal Muscles of the Domestic Fowl (Gallus Domesticus)," *II International Congress on Muscle Diseases, Perth, Australia*, Excerpta Medica, International Congress Series 237, p. 9 (Abs.).
105. Kinoshita, M. and Cadman, T. E. (1968), "Myotubular Myopathy," *Arch. Neurol.* (*Chic.*), **18**, 265–271.
106. Kitiyakara, A. and Angevine, D. M. (1963), "A Study of the Pattern of Postembryonic Growth of M. Gracilis in Mice," *Devel. Biol.*, **8**, 322–340.
107. Knappeis, G. C. and Carlsen, F. (1962), "The Ultrastructure of the Z-disc in Skeletal Muscle," *J. Cell Biol.*, **13**, 323–335.
108. Konigsberg, I, R. (1963), "Clonal Analysis in Myogenesis," *Science*, **140** 1273–1284.
109. Konigsberg, I. R., McElvain, N., Tootle, M. and Herrmann, H. (1960), "The Dissociability of Deoxyribonucleic Acid Synthesis From the Development of Multinuclearity of Muscle Cells in Culture," *J. biophys. biochem. Cytol.*, **8**, 333–343.
110. Landon, D. N. (1966), "Electron Microscopy of Muscle Spindles," in *Control and Innervation of Skeletal Muscle*, pp. 96–110 (B. L. Andrew, Ed.). Edinburgh and London: Livingstone.
111. Landon, D. N. (1970), Personal communication.
112. Larson, P. F., Hudgson, P. and Walton, J. N. (1969), "Morphological Relationship of Polyribosomes and Myosin Filaments in Developing and Regenerating Skeletal Muscle," *Nature* (*Lond.*), **222**, 1168–1169.
113. Larson, P. F., Jenkison, M. and Hudgson, P. (1970), "The Morphological Development of Chick Embryo Skeletal Muscle Grown in Tissue Culture As Studied By Electron Microscopy," *J. Neurol. Sci.*, **10**, 385–405.
114. Levander, G. (1945), "Tissue Induction," *Nature* (*Lond*)., **155**, 148.
115. Lewis, W. H. (1902), "The Development of the Arm in Man," *Amer. J. Anat.*, **1**, 145–183.
116. Lewis, W. H. (1910), "The Development of the Muscular System," in *Manual of Human Embryology*, pp. 454–522 (F. Keibel and F. P. Mall, Eds.). Philadelphia and London: J. B. Lippincott.
117. Lubinska, I. and Zelena, J. (1967), "Acetylcholinesterase at Muscle-tendon Junctions During Postnatal Development in Rats," *J. Anat.* (*Lond.*), **101**, 295–308.
118. MacCallum, J. B. (1898), "On the Histogenesis of the Striated Muscle Fibre, and the Growth of the Human Sartorius Muscle," *Bull. Johns Hopk. Hosp.*, **9**, 208–215.
119. MacConnichie, H. F., Enesco, M. and Leblond, C. P. (1964), "The Mode of Increase in the Number of Skeletal Muscle Nuclei in the Postnatal Rat," *Amer. J. Anat.*, **114**, 245–254.
120. Marchok, A. C. and Herrmann, H. (1967), "Studies of Muscle Development. I. Changes in Cell Proliferation," *Devel. Biol.*, **15**, 129–155.
121. Marinskaja, L. F. (1962), "Histochemical Study of Cholinesterase During Development of Somatic Musculature in the Human Foetus," *Arkh. Anat. Gistol. Embriol.*, **42**, 30–35.
122. Mastaglia, F. L. ahd Kakulas, B. A. (1969), "Regeneration in Duchenne Muscular Dystrophy: A Histological and Histochemical Study," *Brain*, **92**, 809–818.
123. Mastaglia, F. L. and Kakulas, B. A. (1970), "A Histological and Histochemical Study of Skeletal Muscle Regeneration in Polymyositis," *J. Neurol. Sci.*, **10**, 471–487.
124. Mastaglia, F. L., Papadimitriou, J. and Kakulas, B. A. (1970), "Regeneration of Muscle in Duchenne Muscular Dystrophy: An Electron Microscope Study," *J. Neurol. Sci.*, **11**, 425–444.
125. Mastaglia, F. L. and Walton, J. N. (1971), "An Ultrastructural Study of Skeletal Muscle in Polymyositis," *J. Neurol. Sci.*, **12**, 473–504.
126. Mastaglia, F. L., Dawkins, R. L. and Papadimitriou, J. M. (1971), "Morphological Changes in Isogeneic and Allogeneic Grafts of Murine Rectus Abdominis Muscle," in *Proceedings of the II International Congress on Muscle Diseases, Perth, Australia* (B. A. Kakulas, Ed.). Amsterdam: Excerpta Medica. In press.
127. Mauro, A. (1961), "Satellite Cells of Skeletal Muscle Fibres," *J. biophys. biochem. Cytol.*, **9**, 493–495.
128. Mayer, R. F. and Doyle, A. M. (1969), "Studies of the Motor Unit in the Cat. Histochemistry and Topology of Anterior Tibial and Extensor Digitorium Longus Muscles," in *Muscle Diseases*, pp. 159–163 (J. N. Walton, N. Canal and G. Scarlato, Eds.). Amsterdam: Excerpta Medica.
129. Montgomery, R. D. (1962), "Growth of Human Striated Muscle," *Nature* (*Lond.*), **195**, 194–195.
130. Morita, S., Cassens, R. G. and Briskey, G. J. (1970), "Histochemical Localisation of Myoglobin in Skeletal Muscle of Rabbit, Pig and Dog," *J. Histochem. Cytochem.*, **18**, 364–366.
131. Moss, F. P. and Leblond, C. P. (1970), "Nature of Dividing Nuclei in Skeletal Muscle of Growing Rats," *J. Cell Biol.*, **44**, 459–462.
132. Murray, M. R. (1960), "Skeletal Muscle Tissue in Culture," in *Structure and Function of Muscle*, Vol. 1, pp. 111–136 (G. H. Bourne, Ed.). New York and London: Academic Press.
133. Nyström, B. (1967), "Muscle-spindle Histochemistry," *Science*, **155**, 1424–1426.
134. Nyström, B. (1968), "Histochemistry of Developing Cat Muscles," *Acta neurol. Scand.*, **44**, 405–439.
135. Ogawa, Y. (1958), "Development of Skeletal Muscle Protein," *Nature* (*Lond.*), **182**, 1312–1313.
136. Ogawa, Y., Kawahara, T. and Miura, J. (1958), "Serological Determination of Developing Muscle Protein in Chick Embryo," *Nature* (*Lond.*), **181**, 621–622.
137. Okazaki, K. and Holtzer, H. (1965), "An Analysis of Myogenesis *In Vitro* Using Fluorescein-labelled Antimyosin," *J. Histochem. Cytochem.*, **14**, 726–739.
138. Okazaki, K. and Holtzer, H. (1966), "Myogenesis: Fusion, Myosin Synthesis, and the Mitotic Cycle," *Proc. nat. Acad. Sci.* (*Wash.*), **56**, 1484–1490.
139. Pearce, G. W. (1963), "Tissue Culture and Electron Microscopy," in *Research in Muscular Dystrophy*, pp. 75–85. Pitman Press.
140. Pearson, C. M. (1962), "Histopathological Features of Muscle in the Preclinical Stages of Muscular Dystrophy," *Brain*, **85**, 109–120.
141. Penman, S., Scharrer, K., Becker, Y. and Darnell, J. E. (1963), "Polyribosomes in Normal and Poliovirus-infected Hela Cells and Their Relationship to Messenger RNA," *Proc. nat. Acad. Sci.* (*Wash.*), **49**, 654–662.
142. Perkoff, G. T. (1965), "Myoglobin," *Amer. J. Med.*, 527–532 (editorial).
143. Perry, S. V. (1969), "Biochemical Changes During the Development of Skeletal Muscle," in *Muscle Diseases*, pp. 668–675 (J. N. Walton, N. Canal and G. Scarlato, Eds.). Amsterdam: Excerpta Medica.
144. Peter, J. B., Fiehn, W. and Rusdal, L. (1971), "Distinctive Lipid

Composition of Sarcolemma, Fragmented Sarcoplasmic Reticulum and Mitochondria of Skeletal Muscle," *II International Congress on Muscle Diseases, Perth, Australia*, Excerpta Medica, International Congress Series, 237, p. 20 (Abs.).
145. Peterson, E. R. and Crain, S. M. (1970), "Innervation in Cultures of Fetal Rodent Skeletal Muscle by Organotypic Explants of Spinal Cord from Different Animals," *Z. Zellforsch.*, **106**, 1–21.
146. Price, H. M., Howes, E. L. and Blumberg, J. M. (1964), "Ultrastructural Alterations in Skeletal Muscle Fibers Injurvd By Cold, Part 2 (Cells of the Sarcolemmal Tube: Observations on 'Discontinuous' Regeneration and Myofibril Formation)," *Lab. Invest.*, **13**, 1279–1302.
147. Przybylski, R. J. and Blumberg, J. M. (1966), "Ultrastructural Aspects of Myogenesis in the Chick," *Lab. Invest.*, **15**, 836–863.
148. Rebollo, M. A. and Piantelli, A. (1965), "Differentiation of the Skeletal Muscle in the Chicken. VI. The Lipids During Development," *Acta neurol. lat.-amer.*, **10**, 181–188.
149. Reger, J. F. and Craig, A. S. (1968), "Studies on the Fine Structure of Muscle Fibers and Associated and Associated Satellite Cells in Hypertrophic Human Deltoid Muscle," *Anat. Rec.*, **162**, 483–499.
150. Remak, R. (1845), quoted by Przybylski and Blumberg (1966), *Lab. Invest.*, **15**, 836–863.
151. Reznik, M. (1969), "Origin of Myoblasts During Skeletal Muscle Regeneration. Electron Miscroscopic Observations," *Lab. Invest.*, **20**, 353–363.
152. Robbins, N., Karpati, G. and Engel, W. K. (1969), "Histochemical and Contractile Properties in the Cross-innervated Guinea Pig Soleus Muscle," *Arch. Neurol. (Chic.)*, **20**, 318–329.
153. Robbins, N. and Yonezawa, T. (1971), "Developing Neuromuscular Junctions: First Signs of Chemical Transmission During Formation in Tissue Culture," *Science*, **172**, 395–398.
154. Ross, K. F. A. and Hudgson, P. (1969), "Tissue Culture in Muscle Disease," in *Disorders of Voluntary Muscle*, pp. 319–361 (J. N. Walton, Ed.). London: J. & A. Churchill.
155. Ross, K. F. A., Jans, D. E., Larson, P. F., Mastaglia, F. L., Parsons, R., Fulthorpe, J. J., Jenkison, M. and Walton, J. N. (1970), "Distribution of Ribosomal RNA in Fusing Myoblasts," *Nature (Lond.)*, **226**, 545–547.
156. Romanul, F. C. A. and Van der Meulen, J. P. (1966), "Reversal of the Enzyme Profiles of Muscle Fibres in Fast and Slow Muscles by Cross-innervation," *Nature (Lond.)*, **212**, 1369–1370.
157. Schwann, T. (1839), quoted by Przybylski and Blumberg (1966), *Lab. Invest.*, **15**, 836–863.
158. Shafiq, S. A. and Gorycki, M. A. (1965), "Regeneration in Skeletal Muscle of Mouse: Some Electron Miscroscope Observations," *J. Path. Bact.*, **90**, 123–131.
159. Shafiq, S. A., Gorycki, M. A. and Milhorat, A. T. (1967), "An Electron Microscopic Study of Regeneration and Satellite Cells in Human Muscle," *Neurology (Minneap.)*, **17**, 567–574.
160. Shafiq, S. A., Dubowitz, V., De C. Peterson, H. and Milhorat, A. T. (1967), "Nemaline Myopathy: Report of a Fatal Case, With Histochemical and Electron Microscopic Studies," *Brain*, **90**, 817–828.
161. Shafiq, S. A., Gorycki, M. A. and Mauro, A. (1968), "Mitosis During Postnatal Growth in Skeletal and Cardiac Muscle of the Rat," *J. Anat. (Lond.)*, **103**, 135–141.
162. Shainberg, A., Yagil, G. and Yaffe, D. (1969), "Control of Myogenesis *In Vitro* by Ca^{++} Concentration in Nutritional Medium," *Exp. Cell Res.*, **58**, 163–167.
163. Shainberg, A. Yagil, G. and Yaffe, D. (1971), "Alterations of Enzymatic Activities During Muscle Differentiation *In Vitro*," *Devel. Biol.*, **25**, 1–29.
164. Sher, J. H., Rimalovski, A. B., Athanassaides, T. J. and Aronson, S. M. (1967), "Familial Centronuclear Myopathy," *Neurology (Minneap.)*, **17**, 726–742.
165. Shimada, Y. (1971), "Electron Microscope Observations on the Fusion of Chick Myoblasts *In Vitro*," *J. Cell Biol.*, **48**, 128–142.
166. Shy, G. M., Engel, W. K., Somers, J. E. and Wanko, T. (1963), "Nemaline Myopathy: A New Congenital Myopathy," *Brain*, **86**, 793–810.
167. Shy, G. M. and Magee, K. R. (1956), "A New Congenital Non-progressive Myopathy," *Brain*, **79**, 610–620.
168. Singer, K., Angelopoulos, B. and Raniot, B. (1955), "Studies on Human Myoglobin. II. Foetal Myoglobin: Its Identification and its Replacement by Adult Myoglobin During Infancy," *Blood*, **10**, 987–998.
169. Skeate, Y., Bishop, A. and Dubowitz, V. (1969), "Differentiation of Diseased Human Muscle in Culture," *Cell Tissue Kinet.*, **2**, 307–310.
170. Spiro, A. J. and Kennedy, C. (1965), "Hereditary Occurrence of Nemaline Myopathy," *Arch. Neurol. (Chic.)*, **13**, 155–159.
171. Spiro, A. J., Shy, G. M. and Gonatas, N. K. (1966), "Myotubular Myopathy," *Arch. Neurol. (Chic.)*, **14**, 1–14.
172. Spiro, A. J. and Beilin, R. L. (1969), "Human Muscle Spindle Histochemistry," *Arch. Neurol. (Chic.)*, **20**, 271–275.
173. Streler, B., Konigsberg, I. R. and Kelley, J. (1963), "Ploidy of Myotube Nuclei Developing *In Vitro* as Determined With a Recording Double Beam Micro-spectrophotometer," *Exp. Cell Res.*, **32**, 232–241.
174. Stockdale, F. E. and Holtzer, H. (1961), "DNA Synthesis and Myogenesis," *Exp. Cell Res.*, **24**, 508–520.
175. Sugita, H., Masaki, T., Ebashi, S. and Pearson, C. M. (1971), "Protein Composition of Rods in Nemaline Myopathy," *II International Congress on Muscle Diseases, Perth, Australia*, International Congress Series No. 237, p. 17 (Abs.). Amsterdam: Excerpta Medical.
176. Takasu, T. and Hughes, B. P. (1969), "Lactate Dehydrogenase Isozyme Patterns in Human Skeletal Muscle," *J. Neurol. Neurosurg. Psychiat.*, **32**, 175–185.
177. Tello, J. F. (1917), quoted by Adams *et al.* (1962), "Genesis de las terminaciones nerviosas motrices y sensitivas. I. En el sistema locomotor de las vertebrados superiores. Histogenesis-muscular," *Trab. Lab. Invest. biol. (Madrid)*, **15**, 101–199.
178. Tizard, J. P. M. (1969), "Neuromuscular Disorders of Infancy," in *Disorders of Voluntary Muscle*, pp. 579–605 (J. N. Walton, Ed.). London: J. & A. Churchill.
179. Van Linge, B. (1962), "The Response of Muscle to Strenuous Exercise," *J. Bone Jt Surg.*, **44B**, 711–721.
180. Van Wijngaarden, G. K., Fleury, P., Bethlem, J. and Meijer, A. E. F. H. (1970), "Familial Muscle Disease With So-called Myotubes," in *Muscle Diseases, Proceedings of an International Congress, Milan*, 1969, pp. 581–584 (J. N. Walton, N. Canal and G. Scarlato, Eds.). Amsterdam: Excerpta Medica.
181. Volkmann, R. (1893), "Ueber die Regeneration des quergestreiften Muskelgewebes beim Menschen und Säugetier," *Beitr. path. Anat.*, **12**, 233–332.
182. Walker, B. E. (1963), "The Origin of Myoblasts and the Problem of Differentiation," *Exp. Cell Res.*, **30**, 80–92.
183. Walton, J. N. (1956), "Amyotonia Congenita: A Follow Up Study," *Lancet*, **i**, 1023–1027.
184. Walton, J. N. and Adams, R. D. (1956), "The Response of the Normal, the Denervated and the Dystrophic Muscle-cell to Injury," *J. Path. Bact.*, **72**, 273–298.
185. Williamson, E. and Brooke, M. H. (1972), "Myokymia and the Motor Unit," *Arch. Neurol. (Chic.)*, **26**, 11–16.
186. Wohlfart, G. (1937), "Über das Vorkommen verschiedener Arten von Muskelfasern in der Skelettmuskulatur des menschen und einiger säugetiere," *Acta Psychiat. (Kbh)*, suppl. 12, p. 1–119.
187. Yaffe, D. (1971), "Developmental Changes Preceding Cell Fusion During Muscle Differentiation *In Vitro*," *Exp. Cell Res.*, **66**, 33–48.
188. Yaffe, D. and Feldman, M. (1965), "The Formation of Hybrid Multinucleated Music Fibres From Myoblasts of Different Genetic Origins," *Dev. Biol.*, **11**, 300–317.
189. Zacks, S. I. (1964), *The Motor Endplate*. Philadelphia and London: W. B. Saunders.
190. Zhinkin, L. N. and Andreeva, L. F. (1963), "DNA Synthesis and Nuclear Reproduction During Embryonic Development and Regeneration of Muscle Tissue," *J. Embryol. exp. Morph.*, **11**, 353–367.

21. GROWTH AND DEVELOPMENT OF BONY TISSUES

PIERRE ROYER

The growth and anatomical development of the skeleton, the characteristic feature of vertebrates shows three important features.

Firstly, bony tissue develops from its embryonic beginnings either directly from mesenchymal cells (membranous bones; periosteal and endosteal ossification), or from a cartilagenous model, via enchondral ossification. This latter is very active during prenatal life and persists until adulthood in the metaphyses.

Secondly, bony tissue is subject to continuous remodelling throughout life, a balance being struck between osteogenesis (which never stops) and two processes of bone destruction: osteolysis by osteocytes and osteoclastic resorption. This remodelling, which in the adult adapts the bony tissue to its mechanical needs and to the effects of damage, is also present during the period of development. It is this which facilitates alterations of length and shape and structure.

Thirdly, bony tissue is strongly mineralized. In the course of prenatal, perinatal, and postnatal development, mineral content plays an important part in the regulation of the equilibrium between extracellular phosphate and calcium, while it is also very susceptible to the endocrine and nutritional factors impinging on these metabolic pathways.

In the interests of clarity, this presentation will consider the development of bony tissue and of the regulation of calcium metabolism in three separate periods of life: (1) the prenatal period, (2) the perinatal period, and (3) the postnatal period. Reference will be made as much as possible to human development and information coming from the study of other vertebrates will be limited to those aspects which contribute to an understanding of the human.[16,43,126]

PRENATAL DEVELOPMENT

In the human embryo the formation of the trunk reaches completion towards the close of the third week of prenatal life when Wolff's crests appear laterally. At the same level the outline plans of the limbs appear about the 30th day with the appearance of a cellular condensation which arises from the middle of the primitive mesenchyme, without any migration of new cells, and represents the future skeleton of the limbs. The limb buds are formed from a core of condensed mesenchyme covered with an epidermal cap known as the apical ectodermal ridge (AER) (Fig. 1). The two structures are functionally related in a two-way process of induction: the mesenchyme induces the development and maintenance

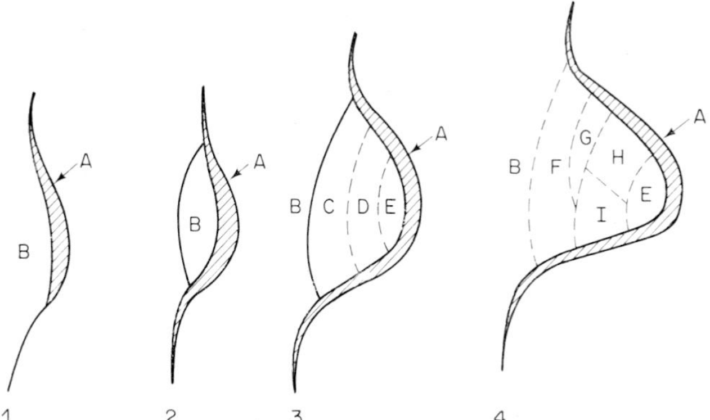

FIG. 1. Development of a limb bud:

A Apical ectodermal ridge
B Primitive mesenchyme
C Stylopode
D Zygopode
E Autopode
F Femur
G Knee
H Tibia
I Fibula

of the AER and it is this which, in turn, gives the mesenchymal cells the "competence" to form the skeletal pattern. "Condensation" begins towards the 40th day. The articular spaces which will delimit the "segments" are present from the 60th day. During this 20 days period, the upper limb grows 2–3 days ahead of the lower limb. The segments of the upper limb appear almost simultaneously, whereas the formation of the proximal division of the lower limb is more precocious than that of its distal part. Later the skeletal components come to assume their definitive shape, structure and mineralization. These events are described in detail in the classical embryological texts.[31,32,88,91,98,130,131]

Early Histogenesis

The way in which the first elements of cartilagenous and bony tissue are laid down is not yet clear. Several processes must be simultaneously involved, viz: condensation of mesoderm, cellular differentiation, and cartilagenous and bony induction.

Mesodermal Condensation[64]

Enchondral or membranous osteogenesis begins with a condensation of mesenchymal cells. It is recognized that which cells take part in the process of condensation is genetically determined.

The physico-chemical factors determining the phenomenon must be numerous; and include the ionic content of the cell and of its microenvironment, as well as the polarity imposed on the cell.[137] The increasing "competence" of the mesenchymal cells of the limb bud and the process of condensation must in some way be correlated. At all events an increase in the density of the cells seems to favour the appearance of cartilage.[67]

There is a considerable synthesis of specific macromolecules during the period of condensation in the intercellular material: the presence of collagen has been shown at a very early stage of histogenesis, when studies with the electron microscope reveal fibrils of 200 Å. in diameter, with a periodic structure, in the basal membrane of the limb bud. It is possible that this collagen may be important to the role of the ectodermal-mesodermal interface. The presence of incompletely sulphated glycosaminoglycans has also been at a very early stage of condensation. It is possible to detect chondroitin-4-sulphate and chondroitin-6-sulphate as well as the enzymatic mechanisms involved in their synthesis very early. These latter enzymes are uridine-diphosphate-N-acetylglycosamine-4-epimerase, uridine-diphosphate-D-glucose-dehydrogenase and sulphating enzymes.[90] The question of whether the fundamental macromolecules of bony tissue, collagen and glycoprotein, play a role in the phenomenon of cellular condensation is still not decided.[41]

Cellular Differentiation

Osteogenic cells are thought to be derived from the primitive mesenchymal reticulum, which is also the origin of haemopoeitic cells. This unitary hypothesis is supported by several pieces of evidence drawn from pathology and biology.[41] Thus the multipotential mesenchymal cell may develop in the direction of the primordial haemopoeitic cells of the bone marrow or towards those cells known as "osteoprecursors" (OPC) or "chondroprecursors" (CPC). OPC's will give rise to osteoblasts and osteocytes, osteoclasts being derived from osteoblasts or directly from OPC's. CPC's will give rise to chondroblasts and chondrocytes. The majority of these morphological and functional specializations seem to be reversible and interchangeable. It is still difficult to be sure that such processes of specialization are linked to a cellular "differentiation" implying a definitive suppression of one part of the genetic information, or to a "modulation" representing partial and reversible repression of these latter, or to both phenomena.[126] Thus OPC's and CPC's whose morphology at this stage is identical, appear at the level of the zone of condensation. They are cells with a large nucleus, an important endoplasmic reticulum, free ribosomes, numerous mitochondria and a poorly developed Golgi apparatus; and they are rich in DNA, RNA, glycogen and alkaline phosphatase. While both the OPC's and CPC's multiply very rapidly, there seems to be some incompatibility between cellular division and specialization, for example between the rate of division of an OPC which is becoming an osteoblast and one which is going to divide again.

Factors which stimulate cellular differentiation or modulation are various. Thus, during the process of enchondral ossification, the hypertrophic chondrocytes send out a signal of unknown nature which stimulates the proliferation of osteoblasts from perivascular mesenchymal cells.

It seems to be established that the direction of differentiation from the common cell line towards chondrogenesis or osteogenesis depends on the synthesis of macromolecules. The synthesis of glycosaminoglycans favours chondrogenesis, and sulphation of chondroitine-sulphate has a clear correlation with hypertrophy of the chondrocyte. Synthesis of tropocollagen and of collagen leads to differentiation in the direction of osteogenesis.[62] The availability of oxygen in the cellular microenvironment is a factor in differentiation. When the oxygen supply is good there will be a tendency towards bone-forming cells; when it is poor the direction will be towards chondrogenesis. All those situations which modify the transport of the oxygen: hypoxia and ischemia; hyperoxia and hypervascularization, may influence the differentiation of the precursor cells in the direction of osteogenesis or of chondrogenesis.

Mechanical stimulation can also have an effect on differentiation, perhaps by means of piezoelectric forces. Increased mechanical stress favours chondrogenesis; its reduction favour osteogenesis. In this context, an elegant hypothesis has been proposed which states that there is a direct connection between mechanical stimulation, oxygen transport, and the preferential synthesis either of glycosaminoglycans or of collagen. These macromolecules finally determine whether cellular differentiation will be towards chondrogenesis or osteogenesis.[62]

The factors regulating macromolecule synthesis in the embryo and fetus are little understood though it seems that parathormone has a powerful stimulating effect on synthesis or glycosaminoglycans by the cartilagenous cells of the calf fetus studied in tissue culture,[69] an effect abolished by actinomycine D. Calcitonin has no action.[85]

Ecto-mesodermal Interaction and Induction Factor

The initiation of skeletal development thus comprises a process of condensation of mesenchymal cells and processes of division, differentiation and/or cellular modulation. It has been shown, *in vivo* and *in vitro*, that this initiation depends on complex interactions between the mesoderm and its endodermal covering.[7] At the stage of the delineation of the limb skeleton, the mesoderm induces the development of the epiblast or AER (apical ectodermal ridge), and this latter can only remain active under the influence of a maintenance factor or AEMF (apical ectodermal maintenance factor). This substance of high molecular weight is produced either by the active mesoderm or by the necrotic zone behind the limb bud and has no zoological specificity. In its turn, it induces the formation of the skeleton from the mesoderm. The primary inducers in the formation of the skeleton of the limbs do not depend on the availability of phenylalanine, in contrast to the inducers involved in visceral ossification which derives from cells of the neural crest, or the mechanism of induction involved with the pharyngeal ectoderm.[134]

The Bone Induction Principle

The embryonic induction principles may be related to the bone induction principle or BIP studied in adults.[125] This principle governs the development of bony tissue from receptor cells even after the end of the growth period: for example, perivascular hypertrophic mesenchymal cells which it is capable of causing to differentiate into osteoblasts, chondroblasts and even haemocytoblasts.

BIP is not bound to the cell but derives from specific proteins of the intercellular matrix of dentine, bony tissue and cartilage, the model which is generally used being lyophylized, decalcified bone. It is interesting that it can equally well be obtained from the epithelium of the gastric fundus, the gall bladder, the urinary tract and the placenta.

It seems that BIP results from the combination of a fundamental substance elaborated by the competent mesenchymal cells with "inducer substrates."[123] BIP is a non-diffusable macromolecular complex, but unlike AEMF it can cross millipore filters. The chemical nature of "induction substrates" is not known but their activity depends on the quaternary structure of the proteins of which they are composed. Induction substrates prepared from dentine or bony matrix induce the formation of bony tissue after brief contact. Those derived from the placenta or the urinary tract epithelium do not have an immediate action.[21] In high dosage, these "induction substrates" allow ectopic bony tissue to appear when injected into rat muscle.[123]

The mode of action of BIP is not known. Two mechanisms have been suggested. The first suggests that it is a transport system for a chemical agent which abolishes the genetic control of osteogenesis. The second is a semi-conducting mechanism transmitting a flux of electrons from the substrate to the cell. A period of 4 days elapses between the intervention of "induction substrate" and differentiation in osteoblasts. This period is necessary for the formation of BIP and for the transmission of the signal for ossification.[124]

There also exists a postnatal inducer principle for chondrogenesis which can be obtained from lyophylized decalcified cartilage and will initiate chondrogenesis in mesenchymal cells. The following cartilages are active in this respect: articular, nasal, costal, xyphoid and tracheal.[125]

The factors regulating BIP are little known. It is known that STH and TSH accelerate the formation of callous and that cortisol reduces it. It has also been possible to demonstrate the same hormonal actions on induction capacity near mesenchymal cells, of allogenic implants of decalcified and lyophylized bones.[65]

Morphogenesis

Primary ossification commences at the beginning of the eighth week of embryonic life. It occurs in membranous bone in the zone of fibrous condensation and in cartilage as regards endochondral ossification. In the latter case, formation of bony tissue is firstly perichondral, then enchondral, except in the vertebral bodies where the order is reversed. Simulated models of morphogenesis have been studied with computers.[37]

Development of the Bony Architecture

From the stage of condensation of cartilagenous cells onwards the growth of the skeletal pattern of the limb takes place rapidly, segmentation corresponding with the future joints. Rudimentary patterns of skeletal components are first defined, each component being made of hypertropic cartilage in the centre and flattened cartilagenous cells at the edges. The cartilagenous core is surrounded by perichondrium formed from mesenchymal cells. Perichondrium consists of an external layer of fibroblasts and an internal layer comprising several groups of cells. This internal layer differentiates centrally into osteoblasts and, becoming osteogenic, is transformed into periosteum. During this time the ground substance becomes metachromatic and fibrils of collagen appear there (Fig. 2).

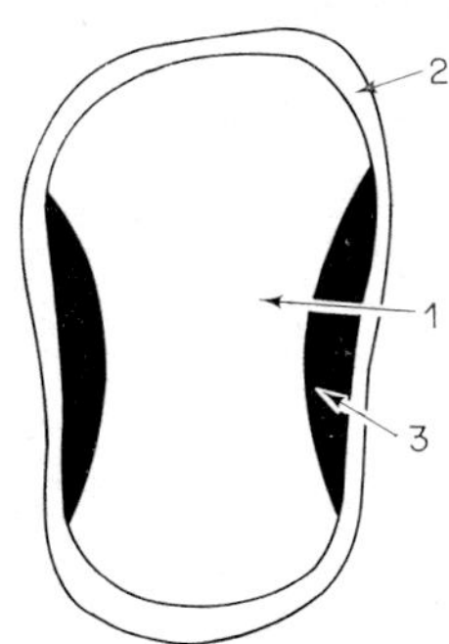

FIG. 2. Primitive cartilagenous maquette of an enchondral bone:
1. Cartilagenous part
2. Perichondrium with 2 layers
3. Periosteum

Thus, the diversity of structure of the three constituent tissues of the initial plan (cartilage, perichondrium and periosteum) is established during early morphogenesis. This process depends on intrinsic influences which act in two ways: (1) as regards cellular phenomena: by the rates of mitosis and of cellular division with hypertrophy of cartilagenous cells which varies from one location to another, and (2) by the differential rates of synthesis of glycosaminoglycans and above all of collagen.

Initially, collagen exists only in the form of chains of alpha-collagen. Later these monomeres become organized into tridimensional polymeres. First fibrils of small diameter (100 Å.) appear; next, the diameter increases progressively; and finally one can discern periodicity. These fibrils may be disposed at random or are already precisely arranged and play a definite morphogenic role. Indeed, in organic culture, the action of collagenase lyses the cartilagenous pattern while hyaluronidase does not affect the anatomical arrangement of the tibia.[41]

Cellular division and hypertrophy, together with the arrangement of collagenous fibres are the early factors in morphogenesis: hormones and vitamins only intervene later. The development of bone marrow and of organs near the components of the skeleton are important for certain bones. The role of mechanical forces is minimal in morphogenic prenatal morphogenesis, except as regards architectural details like the areas of tendon insertion.

Growth of a Long Bone

After the rudimentary pattern is established, how can postnatal morphogenesis be followed? An interesting system for study which has been used for a long time[33] is the development of the long bone which has been described in detail by different authors.[17,77] Nevertheless, a number of features are not clear and their interpretation is sometimes contradictory. Two recent studies will be summarized by way of example.

(a) Morphogenesis of a Metatarsal in the Rat.[72] In this study micrographic and histological evidence permits the stages of development of a metatarsal to be described in seven parts:

1. A centre of calcification (and not of ossification) appears in the *centre* of the cartilagenous maquette (Fig. 3).
2. When this zone of calcified cartilage comes into contact with the perichondrium it induces the formation of "marginal membrane," a deep calcified zone (not ossified) of the perichondrium.
3. At the site of the calcified marginal membrane, periosteal bone is next formed.
4. Primary resorption, the formation of bony tissue in the calcified cartilagenous matrix, and secondary resorption end with the formation of enchondral bone and of the medullary canal and with the division of the marginal membrane into two parts, proximal and distal, separated by periosteal bone. These parts are the perichondral bars which limit the metaphyses (Fig. 4).
5. It is the perichondral bar and not periosteal bone which undergoes the modelling resorption of Hunter under the influence of a group of cells outwith the bar. The metaphyses evolves toward maturity.
6. The epiphyseal centre of ossification appears and the growth of cartilage becomes organized between this point and the metaphyses.
7. Diaphysis, metaphysis and epiphysis grow with their own particular characteristics. However, the formation of definitive bone comprises: the integration of the metaphysis in diaphyseal cortex with progressive displacement from the point of integration towards the epiphysis and the integration of the epiphysis with the diaphysis by the disappearance of growth cartilage and the surrounding of the diaphyseal cortex with epiphyseal spur.

(b) Prenatal Development of the Human Humerus.[58] From a radiographic and histological study of 40 pairs of humeri from human embryos and fetuses, whose length ranged from 26–342 mm. (55–252 days), the following facts have been deduced:

1. A "rod" of primary bone is demonstrable very early and from the 27 mm. stage (55 days) it extends along the middle third of the length of the humerus. Primary resorption of this "rod" begins at the end of the embryonic period.
2. Enchondral ossification begins at the 37 mm. stage, at the proximal and distal extremities.
3. The formation of periosteal bone grows in length and towards the 18th week overflows a millimetre beyond the zone of growth of the extremities.
4. Thus, enchondral ossification and periosteal

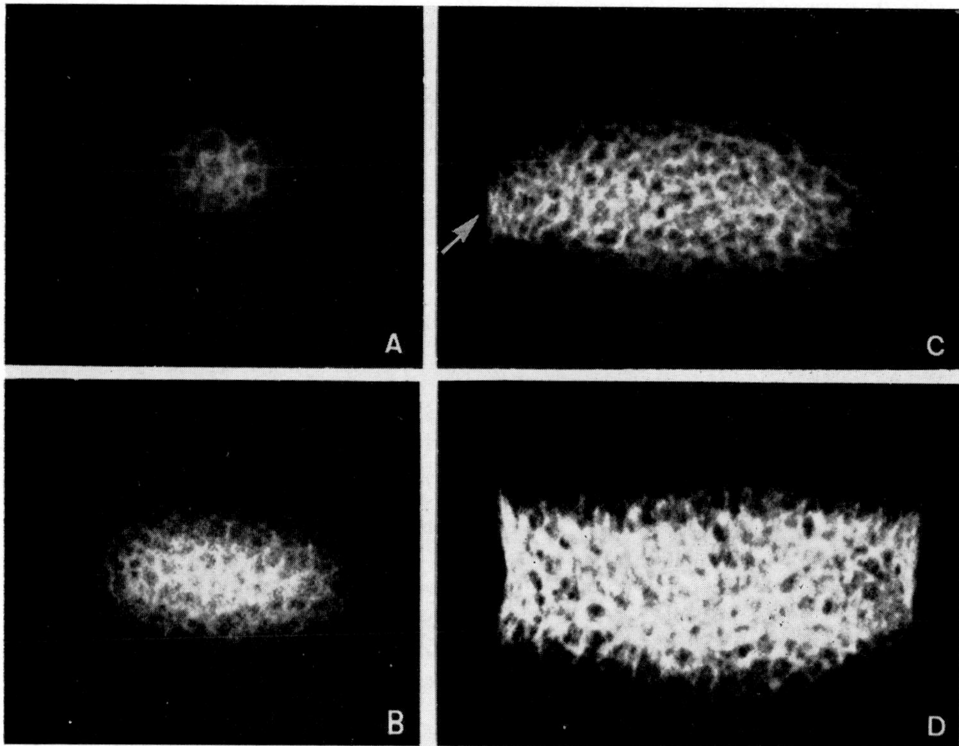

FIG. 3. X-ray showing a centre of calcification in a cartilagenous maquette of long bone (*by kind permission of M. Juster.*)

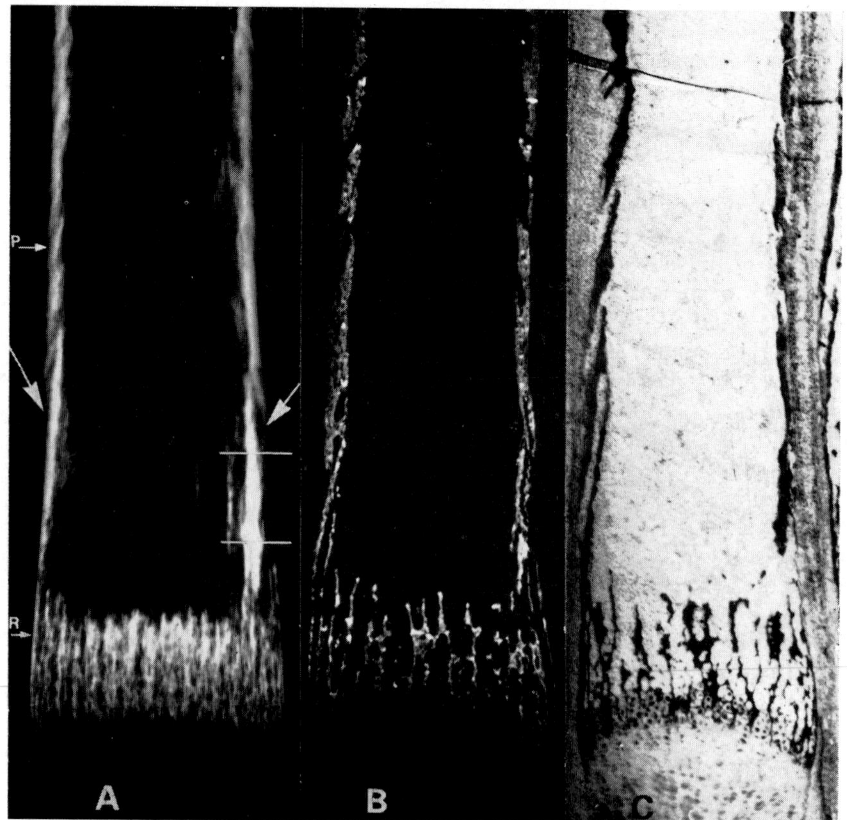

FIG. 4. X-ray appearance of the perichondral bar and the periosteal bone of a rat metatarsus (*by kind permission of M. Juster.*)

ossification are harmonious and at birth represent 79 per cent of the length of the humerus.

5. Trabeculation of the primary bone commences in the embryonic period. Fusion of the sections of enchondral and periosteal origin begins about 61 mm. (76 days). The medullary canal appears in bipolar fashion: at 73 mm. (82 days) at the proximal extremity and at 113 mm. (100 days) at the distal extremity.

Structure, Weight, Density

The formation of bony tissue thus commences towards the eighth week of human embryonic life.

(a) **The Structure of Fetal Bone** differs from that observed after birth. Embryonic bone is characterized by an irregular arrangement of collagenous fibres which give it a felted appearance, by a high degree of mineralization and by a great number of large osteocytes. In the cortex of long bones the irregular bands of osseous tissue are separated by spaces containing vascularized connective tissue. Near term, these spaces become covered with beds of lamellar bone. Lamellar bone is much less mineralized and it is poorer in osteocytes which are somewhat smaller. Thus, lamellar bone is formed along the length of the embryonic bone. It becomes organized in cylindrical structures which are the primary osteones. The result of this is a very compact cortex in fetal bone.

It is striking how little osseous remodelling occurs during prenatal life. But loss of bone is enough to assure the external form of the bone and the appearance of the medullary canal. The medullary canal in the middle part of the human femur doubles its diameter, between the third month and the end of prenatal life, while the external diameter of the bone is multiplied by 8. Internal remodelling at the level of the endosteum, does not begin until the last month of prenatal life.[116]

(b) **Study of the Weight of Bones and of the Skeleton** during fetal life has given rise to some interesting findings. In the adult there is good correlation between the height of an individual, the weight of his skeleton and the weight and length of his femur. Recently a study was made of the dried and defatted skeletons of 124 fetuses of both sexes whose gestational age ranged from 16–44 weeks and regression equations were calculated to estimate the correlation between the weight of the skeleton and the age, the weight at birth, fetal length and the weight and length of certain bones: femur, humerus, tibia and radius. The weight of a long bone gives a better estimate of total skeletal weight than the other parameters. There are no ethnic or sex differences in the weights of bones, of limb bones or of complete skeleton. By contrast, the length of the bones is greater in black children than in caucasians, and the ratio of femur length to humerus length or of tibial length to humerus length is greater in girls than in boys.[120] (Fig. 5)

(c) **The Density of Fetal Bone** can be expressed as the ratio of the weight of dry defatted bone to the volume of the bone measured by the quantity of water displaced. The mean density decreases in the following order for four long bones: radius, humerus, tibia, femur. The density increases with fetal age contrary to what is observed during postnatal life.[122]

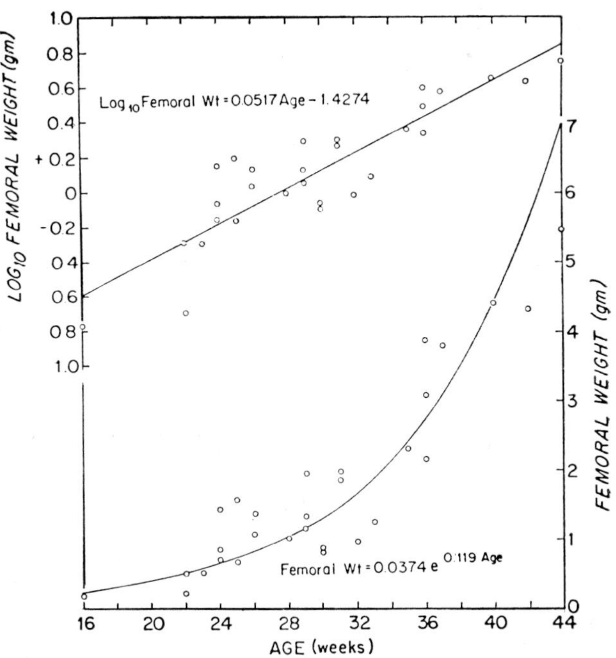

Fig. 5. Comparison of fitted regression lines in White male series: the exponential growth curve relating femoral weight to age and its transformation to a straight line relating logarithms of the same femoral weights to age.[120]

Mineralization

Precise data has been acquired from chemical analysis of the mineral compartment of human fetal bones. During the last month of prenatal life the water content of bone diminishes. The magnesium, sodium and chloride content of the ash also falls. The quantities of citrate and carbonate rise from the 28th week of gestation until birth. Although embryonic bone already contains calcium it is well known that this accumulates primarily in the 4 last months of fetal life: between 2 and 3 g. at 5 months, 5–6 g. at 6 months, 9 g. at 7 months, 15 g. at 8 months and about 30 g. at birth. The calcium: phosphorus ratio remains constant and the phosphorus content of the skeleton passes from 1 or 2 g. at 5 months to 18 g. at birth. The accumulation of calcium is almost parallel to that of fetal weight. However, the calcium content per kilogramme body weight has a tendency to reduce during the 6th and 7th month and to rise during the 8th and above all the 9th month. It seems quite clear that premature birth deprives the newborn of an important fraction of its calcium and phosphorus content.

Biophysical Aspects

The predominant crystal in bone is a hydroxyapatite. The crystals are orientated along the mature collagen fibrils. It is possible, however, that some part of the mineral material is deposited in an amorphous form and that at the beginning of crystalization the first crystals are octophosphates of calcium. The biophysical aspects of bone mineralization are far from clear.[24]

Human fetal bone has been studied in detail by quantitative microradiography, X-ray microdiffraction, polarized microscopy of the matrix, and X-ray diffraction. These researches have led to certain conclusions concerning the formation and growth of fetal bone, for which the model chosen has been the femur.

1. Newly formed bone is strongly mineralized and shows characteristic aspects of hydroxyapatites by X-ray diffraction from the outset.

2. The mineral content of fetal bone tissue accumulates rapidly during the 3 weeks following its appearance, then remains almost constant until birth. The "coefficient of linear absorption" which reflects the degree of mineralization of bony tissue is 95 for adult bone and 85 for prenatal bone. It can reach 100 in the fetus in the regions of enchondral and periosteal ossification.

3. The rapid increase of mineralization in the fetal skeleton is accompanied by an elongation of the apatite crystals whose length is 160 Å. at 15 weeks and reaches 220 Å. at full term.

4. The first crystals formed in fetal bone are not orientated in the same pattern as the collagenous matrix. One or two weeks after their appearance there begins to appear an arrangement which follows the longitudinal axis of the collagen fibrils. The factors which determine this orientation depend more on the matrix than on the crystals.

5. The rapid progress in the degree of mineralization of fetal bone is dominated by the growth in length of the crystals. It is still not known which factors limit mineralization, but these are doubtless something to do with the matrix, and are probably the same factors which limit the growth in length of the crystals.[128]

Metabolic Aspects

It is necessary to consider the process of mineralization of bony tissue during prenatal life in the context of the more general phenomenon of the regulation of calcium and phosphorus metabolism at this time. Three factors enter into this regulation and into the mineralization of the fetal skeleton: the mineral metabolism of the mother, the placenta's own activity and the endocrine regulation of the fetus itself.

Earlier studies had led to the belief that in the immature human fetus, serum calcium was normal while the concentration of inorganic phosphorus in the serum was high, as much as 14·8 mg./100 ml.[36]

In fact, it has now been demonstrated unequivocably that in several animal species, in particular in the sheep, fetal serum calcium (6·73 $\pm$ 0·64 mequiv./l.) is higher than maternal serum calcium (4·23 $\pm$ 0·62 mequiv./l.).[6] The same has been shown for ultrafilterable calcium. The serum phosphorus is very high in the fetus; urinary secretion of phosphorus is small; and the percentage of tubular reabsorption of phosphorus (TRP) is in the neighbourhood of 100 per cent. Thus the fetus, in comparison with its mother, is in a state of hypercalcaemia and of hyperphosphataemia. Anomalies of maternal mineral metabolism, whether they be of nutritional or endocrine origin, must needs have an influence on the fetal calcium and phosphorus but there is not a strict correlation between the fetus and the mother in this regard.[28]

It follows that the role of the placenta and that of the fetus' own endocrine regulation are important.

(a) Placenta. The existence of bidirectional transport of calcium across the placenta has been demonstrated. When calcium is injected into the mother or into the fetus, it enters the amniotic fluid; by distinction calcium injected into the amniotic fluid only goes into the fetus.[132]

The existence of a serum calcium level higher by 1 or 2 mg. per 100 ml. of serum in the fetus than in the mother suggests that there is active transport of calcium from the mother to the fetus at the level of the placenta. The nature of this active transport (the calcium pump) is unknown but it obviously attenuates the consequences for fetal serum calcium of any fall in maternal calcaemia.

In the guinea pig it has been demonstrated that the serum phosphorus of the mother is the principal source of inorganic phosphorus for the fetus. Perhaps the very high level of serum phosphorus in the fetus depends, as with calcium, on an active process of placental transport. At all events, it is likely that the fetus's own homeostatic mechanisms play a fundamental role in this situation.[46]

(b) Parathormone. The parathyroid glands are derived from the endoderm of the 3rd and 4th pharyngeal pouches. In man these glands arise in the region of the dorsal zone of these pouches. The upper glands come from the 4th pharyngeal pouches. The 3rd pouches give rise to the inferior parathyroids and in their ventral part to the thymus.

It is established that the parathyroids of a human fetus of 12–13 weeks are functional. They induce the resorption of parietal bone in the rat when the two tissues are cultivated *in vitro* on the chorioallantoic membrane of the chick embryo.[110]

The response of the fetus to parathormone has been studied in the rat fetus deprived of parathyroids by decapitation in which the blood calcium fall and returns to normal following the injection of 5 USP units of parathormone. In the intact rat fetus the same dose of parathormone produces a net rise of blood calcium 4–16 hours after the injection, disappearing after 24 hours; and a fall in the blood phosphorus. Injection of a large dose of parathormone into the pregnant female (100 USP) produces no modification of the fetal blood calcium which suggests that the hormone does not pass or passes very little across the placenta from mother to fetus.[56]

In the 21-day rat fetus, circulating parathormone can be bound and rendered inactive by subcutaneous injection of serum anti-parathormone. The hypocalcaemia and hyperphosphataemia which result from this seem to indicate that the parathormone in fetal plasma, whose origin is undoubtedly fetal, plays a role in the homeostasis of blood levels of calcium and of phosphate.[49]

It has been established in the lamb that the renal response to parathormone is of the same type as in the adult. The normal fetus exhibits a very high blood phosphorus level with practically no phosphorus in the urine, and the percentage of tubular reabsorption of phosphorus is very high.

The administration of an extract of parathyroid by continuous perfusion (0·1 International units/kg./min.) lowers the blood phosphorous and the PTR.[113] This can be interpreted as meaning that the high concentration of calcium in fetal serum, maintained by a placental mechanism, inhibits parathyroid function during prenatal life. This functional parthyroid insufficiency could be an explanation for the high blood phosphorous level. It is possible that the hypercalcaemic situation involves an increased secretion of fetal calcitonin which would explain the poor bony response to parathormone in the lamb.[6]

Maternal hyperparathyroidism is often associated with a prolonged hypocalcaemia in human newborn infants.[43] Occasional clinical observations on children born of mothers with untreated hypoparathyroidism show that these infants present with neonatal hypercalcaemia and bony lesions compatible with a diagnosis of hyperparathyroidism. In some cases maternal tetany has ceased to be troublesome during the pregnancy. As it is unlikely that parathormone crosses the placenta, it must be agreed that it is the calcium concentrations of the mother which are involved in the hypoparathyroidism of the fetus, and that the high fetal blood calcium level which sometimes correct the maternal hypocalcaemia.[220]

Removal of both the thyroid and the parathyroid of the rat on the 3rd day of gestation leads on the 21st day of gestation to a weight deficit in the fetus, a lowering of fetal blood calcium and a rise in fetal blood phosphorus. The weight of the fetal parathyroid glands in terms of fetal body weight are increased by 50 per cent compared with controls.[52]

In conclusion certain facts can be stated. Fetal parathyroids can elaborate parathormone very early in prenatal life. In the normal state, the high concentration of fetal blood calcium maintained by the placenta prevents the parathyroids from being stimulated, and this explains in part the high blood phosphorus and the very low urinary excretion of phosphorus. The renal response to parathormone in the lamb during fetal life is excellent. Bone responds very little but does so to some extent. Maternal hypoparathyroidism in the human female and in the rat produces a parathyroid hyperplasia in the fetus, secondary to the diminished transfer of calcium. Parathormone crosses the placental barrier very poorly or not at all.

(c) Calcitonin. The cells which secrete calcitonin are provided with numerous mitochondria and are rich in alphaglycerophosphate-dehydrogenase. In birds and fishes they are found in a separate organ: the ultimobranchial body. In mammals, they constitute the parafollicular cells or C cells of the thyroid; they exist, sometimes, in small number in the thymus and the parathyroids. The development of these cells from the pharyngeal pouches has given rise to some interesting studies. In the chick the ultimobranchial body develops from the 5th pouch. Using the technique of orthotopic grafts of neural tube taken from the quail and grafted into chick embryos, it has been shown that the origin of the calcitonin cells is from the cells of the neural crest which come secondarily to colonize the epithelium of the 5th pharyngeal pouch.[79,99]

In vitro studies on explants of embryonic bone have not been able to demonstrate an anti-osteolytic action of calcitonin, contrary to what occurs *in vivo* in man or in mature animals. However, the possibility that calcitonin has an action on the fetal skeleton has recently given rise to some interesting findings. The injection of large doses of pig calcitonin into pregnant rats does not involve any modification of total hydroxyproline in the fetal serum and only produces a small alteration in fetal blood calcium levels which is certainly secondary to the severe hypocalcaemia obtained in the mother. Studies of the movements of ^{47}Ca do not support the idea that calcitonin injected into the mother has an action on the fetus. The presence in adult rats of a serum factor which inactivates calcitonin is well known. This has been looked for in the fetus and it has been found that it exists but is much less powerful than in later life. It therefore seems inconceivable that any transplacental passage of calcitonin occurs from the mother to the fetus.[132]

A series of experiments using the rat fetus has made it possible to establish some important facts. The injection of calcitonin labelled with ^{125}I either into the mother or into the fetus shows the absence of any transplacental passage in either direction. The rate of disappearance of calcitonin labelled with ^{125}I is more rapid in the adult than in the fetus, when the same quantity is given in terms of body weight. *In vitro* the supernatant of a placental homogenate inactivates calcitonin. Injection of calcitonin into the rat fetus at 21 days lowers its blood calcium and its blood phosphorus; these changes being less noticeable in younger fetuses.[51,53,54,55] It therefore seems unlikely that maternal calcitonin crosses the placenta. The fetal skeleton is sensitive *in vivo* to the action of calcitonin and loading of the rat fetus with calcium is capable of leading to the secretion of calcitonin.[50]

(d) Cholecalciferol. It has been known for a long time that the mineralization of the fetal skeleton is closely dependent on the mineral metabolism of the mother:[74,114] for instance, rickets has been observed in the newborn infants of women suffering from osteomalacia.[89] Studies using biological assay techniques in the calf, rabbit and man have shown that the liver, the skin and the plasma were the principal fetal sources of steroids with antirachitic activity.[66]

A recent study using cholecalciferol and 25-OH-cholecalciferol labelled with tritium, has established the following (Fig. 6).

1. That the transplacental passage of cholecalciferol and of its 25-hydroxylated metabolite is certain and rapid.
2. That there exists a state of equilibrium between the fetus and the mother for these two metabolites.
3. That the plasma of pregnant rats and their fetuses contains more of the inactive water-soluble metabolites than that of non-pregnant rats submitted to the same experimental procedure. It is possible that this finding may be secondary to the particular steroid metabolism obtaining in the fetus.[61]

Effects on the fetus obtained with high doses of vitamin D administered during gestation have been described. In the pregnant rat, elevated doses of vitamin D produce a diminution in fetal weight. The total fetal calcium and phosphorus

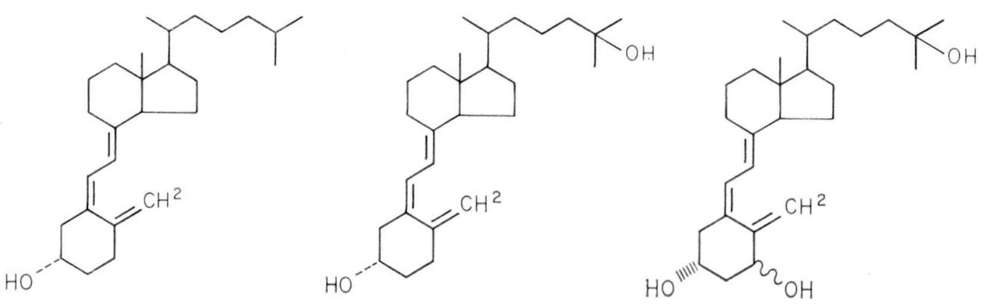

FIG. 6. Chemical formula of cholecalciferol and its derivatives:
1. cholecalciferol
2. 25–OH-cholecalciferol
3. 1–25-dihydroxycholecalciferol

and that of its skeleton are reduced.[97] As regards cartilage few changes are noticed: viz. a reduction of the proliferative and hypertrophic zones, with increased osteoblastic activity. It is known that in transplacental cortisol intoxication of the rat fetus, the ground substance and cartilage cells are very altered. Although some antagonism between cortisol and vitamin D is recognized in postnatal life, transplacental intoxication with vitamin D considerably accentuates the lesions provoked by cortisol in the fetus.[96] It is interesting that supravalvular stenoses of the aorta can be produced in fetal rabbits by an overdose of vitamin D to their pregnant mothers.[45] Since such stenoses occur in idiopathic hypercalcaemia with an elfin facies possible resulting from a disturbances of cholecalciferol metabolism during gestation.

In Conclusion, three factors seem to be involved in the mineralization of the skeleton and in prenatal calcium metabolism. The first is the mineral metabolism of the mother with its nutritional component and its own endocrine regulation. Second is the placenta which permits, on the one hand, the passage of cholecalciferol and of its 25-hydroxylated derivative; on the other hand, the bidirectional transference of calcium and phosphorus with an active calcium pump mechanism maintaining fetal calcium at a level 1 or 2 mg./100 ml. above the maternal blood calcium. The third factor is the endocrine regulation of the fetus itself which, as far as parathormone and calcitonin are concerned, seems to possess the capability of synthesizing these hormones very early and of regulating their secretion and distributing them to the principle target organs: the bony tissue and the kidney.

Anomalies of calcium metabolism—hypocalcaemia or hypercalcaemia—in the mother and fetus have an influence not only on the mineralization of the skeleton but on the development of other factors: weight and the state of the hair.[38]

Hydroxyproline excretion

Hydroxyproline is a characteristic amino acid of collagen and in particular of collagen of bony tissue. It is excreted in the urine both in a free form and linked with polypeptides, some of which are dialysable. It appears that non-dialysable urinary hydroxyproline derives from the metabolism of soluble collagen.

The level of total hydroxyproline in amniotic fluid towards the 28th week of gestation has reached concentrations of from 6–14 mg./l., falling to from 2–4 mg./l. towards the 34th week. From the 36th to the 40th week the concentration is between 0·2 and 4·5 mg./l.: concentrations of less than 2 mg./l. are found in high-risk pregnancy and in intrauterine growth retardation.[132a]

During postnatal development, total urinary hydroxyproline expressed in mg./24 hours rises from birth to 2 years of age, becomes stable at about 1 year of age, and then rises progressively to climb much more steeply at the time of puberty (Tables 1 and 2).[72a,b] When these results are expressed as a ratio of hydroxyproline/creatinine, there is a steady increase during the first 2 months of life, then a decrease until 2 years of age, after which it does not change until 12 or 13 years of age when it begins to decrease until 20 years of age (Table 3).[22a] These figures vary according to the authors and the methods of measurement. Thus there exists a positive correlation between the rate of growth and the urinary excretion of hydroxyproline.

TABLE 1

URINARY EXCRETION OF TOTAL HYDROXYPROLINE EXPRESSED IN mg./24h./m^2. BODY SURFACE[72a]

Age	*Number of Subjects*	*Average*	± 2 *S.D.*
0–12 m.	24	115·4	39·8–191
1 year	7	80·5	40·3–120·7
2–10 years	36	63·3	34·1–92·5
11–14 years	25	76·8	40·2–113·4

TABLE 2

URINARY EXCRETION OF HYDROXYPROLINE DURING THE FIRST 60 DAYS OF LIFE[72b]

Age (*Days*)	*Free* *Hdyroxyproline* (mg./24 h.)	*Total* *Hydroxyproline* (mg./24 h.)
1–2	<5	<12
10–14	15–22	50–65
50–60	20–28	65–85

TABLE 3

HYDROXYPROLINE (mg.): CREATININE (g.) RATIO IN URINE (FROM 22[a])

<table>
<tr><th></th><th>Boys</th><th>Girls</th></tr>
<tr><td>2/12–6/12</td><td colspan="2">0·58</td></tr>
<tr><td>1</td><td colspan="2">0·38</td></tr>
<tr><td>3</td><td colspan="2">0·22</td></tr>
<tr><td>5</td><td colspan="2">0·23</td></tr>
<tr><td>7</td><td colspan="2">0·14</td></tr>
<tr><td>9</td><td>0·10</td><td>0·12</td></tr>
<tr><td>11</td><td>0·10</td><td>0·12</td></tr>
<tr><td>13</td><td>0·11</td><td>0·09</td></tr>
<tr><td>15</td><td>0·09</td><td>0·03</td></tr>
<tr><td>17</td><td>0·07</td><td>0·03</td></tr>
<tr><td>19</td><td>0·05</td><td>0·04</td></tr>
</table>

PERINATAL DEVELOPMENT

The perinatal development of calcified tissues and of calcium and inorganic phosphorus metabolism is of very great interest for the understanding of the different clinical incidents which can occur during this period, in particular those related to a lowering of the blood calcium.[92]

Development of the Bony Tissue

Structure

Shortly after birth the remodelling of the cortex of long bones and endosteal resorption, which were not very active before birth, begin to accelerate. During the first year of life an important portion of primary bone is remodelled and the secondary osteones are formed. The diameter of the medullary canal increases and at the end of the first year the cortex of long bones has become relatively thin even though periosteal bone continues to be formed actively. All this has been observed in the tibia, the femur and the metacarpals. A state that has been described in the first weeks of life in which the cortex of the long bones is thick and compact, and associated in almost half the cases (from radiographic evidence) with a splitting of the periostial sheath (lamellar peristosis), has been designated by the term "physiological osteosclerosis of the newborn." A condition often observed between 6 and 15 months of postnatal life, in which the cortex is thin and rich in young osteones and resorption lacunae, is called "physiological osteoporosis of the suckling period." During the second year, the ratio of the diameter of the cortex to the diameter of the entire diaphysis becomes almost constant. It is believed that all the primary bone has been remodelled towards the age of 2 years, and this represents a remodelling of 50 per cent of the bone per annum compared to a rate of 5 per cent in the adult.[116]

During the same period, membranous bones continue their ossification and there is closure of the fontanelles in the vault of the cranium.

Maturation

The concept of maturation of the skeleton will be discussed later. However, it is convenient to state at this stage that it is useful to have certain indices of maturation at birth, these being the head of the humerus, the distal centre of the femur, the proximal centre of the tibia and the cuboid. It has been shown that the following centres are present during the last 2 months of gestation: in boys, the humerus in 78 per cent of cases, the femur in 100 per cent, the tibia in 98 per cent and the cuboid in 91 per cent; in girls: the humerus in 81 per cent the femur and tibia in 100 per cent and the cuboid in 98 per cent. Thus at this stage there is some maturational precocity in girls as a group compared with boys.[4] The prenatal influence of thyroid hormone on these indicators of maturation in the human species is demonstrated by the fact that in cases of fetal athyroidism, these epiphyseal centres and the cuboidal pattern are either not ossified or reach a multiple ossification characteristic of thyroid insufficiency and known as "epiphyseal dysgenesis."[135]

Phosphorus and Calcium Metabolism

During prenatal life the needs of the fetus for calcium and phosphorus are covered by the mother. At birth, at full term, the newborn human skeleton contains about 30 g. of calcium and 18 g. of phosphorus. From the outset of postnatal life, the newborn is dependent solely on his dietary intake; his skeleton is about to be mineralized and to develop very rapidly; his regulatory system is not immediately liberated from the constraints imposed on it by fetal homeostasis.

In cord blood, at the time of birth, the blood calcium is raised (10·7 mg./100 ml.) as is the plasma inorganic phosphorus (5·6 mg./100 ml.). In the hours which follow birth, there occurs a progressive fall of blood calcium (8·5–9 mg./100 ml.) and a progressive rise in the concentration of serum phosphorus (7–8 mg/100 ml.).

The Intestinal Absorption of Calcium[42]

In all those situations (prematurity; babies born of high-risk pregnancy; small-for-dates babies in whom there may be a reduction or difficulty in acquiring an adequate intake of calories) there will be a reduction in the alimentary intake of calcium.

In the normal breast-fed full-term baby, it seems that the percentage absorption (or the coefficient of net digestive utilization) of calcium undergoes a progressive maturation. Thus, the percentages are 27·8 ± 16·5 per cent for babies from 4–7 days old, and from 43·9 ± 13·2 per cent for those between 7 and 10 days.[136] This figure can reach 60 per cent or more after a month.

By contrast, the absorption of calcium is much less good with cows' milk or with modified formulae. There has been some attempt recently to "adapt" cows' milk to the needs of the human newborn by replacing the butter fats by vegetable oils, with the aim of improving lipid absorption and, with this, calcium absorption which is partly related to it. One study which has been made using such milks has shown that faecal loss of calcium in the newborn is influenced by the fatty-acid composition of the milk lipids. A high level of stearate (C_{16}) and of palmitate (C_{18}) increases the calcium loss. These losses are reduced by feeding the same formula rendered poor in stearate and palmitate but rich in oleate. It therefore seems that the long-chain saturated fatty acids are less favourable to the absorption of calcium.[136] Thus it may be important in the neonatal period to take account of this possible cause of tetany, when studying the new milks often described as "adapted" or "humanized," some of which are inseparable from a very poor calcium absorption.[133]

Regulation of Blood Calcium

The fall in blood calcium in the neonatal period is often more profound in the premature infant than in the term infant of the same weight.[100] This suggests that some reduction of the calcium reserves of the skeleton plays an important role. Transitory hypocalcaemia of the newborn, whether or not accompanied by clinical manifestations, has been explained in several ways:

1. Insufficient activity of the parathyroid glands.
2. An insufficient sensitivity of the bones to parathormone.
3. The role of hyperphosphataemia.
4. Rather poor mineralization of the skeleton at birth.

The skeleton at birth is poorly mineralized, the ratio of ash to dry, defatted weight of the bone being half what is found in the adult. It is likely that this newborn skeleton is capable of fixing large quantities of calcium, more so since its rate of remodelling is increasing very quickly.

Parathyroid activity is low at birth and for several days thereafter. The inactive state of the parathyroids in the fetus due to the raised concentration of blood calcium at the end of fetal life, provides indirect evidence that this is so. The response of the neonatal skeleton to parathormone is generally regarded as insufficient and it has been proposed that lamellar bone is more sensitive to parathormone than embryonic bone: on the other hand, the therapeutic use of parathormone in conditions of hypocalcaemia in the newborn is often effective and this lends support to the proposition that the skeletal receptors are not absent.

Finally, the alimentary intake of cows' milk rich in inorganic phosphorus probably plays an important role.

Although the depressor role of hyperphosphataemia on blood calcium levels may still be unclear, it seems certain that the arrival of orthophosphate ions by an enteral or parental route powerfully inhibits osteolysis whether in physiological or pathological conditions. This increased intake in newborn babies fed on cows' milk creates a situation which favours hypocalcaemia, above all when the absorption of calcium is mediocre. The part played by secretory insufficiency of the parathyroid glands can be prolonged for several weeks in certain newborn infants when it reaches the status of "transitory parathyroid insufficiency" in the first months of life. These patients react very well to injections of parathormone, followed by treatment with Vitamin D and a calcium supplement combined with a diet of human breast milk. The treatment can be abandoned after several weeks, without the decline recurring.[116] One has to differentiate these cases from rare examples of chronic hypoparathyroidism in the newborn due to haemorrhage or to congenital absence of the parathyroid glands.[43]

Regulation of Plasma Phosphorus Concentration

Many explanations have been advanced for the high blood level of phosphorus in the neonatal period.

Study of urinary excretion of phosphorus in the newborn has shown that TRP which is very high on the first day, becoming less during the following three days. Phosphaturia, and the ratio: phosphorus clearance/creatinine clearance rises on the first and third day of life after an injection of parathormone, but the renal response to this hormone is not complete.[22] By contrast, by the sixth day the renal response will be essentially similar to that in the adult. The very low glomerular filtration rate explains the difficulties of renal excretion of phosphorus in the newborn.

The urinary excretion of cyclic AMP may be partly regarded as a consequence of the response of the proximal renal tubule to parathormone. This excretion is multiplied two- or three-fold between one and three days of postnatal age in both breast-fed and artificially fed infants. The increased excretion which follows injection of parathormone is five times greater on the third day than on the day of birth.[79a]

Another important factor is the considerable cellular catabolism which accompanies birth, especially in high-risk cases.

Finally, the high inorganic phosphorus content of cows' milk plays an important role as has been known for a long time in that babies fed with cows' milk have a higher blood phosphorus level than those fed at the breast.[47]

It thus seems that in the first two or three days of life, functional parathyroid insufficiency, intense cellular breakdown, and very poor diuresis combine to establish a raised inorganic phosphorus concentration in the plasma. In the following days, the low rate of glomerular filtration does not allow the correction of this situation, above all if an alimentary intake rich in phosphates is ingested in the form of cows' milk. However, it should be noticed that even if one inhibits the intestinal absorption of phosphorus with aluminium hydroxide, tubular reabsorption of phosphates is still further increased.[83] This leads one to think that phosphorus conservation by the newborn kidney reflects a real requirement, since it is increased when there is a much reduced alimentary intake. The regulator mechanism for this action remains unknown. It is possible that the high levels of growth hormone at this time of life which favour tubular reabsorption of phosphorus are important in this regard, but this remains hypothetical.

Other Minerals

It is known that the renal tubule and the intestinal mucosa can recognize and distinguish calcium and strontium during postnatal life. Thus strontium is less well absorbed and more abundantly excreted in the urine than is calcium. It seems that the capacity of the newborn to make this distinction is very reduced in comparison with that which can be observed in the adult.[80]

The metabolism of magnesium in the newborn is important, in relation to that of calcium, since a depletion of magnesium can lead to tetany and can reduce the response to parathormone. A study of 156 full-term newborn babies has shown that on the first day of life, before any feeding has occurred, the concentration of magnesium in the serum is 2·0 ± 0·2 mg./100 ml. This concentration by the fifth day of life has risen slightly in those fed at the breast, falls slightly in babies fed with cows' milk as well as in those who receive vitamin D. In hypocalcaemic children there is a positive correlation between the blood calcium and the magnesium concentration in the serum.[57]

POSTNATAL DEVELOPMENT

Postnatal development of the skeleton represents a combination of three distinct phenomena. The first is growth of the skeleton in length, in volume, and in weight, this growth participates directly in the growth of the stature of the individual and in the modification of bodily segments. The second is skeletal maturation which is no longer a matter of the formation of new tissue, but of the consolidation of bony tissue in its definitive form by the achievement of enchondral ossification; the appearance of epiphyseal centres, ossification of the small bones of the carpus and of the tarsus, and the disappearance of the growth cartilages. The third is the continuous remodelling of bony tissue, a process which persists until adulthood, but is accelerated during the entire period of development. Thus, from birth to adult age, bony tissue continues to mature and to renew itself. Such development involves the systems of periosteal, endosteal and enchondral ossification and the osteolysis systems comprising the periosteocytic and osteoclastic resorption.

Biometrics of Growth in Stature

An account of these events is given in several major works.[4,111,117]

Phenomenology

The development of height is such that for any given age in any given sex the distribution of heights of a population is near gaussian and this makes it possible to calculate a mean and standard deviation. It has been possible to establish the pattern of statural growth by means of longitudinal studies which have permitted the establishment of growth velocity expressions for each age. Growth is not a regular process: the speed of growth per annum is greater than 20 cm. in the first year and 10 cm. in the second; it subsequently falls from 8–5 cm./annum until the prepubertal period during which it climbs back to about 10 cm./annum, after which it rapidly decreases to zero 3 or 4 years after puberty. Individual and sex differences are well known and this makes it possible to understand the role of factors which act on the growth curve either by slowing or accelerating the rate of growth rather than in terms of absolute height. This growth in height is not homogeneous and differential biometry of the segments of the body or of the individual parts of the skeleton has shown variable periods of growth from one part to another. Thus, the growth in length of certain long bones has been described for the radius, the femur, the tibia and the humerus.[121] From a longitudinal study of the growth of 54 normal girls it has been concluded that after the age of 5 years, the lower part of the body follows a constant rate of growth which stops soon after the first menstrual period; the pubertal growth spurt occurs solely in the growth of the upper part of the body; it has been possible to establish mean velocity curves with standard deviations for these two parts of the body showing the greatest rate of growth in the lower part before puberty and the slowest rate after the pubertal growth spurt.[34]

Genetic Factors[109]

Genetic controls of growth in height and of rate of growth is of the multifactorial type. It is unlikely that this genetic control is mediated by hormonal activity. Nevertheless, certain recent studies of the activity of growth hormone, the factor of sulphation and the reaction to insulin leads to the conclusion that pygmies have an anomaly in their cellular sensitivity to growth hormone or to the sulphation factor. The genetic control of bony growth can be appreciated in several situations. There are ethnic differences: negroes grow their lower limbs faster than white people, who in turn grow them more rapidly than the Japanese. There are familial differences: children of large parents are on the average larger than children born from small parents; similarly, familial differences in bony maturation can be observed. Finally, there are sex differences in the rate of growth which is more rapid in girls, and in the final height which is larger in boys.

Studies of chromosomal aberrations have shown that any quantitative modification of the autosomes leads to a net reduction in growth. Illnesses accompanied by anomalies in the number of sex chromosomes seem to show that the differences in height of the two sexes does not appear to be dependent on the Y chromosome, but on inhibitor genes carried by the X chromosome and these only act where there are two of them.

Role of the Environment[109]

It is clear that arrest of growth and maturation of the skeleton, or serious slowing down of these processes is related to environmental factors. The situation can be reversed when these are changed and relapse again when they are reintroduced (dwarfism due to a poor environment). At the same time, a detailed analyses of the different environmental factors acting on growth and maturation of the skeleton is not simple. The following are concerned:

1. Chemical factors.
2. Emotional and psychological factors.
3. Pathological factors, all acute and chronic illness being able to slow or stop growth.
4. Socio-economic factors.
5. Dietary factors.

Hormonal factors are discussed below.

Socio Economic Factors still Remain Uncertain. The best established facts are that town children are larger than country children, that single children are larger than those of large families and that children from a privileged social environment are larger than poorer children.

The role of diet is proved by experiments in which milk

and fruit supplements have been given in schools, accelerating the rate of growth; by the depression of growth norms in wartime; and by modification of the same norms in refugee populations. The dietary factors which have been invoked are the intake calories, proteins, calcium and other electrolytes, and in vitamin C, A and D. These factors act on osteogenesis and/or on the physiology of growth cartilage concerning which their effect will be described.

Mechanical Forces Intervene as Well. Any increase in pressure which can be produced parallel to the axis of growth in length of long epiphyseal bones inhibits the growth in length of these long bones, while diminution of this pressure favours growth. The pressure necessary to stop epiphyseal growth in the child is more than 900 kg. whereas a state of weightlessness is accompanied by an acceleration in the rate of growth in length. It thus appears that mechanical forces, whose action is nil or negligible in the prenatal development of the skeleton, do play a part in determining the shape and architecture of the long bones during postnatal growth and maintain the shape and the resistance of parts of the skeleton in the adult.

The role of mechanical forces has been interpreted in terms of piezo-electricity.[10] Although this theory has been criticized and corrected it provides a reasonable basis for explaining observations found by radiographic techniques of the straightening of shafts which have been bent in osteomalacia and in rickets. This applies equally to the understanding of the demineralizing osteopathies in paralysed people, in patients immobilized in plaster and in subjects subjected to simulated or real weightlessness. It is not known whether the mechanical or electrical forces act the level of the surface of the osteoblast or at the junction between collagen and the hydroxyapatite crystal. It is possible that the synthesis of mucopolysaccharides may be stimulated by mechanical forces: thus, it is raised in joints submitted to significant pressure compared with others and is reduced in cases of paralysis and raised with exercise. In tissue culture the membrane potential of fibroblasts plays a regulatory role in the rate of synthesis of mucopolysaccharides and the chemical type of these latter is preferentially elaborated.[64] Finally it seems that all mechanical forces which reduce the rate of longitudinal growth of the skeleton—and thus affect the statural growth of the individual—by contrast stimulate the apposition of the bone on the diaphysis, thus increasing the thickness of this latter, as well as the density of the bone; such forces also determine the orientation of bony trabeculae in the direction of architectural adaptation to those forces.

Secular Acceleration

Progressive modifications of the rate of growth and maturation of bones occur. In one century, school children have become larger by 10–15 cm., adolescents by 10 cm. and female puberty is more precocious by 3 years. American, British and Swedish figures show that between 1880 and 1950, in each decade there has been an increase of 1·5 cm. in height between 5 and 7 years of age and of 2 cm. at adolescence. It is probable that this phenomenon is not very old and began at the beginning of the nineteenth century, and it has been interrupted during times of war and economic crisis. The causes of secular acceleration in growth are not clear. Improvement in hygiene and nutrition is often invoked, but the phenomena are identical in different social classes. The genetic influence of the opening of human isolates is possible, but this makes it necessary to propose the existence of recessive genes concerned with the slowing of growth.[117]

Homeorrhesis[101]

Normal growth in any given individual follows a curve which corresponds with the mean or which differs from it in a constant fashion by a part or a round number of standard deviations. It is said that a subject follows his growth trajectory or that this latter is canalized. An important fact often observed in animals and in man is that when a pathological cause inhibits growth, the individual departs from his normal growth trajectory. If the cause can be removed the subject rejoins his initial trajectory and to do this he must grow more quickly than a normal subject of the same age (catch-up growth). When he gets back to his normal trajectory, the acceleration disappears and the velocity of growth becomes normal again.[4]

Bone Growth

Growth in length of bone has similar features to that of statural growth. The gaussian distribution of length; the variation according to age of physiological maturation of growth rates in height; phenomena like secular acceleration in height and catch-up growth occur in both cases. Bone growth is equally concerned with a modification in the weight of the skeleton during postnatal development. It has been established in 150 skeletons of subjects aged from 23 days to 22 years how the growth in weight of total skeleton proceeds. This weight has no clear correlation with chronological age nor with the height of the individual. By contrast, there is a good correlation between the total weight of the skeleton and the length of certain bones: the tibia, femur, humerus and radius. Radiographic measurement of the humerus is capable of providing a precise indication of the total weight of the skeleton during postnatal development.[121] The bony mass is defined as the fraction of the total surface of a section of bone occupied by bony trabeculae. The advent of a mechanized technique of reading microradiographs and integrating the surfaces by computer has permitted the analysis of the manner in which the bony mass evolves. In the dorsal vertebrae of a normal adult, the bony mass is about 20 per cent. In the newborn it reaches 40 per cent, but from the age of 4 months arrives at the figure of 20 per cent and is stabilized there. From this age onwards, growth is accomplished without modification of the bony mass at the vertebral level.[138] Chemical examination of the bones of children of 18 months have shown that the proportion of bony tissue in terms of total weight of bone at the level of the vertebrae is about 25 per cent, but there is no information available on the development of this percentage.[35] Bone growth manifests itself by modifications of length, weight and mass, both in membranous bones and long bones.

A number of papers have been written on the process of postnatal growth in man of the membranous bones of the cranio-facial mass bearing on the measurement of the cranial perimeter, the closure of the fontanelle, and of the bony sutures of the cranium, the modifications in the base of the nose, the differential growth of the cranial mass and of the lower maxilla.

Growth of long bones involves two different processes: longitudinal growth which depends above all on the physiology of the growth cartilage; and growth in thickness which depends on sub-periosteal apposition, a system of osteogenesis comparable with that existing in membranous bone.

Longitudinal study of the width of the diaphysis and of the thickness of cortex of the second metacarpal has led to the establishment of longitudinal growth curves which varies with age and sex.[14] At the level of the mid shaft of the tibia a modification in the "cortico-diaphysial ratio," the ratio between the thickness of the cortex and that of the entire diaphysis has been described. This ratio is 0·6 at about the time of birth, falling to about 0·35–0·4 by about 10 months, rising again to $0{\cdot}48 \pm 0{\cdot}09$ at about 16 months and staying at this level subsequently.[12] The width of the diaphysis allows one to appreciate the growth in thickness of long bones radiographically; the cortico-diaphysial ratio allows one to judge the relationship between osteogenesis and bony destruction; it is moreover, possible that there is a relationship between the thickness of cortex and its calcium content.[14]

Bone growth is a biological phenomenon which deserves to be examined from two points of view: one is the physiology of the growth cartilage; the other, the mineralization of the growing skeleton.

Growth Cartilage

The longitudinal postnatal growth of the skeleton depends on the development of the articular cartilage for the epiphyseal centres and on the growth cartilage for the diaphysis. Growth cartilage is therefore the principal organ of growth in length of the skeleton from birth to adult age, which is marked by the disappearance of this cartilage in the human species. The activity of the two growth cartilages of the long bone is unequal: for example, the distal cartilage of the femur develops twice as quickly as the proximal cartilage. In the limbs in man the most active growth cartilages are near the knee in the lower limb and distal to the elbow in the upper limb. Growth cartilage is an organ which functions by means of mechanisms close to or identical with those which control chrondrogenesis and enchondral osteogenesis in the embryo, but it is subject to physical hormonal and nutritional factors peculiar to postnatal life. The structure and function of growth cartilages shows species differences from one animal to another. Reference will be mainly made to growth cartilage of man, rat and rabbit.

Structure and Methods of Study

Growth cartilage is situated between two ossified regions: the epiphyseal centre and the metaphysis. The limit of the latter is the line of ossification. Growth cartilage is formed from a very abundant matrix and from cells. These cells are arranged in five rows working from the epiphyseal centre towards the ossification line.

1. The first row is made of a narrow band of round cells called chondroprecursors (CPC). Each such cell divides to give rise to one other CPC and one chondroblast. This latter generates a cellular clone arranged in a column. Columns are arranged in parallel fashion in the longitudinal axis of the bony part.
2. The proliferative band is made of flattened chondroblasts becoming oval and is the site of intense reactive cellular division.
3. The band of maturation is made of chondrocytes which have a rounded appearance.
4. The hypertrophic band is formed at the summit of the columns and consists of voluminous chondrocytes with vacuolization of their cytoplasm and karyolysis. Here the intercellular matrix is less abundant and deposits of calcium appear.
5. The zone of ossification is the zone of invasion by capillaries from the metaphysis. The osteoblasts derive from such perivascular mesenchymal cells.

The pattern of cellular deployment has been studied in the mandibular condyle of the rat by marking the cells with tritiated thymidine. In the 4 hours following the injection of the label the cells of the proliferative bands and of maturation are labelled. In a progressive fashion, in the seven days which follow, one sees the radioactivity displaced little by little towards the zone of hypertrophy.[13,76]

Histochemical methods and cytoenzymological methods have made it possible to obtain information, in particular by biopsies of growth cartilage of the tibia, about the normal infant or the infant with hereditary or hormonal growth problems. Acid mucopolysaccharides are abundant in the cells and in the matrix of the basal proliferative and upper hypertrophic zones, while they are absent in the lower hypertrophic zone which by contrast is strongly coloured by PAS. Collagen is stained positively in the matrix of the hypertrophic zone and in the osteoid tissue, as are the amino groups in proteins. The cells of the proliferative and hypertrophic zones are rich in RNA and in glycogen. The most easily demonstrable enzymic activities, above all in the hypertrophic zone, are those of acid and alkaline phosphatases, 5-nucleotidase, lactic dehydrogenases, and glucose-6-phosphatase. In the basal and proliferative zone there is evidence of alpha-glycerophosphate-dehydrogenase, leucylamine-peptidase and cysteine-desulphurase.[115]

Functional study of growth cartilage and of the influences which affect it have been made in several ways: either *in vivo* by the line-test technique on the intact, hypophysectomized or thyrohypophysectomized animal, or more recently on the growth cartilage of *in vitro* tissue culture,[125] or on cartilage in cell culture. Whether *in vitro* or *in vivo*, different methods of incorporation have been used as indices: ^{35}S for the synthesis of mucopolysaccharides, tritiated thymidine for that of DNA in the course of mitosis; and ^{14}C proline for collagen.[44]

Functions

Growth cartilage has three main biochemical functions: the synthesis of glycosaminoglycans, and of collagen, and calcification.

The synthesis of chondroitin-sulphate, of keratine-sulphate and of sialic acid occurs rapidly in the calf. ^{35}S appears firstly in the cells, above all in the vesicles of the Golgi apparatus which migrate towards the outside of the chondrocyte so that their content is dispersed outside the cell in 30–70 min. Fifteen hours later, 30 per cent of the ^{35}S is found in the matrix. Thus the synthesis of the glycosaminoglycans take place in the chondrocyte through uridine-nucleotide intermediaries, while sulphation occurs by transfer of 3-phospho-adenosine-5-phospho-sulphate to saccharide acceptors.[126] The synthesis of collagen fibres is likewise demonstrable. It is probable that sub-units are at first associated in the cells with ribosomal aggregates and only pass later into the matrix. In culture, cartilagenous cells produce less collagen than osteoblasts, synthesis being slower and the diameter of the fibrils smaller.[126]

The mechanism of enchondral calcification is less clear. In the dog it is found that 1·5 per cent of the dry weight of growth cartilage consists of calcium, rising to 10 per cent in the zone of calcification. The ^{47}Ca injected into the animal goes first to the hypertrophic zone and only later diffuses into the matrix. It is believed that modification of glyco-protein complexes, and above all the appearance of a sialomucin in the zone of hypertrophic cartilage, furnishes the free anionic sites for metal-binding in particular of calcium.[126]

The Role of Hormones

Compared with embryonic models where intrinsic factors are fundamental, growth cartilage is subject to numerous extrinsic influences, particularly those of hormones.[44]

Thyroxine undoubtedly intervenes in prenatal development since in congenital athyreosis there is a delay in maturation or a dysgenetic appearance of the ossification centres of the knee and of the cuboid and it is probable that growth hormone also plays a part in the prenatal formation of membrane bone. Subjects with an hereditary deficit of growth hormone are of normal length at birth, but exhibit a particular cranio-facial morphology, which persists (flat-nosed dwarfism). Finally, some prominence has been given to the fact that oestrogens may be important, since it is possible to inhibit the growth of cartilage and the synthesis of osteoid in the fetus by administering an anti-oestrogenic compound, ethamoxytriphetrol, to pregnant ewes and to annul this effect by giving oestrogens.[1]

In postnatal life several hormones take a major part in the control of the function of growth cartilage.

(a) Growth Hormone (STH). The zoological specificity, the chemical structure and the radioimmunological dosage of this hormone are known. Human STH is a holoprotein of molecular weight 21,500 comprising a sequence of 187 amino acids with 2 sulphate bridges. It is synthesized in the acidophil cells of the anterior lobe of the pituitary which contains 3–5 mg. It can be assayed biologically by the tibia test and above all by radioimmunological methods. The plasma concentration at birth is raised (10–70 ng./ml.) compared with that found later (0–10 ng./ml.) and even higher values have been found in immature babies.

The physiological secretion of STH is subject to two powerful stimuli: deep diurnal or nocturnal sleep and hypoglycaemia. Certain amino acids, arginine in particular, also have an effect on the secretion. The evidence suggests that the elaboration/secretion of STH depends on a releasing factor, SRF, which has recently been isolated from the sheep, pig and ox hypothalamus and purified; it is a polypeptide of molecular weight 2,500. There also exists an inhibiting factor. The secretion of STH in man can be stimulated by L DOPA, and therefore it seems that the dopaminergic fibres of the medium eminence may be stimulating for the synthesis or liberation of SRF.[18]

The general metabolic effects of STH on protein synthesis, liberation of fatty acids from adipocytes, retention of water and sodium, tubular reabsorption of phosphorus and augmenting of urinary calcium levels are known. It is established that the administration of STH to pituitary dwarfs stimulates the production of a plasma factor which favours hydroxylation of proline[26] and increases the excretion of hydroxyproline in the urine.[68]

The mode of action of STH at cellular level is not known. STH, however, has three known general actions: it favours entry of amino acids into the cell; it increases the syntheses of messenger RNA and ribosomal RNA; and above all, it produces an increase in the synthesis of DNA. This last effect has been demonstrated in the growth cartilage of the hypophysectomized rat.[27]

(b) Sulphation Factor (Somatomedine). The mode of action of STH on growth cartilage has been elucidated:[28] it does not act directly, but through the intermediary of a sulphation factor. *In vitro*, the incorporation of ^{35}S and of tritiated thymidine into the cartilage of hypophysectomized rats in tissue culture cannot be restored on adding STH to the medium. By contrast, such incorporation is restored to normal if serum of normal rats or an extract of serum rich in sulphation factor is put into the medium. The action of this latter lasts for as long as 24 hours and thus permits a more continuous effect than that of STH, whose secretion is above all nocturnal. The sulphation factor seems to circulate in the plasma as a macro-molecular structure, but it is likely that it is a polypeptide of relatively low molecular weight which has been purified.[65] It seems probable that several organs can elaborate sulphation factor under the action of STH; the liver seems to be effective as has been shown by perfusion of the isolated rat liver[82] at microsomal level.[65] The effect of sulphation factor on growth cartilage involves:

1. The replication of chondrocytes as shown by the incorporation of tritiated thymidine.
2. The synthesis of proteins measured by the incorporation of uridine into RNA and amino acids of the chondromucuproteins.
3. The sulphation of chondroitin-sulphate.

It is likely that sulphation factor also mediates the action of STH on other tissues. It seems that sulphation factor may be identical with or resemble very closely that "plasma insulin-like activity" which is not suppressed by anti-insulin antibodies.[65]

Several interesting findings have been adduced in evidence. Thus an activity corresponding with that of sulphation factor at the growth cartilage level has been found in infestation by a parasite: *spirometra mansonoides* though the substance elaborated has only a transitory action which wears off after a month; while amongst pathological conditions an hereditary dwarfism transmitted as a recessive characteristic and having the same phenotype as inherited STH deficiency has been described[78] in which the plasma level of STH is raised, but that of sulphation factor is very low and injections of human growth hormone are without effect.

(c) **Thyroxine.** The thyroid hormones T3 and T4 have a predominant action on osteogenesis while the fundamental role of STH is to act on chondrogenesis. However, in post-natal life, thyroxine plays a part not only in ossification of membranous bones and in skeletal maturation, but equally on cartilagenous growth.

The study of epiphyseal dysgenesis in children and kittens with thyroid insufficiency has brought a curious fact to light. When the quantity of thyroid hormone is insufficient, the orientation and maturation of the columns of cartilagenous cells are anarchic. The penetration of blood vessels is polytopic instead of occurring in the centre of the future epiphyseal centre, and there thus appear several centres of ossification giving the "centre" a fragmented appearance.[135]

Thyroxine also plays a part at the growth cartilage level being necessary for the hypertrophy of chondrocytes and for the vascular invasion at the ossification front.

Thyroxine acts on growth cartilage in close relation with STH. It has been known for a long time that in the hypophysectomized rat STH alone stimulates the proliferation of chondrocytes while thyroxine alone favours the resorption of cartilage at the level of the front of ossification. However, certain studies now suggest that the action of growth hormone is augmented by thyroxine in two ways: the hypertrophic transformation of chondrocytes on the one hand and the activity of the chondroprecursors on the other.[8]

As well as this thyroxine plays a part in the mineralization of the skeleton by accelerating the accretion of calcium and osteolysis and osteoclastic resorption. It also reduces the intestinal absorption of calcium.

(d) **Sex Hormones.**[44,127] Testosterone in small dosage in the rat stimulates the proliferation of growth cartilage cells. Its effect potentiates that of STH. In high dosage, for example 10 mg. a day in the rat, it inhibits cellular proliferation and hastens the disappearance of growth cartilage. Synthetic derivatives, 17-ethyl-19-nortestosterone and oxandrolone have identical effects and produce an increase in the incorporation of ^{35}S into growth cartilage and an osteoblastic and osteocytic proliferation.

Oestradiol in high dosage favours the disappearance of growth cartilage by degeneration of the chondrocytes and vascular proliferation.

(e) **Cortisol.** Cortisol and synthetic corticoids have a powerful action on growth cartilage. Cortisol in approximately physiological dosage reduces the incorporation of ^{35}S and the synthesis of collagen in growth cartilage and this involves a considerable reduction in cells in the proliferated zone and a narrowing of the growth cartilage. It also stops cartilage resorption while stabilizing lysosomal membranes. As a result the line of ossification becomes irregular and the trabeculae of spongy bone which have formed are scarce and surround cartilagenous cells which have not been reabsorbed. This set of actions blocks enchondral growth. The effect of cortisol on rat growth cartilage is modified neither by testosterone nor by oestradiol, but it is suppressed by STH.[126]

The Action of Nutritional Factors

Chronic malnutrition, without any doubt, produces retardation of bony growth and maturation. However, the situation is so complicated that it is difficult to be precise which nutritional factor plays a part and by what mechanism. It seems that the functions of growth cartilage can depend on the supply of oxygen, of certain electrolytes and of several vitamins.[105]

(a) **Oxygenation.** Oxygenation plays an important part in the formation of the embryonic skeleton. It is likely that an optimum level of oxygenation is necessary for the functions of growth cartilage. In order to sustain growth for any length of time *in vitro* a sufficient oxygenation is necessary; otherwise the incorporation of ^{35}S is reduced; but it is also possible that, *in vivo*, a certain degree of sub-oxygenation may be stimulating: indeed in the child, as in the animal, reduction in the circulatory veinous return produces an acceleration of growth in length of the affected limb in comparison with that of the opposite one.

(b) **Electrolytes.** A poor or nil supply of calcium in the presence of a normal supply of vitamin D and phosphorus, produces an osteopenia and a total cessation of statural growth in the dog and the rat, growth recommencing when the diet becomes normal in calcium content.[108] Under the influence of a diet poor in calcium and normal in vitamin D and phosphorus in the rat, growth cartilage is apparently normal though a little thicker and the line of ossification is regular. From the histological point of view, therefore, it does not seem that isolated calcium deficiency modifies growth cartilage.[87]

In the growing rat, a deficit in sodium produces osteoporosis of a predominantly metaphyseal and periosteal distribution with reduced cellular activity and there is thinning of the growth cartilage, its proliferative and hypertrophic zones being reduced in height to 2 or 3 cells. However, the inanition which accompanies sodium deficit is perhaps the cause of these anomalies since they are also found in control rats consuming a diet equivalent in calories and proteins to that of the sodium-deficient rats. The diminution in the number of cells of the columns of growth cartilage is, however, more pronounced in the rats deficient in sodium.[139]

Potassium deficiency in the weanling male rat produces a cessation of bone growth, osteoporosis, and a halt in chondrogenesis while the growth cartilage is very narrowed.

This dimunition in thickness occurs particularly in the proliferated zone, which only contains two or three rows of cells, while the hypertrophic zone is normal.[23]

(c) Vitamins. *Vitamin A* affects the functions of growth cartilage. It seems that a deficiency can reduce growth cartilage activity, but it is mainly the effects of excessive doses which have been studied. Vitamin A in excessive dose inhibits the incorporation of ^{35}S and reduces the synthesis of hydroxyproline. It is known, moreover, that it increases the permeability of lysosomal membranes and permits the liberation of acid hydrolases, an effect which has been observed in cartilagenous cells both *in vivo* and *in vitro* and is retarded by cortisol.[30]

Vitamin C encourages the synthesis of collagen by favouring hydroxylation of proline by microsomes and the synthesis of glycosaminoglycans by stimulating the incorporation of glucose into galactosamine. In the absence of ascorbic acid, the cellular columns continue to grow in the growth cartilage. The matric calcifies but osteoid does not form.

A point still open for discussion is whether *Vitamin D* and its active derivatives, mono- or dihydroxylated, have a direct action on growth cartilage. It has been demonstrated that tritiated cholecalciferol after injection into an animal is avidly fixed by the cartilagenous cells of the proliferative zone but not by the cells of the hypertrophic zone.[73] What is certain, is that in the absence of vitamin D one does not see any calcification either of the matrix of the hypertrophic cartilage nor of the osteoid tissue. This failure of calcification has been attributed to an insufficient availability of extra cellular calcium as a result of a defect of intestinal absorption; but in addition lack of an action of vitamin D or of its active derivatives on mobilization of calcium at the level of deep bone has to be considered and perhaps also a deficit of a vitamin dependent serum factor favouring the incorporation of calcium in the skeleton.

Mineralization and Postnatal Development

The skeleton of the full-term newborn infant contains 30 g. calcium and 18 g. phosphorus: the skeleton of an adult contains more than 1000 g. calcium and 600 g. phosphorus. The development of the skeleton thus involves the retention of about 1 kg. of calcium. This occurs throughout the whole period of statural growth, but at different rates at different times and in an irregular fashion. The skeletal content of calcium increases by 70 g. a year from 0–2 years, 20–25 g. from 2–8 years, by 50 g. a year from 8–10 years and by 80–100 g. a year from 10–18 years of age.

Nutritional Aspects

The accumulation of calcium in the skeleton during development involves a very marked positive calcium balance during infancy and adolescence, a fact established in spite of critics who have questioned it, by the technique of stable calcium balance.[107] Such a balance represents the alimentary supply less losses in the faeces, urine and sweat. The metabolic needs for calcium, in order to assure the mineralization of the skeleton, are 1 kg. over 18–20 years—say, an average of 140–160 mg. a day or between 20 and 30 mg./kg./day in the first years of life, falling to 5–10 mg./kg./day later. Normal calcium excretion in the urine is, in the majority of children, between 1 and 6 mg./kg./day which represents an obligatory loss which is little related to the alimentary supply. The sum of the metabolic needs for growth and the loss of calcium in the urine represents the daily quantity which must be absorbed by the intestine from the food. This amount is from 10–35 mg./kg./day according to age during the period of skeletal development.

Intestinal Absorption of Calcium can be calculated by the balance technique, which makes it possible to evaluate the net coefficient of digestive utilization of calcium (CDU), or by using radioactive markers which allow the study of true absorption. The net CDU for calcium varies with age; it is strikingly higher in the child (30–40 per cent) than in the adult (20 per cent). It depends on the nature of the foodstuffs being more than 60 per cent in the suckling child fed with mother's milk and between 20 and 30 per cent in the baby fed with cows' milk. It is much influenced by the other constituents of the diet, but above all by the availability of cholecalciferol which markedly increases absorption. Finally, it depends on factors concerned with adaptation to the alimentary supply of calcium.

The problem of *adaptation* of net calcium absorption to the alimentary supply is well understood. The geographical distribution of the alimentary consumption of calcium shows the existence of four world zones: North America and Europe, where the daily ration is more than 900 mg.; Latin America and Southern Europe, where it is from 650–800 mg.; South Africa, the Middle East and India, where it is between 350 and 500 mg.; and Japan, where it is 350 mg. or less.[95] The consumption of calcium also varies in these countries according to the socio-economic level and the habits of particular families. It has been established in various circumstances that the net CDU for calcium varies inversely with the usual alimentary supply. Further, it has been demonstrated in the adult that in an individual, a rapid or a slow adaptation to variations of alimentary supply can be observed.[84] After a period of low calcium intake (less than 50 mg./day), or during the period of recovery from deficiency rickets, the net CDU of calcium in the child may surpass 60 per cent; and we have found that the phenomenon may be prolonged one or two weeks until the metabolic needs for calcium have been met. The existence of a signal governing the relationship between metabolic need for calcium and the percentage of alimentary calcium absorbed by the intestine has been hypothesized for a long time, and has been given the name "endogenous factor."[93]

These facts show that the meeting of the considerable metabolic needs created by the development and mineralization of the skeleton may be met despite very varied levels of alimentary supply. The "recommended practical requirements" have been set out by a group of experts of WHO-FAO[95] for the period of postnatal development of the skeleton. These are (daily); from 500–600 mg. from 0–12 months, from 400–500 mg. from 1–9 years, from 600–700 mg. from 10–15 years and from 500–700 mg. from 16–19 years. In the opinion of this group, there is no reason to believe that supplies a little short of these figures or frankly in excess of them can be harmful; these recommended levels represent an optimum:[95]

It seems to be well established that calcium deficiency limits bony growth.[108] The addition of calcium lactate to the diet of underfed Indian schoolchildren made it possible to increase their height.[5] In growing animals, dogs and rats, a diet poor or lacking in calcium but normal in vitamin D produces a total arrest of growth in stature with recovery when the supply of calcium becomes normal again. Besides the arrest of growth, maturation of the skeleton ceases and an osteoporosis appears, associated with intense osteoclastic resorption.[87] It may be that certain growth problems observed in human pathology may in part, or entirely, be linked to a long-standing negative calcium balance due to intestinal malabsorption and/or to excessive urinary excretion of calcium. The relationships between postnatal skeletal development and the availability of calcium are not yet clearly understood. This fact accounts for the defect of growth of the rat fetus of maternal rats kept hypocalcaemic; but in addition it will be recalled that the calcium ion, besides its role in the mineralization of calcified tissues, plays a fundamental role in the permeability of biological membranes, the activation or inhibition of numerous enzymes, and the action of several hormones.

Hormonal Aspects

It is on the developing skeleton that anomalies of mineralization produce the clearest clinical and radiological signs.

The rate of renewal of calcium at the skeletal level corresponds to the two processes of accretion and osteolysis, normally in equilibrium; and it is considerably increased during the period of development compared with that in adults. However, the quantitative expression of this phenomenon is made difficult by criticisms of the methods of compartmental analysis on the one hand, and on the other by the difficulty of finding a valid way of comparing the results obtained in children with those from adults.[43] It is convenient to recall that the rate of renewal of a mineral measured by the radioactive isotopes of calcium; ^{45}Ca or ^{47}Ca, or rather by ^{85}Sr, is much greater than the rate of remodelling of bone, and that the two concepts are different.

The regulation of the serum concentration of calcium or particularly of the concentration of ionized calcium; the concentration of cytoplasmic and mitochondrial calcium; the maintenance of the equilibrium between construction and resorption of bony tissue, and of mineralization and de-mineralization is subject to numerous factors: particularly parathormone, calcitonin and cholecalciferol. Their effect can be particularly important during the period of skeletal development.

(a) **Parathormone** is a polypeptide of molecular weight 3500 made of a sequence of 84 amino acids, the sequence of which is now known. It has zoological specificity. It is produced by the principal cells of the parathyroid glands. Its secretory stimulus is the lowering of ionized calcium in the blood. Its main physiological actions is to raise the blood calcium level, an action which is secondary to that of the osteocytes which favour bony resorption. A lesser physiological effect is to increase phosphodiuresis due to the reduction of tubular re-absorption of phosphorus. The plasma level of parathormone is from 0·3–1·7 ng./ml. in the normocalcaemic subject and its half-life is from 10–20 min. Its cellular action at the level of the target organs produces an augmentation of permeability to calcium ions on the one hand and synthesis of cAMP on the other at the cytoplasmic membrane. These mechanisms together produce an elevation of the intracytoplasmic concentration of calcium, an activation of calcium-dependent enzymes and the appearance of a flux of calcium from the mitochondria towards the cytoplasm.[103]

(b) **Calcitonin** is a polypeptide of molecular weight 3,200 made of a single chain of 32 amino acids in the pig. It is produced by the parafollicular cells of the thyroid in mammals and by the cells of the ultimobranchial body in birds and fishes. It has been synthesized. Its half-life in plasma is 10 min. Its concentration in serum in men is less than 1 ng./ml. Its stimulus for secretion is a rise in blood calcium. Its major physiological role is to block osteolysis and to lower blood calcium and blood phosphorus. It possesses a rapid and transitory phosphodiuretic effect and also one on the diuresis of sodium. At the cellular level it lowers the concentration of intra-cytoplasmic calcium.[81]

(c) **Cholecalciferol** or vitamin D3 is obtained partly from food; partly it is synthesized in the skin under the action of photons in the ultra-violet range of light. It is activated by the liver to 25-OH-cholecalciferol. This latter suffers a second hydroxylation at the level of the kidney which leads to 1-25-dihydroxycholecalciferol. Other active derivatives are known, in particular 24-25-dihydroxycholecalciferol.[29] These active derivatives work like steroid hormones acting mainly on two target organs: the mucosa of the small intestine and the osteocytes where its action facilitates that of parathormone. The cellular mechanism of action seems to be derepression, at the transcriptional level, of the system of synthesis of proteins concerned with the cellular transport of calcium. One of these latter, present in the mucosal cells of the small intestine, is the "calcium binding protein" or CaBP of Wassermann;[129] the other is a calcium dependent ATP-ase of the cytoplasmic membrane.[29]

Thus it seems that parathormone and the derivatives of cholecalciferol raise the concentration of extracellular and intracytoplasmic calcium and that calcitonin has an opposite action. The first two activate osteolysis and the second slows it down. Parathormone depresses calcium balance; cholecalciferol and its derivatives increase it. It is likely that the action of these regulatory factors are important during mineralization of the developing skeleton.

One fact to underline is that the phenomenon of adaptation of the absorption of alimentary calcium to the needs of the organism seems to depend on the elaboration of CaBP- which in turn is dependent on calciferol, and on other transport systems. Recently it has been shown that at the intestinal level, 1-25-dihydroxycholecalciferol was more active on calcium transport than 24-25-dihydroxycholecalciferol. An equilibrium between these two metabolites would permit absorption to be modulated, depending on the blood calcium level and perhaps that of parathormone. This equilibrium system probably represents the so-called "endogenous factor."[19]

The Maturation of the Skeleton

The concept of maturation is different from that of growth of the skeleton. Growth is the creation of new tissues; maturation is the consolidation in their definitive state by calcification of the fibrous and cartilagenous Anlagen of the various parts of the skeleton. This maturation proceeds in three stages:

1. Prenatal maturation, where principally the diaphyseal cartilagenous Anlagen are ossified, as also the cuboid, the epiphyseal centres of the femur, the tibia at the knee and the head of the humerus.
2. Postnatal maturation of infancy when the small bones of the carpus and the tarsus, the vault of the cranium and particularly the epiphyses of the long bones are progressively ossified.
3. The maturation of adolescence when growth cartilage is ossified.[70]

Skeletal maturation has been studied in the child since the beginning of radiology[102] having been developed by Rotche[106] and well defined by Todd and his school.[119] These studies hade led to the description of "maturity indicators" and to the construction of many atlas amongst which one of the most used remains that of Greulich and Pyle.[59]

It quickly appeared that maturation is more rapid in girls than in boys, and that this is already apparent at birth; that it is symmetrical; that it varies between individuals both in its sequence and its speed; and that it is partly linked to heredity, as has been shown by studies in twins.

The whole problem of skeletal maturation has been reviewed in various monographs.[3,60,112,118]

Methods of Study

Longitudinal studies of bony maturation have clearly shown the difficulty of defining "indicators of maturity" on the basis of small numbers of films, generally on the wrist and the hand. Those first used were based on the *date* of appearance of centres of ossification,[109] the *size* of centres of ossification and their description on a four points scale, A, B, C, D,[9] and the *shape* of ossification centres;[59] later values were given according to the degree of maturation of each bone, these figures being added together;[3] and finally systems of weighting[118] were introduced.

What is certain, is that with the use of more and more refined methods, usefulness and speed have been lost in exchange for a more scientific description of phenomena. Based on the information derived from: (1) anthropological study of populations; (2) comparative longitudinal study of growth, of bone maturity and of physiological maturity; (3) study of the pathological deviations (which are more often very gross) methods will be developed which can be relied on in a given context. (Fig. 7).

The Concept of Bone Age

The comparison of bony maturation in cross-sectional studies of populations and in longitudinal studies of individual children has led to the description of so-called "bone age". Bone age is theoretically a clear concept. It corresponds for any individual to the real age of the majority of individuals of the same sex who have reached the same degree of skeletal maturation. In practice, the study of precise indicators of maturation has shown that this idea is still ambiguous. Growth and maturation are two different phenomena; "the bone year" has no precise chronological significance. Thus the bone year of a girl comprises more events than that of a boy. Bony maturation does not proceed at the same speed during development so that, for example, the 13th bone year of a boy belongs on a different scale than the 6th. The speed of maturation is closely correlated neither with chronological age nor with statural age. In pathological states the concept of bone age is still more difficult to analyse.

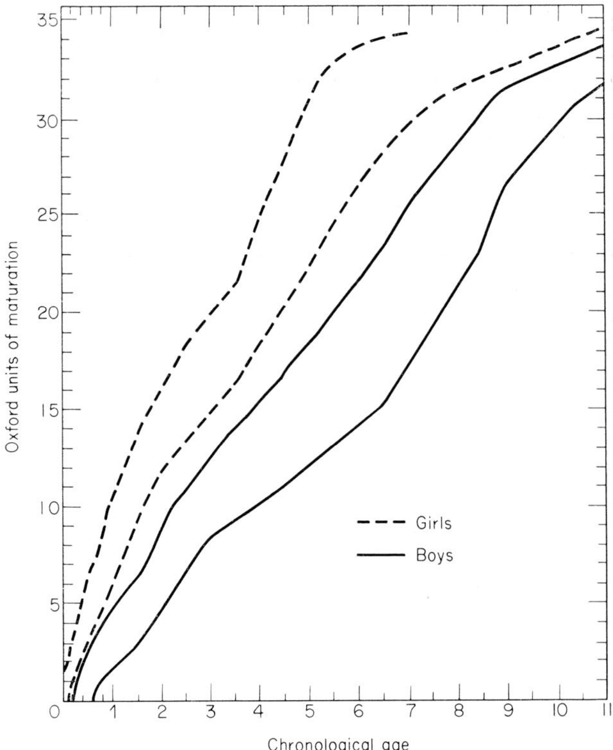

FIG. 7. Comparison of bone age in boys and girls for the ossification of the left wrist and hand (*after Drs. M. Sempe and G. Pedron.*)

However, in spite of these criticisms, the use of bone age to express the level of skeletal maturation has become very widespread for analysing the influences which may act over all on the speed of maturation. No doubt this latter is controlled by genetic factors, as has been shown by the study of twins[40] and by ethnic factors[86] while all the influences which may be brought to bear on growth also often affect maturation; i.e. intake of calories, proteins, and calcium, socio-economic and nutritional factors and ill nesses.[114] Deficiency in thyroid hormone, sex hormones and STH, and an excess of cortisol slow down or stop bony maturation and produce a retardation of bone age.

Physiological Maturation

During the period of postnatal development, an attempt has been made to define the notion of physiological development, in which a number of different functions are concerned. One of the most important facts to bear in mind is the very variable chronological age at which puberty appears and at which growth in size comes to an end. A very close correlation has been discovered between bone age, the date of the first menstrual period in girls, and the age of statural growth. The relationship connecting bone age on the one hand and a phenomenon as precise as the launching of the hypothalamo-hypophyso-gonadic system controlling puberty on the other is not known.

Prediction of Definitive Height

Regular measurement of bone age in comparison with statural age and chronological age makes it possible to retrace the rate of bony maturation in the previous history of a child. These measurements by extrapolation have been utilized to predict the future rhythm of bony maturation and the potential for statural growth as a result of this maturation.

Tables for predicting the adult height as a function of the height and the bone age of the child, measured by means of the atlas of Greulich and Pyle have also been proposed.[11] To be able to make such a prediction would be very useful for interpreting the physiological deviations in height in boys and girls and the precise analysis of the action of certain drugs and of abnormal diets. But it seems clear that one should be very prudent in this regard because of the reservations already made on the significance of bone age, on its lack of purely chronological significance, and on the very large individual variability in the speed of maturation. It is particularly difficult to make reasonable predictions from these data in pathological cases.

Errors of prediction have recently been analysed.[104] It has been confirmed that bone age has no linear relation with chronological age and that the methods of rectilinear extrapolation lead to errors which are more numerous the longer the interval between two assessments of bone age. There has been much less error when measuring bone age by the method of Greulich and Pyle[59] than when using that of Tanner and Whitehouse.[118]

Bony Remodelling

The remodelling of bone goes on throughout life; but it is particularly active during the period of development.

Measurement of the Degree of Remodelling

The degree of bony remodelling has been assessed by different methods. For a historical point of view, the oldest consisted of using red garance (which marks bone during its formation) as a mark of new bone formed in a given time. The marking of such bone by tetracycline, easy to identify because of its fluorescence, is now widely used. Autoradiographs obtained after injection of a radioisotope, for example ^{45}Ca, allows the identification of "hot centres" avidly fixing the isotope in spongy bone and in subperiostial bone and in a diffuse component observed above all in compact bone; also permit one to distinguish the young osteones from older ones.[70,71,77] It has also been possible to measure the rate of renewal in people already contaminated by accidental ingestion of radioactive isotopes, such as, in particular, strontium 90.

Variation in Rate of Renewal

The rate of renewal, per annum, in the adult is from 3 to 5 per cent for the whole skeleton. It varies greatly from one bone to another being about 16 per cent for the clavicle and 8 per cent for the tibia and the femur. It changes greatly with age approximating to 50 per cent per annum during the period of development in the two years following birth. Its maximum rate is about $2\frac{1}{2}$ years of age.[116]

Factors Influencing Remodelling

Bony remodelling, which is very active during the developing period follows two principles: the first, maintenance of skeletal homeostasis, the second, homeostasis of skeletal mineralization. Although it is not easy sometimes to distinguish these two constituent parts, it appears that growth hormone, thyroxine and the hormones of the adrenal cortex mostly influence skeletal homeostasis while parathormone, calcitonin and the hydroxylated derivatives of cholecalciferol influence the homeostasis of mineralization. Nutritional supplies, the state of health, and above all mechanical factors and piezoelectric forces, also play an active role. Those factors which intervene in a general way in postnatal development will, during infancy, thus influence not only the growth and maturation of the skeleton but also its renewal. They do this with more vigour than in the adult because of the greater rapidity of the rate of renewal. This fact explains the extreme frequency of conditions defined on clinical and radiological grounds as "osteoporosis" or "osteosclerosis" in the first years of life.

Structural Aspects

The histological picture of bone remodelling comprises the juxtaposition of zones of bone formation and regions of periosteocytic osteolysis and sometimes of osteoclastic resorption. Where there is spongy bone, one can see in the region of the medullary canal the appearance of lacunae of osteoclastic resorption; these lacunae are covered with beds of osteoblasts destined for the construction of new bone. In compact bone resorption is by osteocytes. During the period of development, remodelling involves transformations of structure and of the architecture of bone tissue. During periods of rapid growth non-lamellar bone is preferentially elaborated; during periods of slow growth a typical lamellar bone arranged circumferentially.

Biochemical Aspects

An understanding of the processes of bony remodelling in biochemical terms is far from complete. Just as during prenatal development, osteogenesis is of two types: the one proceeding directly from a mesenchymal model to bone tissue (membranous bone, periosteal ossification); the other passing through the intermediary of a cartilagenous stage (enchondral ossification). These two types of ossification both involve cellular division, differentiation or modulation and a synthesis of macromolecules and in particular of collagen. One has seen already that principles of bony induction persist in the acellular matrix of adult bone; perhaps they play a physiological role.

It would seem to be established that in postnatal osteogenesis, consumption of oxygen is low compared with that of glucose and that much lactate is formed.[15] On the other hand the breaking down of bone is associated with a high oxygen consumption, an expenditure of energy which is large, and the formation of citrate.

REFERENCES

1. Abdul-Karim, R. (1967), "Fetal Endocrinology. A Review," *J. med. liban.*, **20,** 201–233.
2. Aceto, T., Jr., Batt, R. E., Bruck, E., Schultz, R. B. and Perez, Y. R. (1966), "Intrauterine Hyperparathyroidism: a Complication of Untreated Maternal Hypoparathyroidism," *J. clin. Endocr.*, **26,** 487–492.
3. Acheson, R. M. (1954), "A Method of Assessing Skeletal Maturity from Radiographs," *J. Anat.* (*London*), **88,** 498–508.
4. Acheson, R. M. (1966), "Maturation of the Skeleton in Human development," in *Human development*, pp. 465–502 (F. Falkner, ed.). Philadelphia and London: Saunders.
5. Ackroyd. W. E, and Krishnan, R. S. B. G. (1938), "Effect of Calcium Lactate on Children in a Nursery School," *Lancet*, **i,** 153–155.
6. Alexander, D. P. and Nixon, D. A. (1969), "Effect of Parathyroid Extract in Foetal Sheep," *Biol. Neonat.* (*Basel*), **14,** 117–130.
7. Amprino, R. (1965), "Aspects of Morphogenesis in Children," *Organogenesis*, p. 255 (R. L. Haan and J. Ursprung, eds.). New York: Holt, Rinehart and Winston.
8. Asling, C. W., Tse, F. and Rosenberg, L. L. (1968), "Effects of Growth-hormone and Thyroxine on Sequences of Chondrogenesis in the Epiphyseal Cartilage Plate," in *Growth Hormone*, p. 319–331. A. Pecile and E. Müller, eds.). Amsterdam: Excerpta medica Foundation.
9. Bardeen, C. R. (1921), "The Relation of Ossification to physiological Development," *J. Radiol.*, **2,** 1–8.
10. Bassett, C. A. L. and Becker, R. O. (1962), "Generation of Electrical Potentials by Bone in Response to Mechanical Stress," *Science*, **137,** 1063–1064.
11. Bayley, N. and Pinneau, S. R. (1952), "Tables for Predicting Adult Height from Skeletal Age: Revised for Use with the Greulich-Pyle Hand Standards," *J. Pediat.*, **40,** 423–441.
12. Bernard, J. and Laval-Jeantet, M. (1962), "Le rapport cortico-diaphysaire tibial pendant la croissance", *Arch. franc. Pediat.*, **19,** 805–817.
13. Blackwood, H. J. J. (1966), "Growth of the Mandibular Condyle of the Rat Studied with Tritiated Thymidine," *Archs. oral Biol.*, **11,** 493–500.
14. Bonnard, G. D. (1968), "Cortical Thickness and Diaphyseal Diameter of Metacarpal Bones from the Age of Three Months to Eleven Years," *Helv. paediat. Acta*, **23,** 445–463.
15. Borle, A. B. and Nichols, N. (1960), "Metabolic Studies on Bone *in vitro*. I: Normal Bone," *J. biol. Chem.*, **235,** 1206–1210
16. Bourne, G. H. (1972), "The Biochemistry and Physiology of Bone," in *Development and Growth*, Vol. 3. New York and London: Academic Press. In press.
17. Boyd, E. (1941), *Outlines of Physical Growth and Development*, (—. Burgess, ed.). Minneapolis.
18. Boyd, A. E., Lebovitz, H. F. and Pfeiffer, J. B. (1970), "Stimulation of Human Growth Hormone Secretion by L-DOPA," *New Engl. J. Med.*, **283,** 1425–1429.
19. Boyle, L. T., Gray, R. W. and De Luca, H F. (1971), "Regulation by Calcium of *in vivo* Synthesis of 1-25-dihydroxycholecalciferol and 21-25-dihydroxycholecalciferol," *Proc. nat. Acad. Sci.* (*USA*), **68,** 2131–2134.
20. Bronsky, D., Kiamko, R. T., Moncada, R and Rosenthal, I. M. (1968), "Intrauterine Hyperparathyroidism Secondary to Maternal Hypoparathyroidism," *Pediatrics*, **42,** 606–613.
21. Burdick, F. A. (1968), "Bone Induction," *J. dent. Res.*, **47,** 41–46.
22. Connelly, J. P., Crawford, J. D. and Watson, J. (1962), "Studies on Neonatal Hyperphosphatemia," *Pediatrics*, **30,** 425–432.
22a. Crowne, R. S., Wharton, B. A. and MacCance, R. A. (1969), "Hydroxyproline Indices and Hydroxyproline/Créatinine Ratios in Older Children," *Lancet*, **i,** 395–396.
23. Cuisinier-Gleizes, P., Mathieu, H., Witmer, G., Dulac, H., Herouard, S., Habib, R., Lefebvre, J. and Royer, P. (1964), "Effets de la carence potassique chez le rat sur le squelette, le cholesterol plasmatique, l'histologie des surrénales," *Path. Biol.*, **12,** 1055–1073.
24. Dallemagne, M. J. and Richelle, L. J. (1971), *Inorganic Chemistry of Bone*, Vol. 1. Institute of materials Science, University of Connecticut, U.S.A.
25. Daughaday, W. H. (1971), "Sulfation Factor Regulation of Skeletal Growth. A Stable Mechanism Dependent on Intermittent Growth-hormone Secretion," *Amer. J. Med.*, **50,** 277, 280.
26. Daughaday, W. H. and Mariz, I. K. (1962), "Conversion of $U^{14}C$ to Labelled Hydroxyproline by Rat Cartilage *in vitro*: Effects of Hypophysectomy, Growth Hormone Cortisol," *J. Lab. clin. Med.*, **59,** 741–752.
27. Daughaday, W. H. and Reeder, C. (1966), "Synchronous Activation of DNA Synthesis in Hypophysectomized Rat Cartilage by Growth Hormone," *J. Lab. clin. Med.*, **68,** 357–368.
28. Delivora-Papadopoulos, M., Battaglia, F. C., Bruns, P. E. and Meschia, G. (1967), "Total Protein-bound and Ultrafiltrable Calcium in Maternal and Fetal Plasma," *Amer. J. Physiol.*, **213,** 363–366.
29. De Luca, H. F. (1967), "Mechanism of Action and Metabolic Fate of Vitamin D," *Vitam. Horm.*, **25,** 315–367.
30. Dingle, J. T., Lucy, J. A. and Fell, H. B. (1961), "Studies on the Mode of Action of Excess of Vitamin A: (i) Effect of Vitamin A on the Metabolism and Composition of Embryonic Chick-limb Cartilage Growth in Organ Culture," *Biochem. J.*, **79,** 497–500.
31. Dubreuil, G. (1941), *Embryologie humaine* (Vigot Frères, ed.), 2nd edition, 492 pp.
32. Duhamel, B., Haegel, P. and Pages, R. (1966), "Morphogénèse pathologique," *Des monstruosités aux malformations*, 307 pp. (Masson, ed.). Paris.
33. Duval, M. (1897), *Précis d'histologie* (Masson, ed.). Paris.
34. Duval-Beaupere, G. and Combes, J. (1971), "Segments superieur et inferieur au cours de la croissance physiologique des filles," *Arch. franç. Pediat.*, **28,** 1057–1071.
35. Dyson, E. D. and Whitehouse, W. J. (1968), "Composition of Trabecular Bone in Children and its Relation to Radiation Dosimetry," *Nature*, **217,** 576–578.
36. Economou-Mavrou, C. and McCance, R. A. (1958), "Calcium, Magnesium and Phosphate in Foetal Tissues," *Biochem. J.*, **68,** 573–580.
37. Ede, D. A. and Law, J. T. (1969), "Computer Simulation of Vertebrate Limb Morphogenesis," *Nature*, **221,** 244–248.
38. Fairney, A. and Weir, A. A. (1970), "The Effect of Abnormal Material Plasma Calcium Levels on the Offspring of Rats," *J. Endocr.*, **48,** 337–345.
39. Falkner, F. (1966), *Human Development*, Vol. 1. Philadelphia and London: W. B. Saunders Company.
40. Falkner, F. (1964), "Hereditary and Skeletal Maturation Patterns in Human Twins," Child Development Unit: Report No. 4. Université of Louisville.
41. Fitton-Jackson, S. (1968), "The Morphogenesis of Collagen," in *Treatise on Collagen*, Vol. 2, pp. 34–54 (G. N. Ramachandran, ed.). London and New York: Academic Press.

42. Fomon, S. J., Owen, G. M., Jensen, R. L. and Thomas, L. N. (1963), "Calcium and Phosphorus Balance Studies with Normal Full-term Infants Fed Pooled Human Milk or Various Formulas," *Amer. J. clin. Nutr.*, **12,** 346–357.

43. Fourman, P. and Royer, P. (1970), *Calcium et tissu osseux.* Edition française Flammarion Med., Paris.

44. Franchimont, P. and Denis, F. (1969), "Influence de la somatotrophine, des gonadotrophines et des stéroïdes génitaux sur le métabolisme du cartilage costal du rat," *Rev. franç. Et. clin. biol.*, **14,** 970–976.

45. Friedman, W. F. and Roberts, W. C. (1966), "Vitamin D in the Supravalvular Aortic Stenosis Syndrome. The Transplacental Effects of Vitamin D on the Aorta of the Rabbit," *Circulation*, **34,** 77–86.

46. Fuchs, F. (1957), *Studies on the Passage of Phosphate between Mother and Foetus in the Guinea Pig*, p. 56 (Monograph). Copenhagen: Munksgaard.

47. Gardner, L. I. (1952), "Tetany and Parathyroid Hyperplasia in the Newborn Infant: Influence of the Dietary Phosphate Load," *Pediatrics*, **9,** 534–543.

48. Garel, J. M. (1969), "Dosage biologique de la parathormone chez le jeune rat de 3 jours," *C.R. Acad. Sci.* (Paris), **268,** 2932–2933.

49. Garel, J. M. (1970), "Effet de l'injection d'un serum 'antiparathormone' chez le foetus de rat," *C.R. Acad. Sci. (Paris)*, **271,** 2364–2366.

50. Garel, J. M. (1970), "Action de la calcitonine après surcharge calcique chez le foetus de rat entier ou décapité," *C.R. Acad. Sci.*, **271,** 1560–1563.

51. Garel, J. M. and Dumont, C. (1971), "Vitesse de disparition de la calcitonine porcine chez le foetus de rat," *C.R. Acad. Sci.*, **272,** 1279–1282.

52. Garel, J. M. and Geloso-Meyer, A. (1971), "Hyperparathyroïdisme foetal chez le rat, consécutif á un hypoparathyroïdisme maternel," *Rev. eur. Et. clin. biol.*, **16,** 174–178.

53. Garel, J. M., Milhaud, G. and Jost, A. (1968), "Action hypocalcémiante et hypophosphatémiante de la thyrocalcitonine chez le foetus de rat," *C.R. Acad. Sci. (Paris)*, **267,** 344–347.

54. Garel, J. M., Milhaud, G. and Sizonenko, P. C. (1970), "Inactivation de la calcitonine porcine par différents organes foetaux et maternel du rat," *C.R. Acad. Sci. (Paris)*, **270,** 2469–2471.

55. Garel, J. M., Milhaud, G. and Sizonenko, P. C. (1969), "Thyrocalcitonine et barrière placentaire chez le rat," *C.R. Acad. Sci. (Paris)*, **269,** 1785–1787.

56. Garel, J. M., Pic, P. and Jost, A. (1971), "Action de la parathormone chez le foetus de rat," *Ann. Endocr.*, **32,** 253–262.

57. Gittleman, I. F., Pinkus, J. B. and Schmertzler, E. (1964), "Interrelationship of Calcium and Magnesium in the Mature Neonate," *Amer. J. Dis. Child.*, **107,** 119–124.

58. Gray, D. J. and Gardner, E. (1969), "The Prenatal Development of the Human Humerus," *Amer. J. Anat.*, **124,** 431–445.

59. Greulich, W. W. and Pyle, S. I. (1950 and 1959), *Radiographic Atlas of Skeletal Development of the Hand and Wrist*, 256 pp. London: Oxford Press; California: Stanford Press.

60. Gryfe, C. I., Exton-Smith, A. N., Payne, P. R. and Wheeler, E. F. (1971), "Pattern of Development of bone in Childhood and Adolescence," *Lancet*, **i,** 523–526.

61. Haddad, J. G., Boisseau, V. and Avioli L. V. (1971), "Placental Transfer of Vitamin D_3 and 25-hydroxycholecalciferol in the rat," *J. lab. clin. Invest.*, **77,** 908–915.

62. Hall, B. K. (1970), "Differentiation of Cartilage and Bone from Common Germinal Cells. Part 1: The Role of Acid Mucopolysaccharide and Collagen," *J. exp. Zool.*, **173,** 383–393.

63. Hall, B. K. (1970), "Cellular Differentiation in Skeletal Tissues," *Biol. Rev.*, **45,** 455–484.

64. Hall, B. K. (1971), "Histogenesis and Morphogenesis of Bone," *Clin. Orthop.*, **74,** 249–268.

65. Hall, K. and Uthne, K. (1971), "Some Biological Properties of Purified Sulfation Factor (SF) from Human Plasma," *Acta med. scand.*, **190,** 137–143.

66. Heymann, W. (1937), "Metabolism and Mode of Action of Vitamin D. II: Storage of Vitamin D in Different Tissues *in vivo*," *J. biol. Chem.*, **118,** 371–376.

67. Holtzer, H. (1961), "Aspects of Chondrogenesis and Myogenesis," in *Synthesis of Molecular and Cellular Structure*, (D. Rudnick, ed.). New York: Ronald Press.

68. Jasin, H. E., Fink, C. W. and Ziff, M. (1962), "Relationship between Urinary Hydroxyproline and Growth," *J. clin. Invest.*, **41,** 1928–1935.

69. Jones, H. S. (1970), "The Morphological Effect of Parathyroid Extract upon the Developing Skeleton of the Embryonic Chick," *Amer. J. Anat.*, **127,** 89–99.

70. Jowsey, J. (1960), "Age Changes in Human Bone," *Clin. Orthop.*, **17,** 210–218.

71. Jowsey, J., Kelly, R. J., Riggs, B. L., Bianco, A. J., Jr., Scholz, D. A., and Gershon-Cohen, J. (1965), "Quantitative Microradiographic Studies of Normal and Osteoporotic Bone", *J. Bone Jt. Surg.*, **47A,** 785–806.

72. Juster, M. (1969), "Sur la formation du squelette. IV: Croissance d'un os long. Vue d'ensemble et schéma," *Bull Ass. Anat.* 54° *Congrès*, No. 145, pp. 231–242.

72a. Kivirikko, K. I. and Laitinen, O. (1965), "Clinical Significance of Urinary Hydroxyproline Determinations in Children," *Ann. Paed. FEnn.*, **11,** 148–153.

72b. Klein, L. and Teree, T. M. (1966), "Skeletal Metabolism in Early Infancy: Urinary Hydroxyproline," *J. Pediat.*, **69,** 266–273.

73. Kodicek, E. and Thompson, G. A. (1965), "Autoradiographic Localization in Bones of (1α ^3H) cholecalciferol," in *Structure and Function of Connective and Skeletal Tissue* (S. Fitton-Jackson, S. M. Partridge and G. R. Tristam, eds.), pp. 369–372. London: Butterworths.

74. Korenchevsky, V. and Carr, M. (1923), "The Influence of the Mother's Diet during Pregnancy and Lactation upon the Growth, General Nourishment and Skeleton of Young Rats," *J. Path. Bact.*, **26,** 383–396.

75. Koskinen, E. V. S., Ryoppy, S. A. and Lindhom, T. S. (1971), "Bone Formation by Induction under Influence of Growth Hormone and Cortisone," in *Calcified Tissue* (J. Menzel and A. Harell, eds.), pp. 46–49. New York: Academic Press.

76. Kuhlman, R. E. and McNamee, M. J. (1970), "The Biochemical Importance of the Hypertrophic Cartilage Cell to Enchondral Bone Formation," *J. Bone Jt. Surg.*, **52A,** 1025–1032.

77. Lacroix, P. (1951). *The Organization of Bones.* London: Churchill.

78. Laron, Z., Pertzelan, A. and Mannheimer, S. (1966), "Genetic Pituitary Dwarfism with High Serum Concentrations of Human Growth Hormone: A New Inborn Error in Metabolism," *Israel J. med. Sci.*, **2,** 152–155.

79. Le Douarin, N. (1971), "Demonstration of the Neural Origin of the Glandular Cells of the Ultimobranchial Body in the Avian Embryo," *Endocrinology*, Abstracts, p. 13.

79a. Linarelli, L. G. (1972), "Newborn Urinary Cyclic AMP and Developmental Renal Responsiveness to Parathyroid Hormone," *Pediatrics*, **50,** 14–23.

80. Lough, S. A., Rivera, J. and Comar, C. L. (1963), "Retention of Strontium, Calcium, and Phosphorus in Human Infants," *Proc. Soc. exp. Biol. (N.Y.)*, **112,** 631–636.

81. Macintyre, I. (1970), "Human Calcitonin: Practical and Theoretical Consequences," in *Calcitonin* 1969, pp. 1–13. London: William Heinemann Medical Books.

82. McConaghey, P. and Sledge, C. B. (1970), "Production of 'Sulphation Factor' by the Perfused Liver," *Nature*, **225,** 1249–1450.

83. McCrory, W. W., Forman, C. W., McNamara, H. and Barnett, H. L. (1952), "Renal Excretion of Inorganic Phosphate in Newborns," *J. clin. Invest.*, **31,** 357–366.

84. Malm, O. J. (1958), "Calcium Requirement and Adaptation in Adult Men", *Scand. J. clin. Lab. Invest.*, **10,** suppl. 36.

85. Martin, T. J., Harris, G. S. and Melick, R. A. (1971), "Glycosaminoglycans Secretion by Fetal Cartilage Cells *in vitro.* Effect of Parathyroid Hormone," in *Calcified Tissue* (J. Menczel and A. Harell, eds.), pp. 24–25. New York: Academic Press.

86. Masse, G. and Hunt, E. E., Jr. (1963), "Skeletal Maturation of the Hand and Wrist in West African Children," *Human Biol.*, **35,** 3–25.

87. Mathieu, H., Laval-Jeantet, M., Cuisiner-Gleizes, P., Habib, R., Oligo, N. and Juster, M. (1966), "Effets de doses variables de vitamine D_3 sur la nature de l'ostéopathie provoquée par la carence en calcium chez le Rat en croissance," *Path. Biol.*, **14,** 1117–1134.
88. Maximow, A. A. and Bloom, W. (1948), *A Textbook of Histology*. Philadelphia: W. B. Saunders.
89. Maxwell, J. P. (1935), "Further Studies in Adult Rickets (Osteomalacia and Foetal Rickets," *Proc. roy. Soc. Med.*, **28,** 265–300.
90. Medoff, J. (1967), "Enzymatic Events During Cartilage Differentiation in the Chick Embryonic Limb Bud," *Develop. Biol.*, **16,** 118–143.
91. Murray, P. D. F. (1936), *Bones*. Cambridge University Press.
92. Nesbitt, R. E. L., Jr. (1966), "Perinatal Development," in *Human Development*, p. 123, (F. Faulkner, ed.). Philadelphia: W. B. Saunders.
93. Nicolaysen, R. (1943), "The Absorption of Calcium as a Function of the Body Saturation with Calcium," *Acta physiol. scand.*, **5,** 200–211.
94. Olivier, G. (1962), *Formation du squelette des membres chez l'homme*, Paris: Vigot Frères.
95. O.M.S.–F.A.O. (Groupe d'experts) (1962), *Besoins en calcium FAO*, Report No. 30. Rome, Italy.
96. Ornoy, A. (1971), "Transplacental Effects of Cortisone and Vitamine D_2 on the Osteogenesis and Ossification of Foetal Long Bones in Rats," in *Calcified Tissue*, pp. 208–211 (J. Menczel and A. Harell, eds.). New York: Academic Press.
97. Ornoy, A., Menczel, J. and Nebel, L. (1968), "Alterations in the Mineral Composition and Metabolism of Rat Foetuses and Their Placentas Induced by Maternal Hypervitaminosis D," *Israel J. med. Sci.*, **4,** 827–832.
98. Patten, B. M. (1953), *Human Embryology*. Toronto: Blakiston.
99. Peane, A. G. E. and Polak, S. M. (1971), "Cytochemical Evidence for the Neural Crest Origin of Mammalian Ultimobranchial C Cells," *Histochemie*, **27,** 96–102.
100. Pincus, J. B. and Gittleman, I. F. (1963), "Hypocalcemia During First Week of Life in Mature and Premature Infants," *N.Y. State J. Med.*, **63,** 2502–2506.
101. Prader, A., Tanner, J. M. and von Harnack, G. A. (1963), "Catch-up Growth Following Illness or Starvation. An Example of Development Canalization in Man," *J. Pediat.*, **62,** 646–659.
102. Pryor, J. W. (1907), "The Hereditary Nature of Variation in the Ossification of Bones," *Anat. Rec.*, **1,** 84–88.
103. Rassmussen, H. (1968), "The Parathyroids," in *Textbook of Endocrinology*, pp. 847–965 (R. H. Williams, ed.). New York: W. B. Saunders.
104. Roche, A. F., Eyman, S. L. and Davila, G. H. (1971), "Skeletal Age Prediction," *J. Pediat.*, **78,** 997–1003.
105. Rodahl, K. (1966), "Bone Development," in *Human Development*, pp. 503–509 (F. Falkner, ed.). Philadelphia; London: W. B. Saunders.
106. Rotch, T. M. (1909), "A Study of the Development of the Bones in Childhood by the Roentgen Method, with the View of Establishing a Development Index for the Grading of and the Protection of Early Life," *Trans. Ass. Amer. Physcns.*, **24,** 603–630.
107. Royer, P. (1961), "Explorations biologiques du métabolisme calcique chez l'enfant," *Helv. paediat. Acta*, **16,** 320–346.
108. Royer, P. (1962), "Calcium et croissance," *Rev. franç. Et. clin. biol.*, **7,** 1025–1028.
109. Royer, P. (1972), "La croissance," in *Glandes endocrines*, pp. 307–319 (E. Beaulieu, H. Bricaire and J. Leprat, eds.) Paris: Fammarion Médicine.
110. Scothorne, R. J. (1964), "Functional Capacity of Foetal Parathyroid Glands with Reference to Their Clinical Use as Homografts," *Ann. N.Y. Acad. Sci.*, **120,** 669–676.
111. Sempe, M. and Masse, N. P. (1965), "Méthodes de mesure et résultats. La croissance normale," *Rapport au XX° Congrès des Pédiatres de Langue Française* (Nancy, ed.), Livre 2, 23–95. Expension Scientifique Française.
112. Sempe, P., Sempe, M. and Pedron, G. (1971), *Croissance et maturation osseuse*. Theraplix.
113. Smith, F. G., Tinglof, B. O., Meuli, J. and Borden, M. (1969), "Fetal Response to Parathyroid Hormone in Sheep," *J. appl. Physiol.*, **27,** 276–279.
114. Sontag, L. W., Munson, P. and Huff, E. (1936), "Effects on the Fetus of Hypervitaminosis D and Calcium and Phosphorus Deficiency During Pregnancy," *Amer. J. Child.*, **51,** 302–210.
115. Stanescu, V., Bona, C. and Ionescu, V. (1970), "The Tibial Growing Cartilage Biopsy in the Study of Growth Disturbances," *Acta endocr.*, **64,** 577–601.
116. Steendijk, R. (1971), "Metabolic Bone Disease in Children," *Clin. Orthop.*, **77,** 247, 275.
117. Tanner, J. M. (1962), *Growth at Adolescence*. London: Blackwell.
118. Tanner, J. M., Whitehouse, R. H. and Healy, M. J. R. (1962), *A New System for Estimating the Maturity of the Hand and Wrist, with Standards Derives from 2,600 Healthy British Children. Part II. The Scoring System*. Paris: International Children's Centre.
119. Todd, T. W. (1937), *Atlas for Skeletal Maturation*. Saint Louis: C. V. Mosby.
120. Trotter, M. and Peterson, R. R. (1969), "Weight of Bone During the Fetal Period," *Growth*, **33,** 167–184.
121. Trotter, M. and Peterson, R. R. (1970), "Weight of the Skeleton During Post-natal Development," *Amer. J. phys. Anthrop.*, **33,** 313–324.
122. Trotter, M. and Peterson, R. R. (1970), "The Density of Bones in the Fetal Skeleton," *Growth*, **34,** 283–292.
123. Urist, M. R., Dowell, T. A., Hay, P. H. and Strates, B. S. (1968), "Induction Substrates for Bone Formation," *Clin. Orthrop.*, **59,** 59–96.
124. Urist, M. R., Dowell, T. A. and Hay, P. H. (1968), "Bone Induction and Osteogenetic Competence," *Amer. Zool.*, **8,** 783–795.
125. Urist, M. R., Silverman, B. F., Buring, K. and Dubuc, F. L. (1967), "The Bone Induction Principle," *Clin. Orthop.*, 196è, **53,** 243–283.
126. Vaughan, J. M. (1970), *The Physiology of Bone*. Oxford: Clarendon Press.
127. Visser, H. K. A., Doornbos, L. and Croughs, W. (1966), "Evaluation of the Effects of Hormones and Anabolic Steroids on Height, Growth and Skeletal Maturation: Growth Velocity Plotted Against Chronological and Skeletal Age," *Acta paediat. Acta*, **21,** 631–652.
128. Wallgren, G. (1957), "Biophysical Analysis of the Formation and Structure of Human Fetal Bones. A Microradiographic and X-ray Crystallographic Study," *Acta paediat.*, **46,** Suppl. 113.
129. Wasserman, R. H. and Taylor, A. N. (1966), "Vitamin D_3 Induced Calcium Binding Protein in Chick Intestinal Mucosa," *Science*, **152,** 791–793.
130. Weidenreich, F. (1930), in *Handbuch der Mikroskopischen Anatomie des Menschen* (V. Möllendorf, ed.). Berlin: Julius Springer.
131. Weinmann, J. P. and Sicher, H. (1947), "Bone and Bones," *Fundamentals of Bone Biology*. Saint Louis: C. V. Mosby.
132. Wezeman, F. H. and Reynolds, W. A. (1971), Stability of Fetal Calcium Levels and Bone Metabolism after Maternal Administration of Thyrocalcitonin," *Endocrinology*, **89,** 445–452.
132a. Wharton, B. A., Foulds, J. W., Fraser, I. D. and Pennock, C. A. (1971), "Amniotic Fluid Total Hydroxyproline and Intrauterine Growth," *J. Obstet. Gynaec. Brit. Commw.*, **78,** 791–797.
133. Widdowson, E. M. (1965), "Absorption and Excretion of Fat, Nitrogen, and Minerals from 'Filled' Milk by Babies One Week Old," *Lancet*, **ii,** 1099–1105.
134. Wilde, C. E., Jr. (1955), "The Urodele Neuroepithelium. Part II: The Relationship between Phenylalanine Metabolism and the Differentiation of Neural Crest Cells," *J. Morphol.*, **97,** 313–320.
135. Wilkins, L. (1955), "Hormonal Influences on Skeletal Growth," *Ann. N.Y. Acad. Sci.*, **60,** 763–775.

136. Williams, M. L., Rose, C. S., Morrow, G., Sloan, S. E. and Barness, L. A. (1970), "Calcium and Fat Absorption in Neonatal Perios," *Amer. J. clin. Nutr.*, **23**, 1322–1330.

137. Wilmer, E. N. (1960), *Cytology and Evolution.* New York: Academic Press.

138. Witmer, G. (1969), "Evolution avec l'âge des tailles des espaces et des travées dans l'os spongieux de l'enfant, étudiée par mesure automatique," *Radioprotection*, **4**, 43–64.

139. Witmer, G., Cuisinier-Gleizes, P., Debove, F. and Mathieu, H. (1971), "Osteoporose provoquée par la carence en sodium chez le rat en croissance," *Calc. Tiss. Res.*, **7**, 114–132.

22. THE GROWTH AND DEVELOPMENT OF BONES AND JOINTS: ORTHOPAEDIC ASPECTS

J. TRUETA

INTRODUCTION

As far back as 1727 Stephen Hales[19] mentioned that the long bones grow in length at their ends; his experiments and those in 1743 of Duhamel[11] and John Hunter in 1772 (*see* [24]), confirmed this assertion which has since been repeatedly verified by many workers. The first description of the epiphyseal cartilage in all details was due to Tomes and de Morgan,[54] even if they had been preceded by the less exhaustive work of a few others, but the mechanism of ossification of the epiphyseal cartilage was not fully described until the publication of the classical work of H. Müller.[41] Since then, the behaviour of the growth cartilage under the influence or absence of several hormones alone or in combination (growth hormones from the anterior hypophysis, thyroid glands, androgens, etc.) and vitamins A, D and others, have been intensively investigated and there is not much more in this field that appears to be in immediate need of further elucidation. The effect of pressure upon growth has also been the object of repeated studies, a fact which is understandable, for part at least of the movement of tissue fluid within cartilage is carried to the cells by the pumping action of compression and relaxation of pressure through the growth cartilage. There is nothing peculiar in this, because it is well known that the total lack of vessels of the cartilage tissue such as the hyaline joint cartilage makes its nourishment dependent upon muscular and gravitational pressures, and consequently on the blood flow in bone.

This stimulated the study of some of the characteristics of the vascular supply adjacent to the growth cartilage and of the difference in function which appears to be conferred on the vessels at each side of the columns of cartilage cells.

To make this clear, it may be helpful to remember how the growth cartilage becomes established. Before birth, the long bones are preceded by their cartilage models or "anlages," a German word which is now accepted by many for lack of a better one either in English or French. The first bone appears in the middle of the shaft after vascular penetration. This progresses towards the two ends, and at a particular period of development for each bone. Under normal conditions, the epiphyses begin to ossify either before birth (primary centres of ossification) or some time after birth (secondary centres of ossification). As these epiphyseal centres progress, they constitute the distal limit of the space where the growth cartilage is to be located in each particular bone. The proximal limit is formed by the bone end of the enlarged part of the shaft or metaphysis. This process of progressive imprisonment of the growth cartilage between two bone plates takes a different length of time to be completed for each bone, and on some occasions years are needed for the growth plate to reach full development.

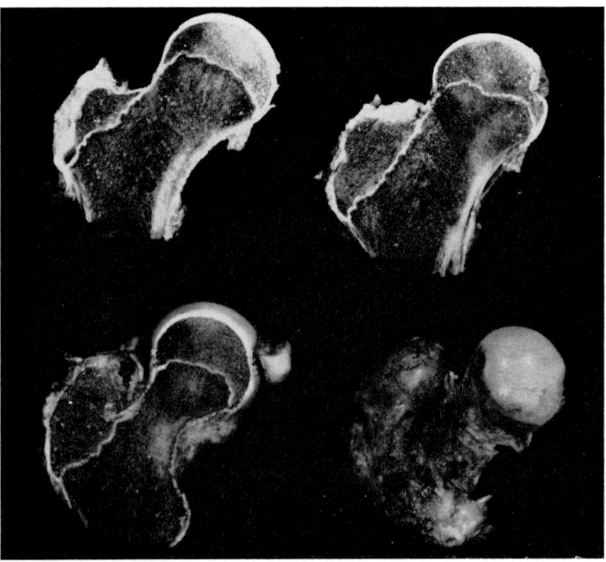

Fig. 1. A single growth cartilage is formed at the proximal end of the femur. Its medial side is under the epiphysis and is subjected to constant but variable pressure. Its outer side is under the apophysis or trochanter major and is subjected to the pull of the abductor muscles.

While it is as yet unknown why each particular bone-end of every mammal has a pre-ordained time for the establishment of the fully developed growth cartilage, it is very likely that this depends mainly on the time taken by the epiphyses to be totally ossified. Thus it may be very important to know why a secondary centre of ossification such as that of the femoral head, appears normally before six postnatal months, while the secondary centre of the trochanter major, covering approximately the outer half of the same growth cartilage as that of the femoral head until its final obliteration at puberty, appears only at the age of four to five years. It is possible that the main reason for this peculiar behaviour of the two epiphyses covering a single growth cartilage depends on the inherited adaptation to the pressure difference between the two epiphyses. The femoral head supports the heaviest joint pressure in the whole body by the combination of gravitation and muscle contraction; while the trochanter apophysis, on the contrary, is subjected to the pull of muscle insertion and no gravity (Fig. 1). This is only mentioned to show how much the growth of any epiphysis is under the influence of such physical forces as pressure. It is certain that for growth in length of long bones the intermittent contribution of pressure of gravity and particularly of muscle contraction are required; however, these need to be accomplished within normal limits for when they are insufficient or absent as after paralytic poliomyelitis, the limbs become shorter and in some severe cases of joint tuberculosis treated by prolonged recumbency and immobilization, premature epiphyseal closure may cause greatly disabling shortening of the affected limb.

The unequal distribution of joint pressure through the growth plate is responsible for the deviation of the bone from its normal pattern as in cases of coxa-vara or valga, genu-valgum or varum, etc. This early influence of the distribution of pressure over the growth cartilage differs very little from that exerted over the joint cartilage which is responsible for the development of degenerative arthritis in late life. There too, the consequences of uneven or excessive pressure over a segment of cartilage interfere with its nutrition and may cause its final disintegration.

THE GROWTH CARTILAGE

The organization of the cartilage cells of the original anlage in close parallel columns to constitute the growth cartilage is the result of two main factors. On the one hand, the repeated cell division and expansion that constantly enlarges the anlage, increases the resistance and thickness of the perichondrium. On the other hand, the development of the secondary nucleus of ossification opposes that of the shaft and forces each new cell to remain flattened on top of its predecessors, thus forming a column. In its constant progression, the vanguard of the vasculature which advances from the middle of the shaft reaches the place where the growth cartilage is to be situated. The rambling vessels then begin to proceed towards the cells in an ordered manner until they become parallel to each other forming large loops. This is due to the calcification of the matrix surrounding the cartilage cells which forms solid pipes round the cells. Soon the vascular loops, now protected by the calcified matrix, can advance in the direction of the epiphysis along the spaces occupied by the cartilage cells, removing the cells at the metaphyseal end of the columns one after the other (Fig. 2).

THE DEVELOPMENT OF THE GROWTH CARTILAGE

At the time of the transformation of the shaft from cartilage to bone, the growth cartilage takes over the responsibility for carrying on skeletal growth. The fulfilment of this function is the responsibility of the narrow layer of cells which, by their repeated division, form the cell columns.

These eminently reproductive cells are commonly referred to as *resting cells*; however, it may be more accurate to call them *germinal cells* for that is their function, namely to engage in the formation of the cell columns.

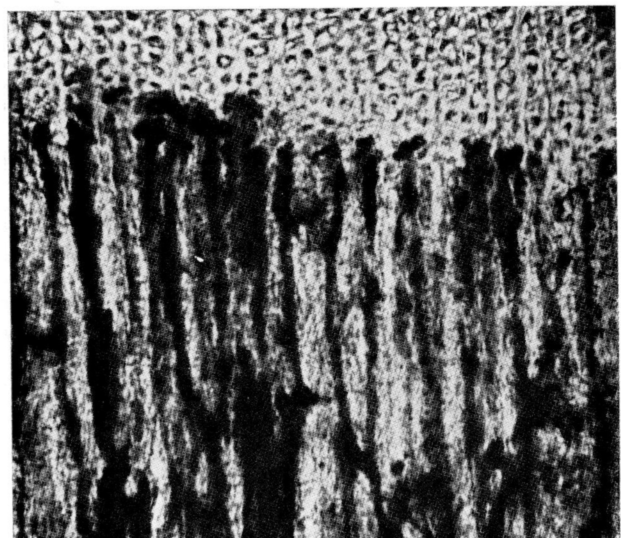

FIG. 2. The long vascular loops at the metaphyseal side of the growth cartilage. They advance towards the degenerating cartilage cells which, after the calcification of the matrix, are removed by the vessels.

THE EPIPHYSEAL PLATE UNDER NORMAL PHYSIOLOGICAL CONDITIONS

For many decades histologists have described the cellular arrangement of the epiphyseal plate and its development from early embryonic life to its final disappearance at the end of puberty. There is no need to enlarge on this anatomical description which forms part of all anatomical works since Müller[41] gave details of the cellular arrangement of the epiphyseal plate and Broca divided the epiphyseal cartilage in two sections: (a) the *chondroid* and (b) the *spongoid.* Only a short reference to it will be made here. In the hundred years which have elapsed, the minute characteristics of the growth plate have been thoroughly investigated and the following may be considered a summary of present views on this important tissue organization.

A fully developed epiphyseal cartilage consists (Fig. 3), from epiphysis to metaphysis, of:

(a) A *terminal area* or bone plate of epithyseal bone limiting the growth cartilage on its epiphyseal side.

(b) The first part of the columnar arrangement of the cartilaginous cells is the *germinal zone* because of its active mitoses, giving rise to its columnar arrangement.

(c) The *proliferative zone* of the cartilaginous cells which are organized in closely arranged columns.

(d) About the middle of the columns of cartilaginous cells these begin to enlarge constituting the *hypertrophic zone.*

(e) The progressive enlargement of the cells and the developing oedema of their protoplasm form the segment of the columns known as the *degenerative zone.*

(f) Finally, the *zone of calcification* where the chondrocyte is removed by the vascular loops.

The expansion of the plate is due to both appositional and interstitial growth. The first is caused by the addition of new cells from the perichondrium while interstitial growth is provided by the division and growth of the chrondrocytes of the germinal and proliferative zones, together with the

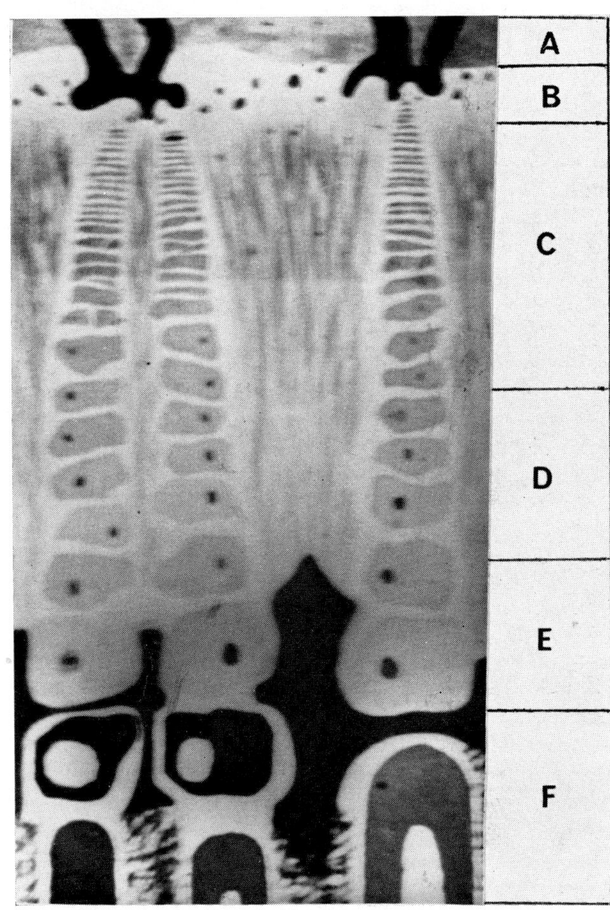

FIG. 3. Scheme of the growth cartilage with its several segments, from the germinal zone to that of the degenerating cells—*a:* bone plate. *b:* germinal zone. *c:* proliferative zone. *d:* hypertrophic zone. *e:* degenerative zone. *f:* vascular zone of calcification.

growth of the cells of the hypertrophic area, the oedema of the cells of the degenerative zone, both inside and outside the cells, and finally, the increase of the ground substance.

While this picture of the cellular anatomy of the growth cartilage is well known, that of the vessels supplying it has been less-well understood. Recent studies by a number of workers have attempted to fill this gap.

The site and position of the germinal layer of cells is genetically conditioned. Each growth cartilage has a topography of its own, depending on the particular bone and the species studied. According to the direction and power of the pressure the cell columns may change their orientation, but not the place they occupy in the particular bone. The metabolic requirements of the germinal cells are greater than those of the chondrocytes which have lost their reproductive capacity. For that reason, they must have a rich supply of transudates close at hand, which means that a profuse vasculature has to be present near the area of the germinal cells. This was shown to be the case by Trueta and Morgan.[61]

Until the epiphyseal ossicle has been well organized and is thus well supplied with blood, the growth cartilage does not become properly active (Fig. 4).

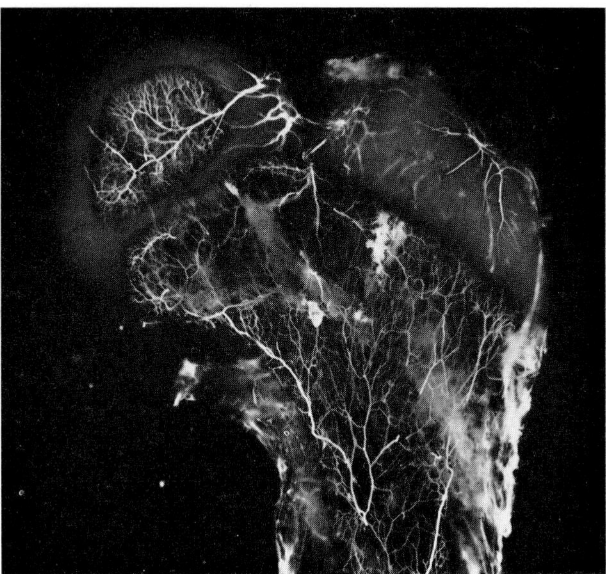

FIG. 4. Microradiograph of a perfused, decalcified proximal extremity of a human femur before the age of two years. The secondary epiphyseal ossicle is already well constituted and its rich sources of nourishment will permit the final organization of the growth cartilage.

The proliferative cells have little cytoplasm and their nucleus appears displaced towards the periphery as if being squeezed by pressure. This part of the columns is known as that of proliferation or palisade and together with the segment of germinal cells, forms approximately half of the growth cartilage.

BLOOD SUPPLY OF THE EPIPHYSEAL PLATE

(a) The Vasculature Supplying the Epiphyseal (E)-side of the Plate

Beginning at the E-side, it is found that the so-called terminal bone plate which covers the growth cartilage is not a continuous layer of bone, but a bone surface widely opened by large gaps through which the E-vessels pass to come into contact with the surface of the germinal zone of the growth plate (Fig. 5). These vessels are, in general, large and tortuous and, after penetrating through the gaps in the terminal plate of bone, loop back through the same gap after extending somewhat over the plate. In general, every vessel covers an area corresponding to from four to six columns of chondrocytes before returning to the epiphysis. In transverse sections, it may be seen that the E-vessels turn back at different levels which correspond to the varying heights at which the columns of chondrocytes begin. We have never seen an E-vessel penetrating between the columns of cells for any appreciable distance but many of these vessels come very close to the germinal cells. They are all thin walled and have the appearance of large capillaries.

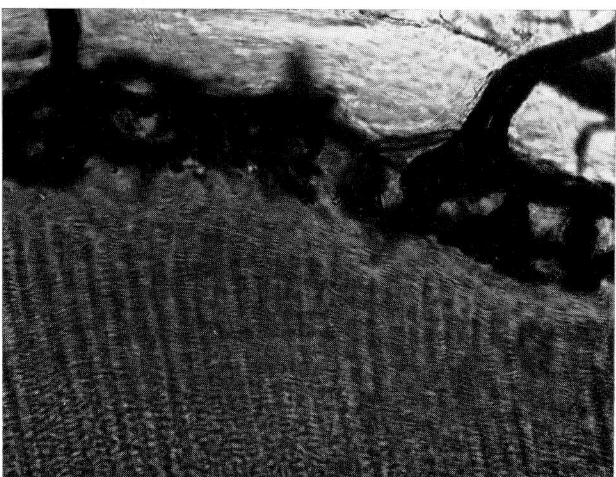

FIG. 5. An enormous, even if unsuspected, blood supply is available to the germinal cells of the growth cartilage.

(b) The Vasculature Supplying the Metaphyseal (M)-side of the Plate

The vascular arrangement adjacent to the growth plate at the M-side follows a completely different pattern. The last ramification of the branches from the nutrient artery (tibia, distal femoral end) or of the M-perforating vessels (proximal femoral plate and parts of the proximal tibial plate) reach the area of metaphysis occupied by the coarse, recently formed bone, at the end of the calcified cartilage; from a branching reticular arrangement the vessels become arranged in parallel lines like the hairs of a brush. Each vessel progresses some distance toward the plate until it loops back with both legs close to each other (Fig. 6). Each vessel runs within the area of one or two columns of degenerated chondrocytes and never seems to break across the wall of ground substance separating the columns. Contrary to

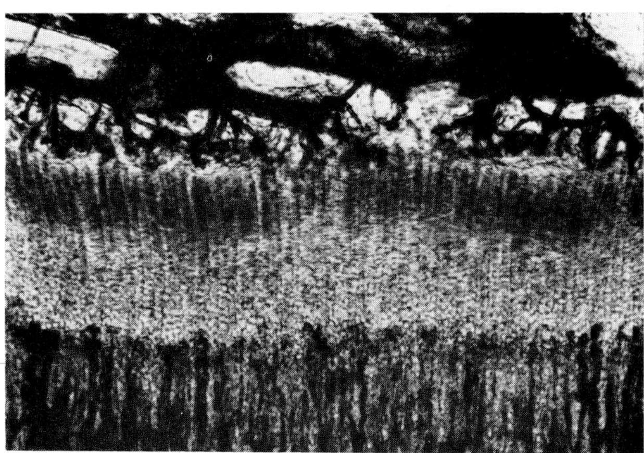

FIG. 6. Perfused upper extremity of a rabbit's tibia showing the striking contrast between the epiphyseal (upper part of the illustration) and its metaphyseal side, where the two arms of the vascular loops are parallel to each other and very close together.

what happens to the vessels at the E-side of the plate, those of the M-side all terminate at approximately the same level which is exactly where the calcification of the degenerating cell starts, at the end of the column. No anastomosis exists between the looping vessels which may be nearly as long as the whole height of the epiphyseal cartilage (Fig. 6).

ROLE OF THE BLOOD AT EACH END OF THE GROWTH PLATE

(a) Role of the Epiphyseal Vessels

It has been shown experimentally that the blood that reaches the plate by the E-vessels is the only source of nourishment for the chondrocytes of the plate. The greatest concentration of transudates must be found near the vessels from which they come, in this case those of the terminal plate of bone of the epiphysis; thus the better-supplied chondrocytes would be those of the germinal and upper part of the proliferative segments of the column. It is suggestive that the segment of hypertrophic cells occurs from the middle of the column onwards and that the degenerative zone is placed even further away from the E-vessels.

If the blood supply to part of the E-side of the plate is suppressed, the cells of the germinal segment undergo complete degeneration and the whole column begins to be filled with dead or dying cells. This degeneration only takes place in areas totally deprived of blood supply (Fig. 7).

(b) Role of the Metaphyseal Vessels

The suppression of blood flow through the M-vessels causes changes to the growth plate totally distinct from those resulting from suppression of epiphyseal blood flow. The cells of the columns remain of normal aspect in their different sections, germinal, proliferative and hypertrophic, but those of the degenerative segment change notably. Instead of the oedematous cells with advanced signs of nuclear degeneration and vacuolization, the cells retain characteristics of the hypertrophic cells. On reaching the level normally occupied by calcified cells, those of the columns in which the M-blood supply has been discontinued do not calcify and are left behind in the metaphysics by the formation of new chondrocytes at the top of the columns; thus, the thickness of the growth plate is increased on occasions to more than three times that of the normal (Fig. 8).

It is interesting that neither the presence nor absence of blood at the M-end of the cartilaginous columns seems to have much influence on preventing or accentuating cell degeneration. What the lack of blood flow at the M-end does is to prevent calcification, the plate taking on the histological characteristics of rickets.

The suppression of blood flow, even if maintained for relatively long periods of time, does not cause any appreciable damage to the chondrocytes apart from preventing calcification at the end of the epiphyseal columns. Shortly after the vessels reach the plate again from the M-side, the whole segment of the column up to the level where calcification normally begins to take place becomes calcified and the height of the growth cartilage is reduced to normal.

It may be concluded from all these observations that the functional role of the vessels adjacent to the E-side of the growth cartilage is purely *nutritional* whereas the role of the vessels reaching the plate from the M-side is that of forming

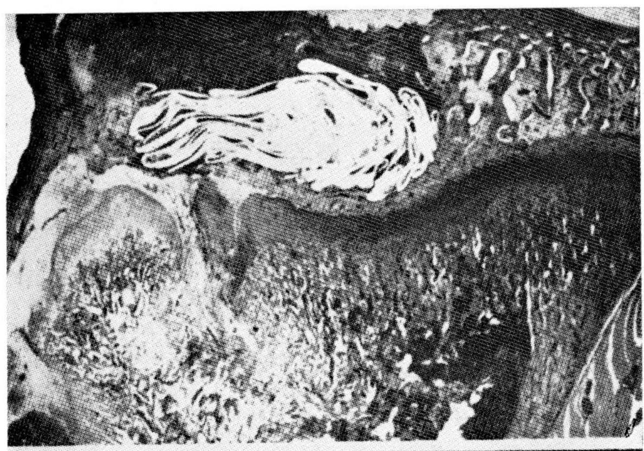

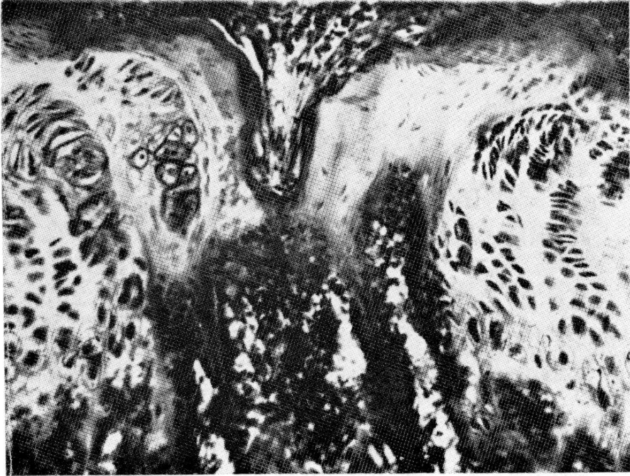

FIG. 7. Three illustrations of the same growth cartilage permanently damaged by the interruption of its epiphyseal blood supply. Note in the lowest figure the complete degeneration of the cartilage corresponding to the zone of ischaemia.

bone. The evidence so far gathered on any nutritional property of these M-vessels is very scanty and unconvincing. In spite of their resemblance to the loops supplying the calcified zone of the articular cartilage,[60] whose function appears to be mainly nutritional, those vascular loops at the M-side of the plate appear to have the unique function of cell removal and osteoblast formation. For as long as the growth plate separates the two systems of vessels here described, an anastomosis only exists between the two vascular systems as the periphery of the cartilage through perichondral vessels. The role of these anastomoses is not yet well understood, but they may in a certain way act as regulating channels which would contribute to the survival of the epiphyses—and possibly of the growth cartilage—in cases of severe epiphyseal damage to the main source of E-blood, as in Perthes' disease.

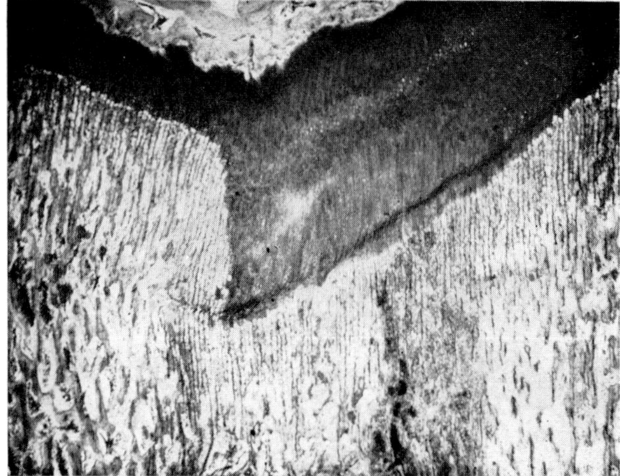

FIG. 9. Growth cartilage of the proximal end of a rabbit's tibia made about four times bigger by the experimental interruption of the blood flow to its metaphyseal side, which may be seen in the upper picture. The impossibility for the vascular loops to progress allows the preservation of the hypertrophic cells while new chondroblasts are added at the epiphyseal end of the cell columns.

In general it may be concluded that the function and persistence of the growth cartilage will mainly depend on the way in which both systems of vessels discharge their function. If an increase in E-blood flow before puberty causes an acceleration of cell division at the top of the cartilaginous column, a corresponding increase of the M-blood flow would cause an acceleration in bone formation. If a short-lived anaemia or momentary ischaemia affected the E-blood flow while no reduction of blood circulation occurred in the M-side of the plate, the addition of cells along the columns could be brought to a standstill while the process of calcification working repeatedly over the same matrix would cause a much denser calcification, leading to lines of arrested growth visible in the radiographs as described by Harris.[20]

It is probable that the endocrine control of growth involves a balance between growth hormone from the hypophysis and the sexual and adrenal hormones. These work independently on the cells at the two ends of the columns, the growth hormone activating cell division at the reproductive E-zones and the sexual hormones helping calcification at the M-zone. Thus it could be that both hormones had some direct cellular action which is conveyed through the vessels at each side of the plate. But so far the evidence for this hypothesis is insufficiently convincing.

As a summary, it may be said that the integrity of the blood flow to both sides of the plate is most important for normal function and that either an increase (hyperaemia) or a decrease (anaemia or ischaemia) can cause changes in the rate of growth in the whole plate or only in segments of it, which may cause irregular growth and subsequent bone deformities.

CHANGES IN THE GROWTH PLATE CAUSED BY INTERRUPTING THE BLOOD FLOW TO THE SHAFT

It has been stated that the E-system of vessels is relatively independent from that of the rest of the bone except for the small perichondrial anastomoses. By contrast, the M-system of vessels is intimately linked with that of the rest of the long bone, namely the nutrient artery, the perforating vessels of the metaphysis and their periosteal vessels (Fig. 9).

For many years, it has been known that these different sources of blood to the bone have intimate connections between them.[29,32,36,56]

When any of these vascular sources are interrupted, the remaining systems of vessels multiply. Thus when the nutrient artery and the periosteal vessels are interrupted, the perforating vessels increase both in number and in thickness. That is what happens in every fracture of the shaft of long bones, since these always affect the nutrient artery and many periosteal vessels. It is thought that the increase in the vascularity of the epiphysis in such cases may be responsible for the acceleration in growth which has been noticed in many shaft fractures in children, especially when the factor stimulating the increase in blood flow (namely, the removal of the obstruction of the bone-marrow cavity by callus) lasts for a long enough period. The result is an increase in growth rate which ceases precisely as soon as the remoulding of the callus ends. For this reason overlapping fractures of the shaft cause the greatest acceleration in the rate of growth.[55] It has also been observed since the time of Ollier[43] that a frequent sequel of acute haematogenous osteomyelitis is an increase in the rate of growth of the affected bone (Fig. 10). In an investigation of late results obtained in 100 cases of acute osteomyelitis[61] it was found that 32 cases had some increase in growth and that the factor common to all of them was that the bone infection had affected the mid shaft, and sometimes even extended towards both metaphyses. No case of overgrowth was

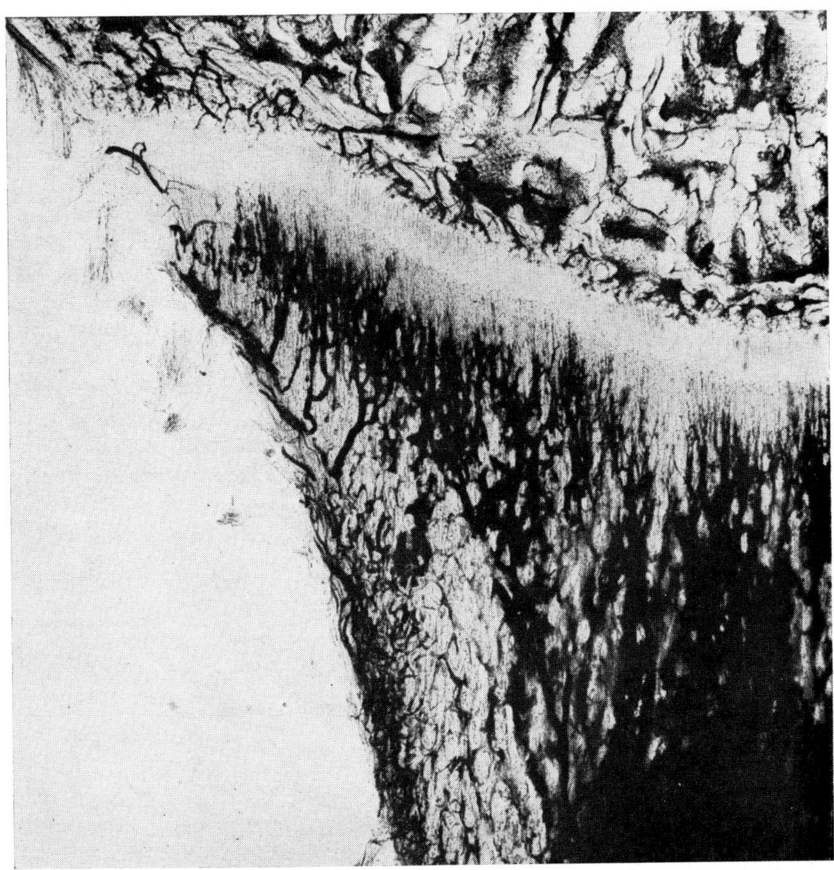

FIG. 9. Perfused upper extremity of a rabbit's tibia. The central part of the metaphysis appears supplied by the terminal branches of the nutrient artery. The left side of the illustration shows multiple perforating vessels and the rich vascularity penetrating the cortex from the periosteal region.

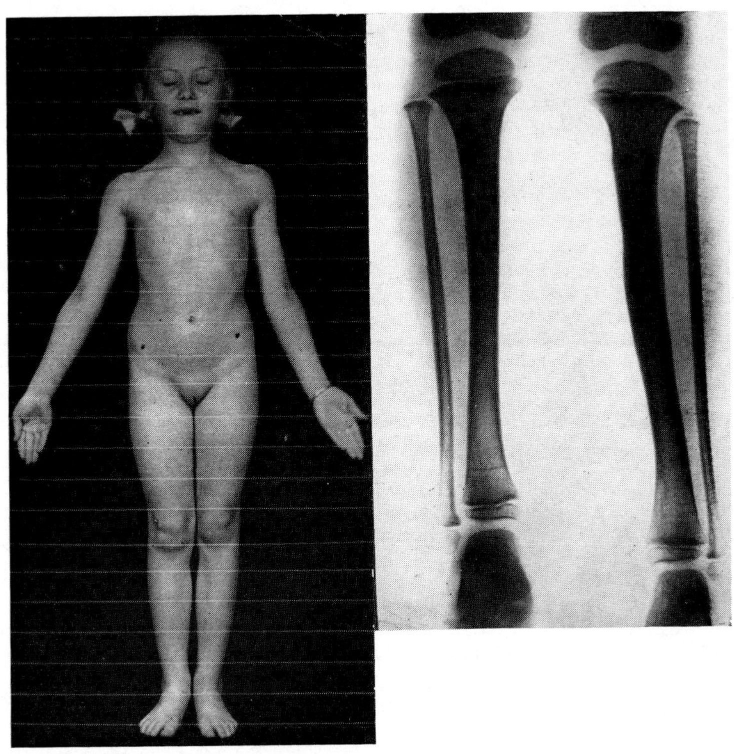

FIG. 10. Acceleration of growth caused by osteomyelitis of the tibia in a girl of seven years. Note that the increase in length affects almost exclusively the diseased bone.

found when the osteomyelitis had affected the metaphysis only. The conclusion was that, as in fractures, the remoulding of bone structure following the obstruction of the bone-marrow cavity caused changes in blood flow in the still patent vessels of the metaphysis, which was in turn responsible for cumulative overgrowth through their connections with the E-vessels. The anastomoses described above between epiphyseal and metaphyseal vessels may account for the over-activity of the proliferative cells of the growth plate.

EFFECT OF PRESSURE THROUGH THE EPIPHYSEAL PLATE

Apart from circulation factors (related to both the vessels and the quality of the blood) the transmission of stresses and strains through the epiphyseal cartilage is the most important factor regulating the growth of long bones. The fact that the growth plates in children more than two years of age are placed between two masses of bone—the epiphysis and the metaphysis—suggests that the cartilage cells must be very resistant to pressure. They must be able to bear both the weight of the growing child and the compression caused by muscular contraction without being disturbed.

In the literature on the nutrition and metabolism of joint cartilage[3,7,21,27,42,55] the mechanism of fluid penetration by diffusion into and expression from the cartilage, has been studied. The general view is that the distribution of fluid by imbibition or through canals is greatly favoured by and, indeed almost dependent on, the fluctuating pressure which effects a pumping action resembling that of a submerged sponge being compressed and distended intermittently. Thoma[53] considered that stress and strain amounting to 6·6 g./mm.^{2} may stimulate growth in long bones of the human.

There have been many investigations into whether compression of the epiphyseal plate which does not arrest growth has any ultimate effect on the rate of growth. Hueter[26] and Volkmann[64] maintained that excessive pressure causes retardation of growth, but Wolff[69] supported opposite views, thinking that growth is stimulated by pressure through the growth plate.

In 1901 Mass,[37] encasing the knees of animals in plaster in marked valgus position, found an increase in height of the growth plate of the tibia of the compressed outer side. Stieve[51] showed that compression increases the thickness of bone but not its length. Müller[42] performed resection of one of the forearm bones and saw that the growth plate of the remainder enlarged, having the histological appearance of rickets. Gelbke[16] studied the inhibition and atrophy which may be caused to the epiphyseal cartilage by great pressure. Pottorf[47] obtained early fusion of the growth cartilage in an immobilized limb of a dog and Howell[25] found shortening of 5·5 mm. in a humerus of a puppy in which the brachial plexus had been divided; but in this animal no difference in fusing time of the growth plate was observed. These and other observations confirm that absence or diminution of pressure interferes with the health and activity of the growth plate, as was also shown by Gill[17] in tuberculosis, and by Geiser[15] in immobilization.

Strobino *et al.*,[52] using calves, added evidence to the findings of Haas,[18] confirmed by Blount and Clark,[6] that a strong compressing force may totally arrest growth for a period of more than six months (equivalent to 3 or 4 years in man) without the cartilage losing the capacity for resuming normal growth if this compression is discontinued. These authors have claimed that there is an "all or none" law of growth in respect to compression forces when these are beyond physiological limits. They consider that for the upper plate of the calf's tibia this value is 45 lb./in.^{2} of cross section, which corresponds approximately to slightly less than the total weight of the animal. This is not a surprising finding, since it is considered that even in quadrupeds it is possible for the weight of the animal to be concentrated mainly in one limb in motion and particularly in running. This figure to arrest growth would correspond to 37 g./mm.^{2} If both Thoma and Strobino *et al.* were right, the appropriate amount of pressure for the growth cartilage should lie between 7 and 37 g./mm.^{2}

The compressed bone recovers its normal length once the compressing force has been removed. There are other authors who are not so convinced as to the existence of the "all or none" law of growth and think that slight or even intermittent pressure can slow-up or hinder growth.[1]

It is now known that sustained and firm compression causes an enlargement of the epiphyseal cartilage corresponding to the area of increased pressure. Histologically, the columns preserve their normal aspect in their several sections except in the segments corresponding to the hypertrophic and degenerating cell segments which become enlarged on occasions about six or eight times (Fig. 11). This appears to be due to a failure of calcification of the degenerating cells. The vascular pattern under these conditions shows that while the E-vessels are still permeable, the M-vessels are not filled near the plate, thus reproducing the condition found when the blood flow is interrupted. The calcification of the degenerating epiphyseal cells occurs shortly after the compressing force is removed and the cartilage resumes its normal appearance. It has been also found that when the pressure exceeds a certain limit and it is exerted uninterruptedly for seven or more days, disorganization of the cellular columns occurs, the staining of the cells alters and the division among the sections of the columns becomes blurred. The height of the growth plate decreases to below normal. Finally, vessels invade this area and bone bridges across the plate are formed.

These severe degenerative changes occur only when the pressure interferes with the blood flow at the E-side of the plate. The characteristics of bone growth seem to be related to the amount of suffering of the cartilage, and thus to the degree of interference with its blood supply. Experimentally, it has been found that the animals in which the growth is less affected are those that had the excessive pressure acting for shorter periods of time, whereas those with more severe shortenings are the animals which have been subjected to more prolonged periods of pressure.

It may be concluded from all these observations that pressure, while necessary to maintain the normal metabolism of the growth plate, must be within moderate limits and also acting intermittently. The other observation is that provided the E-side of the plate and its blood supply remain unaffected, the changes caused by excessive pressure on the M-side will tend to regress when the compressing force is removed.

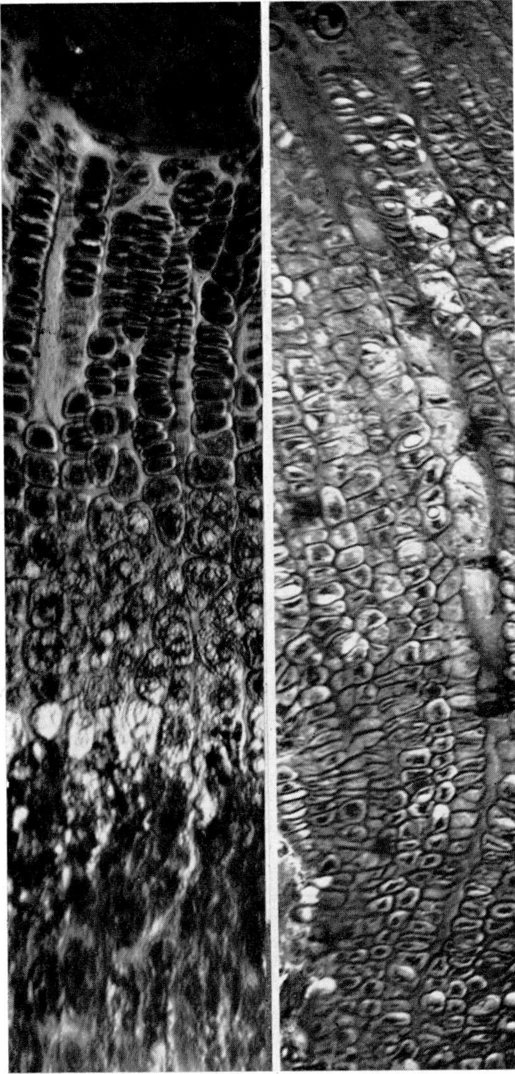

FIG. 11. Experimental rickets in the rat. On the left, a control growth cartilage from the upper extremity of the tibia. On the right, the permanency of the hypertrophic cells increases enormously the length of the cell columns and is due to the prevention of the vascular progress at the metaphyseal side, for the vessels are incapable of advancing in the absence of calcification.

Finally, no *increase* in length has been found which could be attributed to excessive pressure. From all this, it seems clear that persistent excessive pressure either has no influence on growth, or when it has any, it is an inhibitory factor.

THE MODELLING EFFECT OF MECHANICAL FORCES

Fell and Robison[13] demonstrated that the location of bones and joints is genetically conditioned. Isolated rudiments of rats' femora grown in tissue culture developed with the general shape of femora even if their final form was not exactly that of the normal. The absence of blood flow and of normal pressures was responsible for the changes.

The upper femoral architecture was found by Ward[66] to be similar to that of a bracket. Later, Culmann[9] noted that the design of the trabecular architecture of the upper femoral extremity resembles that of a Fairbairn crane. Together with Mayer[39] they explained the formation of the trabecular architecture and put forward the trajectorial theory of bone structure which considers that the trabeculae are materialized trajectories. Wolff,[68] Roux,[48] and Koch[31] agreed with this. Thoma,[53] Jansen[28] and Carey[8] attributed to pressure the role of directing the configuration of the spongiosa. Thoma showed that the determining role of pressure is bound up not only with the quantity of the load but also with the period of time during which it is acting. It is believed that the duration of weight-bearing, habits of stance and the relatively restricted joint usage of adult life as opposed to those of youth and adolescence, may explain the tendency to increasing definition of the pressure system in the mature man.

Many studies are available of the forces acting upon bone. Evans and Lissner,[12] using the "Stresscoat" lacquer method as a means of visualizing strains or linear deformations, determined the tensile strains of the femur under static vertical loading. The forces are of two opposite main types, compression and tensile forces. Benninghoff,[4,5] studying the course of the fibre bundles in lamellae, found that the general direction of the fibres as well as that of the osteons, was parallel to the axis of the long bones except near the area of tendon attachments. He thought that the increase in bone density was due to the condensation of trajectoral lines in a smaller area. It has been objected that if this was the case, the cancellous bone of the metaphysis would change into a solid mass of bone. It is well known that these strictly mechanical concepts of bone structure are not sufficient to explain the reason for the particular shape and direction of the trabeculae and that the constant action of bone remodelling plays a most active part in the final characteristics of bone structure. Even in the thickest bone, such as the calcar femoralis of man, the crystals of hydroxyapatite responsible for its strength are deposited around the vascular canals. The osteocytes survive owing to the persistence of the canalicular system through which the cytoplasmic expansions connect each osteocyte with its neighbours. The canaliculi extend in all directions until they finally open in a marrow space where the more superficial osteocytes remain attached to the corresponding osteoblasts (Fig. 12). Several workers[2,14] believe that bone generates an electric current when it is mechanically deformed and that this current acts as a pump to promote the ebb and flow of ions and charge molecules fundamental to its nutrition. If a metaphysis were considered as a sponge subjected to compression in one axis, the small spaces of its inner structure which were placed on the line of compression would be those more greatly reduced in height. Similarly in bone, the canaliculi crossing the line of compression at or near 90 degrees are those subjected to the greatest reduction and tend to obliterate more energetically and more often than any of the canaliculi running in other directions. It is probable that this obliteration alters the enzyme production

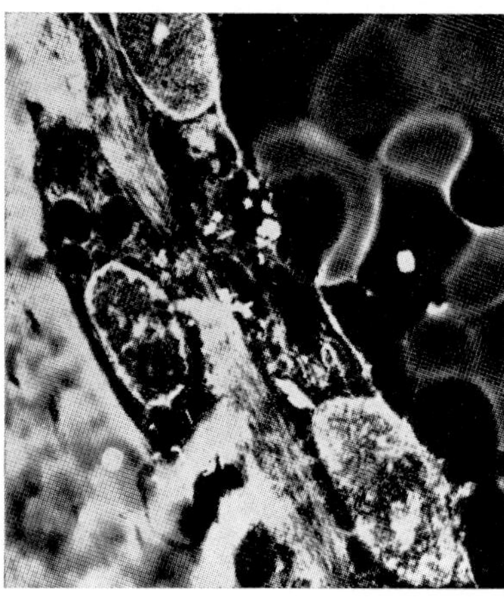

FIG. 12. Electron microscope. A vessel with several red corpuscles in it. Note two endothelial cells and the intercellular membrane connected to an osteoblast on the way to becoming encircled by calcified matrix, thus becoming an osteocyte.

by the osteoblast-osteocyte units along the lines of obliterated canaliculi on the line of maximal compression. Under these stimuli, the osteogenetic cells become active, deposit osteoid matrix and are incorporated in a new lamella. The writer thinks this is the way thickening of the lamellae in the direction of maximum pressure occurs.[59] Currey,[10] studying the stress-concentrating properties in bone, has found that transversely situated canaliculi constitute areas of potential weakness.

The consistency with which bone thickening follows the line of maximum compression makes it possible to reconstruct with impressive exactitude, the stance and posture of any fossil vertebrate, including man, by the direction of the

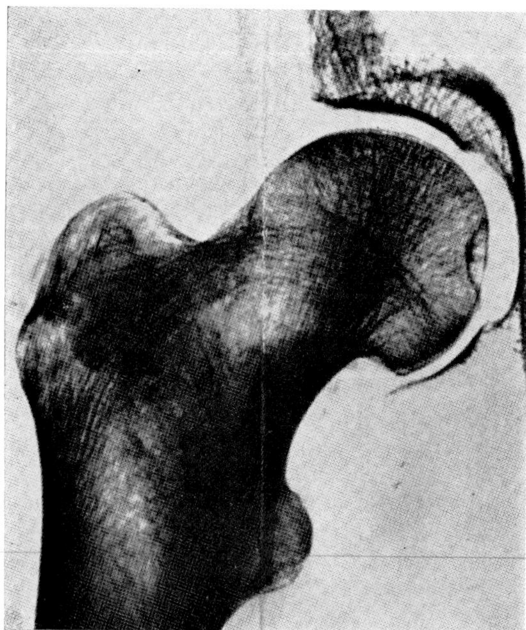

FIG. 13. Thickening of trabeculae is motivated only by pressure. Note that the transversely placed trabeculae often named "tensional trabeculae" are also formed due to pressure of the femoral head against the lower segment of the acetabulum.

thickest trabeculae in the bone extremities. Volkhoff[65] was the first to use radiography to determine the standing attitude of early primates and of man. Against the old belief that tension as well as compression may cause thickening of trabeculae, there is now ample evidence that only compression is responsible for increase in thickness and number of bone trabeculae as is well shown in the proximal extremity of the femur (Fig. 13).

HORMONAL ACTION ON GROWTH CARTILAGE

Since all the endocrine glands have the property of influencing each other's activity in various, and occasionally opposite, ways, the action on growth of most of the known hormones has been investigated. It has been found that two of them are mainly responsible for the behaviour of the growth cartilage. The first and most important of all is the somatotrophic or growth hormone, one of the six hormones already isolated from the anterior hypophysis. There is ample experimental evidence of the changes that the withdrawal of growth hormone causes in the epiphyseal cartilage. It is well established that the changes caused in young laboratory animals by the removal of the anterior pituitary gland occur mainly in the germinal and proliferative zones, as a consequence of which the cell columns become much shorter than normal (Fig. 14). Conjointly, the vascular progression at the M-side of the growth cartilage is arrested. As the removal of the pituitary gland decreases the vascularity at both sides of the growth cartilage this may be, at least in part, responsible for the slowing down of the mitotic activity of the germinal and proliferative cells of the growth cartilage.

Another responsibility of the somatotrophic hormone is to regulate the secretion of the thyrotrophic hormone, in this way acting, even if indirectly, on growth, for the thyroid hormone is essential for the development of bone to such a degree that hypothyroidism in childhood may be excluded when linear growth and particularly skeletal maturation are normal. In the athyrotic cretin diagnosed shortly after birth, it is possible to say that the thyroid deficiency was present during fetal life if the knee and the cuboid centres are absent. The epiphyseal disgenesis caused by the deficiency of thyroid hormone may be confused with an osteochrondritis of the hip, but differs from it by the fact that the latter affects only the hip joint in 90 per cent of the cases whereas epiphyseal disgenesis alters both hips together with other epiphyses. Skeletal maturation in hypothyroidism is often more retarded than linear growth, though on occasions they may be coincidental. The fusion of epiphyses is also delayed. If a child has both normal height increments and skeletal maturation, it can be denied that he suffers from thyroid deficiency. The developing skeleton is very sensitive to thyroxine deficiency, but in the absence of any other sign of thyroid deficiency, retardation of growth and maturation must be ascribed more to reduced pituitary function than to any direct damage from thyroid deficiency on the cartilage-versus-bone process underlying the mechanism of growth.

Androgens in the form of *testosterone* propinate in large doses causes shortening of bodies, tails, tibiae and femora

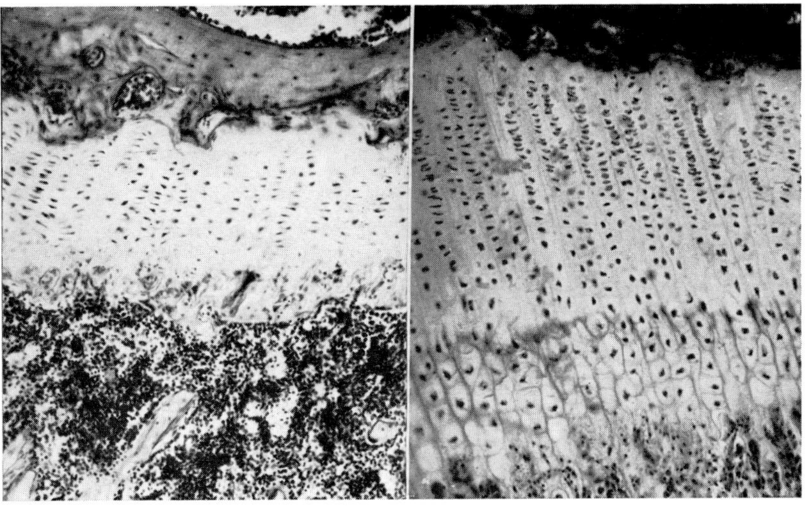

FIG. 14. Growth cartilage of a rat's tibia after hypophysectomy. On the right, the growth cartilage of a normal, control animal with cell columns nearly three times as long.

and reduces substantially the height of the growth cartilage of rats which become atrophic (Fig. 15). In rats given oestrogen-treated milk new endosteal bone appears and almost the whole of the metaphysis becomes solid.

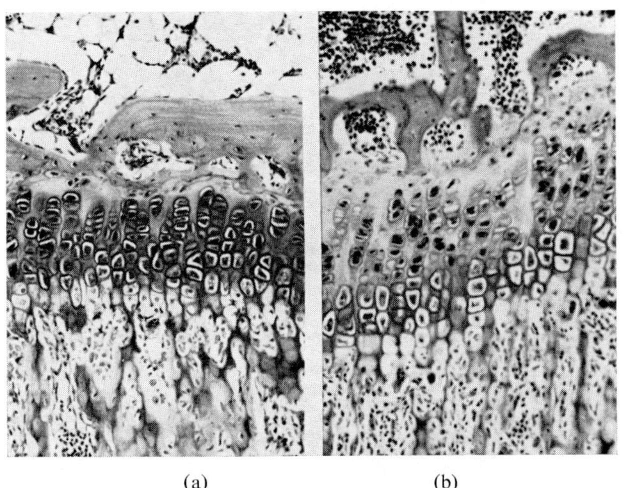

(a) (b)

FIG. 15(a). Proximal epiphyseal cartilage of a rat's tibia after receiving 40 mg. of testosterone proprionate during 40-days. The columns are much shortened in particular at their germinal and proliferative segments. (b) Control from the same litter.

It is now thought that the increase in sexual hormones occurring at puberty, in particular testosterone, inhibits the production of growth hormone which reduces the activity of the germinal and proliferative segments of the epiphyseal cartilage and, consequently, inhibits growth. This results in the final fusion by vascular invasion of the growth cartilage.

VITAMINS AND SKELETAL DEVELOPMENT

Three are the vitamins especially intimately related to skeletal development: Vitamins A, C and D.

Vitamin A

Mellanby[38] found in dogs that vitamin A deficiency thickens bone and reduces the marrow spaces. Remodelling of bone ceases to operate. Skeletal growth ceases whereas appositional growth of periosteal origin continues until inanition supervenes. The thickening of the periosteal bone tends to close many vascular foramina and that causes interference with the blood supply.

Vitamin A is necessary for the metabolism of cartilage and bone cells and its deficiency affects growth to a variable degree depending on the age and species studied.

Vitamin C

Ascorbic-acid deficiency causes an irregular arrangement of the rows of cartilage cells in the epiphyseal and rib cartilages, and a pronounced persistence of the zone of calcification in the form of a network of trabeculae of calcified tissue. The vessels are very sparse and osteoblasts are few or non-existent. Consequently no new bone is formed. Subperiosteal haemorrhages are characteristic of the condition. The bones are fragile in the adult and this explains the frequency of fractures in vitamin C deficiency. It is now known that both the amount of soluble collagen and the synthesis of collagen are decreased in scurvy.

Vitamin D

The study of rickets is a classic chapter in medical research. Deficiency of vitamin D inhibits the mechanism of calcification and affects the blood supply adjacent to the growth cartilage in such a way that the vascular loops at the metaphyseal side of the growth cartilage cease their progression and cannot remove the hypertrophic cells of the cartilage, thus causing what may be an enormous increase in height of the cell columns (*see* Fig. 11).

Calcium deficiency may be brought about by dietary insufficiency of vitamin D, by the insufficiency of calcium and phosphates, singly or together. Acidity of the gut tends to enhance absorption, while disorders of fat metabolism such as occur in coeliac disease, prevent intestinal absorption of vitamin D and calcium and is often the cause of rickets.

Rickets and its adult variant, osteomalacia, may be genetically conditioned causing "vitamin-resistant rickets" which occurs despite a normal intake of the vitamin and calcium in the diet. In these cases the vitamin D deficiency may be accompanied by renal tubular damage.

The administration of very high doses of vitamin D is required to control the deficiency. It is thought that vitamin D acts upon the enzymes of the Kreps cycle, and that in this respect the vitamin complements the action of parathyroid hormone.

SUMMARY

The main factors controlling joint and bone growth are: first the genetic message, to which blood flow and the action of pressure are soon added, the former supplying the required nutrients, minerals, hormones and vitamins to the growth cartilage.

DISTURBED GROWTH

In the following section, several of the conditions caused by disturbed growth will be referred to. Congenital Coxa Vara, Congenital Dislocation of the Hip (CDH), Coxa Plana, Genu-Valgum, Slipped Epiphysis and Osteochondritis of the Spine (Scheuermann's Disease), are shown as examples of growth disturbances among the many conditions which load the orthopaedic field.

Congenital Coxa Vara

The reduction of the neck-shaft angle to less than 125–135 degrees can occur at any age before fusion of the upper femoral epiphysis. We shall here refer to the congenital or infantile type only. It is usually bilateral and of unknown aetiology. A delay in the ossification of the femoral head which normally takes place between 4 and 6 months of age, would cause excessive compression of the cartilaginous anlage at the medial side of the epiphysis, thus inhibiting cell multiplication there and in extreme circumstances even decreasing the blood flow to that particular area. This would cause uneven growth, the outer side of the growth cartilage adding more cells and thus more bone than its medial side. The proximal extremity of the femur has only a single growth cartilage even if only the half situated under the femoral head is subjected to increasing pressure. As coxa vara never affects the growth of the trochanter, its increment in length remains normal whereas the growth of the epiphysis becomes progressively reduced, particularly in its medial portion. The result is a tendency of the femoral head to rotate round its centre, the lateral aspect moving upwards while its medial side moves downwards. The immediate result from this unbalanced growth is a weakness of the trabecular system corresponding to the medial side of the femoral neck. This constitutes an added disturbance also tending to deform the femoral neck and head in varus. The combination of these several factors explains the resistance of coxa-vara to improvement by most of the surgical procedures which have been tried. In severe cases the premature closure of the growth cartilage places the whole process at the mercy of the continuous growth of the trochanter major which forces the head to increase its rotation downwards.

Osteotomy below the base of the femoral neck to place the shaft in extreme abduction is the only surgical approach to the deformity. Pauwels[46] has devised an osteotomy with the purpose of reinforcing the inner side of the femoral neck which has given rewarding results.

CDH (Congenital Dislocation of the Hip)

The condition known by the initials CDH ought to be called Infantile Dislocation of the Hip for the departure of the femoral head from the acetabulum does not occur in the fetal stage of development but weeks or months after birth. The only exceptions are those who suffer great embryonic disturbances such as arthrogryposis or spina bifida.

A genetic factor in the production of the condition cannot be denied since there is a 4- to 5-fold sex predominance of females in all the statistics regardless of the peoples concerned. Some have considered that the female propensity to dislocating her hip was due to the inclination of the acetabula and others have found that Sudanese women, among whom the condition is almost unknown, have deeper acetabula than white women, which could make the femoral head more stable. As the activity of the femoral head is the real factor in shaping the acetabulum, the reduction or suppression of the appropriate joint pressures alters the maturation of the chondroblasts and ossification is delayed. The delayed ossification of both the femoral epiphysis and the ilium near the acetabulum, causes the sloping appearance in what is named the acetabula roof (Fig. 16). These changes are the bases for the so-called "hip displesia." Later, if the head really emigrates out of the socket, the pressure it exerts upon the lateral and superior aspect of the cartilaginous acetabulum causes an identation which, in becoming ossified, gives origin to the "false acetabulum."

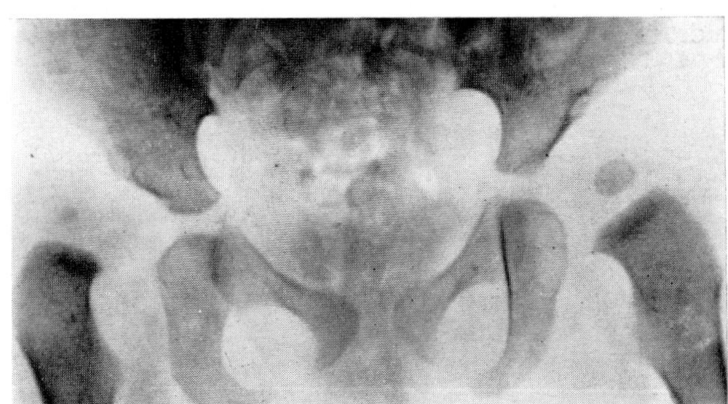

FIG. 16. Slipping appearance of the acetabular roof before the ossification of the ilium in a bilateral dislocation of the hip.

It is undeniable that in certain human communities there is a tendency to "weak" hip joints which dislocate, but the causes that bring the femoral head out of the acetabulum are all extrinsic and thus controllable. Teratological disorders are, of course, excluded.

It has been shown by several authors and in particular by Ortolani[44,45] that for the femoral head to move out of the acetabulum, the capsule and the powerful anterior ilio-femoral ligament should become weakened. Many studies of the relationship of post-natal posture and the rate of hip dislocation have been carried out and there is now an almost general agreement that the people who keep their young infants with the legs tied together are those who suffer the highest incidence of dislocation. On the other hand, those who allow their children to keep their legs fully mobile, and even more those in which the mothers carry their children on their back or side, with the child's lower limbs fully abducted, are among the lowest in incidence of dislocation.

What should be called Infantile Dislocation of the Hip (IDH) offers clear evidence of the misshaping effect of wrong pressures in early life when the child is fully engaged in the process of ossification.

Coxa Plana

Coxa plana, juvenile osteochondritis of the hip or Perthes' disease is a condition which often causes severe growth disturbances, following the reduction or suppression of the blood flow to the proximal femoral epiphysis. The mechanism by which the vascular interference occurs is still unknown and a variety of hypotheses have been put forward to explain it. The condition is mentioned here as an example of growth disturbance caused by interference with the blood supply of an epiphysis at the age of active growth, that is from 4–8 years.

For a reason which is still unknown, the sex distribution of coxa plana is about 4 males to 1 female, almost the reverse of IDH. From 10–15 per cent of cases are bilateral. That the disease causes a partial necrosis of the femoral head has been demonstrated by repeated biopsies obtained during the first months of the disease. While the process has a relatively rapid onset, it takes years to return to the normal or almost normal condition. Permanent alteration of the growth of the epiphysis may be caused by the severity of the ischaemia and the length of time that the growth cartilage is left without effective blood flow to its epiphyseal side. It is possible that the vascular damage is caused by trauma or a joint effusion which compresses the lateral epiphyseal vessels of the femoral head at the time they are the main, if not the only, suppliers of blood to the epiphysis. The negro child is much less prone to suffer from coxa plana and there is some evidence that he has a richer bloodflow in the femoral head than the white child.

When severe interference with the blood-flow to the epiphysis persists for several days, the growth cartilage may be permanently damaged. A type of coxa vara of the maturing child may occur causing important deformities and early hip arthritis (Fig. 17).

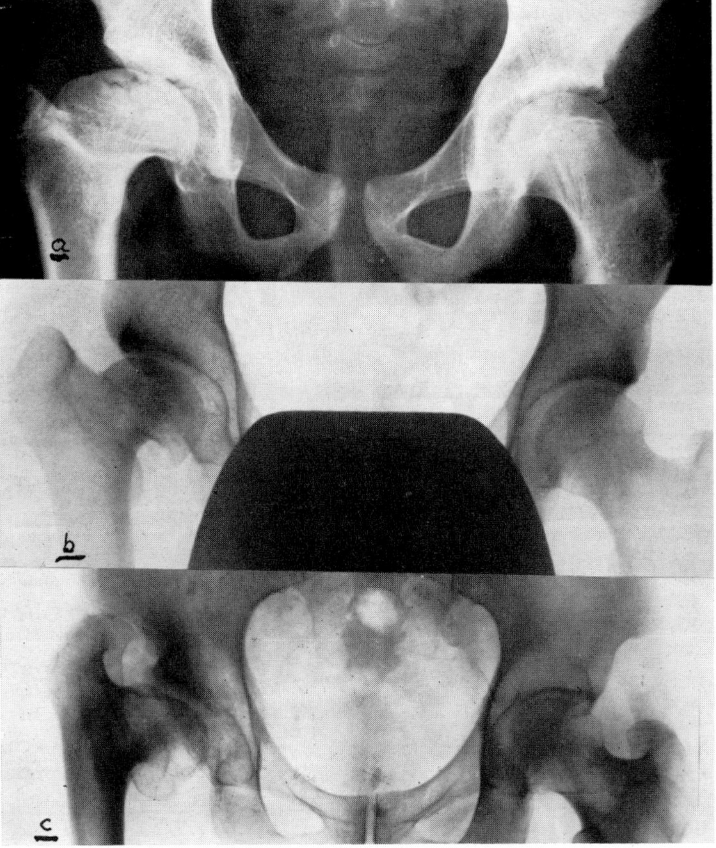

FIG. 17. Bad case of coxa-plana that caused persistent epiphyseal ischaemia and destroyed the growth cartilage. A severe coxa-vara resulted.

Genu-Valgum

The most frequent deformity of the knee joint in the young child is genu-valgum, while genu-varum is extremely rare now that rickets (its usual causative condition) is generally prevented. The reason for the predominance of genu-valgum in early life is probably related to the fact that in the human embryo the medial femoral condyle develops before the lateral condyle and later this catches up and takes an equal part in carrying the weight of the body. If the distribution of the knee pressures is excessively displaced towards the lateral side of the joint, the foot also takes up a valgus position. From then on, the inhibition of growth of the outer half of the two growth cartilages adjacent to the knee tends to increase the valgus angulation centred in the knee. Fortunately, in most cases the development of the outer femoral condyle results in a decrease of the valgus deviation and if the foot is supported from below to suppress its valgus and a night splint of the Mermaid type places both legs together in the appropriate manner, restoration of the correct shape of the legs is usually obtained.

Slipping of the Upper Femoral Epiphysis

The upper femoral epiphysis may become separated by violent trauma at any age before fusion of the growth cartilage. However, the entity discussed in this section occurs only in the pre-adolescent and adolescent period of boys and girls. The distribution of the condition has a ratio of 2 boys to 1 girl. The age of girls extends from 11–13 and exceptionally 14, and that of the boys from 12–16. Many causes have been suggested for the break of the epiphyseal cartilage, an intriguing event which affects only a small proportion of young people compared with the number of those who reach maturation without any trouble. The rupture of the cartilage takes place always through the area of vascular erosion at the M-side of the epiphyseal cartilage where calcification of the matrix but no real ossification has occurred (Fig. 18).

Three factors have been invoked to explain the crack. The first one is the weight of the child which is thought to be too heavy to be supported even by normally calcified cartilage. The second factor is supposed to be some endocrine imbalance which would weaken the strength of the cartilage, and the third, an abnormal inclination of the growth cartilage, which would make it vulnerable to shearing forces. None of these factors has been found to be present in a sufficient number of cases to be accepted as the cause of the initial crack in the growth cartilage. The number of patients with bilateral slipping strongly suggests that the people affected present some unknown weakness in their upper femoral epiphyses.

In the study of the vascular pattern of the upper femoral extremity performed by the author,[56] it was found in specimens of perfused adolescents of both sexes that a peculiar dilatation of the sinusoids and vascular loops of the metaphyseal side of the cartilage took place. This hypervascularity has been seen to occur at the age of 11 years in girls and at 12 years in boys. It is still evident near the time of epiphyseal fusion. It cannot be present without an enlargement of the narrow bonny-marrow spaces in the area of vascular invasion of the growth cartilage. It is this, in all probability, that is the factor that weakens the resistance of the calcified zone of the epiphyseal cartilage, which is the zone of intersection between the end of the cartilage and the beginning of the metaphysis (Fig. 19).

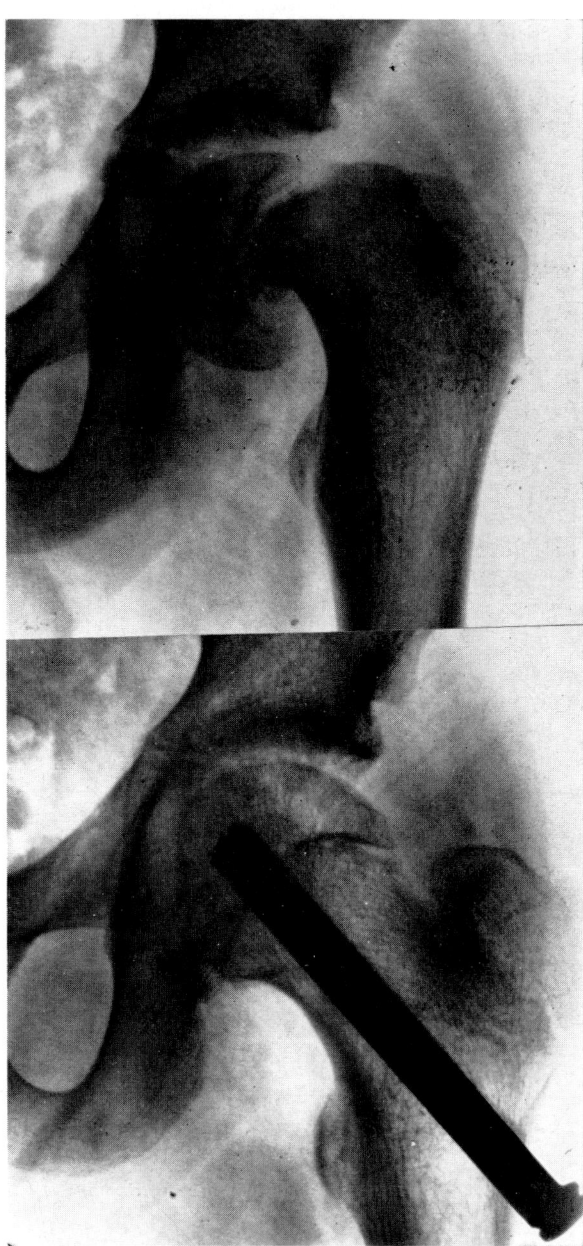

FIG. 18. Slipped upper femoral epiphysis with concurrent displacement and its correct reduction and fixation.

The vascular activity at this age is related to the final increase of the rate of cell division in the germinal and proliferative segments of the columns, at the time of the last growth spurt preceding the fusion of the epiphysis. It has been described before that the role of the M-vessels is that of removing the hypertrophic cells, and while more cells are added to the columns, more energetic vascularity is required to remove them. The reason why in some adolescents this vascular overactivity reaches a dangerous point while in others it does not, must depend on one of the other factors already mentioned, among them overweight.

After the crack, the immediate tendency of the femur to become adducted forces its upper margin against the outer

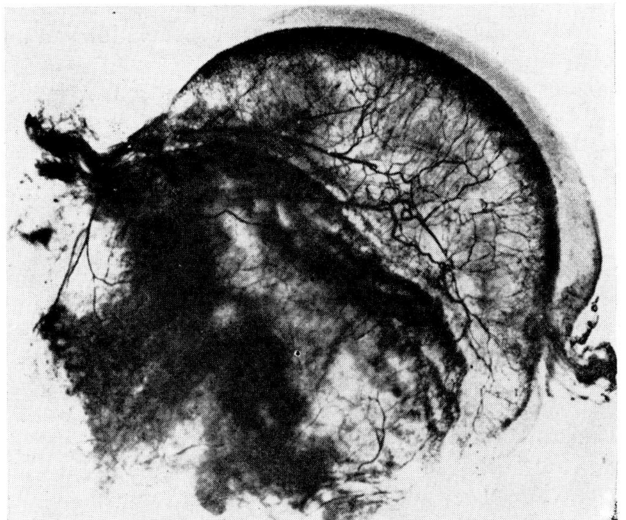

FIG. 19. Remarkable vascularity of the femoral head at the age of 12–14 years, located at the metaphyseal side of the growth cartilage.

half of the epiphyseal fracture surface, causing downward and backward tilt of the epiphysis.

It must be said that any adolescent of either sex who, without signs of sepsis, complains of pain in the groin, buttocks, thigh or knee, or limps without any apparent reason, must be suspected of suffering from epiphysiolysis.

This condition is an example of a severe alteration caused by disproportion between the forces acting upon the hip joint and the capacity to resist them at the time preceding the fusion of the growth cartilage.

Scheuermann's Disease (Vertebral Epiphysitis)

One of the best examples of bone and joint deformity due to abnormal distribution of pressure upon a growing epiphysis is found in the vertebral column. In 1930 Scheuermann[49] described the deformity occurring in the spine at the time of puberty, consisting in an increase of the normal thoracic kyphosis, accompanied by drooping shoulders, prominent scapulae and a flat chest. It has been noted that in all the youngsters affected by this condition the hamstrings are unduly tight and do not allow the pelvis, and therefore the sacrum, to rotate upwards on a transverse axis when the spine is brought to flull flexion as in attempting to touch the floor with the hands while the knees are kept in extension. This limitation of forward movement by the lower segments of the spine is partially compensated by an increase of the normal kyphosis in the thoracic segment.

The development of the deformity occurs when the ossification of the cartilage equivalent to the epiphysis of the long bones appears in the vertebral bodies. It has been due mainly to the recent work of J. Mineiro[40] on the development of the spine and its vasculature that we know the details of the maturation of the human spine. The first ossification of the spine occurs early in fetal development and it is well seen in radiographs of fetuses of 50 mm. The progress of this primary ossification is slow and it is only at the ages of 12–17 that the secondary ossification of the cartilage corresponding to the vertebral epiphysis takes place, as usual a couple of years earlier in girls than in boys. The final fusion of the secondary nucleus to the primary ossicle of the body occurs at the ages of 20 and 21 years.

The disturbance of the ossification process known as osteochondritis of the spine is shown by the fragmentation of the epiphyseal ossicle only in its anterior or ventral aspect. This may be due, as in coxa plana, to interference with the blood supply of the epiphyseal nucleus in its anterior part, as this is precisely the region where the maximum pressure is exerted in the standing position and particularly when playing games. As the youngster matures, the progressive forward displacement of the centre of gravity further increases the pressure until it inhibits the growth of the anterior half of the vertebral body and ends by causing the permanent wedging of the thoracic vertebrae. From then on, the deformity becomes irreparable.

The prevention of this condition depends on its diagnosis before the secondary nucleus becomes severely disrupted, that is at the time the forward stooping is developing.

The only successful treatment is a period of recumbency in a plaster bed. The apex of the kyphos must rest on a progressively raised hard pillow or on the hinges of the plaster shell.

Many have attributed forward wedging of the spine to shorter hamstrings, so that the lengthening of those muscles by repeated distraction or by surgery has been recommended; but even in those cases a period of recumbency is unavoidable in order to succeed. In the non-treated cases, early degenerative disease of the spine is a common event (Fig. 20).

CONCLUSIONS

It may be evident from the foregoing considerations that apart from the genetic message—and on many occasions even despite it—nutritional factors including the blood-flow to the skeleton, and the characteristics of the forces acting upon bone and joint, are responsible for the final shape of the human body. For this reason, supervision of the child's posture and habits of stance at regular intervals is imperative to reach maturity with a normal frame.

THE VASCULAR ANATOMY AND THE THREE TYPES OF HAEMATOGENOUS OSTEOMYELITIS

It is well known that acute haematogenous osteomyelitis varies in its clinical characteristics according to the age of the patient; thus, osteomyelitis of the infant, child and adult constitute three separate clinical entities with few features in common apart from the generalized, or septicaemic, phase of the disease from which they all suffer.

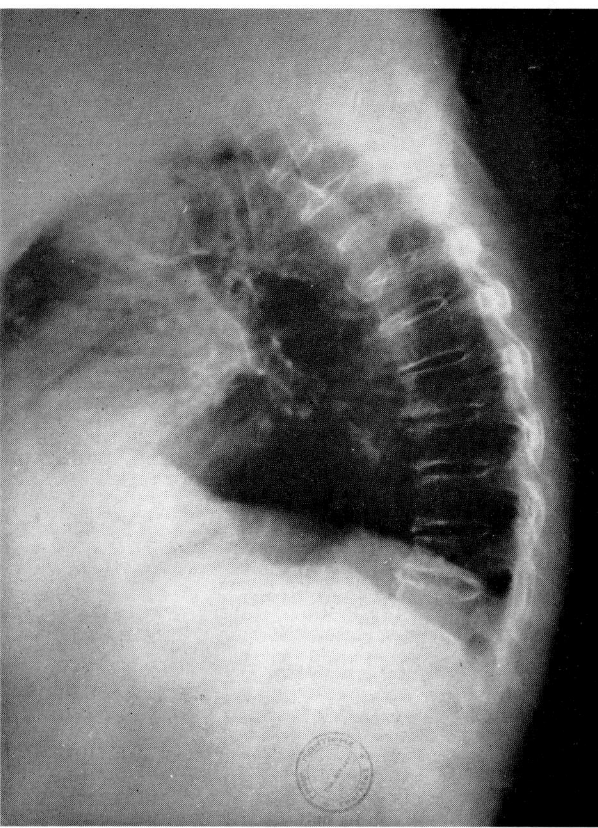

FIG. 20. Early osteoarthritis of the thoracic spine in an untreated osteochondritis.

In a systematic study of acute haematogenous osteomyelitis since 1944 we treated 225 patients. This experience will be used here to summarize the main clinical features of these three types of osteomyelitis. I will begin by mentioning the main clinical features of the disease in childhood, which in osteomyelitis covers the span of life between one and sixteen years inclusively. This is followed by a summary of the disease in the infant and in the adult.

Severity of Acute Osteomyelitis

It is well recognized that acute haematogenous osteomyelitis is a disease in which the majority of contributing factors vary, including the nature and pathogenesis of the causal organism. Thus, whereas the prevalent bacteria in the older age-groups—the child and the adult—is the coagulase-positive *staphylococcus pyogenes aureus*, the *streptococcus pyogenes* appears responsible for most acute bone infections in infants. The almost general agreement existing at present on the severity and clinical characteristics of the three age types is not accompanied by an equal consensus of opinion regarding the factors responsible for them.

In the following paragraphs, we offer an explanation for the diversity of clinical characteristics of acute osteomyelitis in the three ages in which they are grouped. No similar explanation has been found in the medical literature.[58]

Localization of Pathogenic Bacteria

Since the early experiments of Lexer[35] it has been generally accepted that the nutrient artery is the main route for bacteria causing osteomyelitis, even if other bone vessels cannot be excluded as a route for the infecting organisms. From the experiments of Koch[30] we know that an intravenous injection of bacteria localizes in the metaphyseal veins in the bone only two hours after inoculation and that a focus of infection may develop there.

Hobo[23] showed the part played by the vascular arrangement adjacent to the metaphyseal side of the growth plate in causing the localization of the pathogenic bacteria in children. His diagram is based on observations of the normal structure of the vessels in that region.

In his studies of experimental infection, Star[50] showed that the organisms responsible for the bone infection were carried by the blood stream until they reached what is referred to as "the finer capillaries of the juxtaepiphyseal region of a long bone," but he attributed the infection to the lowering of an undetermined "general resistance" of the patient. Wilensky[67] pointed out the importance of what he called the fixation points of the disease and supported the views of Hobo on the vascular responsibility in the onset of the infection. Finally, Leveuf[34] denied that the disease in the child was initially localized in the metaphysis, as suggested by Lannelongue[33] in 1879, and favoured the hypothesis of thrombosis of the main trunk of the nutrient artery from the onset of infection, as had been suggested by Hartmann[22] as early as 1855.

We are not aware of proper mention being made by any author of the fact that the vascular pattern of the long bones occurring during the first year of life, during childhood, and at puberty, is responsible for each of the three types of acute osteomyelitis. It is our purpose here to suggest that it is precisely the changing vascular arrangement at each age limit which explains the diverse clinical picture of acute osteomyelitis in every one of the age groups in which it presents itself.

Acute Osteomyelitis in Children

The vascular studies carried out in the Nuffield Orthopaedic Centre have repeatedly shown that the capillaries adjacent to the growth cartilage in its metaphyseal side are, apart from a very narrow fringe at the periphery of the cartilage, the last ramifications of the nutrient artery; these, after turning down in acute loops (Fig. 21), reach a system of large sinusoidal veins responsible with others for the haemopoietic activity of the bone marrow (Fig. 22). It is here that the blood flow slows down and that the pathogenic bacteria, particularly the coagulase-positive *staphylococcus aureus*, finds its ideal medium for development.

The system of blood lakes, beginning at the end of the capillary loop, spreads through the whole of the metaphysis in a pattern exactly corresponding to that of the distribution of bone sepsis in the early stages of osteomyelitis.

The peripheral branches of the nutrient artery, erroneously labelled end-arteries, are secondarily thrombosed by spreading infection from the venous side of the loops.

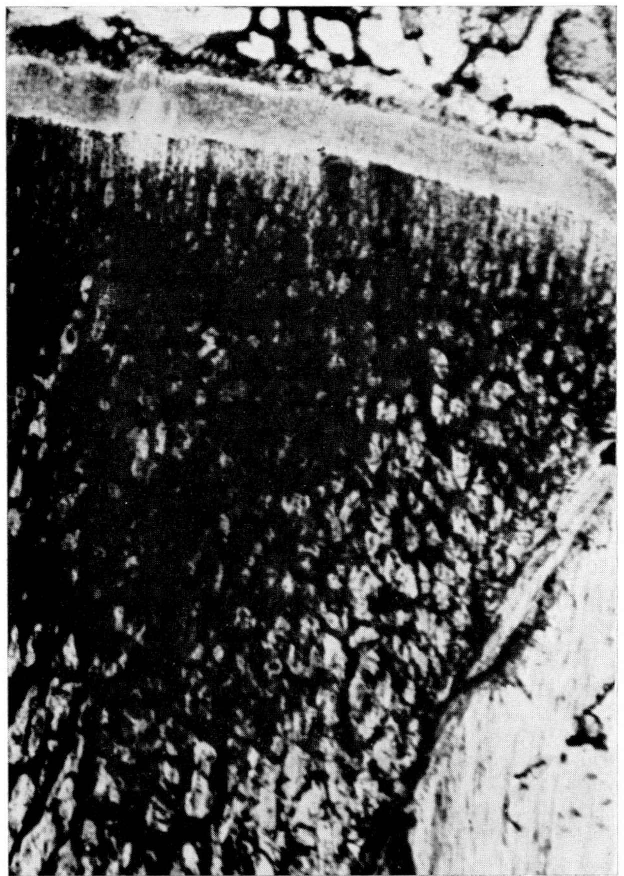

FIG. 21. The long metaphyseal loops after turning back from the degenerative cell layer of the growth cartilage end in the sinusoidal lakes of the metaphysis shown in the following picture.

Eventually the nutrient artery itself is thus occluded. Bone infection does not occur initially along the periosteal and metaphyseal vessels because none of them has a system of vascular loops proximal to venous sinusoids like those distributed at the periphery of the growth cartilage.

In a study of the changes of the vascular pattern of the human upper femoral epiphysis during growth,[56] it was found that the vascular barrier represented by the growth cartilage is first obvious at the age of eight months and is definitely established before the eighteenth month, except for some peripheral vascular connections between epiphysis and metaphysis. Thus, from the point of view of the vascular anatomy, the infant becomes a "child" at the age of one year.

The extensive involvement of the metaphyseal veins in acute osteomyelitis of the child causes early oedema. Transudates expand towards the surface of the bone across the cortex where it is thinnest, over the distal part of the metaphysis, and here the periosteum is raised from the cortex, disrupting all vascular connections between them. Soon, pus follows the oedema and the periosteum lays down a new layer of bone—the involucrum—at some distance from the cortex, visible after a few days on a radiograph. In another study, we have found evidence of the mechanism of involucrum formation. The early deprivation of blood to the inner half of the cortex by the thrombosis of the nutrient artery, followed soon after by the interruption of the blood supply to the outer half of the cortex which accompanies the lifting of the periosteum, is responsible for the large cortical sequestra that are typical of osteomyelitis in the child.

On the other hand, the isolation of the epiphysis from the metaphysis caused by the epiphyseal plate provides protection both for the epiphysis itself and for the joint, and explains the rarity of joint infections and epiphysitis with growth inhibition in children, even if early treatment is defective.

Summary

The aim of the surgeon in treating early acute haematogenous osteomyelitis in children should be to protect the

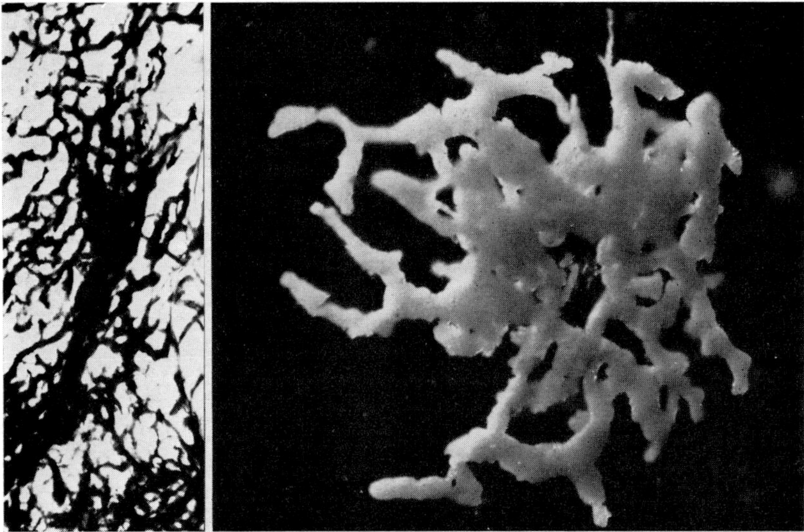

FIG. 22. The sinusoids of the metaphysis where the blood collects is an ideal site for the development of pyogenic bacteria as well as for the reproduction of tumor cells later in life.

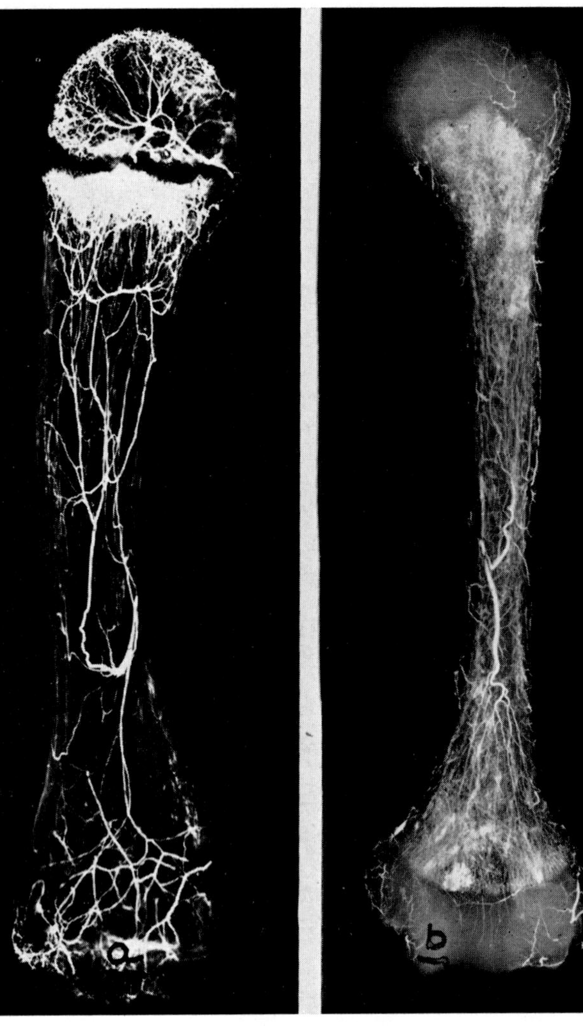

Fig. 23. In *a*, the vascular pattern of a metacarpal bone of a child showing the total separation of the blood flow to the epiphysis from that of the shaft, the growth cartilage acting as a barrier. In *b*, the vascular pattern of the humerus of a recently born infant, with the ascending vessels which join the metaphysis with the cartilagenous epiphysis. There is no protective barrier here.

blood supply to the outer side of the cortex to prevent the formation of an involucrum which would leave the cortex separated from its periosteum and cause sequestration.

In the child the disease tends to be more dangerous to life than to limb, for it may cause severe generalized toxaemia by massive absorption of toxins from the whole of the shaft. It seldom causes permanent damage to growth. On the contrary, in over 30 per cent of the cases studied in children, growth was stimulated by the increased vascularity of the metaphyseal side of the growth plate.

Acute Osteomyelitis in the Infant

The most important characteristic of acute osteomyelitis in the infant is the local severity of the disease. A particularly severe group occurs in the new born, infected from the umbilicus. It is the conviction of the writer that the more outstanding clinical features of the disease at this age should be attributed to the fetal vascular arrangement that persists in some bones up to the age of one year, with local variations corresponding to the time of full development of the epiphyseal bone nucleus (Fig. 23).

From the time in the embryo when the ossification of the central part of the shaft of the long bones has started, the perichondral vessels progress towards the two ends of the cartilaginous "anlage" in a tortuous way, turning back when they reach the still unossified cartilaginous ends of the bone. From the last stages of intra-uterine life up to the first six months, in some epiphyses, when the growth cartilage is established but not yet limited by bone on the epiphyseal side, vessels from the metaphysis penetrate the end of the "anlage" perforating the pre-existing growth plate. At their ends those vessels expand, forming large venous lakes resembling metaphyseal sinusoids. They are situated close to the surface of the epiphysis. This explains the frequency of infections of the joint and of the epiphyseal side of the preliminary growth cartilage in the infant.

In experimental work in the Nuffield Orthopaedic Centre[57] it was shown that any severe damage to the cells at the epiphyseal side of the growth plate is irreparable;

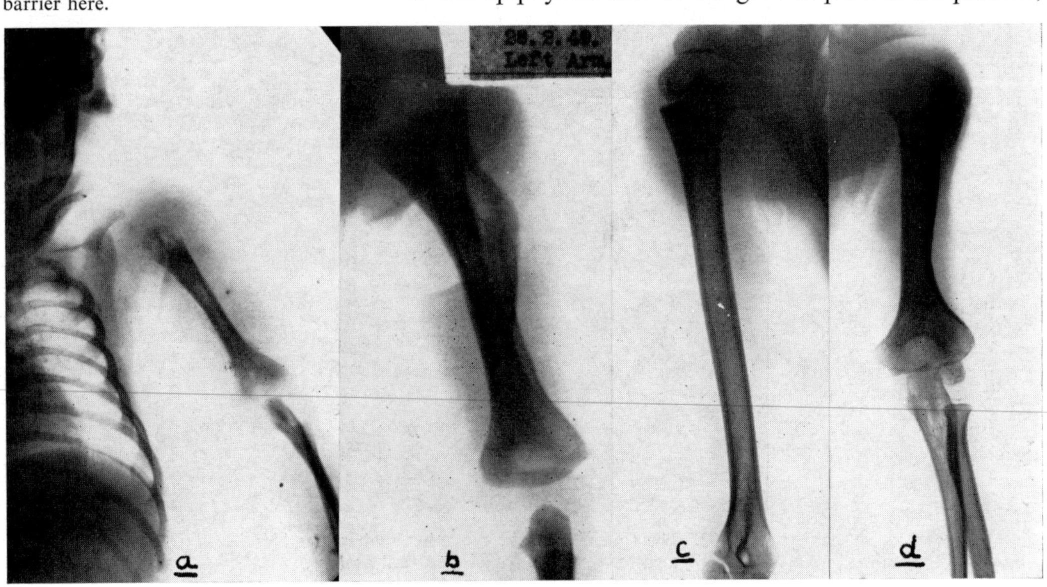

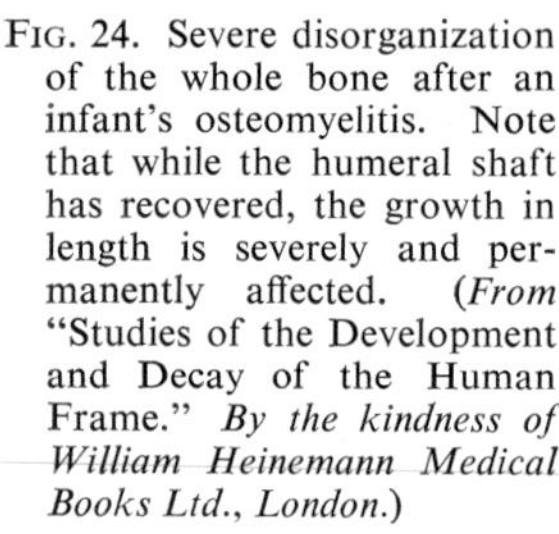
Fig. 24. Severe disorganization of the whole bone after an infant's osteomyelitis. Note that while the humeral shaft has recovered, the growth in length is severely and permanently affected. (*From* "Studies of the Development and Decay of the Human Frame." *By the kindness of William Heinemann Medical Books Ltd., London.*)

thus, both joint damage and arrest or disorganization of growth are the consequences of the spread of bacteria to the ends of the nutrient artery in very early life (Fig. 24).

Another characteristic of osteomyelitis in the infant is the profuse involucrum formation, sometimes monstrously large. But, contrary to the severity of the epiphyseal lesion, the bulging new bone along the shaft represents only a transient alteration of which no trace will remain in later life (Fig. 25).

The extreme richness of blood flow through the periosteal vessels and the fertility of the cambium layer of the periosteum are responsible both for the early exuberant reactions and for the extraordinary remodelling that occurs in succeeding years.

Acute Osteomyelitis in the Adult

The acute haematogenous osteomyelitis of the long bones in adults is rare. On occasions acute haematogenous osteomyelitis occurs in the adult but is usually localized to the short bones, particularly the vertebrae, following infections of the pelvis.[62]

The main features of the condition in adults are the rapid spread along the whole length of the bone, the frequency of joint infections, the lack of large sequestration, and instead the irregular atrophy of the cortex, and the limited involucrum formation. All this leads to large extraperiosteal abscesses and chronic discharging sinuses when there has not been proper treatment from the early stages.

In the adult, as in the other types, the typical features of the disease may be attributed to the peculiarities of the vascular arrangement following the fusion of the growth cartilages. By the progressive penetration of the growth cartilage by metaphyseal vessels, its height is reduced until finally vascular connections are established between the epiphyseal and metaphyseal system of vessels. From then on, the blood in the nutrient artery reaches the surface of the epiphysis through large anastomoses; thus bacteria penetrating the nutrient artery may be brought to the vascular loops under the articular cartilage[60] and spread the infection into the joint.

The fibrosis of the periosteum in the adult and its adhesion to the cortex make its detachment by pus more difficult; this prevents the formation of subperiosteal abscesses and thus preserves the blood supply to the outer half of the cortex. Consequently, large sequestra are not formed. Instead, the rapid and progressive cortical absorption may allow a fracture to occur if no protection is used. The tendency to chronic infection in the marrow, from phlebitis within the bone, and joint infection are the two main factors responsible for the crippling severity of the condition in the adult. The lack of reparative capacity apparent after the fusion of the epiphysis makes chronic infection the most frequent sequel of acute osteomyelitis in the adult.

Discussion

It is beyond the purpose of this contribution to enlarge on therapeutic considerations, but it may not be out of place to suggest some lines of treatment which are supported as much by anatomical vascular research—the object of this contribution—as by long years of clinical study of acute osteomyelitis.

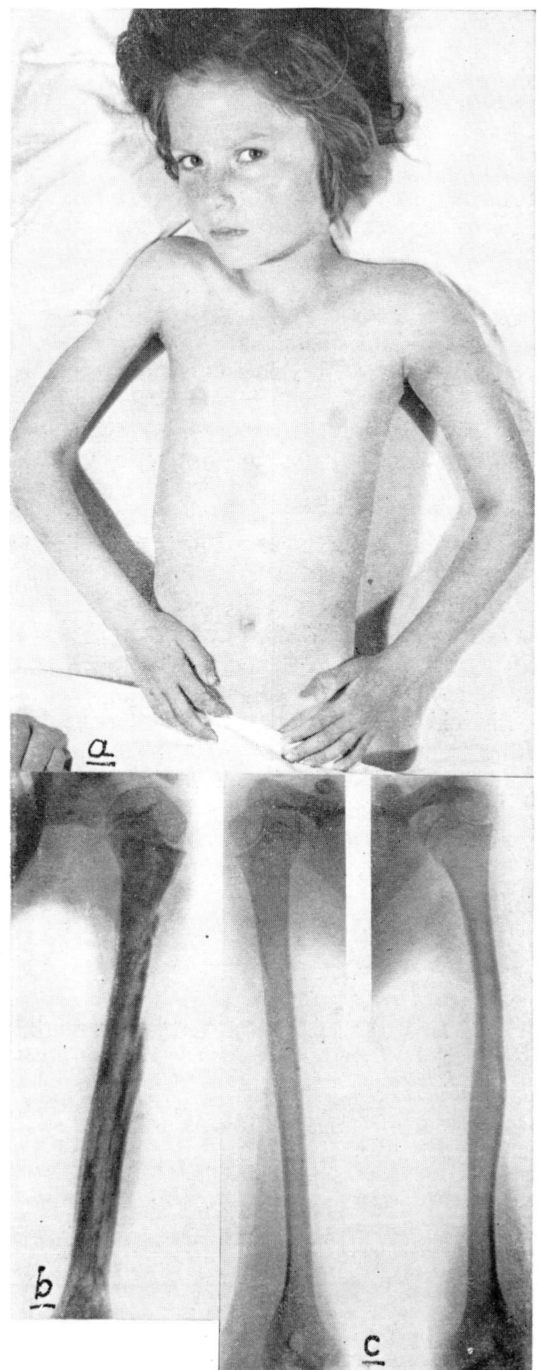

FIG. 25. Severe acute haematogenous osteomyelitis of the left humerus affecting the whole shaft in a girl of seven years of age. Note the complete restitution of the shaft. The only remaining anomaly is the greater length of the affected bone. (*From* "Studies of the Development and Decay of the Human Frame." *By the kindness of William Heinemann Medical Books Ltd., London.*)

Specific antibiotic treatment instituted as early and as radically as possible must be the main aim of any treatment of acute haematogenous osteomyelitis in any of its three age forms. If started soon enough, it may control the infection before severe vascular damage has been caused: (1) in the epiphyseal "anlage" and joint in the infant, (2) in the cortex of the shaft in the child, and (3) in the joint and bone marrow of the adult, these being the most commonly and severely affected regions in the three types of bone infection.

When some delay in the antibiotic treatment occurs, frequently because the appropriate antibiotic is not available, or known, the main object of the treatment must be to reduce vascular damage to the utmost. Early, effective, radical aspiration, or preferably incision and lavage of the affected joint in the infants and adults, and splitting of the periosteum, are the most conservative procedures for the preservation of what still may remain of the blood flow in the affected bone and joint. One thing must never be forgtten, and this is that no antibiotic will ever reach the foci of infection without the preservation of some local blood flow.

The vascular anatomy may also explain the predominance of the streptococcal infection in infancy and the staphylococcal in childhood. In early life, bone infection has been rightly compared to a cellulitis and a germ such as the streptococcus aureus, the common aggressor of the bone in childhood, needs for its development a stagnant or moderately active circulation such as that in the venous sinusoids under the growth plate. It may well be that the rarity of streptococcal bone infection in children is not so much due to a lack of streptococcal bacteraemia at the age as to the incapacity of this germ to localize in the metaphyseal sinusoids; this is, as yet, mere conjecture, but we consider it highly possible.

REFERENCES

1. Arkin, A. M. and Katz, F. S. (1956), "The Effects of Pressure on Epiphyseal Growth; Mechanism of Pressure on Growing Bone", *J. Bone Jt. Surg.*, **38A**, 1056.
2. Bassett, C. A. L. and Baker, R. D. (1962), "Generation of Electric Potentials by Bone in Response to Mechanical Stress", *Science*, **137**, 1063.
3. Bennett, G. A., Bauer, W. and Maddock, S. J. (1932), "Study of Repair of Articular Cartilage and Reaction of Normal Joints," *Amer. J. Path.*, **8**, 499.
4. Benninghoff, A. (1925), "Spaltlinien am Knocken, eine Methode zur Ermittlung der Architektur platter Knocken," *Verh. Anat.* Gess, **34**, 189.
5. Benninghoff, A. (1930), "Uber Deitsysteme der Knochencompakta. Studien zur Architektur der Knocken," 3, *Morph. Jb.*, **65**, 11.
6. Blount, W. P. and Clark, G. R. (1949), "Control of Bone Growth by Epiphyseal Stapling," *J. Bone Jt. Surg.*, **31**, 464.
7. Brodin, H. (1955), "Longitudinal Growth. The Nutrition of the Epiphyseal Cartilage and the Local Blood Supply," *Acta Orthop. Scand.*, suppl. XX.
8. Carey, E. J. (1921), "Studies on the Dynamics of Histogenesis. Compression between Accelerated Growth Centres of the Segmental Skeleton as a Stimulus to Joint Formation," *Amer. J. Anat.*, **29**, 93.
9. Culmann (*see Meyer*, 1867).
10. Currey, J. D. (1962), "Stress Concentration in Bone," *Quart. J. micr. Sci.*, **103**, 111.
11. Duhamel, H. (1742), "Sur le développement et la crue des os des animaux", *Hist. et Mem. Acad. des Inscrip. et Belles Lettres*, **2**, 481.
12. Evans, F. G. and Lissner, H. R. (1948), "Stresscoat Deformation Studies of Femur Under Static Vertical Loading", *Anat. Rec.*, **109**, 159.
13. Fell, H. and Robison, R. (1929), "The Growth, Development and Phosphatase Activity of Embryonic Avian Femora and Limb Buds Cultivated *in vitro*," *Biochem. J.*, **23**, 767.
14. Fulcada, E. and Yasuda, I (1957), *Nippon Seirigaku Zasshi*, **12** 1158.
15. Geiser, M. (1957), "Muskelaktion bei der posttraumatischen Osteoporose," *Arch. Orthrop. Unfall-Chir.*, **49**, 268.
16. Gelbke, H. (1951), "The Influence of Pressure and Tension on Growing Bone in Experiments with Animals," *J. Bone Jt. Surg.*, **33A**, 947.
17. Gill, G. G. (1944), "The Cause of Discrepancy in Length of the Limbs Following Tuberculosis of Hip in Children", *J. Bone Jt. Surg.*, **26**, 272.
18. Haas, S. L. (1945), "Retardation of Bone Growth by a Wire Loop," *J. Bone Jt Surg.*, **27**, 25.
19. Hales, S. (1727), *Vegetable Statics*. London: Innys & Woodward.
20. Harris, H. A. (1933), *Bone Growth in Health and Disease*, London: Humphrey Mildford, Oxford University Press.
21. Harrison, M. H. M., Schajowicz, F. and Trueta, J. (1953), "Osteoarthritis of the Hip: a Study of the Nature and Evolution of the Disease," *J. Bone Jt. Surg.*, **35B**, 598.
22. Hartmann, F. (1855), "Nekrose, herbeigefürht durch Verstopfung des Foramen nutritium," *Virchows Arch. path. Anat.*, **8**, 114.
23. Hobo, T. (1921), "Zur Pathogenese der akuten haematogenen Osteomyelitis," *Acta Sch. med. Univ. Kioto*, **4**, 1.
24. Home, E. (1835), in J. F. Palmer's *The Works of John Hunter, F.R.S.*, Vol. 1, p. 502. London: Longman, Rees, Orme, Brown, Green and Longman.
25. Howell, J. A. (1917), "An Experimental Study of the Effect of Stress and Strain on Bone Development," *Anat. Rec.*, **13**, 233.
26. Hueter, C. C. (1862), "Anatomische Studien an den Extremitätengelenken Neugeborener und Erwachsener," *Virchows Arch.*, **25**, 572.
27. Ingelmark, B. E. and Ekholm, R. (1948), "Study on Variations in Thickness of Articular Catilage in Association with Rest and Periodical Load: Experimental Investigation on Rabbits," *Upsala Läk Fören.* Föhr., **53**, 61.
28. Jansen, M. (1920), *On Bone Formation in Relation to Tension and Pressure*. London: Longman Green and Co.
29. Johnson, R. W. (1927), "A Physiological Study of the Blood Supply of the Diaphysis," *J. Bone Jt. Surg.*, **9**, 153.
30. Koch, J. (1911), "Untersuchungen über die Lokalisation der Bakterien, das Verhalten des Knochenmarkes und die Veränderungen der Knochen, insbesondere der Epiphysen, bei Infektionskrankheiten," *Z. Hyg. Infektkr.*, **69**, 436.
31. Koch, J. C. (1917), "Laws of Bone Architecture," *Amer. J. Anat.*, **21**, 177.
32. Langer, E. (1876), "Uber das Gefässystem der Röhrenknoche," *Dentschr. Akad. Wiss. Wien.*, **36**, 1.
33. Lannelongue, O. (1879), "De l'ostéomyelite aiguë pendent la croissance", Paris.
34. Leveuf, J. (1947), "Les Lésions initiales de l'osteomyelite aiguë," *Revue d'Orthopédie*, **33**, 177.
35. Lexer, E. (1896), "Experimente über Osteomyelitis," *Langenbecks Archiv für klinische Chirurgie*, **53**, 266.
36. Lexer, E., Kuliga, P. and Turk, W. (1904), *Untersuchungen der Knochenarterien mittelst Röntgenaufnahmen injizierter Knochen und ihre Bedeutung für Einzelne pathologische Vorgänge am Knochensysteme*. Berlin: A. Hirschwald.
37. Maas, H. (1901), "Über mechanische Störungen des Knochenwachsthums," *Virchows Arch.*, **163**, 185.
38. Mellanby, E. (1941), "Skeletal Changes Affecting Nervous System Produced in Young Dogs by Diets Deficient in Vitamin A," *J. Physiol.*, **99**, 467.
39. Meyer, G. H. (1867), "Die Architektur der Spongiosa," *Arch. Anat., Physiol. wiss. Med.*, **34**, 615.
40. Mineiro, G. (1965), *Coluna Vertebral Humana. Algunos aspectos da sua estrutura e vascularizacao.* Lisboa.
41. Müller, H. (1858), "Über die Entwickelung der Knochensubstanz

nebst Bemerkungen über den Bau rachitischen Knocken," *Wschr. wiss. Zool.*, **9**, 147.

42. Müller, W. (1922), "Experimentelle Untersuchungen über mechanisch bedignte Umbildungsprozesse am wachsenden und fertigen Knochen und ihre Bedeutung für die Pathologie des Knochens, insbesondere die Epiphysen störungen bei rachitisähnlichen Erkrankungen," *Beitr. klin. Chir.*, **127,** 251.
43. Ollier, L. (1867), *Traité experimental et clinique de la régéneration des os et de la production artificielle du tissu osseux*. Paris : Masson et Fils.
44. Ortolani, M. (1948), *La lussazione congenita dell' anca*. Bologna: Capelli.
45. Ortolani, M. (1963), "Les nouveaux problèmes de la luxation congénitale de la hanche," *Rev. Med.-Numéro Inter, Rheumatol.*, 4 Année, 468.
46. Pauwells, F. (1936), "Zur Therapie der Klinischen Cox-Vara," *Z. Orthop.*, **64** (Kongressband).
47. Pottorf, J. L. (1916), "An Experimental Study of Growth in the Dog," *Anat. Rec.*, **10**, 234.
48. Roux, W. (1885), "Beiträge zur Morphologie und funktionellen Anpassung," *Arch. Path. Anat. Physiol.*, **9,** 120.
49. Scheuermann, H. (1921), "Kyphosis dorsalis juvenilis," *Zischr. f. Orthop. Chir.*, **41,** 305.
50. Starr, C. L. (1922), "Acute Hematogenous Osteomyelitis," *Arch. Surg.*, **4,** 567.
51. Stieve, H. (1927), "Versuche über die Tätigskeitsanpassung langer Röhrenknochen; der Einfluss stärkerere Inansprunchnahme auf die Länge und Dicke der Mittelfussknochen und Zehenglider am Hinterlaufe des Kaninches," *Arch. Entw. Mech. Org.*, **110,** 528.
52. Strobino, L. J., Colonna, P. C., Brodey, R. S. and Leinback, T. (1956), "The Effect of Compression on the Growth of Epiphyseal Bone," *Surg. Gynec. Obstet.*, **103,** 85.
53. Thoma, R. (1907), "Synostosis sutturae sagittalis dranii. Ein Beitrag zur Lehre von dem Interstitiellen Knochewachstum," *Virchows Arch.*, **188,** 248.
54. Tomes, J. and De Morgan, C. (1853), "Observations on the Structure and Development of Bone," *Philosophical Transactions of the Royal Society of London*, **143,** 109.
55. Trueta, J. (1953), "Regeneration of Bone and Cartilage," *XV Congrès Soc. Inter. Chir. Lisbonne*, p. 564.
56. Trueta, J. (1957), "The Normal Vascular Anatomy of the Human Femoral Head During Growth," *J. Bone Jt. Surg.*, **39B,** 358.
57. Trueta, J. (1958), "Trauma and bone growth," *Société Internationale de Chirurgie Orthopédique et de Traumatologie.* Septième Congrès International de Chirurgie Orthopédique, Barcelone, 16–21 septembre 1957.
58. Trueta, J. (1959), "The Three Types of Acute Haematogenous Osteomyelitis." *J. Bone Jt. Surg.*, **41B,** 671.
59. Trueta, J. (1968), *Studies of the Development and Decay of the Human Frame.* London: William Heinemann Medical Books.
60. Trueta, J. and Harrison, M. H. M. (1953), "The Normal Vascular Anatomy of the Femoral Head in Adult Man." *J. Bone Jt. Surg.*, **35B,** 492.
61. Trueta, J. and Morgan, J. D. (1954), "Late Results in the Treatment of One Hundred Cases of Acute Haematogenous Osteomyelitis," *Brit. J. Surg.*, **41,** 29.
62. Trueta, J. and Morgan, J. D. (1960), "The Vascular Contribution to Osteogenesis. I: Studies by the Injection Method." *J. Bone Jt. Surg.*, **42B,** 97.
63. Wiley, A. M. and Trueta, J. (1959), "The Vascular Anatomy of the Spine and its Relation to Pyogenic Vertebral Osteomyelitis," *J. Bone Jt. Surg.*, **41B,** 796.
64. Volkmann, R. von (1863), "Zur Histologie der Caries und Osteitis," *Arch. klin. Chir.*, **4,** 437.
65. Volkhoff, O. (1904), *Studien über der Entwickelungemechanic des Primatenskellettes.* Wiesbaden: C. W. Kreidler.
66. Ward, F. O. (1838), *Outlines of Human Osteology.* London: Renshaw.
67. Wilensky, A. O. (1934), *Osteomyelitis. Its Pathogenesis, Symptomatology and Treatment. New York: The Macmillan Company.*
68. Wolff, J. (1870), "Über die innere Architecture der Knochen und ihre Bedeutung für die Frage von Knochenwachstum," *Virchows Arch.*, **50,** 389.
69. Wolff, J. (1892), *Das Gesetz der Transformation der Knochen.* Berlin: A. Hirschweld.

23. THE GROWTH AND DEVELOPMENT OF THE TEETH

E. P. TURNER

INTRODUCTION

The human dentition is described as being diphyodont; that is to say, there are two dentitions, one deciduous and one permanent. In total, during his lifetime, Man may have 52 teeth, 20 teeth in the deciduous dentition and 32 in the permanent dentition. The deciduous dentition commences to erupt at approximately 6 months of age and is complete after about $2\frac{1}{2}$ years. (The dates at which teeth erupt are not precise, and show individual variation—*vide infra.*) At 6–8 years of age shedding of this dentition commences with the lower front teeth, their place being taken by permanent successors. This shedding process gradually progresses in a posterior direction over a period of 6–8 years, each deciduous tooth being followed by a permanent successor. In each half of each jaw the fully developed deciduous dentition comprises two incisor teeth (a central incisor and lateral incisor) a canine tooth and two molar teeth (Fig. 1); thus the Dental Formula for this dentition can be written as follows:

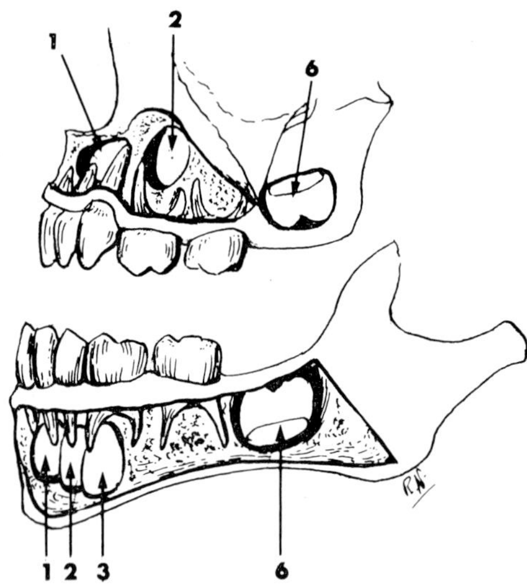

FIG. 1. Maxilla and mandible showing the stage of dental development at approximately $3\frac{1}{2}$-years-of-age. The outer plate of bone has been removed to demonstrate the unerupted developing permanent incisor teeth, lower canine and first molars. The complete deciduous dentition is fully erupted. It will be noted that calcification of

$$\frac{/345}{/\ \ 45}$$

has not commenced. Considerable jaw growth will be necessary to allow the permanent teeth to erupt in their normal position (note for example the present position of $\underline{/2}$ in this specimen.) Growth will also have to take place to provide space for the development and eruption of

$$\frac{/78}{/78}$$

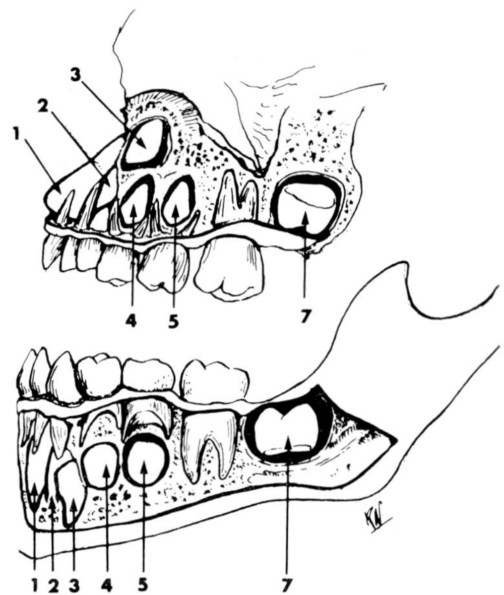

FIG. 2. Maxilla and mandible showing dental development at approximately 7 years of age; note that in this individual $\overline{/1}$ has not yet erupted, but the first permanent molars are in their normal position behind the deciduous molars. Bone has been removed to expose the unerupted developing

$$\frac{/123457}{/123457}.$$

$$I\tfrac{2}{2}\ C\tfrac{1}{1}\ M\tfrac{2}{2}$$

Similarly the permanent dentition comprises two incisors, one canine, two premolars and three molars (Fig. 2) and may be codified as

$$I\tfrac{2}{2}\ C\tfrac{1}{1}\ PM\tfrac{2}{2}\ M\tfrac{3}{3}$$

Thus it will be evident that the permanent incisor, canine and premolar teeth have a deciduous predecessor, but the permanent molars do not. During the period when the deciduous dentition is being shed and the permanent successional teeth are erupting in their place, the dentition will obviously consist of a variable number of deciduous and permanent teeth at any given time, this being referred to as "the mixed dentition".

Turning now to a more detailed consideration of the teeth, it is common knowledge that each tooth has a crown covered by enamel, that the body of the tooth consists of dentine and the root surface is covered by a thin layer of bone-like material named cementum. In the centre of the tooth there is pulp tissue containing blood and lymph vessels and sensory nerve elements. The tooth is "slung" in the alveolar bone by the periodontal membrane, a collagenous ligament attached to the root surface by the cementum and to a thin layer of compact bone lining each tooth socket

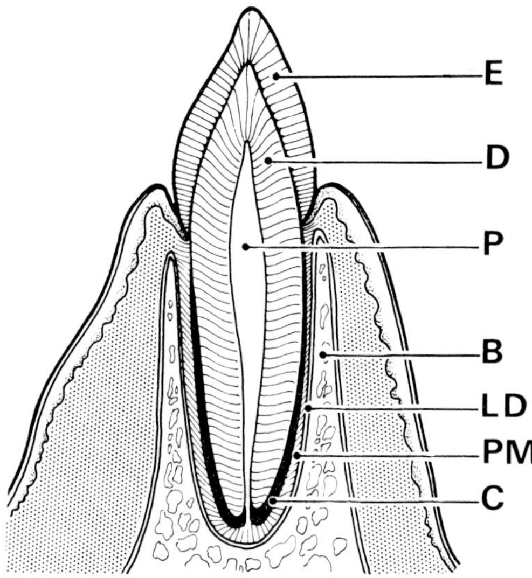

FIG. 3. Diagram of a fully developed erupted tooth.

E: Enamel
D: Dentine
P: Pulp
B: Alveolar bone
LD: Lamina dura
PM: Periodontal membrane
C: Cementum

in the alveolus, known as the lamina dura (Fig. 3). Although this ligament is very thin it permits of limited tooth movement. The incisors and canines of both dentitions have a single root, the upper molars have three roots (one palatal and two buccal) and lower molars have two roots (one anterior and one posterior). The premolar teeth are usually single rooted except for the upper first premolar, which may have one buccal and one palatal root. Certain salient features are described which help to distinguish between the gross appearance of deciduous and permanent teeth. Briefly these are as follows:

(i) Deciduous teeth are smaller than the permanent teeth in each individual.[7] (It is perhaps important to note that between individuals there is quite a wide variation in size of teeth such that in rare instances the second deciduous molar in one person may be equivalent in size to the first permanent molar in another unrelated person.)

(ii) The enamel in deciduous teeth appears whiter than the enamel in permanent teeth.

(iii) The crowns of deciduous teeth are more bulbous and the necks of the teeth are more constricted.

(iv) The roots of deciduous teeth are markedly divergent compared with permanent teeth.

Attrition is the term given to the wearing away of one tooth by an opposing tooth, such that the incisive edges or molar cusps may diminish due to wear. This may be seen to a quite remarkable degree in the deciduous dentition, but it is most unlikely to be encountered affecting permanent teeth to any extent before adulthood. The cutting edge of incisor and canine teeth is termed the incisal edge. The palatal or lingual crown surface of these teeth is called the cingulum. Premolars and deciduous and permanent molars possess a "biting" or occlusal surface, this surface being divided up into a characteristic pattern by "grooves" (or "fissures"), the raised areas adjacent to the grooves being called cusps.

It is important to remember that after a tooth erupts the enamel is removed from communication with body tissue in the metabolic sense, and from the point of view of this discussion can be regarded as inert and therefore incapable of repair or physiological alteration. Although dentine and cementum can to some extent be repaired by the cells of the pulp and periodontal membrane respectively, and although both tissues, particularly the dentine, continue to be laid down (albeit slowly) throughout life, neither tissue is "labile" in the sense that much of the bone structure is undergoing a continuous ebb and flow of dynamic metabolic exchange. In the metabolic sense teeth are unaffected by the agencies that can cause profound changes in bone, e.g. primary hyperparathyroidism.

TOOTH DEVELOPMENT

For a detailed account of tooth development the reader is referred to one of the many excellent works on this subject.[14] A general account of this process is included here with special emphasis on those features which are significant in the interpretation of intercurrent disturbance or disease. The whole process of development of the dentition takes place during the first 20 years of life and provides a tissue system which may be used to evaluate physiological age. The foundations of the dental apparatus are laid down at the end of the second month of fetal life, and from that time until the roots of the third permanent molars are fully developed, at about the age of 21 years, this apparatus is in a continuous state of change. It is some of these changes, such as root resorption of deciduous teeth, or root growth in permanent teeth, that can be used as markers to estimate age.

It is important to appreciate that enamel is derived from epithelium, and that generalized metabolic, developmental or genetically determined disturbances of ectodermal structures may affect the enamel (e.g. Ectodermal Dysplasia). The dentine and cementum are of mesodermal origin and may be similarly altered in some way during development (e.g. Osteogenesis Imperfecta).

At about the 6th week of intrauterine life a change occurs in the oral mucosa overlying the developing jaws in the region where later the teeth will be situated. This change is characterized by a proliferation of the epithelial cells to form a continuous band in this area, which divides into two as growth proceeds, such that in cross section it resembles an inverted letter V. The outer division eventually leads to the formation of the buccal and labial sulcus which separates the lips and cheeks from the alveolus; the inner division forms the "dental lamina" or "true tooth band" and it is from this structure that the teeth develop. At about the 8th week of fetal life eight localized swellings occur towards the lower edge of the dental lamina in each jaw, at the sites where the deciduous incisors, canine and first molars will develop (Fig. 4). Some weeks later a

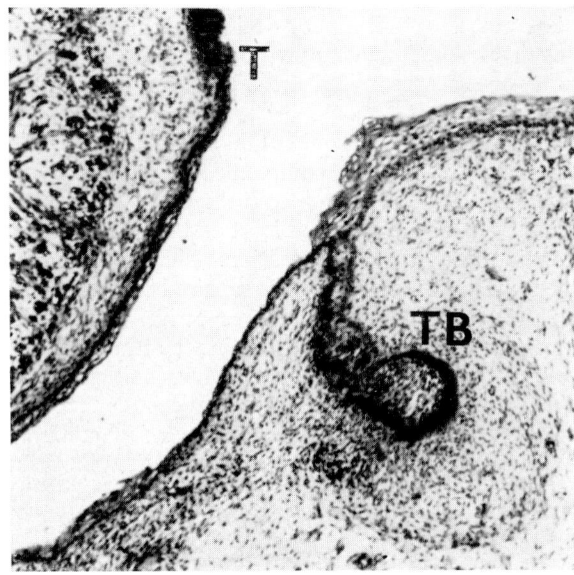

FIG. 4. Coronal section of a deciduous lower molar tooth-germ at the Bud stage of enamel organ development.

Human fetus
T: Tongue
TB: Tooth bud

similar change occurs at the site of the second deciduous molar and then the first permanent molar. These localized areas of epithelial proliferation are referred to as enamel organs. Any indication of the primordial changes which presage the development of the permanent dentition are not evident until a much later stage (the 16th–20th week *in utero*). Continued growth of the epithelium at these sites alters the shape of the epithelial bud such that in longitudinal section it is cap shaped and is known as the Cap Stage of enamel organ development (Fig. 5). From the inception of this phase, progressive changes become apparent in the mesoderm adjacent to the undersurface of the epithelium, manifested by an increase in the density of connective tissue cells in the area. This appears to be an inductive effect by the epithelium, which ultimately leads to the formation of the dental papilla, the name given to the mesodermal element of the toothgerm responsible for the formation of dentine and pulp. From this element the tooth follicle also arises; this is a connective tissue sac surrounding the toothgerm which later has a role in the formation of the supporting tissue of the tooth, to be described below.

Growth along the periphery of the enamel organ alters its shape, making the inner surface deeply concave and enclosing most of the dental papilla. This is known as the Bell Stage in enamel organ development and it is during this period that significant changes occur which will determine the morphology of the tooth crown (Fig. 6). It is

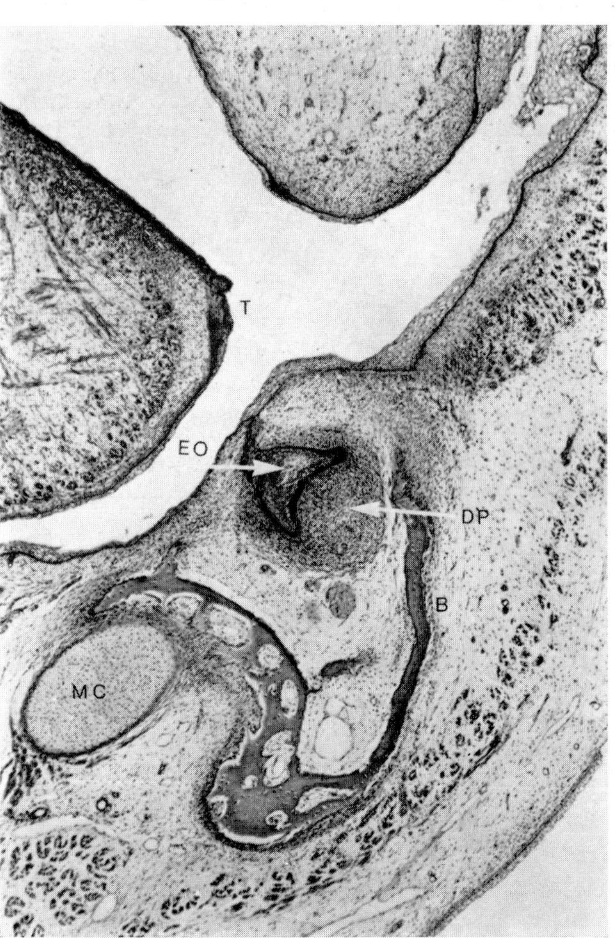

FIG. 5. Coronal section of a human fetal mandible showing $\overline{|D}$ tooth-germ at the Cap stage of development. (×11)

T: Tongue
EO: Enamel organ
DP: Dental papilla
B: Bone of developing mandible
MC: Meckel's cartilage.

believed and there is evidence to support the view, that the inner concave surface of the enamel organ (the inner enamel epithelium) folds as it increases in size, to form the pattern of the toothcrown, by a process of differential mitotic activity (Fig. 7). Another very important function of the inner enamel epithelium is to provide the cells (ameloblasts) which are concerned with enamel formation (Fig. 8). The formation of a tooth of a particular size and morphology at a specific site in the jaw is controlled by the neural crest. A basement membrane is present separating the inner enamel epithelium from the surface of the dental papilla.

This membrane forms the dividing line between the epithelial and connective tissue component of the fully developed and calcified tooth, which at that final stage is termed the amelo-dentinal junction. It will be evident from this observation that to form the enamel matrix, the inner enamel epithelium will have to retreat from the basement membrane in an outwards direction, and the specialized cells on the surface of the dental papilla which participate in dentine formation (the odontoblasts) will have to retreat in an inwards direction (Fig. 9). Initially of course the ameloblast layer and odontoblast layer lie directly adjacent to each other separated only by the basement membrane. The formation of these cells and the commencement of matrix formation follows a definite protocol. The inner enamel epithelium forms the ameloblast layer which then has an inductive effect on the surface cells of the dental papilla to form the odontoblast layer. This layer is the first to form calcified tooth substance—the dentine (Fig. 10). As soon as a small amount of dentine has been laid down and a "foundation" has been formed, then enamel matrix formation commences (Fig. 11). This sequence is followed throughout tooth development, with dentine deposition lying slightly ahead of the other developing tissues. The process of calcification of the dental tissues appears to differ in pattern. In enamel, final calcification of a particular area of matrix does not take place until matrix has been laid down corresponding to the full thickness in that area of the enamel. Matrix formation and subsequent calcification does not occur over the whole crown at once, but commences at the highest point of the developing crown and progresses towards the neck of the tooth, in incremental layers. This is of considerable significance regarding minor isolated episodes of disturbance either of matrix formation or calcification, because such episodes will cause a permanent defect in the tooth structure, and constitute a "marker" of the generalized systemic disturbance at that stage of development. If this is mild it

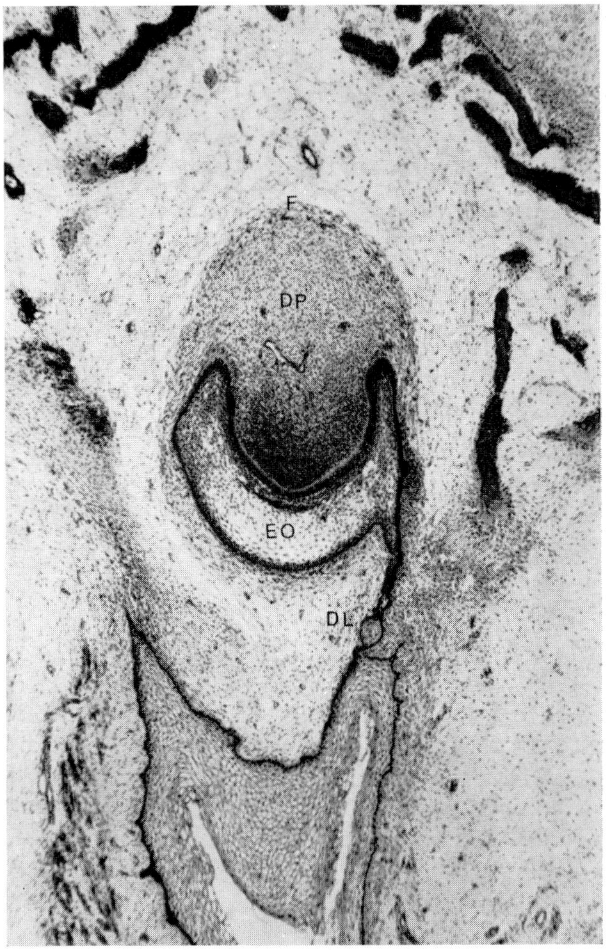

FIG. 6. Coronal section through D/ tooth-germ in a human fetus, where the enamel organ is at the Bell Stage of development. The cells of the dental papilla are densely packed and this structure shows increased vascularity. (×30)

EO: Enamel organ
DP: Dental papilla
F: Developing tooth follicle.

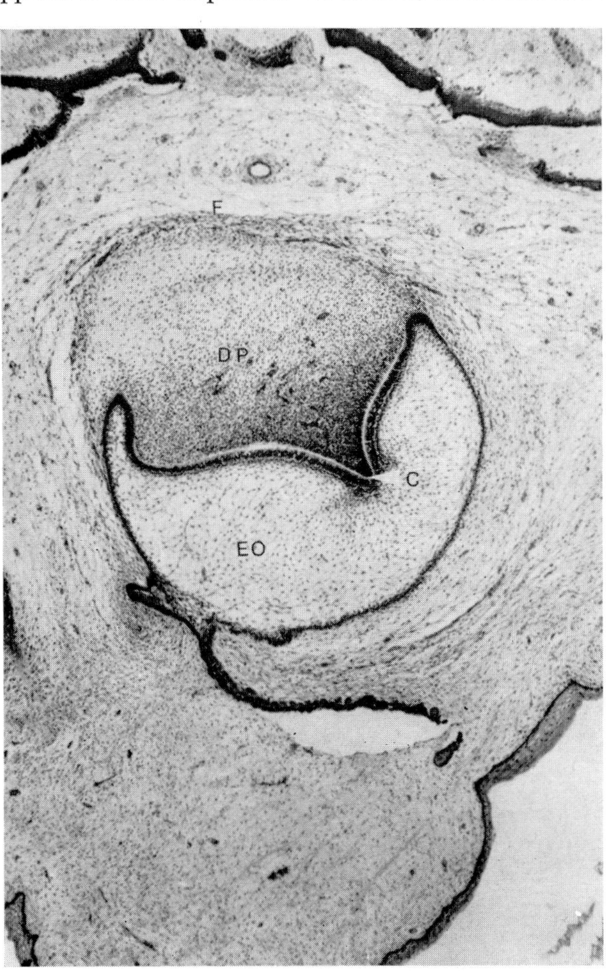

FIG. 7. Coronal section of /E toothgerm in a human fetus. The inner enamel epithelium is folding to form the contour of the tooth surface; in this section a buccal cusp has commenced to form at C. (×60)

EO: Enamel organ
DP: Dental papilla
F: Developing tooth follicle.

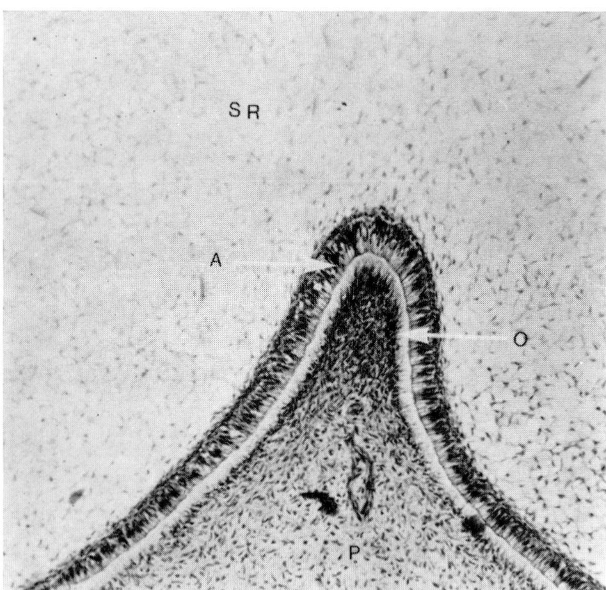

FIG. 8. Section through the tip of a developing molar cusp. At the highest point the columnar ameloblasts are evident (A); the early odontoblasts can be seen opposite (B) whereas in the lower part of the picture these cells are only partly differentiated. (×80)

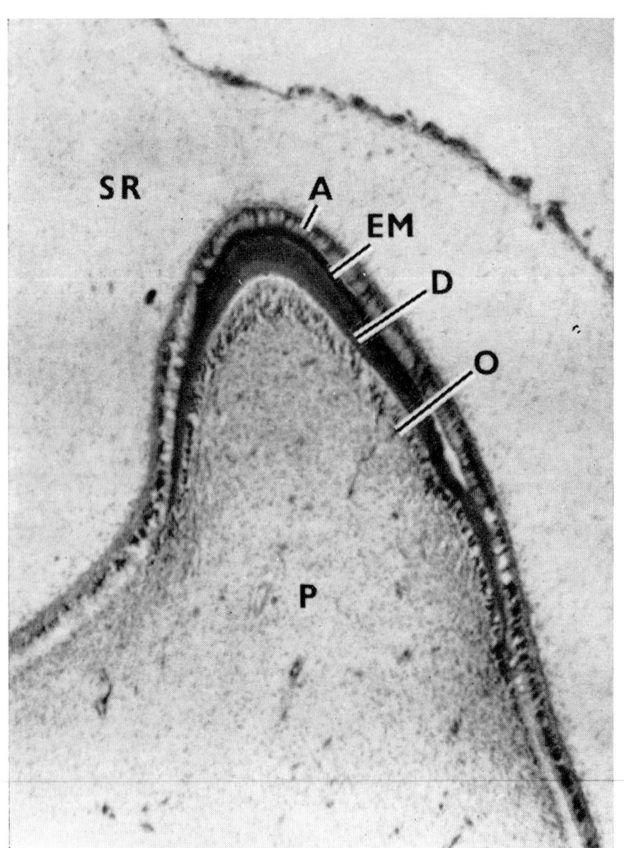

FIG. 9. Section showing the initial formation of enamel matrix at the tip of a molar cusp. (×200)

SR:	Stellate reticulum	D:	Dentine
A:	Ameloblast cells	O:	Odontoblast cells
EM:	Enamel matrix	P:	Dental papilla

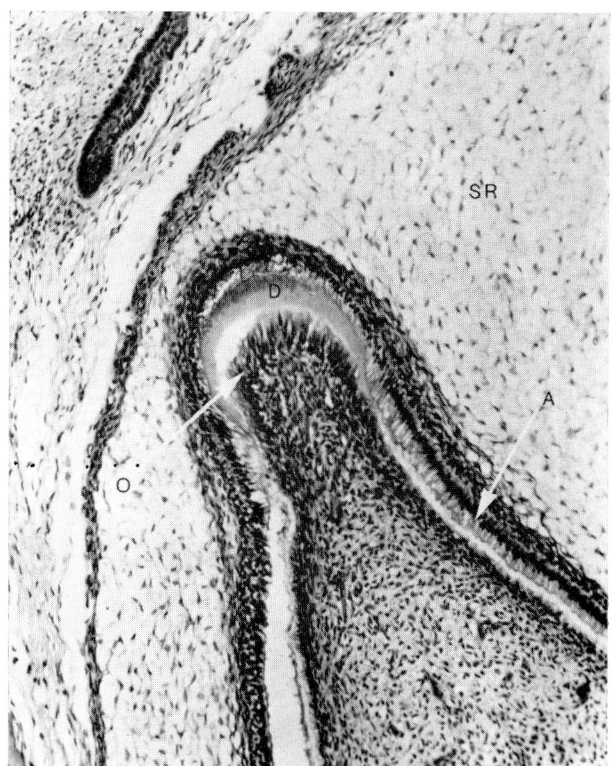

FIG. 10. Coronal section through the tip of a developing molar cusp showing the first layer of dentine (D) being laid down by the odontoblast cells (O). (×150)

A:	Ameloblasts	O:	Odontoblast cells
SR:	Stellate reticulum	D:	Dentine

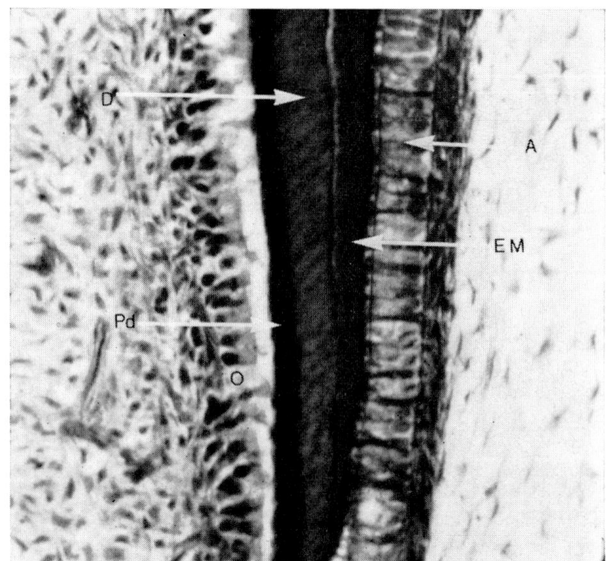

FIG. 11. Section through a developing cusp showing early formation of enamel matrix (EM) laid down on the "foundation" provided by the previously formed first layers of dentine. (×400)

D:	Dentine
PD:	Predentine
O:	Odontoblast cells
A:	Ameloblast cells
EM:	Enamel matrix.

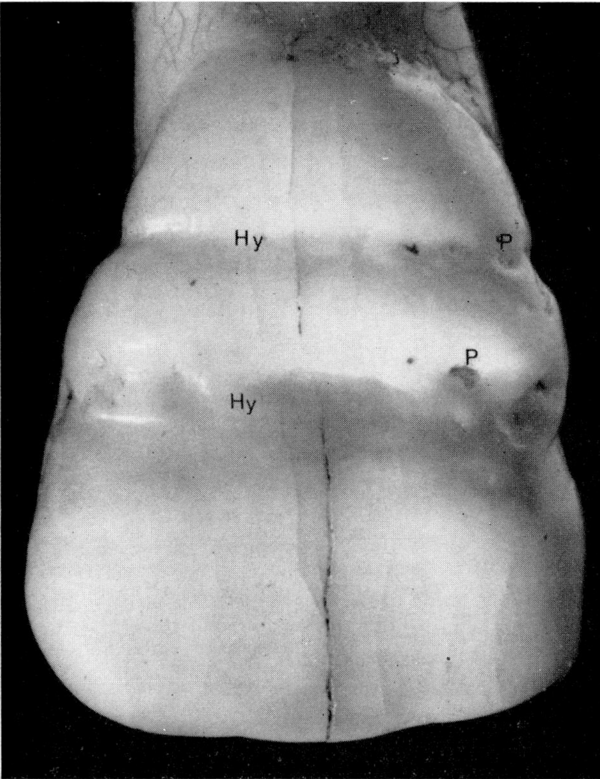

FIG. 12. Macrophotograph of 1/ extracted from a patient who suffered from exanthematous disease at the age of 1½ years and 2 years respectively. On each occason the severe systemic disturbance has resulted in the formation of a hypoplastic band across the crown, which was developing during this period.

Hy: Hypoplastic band
P: Hypoplastic pits

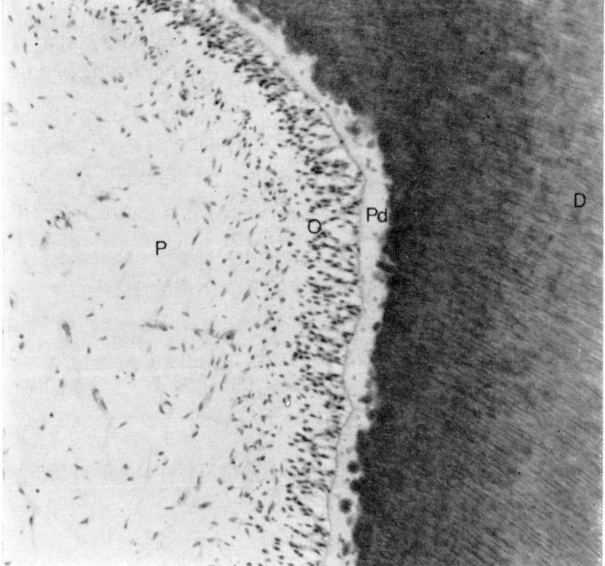

FIG. 13. Section illustrating part of the pulp surface in a fully developed tooth. The pale staining layer of uncalcified predentine is present above the odontoblast layer. (×150)

P: Pulp
O: Odontoblast cells
PD: Predentine
D: Dentine

may only be evident microscopically; if it is severe the defect will be visible clinically (Fig. 12). The pattern of dentine formation is similar, but calcification is different to that of enamel. In this tissue the matrix calcifies shortly after it has been laid down. The thin band of uncalcified matrix above the odontoblast layer is called pre-dentine (Fig. 13).

The dentine is laid down rhythmically in incremental layers, in a similar manner to the enamel. Both tissues

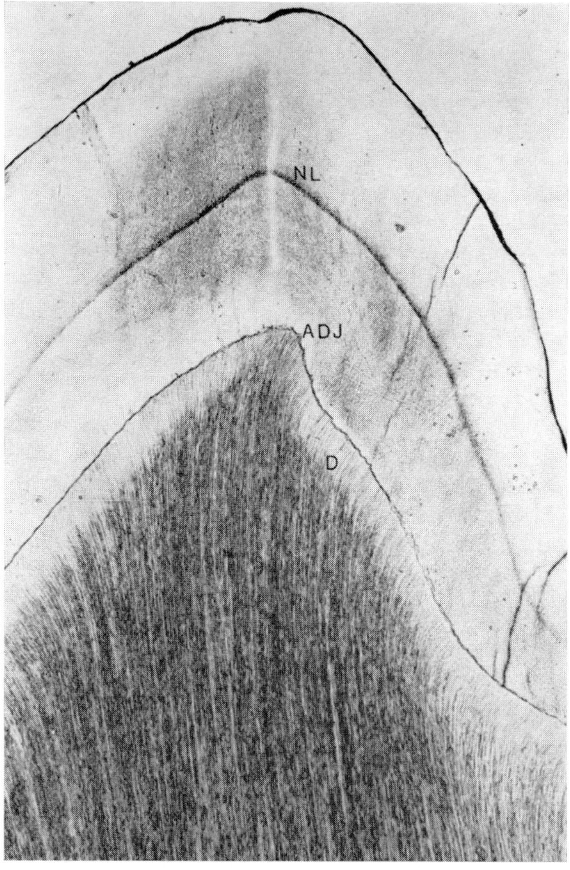

FIG. 14. Longitudinal unstained ground section showing part of the cusp of a lower deciduous molar viewed in transmitted light. The thin dark band (NL) depicts the Neonatal Line.

ADJ: Amelo-dentinal junction
D: Dentine

show incremental bands when ground sections are studied microscopically. At birth, the alteration in the infant's support mechanism causes an exaggerated incremental line to form in both enamel and dentine of the deciduous dentition, this being known as the Neonatal Line (Fig. 14). This represents the dividing line between the part of the tooth formed pre-natally and post-natally. As will be seen later, this Neonatal Line may be significant in the study of neonatal developmental dental abnormalities.

When development of the toothcrown is nearing completion the cells at the rim of the enamel organ proliferate and grow downwards for a short distance into the connective tissue; this extension is known as the "sheath of Hertwig". The function of this structure is to outline the shape of the root or roots. Again this epithelium exerts an inductive influence on the connective tissue to form the dentine of the root. The process of root development takes about 1½–2 years for single rooted teeth and up to 3 years for molar roots to complete. Remnants of the sheath of Hertwig persist in the periodontal membrane as isolated epithelial residues and are sometimes involved in the pathological change, e.g. dental cyst formation.

THE DEVELOPMENT OF THE PERIODONTAL MEMBRANE

The periodontal membrane is the name given to the collagenous ligament which "slings" the erupted tooth in its bony alveolar socket, and allows very limited movement of the tooth within the socket during mastication. In a fully erupted functional tooth the membrane is 0·1–0·33 mm. wide. The collagenous fibres which constitute the membrane are arranged in groups which have an identifiable orientation in relation to the tooth and are termed the Principal Fibres; each group subserves a different function to counteract the various forces which may be applied to a tooth. The fibres between these groups support blood vessels, nerves and lymphatics and are termed "Interstitial Fibres". The periodontal fibres are attached to the root surface by becoming included in the cementum during development; they are attached to the jaw by the thin layer of compact bone which lines the alveolar socket. The membrane develops from the tooth follicle just prior to and during eruption, the fibres of the membrane orientating from the follicular connective tissue cells. The position of a tooth in the jaw is not static and alteration in position occurs under the normal circumstances of development of the dentition and in some abnormal circumstances as well (e.g. the premature loss of a tooth allowing the ajacent teeth to drift towards one another, thus diminishing or even occupying the space previously taken up by a tooth). Consequently the periodontal membrane is not static either and appears well able to adapt to tooth movement in the jaw by the replacement of cells and reattachment of fibres to the tooth by further cementum deposition and bone deposition on the socket wall. Similarly during orthodontic treatment, when a force is applied to a tooth, the unit can be moved without untoward results partly on account of this "plasticity" of the periodontal membrane and supporting bone.

ERUPTION

The mechanism of tooth eruption is not fully understood. It appears to be the result of a combination of different factors, the important considerations being those of changing dimension of the maturing collagen fibrils of the developing periodontal membrane, alveolar bone growth and root growth in the developing tooth. There is good experimental evidence to support the view that certainly a stage in the process is due to the "pull" of the developing periodontal membrane. It will be appreciated that during the period of tooth development, jaw development is proceeding *pari passu* and in the process the tooth is to some extent "carried" to its functional position as a result of bone growth. Finally, it is not difficult to appreciate that the developing (and therefore lengthening) root may also serve to "push" the tooth towards its eruptive position. None of these factors, considered in isolation, provides a satisfactory explanation. For example, although root growth may appear to be the reason, in fact the distance moved by an erupting tooth does not necessarily correspond to the final root length. Approximately ½–¾ of the root has developed when a tooth erupts. Root development does not properly begin until the teeth start their movement towards the mouth cavity.

When the erupting toothcrown nears the surface, the epithelial residuum of the enamel organ covering the enamel (the reduced enamel epithelium) unites with the deep layers of the oral epithelium; this union is of special significance for two reasons. First, the epithelial cells break down over the crown cusp tips at the site of the union and allow a pathway for the final emergence of the tooth into the mouth. In the case of molars not all the cusps may appear at the same time initially, perhaps only one or two being evident clinically at the earliest stage of eruption. (This may allow infection to gain access to the deeper tissues resulting occasionally in pericoronal inflammation around a partly erupted tooth crown). Secondly this union is the initial stage in the development of the attachment of the gum tissue to the tooth surface, ultimately forming the "epithelial attachment" of the "gingival margin" at the neck of the tooth. Once this breaks down, unless treatment is instituted, a creeping destruction of the supporting tissues (periodontal membrane and later alveolar bone) takes place, which is the clinical condition termed pyorrhoea, and one of the commonest reasons for the early extraction of teeth.

PHYSIOLOGICAL TOOTH RESORPTION

The time of normal physiological loss of a deciduous tooth can be viewed in two ways, either in loose relationship to the order of eruption of this dentition or alternatively in relation to the times of eruption or stage of development of the permanent tooth successor to each deciduous tooth; probably the latter is more significant, as will be seen. For example if there is agenesis of the permanent successor, root resorption is delayed, but nevertheless takes place more slowly. Osteoclastic resorption usually commences at the tip of the root on a side which lies adjacent to the permanent successor and frequently when the bone partition between the permanent erupting crown and the deciduous root surface has resorbed the crown follicle impinges directly against the root[5] (Fig. 15). Thus resorption may proceed along a surface and occurs in an irregular pattern. Furthermore the process takes place sporadically such that it may be active in one region of the resorptive area, but quiescent in another. Frequently during the quiescent periods a minor degree of repair takes place, in the form of cementum deposition on the resorbed surface, with concomitant reattachment of periodontal fibres. Clinically this may result in the curious situation where a deciduous tooth may be mobile one day, but a day or two later it appears to have "tightened up" and is firm and non-mobile. Even where the roots have completely disappeared and the crown is a shell on the gum surface, it is remarkable on clinical examination how firmly it is attached. In many teeth the pulp also remains intact within the remaining tooth, or it may undergo fibrosis. Secondary dentine formation (in the absence of pathology such as caries) does not obliterate the residual pulp chamber.

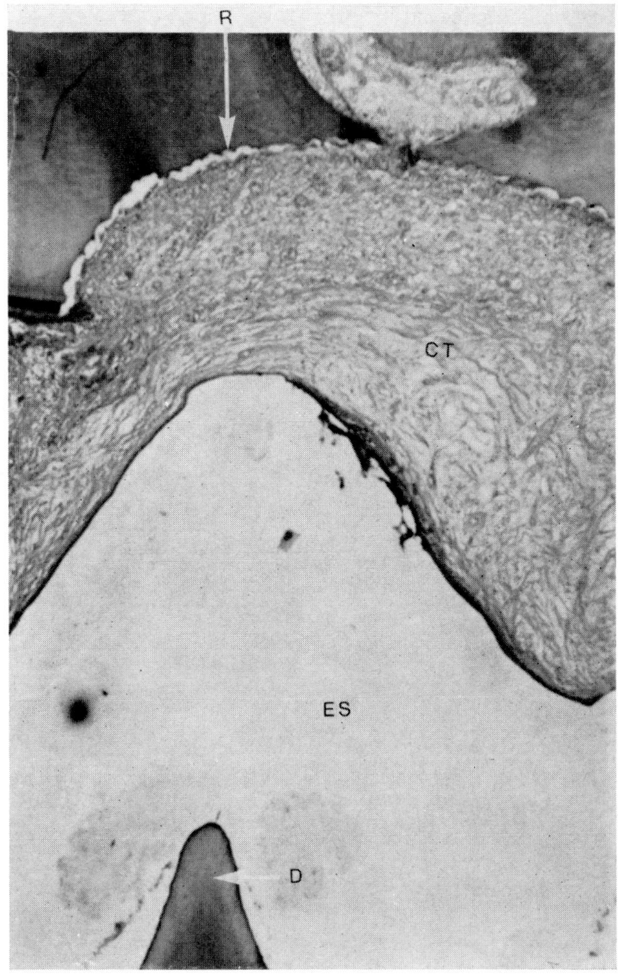

Fig. 15. Section showing resorption (R) of a deciduous molar root caused by the erupting successional premolar tooth. (×100)

ES: Enamel space (The enamel dissolves during preparation of the tissue for sectioning).
D: Dentine
CT: Fibrous connective tissue.

ERUPTION AND EXFOLIATION OF THE DECIDUOUS DENTITION

Surveys of the eruption times of deciduous teeth have yielded somewhat variable results, which emphasises the fact that there is quite marked variation between individuals in this respect. Longitudinal surveys are preferable to cross sectional because they take this factor into account, although of course they take a longer period to complete and more frequent observations have to be made. Data frequently quoted in text-books of dental anatomy is not always based on the results of the most comprehensive surveys available. The average pattern of eruption sequence may be expressed as follows:

	A	B		D	C		E
A			B	D	C	E	

From this simple chart it is evident that usually the first tooth to erupt in the infant's mouth is the lower central incisor, and the last is the upper second molar. The upper central and lateral incisors are usually the second and third teeth to emerge followed by the first molar and then the canine, but there is no general order between the upper and lower jaw concerning these latter two teeth. There is some evidence to indicate that there may be small racial differences in the chronology of eruption.[11] The evidence is conflicting with reference to an overall sex difference (girls' teeth erupting ahead of boys') and between jaws (lower jaw before upper jaw) and in one instance[8] between sides of the mouth (left side before right side). However, having noted these points, it is essential for clinical practice to have a "working chronological chart" based on the available data, bearing in mind the pattern of eruption set out above regarding the actual sequence within the date ranges.

It is generally conceded that a deciduous tooth does not erupt before the age of 4 months and that the deciduous dentition is usually fully functional by about $2\frac{1}{2}$ years of age.

Upper	A	erupts at	7–10 months
	B	erupts at	9–11 months
	D	erupts at	12–16 months
	C	erupts at	16–20 months
	E	erupts at	20–30 months
Lower	A	erupts at	5–7 months
	B	erupts at	10–12 months
	D	erupts at	12–16 months
	C	erupts at	16–20 months
	E	erupts at	20–28 months

Shedding of the deciduous dentition commences about the age of 5 years (5 years in girls and 5 years 6 months in boys).[11] Tooth resorption in the mandible is usually ahead of the maxillary teeth; the process is complete at about $13\frac{3}{4}$–$14\frac{3}{4}$ years.[11] In the absence of extraneous factors (e.g. local inflammation or dental abnormality) deciduous tooth resorption provides a means of establishing physiological age. This process has been studied and carefully catalogued by several observers.[3,12] If the deciduous teeth are not exfoliated at the correct stage, this may influence the time and path of eruption of the permanent successional tooth and lead to malocclusion ultimately.

Nanda[12] studied resorption of the deciduous dentition employing the method of periodic radiographic examinations in 720 Lucknow school-children between the ages of 6 and 12 years, and compared these results to a similar study in American children. The pattern of resorption during this 6-year period is shown in Fig. 16 based on Nanda's findings. The rate of resorption of the dentition is shown in Fig. 17. This data is compared with similar findings in the American studies, and shown in Fig. 18. It will be noted from Fig. 18 that generally speaking the American group were more advanced than their Indian counterparts. Nanda speculates that this discrepancy may result from the fact that the Lucknow sample was derived from a less privileged socio-economic group and suffered lack of proper nutrition, greater frequency of illness and poor health associated with large families, poor housing and a low standard of living.

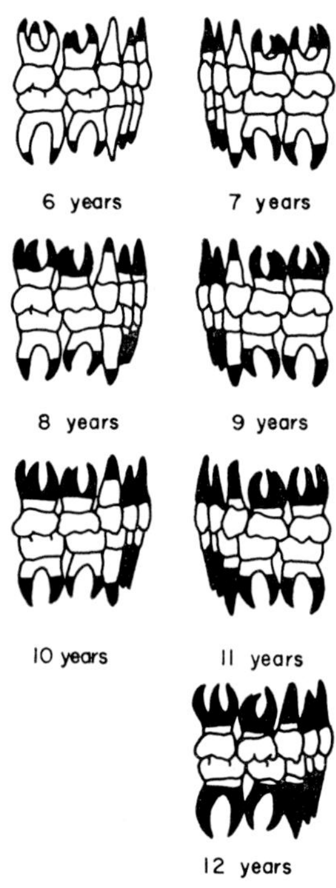

Fig. 16. Diagram illustrating the pattern and progression of root resorption in the deciduous dentition during the age period 6–12 years.[12]

Occasionally a deciduous tooth, particularly a molar, or canine, may be retained in the dental arch for a long period after normally it should have exfoliated. This may ccur for the following reasons:

(1) The successional permanent tooth may have failed to erupt, or has erupted in an abnormal position. This particularly applies to the upper canine tooth.

(2) The successional tooth may fail to develop. This most commonly affects the mandibular second premolar or upper lateral incisor.[4]

(3) Fusion of the partly resorbed deciduous root to the alveolar bone, thus anchoring the tooth to the bone, and referred to as ankylosis. This is usually seen affecting the lower second deciduous molar, and occasionally this may be accompanied by a local retardation of alveolar bone growth. The adjacent alveolar bone continues to grow normally, resulting in a generalized movement of the surrounding dentition, whilst the retained deciduous tooth remains stationary. This causes the occlusal surface of this tooth to lie below the general level of the adjacent teeth. Such a retained deciduous tooth is then referred to as a "submerged" tooth.

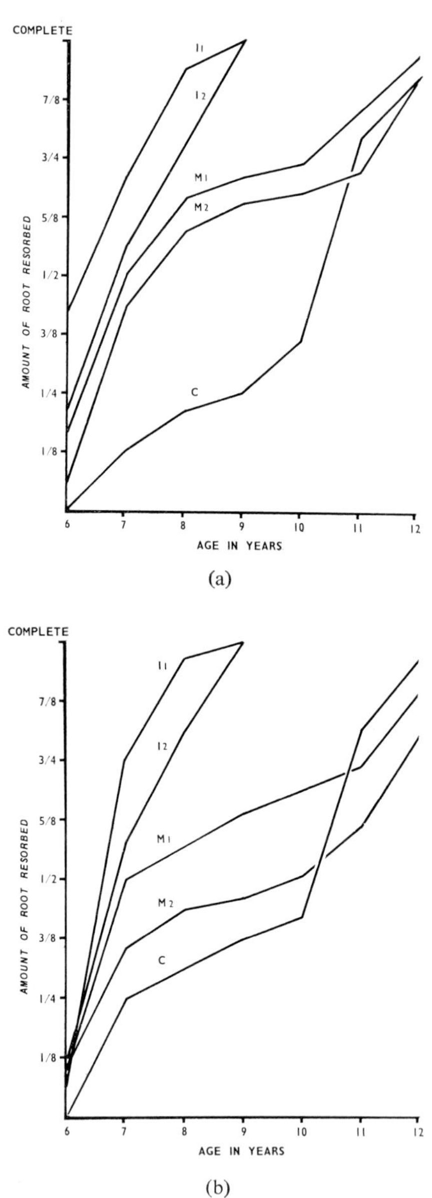

Fig. 17(a) and (b). Rate of root resorption of maxillary deciduous teeth (a) and mandibular deciduous teeth (b).[12]

THE MIXED DENTITION AND ERUPTION OF THE PERMANENT DENTITION

It is important to appreciate that the overall dimensions of the permanent teeth are greater than those of the deciduous dentition. Also there is quite a degree of variation between individuals in these measurements. This means that before eruption and in the absence of genetic imperfections these larger permanent crowns have to be accommodated in the child's jaw, which is of course still

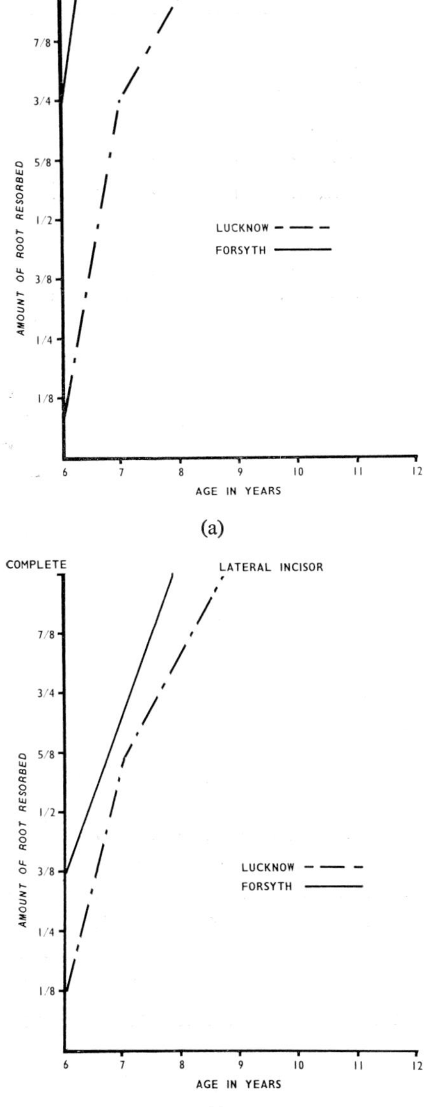

(a)

(c)

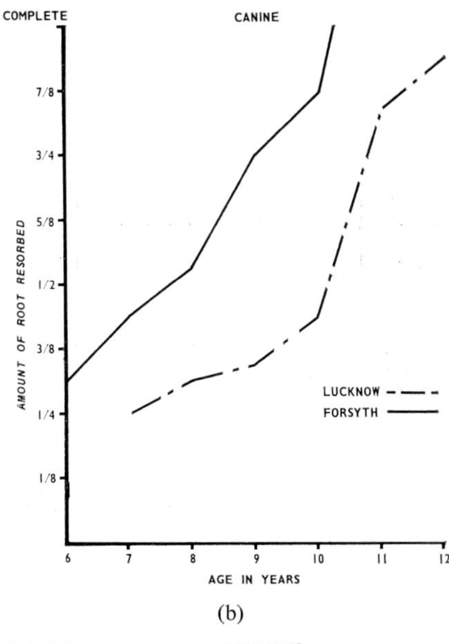

(b)

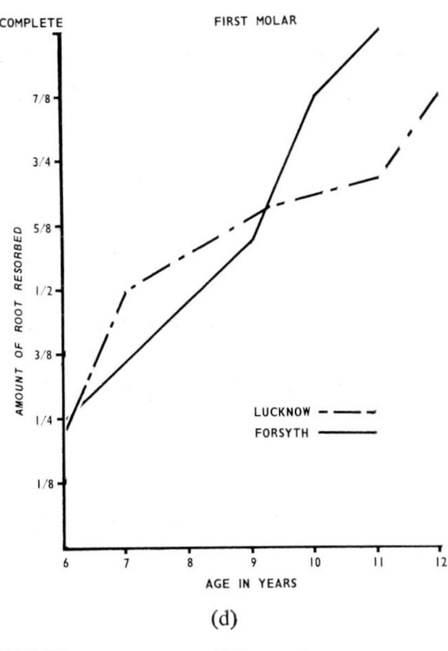

(d)

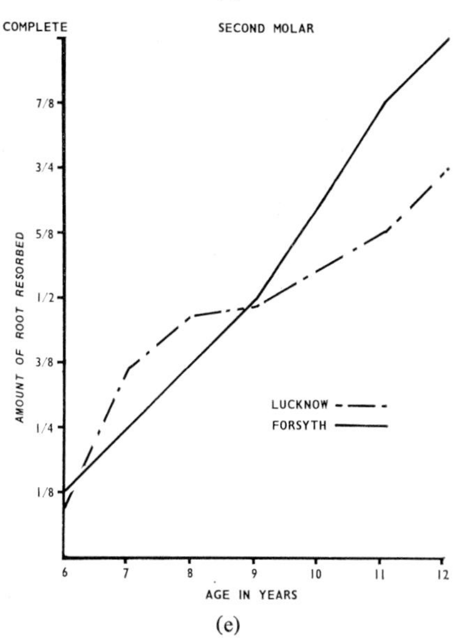

(e)

FIG. 18. Rate of root resorption of deciduous mandibular teeth of children in Lucknow, India, compared with that of children in Boston, U.S.A.[12]

developing and has not reached adult size. The development of the permanent teeth can be summarized as follows:

	Tooth germ formed	*Calcification commences*	*Crown complete*		*Eruption*
Incisors	I.U. life	4–5 years	4–5 years		6–8 years
Canine	7–8 months I.U.	6–7 years	6–7 years	U	11–12 years
				L	9–10 years
Premolars		1½–2½ years	5–7 years		10–12 years
Molar 1	6 months I.U. life	Birth	2½–3 years		6 years
Molar 2	6 months postnatal	2½– 3 years	7–8 years		12 years
Molar 3	6 years postnatal	7–10 years	12–16 years		17–21 years

It is evident from this that the period is variable during which the fully developed crowns remain unerupted. The position of the unerupted permanent teeth alters in relationship to the roots of the erupted deciduous teeth, concomitant with jaw growth. It may be noted clinically that in the infant of about 3 years of age the deciduous teeth lie close together, but later these teeth become spaced due to jaw growth.

The permanent anterior teeth do not erupt directly into the site vacated by the deciduous predecessors, but lie outside the arc of the deciduous dentition. Their path of eruption lies obliquely outwards as well as downwards, such that the incisive edges form the arc of a wider circle than the apices of the roots. The reason for this is the greater width of the permanent teeth in comparison with the deciduous teeth, causing them to require more space. In fact the position may not be straightforward clinically and shortly after eruption the incisors, particularly the lower incisors are imbricated (i.e. they partially overlap each other), often causing the child's parent to seek advice. However as bone growth proceeds and the arc of the jaws increases more space is created and the arrangement of these teeth becomes more orderly, other factors being equal.

To overcome this accommodation problem before they erupt the crowns of the unerupted permanent incisors and canines are imbricated, the lateral incisors in both jaws being more lingually situated than the adjacent teeth. At about 6 years of age the first molars are usually the first permanent teeth to erupt, followed by the lower and then the upper incisors, after which the premolars and canines appear. Just as the deciduous first molar formed a buttress for the erupting deciduous dentition, so the first permanent molars do likewise, which is particularly important during the period when the deciduous anterior teeth are being shed and replaced. Furthermore it is important that the deciduous molars are not lost on account of disease long before the premolar teeth commence to erupt. These deciduous teeth maintain the space between the first permanent molar and the anterior teeth. If the deciduous molars are removed prematurely, the first permanent molar will "drift" anteriorly, causing a reduction in the available space for the premolars so that when they erupt there is insufficient room to accommodate them, and malocclusion and overcrowding results.

The average order of eruption of the permanent teeth can be expressed as follows:

$$\frac{M_1 \quad I_1\ I_2\ / \quad P_1\ P_2\ C \quad M_2\ / \quad M_3}{M_1 \quad I_1\ I_2 \quad /\ C\ P_1\ P_2 \quad M_2 \quad /\ M_3}$$

The vertical lines represent a time interval between the eruption of the groups of teeth so divided, and serve to emphasize that the teeth do not erupt in a steady continuous sequence, but rather there are spurts of activity followed by inactive periods, the lines representing a period of inactivity.

DEVELOPMENTAL DISTURBANCES OF THE TEETH AND DENTITION

Disturbances of tooth development are considered in this section with special reference to their significance in the various processes of normal development. It is interesting to note that comparatively recently a study of developmental enamel disorders provided information towards an understanding of normal enamel calcification. It must be stressed that this section is not intended to be a treatise on developmental abnormalities of teeth.

Hereditary Disturbances in Tooth Development

The different types of genetically determined developmental abnormalities of enamel are usually grouped under the generic heading of Amelogenesis Imperfecta. Basically there are two types. In the first category the enamel appears to be normal in quality, but deficient in quantity (Hereditary Enamel Hypoplasia). This results in teeth having sharp pointed cusps which lack the protection afforded by enamel of normal thickness and leads to excessive wear and a somewhat unsightly appearance. The second type is manifested by enamel which is normal in quantity but poor in quality (Hereditary Enamel Hypocalcification). In this condition the "maturation" or hardening process of developing enamel is disturbed in some way, such that the enamel is soft. As would be expected, it is readily worn away, which again results in an unsightly appearance and also allows considerable and premature dentine wear. It is not unusual in this condition for the teeth to be worn down to gum level. In less severe cases the softened enamel appears to be porous and becomes stained an unsightly brown colour. This condition may affect both the deciduous and permanent dentitions. These conditions support the premise that enamel formation is a two stage process. In the first stage, enamel matrix is laid down accompanied by the deposition of soluble calcium salts; in the second stage (when the full thickness of the enamel matrix has been laid down in a particular area) a "maturation" process takes place whereby organic material is removed, inorganic material is laid down and the enamel becomes hard. In Hereditary Enamel Hypoplasia it appears that matrix formation is deficient but maturation occurs, resulting in a thinned layer of hard enamel, whereas in Enamel Hypocalcification the full thickness of enamel matrix forms, but maturation is defective and the enamel fails to "harden." This group of abnormalities affects the enamel only, the other (connective tissue) components of the tooth develop normally, although there are occasional unconvincing reports of combined ectodermal/mesodermal disturbance.

Hereditary disorder of dentine development is known as Dentinogenesis Imperfecta (sometimes referred to clinically as Hereditary Brown Opalescent Dentine). In this condition the abnormality appears to be due to atrophy of the odontoblasts. The pulp chamber becomes reduced in size and is finally obliterated by a curious calcified structure which lacks dentine tubules and contains cellular inclusions; the roots of these teeth are short and stunted. When this defective dentine is exposed by wear, attrition is more extensive than occurs in normal teeth. Dentinogenesis Imperfecta may either present alone or in association with Osteogenesis Imperfecta, and may involve both the deciduous and permanent dentitions. Presumably the odontoblasts are defective in a manner similar to the defect of the osteoblasts in Osteogenesis Imperfecta.

Downs Syndrome

Johnson *et al.*[6] found prominent arrest lines in ground sections of teeth in 75 per cent of specimens examined from children with Down's syndrome. These lines were present throughout the pre-natal enamel from the commencement of calcification to birth. The neonatal line was wide and deeply pigmented. Similar arrest lines were also prominent during the post-natal period. These microscopic changes in tooth structure indicate a series of recurrent minor disturbances in general growth which are permanently recorded in the enamel and dentine and in a sense may be regarded as exaggerated incremental lines in the same way that the neonatal line is an exaggerated incremental line.

It is pertinent at this point to underline the basic difference between the two groups of hereditary conditions described so far. In Amelogenesis and Dentinogenesis Imperfecta it appears that there is an innate defect of the group of cells concerned with the production of a specific tissue (i.e. enamel or dentine) and consequently all the tissue is defective on this account. However in Downs Syndrome these cells are normal but their function is periodically upset due to a disturbance outside the tooth forming tissues. These latter teeth also serve to illustrate the point made earlier that systemic disturbances which affect the tooth forming tissues result in a permanent chronological record of the event in the tooth structure.

The enamel may also be affected by congenital ectodermal disease, for example, in Epidermolysis Bullosa or Congenital Ichthyosis, although there are few case reports of dental changes in these rare conditions. An apparently puzzling feature in some of these cases is deformity or even absence of roots. When it is remembered that root morphology is outlined by epithelial extensions from the enamel organ (the sheath of Hertwig) which provides the appropriate stimulus to the connective tissue to produce the root dentine, it is readily evident that epithelial abnormalities may affect root formation.

Cerebral Palsy

Both the teeth and the nervous system are derived from the embryonic ectoderm. There are a number of surveys reported which demonstrate a link between cerebral palsy and hypoplasia of the enamel (occasionally there may be dentine involvement). The type of hypoplasia appears to be variable and furthermore this dental abnormality does not invariably accompany such lesions of the nervous system; in fact Pindborg[13] indicates a range between 24 and 54 per cent in a brief review of the reported cases by seven groups of authors (five in the U.S.A., one in Canada and one in Sweden). This type of hypoplasia is characterized by localized bands of thinned enamel around the crown or pitting of the enamel surface; these defects are evident on clinical examination of the teeth. Alternatively tooth morphology may be normal, but in ground sections there may be microscopic defects in the form of exaggerated incremental lines.

One group of Scandinavian investigators[1] suggest that microscopic examination of sectioned teeth from children showing minimal brain dysfunction may be helpful in the differential diagnosis between neurotic and primary organic behaviour disorders. The results indicate that children with minimal brain dysfunction have enamel changes comparable with those of cerebral palsied children. Furthermore the authors state that to some extent it has been possible to estimate the time when the CNS damage occurred by studying the position of the changes in the tooth. Martin Thompson and Castaldi[9] found clinical evidence of enamel defects in one-third of 77 cases of children with cerebral palsy; the teeth were not examined microscopically.

It appears from the position of these lesions that they commence early in pregnancy and the cause appears to be active intermittently and not continuously. The study of ground sections to compute the pre-natal age of the patient at the stages when these hypoplastic defects are present in the tooth may be important in the elucidation of the aetiology of neurological disorders and mental defects.

Neonatal Hypoplasia

This affects the deciduous dentition only with the occasional exception of the first permanent molar. On account of the nature of damage to the enamel in this type of hypoplasia, this may partly fracture off before the paediatrician notices the defect is present. The association that exists between kernicterus in new born infants and the occurrence of enamel hypoplasia and/or pigmentation is well known. The site and severity of the dental changes appears to be related to the circumstance of the underlying systemic condition. The extent of the defect is of course directly related to the stage of development of the teeth and the period during which the systemic disturbance occurred. Usually this means that the incisal region of the deciduous anterior teeth and sometimes the first molar show hypoplasia. Because of the variation in severity of the dental hypoplasia in children with a history of haemorrhagic disease of the newborn Miller & Forrester[10] divided the extent of this hypoplasia into four groups:

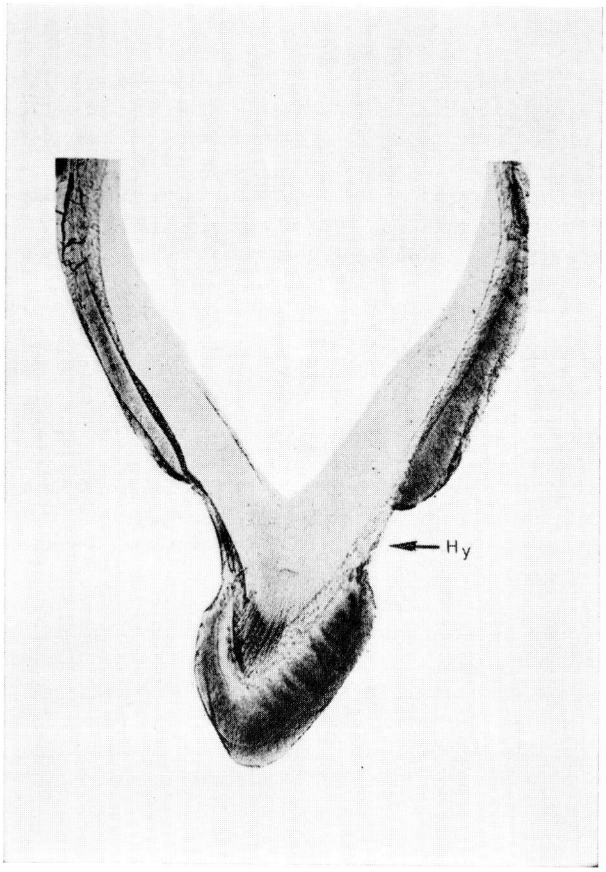

FIG. 19. Longitudinal ground section of a lower deciduous canine showing the deep groove of neonatal hypoplasia.[10] Hy: Hyplastic groove. (×15)

Group 1: Children with normal teeth and no evidence of pigmentation or hypoplasia.

Group 2: Children with intrinsic staining of the dentine without evidence of hypoplasia in the enamel.

Group 3: Children with severe enamel hypoplasia and green staining of the dentine; in addition the dentine shows slight interruption of the dentinal tubules in the area of the green stain.

Group 4: Children with enamel and dentine hypoplasia at the level of neonatal formation but with no pigmentation of the dentine. The last two groups exhibited signs of neurological damage.

Miller observed that where hypoplasia occurs it appears that only those ameloblasts present at the amelodentinal junction at birth were affected and failed to produce normal enamel. Thus the pre-natal enamel and enamel formed subsequent to the infant's recovery was found to be normal; the local failure to form enamel during the neonatal period results in a notch or ring around the toothcrown (Fig. 19). In prematurely born children who suffered kernicterus the hypoplasia was different in character and it was found that the post-natal buccal enamel often broke away at the neonatal line (Fig. 20). Miller suggests that this may be due to a difference in susceptibility of the ameloblasts or the matrix at the two ages, i.e. full term gestation and 7 months' gestation.

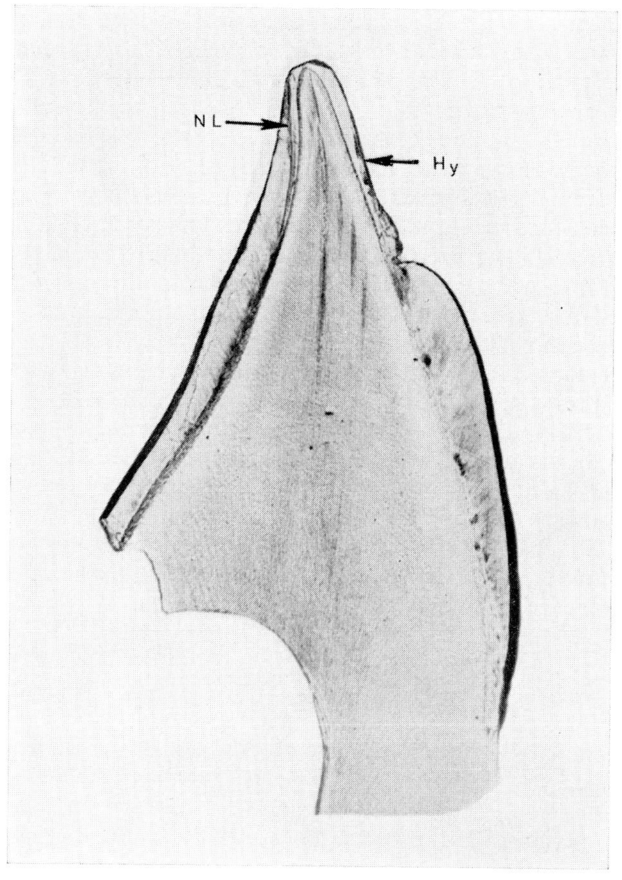

FIG. 20. Longitudinal ground section, lower deciduous lateral incisor, showing enamel hypoplasia in a prematurely born child.[10] (×20)

NL: Neonatal line
Hy: Hypoplastic enamel.

In Miller's Group 2 hypoplasia, where there was intrinsic staining of the dentine without enamel hypoplasia, the green pigmentation varied only in intensity but not in location. Ground sections of these teeth showed the pigment present as a band in the dentine corresponding to the incremental layers formed in the neonatal period. Miller aptly describes the appearance of this band as "a green cap sandwiched between the pre-natal and post-natal dentine". The translucency of the enamel allows the green colour to be seen clinically. In this condition it appears that the severity of the dental changes are roughly proportional to the degree and duration of the jaundice. In mild haemolytic jaundice the level is low and the period transient such that no dental changes occur. Increase in bilirubin level leads to its incorporation in the tooth structure, particularly the dentine (and its subsequent oxidation to biliverdin), causing green pigmentation but no structural

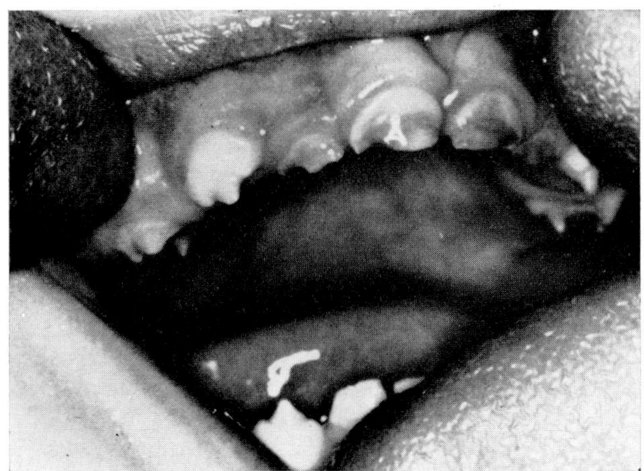

FIG. 21. Neonatal Hypoplasia in a premature child, illustrating hypoplastic grooving of $\frac{C|}{C|}$.

damage. In more severe jaundice enamel formation is disturbed, at the first stage to cause an accentuated neonatal line, but with increased jaundice enamel formation may be temporarily arrested, causing a ringed notch in the crown.

Miller[10] and others have shown that normal premature children may show quite severe enamel hypoplasia clinically. In some instances the post-natal enamel flakes off leaving a marked defect (Fig. 21).

Tetracyclines and Teeth

Since the introduction of tetracycline antibiotics in the 1950's there have been reports of tooth discolouration resulting from the prescription of this group of drugs to children during the period of calcification of both the deciduous and permanent dentition. Tetracycline chelates calcium to form a tetracycline orthophosphate complex which fluoresces in ultra-violet light and in daylight is yellow, grey or brown, depending upon the type of tetracycline prescribed. As tetracycline will cross the placental barrier, administration of the antibiotic during late pregnancy will cause discoloration of the primary dentition even in small doses. The risk of discolouration appears to be highest in children receiving long term continuous prophylaxis or regular courses of the drug. The degree of discoloration appears to be related to the level of dosage per kilogramme body weight, high short term dosage being capable of causing marked clinical discoloration if deposition occurs in the developing crown. Thus the site of deposition and amount of antibiotic in the tooth is important, and thirdly the state of the tetracycline molecule in the tooth is significant (see below). In longitudinal ground sections of pigmented teeth examined in ultra-violet light, the site of deposition of the drug shows as a narrow band of brilliant yellow colouration in the dentine, with chronological correspondence between the stage of tooth formation and the time of dosage. A similar but fainter band may be seen in the enamel; however, generally this fluorescence is more striking in the dentine (similar to that in bone). It has been shown that although rapid uptake of tetracycline occurs in forming enamel, this fluorescence disappears with maturation, except in the cervical enamel. If tetracycline is given over a period of time a series of closely related fluorescent bands will be evident in an incremental pattern, corresponding with continued growth of the tooth. Although there are no detailed reports, mention has been made in some general articles on the subject that where pigmentation was severe deciduous canines and molars had sharp cusps due to "faulty" enamel formation. However it is likely that in fact this hypoplasia was of some other cause than tetracycline administration (e.g. premature birth) and therefore such reports of hypoplasia should be accepted cautiously. The clinical appearance of the discolouration varies according to the type of tetracycline given to the patient; chlortetracycline produces a grey brown tint. Dimethylchlortetracycline, oxytetracycline, clomocycline and tetracycline cause yellow pigmentation. After exposure to sunlight this changes to a brown colour, possibly on account of the formation of an oxidation product. When this forms, ultra violet light fluorescence is considerably reduced. Oxytetracycline or tetracycline are said to cause the least staining and therefore represent the drug of choice from mid-pregnancy to age 7 years, when calcification of the deciduous dentition and anterior permanent teeth is complete.

Fluorosis

All natural drinking water contains a trace of fluoride, and it was first observed about 30 years ago in the United States that up to a certain concentration the level of natural fluoride in drinking water was inversely proportional to the incidence of dental caries. Since that time this observation has been confirmed in many parts of the world, including the British Isles. It has been found that the optimum concentration which will confer protection to the teeth and at the same time allow a substantial margin of safety, is one part of fluoride to one million parts of water (1 p.p.m.) in countries of temperate climate. For maximum protection the water must be drunk from birth, such that the fluoride ion becomes incorporated in the calcified tooth substance. It will be evident of course that there are appreciable quantitative differences in the amount of water consumed by an individual in a warm country as compared with a cold one, and if the bodily concentration of fluoride is high, this may have an effect on the structure of the teeth, as will be seen below.

In simple terms, the inorganic constituent of tooth substance is mainly composed of calcium hydroxyapatite. Substitutions can take place in the apatite structure without altering the characteristic features of this compound, and where F^- ions are available these occupy the OH^- positions, such that calcium fluorapatite is formed

$$Ca_{10}(PO_4)_6(OH)_2 \longrightarrow Ca_{10}(PO_4)_6F_2$$

It is this compound that resists destruction by the carious process. However, excessive fluoride intake can lead to disturbance of normal tooth formation, resulting in the condition known clinically as "dental fluorosis" or "mottled enamel" (the latter term having now fallen into disfavour). Dental fluorosis is characterized by lustreless opaque enamel which may have white or brownish areas or striations and in severe cases the enamel surface may show pitting. Investigation has shown that a fluoride concentration of 1·5 p.p.m. does not alter the appearance of the enamel; where it is more than 6 p.p.m. there are brown bands and opaque areas often accompanied by microscopic enamel surface defects. In areas of higher concentration macroscopic pitting occurs. For reasons which are not understood, the severity of the fluorosis varies between different groups of teeth even though the fluoride concentration of the water is constant. Premolars are the most severely affected followed by second molars, maxillary incisors, canines, first molars and mandibular incisors. The highest natural levels of fluoride are found in the South African Republic (up to 53 p.p.m. F in drinking water) and in Tanzania (up to 45 p.p.m.). Animal experiments demonstrating fluorosis show the ameloblasts react to the fluoride by reducing in height and in severe intoxication there is cystic degeneration of the enamel organ, resulting in structural defects in the fully formed enamel.

Susceptibility to Dental Caries

There is evidence based on extensive animal studies to support the belief that dental caries is a transmissible infectious disease. It is important to emphasize however that this condition is not governed by one factor alone. A small number of the population defy all the factors considered to predispose to dental caries and are inherently immune from the disease, even though they may consume a diet which is soft and rich in fermentable carbohydrate, their standard of oral hygiene is poor, and so on. This complex subject can be considered from three aspects, namely the genetic aspect, the oral environment and the nature of the teeth and their arrangement in the dental arch. Before discussing these factors in more detail it may be useful to first outline briefly the main features of the carious process, as it is understood at present. The enamel is almost wholly inorganic in composition (95 per cent) and decalcification is the main feature of carious attack on this tissue. The acid soluble portion of the sparse organic matrix appears to be significant in the early stages of a developing lesion, to be followed by decalcification. Dentine, on the other hand, contains a higher organic component (about 20 per cent by weight) which means that not only decalcification but proteolysis also takes place. Fermentable carbohydrate in the diet is hydrolysed to form lactic acid by micro-organisms present in a thin dense layer termed "plaque," adherent to the tooth surface; lactic acid is believed to be the principal cariogenic agent. In carious dentine some organisms also produce proteolytic enzymes which digest the already decalcified matrix in the affected area. Expressed in these simple terms, the process appears straightforward, but there are many subtle agencies to consider which have a profound bearing on the incidence of this disease in each individual.

The results of animal experiments and human studies indicate that genetic factors may be significant; these appear mainly to be concerned with inherited characteristics of the teeth. Human twin studies have produced disparate results, although some of these purport to detect significant genetic effects. Racial and ethnic group studies provide some supporting evidence, although for analytical purposes it is very difficult to separate the effects of environment from genetic factors. Based on racial, sibling and twin studies, there is good evidence to show genetic factors influence cusp pattern and crown morphology. The strongest evidence however comes from animal studies, where inbred lines of caries-susceptible and caries-resistant rats have been developed.

Turning now to the oral environment, it has been shown that the bacterial flora of the mouth, the nature and constituents of the diet, and the properties of the saliva have each a significant role and effect on the incidence of caries. Efficient oral hygiene and topical application of fluoride will also influence the process. There is a variation in susceptibility between the teeth themselves in different regions of the same mouth and different surfaces of the same tooth.

Gnotobiotic animals do not develop caries when fed a richly fermentable carbohydrate diet; however when the animal is inoculated, for example, with a streptococcus from another animal, caries will develop. Concerning the diet, there is ample experimental evidence to show the significance of fermentable carbohydrate in producing a high caries incidence, coupled with similarly conclusive group human studies where eating habits could be either accurately observed or accurately controlled. Patients invariably develop extensive caries when the secretion of saliva has diminished (for example where destruction of the salivary glands has followed radiotherapy). The physical nature of the diet is significant, a so-called "detergent" diet being the least likely to encourage caries. Ideally this type of diet is coarse and fibrous, and by its physical nature it does not adhere to the tooth surface and may even "scrub" or cleanse plaque off this surface during mastication. In addition such a diet induces an increased salivary flow. There is evidence which indicates that a rapid flow of saliva and low viscosity saliva tend to be associated with reduced caries incidence. Another factor is the buffering capacity of the saliva, which will tend to neutralize the fall in plaque pH. Thus a well buffered copious saliva of low viscosity will contribute towards modifying caries experience. Saliva contains opsonins and lysozyme, and it has been suggested that the salivary antibacterial activity of caries-free individuals is higher than in the caries-prone. Considering now the actual teeth and their relative arrangement in the dental arch, caries rarely presents on a smooth "self cleansing" surface, and is most likely to occur in a rough or pitted area or a fissure. Where two teeth lie in close contact, the contact area is difficult to clean, thus the plaque and food debris are "sheltered," which allows the caries to proceed with less interference from external agents. At present there is no explanation to the obvious question whether there is a difference in biochemical structure between carious and non-carious teeth. Apart from fluoride concentration, no constituent of enamel is definitely known to be related to caries resistance in man, although considerable research has been carried out on this subject. One of the reasons for this is the difficulty of defining accurately what is a caries susceptible and a caries resistant tooth. Spacing between teeth, where it is sufficiently wide to allow cleansing of the interproximal surface to take place, reduces the possibility of a lesion occurring as compared with areas of contact.

This brief summary of the main considerations in the incidence of dental caries illustrates the multiplicity of factors which are concerned in the process. There is no doubt that if the average child practises a good oral hygiene regimen and the diet is controlled with respect to fermentable carbohydrate, the incidence of caries will be lower than otherwise. This fact is borne out by the situation as it affects the children of members of the dental profession, who have been shown to have a lower caries incidence compared with the general population.[2]

REFERENCES

1. Bergman, G., Bille, B. and Lyttkens, G. (1965), "Tooth Ring Analysis in Minimal Brain Dysfunction," *Lancet*, **i**, 963.
2. Bradford, E. W. and Crabb, H. S. M. (1961), "Carbohydrate Restriction and Caries Incidence," *Brit. dent. J.*, **iii**, 273–279.
3. Fanning, E. (1961), "Longitudinal Study of Tooth Formation and Root Resorption," *N.Z. dent. J.*, **57**, 202–217.
4. Fass, E. N. (1969), "Chronology of Growth of the Human Dentition," *J. Dent. Child.*, **36**, 391–401.
5. Furseth, R. (1960), "Resorption of Deciduous Teeth," *Arch. oral Biol.*, **13**, 417–431.
6. Johnson, N. P., Watson, A. O. and Massler, M. (1965), "Tooth Ring Analysis in Mongolism," *Aust. J. dent.*, **10**, 282–286.
7. Lavelle, C. L. B. (1968), "Comparison of the Deciduous Teeth and Their Permanent Successors," *Dent. Pract.*, **18**, 431–433.
8. Lysell, L., Magnusson, B. and Thilander, B. (1962), "Time and Order of Eruption of Primary Teeth," *Odont. Revy*, **13**, 217–234.
9. Martin, J. K., Thompson, M. W. and Castaldi, C. R. (1960), "A Study of Clinical History, Tooth Enamel and Dermal Patterns of Cerebral Palsy," *Guy's Hosp. Rep.*, **109**, 139–146.
10. Miller, J. and Forrester, R. M. (1959), "Neonatal Enamel Hypoplasia," *Brit. dent. J.*, **106**, 93–104.
11. Nanda, R. S. (1960), "Eruption of Human Teeth," *Amer. J. Orthodont.*, **46**, 363–378.
12. Nanda, R. S. (1969), "Root Resorption of Deciduous Teeth in Indian Children," *Arch. oral Biol.*, **14**, 1021–1030.
13. Pindborg, J. J. (1970), "Disturbances in Tooth Formation: Etiology," in *Pathology of the Dental Hard Tissues*, pp. 175–177. Copenhagen: Munksgaard.
14. Scott, J. H. and Symons, N. B. B. (1971), *Introduction to Dental Anatomy*. Edinburgh and London: Livingstone.

24. CLEFT LIPS AND PALATES

AMBROSE JOLLEYS

INCIDENCE

In Western Europe the incidence is about 1:600 live-births. One-third are confined to the lip (CL), and about one-quarter to the palate (CP) and in the remaining 42 per cent the cleft involves the lip and palate (CLP).

EMBRYOLOGY

The long held concept of the development of the mid-third of the face supposed the formation of three processes of mesoderm covered by ectoderm. They were considered to grow and fuse together with the disappearance of the ectoderm at the lines of fusion, leaving spaces between them which became the oral and nasal cavities. Abnormal clefts resulted if fusion failed to occur.

Recent work has led to the concept of the primary and secondary palates. Development of the primary palate begins in the third week of intra-uterine life. Below the bulging forebrain there is the oral pit, at the bottom of which is the stomodaeum. The cephaled rim of this pit forms a fold of ectoderm into which migrate three processes of mesoderm which then fuse. At the fourth week 2 olfactory pits appear and burrow up and back until they rupture into the naso-oral cavity. Failure of growth of one or more of the mesodermal processes leads to a lack of fusion, and development of the face causes a distraction of the ectoderm which breaks down.

The secondary palate which corresponds to the true palate develops between the seventh and twelth weeks as two shelves of mesoderm covered by ectoderm. At first they hang down on either side of the tongue, and then they swing up and grow together medially above the tongue, fusing together from before backwards.

Clefts of the secondary palate result from failure of this fusion because of insufficient mesoderm or because the tongue remains in the cleft. In some conditions, such as oxycephaly, the width is too great to be bridged.

CLASSIFICATION

The most commonly used classification relates the cleft to the alveolus.

Group I. Pre-alveolar clefts (Harelip only). These may be unilateral, bilateral or rarely median. If incomplete there is a bar of skin across the nostril floor.

Group II. Post-alveolar clefts (Palate only).

Group III. Alveolar clefts. They are usually complete and involve the lip, alveolus and palate.

On the basis of the newer embryological concepts the following classification is also used:

Clefts of the Primary Palate—cleft lip with occasional extension into the alveolus.

Clefts of the Secondary Palate—Palate only.

Clefts of the Primary and Secondary Palates.

Micrognathism

Many post-alveolar clefts are associated with under-development of the mandible and in one-fifth it is bad enough to cause difficulty with breathing which is aggravated by feeding.

Other Anomalies

Apart from the effects of the cleft many other anomalies of various types are seen. Poor mental development is frequent, especially with CPs when it occurs in about 14 per cent. The incidence is higher in cases where there is no family history of similar trouble.

CAUSATION

The literature on the causation of clefts is extensive but confusing, and it is clear that there must be multiple factors. It is necessary to consider separately those cases where the cleft exists as an isolated phenomenon from those in which the cleft is one of many abnormalities.

Genetic Factors

Identifiable chromosomal abnormalities have been found only as part of some general condition, such as Patau's, or Edward's or Down's syndromes.

Family History

On the other hand there is a clear family tendency particularly when the cleft is the sole deformity. It is present in 37 per cent of cases with CLP, and in 19 per cent with CP In surveys of this nature it is clear that CP, which is commoner in females, is genetically different from CLP, which is more common in males.

The pattern suggests that a single gene factor is not involved, except in a few families with CPs accompanied by pits in the lower lip, which are inherited in a dominant manner.

Environmental Factors

The fact remains that there are a great number of clefts without a family history and without another defect. Many teratogenic agents have been shown to cause clefts in experimental animals but they do not appear to play any significant part in humans. The occasional case has been described following steroid treatment or irradiation of the mother.

GROWTH OF THE FACE

Bony growth occurs at the sutures and by sub-periosteal deposition. The main area of growth is in the nasal septum and it pushes the mid-third of the face downwards and forwards. In a unilateral cleft the pre-maxilla is unattached at one side and it must rotate away from the cleft and the nasal septum will bend. In bilateral clefts the whole pre-maxilla becomes anteriorly displaced.

Union of the soft tissue, by operation, moulds the bony segments either in a beneficial or sometimes a harmful way, and care is necessary both in the timing and in the nature of the operation to get the best result.

RHINITIS AND OTITIS MEDIA

Rhinitis is caused by the leakage of food and saliva into the nose. The incidence of otitis media is high and it appears in early infancy in most cases. Persistence results in hearing defects of 10–15 decibels in half the cases and really serious problems in 10–15 per cent of cases. Apart from the rhinitis there is evidence of abnormal function of the Eustachian tube.

SPEECH

Defects in the mechanisms of speech result if the velum is still cleft, too short, too stiff or paralysed. Sound leaks into the nose and results in excessive nasal intonation. Pressure cannot be developed in the mouth and it is impossible to produce certain consonants. Irregularities of the teeth and poor tongue movements interfere with the formation of sibilants.

TREATMENT

Nursing Care

Apart from cases with micrognathos, feeding and breathing do not cause great problems. The least trouble is experienced with CLs, and breast feeding may sometimes be possible. When the palate is cleft, food tends to return down the nose and attacks of coughing and cyanosis may occur, and breast feeding is impossible. Milk must be given slowly using a soft teat with a large hole or a spoon. The baby must be held as erect as possible and winded frequently. Special teats with flanges are also available. It is likely that sucking movements will improve the muscular development of the tongue and lips and the speech. After the feed the mouth and nasal passages are washed out by giving a drink of sterile water. Feeding becomes easier with semi-solids.

Aims of Surgery

The treatment of a harelip is solely to obtain a good cosmetic result, and with a post-alveolar cleft to produce normal speech function. When the cleft is complete the appearance, dental development and occlusion, speech and growth have all to be considered and to a degree there is conflict between these aims, but speech must have priority.

Pre-operative Orthodontic Treatment

Intra-oral appliances may be used for a number of purposes before operation:

(a) Feeding is facilitated by thin appliances worn at the time.

(b) In the treatment of micrognathos.

(c) To reduce the width of the cleft. A plate will reduce the upward pressure of the tongue and will allow the edges of the palatal shelves to grow and also to become more horizontal.

(d) To correct the position of the alveolar segments. They can be designed to bring pressure to bear on selected areas and mould the segments by rotational movements about a vertical axis. The forward growth in the mid-line can also be restrained. To be successful the treatment must be applied during the period of maximum growth in the first 3 months of life. After correction the repair of the lip is facilitated and the results are improved. There is also some evidence that the deciduous dentition and occlusion are better.

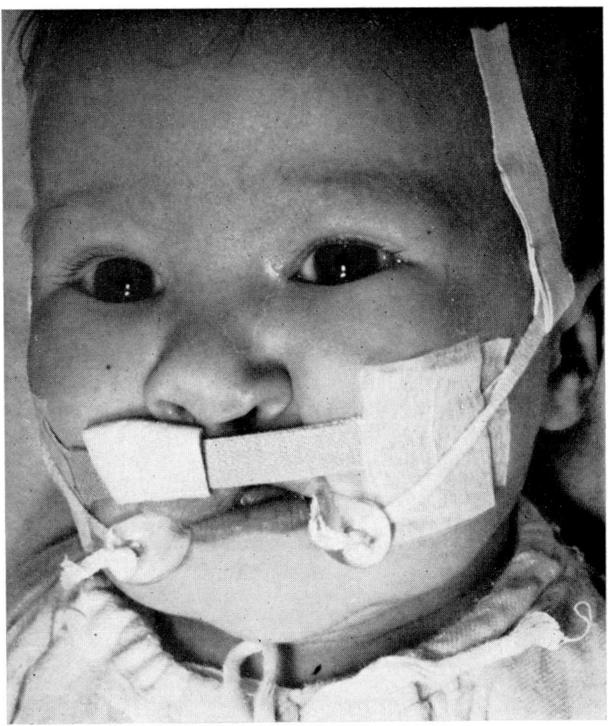

FIG. 1. Child undergoing pre-operative orthodontic treatment with an intra-oral appliance and external pressure provided by elastic strapping.

Surgery

The programming and methods of surgical correction are matters of controversy. It is usual to wait until the baby weighs 4·5 Kgms. and haemolytic streptococci must be eliminated from the nose and mouth. If the cleft is confined to the lip it is repaired at 6 months of age. When it is part of a complete cleft the lip and alveolar gap are closed earlier at about 3 months.

Closure of the lip in the newborn has been tried and abandoned.

Closure of the palate is undertaken by most surgeons before the child begins to talk. It is necessary to incise the edges of the cleft and to make relieving incisions on each side before the cleft can be drawn together. Approximation of the muscular layers is important. As early closure reduces the growth of the mid-third of the face, operation is delayed in some centres until the age of 5–6 years, at which time seven-eights of the growth has occurred.

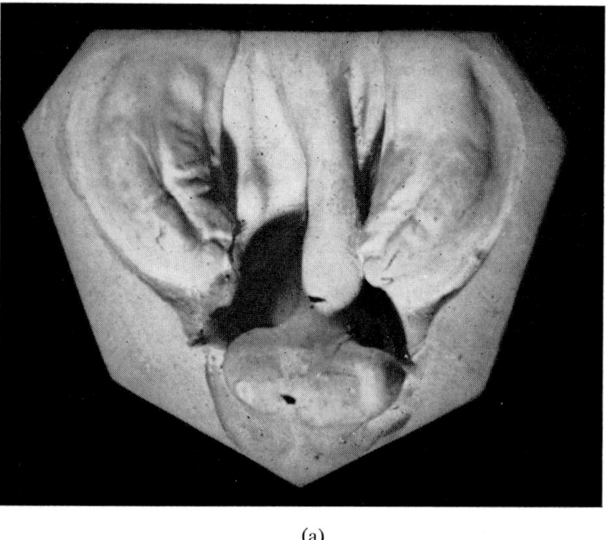

(a)

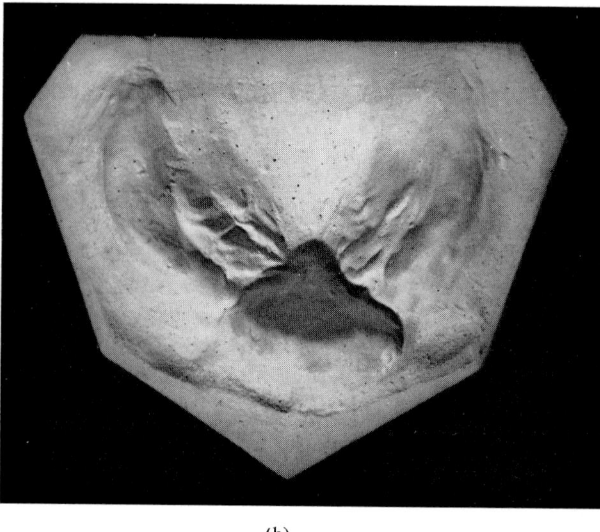

(b)

Fig. 2. Correction of the bony deformity achieved by pre-operative orthodontics. (a) Model of the upper jaw at birth showing the anterior displacement of the premaxilla. (b) At three months of age considerable improvement has been obtained.

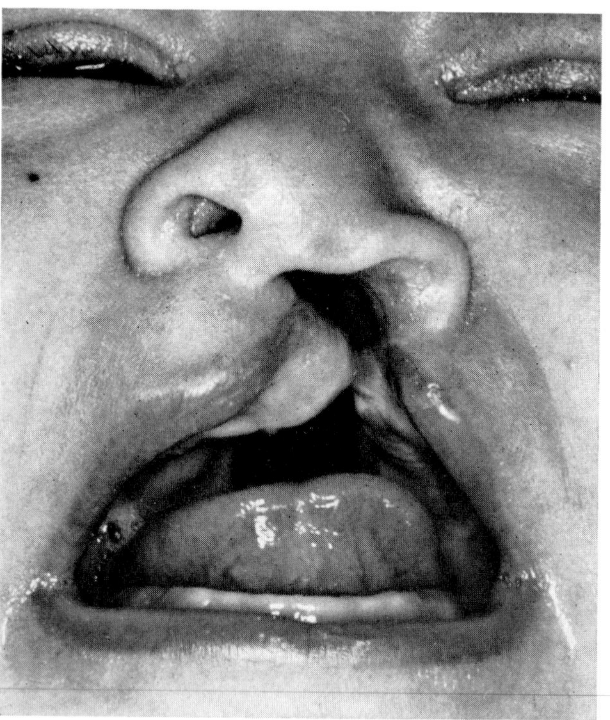

(a)

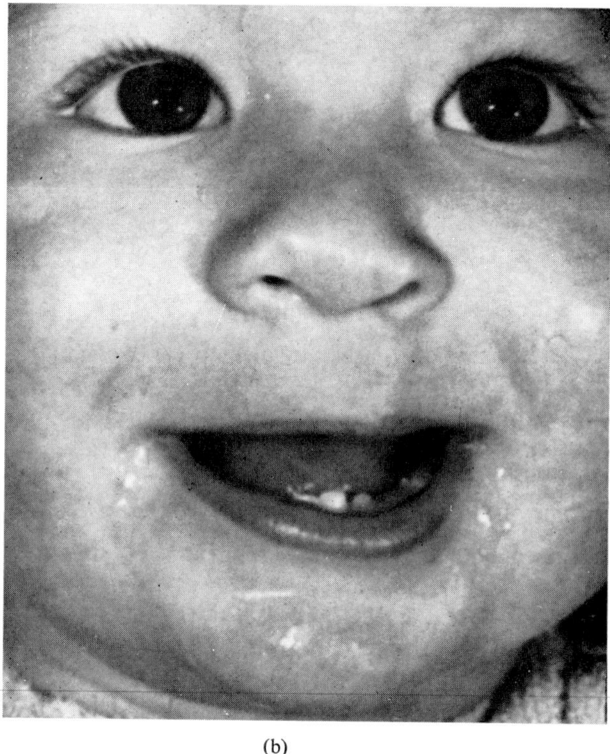

(b)

Fig. 3. Correction produced by the combination of pre-operative orthodontic treatment and operation. (a) The typical deformity of a unilateral complete cleft. The midline is deviated away from the cleft and the premaxilla is tilted. The alar cartilage is concavo-convex. (b) After treatment the midline of the nose and the shape of the cartilage have been corrected.

Bone-grafting

The grafting of bone into the cleft to fill possible deficiencies has always seemed an attractive proposition. It was thought that this would stabilise the arch and growth forces would be more normal. In fact, if it is done in infancy the growth of the jaw is inhibited. Grafting in later childhood does not appear to have any advantages either.

Cleft Palate with Micrognathos

Many of these cases must be nursed in hospital with skilled care and suction apparatus. In most it is advisable to fit a plate to keep the tongue out of the cleft and to use the semi-prone position. Secretions drain out of the mouth readily, and the cleft becomes smaller. Normal feeding stimulates the lower jaw to grow and the baby soon overcomes its difficulties.

In a few severe cases additional treatment is needed, and a great number of methods are advocated.

(a) Surgery to pull the tongue forward and suture it to the lower lip. Simple holding stitches through the tongue pull out in a day or two.

(b) The baby may be nursed entirely prone in a frame which also supports the head. The chin and tongue fall forwards and the saliva runs out of the mouth, giving a freer airway.

(c) Intra-oral appliances can be fashioned so that they not only hold the tongue forwards but also maintain an airway into the hypopharynx.

Airways seem to be the most satisfactory and surgical methods the least satisfactory. Oral feeding tubes or gastrostomies occasionally have to be used.

As the child grows the mandible has an increased growth spurt and the problems disappear over a few months and normal feeding and breathing is attained by 6 months of age.

Pharyngoplasty

In addition to repair of the palate other procedures have been evolved to help close the oropharyngeal space. Some bring forward the posterior wall of the pharynx by plastic techniques or by the insertion of cartilage or some other inert substance behind the wall. Flaps of mucosa can also be placed across the gap. These procedures are no longer undertaken at the same time as the palate repair, but are available for older children if the results are poor. However, the cases must be carefully selected because other factors such as mental retardation contribute to the bad results.

RESULTS

The results can be assessed in a variety of ways, but the speech result is the most important. Its accurate measurement is impossible and different workers have used different criteria and terms.

It is generally agreed that the results following post-alveolar clefts are the best and between 60 and 80 per cent have excellent or easily intelligible speech, with the great majority being quite normal. The poor results are largely accounted for by poor mental development or by severe hearing loss. Fourteen per cent of this group have I.Qs. below 70. The incidence of mentally retarded in the micrognathic group is greater and if this fact is allowed for the results are no worse.

The longer the cleft the worse the result and after CLPs only about 55 per cent have an acceptable result. It is best to begin speech therapy where necessary during the fifth year.

REFERENCES

Burston, W. R. (1958), "The Early Orthodontic Treatment of Cleft Palate Conditions," *Dent. Practitioner*, **9**, 41.

Drillien, C. M., Ingram, T. T. S. and Wilkinson, E. M. (1966), "The Causes and Natural History of Cleft Lip and Palate," Edinburgh: Livingstone.

Fogh-Andersen, P. (1942), "The Inheritance of Harelip and Cleft Palate," Thesis. Copenhagen: Arnold Busck.

Fogh-Andersen, P. (1961), "The Incidence of Cleft Lip and Cleft Palate; Constant or Increasing," *Acta chir. scand.*, **122**, 106.

Fraser, G. R. and Calnan, J. S. (1961), "Cleft Lip and Palate; Seasonal Incidence, Birth Weight, Birth Rank, Sex, Site, Associated Malformations and Parental Age," *Arch. Dis. Childh.*, **36**, 420.

Johanson, B. and Ohlsson, A. (1961), "Bone Grafting and Dental Orthopaedics in Primary and Secondary Cases of Cleft Lip and Palate," *Acta chir. scand.*, **122**, 112.

Jolleys, A. (1966), "Micrognathos," *J. Paed. Surg.*, **1**, 460.

Jolleys, A. and Robertson, N. R. E. (1972), "A Study of the Effects of Early Bone Grafting in Complete Clefts of the Lip and Palate," *Brit. J. plast. Surg.*, **25**, 229.

Kernahan, D. A. and Stark, R. B. (1958), "A New Classification for Cleft Lip and Cleft Palate," *Plast. reconstr. Surg.*, **22**, 435.

Mackeprang, M. and Hay, S. (1972), "Cleft Lip and Palate; A Mortality Study," *Cleft Palate J.*, **9**, 51.

Masters, F. W. *et al.* (1960), "The Prevention and Treatment of Hearing Loss in the Cleft Palate Child," *Plast. reconstr. Surg.*, **25**, 503.

Reidy, J. P. (1960), "Cleft Lips and Palates; A Survey of 370 Cases," *Brit. J. plast. Surg.*, **12**, 215.,

Stark, R. B. (1950), "The Pathogenesis of Harelip and Cleft Palate," *Plast. reconstr. Surg.*, **13**, 20.

Tonbury, G. (1950), "Zum Problem der Gesichtsentwicklung und der Genese der Hesenscharte," *Acta anat.*, **11**, 300.

25. THE FUNCTION AND DEVELOPMENT OF ADIPOSE TISSUE

DAVID HULL

INTRODUCTION

Adipose tissue is one of the last specific tissues to develop. The structure as we know it in man is found only in the higher animals, birds and mammals. Birds and mammals differ from lower species in that they are homeothermic. This association of controlled energy storage and thermoregulation may not be fortuitous, for homeothermy would be difficult without an adequate store of fuel. Energy storage and homeothermy together give higher animals independence over a wide range of climatic conditions.

Although it is one of the last specific tissues to develop, adipose tissue has a relatively simple structure. It is formed of a single cell type set in a rich capillary bed and a generous network of nerves. In the past, its simple structure was one of the factors which tempted biologists into believing that it was inactive. This is far from the truth. The thin rim of cytoplasm around the fat globule is as actively concerned with the exchange of metabolites as the cytoplasm of the lung alveolar or renal tubular cells.

The primary functions of adipose tissue are the formation, storage and supply of fatty acids. Although these processes are obviously interrelated, they are not interdependent. At some sites, adipose tissue is concerned with storage and plays little part in energy exchange, whereas in others it is more actively concerned with energy balance and the supply of fatty acids. For this reason, the two activities of energy homeostasis and energy storage will be considered separately.

There is one form of adipose tissue, brown adipose tissue, which, at least in one stage of its development, does not have as its primary function the storage and supply of fatty acids. It has the specific function of producing heat to maintain thermal stability. In this tissue the two functions of energy homeostasis and homeothermy are closely linked. Thermogenic brown adipose tissue is not found in all mammals and it plays little part in thermoregulation in the adult of most species. However, in many newborn mammals particularly those with poor muscle development at birth, thermogenesis in brown adipose tissue is of major importance. These species include mice, rats, rabbits, lambs and man. It had been noted that the newborn of these species rarely shivered but that they had a good thermogenic response to cold exposure. It was the search for the site of this non-shivering thermogenesis that led to the discovery of the thermogenic role of adipose tissue.

I. THERMOGENESIS

The Distinct Characteristics of Brown Adipose Tissue

At the beginning of this century morphologists argued about the origin of adipose tissue. One group held that non-specific fibroblasts stored fat and thus formed adipose tissue in the presence of excess fat. The other held that only specific adipose cells had this capacity. Recently, the latter view has become generally accepted (for review *see* Wasserman, 1965).[97] In contrast it has long been appreciated that multilocular or brown adipose tissue has distinct developmental and morphological characteristics.[94] In the literature this form of adipose tissue has been described under many names.[1] For example, it has been called the intrascapular gland, for the lobes in the intrascapular region are the most obvious in many species but this is not so in man. The comparative anatomy has been extensively reviewed.[83] It has been called the hibernating gland for it is prominent in hibernating animals and it is, in fact, an important site of heat production during arousal. It has been called glandular adipose tissue for its microscopic structure resembles other endocrine glands. So far, attempts to extract active agents have failed, nevertheless this possibility is still being seriously considered.[52] It has also been called primitive or embryonal fat because it resembles one of the phases through which white adipose tissue passes during development.

Confusion arose because of its name "multilocular fat". In many states, and especially when brown adipose issue is playing its thermogenic role, it can be distinguished from white adipose tissue by light microscopy (Fig. 1). Characteristically each cell contains many fat vacuoles and the numerous large mitochondria give the cytoplasm a granular appearance. In contrast, white adipose tissue has a signet ring appearance with one large central vacuole. However, during its development white adipose tissue also may pass through a multilocular phase[88] though at this time the developing white adipocyte is much smaller than the mature multilocular brown adipose cell. When the plane of nutrition is high and the call for thermogenesis is low the fat vacuoles in brown adipose tissue increase in size and decrease in number until one large vacuole is formed and the cell has the signet ring appearance similar to that of a white adipose cell.

FIG. 1. Diagrammatic representation of the histological appearance of the cells of brown and white adipose tissue in an early stage in development and, in the mature form, when replete and when relatively depleted of fat.

The difference seen with light microscopy are more evident on electron microscopic examination (Fig. 2). The large complex mitochondria can easily be seen filling the cytoplasm in close proximity to the fat vacuoles.[56,7]

Another feature which distinguishes white from brown adipose tissue is its anatomical distribution. Brown adipose tissue is found only in certain sites. The main deposits are found around the arteries in the neck, with fingers of tissue extending through the thoracic inlet into the mediastinum and below the clavicles into the axilla (Fig. 3). In the thorax, thin strips of tissue spread out with the intercostal vessels and the internal mammary arteries. Further islands of tissue may be found in the posterior peritoneum and around the kidneys.[26] In many species there are also prominent and distinct lobes of brown adipose tissue in the interscapular region of the back. In man, such lobes can be seen below the more familiar white adipose tissue but they are by no means prominent and form only a small percentage of total mass. Nevertheless, by virtue of their unusual venous drainage they may have a special role to play.[92,3]

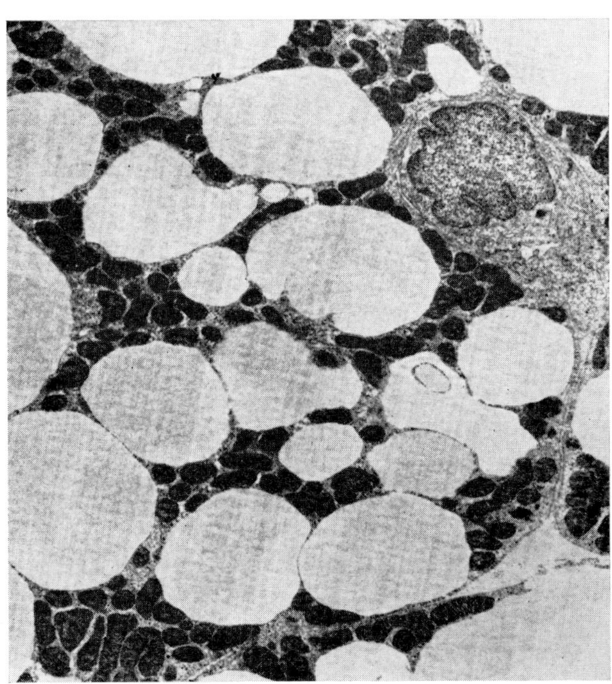

FIG. 2. An electron micrograph of brown adipocyte showing the numerous large complex mitochondria around fat vacuoles. (×3,900)

The third feature which distinguishes brown from white adipose tissue is its function. Only brown adipose tissue

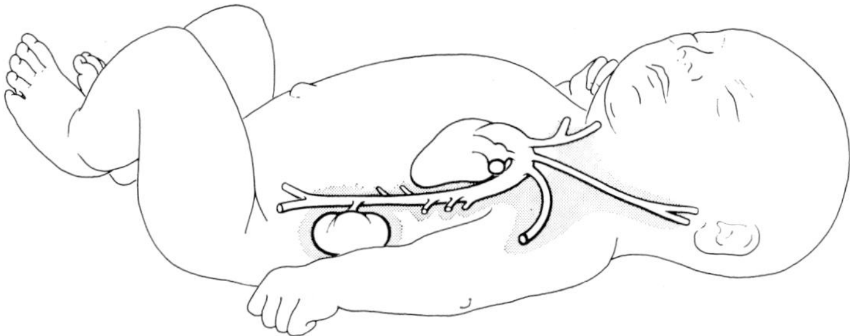

FIG. 3. An illustration of the distribution of brown adipose tissue around the major arteries.

has the capacity to produce extra heat in response to cold exposure. In every situation where brown adipose tissue has been found and investigated it has been shown to do so. White adipose tissue, like all living tissue, releases heat as a by-product of its metabolic activity, but it has not been shown specifically to release extra heat in response to cold. There can be no doubt that in certain species, including man, a thick layer of subcutaneous fat adds to the thermal insulation but fat it not a particular good insulator. Fur is far better. Thus, although white adipose tissue may have some features of an electric blanket its properties in this regard are an inevitable secondary consequence of its anatomical distribution and biochemical activity. Neither adjusts either acute or prolonged cold exposure to assist in thermoregulation. Indeed in certain circumstances these properties of white adipose tissue may be undesirable.

The Demonstration of Thermogenesis in Brown Adipose Tissue

The observations that brown adipose tissue had a high metabolic rate *in vitro* and that it hypertrophied during prolonged cold exposure led Smith in 1961[90] to postulate that it might be an organ of heat production. This was demonstrated by placing thermocouples over the tissue and comparing its temperature with rectal temperature in hibernating animals during arousal from hibernation,[89,91] and newborn rabbits[26] and later adult rats[30] and newborn infants during cold exposure.[87] Differential tissue temperatures do not necessarily indicate that thermogenesis is a specific biological function of the hotter tissue. The effects of surgical excision of brown adipose tissue and the direct measurements of tissue blood flows provided further supporting evidence in animals;[57,46] whilst in man the finding of fat depleted brown adipose tissue in infants dying of cold injury gave strong support for the view that brown adipose tissue was important in man as well as animals.[3] Subsequently, many investigations have confirmed that brown adipose tissue is an organ of heat production.[36,79,84]

The Characteristics of the Heat Organ

It is fascinating to compare this biological system of heat production with domestic oil-fired central heating. Oil-fired central heating requires a regular external source of fuel, a local storage unit, and a boiler in which the burners and the transmission medium (in most domestic systems this is water which may be under high or low pressure) are brought together. Ignition is electrically controlled and the time the burners are "on" is determined by the temperatures recorded by thermostats in different parts of the building, and in the flow line of the transmission medium. Simple on-off systems are commonly employed, the *rates* of heat production are not adjusted to thermal requirements. The thermal capacity of the boiler is chosen to meet thermal needs of the building.

In the body's oil-fired central heating, the external source of fuel is fat and carbohydrate in food. The local storage units of fuel are the many fat vacuoles within each cell, the burners are the numerous mitochondria which surround each vacuole. Instead of a single boiler, the biological central heating has many thousands of small boilers which lag the pipes carrying the transmission medium, blood. Ignition is induced by noradrenaline released at the sympathetic nerve endings and the sympathetic nerves also carry the efferent arm of the body's thermostatic control. However, not only can the body switch on extra heat production it can also adjust the rate of heat production according to requirements.

The Fuel Supply

The fat stored in brown adipose tissue has a similar fatty acid constitution to triglyceride stored at other sites. Before triglyceride can be metabolized in any cell, whether it is the liver, muscle, brown or white adipose tissue, it must be hydrolysed into its constituent parts of fatty acid and glycerol (Fig. 4). The glycerol is released from the white adipose tissue cell for the cytoplasm does not contain the enzyme glycerol-kinase which is necessary to convert glycerol to α-glycerol phosphate which is an essential step if glycerol is to be re-used for esterification of fatty acid. The position with respect to brown adipose tissue is not clear. Glycerol-kinase has been found in the brown adipose tissue of adult animals[25] but is has proved difficult to demonstrate significant activity, although it is present, in brown adipose tissue of newborn mammals immediately after birth.[26,64] Its presence does not appear to be essential for thermogenesis. However, brown adipose tissue of newborn rabbits appears to have some other way of utilizing glycerol.[40] Liver cells, rich in glycerol-kinase, quickly convert glycerol to glucose. The many fat vacuoles within each cell present a large surface area to the mitochondria and this structural arrangement may be important. However, it is not essential for the tissue can continue to produce heat when depleted of fat by drawing fatty acids from the circulation.[40]

Even when the tissue is full of fat and in the fasting state, it continues to draw glucose from the circulation and the rate of uptake increases with the rate of heat production. This uptake is relatively more important when the tissue is depleted of fat. It may be that a small supply of glucose is required for the heat production from fatty acids. Glucose alone appears unable to support thermogenesis.[39]

The Burners

All cells derive most of their energy from biological oxidation within mitochondria. The mitochondria in brown adipose tissue are unique for they release chemical energy directly as heat. How do they do this?

There is no reason to believe that fatty acid oxidation follows a different pathway in the brown adipocyte from that in any other cell. The fatty acids are first "activated" to acyl CoA and then carbon molecules are broken off in pairs to form acetyl CoA. This process, called β-oxidation, involves a complex of enzymes which are structurally related in the mitochondria to the enzymes of the respiratory chain. The acetyl CoA enters the citric acid cycle for further oxidation to CO_2.

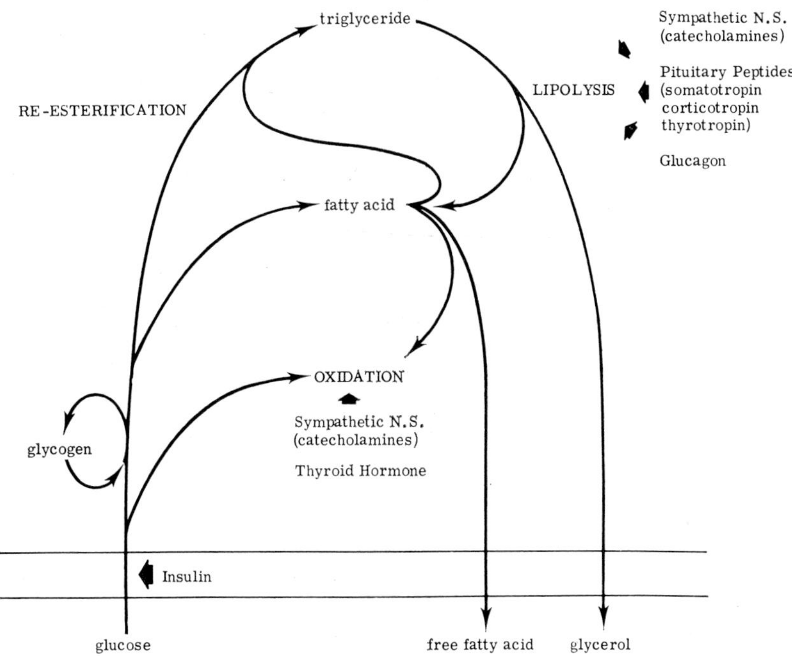

FIG. 4. Some important metabolic pathways in the adipose cell.

In mitochondria the elaborate structured series of respiratory enzymes, nicotinamide dehydrogenases, flavoproteins, cytochromes, etc., ensure that the chemical energy released by oxidation of food is captured in high energy phosphate linkages. This process of coupled oxidative phosphorylation is highly efficient compared to most man-made systems of energy transfer. Nevertheless, there is inevitably some loss of energy as heat. The high-energy linkages provide the energy which drives the cell's vital activities: muscle contraction, active transport, nervous excitation, growth, etc. When the body is at rest, all the chemical energy derived from the catabolism of food, which is initially converted to high energy linkages and then released to drive biological systems, is finally lost as heat. For this reason, the total body oxygen consumption at rest can be related to total body heat production.

Theoretically, the burners in the brown adipose cell could release chemical energy as heat by using linked high-energy phosphate bonds produced by coupled oxidative phosphorylation to drive biologically useless cycles of chemical changes. For example, it could be used for the continuous break-down and resynthesis of triglyceride. This mechanism was one of those originally suggested, but subsequent studies have failed to demonstrate a high rate of triglyceride re-sterification during thermogenesis.[66,64] Another possibility is that in some way the process of oxidative phosphorylation is uncoupled and therefore highly inefficient.[79] Various hormones, i.e. thyroxin, as well as drugs are known to effect uncoupling. It has been shown that fatty acids may act in this way. Therefore it has been postulated that the intracellular release of fatty acids leads to uncoupling and initiates the thermogenic process.[79] It is as well that they do not have this action in other cells of the body! This is a facet of cell biology of great theoretical interest which awaits further clarification.

Transmission

The transmission medium for the body's oil-fired central heating is blood. The individual boilers are located deep within the body around the central arteries. This ensures that the blood leaving the heart is warmed as it passes to the periphery, particularly to the head. In engineering terms, it is a "medium pressure" system!

However, the body also had a "low pressure" system for the unusual venous drainage from the interscapular pads that passes via the external to the internal posterior vertebral venous plexuses and then to the internal and external enterior vertebral venous plexuses before entering the azygos veins within the thorax (Fig. 5). This system will have the effect of keeping the vital centre in the upper spinal cord warm in cold environmental conditioning.[92,3]

In domestic central heating the boilers burn at high temperatures. Brown adipose tissue temperatures rarely rise more than one or two degrees above those of the other internal organs of the body. This is due to the cooling influence of its exceptional vascular bed. Each cell appears to be surrounded by a network of capillaries. In the newborn rabbit, and probably also the human infant, when the tissue produces heat it takes a considerable portion of the cardiac output.[46] Its blood supply expressed per gram tissue exceeds by far that of white adipose tissue or indeed of any other major organ of the body. One of the effects of this considerable circulation is that the heat the tissue produces is rapidly carried away. To produce heat, the tissue requires a large supply of oxygen. Whether it is the tissues' need of oxygen or whether it is a need to keep the tissue cool or a combination of both, which determines the local tissue blood flow remains to be defined.

The control of the blood supply to brown adipose tissue is all the more fascinating in the light of recent

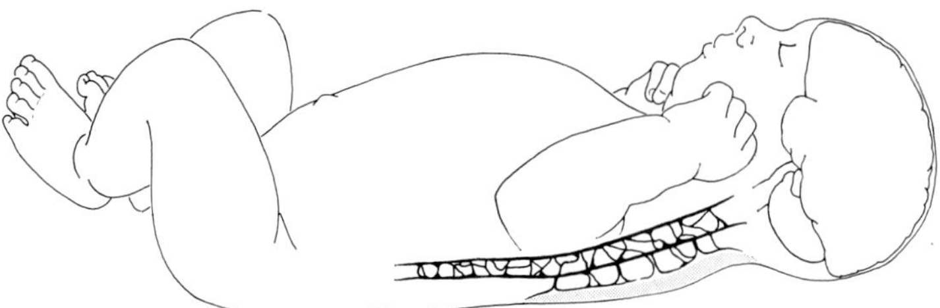

FIG. 5. An illustration of the unusual venous drainage of the interscapular pads of brown adipose tissue. This arrangement ensures that the vital nerve centres in the upper spinal cord will be kept preferentially warm in cold conditions.

morphological studies[128] demonstrating that the sympathetic nerve supply to the vessels is distinct from that of the cells. The latter are innervated by short post-ganglionic fibres arising from peripheral ganglion in the tissue.

Control of Thermogenesis

Non-shivering heat production is rapidly and delicately adjusted to ambient and body temperatures. This in itself suggests that it is under nervous control. Animal studies have demonstrated that the efferent impulses from the thermoregulatory centres pass via the sympathetic nervous systems.[59,26] These impulses release noradrenaline from the nerve-endings around the cells and the noradrenaline in turn initiates thermogenesis (Fig. 6).

The efferent channel of thermoregulation is different in the newborn from that in adults. In the latter shivering is considered to be the main source of thermoregulatory heat. It would be instructive to know more about the central adjustments with aging as shivering thermogenesis becomes of increasing importance.[17]

Ignition

Various lipolytic hormones as well as noradrenaline, initiate thermogenesis. They all activate cyclic adenosine monophosphate which in turn is known to induce intracellular lipase activity. Tissue lipases in turn stimulate hydrolysis of triglyceride, releasing fatty acid and glycerol into the intracellular compartment (Fig. 4). Fatty acids, by their uncoupling effect, may lead to more heat production and may well accelerate oxidation but the extent to which they are able to do this is uncertain.

Studies on brown adipose tissue depleted of fat have shown noradrenaline to be equally effective in inducing thermogenesis in tissue without triglyceride stores.[40] Here the initial process cannot be intracellular hydrolysis. Noradrenaline in some way can directly initiate oxidation. This is consistent with the observation that not all lipolytic agents stimulate thermogenesis,[23] and the fact that the rate of fatty acid and glycerol release can vary independently of the rate of thermogenesis.[40]

Thermal Requirements and Thermal Capacity

Many investigators over the last few years, following the pioneering studies of Brück,[16] have documented the thermal *capacity* of infants of different gestations and at different ages.[47] Others have investigated the effects of disease on thermal control. Of equal interest and importance is the excellent series of studies by Day in the 1940s[27] and Hey and his co-workers[48] more recently which have established the thermal *requirements* of infants of different ages and body weights under different environmental conditions. They have evaluated the effects of nursing infants in incubators,[50] of varying thermal insulation with clothing,[51] and the cooling effects of exchange transfusions as performed under the current clinical circumstances.[49] Ample data is now available to calculate the "thermal capacity" requirements of healthy and sick infants.

A healthy 3 kg infant can probably increase his metabolic

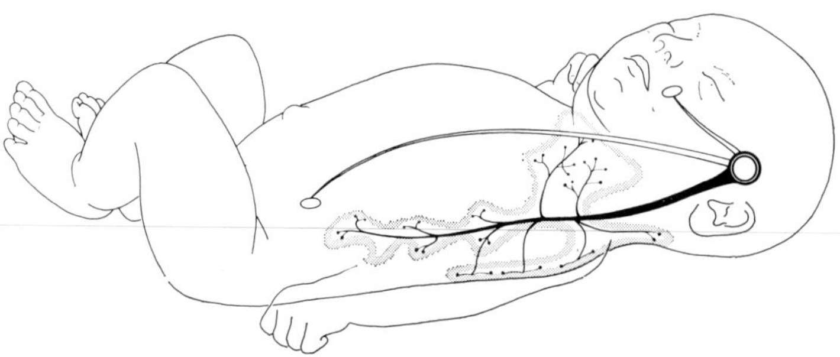

FIG. 6. An illustration of the nervous control of the heat organ. Deep body and superficial sensors inform the brain centres of ambient temperatures. Impulses passing via the sympathetic nerves adjust the rate of heat production and tissue blood flow in the heat organ according to requirements.

rate from a basal level requiring the consumption of oxygen at a rate of 6 ml.O_2 kg./min. to a maximum of 15 ml.O_2 kg./min. As there have been no direct measurements of the thermal capacity of brown adipose tissue in humans nor any accurate measurements of the amounts of tissue present, it is difficult to estimate what fraction of the extra heat is produced in brown adipose tissue. However, if it is assumed that the brown adipose tissue in the infants has the same capacity per gram of tissue to produce heat as that of the newborn rabbit, then the amount that can be recognized easily in the human infant could support well over half of the observed increase.

The heat organ needs a continuous supply of oxygen and a readily available source of fuel. Thus, there are two situations in which the thermal capacity of the tissue might be compromised. The first is when there is a shortage of oxygen, the second when there is a shortage of fuel.

Long before brown adipose tissue was shown to be the site of non-shivering heat production in newborn animals, it was known that relatively mild asphyxia reduced the increase in newborn mammals' metabolic rate following cold exposure. No such effect occurs in adults with comparable degrees of hypoxia. It was postulated that this selective inhibition might be a protective mechanism, for the asphyxiated newborn mammal survives longer at lower temperatures. However, the response is open to a simple explanation. Under *normal* conditions brown adipose tissue, when maximally producing heat, extracts most of the oxygen from the perfusing blood. It is therefore more vulnerable than other tissues of the body to small falls in the perfusing arterial oxygen content.

In acute starvation, animal investigations suggest that the tissue would continue to produce heat until its fat stores in both brown and white adipose tissue are depleted.[58] Prolonged undernutrition has a different effect. Brown adipose tissue decreases in quantity although its percentage fat content may remain unchanged. With the decrease in quantity, there is a fall in the tissues' thermal capacity.[4] In malnourished infants, hypothermia is a common and sometimes lethal complication, their capacity to produce heat is greatly reduced and their brown adipose tissue is shrunken and the cells depleted of granules.[3]

After both acute starvation or low-plane nutrition, even if blood sugar has fallen to low levels, brown adipose tissue still continues to take some glucose from the circulation. This may in part explain the known association of hypoglycaemia and hypothermia, and it emphasises the need to keep infants warm and thus avoid any unnecessary drain on the supply of glucose.

The Rise and Fall of Thermogenesis in Adipose Tissue

Brown adipose tissue usually develops before white adipose tissue. It fills with fat before birth in most species. This is not true of the rat, which has a very poor thermogenic response to cold until feeding has been established. After birth the tissue forms a decreasing percentage of the body weight until it reaches a certain size, when it continues to grow in proportion with the rest of the body. Growth curves based on data from rabbits is shown in Fig. 7.

In utero, the developing fetus enjoys the maternal homeothermy without paying the price. It is doubtful, even if it were needed, that brown adipose tissue could produce heat *in utero*. The perfusing oxygen concentration is probably too low. However, the tissue produces heat within minutes of birth and soon reaches its maximal capacity.[39]

Over the next few weeks the thermal capacity probably remains unchanged. It may even increase a little. The cell of brown adipose tissue in the human infant increases in size and complexity. However, as the body as a whole grows at a faster rate than the tissue and the tissue's thermal capacity becomes relatively less effective, a factor

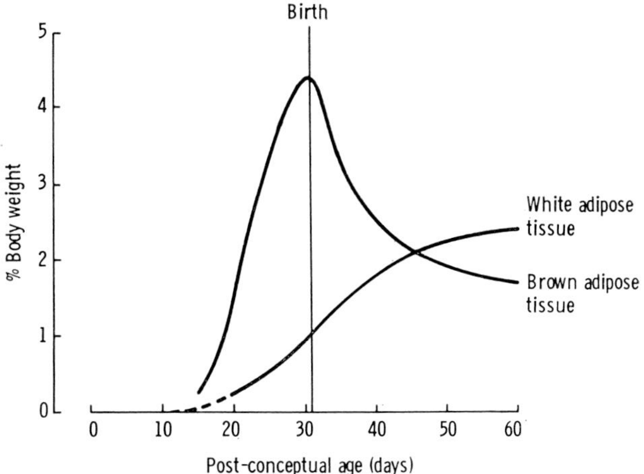

FIG. 7. Growth curves of brown and white adipose tissue in the rabbit as a percentage of the body weight. In absolute terms both tissues increase in weight until maturity.

which is balanced in part by the improved surface area–body weight ratio and increasing thermal insulation. But with increasing age and the establishment of milk feeding the call for extra heat production falls, brown adipose cells become unilocular, and its thermal capacity gradually withers away. Neither the determinants nor the mechanisms of this sequence of events are understood, but in a number of animals their timing has been documented.[86,18,4] Similar data are not available for the human.

One factor which influences the *rate* of disappearance is the ambient temperature. Continuous cold exposure increased the thermal capacity of brown adipose tissue in young rabbits,[41] but how long prolonged cold exposure from birth can delay the fall of the tissues thermal capacity has not been studied.

What is the function of brown adipose tissue in the adult? As we shall see, there is some evidence to suggest that it becomes an active unit of fatty acid supply.

ENERGY HOMEOSTASIS

All the cells of the body require fuel for oxidation. After a meal when glucose is available, glucose is preferred, but with fasting most cells will preferentially burn ketone bodies and fatty acids. Even in a well-fed state most extra demands for energy for muscular work or thermogenesis are usually met by fatty acids. Certain tissues, of which the brain and red cells are the more important, principally use glucose but they can use other metabolites, in particular, ketone bodies and glycerol.

At one time the liver was considered to be the key organ concerned with modulating the supply of fuel, and indeed it is of major importance. However, of equal importance is the massive adipose organ which clears the circulation of excess glucose and circulating triglyceride and is the major site of fatty acid supply. This take-up and supply system, like most biological systems, is in dynamic equilibrium and moves in one direction or another depending on a multitude of ambient factors.

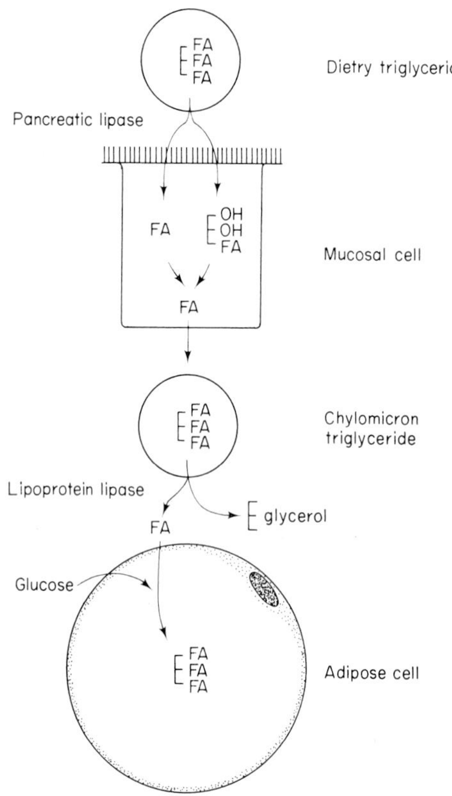

FIG. 8. The transport of dietary fat to the adipose store.

Lipid Traffic

Chylomicron

Pancreatic lipase present in the lumen of the intestine breaks down dietary fat in part to fatty acids and glycerol and in part to the partially split products of monoglycerides and diglycerides. Within the intestinal mucosal cell the break down of the split products is completed before the liberated fatty acids pass to the internal border of the cell where they are re-esterified to triglyceride and pass into the lacteals parcelled with protein and a little phospholipid as chylomicron.

The chylomicron enter the systemic circulation via the thoracic duct and disappear within a few minutes. Some may be temporarily lodged in the liver but the majority are cleared by the peripheral tissues, particularly by adipose tissue (Fig. 8). The rate of chylomicron clearage is closely correlated with the activity of a lipoprotein lipase which is sited in the wall of the capillary endothelial cell.[82] Heparin, which stimulates a sharp rise in lipoprotein lipases activity, also accelerates the clearage of chylomicron from the circulation. The biological role, if any, of this action of heparin is not clear. Lipoprotein lipase must not be confused with the lipases which initiate the intracellular release of fatty acid.

How the fatty acids released in the capillaries are transported into the cell is not certain. Evidence suggests that they travel by "pinocytosis" through the smooth endoplastic reticulum.[99] After they have entered the adipose cell they are re-esterified to triglyceride by linkage with glycerol phosphate which, in white adipose tissue, is derived from glucose.

The glycerol released at the endothelial cell border is cleared from the circulation by any tissue containing glycerol kinase, i.e. liver and kidney.

Lipogenesis

Some of the carbohydrate in the diet also passes through adipose tissue before it is used to provide energy. With a rise in circulating concentrations, glucose enters the body cells at an increased rate under the influence of insulin. In adipose tissue it is converted by the process called lipogenesis to fatty acid. Under anaerobic conditions *in vitro* lipogenesis has been shown to occur within mitochondria by a reversal of β-oxidation. However, under physiological conditions lipogenesis probably occurs in a different place, in the *soluble* fraction of the cytoplasm, and via a different sequence. This pathway has been demonstrated in the liver, brain and mammary gland as well as adipose tissue.

The first step is within the mitochondria. The carbohydrate is oxidized to acetyl CoA but, as acetyl CoA cannot pass through the mitochondrial wall, it is condensed with oxaloacetate to form citrate which diffuses easily into the extra-mitochondrial department where it undergoes cleavage back to acetyl CoA. Here acetyl CoA is carboxylated to malonyl CoA. The enzyme, acetyl CoA carboxylase, like other carboxylases, requires the co-enzyme biotin. The malonyl and acetyl CoA are linked together to form a C_4 molecule. Then C_2 units are added via further malonyl CoA linkages until the long chain fatty acid is formed. Lipogenesis from glucose leads to the preferential formation of C_{16} fatty acids palmitic (16:0) and palmitoleic (16:1) fatty acids.

The rate-limiting step is probably the initial carboxylation of acetyl CoA. One factor which is known to limit the activity of the carboxylase is the end product of the process, acyl CoA. If acyl CoA accumulates, either due to delay in esterification to triglyceride or because fatty acids enter the extra-mitochondrial compartment of the cell cytoplasm from another source, then lipogenesis is inhibited.

Lipolysis

The function of adipose tissue is not only to store fatty acids but also to release them on demand (Fig. 9). The insoluble triglyceride is broken down by hydrolysis to one molecule of glycerol and three molecules of fatty acids

(Fig. 4). With increased mobilization there is increased pinoctosis in the adipocyte cytoplasm again suggesting transport via the smooth endoplasmic reticulum. When the free fatty acids reach the circulation they are bound to albumin for transport. It is thought that the intracellular concentration of fatty acid determines the rate of entry into the circulation and the level in the circulation determines the rate of uptake by other cells. This implies that fatty acid supply is largely determined by the rate of hydrolysis. However, there is some evidence that the situation may be more complex.

Once in the blood stream the fatty acids are quickly cleared. They have a half-life of two or three minutes. The turn-over rate is very high and the circulating concentrations compared to those of glucose are low.

Excess fatty acids appear to be cleared by the liver where they are converted to acyl CoA and then, according to circumstances, they may be oxidized or re-esterified to triglyceride. The triglyceride may be stored as such in the liver or released into the circulation as endogenous triglyceride. Endogenous triglyceride enters the blood stream as a lipoprotein of very low density and it is handled by the rest of the body in a way similar to chylomicron.

Ketosis

The fatty acids which are oxidized in the liver are broken down to acetyl CoA and then they may be either oxidized via the citric acid cycle to CO_2 with a high energy yield, or converted to ketone bodies, aceto-acetate and β-hydroxybutyrate, with only a low energy yield. When the uptake of free fatty acids is high, less enters the citric acid cycle and more ketone bodies are produced, so that the total energy production is unchanged. Ketonogenesis may be a mechanism which allows the liver to oxidize large quantities of fatty acids without increasing its total energy output.[71] Fatty acids are not the only substrate for ketone body formation.

Ketone bodies are not easily oxidized in the liver and therefore they pass into the circulation. From the circulation, they are freely taken up by the other tissues of the body including the brain at a rate dependent on the circulating level. In other organs, in contrast to the liver, ketone bodies are readily oxidized for energy in preference to both glucose and free fatty acids. In starvation they are an important channel whereby the brain obtains energy from fatty acids.[76] Studies on suckling rats suggest that they are also a major fuel of the brain under normal conditions.[46]

Blood Lipids

To end this section on lipid traffic, some mention must be made of the circulating lipids (Table 1). The active unit of energy supply, free fatty acids or non-esterified fatty acids form a small fraction of the total circulating lipid. Endogenous triglycerides from the liver are present in far larger amounts and further triglycerides in the form of chylomicron are found after a meal. Two other groups of lipids, cholesterol esters and phospholipids are also present in much greater quantities than free fatty acids.

Lipids by definition are insoluble in water. To make them less hydrophobic and more suitable for transport in a water-based medium, various lipoprotein complexes are formed. Fatty acids link with albumin in a union containing far more protein (99 per cent) than lipid and thus form a complex of relatively high density. The other lipids form complex macromolecules with two groups of protein called A and B apoprotein because, electrophorecically, they move like α- and β-globulin.

The serum lipoproteins are currently classified according to their density and their electrophoretic behaviour.[68] On

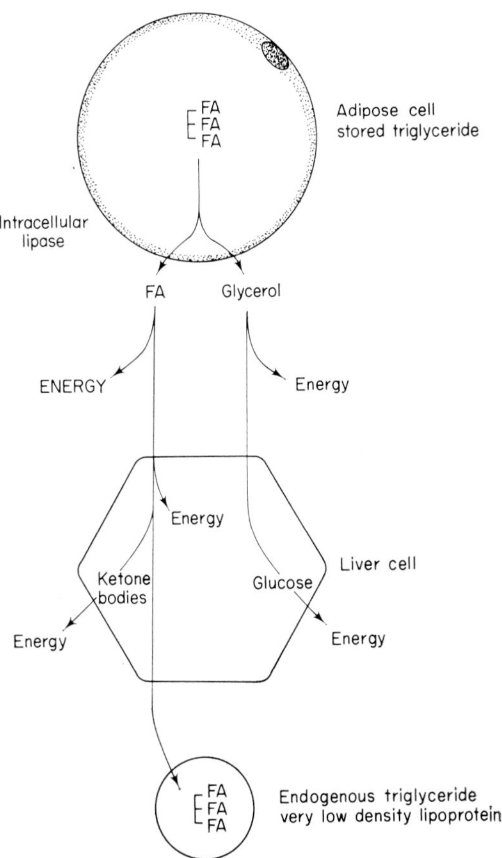

FIG. 9. The mobilization of fatty acids. The by-products, glycerol, glucose and ketone bodies, provide an energy source for the brain.

ultra centrufigation the lightest complexes, chylomicron, float to the top. Chylomicron are 99 per cent lipid, the majority of which is triglyceride and most of the remainder is phospholipid. The next are very low density lipoprotein formed largely in the liver from fatty acids but they may also be formed in the bowel. This fraction contains 93 per cent lipid of which a little over half is triglyceride, with about 20 per cent phospholipid and 15 per cent cholesterol ester. The proteins are a mixture of the α- and β-type. In the next group, low-density lipoprotein, cholesterol esters form nearly half of the lipid component, the remainder is a mixture of triglyceride and phospholipid. The protein is predominantly β-lipoprotein. The high-density lipoprotein falls between low-density liproprotein and albumin-fatty acid complexes and they contain between 30 to 60 per cent protein (mainly α-lipoprotein) and the predominant lipid is phospholipid but the other lipide, triglyceride

TABLE 1

BLOOD LIPIDS (APPROXIMATE)

Fraction	*Source*	*Protein* (%)	*Total lipid* (%)	*Percentage of total lipid*				
				Triglyceride	*Phospholipid*	*Cholesterol ester*	*Cholesterol-free*	*Free fatty acid*
Chylomicron	Intestine	1	99	88	8	3	1	—
Very low density lipoprotein	Liver and intestine	7	93	56	20	15	8	1
Low density lipoprotein	Liver and intestine	10–20	80–90	13–39	26–28	34–48	9–10	1
High density lipoprotein	Liver	30–60	40–70	13–16	43–46	29–31	6–10	0–6
Albumin—fatty acid	Adipose tissue	99	1	—	—	—	—	100

and cholesterol together form over 50 per cent of the lipid content.

There are a variety of rare inherited diseases associated with deficiencies or excess of these lipoproteins, and abnormal levels are found as a secondary effect in a number of disorders.[68]

Control of Energy Homeostasis

With fasting the supply of glucose from the bowel falls. The circulating level is maintained initially by glycogenolysis in the liver, and then by gluconeogenesis from amino acids and glycerol. With the fall in glucose supply, glucose uptake by adipose tissue falls and the release of fatty acids increases. Energy metabolism in peripheral tissues turns to fatty acids as its energy source[77] with the exception of the brain and red blood cells, which continue to rely on glucose but are also able to use other substrates like glycerol. With prolonged starvation the rate of releases of fatty acids exceeds their rate of utilization. The liver mops up the excess which for reasons given above, it release after partial oxidation as ketone bodies.

The whole system has its own feed-back mechanism, one aspect of which is highlighted in the "fatty acid–glucose cycle". The mechanisms which initiate and determine the magnitude of changes in energy homeostasis are not fully understood. Insulin appears to play a major part in the response to starvation, but the lipolytic hormones may also be important. The sympathetic nervous system is the efferent pathway for the emergency supply of energy substrate in response to stress, exercise and cold exposure but it may also play some part in the response to starvation.

Fatty Acid–glucose Cycle

The observations that fatty acids or their metabolites, ketone bodies, inhibit the uptake and oxidation of glucose by the peripheral tissue (particularly muscle), and that glucose uptake by adipose tissue inhibited fatty acid release suggested a feed-back self-regulating system.[31,80] This relationship would explain the association of impaired sensitivity to insulin, reduced glucose tolerance, poor conversion of glucose to glycogen (but not pyruvate) in muscle, with high circulating levels of free fatty acids, all of which may be found in a variety of conditions including starvation, carbohydrate deprivation, diabetes, excess growth hormone, excess of certain steroids and also paradoxically in certain obese states. This valuable concept has emphasized some of the consequences of high circulating free fatty acids, but its role as a "controlling" mechanism must not be over-emphasized. It is one of the features of the body's energy homeostasis. Adjustments of the magnitude and direction of these changes must be based on genetic construction and environmental experiences, which exert their influence on the balance via hormonal and nervous mechanisms.

The Role of Insulin

In man, it is generally considered that insulin is the major hormone controlling energy homeostasis and its main site of action may well be adipose tissue.[19] With a carbohydrate feed the glucose levels rise and stimulate the release of insulin. Insulin acting on the cell membrane increases the uptake of glucose and thus indirectly the rate of lipogenesis in adipose tissue, but it may also directly encourage lipogenesis.[38] Another effect of insulin is to inhibit fatty-acid release. It has been suggested that this is secondary to increased glucose uptake, but there is also evidence demonstrating a direct action on lipase activity. Also, recent studies in brown adipose tissue *in vivo* have shown that insulin has an important and direct inhibiting action on the transport of fatty acids to and from the cells.[42] By inhibiting fatty-acid release it will increase the rate of re-esterification and reduce the rate of lipolysis.

On peripheral tissues (e.g. muscle) insulin increases glucose uptake and encourages glucose oxidation. It also encourages amino-acid uptake and inhibits proteolysis.

With starvation, insulin levels fall and as a consequence fuel reserves are mobilized, fatty acids from adipose tissue, and amino acids from muscle. In the liver amino acids are converted to glucose, a process which is acutely sensitive to a small rise in glucose and insulin levels.

Insulin sensitivity is increased with exercise and in disease states associated with hypopituitarism, and hypoadrenalism[73] and decreased in obesity, trauma, pregnancy, acromegaly, certain hyperadrenal states and possibly intransient hyperglycaemia of the newborn.

Sympathetic Nervous System and Lipolytic Hormones

The sympathetic nervous system could exert its effects over adipose tissue directly by releasing noradrenaline close to the cells or indirectly by controlling the peripheral blood flow. Noradrenaline released at sympathetic nerve-endings is a powerful lipolytic agent. It is interesting to note that this action of noradrenaline is inhibited by drugs which block β-receptor activity. This system is probably the principal efferent channel leading to fatty-acid mobilization in response to sudden exercise, cold exposure and stress. But it could also have a continuous "tone" effect which varies with the plane of nutrition.

In fasting, the increase in rate of release of fatty acids is in part due to an increase in the arterio-venous difference across the tissue and in part due to an increase in blood flow through it.[124,43] Very little is known of the factors which control blood flow, but obviously the sympathetic nervous system could be of major importance. Denervated tissue slowly fills with fat. As free fatty acids require albumin for transport, blood flow clearly has, at the least, a permissive role. Separate systems of nerves supply the adipose tissue cell and vessels and the two mechanisms may work independently.

Many other hormones, other than catecholamines, including glucagon and the pituitary peptides, growth hormone, corticotrophin and a lipid mobilizing factor, have been shown to stimulate lipolysis in adipose tissue *in vitro* and to cause a rise in circulating free fatty acids when injected *in vivo*. The physiological significance of these findings is not clear.

Energy Homeostasis in the Fetus

The fetus enjoys the benefits of the mother's thermal and energy homeostasis. It does not experience cold or starvation. Free fatty acids although they can cross the placenta (indeed the essential fatty acids must) do not appear to do so in significant amounts. Thus glucose is probably the main source of cellular energy and the stored triglyceride is probably formed by lipogenesis from glucose. The evidence is indirect: the R.Q. of the fetus is close to 1 and the fatty acids formed in adipose tissue are those normally produced by lipogenesis from glucose and not those matching the maternal circulating lipids.[61]

There is no evidence as yet that lipolysis occurs to any significant degree under normal conditions. The circulating levels of fatty acids are low. However, some lipolysis must take place, for the fatty-acid pattern of the fetal free fatty acids matches that of the fetal stored triglyceride and not that of the maternal circulating lipids. No chylomicron are found in the fetal circulation, endogenous levels of triglyceride are low cholesterol phospholipid levels are less than half maternal levels. The values do not differ in relation to race, sex, age or nutritional status of the mother, or the gestation or type of delivery of the infact.

The fetus, by virtue of its circumstances, is largely glucose committed. This creates an interesting situation with respect to insulin activity. By the eleventh week of pregnancy insulin can be found in the islet cells[81] and then in the circulation. In the latter part of pregnancy when fetal glucose rises so does the insulin level.[24,75] Fetal blood sugars which reflect the maternal levels, are high in infants of diabetic mothers and this presumably is responsible for the hypertrophy of the fetal islets.[34] What does insulin do? At present both animal investigations and clinical observations give conflicting answers.[67,8,21,62] Early studies showed that insulin injections into the fetus increased the lipid content of fetal adipose tissue suggesting that insulin by some mechanism draws more glucose across the placenta. Insulin does not cross the placenta either way.

What happens in the undernourished fetus when the placenta presumably does not permit transmission of adequate amounts of nutrient? Such infants are characteristically long and thin with reduced subcutaneous fat and small livers with depleted glycogen stores. The fat stores may be small because there is less glucose for storage or because it has been mobilized. There is little evidence to suggest either possibility. If there was increased mobilization one might anticipate a fatty liver and higher circulating levels of lipids but these have not been observed. On the other hand, their circulating fatty acids rise more rapidly after birth.

In contrast, in infants of diabetic mothers, the increased level of maternal blood sugar increases the transfer of glucose across the placenta which in turn increases the adipose tissue mass but also increases growth. The role of insulin in these changes is still not clear.[34] Insulin's action increasing growth[11] is probably independent of its action on glucose or lipid transport. However, it is also possible that the generous supply of glucose itself is responsible for an increase in growth. Excess feeding of newborn rabbits led to bigger animals, not to obese ones, an effect which if it operates at all in the developing human, does so to only the slightest degree after birth, but it may well operate at an earlier stage in development.

Adjustments following Birth

After birth the infant experiences many new and powerful sensations. Evaporative water loss invariably leads to cold exposure and a fall in colonic temperature. This is a strong stimulus for lipid mobilisation. With the metabolic awakening which occurs as the infact adjusts to extra-uterine life, as the lungs, kidneys and bowels begin to provide the services which had been performed by the placenta, the metabolic requirements rise. With the interruption in the supply of glucose the respiratory quotient falls. In the presence of all these changes the levels of free fatty acids rise, indicating an increase in rate of mobilization which more than compensates for the increase in the rate of utilization. The rise varies with the clinical state of the infant and the ambient conditions.[78,72] The rise is greater in small for dates infants,[5] and less in infants of diabetic mothers.[61] The rise is greater in infants exposed to cooler environments and rises even further if hypothermia occurs.

Fatty acid mobilisation after birth is probably a response to stress rather than starvation. Therefore, the response is probably mediated via the sympathetic nervous system rather than through insulin. Growth hormone may make a contribution[101] particularly in infarcts who were undernourished towards the end of pregnancy.

Over the first 24 to 48 hours the blood sugar level falls. The fall is greater in undernourished infants and in infarcts of diabetic mothers.[70] The mechanisms responsible for these changes has been a matter for much investigation and speculation. This author currently favours the view that there is a delay in the adjustment in mitochondrial activity in all tissues to fatty acid and keto-acids as a form of cellular energy. As a consequence the infant's energy requirements are greater than its ability to supply extra glucose despite considerable glycogen stores and the ability to convert amino-acids by gluconeogenesis. Studies on newborn rats[100] and puppies[12] indicate that the myocardium may initially have a limited capacity to oxidize fatty acids. This observation is consistent with the finding that excess fat is found stored peripherally in active muscle groups and in the liver, in increasing concentrations after birth. The phenomenon is more marked in dysmature infants but is not found in stillbirths whether undernourished at birth or not.[2]

TABLE 2

SERUM CHOLESTEROL AND PHOSPHOLIPID IN THE FIRST YEAR OF LIFE

(from Darmady, J. M., Fosbrooke, A. S. and Lloyd, J. K. Institute of Child Health, London, to be published)

	Total Cholesterol (mg/100 ml ± 1 SD)	*Phospholipids* (mg/100 ml ± 1 SD)
Birth	78 ± 28	105 ± 26
1 week	155 ± 31	192 ± 34
6 weeks	155 ± 31	192 ± 30
4 months	184 ± 36	207 ± 32
8 months	196 ± 38	199 ± 33
1 year	191 ± 36	217 ± 35

Although the serum lipid levels, cholesterol and phospholipid, are low at birth they rise rapidly over the first week with the introduction of milk feeding and then more slowly over the first year of life (Table 2). Breast-fed babies tend to have highest levels, whereas babies fed with milk containing vegetable oils have the lowest. Significantly high cord values are present in infants of diabetic mothers and infarcts found later to have the heterozygous form of familial hypercholesterolaemia.

ENERGY STORAGE

To this point, we have been concerned with the activity of the adipocyte cytoplasm. In the first section with its oxidative metabolism, in the second section with its role in the formation of triglyceride and its modulated supply as fatty acids. In this section attention will be focused on adipose tissue as an organ of storage. The adipose organ in normal adult man ranges from about 15 per cent to 40 per cent of the body weight and the woman from 25 per cent to 50 per cent. It is surprising in view of its size that it has not been studied with far greater interest.

On average, man eats about 150 grams of fat each day, about 50 kg. per year and possibly about 3,500 kg. in a lifetime. On average a young man stores about 10 kg., thus his adipose tissue holds the equivalent of 20 per cent of his yearly intake. Wild animals store surprisingly little fat, for food supplies are usually too limited and indeed if there were more food, there would be more animals (one exception is the aquatic mammals). In this setting, as the lion moves from one killing to another, or the camel crosses the desert, it is not difficult to appreciate the value of a storage organ, and that, within anticipated experience, it may from time to time become severely depleted.

Man's problem is different. In most Western societies food is plentiful and eating is a pleasure. How, in these circumstances, does the adipose organ avoid becoming over full? The fact that the adipose organ stays a relatively constant fraction of the body weight for any one individual despite varying food intakes and work loads indicates some controlling systems. Some factors do, indeed must, influence the appetite, the net absorption of food, and the efficiency of biological oxidation. A little increase in the fraction of uncoupling of oxidative phosphorylation could rapidly burn-off excess food (for example in thyrotoxicosis!). But surprisingly little is known of the mechanisms involved in determining the adipose organ size. With persistent forced feeding the mechanisms are invariably overpowered, and obesity usually results, but I have been impressed by the clinical observation in infants that some respond to overfeed by vomiting, other by food refusal, others by frequent loose stools, and others by becoming fat.

It would appear that the number of adipocytes present in adults varies greatly from one individual to another[9] but within an individual, the number remains fixed from puberty. No change in number occurs with over-eating or starvation in either adults[85] or children.[14] Evidence also suggests that the final number of cells present in adults is already determined much earlier in life, although the absolute number of cells continues to increase until puberty (Fig. 10).[14] It is not surprising therefore that there is currently considerable interest in the early development of the adipose organ.

Early Development and Growth of White Adipose Tissue

In the fetus, adipose tissue develops around young capillary shoots from the arterioles lying beneath the dermis. This occurs at many sites at once in the third to fourth month of pregnancy and the tissue begins to to accumulate fat soon afterwards.[97] At term the fat forms about 10 per cent of the body weight and this is more than enough to support the infant's total maintenance requirements for the first month or so of life. In this respect, as in many others, the human infant differs from most other mammalian species. The newborn pig and rat have virtually no

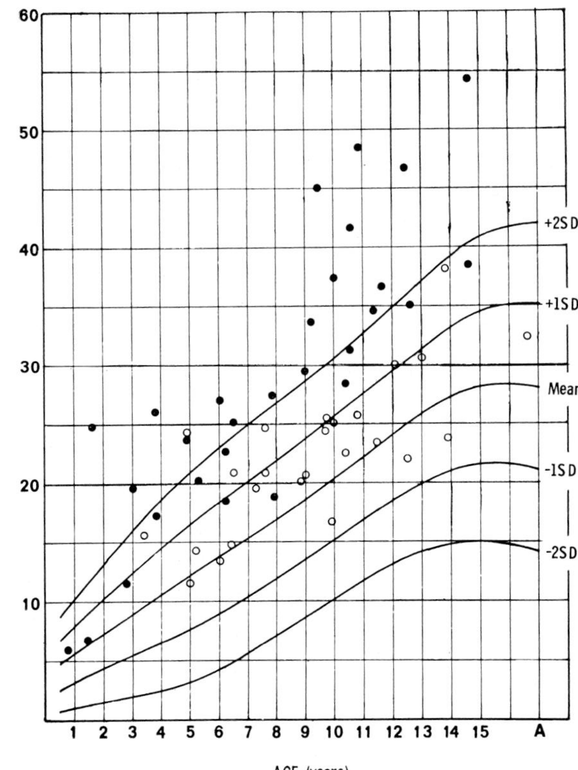

FIG. 10. The lines show the mean ± 1 and 2SD of the total number of fat cells at different ages (from Brook 1972.)[14] The empty circles show the total number of fat cells found in obese children, who according to history, developed obesity after the first year of life. The full circles show the total number of fat cells in obese children who developed obesity during the first year of life. This data supports the suggestion that early obesity leads to an increase in cell number and size whereas late obesity leads to an increase in cell size only (from Brook, C. G. D., Lloyd, J. K. and Wolff, O. H., 1972.)[15]

fat stored at birth in adipose tissue and they are very dependent on the early establishment of milk feeding However, it is the habit of many newborn mammals either to feed continuously or to take such large feeds of milk at a time so that their stomachs are never empty of milk. The milk may contain anything from 5–30 per cent of its weight as fat. Thus the bowel, under normal conditions, serves the newborn as a constant and reliable source of fat until milk feeding ceases. Readers interested in the comparative physiology of milk feeding are referred to an excellent review by Widdowson.[98]

At birth, in term infants, the fat content of adipose tissue is about 40 per cent and thus if adipose tissue contains most of the body fat the adipose organ forms 28 per cent of the body weight.[6]

Over the next four months the human infant doubles his body weight and, like the baby seal, grows fat! Fomon's careful calculations,[35] based on the best available evidence, indicate that in the 4-month-old "reference" male infant over 26 per cent of the body weight is fat and it is probable therefore that about half his body weight is formed of the adipose organ. But it may vary from 40–70 per cent!

By one year of age the infant has increased his birth weight threefold, the body fat has increased sixfold to be about 20 per cent of the body weight and there it remains throughout childhood. With increasing age, however, the fat content of adipose tissue gradually increases from 60–80 per cent, so the adipose organ forms a slightly decreased fraction of the body weight until puberty when in men it may fall slightly, whereas in girls there is another increase.

This is reflected by changes in skin fold thickness.[93] There is a steady increase in skinfold thickness in both sexes until 9 months of age, when it flattens out and fluctuates only slightly for the next seven years. In boys there is a brief pre-adolescent increase which may, when exaggerated, amounts to obesity, and then a slight fall during adolescence. In contrast, girls gain fat in adolescence and women have more fat than men.

Fat Cell Size and Number

The development of techniques which measure the fat content per cell and permit the calculation of the number of fat cells in the body has added considerably to our understanding of adipose organ growth in man.[53,54] It has been shown that rats reared in small litters and therefore well fed, had more fat cells than rats reared in larger litters and therefore not well fed during the crucial early days of life.[65] Similarly in man, over-feeding in the early months may lead to increases in cell number. Obese children, like obese adults,[10,15] fall into two groups. Some have increases in both cell size and number and some have increases in cell size alone. Those with increased cell numbers had been obese in the first months of life[15] (Fig. 10). On the other hand, infants of low birth weight for their gestational age have fewer fat cells at birth (C. G. D. Brook, personal communication). The extent to which this effect of malnutrition is reversible remains to be demonstrated. This data suggests that the availability of excess food over a limited sensitive period when rapid cell division takes place may have a lasting influence on the number of adipocytes. On the other hand, the possibility that other factors play a dominant role has not been excluded. It could be that those who become obese with increased cell division in the first months of life do so because of some inherited tendency. If the availability of food is the sole determining factor, then one would expect infants of diabetic mothers to have *invariably* more cells and to remain obese. Although some infants of diabetic mothers do subsequently become obese, many do not.[33]

Factors Influencing Adipose Organ Growth

Before discussing obesity, it is relevant to consider the factors which might be expected to influence adipose cell growth and size. As we have seen the metabolic functions of adipose tissue are lipogenesis, fatty acid supply, and lipid storage; brown adipose tissue has the added function of thermogenesis to cold exposure. Increased biological demand for any of these activities during development might lead to an increase in cell number (hyperplasia) or an increase in individual cell capacity (hypertrophy). Evidence given above, indicates that excess food for storage increases cell number and later cell size. Increased call for thermogenesis leads to an increase in cell size and number in brown adipose tissue of adult mammals. To date, no one has studied the effects of cold exposure in the newborn on the growth of brown adipose tissue in terms of cell number and size. In contrast, increased exchange of fat, uptake and release, as stimulated by increasing the metabolic rate of young growing rabbits by continuous cold exposure led to a prolonged reduction in the white adipose organ size.[44] Our knowledge of the external factors and the biological mechanisms which influence adipose tissue growth is, to say the least, sketchy.

Obesity

Obesity is a reflection of man's success in controlling his external environment. Excess fat may be so gross that it greatly restricts the individual's daily activities as well as predisposes to a wide range of diseases which lead to an early death. Moderate obesity may have a similar long-term outlook although its daily burden is slight. Fat children tend to grow into fat adults and the hazards of heart disease and diabetes appear to be greater if obesity began in childhood.[55] Infants who have excessive weight gain in the first few months of life are more likely to become obese later.[32] Thus it may well be as important to recognize early obesity and treat with the same thoroughness as we approach an infant with diabetes.

The simplest way to assess obesity is to determine the excess weight over the expected for the individual's height. This has obvious errors. A squat short muscular type might be considered obese when he is not, whereas a tall narrow type could be obese without exceeding his overweight allowance. An alternative method is to measure skin-fold thickness at a number of sites and to make calculations from these. This technique in adults[63] and children[13] correlates much better than excess weight over ideal, with measurement of total body fat based on total body water measurements and estimated lean body mass. Normal data of skin fold thickness is available for children of all ages.[93]

Obesity is associated with a number of biochemical changes. The glucose clearance is abnormal, the glucose cencentration is slow to return to fasting levels in both obese children and adults. The circulating levels of insulin are high[22] and there is relative insulin insensitivity possibly due to the presence of insulin antagonists.[96] Resting free fatty acid levels are raised but the rise in blood levels during a fast is less in obese than non-obese subjects. With the raised resting levels of fatty acids, one might expect increased liver clearage and thus the production of more endogenous triglyceride and more low-density lipoprotein in the circulation. Higher levels have been reported in obesity in adults and children, but others have found normal levels in children.[14] An increased peripheral utilization could match the increased production.

Obese children on the whole tend to be tall for their age,[102] which is largely explicable on the basis of accelerated bone age.[74] Obesity in the first year of life is more likely to be associated with tallness,[14] but their final height is not greater than the expected.[69] They tend to have a decrease in the release of growth hormone with stimulation.[20] However, whether the excess growth is due to the stimulating effects of insulin, growth hormone or some other factor remains to be discovered.

The hyperinsulinism, excess resting growth hormone release, and high circulating levels of lipids all revert to normal soon after the commencement of a reducing diet and long before the fat cells have returned to a normal size.[60,37] Thus although hyperinsulinism is correlated with cell size in obese individuals this is not a dependent relationship. Nor can it be argued on this evidence that hyperinsulinism is a contributory cause of obesity.

Lipodystrophy

One disease which falls under this heading, congenital total lipodystrophy, is of considerable theoretical interest for the infants loose the little fat they have at birth over the first few months of life and they present, usually in the first year of life, because their loss of fat gives the impression of failure to thrive or because of their unusual appearance. The adipose organ is present but contains little or no fat. It would appear that both its storage and its turnover activities are suppressed for there is little evidence of pinocytosis in its cytoplasm (B. Lake and D. Hull, unpublished observation). Thus, these children grow without an effective adipose organ. With increasing age, their livers enlarge to take over the storage and supply role of adipose tissue although biopsies of the liver have shown that some are overfull with fat whereas others are overfull with glycogen. As might be expected there is a compensatory increase in circulating insulin levels and relative insulin insensitivity. A diabetic state develops in later childhood or early adult life. Initially they grow rapidly but their final height is below normal.

Adipose Organs

From a consideration of clinical syndromes associated with obesity, it is obvious that the behaviour of the adipose organ is by no means uniform in its response to hormonal changes. The adiposity of a hypothyroid infant or a child with the Laurance–Moon–Beidl or Prader–Villi syndrome is characteristically different from that following prolonged steroid therapy. Again a superficial review of the comparative physiology of the adipose organ brings to light a variety of situations where the adipose tissue at certain sites has its own peculiar activities, i.e. the hump of a camel, the buttocks of the Hottentot woman. With prolonged starvation, adipose tissue at certain sites withholds its stores of fat for as long as possible. At these sites, adipose tissue is usually playing a space-occupying role, for example in the bone marrow, the orbit of the eye and the sucking pad of the infant. It would be instructive to know if this retention of fat is due to the peculiarity of the adipose cell of the influence of local factors.

The conclusion that the adipose tissue at some sites is more concerned with storage where at others it is more concerned with supply follows the observation that the circulating free fatty acid more quickly reflects changes in dietary fatty acid composition than does stored triglyceride in subcutaneous fat. Dole[39] calculated from the time it took circulating lipids (as opposed to adipose tissue lipids) to equilibrate with a change of fatty acid in the diet that only 10 per cent of the adipose tissue mass was actively engaged in fatty acid exchange. This 10 per cent could either be 10 per cent of each adipocyte or 10 per cent of the adipose tissue mass or a mixture of both.

One major factor determining adipose tissue uptake and release is the perfusion of blood. If fatty acid release is determined by the concentration gradient between cell and plasma and by the availability of blood albumin binding-sites, then the rate of blood flow is critical. Thus the 10 per cent active fat may be the most vascular.

The form of adipose tissue with the most generous blood supply is brown adipose tissue. Although its thermogenic function falls with increasing age, the tissue persists and still has a high flow rate in adult life. It may be that brown adipose tissue is the active fat of the adult.[43]

CONCLUSION

In this review I have highlighted some of the many fascinating facets of adipose tissue biology which have been reported in the last few years. For the purposes of description the various aspects of adipose tissue function have been artificially divided into lipogenesis, serum triglyceride clearance, triglyceride storage, fatty acid oxidation and fatty acid mobilization. The mechanisms involved in these reactions are incompletely understood, the importance of by-products, i.e. glycerol, ketone bodies, etc., are only just beginning to be appreciated. Many hormones have been shown to influence energy homeostasis but their biological role awaits further evaluation and insulin works in so many ways at so many different places that its net achievements are not always obvious.

REFERENCES

1. Afzelus, B. A. (1970), "Brown Adipose Tissue, Its Gross Anatomy, Histology and Cytology," pp. 1–32. In: *Brown Adipose Tissue*, edited by Lindberg, O. New York: American Elsevier Publishing Co. Inc.
2. Aherne, W. (1965), "Fat Infiltration in the Tissues of the Newborn Infant," *Arch. Dis. Childh.*, **40**, 406–410.
3. Aherne, W. and Hull, D. (1966), "Brown Adipose Tissue and Heat Production in the Newborn Infant," *J. Path. Bact.*, **91**, 223–234.
4. Alexander, G., Bell, A. W. and Williams, D. (1970), "Metabolic Response of Lambs to Cold. Effects of Prolonged Treatment with Thyroxine and of Acclimation to Low Temperatures," *Biol. Neonat.*, **15**, 198–210.
5. Anagnostakis, D. E. and Lardinois, R. (1971), "Urinary Catecholaminy Excretion and Plasma NEFA Concentration in Small-for-date Infants," *Pediatrics*, **47**, 1000–1009.
6. Baker, G. L. (1969), "Human Adipose Tissue Composition and Age," *Am. J. clin. Nutr.*, **22**, 829–835.
7. Barnard, T. and Skala, J. (1970), "The Development of Brown Adipose Tissue," pp. 33–72. In: *Brown Adipose Tissue*, edited by Lindberg, O. New York: American Elsevier Publishing Co. Inc.
8. Basset, J. M. and Thornburn, G. D. (1971), "The Regulation of Insulin Secretion by the Ovine Foetus in Utero," *J. Endocr.*, **50**, 59–74.
9. Bjorntorp, P., Bengtsson, C., Blohme, G. *et al.* (1971), "Adipose Tissue Fat Cell Size and Number in Relation to Metabolism in Randomly Selected Middle-aged Men and Women," *Metabolism*, **20**, 927–935.
10. Bjorntorp, P. and Sjostrom, L. (1971), "Number and Size of Adipose Tissue Fat Cells in Relation to Metabolism in Human Obesity," *Metabolism*, **20**, 703–713.
11. Blazquez, E., Montoya, E. and Quijada, C. L. (1970), "Relationship Between Insulin Concentrations in Plasma and Pancreas of Foetal and Weanling Rats," *J. Endocr.*, **48**, 553–561.
12. Brever, E., Borta, E., Ziatos, L. and Pappova, E. (1968), "Developmental Changes of Myocardinal Metabolism," *Biol. Neonat.*, **12**, 54 and 64.
13. Brook, C. G. D. (1971), "Determination of Body Composition of Children from Skinfold Measurements," *Arch. Dis. Childh.*, **46**, 182–185.
14. Brook, C. G. D. (1972), "Obesity in Childhood," M.D. Thesis. University of Cambridge.
15. Brook, C. G. D., Lloyd, J. K. and Wolff, O. H. (1972), "Relation Between Age of Onset of Obesity and Size and Number of Adipose Cells," *Br. Med. J.*, **2**, 25–27.
16. Brück, K. (1961), "Temperature Regulation in the Newborn Infant," *Biol. Neonat.*, **3**, 65–119.
17. Brück, K. (1970), "Nonshivering Thermogenesis and Brown Adipose Tissue in Relation to Age, and Their Integration in the Thermoregulatory System," pp. 117–152. In: *Brown Adipose Tissue*, edited by Lindberg, O. New York: American Elsevier Publishing Co. Inc.
18. Brück, K. and Wünnenberg (1966), "Influence of Ambient Temperature on the Process of Replacement of Non-shivering Thermogenesis during Post-natal Development," *Fed. Proc.*, **25**, 1332–1337.
19. Cahill, G. F. (1971), "Physiology of Insulin in Man," *Diabetes*, **20**, 785–799.
20. Carnelutti, M., Jose del Guercio, M. and Chiumello, G. (1970), "Influence of Growth Hormone on the Pathogenesis of Obesity in Children," *J. Pediat.*, **77**, 285–293.
21. Chez, R. A., Mintz, D. H. and Hutchinson, D. L. (1971), "Effect of Theophylline on Glucagon and Glucose-mediated Plasma Insulin Responses in Subhuman Primate Fetus and Neonate," *Metabolism*, **20**, 805–815.
22. Chiumello, G., Jose del Guercio, M., Carnelutti, M. and Bidone, G. (1969), "Relationship Between Obesity, Chemical Diabetes and β-Pancreatic Function in Children," *Diabetes*, **18**, 233–243.
23. Cockburn, F., Hull, D. and Walton, I. (1967), "The Effect of Lipotype Hormones and Theophylline on Heat Production in Brown Adipose Tissue *in vivo*," *Bri. J. Pharm. & Chemother.*, **31**, 568–577.
24. Cordero, L., Grunt, J. A. and Anderson, G. G. (1970), "Fetal Response to Glucose Infusion: How much Credit Does the Fetal Pancreas Deserve?" *Pediatrics*, **46**, 155–156.
25. Cottlee, W. H. (1970), "The Innervation of Brown Adipose Tissue," pp. 155–178. In: *Brown Adipose Tissue*, edited by Lindberg, O. New York: American Elsevier Publishing Co. Inc.
26. Dawkins, M. J. R. and Hull, D. (1965), "The Production of Heat by Fat," *Sci. Am.*, **213**, 62–67.
27. Day, R. (1943), "Respiratory Metabolism in Brown Adipose Tissue in Infancy and in Childhood. Regulations of Body Temperature in Premature Infants," *Am. J. Dis. Child.*, **65**, 376.
28. Derry, D. M., Schonbaum, E. and Steiner, G. (1969), "Two Sympathetic Nerve Supplies to Brown Adipose Tissue of the Rat," *Can. J. Physiol. Pharmacol.*, **47**, 57–63.
29. Dole, V. P. (1965), "Energy Storage," pp. 13–18. In: *Adipose Tissue*, edited by Renold, A. E. and Cahill, G. F. Jr. Washington D.C.: American Physiological Society.
30. Donhoffer, S., Sardy, F. and Szegiali, G. (1964), "Brown Adipose Tissue and Thermoregulatory Heat Production in the Rat," *Nature, Lond.*, **203**, 765–766.

31. Editorial, *Lancet* (1971), "The Glucose Fatty-acid Cycle," *Lancet*, **2,** 479.
32. Eid, E. E. (1970), "Follow-up Study of Physical Growth of Children Who Had Excessive Weight Gain in the First Six Months of Life," *Br. Med. J.*, **2,** 74–77.
33. Farquhar, J. W. (1969), "Prognosis or Babies Born to Diabetic Mothers in Edinburgh," *Arch. Dis. Childh.*, **36,** 44–48.
34. Farquhar, J. W. (1970), "Islets, Insulin and Hypoglycaemia of Infants of Diabetic Mothers," *Postgrad. med. J.*, **46,** 593–599.
35. Fomon, S. J. (1967), "Body Composition of the Male Reference Infant During the First Year of Life," *Pediatrics, Springfield*, **40,** 863–870.
36. Grausz, J. P. (1970), "Interscapular Skin Temperatures in the Newborn Infant," *J. Pediat.*, **76,** 752–756.
37. Grey, N. and Kipnis, D. M. (1971), "Effeet of Diet Composition on the Hyperinsulinemia of Obesity," *New Engl. J. Med.*, **285,** 827–831.
38. Halperin, M. L. and Robinson, B. H. (1971), "Mechanism of Insulin Action on Control of Fatty Acid Synthesis Independent of Glucose Transport," *Metabolism*, **20,** 78–86.
39. Hardman, M. J., Hey, E. N. and Hull, D. (1969), "The Effect of Prolonged Cold Exposure on Heat Production in New-born Rabbits," *J. Physiol., Lond.*, **205,** 39–50.
40. Hardman, M. J. and Hull, D. (1970), "Fat Metabolism in Brown Adipose Tissue *in vivo*," *J. Physiol., Lond.*, **206,** 263–273.
41. Hardman, M. J. and Hull, D. (1971), "Effect of Environmental Conditions on the Growth and Function of Brown Adipose Tissue," *J. Physiol., Lond.*, **214,** 191–199.
42. Hardman, M. J. and Hull, D. (1972), "The Action of Insulin on Brown Adipose Tissue *in vivo*," *J. Physiol., Lond.*, **221,** 85–92.
43. Hardman, M. J. and Hull, D. (1973), *J. Physiol., Lond.* (in press).
44. Hardman, M. J., Hull, D. and Oyesiku, J. (1970), "The Growth of Brown and White Adipose Tissue," *Biol. Neonat.*, **16,** 354–361.
45. Hawkins, R. A., Williamson, D. H. and Krebs, H. A. (1971), "Ketone-body Utilization by Adult and Suckling Rat Brain *in vivo*," *Biochem. J.*, **122,** 13–18.
46. Heim, T. and Hull, D. (1966), "Blood Flow and Oxygen Consumption of Brown Adipose Tissue of New-born Rabbits," *J. Physiol., Lond.*, **186,** 42–55.
47. Hey, E. N. (1969), "The Relationship Between Environmental Temperature and Oxygen Consumption in the New-born Baby," *J. Physiol., Lond.*, **200,** 589–603.
48. Hey, E. N. (1971), "The care of babies in incubators." In: *Recent Advances in Paediatrics*, 4th Ed., edited by Gairdner, D. and Hull, D. London: J. & A. Churchill.
49. Hey, E. N., Kohlinsky, S. and O'Connell, B. (1969), "Heat Losses From Babies During Exchange Transfusion," *Lancet*, **1,** 335–338.
50. Hey, E. N. and Mount, L. E. (1967), "Heat Losses From Babies in Incubators," *Arch. Fis. Childh.*, **42,** 75–84.
51. Hey, E. N. and O'Connell, B. (1970), "Oxygen Consumption and Heat Balance in the Cot-nursed Baby," *Arch. Dis. Childh.*, **45,** 335–343.
52. Himms-Hagen, J. (1969), "The Role of Brown Adipose Tissue in the Calorigenic Effect of Adrenaline and Noradrenaline in Cold-acclimated Rats," *J. Physiol., Lond.*, **205,** 393–403.
53. Hirsch, J. and Gallian, E. (1968), "Methods for the Determination of Adipose Cell Size in Man and Animals," *J. Lip. Res.*, **9,** 110–119.
54. Hirsch, J., Knittle, J. L. and Salans, L. B. (1966), "Cell Lipid Content and Cell Number in Obese and Non-obese Humans, *J. clin. Invest.*, **45,** 1023.
55. Hueunemann, R. L. (1968), "Consideration of Adolescent Obesity as a Public Health Problem," *Public Health Rep.*, **83,** 491–495.
56. Hull, D. (1966), "The Structure and Function of Brown Adipose Tissue," *Br. Med. J.*, **22,** 92–96.
57. Hull, D. and Segall, M. M. (1965), "The Contribution of Brown Adipose Tissue to Heat Production in the Newborn Rabbit," *J. Physiol., Lond.*, **181,** 449–457.
58. Hull, D. and Segall, M. M. (1965), "Heat Production in the Newborn Rabbit and the Fat Content of the Brown Adipose Tissue," *J. Physiol., Lond.*, **181,** 467–477.
59. Hull, D. and Segall, M. M. (1965), "Sympathetic Nervous Control of Brown Adipose Tissue and Heat Production in the Newborn Rabbit," *J. Physiol., Lond.*, **181,** 458–467.
60. Kalkhoff, R. K., Kim, H. J., Cerletty, J. *et al.* (1971), "Metabolic Effects of Weight Loss in Obese Subjects. Changes in Plasma Substrate Levels, Insulin and Growth Hormone Responses," *Diabetes*, **20,** 83–91.
61. King, K. C., Adam, P. A. J., Laskowski, D. E. *et al.* (1971), "Sources of Fatty Acids in the Newborn," *Pediatrics*, **47,** 192–198.
62. King, K. C., Butt, J., Roivio, K. *et al.* (1971), "Human Maternal and Fetal Insulin Response to Arginine," *New Engl. J. Med.*, **285,** 607–612.
63. Kjelberg, J. and Reizenstein, P. (1970), "Body Composition in Obesity," *Acta med. scand.*, **188,** 161–169.
64. Knight, B. L. and Myant, N. B. (1970), "A Comparison Between the Effects of Cold Exposure *in vivo* and of Noradrenaline *in vitro* on the Metabolism of the Brown Fat of New-born Rabbits," *Biochem. J.*, **119,** 103–111.
65. Knittle, J. L. and Hirsch, J. (1968), "Effect of Early Nutrition on the Development of Rat Epididymal Fat Pads: Cellularity and Metabolism," *J. clin. Invest.*, **47,** 2091–2098.
66. Kornacker, M. D. and Ball, E. G. (1968), "Respiratory Processes in Brown Adipose Tissue," *J. biol. Chem.*, **243,** 1638–1644.
67. Little, W. A., Nasser, D. and Spellacy, W. N. (1971), "Carbohydrate Metabolism in the Primate Fetus. Studies of the Placental Gradient for Glucose and Insulin in Response to Intravenous Saline, Glucose and Glucagon Injections," *Am. J. Obstet. Gynec.*, **109,** 732–743.
68. Lloyd, J. K. (1968), "Disorders of the Serum Lipoproteins. i. Lipoprotein Deficiency States. ii. Hyperlipoproteinaemic States," *Arch. Dis. Childh.*, **43,** 393–404 and 505–515.
69. Lloyd, J. K., Wolff, O. H. and Whelan, W. S. (1961), "Childhood Obesity: A Long-term Study of the Height and Weight," *Br. Med. J.*, **2,** 145–148.
70. Lubchenco, L. O. and Bard, H. (1971), "Incidence of Hypoglycemia in Newborn Infants Classified by Birth Weight and Gestational Age," *Pediatrics*, **47,** 831–838.
71. Mayes, P. (1971), "Metabolism of Lipids," pp. 263–302. In: *Review of Physiological Chemistry*, 13th Ed., edited by Harper, H. A. Oxford and Edinburgh: Blackwell Scientific Publications.
72. Melichar, V., Novak, M., Zoula, J., Hahn, P. and Kobdovsky (1966), "Energy Sources in the Newborn," *Biol. Neonat.*, **9,** 298–306.
73. Merimee, T. J., Felig, P., Marliss, E. B., Fineberg, J. E. and Cahill, G. F., Jr. (1971), "Glucose and Lipid Homeostasis in the Absence of Human Growth Hormone," *J. clin. Invest.*, **50,** 574–582.
74. Mossberg, M. A. (1948), "Obesity in Children," *Acta paediat. Stockh.*, **35,** Supplement II, pp. 1–122.
75. Obenshain, S. S., Adam, P. A. J., King, K. C. *et al.* (1970), "Human Fetal Insulin Response to Sustained Maternal Hyperglycemia," *New Engl. J. Med.*, **283,** 566–570.
76. Owen, O. E., Morgan, A. P., Kemp, H. G., Sullivan, J. M., Herreta, M. G. and Cahill, G. F., Jr. (1967), "Brain Metabolism During Fasting," *J. clin. Invest.*, **46,** 1589–1595.
77. Owen, O. E. and Reichard, G. A. (1971), "Human Forearm Metabolism During Progressive Starvation," *J. clin. Invest.*, **50,** 1536–1545.
78. Perrson, B. and Gentz, J. (1966), "The Pattern of Blood Lipids, Glycerol and Ketone Bodies During the Neonatal Period, Infancy and Childhood," *Acta paediat. Stockh.*, **55,** 353–362.
79. Prusiner, S., Cannon, B. and Lindberg, O. (1970), "Mechanisms Controlling Oxidative Metabolism," pp. 283–318. In: *Brown Adipose Tissue*, edited by Lindberg, O. New York: American Elsevier Publishing Co. Inc.
80. Randle, P. J., Garland, P. B., Hales, G. N. *et al.* (1963), "The Glucose Fatty-acid Cycle. Its Role in Insulin Sensitivity and

the Metabolic Disturbances of Diabetes Mellitus," *Lancet*, **1**, 785–789.

81. Rastogi, G. K., Letarte, J. and Fraser, T. R. (1970), "Immunoreactive Insulin Content of 203 Pancreases from Foetusus of Healthy Mothers," *Diabetologia*, **6**, 445–446.
82. Robinson, D. S. (1965), "The Clearing Factor Lipase Activity in Adipose Tissue," pp. 295–299. In: *Adipose Tissue*, edited by Renold, A. E. and Cahill, G. F., Jr. Washington D.C.: American Physiological Society.
83. Rowlatt, U., Mrosovsky, N. and English, A. (1971), "A Comparative Survey of Brown Fat in the Neck and Axilla of Mammals at Birth," *Biol. Neonat.*, **17**, 53–83.
84. Rylander, E. (1972), "Age Dependent Reactions of Rectal and Skin Temperatures of Infants During Exposure to Cold," *Acta paediat. Stockh.*, **61**, 1–9.
85. Salans, L. B., Knittle, J. L. and Hirsch, J. (1968), "Role of Adipose Cell Size and Adipose Tissue Insulin Sensitivity in the Carbohydrate Intolerance of Human Obesity," *J. clin. Invest.*, **47**, 153–165.
86. Scopes, J. W. and Tizard, J. P. M. (1963), "The Effect of Intravenous Noradrenaline on the Oxygen Consumption of Newborn Mammals," *J. Physiol., Lond.*, **165**, 305–326.
87. Silverman, W. A., Zamelis, A., Sinclair, J. C. and Agate, F. J. (1969), "Warm Nape of the Newborn," *Pediatrics, Springfield*, **33**, 984–987.
88. Smalley, R. L. (1970), "Changes in Composition and Metabolism During Adipose Tissue Development." pp. 73–96. In: *Brown Adipose Tissue*, edited by Lindberg, O. New York: American Elsevier Publishing Co. Inc.
89. Smalley, R. and Dryer, R. (1963), "Brown Fat: Thermogenic Effect of Arousal From Hibernation in the Bat," *Science, N.Y.*, **140**, 1333.
90. Smith, R. E. (1961), "Thermogenic Activity of the Hibernating Gland in the Cold Acclimated Rat," *Physiologist, Wash.*, **4**, 113 (Abstract).
91. Smith, R. E. and Hock, R. J. (1963), "Brown Fat: Thermogenic Effector of Arousal in Hibernators," *Science, N.Y.*, **140**, 199–200.
92. Smith, R. E. and Roberts, J. C. (1964), "Thermogenesis of Brown Adipose Tissue in Cold-acclimated Rats," *Am. J. Physiol.*, **206**, 143–148.
93. Tanner, J. M. and Whitehouse, R. H. (1962), "Standards for Subcutaneous Fat in British Children," *Br. Med. J.*, **1**, 446–450.
94. Toldt, C. (1970), "Contribution to the Histology and Physiology of Adipose Tissue," *Sber Akad. Wiss. Wein. Mathematischnaturwissenschaftliche Klasse*, **62**, 445.
95. Trebble, D. B. and Ball, E. G. (1963), "The Occurrence of Glycerolkinase in Rat Brown Adipose Tissue," *Fedn. Proc. Fedn. Am. Socs. exp. Biol.*, **22**, 357.
96. Vallance-Owen, J. and Lilley, M. D. (1961), "Insulin Antagonism in the Plasma of Obese Diabetics and Pre-diabetics," *Lancet*, **1**, 806–807.
97. Wasserman, F. (1965), "The Development of Adipose Tissue," pp. 87–100. In: *Adipose Tissue*, edited by Renold, A. E. and Cahill, G. F., Jr. Washington D.C.: American Physiological Society.
98. Widdowson, E. M. (1970), "Harmony of Growth," *Lancet*, **1**, 902–905.
99. Williamson, J. R. and Lacy, P. E. (1965), "Structural Aspects of Adipose Tissue," pp. 201–210. In: *Adipose Tissue*, edited by Renold, A. E. and Cahill, G. F., Jr. Washington D.C.: American Physiological Society.
100. Wittelis, B. and Bressler, R. (1965), "Lipid Metabolism in the Newborn Heart," *J. clin. Invest.*, **44**, 1639–1646.
101. Wolf, H., Stubbe, P. and Sabata, V. (1970), "The Influence of Maternal Glucose Infusions on Fetal Growth Hormone Levels," *Pediatrics*, **45**, 36–42.
102. Wolff, O. H. (1955), "Obesity in Childhood," *Jl. Med.*, **24**, 109–123.

26. SEXUAL DIFFERENTIATION IN THE FETUS AND NEWBORN

H. K. A. VISSER

"When a woman gives birth to an infant that has no well-marked sex, calamity and affliction will seize upon the land; the master of the house shall have no happiness ."

Babylonian stone tablet 1700 B.C. (1)

INTRODUCTION

Having delivered her child, every mother asks the question: is it a boy or a girl? After inspection of the external genitalia, the doctor or midwife will in general have no problems answering this question, but what are the differences between boys and girls at birth, and are there other ways, apart from inspection of the external genitalia, to determine the sex of the newborn?

As a group, boys are somewhat taller and heavier than girls, differences being 1–3 per cent in length and 4 per cent in weight, though obviously there are large individual differences and it is important to know gestational age as exactly as possible. Girls are more advanced in skeletal development. This becomes apparent during the intrauterine period; at birth the difference is some weeks; and during further growth and development this increases to about 2 years when puberty starts. At birth there are small differences in pelvic bone conformation between both sexes. Furthermore there are differences in body composition: in girls the percentage of total body fat is somewhat greater, of total body water somewhat smaller. It is clear that these criteria cannot be used for differentiating sex in the individual newborn!

There remains to us the investigation of internal organs: at birth gonads and internal genital ducts are typical for both sexes: and—last but not least—investigation of sex chromosomes. During recent years relatively simple techniques have been developed for routine chromosomal analysis in the human, skin cells and leucocytes being the tissues usually used for culture Boys have 23 pairs of chromosomes: 22 pairs of autosomes, 1 pair of sex chromosomes (XY). Girls have 22 pairs of autosomes and 1 pair of sex chromosomes (XX).

Using simple staining techniques 20–50 per cent of cells from the buccal mucosa of a normal female show densely staining sex chromatin mass adjacent to the nuclear membrane. Nuclear sex chromatin is present when at least two X chromosomes are found in the nuclei of the cells by chromosomal analysis (normal females and abnormal individuals with two or more X chromosomes). Nuclear sex chromatin is absent when only one X chromosome is present (normal males and abnormal individuals with only one X chromosome). It is generally accepted that only one X chromosome is genetically "active"; the "inactive" X chromosomes being visible as sex chromatin bodies. The total number of X chromosomes in the cell is given by the number of chromatin bodies per nucleus plus one. Sex chromatin analysis does not provide any direct information on the Y chromosome. In patients with abnormalities of sexual differentiation detailed chromosomal analysis is required.

Not only cytogenetics but experimental embryology, experimental endocrinology, steroid biochemistry and—last but not least—clinical medicine have contributed to the rapid increase in our knowledge about sexual differentiation during the last decades. A greater part of our information has been derived from animal experiments but the results of these experiments can very often, though not always, be applied to the human. Careful clinical and laboratory investigations of patients with these—relatively rare—"experiments of nature" have enriched our knowledge of heredity and variation as these operate in populations, and also of the role of the genetic material versus environmental factors in controlling the growth and development of the individual. Patients with these disorders, until recently tragic and unhappy individuals, can now usually be treated. With proper treatment (hormonal substitution, surgical reconstruction, psychological counselling) they are now able to grow up as males and females with their own identity and capable of achieving satisfactory (sexual) relationships, although very often they will not produce children.

THE ROLE OF THE Y CHROMOSOME IN THE DEVELOPMENT OF THE FETAL TESTIS

The structure of the undifferentiated gonad is identical in male (XY) and female (XX) embryos until the 7th week. During the 7th week in the XY embryo the medullary tissue of the undifferentiated gonad begins to develop into a fetal testis. About 2 weeks later in the XX embryo the cellular cortex starts to differentiate into a fetal ovary.

Interstitial cells of Leydig are visible at about 8 weeks and it is generally accepted that their secretions are responsible for further male differentiation of genital ducts and external genital organs.

THE ROLE OF THE FETAL TESTIS IN THE DEVELOPMENT OF GENITAL DUCTS AND EXTERNAL GENITAL ORGANS

Undifferentiated external genital organs are identical in XY and XX embryos at the 7th–8th week. Internal genital ducts also are identical at this time: Müllerian and Wolffian ducts being present in both sexes. The Müllerian duct is the anlage for the Fallopian tubes, uterus and upper part of the vagina. The Wolffian duct develops into epididymis, ductus deferens and seminal vesicles. Both internal and external genital organs differentiate during the 8th–12th week and the fetal testis has a decisive role in determining the direction of development. Our knowledge in this field is mainly based on the brilliant animal experiments of Jost and co-workers in Paris.[17]

The fetal testis acts in three ways; it induces development of the external genital organs; it stimulates differentiation of the Wolffian ducts; and it inhibits differentiation of the Müllerian ducts. Induction of the development of the male external genital organs is an androgenic hormonal effect that can be reproduced by administering testosterone. In castrated XX and XY fetuses systemic administration of testosterone to the pregnant mother or the fetus is followed by male differentiation of external genitalia. Physiologically the substance most probably responsible is testosterone, secreted by the Leydig cells of the fetal testis. When a male fetus is castrated, external genital organs develop along female lines; the Wolffian duct disappears and the Müllerian duct develops. Female development of internal and external genital organs does not occur only in the presence of an ovary, but also when no ovary is present. Removal of gonads in both XX and XY embryos is followed by differentiation along female lines. Early removal of one gonad in the XY fetus leads to Müllerian development on that side, while the Wolffian duct develops normally (with disappearance of the Müllerian duct) on the side on which the testis remains intact. When a testosterone propionate crystal was implanted *locally* on the side where the testis was missing, development of the Wolffian duct could be induced but the Müllerian duct did not disappear. This effect could not be reproduced by *systemic* administration of testosterone.

Thus Jost's experiments have shown that male duct differentiation is promoted by a factor that is secreted by the fetal testis and acts unilaterally. The effect cannot be reproduced by systemic injections of testosterone. For this reason some investigators have argued that the "duct male organizing substance" is not a common androgenic steroid; however testosterone secreted by the Leydig cells of the fetal testis probably will be present locally, around the testis, in higher concentrations than can be achieved by systemic injections of testosterone.

Apparently for the differentiation of the Wolffian duct a relatively high concentration of testosterone is needed locally, while much lower peripheral concentrations of testosterone induce development of male external genital organs.

Inhibition of the development of Fallopian tubes and uterus from the Müllerian ducts and subsequent disappearance of this anlage cannot be reproduced by testosterone. The factor involved is still unknown; it certainly is not an androgen.

THE ROLE OF ANDROGENIC HORMONES IN THE SEXUAL DIFFERENTIATION OF THE CENTRAL NERVOUS SYSTEM: IMPRINTING OF PSYCHOSEXUAL DIFFERENTIATION OF THE BRAIN

Maturation of gondal secretory function requires the activity of both gonadotropins, LH (luteinizing hormone) and FSH (follicle-stimulating hormone) in both sexes. However, there is a great difference in the secretory pattern of the gonadotropins in the mature adult male and female. In the male, plasma concentrations of FSH and LH are relatively constant. In the normal adult female there is a typical cyclic pattern. During the first part of the follicular phase (around the 12th day before ovulation) there is a rise in FSH, followed by a decline and then a rise again, together with a sharp increase of LH at the time of ovulation. Both values subsequently decrease to low levels. There is a typical increase of plasma estradiol during the follicular phase with a peak just prior to ovulation, and an increase of both estradiol and progesterone during the luteal phase. Both steroids are secreted by the corpus luteum. Animal experiments have demonstrated that the control of cyclic release of gonadotropins by the pituitary gland is exercised from the hypothalamus. The pituitary gland itself is bipotential: the pituitary of a male adult rat when grafted under the hypothalamus of an adult female rat will be able to release gonadotropins cyclically.

During recent decades experimental endocrinologists have been very interested in the effect of sex hormones on the early differentiation of the central nervous system. The actions of sex hormones on the brain have been studied in great detail by Harris and co-workers at Oxford.[15] On the basis of many experiments there is now good evidence that in several animals (rat, rabbit, dog, monkey) the male sex hormone has a decisive role in determining the psychosexual differentiation of the brain.

In the rat there is a critical period (a few days before birth until ten days after birth) during which the central nervous system becomes sexually differentiated.[2,3,15,25,29,30] In the male animal there is differentiation along male lines, so in adults there is continuous non-cyclic release of gonadotropins by the hypothalamo-pituitary system and sexual behaviour is typically male. In the female animal when adult there is the female type of discontinuous, cyclic release of gonadotropins and a typically female type of sexual behaviour.

When male rats are castrated during the first days of life, a female type of brain differentiation can be demonstrated in adult life. Ovarian implants in such animals form corpora lutea in a normal female manner and there is cyclic release of gonadotropins. Administration of estrogens and progesterone is followed by the female type of sexual behaviour.

Administration of testosterone to the female rat during the critical period of brain differentiation leads to a "male type" central nervous system. One single injection of 1 μg. testosterone given to the newborn female rat causes sterility in the adult. Ovaries in such animals do not show cyclic variations in activity, but usually develop follicular cysts. Gonadotropin secretion apparently is of a non-cyclic type. These late effects of testosterone given to the young female rat have been called the "early-androgen syndrome."

In experiments using electrical stimulation Barraclough and Gorski[2] localized the androgen-sensitive region in the preoptic area of the hypothalamus. Electrical stimulation of this area causes ovulation in normal female adult rats but not in "androgen-sterilized" rats. Barraclough and Gorski suggest that this area controls the cyclic discharge of gonadotropins to cause ovulation. In androgen-treated female animals LH secretion could be induced by electrical stimulation of the median eminence in the ventromedial area of the hypothalamus. According to Barraclough and Gorski this area is responsible for tonic discharge of small amounts of gonadotropin (LH), which maintain estrogen secretion but can not independently initiate ovulation. In the male this area is involved in the feedback-control of LH release by circulating androgens.

Although one must be very cautious in applying the results of such animal experiments to the human situation, and in the human such control-areas have not been anatomically localized, the same system of dual hypothalamic control of secretion of gonadotropins is probably operating in the female. There is no evidence that in the human excess of androgens at early age causes sterility: thus female patients treated for congenital adrenal hyperplasia usually have normal ovarian function at adolescence, though in some of these patients cystic ovaries have been reported. It is possible that the critical period for "androgen sterilization" in the human is at a much earlier period in relation to birth. The comparable period of human brain growth to the critical one in rats would be almost entirely fetal spanning the second and third human trimester (*see chapter* Dobbing), also the androgen concentrations required may be higher. It is not known for certain if early imprinting of the brain by androgens also applies to the human being or will affect sexual behaviour at adult age. Psychosexual development in man is a highly complex process, and depends on genetic, neurohormonal, social-cultural and other environmental factors. However, as will be discussed later in this chapter, there is some evidence that in the human species there is some effect on an individual's gender indentity and psychosexual orientation of the early influence of fetal androgens on the brain.

In summary: in several animals (amphibians and mammals) the male hormone is the dominant inductive substance acting on the genital tract and the brain (hypothalamus). The presence of testosterone induces, in both genetic males and females, a male type genital tract and a male type brain. In the absence of testosterone (in the normal female or after gonadectomy in both sexes) a female genital tract and a female type brain develop. These events are schematically presented in Figs. 1 and 2.

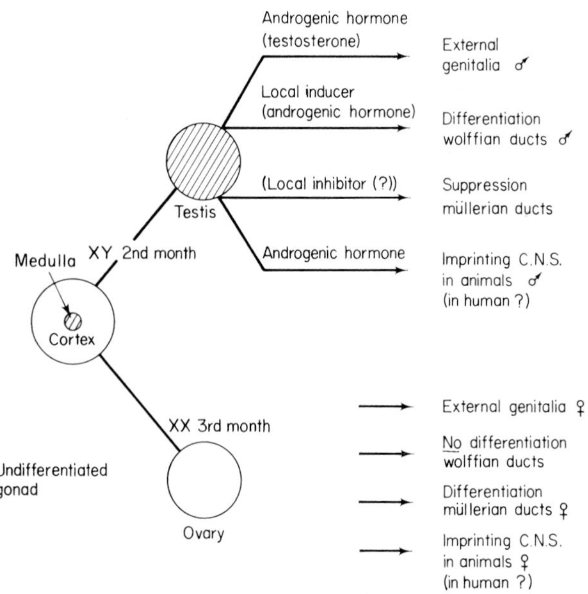

FIG. 1. Schematic presentation of male and female sexual differentiation.

Detailed analysis of the various abnormalities in sexual differentiation has demonstrated that many—if not all—findings of Jost's animal experiments can be applied to the human species. However, the spectrum of abnormalities in sexual differentiation in the human is so large that

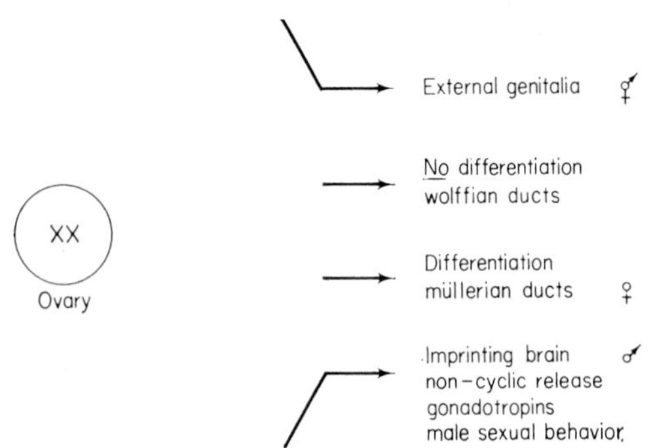

FIG. 2. Effects of androgens (testosterone) on sexual differentiation in female rat. (Harris (15), Barraclough (2) (3), v.d. Werff ten Bosch (29) (30) a.o.) Administration of androgens to fetus before birth or directly after birth.

at this moment it is not yet possible to explain the many variations in one "all-embracing" theory. Tables 1, 2, 3 and 4 present a classification of those abnormalities of sexual differentiation most frequently seen in the human. This classification has been discussed by several authorities,[27,36] and from a pragmatic and didactic standpoint it has great usefulness.

TABLE 1

CLASSIFICATION OF ABNORMALITIES IN SEXUAL DIFFERENTIATION

I Abnormalities in gonadal differentiation	Usually abnormal sex chrosomes
II Female pseudohermaphroditism	Normal XX Karyotype Ovaries and internal genital ducts normal Abnormal external genitalia: From mild clitoral hypertrophy to cryptorchid male
III Male pseudohermaphroditism	Normal XY Karyotype Testes and genital ducts normal Abnormal external genitalia: From mild hypospadias to complete female
IV Unclassified abnormalities	

ABNORMALITIES IN GONADAL DIFFERENTIATION (TABLE 2)

Congenital defects in gonadal differentiation are usually associated with anomalies of the sex-chromosomes. For an extensive discussion of this group of disorders the reader is referred to a number of review articles.[26,27,36]

The male-determining function of the Y chromosome has been questioned, since about 30 *XX males* have been reported. This remarkable phenomenon of XX males is not well explained (*see* Polani[26]). Testes in these individuals are histologically abnormal, as in Klinefelter's syndrome.

TABLE 2

SUMMARY OF MOST FREQUENT ABNORMALITIES IN GONADAL DIFFERENTIATION

External Genitalia	*Sex-Chromosomes*	*Clinical Syndrome*
Male	XXY XX XY	Klinefelter's Syndrome XX-males (?) Congenital absence of testes
Female	XO (70–80%) XX (one X-chromosome abnormal) XO/XX XO/XY	Turner's syndrome (varying clinical syndrome with dysgenesis of gonads)
Female	XX XY	Pure gonadal dysgenesis
Ambiguous	XO/XY XY (abnormal Y-chromosome)	Mixed gonadal dysgenesis
Ambiguous	XX (50%) XY XX/XY	True hermaphroditism

It is possible that in these patients the Y chromosome, essential for testis determination, is hidden in some cell lines that have not been detected; other hypotheses are Y loss from an XXY zygote and transfer (translocation) of the male-determining genetic material from the Y chromosome to the X chromosome transmitted from the father to the patient-son. Yet another theory is that the phenomenon of male phenotype in XX individuals is genetically determined by a mutant autosomal gene which overrides the effect of two XX chromosomes.

Anorchia, or congenital absence of the testes, is a relatively rare disorder, but it has to be included in the differential diagnosis of bilateral cryptochidism. As there is normal male differentiation of internal and external genitalia in these boys, the testes must have been present until the 4th month of fetal life. No satisfactory explanation has been advanced to explain the disappearance of the testes in these patients (prenatal torsion with atrophy?).

In the typical *Turner syndrome* external genitalia are completely female.

The syndrome of *pure gonadal dysgenesis* is rare. In these patients with either XX or XY karyotype the various clinical signs of the Turner syndrome are absent.

Patients with *mixed gonadal dysgenesis* have ambiguous external genital organs. Karyotype of these patients is usually XO/XY. In some variants of this syndrome an abnormal Y chromosome has been found. Recently we observed such a patient who was operated on for a unilateral inguinal hernia. There was hypospadias of minimal degree in an otherwise normal boy. On the side of the inguinal hernia the testis was completely absent; instead a rudimentary Fallopian tube and uterus was found. Apparently no differentiation of the Wolffian duct had occurred. On the contralateral side a normal testis had descended; internal genital organs were completely male. Chromosomal analysis revealed an XY-deleted karyotype. A minute Y chromosome was present; the rest must have been lost during the first cell divisions. Such patients have been described in the literature.

Two patients reported by Jacobs and Ross[16] were phenotypically completely female. Both had bilateral streak gonads, but the typical "Turner phenotype" was absent and they were of normal stature. Chromosomal analysis demonstrated an XY-isochromosome karyotype, the short arm of the Y chromosome being lost. On the basis of these and other observations it has been suggested that the male-determining genes are located on the short arm of the Y chromosome. Apparently the genetic material on the long arm of the Y chromosome prevents the development of typical Turner signs (such as short stature) that are present in patients with XO karyotype.

From birth to puberty girls (XX) are advanced in skeletal maturity when compared with boys (XY) of the same chronological age. This progressive sex-difference in skeletal development is not associated with the presence of one extra X chromosome in girls, but rather with the presence of the Y chromosome in boys. Tanner *et al.*[31] investigated skeletal development in XO girls and XXY boys. XXY individuals had a skeletal age corresponding to normal XY boys, and XO individuals had a rate of skeletal maturation corresponding to normal XX girls. Apparently genes on the Y chromosome are the cause of the retardation in skeletal development.

FEMALE PSEUDOHERMAPHRODITISM (TABLE 3)

The most common and well known "experiment of nature" which leads to female pseudohermaphroditism is the adrenogenital syndrome (congenital adrenal hyperplasia). This autosomal recessive hereditary disorder is a classic example of an inborn error of metabolism and represents the clinical expression of a hereditary defect in the biosynthesis of cortisol.[5,6,14,34]

TABLE 3

FEMALE PSEUDOHERMAPHRODITISM

(Abnormal development of genitalia with normal sex chromosomes XX and normal ovaries)

External Genitalia	*Clinical Syndrome*
Ambiguous (or cryptorchid male)	Congenital adrenal hyperplasia Transplacental steroids— exogenous maternal tumor

Figure 3 is a schematic presentation of the congenital (hereditary) defects in the biosynthesis of steroids in adrenal gland and testis which have been reported up to this moment. An impaired biosynthesis of cortisol will ultimately lead to compensatory hypertrophy of the adrenal cortex by excessive ACTH secretion via the negative

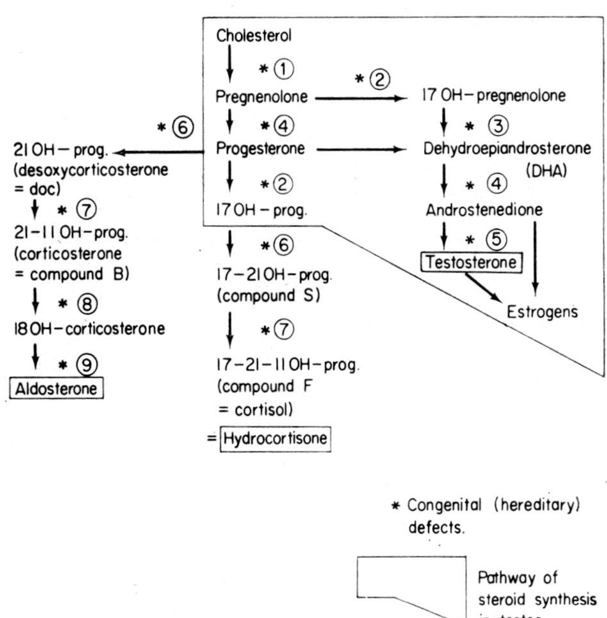

FIG. 3. Biosynthesis of steroid hormones in adrenal glands and testes.

feedback between the anterior pituitary gland (ACTH) and the adrenal cortex (cortisol). The typical clinical symptoms in affected patients are caused by excessive secretion of adrenal androgens associated with the most common variants of congenital adrenal hyperplasia: the 21- and 11-hydroxylation defects. In XX patients the increased elaboration of androgenic substances (dehydroepiandrosterone, androstenedione and also testosterone) during embryonic life results in varying degrees of virilization of the external genital organs. Figure 4 shows a common variant. There is hypertrophy of the clitoris, variable fusion of the labioscrotal folds and a persistent urogenital sinus. In the labiae majora (it looks like the scrotum in boys) no gonads are palpable. Figure 5 illustrates the effects of androgenic steroids on sexual differentiation in XX patients with congenital adrenal hyperplasia. Normal ovaries are present; the internal duct system has developed normally. It seems that local concentrations of androgens are too low to differentiate the Wolffian duct. In extreme cases of virilization a complete penile urethra can be found. In these female (XX) babies diagnosis becomes extremely difficult since they have the appearance of true male babies with cryptorchism. In all cases of ambiguous external genitalia and in all "normal" male babies with bilateral cryptorchism it is wise to carry out the simple test for sex chromatin.

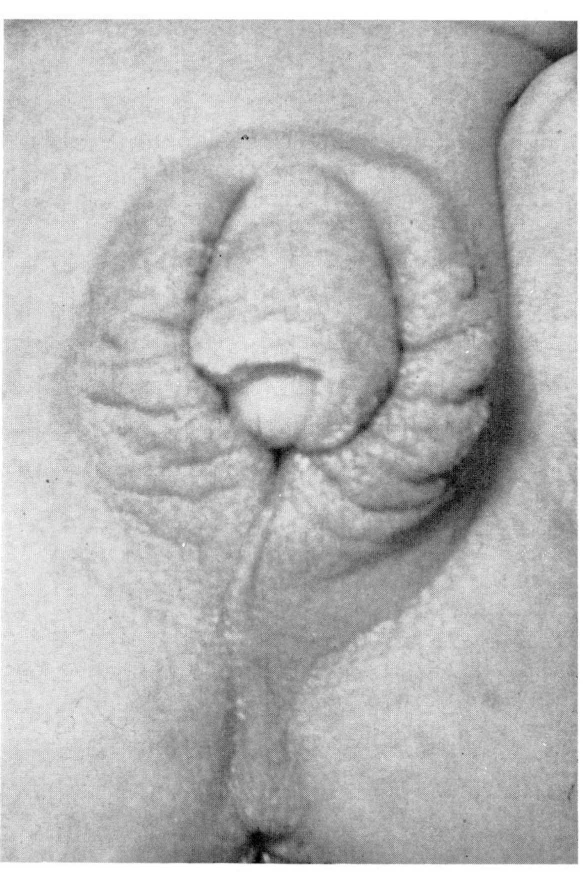

FIG. 4. External genitalia in a girl (XX) with congenital adrenal hyperplasia due to 21-hydroxylase deficiency.

The same abnormalities of external genitalia in the XX fetus can be produced by transplacental passage of steroids from mother to fetus. Many XX babies with varying degrees of virilization of external genitalia were born in the 1950's when habitual or threatened abortion was treated with synthetic progestational agents with androgenic activity.[35]

In rare cases masculinization of the XX fetus is caused by transplacental passage of steroids that are produced by a maternal tumor. Recently Mürset and co-workers[21] described a child with XX karyotype and complete male external genitalia. Gonads were not palpable. The mother was slightly hirsute, but had no complaints. Further steroid analysis revealed an androgen-producing adrenal tumor in the mother which had apparently been active during the gestation of this child.

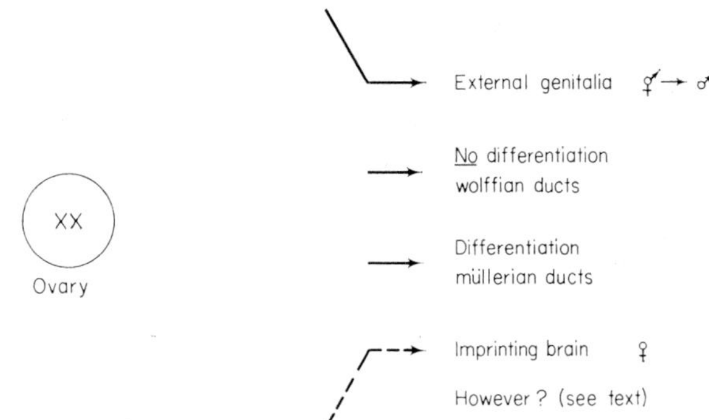

FIG. 5. Effects of androgenic steroids on sexual differentiation in human female (female hermaphroditism).
(*a*) congenital adrenal hyperplasia
(*b*) transplacental steroids (exogenous; maternal tumour).

In western countries congenital adrenal hyperplasia is one of the most common inborn errors of metabolism. Incidence of heterozygous carriers is about 1 in 50.

With proper steroid treatment in these patients a normal pattern of growth and development can be maintained. Surgical correction of the external genitalia in the female (XX) patient should be done in the first year of life.

MALE PSEUDOHERMAPHRODITISM (TABLE 4)

The persistent oviduct syndrome in an otherwise normal man is very rare. It can be explained by a congenital

TABLE 4

MALE PSEUDOHERMAPHRODITISM

(Abnormal development of genitalia with normal sex chromosomes XY and normal testes)

External Genitalia	*Clinical Syndrome*
Male	Persistent oviducts
Female	Testicular feminization
Ambiguous (or complete female)	Congenital abnormalities in biosynthesis of testosterone

defect in the production of the Müllerian duct-suppressing factor by the fetal testis (Fig. 6).

One of the most remarkable abnormalities in sexual differentiation is the syndrome of testicular feminization (Fig. 7). In these individuals with XY karyotype external genitalia are completely female. At puberty there is normal breast development. Pubic and axillary hair usually is scanty, and can be completely absent. Internal genital ducts demonstrate incomplete differentiation of the

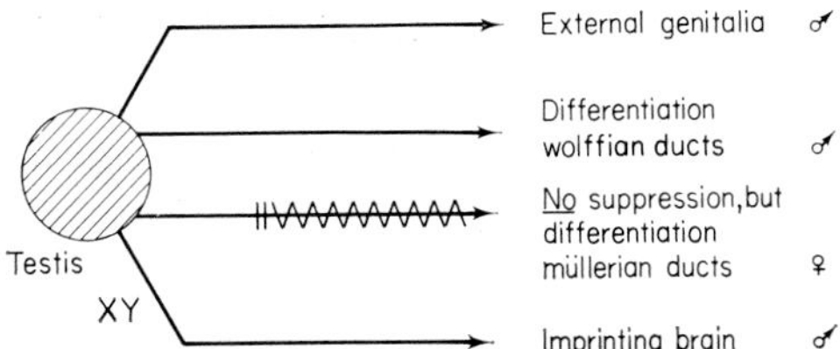

Fig. 6. Effects of "no suppression of Müllerian ducts" in otherwise normal man. (persistent ovidyct syndrome; congenital defect in synthesis of local inhibitor?)

Wolffian ducts. Müllerian ducts are suppressed, but remnants of Fallopian tubes can be found. Production of androgens by the testes is normal for age. Individuals with testicular feminization behave as normal girls during childhood and at a later age sexual behaviour is completely female. The syndrome can be explained by end-organ resistance to androgen stimulation. Administration of testosterone to these patients does not produce symptoms of virilization.

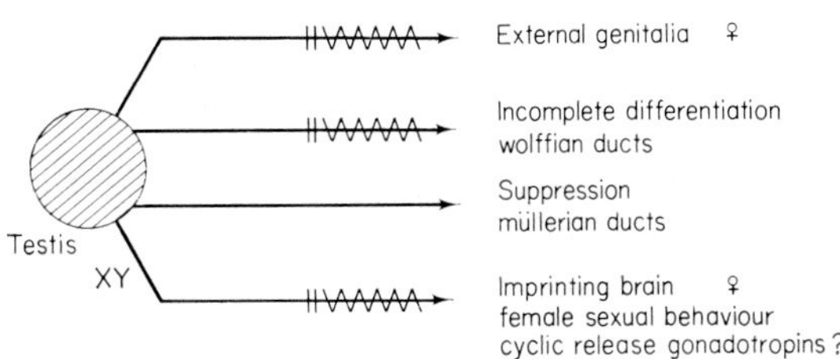

Fig. 7. Effects of "end-organ resistance" to androgens on sexual differentiation in testicular feminization syndrome.

During recent years Neumann and co-workers[23] were able to reproduce in animal experiments all symptoms of the testicular feminization syndrome by using the new anti-androgenic steroid cryproterone-acetate. This steroid competes with androgens at the end-organ level. In these experiments the normal male-type differentiation of the hypothalamus in genetically male animals could be prevented. Treatment of pregnant rats during the second half of gestation and of their newborn animals during the first three postnatal weeks with cyproterone-acetate resulted in the development of female type external genitalia in the male offspring. Following castration and ovarian implantation in such adult animals cyclic changes in the vaginal mucosa were found, indicating female-type imprinting of the central nervous system. These adult animals showed typical female sexual behaviour (Fig. 8).

Theoretically one could expect congenital hereditary defects in the biosynthesis of testosterone in the fetal testis as a cause of abnormalities in sexual differentiation. Such defects have now been reported. Figure 3 illustrates the five different defects in the biosynthesis of testosterone that have been described. Recently we described evidence for deficient 20α-cholesterol hydoxylase activity in the adrenal tissue of a patient with lipoid adrenal hyperplasia.[8] The external genitalia in female (XX) patients with this disorder are moderately or not virilized; the external genitalia in male (XY) patients are either completely female or ambiguous.

By selective inhibition with chemical compounds of different steroidogenic enzymes in the biosynthesis of cortisol and testosterone, animal models have been produced with the same enzymatic deficiencies and abnormalities in sexual differentiation as are found in the human.[5,13] In genetically male animals hypospadias were found, in genetically female animals the typical syndrome of virilization of the external genitalia. The adrenal glands of these animals were hyperplastic. An artificial model of

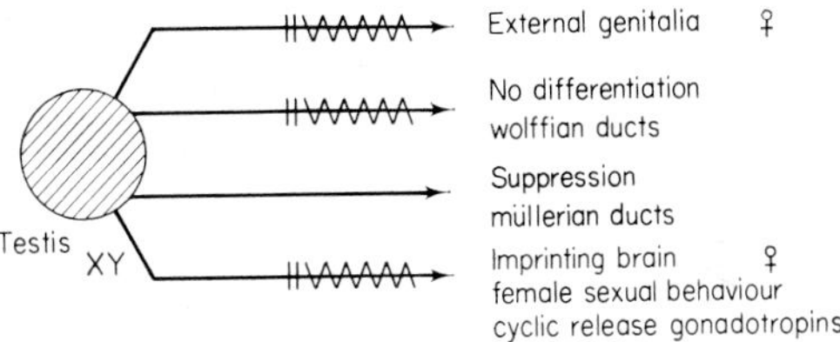

Fig. 8. Effects of anti-androgen (cyproterone-acetate) on sexual differentiation in male rat (Neumann *et al.* 23) (administration to mother during pregnacy 13th–22nd day and during 3 weeks after birth to male young). Syndrome of feminized male rats.

lipoid adrenal hyperplasia could be produced in the rat by giving the pregnant mother aminoglutethimide. Such experimental models of diseases which are found in the human species will be of great help in further research: they will enlarge our knowledge and may lead to practical results in the treatment of patients.

Let us now return to the question whether there is some evidence for "early sexual imprinting of the brain" in the human during a critical period before or directly after birth. A number of most interesting studies have been reported by Money and co-workers.[19,20] They studied sexually dimorphic behavioural characteristics in several groups of patients with abnormalities in sexual differentiation: interest in reproduction and genital morphology; romance, marriage and maternalism; cosmetic interests, physical energy and tomboyism. Adults were studied with attention to marriage and maternalism, including attitudes towards home-making, marital role, pregnancy and delivery and raising a family.

Patients with the androgen-insensitivity syndrome (testicular feminization) and patients with Turner's syndrome were found to be clearly and unmistakably feminine. Money and co-workers state that "neither a second X chromosome nor a fetal ovary is essential to the subsequent differentiation of a perfectly normal female gender identity." In contrast, in two other groups of XX patients (ages up to 14 years) with female pseudohermaphroditism the behavioural pattern was found to be not typically feminine. One group were girls with progestin-induced hermaphroditism (the mothers were treated with progestin-like steroids during pregnancy), the other group were girls with treated congenital adrenal hyperplasia. In these patients a degree of tomboyishness of behaviour was noted. The patients in comparison with controls showed a much higher incidence of interest in masculine-associated clothing and toy preference and very little interest in infant care and feminine-associated clothing and toys. In general, the patients considered themselves and were considered tomboys. Their tomboyism however did not exclude conceptions of eventual romance, marriage and motherhood. Money and co-workers discuss the possibility that the tomboyish traits are the result of an androgen effect on the brain during early fetal life.[9,10,12,19]

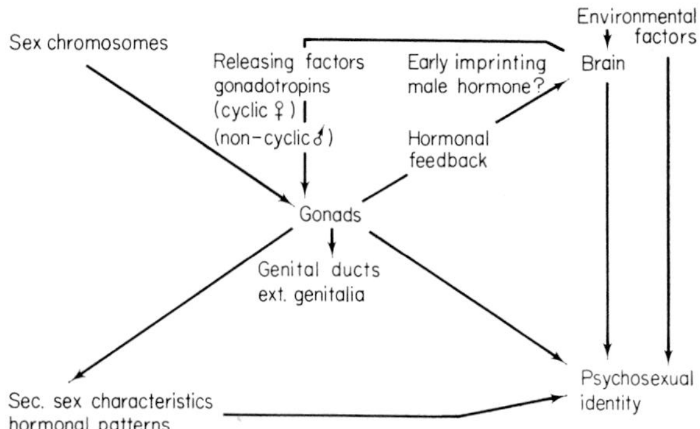

FIG. 9. Schematic presentation of the mechanisms of development of sexual differentiation and gender identity in the human.

In a group of 23 women with late-treated adrenogenital syndrome they found in some women feminine behaviour without masculine tendencies; in others they found evidence for sexually dimorphic behaviour.[11] It is most difficult to exclude the social-cultural and other environmental factors in these late-treated patients. It should be emphasized, as Money and co-workers also point out, that psychosexual orientation and gender identity in the human develop as a result of a complex pattern of genetic, neurohormonal and social-environmental factors. The overruling effect of environmental factors on the development of gender identity can be illustrated by experience with several types of children with abnormalities of external genitalia. Patients with the same karyotype and the same type of abnormality have been reared as boys and girls after proper surgical correction and hormonal treatment. In these patients gender identity follows the sex of assignment in spite of contradictory genetic and gonadal sex and in spite of eventual imprinting of the brain during fetal life.

In a group of 70 patients with congenital adrenal hyperplasia, male and female, Money and Lewis[18] found 60 per cent having an IQ of 110 and above, as compared to only 25 per cent in the ordinary population. Of 10 girls, ages 3–14 years, who had been exposed to androgens *in utero*, due to treatment of the mother with synthetic progestins, 6 had an IQ of 130 or more and none fell below 100. The authors speculate about an effect of androgens on the brain (intelligence) during a critical period of embryonic life.[20]

Figure 9 summarizes the mechanisms of development of sexual differentiation and gender identity in the human. In the end we have to conclude that the question "is it a boy or a girl?" can sometimes be a very difficult question indeed!

REFERENCES

1. Ballantyne, J. W. (1894), "The teratological Records of Chaldea," *Teratologia*, **1**, 127–142.
2. Barraclough, C. A. and Gorski, C. A. (1961), "Evidence that the Hypothalamus is Responsible for Androgen-induced Sterility in the Female Rat," *Endocrinology*, **68**, 68–79.
3. Barraclough, C. A. (1966), "Modification of the CNS Regulation of Production after the Exposure of Prepubertal Rats to Steroid Hormones," *Recent Progr. Hormone Res.*, **22**, 503–540.
4. Bongiovanni, A. M. (1961), "Unusual Steroid Pattern in Congenital Adrenal Hyperplasia: Deficiency of 3β-hydroxy Dehydrogenase," *J. clin. Endocr.*, **21**, 860–863.
5. Bongiovanni, A. M., Eberlein, W. R., Goldman, A. S. and New, M. (1967), "Disorders of Adrenal Steroid Biogenesis," *Recent Progr. Hormone Res.*, **23**, 375–439.
6. Bongiovanni, A. M. (1972), "Disorders of Adrenocortical Steroid Biogenesis. The Adrenogenital Syndrome Associated with Congenital Adrenal Hyperplasia," in *The Metabolic Basis of Inherited Disease*, pp. 857–885, (J. B. Stanbury, J. B. Wyngaarden and D. S. Fredrickson, Eds.). New York: McGraw-Hill.
7. Degenhart, H. J., Frankena, L., Visser, H. K. A., Cost, W. S. and van Seters, A. P. (1966), "Further Investigations of a New Hereditary Defect in the Biosynthesis of Aldosterone: Evidence for a Defect in 18-hydroxylation of Corticosterone," *Acta physiol. pharmacol. neerl.*, **14**, 1–2.
8. Degenhart, H. J., Visser, H. K. A., Boon, H. and O'Doherty, N. J. (1972), "Evidence for Deficient 20α-cholesterol-hydroxylase Activity in Adrenal Tissue of a Patient with Lipoid Adrenal Hyperplasia," *Acta endocr.* (*Kbh.*), **71**, 512–518.
9. Ehrhardt, A. A. and Money, J. (1967), "Progestin-induced Hermaphroditism: IQ and Psychosexual Identity in a Study of 10 girls," *J. of Sex Res.*, **3**, 83–100.
10. Ehrhardt, A. A., Epstein, R. and Money, J. (1968), Fetal Androgens and Female Gender Identity in the Early-treated Adrenogenital Syndrome," *Johns Hopk. Med. J.*, **122**, 160–167.
11. Ehrhardt, A. A., Evers, K. and Money, J. (1968), "Influence of Androgen and Some Aspects of Sexually Dimorphic Behaviour in Women with the Late-treated Adrenogenital Syndrome," *Johns Hopk. Med. J.*, **123**, 115–122.
12. Ehrhardt, A. A., Greenberg, N. and Money, J. (1970), "Female Gender Identity and Absence of Fetal Gonadal Hormones: Turner's Syndrome," *Johns Hopk. Med. J.*, **126**, 237-248.
13. Goldman, A. S. (1970), "Animal Models of Inborn Errors of Steroid Genesis and Steroid Action," in *21st Colloquium der Gesellschaft fur Biologische Chemie*, pp. 389–436. Berlin: Springer Verlag.
14. Hamilton, W. (1972), "Congenital Adrenal Hyperplasia. Inborn Errors of Cortisol and Aldosterone Synthesis," *Clinics in Endocrinology and Metabolism*, **1**, 503–547.
15. Harris, G. W. (1964), "Sex Hormones, Brain Development and Brain Function," *J. clin. Endocr.*, **75**, 627–647.
16. Jacobs, P. A. and Ross, A. (1966), "Structural Abnormalities of the Y-chromosome in Man," *Nature*, **210**, 352–355.
17. Jost, A. (1958), Embryonic Sexual Differentiation (Morphology, Physiology, Abnormalities)," in *Hermaphroditism, Genital Anomalies and Related Endocrine Disorders*, pp. 15–60 (H. W. Jones and W. W. Scott, Eds.). Baltimore: Williams and Wilkins.
18. Money, J. and Lewis, V. (1966), "IQ, Genetics and Accelerated Growth: Adrenogenital Syndrome," *Bull. Johns Hopk. Hosp.*, **118**, 365–373.

19. Money, J., Ehrhardt, A. A. and Masica, D. N. (1968), "Fetal Feminization Induced By Androgen Insensitivity in the Testicular Feminizing Syndrome: Effect on Marriage and Maternalism," *Johns Hopk. Med. J.*, **123,** 105–114.

20. Money, J. (1971), "Pre-natal Hormones and Intelligence: A Possible Relationship," *Impact of Science on Society*, **21,** 285–290.

21. Murset, G., Zachmann, M., Prader, A., Fischer, J. and Labhart, A. (1970), "Male External Genitalia of a Girl Caused by a Virilizing Adrenal Tumor in the Mother," *Acta Endocr.* (*Kbh.*), **65,** 627–639.

22. Neher, R. and Kahnt, F. W. (1966), "Gonadal Steroid Biosynthesis *In Vitro* in Four Cases of Testicular Feminization," in *Androgens in Normal and Pathological Conditions*," pp. 130–136. (A. Vermeulen, Ed.). Amsterdam: Excerpta Medica Foundation.

23. Neumann, F., Von Berswordt-Wallrate, R., Elger, W., Steinbeck, H., Hahn, J. D. and Kramer, M. (1970), "Aspects of Androgen-dependent Events as Studied by Antiandrogens," *Recent Progr. Hormone Res.*, **26,** 337–405.

24. New, M. (1970), "Male Pseudohermaphroditism Due to 17α-hydroxylase Deficiency," *J. clin. Invest.*, **49,** 1930–1941.

25. Pfeiffer, C. A. (1936), "Sexual Differences of the Hypophyses and Their Determination by the Gonads," *Amer. J. Anat.*, **58,** 195–226.

26 Polani, P. E. (1972), "Errors of Sex Determination and Sex Chromosome Anomalies," in *Gender Differences. Their Ontogeny and Significance*, pp. 13–39. (C. Ounsted and D. C. Taylor, Eds.) Edinburgh and London: Churchill Livingstone.

27. Prader, A. (1971), "Störungen der Geschlechtsdifferenzierung (Intersexualität)," in *Klinik der inneren Sekretion*, pp. 730–762, (A. Labhart, Ed.). Berlin: Springer Verlag.

28. Saez, J. M., de Peretti, E., Morera, A. M., David, M. and Bertrand, J. (1971), "Familial Male Pseudohermaphroditism with Gynaecomastia Due to a Testicular 17-ketosteroid Reductase Defect. I. Studies *In Vivo*," *J. clin. Endocr.*, **32,** 604–610.

29. Swanson, H. E. and Van der Werff ten Bosch, J. J. (1963), "Sex Differences in Growth of Rats, and Their Modification by a Single Injection of Testosterone Propionate Shortly After Birth," *J. Endocr.*, **26,** 197–207.

30. Swanson, H. E. and Van der Werff ten Bosch J. J. (1964), "The 'Early-androgen' Syndrome; Differences in Response to Pre-natal and Postnatal Administration of Various Doses of Testosterone Proportionate in Female and Male Rats," *Acta endocr.* (*Kbh.*), **47,** 37–50.

31. Tanner, J. M., Prader, A., Habich, H. and Ferguson-Smith, M. A. (1959), "Genes on the Y-chromosome Influencing Rate of Maturation in Man: Skeletal Age Studies in Children with Klinefelter's (XXY) and Turner's (XO) Syndromes," *Lancet*, **ii,** 141–144.

32. Ulick, S., Gautier, E., Vetter, K. K., Markello, J. R., Yaffe, S and Lowe, C. U. (1964), "An Aldosterone Biosynthetic Defect in a Salt-losing Disorder," *J. clin. Endocr.*, **24,** 669-673.

33. Visser, H. K. A. and Cost, W. S. (1964), "A New Hereditary Defect in the Biosynthesis of Aldosterone: Urinary C21-corticosteroid Pattern in Three Related Patients with a Salt-losing Syndrome Suggesting an 18-oxidation Defect," *Acta endocr.* (*Kbh.*), **47,** 589–612.

34. Visser, H. K. A. (1966), "The Adrenal Cortex in Childhood," *Arch. Dis. Childh.*, **41,** 2–16 (Part 1); **41,** 113–136 (Part II).

35. Wilkins, L. (1960), "Masculinization of the Female Fetus Due to the Use of Orally Given Progestins," *J. Amer. med. Ass.*, **172,** 1028–1033.

36. Van Wyk, J. J. and Grumbach, M. M. (1968), "Disorders of Sex Differentiation," in *Textbook of Endocrinology*, pp. 537–612 (R. H. Williams, Ed.). Philadelphia: Saunders.

37. Zachmann, M., Hamilton, W., Völlmin, J. A. and Prader, A. (1971), "Testicular 17, 20-desmolase Deficiency Causing Male Pseudohermaphroditism," *Acta endocr.* (*Kbh.*), suppl., **155,** 65 (abstract).

FURTHER READING

Diamond, M. (1965), "A Critical Evaluation of the Ontogeny of Human Sexual Behaviour," *Quart. Rev. Biol.*, **40,** 147–175.

Money, J. and Ehrhardt, A. (1973), *Man and Woman, Boy or Girl. Differentiation and Dimorphism of Gender Identity from Conception to Maturity.* The Johns Hopkins University Press. In press.

Ounsted, C. and Taylor, D. C. (Eds.) (1972), *Gender Differences. Their Ontogeny and Significance.* Edinburgh and London: Churchill Livingstone.

Visser, H. K. A. (1973), "Some Physiological and Clinical Aspects of Puberty," *Arch. Dis. Childh.*, **48,** 169–182.

27. THE DESCENT OF THE TESTIS

C. G. SCORER

The normal fetus

Descent of the testis

The time of descent

Boyhood, retraction and puberty

Anomalies of development

The testis
The epididymis
Peritoneal relations of the testis and epididymis
The processus vaginalis
Failure of descent

The management of the undescended testis

The transit of the testis from the abdomen into the bottom of the scrotum is a vital part of human development and essential biologically for the continuation of the human race.

If both testes remain within or just outside the peritoneal cavity after puberty, sterility of the man is apparently certain. It is difficult to find any clear record of paternity in such a case although many are claimed by the older writers. Moreover, histological differentiation of sperm-forming cells is arrested at an early stage when the testis fails to descend.

The description of descent of the testis which follows is based both on personal observations and on the writings of embryologists and anatomists. Facts about anomalies of development and descent are again culled from personal observations, but, far more, from a wide variety of sources in medical literature. References on any particular subject are to be found in a book recently published by the author in collaboration with Mr. Graham Farrington.[3]

THE NORMAL FETUS

From the 3rd to the 7th month the testis lies within the abdominal cavity just above and external to the internal inguinal ring. Postero-laterally is the iliacus muscle (Fig. 1).

The testis is a retroperitoneal organ which projects into the peritoneal cavity and has acquired a covering of peritoneum. This covering is very closely applied to the front, two sides and superior part of the testis. It forms what is subsequently called the tunica albuginea of the testis and it is impossible to dissect it from the underlying glandular tissue.

The gubernaculum is attached very firmly to the lower pole of the testis along an obliquely placed white line. It is an undifferentiated mesenchymatous structure, tubular in shape, tough in consistence and, at this stage, at least twice the length of the testis. Its diameter is slightly larger than that of the testis and the two together permanently retain their intimate connection (Fig. 2).

The testis, as mentioned, lies within the abdomen but the tip of the gubernaculum rests beneath the skin in front of the pubic bone on one side of the genital eminence. The abdominal muscles develop in such a way that they envelop the tubular gubernaculum, leaving the upper end within the

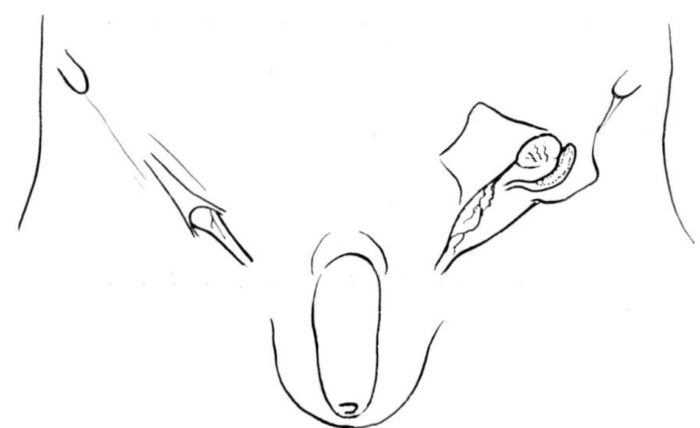

FIG. 1. The testes before descent in a foetus 7 months old. The right side shows the tip of the gubernaculum protruding through the external inguinal ring. The left shows the testis within the abdomen beneath the abdominal muscles.

abdomen but the lower protruding into the subcutaneous tissues. Thus the gubernaculum occupies an oblique tunnel through the muscle layers which comes to be known later as the inguinal canal (Fig. 3). The pathway for descent through the muscle layer is preserved until the time comes for movement to begin.

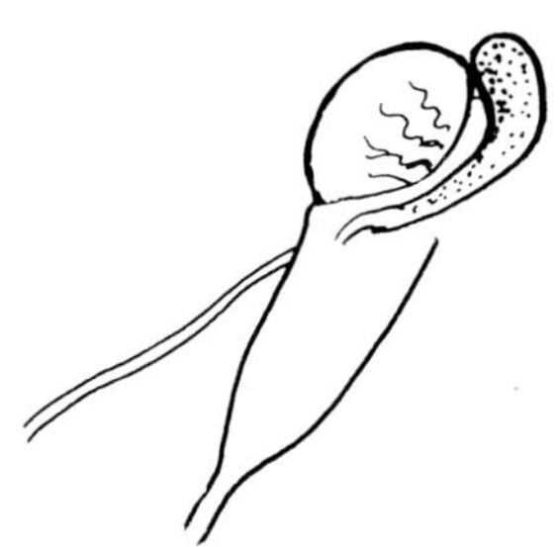

FIG. 2. The relative position of testis, epididymis, vas and gubernaculum before descent.

Two more anatomical points are important. The peritoneum covering the anterior surface and two sides of the testis passes on to the upper half of the gubernaculum to which it is also densely adherent. It dips into the inguinal canal forming a small empty pouch like a fob-pocket. This close adherence of peritoneum to testis and gubernaculum means that the peritoneum must be drawn down when descent occurs.

From the very earliest stages of development the epididymis (arising from the Wolffian duct) lies on the postero-lateral side of the testis and communicates with it at its upper pole by a dozen or so small tubules. The epididymis is closely applied to the lateral border of the testis and is, at this stage, relatively larger than in subsequent years. It tapers towards its lower end, disappears into the substance of the gubernaculum below the testis (Fig. 3) and re-appears on the medial side posteriorly as the vas deferens to pass downwards into the pelvis towards the base of the bladder.

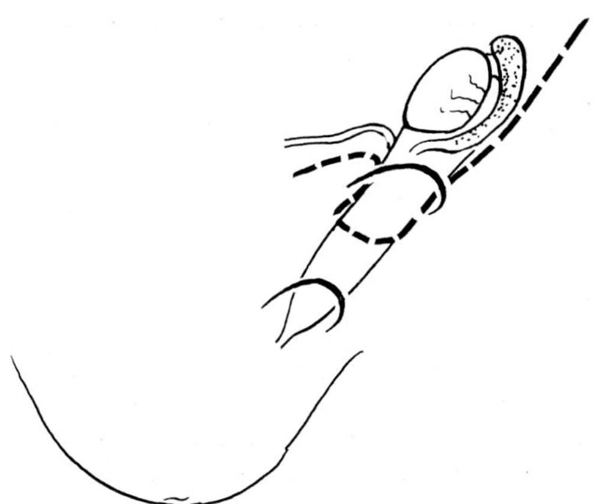

FIG. 3. The disposition of the peritoneum in relation to the gubernaculum and the inguinal canal before descent.

DESCENT OF THE TESTIS

When the time for descent has arrived a marked increase in vascularity of the gubernaculum can be noticed.

The three parts of the single unit, gubernaculum, testis and epididymis, together move down in the canal. The gubernaculum, being of the same diameter as the testis and epididymis together, there is no difficulty in the transit of the two main organs through the prepared tunnel. The three structures retain precisely their relative positions during descent.

Initially the scrotum is a rudimentary, empty container with a corrugated surface but it enlarges as the testis descends from the canal into the subcutaneous tissue and forms a sac ready to receive it. The scrotum continues to enlarge as the testis descends lower into the scrotum.

As soon as the testis has emerged from the external inguinal ring it becomes larger. In addition it changes from an elongated oval to a more spheroid shape. Both of these changes mean that a normally developing testis cannot re-enter the inguinal ring a few days after it has emerged (Fig. 4a).

Descent continues until the testis is well clear of the pubic region and lying free at the bottom of a capacious scrotal cavity. In new-born babies of maturity it will be 4·0 to 7·0 cm. from the pubic tubercle and in boyhood it normally lies at a distance of 8·0 to 9·0 cm. until pubertal changes begin.

The fixed anatomical arrangement of the organs before descent has begun means that there are four changes which take place during descent.

1. The gubernaculum, so obvious and so well developed immediately before descent, begins to atrophy once the testis has reached the scrotum. It becomes shorter, more gelatinous in appearance and ultimately assumes a white opaque appearance. This final degeneration takes some months to be completed. The oblique white fibrous attachment of the gubernaculum can be seen for the rest of life (Fig. 5), and may provide a helpful diagnostic index to the axis of the mature testis. The gubernaculum does not normally become adherent to the bottom of the scrotum; if it did the testicular retraction of boyhood would not be possible without drawing in the scrotal skin.

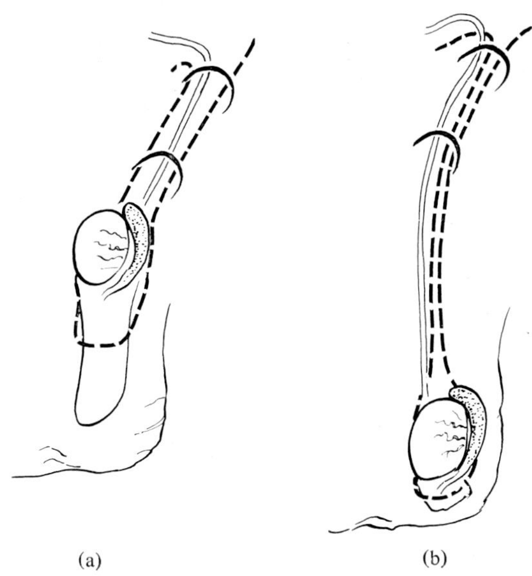

(a) (b)

FIG. 4(a). The testis with its drawn-out peritoneal sleeve entering the top of the scrotum. (b) The peritoneal sleeve (processus vaginalis) is becoming narrower before it becomes absorbed. The gubernaculum is becoming atrophic. The testis has fully descended.

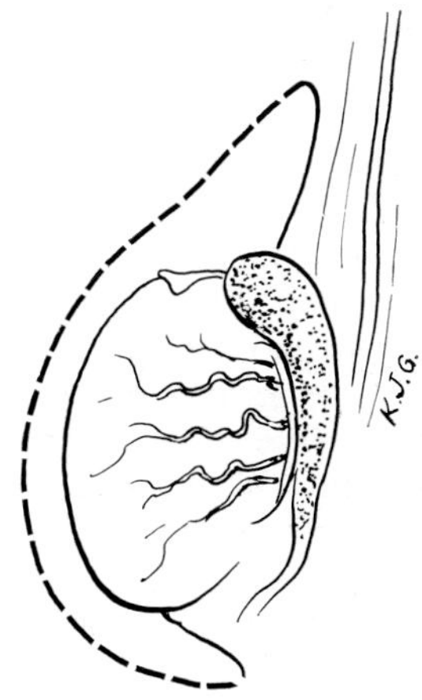

FIG. 5. The adult testis with its atrophic gubernacular remnant at its lower pole, its closely applied epididymis and the closed-off peritoneal sac around it (tunica vaginalis.)

2. The artery, veins and nerves supplying the testis must elongate rapidly to allow free descent. A thin covering of muscle, the cremaster or suspensory muscle,

is drawn down around the vascular bundle. It forms a series of arcades or loops of fibres stretching out from the inner layers of the abdominal muscles down to the testis to envelop it anteriorly. Its action is to draw the testis from the scrotum back into the groin when the genital area is stimulated.

3 The epididymis moves down alongside the testis. As it passes through the canal and into the scrotum the vas necessarily becomes pulled down too and elongates at the same time. It lies postero-medial to, but separate from, the vascular bundle.

4. The processus vaginalis is the name given to the peritoneal sheath lying on the front and two sides of the gubernaculum, testis, epididymis and vascular bundle. As mentioned above, the close attachment of the peritoneum to the three organs is characteristic of the fetal arrangement.

As descent occurs the peritoneum is necessarily drawn down into the canal and scrotum and lies, like a long sleeve, in front of the vascular bundle and vas deferens. The leading part of the sleeve, or empty peritoneal sheath, precedes the descent of the testis for it is attached to the gubernaculum well below the testis (Fig. 4b).

Normally the processus vaginalis disappears shortly after full descent has been achieved. It becomes absorbed from above down leaving only a small empty pouch covering the front and sides of the testis and epididymis and the atrophied gubernaculum. This peritoneal remnant is the tunica vaginalis of the testis.

THE TIME OF DESCENT

The testis descends into the scrotum at about the 7th-8th month of fetal life and when the weight of the fetus is between 1,500 g. and 2,750 g. weight.

Descent is a fairly rapid process—at least through the canal and upper part of the scrotum. This can be shown by watching testicular descent from day to day in a premature infant. It is evident, however, that descent continues and, with it, scrotal development in the first few months after birth. By the end of six months, at the latest, stability has been reached, but then other influences begin to appear.

If fully mature new-born boys are examined at birth, between 3 and 4 per cent will be found to have one or both of the testes undescended. If these boys are watched, full descent will occur in some of them but in the remainder it will be incomplete or may fail altogether. If full descent has not occurred within the first three months of life in a full term infant there is no evidence to suggest it ever will take place. Descent is an incident of the late uterine period which may be carried over briefly after birth but thereafter it ceases.

BOYHOOD, RETRACTION AND PUBERTY

The scrotum of the new-born boy is relatively larger than at any other time of life; it may reach half way down the thigh. Examination of its contents is easy.

By the end of the first year the baby has gained a substantial covering of subcutaneous fat especially in the pubic area and thighs. In addition, retraction of the testis towards the groin, which is absent at birth, has begun to take place. Examination of a restless infant between the ages of 9 and 24 months to determine the exact position of the testes is often a futile procedure.

When the boy reaches the age of 3 or 4 years he is becoming relatively slimmer and the testes can then be felt provided that retraction does not cause them to disappear into the groin. The phenomenon of retraction is difficult to explain except as a protective reflex against damage but, granted this possibility, many mysteries are associated with it. Why, for instance, can it be so persistent without any apparent initiating cause? It reaches its maximum between 5 and 10 years of age and disappears just before puberty. Very rarely it does occur spontaneously in adults.

In its lesser manifestation it is a momentary or temporary drawing up of the testis on stimulation of the skin of the thigh, or even on uncovering the scrotum before examination. The full picture is one of apparently permanent residence of one or both testes in the subcutaneous tissues in front of, or above, the external inguinal ring, yet such a boy may be known to have had full descent at birth. Patience on the part of the doctor will be rewarded. The testis will drop before puberty and will develop normally.

When is retraction not retraction but failure of descent? This is often a question of vital importance. There is one infallible guide and one useful pointer. If the testes were known to be fully descended at birth then the case must be one of retraction—hence the importance of a competent examination of the testes at birth with a record made or the parents informed. If the scrotum is well formed and of equal capacity on each side then the case is probably one of retraction. If both these tests are equivocal there is no sure way of diagnosis between high retraction and failure of descent although repeated examinations in favourable surroundings may sooner or later provide the answer.

At puberty the first obvious change is an enlargement of the testes followed by the appearance of pubic hair. Next, a progressive enlargement of all parts of the external genitalia takes place, penis, scrotum and testes. The testes increase in weight some twenty times and come to lie at a much lower level relative to the pubic crest. From infancy to puberty the position of the testis is constantly 8·0–9·0 cm. from the pubic crest. After puberty, as a result of a generalized enlargement of all organs, the testes lie 12 15 cm. from the crest and as years pass may be still lower.

ANOMALIES OF DEVELOPMENT

During the intricate development of the testis from its earliest to its final stages there is the possibility of failure or defect at many points.

The Testis

One or both testes may fail to arise from the intermediate cell mass, or, having arisen, may become atrophied in subsequent weeks owing to loss of blood supply. Unilateral anorchia is not very uncommon being found in more than 3 per cent of all cases operated on for failure of descent. Bilateral anorchia is very rare and leads to eunuchoid (or lack of male sexual) characteristics after puberty.

Poor development of the germ cells in the testis (dysgenesis) may be associated with failure of descent on one or both sides and, of course, increases the likelihood of subsequent infertility.

The testis on one side may be in two parts (duplication) or may cross over the midline to emerge from the opposite external ring (crossed ectopia). Both are very rare anomalies.

The Epididymis

The epididymis and vas together form a very long and complex tube. It is not surprising that obstructions and defects often occur. If, as a result, sperm cannot be transmitted from the testis the man's fertility will be depressed. If both sides are defective he may be sterile.

A lengthened or kinked epididymis is often found during an operation on an undescended testis. Moreover, the junction between testis and epididymis may be weak and tenuous owing to the length of the gap between the two organs.

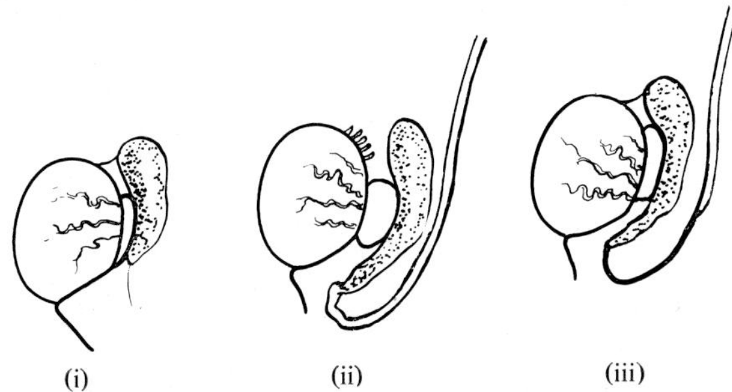

FIG. 6. Common Epididymal Defects.

(i) Failure of development of the lower half of the epididymis and the vas deferens.
(ii) Vasa efferentia ending blindly.
(iii) Failure of canalization of the vas.

Most epididymal faults are noticed during operations on subfertile men. The commonest is an absence of part of the vas deferens including, sometimes, part of the epididymis.[2] When the structures appear normal to naked-eye examination there may still be an obstruction of the lumen where the epididymis joins the vas or a failure of connection between the testis and the epididymis (Fig. 6).

Such defects cannot usually be detected by palpation of the organs through the scrotal wall; a direct inspection by surgical operation is necessary in order to establish a diagnosis.

Peritoneal Relations of the Testis and Epididymis

If the testis, instead of protruding into the peritoneal cavity from behind, it projected into it on a mesentery it is particularly liable to undergo torsion at puberty. Normally the testis is covered on the front, two sides and above by peritoneum and has a bare area posteriorly. If it lies free in the peritoneal cavity on a mesentery this area becomes negligible in size and the testis can move freely on a peritoneal suspension (Fig. 7).

When the testis descends into the scrotum, owing to its

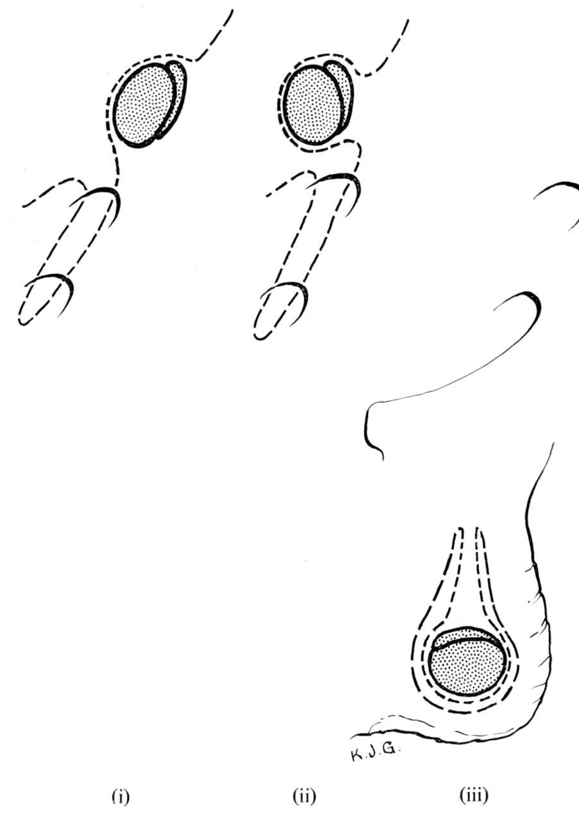

FIG. 7. Peritoneal Relations of the testis to show the anatomy of torsion.

(i) The normal undescended testis.
(ii) The testis projecting into a mesentery before descent.
(iii) After descent the mesentery lengthens and the testis lies horizontally. (The interrupted line represents the peritoneum.)

mobility it no longer lies in a vertical disposition but falls forward to hang horizontally or even upside down. With the increase in size of the testis at puberty rotation is particularly prone to occur and, if not relieved within a very short time, infarction will occur with total loss of the testis.

The Processus Vaginalis

By far the commonest abnormality associated with descent of the testis is a failure of absorption of the peritoneal sleeve after it has been drawn down into the scrotum with the descending organs. Inguinal hernias are very frequently seen after birth, some may disappear spontaneously, some remain empty and cause no trouble until boyhood or early adult years but some are so wide at the neck that abdominal contents easily enter. Obstruction is frequent and, occasionally, strangulation. A partial closure of the sac at the upper end, leaving a small communicating channel, allows a collection of peritoneal fluid around the testis or in the cord. A transient neonatal hydrocele is found in nearly 10 per cent of all new-born boys.

Failure of Descent

In full-term new-born boys at birth over 97 per cent have both testes well down in the scrotum. In the first three months after birth some testes, delayed in descent, will reach the bottom of the scrotum. After this time there is no evidence that an incompletely descended testis will ever reach the bottom of the scrotum. The true incidence of failure of descent of one or both testes is probably just under 1 per cent in all males over 1 year of age.

Why does the testis fail to descend? We do not know. Perhaps the more important question is—How does the testis normally descend?

Many suggestions have been made in past centuries as to how the testis moves from the abdomen into the scrotum.

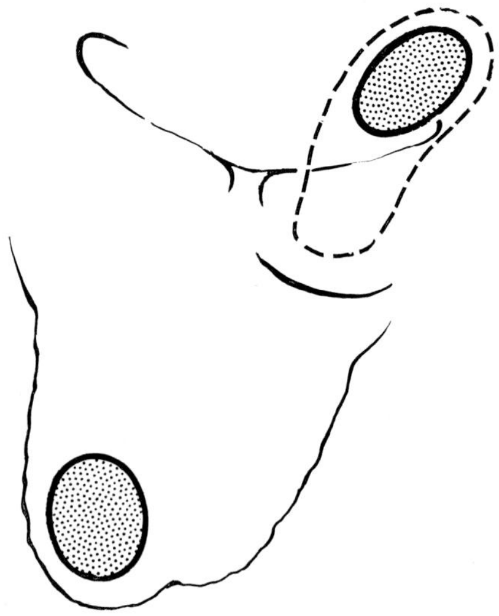

FIG. 8. The obstructed testis whose pathway of descent is blocked by a fascial barrier.

Increasing abdominal pressure may push it out of the canal. Growth of the gubernaculum may draw it towards the scrotum. If the gubernaculum is attached to the lower pole of the scrotum its contraction may draw the testis down. Chemotaxis may cause the gubernaculum and testis to move into the scrotum. Hormones stimulate the movement of the testis. Such theories as these are either untenable logically or are not susceptible of proof.

Failure of descent has also been attributed to many causes. The testicular artery or the vas is too short to allow descent. The testis is too large to enter the canal. The peritoneum is fibrotic and will not extend. The scrotum fails to enlarge. Fascial bands impede the way. Hormones are deficient. And so on. There are only two firmly established facts. The first is that the undescended testis and its epididymis are often found to be anatomically and histologically different from the opposite normal testis. The epididymis is often misshapen or elongated. It seems that the undescended testis is often itself an ill-developed structure and its gubernaculum tenuous and poor in quality. In other words, the testis fails to descend because it is an abnormal organ. Teleologically speaking, nature protects the species from the possible perpetuation of deformity by not allowing the testis to descend.

The second fact is that the pathway to the scrotum is often obstructed. Most frequently there is a condensation of Scarpa's fascia placed like a hammock below the external inguinal ring and so barring the entry of the testis into the scrotum.[1] The testis is obstructed in its descent at this level and so remains above the pubic bone in the superficial inguinal pouch (Fig. 7). It is significant that in such cases the anatomy and histology of the testis and its other components are normal and operative treatment is effective in bringing it to its rightful place in the scrotum.

Occasionally fascial barriers deflect the testes to an ectopic position in the perineum, in front of the penis or into the femoral ring. Such deformities are equally amenable to surgical treatment.

THE MANAGEMENT OF THE UNDESCENDED TESTIS

An analysis of cases of failure of descent shows that some are to be found high in the scrotum and some in the inguinal region in front of the external inguinal ring. A few lie within the inguinal canal and a still smaller number in the abdomen.

If no treatment is given the testis will remain in the same position throughout life. Moreover, it will fail to mature histologically. The further away the testis is from the bottom of the scrotum the greater the degree of cellular arrest or atrophy. In addition, the undescended testis is more prone to malignant degeneration and the higher the testis the more likely is such a change. Torsion may occur in the undescended testis (although much less commonly than in the scrotal one). Hernia is an almost invariable accompaniment of the undescended testis especially in the early months of life.

For these reasons there are good grounds for advising operative treatment to bring the testis, if possible, to its proper position. The hernia can be cured, torsion prevented, and histological development given the best conditions in which to occur. There is evidence that bringing the testis into the scrotum does not prevent malignant change from occurring but at least the enlarged testis will be easily seen and easily removed.

Operation is best done early in life. If done before 5 years of age histological development will continue, if later, arrest of development cannot be reversed. By puberty it is too late. Both psychologically and physically operation is better done either between 3 and 6 months of age or between 4 and 5 years.

Good results from surgical treatment are to be expected if the testis lies high in the scrotum or in the superficial inguinal region. A favourable position can be made for the testis low in the scrotum and it is known that in theseicases histological development continues. With the canalicular or intra-abdominal testis results of treatment are in general disappointing. A second operation can seldom improve on the first. Orchidectomy may be done in the boy when the testis is obviously defective and cannot be brought down. It should certainly be done in the adolescent for no undescended testis should be left in the abdomen or in the canal after puberty.

REFERENCES

1. Browne, D. (1938), "The Diagnosis of Undescended Testicle," *Brit. med. J.*, **2**, 168–171.
2. Girgis, S. M., Etriby, A., El-Hefnawy, H. and Kahil, S. A. (1969), "Testicular Biopsy in Azoaspermia. A Review of the Last Ten Years Experience of over 800 Cases," *Fertil. and Steril.*, **20**, 467–477.
3. Scorer, C. G. and Farrington, G. H. (1971), *Congenital Deformities of the Testis and Epididymis*. London: Butterworth.

28A. THE GROWTH AND DEVELOPMENT OF THE ENDOCRINE GLANDS—ADRENAL CORTEX

CONSTANCE C. FORSYTH

THE ANATOMY OF THE ADRENAL CORTEX

Full details of the anatomy of the adrenal cortex are given by Symington.[90] The rudiments of the adrenal cortex, which is derived from the mesoderm of the coelomic epithelium and the adjacent mesenchymal cells, begin to form in the fetus at the 6th week of gestation and grow to become a relatively large endocrine organ, which differentiates into a broad fetal zone next to the medulla of the gland and a thin subcapsular zone, the adult zone. The adrenal medulla has a common origin with the elements of the sympathetic nervous system in primitive neuroectoderm and is functionally a separate organ from the adrenal cortex although both are enclosed by a common capsule. The adrenal gland in the pre-viable fetus of 16–20 weeks' gestation consists of a narrow adult zone and a prominent fetal zone (Fig. 1). The adult zone consists of small cells with a dense nucleus and scanty cytoplasm with a few lipid globules. In contrast the cells of the fetal zone are large with a dense nucleus and more abundant cytoplasm in which lipid is present. In the mature stillborn fetus, the adult zone has increased in thickness to make up about 20 per cent of the total adrenal cortex and the fetal zone shows congestion and haemorrhage but very little degenerative change. In adrenal glands from newborn infants dying within a few days of birth, signs of degeneration of the fetal zone are already evident. Studies of infants dying between the 4th and 35th day of life show marked cellular degeneration and narrowing of the fetal zone whereas the adult zone has increased in size to make up about 50 per cent of the cortex (Fig. 2). The further development of the adrenal cortex is less clearly defined because of the paucity of post-mortem material so that it is not known exactly when the fetal zone finally disappears nor when the adult zone differentiates into the zona glomerulosa, zona fasciculata and zona reticularis. It is, however, likely that the latter occurs during the 1st year of life. In the gland of the young child the zona glomerulosa completely encloses the zona fasciculata, but in the adult gland the zona glomerulosa has become focal in distribution so that in some areas the zona fasciculata is directly adjacent to the capsule. From post-mortem studies, the average combined weight of both adrenal glands at birth is 10 g. falling to 6 g. at the end of the 1st week of life and 5 g. at the end of the 2nd week due to degeneration of the fetal zone. Thereafter it gradually increases, with a period of more rapid growth at puberty, to the average level in adults of 13 g. The weight of the adrenal glands is directly related to the body weight of the individual.

In the adult, the cortex constitutes about 90 per cent and

the medulla about 10 per cent of the adrenal gland. The adrenal cortex and medulla are surrounded by a common capsule and the glands lie in relation to the upper poles of the kidneys embedded in fat. Accessory adrenal glands may be present consisting usually of cortex only. They lie near the kidneys or in the retroperitoneal area or in relation to the organs of reproduction. Very occasionally heterotopic adrenal tissue is found in sites outwith the normal embryonic distribution. The adrenal glands are vascular

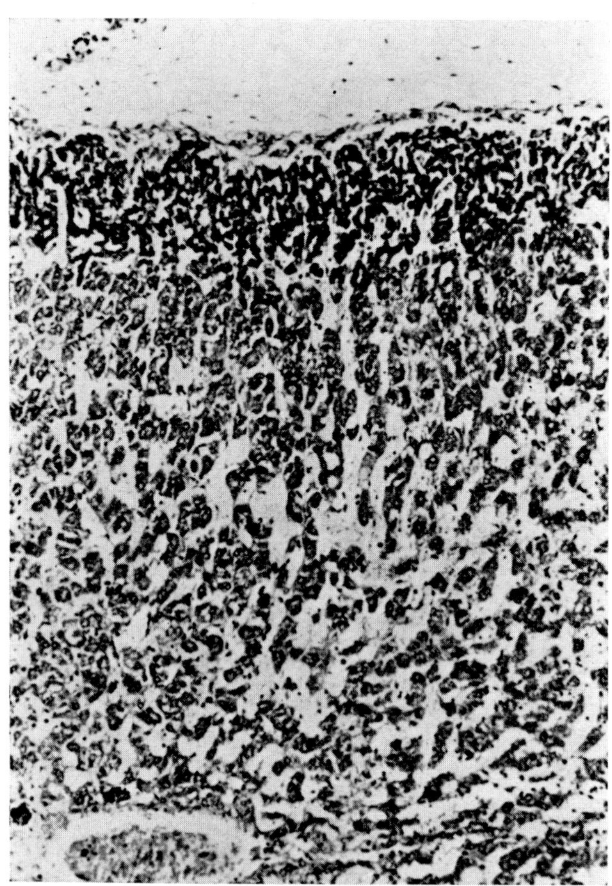

FIG. 1. Fetal adrenal cortex at 16 weeks' gestation. The narrow adult zone is shown above and the rest of the section is fetal zone. H and E (×82) (from Symington, T., 1969. Functional Pathology of the Human Adrenal Gland. E and S. Livingstone Ltd., Edinburgh and London.)

having an abundant arterial blood supply. The main effluent collects in the central veins but there is an alternative drainage route in the form of emissary veins which can enlarge in emergency. It is accepted that there is no innervation of the adrenal cortex in marked contrast to the medulla which is richly innervated. Adrenal lymphatics are known to be present but there is lack of agreement regarding their distribution. For many years it has been accepted that the adrenal cortex is divided into three zones, the zona glomerulosa, the zona fasciculata and the zona reticularis; a concept which is diagrammatically represented in Fig. 3. However, the three classical zones are rarely clearly demarcated in normal human adrenal glands. The cells of the zona glomerulosa have small, dark-staining nuclei and scanty lipid-containing cytoplasm. There is no sharp dividing line between the zona glomerulosa and the zona fasciculata and in sections of normal adult adrenal glands the zona fasciculata extends outwards to the capsule in those areas where no zona glomerulosa can be defined. Most of the adrenal cortex consists of the zona fasciculata. Its cells are arranged in long regular columns and, in the non-stressed gland, are filled with large lipid globules. The change from the lipid-containing cells or clear cells of the zona fasciculata to the compact cells of the zona reticularis is clear cut. The cells of the zona reticularis are arranged in alveoli separated by prominent thin-walled sinuses and they have granular eosinophilic cytoplasm with only a small lipid content. In the resting state, mitotic cell division takes place in the zona reticularis but not in the zona fasciculata. With regard to the site of formation of the adrenocortical hormones, aldosterone is formed by the cells of the zona glomerulosa largely independent of ACTH stimulation. Cortisol, corticosterone, the adrenal androgens and oestrogens are formed by the zona reticularis and the zona fasciculata which act as a single functional unit.

Changes in the structure of the adrenal cortex are seen due to stress prior to death or due to the administration of ACTH to patients before the therapeutic removal of an adrenal gland. In the resting state, the zona fasciculata acts as an inactive storage zone of lipid steroid precursor, which is readily available in times of acute stress. The effect of more prolonged stress is to increase the weight of the adrenal gland as a whole and to produce an apparent widening of the zona reticularis at the expense of the zona fasciculata, because of a change in the clear cells of the zona fasciculata to compact cells, indistinguishable in their reactions from the compact cells of the zona reticularis, extending outwards from the interface between the two zones. This may leave a narrow rim of clear cells at the surface of the gland or, under stronger stimulation, all of the clear cells of the zona fasciculata may become compact. The vascular arrangement of the human adrenal gland is such that ACTH is continually in contact with the zona reticularis and, in times of stress, can be brought into contact with the zona fasciculata at the interface between the two zones. The immediate effect of endogenous or exogenous ACTH is to release steroid hormones from precursor steroids stored in the clear cells of the zona fasciculata and its long term effect is to increase the number of enzymatically active compact cells to allow production of increased quantities of steroids.

THE PHYSIOLOGY OF THE ADRENAL CORTEX

Full details of the physiology of the adrenal cortex are given in various textbooks.[37,38,49]

The Control of Adrenocortical Function

Nervous impulses from higher centres stimulate the median eminence of the hypothalamus to produce Corticotrophin Releasing Factor (CRF), which is transported

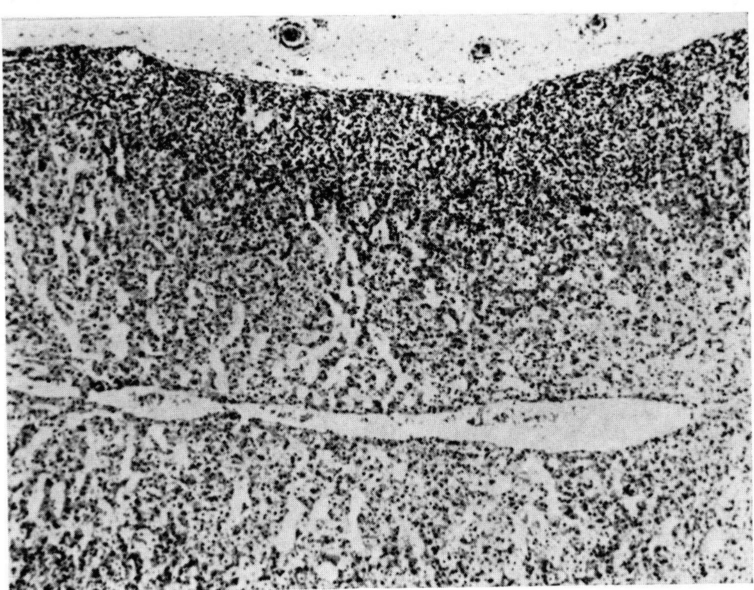

FIG. 2. Neonatal adrenal cortex—4–35 days. The adult zone constitutes above half the width of the cortex. The fetal zone is narrower and cell degeneration is a marked feature. H and E (×34) (from Symington, T., 1969. Functional Pathology of the Human Adrenal Gland. E and S. Livingstone Ltd., Edinburgh and London.)

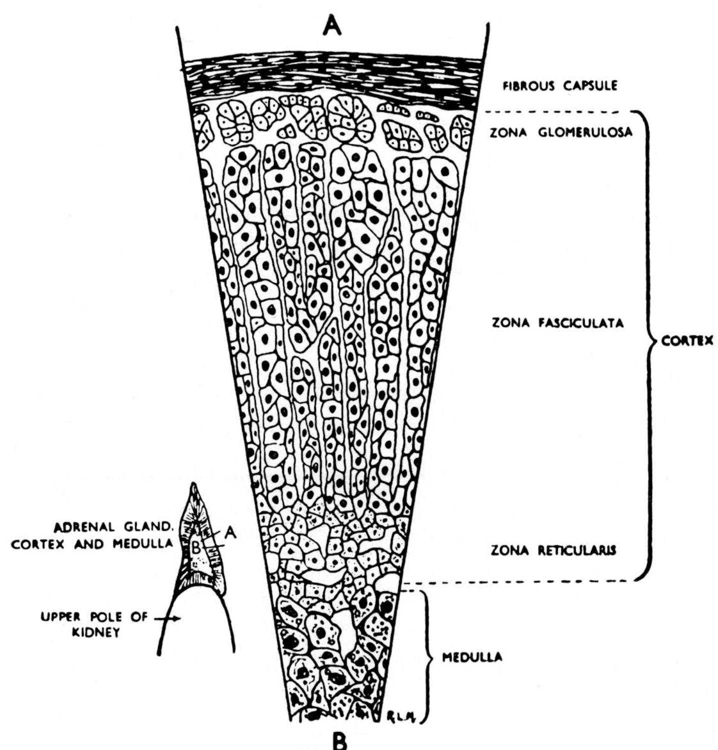

FIG. 3. Diagram of adrenal gland showing differentiation into medulla and cortex, the latter itself being divided into three zones not clearly demarcated from one another. The part of the gland from which the section was taken is shown alongside (AB) (from Bell, G. H., Davidson, J. N. and Scarborough, H., 1968. Textbook of Physiology and Biochemistry, 7th Edition, E. and S. Livingstone Ltd., Edinburgh and London.)

to the anterior pituitary gland by a vascular connection (Fig. 4). The chemical nature of CRF has not been completely elucidated but it may be a polypeptide similar to vasopressin. The anterior pituitary gland secretes corticotrophin (ACTH), which is transported by the blood stream to the adrenal cortex, where ACTH stimulates the production of the corticosteroids and the adrenal androgens. The level of cortisol production is involved in a feedback mechanism in that cortisol inhibits the hypothalamic release of CRF. This mechanism maintains a normal level of cortisol secretion, but during stress it is overcome by excitatory impulses from the hypothalamus leading to an increased cortisol secretion rate. The activity of the higher centres varies throughout the 24 hr., leading to fluctuations in ACTH and cortisol production which occur within the

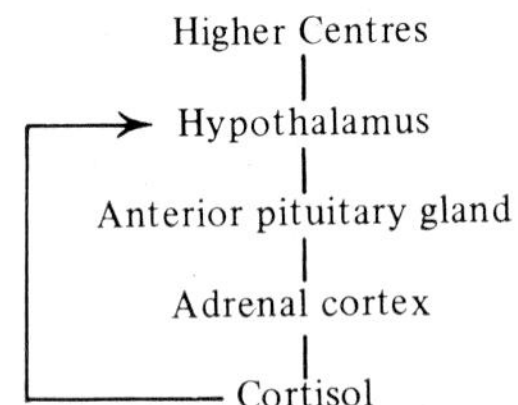

FIG. 4. The control of adrenocortical function.

broader pattern of the normal diurnal variation, characterized by levels of plasma ACTH and plasma cortisol which are higher in the morning than in the late evening. The diurnal variation depends upon sleeping and waking activity and differs in timing in night-shift workers[65] and, as expected, it differs in infants.[41,52] Light does not appear to affect the rhythm directly as it is preserved in blind persons living in normal households. However, it may be abnormal in disorders of the central nervous system specifically affecting the hypothalamus. Determination of the diurnal rhythm may be of value clinically. When the Mattingly method[63] is used to measure plasma "cortisol" or, more correctly, the "11-hydroxy-corticosteroids," under normal circumstances, the 8–9 am.. level varies between 10 μg. and 25 μg./100 ml. and the 10 p.m. to 12 midnight level is less than 12 μg./100 ml. The diurnal variation is considered normal if the evening value is half the morning value or less than 10 μg./100 ml. whichever is lower.[16]

ACTH stimulates the conversion of cholesterol to pregnenolone in the synthetic pathway of the adrenocortical steroids. ACTH is a straight-chain polypeptide consisting of 39 amino acids of which 1–24 are responsible for its biological effects. The amino acid sequence 1–13 is identical in α-Melanocyte-Stimulating Hormone (α-MSH), which is also secreted by the anterior pituitary gland and has greater biological significance in the lower animals than in man. The structural similarity explains the pigment-producing properties of ACTH. If injected intravenously, ACTH rapidly disappears from the circulation and in man, the plasma half-life is approximately 15 min. The molecule breaks down readily so that the urinary excretion is negligible.

As already described, ACTH controls the secretion of cortisol and it also controls corticosterone production. Its effect on the adrenal 17-oxosteroids is less consistent, and a poorer response of 17-oxosteroid excretion following ACTH is seen in children, who normally excrete very small amounts of adrenal androgens, than in adults. These findings could be due to differences in the response of the metabolic pathways concerned. As will be discussed on page 494, hormones from the gonadal axis may begin to affect the adrenal androgen pathway a few years before puberty leading to an increasing excretion of adrenal androgens until adult levels are reached. The administration of ACTH stimulates the output of aldosterone, although the pathway is not very sensitive and the effect is transitory, even if ACTH administration is continued for several days. It seems likely that changes in the plasma sodium concentration and in the blood volume, acting indirectly through the renin-angiotensin mechanism, are mainly responsible for the control of aldosterone secretion, with ACTH playing a subsidiary role. The regulatory effect of changes in the plasma potassium concentration, in contrast, appears to operate directly on the adrenal cortex. A low plasma sodium level and a reduced blood volume stimulate the juxtaglomerular cells of the kidney to produce the enzyme renin. When released into the circulation it leads to the formation of angiotensin I, which is further converted to angiotensin II. Angiotensin II stimulates the adrenal cortex to produce aldosterone, as well as having an independent role in the maintenance of blood pressure. Aldosterone acts on the distal tubule of the kidney to promote reabsorption of sodium in exchange for potassium and hydrogen ions.

Adrenal Steroid Synthesis

In the blood the parent steroids, synthesized by the adrenal cortex, are present in a free, biologically active form or as inactive protein-bound steroids or as inactive salts, for example dehydroepiandrosterone sulphate (DHAS). The free steroids act on many tissues and are metabolized, particularly in the liver, to steroid derivatives which may or may not retain biological activity whereas the protein-bound steroids are protected from degradation and act as a reserve for the free steroid pool. By far the greater proportion of the steroid derivatives are excreted in the urine conjugated as glucuronides or sulphates, which are more freely soluble in water than unconjugated steroids.

The basic corticosteroid formula with 21 carbon atoms is shown in Fig. 5, with the conventional lettering of the steroid rings and numbering of the carbon atoms. The 17-oxosteroids have an oxo group at C_{17} and have 19 carbon atoms since they do not possess the side chain. The principal pathways of adrenal steroid synthesis are illustrated in Fig. 6 and the corresponding steroid formulae in Fig. 7. Cholesterol is synthesized from acetate by the adrenal cortex but cholesterol from other sources, for example the liver, is also utilized. By a series of enzyme reactions, namely those of 20α-hydroxylase, 22-hydroxylase and 20, 22 desmolase, cholesterol is converted to Δ_5-pregnenolone. This stage of the metabolic pathway is stimulated by ACTH. On the cortisol pathway, progesterone is formed from Δ_5-pregnenolone by the action of the enzymes 3β-hydroxy-dehydrogenase and Δ_5–Δ_4 isomerase. The enzyme 17α-hydroxylase leads to the formation of 17α-hydroxy-progesterone, then 21-hydroxylase yields 11-deoxy-cortisol and finally 11β-hydroxylase yields cortisol. The enzyme 11-dehydrogenase converts

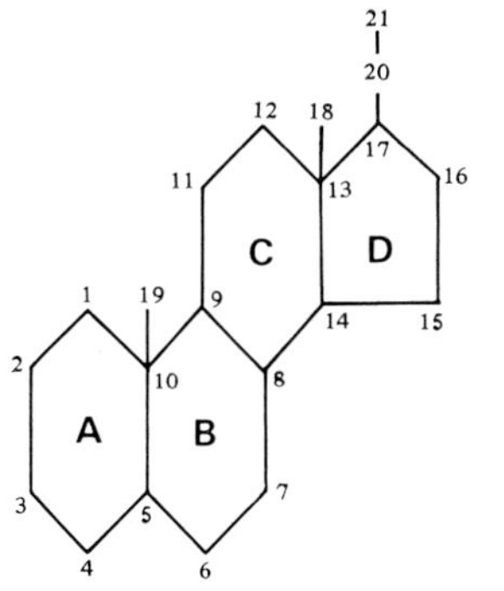

Steroid skeleton with conventional lettering of rings and numbering of carbon atoms

FIG. 5. Steroid skeleton.

cortisol to cortisone, the reaction being readily reversible. On the corticosterone pathway, 17-hydroxylation does not occur. The enzyme 21-hydroxylase leads to 11-deoxy-corticosterone and 11β-hydroxylase to corticosterone. The enzyme 11-dehydrogenase converts corticosterone to 11-dehydrocorticosterone, the reaction being readily

followed by the formation of DHA by the removal of the side chain, becomes more important. The greater proportion of DHA becomes linked with sulphate but some is converted to Δ_4-androstenedione by the action of 3β-hydroxy-dehydrogenase and Δ_5-Δ_4 isomerase. In addition to the above steroids, the adrenal cortex is capable of synthesizing small quantities of testosterone and oestrogens. Little steroid is stored in the adrenal cortex so the rate of synthesis is tantamount to the rate of secretion.

Adrenal Steroids in the Blood

The protein-binding of adrenal steroids has been studied particularly in relation to cortisol. Cortisol is bound mainly to a specific glycoprotein, Corticosteroid Binding Globulin or transcortin but some is bound to albumin. As previously mentioned, the protein binding of cortisol inactivates it but the process is reversible. In normal non-stressful circumstances most of the plasma cortisol is protein-bound although in newborn infants the unbound fraction occupies a far greater proportion of the total plasma cortisol than in the adult. Transcortin has a high affinity for cortisol but it has a low total binding capacity of the order of 25 μg./100 ml. If the plasma level exceeds this, some cortisol will be bound to albumin, but an increasing amount will remain in the free, biologically active form. Corticosterone is also bound to Corticosteroid Binding Globulin, the affinity of the protein being much the same for corticosterone as for cortisol. Aldosterone is bound mainly to albumin, but relatively much less is in the

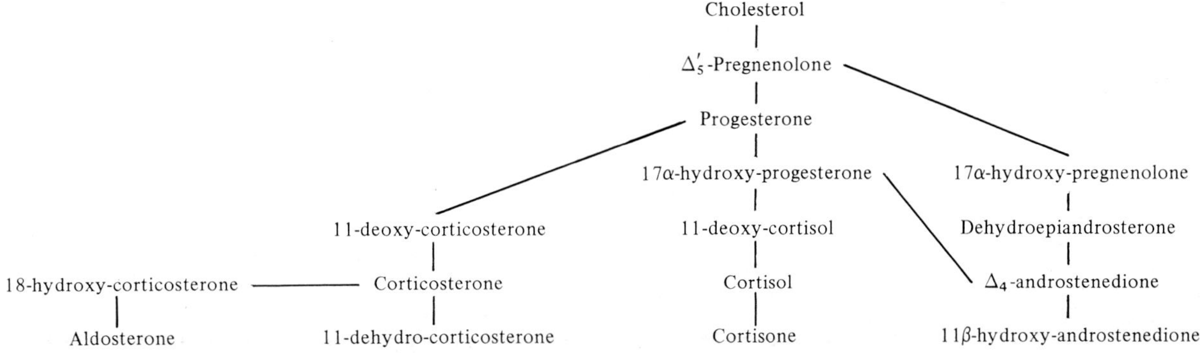

FIG. 6. Principal pathways of adrenal steroid synthesis.

reversible. On the aldosterone pathway from corticosterone, 18-hydroxylase leads to 18-hydroxy-corticosterone and finally 18-dehydrogenase yields aldosterone. The synthesis of adrenal androgens during childhood probably differs from that in adult life. Before puberty, greater utilization is made of the pathway from progesterone by the action of 17α-hydroxylase to 17α-hydroxy-progesterone followed by conversion to Δ_4-androstenedione by the removal of the side chain. 11β-hydroxy-androstenedione is formed from Δ_4-androstenedione by the action of 11β-hydroxylase. As puberty approaches, the formation of DHA increases and the pathway Δ_5-pregnenolone by the action of 17α-hydroxylase to 17α-hydroxy-pregnenolone,

bound form than is the case with cortisol and corticosterone. A small quantity of free DHA is present in the plasma, but the greater proportion is in the form of DHA sulphate, which is biologically inactive.

The Metabolism and Excretion of Adrenal Steroids

Cortisol (Compound F) and cortisone (Compound E) are readily interchangeable and the metabolites of cortisol excreted in the urine are derived directly from cortisol itself or from cortisone. All biologically active corticosteroids have an oxo group at C3 and a double bond in the 4:5 position. The major steps in the degradation to

Cholesterol

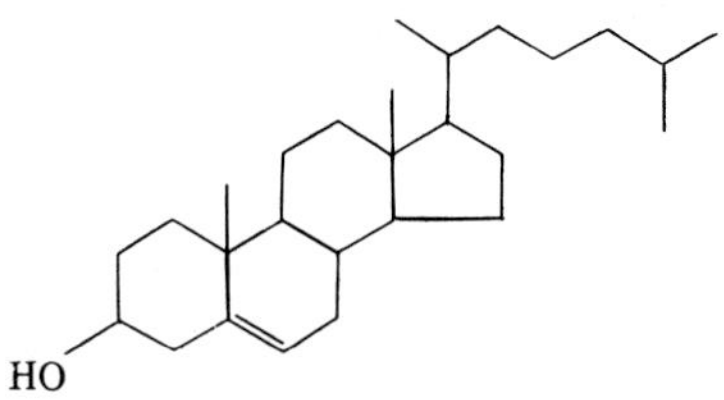

HO

11-deoxy-cortisol
(Compound S)

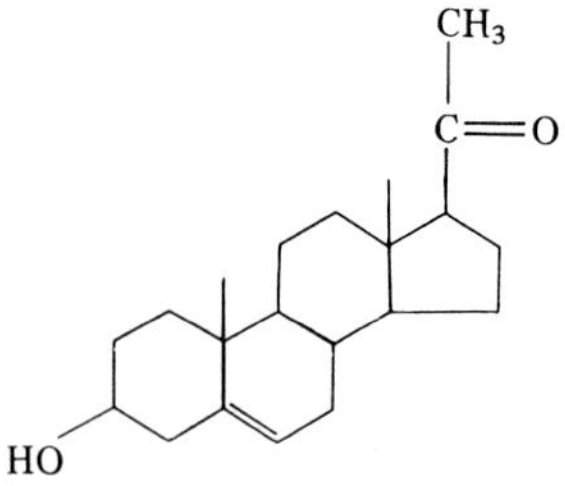

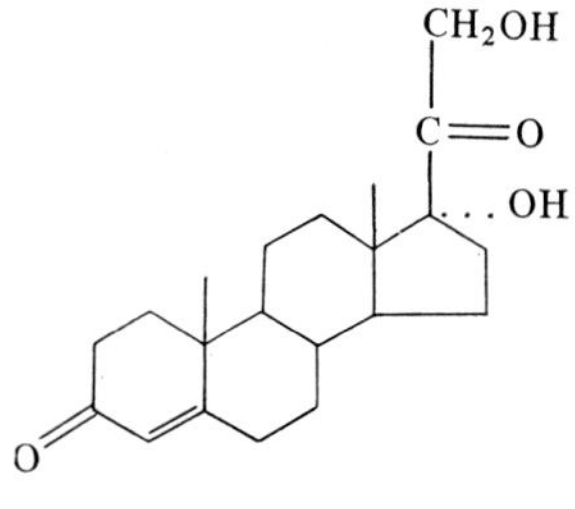

CH_2OH
C=O
. . OH
O

CH_3
C=O

Δ_5-Pregnenolone

HO

Cortisol
(Compound F)

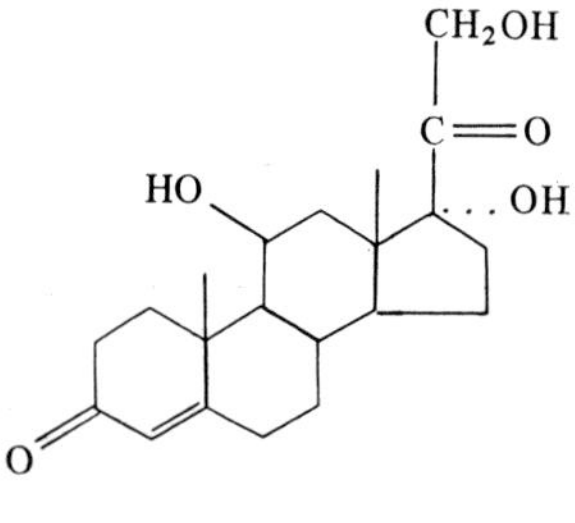

CH_2OH
C=O
HO
. . OH
O

CH_3
C=O

Progesterone

O

Cortisone
(Compound E)

CH_2OH
C=O
O
. . . OH
O

CH_3
C=O
. . . OH

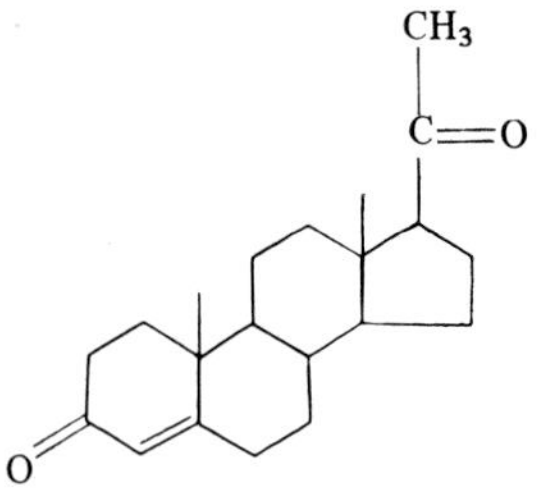

17α-hydroxy-progesterone

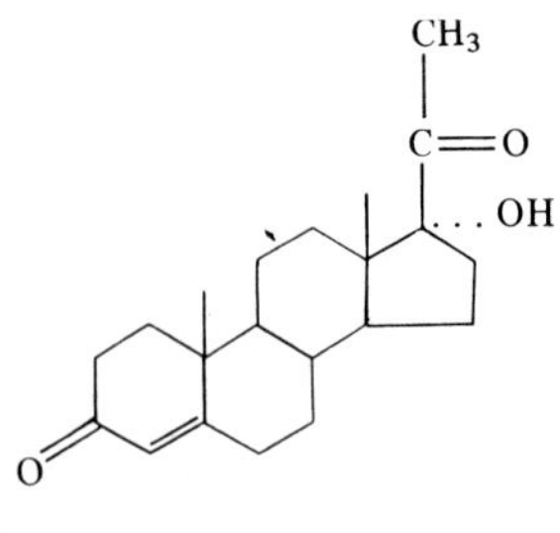

O

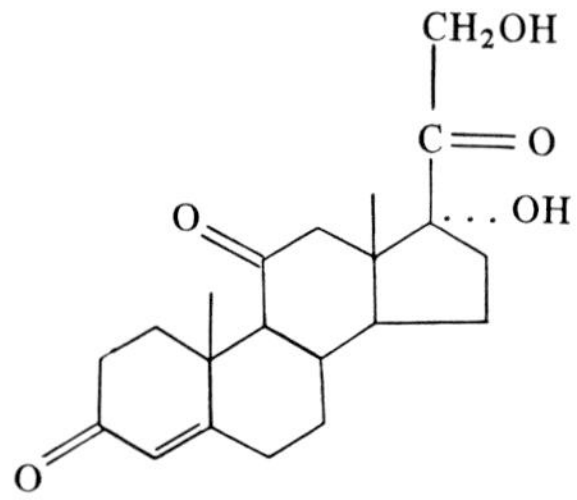

11-deoxy-corticosterone
(DOC)

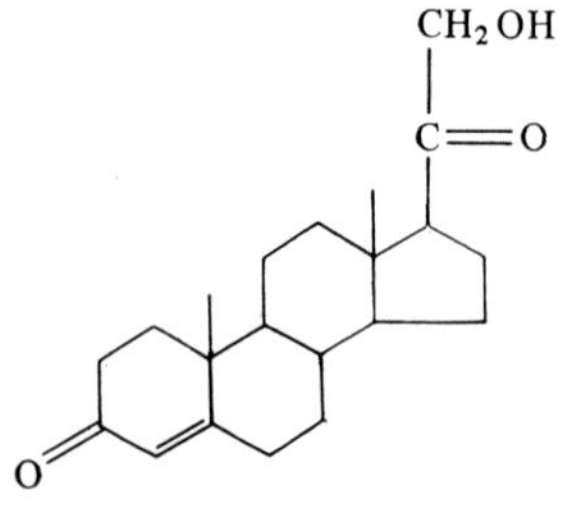

CH_2OH
C=O
O

(a

(b)

FIG. 7. Formulae of

steroids in Fig. 6.

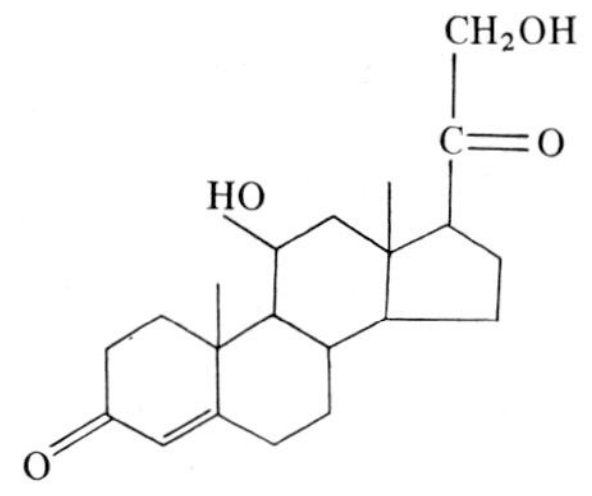

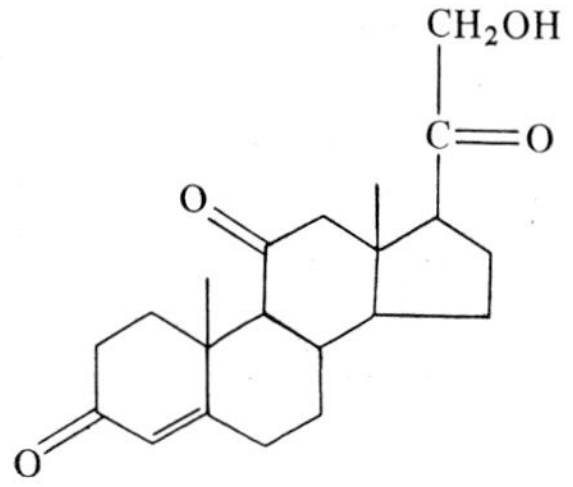

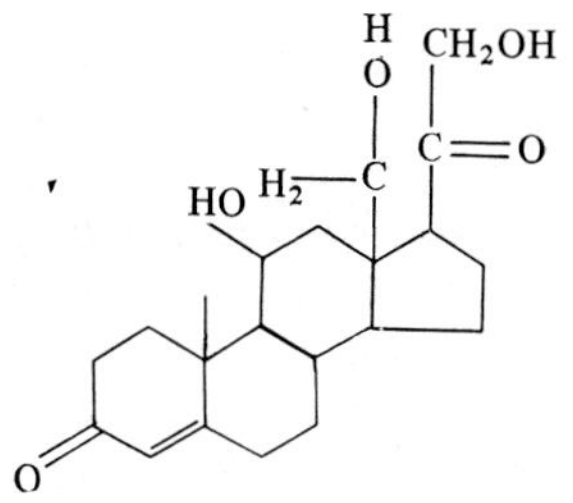

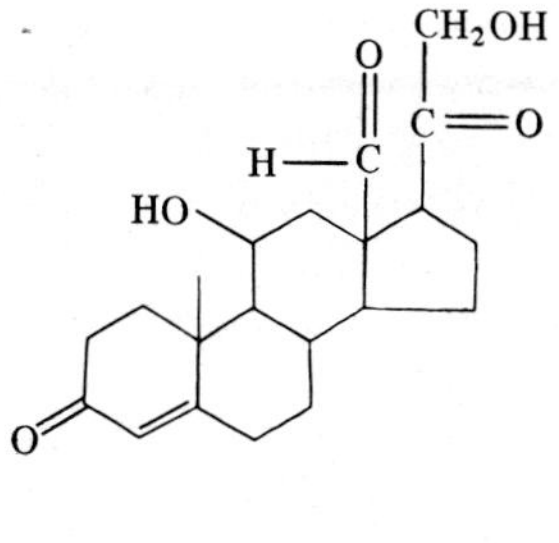

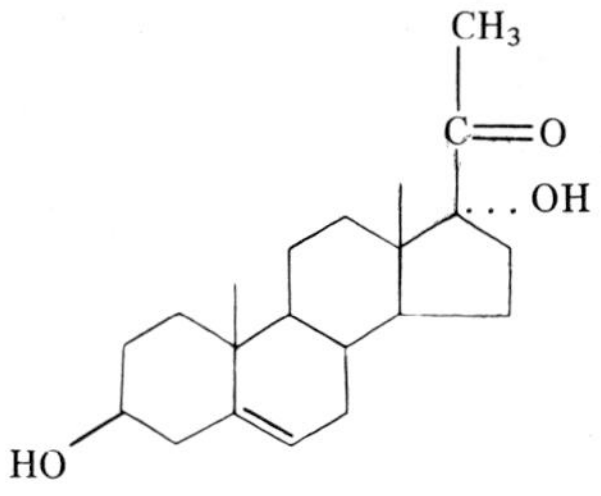

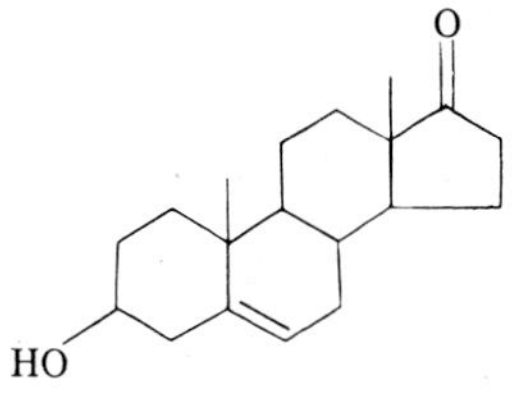

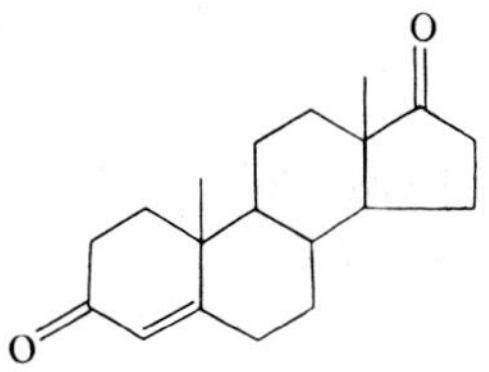

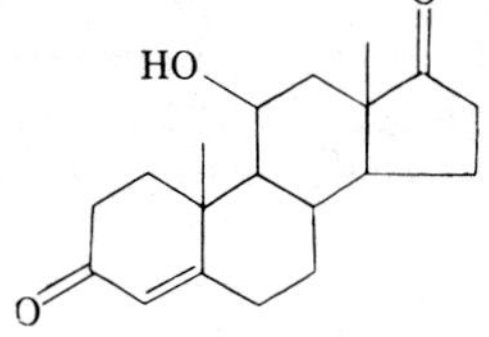

inert metabolites are reduction of ring A, with hydroxylation of the oxo group at carbon atom 3, followed by reduction at carbon atom 20. The first step leads to the addition of 4 hydrogen atoms and the formation of the tetrahydro derivatives. The second step leads to the formation of the hexahydro derivatives by the addition of 2 more hydrogen atoms to the molecule. These hexahydro derivatives are the cortols and the cortolones. Finally, the removal of the side chain at carbon atom 17 leads to the formation of 11-oxy-17-oxosteroids. In children, the major proportion of the 11-oxy-17-oxosteroids arises from cortisol but during puberty and adolescence an increasing contribution is made by adrenal androgens. The tetrahydro or α-ketolic metabolites of cortisol are tetrahydro-cortisol (THF), allo-tetrahydro-cortisol (allo-THF) and tetrahydro-cortisone (THE). Allo-THE is unstable and rapidly converts to allo-THF. The term α-ketol refers to the presence of a $C_{21}\alpha$-hydroxy group and a C_{20}-oxo group on the side chain of the molecule. These groups are necessary for the blue tetrazolium colour reaction which is often used in the determination of the α-ketolic metabolites of cortisol and corticosterone. THF and allo-THF are stereo-isomers, their different terminology depending on the spatial orientation of the hydrogen atom at carbon atom 5 at the ring junction A:B. The spatial orientation of the methyl groups is always taken as β. Therefore, if the hydrogen atom at carbon atom 5 is on the same side of the molecule as the methyl group, the compound is described as 5β and if on the opposite side as 5α. The α-ketolic metabolites of cortisol are excreted in the urine either as free steroids or conjugated as glucuronides or sulphates but the sulphates account for only a small fraction of the total. It has been estimated that in human subjects 95 per cent of a dose of radio-active cortisol is excreted in the urine and only 5 per cent in the bile. Very little, less than 1 per cent, is excreted in the urine as cortisol itself, the rest being in the form of the cortisol metabolites mentioned above. Corticosterone (Compound B) and 11-dehydro-corticosterone (Compound A) are readily interchangeable. Both corticosterone and Compound A have tetrahydro derivatives. As there is no hydroxyl group at C_{17}, no cleavage of the side chain takes place. The chief derivative of aldosterone is tetrahydro-aldosterone, which is conjugated with glucuronic acid prior to excretion.

DHA is excreted chiefly as DHA sulphate. It is present in very small quantity before the commencement of puberty and increases rapidly thereafter. As previously described, DHA may be converted to Δ_4-androstenedione. Following the saturation of ring A, Δ_4-androstenedione is excreted as the 5α-stereo-isomer androsterone and 5β-stereo-isomer aetiocholanolone. 11β-hydroxy-androstenedione is excreted as 11β-hydroxy-androsterone. 11-oxo-androstenedione, which is inter-convertible with 11β-hydroxy-androstenedione, is excreted as 11-oxo-androsterone.

The liver and other tissues, by taking part in the metabolic degradation of the steroids, regulate their excretion and hence also influence their concentration in the blood. The rate of metabolism may be studied by giving an intravenous injection of a trace amount of a radio-actively labelled steroid and then following the disappearance of the radio-activity from the plasma. The time required for half of the plasma radio-activity to disappear is known as the half-life of the steroid in the particular circumstances. Under normal conditions, the half-life of cortisol is about 80 min., whereas that of aldosterone is about 33 min. The difference is largely due to the much greater degree of protein binding of cortisol compared to aldosterone.

The Assessment of Adrenocortical Function

When a patient presents with a suspected disorder of adrenocortical function, the investigations should include a careful neurological examination to establish the integrity of the central nervous system, and it is often necessary to check the function of the other endocrine glands as well as that of the adrenals.

Assessment of adrenocortical function in the laboratory may be made by studies of urine or of plasma. If estimations of the steroid metabolites excreted during a 24-hr. period are made, it has to be remembered that such estimations reflect not only the adrenal secretion of steroids but also their subsequent metabolic fate. The common methods in routine use estimate groups of steroid compounds. The 17-oxosteroid assay[64] (17-ketosteroid assay) measures the C_{19} steroids with an oxo group at C_{17}. The 17-oxosteroids are derived from the adrenal cortex and also, after puberty, from the testes in male subjects. The limitations of this assay in the assessment of adrenal androgens during childhood are discussed elsewhere. The 17-hydroxy-corticosteroid assay[39] is the most widely used method for the estimation of C_{21} steroids in Great Britain. It measures the metabolites of cortisol, including the cortols and cortolones, and pregnanetriol but it does not estimate corticosterone. In the U.S.A., the Porter-Silber method is more widely used. It measures the metabolites of cortisol but not the cortols and cortolones and pregnanetriol. It does not estimate corticosterone. As expected, the results for the Porter-Silber assays are lower than for the 17-hydroxy-corticosteroids.

In the diagnosis of 21-hydroxylase deficiency, it is useful to estimate the 24 hr. excretion of pregnanetriol, the major urinary metabolite of 17α-hydroxy-progesterone or, as an alternative procedure in the diagnosis of 11β-hydroxylase deficiency and 21-hydroxylase deficiency, the 11-oxygenation index may be used. This index is the ratio of the 17-hydroxylated corticosteroids and their metabolites, which have not been 11-hydroxylated (the cortisol precursors) to those which have (cortisol and cortisone). In 11β-hydroxylase deficiency, 11-deoxy-cortisol and its metabolites accumulate and greatly increase the index. In the commoner 21-hydroxylase deficiency, 17α-hydroxy-progesterone and its metabolites increase the index. This method may be applied to random samples of urine which is advantageous in young children. However, the precise diagnosis of the enzyme defect present in adrenal hyperplasia requires a study of the individual urinary steroids.

Estimation of aldosterone in the urine is difficult owing to the very small amount present. The best method, known as the double isotope technique, depends upon the simultaneous use of two radio-active isotopes. This is not a routine procedure and is necessary only occasionally in paediatric practice, for example in the diagnosis of very rare inborn errors of metabolism affecting aldosterone synthesis.

The isolation and quantitation of specific steroids in the urine is usually carried out by chromatographic techniques. Four main methods are in use at the present time, column chromatography, paper chromatography, thin layer chromatography and gas liquid chromatography. Details of a study of the individual steroids excreted in the urine of infants, children and adolescents, based on paper chromatography, are given on pages 488–493.

Determinations of plasma steroid levels have been used less frequently in the assessment of adrenocortical function because of the methodological difficulties and the disadvantage that plasma levels reflect only the moment of time at which the sample was taken. Methods for plasma cortisol estimation used in routine laboratories such as that described by Mattingly[63] or the Porter-Silber method are not specific for cortisol. This must be remembered, particularly if an abnormality in the synthesis of cortisol is suspected as in adrenal hyperplasia. The Mattingly method[63] estimates both cortisol and corticosterone by their fluorescence after treatment with sulphuric acid and the term plasma "11-hydroxy-corticosteroids" is therefore more accurate than plasma "cortisol." This is particularly true in young children where corticosterone is more prominent than in later life. Tetrahydro-cortisol, 11-deoxy-cortisol and cortisone do not fluoresce significantly, but 21-deoxy-cortisol, which accumulates in adrenal hyperplasia, may affect the level of the Mattingly assay. The Porter–Silber colorimetric method, usually termed the plasma "17-hydroxy-corticosteroids," estimates cortisol, cortisone and 11-deoxy-cortisol but not corticosterone. A newer technique for the estimation of plasma cortisol[71] is more sensitive than that of Mattingly and has the advantage that only small volumes of plasma are required, for example 0·1 ml. as compared to 1–2 ml. for the Mattingly technique. The method estimates cortisol and corticosterone by competitive protein binding with Corticosteroid Binding Globulin. Radio-immunoassay methods on small plasma samples are under trial at the present time for cortisol, corticosterone, aldosterone, DHA, androstenedione and testosterone. There is a radio-immunoassay technique available also for the measurement of plasma ACTH. It is likely that the use of these new methods will lead to significant advances in knowledge.

Determination of the secretion rate of cortisol has been established as a routine test in the investigation of adrenocortical function in adults, but its use in children has been restricted in Great Britain by a recommendation of the Medical Research Council. The technique depends upon the principle of isotope dilution in which an administered dose of radioactive steroid becomes diluted by the natural secretion of the steroid by the patient. A metabolite of the injected steroid, derived exclusively from it, is isolated from a 24 hr. sample of urine and estimated for the proportion of radio-activity present. In the determination of the secretion rate of cortisol, either tetrahydro-cortisol or tetrahydro-cortisone may be used. The metabolite is quantitated accurately and its radioactivity is measured. By this means its specific activity, the radioactivity in counts/minute/mg., is calculated. The secretion rate in mg./24 hr. is the dose administered, in counts/minute, divided by the specific activity of the metabolite, in counts/minute/mg. The normal average secretion rate for cortisol in adults is approximately 20 mg./24 hr. In infants, the cortisol secretion rate is equivalent to that of adults when expressed on the basis of surface area. The average secretion rate and one standard deviation values are $11{\cdot}8 \pm 2{\cdot}5$ mg./m.^{2}/24 hr.[51] The technique for the estimation of the aldosterone secretion rate is very much more difficult. In adults the normal rate is approximately 125 μg./24 hr. For research purposes, secretion rates have been determined also for corticosterone and for the adrenal androgens.

Although hypoadrenalism may be suspected from the results of the group assays in 24 hr. samples of urine or from plasma estimations, it is essential to use a stimulation test in order to make this diagnosis accurately. Basal values for the 17-hydroxy-corticosteroid excretion in 24 hr. for normal children and then following injections of intramuscular ACTH have been determined for use in routine laboratories.[24] More recently the use of the synthetic ACTH "Synacthen" has been advocated and the rise in plasma cortisol estimated in preference to that of the urinary 17-hydroxy-corticosteroids.[8] ACTH tests give an indication of the ability of the adrenal cortex to respond to stimulation and, even if normal resting levels are obtained in hypoadrenal states, a poor response to ACTH will establish the diagnosis. Where hypopituitarism is suspected, the determination of ACTH levels in the plasma may be of value in the future, when the method is established routinely. However, at the present time, after the ability of the adrenal cortex to respond to ACTH has been ascertained, the integrity of the hypothalamic-pituitary-adrenal axis is tested by the use of metyrapone which blocks 11β-hydroxylase activity in the synthetic pathway to cortisol. This leads to a reduced cortisol secretion, which is followed by release of the hypothalamus from the feedback mechanism and therefore ACTH production is increased provided the anterior pituitary is intact. The resulting stimulation of the adrenal cortex produces a large output of 11-deoxy-cortisol which is estimated in the urinary 17-hydroxy-corticosteroid assay. Some centres use levels of plasma 17-hydroxy-corticosteroids based on the Porter–Silber reaction in preference to the urinary 17-hydroxy-corticosteroid output for this test. If it is decided to test the reaction of the hypothalamic-pituitary-adrenal axis to a stressful stimulus, the insulin hypoglycaemia test is usually used and the response of plasma cortisol determined in relation to the fall of blood glucose. In the rare circumstance of Cushing's syndrome being suspected in a child, the integrity of the feedback mechanism may be determined by the use of pharmacological doses of dexamethasone. If excessive pituitary activity is present, a failure of suppression is demonstrated. This test is conveniently carried out in combination with the determination of the diurnal variation in plasma cortisol which is lost in Cushing's syndrome.

Inborn Errors of Metabolism Affecting the Adrenal Cortex

Various inborn errors of metabolism affect the adrenal cortex, details of which are available in paediatric textbooks[26,47,99] and in recent review articles.[14,76] The pathways of adrenal steroid synthesis may be inhibited by a reduction of enzyme activity affecting 21-hydroxylase, 11β-hydroxylase, 17α-hydroxylase or 3β-hydroxydehydrogenase. The pathway to aldosterone may be affected by lack of 18-hydroxylase or of 18-dehydrogenase. Interference with the synthetic pathway to all of the corticosteroids and androgens may result from deficiency of the 20, 22 desmolase enzyme necessary for the conversion of cholesterol to Δ_5-pregnenolone.

In 21-hydroxylase deficiency there is an accumulation of 17α-hydroxy-progesterone, leading to the excretion of its derivative pregnanetriol in large quantities in the urine. However, in very young infants the pregnanetriol excretion may not be raised, as it is in older infants and children with this type of adrenal hyperplasia, because of differences in the metabolism of 17-hydroxy-progesterone early in life. On account of this, the determination of the plasma level of 17-hydroxy-progesterone may be useful[7] and an ACTH test may be necessary when the infant is older to determine the exact nature of the enzyme defect.[87] Adrenal hyperplasia due to 21-hydroxylase deficiency leads to an impaired production of cortisol and, in about 30 per cent of patients, there is interference also with the formation of 11-deoxycorticosterone and of aldosterone, leading to a salt-losing state. The response to stress is inadequate and, for example, simple infections such as measles may prove fatal if therapeutic cortisol in excess of the maintenance dose is not supplied promptly. In 21-hydroxylase deficiency the release of the hypothalamus from the feedback inhibitory effect of normal cortisol levels leads to an increased secretion of ACTH, which stimulates the unaffected androgen pathway to produce an excess of androgens. Male affected infants look normal at birth but, if they survive untreated, they will become virilized, with penile enlargement and growth of pubic hair by about the age of 3 years. Untreated female affected infants also become virilized during childhood or, in severer enzyme deficiency, masculinization occurs in the female fetus and the infant's sex at birth may have to be determined by chromosome studies. If the maintenance dose of cortisone is inadequate to suppress excessive androgen secretion, the children grow excessively rapidly and show an advanced bone age and advanced muscular development. The epiphyses close early, however, and they are small in stature in adult life relative to the normal population.

Cortisol production is impaired in 11β-hydroxylase deficiency. In this condition, 11-deoxy-cortisol (Compound S) accumulates and is excreted in the urine as tetrahydro-11-deoxy-cortisol (THS). The aldosterone pathway is also affected and 11-deoxy-corticosterone (DOC) accumulates and is excreted as the tetrahydro derivative. Both Compound S and DOC are salt-retaining and their excess usually leads to hypertension in affected individuals. Virilization occurs for similar reasons to those detailed for 21-hydroxylase deficiency.

The secretion of cortisol is reduced in 17α-hydroxylase deficiency which, however, leads to excessive production of corticosterone and aldosterone as these steroids do not require the enzyme for their synthesis. Patients, therefore, show salt retention and hypertension. The androgen pathway is affected by the failure of 17α-hydroxylation so that there is a marked reduction of adrenal androgen and testicular androgen synthesis. Female infants look normal at birth but genetic male infants have a female phenotype because of interference with testosterone production in the fetal testes. In later life, adolescent girls fail to show the feminizing changes of puberty, as the 17α-hydroxylation defect affects the oestrogen synthetic pathway which is mediated through androstenedione.

A deficiency of 3β-hydroxy-dehydrogenase leads to a defect in the synthesis of cortisol, corticosterone, aldosterone and of Δ_4-androstenedione in the adrenal cortex. It also interferes with the production of testosterone in the testes. Patients suffer from severe salt loss. Female infants look normal or slightly virilized at birth due to the excess of DHA which is produced. Male infants are incompletely masculinized. There is accumulation of Δ_5-pregnenolone which is excreted in the urine as Δ_5-pregnenetriol and of DHA which is present in excess in the urine, along with other Δ_5 steroids.

Defects in the metabolic pathway from corticosterone to aldosterone have been described. If 18-hydroxylase enzyme is deficient, corticosterone accumulates[29,48,97] and if 18-dehydrogenase is deficient, 18-hydroxy-corticosterone accumulates.[28,80,95] In both types of defect spontaneous improvement has been reported. As the children grew older, therapy was no longer required.

A metabolic defect in the pathway between cholesterol and Δ_5-pregnenolone, possibly due to deficiency of 20, 22 desmolase enzyme, causes the condition known as congenital lipoid hyperplasia, in which the adrenal cortex is full of accumulated cholesterol when examined histologically. There is diminished production of cortisol, corticosterone, aldosterone and the adrenal and testicular androgens with severe salt loss and lack of masculinization of male newborn infants.

THE PHYSIOLOGICAL ACTIONS AND PHARMACOLOGICAL USES OF ADRENOCORTICAL STEROIDS AND ACTH

The Physiological Actions of Adrenocortical Steroids

Androgens

DHA, Δ_4-androstenedione, 11β-hydroxy-androstenedione, androsterone and 11β-hydroxy-androsterone are weakly androgenic in comparison with testosterone, whereas aetiocholanolone and 11β-hydroxy-aetiocholanolone have no androgenic properties.

The androgens have growth promoting and masculinizing effects. The anabolic effect of androgens may be demonstrated by balance studies showing their promotion of nitrogen and mineral retention. The increase in the growth rate of children is accompanied by a disproportionate advance in the maturation of skeletal muscle and in bone age leading to early closure of the epiphyses and small stature in adult life. This situation arises due to excessive androgenic activity of adrenal origin in adrenal hyperplasia, as mentioned elsewhere, if adequate suppression of the androgen secretion is not achieved therapeutically. If sensitive methods are used, a reduction in the excretion of androgens before puberty can be detected in Addison's disease[40] but there are no clinically recognizable consequences.

In males, androgens stimulate the growth of the sex organs and the development of the secondary sexual characteristics. These changes occur normally at puberty due to the action of the gonadotrophic hormones and testosterone. Precocious sexual development due to an excessive secretion of adrenal androgens is seen in untreated or under-treated adrenal hyperplasia. However, the testes do not enlarge, as testicular growth is chiefly due to the growth of the tubules which requires stimulation by Follicle Stimulating Hormone (FSH), and this is an important point in the clinical differentiation between precocious sexual development of adrenal origin and that seen due to excess secretion of gonadotrophic hormones and testosterone. The latter condition of true precocious puberty is associated with testicular enlargement and the formation of mature spermatozoa.

In females, the adrenal cortex is virtually the only source of androgens. Plasma levels of Δ_4-androstenedione are higher in women than in men and androsterone is excreted in greater relative amounts than aetiocholanolone. Some testosterone is formed by the peripheral conversion of Δ_4-androstenedione in the tissues but the plasma levels of testosterone are always very much lower than in men. The increased androgen production from the adrenal cortex at puberty stimulates the growth of axillary and pubic hair, but in normal circumstances no virilization takes place. However, in adrenal hyperplasia there may be masculinization of the fetus or, in less severe enzyme defects, virilization may present during childhood, if the condition is not adequately treated.

Androsterone, which is a mild androgen, also has an effect in lowering blood cholesterol. It does not act as a pyrogen, like the 5β-stereo-isomer aetiocholanolone. If aetiocholanolone is administered intramuscularly to humans, it causes an acute inflammatory response locally and a rise in body temperature. The part played by this steroid and others, also known to be pyrogenic, in various naturally occurring febrile states, has not yet been clarified.

Corticosteroids

The adrenal cortex is an organ of homeostasis with constant fluctuations in its secretory activity in response to changes in the environment. Corticosteroids regulate the rate at which various biochemical processes proceed in tissue cells, their actions being inter-related with those of other hormones. The most important corticosteroids are cortisol, corticosterone and aldosterone. Cortisol is interconvertible with cortisone and, along with corticosterone, these steroids are sometimes termed the glucocorticoids, whereas aldosterone is considered the most important of the mineralocorticoids. Such terminology is misleading as all of these steroids promote the accumulation of liver glycogen and the retention of sodium, the distinction between them being one of degree. Cortisol has the greatest effect on liver glycogen deposition followed by corticosterone and finally aldosterone. On the other hand, cortisol has the least sodium retaining effect, that of corticosterone being considerably greater and that of aldosterone being infinitely greater.

The glucocorticoids influence carbohydrate, protein and fat metabolism. The increased storage of liver and muscle glycogen involves the conversion of protein into carbohydrate. Where this catabolic action is exaggerated, as in Cushing's syndrome, or in prolonged corticosteroid therapy, there is wasting of skeletal muscle and reduction of the protein matrix of the bones leading to osteoporosis. The glucocorticoids help to maintain a normal plasma glucose concentration, thus protecting the body from the effects of starvation. They tend to decrease the sensitivity of the tissues to insulin. The glucocorticoids enhance the mobilization of fat from peripheral fat depots, which is stimulated by adrenaline and noradrenaline, and they enhance the lipolysis characteristic of the action of growth hormone. However, while fat is lost from the limbs due to the action of glucocorticoids, it is gained over the face, neck, chest and abdomen because of a difference in the response of the fat depots in various parts of the body.

Aldosterone is the most potent, naturally occurring, mineralocorticoid. It maintains the circulatory blood volume and the blood pressure by causing retention of sodium and water. Signs of a deficiency of mineralocorticoid activity are found in Addison's disease, whereas in Conn's syndrome the excess secretion of aldosterone leads to sodium retention in the renal tubules at the expense of potassium and hydrogen ions, a loss of body potassium, a tendency to depletion of the intracellular fluid and a loss of hydrogen ions which may lead to alkalosis.

The effects of large doses of cortisol have been studied to further knowledge regarding the use of cortisol or its analogues therapeutically. Pharmacological doses of cortisol lead to suppression of the inflammatory response and a general reduction in lymphoid tissue. The early manifestations of inflammation, which include capillary dilatation, oedema, deposition of fibrin and the migration and activation of phagocytes are inhibited, as well as the later responses of capillary and fibroblast proliferation and tissue scarring. This effect may be due to the local action of cortisol on tissue cell metabolism and one speculation is that it promotes the containment within the lysozomes of enzymes which are necessary for the normal inflammatory response. The suppression occurs whether the inflammatory response is due to infection, trauma, allergy or an immune reaction. It takes place after the tissue damage has occurred, as cortisol does not prevent antibody formation or the union of antigen with antibody or the release of histamine from sensitized cells. Cortisol produces a striking diminution in the quantity of lymphoid tissue in the lymph glands, spleen and thymus and there is a fall in the lymphocyte count in the blood. The eosinopenia due to cortisol, is striking and well recognized. In contrast, cortisol has a stimulant effect on neutrophil polymorphs and red blood cells.

Relatively little is known, however, about the normal biological actions of cortisol at cellular level and the role of the adrenal cortex in relation to host resistance in acute and chronic infections and other forms of stress. The complexity of the problem is due to the capacity of adrenocortical hormones to influence virtually every organ system, defence mechanism and biochemical pathway that might participate in the host response. In a recent review of the role of adrenocortical function in infectious illness[9] the following facts emerge. During an acute generalized infection there is a relatively limited increase in adrenocortical function associated with an increase in the 17-hydroxycorticosteroid excretion to about three or four times the normal level and, in addition, the diurnal variation of plasma cortisol is lost. In protracted infections adrenocortical function may return to basal levels or it may even show depression. Changes in the metabolic degradation of adrenal steroids in the liver and other tissues have been noted, leading to an increased half-life of cortisol and the possibility of differences occurring in the protein binding of cortisol remains to be explored. It has been known for some time that both the hypofunction of the adrenal cortex in Addison's disease and the hyperfunction in Cushing's syndrome are deleterious to host resistance to infection. Elucidation of the mechanism by which normal adrenocortical responsiveness is protective is a challenge for future research.

The Pharmacological Uses of Adrenocortical Steroids

For details of the pharmacological uses of adrenocortical steroids or their analogues, readers are referred to standard paediatric textbooks[44,74,88] or a textbook of pharmacology.[45]

Androgens

Adrenal androgens are not employed therapeutically, the anabolic steroids on the market being derivatives of testosterone. Testosterone is one of the most potent anabolic steroids known, but it is also strongly virilizing and in children it causes a disproportionate advance in bone age, producing early epiphyseal closure and small stature in adult life. The pharmaceutical industry has produced derivatives of testosterone which are less virilizing but have an anabolic effect. In the past, such androgen preparations have been employed for their growth promoting properties in children suffering from hypopituitarism, but this treatment has now been superseded by the use of human growth hormone. It is very doubtful whether androgen preparations should ever be used for the treatment of children of small stature of ill-defined aetiology. It is not usual to give replacement therapy for lack of adrenal androgens, for example in Addison's disease. There is a limited use for androgens in an attempt to reduce the osteoporosis consequent upon prolonged corticosteroid therapy and, in certain types of hypoplastic anaemia and aplastic anaemia, androgens may be useful for their stimulant effect on the production of red blood cells, platelets and white cells. Such therapy may be hazardous as clinical observations suggesting a relationship between the development of hepatocellular carcinoma and long-term therapy with androgenic-anabolic steroids have been reported recently.[50a]

Corticosteroids

The most logical use of cortisol (hydrocortisone) is for replacement therapy in hypoadrenal states, such as Addison's disease. In adults, the estimated secretion rate of cortisol is of the order of 20 mg. daily but, because it is not possible to mimic the normal diurnal variation of cortisol, nor for the patient to produce extra cortisol in response to stressful circumstances, the maintenance dose used is higher than this in clinical practice. Oral cortisone is the drug of choice, as it is freely convertible to cortisol in the body, and, in addition, it is usual to administer a mineralocorticoid orally such as 9α-fluorocortisol acetate. Addison's disease in children is treated in a similar manner with smaller doses of the drugs according to body size. In the treatment of children with adrenal hyperplasia, for example due to 21-hydroxylase deficiency, larger doses of cortisone are required as, in addition to replacement therapy, it is necessary to suppress the excess androgen production. These children may also require 9α-fluorocortisol acetate therapy if they show a salt losing tendency.

Analogues of cortisol, for example prednisone or prednisolone, are used in a variety of conditions in childhood. It is important not to exceed the smallest effective dose and to reduce the corticosteroid slowly when the course of treatment is completed to allow some recovery of the hypothalamic-pituitary-adrenal axis before the drug is completely withdrawn. Undesirable side effects may be reduced by giving the corticosteroid on alternate days whenever possible, or by giving it only on three consecutive days each week.[57] Corticosteroids may be used for their anti-inflammatory properties in a number of conditions due to allergy or an abnormality of the immune mechanism, for example, asthma, eczema, rheumatoid arthritis, rheumatic fever, the nephrotic syndrome, systemic lupus erythematosus or ulcerative colitis. They may also be useful in acquired haemolytic anaemia or to stimulate platelet production in idiopathic thrombocytopenic purpura. In the latter condition, the decreased capillary permeability produced by steroid therapy is also of value. Along with other drugs, they have a place in the treatment of acute lymphoblastic leukaemia and, to a lesser extent, of other leukaemias of childhood.

When they are used for a prolonged period it is important to watch for the development of osteoporosis, particularly in the spine, and to keep a record of the child's height in order to detect retardation of growth. Other side-effects of therapy are the development of obesity, with deposition of fat in the face, neck and trunk in particular, and a tendency to hypertension and oedema. Cataract and myopathy may occur. The lowering of host resistance to infection by bacteria, fungi and viral agents may be sufficiently serious to merit the withdrawal of the drug especially when there is no known antibiotic therapy available for the infection in question. Diabetes mellitus, peptic ulceration and undesirable psychological effects are less common in children than in adults.

The Physiological Actions and Pharmacological Uses of ACTH

ACTH (corticotrophin) stimulates the secretion of cortisol and corticosterone and, to a lesser extent, of adrenal androgens, but it has very little effect on aldosterone production. The pharmacological effects of ACTH are therefore chiefly due to the increased secretion of cortisol by the patient's adrenal glands. It is given intramuscularly because the polypeptide molecule is destroyed by the proteolytic enzymes of the gastro-intestinal tract and, following its injection, it is readily metabolized the urinary excretion being negligible. The clinical effects of ACTH may be prolonged by the inclusion of gelatin in the preparation because of the resultant delay in the rate of absorption. Until recently ACTH was prepared from animal sources but synthetic polypeptides are now available, containing the amino-acid sequence 1–24, which have similar biological activity and are less liable to produce allergic reactions. The most common use for ACTH is as a diagnostic agent in stimulation tests to check the reserve of adrenocortical function, for example, in Addison's disease. For therapeutic purposes cortisol analogues are usually used in preference to ACTH, as they are active when given orally and lead to a lesser degree of sodium retention and potassium loss.

The side effects of ACTH therapy are similar to those previously mentioned for corticosteroids. It was claimed some years ago, however, that ACTH therapy caused much less interference with the growth of children than had been noted with prednisone or prednisolone.[42] Further work has supported this claim[101] but it now seems likely that the difference between the two methods of treatment is due to the fact that maintenance ACTH therapy used intermittently has been compared with continuous daily corticosteroid therapy. If long-acting ACTH preparations are given sufficiently frequently to produce continuous suppression of the hypothalamic-pituitary-adrenal axis, inhibition of growth takes place, whereas, if corticosteroids are administered intermittently, for example, on an alternate day basis, interference with growth may be avoided. Suppression of the hypothalamic-pituitary-adrenal axis may be accompanied by interference with the normal production of pituitary growth hormone. It has been reported recently that continuous therapy with ACTH or corticosteroids leads to almost complete disappearance of the normal peaks of plasma human growth hormone observed during a 24 hr. period.[78] During continuous corticosteroid therapy, the output of adrenal androgens is depressed along with that of cortisol from the patient's adrenal glands and during ACTH therapy the glands will produce a much more marked increase in cortisol secretion than in androgens, particularly in childhood. An imbalance of the action of cortisol or its analogues and that of adrenal androgens may lead to direct inhibition of the growth of bone and muscle. However, attempts to stimulate growth by the use of human growth hormone or anabolic steroids along with the régime of corticosteroid therapy have not met with success. It is therefore recommended that, as well as using the smallest effective dose of ACTH or corticosteroid for the control of the disease in question, the drugs should be given in such a way as to minimize the suppression of the hypothalamic-pituitary-adrenal axis as far as possible. The use of oral corticosteroids on alternate days, or on three days each week, is preferable from the child's point of view to parenteral ACTH therapy if the disease can be controlled satisfactorily, but in some circumstances it may be better to use ACTH. Once the course of therapy has been completed, the hypothalamic-pituitary-adrenal axis will recover over a period of months, proportional to the intensity and duration of the course of treatment. Provided the disease process is by then relatively inactive, catch-up growth ensues and therefore interference with growth during therapy is not very serious, if it is continued for only 1 or 2 years and is complete before the growth spurt at puberty takes place. If, however, an intensive and more prolonged course of treatment is necessary, some interference with growth is virtually inevitable due to the therapy in addition to that resulting from the chronic disease in question.

THE DEVELOPMENT OF ADRENOCORTICAL FUNCTION IN THE FETUS, NEONATE AND YOUNG INFANT

Adrenocortical Function in the Fetus

There are several reviews of fetal adrenocortical function.[18,43,61] The fetal adrenal cortex begins to form at the 6th week of gestation and it grows to become a relatively large endocrine organ consisting of a broad fetal zone next to the medulla of the gland and a thin subcapsular zone, known as the adult zone. In the previable fetus the adult zone is very narrow in comparison with the fetal zone, but by the time of birth it has increased in thickness to make up about 20 per cent of the total adrenal cortex. After birth it gradually develops into the permanent adult cortex whereas the fetal cortex undergoes rapid degeneration. During the past decade there have been considerable advances in knowledge of the function of the fetal and adult zones of the adrenal cortex during fetal life, in the newborn period and in early infancy, which go a long way towards explaining the dramatic anatomical changes which have been recognized for many years.

The Fetal Zone: The Feto-Placental Unit

The concept of a feto-placental unit was initially proposed by Diczfalusy, based on the results of experiments performed on human pre-viable fetuses.[33] Further information has accumulated over the years and there is good evidence that all the major features established at mid-term persist until the time of delivery.[34,35] The clinical importance of the concept is demonstrated in a recent review of its application to the assessment of fetal health by the analysis of maternal urinary steroids.[82] Neither the placenta nor the fetus alone has all the enzyme systems necessary to synthesize the large quantity of oestrogens characteristic of pregnancy. They fulfil this function by complementing each other by the mutual transport of intermediate steroids between them. A simplified outline of the pathways of steroid synthesis in the feto-placental unit is given in Fig. 8 and the formulae of the steroids in Fig. 9. Cholesterol, derived from the mother, is the main precursor of both progesterone and the oestrogens. It is converted by the placental trophoblast to pregnenolone. Pregnenolone acts as substrate for the production of progesterone by the placenta and for the production of oestrogen precursor steroids by the fetus. The progesterone formed in the placenta passes to the mother where it is converted to pregnanediol prior to excretion. The level of urinary pregnanediol shows a steady rise throughout pregnancy until the last month when the curve flattens. Some of the progesterone formed in the placenta passes to the fetus where it is utilized by the fetal adrenal glands in the production of cortisol and corticosterone. The fetal zone of the adrenal glands has virtually no ability to convert pregnenolone to progesterone because of a deficiency of the enzyme 3β-hydroxy-dehydrogenase but the adult zone shows a gradual increase in 3β-hydroxy-dehydrogenase activity so that, by the time of birth, the normal infant is capable of independent survival in that the enzymes necessary for the entire synthetic pathway to cortisol, corticosterone and aldosterone are present. Nevertheless, the placental supply of progesterone may be of importance during fetal life in the synthesis of the corticosteroids. Progesterone passing to the fetus which is not utilized in this manner is hydroxylated to various metabolites in the fetal liver.

Whereas progesterone is formed chiefly in the placenta, the synthesis of oestriol, which is mainly responsible for the increased output of oestrogens in the maternal urine during pregnancy, depends to a large extent upon the activity of the fetal adrenal glands and the fetal liver. Pregnenolone passes from the placenta to the fetus where it is converted to pregnenolone sulphate, then hydroxylated to 17-hydroxy-pregnenolone sulphate and finally dehydroepiandrosterone (DHA) sulphate, which is biologically inactive, is formed by scission of the side chain. These reactions take place in the fetal adrenal glands. Some of the DHA sulphate returns to the placenta but most of it is hydroxylated to 16α-hydroxy-DHA sulphate by the fetal liver. This steroid crosses to the placenta where it is hydrolysed by placental sulphatase to free 16α-hydroxy-DHA which is then converted to oestriol prior to excretion in the maternal urine. Free DHA in the placenta is derived approximately equally from the DHA sulphate supplied by the mother and that from the fetus. It is converted to oestrone and oestradiol which pass to the mother. A small amount of oestriol is formed and, finally, the oestrogens are excreted in the maternal urine. Oestrone and oestradiol are synthesized almost equally from maternal and fetal sources of DHA but oestriol is virtually entirely derived from the fetus, through the precursor steroid 16α-hydroxy-DHA. In the urine of women who are not pregnant, the ratio of oestrone to oestradiol to oestriol is 1·1 to 0·3 to 1·1, whereas at the end of pregnancy the ratio is 1·0 to 0·4 to 22. Of the three oestrogens, oestradiol has the greatest biological activity followed by oestrone, whereas oestriol is only weakly oestrogenic. One of the important actions of progesterone is to inhibit myometrial activity but oestrogens oppose this effect by lowering the threshold of excitability of the myometrium. As might be expected, when there is marked impairment of total oestrogen synthesis due to an abnormality of the fetal adrenal glands, the onset of labour is usually delayed.

A study of maternal pregnanediol excretion may be of value in suspected placental insufficiency, but the flattening of the curve, which normally occurs during the last month of pregnancy, limits its usefulness as a measure of placental function during this period. On the other hand, in normal circumstances, the excretion of oestriol, which monitors fetal as well as placental activity, continues to rise until term and serial measurements of urinary oestriol have therefore proved of great value in assessing fetal welfare, particularly in pre-eclamptic toxaemia, when it may be desirable to expedite delivery. There is a correlation between maternal urinary oestriol levels in the last week of gestation and the birth weight of the infant.[27] Women, whose infants show severe intra-uterine growth retardation, have low levels of oestriol excretion, and it is of interest that the excretion may be even lower than would be expected with truly premature infants of the same weight. This suggests a greater relative reduction in the growth of the fetal adrenal glands in light-for-dates infants than in their total body weight. In anencephaly, the fetal zone of the adrenal cortex is atrophic and the oestriol excretion in the maternal urine is reduced to about 10 per cent of the normal pregnancy value, whereas the pregnanediol excretion is unaffected. Low maternal urinary oestriol levels have been noted also in association with fetal adrenocortical hypoplasia.[21] Conversely, in adrenocortical hyperplasia, due to 21-hydroxylase deficiency, associated with stimulation of the androgen pathway of the fetal adrenals from the 3rd or 4th month of pregnancy, leading in the female to masculinization of the fetus, the maternal urinary oestriol levels have been shown to be abnormally high.[19] Suppression of fetal adrenocortical function as a result of corticosteroid administration to the mother for therapeutic purposes is rare unless large doses are used. Corticosteroids cross the placenta and reduce the output of fetal ACTH resulting in hypofunction of both the fetal and adult zones of the adrenal cortex. Hypoplasia of the adrenal glands has been found at post-mortem in infants born to women who have received high dosage corticosteroid therapy for several weeks prior to delivery and to women with untreated Cushing's syndrome. Depression of the function of the fetal zone leads to a reduction of maternal urinary oestriol excretion and of the level of dehydroepiandrosterone sulphate in maternal and cord blood.[18]

There is good evidence that the fetal hypothalamic-pituitary-adrenal axis is active from about the 3rd or 4th month of pregnancy and that the secretion of ACTH from the fetal pituitary gland stimulates the fetal as well as the adult zone of the adrenal cortex. However, after birth, although the hypothalamic-pituitary-adrenal axis remains active, the fetal zone undergoes rapid degeneration. Therefore some other factor, or factors, must play a part in maintaining the integrity of the fetal zone before birth.

Mother
Placenta
Fetus
Cholesterol
Pregnenolone
Pregnenolone sulphate
Cortisol
Corticosterone
Progesterone
Metabolites
Pregnanediol
Progesterone
17α-hydroxy-pregnenolone sulphate
DHA sulphate
DHA
DHA sulphate
Oestrone
Oestradiol
Oestriol
Oestrone
Oestradiol
16α-hydroxy-DHA
16α-hydroxy-DHA sulphate
Oestriol
Oestriol

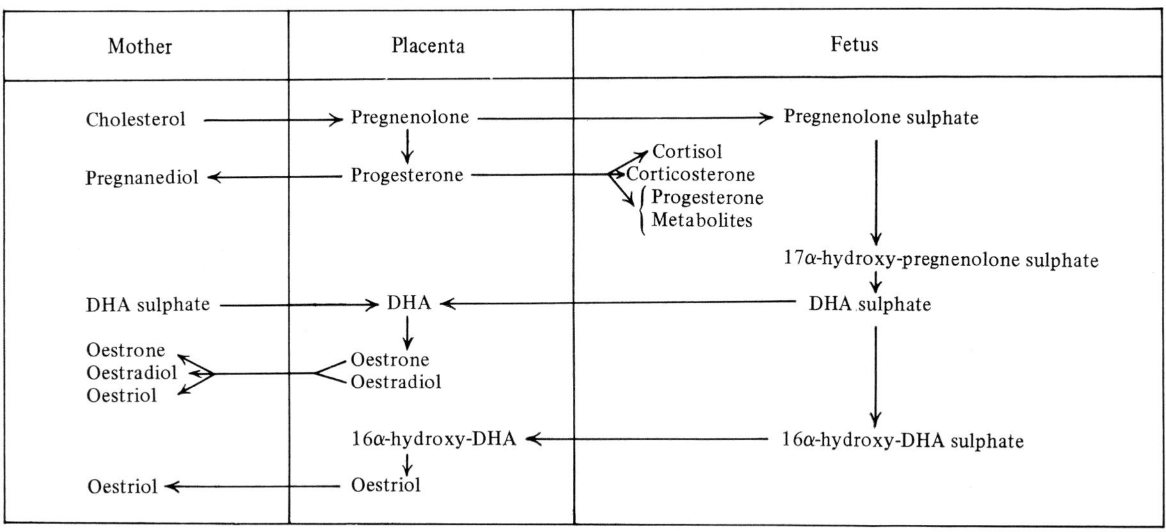

FIG. 8. Pathways of steroid synthesis in the feto-placental unit. (Adapted from Liggins, G. C. (1970), "Foetal Endocrinology," in *Scientific Foundations of Obstetrics and Gynaecology*, Ed. Elliot E. Phillipp. Heinemann Medical Books Ltd.)

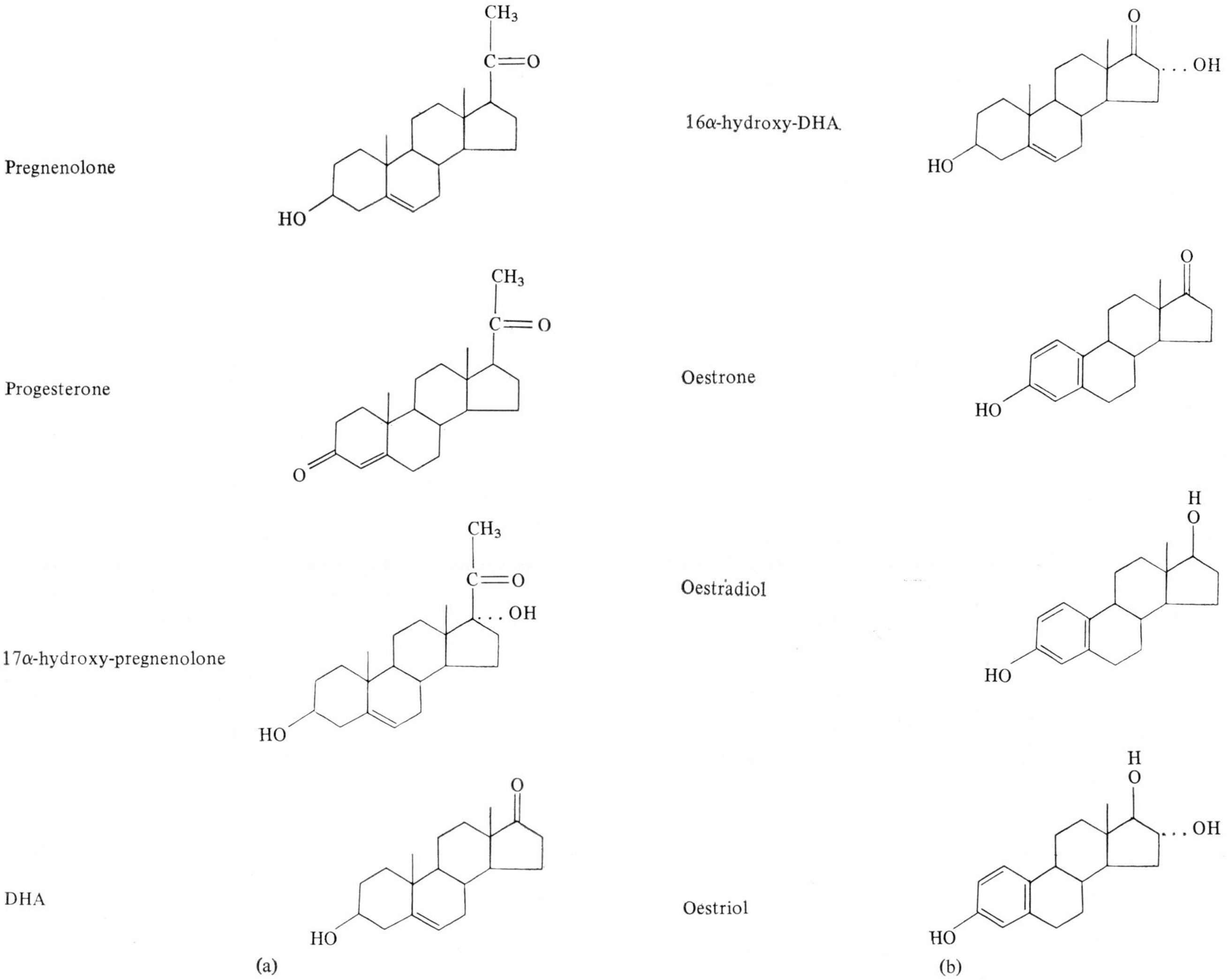

Pregnenolone
Progesterone
17α-hydroxy-pregnenolone
DHA
(a)
16α-hydroxy-DHA
Oestrone
Oestradiol
Oestriol
(b)

FIG. 9. Formulae of steroids synthesized in the fetoplacental unit.

Chorionic gonadotrophin or oestrogens, possibly by stimulating the production of Luteinizing Hormone from the fetal pituitary gland may participate in the maintenance of the fetal zone, or alternatively, large quantities of pregnenolone substrate from the placenta may be necessary for its continued survival.

The Adult Zone

(a). **The Synthesis of Corticosteroids.** While the part played by the fetal zone of the adrenal cortex in relation to the production of oestrogens has been established, knowledge of the function of the adult zone during fetal life is incomplete. By the time of birth, the adult zone is capable of synthesizing adequate mineralocorticoids and glucocorticoids for the independent survival of the infant. If it is assumed that the placenta regulates water and electrolyte balance for the fetus, it appears unlikely that fetal synthesis of aldosterone is of importance during intra-uterine life. The finding of normal electrolyte homeostasis at the time of birth in infants with the salt-losing type of adrenocortical hyperplasia supports this conclusion. Similarly, it seems unlikely that the fetal synthesis of cortisol is important in terms of intra-uterine survival, as infants with congenital adrenal hypoplasia and a low cortisol output show no evidence of glucocorticoid deficiency at birth.

(b). **The Initiation of Labour.** In recent years, it has been suggested that the adult zone of the fetal adrenal cortex, by its production of corticosteroids, plays an important role in the initiation of labour. This theory is based on experiments on pregnant sheep in which it was shown that destruction of the fetal pituitary gland led to prolonged gestation.[60] Post-mortem examination of the lambs after birth revealed marked adrenocortical hypoplasia, suggesting that the fetal pituitary gland normally contributed to the mechanism involved in the onset of parturition, by means of a trophic hormone influencing the adrenal cortex. It was shown, in addition, that bilateral adrenalectomy of the fetal lamb led to prolonged gestation and, conversely, that the infusion of large doses of ACTH into fetal lambs resulted in spontaneous parturition before term. It was found in further experiments that the infusion of cortisol or dexamethasone into fetal lambs led to their early delivery but that the infusion of 11-deoxycorticosterone had no effect. It was therefore concluded that the hormone affecting the onset of labour was a glucocorticoid rather than a mineralocorticoid.[59] As the effective dose of cortisol was much larger than the 24 hr. secretion rate in fetal lambs, it was concluded that the mode of action of cortisol in inducing premature labour was pharmacological rather than physiological in these experiments. However, recent work has shown that the rate at which the sheep fetus is producing cortisol at the end of gestation is adequate to produce parturition when compared with the amounts of steroid which have to be infused into the fetal compartment in the sheep.[73a]. The theory was proposed that the onset of parturition in pregnant sheep was the result of an increased secretion of cortisol brought about by stimulation of the fetal hypothalamus by the maturing higher centres in the brain, leading to increased stimulation of the pituitary gland to produce ACTH. It was postulated that the resultant increased secretion of cortisol might lead to a diminution in the secretion of progesterone and hence a reduction in its inhibitory effect on myometrial activity. However, other experimental observations conflict with this hypothesis. For example, removal of the fetus but not the placenta from rats, mice and from rhesus monkeys results in the placenta being delivered at the normal time of parturition for the species.[96]

There is circumstantial evidence that activity of the human fetal hypothalamic-pituitary-adrenal axis may influence the initiation of parturition. Prolongation of pregnancy occurs frequently in mothers carrying anencephalic infants, provided there is no complication such as hydramnios. In this condition the fetal hypothalamus is absent and the anterior pituitary gland and adrenal glands show hypoplasia. Their mothers have low levels of oestriol excretion indicating hypofunction of the fetal zone of the adrenal cortex. In a detailed study of anencephaly, not associated with hydramnios, it was found in general that the greater the prolongation of pregnancy beyond term, the smaller the size of the fetal adrenal glands.[4] Prolongation of pregnancy has been reported also in congenital adrenal hypoplasia, a condition in which there is a marked diminution in cortisol production.[83] In adrenal hyperplasia due to 21-hydroxylase deficiency the length of gestation has been shown to be normal.[79] In this condition cortisol production rates may be in the lower part of the normal range, so that a normal length of gestation might be expected. Finally, the reverse situation, namely an association between generalized hyperplasia of the fetal adrenal glands of unknown aetiology with unexplained premature labour has been reported.[3] The possibility that activity of the fetal hypothalamic-pituitary-adrenal axis initiates parturition in human beings is of great interest but considerable further research is necessary to define by what mechanism the onset of parturition is influenced.

(c). **The Stimulation of Surfactant Activity.** In the experiments on pregnant sheep, a further interesting finding in the lambs born prematurely, due to the infusion of ACTH or corticosteroids, was the advanced development of lung surfactant for their stage of gestation.[59] Cortisol administered to immature animals has been shown to induce precocious activity of a variety of enzymes and this might explain the accelerated appearance of surfactant. The effect has been demonstrated also in rabbits as cortisol, or one of its analogues, injected into fetal rabbits led to acceleration of the maturation of the respiratory epithelium and of the synthesis of surfactant.[53 70] Circumstantial evidence in favour of fetal production of cortisol stimulating the development of surfactant during human pregnancy is provided by the frequency of respiratory distress in infants suffering from congenital adrenal hypoplasia or adrenal haemorrhage. Further, it has been shown that the adrenal glands from infants dying of hyaline membrane disease were significantly lighter in weight than those of infants dying from other causes in the neonatal period, and a decrease in the number of cells in both the fetal and adult zones of the adrenal cortex was demonstrated.[73] Thus impaired adrenal function, due to congenital adrenal hypoplasia, adrenal haemorrhage or a decrease in the number of cells in the adrenal cortex, may favour the development of hyaline membrane disease.

In theory, therefore, it might be advantageous, in the management of premature infants and light-for-dates infants, to stimulate surfactant activity prophylactically by the use of ACTH, cortisol or a cortisol analogue in the mother before delivery or in the infant shortly after birth. A controlled trial of the use of 12 mg. of betamethasone IM in mothers prior to premature delivery has been reported recently.[61a] All were delivered before 37 weeks' gestation, 213 spontaneously and 69 following induction of labour. With regard to the incidence of the respiratory distress syndrome, there was a significant reduction in treated infants compared to controls, provided treatment had been given to the mothers at least 24 hr. before delivery and that the infants were of less than 32 weeks' gestation. The severity of the respiratory distress syndrome was reduced in infants delivered spontaneously. The early neonatal mortality of 3·2 per cent in the treated group compared with 15 per cent in the control group showed a difference which was statistically significant. The fact that therapy had to be given at least 24 hr. before delivery led the authors to speculate that the treatment of infants after birth would not be effective. It was noted that the use of corticosteroids in pregnancies complicated by severe hypertension, oedema and proteinuria might increase the risk of fetal death but that there was sufficient evidence of beneficial effect on infant lung function to justify further trials. A controlled trial of the use of hydrocortisone in 44 infants suffering from the respiratory distress syndrome has also been reported recently.[5a] Two doses of 15 mg./kg. were administered to each infant through an umbilical artery catheter and levels of plasma total corticosteroids up to 1,000 μg./100 ml. were recorded by the competetive protein binding technique of Murphy. It was concluded that the treatment was ineffective in altering the course and prognosis of the disease. It was speculated that therapy postnatally was too late in view of the period of 24–48 hr. necessary for corticosteroids to induce the synthesis of surfactant.

The use of large doses of corticosteroids antenatally or postnatally might increase the risk of infection in the infant and, in addition, there might be detrimental effects on organ growth not immediately apparent. Recent experimental work involving the giving of a single large dose of dexamethasone or cortisol to immature rats led to interference with the growth of the rat and with the development of the brain, particularly the cerebellum, where a very rapid rate of cell formation takes place during early post-natal life. No ill-effects were noted when physiological doses of cortisol of the order of 1 mg./kg. of body weight daily were given. This work raises the possibility that the use of large doses of corticosteroids might affect the developing brain of the human infant but that it might be quite safe to use physiological doses of cortisol.[32] It is not known, however, whether such lower doses of cortisol would stimulate surfactant activity.

Steroids in Cord Blood

In pregnant women the total plasma cortisol levels, which include free and protein-bound cortisol, are higher than in non-pregnant women because of an increase in the protein-bound cortisol fraction resulting from the high level of plasma transcortin during pregnancy. In spite of the high total plasma cortisol levels, the free cortisol levels and the cortisol secretion rates are of the same order as those of non-pregnant women. In newborn infants the plasma transcortin levels are lower than in older children or adults and very much lower than in their mothers. It is therefore not surprising that the total plasma cortisol in the newborn infant is about one-third that of the mother. However, the free cortisol level is similar to that of the mother and the cortisol secretion rate at least equals that of adults when expressed on the basis of surface area.[51]

It has been known for many years that cortisol may cross the placenta from the mother to the fetus or from the fetus to the mother, from experiments carried out at mid-gestation. However, the details of transplacental transfer of cortisol between the mother and her infant during the latter half of pregnancy have not been elucidated, because of the ethical deterrent to the use of radio-active isotopes at a time when the fetus is viable. Mothers delivered by the vaginal route show a greater rise in plasma cortisol than those delivered by elective Caesarean section. The plasma levels of infants born vaginally are also higher than in those delivered by elective Caesarean section. It has been suggested that transfer of cortisol from the mother to the fetus during delivery occurs but, on the other hand, vaginal delivery might be more stressful to the infant as well as to the mother and hence provoke a response from the infant adrenal glands.

The cortisol:cortisone ratio in cord blood is 0·7:1 whereas in the maternal blood this ratio is 11:1. The high level of cortisone in cord blood may be due to activity of 11β-dehydrogenase from the placenta which converts cortisol to cortisone. After birth the low cortisol:cortisone ratio persists for about 2 weeks. The level of corticosterone in cord blood is also high and the excretion of corticosterone remains elevated during the neonatal period, infancy and early childhood reaching a steady level relative to body weight by the age of 4 years.

The 17-oxosteroids are higher in cord blood than in maternal blood and the level falls off rapidly during the 1st week of life. Cord blood also contains oestrogens and progesterone and precursor steroids, for example 3β-hydroxy-Δ_5-steroids, many of which are thought to be derived from the fetal zone of the adrenal cortex.

Adrenocortical Function in the Neonate and Young Infant

Steroids in Plasma and Urine

A recent study of plasma cortisol levels in the neonatal period, based on a competitive protein-binding technique, has demonstrated that cord levels of cortisol are generally higher and show a wider range than subsequently during the 1st week of life.[89] The mean value for the plasma cortisol in the cord blood of full-term infants was approximately 30 μg./100 ml. and it dropped to approximately 10 μg./100 ml. by the end of the first 24 hr. of life remaining approximately the same thereafter during the 1st week. It was postulated that the high cord level reflected either a transfer of free cortisol from the mother to the infant or an increased fetal adrenocortical activity in response to the stress of delivery.

In spite of low transcortin levels and therefore low protein-binding, the half-life of cortisol has been shown to be prolonged in the neonatal period in comparison with that of older children and adults. Immaturity of the liver leading to a slower reduction of ring A, which is necessary for the formation of tetrahydro and hexahydro metabolites, and slower conjugation of these metabolites with glucuronic acid are thought to contribute to the prolonged half-life. The infant forms water soluble derivatives of cortisol, for example 6β-hydroxy-cortisol, which are excreted without conjugation by the kidneys and, to some extent, this overcomes the difficulties in the degradation and conjugation of cortisol during this period of life.

Several years ago careful qualitative and quantitative determinations of the individual neutral steroids in the urine were made as a basis for a study of the response of newborn infants to stress.[20] The estimations were carried out on 24 hr. urine samples from healthy male infants aged between 1 and 6 days, by a method based on paper chromatography using Bush solvent systems. Steroids of the 17-oxosteroid group were estimated by their reaction with Zimmermann reagent and the corticosteroids by their reduction of blue tetrazolium and by their sodium fluorescence. The excretion pattern in the urine of newborn infants was found to be very different from that in adult urine or maternal urine. Many unidentified steroids were present and several steroids, which are prominent in adult urine, were either present in only small quantities in the urine of the newborn infant or were completely absent.

At the time of the study it was known that the 17-oxosteroid excretion was high for the first few days of life and then fell steeply during the 1st week. Detailed examination of the Zimmermann-reacting chromogens, contributing to the 17-oxosteroid group assay, revealed that the three major 11-deoxy-17-oxosteroids, namely DHA, aetiocholanolone and androsterone present in adult urine were virtually absent from infant urine. On the other hand, several unknown steroids were present in this fraction which disappeared by the 6th day of life. The four major 11-oxy-17-oxosteroids found in adult urine namely 11β-hydroxy-aetiocholanolone, 11β-hydroxy-androsterone, 11-oxo-aetiocholanolone and 11-oxo-androsterone were detected in the urine of infants. However, in this fraction also, there were unknown steroids which disappeared during the 1st week of life.

Previous to the study it had been established that the 17-hydroxy-corticosteroid excretion remained virtually unchanged during the 1st week. When the corticosteroid excretion estimated by the reduction of blue tetrazolium was examined in detail, further differences from adult urine emerged. 6β-hydroxy-steroids were detected in considerable quantities whereas tetrahydro-cortisol (THF) and tetrahydro-cortisone (THE) were present only in small amounts. There were a number of blue tetrazolium-reducing steroids which at the time were not identified. In the light of present knowledge, these probably included allo-THF, tetrahydro-corticosterone (THB), allo-THB and tetrahydro-11-dehydro-corticosterone (THA) as well as 3β-hydroxy-Δ_5-steroids representing synthetic intermediates on the pathways to cortisol and corticosterone. These steroids persisted in the urine during the 1st week of life. Steroids with properties corresponding to that of 6β-hydroxy-cortisol, cortisol, cortisone and corticosterone were detected by their sodium fluorescence. It was noted that corticosterone was present in neonatal urine in greater quantity than cortisol. A steroid reacting with blue tetrazolium found in the 11-oxy-17-oxosteroid fraction was provisionally identified as 21-hydroxy-pregnenolone. Its excretion remained unchanged during the first 6 days of life. Later work proved the provisional identification to be correct.[12]

In view of the marked differences in steroid metabolism in newborn infants in comparison with adults, it was pointed out that the group assay methods designed to measure the principal metabolites in adult urine were unsuited to a study of the urine of newborn infants.

Since this early paper, a great deal of further work on steroid metabolism in the newborn infant and in early infancy has been carried out using methodology specially designed for the purpose. Many of the unknown steroids have been identified and it is now possible to give a theoretical explanation of the findings.[67,68] In the neonatal period the steroids in infant urine are derived from three sources. There are steroids which have come from the placenta associated with the metabolism of progesterone and the oestrogens. There are the 3β-hydroxy-Δ_5-steroids produced by the fetal zone of the adrenal cortex, for example DHA and 16α-hydroxy-DHA, which in fetal life act as precursors of progesterone and the oestrogens, particularly oestriol. Finally, there are the urinary metabolites of steroids produced by the adult zone of the adrenal cortex, namely cortisol, corticosterone, aldosterone, DHA and androstenedione and 3β-hydroxy-Δ_5-steroids produced by the adult zone, because of a relative lack of 3β-hydroxy-dehydrogenase, which persists for the first 6 months of life.

As expected, steroids derived from the placenta virtually disappear from infant urine during the 1st week of life. The 3β-hydroxy-Δ_5-steroids from the fetal zone of the adrenal cortex, with its marked deficiency of 3β-hydroxy-dehydrogenase, continue to be produced during its period of viability. They fall off rapidly during the 1st month of life to about a fifth of the quantity present during the first few days. It is at present unknown whether these steroids have a biological function during early infancy or whether they represent only the vestigial remains of a system of metabolism designed for intra-uterine life.[69] By the time of birth, the production of cortisol, corticosterone and aldosterone by the adult zone is adequate for survival and the urinary metabolites of these steroids gradually increase as the infant grows. Corticosterone excretion is greater relative to body weight during early infancy and up until the age of 4 years than in later childhood and adolescence.

DHA, aetiocholanolone and androsterone are present in very small amounts in the urine of infants and young children. The urine of infants contains 21-hydroxy-pregnenolone and other 3β-hydroxy-Δ_5-steroids probably derived from the adult zone of the adrenal cortex until the deficiency of 3β-hydroxy-dehydrogenase is overcome by the age of 6 months. Thereafter adult pathways of metabolism are fully established. The contribution of the fetal zone to the excretion of 3β-hydroxy-Δ_5-steroids, which is considerable in early infancy, is mentioned above. Because of these differences in metabolism, use should be made of the special methodology now available in the investigation of adrenal steroid metabolism before the age of 6 months.

The Neonatal Response to Stress

It is likely that the hypothalamic-pituitary-adrenal axis is active during fetal life, but the mechanism of cortisol production in the fetus is not fully understood. The fetus may receive cortisol, synthesized by the maternal adrenal glands, across the placenta and, in addition, progesterone passes to the fetus from the placenta and acts as substrate for cortisol synthesis. Nevertheless, by the time of birth, the fetus has developed the ability to form sufficient cortisol for survival and must possess the enzyme 3β-hydroxy-dehydrogenase in sufficient quantity for the purpose.

Initial doubts regarding the adequacy of adrenocortical function in the neonatal period arose from the knowledge that the adrenal glands degenerated very rapidly after birth. Later, however, it was realized that the degeneration affected only the fetal zone, but doubts still existed regarding the adequacy of the hypothalamic-pituitary-adrenal response to stress in newborn infants, in comparison with children and adults, because of the known differences in steroid metabolism. In view of this the following study was undertaken of the response to stress in normal, premature and light-for-dates male infants.[22] If the clinical course was entirely satisfactory the infants were considered normal or unstressed. They were classified as stressed on account of asphyxia immediately after birth or, in the case of premature or light-for-dates infants, if they suffered from respiratory distress. A few full-term infants requiring exchange transfusion for rhesus incompatibility were included. The individual neutral steroids in the 24 hr. urine samples were estimated by the method outlined in a previous paper.[20] The value for the total blue tetrazolium-reducing steroids was obtained by adding together the quantities of the various individual steroids giving this reaction. It was postulated that the value for the total blue tetrazolium-reducing steroids was likely to reflect the corticosteroid secretory activity of the adrenal cortex and in order to compare results from infants of low and normal birth weight the excretion was expressed in μg./kg. of birth weight/24 hr.

The basal levels of excretion of the blue tetrazolium-reducing steroids, averaged for the first 3 days of life, in unstressed full-term, premature and light-for-dates infants, was the same when the results were compared on a statistical basis. There was therefore no evidence of frank hypo-adrenocorticism in any of the three groups. An increased excretion of blue tetrazolium-reducing steroids in response to stress was found in several infants of each category during the first 3 days of life. When the results were submitted to statistical analysis by Student's t test, the increase in the excretion in full-term and premature infants was statistically significant but that in the light-for-dates infants was not. The full-term infants also showed a statistically significant corticosteroid response to stress on the 6th day of life. By that time the number of premature infants studied was too small for statistical analysis. There were enough light-for-dates infants for analysis but no significant corticosteroid response was found. In summary, certain infants of the full-term, premature and light-for-dates categories showed an increased excretion of blue tetrazolium-reducing steroids in response to stress, whereas other infants did not. Taking the groups as a whole, the full-term group showed a response to stress on the first 3 days of life and on the 6th day of life which was statistically significant and the premature group showed a response to stress on the first 3 days of life which was statistically significant, but the number of premature infants on day 6 was too small for analysis. The light-for-dates group did not show a significant response to stress either during the first 3 days of life or on the 6th day.

Light-for-dates infants are undernourished *in utero* and may suffer in other ways from placental insufficiency. There is evidence of depression of function of the fetal zone in, for example, pre-eclamptic toxaemia when a low oestriol excretion is found in the maternal urine. Recent work has demonstrated that light-for-dates infants show a persistence of impaired fetal zone function during the neonatal period.[25] Twenty-four hour samples of urine were collected from a group of normal infants and from infants whose mothers had shown a low oestriol excretion prior to delivery. No difference was found in the excretion of DHA in the two groups of infants but only very small amounts were detected. Very much larger quantities of 16α-hydroxy-DHA and 16-keto-androstenediol were present and the excretion of both of these steroids was significantly lower in the infants whose mothers had shown a low oestriol excretion. In an investigation of fetal adrenal weights in relation to the time of parturition, it was established that the adrenal glands of infants born to mothers who had suffered from pre-eclamptic toxaemia weighed less than those of infants dying from unknown causes or from ante-partum haemorrhage and that this finding was statistically significant when the results for the three groups of infants were standardized for their birth weight and gestational age.[3] It is therefore likely that the poor response to stress demonstrated in light-for-dates infants is due to hypo-function of the adult zone of the adrenal cortex, resulting from placental insufficiency, which persists in the neonatal period. Recent experimental work in rats has confirmed the concept that previously undernourished newborn animals, although they may show a similar basal cortico-steroid excretion to that of normal animals, respond less well to stressful stimulation.[1a]

The level of excretion of the blue tetrazolium-reducing steroids in stressed infants corresponded to two, three or four times that of the normal infants. It was therefore suggested that therapy of the order of 5–7·5 mg. of cortisol daily might be given to newborn infants, such as light-for-dates infants, showing a poor adrenal response to stressful situations.[22] On the basis of a small series, it has been claimed that the giving of physiological doses of cortisol to mothers suffering from pre-eclamptic toxaemia and to their infants after birth improved the survival rate of the infants.[72] The benefit to the infants was thought to be due to an increase in their capacity to withstand non-specific stress. The possibility that such therapy might also induce surfactant activity comes to mind. Unfortunately, as discussed previously, current experiments suggest that the induction of surfactant activity requires pharmacological doses of corticosteroids and the deleterious effects of such therapy to the newborn infant might outweigh the possible advantages.

Infants of diabetic mothers are at risk *in utero* and in the immediate neonatal period. Provided there is no placental insufficiency, hyperfunction of the infant's adrenal cortex may occur in response to fluctuating blood sugar levels *in utero* and hypoglycaemia after birth. It is likely that hyperadrenocorticism contributes, along with the increased secretion of insulin by the fetal pancreas, to the excess of body fat and the plethora of the infants at birth. It was shown some years ago that the total blue tetrazolium-reducing corticosteroids were raised, when calculated per kg. of birth weight, in the 24 hr. urine samples from infants of diabetic mothers, during the first 3 days of life, in comparison with normal infants and infants of pre-diabetic mothers, in whom abnormalities of blood sugar level were minimal. All of the infants studied were making satisfactory clinical progress.[21a] However, in a paper published the same year, the cortisol production rates in infants of diabetic mothers 4–6 days after birth were reported to be similar, when corrected for surface area, to those found in healthy control infants.[1] The suggested fetal adrenocortical response to fluctuant blood sugars would therefore appear to diminish during the 1st week of life in infants under careful medical care.

THE DEVELOPMENT OF ADRENOCORTICAL FUNCTION DURING INFANCY, CHILDHOOD AND ADOLESCENCE

The early studies of adrenocortical function during childhood and adolescence were based on assays of groups of steroids in 24 hr. urine samples. Of these, the largest and most recent series showed that the 17-oxosteroids rose gradually in early childhood and more steeply during adolescence, whereas the 17-hydroxy-corticosteroids rose steadily throughout childhood.[54] For detailed study of the changing pattern of excretion of adrenocortical metabolites during infancy, childhood and adolescence, more information was later obtained from the measurement of the individual steroids in urine. Modern chromatographic methods were employed in several centres for this purpose.[10,13,62,92,94] The results, with regard to the excretion pattern of the various steroids and the relative quantities of one steroid metabolite in relation to another, have proved to be broadly similar to those compiled recently by Dr. D. C. L. Savage and myself, and details of our study will now be given, as it is the most comprehensive to date.[86]

Thirteen steroid metabolites in the 24 hr. urine samples from 62 normal infants, children and adolescents and, for comparison, from 8 adults were estimated. The 17-hydroxy-corticosteroids and the 17-oxosteroids were determined on the same samples. The subjects' heights and weights were in the normal range, between the 3rd and 97th percentile, and the bone ages were within 1 year of the chronological age. The method involved the extraction and hydrolysis of the steroids, followed by their purification and final separation by paper chromatography using Bush systems. The steroids were quantitated on the paper following reactions with Zimmermann reagent for the 17-oxosteroids or blue tetrazolium reagent for the corticosteroids. An internal radio-active recovery technique was incorporated so that the results would be comparable over a period of years.

TABLE 1

Individual Steroids	*Group*
Dehydroepiandrosterone Aetiocholanolone Androsterone	11-deoxy-17-oxosteroids
11β-hydroxy-aetiocholanolone 11β-hydroxy-androsterone 11-oxo-aetiocholanolone 11-oxo-androsterone	11-oxy-17-oxosteroids
Tetrahydro-cortisol Allo-tetrahydro-cortisol Tetrahydro-cortisone	α-ketolic metabolites of cortisol
Tetrahydro-corticosterone Allo-tetrahydro-corticosterone Tetrahydro-11-dehydro-corticosterone	α-ketolic metabolites of corticosterone

The 13 steroids which were estimated are listed in Table 1 and their formulae are shown in Fig. 10. They are grouped under four headings, the 11-deoxy-17-oxosteroids, the 11-oxy-17-oxysteroids, the α-ketolic metabolites of cortisol and the α-ketolic metabolites of corticosterone. The 11-deoxy-17-oxosteroid results are for the free steroids and the glucuronide and sulphate conjugates added together. The 11-oxy-17-oxosteroid results and those for the cortisol and corticosterone metabolites are for the free and glucuronide conjugates added together. As the sulphate conjugates represented such a small proportion of the total, they were omitted.

The 17-oxosteroid block assay[64] measures the 11-deoxy-17-oxosteroids and the 11-oxy-17-oxosteroids. The results obtained in the routine steroid laboratory in mg./24 hr. are shown in Fig. 11. In this graph, and in those following, the

Dehydroepiandrosterone (DHA)

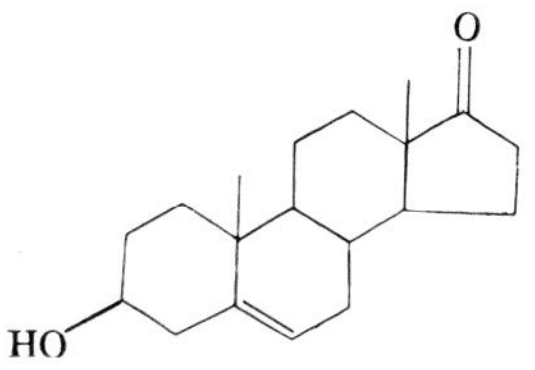

Aetiocholanolone

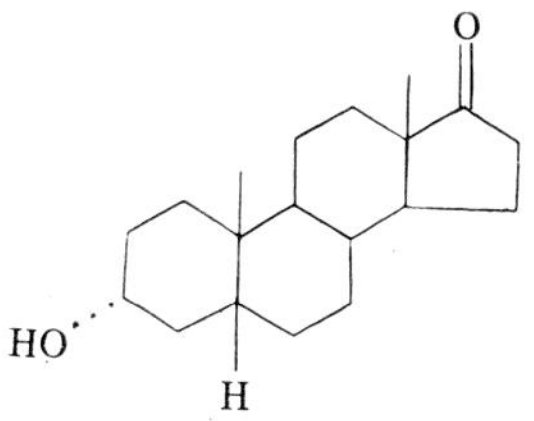

Androsterone

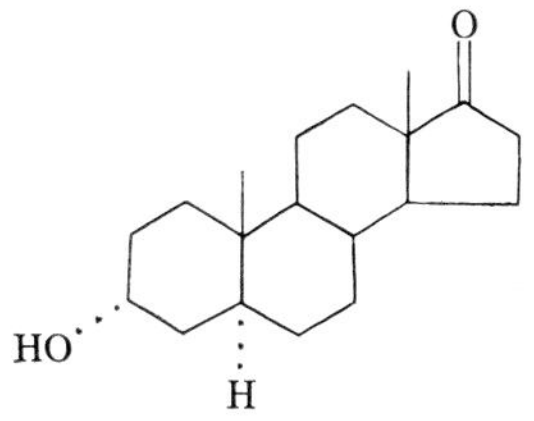

11β-hydroxy-aetiocholanolone

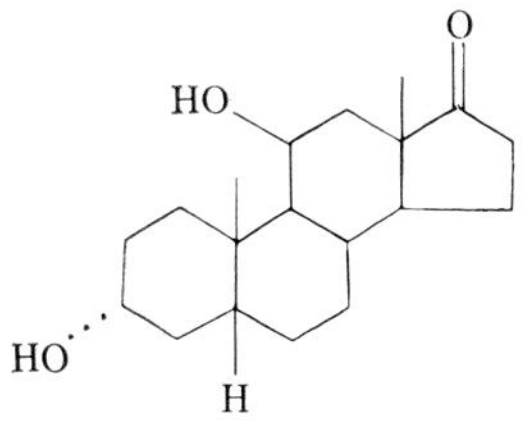

11β-hydroxy-androsterone

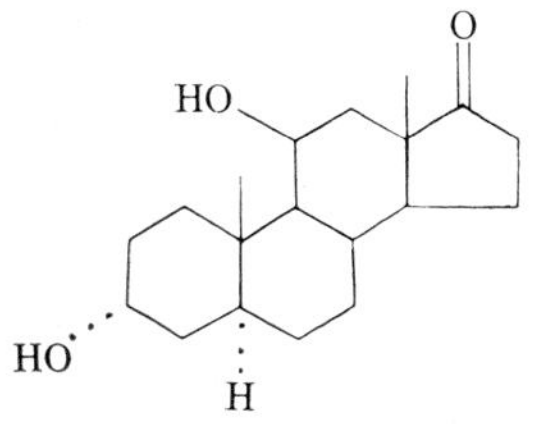

11-oxo-aetiocholanolone

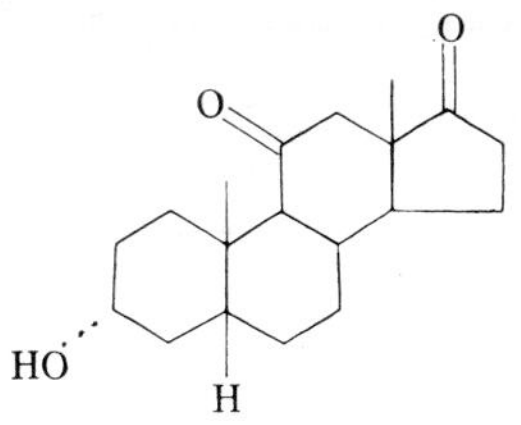

11-oxo-androsterone

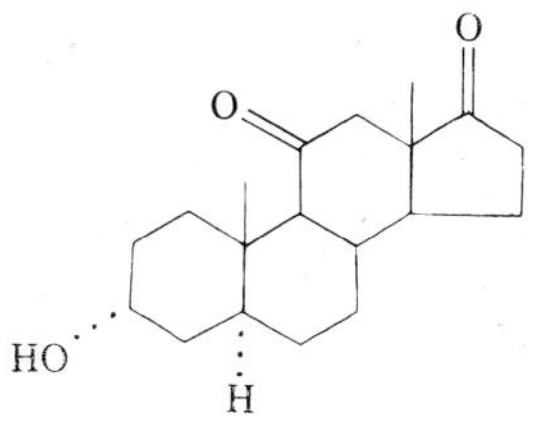

Tetrahydro-cortisol (THF)

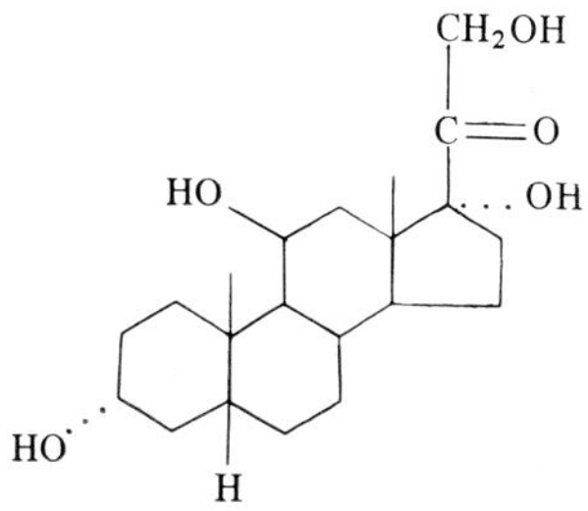

Allo-tetrahydro-cortisol (Allo-THF)

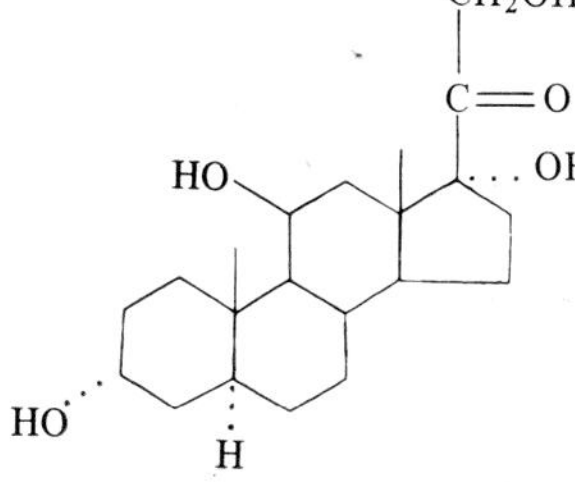

Tetrahydro-cortisone (THE)

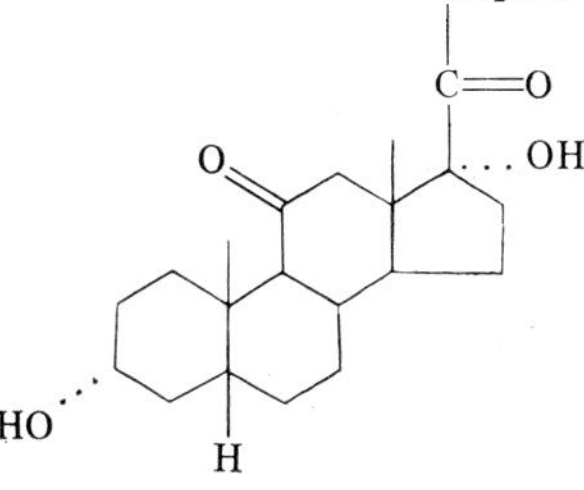

Tetrahydro-corticosterone (THB)

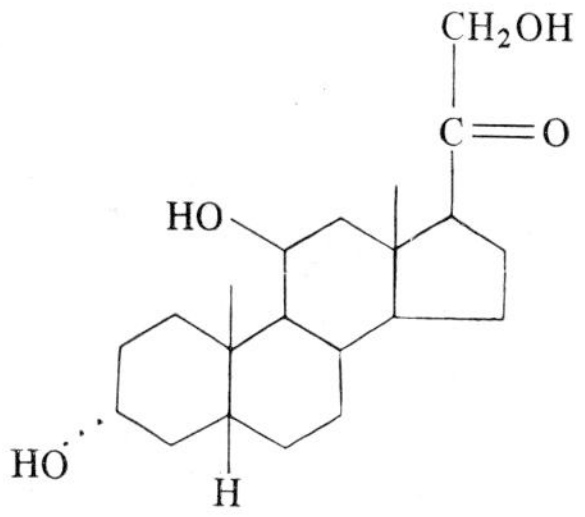

Allo-tetrahydro-corticosterone (Allo-THB)

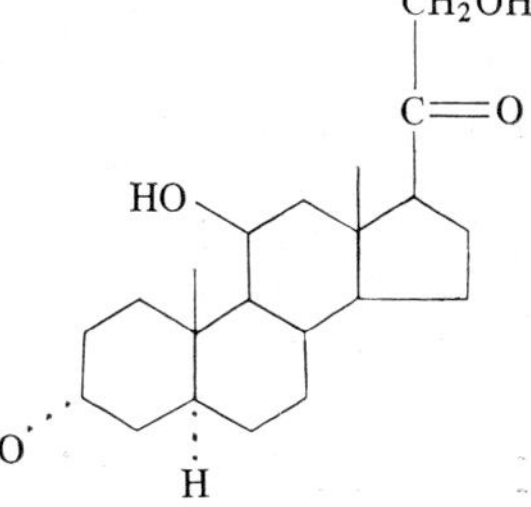

Tetrahydro-11-dehydro-corticosterone (THA)

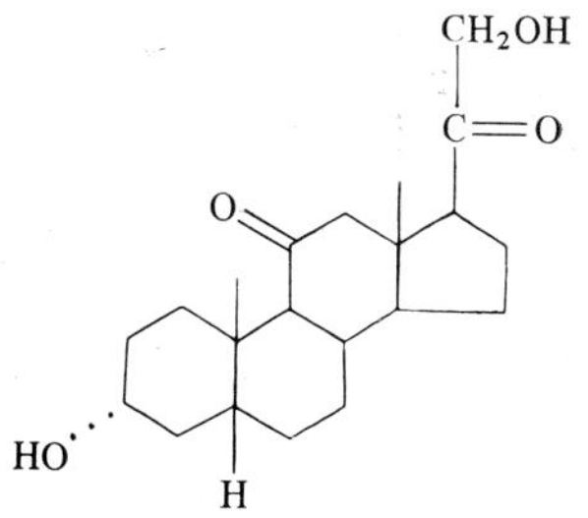

FIG. 10. Formulae of steroids in Table 1.

males are shown as closed circles and the females as open circles. The centre line represents the mean value and the outer lines represent plus and minus two standard deviations from the mean. The lines are smooth curves calculated from the individual results by the medical statistician. The mean and two standard deviation curves are calculated for the age groups 0–1 year to 10–11 years, and 11–12 years to 17–18 years separately. A gradual rise in excretion of the 17-oxosteroids during childhood is seen, and it is followed by a steeper rise in adolescence which continues to a mean adult level of 8·8 mg./24 hr.

The 11-deoxy-17-oxosteroids are the urinary metabolites of DHA and androstenedione and accurately reflect the adrenal androgen excretion in boys and girls before puberty, (Fig. 12). In adult males, testosterone makes a contribution to these steroids but they are still predominantly derived from adrenal androgens and in women they are virtually entirely derived from adrenal androgens. The excretion of the 11-deoxy-17-oxosteroids in μg./24 hr. is shown in Fig. 13. The mean and two standard deviation curves are calculated for the age groups in the same way as for the 17-oxosteroids mentioned above. A rise in excretion begins at the age of 7 years and after the age of 11 years it becomes dramatic and continues beyond the age of 18 years until the adult level of 3,400 μg./24 hr. is reached. When the excretion of DHA, aetiocholanolone and androsterone are compared individually, the excretion of DHA is seen to be very much less in quantity than that of the other two steroids of which androsterone is dominant. DHA is, however, undoubtedly present by 6 years of age and increases sharply after the age of 11 years, when it is excreted chiefly in the form of DHA sulphate. Androsterone, the 5α steroid, increases at a slightly faster rate than aetiocholanolone, the 5β steroid, during adolescence.

The 11-oxy-17-oxosteroids are derived from the adrenal androgens and also from cortisol by scission of the side chain, (Fig. 12). Androstenedione via 11-oxo-androstenedione contributes to 11-oxo-androsterone and via 11β-hydroxy-androstenedione to 11β-hydroxy-androsterone. Allo-THF via allo-cortol contributes to 11β-hydroxy-androsterone, THF via cortol contributes to 11β-hydroxy-aetiocholanolone, and THE via cortolone contributes to 11-oxo-aetiocholanolone. The derivation of the 4 urinary metabolites is therefore as follows, 11-oxo-androsterone is derived from androstenedione; 11β-hydroxy-androsterone is derived from androstenedione and cortisol; 11β-hydroxy-aetiocholanolone and 11-oxo-aetiocholanolone are derived from cortisol only. The 11-oxy-17-oxosteroids thus include metabolites of both androstenedione and cortisol. The contribution from cortisol metabolites compared to adrenal androgens is relatively greater in prepubertal children than in adults, as the stimulation of the androgen pathway which occurs at puberty has not yet taken place. The excretion of 11-oxy-17-oxosteroids in μg./24 hr. is shown in Fig. 14. A gradual rise occurs throughout childhood and it continues to adult life when the mean value is 2,200 μg./24 hr. Of the individual 11-oxy-17-oxosteroids, 11-oxo-aetiocholanolone is dominant and 11-oxo-androsterone is excreted in very small quantity. 11-hydroxy-androsterone, the 5α steroid, increases slightly faster than 11-hydroxy-aetiocholanolone, the 5β steroid, during adolescence.

The total excretion of 11-deoxy-17-oxosteroids and 11-oxy-17-oxosteroids is compared with the 17-oxosteroid group assay in the same samples of urine in Fig. 15. It is evident that there is a considerable gap representing non-steroid chromogens measured by the 17-oxosteroid block assay. The gap is particularly marked in younger children, but represents about 30 per cent of the total, even in adults.

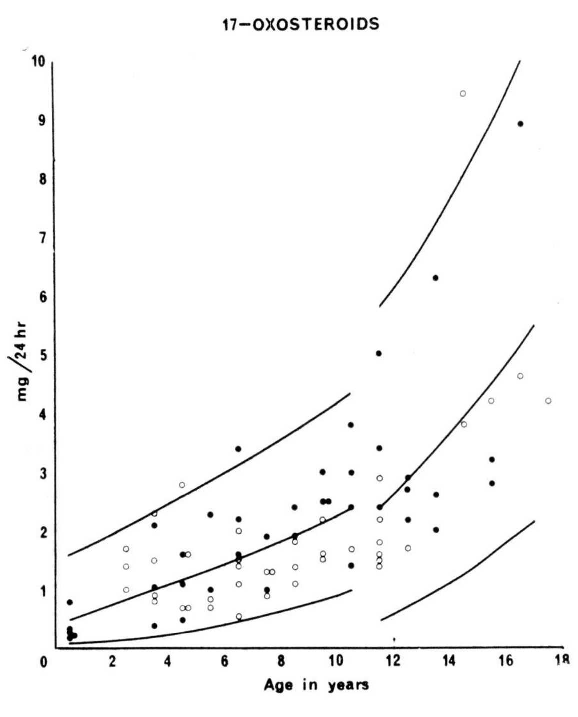

FIG. 11.

The 17-hydroxy-corticosteroid assay[39] measures the α-ketolic metabolites of cortisol plus the cortols and cortolones, but it does not detect the corticosterone metabolites as they do not possess a 17-hydroxyl group. The results obtained in the routine steroid laboratory in mg./24 hr. are shown in Fig. 16. The 17-hydroxy-corticosteroids show a steady rise throughout childhood and adolescence and a further rise to the adult level of 10·2 mg./24 hr.

The α-ketolic metabolites of cortisol reflect the cortisol output by the adrenal gland. The other major metabolites of cortisol, the cortols and cortolones are, however, not detected by the method used. The α-ketolic metabolites of cortisol in mg./24 hr. are shown in Fig. 17. They show a steady rise with increasing age and the metabolites continue to rise to an average adult level of 6·8 mg./24 hr. A study of the individual α-ketolic metabolites of cortisol shows that THE is the dominant steroid throughout childhood. It remains the dominant steroid in adult life. Allo-THF, the 5α steroid, has a higher excretion relative to the total tetrahydro derivatives of cortisol in early childhood and during adolescence than in the middle years of childhood.[85]

The α-ketolic metabolites of corticosterone reflect corticosterone output and, as with cortisol, the hexa-hydro

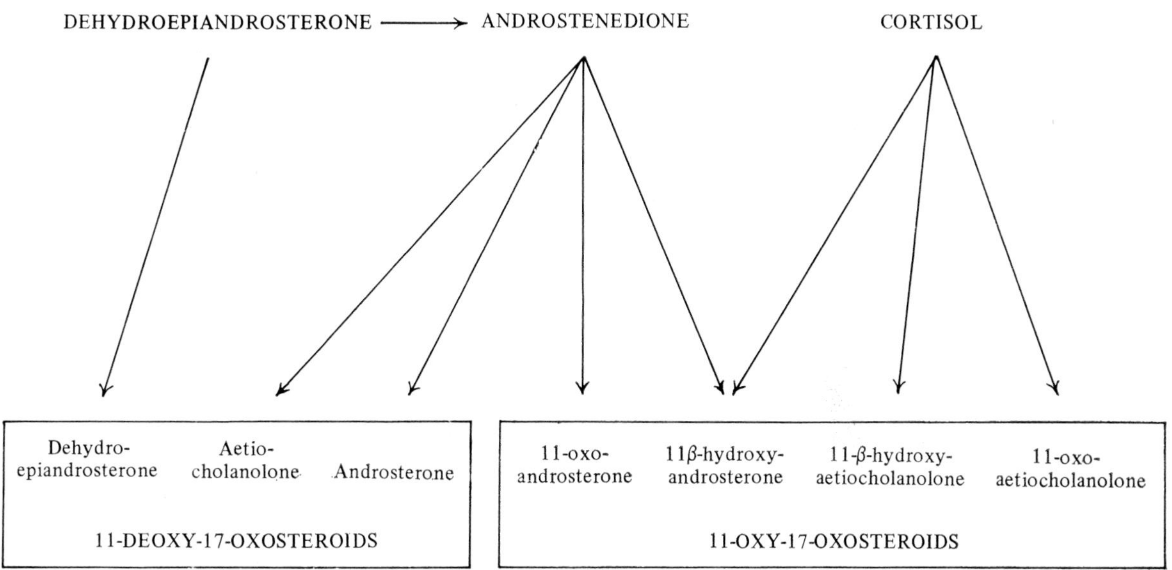

FIG. 12. The derivation of the individual 17-oxosteroids.

derivatives are not detected by our method. The α-ketolic metabolites of corticosterone in μg./24 hr. are shown in Fig. 18. A slight rise occurs throughout childhood and continues to an average adult level of 570 μg./24 hr. The dominant metabolite is allo-THB both in childhood and in adult life.

The 5α and 5β steroid metabolites are formed chiefly in the liver according to the relative activity of the 5α and 5β reductase enzyme systems. It is of interest that the 5α steroids of the 17-oxosteroid group are androgenic, whereas the 5β steroids are not. The 5α/5β ratios are shown in Table 2 in relation to the age groups under 1 year, 1–6 years, 7–10 years, 11–17 years and in adult life. The urine collections under 1 year of age were made from male infants, the youngest being 6 months old. The 5α/5β ratios are high under 1 year of age for the 17-oxosteroids and for the α-ketolic metabolites of cortisol. The ratio of androsterone to aetiocholanolone shows a rise between the 7–10 age group and the 11–17 age group. The ratio of 11β-hydroxy-androsterone to 11β-hydroxy-aetiocholanolone shows a

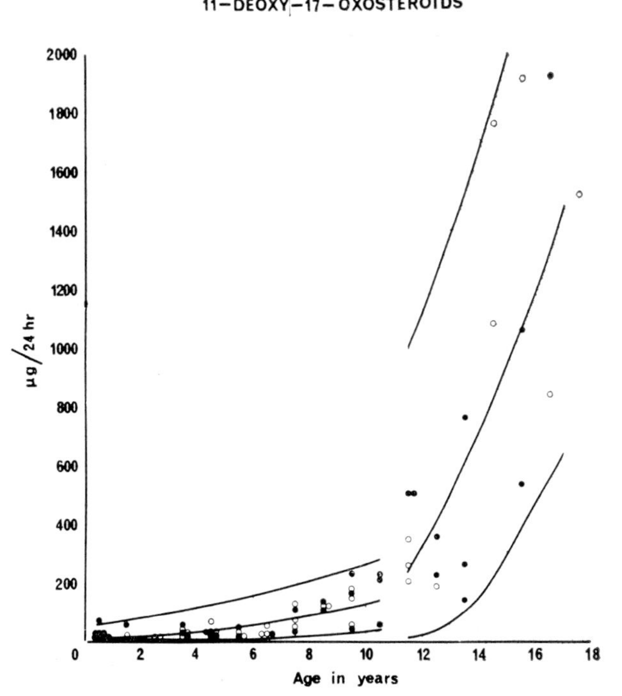

FIG. 13.

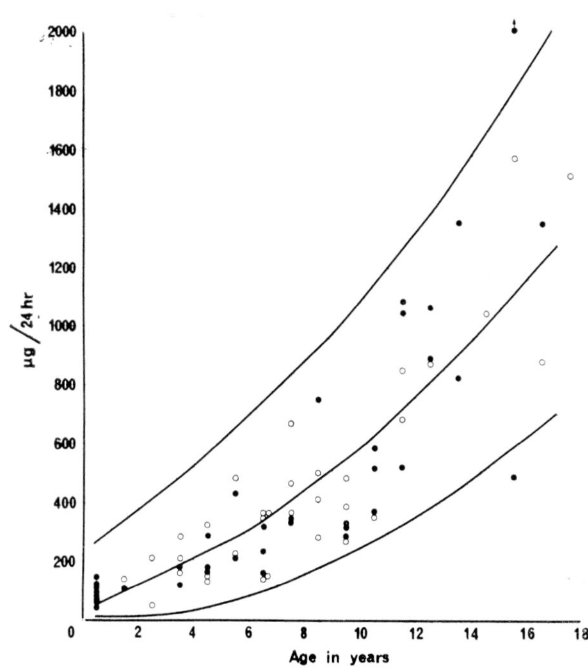

FIG. 14.

consistent rise from the 1–6 age group to adult life. The ratio of the total 5α 17-oxosteroids to the total 5β 17-oxosteroids also shows a consistent rise from the 1–6 age group to adult life. The rise of the 5α/5β ratio for the total

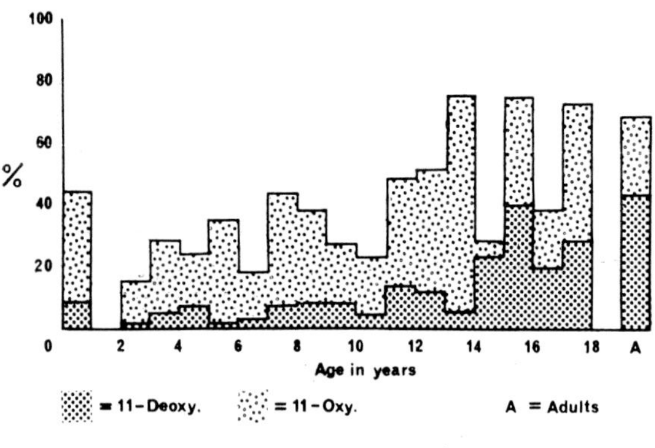

FIG. 15.

17-oxosteroids estimated by the method from the age of 1–17 years is statistically significant ($p < 0{\cdot}001$). The ratio of allo-THF to THF shows a rise between the 7–10 age group and the 11–17 age group. When the results in

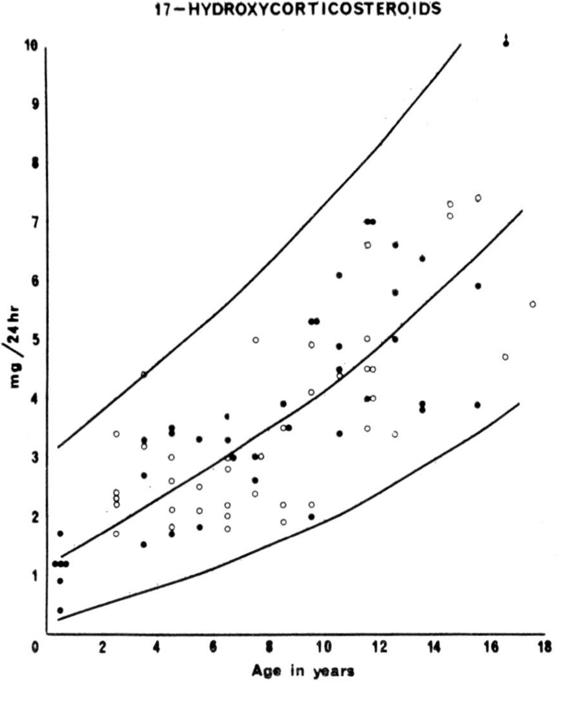

FIG. 16.

girls and boys are analysed separately the rise in all four 5α/5β ratios is shown to occur earlier in girls than in boys.

The significance of change with age in the 24 hr. steroid excretion standardized for height, weight, surface area and creatinine excretion is shown in Table 3. This has been tested by determining whether the regression co-efficient from infancy to adulthood is significantly different from zero using Student's t test. There is a significant change with age where the p values are less than 0·05 and, conversely, no significant change with age where the p values are greater than 0·05.

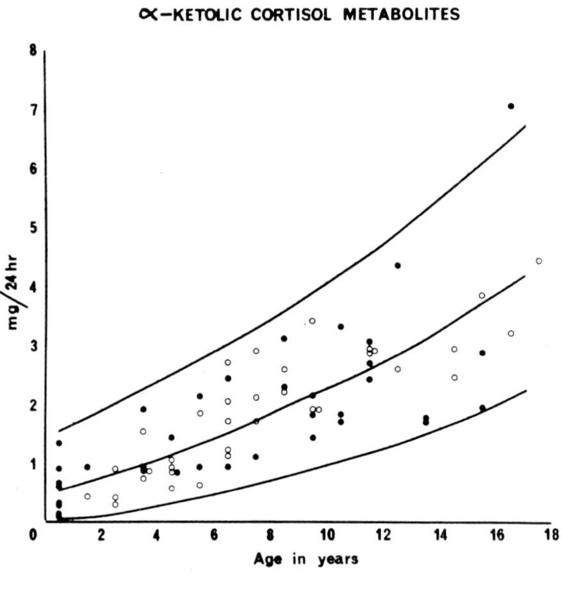

FIG. 17.

The 17-oxosteroids, 11-deoxy-17-oxosteroids and 11-oxy-17-oxosteroids show a rise with age when standardized for height, weight or surface area. The 17-oxosteroids show no change with age when standardized for creatinine excretion. However, the 11-deoxy-17-oxosteroids rise when standardized in this way and, as this group of steroids

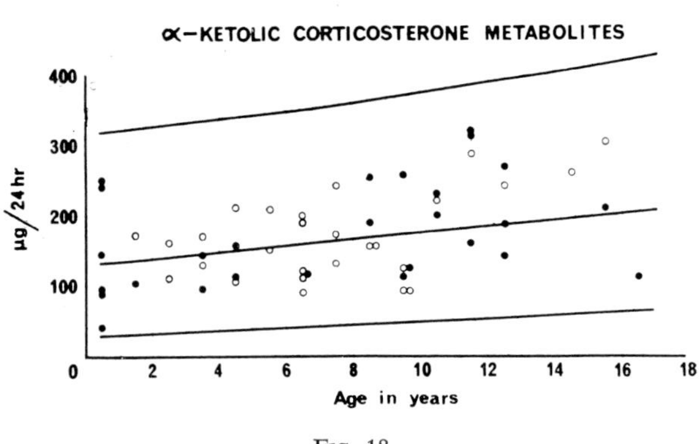

FIG. 18.

reflects adrenal androgen excretion more accurately, it is unlikely that adrenal androgen activity bears a meaningful relationship to the creatinine excretion. The 17-hydroxy-corticosteroids and the α-ketolic metabolites of cortisol show no change with age when standardized for body weight, but a change is noted when they are standardized for height, surface area or creatinine excretion. The correlation of the α-ketolic metabolites of cortisol with body weight is illustrated in Fig. 19. The corticosterone metabolites/100 kg. of body weight show a fall during the

TABLE 2

CHANGES IN THE $5\alpha/5\beta$ RATIOS WITH AGE

Age Group / *Years*	*Androsterone* / *Aetiocholanolone*	*11β-hydroxy-androsterone* / *11β-hydroxy-aetiocholanolone*	*Total 5α 17-oxosteroids* / *Total 5β 17-oxosteroids*	*Allo-*THF / THF
Under 1	2·6	6·9	0·8	2·2
1–6	1·2	1·4	0·4	1·0
7–10	1·2	1·6	0·5	0·7
11–17	1·4	1·7	0·7	1·1
Adults	1·2	3·0	1·0	0·7

TABLE 3

THE CORRELATION OF THE 24 hr. STEROID EXCRETION WITH HEIGHT, WEIGHT, SURFACE AREA AND CREATININE EXCRETION

Steroid Group	*Age Range Years*	*Height per* 100 cm.	*Weight per* 100 kg.	*Surface Area per* m²	*Creatinine Excretion per* g.
17-oxosteroids	0–1 to Adult	$p < 0{\cdot}001$	$p < 0{\cdot}01$	$p < 0{\cdot}001$	$p > 0{\cdot}05$
11-deoxy-17-oxosteroids	0–1 to Adult	$p < 0{\cdot}001$	$p < 0{\cdot}001$	$p < 0{\cdot}001$	$p < 0{\cdot}001$
11-oxy-17-oxosteroids	0–1 to Adult	$p < 0{\cdot}001$	$p < 0{\cdot}001$	$p < 0{\cdot}001$	$p < 0{\cdot}025$
17-hydroxy-corticosteroids	0–1 to Adult	$p < 0{\cdot}001$	$p > 0{\cdot}1$	$p < 0{\cdot}001$	$p < 0{\cdot}001$
Cortisol metabolites	0–1 to Adult	$p < 0{\cdot}001$	$p > 0{\cdot}2$	$p < 0{\cdot}001$	$p < 0{\cdot}025$
Corticosterone metabolites	4 to Adult	$p < 0{\cdot}001$	$p > 0{\cdot}5$	$p < 0{\cdot}025$	$p < 0{\cdot}01$

first 4 years of life. It has been recognized for some time that corticosterone is excreted in relatively large quantities by infants and young children. From the age of 4 years, however, the excretion of the corticosterone metabolites

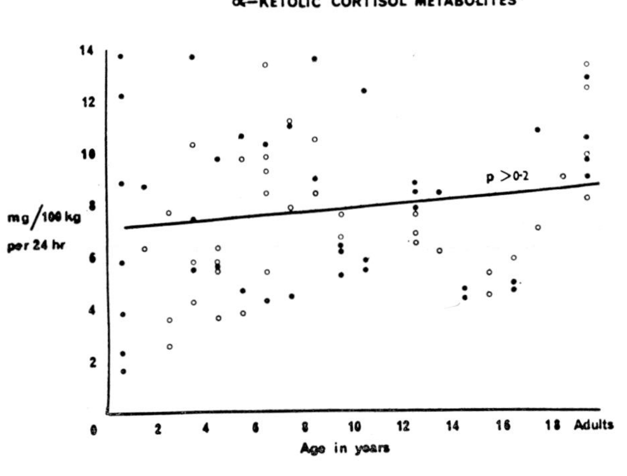

FIG. 19.

is related to body weight in a similar manner to that of the cortisol metabolites.

The implications of these results will now be discussed in relation to adrenocortical function during infancy, childhood and adolescence. The limitations of the 17-oxosteroid block assay in measuring adrenal androgen excretion during childhood are due partly to lack of specificity of the method, as demonstrated, and partly to the contribution to the 11-oxy-17-oxosteroid component from metabolites of cortisol, which play a more prominent part in childhood than in adult life. The 17-oxosteroid excretion shows a gradual rise in early childhood, followed by a steeper rise in adolescence. The 11-oxy-17-oxosteroid excretion shows a gradual rise throughout childhood and adolescence, reflecting the mixed origin of this group of steroids from adrenal androgens and from cortisol. The best reflection of adrenal androgen excretion is shown by the 11-deoxy-17-oxosteroids. There is a very low output before the age of 7 years and thereafter a gradual increase for about 4 years followed by a very rapid rise from the age of 11 years until the adult level is reached. DHA is excreted in much smaller quantity than androsterone and aetiocholanolone, but it is, nevertheless, clearly detectable by the age of 6 years and the output rises abruptly at puberty. The steep rise in the total 11-deoxy-17-oxosteroid excretion greatly exceeds what might be expected in relation to the growth spurt associated with puberty, as the rise persists when the results are calculated in terms of the height, weight, surface area or creatinine excretion of the individuals. The height spurt in the average girl occurs between 10½ and 14 years, breast development between 11 and 15 years and the development of pubic hair between 11 and 14 years. The height spurt in the average boy occurs between 12½ and 16 years, genital development between 11½ and 15 years and the development of pubic hair between 12 and 15 years.[91] It is evident that the rise in adrenal androgen output, which begins at the age of 7 years, precedes these changes, and it continues beyond them, as adult levels of 11-deoxy-17-oxosteroid excretion exceed those at the age of 17–18 years.

The $5\alpha/5\beta$ ratios of the 17-oxosteroids change in relation to age reflecting alterations in the metabolism of the steroids taking place mainly in the liver. The $5\alpha/5\beta$ ratios are higher under 1 year of age and from a few years before the clinical onset of puberty onwards, than during the middle years of childhood and the rise in relation to puberty occurs earlier in girls than in boys. There is evidence that testosterone stimulates the 5α-reductase enzyme system in pre-pubertal boys[94] and an increase in the $5\alpha/5\beta$ ratios occurs in precocious puberty.[11,46,93] The high $5\alpha/5\beta$ ratios are found in infant boys at a time when the Leydig cells of the testes show hyperplasia, associated with relatively high levels of plasma testosterone[15,30] and of Luteinizing Hormone.[17] The giving of parenteral testosterone to infant boys has a similar effect on the $5\alpha/5\beta$ ratios as that shown in older boys before puberty and the effect lasts for several months.[94]

The 17-hydroxy-corticosteroid block assay is more accurate for its purpose than the 17-oxosteroid assay. The 17-hydroxy-corticosteroid excretion and the α-ketolic metabolites of cortisol both show a steady rise throughout childhood and adolescence which is proportional to the increase in body weight of the growing individuals, as the correlation between the steroid levels and body weight is statistically significant. A correlation of the 17-hydroxy-corticosteroid output, measured by the Porter-Silber method, with surface area has been reported, the average output from infancy to adult life being expressed as $3{\cdot}1 \pm 1{\cdot}1$ mg./m²/24 hr.[98] Other reports, however, based on a variety of methods, have favoured a relationship to body weight either in children and adolescents[77] or in adults.[31] The secretion rate of cortisol between 4 months and 20 years of age has been shown, on the basis of surface area, to be similar to that of adults between 20 and 48 years,[51] the average and one standard deviation values established for 48 subjects being $11{\cdot}8 \pm 2{\cdot}5$ mg./m²/24 hr. No matter which of these parameters is accepted, however, the fundamental concept that the excretion of the 17-hydroxy-corticosteroids and of the α-ketolic metabolites of cortisol corresponds to the increase in body size of the individual remains the same. The α-ketolic metabolites of corticosterone are excreted in relatively greater amounts in infancy and early childhood. The biological significance of this is unknown. A correlation with body weight is found after the age of 4 years, from which time the excretion of corticosterone metabolites parallels that of cortisol metabolites, though at a very much lower level. The $5\alpha/5\beta$ ratio of the α-ketolic metabolites of cortisol is higher under 1 year of age in infant boys; and later, in both girls and boys in relation to puberty than during the middle years of childhood. This might be due to the effect of testosterone in boys or the increased adrenal androgen secretion in girls on the 5α and 5β reductase systems in the liver.[94] No biological significance of the changes is known, as the metabolites of cortisol are inactive.

The rise in adrenal androgen excretion and the changes in the $5\alpha/5\beta$ ratios of the 17-oxosteroids are generally considered to be related to puberty as both occur early in children presenting with precocious puberty.[11,46] However, neither the biological significance of the increased adrenal androgen output nor the mechanism of the rise is fully understood.

In adult women the adrenal cortex is virtually the only source of androgens. Some peripheral conversion of androstenedione to testosterone occurs and it is of interest also that the mildly androgenic steroid androsterone is excreted in relatively greater quantity in women than in men, when compared with the inactive androgen aetiocholanolone. In men adrenal androgens are of little biological importance in comparison with the powerful androgen testosterone, but, nevertheless, adrenal androgens contribute precursor steroids in the synthesis of testosterone. They may provide substrate also in the synthesis of oestrogens. On theoretical grounds the increase in adrenal androgens, in view of their anabolic action, might contribute towards the growth spurt at puberty.

The mechanism of the rise in adrenal androgen output will now be considered in the context of puberty as a whole. The onset of puberty is associated with rapid body growth and the appearance of secondary sexual characteristics. Laboratory investigation shows a steep rise in the adrenal androgens and in the levels of the pituitary gonadotrophic hormones. Luteinizing Hormone (LH) stimulates the gonads to produce testosterone or oestrogens and Follicle Stimulating Hormone (FSH) leads to the maturation of spermatozoa or ova. An attractive hypothesis for the mechanism of the onset of puberty is that the hypothalamus alters in its sensitivity to the feedback mechanism of the gonadal hormones as the child grows older.[36] Before the onset of puberty, the hypothalamus is extremely sensitive to very low levels of circulating testosterone or oestrogens which inhibit the output of pituitary gonadotrophic hormones. At the time of the commencement of puberty there is a decreased sensitivity of the hypothalamus to the feedback mechanism so that the output of gonadotrophic hormones is increased. This hypothesis has recently been strengthened by the demonstration that clomiphene inhibits the release of pituitary gonadotrophic hormones before puberty in extremely small doses but that larger doses are required near the onset of puberty.[56,81]

The relationships between the output of the pituitary gonadotrophic hormones, plasma testosterone, testicular size, bone age and the clinical changes of puberty have been established.[5] However, the connection between these clinical and hormonal changes and the stimulation of the adrenal androgens which occurs before the clinical signs of puberty appear, is not understood. In view of the fact that the corticosteroids do not show the sharp increase seen in the adrenal androgens in relation to puberty, it is evident that a marked rise in ACTH itself cannot be responsible.[97a] The possibility that an anterior pituitary hormone, possibly LH, might have a stimulatory effect on the adrenal cortex as well as the gonads was suggested many years ago.[2] A rise of plasma or serum LH has been demonstrated at puberty,[5,58] and some writers have suggested that plasma or serum levels of LH may begin to rise a few years before the clinical signs of puberty appear[6,50,84,100] and the output of LH in the urine has been noted by others to rise gradually from the age of about 6 years.[17] Recent *in vitro* experiments[66] have confirmed that the production of androstenedione in human adrenal tissue slices is increased by the presence of pituitary and gonadotrophic hormone preparations. The timing would therefore appear to be correct for LH to play a role in the stimulation of adrenal androgen production. However, some evidence is contrary to this concept in that premature adrenarché is not associated with a rise in LH,[84] certain gonadal deficiency states associated with elevated levels of LH show no evidence of stimulation of adrenal androgens[84] and, in addition, neither castration, characterized by high levels of gonadotrophic hormone nor the administration of gonadotrophic hormone to adult eununchs leads to an increase in adrenal androgens.

Another hypothesis for the increase in adrenal androgen output at puberty is that steroids of gonadal origin, either androgens or oestrogens, directly stimulate adrenal androgen production.[18,23] It is based on the supposition, suggested by work *in vitro*,[55] that these hormones inhibit the action of the adrenal enzyme 3β-hydroxy-dehydrogenase, in such a manner that the pathway to the adrenal androgens via DHA is less inhibited than the pathway to the corticosteroids. This may depend on the existence of two separate enzyme systems for C_{19} and C_{21} substrates.[75] Occasionally, congenital adrenal hyperplasia first presents at puberty when the previously mild cortisol deficiency becomes more pronounced. In healthy individuals a rise in ACTH might be postulated at puberty to offset the inhibition of the cortisol pathway, as cortisol deficiency does not develop at this time in normal circumstances. The giving of parenteral testosterone to pre-pubertal boys led to a rise in output of the 11-deoxy-17-oxosteroids and the 11-oxy-17-oxosteroids as well as to an increase in the $5\alpha/5\beta$ ratios of the 17-oxosteroids but no increase in cortisol metabolites was found.[94]

It seems probable, from the evidence given, that LH and the gonadal hormones, possibly acting synergistically, are involved in the stimulation of adrenal adrogens in relation to puberty. Clarification of the timing of the adrenal androgen increase in relation to the timing of the growth spurt, the progressive stages of puberty, the rise in plasma LH, FSH, testosterone and oestrogens would require a longitudinal study from the age of about 5 years throughout childhood and adolescence to adult life in a substantial number of individuals. It would be of interest to follow plasma ACTH and growth hormone levels in the same subjects.

The changes in adrenal steroid excretion during infancy, childhood and adolescence may be summarized as follows. Adrenal 11-deoxy-17-oxosteroid excretion is very low during early childhood then it rises slowly from the age of about 7 years. After 11 years there is a very steep increase which continues throughout adolescence until adult levels are reached and the increase is much greater than could be explained on a body weight basis. Differences in the metabolic degradation of 17-oxosteroids, chiefly in the liver, lead to a relatively high level of the biologically active 5α-androgenic steroids in early infancy and again at puberty. The physiological significance of these quantitative and qualitative changes in adrenal androgen excretion are not fully understood. It is likely, however, that they are related to activity of the gonadal axis. The excretion of the metabolites of cortisol and of corticosterone, after the age of 4 years, increases in direct proportion to the body weight of the individuals during childhood and adolescence. The biological significance of the relatively high corticosterone excretion in infancy and early childhood is unknown.

ACKNOWLEDGEMENTS

I am grateful to Professor J. L. Henderson for encouragement to undertake the writing of this chapter. I am particularly indebted to Dr. D. M. Cathro, Dr. D. C. L. Savage and Mrs. J. Cameron who have worked closely with me on various research schemes related to adrenocortical function over the past ten years. The Scottish Hospital Endowments Research Trust provided financial support for the work from this Department referred to on pages 486–488 and the Medical Research Council for that referred to on pages 488–493. I wish to thank Miss M. C. K. Browning, Dr. W. R. McWhirter, Dr. F. L. Mitchell, Professor T. Symington, Professor A. C. Turnbull, Dr. C. H. M. Walker and Dr. S. G. F. Wilson for their criticism of the text and Mr. J. C. G. Pearson for the statistical analyses, Mr. T. King, Mr. S. C. Turner and Mr. A. R. Whytock for photographic assistance and Mrs. J. Duncan and Mrs. B. Forsyth for typing the script.

REFERENCES

1. Aarskog, D. (1965), "Cortisol in the Newborn Infant," *Acta paediat. scand.*, suppl. 158.

1a. Adlard, B. P. F. and Smart, J. L. (1972), "Adrenocortical Function in Rats Subjected to Nutritional Deprivation in Early Life," *J. Endocr.*, **54**, 99–105.

2. Albright, F. (1947), "The Effect of Hormones on Osteogenesis in Man," *Recent Progr. Hormone Res.* **1**, 293–353.

3. Anderson, A. B. M., Laurence, K. M., Davies, K., Campbell, H. and Turnbull, A. C. (1971), "Fetal Adrenal Weight and the Cause of Premature Delivery in Human Pregnancy," *J. Obstet. Gynaec. Brit. Commonw.*, **78**, 481–488.

4. Anderson, A. B. M., Laurence, K. M. and Turnbull, A. C. (1969), "The Relationship in Anencephaly Between the Size of the Adrenal Cortex and the Length of Gestation," *J. Obstet. Gynaec. Brit. Commonw.*, **76**, 196–199.

5. August, G. P., Grumbach, M. M. and Kaplan, S. L. (1972), "Hormonal Changes in Puberty: III. Correlation of Plasma Testosterone, L.H., F.S.H., Testicular Size and Bone Age with Male Pubertal Development," *J. clin. Endocr.*, **34**, 319–326.

5a. Baden, M., Bauer, C. R., Colle, E., Klein, G., Tauesch, H. W. and Stern, L. (1972), "A Controlled Trial of Hydrocortisone Therapy in Infants with Respiratory Distress Syndrome," *Pediatrics*, **50**, No. 4, 526–534.

6. Baghdassarian, A., Guyda, H., Johanson, A., Migeon, C. J. and Blizzard, R. M. (1970), "Urinary Excretion of Radioimmunoassayable Luteinising Hormone (L.H.) in Normal Male Children and Adults, According to Age and Stage of Sexual Development," *J. clin. Endocr.*, **31**, 428–435.

7. Barnes, N. D. and Atherden, S. M. (1972), "Diagnosis of Congenital Adrenal Hyperplasia by Measurement of Plasma 17-hydroxy-progesterone," *Arch. Dis. Childh.*, **47**, 62–65.

8. Barnes, N. D., Joseph, J. M., Atherden, S. M. and Clayton, B. E. (1972), "Functional Tests of Adrenal Axis in Children with Measurement of Plasma Cortisol by Competitive Protein Binding," *Arch. Dis. Childh.*, **47**, 66–73.

9. Beisel, W. R. and Rapoport, M. I. (1969), "Inter-relations Between Adrenocortical Functions and Infectious Illness," *New Engl. J. Med.*, **280**, 541–546 and 596–604.

10. Berger, H., Fink, M., Fritz, H. J., Gleispach, H., Heidemann, P. and Wolf, J. (1970), "Normal Values for the Various 17-oxosteroids, Pregnanes and Testosterone Excreted in the Urine of Healthy Boys and Girls," *Z. klin. Chem. u. klin. Biochem.*, **8**, 354–360.

11. Bertrand, J., Loras, B., Saez, J., Forest, M., de Peretti, E. and Jeune, M. (1965), "Puberté précoce au cours d'une insuffisance surrénale chronique. Nouvel example d'endocrinopathie complexe par entrainement?" *Sem. Hôp Paris*, **41**, 2892–2897.

12. Birchall, K. and Mitchell, F. L. (1965), "The Identification of 21-hydroxy-pregnenolone in the Urine of Newborn Infants," *Steroids*, **6**, 427–436.

13. Blunck, W. (1968), "Die α-ketolischen cortisol-und corticosteron metaboliten sowie die 11-oxy-und 11-desoxy-17-ketosteroide im Urin von Kindern," *Acta endocr. Copnh.*, **59**, suppl. 134, 9–112.

14. Bongiovanni, A. M., Eberlein, W. R., Goldman, A. S. and New, M. (1967), "Disorders of Adrenal Steroid Biogenesis," *Recent Progr. Hormone Res.*, **23**, 375–449.

15. Boon, D. A., Keenan, R. E., Slaunwhite, W. R. and Aceto, T. (1972), "Conjugated and Unconjugated Plasma Androgens in Normal Children," *Pediat. Res.*, **6**, 111–118.

16. Browning, M. C. K. (1972). Personal communication.

17. Buckler, J. M. H. and Clayton, B. E. (1970), "Output of Luteinising Hormone in the Urine of Normal Children and those with Advanced Sexual Development," *Arch. Dis. Childh.*, **45**, 478–484.

18. Cathro, D. M. (1969), "Adrenal Cortex and Medulla," in *Paediatric Endocrinology*, pp. 187–327 (D. Hubble, Ed.). Oxford and Edinburgh: Blackwell Scientific Publications.

19. Cathro, D. M., Bertrand, J. and Coyle, M. G. (1969), "Antenatal Diagnosis of Adrenocortical Hyperplasia," *Lancet*, **i**, 732.

20. Cathro, D. M., Birchall, K., Mitchell, F. L. and Forsyth, C. C. (1963), "The Excretion of Neutral Steroids in the Urine of Newborn Infants," *J. Endocr.*, **27**, 53–75.

21. Cathro, D. M. and Coyle, M. G. (1967), "Adrenocortical Function in Newborn Infants of Low Birth Weight," *Excerpta med. (Amst.)*, International Congress Series, **132**, 688–694.

21a. Cathro, D. M. and Forsyth, C. C. (1965), "Excretion of Corticosteroids by Infants of Diabetic and Pre-diabetic Mothers," *Arch. Dis. Childh.*, **40**, 583–592.

22. Cathro, D. M., Forsyth, C. C. and Cameron, J. (1969), "Adrenocortical Response to Stress in Newborn Infants," *Arch. Dis. Childh.*, **44**, 88–95.

23. Cathro, D. M., Saez, J. M. and Bertrand, J. (1971), "The Effect of Clomiphene on the Plasma Androgens of Prepubertal and Pubertal Boys," *J. Endocr.*, **50**, 387–396.

24. Clayton, B. E., Edwards, R. W. H. and Renwick, A. G. C. (1963), "Adrenal Function in Children," *Arch. Dis. Childh.*, **38**, 49–53.

25. Cleary, R. E. and Pion, R. (1969), "Relationship of C_{19} Steroid Excretion in the Newborn to Maternal Urinary Estriol," *Amer. J. Obstet. Gynec.*, **104**, 166–171.

26. Cooke, R. E. (1968), *The Biologic Basis of Pediatric Practice*. New York, Toronto and London: McGraw-Hill, Inc.

27. Coyle, M. G. and Brown, J. B. (1963), "Urinary Excretion of Oestriol During Pregnancy," *J. Obstet. Gynaec. Brit. Commonw.*, **70**, 225–231.

28. David, R., Golan, S. and Drucker, W. (1968), "Familial Aldosterone Deficiency: Enzyme Defect, Diagnosis, and Clinical Course," *Pediatrics*, **41**, 403–412.

29. Degenhart, H. J., Frankena, L., Visser, H. K. A., Cost, W. S. and van Seters, A. P. (1966), "Further Investigation of a New Hereditary Defect in the Biosynthesis of Aldosterone: Evidence for a Defect in 18-hydroxylation of Corticosterone," *Acta physiol. pharmacol. néerl.*, **14**, 88–89.

30. Degenhart, H. J., Visser, H. K. A. and Wilmink, R. (1970), "Excretion and Production of Testosterone in Normal Children, in Children with Congenital Adrenal Hyperplasia and in Children with Precocious Puberty," *Pediat. Res.*, **4**, 309–317.

31. De Moor, P., Steeno, O., Meulepas, E., Hendrikx, A., Delaere, K. and Ostyn, M. (1963), "Influence of Body Size and of Sex on Urinary corticoid Excretion in a Group of Normal Young Males and Females," *J. clin. Endocr. Metab.*, **23**, 677–683.

32. De Souza, S. W. and Adlard, S. P. F. (1973), "Growth of Suckling Rats after Treatment with Dexamethasone or Cortisol: Implications for Steroid Therapy in Human Infants," *Arch. Dis. Childh.* In press.

33. Diczfalusy, E. (1964), "Endocrine Functions of the Human Foeto-placental Unit," *Fedn. Proc. Fedn. Amer. Socs. exp. Biol.*, **23**, 791–798.

34. Diczfalusy, E. (1969), "Steroid Metabolism in the Human Foeto-placental Unit," *Acta endocr.*, **61**, 649–664.

35. Diczfalusy, E. and Mancuso, S. (1969), "Oestrogen Metabolism in Pregnancy," in *Foetus and Placenta* (A. Klopper and E. Diczfalusy, Eds.). Oxford and Edinburgh: Blackwell Scientific Publications.

36. Donovan, B. T. and Van Der Werff Ten Bosch, J. J. (1966), *Physiology of Puberty*, pp. 38–75, Baltimore: Williams and Wilkins.

37. Dorfman, R. I. and Ungar, S. (1965), *Metabolism of Steroid Hormones*. London: Academic Press.

38. Eisenstein, A. B. (1967), *The Adrenal Cortex*. Boston: Little Brown and Co.

39. Few, J. D. (1961), "A Method for the Analysis of Urinary 17-hydroxy-corticosteroids," *J. Endocr.*, **22**, 31–46.

40. Forsyth, C. C., Forbes, M. and Cumings, J. N. (1971), "Adrenocortical Atrophy and Diffuse Cerebral Sclerosis," *Arch. Dis. Childh.*, **46**, 273–284.

41. Franks, R. C. (1967), "Diurnal Variation of Plasma 17-hydroxycorticosteroids in Children," *J. clin. Endocr. Metab.*, **27**, 75–78.

42. Friedman, M. and Strang, L. B. (1966), "Effect of Long-term Corticosteroids and Corticotrophin on the Growth of Children," *Lancet*, **ii**, 568–572.

43. Gardner, L. I. (1969), "Disorders of the Adrenal Cortex," in *Endocrine and Genetic Diseases of Childhood* (L. I. Gardner, Ed.). Philadelphia and London: W. B. Saunders Company.

44. Gellis, S. S. and Kagan, B. M. (1970), *Current Pediatric Therapy*, 4th edition. Philadelphia and London: W. B. Saunders Company.

45. Goodman, L. S. and Gillman, A. (1970), *The Pharmacological Basis of Therapeutics*, 4th edition, pp. 1604–1642. London and Toronto: The MacMillan Company.

46. Gupta, D. and Zimprich, H. (1966), "Steroid Excretion Patterns in Three Cases of Idiopathic Precocious Puberty," *Helv. paediat. Acta*, **21**, 250–260.

47. Hubble, D. (1969), *Paediatric Endocrinology*. Oxford and Edinburgh: Blackwell Scientific Publications.

48. Jean, R., Legrand, J. C., Meylan, F., Rieu, D. and Astruc, J. (1969), "Hypoaldosteronisme primaire par anomalie probable de la 18-hydroxylation," *Arch. franc. Pédiat.*, **26**, 769–777.

49. Jenkins, J. S. (1968), *An Introduction to Biochemical Aspects of the Adrenal Cortex*. London: Edward Arnold Ltd.

50. Johanson, A. J., Guyda, H., Light, C., Migeon, C. J. and Blizzard, R. M. (1969), "Serum Luteinising Hormone by Radio-immuno-assay in Normal Children," *J. Pediat.*, **74**, No. 3, 416–424.

50a. Johnson, F. L., Feagler, J. R., Lerner, K. G., Majerus, P. W., Siegel, M., Hartmann, J. R. and Thomas, E. D. (1972), "Association of Androgenic-anabolic Steroid Therapy with Development of Hepatocellular Carcinoma," *Lancet*, **ii**, 1273–1276.

51. Kenny, F. M., Preeyasombat, C. and Migeon, C. J. (1966), "Cortisol Production Rate. 2. Normal Infants, Children and Adults," *Pediatrics*, **37**, 34–42.

52. Klevit, H. D. (1966), "Diurnal Rhythmicity of Corticosteroid Secretion in the Newborn," Communication—Meeting of the Society for Pediatric Research, Atlantic City, N.J.

53. Kotas, R. V. and Avery, M. E. (1971), "Accelerated Appearance of Pulmonary Surfactant in the Fetal Rabbit," *J. appl. Physiol.*, **30,** No. 3, 358–361.

54. Knorr, D. (1965), "Untersuchungen zur altersabhängigkeit der ausscheidung einzelner chromatographisch getrennter steroide während des kindes und reifungsalters," in *Fortschritte der Pädologie*, **1,** 109–123, (F. Linneweh, Ed.). Berlin, Heidelberg and New York: Springer.

55. Kowal, J., Forchielli, E. and Dorfman, R. I. (1964), "The Δ_5-3β-hydroxy-steroid Dehydrogenase of Corpus Luteum and Adrenal. II. Interaction of C_{19} and C_{21} Substrates and Products," *Steroids*, **4,** 77–99.

56. Kulin, H. E., Grumbach, M. M. and Kaplan, S. L. (1972), "Gonadal-hypothalamic Interaction in Prepubertal and Pubertal Man: Effect of Clomiphene Citrate on Urinary Follicle-stimulating Hormone and Luteinising Hormone and Plasma Testosterone," *Pediat. Res.*, **6,** 162–171.

57. Lange, K., Strang, R., Slobody, L. B. and Wenk, E. J. (1957), "The Treatment of the Nephrotic Syndrome with Steroids in Children and Adults," *Arch. intern. Med.*, **99,** 760–770.

58. Lee, P. A., Midgley, A. R. and Jaffe, R. B. (1970), "Regulation of Human Gonadal Trophins. VI. Serum Follicle Stimulating and Luteinising Hormone Determination in Children," *J. clin. Endocr.*, **31,** 248–253.

59. Liggins, G. C. (1969), "Premature Delivery of Foetal Lambs Infused with Glucocorticoids," *J. Endocr.*, **45,** 515–523.

60. Liggins, G. C. (1969), "The Foetal Role in the Initiation of Parturition in the Ewe," in *Foetal Autonomy*, pp. 218–231 (G. E. W. Wolstenholme and M. O'Connor, Eds.). London: J. & A. Churchill Ltd.

61. Liggins, G. C. (1970), "Foetal Endocrinology," in *Scientific Foundations of Obstetrics and Gynaecology* (E. E. Philipp, Ed.). Heinemann Medical Books Ltd.

61a. Liggins, G. C. and Howie, R. N. (1972), "A Controlled Trial of Antepartum Glucocorticoid Treatment for Prevention of the Respiratory Distress Syndrome in Premature Infants," *Pediatrics*, **50,** No. 4, 515–525.

62. Loras, B., Roux, H., Cautenet, B., Ollagnon, C., Forest, M., de Peretti, E. and Bertrand, J. (1966), "Determination of the 17-ketosteroids in Children of Various Ages by Paper Chromatography," in *Androgens in Normal and Pathological Conditions*, pp. 93–100 (A. Vermeulen and D. Exley, Eds.). Amsterdam: Excerpta Medica.

63. Mattingly, D. (1962), "A Simple Fluorimetric Method for the Estimation of Free 11-hydroxycorticosteroids in Human Plasma," *J. clin. Path.*, **15,** 375–379.

64. Medical Research Council Committee on Clinical Endocrinology (1963), "A Standard Method of Estimating 17-oxosteroids and Total 17-oxogenic Steroids. An Interim Recommendation," *Lancet*, **i,** 1415–1419.

65. Mills, J. N. (1968), "Circadian Rhythms," in *A Companion to Medical Studies*, vol. 1, 44.1–44.8 (R. Passmore and J. S. Robson, Eds.). Oxford and Edinburgh: Blackwell Scientific Publications.

66. Milner, A. J. and Mills, I. H. (1970), "Effects of Human Pituitary Extracts on Androgen Biosynthesis by Human Adrenals *In Vitro*," *J. Endocr.*, **48,** 379–387.

67. Mitchell, F. L. (1967), "Steroid Metabolism in the Feto-placental Unit and in Early Childhood," *Vitam. and Horm.*, **25,** 191–269.

68. Mitchell, F. L. and Shackleton, C. H. L. (1969), "The Investigation of Steroid Metabolism in Early Infancy," *Adv. Clinical Chem.*, **12,** 141–215.

69. Mitchell, F. L., Shackleton, C. H. L., Gustafsson, J. A. and Sjövall, J. (1970), "3β-hydroxy-Δ_5 Steroids in the Perinatal Period," *Excerpta Medica*, International Congress Series, No. 219, Hormonal Steroids, pp. 534–540.

70. Motoyama, E. K., Orzalesi, M. M., Kikkawa, Y., Kaibara, M., Wu, B., Zigas, C. J. and Cook, C. D. (1971), "Effect of Cortisol on the Maturation of Fetal Rabbit Lungs," *Pediatrics*, **48,** 547–555.

71. Murphy, B. E. P. (1967), "Some Studies of the Protein-binding of Steroids and Their Application to the Routine Micro and Ultra-micro Measurement of Various Steroids in Body Fluids by Competetive Protein-binding Radioassay," *J. clin. Endocr. Metab.*, **27,** 973–990.

72. Musson, F. A. (1968), "Pre-operative Hydrocortisone and Fetal Survival Following Early Elective Caesarean Section for Severe Pre-eclamptic Toxaemia," *J. Obstet. Gynaec. Brit. Commonw.*, **75,** 1134–1137.

73. Naeye, R. L., Harcke, H. T. and Blanc, W. A. (1971), "Adrenal Gland Structure and the Development of Hyaline Membrane Disease," *Pediatrics*, **47,** 650–657.

73a. Nathanielsz, P. W., Comline, R. S., Silver, M. and Paisey, R. B. (1972), "Cortisol Metabolism in the Fetal and Neonatal Sheep," *J. Reprod. Fert.*, suppl. 16, 39–59.

74. Nelson, W. E. (1969), *Textbook of Pediatrics*. Philadelphia, London and Toronto: W. B. Saunders Company.

75. Neville, A. M., Webb, J. L. and Symington, T. (1969), "The *In Vitro* Utilization of 4-^{14}C-dehydroiso-androsterone by Human Adrenocortical Tumours Associated with Virilism," *Steroids*, **13,** 821–833.

76. New, M. I. (1968), "Congenital Adrenal Hyperplasia," *Pediatric Clinics of North America*, **15,** No. 2, 395–407.

77. Norval, M. A. and King, N. (1950), "A Biometric Study of the Excretion of Corticosteroids in Children in Relation to Age, Height and Weight," *Biometrics*, **6,** 395–398.

78. Pantelakis, S. N., Sinaniotis, C. A., Sbirakis, S., Ikkos, D. and Doxiadis, S. A. (1972), "Night and Day Growth Hormone Levels During Treatment with Corticosteroids and Corticotrophin," *Arch. Dis. Childh.*, **47,** 605–608.

79. Price, H. V., Cone, B. A. and Keogh, M. (1971), "Length of Gestation in Congenital Adrenal Hyperplasia," *J. Obstet. Gynaec. Brit. Commonw.*, **78,** 430–434.

80. Rappaport, R., Dray, F., Legrand, J. C. and Royer, P. (1968), "Hypoaldostéronisme congénital familial par défaut de la 18-OH-déhydrogénase," *Pediat. Res.*, **2,** 456–463.

81. Reiter, E. O. and Kulin, H. E. (1972), "Sexual Maturation in the Female," *Pediatric Clinics of North America*, **19,** No. 3, 581–603.

82. Reynolds, J. W. (1970), "Assessment of Fetal Health by Analysis of Maternal Steroids," *J. Pediat.*, **76,** 464–469.

83. Roberts, G. and Cawdery, J. E. (1970), "Congenital Adrenal Hypoplasia," *J. Obstet. Gynaec. Brit. Commonw.*, **77,** 654–656.

84. Root, A. W., Moshang, T., Bongiovanni, A. M. and Eberlein, W. R. (1970), "Concentrations of Plasma Luteinising Hormone in Infants, Children and Adolescents with Normal and Abnormal Gonadal Function," *Pediat. Res.*, **4,** 175–186.

85. Savage, D. C. L., Forsyth, C. C., McCafferty, E. and Cameron, J. (1969), "Individual Corticosteroids in the Urine of Children," *J. Endocr.*, **44,** 453–454.

86. Savage, D. C. L., Forsyth, C. C., McCafferty, E. and Cameron, J. (1973), "Individual Adrenal Androgens and Corticosteroids in the Urine of Normal Children and Adolescents," To be published.

87. Shackleton, C. H., Mitchell, F. L. and Farquhar, J. W. (1972), "Difficulties in the Diagnosis of the Adreno-genital Syndrome in Infancy," *Pediatrics*, **49,** 198–205.

88. Shirkey, H. C. (1968), *Pediatric Therapy*, 3rd edition, Mosby, Saint Louis.

89. Stevens, J. F. (1970), "Plasma Cortisol Levels in the Neonatal Period," *Arch. Dis. Childh.*, **45,** 592–594.

90. Symington, T. (1969), *Functional Pathology of the Human Adrenal Gland*. Edinburgh and London: E. & S. Livingstone Ltd.

91. Tanner, J. M. (1970), "Puberty and Adolescence," in *Child Life and Health*, 5th edition, pp. 188–208 (R. G. Mitchell, Ed.). London: Churchill.

92. Tanner, J. M. and Gupta, D. (1968), "A Longitudinal Study of the Urinary Excretion of Individual Steroids in Children from 8 to 12 years Old," *J. Endocr.*, **41,** 139–156.

93. Teller, W. (1965), "Urinary Steroid Patterns in Different Kinds of Precocious Puberty," *Acta endocr., Copenhagen*, suppl. 101, 26.

94. Teller, W. M. (1967), "Die ausscheidung von C_{19}-und C_{21}-steroiden im harn unter normalen und pathologischen bedingungen der entwicklung und reifung," *Z. ges. exp. Med.*, **142,** 222–296.

95. Ulick, S., Gautier, E., Vetter, K. K., Markello, J. R., Yaffe, S. and Lowe, C. U. (1964), "An Aldosterone Biosynthetic Defect in a Salt-losing Disorder," *J. clin. Endocr. Metab.*, **24,** 669–672.

96. Van Wagenen, G. and Newton, W. H. (1943), "Pregnancy in the Monkey after Removal of the Fetus," *Surg. Gynec. Obstet.*, **77,** 539–543.

97. Visser, H. K. A. and Cost, W. S. (1964), "A New Hereditary Defect in the Biosynthesis of Aldosterone: Urinary C_{21}-corticosteroid Pattern in Three Related Patients with a Salt-losing Syndrome, Suggesting an 18-oxidation Defect," *Acta endocr., Copenhagen*, **47,** 589–612.

97a. Visser, H. K. A. (1973), "Some Physiological and Clinical Aspects of Puberty," *Arch. Dis. Childh.*, **48,** 169–182.

98. Wilkins, L. (1965), "Adrenal Cortex: Hormones and Their Actions," in *The Diagnosis and Treatment of Endocrine Disorders in Childhood and Adolescence*, 3rd edition, pp. 342–367 (L. Wilkins, Ed.). Illinois, U.S.A.: Thomas, Springfield.

99. Wilkins, L. (1965), *The Diagnosis and Treatment of Endocrine Disorders in Childhood and Adolescence*, 3rd edition. Illinois, U.S.A.: Thomas, Springfield.

100. Winter, J. S. D. and Fainan, C. (1972), "Pituitary-gonadal Relations in Male Children and Adolescents," *Pediat. Res.*, **6,** 126–135.

101. Zutshi, D. W., Friedman, M. and Ansell, B. M. (1971), "Corticotrophin Therapy in Juvenile Chronic Polyarthritis (Still's Disease) and Effect on Growth," *Arch. Dis. Childh.*, **46,** 584–593.

28B. GROWTH AND DEVELOPMENT OF THE ADRENAL MEDULLA

WALTER M. TELLER

INTRODUCTION

In lower vertebrates the adrenals consist of two separate organs, the "interrenal" and the "suprarenal" organ. Mammals including man reveal a fusion of these two organs to form one endocrine gland, which consists of two parts. The outer layer (cortex) is responsible for the production and secretion of steroid hormones; the inner portion, the so-called medulla, secretes catecholamines. The latter hormones are chemically derived from *o*-dioxybenzene or (brenz) catechol. Its main representative is adrenaline (epinephrine) which was the first hormone to be isolated (Oliver and Schäfer in 1894), chemically identified (Takamine and Aldrich in 1901) and synthesized (Stolz in 1904). The classic work on the physiology of the catecholamines was done by Cannon in 1914, who realized that they are responsible for emergency reactions ("fright, fight, flight").

During growth and development from the fetal through the adult stage the adrenal medulla undergoes distinct changes which became known only fairly recently when sensitive chemical methods for the detection and determination of catecholamines became available. Few authors have presented reviews on the subject of adrenal medullary function in childhood.[8,18,51] Therefore it seems justified to collect the presently available data on the physiology and pathology of adrenal medulla with particular emphasis on aspects of its growth and development.

DEVELOPMENT OF ADRENAL MEDULLA AND OTHER CHROMAFFIN TISSUES

The adrenal medulla is derived from the sympathetic nervous system. During an early stage of embryonic life, around the seventh week) neuroblasts migrate from the neural crest through the adrenal cortical tissue and congregate at its centre. Slowly they differentiate into polyhedral chromaffin cells. Other chromaffin cells develop at various places around the aorta and in the skin. They are also found around nerves and blood vessels and throughout the alimentary tract. They contain granules which stain blue with ferric chloride or brown with salts of chromic acid—a property which is the basis for their collective term "chromaffin tissues." During early fetal life and childhood, chromaffin cells are rather abundant. By the second year of life they atrophy, although their main aggregation remains detectable for some more years as the organ of Zuckerkandl.

BIOSYNTHESIS AND METABOLISM OF CATECHOLAMINES

Granules within chromaffin cells contain catecholamines. Their main representatives are dopamine, noradrenaline (norepinephrine) and adrenaline (epinephrine) (Fig. 1). Chemically these compounds are derived from catechol. Besides chomaffin tissues, sympathetic nerve-endings also produce catecholamines, mainly noradrenaline. In the

Catechol Dopamine Noradrenaline Adrenaline

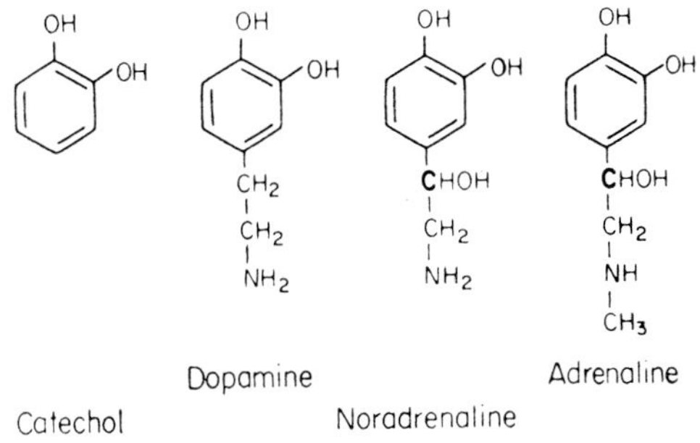

FIG. 1. The formulae of catechol and the catecholamines.

adrenal medulla adrenaline and noradrenaline are probably synthetized in different cells (A-cells→adrenaline; NA-cells → noradrenaline); however, this has not been definitely proved. Fresh human adrenal glands contain adrenaline and noradrenaline in the ratio of 4:1. The granules in the chromaffin cells are essential for the synthesis of the catecholamines (Fig. 2).

The hydroxylation of dopamine occurs in the granules. This catecholamine is formed from tyrosine by hydroxylation and decarboxylation. The biosynthetic pathway is similar in the adrenal medulla and in the nerve endings. The conversion of noradrenaline to adrenaline, however, occurs only in the cytoplasm of the adrenal medullary cells. Hydrocortisone (cortisol) coming from the adjacent adrenal cortex is apparently essential for optimal activity of the N-methyl transferase enzyme. Cortisol could therefore act as a regulator of adrenaline synthesis.[36]

The secretion of catecholamines from adrenal medulla and sympathetic nerves is controlled by nerves, which receive their impulses from subcortical and probably non-hypothalamic brain centres and sympathetic preganglionic fibres. Angiotensin II and bradykinin also contribute to adrenal medullary secretion. The release and physiological effects of catecholamines are rapid. The mechanism of secretion seems to be the following: acetylcholine released from the preganglionic fibres causes an increased calcium influx into the cell and into the intracellular granules. This results in a release of the entire contents of the granules, i.e. catecholamines, protein and ATP. The membranes of the empty granules remain as residues which are gradually filled up again.

In general, more noradrenaline than adrenaline is secreted into the blood stream. The ratio is roughly 5:1. The major portion of noradrenaline comes from the sympathetic nerve endings and appears to be secreted almost continuously, thus influencing the basic tone of the vascular system.

Both adrenaline and noradrenaline are rapidly metabolized, lasting only a few seconds in the circulating blood. The initial step is methylation of the 3-hydroxyl group which is catalysed by the enzyme catechol-*o*-methyl transferase

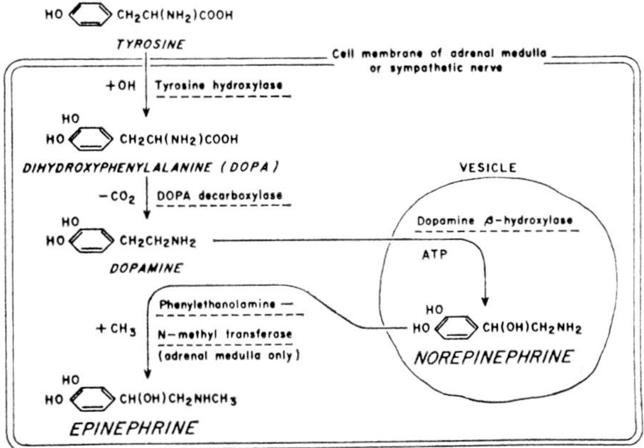

FIG. 2. Biosynthesis of noradrenaline and adrenaline in the adrenal medulla and sympathetic nerve. Enzymes are underlined by broken lines (from Sawin, 1969.)[39]

(Fig. 3). It results in the formation of metanephrine and normetanephrine. These compounds may then be conjugated and excreted as such, or both may be oxidized by monoamine oxidase to form the same compound, vanillyl mandelic acid (VMA or 3-methoxy-4-hydroxymandelic acid).

In the urine, only 2–5 per cent of the secreted catecholamines are recovered unchanged. Of this, 80–85 per cent is noradrenaline. About 20 per cent of the catecholamines metabolized are found in the urine as metanephrine and normetanephrine. Thirty to fifty per cent are excreted as VMA. The assessment of catecholamine secretion and excretion can be made by estimating the various metabolites in the urine, particularly VMA, or by determining the unchanged catecholamines in the urine.

BIOLOGIC ACTIONS OF CATECHOLAMINES

There are a number of sites of action of catecholamines. The main effects are listed in Table 1. Ahlquist[1] proposed two different kinds of receptor sites in the tissues that respond to catecholamines. The alpha (α)-receptor responds to noradrenaline resulting in contraction of smooth muscles in blood vessels, while the beta (β)-receptor responds to adrenaline causing relaxation of smooth muscles. In the course of time, drugs have been developed which specifically block the noradrenaline-induced vasoconstriction and are thus called α-adrenergic blocking agents; other drugs, which prevent vasodilation after adrenaline, were named

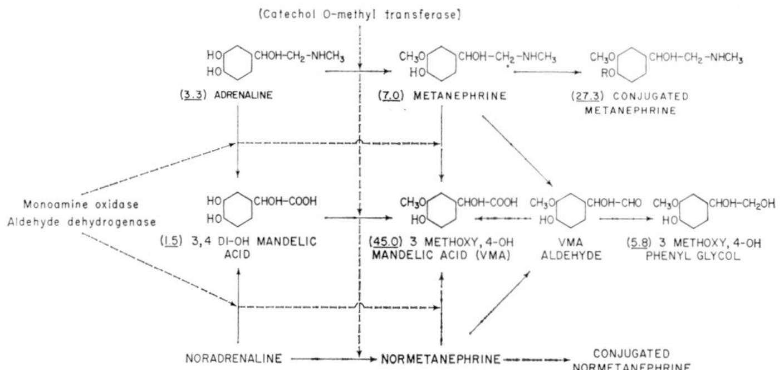

FIG. 3. Metabolic fate of catecholamine hormones. The numbers in parentheses signify the per cent of an administered dose of labelled adrenaline that appeared in the urine in the form indicated. Monoamine oxidase and aldehyde dehydrogenase both participate in the reactions indicated by upper and lower arrows, (from Axelrod, 1960.)[4]

TABLE 1

COMPARISON OF THE BIOLOGICAL EFFECTS OF ADRENALINE AND NORADRENALINE (ACCORDING TO CATHRO, 1969)[8]

	L-Adrenaline Effect	*L-Noradrenaline Effect*
Heart rate	Increase	Decrease
Cardiac output	Increase	Variable
Total peripheral resistance	Decrease	Increase
Blood pressure	Systolic rise only	Systolic and diastolic rise
Respiration	Stimulated	Stimulated
Skin vessels	Constriction	Less constriction
Muscle vessels	Dilation	Constriction
Bronchioles	Dilation	Less dilation
Eosinophil count	Increase	No effect
Metabolism	Increase	Slight increase
Oxygen consumption	Increase	No effect
Blood sugar	Increase	Slight increase
Plasma-free fatty acids	Increase	Increase
Central nervous system	Anxiety	No effect
Uterus in late pregnancy (*in vivo*)	Inhibition	Stimulation
Renal vessels	Vasoconstriction	Vasoconstriction

β-adrenergic blocking agents. By extension, various other nonvascular actions of adrenaline and noradrenaline were classified as α- or β-type, largely by determining which type of blocking-agent inhibits the action (Table 2). This classification must not be taken too rigidly since some reactions are both, α- and β-stimulated (e.g. motility of the gastrointestinal tract). Nevertheless, it does help in understanding many of the major effects of catecholamines.

In many instances not involving the blood vessels, an α-adrenergic response is ultimately an inhibitory one and associated with lower cyclic AMP synthesis, while β-adrenergic responses are stimulatory and the tissues show evidence of increased synthesis of cyclic AMP. The effects of catecholamines are optimal only in the presence of cortisol and thyroid hormones. It seems likely that thyroid hormone enhances the ability of catecholamines to stimulate cyclic AMP synthesis (in β-adrenergic responses) while cortisol somehow allows the cyclic AMP to act as a stimulant.

TABLE 2

CLASSIFICATION AND RESPONSES OF VARIOUS EFFECTOR ORGANS TO ADRENERGIC STIMULI (FROM EPSTEIN, S. E. AND BRAUNWALK, E., 1966)[113]

Effector Organ	*Receptor Type*	*Response*
Heart:		
Sinoatrial node	β	Increase in heart rate
Atrioventricular node	β	Increase in conduction velocity and shortening of refractory period
Atria	β	Increase in contractility
Ventricles	β	Increase in contractility
Smooth muscle:		
Blood vessels to skeletal muscle	(1) α (2) β	(1) Contraction—constriction (2) Relaxation—dilatation
Blood vessels to skin and mucosa	α	Contraction
Bronchial muscle	β	Relaxation
Gastrointestinal tract:		
Mobility		
Stomach	β	Decrease
Intestine	α and β	Decrease
Spincters:		
Stomach	α	Contraction
Intestine	α	Contraction
Urinary bladder:		
Detrusor	β	Relaxation
Trigone and sphincter	α	Contraction
Eye:		
Radial muscle: iris	α	Contraction—mydriasis
Ciliary muscle	β	Relaxation—"negative" accommodation

ADRENAL MEDULLARY FUNCTION AND CATECHOLAMINE EXCRETION AT DIFFERENT AGES

Fetus

The cells of the fetal adrenal medulla synthesize and store little or no adrenaline and the fetal chromaffin system produces noradrenaline almost exclusively. This pertains

TABLE 3

PROPORTION OF NORADRENALINE IN THE ADRENAL GLANDS OF SOME FETAL, NEWBORN AND ADULT ANIMALS, EXPRESSED AS A PERCENTAGE OF TOTAL CATECHOLAMINE CONTENT. (FIGURES FOR POST-MORTEM MATERIAL—SOME ANOXIA—IN ITALICS (FROM COMLINE AND SILVER, 1966)[12]

Species	*Gestational Age (Expressed as a Percentage of Total Duration)*					*New-born*		*Adult*
	33	50	60	75	Term	0–2 days	2 weeks	
Man	 *100*	*100* *90*	*100* *86*	*100* —	*83* —	*92* *76*		 7–16 13
Rat				(Catechols absent) 56	57 49	44 15 46	36 15	16 15
Guinea-pig	100 (fetal age unspecified)				33	66 19	40 —	3 0
Cat			 70	100	—	64 82		50 38 8–87
Rabbit				70 *ca* 50 100 (fetal age unspecified)	12 17	23 — 50–90–43* 38	— — 16 (1 week)	 — 2 0
Calf			*69*	*62*	*50*	49	33	21–25
Lamb			55 *52*	58 *47*	42 *30* }	33 (throughout new-born period)		15–29

* Consecutive changes between 1 hr. and 2 days after birth.

to man particularly. Other mammals show various proportions of adrenaline in their adrenal medullae (Table 3).[12,22] With advancing age the relative content of noradrenaline in adrenal glands invariably decreases. As the medullary cells mature, adrenaline appears in specific cell groups and the distinction can be made between noradrenaline-(NA) and adrenaline-(A) producing cells (Fig. 4). Coupland[11] and Jost[27] have reviewed the evidence that adrenocortical hormones may stimulate the development in the fetus of the methylation step converting noradrenaline into adrenaline within medullary cells but not in extra-adrenal chromaffin cells.

The physiological role of catecholamines in the fetus is largely unknown. They may exert an effect on the calibre of cord and placental vessels, thus regulating the blood flow within the feto-placental unit. Furthermore, it has been debated whether noradrenaline helps to protect the fetus from hypoglycaemia following delivery. Fetally malnourished infants (small-for-dates infants *with* hypoglycaemia) failed to recover from insulin-induced hypoglycaemia and to increase catecholamine excretions.[45] In another study, however, small-for-dates infants, both with and without hypoglycaemia, were shown to respond to hypoglycaemia with a 3- to 4-fold increase of noradrenaline and a 5- to 6-fold increase of adrenaline excretion in the urine.[3] It is generally accepted that noradrenaline increases oxygen consumption and plays an important role in thermo-regulation in early infancy.[8,43] Brown adipose tissue from rabbits generated heat on infusion of noradrenaline. Although the rate of glycerol release was high, there was no increase of free fatty acids.[20]

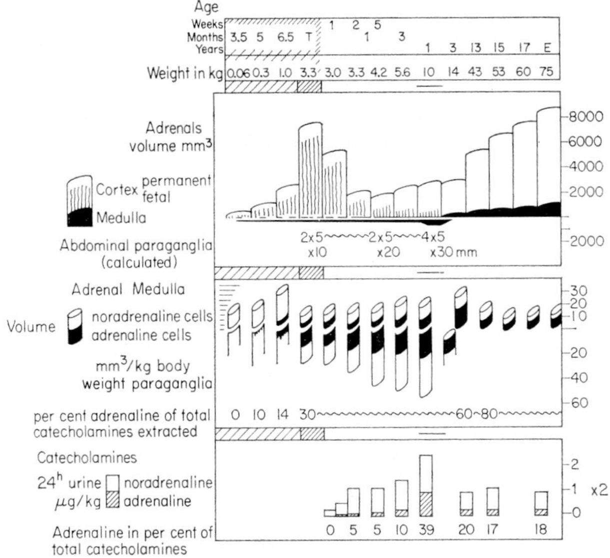

FIG. 4. Synopsis of growth and functional development of adrenal cortex and medulla (from Zeisel, 1959.)[50]

Neonate

As already shown in Table 3 and Fig. 4 the adrenal medulla of the human neonate synthesizes and stores predominantly noradrenaline. The urinary excretion of catecholamines in full-term and premature infants was studied by Nicolopoulos *et al.*[34] On the first day of life the excretion of dopamine by premature infants was less than that by full-term infants. On the fifteenth day excretion by the premature infants had more than tripled in amount, whereas that by the full-term infants had increased only by 50 per cent. The excretion of noradrenaline showed the following: on the first day, it was about one-third of the amount excreted by full-term infants. On the fifteenth day it still remained lower than the amount excreted on the first day by the full-term infants. The amount of adrenaline excreted differed only very slightly between premature and full-term infants. On the fifteenth day, excretion by both groups had increased so that the amounts were about equal. Other authors[42] determined adrenaline and noradrenaline in the urine of male prematures. The maximum excretion was found between the sixteenth and twentieth day of life. Noradrenaline predominated (about 90 per cent) On calculating the excretion of both compounds per kg bodyweight, during the first days of life, noradrenaline was excreted by prematures in the same amount as in adults. Later on, it increased 2–3 fold. Calculated on the basis of body surface, the excretion of noradrenaline was less than in adults. It reached adult levels by fourteen days of life.

The mode of delivery influences the catecholamine content of the initially voided urine of newborns.[24] By bioassay highest values were found after forceps delivery while the lowest values occurred after caesarean section. Also asphyxiated newborns have an increased "pressor activity" in their urine.[23]

In certain metabolic processes catecholamines play an important role during the neonatal period: Chemical thermogenesis is mediated by an increased secretion of noradrenaline.[43] It is associated with an increased oxygen consumption and elevated levels of nonesterified fatty acids in plasma.[41] Cold exposure stimulates the metabolism of brown adipose tissue as does the infusion of noradrenaline. Interestingly the noradrenaline response to cold is not seen in the newly hatched domestic chick, newborn pig or newborn calf, all of which are animals that appear to lack brown fat.[2] Small-for-dates infants are capable of mobilizing their fat stores and releasing catecholamines.[3] It is suggested that their stores of brown fat are within normal ranges.

The response of human adipose tissue to adrenaline and noradrenaline changes in the course of postnatal development. The release of free fatty acids per unit of adipose tissue increases with age while glycerol decreases.[35] This different response at various ages can be explained by a more rapid oxidation in the newborn of fatty acids within adipose tissue. In this way, the newborn has a swift thermogenic response to cold exposure. Postural changes also result in an increased urinary excretion of catecholamines in the newborn (predominantly noradrenaline).[21] During later life, the elevated ratio noradrenaline/adrenaline drops.

Older Child and Adult

Only a few large-scale studies are available on the excretion of catecholamines and their metabolites during childhood through adulthood (reviews by Zeisel,[50,51] Clark *et al.*,[9] Voorhess,[48] Gitlow *et al.*[16]).

The data obtained by Voorhess[48] for the urinary excretion per 24 hr. of adrenaline, noradrenaline, vanillylmandelic acid and dopamine are given in Figs. 5–8. It is readily apparent that the excretion of above compounds increases in the course of childhood. Adult levels are reached by 10 years of age.

TABLE 4

URINARY EXCRETION OF CATECHOLAMINES AT VARIOUS AGES[48]

	Adrenaline ((μg./24 hr.)	*Noradrenaline* (μg./24 hr.)	*VMA* (μg./24 hr.)	*Dopamine* (μg./24 hr.)
1st week	0·5–1	10	500–1,000	20–80
1 year	1–2	10	500–1,000	50–100
10 years	2–8	20–70	2,000–4,000	100–200
50 years	3–5	30–50	2,500–3,000	200–400

In contrast to urinary 17-oxysteroid and 17-hydroxycorticosteroid levels, which decrease in older age, the catecholamine excretion is as high in persons around 50 years of age as in pre-adolescents. Whether there is any causal relationship to the increase of blood-pressure with advancing age remains to be proved. Throughout life, no sex difference in catecholamine excretion was found. Considerable variations of values arise from incomplete 24-hour urine collections. It was therefore proposed that excretion of a specified catecholamine should be expressed in μg./mg. of creatinine. On this scale, there is a linear decrease of catecholamine excretion from infancy through adulthood.[16] McKendrick and Edwards[32] discovered a circadian rhythm in the excretions of VAM, with a maximum in the afternoon. This finding points to the desirability of assays being performed only on complete 24-hour urine samples. The determination of various catecholamines and their metabolites is influenced considerably by certain dietary constituents, which therefore have to be rigidly excluded during the time of urine collections. Bananas and walnuts contain noradrenaline, serotonin and dopamine. Ice cream sometimes has a high vanilla content. The chromatographic and electrophoretic techniques for VMA and homovanillic acid estimations are readily disturbed by substances in tea and coffee as well as by ice cream, custard, chocolate and vanilla-flavoured foods. Citrus fruits and pineapple give rise to homovanillic acid. Also drugs like aspirin, sulpha drugs, penicillin, methyldopa and tetracyclines may interfere in these determinations.

CATECHOLAMINE EXCRETION UNDER PATHOLOGICAL CONDITIONS

In a number of illnesses an abnormal urinary excretion occurs of a single or several catecholamines. In several

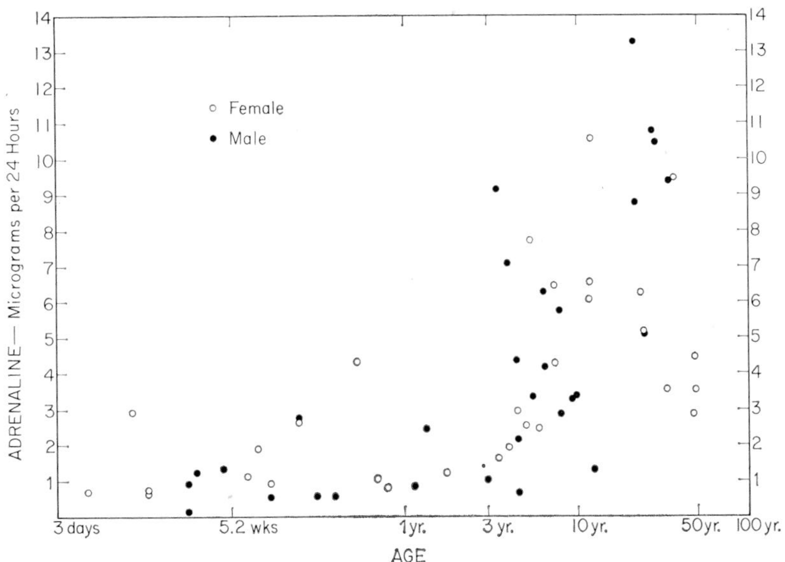

FIG. 5. Daily urinary excretion of adrenaline by male and female subjects of various ages (from Voorhess, 1967.)[48]

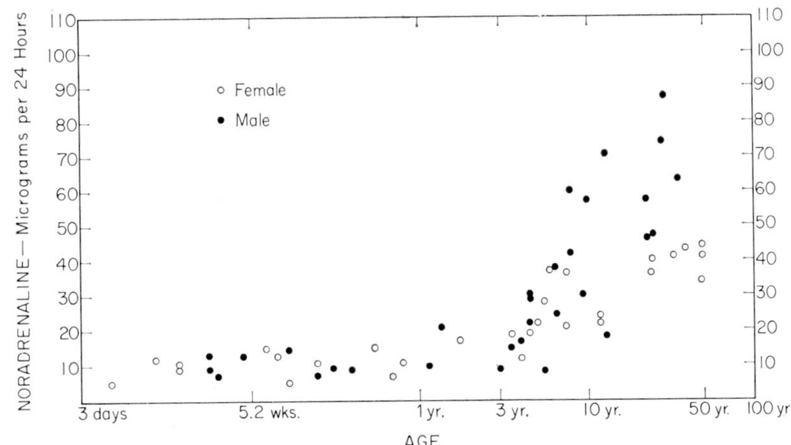

FIG. 6. Daily urinary excretion of noradrenaline by male and female subjects of various ages (from Voorhess, 1967.)[48]

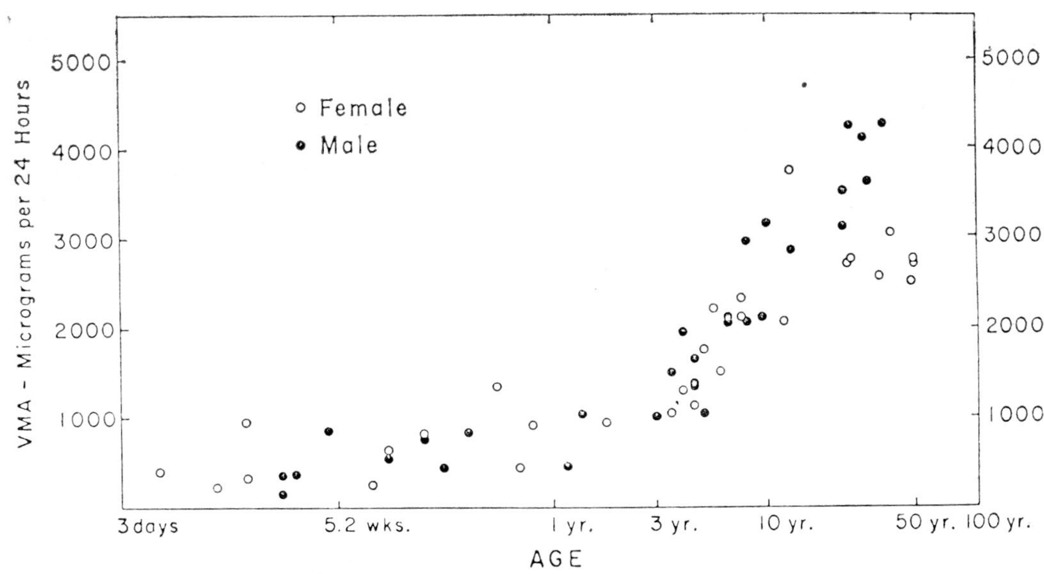

FIG. 7. Daily urinary excretion of VMA by male and female subjects of various ages. (from Voorhess, 1967.)[48]

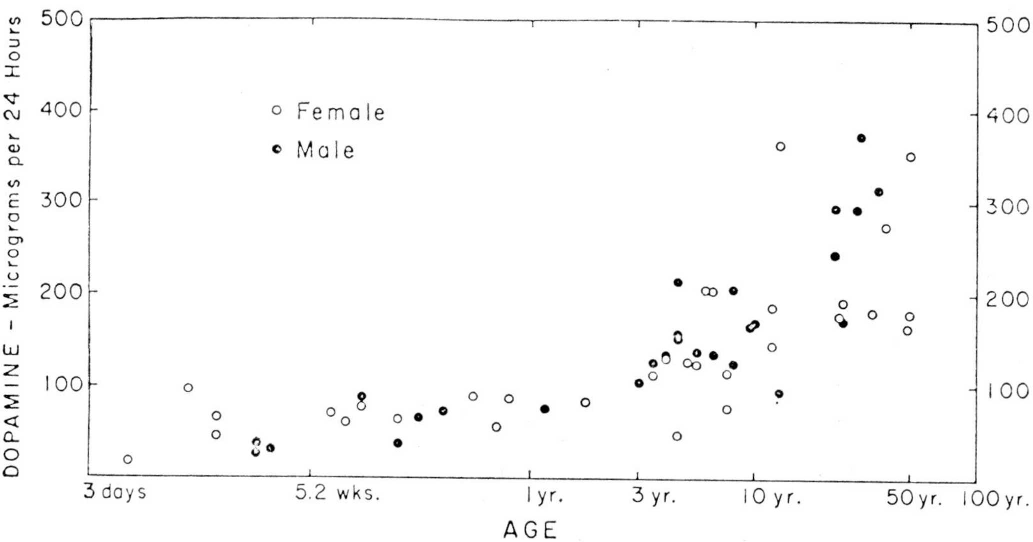

FIG. 8. Daily urinary excretion of dopamine by male and female subjects of various ages (from Voorhess, 1967.)[48]

instances, these findings are considered to be etiologically related to the disease state.

Hypoxia

The responses to asphyxia in the fetus and newborn can be separated into a direct response which consists largely of secretion of noradrenaline and a nervous response which causes the secretion of both adrenaline and noradrenaline. The latter response is independent of impulses from the spinal cord which was shown by section of the spinal cord at the first cervical segment. In adults asphyxia acts primarily on the central nervous system, and the secretion from the adrenal medulla is mediated largely via the nervous response route.[12]

A recent investigation[37] confirmed previous studies that newborn infants respond to hypoxia with a relatively diminished secretion of adrenaline.

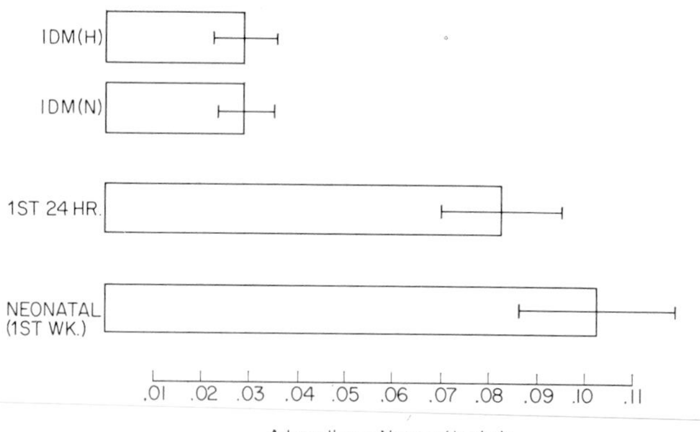

FIG. 9. Urinary adrenaline excretion rates. (Mean and and standard error shown for each group.) IDM (H), infants of diabetic mothers in hypoglycemic periods, IDM (N), infants of diabetic mothers in normoglycemic periods, compared to levels of both first 24-hour and neonatal controls. All values in nanograms per kilogram per minute. (From Stern *et al.*, 1968.)[44]

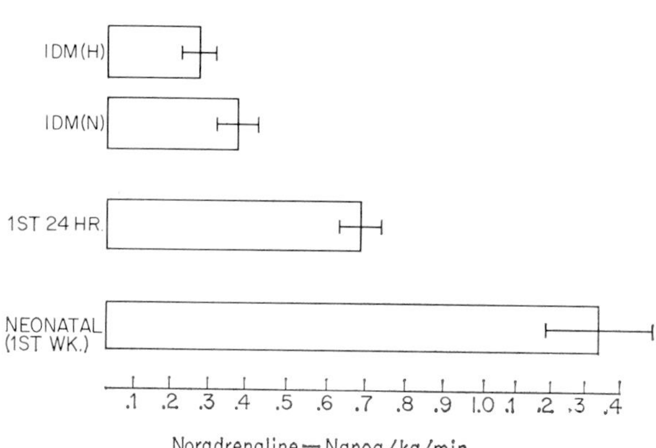

FIG. 10. Urinary noradrenaline excretion rates. (Mean and standard error shown for each group.) IDM (H), infants of diabetic mothers in hypoglycemic periods, and IDM (N), infants of diabetic mothers in normoglycemic periods, compared to levels for both first 24-hour and neonatal controls. Values in nanograms per kilogram per minute. (From Stern *et al.*, 1968.)[44]

Infants of Diabetic Mothers (IDM)

In newborns hypoglycaemia usually results in an increased release of adrenaline. In infants of diabetic mothers, however, severe hypoglycaemia (blood sugar-level below 20 mg./100 ml.) may be related to a failure of adrenaline release as indicated by the failure to detect adrenaline in the 24-hour urine specimen.[31] In contrast, in IDM with moderate hypoglycaemia (blood sugar-level above 10 mg./100 ml.) the mean 24-hour urinary excretion of adrenaline rose above the levels seen in normal newborn infants.[31] Stern *et al.*[44] found a marked reduction of adrenaline and epinephrine excretion in IDM regardless of whether these infants were hypo- or normoglycaemic. The control groups consisted of 7 infants during their 1st day and 7 infants during their 1st week of life (Figs. 9 and 10). These results are suggestive of an adrenal medullary exhaustion phenomenon consistent with the assumption that the hypoglycaemic episodes in IDM are of long-standing (intra-uterine) duration.

Familial Dysautonomia

Gitlow *et al.*[15] studied the excretion of vanillylmandelic acid (VMA), 3-methoxy-4-hydroxyphenylethyleneglycol (HMPG), total metanephrines (TM), normetanephrine (NM) and homovanillic acid (HVA) in 52 patients with familial dysautonomia and 180 normal subjects. Patients with familial dysautonomia were found to excrete elevated quantities of HVA, diminished quantities of VMA and HMPG, and normal amounts of TM and NM in comparison with normal subjects. The excretion of the sum of the deaminated catecholamine metabolites proved to be more aberrant in familial dysautonomia than any other single biochemical parameter measured. These findings are compatible with an abnormality in catecholamine synthesis rather than in release.

Other Pathological Conditions

It can easily be understood that disturbances in the production of tyrosine may lead to abnormal catecholamine excretion (*see* Fig. 2). Indeed the excretion of VMA was found to be diminished in *phenylketonuria*.[10,26] In the *hypoglycaemia* of fetal malnutrition the normal increase of adrenaline excretion did not occur and the infants were unable to recover from insulin-induced hypoglycaemia.[45] A certain group of children fail to respond to hypoglycaemic episodes with an increase in their adrenaline output ("Broberger type" of idiopathic hypoglycaemia).[17,40] The pathogenesis of this type of idopathic hypoglycaemia could be related to a delayed maturation of the adrenal medulla and, because of this, a decrease in the ability of the adrenal gland to synthesize adrenaline. According to the earlier work of Hökfelt,[22] the fetal adrenal gland in man contains very little or no adrenaline. Following birth, there is a gradual increase of this substance. In disease states such as "idiopathic" hypoglycaemia the increase may be delayed.

Adrenocorticotrophic (ACTH) deficiency can result in adrenal medullary unresponsiveness.[25] This clinical finding seems to be the *in vivo* analogue to the experimental finding that glucocorticoids are necessary for optimal activity of the enzyme phenylethanolamine-N-methyl transferase.

Diseases which result in *conditions of prolonged stress* are conceivably associated with an increased urinary excretion of catecholamines. It has been described in acrodynia ("pink disease"),[19] congenital cyanotic heart-disease,[14] heart-failure,[30] chronic anaemia,[33] and nephrotic syndrome.[29] In connection with various types of dental treatment the excretion of adrenaline rose, especially after extraction therapy, while the noradrenaline levels remained unchanged.[47] A normal catecholamine metabolism was found in Down's syndrome,[28] although the metabolism of serotonin is apparently disturbed.

TUMORS OF NEURAL CREST ORIGIN

Depending on the tissue of origin, two kinds of tumours have to be considered: the phaeochromocytoma, arising from chromaffin tissue inside or outside the adrenal medulla, and the neuroblastoma derived from sympathetic nerve cells. Chromaffin and sympathetic nervous tissues have in common the same progenitor, the primitive sympathogone cell. A competent analysis of a large patient material was given by Clark *et al.*[9]

Phaeochromocytoma

Less than 5 per cent of the reported cases have occurred in children. The tumour may occur at any age (review *see* Zeisel.[51]

Eighty per cent of phaeochromocytomas arising in the adrenal medulla are associated with increased secretion of adrenaline, whereas 20 per cent of medullary phaeochromocytomas and all those occurring in extra-adrenal sites are associated with increased secretion of noradrenaline only. This fact may be used in the differential diagnosis regarding the location of the tumour. In children phaeochromocytomas tend to secrete catecholamines more or less continuously. This results in a sustained hypertension contrary to the situation in tumours of chromaffin tissue occurring in the adult. This fact renders pharmacological provocation tests almost unnecessary in children. In more than 90 per cent of cases the diagnosis of phaeochromocytoma can be established beyond doubt by estimation of catecholamines and their metabolites in a single 24-hour urine specimen.

Not infrequently, a phaeochromocytoma is associated with neurofibromatosis. Besides this a positive family history points to the involvement of genetic factors.

Thus, whenever a tumour of chromaffin tissue is diagnosed, family members should be screened. Multiple tumours are particularly common in familial cases. Associations of phaeochromocytomas have also been recorded with thyroid carcinoma, von Hippel–Lindau's disease, and cyanotic congenital heart-disease (for review *see* Ref. 8).

Attempts were made to correlate catecholamine excretion patterns with the electron microscope picture of phaeochromocytomas.[38] In children, the type of tumour which predominates shows low storage and high turnover of catecholamines. These are released continuously.

Neuroblastoma

This includes a variety of neural crest tumours: the highly malignant sympathogonioma, the neuroblastoma in the narrow sense and the fairly matured ganglioneuroma. The latter is usually benign.

Neuroblastomas belong to the most frequent tumours of infancy and early childhood. They may arise anywhere in the sympathetic nervous system. The most frequent site, however, is the adrenal medulla. Bachmann[5] has analysed 1,030 cases from the world literature. Most neuroblastomas produce catecholamines and therefore must be considered to be endocrinologically active tumours. The patients not infrequently show clinical effects of the abnormal secretion such as hypertension and profuse sweating.

Catecholamine metabolism in neuroblastoma has been reviewed repeatedly,[7,8,9,51] Barontini de Gutierrez Moyana *et al.*[6] analysed forty children with tumours derived from the neural crest. The urinary excretion of vanillyl mandelic acid, noradrenaline and dopamine was abnormally high. Raised dopamine and homovanillic acid excretion in the presence of a tumour of the neural crest is strong evidence in favour of malignancy. Normal urinary catecholamine excretion, however, does not exclude the presence of neuroblastoma.[49]

According to von Studnitz[46] increased excretion of dopamine is as characteristic of neuroblastoma as elevated urinary levels of VMA are pathognomonic of phaeochromocytoma.

REFERENCES

1. Ahlquist, R. P. (1967), "Development of the Concept of Alpha and Beta Adrenotropic Receptors," *Ann. N.Y. Acad. Sci.*, **139**, 549–552.
2. Alexander, G. (1969), "The Effect of Adrenaline and Noradrenaline on Metabolic Rate in Young Lambs." *Biol. Neonat.*, **14**, 97–106.
3. Anagnostakis, D. E. and Lardinois, R. (1971), "Urinary Catecholamine Excretion and Plasma NEFA Concentration in Small for Date Infants," *Pediatrics*, **47**, 1000–1009.
4. Axelrod, J. (1960), in *Adrenergic Mechanisms*, Ciba Foundation Symposium (J. R. Vane, G. E. W. Wostenholme and M. O'Connor, eds.). Boston: Little, Brown & Co.
5. Bachmann, K. D. (1962), "Das Neuroblastoma sympathicum; Klinik and Prognose von 1030 Fällen," *Z. Kinderheilk.*, **86**, 710–724.
6. Barontini De Gutierrez Moyana, M., Bergada, C. and Becu, L. (1970), "Catecholamine Excretion in Forty Children with Sympathoblastoma," *J. Pediat.*, **77**, 239–244.
7. Bohuon, C. (1968), "Catecholamine Metabolism in Neuroblastoma," *J. Pediat. Surg.*, **3**, 114–118.
8. Cathro, D. M. (1969), "The Adrenal Cortex and Medulla," in *Paediatric Endocrinology*, pp. 187–327 (D. Hubble, ed.). Oxford, Edinburgh: Blackwell.
9. Clark, A. C. L., Moore, A. E. and Niall, M. (1965), "Metabolites of Catecholamines in the Urine of Children with Tumours of Neural Crest Origin," *Aust. Paediat, J.*, **1**, 42–55.
10. Cession-Fossion, A., Vandermeulen, R., Dodinval, P. and Chantraine, J. M. (1966), "Elimination urinaire de l'adrénaline, de la noradrénaline et de l'acide vanillyl-mandelique chez les enfants oligophrènes phénylpyruviques," *Path. Biol. (Paris)*, **14**, 1157–1159.
11. Coupland, R. E. (1965), *The Natural History of the Chromaffin Cell*. London: Longmans, Green & Co. Ltd.
12. Comline, R. S. and Silver, M. (1966), "Development of Activity in the Adrenal Medulla of the Foetus and Newborn Animal," *Brit. Med. Bull.*, **22**, 16–20.
13. Epstein, S. E. and Braunwald, E. (1966), "Beta-adrenergic Receptor Blocking Drugs," *New Engl. J. Med.*, **275**, 1106–1112, 1175–1183.
14. Folger, G. M., Jr. and Hollowell, J. G. (1972), "Excretion of Catecholamine in Urine by Infants and Children with Cyanotic Congenital Heart Disease," *Pediat. Res.*, **6**, 151–157.
15. Gitlow, S. E., Bertani, L. M., Wilk, E., Li, B. L. and Dziedzic, S. (1970), "Excretion of Catecholamine Metabolites by Children with Familial Dysautonomia," *Pediatrics*, **46**, 513–522.
16. Gitlow, S. E., Mendlowitz, M., Wilk, E. L., Wilk, S., Wolf, R. L. and Bertani, L. M. (1968), "Excretion of Catecholamine Catabolites by Normal Children," *J. Lab. clin. Med.*, **72**, 612–620.
17. Goodall, McG., Cragan, M. and Sidbury, J. (1972), "Decreased Epinephrine Excretion in Idiopathic Hypoglycemia," *Amer. J. Dis. Child.*, **123**, 569–571.
18. Greenberg, R. E. (1969), "The Physiology and Metabolism of Catecholamines," in *Endocrine and Genetic Diseases of Childhood*, pp. 762–779 (L. I. Gardner, ed.). Philadelphia and London: Saunders.
19. Hamza, B. and Meherzi, H. (1965), "Acrodynie mutilante avec troubles de métabolisme des amines pressives," *Sem. Hop. Paris*, **41**, 2603–2605.
20. Hardman, M. J., Hull, D. and Milner, A. D. (1971), "Brown Adipose Tissue Metabolism *In Vivo* and Serum Insulin Concentrations in Rabbits Soon After Birth," *J. Physiol.*, **213**, 175–183.
21. Hintze, A. and Kreppel, E. (1966), "Uber den Einfluβ der Lageänderung auf Herzfrequenz, Blutdruck und Katecholaminausscheidung im Harn bei Säuglingen, Kleinkindern und älteren Kindern," *Klin. Wschr.*, **44**, 1071–1076.
22. Hökfelt, B. (1951), "Noradrenaline and Adrenaline in Mammalian Tissues; Distribution under Normal and Pathological Conditions with Special Reference to Endocrine System," *Acta physiol. scand.*, **25**, Suppl. 92, 1–34.
23. Holden, K. R., Young, R. B., Piland, J. H. and Hurt, W. G. (1972), "Plasma Pressors in the Normal and Stressed Newborn Infant," *Pediatrics*, **49**, 495–503.
24. Howard, W. F., McDevitt, P. I. and Stander, R. W. (1964), "Catecholamine Content of the Initial Voided Urine of the Newborn," *Amer. J. Obstet. Gynec.*, **89**, 615–618.
25. Hung, W. and Migeon, C. J. (1968), "Hypoglycemia in a Two-year-old Boy with Adrenocorticotropic Hormone (ACTH) Deficiency (Probably Isolated) and Adrenal Medullary Unresponsiveness to Insulin-induced Hypoglycemia," *J. clin. Endocr.*, **28**, 146–152.
26. Jones, W. P. G. (1965), "Circulatory Collapse Associated with Defective Catecholamine Metabolism," *Hawaii med. J.*, **25**, 101–105.
27. Jost, A. (1966), "Problems of Fetal Endocrinology: The Adrenal Glands," *Recent Progr. Hormone Res.*, **22**, 541–569.
28. Keele, D. K., Richards, C., Brown, J. and Marshall, J. (1969), "Catecholamine Metabolism in Down's Syndrome," *Amer. J. ment. Defic.*, **74**, 125–129.
29. Kelsch, R. C., Light, G. S. and Oliver, W. J. (1972), "The Effect of Albumin Infusion upon Plasma Norepinephrine Concentration in Nephrotic Children," *J. Lab. clin. Med.*, **79**, 516–525.
30. Lees, M. H. (1966), "Catecholamine Metabolite Excretion of Infants with Heart Failure," *J. Pediat.*, **69**, 259–265.
31. Light, I. J., Sutherland, J. M., Loggie, J. M. and Gaffney, T. E. (1967), "Impaired Epinephrine Release in Hypoglycemic Infants of Diabetic Mothers," *New Engl. J. Med.*, **277**, 394–398.
32. McKendrick, T. and Edwards, R. W. H. (1965), "The Excretion of 4-hydroxy-3-methoxy-mandelic Acid by Children," *Arch. Dis. Childh.*, **40**, 418–425.
33. Matsaniotis, N., Beratis, N. and Economou-Mavrou, C. (1968), "Urinary Vanillyl-mandelic Acid (VMA) Excretion by Chronically Anaemic Children," *Arch. Dis. Childh.*, **43**, 372–376.
34. Nicolopoulos, D., Agathopoulos, A., Galanakos-Tharouniati, M. and Stergiopoulos, C. (1969), "Urinary Excretion of Catecholamines by Full Term and Premature Infants," *Pediatrics*, **44**, 262–265.
35. Nowak, M., Melichar, V. and Hahn, P. (1968), "Changes in the Reactivity of Human Adipose Tissue *In Vitro* to Epinephrine and Norepinephrine During Postnatal Development," *Biol. Neonat.*, **13**, 175–180.
36. Parvez, H. and Parvez, S. (1972), "Effects of Metopirone on Urinary Excretion of Adrenaline, Noradrenaline and Vanylmandelic Acid in Different Physiological Conditions. The Possible Role of Adrenal Cortex in Catecholamine Degradation," *Horm. Metab. Res.*, **4**, 398–402.
37. Pribylová, H. and Herzmann, J. (1972), "Zur adrenalen Reaktion auf die Hypoxie des Neugeborenen," *Klin. Pädiat.*, **184**, 225–228.
38. Rosenthal, I. M., Greenberg, R., Goldstein, R., Kathan, R. and Cadkin, L. (1966), "Catecholamine Metabolism in a Pheochromocytoma. Correlation with Electron Micrographs," *Amer. J. Dis. Child.*, **112**, 389–395.
39. Sawin, C. T. (1969), *The Hormones. Endocrine Physiology*. London: J. & A. Churchill Ltd.
40. Segall, M. M. (1967), "Spontaneous Hypoglycaemia with Failure to Increase Adrenaline Output," *Proc. roy. Soc. Med.*, **60**, 1004.

41. Schiff, D., Stern, L. and Leduc, J. (1966), "Chemical Thermogenesis in Newborn Infants: Catecholamine Excretion and the Plasma Non-esterified Fatty Acid Response to Cold Exposure," *Pediatrics*, **37**, 577–582.

42. Schreiter, G. and Gawellek, F. (1966), "Die Katecholaminausscheidung bei Frühgeborenen," *Pädiat. Grenzgeb.*, **5**, 361–372.

43. Stern, L., Lees, M. H. and Leduc, J. (1965), "Environment, Temperature, Oxygen Consumption, and Catecholamine Excretion in Newborn Infants," *Pediatrics*, **36**, 367–373.

44. Stern, L., Ramos, A. and Leduc, J. (1968), "Urinary Catecholamine Excretion in Infants of Diabetic Mothers," *Pediatrics*, **42**, 598–605.

45. Stern, L., Sourkes, T. L. and Raiha, N. (1967), "The Role of the Adrenal Medulla in the Hypoglycemia of Foetal Malnutrition," *Biol. Neonat.*, **11**, 129–136.

46. Studnitz, W. von (1966), "Chemistry and Pharmacology of Catecholamine-secreting Tumours," *Pharmacol. Rev.*, **18**, 645–650.

47. Thilander, B. and Thilander, H. (1969), "Catecholamine Excretion in Children in Connection with Various Types of Dental Treatment," *Acta odont. scand.*, **27**, 199–203.

48. Voorhess, M. L. (1967), "Urinary Catecholamine Excretion by Healthy Children. I: Daily Excretion of Dopamine, Norepinephrine, Epinephrine, and 3-methoxy-4-hydroxy-mandelic Acid," *Pediatrics*, **39**, 252–257.

49. Voorhess, M. L. (1971), "Neuroblastoma with Normal Urinary Catecholamine Excretion," *J. Pediat.*, **78**, 680–683.

50. Zeisel, H. (1959), "Das Nebennierenmark," In *Die physiologische Entwicklung des Kindes*, pp. 437–447 (F. Linneweh, ed.). Berlin-Göttingen-Heidelberg: Springer.

51. Zeisel, H. (1971), "Das Nebennierenmark," in *Handbuch der Kinderheilkunde*, Band I/Teil 1, pp. 328–343 (H. Opitz and F. Schmid, eds.). Berlin-Heidelberg-New York: Springer.

28C. THE GROWTH AND DEVELOPMENT OF THE ENDOCRINE PANCREAS

R. D. G. MILNER

This chapter is concerned primarily with the growth and development of the human endocrine pancreas. Aspects of endocrine pancreatic function which are of importance to paediatricians but which are not directly related to the development of the organ will not be considered in detail. For example, diabetes mellitus in childhood has been reviewed recently[42] as has the question of hypoglycaemia in infancy and older children.[10] On the other hand, some aspects of endocrine pancreatic development are well documented in experimental animals but incompletely or not at all in man.[78] The results of animal experiments will be described when relevant to an overall appreciation of the development of the organ.

Our understanding of the development of the endocrine pancreas is unbalanced. More is known about insulin than the other hormones secreted by the islets of Langerhans because of the clinical importance of diabetes mellitus. This is particularly true with regard to the functional maturation of the beta cell; the morphological development of the different cells comprising the islet has been studied longer and more evenly than has their physiological role in fetal and post-natal life. The development of an immunoassay for pancreatic glucagon has made it possible to describe something of the physiology of this hormone. Future work will determine if information which is applicable to the adult can be extrapolated back to infancy and the perinatal period. Knowledge regarding the development of other hormones which may be secreted by the endocrine pancreas, such as gastrin, is rudimentary.

ANATOMY

Classical descriptions of the morphological development of the islets of Langerhans state that two "generations" of islets occur during the fetal life of many mammals: a primary generation which grows out from the solid cords of cells that will form the primitive pancreatic tubules and a second generation that appears after the acini have formed. Little is known of the origins of the stem cells destined to become the endocrine cells of the islet. They may be endodermal in origin and capable of development into endocrine or exocrine tissue or they may have migrated to the anlage from another site in the embryo such as the neural crest.[58] In the rat there is evidence that a potential for acino-insular transformation persists into postnatal life[66] and beta cell division can occur to a limited degree in animals subjected to dietary stress.[39]

There is only one definite description of the development of two generations of islets in the human pancreas.[41] The first generation is thought to arise from the primitive ducts at the eighth week and the second generation grows from the terminal ducts during the third month of intrauterine life. Alpha cells have been reported to be the first endocrine cells to appear at nine weeks, followed by delta and then beta cells at 10·5 weeks.[40] Earlier reports agree that alpha, beta and delta cells can be recognized at this stage of development but do not opine on the order of appearance of the different cell types.[9,31] The spatial and numerical relationship of the alpha and beta cells changes through the second and third trimesters. In fetal life alpha cells are always more numerous than beta cells but by term the proportion of alpha to beta cells is approximately unity.[64] The alpha: beta cell ratio continues to fall in postnatal life so that in the adult it is between 1:3 and 1:9.[47] It is not known if the changing ratio is due to a relatively constant number of alpha cells and an increasing number of beta cells in each islet. An alternative explanation is that degeneration of alpha cells takes place in the last three months of intrauterine life.[15] The physiological significance of such an involution, if in fact it does occur, is unknown. Early in pregnancy the alpha and beta cells exist in adjacent clusters in a bipolar islet. Later the beta cells are enveloped by the alpha cells in a mantle islet and after 30 weeks the various cell types become intermingled and the islet becomes histologically similar to that seen in the adult.[59]

INSULIN

Insulin is present in the pancreas from the eleventh week of fetal life and the concentration increases with advancing gestational age.[67] The pancreatic insulin content in fetuses of well controlled diabetics is greater than that of comparable normal fetuses. In man, as in other species, the fetal pancreatic insulin concentration is greater than that in the adult. Whether this is the result of increased concentrations of insulin in the fetal islets or disproportionate postnatal development of the exocrine pancreas is not known.

Insulin secretion *in utero* has been studied by the intravenous injection of potential stimuli in fetuses at operation for the termination of pregnancy. Under these conditions, neither glucose nor arginine stimulates insulin release between the thirteenth and nineteenth week of fetal life.[3,36,55] Insulin has been detected in the amniotic fluid after the sixteenth week in concentrations similar to those found in normal adult blood.[12] It is not known for certain if the insulin in amniotic fluid is of fetal or maternal origin. Injections of glucose into the mother do not produce meaningful changes in amniotic fluid insulin concentration.

The sampling of blood from the fetal scalp for measurement of glucose and insulin during labour, before and after giving the mother glucose intravenously has confirmed the results of earlier work on plasma insulin levels in the mother and baby at the moment of birth.[53] Intravenous glucose given to the mother during labour causes maternal and fetal hyperglycaemia. Maternal plasma insulin levels rise promptly but the fetus responds with a small and delayed rise in plasma insulin. The various metabolic, neural and hypoxic stresses on the fetus associated with labour make the physiological significance of observations recorded at this time difficult to interpret.

The human placenta has been reported to have a limited permeability for insulin in both directions or from fetus to mother only but the balance of evidence suggests that the placenta is impermeable or of such limited permeability that the insulin transported is of no functional importance.[3,74]

Glucose is the stimulus which has been used most often in the newborn to test insulin secretion and conclusions have been drawn, mistakenly, regarding the functional competence of the beta cell from these studies alone. The view is commonly held that the endocrine pancreas of the neonate is immature because the baby disposes of an intravenous glucose load more slowly than the adult and has a smaller rise in plasma insulin for a given glucose challenge. Insulin secretion is but the final common response to a number of stimulatory signals. For example there is evidence that the way in which glucose, amino acids such as leucine and arginine and hormones such as glucagon act on the beta cell may differ.[54] Therefore the finding that glucose is an indifferent stimulus for insulin secretion in the newborn is a narrow base from which to conclude that the neonatal beta cell is functionally immature. Contrary evidence has been obtained *in vivo* and *in vitro*.

Grasso and his colleagues have made a number of important contributions regarding insulin secretion by premature infants. Babies aged 7–18 h. and of birth weights 1,610–2,380 g. were given glucose or essential amino acids via the umbilical vein.[27] Glucose caused a small rise in plasma insulin, but the mixture of nine essential amino acids or arginine alone caused a large rise in plasma insulin. The infusion of 0·4 μg. glucagon or 0·5 mg. theophylline/min. caused no change in blood glucose or plasma insulin, but when both substances were given together there was a progressive rise in both blood glucose and plasma insulin.[26] More recently an analagous study has been performed with glucose and a mixture of amino acids.[25] A rapid injection of glucose (1·25 g.) or of an amino acid mixture (1·25 g.) caused a small rise in serum insulin, but when the glucose and amino acids were given together they constituted a potent stimulus for insulin secretion. The mechanism by which glucose acts on the beta cell of the premature infant is complex. As described above, if glucose is injected acutely it is a poor stimulus of insulin secretion. If on the other hand an infusion of glucose which raises the blood glucose of the infant from 40 to 80 mg./100 ml. is given for 60 min. before the acute injection of glucose, the infusion does not change the serum insulin level but the acute injection becomes a potent stimulus of insulin secretion (S. S. Grasso, personal communication). The full term normal infant responds to intravenous glucagon with a prompt rise in plasma insulin levels.[29,55]

By using pieces of human fetal pancreas obtained at hysterotomy for therapeutic abortion it has been possible to study insulin secretion *in vitro*. The tissue came from fetuses of 14–24 weeks' fetal age. At no age studied did glucose stimulate insulin secretion.[48] This failure was not due to incompetence of the beta cell because ionic stimuli such as potassium and barium or stimuli which act by causing a rise in intracellular concentrations of cyclic adenosine monophosphate (cAMP) were effective.[49] Leucine stimulated insulin release from 14–20 weeks, whereas arginine was effective only on tissue taken from the larger fetuses. By this type of approach an attempt can be made to define the development of different pathways of stimulation of insulin secretion. Viewed teleologically, it might be physiologically meaningful for amino acids and not glucose to control the release of insulin *in utero*. The normal fetus lives in an environment in which blood glucose levels fluctuate little and are under maternal control. There is little need of fetal insulin for glycoregulation. If the function of insulin *in utero* is to promote the cellular uptake of amino acids and stimulate protein synthesis and if insulin secretion is stimulated physiologically by amino acids the hormone could play a part in the control of fetal growth. In this context it is interesting that the release of insulin per unit weight of human pancreas incubated *in vitro* under basal conditions was found to increase as a function of gestational age from week 15–24.[5]

Maternal Diabetes Mellitus

The abnormal development of the fetal beta cell and the perinatal consequences of diabetic pregnancy have been studied intensively and have been recently reviewed in detail.[77] The fetus of a diabetic women well controlled with insulin has blood glucose levels which reflect those of the mother. One consequence of intermittent fetal hyperglycaemia is hypertrophy and hyperplasia of the islets of Langerhans and an increase in fetal pancreatic insulin content.[11,67] The insulin used to treat diabetes comes from other species and stimulates antibody production by the diabetic woman. Some of the antibodies cross the placenta and, reacting with the insulin secreted by the fetus, make the measurement of this by immunoassay difficult. An antibody-antigen reaction at the islet cells may be responsible for eosinophilic infiltration and fibrosis of the fetal islets which has been termed sub-acute interstitial pancreatitis.[43] Hypersecretion of insulin occurs *in utero* and causes lipogenesis which is responsible, at least in part, for the cherubic appearance of some infants born to diabetic women. Clinically there appears to be an inverse relationship between the quality of maternal diabetic control and the degree of obesity of the offspring. It is tempting to deduce that the more normal birthweight of the infant of the well controlled diabetic is the consequence of maternal normoglycaemia and less fetal hypersecretion of insulin.

Hyperinsulinaemia persists following birth and is responsible for the very rapid fall in blood glucose levels of infants of diabetic mothers. The infants of diabetic women treated by diet alone have postnatal hypoglycaemia intermediate in severity between that of normal infants and that of infants born to insulin-treated diabetics.[45] When challenged acutely with intravenous glucose infants of diabetic women have a higher plasma insulin reponse and faster glucose disappearance rate than normal.[7] When the glucose is given by prolonged infusion to produce a sustained hyperglycaemia the difference between the two groups disappears.[35] In one study the long-term effect of maternal diabetes on the beta cell function of the offspring was studied. Six of nine two-year-old infants born to diabetic women had abnormally high blood glucose responses to intravenous glucose. In four this was associated with hyperinsulinaemia and in two hypoinsulinaemia.[73]

The infant of a diabetic woman treated with oral sulphonylureas during pregnancy may pose a particular clinical problem.[2] In this case the fetus is exposed not only to hyperglycaemia but also to the sulphonylurea drugs which cross the placenta. Such an infant is born hyperinsulinaemic and with therapeutic circulating levels of an insulinotropic drug which is degraded slowly because of the immaturity of the neonatal liver. These babies may suffer profound intractable hypoglycaemia for which treatment by exchange transfusion may be necessary to remove the drug and restore the blood glucose level to normal.[34] Glucose tolerance tests on these babies have resulted in the highest plasma insulin levels so far recorded in the newborn. Although not all such infants become hypoglycaemic it seems prudent to avoid maternal therapy which may have serious neonatal consequences.

Erythroblastosis Fetalis

Infants with erythroblastosis fetalis have hyperplasia of the islets of Langerhans. Careful study of the islets has shown that although they are large like those of infants of diabetic women they differ in that the types of cells making up the islet are present in normal proportions, whereas in the islets of infants born to women with diabetes there is a preponderance of beta cells.[71] Erythroblastotic infants have a high pancreatic insulin content and may have high plasma insulin levels at birth and in the succeeding hours.[13,17] They may suffer as a consequence symptomatic hypoglycaemia in the early hours of life.[8] In both term and premature erythroblastotic infants there is increased urinary insulin excretion.[65] In term infants, but not in prematures, the amount of insulin excreted in the urine appears to be related to the severity of the haemolytic process as judged by the cord haemoglobin. Hypoglycaemia in the first day of life may result and is more probable in the premature than the term baby. Babies with haemolytic disease are at risk from hypoglycaemia immediately following exchange transfusion.[62] If blood preserved with citrate and glucose is used the infant develops high blood glucose and plasma insulin levels by the end of the procedure. At the moment the transfusion stops the baby is in a metabolic situation akin to that of the baby of the diabetic mother when the umbilical cord is cut, but without the energy reserves of such an infant. A rapid fall in blood glucose can occur and and hypoglycaemia should be considered in the analysis of any symptoms occurring in the immediate post-transfusion period.

The mechanism responsible for pancreatic hyperplasia is not understood. The erythroblastotic fetus does not appear to be hyperinsulinaemic *in utero* for such babies are rarely obese. Two suggestions have been made concerning abnormal endocrine pancreatic development in erythroblastosis fetalis and common to both is the idea that the life of insulin *in utero* is shortened. The placenta is known to be a site of active insulin degradation and it has been suggested that placental hyperplasia in erythroblastosis fetalis causes increased destruction of insulin and thereby compensatory hypersecretion.[63] An alternative hypothesis is that haemolysis causes raised circulating levels of glutathione which split the disulphide bonds linking the A and B chains of insulin.[68]

Anencephaly

Insulin secretion in the human anencephalic has aroused little interest among investigators and yet is proving important in extending out understanding of factors controlling the development of the endocrine pancreas. A clue that the adenohypophysis might be concerned with the endocrine pancreas *in utero* came from a comparison of the morphology of the pancreas and the hypothalamo-hypophyseal system in anencephalics.[72] A functional hypophysis is not necessary for normal development of the endocrine pancreas to occur. However, in anencephalics born to women with a reduced glucose tolerance there is a difference in the endocrine pancreas between those without a hypothalamo-hypophyseal system and those with a functional hypophysis. Anencephalics with an intact adenohypophysis resemble intact infants born to women with abnormal glucose tolerance in that they have a high percentage of endocrine tissue in the pancreas, a high percentage of beta cells in the islets of Langerhans and a raised umbilical cord plasma insulin level. Anencephalics without a hypothalamo-hypophyseal system born to women with an abnormal glucose tolerance do not show these changes. Further evidence that cephalic factors may influence the development of the endocrine pancreas comes from work with rabbits. Rabbit fetuses decapitated *in utero* on day 24 have higher plasma insulin levels on day 29 than control littermates.[30] Pancreas taken from the decapitated animals secretes more insulin *in vitro* in medium with a low or a high extracellular glucose concentration, indicating that removal of the head has a direct effect on insulin secretion. The mechanism by which the head influences the endocrine pancreas could be neural or humoral or both. The work with human anencephalics suggests that endocrine factors are important as does the report that injection of decapitated rabbit fetuses with ovine growth hormone restores the pancreatic insulin content to normal.[33]

Transient Neonatal Diabetes Mellitus

This condition is most likely to occur in infants aged less than six weeks and is usually acute in onset, the infant presenting with the classical physical signs of polyuria, glucosuria, severe dehydration and marked hyperglycaemia. Ketonaemia may occur but ketonuria is uncommon. Nearly all infants who have transient neonatal diabetes are small for their gestational age and the onset of diabetes is not uncommonly preceded by hypoglycaemia which is probably the consequence of low hepatic glycogen stores. Temporary neonatal diabetes differs from classical diabetes mellitus only in running a self-limiting course.[19] Although insulin resistance has been proposed as an aetiological factor it seems more likely that the condition is due to delay in the development of beta cell function. The infants are insulin sensitive and although the dose regime of 1–3 units insulin per kg. body weight per day may seem appreciable when extrapolated on the basis of body weight to the adult it should not be forgotten that much of the insulin given to the baby is lost in the urine.[52]

Insulinoma in the Newborn

Insulinoma in the newborn is a very rare condition but one which is noteworthy in a review of the development of the endocrine pancreas because it illustrates certain features which differ from hyperinsulinaemic states in later life. In a spate of case reports which have appeared in recent years[18,24,60,65,75] the following characteristics have been noteworthy. The infant is profoundly and persistently hypoglycaemic. Plasma insulin levels are often within the normal range. Diazoxide is ineffective in controlling the hypoglycaemia. At operation either a discrete insulinoma is found in the body and tail or the head of the pancreas or there may be a proliferation of beta cells outside the islets of Langerhans, termed nesidioblastosis. These features are not as strange as they might seem when viewed in the light of current knowledge of the development of the beta cell. In infants with insulinomas, insulin secretion is not likely to be governed by extracellular glucose concentrations since the normal beta cell is not sensitive to glucose at this stage of development. By the same token diazoxide, an inhibitor of insulin secretion which works on the glucose pathway, would not be expected to be effective. Appreciation of these unusual features of neonatal insulinoma is important, for the condition although rare may be lethal or permanently crippling if inadequately treated, whereas neurological normality may be the end result of early diagnosis and prompt treatment.

"Small-for-dates" Infants

Many infants who are born small for their gestational age are commonly regarded as having been malnourished *in utero*. Postnatal undernutrition is associated with hyposecretion of insulin and it has been assumed that infants undernourished *in utero*, respond in the same way. Recent studies have demonstrated heterogeneity among small for dates infants some of whom secrete inappropriately large amounts of insulin in response to glucose or glucagon.[37,48] The oversecretion of insulin disappears during the early weeks of life. Its significance is not understood but appreciation of the phenomenon is important in the management of the symptomatic hypoglycamiae which some of these infants suffer.

GLUCAGON

Much less is known about the functional development of the alpha cell partly because the measurement of glucagon has caused more technical problems than that of insulin. Fewer facts mean that what is written here about glucagon is culled mainly from work on other species whereas what was written about the development of the beta cell was taken mainly from work on man.

α_2 cells are present in the human fetal pancreas from the eighth week of gestation and glucagon has been extracted from the pancreas of a fetus of 50 days' gestational age.[61] The human placenta is impermeable to glucagon[1] and the glucagon which has been detected in fetal blood from the fifteenth week of gestation must therefore be of fetal origin[6]. From the tenth to the twenty-sixth week of intrauterine life the concentration of glucagon per unit weight of pancreas increases five-fold.[6] Glucagon has been demonstrated immunochemically in the fetal and neonatal pancreas of other species also. In the sheep the hormone is detectable from a gestational age of 93 days (0·65 gestation). The concentration of the hormone rises to a peak at 100–110 days and then falls in the latter part of pregnancy.[4]

The perinatal physiology of glucagon secretion has been studied most intensively in the rat. Fetal rat pancreas contains α_2 cells and glucagon from day 18·5 of gestation (term is 22 days).[23,57] The rat placenta is impermeable to radioactive glucagon.[20] The concentration of glucagon in the pancreas rises gradually during the last three days of gestation whereas the fetal plasma glucagon concentration remains steady from day 18·5 to day 19·5, rises significantly on day 20·5 and falls again on day 21·5.[20] The fall in the last day of intrauterine life is associated with a rise in blood glucose level. Following birth the plasma pancreatic glucagon rises threefold in 20 min. and then returns at the age of 2 h. to levels similar to those at birth. These changes are associated with hypoglycaemia and precede an increase in liver phosphorylase activity and fall in heptatic glycogen content which occurs by the age of 2 h. when blood glucose levels have returned to normal.[22] Glucagon secretion is stimulated by noradrenaline and the signal for glucagon release following birth of the rat could be a metabolic one acting directly on the α_2 cell or a neural signal arising as a consequence of the stress of birth or from metabolic changes associated with birth. Recent evidence indicates that the α_2 cell is functionally competent in the rat fetus also.[20] Acute fetal hyperglycaemia or hypoglycaemia has no effect on fetal plasma glucagon levels. Chronic fetal hypoglycaemia, caused by fasting the mother or giving insulin to the fetus, is associated with a rise in the concentration of plasma glucagon. Exogenous glucagon given to rat fetuses causes hyperglycaemia.[21,28] Acute stimuli of glucagon secretion by the rat fetus *in utero* include arginine and noradrenaline.[20] The physiological significance of stimulation by arginine remains unclear but that caused by noradrenaline could play an important role in the provision of energy during the birth process.

In vitro studies have shown that glucagon secretion is stimulated from pieces of neonatal rat pancreas by arginine and is inhibited by octanoic acid.[14] The response of the tissue is age dependent, stimulation and inhibition of glucagon secretion being observed on the first two days of life and on days 10 and 20 but not between days three and seven. Glucagon secretion from neonatal rat pancreas is not inhibited by high extracellular glucose concentrations at one, four or ten days of age although glucose is a potent inhibitor of glucagon secretion in the adult rat. This is of interest because glucose does not become an effective stimulus to insulin secretion in the rat until the third to fifth day postnatally and it poses the question of whether a glucose receptor develops in the beta and alpha cells at a time when intake of nutrient via the gastro-intestinal tract is safely established. The age dependent changes in glucagon release and the observation that adipocyte sensitivity to exogenous glucagon is also age dependent[45] in the rat suggests that the physiological role of the hormone in the perinatal period may be complex.

The role of glucagon in the perinatal period of the rat has been considered in some detail because these studies form the best model available for other species at the present time. In man plasma glucagon levels have been measured at birth and in the hours following. At birth levels in the umbilical artery and vein and in maternal peripheral venous blood are similar and range between 122 and 170 pg./ml.[32,50] No difference was observed between normal full term infants delivered vaginally or by caesarian section but infants with fetal distress had much higher levels of glucagon in umbilical blood (239–254 pg./ml.)[32] Two hours after birth the peripheral venous plasma glucagon level of normal infants had risen significantly to 188 pg./ml. whereas the level in maternal blood had fallen to 83 pg./ml.[32] Much higher levels of glucagon were found in the portal vein of fasted infants of normal or diabetic mothers aged 6–24 h.[44] The differences may be due to the site of sampling, immunoassay methodology or they may be physiological and indicate an important hyperglucagonaemia in the first day of life of the human newborn. Glucose given intravenously at the age of 24 h. did not suppress plasma glucagon levels[44] but glucose given with exogenous insulin causes a fall in the concentration of glucagon in portal venous blood (A. L. Luyckx, personal communication). In fasted infants aged 1–3 days high portal vein plasma glucagon levels were observed despite the blood being collected in the absence of a kallekrein-inhibitor which prevents glucagon destruction *in vitro*.[16] No significant difference was noted between normal term, premature or small-for-dates infants in a thermo-neutral environment or upon exposure to a cool environment.[16] Blood taken from infants with erythroblastosis fetalis under comparable conditions had a higher glucagon concentration and the hyperglycaemia occurring during exchange transfusion failed to suppress glucagon secretion.[51] This finding is in keeping with the observation that the hyperplasia of the islets in erythroblastosis appears to affect alpha and beta cells equally. The intravenous injection of exogenous glucagon in pharmacological doses causes a prompt rise in plasma insulin and glucose[55] whereas the injection of a smaller dose (1 μg.) causes a comparable rise in plasma insulin but a much smaller rise in blood glucose.[29]

These few studies of glucagon secretion by the human newborn have similarities to those in the rat insofar as the plasma concentration rises in both species following birth and it is possible that in the distressed fetus the signal for glucagon secretion may be neural. It appears likely that the hormone may play an important role in metabolic adjustments occurring in the perinatal period.

SUMMARY

Although the islet of Langerhans of the term human fetus resembles that of the adult histologically it is functionally very different. So many of the actions of insulin and glucagon are interrelated that it may be more meaningful to consider each hormone as one facet of a single control mechanism than alone.[70] A full appreciation of the development of the endocrine pancreas will only be achieved however when the results reviewed here are meaningfully integrated with what is known about the intermediary metabolism of the fetus and newborn infant.[76]

REFERENCES

1. Adam, P., King, K., Schwartz, R. and Teramo, K. (1972), "Human Placental Barrier to Glucagon-I-125 Early in Gestation," *J. clin. Endocr. Metab.*, **34,** 772–783.
2. Adam, P. A. J. and Schwartz, R. (1968), "Should Oral Hypoglycaemic Drugs be Used in Pediatric and Pregnant Patients?" *Pediatrics*, **42,** 819–923.
3. Adam, P. A. J., Teramo, K., Räiha, N., Gitlin, D. and Schwartz, R. (1969), "Human Fetal Insulin Metabolism Early in Gestation. Response to Acute Elevation of the Fetal Glucose Concentration and Placental Transfer of Human Insulin-I-131," *Diabetes*, **18,** 409–416.
4. Alexander, D. P., Assan, R., Britton, H. G. and Nixon, D. A. (1971), "Glucagon in the Foetal Sheep," *J. Endocr.*, **51,** 597–598.
5. Ashworth, M. A., Leach, F. N. and Milner, R. D. G. (1973), "Development of Insulin Secretion in the Human Foetus," *Arch. Dis. Childh.* In press.
6. Assan, R. and Boillot, J. (1971), "Pancreatic Glucagon and Glucagon Like Material in Tissues and Plasma from Human Foetuses 6–26 Weeks Old," in *Metabolic Processes in the Foetus and Newborn Infant*, pp. 210–219 (J. H. P. Jonxis, H. K. A. Visser, and J. A. Troelstra, eds.). Leiden: Stenfert Kroese NV.
7. Baird, J. D. and Farquhar, J. W. (1962), "Insulin Secreting Capacity in Newborn Infants of Diabetic Women," *Lancet*, **1,** 71–74.
8. Barrett, C. T. and Oliver, T. K., Jr. (1968), "Hypoglycemia and Hyperinsulinism in Infants with Erythroblastosis Foetalis," *New Engl. J. Med.*, **278,** 1260–1263.
9. Björkman, N., Hellerström, C., Hellman, B. and Petersson, B. (1966), "The Cell Types in the Endocrine Pancreas of the Human Foetus," *Z. Zellforsch. mikrosk. Anat.*, **72,** 425–445.
10. Bower, B. D. (1969), "Hypoglycaemia," in *Paediatric Endocrinology*, pp. 463–478 (D. Hubble, ed.). Oxford: Blackwell.
11. Cardell, B. S. (1953), "Infants of Diabetic Mothers, a Morphological Study," *J. Obstet. Gynaec. Br. Emp.*, **60,** 834–853.
12. Casper, D. J. and Benjamin, F. (1970), "Immunoreactive Insulin in Amniotic Fluid," *Obstet. Gynaec.*, **35,** 389–394.
13. Driscoll, S. G. and Steinke, J. (1967), "Pancreatic Insulin Content in Severe Erythroblastosis Fetalis," *Pediatrics*, **39,** 448–450.
14. Edwards, J. C., Asplund, K. and Lundqvist, G. (1972), "Glucagon Release From the Pancreas of the Newborn Rat," *J. Endocr.* In press.
15. Emery, J. L. and Bury, H. P. R. (1964), "Involutionary Changes in the Islets of Langerhans," *Biol. Neonat.*, **6,** 16–25.
16. Fekete, M., Milner, R. D. G., Soltész, Gy., Assan, R. and Mestyàn, J. (1972), "Plasma Glucagon, Thyrotropin, Growth Hormone and Insulin Response to Cold Exposure in the Human Newborn," *Acta pediat. scand.*, **61,** 435–441.
17. From, G. L. A., Driscoll, S. G. and Steinke, J. (1969), "Serum Insulin in Newborn Infants with Erythroblastosis Foetalis," *Pediatrics*, **44,** 549–553.
18. Garces, L. Y., Drash, A. and Kenny, F. M. (1968), "Islet Cell Tumor in the Neonate," *Pediatrics*, **41,** 789–796.
19. Gentz, J. C. H. and Cornblath, M. (1969), "Transient Diabetes of the Newborn," *Advanc. in Pediat.*, **16,** 345–363.
20. Girard, J., Assan, R. and Jost, A. (1973), "Glucagon in the Rat Foetus," in *Proceedings of the Sir Joseph Barcroft Centenary Symposium Cambridge*, pp. 456–461 Cambridge University Press.
21. Girard, J. and Bal, D. (1970), "Effects du Glucagon-zinc sur la Glycémie et la Teneur en Glycogène du Foie Foetal du Rat en fin de Gestation," *C. R. Acad. Sci. (Paris)*, **271,** 777–779.
22. Girard, J., Bal, D. and Assan, R. (1972), "Glucagon Secretion During the Early Postnatal Period in the Rat," *Horm. Metab. Res.*, **4,** 168–170.
23. Girard, J., Bal, D., Assan, R. and Jost, A. (1973), "Hormones and Glycemia During the Perinatal Period in the Rat," in *Hormonal Factors in Individual Development* (M. B. Mitskevich, ed.). Moscow.
24. Grant, D. B. and Barbor, P. R. H. (1970), "Islet Cell Tumour Causing Hypoglycaemia in a Newborn Infant," *Arch. Dis. Childh.*, **45,** 434–436.
25. Grasso, S., Messina, A., Di Stefano, G., Vigo, R. and Reitano, G. (1973), "Insulin Secretion in the Premature Infant: Response to Glucose and Amino Acids," *Diabetes.* In press.
26. Grasso, S., Messina, A., Saporito, N. and Reitano, G. (1970), "Effect of Theophylline, Glucagon and Theophylline Plus Glucagon on Insulin Secretion in the Premature Infant," *Diabetes*, **19,** 837–842.
27. Grasso, S., Saporito, N., Messina, A. and Reitano, G. (1968), "Serum Insulin Response to Glucose and Amino Acids in the Premature Infant," *Lancet*, **2,** 755–756.
28. Hunter, D. J. S. (1969), "Changes in Blood Glucose and Liver Carbohydrate after Intrauterine Injection of Glucagon into Foetal Rats," *J. Endocr.*, **45,** 367–374.
29. Hunter, D. J. S. and Isles, T. E. (1972), "The Insulinogenic Effect of Glucagon in the Newborn," *Biol. Neonat.*, **20,** 74–81.
30. Jack, P. M. B. and Milner, R. D. G. (1973), "Cephalic Factors Influencing the Development of Insulin Secretion," *J. Endocr.* In press.
31. Jirasek, J. E. (1965), "Die Histogenese und Histochemie der Beta-Zellen der Langerhensschen Inseln im Pancreas Menschlicher Embryonen," *Acta histochem.*, **22,** 62–65.
32. Johnston, D. I. and Bloom, S. R. (1973), "Plasma Glucagon Levels in the Full-term Human Infant and the Effect of Anoxia," *Arch. Dis. Childh.* In press.
33. Kervran, A., Jost, A. and Rosselin, G. (1970), "Insulin Contents in Plasma and Pancreas of Foetal Rabbits Experimental Variations," *Diabetologia*, **6,** 51.
34. Kemball, M. L., McIver, C., Milner, R. D. G., Nourse, C. H., Schiff, D. and Tiernan, J. R. (1970), "Neonatal Hypoglycaemia in Infants of Diabetic Mothers given Sulphonylurea Drugs in Pregnancy," *Arch. Dis. Childh.*, **45,** 696–701.
35. King, K. C., Adam, P. A. J., Clemente, G. A. and Schwartz, R. (1969), "Infants of Diabetic Mothers: Attenuated Glucose Uptake without Hyperinsulinaemia during Continuous Glucose Infusion," *Pediatrics*, **44,** 381–392.
36. King, K. C., Butt, J., Raivic, K., Räiha, N., Roux, J., Teramo, K., Yamaguchi, K. and Schwartz, R. (1971), "Human Maternal and Foetal Insulin Response to Arginine," *New Engl. J. Med.*, **285,** 603–607.
37. LeDune, M. A. (1972), "Intravenous Glucose Tolerance and Plasma Insulin Studies in Small for Dates Babies," *Arch. Dis. Childh.*, **47,** 111–114.
38. LeDune, M. A. (1972), "The Response to Glucagon in Small for Dates Hypoglycaemic Newborn Infants," *Arch. Dis. Childh.*
39. Like, A. A. and Chick, W. L. (1969), "Mitotic Division in Pancreatic Beta Cells," *Science*, **163,** 941–943.
40. Like, A. A. and Orci, L. (1972), "Embryogenesis of the Human Pancreatic Islets: A Light and Electron Microscopic Study," *Diabetes*, suppl. 2, **21,** 511–534.
41. Liu, H. M. and Potter, E. L. (1962), "Development of the Human Pancreas," *Arch. Path.*, **74,** 439–452.
42. Lloyd, J. K. and Wolff, O. H. (1969), "Diabetes Mellitus," in *Paediatric Endocrinology*, pp. 441–462 (D. Hubble, ed.). Oxford: Blackwell.
43. Logothetopoulos, J. and Bell, E. G. (1966), "Histological and Autoradiographic Studies of the Islets of Mice Injected with Insulin Antibody," *Diabetes*, **15,** 205–211.
44. Luyckx, A. S., Massi-Benedetti, F., Falorni, A. and Lefebvre, P. J. (1972), "Presence of Pancreatic Glucagon in the Portal Plasma of Human Neonates. Differences in the Insulin and

Glucagon Responses to Glucose between Normal Infants and Infants from Diabetic Mothers," *Diabetologia*, **8**, 296–300.
45. Manganiello, A. B. and Vaughan, B. C. (1972), "Selective loss of Adipose Cell Responsiveness to Glucagon with Growth in the Rat," *J. Lipid Res.*, **13**, 12–17.
46. McCann, M. L., Chen, C. H., Katigbak, E. B., Kotchen, J. M., Likly, B. F. and Schwartz, R. (1966), "Effects of Fructose on Hypoglucosemia in Infants of Diabetic Mothers," *New Engl. J. Med.*, **275**, 1–7.
47. McLean, N. and Ogilvie, R. F. (1955), "Quantitative Estimate of Pancreatic Islet Tissue in Diabetic Subjects," *Diabetes*, **4**, 367–376.
48. Milner, R. D. G., Ashworth, M. A. and Barson, A. J. (1972), "Insulin Release from Human Foetal Pancreas in Response to Glucose, Leucine and Arginine," *J. Endocr.*, **52**, 497–505.
49. Milner, R. D. G., Barson, A. J. and Ashworth, M. A. (1971), "Human Foetal Pancreatic Insulin Secretion in Response to Ionic and other Stimuli," *J. Endocr.*, **51**, 323–332.
50. Milner, R. D. G., Chouksey, S. K., Mickleson, K. N. P. and Assan, R. (1973), "Plasma Pancreatic Glucagon and Insulin Glucagon Ratio at Birth," *Arch. Dis. Childh.* In press.
51. Milner, R. D. G., Fekete, M. and Assan, R. (1972), "Glucagon, Insulin and Growth Hormone Response to Exchange Transfusion in Premature and Full Term Infants," *Arch. Dis. Childh.*, **47**, 186–189.
52. Milner, R. D. G., Ferguson, A. W. and Naidu, S. H. (1971), "Aetiology of Transient Neonatal Diabetes," *Arch. Dis. Child.*, **46**, 724–726.
53. Milner, R. D. G. and Hales, C. N. (1965), "Effect of Intravenous Glucose on Concentration of Insulin in Maternal and Umbilical Cord Plasma," *Brit. med. J.*, **1**, 284–286.
54. Milner, R. D. G. and Hales, C. N. (1970), "Ionic Mechanisms in the Regulation of Insulin Secretion," in *The Structure and Metabolism of the Pancreatic Islets*, pp. 489–494 (S. Falkmer, B. Hellman and I.-B. Täljedal, eds.). Oxford: Pergamon.
55. Milner, R. D. G. and Wright, A. D. (1967), "Plasma Glucose, Nonesterified Fatty Acid, Insulin and Growth Hormone Response to Intravenous Glucagon in the Newborn," *Clin. Sci.*, **32**, 249–255.
56. Obenshain, S. S., Adam, P. A. J., King, K. C., Teramo, K., Raivo, K. O., Räiha, N. and Schwartz, R. (1970), "Human Foetal Insulin Response to Sustained Maternal Hyperglycemia," *New Engl. J. Med.*, **283**, 566–570.
57. Orci, L., Lambert, A. E., Rouiller, C., Renold, A. E. and Samols, E. (1969), "Evidence for the Presence of A-cell in the Endocrine Foetal Pancreas of the Rat." *Horm. Metab. Res.*, **1**, 108–110.
58. Pearse, A. G. E. (1969), "The Cytochemistry and Ultrastructure of Polypeptide Hormone-producing Cells of the APUD Series and the Embryologic, Physiologic and Pathologic Implications of the Concept," *J. Histochem. Cytochem.*, **17**, 303–313.
59. Robb, P. (1961), "The Development of the Islets of Langerhans in the Human Foetus," *J. exp. Physiol.*, **46**, 335–343.
60. Salinas, Jr., E. D., Mangurten, H. H., Roberts, S. S., Simon, W. H. and Cornblath, M. (1968), "Functioning Islet Cell Adenoma in the Newborn. Report of a Case with Failure of Diazoxide," *Pediatrics*, **41**, 646–653.
61. Schaeffer, L. D., Wilder, M. W. and Williams, R. H. (1971), "Insulin and Glucagon Release from Human Foetal Pancreas Slices *In Vitro*," *Diabetes*, suppl., **20**, 326–327.
62. Schiff, D., Aranda, J. V., Colle, E. and Stern, L. (1971), "Metabolic Effects of Exchange Transfusion. II Delayed Hypoglycaemia Following Exchange Transfusion with Citrated Blood," *J. Pediat.*, **79**, 589–594.
63. Schiff, D. and Lowy, C. (1970), "Hypoglycemia and Excretion of Insulin in Urine in Haemolytic Disease of the Newborn," *Pediat. Res.*, **4**, 280–285.
64. Schultze-Jena, B. S. (1953), "Das Quantitative und Qualitative Inselbild Menschlicher Feten und Neugeborener," *Virchows Arch. Path. Anat.*, **323**, 653–663.
65. Schwartz, J. F. and Zwiren, G. T. (1971), "Islet Cell Adenomatosis and Adenoma in an Infant," *J. Pediat.*, **79**, 232–238.
66. Sétáló, G. (1971), "Light Microscopic Demonstration of Acinoinsular Transformation," *Acta Morph. Acad. Sci. Hung.*, **18**, 359–369.
67. Steinke, J. and Driscoll, S. (1965), "The Extractable Insulin Content of Pancreas from Foetuses and Infants of Diabetic and Control Mothers," *Diabetes*, **14**, 573–578.
68. Steinke, J., Gries, F. A. and Driscoll, S. G. (1967), "*In Vitro* Studies of Insulin Inactivation with Reference to Erythroblastosis Fetalis," *Blood*, **30**, 359–363.
69. Unger, R. H. (1971), "Glucagon Physiology and Pathophysiology," *New Engl. J. Med.*, **285**, 443–448.
70. Unger, R. H. (1971), "Glucagon and the Insulin Glucagon Ratio in Diabetes and other Catabolic Diseases," *Diabetes*, **20**, 834–838.
71. Van Assche, F. A. and Gepts, W. (1971), "The Cytological Composition of the Foetal Endocrine Pancreas in Normal and Pathological Conditions," *Diabetologia*, **7**, 434–445.
72. Van Assche, F. A., Gepts, W. and DeGasparo, M. (1970), "The Endocrine Pancreas in Anencephalics. A Histological, Histochemical and Biological Study," *Biol. Neonat.*, **14**, 374–388.
73. Velasco, M. S. A. and Paulsen, E. P. (1969), "The Response of Infants of Diabetic Women to Tolbutamide and Leucine at Birth and to Glucose and Tolbutamide at Two Years of Age," *Pediatrics*, **43**, 546–558.
74. Wolf, H., Sabata, V., Frerichs, H. and Stubbe, P. (1969), "Evidence for the Impermeability of the Human Placenta for Insulin," *Horm. Metab. Res.*, **1**, 274–275.
75. Yakovac, W. C., Baker, L. and Hummeler, K. (1971), "Beta Cell Nesidioblastosis in Idiopathic Hypoglycemia of Infancy," *J. Pediat.*, **79**, 226–231.

FURTHER READING

76. Adam, P. A. J. (1971), "Control of Glucose Metabolism in the Human Foetus and Newborn Infant," *Adv. Metab. Disorders*, **5**, 184–275.
77. Baird, J. D. (1969), "Some Aspects of Carbohydrate Metabolism in Pregnancy with Special Reference to the Energy Metabolism and Hormonal Status of the Infant of the Diabetic Woman and the Diabetogenic Effect of Pregnancy," *J. Endocr.*, **44**, 139–172.
78. Pictet, R. and Rutter, W. J. (1972), "Development of the Endocrine Pancreas," in *Handbook of Physiology, Volume on Endocrinology*, (N. Freinkel and D. Steiner, eds.).

28D. THE GROWTH AND DEVELOPMENT OF THE THYROID

WELLINGTON HUNG

INTRODUCTION

The thyroid is an endocrine gland which produces the thyroid hormones, thyroxine (T_4) and triiodothyronine (T_3). The classic action of the thyroid hormones is to regulate the rate of cellular oxidation in virtually all tissues. Thyroid hormones are essential for normal growth and development to occur particularly during periods of rapid growth.

The present discussion reviews the growth and development of the thyroid gland in the fetus, newborn infant, child and adolescent.

NORMAL ANATOMY

The thyroid is a bilobed symmetrical, firm, smooth organ. The two lobes are connected by the isthmus. The name "thyroid" is derived from a Greek word meaning "shield". The isthmus usually overlies the region of the second to fourth tracheal cartilages. The pyramidal lobe, if present, is a midline superior projection from the isthmus. The right lobe of the thyroid is often the larger of the two lobes in children.[76] The right lobe also tends to enlarge more than the left lobe in disorders associated with diffuse increase in size.

The weight of the "normal" thyroid gland in children varies from one region of the world to another and appears to be greater in areas of relative iodine deficiency. Within the United States, regional variations are encountered.[42] Since weight is an important criterion in the pathologic diagnosis of goiter, these regional variations as well as variations associated with age must be recognized. Table 1 summarizes the weight of the thyroid gland at various ages.

EMBRYONIC DEVELOPMENT

The median part of the thyroid gland originates in the embryo during 3–4mm. stage by proliferation and invagination of the medial endoderm of the foregut or the floor of the pharynx, at the level of the first and second pharyngeal pouches.[6] Although some controversy exists, most investigators believe that the lateral thyroid anlage, from the area of the fourth pouch, becomes incorporated into the median thyroid anlage to contribute a small proportion of the final thyroid parenchyma. The thyroid anlage becomes elongated and enlarges laterally, to become bilobed with the pharyngeal region contracting to become a narrow stalk, the thyroglossal duct. This duct subsequently atrophies, leaving at its point of origin on the tongue, a depression known as the foramen cecum. Normally, the thyroid continues to grow and simultaneously migrates caudally. By the end of the seventh week of gestation, the developing thyroid becomes crescentic in shape and is located at the level of the developing trachea. At this time the thyroid lobes, one on each side of the trachea, are connected in the midline by a very narrow isthmus of developing thyroid tissue. A pyramidal lobe of the thyroid can result from retention and growth of the lower end of the thyroglossal duct. Usually the pyramidal lobe undergoes gradual atrophy.

The parathyroid glands are derived from the third and fourth pharyngeal pouches. The ultimobranchial body is derived from a portion of the fourth pharyngeal pouch although some investigators consider that it is derived from the fifth pharyngeal pouch.[6] Recent evidence indicates that the ultimobranchial body migrates to the thyroid, where it gives rise to the C cells of the thyroid gland.[59] There is growing evidence that these C cells are the source of calcitonin.[27] Calcitonin is a peptide which has hypocalcemic action in animals but its role in calcium homeostasis in man is as yet unclear.

ANOMALOUS DEVELOPMENT

Variations involving the development of the thyroid gland are of two types:

(a) failure of the thyroid gland to develop, and

(b) differentiation in abnormal locations, including persistence of a thyroglossal duct or tract. Newborn infants in the first group are athyreotic because the embryonic area fails to differentiate into thyroid tissue.

In the second group, most of the anomalies found cephalad to the normal position of the thyroid isthmus and represent an arrest in the usual descent of part or all of the thyroid tissue to the usual location. Fragments of thyroid tissue which become separated from the lateral part or upper pole of the thyroid lobes may be found near the carotid artery or the jugular vein. Occasionally, the entire gland or parts of it descend more caudad into the mediastinum or pericardium. With increased development of ectopically placed thyroid tissue, the usual main gland may be absent. The amount of ectopic thyroid tissue which is present is usually of an insufficient quantity to prevent hypothyroidism. Ectopic placement of thyroid glands is an important etiologic factor in the pathogenesis of nongoitrous sporadic cretinism and hypothyroidism in pediatrics. Ectopic thyroid glands must be included in the differential diagnosis of midline lingual and sublingual masses in hypothyroid as well as euthyroid children.[39] Ectopically placed thyroid tissue can respond to stimulation by TSH by increasing in size. The location of ectopically placed typroid tissue can often be demonstrated with the use of radioisotopes such as radioactive iodine or pertechnetate on scintiscanning.

As mentioned previously, the thyroglossal duct usually atrophies completely. Not infrequently, however, it may fail to atrophy, remaining as a cystic mass in the midline of the neck, somewhere between the base of the tongue and the hyoid bone. A thyroglossal cyst should be considered in any patient presenting with an enlarging cystic mass in the midline of the neck. Occasionally, such cysts may contain a sufficient amount of thyroid tissue capable of concentrating radioactive isotopes for this to be demonstrable on scintiscanning. Such cysts should be removed surgically.

HISTOLOGIC AND FUNCTIONAL DIFFERENTIATION OF THE FETAL PITUITARY AND THYROID GLAND

The cytologic differentiation of the pituitary gland begins at approximately 8 weeks of gestation,[58] and PAS positive basophiles are first detected at approximately 9 weeks of gestation.[71] Thyroid-stimulating hormone (TSH) is produced and stored in the basophilic cells of the anterior pituitary gland.

Three general periods of development of the human fetal thyroid gland have been described by Shepard.[74] The precolloid stage takes place from approximately the 47th to 72nd day of gestation; the initial colloid period from the 73rd to 80th day of gestation; and the follicular growth or maturation period from the 80th day until term. Synthesis of thyroglobulin and iodination of thyroid proteins have been detected at 4 weeks[29] and 11 weeks of gestation,[73] respectively, so that the initiation of these processes appears to be independent of the hypothalamic-pituitary axis. Shepard[74] has demonstrated ^{131}I uptake by the human fetal thyroid gland at about 74 days of gestation. It has also been shown that the primate's fetal thyroid gland concentrates radioactive iodine 10 times greater than the mother's thyroid gland when the concentration is calculated on a weight basis.[64] This is of importance since maternal administration of therapeutic amounts of radioactive iodine after the 70th day of gestation can result in fetal radiothyroidectomy and severe congenital hypothyroidism.

HYPOTHALAMIC-PITUITARY-THYROID INTERRELATIONSHIP

The concentration of thyroid hormones in blood is controlled by a dynamic control system involving the hypothalamus and the pituitary and thyroid glands. This relationship is schematically presented in Fig. 1. Thyrotropin-releasing factor (TRF) from the hypothalamus stimulates the release of TSH, the major regulator of thyroid hormone formation and release: thyroid hormones, in turn, restrain TSH secretion at the anterior pituitary level.

Advances in methodology have largely been responsible for the newer data on TSH secretion by the human pituitary gland. These advances are the development of the radioimmunoassay of human TSH and the discovery of the structure of TRF leading to its synthesis—the first hypothalamic neurohormone to be synthesized.

It has been postulated that the median eminence of the hypothalamus has nerve endings that contain TRF.[69] TRF diffuses into the capillary plexus of the median eminence and is carried by the veins of the pituitary stalk, the hypophyseal portal circulation, to the sinusoids of the anterior pituitary gland, where it effects the release of TSH. The mechanism by which TRF exerts its action on the pituitary gland is poorly understood. It appears to stimulate both release of preformed TSH and synthesis of new TSH. TRF-induced release of TSH requires energy and may be mediated by increased adenyl cyclase activity.

Administration of thyroid hormones blocks the releasing action of TRF on the pituitary gland. There is experimental evidence that thyroid hormones stimulate the formation of an inhibitor of TRF action. Whether thyroid hormones also act at the hypothalamus or elsewhere in the nervous system to inhibit TRF secretion is not known.

Purification of TRF from porcine hypothalami[5] and from ovine hypothalami[9] revealed that TRF in both species is a tripeptide whose structural formula is L-pyroglutamy-L-histidyl-L-proline amide. Available evidence indicates that human TRF has an identical structure.[62] The most promising clinical application of TRF is the evaluation of altered TSH secretory reserve in diseases involving the anterior pituitary gland, infundibular stalk or hypothalamus. The availability of TRF now makes it possible to distinguish between hypothalamic and pituitary causes of hypothyroidism. The response to TRF appears specific for TSH and TRF does not increase plasma levels of other anterior pituitary hormones[2] except perhaps prolactin.

Serum TSH levels increase within 10 min. after the intravenous administration of TRF, peak at 20–45 min., then subside rapidly to be gone from the circulation 120–240 min. after injection.[10]

TSH has a molecular weight of about 28,000. TSH circulates without binding to any particular plasma component. It acts on the protease and peptidase enzymes to stimulate the breakdown of thyroglobulin and the release of thyroxine. TSH also stimulates intermediary thyroid metabolism, eventually leading to synthesis of more thyroid hormones and cellular hypertrophy.

OTHER TSH-LIKE SUBSTANCES

A TSH has been extracted from normal human placentas.[36] This substance, human chorionic TSH, is similar to pituitary TSH in its molecular size and its duration of action in the mouse bioassay. It bears a closer immunologic resemblance to bovine than to human pituitary TSH. The role of chorionic TSH in the control of thyroid function in the mother or fetus is unknown. If it were secreted in an autonomous manner during pregnancy, one might expect the levels of pituitary TSH to be undetectable, but levels of pituitary TSH in the mother appear to be normal.[24–25,28–37]

A long acting thyroid stimulator (LATS), a 7S gamma globulin, has been discovered in the blood of patients with hyperthyroidism.[1] LATS is probably secreted by plasma and/or lymphoid cells. LATS differs in several respects from TSH. It is antigenically different. The sedimentation constant of TSH is 4S, whereas LATS associates with 7S gamma globulins. The biological half-life in humans for TSH is approximately 30 min. while that for LATS is approximately 25 days. In mice given radioactive iodine to label the thyroid gland, intravenous injection of TSH causes a peak release of radioactive iodine between 2 and 3 hr. after injection while LATS causes a peak of blood radioactivity between 8 and 16 hr. after injection. Of prime interest to pediatricians is the fact that LATS crosses the placenta while TSH does not. There is a very strong indication that LATS is responsible for transient neonatal hyperthyroidism.[53]

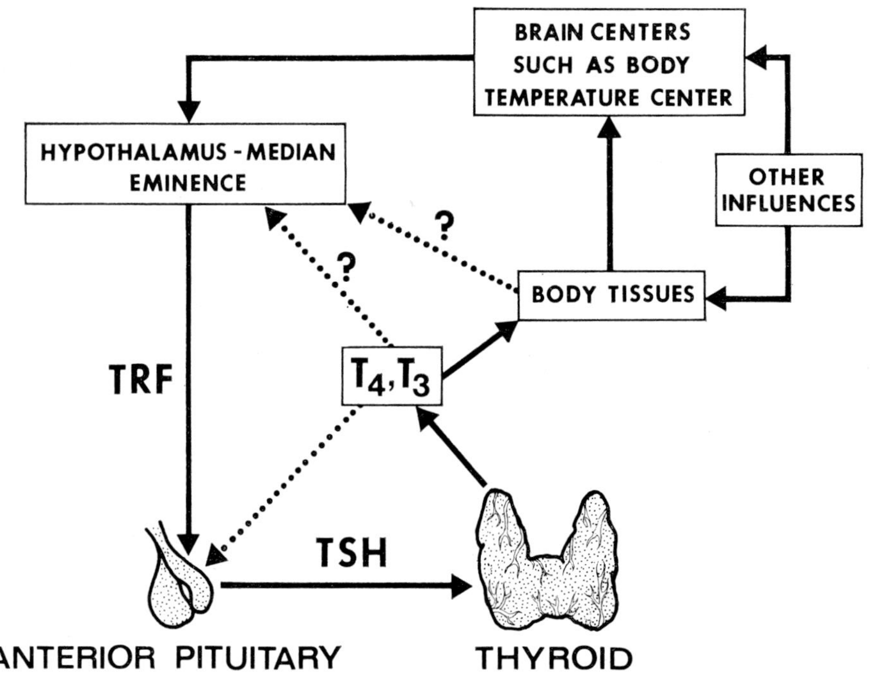

FIG. 1. Hypothalamic-Pituitary-Thyroid Interrelationships

BIOCHEMISTRY AND PHYSIOLOGY OF THYROID HORMONES

Iodine and amino acids are essential substrates for the formation of the thyroid hormones, 3, 5, 3′, 5′-tetraiodothyronine or thyroxine (T_4), and 3, 5, 3′-triiodothyronine (T_3). After iodine is absorbed from the gastrointestinal tract, it enters the iodine pool of the body. From this pool iodine is removed by trapping in the follicular cells of the thyroid gland and through urinary excretion. Immediately after entrance of iodide into the thyroid, iodination of organic compounds occurs. This is dependent upon oxidation of iodide to iodine. Sequential iodination of thyroglobulin-contained tyrosine molecules, first at the 3 and then at the 5 position, promptly occurs to form monoiodotyrosine (MIT) and diiodotyrosine (DIT). These idoinated tyrosines, which are component parts of thyroglobulin, couple with the release of alanine and the formation of T_4 and T_3.

Proteases and peptidases digest thyroglobulin, a complex protein molecule with a molecular weight of 600,000, and consisting of amino acids connected in peptide linkage, releasing iodotyrosines and iodothyronines. A dehalogenase enzyme acts upon the "free" MIT and DIT to release iodine and tyrosine, both of which are probably reincorporated in the synthesis of thyroid hormones. A diagram of the pathway of synthesis of the thyroid hormones is present in Fig. 2: each step is probably enzymatically dependent.

Before proceeding further it is important to review the

methods available for the laboratory evaluation of thyroid function. The PBI measures the iodine in serum which is precipitated with protein. Its determination include MIT, DIT, T_4, T_3 and abnormal iodinated proteins. Organic iodides and high concentrations of inorganic iodies will lead to spurious elevations. The BEI is slightly more specific than the PBI in that it measures T_4 and T_3, but does not include iodoprotein, iodotyrosines or inorganic iodide present in serum and is still subject to contamination by organic iodides. The T_4-by-column determination involves the use of an ion exchange resin for separating the T_4 and T_3 from other iodine-containing material in the serum. It has the added advantage of excluding many, though not all, organic iodide contaminants. The problem of iodine contamination has been eliminated by the introduction of the competitive protein-binding technique for the determination of thyroxine (T_4-CPB). It is a specific and sensitive determination but depends on the thyroxine-binding globulin (TBG) concentration in the serum (as do the previously mentioned determinations). If the TBG level is altered by drug therapy such as estrogen administration, which increases the TBG level, or is altered by different clinical states, the resulting T_4-CPB value will be elevated. Similiarly, the TBG level may be decreased as a consequence of hypoproteinemia, as in the nephrotic syndrome, or by androgen administration, and in these circumstances the PBI, BEI or T_4-CPB values will all be low. In clinical situations where the TBG concentration is abnormal a free thyroxine determination may be obtained. The free T_4 determination is a new sophisticated procedure which measures the concentration of unbound T_4. The test depends on the ability of unbound T_4 to pass a semipermeable membrane during dialysis or ultrafiltration. Serum is enriched with a very low concentration of ^{131}I-labeled T4 and the latter is employed to determine the proportion of endogenous T_4 that is free to traverse the membrane.

The erythrocyte or resin T_3 uptake test is an *in vitro* test which measures the degree of unsaturation of TBG binding sites and does not measure the thyroid hormones themselves. In the resin T_3 uptake test, radioactive T_3 is incubated with the patient's serum, and after equilibrium has been established, the portion of radioactive T_3 not bound to TBG is removed by a resin. A determination is then made of either the amount of radioactive T_3 bound by the resin or the amount remaining in the supernate. When the serum TBG is more saturated such as in hyperthyroidism or has more binding sites occupied by competing agents such as diphenlhydantonin, more radioactive T_3 will be adsorbed by the resin and a high T_3 uptake value is obtained. The converse is true in hypothyroidism or when medications such as estrogens are administered.

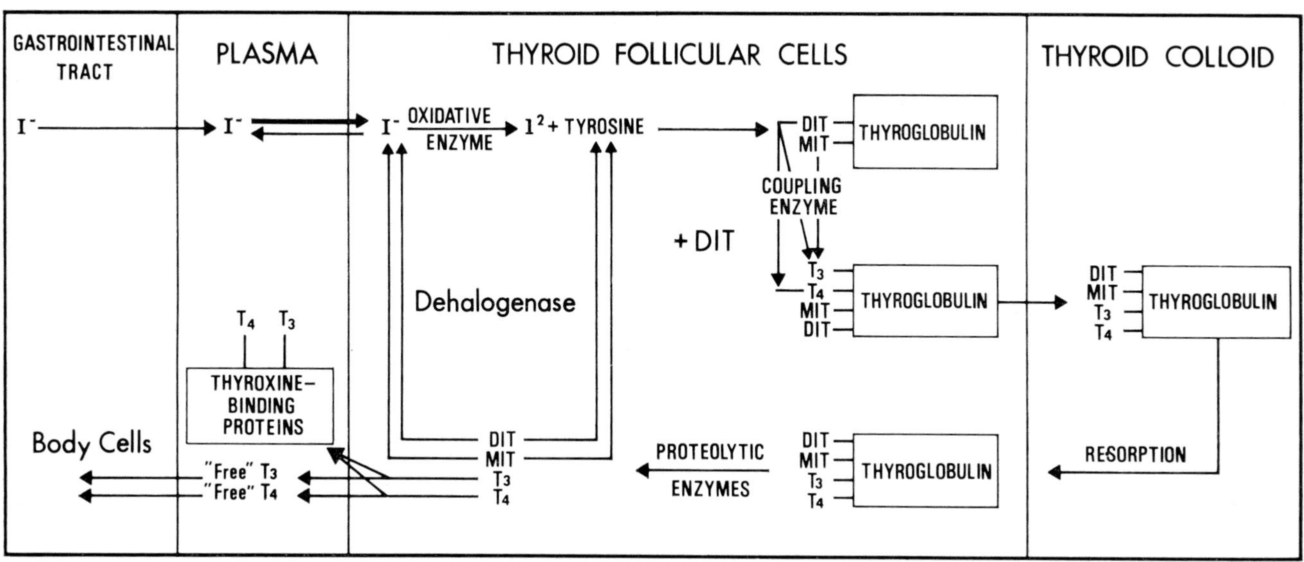

FIG. 2. Diagram of the Biosynthesis of the Thyroid Hormones

Under normal circumstances only T_4 and sometimes T_3 circulate in the serum. Thyroid hormones are almost entirely bound to plasma proteins: less than 0·1 per cent of circulating T_4 and less than 1 per cent of T_3 is in the free (unbound) state.[41] Presumably, the level of free hormone is the main modulator of TSH secretion. Thyroxine is bound to three serum proteins:

(a) TBG, which migrates electrophoretically between the α_1- and α_2-globulins,

(b) thyroxine-binding prealbumin (TPBA), which migrates anodally to albumin during electrophoresis, and

(c) albumin.

The most important of these is TBG, which has the greatest affinity or binding power for thyroxine but the least capacity, since only 20–25 μg is bound per 100 ml. of serum. TBPA has less affinity but greater capacity, 120 μg./100 ml. of serum, and albumin has the least affinity but a physiologically infinite capacity. We have previously mentioned that the circulating thyroxine, as measured by the PBI, BEI, or T_4-CPB determinations is largely dependant upon the TBG capacity. In contrast to thyroxine, triiodothyronine is only loosely bound to TBG. It also binds to albumin but not to TBPA.

FETAL HYPOTHALAMIC-PITUITAR-THYROID INTERRELATIONSHIP

The pituitary-thyroid feed-back system in the fetus and in the mother appear to function independently of each other. Experimentally, it has been shown that maternal and fetal thyroid-stimulating hormones, although active, do not cross the placenta[43,62] Recent data indicate that TSH can be detected by radioimmunoassay in the fetal pituitary gland[28] and in fetal blood[25] at 12 weeks of gestation. There is a progressive increase in fetal pituitary TSH content from 12–24 weeks, and an increase in fetal serum TSH so that term serum levels are reached by 16 weeks of gestation.[31] These changes are possibly brought about by maturation of the hypothalamic neuroendocrine system during this stage of development.

Synthesis of thyroglobulin and iodination of thyroid proteins have been detected at four weeks and 11 weeks of gestation, respectively, so that the initiation of these processes appears to be independent of the hypothalamic-pituitary axis.[29]

Protein-bound iodine has been detected in human fetal serum as early as 13 weeks gestation. Thyroxine as determined by competitive-protein binding and free T_4 have been detected in fetal serum at 78 days gestation.[31] Thyroxine in the serum thus appears approximately one week after the fetal thyroid gland is capable of forming iodothyronines. Serum T_4 and free T_4 levels increase during the 11–24 weeks of gestation.[31] TBG and TBPA have been identified in human fetal serum as early as 74 days gestation. TBG concentrations increase progressively to term. Transplacental passage of estrogens probably contributes to the high serum TBG level in the fetus late in pregnancy.[70] Thus, the increase in fetal serum PBI and T_4 during the latter part of gestation is an effect in part of a rise in TBG levels. The free T_4 concentration increases progressively in fetal serum during the latter half of gestation and at term exceeds the maternal concentration.[23] The normal maternal-fetus thyroid hormone relationships at term are depicted in Fig. 3.

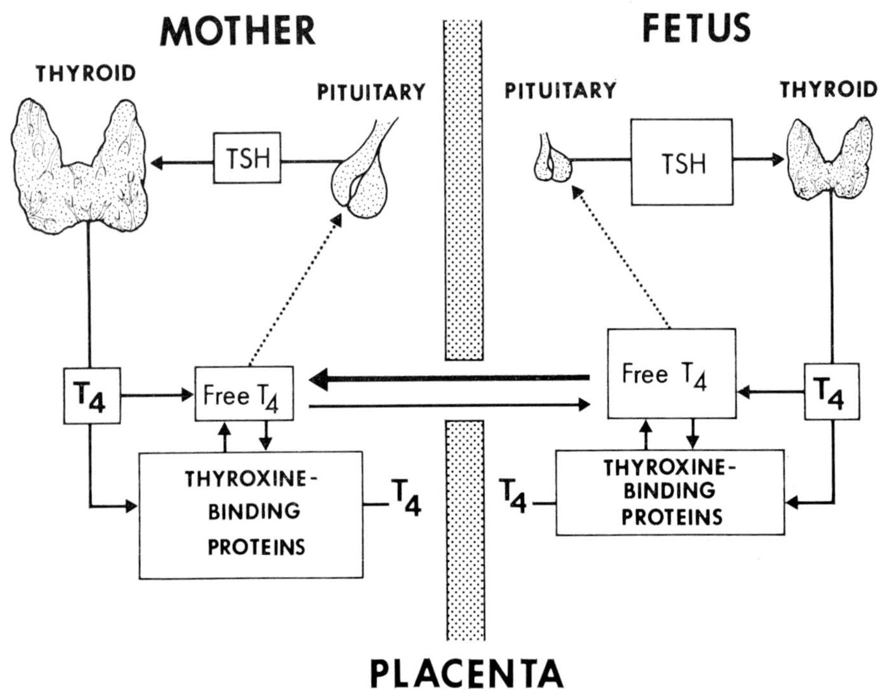

FIG. 3. Schematic Diagram of the Normal Maternal-fetal Thyroid Hormones Relationships.

The role of maternal thyroid hormones in very early fetal development is unknown. In humans, the placenta early in pregnancy is almost impermeable to thyroxine.[57] During the first trimester, the total thyroid hormone needs of the developing embryo must be largely or entirely derived from maternal sources or alternatively, neither fetal nor maternal thyroxine is necessary for early fetal growth. During the second and third trimesters, the fetus becomes more capable of autonomous thyroid hormone synthesis and placental permeability to the thyroid hormones increases.[21,32,67] Maternal thyroid hormone therefore potentially becomes available to the fetus near term. Another barrier to transplacental passage of maternal thyroid hormone to the fetus is the high maternal TBG concentration. Although maternal thyroid hormone may be available to the fetus late in pregnancy it may be inadequate to protect the athyreotic fetus from retardation in osseous and brain maturation.

In humans, the feed-back mechanism between the pituitary and thyroid glands is apparently well established before the 5th fetal month, for a goiter has been reported in the fetus of a thiouracil-treated mother who aborted after 5 months' gestation.[13] The fetal hypothalamic-pituitary-thyroid system apparently is not suppressible by normal or high normal thyroxine levels whereas similar free T_4 in normal children are able to suppress TSH release.

Defective thyroid function and fetal hypothyroidism can result from a number of causes. These include failure of embryonic development of the thyroid gland; ectopically placed thyroid glands; maternal iodine deficiency; inhibition of the synthesis of the thyroid hormones due to transplacental passage of anti-thyroid medications; and deficiency of one of the several enzymes necessary for synthesis of the thyroid hormones.

Recent studies have shown that thyroid antibodies can occur in different thyroid disorders. The demonstration of autoimmunization as a cause of thyroid disease suggested that sporadic athyreotic cretinism might be etiologically related to an autoimmune process. Blizzard and his group[4] demonstrated that 25 per cent of mothers of cretins have circulating antibodies. Antithyroid antibodies can cross the placenta disappearing from the newborn's circulation during the first 2–4 months of life. He also studied cretins born to mothers with and without circulating thyroid antibodies and found that their infants were sometimes normal even though circulating antibodies had crossed the placenta. These studies suggest that some cases of athyreotic cretinism are associated with maternal autoimmune disease of the thyroid, but that circulating antibodies are not destructive to fetal thyroid.

A deficiency in one of the enzymes responsible for synthesis of the thyroid hormones results in congenital goitrous cretinism. The thyroid gland is anatomically normal but enlarged in response to stimulation with TSH which is released through the feed-back mechanism involving the pituitary and thyroid glands. The increase in TSH which occurs in utero may cause a fetal goiter. Not infrequently however, thyroid enlargement, accompanied by signs of hypothyroidism, is not found until later in life. One should remember that enzymatic defects in synthesis of thyroid hormones are generally inherited in an autosomal recessive pattern, and that therefore one of four siblings would be expected to be affected.

In the absence of fetal thyroid function some protective effect from the mother's thyroid occurs, since some thyroid hormone does cross the placenta late in pregnancy. This presumably accounts for the absence of the stigmata of congenital hypothyroidism in the infant until several weeks have passed. Maternal protection is clearly not complete, however, since in utero delay in osseous maturation is frequently found: the high incidence of damage to the central nervous system probably reflects fetal lack of thyroid hormone.

NEONATAL THYROID FUNCTION

At birth the fetal and maternal T_4 levels are within 1·5–2·0 $\mu g\%$ of each other.[11] The changes in thyroid function which occur with age are summarized in Table 1. Some investigators have found higher mean PBI and BEI values in maternal blood at delivery than in cord blood[21,52] while others have found no differences.[7,14,21,53] The serum PBI and BEI levels in newborn infants increase progressively with weight and gestational age.[51,61] These changes are thought to be due, in part, to increased TBG concentrations. TBPA levels are low in the newborn and probably play a minor role in thyroid hormone transport at this time of life.[14,61]

Shortly after birth an increase in thyroid activity becomes apparent. Twenty-four hour thyroidal uptake of ^{131}I average around 70 per cent during the first 2 days of life and then decrease rapidly to 10–40 per cent by 5 days of age.[19] The PBI and BEI levels in the sera of newborn term infants increase progressively following birth.[12,23,61,63] Peak values for PBI of 8–16 $\mu g\%$ are observed within 48 hr. of birth. Similar increments in PBI levels are seen in the sera of premature newborns, but the peak levels are significantly lower than those found in term infants.[14] The PBI concentrations decrease after the first week of life so that by the 6th to 12th week of life, the concentrations are the same as those seen in normal children.[12] The BEI concentration in newborns may increase 80 per cent over the cord concentrations, as high as 10 $\mu g\%$ by the 5th day of life. After the 5th day of life values decline and they approach "normal" levels by 20 days of age.[63]

The increases in serum thyroid hormones following birth are associated with a marked increase in T_3 erythrocyte uptake,[22,50] and free T_4 concentration.[52] The T_3 erythrocyte values reach their peak by the 4th to 9th day of life falling subsequently to within the adult range by 6–9 weeks of life. The elevation of erythrocyte T_3 uptake is more marked and more prolonged in the premature infant. All of the changes described in the neonatal period are associated with a marked increase in serum TSH concentration during the early neonatal period.

In the newborn infant there is a large increase in serum TSH concentration at the time of birth. The increase is probably already occurring at the time of delivery, or existed previously in utero, because TSH levels of umbilical cord blood are higher than those of maternal blood, the mean difference in various studies being 2·8–5·6 $\mu U/ml.$[24,37] An acute increase in TSH levels occurs within the first minutes of life. TSH levels in cord sera range between 2·1 and 10·7 $\mu U/ml.$, and peak values between 25 and 183 $\mu U/ml.$ are noted between 15 and 30 min. following delivery.[11] Thereafter the serum TSH levels gradually decrease to normal childhood levels by 48–72 hr. of life.[24] Beyond the newborn period, serum TSH levels do not appear to change very much with age.

The explanation for this striking increase in TSH levels is obscure. The stress of vaginal delivery is not the stimulus for TSH secretion, since babies born by cesarean section present the same TSH release phenomenon.[24] There is evidence that the increase in TSH levels, at least in part, may be due to the drop in body temperature experienced by the newborn during the first hours of life.[22] These same investigators have shown that prevention of neonatal cooling minimizes the usual marked increase in PBI on the first 2 days of life. In addition, they have demonstrated that acute cooling of the newborn at 3 hr. of age evokes a further increase in serum TSH concentration.[24] Warming

TABLE 1

THYROID FUNCTION VALUES AT DIFFERENT AGES

Age	*Thyroid Weight* gms.	*Protein-bound Iodine* μg%		BEI or T_4-by *column* μg%		*Free* T_4 ng%	*Thyroxine-binding Globulin* μg%		TSH U units/ml.		T_3 *Uptake Test* %		*Age*
	Mean ± S.D. (a)	*Mean* ± S.E.	*Range*	*Mean* ± S.D.	*Range*	*Mean* ± S.D.	*Mean* ± S.D.	*Range*	*Mean* ± S.D.	*Range*	*Mean* ± S.D.	*Range*	
Maternal		7·4 ± 0·4 (c)	5·9–10·0 (c)	14·2 ± 2·6 (a)		3·37 ± 0·64 (b)	46·3 ± 14·1 (b)		2·0 ± 1·3 (a)				Maternal
Cord		6·8 ± 0·4 (c)	4·5–9·4 (c)	12·6 ± 4·0 (a)		3·57 ± 0·84 (b)	24·7 ± 5·1 (b)		3·5 ± 2·5 (a)		16·3 (j)		Cord
		Mean ± S.D. (e)											
Newborn	1·5 ± 0·7	8·3 ± 2·4			7·2–15·2 (g)	5·4 ± 0·3 (d)							Newborn
12–24 hr.		10·1 ± 1·4								8·6–18·0 (b)			12–24 hr.
1–3 days		12·0 ± 2·4				8·6 ± 0·4 (d)				5·0–16·0 (b)			1–3 days
3–7 days		10·9 ± 1·8		9·9 ± 2·1 (i)	7·3–9·9 (g)						19·8 (j)		3–7 days
1–5 weeks	1·4 ± 0·6	7·4 ± 1·8		4·6 ± 0·32 (i)							17·5 (j)		1–5 weeks
6–12 weeks		6·9 ± 1·8										11·2–23·7 (k)	6–12 weeks
12–52 weeks	2·0 ± 0·9	6·3 ± 1·0									13·2 (j)		12–52 weeks
		Mean* (f)		Mean ± S.E. (h)		Mean ± S.E.							
0·1–2 years	2·6 ± 1.4	6·30		6·15 ± 0·21							1–2 years 22·5 ± 6·3 (k)	1–2 years 14·6–32·9 (k)	0·1–2 years
2–4 years	3·9 ± 2	6·15		6·01 ± 0·19							17·6 ± 5·5 (k)	8·9–21·4 (k)	2–4 years
4–6 years		6·05		6·04 ± 0·18									4–6 years
6–8 years	5·3 ± 2·1	5·75		5·64 ± 0·22			25 ± 0·01 (l)	19–32 (l)			15·8 ± 2·3 (k)	11·8–21·7 (k)	6–8 years
8–10 years		5·55		5·38 ± 0·12						<1·25–7·0 (b)			8–10 years
10–12 years	9·6 ± 5·1	5·25		4·99 ± 0·09		5·3 ± 0·4 (d)							10–12 years
12–14 years		4·95		4·79 ± 0·08							17·2 ± 2·8 (k)	13·8–22 2 (k)	12–14 years
14–16 years	14·2 ± 5·2	4·85		4·81 ± 0·07									14–16 years
16–18 years		4·90		5·00 ± 0·09									16–18 years

* Values given are for males, values for females are approximately 0·2 μg% higher (f).

Sources of data: a = ref. 42; b = ref. 11; c = ref. 24; d = ref. 52; e = ref. 12; f = ref. 26; g = ref. 51; h = ref. 56; i = ref. 63; j = ref. 50; k = ref. 45; l = ref. 33

TABLE 2

THYROID FUNCTION VALUES RELATED TO DEVELOPMENT STAGE IN ADOLESCENT MALES

	Stages of Sexual Maturation				
	1	2	3	4	5
Protein-bound iodine (A) (μg%, mean ± S.E.)	5·3 ± 0·2	5·1 ± 0·3	4·7 ± 0·2	5·2 ± 0·2	5·0 ± 0·2
T_4 iodine (B) (μg%, mean)	5·0	3·6	3·6	3·8	4·5
Free T_4 (C) ng%, mean)	2·2				2·0
Thyroxine-binding globulin (A) (μg%, mean ± S.E.)	24 ± 0·7	24 ± 1·0	20 ± 1·2	21 ± 0·6	21 ± 0·7
TBPA (A) (μg%, mean ± S.E.)	190 ± 8	203 ± 8	241 ± 13	233 ± 9	266 ± 21
T_4 half-life (D) (days)			5·32		5·82

Sources of data: (A) = ref. 30; (B) = ref. 68; (C) = ref. 41; (D) = ref. 38.

the newborn just after birth does not prevent the TSH peak from occurring. A satisfactory explanation of the acute TSH release phenomenon observed immediately following birth awaits further study.

The changes in thyroid function in the newborn discussed above have an application of practical importance in the early diagnosis of hypothyroidism in the newborn and provide a basis for the proper interpretation of function tests in this period of life.

THYROID FUNCTION DURING INFANCY AND CHILDHOOD

In early infancy the mean PBI concentration is about 6·3 μg%.[12] The serum concentrations decrease progressively to a mean value of approximately 5·3 μg% until adolescence begins.[20] The mean PBI of females exceeds that of males by approximately 0·2 μg%.[56] The normal range for BEI concentration in children up to 10 years of age is *higher* (mean for boys, 5·6 μg%; mean for girls 5·4 μg%) than for adults (mean for men 5·0 μg%; mean for women 4·5 μg%).[49]

During infancy and childhood the free T_4 concentrations[52] and erythrocyte T_3 uptake values[20,45] are higher than those observed in normal adults. It has been previously mentioned that the erythrocyte uptake of T_3 is a reflection of the binding capacity of the serum protein carriers for thyroid hormones. Thus, uptake is greater when binding capacity is reduced. It has been demonstrated that in children 2–12 years of age the measured T_4-binding capacity of TBG is higher than in young adults, and the binding capacities of TBPA varied inversely.[7]

Beyond the newborn period, TSH levels do not appear to change very much with age. There does not appear to be any sex-dependent variation in serum TSH.[37] The use of TRF in evaluating TSH release from the anterior pituitary gland has been discussed earlier. TRF is a rapid and potent stimulus of pituitary TSH release in normal children and provides a means of distinguishing between hypothalamic and pituitary causes of hypothyroidism.[10] Serum TSH levels in normal children, 5–12 years of age, have been reported to range from undetectable levels to 7·0 μU/ml.[11]

THYROID FUNCTION DURING ADOLESCENCE

Thyroid function during adolescence has been studies in relation to chronological age as well as to the stage of sexual maturation. The most commonly used method of staging of sexual maturation is that of Tanner.[80] All ratings are on a scale of 1 to 5, stage 1 represents the prepubescent state; stage 3 represents a period of intense rapid growth and development; while stage 5 represents the end of the adolescent growth spurt. It should be remembered that not all adolescents at the same chronological age are at the same stage of sexual maturation. It therefore may be more appropriate to correlate thyroid function with the degree of sexual maturation rather than with chronological age during adolescence (Tables 2 and 3).

The PBI concentrations in adolescence decrease to nadir values at 12–14 years of age.[56] The PBI concentrations

TABLE 3

THYROID FUNCTION VALUES RELATED TO DEVELOPMENTAL STAGE IN ADOLESCENT FEMALES

	Stages of Sexual Maturation				
	1	2	3	4	5
Protein-bound iodine (A) (μg%, mean ± S.E.)	6·2 ± 0·4	5·2 ± 0·2	5·2 ± 0·2	5·1 ± 0·3	5·5 ± 0·4
T_4 iodine (B) (μg%)	5·2	4·5	4·6	4·3	4·5
Thyroxine-binding globulin (A) (μg%, mean ± S.E.)	26 ± 2·3	25 ± 1·4	23 ± 0·7	24 ± 1·5	22 ± 1·1
TBPA (A) (μg%, mean ± S.E.)	181 ± 14	219 ± 1	203 ± 11	266 ± 15	245 ± 18

Sources of data: (A) = ref. 30; (B) = ref. 68.

subsequently rise to adult levels from 14–16 years of age. The PBI and T_4 concentrations are lower in the adolescent male than in the adolescent female at comparable ages.[30,68] The nadir value is reached in adolescent boys at stage 3 of sexual maturation and rise at stage 5 as maturity is completed. The lowest level of T_4 is associated with the period of greatest maturation in the adolescent growth spurt. The nadir value in adolescent girls is reached at stage 4 of sexual maturation. Free T_4 concentrations are decreased in adolescents as compared to adults, and particularly at stage 5 of sexual maturation.[47]

A decline in TBG and increase in TBPA capacities occur during the transition from adolescence to the adult stage.[16,30,47] Males at stage 1 of sexual maturation have reduced TBPA maximal binding capacity and blood concentration of TBPA.[47] TBPA-binding capacities in adolescent males 13–16 years of age[15] and at stage 1 of sexual maturation[41] are lower than those of normal adults. These levels rise by 17–18 years of age[16] and stage 5 of maturation[47] and are near the values of normal adults. It would seem, therefore, that significant low TBPA-binding capacities coincide with the growth spurt in the adolescent. As sexual maturation is completed in the adolescent, the value of TBPA approaches that of the normal adult. The serum concentration of T_4 change directly with the changes in TBG binding capacity. In view of the fact that hormones with predominantly androgenic or anabolic activity decrease the binding activity of TBG and tend to increase that of TBPA,[8] it may be that such age-related changes in the binding proteins are related to changes in gonadal activity which occur during adolescence.

The mean biological half-life of thyroxine in the serum of children is approximately 4·9 days[33] and for adolescents approximately 5·3 days.[38] The biological half-life of triiodothyronine in the serum of children is approximately 1·6 days,[38] that for adolescents has not been determined. The mean biological half-life of thyroxine in the serum of adults is 6·7 days and that for triiodothyronine is 2·6 days.[77] The decreased affinity of the serum proteins for tiriodothyronine as compared to thyroxine probably accounts for the difference in half-life between these two thyroid hormones.

CLINICAL MANIFESTATIONS OF SOME THYROID GLAND DYSFUNCTIONS

The thyroid hormones act upon various enzyme systems to affect the expenditure of total body energy. As a result of the actions of thyroid hormones on enzyme systems and metabolic processes the functions of various organ systems increase with excesses and decrease with deficiencies of the thyroid hormones. The cardiac output and heart rate are increased with hyperthyroidism and decreased with hypothyroidism. The renal glomerular filtration rate, plasma flow, and water excretion are decreased in hypothyroidism and increased in hyperthyroidism. The central nervous system has altered physiologic responses to thyroid deficiency or excess.

Hypothyroidism

Newborns with hypothyroidism may differ, depending on the severity and duration of the condition prior to diagnosis and treatment. Severe mental retardation as well as neurologic *sequelae* such as ataxia, incoordination, and convulsions are not uncommon in severely affected newborns, whereas those newborns with mild hypothyroidism may have moderate mental retardation and no neurologic *sequelae*.[75] In complete athyrotic newborns, symptoms may be present at birth but more commonly appear within the first or second month of life. The infant appears inactive, feeds poorly and is constipated. The skin is pale, cool and has a dusky appearance. The facial features become coarse and puffy and the tongue broad and thick. When there are less complete degrees of congenital hypothyroidism these characteristics and easily recognizable features may not appear for many months and there may be great retardation in growth and development.

Patients who develop hypothyroidism during later childhood or during adolescence differ considerably from the newborns with hypothyroidism and from each other depending on the stage of development which they had attained before the onset of the hypothyroidism. Symptoms usually appear gradually over a number of years. There is a slowing up of the general activities and energy and frequently there is loss of appetite and constipation. Growth and development come almost to a standstill and the child retains the juvenile appearance which he presented at the onset of the hypothyroidism. Sexual maturation fails to progress the hypothyroid adolescent. In spite of some physical and mental sluggishness mental impairment is rare when hypothyroidism begins after two years of age.[75]

The dosage of desiccated thyroid or one of its analogues in treating hypothyroidism is determined by both the age and clinical condition of the patient. Desiccated thyroid which has been standardized, sodium L-thyroxine and triiodothyronine are available for use as therapy. Synthetic preparations such as sodium L-thyroxine may be used if one doubts the potency of the desiccated thyroid preparation, but we do not believe that it has any other special virtue. Triiodothyronine which acts more quickly and has a shorter half-life than does either desiccated thyroid or sodium L-thyroxine may be dangerous because of its rapidity of action especially in the very young myxedematous infant.

The objective of treatment is to establish euthyroidism as rapidly as is safe for the patient. In the very young infant, one usually begins therapy with desiccated thyroid in a daily dose of 15 mg. and this is increased by increments of 15 mg. approximately every 7 days. In the grossly myxedematous young infant, therapy may have to begin with a dosage of 8 mg. daily. In infants under one year of age daily doses of 45–60 mg. are usually adequate to maintain euthyroidism as judged by normal growth, development and activity. The ultimate dose is determined on the basis of the clinical state and normal thyroid function tests. The PBI levels remain in the normally accepted range when euthyroidism is achieved with desiccated thyroid. In the older child, the initial dose may be 30 mg. daily. Children between 1 and 3 years of age usually require 75–120 mg. daily and older patients may need 150–180 m g. daily. When treatment is adequate, physiologic evidence of hypothyroidism disappear rapidly.

Sodium L-thyroxine may be used and each 0·1 mg. is equivalent to approximately 60 mg. of desiccated thyroid. When sodium L-thyroxine therapy, the PBI may be as high as 10–14 $\mu g\%$ when the patient is euthyroid. We believe that the use of triiodothyronine offers little therapeutic advantage over the other available thyroid hormones. As stated above, it may be dangerous in the severely myxedematous patient because it can restore a patient to a euthyroid level more rapidly than his myxedematous heart can tolerate. With triiodothyronine therapy, the PBI is 1–2 $\mu g\%$ when the patient is euthyroid.

It should be emphasized that approximately 75 per cent of patients with lingual thyroid glands do not have any other functional thyroid tissue. It is most likely that goiter formation in an ectopic thyroid occurs when the circulating level of thyroid hormones become insufficient to meet the metabolic demands of the body. This insufficiency results in increased TSH release and secondary thyroid hypertrophy. The patient may appear to be clinically euthyroid but may be biochemically hypothyroid.

All euthyroid as well as hypothyroid patients with ectopic thyroid glands should have a trial of full replacement thyroid hormone therapy before excision of the thyroid tissue is contemplated.[39] Thyroid hormone therapy should prevent hypertrophy and hyperplasia by decreasing TSH release and stimulation. Surgery should be reserved for those patients in whom dysphagia or dysphonia fail to respond to adequate thyroid hormone therapy or in those patients with secondary ulceration or hemorrhage in their ectopically placed thyroid glands.

Hyperthyroidism

It has been previously mentioned that LATS is thought to be causally related to neonatal hyperthyroidism. In every instance of this rare condition the mother has been hyperthyroid during pregnancy or gives a past history of hyperthyroidism.[79] The clinical features of neonatal hyperthyroidism may include prematurity, goiter, exophtahlmos, hyperirritability, congestive heart failure, jaundice, hepatosplenomegaly and thrombocytopenia.[18] It is impossible to state the role LATS plays in the cause of the jaundice, hepatosplenomegaly or thrombocytopenia.

The onset of manifestations of hyperthyroidism in the newborn can be variable. The infant may be hyperthyroid at birth or may rarely become so as late as six weeks after delivery. Not all of the signs mentioned above have been present in each reported hyperthyroid newborn. Treatment of the disease and its complications may be required during the active stage of the hyperthyroidism. The disease in the newborn is self-limited, and the rate of disappearance of the signs of neonatal hyperthyroidism is consistent with the half-life of LATS and of passively transferred maternal antibody.[79]

The presenting symptoms in the child or adolescent with hyperthyroidism usually include loss of weight, nervousness, irritability, emotional lability, deterioration in school performance, weakness, palpitations, heat intolerance and an increased number of bowel movements. Exophthalmos, tachycardia, a widened pulse pressure, goiter and tremors of outstretched extremities are frequently present. In girls menstrual irregularities are not uncommon. As was mentioned in the discussion of hypothyroidism, the presenting findings in hyperthyroidism also differ, depending on the severity and duration of the condition prior to diagnosis.

Effects of Malnutrition

The tendency of malnutrition to alter the function of various endocrine glands has been observed in both human beings and experimental animals. Malnutrition, if severe, and whether produced by starvation or by malabsorption, is associated with low plasma proteins, including the thyroxine-binding proteins. Coincident with this the PBI and T_4 levels are depressed.[44] Malnutrition may also be associated with functional hypopituitarism:[60] thus thyroidal uptake of^{131} is often below normal, suggesting that TSH production is depressed;[66] the thyroid gland is smaller in the malnourished infant than in the normal infant.[78] But there is absence of histological changes suggesting that thyroid function may be unchanged even in fatal cases of malnutrition.[78] It is important to note that hypothyroidism is not present clinically in malnutrition.

Effects of X-irradiation

Increased sensitivity of infants' and children's thyroid glands to the development of neoplastic changes from radiation exposure has been amply demonstrated. A series of retrospective and prospective studies have clearly shown the causal relation of irradiation of the head and neck in infants and children to the later development of thyroid cancers, adenomas, and nodules.[17,34–35,65] It has been pointed out that cell division in the growing thyroid gland of the infant and child may be a factor in this increased sensitivity to irradiation.[15] On the average, 3–4 cell divisions are assumed to occur as the infant thyroid gland grows to adult size.[54] It thus seems reasonable to consider the enhanced carcinogenic effect of irradiation in children to be due to the division of cells whose nuclei have previously been injured by radiation. Presumably, the adult gland would not be as prone to such radiation effects, because cell division is not believed to occur normally in the mature gland.[46]

Abbreviations

BEI	Butanol-extractable iodine
DIT	Diiodotyrosine
LATS	Long-acting thyroid stimulator
MIT	Monoiodotyrosine
PBI	Protein-bound iodine
T_3	Triiodothyronine
T_4	Thyroxine
T_4-CPB	Thyroxine as measured by competitive-protein binding

TBG Thyroxine-binding globulin
TBPA Thyroxine-binding prealbumin
TRF Thyrotropin-releasing factor
TSH Thyroid-stimulating hormone

REFERENCES

1. Adams, D. D. (1958), "Presence of Abnormal Thyroid-stimulating Hormone in Serum of Some Thyrotoxic Patients," *J. clin. Endocr. and Metab.*, **18,** 699–712.
2. Anderson, M. S., Bowers, C. Y., Kastin, A. J., Schalch, D. S., Schally, A. V., Synder, P. J., Itiger, R. D., Wilber, J. F. and Wise, A. J. (1971), "Synthetic Thyrotropin-releasing Hormone: A Potent Stimulator of Thyrotropin Secretion in Man," *New Engl. J. Med.*, **285,** 1279–1283.
3. Andreoli, M. and Robbins, J. (1962), "Serum Proteins and Thyroxine-protein Interaction in Early Human Fetuses," *J. clin. Endocr. and Metab.*, **41,** 1070–1077.
4. Blizzard, R. M., Chandler, R. W., Landing, B. H., Pettit, M. D. and West, C. D. (1960), "Maternal Autoimmunization to Thyroid as a Probable Cause of Athyrotic Cretinism," *New Engl. J. Med.*, **263,** 327–336.
5. Bowers, C. Y., Schally, A. V., Enzmann, F., Boler, J. and Folders, K. (1970), "Porcine Thyrotropin Releasing Hormone is (Pyro) Glu-His-Pro(NH_2)," *Endocrinology*, **86,** 1143–1153.
6. Boyd, J. D. (1964), "Development of the Human Thyroid Gland," in *The Thyroid*, pp. 9–31 (R. Pitt-Rivers and W. R. Trotter, Eds.). Washington: Butterworth & Co.
7. Braverman, L. E., Dawner, N. A. and Ingbar, S. H. (1966), "Observations Concerning the Binding of Thyroid Hormones in Sera of Normal Subjects of Varying Ages," *J. clin. Invest.*, **45,** 1273–1279.
8. Braverman, L. E., Foster, A. E. and Ingbar, S. H. (1967), "Sex-related Differences in Binding in Serum of Thyroid Hormones," *J. clin. Endocr. and Metab.*, **27,** 227–232.
9. Burgus, R., Dunn, T. F., Desiderio, D. M., Ward, D. N., Vale, W., Guillemin, R., Felix, A. M., Gillessen, D. and Struder, R. O. (1970), "Biological Activity of Synthetic Polypeptide Derivatives Related to the Structure of Hypothalamic TRF," *Endocrinology*, **86,** 573–582.
10. Costom, B. H., Grumbach, M. M. and Kaplan, S. L. (1971), "Effect of Thyrotropin-releasing Factor on Serum Thyroid-stimulating Hormone: An Approach to Distinguishing Hypothalamic from Pituitary Forms of Idiopathic Hypopituitary Dwarfism," *J. clin. Invest.*, **50,** 2219–2225.
11. Czerichow, P., Greenberg, A. H., Tyson, J. and Blizzard, R. M. (1971), "Thyroid Function Studies in Paired Maternal-cord Sera and Sequential Observations of Thyrotropic Hormone Release During the First 72 hr. of Life," *Pediat. Res.*, **5,** 53–58.
12. Danowski, T. S., Johnston, S. Y., Price, W. C., Mickelvy, M., Stevenson, S. S. and McCluskey, E. R. (1951), "Protein-bound Iodine in Infants from Birth to One Year of Life," *Pediatrics*, **7,** 240–244.
13. Davis, L. and Forbes, W. (1944), "Effect of Anti-thyroid Drugs on the Fetus," *Lancet*, **2,** 740–742.
14. Denayer, P. H., Malvaux, P., Van Den Schrieck, H. G., Beckers, C. and De Visscher, M. (1966), "Free Thyroxine in Maternal and Cord Blood," *J. clin. Endocr. and Metab.*, **26,** 233–235.
15. Doniach, I. (1958), "Experimental Induction of Tumors of Thyroid by Radiation," *Brit. med. Bull.*, **14,** 181–183.
16. Dreyer, D. J. and Man, E. B. (1962), "Thyroxine-binding Proteins and Butanolextractable Iodine in Sera of Adolescent Males," *J. clin. Endocr. and Metab.*, **22,** 31–37.
17. Duffy, B. J., Jr. and Fritzgerald, P. J. (1950), "Thyroid Cancer in Childhood and Adolescence: Report of 28 Cases," *Cancer*, **3,** 1018–1032.
18. Elsas, L. J., Whittemore, R. and Burrow, G. N. (1967), Maternal and Neonatal Graves' Disease," *J.A.M.A.*, **200,** 250–252.
19. Fisher, D. A., Oddie, T. H. and Burroughs, J. C. (1962), "Thyroidal Radioiodine Uptake Rate Measurement in Infants," *Amer. J. Dis. Child*, **103,** 738–749.
20. Fisher, D. A., Oddie, T. H. and Wait, J. C. (1964), "Thyroid Function Tests. Findings in Arkansas Children and Young Adults," *Amer. J. Dis. Child.*, **107,** 282–287.
21. Fisher, D. A., Lehman, H. and Lackey, C. (1964), "Placental Transport of Thyroxine," *J. clin. Endocr. and Metab.*, **24,** 393–400.
22. Fisher, D. A. and Oddie, T. H. (1964), "Neonatal Thyroidal Hyperactivity: Response to Cooling," *Amer. J. Dis. Child,*. **107,** 574–581.
23. Fisher, D. A., Odells, W. D., Hobel, C. J. and Garza, R. (1969), "Thyroid Function in the Term Fetus," *Pediatrics*, **44,** 526–535.
24. Fisher, D. A. and Odell, W. D. (1969), "Acute Release of Thyrotropin in the Newborn," *J. clin. Invest.*, **48,** 1670–1677.
25. Fisher, D. A., Hobel, C. J., Garza, R. and Pierce, C. A. (1970), "Thyroid Function in the Preterm Fetus," *Pediatrics*, **46,** 208–216.
26. Fisher, D. A. (1971), "Thyroid Function Test," in *The Thyroid*, pp. 292–296 (S. C. Werner and S. H. Ingbar, Eds.). New York: Harper & Row.
27. Foster, G. V., MacIntyre, I. and Pearse, A. G. E. (1964), "Calcitonin Production in the Mitochrondion-rich Cells of the Dog Thyroid," *Nature*, **203,** 1029–1040.
28. Fukunchi, M., Inoue, T., Abe, H. and Kumahara, Y., "Thyrotropin in Human Fetal Pituitaries," *J. clin. Endocr. and Metab.*, **31,** 565–569.
29. Gıtlin, D. and Biasucci, A. (1969), "Ontogenesis of Immunoreactive Thyroglobul in the Human Conceptus," *J. clin. Endocr. and Metab.*, **29,** 849–853.
30. Goldsmith, R. E., Rauh, J. L., Kloth, R. and Dahlgren, J. (1967), "Observations on the Relationship Between the Maximal Thyroxine Binding Capacities of Thyroxine-binding Interalpha Globulin and Thyroxine-binding Prealbumin, the Serum Protein-bound Iodine Concentration and Sexual Maturity in Adolescents," *Acta Endocr.*, **54,** 495–504.
31. Greenberg, A. H., Czernichow, P., Reba, R. C., Tyson, J. and Blizzard, R. M. (1970), "Observations on the Maturation of Thyroid Function in Early Fetal Life," *J. clin. Invest.*, **49,** 1790–1803.
32. Grumbach, M. M. and Werner, S. C. (1956), "Transfer of Thyroid Hormone Across the Human Placenta at Term," *J. clin. Endocr. and Metab.*, **16,** 1392–1395.
33. Haddad, H. M. (1960), "Studies on Thyroid Metabolism in Children," *J. Pediat.*, **57,** 391–398.
34. Hagler, S., Rosenblum, P. and Rosenblum, A. (1966), "Carcinoma of the Thyroid in Children and Young Adults: Iatrogenic Relation to Previous Irradiation," *Pediatrics*, **38,** 77–81.
35. Hempelmann, L. H. (1968), "Risk of Thyroid Neoplasma After Irradiation in Childhood," *Science*, **160,** 159–163.
36. Hershmann, J. M. and Sternes, W. R. (1969), "Extraction and Characterization of a Thyrotopic Material from the Human Placenta," *J. clin. Invest.*, **48,** 923–929.
37. Hershmann, J. M. and Pittman, J. A., Jr. (1971), "Utility of the Radioimmunoassay of Serum Thyrotropin in Man," *ann. Int. Med.*, **74,** 481–490.
38. Hung, W., Gancayco, G. P. and Heald, F. P. (1965), "Radiothyroxine Metabolism in Euthyroid Adolescent Males in Different Stages of Sexual Maturation," *Pediatrics*, **35,** 76–81.
39. Hung, W., Randolph, J. G., Sabitini, D. and Winship, T. (1966), "Lingual and Sublingual Thyroid Glands in Euthyroid Children," *Pediatrics*, **38,** 647–651.
40. Hung, W. (1969), "Effect of Maternal Thyrotoxicosis on the Fetus and Newborn," *J. nat. med. Ass.*, **61,** 70–73.
41. Ingbar, S. H., Braverman, L. E., Dawber, N. A. and Lee, G. Y. (1965), "A New Method for Measuring Free Thyroxine in Human Serum and an Analysis of the Factors That Influence its Concentration," *J. clin. Invest.*, **44,** 1679–1689.
42. Kay, C., Abrahams, S. and Mclain, P. (1966), "The Weight of Normal Thyroid Glands in Children," *Arch. Path.*, **82,** 349–352.
43. Knobil, E. and Josinovich, J. B. (1959), "Placental Transfer of Thyrotrophic Hormone, Thyroxine, Triiodothyronine and Insulin in the Rat," *Ann. New York Acad. Sci.*, **75,** 895–904.

44. Krieger, I. and Good, M. H. (1970), "Adrenocortical and Thyroid Function in the Deprivation Syndrome," *Amer. J. Dis. Child.*, **120**, 95–102.

45. Kunstadter, R. H., Buchman, H., Jacobson, M. and Oliner, L. (1962), "The Thyroid in Children. 11. *In Vitro* Erythrocyte Uptake of Radioactive L-triiodothyronine," *Pediatrics*, **30**, 27–31.

46. Leblond, C. P. and Walker, B. E. (1956), "Renewal of Cell Populations," *Physiol. Rev.*, **36**, 255–276.

47. Malvaux, P., De Nayer, P. H., Beckers, C., Van Den Schrieck, H. G. and De Visscher, M. (1966), "Serum Free Thyroxine and Thyroxine Binding Proteins in Male Adolescents," *J. clin. Endocr. and Metab.*, **26**, 459–462.

48. Man, E. B., Pickering, D. E., Walker, J. and Cooke, R. E. (1952), "Butanolextractable Iodine in the Serum of Infants," *Pediatrics*, **9**, 32–37.

49. Man, E. B. (1962), "Differences in Serum Butanol-Extractable Iodines (BEIs) of Children, Men and Women," *J. Lab. clin. Med.*, **59**, 528–532.

50. Marks, J., Wolfson, J. and Klein, R. (1961), "Neonatal Thyroid Function: Erythrocyte T_3 Uptake in Early Infancy," *J. Pediat.*, **58**, 32–38.

51. Marks, A. N. and Man, E. B. (1965), "Serum Butanol-extractable Idione Concentrations in Prematures," *Pediatrics*, **35**, 753–758.

52. Marks, J. F., Hamlin, M. and Zack, P. (1966), "Neonatal Thyroid Function. 11. Free Thyroxine in Infancy," *J. Pediat.*, **68**, 559–561.

53. McKenzie, J. M. (1964), "Neonatal Graves' Disease," *J. clin. Endocr. and Metab.*, **24**, 660–668.

54. Mochizuki, Y., Mowafy, R. and Pasternack, B. (1963), "Weights of Human Thyroids in New York City," *Health Physics*, **9**, 1299–1301.

55. Odell, W. D., Utiger, R. D., Wilber, J. F. and Condliffe, P. G. (1967), "Estimation of the Secretion Rate of Thyrotropin in Man," *J. clin. Invest.*, **46**, 953–959.

56. Oddie, T. H. and Fisher, D. A. (1967), "Protein-bound Iodine Level During Childhood and Adolescence," *J. clin. Endocr. and Metab.*, **27**, 89–92.

57. Osorio, C. and Myant, N. B. (1960), "The Passage of Thyroid Hormone From Mother to Foetus and its Relation to Foetal Development," *Brit. med. Bull.*, **16**, 159–164.

58. Pearse, A. G. E. (1952), "The Cytochemistry and Cytology of the Normal Anterior Hypophysis Investigated by the Trichrome-periodic and Acid-Schiff Method," *J. Path. Bact.*, **64**, 811–826.

59. Pearse, A. G. E. and Carvalheira, A. F. (1967), "Cytochemical Evidence for an Ultimobranchial Origin of Rodent Thyroid C Cells," *Nature*, **214**, 929–930.

60. Perloff, W. H., Lasche, E. M., Nodine, J. H., Schneeberg, N. G. and Vieillard, C. B. (1954), "The Starvation State and Functional Hypopituitarism," *J.A.M.A.*, **155**, 1307–1313.

61. Perry, R. E., Hodgman, J. E. and Starr, P. (1965), "Maternal, Cord and Serial Venous Blood Protein Bound Iodine, Thyroid Binding Globulin, Thyroid-binding, Albumin and Prealbumin in Premature Infants," *Pediatrics*, **35**, 759–764.

62. Peterson, R. R. and Young, W. C. (1952), "The Problem of Placental Permeability for Thyrotropin, Propylthiouracil and Thyroxine in the Guinea Pig," *Endocrinology*, **50**, 218–225.

63. Pickering, D. E., Kontaxis, N. E., Benson, R. C. and Meechan, R. J. (1958), "Thyroid Function in the Perinatal Period," *Amer. J. Dis. Child.*, **95**, 616–621.

64. Pickering, D. R. and Kontaxis, N. E. (1961), "Thyroid Function in the Fetus of the Macque Monkey: 11. Chemical and Morphologic Characteristics of the Foetal Thyroid Gland," *J. Endocr.*, **23**, 267–275.

65. Pincus, R. A., Reichlin, S. and Hempelmann, L. H. (1967), "Thyroid Abnormalities After Radiation Exposure in Infancy," *Ann. Intern. Med.*, **66**, 1154–1164.

66. Powell, G. F., Brasel, J. A., Raiti, S. and Blizzard, R. M. (1967), "Emotional Deprivation and Growth Retardation Stimulating Idiopathic Hypopituitarism. 11. Endocrinologic Evaluation of the Syndrome," *New Engl. J. Med.*, **276**, 1279–1283.

67. Rait, S., Holzmann, G. B., Scott, R. L. and Blizzard, R. M. (1967), "Evidence for the Placental Transfer of Triiodothyronine in Human Beings," *New Engl. J. Med.*, **277**, 456–459.

68. Rauh, J. L., Knox, M. D. and Goldsmith, R. (1964), "Effect of Sexual Maturity in the Serum Concentration of 'Hormonal' Iodine in Adolescence," *J. Pediat.*, **64**, 697–700.

69. Reichlin, S. (1966), "Control of Thyrotropic Hormone Secretion," in *Neuroendocrinology*, pp. 445–536 (L. Martini, and W. F. Ganong, Eds.). New York: Academic Press.

70. Robbins, J. and Nelson, J. H. (1958), "Thyroxine-binding by Serum Protein in Pregnancy and in the Newborn," *J. clin. Invest.*, **37**, 153–159.

71. Rosen, F. and Ezrin, C. (1966), "Embryology of the Thyrotroph," *J. clin. Endocr. and Metab.*, **26**, 1343–1345.

72. Schally, A. V., Arimura, A., Bowers, C. Y., Wakabayashi, I., Kastin, A. J., Redding, T. W., Mittler, J. C., Nair, R. M. G., Pizzolato, P. and Segal, A. J., "Purification of Hypothalamic Releasing Hormones of Human Origin," *J. clin. Endocr. and Metab.*, **31**, 291–300.

73. Shepard, T. H. (1967), "Onset of Function in the Human Fetal Thyroid: Biochemical and Radioautographic Studies From Organ Culture," *J. clin. Endocr. and Metab.*, **27**, 945–958.

74. Shepard, T. H. (1968), "Development of the Human Fetal Thyroid," *Gen. Comp. Endocr.*, **10**, 174–181.

75. Smith, D. W., Blizzard, R. M. and Wilkins, L. (1957), "The Mental Prognosis in Hypothyroidism of Infancy and Childhood," *Pediatrics*, **19**, 1011–1022.

76. Spencer, R. P. and Banever, C. (1970), "Human Thyroid Growth: A Scan Study," *Invest. Radiol.*, **5**, 111–116.

77. Sterling, K., Lashof, J. C. and Man, E. B. (1954), "Disappearance From Serum of I-131-labelled L-thyroxine and L-triiodothyronine in Euthyroid Subjects," *J. clin. Invest.*, **33**, 1031–1035.

78. Stirling, G. A. (1962), "The Thyroid in Malnutrition," *Arch. Dis. Childh.*, **37**, 99–102.

79. Sunshine, P., Kusumoto, H. and Kriss, J. P. (1965), "Survival Time of Circulating Long-acting Thyroid Stimulator in Neonatal Thyrotoxicosis: Implications for Diagnosis and Therapy of the Disorder," *Pediatrics*, **26**, 869–876.

80. Tanner, J. M. (1962), *Growth at Adolescence*. Oxford: Blackwell Scientific Publications.

29. THE DEVELOPMENTAL BIOLOGY OF THE SKIN

E. J. MOYNAHAN

INTRODUCTION

The development of the skin receives rather cursory treatment in the standard textbooks of human anatomy and embryology and fares little better in those devoted to dermatology and paediatrics. Certain aspects of the subject are more fully dealt with in special monographs but a comprehensive presentation of the development of the skin incorporating recent advances which the advent of the electron microscope and the application of newer techniques have brought does not yet exist in any language. The need for such a treatise becomes more urgent with the increasing importance of inherited and developmental disorders in current clinical practice and the frequency with which skin changes contribute to their presentation. Further, the introduction of amniocentesis as an aid to pre-natal diagnosis will demand a greater knowledge of the ontogeny of the skin, since cells shed from the skin of the conceptus contribute largely to the cytology of the fluid obtained by the procedure.

Molecular biology now inspires an increasing number of developmental biologists in the study of morphogenesis and cell differentiation which are the central unsolved problems of present day biology. The solution of these problems will have incalculable effects on future medical practice, bringing the prospect of our being able to correct many inherited and developmental defects including degenerative and neoplastic disease later in life. The task they face is a daunting one because development is an extremely complex phenomenon whereby the single celled zygote becomes transformed into a many celled adult organism, composed of different tissues and organ systems. At the cellular level alone, no fewer than six fundamental processes are involved in achieving this end. These are—(i) growth, (ii) cell division or cleavage, (iii) cell movement, (iv) differentiation, (v) laying down of extra-cellular matrix and (vi) cell death. It is through these, and the factors (genetic and epigenetic) that control them, that the definitive form and functions of the adult organism are attained.

Developmental biology is very much concerned with the pathways by which this goal is reached. Genetic and epigenetic (including environmental) factors interact throughout development, which is continuous through the life of the individual. Irregularities arise in the course of those interactions; embryonic structures and organs vary as to the time of their first appearance, which if the irregularity is slight may be of little consequence but may result in congenital defect if the delay or premature appearance is sufficient to disturb an important developmental sequence. Tissues may be produced in excess of need or structures may persist after they have fulfilled their embryonic functions. Such "accidents" in development are sometimes referred to by Waddington[29,30] as developmental "noise" and in most cases would appear to be the consequence of the inevitable imprecision, albeit usually minor, of most living processes. Many minor congenital defects are the result of developmental "noise" and prominent among these are the commoner birth marks.

The embryo is most vulnerable to epigenetic events at the time of major morphogenetic movements and of organogenesis, especially during the sequential differentiation of embryonic tissues during blastocyst formation, gastrulation and neuralation. These have been aptly termed "epigenetic crises" and the embryo may well perish or continue development at the price of serious malformations of a major organ or system, including the heart and great vessels, the central nervous system, or the skeletal system, in many of which the skin may also participate. Multi-system defects of this type may follow infection of the embryo by rubella virus during early stages of pregnancy, while the unfortunate victims of the thalidomide epidemic display the effects of a teratogenic agent, in whom the skin manifestations (telangiectasia of the glabella, upper eyelids, nose and the upper lip) were sufficiently distinctive to separate it from phocomelia due to other causes and which Fanconi was perspicacious enough to recognize.

EMBRYOLOGY AND ONTOGENY

Embryogeny

The development of the individual may be said to begin with the fertilization of the ripe ovum by the sperm, an event which takes place at or near the infundibulum of the fallopian tube in most mammals, including man. Fertilization restores the full diploid complement of chromosomes in the zygote, determines the sex of the individual, and initiates cleavage. The fertilized ovum (zygote) is a large cell surrounded by a clear apparently structureless membrane, the zona pellucida, which serves to hold together and limit the overall volume occupied by the cells which are produced during cleavage by cell division (mitoses) of the zygote and its descendants. This increase in the number of cells is accompanied by progressive decrease in cell-size until a closely packed mass of cells, 32 or more, the morula, enveloped by the zona pellucida, is produced. The zona pellucida is believed to be comprised largely of acid mucopolysaccharides which may later serve to take up water as the blastocyst is formed. Important changes take place in the cells (blastomeres) during cleavage, to render them mobile—a crucial step, without which the morphogenetic movements and cell re-arrangements essential for further development cannot take place. The first contact of the sperm with the cell membrane of the egg is said to activate the egg, evidenced by changes in the cortex and cytoplasm of the latter. The cortical changes differ in different mammals and are concerned with the prevention of polyspermy and need not detain us. The most important event would seem to be the unblocking of the protein synthesizing mechanism, for the details of which the reader is referred to Davidson's excellent review.[10] There is now considerable evidence that messenger RNA is present in abundance but masked, possibly by combination with a protein, since trypsin will remove this inhibition. During cleavage protein synthesis remains low, but it increases tenfold with the formation of the blastocyst in the rabbit, while nucleoli are present throughout cleavage in the mouse in which synthesis of new ribosomal RNA apparently takes place after the eight-celled stage. Treatment with actinomycin D which specifically inhibits the synthesis of ribosomal RNA will prevent cleavage in mouse and rabbit embryos.

The appearance of the nucleoli in the rat embryo is followed by changes in the morphology of the ribosomes in the cytoplasm, which are arranged linearly at first and later assume a rosette-like assembly or remain as polyribosomes. Much of the energy required by the early embryo is provided by metabolism of carbohydrates, especially glycogen, different pathways being followed at different stages. Thus in the first 3 days, the hexose-monophosphate shunt is the pathway followed, but in the later stages the Krebs cycle (tricarboxylic acid cycle) is the final common pathway of oxidation. Glycogen is normally absent from the mature epidermis although it may reappear in certain pathological states.

Gastrulation and Neurulation

Gastrulation is the best known morphogenetic movement in animals. It has been most studied in amphibia and sea-urchins, although the movements differ greatly in the higher vertebrates. Successful completion of gastrulation is vital for the developing embryo, as it is through the movements of cells rather than by differential growth or mitotic activity that the embryo redistributes the cells in early development and thereby establishes the three primary germ layers. Neurulation, by which the neural tube is developed, is another crucial morphogenetic movement, disturbance of which may result in the birth of an anencephalic infant in the severest cases that survive to term or a mild spina bifida occulta with its associated satyr's or faun's tail tuft of hair in the human infant. Holtfreter[15] was first to establish that the non-cellular material exudate coating the egg plays a significant but until then unsuspected role in gastrulation by holding the cells together and co-ordinating their movements; these begin soon after the appearance of microfibrils and microtubules in those cells destined to move. Microtubules and microfilaments, which probably contain a system not unlike the actin-myosin complex of muscle cells, also play a part in determining the shapes of cells.

Gastrulation in man and other higher vertebrates differs from that of amphibia and birds because of the much greater quantity of yolk in these latter forms. The primitive streak takes the place of the blastopore, through which ectodermal cells move to form the notochord and the mesoderm; instead there is a heaping up of ectodermal cells at the tail end of the human embryonic disc on the 15th day so as to form the primitive streak. From there cells move laterally between the ectoderm and endoderm to form the third primary germ layer of the embryo to make up the intra-embryonic mesoderm. In addition, mesoderm also arises from the prochordal plate, the neural crest (ectomesenchyme) and the trophoblast (extra embryonic mesoderm).

The mesoderm of the prochordal plate plays a fundamental role in the initial differentiation of the ectoderm into epidermis and neural plate; from then onwards the mesoderm determines the modality of the overlying epidermis. This property of the mesoderm persists throughout life; for as every plastic surgeon knows, skin grafts retain the characters of the donor site.

By the 6th week the head ectoderm exhibits a close approximation of the lateral plasma membranes of adjacent cells which appear to fuse near their free borders. These cells contain the full complement of organelles including mitochondria, rough endoplasmic reticulum, free ribosomal particles and single-membraned limited bodies which may be lysosomes. Membranes of the Golgi apparatus are also evident while fairly massive deposits of glycogen are characteristic features of these cells. At this stage too, very fine fibrils may be seen, characteristically on the inner surface of the basal cell membrane and the upper portion of the lateral cell membrane, while a poorly demarcated zone of electron dense, probably also fibrillar material, may be seen on the mesodermal aspect of the basal cell membrane.

Mesodermal cells at this stage are widely dispersed and fairly sparse except immediately beneath the ectoderm. They are elongated thin cells and possess conspicuous nuclei as well as the usual complement of organelles. Long slender processes extend from them by means of which they make contact with their fellows.

After the establishment of the mesoderm the presumptive area of the nervous system differentiates from the rest of the ectoderm as the neural plate. The ectodermal epithelium of the neural plate thickens with further concentration of the epithelium, meanwhile the cells of the neural plate develop microfibrils following which they become elongated and arrange themselves into a columnar epithelium. This clearly distinguishes them from the cells of the epidermis which is now made up of two layers of flattened cells.

Soon the edges of the neural plate become thickened and elevated as the neural folds. These rise higher and eventually make contact in the mid-line and fuse to form the neural tube and thus complete neurulation.

Ontogeny of the Epidermis

The epidermis segregates from other parts of the ectoderm (neural plate and neural crest) as we have seen during the process of neuralation. Although most of it becomes the epidermis of the skin, a number of other structures are derived from it. These include the skin appendages, hair follicles, sweat glands, sebaceous glands and nails; but other important structures in association with the nervous system and the special senses, are also derived from the epidermis. These appear at various sites as plate shaped thickenings of the epidermis known as placodes. The ganglia of the cranial nerves are derived in part from these placodes both olfactory and auditory, as well as the lens and other ocular structures are also epidermal derivatives. These placodes deserve special mention because disturbances in the organogenesis of the skin are often associated with disturbed growth and development of the organs of special sense, particularly the eyes, though ear defects may accompany disturbances in pigmentation.

Development of the Eye

Disturbance in the organogenesis of the eye frequently accompanies disturbance in the development of other structures and tissue of ectodermal origin, including the epidermis and its derivatives. To begin with the eye rudiment is in no way distinct from the rest of the neural or medullary plate, but with the aid of vital stains two zones can be identified at the anterior margin of the neural plate where it borders on prospective fore- and mid-brain and lies on very active mesoderm. These zones become transformed into vesicles which increase in size until they come into contact with the ectoderm and induce the formation of the lens; this at first is made up of a hollow spherical vesicle, the anterior end of which retains the character of a simple epithelium and forms the anterior capsule of the lens; the remainder being transformed later into lens fibre.

Meanwhile the external wall of the optic vesicle invaginates to become the optic cup, the inner layer of which becomes the retina, and the external layer of which gradually accumulates melanin. The vitreous develops as a space between the posterior surface of the developing lens and the inner layer of the optic cup, and it is at first free of mesenchyme; but as invagination of the optic cups proceeds the space increases in size and becomes filled with a reticulated jelly composed largely of mucopolysaccharides. The optic nerve fibres grow back from the retina to the optic stalk in association with the vessels of the optic disc.

Nose (Olfactory Placodes)

Primordia of the nose appear as two ectodermal thickenings, the olfactory or nasal placodes, situated above the stomadaeum, just below and to either side of the forebrain. The placodes then become depressed as the mesoderm proliferates, to form the olfactory pits. As growth continues the olfactory epithelium comes to occupy the medial and lateral walls of the upper part of the nasal cavity and the neuroblasts which it contains differentiate into nerve cells which then grow inwards to the cerebral hemispheres often penetrating the cartilaginous nasal capsule on the way. Later in development, the olfactory nerve fibres become separated into bundles by the cribriform plate of the ethmoid. The fibres of olfactory nerves differ from all other nerves in that they arise solely from the placodes and these cell bodies remain wholly within the olfactory epithelium; in this respect it is remarkable that there are no syndromes in which the olfactory epithelium and the skin form part—in marked contrast with the frequency with which skin and structures derived from the optic and auditory placodes are associated in developmental and inherited defects.

The Auditory Placode

The auditory placode from which the internal ear is derived resembles closely the olfactory placode and it too, is converted by invagination into a sac. This eventually closes to form the ear vesicle from which the labyrinth is developed, through differential expansion of the vesicle. Mesenchyme cells then surround it to give rise later to cartilage as protection to the inner ear. Mesenchyme of neural crest origin is also present and the neural crest gives rise to the bi-polar cells of the auditory nerve as well. It is not surprising therefore to find that many inherited and development disorders of the skin, especially those involving pigmentation, are associated with deafness and other auditory defects.

The Neural Crest

The neural crest, as the ultimate source of the pigmented cells of the skin, hair and eyes (other than the pigmented epithelium of the retina) demands very special consideration. It is a transient embryonic structure which arises in close association with the developing neural tube, and begins with thickening of the ectoderm at the edge of the neural plate, and as the latter folds, these thickened edges gradually approach each other to fuse and thus form the neural tube; certain cells fail to participate in this fusion and the crest is then seen as a ribbon of these cells lying dorsal to the neural tube. Very soon after each segment of the crest has been formed, its cells begin to migrate to all parts of the developing embryo, in a wave-like fashion cephalo-caudally, so that cells may be seen to migrate from the anterior portion of the crest at the same time as the caudal regions of the crest are being formed.

The neural crest gives rise to (i) the pigment cells (melanocytes) of the skin, hair, eyes (except the pigmented epithelium of the retina), meninges and elsewhere but *not* those cells which synthesize melanin within the brain itself, e.g. substantia nigra, (ii) posterior root ganglia and associated sensory neurones, (iii) the autonomic nervous system including sympathetic and parasympathetic ganglia and nerves, (iv) the adrenal medulla, (v) some oligodendroglia, Schwann cells and the leptomeninges among the supportive cells of the CNS, (vi) certain of the ganglia associated with the cranial nerves as well as the cranial parasympathetic ganglia, (vii) the bi-polar cells of the VIII nerve, (viii) the ecto-mesenchyme of the head including the visceral cartilages and membrane bones, (ix) the odontablasts.

Migration of neural crest cells is influenced not only by the built-in programme of the cell itself, but also by the structure and nature of the environment in which the cell finds itself. It is not yet known whether the ultimate fate of any given crest cell is determined before migration takes place, but it is certain that many cells may fail to reach their destination, both in normal and pathological development, well demonstrated in human prebaldism where there is a total absence of melanocytes from extensive areas of skin in the ventral surface of trunk and limbs.

A fuller understanding of the factors governing the localization and behaviour of migrant cells from the crest would throw light on the histogenesis of the common pigmented mole as well as syndromes such as neurofibromatosis, tuberous sclerosis and the lentiginoses associated with cardiomyopathy[26] to name but a few of the inherited disorders in which crest derivatives are playing a part.

The Melanoblast (see Fig. 1)

The early neural crest cells are indistinguishable from the other dorsal cells of the embryo either in shape or behaviour. They are freely mobile and will not aggregate or adhere to each other; they move by the extension of colourless, clear cytoplasmic lobopodia. Holtfreter[15] has made a careful study of these activities and noticed a significant change which takes place in the locomotive behaviour of the cells during differentiation. The blunt pseudopodia gradually cease to form and are replaced by long, thin filopodia, which marks the end of differentiation. Wilde[32] reminds us that all cells of the embryo, except macrophages, possess the property of forming lobopodia which in turn are replaced by filopodia and *in vitro* lobopodial forms usually give way to filopodia after 2–3 days in culture. This continues in the case of melanoblasts until major synthesis of melanin has begun. With the slowing down of movement in the melanoblast, discrete yellowish-brown, uniformly sized granules are synthesized, at first in parallel rows in the perinuclear region of the cell, while with further development the granules are found further and further away from the nucleus. The cells meanwhile become dendritic; and when this takes place, the filopodia are withdrawn. It should be noted that the melanoblast does not produce tyrosinase nor, consequently, melanin, during migration, and that differentiation in this, as in other cell lines, is under genetic control at every step. Genes control the number and distribution of melanocytes, the *morphe* of the cell and its organelles, including melanosomes, the colour of melanin, and its release into the melanosomes.

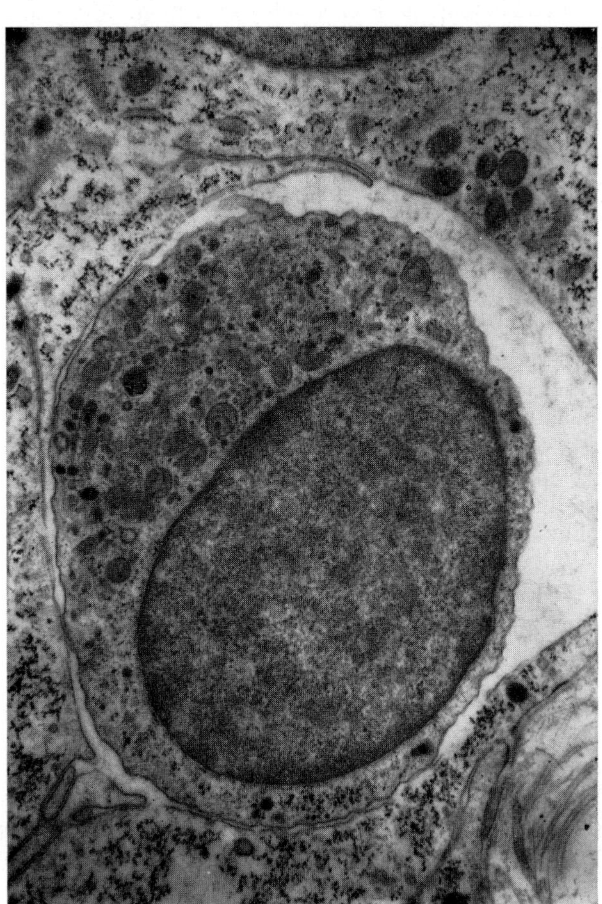

Fig. 1. Melanocyte in basal layer of epidermis of 14 week human fetus. The space between it and surrounding cells is indicative of its recent arrival in the epidermis. Immature melanin granules (melanosomes) are present in the cytoplasm. ×28,500. (A. S. Breathnach.)

The Melanosome

Melanosomes are complex organelles made up of subunits of fibrillar protein assembled and arranged inside membrane bound vesicles to form lamellar matrices within which the enzyme tyrosinase is embedded. Synthesis and deposition of melanin will continue, under appropriate conditions, until the melanosome is fully pigmented and tyrosinase activity is brought to a halt. The organization of the matrix of the melanosome, as well as the pattern of melanin deposition, is controlled by several different genes. The melanocyte is probably second only to the erythrocyte, with respect to our knowledge of its biology. More than 70 genes have been identified which affect coat colour in the house mouse alone and the number of inherited pigmentary disorders in man has been steadily mounting. Many of the genes concerned display pleiotropy, while other neural crest elements often participate in the phenotypic expression of the mutant gene. Thus, absence or gross defect in the enzyme tyrosinase which is essential for the hydroxylation of tyrosine to dihydroxy phenylalanine (DOPA), and for its further oxidation and polymerization to melanin, is responsible for albinism.

"White spotting" is not uncommon in man as well as other mammals and lower vertebrates. White spotting may result from one or several developmental causes, including failure of migrating melanocytes to attain their definitive goals in the skin or other structure. This could be intrinsic to the melanoblast itself, as an example of in-built cell death (thanatotropy), or the target tissue might not permit the entry or survival of the melanoblast. Either event may be responsible for the total absence of melanocytes from certain mid-line regions such as blazes, white forelock and the like in human piebaldism.

White macules, characteristically resembling the leaves of the mountain ash in shape and size, are present at birth in the great majority of individuals carrying the gene for tuberous sclerosis, in some of whom this may be the only phenotypic expression of the gene. Occasionally metameric or zosteriform areas of skin may be devoid of pigment with or without the more typical white macules. These areas contain melanocytes which are morphologically normal and contain well-formed melanosomes, but lack or exhibit depressed activity of the enzyme tyrosinase. In this respect they resemble albinism; however, the lack of enzyme activity is usually not total and pigmentation may take place later in life. Such lesions may well stem from single cells which give rise to clones of cells that have inherited the defect, as suggested by Mintz.[20]

Histogenesis of the Epidermis

Early Stages —Periderm (Figs. 2–5)

The epidermis proper may be said to begin when two layers of cells have differentiated from the ectoderm at the end of neuralation. The more superficial layer forms the periderm (trichoderm) and lies on the basal or germinative layer. The periderm is an embryonic or fetal structure which almost certainly plays a very important part in the metabolic interchanges that take place between the developing epidermis and the amniotic fluid. This is clearly indicated by the presence of microvilli on its amniotic surface, while the presence of pinocytotic vesicles points towards active absorption or excretion. Furthermore, histochemical studies have revealed in the chick and rat embryo that alkaline phosphatase activity is well marked in the periderm until the dermal vessels make their appearance. As soon as this occurs alkaline phosphatase activity ceases and the microvilli and pinocytotic vesicles disappear from the periderm.[24] Normally, the periderm should be shed well before term, but occasionally it may be present at birth, enclosing the baby in a keratinized cocoon.

The so-called collodion baby is the commonest example of this, but exceptionally, keratinization may be very marked so that the baby may superficially exhibit the so-called Harlequin features. However, the mouth and nostrils are usually free and it is a comparatively simple task to open up and remove the thickened periderm. The periderm may persist and keratinize in several of the inherited disorders of keratinization including the more severe forms of ichthyosis. The cells forming the periderm initially have

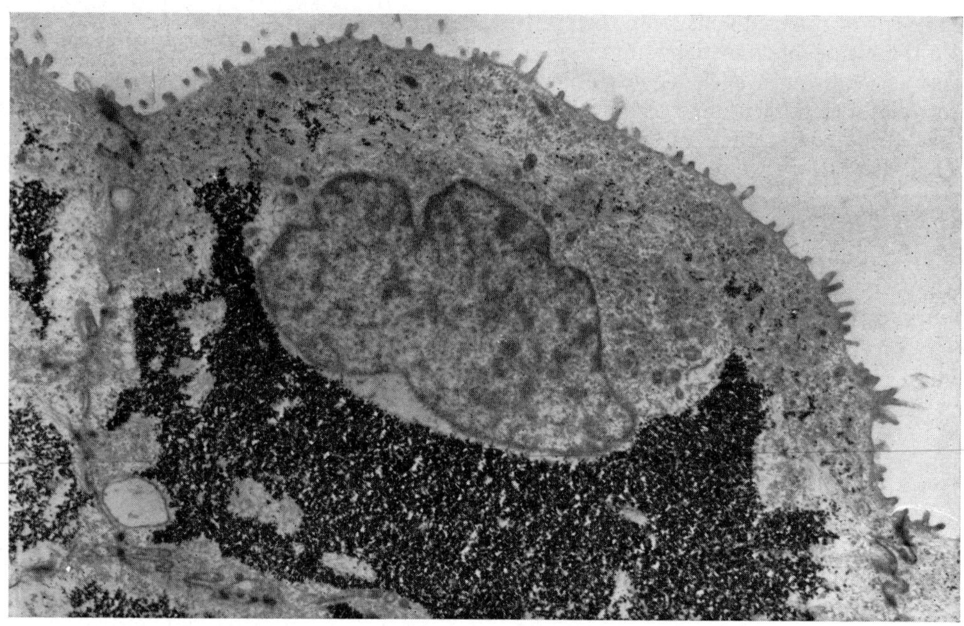

FIG. 2. Periderm cell from back of 11 week human fetus. Note surface microvilli and large deposit of glycogen below the nucleus. ×7,460. (A. S. Breathnach.)

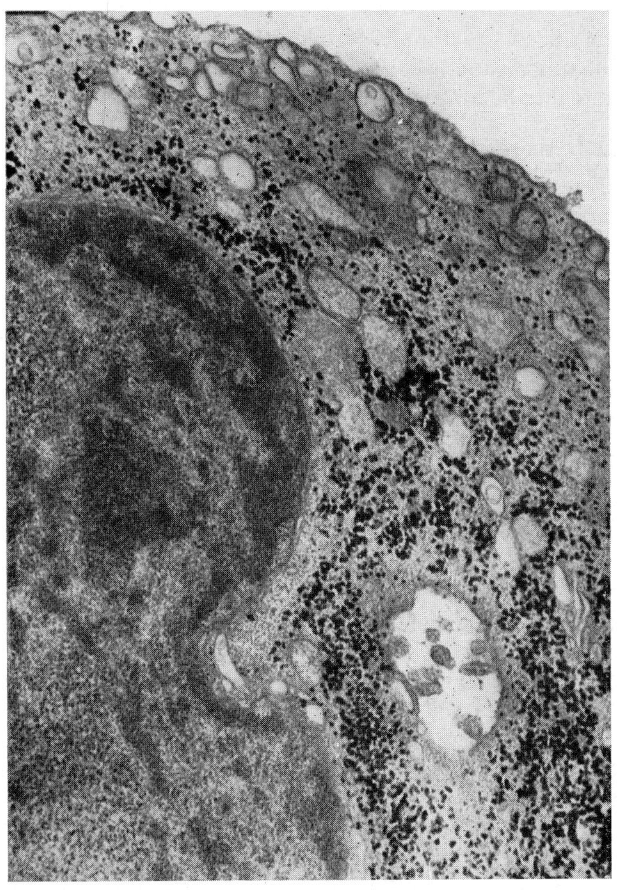

FIG. 3. Periderm cell from arm of 16 week human fetus. Note membrane-limited vesicles and scattered glycogen particles in the cytoplasm. ×28,370. (A. S. Breathnach.)

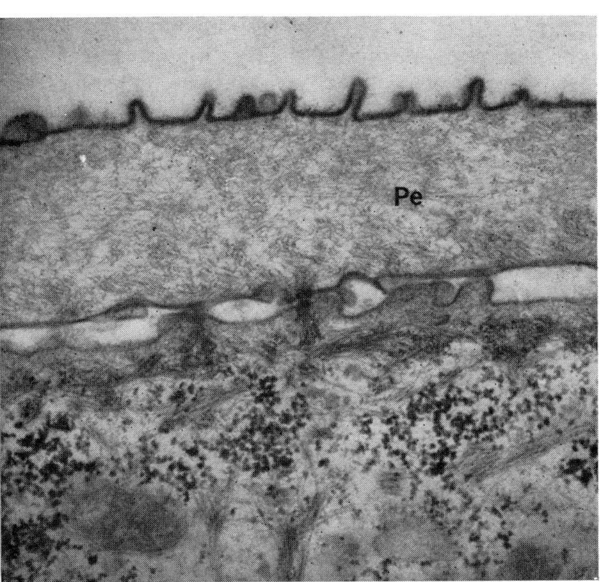

FIG. 4. Transformed periderm cell, and uppermost cell of unkeratinized definitive epidermis from skin of 21 week human fetus. ×18,570. (A. S. Breathnach, *J. invest. Dermat.*, 1971.)

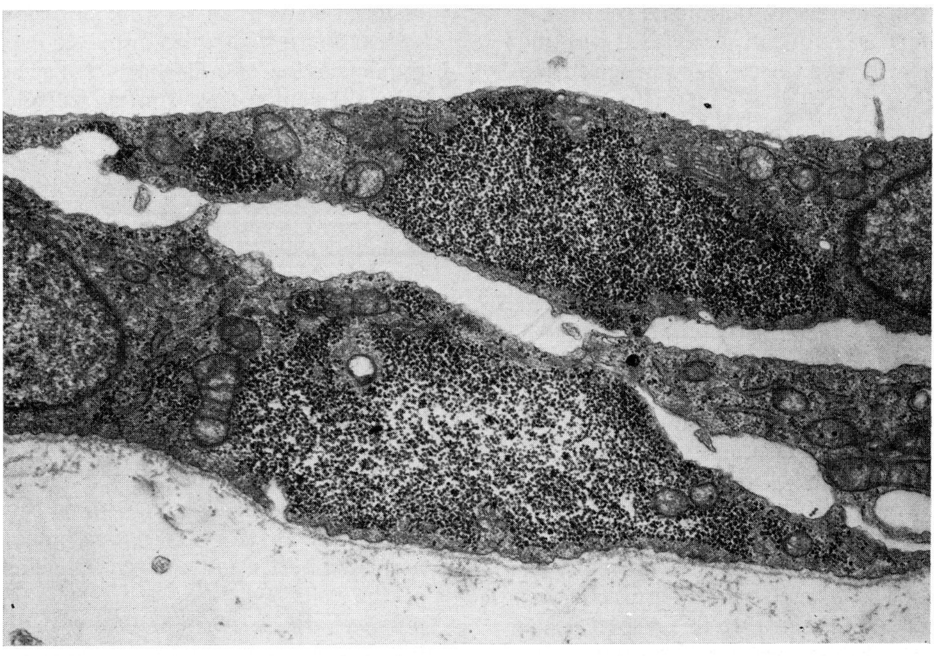

FIG. 5. Bilaminar epidermis from head of 6 week human fetus. At this stage the epidermis consists of a superficial layer of periderm cells, and a deeper layer of germinative cells. ×17,930. (Breathnach and Robins, *Brit. J. Derm.*, 1969.)

a flattened shape but as development proceeds they tend to become wider over the central part of the cell on its amniotic surface. Simultaneously the surface microvilli increase in number and size. The cell organelles at this stage (11 weeks) are principally confined to the supra nuclear compartment which is relatively free from glycogen—in marked contrast to the cytoplasm below the nucleus where large deposits can be seen. A Golgi apparatus is present but not conspicuous and the mitochondria are few in number.

Mitoses are frequently observed in the periderm and this establishes beyond doubt that it is an independent structure maintained by the mitotic activity of its own cells. As ontogeny proceeds the elevation on the surface of the periderm becomes irregular and indentations are seen to appear in the plasma membrane which, by undermining the elevation, result in the formation of spherical protrusions that are connected to the cell by pedicles. Most of the glycogen is still to be found below the nucleus at this stage but increased amounts are seen in the supra nuclear compartment as development proceeds. At this stage junction between adjacent peridermal cells is evident. Later in development the changes mentioned above become more pronounced and some of the spherical swellings eventually detach and float free in the amniotic fluid. Glycogen is now present above the nucleus which begins to become indented, a sign of senescence of the cell. It is worth emphasizing that while these changes are taking place vesicles and microvilli become increasingly prominent; and another feature worthy of notice is the appearance of desmosomes at the junction between the periderm and the underlying intermediate cell layer of the epidermis.

Filaments tend to be concentrated around the nucleus of the periderm cell and also deep to the surface membrane. Little is known concerning the origin of the vesicles nor their contents, which are a feature of the older periderm; they may be concerned with the absorption of fluid from the amnion. Fine filaments are frequently associated with the surface of the microvilli and there is some electron–histochemical evidence that these contain mucopolysaccharides which it has been suggested correspond with the mucous coat found in fully developed amphibian epidermis. Should this be so, then the periderm is the most likely source. In this respect it should be borne in mind that chick and human epidermis will undergo mucous metaplasia when cultured in media containing excess vitamin A. There can be little doubt that the periderm plays an important physiological role especially during the 4th month of gestation and is not merely a passive protective layer for the developing skin.

Finally, the progressive loss of the spherical protrusions not only leads to a thinning of the periderm as a whole, but the individual cells progressively lose vesicles and there is a reduction in size of the organelles with shortening of microvilli. The cytoplasm of the cells becomes electron translucent with an apparently granular matrix, which however can be seen to consist of fine filaments; glycogen disappears; and the plasma membrane thickens. In this respect it has been compared with the stratum corneum of the amphibian epidermis which is also exposed to a fluid medium. It remains to be determined what factors are responsible for the transformation of the periderm into a persistent keratinized structure resembling the horny layer of terrestrial animals in the collodion baby and other more striking anomalies of cornification.

The Desmosomes

Desmosomes play a considerable part in determining the shape of the cell surface and at the same time contribute to the internal scaffolding of the epidermal cell by providing an attachment plate for the tonofibrils. However, some workers hold that the tonofilaments which make up the tonofibrils are not inserted into the desmosome itself but instead loop back into the cytoplasm after making contact with them. Desmosomes herald their presence with an increased electron density of the cell membrane at certain sites which is followed by the appearance of bands of increasing density between the membranes of contiguous cells. This in turn is followed by the appearance of filaments in association with the inner surface of the desmosome. Early in the differentiation of the epidermis these changes are first seen at the adhering edges of adjacent cells, at their free surfaces; indeed, this is an essential first step in the ontogenesis of any epithelium, and it seems likely that certain important changes take place in the permeability of the cells concerned when this happens. Further development brings more contacts which are made in zipper-like fashion until the cells concerned have formed contact with their neighbours all along their lateral surfaces. When this is complete, and the cells are all closely aggregated, the molecular ecology forming the external surface of the tissue will differ from that of the cells beneath and this has important consequences for their subsequent differentiation. An essential step in the development of the epidermis is the formation of the basal lamina (basement membrane). This is accomplished by the laying down of a continuous sheet of material made up of very fine fibrils, which, however, may appear amorphous when displayed in plan: it is the site for the deposition of collagen or collagen-like fibrils. Tissue and organ culture experiments have demonstrated that the establishment of a basal membrane is essential for the maintenance of the orientation of the epithelial cells as well as their mitotic activity. It is no longer disputed that mesodermal mesenchyme commands the behaviour of the adjacent epidermis, including the rich intricate patterning of its horny layer and the sculpturing of the undersurface of the epithelium.

The basal lamina has been considered by some to be a molecular sieve capable of regulating selective interchanges between the epidermis and the dermis which influence cytodifferentiation. Support for this notion comes from studies of epidermal tumours including human squamous cell carcinoma, in which dilated bladder-like herniations of the cytoplasm through gaps in the basal lamina are sometimes seen. The cytoplasm is homogenous both in the herniated protrusion and the immediately adjacent region of the cell, suggesting that the basal lamina not only polarizes the basal cell and restricts its downward growth, but clearly influences the metabolism and fine structure of at least part of the cell.[23]

The basal membrane is characterized by the presence of

localized areas of increased electron density sited precisely opposite similar local densities in the cell membrane of the basal cell immediately above, while deep to the basal lamina two systems of fibrils are clearly distinguished, the finer fibrils (100–200 Å.) forming an irregular mesh in which larger fibrils (250–240 Å.) are enmeshed. The former are probably reticular and composed of tropocollagen while the larger represent slightly older collagen in which more cross-linkage has occurred. The source of collagen in all vertebrate embryos is thought to be the fibroblast but there is some evidence that epithelial cells may secrete it as well.

Establishment of a Multi-layer Stratified Epidermis

One or more intermediate layers of cells begin to appear between the periderm and the basal layer but the time and rate at which this occurs differs considerably throughout the embryo, though it follows the general rule of development. This tends to be more advanced in cephalic regions than those further back. The first sign of an intermediate layer of cells is evident on the face—the eyebrows, lips and nose, and it appears progressively later on the back, abdomen and limbs. The intermediate cells to begin with are flattened and lie parallel with the surface. Close interlocking between the cells of all layers of the epidermis proper develops quickly with the production of many more desmosomes. Once again large deposits of glycogen are to be seen in cells at all levels. By the 12th week, as further layers are established, small rounded cells with relatively little glycogen are seen with increasing frequency both in the basal layer and above, including melanocytes and Langerhans cells. The latter may be seen at levels above the basal layer whereas melanocytes are strictly confined to the basal layer.

The Horny Layer

Epidermal differentiation is complete with the development of the stratum corneum composed of layers of flattened more or less fully keratinized cells 0·5–0·8 mμ. thick and 30 μm. in diameter. The number of layers varies very considerably, ranging from a few on the eyelids to several hundreds on the palms and soles. The cells forming the horny layer are tightly bound together as befits its function as a barrier to physical chemical and biological insults. The ultra-structure of the horny layer varies considerably both in density and the presence of loose fibrils, but these changes may be artefacts. It is generally accepted that the final stage of differentiation of the keratinocytes is represented by filaments possibly derived from tonofibrils which, with the amorphous substance from keratohyalin, give rise to an ordered pattern, the so-called keratin pattern.[11]

Histogenesis of Hair Follicles (Fig. 6)

The first hair anlagen appear towards the end of the second or early in the 3rd month and are seen on the eyebrows, upper lip and chin, but general development of the hair does not begin until the 4th month. Primary hair germs begin to form more or less simultaneously and are fairly evenly placed. The first sign is a crowding together of nuclei in the basal layer at certain sites in the epidermis while it is still composed of only two layers, the basal layer and the periderm; but by the time secondary follicles appear, the epidermis is usually multi-layered and keratinization may already have begun. Some workers suggest that mesodermal nuclei may accumulate at the site of the presumptive hair germ before the epidermal changes. It would seem that neighbouring cells are drawn into the hair germ and the follicle later grows by mitotic division of its

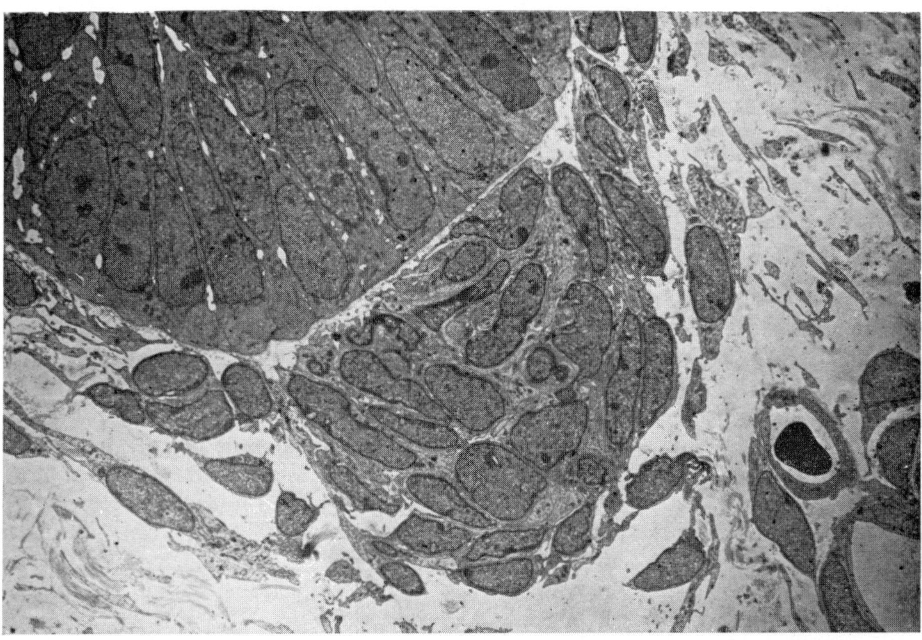

FIG. 6. Hair-bulb and dermal papilla from scalp of 16 week human fetus. ×2,660. (Robins and Breathnach, *J. Anat.*, 1969.)

own cells. Further primary centres are formed and finally secondary follicles to make up the typical hair group.

Bulbous Peg Stage

As growth of the follicle continues, differentiation sets in and the advancing end of the solid column of cells now becomes bulbous so as to envelop part of the mesodermal material which has been pushed before it, during its descent, towards the subcutis. The mesodermal material now consists of the ovoid papilla which lies inside the hollowed-out bulb of the follicle and the papillary pad of mesoderm which lies immediately below the bulb.

Simultaneously, solid epidermal swellings develop on the posterior side of the follicular column. The lower one always remains solid, and its cells grow rich in glycogen with those of the rest of the follicle. This lower bulge although inconspicuous in adults is quite prominent in embryonic life. It disappears earlier and is larger than the more superficial swelling which is the anlage of the sebaceous gland, appearing as a rounded knob, the central cells of which soon begin to accumulate lipid and appear foamy in paraffin section with the light microscope. A solid cord of elongated cells extends backwards from the epidermis to constitute the anlage of the hair tract, in the upper cutis, along which the hair eventually emerges. This consists of two parts, the epidermal (hair-canal) and the sub-epidermal or infundibular parts. Coarse filaments characterize the cells of the hair tract which are the first cells to keratinize in the body—a transient but constant feature of fetal differentiation. The last structure associated with hair follicles is the erector pili muscle, which appears as a row of mesodermal cells which extends downward towards the bulge to which it becomes attached.

Large dendritic cells laden with pigment granules are present in the upper half of the bulb, above the "critical level" of Montagna,[21,22] as the border between indifferent matrix and differentiating cells of the hair and root-sheath. In contrast to adult conditions, there are also scattered melanocytes in the lower half of the bulb and in the outer root-sheaths for some distance above the bulb. Capillary blood vessels approach the follicle near its lower end and lie between the fibroblasts of the papillary pad and around the bulb, but none within the papilla. The border between mesodermal and ectodermal cells, always outlined by a thin PAS positive membrane, soon becomes accentuated with the appearance of the vitreous membrane. Using the electron microscope, the cells of the hair germ can be distinguished from the adjacent basal cells as they appear to contain more organelles, but those of the dermal papilla can not be distinguished from their neighbours in the mesoderm at this stage. With the electron microscope the advancing basal end of the hair peg is seen to be flattened and to press against the more densely packed cells of the dermal papilla; these are connected with two or three layers of mesenchymal cells which now envelop the entire peg. The outer cells of the peg are arranged radially through its long axis while the basal cells present a palisade appearance. The central cells are more rounded and less tightly packed and contain glycogen deposits. By the 16th week presumptive hair cone and presumptive outer root-sheath cells can be distinguished. The former are narrower and more elongated and contain trichohyalin granules. These are invariably associated with filaments which appear to join the granules; these filaments are present before the granules appear. The origin of trichohyalin as well as its chemistry is still obscure.

Trichohyalin rapidly accumulates in the peripheral cells of the hair cone and two layers of cells loaded with granules may be seen surrounding the central less differentiated cells. These constitute the Henle and Huxley layers of the inner root sheath, which with further development become completely transformed. During this process the filaments are arranged more loosely with islands of ribosomes between them, trichohyalin granules disappear completely and the plasma membrane of the cells is thickened; the nucleus loses its membrane and clumping of the chromatin gives rise to granular patches of varying densities. This marks the final differentiation of the inner root-sheath cells.

Studies of the fine structure of these granules have revealed that they are aggregates of particles which are closely associated with the filaments giving rise to the notion that they were responsible for their production. Indeed, a possible chemical link between them is indicated by the finding that filaments of the inner root sheath are rich in citrulline while the fibrils are arginine rich.[269] Citrulline has been found to be directly derived from arginine. The three layers grow at different rates and it is thought that this may be important in the shaping of the hair. The inner root sheath does not emerge from the follicle with the growing hair; instead it disappears presumably through the action of proteolytic enzymes which must possess the property of degrading keratin. This takes place at the level at which sebaceous secretion gains access to the hair canal and it has been suggested that the enzymes concerned with the removal of the inner root sheath are derived from lysosomes of the sebaceous cells. The keratinolytic enzymes have been placed in the outer root sheath because degradation begins at the surface of cells of Henle's layers adjacent to the outer root sheath. Protrusions of the cell membranes into the outer root-sheath cells can be seen and this had led to the suggestion that resorption of the cell constituents may take place through them.

The process leads to a progressive thinning of the cells from the inner root sheath which then slough off together with a few cells of the outer root sheath.

Cuticle of the Hair

The cells of the cuticle of the hair which are present in the upper bulb exhibit an undifferentiated appearance at this level, in striking contrast to the dense granules prominent at a higher level. These are concentrated mainly along the plasma membrane facing the inner root sheath and begin to appear above or at the level of transformation of Henle's layer. The granules become larger as they ascend the follicle and ultimately join together to form a continuous electron dense zone.

Medulla

This forms the central core of the hair shaft and is made up of cells arising near the dermal papilla. Spherical granules begin to appear in the cytoplasm as the cells ascend the follicle. In addition bundles of filaments and many apparently empty vesicles are to be seen. Glycogen is abundant as well. With further ascent the medullary granules increase in size and number and they too join together, at the same time the vacuoles increase in size and the mitochondria and nucleus begin to degenerate so that the cell becomes completely transformed into a structure containing what appears to be empty vacuoles surrounded by an amorphous electron dense granular matrix. The cells of the medulla are then found to be wedged between cortical cells somewhat like the rungs of a ladder. An important chemical feature in which the medulla resembles the inner root sheath is the presence of citrulline rich protein.

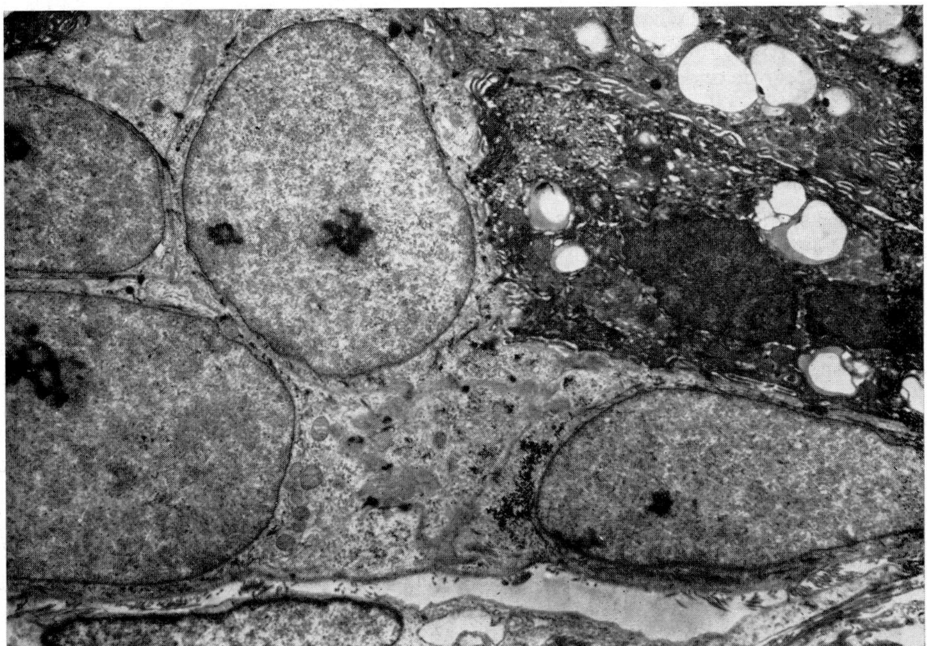

FIG. 7. Portion of peripheral zone of developing sebaceous gland from skin of 24 week human fetus. Lipid-containing vacuoles are present in the more centrally situated cells. ×4,660. (A. S. Breathnach.)

Pilar Canal—or Hair Canal

Just below the entrance of the duct of the sebaceous gland into the follicle, the hair separates from the inner root sheath and lies free in the pilar or hair canal; the wall of this canal is quite thick and the lumen is bounded by the inner root sheath which is undergoing rapid disintegration and fragmentation such that the exact boundaries between the outer and inner sheath are difficult to distinguish.

The cells which give rise to the infundibular and sub-infundibular part of the hair tract are characterized by coarse bundles of filaments which run through the whole length of the cell and by the presence of membrane coating granules in the infundibulum. Morphogenetic cell death is also a feature of the development of the hair tract, the central cells of which undergo rapid keratinization after acquiring keratohyalin. A lumen appears in the central mass of cornified cells and this is soon followed by the appearance of the tip of the growing hair, which is made up of cells of the inner root sheath. Ultrastructural appearances at the interface between keratinized and non-keratinized cells in the infundibulum resemble closely those seen in the space between the granular layer and the horny layer of the surface epidermis, in which membrane coated lamellar granules are prominent. In view of the frequency with which follicular hyperkeratosis forms part of the clinical presentation of many disorders, both genetic, such as pityriasis rubra pilaris, or epigenetic, such as the phrynoderma of vitamin A deficiency or the early lesions of scurvy, it is of more than passing interest that the cells of the infundibulum of the hair follicle are the first in the epidermis to keratinize.

Ontogeny of the Sebaceous Gland (Fig. 7)

The anlage of the sebaceous gland is first recognizable as a bulge on the posterior aspect of the follicle immediately below the point where the follicle joins the basal layer of the epidermis. The cells forming this bulge are in no way distinguishable to begin with from the neighbouring cells of the follicle. Cells soon begin to accumulate further downwards into the dermis. The central cells of the bulge are seen to become foamy as a result of the accumulation of lipids into droplets, while those on the periphery contain glycogen granules. Further development leads to budding to form the multi-acinar gland.

Sebaceous differentiation in its various stages can best be demonstrated in the fully mature gland, already present on the face of the fetus at 24 weeks. Peripheral cells are seen to rest on a basal lamina and show little difference from those at the periphery of the primordium at an earlier stage;

others differ considerably, having a less dense cytoplasm, glycogen granules that are breaking up, and the presence of small vesicles around the nucleus with very few lipid vacuoles. Their cytoplasm is rich in mitochondria. As differentiation proceeds and the cells move towards the central part of the acinus, they contain more lipid vacuoles, both mitochondria and ribosomes also increase in number. Lipid droplets are now evident in increasing numbers and appear to lie free in the cytoplasm, while the Golgi apparatus, which at earlier stages in differentiation was inconspicuous, is now prominent. It is thought that the lipid vacuoles and the Golgi apparatus play the most important role in the synthesis of the sebum. When fully differentiated the cell becomes loaded with lipid droplets which are separated by narrow bands of cytoplasm containing a few vesicles and mitochondria. These disintegrate and the sebum then begins to flow into the hair canal to reach the surface of the epidermis.

The Sebaceous Duct

The sebaceous duct forms within that portion of the gland which joins the hair follicle. At first it consists of typical lipid containing cells which communicate with the hair canal; the cells forming the centre then break down while those forming the periphery of the duct proceed to cornify and exhibit dense concentrations of filaments and irregular masses indicative of subsequent keratinization. With the disappearance of the central cells the lumen becomes patent.

Sebaceous Activity in Fetal and Post-natal Life

The sebaceous glands are active in the later months of intra-uterine life and make their contribution to the vernix caseosa which covers the skin surface at birth. Shortly after birth the glands reduce in size and remain relatively inert until the advent of puberty, which is often ushered in, especially in Caucasians, by a marked increase in sebaceous activity. Human skin differs from that of most mammals not only structurally but biochemically, especially with respect to steroid metabolism, so that it is not surprising to find that there are very marked differences between the various races and even within families. Acne, which is now the commonest medical disorder of the Caucasian adolescent and 'teenager, is relatively rare and nearly always less severe in Mongolian populations. It seems clear that skin is a target for androgens. Histochemical studies[1,2] subsequently established that hydroxy-steroid dehydrogenase activities were confined to sebaceous glands in the areas in which acne is prone to develop. It was later found that human skin would convert testosterone into 5-dihydro-testosterone, which is several times more potent an androgen,[12] and that the inert steroid dehydro-epi-androsterone (DHA) could be converted into testosterone[7] in the skin of young men but not in female skin. The investigation of steroid metabolism in the skin has entered a very active phase and it is to be hoped that it will bear fruit in the shape of a rational, tailor-made remedy for the bane of so many young people's lives. It should also throw light on "cradle-cap" and its accompanying dermatoses, hitherto masquerading as so-called "seborrhoeic eczema." It is clear too, that despite most text-book accounts, Leiner's disease is not just a more troublesome and extensive "seborrhoeic dermatitis of infancy," but the consequence of a serious inherited immune deficit affecting complement which usually terminates fatally.[19]

We are still remarkably ignorant of the changes that take place in the composition of the sebum, especially in the new born and young infant, *vis-à-vis* its antimicrobial capacity. It has of course been long known that puberty is accompanied by "spontaneous" cure of scalp ringworm, but why this is so is not entirely established. It has been found that a diet rich in carbohydrate will produce quite marked changes in the lipid composition of the sebum of healthy medical students. It has also been found that there is a very marked sex difference in the amount of cholesterol in the sebum from girls and young women, and that this varies with the menstrual cycle.

Apocrine Glands

The apocrine glands develop in association with the hair follicles in certain limited regions of the skin surface, principally the axillae, pubic and perineal regions, although isolated follicles or groups of follicles may bear them. The breast is of course an apocrine gland, and apocrine secretion occurs in the ceruminous glands of the external auditory meatus and the ciliary glands of the eyelids (which may be involved in certain inherited cystic disorders).

The anlage of the apocrine gland resembles that of the sebaceous gland, but appears later and forms a lumen at an early stage in its development, possibly presaged by the appearance of vesicles in the central cells. Shortly after this, the cells develop desmosomes and tight junctions and bear microvilli on their free surface; mitochondria and granules of varying size, structure and electron-density can be seen with the cytoplasm of the luminal cells.

The apocrine glands do not develop fully until puberty, when they are found to consist of a coiled secretory part and a straight duct which opens directly into the hair canal. The duct is identical structurally with that of an eccrine sweat gland, while each coil is lined by secretory cells, surrounded by a layer of myoepithelial cells—separated, as usual, from the collagen of the dermis by a readily distinguishable basal lamina. The secretory (juxta-luminal) cells contain granules of different sizes and electron-density mainly in the upper compartment of the cell, while apical caps of cytoplasm (from which the type of secretion derives its name) project into the lumen. Recent ultra-structural studies suggest that the notion that the apical cap is somehow pinched off and shed with its contents into the lumen of the gland is erroneous; indeed the conspicuous presence of microvilli, which are the hallmarks of secretion and/or absorption, virtually rules out that mode of secretion. However, as Breathnach comments,[3] little interest has been taken in these glands to date.

Langerhans Cells

Langerhans cells have been the centre of controversy for many years, but it now seems clear that they are not "effete" melanocytes en route to ultimate desquamation, as was previously thought.[17] They are found in the epidermis in all non-human primates, and those in the African Lorisidae exhibit alkaline phosphatase activity suggesting that they have some important biological function. They are dendritic cells, usually seen above the basal layer, but can easily be distinguished from keratinocytes by their lack of desmosomes and tonofilaments, and from melanocytes because the melanosomes are absent. They possess a very indented nucleus and a characteristic organelle, *the Langerhans granule*, which is made up of an outer limiting membrane and a central lamella. Racquet-shaped structures in which the limiting membrane is expanded at one end are also evident, and vesicles which almost certainly represent cross sections of the expanded portion of the racquet-shaped bodies. It has been suggested that these cells may be of mesenchymal origin.

Merkel Cells (Fig. 8)

Merkel cells are specialized cells evident in the basal layer of the epidermis characterized by the presence of round dense granules mainly on the side opposite to the Golgi apparatus. The Merkel cell is connected to neighbouring keratinocytes by desmosomes. Merkel cells are closely associated with neurites especially in the skin of the digits and are thought to function as a touch receptor. The specific granules are about 1,000 Å. in diameter limited by a membrane. Fine filaments are present in the cytoplasm of the cells and are associated with the inner aspect of the desmosomes which connect the cell to neighbouring keratinocytes. However, hemidesmosomes are not seen on the basal plasma membrane of the Merkel cell and this distinguishes them from keratinocytes. The source and biogenesis of Merkel granules remains unknown and their precise function remains obscure although it has been suggested that they may be secretory in function.

Mammary Glands

The earliest stage in development of breasts is the appearance of paired thickening on either side of the body wall from base of the fore limb bud to the region medial to the hind limb bud. These mammary ridges are barely visible at 7 mm. stage and the caudal two-thirds disappears so as to leave a single pair of thickenings situated about the middle of the cephalic third of the ridge. The primordia of the breasts arise as a superficial layer of flattened cells and a deeper cuboidal layer. As development proceeds the primordia penetrate the underlying mesenchyme and give rise to approximately 20 secondary sprouts around which fat cells begin to gather. These become canalized in the later weeks of gestation, and their ducts open into an epidermal pit, which is raised at or soon after full term by proliferation of the secondary mesoderm to produce the nipple. Congenital amazia may occur as an isolated abnormality; it is also found in the Hutchinson–Gilford form of progeria. Polythelia is much commoner than polymastia and also occurs in non-human primates.

Ontogeny of Epidermal Ridges and Skin Creases

Although considerable attention has been paid to the variations in pattern that may be found in the dermatoglyphics of palmar and plantar skin, the pattern exhibited by the rhomboids and other polygons on the external surface of the epidermis, as well as the sculpture of its undersurface, has been virtually ignored. Yet each region of skin displays a pattern peculiar to itself; furthermore the pattern once established remains unchanged throughout the life of the individual and skin transplanted from one region to another retains the patterning of the donor site.

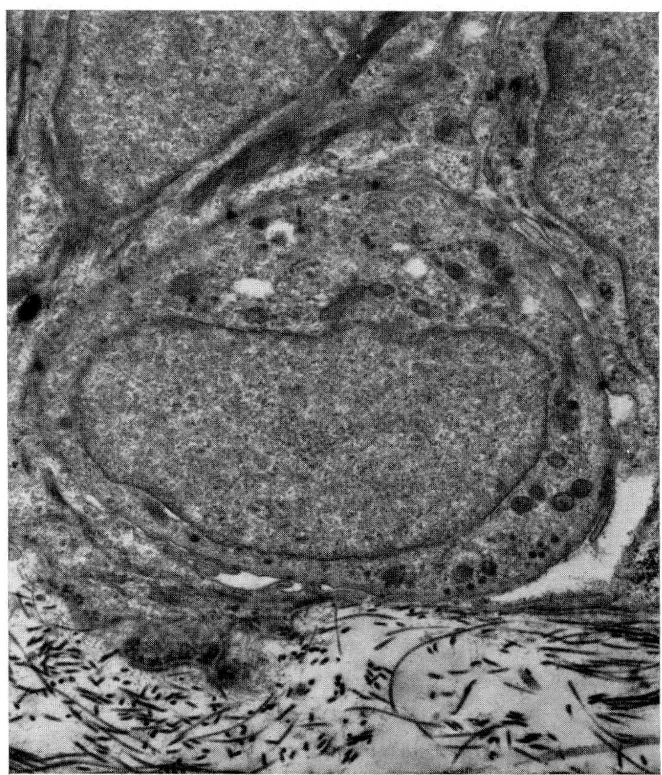

FIG. 8. Merkel cell in basal layer of epidermis of finger of 21 week human fetus. 9,860. (Breathnach, *J. invest. Dermat.*, 1971.)

Regional differences in the architecture of the epidermal ridges and papillae are related to the arrangement of hair follicles and sweat glands, with the sweat pores and ducts assuming a clock-dial pattern. The epidermal ridges tend to radiate towards sweat ducts, but those in relation to hair follicles are arranged as rosettes. Occasionally, the ridges are arranged concentrically about both, such that those round the sweat glands resemble cockades.

The skin shows considerable differences at different sites; the hair follicles vary in number, size and rate at which the hair grows. There are striking differences, too, in the texture and other properties of the hairs produced: thus coarse hairs are found in the eyebrows and the beard, pubic and axillary hairs after puberty, while the hair of the forehead is comprised of very fine down. There are virtually no epidermal ridges between the hair follicles of the head, cheeks and upper lip, whereas they are well developed on the forehead, scalp, chin and ear. The ridges display a very characteristic diamond-shaped pattern in the eyelids, where they often join the wall of the hair canal, and may sub-serve the function of attachment of the follicle to the epidermis. They do not join the sweat ducts but tend to encircle them instead.

The epidermal ridges of the under surface of the chest and back are arranged like a cobweb, in contrast to the parallel arrangement on the skin of the anterior abdominal wall. Obesity destroys the overall reticular pattern which is broken up into isolated parallel ridges separated by a completely flat epidermis.

The first evidence of the development of ridges is the appearance on the under surface of the digital epidermis about the 11th or 12th week of slight thickenings which soon develop into ridges in association with the developing sweat gland and duct. Surface ridges are not evident until those beneath are well developed and they are superimposed on the sweat gland folds, between which depressions are formed such that they correspond with the furrows on the outer surface. The system of dermal ridges is well established by the end of the 5th month of fetal life. On the palms and soles the ridges first appear in association with pads common to and more prominent in the other mammalia. Those on the hands precede those on the feet by approximately 2 weeks.

The mechanisms controlling pattern development are still hotly debated, but it is clear that the fetal mounds or pads must influence pattern leading to loops or whorls; otherwise ridges tend to be at right angles to the long axis of limb or digit. It has been held by some that the ridges result from tension in the skin, but this really explains nothing, while others hold that the ridges follow the line of least curvature which would account very well for loops and triradia.[8,9,14] Chromosomal anomalies, especially trisomy, have profound effects on the pattern; the Simian crease of Down's syndrome has been recognized for a long time and in fact is normal on the palms and soles of many species of monkey.

The Development of the Blood Vessels of the Skin

The earliest sign of development of the vasculature of the skin is the formation of networks of vessels in the subcutaneous tissues of the embryo, from which the dermal vasculature proper develops and from which the definitive blood vessels of the skin ultimately differentiate. The primordial arteries stem from the intersegmental arteries which link the aorta with the subcutaneous vascular plexuses and are first seen during the 4th week (CR = 3–4·5 mm.). Parts of these primordial vessels are themselves plexiform and anastomoses between them may be of importance in their final differentiation and fate.

The cutaneous arteries enter the dermis from the subcutis to give rise to a deep plexus from which branches arise and ascend to the upper dermis; there small twigs are given off which gradually lose their muscle coat (meta-arterioles) to be surrounded by pericytes and finally to consist of the simple endothelial tubes which form the capillary loops of the papillary layer of the dermis. The veins draining the same region also form two plexuses—superficial and deep, which are nearer to the surface than the corresponding arterial vessels. The transition between the different segments of the microvasculature of the skin makes it difficult to identify each element, and it may be impossible to be sure that a given vessel with a muscular coat is a small arteriole or a collecting vessel, even when viewed with the electron microscope.

It is clear from the work of Zweifach[34] that the microvasculature of the skin is made up of arterial and venous arcades which are linked by inter-connecting vessels as well as by the direct arterio-venous shunts associated with glomus bodies. The number of capillaries and the elaborate nature of the microvasculature of the skin is far beyond that required for the metabolic needs of the dermis and epidermis and its appendages: indeed, the blood supply to the skin is some 20 times that required to supply its metabolic needs. This excess of vessels serves for thermo-regulation and also helps to maintain overall vascular tone.

At birth there is a profound change from the uniformly warm aqueous environment of the amniotic cavity to that of the changing temperature and humidity of the infant's new surroundings. There is a striking increase in the number of capillaries in the uppermost layers of the dermis during the first weeks of extra-uterine life which is accompanied by the maturation of the vessels already present at birth as demonstrated by their increased sensitivity to vasoactive agents such as adrenalin and histamine. Premature infants require higher concentrations of these vasoactive agents than full term infants to evoke the appropriate response but they mature and adapt quickly to their new environment. It is during this period that the common strawberry mark (cavenous haemangioma) begins to appear and it is tempting to suggest that these birth marks are in some way associated with the angioneogenesis which takes place in the skin of the normal new born; however, the 3 to 1 preponderance of girls over boys with respect to the incidence of strawberry marks suggests that other factors must play their part in their pathogenesis. Enzyme histochemical studies of these lesions have revealed that the vascular elements of which they are comprised lack alkaline phosphatase active—in contrast to functioning capillaries which display marked activity of this enzyme.[28]

The epidermal appendages, sweat glands, and pilosebaceous follicles have quite elaborate networks of small vessels associated with them, and it is of some interest that hair follicles, as they develop, grow towards a pre-formed plexus of vessels and nerves. The micro-vasculature of the hair follicle also displays changes during the hair cycle; the plexus of vessels associated with the lower portion of the follicle virtually disappears during catagen and telogen, only to be re-established during anagen.

Histogenesis of the Nails (Fig. 9)

The nails first appear at the tips of the digits towards the end of the 3rd month, as epidermal thickenings which migrate to the dorsum of the digit and carry with them branches from the palmar (or plantar) nerves. The skin bearing the nails betrays its origin also by its involvement in several of the inherited disorders affecting palmar (or plantar) epidermis. The primary nail fields lodge in a shallow depression, which is produced by differential growth in the fields which lags behind that of the neighbouring skin; growth of cells proximally produces the nail root or matrix beneath the eponychium. Nail growth is very slow during fetal life and the free margin of the nail rarely reaches the tip of the digit before full term.

around the nucleus, but soon come to be restricted mainly to the sub-nuclear compartment of the cells, away from the free surface with its microvillous processes and the vesicles of the supra-nuclear compartment. With further development glycogen appears in increased amounts in the supranuclear compartment, especially at that stage when indentations appear in the nucleus indicating its senescence and impending disappearance.

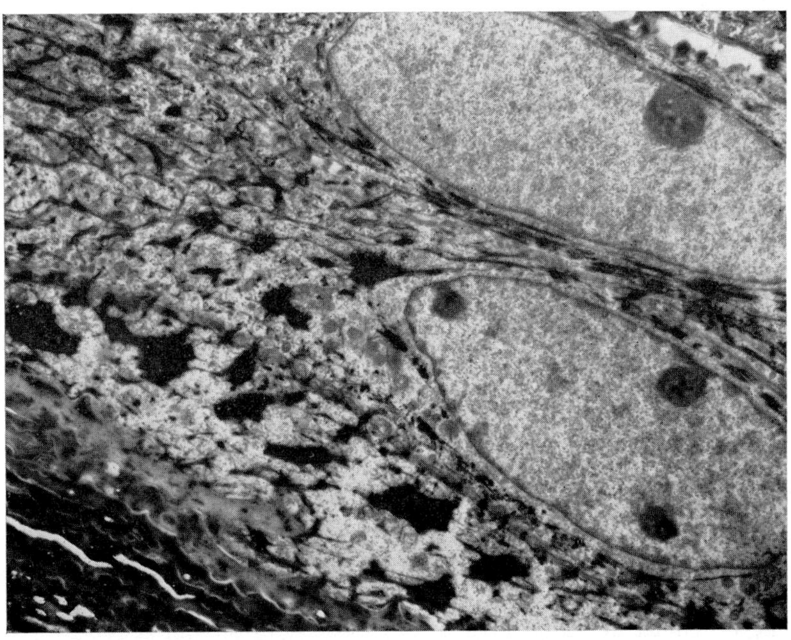

FIG. 9. Longitudinal section of nail organ of finger of 16 week human fetus. The nail plate is seen at the lower left corner of the field, and dorsal to it, cells of the proximal nail fold. ×6,660. (A. S. Breathnach.)

At the ultrastructural level the nail primordium is seen to consist of a plate of epidermal cells inserted somewhat obliquely into the dermis overlying the terminal phalanx of the digit. The epidermal plate constitutes the nail field from which deeper cells proliferate to produce the cells which undergo keratinization as they reach the surface to form the nail plate.

BIOCHEMICAL ASPECTS OF THE DEVELOPING SKIN

Glycogen and the Developing Skin

Glycogen figures prominently, when appropriate lead stains are used, in electron micrographs of the epidermal cells in the early stages of development. It is deposited as particles which may appear singly or as rosettes which may be solitary or grouped. Glycogen disappears from the normal keratinocyte in the fully mature epidermis, but it may be found in epidermal cells in certain disease states in later (post-natal) life. It remains a normal cell constituent of eccrine sweat glands, sebaceous glands and the outer root sheath of the hair follicle.

Large glycogen deposits are also found in cells of the periderm, where at first they are seen to be distributed all

During the hair germ stage of development the entire epidermis is laden with glycogen but the epidermal cells lose their glycogen. Synchronously with this a basal lamina appears, and oxygen consumption rises as metabolism proceeds.

THE STRUCTURAL PROTEINS OF THE SKIN

Biogenesis of Keratin

Ultra-structure of Keratinocytes

The basal layer of the epidermis is 1 cell thick and rests on an electron-lucent layer. The basement membrane or basal lamina which is a continuous structureless layer about 500–700 Å. closely follows the basal surface of the epidermal cells from which it is separated by an intervening space of constant width about 500 Å.

The cytoplasm of the basal cell contain fine filaments of low electron density and approximately 50 Å. in diameter which often occur in bundles (tonofilaments or tonofibrils). They tend to lie in a basal-apical direction but they anastomose and spread across the cell as well. The nuclei are usually oval and there is a perinuclear zone free of fibrils. The filaments and fibrils are often attached to modified desmosomes on the base of the cell and may constitute the basal attachment device of Selby.[27] The Golgi apparatus is poorly developed in the basal cell but other organelles are present. As the daughter cells of the basal layer ascend the epidermis, the fibrils increase in number and stain more deeply until they reach the granular layer, which in the human is about 2–3 cells thick. Here the shape of the cell changes to that of a long thin lens and electron dense bodies of keratohyalin now become conspicuous; at high magnification they are seen to be made up of fine filaments. As the cells move towards the surface there is an abrupt transition to the horny squame which is now almost completely filled with keratin. This is seen to comprise fibres about 70 Å. in diameter embedded in an electron dense matrix. The precise role and composition of keratohyalin is still disputed: some workers think that the keratohyalin granules are transformed into keratin,[18] while Brody[4] and Odland[25] think that the protein associated with the filaments of the keratohyalin granules is the matrix of the final keratin comp ex of the horny layer.

There are a number of inherited disorders of keratinization, but little is known of their developmental pathology.

Biogenesis of Collagen

Collagen is synthesized by the fibroblasts of the dermis and is laid down in the intercellular ground substance, comprising acid mucopolysaccharides and protein which are also synthesized by the fibroblasts. Collagen is the most abundant molecular species in the vertebrate phylum and a major portion of the total body content is present in the adult dermis. The molecule is shaped like a small rod 2,900 Å. in length and 14 Å. in diameter, made up of 3 polypeptide chains which are interwoven to form a triple helix. Each chain forms a spiral, with glycine residues on the inside and proline/hydroxyproline as well as the polar amino acids on the outside. The whole is held together by hydrogen bonds. Collagen is not metabolically inert but much of its metabolism takes place outside the cell. Collagen is soluble in dilute salt solutions and dilute acids, but the molecules will soon aggregate to form microfibrils through co-valent cross links between lysyl residues. The extra-cellular molecular environment largely determines whether this will take place, as well as the number of such cross-links. The presence of chondroitin sulphates appear to be essential for collagen fibrillogenesis. It has been established that the lysyl residues in positron 5 are first oxidized to the semialdehyde of l-aminoadipic acid, after which the link between adjacent chains is forged by an aldol condensation between the two aldehydes followed by dehydration. These bonds in common with others within the same molecule contribute to its topology.

Head to tail bonds as well as cross-links render the collagen molecule insoluble and it seems likely that the quarter "staggering" of arrays of collagen, which gives rise to the characteristic banding seen with the electron microscope, results from side-to-side cross linkage. Collagen is first recognizable in the human skin about the 9th week of gestation and steadily increases throughout development, largely at the expense of the ground substance. The degree of solubility is neither uniform nor constant throughout the dermis. The dermis in common with other collagenous tissue produces one or more enzymes (collagenases capable of degrading collagen); these appear to be synthesized *de novo* and are not stored in an inactive form within the cell. There is increased collagenase activity in certain inherited bullous diseases such as the dystrophic forms of epidermolysis bullosa as well as in acquired conditions such as periodontal disease.

Biogenesis of Elastin

Elastic fibres appear as yellow wavy elements which branch and anastomose freely. Deep in the dermis the fibrils tend to be condensed into flattened bands whereas free fibrillar clumps are found in the papillary layer of the dermis. In both regions, however, the elastic fibres are interconnected to form a network which enmeshes the collagen bundles. No free ends of elastic fibres are to be found anywhere in the dermis as they are all joined to each other. Estimates of the amount of elastic fibres in the tissue vary with the method employed to identify them but approximately 3 per cent of the skin on unexposed surfaces of the body such as the abdomen seems to be the mode. There is marked increase in the elastin of exposed areas but this may well be due to the presence of another compound which differs in many respects from elastin. Elastin undergoes considerable changes in chemical composition with age. Microfibrils are the first to appear in the fetus but as development continues an increasing amount of amorphous matrix appears to be deposited on them which largely obscures the fibrils as the tissue matures. Human skin is rich in elastic fibres which help to anchor the epidermis to the dermis, a function normally performed by the hair follicle in most mammalian species.

Chemically, elastin resembles collagen in that 30 per cent of the residues are glycine. It also has a relatively high content of proline, but here the resemblance ceases. Lysyl residues are, however, present and these undoubtedly contribute to the cross-linkages between the polypeptide chains forming the molecules.

Chalones in Developing Skin

A feature of development is the severe restrictions imposed on the pluripotent genome of the zygote and the blastomeres. It is a matter of common knowledge that the tissues of the normal healthy adult mammal maintain a constant mass. However, in a tissue like the epidermis, from which effete cells are shed continuously throughout life, those lost must be replaced by mitotic division of cells in the basal layer. There must be some mechanism by which the mitotic rate is controlled and homeostatis of the tissue is maintained.

Bullough and Lawrence[5,6] have proposed that there are substances, which are termed chalones, which prevent cell division when they are present in appropriate amounts in the cells of the tissue concerned. Chalones are tissue specific, but not species specific, and are thought to be glycoproteins of low molecular weight. They further postulate that there is a critical period in the life of the cell when a choice is made to divide or become functional. It has been known for a long time that cells often pass through a period of intense mitotic activity before they differentiate. Bullough[5,6] has termed this critical period, when the decision is made, the dicophase. When a basal cell divides, the two daughter cells at first lie side by side. It is thought that pressure builds up in the layer forcing one of the daughter cells upwards to replace those shed. The cell now finds itself in a very different environment; in particular it has lost contact with the basal lamina, and with it the exchange of information that normally takes place between the cells of the basal layer and the subadjacent dermis. It is through these chemical and physical exchanges that key regions of the epidermal cell genome are switched on and off. It is difficult in the light of present knowledge to apply the Monod-Jacob model of the genome which has proved so useful for prokaryotes, with its concept of the operon working through repressor and regulator genes, to mamallian cell systems, but Bullough suggests that there may be a "mitosis" operon and a "tissue operon" with the tissue specific chalones serving as the prime agent in tissue regulation. Adrenalin enhances the inhibitory action of the chalone on mitosis, and this tempts one to speculate on the role of cyclic 3′.5′ AMP in these events.

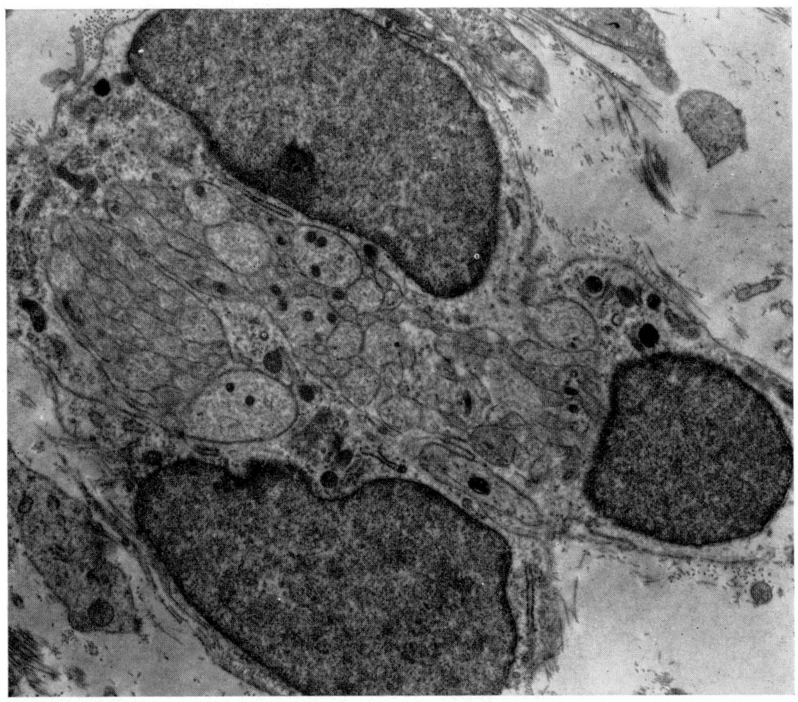

FIG. 10. Developing nerve from skin of 14 week human fetus. Three Schwann cells are seen enveloping groups of neuraxons. ×8,400. (A. S. Breathnach.)

The duration of mitosis varies considerably, not only from tissue to tissue, but also from time to time. There is also an intrinsic circadian rhythm in the epidermis which influences mitosis; cell division being maximal during mid-sleep. The occurrence of congenital skin defects, especially of the vertex, raises some very interesting questions. It is true that some defects are associated with chromosomal anomalies, in particular with trisomy of the "D group"; but in most cases the defect occurs in an otherwise normal infant. It is particularly intriguing that such defects epithelialize and form a firm scar after birth, whereas there is no attempt at repair of the defect during intra-uterine life. It is difficult to interpret this in terms of chalones. On the other hand, certain inherited disordeir of keratinization characterized by increased mitotic activtys of the epidermis, such as the bullous and non-bullous variants of congenital ichthyosiform erythroderma, may well prove to be chalone deficiency disorders. Dermatomegaly, in which there is circumscribed or regional "overgrowth" of dermal as well as epidermal tissue, is also difficult to reconcile with a disturbance in chalone activity, especially as Bullough postulates separate specific chalones for sebaceous glands and other epidermal appendages.

ONTOGENY OF PERIPHERAL NERVES IN SKIN (Fig. 10)

His[13] recognized long ago that the neural crest was a "Zwischenstrang" between presumptive epidermis and the neural tube and that it was the source of the sensory component of the peripheral nervous system, including the spinal ganglia and some of the cranial nerves. The motor nerves, on the other hand, arise from cells in the ventral part of the neural tube from whence they throw out non-medulated axons which eventually terminate in the appropriate muscles, presumably guided to their destination by contact. The fibres of the spinal ganglia on the other hand are myelinated, the latter being produced by the Schwann cells (also derived from the crest) which are invariably associated with the axons of the cells of the dorsal root ganglia.

The dermal neural network is not only well developed in the human scalp but is also well formed here as elsewhere, before the hair follicles make their appearance and these networks represent the first ordered structures to be seen in the vertebrate dermis.[33] Nerve fibres are to be found at the tip of the primordium of the hair follicle in the 4th month, but they do not enmesh the follicle itself until the hair peg invaginates the dermal nerve plexus in its downward path to the lowermost part of the dermis, when it is wrapped by axon filaments in the process. Should the follicle perish for any reason, the nerve nets coil to form endings very like those seen in glabrous skin. The same transformation of the nerve-net associated with the hair follicle of the balding human male takes place when the follicle no longer produces terminal scalp hair. There has been an evolutionary trend in the Primate Order towards progressive loss of pelage, especially of the face and scalp, which suggests that by becoming naked man ceased to be an ape, thanks to the increase in sensory nerve-endings. There must have been a corresponding increase in his cerebral cortex to deal with the increased in-put of information that nakedness brings.

The innervation of the hair follicle conforms to an overall pattern in which stem fibres ascend along the side of the follicle and then sprout into terminal axoplasmic filaments to surround the follicle. A palisade of nerve filaments forms just below the level at which the sebaceous gland duct enters the hair canal, due to the looping back of nerve fibrils. As mentioned above, in male type baldness the nerve end organs are preserved but migrate to the undersurface of the epidermis.

The introduction of techniques for demonstrating cholinesterases has enabled workers to demonstrate nerve fibres with considerable ease, and it is now established that delicate intra-epidermal nerve endings are present in the fetus, especially on the volar surface of the digits.

The cutaneous arteries and arterioles are richly endowed with autonomic nerves (also derived from elements from the neural crest) and nerves may be seen in the media of these vessels. The arterio-venous anastomoses are also richly supplied with nerves and they appear in the fingers as early as the 18th week.

Several of the end organs, such as Meissner's corpuscles, contain a large amount of pseudo-cholinesterase;[16] and it is of some interest that the enzyme has been demonstrated in nerves leaving these corpuscles in the fetus, but not the adult. Paccinian corpuscles also exhibit strong cholinesterase activity. The genital corpuscles of the glans penis and prepuce in the male and the labia and clitoris of the female also contain large amounts of pseudo-cholinesterase, while genital skin also contains many "cholinesterase" nerve fibres in the papillary layer which end free in the epidermis.

The sweat glands are well supplied with nerves which are seen round the secretory cells of the glands. These, unlike the fibres round apocrine glands, are strongly cholinesterase positive, but apocrine fibres may show enzyme activity in Negroes.[21,22]

This absence of cholinesterase from the nerves of apocrine glands is a feature in those glands on the general body surface of many primates, but those in special sites, including the axilla in man's near relatives the chimpanzee and the gorilla are enmeshed by cholinesterase positive nerves.

No convincing evidence has yet been obtained that sebaceous glands are supplied with nerves.

Dermal nerve networks vary with the density of the pelage, where hair follicles are few, the neural networks are frequent and there are more specialized nerve endings just below the epidermis in glabrous skin.[21,33]

Brief mention of some aspects of the developmental pathology of the neural crest and its derivatives would not be out of place here. It seems clear that the neural crest cells are pluripotent during migration and particularly labile in early development[31] and that the environment of the cells plays a dominant role in differentiation. It is tempting to speculate that the common pigmented mole may result from some epigenetic event that allows a clone of cells to attempt for form Schwann cells, neural cells and atypical pigment producing cells. Piebaldism in man results from failure of neural crest cells to arrive and/or survive in the totally non-pigmented areas, such as the frontal blaze. The genesis of *café au lait* patches in neurofibromatosis might be "built in" to the migrant crest cells or result from local tissue changes.

ACKNOWLEDGEMENT

My thanks are due to Professor A. S. Breathnach, St. Mary's Hospital Medical School, for his kind gift of the electron micrographs.

REFERENCES

1. Baillie, A. H., Thomson, J. and Milne, J. A. (1966), "The Distribution of Hydroxysteroid Dehydrogenase in Human Sebaceous Glands," *Brit. J. Derm.*, **78,** 451–457.
2. Baillie, A. H., Calman, K. C. and Milne, J. A. (1965), "Histochemical Distribution of Hydroxysteroid Dehydrogenases in Human Skin," *Brit. J. Derm.*, **77,** 610–616.
3. Breathnach, A. S. (1971), *An Atlas of the Ultra-structure of Human Skin.* London: J. & A. Churchill.
4. Brody, I. (1959), "An Ultrastructural Study of the Role of the Keratohyalin Granules in the Keratinization Process," *J. Ultrastr. Research*, **3,** 84–104.
5. Bullough, W. S. and Laurence, E. B. (1960), "The Control of Epidermal Mitotic Activity in the Mouse," *Proc. roy. Soc. B.*, **151,** 517–536.
6. Bullough, W. S., Laurence, E. B., Iversen, O. H. and Eljo, K. (1967), "The Vertebrate Epidermal Chalone," *Nature*, 214, 578–580.
7. Cameron, E. H. D., Baillie, A. H., Grant, J. A., Milne, J. A. and Thomson, J. (1966), "Transformation *in vitro* of (7-α-^{3}H) Dehydroepiandrosterone to (^{3}H) Testosterone by Skin from Men," *J. Endocrin.*, **35,** *Proc. soc. Endocr.*, xix–xx.
8. Cummins, H. (1964), "Dermatoglyphics: A Brief Review," in *The Epidermis*, pp. 375–386 (W. Montagna and W. C. Lobitz, Eds.). New York and London: Academic Press.
9. Cummins, H. and Midlo, C. (1943), *Finger Prints, Palms and Soles.* Philadelphia: Blakiston.
10. Davidson, E. (1968), *Gene Activity in Early Development.* New York: Academic Press.

11. Frithjof, F. and Wersaal, J. (1965), "A Highly Ordered Structure in Keratinizing Human Oral Epithelium," *J. Ultrastr. Research*, **12,** 371–9.
12. Gomex, E. C. and Hsia, S. L. (1966), "Studies on Cutaneous Metabolism of Testosterone–4^{14}C," *Fed. Proc.*, **25,** 282.
13. His, W. (1866), *Untersuchungen uber die erste Anlage des Wirbeltierleibes. Die erste Entwicklung des Huhnchens im Ei.* Leipzig.
14. Holt, S. B. (1960), "Genetics of Dermal Ridges," *Ann. Human Genetics (London)*, **24,** 253–269.
15. Holtfreter, J. (1953), "A Study of the Mechanics of Gastrulation," *J. exp. Zool.*, **94,** 261–315.
16. Hurley, H. J. and Mescon, H. (1956), "Cholinergic Innervation of the Digital Arteriovenous Anastamoses of Human Skin," *J. appl. Physiol.*, **9,** 82–84.
17. Medawar, P. B. (1953), "The Micro Anatomy of the Mammalian Epidermis," *Quart.* J. *micr. Sci.*, **94,** 481–506.
18. Mercer, E. H. (1965), "Intercellular Adhesion and Histogenesis" in *Organogenesis*, pp. 29–53 (de Haan and Urspring, H., Eds.). New York: Holt, Rinehart & Winston.
19. Miller, J. R. and Giroux, J. (1966), "Dermatoglyphics in Pediatric Practice," *J. Pediat.*, **69,** 302–12.
20. Mintz, B. (1967), "Gene Control of Mammalian Pigmentary Differentation. 1. Clonal Origin of Melanocytes," *Proc. nat. Acad. Sci.*, **58,** 344–351.
21. Montagna, W. (1960), "Cholinesterases in the Cutaneous Nerves of Man," *Advanc. biol. Skin*, **1,** 74–87.
22. Montagna, W. (1962), *The Structure and Function of the Skin*, 2nd edition. New York and London: Academic Press.
23. Moynahan, E. J. (1971), "The Fine Structural Changes in the Basement Membrane and Tumour Cells of Squamous Cell Carcinoma in Human Skin, *Annal. Ital. Derm. clin. et sper.*, **25,** 200–203.
24. Moynahan, E. J., Sethi, N. and Murray Brookes (1972), "Histochemical Observations on Developing Rat Skin," *J. Anat.*, **111,** 427–435.
25. Odland, G. F. (1958), "The Fine Structure of the Inter-relationship of Cells in Human Epidermis," *J. Biophys. Biochem. Cytol.*, **4,** 529–538.
26. Polani, P. E. and Moynahan, E. J. (1972), "Progressive Cardiomyopathic Lentiginosis," *Quart. J. Med.*, No. 162, **41,** 205–225.
26a. Rogers, G. E. (1964), *Structural and Biochemistry Features of the Hair Follicle in the Epidermis.* (W. Montagna and W. C. Lobitz, Eds.). Academic Press.
27. Selby, C. C. (1955), "An Electron Microscopy Study of the Epidermis of Mammalian Skin in their Sections. I. Dermo-epidermal Junctions and Basal Cell Layer," *J. Biophys. Biochem. Cytol.*, **1,** 429–444.
28. Sethi, N. K. (1971), Ph.D. Thesis, University of London.
29. Waddington, C. H. (1956), *Principles of Embryology.* London. Allen & Unwin.
30. Waddington, C. H. (1962), *New Patterns in Genetics and Development.* New York and London: Columbia University Press.
31. Weston, J. A. (1970), "The Migration and Differentiation of Neural Crest Cells," *Adv. in Morphogenesis*, **8,** 41–114.
32. Wilde, C. E. (1961), "The Differentiation of Vertebrate Pigment Cells," *Adv. in Morphogenesis*, **1,** 267–300.
33. Winkelmann, R. (1960), "Similarities in Cutaneous Nerve End Organs," in *Adv. in Biol. Skin*, **1,** 48–62.
34. Zweifach, B. W. (1959). "The Microcirculation of the Blood," *Scient. Amer.*, **200,** 54.

FURTHER READING

Blandau, R. J. (1971), *The Biology of the Blastocyst.* University Chicago Press.

Brachet, J. (1970, "Quelques problemes actuel en embryologie moleculaire," *Annee biologique*, **9,** 619–669.

Curtis, A. S. G. (1967), *The Cell Surface: Its Molecular Role in Morphogenesis.* New York: Academic Press.

Ebert, J. D. (1965), *Interacting Systems in Development.* Holt, Rinehart and Winston.

Gluckmann, A. (1951), "Cell Deaths in Normal Vertebrate Ontogony," *Biol. Rev.*, **26,** 59–86.

Hamilton, W. J. (1949), "Early Stages of Human Development," *Ann. Roy. Coll. Surg. Eng.*, **4,** 281–294.

Hamilton, W. J., Boyd, J. D. and Mossman, H. (1972), *Human Embryology*, 3rd edition. Cambridge: Heffer.

Hashimoto, K., Gross, B. G., Nelson, R. and Lever, W. F. (1966), "The Ultra-structure of the Skin of Human Embryos III. The Formation of the Nail in 16–18 Week Old Embryos," *J. Invest. Derm.*, **47,** 205–217.

Holt, S. B. (1960), "Genetics of Dermal Ridges," *Ann. Human Genetics (London)*, **24,** 253–269.

Horstadius, S. (1950), *The Neural Crest.* London: Oxford University Press.

Kenshalo, D. R. (Ed.) (1968), *The Skin Senses.* C. C. Thomas.

Mercer, E. H. (1961), *Keratin and Keratinization.* Oxford: Pergamon.

Miller, J. R. and Giroux, J. (1966), "Dermatoglyphics in Pediatric Practice," *J. Pediat.*, **69,** 302–312.

Penrose, R. L. (1973), "Fingerprints and Palmistry," *Lancet*, **i,** 1239–1242.

Pinkus, H. (1938), "Embryology of Hair," in *The Biology of Hair Growth*, W. (Montagna and R. A. Ellis, Eds.). New York: Academic Press.

Saunders, J. W. (1966), "Death in Embryonic Systems," *Science N.Y.*, **154,** 604–612.

Thorp, F. K. and Dorfman, A. (1967), "Differentiation of Connective Tissue," *Topics in Develop. Biol.*, **2,** 151–190.

Urspring, H. (1963), "Development and Genetics of Patterns," *Amer. Zool.*, **3,** 71–86.

Wilde, C. E. (1961), "The Differentiation of Vertebrate Pigment Cells," *Adv. in Morphogenesis I*, 267–300.

Wolff, K. (1967), "The Fine Structure of the Langerhans Cell Granule," *J. Cell. Biol.*, **35,** 468–473.

Zelickson, A. S. (1965), "The Langerhans Cell. *J. Invest. Derm.* **44,** 201–212.

30. THE DEVELOPMENT OF THE SWEAT GLANDS AND THEIR FUNCTION

V. SCHWARZ

ANATOMY

The main function of the eccrine gland—the delivery of water to the body surface—is well served by its anatomy and mechanism of action. Deeply embedded in the lower strata of the dermis or the subcutaneous tissue is the sweat coil (C, Fig. 1),[7] a tube closed at one end and lined by a single layered epithelium consisting of two types of cells. One (A) is believed to produce the aqueous salt solution, the other (M) mucus, which together make up the precursor fluid. The duct begins in the coiled portion of the gland where it is in close proximity to the secretory epithelium, a circumstance which may be important in the secretion of NaCl into the lumen and its re-absorption by the ductal cells. The latter are arranged in two layers, all the way up through the dermis. The whole gland, secretory coil and duct, is amply supplied with blood vessels and nerve fibres.

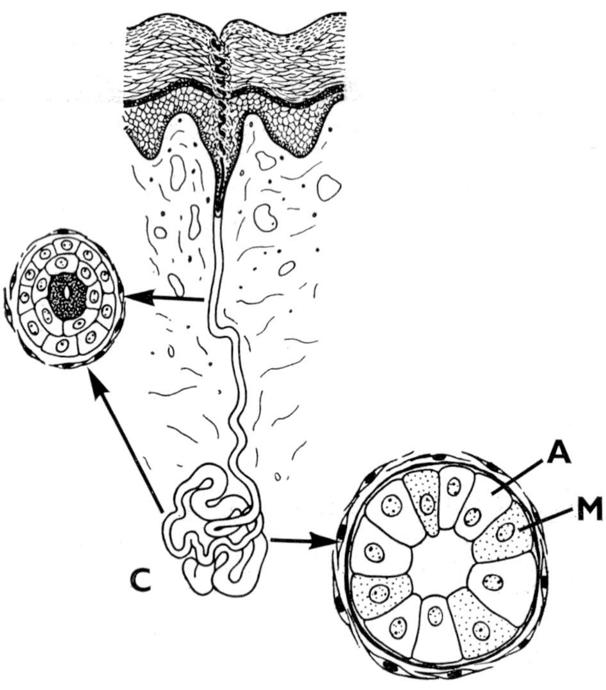

FIG. 1. Anatomy of eccrine gland. (After J. S. Weiner and K. Hellmann (1960), *Biol. Rev.*, **35**, 141.)

FUNCTION

Human sweat glands are recognized to have at least two functions. The eccrine glands, which are widely scattered over all parts of the body, are unique in the animal kingdom in their capacity to produce a copious, dilute secretion which on evaporation dissipates sufficient heat to confer unrivalled adaptability to climatic conditions. Other eccrine glands, situated on the palms and the soles, secrete smaller volumes of a fluid which heightens tactile perception and improves the grip. The function of the apocrine glands which cluster in certain areas (axillary, inguinal, circum-areolar etc.) is probably vestigial in man, in contrast to the social, sexual and territorial role played by their fore-runners in other mammals.[7]

STIMULATION

The sweat glands respond to stimuli appropriate to their physiological function: thus palmar sweating is evoked by mental and emotional stimuli and is largely independent of heat. The sympathetic chain supplies these and other sweat glands, and although the nerves are undoubtedly cholinergic, adrenaline as well as acetylcholine triggers secretion. The eccrine glands on the general body surface are called into play by sympathetic stimuli originating in the heat regulatory centre of the hypothalamus, whereas those of the axillae and of the forehead secrete in response to both psychic and thermal stimuli. Apocrine glands also possess an autonomic innervation, but they appear to be mainly under control of circulating adrenaline.[7]

MECHANISM OF SWEAT FORMATION

Precursor fluid is probably formed by active transport of sodium into the lumen, accompanied by passive movement of water and chloride. The isotonic or slightly hypertonic fluid passes through the proximal, coiled portion of the duct where much of the NaCl is reabsorbed, and thence through the straight, distal duct where some Na is exchanged for K under the influence of aldosterone. The sweat appearing on the body surface is, therefore, always hypotonic its main solid component being NaCl, with some lactate, K and urea, and smaller amounts of a few other substances. The concentrations of only two of these components, NaCl and KCl, show any significant changes in the course of development or in disease. The sweat duct has a limited capacity for re-absorbing NaCl and the fraction of precursor fluid sodium reaching the skin surface therefore depends on the load, i.e. the secretory rate. At low rates of formation of precursor fluid the amount of Na presented to the duct cells is less than their reabsorptive capacity and hence little will appear in the surface sweat. As the rate increases, the reabsorptive capacity is ultimately exceeded and the sodium concentration of the sweat rises.[4] It follows that in adults, whose need to remove excess heat must be met by fewer glands per unit body surface than in children, and whose output per gland is, therefore, greater, the surface sweat contains more sodium. Thus we find a progressive increase in sweat sodium from 5–20 mequiv./l. at birth to levels as high as 120 mequiv./l. in adults (Table 1).[3]

TABLE 1

SODIUM CONTENT OF SWEAT AT DIFFERENT AGES

(From C. C. Lobeck and D. E. Huebner (1962), *Paediatrics*, **30**, 172)

Age	*Na (mequiv./l.)*
1–12 months	3·8–20·1
1–5 years	6·1–38·0
6–10 years	7·1–46·5
11–19 years	5·3–61·3
20–60 years	9·5–96·4

The K concentration falls as the sweating rate rises (for reasons not well understood) and it is also controlled by aldosterone. Thus the greater salt intake of adults, which depresses aldosterone secretion, is one of the major causes of higher sweat sodium levels than those of children (Table 2).[5]

TABLE 2

EFFECT OF SALT INTAKE ON Na CONTENT OF ADULT SWEAT

(From C. B. Sigal and R. L. Dobson (1968), *J. invest. Derm.*, **50**, 451)

	Sweating rate (mg./sq. cm./min.)	*Salt intake*	*Sweat* Na (mequiv./l.)
Subject A	2	low	20
		high	70
Subject B	8	low	50
		high	100

GLAND DEVELOPMENT

The eccrine glands of the general body surface begin to develop only in the 22nd fetal week—later than the palmar or apocrine glands. By the 24th week the density of glands distinguishable histologically (e.g. on the thigh) reaches a peak from which it declines subsequently as a consequence of growth, the total number of glands on the body remaining constant at 2–3 $\times$ 10^6 (Table 3).[6]

It is to be expected, therefore, that in the adult the gland density will be greatest on the forehead (300–400 $cm.^{-2}$) which grows less than other parts of the body. On the arm the density is inversely related to the circumference and one finds fewer glands on the upper compared to the lower forearm and on the muscular limbs of the manual workers compared to the more slender limbs of people with less developed muscles.

TABLE 3

DENSITY OF SWEAT GLANDS ON THIGH. HISTOLOGICAL COUNT

(From G. Szabo in *Adv. Biol. Skin.*, III. Eccrine Sweat Glands and Eccrine Sweating. Eds. W. Montagna, R. A. Ellis and A. F. Silver)

Age	*No. of glands/sq. cm. ± S.E.M.*
24-week fetus	2,970 ± 610
7-month fetus	1,730 ± 70
Full-term baby	1,560 ± 50
11–18-month baby	500 ± 80
Adult	120 ± 10

The fetal glands are inactive, possibly owing to hydration of the skin and consequent compression of the ducts. Since a visible miliaria, which normally develops if glands are stimulated under conditions of skin hydration, is not observed at birth, it would seem likely that no stimulation occurs *in utero*. A "sweat rash" often develops soon after birth, however, at a time when the glands become active.

FUNCTIONAL MATURATION

Premature babies of 30–34 weeks gestational age do not sweat in the first 14 days after birth, while those between 34 and 38 weeks produce only small volumes of sweat even in response to local injection of acetylcholine (a more powerful stimulus than warming to a rectal temperature at 37·8°). Thereafter sweat volume, maximum secretory rate and duration of response increase rapidly, first on the forehead and temples, later on the chest and arms, and finally on the legs.[1]

This increase in glandular activity may reflect a rising level of sympathetic stimulation and a greater responsiveness to pharmacological agents. In this context it is interesting that infants with congenital defects of the brain show no sweat response either to thermal or to massive pharmacological stimulation despite the histologically normal appearance of the sweat glands, the skin and the innervation. Two full-term infants with lumbar meningomyeloceles and complete flaccid paralysis of the legs have been reported to show a normal sweat response on the arms, with no response to chemical or thermal stimuli on the legs.[1] It seems, therefore, that function of the glands depends on intact central innervation.

The number of active glands reaches a maximum at two years but many remain incapable of secreting throughout life, although they appear anatomically normal.[2] Apocrine glands deviate from this pattern in reaching their functional maturity at puberty. The progressive activation during the first two years of life is able to maintain the thermoregulatory capacity of the eccrine glands against the background of a rapidly decreasing gland density engendered by growth. Not only do hitherto inactive glands become capable of producing sweat but the secretory response of each gland to a given stimulus increases. Thus babies may have five or six times the number of active glands per $cm.^2$ of thigh found in an adult, but the output per gland is only a third of the volume produced by mature glands in response to the same dose of intradermal acetylcholine.[1]

In normal adults sweating increases during sleep, which has been interpreted as indicating a heightened excitability of the thermal sweat centre due to loss of stimuli from an inhibitory centre in the cortex. In children the inhibition may be absent even in the waking state and this may account for their greater propensity, compared to adults, to sweat in the winter or at cooler ambient temperatures. At puberty some control mechanism seems to come into play which inhibits sweat gland activity, unless the body is exposed to high temperatures, thus ensuring more adequate thermoregulation and avoiding useless perspiration.[2]

CYSTIC FIBROSIS

Sweat electrolyte levels are affected by a number of pathological conditions, foremost of which is Cystic Fibrosis. The high sweat sodium (in excess of 70 mequiv./l.), widely regarded to be pathognomonic for this disease in babies and young children, is generally attributed to a failure of ductal reabsorption. A similar, though quantitatively lesser defect manifests itself in children heterozygous for Cystic Fibrosis. Since the sweat test is often the ultimate arbiter in the diagnosis of this disease, an appreciation of the factors which bear on the sodium concentration in the sweat—age, secretion rate, salt intake and other factors associated with altered aldosterone secretion—is important. In this context it should be borne in mind that the sodium loss in diarrhoea and the malnutrition due to malabsorption, so commonly found in this disease, promote an increase in aldosterone secretion which may lower the Na and raise the K concentrations in the sweat. As the clinical symptoms improve or disappear with treatment, so the sweat Na tends to *rise* and the K to *fall*. Whether inadequate perfusion affects the proportion of precursor fluid Na reabsorbed by the sweat duct in the manner seen in the nephron is as yet unknown, but it is possible that abnormal reabsorption of the ion, secondary to haemodynamic or other disturbances, may be a further complicating factor in the diagnosis of Cystic Fibrosis by the sweat test.

REFERENCES

1. Foster, K. G., Hey, E. N. and Katz, G. (1969), "Response of Sweat Glands of Neonates to Thermal Stimuli and to Intradermal Acetylcholine," *J. Physiol. (Lond.)*, **203**, 13.
2. Kuno, Y. (1956), *Human Perspiration*. Springfield: Thomas.
3. Lobeck, C. C. and Huebner, D. E. (1962), "Effect of Age, Sex and Cystic Fibrosis on Na and K Content of Human Sweat," *Pediatrics*, **30**, 172.
4. Schwartz, I. L. and Thayson, J. H. (1956), "Excretion of Sodium and Potassium in Human Sweat," *J. clin. Invest.*, **35**, 114.
5. Sigal, C. B. and Dobson, R. L. (1968), "The Effect of Salt Intake on Sweat Gland Function," *J. invest. Derm.*, **50**, 451.
6. Szabo, G. (1962), "The Number of Eccrine Sweat Glands in Human Skin," in *Advances in Biology of Skin. III*, p. 3. (W. Montagna, R. A. Ellis and A. F. Silver, Eds.). Oxford: Pergamon Press.
7. J. S. Weiner, and K. Hellmann (1960), "The Sweat Glands," *Biol. Rev.*, **35**, 141.

31. EMBRYOLOGY OF THE CENTRAL NERVOUS SYSTEM

RONALD J. LEMIRE

The traditional division of life into embryonic, fetal and postnatal periods has drawbacks when one refers to the development of the central nervous system (CNS). The period of "embryogenesis" extends beyond birth for some of its components and into fetal life for many. The present chapter will disregard this artificial barrier in some cases and attempt to discuss the early differentiation of the structure under consideration, irrespective of gestational age. Likewise, it will emphasize the morphological aspects of development and especially those referable to structural malformations of concern to the clinician dealing with newborns and infants.

Before proceeding directly to a discussion of CNS development, three sections will be presented briefly which may seem unrelated to the main topic. However, since much of the remaining chapter will refer to items mentioned in these sections it is hoped they will provide additional background information. These topics include Streeter's Horizons of embryonic growth, Hausman's division of the nervous system and a classification of teratogenic mechanisms.

INTRAUTERINE GROWTH

The presentation of early CNS development will be based on rather precise periods with which the reader should be familiar. At the present time, the stages of development of the human embryo have been succinctly defined by the morphological "Horizons" of the late Dr. George L. Streeter (1951).[10,31] In addition to numerous contributions to the field of human neuroembryology, he provided a framework of early embryonic growth that has been widely used in recent years. It is adaptable for use in the morphological study of the CNS as well as most other systems in the body.

Table 1 is a representation of development in the 23 stages ("Horizons") of human embryonic growth. The gestational age information for the embryonic period is taken from different sources[11,13] which reflect more current thoughts on dating. Since gestational age figures will continue to be revised as new data are available, the present chapter will utilize the "Horizons" for the classical embryonic period, and crown-rump length (CR) thereafter. Each Horizon of growth encompasses 1–3 days and is defined by the fact that all embryos fitting within it have identical features of morphological development. Many of these features are externally apparent while others are identifiable microscopically.

DIVISIONS OF THE CNS

There are several ways of documenting the development of the CNS, but developmentally the brain and spinal cord are so complex that it is difficult to have an embryological classification that is meaningful during postnatal life. Hausman (1961) has, however, provided usable landmarks which are adaptable to most periods of CNS development including adults. The newborn nervous system can be divided into segmental, suprasegmental and intra-/intersegmental components. Although this has wider application if discussed from a physiological basis, it nevertheless is adaptable to many morphological considerations. We will now briefly discuss this segmentation and then return to it again later in the chapter.

Segmental Structures

Starting with the rostral end of the *spinal cord* and proceeding caudally, a series of segments, as defined primarily by levels of motor and sensory nerves, is readily appreciated. Any function that relates entirely to a given level is

TABLE 1

STREETER'S HORIZONS OF HUMAN EMBRYONIC DEVELOPMENT

Horizon	*Gestational Age (days)*	*CR Length (mm)*	*Selected Representative Feature*
I	0–1 (1)[1]	—	One cell stage
II	2–3 (2–3)	—	Segmenting egg
III	4–5 (4–5)	—	Free blastocyst
IV	6 (5–6)	—	Implanting ovum
V	7–11 (7–12)	—	Ovum implanted, but still avillous
VI	12–14 (13–15)	—	Primitive villi, distinct yolk sac
VII	15–17 (15–17)	0·3–0·35	Branching villi, axis of germ disk defined
VIII	18 (17–19)	0·5–1 (0·5)	Hensen's Node, primitive groove
IX	20 (19–21)	1–1·5 (0·5–2)	1–3 somites, neural folds, elongated notochord
X	22 (22–23)	1·5–2 (1·5–2·5)	4–12 somites
XI	24 (23–26)	2·5–3 (2–3·5)	13–20 somites
XII	26 (26–30)	3–4 (3–5·5)	21–29 somites
XIII	28 (28–32)	4–5 (4–6)	Otic invagination closed
XIV	32 (31–35)	5–7 (5–8)	Indentation of lens vesicle
XV	34½ (35–38)	7–8 (6–9)	Lens vesicle closed
XVI	37 (37–42)	8–11 (7–12)	Early retinal pigment
XVII	40 (42–44)	11–13·6 (11–15)	Digital rays in hand
XVIII	43 (44–48)	14–16 (13–19)	Digital rays in hand notched
XIX	45 (48–51)	17–20 (16–20)	Digital rays in foot
XX	47 (51–53)	21–23 (18–23)	Arms slightly bent at elbow
XXI	48½ (53–54)	22–24 (21–25)	Hands slightly flexed at wrists
XXII	50 (54–56)	25–27 (23–28)	Hands overlap in front
XXIII	52 (56–50)	28–30 (28–32)	Forearm rises to or above level of shoulder

[1] Gestational ages and crown-rump lengths appearing in parentheses ( ) are those of Jirásek (1971) derived from therapeutic abortions.

an intrasegmental component. Within the skull, morphological segmentation of the brain can be found in the brain stem. The *midbrain* (MB) is that portion between the pons and the mammillary bodies, and contains the nuclei of cranial nerves III and IV. The remaining brainstem, between the midbrain and spinal cord, is termed the *hindbrain* in which subdivisions of anterior, middle, and posterior can be made. The *anterior hindbrain* (AHB) extends from the midbrain to a level approximately one-half the distance through the pons and contains the nucleus of cranial nerve V. The caudal half of the pons marks the extent of the *middle hindbrain* (MHB), containing nuclei of cranial nerves VI, VII, and VIII. The *posterior hindbrain* (PHB), between the MHB and the C-1 segment of the spinal cord, contains the nuclei of the remaining cranial nerves (the accessory nerve is actually located in the upper cervical segments).

Suprasegmental Structures

The *forebrain*, *colliculi* and *cerebellum* are considered by Hausman to be suprasegmental structures. In general, there is at least one connecting link from each segment to each suprasegmental part.

Intra-/Intersegmental Structures

This component of the divisions of the newborn CNS actually has more application to function than structure. They are the various nerve fibers and tracts that relate to function within a segment (intrasegmental) or between segments and suprasegments (intersegmental). They are only mentioned for completeness and the interested reader is referred to Hausman for further information.

The above divisions of the nervous system are a gross simplification and are mentioned in order to provide a framework on which the embryonic subdivisions can be discussed later. They may be confusing to those who have already acquired a more sophisticated knowledge of the CNS but may offer some simplicity to others. Figure 1 shows the scheme of a nervous system so divided.

MECHANISMS OF TERATOGENESIS

One approach to the study of normal embryogenesis is the study of spontaneous and (in other animal species) experimentally induced malformations. It is beyond the scope of this chapter to discuss experimental teratology of the nervous system, and the interested reader is referred to an excellent recent book on the subject by Kalter (1968). However, since the discussion in this chapter will frequently mention various mechanisms by which malformations arise, it seems important to list them. For each malformation there is a time after which a potentially teratogenic insult will not produce that specific malformation (termination period). Some publications have disregarded this principle, and their formulations of cause and effect have been questioned. A review of the embryology of the system involved will avoid this pitfall and

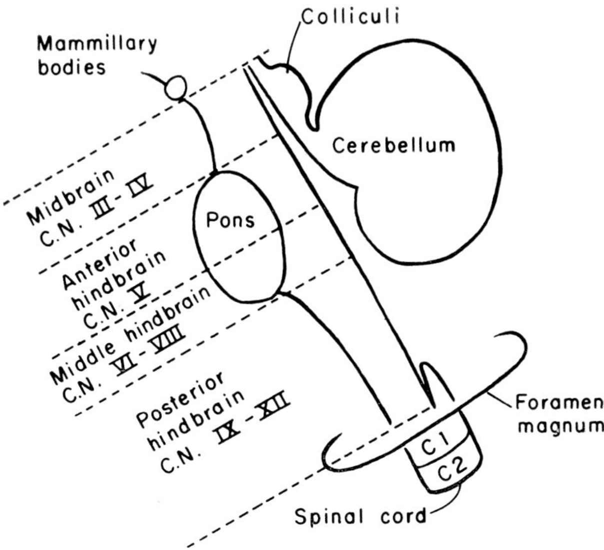

FIG. 1. Schematic representation of the segmentation of the brainstem and upper spinal cord (modified from Hausman). These landmarks are especially useful in defining morphology in the embryo as it relates to postnatal life.

spare clinicians the possibility of conveying false information to parents of patients with malformations.

Table 2 presents a classification of types of teratogenic mechanisms that can be considered responsible for many

TABLE 2

CLASSIFICATION OF MECHANISMS OF TERATOGENESIS[1]

I. *Arrest in Development* (Abnormally decreased development)
   - A. Absence or decrease in initiating stimulus (inductor)
   - B. Absence or decrease in response
   - C. Decrease in both stimulus and response

II. *Excessive Development* (Abnormally increased development)
   - A. Excessive stimulus
   - B. Excessive response

III. *Anomalous Structural Development*
   - A. Intrinsic (In spite of normal stimulus and response)
   - B. Extrinsic (Secondary to anomalies of surrounding tissue)

IV. *Anomalous Functional Development*
   - A. Intrinsic
   - B. Extrinsic

V. *Degeneration*
   - A. Failure of normal degenerative process
   - B. Excessive normal degenerative process
   - C. Degenerative process secondary to extrinsic stimulus

[1] Classification modified from Zwilling (1955).

malformations of the CNS. Several are based on an arrest in development, i.e. that, regardless of cause, the structure does not grow beyond a given point. A phase that is considered normal at that particular time will persist to become an anomaly at any point in time thereafter. The term "agenesis" is frequently applied to many such malformations of a selected part of the nervous system and represents the severest form of a developmental arrest. For obvious reasons it seems unlikely that any human specimen with agenesis of the entire nervous system will ever be recovered. Rather than discussing clinical examples of each category in Table 2 at this time (they will be related to various subjects presented later in the chapter) a few remarks will be made about other factors found to be teratogenic to the human nervous system. There is an apparent interaction between heredity and environment in both normal as well as abnormal growth of the CNS: thus, studies of twins have shown that one of an identical pair can have a normal CNS, the other a malformation; and likewise, both non-identical twins can have a similar CNS lesion, as of course can identical twins. In some areas with increased inbreeding the incidence of certain malformation (e.g. anencephaly) can be increased, an apparent effect of genes; but it can also be argued that they are exposed to the same environmental teratogens. If one looks at other specific anomalies associated with clinical syndromes, there is no question of an underlying genetic basis. Likewise, there is little disagreement that such environmental factors as ionizing radiation, viral infections (rubella, cytomegalovirus, herpesvirus), drugs (aminopterin), and social class (presumably inadequate nutrition and hygiene) can be factors involved in the production of certain CNS malformations in humans.

In the preceding discussions we have considered general embryonic growth, morphological divisions of the CNS and mechanisms of teratogenesis. With this background information we can now turn to specific details regarding development of the nervous system. The major emphasis will be on the embryonic period but, as previously mentioned, it will be necessary in part to discuss later periods as well.

FIRST PHASE OF NEURAL TUBE FORMATION: NEURULATION

Induction of the Neural Plate

For obvious reasons little is known about the factors involved in induction* of the neural plate in man. Since the pioneering work by Hans Spemann (1962) in amphibians, this aspect of experimental embryology has expanded rapidly but some controversy still exists about neural tube induction. There is evidence to support the concept of regional inducers, but the notochord, which is in direct contact with the neural plate, is felt by many to play an inductive role. During Horizon VII (15–17 days), the axis of the germ disc is determined, followed in Horizon VIII (18 days), by Hensen's node and primitive groove. It would be during this latter stage that any inductive influences take place, as the neural plate is then first formed by a thickening of ectodermal cells on the dorsal aspect of the embryo. Hensen's node marks the caudal extent of this neural plate and the primitive groove, which lies even

* "Induction" is a term frequently used to indicate the capacity of one tissue to effect a transformation of another tissue into a specific organized entity, i.e. the influence of the former directly affects the differentiation of the latter, and without its presence the latter would not form.

further caudal to the node, should not be confused with the neural groove which follows at a later Horizon. The induction of the neural plate marks the onset of a process called neurulation. If an arrest in development occurs during this time the embryo usually undergoes spontaneous abortion soon thereafter, with a condition known as *total dysraphism*. Most of these specimens are undoubtedly passed without being recognized as they are rarely found. The smallest human embryo being thus reported had progressed only to the next stage, that where neural folds were present.

Neural Folds

During Horizon IX (20 days) when the embryo has 1–3 somites, the first folding of the neural plate takes place, thus producing neural folds and a neural groove. The *mechanism of neurulation* has been of interest to embryologists for over a century with most studies having been done in amphibian and chick embryos. Some feel that *differential mitoses* within the neural plate and folds (i.e. more in the ventral portions) produce indentation and folding. Other studies have shown that there is neither a differential in cellular mitoses or increase in cellular size, and, therefore, this hypothesis has been questioned. However, there is evidence to suggest that the ratio of cells to surface area changes markedly, and, therefore, mitotic activity does seem to have at least a secondary role.

Some experiments dealing with *alterations in cell size* have suggested this factor may have an important influence. As mentioned above, other investigators have not been able to demonstrate size-related changes.

The role of *change in relative tensions on each side of the neural plate* is attractive from a mechanistic standpoint. Thus if there is increased tension on the lumen side and a relative decrease on the external side, an infolding can occur. There is evidence to suggest that *contractile filaments* are present within the cell membranes on the lumen side and that these are important in the process of neurulation by changing the actual shape of the cells. Although measurements of the forces produced during neurulation have been made, they have not resolved the question at the present time.

The fact that the *notochord* is probably involved is evidenced by electron microscopic studies in chick embryos which have shown that there are indentations of the neuroectoderm at regular intervals by the notochord. This occurs transiently and just precedes the onset of neural folding. Other studies have demonstrated that the final shape of the various portions of the neural tube (i.e. gray and white matter; central canal) can be influenced by the presence or absence of notochord. It has likewise been shown that in some species removal of the notochord can be associated with incomplete neurulation, while in others the neural tube will close, but in an anomalous manner.

As previously mentioned, all experimental studies have been done in lower forms and their applicability to humans is unknown at the present time. The study of factors involved in causing the neural plate to fold remains one of the most fundamental challenges in neuroembryology and is of major importance in relating teratogenic influences to non-closure of the neural tube. Probably no single factor is independent of others, and the experimental evidence suggests that neuroectodermal cells, notochord, and surrounding mesoderm have some role in neurulation. It is pertinent to realize that not only is neurulation dependent on mesoderm but that normal development of mesoderm is dependent on neuroectoderm. This interdependence explains why anomalies in the one are so commonly associated with maldevelopment in the other.

Should an arrest in development occur during Horizon VIII such that the neural folds fail to form, or even during the next stage, fail to fuse; then total dysraphism results. The youngest totally dysraphic human embryo reported had grown beyond this stage in spite of the fact that there was no fusion of the neural folds. It was 2·75 mm greatest length and had 14 somites[4] (which would correspond with Horizon XI).

Fusion of the Neural Folds

When the embryo has acquired approximately 6–7 somites, the neural folds begin to fuse at the 3rd somite level. This then marks Horizon X (4–12 somites: 22 days) embryos, and by the end of this stage the fusion extends from the level of the otic placode (rhombencephalon) to the 12th somite. Even though they are quite extensive, there now exist two openings, a rostral one termed *anterior neuropore* and caudally, the *posterior neuropore*. These two openings represent the key to certain malformations of the nervous system of clinical importance, *anencephaly* and *myelomeningocele*.

The mechanism of fusion of neural folds is worthy of brief comment as this has likewise been a topic of controversy for many years. At the point of contact of the neural folds, the superficial ectoderm approximates and fuses just before or coincident with the fusion of the neuroectoderm. At this dorsal point the neural tube remains in contact with the superficial ectoderm by means of a cellular aggregate which does not have the radial orientation of the neuroectodermal cells.[6] These cells are termed *neural crest* cells, and will later contribute to the sensory system (dorsal root ganglia) as well as sympathetic neuroblasts. While these neural crest cells migrate first laterally then ventrally around the outside of the neural tube, the neuroectoderm fuses dorsally, and a cleft appears between it and the superficial ectoderm. About this same time the notochord, which has been in direct contact with the ventral neural tube, begins to separate. There is no one time in which all of these events take place since neural fusion starts in one place to progress both rostrally and caudally.

Notochord

Although the possible role of the notochord in induction has been mentioned above, its further differentiation is deserving of comment. Originating as a midline cellular process from Hensen's node it continues to advance beneath the ectoderm in a rostral direction. The point at which this process stops is just caudal to the future sella turcica where it provides a midline landmark for *prechordal* and *parachordal* mesoderm, both important in the formation of different parts of the cranial base. In its caudal extent it blends into Hensen's node and later (see second phase of caudal neural tube formation) into the undifferentiated caudal cell mass. The fate of the notochord is somewhat controversial, but it eventually contributes to part of the basioccipital bone in the skull and the nucleus pulposus of the intervertebral discs. Therefore it presumably plays an important role both in the development of the nervous system and its supporting structures. Clinically two types of *notochordal anomalies* are found, one involving cleft vertebrae and the second, embryonic tumors called chordomas. The pathogenesis of the latter is of embryonic origin and possibly arises secondary to persistent adhesions between the notochord and neural tube. These most commonly occur at the base of the skull and in the coccygeal region.

Closure of the Anterior Neuropore

The rostral opening of the neural tube (anterior neuropore), in a period of approximately 2–3 days following initial fusion of the neural folds in Horizon X (22 days),

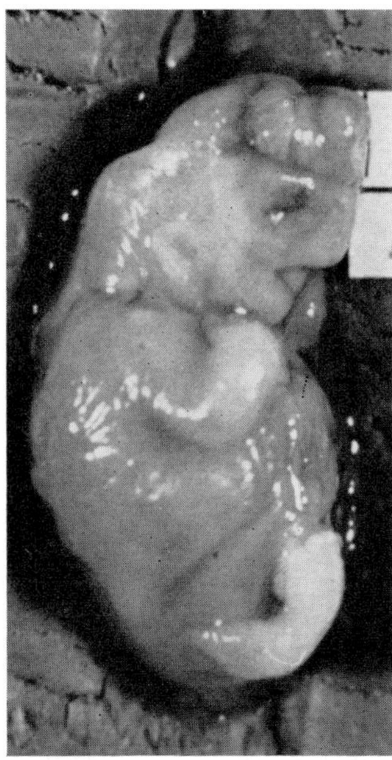

FIG. 2. Typical embryo with anencephaly, slightly macerated and measuring 20·5 mm. CR length (46-days). Note the exposed neural tissue on the head. Serial microscopic sections showed myeloschisis of the cervical region in addition to anomalies of the eyes such as rudimentary optic stalks. The mother had a severe viral illness beginning 24-days later.

gets progressively smaller and closes in Horizon XI (24 days). This process is undoubtedly one of the most important single events in the embryogenesis of the human nervous system since if all or any portion fails to close, a lethal spectrum of anomalies result. At this point we will

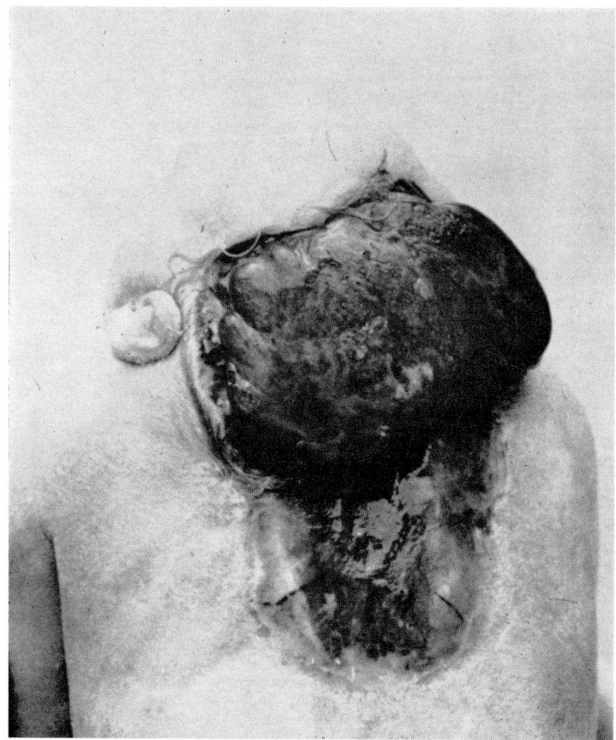

FIG. 3. Posterior view of anencephalic with accompanying myeloschisis of the cervical and thoracic cord. This type is described variously as craniorachischis and anencephaly with spinal retroflexion. The extent of involvement in this full-term fetus is similar to that in the embryo shown in figure 2.

depart from normal embryology and consider the *sequelae of a persistent anterior neuropore*.

Depending on the extent of the opening of the skull and/or cervical spine (Figs. 2–5), a variety of terms are employed. They are frequently grouped under the terms anencephaly, cranioschisis, craniorachischis, or acrania.

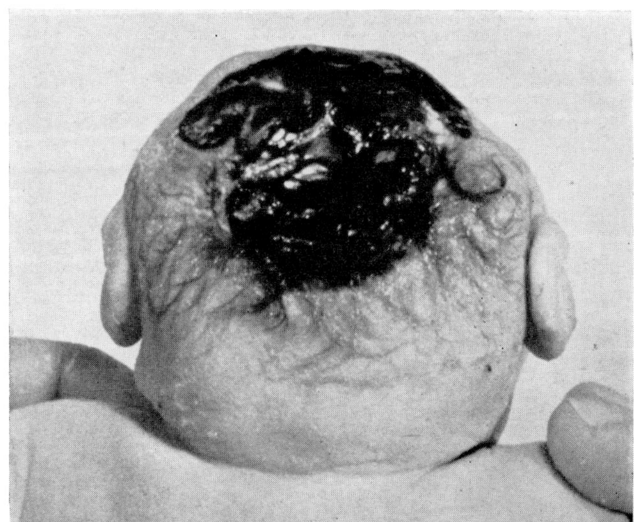

FIG. 4. posterior view of a full-term anencephalic to which the terms meroacrania and cranioschisis are frequently applied. Unlike figures 2 and 3 the defect does not extend to the level of the foramen magnum.

In each situation some portion of the cephalic neural folds, and therefore the developing brain is directly exposed to the amniotic cavity for the remainder of gestation. It is perhaps fortunate that a large number of embryos so affected undergo spontaneous abortion since the incidence of these malformations is already high (5–6 per 1,000 live births in some areas of the world) in newborns. From the scientific viewpoint the anencephalic specimen offers some of the most fascinating dilemmas regarding abnormal growth phenomena. An example is that for many years there was disagreement as to whether or not a pituitary gland was present. It has been shown that most anencephalics do indeed have a pituitary gland, although it is usually small. However, one recent study[21] separated anencephalics into two groups the first of which had pituitaries, normal (or prolonged) gestations, and normal body weights (when corrected for absence of brain). The second group lacked pituitary glands (or they were markedly hypoplastic), had premature births, and subnormal body weights. It is suggested that the prematurely born anencephalic with severe growth retardation (second group above) may be so affected because of decreased growth hormone. Likewise the adrenal glands seem to develop normally until midway through gestation, but thereafter become markedly atrophic. Nearly all other major organs are also small, with an absolute decrease in numbers of cells, except for the thymus which is frequently enlarged. Of equal interest is the fact that in most cases a disproportionate increase in the growth of the upper extremities is found relative to the legs. A rostral-caudal gradient exists such that the upper arms are the most hypertrophied, forearms next and hands least. Another interesting feature is an increased incidence of a sternalis muscle which is uncommon in normal newborns. Likewise an increased size of the mandible is found in some cases. Very little is known about these unusual growth characteristics, and this is an area worthy of further study as it undoubtedly has more general application than to anencephalus alone. The CNS in the term anencephalic is perhaps not as interesting as one might expect. Over the course of intrauterine life the brain usually becomes a hemorrhagic mass of scar tissue with mixtures of neural elements and meninges which are frequently distorted.

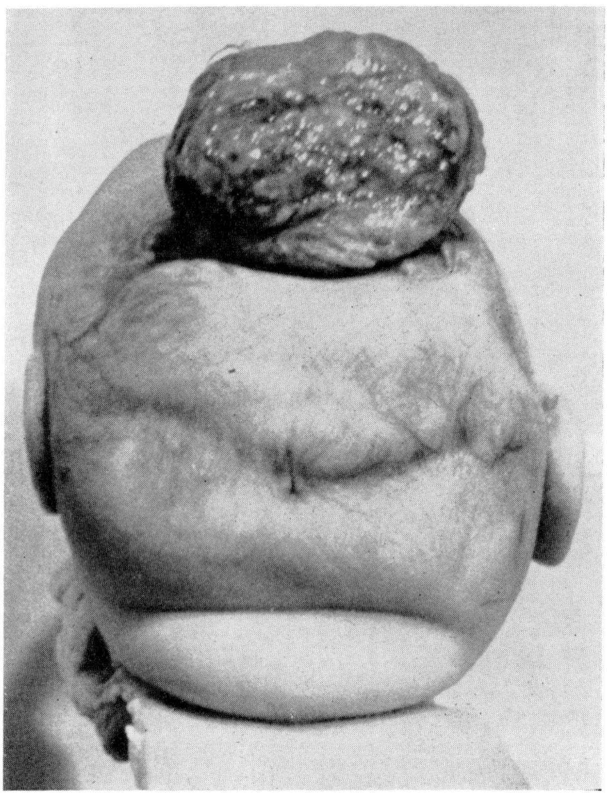

Fig. 5. Another example of a full-term anencephalic as viewed posteriorly. This case which lived one month is similar to that in figure 4 except that not as much of the cortex has been eliminated during intrauterine life. In experimental animals this is frequently termed exencephaly. The specimens shown in figures 2–5 are thought to represent varying degrees of failure of fusion of the cephalic neural folds.

Closure of the Posterior Neuropore

When the posterior neuropore closes in Horizon XII (21–29 somites: 26 days), the first phase of neural tube formation is completed. This marks the first time that neural tissue is not in direct contact with the amniotic cavity, and the neural tube is entirely closed. It is thought that the final closure is at the 25th somite level which would be about the L1–L2 vertebral segment (for purpose of calculation it should be mentioned that the first four somites contribute to the occipital bone). *Failure of closure at the posterior neuropore* is the most popular theory relating to the formation of caudal myelomeningoceles (myeloceles, spina bifida cystica, myeloschisis), a common malformation in embryos (Fig. 6) and newborns. There is little question that descriptive[17] and experimental[33] evidence favors this mechanism, but alternative theories should also be mentioned. Rather than separating the specific hypotheses relating to anencephaly and myelomeningocele since they are in a sense the same lesion at opposite ends of the neural tube, they will be presented together. Firstly, there is one point with respect to the theory of nonclosure of neural folds which relates to the presence of excessive neural tissue.[23] If one looks at a series of human embryos with myeloschisis, about one-half have "overgrowth" of neural tissue (Fig. 7). Some feel this abnormal proliferation is the primary reason the neural folds do not close, i.e. that neural tissue causes an abnormal eversion of the folds. Opponents of this hypothesis acknowledge that overgrowth of neural tissue may be present but claim it is secondary, i.e. that the fact the neural folds do not close permits the neural tissue to overgrow. The nature of the overgrowth is not always an absolute increase in tissue, but may be more related to abnormal position, lack of normal cellular orientation and derangements in the external limiting membrane. In some experimental studies the same overgrowth of neural tissue is found, and the further definition of whether it is primary or secondary will undoubtedly be forthcoming with further experiments in animals.

The second major hypothesis is that the neuropores undergo normal closure, and the neural tube then reopens thereafter. This can either be due to a subsequent "blow out" secondary to increased intralumenal pressure or by "neuroschisis". In the first situation it has been stated that if the thin rhombencephalic roof (discussed later in chapter) becomes impermeable to the passage of fluid, a condition of hydrocephalomyelia may result and cause the neural tube to rupture.[7] In the case of neuroschisis there is a lack of integration of the opposing dorsal neural folds (under an intact ectoderm), and a cleft appears which allows the escape of fluid under the ectoderm with subsequent rupture of the latter. The neuroschisis hypothesis[22] is recent and based on the frequent finding of such neural clefts in a large series of sectioned human embryos. Although it has yet to be confirmed in other descriptive or experimental studies, this hypothesis must at present certainly be regarded as an important possibility.

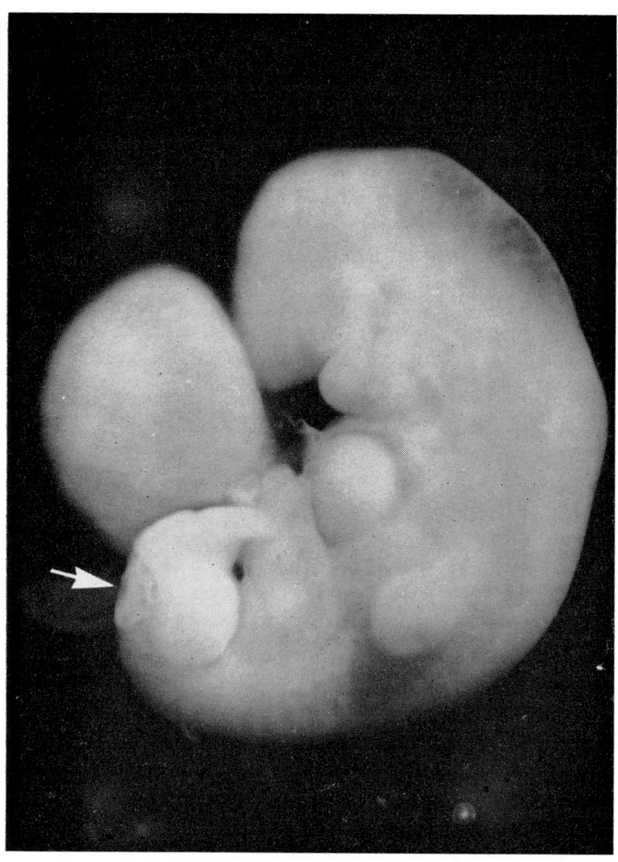

FIG. 6. Lateral view of a 5·5 mm. CR length, Horizon XIV (32-day), human embryo with caudal myeloschisis, the precursor of the common myelomeningocele. Many feel this defect arises as a result of the posterior neuropore failing to close in Horizon XII. Arrow indicates the site of the myeloschisis.

An equally enticing hypothesis (which would relate to an open system) is that the primary defect is not in the neuroectoderm but rather in mesoderm.[20] It has been shown in experimental embryos that in the area adjacent to an area of myeloschisis there is necrosis of the somites. This lack of integrity of the surrounding (and supporting) tissue can be a deterrent to closure of the neural fold.

A final hypothesis, unfortunately not very popular at present, relates the defect to abnormal vasculature in the area.[32] This was proposed more specifically for anencephaly and is based on the findings of anomalous vessels in larger anencephalics which were studied after injection of the vascular system. The major question, like the one on overgrowth, is whether or not these abnormal vessels are primary or secondary.

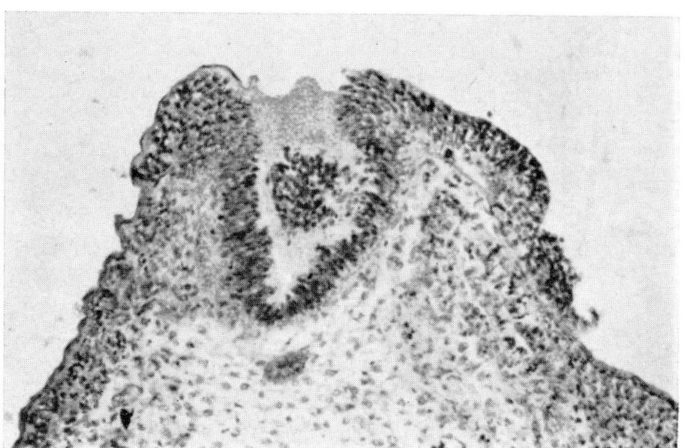

FIG. 7. Microscopic section of embryo in figure 6 showing "overgrowth" of neural tissue. The ectoderm on the right can be seen to continue under a tongue of tissue which is attached to that of the unclosed neural folds. This section also shows a proliferation of nervous tissue into the neural groove.

It is not unreasonable to assume that several different modes of pathogenesis may produce myelomeningoceles, but at the present time many investigators probably favor nonclosure of the posterior neuropore. If this is true, the defect would presumably arise in Horizon XI or XII (24–26 days).

To summarize what has happened during the process of neurulation (first phase of neural tube formation) we have found that it takes place between Horizon VIII, when the neural plate is first formed, and Horizon XII when the posterior neuropore closes. This occurs between the 18th and 26th gestational days after which the neural tissue is no longer in contact with the amniotic cavity. To provide a rough estimate, neurulation accounts for the development of the neural tube only to the level of L1–L2 caudal to which it must develop by a different mechanism. From the standpoint of anomalies, total dysraphism would relate to an onset prior to Horizon X (first fusion of neural folds), anencephaly prior to Horizon XI (closure of anterior neuropore), and myelomeningocele prior to Horizon XII (closure of posterior neuropore).

It is obvious that there are pitfalls when one divides the development of the CNS into phases, since what works well for one area does not fit another. Therefore the following discussion of the second and third phases of neural tube development will actually apply only to the caudal neural tube after which we will again return to specific areas of the brain.

SECOND PHASE OF CAUDAL NEURAL TUBE FORMATION: CANALIZATION

As stated above, the process of neurulation does not account for all of the caudal neural tube. Once the posterior neuropore closes there are no longer neural folds and for the first time the entire neural tube is covered by ectoderm (skin). The process by which there is continued growth caudally is termed *canalization*. To appreciate this rather complex mechanism we must first understand what has happened to some of the previous landmarks. You will recall that Hensen's node marked the rostral boundary of the primitive groove which gave the embryo its initial orientation and that the notochord and neural plate (groove and tube) arose from tissue rostral to Hensen's node. As these tissues differentiated during the process of neurulation, Hensen's node and the primitive streak underwent a relative regression, a process now well understood in chick embryos. During that period a tail fold is formed within which there exists an *undifferentiated caudal cell mass*. It is from those cells placed dorsally, in approximation to the area of the posterior neuropore, that the remainder of the neural tube will form. Other portions of this group of cells will differentiate into important embryonic structures such as the kidney and because they have the ability to form various tissues they are referred to as totipotent.

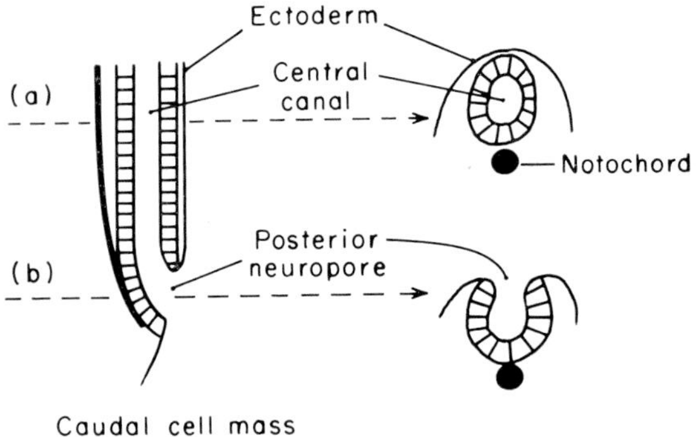

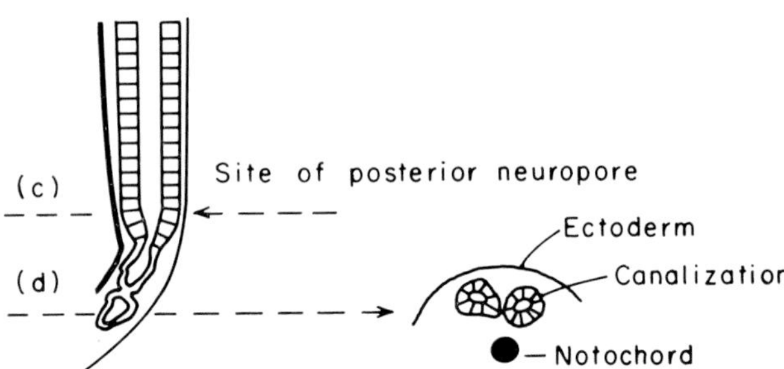

FIG. 8. A highly schematic representation of the difference between neural tube formed by neurulation (top diagrams) and canalization (bottom diagrams). *Top:* At the left is a sagittal section of the caudal neural tube of a Horizon XII (26-day) embryo showing a portion in which fusion of the neural folds has taken place (at the level of "a") and the open posterior neuropore (at the level of "b".) The two diagrams at the right represent coronal sections of these areas. *Bottom:* At the left is a sagittal section of the caudal neural tube of a Horizon XIII (28-day) embryo in which case a section through the level of "c" represents the site of the now closed posterior neuropore in which case it would appear the same as the section through "a" in the top diagram. Section "d" is through the caudal cell mass where canalization is occurring. Unlike neurulation this takes place under an intact ectoderm.

Canalization is not well understood in the human embryo and it undoubtedly differs from that in chicks.[25] The following comments will not differentiate them, however, the basic process being similar, i.e. by some manner a tube is formed out of a solid mass of cells. Probably beginning late in Horizon XII (26 days) or in Horizon XIII (28 days) small vacuoles appear in the caudal cell mass. Those adjacent to each other then gradually coalesce to form larger vacuoles which in turn unite with others, etc. At some point one of these channels makes contact with the central canal of the neural tube previously formed by neurulation. Once this contact is made there is a progressive radial orientation around the lumen of cells which have now differentiated toward ependyma (Fig. 8).

The process of canalization results in many variations in the morphology of the caudal neural tube between Horizons XIII (28 days) and XX (47 days).[18] There can be accessory lumina located in a dorso-ventral (Fig. 9) or lateral plane (Fig. 10). In most cases the main central canal is easy to identify, but occasionally the split tube is nearly identical and both have differentiated to the same degree. It is interesting that this region is also the site of numerous cells undergoing mitosis and others necrosis. As the tube elongates intraluminal cellular proliferations occur both in the form of discrete masses (Fig. 11) and folds. The significance of these cellular masses has not been explained.

It is difficult to define accurately when the human caudal neural tube completes the lengthening process during its second phase. A comprehensive descriptive study showed segmentation to 38–39 with additional non-vertebrated tail in an 11 mm CR embryo[16] (corresponding to Horizon XVI–XVII: 37–40 days). Since some rostral somites are being incorporated into the occipital bone during this period (and therefore disappearing), an accurate "total count" is difficult even in a serial descriptive study. Likewise somite counts reflect mesodermal structures and the number of neural tube segments is more accurately determined by such factors as motor roots and sensory ganglia. It is sufficient to say that a significant component of the entire neural axis differentiates during the second phase of neural tube formation and that this tube is always covered by intact ectoderm. Although the manner in which it develops is still not entirely worked out there seems to be a lack of precision as is seen during the process of neurulation. This is evidenced by the numerous variations in morphology found in this region in sectioned human embryos which are otherwise normal. It likewise helps explain the heterogeneous group of anomalies found in newborns[19] when it is recalled that they all originated from one group of cells showing no initial definition.

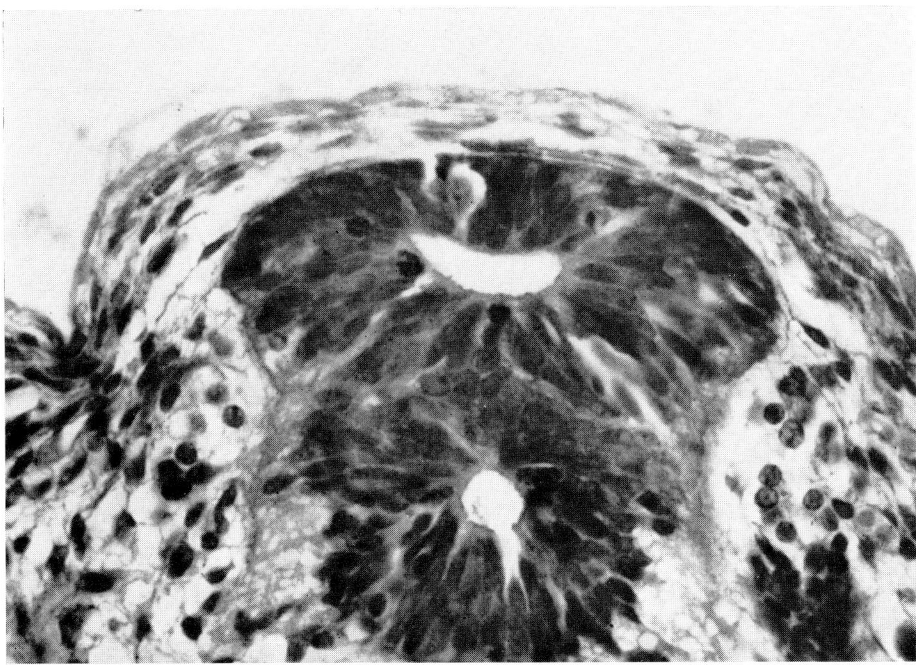

FIG. 9. Microscopic section of the caudal neural tube in a Horizon XVII, 14 mm. CR (40-day) human embryo. Note the two separate lumina (which connect with each other in other sections) each with ependyma oriented around them. The more dorsally placed lumen connects with the main central canal.

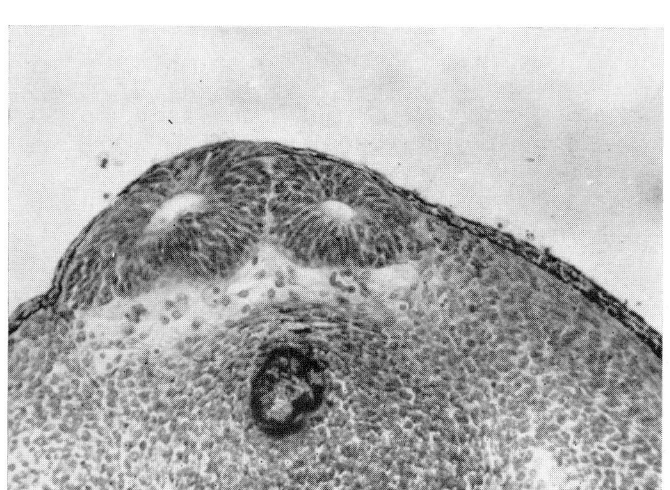

FIG. 10. In contrast to the embryo shown in figure 8, this Horizon XIX, 18 mm. CR (45-day) specimen demonstrates two laterally placed lumens both of which connect with the main central canal rostrally. Note the radial orientation of ependyma around each lumen, the more ventrally placed notochord and the continuous ectoderm dorsally. This section also demonstrates the lack of differentiation of other cells in the area which make up part of the caudal cell mass from which this portion of the neural tube originated.

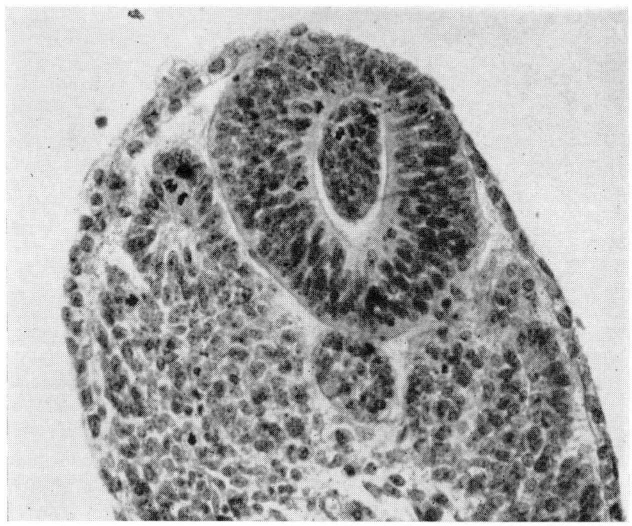

FIG. 11. The caudal neural tube of a Horizon XV, 9 mm. CR (34-day) embryo showing a proliferation of ependymal cells into the lumen (compare with the similar mass in figure 7 which originated from a more rostral segment). Like the embryos of figures 9–10 ectoderm covers the neural tube dorsally. Unlike figure 10 there is more differentiation of surrounding structures and the notochord is in contact with the neural tube. Although this section is taken from a more rostral area and therefore cannot be compared directly, it perhaps illustrates the variability that is seen in neural tube formed from the caudal cell mass.

THIRD PHASE OF CAUDAL NEURAL TUBE FORMATION: RETROGRESSIVE DIFFERENTIATION

At the end of the period of canalization the neural tube has developed more segments than are found in the newborn. Segmentation of the nervous system and vertebral column are two entirely different things but up to this point there has been a close association between them, i.e. it has been convenient to use somites as markers for neural tube development. To understand the further development of the caudal neural tube we will now refer to neural and vertebral structures as separate entities. Likewise to be able to relate development to anomalies that are found in the caudal neural tube it is also important to have some understanding of the development of the meninges. These three entities, neural tube, vertebrae and meninges will be discussed in this section, but separately.

Neural Tube

Commencing between Horizons XVII (40 days) and XXI (48 days) the caudal neural tube (actually only that part formed by canalization) undergoes a regression referred to as *retrogressive differentiation.* The mechanisms are not all well understood, but by cellular necrosis and atrophy most of this tube is transformed into the *filum terminale*, a band of fibrous tissue. This well known structure is eventually located between a small but persistent dilatation of the central canal, the *ventriculus terminalis* (proximal) and a rudimentary ependymal cavity, the *coccygeal medullary vestige* (distal).

The primordium of the ventriculus terminalis is first seen in Horizon XXI (48 days) and is identifiable in serially sectioned human embryos if one follows the neural tube caudally to a point where there is no distinction between ependymal and mantle layers. Just beyond this area the central canal enlarges, then narrows, and the central canal within these limits is called the ventriculus terminalis. It becomes the proximal marker for the filum terminale and is located at the caudal limit of the conus medullaris. In Horizon XXIII (52 days) it is at coccygeal segment 2–3; at 70 mm. CR (75 days), sacral segments 2–3; and at 250 mm. CR (180 days), lumbar segments 2–3. In contrast, the coccygeal medullary vestige is located at the level of coccygeal segment 5 at the end of the embryonic Horizons and remains there throughout gestation. From the above it can be seen that the filum terminale gradually elongates and actually represents embryonic neural tube that has undergone regression. Even though most of it becomes fibrous tissue small ependymal rests persist within it throughout life. The mechanism by which these various components of the caudal neural tube undergo retrogressive differentiation has been well documented at the descriptive level.[15,30] As with the period of canalization there are numerous opportunities for anomalous development. Before these are mentioned a brief discussion of general aspects of vertebral and meningeal development will be presented because these structures play a prominent role in anomalies of this region as well as others.

Vertebral Column

Although a detailed discussion of the development of the vertebrae is beyond the scope of this chapter a certain basic knowledge is helpful in understanding many malformations of the neural tube. As with other parts of the neuroaxis the vertebral column differentiates in a rostral-caudal fashion and therefore the following comments are only indicative of one area at varying points in time.

Sensenig (1949) divides vertebral development into the following periods:

A. *Period of Membrane Formation*

Stage I:	Horizons X, XI, XII	(22–26 days)
Stage II:	Horizons XIII, XIV	(28–32 days)
Stage III:	Horizons XV, XVI	(34–37 days)

B. *Period of Cartilage Formation*
Horizon XVII to 50 mm. CR (40–64 days)

C. *Period of Bone Formation*

During Stage I, as early as 7 somites (Horizon X), sclerotomic cells migrate ventral-medially toward the notochord. These will contribute to the vertebral bodies and intervertebral discs. Initially these cells cannot surround the notochord as the latter is a contact with the neural tube dorsally and the gut ventrally. By the end of Horizon XI (24 days) the notochord begins to separate from both thus forming *epi- and sub-chordal spaces*. Sclerotomic cells are found in these spaces by the end of Horizon XII (26 days), as well as some initial migration dorsally around the neural tube. Each vertebra is eventually formed by the fusion of the cells from the caudal half of one somite with the rostral half of the next. This midline segmentation of a somite is brought about by the appearance of a *sclerotomic fissure*.

In addition to a more rapid proliferation and migration of sclerotomic cells (both ventral-medial and dorsal), Stage II is marked by prominent growth of the neural crests. This is also the stage when spinal nerves are formed, these of course are also involved in the formation of the vertebral column in that the latter must develop outlet foramina for them. Both the epi- and sub-chordal areas increase slightly in size.

It is during Stage III that the membranous vertebrae takes on the appearance of a definite structure if viewed in coronal section, i.e. the primary centra, discs, neural and articular processes can be identified. However, on a longitudinal basis the sclerotomic cells appear as a continuous mass, separated only at brief intervals by the sclerotomic fissures and intersegmental vessels. Therefore, the final segmentation of the vertebral column has not been defined by this time (Horizon XVI: 37 days).

Chondrification begins in the vertebral central body in Horizon XVII (40 days) and the arches in Horizon XVIII (43 days). By Horizon XIX–XX (45–47 days) (the previously mentioned end of the 2nd phase of neural tube formation) the centra and arches are well chondrified. However, the arches are actually not completely formed at this time and lack any definite structure on the dorsal and dorso-lateral aspects of the neural tube. Therefore we now have a situation in which the vertebral development is completed to the stage at which the anomalies generally encompassed by the term *spina bifida occulta* are found, i.e. a defective fusion of the lamina dorsally. Since this point in time provides the framework for the later discussion of anomalies no further comments on the development of the vertebrae will be made except to note Sensenig's statement "in embryos of 50 mm CR (64 days) the arches are almost united across the dorsal surface of the spinal cord in the upper cervical region, in contact in the lower cervical region and completely fused in the thoracic and upper lumbar regions."

Meninges

Between the neural tube and the vertebral canal the embryo has a space filled with loose mesenchymal tissue which is known as the *meninx primitiva*. It is within this tissue space that the three meninges develop; the *pia mater* next to the neural tube, the *dura mater* next to the wall of the vertebral canal and the *arachnoid* between them.

It was previously thought that much of the meninges arose from the neural crest, but in the human embryo this does not seem to be the case. In Horizons XI–XII (24–26 days) a single layer of cells, continuous with the neural crests dorsally, is found closely approximated to the neural tube.[28] They are evidently not neural crest cells but rather precursors of the pia mater. Actually the pia does not become a well defined membrane until about Horizon XXIII (52 days), but some differentiation is found as early as XVI (37 days). The dura mater begins to be recognizable during Horizons XVII–XVIII (40–43 days) along the inner surface of the sclerotomic cellular concentrations making up the bodies (primitiva centra) and intervertebral discs. It presumably arises from the same sclerotomic cells (possibly in part from the meninx primitiva) and by Horizon XXIII (52 days) is continuous around the entire neural tube. It is not until much later, however (about 50 mm CR: 64 days), that its separation from the inner wall of the vertebral canal is complete. There is some disagreement as to when the spinal arachnoid separates from the dura, with estimates from late fetal life to after birth. In our own series of fetuses it has been observed by 180 mm CR (138 days). The meninges of the skull differ from those of the spinal canal, especially the dura mater which always remains more closely approximated in the former.

The above discussion of the development of the vertebral column and meninges was provided to show that important aspects of their differentiation take place during the phases of neural tube formation occurring after closure of the posterior neuropore. It is not surprising that numerous lesions that are found over the lower spine involve them as well as neural tube. With this in mind, a discussion of some of these lesions follows.

ANOMALOUS DEVELOPMENT ARISING DURING THE SECOND AND THIRD PHASES OF CAUDAL NEURAL TUBE FORMATION

It is easy to appreciate the variation of anomalies that arise in the caudal neural tube if one knows the embryology. The main thing to recall is the fact that after closure of the posterior neuropore in Horizon XII (26 days), the neural tube is covered with ectoderm. Many skin-covered caudal lesions arise from neural tube derived from the undifferentiated caudal cell mass. It is more uncertain as to whether or not they arise during the 2nd or 3rd phases of caudal neural tube formation and therefore no attempt will be made to separate these periods with respect to a specific lesion.

Myelocystoceles, also known as myelocystomeningoceles, are large cystic masses over the caudal spine found in association with cloacal extrophy. Although multiple cysts are frequently present at least one will be lined by ependyma. This is indicative of either a localized hydromyelic dilatation of the central canal or perhaps a dilated non-connecting vacuole formed during the canalization process. In addition to the cysts there are usually extensive anomalies of the lumbar spine and sacrum.

The spectrum of *lumbosacral lipomas* includes superficial fatty masses under the skin which have no connections with the spinal canal, and those that have a large intradural component. The latter type is frequently found with connection to the cauda equina and/or conus medullaris from a superficial mass by a fibrous stalk which traverses a bifid spinous process.

Although *meningoceles* can occur anywhere along the neuroaxis, a significant percentage of them are found in the lumbosacral region. They are possibly a later arising lesion involving prolapse of the dura-arachnoid complex through a nonfused dorsal spinous process.

Diastomatomyelia is a term applied to a spinal cord that is split in some portion. Most cases can be grouped on the basis of whether or not each cord is invested in a separate dural sheath or both contained within one.[12] In the latter situation no septum exists between the split cords and the cords rejoin caudally to become single. In the other group (both having separate dura) there is a fibrous septum between them.

Although they are somewhat peripheral to a discussion of the embryology of the CNS, there are two other important clinical entities that are derived from the caudal cell mass of interest to problems of the nervous system. The first represents embryonic tumors found in that region, especially *sacrococcygeal teratomas*. These arise in the anterior sacrococcygeal region and almost all have nervous tissue, a significant percentage being ependyma. That the coccygeal medullary vestige may play a role is evidenced by the fact that there is a high incidence of postoperative malignant degeneration if the coccyx is not resected at the time the tumor is removed. Other CNS related embryonic tumors found in that region include neuroblastoma, ependymoma, and glioma. One of the more important areas linking the fields of oncology and embryology involves the fact that embryonic "rests" have a propensity to form neoplasms.

Another area of clinical interest in the caudal cells mass involves the development of the sacrococcygeal vertebrae. It has been previously mentioned that sacral anomalies are found in association with myelocystoceles. There is also now a well known association between *sacral agenesis* and being the infant of a diabetic mother.

In viewing the above types of anomalies, all arising from the caudal cell mass, it is easy to see that several different mechanisms of teratogenesis (Table 2) are needed to explain them. For example, sacral agenesis can result from an arrest in development, lumbosacral lipomas from anomalous structural development and sacrococcygeal teratomas from excessive development.

SUMMARY OF EMBRYONIC SPINAL CORD DEVELOPMENT

Since the remainder of the chapter will deal with development of the brain it might be worthwhile to summarize what has and has not been said about development of the

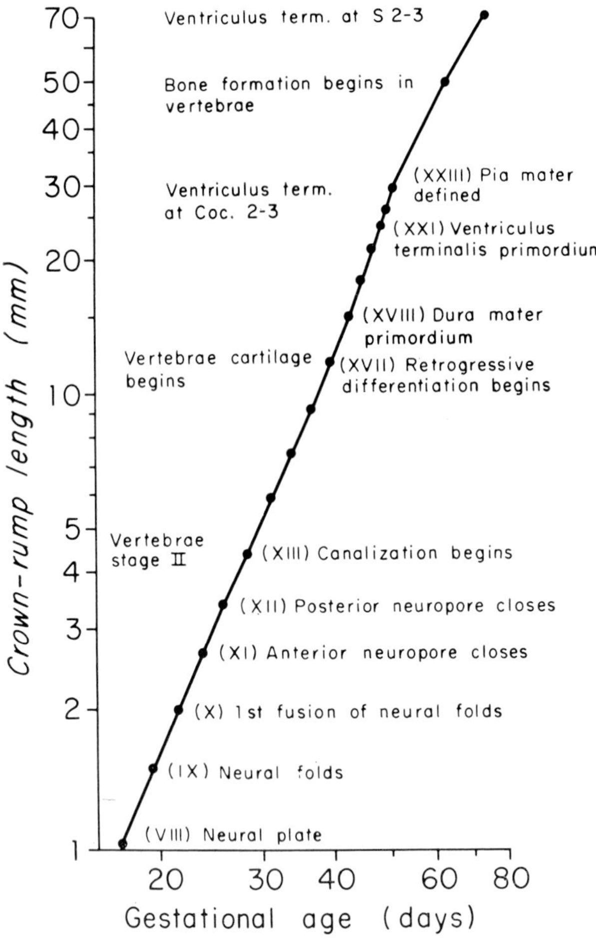

FIG. 12. This diagram represents a few selected events in the development of the portion of the neural tube that will form the spinal cord and that portion of the rostral neural tube applicable to defects in neurulation. The ordinate gives approximate crown-rump lengths (log-log scale) and the abscissa, approximate gestational age (log scale). The lower points on the growth line indicate Streeter's Horizons, some of which are noted by Roman numerals.

spinal cord (some of the features are depicted in Fig. 12 which shows their relationship in time). The phases of development were somewhat arbitrarily divided into three parts, (1) *neurulation*, which takes place between the time neural plate appears (Horizon VIII: 18 days) until the posterior neuropore closes (Horizon XII: 26 days); (2) *canalization*, from Horizon XII (26 days) until the cord reaches its greatest extent of development caudally (approximately Horizon XVII: 40 days); and (3) *retrogressive differentiation*, beginning after canalization is completed and continuing well into fetal (even postnatal) life. The reason for selecting these as phases is based on the fact that each is an entirely different process, as well as being separated in time. From the clinical viewpoint these phases are also helpful in defining when certain malformations of the neural tube arise. For example, lesions over the spine can be classified as to whether or not they are covered by intact skin. The typical myelomeningocele is not covered by skin and most likely arises during neurulation (Horizon XI–XII), whereas lumbosacral lipomas (covered by intact skin) arise after this time. In the search for potential teratogenic influences an understanding of normal embryogenesis is important. The discussion has also noted that the development of the vertebral column and meninges are so closely interrelated to neural tube development that a basic knowledge of their differentiation is equally important.

Another feature with which the reader should be aware is that other aspects of spinal cord development have not been discussed. These include recent studies relating to cellular kinetics (cell division and migration), differentiation of cell types and early myelination. Likewise no mention has been made of either spinal nerves or ganglia. The omission of these topics is consistent with the intent to provide a chapter based on gross morphology, especially as it relates to more common clinical problems.

THE EMBRYONIC BRAIN

Thus far the present chapter has mainly discussed the development of that part of the neural tube that will give rise to the spinal cord. During this same period of time (Horizons X–XXIII) there are significant changes in the portion of the CNS that will lie within the skull. In order to present its development in a meaningful manner it is necessary to introduce another set of terms.

The *primary embryonic brain vesicles* are divided initially into three parts: (1) the prosencephalon (forebrain) which is subdivided into the telencephalon and diencephalon, (2) mesencephalon (midbrain), and (3) rhombencephalon (hindbrain) with its subdivisions, metencephalon and myelencephalon. The following discussion will mainly emphasize the development of each of the above during the Horizon period,[1,10,31] but selected comments will be made about differentiation into the fetal period as well.

Prosencephalon (Forebrain)

This most rostral portion of the neural tube actually contributes to most of the intracranial contents of the newborn baby, and its differentiation is remarkable in the sense that many types of processes are involved in arriving at its final stage. To begin with there are two other systems involved (olfactory and optic) that are not strictly within either of its two major subdivisions (telencephalon and diencephalon) mentioned above. However, they are intimately related with them during early development and some authors choose to discuss them within one or the other. In the present chapter they will be separated for simplicity and therefore the development of four components of prosencephalon will be followed.

The first indication of forebrain development appears during Horizon X (22 days) at a time when the head fold of the embryo begins to elevate. The cephalic neural folds are widely open and near their rostral portion a small groove, the *optic sulcus*, appears bilaterally. During Horizon XI (24 days), the stage during which the anterior neuropore closes, this sulcus becomes a forebrain protrusion, known as the *optic evagination*. Other features of this stage include some differentiation of the diencephalon in the form of primordia of both thalamus and mammillary recess (the diencephalon eventually differentiates into four major areas, the epithalamus, dorsal thalamus, ventral thalamus and hypothalamus).

The primordium of the *olfactory epithelium* appears in Horizon XIII (28 days) and *indentation of the lens vesicle* in XIV (32 days). In Horizon XV (34 days), the prosencephalon can finally be subdivided into telencephalon (cerebral vesicles) and diencephalon. The *epiphysis* (pineal) also appears during this stage. Initially the telencephalic walls are of uniform thickness, but during Horizon XVI (37 days) they show some differentiation into the *primordium hippocampi* and *corpus striatum* (which will give rise to the basal ganglia). The site of the olfactory bulb is marked during XVI by cells between the olfactory pit and telencephalon. During this same stage the four areas of the thalamus mentioned above can be distinguished with the hypothalamus being most developed. In Horizon XVII (40 days) there is focal increase in vascularity marking the future sites of the *choroid plexus* bilaterally. The cerebral hemispheres show rapid growth, now overlapping the mesencephalon.

By Horizon XIX (45 days) there is marked differentiation of the diencephalon. The epithalamus "includes roof plate, stria medullaris, epiphysis and habenular complex". Likewise there is comparable definition of other thalamic structures. Optic fibers are found at the primordium of the *optic chiasm* in Horizon XX and another change at this time is elongation of the hypothalamus.

Near the end of the embryonic period, Horizon XXII (50 days), the cerebral hemispheres are thin walled with no sulci or gyri and dorsally and the *lamina terminalis* is the only structure uniting them. The corpus striatum consists of medial and lateral lobes, and overlying them a few cells are present indicating the beginning of differentiation of the cerebral cortex. It can be seen that the cerebral cortex is still in a remarkably primitive state at the point when an embryo becomes a fetus. This is an example of the limitations imposed when discussing the embryology of the CNS based on the classical embryonic period. The main point to be made is that the features of the cerebral cortex that are frequently of importance to the clinician arise *after* the embryonic Horizons. An example of this is the external cortical patterns which differentiate during the fetal period (Table 3 and Figs. 13–14).

TABLE 3

APPROXIMATE TIMES OF APPEARANCE OF CEREBRAL FISSURES AND SULCI

Fissure or Sulcus	*CR (mm)*	*Approximate Age (mo.)*
Hippocampal Rhinal	80–95	$2\frac{1}{2}$–3
Calcarine	125	$3\frac{1}{3}$
Sylvian	140	$3\frac{1}{2}$
Parieto-Occipital Central Olfactory	170	$4\frac{1}{3}$
Frontomarginal Interparietal Postcentral Superior and Inferior Frontal Callosomarginal	210	$5\frac{1}{4}$
Collateral Superior and Inferior Precentral Postcentral Superior Temporal Orbital	225	$5\frac{1}{2}$

Numerous *anomalies of forebrain development* are of clinical importance. Superficially the cortey may have few or no gyri (*lissencephaly*), too many small gyri (*polymicrogyria*), or large gyri (*macrogyria*). There may be abnormal communications between ventricles and subarachnoid space associated with apparent cysts (*porencephaly*) or no cortex at all (*hydranencephaly*). Outflow of cerebrospinal fluid (CSF) from the ventricles may be blocked by a variety of causes with resultant dilatation of the ventricles and thinning of the cortical mantle (*hydrocephaly*). In general when anomalies of forebrain are present they are associated

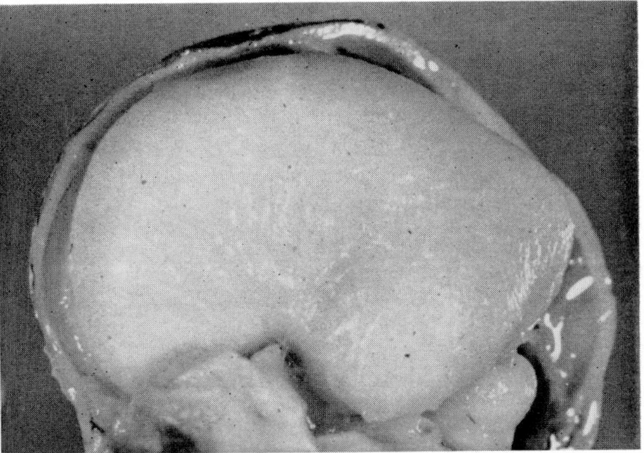

FIG. 13. Lateral view of left cerebral hemisphere (telencephalon) in a 105 mm. CR (92-day) length fetus (3 months). No fissures or sulci are apparent in this view.

with malformations of other parts of the CNS or other systems of the body.

From the numerous pathologic entities two will be discussed briefly to illustrate opposite ends of the spectrum of anomalies. The first, *holoprosencephaly*,[3,5] actually has many varieties, the simplest of which is unilateral or bilateral absence of the olfactory tracts. This is sometimes referred to as *arhinencephaly* and it may be the only defect present. Absence of the olfactory tracts may be associated with more severe forebrain anomalies such as a noncleaved hemisphere containing a single ventricle without a septum pellucidum or corpus callosum. Various terms are applied to the different forms of this spectrum of anomalies and it is of interest that in many cases the cerebral malformation

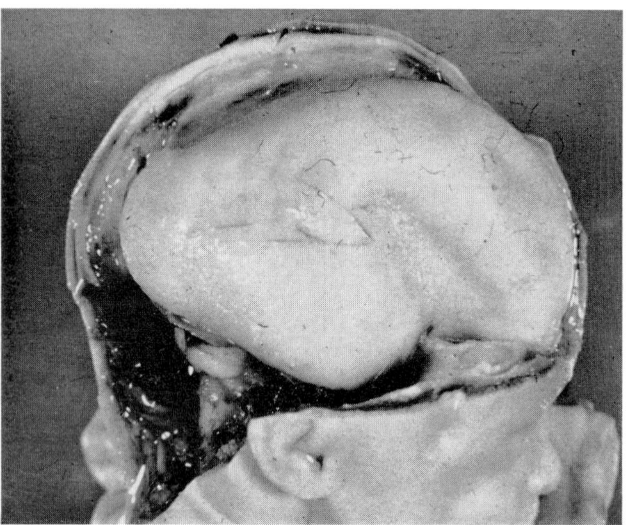

FIG. 14. Lateral view of cerebral hemisphere in a 142 mm. CR length (112-day) fetus (3½ months). The first indication of the Sylvian fissure and insula are seen about this time.

can be predicted by facial features (hypotelorism, median cleft lip, hypoplasia of philtrum, nostrils). Next in severity to simple absence of the olfactory tracts is a situation where bilateral cleft lip is associated with hypoplasia of the philtrum, flattening of the nose and orbital hypotelorism. The cortex is usually small (micrencephaly) and may be fused in the frontal region. In all stages beyond this there is microcephaly, alobar holoprosencephaly, and hypotelorism. The face may exhibit a flat nose associated with a median cleft lip or may have no cleft lip but a single midline infraorbital proboscis-like nose containing a single nostril (*cebocephaly*). *Premaxillary agenesis* is intermediate between cebocephaly and ethmocephaly. *Ethmocephaly* differs from cebocephaly in that the proboscis is supraorbital and the orbits closer together, but unfused. In *cyclopia* which is the last stage, there now being varying degrees of orbital fusion (including single orbit). The more severe types of this spectrum are rare while the milder ones are commonly associated with 13 trisomy or 18 p-syndrome.

Although the present chapter has not covered the development of the face, it is easy to appreciate that the above defects do arise during the embryonic Horizons if one considers the prosencephalic anomalies alone. Experimental evidence, such as removing the telencephalon in chick embryos of 6–7 somites[25] supports human descriptive evidence of early onset. With respect to the classification of teratogenic mechanisms (Table 2), these defects are most likely within the "arrest in development" category.

The second example of a malformation involving forebrain development, arising much later during the fetal period, is *hydranencephaly*. It is most likely an example of "degeneration secondary to an extrinsic stimulus" (Table 2). Based on published neuropathological studies there are variations of forebrain remnants present. Usually the cranium is filled with CSF contained within leptomeninges or a gliotic membrane with a scattering of identifiable cortex and ependyma. Basal ganglia, usually hypoplastic, are present as are midbrain and hindbrain structures. The point is that ample evidence exists that the telencephalon has developed and that at some point during fetal life, degenerated. There are numerous theories of causation such as vascular anomalies or thromboses, and infection, but as yet there is no unifying theme. It has occurred in twin pregnancies, although quite rarely. Possibly several pathogenetic mechanisms can produce the same end result.

The above examples of anomalous forebrain development, holoprosencephaly and hydranencephaly are selected for two reasons. Firstly they are both easy to diagnose in the newborn period if the clinician performs a good physical examination (the former by facial features, the latter by transilluminating the skull). Secondly, they provide examples that anomalies can arise by entirely different teratologic mechanisms, widely spaced in time and affecting a similar part of the developing brain.

Mesencephalon (Midbrain)

In Horizon X (22 days) only one midbrain neuromere exists, whereas in XI (24 days) there are two. By Horizons XII–XIII (26–28 days) the *tectum* and *tegmentum* are defined as general areas and the sulcus limitans is present from the midbrain caudally. During Horizon XIV (32 days) a few fibers of cranial nerves (C.N.) III and IV can be identified and their nuclei are identifiable in the tegmentum during Horizon XV (34 days). The *superior and inferior colliculi* are defined during Horizon XVIII (43 days).

There are two anomalies of the midbrain region that come under clinical consideration both of which are part of the Arnold-Chiari complex. These are *atresia of the aqueduct of Sylvius* and *beaking of the colliculi*. Both are considered secondary to more generalized problems with the CNS and would be examples of "extrinsic anomalous structural development" (Table 2).

Rhombencephalon (Hindbrain)

Like the forebrain, the development of the hindbrain is one of the most complicated processes of the CNS. There are initially seven neuromeres (rhombomeres) whose lumen (the 4th ventricle) is covered by a thin roof plate consisting of a single layer of cells. To establish early points of reference that are meaningful to the final product is difficult and rather than pursuing the discussion in the sequence of specific Horizons as in previous sections of the chapter, it will be related to relationships of parts. The *metencephalon*, mainly derived from rhombomere 1 will differentiate into the *cerebellum* dorsally, whereas one ventral portion will contribute to the *pons*. It extends from the mesencephalic-metencephalic isthmus, where the dorsal decussation of C.N. IV occurs, to the level of the *pontine flexure*, which is apparent ventrally by Horizons XVIII–XX (43–47 days). Although the early identification of the cerebellum is present in the form of rhombic lips during Horizons XIV–XV (32–34 days) its main differentiation takes place during the fetal (Table 4) and early

TABLE 4

DEVELOPMENT OF THE CEREBELLAR VERMIS

Lobule (rostral to caudal)	*Fissure*	*CR (mm)*	*Approximate Age (mo.)*
(Anterior Medullary Velum)		60	$2\frac{1}{3}$
Lingula		105–120	$3–3\frac{1}{3}$
	Precentral	105–120	$3–3\frac{1}{3}$
Central		105–120	$3–3\frac{1}{3}$
	Preculminate	78–87	$2\frac{1}{2}$
Culmen		78–87	$2\frac{1}{2}$
	Primary	72–78	$2\frac{1}{2}$
Declive		130–145	$3\frac{1}{2}$
	Posterior Superior	130–133	$3\frac{1}{2}$
Folium		130–145	$3\frac{1}{2}$
	Horizontal	132–145	$3\frac{1}{2}$
Tuber		132–145	$3\frac{1}{2}$
	Prepyramidal	87–114	3
Pyramis		105–114	3
	Secondary	105–114	3
Uvula		105–114	3
	Postero-lateral	45–53	2
Nodulus		105–114	3
(Taenia)		22	$1\frac{1}{2}$
(Posterior Medullary Velum)		127	$3\frac{1}{3}$

postnatal periods. Further discussion of the cerebellum will be presented later. The remainder of the hindbrain is termed the *myelencephalon*, extends from the pontine flexure to the first cervical segment, and contributes to the *medulla oblongata*. The second rhombomere is associated with C.N. V, and from the segmental standpoint is labelled the anterior hindbrain (AHB). The nucleus of C.N. V is first seen in Horizon XI (24 days). The middle hindbrain (MHB) segment is derived from rhombomeres 3 and 4 (with C.N. VI probably arising in the 3rd, C.N. VII–VIII the 4th). The nuclei of these cranial nerves are identifiable in Horizon XI. Rhombomeres 5–7 make up the posterior hindbrain (PHB) segment with C.N. IX (and the otic vesicle) being associated with rhombomere 5, C.N. X with 6 and 7, and C.N. XI–XII with 7). Various fibers and nuclear cell groups of these cranial nerves are found in Horizons XII–XIV.

Anomalies of the rhombencephalon are more commonly grouped under the term posterior fossa malformations as the entire hindbrain lies in this portion of the skull (Fig. 15). Two malformations of the hindbrain, Arnold-Chiari and Dandy-Walker, are well known to clinicians dealing with children. A short discussion of these will be presented as being representative of maldevelopment of this portion of the brain.

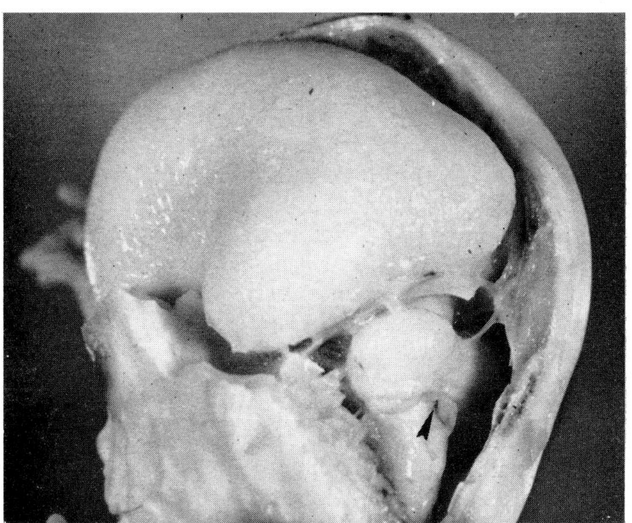

FIG. 15. Posterior fossa of 105 mm. CR (92-day) human fetus (3 months) as viewed from posterior-lateral position. The skull on this side has been removed and the cerebellum and medulla can be seen to lie below the tentorium (part of which was removed with the skull). The position of the foramen of Magendie is marked by the arrow.

Arnold-Chiari Malformation[24]

This is a variable complex consisting of anomalies of hindbrain, midbrain, forebrain, spinal cord and supporting structures of the CNS as listed below:

Structure	*Anomalies*
Hindbrain	Cerebellar vermis displaced
	Medulla kinked
Midbrain	Tectum beaked
	Aqueductal stenosis (or forking)
Forebrain	Polymicrogyria
	Hydrocephalus
Spinal Cord	Myelomeningocele
	Hydromyelia
	Diastematomyelia
Supporting structures	
Skull	Craniolacunia
	Hypoplasia of tentorium and falx
Vertebrae	Spina bifida
	Hemivertebrae

Virtually all patients with myelomeningocele have some features of the Arnold-Chiari complex. However, the Arnold-Chiari malformation itself is commonly used in reference to the downward displacement of the posterior vermis (midline) of the cerebellum through the foramen magnum, i.e. a developmental hindbrain herniation. Most commonly only the uvula and nodulus are involved, but in severe cases the pyramids may also be found displaced. Numerous theories have been put forth to explain the pathogenesis of this malformation. Some are based on the concept of pressure changes such as hydrocephalus of the lateral ventricles causing pressure and downward displacement on the hindbrain from above. Others have invoked mechanical factors, e.g. that the distal cord is tethered at the site of the myelomeningocele and pulls the hindbrain down as the embryo grows. These and numerous other hypotheses have been discussed in detail by Peach (1965) who feels the pathogenesis can best be explained on the basis of an arrest in development at the time the pontine flexure occurs. Although an attractive explanation of the various components of the Arnold-Chiari malformation it fails to explain the fact that experimentally the defect can be produced after this period in time. It is unusual that so common a defect, for which there are experimental models still promotes controversy regarding its pathogenesis, and is therefore an area deserving still more experimental and descriptive work.

Dandy-Walker Malformation

This is another hindbrain anomaly that is presently controversial from the standpoint of pathogenesis. Clinically the patient presents with an enlarging head (hydrocephalus) and increased transillumination over the occiput. Air contrast studies confirm the presence of cystic dilatation of the fourth ventricle. Pathological examination reveals the cerebellum to be extremely hypoplastic (especially the vermis) and unlike the vermis of the Arnold-Chiari, all lobules are involved to some degree (in some cases the posterior vermis is most affected). Likewise the posterior fossa malformation (and secondary changes such as hydrocephalus of the lateral and third ventricles) is frequently the only one present, i.e. there is no constant association with lesions such as myelomeningocele, etc. The roof of the cystic fourth ventricle is covered by a thin membrane consisting of ependyma, pia mater and connective tissue as well as choroid plexus which, though easily identifiable, is displaced caudally.

The search for the pathogenesis of this malformation has led to interesting studies regarding the normal embryogenesis of the fourth ventricle and its outlet foramina (Magendie and Luschka). One theory of the pathogenesis of the Dandy-Walker malformation has proposed that failure of development of these foramina produced the dilated fourth ventricle by not allowing the escape of CSF. Although an attractive hypothesis, most cases do not have this finding while other cases, in which atresias of the foramina have been found, do not have the Dandy-Walker malformation. This is a clear example of how a knowledge of the normal development of this region enables one to avoid pitfalls in making hypotheses, such as the one above. In the earlier discussion of the rhombencephalon it was pointed out that the cerebellum is derived from the rhombic lips of the metencephalon, thus originating as bilateral structures which gradually fuse together (at approxiamtely 40 mm CR: 58 days, the midline portion being referred to as the vermis (Table 4). During this initial period of time (i.e., during the "Horizon" phase) the cerebellum actually lies within the fourth ventricle, the extraventricular portion arising with further differentiation during fetal life. The roof of the fourth ventricle is found to differentiate into two main components, (1) the area membranacea superior (AMS), and (2) area membranacea inferior (AMI). It is these structures that we will now focus on briefly (Fig. 16). The AMS is that portion of the roof of the fourth ventricle lying between the cerebellum and the more caudal choroid plexus of the fourth ventricle (also a paired structure). Its internal surface is lined by cells continuous with, and histologically similar to ependyma, and this layer of cells blends into the choroid plexus caudally. The cellular structure of the AMI (which is that portion of the

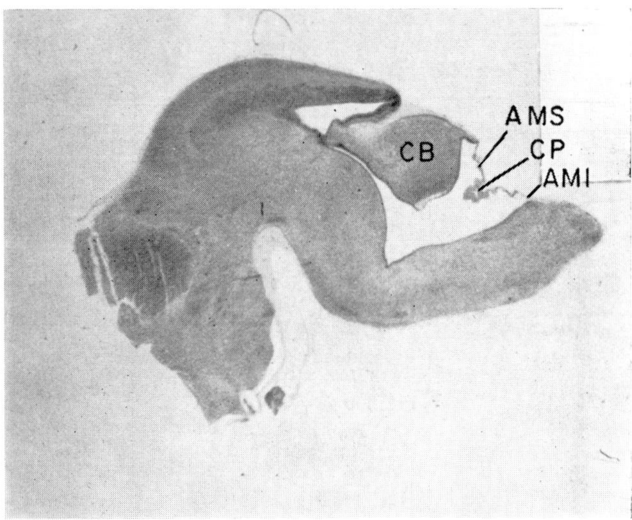

FIG. 16. Sagittal section of hindbrain of 53 mm. (66-day) CR human fetus showing cerebellar vermis (CB), area membranacea superior (AMS), choroid plexus (CP) and area membranacea inferior (AMI.)

roof extending from the choroid plexus to the obex) is markedly different, being both thinner and not cuboidal in nature (Fig. 17). This membrane clearly does not resemble ependyma and is the site through which the foramen of Magendie will develop. As differentiation progresses (through approximately 80 mm CR: 80 days) the AMS becomes relatively small as compared to the AMI. This is because of the gradual involution of the posterior vermis whereby the choroid plexus eventually comes to lie under the cerebellum within the fourth ventricle. With the knowledge of the development of these structures we can now approach the problem of when the foramen of Magendie develops in the AMI and thereby when another important phase occurs in the development of the embryonic neural tube. Earlier in the chapter it was noted that the neural tube was open until closure of the posterior neuropore in Horizon XII (26 days) at which time no further contact with the amniotic cavity was present. It becomes apparent that when the choroid plexus and ependyma begin secreting CSF within the lumen of this tube mechanisms must arise either to absorb or release it. It is remarkable that earlier studies on human fetuses consistently related development of the foramen of Magendie to a later stage (130 mm CR: 105 days) or avoided the issue entirely. It has recently been shown that indeed there are openings in this area occurring between 20–30 mm CR length (45–52 days),[2] i.e., during the later Horizons and therefore the foramen of Magendie provides the necessary exit for CSF at a theoretically appropriate time. Interestingly, the lateral foramina of Luschka may not appear until somewhere between 195–220 mm CR (148–162 days) and undoubtedly are less significant in the early embryonic-fetal CSF pathway. With a knowledge of the sequence of events in the development of the fourth gentricle we can now return to the question of the pathovenesis of the Dandy-Walker malformation. For rather obvious reasons it is difficult to conceive of a situation whereby the foramen of Magendie would not initially form when one considers the delicate nature of the AMI. However, the possibility that it might secondarily be obstructed by scarring from such phenomenon as infection or hemorrhage should be considered. These could conceivably occur midway through gestation and with subsequent increased pressure cause dilatation of the fourth ventricle and retardation of growth in the cerebellum. There are no data to support the above hypothesis and it is offered only as an example of how a secondary pathological process might, during fetal life, produce a situation that after birth would appear to be an embryonic event. Clearly the suggestion that the Dandy-Walker malformation is not necessarily related to atresia of the foramen of Magendie is probably true. However, the reason given—that it is because the anomaly arises prior to the development of that foramen—is incorrect.

It should be noted that not all cysts within the posterior fossa represent the Dandy-Walker malformation. Retrocerebellar "arachnoidal" cysts not involving the fourth ventricle can occur.[8] Likewise numerous other less common malformations of hindbrain structures such as unilateral cerebellar hypoplasia, absence of the vermis and even accessory lobes of cerebellum occur within the spectrum of anomalies, none of which will be discussed.

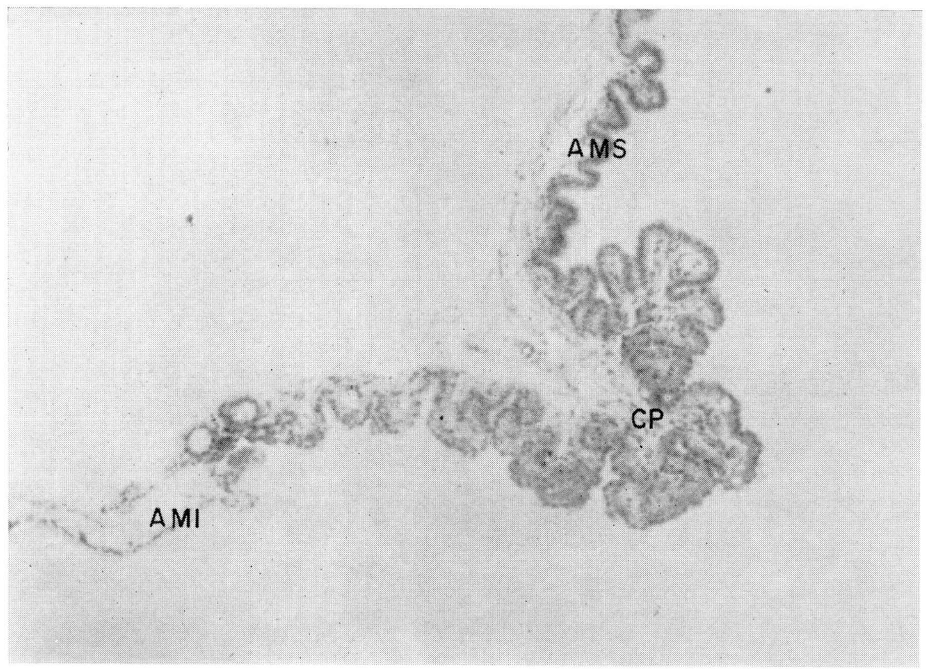

FIG. 17. The roof of the early fetal fourth ventricle (which is to the right) consists of choroid plexus (CP) attached rostrally to the AMS and caudally to the AMI (see text and figure 16.) Note the ependymal characteristic of the AMS as compared with the flattened thin cells making up the AMI.

SUMMARY

The present chapter has attempted to depart from more traditional lines in discussing the embryology of the central nervous system in humans. In doing so it suffers from many gaps if considered from the viewpoint of either the neuroembryologist or pediatrician. Many exciting areas, such as radioautographic studies dealing with cellular kinetics of ependyma and cortex have been deliberately omitted as they still lack direct clinical application. Likewise omitted, but equally important, are studies that have been conducted in lower species with various nervous system teratogens. Truly the forefront of the scientific basis of pediatrics is beyond gross morphology but at the present time basic concepts may still be derived from this older approach, certainly as viewed by the clinician. For over two centuries good morphological studies have been done on the developing human nervous system, but too few have addressed themselves to a specific clinical problem.

To summarize some of the salient points discussed above it can be said that:

1. The "embryology" of the CNS covers the entirety of gestation, and actually extends beyond birth. The teratogenic period is therefore not limited to the classical "first trimester".

2. The primary embryonic divisions of the neural tube (prosencephalon, mesencephalon, rhombencephalon and spinal cord, with their various subdivisions) can be transformed into a more clinically applicable system postnatally in the form of segmental and supersegmental structures.

3. The spinal cord has at least three distinct periods of development: phase 1, neurulation; phase 2, canalization; and phase 3, retrogressive differentiation. The first two relate to the classic periods (Horizons of embryonic development), whereas the latter continues throughout gestation.

4. The neural tube is first open, closes completely in Horizon XII (posterior neuropore), then reopens during Horizons XX–XXIII (foramen of Magendie).

5. The development of the supporting structures of the CNS, vertebral column and skull, although only briefly discussed, are important considerations in the development of numerous anomalies found in infants.

The care of the child with a central nervous system malformation frequently has a devastating effect on family and physician alike. It may be fortunate that most fetuses with severe anomalies die *in utero*, many never being seen. In this regard one must use discretion when counselling families on recurrence risks and in remarks relating to pathogenesis. Too often statements regarding cause and effect are carried through numerous publications without anyone questioning their validity based on a knowledge of embryogenesis. Many of the important facts are known and recorded, but unfortunately remain buried in the literature of many languages and are therefore unavailable to most clinicians.

ACKNOWLEDGEMENTS

The author wishes to acknowledge the National Foundation—March of Dimes, MCHS MR training grant, project 913 and NIH grant HD-00836 for supporting this manuscript.

REFERENCES

1. Bartelmez, G. W. and Dekaban, A. S. (1962), "The Early Development of the Human Brain," *Carnegie Inst. Contrib. Embryol.*, **37**, 13–32.
2. Brocklehurst, G. (1969), "The Development of the Human Cerebrospinal Fluid Pathway with Particular Reference to the Roof of the Fourth Ventricle," *J. Anat.*, **105**, 467–475.
3. Cohen, M. M., Jr., Jirásek, J. E., Guzman, R. T., Gorlin, R. J. and Peterson, M. Q. (1971), "Holoprosencephaly and Facial Dysmorphia: Nosology, Etiology and Pathogenesis," *Birth. Def. Orig. Art. Ser.*, **7**, 125–135.
4. Dekaban, A. S. and Bartelmez, G. W. (1964), "Complete Dysraphism in 14 Somite Human Embryo," *Amer. J. Anat.*, **115**, 27–42.
5. DeMyer, W., Zeman, W. and Palmer, C. G. (1964), "The Face Predicts the Brain: Diagnostic Significance of Median Facial Anomalies for Holoproscencephaly (Arhinencephaly)," *Pediatrics*, **34**, 256–263.
6. diVirgilio, G., Lavenda, N. and Worden, J. L. (1967), "Sequence of Events in Neural Tube Closure and the Formation of Neural Crest in the Chick Embryo," *Acta anat.*, **68**, 127–146.
7. Gardner, W. J. (1960), "Myelomeningocele, the Result of Rupture of the Embryonic Neural Tube," *Cleveland Clin. Quart.*, **27**, 88–100.
8. Gilles, F. H. and Rockett, F. X. (1971), "Infantile Hydrocephalus: Retrocerebellar 'arachnoidal' cyst," *J. Pediat.*, **79**, 436–443.
9. Hausman, L. (1961), *Illustrations of the Nervous System. Atlas III.* Springfield: Thomas.
10. Heuser, C. H. and Corner, G. W. (1957), "Developmental Horizons in Human Embryos. Description of Age Group X, 4 to 12 Somites," *Carnegie Inst. Contrib. Embryol.*, **36**, 29–39.
11. Iffy, L., Shepard, T. H., Jakobovits, A., Lemire, R. J. and Kerner, P. (1967), "The Rate of Growth in Young Human Embryos of Streeter's Horizons XIII–XXIII," *Acta anat.*, **66**, 178–186.
12. James, C. C. M. and Lassman, L. P. (1964), "Diastematomyelia: A Critical Survey of 24 Cases Submitted to Laminectomy," *Arch. Dis. Childh.*, **39**, 125–130.
13. Jirásek, J. E. (1971), *Development of the Genital System and Male Pseudohermaphroditism*, p. 5 (M. M. Cohen, Jr., Ed.). Baltimore: Johns Hopkins Press.
14. Kalter, H. (1968), *Teratology of the Central Nervous System*, Chicago: University Chicago.
15. Kernohan, J. W. (1925), "The Ventriculus Terminalis: Its Growth and Development," *J. comp. Neurol.*, **38**, 107–125.
16. Kunitomo, K. (1918), "The Development and Reduction of the Tail and of the Caudal End of the Spinal Cord," *Carnegie Inst. Contrib. Embryol.*, **8**, 161–198.
17. Lemire, R. J., Shepard, T. H. and Alvord, E. C., Jr. (1965), "Caudal Myeloschisis (Lumbo-sacral Spina Bifida Cystica) in a Five Millimeter (Horizon XIV) Human Embryo," *Anat. Rec.*, **152**, 9–16.
18. Lemire, R. J. (1969), "Variations in Development of the Caudal Neural Tube in Human Embryos (Horizons XIV–XXI)," *Teratol.*, **2**, 361–370.
19. Lemire, R. J., Graham, C. B. and Beckwith, J. B. (1971), "Skin-covered Sacrococcygeal Masses in Infants and Children," *J. Pediat.*, **79**, 948–954.
20. Marin-Padilla, M. and Ferm, V. H. (1965), "Somite Necrosis and Developmental Malformations Induced by Vitamin A in the Golden Hamster," *J. Embryol. Exp. Morph.*, **13**, 1–8.
21. Naeye, R. L. and Blanc, W. A. (1971), "Organ and Body Growth in Anencephaly," *Arch. Path.*, **91**, 140–147.
22. Padget, D. H. (1970), "Neuroschisis and Human Embryonic Maldevelopment," *J. Neuropath.*, **29**, 192–216.
23. Patten, B. M. (1953), "Embryological Stages in the Establishing of Myeloschisis with Spina Bifida," *Amer. J. Anat.*, **93**, 365–395.
24. Peach, B. (1965), "The Arnold-Chiari Malformation," *Arch. Neurol.*, **12**, 527–535.
25. Rogers, K. T. (1964), "Experimental Production of Perfect Cyclopia by Removal of the Telencephalon and Reversal of Bilateralization in Somite-stage Chicks," *Amer. J. Anat.*, **115**, 487–508.
26. Romanoff, A. L. (1960), *The Avian Embryo*, pp. 212–221. New York: Macmillan.
27. Sensenig, E. C. (1949), "The Early Development of the Human Vertebral Column," *Carnegie Inst. Contrib. Embryol.*, **33**, 23–41.
28. Sensenig, E. C. (1951), "The Early Development of the Meninges of the Spinal Cord in Human Embryos," *Carnegie Inst. Contrib. Embryol.*, **34**, 145–157.
29. Spemann, H. (1962), *Embryonic Development and Induction.* New York: Hafner.
30. Streeter, G. L. (1919), "Factors Involved in the Formation of the Filum Terminale," *Amer. J. Anat.*, **25**, 1–11.
31. Streeter, G. L. (1951), *Developmental Horizons in Human Embryos. Age Groups XI to XXIII*, Embryology Reprint Vol. II. Washington, D.C.: Carnegie Inst.
32. Vogel, F. S. (1961), "The Anatomic Character of Vascular Anomalies Associated with Anencephaly," *Amer. J. Path.*, **39**, 163–174.
33. Warkany, J., Wilson, J. G. and Geiger, J. F. (1958), "Myeloschisis and Myelomeningocele Produced Experimentally in the Rat," *J. comp. Neur.*, **109**, 35–64.
34. Zwilling, E. (1955), "Teratogenesis," in *Analusis of Development*, pp. 699–719 (B. H. Willier, P. A. Weiss and V. Hamburger, Eds.). Philadelphia: Saunders.

32. THE LATER DEVELOPMENT OF THE BRAIN AND ITS VULNERABILITY

JOHN DOBBING

INTRODUCTION

The developing brain, from the time of birth until maturity, is subject to a number of different types of pathology, many of which have been reasonably well understood for many years. In the first trimester of gestation various teratological agents may interfere with the many sensitive processes of central nervous system embryology leading to gross malformation. Cardinal characteristics of this pathology are that the timing of the insult must be precise in relation to embryological events, and the consequent malformation is often gross and irrecoverable. Later, throughout the third gestational trimester and during the perinatal period, a pathology of focal lesions may occur in the brain as a result of the tissue's differential susceptibility to many of the hazards of this period of life, such as hypoxia and hypoglycaemia. This is essentially a focally destructive pathology whose irreversibility stems from this tissue's incapacity for repair.

The quantitative aspects of brain growth with which this chapter is concerned are associated with yet another type of pathology. It seems that such is the complexity and rapidity of growth of the brain during its growth spurt period, that mere retardation of the rate of development may be sufficient to dislodge the intricate components of the growth programme away from their delicately ordained interrelationships; and this results in distortion and deficits in the ultimate mature organ. Thus in this pathology there is no gross anatomical anomaly, nor any destructive lesion, and for this reason it is unlikely that there will be localizing signs of the kind which are usually sought by developmental and adult neurologists.

The concept of a "distortion" pathology of growth disorders is not by any means new in other systems. It has long been realized that the different tissues of the growing body react differently to growth restriction, some being comparatively spared and others comparatively severely affected. The result following rehabilitation is frequently a distorted bodily configuration, bones and teeth (for example) showing signs of permanent distortion while organs such as liver apparently recover completely. If the brain can be regarded as being just as complete and heterogeneous *within itself* as is the body as a whole, it is not difficult to imagine how a similar distortion of component interrelationships can result from mere growth retardation during its rapid phase of growth. Not only may certain processes (*e.g.* myelination) be differently susceptible from others (*e.g.* cerebellar neuronal multiplication), but they are also differently timed in relation to the insult; and for all of these general reasons ultimate, permanent, quantitative distortions are scarcely surprising.

The brain growth spurt period is also likely to be similarly susceptible to such insults as inborn metabolic error. The period is one of extraordinary biochemical activity within the tissue, associated with the rapid emergence of new structure and function. Many of the new cellular and non-cellular components of the developing brain are synthesized within the organ itself from quite simple components, the "barrier" to whose entry is temporarily "lifted" at this time; and an extraordinary range of synthetic pathway facilities is transiently and powerfully available, some of which are not present beforehand, and cannot be resurrected subsequently. (It is commonly and erroneously supposed that the phenomenon loosely known as the "blood-brain barrier" *develops* with increasing age. In fact for many substance, *e.g.* dyestuffs, it is always closed, even in early fetal life; while for others (*e.g.* labelled phosphate) it is only transiently "open" during the brain growth spurt period[10]). It is scarcely surprising, therefore, that a breakdown of supplies as in poor nutrition, or distortion of biochemical mechanisms as in the inborn errors finds an easy opportunity at this particular period to disturb the proper achievement of normal brain growth.

There are many obvious reasons, most of them ethical, why this new variety of neuropathology will always be difficult to substantiate in the human species. It must therefore be largely inferred, partly from animal experiment, and partly from observation of developing, living human children. It is a particular handicap to the study of these things that they should be ultimately concerned with the uniquely human attributes of higher mental function, but that they will always be mainly substantiated in animal species. For this reason the question of inter-species extrapolation must be studied here as a primary objective to an extent which probably applies to no other branch of experimental pathology.

This chapter will therefore not conceal its extreme dependence on animal experiment. After describing the experimental evidence, the problem of transference of conclusions from animals to man will then be discussed, with an account of our knowledge of the human brain growth spurt in the same quantitative terms as those used in accumulating the experimental data.

THE BRAIN GROWTH SPURT

The brain growth spurt is arbitrarily defined as that transient period of growth when the brain is growing most rapidly. It is most easily illustrated in a short life-span species such as the rat in which the whole period happens to be postnatal. It is sometimes convenient to portray it as a velocity curve (Fig. 1).

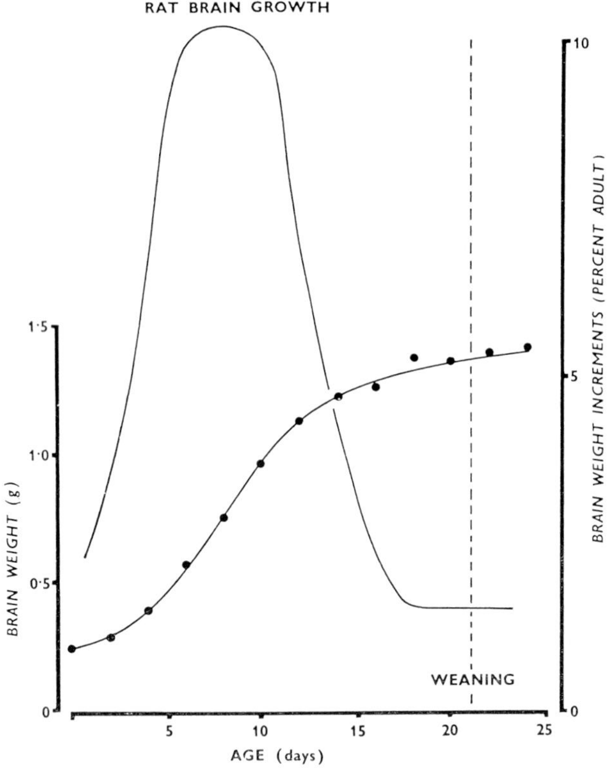

FIG. 1. The brain growth spurt illustrated as a characteristic sigmoid weight curve and its derived velocity curve. In the rat, as shown here, it is entirely postnatal (see Fig. 4).

It is one of the general features of brain growth throughout the mammalian species that adult neuronal cell *number* is almost accomplished before the major phase of glial (spongioblast) multiplication begins; and the brain growth spurt itself does not begin until towards the end of the phase of neuroblast multiplication, adult neuronal cell number having already been accomplished (Fig. 2). (This general statement has exceptions in the granular neurons of the cerebellum and a small minority of other neurons in other regions). The very substantial phase of cell multiplication occupying the first part of the brain growth spurt period is therefore mainly glial. In fact it is mainly oligodendroglial, and is succeeded by a period of rapid myelination occupying the second half of the period. This sequence results from the fact that it is the oligodendroglial cells which synthesize the myelin materials and form the myelin sheaths from their cell membranes[2,8]. The growth spurt ends as the rapid phase of myelination draws to a close. This is not, of course, to say that all myelination has ceased, since histological studies show that some fibres may still be found to be myelinating much later. It is simply that the main quantitative bulk of myelination is accomplished by the end of the brain growth spurt. From this stage onward there is some gradual further growth of the brain until maturity, followed, it is said, by some ultimate regression with senility.

It is impossible to portray these events quantitatively using histological counting procedures because of the extremely large numbers involved in any single histological section, and the enormous number of serial sections which would be required to examine even one brain region. It is therefore necessary to use chemical indices of structure, such as DNA content for cell number and myelin lipid content for myelination. Although much specificity is lost (*e.g.* DNA estimation does not distinguish one cell type from another), many brains can be analysed in a few hours, any one of which could only be imperfectly examined histologically in many months. A discussion of the meaning and validity of the chemical indices will be found elsewhere[7].

Using these methods, velocity curves can be drawn of cell multiplication and brain lipid accumulation as shown in Fig. 3 where their relation to the brain weight growth spurt can be seen. The figure also illustrates that the bodily growth spurt is later than that of the brain, and this is a common mammalian pattern.

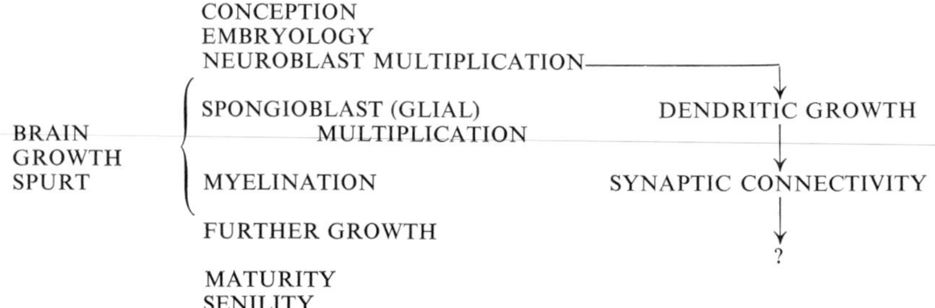

FIG. 2. A greatly simplified scheme to describe the common mammalian pattern of brain growth (see text).

One of the problems of this type of description of brain growth is that only certain anatomical structures can be quantitated, and *it may be that these are not the ones which matter.* Thus it is unlikely that any great intellectual limitation will be imposed by a small deficiency of glial cells or of myelin laminae *per se.* It is much more likely that normal function depends on degree of dendritic branching of neurons and synaptic connectivity. Here again the techniques of quantitative histology for counting these important structures are much too laborious, but unfortunately in this case we do not yet have chemical index techniques that can easily be applied to a large experimental series. It is almost certain, however, that these important developmental processes also underlie the brain growth spurt period as indicated in Fig. 2. This further development of neurons cannot antedate the growth spurt period since it cannot begin before the neurons have themselves arrived and differentiated. We are thus led to conjecture that changes which can be brought about by (somatic) growth restriction during the brain growth spurt and which can be measured, may be analagous to others which are probably more important, but which we cannot measure. Brain cell number is no necessary index of intellectual excellence, any more than is brain size within the reasonable limits of normal distribution.

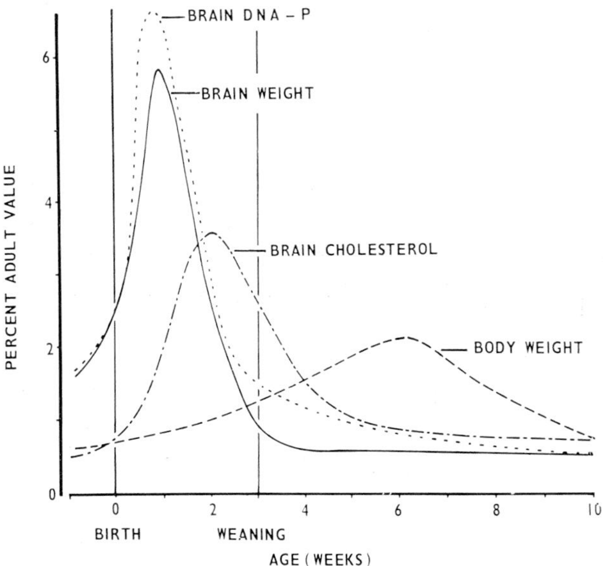

FIG. 3. Velocity curves showing three parameters of brain growth in the rat, and their relationship to the later bodily growth spurt.[15]

INTERSPECIES EXTRAPOLATION

Using these rather crude quantitative methods the brain growth of several animal species as well as that of man has been described, and we can now lay down certain rules for transferring information obtained in any one species to any of the others.

Firstly the general sequence of brain growth outlined in Fig. 2 shows no species differences. Secondly the anatomical units of which the brain is composed show no important interspecies differences. A rat neuron has much the same composition and even the same electrical properties as that of man. The myelin shows only minor compositional differences between the species. The only two important differences are (a) in the complexity of the final product, but, more importantly for our present purposes, (b) the *timing* of the brain growth spurt in relation to birth. This is only another way of saying that some species are more mature at birth than others, and this is illustrated in Fig. 4 where the brain growth spurts of pigs, guinea pigs, rats and man are drawn as velocity curves in relation to birth.

Figure 4 shows how impossible it is to speak meaningfully, for example, of "the neonatal brain" without specifying the species and knowing that particular species' brain growth characteristics. This apparently academic zoological argument is extremely important to the paediatric topic which is the subject of this chapter since without it one cannot appreciate the validity or otherwise of much of the paediatric research literature in the field. There are many gross errors of reasoning which stem from not observing the general rule that in comparing the developing brains of one species with those of another, *stages (of brain development) must be compared, not ages.* Normal brain growth curves are quite uninfluenced by normal birth, and thus productive comparisons can perfectly well be made between (for example) the guinea pig brain at the time of its peak velocity, which is fetal, and the rat brain at *its* peak velocity, which is postnatal, and the human brain at its own peak, provided we know when the latter occurs.

Only one particularly common error of interspecies extrapolation will be mentioned to illustrate the above point.

Rats, since they are born so immature, pass through their neuronal cell multiplication phase during the last one third

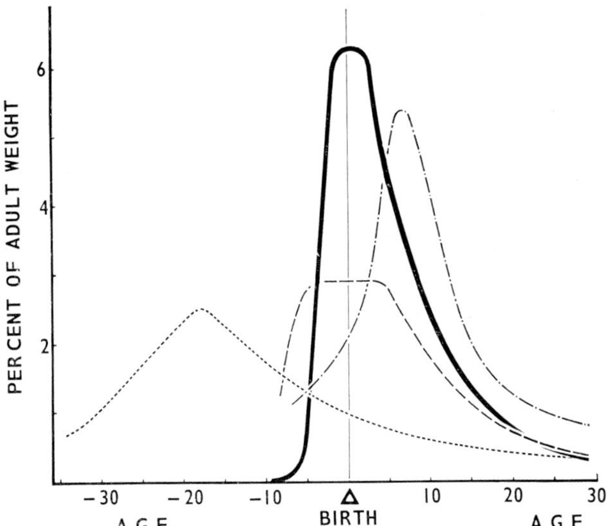

FIG. 4. Velocity of human brain growth (wet weight) compared with that in other species. Prenatal and postnatal are expressed as follows:

human	————	in months[16]
guinea pig	- - - - - - - - -	in days[14]
pig	— — — — — —	in weeks[9]
rat	—·—·—·—·—	in days[15]

of their gestational life. Since this is the only period of pregnancy when nutritional growth restriction can be imposed on a fetus by reasonable undernutrition of the mother, it is scarcely surprising that the newborn rat, born at term of an undernourished mother, is nutritionally small-for-dates, and has a smaller brain *with fewer cells in it;* and because neurons are virtually the only cells present in the brain at this immature stage of development, the undernourished newborn rat's brain cell deficit is necessarily neuronal, not glial.

Extensive research projects in underprivileged human populations have been erroneously based on an uncritical extrapolation of this perfectly respectable result in rats, entirely ignoring the fact that the human baby is born at a much more advanced stage of brain development. Thus the phase of multiplication of human brain neurons occurs well before the beginning of the third trimester (see below), and at a period of fetal life which is *not* subject to growth restriction when the mother is malnourished. There are probably fewer "cells" in the brains of nutritionally small human neonates, *but the deficit will be of glial, not neuronal cells*, since it is only glial cells which are importantly multiplying when the human fetus is growth-restricted by maternal food deprivation. This is not to say that no important brain growth processes occur and may be damaged during human fetal third trimester life, but simply that achievement of neuronal *number* cannot be one of them[12].

The differences in maturity at birth between the different species are probably important to other aspects of interspecies extrapolations besides those in developing brain research. Throughout many of the chapters of this book, differences in perinatal stages of development between man and laboratory animals are referred to in different systems. In many cases these would repay re-examination using brain maturity as an index of developmental age at birth. If the newborn rat, rabbit or mouse is regarded as equivalent to an eighteen week human fetus; and a newborn guinea pig as a 2–3 year-old human child, some of the extrapolation problems appear to be resolved. This is likely to be a helpful approach for any aspect of any tissue's developing function except those which are directly related to the event of birth itself. Stages, not ages are important to the whole subject of interspecies extrapolation between developing mammals.

GROWTH RESTRICTION DURING THE BRAIN GROWTH SPURT

Long-term Effects on Somatic Growth

Long before the effects on the *brain* of growth restriction during its growth spurt were discovered, the effects on *somatic* growth were already demonstrated. It is a curious, and perhaps highly significant feature of these studies that permanent *somatic* stunting, which resists all nutritional rehabilitation, can only usually be imposed by growth restriction during the *brain* growth spurt. Growth restriction during the somatic growth spurt, which is later (Fig. 3) is promptly recoverable through a typical "catch-up" trajectory on release of the growing animals from the restraint. It can also be shown that growth restriction of a realistic degree imposed *before* the brain growth spurt need have no irretrievable influence on bodily growth provided the succeeding brain growth spurt period is covered by adequate nutrition and growth.

There are many implications of this finding both for academic, hypothetical ideas concerning somatic growth-control by the brain as well as for practical human affairs. The topic has no further place in this chapter, except to emphasize again that extrapolation between species must observe the following three "unities": growth restriction must be of similar degree, of similar duration, and above all at a similar developmental stage for comparisons between humans and animals to be valid. The duration factor is important, since it leads to the supposition that in man, as in other animals, a major proportion of the human brain growth spurt (see below) must probably be growth-restricted to produce similarly permanent somatic growth deficits, although the restriction need not necessarily be severe.

Short-term Effects on Brain Growth

These may well be less interesting than the long term irretrievable effects to be outlined later. The time is probably past when the concurrent effects of malnutrition need be studied in all their patho-physiological detail, since this type of study is now known to have been comparatively unproductive in helping to understand the aetiology, prevention, or even the treatment, rehabilitation or cure of nutritional disease. It is still important, however, to investigate which of the changes outlast attempts at rehabilitation, and if these can be shown to be due to undernutrition at particular periods of growth, practical prophylactic measures in the "at risk" population or child can then be taken.

Nevertheless two types of finding will be described in the infant during the course of his malnutrition which may help to elucidate the mechanism by which the ultimate deficits in his brain structure and function are brought about. These describe apparently paradoxical effects. The first shows how the development of functional neurological achievement is *delayed* by nutritional growth restriction; the second implies that major general features of physical growth in the brain *cannot be delayed*, but must occur at pre-ordained ages even if environmental conditions are not good.

Reflex ontogeny in the suckling rat occurs in a sequence which remarkably resembles the developmental pattern in humans, bearing in mind that birth in the rat is developmentally equivalent to the mid-term human fetus, 5–7 postnatal rat days of age is equivalent to human term and the weanling rat at three postnatal weeks is equivalent to the 2 year-old human child. Somatic growth restriction during this period delays the arrival of many of the various milestones of neurological competence[24], just as it is reported there are similar delays in human babies[29]. Since these are "all-or-none" phenomena which eventually do happen even in the growth-retarded, it is impossible to comment on any ultimate deficit. It can only be conjectured that such delays may have long-term consequences by analogy with the consequences of similar delays in educational attainment. Thus it can presumably be ultimately deleterious to delay educational achievement beyond the age which is appropriate, and the same may be true of reflex and other "milestone" ontogeny.

In marked contrast there seems little doubt that the gross parameters of physical growth at this same time cannot be delayed. Fast and slowly growing animals alike must undergo their phases of brain cell division, myelination and growth in brain weight at fixed, identical chronological ages as if they have a once-only opportunity to do so[15]. The consequences in the brain of poor environmental conditions which reduce the somatic growth rate at this time are that the *extent* of these processes is reduced: and since there is no catch-up facility in the brain once its growth spurt is over, the ultimate result is gross deficit. This is illustrated for the (glial) cell division phase in Fig. 5, in which it can be seen that the *timing* of the cell multiplication velocity curve is unaltered by growth restriction. The velocity is at all points merely reduced. This type of finding may have important implications for temporarily deprived human populations for whom nutritional and other aid is too little for any individual if it is evenly distributed. Should it perhaps be concentrated in adequate amounts at those ages at which children currently undergoing their brain growth-spurts? Certainly the evidence suggests that recovery from insult is possible if it is inflicted on older children, but less so if it occurs before the human brain growth spurt ends[4] (see below). Similar considerations may have a bearing on such paediatric problems as the timing and duration of dietary therapy for inborn metabolic errors and the timing of treatment of other growth-retarding pathologies.

Long-term Effects on Brain Growth

These will only be briefly enumerated here, since they are fully described in the relevant experimental literature[17]. In all cases mentioned they can only be achieved by growth restriction throughout the vulnerable period of the brain growth-spurt, though the restriction does not have to be severe. Also all of these features have been observed in adult rats whose post-weaning (equivalent to post-human two-year-old) environment following their early undernutrition has been unrestricted.

(1) Firstly, and associated with the permanent stunting of bodily growth, the brain is found to be small. More importantly it is smaller than would be appropriate even for their reduced body weight, and this therefore constitutes a true microcephaly[15]. The same probably occurs in human children[6].

(2) All parts of the brain are not reduced to the same extent. For example the cerebellum is much more reduced in weight than is the rest of the brain[13]. This is almost certainly attributable to the cerebellum's peculiar growth characteristics. In humans as well as in animals it grows much faster, although at the same time as the rest of the brain (see below)[16]. Thus, on the assumption that long-term vulnerability is related to speed of early growth, restriction of the whole growing brain would be expected to affect the part which grows fastest: and so it does. This differential effect on the cerebellum is also associated in animals with a detectable clumsiness[19]. It is therefore possible that some human clumsiness may be of similar aetiology. The cerebellar growth disorder does not include any focal lesions nor any easily detectable alteration of shape and would therefore easily

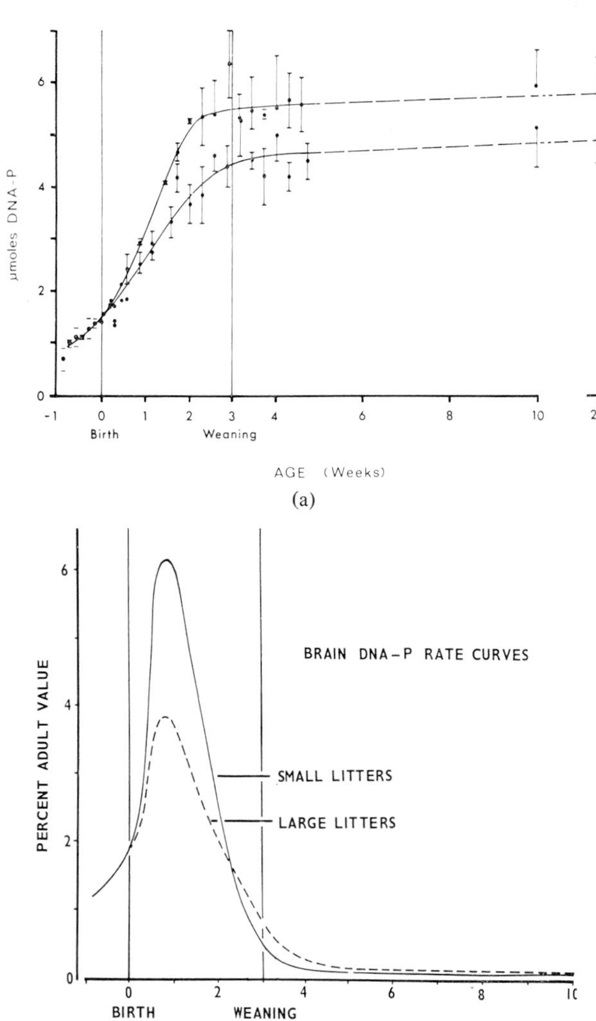

FIG. 5(a). Whole brain DNA-P for slowly growing (lower line) and fast growing (upper line) rats plotted by computer against age. (b) Velocity curves constructed from the curves in 5(a).[15]

escape the pathologist's notice if examined by conventional post-mortem techniques. It can only be shown whether it occurs in human brains when pathologists begin to weigh the cerebellum separately and express it as a proportion of the whole brain; or by laborious quantitative histology, as will be mentioned next.

(3) Histologically it is possible to detect a differential absence of granular neurons in the cerebellum by appropriate quantitative techniques[13]. Also there appears to be a loss of cerebral cortical neurons in certain

layers. These are further examples of the fact that distortion (in this case of the histological architecture) accompanies mere quantitative deficit.

(4) The deficit in brain lipids is greater than that expected from the reduction in brain size[11]. The lipid picture is further distorted by there being a differential reduction specifically in myelin lipids[5].

(5) It has been suggested that the number of synapses per cortical neuron is substantially reduced[3]. If this can be substantiated it is probably the most significant finding to date. Unfortunately the quantitative histological techniques involved are almost heroic and judgement should probably be suspended until the matter can be even more substantially investigated.

(6) This is not the place to discuss the behavioural consequences of early growth restriction. There are formidable difficulties in interpretation of animal behavioural experiments, some of which are discussed elsewhere[17]. In the human field a large literature presents even more complex interpretive problems which are probably best discussed in relation to a recent study of Jamaican children[18,22]. However there are some striking alterations of higher mental function in both human and other animal species, which seem to persist, following early growth restriction correctly timed.

It is by no means clear at the time of writing whether the effects on higher mental function are mediated through such physical brain deficits and distortions as have been mentioned above, whether they result from altered endocrine settings including those known to produce permanent alterations of sexuality and aggression at this same early period, whether they are related to differences induced in the "stress" response as measured by alterations in circulating steroid, or whether by a combination of several of these things. The important concept of early influences on later achievement is still a nebulous one in nearly all branches of paediatric research, but it is likely to be one of the most rewarding in the next half century, and nowhere more so than in the field of developing intellect and personality. For the present our next enquiry must concern the timing and nature of the *human* brain growth spurt, in order to begin our conjectures about the possible meaning of the experimental results for man.

THE HUMAN BRAIN GROWTH SPURT

If one wishes to describe these later stages of human growth in the same quantitative terms as have been used to investigate the effects of restriction on developing animal brains, the voluminous pathological literature is very little help. It is even difficult to construct a smooth growth curve for brain weight in which fetal merges convincingly with postnatal brain weight. The following is a new attempt to describe normal human brain growth quantitatively, and especially to delineate the age limits of the human brain growth spurt. This is a particularly necessary step in the argument because of the species differences in the timing of brain growth mentioned above.

The first problem, which is less difficult to overcome than might at first appear, is how to draw a normal growth curve from data obtained from dead human brains. The material must necessarily be cross-sectional rather than longitudinal, and this can only partly be compensated for by collecting a sufficient number of specimens to portray the magnitude of the variance at each age. In addition brains were carefully selected from fetuses and children who appeared to show no serious deviations from normal somatic growth, and no brain was accepted which showed any conspicuous neuropathology.

Fetal brains of the late first and early second trimester were from induced abortions which can be presumed normal. Third trimester brains were accepted if the *body* weight fell within *one* standard deviation of the expected weight for gestational age. Postnatal brains were from children dying acutely following accidents or very brief illness. Furthermore only those parameters were measured which show no post-mortem alteration in the inevitable interval between death and the availability of the specimen. One-hundred-and-forty-eight complete human brains, ranging in age from 10 gestational weeks to adulthood, were divided into three gross regions, "forebrain", "cerebellum" and "stem", were weighed and investigated for DNA, water and cholesterol content. More detailed findings are reported elsewhere[16].

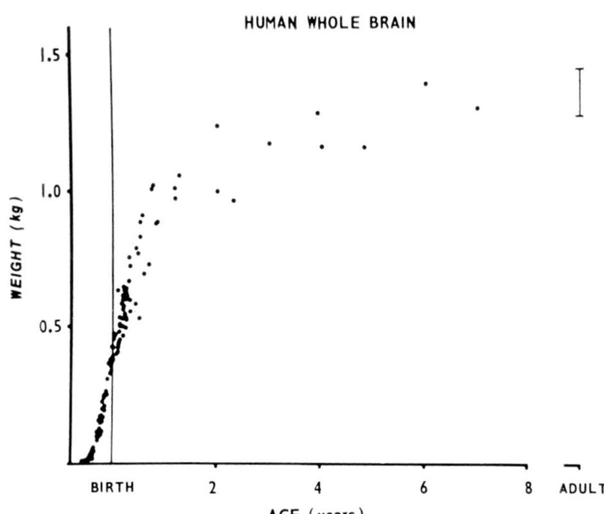

FIG. 6. Whole human brain weight from 10 gestational weeks to adulthood.[16]

Brain Weight

Growth in weight is shown in Fig. 6. The familiar sigmoid growth curve commences its upward inflection in mid-pregnancy and seems to begin to level out between one and two years of postnatal age. Definition of the end-point of the human brain growth spurt is difficult in this and in subsequent figures partly because of an extreme scarcity of specimens from children over one year of age, and partly because the transition between the steep part of the growth spurt and its levelling out is rather gradual. For these reasons the temptation to draw subjective lines through the data has been resisted. However it seems clear from Fig. 6 that, in terms of weight alone, the human brain growth spurt runs from mid-pregnancy to about eighteen months of postnatal age. On this calculation not much more than one sixth of it is fetal, and in cases where fetal growth restriction is confined to the last trimester, no more than six-sevenths of the vulnerable period are postnatal.

Brain Weight/Body Weight Ratio

The ratio of brain weight to body weight was once considered to be a useful guide to whether a birth weight was small for the gestational age. This was when all small-for-dates babies were thought to be "malnourished" during the third trimester, and was based on the fact (and the finding

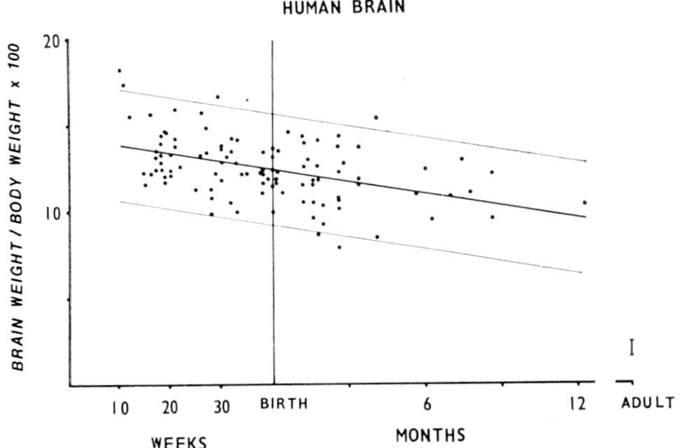

FIG. 7. Ratio of brain weight to body weight in developing human brain.[16]

in some such babies) that undernutrition affects the body weight more than the brain weight. This is the effect of "brain sparing", well known to developmental nutritionists. It should be clearly borne in mind, however, that although the brain, like bone and genital development, certainly is less affected than other tissues, *it is still affected*, and its degree of affection is more important than its "sparing".

Unfortunately the ratio of brain weight to body weight is of little use in making clinical judgments, even in those babies whose intrauterine growth has been slowed by a failure of supply. This is because, as seen in Fig. 7, it is subject to too great a variance in a normal population. The ratio is one of the brain parameters which falls with increasing age in all species. It does so more gradually in the slowly growing human than in some others.

Cellularity

Cellularity is a concentration expression, and may mean number of cells per microscope field, or amount of DNA per unit weight of tissue. It is to be distinguished carefully from total number of cells per anatomical region.

The cellularity of the human forebrain (and hence of the whole brain, since forebrain is much the largest proportion) *falls* with increasing fetal age, even though the *total number* of cells is rising rapidly at the same time (Fig. 8). This overriding dilution effect must be due to the relatively faster arrival of cell substance (and non-cellular myelin) than the already fast rate of cell multiplication; and the steep fall

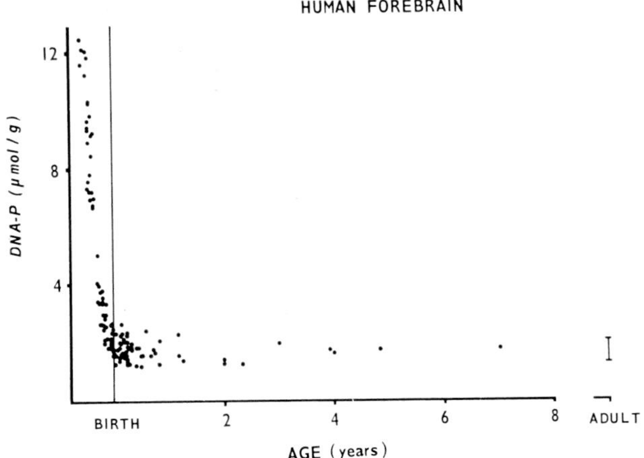

FIG. 8. *Concentration* of DNA-P per unit fresh weight, equivalent to *cellularity* (see text) in human forebrain.[16]

in cellularity makes this parameter a difficult one to consider. The difficulty is compounded by the concurrent paradoxical *rise* in cellularity of the cerebellum (Fig. 9). This is entirely consistent with the extraordinarily rapid

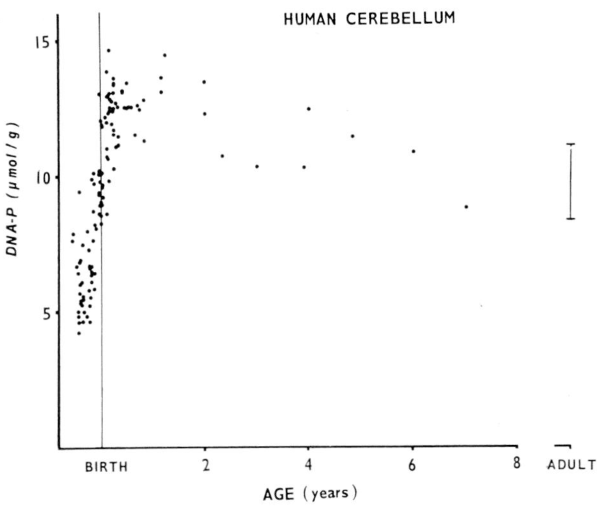

FIG. 9. *Concentration* of DNA-P per unit fresh weight, equivalent to *cellularity* (see text) in human cerebellum.[16]

rate of growth of the cerebellum relative to that of the brain as a whole, and the comparatively small average size of adult cerebellar cells: so that the dilution effect seen in the forebrain is doubly defeated. The mixture of apparently opposite growth characteristics within the brain makes *cellularity* a difficult parameter to consider.

Total Cell Number

This is a much easier parameter to understand, although, as before, the whole brain, or a whole anatomically defined region must be available for its quantitation. Histological heterogeneity forbids the use of fragments or biopsy specimens. Figure 10 shows the total DNA in the human forebrain, from which it can be estimated that cell multiplication does not begin to draw to a close until well into the

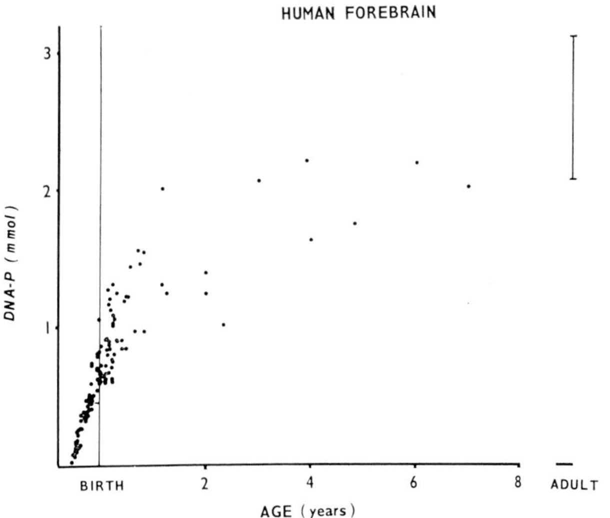

FIG. 10, Total DNA-P, equivalent to total cell number in human forebrain.[16]

second postnatal year. At this time total cell number is still substantially less than its adult value. Previous conclusions based on reports that adult brain cell number is

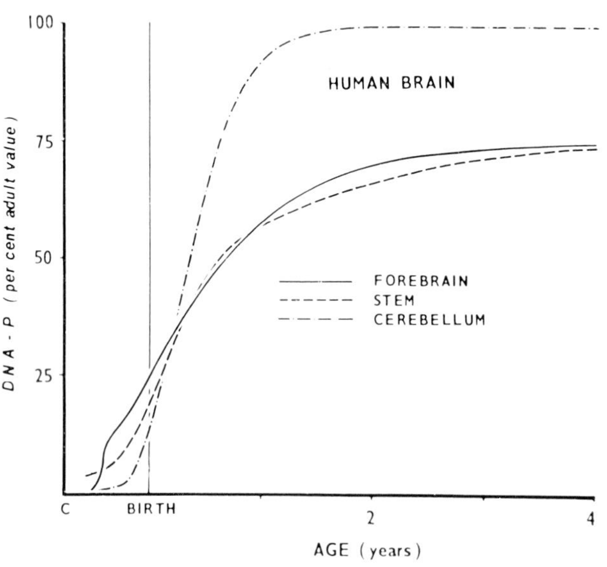

FIG. 11. Comparative values for total DNA-P, equivalent to total numbers of cells, in three human brain regions. Values have been calculated as a percentage of the adult value.[16]

attained by five postnatal months[26] therefore require drastic revision.

Cell multiplication in the three major brain regions is compared in Fig. 11. In this instance smoothed lines have been drawn subjectively through the points. The exceptional growth characteristics of the human cerebellum, comparable with the same phenomena in other animal species, are readily seen. It is frequently and erroneously stated that the cerebellum grows 'later" than the rest of the brain. Figure 11 shows on the contrary that although its cells do begin to multiply later, it achieves its adult dimensions much earlier. The cerebellum therefore grows very much faster through a shorter period but broadly *concurrently* with the other parts of the brain. Indeed it has achieved its adult number of cells by about fifteen postnatal months, an age when the rest of the brain is only about sixty-five per cent of the way towards adult quantities. The same peculiarities of cerebellar growth can be seen in its rate of myelination, and its growth in weight. It is these similarities with cerebellar growth in other animals which lead to the question whether the same differential vulnerability exists in humans, with the same functional consequences.

Myelination

There are several chemical indices which are useful for measuring the process of myelination quantitatively. The most specific for myelin are the hexose-containing lipids cerebroside and sulphatide[8]. Cholesterol, however, is a much easier lipid to estimate reliably in very large numbers of samples, and although it is much less specific, its accumulation does bear a constant relation to that of cerebroside,

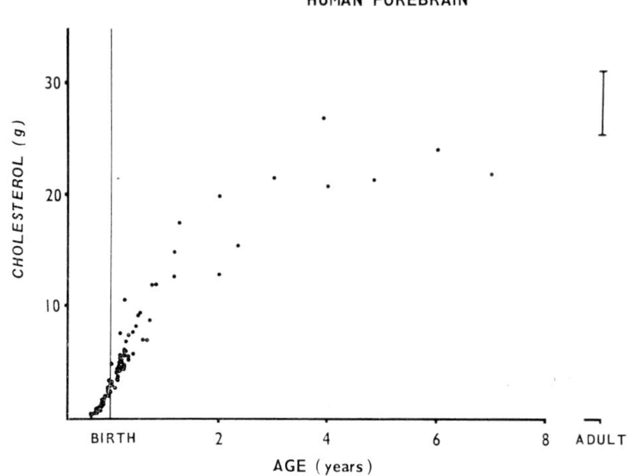

FIG. 12. Cholesterol content of human forebrain, an index of myelination (see text).[16]

arriving before the cerebroside does. As mentioned earlier, the spurt in cholesterol synthesis follows that of glial cell multiplication, since it is synthesized by them, and it therefore occupies the later phases of the brain growth spurt.

Figure 12 shows its increase in human forebrain, and it will be seen that although its end-point is not very well defined, there is still quite a rapid rise almost to four years of age, followed by a very gradual rise to adult levels. The growth spurt proper, which includes myelination, may therefore in this sense be considered to continue well into the fourth year.

Neurons and Glia

It has already been mentioned in describing the general sequential pattern of mammalian brain growth that the major phase of neuronal multiplication occurs before the numerically larger phase of glial multiplication, so that an adult *number* of neurons is achieved very early, except for special cases in certain regions. Theoretically therefore, any growth curve showing the increase in numbers of cells of all types should exhibit two consecutive phases of cell division. Such a phenomenon has not been demonstrated in any of the small laboratory species studied, although it was in these species that the phenomenon was first described by histologists. It now appears that the failure to show the two phases in "DNA counts" may be due to the short life-span and the consequent rapidity of developmental progress in the smaller species, in whom such events take only a few hours or days to occur. It would thus require almost hourly monitoring of conception time, and much more frequent observations on aspects of later development to reveal the two phases of cell multiplication. However, in humans and other slowly-growing species, such as the cow, the time scale is much more extended, and it so happens that humans are the first slowly-growing species whose brain growth has been quantitatively described using "DNA counts." Thus the two phases of brain cell division have been quantitatively revealed for the first time in ourselves.

Figure 13 shows a "high power view" of the earlier stages of the data already shown in Fig. 10. Cell multiplication clearly occurs in two quite distinct phases with a remarkably sharp cut-off point at eighteen weeks of gestation. It seems almost certain that the period from ten to eighteen weeks is the major period of human neuroblast multiplication, differentiation to non-dividing neurons occurring towards the end of this time. Glial division then takes over, and occupies the remainder of the multiplicative phase until well into the second postnatal year.

This finding raises new issues concerning hypotheses of developing brain vulnerability. There can be no question that maternal environmental factors such as her under-nutrition during pregnancy would not begin seriously to retard fetal growth until the early third trimester. The same may be so of many of the obstetric pathologies which affect placental sufficiency, so that in general it may well be that fetal growth retardation of the kind which is due to a restriction of supplies to the fetus will always spare the much earlier neuronal multiplication phase in humans[12]. Such later restrictions will equally certainly *not* spare the subsequent dendritic growth of the newly arrived neurons, nor the establishment of the network of synaptic connectivity; and, as has already been said, these may be functionally more important processes than the mere accomplishment of neuronal *number*.

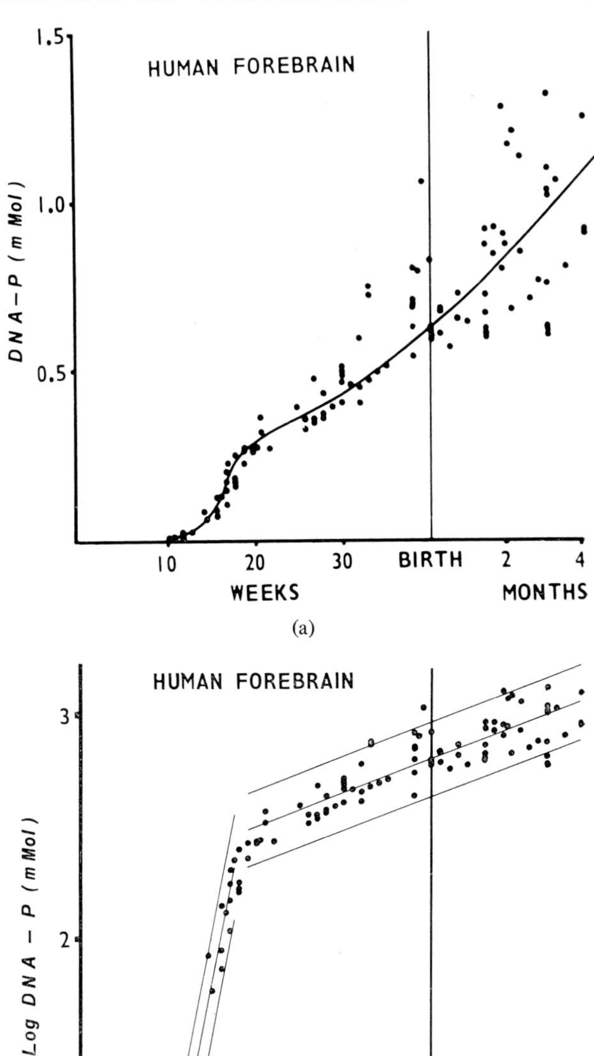

FIG. 13. Total DNA-P, equivalent to total cell number, in the human forebrain from 10 gestational weeks to 4 postnatal months, showing the two-phase characteristics of prenatal cell multiplication. Figure 13(b) is a semi-logarithmic plot of the same data as appears in figure 13(a) to show the sharp separation of the two phases at 18 gestational weeks. Regression lines with 95 per cent confidence limits are added.[16]

Water

Just as in other developing tissues, the water content of the brain falls during development. Its fall is similar to the reciprocal of the concomitant increase in lipids and is illustrated in Fig. 14.

The clinical importance of Fig. 14 is related to the controversy whether true cerebral oedema can occur in the human newborn baby. Certainly it cannot be satisfactorily diagnosed clinically although it is often presumed in babies showing various neurological signs. Unfortunately the post-mortem diagnosis is equally questionable, largely due to the steepness of the fall shown in the figure. No pathologist can carry in his mind a memory for such rapidly changing brain consistency at this age; and even if he measured brain water he would find it difficult with this degree of steepness to pronounce on a given brain's normality: the variance can be so easily increased by small errors in estimating perinatal age. Further, the other aids to post mortem diagnosis in adult brain oedema are of little use

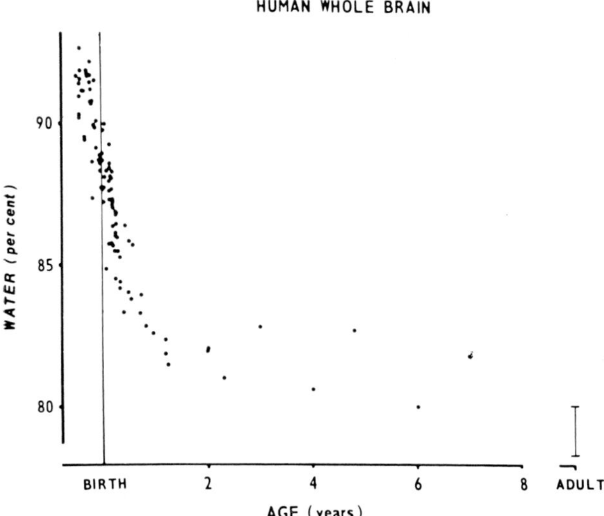

FIG. 14. Water content of human brain during development.[16]

in the newborn. Flattening of gyri when the consistency is so wet anyway, and swelling of the forebrain white matter when there is so little of it at this age are both unhelpful. Quite a sensitive index in experimental oedema of developing brain is the altered sodium: potassium ratio, and the question might be explored whether an estimation of these cations in cerebrospinal fluid might be a useful diagnostic test in the living. The altered ratio is presumably a reflection of impairment of homeostatic pump mechanisms for sodium and potassium and the sensitivity of the ratio is due to the brain levels moving in opposite directions during asphyxial brain oedema.

HAZARDS OF NEURONAL MULTIPLICATION IN HUMANS

How can neuronal multiplication be threatened in the human fetus? We can probably assume that such threats will have to be substantial if they are to be important. Further, since the neuronal number is ultimately heavily outweighed by glial number, even a substantial neuronal number deficit will be difficult or impossible to distinguish by total cell "DNA counts" in the mature brain, and would only be seen after very laborious quantitative histology. It would not be obvious on standard neuropathological examination.

The following is an incomplete list of the kinds of adverse factors, most of them comparatively uncommon, which may be expected to defeat the high degree of protection normally surrounding the fetus during the period of human neuronal multiplication.

(1) X-irradiation and other radioactive exposure. It is remarkable that the large numbers of cases of severe microcephaly with mental retardation in populations surviving the atomic bombs dropped on Hiroshima and Nagasaki were nearly all exposed to the radioactivity at a circumscribed phase of fetal life: between ten and eighteen gestational weeks[21], and although it must be admitted that this is probably a period of important development along many parameters other than neuronal cell multiplication, the resemblance between the sensitive period of fetal exposure to severe atomic irradiation and the data in Fig. 13b is sufficiently striking to raise the question of a causal relationship. The same query must also, therefore, arise regarding diagnostic and especially therapeutic X-irradiation.

(2) Viral infections of the fetus, principally rubella, are often present and effective throughout this time, and may lead to microcephaly.

(3) Chromosomal anomalies are obviously present, when they occur, throughout this period. There has been a suggestion[1] that two factors associated with chromosomal derangement may lead to serious alteration of neuronal cell number: firstly the elongation of mitotic interval and hence the slowing of mitosis in certain chromosome anomalies, together with, secondly, the strictly chronological determination of neuroblast differentiation at a certain *age*, an event which normally brings the phase of neuroblast multiplication to an end. At least in theory these two factors could combine to reduce neuronal numbers, but it is, of course, quite unknown whether such reduction is ever significant.

(4) Other congenital anomalies are associated with a variety of fetal growth retardation which, unlike the "malnutritional" type, probably operates throughout gestation and will therefore be present even during the first and second trimesters. Indeed any such modification of the whole "growth programme" may possibly lead to some reduction in neuronal number.

(5) The occasional mother with high plasma levels of phenylalanine or other metabolic error will expose her fetus to her own derangement at this time. The poor outlook for such pregnancies may be related to the common failure to institute dietary control until later than the 10–17 weeks period. In the present state of knowledge it would clearly be wise to control maternal phenylalanine levels from an earlier stage of a planned pregnancy.

(6) Maternal medication at this time must also be considered a possible hazard to dividing neuroblasts, especially prolonged steroid therapy which is known in experimental animals to reduce brain cell division at comparable stages of development.

(7) The question of much "unclassified" mental retardation is entirely open, and it may finally be wondered whether its origin may not be found in this "middle" period of brain growth.

Thus there are at least two possible periods of brain vulnerability to growth restriction: the first, and probably less common, which has just been discussed, related to the 10–17 week period of neuronal multiplication; and second, the much more recognized later period of the brain growth spurt during which the processes at risk probably include dendritic arborization, establishment of synaptic connectivity, and myelination.

CELL SIZE AND CELL NUMBER

An extremely useful concept relating to catch-up potential following growth retardation has been enunciated by Winick and Noble[27]. It is based on the general truth that all tissues pass through two overlapping phases of growth: an early hyperplastic phase of cell multiplication and a later hypertrophic one of growth in cell size. Winick and Noble suggested that growth restriction during the first phase led to an irrecoverable reduction in cell number, but that reduction in cell size caused by restriction during the second phase was recoverable. There seems little doubt about the general applicability of this idea, although it may possibly have been too uncritically applied to such tissues as adipose tissue during babyhood. Certainly it is difficult to apply to the brain, largely due to this organ's extreme histological heterogeneity. It is not clear, for example, what cell size means to a neuron. Does it apply to the cell body? And if so does it matter? Or does it apply to the whole cell including both its complex dendritic tree and its sometimes enormously long axon? It presumably does not apply to axonal length, so would axonal thickness be involved? The usual indices for measurement of cell size, the amount of protein per unit quantity of DNA, are also manifestly unreal in the brain where the (axonal) protein in any given area such as the stem is in no way anatomically related to much of the DNA of the same area, but to the relevant cell bodies in another part of the brain altogether. Nor can the exclusion of all but cell number from permanent reduction, as suggested by a strict interpretation of the Winick and Noble hypothesis, be held to account for such demonstrable ultimate deficits in the brain as those in non-cellular myelin or synaptic connectivity. It is, of course, very likely that their concept may apply to glial cell number and glial cell size in malnourished human infants. Indeed the deficit in brain cell number in such few specimens as have been examined from underprivileged communities is probably exclusively a glial deficit due partly to the later appearance of glial cells and partly to the comparatively late timing of the nutritional growth restriction in these children.

The histological heterogeneity of the brain and spinal cord probably deprives the simple cell number/cell size concept of much of the usefulness for which it has become renowned in such homogeneous tissues as liver and muscle.

GENERAL COMMENTS ON BRAIN GROWTH-SPURT VULNERABILITY

So far vulnerability has been discussed almost entirely in relation to nutritional growth restriction. One question which arises is whether lack of any particular nutriment is more likely than any other to produce the ultimate deficits and distortions outlined earlier; or whether it is likely to be the mere fact of growth restriction at such a complex and rapid period of growth. The chances seem very high that it is the latter.

If this be true, there can be a good deal of reconciliation between the various researching factions, each with its own favourite nutritional culprit affecting brain growth. Whether the dietary deficit be one of mere quantity of food, or one specifically of protein, a particular amino acid, a range of essential fatty acids, iron, zinc or folic acid, it is an attractive unifying hypothesis that the final-common-path feature bearing on the developing brain is the growth restriction that all these dietary deficits may produce.

Such a unifying hypothesis furthermore admits into the aetiology of poor brain growth all the non-nutritional or secondarily nutritional growth retarding conditions, provided they operate on the growth programme for a substantial part of the brain growth spurt period.

It is possible, in favour of this unifying hypothesis, that nutritionists have greatly exaggerated the dependence of the growing brain on single articles of diet. As has been emphasized before, the brain has a remarkable facility for abstracting its needs from the circulating pool of precursor substances, often quite normally against a large unfavourable gradient. Moreover the brain's needs are quantitatively very small compared with the size of the total pool, and it seems most unlikely that its own growth will often be limited by the availability to it of any single nutriment. However, the brain is an integral part of the whole somatic growth plan, and it seems a much more acceptable concept that it is secondarily at risk whenever the whole plan is restricted during the extremely delicate period of its growth spurt. In this way the comparatively early timing of this period, compared with that in other tissues, may be the most important factor to consider.

SMALL-FOR-DATES BABIES, MALNOURISHED OR OTHERWISE

Where these are growth retarded only during the last trimester, including those retarded by maternal smoking, and where they exhibit good catch-up growth on being liberated by birth from their restraint, the general vulnerable period hypothesis would predict no very deleterious effects on final outcome. Where, however, such growth-retarded babies are born into an external environment (or into any continuing restraint-pathology) which leads to further growth restriction during the first two postnatal years, then poor brain growth may be expected.

Thus, for example, it may be unprofitable for epidemiologists to look into the intellectual outcome simply of "small-for-dates" babies. Rather a group should be separately and particularly considered in whom a major part of the brain growth spurt period was blanketed by growth restriction. Such restrictions would include (see below) restrictions on stimulus of an emotional or "intellectual" nature and would certainly include those mentioned in chapter (McCarthy).

By a similar reasoning, it could well be misleading to

look for diminished intellectual performance in *all* children underfed at some time during their infancy. The key to the problem will almost certainly, and once again involve the three "unities" of developmental undernutrition mentioned earlier: they should have been growth retarded for a substantial part of the whole vulnerable period, to a given degree of severity, but above all at the correct stage of brain growth before they are expected to show ultimate deficit. Add to these variables the enormous and well-documented non-nutritional factors in the external environment which may greatly *add to or compensate for* the nutritional difficulty, and it will not be surprising that the literature abounds with confusing and conflicting evidence from differently selected samples in different parts of the world.

MATERNAL SLIMMING

Attempts to reduce maternal weight or maternal weight-gain during pregnancy by dietary means are widespread in many affluent societies. The obstetric motives are various and confused. For some obstetricians the extra weight-gain in toxaemic conditions, which is mainly due to abnormal water retention, is mistakenly equated with that usually due to over-eating; and it is wrongly supposed that it can be "countered" by reducing food intake in a mother whose fetus may be already suffering from an insufficient supply. For others the opportunity afforded by the mother's "captivity" during pregnancy for curing her of all her vices is irresistable. The smoking mother is advised to stop, and this seems sensible in the interest of the fetus; but the overweight mother is, for similar sorts of reasons, put on a reducing diet at the very time she needs to be well fed, and this is probably to be deplored. In some affluent cultures it is even still customary to reduce maternal intake with the express intention of reducing fetal growth so that delivery may be more comfortable, and this must be reprehensible.

In underprivileged communities where the commonest cause of slowed intrauterine growth is widespread maternal malnutrition, it is easy to show that adequate maternal nutrition will restore "normal" birth weight in the same small mother who has already born several low-birth-weight babies. Ethnic influences on birth weight are therefore far from exclusive and should not be accepted as major ones until shown to persist in the presence of an adequate nutritional environment during pregnancy.

CONCLUSIONS

The case has been argued for a particular kind of vulnerability of the developing brain to growth restriction during its growth spurt period; and for a special variant of this, which is likely to be much less common, but perhaps more severe, during a separate, still earlier stage of brain growth when neuronal multiplication is occurring.

None of the demonstrable physical consequences of growth restriction at this time would be of any significance if they had no behavioural or functional consequences; but evidence for the latter has accumulated and is now compelling[22]. In spite of the academic handicap of our ignorance of the physical basis of higher mental function, there seems little doubt that it does have a considerable physical basis in the brain and that its development can be significantly spoiled by poor environmental conditions during certain growth periods. None of this denies the supreme contribution of the non-nutritional, less tangible environment of the growing fetus and baby within the family, the relative importance of which is now beginning even to be measured[23]. Achievement may be considered to be the algebraic sum of positives and negatives in the total developmental environment. The demonstration that the human brain growth spurt is much more postnatal than was formerly thought creates a new opportunity to ensure one important positive in the calculation, by actively promoting good bodily growth at the time when this most important organ is passing through its own vulnerable period of growth.

ACKNOWLEDGEMENTS

I particularly wish to thank my colleague Jean Sands who was responsible for most of the research work referred to here. The research programme was supported by the Medical Research Council and the National Fund for Research into Crippling Diseases, both of Great Britain.

Figures 6–14 are reproduced by kind permission of the Editors, *Archives of Disease in Childhood.*

REFERENCES

1. Barlow, P. (1973), "The Influence of Inactive Chromosomes on Human Development," *Humangenetik*, **17,** 105–136.
2. Benstead, J. P. M., Dobbing, J., Morgan, R. S., Reid, R. T. W. and Payling Wright, G. (1957), "Neurological Development and Myelination in the Spinal Cord of the Chick Embryo," *J. Embryol. exp. Morph.*, **5,** 428–437.
3. Cragg, B. G. (1972), "The Development of Cortical Synapses During Starvation in the Rat," *Brain*, **95,** 143–150.
4. Cravioto, J. and De Licardie, E. R. (1970), "Mental Performance in School Age Children: Findings after Recovery from Early Severe Malnutrition," *Amer. J. Dis. Child.*, **120,** 404–410.
5. Culley, W. J. and Lineberger, R. D. (1968), "Effect of Undernutrition on the Size and Composition of the Rat Brain," *J. Nutr.*, **96,** 375–381.
6. Davies, P. A. and Davis, J. P. (1970), "Very Low Birth Weight and Subsequent Head Growth," *Lancet*, **ii,** 1216–1219.
7. Davison, A. N. and Dobbing, J. (1968), "The Developing Brain," in *Applied Neurochemistry*, pp. 253–286 (A. N. Davison and J. Dobbing, Eds.). Oxford: Blackwell.
8. Davison, A. N. and Peters, A. (1970), *Myelination.* Springfield: Thomas.
9. Dickerson, J. W. T. and Dobbing, J. (1967), "Prenatal and Postnatal Growth and Development of the Central Nervous System of the Pig," *Proc. roy. Soc. B*, **166,** 384–395.
10. Dobbing, J. (1968a), "The Blood-brain Barrier," in *Applied Neurochemistry*, pp. 317–331 (A. N. Davison and J. Dobbing, Eds.). Oxford: Blackwell.
11. Dobbing, J. (1968b), "Vulnerable Periods in Developing Brain," in *Applied Neurochemistry*, pp. 287–316. (A. N. Davison and J. Dobbing, Eds.). Oxford: Blackwell.
12. Dobbing, J. (1973), "The Developing Brain: A Plea for More Critical Interspecies Extrapolation," *Nutr. Rep. Int.* In press.
13. Dobbing, J., Hopewell, J. W. and Lynch, A. (1971), "Vulnerability of Developing Brain: VII. Permanent Deficit of Neurons in Cerebral and Cerebellar Cortex Following Early Mild Undernutrition," *Exp. Neurol.*, **32,** 439–447.

14. Dobbing, J. and Sands, J. (1970), "Growth and Development of the Brain and Spinal Cord of the Guinea Pig," *Brain Res.*, **17,** 115–123.
15. Dobbing, J. and Sands, J. (1971), "Vulnerability of Developing Brain: IX. The Effect of Nutritional Growth Retardation on the Timing of the Brain Growth-spurt," *Biol. Neonat.*, **19,** 363–378.
16. Dobbing, J. and Sands, J. (1973), "The Quantitative Growth and Development of the Human Brain," *Arch. Dis. Childh.* **48,** 757–767.
17. Dobbing, J. and Smart, J. L. (1973), "Early Undernutrition, Brain Development and Behaviour," Clinics in Developmental Medicine, No. 47. Ethology and Development (S. A. Barnett, Ed.). London: Heinemann.
18. Hertzig, M. E., Birch, H. G., Richardson, S. A. and Tizard, J. (1972), "Intellectual Levels of School Children Severely Malnourished During the First Two Years of Life," *Pediatrics*, **49,** 814–824.
19. Lynch, A. and Dobbing, J. (1974), "Clumsiness in Adult Rats Undernourished or X-irradiated in the Suckling Period." In preparation.
20. Michaelis, R., Schulte, F. J. and Nolte, R. (1970), "Motor Behaviour of Small for Gestational Age Newborn Infants," *J. Pediat.*, **76,** 208–213.
21. Miller, R. W. and Blot, W. J. (1972), "Small Head Size After *In Utero* Exposure to Atomic Radiation," *Lancet*, **ii,** 784–787.
22. *Pan American Health Organization Scientific Publication No. 251* (1972), "Nutrition, the Nervous System and Behaviour."
23. Richardson, S. A. (1972), "Ecology of Malnutrition: Non-nutritional Factors Influencing Intellectual and Behavioural Development," *Pan American Health Organization Scientific Publication No. 251*, 101–110.
24. Smart, J. L. and Dobbing, J. (1971), "Vulnerability of Developing Brain: VI. Relative Effects of Fetal and Early Postnatal Undernutrition on Reflex Ontogeny and Development of Behaviour in the Rat," *Brain Res.*, **33,** 303–314.
25. De Souza, S. W. and Dobbing, J. (1972), "Some Effects of Acute Anoxia and Prolonged Asphyxia on Rat Brain," *Exp. Neurol.*, **37,** 340–346.
26. Winick, M. (1968), "Changes in Nucleic Acid and Protein Content of the Human Brain During Growth," *Ped. Res.*, **2,** 352–355.
27. Winick, M. and Noble, A. (1966), "Cellular Response in Rats During Malnutrition at Various Ages," *J. Nutr.*, **89,** 300–306

33. DIFFERENTIATION, GROWTH AND DISORDERS OF DEVELOPMENT OF THE VERTEBROSPINAL AXIS

A. J. BARSON

The paediatrician's practice revolves around problems which result from the disruption of differentiation and growth by disease. These three processes—differentiation, growth and disease—are interdependent to such a degree that their discussion in isolation is always to a certain extent artificial. This chapter concerns the relationship of these three processes to the vertebrospinal axis. This structure is comprised of two basic components which are also mutually dependent. They are the vertebral column derived from embryonic mesoderm, and the spinal cord derived from the neuroectoderm. We will therefore be involved with three processes and two structures all of which have a profound influence on one another.

The vertebrospinal axis is distinct in that it is the first organ to differentiate in the embryo. Because of this and because of its superficial anatomical position it has probably been the subject of more detailed investigation than any other component of the early embryo. It is unique also in being the structure most commonly subject to malformations, for example anencephaly and spina bifida, and these are often incompatible with extended life. However the features of development and maldevelopment which are illustrated by the vertebrospinal axis are by no means peculiar to it.

DIFFERENTIATION

Primary Induction

During the process of gastrulation the cells of the blastopore lip undergo an orderly migration toward the interior of the gastrula and insinuate their way between the overlying ectoderm and the endoderm beneath to form the mesodermal mantle. The ectoderm above the migrant cells is the presumptive neural plate in which there soon forms the neural groove. This closes during the process of neurulation to become the neural tube which then sinks down beneath the surrounding surface ectoderm to be enclosed by the paired mesodermal neural processes, or presumptive spinal laminae.

If the cells from the blastopore lip are prevented from coming into contact with the cells of the presumptive neural plate, neurulation will not occur. Cells from the lip of the blastopore are said to "induce" a change in the differentiated state and the growth rate of certain cells in the ectoderm of the gastrula which leads ultimately to the formation of a primitive spinal cord. The phenomenon is by no means a simple one since inductors from both paraxial mesoblast and notochord are required[16] and the sequence, timing and location of their presence is all important. The spinal cord itself in the course of its own development is in turn responsible for inductive processes necessary for the normal differentiation of adjacent mesodermal structures. These "interactive" or "inductive" processes are worth defining.[19] "Inductive interaction takes place whenever in development two or more tissues of different history and properties become intimately associated and alteration of the developmental course of the interactants results."

The phenomenon of embryonic induction was first demonstrated by Spemann in 1901 in the formation of the amphibian lens under the influence of the optic vesicle. Spemann later[35] performed certain classic experiments on the induction of neural plate in gastrula ectoderm by the underlying chordamesoderm. This has become known as "primary embryonic induction" and it is typical in many of its features of inductive events which have been described in relation to the differentiation of other tissues.

Spemann dissected out the presumptive neural plate area from the gastrula of a newt and transplanted it onto the ventral aspect of another embryonic newt at the same stage of development. The transplant formed normal belly epidermis as was appropriate to its new surroundings. If the experiment was repeated on a slightly older gastrula, the graft was seen to differentiate into an extra neural plate on the belly of the host. These experiments illustrate how the central nervous tissue is "determined" during the short interval between the two embryonic stages studied. Ectoderm which is initially totipotent has its differentiative capacities progressively restricted by inductive events. Simultaneously its ability to respond to inductive stimuli, or its "competence" is also gradually limited. Competence may be lost before any overt morphological change is observed. Hence in the second of these two experiments the graft was committed to differentiate into neural plate despite the opposing inductive influences of its new surroundings.

The blastopore lip is often termed the "primary organizer." At the conclusion of neural plate development secondary inductors are formed in different parts of the neural plate which stimulate the development of eyes, nasal pits, ear vesicles, etc. To put this another way, after primary induction the competence of the ectodermal cells is restricted to the differentiation of nervous tissue. Further differentiation is possible but over a much smaller range than the originally totipotent cells. When full maturity is attained competence to react to inductors derived from adjacent unlike tissues is lost. However the differentiative state of the ectodermal cells has to be carefully controlled and maintained in relation to other organs. The role of induction therefore depends on the developmental state of the responding tissue. The inductor may initially cause selection of one particular pathway to the exclusion of others. Later an inductor may be required to stabilize and support a tissue which is already determined. In mature tissue the environment of the cell consists of like cells which collectively interact to maintain a stable differentiated state.

To return to the phenomenon of primary induction there are further experiments which are informative. If certain materials are interposed between the archenteron roof and the presumptive neural plate, induction is prevented, providing this is done before the ectoderm has been determined. Destruction of either inductor tissue or the responding tissue will of course prevent neurulation. Not only must the inducing tissue be in close proximity to the responding component but synchronization of the interactive process is also necessary. If the presumptive neural plate region is aged outside the embryo beyond the time when primary induction normally occurs, it completely loses its ability to respond to an inductive stimulus. Hence the competence of a tissue is dependent not only upon its degree of differentiation but also its age.

Something of the nature of the inductive stimulus can be demonstrated by further experiments. It is possible to bring about neuralization of competent amphibian ectoderm in the absence of any kind of organic material. Mechanical trauma, low osmolarity, high pH, ammonia, urea, alcohol and certain inorganic ions have all been shown to precipitate "autoneuralization."[8,22,45] Although this suggests that non-specific factors are involved in induction it is difficult to reconcile such observations with the specific nature of normal tissue differentiation cited in the experiments above.

It is also possible to show that in some circumstances killed tissues may retain their capacity to induce neuralization and that it is possible to incorporate the inductive factor within a piece of agar.[9] If agar is brought transiently into contact with amphibian neural plate in the late gastrula stage, it may then be employed to induce a secondary neural plate if it is implanted into a younger gastrula. These experiments suggested the natural occurrence of a diffusible inductor substance[11] and that actual cell contact between inducing and responding tissues was not necessary. More recently it has been shown[29] that neuralization between chorda mesoderm and overlying ectoderm will occur when the two are separated by a millipore filter 25 μ thick with an average pore size of 0·8 μ. Neuralization has been demonstrated in the chick embryo when the interactants were separated by a millipore filter with an average pore size of 0·45 μ.[17,18] A neuralizing effect becomes markedly weaker with pore sizes smaller than this.

It is not necessary for the inductor to be in constant contact with the ectoderm whilst neuralization is taking place. A limited period of time is required for the ectoderm to be determined after which neuralization will proceed even in the absence of the inducing tissue. This "minimum induction time" has been found to be 2–4 hr. in amphibians[38] and 6–8 hr. in the chick.[27]

It is erroneous to think of neuralation as a single process which is uniform in its effect throughout the embryonic axis. It has long been known[33,34] that the more cranial part of the blastopore lip in the young gastrula induced forebrain structures, whereas the more caudal part led of the induction of trunk and tail structures. The inductor substances within the invaginating dorsal lip appeared to possess a craniocaudal sequence which reproduced itself in the axial differentiation of the central nervous system. It was originally considered that this was a reflection of a quantitative gradient of a single inductor,[12] but experiments with heterogenous inductors have strongly suggested that neuralation requires more than one inductive factor. The inductive specificity of different regions of the blastopore lip has been mimicked by the isolation of inductor substances with a predominantly forebrain or with a predominantly spinocaudal site of action. Spinocaudal induction, however, requires the combined action of "neuralizing" and "mesodermalizing" inductors.

For example it is known that an extract of guinea pig liver applied to amphibian gastrula will lead to the induction of forebrain structures and corresponding sense organs and placodes. On the other hand guinea pig bone marrow induces the formation of trunk somites, notochord, nephric tubules and blood cells and is consequently regarded as a pure mesodermalizing inductor. When this mesodermalizing inductor is applied in isolation spinal cord structures are rarely differentiated. When the guinea pig marrow and liver are combined spinal cord can be induced in the great majority of gastrulae.

A similar phenomenon can be demonstrated when He La cells are chosen for the inductor material.[30] These cells appear to contain both neuralizing and mesodermalizing inductors. When applied to young gastrulae of Triturus vulgaris, somites and spinal cord differentiate. If the cultured He La cells are applied after being heated in a water bath at 70°C. for 30 min., the mesodermalizing factor is destroyed leaving the neuralizing factor to act alone. Heated He La cells therefore induce predominantly forebrain structures. By gradually increasing the proportion of non-heated He La cells, hindbrain rather than forebrain is induced and then the spinal cord is induced more frequently than hindbrain structures. Hence a progressive increase in the tissue which induces the formation of mesoderm results in a caudal shift in the nature of the neural structures induced by the neuralizing principle.

These experiments with heterogenous inductors suggest that the regional specialization of the central nervous system is controlled by the interaction of two types of predetermined cells. Recently[39] it has been shown that regional neuronal specialization can be achieved by mixing proportions of the embryo's own cells. Thus Triturus neurulae cells of the presumptive forebrain region and axial mesoderm have been disaggregated and then recombined in different ratios. The differentiation of the central nervous system was then assessed after subsequent cultivation. An increase in the proportion of mesodermal cells increased the frequency of differentiation of caudal central nervous tissue structures, with a corresponding decrease in the formation of forebrain structures.

We may summarize the results of these latter experiments with what has come to be known as the "two gradient hypothesis". According to this primary induction requires two active principles. One of these controls neuralization of ectoderm, and if acting alone induces only forebrain structures. It is thermostable, soluble in petroleum and ether and dialysable. Tissue fractionation has demonstrated its presence in the ribonucleoprotein fraction although it is apparently not inactivated by ribonuclease.[21] The other inductor leads to the determination of mesodermal structures. It is insoluble in organic solvents, thermolabile and non-dialysable and is probably a protein of relatively low molecular weight.[37] Both these inductors are strongest in the dorsal midline of normal inductor tissue and weaker ventrally. The mesodermalizing inductor, however, is lacking in the most anterior part corresponding to the region of the prechordal plate, but it gradually increases in a caudal direction. As a consequence of the combined action of these two principles, different hindbrain and spinocaudal structures are induced.

We may conclude this account of the mechanism of primary induction with two observations made at an ultrastructural level.

Firstly the electron microscope has been used to search the space between the inducing mesoderm and the responding ectoderm for the passage of inductor material. In both Xenopus[36] and chick[10] gastrulae, neuralation is accompanied by the appearance of granules between these two germ layers which gradually disappear in a cephalocaudal sequence being replaced by filamentous material. That these subcellular changes are the morphological counterpart of the inductive process is as yet circumstantial.

The second type of ultrastructural observation concerns the discovery of fine filamentous structures in a variety of animal and plant cells which appear to have a contractile function. These contractile microfilaments are approximately 40–60 Å in diameter and they have been shown to be present in the cells of the amphibian embryonic medullary plate.[1] These filaments are arranged in a "purse-string" at the more superficial end of each cell forming the initially flat neural plate. Contraction of the filaments alters the overall shape of the lining neural plate cells from a columnar to a pyramidal form. Because of the adhesion of the cells to one another the collective effect of this is an invagination of the surface and the formation of the neural groove. These neural microfilaments have also been demonstrated in the chick embryo in this laboratory (Fig. 1). These filaments are thought to have a similar role in the invagination of the flat lens placode to form the lens cup[44] and also in individual cell movements in a wide variety of situations.[43]

Chondrogenesis

The process of primary induction illustrates how the differentiation of ectodermal structures is dependent on the inductive influence of the adjacent mesoderm. Chondrogenesis on the other hand shows how the differentiation of mesoderm is in turn dependent upon ectodermal tissue.

If three or four segments of embryonic spinal cord are removed from the tail bud of an embryo, the somite cells in the region deficient in the spinal cord will not form cartilaginous neural arches. Conversely when segments to spinal cord are grafted into an area where somites normally form muscle, presumptive muscle cells are diverted into forming cartilaginous vertebral column. This experiment has been performed *in vivo* and *in vitro* in fish, frog, chick and mouse embryos.[23]

Both the notochord and the spinal cord appear to be necessary for chondrogenesis but play rather different roles. Although extirpation of spinal cord leads to deficient neural arches, cartilaginous vertebral centra form normally. Removal of notochord however results in impaired formation of the vertebral centra, but the neural arches are not affected.[42] The notochord and spinal cord are not entirely independent in their inductive influence, because in the salamander and the chick, spinal cord in the absence of notochord leads to a precocious development of centrum cartilage. In no circumstances will notochord induce neural arch cartilage.

If embryonic somites from chicks of $2\frac{1}{2}$–3 days incubation are grown on a fibrin clot ro nutrient agar, no or very little cartilage will form. Somites from older embryos grown in the absence of spinal cord and notochord will form cartilage since they have been previously determined by the influence of inductors. The fact that the pre-induced somites from the younger embryos are capable of forming some cartilage—a capacity that can be enhanced to some degree with appropriate culture conditions—strongly suggests that induction is a phenomenon which stimulates and stabilizes a pre-existing pattern or gene activity. Induction does not necessarily create a new synthetic pathway in the responding tissue but rather encourages the phenotypic expression of an already present, covert differentiation.[20] It must be emphasized that not all cells possessing enzymes necessary for the synthesis of cartilage are capable of being induced to do so. The competence of a tissue to respond to chondrogenic inductors is very specific. Chondrogenesis differs from primary induction in that presumptive cartilage cells will not respond to heterogenous inductors. Chondrogenic inductors seem peculiar to spinal cord and notochord and moreover the cartilage formed in response to these two tissues is morphologically different.[14]

Chondrogenesis observed in tissue culture mimics the *in vivo* situation with regard to the spatial relationship of the cartilage to the source of the inductor. Thus spinal cord cultured with somites induces chondrogenesis at some distance from the surface of the neural tissue. Moreover this appears to be a property of the ventral rather than the dorsal half of the spinal cord. In cultures of somites and notochord a single large mass of cartilage forms around the notochord. Destruction of the notochordal sheath without killing the notochordal cells results in the loss of this inductive property.[23] As with primary induction the secretion of inductor substances and the ability of the target tissue to respond is both transient. The gradual loss in the ability of the somites to respond to chondrogenic inductors coincides with, and is probably related to, their involvement with the synthesis of myosin and actin. All other embryonic neural tissues such as dorsal spinal cord, medulla, spinal ganglia and peripheral nerves, fail to induce cartilage at any time.

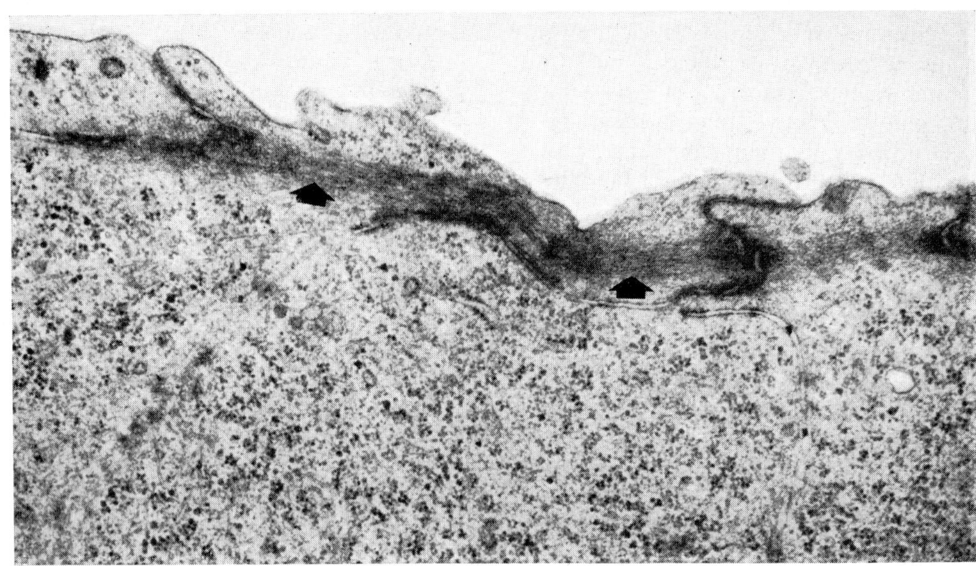

FIG. 1. Microfilaments (arrowed) arranged along the superficial poles of the cells lining the neural groove in a chick embryo. ×18,300.

Transfilter experiments[26] with spinal cord and somites on either side of a millipore filter have shown that the cord has to be in contact with the filter (20 μ thick) for a minimum of 10 hr. Thereafter there is a silent period before the histological appearance of cartilage cells. This lasts for approximately 4 days during which time the continuous presence of the inducer on the filter is unnecessary.

The perchloric acid extract or the nucleotide eluate from three day chick spinal cords and notochords has been found to be chondrogenically active. When added to young somites the incidence of cartilage formation is comparable to that obtained with intact inducing tissues. Unlike the work on primary induction these chondrogenic inducing substances have been extracted from tissues actually acting as inductors in normal development. It is thought that the active components involved may in some cases be relatively small molecules.

GROWTH

Although we have discussed embryonic induction in terms of the determination of clones of cells along separate lines of differentiation, it must be understood that inductive interactions are involved in other kinds of embryonic processes. Interactive mechanisms are operative in cellular proliferation, cell migration, cell death and morphogenesis. A multitude of signal substances are probably necessary for these phenomena, and indeed many are probably involved in even a single interactive process.[29] Taken together these complex interactions manifest themselves in the normal, carefully regulated and balanced growth of the individual. Bearing in mind therefore that cellular interaction is not confined to the early differentiation of the components of the vertebrospinal axis we will turn to a consideration of the growth of the spinal cord and vertebrae in later intrauterine life after the initial period of organogenesis.

In some respects the growth of the spine cannot be considered apart from the growth of the embryo as a whole. Body growth tends to follow what has been termed the "law of developmental direction."[31] This states that in the long axis of the body growth and differentiation appears first in the head region and progresses caudally; development in the transverse plane begins in the mid-dorsal region and proceeds lateroventrally, and in the limbs proximodistally. Thus the head represents about one-half of the body length in the 2nd gestational month, about one-quarter at birth and between 6–8 per cent at maturity. The trunk is always slightly in advance of pelvic growth. The arms remain at 8–9 per cent of the body weight from birth to maturity, but the legs which are about 15 per cent of the body weight at birth increase to 30 per cent by maturity.

One might anticipate that the spinal column would show a similar craniocaudal progression in its rate of differentiation and growth. In fact this only holds true for the first 3 or 4 weeks of embryonic life whilst neuralation is incomplete and the spinal regions are presumptive only. In the 2nd and 3rd fetal months the cervical and sacrococcygeal regions form the greater part of the vertebral column, respectively constituting the head and tail folds. The formation of these two curvatures requires a growth spurt at each extremity of the embryonic axis relative to the thoracic region. Later the coccygeal spine atrophies and the tail fold becomes less pronounced.

The development of the neural tube follows a similar pattern. The margins of the neural groove become fused first in the cervical region, and closure spreads thence cranially and caudally *pari passu* with the growth of the head and tail folds. Complete enclosure of the neural tube by mesoderm and chondrification of the laminae occurs first in the lower thoracic and upper lumbar regions.[25] Fusion of the cartilaginous processes takes place from about 11 weeks (50 m.m.) onwards. The centres of ossification for the neural arches begin in the upper cervical region in the 2nd month and spread to involve the most caudal arches by the 5th or 6th month. On the other hand the centres of ossification of the vertebral bodies appear just after those for the arches but initially in the lower thoracic and first lumbar segments. The law of developmental direction does not therefore hold true for the differentiation of spinal column.

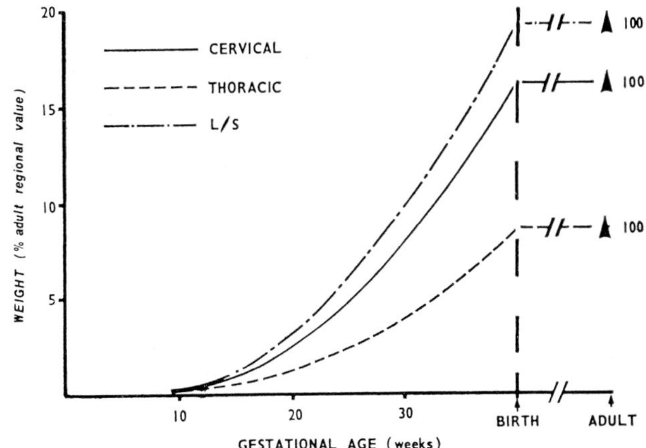

GRAPH I. Cervical, thoracic and lumbosacral spinal cord weights as a percentage of their adult regional values plotted against gestational age.

The characteristics of regional growth of the spinal column from the 10th gestational week to birth is illustrated in Graphs I–III. They depict the mean values of a series of normal spinal cords examined in this laboratory. Only cords from infants whose brain weight and body weight were within one standard deviation for the age by dates were accepted for the study. They were compared with ten control adult cords.

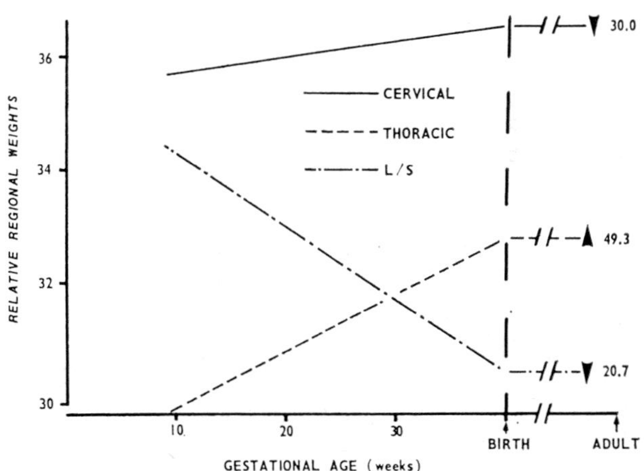

GRAPH II. Cervical, thoracic and lumbosacral cord weights expressed as a percentage of the total for their gestational age.

The cords were divided into cervical, thoracic and lumbosacral regions which because they represent differing numbers of vertebral segments cannot be equated directly

However their growth rates may be related by plotting their weights as a percentage of the mean adult weight for their particular region (Graph I). All parts of the cord increase in weight progressively more rapidly throughout gestation, but the thoracic cord is appreciably slower than that at either extremity of the spinal axis. Although data are lacking for the post-natal period it seems likely that the thoracic cord is the last to achieve its mature weight.

The changing relationships of the three regions to each other during gestation is shown in Graphs II and III. Here the regional weights and lengths are plotted as a percentage of the whole cord at each gestational age. It must be emphasized again that this is a comparison of regions which are embryonically unequal, viz. eight cervical, twelve thoracic and ten lumbosacral segments. Nevertheless the rôles played by the regions in the constitution of the cord is clearly widely different.

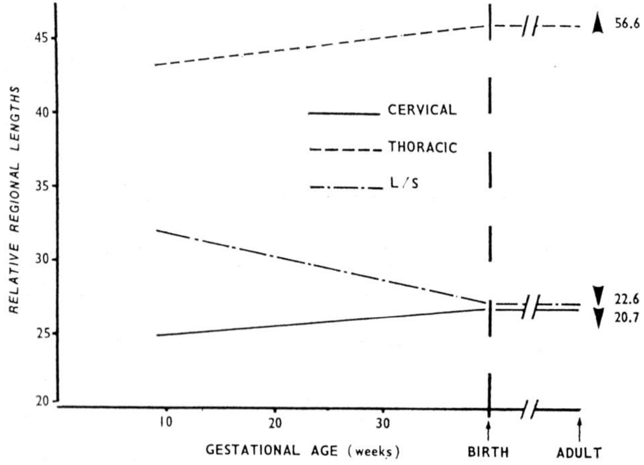

GRAPH III. Cervical, thoracic and lumbosacral cord lengths expressed as a percentage of the total for their gestational age.

At 10 weeks the thoracic cord is the lightest but the longest region. It must necessarily therefore be the thinnest. It always remains the longest of the three portions. Its weight overtakes the lumbosacral cord by about 30 weeks, and although it does not exceed the cervical cord at birth, it does so in adult life. The reason for the intrinsically slower intrauterine growth rate of the thoracic cord is now apparent. The function of the thoracic cord is to supply length to the cord as a whole, and this necessity is paramount in infancy and childhood. On the other hand the cervical and lumbosacral segments are intimately concerned initially with the elongation required for the development of the head and tail folds and then with the innervation of the upper and lower limbs. Hence below 8 weeks when the head and tail folds are most pronounced the cervical and lumbosacrococcygeal regions are longer than the thoracic.[31] Thereafter the thoracic cord becomes longer and the development of the limb buds demands that the cervical and lumbosacral cord grows more by weight than by length.

The cervical and lumbosacral lengths approximate towards each other throughout gestation. The lumbosacral cord loses ground in terms of both relative length (Graph III) and weight (Graph II). As the lumbosacral cord is intrinsically greater by two segments than the cervical cord this process is even more significant than is evident from the graphs.

At this point it is illuminating to compare the growth characteristics of the spinal cord with the vertebral column. The cord and the column are of equal length until the 9th gestational week (30 m.m.). Thereafter the axial elongation of the mesodermal structures is more rapid than the lengthening of the cord, so that the termination of the cord moves cranially. This apparent ascent of the cord is most marked between the 9th and the 19th week by which time the conus medullaris is opposite the 4th lumbar vertebra. There is then a slower ascent with the cord ending approximately opposite the lower border of the 2nd lumbar vertebra at term, attaining the "adult" level about 2 months post-natally (Graph IV).[6]

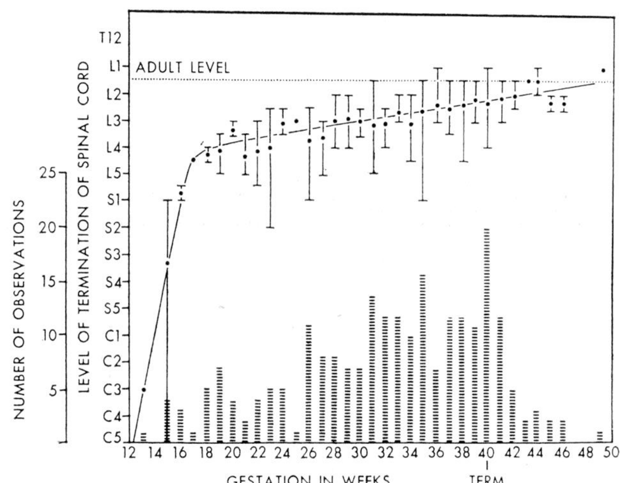

GRAPH. IV. Level of termination of the spinal cord plotted against gestational age. Ranges and mean values are indicated. The block graph represents the number of observations made in each gestational week. (By courtesy of *J. Anat.*, (1970) **106**, 489–497.)

In terms of the skeletal axis the cervical region is longer than the lumbar in the young embryo, becoming equal between the 6th and 8th months. Thereafter the lumbar region slightly exceeds the cervical.[2] The overall differential in axial elongation between the cord and the column is greatest from 9–19 weeks *in utero*, but 8 weeks after birth it becomes equal and remains so throughout the years of childhood.

A consequence of this growth differential is that the spinal nerve roots must necessarily assume a caudal angulation to attain their appropriate intervertebral foramina. This angulation becomes progressively more marked from the cervical to the sacral nerve roots. Since all the roots originally pass laterally directly at right angles from the cord, their angulation is a precise reflection of the elongation of neuroectoderm and mesoderm relative to each other.

It might be anticipated that the roots would remain at right angles to the axis of the cord until ascent of the cord was manifest at the 9th week. In fact in a 7-week embryo

Cl to C4 roots slope caudally, though in a graduated manner so that C5 is at a right angle.[3] This may be accounted for on the basis of the head fold requiring a longer outer spinal cord than the inner axial mesoderm. A similar phenomenon occurs with the nerve roots in relationship to the tail fold. After the 9th week the enormous elongation of the spinal axis masks the effect of the embryonic curvatures. The angulation of the roots then reflects the degree to which the cord segments are shorter than the vertebrae, bearing in mind that the cervical extremity of the cord is anchored to the brain which is immobilized within the cranium. Displacement of the cord with differential growth can only be manifest in one direction, and all the spinal roots become directed caudally.

ABNORMAL DEVELOPMENT

It is not within the scope of this chapter to give a detailed anatomical account of all the anomalies of development to which the vertebrospinal axis is subject. However having discussed the inter-relationship of mesoderm and ectoderm during the differentiation and growth of the spine it is relevant to cite some examples where these processes are derranged.

By far the most common maldevelopment of the spine are the various manifestations of "dysraphia" in which either the mesoderm or the neural tube, or both, have failed to meet in the dorsal mid-line. At the cephalic extremity this may result in anencephaly, and in the spinal region in spina bifida and a spinal myelocoele. It is a common misapprehension to regard these defects as being exactly similar to other common arrests of closure, for example, cleft lip and palate or cardiac septal defects. A little knowledge of the pathology of craniospinal dysraphia soon reveals that this is far too simple an explanation.

Figure 2 shows a portion of a chick's neural tube which has failed to close at a stage of development approximately equivalent to the 5th gestational week in the human, that is to say at a time when the neural tube ought to be completely formed. It cannot be said that closure has been prevented by a failure of growth neuroectoderm, which on the contrary is abundant. Excessive growth of the open portion of the neural plate has also been observed in the rat[41] and in the occasional human dysraphic embryo available for examination at a very early age.[28] Whether such overgrowth is a cause or a consequence of the dysraphia cannot be answered, but such a feature has not been recorded with a cleft lip or ventricular septal defect. The overgrowth of neuroectoderm is not so apparent in the full term fetus because it degenerates during the 8 months of gestation after its initial formation. This accounts for the small quantity of cerebral tissue seen in anencephalic infants at term.[40]

Growth is a three dimensional process so that an excess of spinal cord ought not only to be apparent from pouting of tissue above the surface of the area of dysraphia but also from an increase in length of the cord. As at this age the cord extends throughout the whole of the column the only way in which an excessive length of the cord can be accommodated is by bending the spinal axis and exaggerating the normal dorsal convexity of the embryo. Since spinal myelocoeles usually involve the lumbar region this is a possible cause of the congenital lumbar kyphos which affects about a quarter of all infants with spina bifida.[4,5] The spinal dentate ligaments are of neuroectodermal origin and it is interesting that the dentate ligaments on either side of a myelocoele are commonly enlarged to several times their normal size.[5]

An alternative hypothesis to account for congenital lumbar kyphosis is to suppose that the normal axial elongation of the mesoderm is inhibited, and that in addition to creating an abnormal spinal curvature it also inhibits the closure of the neural tube. Experimentally in both the chick[15] and the mouse[24] it has been alleged that stunting of the longitudinal growth of the chorda-mesoderm precedes dysraphia of the neural tube.

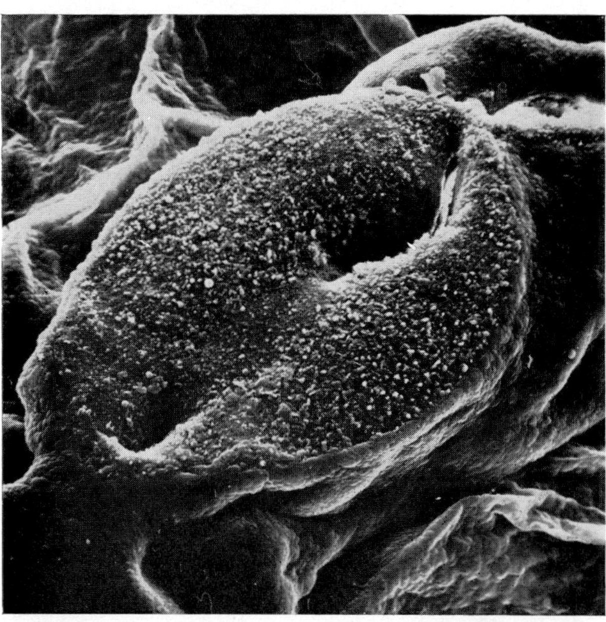

FIG. 2. Scanning electron micrograph of the hind brain region of chick embryo at 50 hours incubation showing an area of dysraphia. The neural canal opens into the defect at the cranial and caudal extremities. ×190.

Human spina bifida is almott invariably accompanied by multiple circular or ovoid defects in the membrane bones of the skull vault termed craniolacunia. On a radiograph these are often clearly visible as numerous coalescing areas of decreased bone density (Fig. 3). Craniolacunia are not related to increased intracranial pressure since they are present at birth in the absence of hydrocephalus and have usually disappeared by 3 months of age despite its onset. It is difficult to regard craniolacunia other than an inherent defect of mesodermal growth.

The Arnold-Chiari malformation (Fig. 4) is characterized by a tongue-like prolongation of cerebellum through the foramen magnum and an elongation and kinking of the medulla oblongata. Like craniolacunia it is almost always present with a spinal myelocoele. The posterior fossa of such infants is abnormally small but whether this is a cause or a result of the malformation can only be a matter of speculation. However if it were entirely due to excessive growth of the cerebellum and medulla one would expect an abnormally large posterior fossa.

Yet another example of a derangement in relative growth of the two germ layers comes from a consideration of the angulation of the spinal nerves in spina bifida. These characteristically take an upward course in the cervical region when there is an Arnold-Chiari malformation (Fig. 4) and also pass upwards immediately on the cranial side of a spinal myelocoele (Fig. 5). Although some ascent of the conus medullaris has usually occurred in an infant with spina bifida, the termination of the cord is often abnormally low.[5,6] It follows from earlier discussion in this chapter that because the angulation of the nerve roots is an indicator of the elongation of cord and vertebral column relative to one another, an upward deviation may only be accounted for on the basis of the spinal cord growing relatively too fast or the vertebral column growing relatively too slowly. The fact that the nerves commonly pass upwards in the cervical region, downwards in the thoracic, upwards in the lumbar region at the level of a myelocoele and downwards again in the lower lumbar and sacral regions indicates that growth rates are derranged at least in two separate levels of the vertebrospinal axis.

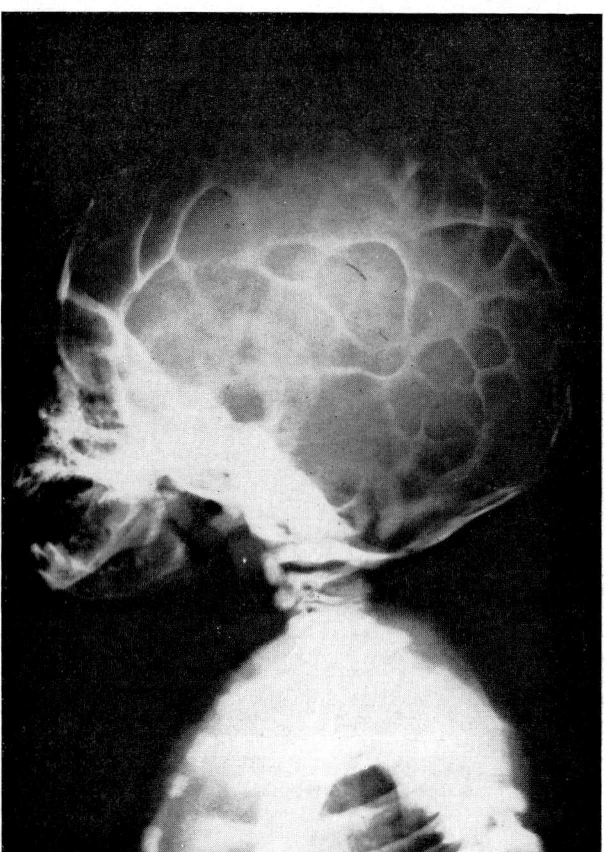

FIG. 3. Lateral radiograph of the skull of a newborn infant with craniolacunia.

It is possible that this dates back to an incoordination in the elongation of the axial mesoderm and neuroectoderm when the head and tail folds form during neuralation.

Finally unlike any other of the common malformations craniospinal dysraphia is invariably accompanied by anomalies of differentiation and growth in the form of hamartomata. Hypertrichosis, pigmentation and haemangiomata are commonly seen surrounding the skin defect. The exposed meninges are characteristically a brighter red than normal pia-arachnoid because of the excessive numbers of blood vessels present, even in the absence of inflammation. Lipomata are also common and if a sufficiently diligent search is made they may be demonstrated in nearly three-quarters of all dysraphic spinal cords.[13] The caudal extremity of the spinal column is particularly prone to teratomatous growths and large subcutaneous lipomata which extend through defective lumbosacral spinal laminae (Fig. 6). Related to this latter condition is the fact that lipomata of the filum terminale occur in 1 per cent of all normal infant spinal cords (Fig. 7).[7] Just as anomalies of axial elongation of cord and vertebral column represent failure of the normal interactive growth control mechanisms relative to each other, so these hamartomatous growths represent a

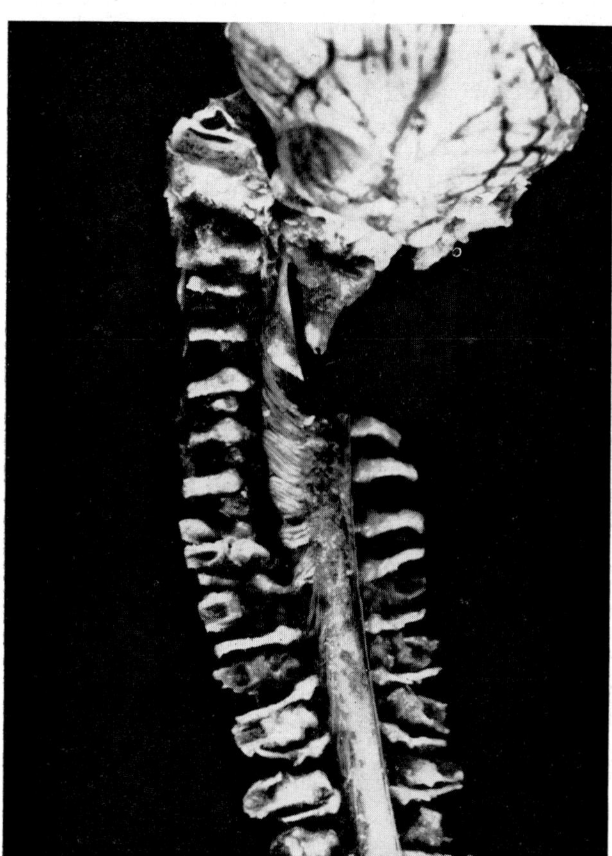

FIG. 4. Arnold-Chiari malformation. Black paper has been inserted between the cerebellar tongue and the cervical cord. The cervical nerve roots are directed upwards cranially and downwards caudally. ×1·5. (By courtesy of *Develop. Med. Child Neurol.* 1970.)

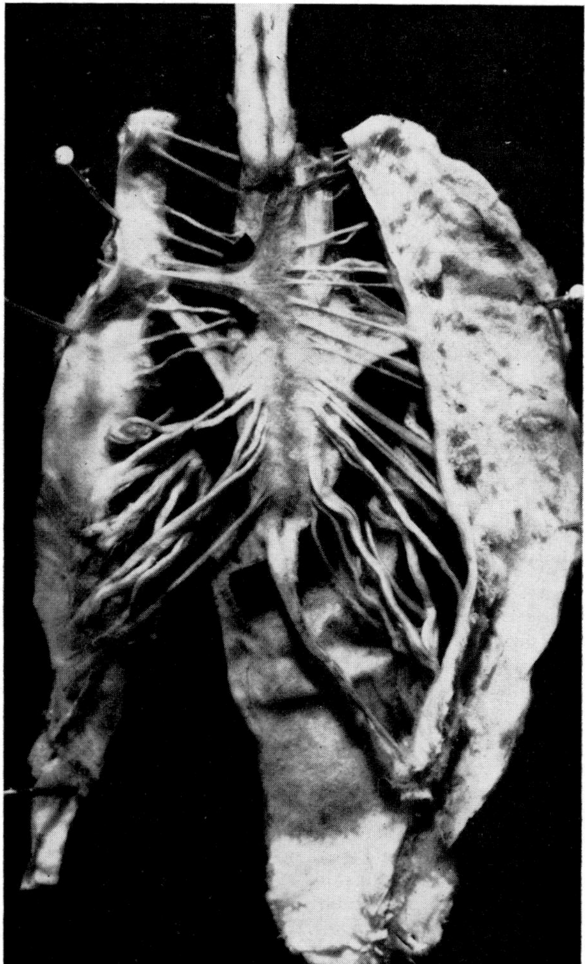

FIG. 5. Ventral aspect of a lumbar myelocoele revealed by a sagittal incision through the dura mater. The nerve roots irradiate outwards from the centre of the myelocoele, the more cranial roots passing upwards, those adjacent to the consus medullaris passing downwards. ×1·5.

failure in the influence of inductors limiting the proliferation of particular tissue components.

We may conclude by observing that malformations of the vertebrospinal axis are unique because of the frequency with which they cause, or are caused by, derrangements in relative growth rates of two embryonic germ layers. This is a reflection of the interactive dependence of these germ layers during early embryogenesis. There is no other structure where differentiation, growth and disease are so clearly interdependent. It is this that is the particular interest, concern and province of the paediatrician.

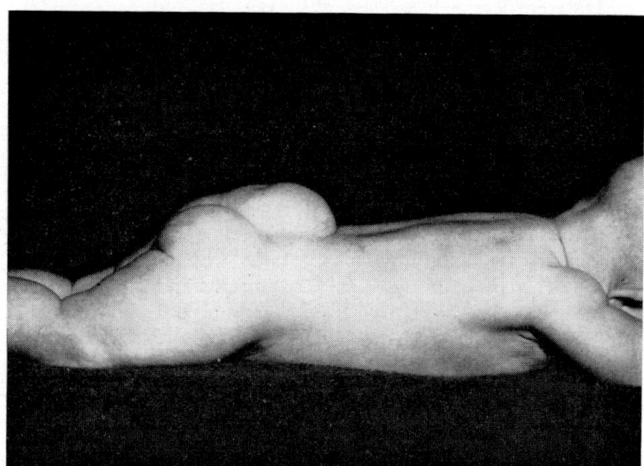

FIG. 6. Large subcutaneous lipoma in an infant with lumbosacral spina bifida. The lipoma was continuous with the filum terminale.

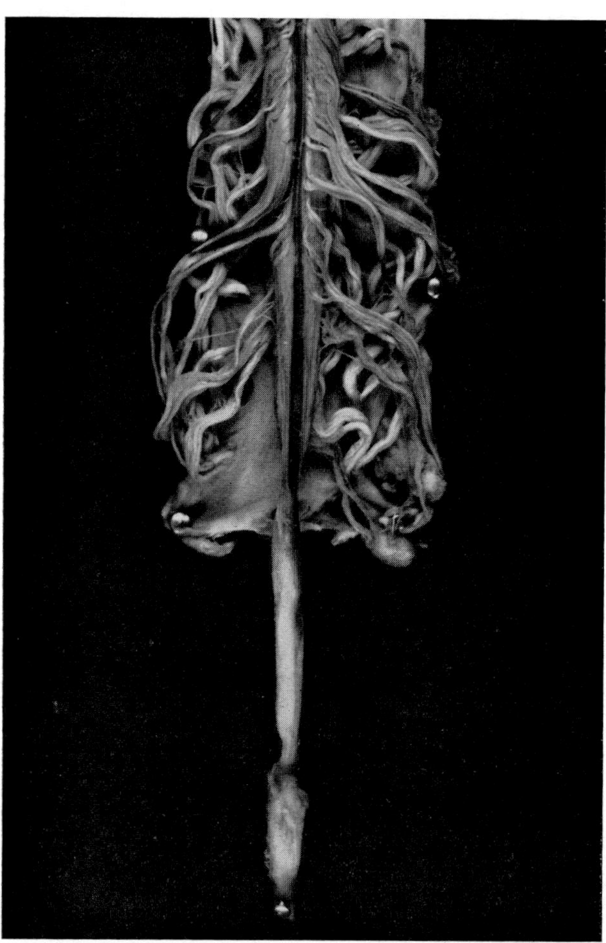

FIG. 7. Lipoma of the filum terminale in a newborn infant. There was no spina bfida or symptoms attributable to it. (By courtesy of *J. Path.*, (1970) **104**, 141–144.)

SUMMARY

1. The early differentiation of the vertebrospinal axis is described and the interactive roles of the ectoderm and mesoderm during primary induction and chondrogenesis are outlined.

2. The characteristics of growth of the vertebrospinal axis in later intrauterine life are discussed in terms of both regional growth and of growth of spinal cord relative to the vertebral column.

3. Some of the features of craniospinal dysraphia are examined to illustrate how normal growth relationships of neuroectoderm and axial mesoderm may become disturbed.

ACKNOWLEDGEMENTS

My thanks are due to Mrs. P. Portch for technical assistance in the provision of the electron microphotographs for Figs. 1 and 2 and to Miss J. Sands for assistance with the data depicted in Graphs I, II and III.

REFERENCES

1. Baker, P. C. and Schroeder, T. E. (1967), "Cytoplasmic Filaments and Morphogenetic Movement in the Amphibian Neural Tube," *Develop. Biol.*, **15,** 432–450.
2. Ballantyne, J. W. (1892), "The Spinal Column in Infants," *Edinb. med. J.*, **37,** 913–922.
3. Barry, A. (1956), "A Quantitative Study of the Prenatal Changes in Angulation of the Spinal Nerves," *Anat. Rec.*, **126,** 97–110.
4. Barson, A. J. (1965), "Radiological Studies of Spina Bifida Cystica. The Phenomenon of Congenital Lumbar Kyphosis," *Brit. J. Radiol.*, **38,** 294–300.
5. Barson, A. J. (1970), "Spina Bifida: the Significance of the Level and Extent of the Defect to the Morphogenesis," *Develop. Med. Child. Neurol.*, **12,** 129–144.
6. Barson, A. J. (1970), "The Vertebral Level of Termination of the Spinal Cord During Normal and Abnormal Development," *J. Anat.*, **106,** 489–497.
7. Barson, A. J. (1971), "Symptomless Intradural Spinal Lipomas in Infancy," *J. Path.*, **104,** 141–144.
8. Barth, L. G. and Barth, L. J. (1964), "Sequential Induction of the Presumptive Epidermis of the Rana Pipiens Gastrula," *Biol. Bull.*, **127,** 413–427.
9. Bautzmann, H., Holtfreter, J., Spemann, H. and Mangold, O. (1932), "Versuche zur analyse der induktionsmittel in der embryonalentwicklung," *Naturwissenschaften*, **20,** 971–974.
10. Bellairs, R. (1959), "The Development of the Nervous System in Chick Embryos, Studied by Electron Microscopy," *J. Embryol. exp. Morph.*, **7,** 94–115.
11. Brachet, J. (1950), in *Chemical Embryology.* New York: Wiley (Interscience).
12. Dalcq, A. (1960), in *Fundamental Aspects of Normal and Malignant Growth*, pp. 305–494 (W. W. Nowinski, Ed.). Amsterdam: Elsevier.
13. Emery, J. L. and Lendon, R. G. (1967), "Lipomas of the Cauda Equina and Other Fatty Tumours Related to Neurospinal Dysraphism," *Develop. Med. Child. Neurol.*, suppl. 20, 62–70.
14. Flower, M. and Grobstein, C. (1967), "Interconvertibility of Induced Morphogenetic Responses of Mouse Embryonic Somites to Notochord and Ventral Spinal Cord," *Develop. Biol.*, **15,** 193–205.
15. Gallera, J. (1951), "Influence de l'atmosphere artificiellement modifee sur le developpement embryonnaire du poulet," *Acta anat.*, **11,** 549–585.
16. Gallera, J. (1966), "Le pouvoir inducteur de la chorde et du mesoblaste parachordal chez les oiseaux en fonction du facteur temps," *Acta anat.*, **63,** 388–397.
17. Gallera, J. (1967), "L'induction neurogene chez les oiseaux. Passage du flux inducteur par le filtre millipore," *Experientia*, **23,** 461–462.
18. Gallera, J., Nicolet, G. and Baumann, M. (1968), "Induction neurale chez les oiseaux a travers un filtre millipore: etude au microscope optique et electronique," *J. Embryol. exp. Morphol.*, **19,** 439–450.
19. Grobstein, C. (1956), "Inductive Interaction in Development," *Adv. Cancer Res.*, **4,** 187–236.
20. Grobstein, C. (1967), "Mechanisms of Organogenetic Tissue Interaction," *Nat. Cancer Inst. Monogr.*, **26,** 279–299.
21. Hayashi, Y. (1959), "The Effect of Ribonuclease on the Inductive Ability of Liver Pentose Nucleoprotein," *Develop. Biol.*, **1,** 247–268.
22. Holtfreter, J. (1947), "Neural Induction in Explants which have Passed Through a Sublethal Cytolysis," *J. Exp. Zool.*, **106,** 197–222.
23. Holtzer, H. (1960), "Interaction of Spinal Cord and Cartilage," in *19th Symposium on Development and Growth. Synthesis of Molecular and Cellular Structure.* New York: Ronald Press.
24. Hsu, C. Y. and van Dyke, J. H. (1948), "An Analysis of the Growth Rates in Neural Epithelium of Normal and Spina Bifidous (Myeloschisis) Mouse Embryos," *Anat. Rec.*, **100,** 745.
25. Keibel, F. and Mall, F. P. (1910), *Manual of Human Embryology*, Vol. 1, p. 331. Philadelphia: Lippincott.
26. Lash, J., Holtzer, S. and Holtzer, H. (1957), "An Experimental Analysis of the Development of the Spinal Column. VI. Aspects of Cartilage Induction," *Exptl. Cell Res.*, **13,** 292–303.
27. Leikola, A. and McCallion, D. J. (1967), "Time Required for Heterogeneous Induction in Chick Embryo Ectoderm," *Experientia*, **23,** 869–870.
28. Patten, B. M. (1953), "Embryological Stages in the Establishing of Myeloschisis with Spina Bifida," *Amer. J. Anat.*, **93,** 365–395.
29. Saxen, L. (1961), "Transfilter Neural Induction of Amphibian Ectoderm," *Develop. Biol.*, **3,** 140–152.
30. Saxen, L. and Toivonen, S. (1961), "The Two-gradient Hypothesis in Primary Induction. The Combined Effect of Two Types of Inductors Mixed in Different Ratios," *J. Embryol. exp. Morph.*, **9,** 514–533.
31. Scammon, R. E. (1933), "Developmental Anatomy," in *Morris' Human Anatomy. A Complete Systematic Treatise*, 9th edition, pp. 25–31 (C. M. Jackson, Ed.). Philadelphia: Blakiston.
32. Spemann, H. (1901), "Uber korrelationen in der entwicklung des auges," *Verh. Anat. Ges. Bonn.*, **15,** 61–79.
33. Spemann, H. (1927), "Neue arbeiten uber organisatoren in der tierschen entwicklung," *Naturwissenschaften*, **15,** 946–951.
34. Spemann, H. (1931), Über den anteil von implantat und wirtskeim an der orientierung und beschaffenheit der induzierten *embryonalanlage*," *Arch. Entwicklungsmech. Organ.*, **123,** 389–517.
35. Spemann, H. and Mangold, H. (1924), "Uber induktion von embryonalanlagen durch implantation artfremder organisatoren," *Archiv. fur mikroskop. Anat. Entwicklungsmech.*, **100,** 599–638.
36. Tarin, D. (1972), "Ultrastructural Features of Neural Induction in Xenopus Laevus," *J.Anat.*, **111,** 1–28.
37. Tiedemann, H. (1967), in *The Biochemistry of Animal Development*, Vol. 2, pp. 3–55 (R. Weber, Ed.). New York: Academic Press.
38. Toivonen, S. (1958), "The Dependence of the Cellular Transformation of the Competent Ectoderm on Temporal Relationships in the Induction Process," *J.Embryol. exp. Morphol.*, **6,** 479–485.
39. Toivonen, S. and Saxen, L. (1968), "Morphogenetic Interaction of Presumptive Neural and Mesodermal Cells Mixed in Different Ratios," *Science, N.S.*, **159,** 539–540.
40. Warkany, J. (1959), "Experimental Production of Congenital Malformations of the Central Nervous System," in *Proc. 1st Internat. Conf. on Mental Retard.*, p. 24 (P. W. Bowman and H. Mautner, Eds.). New York: Grune & Stratton.
41. Warkany, J., Wilson, J. G. and Geiger, J. F. (1958), "Myeloschisis and Myelomeningocele Produced Experimentally in the Rat," *J. comp. Neurol.*, **109,** 35–64.
42. Watterson, R. L., Fowler, I. and Fowler, B. J. (1954), "The Role of the Neural Tube and Notochord in the Development of the Axial Skeleton in Chicks," *Amer. J. Anat.*, **95,** 337–400.
43. Wessels, N. K., Spooner, B. S., Ash, J. F., Bradley, M. O., Luduena, M. A., Taylor, E. L., Wrenn, J. T. and Yamada, K. M. (1971), "Microfilaments in Cellular and Developmental Processes," *Science*, **171,** 135–143.
44. Wrenn, J. T. and Wessells, N. K. (1969), "An Ultrastructural Study of Lens Invagination in the Mouse," *J. exp. Zool.*, **171,** 359–368.
45. Yamada, T. (1950), "Dorsalization of the Ventral Marginal Zone of the Triturus Gastrula. 1. Ammonia Treatment of the Medio-ventral Marginal Zone," *Biol. Bull.*, **98,** 98–121.

34. THE NEUROLOGICAL DEVELOPMENT OF THE NEONATE

F. J. SCHULTE

In discussing the functional development of the neonatal nervous system three aspects have to be considered.

(1) Motor development. Since spontaneous muscle activity and reflexes have been extensively studied in human neonates for almost one hundred years, a great wealth of data on these subjects has accumulated.

(2) Development of bioelectric brain activity and the sleep–wakefulness cycle. Recently we have become aware of the fact that the development of consciousness, arousal, responsiveness and the corresponding bioelectric activity of the cerebral cortex is a most sensitive indicator of brain maturation.

(3) Psychophysiological studies. In the past few years the infant's abilities to perceive the world around him have been reinvestigated with great success. Conditioning experiments and studies on expectation and surprise have revealed that the newborn infant is much more intelligent than expected.

Only the first two aspects of central nervous system maturation will be discussed in this chapter.

SENSORY-MOTOR FUNCTION OF THE PRE-TERM AND FULL-TERM NEWBORN INFANT

In the adult mammal, including the human, motor control has its representation at different levels of the central nervous system. Since Sherrington's[241] basic experiments, a great wealth of data on spinal function has been accumulated, thus allowing for a detailed description of motor control at that level. For the study of the newborn this is particularly advantageous since the motor behaviour of the newborn seems to be largely under the control of the spinal cord and medulla. On the other hand, our limited knowledge of neurophysiological mechanisms of higher motor control, even in adults, may well have led us to overestimate grossly the significance of the spinal cord for neonatal motor function.

The sensory-motor responses of the newborn are highly dependent upon external conditions and the level of CNS excitation at any particular time. Such environmental factors as temperature, light and noise are important in determining these responses. For the neurophysiological analysis of behaviour as well as for the clinical neurological evaluation of the newborn, it is especially important to take into account the general activity level—the internal state of arousal or excitation—of the nervous system. Prechtl and co-workers have studied comprehensively the influence of sleep and wakefulness upon sensory-motor functions of the newborn. In Prechtl and Beintema's[203] invaluable and widely-used manual for the neurological examination of the newborn, it is recommended that the "state" of the infant be assessed and recorded at the beginning and throughout the course of the examination.[192,270] The alterations in sensory-motor function that occur during the different phases of sleep are very complex (*see* page 601). The descriptions given here of the sensory-motor behaviour of the normal full-term newborn refer in general to awake children who are not crying while being examined.

Developmental Physiology of the Neuromuscular Junction

The human embryo begins to make movements at a gestational age of $7\frac{1}{2}$ weeks.[131] Bergström and Bergström[20] were able to demonstrate electromyographic activity in 70-day-old fetuses. By this age one is able to identify primitive motor nerve endings in a few muscles, predominantly those of the face and trunk. By 11 weeks gestation, the motor nerve fibres have made contact with the muscle cells of the biceps, and by 12 weeks they have reached the fingers and toes. Not until the 26–28th week of pregnancy do the motor nerve endings differentiate to form the eventual endplates and this process is far from complete at term. The neuromuscular synapses of the tongue, diaphragm and intercostal muscles are by then already highly differentiated, whereas in the extremities and especially in the muscle of the foot, the development of the mature, complicated endplate structures is still in progress.[112,131] These signs of morphological immaturity have stimulated a number of electrophysiological investigations designed specifically to test neuromuscular

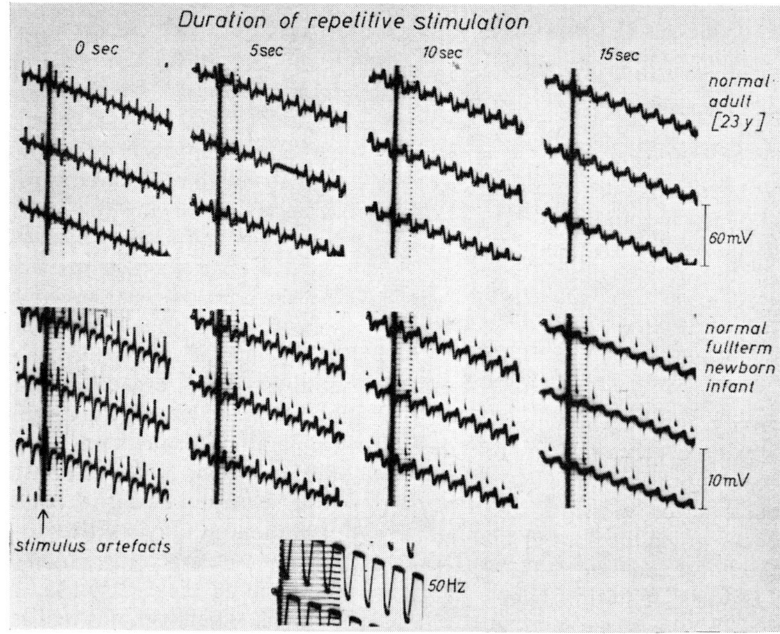

FIG. 1. Muscle action potentials elicited by repetitive motor nerve stimulation. With repetitive motor nerve stimulation, the amplitude of the action potential decreases; this effect is more marked in newborn infants than in adults. (From Schulte and Michaelis, 1965, *Klin. Wschr.*, **43**, 295–300. *Courtesy of Springer-Verlag.*)

transmission in normal, full-term newborns.[23,43,235] The neuromuscular transmission of a series of stimuli at a relatively high frequency is limited in the neonate compared with adults and the required period of endplate recovery is longer (Fig. 1). The immaturity of the endplate in full-term newborn infants is probably of no functional importance. In very immature infants, sustained muscle contraction would possibly be limited by poor neuromuscular transmission of repetitive stimuli. In preterm infants, moreover, spinal motoneurons do not yet have the capability of sustained repetitive discharges with high frequency.

Spinal Cord Motoneurons and the Muscle Spindles

The efferent innervation of skeletal muscles (Fig. 2) is furnished by ventral horn motoneurons with different axonal calibres. The larger A alpha type motoneurons

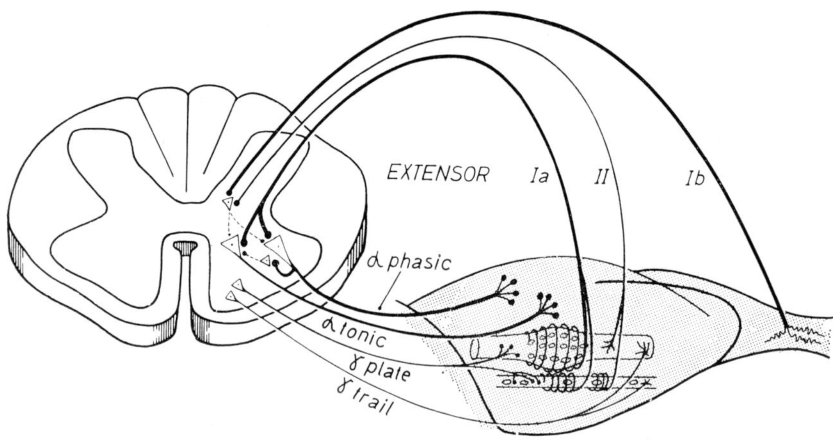

FIG. 2. Diagram of important pathways in the spinal motor system for extensor muscles. Solid lines, excitatory connections; dashed lines, inhibitory connections. α-phasic, phasic α-motoneurones which activate skeletal muscles and generally cause fast movements by means of short bursts of action potentials. α-tonic, tonic α-motoneurones which activate skeletal muscles for longer periods of contraction by means of a series of repetitive action potentials. While still within the grey matter, axon collaterals of the α-motoneurones activate Renshaw cells which act as inhibitors of α-motoneurones. γ-plate and γ-trail, fusimotoneurones innervating muscle fibers within the muscle spindles (intrafusal muscle fibers). Ia, II, Ib, sensory afferent nerve fibres of muscle receptors activated by stretch. (From Schulte, 1968, *In* Bushe, K. A., and P. Glees, eds. *Die Elektromyographie. Courtesy of Hippokrates Verl., Stuttgart.*)

have a more phasic, the smaller ones a more tonic discharge pattern.[72,107,111] The smaller motoneurons, with axons of the A gamma type, are not directly engaged in muscle contraction and limb movement but rather activate muscle fibres within muscle spindles. These gamma efferents or fusimotoneurons supplying the intrafusal muscle fibres enhance the afferent discharge frequency of the stretch receptors and thereby increase their sensitivity to stretch.[29,136,145,149] Spiral or semispiral sensory endings of group Ia and group II nerve fibres are twisted around the intrafusal muscle cells. Group Ia fibre afferents produce monosynaptic excitation of the homonymous alpha-motoneurons while inhibiting motoneurons of antagonistic muscles, thus forming the proprioceptive reflex arc.[71,138,156,157,169,170] The group II fibre afferents, however, are monosynaptically connected only with flexor motoneurons, whereas even homonymous extensor motoneurons are inhibited via interneurons.[73,146]

The Golgi tendon organ group Ib afferents are connected with homonymous alpha-motoneurons via inhibitory interneurons, thus producing what is called "autogenetic inhibition."[106]

No information is available concerning gamma innervation and intrafusal activity in human infants, the data being extremely sparse even for human adults. In kittens, the intrafusal activity maintained by gamma innervation of muscle spindles seems to be less sustained than it is in adult cats.[242,243] This would imply decreased afferent muscle spindle activity and thus diminished depolarization pressure (i.e. excitatory drive) on the motoneurons.

Proprioceptive response by way of sensory Ia fibres, originating in annulospiral endings of the muscle spindle and forming the afferent pathway of the feed-back circuit illustrated in Fig. 2, is also found to be deficient in the newborn kitten. Maximal muscle spindle discharge frequency and its maintenance over a long period of time is severely restricted in the newborn kitten when compared with the adult animal.[244] Both the lack of gamma-efferent support and the peculiar membrane properties of the immature receptor end-organ may account for the lack of tonicity in the afferent muscle spindle discharge pattern. This in turn implies low alpha-motoneuron activity and skeletal muscle hypotonia.[236,245]

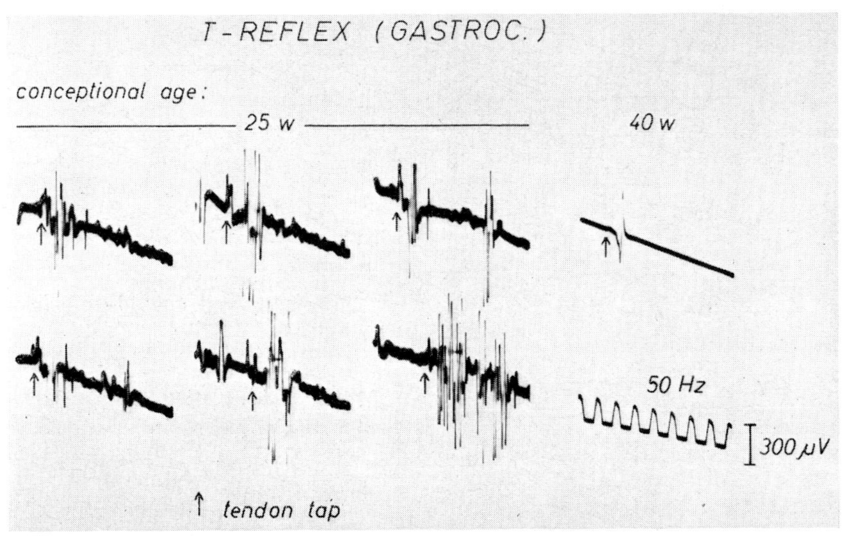

FIG. 3. The monosynaptic stretch reflex elicited by a tendon tap in a preterm infant (25 weeks of menstrual age) consists of a burst of impulses rather than of one compound muscle action potential. (From Schulte *et al.*, 1969. *In* Robinson, R. J., ed.] *Brain and Early Behaviour. Courtesy of Academic Press, Inc., London.*)

Proprioceptive Reflexes of the Newborn: Phasic T and H Reflexes

A brisk tap on a tendon results in a stretch of the muscle and its muscle spindle receptors. Excitation of the receptors leads to activation of alpha motoneurons by way of sensory afferents, and a quick muscle twitch which is called a T (Tendon) or stretch reflex. The same reflex can be elicited by electrically stimulating the afferent nerve and it is then called an H[117] reflex. All phasic, proprioceptive reflexes can be obtained in the newborn infant provided the infant is not asleep and particularly not in active or rapid eye movement (REM) sleep (*see* p. 0).[25,240,254] In both animal and human adults and newborns, muscle stretch reflexes are diminished or even abolished during active sleep.[99,100,114,115,206] This fact has led to considerable confusion in paediatric textbook literature concerning stretch reflexes. Since the examination of the newborn infant is sometimes inadvertently carried out while the subject is almost asleep, many authors have erroneously concluded that newborns do not demonstrate certain stretch reflexes. Even in the youngest preterm infant which we were able to study (25 weeks gestational age), proprioceptive reflexes in the quadriceps could be elicited by tendon tap;[233] the reflex response, however, consisted of a burst of unsynchronized impulses (Fig. 3) rather than a single compound muscle action potential such as is usually seen in newborn infants beyond 30 weeks gestation.

The latency period between electrical stimulation of, for instance, the tibial nerve, and the H reflex response is composed of the sensory nerve conduction time from the popliteal fossa to the spinal cord and from there to the muscle, the synaptic delay in both spinal cord and neuromuscular junction, and finally the time taken for the muscle action potential to reach the recording electrode. The synaptic delay amounts to about 1 m./sec. only. Although nerve conduction velocities in the newborn are only about half those of the adult, due to incomplete myelination, the conduction times for the peripheral reflex arcs are nevertheless somewhat shorter in the newborn because the conduction distances are less (Fig. 4).

This finding demonstrates the significance of myelination on the development of psychomotor functions. We think that the low degree of myelination and the slow conduction rate in the immature nervous system have little bearing upon the functional incapacity of newborn infants in whom the interneuron and the neuromuscular distances are shorter, thus more than compensating for the low speed.

Nerve Conduction Velocity

Since the myelin sheath first reaches its final thickness in the course of postnatal development, nerve conduction velocities in warm blooded animals are lower in the fetus and newborn than in the adult.[258] Comparative measurements have been carried out in chickens[37] and cats[75,242] as well as in human premature and newborn infants.[25,26,42,68,69,89,90,179,209,210,217,237,254]

Based on age estimations derived from menstrual histories in accord with findings at regular prenatal examinations, we were able to establish a quantitative relationship between nerve conduction time and conceptional age (gestational age plus age from birth), the entire range from 25–40 weeks being included. Figure 5 illustrates the relationships for the ulnar and tibial nerves.

During the final 4 weeks of normal gestation the nerve conduction velocity of the ulnar nerve increases by approximately one metre per week.[231] Prior to this, the rate of increase is greater; subsequently it is less. Throughout childhood values for the tibial and peroneal nerves are slightly below those obtained from the ulnar and median nerve. When the gestational age of a newborn is not known, one can obtain an estimate by measuring nerve conduction velocities. Because of the rather great variance, the accuracy of this estimate for an individual baby is not better than with external characteristics;[83] a great advantage, however, is that in contrast to every other method nerve conduction velocity is entirely independent of pathology. Small-for-gestational-age infants of toxaemic mothers, and large-for-gestational-age infants of diabetic mothers as well as newborns suffering from perinatal hypoxia or traumatic brain damage or hydrops fetalis have a nerve conduction velocity, appropriate for their conceptional age.[231,237] When comparing two groups of infants, the mean and standard deviation of ulnar nerve conduction velocity are excellent parameters for checking whether the conceptional ages are similar, correspondence of nerve conduction velocities in normal and abnormal groups of infants indicating that their conceptional ages

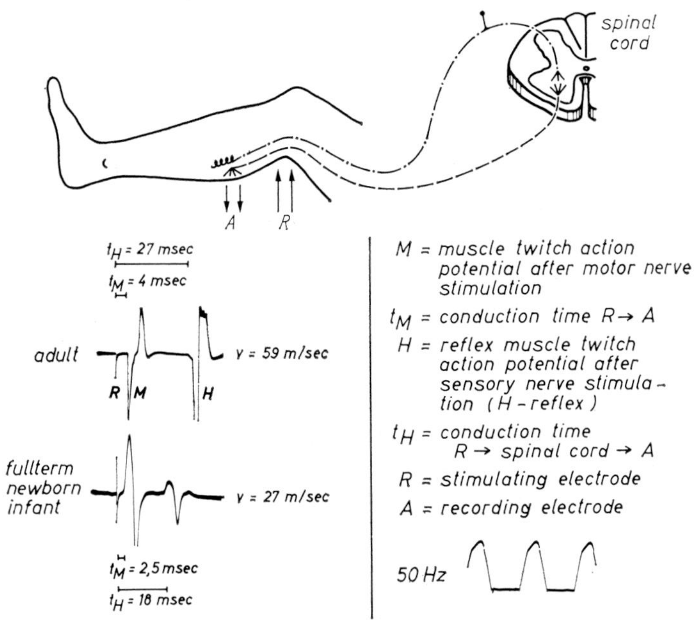

FIG. 4. The motor nerve conduction velocities and reflex times of an adult human subject compared with those of a normal, full-term newborn infant. Although motor nerve conduction velocity is significantly lower in the newborn infant, reflex times are shorter than in the adult because of the smaller distances. (From Schulte, 1968, *Fortschritte der Paedologie. Courtesy of Springer-Verlag.*)

must have been nearly the same. This is an important prerequisite for further comparison of many other kinds of data.

The normal nerve conduction velocities found in small-for-gestational-age infants of toxaemic mothers indicates that even severe chronic fetal distress and growth retardation do not alter the conduction velocity of peripheral nerves in spite of the biochemical effects of early malnutrition on central nervous system myelination.[47,54] Two explanations can be offered for this conflict of evidence: (1) in peripheral nerves myelination may be less affected by early malnutrition than in the central nervous system; or (2) minor alterations in the constitution of myelin may not alter the axonal conductivity.

Only in cases of spina bifida is neonatal nerve condition velocity reduced in the lower extremities.[35,179] Either this is a consequence of chronic irritation to the exposed motoneurons and their axons, or it results from a deficiency in myelination representing an inherent aspect of the anomaly itself.

Muscle Tone

The use of the term "muscle tone" is considered unjustified by some for lack of an adequate definition. In clinical terms muscle tone or tonus is the resistance against passive movement. With such a definition one must remain consciously aware of the fact that muscle tone comprises both cellular and contractile components.

The plastic, cellular component is in no way limited to muscle cells and their properties. The condition of the skin, of the subcutaneous fat tissue and of the connective tissue also determines the cellular resistance against stretch and movement. This component in fact plays a particularly important role in newborn neurology: for example, infants with scleredema, show marked resistance to passive movement of an extremity even when motoneuron activity level is at a minimum.

The contractile component of muscle tone can be assessed by electrophysiological measurements; it is defined in terms of the recorded electrical activity of the motor units of a given muscle. This motor activity can be constantly tonic or phasic or rhythmic, or any combination of these. Contractile muscle tone and movement necessarily arise out of each other.[252] Movements of the extremities as well as tetanic contractions of muscles are the result of tonic, phasic and rhythmic discharges of groups of motoneurons. Sherrington[241] demonstrated not only that the continuous input of efferent impulses from the ventral horn neurons was responsible for muscle contractions and for tone, but also that the constant return of afferent impulses from the stretch receptors of the muscle regulates the activity of the motoneurons and thereby maintains the contractile components of muscle tone.

The mature human newborn favours a flexed position of his extremities as does the young monkey.[196,218,219,220,221,224,273] Prechtl and Knol[204] studied the consistent absence of flexor positioning of the lower extremities that

	N. ulnaris					N. tibialis				
	n	conceptional age [weeks]	weight (g)	conduction velocity [m/sec]	ß (p = 0,05)	n	conceptional age [weeks]	weight (g)	conduction velocity [m/sec]	ß (p = 0,05)
term	19	40,6 ± 0,61	3345 ± 349	✱▲ 30,4 ± 3,40	31,87 28,82	15	40,5 ± 0,20	3355 ± 316	✱▲ 25,8 ± 2,0	26,85 24,82
small for dates	16	40,3 ± 1,58	2068 ± 183	▲ 32,4 ± 7,25	35,95 28,85	24	40,7 ± 1,78	2139 ± 231	▲ 23,68 ± 4,02	25,29 22,07
preterm	17	35,8 ± 1,64	2129 ± 243	✱ 25,9 ± 4,08	27,87 24,0	20	36,3 ± 1,56	2224 ± 219	✱ 18,6 ± 3,71	20,26 17,0
				✱ t = 4,520 p<0,001 ▲ t = 3,360 p<0,005					✱ t = 5,934 p<0,001 ▲ t = 6,516 p<0,001	

FIG. 5. Statistic analysis (t test) of nerve conduction velocity in normal; full-term; preterm; and full-term,small-for-date infants. In each group the mean values and first standard deviations are given for conceptional ages and body weights at the time of examination and for both ulnar and tibial nerve conduction velocities. In addition, the confidence interval for the mean value of the conduction velocities is indicated under β when the probability is 95 per cent ($p = 0{\cdot}05$). Statistically significant differences in ulnar or tibial nerve conduction velocities among the three groups of infants are indicated by and + with the corresponding t values and the level of probability (p). (From Schulte *et al.*, 1968c, *Pediatrics*, **42**, 17–26.)

one finds in infants born by the breech. Not only did they find a predominance of extensor activity in both positioning and spontaneous movements of the legs in a large number of frank breech babies, but they also demonstrated an absence of flexor reflex response to painful stimuli applied to the foot sole (withdrawal reflex) and an actual enhancement of the extensor reflex elicited by dorsiflexion of the foot (magnet response). These findings suggest that the normal flexion pattern of the mature newborn is induced by forced positioning *in utero*.

Other theories have been advanced to explain the preferred flexed posture of mature newborn infants. A temporal difference in the development of the gamma muscle spindle system, with earlier gamma efferent innervation of the flexor muscles, could be postulated. Electromyographic studies do show strong and long-lasting myotonic flexor activity in a number of neonatal reflexes such as the Moro, recoil of the forearms, and traction responses, whereas the extensors receive only short-lasting innervation during comparable movements.[228,229] Moreover, for flexor motoneurons both primary and secondary muscle spindle afferent impulses are excitatory, whereas, extensor motoneurons are connected with secondary muscle spindle fibres via inhibitory interneurons. A preponderance of excitatory afferent impulses to the flexor muscles might thus result. Such a dominance of excitatory receptor afferents from the periphery with the appropriate flexor posturing is important for the vital pattern of the withdrawal reflex. In contrast, proprioceptive, anti-gravitational reflexes match the pattern of tonic innervation of the extensors maintained by primary muscle spindle afferents. The flexor or withdrawal reflex pattern develops in advance of the antigravitational reflexes. It is also possible that as well as the early development of a strong peripheral excitatory drive for the flexor motoneurons the early maturation of the globus pallidus and a temporary absence of strial inhibition favour the flexor pattern of extremity posture.[87]

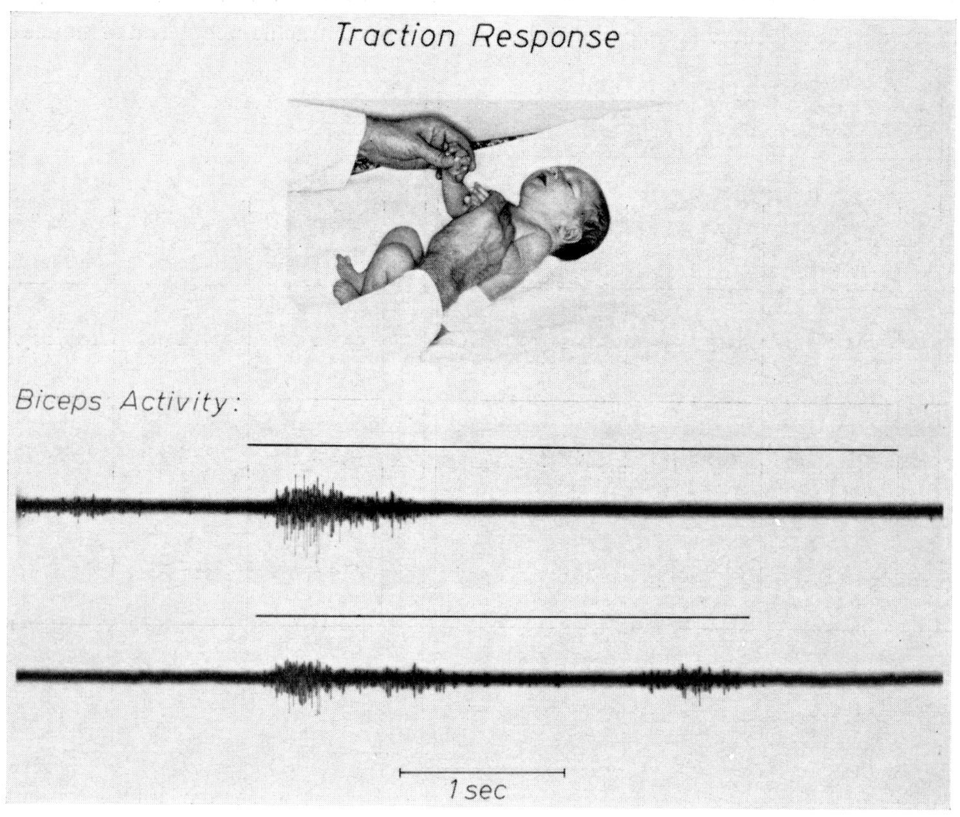

Fig. 6. Top, the elbows remain flexed while the infant is pulled to a sitting position. Bottom, the electromyogram of biceps muscle activity during two traction responses (traction indicated by a bar). (From Schulte 1970, *In* Stave, U., ed., *Physiology of the Perinatal Period*, Vol. 2. *Courtesy of Appleton-Century-Crofts Meredith Corporation, New York.*)

Tonic Myotactic Reflexes

In the normal adult human a slow, gradual muscle stretch does not lead to an increased resistance to passive movement. The afferent drive from the muscle stretch receptors remains subthreshold and motoneurons are not activated to any substantial degree. In contrast, tonic myotactic reflexes, i.e. increasing resistance against gradual stretching, can be elicited in healthy full-term newborn infants in almost all flexor and many extensor muscles.[4,5,6,7,196] A great number of the so-called "primitive reflexes" depend upon the tonic myotactic reflex activity of the newborn. In the wakeful full-term infant an extension of the lower arms is followed by a rather quick recoil into the flexed position (Fig. 6). If an infant lying on his back is pulled up by his hands into the sitting position the arms remain flexed (Fig. 7). The palmar grasp can be reinforced by gradually extending the baby's fingers. A newborn infant who is held in the standing position usually activates hip and knee extensors if his body weight is allowed to act on these muscles. The motoneuron activity demonstrated electromyographically during traction and recoil manoeuvre provides clear evidence that the phenomenon is a spinal reflex rather than the consequence of the elastic properties of muscles and ligaments. In accordance with flexor preponderance and our explanation for it given in the preceding section, tonic myotactic reflexes are more easily obtained in flexor than in extensor muscles. They are difficult to demonstrate in infants of less than 34 weeks gestational age, yet are normally present by 36 weeks.[3,172,219,224]

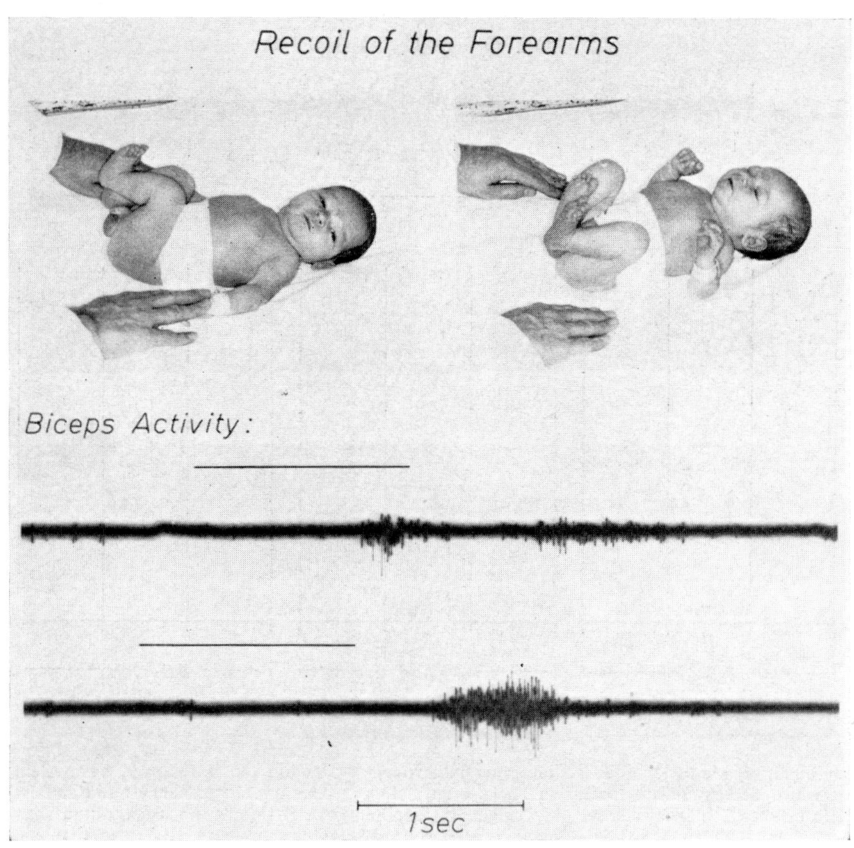

FIG. 7. Stretch and release of the forearms is followed by a quick recoil due to biceps muscle activity. Stretching of the elbows is indicated by a bar; the biceps electromyogram of two recoils is given below. (From Schulte 1970. *In* Stave, U., ed., *Physiology of the Pertinatal Period*, Vol. 2. *Courtesy of Appleton-Century-Crofts Meredith Corporation, New York.*)

Spinal Inhibition

"No excitation without inhibition." This basic rule of central nervous activity holds also for neonatal spinal motor activity. The monosynaptic, compound reflex action potential, as well as any synchronous burst of montoneuron activity, is followed by a short period of more or less complete inhibition. This is indicated by a silent period in the background activity and is called "Innervationsstille."[117,118] Spinal motoneuron inhibition is assured by several mechanisms (Fig. 2):

(1) Each spike potential is followed by membrane hyperpolarization due to a postexcitatory increase in membrane permeability for potassium. This membrane shift is called "positive afterpotential."

(2) Each motoneuron action potential, before leaving the grey matter of the spinal cord, activates Renshaw cells, interneurons which inhibit the adjacent motoneurons. This pathway represents an intraspinal, inhibitory feedback mechanism, and has been shown to be active already in newborn kittens.[183]

(3) The reflex muscle twitch activates Golgi tendon organs, the afferent impulses of which inhibit spinal motoneurons via interneurons. This pathway represents a musculospinal inhibitory feedback mechanism and is called "autogenetic inhibition."

(4) Muscle spindle afferents are silenced by the reflex shortening of the muscle; thus, part of the continuous afferent drive of spinal motoneurons from peripheral sources is eliminated for a short period while the muscle is in contraction.

(5) Afferent fibres from both supraspinal and peripheral sources branch-off from collaterals before reaching the spinal motoneurons, and terminate as end-organs attached to presynaptic excitatory nerve fibres. Action potentials reaching these presynaptic end-organs depolarize the underlying nerve fibres and thereby diminish the amplitude of the action potentials travelling along them. This in turn leads to a diminished amount of transmitter substance being secreted at the axodendritic motoneuronal synapses. The mechanism as a whole is called "presynaptic inhibition."[71,73a] Thus, synaptic excitation of spinal motoneurons concomitantly produces presynaptic inhibition of the adjacent ventral horn cells.

The duration of the silent period subsequent to a synchronous burst of motoneuron discharges is dependent upon the amount of background activity, i.e. the depolarization pressure on spinal motoneurons.[240] The duration of the silent period decreases from greater than 100 to less than 20 m./sec. with increasing background activity (Figs. 8 and 9). This indicates that spinal inhibitory mechanisms can in part be outweighed by supra- or intraspinal excitatory drive.[187]

The duration of the silent period, i.e. the degree of inhibitory influence upon spinal motoneurons subsequent to the monosynaptic stretch reflex, increases with gestational age (Fig. 9). The duration of the silent period in full-term newborn infants is only slightly, if at all, shorter than in older children or adults. The minimal duration of the silent period, obtained during very strong supraspinal motoneuron excitation, is roughly equal in all age groups including very young preterm infants.[233] This observation is consistent with the hypothesis that a minimum degree of postexcitatory inhibition, possibly related to some basic membrane phenomena explained under (1) on p. 593 develops quite early, being present in preterm infants of 30 weeks gestation. It is rather the surplus inhibition due to the more complex, computational synaptic mechanisms explained under (2–5) on p. 593 which increases with gestational age.

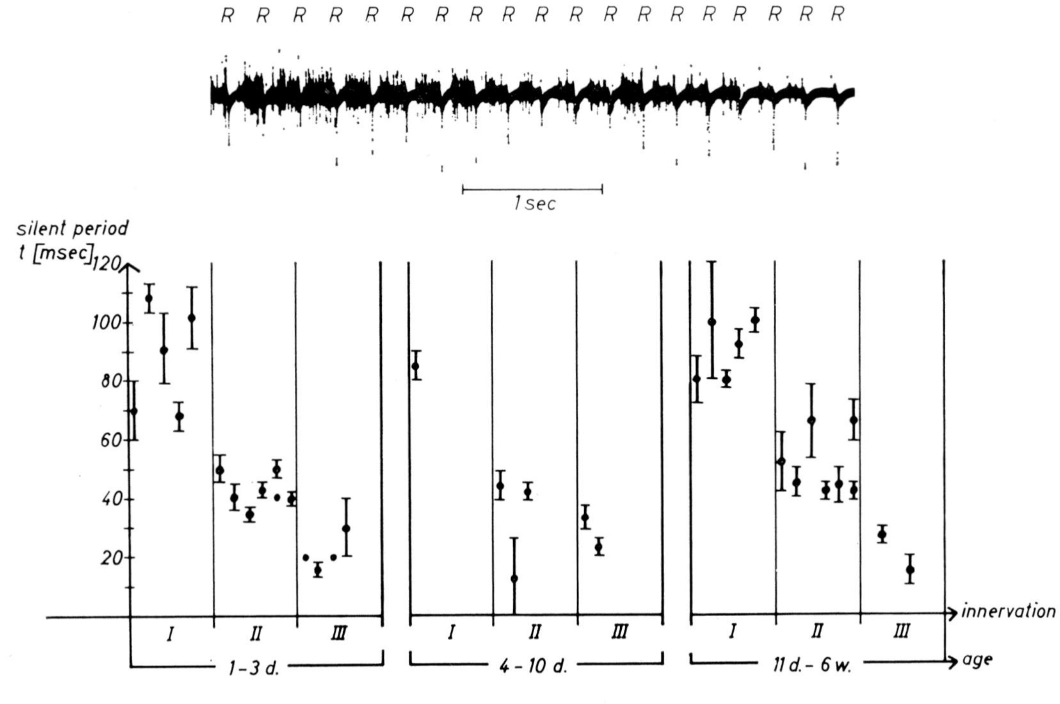

FIG. 8. Each quadriceps muscle reflex action potential evoked by tendon tap is followed by a silent period, the duration of which decreases with increasing background activity. The amount of background activity is indicated by I to III. I (weak), sparse activity, only single action potentials. II (moderate), background activity with one action potential immediately followed, sometimes even superimposed by another; III (strong), maximum activity with action potentials superimposing each other. The silent period is measured from the end of the reflex action potential to the recurrence of the background activity. Changes in the duration of the silent period which are possibly dependent on age were not statistically evaluated for the time after term-birth. (From Schulte 1970. *In* Stave, U., ed., *Physiology of the Perinatal Period*, Vol. 2. *Courtesy of Appleton-Century-Crofts Meredith Corporation, New York.*)

Rhythmic Motoneuron Activity

Rhythmic instead of tonic, i.e. sustained motoneuron activity occurs in some infants, particularly as part of the Moro reaction pattern or subsequent to phasic stretch reflexes (Fig. 10). Similar rhythms frequently occur spontaneously, particularly when the infant is crying. These rhythms show all of the neurophysiological characteristics of clonus rather than tremor.[240] Thus, the frequently seen rhythmic movements of the extremities and

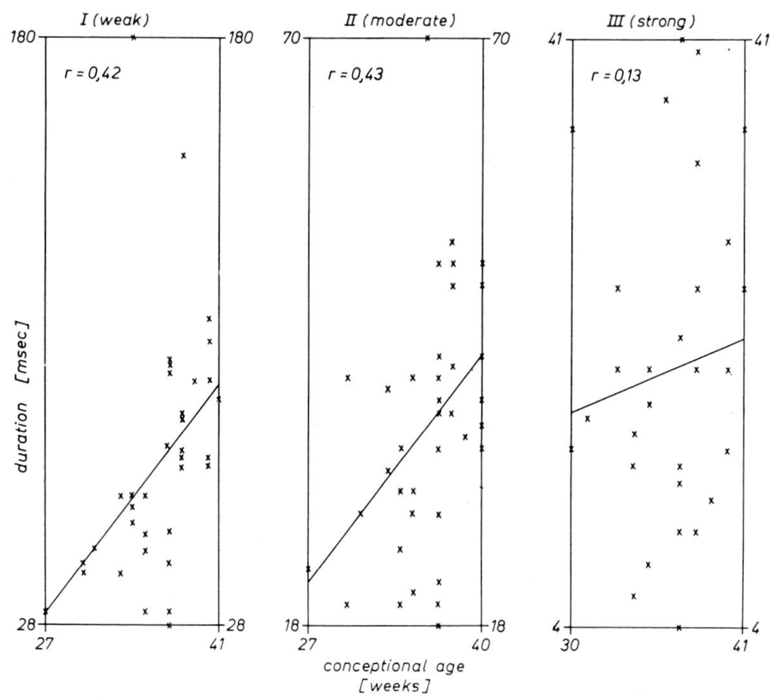

FIG. 9. The duration of the postreflex silent period (muscular quadriceps) is dependent upon background muscle activity (weak, moderate, strong), and it increases slightly with conceptional age. The Pearson correlation coefficient r is 0·42 during weak and 0·43 during moderate background activity. However, the duration of the silent period, subsequent to a monosynaptic reflex and elicited during strong muscle contraction, shows only little variation with age.

the jaw in human neonates are repetitive muscle stretch reflexes. In preterm infants of less than 34 weeks gestational

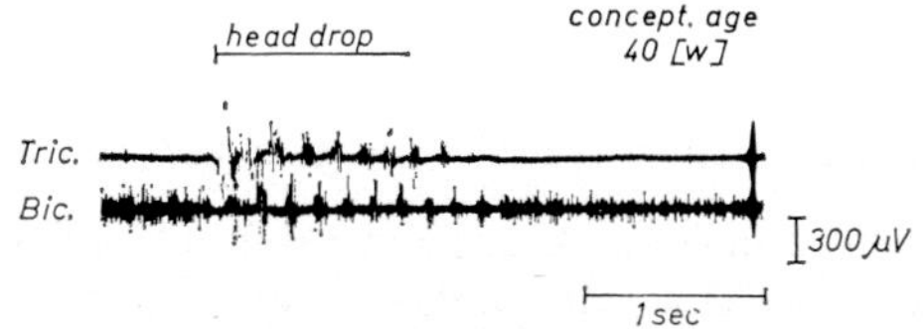

		infants with rhythmic MORO response	% of rhythmic activity Triceps	Biceps
preterm 34-38 w concept. age	27	9 (33 %)	28	22
term 39-41 w concept. age	17	5 (28 %)	23	10
hyperexcitable term	7	7 (100%)	65	85
small for dates abnormal gestation	15	8 (53,2%)	30	22,5

FIG. 10. In some newborn infants, particularly in hyperexcitable babies, the Moro response consists of rhythmic, rather than tonic, motoneurone discharges.

age, the rhythmic activity in arm and leg muscles is quite irregular. As infants become more mature, their histograms show increasing regularity (Fig. 11). Both the amount and the regularity of rhythmic motoneuron activity increases under some abnormal conditions. Particularly in hypertonic or hyperexcitable infants, rhythmic activity predominates. The clonus frequency is higher in the jaw muscles (10–12/sec.) than it is in arm and leg muscles (5–8/sec.).[228] The length of the reflex arc might have something to do with this. On the other hand, the spontaneous discharge frequency in single motoneurons originating from cranial motor nuclei is higher than that from spinal nuclei.[225]

Cutaneous Afferents and Exteroceptive Reflexes of the Newborn Infant

Stimulation of cutaneous sensory receptors gives rise via multiple interneurons to a more or less stereotypic activation of spinal motoneurons—the exteroceptive, polysynaptic reflexes. Reactions of this type are numerous, and they form an essential part of the neurological examination of newborn infants as well as of adults. They will not be described here, since they have been extensively discussed in the recent past.[229] In general the tendency for all exteroceptive reflexes, to irradiate is greater in more immature subjects.[22,127]

In the newborn there seems to be a principle difference in the manner of response of proprioceptive and exteroceptive reflexes during sleep. Whereas proprioceptive reflexes are diminished in active or rapid eye movement (REM) sleep, exteroceptive reflexes are either diminished during the wakeful state and two types of sleep. In particular, the motor responses to nociceptive stimuli, e.g. abdominal wall and Babinski reflexes, are found to be surprisingly independent of the infant's behavioural state.[152,206]

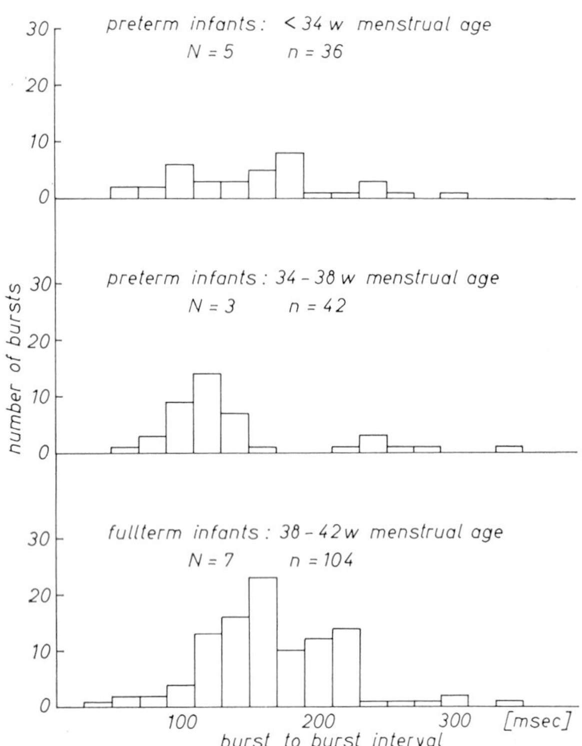

FIG. 11. Interval histograms of motoneurone bursts. The rhythmic motoneurone discharges in the course of a Moro reflex are more regular in full-term than in very immature preterm infants. (From Schulte 1970. *In* Stave, U., ed., *Physiology of the Perinatal Period*, Vol. 2. *Courtesy of Appleton-Century-Crofts Meredith Corporation, New York.*)

Vlach and co-workers[257,261] have been able to delineate a number of general rules regarding exteroceptive reflex response in premature and full-term newborn infants. Tactile stimulation of the skin over a muscle or muscle group activates motoneurons and elicits a reflex motor response that occurs only at the site of stimulation. The activation and response is stronger with stimulation of skin over flexor than over extensor muscles, and the area of skin over which a response can be elicited is larger for the flexors than for extensors. It seems to be a general rule that, as the newborn develops and becomes older, these zones become progressively smaller and more circumscribed.

Brain Structures and Neonatal Motor Behaviour

The Cerebellum. The cerebellum as a whole has no direct connection with the spinal motoneurons, so that its influence is one of regulating and stabilizing rather than executing movements. As far as one can judge from the literature, the cerebellum is of little significance for neonatal motor behaviour. Complete absence of the cerebellum, not easy to detect even later in life, can be present in a completely asymptomatic newborn. However, its destruction at a later stage usually results in dysregulation of muscle tone and posture and an inability to perform voluntary, skilled movements.

The Basal Ganglia. Ever since Foerster[87] coined the word "Pallidumwesen" in 1913, neonatal motor behaviour has been presumed to be primarily under the influence of pallidal neurons. Flexor posturing, climbing movements and the recurrence of grasp and palmomental reflexes in adults with cortical and striatal lesions probably represent pallidal influences upon spinal motoneurons. It is widely assumed that these motor phenomena disappear when the pallidum comes under striatal control.[196] Orthner and Roeder[185] found a similarity between certain stages of infantile motor development and extrapyramidal motor disturbances in adults before and after stereotactic operations. These authors hypothesize that the choreoathetotic kicking-about of the newborn infant represents a pallidal pattern which is replaced some weeks later by more ballistic movements under the influence of the corpus Luys. Interestingly enough, the nucleus niger becomes pigmented only when extrapyramidal motor skills are almost fully developed at around 3 or 4 years of age even though local myelination occurs as early as 2 or 3 months after term birth. According to Hassler,[110] the nucleus niger has a direct regulating and desynchronizing effect on spinal neurons. For many developmental neurophysiologists it does not seem justified to compare the motor activity of the newborn with similar patterns of severely traumatized adults. The motor behaviour of the newborn infant—if not unfairly studied under very restricted conditions—is already much too complex to be assigned only to certain brain structures.

Evidence of Cortical Motor Control in the Newborn Infant

Peiper[196] concluded that neonatal motor behaviour was entirely subcortical, although he was constantly searching for evidence of cortical nerve cell activity. EEG and evoked response studies have shown that bioelectric brain activity does change with certain behavioural states and during reactions to stimuli, thus indicating that the cortex at least takes part in these various states and response patterns. Dendritic arborization of Betz cells in the cerebral cortex, although occurring mainly postnatally, begins before birth, starting first in the motor area representing the trunk.[208] The myelination of pyramidal tract fibres is initiated before birth, and it is possible to elicit isolated movements in the toes and fingers by electrically stimulating unclassified cortical brain tissue in newborn infants with exencephaly (unpublished observation). Cortical lesions due to pre- or peri-natal insult, and later confirmed by radiographic studies, are sometimes clinically evident in the newborn period if a careful neurological examination is performed. Finally, cortical convulsive potentials registered in the EEG during neonatal seizures can often be demonstrated to occur synchronously with peripheral muscle contractions.

Admittedly, all these factors are hardly convincing evidence of cortical influence upon normal neonatal motor behaviour. On the other hand, in view of our present knowledge that behavioural mechanisms are the end result of all computational processes in a countless number of neuronal feedback circuits, it would be illogical to assume that well-documented cortical activity should have no influence upon a newborn infant's motor behaviour.

The Development of Somatomotor Function

The First Period—Up to 28 Weeks Gestational Age

The stages of development during this first period of gestation up to the 28th week remain largely obscure for humans since infants born alive during this period generally survive only briefly. The limited information available stems from observations made on live abortuses or fetuses obtained by way of Caesarean section secondary to ectopic pregnancy.[20,27,86,104,121,122,123,124,125,126,131,132,133,134,173,174,175] Comparable observations on animals are much more abundant, but because of varying rates of development and differences in length of gestation, only approximate comparisons can be made.

Actual reflex activity begins with the exteroceptive reflexes, first elicitable in the trigeminal region with sensory stimulation to the lips. Not until $9\frac{1}{2}$ weeks gestational age can one observe motor responses distal to the point of stimulation; these are mass movements with flexion of contralateral neck trunk muscles. At 12 weeks the embryo actually turns with lip and head movements towards the source of the stimulus; a little later he makes his first sucking movements. Thus, the reflex movements associated with the uptake of food develop out of the more global pattern of skin reflexes. As indicated above, the trigeminal area leads in the development of exteroceptive reflexes. Out of this temporal lead develops a later one of quality as well. The palmar region follows the oral area in the earliest development of exteroceptive reflexes, and it remains a very sensitive skin area even later. At $12\frac{1}{2}$ weeks one observes the first components of the grasp reflex. At about the same time movements of the lower extremities can be elicited by stimulation of the genital region. A withdrawal reflex response of the lower extremities can be obtained at 16 weeks by stimulating the soles of the feet.

The movements of the embryo and young fetus have a peculiar character. They are phasic, which means that innervation is of short duration; they are little influenced by other factors; and they are only minimally inhibited from secondary afferent sources. In summary, they are widely irradiating, poorly differentiated and always uniform in pattern. The duration of muscle contraction itself, however, is rather long; increments and decrements occur slowly.[19,20,21]

Coinciding with the appearance of exteroceptive reflexes in the 10th gestational week is the generation of electrical activity in the brain stem. Electrical responses in the pontine structures of the human fetus following cutaneous stimulation of the oral region can be detected in the 14th week. However, these evoked potentials fatigue rapidly.[20]

The development of the sensory receptor end-organs is in no way complete when exteroceptive reflexes first appear. It is during the 10th week of gestation that the very first nerve fibres reach the epithelium of the lips, their endings being still totally undifferentiated. Primitive, disc-shaped sensory terminals develop during the 14th week. The Meissner and Pacinian corpuscles are not formed until the 26th and 30th week respectively.[16,41,112,119,197]

The proprioceptive or muscle stretch reflexes develop later than the exteroceptive reflexes in animals and man. The gastrocnemius stretch reflex is barely elicitable at 13 weeks gestation;[20] it is routinely present in human fetuses around the 16th week. The development of muscle stretch receptors, namely muscle spindles, begins at 14 weeks in facial and respiratory muscles.[112] Initially, primitive end-organs known as "prespindles" are formed. Not until 24–26 weeks of gestation are the final muscle spindles complete with their complex anatomical structures (*see* p. 588).

Reciprocal effects of excitation and inhibition can first be observed at 18 weeks.[20] By this age, the gastrocnemius stretch reflex can be inhibited by simultaneous stimulation of the sole of the foot. Alterations in exteroceptive reflex patterns following combined stimulation at different locations (e.g. on the face and the hand) were demonstrated by Humphrey and Hooker[133,134] initially at 14 weeks gestational age.

Respiratory movements subsequent to hypoxia can first be seen as early as the 12th week; at 19 weeks they appear routinely under these circumstances.

The Second Period—from 28–40 Weeks Gestation

The stages of development during this second period of gestation between the 28th and 40th week can be followed closely with premature infants. St.-Anne Dargassies,[219,222,223,224] has presented evidence that neurological development is mainly dependent upon gestational age, while being largely independent of postnatal age. As far as neurological behaviour is concerned, it matters little whether an infant with a conceptional age of 40 weeks reached this age *in utero* or spent a later portion of the time as a premature. We think it likely, however, that very precise behavioural analysis will uncover more and more differences between the two, even though the findings of St.-Anne Dargassies have basically been confirmed.[10,34,212] It is thus possible to determine conceptional age on the basis of the neurological examination provided the infant is healthy. Almost every kind of central nervous system pathology and many other diseases, such as electrolyte disturbances, can alter the infant's motor behaviour. A number of neonatal reflexes are especially useful in determining gestational age in normal newborns since their development proceeds in spurts at particular time periods during gestation rather than showing continual progression

(Fig. 12).[38,82] As an example, the developmental changes of the Moro reflex will be discussed in greater detail.[234]

In preterm infants of less than 35 weeks gestational age the Moro response consists of a brisk extension and abduction of the upper extremities. Flexion and abduction is either missing or incomplete (Fig. 13). It is only after 35 weeks of gestational age that an infant develops the characteristic flexion posture of the full-term newborn, and concomitantly the extension and abduction component decreases whereas the flexion and abduction portion of the Moro response increases.

In spite of the high degree of variability in the Moro response pattern, a statistically significant decrease in the triceps/biceps activity ratio can be demonstrated with increasing age. Using electromyographic analysis, it can also be shown that the final flexor predominance of the Moro response pattern is the result of increasing flexor muscle activity with age and not a decrease in extensor activity (Fig. 14).

Neurophysiological studies of motor behaviour in unclassified groups of small-for-gestational-age newborn infants have led some authors to believe that the development of the fetal brain progresses independently of unfavourable gestational circumstances. However, more recent studies suggest that the motor behaviour of small-for-gestational-age infants is in fact different from that of normal-weight full-term infants.[82,172,176,239] The basic concept that brain development depends on age from conception, rather than on age from birth or body weight, still stands. However, more sophisticated methods of study, combined with an appropriate subdivision of small-for-gestational-age infants, have enabled us to detect consistent delay or abnormality in the motor behaviour of small-for-gestational-age infants compared with normal infants of the same gestational age. Muscle tone and general excitability are lower than normal, resembling in some respects the motor behaviour of preterm infants (Fig. 15). The Moro reflex also can show an immature pattern in full-term, small-for-gestational-age newborn infants (Fig. 16).

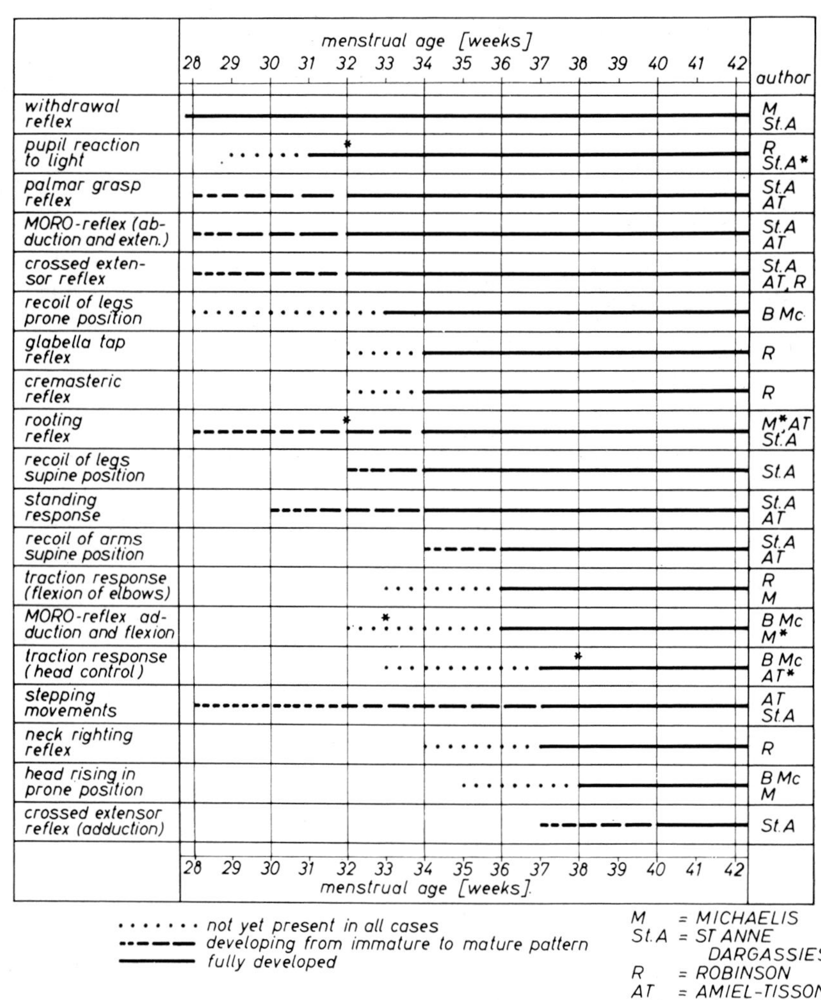

FIG. 12. The developmental sequence of various reflexes and motor automatisms. (Data compiled by R. Michaelis according to Amiel-Tison, Babson and McKinnon, Michaelis, Robinson and Saint Anne-Dargassies.) See also page 619.

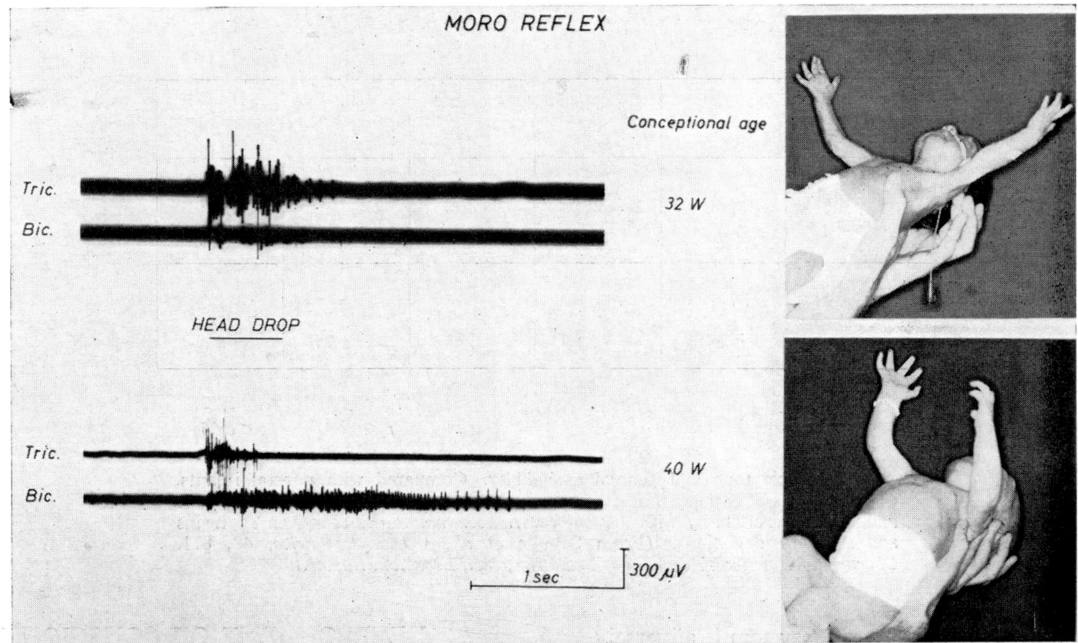

FIG. 13. At 32 weeks menstrual age, the Moro response consists of the extension and abduction of the upper extremities. With increasing maturity, both extension and abduction decrease, while adduction and flexion become more prominent. EMG activity, subsequent to the head drop, starts in the triceps muscle and is outlasted by the biceps in full-term newborn infants. (From Schulte *et al.*, 1968a, *Develop. Psychobiol.*, **1**, 41–47. *Courtesy of John Wiley and Sons, Inc.*)

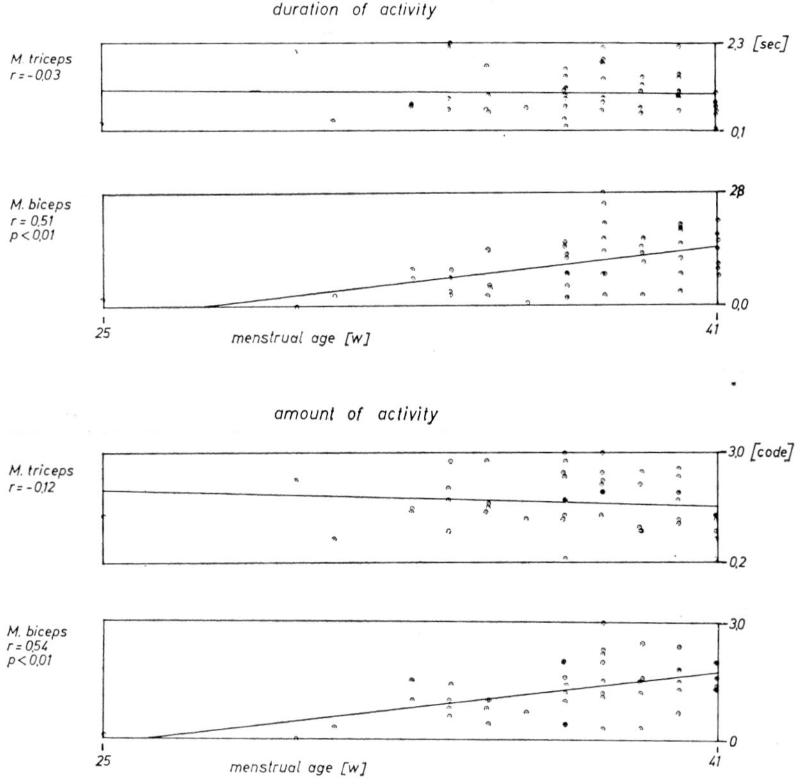

FIG. 14. Moro reflex. Regression lines for the amount and duration of biceps activity rise with increasing menstrual age; the product-moment correlation is significant. Triceps activity shows no significant alteration with age. (From Schulte *et al.*, 1968a. *Develop. Psychobiol.*, **1**, 41–47. *Courtesy of John Wiley and Sons, Inc.*)

MUSCLE TONE AND GENERAL EXCITABILITY

	gestational age [w]	conceptional age [w]	birth weight [g]	muscle tone score	excitability score
control infants N = 21	39,0 ± 1,7	40,0 ± 1,7	3 174 ± 478	24,1 ▲ ± 3,0	36,6 ● ± 2,7
small for gest. age. infants of toxemic mothers N = 21	39,0 ± 1,8	40,2 ± 1,9	2 158 ± 322	19,0 ▲ ± 8,5	30,8 ● ± 9,3

▲ $\hat{t} = 2{,}58$, $p < 0{,}05$ ● $\hat{t} = 2{,}72$, $p < 0{,}05$

FIG. 15. Muscle tone and general excitability. Compared with normal infants. SGA neonates of toxemic mothers have significantly lower scores for muscle tone and general excitability with a greater variance. All values are given as means and standard deviations. (From Schulte *et al.*, 1971b. *Pediatrics*, **48**, 871. *Courtesy of American Academy of Pediatrics, Inc., Evanston, Illinois.*)

The maturation of the fetal nervous system is adversely affected by intra-uterine malnutrition. Recent investigations into the biochemical results of malnutrition during intra-uterine development have shown defective myelination[54] as well as neurocellular growth retardation.[55,268,269,274] That the neurophysiological abnormalities might be the functional correlate of brain cell reduction and myelination deficit is an unproven though stimulating hypothesis.

DEVELOPMENT OF CONSCIOUSNESS AND ITS BIOELECTRICAL CORRELATES

Studies concerning newborn consciousness are particularly problematical. Peiper[196] has exhaustively related the efforts of philosophers and psychologists from Herodot to Freud to explore the psyche of newborn infants. Through the influence of Peiper, Andre-Thomas and St.-Anne Dargassies, Prechtl, Wolff, Papoušek, Bower and others,

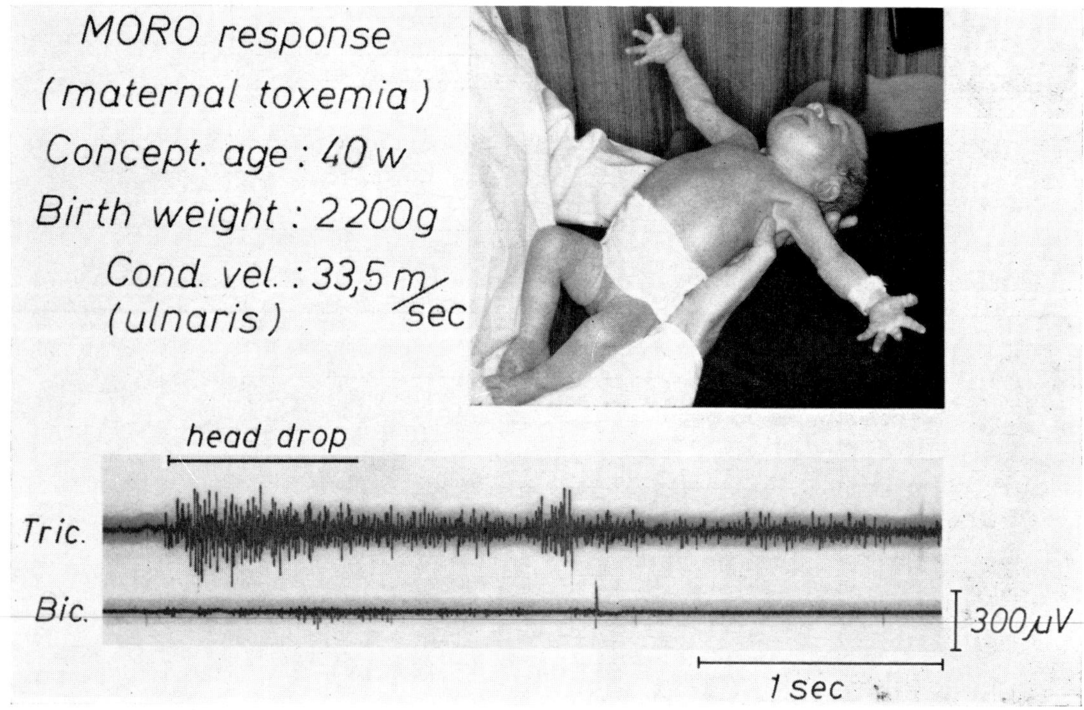

FIG. 16. The Moro reflex of this full-term small-for-gestational-age infant with maternal toxemia is, as an example, quite immature with predominant abduction and extension. In the electromyogram the biceps activity is almost absent and not-as in normal full-term infants—out-weighting and out-lasting the triceps activity. Ulnar nerve conduction velocity and the EEG during sleep were consistent with a conceptional age of 40 weeks or older. (From Schulte *et al.*, 1971b. *Pediatrics*, **48**, 871. *Courtesy of American Academy of Pediatrics, Inc. Evanston, Illinois.*)

research into the psychology of infants has become behavioural in its orientation and philosophical discussion concerning consciousness has been replaced with experimentation including bioelectric assessment of brain activity. This approach followed the discovery by Magoun and Moruzzi and their associates that the reticular formation of the brain stem represents the crucial area for regulating excitatory and inhibitory influences upon both the spinal cord and the cortex thereby decisively affecting brain mechanism including sleep and wakefulness as well as muscular activity.[161,162,180,181,182,211,215,248,249]

The analysis of bioelectric activity with simultaneous observation of behaviour has in recent years led to a wholly new concept of the basic mode of function of the central nervous system. The classical stimulation and denervation experiments were conceived out of the notion that the brain operated in a deterministic fashion under the rule of specific centres. With the introduction of cybernetic theory and computers, and with the investigation of various model synapses, this deterministic concept was replaced by another one in which the CNS was held to operate on the basis of probabilities.[31,32,33] At the synapse, excitatory and inhibitory afferent impulses arising from various sources are totaled millisecond for millisecond and the sum determines the actual reaction of the individual cell, the cell aggregate and an entire system.

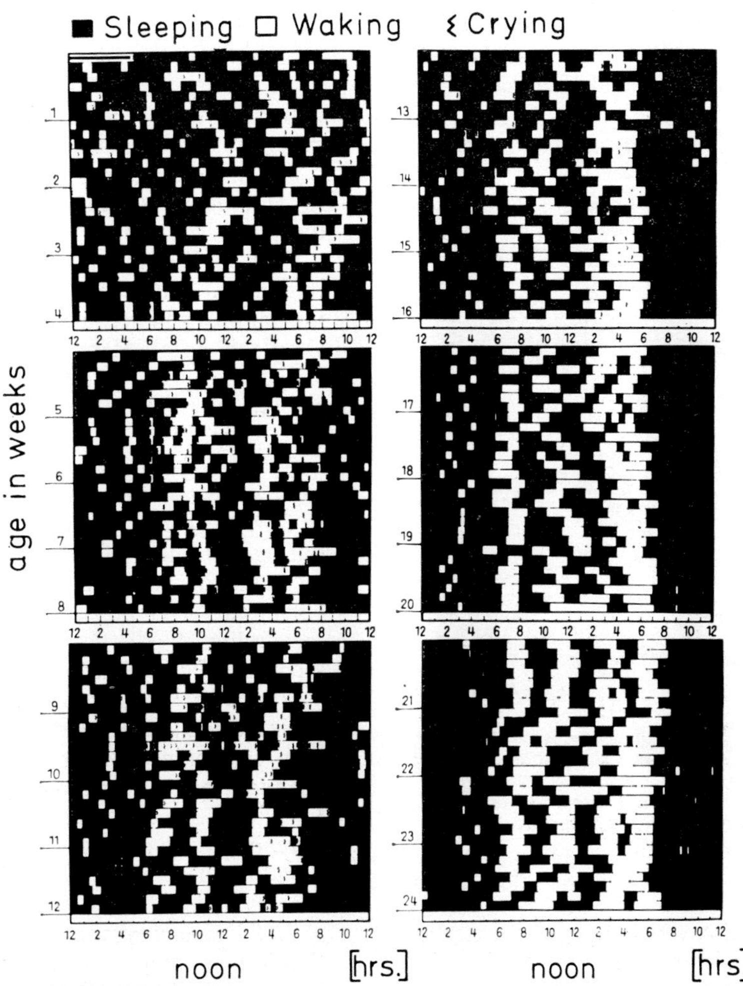

FIG. 17. Behaviour-Day-Chart. Sleeping, waking and crying time of healthy infants. (From Parmelee 1961, *Acta Paed. Scand.*, **50**, 160–170. *Courtesy of Almqvist and Wiksells, Uppsala.*)

Sleep Behaviour

The development of a sleep–wakefulness cycle in preterm and full-term neonates as well as in infants and children has been studied namely by Parmelee and his co-workers (for complete review of literature *see*[150]). As graphically characterized in Fig. 17, periods of sleep and wakefulness are initially disorganized, alternating at short intervals. From the 4th week after full term birth on, the periods become longer, and sleeping or being awake is referred during certain times of day. Fifteen weeks after full term birth a constant periodicity has developed. A full-term newborn infant sleeps an average of 15–18 hr. a day. The individual periods of sleep last at the most 4–5 hr., awake periods a maximum of 2–3 hr. Thus postnatal development consists of a reduction in the total amount of sleep, lengthening of the sleep and wakefulness periods, and a shift from day-time to night-time sleeping.

Sleep is not uniform. As early as 1891/1892 Czerny observed irregular pulsation of the anterior fontanelle in sleeping infants which appeared in a cyclic fashion alternating with phases of completely regular fontanelle pulsations. Cyclic alteration in the depth of sleep and the intensity of motor activity were later described by Irwin,[138] Wagner,[259,260] Gesell and Amatruda[95] as well as Eckstein and Paffrath.[74] In 1913, Zipperling[275] reported a "peculiar type of motor excitatory state" in sleeping preterm infants which he labelled "Stäupchen." He observed that shortly after falling to sleep the preterm infant would go through 15–60 min. periods with very rapid eye movements and other muscular twitchings. Aserinsky and Kleitman[9] and

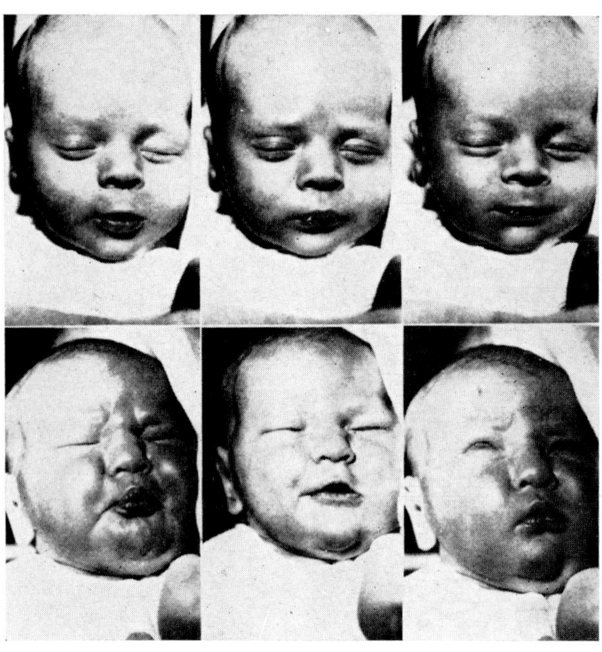

FIG. 18. Sleeping infants during REM sleep. (From Joppich and Schulte 1968, *Neurologie des Neugeborenen. Courtesy of Springer Verlag, Heidelberg.*)

Dement and Kleitman[50] rediscovered these phenomena, quantified the data and made them known worldwide under the heading of "rapid eye movement" or REM sleep. Following the suggestion of Dreyfus-Brisac we have chosen to label REM sleep "active" and sleep without eye movements "quiet" sleep (non-REM: NREM).

In sleeping adults, a cycle of the two types is completed in approximately 90 min.; it invariably begins with quiet sleep. About 20 per cent of total sleep in healthy adults is active (REM) sleep, and it is mainly after wakening from REM sleep that subjects can recall dreams.

Many neurophysiological and biochemical phenomena are associated with the different phases of sleep. In quiet sleep, breathing and heart rate are quite regular, whereas in active sleep they are irregular and somewhat accelerated.[213,247,270] The cerebral blood flow[143] and brain temperature increase during active sleep.

A large number of fine movements of fingers, toes, extremities and face occur in active sleep, especially in the case of preterm and full-term newborn infants. Tcheng and Laroche,[253] Petre-Quadens,[198] as well as Joppich and Michaelis[140] observed that preterm and full-term newborn infants smile and grimace during this phase of sleep (Fig. 18). We assume these facial movements are not an expression of psychic processes comparable to the later-appearing conscious smiling, but rather represent irradiation of rhombencephalic excitation which include the motor nuclei of cranial nerves. Eye movements are also interpreted in the same fashion. Prechtl and Lenard[205] have hypothesized that the rapid eye movements which occur in a complex random pattern, are the result of random noise in the vestibular nuclei caused by deprivation of patterning sensory inflow, for inhibition of various afferent pathways accompanies bursts of rapid eye movements.

Spinal motoneuron excitability responsible for tendon or H reflexes is extinguished by supraspinal inhibition during active sleep.[12,91,92,93,97,98,99,100,114,115,144,206]

Only ineffective, short muscle contractions escape the inhibition. Whereas certain muscle groups, e.g. the submental musculature, are tonically innervated during quiet sleep, this sustained innervation is obliterated during active sleep.[61,139,139a,188] Polysynaptic or exteroceptive reflexes are almost totally absent in newborns during periods of quiet sleep.[206]

Armstrong and associates[8] found gastric juice secretion to be increased during active sleep. Penile erection occurs in 30–50 per cent of all male subjects, including infants, during this phase of sleep.[85] The osmolarity of the urine increases during active sleep, probably as a result of enhanced ADH production and excretion of adrenaline metabolites.[165,166] During quiet sleep, there is increased secretion of growth hormone.[120]

Jouvet[141,141a] proposed that the raphe nuclei of the brain stem of the cat constitute a system—a "sleep lobby"—with serotonin as a transmitter, which when activated produces quiet or slow-wave or NREM sleep.[30,101,141,168,216] The locus coeruleus, on the other hand, with norepinephrine as a transmitter, would produce active or paradoxical or REM sleep. However, the experiments of Wyatt *et al.*[221,272] with parachlorphenylalanine as well as with 5-hydroxytryptophan would lead one to conclude that in man, quite contrary to some experimental animals, serotonin facilitates REM sleep.

There has been much speculation as to the significance of the two so essentially different stages of sleep. The hypothesis proposed by Oswald[186] seems especially plausible. According to Oswald, active sleep is accompanied by increased protein synthesis in the brain. Supporting this are the enhanced cerebral circulation and brain temperature during active sleep. This hypothesis helps to explain the fact that the duration of active sleep is relatively increased in newborn infants. According to this theory active sleep is a condition "chiefly for brain repair," and is therefore of great importance in the process of learning. Mentally retarded children and adults often exhibit relatively little active sleep.[81,191] The function of quiet sleep in contrast is "for bodily restitution." This concept is in agreement with the fact that the proportion of quiet sleep increases following strenuous physical work.[11,113]

Why Should the Paediatrician Follow the Rapidly Expanding Literature on Sleep?

Alternations between active and quiet sleep are also observed in preterm and full-term newborn infants.[49,213] With 50–60 per cent active sleep they spend relatively and absolutely much more time in this sleep state than do adults.[51,103,178,190,198] In preterm infants, there occur long periods in which it is impossible to determine with certainty which of the two types of sleep is present: transitional or ill-defined sleep.[52,53,189] In the case of very immature and previable infants of less than 27 weeks gestational age, sleep states cannot be classified in one of the two categories.[60] It appears that active sleep is the first to become manifestly organized, whereas quiet sleep follows later. In the course of postnatal development active sleep in increasingly displaced by quiet sleep.[250]

Figures 19 and 20 illustrate segments of polygraph recordings during quiet and active sleep of a full-term newborn infant. The rhythmic alternations between the two phases of sleep are illustrated in Fig. 21. The transition from quiet to active sleep occurs quite abruptly, whereas active sleep changes into quiet sleep more gradually; the entirety takes on a sawtooth pattern of fluctuation. The analysis of sleep behaviour has become an important tool for neurophysiological studies in both normal and abnormal infants.[61] It seems as if neonatal studies of this kind are particularly helpful, for the nervous system of the newborn offers so few alternatives for a detailed evaluation. The quite dramatic development of all parameters classifying sleep states between 26 and 53 weeks of conceptional age offers the unique possibility of assessing the infant's neurological maturity and, in longitudinal studies, for evaluating the infant's developmental progress.

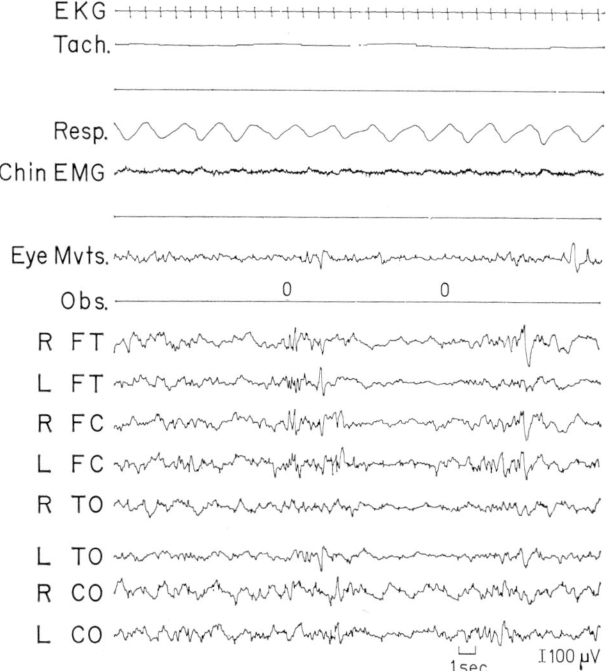

FIG. 19. Polygraphic recording of quiet sleep in a normal full term newborn infant. Observation (Obs) O indicates the infant did not move during this period of 20 seconds. Eye movements were recorded as an electro-oculogram. (Parmelee *et al.*, 1968. *In* Kellaway, P. and I. Petersén, eds. *Clinical Electroencephalography of Children. Courtesy of Almqvist and Widsells, Stockholm.*)

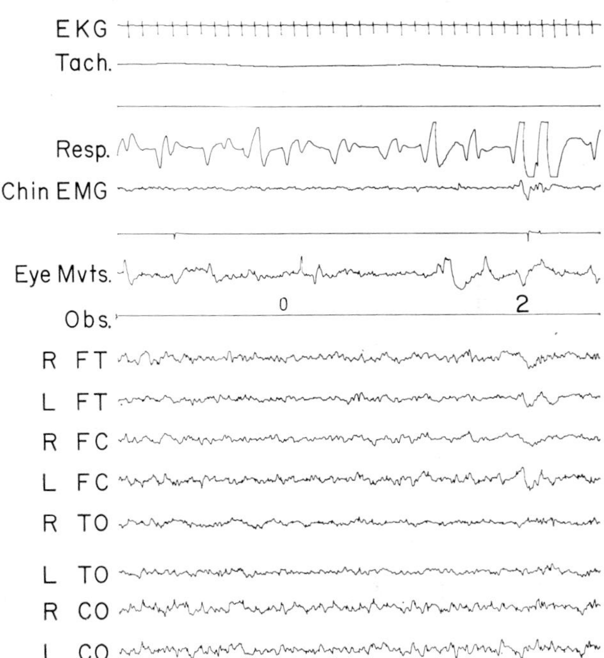

FIG. 20. Polygraphic recording of active sleep in a normal full term newborn infant. Observation (Obs) 2 indicates that there was a small body movement at this time. (Parmellee *et al.*, 1968. *In* Kellaway, P. and I. Petersén, eds. *Clinical Electroencephalography of Children. Courtesy of Almqvist and Widsells, Stockholm.*)

The coordination of the various parameters of a given sleep state, particularly the homeostasis of quiet sleep over a certain period of time, seems to be extremely vulnerable. It is only in the last few weeks before term that the infants are able to sustain quiet sleep with all its characteristics (regular respiration and heart rate, no body or eye movements, tonic submental muscle activity, high voltage *tracé alternant* EEG). With various kinds of pre- or perinatal pathology the neonatal brain loses this recently acquired ability to coordinate all these parameters and to maintain the still very labile state of quiet sleep for a normal period of 10–15 min.

The degree of dissociation of the various behavioural parameters in abnormal newborn infants extends from very minor deviation to complete absence of any cycling behaviour, thus indicating the severity of central nervous system damage.[177,190,202,233,234] In infants of diabetic mothers, for instance, quiet sleep is sometimes poorly defined with occasional eye movements and respiration remains more irregular with abnormally high frequencies.

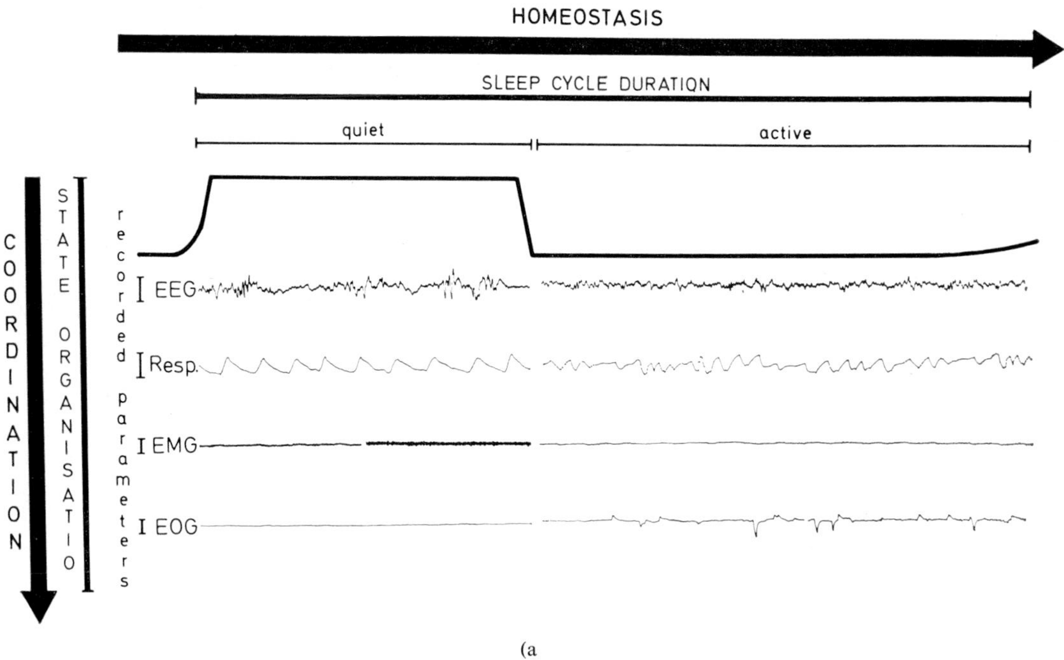

(a

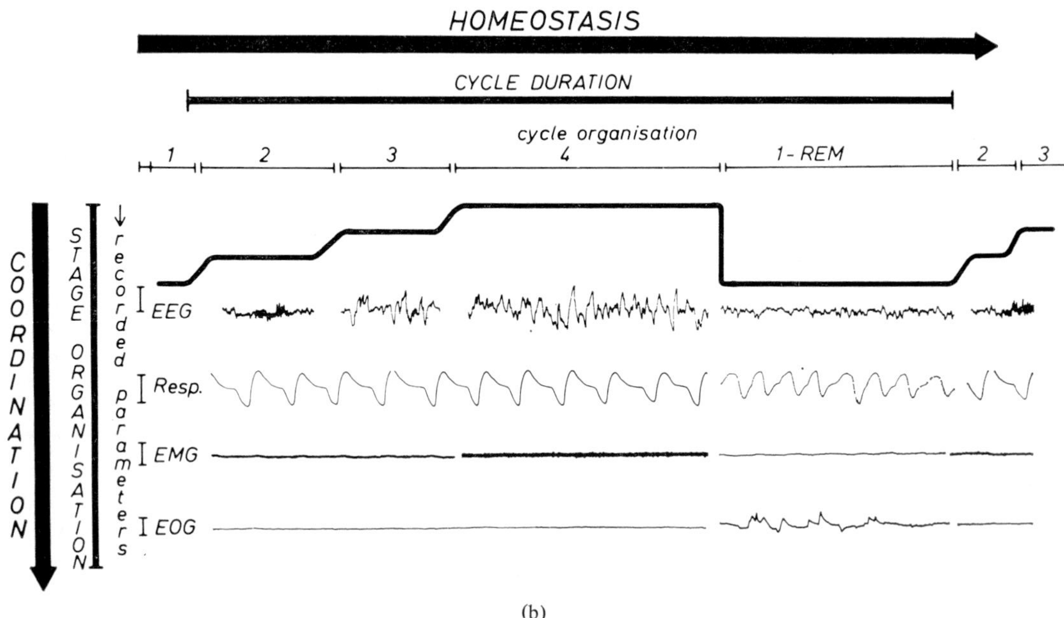

(b)

FIG. 21. The maintenance of certain sleep states over a period of time is called homeostasis. The state-appropriate function of all systems, is called coordination (Lenard, 1970). Active sleep with irregular respiration and rapid eye movements (REM). Quiet sleep with regular respiration and tonic muscle activity in the electromyogram of the submental muscles. Each state (active or quiet sleep) is characterized by certain parameters, only a few of which are depicted in this schematic diagram. Many biochemical and endocrine functions are also changing with sleep states. (a) In the neonate, quiet sleep is uniform. (b) In older infants quiet sleep can be subdivided in three different stages.

This is the characteristic sleeping behaviour of more immature infants. Some small-for-gestational-age newborn

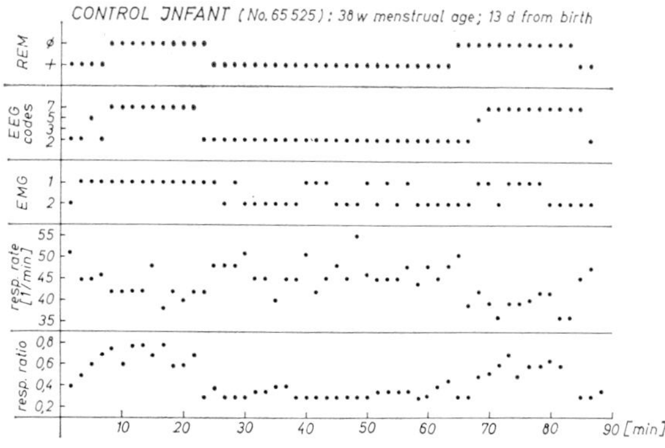

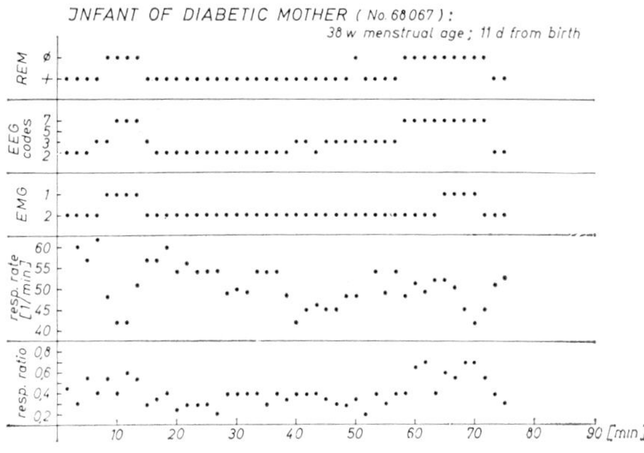

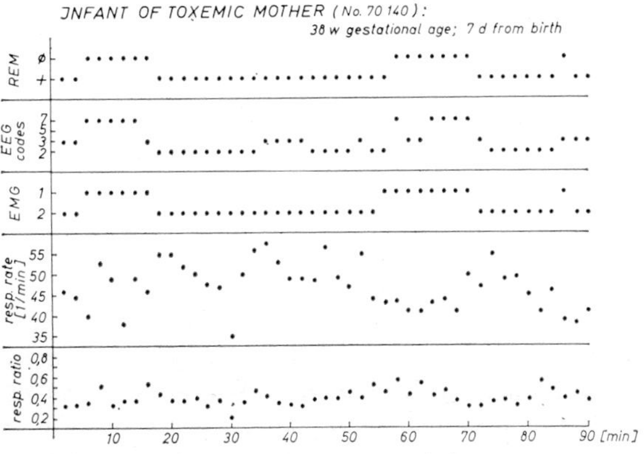

FIG. 22. Compiled polygram of one normal, one infant of diabetic mother and one small-for-gestational-age newborn infant. In the abnormal infants the durations of the two quiet sleep periods are shorter. Moreover, in the abnormal infants the EEG patterns are inconsistent and the respiration remains irregular during quiet sleep. REM: Ø = absent; + = present. EEG codes: (Fig. 1). EMG: 1 = tonic submental muscle activity; 2 = phasic or absent submental muscle activity. Respiration ratio: shortest/longest breath-to-breath interval within 20-sec epoch. (*Courtesy of Schulte et al.*, 1971a., *Neuropädiatrie*, **4**, 439. *Hippokrates Verlag, Stuttgart.*)

infants of toxaemic mothers also show a disturbed sleeping behaviour with poorly co-ordinated quiet sleep (Fig. 22).

The Spontaneous Electroencephalogram of the Newborn Infant

Historical Review. Berger[17] was the first to record human electroencephalograms (EEG), following the much earlier discovery of bioelectric cerebral activity in animal experiments by Caton[40] and by Beck.[15] Berger[18] in fact himself recorded an EEG from a 35-day-old infant. Smith,[246] Loomis and co-workers,[148] and Lindsley[154] were the first authors to deal with the development of the EEG in young infants. They noted that the dominating frequency of voltage fluctuations in the EEG of the newborn is lower than in children and adults. Hughes and associates[129,130,130a] made the first frequency analysis of the electroencephalogram of sleeping newborn babies. Gibbs and Knott[96] as well as Bartoshuk[14] published voltage/frequency analyses from both preterm and full-term newborn infants. Hughes *et al.*,[130a] Mai *et al.*[162a] and Mai and Schaper[163,164] described the discontinuous character of the EEG of preterm infants. Schroeder and Heckel[227] were the first to describe the typical sleep EEG of the newborn with its groups of high amplitude sharp waves against a background of lower voltage activity. They named these paroxysmus "Schlafgruppen." In 1950 began the systematic investigation of the EEG of preterm and full-term newborn infants during the different stages of sleep by Dreyfus-Brisac and Fischgold and their co-workers.[56,57,58,58,62,63,64,65,66,84,251] The findings of the Paris school have been substantiated and extended.[36,37,76,184,193,195]

Bioelectric Brain Development. The development of the EEG in preterm and full-term newborn infants is basically dependent upon conceptional age. Birth weight and age from birth are less important factors. Prior to 28 weeks conceptional age the EEG allows for no clear discrimination between wakeful and sleeping states or the different phases of sleep.

At 30 weeks, the brain wave pattern during *active sleep* is one of slow, high amplitude delta waves with superimposed small beta sharp waves. With increasing age the slow and ultra-slow waves disappear and by about 38-40 weeks, at the time of term delivery, a continuous rhythm of 5–8 c./sec. waves predominates. By 48–52 weeks, intermediate waves with a frequency of 3–6 c./sec. determine the brain wave pattern during active sleep and thereafter very few further changes occur during the course of development.

In *quiet sleep*, the bioelectrical activity of the cerebral cortex remains discontinuous up to 42 weeks conceptional age. At approximately 32 weeks, along with phases of low or absent voltage production (the so-called "black-outs"), there appear bursts of high-amplitude delta or theta waves every 10–15 sec. which are superimposed on small beta sharp waves.[194] A 36–38 weeks conceptional age, the bursts of activity become less pronounced and the activity between these bursts gradually increases. The Paris school under Dreyfus Brisac offered the name "*tracé alternant*" and this term has subsequently gained general acceptance. The *tracé alternant* pattern is still easily recognized at 40 weeks, is barely distinguishable at 42 weeks and is no longer visible at 46 weeks. At 50 weeks

10 weeks after full term birth, sigma rhythms (10–14 sec.) or so-called "sleep spindles" appear imbedded in the continuous theta-delta activity.[151,171,233]

Figure 23 illustrates characteristic EEG patterns as seen in sections of polygraphic sleep recordings during active and quiet sleep from 28–52 weeks conceptional age. The descriptions of the various EEG patterns based on visual analysis are not easily compared with the power spectra obtained by means of modern computer analysis of the neonatal electroencephalograms (Fig. 24). With use of the all the minor differences[61] that exist between two infants of equal conceptional age but different gestational ages at birth.

All these electroencephalographic studies have led to the concept that fetal brain development is dependent on conceptional age rather than on body-weight. Basically this concept is correct and well supported by anatomical studies.[147] However, compared with control infants, the EEG patterns of small-for-gestational-age infants are significantly less mature in both active and quiet sleep.[62a,233]

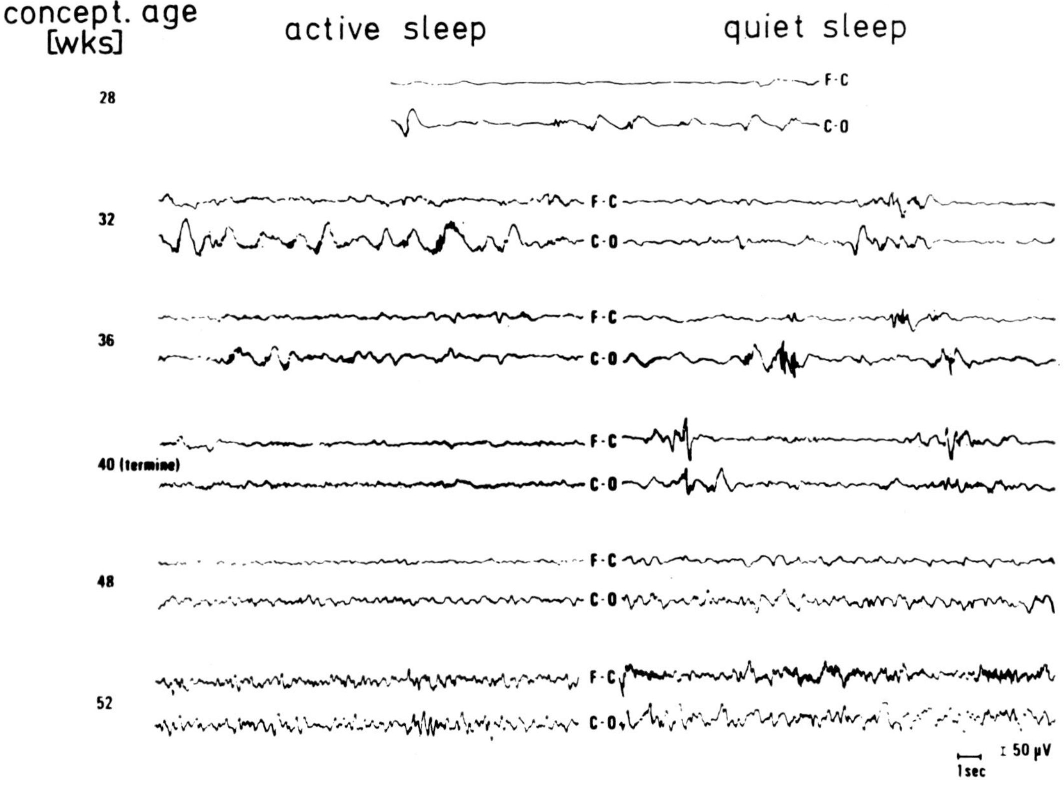

FIG. 23. EEG pattern development during active and quiet sleep from 28–52 weeks conceptional age (From Joppich and Schulte, 1968. *Neurologie des Neugeborenen. Cortesy of Springer Verlag, Heidelberg.*)

latter method, the very slow delta waves predominate in all stages of sleep and at every conceptional age.[202,232] For the detection of fine differences among certain bioelectrical patterns, visual interpretation is still superior to computer analysis; this is due to hitherto inadequate programming of computers for pattern analysis.

The waking EEG appears somewhat similar to that during active sleep, yet differences between the two are discernible in mature newborns. The very rhythmic theta waves are not found in the infant when awake; instead, the EEG is rather flat and polymorphic.

The EEG patterns recorded during wakefulness and during the various phases of sleep are typical for the conceptional age of an infant. A neonate born at 30 weeks gestation traverses outside the uterus, in approximately the same temporal sequence, all the bioelectrical activity patterns that are seen in infants born at 34, 36 or 38 weeks.[193] However, it is quite possible that present-day methods are simply not sensitive enough to detect and to quantify

Thus, conceptional age is therefore frequently underestimated in growth-retarded infants, whereas the estimation is more accurate in normal babies. Whatever the cause and the interpretation of these findings may be, the broad statement that nervous system maturation progresses independently of the nutritional status of the fetus is no longer acceptable. The biochemical and anatomical findings of Dobbing,[54,55] Widdowson,[264] Zamenhof *et al.*[274] and Winick[266] on brain development after fetal malnutrition may well have a functional correlate.

The maturation of the EEG has its anatomical and bioelectrical correlates in the process of dendritic branching and in the formation of intracortical axodendritic synapses. The transmission of impulses from one neuron to the other is probably rendered possible by metabolic processes in the oligodendroglia.[2,88,226] Synaptic impulse transmission is associated with electrical voltage fluctuation at the dendritic membrane. According to the present concurring opinions of Caspers,[39] Purpura,[207] Eccles,[70] Grundfest,[109] Jung[142] and Creutzfeld and associates,[44] the electroencephalogram represents the algebraic sum of all synaptic potentials in the dendritic structures of the cerebral cortex.

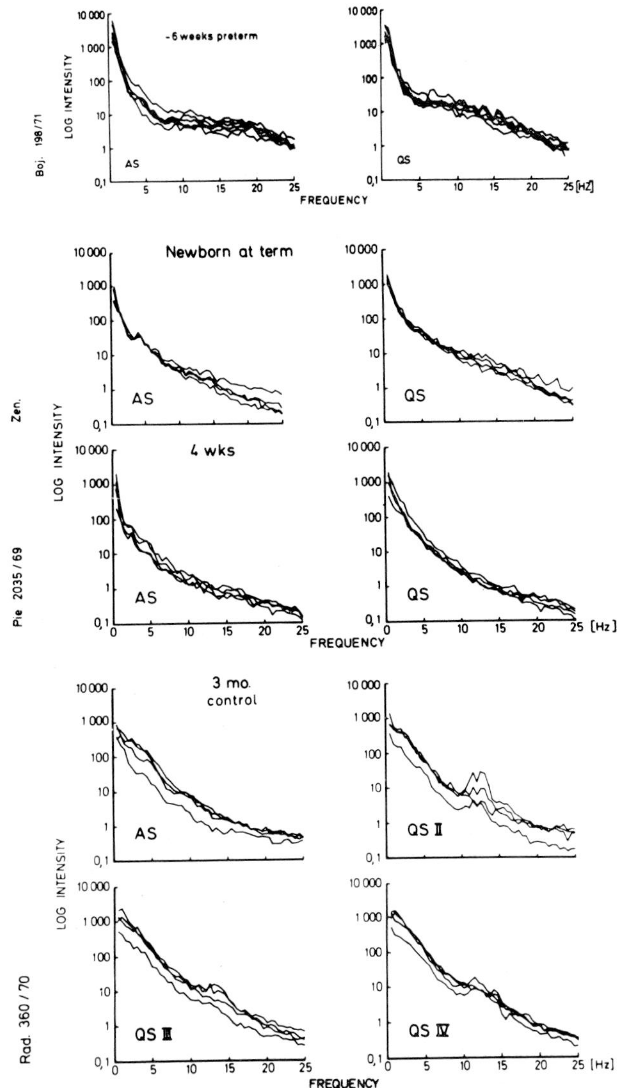

FIG. 24. Autospectrograms of EEGs during various sleep states and stages. As = active sleep. QS = quiet sleep. For infants younger than one month no attempt was made to differentiate quiet sleep stages II, III and IV. Abscissa: frequency in Hertz (c/s) Ordinate: logarithm (base 10) of intensity, units proportional to uV^2. The four (or six) lines on each graph represent various EEG leads: FP_2—C_4, FP_1—C_3, C_4—O_2, C_3—O_1, O_2—T_4 and O_1—T_3.) Two developmental steps seem to occur rather constantly: (1) The relative decrease of power above 5 c/s during the last weeks before term birth; (2) the occurrence of 12–14 c/s sleep spindle activity with a high interhemispheric coherence at about 10 weeks after term birth, their increase to a peak power at about 6–8 months, and subsequent decrease.

Evoked Potentials in the Cerebral Cortex

Visual, auditory and sensory stimuli can produce potential shifts in the spontaneous EEG which are evident either by simple visual analysis of the electroencephalogram or with the help of an appropriately programmed computer (computer for average transients). Such voltage changes resulting from external stimuli are called evoked potentials. Subsequent to photic stimulation, evoked potentials can be identified over the occipital region in the EEG of all full-term newborns and many prematures. They represent responses to stimuli reaching the visual receptive cortex area.[48,77,79,80,128] A photically evoked potential usually shows an initial positive phase followed by a negative one. In immature infants the initial positive phase is often absent.[255] Furthermore, the amplitude and size of the photically evoked potentials from the cerebral cortex increase with conceptional age, probably due to progressing dendrite ramification. The latency in appearance of the potentials following photic stimulation amounts to approximately 210–230 m./sec. in preterm infants of 29 weeks conceptional age and 120–180 m./sec. in full-term newborns.

Rhythmic, stroboscopic stimulation with a frequency of 2–3 flashes per second results in synchronization of the EEG waves with the light stimulus (photic following) in 50 per cent of all full-term infants.[102] Approximately 50 per cent show flattening of the EEG and 35 per cent demonstrate vertex-negative potentials, which actually correspond to K-complexes of the adult EEG.[46,78,167] The responsiveness to repetitive visual stimulation increases markedly during the first 5 months of life[256]

In the EEG of preterm infants of more than 32 weeks of conceptional age loud noises produce a flattening of spontaneous activity, polymorphic theta-delta waves and/or vertex-negative waves of a few seconds duration.[65,66]

Soft clicks result in evoked potentials so small that they can only be identified after summation with the help of a computer.[13,105,262] When 50–150 stimulus responses from the cerebral cortex of newborns both preterm and full-term are summated, a complex evoked potential results with at least 2, but often as many as 5 waves with different latencies (Fig. 25). Preterm infants beyond 32 weeks conceptional age demonstrate auditory evoked potentials from the cerebral cortex;[230] however, these differ from those of full-term newborns in their form and latency.[1,108,230] The auditory evoked potential does not represent a specific response of the auditory receptive cortex area: rather, it is a nonspecific bioelectric arousal phenomenon projected towards the cerebral cortex and in particular the region of the vertex.[24] Such evoked potentials are nevertheless useful as a hearing test in young infants.

Hutt *et al.*[137] and Lenard *et al.*[153] found that the likelihood of an evoked auditory response in the human newborn was best for sine waves, less probable for voices and least for square-wave stimuli. Furthermore, sounds with low frequency are the most effective. Thus, the human voice qualifies as a potent alerting stimulus for the newborn, and this fact may well carry important implications for the formation of human bonds of affection.

The amplitude of evoked potentials is smaller in active sleep than in quiet sleep or wakefulness for newborns, just as it is in adult humans and animals.[45a,262,263,265,266,267] This reduction in amplitude is generally explained in terms of "occlusion": The neurons of the reticular formation are occupied during active sleep and are thus unable to transmit with full strength the synchronous, afferent impulses to the cortex.[263] We have reason to modify this interpretation[1] and think that the height of the evoked potentials is largely dependent upon the amplitude of the spontaneous EEG itself, an interpretation which is

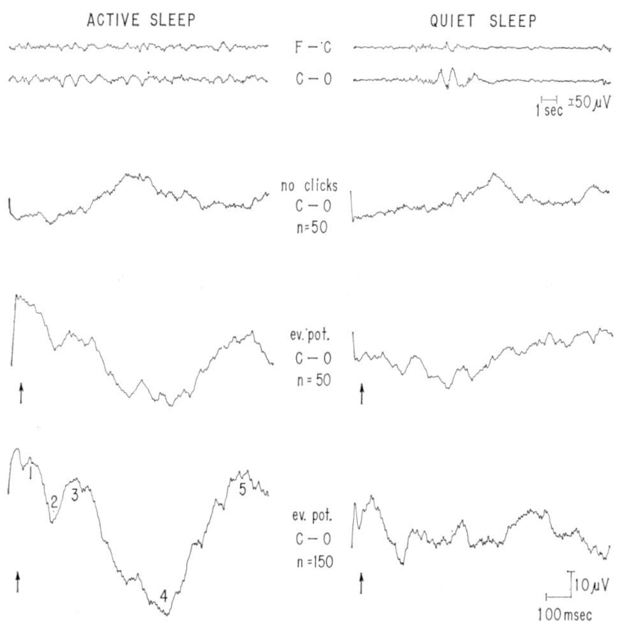

FIG. 25a. Acoustically evoked responses in a premature infant obtained during quiet sleep and active sleep using 50 and 150 clicks. The peaks are more prominent in active sleep. Upper two tracings show the background EEG.

not necessarily incompatible with the above-mentioned occlusion theory.

The newborn's response to auditory or other stimuli is not limited to the evoked potentials of the cerebral cortex. Changes in heart rate, respiratory rate and galvanic skin resistance have also been recorded and likewise successfully applied as response indicators in the audiometric testing of newborns.[28,45,155,201]

Perspectives

In recent years, the advancement of knowledge in our understanding of brain mechanisms has come up against a considerable difficulty: Research into the nervous system is following three different lines with three differently educated investigators:

(1) Investigators who are thoroughly trained in modern neuroanatomy, neurophysiology and clinical neurology have usually a great depth of knowledge about how the nervous system functions but they know strikingly little about the single biochemical steps which are certainly the basis of every neuronal mechanism.

(2) Biochemists who—usually late in their training—turn to neurochemistry quite frequently could not care less about nerve tracts and bioelectric brain phenomena. They are as meticulous with molecules and chromatography as they are sometimes crude in their neurophysiological reasoning.

(3) Behaviourists and psychologists have perhaps the broadest understanding of what the brain really does

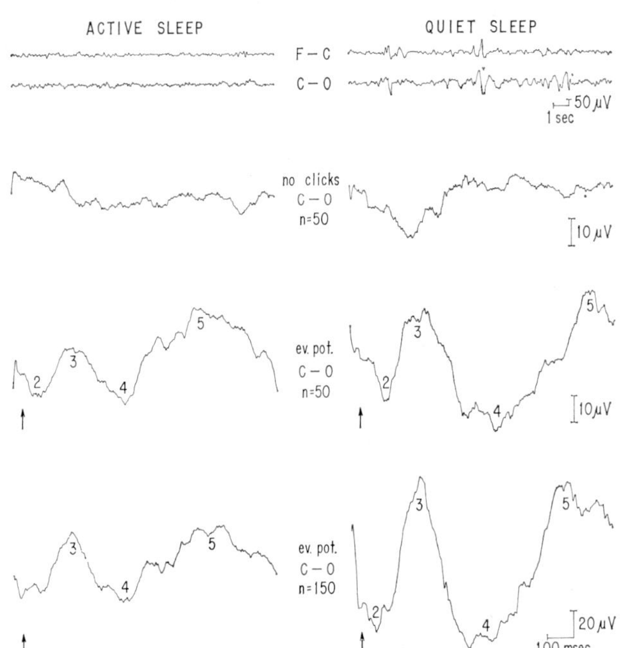

FIG. 25b. Acoustically evoked responses in a full term newborn infant during quiet sleep and active sleep. Top two tracings show the background EEG samples. (F-C = fronto-central; C-O = central-occipital). Fifty 1 sec samples averaged without clicks ("no clicks") show no patterning of the peaks. Increasing the number (n) of clicks from 50–150 enhances the peaks. Arrows: stimulus presentation. Note vertical scale differences between upper two and lower tracings. (Akiyama *et al.*, 1969. *Electroenceph. clin. Neurophysiol.*, **26**, 371–380. *Courtesy of Elsevier Publishing Company, Amsterdam.*)

but their application of neurophysiological techniques, for instance EEG, evoked responses and EMG is often very naïve.

I have the feeling that all three groups of investigators who are interested in the developing nervous system do not listen to each other and I would like to show this with myelination as an example.

In 1920 Flechsig propounded the idea that myelination of nerve tracts is the basis of psychomotor development. A little later it was A. Gesell[95] who actually initiated wide scale research into the psychological, intellectual and motor development of the child. In the last 50 years a great wealth of data has been accumulated in these two fields and we now know that myelination can hardly be responsible for major steps of motor (let alone intellectual) development since both may occur when myelination is already completed. They mainly do occur when the very little more myelin still to come is only that which would be required for an increase in conduction velocity in order to compensate for increasing distances with growth. Nevertheless neurochemists, who quite recently fell in love with brain lipids and myelin, do not hesitate to attribute to defects in myelination a wide variety of conditions responsible for almost everything they find lacking in nervous function.

A true correlative neurophysiological, biochemical and behavioural approach is needed to build up a body of knowledge about nervous activity which could be used for dealing with the development of children, both normal and abnormal.

REFERENCES

1. Akiyama, Y., Schulte, F. J. Schultz, M. A. and Parmelee, A. H. (1969), "Acoustically Evoked Responses in Premature and Full-term Newborn Infants," *Electroenceph. clin. Neurophysiol.*, **26,** 371–380.
2. Aladjalova, N. A. (1964), "Slow Electrical Processes in the Brain," in *Progress in Brain Research*, Vol. 7, pp. 1–243. Amsterdam: Elsevier Publ.
3. Amiel-Tison, C. (1968), "Neurological Evaluation of the Maturity of Newborn Infants," *Arch. Dis. Childh.*, **43,** 89–93.
4. André-Thomas, A. and Ajuriaguerra, J. (1949), *Etude sémiologique du tonus musculaire*. Paris: Flammarion.
5. André-Thomas, A., Chesni, Y. and Autgaerden, S. (1954), "A propos de quelques points de sémiologie nerveuse du nouveau-né et du jeune nourrisson. Exploration de quelques afférence. Reaction aux excitation digitales et palmaires. Rythme, inhibitions de réflexes. Aptitude statique et locomotrice des membres superieurs. Affect et affectivité," *Presse méd.*, **62,** 41–44.
6. André-Thomas, A. and Hanon, F. (1947), "Les premiers automatismes," *Rev. neurol.*, **79,** 641–648.
7. André-Thomas, A. and St. Anne-Dargassies, S. (1952), *Etudes neurologiques sur le nouveauné et le jeune nourisson.* Paris: Masson & Cie.
8. Armstrong, R. H., Burnap, D., Jacobson, A., Kales, A., Ward, S. and Golden, J. (1965), "Dreams and Gastric Secretion in Duodenal Ulcer Patients," *New Physician*, **14,** 241–243.
9. Aserinsky, E. and Kleitmann, N. (1955), "A Mobility Cycle in Sleeping Infants as Manifested by Ocular and Gross Bodily Activity," *J. appl. Physiol.*, **8,** 11–18.
10. Babson, S. G. and Mckinnon, C. M. (1965), "A Preliminary Report on the Neuromuscular Milestones in Premature Infant Development," 13th Annual Meeting of the Western Society for Pediatric Research, Portland (Oregon).
11. Baekeland F. and Lasky, R. (1966), "Exercise and Sleep Patterns in College Athletes," *Percept. Mot. Skills*, **23,** 1203–1207.
12. Baldissera, F., Broggi, G. and Mancia, M. (1964), "Spinal Reflexes in Normal Unrestrained Cats During Sleep and Wakefulness," *Experientia* (*Basel*), **20,** 577.
13. Barnet, A. B. and Goodwin, R. S. (1965), "Averaged Evoked Electroencephalographic Responses to Clicks in the Human Newborn," *Electroenceph. clin. Neurophysiol.*, **18,** 441–450.
14. Bartoshuk, A. K. and Tennant, J. M. (1964), "Human Neonatal EEG Correlates of Sleep-wakefulness and Neural Maturation," *J. Psychiat. Res.*, **2,** 73–83.
15. Beck, A. (1890), "Oznaczenie lokalizacyi w mozgn rolzenin za pomoca elektry czynch." Thesis, Krakau Univ., Jagiellonski.
16. Beckett, E. B., Bourne, G. H. and Montagna, W. (1956), "Histology and Cytochemistry of Human Skin. The Distribution of Cholinesterase in the Finger of the Embryo and the Adult," *J.* (*Physiol.* (*Lond.*), **134,** 202–206.
17. Berger, H. (1929), "Über das Elektroencephalogramm des Menschen," *Arch. Psychiat. Nervenkr.*, **87,** 527–570.
18. Berger, H. (1932), "Über das Elektroencephalogramm des Menschen. IV. Mitteilung," *Arch. Psychiat. Nervenkr.*, **97,** 6–26.
19. Bergström, R. M. (1962), "Prenatal Development of Motor Functions. A Study of the Intrauterine Guinea-pig Foetus in the Conscious, Pregnant Animal," *Ann. Chir. Gynaec. Fenn.*, suppl. 112, **51,** 1–48.
20. Bergström, R. M. and Bergström, L. (1963), "Prenatal Dvelopment of Stretch Reflex Functions and Brain Stem Activity in the Human," *Ann. Chir. Gynaec. Fenn.*, suppl. 117, **52,** 1–21.
21. Bergström, R. M., Hellström, P. E. and Stenberg, D. (1961), "Prenatal Stretch Reflex Activity in the Guinea-pig," *Ann. Chir. Gynaec. Fenn.*, **50,** 458–466.
22. Bergström, R. M., Hellström, P. E. and Stenberg, D. (1962), "Studies in Reflex Irradiation in the Foetal Guinea-pig, *Ann. Chir. Gynaec. Fenn.*, **51,** 171–178.
23. Bernuth, H. and Mortier, W. (1971), "Die neuromuskuläre Entwicklung in Abhängigkeit von Geburtsgewicht und Menstruationsalter," *Mschr. Kinderheilk*. In press.
24. Beyer, C. and Sawyer, Ch.H. (1964), "Effects of Vigilance and Other Factors on Non-specific Acoustic Responses in the Rabbit," *Exp. Neurol.*, **10,** 156–169.
25. Blom, S. and Finnström C. (1968), "Motor Conduction Velocities in Newborn Infants of Various Gestational Ages," *Acta paediat. scand.*, **57,** 377–384.
26. Blom, S. and Finnström, O. (1971), "Studies on Maturity in Newborn Infants. V. Motor Conduction Velocity," *Neuropädiatrie*, **3,** 129–139.
27. Bolaffio, M., and Artom, G. (1924), "Richerche sulla fisiologia del sistema nervosa del feto umano," *Arch. Sci. biol.*(*Bologna*), **5,** 457–487.
28. Bordley, J. E., Hardy, W. G. and Richter, C. P. (1948), "Audiometry with the Use of Galvanic Skin Resistance Response. A preliminary report," *Bull. Johns Hopk. Hosp.*, **82,** 569.
29. Boyd, J. A. (1962), "The Nuclear-bag Fibre and Nuclear-chain Fibre Systems in the Muscle Spindles of the Cat," Symposium on Muscle Receptors. Hong Kong: University Press.
30. Bradley, P. B. (1958), "The Effects of 5-hydroxytryptamine on the Electrical Activity of the Brain and on Behaviour in the Conscious Cat," In 5-Hydroxytryptamine, pp. 214–220 (G. P. Lewis, Ed.). London: Pergamon Press.
31. Brazier, M. A. B. (1962), "The Analysis of Brain Waves," *Sci. Amer.*, 142–153.
32. Brazier, M. A. B. (1964), "Stimulation of the Hippocampus in Man Using Implanted Electrodes," in *Brain Function*, Vol. II, pp. 299–310. Berkeley and Los Angeles: University Calif. Press.
33. Brazier, M. A. B. (1964), "The Electrical Activity of the Nervous System," *Science*, **146,** 1423–1428.
34. Brett, E. M. (1965), "The Estimation of Foetal Maturity by the Neurological Examination of the Neonate," *Clinics inDevelop. Med.*, pp. 105–117, No. 19, Publ. Spastics. Soc. Med. Education. London: W. Heinemann Medical Books.
35. Brown, B. H., Porter, R. W. and Whittaker, G. E. (1968), "Nerve Conduction Measurements in Spina Bifida Cystica," *Develop. Med. Child Neurol.*, suppl., **15,** 70–73.
36. Canova, G. and Cossandi, E. (1956), "The EEG of the Premature Newborn," *Riv. Clin. pediat.*, **58,** 51–62.
37. Carpenter, F. G. and Bergland, R. M (1957), "Excitation and Conduction in Immature Nerve Fibers of the Developing Chick," *Amer. J. Physiol.*, **190,** 371–376.
38. Casaer, P. and Akiyama, Y. (1970). "The Estimation of the Postmenstrual Age: A Comprehensive Review," *Develop. Med. Child Neurol.*, **12,** 697–729.
39. Caspers, H. (1959), "Über die Beziehungen zwischen Dendritenpotential und Gleichspannung an der Hirnrinde," *Pflügers Arch. ges. Physiol.*, **269,** 157–181.
40. Caton, R. (1875), "The Electrical Currents of the Brain," *Brit. med. J.*, **2,** 278.
41. Cauna, N. (1956), "Structure and Origin of the Capsule of Meissner's Corpuscle," *Anat. Rec.*, **124,** 77–93.
42. Cerra, D. and Johnson, E. W. (1962), "Motor Nerve Conduction Velocity in Premature Infants," *Arch. phys. Med.*, **43,** 160–164.

43. Churchill-Davidson, H. C. and Wise, R. P. (1963), "Neuromuscular Transmission in the Newborn Infant," *Anesthesiology*, **24,** 271–278.

44. Creutzfeldt, O. D., Fuster, J. M., Lux, H. D. and Nacimiento (1964), "Experimenteller Nachweis von Beziehungen zwischen EEG-Wellen und Aktivität corticaler Nervenzellen," *Naturwissenschaften*, **51,** 166–167.

45. Crowell, D. H., Davis, C. M., Chun, B. J. and Spellacy, F. J. (1965), "Galvanic Skin Reflex in Newborn Humans," *Science*, **148,** 1108–1111.

45a. Dagnino, N., Favale, E., Loeb, C. *et al.* (1965), "Sensory Transmission in the Geniculostriate System of the Cat." *J. Neurophysiol.*, **28,** 443–456.

46. Davis, H., Davis, P. A., Loomis, A. L., Harvey, E. N. and Hobart, G. (1939), "Electrical Reactions of the Human Brain to Auditory Stimulation During Sleep," *J. Neurophysiol.*, **2,** 500–514.

47. Davison, A. N. and Dobbing, J. (1966), "Myelination as a Vulnerable Period in Brain Development," *Brit. med. Bull.*, **22,** 40–44.

48. Dawson, G. D. (1947), "Cerebral Response to Electrical Stimulation of Peripheral Nerve in Man," *J. Neurol Neurosurg. Psychiat.*, **10,** 137–140.

49. Delange, P. C., Cadilhac, J. and Passouant, P. (1961), "Etude EEG des Divers stades du sommeil de nuit chez l'enfant. Considerations sur le stade IV ou d'activité electrique," *Rev. neurol.*, **105,** 176–181.

50. Dement, W. and Kleitman, N. (1957), "Cyclic Variations in EEG During Sleep and Their Relation to Eye Movements, Body Motility and Dreaming," *Electroenceph. clin. Neurophysiol.*, **9,** 673–690.

51. Dittrichová, J. (1966), "Development of Sleep in Infancy," *J. appl. Physiol.*, **21,** 1243–1246.

52. Dittrichová, J. and Lapackova, V. (1965), "Transition Period from Wakefulness to Sleep in Young Infants," *Activ. nerv. sup. (Praha)*, **7,** 11–18.

53. Dittrichová, J. and Mares, P. (1965), "Sleep Cycles in Infancy," *Activ. nerv. sup. (Praha)*, **7,** 143–144.

54. Dobbing, J. (1965/66), "The Effect of Undernutrition on Myelination in the Central Nervous System," *Biol. Neonat.*, **9,** 132–147.

55. Dobbing, J. (1971), "Undernutrition and the Developing Brain: The Use of Animal Models to Elucidate the Human Problem," in *Normal and Abnormal Development of Brain and Behaviour*, (G. B. A. Stoelinga and J. J. van der Werff ten Bosch, Eds.). Leiden University Press.

56. Dreyfus-Brisac, C. (1957), "Activité électrique cérébrale du foetus et du trés jeune prématuré." *Ive. Congr. Int. Electroenceph. Neurophysiol.*, pp. 163–171 (Clin. Acta Med. Belg., Eds.). Bruxelles.

57. Dreyfus-Brisac, C. (1962), "The Electroencephalogram of the Premature Infant," *World Neurol.*, **3,** 5–15.

58. Dreyfus-Brisac, C. (1964), "The Electroencephalogram of the Premature Infant and Full-term Newborn. Normal and Abnormal Development of Waking and Sleeping Patterns," in *Neurological and Electroencephalographic Correlative Studies in Infancy*, pp. 186–207. New York: Grune & Stratton.

59. Dreyfus-Brisac, C. (1965), "Sleep of Premature and Full-term Neonates. A Polygraphic Study," *Proc. roy. Soc. Med.*, **58,** 6–7.

60. Dreyfus-Brisac, C. (1968), "Sleep Ontogenesis in Early Human Prematurity From 24 to 27 Weeks of Conceptional Age," *Develop. Psychobiol.*, **1,** 162–169.

61. Dreyfus-Brisac, C. (1970), "Ontogenesis of Sleep in Human Prematures After 32 Weeks of Conceptional Age." *Develop. Psychobiol.*, **3,** 91–121.

62. Dreyfus-Brisac, C., Flescher, J. and Plassart, E. (1962), "L-"L-électroencéphalogramme: Critére d'âge conceptionnel du nouveau-né à terme et prématuré," *Biol. Neonat.*, **4,** 154–173.

62a. Dreyfus-Brisac, C. and Minkowski, A. (1968), "Electroencephalographic Maturation and Low Birth Weight," *Clinical Electroencephalography of Children*, pp. 49–60 (P. Kellaway and I. Petersén, Eds.). Stockholm: Almqvist & Wiksell.

63. Dreyfus-Brisac, C., Samson-Dolfuss, and Fischgold, H. (1955a), "Cerebral Electrical Activity in Premature and Newborn Infants," *Sem. Hôp. Paris*, **31,** 1783–1790.

64. Dreyfus-Brisac, C., Samson-Dolfuss, D. and Fischgold, H. (1955b), "Technique de l'enregistrement EEG' du prématuré et du nouveau-né," *Electroenceph. clin. Neurophysiol.*, **7,** 429–432.

65. Dreyfus-Brisac, C., Fischgold, H. Samson-Dolfuss, D., St. Anne-Dargassies, Ziegler, T., Monod, N. and Blanc, C. (1956), "Veille, sommeil et réactivité sensorielle chez le prématuré, le nouveau-né. Activité electrique cerébrale du nourisson," *Electroenceph. clin. Neurophysiol.*, suppl., **6,** 417–440.

66. Dreyfus-Brisac, C., Samson-Dolfuss, D. and Monod, N. (1956), "The Electrical Activity of the Brain in Mature and Premature Infants," *Electroenceph. clin. Neurophysiol.*, **8,** 171.

67. Dreyfus-Brisac, C., Monod, N., Parmelee, A. H., Prechtl, H. F. R. and Schulte, F. J. (1970), "For What Reasons Should the Pediatrician Follow the Rapidly Expanding Literature on Sleep? A Panel Discussion on Sleep Cycles in Newborn Infants," *Neuropädiatrie*, 349–350.

68. Dubowitz, V., Whittaker, G. F., Brown, B. H. and Robinson, A. (1968), "Nerve Conduction Velocity. An Index of Neurological Maturity of the Newborn Infant," *Develop. Med. Child Neurol.*, **10,** 741–739.

69. Dunn, H. G., Buckler, J. and Morrison, G. C. *et al.* (1964), "Conduction of Motor Nerves in Infants and Children," *Pediatrics*, **34,** 708–727.

70. Eccles, J. C. (1957), "Interpretation of Action Potentials Evoked in the Cerebral Cortex," *Electroenceph. clin. Neurophysiol.*, **3,** 449–464.

71. Eccles, J. C. (1964), *The Physiology of Synapses*. Berlin-Göttingen-Heidelberg: Springer.

72. Eccles, J. C., Eccles, R. M. and Lundberg, A. (1957), "The Convergence of Monosynaptic Excitatory Afferents on to Many Different Species of Alpha Motneurones," *J. Physiol.*, **137,** 22–50.

73. Eccles, R. M. and Lundberg, A. (1959), "Synaptic Actions in Motoneurones by Afferents Which May Evoke the Flexion Reflex," *Arch. ital. Biol.*, **97,** 199–221.

73a. Eccles, R. M. and Willis, W. D. (1962), "Presynaptic Inhibition of the Monosynaptic Reflex Pathway in Kittens," *J. Physiol. (Lond.)*, **165,** 403–420.

74. Eckstein, A. and Paffrath, H. (1928), "Bewegungsstudien bei frühgeborenen und jungen Säuglingen," *Z. Kinderheilk.*, **46,** 595–610.

75. Ekholm, J. (1967), "Postnatal Changes in Cutaneous Reflexes and in the Discharge Pattern of Cutaneous and Articular Sense Organs. A Morphological and Physiological Study in the Cat," *Acta Physiol. scand.*, suppl., **297,** 1–130.

76. Ellingson, R. J. (1958), "EEG of Normal, Full-term Newborns Immediately After Birth. With Observations on Arousal and Visual Evoked Responses,' *Electroenceph. clin. Neurophysiol.*, **10,** 31–50.

77. Ellingson, R. J. (1960), "Cortical Electrical Responses to Visual Stimulation in the Human Infant," *Electroenceph. clin. Neurophysiol.*, **12,** 663–667.

78. Ellingson, R. J. (1964), "Cerebral Electrical Responses to Auditory and Visual Stimuli in the Infant (Human and Subhuman Studies)," in *Neurological and Electroencephalographic Correlative Studies in Infancy*, pp. 78–116. Grune & Stratton, Inc.

79. Engel, R. (1964), "Electroencephalographic Response to Photic Stimulation and Their Correlation with Maturation," *Ann. N.Y. Acad. Sci.*, **117,** 407–414.

80. Engel, R. and Butler, B. V. (1966), "Rassische und geschlechtliche Unterschiede in der elektroenzephalographischen Lichtreizlatenz beim Neugeborenen," *Fortschr. Med.*, **84,** 411–415.

81. Feinberg, I., Braun, M. and Schulman, E. (1969), "EEG

Sleep Patterns in Mental Retardation," *Electroenceph. clin. Neurophysiol.*, **27**, 128–141.

82. Finnström, O. (1971), "Studies on Maturity in Newborn Infants III. Neurological Examination," *Neuropädiatrie*, **3**, 72–96.
83. Finnström, O. (1972), "Studies on Maturity in Newborn Infants. II. External Characteristics," *Acta Paediat. scand.*, **61**, 24–32.
84. Fischgold, H., Dreyfus-Brisac, C., Monod, N., Samson-Dolfus, D., Kramarz, P. and Blanc, Cl. (1955), "L'électroencephalogramme au cours de la maturation cérébrale Aspects physiologiques," in *XVIIe Congr. de l'Assoc, des Pediat. de langue francaise.* (Dehan Montpellier, Ed.), pp. 1–66.
85. Fisher, C., Gross, J. and Zuch, J. (1965), "Cycle of Penile Erections Synchronous with Dreaming (REM) Sleep. Preliminary Report," *Arch. gen. Psychiat.*, **12**, 29–45.
86. Fitzgerald, J. E. and Windle, W. F. (1942), "Some Observations on Early Human Fetal Movements," *J. comp. Neurol.*, **76**, 159–167.
86a. Flechsig, P. (1920), *Anatomie des menschlichen Gehirns und Rückenmarks auf Myelogenetischer Grundlage*, pp. 121–136. Leipzig: G. Thieme.
87. Foerster, O. (1913), "Das phylogenetische Moment in der spastischen Lähmung," *Berl. klin. Wschr.*, **1**, 1217–1255.
88. Galambos, R. (1961), "A Glia-neural Theory of Brain Function," *Proc, nat. Acad. Sci.* (*Wash.*), **47**, 129–136
89. Gamstorp, I. (1963), "Normal Conduction Velocity of Ulnar, Median and Peroneal Nerves in Infancy, Childhood and Adolescence," *Acta paediat. scand.*, suppl., **146**, 68–76.
90. Gamstorp, I. and Shelburne, S. A., Jr. (1965), "Peripheral Sensory Conduction in Ulnar and Median Nerves of Normal Infants, Children, and Adolescents," *Acta paediat. scand.*, **54**, 309–313.
91. Gassel, M. M., Marchiafava, P. L. and Pompejano, O. (1964), "Tonic and Phasic Inhibitions of Spinal Reflexes During Deep, Desynchronized Sleep in Unrestrained Cats," *Arch. ital. Biol.*, **102**, 471–479.
92. Gassel, M. M., Marchiafava, P. L. and Pompejano, O. (1965a), "An Analysis of the Supraspinal Influences Acting on Motoneurones During Sleep in the Unrestrained Cat," *Arch. ital. Biol.*, **103**, 25–44.
93. Gassel, M. M., Marchiafava, P. L. and Pompejano, O. (1965b), "Activity of the Red Nucleus During Deep Desynchronized Sleep in Unrestrained Cats," *Arch. ital. Biol.*, **103**, 369–396.
94. Gassel, M. M. and Pompejano, O. (1965), "Fusimotor Function During Sleep in Unrestrained Cats," *Arch. ital. Biol.*, **103**, 347–368.
95. Gesell, A. and Amatruda, C. J. (1945), *The Embryology of Behaviour*, pp. 289–297. Paul Hobber, New York and London: Harper.
96. Gibbs, F. A. and Knotts, J. R. (1949), "Growth of the Electrical Activity of the Cortex," *Electroenceph. clin. Neurophysiol.*, **1**, 223–229.
97. Giaquinto, S., Pompejano, O. and Somogyi, I. (1963a), "Reflex Activity of Extensor and Flexor Muscles Following Muscular Afferent Excitation During Sleep and Wakefulness," *Experientia*, **19**, 481–482.
98. Giaquinto, S., Pompejano, O. and Somogyi, I. (1963b), "Supraspinal Inhibitory Control of Spinal Reflexes During Natural Sleep," *Experientia*, **19**, 652–653.
99. Gianquinto, S., Pompejano, O. and Somogyi, I. (1964a), "Supraspinal Modulation of Heteronymous Monosynaptic and of Polysynaptic Reflexes During Natural Sleep and Wakefulness," *Arch. ital. Biol.*, **102**, 245–281.
100. Giaquinto, S., Pompejano, O. and Somogyi, I., (1964b), "Decending Inhibitory Influences on Spinal Reflexes During Natural Sleep," *Arch. ital. Biol.* **102**, 282–307.
101. Glässer, A. and Mantegazzini, P. (1960), "Action of 5-hydroxytryptamine and 5-hydroxytryptophan on the Cortical Electrical Activity of the Midpontine Pretrigeminal Preparation of the Cat With and Without Mesencephalic Hemisection," *Arch. Ital. Biol.*, **98**, 351–366.
102. Glaser, G. H. and Levy, L. L. (1965), "Photic Following in the EEG of the Newborn," *Amer. J. Dis. Child.*, **109**, 333–337.
103. Goldie, L. (1965), "Sleep Cycles in Premature Infants," *Develop. Med. Child Neurol.*, **7**, 317–319.
104. Golubewa, E. L. Shulejkina, K. V. and Vainstein, I. I. (1959), "The Development of Reflex and Spontaneous Activity of the Human Fetus During Embryogenesis," *Akush. i. Ginek.*, **3**, 59–71.
105. Goodman, W. S., Appleby, S. V., Scott, J. W. and Ireland, P. E. (1964), "Audiometry in Newborn Children by Electroencephalography," *Laryngoscope*, 1316–1328.
106. Granit, R. (1950), "Reflex Selfregulation of Muscle Contraction and Autogenetic Inhibition," *J. Neurophysiol.*, **13**, 351–372.
107. Granit, R., Henatsch, H. D. and Steg, G., (1956), "Tonic and Phasic Ventral Norn Cells Differentiated by Post-etanic Potentiation in Cat Extensors." *Acta physiol. scand.*, **37**, 114–126.
108. Graziani, L. J., Weitzman, E. D. and Velasco, M. S. (1968), "Neurologic Maturation and Auditory Evoked Responses in Low Birth Weight Infants," *Pediatrics*, **41**, 483–494.
109. Grundfest, H. (1961), "The Interpretation of Electrocortical Potentials," *Ann. N.Y. Acad. Sci.*, **92**, 877–889.
110. Hassler, R. (1964), "Pathologische Grundlagen der Klinik und Behandlung extrapyramidaler Erkrankungen," *Klin. Wschr.*, **42**, 404–409.
111. Henatsch, H. D. and Schulte, F. J. (1958), "Reflexerregung und Eigenhemmung tonischer und phasischer Alpha-Motoneurone während chemischer Dauererregung der Muskelspindeln," *Pflügers Arch. ges. Physiol.*, **268**, 134–147.
112. Hewer, E. E. (1955), "Development of Nerve Endings in Human Fetoes," *J. Anat.* (*Lond.*), **69**, 369–379.
113. Hobson, J. A. (1968), "Sleep After Exercise," *Science*, **162**, 1503–1505.
114. Hodes, R. and Dement, W. C. (1964), "Depression of Electrically Induced Reflexes in Man During Low Voltage EEG Sleep," *Electroenceph. clin. Neurophysiol.*, **17**, 617–629.
115. Hodes, R. and Gribetz, J. (1962), "H.-reflexes in Normal Infants: Effects of Sleep, Age and Phenobarbital on These Electrically Induced Reflexes," *Amer. J. Dis. Child.*, **104**, 490–498.
116. Hodes, R. and Gribetz, J. (1962), "H.-reflex in Normal Infants: Depression of These Electrically Induced Reflexes in Sleep." *Proc. Soc. Exp. Biol. Med.*, **110**, 577–580.
117. Hoffmann, P. (1922), "Untersuchungen über Eigenreflexe (Sehenreflexe) menschlicher Muskeln," Berlin: Springer.
118. Hoffman, P. (1934), "Die physiologischen Eigenschaften der Eigenreflexe," *Ergebn. Physiol.*, **36**, 15–108.
119. Hogg, I. D. (1941), "Sensory Nerves and Associated Structures in the Skin of Human Fetuses of 8 to 14 Weeks of Menstrual Age Correlated with Functional Capability," *J. comp. Neurol.*, **75**, 371–410.
120. Honda, Y., Takahashi, K., Takahashi, S., Azumi, K., Irie, M., Sakuma, M., Tsushima, T. and Shizume, K. (1969), "Growth Hormone Secretion During Nocturnal Sleep in Normal Subjects," *J. clin. Ednocrinol. Metab.*, **29**, 20–29.
121. Hooker, D. (1938), "The Origin of Grasping Movement in Man," *Proc. Amer. phil. Soc.*, **79**, 597–606.
122. Hooker, D. (1939), *A Preliminary Atlas of Early Human Fetal Activity*. Pittsburgh (Penn.). U.S.A., privately published by the author.
123. Hooker, D. (1944), *The Origin of Overt Behavior*, 38 pp. Ann. Arbor University of Michigan Press.
124. Hooker, D. (1952), *The Prenatal Origin of Behavior*, viii+ 143 pp., 18th Porter Lecture Series. Kansas: University of Kansas Press.
125. Hooker, D. (1954), "Early Human Fetal Behavior, with a Preliminary Note on Double Simultaneous Fetal Stimulation," *Res. Publ. Ass. nerv. ment. Dis.*, **33**, 98–113.
126. Hooker, D. (1958), "Evidence of Prenatal Function of the Central Nervous System in Man,"
127. Hopf, H. C., Hufschmidt, H. J. and Ströder, J. (1964), "Über die 'Ausbreitungsreaktion' nach Trigeminusreizung beim Säugling," *Ann. Paediat.* (*Basel*), **203**, 89–100.

128. Hrbek, A. and Mares, P. (1964), "Cortical Evoked Responses to Visual Stimulation in Full-term and Premature Newborns," *Electroenceph. clin. Neurophysiol.*, **16**, 575–581.
129. Hughes, J. G., Davis, B. C. and Brennan, M. L. (1948), "Electroencephalography of the Newborn," *Amer. J. Dis. Child.*, **76**, 503–512.
130. Hughes, J. G., Ehemann, B. and Hill, F. S. (1949), "EEG of Newborn, Studies on Normal Full Term Infants While Awake and While Drowsy," *Amer. J. Dis. Child.*, **77**, 310–314.
130a. Hughes, J. G., Davis, B. C. and Brannan, M. L. (1951), "Electroencephalography of Newborn Infant; Studies on Premature Infants," *Pediatrics*, **7**, 707–712.
131. Humphrey, T. (1964), "Some Correlation Between the Appearance of Human Fetal Reflexes and the Development of the Nervous System," in *Progress in Brain Research*, Vol. 4. Amsterdam: Elsevier Publ. Co.
132. Humphrey, T. (1970), "Reflex Activity in the Oral and Facial Area of the Human Fexus," in *2nd Symposium on "Oral Sensation and Perception,"* pp. 195–233. (J. F. Bosma, Ed.). Springfield: Thomas.
133. Humphrey, T. and Hooker, D. (1959), "Double Simultaneous Stimulation of Human Fetuses and the Anatomical Patterns Underlying the Reflexes Elicited," *J. comp. Neurol.*, **112**, 75–102.
134. Humprey, T. and Hooker, D. (1961), "Human Fetal Reflexes Elicited by Genital Stimulation," *Proceedings of the VIIth Int. Congr. of Neurology, Rome*, **2**, 473–488.
135. Hunt, C. C. (1955), "Relation of Function to Diameter in Afferent Fibres of Muscle Nerves," *J. gen. Physiol.*, **38**, 117–131.
136. Hunt, C. C. and Paintal, A. S. (1958), "Spinal Reflex Regulation of Fusimotor Neurones," *J. Physiol. (Lond.)*, **143**, 195–212.
137. Hutt, S. J., Hutt, C., Lenard, H. G., v. Bernuth, H. and Muntjewerff, W. J. (1968), "Auditory Responsivity in the Neonate," *Nature*, **218**, 888–890.
138. Irwin, O. C. (1932), "Distribution of Amount of Motility in Young Infants Between 2 Nursing Periods," *J. comp. Psychol.*, **14**, 429–445.
139. Jacobson, A., Kales, A., Lehmann, D. and Hoedmaker, F. S. (1964), "Muscle Tonus in Human Subjects During Sleep and Dreaming," *Exp. Neurol.*, **10**, 418–424.
139a. Jacobson, A., Kales, A., Lehmann, D. *et al.* (1965), "Somnambulism: All-night Electroencephalographic Studies," *Science*, **148**, 975–977.
139b. James, A. (1958), Lecture on "The Evolution of the Human Brain," Jan. 1957, pp. 1–41. New York: American Museum of Natural History.
140. Joppich, G. and Michaelis, R. (1967), "Über zerebrale Aktivitäten bei Neugeborenen und jungen Säuglingen," *Dtsch. med. Wschr.*, **92**, 2295–2302.
141. Jouvet, M. (1967), "Mechanisms of the States of Sleep: A Neuropharmacological Approach," in *Sleep and Altered States of Consciousness*, pp. 86–126 (S. S. Kety, E. V. Evarts and H. L. Williams, Eds.). Baltimore: The Williams & Wilkins Co.
141a. Jouvet, M. (1969), "Biogenetic Amines and the States of Sleep." *Science*, **163**, 32–41.
142. Jung, R. (1963), "Hirnpotentialwellen, Neuroentladungen und Gleichspannungsphänomene," in *Jenenser EEG-Symposion. 30 Jahre Elektroenzephalographie*, pp. 54–81. Berlin: VEB Verlag Volk und Gesundheit.
143. Kanzow, E., Krause, D. and Kuhnel, H. (1962), "Die Vasomotorik der Hirnrinde in den Phasen desynchronisierter EEG Aktivität im natürlichen Schlaf der Katze," *Pflugers Arch. ges. Physiol.*, **274**, 593–607.
144. Kubota, K., Iwamura, Y. and Niimi, Y. (1964), "Monosynaptic Reflex and Natural Sleep in the Cat," *Experientia*, **20**, 316–317.
145. Kuffler, S. W., Hunt, C. C. and Quilliam, J. P. (1951), "Function of Medullated Small-nerve Fibers in Mammalian Ventral Roots: Efferent Muscle Spindle Innervation," *J. Neurophysiol.*, **14**, 29–54.
146. Laporte, Y. and Bessau, P. (1959), "Modification d'exitabilité de motoneurones homonymes provoqués par l'activation physiologique de fibres afférentes d'origine musculaire du groupe. II," *J. Physiol. (Paris)*, **51**, 897–908.
147. Larroche, J. C. (1962), "Quelques aspects anatomiques du dévelopment cérébral," *Biol. Neonat.*, **4**, 126–153.
148. Ledebur, I. X. and Tissot, R. (1966), "Modification de l'activité électrique cérébrale du lapin sous l'effet de microinjections de précurseurs des monoamires dans les structures somnogénes bulbaires et pontiques," *Electroenceph. clin. Neurophysiol.*, **20**, 370–381.
149. Leksell, L. (1945), "The Action Potential and Excitatory Effects of the Small Ventral Root Fibres to Skeletal Muscle," *Acta physiol. scand.*, **10**, suppl. 3, 1–84.
150. Lenard, H. G. (1970a), "Sleep Studies in Infancy," *Acta paediat. scand.*, **59**, 572–581.
151. Lenard, H. G. (1970b), "The Development of Sleep Spindles in the EEG During the First Two Years of Life," *Neuropädiatrie*, **1**, 264–276.
152. Lenard, H. G., v. Bernuth, H. and Prechtl, H. R. R. (1968), "Reflexes and Their Relationship to Behavioural State in the Newborn," *Acta paediat. scand.*, **57**, 177–185.
153. Lenard, H. G., v. Bernuth, H. and Hutt, S. J. (1969), "Acoustic Evoked Responses in Newborn Infants: The Influence of Pitch and Complexity of the Stimulus," *Electroenceph. clin. Neurophysiol.*, **27**, 121–127.
154. Lindsley, D. B. (1938), "Electrical Potentials of the Brain in Children and Adults," *J. gen. Psychol.*, **19**, 285–306.
155. Lipton, E. L., Steinschneider, A. and Richmond, J. B. (1965), "The Autonomic Nervous System in Early Life," *New Engl. J. Med.*, **273**, 147–154 u. 201–208.
156. Lloyd, D. P. C. (1946), "Facilitation and Inhibition of Spinal Motoneurons. Integrative Pattern of Excitation and Inhibition in Two-neuron Reflex Arcs," *J. Neurophysiol.*, **9**, 421–444.
157. Lloyd, D. P. C. and Chang, H. T. (1948), "Afferent Fibers in the Muscle Nerves," *J. Neurophysiol.*, **11**, 199–207.
158. Loomis, A. L., Harvey, E. N. and Hobart, G. A. (1937), "Cerebral States During Sleep, as Studied by Human Brain Potentials," *J. exp. Psychol.*, **21**, 127–144.
159. Nolte, R., Schulte, F. J., Michaelis, R. and Jürgens, U. (1968), "Power Spectral Analysis of the Electroencephalogram of Newborn Twins in Active and Quiet Sleep," in *Clin. Electroenceph. of Children* (P. Kellaway and I. Petersen, Eds.). Stockholm: Almquist & Wiksell.
160. Nolte, R., Schulte, F. J., Michaelis, R., Weisse, U. and Gruson, R. (1969), "Bioelectric Brain Maturation in Small-for-dates Infants," *Develop. Med. Child Neurol.*, **11**, 83–93.
161. Magoun, H. W. (1954), *The Waking Brain*. Springfield (I11.): Charles C. Thomas.
162. Magoun, H. W. and Rhines, R. (1946), "Inhibitory Mechanism in the Bulbar Reticular Formation," *J. Neurophysiol.*, **9**, 165–171.
162a. Mai, H., Schütz, E. and Müller, M. W. (1951), "Über das Electroencephalogramm von Frühgeburten," *Ztschr. Kinderh.*, **69**, 251–261.
163. Mai, H. and Schaper, G. (1953a), "Beitrag zur Klinik der Hypothyreose. Studien über die nach langer Thyreodidinbehandlung erreichte Intelligenz und über das Verhalten des Hirnstrombildes," *Ann. Paediat. (Basel)*, **180**, 65–97.
164. Mai, H. and Schaper, G. (1953b), "Elektrencephalographische Untersuchungen an Frühgeborenen," *Ann. Paediat. (Basel)*, **180**, 345–365.
165. Mandell, A. J. and Mandell, M. P. (1965), "Biochemical Aspects of Rapid Eye Movement Sleep," *Amer. J. Psychiat.*, **122**, 391–401.
166. Mandell, A. J. and Mandell, M. P. (1969), "Peripheral Hormonal and Metabolic Correlates of Rapid Eye Movement Sleep," *Exp. Med. Surg.*, **27**, 224–236.
167. Marcus, R. E., Gibbs, E. L. and Gibbs, F. A. (1949), "Electroencephalography in the Diagnosis of Hearing Loss in the Very Young Child," *Dis. nerv. Syst.*, **10**, 170–173.
168. Matsumoto, J. and Jouvet, M. (1964), "Effects de réserpine,

DOPA et 5 HTP sur les deux états de sommeil," *C. R. Soc. Biol. (Paris)*, **158,** 2137–2140.

169. Matthews, B. H. C. (1933), "Nerve Endings in Mammalian Muscle," *J. Physiol. (Lond.)*, **78,** 1–53.

170. Matthews, P. B. (1964), "Muscle Spindles and Their Motor Control," *Physiol. Rev.*, **44,** 219–288.

171 Metcalf, D. R. (1970), "EEG Sleep Spindle Ontogenesis," *Neuropädiatrie*, **1,** 428–433.

172. Michaelis, R., Schulte, F. J. and Nolte, R. (1970), "Motor Behaviour of Small for Gestational Age Newborn Infants," *J. Pediat.*, **76,** 208–213.

173. Minkowski, M. (1921), "Über Bewegungen und Reflexe des menschlichen Foetus während der ersten Hälfte seiner Entwicklung," *Schweiz. Arch. Neurol. Psychiat.*, **8,** 148–151.

174. Minkowski, M. (1923), "Zur Entwicklungsgeschichte, Lokalisation und Klinik des Fußsohlenreflexes," *Schweiz. Arch. Neurol. Psychiat.*, **13,** 475–514.

175. Minkowski, M. (1928), "Neurobiologische Studien am menschlichen Foetus," in *Handbuch der biologischen Arbeitsmethoden*, Abt. 5, Teil 5B, Heft 5, Ser. Nr. 253, pp. 511–618 (E. Abderhalden, Ed.), Berlin and Vienna: Urban & Schwarzenberg.

176. Minkowski, A., Larroche, J. C., Vignaud, J. and Dreyfus-Brisac, C. *et al.* (1966), "Development of the Nervous System in Early Life," in *Human Development*, pp. 254–257, (F. Faulkner, Ed.). Philadelphia: W. B. Saunders.

177. Monod, N., Eliet-Flescher, J. and Dreyfus-Brisac, C. (1967), "Le sommeil du nouveau-né et du prématuré. III. Les troubles de l'organisation du sommeil chez le nouveau-né pathologique: Analyse des études polygraphiques," *Biol. Neonat.*, **11,** 216–247.

178. Monod, N., and Pajot, N. (1965), "Le sommeil du noveau-né et du prématuré, *Biol. Neonat.*, **8,** 281–307.

179. Mortier, T. and v. Bernuth, H. (1971), "The Neuralinfluence on Muscle Development in Myelomeningocele: Histochemical and Electrodiagnostic Studies," *Develop. Med. Child Neurol.*, suppl., **25,** 82–89

180. Moruzzi, G. (1960), "Synchronizing Influences of the Brain Stem and the Inhibitory Mechanisms Underlying the Production of Sleep by Sensory Stimulation," (H. H. Jasper and G. D. Smirnow, Eds.), Moscow Colloquium (1958), *Electroenceph. clin. Neurophysiol.*, suppl. 12, **13,** 231–256.

181. Moruzzi, G. (1964), "Reticular Influences on the EEG," *Electroenceph. clin. Neurophysiol.*, **16,** 2–17.

182. Moruzzi, G. and Magoun, H. W. (1949), "Brain Stem Reticular Formation and Activation of EEG," *Electroenceph. clin. Neurophysiol.*, **1,** 455–473.

183. Naka, K. I. (1964), "Electrophysiology of the Fetal Spinal Cord. II. Interaction Among Peripheral Inputs and Recurrent Inhibition," *J. gen. Physiol.*, **47,** 1023–1038.

184. Okomoto, Y. and Kirikae, T. (1951), "EEG Studies on Brain of Foetus, of Children of Premature Birth and Newborn, Together with a Note on Reactions of Foetus Brain Upon Drugs," *Folia psychiat. neurol. jap.*, **5,** 135–146.

185. Orthner, H. and Roeder, F. (1969), *Die Entwicklung der Motorik beim Menschen.* In press.

186. Oswald, I. (1969), "Human Brain Protein, Drugs and Dreams," *Nature*, **223,** 893–897.

187. Paillard, J. (1955), "Les formed musculaires d'expression de la vigilance et leur traduction expérimentale," in *Réflexes et régulations d'origine proprioceptive chex l'homme*, (J. Paillard, Ed.). pp. 293–316. Arnette Paris.

188. Parmeggiani, P. L. and Zancco, G. (1963), "A Study on the Bioelectrical Rhythms of Cortical and Sub-cortical Structures During Activated Sleep," *Arch. ital. Biol.*, **101,** 385–412.

189. Parmelee, A. H. (1961), "Sleep Patterns in Infancy. A Study of One Infant from Birth to Eight Months of Age," *Acta paediat. scand.*, **50,** 160–170

190. Parmelee, A. H., Wenner, W. H., Akiyama, Y. and Flescher, J. (1964), "Electroencephalography and Brain Maturation," in Symposium on Regional Maturation of the Nervous System in Early Life, Council for International Organization of Medical Sciences, CIOMS. Paris, December 3–5.

191. Parmelee, A. H., Wenner, W. H. and Schulz, H. R. (1964), "Infant Sleep Patterns: From Birth to 16 Weeks of Age," *J. Pediat.*, **65,** 576–582.

192. Parmelee, A. H., Wenner, W. H., Akiyama, Y., Schultz, M. and Stern, W. (1967), "Sleep States in Premature Infants," *Develop. Med. Child Neurol.*, **9,** 70–77.

193. Parmelee, A. H., Schulte, F. J., Akiyama, Y., Wenner, W. H., Schultz, M. A. and Stern, E. (1968), "Maturation of EEG Activity During Sleep in Premature Infants," *Electroenceph. clin. Neurophysiol.*, **24,** 319–329.

194. Parmelee, A. H., Akiyama, Y., Stern, E. and Harris, M. A. (1969), "A Periodic Cerebral Rhythm in Newborn Infants," *Exp. Neurol.*, **25,** 575–584.

195. Passounant, P., Cadilhac, J. and Ribstein, M. (1960), "EEG During Cerebral Maturation," *Montpellier med.*, **57,** 138–154.

196. Peiper, A. (1963), *Die Eigenart der kindlichen Hirntätigkeit.* Edition Leipzig.

197. Peréz, R. M. and Peréz, A. P. R. (1932), "L'évolution des terminaisons nerveuses de la peau humaine," *Trav. Lab. Rech. biol. Univ. Madr.*, **28,** 61–73.

198. Petre–Quadens, O. (1966), "On the Different Phases of the Sleep of the Newborn with Special Reference to the Activated Phase, or Phase d. *J. Neurol. Sci.*, **3,** 151–161.

199. Petre-Quadens, O. and Jouvet, M. (1966), "Paradoxical Phase of Sleep in the Mentally Retarded," *J. Neurol. Sci.*, **3,** 608–612.

200. Petre-Quadens, O. and Laroche, J. L. (1966), "Sommeil du nouveau-né: phases paradoxales spontanées et provoquées," *J. Psychol. norm. path.*, 19–27.

201. Pratt, K. C. (1954), "Neonate," in *Manual of Child Psychology*, 2nd edition. (L. Carmichael, Ed.). New York: John Wiley & Sons.

202. Prechtl, H. F. R. (1968), "Polygraphic Studies of the Full-term Newborn: II. Computer Analysis of Recorded Data," in *Studies in Infancy* (M. Bax and R. C. MacKeith, Eds.), Clinic in Developmental Medicine 27. London: S.I.M.P./Heinemann.

203. Prechtl, H. F. R. and Beintema, D. (1964), *The Neurological Examination of the Newborn.* London: Heinemann Medical Books Ltd.

204. Prechtl, H. F. R. and Knol, A. R. (1958), "Der Einfluß der Beckenedlage auf die Fußsohlenreflexe beim neugeborenen Kind," *Arch. Psychiat. Z. ges. Neurol.*, **196,** 542–553.

205. Prechtl, H. F. R. and Lenard, H. G. (1967), "A Study of Eye Movements in Sleeping Newborn Infants," *Brain Research*, **5,** 477–493.

206. Prechtl, H. F. R., Vlach, V., Lenard, H. G. and Grant, D. K. (1967), "Exteroceptive and Tendon Reflexes in Various Behavioural States in the Newborn Infant," *Biol. Neonat.*, **11,** 159–175.

207. Purpura, D. P. (1959), "Nature of Electrocortical Potentials and Synaptic Organizations in Cerebral and Cerebellar Cortex," *Int. Rev. Neurobiol.*, **1,** 47–163.

208. Rabinowicz, T. (1964), "The Cerebral Cortex of the Premature Infant of the 8th Month," *Prog. Brain Res.*, **4,** 39–86.

209. Radtke, H. W. (1969), "Motorische Nervenleitgeschwindigkeit bei normalen Säuglingen und Kindern," *Helv. paediat. Acta*, **24,** 390–398.

210. Raimbault, J. and Laget, P. (1963), "Etude de la vitesse de conduction des fibres nerveuses chez le jeune enfant," *Rev. Neurol.*, **108,** 204–209.

211. Rhines, R. and Magoun H. W. (1946), "Brain Stem Facilitation of Cortical Motor Response," *J. Neurophysiol.*, **9,** 219–229.

212. Robinson, R. J. (1966), "Assessment of Gestational Age by Neurological Examination," *Arch. Dis. Childh.*, **41,** 437–447.

213. Roffwarg, H., Dement, W. and Fischer, C. (1964), "Preliminary Observations of the Sleep Dream Patterns in Neonates, Infants, Children and Adults," in *Problems of Sleep Dream in Children.* pp. 60–72 (E. Harms, Ed.). Pergamon Press.

214. Roffwarg, H. P., Muzio, J. N. and Dement, W. C. (1966), "Ontogenetic Development of the Human Sleep-dream-cycle," *Science*, **152,** 604–619.

215. Rossi, G. F. and Zanchetti, A. (1957), "Brain Stem Reticular

Formation. Anatomy and Physiology," *Arch. ital. Biol.*, **95**, 199–535.

216. Rothballer, A. B. (1957), "The Effect of Phenylephrine, Methamphetamine, Cocaine, and Serotonin Upon the Adrenaline-sensitive Component of the Reticular Activating System," *Electroenceph. Clin. Neurophysiol.*, **9**, 409–417.

217. Ruppert, E. S. and Johnson, E. W. (1968), "Motor Nerve Conduction Velocities in Low Birth Weight Infants," *Pediatrics*, **42**, 255–260.

218. Saint-Anne Dargassies, S. (1954), "Méthode d'examin neurologique sur la nouveau-né," *Etud. Neonat.*, **3**, 101.

219. Saint-Anne Dargassies, S. (1955), "La maturation neurologique du prématuré," *Rev. Neurol.* (*Paris*), **93**, 331–340.

220. Saint-Anne Dargassies, S. (1957), "A propos d'un enfant né au 6ème mois de la gestation," *Etud. Neonat.*, **6**, 11–24.

221. Saint-Anne Dargassies, S. (1962), "Le nouveau-né à terme: Aspect neurologique," *Biol. Neonat.*, **4**, 174–200.

222. Saint-Anne Dargassies, S. (1964a), "Introduction à la sémiologie du développement neurologique du nourrisson normal. 1. Conceptions générales," *J. Neurol. Sci.*, **1**, 160–177.

223. Saint-Anne Dargassies, S. (1964b), "Introduction à la sémiologie du développement neurologique du nourrisson normal. 2. Méthode d'exploration neurologique," *J. Neurol. Sci.*, **1**, 578–585.

224. Saint-Anne Dargassies, S. (1966), "Neurological Maturation of the Premature Infant of 28–41 Weeks Gestational Age," in *Human Development* (F. Faulkner, Ed.). Philadelphia: W. B. Saunders Co.

224a. Samson-Dollfus, D. (1955), *L-électro-encéphalogramme du prématuré jusqua l'age de trois mois et du nouveau-né a term.* Paris: Imp. R. Foulon.

225. Schaefer, K. P. (1965), "Die Erregungsmuster einzelner Neurone des Abducens-Kernes beim Kaninchen," *Pflügers Arch. ges. Physiol.*, **284**, 31–52.

226. Scheibel, M. and Scheibel, A. (1958), "Neurons and Neuroglia Cells as Seen with the Light Microscope," in *Symp. Biology of Neuroglia*, pp. 5–10. Springfield.

227. Schroeder, C. and Heckel, H. (1952), "Zur Frage der Hirntätigkeit beim Neugeborenen," *Geburts. u. Frauenheilk.*, **12**, 992–999.

228. Schulte, F. J. (1964), "Reflex Activation and Inhibition of Spinal Motoneurones of the Newborn, in *Symp. Neurol. Newborn* (April). Roma.

229. Schulte, F. J. (1970), "Neonatal Brain Mechanisms and the Development of Motor Behaviour,' in *Physiology of the Perinatal Period*, **9**, 797–841 (U. Stave, Ed.). New York: Appleton-Century-Crofts.

230. Schulte, F. J., Akiyama, Y. and Parmelee, A. H. (1967), "Auditory Evoked Responses During Sleep in Premature and Full-term Newborn Infants," *Electroenceph. clin. Neurophysiol.*, **23**, 97.

231. Schulte, F. J., Albert, G. and Michaelis, R. (1969), "Gestationsalter und Nervenleitgeschwindigkeit bei normalen und abnormen Neugeborenen," *Dtsch. med. Wschr.*, **94**, 599–601.

232. Schulte, F. J. and Bell, E. F. "Bioelectric Brain Development. An Atlas of EEG Power Spectra in Infants and Young Children," *Neuropädiatrie*. In press.

233. Schulte, F. J., Hinze, G. and Schrempf, G. (1971a), "Maternal Toxemia, Fetal Malnutrition and Bioelectric Brain Activity of the Newborn," *Neuropädiatrie*, **4**, 439–460.

233a. Schulte, F. J., Linke, I., Michaelis ,R. and Nolte, R. (1969b), "Excitation, Inhibition, and Impulse Conduction in Spinal Motoneurones of Preterm, Term and Small-for-dates Newborn Infants," in *Brain and Early Behaviour*, pp. 87–114 (R. J. Robinson, Ed.). London: Academic Press Inc.

234. Schulte, F. J., Lasson, U., Parl, U., Nolte, R. and Jürgerns, U. (1969), "Brain and Behavioural Maturation in Newborn Infants of Diabetic Mothers. Part II: Sleep Cycles," *Neuropädiatrie*, **1**, 36.

235. Schulte, F. J. and Michaelis, R. (1965), "Zur Physiologie und Pathophysiologie der neuromuskulären Erregungs-Übertragung beim Neugeborenen," *Klin. Wschr.*, **43**, 295–300.

236. Schulte, F. J., Michaelis, R., Linke, I. and Nolte, R. (1968a)› "Electromyographic Evaluation of the Moro Reflex in Preterm, Term and Small-for-dates Newborn Infants," *Develop. Psychobiol.*, **1**, 41–47.

237. Schulte, F. J., Michaelis, R., Linke, I. and Nolte, R. (1968b), "Motor Nerve Conduction Velocity in Term, Preterm, and Small-fordates Newborn Infants," *Pediatrics*, **42**, 17–26.

238. Schulte, F. J., Michaelis, R., Nolte, R., Albert, G., Parl, U. and Lasson, U. (1969), "Brain and Behavioural Maturation in Newborn Infants of Diabetic Mothers. Part I: Nerve Conduction and EEG Patterns," *Neuropädiatrie*, **1**, 24–35.

239. Schulte, F. J., Schrempf, G. and Hinze, G. (1971), "Maternal Toxemia, Fetal Malnutrition, and Motor Behaviour of the Newborn," *Pediatrics*, **48**, 871–882.

240. Schulte, F. J. and Schwenzel, W. (1965), "Motor Control and Muscle Tone in the Newborn Period. Electromyographic Studies," *Biol. Neonat.*, **8**, 198–215.

241. Sherrington, C. S. (1948), *The Integrative Action of the Nervous System.* New Haven: Yale University Press.

242. Skoglund, S. (1960a), "On the Postnatal Development of Postural Mechanisms as Revealed by Electromyography and Myography in Cecerebrate Kittens," *Acta physiol. scand.*, **49**, 299–317.

243. Skoglund, S. (1960b), "The Spinal Transmission of Proprioceptive Reflexes and Postnatal Development of Conduction Velocity in Different Hindlimb Nerves in the Kitten," *Acta physiol. scand.*, **49**, 318–329.

244. Skoglund, S. (1960c), "The Activity in Muscle Receptors in the Kitten," *Acta physiol. scand.*, **50**, 203–221.

245. Skoglund, S. (1969) "Growth and Differentiation, with Special Emphasis on the Central Nervous System," *Ann. Rev. Physiol.*, **31**, 19–42.

246. Smith, J. R. (1937), "The EEG During Infancy and Childhood," *Proc. Soc. exp. Biol.* (*N.Y.*), 384–386.

247. Snyder, F., Hobson, J., Morrison, D. and Goldfrank, F. (1964), "Changes in Respiration, Heart Rate and Systolic Blood Pressure in Relation to Electroencephalographic Patterns of Human Sleep," *J. appl. Physiol.*, **19**, 417–422.

248. Sprague, J. M. and Chambers, W. W. (1953), "Regulation of Posture in Intact and Decerebrate Cat," *J. Neurophysiol.*, **16**, 451–463.

249. Sprague, J. M. and Chambers W. W. (1954), "Control of Posture by Reticular Formation and Cerebellum in the Intact, Anesthetized and Unanesthetized in the Decerebrated Cat," *Amer. J. Physiol.*, **176**, 52–54.

250. Stern, E., Parmelee, A. H., Akiyama, Y , Schultz, M A. and Wenner, W. H. (1969), "Sleep Cycle Characteristics in Infants," *Pediatrics*, **43**, 65–70.

251. Sureau, M., Fischgold, H. and Capdevielle, G. (1950), "L'EEG du nouveau-né: normal et pathologique," *Electroenceph. clin. Neurophysiol.*, **2**, 113–114.

252. Takano, K. (1966), "Phasic, Tonic and Static Components of the Reflex Tension Obtained by Stretch at Different Rates," in *Nobel Symposium I: Muscular Afferents and Motor Control*, pp. 461–463 (R. Granit, Ed.). Stockholm: Almquist & Wiksell.

253. Tcheng, F. C. Y. and Laroche, J. L. (1965), "Phases de sommeil et sourires spontanes," *Acta Psychol.* (*Amst.*), **24**, 1–28.

254. Thomas, J. E. and Lambert, E. H. (1960), "Ulnar Nerve Conduction Velocity and H-reflex in Infants and Children," *J. appl. Physiol.*, **15**, 1–8.

255. Umezaki, H. and Morell, F. (1970), "Developmental Study of Photic Evoked Responses in Premature Infants," *Electroenceph. clin. Neurophysiol.*, **28**, 55–63.

256. Vitová, Z. and Hrbek, A. (1970), "Ontogeny of Cerebral Responses to Flickering Light in Human Infants During Wakefulness and Sleep," *Electroenceph. clin. Neurophysiol.*, **28**, 391–398.

257. Vlach, V. (1968), "Some Exteroceptive Skin Reflexes in the Limbs and Trunk in Newborn," in *Studies in Infancy*, pp. 41–55, Clinics in Developmental Medicine 27. London: S.I.M.P./Heinemann.

258. Wagner, A. L. and Buchthal, F. (1972), "Motor and Sensory

Conduction in Infancy and Childhood: Reappraisal," *Develop Med. Child. Neurol.*, **14,** 189–216.

259. Wagner, I. F. (1937), "The Establishment of a Criterion of Depth of Sleep in the Newborn Infant," *J. genet. Psychol.*, **.1,** 17–59.

260. Wagner, I. F. (1939), "Curves of Sleep Depth in Newborn Infants," *J. Genet. Psychol.*, **55,** 121–135.

261. Weinmann, H. M., Meitinger, Ch. and Vlach, V. (1969), "Polygraphische Untersuchungen exterozeptiver Reflexe bei Frühgeborenen," *Z. Kinderheilk.*, **107,** 74–86.

262. Weitzmann, E. D., Fischbein, W. and Graziani, L. (1965), "Auditory Evoked Responses Obtained from the Scalp Electroencephalogram of the Full-term Human Neonate During Sleep," *Pediatrics*, **35,** 458–462.

263. Weitzmann, E. D. and Kremen, H. (1965), "Auditory Evoked Responses During Different Stages of Sleep in Man," *Electroenceph. clin. Neurophysiol.*, **18,** 65–70.

264. Widdowson, E. M. (1971), "Effects of Early Malnutrition on General Development in Animals," in *Normal and Abnormal Development of Brain and Behaviour*, pp. 39–49 (G. B. A. Stoelinga and J. J. van der Werr ten Bosch, Ed). Leiden University Press.

265. Williams, H. L., Hammack, J. T., Daly, R. L., Dement, W. C. and Lubin, A. (1964), "Responses to Auditory Stimulation, Sleep Loss and the EEG Stages of Sleep," *Electroenceph. clin. Neurophysiol.*, **16,** 269–279.

266. Williams, H. L., Morlock, H. C., Morlock, J. V. and Lubin, A. (1964), "Auditory Evoked Responses and the EEG Stages of Sleep," *Ann. N.Y. Acad. Sci.*, **112,** 172–181.

267. Williams, H. L., Tepas, D. J. and Morlock, H. C. Jr. (1962) "Evoked Responses to Clicks and Electroencephalographic Stages of Sleep in Man," *Science*, **138,** 685–686.

268. Winick, M. (1969), "Malnutrition and Brain Development," *J. Pediat.*, **74,** 667–679.

269. Winick, M. (1970), "Cellular Growth in Intrauterine Malnutrition," *Pediat. Clin. N. Amer.*, **17,** 69–78.

270. Wolff, P. H. (1959), "Observations on Newborn Infants," *Psychosom. Med.*, **21,** 110–117.

271. Wyatt, R. J., Engelman, K., Kupfer, D. J., Scott, J., Sjoerdsma, A. and Snyder, F. (1969), "Effect of Para Chlorophenylalanine on Sleep in Man," *Electroenceph. clin. Neurophysiol.*, **27,** 529–532.

272. Wyatt, R. J., Zarcone, V., Engelman, K., Dement, W. C., Snyder, F. and Sjoerdsma, A. (1971), "Effects of 5-Hydroxytryptophan on the Sleep of Normal Human Subjects," *Electroenceph. clin. Neurophysiol.*, **30,** 505–509.

273. Yerkes, R. M. and Yerkes, A. W. (1929). *The Great Apes.* New Haven: Yale University Press; London: Humphrey Milford, Oxford University Press.

274. Zamenhof, S., van Marthens, E. and Margolis, F. L. (1968), "DNA (Cell Number) and Protein in Neonatal Brain: Alteration by Maternal Dietary Protein Restriction," Science, **160,** 322–323.

275. Zipperling, W. (1913), "Über eine besondere Form motorischer Reizzustände bei Neugeborenen," *Z. Kinderheilk.*, **5,** 31–40.

35. THE NEUROLOGICAL DEVELOPMENT OF THE INFANT

BERT C. L. TOUWEN

INTRODUCTION

This chapter is devoted to a discussion of the developmental expansion of the infant's neurological repertory. The neurological repertory denotes the manifestations of nervous activity which can be evaluated by a neurological examination, and which form a part of the infant's behavioural repertory which in turn may be assessed by a developmental examination. Although a wide overlap undoubtedly exists between a neurological and a developmental assessment, and although the one is indispensable to the other, they should be distinguished as they basically subserve different aims.

The developmental assessment is used to measure an infant's achievements in different functional areas. Comparing the achievement with preset age norms, it is possible to conclude that a retarded or an accelerated or age-appropriate developmental course of achievement exists. Development in this connotation is defined as an increase in the number of abilities which result from an interaction between nervous system properties and environmental experiences. Besides this aspect of achievement the developmental examination aims also at a description of the quality of the behaviour, though the interpretation of quality remains within the terms of age-appropriate development.

The neurological assessment is used to evaluate the manifestations of nervous activity, in order to give a judgement of the integrity of neural mechanisms. Thus the results of the neurological examination subserve an interpretation of the quality of the underlying neural mechanisms; besides this an assessment can be made of neurological development in relation to age. There need be no complete correspondence between the results of a developmental and a neurological assessment, since the neural mechanisms analysed in the neurological examination are naturally implicated but not necessarily reflected in functional development. For instance a mildly diplegic child may show age-appropriate manual abilities, and may even walk at a reasonably expected age, so that he may pass a strictly developmental assessment as belonging to a developmentally normal group of children. The neurological examination will nevertheless demonstrate impairment of the quality of movements, such as for instance a slight ataxia at voluntary reaching and gait abnormalities.

DEVELOPMENT VERSUS MATURATION

Terms like functional development and maturation are often used as synonyms, which easily leads to confusing concepts regarding the infant's properties. Both terms demonstrate an ongoing process, but while development reflects an increase of functional abilities, maturation describes the changes which occur in the underlying physical structure. For example, in the nervous system maturation is a property of the nervous tissue, development being the result of the interaction between maturation and environmental influences. Much of the confusion arose from the application of adult standards to phenomena in infants. Certainly an infant is in many instances less developed than an adult. As far as maturation is concerned however, it may be argued that the infantile nervous system is at any age perfectly mature for its own purpose, i.e. for the timely needs of the infant. The infant is not an immature or an impaired adult, irrespective of how much less developed he may be.

MATURATION AND LEARNING

Functional development is not exclusively dependent on genetically determined maturation. Gesell's maturation hypothesis[26] in which the increase of the infant's functional abilities was thought to be based mainly on preset genetic programming, cannot be maintained. This was pointed out by Conolly in a concise discussion of the problem of the relation between genetically based maturation and environmentally dependent experience.[10]

Even processes which have been considered to be based on genetically based maturation need not be solely genetically determined, as Rosenzweig claims to have demonstrated in rats.[67] Rats, which were kept in an enriched laboratory environment for thirty days from weaning onwards showed a significant weight gain of their brains compared with animals reared in a normal laboratory environment. This weight gain reflected an increase in cell volume and biochemically greater enzyme activity. Animals reared in impoverished laboratory environments showed the reverse. A less controversial example may be the modifications of brain growth and reflex ontogeny which can be induced by nutritional growth retardation (*see* Chapter Dobbing).

Tabary and Tardieu conclude after a discussion of the morphological and neurological properties of the infant's nervous system that the degree of maturation in itself may not be sufficient to explain a concurrent lower degree of motor development. In their opinion the brain should be considered capable of manifesting many more activities than are demonstrated in the infant's motor behaviour, and they conclude that experience and learning are necessary for the nervous system to display its potential.[71] Piaget holds that maturation of the CNS only opens up the possibility for new responses and functional development, but does not result in the actualization of any given response unless appropriate environmental circumstances are available (cited by [24]). However there is not a dichotomy between maturation of the nervous system and learning and experience, but rather an intimate interplay between genetic and environmental factors, which results in functional development.[3] The claim of revalidation therapy that training and exercise may improve functional development which is impaired by structural damage during maturation[440] is based on the compensatory influence of particular environmental stimulations. On the other hand it is stated that institutionalized infants show a retarded functional development compared with infants reared in ordinary family-circumstances, although no signs of neurological impairment are present.[5,59,60]

One should however clearly distinguish between long-term and short-term effects of these types of environmental deprivation. O'Connor argued in a critical review of the literature that although there was good evidence for a short-term effect of change of parent and/or home environment, long-term effects were virtually non-existent unless long-term privation of social and maternal stimuli had taken place.[52] Kagan's observations (cited by Chedd), on a tribe of Indians in Guatemala, who neglected their infants during the first years of life, except as far as feeding was concerned, are in agreement with O'Connor's opinion. The infants were functionally severely retarded at the end of their first year, but did not show any significant differences with non-neglected children at school age, either in somatic, or in emotional or cognitive development. Apparently they catch up as soon as they start to explore their environment independently, and supply themselves in this way with sufficient environmental stimulation.[9]

An acceleration of development by environmental stimulation was reported by Zelazo *et al.* who found that daily exercises of stepping movements especially during the first eight weeks of life resulted in maintenance of stepping and an earlier onset of walking unsupported. This period in which automatic stepping movements can usually easily be elicited, constitutes in their opinion a critical period for the success of the exercise.[84] Also Koch reported early functional motor development as a result of early exercise and training of infants.[39]

The significance of the quality of the environment for functional development was further clearly demonstrated by White and Held, who reported that increased handling and enrichment of the environment resulted in an increased rate of development in institutionalized infants.[79,80] The same study however, showed that enrichment before the age of six weeks resulted in a standstill or even a regression of the infants' functional behaviour. This suggests that the nervous system must have reached a certain degree of maturation before it can make use of environmental stimulation. This is another example of the fact that there are critical periods during the maturation of the nervous system, during which the effects of environmental input, such as stimulation, or biochemical agents, are most pronounced.[14,15,47]

As an example of a laboratory experiment demonstrating the importance of environmental feedback in the development of a behavioural repertory, the work of Hein, Held and Gower in kittens should be mentioned. After covering one eye in intact animals, the visually guided behaviour acquired by the open eye turned out not to be transferred to the unused eye.[32] Sander reported on the interplay between individual characteristics and environmental stimulation in very young infants. Twenty-four hour recordings of motility and crying in relation to caretaking manoeuvres during the first month of life, showed clearcut influences of the caretaking procedure on the final behavioural configuration, as well as large inter-individual variation, to which genetic determinants undoubtedly contribute.[69]

On the other hand, Tanner states "that there is every reason to believe that the higher intellectual abilities (and appearance of function, for that matter) appear only when maturation of certain structures or cell assemblies, widespread throughout the cortex, is complete".[73]

It can be concluded that the nervous system needs a particular degree of maturation in order to be able to generate particular functional phenomena, but that this degree of maturation is on the whole higher at any given time than the level of functional development would suggest. Training may be effective to a certain extent, and learning and experience play an important role in the achievement of functional abilities. The question of how the process of learning takes place in normal circumstances, remains unanswered, however, and it is quite possible that this in itself is genetically determined. In this respect it should be remembered that insults such as, for instance, infectious diseases and traumata, or hospitalization, may lead to a standstill or even a temporary regression in functional development in some infants, while in others this has no influence at all.

DEVELOPMENTAL TESTS

Developmental tests were originally designed in order to assess the mental abilities of the infant and to predict later intellectual functioning.[25,35,37] The reasoning was that adequate functional development during infancy reflected the potential of the CNS for later development. For this purpose the infant's behaviour at each age was divided into categories such as motor, adaptive, language and social-personal behaviour, and for each category a number of test items was designed that measure specific abilities. Well-known developmental tests are Gesell's developmental scale,[25] Cattell's Mental test for Infants and Young Children[8] and the Bayley Scales for Infant Development,[2] while the Denver test[20,21,22,23] is only a screening instrument. In England Griffith's Abilities of Babies[31] and Francis Williams' introduction of the Bayley Scales[19] and in the German language area Bühler-Hetzer's Kleinkindertests[7] should be mentioned. The age norms given in these tests show conspicuous differences for apparently the same abilities. There are various reasons for these differences. Standardization of technique, sampling and recording, and operational definition of test items, often differ considerably. Moreover, cultural differences have substantial influence, as has been repeatedly shown for motor development.[27,28,29,30,34,42] This means that each developmental test must be standardized anew before it can be used in another country. The predictive value of the results of developmental tests for later mental functioning has been challenged.[33,68] The value of gross motor developmental testing especially is small in this respect, but is nevertheless vital for assessment of neurological integrity.[35,37]

The value of developmental assessment for the neurological examination was already underlined by Gesell, who advised qualitative assessment of test-items besides the testing of final achievement, but was not able to construct his scales adequately for this purpose. Knobloch and Pasamanick used Gesell's scales for the construction of their Developmental Screening Inventory for Infants, which they claim is meant to detect not only retarded but also neurologically impaired infants.[38] Illingworth introduced the Gesell scales in England and adapted the age norms from his experience, stressing their value for neurological diagnosis besides developmental assessment. As in his view neurological and developmental assessment are inseparably related, he paid extra attention to the development of neurological phenomena in addition to development of functional abilities.[35] The use of neurological items such as the Moro response, grasp reflexes, tonic neck reflexes etc. as developmental items, without paying attention to qualitative changes during their developmental course, which is the case when these so called infantile responses are only scored as present or absent at consecutive age levels, does not constitute a neurological examination, however. The same remark can be made about the Denver Developmental Screening test, which contains many neurological as well as developmental items, but which has the advantage of offering percentiles for the ages of achievement of abilities, e.g. disappearance of infantile responses.[20,21,22,23]

Neither the Knobloch-Pasamanick, nor the Denver-scales pretend to offer more than a screening method. They are only meant to arouse the suspicion of the examiner about the condition of the tested infant, so that full and comprehensive assessment can follow, if necessary. In practice however, such screening tests often turn out to be used as final diagnostic instruments, which, it must be stressed, they are definitely not.

Table 1 summarizes the age norms for some motor and language development items, as given by different authors. The differences are considerable. Well established population norms for unequivocally operationally defined developmental items, based on longitudinal studies are clearly needed. The only good norms available at the moment seem to be those given by Neligan and Prudham on sitting, walking and language development[51] (Fig. 1).

TABLE 1

NORMAL VALUES (MEDIANS) FOR SOME DEVELOPMENTAL ABILITIES ACCORDING TO DIFFERENT AUTHORS (IN MONTHS)

Developmental Ability	*Gesell*[25]	*Knobloch**[38]	*Bayley*[2]	*Cattell*[8]	*Bühler*[7]	*Griffiths*[31]	*Illingworth*[35]	*Denver*[20]	*Neligan*[51]
Head-control	4–5	3–5	2·8	3	2–3	4	3·5–4	2·9	
Sits alone	8–9	8–9	6·9		9·5	8–9	8–9	5·5	6·4
Stands with support	8–9	7–9	8–9			11		5·8	
Stands alone	13–14	13–14			13–15	13		11·5	
Walks alone	15–18	15	11·8		15–18	14	13	12·1	12·8
Creeps on all fours	9–10	9–10				12	10		
Pincer grasp	11–12	11–12	9	11		9	11	10·7	
Speaks 2–3 clear words	12	12	14·5	12		12	12	12·8	12·4

* Using Gesell's norms.

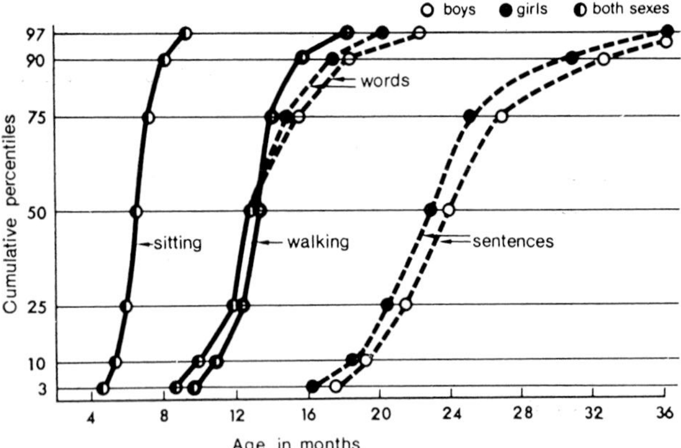

FIG. 1. Cumulative percentile curves for four standard developmental milestones, derived from a longitudinal population study.[51]

In Table 2 Neligan's data are presented together with the comparable norms offered by the Denver Developmental Screening Test.

TABLE 2

25–90 PERCENTILE RANGES FOR SOME DEVELOPMENTAL ABILITIES, ACCORDING TO THE DENVER SCALES AND TO NELIGAN AND PRUDHAM[51] (IN MONTHS)

Developmental Ability	*Denver*[20]	*Neligan*[51]
Head control	1·5– 4·2	
Sits alone	4·8– 7·8	5·8– 8·1
Stands with support	5·0–10·0	
Stands alone	9·8–13·9	
Walks alone	11·3–14·3	11·8–15·8
Pincer grasp	9·4–14·7	
Speaks 2–3 clear words	11·8–20·5	11·5–18·0

NEUROLOGICAL ASSESSMENT

As stated in the introduction, the neurological examination aims at an evaluation of neural mechanisms which underlies sensori-motor behaviour. In the neurological examination the way in which an infant performs a task or achieves an ability is more important than the ultimate achievement-level.

If functional development is a result of the interaction between maturational processes and environmental influences, it may be argued that many of the neurological phenomena analysed in the neurological examination are much less affected by learning and experience. It is difficult to understand how, for instance, the developmental course of the Moro reaction or of the palmar grasp response can directly be influenced by learning. Nevertheless other neurological items, such as supporting-reactions or parachute reactions, may easily be influenced by other factors besides maturation.

In the infant many responses and reactions can be elicited which resemble neurological signs in adult neurological patients, and which are well known to neurophysiologists from animal experiments (grasp reflexes, tonic neck reflexes, supporting reactions). This has led to the idea that these infantile responses are primitive reactions, which in the course of ontogeny disappear as a result of inhibition by higher cortical control functions. In the case of neurological disorders or aging,[58] according to this concept, the higher control functions would be impaired, so that the infantile reactions reappear as release phenomena. Such a concept tends to equate mechanisms in a pathological adult nervous system and in specifically manipulated nervous systems of (adult) animals with those of a normal nervous system in healthy infants. This is fallacious reasoning, as the infantile nervous system is qualitatively quite different from the adult nervous system. It is possible and even probable that a neurological sign in a brain damaged infant such as an obligatory asymmetric tonic neck reflex, is based on analogous impaired neural mechanisms, as in an adult patient. It is highly improbable, however, that the asymmetric tonic neck response which may frequently be observed in the two-or-three-month-old healthy infant is based on the same mechanisms. This is evident as soon as one observes the difference between the response in the healthy infant, in whom it is never obligatory and consistent and in the damaged infant or older patient, who shows a poor, stereotyped response. Neurological phenomena which are present during normal infantile development

into account the normal values arranged in percentile distributions, is offered by Zdańska and Wolański.[83] (Fig. 5.)

Something must be said about standardization of the technique.[62,63] Behavioural state, degree of alertness or

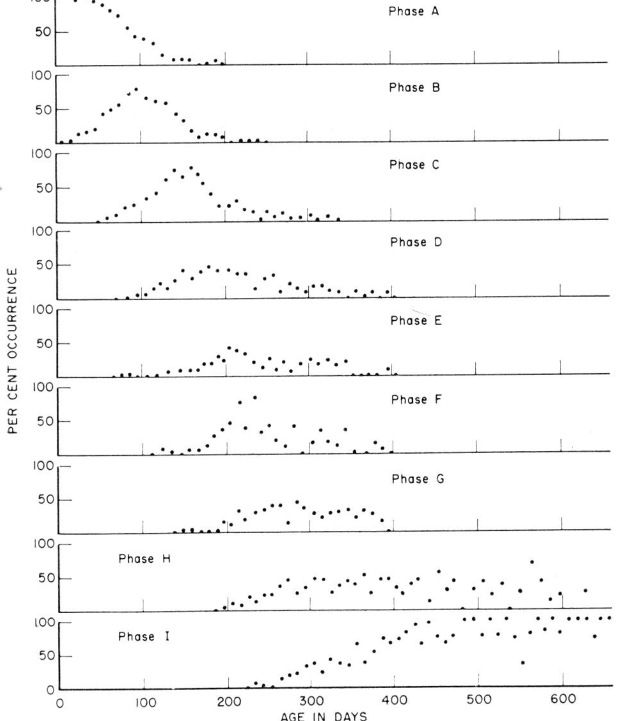

FIG. 3. Percentage distribution of each of the nine phases of prone progression (fig. 2) in a group of 82 infants.[44]

fatigue, environmental variables such as room temperature, number of persons present, character of the room in which the assessment is carried out, all influence the results of the examination, as does also the position in which the infant is assessed. Very young infants may be easily examined when lying on an examination table. From about six months onwards the mother's lap is preferable for most of the examination, as this will make the infant more co-operative. In both instances it is essential to keep the infant's position symmetrical, regarding the posture of head, trunk and extremities. As the co-operation of the infant to a large extent determines whether he can be assessed at all—neither observation of posture and spontaneous motility, nor an evaluation of the sensori-motor apparatus and responses such as the Moro response or supporting reactions is possible in a crying or otherwise upset infant—the infant needs sufficient time to adapt to the environment and to the examiner. This may often prolong the session, especially in the case of infants of about nine months of age, who are frequently afraid of strangers and unfamiliar surroundings.

SOME REMARKS ON DIFFERENTIAL DIAGNOSIS

Although an extensive discussion of neurological disorders and their symptomatology falls outside the scope of this chapter, some suspect findings which can be meaningful for early diagnosis during infancy may be discussed.

The results of the neurological examination may be broadly divided into two categories: results which are indicative of a purely functional retardation in development without specific evidence of neural damage, and on the other hand results justifying a diagnosis of dysfunction of neural mechanisms. Considering the large variability—both within and between individuals—in rate of development of different functional abilities, it is not surprising that the diagnosis of a functional retardation is not easy. Such a diagnosis requires at least two examinations at an interval of some six weeks, so that the developmental rate can be evaluated. This approach often offers more conclusive information than a determination of the achievement level. Moreover, as neurological retardation is in the majority of cases accompanied by mental retardation, a

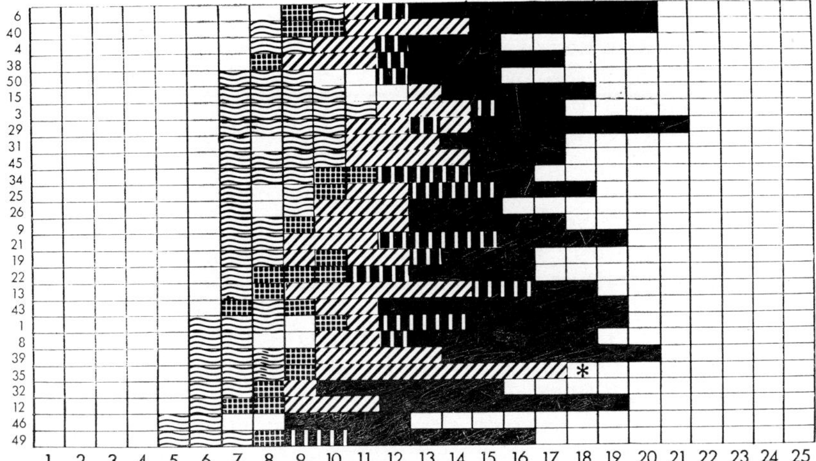

FIG. 4. Developmental course of locomotion in prone position in 27 boys.[75] Key: Wave pattern = abdominal creeping, wriggling, pivoting; grid pattern: crawling with help of arms only; diagonal pattern = crawling with help of arms and legs; vertical pattern = creeping on all fours with frequent return to abdominal crawling; solid areas = consistently creeping on all fours.

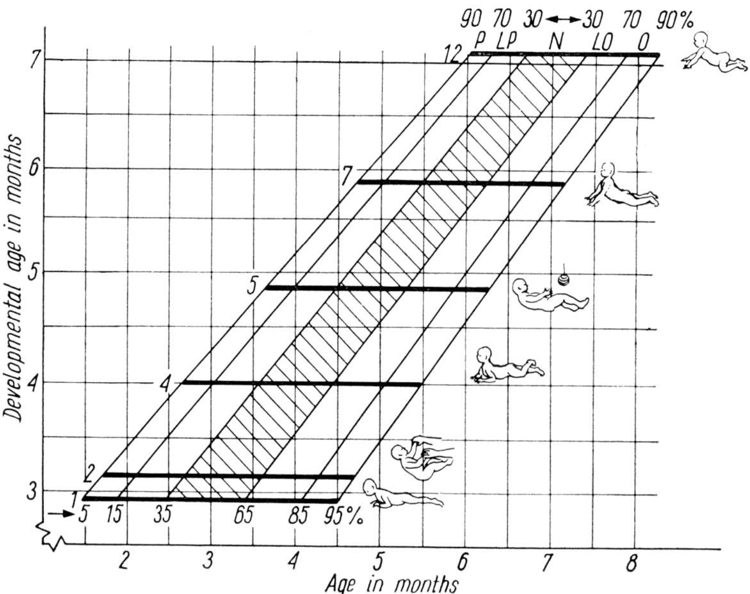

FIG. 5. Percentile grid for the evaluation of 6 stages of the development of head and trunk movements.[83] Key:

N = average (35–65 percentile)
LP = 15–35 percentile = slightly advanced.
LO = 65–85 percentile = slightly retarded.
P = 5–15 percentile = considerably advanced.
O = 85–95 percentile = considerably backward.

developmental assessment is necessary in order to test capacities not evaluated in the neurological examination.

A description of overt signs of neurological impairment and their significance may be found in clinical texts.[11,17,18,35,36,50,56,62,74] In the following paragraphs only some easily overlooked signs will be mentioned, such as may arouse the suspicion of the examiner and label the infant as being at risk of neurological disturbance.

MOTILITY

A paucity of spontaneous movements is an easily overlooked early sign of nervous dysfunction. A lack of initiative both in daily activities and in the acquisition of new abilities should always arouse the suspicion of neurological impairment in otherwise seemingly normal and alert infants. The differential diagnosis from retardation is often difficult, the more so as combinations often occur. Here a developmental assessment can be of great value.

Asymmetries in spontaneous or provoked motility are always suspicious of impairment of neural mechanisms, whatever the age of the infant. Although many infants show a preference for one hand, in most cases the right, at the end of the first year, this never leads to a consistent neglect of the other hand in a healthy infant.

Lateralized stereotyped hand or leg postures, such as for instance a closed fist on one side during use of the other hand, are often indicative of hemiplegia, as is the case with a differential developmental rate of motor functions between the arms or legs of both sides. Of clinical significance are the observations of Robson on plagiocephalic infants and shufflers.[64,65,66] The former may develop transient asymmetric walking patterns which gradually disappear during the second year of life. Although shuffling may occur in healthy infants, it should arouse the suspicion of hypotonia and the development of diplegia.

Dyskinesia such as choreoathetosis may easily escape notice, especially in the early stages. There is no uniform time course in dyskinesia. The time of first appearance may vary from the second half of the first year of life to preschool age. In the majority of cases it is preceded by hypotonia, often accompanied by psychomotor retardation. Here the behavioural state of the infant is extremely important, as early signs of dyskinesia may easily escape notice in a resisting, upset infant. Defects in co-ordination are often preceded by hypotonia, and can only be evaluated at an age at which the infant is able to manipulate objects and/or has mastered some degree of locomotion. In the case of co-ordination deficits the development of these abilities is retarded, and, even more important, it runs a different developmental course than is seen in normal infants.

HYPO- AND HYPERTONIA

Hypertonia is always an important sign of nervous dysfunction, but the differentiation from normal resistance against passive movements may be difficult. The normal vigorous and strong movements of the healthy infant during the first months of life should not be called hypertonia, as is often done by French authors.[1,70] Although in the actively moving infant an increased resistance against passive movements may be found, this so-called hypertonia immediately disappears as soon as the infant is quiet and relaxed, in contrast to pathologically increased resistance against passive movements. The latter is moreover usually accompanied by paucity of movements and stereotyped movement patterns.

The differential diagnosis of hypotonia is extensive (Table 4). Slight hypotonias are quite frequently found, often without much clinical significance, and disappear with further development of the infant. The presence of abnormal postural reactions such as head lag in sitting posture but not in prone position, or active extension of the legs on vertical suspension and swaying to and fro in vertical suspension, should arouse the suspicion of cerebral palsy. An early sign of significant hypotonia is the finding that the child when kept in vertical suspension supported under the shoulders, slips through the examiner's hands. Hypotonia which is not accompanied by deviant postural reactions and abnormal muscle reflex patterns may result from non-specific neurological diseases, muscle diseases or mental retardation. The syndrome of benign hypotonia is rare.[53] Slight asymmetries in active and passive resistance against passive movements should be interpreted very cautiously. As a general rule asymmetries which may result in hemiplegia are found much earlier on observation of spontaneous posture and voluntary motility than on the examination of the muscular apparatus. The majority of hemiplegias become manifest at an age at which the infant starts to show locomotor progression and manipulative abilities. Before that age hypotonia is often the only finding, and it may be of the same degree on both sides of the body. This example shows that abnormal neurological symptoms may also undergo changes during development, although they need not be based on a progressive brain lesion. These changes in neurological symptomatology may be caused by the developmental changes occurring in the unimpaired brain areas, but are also dependent on the site and type of the lesion. A cortical lesion for instance may remain latent as long as the particular cortical area which is damaged is not itself necessary for adequate functioning. This very often complicates the procedure of neurological diagnosis during infancy and early childhood.

Table 4

A: Metabolic and infectious disorders which may secondarily affect the neuromuscular apparatus.
B: Disorders of the C.N.S. including myelopathies.
C: Disorders of anterior horn cells.
 1. Infantile spinal muscular atrophy (Werdnig Hoffman)
 2. Poliomyelitis and related viral disorders.
D: Disorders of peripheral nerves.
 1. Guillain-Barré syndrome.
 2. Familial forms of peripheral neuropathy.
E: Disorders of neuromuscular junction—myasthenia gravis.
F: The primary myopathies.
 1. Muscular dystrophies
 2. Inflammatory myopathies
 3. Congenital non-progressive myopathy syndrome
 4. The myotonic syndrome
 5. The periodic paralyses.
G: Skeletal, tendinous, and ligamentous disorders.

Causes of congenital and infantile neuromuscular weakness (Munsat and Pearson, 1967)[50].

CONCLUSION

In conclusion it can be stated that for a proper analysis of the developing infant nervous system both developmental and neurological assessment are required. Reviewing the available methods, however, one is confronted with many difficulties. Many developmental tests are available, but they often differ so much in the way they are performed that results are not easily compared. Moreover cultural differences must be taken into consideration for the interpretation of the findings. Longitudinally collected population norms are needed.

For a proper neurological evaluation of the infant's development the developmental course of the manifestations of neural mechanisms must be investigated. This requires primarily an appreciation of the infant's nervous system as qualitatively different from the adult nervous system, so that neurological findings, collected with help of standardized and age-specific techniques can be analysed in a proper frame of reference. Longitudinally collected normal data for unequivocally defined neurological items are still scarce. More analysis of the interrelationship of items, and evaluation of the different subsystems of the nervous system, and their developmental course, are required in order to get insight into how the infant's brain works and develops. For the differential diagnosis of neurological impairment it should be remembered that both normal and abnormal neurological symptoms show a developmental course, which may change the clinical appearance considerably. This is an example of the general problem in paediatric neurology that symptoms in infancy and childhood may change although the underlying lesion may be non-progressive, due to the rapid development of the brain. It stresses the need of normative data and age-specific techniques of examination.

ACKNOWLEDGEMENTS

My thanks are due to Prof. Dr. H. F. R. Prechtl, and to Drs. A. F. Kalverboer and M. J. O'Brien, for their help in the preparation of this manuscript.

Some of the data on which this paper is based are derived from a project which was supported by a grant from the Organization for Health Research T.N.O. (the Netherlands).

REFERENCES

1. André-Thomas and Saint-Anne Dargassies, S. (1952), *Etudes neurologiques sur le nouveau-né et le jeune nourisson*. Paris: Masson et Cie.
2. Bayley, N. (1969), *Bayley Scales of Infant Development: Birth to Two Years*. New York: Psychological Corporation.
3. Bekoff, M. and Fos, M. W. (1972), "Postnatal Neural Ontogeny: Environment-dependent and/or Environment-expectant?" *Developm. Psychobiol.*, **5**, 323–341.
4. Bobath, B. (1967), "The very Early Treatment of Cerebral Palsy," *Dev. Med. Child. Neurol.*, **9**, 373–390.
5. Bowlby, J. (1952), *Maternal Care and Mental Health*, W.H.O. Monograph Series, No. 179. Geneva: World Health Organization.
6. Brain, R. and Wilkinson, M. (1959), "Observations on the Extensor Planter Reflex and its Relationship to the Functions of the Pyramidal Tract," *Brain*, **82**, 297–320.

7. Bühler, Ch. and Hetzer, H. (1932), *Kleinkindertests*. München: Barth (Shortened Edition, 1953).
8. Cattell, P. (1940, 1960), *The Measurement of Intelligence of Infants and Young Children*. New York: Science Press, 1940; Psychological Corporation, 1960.
9. Chedd, G. (1973), "Will the Mind Flourish Despite Neglect?" *New Scientist*, **11,** 71–72.
10. Conolly, K. J. (1970), "Skill Development: Problems and Plans," in (K. J. Conolly, Ed.). *Mechanisms of Motor Skill Development*, pp. 3–17. London, New York: Academic Press.
11. Dekaban, A. (1959), *Neurology of Infancy*. London: Bailliere, Tindall and Cox.
12. Dietrich, H. F. (1957), "A Longitudinal Study of the Babinski and Plantar Grasp Reflexes in Infancy," *Amer. J. Dis. Child.*, **94,** 265–271.
13. Dileo, J. H. (1967), "Developmental Evaluation of Very Young Infants," in *The Exceptional Infant. I: The Normal Infant*, pp. 121–142 (J. Hellmutt, Ed.). Seattle, Washington: Special Child Publ.
14. Dobbing, J. (1970), "Undernutrition and the Developing Brain: the Use of Animal Models to Elucidate the Human Problem," in *Normal and Abnormal Development of Brain and Behaviour*, pp. 20–39. (G. B. A. Stoelinga and J. J. v.d. Werff ten Bosch, Eds.). Leiden University Press.
15. Dobbing, J. (1970), "Undernutrition and the Developing Brain," *Amer. J. Dis. Child.*, **120,** 411–415.
16. Dreier, Th. and Wolff, P. H. (1972), "Sucking, State and Perinatal Distress in Newborns," *Biol. Neonat.*, **21,** 16–24.
17. Dubowitz, V. (1969), "The Floppy Infant," *Clin. Dev. Med.*, **31.** London: The Spastics Society with Heinemann.
18. Ford, F. R. (1966), "Diseases of the Nervous System in Infancy, Childhood and Adolescence," 5th edition. (Thomas, Ed.). Springfield, Illinois.
19. Francis-Williams, J., and Yule, W. (1967), "The Bayley Infant Scales of Mental and Motor Development. An Exploratory Study with an English Sample," *Develop. Med. Child Neurol.*, **9,** 391–401.
20. Frankenburg, W. K. and Dodds, J. B. (1967), "The Denver Developmental Screening Test," *J. Pediat.*, **71,** 181–191.
21. Frankenburg, W. K., Goldstein, A. D. and Camp, B. W. (1971), "The Revised Denver Developmental Screening Test: its Accuracy as a Screening Instrument," *J. Pediat.*, **79,** 988–995.
22. Frankenburg, W. K., Camp, B. W. and Van Natta, P. A. (1971), "Validity of the Denver Developmental Screening Test," *Child Developm.*, **42,** 475–485.
23. Frankenburg, W. K., Camp, B. W., Van Natta, P. A., Demarsseman, J. A. and Voorhees, S. F. (1971), "Reliability and Stability of the Denver Developmental Screening Test," *Child Developm.*, **42,** 1315–1325.
24. Freedman, D. A. and Cannady, C. (1971), "Delayed Emergence of Prone Locomotion," *J. nerv. ment. Dis.*, **153,** 108–117.
25. Gesell, A. and Amatruda, C. S. (1947; reprinted 1969), *Developmental Diagnosis*. New York: Harper and Row.
26. Gesell, A. (1954), "The Ontogeny of Infant Behaviour," in *Manual of Child Psychology* (L. Carmichael, Ed.). London: Wiley.
27. Goldberg, S. (1972), "Infant Care and Growth in Urban Zambia," *Human Develop.*, **15,** 77–89.
28. Grantham-McGregor, S. M. and Back, E. H. (1971), "Gross Motor Development in Jamaican Infants," *Develop. Med. Child Neurol.*, **13,** 79–87.
29. Grantham-McGregor, S. M. and Back, E. H. (1971), "Developmental Assessment of Jamaican Infants," *Develop. Med. Child Neurol.*, **13,** 582–589.
30. Greenfield, P. M. (1972), "Cross-cultural Studies of Mother-infant Interaction: Towards a Structural-functional Approach," *Human Develop.*, **15,** 131–138.
31. Griffiths, R. (1954), *The Abilities of Babies*. University of London Press.
32. Hein, A., Held, R. and Gower, E. C. (1970), "Development and Segmentation of Visually Controlled Movement by Selective Exposure during Rearing," *J. comp. physiol. psychol.*, **73,** 181–187.
33. Hindley, C. B. (1960), "The Griffiths Scale of Infant Development: Scores and Predictions from 3–18 Months," *J. Child Psychol. Psychiat.*, **1,** 99–112.
34. Hindley, C. B., Filliozat, A. M., Klackenberg, G., Nicolet-Meister, D. and Sand, E. A. (1966), "Differences in the Age of Walking in Five European Longitudinal Samples," *Hum. Biol.*, **38,** 364–379.
35. Illingworth, R. S. (1966), *The Development of the Infant and Young Child, Normal and Abnormal*, 3rd edition. Edinburgh and London: Livingstone.
36. Illingworth, R. S. (1966), "The Diagnosis of Cerebral Palsy in the First Year of Life," *Develop. Med. Child Neurol.*, **8,** 178–194.
37. Knobloch, H. and Pasamanick, B. (1963), "Predicting Intellectual Potential in Infancy," *Amer. J. Dis. Child*, **106,** 43–51.
38. Knobloch, H., Pasamanick, B. and Sherard, E. S., Jr. (1966), "A Developmental Screening Inventory for Infants," *Pediatrics*, suppl., **38,** 1095–1108.
39. Koch, J. (1969), "The Influence of Early Motor Stimulation on Motility and on Mental Development in Infancy," *Act. Nerv. Sup.* (*Praha*), **11,** 312–313.
40. Köng, E. (1966), "Very Early Treatment of Cerebral Palsy," *Develop. Med. Child Neurol.*, **8,** 198–202.
41. Lamote de Grignon, C. (1955), "La dissolution du réflexe de Moro et son integration dans la conduite du nourisson," *Revue Neurologique*, **93,** 217–225.
42. Lewis, M. and Wilson, C. D. (1972), "Infant Development in Lower-Class American Families," *Human Develop.*, **151,** 112–127.
43. Linden, J. (1969), "Der Greifreflex des Fusses und seine Bedeutung in der Reihenfolge Cerebraler Abbauerscheinungen," *Der Nervenarzt.*, **40,** 497–500.
44. McGraw, M. B. (1943), *The Neuromuscular Maturation of the Human Infant* (repr. ed. 1969). New York: Hafner.
45. Milani-Comparetti, A. and Gidoni, E. A. (1967), "Pattern Analysis of Motor Development and its Disorders," *Develop. Med. Child Neurol.*, **9,** 625–630.
46. Milani-Comparetti, A. and Gidoni, E. A. (1967), "Routine Developmental Examination in Normal and Retarded Children," *Develop. Med. Child Neurol.*, **9,** 631–638; 766.
47. Miller, N. E. (1968), "The Brain's Critical Periods," *Impact Sci. Soc.*, **18,** 157–167.
48. Mitchell, R. G. (1960), "The Moro Reflex," *Cerebral Palsy Bull.*, **2,** 135–141.
49. Mitchell, R. G. (1962), "The Landau Reaction (Reflex)," *Develop. Med. Child Neurol.*, **4,** 65–70.
50. Munsat, T. L. and Pearson, C. M. (1967), "The Differential Diagnosis of Neuromuscular Weakness in Infancy and Childhood. I. Non Dystrophic Disorders," *Develop. Med. Child Neurol.*, **9,** 222–230; II. "Dystrophic Myopathies," *Develop. Med. Child Neurol.*, **9,** 319–328.
51. Neligan, G. and Prudham, D. (1969), "Norms for Four Standard Developmental Milestones by Sex, Social Class and Place in Family," *Develop. Med. Child Neurol.*, **11,** 413–422.
52. O'Connor, N. (1971), "Children in Restricted Environments," *Psychiatria, Neurologia, Neurochirurgia*, **74,** 71–77.
53. Paine, R. S. (1963), "The Future of the 'Floppy Infant', a Follow-up Study of 133 Patients," *Develop. Med. Child Neurol.*, **5,** 115–125.
54. Paine, R. S. (1964), "The Evolution of Infantile Postural Reflexes in the Presence of Chronic Brain Syndromes," *Develop. Med. Child Neurol.*, **6,** 345–361.
55. Paine, R. S., Brazelton, T. B., Donovan, D. E., Drorbaugh, J. E., Hubbell, J. P. and Sears, E. M. (1964), "Evolution of Postural Reflexes in Normal Infants and in the Presence of Chronic Brain Syndromes," *Neurology* (*Minneapolis*), **14,** 1036–1048.
56. Paine, R. S. and Oppé, T. E. (1966), "Neurological Examination of Children," *Clin. Dev. Med.*, **20/21.** London: Spastic Society with Heinemann.
57. Parmelee, Jr., A. H. (1964), "A Critical Evaluation of the Moro Reflex," *Pediatrics*, **33,** 773–788.
58. Paulson, G. and Gottlieb, G. (1968), "Developmental Reflexes: the Reappearance of Foetal and Neonatal Reflexes in Aged Patients," *Brain*, **91,** 37–52.

59. Pechstein, J. (1968), "Entwicklungsphysiologische Untersuchungen an Säuglingen und Kleinkindern in Heimen. Beitrag zur Frage der Frühkindlichen Deprivation," *Mschr. Kinderheilk.*, **116**, 372–373.

60. Pechstein, J. (1968), "Frühkindliche Deprivation durch Massenpflege," *Fortschritte der Medizin*, **86**, 409–412.

61. Poeck, K. (1968), "Die Bedeutung der Reizqualität für die Greifreflexe beim menschlichen Neugeborenen und Säugling," *Deutsche Zschr. Nervenheilk.*, **192**, 317–327.

62. Prechtl, H. F. R. and Beintema, D. J. (1964), "The Neurological Examination of the Full-term Newborn Infant," *Clin. Dev. Med.*, **12.** London: Spastics Society with Heinemann.

63. Prechtl, H. F. R. (1972), "Strategy and validity of early detection of neurological dysfunction," in *Mental Retardation: Prenatal Diagnosis and Infant Assessment*, pp. 41–47 (C. P. Douglas and K. S. Holt, Eds.). London: Butterworths.

64. Robson, P. (1968), "Persisting Headturning in the Early Months: some Effects in the Early Years," *Develop. Med. Child Neurol.*, **10**, 82–92.

65. Robson, P. (1970), "Shuffling, Hitching, Scooting or Sliding. Some Observations in 30 Otherwise Normal Children," *Develop. Med. Child Neurol.*, **12**, 608–617.

66. Robson, R. and Mackeith, R. C. (1971), "Shufflers with Spastic Diplegic C.P. A Confusing Clinical Picture," *Develop. Med. Child Neurol.*, **13**, 651–659.

67. Rosenzweig, M. R., Bennett, E. L. and Diamond, M. C. (1972), "Brain Changes in Response to Experience," *Sci. Amer.* **226**, No. 2, 22–30.

68. Rutter, M. (1970), "Psychological Development—Predictions from Infancy," *J. Child Psychol. Psychiat.*, **11**, 49–62.

69. Sander, L. W. (1969), "Regulation and Organization in the Early Infant Caretaker System," in *Brain and early behaviour*, pp. 311–332 (R. J. Robinson, Ed.). London, New York: Academic Press.

70. Saint-Anne Dargassies, S. (1972), "Neurodevelopmental Signs during the First Year of Life," *Develop. Med. Child Neurol.*, **14**, 235–264.

71. Tabary, J. C. and Tardieu, G. (1967), "Etude critique de l'interprétation de l'évolution motrice de l'enfant normal avec application à l'infirmité motrice cérébrale, maturation et apprentissage," in *Les feuillets de l'infirmité motrice cérébrale, chapitr. IV. A*, pp. 1–35. Paris: Association Nation des IMC.

72. Taft, L. T. and Cohen, H. J. (1967), "Neonatal and Infant Reflexology," in *The Exceptional Infant I: The Normal Infant*, pp. 79–120 (J. Hellmuth, Ed.). Seattle, Washington: Special Child Publ.

73. Tanner, J. M. (1970), "Physical Growth," in *Carmichael's Manual of Child Psychology*, 3rd edition, pp. 77–157 (P. H. Mussen, Ed.). New York, London: Wiley.

74. Tizard, J. P. M. (1969), "Neuromuscular Disorders in Infancy," in *Disorders of voluntary muscle*, 2nd edition (J. N. Walton, Ed.). London: Churchill.

75. Touwen, B. C. L. (1971), "A Study on the Development of Some Motor Phenomena in Infancy," *Develop. Med. Child Neurol.*, **13**, 435–446.

76. Twitchell, Th.E. (1970), "Reflex Mechanisms and the Development of Prehension," in *Mechanisms of Motor Skill Development*, pp. 25–38 (K. Conolly, Ed.). London, New York: Academic Press.

77. Vassella, F. and Karlsson, B. (1962), "Asymmetric Tonic Neck Reflex," *Develop. Med. Child Neurol.*, **4**, 363–369.

78. Vassella, F. (1968), "Die neurologische Untersuchung des Säuglings und Kleinkindes," in "Aspekte der pädiatrische Neurologie" (F. Vassella, Ed.), *Päd. Fortbildungskurse*, **24**, 1–22. Basel, New York: Karper.

79. White, B. L. and Held, R. (1966), "Plasticity and Sensorimotor Development in the Human Infant," in *The Causes of Behavior: Readings in Child Development and Education. Psychology* (2nd edition) (J. F. Rosenblith and W. Allensmith, Eds.). Boston: Allyn and Bacon.

80. White, B. L. (1967), "An Experimental Approach to the Effects of Experience on Early Human Behavior," in "Minnesota Symposium on Child Psychology" (J. P. Hill, Ed.). *Univ. Minnesota Press, Minneapolis*, **1**, 201–225.

81. Zappella, M. (1966), "The Placing Reaction in the First Year of Life," *Develop. Med. Child Neurol.*, **8**, 393–401.

82. Zappella, M. (1967), "Placing and Grasping of the Feet at Various Temperatures in Early Infancy," *Pediatrics*, **39**, 93–96.

83. Zdańska-Brińcken, M. and Wolański, N. (1969), "A Graphic Method for the Evaluation of Motor Development in Infants," *Develop. Med. Child Neurol.*, **11**, 228–241.

84. Zelazo, Ph.R., Zelazo, N. A. and Kolb, S. (1972), "'Walking' in the Newborn," *Science*, **176**, 314–315.

36. THE BEGINNINGS AND FRUITION OF THE SELF—AN ESSAY ON D. W. WINNICOTT

MASUD KHAN, JOHN A. DAVIS AND MADELEINE E. V. DAVIS

Historical Introduction

Nature and function of maternal provision

Early psychic functioning
- Integration and unintegration
- Personalization
- Object relating

Reality adaptation

Innate morality

HISTORICAL INTRODUCTION

To evaluate Dr. Donald Winnicott's contributions to the study of human nature one has to see them in the context of a certain climate of psychiatric and psychoanalytic research both locally in the British Psychoanalytic Society and generally in the European culture following the revolutionary work of Freud. The same cultural forces and factors in the nineteenth century that crystallized the genius of Karl Marx actualized that of Sigmund Freud. Both thinkers were reacting against and trying to remedy the progressive alienation of the individual both from himself and from his fellow men under the impact of the mammoth growth of technology and the rapid wealth and acute misery that it had created (cf. Mézaros, 1970),[13] yet no two thinkers reacting to the same cultural factors sought such different routes and remedies as Marx and Freud.

Freud was a militantly private individual and both from personal reasons and from his medical education sought to understand the predicament of the individual in terms of the individual himself and what constituted the facts of his psychic, emotional and sexual life. Freud has left us a vivid account of his struggle with himself towards finding his bearings in this dark and mysterious domain of human experience in his correspondence with Fliess (Freud, 1954).[6] By the very nature of his search Freud was compelled to isolate the individual, following the model of medical and surgical patients, in order to examine and establish the nature and dynamics of the processes within him. That which was a private and historical necessity to Freud, institutional psychoanalysis turned into dogma. It made out that psychoanalytic discoveries of Freud were entirely self-generating and unamenable to any other influence from the neighbouring disciplines. Freud's official biographer, Ernest Jones (1953–7)[12] maximalized this bias in evaluating Freud's way of thinking. It is true that Freud had deliberately and advisedly dissociated himself from the cacophany of socio-literary trends rife at the end of the nineteenth century with their rather vehement, and often misguided, prejudice that man was the victim of his social environment and its morality. But the fact that Freud wilfully succeeded in pursuing his own insights and disregraded the intellectual ferment of his time should not mislead us to believe that he was not influenced by them. Trilling (1955),[17] Rieff (1959),[15] and more recently Johnston (1972)[11] have made significant contributions towards a historical understanding of the cultural influences that are inherent in Freud's way of thinking.

The one overruling bias of his century that Freud could never shed was to try to explain the human individual on the model of a machine; that is, as an isolate, determined in its functioning by the dynamics built into it. As psychoanalysis evolved and enlarged its scope it ran into two basic difficulties: first that the temperament of each individual who came to psychoanalysis conditioned his style of assimilating its basic theories as postulated by Freud, and second that as psychoanalysis travelled outside Vienna the impact of the cultures in which it was practised dynamically changed its character. For example, in the United States of America it became more pragmatic, in France more intellectual and in England more empirical. Hence all the squabbles that have chequered and enriched the course of the International Psychoanalytic movement (cf. Ellenburger, 1970).[2]

Freud never claimed that he had discovered either the unconscious or introspection as a means of knowing oneself. Starting with Rousseau in particular, and all through the nineteenth century, writers and philosophers had sought various means of transcending the confines of merely conscious self-awareness and have left us detailed accounts of their often macabre experiments with extending self-awareness (cf. Whyte, 1960[18]; Hayter, 1971[9]; Girard, 1963[8]). Freud's unique contribution was that he invented a new way of making the unconscious accessible to consciousness and this revealed characteristics of unconscious mental functioning hitherto unknown in epistemology. By establishing an exclusive private physical setting (the analytic situation) where one person could speak about himself to another without constraint, Freud made it possible for quite a different type of relationship and communication to actualize. The clinical data that accrued from this way of relating and communicating (the transference) enabled Freud to construct all his theories about infantile sexuality and the complex way the human psyche operates. One basic inference from these researches was that the psyche has laws peculiar and specific to its functioning and no matter what the familial and socio-economic conditions may be, each individual internalizes these factors subjectively and constructs his own psychic life according to his own endowment. The emphasis hence was on the nature and quality of the subjective assimilation of the lived experience and its elaboration through fantasy systems, both in order to master it and to extend it. The unconscious fantasy systems, as a way of coping with the biological instinctual inner needs and the demands of external reality thus became the chief area of psychoanalytic research.

In the early 'twenties a new dimension in clinical research was added to the analytic treatment of adults: namely that of child analysis. Anna Freud in Vienna and Melanie Klein in Berlin started this speciality of analytic work and soon extreme differences of approach became apparent in their handling of the child patient (cf. Smirnoff, 1972)[16]. Melanie Klein (1932)[10] insisted that there was no difference of technique involved and the child's unconscious fantasies were as readily amenable to the analytic process through the play technique as those of the adult through verbal free association. Anna Freud (1927)[4] argued that the child's immature ego functioning and *actual* dependence on the parental objects entailed modification of the classical analytic technique. The issue rapidly took a political turn and the conflict for the time being was resolved by Ernest Jones inviting Melanie Klein to teach in London.

Melanie Klein came to London in the late 'twenties, and the next two decades of research in the British Psychoanalytic Society were predominantly inspired by her researches. It was her work which enabled psychoanalytic theory in this country to transcend the boundaries placed upon it by its almost exclusive concern with Oedipal relationships and with the libidinal fixation points. This concern had hitherto led to the very careful choice of the patient for psychoanalysis, only those labelled "psychoneurotic" being thought of as suitable for this treatment. But Klein, in her analyses went (in Winnicott's words) "deeper and deeper into the mental mechanisms of her patients and then . . . applied her concepts to the growing baby".[19] Her original contribution to psychoanalytic theory shifts the emphasis from a three-body relationship (Oedipal) to a two-body relationship, that between the infant and the mother. It is concerned with the aetiology of illnesses associated with depression, and, in so far as the two-body relationship founders, with that of schizophrenia. Henceforward, it became possible for experienced analysts to use the psychoanalytic method to help patients whose illness was at root psychotic and to derive from these analyses material relating to the development of the Self from earliest infancy.

It was Winnicott's belief that:

> "Elucidation of the earliest stages of emotional development must come chiefly through psychoanalysis, psychoanalysis being by far the most precise instrument, whether it be used in the analysis of small children or of regressed adults or of psychotics of all ages or of relatively normal people who make temporary or even momentary regressions. Within the psychoanalytic framework there is opportunity for an infinite variety of experience, and if from various analyses certain common factors emerge, then we can make definite claims."[20]

This is not to say that Winnicott eschewed the role of direct observation. He came to psychoanalysis through paediatrics, and it was through observation and history-taking as a paediatrician that he first felt the limitations of classical psychoanalytic theory, and so sought out and became for a time the pupil of Melanie Klein. In his writings we find his conceptual structures continually pegged down to actual observations of infants with their mothers and of small children as well as to clinical descriptions of patients of all ages. But "direct observation is not able of itself to construct a psychology of early infancy."[21]

Winnicott sustained the dialogue between paediatrics and psychoanalysis across four decades. His first book, entitled *Clinical Notes on Disorders of Childhood* (1931) is concerned with the care and cure of children as is his last, *Therapeutic Consultations in Child Psychiatry* (1971). Perhaps it is in this sphere, and particularly in the therapeutic interview with children, that his unique talent for communicating with and relating to (while always respecting) the inner core of human beings was recognized by those who sought his help, and will be sorely missed. Something of it, fortunately, remains permanent in his written works. It is nevertheless a fact that any child brought to him for psychotherapy, as well as any adult in analysis with him, was receiving the benefit of, and contributing to, a complex and consistent theoretical structure built up through years of scrupulously conducted analytic work.

NATURE AND FUNCTION OF MATERNAL PROVISION

Winnicott's most revolutionary gesture is epitomized by his statement at the Scientific Meeting of the British Psychoanalytic Society in 1940: "THERE IS NO SUCH THING AS AN INFANT." Later on he explained in a footnote: "meaning, of course, that whenever one finds an infant one finds maternal care, and without maternal care there would be no infant".

The conception in itself was not new, and Winnicott was aware of this, as he himself quotes Freud's significant passage from *Formulations on the Two Principle of Mental Functioning* (1911):

> "It will be rightly objected that an organisation which was a slave to the pleasure principle and neglected the reality of the external world could not maintain itself alive for the shortest time, so that it could not have come into existence at all. The employment of a fiction like this, is, however, justified when one considers that the infant—provided one includes with it the care it receives from its mother—does almost realise a psychical system of this kind."[5]

But in order to work out his theories at the time, Freud had to disregard the nature and character of "the care it (the infant) receives from its mother."

For Winnicott the crux of the matter was that "the infant and the maternal care together form a unit," and it was towards the understanding of the psychodynamics of this unit that he devoted all his energies of mind and clinical labours.

In the first of *Nine Broadcast Talks*, entitled *The Ordinary Devoted Mother and Her Baby* (Autumn, 1949), Winnicott states his position with colloquial and explicit candour:

> "If human babies are to develop eventually into healthy independent and society-minded adult individuals they absolutely depend on being given a good start, and this good start is assured in nature by the existence of the

bond between the baby's mother and the baby, the thing called love. So if you love your baby the baby is getting a good start.

"Let me quickly say that I'm not talking about sentimentality. You all know the kind of person who goes about saying, 'I simply *adore* babies.' But you wonder, do they love them? A mother's love is a pretty crude affair. There's possessiveness in it, there's appetite in it, there's a 'drat the kid' element in it, there's generosity in it, there's power in it, as well as humility. But sentimentality is outside it altogether and is repugnant to mothers."[22]

Winnicott defines in this context the role of the father as well:

"Fathers come into this, not only by the fact that they can be good mothers for limited periods of time, but also because they can help protect the mother from whatever tends to interfere with the mother-infant bond, which is the essence and very nature of child care. . . .[22] This is where the father can help. He can help provide a space in which the mother has elbow room. Properly protected by her man the mother is saved from having to turn outwards to deal with her surroundings at the time when she is wanting so badly to turn inwards, when she is longing to be concerned with the inside of the circle which she can make with her arms, in the centre of which is the baby. This period of time in which the mother is naturally preoccupied with the one infant does not last long. The mother's bond with the baby is very powerful at the beginning and we must do all we can to enable the mother to be a mother preoccupied with her baby at the time when it is natural, which is at the beginning."[23]

These passages establish three facts: one, that a baby needs its mother; two, that a mother enjoys taking care of her baby; and three that the bond between the two is facilitated and protected by the presence of the father. By the very nature of its clinical material most analytic writings give one the impression that the whole business of being an infant is frought with terrible predicaments. It is one of the salutary implications of Winnicott's researches that infant rearing can be an exciting and happy experience for all concerned, and furthermore that nature has allowed for it to be so. The endless complications that can arise should not blind us to the ordinary naturalness of parents who enjoy rearing their infant to health and maturity, nor to their adequacy to do so.

The most comprehensive statement of Winnicott's theory of infant care is given in his paper *The Theory of the Parent–Infant Relationship* (1960). For Winnicott *dependence* is the *core* of the infant's experience of infant care, and he makes his stand *vis-à-vis* the issue of inherited potential of the infant explicit:

"Infants come into being differently according to whether the conditions are favourable or unfavourable. At the same time, conditions do not determine the infant's potential. This is inherited, and it is legitimate to study this inherited potential of the individual as a separate issue, provided always that it is accepted that the inherited potential of an infant cannot become an infant unless linked to maternal care."[24]

The inherited potential of the infant includes an innate tendency towards growth and development, but its realization depends on the facilitating infant care and maternal environment. Winnicott classifies satisfactory parental care in three overlapping stages:

"(a) Holding.

"(b) Mother and infant living together. Here the father's function (of dealing with the environment for the mother) is not known to the infant.

"(c) Father, mother, and infant, all three living together."[24]

The concept of "holding" is crucial to our understanding of Winnicott's theories of infant care. He extends the ordinary use of the word which denotes the actual physical holding of the infant to include "the total environment provision prior to the concept of *living with*."[24] For him it is a "three dimensional or space relationship,"[24] to which time is gradually added, and his qualifying statement is important:

"This (holding) overlaps with but is initiated prior to, instinctual experiences that in time would determine object relationships. It includes the management of experiences that are inherent in existence, such as the completion (and therefore the non-completion) of processes, processes which from the outside may seem to be purely physiological but which belong to infant psychology and take place in a complex psychological field, determined by the awareness and the empathy of the mother."[24]

In the holding phase the infant is maximally dependent. Through the maturational processes this dependence changes in character and Winnicott distinguishes three types of dependence:

"(i) Absolute Dependence. In this state the infant has no means of knowing about the maternal care, which is largely a matter of prophylaxis. He cannot gain control over what is well and what is badly done, but is only in a position to gain profit or to suffer disturbance.

"(ii) Relative Dependence. Here the infant can become aware of the need for the details of maternal care, and can to a growing extent relate them to personal impulse, and then later, in a psychoanalytic treatment, can reproduce them in the transference.

"(iii) Towards Independence. The infant develops means for doing without actual care. This is accomplished through the accumulation of memories of care, the projection of personal needs and the introjection of care details, with the development of confidence in the environment. Here must be added the element of intellectual understanding with its tremendous implications."[24]

Winnicott's stand on the issue of the role of dependence in the infant's experience of holding through maternal care made his whole approach to this area of analytic theorizing divergent from that of Melanie Klein.

"There is nothing in Klein's work that contradicts the idea of absolute dependence, but there seems to me to be no specific reference to a stage at which the infant exists only because of the maternal care, together with which it forms a unit."[24]

Winnicott also questions Freud's hypothesis of hallucinatory wish-fulfilment in early infancy:

"At this point, it is necessary to look again at Freud's statement quoted earlier. He writes: 'Probably it (the baby) hallucinates the fulfilment of its inner needs; it betrays its pain due to increase of stimulation and delay of satisfaction by the motor discharge of crying and struggling, and then experiences the hallucinated satisfaction.' The theory indicated in this part of the statement fails to cover the requirements of the earliest phase. Already by these words reference is being made to object relationships, and the validity of this part of Freud's statement depends on his taking for granted the earlier aspects of maternal care, those which are here described as belonging to the holding phase. On the other hand, this sentence of Freud fits exactly the requirements in the *next* phase, that which is characterised by a relationship between infant and mother in which object relationships and instinctual or erotogenic-zone satisfactions hold sway; that is, when development proceeds well."[24]

The reason why it is important to state Winnicott's concept of the infant's experience in the stage of absolute dependence at such length in relation to Freud and Klein is that for Winnicott the difference between need-satisfaction and wish-fulfilment was a very fateful one. He makes this explicit indistinguishing between ego-needs and id-needs:

"It must be emphasized that in referring to the meeting of infant needs I am not referring to the satisfaction of instincts. In the area that I am examining the instincts are not yet clearly defined as internal to the infant. The instincts can be as much external as can a clap of thunder or a hit. The infant's ego is building up strength and in consequence is getting towards a state in which id-demands will be felt as part of the self, and not as environmental. When this development occurs, the id-satisfaction becomes a very important strengthener of the ego, or of the True Self; but id-excitements can be traumatic when the ego is not yet able to include them, and not yet able to contain the risks involved and the frustrations experienced up to the point when id-satisfaction becomes a fact."[25]

The change from the classical position is summed up in this sentence: "id-relationship . . . is a recurring complication in what might be called ego life."[26]

The growth in the infant at the stage of absolute dependence, then, is nurtured and facilitated by the empathic care of the mother, a function which Winnicott defines as:

"Holding:

"Protects from physiological insult.

"Takes account of the infant's skin sensitivity, visual sensitivity, sensitivity to falling (action of gravity) and of the infant's lack of knowledge of the existence of anything other than the self.

"It includes the whole routine of care throughout the day and night, and it is not the same with any two infants because it is part of the infant, and no two infants are alike.

"Also it follows the minute day-to-day changes belonging to the infant's growth and development, both physical and psychological."[24]

If the holding provision is adequate, then it, in time, forms the basis for the infant's first object relationships and his first experiences of instinctual gratification. This early stage of maximal adaptation on the part of the mother begins to give way to a graduated failure of maternal care fitting in with the increasing maturity of the infant:

"The next stage, that of relative dependence, turns out to be a stage of adaptation with a gradual failing of adaptation. It is part of the equipment of the great majority of mothers to provide a graduated de-adaptation, and this is nicely geared to the rapid developments that the infant displays. For instance, there is the beginning of intellectual understanding, which develops as a vast extension of simple processes, such as conditioned reflexes. (Think of an infant expecting a feed. The time comes when the infant can wait a few minutes because noises indicate that food is about to appear. Instead of simply being excited by the noises, the infant uses the news item in order to be able to wait.)"[27]

The whole issue hinges here on a "steady presentation of the world to the infant."[27] It is in this context that we should now examine another concept of Winnicott's, namely that of *impingement*.

The concept of trauma is a very well established one in psychoanalytic literature. Freud had postulated clearly and definitively the role of repressed traumatic experiences in the aetiology of hysteria and Otto Rank had, some two decades later, postulated the concept of birth trauma. Winnicott offers us quite a new way of approaching the role of traumata in early infancy in his concept of impingement. To start with he does not consider the birth experience traumatic as such. He discusses the issue at length in his paper "Birth Memories, Birth Trauma and Anxiety" (1949), and his own view is clearly stated.

". . . in the natural process *the birth experience is an exaggerated sample of something already known to the infant*. For the time being, during birth, the infant is a reactor and the important thing is the environment; and then after birth there is a return to a state of affairs in which the important thing is the infant, whatever that means. In health, the infant is prepared before birth for some environmental impingement, and already has had the experience of a natural return from reacting to a state of not having to react, which is the only state in which the self can begin to be. This is the simplest possible statement that I can make about the normal birth process. It is a temporary phase of reaction and therefore loss of identity, a major example, for which the infant has already been prepared, of interference with the personal 'going along,' not so powerful or so prolonged as to snap the thread of the infant's continuous personal process."[28]

For Winnicott the most important thing about impingements is that they compel the infant to *react*. At the very earliest stage of emotional development, he says,

> ". . . it is necessary not to think of the baby as a person who gets hungry, and whose instinctual drives may be met or frustrated, but to think of the baby as an immature being who is all the time *on the brink of unthinkable anxiety*. Unthinkable anxiety is kept away by this vitally important function of the mother at this stage, her capacity to put herself in the baby's place and to know what the baby needs in the general management of the body, and therefore of the person. Love, at this stage, can only be shown in terms of body care, as in the last stage before full-term birth.
>
> "Unthinkable anxiety has only a few varieties, each being the clue to one aspect of normal growth.
>
> (1) Going to pieces.
> (2) Falling forever.
> (3) Having no relationship to the body.
> (4) Having no orientation.
>
> "It can be said that good-enough ego-coverage by the mother (in respect of the unthinkable anxieties) enables the new human person to build up a personality on the pattern of a continuity of going-on-being. All failures (that could produce unthinkable anxiety) bring about a reaction of the infant, and this reaction cuts across the going-on-being. . . . The infant whose pattern is one of fragmentation of the line of continuity of being has a developmental task that is, almost from the beginning, loaded in the direction of psychopathology."[29]

To this should be added a complementary statement:

> "Impingements may be met and dealt with by the ego-organisation, gathered into the infant's omnipotence and sensed as projections. On the other hand, they may get through this defence in spite of the ego-support which maternal care provides. Then the central core of the ego is affected, and this is the very nature of psychotic anxiety. In health the individual soon becomes invulnerable in this respect, and if external factors impinge there is merely a new degree and quality in the hiding of the central self. In this respect, the best defence is the organisation of a false self. Instinctual satisfactions and object relationships themselves constitute a threat to the individual's personal going-on-being. Example: a baby is feeding at the breast and obtains satisfaction. This fact by itself does not indicate whether he is having an ego-syntonic id-experience, or, on the contrary, is suffering the trauma of a seduction, a threat to personal ego continuity, a threat by an id-experience which is not ego-syntonic, and with which the ego is not equipped to deal."[24]

From Winnicott's writings, then, we may make a classification of impingement thus:

1. *Traumatic impingement* which leads to the unthinkable anxieties, with which neither the mind nor the ego can cope.
2. *Intrusive impingement* which demands defence and is dealt with by dissociation and the organisation of a false self.
3. *Relative impingement* which is allowed for by the state of development. The result is increment.

From all this emerges with even greater clarity the importance of the function of holding which is the concern of the "ordinary devoted mother." Many analysts and others from neighbouring disciplines have accused Winnicott of either sentimentalizing the role of the mother or exaggerating its importance. It is as well to remember that when Winnicott talks of the "ordinary devoted mother" he is employing a complex metaphor that assumes a variety of agents and factors: the society, the family, the father and his wife (the mother), and the non-human environment which the mother has to modify for and initiate to her infant. Criticism of his position led Winnicott to stating what enabled a particular mother to meet the needs of her particular infant. In his paper, *Primary Maternal Preoccupation* (1956), he gives us a moving and detailed account of what prepares and equips a mother for her role of "holding":

> "It is my thesis that in the earliest phase we are dealing with a very special state of the mother, a psychological condition which deserves a name, such as Primary Maternal Preoccupation. I suggest that sufficient tribute has not yet been paid in our literature, or perhaps anywhere, to a very special psychiatric condition of the mother, of which I would say the following things:
>
> It gradually develops and becomes a state of heightened sensitivity during, and especially towards the end of, pregnancy.
>
> "It lasts for a few weeks after the birth of the child.
>
> "It is not easily remembered by mothers once they have recovered from it.
>
> "I would go further and say that the memory mothers have of this state tends to become repressed. . . .
>
> "I do not believe that it is possible to understand the functioning of the mother at the very beginning of the infant's life without seeing that she must be able to reach this state of heightened sensitivity, almost an illness, and to recover from it. . . . I have implied this in the term 'devoted' in the words 'ordinary devoted mother' (Winnicott, 1949). There are certainly many women who are good mothers in every other way and who are capable of a rich and fruitful life but who are not able to achieve this 'normal illness' which enables them to adapt delicately and sensitively to the infant's needs at the very beginning; or they achieve it with one child but not with another. Such women are not able to become preoccupied with their own infant to the exclusion of other interests, in the way that is normal and temporary. It may be supposed that there is a 'flight to sanity' in some of these people. Some of them certainly have very big alternative concerns which they do not readily

abandon or they may not be able to allow this abandonment until they have had their first babies. When a woman has a strong male identification she finds this part of her maternal function most difficult to achieve, and repressed penis envy leaves but little room for primary maternal preoccupation.

"In practice the result is that such women, having produced a child, but having missed the boat at the earliest stage, are faced with the task of making up for what has been missed. They have a long period in which they must closely adapt to their growing child's needs, and it is not certain that they can succeed in mending the early distortion. Instead of taking for granted the good effect of an early and temporary preoccupation they are caught up in the child's need for therapy, that is to say, for a prolonged period of adaptation to need, or spoiling. They do therapy instead of being parents."[30]

EARLY PSYCHIC FUNCTIONING

We have already quoted Winnicott's statement that "direct observation is not able of itself to construct a psychology of early infancy." To do this, he has used psychoanalysis, but "one of the difficulties of our psychoanalytic technique is to know at any one moment how old a patient is in the transference relationship." It is not yet possible to point to an early emotional achievement and say with certainty that it belongs to these or those months of age. Moreover, these achievements are not necessarily clear-cut and consecutive: each overlaps and is dependent on others, so that all that can be claimed is that:

> ". . . these developments . . . can be seen in the first year, though of course nothing is established at the first birthday, and almost all can be lost by a breakdown of environmental provision after that date, or even through anxieties that are inherent in emotional maturation."[31]

Conversely,

> ". . . most of the processes that start up in early infancy are never fully established, and continue to be strengthened by the growth that continues in later childhood, and indeed in adult life, even in old age."[44]

The theme that holds together all Winnicott's ideas on early development, and forms the basis for them, like the warp in a piece of woven cloth, is that of the "good-enough mother," with all that this phrase implies. This is the *sine qua non* of all steps towards emotional maturity.

Integration and Unintegration

Integration of the ego is the process by which an infant becomes a unit—"I am." "Ego-functioning needs to be taken as a concept that is inseparable from the existence of the infant as a person." It is basic to Winnicott's theory that instinctual experiences, which form the springboard for a relationship with reality, can have no meaning without ego-functioning, because without it "the infant is not yet an entity having experiences." The start of the person "is when the ego starts." Integration, then, is rudimentary in psychological development.[29]

> "It is useful to think of the material out of which integration emerges in terms of motor and sensory elements, the stuff of primary narcissism. This would acquire a tendency towards a sense of existing. Other language can be used to describe this obscure part of the maturational process, but the rudiments of an imaginative elaboration of pure body-functioning must be postulated if it is to be claimed that this new human being has started to be, and has started to gather experience that can be called personal."[29]

Integration is only possible when the infant gets "ego-support from the mother's actual adaptive behaviour"[29]—another way of describing the function of "holding" previously mentioned. This ego-support allows the infant to become integrated, and, insofar as it can be taken for granted, it allows for a state of "unintegration." The concept of unintegration is important in Winnicott's theoretical structure. For him, it is the forerunner of the "Capacity to Be Alone," which is "one of the most important signs of maturity in emotional development."[26]

> "We need to be able to speak of an unsophisticated form of being alone, and . . . even if we agree that the capacity to be truly alone is a sophistication, the ability to be truly alone has its basis in the early experience of being alone in the presence of someone. Being alone in the presence of someone can take place at a very early stage, when the *ego immaturity is naturally balanced by ego-support* from the mother. In the course of time the individual introjects the ego-supportive mother and in this way becomes able to be alone without frequent reference to the mother or mother symbol."[26]

The necessity of the Capacity to Be Alone is stated in the following passage:

> "It is only when alone (that is to say, in the presence of someone) that the infant can discover his own personal life. The pathological alternative is a false life built on reactions to external stimuli. When alone in the sense that I am using the term, and only when alone, the infant is able to do the equivalent of what in an adult would be called relaxing. The infant is able to become unintegrated, to flounder, to be in a state in which there is no orientation, to be able for a time to exist without being either a reactor to an external impingement or an active person with a direction of interest or movement. The stage is set for an id-experience. In the course of time there arrives a sensation or an impulse. In this setting the impulse will feel real and be a truly personal experience.
>
> "It will now be seen why it is important that there is someone available, someone present, although present without making demands; the impulse having arrived, the id-experience can be fruitful, and the object can be a part or the whole of the attendant person, namely the mother. It is only under these conditions that the infant can have an experience which feels real. A large number

of such experiences forms the basis for a life that has reality instead of futility. The individual who has developed the capacity to be alone is constantly able to rediscover the personal impulse, and the personal impulse is not wasted because the state of being alone is something which (though paradoxically) always implies that someone else is there."[26]

Winnicott uses a special term for the relationship between the infant and its mother at this crucial time when the infant's ego is given support by the mother's. He calls it "ego-relatedness," and suggests that it is the "stuff out of which friendship is made," and that it forms the basis for "highly satisfactory experiences" such as may be obtained in listening to music or poetry.

Personalization

"Personalization" is the word used by Winnicott to describe "the establishment (in the infant) of a psycho-somatic union."[29]

> "In favourable circumstances the skin becomes the boundary between the me and the not-me. In other words, the psyche has come to live in the soma and an individual psycho-somatic life has been initiated."[29]

This state of affairs has its clinical manifestations:

> "The neurologist would say that body-tone is satisfactory, and would describe the infant's co-ordination as good. . . . Even in health, the infant of one year is firmly rooted to the body only at certain times. The psyche of a normal infant may lose touch with the body, and there may be phases in which it is not easy for the infant to come suddenly back into the body, for instance, when waking from deep sleep. Mothers know this, and they gradually wake an infant before lifting him or her, so as not to cause the tremendous screaming of panic which can be brought about by a change of position of the body at a time when the psyche is absent from it. Associated clinically with this absence of the psyche there may be phases of pallor, times when the infant is sweating and perhaps very cold, and there may be vomiting. At this stage the mother can think her infant is dying, but by the time the doctor has arrived there has been so complete a return to normal health that the doctor is unable to understand why the mother was alarmed."[31]

It is in the context of personalization that the concept of "handling," a part of the broader concept of "holding," comes into its own.

> "Handling describes the environmental provision that corresponds loosely with the establishment of a psycho-somatic partnership. Without good-enough active and adaptive handling the task from within may well prove heavy, and indeed it may actually prove impossible for this development of a psychosomatic inter-relationship to become properly established."[29]

In failure to achieve personalization Winnicott saw the aetiology of some psycho-somatic illnesses:

> "Psycho-somatic disease is sometimes little more than a stressing of this psycho-somatic link in face of a danger of a breaking of the link; this breaking of the link results in various clinical states which receive the name of 'depersonalisation'."[32]

Object Relating

Integration and personalization in the infant lead to object relating. The word "object" in the psychoanalytic context has to be given its particular meaning as the opposite of "subject." It can be a confusing word, because it nearly always refers to a person or part of a person. Thus the phrase "object relationship" can nearly always be replaced by the phrase "personal relationship."

It could be said that the whole of classical psychoanalytic theory is concerned with object relating. Winnicott's own contributions, however, were made in respect of its initiation and early development.

> "The initiation of object-relating is complex. It cannot take place except by the environmental provision of object-presenting, done in such a way that the baby creates the object. The pattern is thus: the baby develops a vague expectation that has origin in an unformulated need. The adaptive mother presents an object or a manipulation that meets the baby's needs, and so the baby begins to need just that which the mother presents. In this way the baby comes to feel confident in being able to create objects and to create the actual world. The mother gives the baby a brief period in which omnipotence is a matter of experience. It must be emphasised that in referring to the initiating of object-relating I am not referring to id-satisfactions and id-frustrations. I am referring to the preconditions, internal to the child as well as external, conditions which make an ego-experience out of a satisfactory breast feed (or a reaction to frustration)."[29]

It will be seen that this is very like Freud's statement quoted earlier: however, the substitution of the word "create" for "hallucinate" is critical.

Winnicott's theory of early object-relating was given a new dimension towards the end of his life. In the course of an analysis a dissociation was forced upon his attention: the dissociation between the male and female elements in the personality of his patient. He writes

> "Here then I found myself with a new edge to an old weapon, and I wondered how this would or could affect the work I was doing with other patients, both men and women, or boys and girls. I decided, therefore, to study this type of dissociation."[33]

His conclusions are fascinating in the light of recent research, carried out in mammals, concerning the relation between hormones and sexual behaviour. It has been found in this research that whereas being sexually attractive has to do with the presence of female sex hormones, sexual activity itself, which includes the activity of the male and the acceptance and participation of the female, is related to the presence of male hormones (cf. Everitt and Herbert, 1972).[3]

Freud's theory of the origin of sexuality went very close to this:

"There is only one libido, which serves both the masculine and feminine sexual functions. To it itself we cannot assign any sex; if, following the conventional equation of activity and masculinity we are inclined to describe it as masculine, we must not forget that it also covers trends with a passive aim" (Freud, 1933).[7]

Winnicott, in considering primitive object relating in terms of his hypothesis of the pure male and female elements in the human infant, went even closer.

"These considerations have involved me then in a curious statement about the pure male and the pure female aspects of the infant boy or girl. I have arrived at a position in which I say that object-relating in terms of *this pure female element has nothing to do with drive* (*or instinct*). Object-relating backed by instinct drive belongs to the male element in the personality uncontaminated by the female element. This line of argument involves me in great difficulties, and yet it seems as if in a statement of the initial stages of the emotional development of the individual it is necessary to separate out (not boys from girls but) the uncontaminated boy element from the uncontaminated girl element. . . .

"The study of the pure distilled uncontaminated female element leads us to BEING, and this forms the only basis for self-discovery and a sense of existing (and then on to the capacity to develop an inside, to be a container, to have the capacity to use the mechanisms of projection and introjection and to relate to the world in terms of introjection and projection).

"At the risk of being repetitious I wish to restate: when the girl element in the boy or girl baby or patient finds the breast it is the self that has been found. If the question is asked, what does the girl baby do with the breast?—the answer must be that this girl element *is* the breast and shares the qualities of breast and mother and is desirable. In the course of time, desirable means edible and this means that the infant is in danger because of being desirable, or, in more sophisticated language, exciting. Exciting implies: liable to make one's male element *do* something. In this way a man's penis may be an exciting female element generating male element activity in the girl. But (it must be made clear) no girl or woman is like this; in health, there is a variable amount of girl element in a girl, and in a boy."[33]

The possible corroboration of psychoanalytic theory by biological experiment would certainly not have surprised Freud, who sought such corroboration everywhere. But it could be said of Freud, speaking in terms of male and female elements, that his theoretical system concerned itself with the male element, whereas the "ego-psychologists" have been seeking a formulation akin to that of the pure female element. This formulation can be seen as a development of Winnicott's concept of a state of "ego-relatedness"; as an explanation of this state carried as far as possible to its origins: as such it is central to his psychology. In his own words, "After being—doing and being done to. But first, being."

Three processes, then, integration, personalization and object-relating, are the axes of the development of the Self. It is in failure in maternal adaptation at this early stage that the aetiology of personality distortion may be found. Winnicott indicates:

"(1) Distortions of the ego-organisation that lay down the basis for schizoid characteristics" (including latent schizophrenia and infantile schizophrenia in those cases where "there is no evidence of neurological defect or disease"), and

"(2) The specific defence of self-holding, or the development of a caretaker self and the organisation of an aspect of the personality that is false (false in that what is showing is a derivative not of the individual but of the mothering aspect of the infant-mother coupling). This is a defence whose success may provide a new threat to the core of the self though it is designed to hide and protect this core of the self."[29]

REALITY ADAPTATION

A passage from Winnicott's paper *The Child in Health and Crisis*, presented at an American Psychoanalytic Institute, is pertinent here. The sentiments expressed could be said to be an essential part of his personal philosophy which (as he would have been the first to admit) influenced the character of his theoretical structure.

"Immediately I want to put in a word to counteract any impression I may have given that health is enough. We are not only concerned with individual maturity and with the freedom of individuals from mental disorder or from psycho-neurosis; we are concerned with the richness of individuals in terms not of money but of inner psychic reality. Indeed, we often forgive a man or woman for mental ill-health or for some kind of immaturity because that person has so rich a personality that society may gain much through the exceptional contribution he or she can make. May I say that Shakespeare's contribution was such that we would not mind much if we found that he was immature, or homosexual, or anti-social in some localised sense. This principle can be applied in a broad way and I need not labour the point. A research project, for instance, might show by significant statistics that infants who are bottle-fed are physically healthier and even, perhaps, less liable to mental disorder than those who are not. But we are concerned also with the richness of the breast-feeding experience in comparison with its alternative, if this affects the richness of the personality potential in the infant now grown to childhood and to adult life.

"It is enough if I have made it clear that we aim at providing more than healthy conditions to produce health. Richness of quality rather than health is at the top of the ladder of human progress."[34]

In this passage, Winnicott makes use of the concept of "inner psychic reality." This is, of course, an idea as old as the hills; Winnicott calls it "Freud's concept . . . that was clearly derived from philosophy." He clarifies the idea in these words:

> "Of every individual who has reached to the state of being a unit with a limiting membrane and an outside and an inside, it can be said that there is an inner reality to that individual, an inner world that can be rich or poor and can be at peace or in a state of war."[35]

This inner reality is responsible for the individual's unique personality, or Self. It is contrasted with external, or "shared" reality, with which the infant gradually comes to terms. This process of coming to terms with reality is expressed in Winnicott's writings as a transition from primitive object-relating (where the infant and the object or the part object are one) to the capacity to use an object. The capacity to use an object means that the object is "objectively perceived," is seen as "not me" and has a "property of having been there all the time." This process occurs concurrently with, and owes its success to, the mother's gradual failure in adaptation. The idea is illuminated by a clinical description:

> "In clinical terms: two babies are feeding at the breast. One is feeding on the self, since the breast and the baby have not yet become (for the baby) separate phenomena. The other is feeding from an 'other than me' source, or an object that can be given cavalier treatment without effect on the baby unless it retaliates. Mothers, like analysts, can be good or not good enough; some can and some cannot carry the baby over from relating to usage."[36]

Winnicott's most original contribution to the study of human nature was made in terms of this transition from relating to usage. His original hypothesis was put forward in a paper published in 1953 called *Transitional Objects and Transitional Phenomena.* It had immense implications for him, and was the subject of his last book, *Playing and Reality*.

The original hypothesis is based on very sensitive and simple direct observation. It hinges on what Winnicott calls the "First not-me Possession", and he traces the evolution of this possession from very primitive forms of relating thus:

> "There is plenty of reference in psychoanalytic literature to the progress from 'hand to mouth' to 'hand to genital,' but perhaps less to further progress to the handling of truly 'not-me' objects. Sooner or later in an infant's development there comes a tendency on the part of the infant to weave other-than-me objects into the personal pattern. To some extent these objects stand for the breast, but it is not especially this point that is under discussion.
>
> "In the case of some infants the thumb is placed in the mouth while fingers are made to caress the face by pronation and supination movements of the forearm. The mouth is then active in relation to the thumb, but not in relation to the fingers. The fingers caressing the upper lip, or some other part, may be or may become more important than the thumb engaging the mouth. Moreover, this caressing activity may be found alone, without the more direct thumb-mouth union.
>
> "In common experience one of the following occurs, complicating an auto-erotic experience such as thumb-sucking:
>
> (i) with the other hand the baby takes an external object, say a part of a sheet or blanket, into the mouth along with the fingers; or
>
> (ii) somehow or other the bit of cloth is held and sucked, or not actually sucked; the objects used naturally include napkins and (later) handkerchiefs, and this depends on what is readily and reliably available; or
>
> (iii) the baby starts from early months to pluck wool and to collect it and to use it for the caressing part of the activity; less commonly the wool is swallowed, even causing trouble; or
>
> (iv) mouthing occurs, accompanied by sounds of 'mum-mum', babbling, anal noises, the first musical notes, and so on.
>
> "One may suppose that thinking, or fantasying, gets linked up with these functional experiences.
>
> "All these things I am calling *transitional phenomena.* Also, out of this, if we study any one infant, there may emerge some thing or some phenomenon—perhaps a bundle of wool or the corner of a blanket or eiderdown, or a word or tune, or a mannerism—that becomes vitally important to the infant for use at the time of going to sleep, and is a defence against anxiety, especially anxiety of depressive type. Perhaps some soft object or other type of object has been found and used by the infant, and this then becomes what I am calling a *transitional object.* This object goes on being important. The parents get to know its value and carry it around when travelling. The mother lets it get dirty and even smelly, knowing that by washing it she introduces a break in continuity in the infant's experience, a break that may destroy the meaning and value of the object to the infant.
>
> "I suggest that the pattern of transitional phenomena begins to show at about four to six to eight to twelve months. Purposely I leave room for wide variations."[35]

Winnicott sums up the special qualities in the relationship of the infant to the transitional object thus:

> "1. The infant assumes rights over the object, and we agree to this assumption. Nevertheless, some abrogation of omnipotence is a feature from the start.
>
> "2. The object is affectionately cuddled as well as excitedly loved and mutilated.
>
> "3. It must never change, unless changed by the infant.
>
> "4. It must survive instinctual loving, and also hating and, if it be a feature, pure aggression.
>
> "5. Yet it must seem to the infant to give warmth, or to move, or to have texture, or to do something that seems to show it has vitality or reality of its own.

"6. It comes from without from our point of view, but not so from the point of view of the baby. Neither does it come from within; it is not a hallucination.

"7. Its fate is to be gradually allowed to be decathected, so that in the course of years it becomes not so much forgotten as relegated to limbo. By this, I mean that in health the transitional object does not 'go inside' nor does the feeling about it necessarily undergo repression. It is not forgotten and it is not mourned. It loses meaning, and this is because the transitional phenomena have become diffused, have become spread out over the whole intermediate territory between 'inner psychic reality' and 'the external world as perceived by two persons in common,' that is to say, over the whole cultural field."[35]

So we return to the contrasting concepts of inner and shared reality and can state the theoretical position of the transitional object. It is Winnicott's thesis that it belongs to the realm of illusion.

> "From birth, therefore, the human being is concerned with the problem of the relationship between what is objectively perceived and what is subjectively conceived of, and in the solution of this problem there is no health for the human being who has not been started off well enough by the mother. *The intermediate area to which I am referring is the area that is allowed to the infant between primary creativity and objective perception based on reality-testing.* The transitional phenomena represent the early stages of the use of illusion, without which there is no meaning for the human being in the idea of a relationship with an object that is perceived by others as external to that being."[35]

For Winnicott, then, "illusion is at the basis of experience," and so the intermediate realm between inner and shared reality is also called by him "the area of experiencing." Enrichment of the self or personality can come only through experience, and as early as 1945 Winnicott wrote:

> ". . . the enrichment of fantasy [which in this context can be taken as synonymous with inner reality] with the world's riches depends on the experience of illusion. It is interesting to examine the individual's relation to the objects in the self-created world of fantasy. In fact there are all grades of development and sophistication in this self-created world according to the amount of illusion that has been experienced, and so according to how much the self-created world has been unable or able to use perceived external world objects as material."[37]

Or, to put it in other words,

> ". . . the infant's growth takes the form of a continuous interchange between inner and outer reality, each being enriched by the other.
>
> "The child is now not only a potential creator of the world, but also the child becomes able to populate the world with samples of his or her own inner life. So, gradually, the child is able to 'cover' any external event, and perception is almost synonymous with creation. Here again is a means by which the child gains control over external events as well as over the inner workings of his or her own self."[27]

In 1946 Winnicott wrote in the *New Era in Home and School*,

> "Put a lot of store on a child's ability to play. If a child is playing there is room for a symptom or two, and if a child is able to enjoy playing, both alone and with other children, there is no very serious trouble afoot. If in this play is employed a rich imagination, and if also pleasure is got from games that depend on exact perception of external reality, then you can be fairly happy, even if the child in question is wetting the bed, stammering, displaying temper tantrums, or repeatedly suffering from bilious attacks or depression. The playing shows that this child is capable, given reasonably good and stable surroundings, of developing a personal way of life, and eventually of becoming a whole human being, wanted as such, and welcomed by the world at large."[38]

It will be seen from this piece of advice that playing for Winnicott also belongs to the middle realm of illusion, to the "potential space" between the individual and the environment. It is an extension of the use of transitional phenomena. Though the idea of playing has been much used by the psychoanalysts, as has the actual play itself in child analysis, Winnicott argues that "playing needs to be studied as a subject on its own, supplementary to the concept of the sublimation of instinct."[39] To him, playing includes the following characteristics:

> (a) To get to the idea of playing, it is helpful to think of the *preoccupation* that characterises the playing of a young child. The content does not matter. What matters is the near withdrawal state, akin to the *concentration* of older children and adults. The playing child inhabits an area that cannot be easily left, nor can it easily admit intrusions.
>
> (b) This area of playing is not inner psychic reality. It is outside the individual, but it is not the external world.
>
> (c) Into this play area the child gathers objects or phenomena from external reality and uses these in the service of some sample derived from inner or personal reality. Without hallucinating the child puts out a sample of dream potential and lives with this sample in a chosen setting of fragments from external reality.
>
> (d) In playing, the child manipulates external phenomena in the service of the dream and invests chosen external phenomena with dream meaning and feeling.
>
> (e) There is a direct development from transitional phenomena to playing, and from playing to shared playing, and from this to cultural experiences.
>
> (f) Playing implies trust, and belongs to the potential space between (what was at first) baby and mother-figure, with the baby in a state of near-absolute dependence, and the mother-figure's adaptive function taken for granted by the baby.
>
> (g) Playing involves the body:
>
> (i) because of the manipulation of objects

(ii) because certain types of intense interest are associated with certain types of bodily excitement.

(h) Bodily excitement in erotogenic zones constantly threatens playing, and therefore threatens the child's sense of existing as a person. The instincts are the main threat to play as to the ego; in seduction some external agency exploits the child's instincts and helps to annihilate the child's sense of existing as an autonomous unit, making playing impossible (cf. Khan, 1964).

(i) *Playing is essentially satisfying*. This is true even when it leads to a high degree of anxiety. There is a degree of anxiety that is unbearable and this destroys playing.

(j) The pleasurable element in playing carries with it the implication that the instinctual arousal is not excessive; instinctual arousal beyond a certain point must lead to:

(i) climax;
(ii) failed climax and a sense of mental confusion and physical discomfort that only time can mend;
(iii) alternative climax (as in provocation of parental or social reaction, anger, etc.).

Playing can be said to reach its own saturation point, which refers to the capacity to contain experience.

(k) Playing is inherently exciting and precarious. This characteristic derives *not* from instinctual arousal but from the precariousness that belongs to the interplay in the child's mind of that which is subjective (near-hallucination) and that which is objectively perceived (actual, or shared reality).[39]

Winnicott's description of playing finds support in Piaget's description of "symbolic play":

"Obliged to adapt himself constantly to a social world of elders whose interests and rules remain external to him, and a physical world which he understands only slightly, the child does not succeed as we adults do in satisfying the affective and even intellectual needs of his personality through these adaptations. It is indispensable to his affective and intellectual equilibrium, therefore, that he have available to him an area of activity whose motivation is not adaptation to reality, but, on the contrary, assimilation of reality to the self, without coercions or sanctions. Such an area is play, which transforms reality by assimilation to the needs of the self, whereas imitation (when it constitutes an end in itself) is accommodation to external models."[14]

Of course Piaget acknowledges his debt to Freud, but in this particular instance both he and Winnicott are seeking a formulation beyond classical concepts of the use of play. Considering the difference in approach between the epistemologist and the psychoanalyst the similarity of their conclusions is striking. But whereas for Piaget the "symbolic play" of the child is carried over to the adult state only in dream (the symbolism of the dream being analogous to the symbolism of play), for Winnicott playing itself continues to be that part of living through which the individual feels his life to be worthwhile.

"It is in playing and only in playing that the child or adult is able to be creative and to use the whole personality, and it is only in being creative that the individual discovers the self."[39]

The theme of creativity is continued thus:

"I am hoping that the reader will accept a general reference to creativity, not letting the word get lost in the successful or acclaimed creation but keeping it to the meaning that refers to a colouring of the whole attitude to external reality.

"It is creative apperception more than anything else that makes the individual feel that life is worth living. Contrasted with this is a relationship to external reality which is one of compliance, the world and its details being recognised but only as something to be fitted in with or demanding adaptation. Compliance carries with it a sense of futility for the individual and is associated with the idea that nothing matters and that life is not worth living. In a tantalising way, many individuals have experienced just enough of creative living to recognise that for the most of their time they are living uncreatively, as if caught up in the creativity of someone else, or of a machine.

"This second way of living in the world is recognised as illness in psychiatric terms. In some way or other our theory includes a belief that living creatively is a healthy state, and that compliance is a sick basis for life. There is little doubt that the general attitude of our society and the philosophic atmosphere of the age in which we happen to live contribute to this view, the view that we hold here and that we hold at the present time. We might not have held this view elsewhere and in another age."[33]

So, for Winnicott, the value to each individual of his being alive rests in the intermediate area of illusion between the inner and shared realities; in the content of the "potential space" between the self and the environment where an infinitely variable exchange can take place. The potential space, like the Capacity to Be Alone, is founded on body experiences rather than on body functioning. "These experiences belong to object-relating of a non-orgiastic kind, or to what can be called ego-relatedness, at the place where it can be said that *continuity* is giving place to *contiguity*."[40] The potential space is the "common ground" between the infant and the mother in this state of "ego-relatedness." It is that which "initially both joins and separates the baby and the mother when the mother's love, displayed or made manifest as human reliability, does in fact give the baby a sense of trust or of confidence in the environmental factor."[40]

The potential space is an area of experiencing, where the individual can draw from "the common pool of humanity" in terms of cultural experiences which "provide the continuity in the human race that transcends personal existence."[40] It is also an area of doing. In the first object relations, before the "me" becomes separated from the "not-me," the mother, through sensitive adaptation to her infant's needs, allows the infant a "brief experience of omnipotence." In the potential space this experience is transmuted, through the use of transitional phenomena and through the playing of the child, into the ability to live creatively, to discover and rediscover the Self, and to give something of the Self back to the world.

INNATE MORALITY

In view of Winnicott's theories concerning reality adaptation, it is not surprising that he takes the following stand on morality:

> "The fiercest morality is that of early infancy, and this persists as a streak in human nature that can be discerned throughout an individual's life. Immorality for the infant is *to comply at the expense of the personal way of life.* For instance, a child of any age may feel that to eat is wrong, even to the extent of dying for the principle. Compliance brings immediate rewards and adults only too easily mistake compliance for growth. The maturational processes can be by-passed by a series of identifications, so that what shows clinically is a false, acting self, a copy of someone perhaps; and what could be called a true or essential self becomes hidden, and becomes deprived of living experience. This leads many people who seem to be doing well eventually to end their lives which have become false and unreal; unreal success is morality at its lowest ebb as compared with which a sexual misdemeanor hardly counts."[41]

In other words, morality as understood by mature adults in our society can only be true morality insofar as it becomes a part of inner reality and is a manifestation of the True Self. In this case it is characterized by spontaneity. The exo-skeletal morality of the False Self, of compliance (which is immorality), is likely to break down into failure.

The concept of the immorality of the False Self was made particular use of in Winnicott's explanations of the behaviour of adolescents:

> "It is a prime characteristic of adolescents that they do not accept false solutions. This fierce morality on the basis of the real and the false belongs also to infancy and to illness of schizophrenic type.
>
> "The cure for adolescence is the passage of time, a fact which has very little meaning for the adolescent. The adolescent looks for a cure that is immediate, but at the same time rejects one 'cure' after another because some false element is detected.
>
> "Once the adolescent can tolerate compromise, he or she may discover various ways in which the relentlessness of essential truths can be softened. For instance, there is a solution through identification with parent figures; or there can be a premature maturity in terms of sex; or there can be shift of emphasis from sex to physical prowess in athletics, or from the bodily functions to intellectual attainment or achievement. In general, adolescents reject these helps, and instead they go through a sort of *doldrums area*, a phase in which they feel futile and in which they have not yet found themselves. We have to watch this happening. But a total avoidance of these compromises, especially of the use of identifications and vicarious experience, means that each individual must start from scratch, ignoring all that has been worked out in the past history of our culture. Adolescents can be seen struggling to start again as if they had nothing they could take over from anyone. They can be seen to be forming groups on the basis of minor uniformities, and on the basis of some sort of group adherence which belongs to locality and to age. Young people can be seen searching for a form of identification which does not let them down in their struggle, *the struggle to feel real*, the struggle to establish a personal identity, not to fit into an assigned role, but to go through whatever has to be gone through. They do not know what they are going to become. They do not know where they are, and they are waiting. Because everything is in abeyance, they feel unreal, and this leads them to do certain things which feel real to them, and which are only too real in the sense that society is affected."[42]

The origins of behaviour patterns in adolescence are elsewhere described in greater depth by Winnicott, particularly in relation to the environmental provision in infancy. He has much to say, for instance, about the anti-social tendency and its aetiology in early deprivation, and why it is so manifest in adolescence. In 1945 Winnicott wrote that it was important to him "that living things could be examined scientifically, with the corollary that gaps in knowledge and understanding need not scare me."[43] We think he has helped all who have to do with adolescents in this particular way by extending his theories to include his sensitive observations of the adolescent scene. His explanations also cover the adult's reactions of exasperation and even fear, and deal with the adolescent's need to be confronted. What emerges is a firmly rooted optimism for those who are passing through the "doldrums," and, through them, for future generations.

Morality in the context of the True and False Self is not, of course, Winnicott's whole statement about the growth of morals, but it is basic to further development. An important part of his statement can be found in his explanation of the origins of the "Capacity for Concern." The "Capacity for Concern" is a concept arising out of Melanie Klein's work in which she came to recognize the crucial importance of the need for reparation. It is very briefly stated in the following passage:

> "At this stage to which I refer now there is a gradual build-up in the child of a capacity to feel a sense of responsibility, that which is at base a sense of guilt. The environmental essential here is the continued presence of the mother or mother-figure over the time in which the infant and child is accommodating the destructiveness that is part of his make-up. This destructiveness becomes more and more a feature in the experience of object relationships, and the phase of development to which I am referring lasts from about six months to two years, after which the child may have made a satisfactory integration of the idea of destroying the object and the fact of loving the same object. The mother is needed over this time and she is needed because of her survival value. She is an environment-mother and at the same time an

object mother, the object of excited loving. In this latter role she is repeatedly destroyed and damaged. The child gradually comes to integrate these two aspects of the mother and to be able to love and to be affectionate with the surviving mother at the same time. This phase involves the child in a special kind of anxiety which is called a sense of guilt, guilt related to the idea of destruction where love is also operating. It is this anxiety that drives the child towards constructive or actively loving behaviour in his limited world, reviving the object, making the object better again, rebuilding the damaged thing. If the mother-figure is not able to see the child through over this phase then the child fails to find or loses the capacity to feel guilt, but instead feels crudely anxious and this anxiety is merely wasteful. . . .

"Here is an essential stage in child development, and it has nothing to do with moral education except that if this stage is successfully negotiated the child's own and personal solution to the problem of destruction of what is loved turns into the child's urge to work or to acquire skills. It is here that the provision of opportunity, and this includes the teaching of skills, meets the child's need. But the need is the essential factor, and the need arises out of the child's establishment within the self of a capacity to stand feeling guilt in regard to destructive impulses and ideas, to stand feeling generally responsible for destructive ideas, because of having become confident in regard to reparative impulses and opportunities for contributing in. This reappears in a big way at the period of adolescence, and it is well known that the provision of opportunity for service for young people is of more value than moral education in the sense of teaching morals."[41]

The idea that at first the infant does not integrate the different aspects of the mother (environment-mother and object-mother) has recently been given physiological basis through experimental psychology. It has been shown to be probable that the world of the very young infant is overpopulated because his perception of objects is spatial: if an object moves from one place to another it has become two. Infants under twenty weeks of age when presented with two or three mirror images of their mother, while recognizing the mother in all the images, did not appear to perceive them as belonging to the same person. Older infants did, and were quite upset by this presentation, because, it is argued, they "know that they have only one mother" (Bower, 1971).[1]

It must, however, be said that the idea of an observable change taking place in the infant in relation to his mother at about five to six months is not new to those concerned with the psychology of the infant. Winnicott had come to the conclusion in 1945 that at this stage

"the infant assumes that his mother also has an inside, one which may be rich or poor, good or bad, ordered or muddled. He is therefore starting to be concerned with the mother and her sanity and her moods. In the case of many infants there is a relationship as between whole persons at six months."[37]

It can be seen that this stage in the infant's development coincides with the beginning of his being able to use an object, and therefore to give it "cavalier treatment." Winnicott came to his conclusion about the change in the infant's view of the mother by simply observing again and again how a baby of this age, when given a spatula to play with in his out-patient clinic, started "deliberately dropping the object as part of his play with it."[37] The observation was incorporated in, and enlarged, his developing theories. It was typical of him in his work as an analyst and a physician that he provided the appropriate setting, the environment which did not permit intrusive impingements, and was always prepared to wait for the spontaneous word or act.

This, then, is our attempt to describe the personal contributions made by Dr. Winnicott to the study of human nature. It is necessarily incomplete, and, in the face of his own writings, inadequate.

There is something which emerges from these writings taken as a whole. It could be stated in terms of the meaning attached to the word "science." It sometimes seems that the meaning is becoming so narrow as to be almost equivalent to technology, and many potentially rich fields are impoverished by this narrowness. There is no more the feeling of a pioneering spirit, and the climate of thought is such that one wonders if our culture can produce among our contemporaries a single thinker approaching the stature of Darwin or Marx or Freud. The writings of Winnicott lead us to the conclusion that this is not impossible. His "psychology of early infancy," so painstakingly built up, in his own words, "by the observation of facts, by the building of theory and the testing of it, and by modification of theory according to the discovery of new facts,"[43] touches the whole of mental functioning and its implications for our life today. Like the great thinkers of the nineteenth century, he had the courage to look these implications squarely in the face. For this we are in his debt as we are in theirs.

REFERENCES

1. Bower, T. G. R. (1971), "The Object in the World of the Infant," *Scientific American*, **225**, 4.
2. Ellenberger, F. (1970), "The Discovery of the Unconscious," *The History and Evolution of Dynamic Psychiatry*. London: Allen Lane The Penguin Press.
3. Everitt, B. J. and Herbert, J. (1972), "Hormonal Correlates of Sexual Behaviour in Sub-Human Primates," *Danish Medical Bull.*, **19**, 8.
4. Freud, Anna (1927), *The Psycho-analytical Treatment of Children*. London: Imago 1946.
5. Freud, S. (1911), *Formulations on the Two Principles of Mental Functioning*, Standard Edition XII, p. 220.
6. Freud, S. (1954), "The Origins of Psycho-analysis," *Letters to Wilhelm Fliess, Drafts and Notes:* 1887–1902. London: Imago.
7. Freud, S. (1933), "Femininity," in *The Complete Introductory Lectures on Psycho-Analysis*, p. 595. Translated and edited by James Strachey 1963. London: George Allen and Unwin.
8. Girard, Alain (1963), *Le Journal Intime*. Paris: Presses Universitaires de France.
9. Hayter, Alethea (1971), *Opium and the Romantic Imagination*. London: Faber Papercovered Editions.

10. Klein, Melanie (1932). *The Psycho-analysis of Children.* Revised Edition 1949. London: The Hogarth Press and the Institute of Psycho-analysis.
11. Johnston, M. (1972), *The Austrian Mind. An Intellectual and Social History* 1848–1938. Los Angeles: University of California Press.
12. Jones, E. (1953–7), *The Life and Work of Sigmund Freud.* London: Hogarth Press.
13. Mezaros, I. (1970), *Marx's Theory of Alienation.* London: Merlin Press.
14. Piaget, J. and Inhelder, B. (1969), "The Semiotic or Symbolic Function," in *The Psychology of the Child*, pp. 57–58. London: Routledge & Kegan Paul.
15. Rieff, P. (1959), *Freud. The Mind of the Moralist.* London: Victor Gollancz Ltd.
16. Smirnoff, V. (1971), *The Scope of Child Analysis.* London: Routledge and Kegan Paul.
17. Trilling, L. (1955), *Freud and the Crisis of Culture.* Boston: The Beacon Press.
18. Whyte, L. L. (1960), *The Unconscious Before Freud.* Social Science Paperbacks.
19. Winnicott, D. W. (1965), "On the Kleinian Contribution," in *The Maturational Processes and the Facilitating Environment*, pp. 171–178. London: Hogarth Press and the Inst. P.A. Library.
20. Winnicott, D. W. (1958), "Psychoses and Child Care," in *Collected Papers: Through Paediatrics to Psycho-Analysis*, pp. 219–228. London, Tavistock, New York: Basic Books.
21. Winnicott, D. W. (1965), "Direct Child Observation," in *The Naturational Processes and the Facilitating Environment*, pp. 109–114. London: Hogarth Press and the Inst. P.A. Library.
22. Winnicott, D. W. (1957), "A Man Looks at Motherhood," in *The Child and the Family: First Relationships*, pp. 3–6. London: Tavistock Publications.
23. Winnicott, D. W. (1957), "The Baby as a Going Concern," in *The Child and the Family: First Relationships*, pp. 13–17. London: Tavistock Publications.
24. Winnicott, D. W. (1965), "The Theory of the Parent-Infant Relationship," in *The Maturational Processes and the Facilitating Environment*, pp. 37–55. London: Hogarth Press and the Inst. P.A. Library.
25. Winnicott, D. W. (1965), "Ego-Distortion in Terms of the True and False Self," in *The Maturational Processes and the Facilitating Environment*, pp. 140–152. London: Hogarth Press and the Inst. P.A. Library.
26. Winnicott, D. W. (1965), "The Capacity to Be Alone," in *The Maturational Processes and the Facilitating Environment*, pp. 29–36. London: Hogarth Press and the Inst. P.A. Library.
27. Winnicott, D. W. (1965), "From Dependence Towards Independence in the Development of the Individual," in *The Maturational Processes and the Facilitating Environment*, pp. 83–92. London: Hogarth Press and the Inst. P.A. Library.
28. Winnicott, D. W. (1958), "Birth Memories, Birth Trauma and Anxiety," in *Collected Papers: Through Paediatrics to Psycho-Analysis*, pp. 174–193. London, Tavistock, New York: Basic Books.
29. Winnicott, D. W. (1965), "Ego Integration in Child Development," in *The Maturational Processes and the Facilitating Environment*, pp. 56–63. London: Hogarth Press and the Inst. P.A. Library.
30. Winnicott, D. W. (1958), "Primary Maternal Preoccupation," in *Collected Papers: Through Paediatrics to Psycho-Analysis*, pp. 300–305. London, Tavistock, New York: Basic Books.
31. Winnicott, D. W. (1964), "The First Year of Life," in *The Family and Individual Development*, pp. 3–14. London: Tavistock Publications.
32. Winnicott, D. W. (1965), "The Mentally Ill In Your Case Load," in *The Matu Rational Processes and the Facilitating Environment*, pp. 217–229. London: Hogarth Press and the Inst. P.A. Library.
33. Winnicott, D. W. (1971), "Creativity and Its Origins," in *Playing and Reality*, pp. 65–85. London: Tavistock Publications.
34. Winnicott, D. W. (1965), "The Child in Health and Crisis," in *The Maturational Processes and the Facilitating Environment*, pp. 64–72. London: Hogarth Press and the Inst. P.A. Library.
35. Winnicott, D. W. (1971), "Transitional Objects and Transitional Phenomena," in *Playing and Reality*, pp. 1–25. London: Tavistock Publications.
36. Winnicott, D. W. (1971), "The Use of an Object," in *Playing and Reality*, pp. 86–94. London: Tavistock Publications.
37. Winnicott, D. W. (1958), "Primitive Emotional Development," in *Collected Papers: Through Paediatrics to Psycho-Analysis*, pp. 145–156. London, Tavistock, New York: Basic Books.
38. Winnicott, D. W. (1957), "What Do We Mean By a Normal Child?" in *The Child and the Family: First Relationships*, pp. 100–106. London: Tavistock Publications.
39. Winnicott, D. W. (1971), "Playing, a Theoretical Statement," in *Playing and Reality*, pp. 38–52. London: Tavistock Publications.
40. Winnicott, D. W. (1971), "The Location of Cultural Experience," in *Playing and Reality*, pp. 95–103. London: Tavistock Publications.
41. Winnicott, D. W. (1965), "Morals and Education," in *The Maturational Processes and the Facilitating Environment*, pp. 93–108. London: Hogarth Press and the Inst. P.A. Library.
42. Winnicott, D. W. (1964), "Adolescence," in *The Family and Individual Development*, pp. 79–87. London: Tavistock Publications.
43. Winnicott, D. W. (1957), "Towards an Objective Study of Human Nature," in *The Child and the Outside World: Studies in Developing Relationships*, pp. 125–133. London: Tavistock Publications.
44. Winnicott, D. W. (1963), "The Development of the Capacity for Concern," in *The Maturational Processes and the Facilitating Environment*, pp. 73–82. London: Hogarth Press and the Inst. P.A. Library.

BIBLIOGRAPHICAL NOTE ON D. W. WINNICOTT

The total writings of Dr. Winnicott are available in ten volumes which can be conveniently divided into two categories: Category A contains the papers addressed to general audiences and Category B assembles papers which are more specialized in their address to psycho-analysts and paediatricians.

A complete bibliography of Winnicott's writings from 1926–1964 is available at the end of his book *The Maturational Processes and the Facilitating Environment.*

The volumes can be categorized in two series as follows:

Category A

1. *The Child and the Family: First Relationships.* (London: Tavistock Publications, 1957.)
2. *The Child and the Outside World: Studies in Developing Relationships.* (London: Tavistock Publications, 1957).
3. *The Child, the Family, and the Outside World.* (Harmondsworth: Penguin Books, 1964. Pelican Book A668.)
4. *The Family and Individual Development.* (London: Tavistock Publications, 1964.)

Category B

5. *Clinical Notes on Disorders of Childhood.* (London: Heinemann, 1931.)
6. *Collected Papers: Through Paediatrics to Psycho-Analysis.* (London, Tavistock, New York: Basic Books, 1958.)
7. *The Maturational Processes and the Facilitating Environment.* (London: Hogarth Press and the Inst. P.A. Library, 1965.)
8. *Therapeutic Consultations in Child Psychiatry.* (London: The Hogarth Press and The Institute of Psycho-Analysis, 1971.)
9. *Playing and Reality.* (London: Tavistock Publications, 1971.)
10. "Fragment of an Analysis," published in *Tactics and Techniques in Psychoanalytic Therapy*, Editor Peter L. Giovacchini. (London: Hogarth Press and The Institute of Psycho-Analysis, 1972.)

It may be useful, however, to single-out a few more significant papers from the above books that provide Winnicott's basic theory. These are itemized below under three headings:

A. *Papers on Mother-Child Relationship*

1948: "Paediatrics and Psychiatry," in Collected Papers.
1948a: "Reparation in Respect of Mother's Organized Defence against Depression," in Collected Papers.
1952: "Psychoses and Child Care," in Collected Papers.
1956: "Primary Maternal Preoccupation," in Collected Papers.
1960: "The Theory of the Parent-Infant Relationship," in *The Maturational Processes.*
1963: "From Dependence towards Independence in the Development of the Individual," in *The Maturational Processes.*

B. *Papers on Early Psychic Development and Ego Pathology*

1935: "The Manic Defence," in Collected Papers.
1945: "Primitive Emotional Development," in Collected Papers.
1949: "Mind and its Relation to the Psyche-Soma," in Collected Papers.
1951: Transitional Objects and Transitional Phenomena," in Collected Papers.
1954: "The Depressive Position in Normal Emotional Development," in Collected Papers.
1956: "The Antisocial Tendency," in Collected Papers.
1958: "Psycho-Analysis and the Sense of Guilt," in *The Maturational Processes.*
1958a: "The Capacity to Be Alone," in *The Maturational Processes.*
1960: "Ego Distortion in Terms of True and False Self," in *The Maturational Processes.*
1963: "The Development of the Capacity for Concern," in *The Maturational Processes.*
1963a: "Communicating and Not Communicating Leading to a Study of Certain Opposites," in *The Maturational Processes.*
1967: "The Location of Cultural Experience," in *The International Journal of Psycho-Analysis*, Vol. 48.
1968: "Playing: its Theoretical Status in the Clinical Situation," in *The International Journal of Psycho-Analysis*, Vol. 49.
1969: "The Use of an Object," in *The International Journal of Psycho-Analysis*, Vol. 50.
1972: "Basis for Self in Body," in *The International Journal of Child Psychotherapy*, Vol. 1, No. 1.

C. *Papers on Technique*

1947: "Hate in the Countertransference," in Collected Papers.
1949: "Birth Memories, Birth Trauma, and Anxiety," in Collected Papers.
1954: "Withdrawal and Regression," in Collected Papers.
1954a: "Metapsychological and Clinical Aspects of Regression within the Psycho-Analytical Set-Up," in Collected Papers.
1955: "Clinical Varieties of Transference," in Collected Papers.
1958: "Child Analysis in the Latency Period," in *The Maturational Processes.*
1960: "Counter-Transference," in *The Maturational Processes.*
1963: "Psychotherapy of Character Disorders," in *The Maturational Processes.*
1963a: "Dependence in Infant-Care, in Child-Care, and in the Psycho-Analytic Setting," in *The Maturational Processes.*
1972: "Fragment of an Analysis."

M. Masud R. Khan

37. GROWTH AND DEVELOPMENT OF THE AUTONOMIC NERVOUS SYSTEM

JENNIFER M. H. LOGGIE

INTRODUCTION

The autononmic nervous system has been extensively studied in adult humans and in animals. Information is now accumulating about its anatomical and functional development in the human fetus and infant. Unfortunately, however, there are still large gaps in our knowledge with respect to the functional maturation of this system in the developing child and in our knowledge of the responses of children of various ages to autonomic drugs.

No attempt will be made to review the basic physiology and pharmacology of the autonomic nervous system here except as they pertain to an understanding of its developmental aspects. Efferent fibres from the central nervous system innervating heart, smooth muscle, and glands, comprise the autonomic nervous system. This system is subdivided into the sympathetic or thoracolumbar and the parasympathetic or craniosacral components. Both components have preganglionic fibres which stimulate ganglion cells and postganglionic fibres which stimulate the end organs. Stimulation is caused by a neurohumoral substance which is released from the nerve ending and which combines with a receptor in the membrane of the innervated cell as the first step leading to the final response.

All nerve endings of preganglionic fibres, postganglionic parasympathetic, and postganglionic sympathetic fibres to sweat glands have vesicles containing acetylcholine which can be released on excitation of the nerve endings. The acetylcholine in cholinergic nerve endings is thought to be synthesized locally by the acetylation of choline in the presence of choline acetylase. Acetylcholinesterase (AChE, specific or true ChE) is present at the neuromuscular junction and is responsible for the hydrolysis of acetylcholine which is released in the process of cholinergic transmission. Butyrocholinesterase (BuChE, nonspecific or pseudo-ChE), which can also hydrolyze acetylcholine, is also present in the central and peripheral nervous systems, liver and other organs. Its physiological function is unknown and, the only reason for mentioning it, is to point out that it exists and that in studies of cholinesterase activity in the developing fetus, its presence is frequently noted.

In postganglionic sympathetic fibres (excluding those to sweat glands), norepinephrine is stored in vesicles at nerve endings. While the synthesis of norepinephrine which occurs in adrenergic nerves can take place in both the neuronal cell body and the nerve ending, under normal conditions the major synthesis probably takes place in the latter location. The primary precursor of norepinephrine, L-tyrosine, is oxidized by tyrosine hydroxylase to L-dopa. L-dopa is then decarboxylated by dopa decarboxylase to dopamine. Vesicles, which originate in the cell body and migrate to the nerve ending, take up dopamine which is then oxidized to norepinephrine by dopamine beta oxidase. The oxidation of tyrosine to dihydroxyphenylalanine (dopa) is the rate limiting step in the synthesis of norepinephrine.

Within the adrenal gland, and any other chromaffin tissue capable of synthesizing epinephrine, the enzyme phenylethanolamine N-methyl transferase, is responsible for the methylation of norepinephrine to epinephrine. There is evidence, which will be discussed later, that corticosteroids exert a direct regulatory effect on the formation of epinephrine from norepinephrine.

Norepinephrine released by stimulation of adrenergic nerves can react with adrenergic receptors, become inactive through methylation by catechol-O-methyltransferase, be carried away by the blood stream or return to the nerve ending.[4,9] Recent evidence indicates that most of the norepinephrine released returns to the nerve ending through an active transport system, so that the need for its *de novo* synthesis is decreased, except during prolonged sympathetic stimulation. Most of the norepinephrine and epinephrine (endogenous or exogenous), which enters the circulation is methylated to normetanephrine or metanephrine respectively by catechol-O-methyltransferase. These metabolites are, in large part, further converted to 3-methoxy-4-hydroxymandelic acid, commonly known as vanillylmandelic acid (VMA). Some of the norepinephrine which is released is probably deaminated intraneuronally by monoamine oxidase. The major metabolite of catecholamines which is excreted in the urine is VMA while homovanillic acid (HVA) constitutes the corresponding degradation product of dopamine metabolism. It should be added, that there is accumulating evidence that dopamine may be the neurohumoral transmitter in some adrenergic nerves.

Acetylcholine stimulates end-organ receptors in heart, smooth muscle and glands. These receptors are known as either muscarinic or "atropine receptors." Acetylcholine also stimulates receptors in ganglion cells and striated muscle fibres and these receptors are known as nicotinic or "hexamethonium receptors." In both instances, the latter term is now considered more specific. The adrenergic receptors are more difficult to characterize. However, it is generally agreed that they can be presently classed as alpha, beta-1 and beta-2. Identification of these receptors is now based primarily on the effects of blocking agents such as phenoxybenzamine (alpha blocking) and propranolol (beta blocking).

The development of the autonomic nervous system, like the development of all other systems, cannot properly be described in a vacuum. It is known, for example, that there are extensive ramifications of the autonomic nervous system above the level of the spinal cord. Some autonomic functions, such as integration of the control of blood pressure and respiration, are known to occur in the medulla oblongata, others are integrated in the hypothalamus. However, no attempt will be made in this review to discuss the development of these central areas of autonomic control. Nor, in general, will the known relationships between catecholamines and other hormones be considered.

The pediatrician is in the unique position of having to recognize at an early age and treat infants with inborn errors of metabolism, chromosomal aberrations and congenital defects. The prescription of drugs for all infants and children is compounded by a lack of information about their efficacy, metabolism and toxicity. Children with inborn errors of metabolism and chromosomal abnormalities may react differently than normal children, of the same age, to various drugs, and the autonomic drugs are not exceptions. For example, children with phenylketonuria are extremely sensitive to epinephrine, and cardiac hyperreactivity has been described after the administration of atropine to patients with Down's syndrome. The responses of children with familial dysautonomia to some autonomic drugs are also quite different from those of normal children.

While phenylketonuria and familial dysautonomia are relatively rare diseases, autonomic drugs are used with some frequency in children of all ages with little information available about potential hazards which may be age related. For example, atropine is used with considerable frequency for premedication prior to surgery and in 1971, Dauchot and Gravenstein described age-related changes in responses to atropine. They found that after atropine, 0·015 mg. of salt per kilogram of body weight administered intravenously in four divided doses at five-minute intervals, atrial arrhythmias occurred with more frequency in children than in adults. In individuals over 13 years of age, maximum slowing of the heart was seen after the first dose of drug, while in younger subjects the slowest heart rates were seen after the second dose. While older children and adults showed no central nervous system effects, children under 6 frequently fell asleep after the second dose of atropine, and sometimes after the first.

Not only are autonomic drugs given with some frequency to children of all ages, they are also administered to pregnant females. Reserpine, for example, was at one time used quite extensively to treat women with pre-eclamptic toxemia. It was found that the offspring of some of these women developed respiratory distress related to nasal obstruction, secondary to reserpine. Nasal stuffiness, an adverse effect of reserpine at all ages, is tiresome for an older individual but may be a life threatening, adverse effect for an obligatory nose breather such as the neonate.

We have reported a paradoxical hypertensive response, associated with tachycardia, in two children under 2 years of age, who accidentally ingested large doses of reserpine. In one patient in whom it was measured, the urinary excretion of catecholamines increased acutely. We postulated that in the young child a quantitative deficiency of intraneuronal enzyme allowed the release of excessive amounts of free catecholamines. A similar pressor response was not seen in an older child thought to have ingested a similar amount of the same drug. In addition, in a recently treated hypertensive three month old child who received methyldopa, we noted marked mottling of the skin and profuse sweating which seemed to disappear within 2–3 days after the drug was discontinued. In many ways the findings in the infant, a child with resected coarctation, resembled those seen in patients with pheochromocytomas. It was our clinical suspicion that the infant could not metabolize methyldopa in a normal fashion. A few spikes of blood pressure were noted during treatment which could not be directly attributed to the drug, since the child was said to be extremely irritable at the time of the measurements. Clearly, a great deal of research needs to be done into the efficacy, toxicity and metabolism of the autonomic drugs in children of all ages.

It is unfortunate that pharmacologic studies cannot often give conclusive answers to the many questions regarding maturation of the autonomic nervous system, and this should be taken into account in interpreting the data presented later. The techniques which are used are often difficult to perform, have a wide margin of error and provide only indirect evidence. Interpreting the fetal effects of autonomic drugs given to pregnant women is especially difficult because of the changes which such drugs may induce in the feto-placental circulation. Finally, while many aspects of autonomic development have been studied in fetal and neonatal animals, results from such experiments cannot usually be directly extrapolated to man.

PRENATAL DEVELOPMENT OF CATECHOLAMINE-STORING CELLS IN PARAGANGLIA AND THE ADRENAL MEDULLA

Chromaffin cells and sympathetic neurons are considered to originate from primitive sympathetic cells which are derived from neurol crest elements. The chromaffin cells show the "chromaffin reaction" which is the old term used to refer to the brown coloration produced by the action of potassium dichromate upon cells which contain norepinephrine or epinephrine. In early developmental studies of the fetus, the presence of the chromaffin reaction was used to determine the appearance time of these catecholamines. It is now accepted that the chromaffin reaction is rather insensitive for demonstrating small amounts of catecholamines.

Since the early 1950's, formaldehyde-induced fluorescence (FIF) has been used for localization of catecholamines in tissues. It is now considered that the demonstration of FIF is a reasonably reliable and specific histochemical method for demonstrating catecholamines, especially when minimal amounts are present, as in the very young fetus. Consequently, recent studies using FIF have demonstrated the presence of catecholamines at an earlier stage of fetal development than older studies, in which the chromaffin reaction was used.

Since the introduction of electron microscopy, the fine structure of the true chromaffin cell has been elucidated. It has been shown, however, that there are cells which are electron microscopically identical to the true chromaffin cell but which do not give a positive chromaffin reaction. Some authors continue to use the term chromaffin cell to include both cell types, others prefer the term "granule-containing cell" when considering structure observed by means of the electron microscope. Hervonen,[5] in a recent extensive thesis, has chosen to use the term "catecholamine-storing cell" when describing the light microscopy of cells in the developing paraganglia and adrenal medulla.

Coupland[2] in 1952 described the prenatal development of the abdominal para-aortic bodies in eighteen human fetuses (8–270 mm.) and five infants who had died within one day of birth. He preferred the term "para-aortic bodies" to "paraganglia," since confusion about the precise meaning of the latter term had arisen in the literature. The para-aortic bodies were defined, in his study, as encapsulated collections of chromaffin cells lying in intimate contact with the sympathetic nervous system and producing a pressor substance. The importance of these structures to the pediatrician is twofold: (1) neural crest tumors may develop wherever chromaffin tissue has existed and (2) the paraganglia, or para-aortic bodies, may have an important endocrine function during intra-uterine life.

In the 8 mm. fetus, Coupland described a few primitive sympathetic cells extending ventrally on both sides of the abdominal aorta but no pre-aortic plexus. A definite pre-aortic plexus existed at the 12 mm. stage of development. Between the 46 and 52 mm. stages, the para-aortic bodies could be divided into a median group, closely related to the aorta and in the mid-line of the pelvis, and two lateral groups which were in close proximity to the adrenal glands, kidneys, ureters and lateral pelvic walls. In the median group, the largest bodies were in close relation to the origin of the inferior mesenteric artery and are known as the organs of Zuckerkandl. While most pheochromocytomas which secrete predominantly epinephrine, are intra-adrenal in location, a few have been described occurring in these organs of Zuckerkandl.

Coupland concluded that, with the exception of the organs of Zuckerkandl, all para-aortic bodies reach their maximum size between the 150 and 270 mm. stages. They may be found in all parts of the abdominal and pelvic prevertebral sympathetic plexuses and sometimes in association with the sympathetic chains. The organs of Zuckerkandl appear to continue to enlarge up to the time of delivery.

At what time the para-aortic bodies finally degenerate is not completely clear. Macroscopic para-aortic bodies are not seen in the adult though Zuckerkandl reported microscopic evidence of degenerated chromaffin bodies in a 39-year-old subject. It has been reported that atrophy of these structures begins after 12–18 months of age but that they may persist up until 5–6 years of age.

Hervonen[5] has described in exhaustive detail the development of the human fetal paraganglia and adrenal medulla as seen by light and electron miscroscopy. In his studies of 200 fetuses of 6–27 weeks gestation (crown rump length 1·2–23 cm.), he also characterized the appearance time of FIF, the vascular supply and the innervation of the paraganglia and adrenal medulla

Development of Formaldehyde-induced Fluorescence

Fluorescing cells were found for the first time within the pre-aortic collections of primitive sympathetic cells of a 7-week-old fetus. Monoamines had not been detected previously in fetuses under 11 weeks (55 mm.), when the chromaffin reaction had been used for their detection. Because of the nature of the fluorescence, the catecholamine present was considered to be norepinephrine. By the end of 8 weeks large extra-adrenal collections of fluorescing cells were found and, regularly, a paired mass of early paraganglionic cells was found at the level of the inferior mesenteric artery. The total mass of para-aortic bodies increased rapidly between the 9th and 12th weeks of gestation and, by 12 weeks, when the fluorescence maximum had been reached, the fluorescent cells were arranged in cords or columns in close contact with capillaries. At the end of the 3rd month, no primitive sympathetic cells were detected in the paraganglia which were comprised entirely of fluorescent cells. After the 14th week of fetal life, only minor changes occurred in FIF or the localization of catecholamine-storing cells.

During the period when the intensity of FIF was increasing rapidly in the paraganglia, small clusters of fluorescing cells appeared along the course of the developing sympathetic plexus and in close contact with the coeliac ganglion.

The appearance of FIF was somewhat delayed in the adrenal gland when compared with the paraganglia. Primitive sympathetic cells were found within the adrenal cortical elements at the age of 8 weeks, at which time fluorescent cells were found only on the medial aspects of the adrenal glands. Fluorescence spread rapidly through the medial half of the adrenal cortex during the 9th week. At this time, fluorescing solitary cells or small groups of cells were scattered through the invasion zone on the medial side of the adrenal and in the central cortical mass, where primitive sympathetic cells were also found. At the end of the 3rd month, large groups of primitive sympathetic cells were seen in the central region of the fetal cortex, surrounded by brightly fluorescent cells. With condensation of these two cell types in the center of the cortical tissue, a clear medullary group of cell clusters was formed.

Primitive sympathetic cells persist in the human adrenal gland beyond term and disappear during the first 3 years of postnatal life. It is believed that new adrenomedullary cells differentiate from these primitive cells after the 12th week of fetal age.

Vascular Organization and its Significance

In paraganglia, highly fluorescent cells were in intimate contact with blood sinusoids or capillaries at even the earliest stages of development. Likewise, in the developing adrenal medulla, catecholamine-storing cells were found on widened medullary sinusoids while the groups of primitive sympathetic cells formed avascular areas. In other words, in both the paraganglia and the adrenal medulla, the development of catecholamine-storing cells was accompanied by the development of a rich capillary network.

The activity of phenylethanolamine-N-methyl transferase, which converts norepinephrine to epinephrine, is thought to be dependent on the presence of hydrocortisone. Steroidogenic activity is probably present in the human fetal adrenal cortex as early as the 7th–8th week of gestation. It has therefore been postulated that the proximity of catecholamine-storing cells to a rich vascular supply allows suitable conditions for both the release of catecholamines from these cells and for humoral stimuli to reach them. Furthermore, it has been suggested that the glucocorticoids may play an important role in determining the direction of differentiation of primitive sympathetic elements.

Ultrastructure of Developing Catecholamine-storing Cells

Studies of the ultrastructure of primitive sympathetic cells showed no specific cytoplasmic changes in fetuses under 8 weeks of age. Since FIF had been demonstrated in the paraganglionic tissue by 7 weeks gestation, indicating the presence of catecholamine, it was assumed that cytoplasmic catecholamine stores were present though not in the form of the granular vesicles found later in development. In extra-adrenal tissue, occasional vesicles were found in the 8-week-old fetus, but no catecholamine granules were found at this stage within the adrenal gland. This difference between paraganglionic and adrenal sympathetic cells was no longer evident by 10–12 weeks.

As catecholamine-storing cells matured in both the paraganglia and the adrenal medulla, the granular vesicles which presumably contain catecholamine, increased markedly in size. Until the 16th week of gestation, granule size was the same in intra- and extra-adrenal sites. After the 16th week, however, granules which were both larger and paler than the earlier population developed in a large number of adrenomedullary cells. Intermediate sized and smaller granules were found to be present in both the adrenals and the para-aortic bodies but no large granules were found in the latter tissue. Hervonen postulates, as others have done, that the large, pale granules, seen only within the adrenal medulla, represent stores of epinephrine, while the smaller granules represent sites of norepinephrine storage.

The age at which the fetal adrenal gland can synthesize epinephrine has been controversial. Various authors who have measured the differential catecholamine content of the adrenal medulla have found markedly differing amounts of epinephrine and norepinephrine at the same gestational age. In 1953, West *et al.* reported that in the human fetus, at about 27 weeks of gestation, no epinephrine could be detected in the adrenal gland. On the other hand, in 1961, Greenberg and Gardner reported that while they could detect no epinephrine in the 11·5 cm. fetus, epinephrine accounted for about 15 per cent of the catecholamine present in the adrenal medulla of the 13 cm. fetus. More recently, using more refined methods, equal concentrations of epinephrine and norepinephrine have been found in the adrenal medulla of the midterm fetus and traces of epinephrine have also been found in the paraganglia of midterm fetuses.

It is of some interest that Greenberg and Gardner found the catecholamine content of human fetal heart, kidney and lung to be roughly similar to the values found in adult members of other species. The percentage of epinephrine in fetal tissues was, in fact, somewhat higher than that measured in adult organs. It is generally presumed that when catecholamines are measurable in fetal organs, a functional adrenergic nerve supply exists.

Development of Innervation

The innervation of the adrenal medulla and paraganglia was studied both by electron microscopy and histochemically, by the demonstration of acetylcholinesterase (AChE) activity. Hervonen makes the assumption that nerve fibres which contain acetylcholinesterase are probably cholinergic in type. This is disputed by other workers who, while conceding that AChE activity is present in all cholinergic neurons, disagree that its presence alone proves that the neuron in question is cholinergic. They feel that the presence of high concentrations of acetylcholine or choline acetylase are the only criteria for definitely identifying a neuron as cholinergic.

In any event, Hervonen found weak AChE activity in the primitive sympathetic trunk of an 8-week-old fetus. A few fibres from the AChE positive pre-aortic network were found invading the medial aspect of the adrenal cortex at this stage of development. By 12 weeks of gestation, a tight network of AChE positive fibres formed a clearly delineated, tetrahedron shaped, primitive adrenal medulla. An AChE positive network of fibres was found in the paraganglia after the 12th week of development.

By electron microscopy, nerve fibres were found within the adrenal cortical elements after the 7th week of development. The paraganglia maintained a sparse supply of nerve fibres in the fetuses studied, with only solitary axons or bundles of axons present after the age of 10 weeks. Synapses were always found on the adrenomedullary cells after the 12th week and were morphologically mature after the 14th week. No synaptic contacts could be demonstrated in paraganglionic tissue. The increasing numbers of mature synaptic profiles found in the adrenal medulla suggested that a synaptic form of transmission was functional after the first trimester of pregnancy. The paraganglia, on the other hand, lacked evidence of functional innervation during the first two trimesters of pregnancy.

Other Aspects of Adrenergic Anatomical Development

Other workers have described various aspects of the anatomical development of the adrenergic nervous system. For example, segmentation of the sympathetic trunk begins in the 10 mm. human embryo, and is well marked throughout the thoracic and lower abdominal regions by 15 mm. In 3–4-month-old fetuses the lumbar sympathetic trunks lie close to each other on the lumbar vertebrae and have well-defined ganglia. By 5 months, the sympathetic trunks show the same irregularity that is seen in adults and the ganglia have frequently fused.

In 1970, Read and Burnstock[12] described the development of adrenergic innervation and chromaffin cells in the gut of 11 human fetuses of ±5–19 weeks gestation (2·5–25 cm. crown rump length) using fluorescence microscopy. Fluorescent nerves were first seen in the esophagus in a fetus aged 10 weeks. The first catecholamine fluorescence detectable in the gut was seen in the region of Auerbach's plexus in fetuses of 9–10 weeks. In one 8-week-old fetus, fluorescence could be detected in Auerbach's plexus in the intestine, only after treatment with norepinephrine. This probably means that developing adrenergic nerves are capable of norepinephrine uptake before they contain enough endogenous norepinephrine to be detected.

Although catecholamine fluorescence was demonstrated by 9–10 weeks gestation in the fetal intestine, co-ordinated peristalsis does not occur in the gut before the 11th week. This may mean that there is not a functional relationship between ganglion cells and adrenergic nerves until after 9 weeks.

FETAL DEVELOPMENT OF THE PARASYMPATHETIC NERVOUS SYSTEM

A review of the anatomical development of the parasympathetic nervous system is made difficult by the fact that, unlike the sympathetic nervous system, the parasympathetic system has no large components like the para-aortic bodies and adrenal medulla which can be studied. In addition, it is not clear that the demonstration of acetylcholinesterase activity in neurons in fetal tissues indicates that such neurons are cholinergic in type. This controversy has been alluded to earlier and should be kept in mind.

Filogamo and Marchisio,[3] who have extensively studied neural development in the embryos of species other than man, have chosen to use the term "acetylcholine system" rather than "cholinergic system." They contend that acetylcholine is not necessarily involved in cholinergic transmission of impulses at synapses, particularly during embryonic development.

It was mentioned previously that some workers have asserted that the presence of high concentrations of acetylcholine or choline acetylase, are the only real criteria for positively identifying cholinergic neurons. Based on their observations, Filogamo and Marchisio have argued that the presence of the acetylcholine system in early neuroblasts does not imply that they will give rise ultimately to cholinergic neurons. This is of interest since in their recent work they have studied the distribution of choline acetylase which has the same distribution as acetylcholine. They hypothesize that in the developing embryo there are two acetylcholine systems, an early or "neuroblast" system and a later or "neuron" system. They suggest that the earlier system is a primitive and peculiar property of the neuroblast which is probably involved in its growth and maturation and which progressively disappears with maturity. This is of some interest, since Burn and Rand in 1965 hypothesized that all autonomic nerves are originally cholinergic and that the adrenergic nerves develop later phylogenetically.

Perhaps it might be fair to say that, if the hypothesis of Filogamo and Marchisio is correct, histochemical demonstrations of the "acetylcholine system" may be valueless in determining cholinergic development during stages of fetal development when neuroblasts, rather than neurons, predominate. Those studies which have utilized the demonstration of AChE as evidence for development of the parasympathetic nervous system in older fetuses, may still prove to be valid.

Development of Parasympathetic Innervation of the Heart

Neuroblasts migrate down the vagi and have colonized the superior aspects of the atria in the 22 mm. human embryo; they are still seen in the 120 mm. fetus. Smith[14] has described the development of the autonomic neurons in the human heart in detail. In the 120 mm. fetus, he found that mature multipolar cells comprised 30 per cent of the cardiac autonomic ganglion cells. At term they represented 90 per cent of this population. Binucleate cells, first noted in the 55 mm. embryo, closely resembled cells which mature into multipolar neurons and this may be the method whereby the number of multipolar neurons in the heart is increased during later development.

It has been disputed whether ganglion cells exist in the ventricles in man. In 4 fetuses at term, an apron of small ganglia has been demonstrated, extending downwards from the atrio-ventricular groove. Small groups of ganglion cells were also occasionally noted in association with the main branches of the coronary arteries. All intrinsic ganglia were subepicardial.

Using histochemical techniques, Taylor and Smith[15] have also demonstrated cholinesterase activity in the human fetal heart between the 35 and 160 mm. crown rump length stages. They found that the ganglia of the fetal heart in the atrial epicardium and atrio-ventricular grooves showed AChE activity. While the epicardial plexus of nerves was present in all of the hearts studied, it was sparse in fetuses smaller than 80 mm. Nerves were prominent in the interatrial and interventricular septa of embryos larger than 100 mm.

Miscellaneous Examples of Parasympathetic Development

The primordium of the submandibular ganglion has been found in a 13 mm. fetus (6 weeks old). However, the adult configuration of the ganglion has not been noted even in term infants. In the tongue, acetylcholinesterase activity has been observed in the 85 mm. embryo. Abundant cholinesterase activity has been found in nerves to sweat glands, in Meissner and pacinian corpuscles, and in the arteriovenous anastomoses in the fingers of fetuses at 16 weeks gestation.

SOME ASPECTS OF THE PHYSIOLOGY AND PHARMACOLOGY OF THE DEVELOPING FETUS AND NEONATE

At what age the components of the autonomic nervous system are functionally mature is not yet known. Nor is it clear what the physiologic role of the paraganglia, which constitute the majority of fetal catecholamine-storing tissue, really is. It has been postulated that this mass of tissue functions as an endocrine organ during intra-uterine life and there is some preliminary evidence that it releases norepinephrine during fetal asphyxia. The ductus venosus and the ductus arteriosus may be controlled by adrenergic mechanisms since contractile responses can be produced in both by catecholamines. Hence, blood flow in the umbilical cord and closure of the ductus arteriosus may be dependent on sympathetic mechanisms.

In 1965, Lipton *et al.*[88] reviewed many aspects of the functional development of the autonomic nervous system in early life. Instead of reiterating the data which they presented, more recent studies of autonomic development will be presented in the following text. The cardiovascular and gastrointestinal systems, as well as pupillary responses, have been relatively well studied during both fetal and early neonatal life. In addition, some data are available concerning the role of the sympathetic nervous system in neonatal thermogenesis, though this remains a confusing area.

Cardiovascular System

The neural responses to acetylcholine and atropine of the isolated atria from a 13-week human embryo have been reported. At a concentration of 1 in 10 million, acetylcholine decreased atrial rate, and at a concentration of 1 in 2·5 million it caused atrial standstill. It should be pointed out that far smaller doses of acetylcholine are required to produce the same effects on adult atria. Atropine blocked the effects of acetylcholine in the fetal preparation. It appears from this experiment that the inhibitory function of the vagus on sinus rate is demonstrable at a very early stage of fetal development.

Many studies of the effects of autonomic drugs on the

fetal cardiovascular system have involved the administration of these drugs to pregnant women. Interpretation of data, obtained from such studies, is difficult since the drugs may induce changes in placental blood flow which may affect the fetus, producing a response which is not really a direct effect of the drug upon the fetus.

Atropine injected into pregnant women during labor has been reported to cause an increase in fetal heart rate of 10–35 beats/min. A similar increase in heart rate was not found in another study when doses of atropine, ranging from 10 to 200 μg., were injected into the umbilical vein at the time of cesarean section. However, in the latter study, scopolamine had been administered to the mothers preoperatively.

It has been argued that the bradycardia, which may occur during uterine contractions, when compression of the fetal head and umbilical cord occurs, is of reflex vagal origin and is not secondary to hypoxia. A similar response can be seen when pressure is exerted on the anterior fontanel of the neonate. Bradycardia, occurring during uterine contractions, can be partially abolished by the administration of atropine to either the mother or fetus.

In a recent study, atropine (0·1–0·6 mg.) was administered directly into the scalps of 5 fetuses. A scalp electrode was used to monitor heart rate electrocardiographically, and it was found that fetal heart rate increased in all subjects. The peak response (mean increase 31 beats/min.) occurred within 15 min. and heart rate started to decrease 55 min. after the administration of drug. As the tachycardia subsided, the normal small variations in fetal heart rate which had been abolished by atropine, began to reappear.

The effects of atropine administered to patients of various ages, including 16 children aged 6 weeks to 13 years, have been discussed (cf. Introduction). Atrial arrhythmias were commoner in patients under 13 years than in older individuals.

The beta-adrenergic blocking drug, propranolol, has been found to decrease fetal heart rate when given to pregnant women. In addition, direct injection of propranolol into an anencephalic fetus, and one apparently normal fetus with tachycardia, resulted in a decrease in heart rate of 30 beats/min. in each one.[13] The cardiovascular effects of both propranolol and atropine probably indicate some sympathetic and parasympathetic reactivity in unborn infants.

Radioactive norepinephrine administered to pregnant women, crosses the placenta and small amounts of labeled drug can be recovered from the urine of the neonate. Transient fetal bradycardia follows the administration of the drug but this may not be a direct effect. However, Karlberg *et al.*[6] have reported the cardiovascular effects of the intravenous infusion of norepinephrine 0·4 μg./kg./min. to 5 full-term infants who ranged in age from 1 to 6 days.

Non-invasive measurements of blood pressure and blood flow are not easy to perform with accuracy in the neonate, but Karlberg and his co-workers were at least able to show reproducible trends in blood pressure and heart rate after the administration of norepinephrine. Blood pressure rose very rapidly after the onset of the norepinephrine infusion and remained elevated throughout the period of drug administration. Bradycardia occurred transiently at the beginning of the infusion, concomitant with the initial increase in blood pressure. It was, however, not sustained and, unlike blood pressure, heart rate returned to pre-norepinephrine levels while the drug was still being administered. This is unlike the response seen in adults in whom bradycardia is sustained as a result of a vagal response to increased baroreceptor activity.

In a group of 30 premature infants, all of whom weighed less than 1,500 gm. at birth, and whose gestational ages were estimated to be 26–34 weeks, 349 episodes of arrhythmia were found in 81 taped electrocardiographic recordings. Since the basic cardiac rhythm in these infants was sinus in nature with sinus arrhythmia, sinus arrhythmia was not included in the tally. Seventy-five per cent of the arrhythmias were sinus bradycardia, with a slowest recorded heart rate of 32 beats/min. Over a quarter of the arrhythmias were associated with startle reactions. As these infants matured, the incidence and severity of arrhythmias diminished. Furthermore, in a group of full-term infants who were similarly studied, a high incidence of arrhythmias was not observed. It is possible that autonomic immaturity in the younger subjects accounted for the difference.

The oculocardiac reflex is usually present in premature and newborn infants as well as in older children. In one report, 68 of 151 premature infants showed a positive oculocardiac response with pronounced P-wave changes in their electrocardiograms. Carotid sinus stimulation is less often positive in both the full term and premature infant and may be variable from day to day in the same infant.

Studies of cold pressor responses and baroreceptor reflexes to tilting have given variable results in the premature and term infant. Likewise, while a normal "adult" type of response has been recorded in newborn infants in response to blood loss, absence of marked heart-rate changes with the withdrawal of up to 10 per cent of the blood volume, has been noted during exchange transfusions. There is no doubt that difficulties in accurately measuring blood pressure, for example, in this age group can produce artifacts in the data. As improved techniques evolve for studying the neonate, important new data should accumulate about the vasomotor regulatory mechanisms which are functional at birth and about their maturation.

Gastrointestinal Tract

The activity of this system is dependent on many extraneural factors so that the role of the autonomic nervous system *per se*, is difficult to study. Boréus has recently published observations of the dose-effect relationships of acetylcholine, and of adrenergic receptor function, in the small intestine of the human fetus.[1,10]

Segments of ileum, from 25 fetuses of 12–24 weeks gestation (6·5–20·5 cm. crown rump length), were tested for their sensitivity to acetylcholine. All segments of ileum, including those from the smallest fetuses examined, contracted promptly when exposed to acetylcholine. The slopes of the dose-effect curves were similar at all ages. As crown rump length increased, the maximum effect which could be obtained with any concentration of acetylcholine also increased, so that during the period of gestation studied, the maximal isometric tension that could be elicited from ileum by acetylcholine increased 20-fold. When the effect of acetylcholine was evaluated against its maximal effect and the shape of the dose-effect curve for individual age groups, it was found that the concentration of acetylcholine required to produce a certain proportion of the maximal response was the same at all fetal ages.

In similar studies, adrenergic receptor function in ileum from 26 human fetuses of about 11½–23½ weeks gestation, was investigated. Isoproterenol was 10 times more active than epinephrine and norepinephrine in producing relaxation of the gut. The effect of these three drugs could be completely blocked by either propranolol or H56/28, both of which are beta-blocking agents. Inhibition of the relaxation of ileum produced by isoproterenol, epinephrine and norepinephrine could not be achieved with the single dose level of phenoxybenzamine which was studied. In a few experiments of combined alpha and beta-blockade, no apparent differences in blockade were noted when the results were compared to those of beta-blockade alone. Because of these results, and because of the fact that methoxamine (used for its supposed pure alpha-stimulating properties), was much less potent than isoproterenol, etc., it was concluded that relaxation of the fetal ileum was due exclusively to beta receptor function. In adult man and in some animals, stimulation of both alpha and beta receptors is considered to be necessary for relaxation of intestinal muscle.

Pupillary Responses in the Premature and Full Term Infant

It has long been known that the pupils of both premature and term infants react to light. Recently, pupillary responses to various autonomic drugs have been reported in 70 infants, ranging in age from prematures of 28 weeks gestation to infants 60 days past term.[7] One drop (±0·2 ml.) of phenylephrine hydrochloride 5 per cent, hydroxyamphetamine hydrobromide 1 per cent, tyramine hydrochloride 2 per cent, or adrenaline bitartrate 1 per cent, was instilled in the eye.

Phenylephrine hydrochloride caused significant mydriasis in all of the infants who were studied, including the youngest who was about 65 days premature. Most premature infants did not respond to hydroxyamphetamine hydrobromide and, in the 6 infants studied, adrenaline bitartrate did not produce mydriasis. With tyramine hydrochloride there was a significant positive correlation between the percentage of mydriasis produced and the gestational age and birth weight. The percentage of mydriasis produced by hydroxyamphetamine correlated positively with only gestational age. With phenylephrine, there was no correlation between the degree of mydriasis and gestational age.

Phenylephrine is a direct acting drug and the fact that it caused mydriasis in all infants, including very immature ones, indicates that end organ receptors are fully functional at an early age. Tyramine and hydroxyamphetamine are indirectly acting adrenergic agents, i.e. they release norepinephrine from nerve endings. The results obtained with these two drugs suggest that, in younger infants, nerve endings are not able to release norepinephrine or are unable to take up tyramine or hydroxyamphetamine. Alternatively, norepinephrine may not be available for release, particularly if membrane immaturity prevents the uptake of its precursors.

Role of the Sympathetic Nervous System in Neonatal Thermogenesis

The factors controlling heat production in the newborn infant are not yet well understood. However, it is believed that the release of endogenous norepinephrine in response to a cool environment is important. While measurements of free catecholamines and their metabolites in the urine do not accurately reflect the functional activity of the sympathetic nervous system, consistent changes in the excretion pattern in a particular illness or situation, are suggestive of changes in sympathetic activity. Increases in the urinary excretion of norepinephrine have been consistently measured after exposure to cool environmental temperatures of newborn infants born at term, but not of premature infants.

In 10 healthy newborn infants, born at 32–40 weeks gestation and weighing 1·2–3·8 Kg., exposed to a cool environment at 6–30 hr. after delivery, oxygen consumption almost doubled and plasma glycerol levels rose significantly. Levels of blood glucose, lactate and free fatty acids did not change significantly and no differences were observed between mature and premature infants. Very similar changes in oxygen consumption and plasma glycerol levels have been observed during infusions of exogenous norepinephrine to newborn infants. In one report, levels of free fatty acids also increased in an infant receiving norepinephrine. In adult man, administration of norepinephrine has been shown to produce increases in free fatty acids and also in blood glucose. The lipolytic effect can be blocked primarily by propranolol, though phenoxybenzamine can also decrease it.

Synthesis, Metabolism and Urinary Excretion of Catecholamines

It is clear that the human fetus can synthesize both norepinephrine and epinephrine from an early age. Furthermore, the newborn infant can respond to various stresses with a selective increase in either norepinephrine or epinephrine excretion. It has already been mentioned that norepinephrine increases in the urine in response to cold. In the normal newborn, as in the normal adult, tilting also results in an increase in free norepinephrine excretion, while insulin-induced hypoglycemia results in an increased urinary excretion of free epinephrine.

How well infants of various ages metabolize free catecholamines, and whether their ability to synthesize unlimited quantities of free amines is restricted in early life, remains uncertain. Normetanephrine, metanephrine and VMA are present in the urine of term and premature infants so that apparently the enzyme systems involved in the degradation of catecholamines are qualitatively normal. Furthermore, when epinephrine is administered parenterally to newborn infants, the amount recovered in the urine is comparable to that recovered in adults.

Voorhess[16] has published values for the 24-hr. urinary excretion of norepinephrine, epinephrine, dopamine and VMA in children of various ages. Although absolute 24-hr. values increased progressively with age, the excretion of free amines and VMA changed very little when the values were expressed as a function of surface area or weight, except for children under 1 year of age. Proportionately more norepinephrine and dopamine were excreted by youngsters who were less than 1 year old.

More recently, it has been found that at least during the first 15 days of life, premature infants excrete significantly less norepinephrine in their urine than full-term infants.[11] Since norepinephrine is apparently important for thermogenesis, the dependence of premature infants on environmental temperature may, in part, be due to a relative inability to produce adequate amounts of norepinephrine. However, it should be recalled, that measured increases in oxygen consumption and plasma glycerol levels have been reported in some premature infants exposed to cold.

The premature infant has also been found to excrete amounts of epinephrine equal to those excreted by term infants, but amounts of dopamine greatly in excess of those excreted by the mature newborn. Increased VMA excretion has also been measured in prematures and this fact, in association with increased dopamine excretion, has led to speculation that more dopamine is metabolized to VMA than to epinephrine and norepinephrine in the immature than in the mature infant. This remains to be proven.

In conclusion, it is clear that our knowledge of the normal development of the human autonomic nervous system is far from complete. Even in those systems, such as the cardiovascular system, where most interest has been shown, studies of autonomic function are incomplete. Abnormalities of the sympathetic nervous system have been postulated to occur in a variety of disease states affecting children, such as asthma, cystic fibrosis and atopic dermatitis, and these will no doubt need to be pursued. Finally, more effort must be expended in studying the effects of drugs, which affect the autonomic nervous system, in children of various ages.

REFERENCES

1. Boréus, L. O. (1967), "Pharmacology of the Human Fetus: Dose-effect Relationships for Acetylcholine During Ontogenesis," *Biol. Neonat.*, **11,** 328–337.
2. Coupland, R. E. (1952), "The Prenatal Development of the Abdominal Para-aortic Bodies in Man," *J. Anat. (Lond.)*, **86,** 357–372.
3. Filogamo, G. and Marchisio, P. C. (1971), "Acetycholine System and Neural Development," *Neurosci. Res.*, **4,** 29–64.
4. Goodman, L. S. and Gilman, A. (Eds.) (1970), *The Pharmacological Basis of Therapeutics*, 4th edition, Chap. 4, pp. 402–601. New York: MacMillan Co.
5. Hervonen, A. (1971), "Development of Catecholamine-storing Cells in Human Fetal Paraganglia and Adrenal Medulla," *Acta Physiol. scand.*, suppl. 368, **83,** 1–94.
6. Karlberg, P., Moore, R. E. and Oliver, T. K. (1965), "Thermogenic and Cardiovascular Responses of the Newborn Baby to Noradrenaline," *Acta Paediat. scand.*, **54,** 225–238.
7. Lind, N., Shinebourne, E., Turner, P. and Cottom, D. (1971), "Adrenergic Neurone and Receptor Activity in the Iris of the Neonate," *Pediatrics*, **47,** 105–112.
8. Lipton, E. L., Steinschneider, A. and Richmond, J. B. (1965), "The Autonomic Nervous System in Early Life," *New Engl. J. Med.*, **273,** 147–153 and 201–208.
9. Loggie, J. M. H. and Van Maanen, E. F. (1972), "The Autonomic Nervous System and Some Aspects of the Use of Autonomic Drugs," Part 1, *J. Pediat.*, **81,** 205–216.
10. McMurphy, D. M. and Boréus, L. O. (1968), "Pharmacology of the Human Fetus: Adrenergic Receptor Function in Small Intestine," *Biol. Neonat.*, **13,** 325–339.
11. Nicolopoulos, D., Agathopoulos, A., Galanakos-Tharouniati, M. and Stergiopoulos, C. (1969), "Urinary Excretion of Catecholamines by Full-term and Premature Infants," *Pediatrics*, **44,** 262–265.
12. Read, J. B. and Burnstock, G. (1970), "Development of Adrenergic Innervation and Chromaffin Cells in the Human Fetal Gut," *Dev. Biol.*, **22,** 513–534.
13. Renon, P., Newman, W. and Wood, C. (1969), "Autonomic Control of Fetal Heart Rate," *Amer. J. Obstet. Gynec.*, **105,** 949–953.
14. Smith, R. B. (1971), "The Development of Autonomic Neurons in the Human Heart," *Anat. Anz.* **129,** 70–76.
15. Taylor, I. M. and Smith, R. B. (1971), "Cholinesterase Activity in the Human Fetal Heart Between the 35 and 160 mm. Crown-rump Length Stages," *J. Histochem. cytochem.*, **19,** 498–503.
16. Voorhess, M. L. (1967), "Urinary Catecholamine Excretion by Healthy Children. Daily Excretion of Dopamine, Norepinephrine, Epinephrine and 3-methoxy-4-hydroxymandelic Acid," *Pediatrics*, **39,** 252–257.

38. THE VISUAL SYSTEM

BRIAN HARCOURT

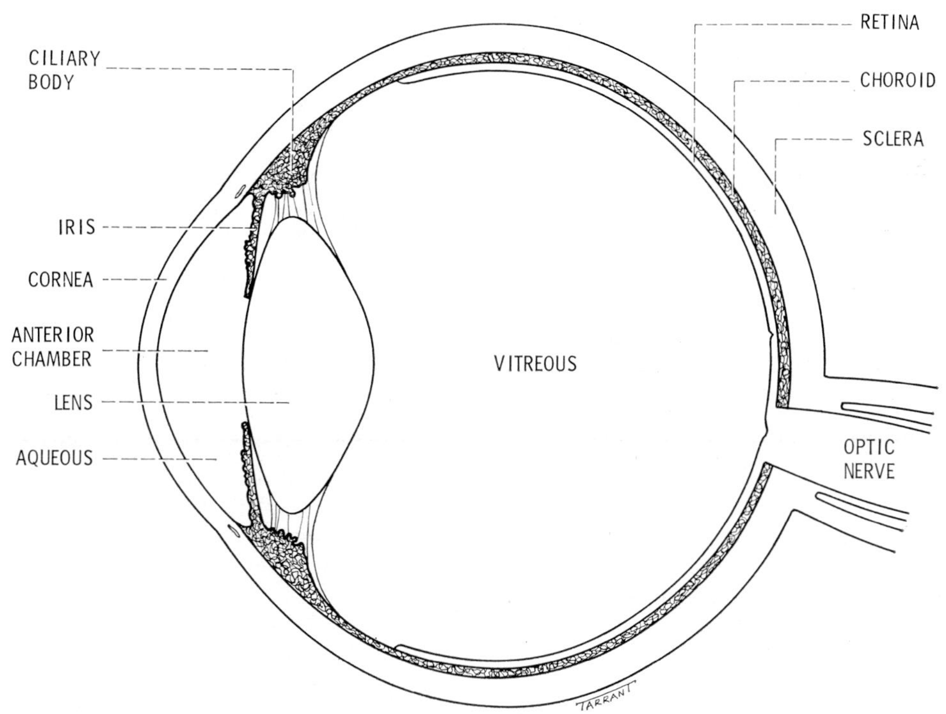

INTRODUCTION

In the process of evolution the response of living things to visible light has developed from a primitive phototropism to an ability to perceive and to interpret complex visual patterns, discriminating their intensity, their form and their colour. Sight is man's dominant special sense and his eyes are his most highly developed sense organs. Furthermore, the neurological connections of the human visual system which allow for binocular stereoscopic perception and interpretation of the visual panorama are immensely complex. Such complexity of necessity implies a very intricate development and it is perhaps surprising that the visual apparatus is anatomically mature within a few months of birth. However, the physiological processes involved in binocular stereoscopic vision take much longer to develop and the binocular reflexes are not fully grounded until the eighth year of life. Understanding of the processes involved in this later development requires some knowledge of simple physiological optics, of the principles of refraction and of the development of refractive errors.

As complexity increases so usually does vulnerability to disruptive influences and the visual system is no exception to this rule. The delicate ocular tissues are vulnerable to adverse external influences especially during the critical period of organogenesis. Hereditarily determined defects in the development of the eyes are also quite common and a knowledge of ocular embryology makes major deformities such as coloboma more easily comprehensible.

A fairly detailed description of normal ocular embryology is therefore followed by discussion of postnatal anatomical and physiological development including refraction, visual acuity and binocular vision. This is succeeded by some description of adverse influences upon the developing visual system both before and after birth. In this respect three disorders are of particular clinical importance. First is infection with rubella virus in the organogenetic embryonic period during the second and third months of pregnancy. Second is the toxic effect of high oxygen concentration upon immature growing retinal blood vessels in the later foetal period of development which may be exhibited by prematurely born babies. Thirdly there is that loss of visual function in an anatomically normal eye, termed amblyopia, which may occur soon after birth as the result of visual sensory deprivation, or later during the first seven years of life in the period of ocular physiological flux or immaturity as the result of acquired squint or of uniocular refractive errors. Understanding of the aetiology, clinical manifestations and treatment of these disorders requires a considerable knowledge of many aspects of ophthalmic development and these are therefore dealt with in some detail in the descriptions which follow.

ANATOMY

Ocular Organogenesis

This is the period during which the specialized tissues are arranged to form the basic elements of the future ocular apparatus. Three embryonic layers contribute to the development of the eyes; the neural ectoderm gives rise to the retina and the optic nerve, the basic light-sensitive visual apparatus. Specialized surface ectodermal derivatives form important portions of the light focussing devices of the eye, while mesoderm differentiates to form ocular muscular, protective, supportive and nutritive elements.

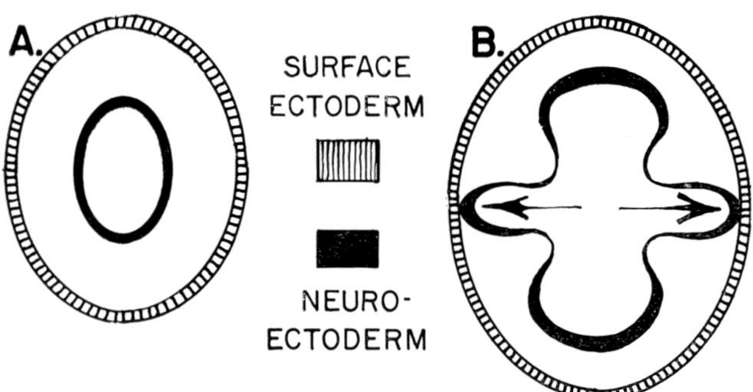

FIG. 1. Transverse sections of the diencephalic portion of the forebrain demonstrating diagrammatically the development of the primary optic vesicles.

The first stage in development of the eyes is the appearance of the **Optic Pits** as small depressions on the surface of the cephalic end of the neural plate in the anterior neural folds by the 2·6 mm. stage (third week). Very shortly afterwards the invagination of neuro-ectoderm leads to the closure of the anterior neuropore, and the cells assembled in the optic pits come to lie in the lateral walls of the diencephalic portion of the developing forebrain (*see* Chapter 31). These cells divide and the neural tissue of each former optic pit region evaginates to form a **Primary Optic Vesicle**, an outgrowth from the lateral aspect of the neural tube which approaches the overlying surface ectoderm at the 4 mm. stage during the fifth week (Fig. 1).

With growth and development of the surrounding mesoderm, the optic vesicle becomes narrowed at its proximal end to a neuro-ectodermal **Optic Stalk**, the open lumen of which continues to connect the vesicle with the forebrain cavity.

The next important stage of development involves the invagination of the optic vesicle to a cup-shaped form. At the 5 mm. stage a deepening depression appears in the distal portion of the surface of the vesicle. This gradually causes a complete invagination of the vesicle and of the distal portion of the optic stalk to form the **Optic Cup** or **Secondary Optic Vesicle** (Fig. 2). The groove or space on the inferior aspect of the cup through which the invagination occurs is termed the **Embryonic Fissure**, which extends from the peripheral rim of the optic cup almost to the forebrain. Through this fissure surrounding embryonic mesoderm is able to migrate into the optic cup and stalk. The fissure is open from the 10 mm. to the 18 mm. stage when it closes without trace in the normal eye (Fig. 3). It is the failure of normal closure which is the cause of the varying degrees of colobomata which can occur as developmental ocular abnormalities (Fig. 4).

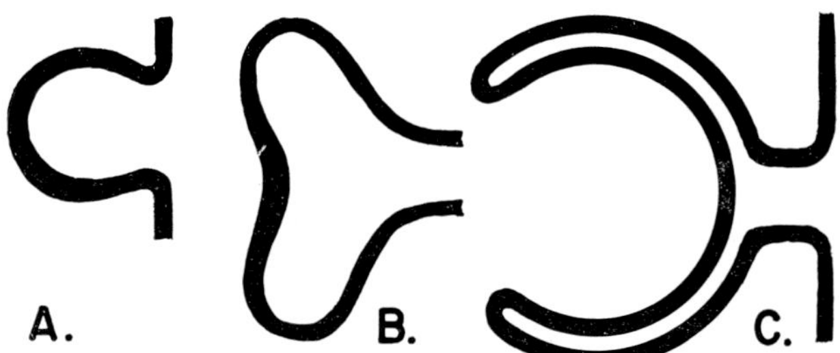

FIG. 2. The primary optic vesicle invaginates to form the optic cup.

While this invagination process is taking place, that

portion of the wall of the optic vesicle which will form the inner surface of the optic cup proliferates to form a number of layers (Fig. 5b) while the outer wall remains as a single cell layer (Fig. 5a). The inner wall will eventually differentiate to form all the elements of the neuro-retina while the outer single cell layer forms the pigment epithelium of the retina. The cavity of the primary optic vesicle does *not* form the cavity of the fully formed eye, but is compressed

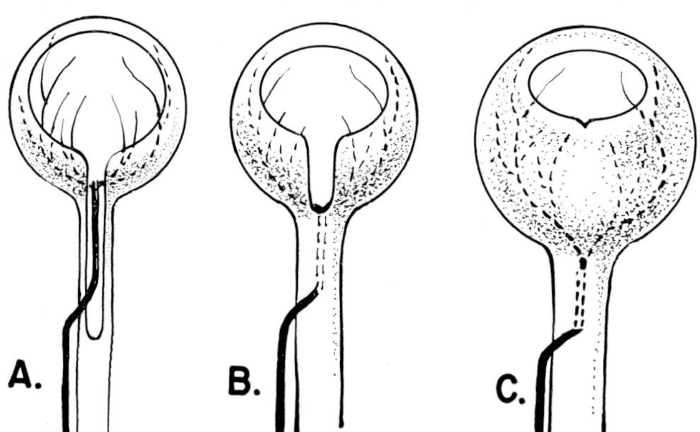

FIG. 3. The invaginating optic cup viewed from below to show various stages in the closure of the embryonic fissure.

into a negligible potential space between these two portions of the retina (Fig. 5). Apart from the region of the optic disc and of the ora serrata at the retinal periphery, firm adhesion between the derivatives of these two primitive embryonic layers never develops, and retinal detachment occurs as a fluid separation between the neuroretina and the pigment epithelium; that is, in the plane of this potential space.

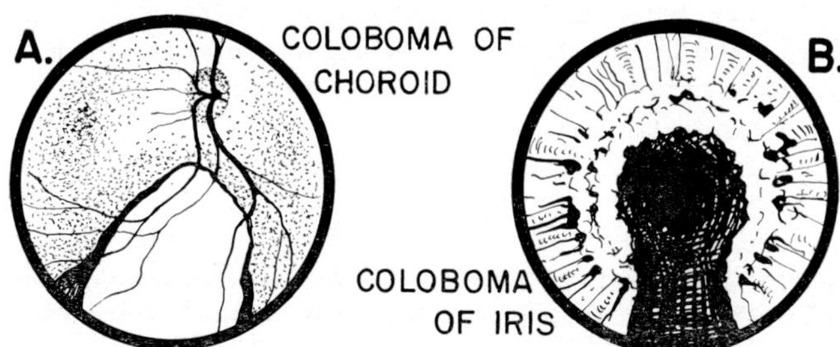

FIG. 4. The major developmental ocular defects termed colobomata are the result of various forms of incomplete closure of the embryonic fissure.

At the time when the distal end of the primary optic vesicle approaches the surface of the embryo (3·2 mm. stage, before the fifth week), a thickening of the overlying surface ectoderm develops termed the **Lens Plate.** As the primary optic vesicle invaginates, so also does the lens plate, forming first a depression, the **Lens Pit,** and later a **Lens Vesicle** which quickly becomes isolated from the surface and lies within the anterior portion of the optic cup (7–9 mm. stage, in the 5th–6th week) (Fig. 6).

While these ectodermal differentiations are occurring, mesodermal tissue also begins to make its contribution to the development of the eye. The surrounding paraxial mesoderm is initially vaso-formative in character and produces a primitive series of undifferentiated blood vessels on the outer surface of the optic cup, and also passing on to its inner surface through the embryonic fissure (Fig. 3). These latter vessels will form the **Hyaloid** embryonic intra-ocular vascular system, and they pass through the fissure

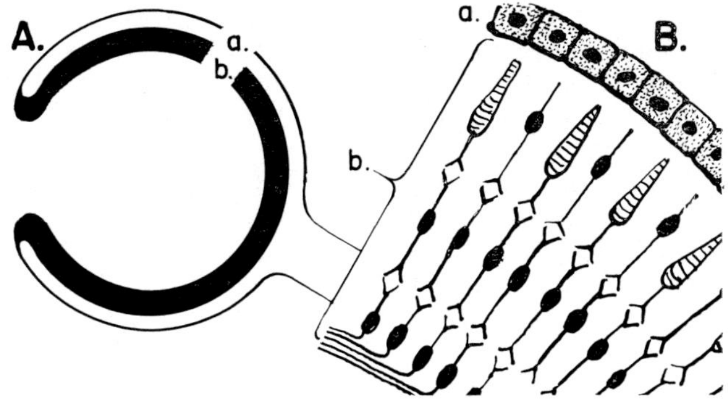

FIG. 5. Development of the retina from the two layers of the optic cup. The inner layer (b) proliferates to form all the component layers of the neuro-retina, whereas the outer layer (a) remains relatively undifferentiated as the pigment epithelium of the retina. Between these two layers lies the remains of the original cavity of the primary optic vesicle.

at the 7–8 mm. stage (5th–6th week). A third series of vessels form around the rim of the cup forming an annular vessel at the 9 mm. stage which links up with the hyaloid system within the cup; all these vessels are derivatives of the carotid vascular system. Paraxial mesoderm is also swept into the optic cup along with the lens vesicle, and

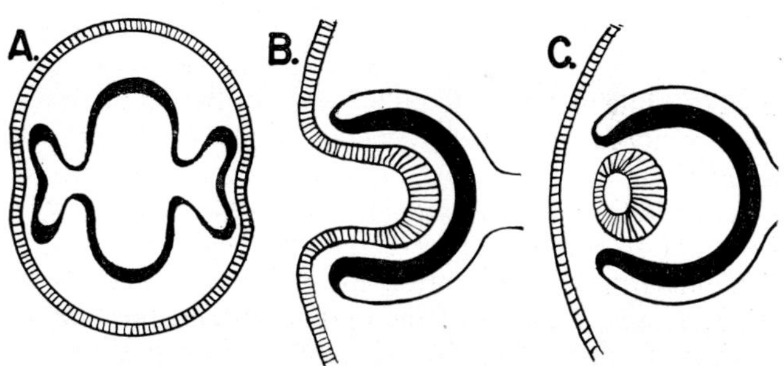

FIG. 6. Diagrammatic representation of the stages in the development of the lens vesicle by invagination of the surface ectoderm overlying the optic cup.

goes to form the stromal tissues of the eye. Surrounding mesoderm forms the vascular and protective outer ocular coats. Paraxial mesoderm forms the upper and inner walls of the orbit, and visceral mesoderm from the maxillary process forms the lower and lateral orbital walls and the stromal tissues of the lower eyelid.

Further Development

(a) Neuroectodermal Derivatives

The Retina. As has already been described, the outer layer of the optic cup remains relatively undifferentiated as a single layer of cells throughout life as the **Retinal Pigment Epithelium**. Pigmentation of the cells occurs first at the 6 mm. stage during the 5th week and is already widespread by the 10 mm. stage at the end of the 6th week. The most essential feature of true albinism is an absence of pigment from this layer. The inner layer of the cup differentiates in a complex fashion to form all the layers of the neuroretina (retinal receptors, rods and cones, bipolar and radial cells, retinal ganglion cells and optic nerve fibres). The minute cilia which are present upon the primitive cells of the primary optic vesicle, as upon all the cells which form the inner surface of the neural tube and of its derivatives, become modified to form one of the most important connecting structures in the outer segments of the retinal receptors.

Ciliary Body Epithelium consists of two layers, the outer being pigmented, which are derived from the forwards proliferation of the rim of the optic cup that commences at the 48 mm. stage.

Iris Epithelium is formed by a yet further anterior proliferation of the optic cup rim. Both layers are pigmented, and from the outer layer derive the sphincter pupillae and dilator pupillae muscles of the iris. The sphincter muscle (unstriated) is first evident at the 65 mm. stage in the 12th week, but the dilator muscle does not begin to develop until the sixth month. This late differentiation explains the extreme difficulty of dilating the pupil in the 28–30 weeks gestation period premature infant.

Optic Nerve. The cells derived from the primitive epithelium of the optic stalk form the glial supporting framework of the nerve, while the optic nerve fibres grow up the stalk from the developing retina to make contact with the cell bodies in the developing lateral geniculate bodies, partially decussating to form the optic chiasma. The optic "nerve" is not, of course, a nerve at all but a tract of white matter, with no Schwann cells, and therefore no capacity for neuronal regeneration (hence the impossibility of envisaging the likelihood of successful whole-eye transplantation operations in the foreseeable future). Myelination of the optic nerve fibres proceeds centrifugally (i.e. outwards from the brain), and does not reach the level of the lamina cribrosa of the optic disc until the time of birth or a little later. Occasionally myelination extends further and appears in patches upon the retinal surface, producing the well-known white feathery appearance which may create a diagnostic problem for the uninitiated. As the retinal layers (Fig. 5) are arranged in vertebrates with the receptors furthest from the light source (the opposite to the apparently more rational situation which exists in invertebrates), any myelination of nerve fibres on the retinal inner surface necessarily produces corresponding areas of complete blindness (absolute scotomata) because of the inability of light to penetrate through to the underlying rods and cones. Furthermore, these scotomata and the white retinal patches may disappear if optic atrophy develops in later life.

(b) Surface Ectodermal Derivatives

The Lens. The posterior epithelial cells of the hollow lens vesicle begin to lengthen from the 10 mm. stage, completely obliterating the lens cavity by the 18 mm. stage in the 7th week, and forming the primary lens fibres which are visible throughout life in the centre of the crystalline lens as the embryonic nucleus. The cells at the lens equator derived from the extremities of the anterior epithelium continue to divide, budding off secondary lens fibres which surround the embryonic nucleus in successive layers, the ends passing from the anterior to the posterior lenticular poles, placed astride the equator like riders. This process continues throughout life, accounting for the ever-increasing size of the lens, for changes in its refractive properties with increasing age and also for the development of senile central lenticular opacities (cataract formation). The opacities are the result of lens fibres dying as the lens nucleus becomes further and further removed from its source of nutrition in the surrounding aqueous humour (a process analogous to the rotting of the central portion of the trunk of elderly trees).

The Corneal Epithelium comes to be 4–5 cells in thickness, but it remains transparent and non-keratinized throughout life, with no glandular appendages.

(c) Mesodermal Derivatives

Choroid. The vascular tissue which envelops the outer surface of the retina supplying nutrition to its outer layers first appears at the 5 mm. stage in the 5th week, and maintains its largely undifferentiated vascular pattern throughout life. Pigmentation commences about the 20th week, which is very much later than the appearance of pigment in the retinal epithelium.

Ciliary Body. Similar highly vascular and pigmented mesodermal tissue forms the stromal core of the ciliary processes and also the unstriated ciliary muscles which will control the process of accommodation.

Cornea, Sclera and Anterior Chamber. Mesodermal cells invade the space between the surface ectoderm and the lens vesicle from the 8 mm. stage during the 6th week to form the stroma and the endothelium of the cornea. Commencing at the 18 mm. stage (7th week), condensation of previously undifferentiated paraxial mesoderm occurs around the vascular choroid and ciliary body forming the sclera; the junction (limbus) between the cornea and the sclera becomes detectable about the 30 mm. stage (8–9 weeks). The anterior chamber first appears as a narrow chink between the corneal endothelium and the mesodermal tissue which lies on the anterior surface of the developing iris epithelium at the 20 mm. stage (end of the 7th week). The cleft continues to extend laterally, but it is not until the fifth month that the angle of the anterior chamber begins to form and to become connected with the Canal of Schlemm through the pores of the trabecular meshwork; the development of these connections which are so important for the correct drainage of aqueous humour and the maintenance of normal intraocular pressure continues until well after birth. The progressive lateral extension of the anterior chamber into the drainage angle in this way is thought to occur by a process of mesodermal cleavage, and a number of developmental anomalies affecting the anterior segment of the eye have recently been grouped together and ascribed to differing degrees of failure of anterior chamber cleavage. These defects range from the most severe in which there is persistent adhesion between the central portion of the anterior mesodermal layer of the iris and of the anterior lens capsule and the central cornea with corneal opacification (central anterior synechiae), to a partial or complete failure of the peripheral portion of the anterior chamber to cleave and to open, with persistent undifferentiated mesodermal tissue in the anterior chamber angle. This latter state of affairs is the classic cause of congenital glaucoma (buphthalmos) and the most effective form of treatment is the rational surgical one of "cleaving" the persistent mesodermal angle tissue with the tip of a fine knife passed across the anterior chamber under microscopic control (goniotomy).

The Ocular Vascular System plays a major part in the development of the eye and shows interesting regressive features, anomalies of which give rise to certain well recognized developmental ocular defects which are difficult to interpret in the absence of an understanding of these processes. Of particular importance is the transient hyaloid vascular system and the tunica vasculosis lentis which together nourish intraocular structures during the period of their active growth, later regressing or disappearing after the development of dependent tissues has been completed.

The **Hyaloid Artery**, a branch of the ophthalmic artery, enters the embryonic fissure at its proximal end and running forwards in its depths reaches the posterior pole of the lens vesicle within the optic cup during the 5th week (Fig. 3). Branches from the anterior portion of the vessel spread over the lens capsule both posteriorly and anteriorly, anastomosing with the annular vessel of the optic cup rim and forming the **Tunica Vasculosus Lentis.** The hyaloid vascular system is at the height of its development at the 50 mm. stage (10–11 weeks) when its branches (vasa hyaloidea propria) fill the optic cup in the primary vitreous (Fig. 7a). Later the vessels atrophy, although remnants of the hyaloid system may persist into adult life causing minor defects of the optic disc (Bergmeister's papilla) or at the posterior pole of the lens (Mittendorf's dot). The "floaters" (muscae volitantes) which are often noted by normal subjects as a sort of frog spawn moving against bright backgrounds such as white paper or the sky, are caused by the visualization of microscopic remnants of the hyaloid vasculature remaining within the adult vitreous body (Fig. 7b). The persistence of the complete hyaloid trunk is occasionally the cause of a very severe functional disorder of the adult eye. The posterior portion of the artery between its insertion into the optic nerve as far as its passage forwards from the optic nerve head persists into adult life forming the trunk of the central retinal artery. The anterior tunica vasculosis lentis develops into the anterior mesodermal leaf of the iris, and atrophies centrally from the fifth month, having formerly formed the pupillary membrane which fills the pupil with vascular tissue. Fine strands spanning the pupil or inserting into the anterior lens capsule in the adult are common minor developmental defects which represent varying degrees of peristence of this membrane into adult life (Fig. 7c).

Recent studies have demonstrated that the retinal blood vessels in man are not formed, as was previously thought, by a process of budding from the hyaloid artery at the optic disc, but independently from primitive mesenchymal cells which have already invaded this area. At the 15–16th week, spindle cells which appear to arise from the walls of the venous channels which accompany the hyaloid artery and from the adventitia of that structure grow from the optic nerve head and invade the nerve fibre layer of the retina. This proliferating primitive vascular mesenchyme spreads peripherally from this central area of the retina in advance of the ingrowing patent blood vessels which finally reach the ora serrata at the periphery of the retina about the time of birth at term. Active retinal vascular growth is then completed (Ashton, 1970). The relation of this normal process of vascular growth to the development of

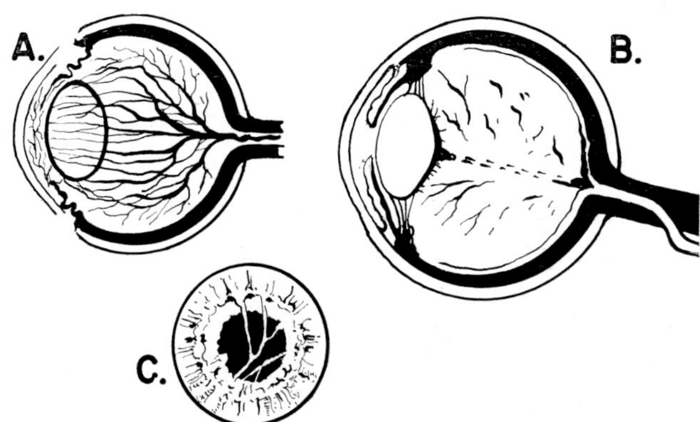

FIG. 7. Development and regression of the fetal ocular vascular system. A. The hyaloid system at the height of its development. B. Remnants of the hyaloid system which may persist into adult life, on the posterior surface of the lens, in the vitreous and on the optic disc. C. Fine strands of persistent pupillary membrane spanning the pupil; they represent a persistence into adult life of remnants of the anterior vascular tunic of the lens.

the retinopathy of prematurity is of the utmost importance, and will be discussed more fully in a subsequent section.

The Eyelids. Initially the eye is separated from the surface only by a thin layer of undifferentiated ectoderm, but during the second month of development, active proliferation of subsequent mesoderm begins to form two eyelid folds covered on both superficial and deep surfaces by ectoderm. The mesodermal tissue of the upper lid derives from the fronto-nasal process in separate medial and lateral portions, and occasionally there is a notch (coloboma) of the upper lid margin due to their incomplete fusion. The lower lid is an upwards extension of the maxillary process. The eyelids fuse temporarily by an epithelial marginal seal in front of the eye at about the ninth week; reopening occurs from the nasal end commencing about the fifth month and is usually complete by the seventh or eighth month, although rarely a partial or complete adhesion of the lid margins may persist until after birth (ankyloblepharon); this condition is, of course, physiological in many young animals such as the kitten and the puppy.

The Lacrimal Gland. This compound racemose exocrine

gland develops from the basal cells of the conjunctiva commencing at the 25 mm. stage (8th week), but it is still not fully developed at birth.

The Lacrimal Drainage Passages. These develop along the course of the cleft between the lateral nasal and the maxillary processes, where a solid rod of ectodermal cells becomes implanted deep to the skin surface. This rod canalizes by disintegration of the central cells, forming the lacrimal canaliculi, lacrimal sac and naso-lacrimal duct. Failure of canalization may occur at any level producing developmental lacrimal drainage defects, but most commonly there is a lack of patency of the lower end of the lacrimal duct at birth and in the first few months of life, leading to a persistently wet and sticky eye. Surgical treatment should be postponed for some months as spontaneous but delayed canalization often occurs up to six months after birth.

Summary of Embryonic Origins of Ocular Tissues

The basic embryological layers give rise to the following structures:

Neural Ectoderm (Optic Cup and Optic Stalk Derivatives)

Pigment epithelium of retina, ciliary body and iris.
Neuroretina.
Optic nerve.
Sphincter and dilator muscles of the pupil (in the iris).

Surface Ectoderm

Corneal epithelium.
Conjunctival epithelium.
Conjunctival and lacrimal glands.
Epithelium of eyelid skin and associated glands.
Epithelium of the lacrimal passages.
The crystalline lens.

Mesoderm

All the other tissues, particularly the blood vessels, sclera, stroma of iris and ciliary body and choroid, stroma and endothelium of cornea, extrinsic ocular muscles, ciliary muscle, and the orbital walls and stromal contents.

Summary of Chronology of Events During Early Ocular Development

5th Week

4–5 mm. Stage. Optic vesicle commences invagination to form the optic cup.

7 mm. Stage. The optic cup is formed by full invagination and the embryonic fissure is open throughout its length with the hyaloid artery commencing to enter it. The lens vesicle is formed from the lens pit.

6th Week

8–9 mm. Stage. The lens vesicle is detached from the surface ectoderm and is covered posteriorly by the tunica vasculosis lentis derived from the hyaloid system.

10 mm. Stage. The outer layer of the optic cup becomes pigmented.

7th Week

15–16 mm Stage. Optic nerve fibres are growing up the optic stalk from retinal ganglion cells. The lens vesicle cavity is completely obliterated by lengthening posterior lens fibres.

17–18 mm. Stage. Scleral condensation is first discernible.

20–21 mm. Stage. The embryonic fissure is completely closed. Nerve fibres have reached the optic chiasma.

8th Week (22–30 mm.)

Corneal stroma appears and the pupillary vascular membrane is complete.

9th Week (30–40 mm.)

The eyeball reaches 1·0 mm. in diameter. The eyelids have formed and are closed in front of the eyes. The ciliary body forms. Muscle fibres are first seen in the mesodermal condensations which are the precursors of the extrinsic ocular muscles.

10th Week (40–50 mm.)

The optic tracts are laid down.

11th Week (50–60 mm.)

The macula area of the retina is first distinguishable. The hyaloid vascular system reaches its most highly developed stage.

12th Week (60–70 mm.)

Iris epithelium develops from the anterior rim of the optic cup. The sphincter pupillae muscle is formed. The canal of Schlemm appears.

Postnatal Development

Compared with most other body organs, the eye is relatively fully developed at birth. It increases threefold in volume between term and adult life, whereas total body volume increases by a factor of twenty. Nearly three-quarters of this postnatal ocular development is completed during the first three years of life, and this is followed by a very slight and steady final growth phase affecting the posterior segment of the eye only, which is usually completed by the age of fifteen years. This precocious growth and development parallels that of other special sense organs and of the brain itself (*see* Chapter 31).

At term the retina is fully developed except for the central foveal region. Myelination of the optic nerve fibres has reached the optic disc, but the optic radiations are still incompletely myelinated. Pigment is usually absent from the iris stroma in Caucasian races at birth, so that the iris is a light blue colour at that stage.

During the first four months of life final differentiation of the foveal retinal receptors (all cones) occurs, and these become directly exposed upon the inner surface of the retina as the result of the migration of the retinal connecting elements towards the surrounding macular zone and the consequent appearance of the foveal pit. By four months there is also full myelination of the optic radiations, and the differentiation of the occipital cortex is also complete; that is, the visual apparatus is anatomically perfected by that stage. The relation of this early completion of development in size and shape of the eye, and in structure of the visual pathways and of the visual cortex will be discussed in terms of the optics and the physiology of vision at a later stage.

The cornea is almost fully formed at birth, being then 10 mm. in diameter compared with 11·5 mm. in adult life; virtually all of this postnatal increment occurs within the first two years. The lens is unique in that it continues to grow throughout life, its mass being 80 mg. at birth, approximately double this at age twenty years, and treble at the age of eighty years. These progressive changes associated with alterations in the shape, pliability and refractive index of the lens have important effects throughout life.

The lacrimal gland is immature at birth, and reflex weeping is usually absent during the first two months of life; psychic weeping does not usually develop until the fourth month after birth, and often not until much later, and it is not known whether this is due to delayed completion of the complex nervous pathways involved.

PHYSIOLOGICAL OPTICS

In order to understand the changes which occur in the dioptric apparatus of the eyes with growth and development it is necessary to examine the basis of ocular refraction. The design of the eye is very similar to that of a camera (Fig. 8), with a pupillary aperture and iris diaphragm, and an otherwise light-excluding covering (the highly pigmented uveal tract—choroid, ciliary body and iris). The "film" of the ocular camera is vastly superior to that of an ordinary camera however, for the retina is able to increase its sensitivity to light (its "speed" in photographic terms) by a factor of over ten thousand on full dark adaptation. The eye also has two separate focussing lenses in its optical system, the cornea and the crystalline lens. The refractive power of the cornea arises as a consequence of its curvature and of the difference in refractive index of the air in front of it compared with the aqueous behind it . . . the refractive power of the cornea is therefore abolished when the eyes are opened under water, and it is for this reason that divers require a face mask retaining the air film in front of the eyes in order to see clearly. The lenticular shape of the crystalline lens and the fact that its refractive index is higher than that of aqueous provides its refractive power. However, the difference in the refractive index is much less between lens and aqueous than between air and aqueous, so that the cornea contributes much more to the total refractivity of the eye than does the lens, although their radii of curvature are relatively similar (the total dioptric power of the eye is approximately +60D, with the cornea contributing +43D and the crystalline lens +17D).

A change in refractive power of the eye, and therefore a change in its focussing is brought about by the process of accommodation in which the refraction of light by the lens is increased by contraction of the ciliary muscle; this relaxes tension on the suspensory ligament and the lens becomes more convex due to its inherent elasticity. This phenomenon allows gaze to be transferred from distant to near objects of regard while at the same time the eye is able to maintain a clear focus.

With increasing age the lens becomes more sclerosed and less easily moulded so that the amplitude of accommodation diminishes. This becomes a serious inconvenience in middle age when a difficulty in reading print becomes manifest even in normal subjects, requiring the prescription of reading glasses; a process termed presbyopia. It is salutary to realize, however, that this process dates from early childhood, with a gradual but progressive retreat of the near point of clear vision from the eyes; at the age of six years the mean amplitude of accommodation in normal

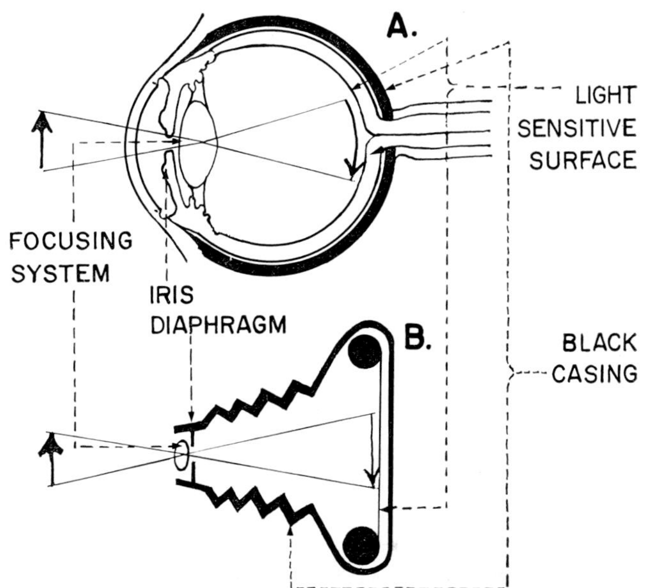

FIG. 8. Simple diagrammatic comparison between the eye and a camera. In each case an inverted image of the object focussed falls on the light-sensitive surface.

subjects is 14 dioptres, and this has already fallen to 11 dioptres by the age of twenty years (the amplitude in younger children is probably greater still, but the subjective responses necessary to assess this accurately require more co-operation than a younger child is able to give).

This description applies to **Emmetropic** eyes, in which a clear image of an object at infinity falls on the subject's retina in the unaccommodated state; in the presence of an error of refraction this ceases to be the case. When the image falls in front of the retina in these conditions the eye is said to be **Myopic** or short-sighted, if it falls behind the eye is **Hypermetropic** or long-sighted (Fig. 9). In the presence of powerful accommodation, hypermetropia can be compensated for by an increased convexity of the lens, but the poor distance visual acuity induced by myopia cannot be compensated for by any such ocular mechanism. The refractivity of the eye depends principally upon the curvature of the cornea and of the lens, and on the axial length of the globe; if the refractive surfaces are too curved or if the eye is too long, myopia will result, while the opposite condition gives rise to hypermetropia.

At birth, the eye is considerably shorter than in adult life, and this would render it highly hypermetropic were it not for the fact that the lens and to a lesser extent the cornea are more markedly convex than in the mature eye, variations which have the opposite refractive effect. Even so, the eye of the newborn is indeed somewhat hypermetropic and this state decreases gradually during the first five years of life, both as the result of growth of the lens which renders it flatter, and of an increase in the axial length of the eye through growth of the posterior segment.

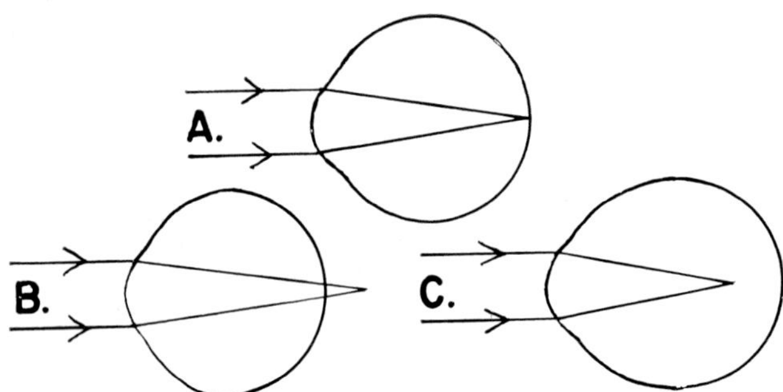

FIG. 9. The basis of axial refractive errors demonstrated by simple ray diagrams of the focussing of a distant object by an eye which is A. emmetropic, B. hypermetropic, and C. myopic.

If the eye is shorter than average, then the subject is hypermetropic, and this refractive error tends to diminish during the period of growth in later childhood. If the eye grows to be longer than average then myopia results, and this refractive error tends to be manifest first around the age of eight to ten years, and to increase during and following puberty, stabilizing and remaining constant when ocular and body growth are completed. Despite earlier claims, there is really no firm scientific evidence that this process is made more severe or is accelerated by excessive reading or other close work at school. The circumstances controlling the axial length of the eye and thus its refractivity can be compared with those influencing the skeletal measurements of the foot; there is no claim that adults with larger than average feet developed this condition because of excessive walking or running in childhood.

The state of emmetropia results from a co-ordination of the three main components of the refractive system of the eye, the dioptric powers of the cornea and of the lens, and the axial length of the globe. Conversely, ametropia results when these factors are inadequately correlated. All three factors follow individual Normal (binomial) population distributions. If each of the three components showed a random variation then the total refractivity of the eye would also follow a Normal distribution, but this is not the case. High degrees of myopia and of hypermetropia are in excess of expectation and lie well outside such a distribution curve, and at the same time there is a marked excess around emmetropia. The former phenomenon is explained by an excessive variation in the axial length of the eye in high degrees of hypermetropia (globe too short) and myopia (globe too long), which lie outside the physiological normal distribution of this component of refraction. Such a phenomenon is analogous to that of the normal height distribution curve, dwarfism and gigantism representing pathological conditions at opposite ends of this scale. The excess of emmetropic subjects indicates that the various contributory refractive elements do not, in fact, vary one from the other in a random fashion, but tend to correlate. Hence, excess length of the eye tends to be associated with a less marked curvature of the cornea and of the lens, and potential refractive errors cancel each other out. Sorsby, Sheridan and Leary (1962) in studying refraction and its components in unselected series of uniovular and of like-sexed binovular twins found a high degree of concordance both in the refraction and the components which contribute to it in uniovular pairs of twins, but not in binovular pairs or in unselected control pairs. These findings indicate strongly that the controlling influences in determining ocular refraction are essentially genetic in nature.

VISUAL FUNCTION

The Development of Form Vision

There are three aspects of vision: the sensation of light, the discrimination of colours and the perception of images due principally to a determination of their shape and size. This last power of "form vision" is certainly the most important aspect of human visual function, and it is particularly the concern of the retinal fovea which has a much more complex relationship with the visual cortex than has the peripheral retina. This was at one time considered as a "one-to-one" relationship between individual retinal cones (the foveal region contains no rods) and the visual cortex, but it is now realized that the relationship is a much more complex one than that, although it is true that the number of nerve fibres carrying information to the brain from each finite group of retinal elements in this region is much greater than in peripheral areas. The classical clinical method of assessing form vision as the maximum degree of visual spatial discrimination is by the subjective assessment of visual acuity using Snellen letter charts or an equivalent test. Illiterate "E" tests or letter or symbol matching tests can be used for the subjective assessment of vision in children as young as three years, but below that age measurement of visual acuity has to be entirely objective, and this poses considerable problems. In the past, discernment of a child's fixation and following responses to visually stimulating moving targets of decreasing size has been used to give some sort of notion of visual acuity in the very young. It is, however, very difficult to correlate the dimensions of such stimuli with the equivalent in Snellen letters.

Recently the phenomenon of optokinetic nystagmus has been utilized in attempting to assess visual acuity in the very young. When a pattern of stripes is moved before the eyes in the visual panorama then the eyes follow an individual stripe through an arc of about 30° and then refix onto the next stripe, producing a regular jerking ocular movement, similar to that observed in subjects looking at passing scenery from a moving train (hence the equivalent term of "railroad nystagmus" which is in use in the United States). In attempting to assess visual acuity objectively by this method moving stripes of graded width are presented to the subject; the width of the narrowest stripe which evokes a following response is then a function of the resolving power of the eye and thus of the visual acuity. This technique has been used recently not only with older infants but also with new-borns in assessing visual acyity.[8]

The traditional view has been that visual acuity in the first few months of life is very poor on account of a number of factors, but principally because the fovea is incompletely developed anatomically, and the eye has a considerable degree of hypermetropia and little ability to accommodate. An acuity of 6/288 at six months was estimated, but more recent work using the results of optokinetic stimulation suggests a visual acuity of roughly 6/240 at birth improving to 6/24 by the age of six months, and 6/18 at one year. All authorities agree that acuity is 6/12 or better at the age of two years, and reaches adult levels of 6/6 around the age of four years in normal subjects. Recent excellent experimental work[10] using the technique of dynamic retinoscopy confirms the traditional view that there is little or no range of accommodation in the newborn, and demonstrates that at that stage the infant maintains a "fixed-focus" at around 20 cm. distance. By the age of four months, however, there is excellent accommodative function with an amplitude of at least twelve dioptres.

Visual acuity in the neonatal period and in early childhood is intimately linked with the refractive state and with the power of accommodation. The blurring of distance vision and the more marked impairment of near vision which hypermetropia induces can be overcome optically by powerful accommodation which increases the refractivity of the eye. In considering refractive errors in the young and their effects upon visual acuity, thought must also be given to the availability of accommodation; that is, the dynamic as well as the static attributes of the ocular dioptric system must be taken into account. In order to remove the accommodative factor from the calculations of refractivity it is necessary to abolish this process temporarily by the instillation of a cycloplegic agent such as atropine to the eye. The retinoscopic findings (the objective method of assessing refractive error) in the unaccommodated state have then to be compared with the results of dynamic retinoscopy. Unfortunately there has as yet been little exploration of this field of investigation, and no adequate figures for normal populations of the very young have been published. The traditional view has been that a considerable degree of hypermetropia was present at birth and that this was eliminated at a rapid rate during the first three years of life and more slowly thereafter to become abolished during teenage. Figures of 5 dioptres of hypermetropia at birth reducing to 2·5 dioptres at three years and to 1 dioptre at eight years have been quoted,[12] but a figure of 2 to 3 dioptres of hypermetropia present at birth, and largely disappearing before the age of puberty probably gives a more accurate assessment of the refractive state in the majority of children.[15] Cook and Glasscock (1951) recorded the refractive findings under cycloplegia in 1,000 newborn infants and found that 25 per cent were myopic, although only to a small degree; the mean refraction was 2·5 dioptres of hypermetropia.

The Development of Binocular Vision

The use of the two eyes together, which allows a combination by the brain of the images presented to the retina of each eye, is controlled by the binocular visual reflexes. These are acquired conditioned reflexes and their development and grounding is spread over a number of years in childhood. Abnormality in their development or in their subsequent function gives rise to squint, one of the commoner disorders of childhood, so that an understanding of the reflex mechanisms is obviously important.

The uniocular fixation reflex orientates the eye so that the image of the object of regard, the most interesting feature in the visual panorama at any moment, falls upon the fovea and the surrounding macula, the most sensitive portions of the retina in terms of form vision. This, like all the visual reflexes, is mediated through the afferent visual pathways, the occipital visual cortex and the brainstem oculomotor centres and cranial nerve nuclei. Of greater complexity is the binocular fixation reflex whereby the image of the object of regard falls on the fovea of both eyes, allowing bifoveal fixation. This function is the basis of binocular vision, for in the normal subject the projection of visual images into space is from the fovea of the two eyes and from surrounding "corresponding" retinal points in the same visual direction, so that a single image of the object of regard is consciously perceived as if by a "cyclopean" eye situated in the middle of the forehead. This fusion of the two retinal images produces only a reinforced two-dimensional view of the visual panorama. The third dimension is supplied by the fact that the two eyes, on account of their spatial separation, view the object of regard from slightly different angles and so exhibit slightly different retinal images. The fusion of these two differing images, falling on retinal points which do not quite correspond, produces the visual perception of depth termed stereopsis. The disparity of the retinal images of a single object increases with proximity, and hence the great importance of good visual acuity at close range. Visual perception is virtually two-dimensional at distances of greater than one hundred feet, and depth perception of distant objects depends upon learned monocular clues such as perspective, light and shade distribution, the haziness of very distant objects, and upon the overlapping of contours, as in an academic painting. In order to view the world in three dimensions, therefore, the subject has to fix both eyes upon the object of regard, and if the object moves, to follow it. The basic reflexes which allow this function are the binocular fixation, refixation and following reflexes, and the convergence reflex. As the eyes track a target moving across the visual panorama the binocular ocular movements are conjugate and the movement is termed a version; as an object approaches the subject the eyes converge in a dysjunctive vergence movement. Combined with convergence there is normally a similar degree of accommodation so that the approaching target is kept in clear focus, and this association, together with the accompanying pupillary constriction is termed the near reflex.

All these visual reflexes are clearly very complex in nature, and from a phylogenetic point of view they are of recent origin, being perfected only in man and the primates. They are mediated through the occipital cortex. It is not therefore surprising that they appear at a chronologically fairly late stage and that they take a considerable period in which to develop into well-grounded conditioned reflexes. It is indeed not until the eighth or ninth year of life that adverse emotional factors are no longer capable of breaking down binocular function. In marked contrast to this are the pupillary light reflexes; these are subcortical unconditioned reflexes and they first appear at the early stage of 29th to 31st week of gestation.[13] These are never deranged or abolished by acquired emotional disturbances. At the same, or at an even earlier stage of development the unconditioned reflex of blink to bright light is first noted. Associated with this is a withdrawal movement avoiding the light. From the thirty-third week, however, a positive response to "soft" light is first noted, the infant turning the head to face a diffusely lit area such as a window.[7]

Fixation and following reflexes can be demonstrated from the first day of the life of the child born at term, although initially the responses are intermittent and poorly sustained, depending very much upon the infant's general state of attention; positive responses are much more easily obtained when the baby is quiet but alert, as often occurs during feeding. Initially the eyes tend to move irregularly and independently (uniocular fixation and following) but within six weeks of birth at term the conjugate binocular reflexes are sufficiently developed for the eyes to fix and follow a bright light, or an interesting target such as the mother's face, synchronously. The binocular fixation reflex is still unsteady at that stage, but becomes gradually better sustained until the age of six months when it is well grounded. At that stage dysjunctive movements have also appeared with the infant's increasing interest in objects close at hand, and binocular convergence reflexes are becoming firmly established in association with the development of accommodation. At a little later stage, corrective fusional movements can be demonstrated if a prism is placed before one eye to produce a horizontal shift in the position of the retinal image, and this compensatory eye movement is not only an indication of the firm desire of the child to maintain binocular fixation even under adverse circumstances, but also a very useful objective clinical test for the presence of binocular function.

ADVERSE INFLUENCES UPON THE DEVELOPMENT OF VISION

Vulnerable Periods in the Development of the Visual System

In the preceding sections the normal development of the visual apparatus from the embryonic stage to adult life has been described. Such a highly organized and complex binocular optical system is particularly liable to functional derangement as well as to organic disorder, and it is the purpose of this section to draw attention to the factors which may give rise to such disorders, and to discuss the stages of development at which they most commonly arise; stages at which the visual system can be considered as being in some critical phase or vulnerable period of development.

Developmental disorders of the visual system are common and extremely varied in character. A great number of these disorders, whether antenatal or postnatal in origin, follow a genetic pattern of inheritance. Approximately 50 per cent of a series of 776 children with severe visual handicaps recently described[4] were considered to be blind mainly as the result of genetically determined factors. In the present context, however, it is acquired factors which are of greater concern. Whilst focussing attention upon the adverse environmental influences which it is thought may affect the visual system deleteriously at critical phases of development, it is to be realized that these factors act against a complex genetically determined background which may profoundly influence their effects.

Adverse Antenatal Influences

That environmental factors may act as teratogenic agents affecting the human foetus to produce congenital ocular deformities has been suspected for many years. Although very large numbers of factors have been theoretically incriminated (drug and chemical toxicities, poor maternal nutrition and avitaminosis, many infections, irradiations and mechanical factors), support for these suppositions by strong scientific evidence is available in only a very small minority of instances, principally ionizing irradiation, thalidomide toxicity and rubella infection. With these exceptions the place of environmental factors during pregnancy in producing ocular defects is extremely difficult to evaluate, and it has to be admitted that, in common with other systems, there is very little knowledge at the present time of the exact aetiology of the vast majority of the congenital deformities which may affect the eyes. The diverse but positively incriminated environmental factors mentioned tend to produce significant ocular damage only when they are active at the critical period of susceptibility, the stage of maximum growth and development; that is during ocular organogenesis in the first three months of pregnancy. Early in this critical stage (4–6 weeks) they tend to produce deformities affecting the eye as a whole, such as anophthalmos, severe microphthalmos and coloboma formation. At a slightly later stage in development (6–9 weeks) similar influences may induce cataract formation and pigmentary retinopathy. If the noxious influence does not exert its effect until later pregnancy when the period of major ocular development is complete, only minor defects result, representing arrests or aberrations in the already established growth of basically normal organs and tissues.

Ionizing Irradiations are the only physical teratogenic agents known with certainty to cause human congenital malformations, including ocular anomalies. The effects of irradiation upon the developing eyes depends upon the time of exposure as has been discussed, but if this occurs in the ocular organogenetic period, anophthalmos, microphthalmos and ocular colobomata have subsequently been reported.[3]

Thalidomide has been reported as a cause of anophthalmos and microphthalmos (Leck and Millar, 1962); it has also been held responsible for varying degrees of defective closure of the embryonic fissure giving rise to colobomata of differing severity.[6]

Rubella Syndrome. The most important contribution to the present understanding of the way in which a maternal infection can adversely affect a developing human embryo dates from the observations of Gregg (1941) that in some cases rubella infection acquired during the first three months of pregnancy was associated with congenital deformities in the off-spring. Further observations confirmed these clinical observations with particular reference to the association of congenital cataracts with microphthalmos, deafness and anomalies of the heart and of the central nervous system.

The diagnosis of congenital rubella may often be made on clinical grounds alone, especially where this obvious association of defects affecting the visual, auditory, cardiovascular and central nervous system exists, and there is a history of maternal rubella. A precise clinical diagnosis is often difficult, however, as sub-clinical infection in the mother can lead to foetal damage. Since the isolation of the rubella virus by Sever, Schiff and Traub (1962) laboratory techniques have been established which make the diagnosis of congenital rubella much more certain. In particular, the demonstration of high levels of rubella antibodies in the child's blood, the finding of raised levels of IgM in the child's serum in the early months of life, and the isolation of rubella virus from the naso-pharynx, urine or cataractous lens tissue of the young affected child are all of great diagnostic value. The discovery of these laboratory methods of diagnosis and the advent of a severe rubella epidemic in 1964 both served to stimulate renewed interest in the disorder, by ophthalmologists as well as by others. In a retrospective study of 105 cases reported from the United States following this epidemic, Geltzer, Guber and Sears (1967) reported that of those children who had positive virus cultures and significant neutralizing antibody titres, 63 per cent exhibited cataracts, 38 per cent had rubella retinopathy, 33 per cent had hypoplasia of the iris, 25 per cent had some degree of microphthalmos, 8 per cent had congenital glaucoma and 2 per cent had iris colobomata. Of the patients who exhibited ocular anomalies, 96 per cent had a cardiopathy of some degree, 50 per cent had hearing loss, 38 per cent were mentally retarded and 13 per cent had a thrombocytopenic purpura. Of great interest in terms of early diagnostic confirmation was the fact that of infants with congenital ocular pathology in this series, 39 per cent yielded positive cultures of rubella virus from the conjunctival sac during the first two months after birth. Live virus has now been cultured from the cataractous lens up to the end of the second year of life in some children affected by congenital rubella. This fact, combined with the inability to dilate the pupil and the small size of the eye in many cases, is responsible for the generally poor results of rubella cataract surgery, instrumentation of the lens commonly being followed by a chronic endophthalmitis with retrolental membrane formation. This is thought to be the result of a reactivation of virus inflammation within the eye at the time of surgery, and techniques such as careful aspiration with a minimal spillage of lens material containing live virus, and also the use of topical anti-viral agents are the methods most likely to improve the results of surgery in the future.

It is perhaps interesting to speculate on the way in which further understanding of the rubella syndrome has tended to undermine its previously unique position in the study of human teratology. It has been known for many years, of course, that other infectious agents, most importantly the Toxoplasma gondii and the Treponema pallidum could pass the placental barrier during pregnancy to infect the unborn infant, and ocular pathology was then a major factor. These infections were also known to have continuing effects throughout pregnancy, often extending beyond birth. Initially, rubella seemed to be unique in that it produced a true teratogenic influence early in pregnancy as a "once-only" affect. It is now known, of course, that the influence of the rubella virus upon the foetus continues throughout the pregnancy and extends into the infantile period of development; indeed some cases have been reported in which cataracts were formed only after birth. Rubella has thus come more to resemble syphilis in the way in which the infectious organism affects the foetus.

Adverse Perinatal Influences

Retrolental Fibroplasia (Retinopathy of Prematurity)

Since its original description by Terry in 1942, this disorder has been clearly defined as an entity which occurs in premature infants of very low birth weight to whom oxygen has been administered in the neonatal period. This specific cause of the disorder was not determined until the early years of the 1950's, and the peak incidence of new cases in this country occurred between the years of 1949 and 1953. Since that time, however, sporadic cases have continued to be reported. The sequence of events which leads to the permanent cicatricial stage of the disorder is now well understood. The developing blood vessels in the peripheral part of the premature infant's retina are very sensitive to oxygen exposure, to high concentrations of this gas leading to occlusion and to disintegration of the small blood vessels of the retina. As a result, when the infant is later removed from an environment of high oxygen concentration the peripheral retina is relatively avascular and therefore hypoxic. The common response of the retina to chronic hypoxia is new vessel formation (for example, after central retinal vein occlusion). As this process ensues, new thin-walled capillaries with supporting fibrous and glial tissue grow inwards from the retina to invade the vitreous body and the retrolental space. Recurrent vitreous haemorrhages may develop, and in the later cicatricial stages of the disorder in its most devastating form, shrinkage of the mass of retrolental fibrovascular tissue leads to traction detachment of the retina and thus to total blindness. Lesser degrees of the disorder, with localized retinal scarring only, but carrying a considerable long-term risk of retinal detachment formation, and sometimes associated with a high degree of myopia, are recognized.

To state that this disorder can easily be prevented by avoiding exposure in the neonatal period to high environmental concentrations of oxygen is to over-simplify the problem; for there seems little doubt that the denial of such therapy to small premature infants with respiratory distress increases perinatal mortality. A major advance in recent years has been the development of techniques for monitoring intra-arterial rather than environmental partial pressures of oxygen in incubated babies. In the presence of inadequate pulmonary exchange, the arterial oxygen concentration may be abnormally low even in the presence of a very high environmental concentration, and it is the former factor only which influences the development of the retinal vasculature. In the sporadic cases of retrolental fibroplasia which continue to be reported, it seems likely that with an opening of the pulmonary vascular bed and a relief of respiratory distress, there may be a sudden and possibly unrecognized increase in the arterial oxygen tension. At present this can be monitored in certain large neonatal units by intermittent arterial pO_2 estimations, but if these are carried out at intervals of greater than six hours during a critical period in the premature infant's progress, it may be that irreversible retinal vascular occlusion can result due to unsuspected toxic oxygen concentrations building up in the intervening periods. The hope, therefore, is for the future development and perfection of techniques which will allow constant, rather than intermittent, monitoring of intra-arterial pO_2. Only then is it likely that new cases of retrolental fibroplasia, an iatrogenic disorder which at one stage became the commonest cause of blindness in childhood in the Western world, may finally cease to be reported.

Adverse Postnatal Influences

Amblyopia

An amblyopic eye is defined as one which is visually defective without exhibiting any evidence of causative disease, and the condition has a very varied aetiology. Clinical and experimental observation, however, delineates two broad categories of the condition. In the first, the amblyopia is acquired, and may be referred to as "amblyopia of extinction", or "functional amblyopia". In this condition the affected eye has developed normal vision initially, but some subsequent process has led to a suppression of vision, and by far the commonest cause of this is the development of a constant uniocular squint, although similar effects may result from uncorrected uniocular refractive errors. In such cases correction of any significant error of refraction and occlusion of the contralateral eye before the age of seven years will almost always lead to the re-establishment of normal visual acuity. Of greater interest in terms of the development of the visual system is the second type of amblyopia which was previously termed "amblyopia of arrest", but has now been renamed "stimulus deprivation amblyopia" or "amblyopia ex anopsia". In this condition there has been some impediment to the normal use of the affected eye since birth, so that a clear optical image has never fallen upon the retina. This state of affairs exists in the presence of dense congenital corneal opacification or of cataract, and also as a consequence of severe unilateral ptosis. It has long been realized that the surgical correction in later life of any factor which denied the early projection of a clear image upon the retina does not lead to any significant improvement in the vision of the affected eye. In the past it was inferred that this was due to a faulty development of macular function in the early months of life. In recent years, however, experimental work on kittens (Wiesel and Hubel, 1965a and b) and on monkeys (Von Noorden, Dowling and Ferguson, 1970) in which one or both eyes were totally occluded during the neonatal period has demonstrated that in these animals at least (and in man by close analogy) the cause of the permanent amblyopia in these circumstances is a postnatal degeneration of previously functioning pathways between the retina and the visual cortex. The prevention of stimulus deprivation amblyopia therefore depends upon the *very early surgical treatment of conditions which severely obscure the retina of the eye*, and this applies most importantly to uniocular ptosis and to cataract. "Very early" means certainly before the end of the first year of life and probably ideally before the age of six months. In the case of uniocular cataract, surgery must be followed by the early fitting of a contact lens to the aphakic eye and by occlusion of the healthy contralateral eye for a prolonged period in order to stimulate the use of the defective eye and so to prevent a permanent amblyopia. This is clearly a formidable undertaking in a young child, so that many ophthalmologists would hesitate to embark on such a course at all in the presence of a completely healthy contralateral eye.

GENERAL READING

Duke-Elder, S. and Cook, C. (1963), *System of Ophthalmology*, Vol. 3: "Normal and Abnormal Development." Part 1: "Embryology." London: Kimpton.

Mann, I. (1964), *The Development of the Human Eye*, 3rd Edition. London: British Medical Association.

REFERENCES

1. Ashton, N. (1970), "Retinal Angiogenesis in the Human Embryo," *British Medical Bulletin*, **26**, 103–106.
2. Cook, R. C. and Glasscock, R. E. (1951), "Refractive and Ocular Findings in the Newborn," *Amer. J. Ophthal.*, **34**, 1407–1413.
3. Francois, J., Hooft, C., De Blond, R. and De Loure, F. (1962), "Embryopathie par radiations ionisantes," *Ophthalmologica (Basel)*, **143**, 163–186.
4. Fraser, G. R. and Friedmann, A. I. (1967), *The Causes of Blindness in Childhood.* Baltimore: The Johns Hopkins Press.
5. Geltzer, A. I., Guber, D. and Sears, M. L. (1967), "Ocular Manifestations of the 1964–65 Rubella Epidemic," *Amer. J. Ophthal.*, **63**, 221–229.
6. Gilkes, M. J. and Strode, M. (1963), "Ocular Anomalies in Association With Developmental Limb Abnormalities of Drug Origin," *Lancet*, **1**, 1026–1027.
7. Goldie, L. and Hopkins, I. J. (1964), "Head Turning Towards Diffuse Light in the Neurological Examination of Newborn Infants," *Brain*, **87**, 665–672.

8. Gorman, J. J., Cogan, D. G. and Gellis, S. S. (1957), "An Apparatus for Grading the Visual Acuity of Infants on the Basis of Optico-kinetics," *Pediatrics*, **19,** 1088–1092.
9. Gregg, N. McA. (1941), "Congenital Cataracts Following German Measles in the Mother," *Trans. ophthal. Soc. Aust.*, **3,** 35–43.
10. Haynes, H., White, B. L. and Held, R. (1965), "Visual Accommodation in Human Infants," *Science*, **148,** 528–530.
11. Leck, I. M. and Millar, E. L. M. (1962), "Incidence of Malformations Since the Introduction of Thalidomide," *Brit. med. J.*, **2,** 16–20.
12. Lyle, T. K. and Bridgeman (1959), *Worth and Chavasse's Squint*, 9th Edition, p. 26. London: Balliere, Tindall and Cox.
13. Robinson, R. J. (1966), "Assessment of Gestational Age by Neurological Examination," *Arch. Dis. Childh.*, **41,** 437–445.
14. Sever, J. L., Schiff, G. M. and Traub, R. G. (1962), "Rubella Virus," *J. Amer. med. Ass.*, **182,** 663–671.
15. Sorsby, A., Benjamin, D. and Sheridan, M. (1961), "Refraction and its Components During the Growth of the Eye From the Age of Three Years," Medical Research Council Special Reports Series, No. 301. London: H.M. Stationery Office.
16. Sorsby, A., Sheridan, M. and Leary, G. A. (1962), "Refraction and its Components in Twins," Medical Research Council Special Reports Series, No. 303. London: H.M. Stationery Office.
17. Terry, T. L. (1942), "Extreme Prematurity and Fibroblastic Overgrowth of Persistent Vascular Sheath Behind Each Crystalline Lens. 1: Preliminary Report," *Amer. J. Ophthal.*, **25,** 203–206.
18. Von Noorden, G. K., Dowling, J. E. and Ferguson, D. C. (1970), "Experimental Amblyopia in Monkeys. 1. Behavioural Studies of Stimulus Deprivation Amblyopia," *Arch. Ophthal. (Chicago)*, **84,** 206–214.
19. Wiesel, T. N. and Hubel, D. H. (1965a), "Comparison of the Effects of Unilateral and Bilateral Eye Closure on Cortical Unit Responses in Kittens," *J. Neurophysiol.*, **28,** 1029–1040.
20. Wiesel, T. N. and Hubel, D. H. (1965b), "Extent of Recovery From the Effects of Visual Deprivation in Kittens," *J. Neuro-Physiol.*, **28,** 1060–1072.

39. HEARING AND BALANCE

INGLE WRIGHT

"The problems of deafness are deeper and more complex, if not more important, than those of blindness. Deafness is a much worse misfortune. For it brings loss of the most vital stimulus—the sound of the voice—that brings language, sets thought astir, and keeps us in the intellectual company of man."

Helen Keller[62]

"No disability presents a greater challenge (than deafness) to the imagination. It is invisible. It cannot be simulated. It is an unseen individual cage,"

Jack Ashley, M.P.[7]

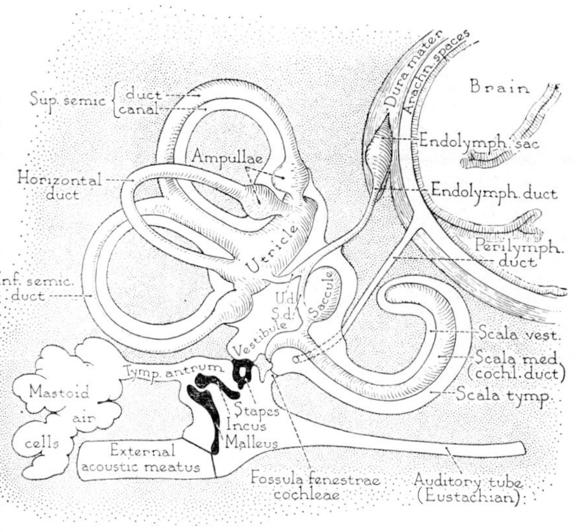

Diagram of general relationships of parts of the adult internal and middle ear and auditory tube; the cochlea is only partly represented as a simple coiled tube. Not to scale.

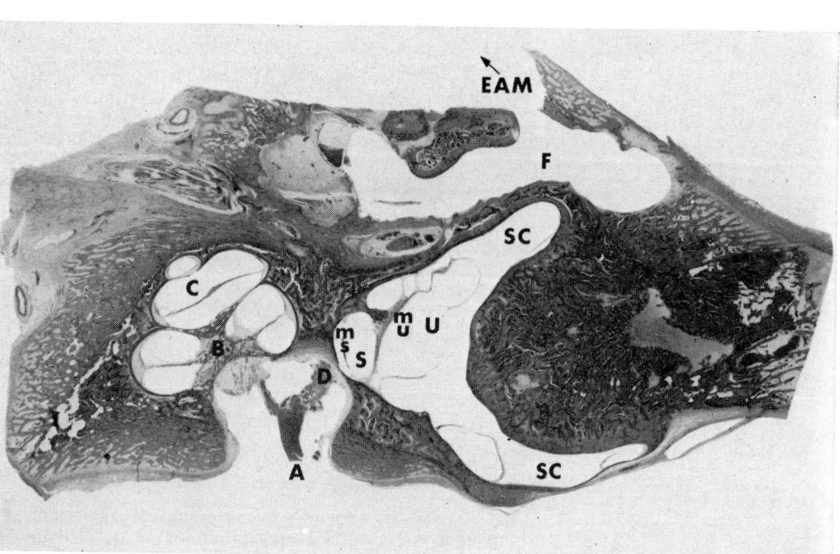

This is a section of a newborn infant's temporal bone. The cochlea and vestibular system are already adult in size. *S* saccule; *U* utricle; *MS* macula of saccule; *MU* macula of utricle; *SC* semicircular canal; *D* Scarpa's ganglion; *B* bony modiolus; *A* auditory division; *EAM* external auditory meatus; *F* middle ear; *C* cochlea. (×3.75)

INTRODUCTION

The classical work in the field of embryology and development of the sensory end-organs of hearing and balance is *The Temporal Bone and the Ear* (1949) by T. H. Bast and B. J. Anson.[12] Since its publication, knowledge of the microanatomy and ultrastructure of the sensory end-organs of hearing and balance has deepened, largely due to the work of Hans Engström[25] and others, in elucidating the role and arrangement of the sensory hair cells (Fig. 1). Impetus for such research has come from diverse fields—space neurophysiology, ototoxicology and the electrophysiology of hearing; while at the same time, advances in biochemical technique, enzyme studies and tissue organ culture, particularly otocyst culture,[44] have begun to make clear some of the processes of cochlear physiology and development. There has been a parallel increase by the use of refined audiometric and electro-physiological techniques in exploration of the eighth cranial nerve and its central connections. In its turn, Engström's[25] refinement of Retzius'[100] (Figs. 2 and 3) surface-preparation technique for use in phase-contrast microscopy has stimulated knowledge of other sensory cells in the tongue[56] and olfactory mucosa.[84,85,86] It has also been applied to study of the cochlea of small animals including the echo-locating fruit-bat.[96,97] This technique involves staining myelin during

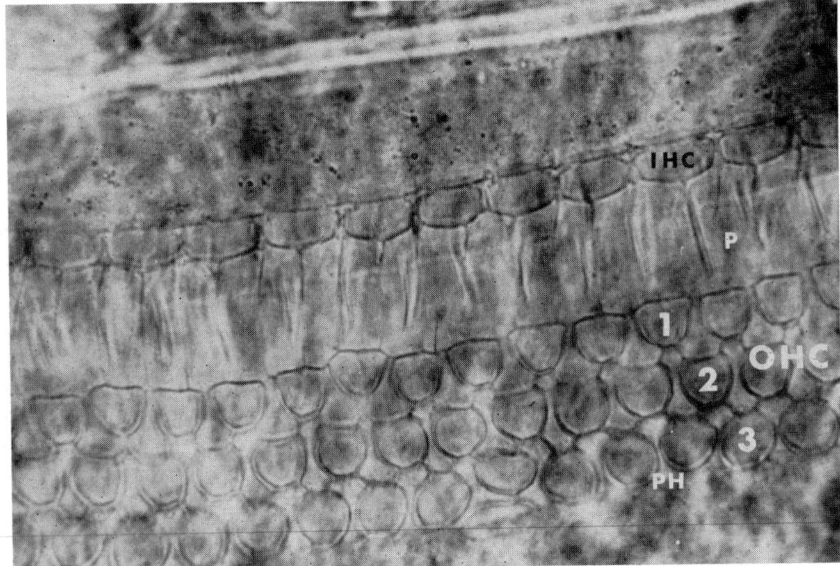

FIG. 1. Sensory hair cells in the organ of Corti from a guinea-pig fetus. This is not a section but a surface preparation. You are looking down on a small segment of the organ of Corti, which is a spiral ribbon. The top row of oval cells are the inner hair cells, *IHC*, below these the pillar cells *P*. The three rows of outer hair cells, *OHC*, are arranged in a characteristic honeycomb pattern in which any irregularity is easily seen. Between the outer hair cells are the supporting "phalangeal" cells, *Ph*. Phase contrast (×675)

osmic-acid fixation, and special stains[74] will also show-up unmyelinated fibres.

The embryology and intrauterine growth of the labyrinth and middle ear in their bony setting are complex. Both are structurally mature before birth. The development of the eighth nerve and its central connections is complete soon after birth and considerably before the age at which the child speaks.[38,114] In fact, the physical development of all the apparatus needed for hearing is nearly complete by the time of birth.

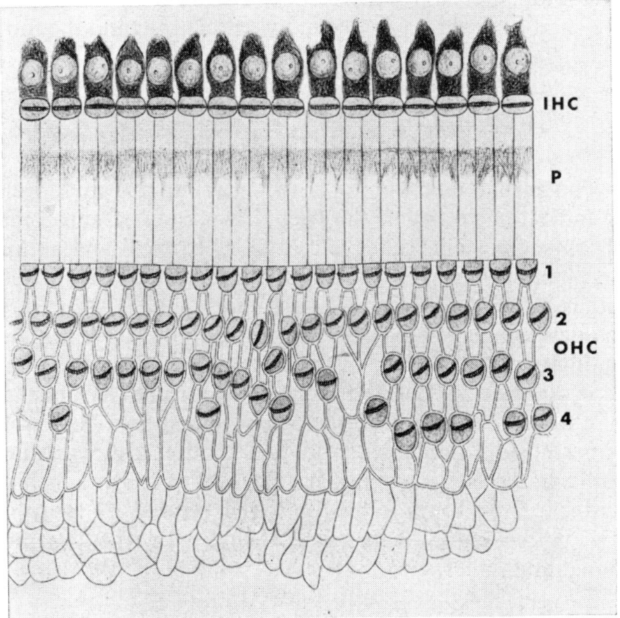

FIG. 2. The surface preparation (Retzius)[100] of a human infant showing both hairs and reticular pattern of the organ of Corti, which is less regular than in the guinea-pig (Fig. 1), and here has 4 rows of outer hair cells, *OHC*. The row of inner hair cells, *IHC*, is seen above, the pillars, *P*, next below, and the outer hair cells below again.

As elsewhere, if a malformation occurs it may be accompanied by other malformations in other parts developing at the same time.[79]

EARLY DEVELOPMENT

The developing embryo is recognizable at the 2 mm. stage (9 somites, 20 post-conception days) as having a primitive brain, a backbone and a tail. A gut of entodermal origin is present. Much ectodermal development lies ahead, but the neuroectoderm is already recognizable as a specialized area developing along its own pathways at the anterior end of the embryonic plate. The adult ear includes tissues developing from all embryonic layers:

Ectoderm	*Mesoderm*	*Entoderm*
Neuroepithelium of organ of Corti, cristae ampullares, and maculae of saccule and utricle	Bone of otic capsule Cartilage Ossicles Muscles	Eustachian or auditory tube and paranasal sinuses Middle ear epithelium
Stria vascularis	Blood vessels Lymph	Inner layer of drum
Skin of Pinna External auditory meatus Outer surface of the drum		

The relations of these layers are complex during embryonic life. Growth in one layer may direct growth in another, as in the likely relationship of the nerve-cells that will supply the various sensory cells to the developing otocyst.[44]

The middle-ear function is transmission of sound from the drum through the ossicular chain to the cochlea. This requires controllable air pressure so that the movement of the bones is not impeded, an intact drum and protection from exterior noxious influences. A somewhat indirect route to the exterior atmosphere exists, the auditory (eustachian) tube leading to the nasopharynx. It is of entodermal origin, as is the middle ear. This, however, makes the middle ear virtually an extension of the upper respiratory tract, and thus prone to the infections of childhood.

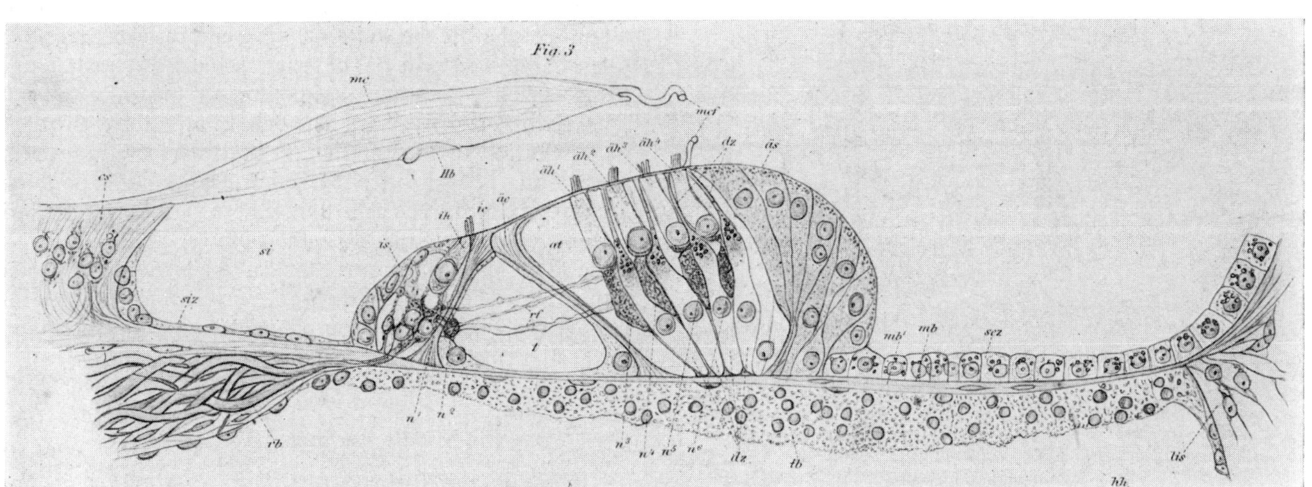

FIG. 3. Cross section of part of the human cochlea (Retzius)[100]. *mc* tectorial membrane; *mcf* Randfasernatz, wavy edge of tectorial membrane, here apparently attached; *ih* inner hair cell; *ic* inner pillar; *ac* outer pillar; *ah* outer hair cells (4 rows apparently present); *t* tunnel; *at* Nuel's space; *dz* Deiter's cells (supporting cells); *äs* Hensen's cells; *cs* limbus. The 4 outer hair cells are here seen in sections; in surface views we look down on them.

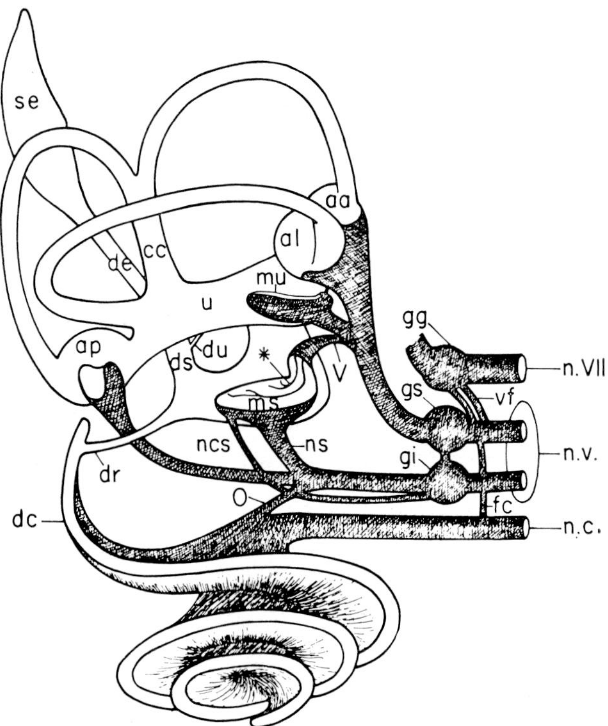

FIG. 4. Diagram of the membranous (otic) labyrinth, showing the divisions of the eighth nerve, with the three end organs: cristae ampullares, maculae, and spiral organ of Corti, shown in greater detail in Figs. 5, 6 and 1 and 2 respectively. *ncs* cochleo-saccular nerve; *ns* saccular nerve; *mu* macula utriculi; *aa* ampulla anterior; *ap* ampulla posterior; *al* ampulla lateralis; *cc* crus commune; *ds* saccular duct; *du* utricular duct; *de* endolymphatic duct; *se* endolymphatic sac; *dr* ductus reuniens; *dc* cochlear duct; *nVII* facial nerve; *nv* vestibular nerve; *nc* cochlear nerve; *gs* superior vestibular ganglion; *gi* inferior vestibular ganglion; *gg* geniculate ganglion; *O* anastomosis of Oort; *fc* facio-cochlear anastomosis; *vf* vestibulo-facial anastomosis. (*Courtesy of H. Lindeman.*)

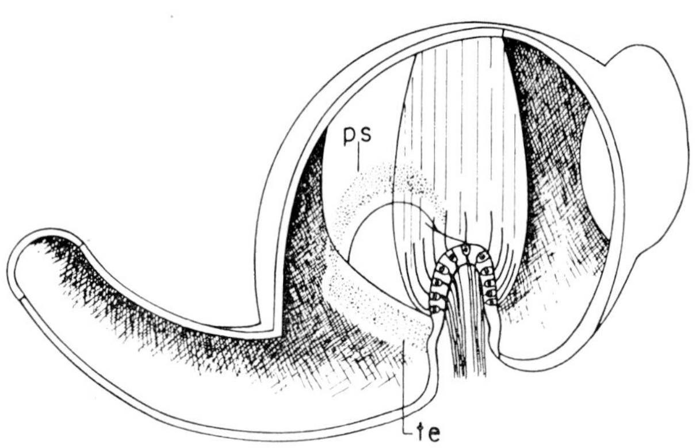

FIG. 5. Schematic drawing illustrating the architecture of the ampulla. The crista, traversing the ampulla, is covered by sensory epithelium. The hairs of the sensory cells protrude into the cupula, which is assumed to extend from the surface of the epithelium to the roof of the ampulla and outwards to the plana semilunata *ps* on the side walls of the ampulla. The transitional epithelium *te* is located at the base of the crista. (*Courtesy of H. Lindeman.*)

It is lined by low ciliated cuboidal cells, with goblet cells and occasional more complex glands.[10] Cells resembling pulmonary Type II are also found. The malleus and incus, ossicles of the middle ear, develop from Meckel's bar (the first branchial arch) the stapedial head and crura from Reichert's cartilage (the second visceral arch) and the footplate from the mesenchyme of the otic capsule.

GENETICS

The normal embryology of the labyrinth and middle ear is under the control of the twenty-two pairs of autosomal chromosomes plus the X and Y pair. Normal and abnormal genetics are fully dealt with in Chapter 1. Where either autosomal or gonosomal abnormality exists, certain maldevelopments have been identified in the labyrinth and middle ear. Gonosomal disturbances have only been associated with hearing defect in Turner's syndrome (XO, phenotypically female) in which there may, in addition, be low-set pinnae, and a minor sensorineural hearing loss.[113] Autosomal anomalies involving disturbances of hearing include trisomy E (trisomy 17–18)[23,66] and trisomy D (trisomy 13–15).[66,91] These are mentioned below with other chromosomal anomalies.

SUMMARY OF DEVELOPMENT OF INNER AND MIDDLE EAR

The Labyrinth: Ectoderm and Mesenchyme

The future otic labyrinth derives from ectoderm. It forms the spaces in the cochlea and semicircular canals which contain endolymph, or otic fluid. The epithelium lining these spaces is very highly specialized, and includes the sensory cells of both divisions of the eighth nerve (Fig. 4), the organ of Corti (Fig. 2), the cristae ampullares (Fig. 5) and the maculae (Fig. 6) of the saccule and utricle. Phylogenetically these are all developments of the lateral line organs and thus we may expect the vestibular system to be complete before the auditory, while clinically it is considered less liable to disease.[38] The stria vascularis is a further highly specialized ectodermal epithelium in the otic labyrinth, overlying a rich capillary network. It probably controls the constitution of the endolymph both by secretion and absorption. The periotic labyrinth will contain the perilymph (periotic fluid). The cells lining these various spaces derive from mesenchyme as does the bony otic capsule and the blood vessels. The periotic labyrinth envelops and protects the otic. (The nomenclature *otic labyrinth* for membranous labyrinth, *periotic* for the channel containing perilymph, was first suggested by Streeter[111,112].)

The Middle Ear and Eustachian Tube

These develop from entoderm; the ossicular chain develops from mesenchyme. The stapes forms from a condensation of mesenchyme at the end of the hyoid bar (second visceral bar) which unites with the mesenchymal condensation that also develops into the otic capsule.

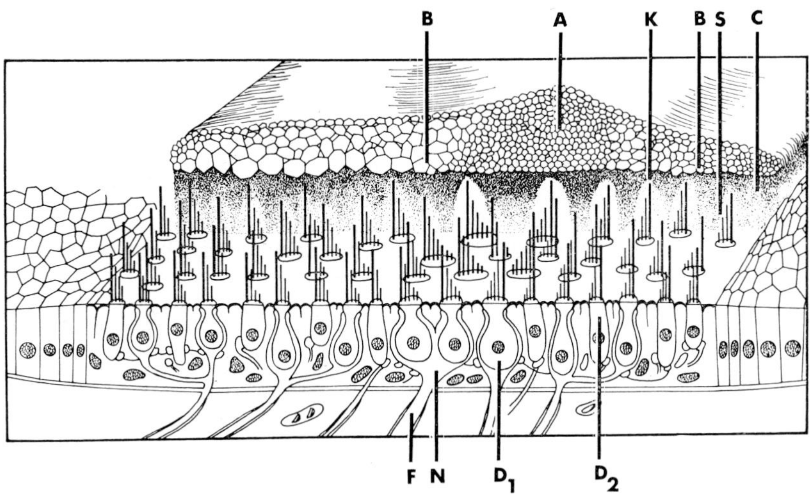

FIG. 6. A *macula* and its statoconial membrane. Regional differences can be shown concerning the thickness of *A* the crystal layer; *B* size of the crystals; *C* structure of the gelatinous substance; *K* and *S* structure of the sensory hairs. Note also the size and density of the sensory cells, and distribution of type 1 *D1* and type 2 *D2* cells; localization of the nucleii within the epithelium; and *N* calyces of the nerve fibres *F*. Note the change in the morphological polarization of the sensory cells in the middle of the striola. (*Courtesy of H. Lindeman.*)

The Eighth Nerve

The cochlear ganglion is spiral (Fig. 7), the cell bodies being within the modiolus (except in trisomy 18,[66] where the modiolus is incompletely developed) (Introductory Illustration B). These are bipolar cells with sensory processes in contact with the sensory hair cells, and central processes running to the brain stem. The vestibular ganglion is in the internal auditory meatus and its cells are also bipolar, with sensory processes round the two types of hair cells of the maculae of the utricle and saccule and of the cristae ampullares.

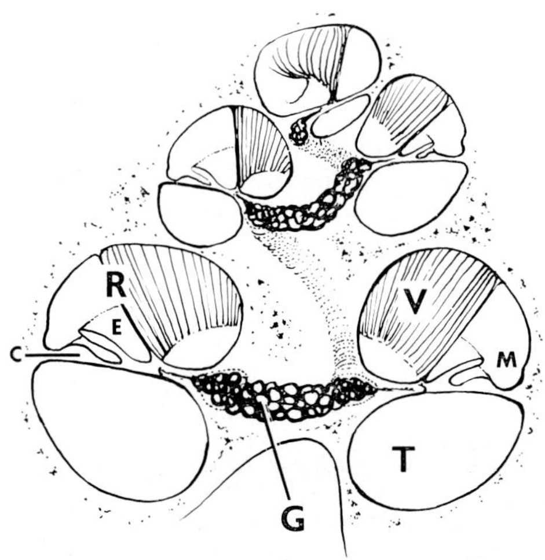

FIG. 7. The spiral ganglion. This chain of cells *G* constituting the cochlear part of the eighth cranial nerve winds up the canal "of Rosenthal" in the modiolus. From these cells, myelinated fibres (not shown) pass towards the organ of Corti *C*. The section shows the three canals: *T* the scala tympani below and *V* scala vestibuli above, both containing perilymph. Reissner's membrane *R*. The scala media *M* (cochlear duct) contains endolymph. The tectorial membrane *E* covers the organ of Corti (seen in detail in Fig. 3). Drawn by R. Neave.

NORMAL DEVELOPMENT

Embryonic Age and Size

Fetal crown-rump lengths in this section are those of Bast and Anson.[12] Where corresponding somite stages, and post-fertilization age in days or weeks, are included, these have been taken mainly from Patten.[92] Post-fertilization days are two or three less than post-coital days, and about 15 less than days from LMP.

The Developing Otocyst

Beginning at about the 2 mm. (9 somite, about 20 days after fertilization) stage, the human embryo shows bilateral ectodermal thickenings at the levels of the middle of the hindbrain. These are the auditory placodes. At 2·4 mm. ($3\frac{1}{2}$ weeks) the placodes have invaginated, forming pits: by the 3·75 mm. ($3\frac{3}{4}$ weeks) stage these are deeper and larger and the ectodermal cells are taller. At 4 mm. (4 weeks) these pits are closed, forming vesicles (otocysts) which are still attached by a stalk to the placode area by the 6 mm. ($4\frac{1}{2}$ weeks) stage.

Meanwhile the vesicles grow and become pear-shaped: at the 6·3 mm. (before 5 weeks post-conception) stage, it is possible to see the beginning of three areas: the upper one-sixth of the pear will form the endolymphatic appendage, and the rest the vestibule and cochlea. The placode area is joined to the sac, no longer separated by a stalk. By 6–7 mm. ($4\frac{1}{2}$ weeks) the different growth rates have made the pear rather crescentic, with placodal epidermis attached at the upper end. The endolymphatic appendage develops first, presumably because of its enormous importance in fish for the rapid control of pressures within the organ of balance.

The otocyst grows, particularly anteriorly (ventrally): a constriction forms by the 8·0 mm. (5 weeks post-conception, 7 weeks post-menstrual) stage, demarcating the endolymphatic appendage from vestibule. The sites of the placodal stalk have disappeared both on the otocyst and on the ectoderm, but up till this stage a nodule is present on the lateral side at the junction of the distal and middle third of the endolymphatic appendage, which represents the site of closure of the auditory pit.

Ventral enlargement of this vestibular part of the otocyst leaves the now lanceolate endolymphatic appendage medial. An invagination comes to separate the appendage from the vestibule (12 mm., 6 weeks post-conception, 8 weeks post-menstrual). The appendage lengthens, expanding medially, and this sac becomes flattened medio-laterally with the free end lying dorsally.

The utriculo-saccular chamber begins to expand laterally and caudally, giving rise to the utricle and, later, the semicircular canals. The ventral or saccular portion develops medially, forming the cochlear anlage by the 13 mm. (6⅓ weeks) stage. Rotation of the otocyst produces a horizontal rather than vertical position for the long axis: hence the semicircular ducts will lie laterally and the cochlea medially. The rotation is clockwise on one side and anti-clockwise on the other.

Chick otocyst culture has shown[33,34,44] that differentiation in isolation can proceed to the point of producing hair cells and complete sensory areas but unless neural elements are included, differentiation will not proceed further. Although cholinesterase activity has not been shown in these cultures, synaptic structures have been found;[46] and acetyl cholinesterase has been identified in 10-day-old mice.[88] It appears that future eighth nerve ganglion-cell centres are removed with the otocyst when embryonic tissue is dissected.

The saccule and the utricle (Introductory Illustration B) will each develop a macula or plaque of hair cells sensitive to movement. The cochlear duct develops from the saccule. It grows as a coiled tube, differentiating to produce the spiral ribbon of sensory cells in the organ of Corti and the secretory epithelium overlying the stria vascularis. Between the mature saccule and the base of the cochlea, lined by flattened epithelium, lies all that remains of the saccular origin of the cochlea, the ductus reuniens (Fig. 4).

The Endolymphatic (Otic) Duct and Sac

In the first half of fetal life, the duct runs straight towards the brain from the mid-region of the otocyst, but greater growth-rates of the brain and dura later carry the dilated sac caudally and it is flattened by pressure. The duct originates from the junction in the otocyst of the utricle and saccule. At first, only a fold divides the common opening, giving a false appearance of separate ducts, but separate ducts do in fact develop later.

After union the duct expands, forming the "sinus", after which it narrows again at the "isthmus," before joining the sac itself, which lies beneath the dura and draining into the venous system.

The sinus is lined by cuboidal epithelium and exhibits varying degrees of rugosity and dilatation in different individuals. It has been considered that the plicate structure of parts of the endolymphatic system indicate physiological activity. In such areas and in the rugosities of the sac, the lining epithelium contains two types of cell[1] which may control pressure by removal or secretion. Phylogenetically, this system was clearly of first importance in the swimming fish, where changing pressure on the fluid which surrounds the lateral line cells needs to be rapidly counteracted.

The Utricle and Saccule

Between the mature semicircular canals and the cochlea lie two cavities, the utricle and saccule. Each bears a macula composed of sensory cells and their supporting cells. The hairs of the sensory cells reach into the otolithic membrane, which is gelatinous and supports the calcareous otoconia (Fig. 6). The peripheral afferent nerve processes run to the nerve cells in the vestibular ganglion in the internal auditory meatus. The central processes run together, forming branches of the vestibular nerve.

By the 25 mm. (7½–8 weeks) stage macular differentiation can be seen, and by 115 mm. (14–15 weeks) the maculae are adult in form. Otolithic membrane is formed at 10 to 11 weeks (50–62 mm.). Figure 8 shows the otic capsule in a 14 weeks fetus.

Semicircular Ducts

The three ducts grow from the utricle and are first seen at the 6–7 mm. (4½ weeks) stage, in the fifth post-conception week, when they appear solid half-moon-shaped discs. By 6–6½ weeks (13·5 mm.) the central parts of the discs have fused together, after which they disappear leaving peripheral ducts. These then grow fast, the posterior duct trebling in size from 10–20 post-conception weeks (from 50–180 mm. fetal length). The superior is slightly smaller, reaching its maximum at the 160 mm. (18 weeks post-conception) stage. The lateral is smallest and slowest, reaching its maximum at the 200 mm. stage (21 weeks post-conception).

At the 15 mm. (6½ weeks) stage when the ducts are newly formed, the surrounding connective tissue forms pre-cartilage, and this is mature cartilage by the 25 mm. stage. It must also be realized that the further and greatest development, the periotic part of the semi-circular canals, involves resorption of cartilage and its replacement by bone.

Each semicircular canal contains a crista in the ampulla at the utricular end (Fig. 5). The crista at first resembles a macula in its development, being seen at 25 mm. (7½–8 weeks) and complete by 20 weeks (185 mm.), but the prominence of the epithelial ridge, topped by a crest of gelatinous material distinguishes it later. Its function, like that of the macula, is of sensitivity to gravity and movement.

Light and electron microscope studies of the epithelium of the crista show that it contains two types of sensory cells, both of which bear one *kinocilium* and several *stereocilia* as in Fig. 9. The type I hair cell is flask-shaped, and seated in a calyx of sensory nerve endings. The type II cell has nerve endings at its base, and is columnar. Both nerves become myelinated after leaving the crista. The hair cells

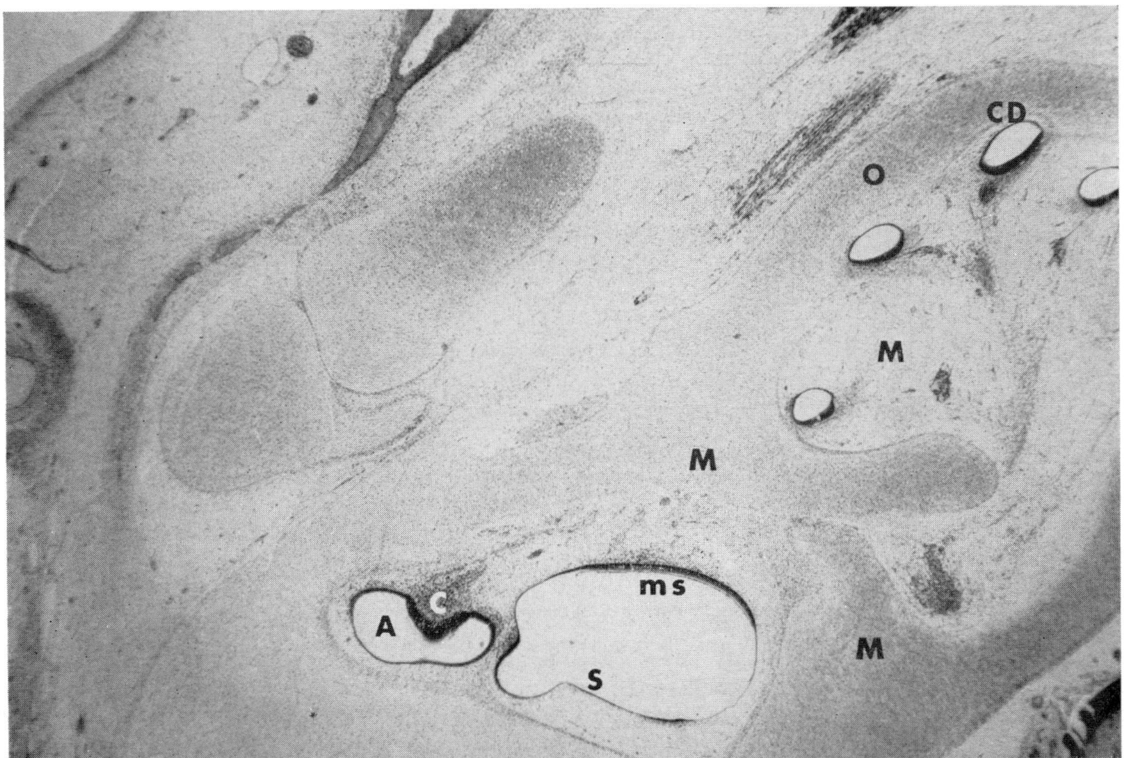

FIG. 8. Photomicrograph showing the otic capsule at 14 weeks: all endolymphatic canals are well developed. The first stages can be seen of mesenchyme removal before perilymphatic channels develop. *O* otic capsule; *CD* cochlear duct; *M* mesenchyme; *S* saccule; *ms* macula of saccule; *A* endolymphatic channel of semicircular canal and ampulla containing crista *C*. See also Fig. 10. (×30)

have supporting cells on either side: these have basal nuclei, and many granules in the upper part of the cell which may have a secretory function. There is a cytoplasmic conden-

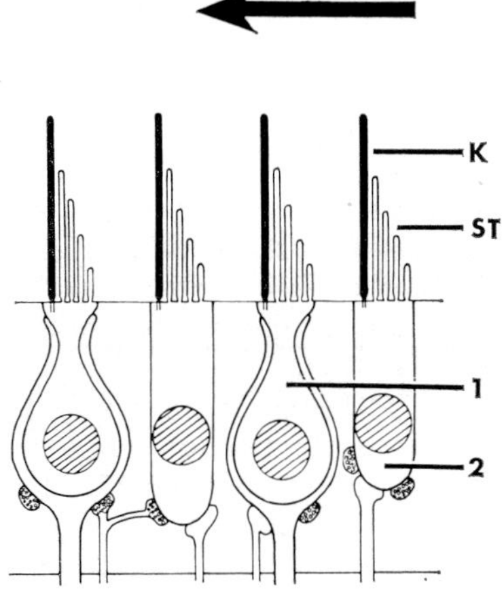

FIG. 9. The two types 1 and 2 of hair cells in the maculae, showing the kinocilium *K* and stereocilia *ST*. Directional stimulus is also illustrated by arrow. (*Courtesy of H. Lindeman.*)

sation at the superficial surface of the hair cells forming the reticular membrane.

The pattern of reticular structure, hair cells and nerve endings, is one which is seen with variations in the vestibular maculae,[70,72] the cristae of the semicircular canals,[87,117] the organ of Corti[25], the taste buds,[56] the retina[105] and the olfactory area.[84,85,86]

In the ampullae, type I cells are mainly on the crest, type II at the edge (Fig. 5). The thicker nerve fibres come from the summit, receiving fibres from several cells. The thinner fibres come from the plexus formed by type II cell fibres. The sensory areas of the cristae are oblong: both types I and II cells are all orientated in one direction, and they are stimulated by one movement. The crista is first seen as a thin gelatinous layer at 10 weeks (50 mm.). It is slightly domed at 15 weeks (100 mm.), and is mature in size and shape by 200 mm. (21 weeks).

The Maculae[69,70,72,117] (Figs. 4, 6)

The development of the sensory cells of the human maculae and of the cristae has not yet been studied in such detail as those of the organ of Corti.[14,15] The first indication of the maculae and cristae is that groups of polygonal cells appear, each cell bearing a kinocilium. Unlike the kinocilia on the cochlear hair cells, these will persist. The bundles of stereocilia on the cells form a different surface pattern from those of the cochlea. (Figures 1, 6, 13.)

The earliest sign of differentiation of the sensory cells from the future supporting cells in these areas is darkening. In the maculae each sensory cell is surrounded by many supporting cells (Fig. 6). The shapes of the sensory areas differ and the distribution of cells differs with each area. There are two types of cell (Fig. 9), as in the cristae, type I,

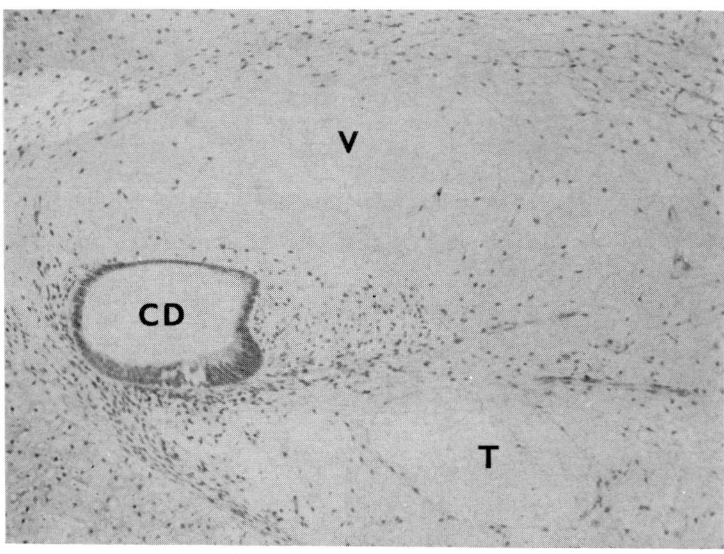

FIG. 10a. Photomicrograph of same section as Fig. 8, showing that the mesenchyme disappears before the perilymph channels appear in the otic capsule. *CD* cochlear duct or scala media; *T* future scala tympani; *V* future scala vestibuli. (×85)

flask-shaped[72] and type II columnar, with stereocilia and kinocilia arranged, according to location, for directional stimuli: these cells may differ in antibiotic sensitivity.[71] The type I cells are phylogenetically younger and more susceptible to poisoning by the aminoglycoside antibiotics kanamycin, streptomycin and gentamycin.[115] The damage caused by these drugs may well be mediated by enzyme and electrolyte changes.[76]

In the macula of the utricle (Fig. 6), which is reniform, the ridge running between the poles (the striola) contains in the guinea-pig mostly type I cells,[117] and these have a larger free surface than around the periphery, where both types occur in equal numbers.

The macula of the saccule contains a similar distribution of sensory hairs. Both maculae are covered by the statoconial membrane, a gelatinous substance first seen at about 10 weeks, and containing crystalline bodies (statoconia) which are calcite crystals. This membrane is thicker, and the crystal bodies are larger, over the striola. Electron microscopy of the statoconia shows pointed irregular ends and curved sides: they may be covered by membrane.[16]

Cochlear Duct (Scala Media)

This begins to be a recognizable entity as a short tubular outgrowth from the antero-medial end of the saccule at the 13 mm. stage (about 6 weeks). It grows along a curved course through mesenchyme and it has accomplished one turn by 20 mm. (7 weeks) and by 30 mm. (8½ weeks) 1¾ turns. The adult 2½ to 2¾ turns of the cochlear spiral are accomplished by 50 mm. (10–10½ weeks), the height of the spiral then being 3 mm., which remains unchanged through life.

Differentiation within this short tube is seen first at its basal end. In Fig. 2 we saw that the organ of Corti when mature contained regular rows of inner and outer hair cells, beneath a tectorial membrane. A tunnel separates the inner and outer cells. The outer cells themselves are separated one from another by supporting cells, the whole having the appearance of a honeycomb (Figs. 1 and 2). During differentiation, this pattern slowly emerges. At 25 mm. (7½ weeks) the cells of the cochlear duct are cuboidal: in cross-section the duct is a flattened oval, showing multi-layered development of cells at the base[12] (Fig. 10). By 62 mm. (10½ weeks) the cochlear duct is more circular in cross-section, and there is a notable difference between the flatter base with thicker epithelium, and the single-layered columnar or cuboidal epithelium of the roof. At the base of the coil, liquefaction has produced a central gap in the floor, where the pillars will be; and the surface cells are covered by a thin gelatinous layer, later to be the tectorial membrane. By 115 mm. (14½ weeks), cross-section of the duct is triangular, and outer hair cells can be seen arranged in orderly fashion (Fig. 10) above the similarly ordered supporting cells. The tunnel of Corti is newly visible in the basal layer. Laterally, the wall shows early signs of stria vascularis epithelium. Medially, the future Reissner's membrane is evident. Mesenchyme disappears before the perilymph channels appear (Fig. 10a).

The sensory cells form from specialized epithelium covering ridges running from the base towards the apex. A surface view of the inner ridge epithelium at the 90 mm. (13 weeks post-conception) stage shows hexagonal cells (Fig. 11), each bearing a kinocilium. The inner hair cells are first distinct 11 mm. from the base as darker cells separated from one another by one kinocilium-bearing cell. At this level, there is no distinction between the hexagonal cells in the outer hair cell area, some of which will become hair cells, some supporting cells. Nearer the base, the outer hair cells are seen as darker, and the inner cells as larger (Fig. 12); between them lie the heads of the inner pillar cells. Stereocilia are present, but the kinocilia disappear before birth except for the basal bodies (Fig. 13).

The supporting cells of the adult contain basal bodies,

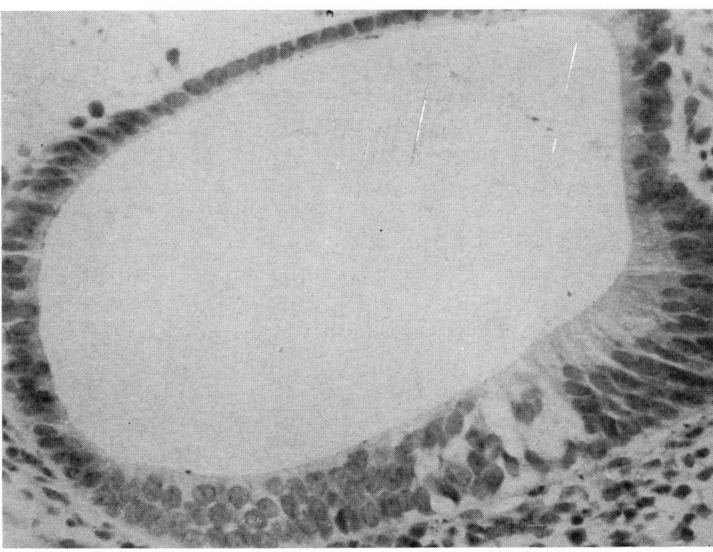

FIG. 10b. Layering of future hair cells above supporting cells in the basal turn of organ of Corti, in the same 14-week fetus. The future tunnel is also evident. (×340)

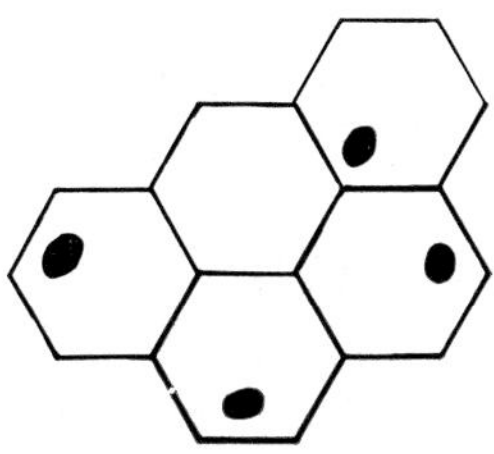

FIG. 11. A surface view of the polygonal cells at the base of the endolymphatic channel. These cells mostly bear a kinocilium. Bredberg[15] has found future inner and outer sensory cells of this sort running along two ridges in the organ of Corti at 3–4 months. Drawn by R. Neave.

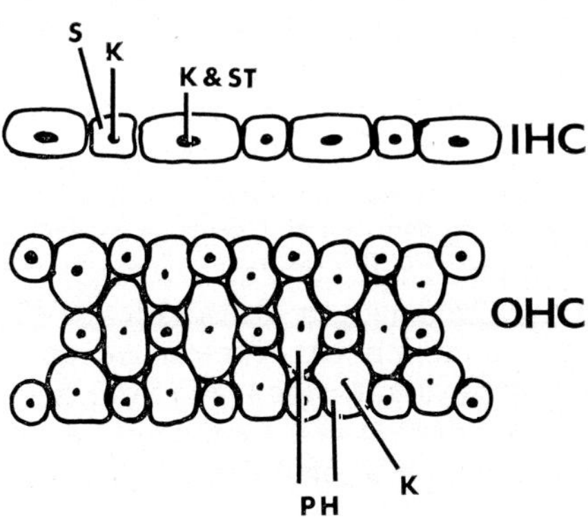

FIG. 12. A surface view of the early differentiation of the fetal organ of Corti. Every cell, which you are looking down on, still bears a kinocilium *K*, here represented by a round dot. The inner hair cells, *IHC*, are in the separate row at the top of the diagram. These are differentiating from their supporting cells, *S*, which are small in comparison, and are assuming adult shape. Stereocilia (hairs), *ST*, arranged in a thick line are becoming apparent on the inner hair cells. Pillar cells between inner and outer bands of hair cells are omitted. The outer hair cells, *OHC*, are rounder than formerly; the supporting cells, *PH*, have become adult in shape. Outer hair cells and supporting cells, *PH*, still bear the kinocilium, *K*, but not stereocilia, *ST*, yet. Drawn by R. Neave.

remains of the fetal kinocilia. In the adult cochlea, as in the macular supporting cells, there is a basal body as the sole remainder of the kinocilium which is positioned on each hair cell nearer to the stria vascularis than are the associated stereocilia.[40,41,117] Stimulation of the cochlear stereocilia is caused by tangential displacement of the tectorial membrane[13]: it is thus possible that functional and

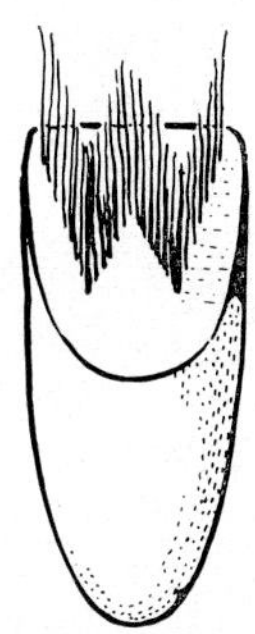

FIG. 13. Three dimensional diagram of a human outer hair cell with "W" pattern of hairs (stereocilia) which are inserted above in the tectorial membrane (Fig. 15). There is now no kinocilium. It has now disappeared from all the hair cells of the organ of Corti. Drawn by R. Neave.

morphological polarization may be correlative in the organ of Corti as well as in the other developments of the lateral line organs. Numerical studies of the hair cells of all these organs have been published.[15,69,70,72]

At 4 months ($16\frac{1}{2}$–19 weeks, 140–170 mm.) the developed sensory cells have reached the apex, and by 5 months (23–24 weeks, 220–230 mm.) they are assuming mature shapes, with the stereocilia arranged in characteristic W patterns (Fig. 13). There are three rows of outer hair cells at this stage. Division may occur during the sixth month (Fig. 23) to produce irregular members of a 4th or 5th row (Fig. 2) and some extra cells in the first three rows. These later

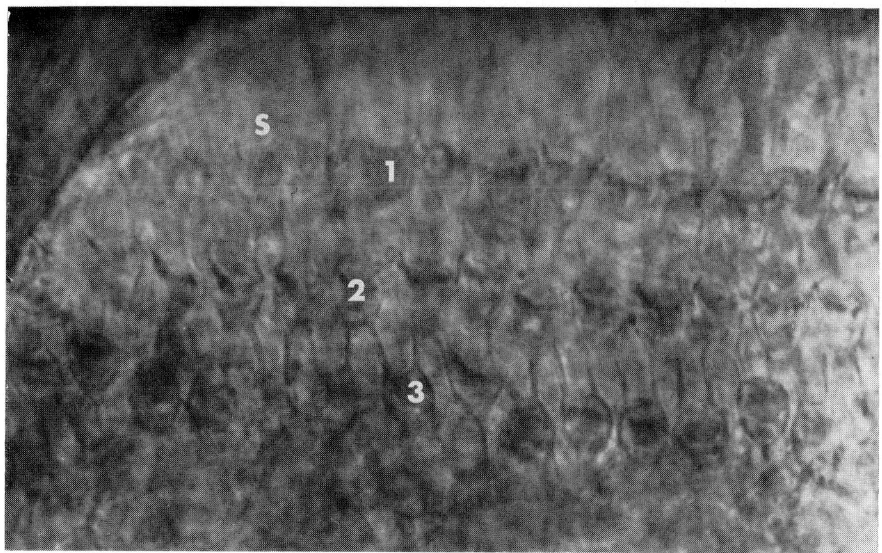

FIG. 14a. Photomicrograph of infant outer hair cell in the organ of Corti. Three rows are present, fairly regularly arranged. In the first (top) row, the stereocilia, *S*, are identifiable singly and resemble eyelashes. In the second and third rows the hairs are less obvious. The reticular pattern is fairly clear. Phase contrast. (×1080)

divisions are responsible for the typical infant appearance of an irregular sensory arrangement (Fig. 14), which often includes 4th and 5th rows of outer hair cells.

At this stage an intracellular space is seen running between the outer pillar cells and the first row of hair cells, thus

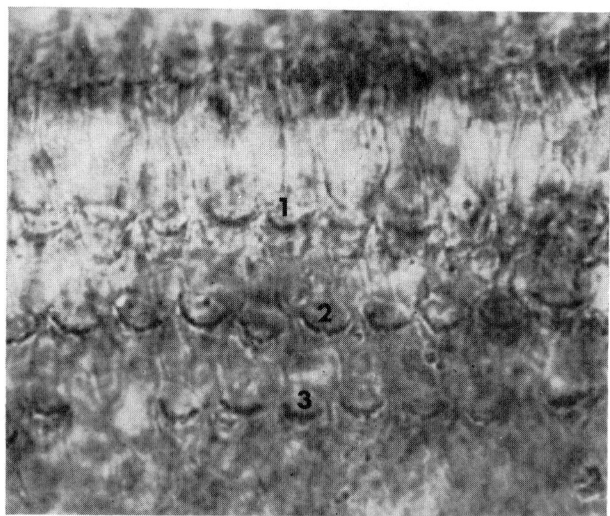

FIG. 14b. Photomicrograph of infant outer hair cells, rows 1, 2 and 3, showing the W-pattern of hairs and faint reticular pattern. One "collapse" figure, due to loss of one hair cell, is seen in row 3 on the left. Phase contrast. (×920)

corresponding to the space of Nuel. A few weeks later[15] the tunnel of Corti develops, between the pillar-cell bases. In the 21-week (200 mm.) fetus the space of Nuel is larger than the tunnel, which is to widen considerably. These spaces do not appear in the apical coil till 24 weeks (230 mm.) or later.

The origin of the fluid in these intercellular spaces of the tunnel has been much discussed, and secretion from cells has been suggested. It is sometimes referred to[24] as Corti-lymph, and has not been conclusively shown to have connection with either endolymph or perilymph.

The Tectorial Membrane

This is first seen as a shadowy gelatinous layer at the 62 mm. ($10\frac{3}{4}$ weeks) stage, lying on the almost undifferentiated cells. Attachment to the limbus is seen by the 90–115 mm. (13–$14\frac{1}{2}$ weeks) stage, but it does not yet reach across the future hair cells except at the base. Finally, the hairs of the outer sensory cell leave imprints, three rows on the "under" surface of the membrane and 4th- and 5th-row cells on the randfasernatz or fibrillary edge (Figs. 3 and 15). The membrane contains osmiophilic fibres. At no time is it covered by cellular membrane.

It has been found[73] that the surface topography of the cat organ of Corti is of mature appearance 3 to 5 weeks after birth. The tectorial membrane is attached until this time at its outer margin to the long microvilli of Deiters cells, the detachment being the last event in the maturation of the cat cochlea beginning at 10 days after birth. This may be related to the finding that cochlear microphonics have been found to attain adult value at 4 to 5 weeks in the kitten, and suggests that the tectorial membrane may exert a protective function until hearing is needed.

The Eighth Cranial Nerve

(1) Cochlear Division (Figs. 4, 7)

The hair cells have sensory nerve endings which may be shared with other hair cells. The innervation of the inner and outer hair cells may account for recognized differences in sensitivity.[110] These nerve fibres run from the cells through the bony spiral lamina and become myelinated on their way to the cells situated in the modiolus. They are bipolar, with the longer process running in the cochlear part of the eighth nerve to the brain stem to reach the central and dorsal cochlear nuclei where they have synaptic junctions with the second neurons. The second neurons, with few exceptions, cross the brain stem, establishing connections with the third neurons. The function of the efferent innervation is not wholly clear.[110]

(2) Vestibular Division

The vestibular system begins similarly with bipolar neurons from the sensory endings in the ampullae and the maculae. The cell bodies lie in Scarpa's ganglion (Introductory Illustration B) in the internal auditory meatus,[11] their processes terminating in the medulla. The second neurons follow complicated courses, both ipsilateral and contralateral, establishing connections with cerebellum, spinal cord and other cranial-nerve nuclei, particularly those connected with eye movement.

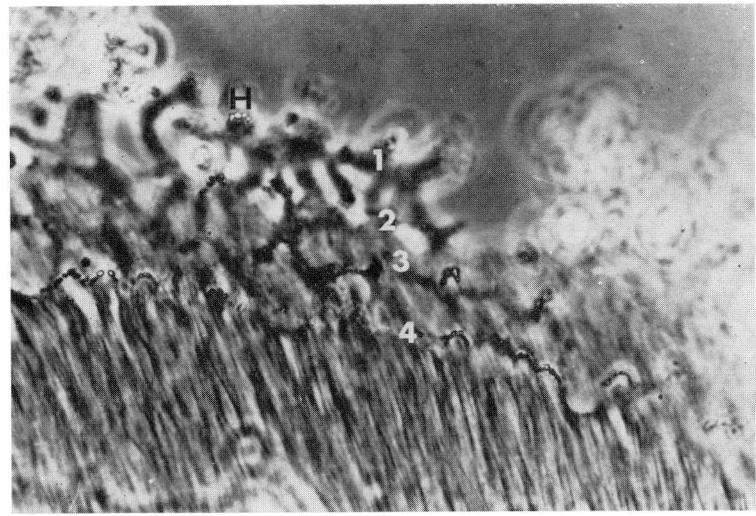

FIG. 15. Photomicrograph showing the under surface of edge of tectorial membrane from infant organ of Corti, showing imprints, *H*, of four rows of hairs from outer hair cells. Phase contrast (×600)

(3) The Cochlear Nuclei

The cochlear nuclei and the rest of the auditory pathway are very highly vascularized, more so than any other part of the central nervous system,[10,20,22,38,67]

The vascularity of the cochlear nuclei of the rat at birth is lower than of some other nuclei: but by 21 days, when hearing is fully functional, it is the most vascularized. The degree of vascularization is thus related to function.

An important consequence of this relationship is the vulnerability of the cochlear nuclei to anoxia and to deprivation of essential nutrients. Histological studies[52] have shown that infants dying from neo-natal asphyxia may have only 50 per cent of the normal quota of cells in these nuclei. Further, of twins, the one exposed to the longer period of anoxia has a lower quota of cells.

The cells of the cochlear nuclei show a different selective vulnerability in hyperbilirubinaemia, where the frequency loss is in the 2,000 Hz. region, from that of anoxia, which results in a high frequency loss.[38]

Dominance of one side has been considered.[9,17,64] It may involve higher metabolism on one side, and thus higher vulnerability.

Rubella, though it primarily damages the end-organ of hearing, presumably affects the rest of the auditory pathway by an overall reduction in cell numbers.

The Bony Modiolus of the Cochlea

This develops in membranous bone and is first seen at 20–21 weeks (185–200 mm.) by which time the otic capsule has begun to ossify. It carries the cochlear part of the eighth cranial nerve. Bundles of collagen fibres appear within the connective tissue modiolus, and by week 23 (220 mm.) all but the apical part is ossified. It is complete by week 25 (240 mm.), as are the spiral laminae and their attachment, the spiral ligament, anchoring the modiolus within the bony otic capsule.

The Periotic Spaces and the Bony Otic Capsule (Fig. 8)

Round the early otocyst (4 mm., 4 weeks) loose mesenchyme is seen: the cells then condense in the vicinity of the otocyst (9 mm., $5\frac{1}{4}$ weeks). By 14 mm. ($6\frac{1}{4}$ weeks) they form a recognizable spherical mass; by 18 mm. ($6\frac{3}{4}$ or 7 weeks) pre-cartilage has formed, particularly in the outer zones of the mass. This is a dense cellular tissue showing marked metachromasia if the ground substance is stained with Alcian blue. Mature cartilage is present in the region of the future otic capsule. Chondrolytic histiocytes, identical with those in fetal epiphyseal plates during the invasion by vascular mesenchyme,[4,12] are found at 12–15 mm. (just over 6 weeks) when vessels appear on either side of the otocyst.[5] At this stage both cellularity and metachromasia diminish, leaving a sharp distinction between the otic cartilage and this loosely cellular tissue surrounding the developing otocyst and its derivative ducts. In this area, the chondrolytic phagocytic histiocytes may be found closely associated with blood vessels: later, 20 mm. (8 weeks), they are more scattered, but in greater numbers. They contain acid phosphatase and non-specific esterase.[5] These changes are first seen at the basal turn of the cochlea and the future vestibule, following later in the canal region (30 mm., beginning of ninth post-conception week). Later, the condensation of the reticular tissue forms a *membrana propria:* within is the open meshwork of the periotic spaces. Further out is fibrous perichondrium and cartilage, seen in the semicircular canals at 73 mm. (11½ weeks). The cartilage of the otic capsule shows the same process from 100–160 mm. (about 14–18 post-conception weeks); here the process is elaborated by bone formation. (The superior semicircular canal may still be translucent for a few months after birth.) Maldevelopments of the capsule occur in some chromosomal anomalies, trisomies 13–15 and 17–18, and other as yet unknown causes.

The periotic ducts and the aqueductus cochleae arise from the periotic labyrinth: also the *fissula ante fenestram* and the *fossula post fenestram.* These two are evaginations or pouches from the periotic (mesenchymal) capsule, seen in the mature bone as fissure and small fossa containing connective tissue and cartilage.

The Scala Vestibuli and Scala Tympani

These structures begin to develop along the anterior and posterior surfaces respectively of the cochlear duct at 8 weeks (25 mm.). Both are larger and nearer to the modiolus than the cochlear duct. A shelf (later to be ossified) separates these structures and the cochlear duct rests on its outer extremity. The anterior surface of the cochlear duct presses against the wall of the scala vestibuli, forming Reissner's membrane. The posterior wall unites with part of the scala tympani to form the basilar membrane. Under these pressures the cochlear duct assumes a triangular section with the anterior stratification modifying to a simple columnar epithelium along Reissner's membrane (65 mm., 11 weeks). By 14 weeks (108 mm.) this latter is cuboidal, later flattening to the squamous type.

Reissner's Membrane

The mature form of epithelial cell in this membrane is seen by electron microscopy to possess microvilli, mitochondria and organelles, suggesting considerable metabolic activity.[8]

The Blood Supply of the Otic Labyrinth

Fetal cochlear vascularization is apparently excessive for the young child, and some involution occurs at about the time of birth.[58] The blood supply of the otic labyrinth comes from the vertebral artery via the internal auditory artery, of which the first branch supplies the saccule, utricle and semicircular canals. Further branches and anastomoses supply cochlea, saccule and ampulla. The third branch forms the spiral artery of the modiolus from which arise the arteries of the spiral sulcus, and in turn the arteries to the stria vascularis and some supply to the bony otic capsule. Venous drainage of the otic labyrinth seems likely to be in part via the venous plexus in the wall of the saccus endolymphaticus and thus direct to the lateral sinus.

The Stria Vascularis

The outer wall of the cochlear duct shows slight differentiation by the 15th week, later assuming the appearance of a glandular epithelium. The dark apical cells are extremely rich in mitochondria[98] and the capillary network beneath them has a slow circulation suggesting that oxygen is not supplied from it by diffusion but via electron transport systems. The epithelial cells have been shown[107,108] to have a rough endoplasmic reticulum, granular material and large mitochondria, all suggestive of great metabolic activity. Basally, the plasma membrane has many projections and is greatly folded round the capillaries.[65]

It is thought[18,35] that the stria vascularis is at least in part the source of otic fluid and of its constituents, which include 12–16 mequiv./l. of sodium and 140–160 mequiv./l. of potassium, with some protein, sugars and amino acids.[98] The periotic fluid contains 130–150 mequiv./l. of sodium and 4–5 mequiv./l. of potassium.[109] The proteins present are pre-albumen, albumen, transferrin, and haptoglobin.[90] The large-molecule substances of the blood and CSF are in lower concentration in perilymph. Enzyme studies have suggested that perilymph is an actively secreted fluid since it has a demonstrable lactic dehydrogenase content, but its origins remain a source of speculation. Active transport may be possible across Reissner's membrane.[98] Differences in electrolyte and other content have been summarized.[50]

The fluid surrounding the cells of the organ of Corti may not be otic fluid (endolymph) nor is it perilymph. Independent sources, such as secretion by supporting cells, have been suggested.[24]

The maculae of the utricle[107] and saccule, and the cristae, contain areas with much-branched epithelial cells in which are seen many mitochondria; these cells are thought to be secretory. They are not the cells described at the periphery of sensory areas,[35] but are additional. They have a greatly increased and folded basal membrane, and between them are large intercellular fluid spaces which may represent the vestibular equivalents of Nuel's space (Fig. 3 "*at*") in the organ of Corti.

MALDEVELOPMENTS

Deafness Associated with Chromosomal Anomalies

Trisomy 13–15 (D): Cochlear and saccular abnormalities have been found in two cases[66] but not in another.[82] In one case, there was replacement of the organ of Corti by fibrous tissue in the basal turn of the cochlea; in another, part of the bony capsule was missing.

Trisomy 18 (E),[66] Trisomy 17–18:[23,91] In one middle ear the bony ossicles and tensor tympani muscle were abnormal and the cochlea had an incomplete bony modiolus with some of the spiral ganglion cells in the internal auditory meatus. The sensory areas of the cochlea and vestibule were normal. This child has responded to sound. On the other side, however, there was a great reduction in the ganglion cells, and few fibres passed to the organ of Corti.

The authors[66] note that these changes resemble those described by Scheibe (1895);[101] but Schuknecht, Igarashi and Gacek (1965)[102] have attributed cochleo-saccular defects to inherited anomaly, viral disease and other causes. Further discussion[103] is available.

Turner's syndrome (XO anomaly) may exhibit a minor sensorineural deafness and low-set pinnae.

One case of XXXXY (chromosomal non-disjunction) is described[60] as having multiple defects including short neck, smallness of size for age, widely set eyes, epicanthic fold and patent ductus arteriosus. All these suggest that deafness should have been excluded since these defects are known associates of malformation of one sort or another of the ear. Unfortunately, no mention was made of defects of hearing.

Inherited Hearing Defects

Fifty-one per cent of those with profound childhood deafness in the U.K. were considered to be suffering from inherited disease.[42]

		Per cent
Genetic Causes:	Recessive	
	With retinitis pigmentosa	7.5
	goitre	3.0
	abnormal ECG	1.0
	Others	26.0
	Dominant	
	With pigmentary anomalies	2.5
	Without " "	10.0
	Sex-linked	1.5
Congenital malformations		2.5
Acquired:	Prenatal	6.0
	Perinatal (including excess of prematurity)	10.0
	Post-natal	30.0
		100.0

This proportion is, in fact, also 51 per 100,000 live births. No hearing loss has been associated with the inborn errors of metabolism, with the exception of the hyperprolinaemias. Examples of association with pigmentary anomalies are seen in one dominant syndrome, Waardenburg's,[37] and one recessive (Usher's syndrome, where malformation of the organ of Corti accompanies retinitis pigmentosa). These account for 7·5 per cent and 2·5 per cent profound childhood deafness respectively accounting for one-fifth of the profound inherited deafness between them. In animals also there is some association between pigmentary anomalies and labyrinthine disturbances.[42,43] Sporadic goitre with sensorineural deafness (Pendred's syndrome) is recessively inherited; the mechanism of hearing loss in some thyroid diseases is partially central, and many sometimes be neural rather than cochlear, and Pendred's syndrome deafness is not really clear. Another recessive syndrome, where the organ of Corti is deficient and has PAS-positive deposits in the stria vascularis, is usually diagnosed when the ECG is seen. This is the Jervell-Lange-Nielsen cardio-auditory syndrome[47,48] where inherited deafness is associated with fainting fits and indeed sudden death. It has been suggested that glycogen metabolism is abnormal, and interferes with conduction in the Bundle of His.

Syndromes inherited as dominants include Alport's hereditary nephritis and sensorineural deafness. There is degeneration of hair cells, damage to the stria vascularis and cyst formation in the spiral ligament:[21] the onset of deafness is not till 10 years of age or more, and is more severe in the males, who usually die in early adult life. In some families, an associated hyperprolinaemia has been found, but the inheritance appears to be independent.

Mention must also be made here of otosclerosis, a middle-ear conductive deafness due to stapedial fixation: in some 12 per cent of cases hearing loss is noted before the age of 16 and in a few as early as 5 or 6 years of age. Inheritance is probably dominant.[80,81]

Osteogenesis imperfecta is often accompanied in adult life by deafness due to ankylosis of the stapedio-vestibular joint. Although clinically and histologically this lesion resembles otosclerosis, it is regarded as a phenocopy rather than a genocopy.[80]

Some of the inherited syndromes of cochlear malfunction are in fact associated with defects in the development of metabolism of other organs. The deafness may not manifest itself for years after birth, as in Alport's syndrome where cochlear and renal tubular function deteriorate.

The Mondini bony cochlear abnormality is one of incomplete development involving incomplete separation of cochlear turns, giving a "scala communis"; it may be familial.[14] The Scheibe "cochleo-saccular degeneration"[14] is sometimes said to be the usual histological finding in autosomal recessive cases[43] but this is difficult to prove, for it somewhat resembles post-mortem autolytic changes. It has also been attributed to post-natal factors.[2,3]

In Usher's syndrome (deafness and retinitis pigmentosa) the saccular changes are usually very severe.

This is a field where post-mortem histopathology is very regrettably not usually obtained, though the removal of temporal bones (Fig. 16) is easy, and the subsequent examination need not be unduly time-consuming. Early fixation as soon after death as possible and refrigeration give best results.[121] Some results may be obtained if the post-mortem is not delayed beyond 6–10 hours after death and the refrigeration has been adequate, but not of the quality obtainable by immediate fixation.

Detection of Carriers of Genes for Deafness

Audiometric identification of carriers of some autosomal recessive genes for deafness has been reported.[6] Further work is greatly needed in this field.

Maldevelopment of the Cochlea Due to Maternal Ototoxic Drugs and Antibiotics

Disturbed development during intrauterine life may follow administration of drugs and ototoxic antibiotics to the mother, with transference to the fetal circulation: quinine[54] and streptomycin[45] are examples of drugs that may destroy fetal hair cells in this way. All other antibiotics and diuretics known to be causes of ototoxicity should be considered

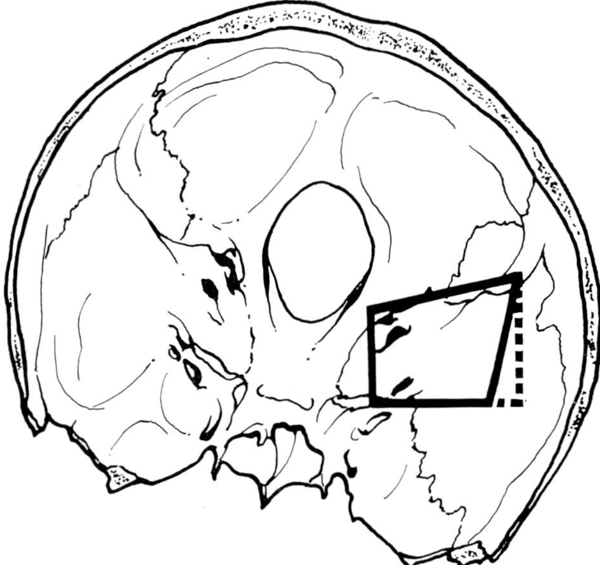

FIG. 16. "Temporal bone" removal at post-mortem takes only a small part of the bone, but it includes the ear drum, middle ear and part of eustachian tube, the cochlea, vestibule and semi-circular canals, and the divisions of the eighth nerve. It will also include the seventh nerve ganglion, beginning in the internal auditory meatus. Cut with a saw or chisel along the lines: the interrupted line would give better clearance of the ear drum and some external auditory meatus, but is difficult to make because of the squamous part of the bone. A depth of 2–3 cms. is adequate: this should include part of the carotid artery and jugular bulb. Drawn by R. Neave.

similarly potent.[123] Thalidomide has been held responsible for complete aplasia of the inner ear following one or two 100 mg. tablets at about the 25th day of embryonic life[59] coinciding with the auditory placodal invagination and formation of early otocyst. Previously, total inner-ear aplasia had been reported only by Michel in 1863.[77]

Maldevelopments Due to Infections *in utero*

Rubella is an intrauterine infection which can produce a "granuloma" of the stria vascularis and also covering of the tectorial membrane with a cellular sheath: the degeneration of the organ of Corti is possibly secondary to such changes, though primary malformation remains a possibility if infection is early enough. Viraemia in the 6th or 7th week after conception has clearly led to changes in the appearance of the organ of Corti and the stria vascularis (Fig. 17): these are most marked when the fetus survives to term,[49] and when the viraemia coincided with cochlear duct growth and early differentiation of neuroepithelium. Sometimes, rubella deafness is unilateral. This has been held to be due to two possible causes: viraemia with sporadic embolism, reaching perhaps one stria vascularis and not the other, or to dissimilar rates of maturation and growth on the two sides.

Congenital syphilis does not cause lesions in the fetus before the 5th month. In a severe case where the infant was stillborn, with a pathological placenta, treponemes were *not* identified[51] in the semicircular canals, but were seen in blood vessels in the temporal bone. In the late-onset form

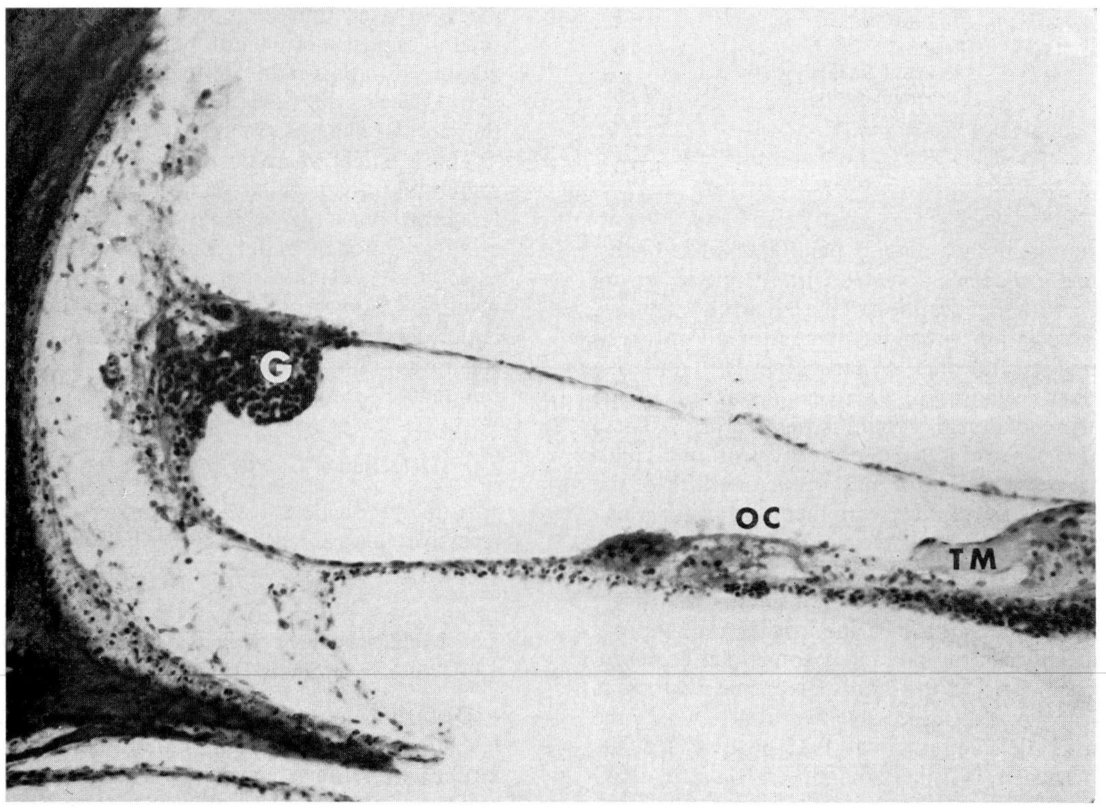

FIG. 17. Rubella. Photomicrograph. A granuloma, *G*, is present at the upper end of the stria vascularis of the upper cochlear turn: other characteristics of congenital rubella are present, in the degenerated organ of Corti, *OC*, and the abnormal tectorial membrane, *TM*, which is covered by cells and is misshapen. (×172)

of deafness following congenital syphilis, the time when the cochlear lesions are sustained is uncertain and is likely to be post-natal.[122]

Maldevelopments of the Middle Ear and Eustachian Tube

These are sometimes associated with mandibular and maxillary maldevelopment. The "Treacher-Collins" syndrome involves mandibular and maxillary dystosis, and the middle-ear ossicles may be defective in sound-conduction; this syndrome is inherited as a dominant. Other maldevelopments may exist associated with other skeletal deformities, for example the Klippel-Feil syndrome with a very short neck. Maldevelopments of the palate may affect the form and patency of the eustachian tubes, leading to obstruction and infections of the middle ear in childhood and later life.[55,93,94] The fact that the human palate is formed by maxillary coalescence as late as the 10th embryonic week allows for unusually prolonged opportunities for growth arrest by harmful influences.[120] It is thus a frequent malformation and it is surprising that deafness has found so little mention in the literature. The deafness is conductive. Two per cent of 401 patients had a congenital malformation of the ear;[106] 39 per cent were deaf, and of these 45 per cent had clinical ear disease. The causes of such obstruction will include lymphoid hyperplasia, tubal stenosis and palatal dysfunction. Experimental work[55] has shown malfunction of the tensor palati to be largely responsible for obstruction once cleft palate is established, and even this may continue after surgery.

The aetiology of cleft palate is likely to be due to interaction of several factors: polygenic inherited factors may confer liability (*see* chapters on Genetics and Cleft Palate). In rats, hypervitaminosis A at the 15–17th days and intrauterine irradiation have been shown to produce the condition.[93,94] Oligohydramnios has also been shown to cause failure of coalescence.

Complete atresia of the ear is rare and has been fully reviewed elsewhere.[2,3]

Maldevelopment and the Sense of Balance

No clinical end-organ dysfunction has been histologically correlated with abnormal or reduced hair cells in the maculae or in the cristae. The aetiology of labyrinthine disturbances with late onset of symptoms[61] is usually stated to be a perilymph-endolymph fistula in congenital syphilis, and may be so in Ménière's disease in which endolymphatic hydrops has been found with some degenerating macular changes.[53]

Vertigo in untreated thyroxin deficiency may be associated with increases in mucopolysaccharides in endolymph and perilymph.[95] No detailed examination of the cells has been possible in a case of epidemic labyrinthitis, but sections showed a "normal labyrinth" a few weeks after the attack.[75] No histopathological description of the labyrinth has been published from cases of motion sickness.

It is to be hoped that more detailed histological studies of such cases will be made. Small anomalies of pattern were noted in human material.[72]

RELATIVE GROWTH PERIODS

The complex of the labyrinth includes little that can be counted or measured easily, and further, insufficient specimens have been available for examination in some stages of fetal life. Nevertheless, it is possible, by reducing photomicrographs from Bast and Anson's monograph[12] to one scale, to derive some information (Figs. 18, 19, 20).

Taking the longest measurement only, we find that the otic vesicle undergoes rapid development for the beginning

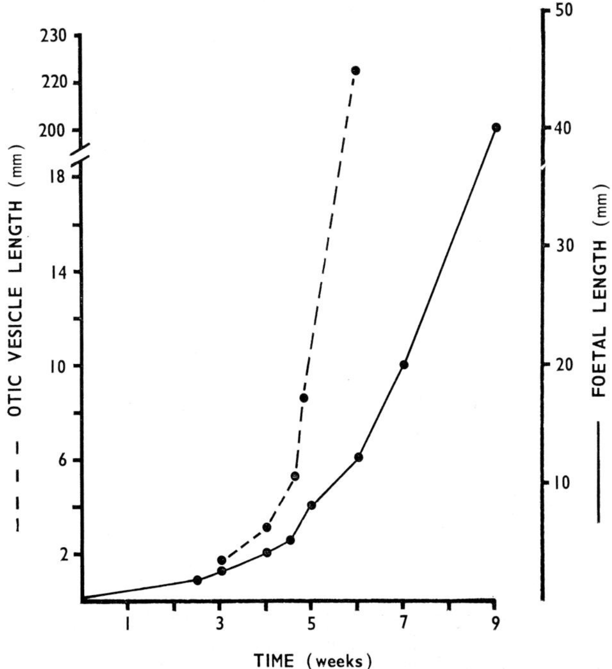

FIG. 18. Growth rate of the otic vesicle, its derivatives and their appendages (Fig. 19) compared with changing fetal length. Derived from Bast and Anson's[12] photomicrographs. The decimal point has been deliberately omitted from the left hand scale, where 230 represents 2.3 mm. Drawn by R. Neave.

of the 4th week, with extraordinarily rapid development of the future endolymphatic appendage, cochlear duct, and utricle and the beginnings of the semicircular canals in the second half of the 5th week. Once established, the growth curves of these appendages resemble that of fetal length.

Numbers of sensory cells in the organ of Corti are not available before the 4th month, but Bredberg[15] has shown (Fig. 21) that length of the organ of Corti progresses on a fairly smooth curve for 8–24 weeks. The inner and outer sensory cells do not increase much between the 17th and 21st week; in the next month, however, increasing numbers appear, particularly in the outer hair cells, where even 4th and 5th row hair cells appear (Figs. 22, 23).

RELATING MORPHOLOGY AND MATURITY TO FUNCTION

Remarkable localization of hearing defects has become possible with human post-mortem material, when previous audiograms were also studied.[15] The precise stages of maturity necessary for function in either hearing or balance are not completely known; nor is the significance of the inner hair cell wholly understood; difference in form and innervation may imply difference in function. The inner hair cells are distinct slightly before outer hair cell differentiation.

Stereocilia are seen on inner and outer hair cells by 5 gestational months, though only kinocilia were visible at 4. At 6 months gestation the whole organ of Corti has widened, particularly in the pillar regions. At the same time, irregularities become more common, and the intercellular spaces larger. Deiter's cells (supporting cells) take on a mature form. A few outer hair cell divisions probably occur, accounting for the 4th and 5th rows of outer hair cells (Fig. 2). At 8 months the organ of Corti is adult in form and size. It seems, however, that function is detectable before this stage in the human fetus at about 26 weeks.[116]

Electrophysiological reaction can be elicited before complete cochlear maturity. The distinction between "precocial" and "altricial" young, indicating mobility or helplessness at birth or hatching, has not been used in the literature of audiology, probably for lack of data. Fluid spaces were found still incompletely developed[68,78] at a stage when sound elicited a response in the opossum. Although afferent nerves in the mouse[63] were present several days before the full development of fluid spaces, action potentials in the eighth nerve were not recordable until the efferent nerves were identifiable. Presumably, both systems are required for function.

The human fetus reacts to sound in the 26th week.[57,116]

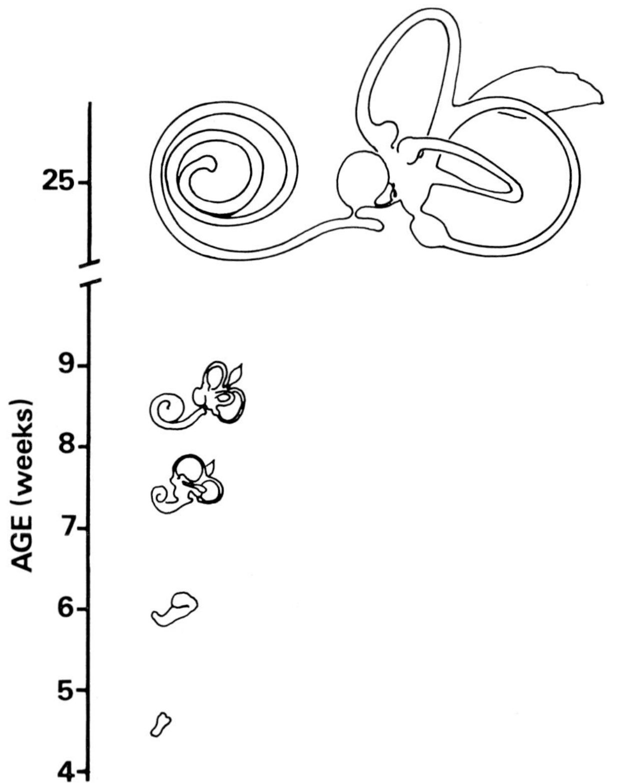

FIG. 19. Redrawn by R. Neave from Bast and Anson[12] to show overall increase in size of the labyrinth during fetal life. (×6.5 approx.)

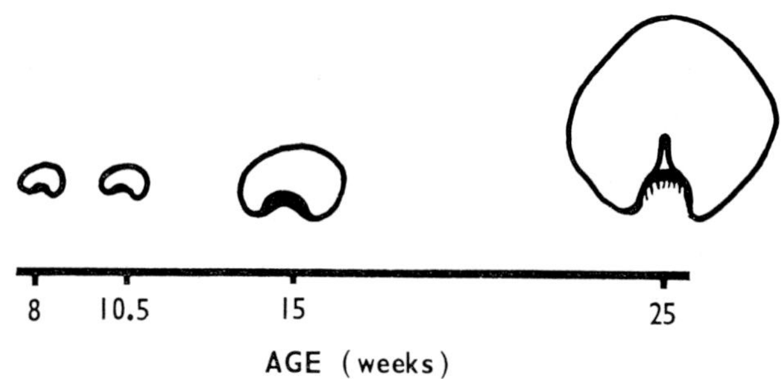

FIG. 20. Increase in size of fetal semi-circular canal, redrawn by R. Neave from Bast and Anson's photomicrographs[12] reduced to one scale. (×8 approx.)

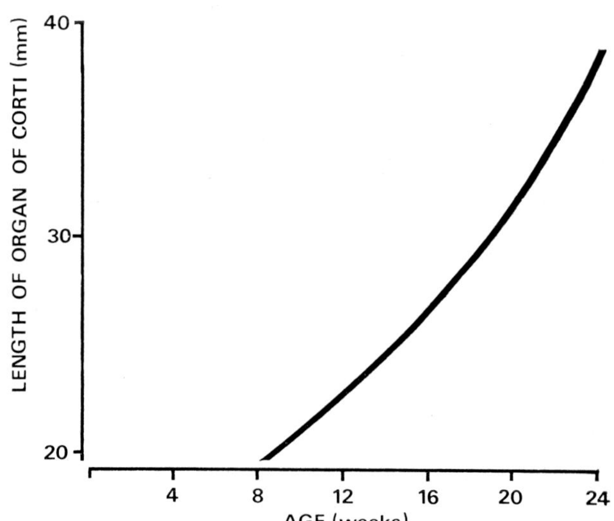

FIG. 21. Growth of fetal organ of Corti. Drawn by R. Neave from Bredberg's[15] measurements of human fetal organ of Corti.

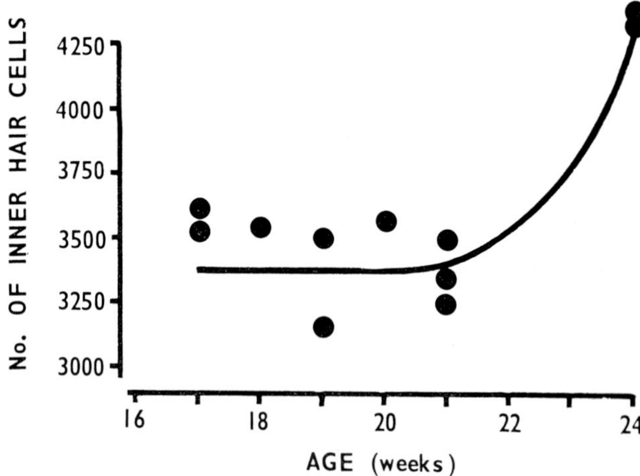

FIG. 22. Multiplication of inner hair cells. Drawn by R. Neave from Bredberg's[15] figures. The number of inner hair cells in the human fetus appear to increase sharply after the 21st week.

Further work is essential to show whether any earlier response could be detected; this could for instance be an important point in deciding on abortion where there is risk of inherited or acquired profound deafness.

Fetal movements in response to tonal sound have been noted[39] at 7–9 months: frequencies of 500 c./s. and 1,000 c./s. were used, at 115 dB. A rise of fetal heart-rate was detected by ECG 2–7 weeks before term, in response to 3,000 c./s. at 110 dB.[57] In two cases of maternal diabetes[83] responses were present at 30 weeks, and their absence at 34 weeks was followed by still-births. Sometimes in still-born premature children there is phalangeal scarring in the

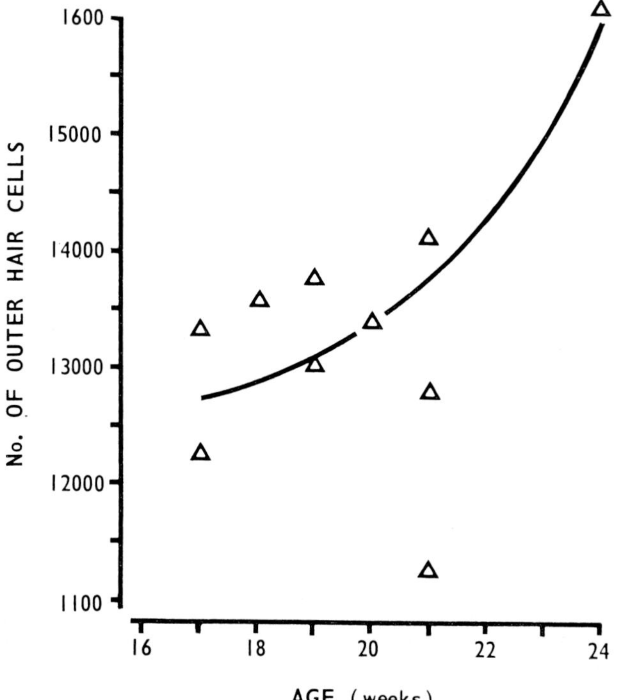

FIG. 23. Multiplication of outer hair cells. Drawn by R. Neave from Bredberg's[15] counts of outer hair cells in the human fetus, showing a steep rise after the 21st week.

cochlear outer hair cells (Fig. 24). Phalangeal scarring among the outer hair cells takes 2 weeks to appear from the time of the impact of noxious influences in animals and presumably the same time in man. It is due to collapse of one or more hair cells, leaving a characteristic collapse figure (Fig. 24).

It must be concluded that much remains to be learnt in the field of prenatal audiology.

POST-NATAL AUDIOLOGY

Anatomical maturity of the cochlea does not of itself guarantee hearing. Many of the factors involved in testing the hearing of older children and adults are due to *learning*. It must be appreciated that a deaf child is not only incapable of appreciating sound: he is also in the state of a normal-hearing child who has been deprived of sound and hence of normal incidental auditory training.[118] A special series of tests has been compiled in which the child gives a recognizable response to sound.[30] These are mainly due to the work of the Ewings.[26–32]

It must also be recognized that infants may be wrongly suspected of deafness owing to lack of knowledge on the part of the tester of the sounds that they might respond to at any given time.

Screening for Deafness at Birth[119]

A neonate does not respond to quiet sounds, and this includes the voice, even if a familiar voice. He will, however, exhibit a startled reaction to loud sounds unless deeply

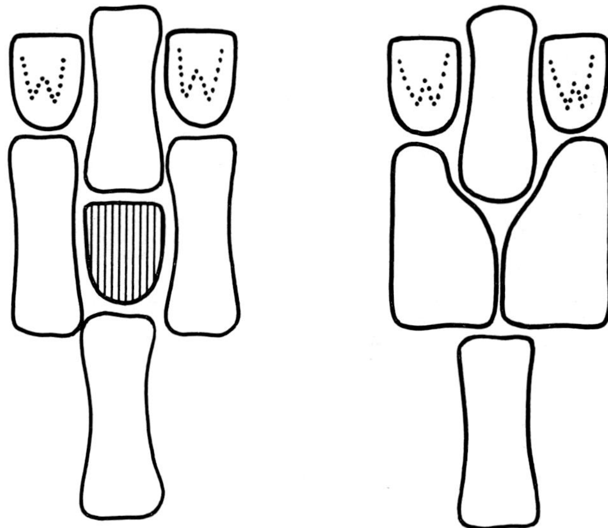

FIG. 24. Formation of "collapse" figures in the organ of Corti, when an outer hair cell (hatched on left) degenerates: the hair pattern is lost, the cell darkens and adjacent supporting cells ("phalangeal cells") begin to fill the gap. Drawn by R. Neave.

asleep after feeding. If this is apparently not present, further tests should be done later.

Later Responses

At 4–5 months the startle reflex may begin to be inhibited: but by now the infant will look once towards an unfamiliar quiet sound, including an unfamiliar voice. A few sounds are familiar and he will look right and left to localize them.

At 6–8 months the startle reflex is no longer present. There are few unfamiliar quiet sounds: he localizes many sounds by turning and looking *once*. This statement should be modified to "turning and looking once *unless inhibited.*" Inhibition may occur because of ignorant testing. Very often, amateur testing by the parents can achieve inhibition of a normal response: the infant is purely Pavlovian, and though he may hear the rustle of a paper bag is not going to turn repeatedly if he is unrewarded.[118]

At 1 year, failure to localize sounds which should be familiar, and in early attempts at speech, should raise suspicion of deafness: so should failure to understand speech or to talk at 2 years.

In general, it is true to say that audiometric patterns are characteristic of certain forms of hearing loss.[36]

The High-risk Register

Where such registers are kept, they are of considerable value in ensuring testing as early as possible, so that those who are deaf can be given the right help early. Congenital malformation registers do not necessarily ensure that a deaf child will be screened[122] and thus detected early. Neither spreads a complete net.

Definitive Tests of Hearing[30,104,114,118,119]

Peepshow play audiometry
Auditory reaction time
Slow cortical EEG response to auditory stimulus
Pure-tone audiograms.

Early detection of partial deafness leads to the use of amplifying aids, which enables a child to benefit from normal auditory training. This is essential. Profound childhood deafness may require very special training very early.

The problems of testing for hearing where other defects such as backwardness are present are dealt with in the STYCAR Handbook.[104]

Many syndromes including deafness are recognized in various general diseases[122] such as the mucopolysaccharidoses, thyroid disorders and numerous familial syndromes, of which only a few are mentioned here. Rarely is satisfactory histopathological description present in the literature: mostly it is still impossible to say with certainty where the lesion is found. Today's techniques make such examination of post-mortem material much more informative: it is now up to the clinicians to obtain autopsies, and inform the pathologists that the temporal bones are wanted. In some cases, prior consultation with the pathologist is essential, and in all cases early fixation.[121]

ACKNOWLEDGEMENTS

It is a pleasure to acknowledge the help I have had from the University Department of Medical Illustration, Manchester. Figures 18–20 are based on photomicrographs by C. H. Bast and B. J. Anson[12] appearing in *The Temporal Bone and the Ear*, and introductory illustration A is taken from the same work, by kind permission of Charles C. Thomas, publisher, Springfield, Illinois. Figures 21–23 are based on Bredberg's[15] cell-counts and measurements.

Figures 4, 5, 6 and 9 are reproduced from H. H. Lindeman's *Morphology of the Sensory Regions of the Vestibular Apparatus* appearing in *Advances in Anatomy, Embryology and Cell Biology*, by kind permission of the publishers, Springer-Verlag, Heidelberg.

REFERENCES

1. Adlington, P. (1967, 1968), "The Ultrastructure and Functions of the Saccus Endolymphaticus," *J. Lar. Otol.*, **81**, 759–776 and **82**, 101–110.
2. Altmann, F. (1949), "Congenital Atresia of the Ear," *Archs. Otolaryng.*, **50**, 759–788.
3. Altmann, F. (1955), "Congenital Atresia of the Ear in Man and Animals," *Ann. Otol. Rhinol. Lar.*, **64**, 824–858.
4. Andersen, H. and Matthiessen, M. E. (1966), "Histiocyte in Human Fetal Tissues, its Morphology, Cytochemistry, Origin, Function and Fate," *Z. Zellforsch.*, **72**, 193–211.
5. Andersen, H., Matthiessen, M. E. and Jorgensen, M. B. (1969), "Growth of Otic Cavities in the Human Fetus," *Acta Otolaryng.*, **68**, 243–249.
6. Anderson, H. and Wedenberg, E. (1968), "Audiometric Identification of Norman Hearing Carriers of Genes for Deafness," *Acta Otolaryng.*, **65**, 535–554.
7. Ashley, Jack, *M.P.* (1970), "A Personal Experience," in *Sensorineural Hearing Loss*, p. 2, CIBA Foundation Symposium. London: J. & A. Churchill.
8. Bairati, A. and Iurato, S. (1964), in *Biochemie des Hörorgans*, p. 17 (S. Rauch, Ed.). Stuttgart.
9. Bakker, D. J. (1969), "Ear Asymmetry with Monaural Stimulation," *Cortex*, **5**, 36–42.
10. Bak-Pedersen, K. and Tos, M. (1971), "The Mucus Glands in Chronic Secretory Otitis-media," *Acta Otolaryng.*, **72**, 14–27.
11. Ballantyne, J. and Engström, H. (1969), "Morphology of the Vestibular Ganglion Cells," *J. Lar. Otol.*, **83**, 19–42.
12. Bast, C. H. and Anson, B. J. (1949), *The Temporal Bone and the Ear*. Springfield: Thomas.
13. Bekesy, G. von (1953), "Description of Some Mechanical Properties of the Organ of Corti," *J. Acoust. Soc. Amer.*, **25**, 770–785.
14. Bredberg, G. (1967), "The Human Cochlea During Development and Ageing," *J. Lar. Otol.*, **81**, 739–758.
15. Bredberg, G. (1968), "Cellular Pattern and Nerve Supply of the Human Organ of Corti," *Acta Otolaryng.*, Supplement 236, 1–135.
16. Carlström, D. and Engström, H. (1955), "The Ultrastructure of Statoconia," *Acta Otolaryng.*, **45**, 14–18.
17. Carr, B. M. (1969), "Ear Effect Variables and Order of Report in Dichotic Listening," *Cortex*, **5**, 63–68.
18. Citron, L., Exley, D. and Hallpike, C. S. (1956), "Formation, Circulation and Chemical Properties of the Otolabyrinthine Fluid," *Brit. med. Bull.*, **12**, 101–104.
19. Craigie, E. H. (1924), "Changes in Vascularity in the Brain Stem and Cerebellum of the Albino Rat between Birth and Maturity," *J. comp. Neurol.*, **38**, 27–48.
20. Craigie, E. H. (1938), "Vascularity in the Brain of the Frog," *J. comp. Neurol.*, **69**, 453–470.
21. Crawfurd, M. D'A. and Toghill, P. H. (1968), "Alport's Syndrome of Hereditary Nephritis and Deafness," *Quart. J. Med.*, **37**, 516–576.
22. Dunning, H. S. and Wolff, H. G. (1937), "Relative Vascularity of Various Parts of the Central and Peripheral Nervous System of the Cat and its Relation to Function," *J. comp. Neurol.*, **67**, 433–450.
23. Edwards, J. H., Harnden, D. G., Cameron, A. H., Crosse, V. M. and Wolff, O. H. (1960), "A New Trisomic Syndrome," *Lancet*, **1**, 787–790.
24. Engström, H. (1960), "The Cortilymph, the Third Lymph of the Inner Ear," *Acta morph. neerl.-scand.*, **3**, 195–204.
25. Engström, H., Ades, H. W. and Andersson, A. (1966), *The Structural Pattern of the Organ of Corti*, pp. 1–166. Stockholm: Almqvist & Wiksell.
26. Ewing, Irene R. and Ewing, A. W. G. (1944), "The Ascertainment of Deafness in Infancy and Early Childhood," *J. Lar. Otol.*, **59**, 309–339.
27. Ewing, Irene R. and Ewing, A. W. G. (1947), *Opportunity and the Deaf Child.* London: University of London Press.
28. Ewing, Irene R. and Ewing, A. W. G. (1954), *Speech and the Deaf Child.* Manchester: Manchester University Press.
29. Ewing, Irene R. and Ewing, A. W. G. (1958), *New Opportunities for Deaf Children.* London: University of London Press.
30. Ewing, A. and Ewing, E. C. (1965), "The Young Deaf Child, Identification and Management," *Acta Otolaryng.* Supplement 206.
31. Ewing, A. and Ewing, E. C. (1967), *Hearing Aids, Lip-reading and Clear Speech.* Manchester: Manchester University Press.
32. Ewing, A. and Ewing, E. C. (1971), *Hearing-impaired Children under Five.* Manchester: Manchester University Press.
33. Fell, H. B. (1928), "Development *in vitro* of Isolated Otocyst of Embryonic Fowl," *Arch. exp. Zellforsch.*, **7**, 69–81.
34. Fell, H. B. and Robison, R. (1929). "The Growth and Develop-

ment and Phosphatase Activity of Embryonic Femoral Limbbuds Cultivated *in vitro*," *Biochem. J.*, **23**, 767–784.

35. Fieandt, H. von and Saxon, A. (1951), "Histological Studies in Endolymph Secretion and Absorption in the Inner Ear," *Acta Otolaryng.*, **40**, 23–31.
36. Fisch, L. (1955), "Aetiology of Congenital Deafness and Audiometric Patterns," *J. Lar. Otol.*, **69**, 479–493.
37. Fisch, L. (1959), "Deafness as Part of an Hereditary Syndrome," *J. Lar. Otol.*, **73**, 355–382.
38. Fisch, L. (1970), "Selective and Differential Vulnerability of the Auditory System," in *Sensorineural Hearing Loss*, pp. 101–126; CIBA Foundation Symposium. London: J. & A. Churchill.
39. Fleischer, K. (1955), "Untersuchungen zur Entwicklung der Innerohrfunktion. Intrauterine Movements of Fetus Following Sound Stimulation. *Z. Laryng. Rhinol. Otol.*, **34**, 733–740.
40. Flock, A. and Wersall, J. (1962), "A Study of the Orientation of the Sensory Hairs of the Receptor Cells in the Lateral Line Organ of Fish, with Special Reference to the Function of the Receptors," *J. Cell. Biol.*, **15**, 19–27.
41. Flock, A. (1964), "Structure of the Macula Utriculi with Special Reference to Directional Interplay of Sensory Responses as Revealed by Morphological Polarisation," *J. Cell. Biol.*, **22**, 413–431.
42. Fraser, G. R. (1964), "Profound Childhood Deafness." *J. Med. Genet.*, **1**, 118–151.
43. Fraser, G. R. (1970). The Causes of Profound Deafness in Childhood," in *Sensorineural Hearing Loss*, pp. 5–40; CIBA Foundation Symposium. London: J. & A. Churchill.
44. Friedmann, I. (1968), "The Chick Embryo Otocyst in Tissue Culture," *J. Lar. Otol.*, **82**, 185–201.
45. Friedmann, I. and Bird, E. S. (1961), "The Effect of Ototoxic Antibiotics and of Penicillin on the Sensory Areas of the Isolated Fowl Embryo Otocyst in Organ Cultures: an Electron-microscope Study," *J. Path. Bact.*, **81**, 81–90.
46. Friedmann, I. and Bird, E. S. (1967), "Electron Microscopic Studies of the Isolated Fowl Embryo Otocyst in Tissue Culture. Rudimentary Kinocilia, Cup-shaped Nerve Endings and Synaptic Bars," *J. Ultrastruct. Res.*, **20**, 356–365.
47. Friedmann, I., Fraser, G. R. and Froggatt, P. (1966), "Pathology of the Ear in the Cardio-auditory Syndrome of Jervell and Lange-Nielsen," *J. Lar. Otol.*, **80**, 451–471.
48. Friedmann, I., Fraser, G. R. and Froggatt, P. (1968), "Pathology of the Ear in the Cardio-auditory Syndrome of Jervell and Lange-Nielsen. Report of a Third Case," *J. Lar. Otol.*, **82**, 883–896.
49. Friedmann, I. and Wright, M. I. (1966), "Histopathological Changes in the Fetal and Inner Ear Caused by Maternal Rubella," *Brit. med. J.*, **2**, 20–24.
50. Groves, J. and Ballantyne, J. (1971), *Scott-Brown's Diseases of the Ear, Nose and Throat*, Vol. 1, Chap. 1, p. 91, 3rd edition. London: Butterworths.
51. Grünberg, K. (1911), "Spirochaetes Found in the Temporal Bone of a Luetic Foetus," *Z. Ohrenheilk.*, **73**, 223–228.
52. Hall, J. G. (1964), "The Cochlea and the Cochlear Nuclei in Neonatal Asphyxia," *Acta Otolaryng.* Supplement 194, 1–93.
53. Hallpike, C. S. and Cairns, H. (1938), "Observations of the Pathology of Ménière's Syndrome," *J. Lar. Otol.*, **53**, 625–655.
54. Harrison, K. (1959), "Causation of Deafness in Childhood," *J. Lar. Otol.*, **73**, 451–460.
55. Holborow, C. A. (1962), "Deafness Associated with Cleft Palate," *J. Lar. Otol.*, **76**, 762–773.
56. Jeppson, P. H. (1969), "Studies on the Structure and Innervation of Taste Buds," *Acta Otolaryng.* Supplement 259, 1–95.
57. Johansson, B., Wedenberg, E. and Westin, B. (1964), "Measurement of Tone Response by the Human Fetus," *Acta Otolaryng.*, **57**, 188–192.
58. Johnsson, Lars-Göran (1972), "Cochlear Blood Vessel Pattern in the Human Fetus and Post-natal Vascular Involution," *Ann. Otol. Rhinol. Lar.*, **81**, 22–40.
59. Jorgenssen, M. B., Kristensen, H. K. and Buch, N. (1964), "Thalidomide-induced Aplasia of the Inner Ear," *J. Lar. Otol.*, **78**, 1095–1101.
60. Joseph, M. C., Anders, J. M. and Taylor, A. I. (1964), "A Boy with Chromosomes," *J. Med. Genet.*, **1**, 95–101.
61. Karmody, C. S. and Schuknecht, H. (1966), "Deafness in Congenital Syphilis," *Archs Otolaryng.*, **83**, 18–27.
62. Keller, Helen (1911), in Letter to J. Kerr Love used as Foreword in his book *The Deaf Child*. London: Simpkin & Co.
63. Kikuchi, K. and Hilding, D. (1965), "The Development of the Organ of Corti in the Mouse," *Acta Otolaryng.*, **60**, 207–222.
64. Kimura, D. (1961), "Some Effects of Temporal Lobe Damage on Auditory Perception," *Canad. J. Psychol.*, **15**, 156–165.
65. Kimura, R. S. and Schuknecht, H. F. (1970), "The Ultrastructure of the Human Stria Vascularis," *Acta Otolaryng.*, **69**, 415–427 and **70**, 301–318.
66. Kos, A. O., Schuknecht, H. F. and Singer, J. D. (1966), "Temporal Bone Studies in 13–15 and 18 Trisomy Syndromes," *Archs Otolaryng.*, **83**, 439–445.
67. Landau, W. M., Freygang, W. H., Rowland, L. P., Sokoloff, L. and Kety, S. S. (1955), "The Local Circulation of the Living Brain, Values in Unanesthetized and Anesthetized Cat," *Trans. Amer. neurol. Ass.*, **80**, 125–129.
68. Larsell, O., McCrady, E. and Larsell, J. F. (1944), "The Development of the Organ of Corti in Relation to the Inception of Hearing," *Archs Otolaryng.*, **40**, 233–248.
69. Lindeman, H. H. (1966), "Cellular Pattern and Nerve Supply of the Vestibular Sensory Epithelia," *Acta Otolaryng.*," Supplement 224, 86–95.
70. Lindeman, H. H. (1969), "Regional Differences in Structure of the Sensory Vestibular Regions," *J. Lar. Otol.*, **83**, 1–17.
71. Lindeman, H. H. (1969), "Regional Differences in Sensitivity of the Vestibular Sensory Epithelia to Ototoxic Antibiotics," *Acta Otolaryng.*, **67**, 177–189.
72. Lindeman, H. H. (1969), "Studies on the Morphology of the Sensory Regions of the Vestibular Apparatus," *Ergebn. Anat. EntwGesch.*, Band 42, Heft 1, 1–113.
73. Lindeman, H. H., Ades, W., Bredberg, G. and Engström, H. (1971), "The Sensory Hairs and the Tectorial Membrane in the Developing Cat's Organ of Corti," *Acta Otolaryng.*, **72**, 229–242.
74. Maillet, M. (1963), Le réactif au tetraoxyde d'osmium-iodure de zinc," *Z. mikr.-anat. Forsch.*, **70**, 397–425.
75. Marshall, J. B. (1955), Letter to *Lancet*, **i**, 458.
76. Mendelsohn, M. and Katzenberg, I. (1972), "Effect of Kanamycin in the Cation Content of (Guinea-pig) Endolymph," *Laryngoscope*, **82**, 397–403.
77. Michel, M. (1863), "Mémoire sur les anomalies congenitale de l'oreille interne," *Gaz. méd. de Strasb.*, ser. 2, **3**, 55–58.
78. Mikaelian, D. and Ruben, R. J. (1965), "Correlations of Physical Observations with Behavioural Responses and with Cochlear Anatomy," *Acta Otolaryng.*, **59**, 450–461.
79. Millon, J. W. (1963), "Timing of Human Congenital Malformations with a Timetable of Human Development," *Develop. Med. Child Neurol.*, **5**, 343–350.
80. Morrison, A. W. (1967), "Genetic Factors in Otosclerosis," *Ann. roy. Coll. Surg.*, **41**, 202–237.
81. Morrison, A. W. and Bundey, S. E. (1970), "The Inheritance of Otosclerosis," *J. Lar. Otol.*, **84**, 921–932.
82. Mottet, N. V. and Jensen, H. (1965), "The Anomalous Embryonic Development Asssociated with Trisomy 13–15," *Amer. J. clin. Path.*, **43**, 334–347.
83. Murphy, K. P. and Smyth, C. N. (1962), Letter in *Lancet*, **i**, 972
84. Naessen, R. (1970), "Identification of Topographical Localization of the Olfactory Epithelium in Man and Other Mammals," *Acta Otolaryng.*, **70**, 51–57.
85. Naessen, R. (1971), "Possible Age Changes in Olfactory Epithelium," *Acta Otolaryng.*, **71**, 49–62.
86. Naessen, R. (1971), "Receptor Surface of the Olfactory Organ," *Acta Otolaryng.*, **71**, 335–348.
87. Nakai, Y. (1970), "Development of the Sensory Epithelium of the Cristae Ampullares in the Rabbit," *Pract. ORL.*, **32**, 268–278.
88. Nakai, Y. (1972), "Fine Structural Localization of Acetylcholinesterase in the Adult and Developing Cochlea," *Laryngoscope*, **82**, 177–187.

89. Palva, T. and Raunio, V. (1967), "Disc Electrophoretic Studies of Human Perilymph and Endolymph," *Acta Otolaryng.*, **63,** 128–137.
90. Palva, T. and Raunio, V. (1967), "Disc Electrophoretic Studies of Human Perilymph," *Ann. Otol. Rhinol. Lar.*, **76,** 23–36.
91. Patau, K., Smith, D. W., Thorman, E., Inhorn, S. L. and Wagner, H. P. (1960), "Multiple Congenital Anomaly Caused by an Extra Autosome," *Lancet*, **i,** 700–793.
92. Patten, B. M. (1968), *Human Embryology*, 3rd edition. New York: McGraw Hill.
93. Poswillo, D. E. (1968), "Cleft Palate in the Rat." *Lab. Anim.*, **2,** 181–190.
94. Poswillo, D. E. (1968), "The Aetiology and Surgery of Cleft Palate with Micrognathia," *Ann. roy. Coll. Surg.*, **43,** 61–88.
95. Poulsen, H. (1966), *Hormones and Connective Tissue* (G. Asboe-Hansen, Ed.). Copenhagen: Munksgaard.
96. Pye, A. (1971), "The Destructive Effect of Intense Pure Tones on the Cochlea of Mammals," *First British Congress in Audiology*, Dundee, to be published in *International Audiology*.
97. Pye, A. (1971), "The Effect of Exposure to Intense Pure Tones on the Hearing Organ of Mammals," *Revista de Acustica*, **2,** 199–203.
98. Rauch, S. (1966), "Membrane Problems of the Inner Ear and Their Significance," *J. Lar. Otol.*, **80,** 1144–1155.
99. Rauch, S. and Köstlin, A. (1958), "Aspects chimiques de l'endolymphe et de la périlymphe," *Pract. ORL* (*Basel*), **20,** 287–291.
100. Retzius, G. (1884), "Das Gehörorgan der Wirbelthiere. Vol II: Das Gehörorgan der Reptilien, der Vogel under der Saugethiere," *Die Centraldruckerei*. Stockholm.
101. Scheibe, A. (1892), "Deaf Mutism with Auditory Atrophy," *Arch. Otol. N.Y.*, **21,** 12–22.
102. Schuknecht, H., Igarashi, M. and Gacek, R. R. (1965), "The Pathological Types of Cochleo-saccular Degeneration," *Acta Otolaryng.*, **59,** 154–170.
103. Schwartz, M. and Becker, P. E. (1964), *Human Genetik*, pp. 248–345 (P. E. Becker, Ed.). Stuttgart: Thieme.
104. Sheridan, M. (1968), *Manual for the STYCAR Hearing Test*, 2nd edition. London: National Foundation for Educational Research.
105. Sjöstrand, F. S. (1953), "Ultrastructure of Retinal Rods and Cones," *J. cell. comp. Physiol.*, **42,** 15–44, 45–70.
106. Skolnik, E. M. (1958), "Otologic Evaluation in Cleft Palate Patients," *Laryngoscope*, **68,** 1908–1949.
107. Smith, C. A. (1956), "Microscopic Structure of the Utricle," *Ann. Otol. Rhinol. Lar.*, **65,** 450–469.
108. Smith, C. A. (1957), "Structure of the Stria Vascularis and the Spiral Prominence," *Ann. Otol. Rhinol. Lar.*, **66,** 520–536.
109. Smith, C. A., Lowry, O. H. and Wu, M. L. (1954), "Electrolytes of Labyrinthine Fluid," *Laryngoscope*, **64,** 141–153.
110. Spoendlin, H. (1967), "The Innervation of the Organ of Corti," *J. Lar. Otol.*, **81,** 717–738.
111. Streeter, G. L. (1918), "The Histogenesis and Growth of the Otic Capsule and its Contained Periotic Tissue-spaces in the Human Embryo," *Carnegie Contrib. to Embr. No. 20*, **7,** 5–54.
112. Streeter, G. L. (1922), "Development of the Auricle in the Human Embryo," *Carnegie Contrib. to Embr. No. 69*, **14,** 111–138.
113. Szpunar, J. and Rybak, M. (1968), "Middle Ear Disease in Turner's Syndrome," *Archs Otolaryng.*, **87,** 34–40.
114. Taylor, I. G. (1964), *Neurological Mechanisms of Hearing and Speech in Young Children*. Manchester: Manchester University Press.
115. Watanuki, K., Stupp, H. F. and Meyer zum Gottesberge, A. (1972), "Toxic Effects of Gentamicin on the Peripheral Vestibular Sensory Organ," *Laryngoscope*, **82,** 363–371.
116. Wedenberg, E. (1965), "The Young Deaf Child: Identification and Management. Prenatal Tests and Hearing," *Acta Otolaryng.* Supplement 206, 26–32.
117. Wersall, J. (1956), "Studies on the Structure and Innervatio of the Sensory Epithelium of the Cristae Ampullares in th Guinea-pig," *Acta Otolaryng.* Supplement 126, 1–85.
118. Whetnall, E. and Fry, D. B. (1964), *The Deaf Child*, pp. 1–237. London: Heinemann.
119. Whetnall, E. (1965), "The Young Deaf Child: Identification and Management," *Acta Otolaryng.* Supplement 206, 52–58.
120. Willis, R. A. (1962), *The Borderland of Embryology and Pathology*. London: Butterworth.
121. Wright, I. (1970), "Complete Examination of a Case of Sensorineural Deafness at Autopsy," in *Sensorineural Hearing Loss*, pp. 69–78, CIBA Foundation Symposium. London: J. & A. Churchill.
122. Wright, I. (1971), *The Pathology of Deafness*, pp. 1–175. Manchester: Manchester University Press.
123. Wright, I. (1973), *Ototoxicity. Proc. roy. Soc. Med.*, **66,** 189–193.
124. Wright, I. (1968), "Late-onset Hearing Loss Due to Congenital Syphilis," *International Audiology*, **7,** 302–310.

40. LINGUISTIC DEVELOPMENT

D. BETTY BYERS BROWN, J. E. J. JOHN, H. L. OWRID and I. G. TAYLOR

THE SOUNDS OF SPEECH

Speech is the primary mode of human communication; it is, much more than writing let alone other aspects of human behaviour such as music and the pictorial arts, the main way in which one person may affect another. The basic communication system in speech has the brain of the speaker as the source of some message, and his vocal mechanism as the transmitter of sounds of varying pressures and frequencies. The stream of sound generated by the transmitter is the signal carried through the air and detected by the ear of the listener. The listener's brain receives information which enables him to interpret the meaning of the message intended by the speaker.

The purpose of this section is to examine some aspects of how the sound signal, which we call speech, works. A discussion of the nature of speech is made difficult because we usually describe it in terms of writing and this leads us to think of speech as something which it most certainly is not, i.e. a sequence of juxtaposed phonemes. A phoneme is a "speech sound" and corresponds to an alphabetic letter in writing. The fact that the written word "man" contains three separate letters may lead people to think of the spoken word "man" as being composed only of three separate phonemes. This is not the case, because *speech is not spoken writing*. Writing is a visual representation of speech—not the other way round.

The Flow of Sound

When man invented writing, he was concerned to produce visible symbols which would represent and enable him to recall speech. Eventually he invented symbols for the component sounds which he could identify in speech. It was a process which took him many millenia ending, for us in Western Europe, with the Latin or Roman alphabet. But our alphabet is not consistent; it cannot be, because twenty-six letters have to represent about forty identifiable sounds in the language. For this reason, phoneticians have invented phonetic alphabets in which each symbol is a phonogram corresponding to a sound. What do the symbols in writing really represent? We may suppose that, in an ideal orthography, each letter would represent a sound in speech—but in saying that one needs to define "a sound in speech." When we examine the stream of sound, the acoustic flow which is speech, one finds that the identification of "a sound," i.e. something discrete, something separate, something with a beginning and an ending is impossible. The spoken word "man" is a continuous, unbroken flow of sound. The problem which has most exercised those concerned with analysing the acoustics of speech has been that of segmentation, of delimiting the parts corresponding to phonemes—and all methods so far devised have been compromises of one kind or another.

Speech is a flow of sound which is continually changing, microsecond by microsecond, reflecting the continually changing positions of our articulators in speech. D. B. Fry of University College, London, was responsible for a remarkable film which allows us to see the movements of the articulators in speech. The film is valuable for many reasons, but in this context its chief value lies in the fact that it shows that the tongue does *not* stand still whilst we make "one sound" and then move to the position for "another sound"—it moves continually and this is why the flow of sound is continually changing in speech. What we can represent by letters or other symbols are those parts of the sound stream during which the rate of change is relatively slow and which are of long enough duration for us to be able to recognize them. The letters ignore the ways in which these elements flow one to another, how they affect one another, how they are mutually modifying. These transitional features in speech are of extremely short duration; so short that we do not consciously hear them. Nevertheless, they contain information which our ears can detect and our brains can interpret. Indeed, the recognition of some phonemes in running speech is more dependent on information which lies at the boundaries *between* phonemes than on that which is contained in the centre—in the phonemes themselves. In the spoken word "man," ordinary listeners recognize only three sounds which are the relatively long, slowly changing parts of the sound flow represented by the letters. These are the phonemes. Nevertheless, we can detect and interpret the much shorter, much more quickly changing sounds which link the three phonemes. In writing, we take no account of these very short elements; writing is a representation based on the long duration elements and not a pictorial representation of the sound flow.

In their learning to talk, children have to learn to interpret not only the long sounds which we consciously hear, but also the extremely short ones of which we are not conscious. Speech is a flow of sound which has been encoded in accord with a set of rules, which is the language, and so the sound is made intelligible. The phonemes, syllables, words and their sequential orders are constrained by the rules and our ability to recognize speech depends on our knowledge of the language. Languages have evolved with a high degree of what communication engineers and linguists call redundancy. Redundant features in language are not unwanted, superfluous, useless features. It is the presence of redundant cues which protects messages from misinterpretation—they reduce the possibility of error. (The choice of the word "redundant" is unfortunate.) Redundancy refers to the fact that in various aspects of language—semantic, syntactic, acoustic—we are presented with many cues in order that we may decode the message. Redundancy means that additional signs are presented or that something is in some way repeated. The redundancy in speech is mainly a product of relationships between the component parts of speech. Indeed, the recognition of speech is not a matter of perceiving absolute physical properties but of relationships between them.

Much of the linguistic code, its relationships and redundancies, have been acquired by the normally hearing child by the age of five years. By that age, he has stored in his brain an immense knowledge of the rules and probabilities of the language. It is knowledge which he has gained without any conscious effort and, although he is unaware of having it, his ability to communicate by speech depends on it. Let us consider some of these features.

Characteristics of Speech Sounds

Vowels are produced by the resonant modification in the oral tract of the sound generated by the vocal cords. Vocal cord vibrations are effectively periodic and the sound they produce is composed of a fundamental frequency and an enormous number of harmonics. The fundamental frequency corresponds to the rate of opening and closing the vocal cords and gives rise to the sense of the pitch of the voice. The harmonics are exact multiples of the fundamental frequency and they fall fairly smoothly in intensity. Components up to 8 kHz. or more may be present. The sound produced by the vocal cords, however, is never heard because in its passage along the oral tract, it is modulated by the resonant cavities of the tract. These resonators reinforce some harmonic frequencies and filter out others. The frequencies which are reinforced are those near to the natural (or resonance) frequencies of the resonating system. The natural frequencies depend on the sizes and shapes of different parts of the tract and these are varied mainly by changes in tongue position and also by changes in lip position. The result is that the sound radiated from the lips, instead of being the wide range of harmonic frequencies falling smoothly in intensity generated by the vocal cords, is composed of energy concentrated into narrow bands of frequencies corresponding to the resonances. These resonant concentrations or peaks of energy are called formants. Although many formants will be present in any vowel sound, its recognition depends mainly on the two lowest ones. They are conventionally labelled F_1 and F_2.

Modern studies of the acoustics of speech are based on spectrography, a technique developed from an instrument originally designed at the Bell Telephone Laboratories to make speech visible for the deaf. A spectrogram relates the frequency components of a sound to time and in the case of vocal cord sound, would show the presence of all harmonic components. Figure 1 shows a spectrogram of the vowels /i/ (as in see), /a/ (as in car) and the diphthong /aI/ (as in my) in isolation. It will be seen that, in the case of /i/, F_1 is low and has its centre at about 200 Hz. F_2 is much higher and has its centre at about 2,250 Hz. In making the vowel /a/, the tongue adopts a different position from that in /i/ and so resonance frequencies are different. It will be seen that F_1 and F_2, instead of being widely separated as in /i/, are much closer together in /a/ and have centres at about 800 Hz. and 1,000 Hz. respectively. A diphthong is made by gliding the tongue from the position for one vowel to that for another and then changing resonance produced by the glide is clearly seen in the movement of the formants on the spectrogram for /aI/.

The recognition of a vowel, however, is not a matter of the absolute values of F_1 and F_2 but of relationships involving them. There are two aspects of this and they are relationships within a particular vowel and relationships between them. Average values of F_1 and F_2 for the vowel /i/ spoken by men, women and children are given as follows by Peterson and Barney:[43]

	Men	*Women*	*Children*
F_1	270	310	370
F_2	2,290	2,790	3,200

It is clear that, in the case of a man, a woman and a child, the actual acoustic events which lead to the recognition of the same linguistic event—the vowel /i/—are very different. In fact, it is the relationship between the formants that matters and not their absolute values. A child in learning to recognize vowels has to learn to perceive these F_1/F_2 relationships and, as Ladefoged and Broadbent[32] have

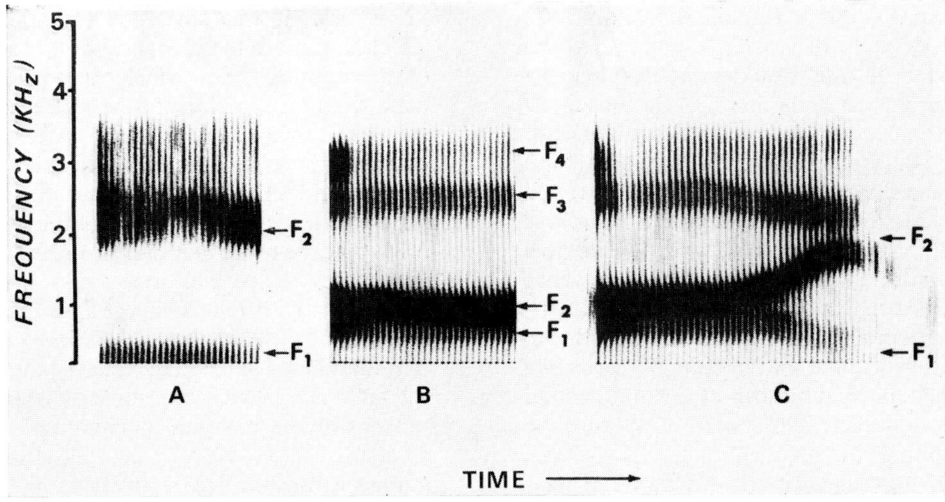

FIG. 1. Spectrograms of (A) the vowel /i/, (B) the vowel /a/ and (C) the diphthong /ai/. Note that F_1 and F_2 in /a/ are so close that they tend to coalesce.

shown, has to learn to set the F_1/F_2 relationship for a particular vowel against the F_1/F_2 relationships of the other vowels in a speaker's vowel system. That a child should, not consciously but intuitively, learn to perceive such relationships is remarkable.

Consonants (other than m, n, ŋ (as in long), 1 and r which are, acoustically, like vowels) are sounds in which the energy is spread randomly over a wide range of frequencies. Some, such as /s/, are noises produced by forcing air smoothly through a narrow constriction for some length of time; others like /t/ are produced explosively and the noise exists for a much shorter time. The range of frequencies over which the noise is spread is different for the different consonants, e.g. the sound of /s/ lies mainly above 4 kHz., while that of /ʃ/ (as in ship), lies mainly below 4 kHz., but above 2 kHz. The recognition of one consonant from another is largely a matter of perceiving the different spectra of their noise.

Redundancy

In the recognition of consonants, however, the spectral information is supplemented by transitions—those sounds which are not consciously heard, which are not represented in writing, but which link the alphabetic sounds. The realization of the significance of the transitions, particularly in the case of the plosive and nasal consonants, is largely the product of work in the Haskins Laboratories in New York. The spoken word "man" is not the sounds /m/ + /æ/ + /n/ spoken so quickly one after the other that we cannot hear the silences between them. The moving of our articulators from the position for /m/ to that for /æ/ occupies a very short period of time during which sound continues. This transitional sound reflects the changing resonance and so the movement of the articulators. The transition of a labial consonant (/m/, /p/, /b/) is different from that of an alveolar consonant (/n/, /t/, /d/) and is different again from that of a velar consonant (/ŋ/, /k/, /g/). The Haskins team have shown that these different transitions, and particularly the transition of F_2, are significant in our recognition of speech. The stylized spectrogram of Fig. 2 summarizes their work. In normal conditions, the transition supplements the information contained in the sound of the consonant; this is an example of acoustic redundancy. It has been shown that there are circumstances in which transition information is of primary significance—for example, in distinguishing between the nasal consonants.

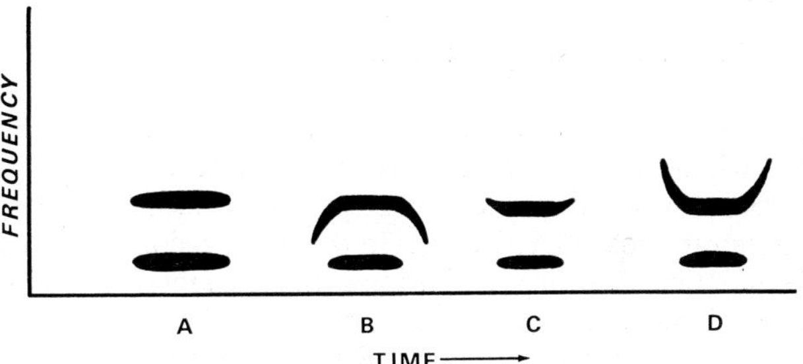

FIG. 2. Stylized spectrograms of a vowel showing (A) F_1 and F_2 but no transitions, (B) transitions of F_2 cueing labial preceding and following consonants, (C) transitions of F_2 cueing alveolar consonants and (D) transitions of F_2 cueing velar aonsonants.

Another example of acoustic redundancy is provided by Denes's[16] important experiment showing how time relationships give cues to voicing in speech. Consonants (other than /m/, /n/, /ŋ/, /1/ and /r/) may be divided into two groups. The sounds of those forming the group of "unvoiced" consonants (/p/, /t/, /k/, /f/, /θ/ (as in thin), /s/, /ʃ/) are composed entirely of aperiodic noise. The sounds of those forming the "voiced" group (/b/, /d/, /g/, /v/, /ð/ (as in then), /z/, /ʒ/ (as in pleasure)) are composed of very similar aperiodic noise to their equivalents in the first group with, in addition, the periodic vibration of the vocal cords. The voicing or not voicing of consonants is an important feature, because it changes the meanings of words as, for example, in pill, bill; feel, veal; kill, gill; seal, zeal. It had long been known that vowel duration varied according to whether or not a consonant with which it was associated was voiced. Denes showed that this feature of relative time was significant in the recognition of voicing when he demonstrated that the word spelt "use" could be interpreted as a noun, /jus/, or a verb, /juz/ entirely on time relationship of vowel and consonant parts and in the complete absence of voicing of the consonant in the verb form. Similarly, John and Howarth[30] showed that relative duration of vowel and consonant segments could determine whether a word was heard as cheap, /tʃip/, or jeep, /dʒip/ even when voicing was absent in the initial consonant of the latter. The importance of time relationships is also demonstrated in Fry's[18] experiments on stress). Stress in speech is dependent on loudness, pitch and duration. Fry showed that in pairs of words like óbject and objéct, the relative durations of first and second syllables were a feature, sufficient on its own, to change the meaning from the noun to the verb.

Redundancy, it has been said earlier, is a matter of relationship between the parts of an utterance whether the parts are shorter: a phoneme or longer: a phrase. Information is contained in one part of an utterance about other parts because speech is not the stringing together of separate, unrelated segments. We have an effective demonstration of this in a pair of recordings of the sentence "when the baby cried his mother kissed him." In making the records, filters were used so that only sounds below 1,000 Hz. have been recorded of what is basically the same material. In one of the recordings, however, instead of being spoken naturally and running smoothly, each syllable has been separated for a brief instant from the next; thus

When–the–ba–by–cried–his–mo–ther–kissed–him

Also, in this recording, the speech is on a monotone. The recording is quite unintelligible; listeners who have experience of filtered speech suggest that it is a recording of filtered monosyllabic words. In the other recording, made in identical filtering conditions, the sentence is spoken naturally with normal flow and normal intonation. Nearly all listeners recognize part of the recording and most recognize the whole of it. What is present in the second recording and absent in the first is the relationship between the parts, a relationship which listeners expect in speech; there is the stress pattern, the intonation pattern and the information in each segment about the segments on either side of it. Filtering to allow only sounds below 1,000 Hz. to be heard is a severe distortion which removes nearly all consonant sound. The consonants are nevertheless recognized in the second version, because of the redundant cues in the acoustic and linguistic pattern.

The significance of time factors and of the relationship between parts in the perception of speech is illustrated by some work on the speech of deaf children. Following spectrographic analysis of deaf children's speech, John and Howarth[29] argued that some of the defects in that speech could be classed as errors of time which destroyed information in the transitions and in the relative durations of components. They suggested that these errors were an important factor in the poor intelligibility of the speech. Typically the approach to improving deaf children's speech had been to concentrate on the articulation of the separate phonemes. It was suggested that this led to utterances which had more the character of bits strung together than of the continuous flow which exists in normal speech. They conducted an experiment in speech teaching in which they concerned themselves *only* with the temporal aspects of the children's speech. The errors in articulation were wholly ignored and all the effort was put into improving the flow, the continuity and the rhythm of the speech so that its timing would be more like that of normal speech. The result was speech which conformed more nearly to the pattern which normal listeners expect and which was significantly more intelligible for them.

Redundancy in language takes many forms. The syntax, the set of rules which determine the sequence of words, also puts us in the position of being able to predict. Before someone speaks, we may be very uncertain of what he is going to say, but progressively as his utterance proceeds, the possible sequences of words become fewer and fewer to the point that we can complete the utterance for him. The recognition of speech is partly a matter of statistics—of our knowledge of what is probable. Given one word of a sentence, the possible word or words which can follow it are constrained. For example, after the word "the," the only classes of words which can follow it are nouns and adjectives and, of these, nouns are the more probable. Many writers have shown that we have ingrained in us a vast store of knowledge of the statistics of the language in terms of letter, word and phoneme order.[19,38,49] We do not need to hear everything in order to understand an utterance. The value of conformity in the syntax is well illustrated by Cherry's[11] analysis of a "nonsense" sentence:

The ventious crapests pounted raditally.

Although this is nonsense, we are able to say that "ventious" is an adjective describing crapests—of which, whatever they may be, there are more than one; pounted is a verb in the past tense and raditally is an adverb. The sentence obeys the code of English in all respects; it is a possible sentence in which a statement is being made. The same may be said of Cherry's French version of the same sentence:

Les crapets ventieux pontaient raditallement.

Shannon[49] has estimated that about 50 per cent of written English is redundant and this may be illustrated by considering how plurality is signalled in the sentence:

These women are training to be teachers.

When this is compared with the singular version, one finds that between sound changes and word changes, there are seven cues to plurality.

A child in learning his language has to acquire an enormous store of knowledge of what Cherry[11] calls "our speech habits." He has to learn to interpret relationships both within and between sounds, even though these relationships are changing rapidly, sometimes very rapidly, in time. He has to learn the redundancies and probabilities in the acoustic and syntactic aspects of the language. The whole business of perceiving speech is indeed very complex and has to be learned. Perhaps the most wonderful aspect of a child's development is his learning intuitively, unconsciously, to recognize and interpret and to produce himself the flow of sound which is speech.

THE DEVELOPMENT OF SPEECH

The infant develops communication skills upon a basis of his early responsiveness to others and his ability to signal his own needs. Both these abilities are revealed very early in infant life. The young infant spends most of his working time looking at people and things, and a strong and developing source of attraction is the adult face. The infant may start to show smiling responses to an adult at around the age of a month and these responses will become more frequent and will be called forth by a variety of stimuli.[48] By three months, the infant may be showing alertness and attentiveness and his responsive behaviour can be increasingly promoted by loving inter-action. If the baby is sickly or damaged, he will not show normal alertness and responsiveness and the absence of these will, quite rightly, be a cause of concern.

Infant Cries

The first infant cry appears, or may be induced, immediately following birth. Wasz-Höckert *et al.*[56] carried out spectrographic and auditory analyses of the infant cry. The birth cry, the pain cry and the hunger cry were shown to have characteristic patterns. They could be distinguished not only from each other, but from the cries of abnormal babies suffering from Downs's syndrome or from brain damage. At about three months, the pleasure cry could be distinguished in the healthy babies. The authors conclude that "the baby is trying to communicate with the adult and it would be churlish not to respond." Certainly the infant cry is a powerful signal to the mother to provide food, comfort or attention and the crying behaviour of the child will be directly influenced by the personality and response of the mother.

The ability to produce, and later to modify, a vocal note is the essential pre-requisite for normal speech. This means that the basic, primitive function of the larynx is adapted for the more sophisticated purpose of communication. The sphincteric action of the larynx operates as a reflex mechanism to seal off the thorax. In the production of the vocal note, air is allowed to escape under pressure from the lungs, setting up vibrations in the vocal cords. These vibrations are affected in number and size by the breath force and also by the length, elasticity and degree of approximation of the vocal cords. In the infant, the larynx is very small and the length of the vocal cords reported by Negus[40] as 3 mm. long at fourteen days; 5·5 mm. at a year. The infant or young child has a piping pitch which he will retain until somewhere between four and five years.

The vocal note is modified in quality by the action of the resonators of the pharynx and oral and nasal cavities. The mobility of the mouth, the tongue, lips and soft palate permit of endless varieties of modification of the vocal note and it is this factor, combined with the ability to organize movements in a patterned and predictable way dictated by the cerebral cortex which allows the development of articulate speech.

The organs of articulation have as their primary function sucking, chewing and swallowing. At first they are dominated by reflex response to stimulation.[20,27,28] With the inhibition of much of this early reflex activity and the appearance of more selected individual movements dependent upon cerebral maturation, it becomes possible for oral patterns to be re-organized and co-ordinated with the vocal note to produce strings of sound or babble. This may be distinguished from the clicks, grunts, lip smacking and other appreciative feeding noises by its sustained and varied nature and the presence of the vocal note. It arises from the interruption of cooing or pleasurable vocalization by movement of lips and tongue which have already experienced sensations of movement and contact from the activities of feeding.

The sucking process demands the sealing of the oral cavity by the lips and the rhythmic peristaltic movements of the tongue which pumps the milk into the mouth and squirts it towards the soft palate. The soft palate seals off the nasal egress and thus milk is driven into the oesophagus. The soft palate will be lowered at intervals to allow for nasal breathing. Thus sucking and breathing are able to continue side by side. (For a full description *see* Gwynne-Evans.[22]) In infants with cerebral palsy, this synergistic activity may not develop. The infant may experience gross difficulty in feeding due to inability to synchronize breathing and sucking. He may also show later difficulties in inhibiting sucking and reflex oral behaviour so that selective speech movements can be made. A brain damaged child's early feeding difficulties are a fair predictor of the difficulties he may encounter in acquiring articulate speech. It is this realization which has prompted speech therapists to devote much attention to feeding and pre-speech skills in the cerebral palsied.

The retention of infantile or abnormal swallowing action may lead to difficulties in the later production of certain speech sounds. Some children continue to swallow with the tongue thrust forward against the lips instead of with the tongue raised to the alveolar as happens with the maturation of the facial musculature and the eruption of the teeth. The tongue consequently tends to take up a consistently forward posture and speech sounds may be acquired upon a basis of simple protrusion and retraction movements instead of the variety of degrees of elevation of the tip, front, back and sides of the tongue upon which distinctive and mature articulation depends. The tongue thrust has been the Waterloo of many a speech therapist who started out to correct a simple lisp. It has caused equal consternation to orthodontists who, confronted by an open bite or mal-approximation of upper and lower dentition may embark upon a series of appliances to re-align the teeth only to be defeated by the unabashed forward displacing movements of the unruly member. Attempts to correct tongue thrust meet with varying success depending upon the strength of the endogenous postures and movement patterns.

Babbling

The infant's ability to produce selective sounds and to imitate the sounds of others is the result of a coming together of several skills and abilities which are dependent upon, and related by, the integrity and maturation of his central nervous system. At first, his utterance depends upon his posture. While he lies supine, he will produce back and nasal sounds. A nasal vowel type "ah" may be heard and the plosive type "g" which can occur as the result of the back of the tongue falling back to make contact with the palate. The nasal continuant sound "ng" may also be produced in this way. Lip sounds may occur in association with feeding and will be used more frequently when the child is able to control his head and hold it in the mid-line, so that the lips can come together symmetrically. As the arms are freed from their reflex action in relation to the movements of the head (a.t.n.r. in particular) there is an increase in hand mouth activity. Objects are taken to the mouth for chewing and exploration and this will be increased as the teeth start to erupt. All this activity stimulates the oral area and the pleasurable sensations are likely to be transferred into babbling.

The amount of babbling and sound play indulged in by healthy babies appears to vary very considerably. Adult re-inforcement by babbling back to the baby seems to have a very stimulating effect, though some observers have reported maximum babbling when the child is lying alone contented after feeding, but not too sleepy. The difference in sound production of babies can be measured even prior to the babbling stage by the recording of vowel type glides in vocalization. The range and inflexion of sounds produced does not only reflect his increased neuro-muscular maturity, but his hearing, imitative ability and very probably his individual propensity for speech acquisition.[21]

Imitative and self imitative oral activity will promote babbling, but to begin with the activity is almost certainly pursued for the sensory pleasure it gives rather than to influence the behaviour of others. Early babbling is non-linguistic. With the development of hearing and thereby the ability to perceive precisely the sound patterns employed by adults in their normal speech, the babbling will take on the prosodic features of the baby's linguistic environment. This is combined with preference for those sounds which are used in the phonological or sound system of the language and constitutes the phenomena called "babbling drift."[8] Evidence has been presented to show that the babbling of Chinese, Dutch and American babies is distinctive and identifiable from the age of six months.[57]

The extent to which babbling is necessary for speech development is not determined. Morley, among others, regards it as a necessary practice stage in the development of independent voluntary control of lips, tongue and palate. Berry[5] questions the relationship of babbling to later development of speech, but perceives it as valuable "as a tuning up and integrating process for the phonating, resonating and articulating organs later to be employed in speech." Modifiable and linguistic babbling certainly demonstrate integrities of tactile, proprioceptive and auditory feedback which are essential in speech development and maintenance.

The Emergence of Speech

A baby will show auditory discrimination early in life by his response to the tones of others. He takes pleasure in a soothing tone and shows fear at a sharp or scolding one. This discrimination will become extended to individual sounds and words. Auditory discrimination differs from auditory acuity in being a learned skill and one that can be assisted by training. It is associated with auditory memory and if outstandingly deficient, the child will have considerable difficulty in acquiring language. He may develop comprehension for overall content, but remain poor on detail, both of sound and syntax.

Comprehension develops gradually in the infant, who makes use of much paralanguage in the interpretation of speech. The expression of the speaker, the situation in which the words appear, the intonation and cadence of the utterance all contain extremely valuable information. A child of eighteen months will rely on this information within which he is able to recognize individual words referring to familiar and often named objects and people. His own speech will reflect the limitations of his ability to appreciate linguistic units. The mean age for the production of the first word is 11 months and words will then be used in a context of jargon-like utterance which employs the intonation of adult speech. The number of words will increase as will the complexity of the syntax and the jargon will disappear. Retention of jargon after the age of two and a half or three should alert attention to possible difficulties of comprehension. A similar warning is contained in the persistence of echolalia or imitative utterance. This, too, may appear as a normal feature in the speech of the young child. At a certain stage the young child may be capable of imitating sentences ahead of his power to comprehend them. The normal child who is constantly experimenting and is listening to the speech of others will move through this stage without difficulty. But the retarded, disturbed or brain damaged child may be reinforced in his echoing speech by a mother anxious that he shows speech progress with the result that utterance becomes disassociated from comprehension. If echoing persists, comprehension is shown to be blocked and should be investigated.

It may be seen that the development of speech is not a simple matter of acquiring sounds, but of being able to appreciate and re-produce sounds in a systematic and flexible manner conforming to linguistic convention. A child who is well able to produce sounds at the simple babbling stage may lack the intellectual ability to re-assemble them for the creation of communicative or symbolic units and thus use them as "free, floating vehicles for the expression of ideas."[20]

Some intelligent children appear to do far less experimenting with speech sounds than others and may move into words and sentences with little sound play and no real baby talk. The use of arbitrary criteria for deciding whether the early speech attempts of a young child fall within normal limits may be dangerous as they can fail to take account of what is suitable to the whole physical and psychological disposition of this particular infant, his character, his relations with his family and the amount of stimulation he is receiving. Nevertheless, scales of sound and word acquisition based on the norm for the population are a very useful guide and will certainly give a framework for speech evaluation. One very important result of the application of standardized tests of articulation and language is the distinction which should emerge between an immaturity and a deviation of utterance. Delayed speech employs a number of features which are appropriate to young children. These features may be unsuitable to the actual age of the individual child, but they do appear somewhere in the emerging speech of normal children. Deviant utterance involves sounds which are not in use among normal speakers in the child's environment. The presence of an extremely marked deviation will, of course, direct the doctor's attention to some physical abnormality. An obvious connection is between nasal emission of air on consonants and defective structure or function of the palate. A very husky vocal note will draw attention to lack of vocal cord approximation or other forms of laryngeal abnormality; the absence of high frequency sounds will demand investigation for hearing loss. Such examples are familiar and indeed obvious.

Within the emerging speech pattern of the child, there may be more sophisticated signs of deviation which can only be detected from a thorough knowledge of normal linguistic structures and development. In normal speakers, the sound or phonological system develops at the same time as the syntactical one. The child attempts new sound combinations as the result of his desire to use more words. Thus he will gradually extend his repertoire of sounds in order to pursue his goal of communication. But he needs to have achieved certain basic sound skills notably consonant/vowel opposition before he can get started on meaningful linguistic units. A normal infant first learns to combine a front nasal consonant and back vowel as in "mama" and a front labial stop or plosive and a back vowel "papa." It is highly unusual and would indeed be abnormal for a child to make use of the back of tongue plosives, "k" and "g," before the front labials, "p" and "b," and the silibants, "s" and "sh," before the lingual plosives, "t" and "d."

In children who have difficulty in acquiring speech, the sound system may not develop sufficiently quickly to allow the child to extend his vocabulary. According to his temperament, he may either refuse to attempt words which he cannot master or he will produce them in the best manner he can. While his attempts usually correspond to some linguistic logic, they are likely to be unintelligible to those around him. It is common for children to replace sounds from a later stage of acquisition with those from an earlier stage. Thus "d" may be used for "g" and also for "j." The word "jug" rendered as "dud" might only constitute a simple immaturity, which the child would eventually transcend. The word "dead" pronounced as "jeg" would, however, transgress several linguistic rules and be considered very deviant by a speech therapist.

In some cases the child's sound structure may be perfectly adequate, but he falls down when it comes to using it to make linguistic changes of tense or plurality. A child who can pronounce the "s" in bus may fail to use it in "bricks" because he has not grasped the relationship between word change and meaning. Any speech evaluation would be ridiculously superficial if it did not take into account the kind of language a child understood and was attempting to use.

There is a very general measure of agreement as to the order of sound acquisition and this can certainly be helpful in trying to assess a child's problem or his progress. Templin's[53] classic study, Certain Language Skills in Children, remains an extremely useful guide. For more recent studies, *see* Morley[39] and Menyuk.[37] Menyuk[37] gives the following simple outline of stages at which gross linguistic performances occur.

Birth	Crying and other physiological sounds
1–2 months	Cooing sounds as well as crying
3–6 months	Babbling as well as cooing
9–14 months	First words as well as babbling
18–24 months	First sentences as well as words
3–4 years	Use of all basic syntactical structures
4–6 years	Correct articulation of all speech sounds in context

Correct articulation, employing complicated sound clusters, occurs well after all the basic syntactical structures have been laid down. The degree of precision expected in this particular area will depend upon dialectal and class as well as individual features. In some regions the substitution of "f" for "th" is almost a regional variation, whereas in others it would appear as an individual immaturity. The sound "r" is subject to a degree of regional variation greater than that of any other sound. It is more commonly used in its strong form in Scotland, where inability to produce it would constitute a defect far earlier than in England where a weak form is more frequently used and labial substitutions are common. In order to acquire the speech sounds of his native language and to use them appropriately, the child has to be able to recognize and produce the distinctive features by which sounds are characterized. These features include voicing, or the presence of vocal cord vibration, nasality, plosion (the stopping and release of the air stream or vocal note) and friction as when the air is forced through a very narrow aperture. The continuing absence of one or more of these features from any child's speech places it outside normal limits and merits investigation.

The child has also to learn the placement of the articulators in the production of sounds. Although, as has been pointed out in the preceding chapter, the total character of a speech pattern is the outcome of movement not static postures, certain positions must be taken up by the lips, tongue, jaw and palate for identifiable sounds to be produced. Until full control has been gained over placement sounds may vary in accuracy, e.g. the sound "s" which requires a high degree of tongue control and of auditory discrimination may move through several transitory stages before it is produced in its adult form. Acceptable variants during the period of speech acquisition are those which show recognition of some of the features of the sound aimed at. The fewer the features common to both sounds, the less acceptable is the infant version.

Ease of placement and degree of perception and discrimination influence the acquisition of speech sounds and there is general agreement as to the order in which they appear. The vowels, which call for open, unobstructed positions of the resonators appear first and are combined with the nasal "m" and the plosives "p" and "b." Then follow the front of tongue plosives "t," "d" and the nasal "n," the back of tongue plosives "h," "g" and nasal "ng." Subsequently emerge the fricative group "f," "v," "s," "z," "sh" and the continuant sounds "l" and "r." The sounds which are last to emerge are those which are made up of more than one position and several features, e.g. "ch."

Clusters of sounds follow the development of single sounds and the time of their emergence is dependent upon their degree of complexity. A child may be seven years old before he can produce the blend "skr," although he may possess all its components in isolated form.

Seven years is an age commonly given for the establishment and integration of the sounds of speech and omissions and distortions occurring after that date are accepted as evidence of persisting speech defects.[10] But it should be pointed out that a child's linguistic difficulties may be heralded several years earlier by the rate and degree of his mastery of sound sequences and the kind of substitutions he employs.

A child who is making no attempt to speak at two years should have his hearing examined and be kept under observation. A child who has no phrases by two and a half will need to be kept under observation and a child with no words may need help, probably in the form of parent guidance. A child who is not using words at three is handicapped and in immediate need of attention, and a child without sentences at that age should be thoroughly investigated. The extent to which intelligibility constitutes a need for treatment will depend upon the child's circumstances, the degree of support and protection offered by the home and the extent to which the child seems to be moving towards intelligibility. In pre-school children, the decision to treat or not will be made by the speech therapist upon individual rather than general criteria. An unintelligible child of school age will be socially and in all probability educationally handicapped and needs help.

A stage of development which can cause parents great concern is non-fluency. This occurs normally in the young child of two and a half to three and a half years who is rapidly acquiring vocabulary and experimenting with new sound combination. It may occur later in children who have started to speak later than average. Parents need to be reassured that the state is normal and transitory or their anxieties and efforts to help will arouse anxiety in the child. His non-fluencies may then change from hesitant, prolonged or repetitive utterance to stammering, with inhibition, tension and avoidance. Any child who is showing speech anxiety and stammering using tense repetitions or avoidance of words needs help no matter what his age.

The development of speech in the young child may be seen to arise from a variety of processes requiring integration and synchronization. The importance of the home influence can hardly be over-estimated. Any attempt to pronounce upon a child's performance must take into account his own intrinsic abilities and rate of development and the quality of his relationships with those who care for him.

SPOKEN LANGUAGE

In this section, the development of language is understood to include the comprehension of words spoken by others as well as the speech of the child himself. Aspects of language are so numerous and its ramifications so extensive that only the major facets have been selected for consideration. At the later stages, a more personal choice has been made of those features which may be determinants of educational and socio-cultural development.

The First Year of Life

Of the first year of life, it is sometimes said that the baby makes more progress than he will later achieve in the rest of his life. Such progress is not immediately evident in his language, but it would be unwise to assume that even the earliest months can be truly described as prelingual.

Babies' Cries

These sounds which have been fully discussed in the previous section indicate that action is required from those who surround the child. They clearly have a fundamental role in communication of vital information between the child and the social group to which he belongs. Yet it is only by a very tenuous thread that they can be linked with the spoken language of the child. In the first days and even the first weeks of life, the sounds are almost entirely indicators of discomfort or at least of lack of equilibrium in the childish organism, and it is significant that the majority of adults react very readily and strongly to the cries of young babies. They cannot normally ignore them for long and if measures to stop the cries are not successful, strong emotions are quickly aroused. A further and related feature is that the baby whose reasons for crying are not removed very soon achieves remarkably high sound levels. In all the baby's cry is one of the most effective demands for attention which he will ever make.

Babbling

The place of babbling in the development of speech sounds has already been discussed. We are concerned here with the part which babbling may play in the emergence of the child's earliest words. David McNeill[34] argues that there is a definite discontinuity at both ends of the babbling period. It is true that the combinations of front consonants with back or neutral vowels, known as babbling, which frequently begin to be heard when the child reaches the age of three months, appear to be initially independent of auditory experience.[31,36] On the other hand, the influence of auditory experience in babbling drift is clearly evident. Moreover, a link between babbling and early words is found in the occurrence in many languages of words, usually nursery words, which are formed according to babbled patterns. Cruttenden[15] has noted typical features in children's formation of many of their first words. The main accented word in the heard sentence is likely to be imitated, the initial consonant of the stressed syllable of that word being reduplicated, so that "biscuit" becomes /bibi/.

The reduplications found in babbling are also frequently encountered in the young child's use of conventional words. A representative recording provides instances of a child of fourteen months repeating the sound pattern /kaka/. This pattern was used by the child to indicate vehicles or car like toys and was clearly a meaningful word for her, yet the repetitions of these two syllables occurring on this recording are virtually identical with those produced in pure babbling. It is as though the child finds satisfaction in the repetition of words in a similar way to that found in the repetition of babbled sounds. Weir's[58] material provides many examples of this process.

It must, nonetheless, be conceded that the first meaningful word which a child utters does not necessarily resemble babble patterns. Children do not take precisely the same steps in the acquisition of language and sometimes the first recognizable word is an attempt to copy the conventional adult term for some object or event which holds special interest for the child. We observe, too, that the proportion of babbled words in children's vocabularies is reduced with remarkable rapidity. Bloom[6] lists the single words spoken by a child of nineteen months during a period of four hours. There are sixty-one different words and only five follow babble patterns. It remains that for many children their babble and their early speech show remarkable similarities to the extent that clear discontinuity between the two is difficult to accept.

The Speech Environment of the Baby

So far we have considered the child's utterances during his earliest life, but equally important are the utterances which are addressed to him and the spoken language which he overhears. Perhaps the most striking feature of the sounds spoken to the young child is the very strong emotional charge which they normally carry. As a rule, the care which is given to the baby in his first year and particularly in the first months of life is accompanied by words and tones of exceptional love and sweetness. For the majority of us, it is true to say that we will never again hear the tones of love as consistently and so constantly addressed to us as we do during those first months.

The utterances to the child during the period up to about nine months are different from later utterances in the type of response which they are expected to evoke from the child. In terms of a reaction which might give evidence of comprehension none, of course, is expected in the earliest weeks and months. What may be expected or hoped for are emotional reactions such as smiling, laughing, quieting if upset and certainly at the babbling stage it is hoped to encourage further babbling. Frequently the babbled patterns used to the child are similar to those used by the child. In this way, a sort of dialogue in sounds takes place. How influential these dialogues are in forming the later sounds produced by the child is a matter for discussion. What seems certain is that the child finds pleasure in the dialogue and in this respect at least the joint activity is likely to forward development. The content of the adult's utterances to the child are likely to be references to the immediate situation or to the immediate past or future. References to the child himself are, of course, frequent and are predominantly to his physical, moral or emotional state. Almost invariably (and in contrast with later childhood!) the comments are favourable or if unfavourable made in a playful way. Question forms are frequent. The units are likely to be short and repetitions abound.

In the second six months of the first year, the child shows much more careful attention to the speech of those in his environment, particularly when the speech is addressed to him. At this stage, the parents are likely to see the first indications of the understanding of their words. Previously, as we have seen, the implications of intonation and intensity are likely to be appreciated by the baby. Loud harsh tones may produce puckering of the lips and crying. Now, for the first time, the words themselves are seen to be the crucial guides to meaning for the child. To give clear evidence of understanding, the child normally has to suit his actions to the words which are spoken. Consequently, parents will often cite such directions or questions as "clap hands," "where's Dolly?" "kiss Teddy" as being the first words understood by the child. It is clear that observable instances of comprehension may be predated by understanding which is not accompanied by observable action. Because of the problems of observing comprehension, it is probable that many instances of comprehension go unnoticed and that many children's understanding of words dates from a point nearer to the eighth or ninth month than to the first birthday.

Linguistic Innovation

We have already touched on the possible origins of some of the child's first words in the development of his babbled sounds. We have also seen that sometimes a child's first word or words are not of the babbled form, but are attempts to say the adult version of a word. There is another interesting group of words which fall into a more individual category. These are words which are used by the child, but which do not exist either in the adult vocabulary or in the generally accepted vocabulary of nursery words. They frequently have a fairly specific meaning and sometimes have the consonant-vowel formation of the babble pattern nursery words. Examples we have noted in this group from our own and colleagues' experience are /ga/ for the process of falling or dropping, /gaka/ meaning "broken" or "undone" /naŋŋaŋ/ (ŋ as in long) meaning "closed, please open." It is possible, of course, that these words are very distant copies of adult forms, but more probably they are individual children's contributions to language which have not been accepted generally by the adult language. Sometimes such words persist for a time in a family. They are important in that they provide early evidence of the creative rather than purely imitative language behaviour of the child.

The Second Year of Life

The period at the commencement of the child's second year of life is often described as the time of the child's first words and for many writers has marked the beginnings of the child's language. As we have seen, the initiation of language for the majority of children is, relative to the child's life span, much earlier.

Holophrases

According to legend, Thomas Carlyle's first remark was the question aimed at a neighbouring cry baby "What ails thee, Jock?" Unlike such infant prodigies, the great majority of the human race express themselves by single words rather than sentences when they begin to express themselves freely in speech. The term holophrases has been given to these words. They have several distinctive characteristics. Firstly, they usually represent features of the child's environment, experience or purposes which are of particular importance to him. In this sense again, the child's development of language is seen to be not purely or even principally imitative, not imposed from without, but originating from within. It is true that patterns of these words will have been provided by the parents, but in many instances parents' utterances will have been determined by a situation in which the child's needs are the centre. Moreover, the parents will have provided many patterns for the child only a very few of which will be initially made use of in his own utterances. Secondly, the holophrases are likely to be those termed contentives—the words, normally nouns, verbs, adjectives, adverbs, which carry the weight of the meaning in a language as opposed to function words, such as articles, conjunctions, pronouns, prepositions, etc. for which the role is grammatical rather than referential. It is significant that the frequency of many function words in language is high, so that the child is likely to have a great deal of experience of hearing such words, for example, "the," "and." Yet frequency of experience does not impose the word in the child's spoken vocabulary. A third feature of the holophrase is that the single word usually carries the meaning of one or more sentences, the meaning of the implicit sentence being conveyed partly by the word and partly by the situation as a whole or particular features of it. Thus "Teddy" may mean "I want Teddy," "Down" may mean "Put me down" or "Put Teddy down."

Speech and Motor Development

To speak purposively requires close attention. This is true for the adult even in relatively casual conversation. The most talkative driver ceases to chat when his driving demands complete concentration. It is thought that the child who is rapidly developing motor skills, particularly the new found ability to walk unaided, is under similar compulsion. The control of his movements, the retention of balance, have not at this stage become automatic, instead they engage his mind to an extent which will rapidly decline as the child becomes more confident of his steps and of his general motor co-ordination. Furthermore, the child's increased mobility brings greatly increased scope for the exploration of his environment. His mounting curiosity and his eagerness for new experiences can now be satisfied by the child independently in many instances of the immediate help of the adult who transported him from place to place. Altogether, the child's motor activities are dominant in his behaviour at this stage of development. We may have here an explanation of the plateau in speech development which has been noted by observers to occur between the appearance of the child's first words and his first expressions in combinations of two or more words. In very many children the acquisition of a small vocabulary of holophrases is followed by an appreciable time lag which may be upwards of three months before the child reaches a further stage in expressive speech.

As the child's speech develops, a further inter-relationship between speech and motor behaviour has been noted.[52] This is the tendency for speech to be concomitant with motor activities in the sense that the child's words are not readily separable from his deeds. The child acts to support his words just as he may also speak to support his actions. In these instances there is for the child's attention a single focus to which all his energies are bent. A similar fixation has been noted in situations in which the normal child's comprehension of speech and his reaction to sounds is being assessed.[52] If a child whose responses to sounds and to speech are being examined engages in manipulation of play material, it may well be that he will give no response to sounds which he will readily react to provided that he is disengaged from motor activities. These features of the young child's behaviour are not without parallel in later stages of childhood and indeed in adult life, but of course, they emerge then as isolated instances whereas, at the stage we are discussing, they are likely to be the rule rather than the exception.

Developing Comprehension of Language

By the age of eighteen months, many children are said by their parents to "understand everything said to them." Such statements are clearly exaggerations and frequently they do not take sufficient account of how much information is carried to the child by their gestures, their looks and by other aspects of the context in which words are spoken to the child.[52] What is clear from studies of the responses of young children to directions spoken in play situations is that provided the vocabulary is related to familiar objects and experiences, a considerable range of understanding of relationships expressed linguistically can be demonstrated. By this stage, in effect, the child who may be uttering single words only, has begun to comprehend the combinations of words which we may rightly term language.

Parents' speech to their children takes account of this fast changing state in the child's comprehension. In contrast to the period before the end of the first year, the parents appreciate that by means of simplification of structure and short phrases and sentences, they will usually be able to communicate readily within the range of the child's experience. The sort of simplifications introduced by parents are exemplified by instances provided by M. M.

Lewis[33] in which, in reporting a child's utterances and responses, he gives the parents' words in the same context:

(a) To child aged 12 months 27 days: "Baby, where's shoe-shoe?"
(b) To child aged 13 months 6 days: "Give Daddy crustie"
(c) To child aged 15 months 3 days: "Baby, have honey"
(d) To child aged 16 months 16 days: "Baby, where's flowers?"

In the above instances, the parents are using a form of simplified speech akin to the later telegraphic speech of the child. Particularly noticeable is the omission of articles at a stage when the child himself is uttering single words or two word combinations. This suggests that parents in simplifying their speech to their children do so broadly proportionately to but in advance of the stage which the child has reached in his own expression. The data provided by Lewis[33] shows that within a few months of the examples quoted above, the parents are no longer using telegraphic sentences, but short sentences which follow conventional grammar as in the following instances:

(a) To child aged 18 months 21 days: "Where are the flowers?"
(b) To child aged 19 months 27 days: "Pick a flower and give it to Daddy."

Two Word Sentences

The stage of holophrases is followed by a briefer period in which the child expresses himself by two word combinations. For the majority of children this stage is reached between eighteen months and two years. The emerging grammar of the child now begins to be evident. Although the grammatical features which two word sentences are capable of evincing are limited, these sentences show similarities to but also some differences from adult patterns. In general word order is similar to that of the adult language at least in those languages in which word order is relatively fixed. There are exceptions, a notably common one being the combination with "all gone"—"all gone milk," etc. The words used in the two word combinations are frequently combinations of words which were used independently at the holophrasic stage, but it has been shown that the two words used by children at this stage really are combinations and not utterances of separate single words. The evidence lies in differing stress patterns of the words which may occur in the two word combinations. Indeed the child may well express differences in meaning by differences in stress. For instance, "Daddy shoe" with stress on the first syllable may mean "That is Daddy's shoe" (and not someone else's) whilst "Daddy shoe" with stress on the last syllable may mean "That is Daddy's shoe" (and not some other object) or even "Daddy is putting on his shoe."

There is further evidence of developing grammar in that the words used in the combinations although appearing as basic or root forms do often begin to show inflection. For example: "Sat wall," meaning "He sat on the wall," where the verb is in the past tense. Some writers have gone so far as to distinguish grammatical classes in the child's two word utterances. They postulate two basic classes "functors" or pivot words which are few, frequently occurring and having a fixed position in the sentence and "contentives" a much wider class of words which correspond particularly to the nouns of later language. Although this analysis throws light on grammatical patterns which do seem to be present at the two word stage, it has been criticized as superficial. Lois Bloom[6] has pointed out that utterances which have different meanings may not be distinguishable by this analysis, nor indeed by any analysis which does not take account of the context in which the words are uttered. She gives as an example the sentence "Mommy sock" which occurred in two contexts: (i) the child picked up her mother's sock and (ii) the child's mother put the child's sock on the child. Evidently any comprehensive account of the child's grammar at this stage will need to seek its information from sources additional to the words themselves.

The Third Year of Life

The second birthday is at a time of rapid change, especially in linguistic expression. Consequently, it is particularly difficult to set chronological limits to the stages of development at this period. Some children will have already passed beyond two word combinations and will be well advanced in telegraphic speech, but for the majority of children this latter stage has only just started or has not yet begun by the time they reach two years of age.

Telegraphic Speech

As Roger Brown[9] observes, the adult who sends a telegram is under financial constraint. The child, he argues, is under planning constraint. There is a limit to the length of utterance which the child can programme and at this stage the limit is very restrictive, between two and four morpheme .

The result in both instances is similar. Those words find place in the message which are important in the transmission of meaning. Words which are not important in this respect are likely to be omitted. The words which appear in the child's telegraphic speech are of the type which he used in his holophrases—nouns, verbs and adjectives, those words which have reference to the external environment, to his experience, and those omitted are the words which are basically grammatical devices. Like many of the two word combinations, telegraphic speech may lack the inflections of conventionally formed sentences.

Examples:

(a) (Parent: "Put the truck where?")
Child: "Put truck window"
(b) Child: "Kathryn no like celery"
(c) Child: "Daddy wash hands"

Brown points out that the words which the child retains have three characteristics. They are the words which the child is likely to have uttered frequently as single words. As we have noted, they are the words which, predominantly, communicate the meaning of a spoken message and thirdly they are words which are likely to be stressed in the spoken sentence. The last point is significant in the light it throws on the way auditory patterns are modified so that they can most effectively convey meaning.

Parents' Expansions of Children's Speech

In the pioneer study by Roger Brown[9] and his co-workers of the language of two young children, the investigators noted the replies of the adults to the children's observations. The responses by parents sometimes took up and presented the child's observation in the conventional grammatical form. Brown says that these expansions of the child's utterances were often checks on what the child said, having the implicit meaning "Is this what you meant?" The expansion usually represented the child's expression in a simple but grammatical adult form. The form, Brown says, which the child himself will use some six months or so later. An interesting point which emerges is that, although the adults involved were highly educated middle class parents, they used expansions in only thirty percent of the possible cases. How important such expansions are in the child's development of grammar is not clear, but it seems probable that they are of only auxiliary influence, when the child's hearing is normal.

Interpreting the Speech of the Young Child

The fact that these parents required a confirmatory check on what the child said throws up an important feature of children's speech which is perhaps at its most prominent during the telegraphic stage. This is the relatively poor intelligibility of many children's speech at this period. Strangers may have extreme difficulty in interpreting the child's speech. For this reason, Brown,[9] in the study referred to, took particular care to select children whose speech was of good intelligibility. Even parents may have problems of interpretation from time to time, although familiarity with the child and with the situations in which his utterances are made obviously helps enormously in the task of interpretation. One factor which helps in the interpretation of the child's speech at this stage is that most of his observations are directed to the immediate present situation, the "here and now." References to the future, apart from the immediate future, are rare. References to the past may be more common and may be to incidents which have impressed the child or are frequently repeated. It happens, of course, that the here and now for the child—his immediate wants are not necessarily evident to the adult witness. It is the child's developing ability to express his wants, intentions, feelings and thoughts which does so much to reduce frustrations, especially as with increasing mobility, individuality and independence, the child's satisfaction is less likely to be provided as a matter of course by his parents.

New Approaches to the Study of Child Language

The period between two and three years sees the development from telegraphic speech to the level at which the child can form a wide range of simple, compound (involving two main verbs) and even complex sentences (with verb subordinate to a main verb) which conform to the patterns of adult grammar. The study of this period in language has received an immense impetus from the theoretical work of Noam Chomsky. Following the writing of Chomsky's Syntactic Structures[12] and Aspects of the Theory of Syntax[13] certain groups who had been influenced by and linked with the new linguistic outlook at Harvard turned their attention to child language partly as a source of evidence for Chomskyan theories, partly to see what light these theories threw upon linguistic development. The studies which initially resulted were of a type in favour earlier in the century, that is to say, they involved the collection of extensive data on individual children. This approach had been abandoned in the twenties and thirties in favour of normative studies in which cross sectional data was obtained, particularly by means of tests on large numbers of children. The return to the earlier method of collecting data did not, however, involve a similar analysis of the data. The earlier studies tended to adopt a global approach and to emphasize the psychological aspects of the child's linguistic growth. The new studies were concerned particularly with the analysis of the data as a source of information at the origins of transformational grammar. Over the last decade, this approach has become the dominant way of studying child language throughout the Western world. Many of the views put forward are still the subject of much discussion and some early "findings" have already been discarded. There is moreover general agreement that knowledge of the development of grammar in terms of fundamental processes is still at only a very tentative stage. Nonetheless, it seems certain that the Chomskyan influence on the study of child language has been and is a particularly creative one. The impetus derived from his work is far from exhausted.

A psychologically radical notion which Chomsky has put forward is that humans have an innate propensity to acquire language. One piece of evidence in favour of this view is the remarkable rapidity with which children move from the stage of expression in single words to expression in the conventional grammar of their native language. When the complexity of the system is considered as measured, for instance, by the difficulty which adults encounter in learning the grammar of another language, the speed of the child's progress is phenomenal. There is one crucial requirement which must be fulfilled without which the rapid progress cannot take place. This requirement is access to auditory experience of language. Without this access, the development of knowledge of the grammar of the native language, is as painstaking a task as it is painless and automatic when access is available. Not only grammar but vocabulary and indeed all aspects of spoken language are subject to likely limitation and retardation where there are limitations on hearing. The innate propensity to acquire language, if it exists, does not enable us to dispense with dependence upon our ears.

One of the most thorough studies of children's expressive language at the telegraphic stage is that by Lois Bloom.[6] A full analysis of the production of three children of just under two years of age sustains the thesis that children follow definite rules in their progress towards conventional grammar. It is true that they make grammatical errors just as adults do by slips of the tongue and in other ways, but these can be distinguished from those other usages of the child which, whilst not conforming to adult grammar, have their clear regularities. One of Bloom's subjects expressed by negation, the following categories:

Non existence—The child unable to find a pocket in a skirt says "No pocket."

Rejection—The child refuses a worn piece of soap in favour of a new tablet. "No dirty soap."

Denial—The child is looking for a toy truck and has been offered a car by her mother. "No truck."

Individuality in the Development of Grammar

Bloom[6] demonstrates that, whilst the children follow regular patterns in moving towards the grammar of their native language, the regularities may differ from child to child. In this and other ways, she makes clear how within the general framework of orderly progression there is scope for individuality in the procedures which the child may adopt. "The emerging grammars," she writes, "proposed for the language of the three children studied were different; a single grammar would not have accounted for the language of all three in any adequate way" (p. 227). There is, too, no question for Bloom but that the language of the child is of the same essential nature as that of the adult and not as has been argued by, for example, David McNeill,[35] an exotic language which then gives way to the language of the environment.

Bloom's material shows that, in spite of the relatively short sentence spans produced by the children, they are already before the age of two years well on the way to expression in phrases which are no longer telegraphic. Indeed, Bloom provides instances of completely well formed sentences by these children. For example, from a child of nineteen months—"Who has that book?" "Kathryn has that book." "Make him sit down." She treats these, however, as stereotype sentences, which are not evidence of the child's own grammatical level of production. This may be disputable, although Bloom had access to much more situational and supportive evidence to back her interpretation. Nevertheless, there is no doubt that many children at the age of two years are, when observed in those situations which allow full scope for their linguistic capacities, ready to produce phrases if not sentences which partake of the grammatical devices of the adult language.

By the time children reach the age of two and a half years, the adult grammar is already widely reflected in the phrases they use. There are, of course, frequent deviations from conventional patterns, but by this stage the deviations themselves often correspond to regular adult forms which the child generalizes inappropriately. Examples: I bringed the basket. I saw some sheeps. Such inappropriate generalizations have long been seen as evidence that the child is following general rules in his learning of the language. As Brown[9] says: "They are mistakes which externalize the child's search for the regularities of English syntax." Further evidence of the compelling force for the child of conformity to rule in language is the observation that children will often revert to an incorrect regular form after having previously adopted the correct irregular version.

Widening Scope of the Child's Language

In expressive language, the third year of life witnesses the immense change from the limited telegraphic utterances of the child at beginning of the third year to the relatively fluent expression in short but conventionally grammatical sentences and phrases of the child of three years of age.

In comprehension, too, the third year sees an immense widening of the child's linguistic range. Although the child of two years understands well those adults who are familiar to him, particularly his mother, when they are speaking about matters which are also the familiar experience of his everyday life, he does not show full comprehension of strangers and he is likely to be unable to follow a conversation which strays far from his immediate experience. At three years, in contrast, many children readily engage in simple conversation with strangers. Indeed, as adult visitors to nursery schools find, a stranger is the object of an interest which is particularly amenable to exploration through questioning and conversation. At the stage of telegraphic speech, much of the child's meaning was only to be inferred from the situation in which the speech was uttered, the child's statements often being either ambiguous or incomplete as statements of the case. Now the child is increasingly capable of formulating his meaning in combinations of words which are sufficiently explicit to be interpretable independently of their context. Moreover, speech is becoming increasingly a means of gaining access to experience which is no longer "here and now," and of recalling and dwelling upon, as well as looking forward to, significant experiences which are no longer present.

At this point, it is helpful to consider the ways in which the child makes use of the language in which he is now becoming so fluent. M. A. K. Halliday[23] has formulated an illuminating account of the different purposes to which children even at the nursery school stage are able to put their language. He has distinguished seven important functions in a child's language. These are:

(i) instrumental (to gain ends);
(ii) regulatory (to control conduct);
(iii) interactional (to mediate relationships between self and others);
(iv) personal (to develop the concept of oneself);
(v) heuristic (to find out);
(vi) imaginative (to create in words and sounds);
(vii) representational (to state the case).

Halliday goes further than other writers who have carried out similar analyses of ways of using language. He argues that children become consciously aware of language as an instrument of extreme flexibility which can be adapted by them the better to serve their ends. Instances from our own experience seem to us to bear out Halliday's view. Here are some examples in which an alteration of a child's normal manner of speech highlights the mode of language which he is employing.

(i) On a recording of a colleague's nephew at the age of two and a half, we hear the toddler switching to a special "baby talk" when he turns to address his baby brother.

(ii) A young child scolds a doll or a pet. To do this, the child frequently adopts the phrases and intonations which reflect those which the adult uses to the child.

(iii) Jean Piaget[44] gives an account of a child who was impressed by the sight of a duck plucked ready for the oven. Later the child was found lying so still upon a sofa that she was thought to be ill. At first she did not answer questions, then said in a *faraway voice:* "I'm the dead duck!"

Most parents of young children will have observed similar occasions on which there has been an unmistakably purposeful selection by the child of a particular usage of language.

Observations and comparisons made many years ago by the Gestalt psychologist, Fritz Heider[26] of the social and play behaviour of young deaf and hearing children have made clear how extensively even very young children are dependent upon spoken language in social situations, and how extreme are the restrictions imposed on the operation and development of normal social interaction by the absence of words.

One most important feature of children's language use is the way words and the sounds of speech are the material of play behaviour. This aspect of child language has been excellently illustrated for older children in the work of the Opies.[41] Play with sounds and language is manifest as a basic tendency of humans from the earliest months of life. We have noticed this already in the repetitions of babbling. The playful noise making: cooing and crowing, of the very young child does not come to any sudden end, but changes its form. The data collected by Ruth Weir[58] in Language in the Crib illustrates the same features for somewhat older infants. From the age of about two and a half years, many children enjoy linguistic play in the form of nursery rhymes, listening intently to the rhymes spoken by adults and older children and frequently joining in final lines or in terminations of lines. What is striking here as B.B.C. programmes such as "Listen with Mother" make clear, is the ability of many young children to sustain continuous listening over relatively long periods, provided that the words and sounds which they hear are suited to their interests. In the Opies' books, we see children of primary school years using language in the battle of the child against the all powerful adult. This tendency, too, is to be found in the younger child. Many children at the nursery school age not only relieve their feelings by verbal abuse of the offending adult, but especially when playing together find great satisfaction in wordy ruderies which are aimed more generally at the world of the grown up. Numerous young children have been hilariously fascinated by adding tags such as "Mrs." to inappropriate words.

Later Developments: Language in Thinking

When normally developing children reach the later pre-school years, by the age of three and a half to four years, they have already achieved the major part of their mastery of the native language. From this time on there will be greater grammatical fluency. The ability to plan and execute longer sentences and sentences of greater complexity will increase, but the most important area of development will from now be in extension of vocabulary. This in turn will lead to increasing efficiency of communication and increasing ability to use words in thinking. Estimates of vocabulary sizes at different ages have varied according to the basis upon which the estimate has been made. The most widely quoted figure and one virtually enshrined by its appearance in the Plowden Report[45] is that made many years ago by A. F. Watts,[57] who suggested on the basis of tests which he had carried out that the recall or expressive vocabulary of children at the normal age of school entry was likely to be of the order of 2,000 words. Watts did not, of course, intend more than an informed guess. His principal object was to counteract the tendency he regarded as prevalent among teachers and others working with children to underestimate grossly the size of children's vocabularies.

The extent to which children and indeed adults make use of language in their thinking has been discussed over the past century at great length and without definite conclusion. Often the discussion has been held up by differing definitions of terms. For example, it might surely be argued that at one level a child is using words in thinking if he shows that he can discriminate between different spoken directions by his appropriate performance of them, something which many children may do before the age of two years. At another level, an interesting distinction has been shown between the thinking of the pre-school child and of the older child in an elegant experimental investigation by Reuben Conrad.[14] Conrad's evidence is drawn from performances on a memory task in which the subject has to recall pictures which he has just seen. Some of the pictures are of objects whose names are known to be readily confused by adults when recalling word lists, for example, rat, hat, cat, etc. The remaining pictures are of objects whose names are not confused in this way. Now the task can be performed purely in terms of the visual image without recourse to the names of the objects, but it is found that older children rely on the names in their recall, a consequence being that their performance is poorer on the set whose names are easily confused. The younger children on the other hand show no indication of employing the names in their recall, although the names of the objects are known to them, and their performance on the two sets of pictures is similar.

It is interesting that Conrad places the beginning of this particular use of words in thinking precisely at the age at which children (in this country) enter school. School was traditionally, and still is to a very great extent, a place where intellectual growth and intellectual education are virtually synonymous with verbal progress. To say this suggests that scholastic success is dependent on language achievement and that conversely scholastic failure might well be associated with, and caused by, factors in language development.

In 1959 Bernstein[3] described two varieties of language which he later called the restricted and the elaborated codes. The two codes differ from each other in their grammar and in their vocabulary and they are linked with social class

reply to a question by Richard Silverman, Noam Chomsky, who is the leading proponent of the innate theory of language acquisition made this comment: "One would expect that unless the appropriate stimulus conditions are realized, the instinctive behaviour would not appear. It may be that the appropriate stimulus condition is hearing enough linguistic noises in your environment. So it just might be that there is no way to tap the system, any more than there is a way of initiating the system of flight in birds without putting them in the situation in which they have to flap their wings."[50]

In respect to the development of the grammar of the language which is the issue with which Chomsky is concerned here, it does seem that the "hearing of enough linguistic noises" is the crucial determinant and that very probably there are thresholds of experience above which the grammar of the language is acquired without great deviance although at later stages than when hearing is normal. Below these thresholds, by contrast, the acquisition of grammar is frequently extremely difficult and the grammatical patterns which are developed may be very deviant from the conventional structures.

However, we must emphasize that the distinction which results is by no means so clear cut as in the case of the "all or none" flight behaviour of a bird to which Chomsky referred. Furthermore, as we have seen, language is not solely grammar. The more important aspect considered from the standpoint of the transmission of meaning—the fundamental role of language—is vocabulary. Here we can perceive nothing but a continuum in the gradation of the handicap. Those children whose linguistic limitations are most severe may at the secondary school stage have vocabularies which are similar in extent to those of normally hearing children who are at the nursery school stage, whilst children with slight impairments of hearing may be found to have retardation in their vocabulary development which is sufficient to place them at a grave disadvantage in many situations in the ordinary primary school.

In order to give a more specific exposition of the relationships between hearing impairment and linguistic development, we may consider the difficulties ensuing from deafness under the following headings: intelligibility of spoken language, linguistic structure (or grammar), vocabulary and reading. There is also the problem of comprehension on the one hand in that the deaf person is handicapped in understanding others, and on the other hand the problem which the deaf person has in expressing himself fluently and intelligibly to other people.

Intelligibility

There are two main difficulties for the hearing impaired child in understanding the speech of others. The first is lack of knowledge of the meanings of the words themselves. The second is the failure to perceive sufficient of the auditory and visible elements of words to interpret them. This is, of course, the situation of the person deafened in adult life whose language is adequate but whose perception is no longer effective. It is clear that in the child the two difficulties react together, the second making the first much more acute. Moreover, it is this interaction which tends to limit the development of the child's language at every stage. It is for this reason that the clear presentation of words in meaningful contexts is essential to the young hearing impaired child. By clear presentation we mean speaking the words so that the child has the fullest opportunity of hearing and of seeing on the speaker's lips as much of the speech elements and of the global patterns as he is capable. By meaningful contexts we mean that the words are presented in situations in which as far as possible there is visible evidence from the circumstances in which they are spoken which will illustrate the meanings of the words. Additionally, the context must be interpretable by, and of interest to, a child of the age in question if the words are to be assimilated by the child.

This initial problem of comprehension must obviously be overcome if the child is to acquire language and to express himself in words. It is complicated by the fact that comprehension especially in the young child cannot be easily observed or assessed. This means that on the one hand, for children who have only slight impairments of hearing, assumptions of understanding are made which in fact over-estimate the child's level of comprehension, whilst on the other hand, for the child with severe deafness, apparent failure to respond to words may cause those who work with the child to despair too readily of his development of any comprehension of words. Each reaction may have unfortunate consequences for the child.

Lack of intelligibility in the speech of a hearing impaired child may be frequent at many degrees of hearing loss whilst the child is very young. The period which most normally hearing children go through in which their speech is difficult to interpret may be lengthened or may come at a later age in the child with a slight or partial impairment of hearing. Most children who have useful hearing for speech will, however, develop speech which is intelligible to a listener who is willing to put a little effort into the task. This is especially true where the listener is in personal conversation with the hearing impaired speaker. When the sufferer has very little or no useful hearing for speech, intelligibility may remain at a level which is difficult for the stranger.

The reason for lack of intelligibility of speech of the profoundly deaf speaker does not appear to reside solely in the lack of clear articulation of consonant sounds or even of vowels. Rhythmic, intonational and stress patterns as well as the speed of utterance appear to be important contributory factors in the intelligibility of deaf children's speech. This is important because these are features of the speech pattern which may be available to children who are unable to discriminate between consonants or even to hear them.

A final point on the problem of intelligibility is that children whose speech may be very difficult or impossible for strangers to interpret may yet be understandable to parents, teachers and others who know the children well. That a child can make himself understood to those people who are most important to him is an appreciable achievement.

The figures on the ability to communicate by speech of fifteen-year-old pupils in schools for the deaf, given in "The Health of the School Child, 1969–1970,"[17] put this problem in clearer perspective. One of the medical officers of the Department of Education and Science interviewed 167 pupils in ten day and ten boarding schools. Three categories of communication level were defined, these together with the percentages of children in each category were as follows:

Intelligible speech	38·9 per cent
Partly intelligible speech	44·9 per cent
No intelligible speech	16·2 per cent

These results show that it was a minority of the children who were not able to communicate with a sympathetic stranger. Furthermore, within this minority only 7 per cent of the children had no additional handicap.

Linguistic Structure

The reason why the acquisition of the structure of the language should present such grave difficulty to profoundly deaf children is not immediately clear. We can, however, distinguish aspects of grammar which certainly contribute to, and may when operating together as they do, be sufficient to explain the difficulty. The first of these features is that many of the indicators (or markers, to use the linguist's term) of grammatical distinctions provide extremely limited auditory and visual information to the person relying on impaired hearing aided by vision. If we compare the differences in sounds between pairs such as the following: the dog, the dogs; the cat, the cats; the ball, a ball; he has fallen, he is falling; he sings, he sang; we see that only very small acoustic differences and very brief movements of the speech organs are responsible for the contrasts. The pairs presented here are typical of many of the slight variations in speech which give rise to grammatical contrasts. The person with impaired hearing is clearly faced with very meagre information in these circumstances.

The second feature of grammar which creates difficulty is that, whereas much of the vocabulary of a language is related in a fairly clear way to the world of visible and tangible experience, this is by no means so evident in the case of the elements of grammar. Consider the following pair of sentences: The black cat was drinking the milk quickly; The milk was quickly drunk by the black cat. Certain words in each sentence—black, cat, drink, milk, quickly, that is nouns, verbs, adjectives and adverbs can be demonstrably linked with what they refer to in non-verbal experience. For function words, however, it is much less easy to link them with the world of the senses. What is it in the external world which corresponds with—the, was, by? The meaning of such words is to a great extent a meaning which only makes sense within the context of the grammar of the language. To take another grammatical feature represented in this pair of sentences, the object of one sentence has become the subject of the other, yet each sentence represents the same events. Consequently we find that whilst the meanings of many words can be demonstrated to the child with impaired hearing, it is very difficult to provide demonstration of the elements and processes of grammar.

A third feature which is more difficult to assess but which appears to be of fundamental importance is one which has been discussed by Bernard Tervoort.[55] Pointing to the temporal nature of experience in the auditory mode, Tervoort draws attention to the fact that the structure of spoken language is essentially a system which consists of temporal relationships. Every sentence has a beginning, a middle and an end, a now, a before and a hereafter. To understand sentences, we must retain mentally the pattern with which they were started. We must also do this in order to finish our own sentences appropriately. The sentence patterns appear to be preserved over the necessary period in our auditory memory. Lack of auditory memory consequent upon lack of auditory experience will thus act to prevent the apprehension and formation of the appropriate grammatical sequences. The implications of Tervoort's ideas have not been fully worked out and in some respects the ideas themselves may seem to be speculative, but they do throw light on possible reasons for the great difficulty in the development of the sequences and relationships of grammar by those who have little access to auditory experience.

The following examples illustrate typical grammatical problems which may be found at differing levels of handicap. The first instance is taken from the language of a child who normally showed few deviations when using everyday constructions. In this instance, in telling a story, she became involved in indirect speech (the old Latin bugbear oratio obliqua!) and found the sequence of tenses too much for her. Consequently she reverted to the simpler direct speech:

> "Then, after, the boy told his mother that—
> He said: 'I have finished my dinner'."

It is clear that the child was not confident of her knowledge of the appropriate pluperfect—"he had finished"—and preferred to recast the sentence to use the perfect tense.

The second instance shows a well developed and complete sentence which is deviant in tense sequence, in the use of the conjunction, and in the verb. It has been pointed out by the Heiders[25] that any variability of form in language is especially likely to create difficulty for hearing impaired children (just as it does for those learning a foreign tongue). The verb is the part of speech which above all the others is subject to great variation in its form.

> "Suddenly he went back to sleep and his wife is very cross with her husband that he sleep very late for his work."

In the next example the sentences retain the conventional sentence patterns but even though they are short and simple, each of them is grammatically deviant.

> "The boy play with match. The mother said: 'Be careful with fire.' Mother go to the shops."

The fourth instance shows the presence of simple phrases but the conventional sentence has not been achieved.

> "The man over, in house."

From the context in which it was produced, the full sentence would have been something like:

> "The man climbs over the window sill and into the house."

Finally, we reach a stage in which the severity of the linguistic handicap is reflected in the fact that neither sentences nor phrases are formed. The single words—global meaning carriers like the holophrases found in the speech of very young normally hearing children are juxtaposed but not related linguistically.

> "Window look open man."

This may represent a sentence such as:

> "The man looks through the window and then opens it."

Two principal methods are employed in teaching the grammar of the language to hearing impaired children. The first of these may be termed the natural method and in it the teaching of the grammar of the language is simply a part of the teaching of the language as a whole. The natural method aims, by the conscious presentation of language to the hearing impaired child, to replicate in so far as possible the situation in which the hearing child develops the grammar of language. That is, by experience of language together with whatever natural capacity for the acquisition of language which man may have.

To be effective the natural method requires great effort from parent and teacher. It demands consistency, it demands constant attention to the task, it demands that no opportunity for turning the child's life experiences into the material of language should be missed. To be wholly successful, it requires, too, that the effort which child and parent are required to make is co-ordinated with a satisfactory adjustment in social relationships. When this method is successful, it leads to the attainment of language which is flexible and which is adapted to the nature of the language of the world of everyday life. It is also a method which can be explained and demonstrated to parents who have no prior knowledge of teaching language, and indeed to parents from virtually the whole range of educational and cultural levels.

The second method attempts to teach to the child the structure of grammar by presenting examples and rules. In this respect, the process is comparable with methods which have been frequently used in the past in the teaching of foreign languages. Generally, it is a method which tends to be restricted to application within the school, since many parents will not be able to teach their children in this more formal way. The method may, of course, be combined with the use of the natural method and it is in these instances in which the most impressive results appear to be achieved, as for example at the Clarke School for the Deaf in Massachusetts. On the whole, whichever method is adopted the outcome appears to be most closely related to the amount and quality of the experience provided for the child.

Vocabulary

As we have pointed out, restriction of vocabulary is likely to be found in groups of hearing impaired children at any level of impairment. That the restriction is not an inevitable accompaniment of hearing loss is shown by the biographical and literary talent of many who have suffered severe deafness from early childhood. Helen Keller is the outstanding example, but there are many others whose vocabularies range far beyond that of the average hearing person.

The most obvious effect of hearing impairment is a general limitation on the extent of vocabulary which may be simply explained by limitation on linguistic experience. Against this background of general impoverishment there are specific aspects of vocabulary which account for particular difficulty, especially for those children who are handicapped by extreme deafness.

One area of difficulty is metaphoric usages. The tendency is for the deaf child to interpret the metaphor literally and to be simply puzzled by it. This is so not simply for the obvious metaphor—He boiled with rage. The words froze on his lips. His face fell—which might well puzzle many normally hearing children. It is also true for many usages whose metaphorical nature are scarcely appreciated. The head of the procession. A sharp wind. A bright boy.

Young normally hearing children are generally able to grasp such meanings without great difficulty, perhaps because they are used to hearing the same word in varying contexts in which the meaning may vary slightly or in some cases appreciably. The deaf child is more likely to interpret the word in terms of its root meaning or of its literal meaning. A similar explanation probably accounts for the limitation in the range of meanings known for a particular word which has been observed in hearing impaired pupils, and which has been examined in respect of commonly known words (such as: point, cover, line) by Mildred Templin.[54]

As might be expected in view of the difficulties which foreign language students encounter in the learning of idomatic usages, these are likely to give difficulty to children with impaired hearing. The principal cause of the difficulty is doubtless the confusion which a literal interpretation of the words of the idiom gives rise to. Examples of such problems are shown in the investigations made on the language of children at the secondary stage by D. C. Wollman.[59]

That limitations in vocabulary are associated with hearing losses of moderate and severe degree is readily observable. What is not so evident from simple observation is that many children whose auditory impairments are of much slighter extent have handicapping limitations of vocabulary. Yet when groups of these children are assessed on measures of vocabulary attainment appreciable retardation has been found. This is illustrated by two recent studies which have examined the extent of this retardation. In the first, a group of thirty-three primary school children attending the audiological assessment clinic in the Department of Audiology and Education of the Deaf were investigated.[42] These children were all attending ordinary schools at the time of testing. They had bilateral deafnesses, the mean hearing loss being just above 40 dB, measured in the better ear. Measures were made of the comprehension of spoken vocabulary of these children. The mean standard score (equivalent to a quotient) was 79·8. Of these children only three showed in their speech any marked deviations from the conventional structures of English grammar. Consequently many of them would not be judged to have a linguistic handicap by one who simply listened to their speech. There was also considerable evidence of retardation in reading in the children in this group.

The second study carried out as a research investigation by Patrick Hamilton[24] avoided the problems of the selected clinic population inherent in the study mentioned above. Hamilton examined the language of two groups of hearing impaired children attending ordinary schools in an industrial area of north-west England, all of whom were of at least average ability as measured by a non-verbal test. One group of thirty children comprised those meeting the criteria in the area who were known to have bilateral perceptive deafnesses. The mean hearing loss of this group was 38 dB. The mean standard score in comprehension vocabulary was 82·76. The second group was randomly selected from a much larger group of children with bilateral, persistent conductive deafnesses. The mean hearing loss for this group was 32 dB. The mean standard score in comprehension vocabulary was 81·8. A group of normally hearing children drawn from the same schools as the hearing impaired children had a mean standard score of 99·2. What is particularly disturbing about these figures is that the children with long-standing conductive deafnesses show a similar retardation to that of the children with perceptive deafness. There are strong indications from the studies referred to here that the vocabulary limitation dates in most instances from the children's pre-school years. In the next section, we will see how the vocabulary limitation of the children with impaired hearing is paralleled by retardation in reading.

Reading

It is a constantly recurring hope that the printed word will be able to compensate the hearing impaired child for the difficulty he encounters with the spoken word. As the Latin tag has it—Vox audita perit, littera scripta manet. The printed word is visible and permanent when contrasted with the fleeting everchanging patterns of spoken language.

It is true that many children with hearing impairments do learn to read well and find in this stable printed word a readily accessible means of developing both their vocabulary and their knowledge of the grammar of the language. Yet for the majority of children with hearing loss reading presents difficulty. Children with extreme deafness encounter extreme difficulty in learning to read fluently, but even those who have much slighter hearing handicaps are likely to be retarded as compared with their normally hearing school fellows. The evidence points to a close link between knowledge of and skill in the uses of spoken language and the capacity to take the initial steps in reading and thereafter to make good progress. This is not, after all, surprising since the printed word is a transformation, although by no means a complete one, of the spoken word, so that the child who is fully conversant with spoken language simply has to break the code to gain access to a message which he is then able to understand because of his previous linguistic knowledge.

This point has been emphasized in a recent research report which has made an exhaustive study of reading methods in use with deaf children at the primary school stage and of the factors which are related to progress in reading.[47] Of the many variables which were examined, the measures in spoken language, comprehension and expression, showed by far the strongest relationship to performance in reading, the test of comprehension of spoken vocabulary being the best single predictor of reading progress.

The severity of the handicap in reading sustained by severely and profoundly deaf children is shown by figures gained from the application of reading tests with pupils in schools for deaf children in this country. Results from studies in other countries, notably the United States, show a similar pattern. Christine Wilkins[47] tested 698 deaf children in schools for the deaf in the United Kingdom using a silent reading comprehension test (Southgate Group Reading Test 2). The mean reading ages of the children in the later stages of the secondary school were not above the age of eight years. Such figures make clear that for the main body of these children, reading has not enabled them to escape the limitations imposed by deafness on the development of their language.

At the other end of the scale of hearing loss, the investigation made by Hamilton[24] which is referred to above confirmed that children whose hearing losses are so slight that they are appropriately attending ordinary primary schools are nevertheless considerably retarded in reading as compared with their class-mates and that this retardation is not to be explained by lack of ability nor by socio-cultural factors. It is almost certain that the cause of the retardation in these instances is the auditory and the associated linguistic handicaps. The reading quotients which Hamilton obtained from both the groups of hearing impaired children referred to above varied between eighty-two and eighty-seven, whilst those for the normally hearing group were just above 100. When one considers how important reading is in determining satisfactory progress in the primary school, still more at the secondary school stage the extent of the disadvantage suffered by these children in comparison with the other children in their schools is very clear and very disturbing.

The facts presented in these pages offer a sombre picture of the handicaps in language and in communication which are the usual consequences of deafness. We have emphasized that these consequences are not inevitable in the sense that there are people who overcome them, but it would be most misleading, by failing to appreciate the severity of the disability, to suppose that changes or manipulations of methods of teaching or of communication could resolve the language problems of severe deafness. Nonetheless we must also recognize that our present provisions and practices are in many ways ineffective in ameliorating the conditions resulting from deafness to an extent which we know can be achieved. Sometimes the obstacle is financial, sometimes a lack of appropriately trained personnel and sometimes a problem of the attitudes of parents, teachers and other professional workers and indeed of that vague, amorphous body, the general public. On the positive side, we can point to the change in the pattern of special educational provision which reflects the increasingly effective use of the hearing and other potentialities of the children in the development of language. This is attested by the number of classes and units for children with impaired hearing which are attached to ordinary schools and which cater for many children who would twenty years ago have been in schools for deaf children. Moreover, there are now frequent instances in the special schools of children who, though severely and profoundly deaf by the evidence of the audiogram, are functioning linguistically as partially hearing children. Even the increasing awareness of the consequences of the slight deafnesses suffered by many children in ordinary schools is a reflection of a more general concern about the handicap of deafness which can lead to improvement for all who are disabled in this way.

REFERENCES

1. Abercrombie, D. (1968), "Paralanguage," *Brit. J. Dis. Comm.*, **3,** 55–59.
2. Bartlett, Sir F. C. (1932), *Remembering*, Cambridge: University Press.
3. Bernstein, B. (1959), "A Public Language: some Sociological Implications of a Linguistic Form," *Brit. J. Sociol.*, **10,** 311–326.
4. Bernstein, B. (1971), *Class, codes and control*, Vol. 1. London: Routledge and Kegan Paul.
5. Berry, M. F. (1969), *Language Disorders of Children*. New York: Appleton-Century-Crofts.
6. Bloom, L. (1970), *Language Development: Form and Function in Emerging Grammars*. Cambridge, Mass.: M.I.T. Press.
7. Board of Education (1938), *Report of the Committee of Inquiry into Problems relating to Children with Defective Hearing*. London: H.M.S.O.
8. Brown, R. (1958), *Words and things*. New York: The Free Press.
9. Brown, R. and Bellugi, U. (1964), "Three Processes in the Child's Acquisition of Syntax," in *New Directions in the Study of Language*, pp. 131–161 (E. H. Lenneberg, Ed.). Cambridge, Mass.: M.I.T. Press.
10. Butler, N., Peckham, K. and Sheridan, M. (1973), "Speech Defects in a National Sample of 7-year-old Children," *Brit. J. Dis. Comm.*, **8,** in press.
11. Cherry, C. (1957), *On Human Communication*. London: Chapman and Hall.
12. Chomsky, N. (1957), *Syntactic Structures*. The Hague: Mouton.
13. Chomsky, N. (1965), *Aspects of the Theory of Syntax*. Cambridge, Mass.: M.I.T. Press.
14. Conrad, R. (1972), "Language Development in Children," in *Proceedings of the International Congress on Education of the Deaf, Stockholm*, 1970. Vol. 1, pp. 71–73. Stockholm: Sveriges Lärarförbund.
15. Cruttenden, A. (1970), "A Phonetic Study of Babbling," *Brit. J. Dis. Comm.*, **5,** 110–117.
16. Denes, P. (1955), "Effect of Duration on the Perception of Voicing," *J. Acoust. Soc. Amer.*, **27,** 761–764.
17. Department of Education and Science (1972), "Health of the School Child," *Report of the Chief Medical Officer of the Department of Education and Science for the years* 1969–1970. London: H.M.S.O.
18. Fry, D. B. (1955), "Duration and Intensity as Physical Correlates of Linguistic Stress," *J. Acoust. Soc. Amer.*, **27,** 765–768.
19. Fry, D. B. (1955), "The Experimental Study of Speech," in *Studies in Communication contributed to the Communication Research Centre, University College, London*, pp. 147–167. London: Secker and Warburg.
20. Gesell, A. (1952), *Infant Development*. London: Hamilton.
21. Greene, C. L. (1972), *The Voice and its Disorders*, 2nd edition revised. London: Pitman.
22. Gwynne-Evans, E. (1972), "The Biological Destiny of the Orofacial Muscles," *Brit. J. Dis. Comm.*, **7,** 110–116.
23. Halliday, M. A. K. (1969), "Relevant Models of Language," *Educ. Rev.*, **22,** 26–37.
24. Hamilton, P. and Owrid, H. L. (1973), "Comparisons of Hearing Impairment and Socio-cultural Disadvantage in Relation to Verbal Retardation." In preparation.
25. Heider, F. and Heider, G. M. (1940), "A Comparison of Sentence Structure of Deaf and Hearing Children," *Psychol. Monogr.*, **52** (232), 42–103.
26. Heider, F. and Heider, G. M. (1941), "The Language and Social Behaviour of Young Deaf Children," *Psychol. Monogr.*, **53** (242), i–56.
27. Illingworth, R. S. (1966), *The Development of the Infant and Young Child*. Edinburgh: Livingstone.
28. Ingram, T. T. S. (1964), *Paediatric Aspects of Cerebral Palsy*. Edinburgh: Livingstone.
29. John, J. E. J. and Howarth, J. N. (1965), "The Effect of Time Distortions on the Intelligibility of Deaf Children's Speech," *Lang. and Speech*, **8,** 127–134.
30. John, J. E. J. and Howarth, J. N. (1963), Unpublished work reported at a meeting of the Acoustics Section of the Physical Society. London.
31. Kampik, A. (1930), "Das Lallen beim taubgeborenen Kinde," *Blätter für Taubst. bldg.*, **43,** 354–356.
32. Ladefoged, P. and Broadbent, D. E. (1957), "Information Conveyed by Vowels," *J. Acoust. Soc. Amer.*, **29,** 98–104.
33. Lewis, M. M. (1957), *How Children Learn to Speak*. London: Harrap.
34. McNeill, D. (1970), *The Acquisition of Language*. New York: Harper and Row.
35. McNeill, D. (1966), "The Capacity for Language Acquisition," in *Language Acquisition* (S. P. Quigley, Ed.). Washington, D.C.: A. G. Bell Association for the Deaf.
36. Mavilya, M. (1972), "Spontaneous Vocalization and Babbling in Hearing-impaired Infants," in *Proceedings of the International Congress on Education of the Deaf, Stockholm*, 1970. Vol. 1, pp. 73–78. Stockholm: Sveriges Lärarförbund.
37. Menyuk, P. (1972), *The Development of Speech*. New York: Bobbs-Merrill.
38. Miller, G. A. (1951), *Language and Communication*. New York: McGraw-Hill.
39. Morley, M. E. (1972), *The Development and Disorders of Speech in Childhood*. Edinburgh: Livingstone.
40. Negus, V. E. (1963), *The Comparative Anatomy and Physiology of the Larynx*, 2nd edition. London: Heinemann.
41. Opie, I. and P. (1959), *The Lore and Language of School Children*. Oxford: Clarendon Press.
42. Owrid, H. L. (1970), "Hearing Impairment and Verbal Attainments in Primary School Children," *Educ. Res.*, **12,** 209–214.
43. Peterson, G. E. and Barney, H. L. (1952), "Control Methods used in a Study of the Vowels," *J. Acoust. Soc. Amer.*, **24,** 175–184.
44. Piaget, J. and Inhelder, B. (1969), *The Psychology of the Child* (Tr. by H. Weaver). London: Routledge and Kegan Paul.
45. [Plowden Report] Department of Education and Science (1967), *Children and their Primary Schools*. London: H.M.S.O.
46. Polanyi, M. (1959), *The Study of Man*. London: Routledge and Kegan Paul.
47. Redgate, G. W. and Palmer, J. (1972), "The Teaching of Reading to Deaf Children: a Research Report." Manchester University, Department of Audiology and Education of the Deaf.
48. Schiefelbusch, R. L., Copeland, R. H. and Smith, J. O. (Eds.) (1967), *Language and Mental Retardation*. New York: Holt, Rinehart and Winston.

49. Shannon, C. E. and Weaver, W. (1949), *The Mathematical Theory of Communication.* Urbana: Illinois University Press.
50. Silverman, S. R. (1972), "Today and Tomorrow in the Education of the Deaf," in *Proceedings of the International Congress on Education of the Deaf, Stockholm*, 1970, Vol. 1, pp. 13–22. Stockholm: Sveriges Lärarförbund.
51. Smith, F. and Miller, G. A. (Eds.) (1966), *The Genesis of Language.* Cambridge, Mass.: M.I.T. Press.
52. Taylor, I. G. (1964), *The Neurological Mechanisms of Hearing and Speech in Children.* Manchester: University Press.
53. Templin, M. C. (1957), *Certain Language Skills in Children.* Minneapolis: University Minnesota Press.
54. Templin, M. C. (1966), "Vocabulary Problems of the Deaf Child," *Internat. Audiol.*, **5**, 349–354.
55. Tervoort, B. T. (1960), "The Effectiveness of Communication among Deaf Children as a Contribution to Mental Growth," in *The Modern Educational Treatment of Deafness* (Sir A. W. G. Ewing, Ed.). Manchester: University Press.
56. Wasz-Höckert, O. *et al.* (1968), *The Infant Cry.* [n.p.]: Heinemann.
57. Watts, A. F. (1944), *The Language and Mental Development of Children.* London: Harrap.
58. Weir, R. H. (1962), *Language in the Crib.* The Hague: Mouton.
59. Wollman, D. C. (1961), "Some Problems Involved in the Application of Secondary Modern Education for Deaf Pupils." Ph.D. thesis, Manchester University.

SECTION IV

SPECIAL TOPICS

41A. PAEDIATRIC ASPECTS OF EPIDEMIOLOGY—THE FREQUENCY OF DISORDERS OF EARLY LIFE

IAN LECK

The study of disease-frequency must be reckoned among the foundations of paediatrics, and this for two main reasons. The first is that the paediatrician needs to have some knowledge of how common particular disorders are, to assist him in differential diagnosis, in establishing the priorities that should be given to different disease problems in research and the development of new medical-care facilities, and in determining the scale on which such research and development should be planned. Secondly, he should know in what way comparisons of disease frequency between different times, places and categories of people can help to show how diseases are caused and may be prevented.

The themes of this chapter are the methods of measuring disease frequency and the information they have yielded about the magnitude of some of the more widespread and severe problems of childhood, with particular reference to total mortality and morbidity and to three manifestations of disordered growth and development—malformation, neoplasia and low birth-weight. The use of data on frequency to explore the causation of some of these problems will be illustrated in Chapter 41B.

It is customary to divide data on disease frequency into those relating only to death (mortality statistics) and those which also cover non-fatal illness (morbidity statistics). Morbidity statistics can be subdivided into those which refer only to contacts with the medical services (health service statistics) and those obtained by questioning or examining whole populations (screening statistics). Screening statistics can relate not only to the frequency of overt disease, but also to quantitative variables such as birth-weight and intelligence quotient which are of medical importance. Statistics of all these kinds have contributed to our knowledge of the frequency of disordered growth and development, and will be illustrated in turn.

MORTALITY STATISTICS

Although mortality statistics are not a complete source of information about frequency (except for the few diseases that are invariably fatal, like anencephaly), they have the advantage over morbidity statistics of being more widely and readily available, since death registration has been compulsory and statistics for all registered deaths have been published for many years in all the developed countries, and in some others. Mortality statistics are also more reliable than morbidity statistics, since death is easier to define than illness; and mortality statistics relating to deaths from all causes are more reliable than those relating to specific diseases, which may be affected by changing fashions in diagnosis. The uses of both total and disease-specific mortality statistics will be illustrated by reviewing firstly the improvement in child health in Great Britain and secondly the differences between this and other countries today, which can only be measured in terms of mortality. Except where stated, the data used are taken from the statistical returns and reviews published weekly, quarterly and annually by the Registrars-General for England and Wales and for Scotland.

Changes in Mortality in Great Britain

When considering mortality in Great Britain it is convenient to discuss mortality from all causes before mortality by cause, and in both cases to distinguish between what is known about the whole period since death registration began and the more-detailed information that is available for the last few decades.

Mortality from all Causes

To compare mortality in different years, we need to divide the number of deaths during each year by an estimate of the number at risk of dying. The most acceptable estimate of the latter for most purposes is the mid-year population, which is the number estimated to be alive on June 30th. In England and Wales, births and deaths have been registered and counted since 1838; and starting from the following Census (in 1841) the mid-year population in each age-group has been estimated annually from the results of the most recent census, and from the numbers of births and deaths recorded subsequently. According to these estimates, the annual death-rate per million at risk at all ages declined from 21,555 in 1841 to 11,742 in 1970.

Figures like these, which relate to deaths at all ages but do not take account of the relative numbers of young and old people in the populations concerned, are known as *crude death-rates*. They are not an adequate measure of how much healthier people are age for age, for at least three reasons. Firstly, they do not allow for the increase in the proportion of elderly people, which would inflate the 1970 death-rate relative to that of 1841. Secondly, they do not show whether it is mainly among the young or the old that mortality has declined. Thirdly, each rate relates only to a single year; and because the death-rates of single years can be affected by short-term phenomena such as epidemics, they are not always typical of the longer periods in which they occur.

The last of these problems can be overcome by adding together the deaths in several adjacent years and dividing the total by the sum of the mid-year populations for these years. The sum of these populations is virtually the same as the number of *person-years* lived during the years in question—i.e. the figure that would be obtained if the amounts of time for which the different members of the population were alive during these years could be added together. The ratio of the number of deaths to the sum of the mid-year populations can therefore be regarded as the death-rate per person per year during the period concerned.

The other limitations of the crude death-rate can only be overcome by the use of *age-specific death-rates*. Except for the first year of life, these are calculated by dividing the number of deaths in each age-group by the number of person-years lived within that age-group. Death in infancy, however, is usually measured by the *infant mortality rate*, which is an estimate of the proportion of children born alive who die within a year of birth. The most widely used estimate is the number of infant deaths in a year or more, divided by the number of live births (children born alive) during the same period. This type of estimate is particularly accurate in countries where most infant deaths occur within a few days of birth (and therefore almost all during the same calendar year). The fact that the infant mortality rate is expressed as a proportion of births makes it rather lower than it would be if related to person-years (since the number of live births is always greater than the number of person-years lived in infancy, which is reduced by neonatal and later infant deaths).

Besides showing how mortality has changed in each age-group separately, age-specific death-rates can be used to calculate the death-rates that would have occurred in the total population at various times such as the 1840s and the 1960s if the population in each age-group at all these times had been the same as in one "standard" year. Rates calculated so as to make them comparable in this respect are described as *age-standardized*. In the present context the standardized death-rate at all ages is not very relevant, since it does not tell us specifically about mortality in children, but there is some interest in comparing the trend of mortality in the adult population with that in children; and the death-rates for all adults in different periods must be standardized for age before they can be compared, since the adult population alone contains a much bigger proportion of elderly people today than it formerly did.

Long-term Trends at 0–15 Years

Age-standardized death-rates for adults and age-specific death-rates for children for the decades since 1841 are shown in Fig. 1. The adult rates have been standardized to the 1961 census population—i.e. they are those that would have occurred in each decade, given the age-specific death-rates observed then, if the population in each age-group had been the same as at the 1961 Census (the last for which complete data are available). The rates are plotted on a logarithmic scale to condense the range to a manageable one without loss of detail at the lowest rates, and to make the slopes for different age-groups comparable; on such a scale the slope between two adjacent points is always the same if the second is a given percentage of the first, regardless of whether they are both high or both low.

Figure 1 shows that the decline in mortality since 1841 has been predominantly a feature of infancy and childhood. The age-specific rates for each age-group under 15 years have fallen to between one-eighth and one-fortieth of what they were. The age-standardized rate for all ages over 15 years, on the other hand, was only halved (although further analysis shows that in adolescents and young adults the improvement was almost as great as in children). The over-fives were the first to manifest a decline—in the 1850s—and the last were infants in their first year—fifty years later. It is, however, likely that not all deaths were registered during the earlier years shown, and as deaths in infancy are the most often missed when registration is incomplete, there may have been an improvement in infant survival during the nineteenth century which was masked by a more complete registration of deaths. In each of the age-groups shown, more than half the total reduction in mortality occurred before the 1930s, although it was in the 1940s and 1950s that the reduction was most rapid in relation to mortality at the time.

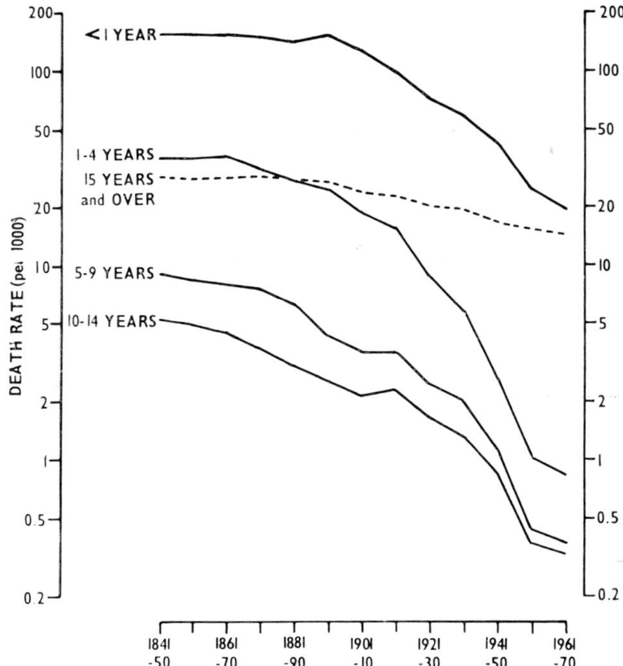

FIG. 1. Decennial infant death rates, age-specific death rates for children, and age-standardized death rates for adults, in England and Wales (quoted or estimated from data published by the Registrar-General, with the adult rates standardized to the 1961 population.)

Between them, the commonly used measures of mortality before one year are based on four mutually exclusive groups of deaths: stillbirths; deaths during the first week after birth (*early neonatal deaths*); deaths between one and four weeks (*late neonatal deaths*); and deaths between four weeks and one year (*post-neonatal deaths*). The first two groups contribute to perinatal mortality, the second and third to neonatal mortality, and the last three to infant mortality. The frequency of each of the four mutually exclusive groups is shown in Fig. 2 for the eight quinquennia for which data on all four groups are available. During these forty years, the ratios of stillbirths and early neonatal deaths to total births fell by half to two-thirds, mainly during the 1940s and 1960s, and the ratios for late-neonatal and post-neonatal deaths fell by four-fifths, mainly between 1945 and 1960. These findings support the grouping together of stillbirths and early neonatal deaths, and suggest that the late neonatal deaths have more in common with the post-neonatal.

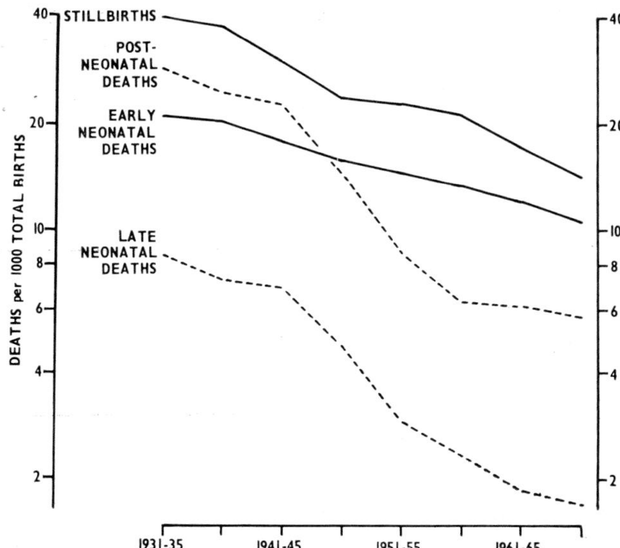

FIG. 2. Quinquennial stillbirth and infant death rates in England and Wales (see text for definitions.)

Recent Trends in Fetal and Infant Mortality

The most closely studied of the rates shown in Fig. 1 has been the infant death-rate, which accounts for most child deaths today. Deaths in early infancy are often analysed separately, since they are more often related to events at birth and earlier than are later infant deaths. At one time, early infancy was usually defined as the first four weeks of life which became known as the *neonatal period*. The *neonatal death-rate* is the number of deaths within four weeks of birth divided by the number of live births during the same period, and the *post-neonatal death-rate* is the number of deaths between four weeks and one year, also divided by the number of live births.

During the last few years, the emphasis in studies of mortality in relation to natal and prenatal factors has shifted to the third trimester of pregnancy and the first *one* week after birth. The inclusion of third trimester fetal deaths in studies of mortality became possible in England and Wales in 1927 with the introduction of registration of stillbirths (children born after the 28th week of pregnancy and showing no sign of life after delivery). At first their frequency was generally measured separately, by the *stillbirth rate*, which is the number of stillbirths divided by the number of *total births* (live and stillbirths added together); but the tendency now is to treat stillbirths and deaths during the first week after birth as a single group, known as *perinatal deaths*. The *perinatal death-rate* is the number in this group divided by the number of total births.

The Contribution of different Diseases to Mortality

When investigating a change in mortality such as the decline over the last century, the next step after examining its relationship to age must be to assess what diseases have contributed to the change. The analysis of deaths or illnesses according to the diseases which cause them is, however, fraught with difficulties, especially when comparing data from widely different times or places, since the disease category to which any death is attributed may depend on the thoroughness with which the patient has been investigated, the diagnostic habits of his doctor, and the overall state of medical knowledge and opinion at the time. A death from congenital heart disease in a baby whose mother has had rubella in early pregnancy, for example, may be certified as due ultimately either to the heart malformation or to maternal rubella, depending on whether the doctor knows that rubella has occurred and that it can cause cardiac defects, and on whether he attaches more importance to morbid anatomy than to aetiology.

To encourage consistency, the World Health Organization publishes the two-volume *Manual of the International Statistical Classification of Diseases, Injuries, and Causes of Death* (commonly known as the *I.C.D.*), on which all countries are encouraged to base their national statistics. The main feature of this manual is a comprehensive classified list of several hundred disease categories, each with a distinctive three-digit code number; and some of these categories are themselves divided into sub-categories, identified by an additional digit which is preceded by a decimal point. Clefts of the lip and palate, for example, are all coded 749, but cleft palate alone is 749.0, cleft lip alone is 749.1, and cleft lip and palate combined is 749.2. The manual also has two other features: an alphabetical index of diagnostic terms giving the code number of the category to which each term is assigned, and several supplementary lists for use in special contexts (including one for analysing perinatal deaths and illnesses) in which diseases that rarely occur in the context in question are grouped together.

Inevitably, the *I.C.D.* is a compromise between the anatomical and aetiological concepts of diagnosis. Its main list is in 17 sections, of which the first and last are defined in terms of aetiology (infective and parasitic diseases first, and accidents, poisonings and violence last) and most of the others in terms of anatomy—and most non-specific and local infections are listed in the anatomical sections. There is, for example, a section headed "diseases of the respiratory system" which includes influenza, pneumonia and bronchitis.

Every ten years or so the *I.C.D.* is revised, the last revision (the eighth) having come into effect in 1968; and even within the currency of one revision, the apparent frequency of different causes of death may be altered by changes in the availability of postmortem and other information, in the diagnostic habits of doctors, and in the ways in which government departments enumerate conditions on the borderline between two diagnoses. For example, between 1962 and 1963 the crude death-rate attributed to *spina bifida* in England and Wales rose by about 30 per cent and the corresponding rate for hydrocephaly fell by 60 per cent, largely because the staff of the Registrar-General then began to enumerate under *spina bifida* all deaths for which both hydrocephaly and *spina bifida* appeared on the death certificate, instead of counting whichever of these conditions was stated to be the primary cause of death.

TABLE 1

PRINCIPAL CAUSES OF DEATH IN EARLY LIFE—ENGLAND AND WALES, 1969

I.C.D. Nos.	*Causes of death*	*Perinatal deaths (per 1,000 total births)*	*Infant deaths after one week (per 1,000 live births)*	*Deaths between 1 and 15 years (per 1,000 living, per year)*	*Stillbirths and deaths under 15 years (per 1,000 total births)**
740–759	Congenital anomalies	4·24	1·92	0·057	6·87
760–772	Complications of pregnancy and childbirth (including maternal, placental and cord conditions)	10·18	0·10	0·000	10·28
776–777	Anoxic and hypoxic conditions, immaturity	5·78	0·18	0·000	5·96
000–136, 466–491	Infective and parasitic diseases, influenza, pneumonia, bronchitis	0·28	3·61	0·084	4·93
140–239	Neoplasms	0·01	0·06	0·074	1·05
800–999	Accidents, poisonings and violence	0·06	0·72	0·153	2·80
All other	Miscellaneous and unknown	2·82	1·14	0·091	5·16
	Total	23·37 (18,886 in 808,192 total births)	7·73 (6,162 in 797,538 live births)	0·459 (4,910 in 10,693,000 person-years)	37·06 (29,954 in 808,192 total births)

* Figures that would apply if all children born in 1969 were subject to age-specific death-rates for 1969.

Although changes in nomenclature and classification may mask or simulate alterations in frequency even when the disease categories analysed are those of the *I.C.D.*, it is strongly recommended that workers should generally use these categories, aggregating or augmenting them where necessary, in preference to developing their own systems independently. Such independent systems are seldom any better than the *I.C.D.*, and make it even harder to compare the results of different studies.

Present-day Mortality By Cause

The frequency in England and Wales of the principal causes of death under 15 years is summarized in Table 1. Malformations are listed first, followed by disorders arising outside the fetus during pregnancy and delivery—notably pre-eclamptic toxaemia, difficult labour, premature separation of the placenta, and compression of the cord. The distinction between deaths from these causes and those in the third group (anoxic and hypoxic conditions and immaturity) is in one sense an artificial one, arising largely from the fact already mentioned that some death certificates give only the morbid anatomy at death and others give the aetiology. This problem is greatest for perinatal deaths, where in a very high proportion of cases the person completing the death certificate may choose to describe either the child's condition at death (e.g. immaturity, growth retardation or birth asphyxia) or the maternal, placental or cord conditions which may have led to premature labour, growth retardation or asphyxia. Necropsy and histology studies suggest that anoxic and hypoxic conditions and immaturity are also the conditions most often certified in neonatal deaths that are really due to pulmonary infection.[11] These conditions and the complications of pregnancy and labour which can produce them are blamed on death certificates for two-thirds of all perinatal deaths, and many of the causes classified as "miscellaneous and unknown" are probably similar.

In view of the mixture of anatomical (or histological) and aetiological information and misinformation that appears on the death certificates of perinatal deaths and that the *I.C.D.* has been designed to accommodate, these records must be considered less rewarding to analyse by cause than the routine data for later deaths, and the rule that analyses of deaths by cause should generally be based on the categories of the *I.C.D.* must be questioned as far as perinatal deaths are concerned. More may be achieved by collecting clinical and pathological summaries of representative series of perinatal deaths, preferably on standard forms, and arranging for each case to be allocated to one carefully defined aetiological or pathological category by a single assessor or team. An attempt was made to do this for three months in Great Britain in the British Perinatal Mortality Survey of 1958. The deaths were analysed according to two main classifications, one of pathological findings[4] and the other of factors that may initiate trains of events ending in death.[1] The second of these was of particular interest since it had already proved its value in the prevention of perinatal deaths (*see* pp. 735–736). It lists four "obstetrical causes" (categories of death which can often be prevented by high standards of obstetric care), and four "environmental causes" (which are less amenable to obstetric intervention but seem to respond to environmental influences). The eight categories and the death-rates ascribed to them in March–May 1958 are shown in Table 2.

Beyond the perinatal period, few deaths are due to disorders of late pregnancy and childbirth (Table 1). Malformations still account for substantial proportions of deaths, both in infants over one week and in older children; but deaths from infections are even commoner, especially between one week and one year when they account for nearly half the total. Accidents also increase in frequency after the first week, and cause nearly one-third of deaths between one and fifteen years. Apart from accidents and infections, neoplasms cause the most deaths during the latter period.

The last column of Table I shows how many children (including stillbirths) out of 1,000 born would die from each cause if they were to experience from late pregnancy to fifteen years the age-specific death-rates observed in 1969. The number of deaths from each cause which would occur before the first birthday in such a group was assumed to be the number of stillbirths and infant deaths per 1,000 total births in 1969; and the numbers in age-groups from one to fifteen years were estimated by multiplying the appropriate age-specific death-rates by the numbers of person-years that the 1,000 children would live while passing through these age-groups. Numbers of person-years were estimated from the Life Table published in the *Registrar-General's Annual Review*, which shows how many children out of 10,000 born alive would still be alive on each birthday to age five and on every fifth birthday thereafter.

With the 1969 rates, death before fifteen years would occur in approximately 37 per 1,000 total births, and three-fifths of these deaths would be perinatal. Nearly half the rest would occur after the end of the first year, when the average annual death-rate is many times lower than in infancy, but the period of exposure is fourteen times as long. Apart from the hazards of late pregnancy and childbirth and their effects, the commonest causes of death overall would be malformations, infections and accidents, in this order.

TABLE 2

ESTIMATED PERINATAL DEATH-RATES FROM VARIOUS CLINICO-PATHOLOGICAL CAUSES IN LEGITIMATE SINGLE BIRTHS—GREAT BRITAIN, MARCH–MAY 1958[1]

Cause	*Perinatal death-rate (per* 1,000 *total births)*
Obstetrical causes	
Toxaemia	4·0
Mechanical causes	4·2
Unexplained death in babies over 2,500 gm.	4·5
Serological incompatibility	1·4
Environmental causes	
Malformation	6·0
Antepartum haemorrhage without toxaemia	4·5
Unexplained death in babies of 2,500 gm. or less	5·7
Miscellaneous	1·6
Total	31·9

Mortality By Cause, Recent Trends

The contributions of different causes to the decline in mortality before fifteen years cannot be analysed comprehensively for England and Wales, since in these countries it is only since 1961 that cause has been among the particulars required when stillbirths are registered. In Scotland, however, this information has been collected and published since 1939, and from that time it is possible to estimate fairly closely the death-rates from the causes listed in Table 1, in spite of the changes in nomenclature and classification that have since occurred. The rates for 1939–41 and 1968–70 are compared in Table 3.

As in England and Wales, the death-rates between one week and fifteen years have declined much more than the perinatal rate. About two-thirds of these reductions, both at 1 week–1 year and beyond, were due to a decline in mortality from infections, which by 1968–70 had fallen to one-eighth of its 1939–41 level at 1 week–1 year, and to one-twentieth at 1–15 years. The rate for malformations, on the other hand, fell by little more than one-third in deaths before

TABLE 3

MORTALITY IN EARLY LIFE IN 1939–41 AND 1968–70—SCOTLAND

Causes of death	*Perinatal deaths* (*per* 1,000 *total births*)		*Infant deaths after one week* (*per* 1,000 *live births*)		*Deaths between* 1 *and* 15 *years* (*per* 1,000 *living, per year*)	
	1939–41	1968–70	1939–41	1968–70	1939–41	1968–70
Congenital anomalies	8·2	5·4	3·9	2·4	0·04	0·07
Complications of pregnancy and childbirth (including maternal, placental and cord conditions)	26·3	9·7	0·7	0·1	0·00	0·00
Anoxic and hypoxic conditions, immaturity	20·4	7·5	4·3	0·2	0·00	0·00
Infective and parasitic diseases, influenza, pneumonia, bronchitis	0·5	0·2	30·0	3·7	1·76	0·09
Neoplasms	0·0	0·0	0·1	0·1	0·04	0·07
Accidents, poisonings and violence	0·0	0·1	1·5	1·5	0·51	0·21
Miscellaneous and unknown	10·6	2·4	10·5	1·2	0·58	0·10
Total	66·0	25·3	50·8	9·3	2·93	0·54

one year, and apparently increased in older children—probably because of more with serious malformations surviving to this age. The causes of death that are commonest today—complications of late pregnancy and labour and their effects before one year, and accidents afterwards—showed reductions of between one-half and two-thirds. The real decline in deaths of obstetric origin may have been rather greater, since there were probably many such in the miscellaneous and unknown group (which showed a more marked decline).

Long-term Trends in Mortality By Cause

Although 1939 is the earliest year for which it is possible to include any of the fetal period when studying causes of death, cause has been recorded on death certificates (which do not, of course, apply to stillbirths) ever since their introduction in England and Wales, in 1838. Although the many changes in diagnostic accuracy, nomenclature and classification rule out a comprehensive analysis of the causes of child mortality over so long a period, most of the common infections of childhood were well-recognized by 1850. It has been shown that from this time meaningful comparisons are possible between the mortality rates ascribed in different periods to some at least of these conditions—intestinal infections, typhus, tuberculosis, scarlet fever and smallpox—which between them declined enough to be credited with the whole of the improvement in mortality at all ages during the next fifty years.[16] The mortality attributed to these and other common infections in children is shown in Fig. 3 for four evenly spaced three-year periods, from the middle and late nineteenth century, the last years before the introduction of chemotherapy, and the most recent years for which data are available.

Even these infections provide examples of changes in what are recognized as disease entities. Typhus and the enteric fevers are now listed separately in the mortality tables but formerly were not, whereas the reverse is true for

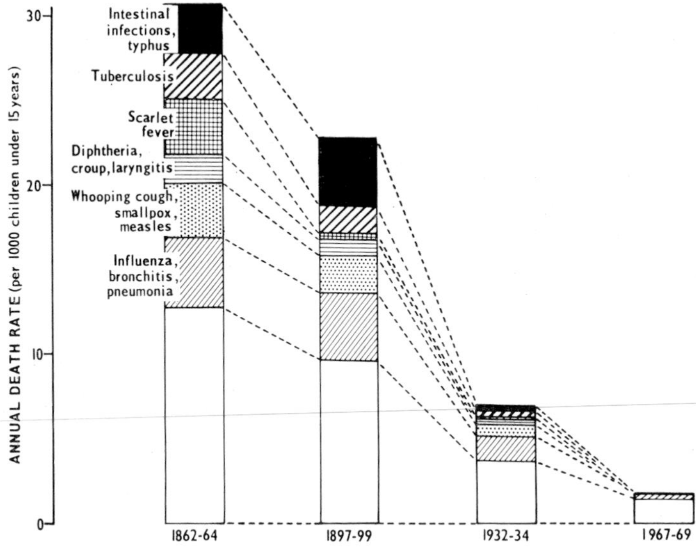

FIG. 3. Secular trend of child deaths from principal infections and other causes in England and Wales.

diarrhoea and enteritis. In the nineteenth century croup was certified in many deaths which today would probably be diagnosed as diphtheria or laryngitis. Influenza, pneumonia and bronchitis form another group of overlapping diagnoses. These diseases which have not always been clearly distinguished have been grouped in the figure, as have whooping-cough, smallpox and measles (which caused fewer deaths each than the other specific infections).

During the late nineteenth century, total mortality from the infections shown only fell in proportion to the rate from all causes: three-fifths of all deaths at both the beginning and the end of this period were attributed to them. The real reduction in infections may have been greater, since there are likely to have been more unrecognized cases of them among the deaths attributed to other and ill-defined causes in 1862–4 than in 1897–9. Scarlet fever accounted for more than half the decline in infections between these dates. Typhus, enteric fever, tuberculosis and smallpox also became less common, but more non-specific intestinal infections were reported.

The main reasons why mortality from some infections should have declined in the nineteenth century have been explored in some detail,[16] and are believed to have been a rising standard of living, and particularly of diet, in the case of tuberculosis; improved cleanliness and sanitation in the case of typhus and the enteric fevers; and the reduction of virulence by genetic changes in the causal organism in the case of scarlet fever. Among other factors which can reduce the frequency of infection, effective specific medical measures were not available at the time, with the exception of smallpox vaccination; and although smallpox virtually disappeared following the introduction of vaccination, this accounted for very little of the total decline in mortality. Genetic increases in human resistance would presumably have occurred if the growth of towns had increased the frequency of exposure to the infections and intensified selection pressure against susceptibility to them, but there is evidence that exposure was also frequent in earlier centuries.

During the present century the decline in total mortality has been much more marked, and all the infections shown have contributed disproportionately to this decline. The rate from all causes is now less than 8 per cent and the rate from infections less than 3 per cent of what it was 70 years ago. Most of this reduction occurred during the first third of the century, when the rate from infections fell by three-quarters. During the middle third it fell by eight-ninths, which although a greater relative decline did less than the earlier fall to reduce the absolute death-rate.

The improvement in the first third of the twentieth century, like that in the nineteenth, must have been largely independent of the introduction of specific medical measures, except for the decline in diphtheria mortality which was probably helped by the use of antitoxin. With this exception, specific agents only began to be used therapeutically in the late 1930s. Undoubtedly these advances have contributed substantially to the decline in mortality since 1935, and especially to the acceleration of this decline in the 1940s and 1950s, which as we have already seen was a feature of all age-groups over one week (Figs. 1 and 2), attributable largely to the infections (Table 3). But most of the decline in infant and child mortality occurred earlier in the century, when the main influences on mortality must have been those described for the nineteenth century, perhaps augmented by the general preventive measures embodied in the school health and maternity and child welfare services.

Epidemiological studies of the causation of perinatal problems (summarized on pp. 728–736) indicate that the decline in perinatal mortality, although largely unrelated to infection, has also resulted from a combination of better living conditions and advances in preventive and curative medicine.

International Differences in Mortality

The susceptibility of child mortality to such varied aspects of the quality of life as nutrition, cleanliness, sanitation and the preventive and curative medical services has led to its widespread use as an index for comparing the overall living standards of different countries. Alternatively, when a country's child mortality is out of line with other measures of national development such as the Gross National Product per head, it may be possible to attribute the excess or deficiency to one particular disease. If so, the country or countries with the higher rate may be able to find ways of controlling the disease by determining why the rate elsewhere is lower.

The main limitations on comparisons like these are two that have already been encountered in studying how mortality in Britain has changed. Firstly, in many countries, especially those in the early stages of development, either the registration of stillbirths, and sometimes even deaths, is not required, or the requirement is often ignored, or there are no known population totals to which the deaths can be related. Secondly, although most countries where cause of death is registered use the *I.C.D.*, there are gross international differences in diagnostic accuracy and nomenclature which can affect the categories under which deaths are enumerated. Many countries have so few doctors that the registration of deaths by laymen is permitted and usual, and many of these deaths are classified as of unknown cause.

Both problems are greatest where perinatal deaths are concerned. In many countries, no fetal deaths are registrable; in others, including Great Britain, registration only applies beyond a certain gestational age, which differs according to country; and a few countries have no age limit. Causes of fetal deaths are recorded in some but not all the countries which register them. Fetal deaths apart, the deaths most often missed in countries where registration is incomplete are those occurring shortly after birth.

For these reasons, the only international comparisons to be illustrated here concern mortality from all causes after the perinatal period in fifteen countries, and mortality by cause (including the perinatal period) for four. The countries chosen along with England and Wales to show mortality by cause are the only three outside the United Kingdom for which data for fetal deaths after twenty-eight weeks as well as for live-born children are readily available. The fifteen for which mortality from all causes is shown are these four countries and the eleven other most populous countries for which overall figures are available. The figures are taken from the *Demographic Yearbook* of the United Nations and the *World Health Statistics Annual* and monthly *Epidemiological and Vital Statistics Report* of the World Health Organization.

Mortality from all Causes by Country

Mortality from all causes in the fifteen countries is shown in Fig. 4 for infants over one week, and in Fig. 5 for children between one and fifteen years old. Both rates are plotted against United Nations estimates of Gross National Product per head to show the close correlation between mortality (especially in infancy) and national development. Each rate varies approximately twenty-fold between the countries shown, and the range if data for the poorest countries were available would probably be two or three times as great. Perinatal death-rates, to judge from those of countries where statistics are thought to be reliable, are probably less variable. In 1967 the perinatal death-rate for the United Kingdom was 25·8/1,000 total births. The highest perinatal death-rate that was claimed to be reliable was 67·2/1,000 in Mauritius, and the lowest were 19·5 in Denmark and 19·6 in Bulgaria. The latter figure is somewhat surprising, since Gross National Product per head for Bulgaria is estimated to be about two-fifths that of the United Kingdom and one-third that of Denmark. Death-rates like this which do not accord with national wealth are, if genuine, perhaps the most likely to yield information that might be used in prevention. Other findings of this kind are the relatively low rate between one week and one year for the Netherlands, and the high rates for Canada and the United States relative to the United Kingdom, especially after one year.

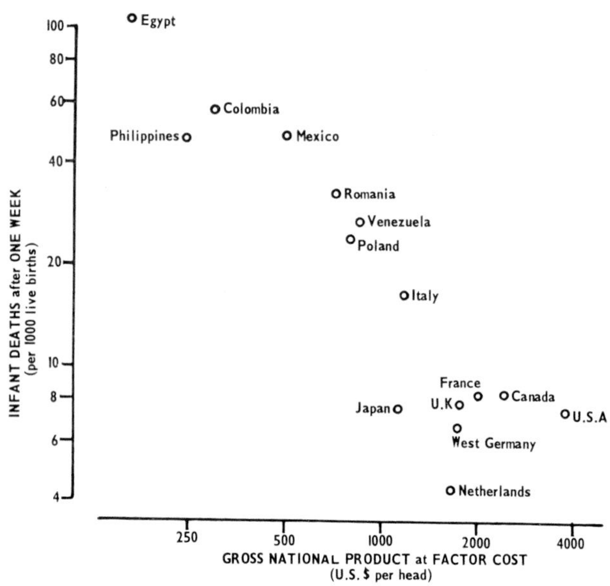

FIG. 4. Estimates of infant mortality after one week and Gross National Product per head for 15 countries during 1967.

Mortality by Cause and Country

The figures for Canada, the Netherlands and England and Wales are analysed by cause in Fig. 6, together with data from Venezuela which show—although not in their extreme form—some ways in which the poorer countries differ from the rich. The same groups of causes have been used as in Tables 1 and 3, except that the miscellaneous causes have been divided into known and ill-defined, and where any group accounted for less than 0·4 perinatal or later infant deaths/1,000 births it has been merged with the miscellaneous defined causes.

The most striking contrasts shown are the much higher rates attributed to infections and deaths of ill-defined or unknown cause in Venezuela than in the other countries. Also, fewer deaths there than elsewhere were attributed to anomalies, but on these data alone one cannot exclude the possibility that this deficiency arose because some children's defects were missed.

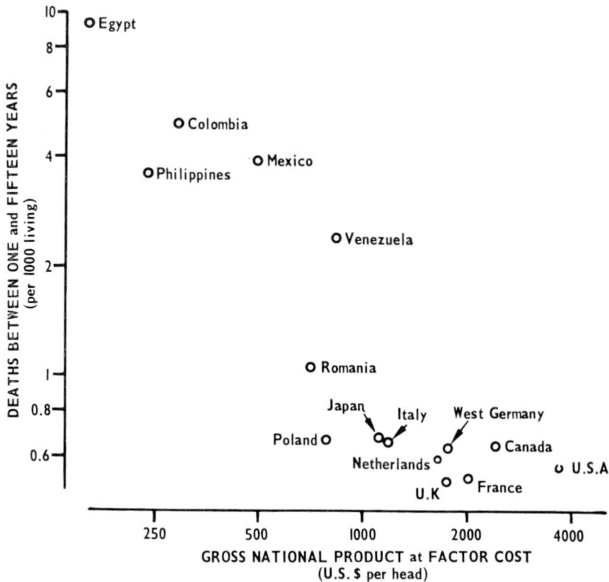

FIG. 5. Estimates of child mortality and Gross National Product per head for 15 countries during 1967.

Among the three developed countries, the mortality from problems arising in late pregnancy and labour was lowest in the Netherlands, which as a result had the lowest perinatal death-rate. Also, as already noted, the Netherlands had an unusually low death-rate during the rest of infancy, which occurred largely because there were very few deaths from infections. The rates for Canada between one week and fifteen years were apparently high because accidental death was more common there. England and Wales had a higher perinatal death-rate from all causes, and from malformations, than the other two developed countries, but a lower 1–15 year death-rate from all causes, especially accidents.

As all these differences between the mortality from specific causes in the three countries were reflected in their overall death-rates, they are likely to be genuine and to repay further

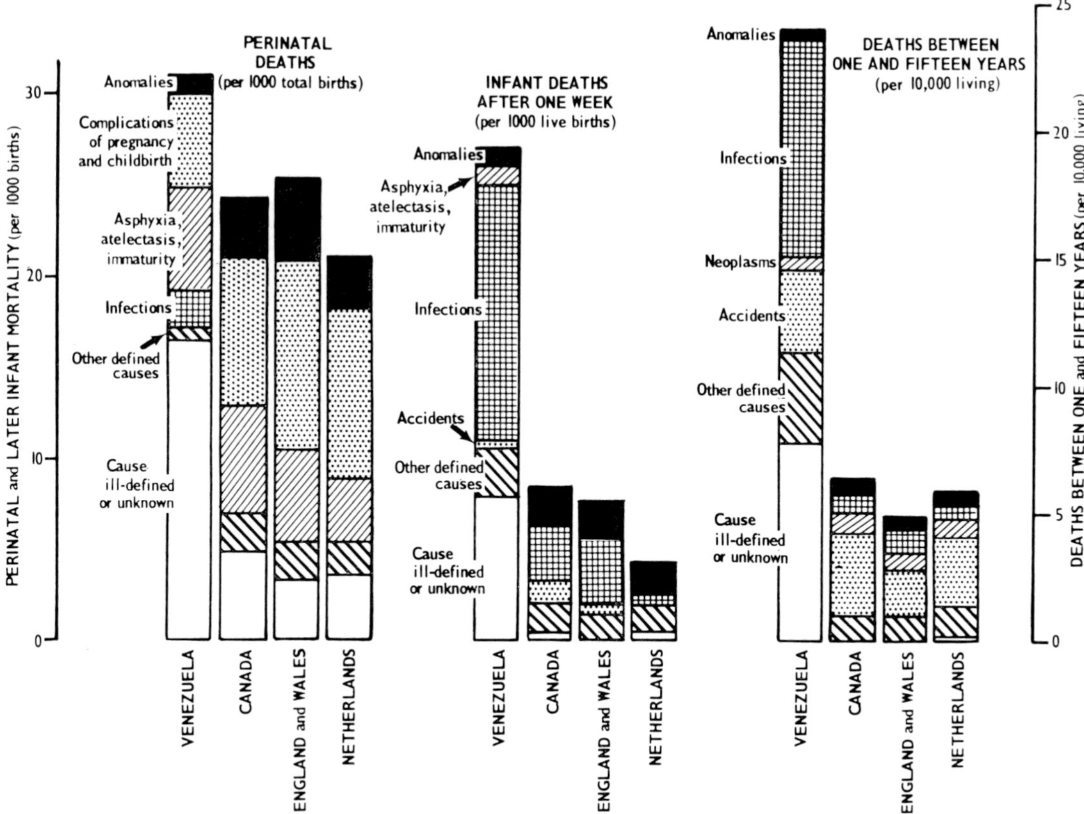

FIG. 6. Principal causes of death in early life in four countries during 1967.

study. For example, if the circumstances which have produced such a low death-rate from infection in the Netherlands could be identified, it might be possible to reduce the rate in other countries by simulating these circumstances there.

MORBIDITY STATISTICS

The mortality differences that have now been described show that the pattern of disease facing the European or North American paediatrician today is very different from that encountered in other countries and centuries. The acute infections, which once dwarfed all other problems because of the many deaths they caused, have shrunk enormously in importance: although some are still common they now only cause death very rarely, and seldom have other lasting effects. Their place as the foremost paediatric problems has been taken by disorders of growth and development, such as those that cause or are caused by malformations, intrauterine growth retardation, short gestation and neoplasms. Many of those affected survive childhood and may make frequent demands on the medical services in the process, not only to stay alive but also to minimize their handicaps. To assess the magnitude of these problems, morbidity as well as mortality data are needed.

It is, however, even more difficult to interpret morbidity than mortality data, for at least three reasons. The first is that the borderline between health and illness is much less objective than between life and death, so that an arbitrary definition of illness has sometimes to be used in deciding what to count. Secondly, diagnostic standards vary even more in the illnesses which patients survive than in those when they die, since in the living the pathological changes are generally less extreme and cannot be inspected as they can at necropsy, and especially when an illness is minor many other aids to diagnosis are also likely to be omitted. Thirdly, morbidity can be summarized statistically in more ways than mortality, since illness, unlike death, has duration, and can happen more than once to the same individual.

In the absence of a sharp dividing-line between health and sickness, two methods of identifying cases of disease have been used in studies of morbidity. One method is to restrict attention to patients making demands on the health and social services or some part of them—e.g. patients consulting their general practitioners, or attending hospital, on account of the disease in question. The other method is to screen everyone in a population, and then either to classify as diseased all those who satisfy certain criteria (e.g. a perforated eardrum), or, if the abnormalities under investigation are extreme values of a quantitative variable (e.g. birth weight), to study how the population is distributed over the whole range of the variable.

These methods of obtaining data are discussed in turn below. The principal methods of summarizing morbidity data statistically are introduced in relation to hospital in-patient statistics, the first example of morbidity data to be discussed.

Studies of Health Service Contacts

The use of health service contacts in the measurement of frequency has two main advantages over screening: economy and simplicity. If diagnostic data on patients using medical services are available or can be collected, it is generally very much more economical to use them than to screen the entire population *de novo*, especially if the disease being studied is rare. It is also simplest for the investigator if he does not have to apply diagnostic criteria of his own but can accept as cases those in whom the relevant disease has been diagnosed on seeking medical attention.

The disadvantages of the method are that some patients in whom the diagnosis is not based on acceptable criteria may be included, and many more in whom it would be acceptable may be missed. Some patients are likely to be incorrectly included or excluded because of misdiagnosis. A greater number will usually be missed because of patients not making use of the agencies from which data are being collected, or because of agencies omitting to complete the records from which cases are ascertained. For example, the frequency of many infectious diseases has long been kept under surveillance in this country by asking doctors to notify every case they attend, but it is well known that some of the resulting figures are underestimates, partly because some cases are not attended by a doctor and also because doctors often fail to notify cases they have attended.

Two examples will be used to illustrate the information yielded by data on health service contacts by children: hospital discharges analysed by cause (illustrating various commonly used statistical indices of morbidity), and cancer incidence statistics (illustrating some sources of error in health service contact data).

Hospital Discharges by Cause

Although general practitioners are involved in the notification of infectious disease, the only contacts of children with the health services for which data are collected and published (in England and Wales) regardless of diagnosis are spells (or periods) in hospital. For many years the Registrar-General's office (now the Office of Population Censuses and Surveys) has conducted the Hospital In-Patient Enquiry, or H.I.P.E., which is based on summaries that hospitals are asked to complete in respect of every tenth hospital in-patient discharge or death (except in psychiatric wards and hospitals). In fact, the proportion of these deaths and discharges for which forms are completed is rather less—9·09 per cent in 1968 (the most recent year for which data are available). The forms are analysed by various attributes including diagnosis, age, sex and length of stay in hospital, and the resulting figures are multiplied by a constant (11·001 in 1968) to obtain estimates for the whole population. Some of the findings are published in an annual *Report on the Hospital In-Patient Enquiry*, which includes one table relating exclusively to children under fifteen years. The information about the frequency of childhood disease given by this table for 1968 is summarized in Table 4.

TABLE 4

PRINCIPAL CAUSES OF HOSPITAL ADMISSION AT 0–15 YEARS: ENGLAND AND WALES, 1968

I.C.D. Nos.	*Causes of admission*	*Deaths and discharges per 1,000 living*	*Average number of beds used daily per 1,000,000 living*
000–136	Infective and parasitic diseases	4·2	156
140–239	Neoplasms	1·0	27
	Diseases of respiratory system:		
460–492	Acute respiratory infections, influenza, pneumonia, bronchitis, emphysema	6·5	124
500	Hypertrophy of tonsils and adenoids	10·2	106
493, 501–519	Other respiratory diseases	2·8	63
520–577	Diseases of digestive system	6·6	121
710–738	Diseases of musculo-skeletal system and connective tissue	1·3	93
740–759	Congenital anomalies	4·8	190
760–779	Perinatal causes	4·0	156
780–796	Symptoms and ill-defined conditions	5·4	92
800–999	Accidents, poisonings and violence	11·0	201
All other	Other causes	14·0	343
	Total	71·8	1,672

The two columns of figures in Table 4 illustrate two of the main methods of analysing morbidity data. The first column gives the number of deaths and discharges in different disease categories per 1,000 living per year. Such numbers measure the frequency of a kind of *event* (discharge from hospital) over a *period* of time. The second column gives the average numbers of hospital beds used daily per 1,000,000 living. These numbers measure the frequency of a kind of *state* (the state of being a hospital in-patient) at an average *point* in time. In the measurement of disease frequency, both approaches are often applied. The type of *event* most commonly enumerated is the onset of a disease, the frequency of which is called its *attack rate*, *inception rate* or *incidence rate* (usually abbreviated to incidence). The frequency of the *state* of suffering from a disease is called its *prevalence*.

Measures of the "Incidence" of Hospitalization

The concept behind incidence, that of measuring the frequency of events, is also illustrated by the mortality statistics described earlier. But discharges from hospital, like most of the other non-fatal events that may be enumerated when studying morbidity, are more complicated than deaths to study because they can happen more than once to the same person. A single case of leukaemia or cleft lip and palate may appear several times in the discharge statistics, so that even the frequency of conditions like these for which hospital admission is almost universal cannot be inferred from the number of hospital discharges ascribed to them. To measure the frequency of onset of such a condition, clearly only one of each child's admissions must be counted, which could only be done using H.I.P.E. data if first admissions were enumerated separately. As they are not, our best sources of information about the numbers of children admitted to hospital (as opposed to numbers of individual admissions) are perhaps surveys in which parents have been asked whether their children have been in hospital for various conditions. Table 5 shows the results obtained in a

TABLE 5

SEVEN-YEAR-OLD CHILDREN WITH A HISTORY OF HOSPITAL ADMISSION[26]

Reasons for hospital admission	*Proportion of cohort admitted* (%)
Tonsils, adenoids	15·5
Abdominal operation	1·4
Repair of hernia	1·9
Other operation (including transfusion)	6·2
Road accident	2·3
Home accident (including burns, scalds, poisoning, injury)	9·3
Other accident or injury	8·3
Illness, investigations or tests	11.7
Other reasons	4·7

survey of this kind which was carried out in the course of the National Child Development Study.[5,26] In this Study an attempt is being made to follow-up every child in Great Britain who was born on March 3–9, 1958. The figures shown relate to 7,985 of these children (all of them single births) for whom the results of a seven-year follow-up by Local Authorities in England and Wales had been received by mid-August, 1965.

When describing such figures, which show the proportion of *individuals* who had experiences of a certain kind, the description should be qualified by the word "persons", and the word "spells" may be used in the same way when describing figures based on the number of *experiences* themselves. The figures in Table 5 could be described as "seven-year hospital admission rates (persons)", and those in the first numerical column of Table 4 as "annual hospital discharge rates (spells)".

Both these sets of figures show the predominance of accidents and of tonsil and adenoid surgery as causes of hospital admission in childhood. But the two sets cannot be compared in detail since they do not cover the same age-range, and one is analysed by medical diagnosis and the other by parents' assessment of the type of care given. Also, one table relates to admissions and the other to discharges—but this difference is more apparent than real, since discharges closely reflect admissions and are documented in preference to them only because it is easier and enables data on final diagnosis, surgery, length of stay and outcome to be included.

Measures of the "Prevalence" of Hospitalization

The average proportion of people who are in any given state such as being diseased or in hospital at a point in time depends on the incidence and the mean duration of the state. If, for example (as happened in 1968), the "incidence" of hospital admission for hypertrophy of tonsils and adenoids was 10,200 per million per year and the average time spent in hospital by those admitted was 3·8 days, the number of days spent in hospital would be 10,200 × 3·8 or 38,760 person-days for every million children in the population. These person-days would be distributed over the 366 days of 1968, so that the average number current on any one day, or average number of hospital beds occupied by this group of patients, would be 36,760 ÷ 366, or 106, per million. The equation may be written algebraically as:

$$p = \frac{in}{d},$$

where p is the average prevalence of the state at a point in time (sometimes known as average *point prevalence*), i is the incidence in a population of standard size (such as one million) during a period of length d days, and n is the mean number of days for which the state lasted in each person in whom it arose.

The prevalence of a state at a point in time is known as "point prevalence" to distinguish it from "period prevalence (persons)" and "period prevalence (spells)". The *period prevalence (persons)* is the number of persons in a standard population who were affected at any time during a defined period. The *period prevalence (spells)* is the number of spells of being affected that were current during any of this time, and is therefore greater than period prevalence (persons) for conditions which may recur. It may be obtained by adding the number of times the conditions arose in the standard population during the period (the incidence) to the number of members of the population who were affected at the time the period began (the point prevalence at that time).

Results and Interpretation of the Hospital In-Patient Enquiry

Neither kind of period prevalence is as useful as point prevalence and incidence for measuring frequency, and the latter two kinds of measures should not be used indiscriminately. Diseases which have the same incidence can differ widely in prevalence, and vice versa, if the duration of one is generally long and the other short. These differences can be illustrated from Table 4. The disease groups listed there are all those to which more than 5 per cent of either discharges or occupied beds were ascribed, except for neoplasms, which are shown separately because of their importance as causes of death although they account for a relatively small proportion of hospital practice. Among the groups listed, hypertrophy of tonsils and adenoids is credited with twice as high a proportion of discharges as of beds, and the reverse is true for diseases of the musculoskeletal system and connective tissue. Accidents come first whichever measure of frequency is used, but are followed by hypertrophy of tonsils and adenoids, respiratory infections and digestive diseases (mainly hernia and appendicitis) in the discharge statistics, and by congenital anomalies, perinatal causes, and infective and parasitic diseases in the figures for bed occupancy.

Prevalence or bed occupancy statistics are more useful than incidence or discharge rates for health service planning, since they reflect the burdens imposed by different diseases on the service and are a guide to the scale on which hospital treatment for each must be made available. Their main limitation for this purpose is that they are biassed in favour of what is currently available. The proportion of children admitted to hospital for adenotonsillectomy is probably affected more by the number of Ear, Nose and Throat consultants and beds in hospital than by the frequency of severe disorders of the tonsils and adenoids.

Incidence rates are of more value than prevalence for studying the causation and prevention of disease. Prevalence is affected by the duration of disease, and therefore by the proportion of patients with the disease who die from it (*case fatality*) and the rapidity of death or recovery, all of which may vary with treatment and other events after the onset of the disease. The incidence of a disease, on the other hand, can only be affected by the factors that influence its development up to the time that it comes to notice. It is, therefore, by the study of incidence that these causal factors are most likely to be identified, and perhaps prevented. But as already indicated, hospital discharge rates (spells) like those shown in Table 4 are not accurate as measures of the incidence rates of the diseases concerned, since they exclude patients not admitted to hospital and include readmissions.

Cancer Incidence

Most of the common disorders of child growth and development—malformations, immaturity, fetal growth retardation, and mental handicap—cannot be identified from hospital statistics in all cases: the mentally handicapped because they are often cared for outside, and the others because some die before they can be admitted to hospital, or are never enumerated as patients in their own right if they are born there. But for malignant neoplasms, one might think that hospital admission would be almost universal and could be made a basis for studies of incidence.

To exploit this possibility, various countries and smaller administrative areas have established cancer registries, to which hospitals are asked to notify the name, address, sex and age of every affected patient, the site and histology of his neoplasm, the date of first hospital attendance, admission or treatment, and sometimes other data. At the registry, each new notification is checked against a register of malignancies already notified, and registered if the case is not found to have been notified before.

The whole of England and Wales is split up between registries run by the Regional Hospital Boards and co-ordinated by the Office of Population Censuses and Surveys, which analyses all the data. The most recent of these data to have been published[12] were for registrations of patients who started treatment in 1963–6, and the Seventh Revision of the *I.C.D.* (which went out of use at the end of 1967) was therefore used to classify them. Figures are, however, available for those who started treatment in 1968, who have been classified according to the current, Eighth Revision. The first column of rates in Table 6 contains estimates of incidence in childhood based on these figures. Benign neoplasms of the central nervous system, pineal, and pituitary, are included because the English registration scheme covers them as well as all malignancies.

TABLE 6

ESTIMATES OF THE FREQUENCY OF NEOPLASMS IN CHILDREN UNDER 15 YEARS

I.C.D. Nos.	*Category of neoplasm*	*Annual incidence per million living:* *England and Wales*, 1968*	*Annual incidence per million living:* *Manchester Hospital Region* 1956–68[31]	*Annual mortality per million living: England and Wales*, 1968*
	Registrable neoplasms (malignant, or arising in the central nervous system, pineal or pituitary)			
170	Bone	4·9	4·9	2·7
171	Connective tissue	3·8	6·1	0·9
189	Kidney	7·6	5·5	4·7
190	Eye	3·1	3·3	0·3
191; 225.0; 238.1	Brain	20·0	18·5 (17·5 malignant)	21·5† (8·8 malignant of brain; 8·0 other malignant) [Brain and Other parts of nervous system combined]
192; 225.1–4, 9; 238.2–5, 9	Other parts of nervous system	7·3	8·8 (8·5 malignant)	
200	Lymphosarcoma, reticulosarcoma	6·0	3·4	5·3
201	Hodgkin's disease	3·2	3·3	0·9
204–207	Leukaemia	26·6	31·4	33·1
Rest of 140–209; 226.2, 3; 239.1 (part)	Miscellaneous	13·8	6·7 (4·9 malignant)	6·7† (6·0 malignant)
All above	Total registrable neoplasms	96·3	91·8 (88·7 malignant)	76·0 (70·7 malignant)
Rest of 210–239	Non-registrable neoplasms	—	10·1	2·8

* Prepared from preliminary tables supplied by the Office of Population Censuses and Surveys, and age-standardized to the average population of the Manchester Region in 1956–68.

† All deaths classified to I.C.D. Nos. 238 and 226 are included under "Brain" and "Miscellaneous" respectively.

Unfortunately these figures cannot be regarded as accurate estimates of incidence in 1968, for various reasons. Firstly, they do not relate specifically to malignancies in which the clinical onset was in 1968, but to those which were first treated then, including some that became apparent in earlier years, and excluding those that appeared in 1968 but were first treated later. Secondly, and more serious, the figures can be shown to suffer from all the defects that have already been mentioned in relation to studies of health service contacts generally: misdiagnosis, and the exclusion of some cases either because the agency that should have notified them (in this instance a hospital) has failed to do so or because they have not been to any such agency.

The Problem of Misdiagnosis

The occurrence of misdiagnosis can be illustrated by comparing routine cancer registry data with the records of the Children's Tumour Registry associated with Manchester University.[20,30] These records deal with the malignant and benign tumours that have arisen since 1954 in children from the Manchester Hospital Region. The treatment of children's tumours in this Region has been largely centralized in a few units, which have close links with the Children's Tumour Registry, so that it is considerably easier for this Registry to ensure that most cases are notified than it is for the average cancer registry of a Regional Hospital Board. Also, the hospital records and histological preparations of most cases notified to the Children's Tumour Registry are reviewed by an expert panel, so that diagnostic accuracy is much greater than in most other registries, which have to rely on diagnostic data abstracted by hospital clerks.

The incidence in 1956–68 of tumours known to the Children's Tumour Registry is shown alongside the 1968 national rates (which have been age-standardized to make them comparable to the Manchester figures) in Table 6. In both series, by far the commonest conditions were leukaemia and tumours of the brain, which accounted for one-third and one-fifth respectively of the registrable neoplasms in the Manchester series.

The biggest differences between the two series are the excesses for connective tissue tumours and leukaemia, and the deficiencies for kidney and miscellaneous tumours and lymphosarcoma, in the Manchester series relative to the national one. The net effect of these differences is to make the Manchester rate for all registrable neoplasms rather lower than the national figure.

Evidence that these differences are to a considerable extent diagnostic in origin has been obtained by comparing the Children's Tumour Registry diagnoses of cases first treated in 1968 with the categories to which they were allocated when notified routinely to the all-age cancer registry of the Regional Hospital Board. Out of ninety-six registrations for which data from both sources were available, the Children's Tumour Registry showed that the all-age cancer registry had registered six that should have been excluded and allocated nine others to the wrong category. It seems reasonable to assume that the national figures in Table 6 are similarly distorted. Apart from the deficiency of leukaemia cases in the national statistics (discussed below), the differences from the Children's Tumour Registry rates that remain after allowing for 6 per cent of national registrations being unacceptable seem likely to be due mainly to some tumours of connective tissue, and of the nervous system apart from the brain (e.g. neuro-blastomas), being classed as kidney and miscellaneous tumours and lymphosarcoma in the national statistics.

In spite of the disturbing effect which diagnostic errors may have on estimates of incidence (and indeed on the death-rates ascribed to different causes), these errors cannot always be eliminated, and it is sometimes necessary to examine data affected by them for variations in incidence when studying aetiology. At the outset of such studies, it is important to consider what effects these and other errors may have on apparent incidence.

The Problem of Deficient Notification

The evidence that some cases of childhood cancer are not notified at all to cancer registries is strongest in the case of leukaemia. Inspection of the age-standardized death-rates for tumours in England and Wales (given in the last column of Table 6) shows that the death-rate from leukaemia was nearly a quarter higher than the incidence reported nationally. As incidence has not declined sharply in recent years, this finding can only indicate that a substantial proportion of leukaemic children are not notified to the cancer registries. This failure to notify is probably a more important reason than diagnostic differences for the deficiency in the incidence of leukaemia reported nationally relative to the Manchester incidence. A genuine difference in incidence may however be responsible for the latter rate being lower than the national *death-rate* from leukaemia, since the death-rate in the Manchester region was lower still (28 per million in 1968).

In contrast to leukaemia, the other tumours listed have national death-rates which are lower than the national incidence rates. It may be concluded that the cancer registration data from which these incidence rates are derived are less useful than mortality data for estimating the frequency of childhood leukaemia in different groups, but preferable for studying other neoplasms. But failure to notify is certainly not confined to leukaemia, and its possible effects must always be borne in mind when using cancer registration data.

The procedure known as Hospital Activity Analysis (H.A.A.), which is being progressively introduced throughout England and Wales, should eventually make it easier to identify cancer patients treated in hospital, and also to collect reliable data on all hospital in-patients. Under this procedure, many of the diagnostic and other data which hospitals have been asked to record on one-tenth of their patients for H.I.P.E., will be abstracted and processed routinely for all cases. As the procedure is routine it is less likely to be overlooked than cancer registration and H.I.P.E. documentation, which as they concern only relatively small minorities of patients can sometimes get forgotten.

Studies Based on Screening

Apart from deaths, hospital admissions are the only health service contacts for which data on the frequency of each diagnosis are published routinely. For a picture of morbidity in childhood that is not confined to such contacts, it is generally necessary to use data obtained by screening whole populations, either as a routine or in special surveys. Routine screening of all or nearly all the child population can be said to take place at birth, when clinical notes are always made by medical or nursing attendants, and again at the school medical examinations at the beginning and end of school life and the test of intellectual ability at ten years to which most English children have in the past been subjected. The conditions on which useful information about frequency can be obtained from these routine sources are mostly quantitative variables like weight and intelligence quotient, and lasting disabilities such as malformations and impaired hearing. To study the frequency of temporary disorders such as infections, special surveys are generally needed.

The fact that data obtained by screening are not limited to the recipients of medical care, and may even include details of disorders previously unknown to anyone, is not their only advantage over health service contact data where studies of disease frequency are concerned. Another asset is that screening data cover not only the affected individuals but also the population from which they are drawn. Given such data, the incidence or prevalence of the condition under study can be computed not only in the population as a whole but also in groups within it, and if the condition involves a quantitative variable such as birth weight the distribution of the population over the whole range of this variable can be analysed. But screening as well as health service contact statistics can be distorted by misdiagnosis, by inadequate reporting, and by some individuals not undergoing the procedure (screening or health-service contact) which generates the data.

The problem of misdiagnosis has perhaps received most attention in connection with the use of simple tests as screening procedures for the presymptomatic detection of disorders such as phenylketonuria in which the aim is to start treatment as early as possible. In recent years, it has been widely accepted that before any such screening procedure is introduced routinely it must be rigorously evaluated from many aspects, including the diagnostic accuracy of the test proposed.[17] Two indices of diagnostic accuracy are used—*specificity*, which is the proportion of individuals with a positive test result who have the relevant disorder, and *sensitivity*, which is the proportion of individuals with the disorder whose test result is positive. When a choice has to be made between tests, more importance is generally attached to sensitivity than to specificity: if a sensitive but not highly specific test is used, further tests must be done to eliminate false positives, but if the screening procedure is justified at all, the resources needed for further testing and the personal hardship this may cause are likely to be much less than would be involved subsequently if a less sensitive test were used and some presymptomatic cases were not diagnosed till later. For example, in screening for phenylketonuria the ferric chloride test for phenylpyruvic acid in urine, which is seldom if ever positive in the normal but may miss 25–50 per cent of cases, has been largely replaced by the Guthrie test for phenylalanine in blood, which seems to miss fewer cases but is less specific, since children without phenylketonuria sometimes have transient phenylalaninaemia.[33] But the considerations that make incomplete specificity matter less than incomplete sensitivity when screening is carried out as a service do not apply, of course, when data obtained by screening are used for research: the diagnosing of defects in children who have none distorts incidence and prevalence just as much as the reverse.

The other sources of inaccuracy in data obtained by screening are inadequate reporting and incompleteness of the population. Inadequate reporting arises mainly under the circumstances already described in connection with data on health service contacts, when the presence of an abnormality has to be notified by completing a record or section of a record that is not otherwise used. An example is the notification of malformations, which doctors and midwives in England and Wales are asked to do by adding particulars of any they observe to the form of notification of birth which is filled in for all infants and sent to the local Medical Officer of Health.

Finally, almost every screening procedure misses some people altogether. Most routine procedures, such as the school medical examinations and tests of intellectual performance, exclude children not at school because of subnormality and some in independent schools. In special surveys, some of those who should be included usually cannot be traced and others refuse to co-operate. The proportion of those intended for inclusion who actually take part is known as the *response rate*. What should be regarded as adequate coverage of the study population varies according to the frequency of the condition being studied, the extent to which frequency is likely to vary between non-respondents and respondents, and the ways in which the data are to be analysed. For most purposes, a 90 per cent response rate is acceptable, and one often has to do the best one can with less.

Malformations are probably the most important group of childhood disorders for which routine screening has been the leading source of information about frequency, and the overall pattern of morbidity in childhood has been studied particularly extensively by special surveys. Birth weight is an example of a quantitative variable which has been much studied over its whole range, by both methods. Because of their intrinsic interest and as examples of the different approaches, all these subjects will be discussed.

Incidence of Malformations

The primary source of data in most studies of the frequency of malformation has been the routine clinical examination of the newborn. Properly used, the results of this examination can provide most valuable information about frequency; but they are highly susceptible to all the errors that have been mentioned—misdiagnosis, inadequate reporting, and failure to screen the whole population.

Diagnostic Difficulties

The most common form of misdiagnosis at birth is not recognizing genuine defects, but the opposite error of diagnosing defects which are not present also occurs. Both errors seem to arise particularly often in relation to congenital heart disease; for example, in one series from Birmingham, England, for 199 children in whom an unequivocal diagnosis of this kind was made shortly after birth and not withdrawn later ("true positives") there were 12 "false positives" in whom such a diagnosis was made initially and later proved incorrect, and 201 "false negatives" whose condition was not diagnosed at first although it became manifest during follow-up.[14] One source of discrepancies, not only like these between findings at different ages, but also between estimates of incidence from different centres, is that health workers vary in what they regard as significant deviations from the normal—in the positioning of the newborn's feet, for example—and in the extent to which they examine patients, including their use of aids to diagnosis such as radiography and necropsy.

Although it is impracticable to enforce consistency on others in these matters, the problem of misdiagnosis as a whole can be much reduced by arranging for all children in the study population to be followed-up in some way, and by making special enquiries when there is reason to question a diagnosis (e.g. if an infant in whom *spina bifida* has been reported does not die or enter hospital).

Inadequate Reporting

Inadequate reporting of malformations observed on examination is most apparent on statutory notifications of births and in material abstracted retrospectively from hospital records. Both in England and Wales and in most of the United States, the statutory forms on which births are notified by doctors and midwives include a space for recording malformations, which is, however, often left blank even when a malformation has been diagnosed. In England and Wales, even anencephaly, the most striking of all common malformations, was found not to appear on the birth notifications of one-quarter of those whose stillbirth or death certificates referred to it,[32] and in the United States it seems to be generally the case that only a minority of the malformations mentioned in the hospital notes of newborn children are recorded on their birth notifications.[18]

Although hospital notes are more reliable than birth notifications, and although more estimates of the frequency of malformation have probably been obtained by abstracting such notes retrospectively than in any other way, even this method is by no means a complete safeguard against inadequate recording. Among estimates obtained in this way, those based on hundreds of thousands of births tend to be much lower than those for populations of ten or twenty thousand.[13] This finding probably reflects variations in the completeness both of the original case notes and of the abstracts, since in the more extensive studies less care is likely to have been taken both in selecting hospitals and in abstracting their records.

It is more satisfactory to collect data prospectively, by arranging for specially designed forms to be completed by the hospital staff or domiciliary midwife when the child leaves their care, preferably for every infant but at least for the malformed, in a community which is compact enough for the investigators to promote accurate filling-in of the forms by personal contact with those responsible.

Incomplete Coverage of the Population

Practically all studies of malformation are based on incomplete coverage of the population in that they do not include very early deaths—abortions and sometimes stillbirths—and many exclude domiciliary births also. The exclusion of abortions and stillbirths makes the frequency of defects appear lower than if all conceptions were covered. Some indication of the extent of the difference is given by recent data on late embryos and early fetuses from pregnancies interrupted artificially.[23] These, which are probably fairly representative of all embryos and fetuses of like age, seem to be affected by severe defects of the central nervous system and mouth several times as often as infants (including stillbirths) born in late pregnancy, from which it may be inferred that most of those affected are aborted spontaneously before then. Studies of spontaneous abortions suggest that the same is true of embryos with chromosomal anomalies.[6]

The exclusion of domiciliary births from studies of frequency tends to inflate the estimates obtained, since some malformations produce obstetrical problems such as hydramnios which can lead to women being delivered in hospital who would otherwise have stayed at home. The effect can be ignored where hospital delivery is almost universal (as in most of the United States) and is becoming less marked in the United Kingdom as this state of affairs is approached; but in, for example, a population in which 61 per cent of births occurred in hospital (Birmingham, England, in 1950–9), malformations were reported in the newborn period in 2·3 per cent of children born in hospital and only 1·9 per cent of the total population.[14]

Studies with Minimal Errors

Although it is not generally practicable to include abortions in studies of the incidence of malformations, there have been several studies of incidence in which attempts have been made to avoid most of the other errors mentioned, by collecting data prospectively on all newborn infants in a community (including stillbirths and domiciliary births) and then following them up. Some results of three such studies which included enough births to yield fairly reliable figures for specific defects are summarized in Table 7.

Neonatal data were collected on special forms for the malformed alone in one of these studies, in Liverpool, and for the normal as well in the other two, in Japan and Birmingham. Follow-up data were obtained in the Japanese study by medical examination of a sample of about 30 per cent of the children at nine months, whereas the English children were followed-up through their contacts with hospitals and some community health services in the early years of life. Information about such contacts was obtained in Liverpool mainly by asking hospital and local health department staff to complete special forms when they saw malformed children, and in Birmingham by checking stillbirth and death registers and the records of local hospital admissions, necropsies, and action taken when children had handicaps which might affect their education.

Although malformations were reported in about one fortieth of each population, the incidence of most individual

TABLE 7

INCIDENCE OF MALFORMATIONS ASCERTAINED FROM MULTIPLE SOURCES

I.C.D. Nos.	*Types of malformations*	*Incidence (per 1,000 total births)*		
		Hiroshima, Nagasaki and Kure, Japan, 1948–54[22]	*Birmingham, England* 1950–54[14]	*Liverpool and Bootle, England* 1960–64[29]
740	Anencephaly	0·6	2·0	3·1
741 (without 740), 743.0	Spina bifida (not occulta nor with anencephaly), encephalocele	0·3	2·5	3·4
742	Congenital hydrocephalus (without spina bifida)	0·4	1·4	0·5
746, 747.0–4	Congenital anomalies of heart and great vessels	7·0	4·2	5·0
749.1, 2	Cleft lip (with or without cleft palate)	2·2	1·4	1·0
752.2	Hypospadias	0·2*	1·8*	2·4*
754 (without 741)	Clubfoot (congenital, without spina bifida)	1·4	5·2	2·7
755.1, 2	Polydactyly, syndactyly	1·3	1·8	1·4
755.6	Congenital dislocation of hip	7·1	0·9	0·7
759.3	Down's disease	0·9	1·6	1·4
	All malformed individuals	24·5	26·7	23·3–23·9†

* Incidence per 1,000 male births.

† Two totals are given for Liverpool, one including and one excluding defects of the jaws, tongue and pharynx, since this group included some conditions which the other series did not.

defects varied by a factor of two or more. Among the conditions listed, which all occurred in more than one per 1,000 births in at least one series, neural tube defects (anencephaly, *spina bifida* and encephalocele) and hypospadias were particularly common in Liverpool, hydrocephaly and talipes in Birmingham, and cleft lip and dislocation of the hip in Japan. The two English figures for each defect are considerably closer to each other than to the Japanese, with two exceptions—hydrocephaly and talipes, the figures for which may have been affected by differences in what was regarded as abnormal and congenital as opposed to normal or acquired. Apart from congenital heart disease, which is not one type of malformation but many, the commonest defects in England and the only ones affecting more than one in 500 infants overall are anencephaly, *spina bifida*, and club-foot. Hypertrophic pyloric stenosis is of similar incidence,[19] but was not included in these surveys since it may arise after birth.

This use of the term "incidence" is of course rather different from its most common meaning, which is the proportion of individuals developing a disease *during a specific time period.* As the latter concept is difficult to apply to congenital conditions, the meaning attached to "incidence" in this context is the proportion of individuals (excluding the aborted) who are *ever* affected. The corresponding statistic for a disease arising after birth is called its *lifetime incidence.* The incidence of a congenital condition is also its prevalence at birth.

Childhood Morbidity

Two kinds of special surveys of disease in communities are commonly distinguished—*cross-sectional, retrospective* or *case-history studies*, and *longitudinal, prospective* or *cohort studies.* In cross-sectional studies, individuals are enrolled and their medical histories or other characteristics ascertained at one and the same time, after the onset of the diseases or other experiences under investigation. In longitudinal studies, individuals are enrolled when these experiences are still in the future and then followed up. To be included in the latter type of study, individuals have usually to have been born during a defined period, and when such a group is followed up it is called a *cohort.*

Our most complete sources of information on childhood morbidity in Britain are cohort studies in which children born within a specified period have been followed up during the next few years by special examinations and parental questionnaires administered by staff of the child health and school health services of Local Authorities. Probably the most detailed study to have been undertaken with the aim of following up an entire cohort in this way was the "Thousand Families Survey" of children born in Newcastle-upon-Tyne in May and June 1947.[21] The basic methods of follow-up were visits by a health visitor about every 10–12 weeks, and examinations by a doctor from the Department of Child Health at King's College, Newcastle (now the University) at 1, 3 and 5 years. The local hospitals provided particulars of children seen there, and parents were encouraged to report illnesses, and additional visits were made in these cases. Out of 1,142 children born, 847 were followed up to 5 years, 49 died, 239 left the city, and only in 7 cases did the parents refuse to take part.

Much larger numbers of children have been surveyed, but in less detail, in follow-up studies of children born in one week during 1946 and one in 1958 throughout Great Britain. A sample of the 1946 cohort (consisting of one-quarter of the children of manual and self-employed workers, and all whose parents were in other occupations) was initially followed up by questionnaires administered by health visitors or school nurses at 2, 4¼ and 6 years and a medical examination by school medical officers at 6 years also.[7] All available members of the 1958 cohort were followed up at age 7, by an educational assessment completed by their teachers, a parental questionnaire administered by health visitors, and a medical questionnaire recording the results of a clinical examination by school medical officers.[5,26]

Sources of Error in Morbidity Surveys

The results of special surveys like these may be affected by two sources of error which have not already been illustrated: inadequate reporting by parents (as opposed to health workers) and the deficient coverage of the population that results when families cannot be traced or will not co-operate. Reporting by parents was probably best in the Newcastle study, in which the frequency of contact with health visitors led to a close personal rapport, as well as enabling events to be recorded when they were still relatively fresh in the mind. Some indication of the effect which such factors may have on reporting is given by the figures in Table 8 for conditions that were examined both in the Newcastle study and in the first national one. The differences between the five-year incidence rates (persons) given for measles, mumps and whooping-cough in the two studies are small in relation to the rates themselves, but the incidence of otorrhoea and prevalence of regular enuresis reported in Newcastle were about twice the national figures. Although parts at least of the differences may be genuine, it seems likely that some parents in the national study had forgotten episodes of otorrhoea, and were more reluctant than the Newcastle parents to admit to enuresis because they did not know the investigators so well. Another factor may have been the use of differently worded questions. To minimize differences of this kind, it is important when drawing up a questionnaire to consider the possibility of using the same questions as previous investigators, and also to test carefully all questions in which there could be a subjective element before using them routinely.

TABLE 8

FREQUENCY WITH WHICH A HISTORY OF CERTAIN DISORDERS DURING EARLY CHILDHOOD WAS OBTAINED IN TWO COHORT STUDIES

Disorder (occurring in first 5 years, except where stated)	*Children with positive history (%)*	
	Born in two months of 1947, *in Newcastle upon Tyne*[21]	*Born in one week of* 1946, *in Great Britain*[7]
Infective illnesses		
Measles	63·8	55·1
Mumps	13·3	19·7
Whooping-cough	45·8	38·5
Otorrhoea	16·2*	6·6**
Developmental conditions		
Regular enuresis	7·1†	3·5–3·6‡
Gross mental retardation	0·6	—
Behaviour difficulties	6·5	—
Convulsions	5·8	—
Speech defects	19·7	—
Squint	6·6	—

* Minimal frequency consistent with published statements that 13·0 per cent of children had a single episode of otitis media; 6·3 per cent had two or more (2·8 on average); and nine-tenths of all episodes involved otorrhoea.

**In first 4½ years.

† At 5 years.

‡ At 4½ years and 6 years respectively.[2]

The problem of incomplete coverage hardly ever arose in the Newcastle study except when children left the district, as 21 per cent did. Only 0·6 per cent were excluded because their parents would not co-operate. In the two nation-wide studies, it was possible to follow up children who left their place of birth for other parts of Great Britain, so that the total proportion lost to follow-up was smaller, but more parents failed to collaborate; for example, 6 per cent of the 1946 cohort were omitted from the 4½-year follow-up because they had emigrated or could not be traced, and 2 per cent because their parents would not be interviewed. Such deficiencies in follow-up can lead to the under-representation both of children from well-to-do homes and of the less-fortunate. Families in which the father is in an occupation of high socio-economic status are the most liable to move to another area—an especial problem in local surveys such as the Newcastle one, in which follow-up to five years was achieved in less than half the children of fathers in Social Class I (the most privileged of the five classes into which occupations are grouped by the Registrar-General for England and Wales).[24] Interviews may, however, sometimes be particularly difficult to arrange with parents in unfavourable circumstances. This explanation was for example advanced when the initial analysis of the seven-year follow-up of the 1958 cohort showed that the children whose parental and medical questionnaires had not been returned within five months of being sent out were below average in the educational assessment.[26]

The Incidence of Common Illnesses in Childhood

Although the Newcastle survey finished twenty years ago and was limited to one industrial town and biassed by removals from the district, there does not seem to have been any more recent or representative study in which children have been followed up with sufficient frequency to obtain a reliable picture of minor morbidity.

The published Newcastle figures cover the five-year incidence (persons) of developmental conditions (Table 8) and the five-year incidence (spells) of other disorders (given in Table 9 for conditions of which there were more than 20 spells per 100 children). The most widespread developmental conditions were speech defects, observed in 20 per cent. Nine-tenths of these children had defective articulation or no speech at 3¾ years, when all children were examined by speech therapists; the rest had stammered at some time. Behaviour defects, convulsions and squints were each noted in 5–7 per cent. Most of the children with convulsions had only one isolated fit or episode of fits, often during an infection, but most of the squints, behaviour problems and speech defects persisted into school life.

The commonest illnesses (Table 9) were severe colds—colds with some constitutional disturbance. Mild colds were recorded even more often, but were not tabulated because of being difficult to define. An average five-year-old child would have had two severe colds, two other respiratory infections, one alimentary infection, two "infectious diseases" in the narrow sense, one other infection, and one significant accident. Accidents were considered significant if they involved injuries sufficiently severe to cause more than transient upset or for which medical advice was sought, substantial falls downstairs, burns and scalds, and the swallowing of poisons or foreign bodies.

TABLE 9

ILLNESS DURING THE FIRST FIVE YEARS IN 847 SURVIVING CHILDREN BORN IN NEWCASTLE UPON TYNE IN 1947[21]

Disorder	*Episodes per* 100 *children*	
Infective and parasitic diseases		
Alimentary infections	93	
Whooping-cough	46	
Chicken-pox, zoster	28	299
Measles	64	
Other infective and parasitic diseases	68	
Diseases of the respiratory system		
Severe colds	191	
Tonsillitis, pharyngitis	63	407
Bronchitis	74	
Other respiratory infections	79	
Other infections		
Otitis media	31	
Miscellaneous staphylococcal infections	40	110
Other infections	39	
Other conditions		
Non-infective skin rashes	29	
Home accidents	46	
Other accidents	40	136
Surgical operations	21	

If this survey were to be repeated today, the main difference would probably be a lower incidence of infectious diseases, notably measles and whooping-cough, which are now combatted by routine immunization. With overcrowded housing less of a problem than it used to be, other infections and home accidents may also have declined.

The Prevalence of Common Handicaps in Childhood

Although the children in the 1946 and 1958 cohort studies have been followed up too infrequently to yield reliable estimates of the incidence of minor disorders, the 1958 cohort has provided more up-to-date and representative data than the Newcastle series on the prevalence of common handicaps. Table 10 shows the conditions that were sought at the seven-year medical examination of the 1958 cohort and either found then or reported by the parents in more than 5 per cent of cases.

Speech defects and squint are the only conditions for which the figures can be compared with those for Newcastle. The proportions in which a positive history was given, which can be described as the reported seven-year incidence rates (persons) of these conditions in the 1958 cohort, were both rather lower than the five-year incidence rates for Newcastle, perhaps again because of inadequate reporting by parents. The transient nature of many cases of the conditions about which parents were asked is reflected by the fact that, except for defects of articulation, the reported seven-year incidence rate of each of these conditions was higher than the proportion in whom it was found on examination (the reported point prevalence).

The most prevalent conditions were dental decay (88 per cent), various signs of upper respiratory tract infection (9–24 per cent), defects of articulation (14 per cent) and visual defects (14 per cent). The prevalence of visual defects

TABLE 10

PROPORTIONS OF SEVEN-YEAR-OLD ENGLISH CHILDREN WITH A HISTORY OF CERTAIN DISORDERS, AND PROPORTIONS IN WHOM THESE DISORDERS WERE OBSERVED ON EXAMINATION, IN 1965[26]

Disorder	*Percentages*	
	History positive	*Examination positive*
Stutter or stammer	6·2	1·1
Other speech defect	10·0	13·9
Tics, habit spasms	5·2	4·0
Squint	6·3	3·1–6·0**
Visual defect	—	13·8
Hearing impairment	10·3	4·9
Signs of past or present otitis media	—	8·8
Nasal obstruction	—	9·0
Nasal or post-nasal discharge	—	9·9
Enlarged cervical lymph nodes	—	24·3
Decayed, missing or filled teeth	—	87·5
Eczema	5·6*	2·8

* Excludes eczema confined to first year.
** Higher figure includes latent squint; lower is for manifest squint only.

(which were not defined in the instructions to the examining doctors) may have been underestimated: apparently only 6 per cent had glasses, but more than 13 per cent of those without glasses were of visual acuity below 6/6 (more than 3 per cent below 6/9) for at least one eye. The proportions exhibiting dental, visual and speech defects all compare unfavourably with the numbers who had received appropriate treatment. According to their parents, only 76 per cent of children had attended a dentist, 13 per cent an eye department or clinic, optician or hospital, and 2 per cent a speech therapist. These observations illustrate the use of prevalence statistics to uncover unmet needs, which is perhaps their main practical value.

Morbidity in Children of very low Birth Weight

The methods illustrated by the above-quoted cohort studies of all children have also been used to assess the morbidity of special groups—e.g. those of very low birth weight, the assessment of whose health if they survive is as essential as the measurement of survival itself for evaluating the methods used in caring for these infants. In one study,[15] children who had been in 19 premature baby units in Great Britain in 1951–53, and whose progress there had been recorded during an earlier enquiry, were traced 6–8 years later with the help of the routine records kept by local health authorities; they were then seen and their mothers and teachers interrogated by health visitors, and medical reports were obtained on those in whom there was any suggestion of abnormality. In another survey,[8] infants discharged from Edinburgh maternity hospitals in 1948–59 were examined regularly until they were seven years old, mostly by a single paediatrician. In both studies the children were also given an intelligence test, and were classified as handicapped if they scored less than 70 or had certain other defects (among which fits and cerebral palsy predominated in both surveys, although the types of defects selected for inclusion were not quite the same in each).

Among surviving children whose birth weight was 3 lb. (1,360 Kg.) or less, the proportion classified as handicapped was about one third in the first survey (which included no births after mid-1953), and the same for children in the second survey who were born in 1948–52. Among children of similar weight born in later years of the second survey, there was an improvement in survival but the proportion of handicapped among the survivors rose above one half—suggesting that innovations in the management of prematurity were only keeping seriously handicapped children alive, and were therefore of doubtful value.

Such findings have increased the emphasis placed on preventing brain-damaging conditions such as hypoxia, hypoglycaemia and hyperbilirubinaemia in very small babies. The results of following up the recipients of this intensified care that have been published to date cannot be compared precisely with the earlier findings, partly because the more recent figures are not based on such a long follow-up, and also because they relate mostly to babies weighing up to 1,500 gm. (instead of 1,360 gm.). The earlier Edinburgh survey did however include children weighing 1,500 gm. or less at birth who were born in 1953–60, and even of these more than half were classified as handicapped on the above criteria[9]—whereas follow-up studies covering the early childhood of babies born at these weights in 1966 onwards in Edinburgh and London suggest not only that the improvement in survival has continued but also that not more than a quarter and possibly less than an eighth of these more recent survivors have any of the handicaps in question.[10,27]

Variations in Birth Weight

With a few exceptions such as impaired visual acuity, the conditions so far mentioned that can be detected by screening are generally regarded as qualitative rather than quantitative deviations from the norm. In reality, all that may be implied when some of these conditions (e.g. positional foot deformities) are diagnosed is that a health worker has the impression that some measurable characteristics (e.g. the angles between the lower leg and the inner and outside sides of the foot) are outside his idea of the normal range; but such impressions are seldom quantified by making exact measurements and diagnosing the relevant condition if these measurements lie beyond a specific threshold.

Immaturity at birth, retarded physical growth thereafter, and intellectual subnormality, are much more generally recognized to be quantitative abnormalities. Three considerations apply particularly to studies of the frequency of such problems. They are firstly the sources of inaccuracy of the measurements recorded; secondly the heterogeneity of the conditions which an abnormal measurement may reflect; and thirdly the artificiality of classifying individuals into normal and abnormal on the basis of whether a measurement is more or less than a fixed threshold.

Sources of Inaccuracy

Isolated readings of most measurements on living things may be rendered misleading by both objective and subjective variations. If a characteristic can vary objectively in an individual, any single reading is likely to be above or below the average for that individual. This objective type of variation cannot affect measurements like birth weight which relate only to one point in time, but is considerable for many other variables such as intelligence test scores. Subjective variation can arise from differences both in the accuracy of the scales used and in the observer's interpretation of what the scales record. Some scales show birth weight to the nearest ounce, and some observers record it in equal detail; others are less precise. When faced with readings midway between two marks on a scale, some observers may record the figure below; others may be influenced by what the two adjacent figures are when they decide which to record, half-pounds being preferred to quarters. Figure 7 shows how subjective variations like these affected the distribution of recorded birth weight in the cohort of children born in one week of 1958 in Great Britain.[3] Instead of the graph rising and falling smoothly on either side of a single peak, as would be expected for so large a population if the data had been based on uniformly accurate measurements, there are three main peaks (for the groups that include babies of 7, 7½ and 8 lbs. respectively), and other irregularities also indicative of a tendency to round-off birth weights to the nearest pound or half-pound. When presenting such a distribution graphically, it is generally best to smooth it by merging adjacent groups—e.g. the 6lb. 9 oz.–6 lb. 12 oz. and 6 lb. 13 oz.–7 lb. groups. Better still, if number preferences are anticipated when a survey is being planned, it may be possible to reduce them by asking for all measurements to be given in completed quarter-pounds, weights that are not an exact number of quarter-pounds being rounded-off to the one below.

Heterogeneity of Quantitative Abnormalities

It is well known that in some children (the "immature") low birth weight is secondary to short gestation, and in others (the "growth-retarded") it is not. An attempt to indicate the characteristics of the two groups separately is made in Fig. 8, in which the solid and open circles refer respectively to children born after less than 38 weeks and after longer periods. The upper part of the figure shows the birth weight distributions of these two groups in the 1958 cohort, in which 6·1 per cent of children weighed 2·5 kg. or less at birth.

Fifty-five per cent of these "under-weight" children were reported to have been born *before 38 weeks*. Short gestation may be regarded as the main direct cause of low birth weight in these 55 per cent.

The distribution for *all* children born *at 38 weeks or later* is

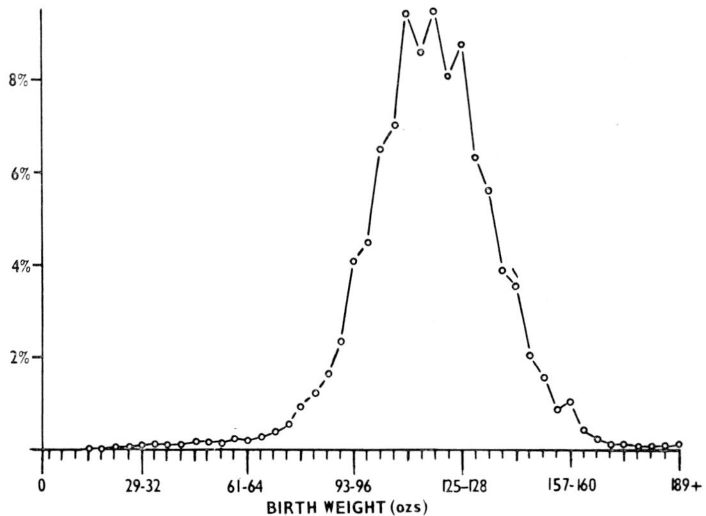

FIG. 7. Percentage distribution by recorded birth weight (in 4 oz. groups) of all British children (singletons, including stillbirths) born in one week of 1958.

almost exactly of the form known to statisticians as Gaussian or "normal", as can be seen by comparing it with the line of dots in the upper part of the figure. This line shows the "normal" distribution corresponding to the observed mean (3·376 kg.) and standard deviation (0·119 kg.). The observed distribution would be expected to follow the "normal" curve if the birth weights of all children born near to term were determined by a multiplicity of small causes, distributed at random in the population and acting some positively and some negatively. From the correspondence between the observed and "normal" distributions, it seems likely that when children born near to term are of low birth weight, it is not generally because of one specific abnormality but because they have an unfavourable assortment of the factors that influence birth weight in the general population.

It also seems to be true of many other quantitative variables that the individuals with extreme values are a heterogeneous group, some affected only by the interaction of a multiplicity of small causes, and others in whom a cause of large effect like short gestation can be specified. For example, the distribution of Stanford-Binet intelligence-test scores in populations provides evidence that the lower end of this distribution also is formed by a mixture of some children whose subnormality is related to the multiplicity of factors that govern intelligence in the general population, and others with specific conditions such as Down's disease, phenylketonuria and brain damage at birth.[25] In all such situations, it is important to distinguish between the different groups whenever possible in studies of frequency and causation.

Inadequacy of Arbitrary Thresholds

The heterogeneity of children with low birth weight and the distributions of the two main groups of affected infants (Fig. 8, upper part) make it difficult to justify the traditional classification of children as "premature" if their birth weight is at or below a threshold of 2·5kg. This weight is far from being either the lower limit of the range for children born near term or the upper limit for the immature. According to Fig. 8 a majority of the children in the topmost of the weight groups traditionally regarded as premature (2·3–2·5 kg.) were born at 38 weeks or later, and more than half the children born before 38 weeks weighed more than 2·5kg. The precise accuracy of these figures may be queried, since gestation length can never be estimated as reliably as birth weight; but there must clearly be considerable overlap between those infants in whom a specific cause of low birth weight such as short gestation can be identified and those affected only by the multiplicity of factors that govern birth weight in the population at large. In other words, there is no aetiologically meaningful threshold between normal and subnormal weight, but only a progressive increase, as one passes from the rather small newborn to the very small, in the proportion in whom specific causes of low birth weight can be demonstrated. The situation in subnormality of intelligence is analogous.[25]

A threshold, of course, may have no aetiological significance and still be clinically meaningful if it marks a sharp transition from normal to increased mortality, morbidity or disability. But the variation in the frequency of such problems with birth weight is not an abrupt change at 2·5 kg. or any other point, but a gradual improvement from below 1 kg. to above 3·5 kg. The lower part of Fig. 8 illustrates this trend in relation to mortality and intellectual performance. The death-rates shown (on a logarithmic scale) were estimated from data collected in the nation-wide British survey of stillbirths and neonatal deaths in three months and total births in one week of 1958.[3,4] Except below 2 kg. mortality was lower at each weight and fell more steeply with increasing weight among infants born near to term than in those born before 38 weeks. It increased beyond 4 kg. in both groups.

The index of intellectual performance that was analysed was the mean score obtained in two verbal reasoning tests taken as a routine during the eleventh year of life by children in Birmingham, England, who had been born in 1950–4.

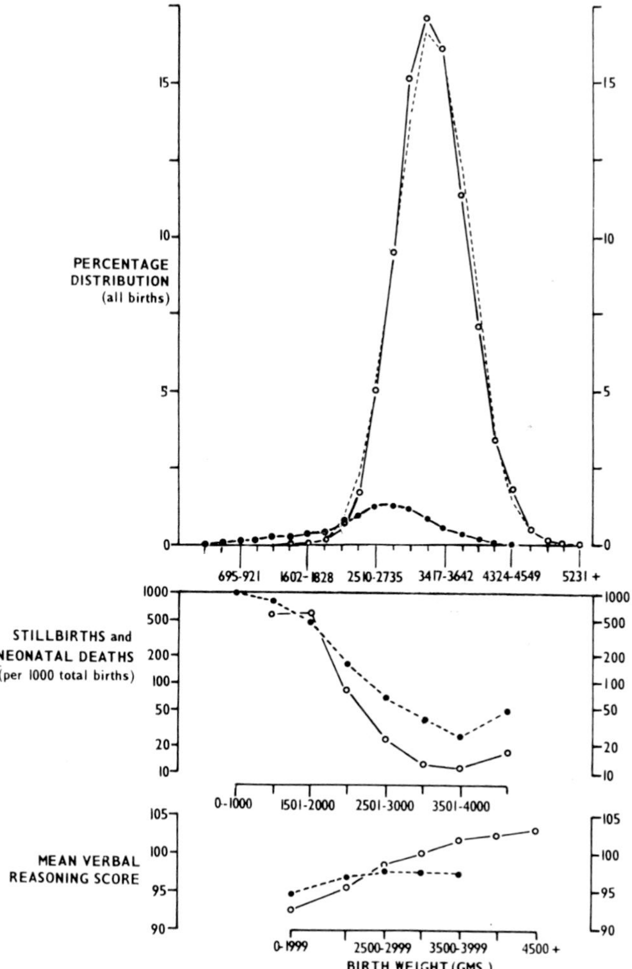

FIG. 8. The frequency, early mortality, and mean verbal reasoning scores (at ten years) of singleton children in different birth weight groups, subdivided into those born after gestations of at least 38 weeks (open circles) and of less (solid circles). The dotted line on the upper graph shows the "normal" distribution corresponding to the mean and standard deviation of the birth weights observed in infants born at 38 weeks or more. (See Text for sources.)

The scores had been adjusted to give a mean of 100 and a standard deviation of 15 for children born in each month. They were linked by computer with other routine data for these children, including birth weight and length of gestation from the last menstrual period, recorded at birth by obstetric hospital staff and domiciliary midwives.[28]

Although mean score did not vary much in the prematurely born, it increased steadily with birth weight over the whole range shown for children born near to term. The aetiological significance of this trend is doubtful; it may not mean that birth weight affects verbal reasoning score, but only that similar influences affect both variables. The importance of the trend in the present context is that it is gradual, and therefore agrees with the mortality data in suggesting that there is no critical birth weight below which health changes abruptly.

When a quantitative character like birth weight has no objective threshold value beyond which aetiology or outcome changes abruptly, there are only relatively few situations in either medical care or research where the use of an arbitrary figure can be justified. In medical care, arbitrary figures may help as a guide to quick decision-making: it might, for example, be suggested that a baby born at home should be transferred to hospital if its birthweight and/or gestation length are low enough to make its chance of dying greater than 10 per cent. In research, the most convenient way to explore the causes or effects of a condition like immaturity may sometimes be to use an arbitrary figure to define an "abnormal" group which is then analysed separately, as in the above discussion of birth weight in which 38 weeks was treated as the lower limit of normal gestation length. But it is generally best, when studying a quantitative variable of medical significance, to begin by a comprehensive examination of how the general population is distributed over the whole range of the variable. If there are differences between groups they can generally be demonstrated more clearly by comparing distributions, or even mean values of the variable for these groups (as was done for verbal reasoning scores in Fig. 8), than by restricting attention to the proportions of individuals with extreme values.

ACKNOWLEDGEMENTS

I am much indebted to Dr. J. K. Steward for data from the Manchester Children's Tumour Registry; to Mr. Frank Cutler for drawing the figures; and to Mrs. Winifred Murray and Mrs. Evelyn Townsend for secretarial help.

REFERENCES

1. Baird, D. and Thomson, A. M. (1969), "The Survey Perinatal Deaths Reclassified by Special Clinico-Pathological Assessment" *and* "The Effects of Obstetric and Environmental Factors on Perinatal Mortality by Clinico-Pathological Causes", in *Perinatal Problems* (Second Report of the British Perinatal Mortality Survey), pp. 200–226 (N. R. Butler and E. D. Alberman eds.). Edinburgh: Livingstone.
2. Blomfield, J. M. and Douglas, J. W. B. (1956), "Bedwetting—Prevalence Among Children Aged Between 4 and 7 years", *Lancet*, **i**, 850–852.
3. Butler, N. R., Alberman, E. D. and Goldstein, H. (1969), "Maternal Factors Affecting Duration of Pregnancy, Birth Weight and Foetal Growth", in *Perinatal Problems* (Second Report of the British Perinatal Mortality Survey), pp. 47–71 and 331–336 (N. R. Butler and E. D. Alberman, eds.). Edinburgh: Livingstone.
4. Butler, N. R. and Bonham, D. G. (1963), *Perinatal Mortality* (First Report of the British Perinatal Mortality Survey). Edinburgh: Livingstone.
5. Davie, R., Butler, N. and Goldstein, H. (1972), *From Birth to Seven* (Second Report of the National Child Development Study: 1958 Cohort). London: Longman.
6. Dhalial, R. K., Machine, A. M. and Tait, S. M. (1970), "Chromosomal Anomalies in Spontaneously Aborted Human Fetuses", *Lancet*, **ii**, 20–21.
7. Douglas, J. W. B. and Blomfield, J. M. (1958), *Children Under Five*. London: Allen & Unwin.
8. Drillien, C. M. (1967), "The Incidence of Mental and Physical Handicaps in School Age Children of Very Low Birth Weight. II," *Pediatrics (Springfield)*, **39**, 238–247.
9. Drillien, C. M. (1968), "Causes of Handicap in the Low Weight Infant," in *Aspects of Praematurity and Dysmaturity* (Nutricia

Symposium), pp. 287–302 (J. H. P. Jonxis, H. K. A. Visser, and J. A. Troelstra, eds.). Leiden, Stenfert Kroese.

10. Drillien, C. M. (1972), "Aetiology and Outcome in Low-Birth-weight Infants," *Develop. Med. Child. Neurol.*, **14**, 563–574.
11. Fedrick, J. and Butler, N. R. (1972), "Accuracy of Registered Causes of Neonatal Deaths in 1958", *Brit. J. prev. soc. Med.*, **26**, 101–105.
12. Hill, G. B., Howitt, L. F. and Soaper, A. (1972), *Cancer Incidence in Great Britain 1963–1966* (Studies on Medical and Population Subjects—No. 24). London: Her Majesty's Stationery Office.
13. Leck, I. and Record, R. G. (1963), "Sources of Variation in the Reporting of Malformations", *Develop. Med. Child Neurol.*, **5**, 364–370.
14. Leck, I., Record, R. G., McKeown, T. and Edwards, J. H. (1968), "The Incidence of Malformations in Birmingham, England, 1950–1959", *Teratology*, **1**, 263–280.
15. McDonald, A. (1967), *Children of Very Low Birth Weight. A Survey of 1128 Children with a Birth Weight of 4 lb (1800 g) or Less* (M.E.I.U. Research Monograph No. 1). London: Spastics Society Medical Education and Information Unit.
16. McKeown, T. and Record, R. G. (1962), "Reasons for the Decline in Mortality in England and Wales During the Nineteenth Century", *Population Studies*, **16**, 94–122.
17. McKeown, T. *et al.* (1968), *Screening in Medical Care: Reviewing the Evidence*. London: Oxford.
18. Mackeprang, M., Hay, S. and Lunde, A. S. (1972), "Completeness and Accuracy of Reporting of Malformations on Birth Certificates", *HMSHA Hlth. Rep.*, **87**, 43–49.
19. MacMahon, B., Record, R. G. and McKeown, T. (1951), "Congenital Pyloric Stenosis: an Investigation of 578 Cases," *Brit. J. soc. Med.*, **5**, 185–192.
20. Marsden, H. B., Steward, J. K., *et al.* (1968), "Problems of Children's Tumours in Britain", in *Tumours in Children* (Recent Results in Cancer Research No. 13), pp. 1–12 (H. B. Marsden and J. K. Steward, eds.). Berlin: Springer.
21. Miller, F. J. W., Court, S. D. M., Walton, W. S. and Knox, E. G. (1960), *Growing Up in Newcastle upon Tyne*. London: Oxford.
22. Neel, J. V. (1958), "A Study of Major Congenital Defects in Japanese Infants", *Amer. J. hum. Genet.*, **10**, 398–445.
23. Nishimura, H. (1970), "Incidence of Malformations in Abortions", in *Congenital Malformations* (Proceedings of the Third International Conference), pp. 275–283 (F. C. Fraser and V. A. McKusick, eds.). Amsterdam: Excerpta medica.
24. Office of Population Censuses and Surveys (1970), *Classification of Occupations 1970*. London: Her Majesty's Stationery Office.
25. Penrose, L. S. (1963), *The Biology of Mental Defect*, 2nd edition. London: Sidgwick & Jackson.
26. Pringle, M. L. K., Butler, N. R. and Davie, R. (1966), *11,000 Seven-Year-Olds* (First Report of the National Child Development Study: 1958 Cohort). London: Longman.
27. Rawlings, G., Reynolds, E. O. R., Stewart, A. and Strang, L. B. (1971), "Changing Prognosis for Infants of Very Low Birth Weight," *Lancet*, **i**, 516–519.
28. Record, R. G., McKeown, T. and Edwards, J. H. (1969), "The Relation of Measured Intelligence to Birth Weight and Duration of Gestation", *Ann. hum. Genet.* (*Lond.*), **33**, 71–79.
29. Smithells, R. W. (1968), "Incidence of Congenital Abnormalities in Liverpool, 1960–64", *Brit. J. prev. soc. Med.*, **22**, 36–37.
30. Steward, J. K. (1973), "Manchester Children's Tumour Registry", in *Modern Radiotherapy—Malignant Diseases in Children* (T. J. Deeley, ed.). London: Butterworth, in press.
31. Steward, J. K. (1973), Personal communication.
32. Weatherall, J. A. C. (1969), "An Assessment of the Efficiency of Notification of Congenital Malformations", *Med. Off.*, **121**, 65–68.
33. Wilson, J. M. G. (1968), "Evaluation of Prescriptive Screening for Phenylketonuria," in *Screening in Medical Care: Reviewing the Evidence*, pp. 97–115 (T. McKeown *et al.*, eds.). London: Oxford.

41B. INSIGHTS INTO THE CAUSATION OF DISORDERS OF EARLY LIFE

IAN LECK

In the last chapter, the methods of measuring disease frequency were illustrated from studies showing the overall frequency of some of the more widespread and severe problems of childhood. But although information about overall frequency is an important aid to medical decision-making, both in differential diagnosis and in the allocation of limited research and service resources, an even greater contribution is the insights into causation and prevention which studies of disease frequency are providing. Such insights cannot be gained simply by inspecting a single estimate of frequency, but only by *comparing two or more figures*—preferably incidence rates—for different times, places or groups of people. Incidence rates are preferred in aetiological studies to statistics of prevalence because, as already indicated (p. 716), prevalence is affected by the factors which govern the course of a disease as well as by those related to its inception.

If a disorder is of unknown aetiology, the epidemiological comparisons which the search for its causes may involve are of various kinds, which may be classified under four heads—descriptive studies, correlative studies of groups, correlative studies of individuals, and experimental studies. *Descriptive studies* are comparisons between the incidence rates of the disorder observed in different periods, places, or categories of individuals defined in terms of the other variables commonly studied by demographers—sex, ethnic group, socio-economic status, parental age and birth rank, for example. Such factors cannot themselves be pathogenic, but may serve as pointers to influences which are.

In *correlative studies of groups*, the incidence rates in people in different periods, places and other circumstances are compared with indices of the exposure of these groups of people to micro-organisms, chemicals, or other influences which might conceivably cause the disorder concerned. The incidence rates of the disorder in the different groups can be expected to be correlated with the groups' exposure to any influence which is causal.

The primary object in *correlative studies of individuals* is to determine whether the disorder and a history of exposure to the suspected cause tend to occur not merely in the same groups but in the same individuals. There are two ways of answering this question. One is to compare persons with and without the disorder in respect of their exposure to the suspected cause. The other is to compare unexposed and exposed persons (the latter sometimes sub-divided into groups differing in intensity of exposure) in respect of incidence of the disorder.

Experimental studies also involve comparing the incidence rates experienced by those unexposed to a suspected cause and those exposed, or by the more lightly and the more heavily exposed. But in correlative studies the comparison is between persons whose levels of exposure have been determined by factors extraneous to the study, and who may therefore differ in many other respects as well, whereas in experimental studies the difference in exposure is created deliberately, by actions aimed at selectively reducing the exposure of some individuals to the suspected cause without making them different in any other way from the more exposed. The most convincing type of experimental study is a randomized trial, akin to those used by clinicians to evaluate different treatments for established disease. In the simplest trials of this type individuals are allocated at random to two groups. In one of these groups, steps are then taken to reduce exposure, and both groups are followed up to see whether the incidence of the relevant disorder is lower in the group with reduced exposure (the "experimental group") than in the other (the "control group").

The ease with which studies of all these kinds can lead to the identification of causes of disorders and methods of prevention is of course affected by the nature of these causes. In discussing sources of variation in birth weight (pp. 723–724) the point was made that extreme values of this and other quantitative variables are sometimes produced by specific causes of large effect, and sometimes by the interaction of a multiplicity of small causes. It is often also helpful to think of both these kinds of causation as possibilities when studying *qualitative* abnormalities of unknown aetiology, although it must be borne in mind that this distinction between unifactorial and multifactorial causation is to some extent artificial: even in a condition like tuberculosis or phenylketonuria which has one specific cause (in these cases a micro-organism and a gene respectively), there are often also other factors such as the genotype of the tuberculosis contact or the diet of the phenylketonuria homozygote which have a bearing on whether the presence of the specific cause leads to clinical disease. But although disorders produced by specific causes may be related to other factors as well, it is generally by action directed at the specific causes that such disorders can most effectively be prevented, and the biggest contribution which epidemiological methods have made to disease prevention has been in identifying and eliminating some of these causes, including many micro-organisms and some nutritional deficiencies.

Disorders caused by combinations of many influences, each of which may contribute only a little to the total effect, often seem to be less rewarding to examine epidemiologically, since influences like these are harder to define, and even if one is defined and eliminated the fact that it is only one of many may mean that only a few cases are prevented. But even in this context the methods of epidemiology, and especially of descriptive epidemiology, can be claimed to have justified themselves, by enabling cases of some disorders of multifactorial aetiology (e.g. perinatal anoxia) to be prevented, and by clarifying the relative aetiological importance of genotype and environment in others (e.g. some common malformations). These descriptive investigations have also given rise to suggestions, now being explored by correlative studies of groups, that even the aetiology of some multifactorially determined conditions (e.g. neural tube defects) may include specific environmental components which affect incidence enough to be worth trying to control.

At the beginning of this century, a great deal of childhood mortality and morbidity was due to infective and nutritional disorders, which are now known to have specific causes. But these diseases have so diminished in importance that the main problems now confronting paediatricians in developed countries are conditions arising during and before birth, most cases of which appear at the present time to have no one specific cause but to be multifactorial in origin. Because of their contemporary importance and the promising results mentioned in the last paragraph, two areas of this field—perinatal mortality in general and the common facial and neural tube defects—are used in what follows to introduce and illustrate the first two of the types of epidemiological enquiry mentioned earlier: descriptive and correlative studies of groups.

The paediatrician must not however allow the apparently multifactorial nature of most contemporary paediatric problems to blind him to the possibility that some of them may eventually prove to have specific causes after all; nor can he assume that further problems caused by specific strains of micro-organisms, methods of treatment or other potential hazards will not arise in the future. During the last few decades many such features of the environment have been shown to be hazardous, often by practising clinicians using epidemiological methods. To help in equipping others to emulate these clinicians, some of the work which led to the incrimination of three of these hazards—rubella epidemics, and the administration of thalidomide to pregnant women and of high concentrations of oxygen to very premature babies—is used in this chapter to illustrate the second two types of epidemiological enquiry: correlative studies of individuals and experimental studies.

As this chapter is primarily concerned with the principal epidemiological *methods* used in studies of causation, rather than with their results, no attempt has been made to deal comprehensively with the epidemiology of the problems discussed. Instead, merely a few epidemiological studies of each of these problems have been picked as examples, because of the methodological points they illustrate and their accessibility or significance as sources of new ideas.

PERINATAL MORTALITY: DESCRIPTIVE STUDIES

From the British mortality statistics already presented (Chapter 41A, Tables 1–3, pp. 708–710) it can be seen that nearly two thirds of all deaths between the 28th week of gestation and the 15th anniversary of birth occur during the perinatal period, and that the commonest clinicopathological causes of these perinatal deaths include malformations, mechanical difficulties during labour, immaturity, and other conditions which together are also responsible, directly or indirectly, for a very large share of the total burden of disease and disability throughout infancy and childhood which the paediatric services exist to treat. In view of the magnitude of the burden which these perinatal problems together impose, and which their prevention would remove, they can be regarded as the most important of all the challenges facing the paediatric epidemiologist today.

Most epidemiological studies in this field have been descriptive in nature: in other words, they have been concerned with the relationship of mortality and morbidity to demographic factors such as time, place, and parental age and class. When a group of conditions as heterogeneous as perinatal deaths is being studied like this, it is of course important that the different conditions in the group should be considered separately as well as together. In this way, information of immediate preventive value is sometimes obtained.

Perinatal mortality differences between times and countries have already been illustrated (pp. 707, 709–710, 712–713). In what follows, examples are given of the differences between places within countries, and between groups distinguished by various parental characteristics. The first aspect to be considered is the relationship of these factors to overall perinatal mortality, and to a few related obstetric and paediatric problems. Following this account, perinatal deaths from different clinico-pathological conditions are analysed separately, and the practical contribution which analyses of this type may make to prevention is illustrated.

There are many sources from which data might be taken to illustrate these points. Some of these sources are routine statistics, like those compiled by the British Registrars General (from which the data in Tables 1 and 3 of Chapter 41A—pp. 708 and 710—were taken). Others are special surveys like the British Perinatal Mortality Survey of 1958 (which yielded the data shown in Table 2 of Chapter 41A—p. 709).

In general, routine statistics have the advantage of being based on larger numbers than most special surveys, but the disadvantages of including fewer clinical and pathological details and being more susceptible to bias by the diagnostic discrepancies to which, as already indicated (pp. 708–709), perinatal death records are particularly prone. In special surveys diagnosis can to some extent be standardized, even when many observers are involved, firstly by providing special questionnaires with precise instructions on what to record, and secondly by having one or more assessors review all these records. The 1958 survey[2,3] was notable for combining these methods with coverage of a very sizeable population. The data used below to demonstrate the epidemiological features of perinatal mortality are mainly from this source.

The 1958 survey was designed to cover all children in Great Britain who were stillborn or died in the neonatal period during March, April and May, and also those born in one week of March (the "control week") who survived. To obtain demographic and clinical data on these children and their parents, clinical questionnaires were distributed in advance to hospitals and Local Health Authorities for completion by their midwives. After checking, the completed forms were passed to the Medical Officers of Health of the Local Authorities, who matched them with the statutory notifications of births and deaths and reminded the midwives to send in questionnaires for any cases in which they had omitted to do so. Clinical questionnaires were eventually obtained for 7,848 (94 per cent) of stillbirths and neonatal deaths in March–May 1958, and for 17,418 (98 per cent) of infants born in the control week. For two-thirds of the 7,848 stillbirths and neonatal deaths, necropsy data were obtained from the pathologists on special questionnaires or as copies of the routine reports.

Of the clinical questionnaires, 6,252 related to legitimate children from single pregnancies who died in the perinatal period. The questionnaires of these children, and summaries of as many necropsy reports on them as had been received, were sent for assessment to the distinguished obstetric team at Aberdeen, Scotland, led by Sir Dugald Baird, who together allocated each death to one of the eight clinicopathological categories listed in Chapter 41A, Table 2 (p. 709). To obtain estimated mortality rates for the population surveyed and for various groups into which it was broken down, the numbers of fetal and neonatal deaths in the survey three months for whom clinical data were available were divided by twelve times the total number of documented births in the same group in the control week, since it was estimated that one-twelfth of the population represented by the deaths was born during this week.

Perinatal Mortality from all Causes

The relationship of overall perinatal mortality to abnormalities of pregnancy and labour such as twinning, toxaemia, antepartum haemorrhage, premature labour, malpresentation and disproportion is so marked as to be clinically obvious. What epidemiological studies such as the 1958 survey have done is to measure the less obvious mortality increases that are found in certain places and classes, and in the children of women of certain ages, parities, heights and habits. Characteristics of these types which are associated with increases in the incidence of a condition are known as *risk factors* for the condition. Frequently, risk factors are interrelated—high maternal age and parity, for instance—so that it is not always enough to consider each variable in isolation. This is often a useful first step, but if variations in incidence are found the investigator must go on to determine whether each variable is affecting incidence independently or whether some effects are merely secondary to others—whether an association with high parity is secondary to one with high maternal age, or vice versa, for example.

In what follows, the results obtained by applying these two approaches to the 1958 survey data are considered in turn. Some of these results were obtained by the original organizers of the survey, who reported on all still-births and neonatal deaths among single births, and others by the Aberdeen team, who studied only perinatal deaths among legitimate single births. Also, the Aberdeen team used their own socio-economic classification of occupations, whereas the other group analysed social status in terms of the Social Classes I–V set out by the Registrar General for England and Wales. Consequently, the perinatal death rates given below relate only to legitimate single births, and are analysed for socio-economic effects by the Aberdeen classification, whereas the stillbirth and neonatal death rates are for all single births and are analysed by Social Class. These differences are however more apparent than real, in view of the small proportions of fetal and neonatal deaths in single births that occurred after the perinatal period (7–8 per cent) and that involved illegitimate children (4 per cent), and the fact that both occupational classifications were based on socio-economic criteria, professional and managerial workers being allocated in each case to the "highest" group and unskilled manual workers to the "lowest."

Apparent Effects of Single Risk Factors on Mortality

Most of the risk factors demonstrated in the 1958 survey were maternal characteristics: residence in the less privileged parts of the country, and in large towns; age or parity at either end of the normal range; low socio-economic status; lack of a husband; short stature; and smoking during late pregnancy.

For the analysis of places of residence, two types of classifications are commonly used in epidemiological studies—one based on region and the other on urbanization. For example, the local authority districts of England and Wales are aggregated into nine Standard Regions in some of the tables produced by the Registrar General and into five categories reflecting degree of urbanization (ranging from conurbations to rural districts) in other tables. In the 1958 survey, a simpler breakdown into three zones and two categories of urbanization was used. The main urban areas—conurbations and county boroughs, where perinatal deaths accounted for 3·3 per cent of births—were compared with all other areas, where the rate was 3·1 per cent. The three zones compared were the relatively wealthy South, centred on London and not including the South West; the less prosperous North, including the north west and extreme north east of England and the whole of Scotland and Wales; and the intervening Central Zone, with intermediate living standards. The perinatal death rate varied from 2·8 per cent in the south to 3·5 per cent in the north.

As may be seen from the top row of histograms in Fig. 1, the excesses of mortality associated with the other risk factors mentioned above were on the whole greater than those associated with residence in the North zone or in large towns.

Apparent Effects of Single Risk Factors on Other Perinatal Problems

In the remainder of Fig. 1, data for the control week births are used to show that the effects of the other risk factors are mediated at least in part through their associations with some of the clinical conditions that increase mortality.

As was illustrated in Chapter 41A, Fig. 8 (p. 725), the striking effect which low birth weight has on mortality is particularly marked in those who are small because of being born early, but is also evident in small children born near to term. Figure 1 shows that the risk factors for early birth are qualitatively the same as for early death—and that the same is true for low birth weight at term (indicative of fetal growth retardation), except that the latter is not associated with high maternal age. Even the quantitative importance of each factor relative to the others is broadly the same for early birth and early death—except for the risk of early delivery being greater for women aged below 20 than above 35, which is the reverse of what the mortality data showed. Gestation length was only recorded for four-fifths of mothers under 20, as opposed to nine-tenths of other mothers, so that the estimated frequency of early births in the former group (which is, as elsewhere, the percentage among births of known gestation only) is relatively unreliable; but other data[20] also suggest that prematurity of this degree is commonest at the bottom of the maternal age range.

Liability to fetal growth retardation also seems to be more affected than the death rate by low maternal age—and by maternal smoking, primiparity, and short stature as well. These four risk factors also appear from the 1958 survey and other studies[41] to have more influence on *mean* birth weight than do the other factors listed, which is probably mainly because they are related to fetal growth, although their relationship to gestation length must also have affected the means.

The clinical conditions through which the effects of risk factors on perinatal mortality may be mediated include not only abnormalities of labour such as premature onset, and fetal conditions such as growth retardation, but also disorders of pregnancy such as pre-eclampsia. Indeed, the associations with early birth and growth retardation which help to make some maternal characteristics into risk factors for perinatal death may themselves be secondary in part to relationships between these characteristics and maternal pre-eclampsia, since this condition can lead both to early birth (including cases induced deliberately) and to retarded growth. The incidence of pre-eclampsia was not analysed by maternal age and parity in as much detail as the other rates examined in Fig. 1, but primiparity and high maternal age again emerged as risk factors. The most powerful risk factor apart from primiparity seemed to be illegitimacy—partly no doubt because three-quarters of the unmarried mothers were primiparae, but perhaps also because a relatively high proportion of them (16 per cent, as compared with 7 per cent of married) were excluded when calculating the incidence of toxaemia, mostly because their records were incomplete. Omissions in the filling in of questionnaires are liable to occur most often when there is nothing positive to report, so that individuals whose questionnaires are completed may include an excess with positive findings, especially if (as with unmarried mothers) the number of incomplete questionnaires is considerable.

Of the other risk factors, maternal height has the same relationship to severe pre-eclampsia as to mortality, short gestation, and retarded fetal growth. Smoking however is quite the reverse, since it seems to reduce the incidence of pre-eclampsia—a surprising finding, but one confirmed by other data.[10] But with this exception, the associations

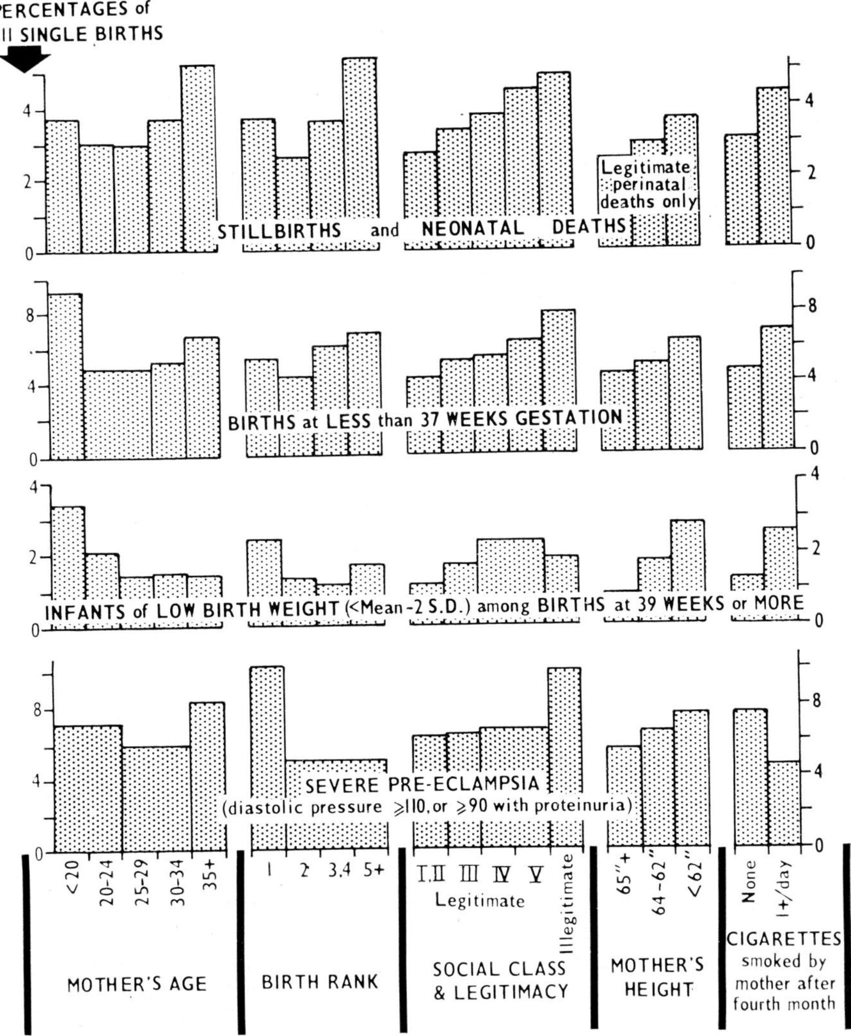

FIG. 1. Indices of frequency of early death, early birth, retarded fetal growth, and severe pre-eclampsia, in various groups of singleton pregnancies in Great Britain at the time of the British Perinatal Mortality Survey of 1958[2,3].

which the risk factors examined have with toxaemia, premature labour and retarded growth suggest that it is at least partly by predisposing to these disorders that the factors influence mortality. Indeed, the influence of smoking can it seems be explained entirely in terms of its effects on gestation length and fetal growth: the smokers' children in the 1958 series do not seem to have differed in mortality from non-smokers' offspring of the same birth weight, suggesting that the overall mortality in smokers' children is higher only because their liability to retarded growth and early birth means that they are over-represented in the low birthweight groups where death is commonest.

Effects of Risk Factors Corrected for Interaction

All the risk factors discussed above are inter-related. In the 1958 survey, mothers whose characteristics included any one of the risk factors of high parity, low socio-economic status, short stature, and residence in northern Britain, were shown to be more likely than average to have each of the other characteristics on this list. Very young mothers also tended to be short and of low socio-economic status, and advanced maternal age goes of course with high parity. Residence in large towns was found to be associated with short stature, and smoking with high parity and low socio-economic status.

When factors that are related to the incidence of a disorder (in this case perinatal mortality) tend to occur together, it cannot be assumed that they all have independent effects on incidence. If one of an interrelated group of factors—e.g. high maternal age—has an independent effect, secondary associations between the other factors—e.g. high birth rank—and the disorder will also tend to occur. In the 1958 study, two main methods that can help to distinguish between independent and secondary associations were used: tabulation, and analysis of variance.

Corrected Mortality Data. Tabulation as a method of separating the effects of two variables on mortality is illustrated in Table 1. Each column of this table refers to a different zone and each row to a different category of urbanization. The perinatal death rate for places in each zone and category of urbanization is shown in the cell where the relevant column and row intersect. The effects of zone and urbanization can be examined more or less separately by looking along the rows and down the columns respectively. Alternatively, the contents of such a table can be presented graphically. Figure 2 shows two tables in this form, the

TABLE 1

PERINATAL MORTALITY IN ZONES AND CATEGORIES OF URBANIZATION[2]

Urbanization	*Zone* (*see p.* 730)		
	South	*Central*	*North*
County boroughs and conurbations	29·0	32·6	37·1
Other districts	26·6	32·4	33·7

intention being to separate the effects of mother's age and parity in the first, and of socio-economic group and mother's height in the second. In each case the slopes of the lines show the influence of one variable of the pair (e.g. age), and the relationship between these lines shows the other (e.g. parity).

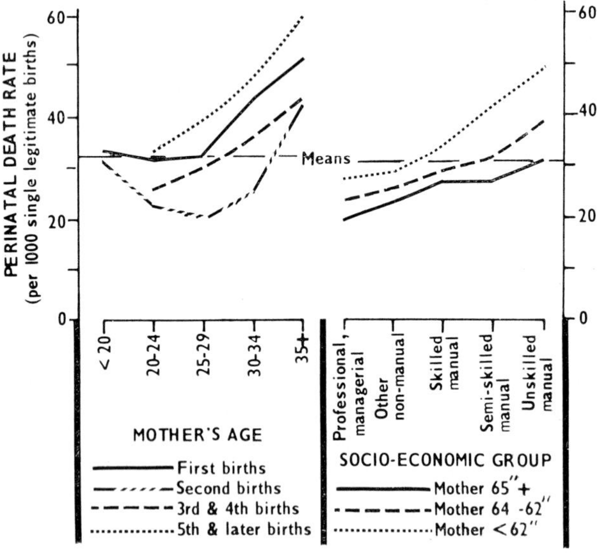

FIG. 2. Perinatal mortality in children with various combinations of parental characteristics: British Perinatal Mortality Survey, 1958.[2]

The pattern most commonly found when two variables which affect perinatal mortality are examined together is that shown for zone and urbanization, and for height and socio-economic status, where the relationship of mortality to each variable is found to be much the same among those who are alike in respect of the other as it is in the general population: in other words, the two risk factors concerned are found to be independent, at least in part. The findings for maternal age and parity, however, are rather more complicated. When either of these variables is examined without taking account of the other, the trend of mortality observed is J-shaped (Fig. 1); but although the parity trend persists in each maternal age group, it is only among second births that a similar trend with maternal age is observed. Among first births there is little change till after 30, when mortality starts to rise; and among third and later births it increases over the whole age range.

Although tabulation is often the simplest and most instructive way of separating the effects of *two* variables, it is less satisfactory when more than two are to be considered

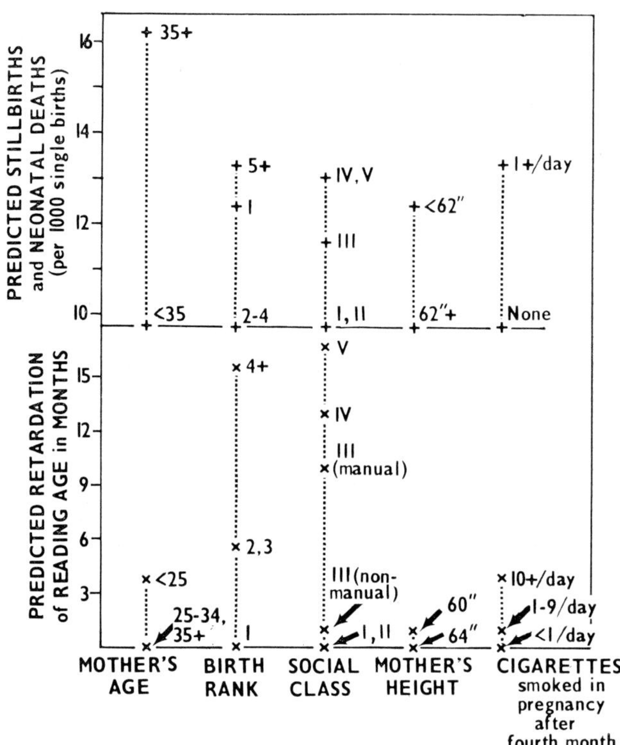

FIG. 3. Results of analyses of variance of early death and of reading age at seven years, for children with various risk factors in the British Perinatal Mortality Survey and National Child Development Study (1958 Cohort.)[2,9] The grades of each variable which had the lowest risk of death and the highest reading age are indicated on the horizontal axes. Mortality estimates for each variable relate to children of mothers without severe pre-eclampsia who were in the grades of lowest risk for all the other variables listed. For reading age, estimates shown are of the retardation in each grade relative to the most favourable grade for the variable concerned, with all other variables held constant.

simultaneously—partly because the numbers in many of the resulting cells may be too small to be relied upon, and partly because three or more dimensions are more difficult to picture, both in the mind and on paper. In the 1958 survey, this problem was approached by using various adaptations of the statistical procedure known as Analysis of Variance to estimate the mortality differences to be expected on average between children differing in respect of one risk factor alone. The upper part of Fig. 3 shows estimates of the effects that various risk factors would have on mortality if present singly in children who in all other respects resembled the most low-risk group distinguished (second, third and fourth births to non-smoking mothers aged under 35, in Social Classes I and II, at least 62 in. tall and without severe pre-eclampsia).

One reservation that applies to both tabulation and the analysis of variance is that neither these nor any other method can completely separate or quantify the effects of different variables if individuals with a *range* of characteristics beyond one point or beween two on a scale (e.g. fifth and later births, mothers aged 25–9) are grouped together. For example, the rise with maternal age in the death rate among fifth and later births need not necessarily mean that maternal age has an independent effect on mortality in the children of grand multiparae. Some such rise is inevitable, given that mortality increases with birth rank, since the proportion of fifth and later births that are of extremely high birth rank rises with maternal age. However, the magnitude of the mortality differences shown in Fig. 3 suggests that all the risk factors concerned have some independent effects.

Corrected Data on Related Problems. The excesses of cases of premature birth, retarded growth and maternal pre-eclampsia noted in association with different risk factors in Fig. 1 may not all be independent. Tabulation of the 1958 data on pre-eclampsia by maternal age and parity showed that the only reason for the decline in incidence between ages under 25 and 25–34 was that fewer of the latter women were primigravidae. The variations in incidence of early birth and retarded growth were not examined as such for independence, but data on mean birth weight (which increases with maternal age, parity, height and socio-economic status and is reduced by toxaemia and smoking) were subjected to an analysis of variance. This analysis suggested that the associations with maternal age and socio-economic status were secondary to the others listed, but that parity, height, smoking and toxaemia had independent effects, which persisted when gestation was held constant and must therefore be due at least in part to differences in fetal growth.

The conclusion that maternal age has no independent effect on birth weight may only apply to the differences between maternal age groups over 20. The children of younger mothers had a high incidence of both early birth and growth retardation (Fig. 1) which made them even lighter than all first births, but this effect was not tested by the analysis of variance since all births to mothers under 25 were treated in this analysis as a homogeneous group—an illustration of the limitations of this method.

As already indicated (p. 720), the survivors born in the control week of the 1958 study were followed up at seven years. The variances of several characteristics measured then have been analysed, with results which illustrate the fact that some risk factors for perinatal death also predispose to developmental retardation and other abnormalities later.[9] The lower part of Fig. 3 shows the variations in reading age which such an analysis predicted would be found in children differing in respect of one risk factor alone. The result for each risk factor was expressed as the average reduction in reading age for children exposed to the factor relative to those in the most favourable grade for the variable concerned. High birth rank, low socio-economic status and maternal smoking appear prejudicial to development as well as to early survival. But the perinatal disadvantages experienced by children who are first-born or have elderly mothers are replaced later by advantages, which are not only developmental but also include relatively low death rates after the neonatal period.[58]

Perinatal Mortality by Cause

Analysis by clinicopathological cause of the variations in perinatal mortality shown for all causes in Table 1 and Fig. 2 produced the results shown in Figs. 4–6. Four of the eight

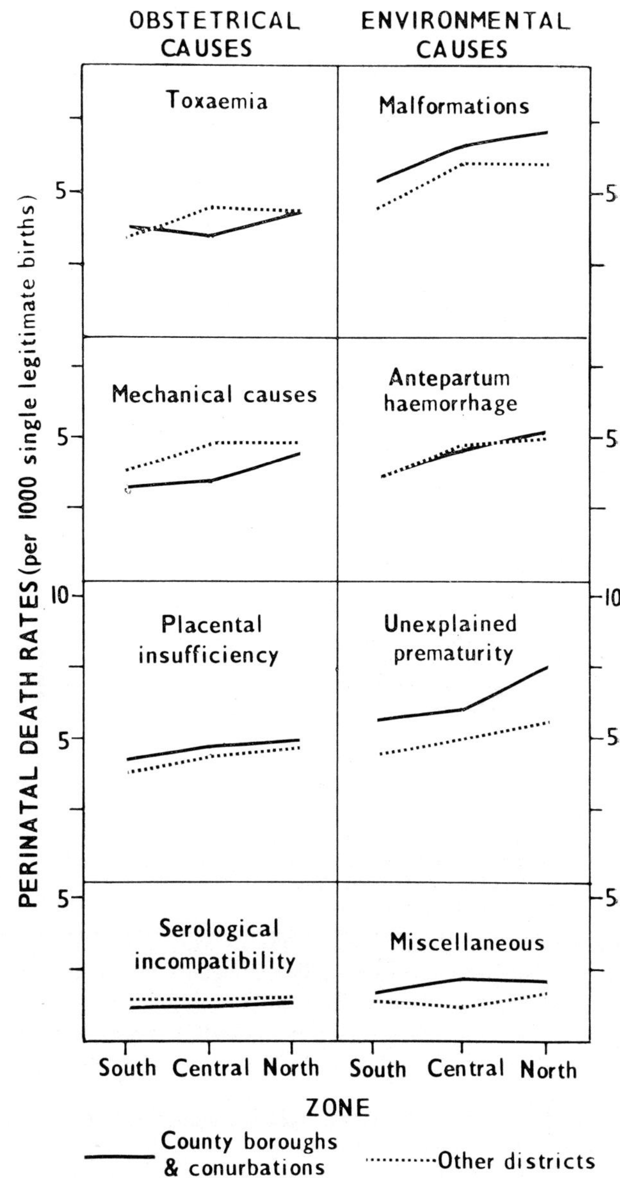

FIG. 4. Perinatal mortality from various causes by zone and urbanization: British Perinatal Mortality Survey, 1958.[2]

clinicopathological conditions are grouped together as "obstetrical" causes, since in these the chances of preventing death by obstetric intervention are relatively good. The other conditions are described as "environmental" causes, since they are more closely associated with environmental deficiencies and do not seem likely to become much less widespread except as maternal living standards improve. The terms "placental insufficiency" and "unexplained immaturity" are used in the figures, as in the 1958 report, to denote unexplained deaths at birth weights of over 2,500 gms. and 2,500 gms. or less respectively. This nomenclature may be criticized on semantic grounds, but is difficult to replace. Figures 4 and 5 show that, not surprisingly, the main "environmental" problems—malformations, antepartum haemorrhage and unexplained prematurity—were the conditions principally responsible for mortality being higher in the north than in the south, and for the

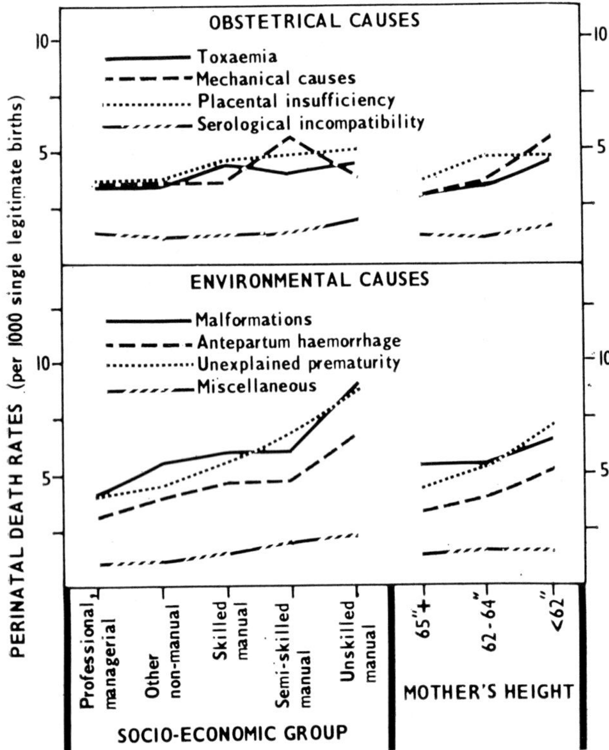

FIG. 5. Perinatal mortality from various causes by father's socio-economic status and mother's height: British Perinatal Mortality Survey, 1958.[2]

associations with socio-economic status and maternal height (except that the association of height with malformation was relatively weak). The corresponding trends for the obstetrical conditions were less marked, except for variations with zone and height in the mortality from mechanical causes.

The fact that mortality was relatively high in large towns was also largely accounted for by causes in the environmental group (Fig. 4). The death rates from some obstetrical causes, on the other hand, were higher outside large towns, especially in the Central Zone—possibly because of the fact that hospital confinement was less common in the less populous areas of the Central Zone than anywhere else. The finding that overall mortality in every zone was higher in the large towns than elsewhere (Table 1) suggests however that the more extensive obstetric hospital facilities which these towns have are insufficient to cancel out the effects of the environmental deficiencies to which the association of urbanization with short stature points.

Figure 6 shows that the main "obstetrical" causes of death—toxaemia, mechanical causes, and placental insufficiency—were largely responsible for the increase of overall

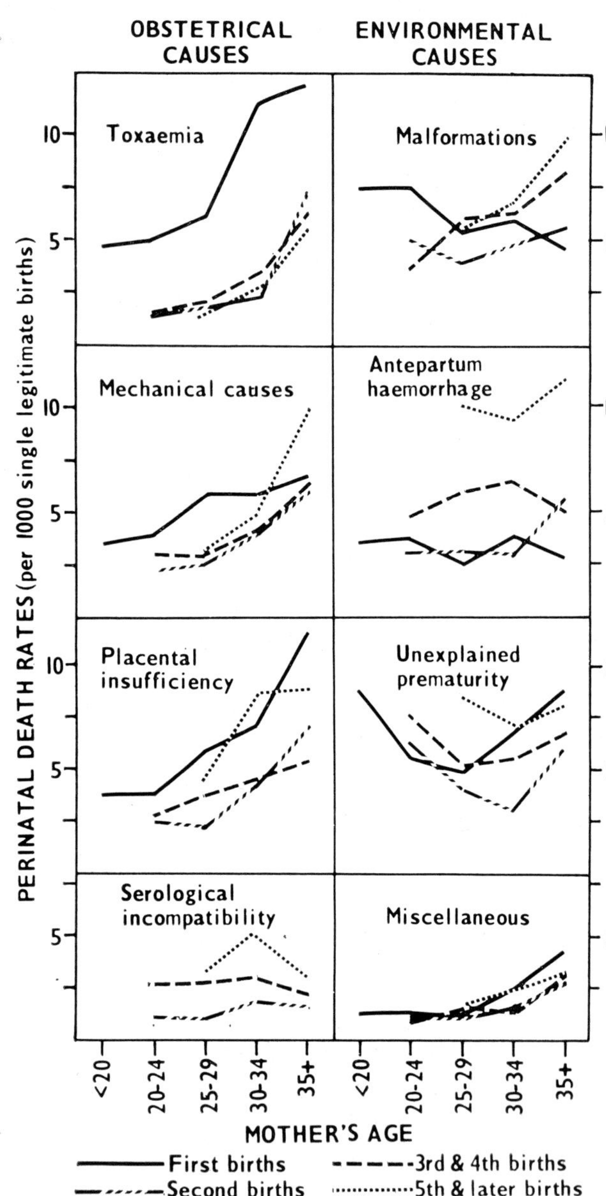

FIG. 6. Perinatal mortality from various causes by mother's age and parity: British Perinatal Mortality Survey, 1958.[2]

mortality with maternal age and its high frequency in first births (Fig. 2). Among the environmental causes, on the other hand, antepartum haemorrhage showed neither of these trends, and for malformations and unexplained prematurity they were limited in their extent. The risk to first births was high only at low maternal ages in the case of malformations, and at high ages in the case of unexplained prematurity. High maternal age was a risk factor for death from malformations only among the higher birth ranks. In unexplained prematurity the variation in mortality with maternal age was U-shaped for every birth rank.

The "environmental" causes were however consistent in contributing to the tendency for overall mortality to increase with birth rank in children who were not firstborn. Serological incompatibility showed a similar increase, but for the other obstetrical causes this trend was either completely absent or largely confined to birth ranks greater than four. The association of multi-parity with "environmental" causes of death may itself be seen as a reflection of the relationship of these deaths to environmental deficiencies, in view of the tendency for women in poor circumstances to have the largest families.

Practical Applications of Perinatal Mortality Statistics

The use of descriptive epidemiological methods to define the risk factors for perinatal death has so far justified itself mainly by enabling the mothers and children in whom these risks are concentrated to be singled out for special care, rather than by identifying specific pathogens which can be eliminated. The clinico-pathological conditions which lead to perinatal death may in many cases not be brought about by specific causes of major effect but by the interaction of a host of variables, many of them related in various ways to the mother's age, parity, and past and present environment. But although epidemiological attempts to disentangle these effects may be unrewarding, many infant lives can be and have been saved by using criteria of risk derived from epidemiological studies to select pregnant women for hospital confinement and, in some cases, obstetric intervention.

Elderly primigravidae are one example of a group whose offspring have benefitted from such an approach. Figure 6 shows that during the 1958 survey an unusually high proportion of these children died from placental insufficiency. When the first births are broken down by gestation length as well as maternal age (Fig. 7), it is seen that in each age group prolonged pregnancy is associated with an increase in mortality from placental insufficiency, and that the main reason for the effect of maternal age on mortality is that with advancing maternal age the increases with gestation length begin earlier and become more extreme.

The clinical precursor of death in these cases is fetal distress. The frequency with which this condition occurs without apparent cause or during difficult labour was shown by epidemiological studies in Aberdeen around 1950[64] to be associated with first pregnancies, prolonged gestation and high maternal age in a similar way to the deaths shown in Fig. 7. This finding led to the introduction of a policy of surgical induction of labour, at or soon after term, to ensure that as many pregnancies as possible, especially in elderly primigravidae, ended before entering the high-risk weeks. Caesarian section was also done more often in these cases, to cut short or avoid the stress of labour.

To illustrate the effectiveness of these measures, the mortality among first births in Aberdeen in the last five years before the measures were taken (1948–52) and the next ten years (1953–62) is compared in Fig. 8. The

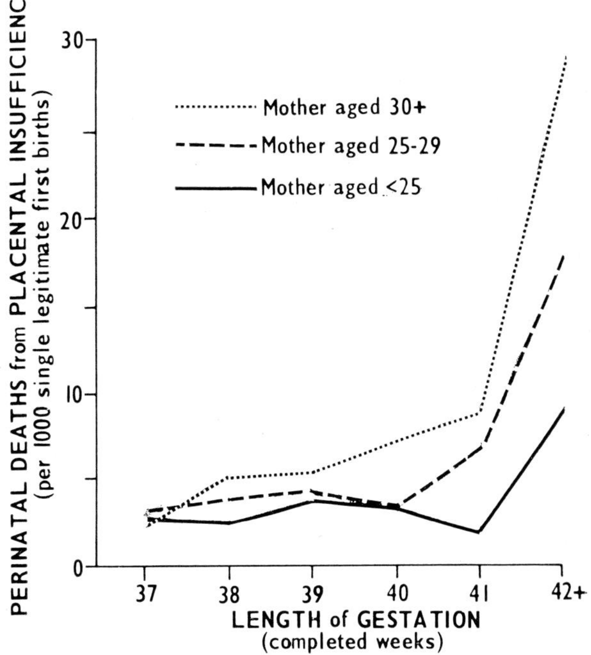

FIG. 7. Perinatal mortality from placental insufficiency in firstborn children, by mother's age and length of gestation: British Perinatal Mortality Survey, 1958.[2]

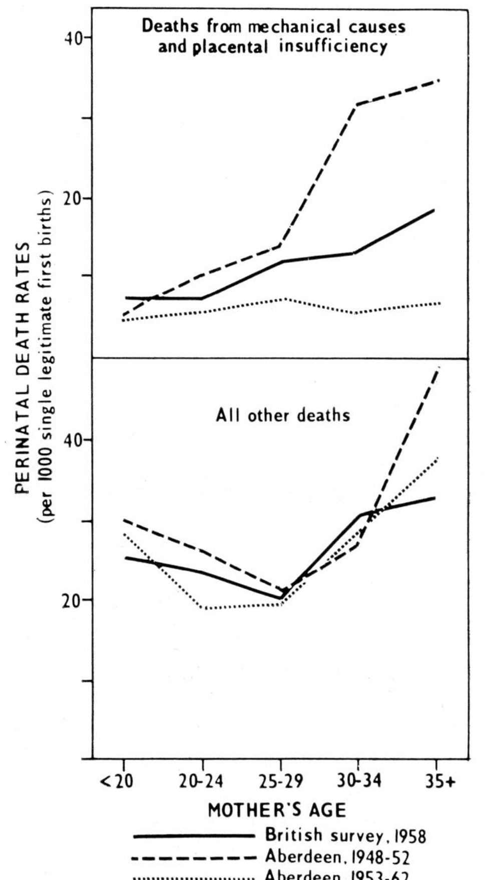

FIG. 8. Perinatal mortality from two groups of causes in three cohorts of firstborn children, by mother's age.[2]

association of maternal age with placental insufficiency and mechanical causes completely disappeared after 1952, leaving a rate in every age group almost level with that previously observed at maternal ages under 20. In Great Britain as a whole, there was apparently still room for considerable improvement in the rate in 1958, when it was quite strongly associated with maternal age and considerably higher than in Aberdeen. The differences between the two Aberdeen rates from other causes and the British one were not nearly so marked. But new ways of preventing some deaths from these causes may well be suggested by epidemiological studies in the future.

SOME COMMON MALFORMATIONS: DESCRIPTIVE AND CORRELATIVE STUDIES OF GROUPS

Malformations are today perhaps the most intractable of all paediatric problems. They cause more deaths during the perinatal period than any of the other clinico-pathological conditions distinguished above (Chapter 41A, Table 2, p. 709); and whereas the overall death rate during late fetal life, infancy and childhood has been reduced to about one-quarter of what it was 30 years ago, the corresponding figure for deaths from malformations now is still two-thirds as high as then (Chapter 41A, Table 3, p. 710). Even this limited reduction has added the disabilities of many children now surviving who would formerly have died (e.g. with spina bifida) to the burden which malformations represent for society.

Incidence rates for common malformations (those found in at least 0·1 per cent of births) were given in Chapter 41A, Table 7 (p. 720). The epidemiology of these conditions, as of perinatal deaths in general, has been explored mainly by descriptive methods. The contrasts in incidence which these methods have disclosed, between children born in different times or places or with different parental characteristics, are however now beginning to be explored by comparing the incidence rates in these different groups with their intake of substances that might be teratogenic—by correlative studies of groups, in other words. Besides showing how in this way descriptive studies can lead to correlative ones, the work on common malformations illustrates how descriptive methods may clarify the relative importance of the roles that genotype and environment in general play in causation.

Descriptive Studies

The descriptive methods by which the aetiological roles of genetic and environmental factors can be clarified include (a) comparisons of the incidence rates found in different communities and (b) studies of the relationship of incidence to time and to parental circumstance within individual communities. Unfortunately, the scope for comparative studies of the incidence of most of the common malformations in different communities is rather limited, since except for a few places the available data relate only to cases diagnosed in obstetric units, where defects of most types are too often overlooked for the findings to be an adequate guide to incidence. The main exception to this generalization is that data collected soon after birth in different communities can usefully be compared in respect of anencephaly, spina bifida and encephalocele, and cleft lip. In the largest series in which age at ascertainment appears to have been studied, these were the only common defects which were apparently diagnosed within two weeks of birth in more than 90 per cent of cases.[30]

Besides covering many communities, the epidemiological studies of these neural tube and lip defects are particularly instructive because of the contrasting results they are yielding, pointing in the case of cleft lip to a predominantly genetic aetiology and in the neural tube defects to one with an important environmental component. These therefore are the only malformations to be considered below, although by no means the only ones in which epidemiological studies have proved rewarding.[6,67]

Studies of Single Communities

The Birmingham study quoted in Chapter 41A, Table 7 (p. 720), which has been extended to cover a population of 406,507 children (including stillbirths) born to city residents in 1950–69,[29] will be taken as an example of the many studies in which incidence has been related to time and to parental circumstances.

Methods of Study. The primary sources of information in this study, both as to malformations and about the demographic characteristics of all the children, were record cards which are filled in by obstetric staff and health visitors and from which punch cards that can be mechanically or electronically analysed are prepared in the Health Department of the city. Additional malformations were ascertained by checking records of contacts with some of the other health services (detailed in Chapter 41A, p. 719).

The incidence of neural tube defects and cleft lip in various subgroups of the Birmingham population is shown in Fig. 9. The data relate to children of all ethnic groups born in 1950–69, except for the distributions by parental social class, which exclude all children born before 1960 and those whose parents were both West Indians. Social class was not recorded for births before 1960, and as West Indians have a low incidence of these defects their inclusion would have tended to depress incidence in the less privileged social classes where they are concentrated. Cleft lip alone has been grouped with cleft lip and palate, and encephalocele with spina bifida—partly to make the data comparable with series from elsewhere in which the more detailed categories were not distinguished, and partly because the distributions seen when these categories are examined separately[29] are in agreement with familial and embryological studies in suggesting that the paired conditions are aetiologically similar.

Some of the groups for which rates are given in Fig. 9 contained only a few thousand births and were therefore likely to include only a handful of cases of each defect. In these circumstances, quite marked variations in incidence often occur at random, and even when a much higher or lower than average rate is found the investigator must ask himself whether the frequency with which variations of at least this magnitude occur by chance (i.e. the statistical probability) is low enough for the observed findings to be regarded as important. In preparing Fig. 9, only the statistical probability associated with each individual finding was estimated, by using the χ^2 test (with Yates's correction) to compare the incidence rate in each group with the rate in all other groups combined. This approach has the disadvantage of not taking account of the sequence in which high and low rates occurred, which may also affect the interpretation of such variations. For example, the monthly variations in the incidence of spina bifida (Fig. 9) must not only be taken more seriously than those for cleft lip because they are more extreme, but also because the highest spina bifida rates occurred in adjacent months (December and January) and so did the lowest (in June and July), whereas the corresponding rates for cleft lip were widely separated—April and December having the highest rates, and January and July the lowest. There are ways of estimating statistical probability which take account of sequence,[11,12] but to introduce them might unduly complicate this account.

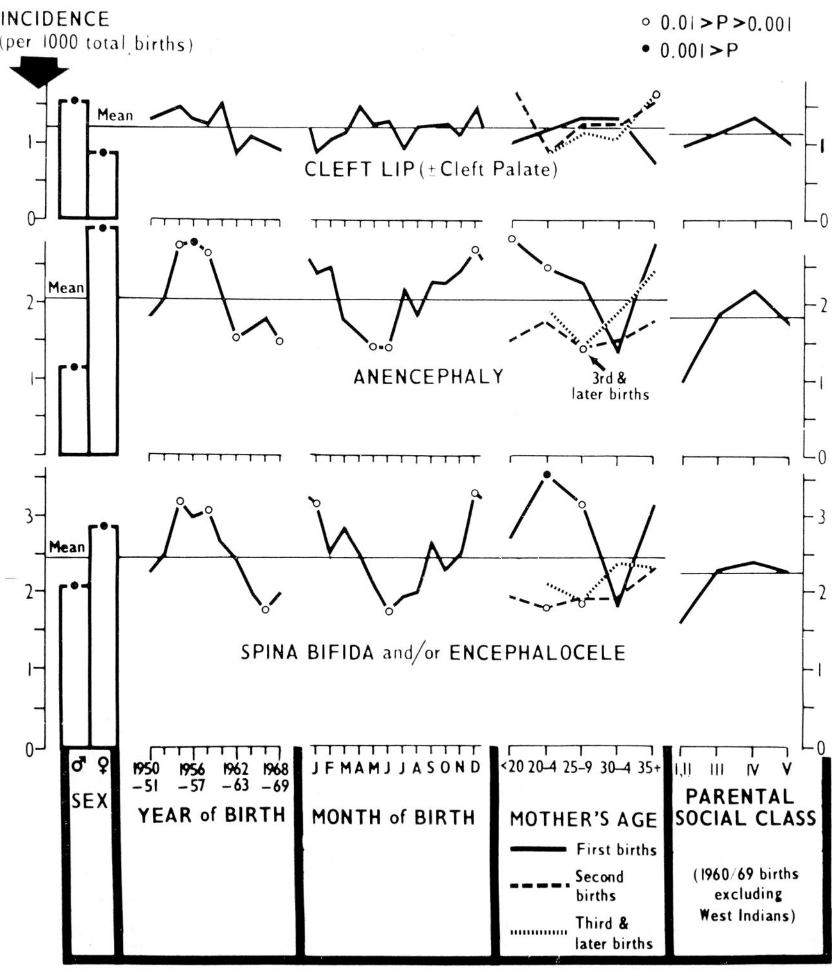

FIG. 9. Incidence of common obvious malformations in various groups of children born in Birmingham, England, in 1950–69.[29] Groups which differed significantly from the rest of the population in respect of incidence were identified by the χ^2 test with Yates's correction.

Results. In the case of cleft lip, the only variations in incidence that were shown to be significant at the 1 per cent level were the high sex ratio and the excess among births of high maternal age and parity. The data do not make it clear whether the latter association is really with age and parity or with age alone: there were so few first and second births to mothers over 35 that the differences in incidence between these and the later births could well have arisen by chance. If the increase with maternal age was not related to parity, it as well as the high sex ratio may have been genetically determined, like the parental age effects observed in some disorders caused by single-gene mutations and trisomies.[45] Conditions like these often produce multiple defects—cleft lip, microphthalmia and polydactyly in d-trisomy, for example;[42] and other surveys in which an increase in the incidence of cleft lip with maternal age has been observed suggest that this increase may be confined to cases with other malformations.[14] Studies distinguishing between the ages of fathers and mothers (which should ideally be done whenever a maternal age effect is found, since the two ages are highly correlated) suggest that the association of cleft lip with maternal age may be secondary to a paternal effect.[19,69]

In contrast to cleft lip, the two categories of neural tube defects seem to be related to all the variables examined, and these relationships are very similar for the two categories. The incidence of both increased during the early 1950's, decreased again after 1959, and was higher in winter than summer, higher in females than males, and relatively low in the professional and managerial classes—although the latter deficiency only becomes significant at the 1 per cent level when data for both categories are combined. Both were particularly common in first births (except apparently to mothers in the early 30's) and uncommon in second births. Their incidence in third and later births was much the same as in second births at maternal ages below 30, but higher at later ages. Broadly similar associations between all these variables and the incidence of anencephaly have been demonstrated in nationwide studies, and appear from these studies to be largely independent of one another.[15,48] Most of these associations are believed to point to the involvement of environmental factors in the aetiology of neural tube defects, although some may merely reflect differences between groups in the proportions of embryos that survive long enough to be born as opposed to being aborted.[29]

One further approach to the descriptive study of individual communities involves determining whether "clusters" of malformations—groups of cases arising at about the same time in the same locality—occur more often than would be expected if they happened only at random. Outbreaks of infectious disease and of environmental pollution by toxic chemicals do not generally happen everywhere at the same time, and malformations too might be expected to show clustering if and when caused by such hazards. Many ways of testing for clustering of malformations have been described, but none as yet that is universally acceptable.[26,36] A few workers have applied some of these methods, largely with negative results, to data for cleft lip, anencephaly and spina bifida in individual communities of sufficient size for their members to be separated by distances of up to a few miles.[14,17]

Comparisons Between Communities

As already indicated (Chapter 41.A, pp. 718–719), the comparability of data on malformations collected in different places is too often impaired by variations in diagnostic criteria, in the completeness of reporting, and in the representativeness of the births surveyed. So far as cleft lip, anencephaly, and spina bifida aperta are concerned, however, diagnosis is relatively easy, and many of the estimates of their incidence now available are from centres where the reporting of defects also is believed to be reasonably complete. These figures are not all representative of the localities from which they came, since some are from hospitals where the women delivered include a higher than average proportion with obstetrical problems, but the effects of this selection on incidence are probably limited. Belfast, for example, has been quoted as a place where these effects are strong, since four-fifths of anencephalic births and only three-fifths of all births there occur in hospital;[59] but the effect this has of making the hospital rate of anencephaly higher by one-third than the community rate, although serious in some contexts, is small in relation to the contrasts between the incidence rates reported from different countries. In places where smaller proportions of births occur in hospitals, the effects of selection could theoretically be greater than in Belfast, but the rates reported by these hospitals are not high enough to suggest that any such trend exists in practice—possibly because the general level of antenatal care in the communities they serve is too low for there to be efficient selection. It therefore seems legitimate to compare broadly the rates observed in different centres.

Methods of Study. Figure 10 summarizes data for 28 series of births, selected because each included more than 10,000 children, all or nearly all of whom were inferred to belong to one broad ethnic group, and who had been screened for all cases of the relevant defects (including those associated with still-birth or with other malformations) by methods which seemed fairly reliable.[29]

Attention was focussed on children of known ethnic group because of the relevance of this variable to the understanding of differences in incidence between places. Such differences may reflect the aetiological influence of either genotype or environment. If genetically determined, they are likely to be most marked between children of different ethnic groups, and to be found even when members of these groups born in the same place are compared. Differences of environmental origin, on the other hand, may be as great between places where the inhabitants are of the same ethnic group as where they are not, but be absent between those of different ethnic groups living in the same place.

The communities represented in Fig. 10 have been grouped according to the primary races that predominated in their ancestry. Latin Americans described as Mestizo or European have been placed in a separate group, since they are of mixed Caucasoid and American Indian ancestry. The points are linked by lines of dashes to show the variability observed within each primary race by place and racial subgroup; and some impression of the effects of primary race itself can be gained by comparing the different lines. Three "places"—Birmingham, Hawaii, and an aggregate of 12 U.S. cities—are each represented by two or more points, which relate to different racial subgroups. These points, and the points for other places where one of the same subgroups occurred, have each been labelled with two initials, the first showing the race and the second the place, so that the rates experienced by populations who differed in respect of only one of these two variables can be compared.

Results. The incidence of cleft lip varies relatively little within each primary race, and much more so between these races, especially if one disregards the isolated point at the upper end of the Caucasoid range (which is based on 11,000 Johannesburg births). The low, moderate and high rates characteristic of Negroids, Caucasoids and Mongoloids respectively were observed even in the places where two primary races were studied. The range for Latin Americans, whose ancestors on the American Indian side were of course probably of Mongoloid origin, lies between the Caucasoid and Mongoloid ranges. All these findings are consistent with the data shown in Fig. 9 in suggesting that the incidence of cleft lip is strongly affected by the genotype, but little if at all by the environment.

The incidence of anencephaly varies very strikingly indeed among the Caucasoids, but not nearly so much within or between the Mongoloid, Negroid and Latin American groups, which are more or less level with the lower end of the Caucasoid range. The findings where members of two or more ethnic groups live in the same places seem to be variable. The defect is uncommon in Negroids even in British and American cities where Caucasoids are relatively often affected, but frequency in Caucasoids seem to be more sensitive to local influences: the incidence in Caucasoids is much closer in Hawaii than in the continental United States to the figures for Mongoloids in Hawaii, and a similar pattern is observed when children of Irish origin born in Birmingham and in Ireland are compared with British children born in Birmingham.

The other neural tube defects vary in frequency between populations in much the same way as anencephaly; but they affect Mongoloids less often, except in Hawaii, where the Mongoloid figures are closer to those observed in United States Caucasoids.

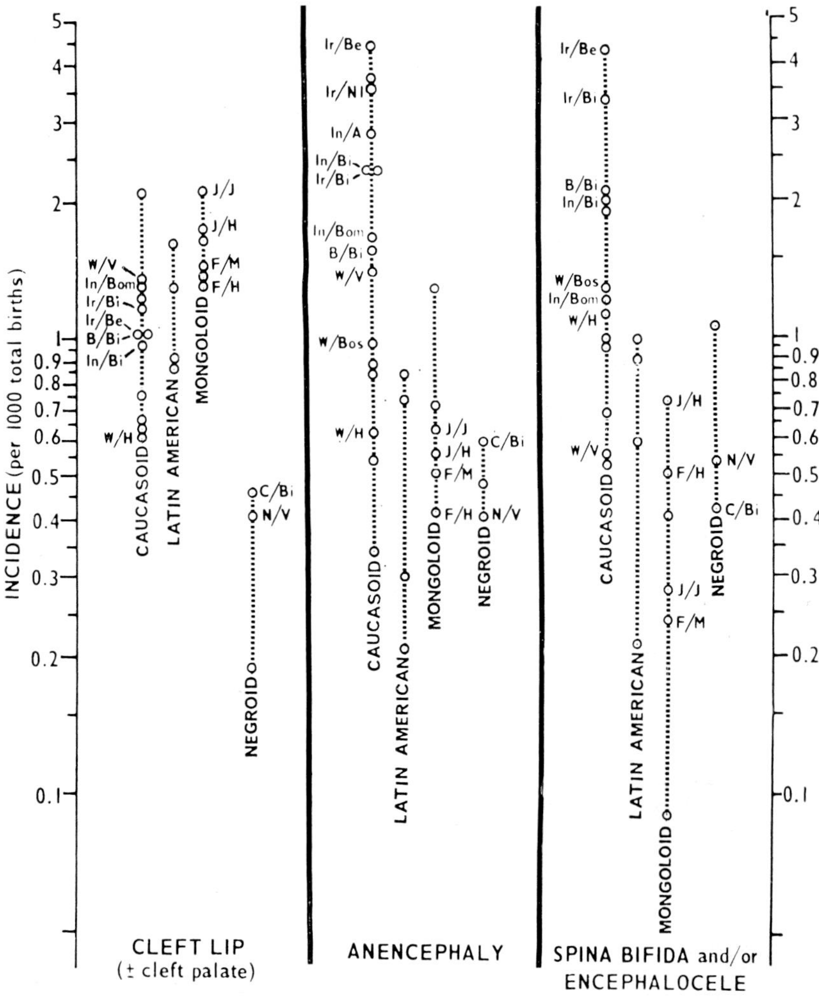

FIG. 10. Incidence of common obvious malformations in series of over 10,000 children of relatively homogeneous ethnic group, plotted logarithmically and aligned according to the primary races that predominated in their ancestry.[29] Points labelled with pairs of initials refer to populations that were represented by two or more series of different ethnic groups, or that were of similar ethnic group to one of these series. The first initial of each pair denotes ethnic group: B(ritish), C(aribbean), F(ilipino), In(dian, Bangladeshi, or Pakistani), Ir(ish), J(apanese), N(egroid American), W(hite American). The second denotes place: A(mritsar, Punjab), Be(lfast, Northern Ireland), Bi(rmingham, England), Bom(bay), Bos(ton, Mass.), H(awaii), J(apanese cities), M(anila), N(orthern) I(reland), V(arious U.S. cities).

Like the variations with time, birth rank, and social class shown in Fig. 9, most data for different places and ethnic groups suggest that the incidence of neural tube defects is affected much more by the environment and less by the genotype than is the case for cleft lip. Findings consistent with this view are the extent to which incidence varies according to place within some primary races (especially the

Caucasoid); the wide overlap between the ranges for different races; and the tendency for the differences between the British and Irish, and between Mongoloids and Caucasoids, to be less when they live in the same place. And although the contrast in incidence between Negroids and some Caucasoids seems to persist even in children born in the same cities so long as the parents are both of one race, the incidence in Birmingham children of European mothers and Caribbean fathers appears to be virtually as high as when both parents are European[29]—suggesting that incidence is not governed by the *child's* genes, but by the effects on the intra-uterine environment of genetic or other characteristics of the *mother* that are race-related.

Correlative Studies of Groups

Although the above and other descriptive studies appear to shed some light on the relative importance of genotype and environment in the aetiology of different defects, they have not so far led to the identification of specific causes in either of these fields. There is now considerable evidence, mainly from studies of the incidence of malformations in patient's relatives, that the genetic component in the aetiology of most malformations involves many genes with cumulative effects. The sum of these effects can be envisaged as a score in respect of which all embryos are normally distributed, the ones at risk of malformation being those whose score exceeds a threshold value.[6] The fact that even monozygotic twins do not always have the same malformations,[6] in spite of occupying the same uterus as well as having the same genes, suggests that the influence of the environment may be equally subtle, and so does the general complexity of embryonic development—in which even the formation of a single structure like the palate may be prevented by extreme variations in any of a considerable number of quantitative variables such as head width.[18] But even if the aetiology of each common defect involves many factors, it seems possible that in the case of neural tube defects some of these factors are environmental influences which are powerful enough to double incidence. If for example the seasonal variations in the frequency of these defects are due to a single influence, it must be one with an effect of this magnitude. There is also a more than two-fold increase in incidence across the British Isles from the South East to the North and West (shown in Fig. 11 for the Standard Regions of England and Wales and for northern and southern Scotland and Ireland) which it has been suggested may have an environmental cause.[60]

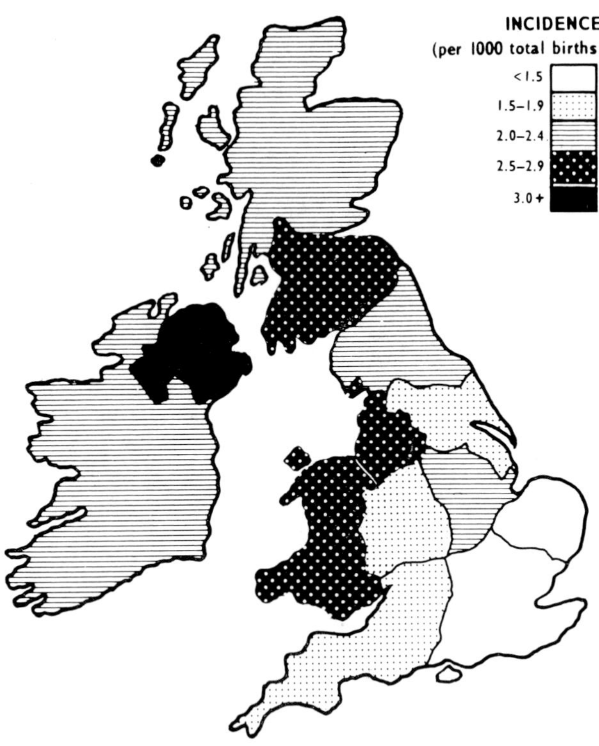

FIG. 11. Regional incidence of anencephaly recorded on stillbirth and infant death certificates in the British Isles: 1965–67.[13]

Perhaps the most obvious variables to explore as causes of these variations are the constituents of food and drink that are affected by season or region; and several correlative studies of groups have recently been carried out in which the incidence of neural tube defects in these groups has been compared with their intakes of calcium (in drinking water), blighted potatoes, and many other foods.

Calcium in Drinking Water

The hypothesis that the level of calcium in drinking water might be important was suggested as a possible explanation for the regional differences in incidence in Great Britain, since in the North and West, where incidence is highest, the water tends to be softer than in the South-East. This hypothesis has been tested by relating the incidence of anencephaly in 58 large towns in England and Wales to the calcium content of their drinking water.[34] Although the coefficient of correlation between these two variables is positive, it can be shown by aggregating the figures for towns with similar calcium levels (Fig. 12) that the incidence

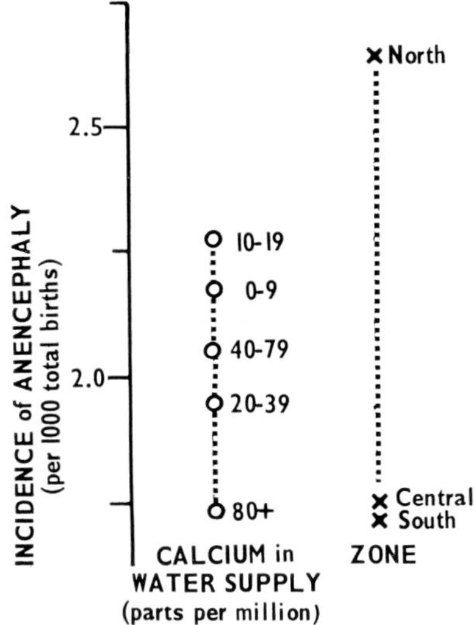

FIG. 12. Perinatal mortality ascribed to anencephaly in county boroughs of England and Wales, grouped by calcium content of water supply and by zone: 1965–67.[34]

of anencephaly does not increase regularly as calcium level decreases, and also that incidence varies less in relation to calcium level than in relation to Zone (as defined on p. 730)—which is the reverse of the pattern expected if the regional differences were secondary to variations in water softness.

Blighted Potatoes

Potatoes first came under suspicion because the amounts consumed, like the incidence of anencephaly, are particularly high in Ireland and among the socially underprivileged, and also because the concentration of the toxic alkaloids (derivatives of solanidine) which potatoes synthesize is probably relatively high in tubers eaten in spring, when the children with the highest seasonal incidence of anencephaly are conceived.[49]

More recently, it has been shown that the production (and by inference the consumption) of potatoes affected by blight in different parts of the world may correlate more closely than total potato production with the incidence rate of

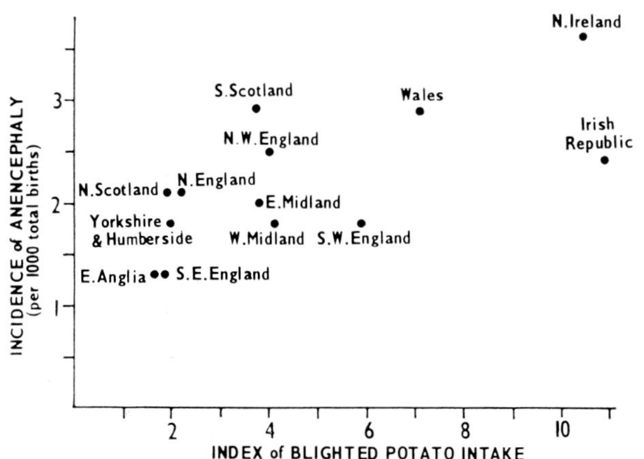

FIG. 13. Relationship of regional incidence of anencephaly in the British Isles (Fig. 11) to an index of blighted potato intake obtained by multiplying weekly potato consumption (Kgs./head) by estimated blight intensity (graded 1, 2, or 3) in each region.[50]

neural tube defects, and various changes in this rate from year to year have been interpreted as reflecting variations of blight intensity.[50,51,52] The most detailed numerical data reported were for the regions of the British Isles shown in Fig. 11, and for the years 1961–8 in England and Wales.

For the regions, total potato consumption per head and crude blight intensity (the latter measured on a three point scale) were given. Figure 13 shows the correlation between the incidence of anencephaly and an index of blighted potato intake (obtained by multiplying blight intensity by potato consumption). The coefficient of correlation is quite low (+0·68), but one factor here is the relatively low incidence of anencephaly reported for the Irish Republic, for which under-reporting (arising from the fact that stillbirth registration is only voluntary in the Republic) may be to blame.

The data given for 1961–8 were the percentages of tubers visibly blighted when harvested each year (0·90–3·33 per cent), which were compared with the incidence rates of anencephaly (corrected for linear trend) among births $1\frac{1}{8}$ years later (1·828–1·913/1,000). In this instance the coefficient of correlation is higher (+0·87), suggesting that most of the year-to-year variability in the incidence of anencephaly could be caused by variations in blight prevalence. Even if this were so, the equation for the regression of the incidence of anencephaly (a) on the prevalence of blight (b) which these data yield ($a = 0{\cdot}0336\, b + 1{\cdot}8007$) predicts that 1·80/1,000 births would still have been affected had there been no blight; but such equations do not always hold good beyond the range of values encountered.

It has been argued from these and other correlative studies of groups that potatoes damaged by disease and long storage may contain teratogens. But such studies are not on their own an adequate basis for drawing firm conclusions, and so far there have been no correlative studies of individuals* or experimental studies on man, although cranial osseous defects have been reported in marmosets whose mothers were fed blighted potatoes.[47]

Other Foods

The relationship of a wide variety of foods to the incidence of anencephaly in England and Wales has recently been explored using estimates of food intake for each quarter in 1961–7, prepared by the Ministry of Agriculture in London.[27] The variations which series of quarterly figures such as these generally exhibit are often thought of as having three components, known as annual, seasonal and residual. The seasonal and annual components are the variations exhibited respectively by the quarterly rates for all years combined and by the annual rates. The residual component embraces all differences between the observed quarterly figures and those that would have occurred if each year's intake had been distributed in the same way between quarters as the intake for all years combined. These three components of the figures for each common food were tested for correlations with the corresponding components of the incidence of anencephaly a few months later. A particularly suggestive correlation involving all three components was found between the intake of cured meats and the incidence of anencephaly six months later (Fig. 14). The main similarities were declines in the *annual* figures after 1963–4; *seasonal* peaks in summer for cured meat intake and in winter for anencephaly; and *residual* deficiencies in the figures for cured meat intake in late 1964 (after a typhoid epidemic transmitted by corned beef) and for anencephaly six months later.

At the time of writing, the lines of research suggested by this analysis have not even been pursued as far as those arising from the association of defects with potatoes: no experiments involving the feeding of cured meat to animals have yet been reported, nor any studies of intake in relation to international differences in the incidence of anencephaly, although intake in England and Wales seems to vary in a similar way to incidence.[27] But despite the gaps in our knowledge, the hypotheses linking neural tube defects to

* Since this chapter was written one report has appeared of a correlative study of individuals, with negative results. Retrospective estimates of potato consumption during pregnancy were obtained from mothers of children with spina bifida and of controls (Clarke, C. A., McKendrick, O. M., and Sheppard, P. M., 1973, Spina bifida and potatoes. *Brit. med. J.*, **iii**, 251–254.

blighted potatoes and cured meat seem to be among the more promising ideas about these defects to have emerged from correlative studies of groups. And the use of these

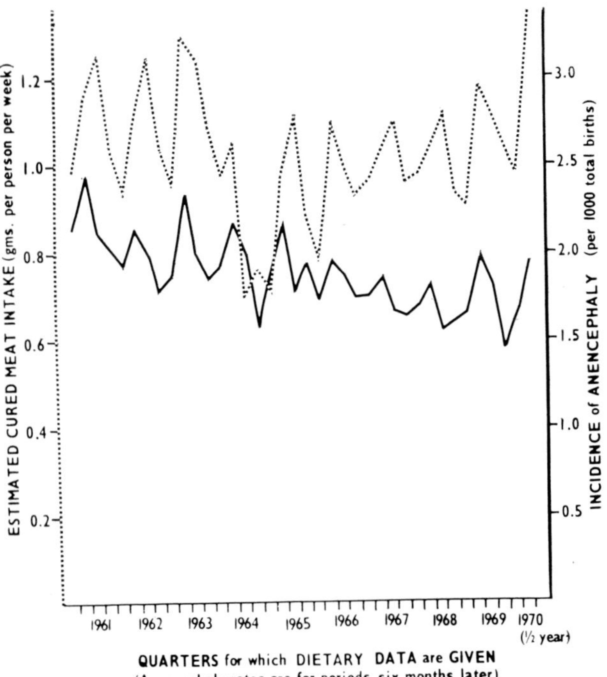

FIG. 14. Quarterly intake of cured meat (dotted line) related to incidence of anencephaly six months later (according to stillbirth and infant death certificates—continuous line) in England and Wales.[27] Cured meat intake was estimated by adding all the corned meat consumed to half the cooked bacon and ham.

examples to illustrate the methods, potentialities and limitations of such studies, which is our main purpose in discussing them here, will remain valid whether or not the hypotheses prove correct.

EFFECTS OF RUBELLA AND THALIDOMIDE: CORRELATIVE STUDIES OF INDIVIDUALS

Epidemiology began as the study of epidemics. During the last century, the developed countries have experienced a great diminution in the impact made by most of the infections traditionally thought of as epidemic diseases, and an enlargement of the scope of epidemiology to cover disease frequency in general. But the finding of causes for epidemic diseases continues to be one of the most obviously productive areas of epidemiological research—largely because diseases that occur in epidemics generally do so as a result of being caused by specific environmental factors which vary in prevalence and which are therefore often relatively easy to identify and—once identified—to eliminate.

Most of the paediatric problems of this kind that have arisen in recent decades—like those in other fields of medicine—were first defined and explored by the descriptive and correlative methods of studying groups that have already been illustrated, but required correlative studies of individuals and experimental studies to solve them finally. From this field, some surveys of the defects now known to be caused by rubella and thalidomide have been selected as examples of correlative studies of individuals, and the experimental approach is illustrated by some controlled investigations of retrolental fibroplasia.

Two Epidemics of Malformations

Two clinicians, N. McA. Gregg in 1941[21] and H.-R. Wiedemann in 1961,[68] first described in print the most obvious features of the syndromes now known to be caused by rubella and thalidomide respectively, and reported that these conditions (especially congenital cataract in Gregg's syndrome and amelia and phocomelia in Wiedemann's) had become relatively common whereas previously they had been very rare. The findings arose out of the clinical practice of these workers and their colleagues, as opposed to covering all the cases in defined populations, and therefore could not be converted into incidence rates as is desirable in epidemiological work. But even when not precisely quantified, comparisons such as by implication these workers made between the frequency of disorders at different times can be regarded as descriptive epidemiology.

Although the epidemics of the two syndromes first came to light in rather similar circumstances, there were various differences between the ways in which their respective causes were found, of which the most important from a methodological viewpoint was in the relative importance of the parts played by correlative studies of groups and of individuals. The relationship of maternal rubella to the epidemic of cataracts was first suggested by what was in effect a correlative study of groups, when Gregg considered whether the cohort or group consisting of all children born during this epidemic had been exposed more than other cohorts to any toxic or infective condition during early prenatal life, and was struck by the fact that there had been a very widespread and severe outbreak of rubella in 1940.[21] The role of correlative studies of individuals in exploring the aetiology of Gregg's syndrome has therefore only been to confirm and quantify an already formulated hypothesis. The hypothesis that the sedative thalidomide was causing amelia and phocomelia, on the other hand, seems to have been first suggested by correlative studies of individuals.[32,37,65]

The studies of individuals by which each syndrome was investigated included surveys of both the kinds distinguished when childhood morbidity in general was discussed (Chapter 41.A, p. 720): *cross-sectional, retrospective or case history studies*, in which the data on events in pregnancy were collected when the defects of which the causation was being studied had already manifested themselves; and *longitudinal, prospective or cohort studies*, in which the antenatal data were recorded before the outcome of the pregnancy was known. It is of course much more expensive, both of time and money, to collect data prospectively than to wait until cases of the disorder can be identified—both because a very large number of individuals in whom the subsequent outcome is normal must generally be surveyed if the yield of abnormalities is to be adequate, and also because follow-up is essential. The extra effort can however be more than justified if histories taken when the sequel is known are liable to be biased by this sequel, which accounts of events in pregnancy often are.

The first retrospective study of each syndrome to be published was one in which only the mothers of affected children were questioned in detail and comparable data were not obtained for other mothers. In 1941, Gregg himself enquired specifically about rubella, with positive results in all but 10 of the 78 cases of cataract he studied.[21] In 1961, detailed antenatal histories for 46 children who had amelia, phocomelia, or certain other limb and ear defects (which had also become more common) were obtained by W. Lenz and K. Knapp, mainly by questioning the mothers (often repeatedly) and their doctors, although records of prescriptions were also consulted when available. Forty-one of these women were said to have taken thalidomide in the first two months of pregnancy.[32]

Without statistics for other pregnancies to compare them with, these figures for cases in which malformations occurred did not formally prove that the defects were associated with rubella or thalidomide. The figures were highly suggestive; but to prove an association of this kind between a disorder and a possible cause, it must be shown either that a higher proportion of individuals with the disorder than of others has been exposed to the "cause," or that a higher proportion of exposed individuals than of others develop the disorder. These requirements were only fully met by subsequent studies, and in rather different ways for the two syndromes, which are therefore considered separately from this point.

The Association between Malformations and Rubella

Three examples of retrospective and prospective studies of the association between rubella and malformations will be described, all of which were concerned with the proportions of exposed individuals—children *in utero* when their mothers had rubella—who developed the malformations. The first study was retrospective. The second and third were both prospective, but in one the basis for regarding women as having had rubella was a positive history, whereas in the other serological evidence was required. The account of these studies is followed by a brief mention of other kinds of evidence that rubella causes malformations.

A Retrospective Survey

The first published data on the incidence of defects among children born after maternal rubella,[61] were obtained by asking all doctors in South Australia to send in details of all pregnancies in which acute exanthemata had occurred. By the time of the first report, 49 cases of maternal rubella had been reported, all preceding births in 1939–42. Thirty-one of the 49 children were said to have one or more defects. Four groups of defects were reported repeatedly: congenital heart disease; cataract or glaucoma; microcephaly or mental defect; and deafness.

Table 2 shows how many of the 18 normal and 31 handicapped children were born after rubella at different stages of pregnancy. Defects were present in all children notified who were born after rubella in the first two months of pregnancy, and half of those where the infection occurred in the third month. As the proportion of all children affected by significant malformations is only of the order of one in 40 (Chapter 41.A, p. 719), it was concluded that malformations were indeed very much commoner than average in children born after maternal rubella, with an incidence in the region of 100 per cent following infections in the first two months of pregnancy.

TABLE 2

RESULTS OF A RETROSPECTIVE STUDY OF CHILDREN BORN AFTER MATERNAL RUBELLA IN PREGNANCY[61]

Month in Pregnancy when Rubella Occurred	*Infants Born*		
	Total Number	*Number Malformed*	*Percentage Malformed*
1st	8	8	100
2nd	17	17	100
3rd	8	4	50
4th	3	1	33
5th and 6th	7	1	14
7th and over	6	—	0

A Prospective Survey Based on a Questionnaire

One of the most extensive studies of this kind was a survey of women in Great Britain who began receiving antenatal care from family doctors, hospitals, or local authority clinics between mid-1950 and the end of 1952.[35] The Medical Officers of Health of all the Local Authorities agreed to arrange for such women to be asked at their first and subsequent antenatal consultations about any illnesses they had experienced. If rubella, measles, mumps, chickenpox or poliomyelitis was mentioned, the patient's doctor was asked to confirm the diagnosis if he had been consulted, and in due course the outcome of pregnancy was noted, and living children were medically examined at birth and one and two years later. Some also had a complete paediatric examination later in childhood, but apart from a high prevalence of impaired hearing no additional defects were found—a fact which testified to the high standard of the original examination.

To serve as a control group, a sample of the women receiving antenatal care at the same time who gave no history of the five virus infections was drawn by selecting those who had themselves been born on the 31st of any month. These "control cases" were followed up in the same way as the cases with a history of infection.

Methods of Analysis. The numbers of abortions and children with defects revealed during the first two years of life by this survey are shown in Table 3, together with the incidence of the defects and three kinds of indices which quantify the increased frequency of abnormal outcomes of pregnancy after rubella—the *relative risk* and *attributable risk* of defects, and the *standardized abortion ratio.*

The *relative risk* of defects after rubella is the increase expressed as a ratio—the ratio of incidence after rubella to incidence in controls—and would therefore be expected to be unity if rubella was unrelated to incidence. The *attributable risk* is the increase expressed as a rate—the difference between the incidence rates after rubella and in controls—which would be expected to be zero if rubella and incidence were unrelated. The attributable risk is probably the more important to the pregnant woman who has had rubella, and to her medical attendants, since when accurate it shows what the chances are, if pregnancy continues, that she will have a child with defects due to rubella. The relative risk may matter more to the student of aetiology, since it helps him to decide whether the association between rubella and malformations is likely to be one of cause and effect. It would be relatively easy to believe in the alternative possibility that the relationship might be indirect—due, that is, to the existence of factors, perhaps in the mother's constitution, which predispose independently to both conditions—if defects were only twice as common in rubella cases as in controls; but higher relative risks make this possibility appear more remote and a causal relationship more likely.

Each *standardized abortion ratio* is the ratio of the observed number of abortions in a group of rubella pregnancies to an estimate of the number that would have occurred in these pregnancies, given the gestational ages from which they were followed up, if they had experienced at each stage of pregnancy the abortion rate observed in the control cases at the same stage. The reason for comparing observed and expected *numbers* of abortions in preference to the abortion *rates* for the rubella and control cases is that the rates were not strictly comparable: the controls were on average observed from earlier in pregnancy than the rubella cases, and would therefore be likely to stand a bigger chance of abortion after coming under observation. The method of comparing observed and expected numbers is also often used when studying the mortality or incidence of a disease in a particular set of people: an *age-sex-standardized mortality ratio* or *incidence ratio* is calculated, which is the ratio of the observed number of deaths or cases in the set to the number that would have occurred if the mortality or incidence rate in each sex and age group of the set had been the same as in the corresponding group of a control or standard population. This method is known as *indirect standardization*, as opposed to *direct standardization* which is exemplified by the use of age-sex-standardized mortality or incidence *rates*. As already indicated (Chapter 41.A, p. 706), the latter are estimates of the rates that would have occurred in different sets if all the members of each set had been distributed between the sexes and age groups in the same proportions as the members of a standard population.

TABLE 3

RESULTS OF A PROSPECTIVE STUDY OF THE OUTCOME OF PREGNANCIES IN WHICH THERE WAS A HISTORY OF RUBELLA[35]

	Spontaneous Abortions			*Total Births*				
Type of Case	Number observed (a)	Number expected[1] (b)	Standardized ratio $\left(\frac{a}{b}\right)$	Number born (c)	Number with defects[2] (d)	% with defects[2] $\left(\frac{100d}{c}\right)$	Attributable risk of defects[2] $\left(\frac{100d}{c} - 2{\cdot}8\right)$	Relative risk of defects[2] $\left(\frac{100d}{2{\cdot}8c}\right)$
Control	92	—	—	5,611	156	2·8	—	—
Rubella (by time of occurrence from onset of last menstrual period):								
1st–4th week	3	1·1	2·7	48	8	16·7	13·9	6·0
5th–8th week	2	1·9	1·1	67	12	17·9	15·1	6·4
9th–12th week	5	1·9	2·6	77	10	13·0	10·2	4·6
13th–16th week	1	1·0	1·0	74	3	4·1	1·3	1·4
17th–28th week	0	1·0	0·0	201	6	3·0	0·2	1·1
29th week and over	—	—	—	96	2	2·1	−0·7	0·7

[1] See text for method of calculation.
[2] Major defects ascertained at 0–2 years.

Results. In the study summarized in Table 3, ten abortions were observed following first-trimester rubella, which although not many were twice the number expected (4·9). Major defects were observed within the first two years of life in 30 (15·6 per cent) of the children (including stillbirths) born after first-trimester rubella, as against 11 (3·0 per cent) of those whose mothers had rubella later. Twenty-four (12·5 per cent) of the first-trimester cases, but only two of the later ones and not more than 0·94 per cent of all the controls, had cataract, congenital heart disease, mental subnormality or deafness, so that the attributable risk of these defects in children born after first trimester rubella was at least (12·5–0·9) or 11·6 per cent, and the relative risk was at least (12·5 ÷ 0·94), or 13·3.

Interpretation. This prospective survey supported the earlier retrospective studies in indicating a close association between certain defects and a history of rubella in early pregnancy, but gave a different impression of the strength of this association: whereas the retrospective data in Table 2 suggested that rubella in the first two months of pregnancy was always followed by the birth of an affected child, the results of the prospective survey (Table 3) seemed to indicate that major defects that manifest themselves within two years of birth were only present in about one-sixth of children whose mothers had rubella when less than two months pregnant. A similar impression of the risk to such children is gained when an overall view is taken of the many other prospective studies in which pregnant women have been questioned and their children examined.[53]

The main reason for the proportions of children affected being much higher in the cases of maternal rubella reported in the retrospective studies was that such events in pregnancy are likely to be remembered—or imagined—much more clearly than usual, by both patients and their doctors, if the outcome is abnormal. One illustration of this memory bias is the fact that among the cases summarized in Table 2, which were all notified in response to a questionnaire sent to doctors in late 1942, 19 of the 31 births of children with defects but only 2 of the 18 normal births after rubella that were recalled by doctors had occurred before 1942. The great merit of prospective surveys is that they are free from memory bias, and are therefore much less likely than retrospective studies to overestimate the incidence of a disease in individuals who have been exposed to a possible cause.

A Prospective Survey Using Serological Data

During the first six months of 1964, an extensive epidemic of rubella occurred in the United States. When this happened, clinical data and blood samples were already being collected during pregnancy from women booked for confinement in 14 university hospitals throughout the United States, as part of a prospective study of the influence of a wide range of prenatal factors on development. Women who attended these hospitals for antenatal care during January–June 1964 were asked additional questions about rubella, and the sera collected in pregnancy from the women with a positive history were tested for antibody to the rubella haemagglutinating antigen. In women for whom serum specimens had been obtained both before and after the reported illness, the diagnosis of rubella was regarded as confirmed if the second but not the first of these sera contained antibody. In women for whom there was no specimen from before the illness, an antibody titre of 128 or greater in a subsequent serum was accepted as confirmation. Standardized examinations of the children from all pregnancies were carried out by trained staff during the first days of life, and again in most cases at four months, eight months, one year and three years.[55,56]

TABLE 4

RESULTS OF A PROSPECTIVE STUDY OF THE OUTCOME OF PREGNANCIES IN WHICH THERE WAS SEROLOGICAL EVIDENCE OF RUBELLA INFECTION[55]

Time when Rubella Occurred	*Pregnancies (Excluding Abortions)*						
	Total Number	*Numbers with Children definitely Affected by Characteristic Defects*					*Percentage with Affected Child*
		Congenital Heart Disease	*Cataract, Glaucoma*	*Microcephaly, Mental and/or Motor Retardation*	*Hearing Loss*	*Total*	
0–28 days before conception	6	1	0	1	0	1	17
After conception:							
1st–13th week	35	5	4	8	5	10	29
14th–26th week	57	2	0	5	5	10	18
27th week and over	21	0	0	0	0	0	0

Results. Table 4 shows the numbers of defects of the types previously known to be associated with rubella that were found in 119 children born after confirmed maternal rubella, of whom 21 were affected by one or more of these defects. The 1964 epidemic also led to the widespread recognition that neonatal disturbances such as hepato-splenomegaly, thrombocytopaenia, and failure to thrive, were common in such children. Each of these disorders was observed soon after birth in 3 or more of the 21, and 4 of them had inguinal hernia.

Although the cases enumerated in Table 4 are too few to give more than the broadest indication of the risks associated with rubella, they suggest that these risks are higher than has been inferred from the results of the earlier surveys in which the diagnosis of rubella was based on clinical data only (as in Table 3). Exact comparisons between these surveys are not possible, since different groupings of the times when rubella occurred were used; but the data in Table 4 for infections from 28 days before to the 13th week after conception and for those during the next 13 weeks may be regarded as approximately comparable to the figures from the earlier survey for the first 16 weeks after onset of the last menstrual period and the next 12 weeks respectively. When the data are split in these ways, the incidence of the defects specified in Table 4 is found to have been 27 per cent following infection during the early weeks and 18 per cent following mid-pregnancy infections in the study using serological data. The corresponding figures for the earlier study were 10 per cent in cases infected during the early weeks, and zero in mid-pregnancy cases.

Interpretation. Two differences in method may have contributed to these discrepancies between the two sets of results. One is the greater rigour and consistency with which the children were examined in the more recent study. Most of the defects found following mid-pregnancy infections probably owed their detection to the quality of this examination procedure, since they tended to be less striking and less often multiple than the ones observed after earlier infections—for example, the two cases of congenital heart disease among them were both of peripheral pulmonic stenosis only.

The other difference to note is that the mothers of the children in the earlier series had only a clinical history suggestive of rubella, whereas in the second series there was also serological evidence of infection. The mothers of the first series, but not of the second, are therefore likely to have included some "false positives"—women in whom the diagnosis of rubella was incorrect. These women would probably have normal children, whose inclusion among those with maternal rubella would decrease the incidence of malformations in this group.

There must also have been some "false negatives"—women who had suffered an unrecognized rubella infection during pregnancy—in the populations from which both series of women with clinical rubella were drawn. As the children of "false negatives" are sometimes affected by defects of the rubella syndrome,[55,56] their inclusion among the children classified as controls (Table 3) would tend to make the incidence of defects in these controls higher than the true rate for children not exposed to rubella.

In other words, both kinds of errors in recording exposure to a hazard—"false negatives" and "false positives"—can make the apparent difference in incidence between exposed and unexposed less than the real difference. Although serological methods of diagnosis can largely overcome this problem as far as rubella is concerned they cannot be used when aetiological factors involving non-infective agents are being tested. In such circumstances one may have to accept that even the best estimates of risk that can be obtained by prospective surveys are liable to be conservative.

Laboratory Findings

Prior to the isolation of the rubella virus in 1962, the case for rubella being a teratogen rested entirely on the epidemiological evidence provided by the above and other correlative studies, the essential point of which was the high relative risk of certain defects after maternal rubella in early pregnancy—a risk whose magnitude seemed to rule out the possibility that the association was merely indirect. This evidence has now been corroborated by two laboratory proofs. These proofs are firstly the finding that all or nearly all children with the rubella syndrome of defects also have rubella antibodies, and secondly the recovery of the rubella virus itself from many of them.[8]

Material from therapeutic abortions has also been studied virologically, with results which suggest that at least 50 per cent of embryos and fetuses become infected with the virus in first trimester maternal rubella—a finding which has led some workers to suggest that the lower estimates of incidence yielded by even the most sophisticated epidemiological studies may be incorrect.[8,53] There are however at least two other possible reasons for the discrepancies. Firstly, experience with other malformations (Chapter 41.A, p. 719) and the increased frequency of spontaneous abortions seen after rubella (Table 3) suggest that a disproportionate number of rubella-damaged embryos and fetuses are aborted, in which case the proportion of infected fetuses among those who survive to be born normally must be less than in early pregnancy. Secondly, it seems that not all infected offspring develop defects: some workers have detected virus and antibody in substantial proportions of clinically normal infants whose mothers had rubella in early pregnancy.[4,46]

The Association between Malformations and Thalidomide

The dramatic increase in the frequency of limb defects which Wiedemann[68] reported in 1961 led several investigators to formulate and investigate the hypothesis that some environmental factor which had recently become more widespread might be to blame. Lenz's retrospective study of mothers of affected children which has already been mentioned (p. 743) was but one of at least three investigations that led independently to incrimination of thalidomide. One of the other enquiries was a retrospective comparison between affected and normal children. The third was a prospective study in which the children of women who had been given thalidomide were compared with other children. Descriptions of these surveys are given below, followed by examples of data from other fields which point to the same conclusions.

A Retrospective Survey

H. Weicker[65] was responsible for the retrospective comparison between affected and normal children by which thalidomide was incriminated. He interviewed the parents of 50 affected children about various factors which might have affected them and their offspring during pregnancy, including drugs and other chemicals used in the home. The ten substances or groups of substances mentioned most frequently by these parents were determined, and two other series of parents—one a control group with normal children, the other a small group whose children had limb deficiencies of types which had not become more common (e.g. absent hands or digits)—were asked whether they had been exposed to these substances during pregnancy. Table 5 shows how often three of the selected items—anti-emetics, hormonal preparations, and thalidomide—were said to have been taken by the 50 mothers of affected children and by 90 controls.

Methods of Analysis. Unlike the table showing retrospective data for rubella and malformations (Table 2), Table 5 does not purport to show the incidence of malformations among children exposed to a teratogen, but rather the incidence of exposure reported among the malformed. Even if the information given was accurate, it would only be possible to calculate the incidence of the characteristic defects in exposed and unexposed children if one knew how many children of these two kinds there were in the population from which the affected individuals were drawn. This information was not available for Weicker's series, which occurred in a population of undetermined size, like most series of hospital patients studied retrospectively.

Although in such circumstances incidence rates and attributable risks cannot be calculated, the relative risk is sometimes estimated. The formula for this estimate is $a_e c_u / a_u c_e$, where a_e and a_u are the numbers of exposed and unexposed affected children, and c_e and c_u the numbers of exposed and unexposed controls. This formula is not strictly accurate except when the proportions of exposed and unexposed individuals in the related population are the same as in the control group, which they tend not to be when a relatively high proportion of those exposed are affected. Nevertheless, the statistic which the formula yields is a useful one for comparing the strengths of different associations between disorders and factors that may cause them, and approximates quite closely to the relative risk when the excess risk in those exposed to the factor (the attributable risk) is only a few per cent. For example, the statistic is 13·9 for the figures for exposure to thalidomide in Table 5. The exact relative risk would have been 13·2, if the affected children had come from a population of 0,000 (which estimates of incidence from other sources suggest is of the right order) and if the proportion of mothers of unaffected children who took thalidomide had been the same for this population as for the controls.

Results and Interpretation. In Weicker's study, the apparent relative risk associated with taking thalidomide was substantially higher than those for any of the other substances about which parents were asked, as is illustrated in Table 5. But it is noteworthy too that the risks were also apparently increased at least two-fold in children whose mothers had taken other drugs, and that thalidomide was not mentioned in most cases—both of which facts can with hindsight be seen to point to the fallibility of patients' memories, which may give rise to even greater difficulties where common drugs are concerned than those encountered in studying rubella and malformations (pp. 744–745). The fact that more mothers of cases than of controls remembered taking various drugs other than thalidomide may be at any rate in part a reflection of the tendency for events preceding abnormal births to be remembered selectively (p. 745). The failure of many mothers of cases to mention thalidomide illustrates how often even their histories may be seriously deficient. The guilt feelings which some women with handicapped children have may even lead them to suppress memories of anything that they believe has caused the handicap—a source of memory bias of the reverse kind to that mentioned above. However, the main reason why more of the mothers of cases in Weicker's series did not at first mention thalidomide seems to have been that the only relevant question they were asked was the general one of what sedatives they had taken, if any—although the controls were asked specifically whether they had taken thalidomide. The cases' mothers were asked specifically about this drug at a later stage (although still before the first suggestions of its teratogenicity were published), and 22 who had not previously mentioned taking it then did so, bringing the total number with a positive history to 34 out of 50, or 68 per cent.[65]

To assist in distinguishing between memory biases and real differences in exposure to possible hazards, retrospective studies should if possible have built into them the kind of internal checks provided in Weicker's enquiry by the inclusion of drugs other than thalidomide and of limb deficiencies of types which had not become more common. If the apparent association between the new syndrome of defects and thalidomide had been due to memory bias, similar associations would probably have been found between this syndrome and other drugs, and between this drug and other defects (unless this syndrome and drug were already reputed to be more closely related than others, which they were apparently not). In fact, no other associations of anything like the strength of that between thalidomide and the new syndrome were found.

TABLE 5

RESULTS OF A RETROSPECTIVE STUDY OF MOTHERS OF MALFORMED AND CONTROL GROUPS OF CHILDREN, CLASSIFIED ACCORDING TO THE HISTORIES THEY GAVE[65]

Type of Drug	*Children Affected by Characteristic Limb Defects*		*Children Not Affected by Characteristic Limb Defects*		*Relative Risk of Characteristic Defects (Approximate Estimate)* $\left(\frac{ad}{bc}\right)$
	Drug Mentioned (a)	*Drug Not Mentioned* (b)	*Drug Mentioned* (c)	*Drug Not Mentioned* (d)	
Anti-emetics	18	32	20	70	2·0
Hormonal preparations	15	35	9	81	3·9
Thalidomide	12	38	2	88	13·9

A Prospective Survey

Without knowing about the German epidemic of limb defects, W. G. McBride[37] suggested from Australia that thalidomide might be teratogenic, after seeing six children with similar defects born at the Sydney Woman's Hospital in 1961, whose mothers' hospital notes showed that these women had been included in a trial carried out at the hospital from early 1960 to mid-1961 to evaluate the effectiveness of thalidomide for treating morning sickness.[39] As all the women who had taken part in this trial could be identified from records made at the time they were given thalidomide, it was possible to carry out in retrospect a study of the association between drug and defects which was methodologically prospective, in that the data on exposure to the suspected cause had been recorded before the outcome was known, and therefore could not be biased by this outcome.

Miscellaneous Studies

When the association between thalidomide taking and limb deficiencies was first demonstrated in individuals, there were some who suggested that it might be merely an indirect relationship, due to the two occurrences having a common cause such as one of the disorders treated by thalidomide. This hypothesis was however quickly rejected—firstly because of the strength of the association, secondly because of animal experiments in which defects were observed in litters whose mothers had been given thalidomide in pregnancy,[57] and thirdly because of correlative studies of groups in man. Studies of the latter kind were needed (as they often are when an association between a disease and a factor that may be causal has been demonstrated in individuals) because the incidence of the defects and the intake of thalidomide in different times and places were likely to be closely correlated if the association in individuals was causal, but not if this association was due to a maternal condition which caused defects regardless of whether it was treated with thalidomide. In fact, very striking contrasts between the incidence of the defects in different countries and cities were found, which correlated closely with thalidomide sales.[28,66] Studies of time trends revealed a similar pattern, illustrated in Fig. 15: where increases in incidence had occurred, they reproduced almost exactly the trend in thalidomide sales nine months earlier, and the withdrawal of the drug in late 1961 was followed by a fall in incidence to near zero. There may be two reasons why the fall shown in Fig. 15 began less than nine months after the drug was withdrawn: firstly, the decline in the drug's popularity earlier in 1961, after it had been found to cause neuropathy in some patients; and secondly, the securing of abortions by some women who had taken it.

TABLE 6

RESULTS OF A PROSPECTIVE SURVEY OF ALL BIRTHS CLASSIFIED ACCORDING TO DATA IN ANTENATAL RECORDS[38]

History	*Number of Children Born* (a)	*Children Affected by Skeletal Defects of Limbs*		
		Number (b)	*Percentage* $\left(\frac{100b}{a}\right)$	*Relative Risk* $\left(\frac{100b}{0{\cdot}24a}\right)$
Thalidomide not prescribed in early pregnancy	21,485	51	0·24	—
Thalidomide prescribed				
1st–8th week from conception	25	10	40	167
9th–16th week from conception	16	4	25	104

Table 6 shows the results of analysing in this way the hospital's records of children born in 1957–62, including those whose mothers were in the trial.[38] Other studies suggest that the duration of some pregnancies at the time of taking thalidomide was over-estimated; but in any case the figures are equivalent to a 140-fold increase in the incidence of *all* bony abnormalities of the limbs following thalidomide usage during the first 16 weeks. The specific types of limb defects observed in association with thalidomide must have had a much lower incidence in other children, and a correspondingly higher relative risk in those whose mothers took the drug. By contrast, the relative risk for the characteristic defects *alone* was only 62 in a later prospective study, undertaken on behalf of the German manufacturers of thalidomide,[54] in which the source of information about drugs taken in early pregnancy was women's recollections shortly before delivery. The difference between the two results probably reflects a failure by some mothers in the German study to recall what they had taken. It thus highlights the fact that histories taken in late pregnancy, although relatively unbiased by the child's condition and therefore preferable to particulars obtained postnatally, cannot generally compete for completeness with records made at the time when teratogenesis can occur. Also, some malformations can produce effects before birth or be diagnosed then, so that even in late pregnancy memory bias is a real possibility.

RETROLENTAL FIBROPLASIA: EXPERIMENTAL STUDIES

Experimental studies, in which individuals whose circumstances have been deliberately modified in some way are compared with controls, have been used much less in the search for causes of disease in man than in the evaluation of methods of prevention and treatment, for which randomized controlled trials are routine. Steps taken to reduce the frequency of diseases by removing or inactivating influences that may cause them (such as the withdrawal of thalidomide and the giving of diphtheria toxoid respectively) can of course be regarded as epidemiological experiments, since they permit the causality of the influence in question to be checked by comparing the individuals in whom it has been suppressed (the experimental group) with those not given this protection (the control group). But often, protective action of this kind is only taken after or shortly before the

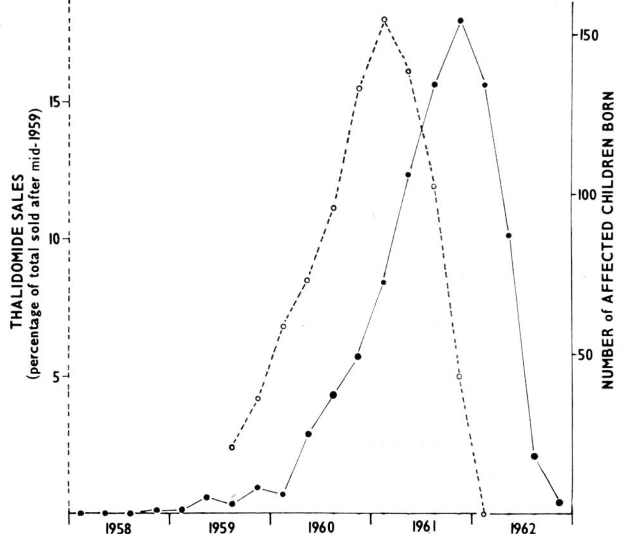

FIG. 15. Quarterly thalidomide sales (interrupted line) and births of children known by Lenz to have had the syndrome described by Wiedemann (continuous line), in West Germany excluding Hamburg.[33]

causal role of the influence becomes established. This was for example the case when thalidomide was withdrawn. It would have been unethical at this stage to withdraw it only from an experimental group while still allowing controls to use it. The only children with whom those conceived after its withdrawal could be compared were therefore those conceived earlier, who were not an ideal control group since they probably differed from their successors in other respects besides thalidomide intake. This kind of comparison is often the only type of experimental study open to the epidemiologist.

There have however been some occasions in epidemiological research when comparisons of randomized experimental and control groups have been used to establish how a condition is caused. Retrolental fibroplasia is one example of a problem tackled in this way.

Features of the Retrolental Fibroplasia Epidemic

In 1942, T. L. Terry[62] described five infants of very low birth weight with an opaque membrane behind the lens of each eye, which he believed to be of postnatal origin and later reported to consist of fibrous tissue.[63] He suggested that the condition might be a new disorder, occasioned by "some new factor . . . in extreme prematurity."

Over the next eight years, this hitherto unknown condition increased in incidence to become a common cause of blindness in infants who weighed less than 2 kg. at birth—so much so that a 50 per cent increase in the frequency of new cases of blindness from all causes in children was observed in some studies of United States data.[23] As well as the change over time, marked differences in incidence between places were noted, and both kinds of variations were eventually found to be highly correlated with the extent to which supplementary oxygen was being given to immature infants.[5,25]

This evidence against oxygen had however the weakness of being based almost exclusively on correlative studies of *groups*—children born at different times or places, who might have differed in many respects apart from exposure to oxygen. There had been no satisfactory studies correlating the incidence of retrolental fibroplasia with the oxygen levels experienced by *individuals* born at the *same* time and place, since such individuals had generally received much the same treatment.

Consequently, although some paediatricians were prepared to restrict the use of oxygen, others had reservations. Other factors had in the past been accused of causing fibroplasia on evidence as convincing to some as that in respect of oxygen, only to be eliminated later. It was also feared that any curtailment of the oxygen supplied to immature infants might have ill effects which would more than outweigh whatever advantages there might be.

A Randomized Controlled Experiment

To resolve the above issues, controlled experiments were instituted. Even before the view that high concentrations of oxygen might damage the eyes had appeared in print, one hospital in Washington, D.C., had begun allocating alternate infants with birth weights under 3·5 lbs. to a "high oxygen" and a "low oxygen" group. When the figures for the first 65 cases to complete the trial showed a lower incidence of retrolental fibroplasia in the "low oxygen" group,[44] a more extensive and sophisticated study[24] was launched by 18 hospitals in the eastern half of the United States.

Methods

Infants born in the 18 hospitals who survived 48 hours were admitted to the trial if they weighed 1·5 kg. or less. This limitation of the study to children of low birth weight makes it an example of the use of high-risk groups in epidemiological research, as a way of reducing the number of individuals who need to be surveyed to obtain an adequate yield of cases.

One out of every three infants was selected, on a statistically random basis, to receive oxygen in concentrations over 50 per cent for at least 28 days ("routine oxygen"), and the rest were nursed in normal air, except for limited amounts of oxygen if their clinical condition demanded it ("curtailed oxygen"). The allocation procedure was separate for each hospital and each of three birth weight groups (1,000 gm. or less, 1,001–1,250 gm., and 1,251–1,500 gm.), to ensure that "routine oxygen" was allocated to one in every three infants within each of these categories as well as in the study as a whole. This process of ensuring that all sections of a population are represented in a sample in proportion to their sizes is known as *stratification*—in this case stratification by hospital and birth weight—and a sample picked in this way is described as *stratified.* When the sample is to be treated in one way and the remainder of the population in another, stratification helps to ensure that the two groups are alike in respect of variables other than the treatment that might influence the outcome. The samples used in sample surveys are also often stratified, since the more closely they represent the population from which they are drawn, the more reliable will be the conclusions about this population that can be drawn from them.

Three months after the start of the 18-hospital trial, the numbers of deaths of infants receiving routine and curtailed oxygen were compared. As the proportions who had died did not differ significantly, it was concluded that routine oxygen had no advantages to balance the eye damage it might cause, and all infants admitted thereafter to the trial were given curtailed oxygen only.

Conclusions

Table 7 summarizes the position when all the infants admitted during the first 6 months of the trial had been followed for 2½ months or more. Strictly speaking, the recipients of routine oxygen should perhaps not have been compared with all those given curtailed oxygen when most of the latter were born and treated at a different time to the former; but the comparison was defended by the workers responsible, on the ground that the incidence rates of retrolental fibroplasia in the recipients of curtailed oxygen in the first and second three months did not differ significantly. The routine oxygen group had more than twice the incidence of retrolental fibroplasia experienced by the group on curtailed oxygen, and the proportion of all infants left with permanent eye damage was four times as high in the former group as the latter.

This epidemiological experiment, and experiments in animals reviewed at the same time,[43] appear finally to have substantiated the hypothesis that retrolental fibroplasia is generally caused by the exposure of immature infants to high concentrations of oxygen, and can be avoided by restricting the oxygen given in these cases.

TABLE 7

INCIDENCE OF RETROLENTAL FIBROPLASIA IN AN EPIDEMIOLOGICAL EXPERIMENT[24]

Eye Condition	*Infants Given Routine Oxygen**		*Infants Given Curtailed Oxygen**	
	Number	*Percentage*	*Number*	*Percentage*
Normal	15	28	172	70
Retrolental fibroplasia:				
Regressed to normal	25	47	58	24
Became cicatricial	13	25	15	6
Total	53	100	245	100

* See text for definitions.

GENERALIZATIONS

Although many a piece of important research into the aetiology of disease in childhood has arisen from a paediatrician's clinical impression that some disease is unusually common in a particular group of children, enough examples have now been given to show that more formal epidemiological methods are needed to test and quantify such impressions and the hypotheses they suggest. In the future, other aetiological problems will no doubt present themselves to paediatricians. To help them to make the best use of epidemiological methods on such occasions, an attempt is made below to review systematically the main issues involved, firstly in obtaining suitable material and then in analysing and interpreting it.

These issues are considered mainly in relation to the studies of *qualitative* disorders already described. Their application to the study of *quantitative* aspects of growth and development has not been spelt out in detail, but should present no special difficulty with either of the approaches already advocated for analysing quantitative data at the close of Chapter 41.A (p. 725): i.e., either the numbers of individuals in whom the variable has a value beyond an arbitrary "threshold" can be analysed in the same ways as if they were patients with qualitative conditions (as was done in Fig. 1 for infants born at less than 37 weeks' gestation, and at weights more than two standard deviations below the mean); or alternatively, comparisons may be made between distributions of different groups of children over the whole range of the variable, or between figures summarizing these distributions (e.g. the mean verbal reasoning scores in Chapter 41.A, Fig. 8, and the estimates of average retardation in reading age in Fig. 3 of the present chapter).

Material Required

All the aetiological studies that have been described were concerned with the occurrence of one characteristic in two or more groups who differed in respect of another. In Weicker's retrospective study of limb defects (Table 5) and some of the correlative studies of neural tube defects (Figs. 13 and 14), groups which differed in their medical condition (cases and controls in Weicker's study; series of births with high and low incidence rates of neural tube defects in the correlative studies of groups) were compared with respect to characteristics that might relate to aetiology. In most of the other studies, groups differing in characteristics of the latter kind (demographic variables in the descriptive studies; exposure to rubella, thalidomide, and supplementary oxygen in the correlative studies of individuals and the experimental studies) were compared in respect of their liability to disorders.

Every type of study therefore involved a study population whose members were classified both by whether they had a disorder and by their status in respect of some other variable. Each correlative study of groups that was mentioned also involved a third variable: the *incidence rates of a disorder* in groups defined in terms of a *demographic variable* (time or place of birth) were compared with the experience of the communities from which these groups came in respect of *another factor* (water hardness, food intake, thalidomide usage, etc.). Details of the latter factors were however obtained from independent, already existing sources. Even in these studies therefore, the initial requirements so far as the study population itself was concerned were simply (i) to select this population; (ii) to ascertain cases of the disorder among its members, and (iii) to determine the status of the affected individuals and the rest of the population in respect of one or more possible risk factors (characteristics that may be associated with the disorder). In what follows, these three requirements are illustrated in turn.

Population Selection

There are three main ways of selecting a population for epidemiological study of the aetiology of a disorder. The first way is to consider one or more natural populations—all children born in one or more places during a defined period or periods, for instance, as in the descriptive studies of perinatal mortality and malformations (Table 1 and Figs. 1–11). The second way is to assemble a group of individuals who have the disorder, and an unaffected group to serve as controls—as in Weicker's retrospective study of limb defects (Table 5). The third way, applicable if a particular factor is suspected of causing a disorder, is to select a group exposed to this factor, and either to take as controls some unexposed individuals (as in the nationwide prospective British study of the effects of rubella—Table 3), or else to present incidence rates for the exposed alone, these being compared by implication with the rates observed in the general population—a fairly acceptable approach if the risk in the exposed is many times the normal (as with rubella, investigated in this way both in the first retrospective study—Table 2—and in the prospective survey with serological diagnosis—Table 4). Studies which make use of the second or third of these three approaches (including most correlative studies of individuals) can be described as case-control studies.

Case-control Series. Cases of disorders and individuals in high risk groups can be selected for the first and second kinds of case-control studies respectively by the same methods as are used to identify them in other epidemiological enquiries, which are mentioned below under "ascertainment of disorders" and "ascertainment of risk factors." Controls for case-control studies may be selected either by sampling as randomly as possible from the natural population to which the affected or high risk individuals belonged (as in the British rubella study—Table 3) or by matching each case or high-risk individual with one other person from this population (or in some surveys more than one) who resembles him or her in certain selected respects. For example, if a perinatal condition was being studied, cases and controls might be matched for date and place of birth. The resulting control group would inevitably be distributed by date and place in the same way as the cases, which is generally an advantage. For example, the comparability of series of cases of malformations and controls matched in this way would not be impaired by variations in diagnostic standards between different times and hospitals, which would affect the two groups equally. Matching has however the disadvantage of sometimes making real differences between cases and the rest of the population seem smaller than they are. For example, if cases of limb defects and matched controls had been collected during the period when the use of thalidomide and the incidence of consequent defects were increasing, matching by date of birth would have led to there being more control births from the end of this period, when thalidomide was most widely used, than from the beginning. Consequently, the proportion of thalidomide takers among the control mothers would probably have been higher (and therefore less different from the figure for mothers of cases) than the proportion for the total population.

Natural Populations. The point has already been made in discussing mortality statistics (Chapter 41.A, pp. 705–713) that children affected by disorders are commonly thought of in relation to two kinds of populations—all births, and all children living. Death rates during the last three months before birth and the first year thereafter are generally expressed as proportions of all births, and so are the incidence rates of congenital and neonatal disorders like those already discussed in this chapter. Overall death rates, age-specific death rates, and the incidence rates of diseases that may arise beyond infancy (e.g. cancer—Chapter 41.A, pp. 716–717), on the other hand, are given in relation either to an estimate of the average number alive at any one time in the relevant age-group, or to a figure (such as person-years lived) based on this number.

In England and Wales, the Annual Statistical Reviews of the Registrar General contain population data of both kinds—the *numbers of births* in every Local Authority, and mid-year population estimates for each age group, region and conurbation which are virtually the same as the average *numbers alive* in these categories. The numbers alive at different ages in smaller populations are enumerated in each decennial Census. The most suitable natural populations to use for epidemiological research are ones for which official data like these are available. By using such statistics the need to collect fresh data on the whole population can sometimes be avoided, or if additional data have to be collected from everyone the numbers covered can be checked for completeness against the official figures (as in the 1958 Perinatal Mortality Survey).

Data on perinatal problems are often collected and related to all births in obstetric hospitals (as in many of the surveys summarized in Fig. 10) instead of in communities, since hospital data tend to be more complete and easily available, especially to clinicians. There is however the risk in such studies that variations in selection for hospital confinement may make it misleading to compare incidence in different groups: for example, the incidence of anencephaly among hospital births may be considerably higher than its overall incidence in groups which include many births outside hospital (p. 738) but not in groups where hospital confinement is universal or nearly so.

For exploring the aetiology of rare disorders, studies of complete natural populations have the disadvantage of needing to be based on much larger numbers than case-control studies if the yield of cases is to be adequate. One refinement by which such numbers are sometimes reduced is to select members of the population in whom a particular risk factor for the disorder is present, and to carry out a prospective survey or experiment on these individuals alone, as in the experimental study of retrolental fibroplasia (Table 7), in which low birth weight was the selecting factor.

Ascertainment of Disorders

The main sources of records from which disorders can be ascertained have been spelt out in some detail in Chapter 41.A, together with the main possible reasons for inaccuracy—deficiencies in coverage of the population supposed to be at risk, in diagnosis, and in reporting what has been diagnosed—against which the user of any of these sources must be on his guard. Listed in order (the most convenient but most incomplete first) the sources are deaths, health service contacts, routine screening, and screening by special surveys. The quickest way either to ascertain the bulk of cases of any type of disorder in a population, or to assemble a series for a case-control study, is generally to use the first of the sources listed that is likely to be reasonably complete —for example, death (including stillbirth) for anencephaly (Figs. 11–14); hospital attendance for cancer (Chapter 41.A, Table 6); routine screening by clinical examination at birth, preferably combined with the preceding sources, for defects like spina bifida and cleft lip which are obvious but not always lethal (Figs. 9–10); and specially arranged screening for the early detection of retrolental fibroplasia (Table 7). But even disorders which could be ascertained from routine hospital or death records are sometimes studied by screening whole populations, as in the British Perinatal Mortality Survey (Table 1, Figs. 1–8), in which the more elaborate approach was needed to determine how both the dead and the surviving children were distributed in respect of various possible risk factors.

Of course, when numbers of deaths, or of positive findings on screening, are divided by totals at risk, the results are not necessarily statistics of incidence (the most informative variable to the student of aetiology) but only of mortality and point prevalence (Chapter 41.A, p. 715) respectively. However, mortality can generally be assumed to vary in the same way as incidence for conditions which usually cause death, as well as for those which are always fatal. For congenital and neonatal disorders, incidence is generally expressed as the proportion of affected among all births, which is the same as the prevalence at birth (Chapter 41.A, p. 720). Estimates of the incidence as well as the prevalence of other conditions may be obtained from screening surveys if questions about medical history are included (Chapter 41.A, Tables 8 and 10). If incidence cannot be determined, the prevalence of the condition in different groups may itself be compared in the search for aetiological factors, although it must be borne in mind that prevalence can vary as much with the average duration of a disease as with its incidence (Chapter 41.A, p. 715).

Ascertainment of Risk Factor Status

Most of the features of individuals that may be examined for possible associations with liability to disorders can be divided into two main groups: firstly the so-called demographic categories (time, place, social class, etc.) which cannot of themselves cause disorders but may be related to risk and so point to causes, and with which descriptive studies are largely concerned; and secondly encounters with micro-organisms and chemicals and other experiences that could be causal themselves, which are examined particularly in correlative and experimental studies. The numbers of individuals in various demographic categories are published for some populations (e.g. regional and seasonal analyses of births in England and Wales, as in Figs. 11–14), and even when such figures are not published they can often be obtained from existing sources for all births, and sometimes for all children living (e.g. the data from records of the Birmingham Health Department used in Fig. 9).

Data on exposure to factors that may be causal, on the other hand, cannot generally be obtained in this way. There are exceptions (such as the records showing which women had taken thalidomide in Sydney, on which Table 6 is based), but usually data of this kind have been sought by questionnaire, both in retrospective enquiries such as Weicker's study of limb defects (Table 5) and—more reliably—in prospective surveys like the British follow-up of rubella in pregnancy (Table 3). More objective methods such as the serological tests for rubella in the American follow-up (Table 4) are sometimes used as well. Demographic data that are not readily available from routine sources may also be collected by questionnaire, as in the British Perinatal Mortality Survey (Table 1 and Figs. 1–8).

A final approach to the investigation of possible causes is that embodied in experimental studies such as that of retrolental fibroplasia (Table 7), in which the level of exposure to the factor in question was not only recorded but set by the investigators.

Methods of Analysis and Inference

As has been repeatedly stressed, the analysis of the material collected in epidemiological studies of causation is largely a matter of comparison—comparison of the frequency distributions of different groups in respect of quantitative or (more often) qualitative characteristics. This comparing of distributions involves both demonstrating and evaluating any differences there may be between them. The conversion of absolute numbers to rates, and the use of tables, figures, and indices such as relative and attributable risks to compare rates, are all ways of demonstrating differences. Evaluation involves considering whether any difference observed could easily have arisen by chance, and if not what may have caused it.

In what follows, the methods of demonstrating differences and of explaining those that are unlikely to be due to chance are briefly reviewed for the kinds of situations that have been described, and some applications of these methods to other situations are mentioned, for the four main types of epidemiological studies in turn. The methods used when considering the possibility of differences being due to chance—mainly tests of significance—are not however described here, since there are many texts on statistical methods for medical workers (some of them listed on p. 757) from which an understanding of these tests and the statistical theory underlying them can be acquired. It is however worth stressing the limitations of the results (usually a value for P, the statistical probability) which the statistical evaluation of differences yields. To realize the limitations, one has only to consider the situation in a game of dice, where the statistical probability of throwing two sixes is one in thirty-six, or approximately 0·03. This statement means that on average this score occurs by chance once in 36 throws—*not* that the odds against this score being a chance occurrence if it *does* occur are 35 to 1. Similarly, a finding that P for a difference between two rates is 0·01 only means that differences of this magnitude or greater occur by chance in 1 per cent of comparisons, and *not* that the odds against the difference being due to chance are 99 to 1—although it may often be reasonable to conclude that some other explanation is more likely than not to be correct.

Descriptive Studies

In the typical descriptive study one is looking for associations between demographic variables and the incidence of a disorder which may suggest aetiological hypotheses. Initially, the relationship of each variable to incidence is generally examined separately (as in Fig. 1 and most of Fig. 9). However, when two or more variables (e.g. maternal age and parity) are inter-related, one may appear to affect incidence because of its association with another—as in pre-eclampsia of pregnancy (Fig. 1), which is commoner under 25 years than at 25–9 purely because its incidence is highest in primigravidae. Therefore, where variables with effects on incidence are related to each other, it is advisable to consider the relationship of each to incidence when the others are held constant. Methods of exploring relationships of this kind include:

(a) tabulation in two or more dimensions, one for each variable (e.g. Table 1), the results of which are often presented graphically (e.g. Figs. 2 and 4–7, and the data on maternal age and parity in Fig. 9);

(b) direct standardization, in which the effects of one variable are explored at a time, by computing a standardized incidence or mortality *rate* for each of the groups that differed in respect of the variable in question (e.g. the age-standardized adult mortality rates for different decades in Chapter 41.A, Fig. 1, p. 707);

(c) indirect standardization, in which the figure computed for each group is a standardized incidence or mortality *ratio* of the number of cases observed to the number expected (e.g. the Standardized Abortion Ratios—standardized for duration of pregnancy at first antenatal visit—in Table 3; q.v. text, p. 744);

(d) analysis of variance—a statistical technique for estimating the contributions of different sources of variation to the total variability, either of measurements from individual to individual or of means or proportions from group to group (Fig. 3).

Combined Risks and Combined Disorders. Besides attempting to separate the effects on incidence of inter-related variables, one has sometimes to consider whether particular combinations of more or less independent variables may be especially common in persons with a disorder—individuals living in the same place being affected at the same time, for example, as in epidemics (p. 738). Also, certain combinations of different disorders may be found to occur more often than one would expect by chance in particular individuals or groups (e.g. Down's syndrome and leukaemia in individuals[40] and anencephaly and spina bifida in families[6]) suggesting that they are related aetiologically.

Parental Age and Parity Effects. Two other problems which call for rather special methods are the interpretation of variations in incidence with parental age and birth rank, and with age and time. Parental age and birth rank effects are complicated by the fact that fertility is related to both: the proportion of children whose parents will never have large families (i.e. are relatively infertile) falls from one birth rank group to the next, and is also lower among children born to young parents than among those of equal birth rank born when their parents were older. Consequently, if the incidence of a disease varies with birth rank and parental age it does not automatically follow that an individual woman's liability to produce an affected child will alter as her age or parity increases; it may sometimes be simply that the more fertile differ in liability from the less fertile. Various ways of approaching these and the other problems which the analysis of maternal age and parity data raises have been described elsewhere.[1]

Cohort Analysis. A question that arises particularly when interpreting data for different times and age groups is whether to attach more importance to the date of onset of a disorder or to the date of birth. With perinatal disorders this is no problem, since the date of birth is generally treated as the date of onset. Among disorders arising later, however, some such as the common specific infections of childhood are caused by factors operating shortly before the time of onset; others have causes more closely related to the time of birth, such as stilboestrol taken in pregnancy and followed 14–22 years later by vaginal adenocarcinoma in the offspring;[22] and the causes of a third group are uncertain, cumulative, or variable in their timing.

A disorder of the first kind is clearly best analysed in relation to time of onset. Its incidence in different years, for example, will show if its cause becomes more or less widespread, and its incidence in different age groups during a single year will show how liability to the disorder varies with age.

Disorders of the second kind, on the other hand, are better analysed in relation to time of birth. For such a disorder, age-specific or standardized rates or ratios for children *born* in different periods (i.e. different cohorts) show more clearly than onsets in different years how the cause has behaved. The effects of age on liability are most clearly shown by the age-specific rates for a single cohort (rates which are of course spread over many years of onset), as opposed to the incidence rates observed in different age-groups in a single year, since rates of the latter kind relate to children born in various years and may therefore be affected by differences in exposure to the cause as well as in age.

In disorders that do not definitely fall into either of the above groups, analyses by date of onset and by cohort may both or either lead to findings of aetiological value, especially in clarifying whether the effects of any specific cause that may be involved are immediate or long-term.

Correlative Studies of Groups

Correlative studies of groups are usually undertaken to determine whether the incidence of a disorder in different demographic categories is correlated with their exposure to one or more factors which it is envisaged might cause the disorder. Both visual and statistical methods are widely used in this type of data analysis. The most usual visual method of presentation is by *scatter diagrams* (e.g. Fig. 13)—except when the incidence rates and exposure levels to be compared are time series (sets of figures for consecutive periods), in which case it is more usual to plot each variable against time and compare the two graphs (e.g. Figs. 14 and 15). The most popular statistical approach is to calculate the *coefficient of correlation*—usually for the two sets of values as they stand, although when time series are compared and there is evidence of independent variations by year and by season (as in Fig. 14) it may be useful to calculate separate coefficients for the annual, seasonal, and residual components of variation (p. 741).

For a full account of the coefficient of correlation a text on medical statistics should be consulted. Briefly, it varies from unity for variables with a completely *linear* relationship (+1 if they increase together and −1 if one rises as the other falls) to zero for variables that are totally unrelated. Variables which are related closely but in a non-linear way may therefore yield a relatively low co-efficient of correlation; and on the other hand, even when the extent to which one variable changes over the normal range for another is only very slight—like the variation in annual incidence of anencephaly with the frequency of potato blight in England and Wales (p. 741)—a high correlation coefficient will result if the relationship is approximately linear. To avoid being misled by such coefficients, it is best only to interpret them after examining the scatter of the individual pairs of findings on which they are based.

When each group in a correlative study includes only a few cases of the disorder that is being studied, random differences between the groups may obscure any correlation there may be between incidence and the suspected cause. One solution then is to combine the data for groups that have had similar amounts of exposure to the suspected cause, and to compare incidence rates in the combined groups—as in Fig. 12, which compares the incidence of anencephaly in five aggregates obtained by grouping together towns with similar levels of calcium in the water supply. Similarly, the suggestion that influenza in pregnancy predisposes the offspring to develop some neoplasms in childhood[16] has recently been explored by combining births in different months into two categories according to whether or not they followed periods when influenza was prevalent. The incidence of neoplasms in the two categories was then compared—with negative results.[31]

Correlative Studies of Individuals

The data yielded by correlative studies of individuals almost always consist essentially of records which enable each individual to be classified simultaneously by whether he has a particular disorder and by his estimated exposure to some factor of possible aetiological importance. So far as their analysis is concerned such data fall into two categories: firstly, data for natural populations (e.g. the Sydney births in Table 6) and for case-control series in which the "cases" are individuals who have been exposed to a suspected cause (e.g. the rubella cases in Tables 2–4); and secondly, data for case-control series in which the "cases" have the disorder (e.g. those with limb defects in Table 5).

When the data are of the first kind, the incidence rates of the disorder in the exposed and unexposed groups can be calculated and compared by the same methods as are applied to demographic categories in descriptive studies (p. 753). The methods of holding other variables constant that were described in the latter context were not however used in the studies of rubella and thalidomide in Tables 2–4 and 6, except for analysing abortions after rubella (Table 3)—probably because the magnitude of the other associations was felt to rule out the possibility that they might be merely secondary to any other variables' effects on incidence. There is also of course no need to allow for such effects when comparing cases and controls that have been matched for the relevant variables.

The situation in case-control series in which the "cases" are patients with the disorder is rather more complicated. Incidence rates for the exposed and unexposed can only be estimated if the cases comprise all the affected individuals in a defined population and the controls are representative of the rest of the population. Otherwise (as in the study quoted in Table 5), the only proportions that can be calculated and compared are the proportions of exposed individuals among cases and controls. The extent to which exposure affects liability to a disorder can only be judged approximately from such results (p. 747).

The biggest source of difficulty in interpreting correlative studies of individuals is however inaccurate reporting.

Records of exposure to factors which may cause disorders are much more liable than demographic data to be inaccurate and (in retrospective studies) biased according to whether the disorder is present. True associations can sometimes be distinguished from the effects of bias if data are collected simultaneously on various disorders and factors which patients might regard as causal, since any real associations are likely to be stronger than the others (like the association between limb deficiencies and thalidomide in Table 5); but a more reliable way of checking noteworthy retrospective survey results is to carry out observations on individuals whose exposures to the suspected cause have been recorded prospectively (p. 744–745).

The most accurate data on exposure to possible causes are of course those collected at the time (e.g. in Table 6) or based on objective criteria such as serological tests (e.g. in Table 4). Given accurate data, the results of correlative studies of individuals can be used not only to demonstrate associations between disorders and possible causes, but also to calculate the attributable and relative risks associated with factors already known to be causal. These calculations may be done separately for individuals exposed at different times (as in Table 3) or to different amounts of a hazard; but such breakdowns—although necessary—are not always completely reliable, since gestation length, for example, is not always estimated accurately.

Experiments and Other Proofs of Causality

If a significant disorder is found repeatedly to be associated with a factor which may be causal and amenable to control, there comes a time when the decision must be taken either to prove by experiment whether this factor is causal, or to accept it as proved on other grounds and take steps to protect all those at risk. There are no firm rules for deciding which course to follow, but the case for accepting an association as causal is particularly strong if it satisfies the following conditions.

Firstly, the risk of the disorder should be at least several times as high in the exposed as in the unexposed, and vary with the intensity or timing of the exposure. To ensure that the association is not due to bias, it should be stronger than those involving other disorders or risk factors studied at the same time. The excess of instances of contact with the risk factor observed in those affected should all have taken place at or before the onset of the disorder. The causal hypothesis proposed should be supported by the results of research in other fields (such as the serological and virological studies and animal experiments mentioned in connection with rubella and thalidomide respectively), and what it envisages should make biological sense, and preferably be analogous to aetiological processes that are already known.

Finally, the link between disorder and risk factor should have been observed not merely in one epidemiological enquiry but in several, preferably of various kinds including studies both of groups and of individuals. If the only sources of evidence linking rubella and malformations had been studies of *groups*, showing that malformations were commoner after rubella epidemics than at other times, one possibility would have been that environmental conditions favouring the spread of this infection had an independent effect on pregnant women which was harmful to their offspring. If on the other hand the only evidence had been from studies of *individuals*, in which the incidence of malformations was found to be higher in children whose mothers had had rubella than in others born at the same time, one explanation could have been that the characteristics which make some women more prone to rubella than others include factors which predispose to malformations in their children regardless of whether the women actually acquire the infection. However, neither of these hypotheses alone can explain both associations, whereas the causal hypothesis does. To demonstrate that both associations occurred and that therefore the causal hypothesis was superior, studies of groups born at different times and of infected and uninfected individuals were both needed.

When an association satisfies all the above conditions, the case for assuming that the risk factor concerned is involved in the causation of the disorder can be considered strong enough to justify attempting to protect all susceptible individuals against this risk without doing an epidemiological experiment first, so long as the likely benefits are not outweighed by what the measures may cost in financial or other terms. Even on more limited evidence like that available when thalidomide was withdrawn, such measures may often be justified if they are easy to take and the effects which it is hoped to prevent are severe. Eventually the measures may themselves lead to the production of stronger evidence, in the form of data on the subsequent incidence of the disorder to compare with what it was before (as in Fig. 15).

It is when the case against a possible cause is not thought strong enough to justify such universal measures that controlled epidemiological experiments are generally carried out. Such experiments are easiest to interpret when based on one natural population of individuals, stratified by any relevant demographic variables (e.g. birth weight and hospital in the retrolental fibroplasia study summarized in Table 7) and then randomly divided into one or more experimental groups who are given protection and a control group who are not. When however the risk factor is one to which all members of any one population must inevitably have much the same exposure, one complete population may have to be given protection and another be kept as a control group, as was done to confirm that too little fluoride in drinking water is aetiologically related to dental caries.[7] In both kinds of studies, the same methods of analysis are used as in correlative case-control studies where the "cases" are individuals who have been exposed to a possible hazard (p. 754); but when different natural populations have been used as experimental and control groups the interpretation of results may be more difficult than with groups from the same population, since the chances of the former groups differing in other respects besides exposure which may affect incidence are greater.

ACKNOWLEDGEMENTS

I am grateful to Professor Alwyn Smith for reading the first draft of this chapter and suggesting various improvements; to Mr. Frank Cutler for drawing the figures; and to

Mrs. Evelyn Townsend and Mrs. Eleanor Richardson for secretarial help.

REFERENCES

1. Barker, D. J. P. and Record, R. G. (1967), "The Relationship of the Presence of Disease to Birth Order and Maternal Age," *Amer. J. hum. Genet.*, **19**, 433–449.
2. Butler, N. R. and Alberman, E. D. (Eds.), (1969), *Perinatal Problems* (Second Report of the British Perinatal Mortality Survey). Edinburgh: Livingstone.
3. Butler, N. R. and Bonham, D. G. (1963), *Perinatal Mortality* (First Report of the British Perinatal Mortality Survey). Edinburgh: Livingstone.
4. Butler, N. R., Dudgeon, J. A., Hayes, K., Peckham, C. S. and Wybar, K. (1965), "Persistence of Rubella Antibody with and without Embryopathy: a Follow-up Study of Children Exposed to Maternal Rubella," *Brit. med. J.*, **ii**, 1027–1029.
5. Campbell, K. (1951), "Intensive Oxygen Therapy as a Possible Cause of Retrolental Fibroplasia: a Clinical Approach," *Med. J. Aust.*, **ii**, 48–50.
6. Carter, C. O. (1971), "Genetics of Common Malformations," in *Recent Advances in Paediatrics*, 4th edition, pp. 527–557 (D. M. T. Gairdner and D. Hull, Eds.). London: Churchill.
7. Committee on Research into Fluoridation (1969), *The Fluoridation Studies in the United Kingdom and the Results Achieved after Eleven Years* (Ministry of Health Reports on Public Health and Medical Subjects No. 122). London: Her Majesty's Stationery Office.
8. Cooper, L. Z. (1968), "Rubella: a Preventable Cause of Birth Defects," in *Intrauterine Infections* (Birth Defects: Original Article Series Vol. 4, No. 7), pp. 23–35 (D. Bergsma, Ed.). New York: The National Foundation—March of Dimes.
9. Davie, R., Butler, N. and Goldstein, H. (1972), *From Birth to Seven* (Second Report of the National Child Development Study—1958 Cohort—with full Statistical Appendix). London: Longman.
10. Duffus, G. M. and MacGillivray, I. (1968), "The Incidence of Pre-eclamptic Toxaemia in Smokers and Non-smokers," *Lancet*, **i**, 994–995.
11. Edwards, J. H. (1958), "A Note on the Interpretation of $n \times 2$ Tables," *Brit. J. prev. soc. Med.*, **12**, 141–146.
12. Edwards, J. H. (1961), "The Recognition and Estimation of Cyclic Trends," *Ann. hum. Genet. (Lond.)*, **25**, 83–87.
13. Elwood, J. H. (1970), "Anencephalus in the British Isles," *Develop. Med. Child Neurol.*, **12**, 582–591.
14. Emanuel, I., Culver, B. H., Erickson, J. D., Guthrie, B. and Schuldberg, D. (1973), "The Further Epidemiological Differentiation of Cleft Lip and Palate: a Population Study of Clefts in King County, Washington, 1956–1965," *Teratology*, **7**, 271–281.
15. Fedrick, J. (1970), "Anencephalus: Variation with Maternal Age, Parity, Social Class and Region in England, Scotland and Wales," *Ann. hum. Genet. (Lond.)*, **34**, 31–38.
16. Fedrick, J. and Alberman, E. D. (1972), "Reported Influenza in Pregnancy and Subsequent Cancer in the Child," *Brit. med. J.*, **ii**, 485–488.
17. Fedrick, J. and Wilson, T. S. (1971), "Malformations of the Central Nervous System in Glasgow: an Examination of the Evidence for Clustering in Space and Time," *Brit. J. prev. soc. Med.*, **25**, 210–215.
18 Fraser, F. C., Walker, B. E. and Trasler, D. G. (1957), "Experimental Production of Congenital Cleft Palate: Genetic and Environmental Factors," *Pediatrics*, **19**, 782–787.
19. Fraser, G. R. and Calnan, J. S. (1961), "Cleft Lip and Palate: Seasonal Incidence, Birth Weight, Birth Rank, Sex, Site, Associated Malformations and Parental Age. A Statistical Survey," *Arch. Dis. Childh.*, **36**, 420–423.
20. Gibson, J. R. and McKeown, T. (1950), "Observations on all Births (23,970) in Birmingham, 1947: I. Duration of Gestation," *Brit. J. soc. Med.*, **4**, 221–233.
21. Gregg, N. M. (1941), "Congenital Cataract following German Measles in the Mother," *Trans. ophthal. Soc. Aust.*, **3**, 35–46.
22. Herbst, A. L., Ulfelder, H. and Poskanzer, D. C. (1971), "Adenocarcinoma of the Vagina: Association of Maternal Stilbestrol Therapy with Tumor Appearance in Young Women," *New Engl. J. Med.*, **284**, 878–881.
23. Ingalls, T. H. (1954), "Epidemiology of Retrolental Fibroplasia: its Etiologic Relation to Pulmonary Hyaline Membrane," *New Engl. J. Med.*, **251**, 1017–1022.
24. Kinsey, V. E. and Hemphill, F. M. (1955), "Etiology of Retrolental Fibroplasia: Preliminary Report of a Co-operative Study of Retrolental Fibroplasia," *Amer. J. Ophthal.*, **40**, 166–174.
25. Kinsey, V. E. and Zacharias, L. (1949), "Retrolental Fibroplasia: Incidence in Different Localities in Recent Years and a Correlation of the Incidence with Treatment given the Infants," *J. Amer. med. Ass.*, **139**, 572–578.
26. Knox, E. G. (1971), "Epidemics of Rare Diseases," *Brit. med. Bull.*, **27**, 43–47.
27. Knox, E. G. (1972), "Anencephalus and Dietary Intakes," *Brit. J. prev. soc. Med.*, **26**, 219–223.
28. Leck, I. (1969), "The Incidence of Limb Defects in Recent Years," in *Limb Development and Deformity: Problems of Evaluation and Rehabilitation*, pp. 248–268 (C. A. Swinyard, Ed.). Springfield: Thomas.
29. Leck, I. (1972), "The Etiology of Human Malformations: Insights from Epidemiology," *Teratology*, **5**, 303–314.
30. Leck, I., Record, R. G., McKeown, T. and Edwards, J. H. (1968), "The Incidence of Malformations in Birmingham, England, 1950–1959," *Teratology*, **1**, 263–280.
31. Leck, I. and Steward, J. K. (1972), "Incidence of Neoplasms in Children born after Influenza Epidemics," *Brit. med. J.*, **iv**, 631–634.
32. Lenz, W. (1961), "Kindliche Missbildungen nach Medikament-Einnahme während der Gravidität?" *Dtsch. med. Wschr.*, **86**, 2555–2556.
33. Lenz, W. (1965), "Discussion (session 5)," in *A Symposium on Embryopathic Activity of Drugs*, pp. 182–185 (J. M. Robson, F. M. Sullivan, and R. L. Smith, Eds.). London: Churchill.
34. Lowe, C. R., Roberts, C. J. and Lloyd, S. (1971), "Malformations of Central Nervous System and Softness of Local Water Supplies," *Brit. med. J.*, **ii**, 357–361.
35. Manson, M. M., Logan, W. P. D. and Loy, R. M. (1960), *Rubella and other Virus Infections during Pregnancy* (Ministry of Health Reports on Public Health and Medical Subjects No. 101). London: Her Majesty's Stationery Office.
36. Mantel, N. (1967), "The Detection of Disease Clustering and a Generalized Regression Approach," *Cancer Res.*, **27**, 209–220.
37. McBride, W. G. (1961), "Thalidomide and Congenital Abnormalities," *Lancet*, **ii**, 1358.
38. McBride, W. G. (1963), "The Teratogenic Action of Drugs," *Med. J. Aust.*, **ii**, 689–693.
39. McBride, W. G. (1965), Personal Communication Cited by Ingalls, T. H. and Klingberg, M. A. (1965), in "Congenital Malformations: Clinical and Community Considerations," *Amer. J. med. Sci.*, **249**, 316–344.
40. Miller, R. W. (1970), "Neoplasia and Down's Syndrome," *Ann. N.Y. Acad. Sci.*, **171**, 637–644.
41. Ounsted, M. (1971), "Fetal Growth," in *Recent Advances in Paediatrics*, 4th edition, pp. 23–62 (D. M. T. Gairdner and D. Hull, Eds.). London: Churchill.
42. Patau, K., Smith, D. W., Therman, E., Inhorn, S. L. and Wagner, H. P. (1960), "Multiple Congenital Anomaly Caused by an Extra Autosome," *Lancet*, **i**, 790–793.
43. Patz, A. (1955), "Experimental Studies," *Amer. J. Ophthal.*, **40**, 174–183.
44. Patz, A., Hoek, L. E. and De La Cruz, E. (1952), "Studies on the Effect of High Oxygen Administration in Retrolental Fibroplasia: I. Nursery Observations," *Amer. J. Ophthal.*, **35**, 1248–1253.
45. Penrose, L. S. (1955), "Parental Age and Mutation," *Lancet*, **ii**, 312–313.
46. Phillips, C. A., Melnick, J. L., Yow, M. D., Bayatpour, M. and

Burkhardt, M. (1965), "Persistence of Virus in Infants with Congenital Rubella and in Normal Infants with a History of Maternal Rubella," *J. Amer. med. Ass.*, **193,** 1027–1029.

47. Poswillo, D., Sopher, D. and Mitchell, S. (1972), "Experimental Induction of Foetal Malformation with 'Blighted' Potato: a Preliminary Report," *Nature, Lond.*, **239,** 462–464.
48. Record, R. G. (1961), "Anencephalus in Scotland," *Brit. J. prev. soc. Med.*, **15,** 93–105.
49. Record, R. G. and Leck, I. (1966). Unpublished work.
50. Renwick, J. H. (1972), "Hypothesis: Anencephaly and Spina Bifida are usually preventable by Avoidance of a Specific but Unidentified Substance present in Certain Potato Tubers," *Brit. J. prev. soc. Med.*, **26,** 67–88.
51. Renwick, J. H. (1972), "Spina Bifida and the Potato," *New Scientist*, **56,** 277–279.
52. Renwick, J. H. (1973), "Diet and Congenital Defects," *Brit. med. J.*, **i,** 172.
53. Robbins, F. C. and Heggie, A. D. (1970), "The Rubella Problem," in *Congenital Malformations* (Proceedings of the Third International Conference), pp. 341–348 (F. C. Fraser and V. A. McKusick, Eds.). Amsterdam: Excerpta medica.
54. Seivers, G. (1964), "Clinical-statistical Studies of the Topical Problem of Congenital Abnormalities," *Arzneimittelforschung*, **14,** 605–655.
55. Sever, J. L., Hardy, J. B., Nelson, K. B. and Gilkeson, M. R. (1969), "Rubella in the Collaborative Perinatal Research Study II. Clinical and Laboratory Findings in Children through 3 Years of Age," *Amer. J. Dis. Child.*, **118,** 123–132.
56. Sever, J. L., Nelson, K. B. and Gilkeson, M. R. (1965), "Rubella Epidemic, 1964: Effect on 6,000 Pregnancies I: Preliminary Clinical and Laboratory Findings Through the Neonatal Period: A Report from the Collaborative Study on Cerebral Palsy," *Amer. J. Dis. Child.*, **110,** 395–407.
57. Somers, G. F. (1962), "Thalidomide and Congenital Abnormalities," *Lancet*, **i,** 912–913.
58. Spicer, C. C. and Lipworth, L. (1966), *Regional and Social Factors in Infant Mortality* (Studies on Medical and Population Subjects No. 19). London: Her Majesty's Stationery Office.
59. Stevenson, A. C., Johnston, H. A., Stewart, M. I. P. and Golding, D. R. (1966), "Congenital Malformations: A Report of a Study of Series of Consecutive Births in 24 Centres," *Bull. World Hlth Org.*, **34,** suppl.
60. Stocks, P. (1970), "Incidence of Congenital Malformations in the Regions of England and Wales," *Brit. J. prev. soc. Med.*, **24,** 67–77.
61. Swan, C., Tostevin, A. L., Moore, B., Mayo, H. and Black, G. H. B. (1943), "Congenital Defects in Infants Following Infectious Diseases during Pregnancy," *Med. J. Aust.*, **ii,** 201–210.
62. Terry, T. L. (1942), "Extreme Prematurity and Fibroblastic Overgrowth of Persistent Vascular Sheath behind each Crystalline Lens: I. Preliminary Report," *Amer. J. Ophthal.*, **25,** 203–204.
63. Terry, T. L. (1942), "Fibroblastic Overgrowth of Persistent Tunica Vasculosa Lentis in Infants Born Prematurely: III. Studies in Development and Regression of Hyaloid Artery and Tunica Vasculosa Lentis," *Amer. J. Ophthal.*, **25,** 1409–1423.
64. Walker, J. (1959), "Fetal Distress," *Amer. J. Obstet. Gynec.*, **77,** 94–107.
65. Weicker, H., Bachmann, K. D., Pfeiffer, R. A. and Gleiss, J. (1962), "Thalidomid-Embryopathie: II. Ergebnisse individueller anamnestischer Erhebungen in den Universitäts-Kinderkliniken Bonn, Köln, Münster und Düsseldorf," *Dtsch. med. Wschr.*, **87,** 1597–1607.
66. Weicker, H. and Hungerland, H. (1962), "Thalidomid-Embryopathie: I. Vorkommen inner- und ausserhalb Deutschlands," *Dtsch. med. Wschr.*, **87,** 992–1002.
67. W.H.O. Scientific Group on Genetic Factors in Congenital Malformations (1970), *Genetic Factors in Congenital Malformations* (World Health Organization Technical Report Series, No. 438). Geneva: World Health Organization.
68. Weidemann, H.-R. (1961), "Hinweis auf eine derzeitige Häufung hypo- und aplastischer Fehlbildungen der Gliedmassen," *Med. Welt*, No. 37, 1863–1866.
69. Woolf, C. M. (1963), "Paternal Age Effect for Cleft Lip and Palate," *Amer. J. hum. Genet.*, **15,** 389–393.

FURTHER READING

Books on statistical and epidemiological methods

i. Hill, A. Bradford (1971), *Principles of Medical Statistics*, 9th edition, 390 pp. London: Lancet.
ii. Castle, Winifred M. (1972), *Statistics in Small Doses*, 216 pp. Edinburgh: Churchill Livingstone.
iii. Bailey, N. T. J. (1959), *Statistical Methods in Biology*, 200 pp. London: English Universities Press.
iv. Bourke, G. J. and McGilvray, J. (1969), *Interpretation and Uses of Medical Statistics*, 162 pp. Oxford: Blackwell.
v. Dunn, O. J. (1964), *Basic Statistics: A Primer for the Biomedical Sciences*, 184 pp. New York: Wiley.
vi. Smart, J. V. (1970), *Elements of Medical Statistics*, 2nd edition, 176 pp. London: Staples.
vii. Armitage, P. (1971), *Statistical Methods in Medical Research*, 504 pp. Oxford: Blackwell.
viii. Oldham, P. D. (1968), *Measurement in Medicine*, 216 pp. London: English Universities Press.
ix. MacMahon, B. and Pugh, T. F. (1970), *Epidemiology: Principles and Methods*, 376 pp. London: Churchill.
x. Witts, L. J. (Ed.) (1964), *Medical Surveys and Clinical Trials: Some Methods and Applications of Group Research in Medicine*, 2nd edition, 368 pp. London: Oxford University Press.

(i) is an excellent introduction, not only to *how* the most widely used statistical techniques are performed but also to *why* and *when* they are of value to the doctor. (ii) (a programmed learning manual) and (iii)–(vi) are other books written for bio-medical workers with no previous statistical knowledge, which describe mostly the same statistical techniques as (i) and a few more (although (ii), (iii), (v) and (vi) do not cover vital statistics), but give less space to introducing and discussing these techniques. For further reading by workers who already have some mathematical or statistical expertise, (vii) is recommended as a more comprehensive account of the statistical methods used in medical research, and (viii) as a critical review of some of these methods and their uses. (vii) includes a more extensive list of books on medical statistics. (ix) and (x) describe and illustrate epidemiological methods.

42. DEVELOPMENT OF CIRCADIAN RHYTHMS IN INFANCY

J. N. MILLS

INTRODUCTION

The study of human circadian (*circa*, *dies*, around a day) rhythms has achieved respectability with the inclusion of a chapter in a standard textbook.[30] This presumes a recognition of the practical importance of these rhythms, but it is also a tribute to the development of reputable methods of statistical assessment. Studies during infancy are few, although most of the useful aspects are as relevant to the infant as to the adult. Admittedly, the difficulties of adjustment of obstinately persistent physiological rhythms to night work or to other abnormal hours of working do not affect the infant; but the difficulties of adaptation to a sudden time-zone transition after long-distance flights are encountered, one must presume, by children who accompany their parents on their travels, though observations in this field are almost non-existent. So far as studies on adults are concerned, a further well-established usefulness is in diagnosis: a temperature which in the evening would be normal might suggest fever if it were recorded in the morning; and a concentration of corticosteroids in the plasma which would be normal at night would in the morning suggest adrenal deficiency, while one entirely normal in the morning would, if recorded in the evening, suggest Cushing's disease. There are also many indications that a disturbance of normal rhythmicity may be an early indication of disease of various kinds, although there is as yet no systematic body of knowledge on this topic.

One reason for sparsity of information about infancy lies in the ethical problem, when one passes from observation to experiment upon a subject who cannot give voluntary assent. The measurements needed to define rhythms are numerous, and often demanding on the subject as well as the experimenter, and the line between the harmless and the hazardous cannot always be clearly drawn; but there are certainly points where what might be scientifically valuable is ethically indefensible, and where information must therefore be obtained upon other species.

It is thus hardly possible to discuss the development of circadian rhythms in infancy without frequent reference to the much larger body of observation and experiment upon adult man, and upon other species. The reader wishing for more information upon human circadian rhythms generally is referred to a recent book,[9] which has an extensive bibliography, and for a fuller discussion of the causal connections between different rhythms to a chapter in another book.[31] There are some specific accounts of the rhythms in infancy.[16,17,20]

By way of introduction, for those unfamiliar with the subject, a simple example may clarify some of the concepts.

It has been recorded that neonates were more restless and slept less by night than by day.[16] Since restlessness is associated with hunger, and sleep with satiety, this nocturnal restlessness was apparently due to the long interval between the last evening feed and the first one in the morning. This is an example of an exogenous rhythm, one which is wholly dependent upon a rhythm in the environment. Such rhythms abound; but they are seldom of great interest, except when the rhythmic manifestation is itself of practical importance, when a knowledge of the external cause may be useful. A noisy infant, disturbing the neighbours, may be kept quiet by an extra nocturnal feed.

Of much greater interest are those rhythms which seem to arise from within the organism, and which are therefore described as endogenous; but the demonstration of endogeneity presents considerable difficulties, since we live in a world in which the alternation of light and darkness, day and night, affect profoundly all the habits of society. Our work, leisure, meals, sleep are all regulated to accord with this external rhythm with a period of approximately 24 hours, and such exogenous rhythmicity is almost inevitable in the lives of mothers or others who tend infants. Only when such external rhythmic influences have been rigorously excluded can we be confident that an observed rhythm has arisen from within the organism.

It has sometimes been assumed that the infant, after a sheltered existence in constant warmth and darkness, emerges suddenly at birth to meet for the first time an environment with a circadian rhythm. This is a fallacy, for some at least of the numerous rhythms in the mother, in her rest and activity as well as in the concentration of numerous constituents of her blood, must penetrate to the infant. It has in fact been shown that some circadian rhythmicity is present in the fetus before birth. For example, the plasma concentration of oestriol in maternal blood, which is believed to be of fetal-placental origin, has, in observations on 25 women over 2 days near the end of pregnancy, been found to fall from 0830 to 1630 hr., and to rise again from this time until 2130 hr.[38] The mean fall, not calculated by the authors, was $48{\cdot}3 \pm 5{\cdot}8\ \mu g/l$, (S.E. of mean), and the subsequent rise $28{\cdot}6 \pm 3{\cdot}6\ \mu g/l$. Records of fetal movements also suggest that these are not randomly distributed around the 24 hours, but are determined in part by the rhythm in the mother's habits.[41]

Fuller observations are possible in other species. The respiratory movements of fetal lambs of 110–142 days gestation have been studied by inserting electromagnetic flowmeters and integrating the rectified signal.[5] In 7 fetal lambs studied in this way over 5–12 consecutive days, there was always a peak in the late evening and a trough in the early hours of the morning (Fig. 1). The peak periods of fetal "breathing" appeared to be associated with high-frequency, low-voltage electrocorticograms, suggestive of REM sleep. Since the ewes were exposed to the usual external rhythmic influences, there is as yet no indication of the origin of this fetal rhythm; but the fact that the timing was similar in all fetuses examined, and related to a particular time of day, shows that it was not endogenous. In 4 other fetal lambs subjected similarly to preliminary intra-uterine surgery,[8] solute-free water clearance by the kidney was maximal around 1000 hr. and fell sharply thereafter to a minimal value between 1500 and 1900 hr.; again, a maternal or other external influence seems probable. It is clear from these several observations that the development of rhythmicity after birth is not solely a result of a first exposure to rhythmicity in the environment.

The distinction between exogenous and endogenous rhythms, though conceptually simple, is often blurred in practice. It has been shown on a wide range of organisms, including men, mice, birds and plants, that when external rhythmic influences are effectively excluded the persistent rhythms have a period departing slightly from 24 hours, perhaps of 23 or 25 hours, so that as time passes they become increasingly out of phase with the alternation of day and night in the world outside. It appears that, like most domestic clocks, the supposed internal clock is not a perfect timekeeper, but needs constant minor adjustment, which is presumably achieved by some aspect of the external rhythms. An endogenous and an external influence thus interact to produce the observed result.

Study of rhythms may be simply by observation, by measurement of the variable to be studied over a sufficient number of cycles, without attempt to determine how far it is endogenous. A further advance is to attempt to exclude the grosser external rhythms, as for example by keeping babies in constant illumination, and feeding either on demand or at regular intervals throughout the 24 hours. More rigorous studies involve a deliberate alteration in the external rhythm, as by life on a 27-hour day or day of other abnormal length, or by shifting the phase, as occurs with a long eastward or westward flight through several time zones. Few observations have been recorded after flights and experimental disturbance of rhythms appears to have been attempted only in rats, in experiments which have as yet been only reported in abstract.[6] The animals were kept, from the time of conception, on a day of 27 hours, 14 hours of light alternating with 13 hours of darkness, and at the age of about 1, 2, or 3 months their activity rhythms were studied in darkness. It is claimed that, over 20 cycles of observation, they adopted activity rhythms with periods of $24\frac{1}{2}$–$25\frac{1}{2}$ hours, longer than did control animals brought up on a normal 24-hour day but substantially short of 27 hours. Whatever interpretation be placed upon these experiments, it does not seem that there was any phase of development at which the external periodicity of 27 hours could impose itself upon the animals' internal timekeeping mechanism. Since most of our knowledge of rhythmicity in infants thus rests upon series of sequential observations, some mention must be made of the methods used to analyse rhythms. The reader wishing a fuller account is referred elsewhere.[40]

The simplest method of study is a comparison between values obtained during the day and during the night, or between values obtained at two points during the 24 hours. This procedure may reveal the existence of a rhythm if the timing is appropriate, or if night and day correspond to the low and high parts of a curve. This is, however, a matter of luck, unless one has previous knowledge of when to expect maxima and minima. For example, when body temperature is continuously recorded in adults maximum values are usually found in the late evening and minima in the small hours of the morning. The rhythm is thus obscured when measurements are only made at bedtime, when temperature has already fallen from its maximum, and on rising in the morning when it is already above its minimum. Similarly, phosphate excretion commonly falls during the latter part of the night and the first hours after waking, and rises sometimes to high values in the afternoon. A clear rhythm may thus be obscured if comparison is made only between excretion during sleep and during the day.

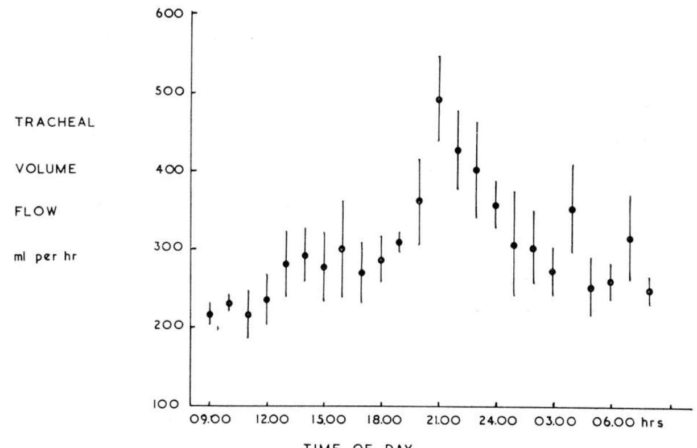

FIG. 1. Tracheal flow rate in a fetal lamb, gestational age 112–117 days, observed over 5 consecutive days, mean and S.E.[5]

A more satisfactory but more laborious technique is to plot individual, or mean, values at frequent intervals over 24 hours, when a rhythm may be obvious. While these and other graphic displays may be informative, they do not permit the ascription of any formal significance levels to the presence or absence of a rhythm, and for the formal analysis of rhythms a variety of mathematical techniques are being increasingly used. Such techniques, in contrast to the mere inspection of graphic displays, have been compared with the use of a microscope rather than the unaided eye. The commonest method of analysis is the fitting of a sine curve, which defines a rhythm in terms of amplitude and phase, and if the curve is obviously non-sinusoidal in shape harmonics may be added. This analysis depends upon a prior assumption of a certain fundamental frequency, usually 24 hours, and the other frequencies which are detected will all be multiples of this. A more elaborate technique, even more heavily dependent upon suitable computer programmes, is to fit independently a large series of sine curves of different periods, and calculate the power spectrum, or variance due to each period or frequency. A power spectrum linear in frequency will give good resolution for rhythms of a few hours but will not readily distinguish between a period of 24 hours and one longer or shorter by an hour or less. By contrast, a spectrum linear in period will discriminate better in the circadian region. Periods may be fitted as close to one another as every 0·1 hour, and in this way a rhythm of period, say, 24·6 hours can be distinguished from one of 24·0 hours. The criterion of goodness of fit is the curve of greatest variance or of the greatest amplitude, or that which reduces the residual variance to a minimum. Very little formal rhythm analysis has yet been published upon human infants, partly again because of the paucity of data.

Yet another technique, entirely independent of the properties of a sine curve, is that of autocorrelation. If a series of observations tends to repeat its form every 24 hours, then, whatever the shape of the curve, each value will be better correlated with the value 24 hours later than with one later by any other interval of time. Clearly, this method is only applicable when observations are made at regular and frequent intervals over several days.

SLEEP, WAKEFULNESS AND ACTIVITY

Records of whether infants are awake or asleep are relatively simple to obtain, granted a sufficiency of patient observers. Alternatively, graphic tracings may be obtained with an actograph. This is a device for recording movements of cot, cage or other domicile, occasioned by movements of its occupant, and has been very extensively employed in studying the activity rhythms of other species. In most studies, infants have been exposed to the customary rhythm of alternating diurnal light and nocturnal darkness which, at least in other species, is a powerful influence in determining physiological rhythms. Feeding patterns have varied: in some studies a night feed has been omitted, thus introducing another important rhythmic circadian influence. In some, feeding has been at regular intervals, three- or four-hourly, throughout the 24 hours. Although, strictly speaking, this is not a circadian influence, there is evidence that such regularity may help to form a rhythm whose period is a multiple of that imposed externally. Studies involving demand feeding are thus more informative. Another influence, seldom mentioned but probably important, is the amount of attention which the infant receives. This is likely to reflect the rhythm of wakefulness and sleepiness of the mother or nurse, and may thus further conduce to the imposition of rhythmicity upon the infant.

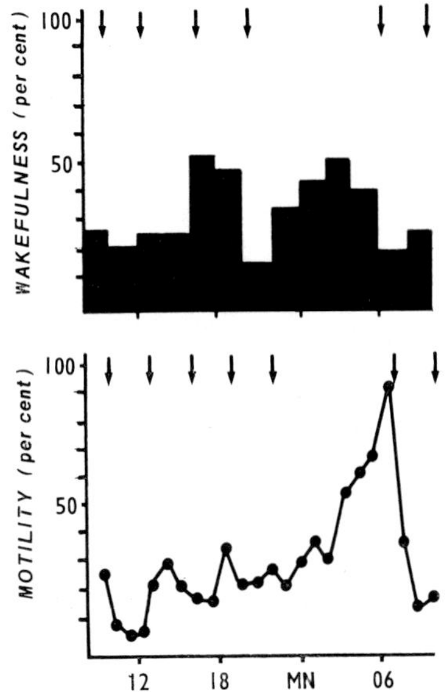

FIG. 2. Percentage of wakefulness and of motility in infants during the first week of life. Arrows indicate times of feeding.[16]

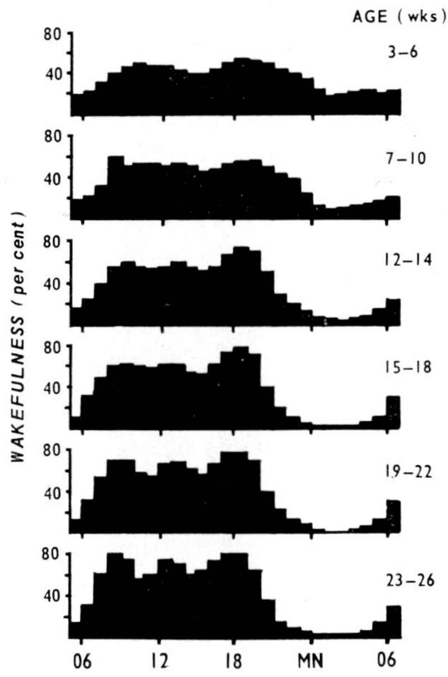

FIG. 3. Percentage of time spent awake in each hour in infants of different age groups.[16]

Calculation, from records of sleep and activity, of the percentage of each 2-hour period spent in sleep[20] indicate that the pattern of nocturnal sleep and diurnal wakefulness is not established during the first week of life (Fig. 2), and the increase of motility during the night suggests further that this is at least in part a consequence of a long interval between feeds. Similar studies over the first 6 months of life[26] (Fig. 3) indicate that the proportion of time awake during the day steadily increases, and the proportion during the night diminishes. It is a reasonable presumption that this rhythm has been imposed upon the infant by its environment.

One interesting study strongly suggests that regularity of treatment is a potent environmental influence in establishing this rhythmicity.[35] For the first 10 days of life, 9 infants were nursed in a communal nursery with regular

4-hourly feeding, and another 9 in a single room with demand feeding by a foster-mother. During the next 18 days all were treated identically, each in a single room with demand feeding by a foster-mother. Those who had spent their first ten days of life in the communal nursery had a more clearly differentiated pattern of diurnal wakefulness and nocturnal sleep than had those nursed on their own throughout (Fig. 4). Exposure to a regular 4-hourly routine had apparently facilitated the development of a 24-hour rhythm. A later paper by the same authors, however,[36] records this effect in female babies only.

There is evidence that this 24-hour rhythm develops more slowly in premature than in full-term infants. Figure 5 shows a computer analysis of the sleep rhythms of full-term and premature infants in different age groups. The various

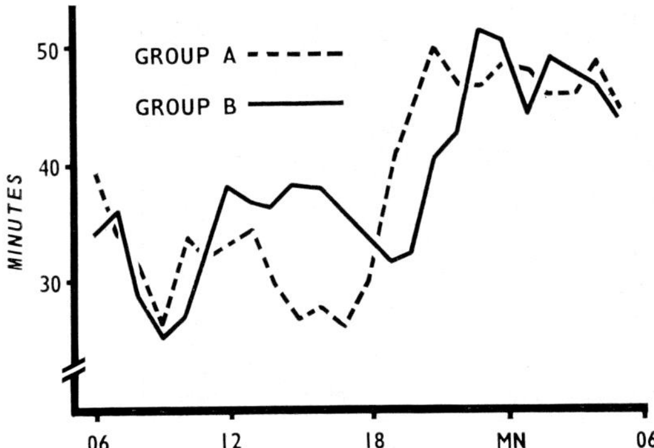

FIG. 4. Mean minutes of sleep in each hour in 2 groups of infants. During the first 10 days of life, Group A wer nursed in a communal nursery and Group B individualy with a foster mother.[35]

harmonics indicated by this programme probably indicate the non-sinusoidal character of the sleep–wakefulness pattern; but the much greater prominence of the 24-hour component in full-term infants than in premature infants, which is obvious in those aged 7 to 13 weeks, probably indicates an earlier adaptation to the external 24-hour rhythm, and thus a maturation of the ability to respond to the external rhythmic influence.

The spontaneous development of rhythmicity in infants not subjected to regular habits of feeding has been observed in several studies.[12,26,28,34] In one of these[34] it has been claimed that even in the first three days of life the longest continuous sleeping periods usually occur between 2300 and 0700 hr. Further details of two such studies are shown in Fig. 6. In the infant represented on the left of this figure, the black and white areas, representing sleep and wakefulness, appear more or less random for the first few weeks. If there is any rhythm, it has a period much less than 24 hours. Some authors in fact describe the infant as "polycyclic," implying the occurrence of many cycles of rest and activity in the course of the 24 hours. From about the 8th to the 14th week the white intervals run at an angle of nearly 45° from the left to the right-hand side. The time when the child becomes wakeful is slightly later every day, indicating a rhythm with a period of about 24·4 hours. After this, the white areas correspond mainly to daytime, but between the 17th and 23rd week they are shifting slightly to the left, indicating a period slightly below 24 hours, and only in the last three weeks is the period indistinguishable from 24 hours.

In the infant represented on the right, there is some indication of a shift to the right between the third and fourteenth day, and back to the left during the following week, suggesting periods of 24·4 and 23·7 hours. From the 4th week, a 24-hour rhythm is apparent, although the diurnal wakefulness is fairly regularly divided by a period of sleep around noon. Both these infants therefore appear

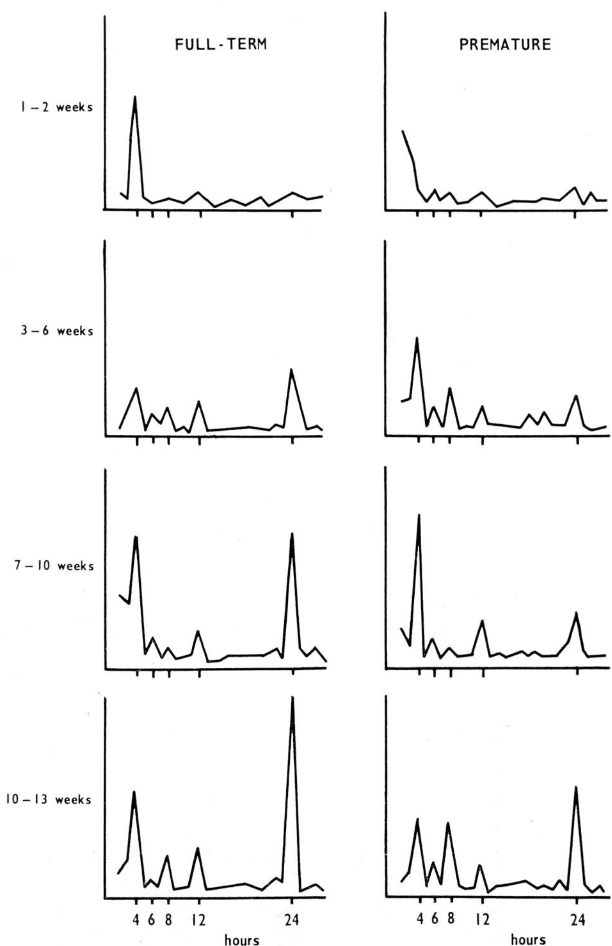

FIG. 5. Spectral analysis of frequency components in the rhythm of sleeping and waking in full-term and premature infants of different ages. Abscissa linear in period.[18]

to have had an endogenous rhythm whose period was not precisely 24 hours, as has often been observed upon adults in isolation. Eventually they adopted a rhythm with a reasonably accurate 24-hour period, and observations upon adults suggest that this was due to the synchronizing effect of some factor in the environment. What was the environmental influence which thus constrained them to a more precise 24-hour rhythm, the one around 4 and the other around 23 weeks of age, is unknown, but the alternation of light and darkness seems a likely guess.

Endogenous rhythms with a period slightly above or below 24 hours have not been observed in all studies; Fig. 7

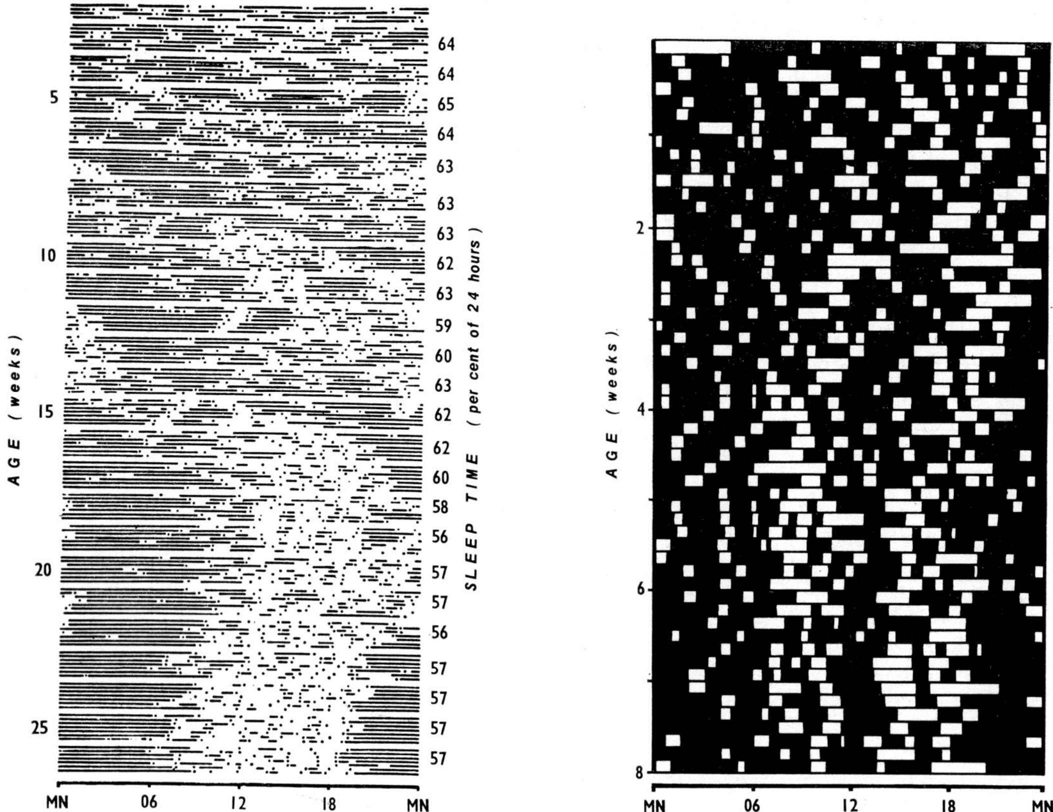

FIG. 6. Sleep-wakefulness distribution of two children, recorded continuously. On left from,[26] on right from.[34] Black indicates sleep; dots on left figure indicate feeds.

shows a record of a child who was demand-fed from the moment of birth. He was the child of the author,[28] so that demand-feeding was known to be practised conscientiously.

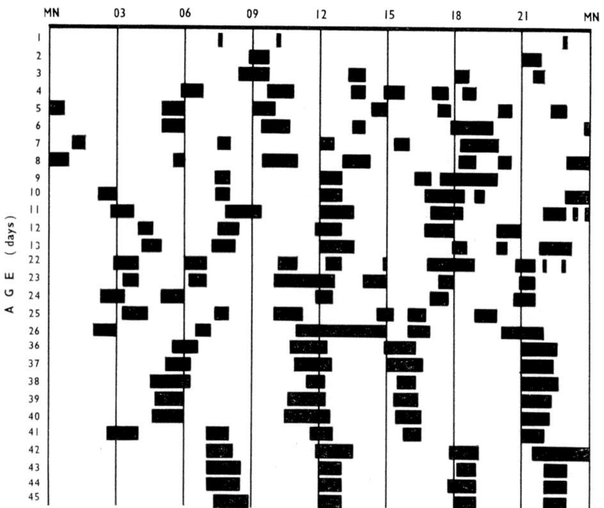

FIG. 7. Times of wakefulness (black) and sleep (white) in an infant fed on demand from birth.[28]

The number of feeds demanded, their timing, and the consequent timing of sleep periods, varied in a nearly random manner during the first month, after which the baby usually demanded 4 feeds a day, distributed nearly evenly over the 24 hours. After the 6th week of life, however, the hours became much more regular and were confined to the hours of daytime. A second child studied in similar detail demanded much more frequent feeds during the early weeks of life, but also eventually demanded only 4 feeds a day, confined to the daytime.

It has already been suggested that the alternation of light and darkness is the most probable external influence inducing this circadian rhythm of diurnal wakefulness and appetite and nocturnal sleep. Of very special interest therefore are observations[28] upon two infants who from the 8th day of life were kept in continuous light and fed on demand. A record from one of these infants is shown in Fig. 8, and the behaviour of the other is stated to have been similar. As with infants exposed to alternating day and night, his demands for food were quite irregular during the first few weeks of life, but by the 8th week he was taking one long sleep of about 8 hours, from 0500 until 1300. He had in fact developed a circadian rhythm, but as he had no indication of the passage of day and night his hours of sleep did not correspond to those of the children outside. At the age of 80 days he was exposed again to the natural alternation of light and darkness, and within 9 days had altered to demanding four feeds at more conventional hours, sleeping from 1930 to 0500 hr. Of even more interest is the observation that his urinary rhythms also altered their timing appropriately. The 24-hour output was divided into diurnal urine, collected from 0600 to 1800 hr., and nocturnal urine from 1800 until 0600 hr. The day-night ratio was below unity for volume and excretion of sodium, potassium, chloride and phosphate immediately before he was removed from continuous light, but after a week of exposure to day and night these ratios were all above unity, as is usual in infants of his age. This study provides the best evidence yet available for the spontaneous development of endogenous circadian rhythm in a human infant. The fact that his habits were so clearly out of phase with the world outside makes it unlikely that some undetected influence, such as nocturnal sleepiness on the part of those nursing him, had penetrated to his nursery.

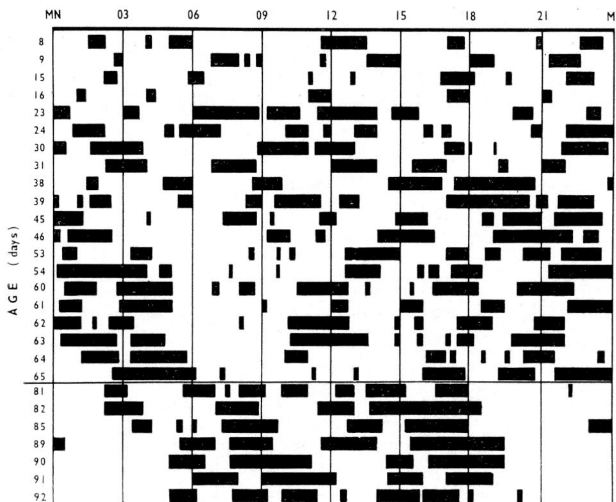

FIG. 8. Times of wakefulness (black) and sleep (white) in an infant who, from the 8th day of life, was kept in isolation in uniform illumination and fed on demand. After he reached the age of 80 days the light was turned out at night and he was exposed to the natural alternation of day and night.[28]

A similar maturation of circadian activity rhythms has been observed in other species. In rats, for example,[2] nocturnal activity begins to exceed diurnal by 21 days of age, and the adult pattern of activity, largely confined to the night, is developed in the 8th week of life. At the same time, the rhythm in 5-hydroxytryptamine (5-HT) content of the brain becomes reversed in phase. Up to the 17th day of life it is high during the hours of darkness, but after this it gradually changes, until the peak level is observed during daylight and the content falls during the hours of darkness. There are also changes in the pattern of noradrenaline content, although this does not reverse its phase as does that of 5-HT. Since functionally different nerve tracts in the brain are known to operate through different synaptic transmitters, these observations suggest that a neurochemical contribution to activity rhythms may in due course be established.

REM SLEEP

In addition to a circadian cycle infants, like adults, show during sleep a more or less regular alternation between orthodox ("passive") and REM ("paradoxical," "active") sleep. At birth, REM sleep occupies about half of the total time of sleep, and only by the age of 4 years has it diminished to around 20 per cent, the value found in young adults. The cycles between different stages of sleep are also considerably shorter, about 50 min. at birth, lengthening to about 75 min. by the age of 4.[15] This is still substantially below the usual adult value of between 90 and 100 min.

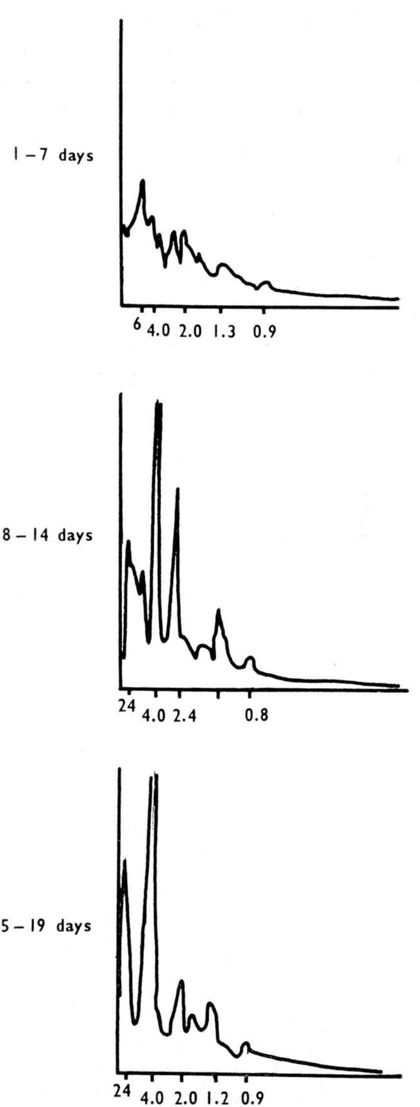

FIG. 9. Spectral analysis of frequency components in the rhythm of eye movements (REM) of a prematurely born infant in the first, second and third weeks of life. Abscissa linear in frequency.[18]

The eye movements are a conspicuous component of the REM sleep of infants, and a detailed study[18] of eye movements in a single premature baby suggests that the periodicity is complex. Figure 9 shows the already mentioned period of slightly under an hour. In addition, other longer periods are ill-defined in the 1st week of life, but in the 2nd and 3rd week several periods from 1 to 4 hours stand out clearly. The 2·4-hour period in the 2nd week, and the 4-hour period in the third week, correspond to the frequency of feeding and are probably simple consequences of this external rhythm, but the other periods have no such obvious cause. In addition, a 24-hour period has emerged clearly by the 3rd week.

Despite much speculation, little is known about the separate functions of REM and deep sleep, nor why the neonate spends such a large proportion of his time in REM sleep. The rhythmic alternation between the two forms, seen in the adult, has been described as a persistence of the polyphasic sleep rhythm of the infant, but this in no sense offers an "explanation" of their rhythmic alternation in either infant or adult.

TEMPERATURE

The circadian rhythm of body temperature has probably received more attention than has that of any other function. Observations upon human adults, and upon other species, were accumulated during the first half of the nineteenth century, but it was only at the beginning of the twentieth century that attention was turned to the human infant. This early literature is reviewed by Aschoff[3] and by Kleitman.[25] Figure 10 is derived from measurements on 78 children[24] on most of whom measurements were made every 4 hours for up to 11 days. Most authors agree that, as is indicated in this figure, there is no consistent circadian rhythm during the first week of life. It is difficult to say with precision when this rhythm first appears, but after the first week it is visible in the mean of a group, and has a timing similar to that in older children. The amplitude of the rhythm then progressively increases at least until the 2nd year, both by an increase of the diurnal peak and by a fall of the nocturnal minimum. By the age of 5 years the pattern is very similar to that in older children or adults.[16] This same development of the temperature rhythm has also been studied in a single infant observed repeatedly during the first 15 months of life;[32] *see also* reference 25.

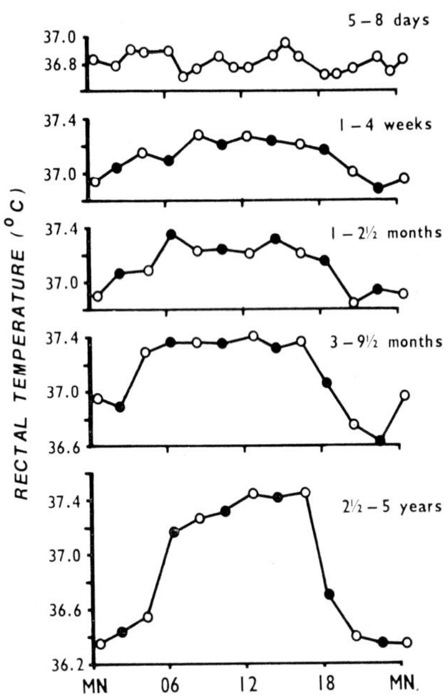

FIG. 10. Mean rectal temperature at different hours in groups of infants of different ages. Except in the youngest group, measurements were made 4-hourly, and the symbols ○ and ● represent different groups, each of 3–18 infants, each observed over 2–11 days.[24]

Some authors also describe alterations in the form of the curve, such as a maximum around midday instead of in the late afternoon, and a double peak. Most of these variations could, however, probably be paralleled by observations upon different individuals in any one age group, and many individual variations are obscured when the mean of several subjects, or even of several days upon the same subject, is presented.

There has been little investigation of the cause of this temperature rhythm in infancy, but in the adult it clearly results mainly from rhythmic changes not in heat production but in heat loss, largely due to alterations in the peripheral circulation. Some observations suggest that these variations, in turn, are due to rhythmic variations in the "set point" in the hypothalamus, the temperature around which this controlling centre thermoregulates. Some indication of this set point can be given by studies of the critical temperature above which substantial sweating begins, or the lower critical temperature below which there is a substantial increase in metabolic rate. These critical points have been measured in human infants of different ages or maturity[21,22] in studies which have indicated the neonatal development of thermoregulatory mechanisms. There has however been no systematic study at different times over the 24 hours which could indicate when these separate regulatory mechanisms assume a circadian rhythm.

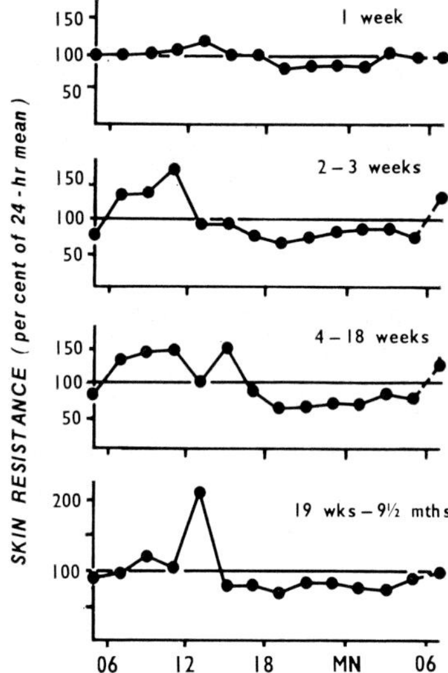

FIG. 11. Mean electrical resistance of skin in groups of infants of different ages. Each group is derived from 19–87 days of observation on 4–16 infants.[16]

An indirect indication of the intensity of sweating is given by a fall in the electrical resistance of the skin. This has been measured systematically at different times of day in infants of different ages; it begins to show a rhythm during the 1st week of life and the amplitude becomes more marked during the 1st year[16] (Fig. 11). This parallel between the developing rhythm in body temperature and an indirect measurement of one important means of heat loss offers some support to the suggestion that the temperature rhythm is, as in adults, mainly dependent upon variations in heat loss rather than in heat production.

There appears to be little evidence upon how far the temperature rhythm develops as a result of exposure to external rhythms, or as a result of a maturation process in the infant. Little detail is in fact given in most published accounts of the external rhythms present, from which one could attempt to assess the importance of the different components. The slow development of a circadian temperature rhythm during the first 3 months of life in infants born prematurely suggests, however, that a maturation process in the infant plays some part.

CIRCULATION

A circadian rhythm has been observed in the pulse rate after the first month of life, and it becomes much more prominent during the second year[16,19] (Fig. 12). In the

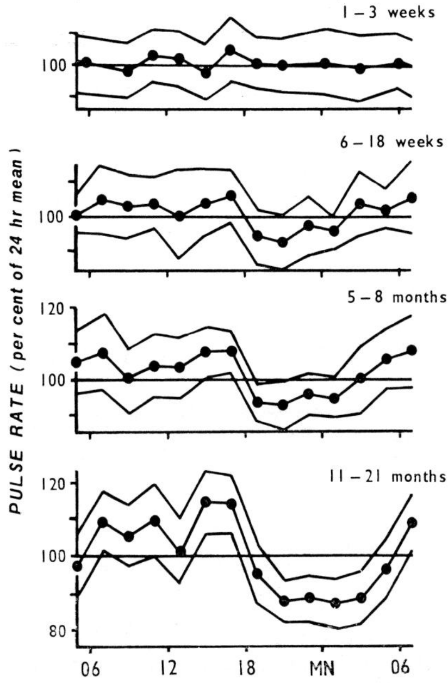

FIG. 12. Pulse rate in infants of different ages, mean and S.D. Each group is derived from 35–359 days of observation on groups of 4–58 infants.[16]

adult, circadian rhythmicity in the pulse rate is largely exogenous, depending upon the alternation of rest and activity, though when these are kept uniform a rhythm sometimes persists which probably results from the rhythm of deep temperature. The cardiac pacemaker is directly temperature-sensitive, and the circadian variation in its frequency is of about the right magnitude for the temperature rhythm. In the infant, rhythm analysis has been performed upon long series of measurements of pulse rate, yielding high frequencies corresponding well to the periodicity of feeding. It would thus seem that, as in the adult, rhythmic variations in the pulse rate are largely exogenous, being at first determined by the pattern of feeding and later by the development of a circadian pattern of rest and activity. Observations upon 12 women during the last month of pregnancy[16] (Fig. 13) indicate a pulse rate in the fetus with no apparent rhythm, although the mothers had a sharp

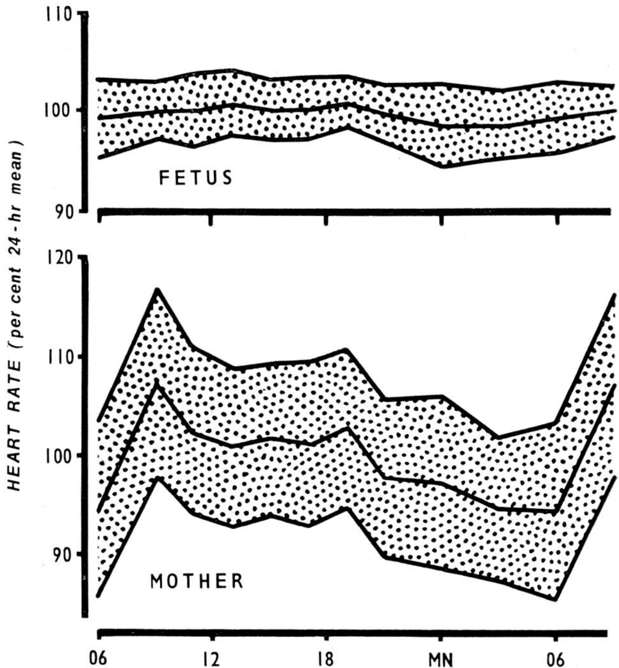

FIG. 13. Nychthemeral variations of heart rate of mother and fetus in last months of pregnancy: mean and S.D.[16]

maximum around 0900 and a gradual fall to a minimum around 0600. Presumably the mothers followed the usual circadian rhythm of rest and activity, which failed to impose any rhythm on the fetus.

A circadian rhythm in blood pressure has been detected in children aged 4 to 13 years.[20] but as in adults this may well be wholely exogenous.

RENAL FUNCTION

Circadian rhythms in renal function are of particular interest since the ability of the infant to sleep without wetting the bed, as of the adult to sleep through without being awakened by a full bladder, are due at least in part to a nocturnal reduction in urine flow.

The development of urinary rhythms throughout infancy and childhood has been observed by means of 4-hourly collections of urine over several days on children divided into a number of broad age groups.[16,20] The same data are used in both these papers, but the age ranges in which they are grouped are not identical. They are chosen in the earlier paper[16] to illustrate the time course for each urinary component, and in the later paper[20] to compare the rhythm in different components at any one time. According to the authors, the circadian rhythm became apparent at different times after birth for different constituents, and the earliest rhythm to appear was that in urine flow (Fig. 14). The day–night differences are said to be statistically significant in a group of 16 children aged between 1 and 5 months, though not in a group of 9 aged 2 or 3 weeks, nor in another group of 12 during the 1st week of life. The method of calculation of statistical significance was to treat samples centred around 0600, 1000, and 1400 as day and those at 1800, 2200 and 0200 as night samples, and to calculate the difference between day and night by a *t*-test. This timing appears appropriate for the older children, but not for the younger groups. Inspection of the published figures suggests that even in the 1st week of life flow was rhythmic, but the maximum was at 1800 and the minimum at 0600, and at 2 or 3 weeks the maximum was at 1400. The appearance is indeed of a rhythm of low amplitude with a late maximum at birth, with the amplitude increasing and the maximum

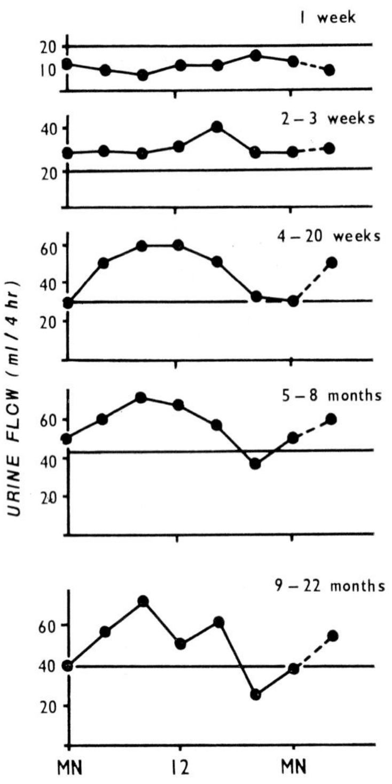

FIG. 14. Mean urine flow in children of different ages. Each group is derived from 24–90 days of observation on 3–16 children.[16]

coming earlier until the age of 5 months. Since the number of observations is substantial, it would be useful if these data were analysed by the more satisfactory methods now available.

The figure shows clearly that any rhythm in the two younger groups was of low amplitude, while in children over one month old there is an obvious rhythm of large amplitude. It may be observed that the two younger groups were being fed 4-hourly, while the night feed was omitted in the older groups. This cannot, however, be a direct cause of the rhythm, since in the group aged 4–20 weeks flow had already fallen to nearly its lowest level before the last evening feed, and was already rising before the first feed in the morning. The time of development of the rhythm in urine flow is of particular interest since there is evidence that in adults an important determinant of the rhythm in urine flow is the osmotic effect of a rhythm in excretion of sodium and potassium. It is claimed,[16] however, that the rhythm in excretion of sodium and potassium, which in older children is roughly synchronous with urine flow (Fig. 15), appeared later than the flow rhythm. This dissociation between rhythms of water and electrolyte excretion is not, however, at all clearly established from the data, and the assertion that a rhythm was present in flow when it was absent in electrolytes must be treated with some caution, particularly as a much earlier emergence of a urinary potassium rhythm has been described[28,29] (Fig. 18 discussed below). There are of course many other factors which may

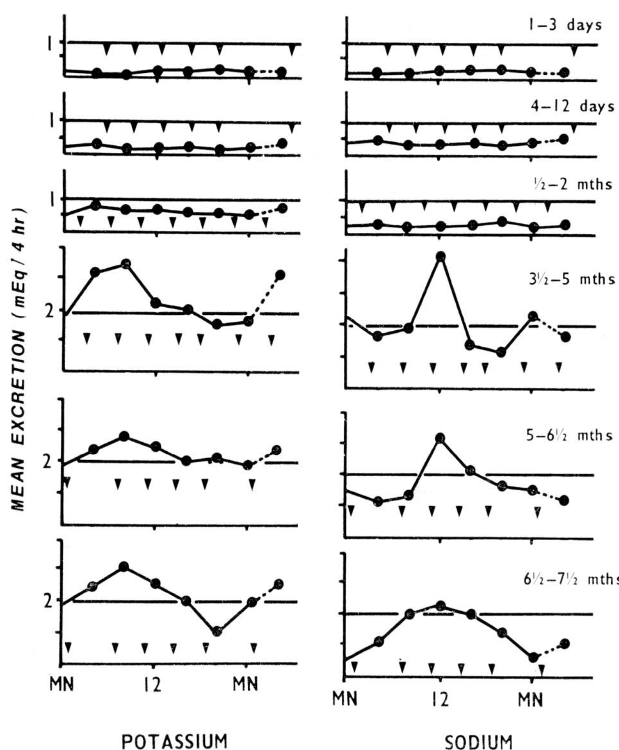

FIG. 15. Mean urinary kation excretion in infants of different ages. Each group is derived from 15–32 days of observation upon 3–9 infants. ▼ times of feeding.[16]

influence urine flow, including the rate of glomerular filtration and the secretions of the adrenal cortex and the neuro-hypophysis, as well as the little-understood effect of variations in external temperature, so we have almost no evidence available to interpret the apparent maturation of a rhythm in urine flow during the first months of life.

In at least some instances of nocturnal enuresis, associated with a failure of development of the usual rhythm in flow,[27] the rhythm in electrolyte excretion has also failed to develop, but a subsequent emergence of a normal electrolyte rhythm has not been accompanied by nocturnal oliguria. The connexion between nocturnal enuresis and urinary electrolyte rhythms thus remains obscure.

A circadian rhythm in the excretion of other urinary constituents is said to emerge later than that of sodium and potassium. That of phosphate, chloride, creatine and creatinine are evident only in groups of infants aged over 16 months.[20] This statement is a little puzzling since the sum of the anions in urine must equal the sum of the kations, and chloride, phosphate, sodium and potassium form a large proportion of the two sorts of ions. Only sulphate and ammonium, of those omitted in this study, are likely to make a considerable contribution. A rhythm of large amplitude in the excretion of sodium and potassium, with roughly uniform excretion of phosphate and chloride, must therefore imply either a high-amplitude rhythm in sulphate excretion, which is unlikely, or a rhythmic excretion of ammonium opposite in phase to that of sodium and potassium. This latter could well be a partial explanation, since a similar inverse relationship is usual in adults; but in the adult, a rhythm in excretion of chloride is usually as clear as that of sodium, and nearly in phase with it. Since no data on chloride excretion are published, it is difficult to comment further.

A rhythm in phosphate excretion is said[20] to be absent during the 1st year of life but present during the 2nd year. Inspection of the published figures certainly shows a rhythm of much greater amplitude in the 2nd year; but it is possible that the statement that no "significant" rhythm is present during the 1st year again derives from the method of calculation of "significance," by looking for a mean difference between excretion during arbitrarily defined "day" and "night." The phosphate rhythm is known to be, in adults, out of phase with that of other urinary constituents, and the published diagram suggests that excretion is minimal at 1800 hr. and maximal at 0200; both these times are included by the authors as "night."

This rhythm in phosphate excretion is little understood even in the adult. The pattern of meals and of activity certainly contribute, and the infant consumes phosphate-rich milk, and lays down phosphate in bone. The rhythmic secretion of cortisol is probably also involved; but since the nature and importance of these contributions is unknown, even in the adult, it would be idle at present to attempt any interpretation in the infant.

The rhythm in creatinine excretion, which in some adults is barely detectable and in others is quite large, probably reflects a rhythm in rate of glomerular filtration, and it is a reasonable supposition that the same is true in the infant when a rhythm develops during the second year of life.

As will be seen, almost all our knowledge of renal rhythms in infancy derives from observation, without any of the environmental control which would be appropriate for more rigorous study. We are thus largely ignorant how far the emergence of rhythms reflects an increasingly well-marked rhythm in the environment, and how far, if at all, the appearance of an endogenous rhythm. Limited observations upon Arctic dwellers suggest that the usual renal rhythms are less marked in people who, for a considerable part of the year, are not exposed to the clearcut alternation of day and night to which all inhabitants of lower latitudes are exposed. This suggests that man has not wholly endogenous renal rhythms. There is, however, one limited piece of work[4] which suggests that the urinary flow rhythm which is observed in infants in normal surroundings during the first year of life becomes endogenous only in the second year. In this study, the 24-hour collection of urine was divided into two aliquots, the day-urine passed between 0600 and 2200 hr. and the night-urine, produced between 2200 and 0600 hr. The ratio of the rate of flow by day to that during the night gives an indication of the presence of a circadian rhythm. In conformity with other findings, a rhythm was absent in infants aged under 1 month, and present in those aged over 2 months; and in one baby, observed on the 30th and 31st days of life and again 12 and 13 days later, the rhythm had developed between these two periods of observation (Fig. 16). Of especial interest,

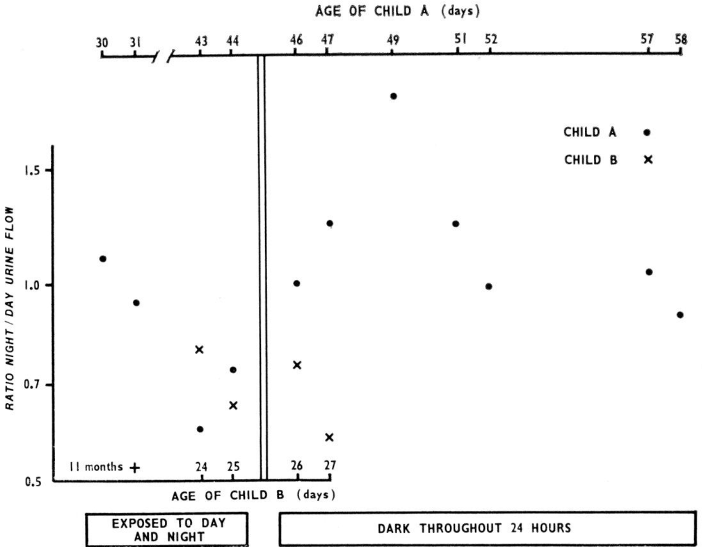

FIG. 16. Ratio of urine flow by night (2200–0600 hr.) to flow by day (0600–2200 hr.) in one child ● in the second, and another × in the twelfth month of life, at first exposed to day and night, and afterwards in darkness for the 24 hours of each observation.[4]

however, were observations upon infants who, after a rhythm had appeared, were kept alone in a dark room for varying periods. These are also shown in Fig. 16, where the existence of the usual rhythm is indicated by a low day–night ratio of urine flow. A baby who by the age of one and a half months was rhythmic when living in a communal nursery, lost his rhythm completely on a series of days during the latter half of this month when he was kept alone in a continuously darkened room. Similar but more fragmentary observations were made upon two other infants aged 2 and 3 months. By contrast, another infant in his 12th month of life was rhythmic when kept alone, and retained this rhythm during 2 further days when he was kept alone in the dark. While this procedure probably does not involve that total exclusion of all exogenous rhythms which is desirable for the rigorous demonstration of an endogenous rhythm, it does strongly suggest that, when urinary rhythm first appears in the 2nd month of life, it is dependent for its continuance upon at least some rhythmic external factors. The alternation of light and darkness may well be of prime importance. However, by the end of the first year this rhythm has become endogenous, persisting during the suspension of external rhythms.

The observations described above[28] upon infants kept in uniform light suggest the emergence of endogenous urinary rhythms early in the 3rd month of life; and the retiming of their phase by exposure to day and night gives further support to the suggestion that light is a major influence. It would be valuable to have these findings published in more detail, for circadian rhythm in electrolyte excretion appears to have developed earlier than in infants exposed to day and night,[20] and a urinary chloride rhythm is said, as one might expect, to have developed at the same time as the sodium and potassium rhythms.

ADRENALS

The circadian rhythm in secretion of cortisol is, in the adult, one of the most stable. Secretion is mainly in the early morning, so that plasma concentration falls at night to a very low level. Recent work, involving collection of blood every 20 minutes, has shown that this rhythm is more complex than had been previously supposed, consisting of a large number of discrete episodes of secretion, each of which is followed by an exponential decline of plasma concentration. These episodes are mainly concentrated in the early morning, though they continue with diminishing frequency into the late afternoon. The "average" circadian pattern of plasma concentration, derived from less frequent sampling on many days or subjects, grossly smooths the pattern that may be observed on any one occasion on a single subject.

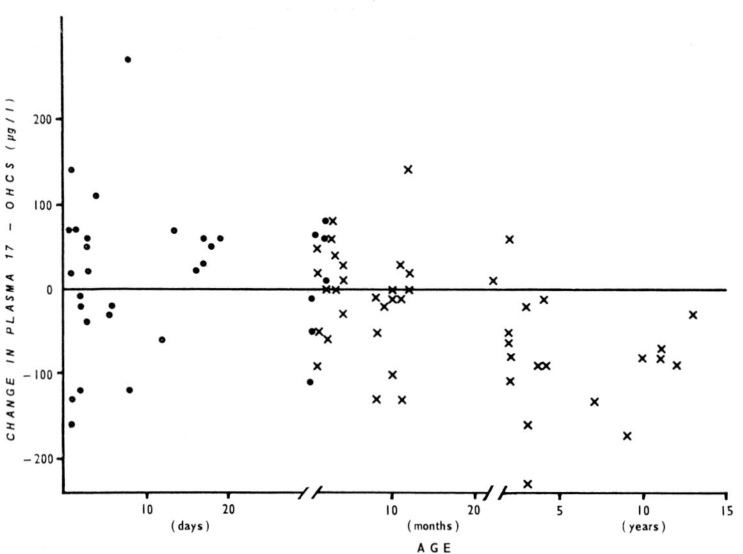

FIG. 17. Change in plasma 17-hydroxycorticosteroid concentration from 0800–2000 hr. in children of different ages ● premature births; × full term births. Note the two changes of scale on the abscissa.[11]

When attempts are made to define the circadian rhythm by analysis of only two blood samples in the 24 hours, there must therefore be a random variation in their difference, dependent upon whether they happen to have been collected at the peak or the trough of one of the short-term oscillations. The development of the rhythm in infants has been studied in this manner, measuring the plasma 17-hydroxycorticosteroid concentration at 0800 and 2000 hr., and it is not surprising that in any age group the variation is large.[11] In babies who were premature both by gestational age and by birth weight, and who were examined when they weighed 2 to $2\frac{1}{2}$ kg., the steroid concentration was on average higher in the evening than in the morning, though the mean difference was quite non-significant, and according to the authors it was only in a group aged between 3 and 13 years that there was a significant mean fall from morning to evening, similar to that seen in adults. Inspection of the original data (Fig. 17) suggests, however, that the adult pattern was probably developed somewhere between the end of the 1st and the 2nd year of life.

Very similar observations have been made in the rat[1] except that the main steroid involved is corticosterone, and the phase of the rhythm is reversed, in accordance with the nocturnal habits of the species. Maturation of the rhythm consisted of the development of a consistently higher steroid level in the afternoon than in the morning. This occurred between the 25th and 30th day of life. At an earlier age, up to 15 days, the adrenals were incapable of responding to exogenous ACTH, but the glands were capable of responding substantially before they became rhythmic.

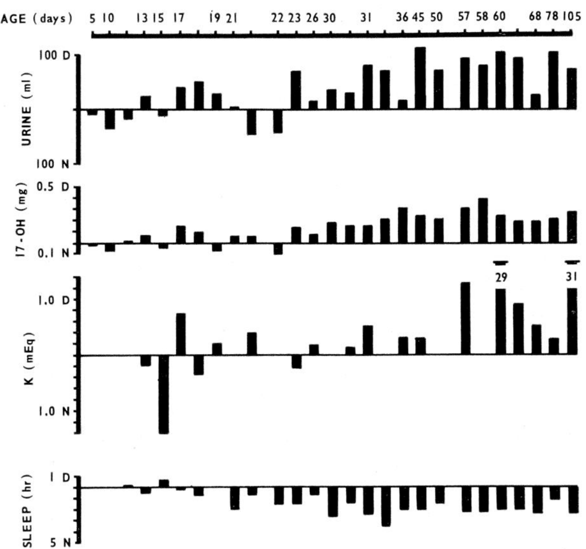

FIG. 18. Difference between diurnal (D, 0600–1800 hr.) and nocturnal (N, 1800–0600 hr.) urinary volume, and excretion of 17-hydroxycorticosteroids and potassium, and in hours of sleep, in infants of different ages. Columns above the line indicate a higher diurnal, and below the line a higher nocturnal, level.[29]

Sampling more frequently than twice in 24 hours would be needed to define steroid rhythms precisely. It would be hard to justify frequent blood-sampling, but an attempt has been made by measuring urinary corticosteroids (Porter-Silber chromogens) in urine samples collected over every 3 hours from 27 infants aged between 5 and 105 days,[29] using a small plastic bag over the penis to facilitate collection. By the fourth week of life the rate of excretion by day (0600 to 1800 hr.) was fairly consistently higher than that by night, as was also the urine flow and excretion of potassium (Fig. 18). This was around the same age as that when nocturnal sleep first regularly exceeded dirunal. When the steroid excretion of each infant was plotted however, no consistent pattern emerged, and all showed at least two excretory peaks in the 24 hours. Measurement of the plasma concentration at 0900 and 1800 hr. in two infants, aged 1 and 2 months, showed the morning concentration much higher in both. This contrasts strikingly with the claim[11] that the rhythm only develops between 3 and 13 years of age; but the numbers were small in both studies and, as has been indicated, two samples in 24 hours is too infrequent for reliable conclusions.

SERUM IRON

Many workers have documented circadian variations in serum iron in adult man. The majority of subjects show a steady fall in concentration from an early morning peak to low values in the evening, though a minority show no regular pattern. This usual pattern of a morning fall is observed more often in children over 3 years of age than in those under 2 years.[37] In another study[42] in which samples were collected every 3 hours, circadian periodicity was observed from 7 months of age onwards, although the timing of the peak was not very consistent. When observations were made for at least a continuous 48 hours, the younger infants, up to 6 months of age, often appeared to show an oscillation of a different period. Out of 91 curves examined in infants of this age group, 55 showed a rhythm with a period close to 24 hours, 11 showed no regular rhythm, and 25 showed a rhythm with either a short period of between 16 and 22 hours, or a long period, between 28 and 34 hours. Though no figures are published, the authors state that the rhythms were perfectly clear, with the time occupied by the fall from maximum to minimum about equal to that from the minimum up to the maximum again. It would be valuable to have this interesting finding confirmed by more formal rhythm analysis, since it suggests the existence of an endogenous rhythm of rather variable period, which in due course becomes entrained to the 24-hour cycle of day and night. There is no obvious external rhythm which could impose a periodicity of 16 or 34 hours, nor have other rhythms in infants been found to follow such periods.

MITOTIC RHYTHMS

While most rhythms are more difficult to study in infants than in adults, that of the mitotic rate in epidermal skin is facilitated by the constant supply of preputial skin, removed at circumcision. Perhaps it is only the need to arrange the operation at unusual hours of day and night, and the tedium of the counting procedure, that has restricted this fruitful field for study. Counts upon 57 prepuces, removed at different hours from infants aged from 6 to 11 days,[10] have revealed a clearcut rhythm. Fitting to the original data the sine curve, which reduces residual variance to a minimum, indicates a maximum mitotic rate at 1925 hr. and a minimum at 0725 hr. This is perhaps the best example of a rhythm, with no obvious cause in any external influence, which is clearly established at the end of the first week of life. The phase is, however, rather different from that of the rhythm demonstrated in adults by punch biopsy of the skin. A similar fit of a sine curve to this data gave a maximum mitotic rate at 0205 hr. and a minimum at 1405 hr. In nocturnal animals, such as rats, the minimum is likewise during the course of the activity period, though this is now during the night; and similar mitotic rhythms have been demonstrated in other tissues, collected by killing the animals at different hours.

The time of appearance of one of these mitotic rhythms, that in the cornea of the rat, has been defined with great precision[14] and the maximum and minimum, at 0700 and 1900 hr., are exactly the reverse in phase to the timing of the preputial mitotic rhythm in human infants. The rhythm appears with remarkable abruptness on the 15th day of life. The rat is born in a more immature condition than is the human infant, and this emergence of mitotic rhythm follows closely the day when the animal's eyes first open. Since, at least in non-human species, the alternation of light and darkness is known to be one of the most important external factors in phasing circadian rhythms, it may well be that this first exposure of the infant rat's retina to such alternation is responsible, via some means as yet unknown, for this emergence of a rhythm in mitotic rate.

In human and other species there is evidence associating the mitotic rhythm with the secretions of the adrenal cortex, but the nature of any causal connexion is not clear. It is therefore of interest[13] that in rats a circadian rhythm in corneal mitoses can be induced by injection of a single dose of dexamethasone at 1500 hr. on the 13th day of life, 2 days before a rhythm would otherwise appear. A similar injection on the 9th day of life is ineffective. It thus appears that some maturation process is operative 2 days before the rhythm becomes overtly manifest. The connexion between activity rhythms and mitotic rhythms is equally obscure. It has been noted already that the phasing of the mitotic rhythms in man and in rat is appropriate for diurnal and nocturnal species respectively. The mitotic rhythm is present, however, in both species at an age when activity is still randomly distributed over the 24 hours. Any causal connexion between these two rhythms must therefore be an indirect one.

TISSUE ENZYMES

It is now known that the concentration of many enzymes in different organs varies circadianly; and such variations are probably responsible for rhythms in, for example, metabolic processes or production of hormones. Observations are necessarily confined to non-human species, since the considerable number of samples needed to define a rhythm would hardly be acceptable by biopsy of even a large organ such as the liver. With other species the usual practice is to attempt to synchronize the rhythms of a large group by exposing them to a rigid routine, particularly in the alternation of light and darkness, and then to kill them in groups at regular intervals throughout one or more nychthemera, or merely at two chosen times, usually 12 hr. apart.

The development of one such rhythm, that of liver tyrosine aminotransferase, has been studied in young rats in this way. Measurements, twice only in the 24 hours,[23] indicated that even on the first and second day of life the enzyme concentration was regularly higher at 1000 than at 2200 hr. After about the 3rd week, the morning values fell and the evening values rose, until by 3 months of age the value at 2200 hr. was about 4 times as high as that at 1000 hr. In a more detailed study, in which measurements were made at 5 points in each 24 hours,[33] no rhythm was found in rats 3 and 5 days old, but a clearcut rhythm, with a peak value at 2400, developed between the 11th and 15th day, corresponding to the time of eye opening. At about the time of weaning during the 4th week, the rhythm became obscured by elevation of the basal value, and a new rhythm of high amplitude emerged, with the highest value now at the onset of the dark period, which in these experiments was at 1700 hr. Corticosterone is known to induce this enzyme, and as has been seen high evening values of corticosterone develop at much the same time as the high evening values of liver tyrosine aminotransferase. The development of regular nocturnal feeding habits, with an increased intake of high-protein solid food instead of the low-protein maternal milk, may also contribute. In addition, there is evidence that the different isoenzymes of the aminotransferase behave differently, both in the development of their rhythmicity and in their response to corticosterone. There appears to be a field wide open for fuller investigation.

CONCLUSIONS

It will be seen that there is a sufficient body of evidence to indicate that different circadian rhythms develop at different times in the human infant, though the actual times can seldom be defined with any precision. Attempts to summarize our knowledge[20] inevitably ignore contradictory findings and imply a spurious precision. It is surprising that one group of workers[7] who have attempted to define the rhythms of temperature, pulse rate, respiratory frequency and blood pressure in 143 subjects aged from 3 months to 21 years have pooled their results to derive a single composite index of circadian periodicity. In this way, much potentially useful information is lost; and since only 4 of the very many circadianly rhythmic variables were studied it is impossible to assert that any such index offers any useful information upon how regularly rhythmic are the subjects at different ages. Even did this index not scatter very widely between individuals, it hardly supports the contention of the authors that circadian rhythmicity is maximal at the age of 6 years.

It is tempting to draw, from their differing times of appearance, tentative inferences about the causal relations between different rhythms. The dangers inherent in inferring causal connexion from such associations have been indicated elsewhere,[31] and they are increased by the uncertainty of the exact time of appearance of rhythms in infancy, and by the fact that the different rhythms have usually been observed in different groups of infants. However, the late emergence of the corticosteroid rhythm is perhaps worthy of note, since in the adult this has been claimed to be the cause of many other rhythms. It has, for example, been invoked as at least partly responsible for mitotic rhythms; but since these are present so soon after birth, at least in the epidermis, a rhythmic production of cortisol cannot readily be held responsible. Whether it could contribute to urinary rhythms must depend, inter alia, upon whether the earlier or later estimates of the dates of emergence of the adrenal rhythm turn out to be correct. The late emergence of an excretory rhythm for creatinine likewise suggests that a rhythm in glomerular filtration rate is not the cause of the rhythms in excretion of sodium and potassium.

As with the adult, we are finally faced with the question whether the human infant is an inherently rhythmic animal; or is rhythmicity merely the consequence of continued exposure to a large variety of rhythmic influences, all following with fair precision a period of 24 hours? Or should we regard the infant as an assembly of different organs each with its own rhythm, and with complex interactions between them? From the substantial substratum of observation, and thin superstratum of experiment, only the most speculative answers can be given. The existence of circadian rhythms at or before birth is of little help, as circadian influences are operating upon the infant even *in utero*. The late development of some rhythms certainly suggests that they are acquired rather than innate, but this is not conclusive evidence. The evidence most suggestive of an external origin of rhythmicity lies in the low amplitude of some rhythms in Arctic dwellers, and in the disappearance of acquired rhythms of urine flow in infants kept continuously in the dark: there is here a clear distinction between the age at which urine flow follows a circadian rhythm wholly dependent upon external rhythmicity, and the later stage when rhythm in urine flow survives the temporary suspension of the obvious external rhythms, as if an internal timing mechanism were, as a result of prolonged exposure to external rhythms, developing the ability to keep time without them. By contrast, evidence suggestive of endogenous rhythms comes from the infants reared on demand-feeding and living in continuous light, and from those instances where the period of the rhythm departs somewhat from 24 hours: the sleep–wakefulness cycles of slightly under or over 24 hours in demand-fed infants, and the serum iron rhythms with periods covering the whole range from 16 to 34 hours.

Further advances are likely to follow the increasing use of computers in analysis of rhythms. Jundell, for example,[24] published all his temperature measurements on 107 infants, taken every 4 hours for up to 11 consecutive days on each infant, and these figures have never been analysed by the methods now available. Further progress is likely to be made in the definition of rhythms of short period in the early weeks of life. Apart from those already mentioned, an "ultradian" rhythm, with 3 maxima in each 24 hours, has been described in the plasma concentration of growth hormone in neonates.[39] Blood samples were collected every 8 hours for 48 hours from 29 premature infants of less than 38 weeks gestation. Sampling began about 48 hours after birth, to avoid the immediate post-natal fluid shifts; and by staggering the time of first sampling, the authors obtained samples at every even hour throughout the 24 from 7 or 8 infants. The composite graph derived in this way from 4 separate groups of infants repeated itself fairly precisely over the second 24 hours of sampling, so the appearance of 3 peaks is not fortuitous. Figure 19 shows the mean results at each hour. The authors' further conclusion, that the rhythm is essentially circadian, is less-securely based, being derived by calculating the values at each time as a percentage of the overall mean of the group; if a rhythm has 3 peaks in 24 hours, the mean of 3 samples at 8-hour intervals is likely to differ significantly from the true 24-hour mean.

This procedure of pooling measurements from different individuals, made at different times, to obtain a composite graph falls short of the ideal; but like the classic observations upon mitoses in preputial skin,[10] it offers a means of collecting valuable data by a simple organization of routine without any stretching of the fine boundary line of the ethically dubious; but for a closer understanding of the causes of these rhythms we are likely to rely increasingly upon observations on non-human species.

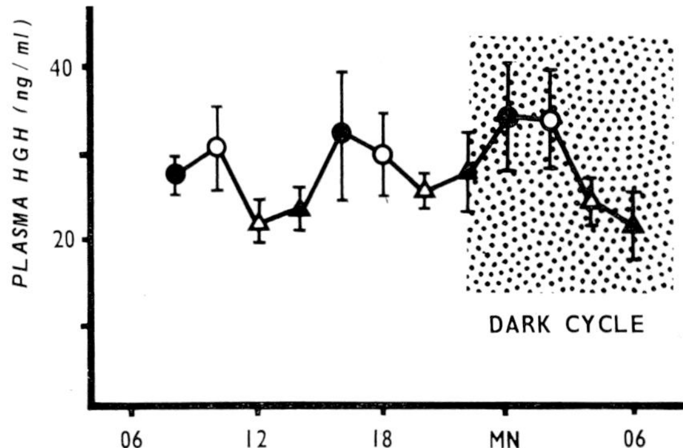

FIG. 19. Mean plasma concentrations of growth hormone in premature infants aged 2–4 days, with S.D. ● group of 8 babies, ○ △ groups of 7 babies, all sampled at 8-hourly intervals on two consecutive days.[3]

ACKNOWLEDGEMENTS

My thanks are due especially to Professor T. Hellbrügge of Munich, and to many others who also have helped me with offprints and by giving me access to work as yet unpublished. Without their help this chapter would give a wholly inadequate picture of the range of work in progress.

REFERENCES

1. Allen, C. and Kendall, J. W. (1967), "Maturation of the Circadian Rhythm of Plasma Corticosterone in the Rat," *Endocrinology*, **80**, 926–930.
2. Asano, Y. (1971), "Maturation of Circadian Rhythm of Brain Norepinephrine and Serotonin in Rat," *Life Sci. Oxford*, **10**, 883–894.
3. Aschoff, J. (1955), "Der Tagesgang der Körpertemperatur beim Menschen," *Klin. Wschr.*, **33**, 545–551.
4. Beyer, P. and Kayser, C. (1949), "Etablissement du rythme nycthéméral de la sécrétion urinaire chez le nourrisson," *C.r. Séanc. Soc. Biol. (Paris)*, **143**, 1231–1233.
5. Boddy, K., Dawes, G. S and Robinson, J. S. (1973), "A 24-hour Rhythm in the Foetus," *Proc. Barcraft Symposium*, pp. 63–66 (R. S. Comline, K. W. Cross, G. S. Dawes and P. W. Nathanielsz, Eds.). Cambridge: University Press.
6. Brown, F. M. (1972), "Circadian Rhythm Modification in Rats by Whole-life Synchrony to a 27-hour day," *Dissertation Abstracts International*, **32B**, 4879–4880.
7. Bryan, G. T. and Overall, J. E. (1970), "A Study of the Development of Human Circadian Periodicity," *Pediat. Res.*, **4**, 63–70.
8. Buddingh, F., Parker, H. R., Ishizaki, G. and Tyler, W. S. (1971), "Long-term Studies of the Functional Development of the Fetal Kidney in Sheep," *Amer. J. vet. Res.*, **32**, 1993–1998.
9. Conroy, R. T. W. L. and Mills, J. N. (1970), *Human Circadian Rhythms*. London: Churchill.
10. Cooper, Z. K. (1939), "Mitotic Rhythm in Human Epidermis," *J. invest. Derm.*, **2**, 289–300.
11. Franks, R. C. (1967), "Diurnal Variation of Plasma 17-hydroxycorticosteroids in Children," *J. clin. Endocr. Metab.*, **27**, 75–78.
12. Gesell, A. (1943), *Infant and Child in the Culture of Today*. Yale: University Press.
13. Goodrum, P. and Cardoso, S. S. (1972), "Establishment of a Circadian Pattern of Mitosis in the Corneal Epithelium of Dexamethasone Treated Immature Rats," *Fed. Proc.*, **31**, 271.
14. Goodrum, P. J., Sowell, J. G. and Cardoso, S. S. (1973), "Characterization of the Circadian Rhythm of Mitosis in the Corneal

Epithelium of the Immature Rat," In *Chronobiology. Proceedings of the International Society for the Study of Biological Rhythms, Little Rock, Ark.*, pp. 31–36 (L. E. Scheving, F. Halberg and J. E. Pauly, Eds.) Tokyo: Igaku Shoin.

15. Hartmann, E. (1968), "The 90-minute Sleep-dream Cycle," *Arch. gen. Psychiat.*, **18,** 280–286.
16. Hellbrügge, T. (1960), "The Development of Circadian Rhythms in Infants," *Cold Spring Harbor Symposia on Quantitative Biology*, **25,** 311–323.
17. Hellbrügge, T. (1968), "Ontogénèse des rythmes circadiaires chez l'enfant," in *Cycles Biologiques et Psychiatrie*, pp. 159–183 (J. Ajuriaguerra., Ed.). Symposium Bel-Air III, Geneva, September 1967. Geneva and Paris: Georg & Co. and Masson & Co.
18. Hellbrügge, T. Unpublished observations.
19. Hellbrügge, T., Lange, J. and Rutenfranz, J. (1956), "Über die Entwicklung von tagesperiodischen Veränderungen der Pulsfrequenz im Kindesalter," *Z. Kinderheilk.*, **78,** 703–722.
20. Hellbrügge, T., Lange, J. E., Rutenfranz, J. and Stehr, K. (1964), "Circadian Periodicity of Physiological Functions in Different Stages of Infancy and Childhood," *Ann. N.Y. Acad. Sci.*, **117,** 361–373.
21. Hey, E. N. and Katz, G. (1969), "Evaporative Water Loss in the New-born Baby," *J. Physiol. (Lond.).* **200,** 605–619.
22. Hill, J. R. and Rahimtulla, K. A. (1965), "Heat Balance and the Metabolic Rate of New-born Babies in Relation to Environmental Temperature; and the Effect of Age and Weight on Basal Metabolic Rate," *J. Physiol. (Lond.)*, **180,** 239–265.
23. Honova, E., Miller, S. A. Ehrenkranz, R. A. and Woo, A. (1968), "Tyrosine Transaminase—Development of Daily Rhythm in Liver of Neonatal Rat," *Science, N.Y.*, **162,** 999.
24. Jundell, J. (1904), Über die nykthemeralen Temperaturs Schwankungen im 1. Lebensjahre des Menschen," *Jb. Kinderheil.*, **59,** 521–619.
25. Kleitman, N. (1963), *Sleep and Wakefulness*, 2nd edition. Chicago and London: University of Chicago Press.
26. Kleitman, N. and Engelmann, T. G. (1953), "Sleep Characteristics of Infants," *J. appl. Physiol.*, **6,** 269–282.
27. Lewis, H. E., Lobban, Mary C. and Tredre, Barbara E. (1970), "Daily Rhythms of Renal Excretion in a Child with Nocturnal Enuresis," *J. Physiol. (Lond.)*, **210,** 42–43.
28. Martin-du-Pan, R. (1970), "Le role du rythme circadian dans l'alimentation du nourrisson," *La Femme et l'Enf.*, **4,** 23–30.
29. Martin-du-Pan, R. and Vollenweider, L. (1967), "L'apparition du rythme circadien des 17-hydroxy-stéroides chez le nourrisson. Sa Modification sous l'effet de la consommation de corticostéroides," *Praxis*, **56,** 138–144.
30. Mills, J. N. (1968), "Circadian Rhythms," in *A Companion to Medical Studies*, Vol. 1, pp. 44: 1–8. (R. Passmore and J. S. Robson, Eds.). Oxford: Blackwell.
31. Mills, J. N. (1973), "Transmission Processes Between Clock and Manifestations," in *Biological Aspects of Circadian Rhythms*, Chap. 2 (J. N. Mills, Ed.). London: Plenum.
32. Mullin, F. J. (1939), "Development of the Diurnal Temperature and Motility Patterns in a Baby," *Amer. J. Physiol.*, **126,** 589.
33. Osawa, K., Abe, T., Muto, Y. and Hosoya, N. (1972), "Development of Circadian Rhythm of Hepatic Tyrosine Aminotransferase in Growing Rats," *Life Sciences*, Part 1, **11,** 693–700.
34. Parmelee, A. H. (1961), "A Study of One Infant from Birth to Eight Months of Age," *Acta Paediat., Stockh.*, **50,** 160–170.
35. Sander, L. W., Stechler, G., Burns, P. and Julia, H. (1970), "Early Mother-Infant Interaction and 24-hour Patterns of Activity and Sleep," *J. Amer. Acad. Child Psychiatry*, **9,** 103–123.
36. Sander, L. W., Julia, H. L., Stechler, G. and Burns, P. (1972), "Continuous 24-hour Interactional Monitoring in Infants Reared in Two Caretaking Environments," *Psychosomatic Medicine*, **34,** 270–282.
37. Schwartz, E. and Baehner, R. L. (1968), "Diurnal Variation of Serum Iron in Infants and Children." *Acta Paediat. Scand.*, **57,** 433–435.
38. Selinger, M. and Levitz, M. (1969), "Diurnal Variation of Total Plasma Estriol Levels in Late Pregnancy," *J. clin. Endocr. Metab.*, **29,** 995–997.
39. Sisson, T. R. C., Root, A. W., Kendall, N., Kechavarz-Olia, L. and Shaw, E. (1973), "Biologic Rhythm of Plasma Human Growth Hormone in Newborns of Low Birth Weight," in *Chronobiology. Proceedings of the International Society for the Study of Biological Rhythms, Little Rock, Ark.* (L. E. Scheving, F. Halberg and J. E. Pauly, Eds.). Tokyo: Igaku Shoin.
40. Sollberger, A. (1965), *Biological Rhythm Research.* New York: Elsevier.
41. Waterhouse, J. M. Unpublished observations.
42. Werner, E. and Gladtke, E. (1970), "Der zirkadiane Rhythmus des Serumeisens bei Kindern," *Dtsch. med. Wschr.*, **95,** 1476–1483.

43. PAEDIATRIC ONCOLOGY

H. B. MARSDEN

GENERAL ASPECTS

Cancer in childhood forms a small part of the overall picture of human neoplasia as can be seen from a study of newly diagnosed cases in England and Wales in 1965.[66] The number for all ages was 141,421, whereas below 15 years of age there were 1,128 registrations.

The importance of this relatively small group may tend to be overlooked when studied in this context, but neoplasia is only second to accidents as a cause of death in children over one year of age in both the United States, and England and Wales.

The sites for tumour development in childhood are very different from those in the adult. The gastrointestinal tract, bronchus and breast are the three most frequent sites in later life whereas such tumours are rarities in Paediatric Oncology.

Relatively short exposure to carcinogens in childhood accounts for some of the variation in incidence of tumours in children and adults and a study of cancer in young patients may yield information on other aspects in the production of human neoplasia.

In addition to the variation between children and adults, the incidence and behaviour of particular tumours show differences throughout infancy and childhood and it is this aspect which will be given particular attention in the present chapter.

The relatively small number of childhood tumours makes it difficult to gain experience regarding their behaviour and treatment, but Manchester University has been fortunate in having a Children's Tumour Registry.

This registry was started in 1953[58] and includes all the children (approximately one million) below the age of 15 years in the Manchester hospital region. There are a number of industrial areas, the largest town being Manchester, with rural districts particularly in the north. The number of cases per year is in the region of one hundred of which approximately one third are leukaemias and this number remains remarkably constant so that at the present time nearly 2,000 cases have been included.

The age of the patient used throughout the chapter is the age at referral to a paediatrician or specialist because of the tumour, this being found to be the most reliable figure.

The association between neoplasia, congenital malformations and chromosomal aberrations has received particular attention in recent years. Genetic factors play a significant part in certain paediatric tumours and, with improvement in treatment, these may become increasingly important. In addition, the presence of a tumour in a patient at an early age makes it easier to obtain information concerning relatives.

Adrenal cortical, Wilm's and hepatic tumours are associated with hemihypertrophy, naevi, macroglossia and omphalocoele and Wilm's tumour and primary hepatic carcinoma have been reported in the same patient.[28]

Genetic factors have been reviewed[2] and pedigrees classified into three main groups:

1. The neoplasm is the only genetic expression as in phaeochromocytoma and retinoblastoma.
2. The tumour is one phenotypic expression of the syndrome as in tumours occurring in Lindau's or von Recklinghausen's disease or the naevoid basal cell carcinoma syndrome.

Figure 1 shows an example of the latter in a boy of 15 years of age who was treated for a medulloblastoma at the age of 2½ years. The patient's father died from a cerebral glioma at the age of 28 years and a cousin had meningocoele and hydrocephalus.

3. Pedigrees in which a solid neoplasm or leukaemia develops in a phenotypic disease state in a proportion of cases. The agammaglobulinaemias, multiple exostoses and tuberous sclerosis are among the syndromes which are included.

Apart from the neoplasias of childhood, it must be remembered that hamartomata are numerically more important and may cause severe incapacitation or death by the extent or situation of the lesion. In an analysis of 1,039 childhood tumours[84] collected, over a 10 year period 64 per cent were found to be benign and more than half of the benign lesions were angiomas, mostly haemangiomas.

Figures 2, 3 and 4 show examples of lymphangioma necessitating amputation and fatal cases with laryngeal and generalized bone involvement. The cystic hygroma of the neck may extend to the mediastinum and this is a feature of right sided lesions.[8]

Vascular naevi are common in childhood and 83 per cent are present at birth.[26]

Those present at birth may be divided into three types.

The telangiectatic naevi are seen over the nape of the neck, the "mark of the stork's beak" and about 5 per cent of these persist.[37] The port wine stain is capillary in nature and may be associated with gigantism or underlying malformations as in the Sturge–Weber syndrome. Cavernous haemangiomata may also be seen at birth and are fully developed when first seen.

The capillary haemangiomata or strawberry naevi which may appear shortly after birth, nearly all develop within six weeks[85] and are seen particularly in premature infants. The majority of lesions regress by 6–12 months of age although some may actively persist until the 10th year.[37] Rapid increase in size may be noted in the strawberry naevi.

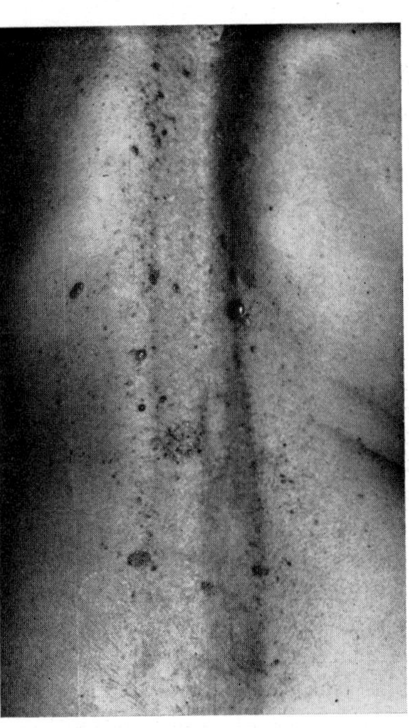

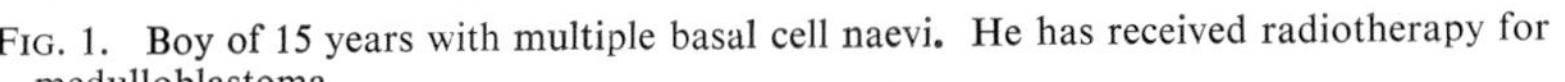

FIG. 1. Boy of 15 years with multiple basal cell naevi. He has received radiotherapy for medulloblastoma.

Haemangiomata may be associated with thrombocytopenia and haemorrhagic episodes in deeply situated lesions may be difficult to control. In the muscles vascular hamartomata are most commonly encountered in the thigh and visceral lesions favour the liver. Arteriovenous malformations are usually encountered later in childhood or in adult life.

The multiple haemangiomatous syndromes include involvement of the skin, mucous membranes, abdominal viscera, nervous tissue and bones.[89]

The pigmented lesions may be classified as benign pigmented naevi, blue naevi and juvenile melanomata to which might be added the mongolian spot. In an analysis of 172 cases[57] there were 149 benign naevi, 7 blue naevi, 11 juvenile melanomata and 5 malignant melanomata.

The malignant melanoma is a rare tumour of childhood with unpredictable behaviour and does not differ from its counterpart in the adult. In an analysis of 1,000 consecutive solid tumours in the Manchester University Children's Tumour Registry there were 2 malignant melanomata. These included a tumour of the buttock in an 8 year old child and a tumour of the cheek in a patient of 15 years of age who is without recurrence 3 years after surgery. Only one other malignant melanoma has been encountered in the C.T.R., the lesion being in the forearm of a 13 year old child who shows widespread metastases 7 years after excision. In the malignant melanomata in the series referred to above,[57] the lesions were found mainly over the head and neck and the authors reviewing 18 cases found 10 tumours in this area with 5 on the cheek.

Malignant change is a feature of the giant pigmented naevus which is a lesion present at birth unlike the benign pigmented naevus. Satellite nodules are associated with these extensive lesions and malignant melanoma may develop in 10 per cent of cases[69] although the incidence may be even higher.

The mongolian spot which is due to delayed disappearance of dermal melanocytes in their migration from the neural crest to the epidermis[86] is present at birth and may darken in the first few weeks of life but fades during childhood. The lesion is more predominantly in the lumbosacral region but is also run over the posterior aspect of the trunk and limbs.

The common benign pigmented naevi are not usually present at birth and may be classified as junctional, intradermal or compound. The intradermal naevus is raised, hairy and is the typical lesion of the adult while the junctional and compound varieties are flat and brown and are more commonly seen in childhood. The naevus arises from cell precursors of the melanoblast and dermal neural elements; the melanoblasts in the junctional layer of the epidermis migrate into the dermis. The persistence of junctional activity after puberty may lead to the development of a malignant melanoma.[1] Benign pigmented naevi develop during childhood and the increased cellular activity at purberty may give rise to difficulties in diagnosis They may regress during adult life apart from pregnancy and steriod therapy and may become pedunculated in old age. In adolescence 20–40 may be present. The regression of naevi is interesting when considered in relation to the halo

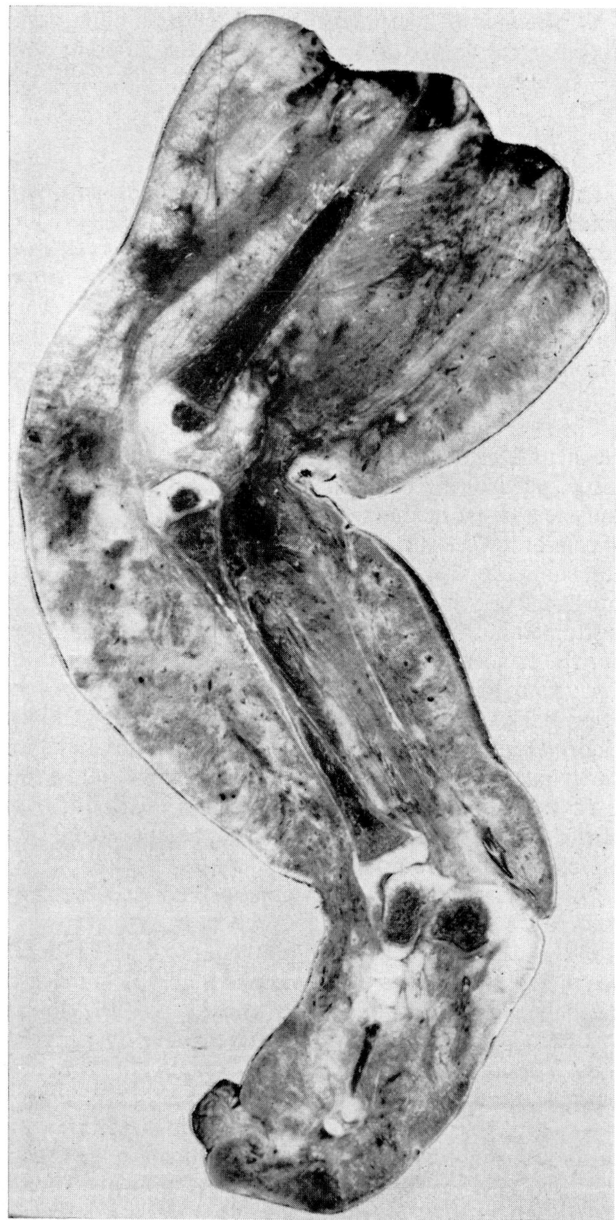

FIG. 2. Large subcutaneous lymphangioma involving the whole of the leg.

naevus which is usually a compound naevus and is seen in children and young adults. There is a collar of depigmentation. The halo naevus is self-limited, regression usually taking place over several months.

The blue naevus is similar in origin to the mongolian spot and the spindle-celled appearance may lead to confusion with a fibromatous tumour or sclerosing angioma. The lesion appears in early childhood and grows slowly during childhood.

The juvenile melanoma is particularly a lesion of childhood, but about 15 per cent are seen in adolescence and adult life.[86] There is little pigment present, and the lesions are predominantly encountered over the head and neck. In the series referred to above,[57] 7 of the 11 juvenile melanomata were in this site, mostly over the cheek, The inflammatory response may give rise to confusion with malignant melanoma on histological examination but the absence of

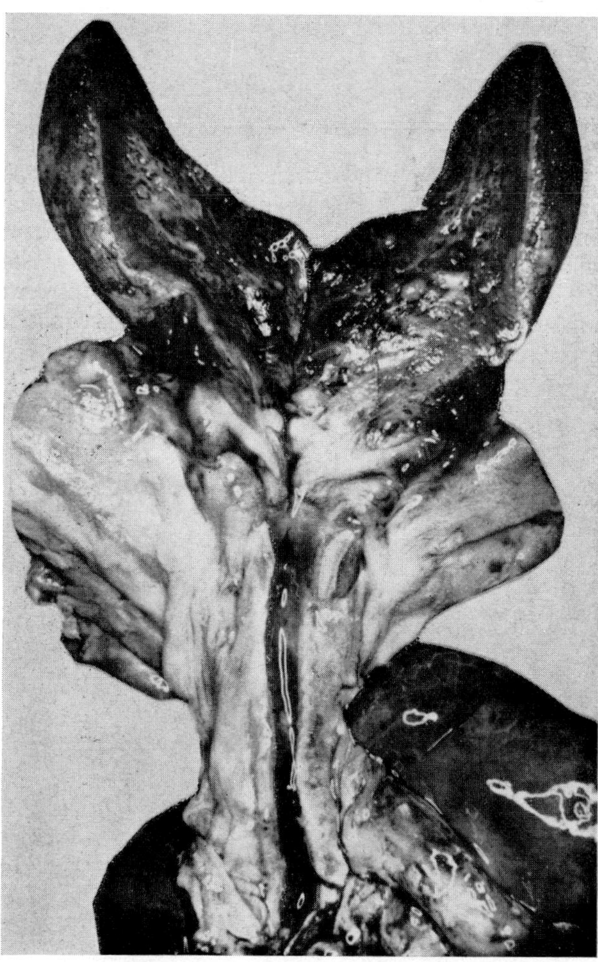

FIG. 3. Lymphangioma of the tongue and larynx causing respiratory obstruction.

epithelial invasion and the negative dopa and tyrosinase reactions may be helpful in diagnosis.

The syndromes of neurofibromatosis and tuberous sclerosis form a bridge between hamartoma and neoplasia in childhood. Neurilemmoma, neurofibroma and neurogenic sarcoma may be found in the former and glioma and glioblastomatosis may develop in the tuberous foci of the latter.

As regards neoplastic disease in children,there is variation in the incidence of different tumours throughout the paediatric range. In addition, the behaviour of particular types of tumour varies when encountered at different ages in childhood.

An analysis of the neoplasms in the first year of life shows a different picture from that seen throughout childhood.

TABLE 1. INCIDENCE OF CHILDREN'S TUMOURS FROM 1953–68 FROM THE MANCHESTER UNIVERSITY C.T.R.

	0–1 *year*	1–15 *years*
Sympathetic	31	84
Leukaemia	24	440
Cerebral	23	284
Retinoblastoma	17	34
Teratoma	17	33
Connective Tissue	17	170
Histiocytosis	14	28
Renal	10	76
Lymphosarcoma and Hodgkin's Disease	0	94

From the table it can be seen that leukaemia is not the commonest form of neoplasia in infancy and lymphosarcoma was not encountered in this age group. Cerebral tumours play a more important part than is generally stated in the 0–1 year age group and the neoplasms of nervous tissue origin, including the retinoblastomas, account for 46 per cent of the cases.

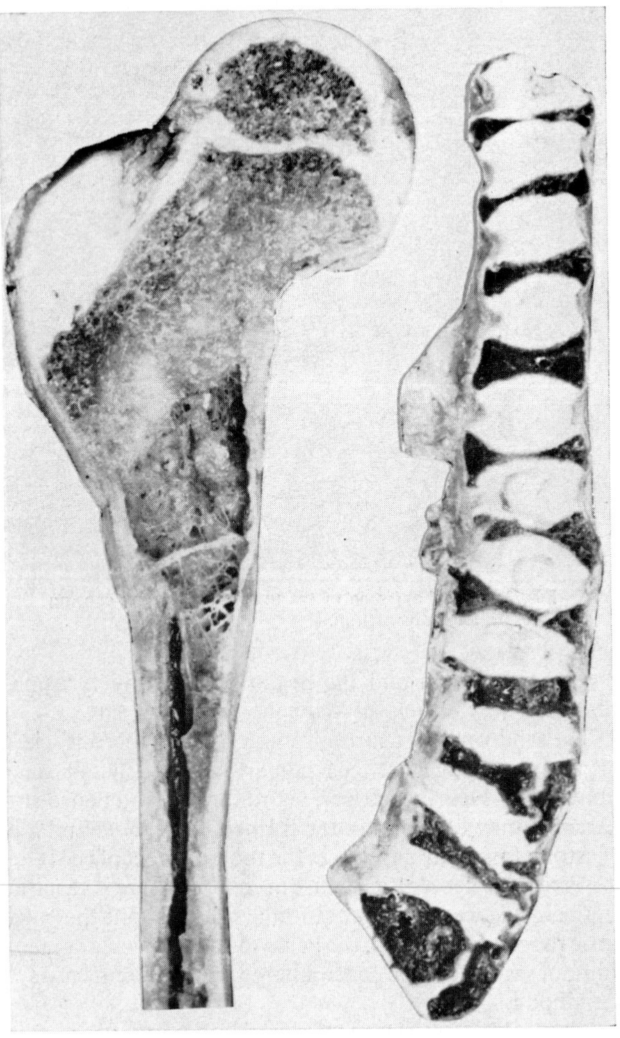

FIG. 4. Lymphangiomatosis of femur and vertebrae. The ribs were also involved and the patient had a lymphangioma of the spleen and cystic hygroma of the neck.

Other childhood tumours not encountered in the first year of life in the present series include Hodgkin's disease, osteosarcoma, Ewing's tumour and gonadal tumours (non teratomatous). Rare examples of such tumours have been encountered in infancy and more recently a Ewing's tumour has been seen by the author in the first year of life.

As already stated, the behaviour of a tumour varies according to the age of the patient and the different types may now be studied.

NEUROBLASTOMA

The neuroblastoma is a tumour of infancy and early childhood. 83 per cent of the Manchester University C.T.R. cases occurred in the first 5 years of life. Occasional cases have, however, been described in the adult.[68] Neuroblastoma, ganglioneuroblastoma and ganglioneuroma form a continuous spectrum, the ganglioneuroma presenting throughout childhood but not usually in the first two years of life.

The neuroblastoma arises from cells which migrate from the neural crest into the concentrations of sympathetic tissue, particularly in the paravertebral abdominal region and the adrenal medulla. The migration or differentiation of primordial cells occasionally occurs in post-natal life and nests of neuroblasts may be found in the adrenal medulla as late as puberty.[45] The primary tumour assessed for all ages is situated in the adrenal gland in about one third of cases, but the incidence of adrenal involvement is higher in the first year of life. There is some indication that the likelihood of primary adrenal involvement decreases as the child gets older. Dumbell tumours, which are partly intraspinal and partly paravertebral, are also seen and the pressure within the spinal canal leads to relatively early presentation. One of the tumours in the series was of dumbell type, and was present in the newborn period.

Neuroblastoma with metastases to bone and liver have been called the Hutchinson and Pepper syndromes respectively. These terms have rather fallen into disuse in recent years, but the spread to liver and bone is, to a certain degree, age dependent. Bone metastases are seen in older children in whom the prognosis is worse, and massive liver involvement is a particular feature in young infants. In the 31 sympathetic tumours under one year shown in Table 1, 11 showed liver involvement and 3 had bone metastases, 2 of the latter being 10 months of age. In an analysis of 212 cases of neuroblastoma from 1942–65 in the California Tumour Registry,[17] it was noted that localized disease was more common in infants and distant metastases were more liable to occur in older children.

Subcutaneous deposits are encountered more frequently in young children, and in one series studied[73] an incidence of 32·3 per cent skin metastases was noted in the newborn, compared with 2·6 per cent of such lesions at all ages.

Multiple subcutaneous ganglioneuromatous nodules with skin pigmentation similar to the von Recklinghausen syndrome are occasionally seen, and the possibility of metastatic neuroblastoma with maturation of the primary tumour has been considered to account for this picture.

The variation in behaviour of the neuroblastoma has

received particular attention. On the one hand, there may be widespread metastases with dissemination of tumour throughout the marrow, while in a relatively small proportion of cases spontaneous regression of the tumour may occur. In the 176 examples of spontaneous regression of tumours which were collected in one review,[23] 29 of the tumours were neuroblastomata.

Apart from regression, in about 5 per cent of the cured cases, maturation takes place and the tumour becomes a benign ganglioneuroma. The concept of "neuroblastoma *in situ*" has been discussed,[4] and it is suggested that this may account for the nodules, or collections of neuroblasts, which

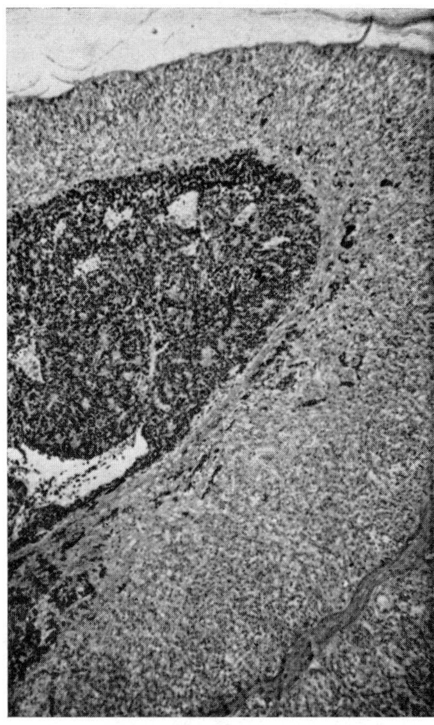

FIG. 5. Neuroblastoma as an incidental autopsy finding in the adrenal medulla. Small groups of cells are noted in the cortex. H and E (×40)

may be an incidental autopsy finding in the adrenal encountered up to the age of 3 months (Fig. 5).

The invasion of vessel walls and extension into the adrenal cortex support the suggestion that the nodules are, indeed, neoplastic and similar lesions may be found in one adrenal, when the other gland is the site of overt neuroblastoma. The incidence of "neuroblastoma *in situ*" is once in every 200–300 autopsies up to the age of 3 months. In the Manchester Hospital region there are approximately 1 million children under the age of 15 years, and the incidence of about 7 new cases of neuroblastoma per year remains remarkably constant. This figure is considerably lower than that given for the incidence of "neuroblastoma *in situ*", so that it is possible that the majority of neuroblastomata do not develop to the stage of production of a macroscopic tumour.

The pure ganglioneuromas are more likely to be seen in older children than the neuroblastoma, and in a study of 10 such tumours the average age was 6 years, with a range between 2–13 years. The ganglioneuroma may be seen in infancy, and more recently a pure ganglioneuroma has been seen in the pelvis of an 8 month old infant.

Three of the sympathetic tumours over the age of one year were phaeochromocytomas as shown in Table 1, and the age of presentation in these cases was 10, 12 and 12 years.

One aspect of neuroblastoma which requires further study is the rare association with acute cerebellar encephalopathy. Opsoclonus, ataxic conjugate movement of the eyes, cerebellar ataxia and myoclonic encephalopathy of infants are terms which have been applied to this condition. In a discussion of this syndrome[6] it has been suggested that cases of acute cerebellar encephalopathy in childhood could be associated with a silent neuroblastoma.

RENAL TUMOURS

In a series of 86 consecutive primary renal tumours in the Manchester University C.T.R., 81 were classified as Wilm's tumour, 2 as mesenchymal nephromas, 1 hypernephroma, 1 papillary carcinoma and 1 vasoformative bone-metastasizing tumour regarded as an angiosarcoma.

The oldest patient with a Wilm's tumour was 11 years of age, and typical histological cases were seen in young infants. Ten tumours were recorded in children under one year of age and, of these, 8 were classified as Wilm's tumour and 2 as mesenchymal nephromas. The survival rate of 50 per cent in the younger patients is better than that for Wilm's tumour cases at all ages, and the behaviour of certain of the infantile tumours differs from typical nephroblastoma.

The term "nephroblastoma *in situ*" has been applied[76] to nodules of neoplastic elements arising in the region of the renal blastema and which are microscopically indistinguishable from Wilm's tumour. The lesions described are larger than the double folds of renal blastema in premature kidneys. The relationship to nephroblastoma requires further study, and in the two cases described the lesions were bilateral and had multicentric subcapsular location. Similar nodules, although more deeply situated in the kidney, have previously been reported.[64] The incidence of bilateral Wilm's tumour lies between 10·3 per cent[39] and 3 per cent[74] but diffuse bilateral involvement of the kidney may be encountered in the neonatal period.

The term congenital mesoblastic nephroma of infancy has been applied[5] to mesenchymal tumours of the kidney with little, or no malignant nephroblastic or epithelial tissue, and a variety of terms including leiomyomatous hamartoma, congenital fibrosarcoma, fibroma and rhabdomyoma have been applied to tumours showing similar histological features in infancy. Such tumours may, in fact, be atypical Wilm's tumours and recent studies[14] lend some support to this concept.

The formation of "S" shaped nephrons may be induced in purely spindle celled renal tumours using organ culture when the tumour tissue is placed in contact with mouse neural tissue. The behaviour and histological appearance of renal tumours encountered in the first year of life in the present series have been studied. There were two purely spindle celled neoplasms regarded as mesenchymal nephroma and occurring in infants of 2 and 3 months of age, although the older case had enlarged glands in the hilum of the kidney. In the 8 tumours classified as nephroblastoma, there were more cellular lesions having a similar spindle celled structure with polygonal cells in addition, and more numerous mitotic figures were encountered towards the end of the first year of life. In some of the tumours the histological appearance, while being undifferentiated, showed a predominance of polygonal cells. A relationship to the mesenchymal nephroma was suggested by the presence of isolated non-neoplastic renal tubules embedded in the tumour.

The Wilm's tumour in infancy may present a spectrum with the spindle celled mesenchymal nephroma at one end, and the typical nephroblastic tumour at the other, and this variation in the renal embryonic tumours may account for the improved prognosis in the first year of life.

CEREBRAL TUMOURS

Cerebral tumours are numerically the most important group of solid neoplasms in childhood. The great majority of these are gliomas and are of three main types, astrocytoma, medulloblastoma and ependymoma. In an analysis of 286 gliomas in children, these tumours accounted for 83 per cent with an incidence of astrocytoma 125, medulloblastoma 76 and ependymoma 36.

Apart from the histologically verified tumours, a number of cases have been included in the Manchester University C.T.R. on the basis of clinical findings alone.

The situation of certain cerebral tumours makes biopsy a hazardous procedure, but the exclusion of such cases gives an incorrect assessment of the incidence of cerebral neoplasms. Some of the "clinical gliomas" have survived for a long time and the diagnosis of a cerebral tumour might be considered to be incorrect in such cases. There is little doubt, however, that children with gliomas may survive for prolonged periods even in the absence of radiotherapy or chemotherapy as can be seen from the following case report:

Case Report

C.C. A girl first seen at the age of 2 years because of weakness of the legs. At that time there was fullness of the retinal vessels, and tremor of the arms. In the following year the child became unable to walk, and started vomiting. Papilloedema was noted at this time and a diagnosis of aqueduct obstruction was made. A by-pass procedure was carried out with great improvement in the child's condition. There were episodes of increased intracranial pressure with vertigo in the ensuing years and the by-pass had to be revised on several occasions. At the age of 20 years, following such an attack, the patient died and at autopsy a low grade astrocytoma was found to be the cause of the aqueduct obstruction (Fig. 6).

The gliomas present throughout childhood with a higher incidence in younger children as shown in (Fig. 7). The incidence is different, however, for the three main types of glioma.

The astrocytomas show considerable variation in their clinical behaviour and histological appearance. At one end of the scale there are low grade, hypocellular tumours with spongioblastic features commonly encountered in the cerebellum and hypothalamus, while diffuse tumours are seen in the brain stem and cerebrum. The diffuse, or adult

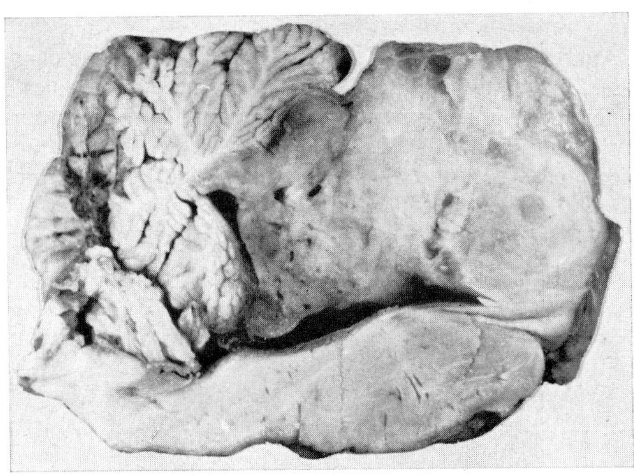

Fig. 6. Astrocytoma in a patient of 20 years. Symptoms had been present from the age of 2 years.

tumours, vary in cellularity and include pleomorphic and highly cellular glioblastomas.

The pontine or brain stem astrocytic gliomas are unusual in young children, and no example was encountered in the first year of life in the present series.

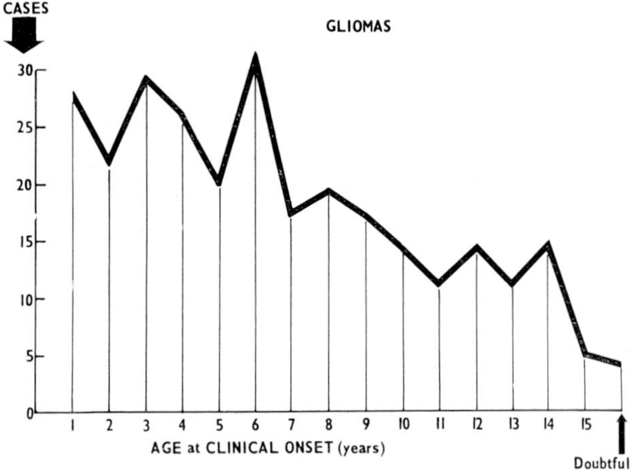

Fig. 7. Graph showing the age incidence of gliomas in childhood.

Medulloblastomas show more constant features, the majority being situated in the cerebellar vermis, and show a tendency to spread through the ventricular system and spinal theca.

Ependymomas are particularly seen in the cerebral and cerebellopontine regions. In the latter case the tumour may extend down the spinal canal or fill the fourth ventricle.

The differences in age incidence between the three main types of glioma are shown in Figures 8, 9 and 10. The tumours in older children are predominantly astroycytomas

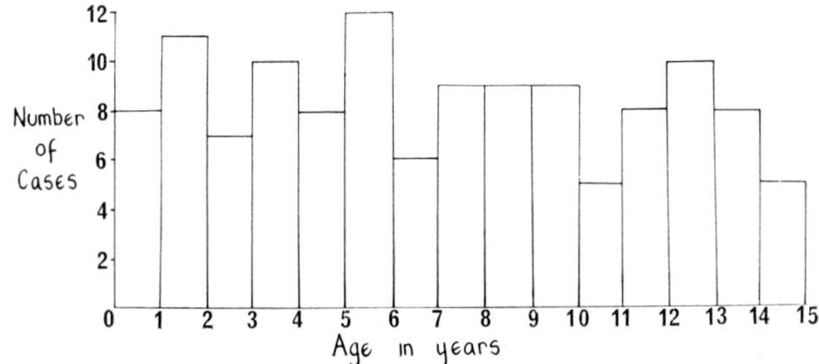

FIG. 8. Histogram showing the age incidence of astrocytoma in childhood. 125 cases.

and after the tenth year there is great probability that a cerebral glioma will be, in fact, an astrocytoma. The incidence shows little variation throughout childhood while the medulloblastoma is commoner in young children but not infants with a peak in the third year of life. The ependymoma is a tumour of early childhood, 75 per cent of the cases being confined to the first 5 years of life.

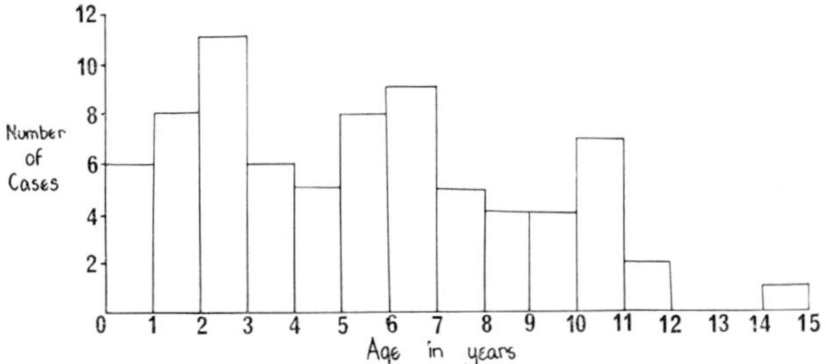

FIG. 9. Histogram showing the age incidence of medulloblastoma in childhood. 76 cases.

Infratentorial tumours are more common than supratentorial in childhood and among the gliomas in the Manchester hospital region, over 70 per cent were below the tentorium. This does not apply to the first year of life, however, and in an analysis of the 23 gliomas in this age group, 11 were supratentorial and 10 infratentorial, with 2 tumours involving both sites. The preponderance of astrocytomas was maintained in the young age group, 13 tumours being of this type with 5 medulloblastomas and 5 ependymomas.

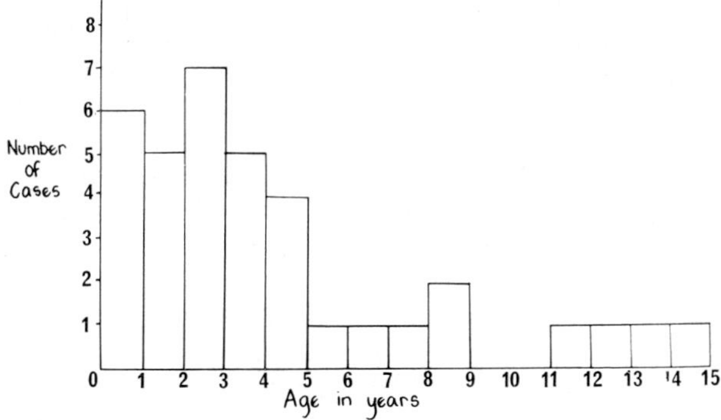

FIG. 10. Histogram showing the age incidence of ependymoma in childhood. 36 cases.

One aspect to be noted in relation to the infantile gliomas is the large size of the tumour in some cases. Fig. 11 shows an example of a supratentorial ependymoma in a young infant which involved the greater part of both cerebral hemispheres.

Apart from the gliomas, the cerebral tumours include

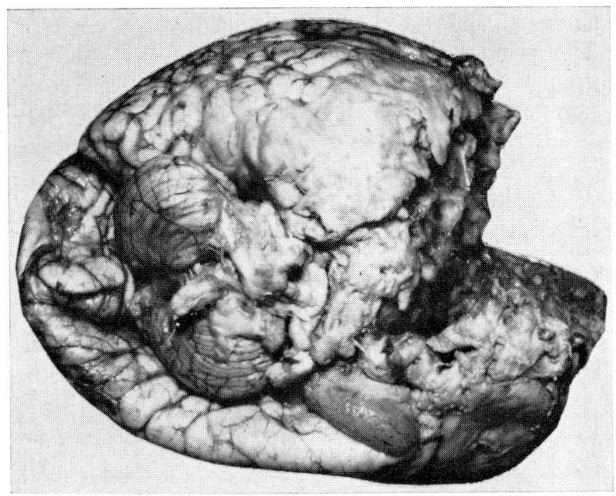

FIG. 11. Large ependymoma in the brain of a young infant. The tumour involved the greater part of both cerebral hemispheres.

craniopharyngiomas which form a relatively small but important group. These developmental tumours may show cellular proliferation and fluid accumulation and incidence is mainly in later childhood.

Figure 12 shows the incidence of craniopharyngiomas over the same period as the group of gliomas already discussed.

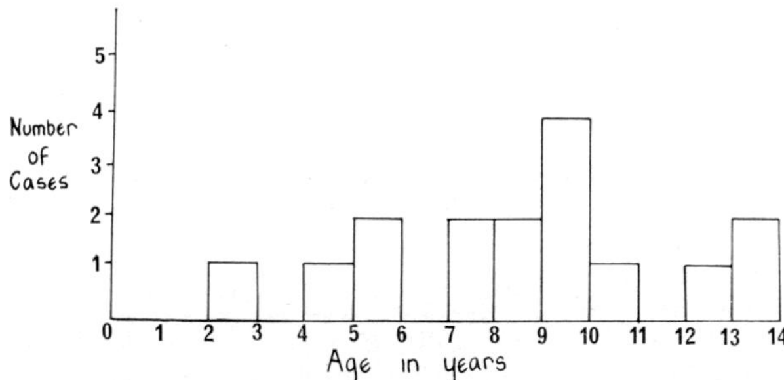

FIG. 12. Histogram showing the age incidence of craniopharyngioma in childhood. 16 cases.

There is a peak in the tenth year, and no case presented in the first two years of life. Although the craniopharyngioma is predominantly seen in children and young adults, 24 out of 68 cases in one series[70] were diagnosed when over 50 years of age, and 9 when over 70 years. It has been noted that the presenting features change with the age group.[7] Defects of vision and increased intracranial pressure predominate in childhood, while sexual immaturity and retarded growth are seen in adolescent cases. In the older patients visual defects are again predominant, and up to half of the elderly group have mental abnormalities. Small stature is recorded in 19 out of a series of 50 craniopharyngiomas in childhood.[60]

The inanition syndrome in infants with anterior hypothalamic neoplasms has been discussed, and 4 cases between the ages of 3 months and 2½ years of age recorded.[88] The authors stress that the signs of hypothalamic disturbance which are seen in older children are not encountered in infants with anterior hypothalamic neoplasms.

The primary hypothalamic locus controlling growth hormone secretion is in the ventromedial nucleus and experimental work in this field has been reviewed.[29]

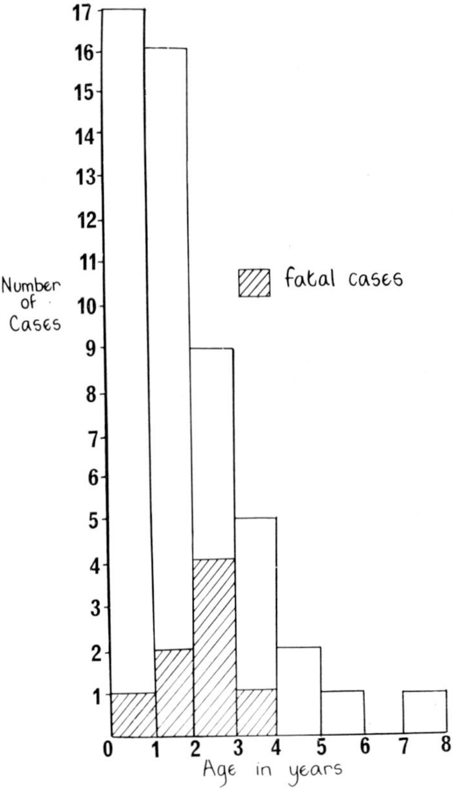

FIG. 13. Histogram showing the age incidence of retinoblastoma in childhood. 51 cases.

Gigantism is exceptionally rare in childhood, excessive growth usually beginning at puberty, and no case has been reported in association with a neoplasm of the hypothalamus.[27] The pituitary tumours giving rise to such symptoms are usually of the acidophil type, but an increase of chromophil cells rather than tumour formation may be encountered. In some cases, however, chromophobe tumours may be present.[71] The picture is further complicated by the occurence of acidophilic pituitary tumours with no sign of somatic overgrowth.[81]

Tumours of the posterior hypothalamus may be associated with precocious puberty.[52,87] In such cases it is suggested that a loss of control of the tuber cinereum may lead to the liberation of excessive amounts of anterior pituitary gonadotrophic hormone. Precocious puberty is only rarely encountered with pinealomas and then when the tumour extends to the tuber cinereum.[38,59]

The genetic aspect of tumours in childhood has been mentioned and, in the present study, gliomata were seen in two sisters in the first few months of life. These cases may be associated with von Recklinghausen's disease, and both the mother and maternal grandfather had pigmented lesions on the back and shoulder.

Genetic factors have been studied more fully in the retinoblastoma and there were 51 examples of this tumour in the Manchester series. The retinoblastoma is virtually confined to childhood and usually presents before 5 years of age (Fig. 13). In a large series of 467 cases,[92] 314 or 67 per cent presented under the age of 3 years compared with 82 per cent in the present series. In the Manchester cases, 17 or 33 per cent were diagnosed in the first year of life and ages of these patients are listed below:

* 4 days
2 weeks
1 months
10 weeks
3 months (5 cases)
4 months (2 cases)
* 5 months
6 months
7 months
8 months (2 cases)
11 months

No retinoblastoma was diagnosed at birth, whereas neuroblastoma with bilateral adrenal tumours and massive hepatic involvement was the cause of one neonatal death and 30 (27 per cent) of neuroblastomas presented in the first year of life.

The epidemiologic characteristics of retinoblastoma have been studied[41] and an increased incidence of mental retardation, associated malformations and neoplasms with evidence of the D deletion syndrome has been found.

CONNECTIVE TISSUE TUMOURS

The three main subdivisions of this group are rhabdomyosarcoma, fibroblastic and bone tumours. These types made up 103 out of a total of 117 connective tissue tumours. These types made up 103 out of a total of 117 connective tissue tumours.[58] The remainder included synovial and lipomatous tumours.

The rhabdomyosarcoma is the most frequently encountered soft tissue malignant tumour in childhood, and is only exceeded numerically by the gliomas, neuroblastoma and renal tumours.

The term rhabdomyosarcoma implies a tumour of striated muscle, and the presence of such fibres is a diagnostic feature in a proportion of the cases. The absence of striations does not exclude such a diagnosis and their detection depends, to a certain degree, upon the diligence with which a search is made for them. In their absence other features such as strap-like cells with nuclei distending the cell to give

* Tumours found on ophthalmoscopic examination because the parents suffered from the disease.

a racquet, or tandem, appearance may be helpful. Some of the tumours have loose tissue with stellate cells resembling embryonic mesenchyme, and the arrangement of cells around spaces or clefts in the alveolar rhabdomyosarcoma may give rise to difficulty in diagnosis, and confusion with the synovial sarcoma arises.

The microscopic structure of the embryonic rhabdomyosarcoma shows features which resemble muscle of the 7–10 weeks foetus and the alveolar type that of the hollow tube stage, while the pleomorphic tumour may be due to dedifferentiation[63] as the pleomorphic cells do not differentiate in tissue culture.

In an analysis of 60 rhabdomyosarcomas, the tumours were classified into the following histological types:

Botryoid	5
Loose embryonic	8
Dense embryonic	23
Alveolar	7
Myoblastic	3
Pleomorphic	13
Mesenchymoma	1

The botryoid or grape-like tumours are similar to the loose embryonic neoplasms but are encountered in submucosal situations in the head or pelvic regions.

Not all such rhabdomyosarcomas are, however, botryoid and Fig. 14 shows a tumour of the bladder extending into the submucosa without grape formation.

The alveolar tumours overlap the dense embryonic group and the presence of alveolar features is to some extent subjective and may depend on the amount of tissue available for microscopic examination. In one study of embryonic rhabdomyosarcoma of the limbs and limb-girdles,[78] alveolar features were noted in 21 out of 61 cases, the finding being pronounced in 9, focal in 7 and 5 showing clusters or clefts in a fibrous stroma. The embryonic rhabdomyosarcomas have been divided into alveolar and botryoid types in another report[44] when 10 per cent were considered to be alveolar.

The pleomorphic tumours are more commonly seen in adults and the majority of such neoplasms in the present series were in older children although the youngest case, an infant of 6 weeks of age, had such a tumour. The pleomorphic tumour was the type usually encountered in peripheral muscles.

The myoblastic tumours in the table showed very marked muscle differentiation, and the mesenchymoma had islands of cartilage in addition to myoblastic features.

The predominant sites for the rhabdomyosarcoma are the head and neck involving the nasopharynx, middle ear and orbit in particular, and the pelvis and retroperitoneal region. Relatively few tumours were encountered in peripheral muscles in the present series, but isolated examples of testicular and bile-duct involvement were noted.

The malignant bone tumours of childhood are predominantly osteosarcomas and Ewing's tumours with 30 and 28 examples of such tumours respectively in an analysis over a 15 year period in the Manchester University C.T.R. The only other common bone lesion was histiocytosis, 22 of the 42 cases in the same period showing osseous involvement.

The nature of Ewing's tumour is not yet understood although, from electron microscopical studies, some clones have the characteristics of the developing myelocyte and a myelogenous origin with growth and spread similar to the myeloma has been considered.[42] The myeloma has a predilection for the vertebrae and sternum unlike the pipe bones in Ewing's tumour, and tends to replace the marrow distending the cortex of the bone, whereas the Ewing's tumour invades the marrow cavity over a localized area and extends widely into the surrounding tissues.

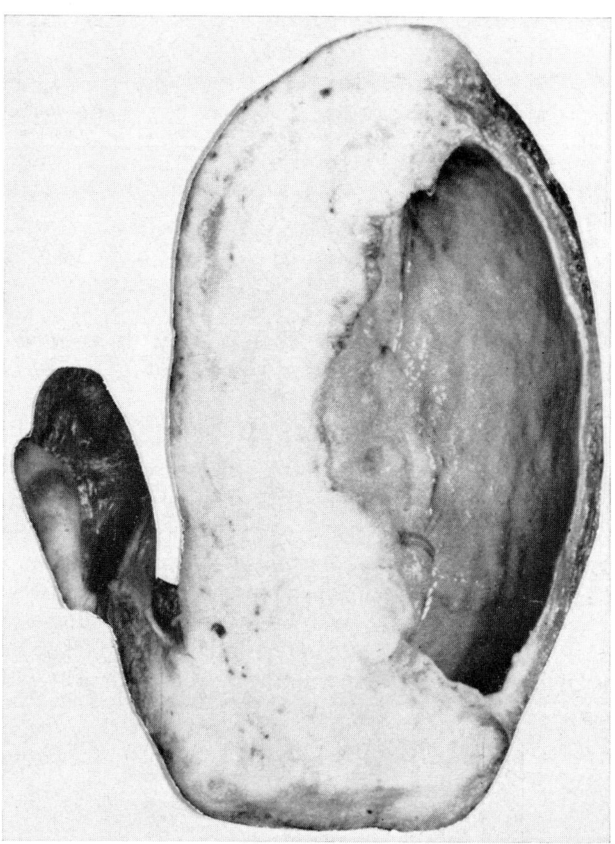

FIG. 14. Rhabdomyosarcoma of the bladder. Although the tumour is submucosal there is little evidence of botryoid formation.

The osteosarcoma is a tumour of older children, no case in the present series presenting under the age of 6 years. Ewing's tumour is encountered over a wider age distribution but is rare in early childhood. No such neoplasm below the age of 2 years is shown in Fig. 15, although a Ewing's tumour in the first year of life has recently been encountered.

The rarity of Ewing's tumour in the first two years of life is very different from the incidence of neuroblastoma with which there may be histological confusion when the latter shows bone metastases. The involvement of a single bone in the first instance, the metastatic spread to the lungs, the prolonged course of the disease and the normal level of catecholamines in the Ewing's tumour, are distinguishing features.

The nature of histiocytosis X is in doubt at the present time, and not all authorities would agree that it is a tumour. In the absence of any known causative agent and having regard to the pathological behaviour, including invasiveness and response to radiation, histiocytosis X has been included. The histological features are varied, giant cells being sometimes present and cases have been referred to the Manchester C.T.R. with an initial diagnosis of Hodgkin's disease to which there is some similarity regarding the neoplastic status of the disease. In this connection, a borderline case between Hodgkin's disease and eosinophilic granuloma has been reported.[32]

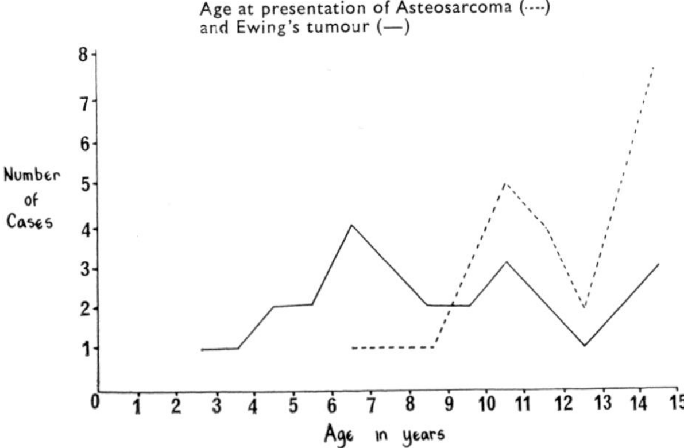

FIG. 15. Graph showing the age incidence at presentation of osteosarcoma and Ewing's tumour in childhood.

Histiocytosis X is found predominantly in infants and young children and the majority of cases occur within the first three years of life as shown in Fig. 16.

The variation in the clinical picture with a range between Letterer-Siwe's disease and eosinophilic granuloma is generally accepted. An attempt has been made to relate the distribution of the lesions with the age of the patient with

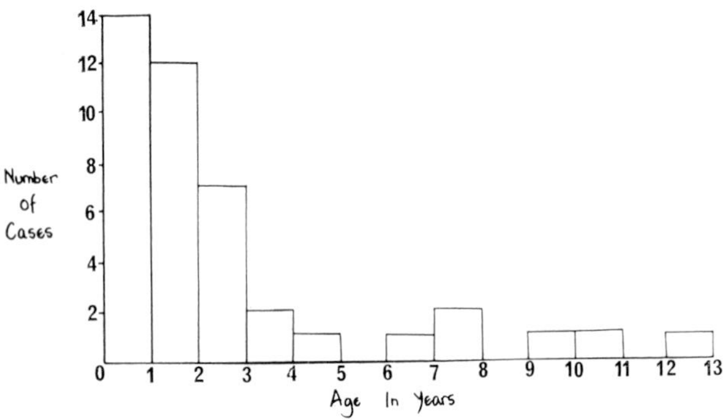

FIG. 16. Histogram showing the age incidence of histiocytosis X in childhood. 42 cases.

little success, although diffuse reticuloendothelial involvement may be a more prominent feature of infancy. There is the same lack of correlation between prognosis and age of the patient up to 5 years. No fatalities were noted after the age of 5 years, but there were few cases in this age range. Involvement of the lung was a bad prognostic feature.

A clinical and histological finding in young infants is the presence of nodules confined to the skin, and which have the microscopic features of histiocytosis X.

METASTATIC TUMOURS IN BONE

Neuroblastoma is by far the most important tumour to show bone metastases in childhood, although this is a finding in other neoplasms. The following table shows the types of tumour encountered in the Manchester University Children's Tumour Registry in which bone metastases developed:

Neuroblastoma
Ewing's tumour
Lymphoma
Osteosarcoma
Retinoblastoma
Medulloblastoma
Wilm's tumour
Synovioma
Lymphoepithelioma
Alveolar soft part sarcoma

The incidence of bone marrow metastases in children with solid tumours has been investigated in a series of 213 cases.[25] Tumour cells were detected in 49 out of 90 neuroblastomas, 5 out of 25 rhabdomyosarcomas, 3 out of 15 retinoblastomas, 2 out of 5 ganglioneuroblastomas and 1 out of 13 miscellaneous sarcomas. No tumour cells were detected in 53 marrow aspirations from 33 cases of Wilm's tumour, although this may occur.[62] In another series[16] in which there were marrow aspirations from 75 cases of children with malignant tumours, positive results were obtained in 21 out of 30 neuroblastomas, 3 out of 15 rhabdomyosarcomas, 1 out of 2 retinoblastomas, 2 out of 6 osteosarcomas and 1 out of 8 Ewing's tumours. In this latter series, all the patients with positive aspirations died within 6 months.

FIBROBLASTIC TUMOURS

The fibroblastic tumours comprize a varied group but are mostly benign in histological appearance and behaviour. The fibrosarcomas show little tendency to metastasize and a figure of 1 in 13 tumours has been suggested for this occurrence.[80] Fibrosarcomas may be found at any age in childhood and may be congenital. There is a tendency to recur after excision, but regression or spontaneous disappearance of the tumour may also be noted in infancy.[77] The tumours may be large and closely applied to bone as in Fig. 17, which shows a fibrosarcoma in the forearm of a young infant which was filling the interosseous space.

Apart from the congenital fibrosarcoma, the term generalized fibromatosis has been applied to fibroblastic nodules thought to be hamartomatous rather than neoplastic which are found in the viscera and soft tissues.[51] Another lesion which is probably hamartomatous and is seen predominantly in male infants is the fibrous hamartoma of infancy[22] in which there are fibrocollagenous and adipose elements.

Digital neurofibrosarcoma of infancy is the term applied to single, or multiple, pea-sized nodules which are fixed to the skin on the lateral aspect of a distal phalanx, and which tend to recur after removal.[40]

In the young child, the juvenile aponeurotic fibroma or fibromatosis particularly involving the palm or sole may give rise to considerable difficulty in treatment, owing to its wide ramification and tendency to recur.

In older children, desmomas may occur and fibrosarcomas have been reported in the deeper tissues and viscera, notably the bronchi and lung.[24] Fibromatous tumours

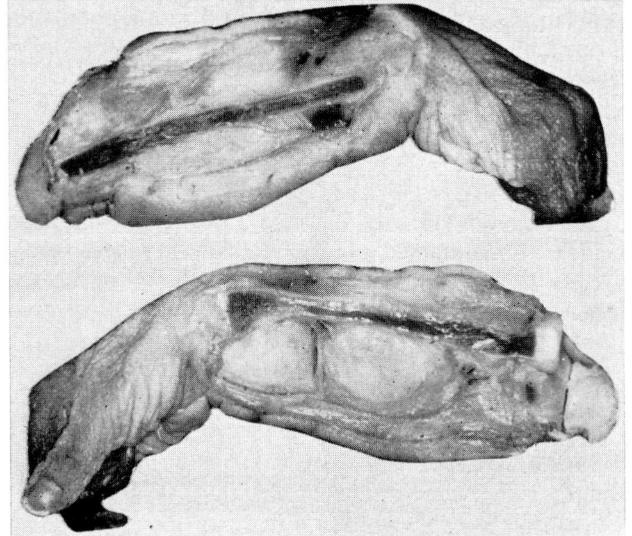

FIG. 17. Interosseous fibrosarcoma in the forearm of a young infant.

have also been noted by the author in the choroid plexus, and 3 similar cases have been reported.[30] In addition, a dural fibroblastic tumour has been encountered in an infant of 7 days. In this latter case there was a history of extracranical subcutaneous tumours in a similar site over 4 generations. Histological information was not available, but the father's "tumour" was a hard, mobile mass situated in the subcutaneous tissue of the left parieto-occipital region, and was considered clinically to be a fibroma.

TERATOMA

Presacral teratoma is the one childhood tumour which is seen more commonly in the female child. Wilm's tumours have approximately equal sex incidence while some groups including medulloblastoma, lymphoma and neuroblastoma show male preponderance.

In the period 1953–68 12 cases of presacral teratoma were encountered, 9 of the patients being girls. Analysis of the 44 cases of teratoma in the C.T.R. during the same period as the tumours already discussed showed involvement of the following sites, and included 31 girls and 13 boys:

Ovary 19
Sacrococcygeal 12 (9 female)
Testis 7
Intracranial 3 (1 female)
Intraspinal 1 (female)
Mediastinum 1 (female)
Heart 1 (male)
Lung 1 (female)
(in one case there were two benign primary tumours involving the ovary and lung)

Other sites involved by teratomata which are recorded in the literature include the stomach,[49] liver,[93] spleen, retroperitoneal[11] and cervical regions. Thirty two cases with tumours in the thyroid and cervical region have been reviewed with reports of 2 additional cases,[34] and in this series the sex incidence was equal.

The hepatic tumours must be distinguished from mixed hepatoblastomas in which mesodermal tissues such as osteoid and cartilage may be found.

The origin of teratomata is still under discussion. Chromosome studies have not yet yielded sufficient information, and nuclear sexing of tumour cells gives equivocal results. Apart from the female gonadal tumours, 40 per cent of testicular and considerably fewer extragonadal tumours possess a chromatin mass resembling a Barr body, and indicating the presence of two X chromosomes. Parthenogenetic development of haploid cells, either by fusion or reduplication, has been suggested as a possible mechanism[50] but most authorities no longer accept this view. The two main hypotheses at the present time propose an origin from regions of embryonic tissue which have escaped from the primary embryonic organizer, or from multipotential germ cells.

Many presacral teratomas have been detected at birth, and such tumours have been noted in the foetus. A tumour in a stillborn infant causing obstructed labour has been recorded.[47] The tumours presenting at birth are more likely to be benign and a figure of 10 per cent malignancy for such cases compared with 33 per cent throughout childhood has been suggested.[20] The benign teratomata in this analysis showed a female preponderance of 4:1, whereas the sex incidence was equal in the malignant tumours.[20] There is some variation in the figure given for the sex incidence of presacral teratoma, 94 per cent of the cases in one series being girls[33] and 13 girls to 1 boy in another[18] but all reports indicate the female preponderance.

The benign nature of the cases which present early in life is supported by the finding that all the 7 surviviors in the present series presented at birth, and 4 of the 5 fatal cases presented in the second year of life. There was one fatal case which presented in the neonatal period, but fibrocystic disease was a more important feature in this patient. All the fatal cases were girls, whereas in this small series the patients presenting at birth had an equal sex incidence.

The only other teratoma apart from the presacral region to present at birth was situated in the heart. The infant showed cyanosis, and a systolic murmur was heard down the left sternal border. Cardiac failure developed, followed by death at the age of 3 weeks. At autopsy a benign teratoma was found to be attached to the wall of the right ventricle with involvement of a tricuspid leaflet, and extension through the pulmonary valve.

Ovarian teratomata are encountered in older children than testicular tumours, as would be expected from their situation. Six of the 7 testicular tumours presented in the first or second year of life, while the age incidence at presentation of the cases of ovarian teratoma is shown in Fig. 18. One testicular tumour was diagnosed at 8 years of age, and it has been pointed out[90] that such neoplasms may be first detected in later childhood. The majority of testicular teratomas, probably about 75 per cent, are histologically benign, and recurrence was not seen in any of the 7 cases in the present series.

Apart from teratoma, the orchioblastoma or adenocarcinoma of the infant testis is the most frequently encountered testicular tumour in childhood while seminoma, Sertoli and Leydig cell tumours are occasionally seen. The increased incidence of both teratoma and seminoma in the cryptorchid testis is recognized, although it is not known whether neoplasia arises from the abnormal situation or, whether failure of descent is due to a defect in the testis itself.

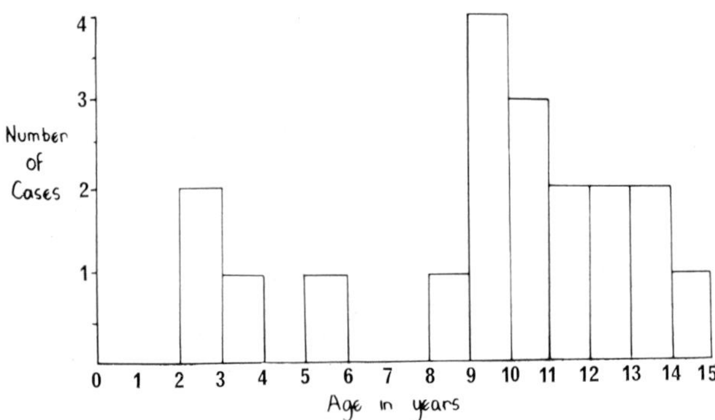

FIG. 18. Histogram showing the age incidence of ovarian teratoma in childhood. 19 cases.

Varying figures have been given for the increased incidence of tumours developing in the cryptorchid testis. An increase of eleven times when compared to the scrotal testis has been reported in one series,[19] and 50 times in another.[31] There is a greater likelihood of malignancy with abdominal than inguinal testis.[10] In addition, there is general agreement that orchiopexy, or spontaneous descent, does not remove the chance of developing tumours in the testis.[83] A teratoma has been recorded in the testis of a 2 month old infant associated with torsion and infarction of the gonad.[35]

Solid tumours in the ovary are rare. In an analysis of 75 cystic and solid ovarian tumours in children collected over a 44 year period at one Centre, the following classification is given:[21]

Benign 63 (84 per cent)

35 Cystic (dermoid) teratomas
26 Simple follicular cysts
1 Granulosa cell tumour
1 Arrhenoblastoma

Malignant 12 (16 per cent)

3 Teratomas
3 Papillary carcinomas
2 Dysgerminomas
2 Embryonal cell carcinomas
1 Granulosa cell carcinoma
1 Choriocarcinoma

LYMPHOMA AND LEUKAEMIA

Leukaemia is the most important malignancy of childhood numerically accounting for 30 per cent of the cases in the Manchester University C.T.R., and with a population of one million children under the age of 15 years, about 30 new cases are registered annually.

The age incidence at presentation of leukaemic patients is shown in Fig. 19.

Relatively few cases present in infancy, but the incidence rises rapidly to a peak in the third year of life. There is then a rather slower fall over the next 7 years, and the lower incidence is maintained up to 40 years of age when a second increase occurs and is maintained in the following two decades.

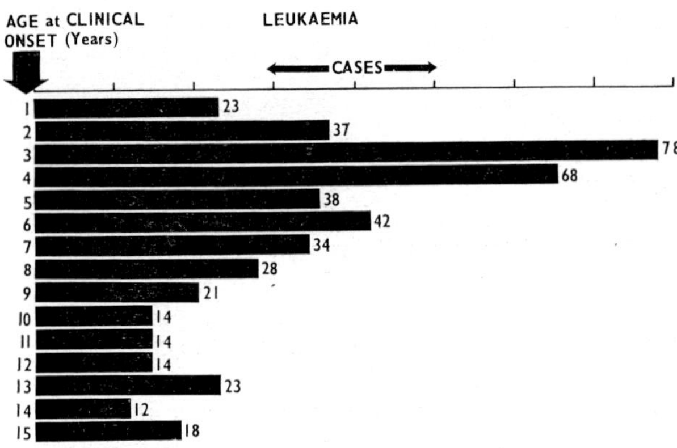

FIG. 19. Histogram showing the age incidence of leukaemia in childhood. 464 cases.

The incidence of lymphosarcoma follows a similar pattern but, whereas leukaemia is relatively uncommon in the first year of life, lymphosarcoma is rare at this age.

The great majority of lymphosarcomas in childhood are diffuse, and only occasional nodular histological variants are encountered. In addition, they are lymphoblastic or lymphocytic in most cases and reticulum cell sarcoma is a relatively rare tumour.

Hodgkin's disease occurs more frequently in later childhood. In the present series no case was seen in the first 2 years of life with small numbers after this age in childhood, and a rise in incidence after the twelfth year.

There has been considerable work on the histological classification of Hodgkin's disease based on the Rye conference[53,54]. The types showing lymphocytic predominance, or nodular sclerosis, have a better prognosis than the mixed cellularity and lymphocyte depleted types. Variations in age, and sex incidence together with differences in the incidence of histological sub-types are encountered in different communities. In the Manchester cases there is a relatively low incidence in childhood with a high proportion of lymphocyte predominant cases, whereas the reverse may be encountered in other communities.[13]

The myeloid, monocytic and myelomonocytic leukaemias do not show the same incidence curve in relation to age as the lymphoblastic types. They are evenly distributed throughout childhood, so that relative preponderance of these types is seen in infants and older children. The response to treatment is less satisfactory in children with leukaemia under the age of 2 years and over the age of 10 years. This does not appear to be due to the relative excess of non-lymphoblastic leukaemias in infancy and later childhood, and the response to treatment in lymphoblastic leukaemia is less satisfactory in these age groups.

3. *C.T.R.* 69/58 *C.O.K.* 2 months. Female. Monocytic leukaemia. Nodules up to one inch in diameter developing over the back, face and scalp. The initial lesions disappeared but others developed over the trunk, and there was lymph node enlargement. A skin biopsy of a nodule showed leukaemic infiltration. There was a left facial palsy due to nerve compression by tumour deposits. (Figs. 20a and b.)

4. *C.T.R.* 39/61 *P.B.* 6 weeks. Male. Lymphoblastic leukaemia. Nodules over the side of the head, present at birth with spread to the trunk later.

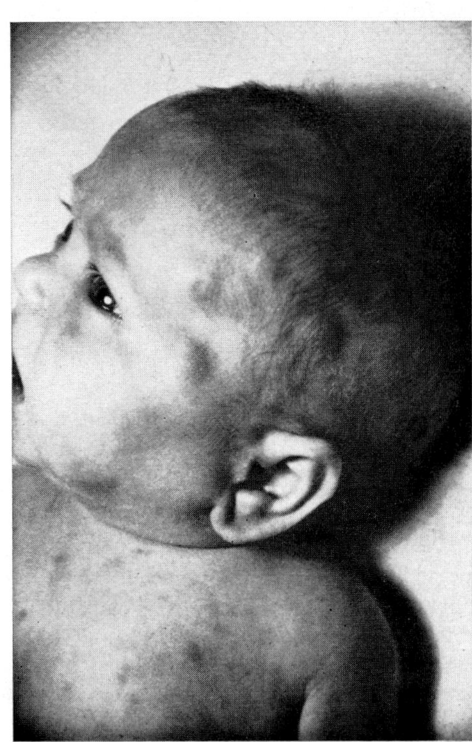

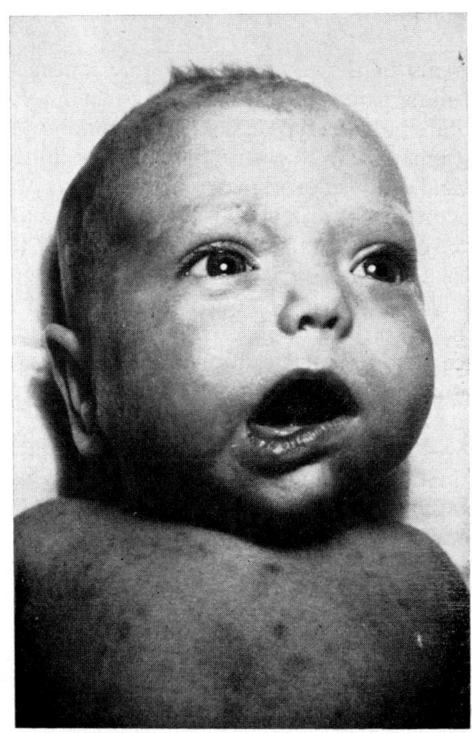

FIG. 20(a and b). Skin nodules in a case of leukaemia in infancy. Facial palsy has developed due to leukaemic infiltration.

One particular aspect of leukaemia in infants is the development of subcutaneous deposits. In an analysis of 447 cases of leukaemia seen over a 15 year period, 22 or about 5 per cent presented in the first year of life. The cytological classification was lymphoid 9, myeloid 6, monocytic 3 and "blast cell" 4, emphasizing the relatively high proportion of myeloid and monocytic types in infancy. Subcutaneous nodules were found in 5 of the infants, and they were the presenting feature in 3 cases. The clinical findings in these cases were as follows:

1. *C.T.R.* 61/54 *P.M.S.* 6½ months. Female. Lymphoblastic leukaemia. Pink nodules appeared on the cheek enlarging after 6 weeks and extending over the scalp, trunk and thighs. There was a papular rash over the back and generalized lymph node enlargement.

2. *C.T.R.* 79/56 *T.H.* 3 months. Male. Lymphoblastic leukaemia. Lump on the scalp enlarging to one inch in diameter with the development of similar nodules over the trunk.

5. *C.T.R.* 10/62 *J.G.* 6 weeks. Female. Monocytic leukaemia. Nodules over the scalp extending to the trunk and eventually disappearing within 4 weeks.

Skin nodules have been reported in a case of congenital myeloblastic-promyelocytic leukaemia.[94] The authors in the paper refer to 50 cases of congenital leukaemia and in the case described, nodules were the presenting feature at birth. In an earlier report,[67] it is pointed out that such nodules may be the first sign in congenital leukaemia. The vascularity of the neonatal skin may play a part in the high incidence of cutaneous infiltration in congenital leukaemia.

Skin involvement is prominent in other malignancies in the neonatal period and infancy. Reference has already been made to the increased incidence of such lesions in young patients with neuroblastoma. The prominence of cutaneous manifestations in histiocytosis in infancy has also been noted, and skin nodules with the histological features of this disease may be found in this age group without evidence of visceral or bone involvement. The cutaneous manifestation of malignancy in infants is a subject which requires further study.

CONCLUSION

Occupational factors such as coal-tar dyes and asbestosis clearly are not relevant in the production of cancer in infancy and childhood. Similarly, smoking as an aetiological agent in bronchial carcinoma, and multiparity in carcinoma of the cervix, are social aspects which are not involved.

The rarity of carcinoma in children is an expression of the unimportance of such factors. In a study of 914 cases of malignancy in childhood, only 39 were classified as carcinomata.[72]

Extrinsic agents in the mother which may affect the foetus require more extensive investigation. The development of adenocarcinoma of the vagina in later childhood in association with maternal stilboestrol therapy is an important example[36] and the position of maternal irradiation as an aetiological factor in the production of childhood malignancy has received attention. It has been suggested that there could be 300–800 additional deaths from malignancy before the age of 10 years among one million children exposed shortly before birth to one rad of ionizing radiation.[79] The importance of maternal irradiation in pregnancy is still under discussion, but it may well play a significant part in the production of childhood malignancy.

One field in which there is little doubt that irradiation plays a part in the aetiology of childhood neoplasia is related to the application of such treatment to the thymus and neck in infancy. There is a higher incidence of such treatment in patients with thyroid carcinoma,[91] and a higher incidence of carcinoma in patients who have received irradiation.[3,48] The interval between irradiation and the development of neoplasia is in the region of 10 years,[65] and this interval is dose related.[9,82]

The incrimination of viruses as aetiological agents has received an impetus from the studies on the herpes-like virus (E.B.V.) in African lymphoma, although the association is not a simple one.

Immature murine type A, and mature type C particles, have been described in 50 per cent of biopsy specimens, and 15 per cent of the plasmas in a report on 149 cases of leukaemia and malignancy of the blood-forming organs.[75] This incidence has not, however, been reported by any other author.

Failure of immunological homeostatic mechanisms as in the hypo-gammaglobulinaemias, are associated with an increased incidence of malignancy ,and in early life associated with developing immunity, and in old age, due to depression of the immune response, there may be particular hazards resulting in neoplastic development.

The position of the childhood fevers in relation to immune surveillance requires investigation. Studies have shown that an attack of measles may reduce homograft immunity for some weeks.[61]

Immunity and genetic predisposition are associated. Apart from the increased incidence of cancer in the autosomal trisomies, particularly mongolism and the Klinefelter syndrome, there is increased tendency to transformation of fibroblasts by oncogenic viruses. Leukaemia in the patient with Down's syndrome tends to occur at an earlier age than in the patient with a normal chromosomal complement, and this applies to malignancies associated with malformations as in Wilm's tumour with aniridia.

It has been suggested that two somatic mutations are involved in the aetiology of unilateral and sporadic cases of Wilm's tumour, and only one in bilateral or familial cases.[46]

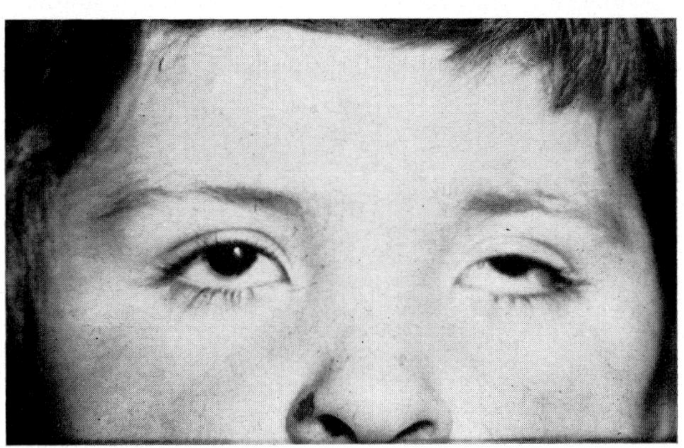

FIG. 21. Aniridia in a girl with Wilm's tumour.

Familial incidence is another field for study, not only with regard to the relatives of the child with cancer, but also to the investigation of certain "cancer families" in which a high incidence of a particular malignancy develops in one sibship. Three cases of leukaemia among 4 siblings have been reported[55] and studies have been made in this field.[56]

Genetic factors, chromosomal and immunological abnormalities, and susceptibility to oncogenic viruses have been described in an Icelandic family in which all the five members of one generation were affected by acute myeloid leukaemia or preleukaemia.[43]

The high concordance rates for monozygotic twins for the development of leukaemia diminishing with increasing age, and the lack of concordance for dizygous twins has led to the suggestion of placental transplantation of leukaemic cells.[12]

One of the striking features in the Manchester University C.T.R. is the constancy of the annual incidence not only of total cases, but also of the numbers of new cases in the particular groups. As regards two of the major groups, namely, leukaemia and gliomas, the incidence is very similar to that encountered in the United States. The low incidence of gliomas in African children has been reported[15] and geographical variation in the incidence of childhood neoplasia is important.

The reasons for the vulnerability of the male child regarding the development of tumours need further investigation.

In conclusion, the aetiological factors in the production of paediatric neoplasia are distinctly different from those encountered in adult life. Furthermore, these factors are acting during the period of growth and development. This, together with the variation in the behaviour of malignancy throughout infancy and childhood, makes paediatric oncology a subject which requires particular attention.

REFERENCES

1. Allen, A. C. and Spitz, S. (1953), "Malignant Melanoma. A Clinicopathological Analysis of the Criteria for Diagnosis and Prognosis," *Cancer*, **6**, 1–45.
2. Anderson, D. E. (1970), *Genetic Concepts and Neoplasia*. A Collection of Papers Presented at the Twenty-third Annual Symposium on Fundamental Cancer Research 1969 at the University of Texas M. D. Anderson Hospital and Tumour Institute at Houston, pp. 85–104. Baltimore: Williams & Wilkins Co.
3. Archer, V. E. and Simpson, R. V. (1963), "Semiquantitative Relationship of Radiation and Neoplasia in Man," *Health Phys.*, **9**, 45–56.
4. Beckwith J. B. and Perrin E. V. (1963), "*In Situ* Neuroblastoma. A Contribution to the Natural History of Neural Crest Tumours," *Amer. J. Path.* **43**, 1089–1104.
5. Bolande R. P., Brough, A. J. and Izant, R. J. (1967), "Congenital Mesoblastic Nephroma of Infancy. A Report of 8 Cases and the Relationship to Wilm's Tumour." *Pediat.*, **40**, 272–278.
6. Bray, P. F., Ziter, F. A. and Lahey, M. E. (1969), "The Coincidence of Neuroblastoma and Acute Cerebellar Encephalopathy." *J. Pediat.*, **75**, 983–990.
7. *Brit. med. J.* (1972), "Craniopharyngiomas. Leading article," **i**, 764.
8. Broomhead, I. W. (1964), Cystic Hygroma of the Neck. *Brit. J. plast. Surg.*, **17**, 225–244.
9. Buschke, F. and Parker, R. G. (1972), *Radiation Therapy in Cancer Management*, p. 182. N.Y. and London: Grune & Stratton.
10. Campbell, H. E. (1942), "Incidence of Malignant Growth of the Undescended Testicle. A Critical and Statistical Study," *Arch. Surg.*, **44**, 353–369.
11. Charles, D. (1953), "Retroperitoneal Teratoma in Infancy," *Arch. Dis. Childh.*, **28**, 147–148.
12. Clarkson, B. D. and Boyse, E. A. (1971), "Possible Explanation of the High Concordance for Acute Leukaemia in Monozygotic Twins," *Lancet*, **i**, 699–701.
13. Correa, P. and O'Conor, G. T. (1971), "Epidemiologic Patterns of Hodgkin's Disease," *Int. J. Cancer*, **8**, 192–201.
14. Crocker, F. S. and Vernier, R. L. (1972), "Congenital Nephroma of Infancy: Induction of Renal Structures by Organ Culture," *J. Pediat.*, **80**, 69–73.
15. Davies, J. N. P. (1968), "Some Variations in Childhood Cancers Throughout the World," *Tumours in Children*, pp. 13–36. (H. B. Marsden, and J. K. Steward, eds.). Berlin, Heidelberg, New York: Springer-Verlag.
16. Delta, B. G. and Pinkel, D. (1964), "Bone Marrow Aspiration in Children with Malignant Tumours," *J. Pediat.*, **64**, 542–546.
17. de Lorimer, A. A., Bragg, K. U. and Linden, G. (1969), "Neuroblastoma in Childhood," *Amer. J. Dis. Child.*, **118**, 441–450.
18. Dillard, B. M., Mayer, J. H., McAlister, W. H., McGarvin, M. and Strominger, D. B. (1970), "Sacrococcygeal Teratoma in Children," *J. Pediat. Surg.*, **5**, 53–59.
19. Dixon, F. J. and Moore, R. A. (1953), "Tumours of the Male Sex Organs," *Atlas of Tumour Pathology*, Section VII, Fascicle 32. Washington D.C.: Armed Forces Institute of Pathology.
20. Donnellan, W. A. and Swenson, O. (1968), "Beningn and Malignant Sacrococcygeal Teratomas," *Surgery*, **64**, 834–846.
21. Ein, S. H. and Darte, J. M. M. (1970), "Cystic and Solid Ovarian Tumours in Children. A 44 Year Review." *J. Pediat. Surg.*, **5**, 148–156.
22. Enzinger, F. M. (1965), "Fibrous Hamartoma of Infancy," *Cancer*, **18**, 241–248.
23. Everson, T. C. and Cole, W. H. (1966), "Spontaneous Regression of Cancer. A Study and Abstract of Reports in the World Medical Literature and of Personal Communications Concerning Spontaneous Regression of Malignant Disease," Philadelphia and London: W. B. Saunders Co.
24. Feldman, P. A. (1957), "Sarcoma of the Lung," *Brit. J. Tuberc.*, **51**, 331–334.
25. Finklestein, J. Z., Ekert, H., Isaacs, H. and Higgins, G. (1970), "Bone Marrow Metastases in Children with Solid Tumours." *Amer. J. Dis. Child.*, **119**, 49–52.
26. Fitzwilliams, D. C. L. (1911), "The Etiology of Naevi. Nerve influence in their causation," *Brit. med. J.*, **ii**, 489–491.
27. Ford, F. R. (1966). *Disease of the Nervous System in Infancy, Childhood and Adolescence*, 5th Ed., pp. 918–927. Springfield, Illinois: C. C. Thomas.
28. Fraumeni, J. F., Jr., Miller, R. W. and Hill, J. A. (1968), "Primary Carcinoma of The Liver in Childhood: An Epidemiologic Study," *J. Nat. Cancer Inst.*, **40**, 1087–1099.
29. Frohman, L. A. (1971), "Hypothalamic Control of Growth Hormone," *Pathobiology Annual*, Vol. 1, pp. 362–364. N.Y.: Appleton-Century-Crofts.
30. Gardner, W. J. and Turner, O. A. (1938), "Primary Fibroblastic Tumours of the Choroid Plexus of the Lateral Ventricles. A Clinicopathological Study of Three Cases," *Surg. Gyncl. Obstet.*, **66**, 804–809.
31. Gilbert, J. B. and Hamilton, J. B. (1940), "Studies in Malignant Testis Tumours III. Incidence and Nature of Tumours in Ectopic Testes," *Surg. Gynec. Obstet.*, **71**, 731–743.
32. Gubler, J. P., Ramon, J. and Moreno, E. (1962), "Hodgkin's Disease, Eosinophilic Granuloma, Hand-Schüller-Christian Syndrome. Apropos of a Borderline Case," *Arch. Franc. Pediat.*, **19**, 1279–1293.
33. Gwinn, J. L., Dockerty, M. B. and Kennedy, R. L. J. (1955), "Presacral Teratomas in Infancy." *Pediat.*, **16**, 239–249.
34. Hajdu, S. I., Faruque, A. A., Hajdu, E. O. and Morgan, W. S. (1966), "Teratoma of the Neck in Infants." *Amer. J. Dis. Child.*, **111**, 412–416.
35. Hansen J. L. (1967), "Tumor of Undescended Testicle in an Infant," *J.A.M.A.*, **199**, 944–945.
36. Herbst, A. L., Ulfelder, H. and Poskanzer, D. C. (1971), "Adenocarcinoma of the Vagina. Association of Maternal Stilobestrol Therapy with Tumour Appearance in Young Women," *New Engl. J. Med.*, **284**, 878–881.
37. Hodgman, J. E., Freedman, R. I. and Levan, N. E. (1971), "Neonatal Dermatology," in *Ped. Clin. of N. Amer.*, Vol. 18, No. 3, pp. 725–733. Philadelphia, London, Toronto: W. B. Saunders Co.
38. Horrax, G. and Wyatt, J. P. (1947), "Ectopic Pinealomas in the Chiasmal Region. Report of 3 Cases," *J. Neurosurg.*, **4**, 309–326.
39. Jagasia, K. H. and Thurman, W. G. (1965), "Congenital Anomalies of the Kidney in Association with Wilm's Tumour," *Pediat.*, **35**, 338–340.
40. Jensen, A. R., Martin, L. W. and Longino, L. A. (1957), "Digital Neuro-fibrosarcoma in Infancy, *J. Pediat.*, **51**, 566–570.
41. Jensen, R. D. and Miller, R. W. (1971), "Retinoblastoma: Epidemiologic Characteristics," *New Engl. J. Med.*, **285**, 307–311.
42. Kadin, M. E. and Bensch, K. G. (1971), "On the Origin of Ewing's Tumor," *Cancer*, **27**, 257–273.
43. Kaur, J., Catovsky, D., Valdimarrson, H., Jensson, O. and Spiers, A. S. D. (1972), "Familial Acute Myeloid Leukaemia with Acquired Pelger-Huët Anomaly and Aneuploidy of C Group. *Brit. med. J.*, **ii**, 327–331.
44. Keyhani, A. and Booher, R. J. (1968), "Pleomorphic Rhabdomyosarcoma," *Cancer*, **22**, 956–967.
45. Kissane, J. M. and Smith, M. G. (1967), *Pathology of Infancy and Childhood*, p. 707. St. Louis: C. V. Mosby Co.
46. Knudson, A. G., Jr., and Strong, L. C. (1972), "Mutation and Cancer: a Model for Wilm's Tumour of the Kidney," *J. Nat. Cancer Inst.*, **48**, 313–324.
47. Langley, F. A. (1968), in *Tumours in Children* (H. B. Marsden and J. K. Steward, eds.). p. 257, Berlin, Heidelberg, New York: Springer-Verlag.
48. Latomette, H. B. and Hodges, F. J. (1959), "Incidence of Neoplasia After Irradiation of the Thymic Region," *Amer. J. Roentgenol.*, **82**, 667–677.
49. Lebreuil, G., Garbe, L. and Payan, H. (1969), "Gastric Teratoma in a Newborn," *Arch. Anat. Path.*, **17**, A.47–A.50.
50. Lennox, B. (1966), in *Recent Advances in Pathology*, 8th Ed., (C. V. Harrison, ed.), p. 46. London: J. & A. Churchill Ltd.
51. Levkoff, A. H., Gonzalez, L. G. and Neher, J. L. (1965), "Congenital Diffuse Fibromatosis. A Case Report," *Pediat.*, **35** 331–333.

52. List, C. F., Dowman, C. E., Bagchi, B. K. and Bebin, J. (1958), "Posterior Hypothalamic Hamartomas and Gangliogliomas Causing Precocious Puberty," *Neurology*, **8**, 164–174.
53. Lukes, R. J., Butler, J. J. and Hicks, E. B. (1966), Natural History of Hodgkin's Disease as Related to its Pathologic Picture," *Cancer*, **19**, 317–344.
54. Lukes, R. J., Craver, L. F., Hall, T. C. *et al.* (1966), "Rye Conference: Report of the Nomenclature Committee," *Cancer Res.*, **26**, 1311.
55. Lundmark, K. M., Thilen A. and Vahlquist, B. (1967), "Familial Leukaemia—Three Cases of Acute Leukaemia in Four Siblings," *Acta paediat. scand.* suppl. **172**, 200–205.
56. Lynch, H. T. (1967), *Hereditary Factors in Carcinoma*, Berlin, Heidelberg, New York: Springer-Verlag.
57. McWhorter, H. E. and Woolner, L. B. (1954), "Pigmented Nevi, Juvenile Melanomas and Malignant Melanomas," *Cancer*, **7**, 564–585.
58. Marsden, H. B. and Steward, J. K. (1968), *Tumours in Children*, p. 197. Berlin, Heidelberg, New York: Springer-Verlag.
59. Matson, D. D. (1969), *Neurosurgery of Infancy and Childhood*, 2nd Ed., pp. 540–543. Springfield, Illinois: C. C. Thomas.
60. Ibid. pp. 544–574.
61. Mellman, W. J. and Wetton, R. (1963), "Depression of the Tuberculin Reaction by Attenuated Measles Virus Vaccine," *J. Lab. clin. Med.*, **61**, 453–458.
62. O'Neill, P. and Pinkel, D. (1968), Wilm's Tumor in Bone Marrow Aspirate," *J. Pediat.*, **72**, 396–398.
63. Patton, R. B. and Horn, R. C., Jnr. (1962), "Rhabdomyosarcoma Clinical and Pathological Features and Comparison with Human Fetal and Embryonal Skeletal Muscle," *Surgery*, **52**, 572–508.
64. Potter, E. L. (1952), *Pathology of the Fetus and Newborn*, pp. 169–170. Chicago: The Year Book Publishers.
65. Raventos A. and Winship, T. (1964), "The Latent Interval for Thyroid Cancer Following Irradiation, *Radiology*, **83**, 501–508.
66. *The Registrar General's Statistical Review of England and Wales, 1965* (1970). Suppl. on Cancer, pp. 28–31. London: H.M.S.O.
67. Reimann, D. L., Clemmens, R. L. and Pillsburg, W. A. (1955), "Congenital Acute Leukemia: Skin Nodules, a First Sign," *J. Pediat.*, **46**, 415–418.
68. Rodewald, H. (1956), "Contribution to the Knowledge of Sympathetic Ganglioneuroblastoma. Cases in a 67 Year Old Man and a 69 Year Old Woman," *Zbl. allg. Path. path. Anat.*, **95**, 194–199.
69. Rook, A. J. Wilkinson, D. S. and Ebling, F. J. G. (1968), *Textbook of Dermatology*, Vol. 1. Oxford: Blackwell.
70. Russell, R. W. F. and Pennybacker, J. B. (1961), "Craniopharyngiomas in the Elderly," *J. Neurol. Neurosurg. Psychiat.*, **24**, 1–13.
71. Russfield, A. B. (1968), in *The Pathology of the Nervous System*, Vol. i, pp. 629–631 (J. Minckler, ed.), New York: McGraw-Hill Book Co.
72. Salas, M. M. (1962), "Pathology of Neoplasms in Childhood Related with those in Adults," *Gac. méd. Méx.*, **92**, 545–553.
73. Schneider, K. M., Becker, J. M. and Krasna, I. H. (1965), "Neonatal Neuroblastoma," *Pediat.*, **36**, 359–366.
74. Scott, L. S. (1955), "Bilateral Wilm's Tumour," *Brit, J. Surg.*, **42**, 513–516.
75. Seman, G. and Seman, C. (1968), "Electron Microscopic Search for Virus Particles in Patients with Leukaemia and Lymphoma," *Cancer*, **22**, 1033–1045.
76. Shanklin, D. R. and Sotelo-Avila, C. (1969), "*In Situ* Tumours in Fetuses, Newborns and Young Infants," *Biol. Neonat.*, **14**, 286–316.
77. Shore, B. R. (1936), "Spontaneous Cure of a Congenital Recurring Connective-tissue Tumor," *Amer. J. Cancer*, **27**, 736–739.
78. Soule, E. H., Geitz, M. and Henderson, E. D. (1969), Embryonal Rhabdomyosarcoma of the Limbs and Limb-girdles. A clinicopathologic Study of 61 Cases," *Cancer*, **23**, 1336–1346.
79. Stewart, A. and Kneale, G. W. (1970), "Radiation Dose Effects in Relation to Obstetric X-rays and Childhood Cancers," *Lancet*, **i**, 1185–1188.
80. Stout, A. P. (1962), Fibrosarcoma in Infants and Children," *Cancer*, **15**, 1028–1040.
81. Sussman, W. (1933), "Pituitary Adenomata," *Brit. med. J.*, **ii**, 215.
82. Toyooka, E. T., Pifer, J. W., Crump, S. L., Dutton, A. M. and Hempelmann, L. H. (1963), "Neoplasms in Children Treated with X-rays for Thymic Enlargement II. Tumour Incidence as a Function of Radiation Factors," *J. nat. Cancer Inst.*, **31**, 1357–1377.
83. Turner, J. H. and Bloodworth, J. M. B., Jr., in *Endocrine Pathology* (J. M. B. Bloodworth, Jr., ed.), pp. 439–440. Baltimore: Williams & Wilkins Co.
84. Vlachos, J. and Matani, S. (1969), "Analysis of 1,039 Childhood Tumours," *Delt. Paidiat. Klin. panep. Athena.*, **16**, 398–412.
85. Walsh, T. S., Jr., and Tompkins, V. N. (1956), "Some Observations on the Strawberry Nevus of Infancy," *Cancer*, **9**, 869–904.
86. Walton, R. G. (1971), "Pigmented Nevi," in *Ped. Clin. of N. Amer.*, Vol. 18, No. 3, pp. 897–923. Philadelphia, London, Toronto: W. B. Saunders Co.
87. Weinberger, L. M. and Grant, F. C. (1941), "Precocious Puberty and Tumors of the Hypothalamus. Report of a Case and Review of the Literature with a Pathophysiologic Explanation of the Precocious Sexual Syndrome," *Arch. intern. Med.*, **67**, 762–782.
88. White, P. T. and Ross, A. T. (1963), "Inanition Syndrome in Infants with Anterior Hypothalamic Neoplasms," *Neurol.*, **13**, 974–981.
89. Willis, R. A. (1958), in *Borderland of Embryology and Pathology*, pp. 341–350. London: Butterworth.
90. Willis, R. S. (1948), in *Pathology of Tumours*, p. 948, London: Butterworth.
91. Winship, T. and Rosvold, R. V. (1961), "Childhood Thyroid Carcinoma," *Cancer*, **14**, 734–743.
92. Wintersteiner, H. (1897), *Das Neuroepithelioma Retinae*, Vienna.
93. Yarborough, S. M. and Evashwick, G. (1956), "Case of Teratoma of the Liver with 14 Year Post-operative Survival," *Cancer*, **9**, 848–850.
94. Zussman, W. V., Khan, A. and Shayesteh, P. (1967), "Congenital Leukaemia. Report of a Case with Chromosome Abnormalities," *Cancer*, **20**, 1227–1233.

44. COLONIZATION OF THE DEVELOPING BODY BY BACTERIA

R. FRASER WILLIAMS

INTRODUCTION

Consideration of data concerning colonization of babies and children by bacteria must be tempered with caution. Studies on bacteria associated with man in disease and in health have been conducted for the past hundred years or so and surveys have been carried out sporadically according to local and contemporaneous interests.

During this period, the technical methods available for bacterial isolation have been refined and extended; the characteristics of population groups from which bacteria are derived are better understood; and associated technical and scientific disciplines have advanced as rapidly as bacteriology itself. Any given survey of bacteria may be difficult to compare with others since the parameters observed will reflect the interpreted status of a genus (including nomenclature and taxonomic location) extant at that time. In bacteriology as in most medical sciences, fashions and exigencies come and go.

Geographical differences may result in wide variations in survey results because of differing climatic, cultural and economic factors. Even surveys conducted within the same country may show considerable variation in the nature of bacterial flora according to seasonal changes in climate and the varying prevalence of coincident viral and bacterial infections.

An additional reservation concerns the far-reaching changes induced in bacterial populations by antibacterial drugs over the past two decades and more. The rapidity of these changes is exemplified by the altered direction of study of hospital infections. During the 1950's and most of the 1960's, major attention was devoted to the very serious problems of staphylococcal carriage and sepsis but, currently, the main concern is with infections caused by Gram-negative "enteric" bacteria.

Bacteria possess astonishingly versatile genetic mechanisms which enable them to adapt with varying rapidity and success to antibiotic challenge and other environmental assaults. Thus changes in the nature of bacterial populations are brought about by external influences and, since these populations interact with each other and with their various habitats, extensive changes in body flora can occur. And these changes are progressively influenced by new measures of infection control in home and hospital, by extended application of mass immunization procedures, by improved dietary and economic standards and by much else besides.

It is with these various reservations in mind that colonization of the developing body by bacteria should be considered.

Bacteria that are present in or on the body may be regarded as "transient" or "resident". Transient bacteria are those that are found only occasionally, whereas the resident bacteria are always present in any given individual or, indeed, in most healthy people. Resident bacteria include such species as *Streptococcus viridans*, which is almost always present in the nasopharynx of healthy people, and by *Escherichia coli* ("coliforms") in the large intestine. Transient bacteria can include such nasally carried organisms as the meningococcus (*Neisseria meningitidis*) and *Staphylococcus aureus*. Carriage rates of meningococci vary according to the prevalence of meningococcal infection while staphylococci are only carried transiently by healthy "occasional carriers".

This discussion will be concerned mainly with resident bacteria, though it is often difficult to distinguish between those that are transient and those regarded as permanent. This distinction is made more difficult by use of antibiotic preparations that may abolish or damage any bacterial population, so that it may subsequently be replaced by another strain or even another species.

In attempting to assess potential pathogenicity of colonizing bacteria—an exercise that was regularly performed in the past—difficulties arise because of the heightened susceptibility of many children to infection by a very wide range of micro-organisms and, as already noted, by altered behaviour of many of the bacteria themselves. For example, children showing genetic defects, especially those involving inadequacy of immune mechanisms and those with malabsorption states, may carry bacterial populations that differ markedly from those found in "normal" children. At the same time, use of cytotoxic drugs, immunosuppressive measures and steroid hormones can lead not only to variations in resident flora, but may foster serious systemic infections by bacteria not formerly regarded as pathiogenic.

All these factors underly he following discussion on bacterial colonization of the healthy developing child.

GENERAL ASPECTS OF BACTERIAL COLONIZATION

Patterns of colonization and the varied bacteria that make up the flora of the body will be discussed in this account in terms of various sites such as intestine, vagina and nasopharynx. Particular attention will be paid to those bacteria that are prominent in the various situations, to those that are of greatest contemporary interest because of their actual or potential behaviour as pathogens, and to those that underline the problems of changing ecology.

But any discussion of bacterial colonization must begin with the newborn baby, for it is in the neonatal period that the basic pattern of colonization is established, and it is at this time also that the infant is most vulnerable to bacteria that do not often harm older children who are healthy.

There is much evidence to show that the newborn baby is colonized very soon after birth. The pattern of colonization will vary according to whether the child is born in hospital or at home, and whether he or she is breast- or bottle-fed. But colonization commences at birth, and the first bacteria to become established may be those encountered in the mother's birth canal.

Thereafter, bacteria derived from various sources quickly become established. The main sources are the skin and nasopharynx of the mother and, to a lesser extent, of nurses and others who handle the baby. Gut bacteria may be acquired from either artificial or breast milk, from the skin of the mother and other intimate contacts, and from the general environment. Some bowel colonizing bacteria may enter by the anal route. The immediate locality of the baby —clothing, bedding, incubator, toilet and feeding utensils, and the surrounding air—all provide their share of micro-organisms.

THE UMBILICUS

The umbilical stump is a wound that can rapidly become colonized with dangerous bacteria and measures to minimize this contingency are an essential part of infant care. The most important organism that colonizes the umbilicus of the newborn baby (and also the skin and the nose) is *Staphylococcus aureus*, and colonization by this bacterium has been intensively studied in the past. Most studies have been concerned with spread of virulent and multiply antibiotic-resistant staphylococci within maternity units, and with evaluation of measures designed to reduce spread, colonization and subsequent infection. Since many of the studies were conducted before the advent of the newer and more efficacious systemic antistaphylococcal preparations, it cannot be assumed that today's colonization rates give an exact parallel.

Nonetheless, the modes of spread within maternity wards[32,39] and the epidemiology of staphylococcal carriage[75] are well understood, and the general principles of infant colonization still hold. Babies are colonized by staphylococci within a few hours or a few days of birth. The sites of colonization progressively are umbilicus, groin, nose and, often, the perineum. Since colonization of the umbilicus is accompanied by colonization of the other sites listed above, it is difficult to separate them in this discussion.

The umbilical stump is a wound which is actually or potentially open, and forms a fertile breeding-ground for staphylococci; but phage group III staphylococci predominate in umbilical colonization, and these are strains that cause infection most commonly in surgical rather than maternity units. (The phage group I strains e.g. 52A/79, 80/81 that do frequently cause maternity ward sepsis—among babies, mothers and staff—are those that generally colonize the nose of the baby, and it is in the nose that the most persistent form of carriage is seen.)

Many reports have described methods for protecting the umbilical wound against colonization by staphylococci; application of hexachlorophene dusting powder, chlorhexidine and spirit, and various methods of covering the wound have been utilized. Usually, staphylococcal colonization of the umbilicus has been reduced or abolished by these means (in conjunction with other coincident antistaphylococcal measures) though some workers have reported resultant higher frequencies of colonization of that site by Gram-negative bacteria. (As well as being colonized by staphylococci and Gram-negative bacilli, the umbilicus may also become heavily colonized with streptococci[49] though subsequent infection of the baby by these bacteria is, surprisingly, an uncommon event).

Many infants do become heavy carriers and disseminators of staphylococci by the second day of life and such babies are more likely to develop subsequent staphylococcal infection than those who harbour comparatively fewer bacteria, or become carriers at a later stage. But it should be remembered that *all* colonized babies can infect themselves as well as others (including the mother) and can also serve as vectors of staphylococcal infection within their own household.

It is sometimes difficult to disentangle "colonization" from "infection." But though a preponderance of babies become colonized with staphylococci of various sorts (including the highly virulent "hospital" varieties) and though these can and usually do spread to other neonates, persistence of carriage through to older ages, and the actual incidence of overt infection in hospital are not consistently and unduly high. A number of studies have suggested that staphylococcal infection (and carriage) is more common in male than in female infants. A consensus suggests that the male preponderance is not great, and a suggestion that this preponderance might be related to circumcision has not been confirmed.

Despite the often alarming picture of widespread and heavy colonization of babies by staphylococci in maternity units, carrier rates decline sharply when the infants leave hospital since the majority of them do not become "permanent" carriers.

COLONIZATION OF THE SKIN

Bacteria colonizing the skin may be of the resident variety in that they may subsequently be constantly isolated and multiply in or on the skin, whereas isolation of transient varieties will vary according to environmental and other factors. (It has been shown, for example, that skin moisture encourages bacterial multiplication, and it has been suggested that the wearing of overlarge plastic pants over the napkin can encourage staphylococcal colonization.[4])

Some bacteria which, strictly speaking, should be classified as transient may be repeatedly isolated through reinfection of the skin from some other carrier site; thus *Staphylococcus aureus* may be constantly showered onto the skin from the anterior nares of a persistent nasal carrier. At the same time, *Staphylococcus aureus* may be truly carried on the skin—"carried" in the sense that the bacteria actively multiply on, and are disseminated from any part of the skin of a persistent carrier, the main site of carriage when it occurs is the perineum.[37,53] The dangers of contamination of clothing by staphylococci dispersed from such a site are obvious. Because of the physiological skin changes that accompany the onset of puberty, there is an increased susceptibility to staphylococcal sepsis at this time; thus a child may suffer a series of boils or carbuncles caused by a staphylococcus that has been present from birth without, hitherto, causing overt infection.

The two most important groups of bacteria found in the skin are, firstly, anaerobic bacteria and, secondly, Gram-positive which, in this respect, include *Staphylococcus albus*, *Staphylococcus aureus*, the non-pathogenic pigmented sarcinae such as *Sarcina lutea*, and *Streptococcus viridans*.

No systematic study of skin colonization by anaerobic bacteria has been found. Nonetheless, it should be pointed out that the skin provides a vast anaerobic medium in which anaerobic bacteria (including facultative anaerobes) can live and multiply. It has been shown[24] that, in the adult at any rate, anaerobic bacteria greatly outnumber aerobic varieties in the skin. Anaerobic bacteria that have been isolated from this source include anaerobic Lactobacilli, micrococci (Gram-positive coagulase negative cocci), anaerobic propionibacteria (such as *P. acnes*) and, occasionally, *Streptococcus pyogenes* which is a facultative anaerobe. These various bacteria, being so commonly distributed, are likely to colonize the newborn skin quite soon after birth.

Staphylococcus albus ("Staphylococcus epidermidis albus"), though it is a common skin bacterium has not been so well studied as the aureus strains. Though it is largely held to be a non-pathogen, some strains cause urinary infection and some cause endocarditis following heart surgery. It may be isolated from the blood of terminal cases of leukaemia, and it is well-known for its ability to infect Spitz–Holter valves. More attention has been directed to the characterization of strains known to have caused recognizable infection than to its colonizing ability. However, it often accompanies *Staphylococcus aureus* and, together with *Streptococcus viridans*, forms a notable component of the healthy infant's skin.

COLONIZATION OF THE GUT

The establishment of bacteria in the gut from birth onwards has been studied since the time of the great German bacteriologist Escherich (1886), who gave his name to the bacteria known today as *Escherichia coli*. A vast literature exists which describes the appearance of very many bacterial species in the faeces of children from the time of birth to older ages. Many of the surveys are difficult to interpret since they were conducted prior to descriptions of refined isolation methods and systems of classification, and they were carried out at times when human populations were more static and before the use of antibiotics caused the rapid genetic modification and selection that obtains today.

It is generally accepted that the gut is sterile for a few hours after birth. A very small minority of workers has suggested that, occasionally, bacteria may be present in the meconium at birth, but these suggestions are far outweighed by the consensus which believes that bacteria do not enter for some hours.[62]

Some four to eight hours after birth, the appearance of a large variety of different bacterial species is seen and these gradually develop as colonizing agents until the formation of the "milk stool," by which time the faecal flora is well established. The varieties of bacteria involved in this initial colonization include micrococci, staphylococci and streptococci. The streptococci include *Streptococcus faecalis* (the Enterococcus) which is found in most normal stools at all ages; *Streptococcus viridans*, which is best known as a member of the upper respiratory tract normal flora; and various haemolytic, though not necessarily very pathogenic, streptococci. Yeasts are represented by *Candida albicans*, the sources of this organism being mainly the mother's mouth and vagina.

A number of bacillary forms can also be isolated. The anaerobic non-sporing *Bacteroides* appear, Lactobacilli are found in large numbers together with "coliforms" (*Escherichia* and *Klebsiella* species). The non-pathogenic *Bacillus* species (especially *Bacillus subtilis*) is present, together with members of the anaerobic *Clostridia*, such as *Clostridium welchii*.

Clostridia are saprophytic bacteria whose natural habitat is the soil where they exist in exceedingly large numbers. They are spore-bearers, and derive energy by breakdown of protein and sugar without utilizing oxygen, so that their role in nature is to act as putrefactive agents. The spores of Clostridia are very hardy, being highly resistant to the effects of heat and disinfectants. Because of their wide distribution in soil, which dries and is blown and carried about, Clostridia can be found literally everywhere; they are therefore commonly present among the normal flora at various sites in the body. (Fortunately, they do not often cause infection in the human since their stringent metabolic demands—dead protein and lack of oxygen—are not often met in the body. They can, however, cause "food poisoning" when foodstuff in which they have been able to grow and produce toxins is ingested).

However, Clostridia are present in human faeces, and they were observed by Escherich; because he was unaware of their anaerobic nature and did not possess the means to grow them, he described their appearance (rods which were often surmounted by spores) and named them "Köpfenbakterien."

From the very beginning the bowel contains a complex microbial flora and this is derived from the mother herself and from the infant's surroundings, including other people and babies within that environment. The bacterial content of the newborn infant's food is of paramount importance in establishing the early pattern of colonization.

From the time of the establishment of these various microorganisms in the gut during the early neonatal period, the subsequent development of the faecal flora depends more upon diet than upon age. So consistent were the findings in this respect that Moro in 1908 enunciated three postulates,[48] and these are summarized below:

1. The intestinal flora depends upon the variety of food taken by the infant.
2. The microscopic picture of the "physiological intestinal flora" is uniform and constant.
3. Any apparent change of flora in the infant gut is not due so much to the introduction of new bacteria but, rather, to the developing predominance of one or two types already present in the gut.

These postulates (and particularly the third) must, of course, be modified in the light of present-day experience, and especially in the case of infants housed in the hospital environment where highly antibiotic-resistant strains and others possessing enhanced invasive and colonizing ability are to be found in abundance. (Moro's prescience in using the term "*physiological* intestinal flora" suggests a delicate insight of things to come.)

However, in the case of *Bacteroides*, *Lactobacilli* and "coliforms," the postulates still hold (except, probably when enteropathogenic serotypes of *Escherichia coli* are introduced into the infant gut with subsequent severe diarrhoeal illness. In this circumstance, the enteropathic strain may be the only "coliform" to be isolated from the gut contents).

The importance of Lactobacilli in the gut of the newborn child is well recognized. The stools of breast-fed infants tend to be rather acid and, in these, Lactobacilli predominate. Lactobacilli are slender Gram-positive rods that do not possess capsules, spores or flagella. An outstanding characteristic is their ability to ferment carbohydrates and produce a high degree of acidity, so that reduction of the pH of a suitable culture medium to 3 or less is not unusual. The Lactobacilli are widespread in nature, and some of them are commensals in man. In the human, the species is represented by *Lactobacillus acidiphilus* (or Döderlein's bacillus) and *Lactobacillus bifidus*, while a third member, *Lactobacillus odontolyticus*, is associated with dental caries.

Cruickshank[20] opined that predominance of Lactobacilli (which, at the time of his study, were referred to as *B. bifidus*) is an important factor in preserving a healthy condition of the intestinal tract in breast-fed infants. This is an opinion which has since been amply confirmed in studies of the well-recognized resistance of breast-fed infants to infantile gastroenteritis.[2,38,58] And breast-fed babies produce acid stools containing a very heavy predominance of Lactobacilli.

Some probable reasons for the increased susceptibility of the bottle-fed baby to gastroenteritis have been discussed.[13] These concern mainly the composition of artificial feeds and the ways in which they differ from human milk, the more rigid timetables usually followed in artificial feeding (which can result in undue periods of starvation) and, ultimately, the composition of the faecal flora, and especially the lactobacillary content with its influence on acid production.

Artificial feeds consist essentially of cow's milk which has been heated in order to denature protein. Subsequent dilution reduces this protein level to that found in human milk, and substances such as sugar, vitamins and iron are added. Artificial feeds, naturally, vary in their composition according to method of manufacture and the nature and proportion of the various additives.

However, artificial feeds differ broadly from breast milk in that the human product contains high lactose and low protein; above all, a low phosphate content precludes any great buffering activity. This paucity of buffering action has been demonstrated by comparative *in vitro* experiments in which mixed cultures of anaerobic lactobacilli and *Escherichia coli* were grown in culture media containing human milk, and media containing different preparations of cow's milk.[13] In the cow's milk mixtures, pH rarely fell below 5·0, while the *Escherichia coli* grew far more rapidly than the lactobacilli; when human milk was included in the incubation mixture, the numbers of *Escherichia coli* fell, lactobacilli grew more rapidly, and the final pH achieved (4·0–4·5) was lower than in the cow's milk mixture. (It has been suggested[36] that human milk contains a special growth factor for Lactobacilli—the "Bifidus Factor"; this was regarded as necessary for adequate growth of a variant of *Lactobacillus bifidus* in artificial culture. The variant studied, however tended to be unstable and lose its requirements for human milk.)

In regard to the starvation periods that may be connected with bottle feeding, together with interim overfeeding, evidence is cited[13] that, in experimental animals at least starvation can lead to increased susceptibility to Gram-negative enteric infections, while overfeeding may predispose to endotoxaemia.

Apart from the gross chemical differences between human and cow's milk, human milk contains a number of constituents which have a direct function in reducing infection in the newborn infant. It has been shown, for example,[14] that human milk contains large quantities of iron-binding protein—consisting mainly of lactoferrin, though a small amount of transferrin is also present. The bacteriostatic effect of samples of human milk against an enteropathic strain of *Escherichia coli* (0111/B4) was related to the unsaturated iron-binding capacity of that milk; saturation of the samples with iron removed the bacteriostatic effect and it was concluded that the iron-binding proteins played an important *in vivo* part in increasing resistance to infantile gastroenteritis.

Furthermore, resistance to infection is conferred by immunoglobulins present in colostrum. Absorption of immunoglobulins by the intestine of newborn infants has been studied in relation to the levels of IgA, IgG and IgM in cord blood and in samples of blood taken subsequently, and comparisons were made between breast- and bottle-fed babies.[40] There were generally higher levels of the three immunoglobulin fractions by the 5th day of life in colostrum-fed infants with a significant increase in the concentrations of IgG, whereas babies who were bottle-fed until the 4th day after birth showed a marked fall in IgG levels.

Nonetheless, it should be noted that not all the immunoglobulins supplied in breast milk may enter the circulation, as it is known that some of them may act as surface antibodies in relation to the gut wall itself[33] and other workers[72] have suggested that high levels of immunoglobulins (particularly of IgA and IgM) in breast milk possibly protect the intestinal tract by directly lysing the bacteria themselves.

Indeed, antibodies may reduce the chance of successful immunization with poliomyelitis vaccine in young babies. Part of this interference is ascribed to circulating antibody derived from the mother during foetal life, and it has been recorded in relation to studies on heat-killed vaccine[50] that cord blood levels of poliomyelitis neutralizing antibodies are similar to those in maternal serum. However, circulating levels in the baby are halved every 21 days or so, and attempted immunization should be delayed until the age of 6 or 9 months.

Antibody action in reducing the rate of infection with living attenuated (Sabin) poliomyelitis vaccine is more prolonged in breast-fed babies;[72] bottle-fed babies demonstrate decreased resistance to vaccine virus very soon after birth, even when there is little detectable change in the levels of circulating antibody.[43] It is likely that the resistance of breast-fed babies comes in part from the antibodies present in the milk and that these act locally in reducing the infectivity of the attenuated poliovirus.

Where bacteria are concerned, it is unlikely that the presence of complement derived from breast milk is a necessary condition for their intraluminal destruction, since milk can be heated to 56°C for 30 min. (a process that inactivates complement) without the bacteriostatic power being abolished.[14] Neither does the addition of N-acetyl-tyrosine (which inactivates the third component of complement)[7] reduce bacteriostatic activity. But, despite the unlikelihood of much active complement—whatever its origin—being present in the human gut,[31] any small amount that is present may participate in bacteriolytic activities.

The action of lysozyme, which is present in large concentration in human milk[35] is, however, of some importance in conferring resistance to gastro-intestinal infection; the lysis of bacteria sensitized by specific antibody is not completed by complement alone, the additional participation of lysozyme being necessary.[71]

Lysozyme is a protein substance present in high concentration in tears, but found also in saliva, mucus, blood and other body fluids, and it is present in practically all human secretions. It destroys bacteria probably by depolymerizing mucopeptides found in the cell walls of most species.[59] A point of some significance when considering the protective effects of breast milk against intestinal infection is that *Escherichia coli* is lysed to some extent by IgM antibody, but in the presence of IgA, lysis will not occur unless lysozyme is present.[1]

Apart from the various protective mechanisms accompanying breast feeding and the optimum nourishment gained from this source, the breast-fed infant enjoys prolonged physical contact with the mother, and often largely with her alone. The important gut-colonizing bacteria are therefore derived mainly from one source; and this source is usually the safest one for the baby.

In the artificially-fed infant, conditions in the gut favour the establishment of a post-weaning type of flora. In other words, the baby acquires bacteria from sundry and random sources—partly because of the particular physiological condition of its bowel, and partly through contact with the variety of people who participate in the bottle feeding process. Thus the bacteriological space available may come to be occupied preferentially by any stray bacteria including those that can be very harmful to young babies.

In breast-fed children, the eventual pattern of bacterial colonization of the gut is determined at the time of weaning. Thereafter, in both naturally-fed and artificially-fed babies, the adult pattern of intestinal flora develops. Now, the stools become more offensive and more anaerobes are present than aerobic bacteria; the anaerobic forms being made up predominantly of *Bacteroides* species, while aerobes consist of *Escherichia coli*, *Klebsiella* and various Gram-positive cocci.[23,73]

Bacteroides is a complex group of non-sporing anaerobic bacteria, the classification and nomenclature of which are still in some dispute. In spite of the great predominance of *Bacteroides* in faeces, they are not routinely isolated in many bacteriological laboratories because they are rather fastidious anaerobes requiring specialized techniques for consistent isolation. (As aetiological agents in clinical disease, they may be found in lesions near the gut, or associated with gut surgery; they are occasionally isolated from blood cultures and they may be a cause of brain abscesses).

Infantile Gastroenteritis

The enteropathogenic serotypes of *Escherichia coli* that are associated with the acute gastroenteritis of infancy can in no sense be regarded as part of the normal flora of the developing child. But the frequency with which they are encountered in paediatric practice, and the sometimes serious and life-threatening consequences of colonization by these bacteria make it necessary to include them in any discussion of gut flora.

Some twenty-odd serotypes associated with diarrhoeal illness in infants have been recognized. These are identified by the specific "O" (somatic) antigens that they possess (together with some other antigenic subdivisions) and they are familiar as, for example, strains 0·55, 0·26, 0·111, 0·114 etc. It should be noted that acquisition of one of these or similar strains does not invariably lead to diarrhoea; conversely, very serious outbreaks of gastroenteritis can be associated with consistent isolation of a particular serotype from affected babies' stools.[41]

Escherichia coli gastroenteritis affects very young infants more frequently than older children the highest incidence and the most serious effects being seen from birth to the age of about 6 months. Young babies acquire the bacteria sometimes from their mothers,[18] from other babies and from their attendants[55] and from the immediate environment.[56] Much can be done to reduce the spread of the bacteria within a hospital unit by meticulous screening of all admissions.[42]

Though most studies of infantile gastroenteritis have been carried out in a hospital environment, the bacteria are by no means concentrated in hospital alone; they may be regarded as being fairly widespread throughout the population. In general, the disease is related to higher social and economic standards, and may be absent or rare in more primitive societies,[47] possibly because breast-feeding is the universal rule in such communities.

But though specific serotypes of *Escherichia coli* are not truly "hospital bacteria" they may well, if introduced into a unit housing a number of small babies, cause many cases of diarrhoea with consequent dehydration. Clearly, the most effective approach is to identify and isolate infected babies, and thus exclude their bacteria from the general ward.

During the past decade or so, the severity of infantile gastroenteritis has generally decreased, though this decline is independent of any improvement in supportive and specific therapy.[63] Indeed, the rationale of antibiotic therapy in this condition is a matter of some controversy, and specific serotypes of *Escherichia coli* resistant to one or more of the antibiotics generally recommended (e.g. neomycin, gentamicin, colistin) have been reported from various parts of the world.

Present-day Variations in Colonization

Colonization of the infant gut by *Staphylococcus aureus* has been well studied, particularly in hospital nurseries. During the 1950's and early 60's, gut colonization was found to be variable, but occurred in about 50 per cent of babies by the 8th day of life whether the babies were breast-fed or not.[6] Such colonization did not lead generally to clinical illness, though the importance of gut colonization as a reservoir of staphylococcal sepsis was well recognized. At the present time, staphylococcal colonization is not a predominating factor in new-born nurseries, possibly due to the greater awareness of the need for aseptic handling of babies, and to the greater availability of efficacious anti-staphylococcal drugs.

A more serious problem is the increased incidence of colonization by Gram-negative bacteria at the present day.[60] This is a trend that is seen particularly in babies that are ill and housed in special units. These infants are often separated from their mothers (who tend to confer Gram-positive bacteria on their babies) and they are kept in special apparatus such as incubators and ventilators. Many Gram-negative bacteria—in contrast to those that are Gram-positive—are spread most readily in moist environments, and are found in humidification apparatus, suction tubes and ventilators. The bacteria spread by these means include *Proteus*, *Klebsiella*, "coliforms" (including, potentially, the enteropathic varieties) and, notably, *Pseudomonas aeruginosa*.

Pseudomonas is a notoriously antibiotic-resistant species which also withstands the action of many disinfectant preparations; it is thus extremely difficult to eradicate from a baby unit, and may be carried and excreted by colonized infants for very long periods. Difficulty in eradication may be compounded by the nature of the equipment used, which may be technically complex as in, for example, an infant incubator. It is unfortunate that these and similar machines are constructed with little but their primary function in mind, small heed being paid in fundamental design to the problems of sterilization. Incorporation of many essential but delicate electrical components, the presence of many interstices and inaccessible areas in these machines renders sterilization a difficult and often ineffectual process—and any incubator becomes heavily contaminated with Gram-negative bacteria after only a few hours' use. A further cause for alarm is the seeming acceptance of contaminated water in the humidifying components of specialized nursing equipment, and this can happen even in those units distinguished for meticulous aseptic observances. Clearly, more positive bacteriological education is required on this point.

The free use of antibacterial drugs strongly influences the pattern of bacteria ultimately established in the infant's gut, particularly where wide-spectrum antibiotics are used for prolonged periods. In these circumstances, virtual sterilization of the bowel can occur with subsequent overgrowth by less desirable (and often antibiotic-resistant) organisms; in this respect, overgrowth by *Staphylococcus aureus* or *Candida albicans* (Monilia) may be more life-threatening than the original infection. Use of antibiotics for shorter periods can produce lesser, but still profound, changes in gut and other colonizing flora, and these possibilities should be considered when selecting antibacterial agents.[26]

It should be remembered that very young infants in general, but especially those that are underweight, premature or displaying any of a variety of congenital defects, are highly susceptible to infection. This susceptibility is often more a reflection of the inadequacy of the host defences than the virulence of the infecting organisms. Thus almost any bacterium colonizing the body may cause serious infection. In view of the wide variety of bacteria that may be encountered, and the differing therapeutic measures that may be required to deal with them, a knowledge of locally colonizing varieties and their sensitivities is an essential prelude to successful treatment. Likewise, the avoidance of situations in which the "normal flora" is likely to be disturbed or those in which superinfections by dangerous strains are likely to occur is an essential part of the correct management of the small child.

COLONIZATION OF THE UPPER RESPIRATORY TRACT

The sectors of the upper respiratory tract which normally harbour bacteria may be divided into the nose, the nasopharynx and the throat. The accessory sinuses are usually regarded as sterile, and bacteria are not found in the bronchi during health.[12] The population of bacteria in the nose and the throat differ from each other, but differ in the proportions of the bacteria found in the two sites rather than in any absolute degree.

At birth, the nasopharynx is sterile but bacterial colonization occurs rapidly during the first 2 days of life and colonization follows a fairly regular pattern. The first bacteria to appear are *Streptococcus viridans*, coliform bacteria, some diphtheroids and non-pathogenic Gram-negative diplococci of the Neisseria group (e.g. *Neisseria catarrhalis*), which are present in the throat of most people throughout life. Pneumococci (also present in "normal" people) and members of the Haemophilus species appear by the 2nd or 3rd day[44] and, less frequently, streptococci.[8]

How the pattern of colonization develops subsequently depends largely upon whether the child is born at home or in hospital and, if in hospital, on the local methods and standards of care and on the use of antibiotics in the unit.

"From the standpoint of infection, it is still more dangerous for a baby to be born in hospital than at home."[19] The risks of staphylococcal colonization and infection of the newborn, and the increasing present-day dangers of contamination by enteric bacteria have been discussed elsewhere in this chapter. No apology is proferred for reiterating the dangers from these groups.

Pseudomonas aeruginosa, *Klebsiella* species, "coliform" bacteria and *Proteus* constitute serious danger to the newborn child in hospital. They can colonize any part of the body and must be included in any discussion of the upper respiratory tract. These bacteria thrive in any moist warm atmosphere, and *Pseudomonas* in particular is found in any equipment requiring a humidification system, such as an incubator.[5]

All these Gram-negative bacteria possess a remarkable ability to develop antibiotic resistance, and it is not surprising that colonization with antibiotic-resistant enteric bacteria is an accompaniment to widespread use of antibiotics in a newborn unit, or that sepsis due to these organisms can be a consequence.[25,60] The increasing problem of serious infection following general use of antibacterial agents has been recognized for some time.[28]

The problem of staphylococcal colonization of the newborn has been fully reviewed,[75,76] and it has been accepted for some time that *Staphylococcus aureus* may be part of the normal flora of the anterior nares of some people. Hospital born babies, however, are at particular risk of acquiring the "epidemic" or "hospital" varieties of staphylococci, in particular type 80/81 which is noted for its virulence in both mothers and babies. Over the years, the consensus of opinion among numerous workers has been that nasal carriage of staphylococci and subsequent sepsis due to that organism are more common among babies born in hospital, though one study[29] reported a higher mortality due to staphylococci among babies born at home.

Nonetheless, it is generally accepted that colonization by antibiotic-resistant bacteria is hazardous and that efforts should be made to minimize this danger in hospital units. From this point of view, the matters that require particular attention are:

(i) A reduction in the number of people who handle the baby and, in this respect, "rooming in" is a procedure to be commended.[52]

(ii) Scrupulous hand-cleansing.

(iii) Measures designed to reduce airborne carriage of bacteria and their dissemination by fomites.

(iv) Careful disinfection of incubators and ventilators.

(v) Restriction—as far as is possible—of antibiotic prescription.

The problems of colonization by staphylococci and enteric bacteria are largely hospital induced. However, colonization of the upper respiratory tract by bacteria that colonize most children whether born in hospital or not must be considered, and these bacteria include potentially serious pathogens such as *Haemophilus influenzae*, *Neisseria meningitidis* and pneumococci.

Most of the upper respiratory tract bacteria are derived initially from the mother, and it has been found[67] that nose, nasopharynx and throat usually remained free from aerobic organisms until the baby had been fed by the mother. Thereafter, of course, bacteria are increasingly acquired through close contact with other people—a process that occurs throughout life.

Thus, after the immediate post-natal period, populations of bacteria may vary from infant to infant, though a given person may show remarkably consistent nasopharyngeal flora over a long period. A typical nasopharyngeal flora will include a mixture of organisms, some predominating in the nose, others in the throat, the distribution in the nasopharynx being intermediate between nose and throat.

Bacteria are less numerous in the nose than in the throat, but include mainly staphylococci (white and golden), meningococci (*Neisseria meningitidis*) and diphtheroids. The mouth and throat harbour mainly streptococci, *Haemophilus influenzae*, *Diplococcus pneumoniae* ("the pneumococcus") and the non-pathogenic *Neisseria*, all of which are present in abundance.

Subsequent development of nasopharyngeal bacterial flora in both children and members of their immediate family depend upon a number of factors. A study of families living in a highly urbanized area of London[11] showed that colds and chronic catarrh were commonest among young children up to the age of 4 years. However, older children attending school were the most effective disseminators of respiratory infection within the family, and the incidence of such illness was related to the degree of overcrowding within a given family.

An analysis of the bacteriological work undertaken during that survey[46] showed that nasal (as opposed to pharyngeal) carriage of pneumococci and *Haemophilus* species tended to decline with increasing age. New strains of pneumococci, once introduced, tended to persist longer in the noses of the children than the adults, and change in the type of pneumococcus carried occurred more often in the children. Carriage of staphylococci and haemolytic streptococci showed the greatest incidence in children of school age.

This feature may be related to the great susceptibility to respiratory infection shown by children starting school for the first time. This is a period, too, when the influence of tonsils and adenoids on the incidence of respiratory tract infection is seen, so that recurrent "tonsillitis" and associated disorders which do not respond to planned therapy and prevention may be an indication for tonsillectomy. But tonsils, especially if they are enlarged, are traditionally regarded as predisposing factors in respiratory infections (and, indeed, in "general debility"), and little regard may be paid to the physiological, developmental and immunological causes of tonsillar enlargement.[34]

Thus tonsillectomy remains one of the most frequent "routine" operations of childhood, and may be undertaken without preceding detailed bacteriological studies, correction of dental sepsis or treatment of infected sinuses.

Haemophilus Influenzae and Related Bacteria

Haemophilus influenzae can prove to be one of the most virulent of bacteria causing infection in childhood. It is therefore of serious import to the clinician and, because of its complexity both as an infecting and a laboratory organism, it poses many problems also for the bacteriologist.

Colonization of healthy children by *Haemophilus influenzae* has been widely studied, but from rather different viewpoints than establishment of staphylococci as colonizing bacteria. Surveys have been conducted since the first description of this species by Pfeiffer in 1890 until the present day. However, these studies have been conducted among more-or-less healthy communities of all ages with especial regard for development of *Haemophilus influenzae* meningitis and respiratory tract infection. But little attention has been directed specifically to the mechanisms, colonization rate and persistence of the species in small children. Furthermore, surveys of healthy individuals have been confined to detection of Haemophilus species in the upper respiratory tract with little regard being paid to the presence of haemophili elsewhere in the body.

From the viewpoint of paediatric practice, especially in the United Kingdom, two general features emerge concerning *Haemophilus influenzae*. The first of these is that it, and related species (such as *Haemophilus parainfluenzae*) are widely distributed in the population among people who are not only healthy, but who remain healthy. The second feature is that *Haemophilus influenzae* can prove to be a very dangerous pathogen indeed in childhood, particularly as a cause of acute epiglottitis, pneumonia and meningitis. Other serious infections include arthritis, cellulitis, osteomyelitis, peritonitis, pericarditis and infections of the middle ear and sinuses; and it may be implicated in urinary tract infection, bacterial endocarditis, conjunctivitis and a variety of minor lesions.

The two seemingly contradictory findings detailed above are largely reconciled by closer consideration of the nature of the haemophili isolated in different circumstances. *Haemophilus influenzae* may exist as both capsulated and uncapsulated forms, and it is the former varieties that are incriminated in serious lesions. The uncapsulated forms are those generally distributed among the population at large. The capsulated varieties can be subdivided serologically into six groups (a–f) on the basis of polysaccharide antigens examined by Pittman[51] and, of these, group b is that most commonly isolated from infections such as meningitis and epiglottitis.

Because a number of surveys were conducted before the significance of capsulation was appreciated, and before the serological subgroups had been identified, the conclusions drawn in the various reports are by no means uniform. Additionally, not all surveys are based on precise identification of *Haemophilus influenzae per se* but may include strains described as "haemophili" or "haemophilic bacteria" so that other strains of Haemophilus may have been included.

A detailed analysis of the various surveys that have been performed is given by Turk and May,[69] who arrive at two general conclusions. The first is that non-capsulated strains of *Haemophilus influenzae* are very commonly present in the upper respiratory tracts of healthy children and adults —a conclusion borne out in any paediatric hospital laboratory. (So commonly is non-capsulated *Haemophilus influenzae* isolated that it may be regarded as virtually a component of the normal flora of the nasopharynx. Carriage rates range from 25–82 per cent in normal people.) The second conclusion is that capsulated strains are far less commonly found in the general population. The carriage rate runs at about 5 per cent or less, and, of these capsulated strains, only a small minority consists of serological type b.

In the light of these conclusions, it is not easy to discern why some children develop serious infections and others do not. The presence of a virulent capsulated strain is obviously a prerequisite, but exposure alone is not the sole prelude to illness. For example, in one particular series of investigations in a residential nursery in Jamaica, an exceptionally high carriage rate of *Haemophilus influenzae*, type b (50 per cent and over) was found among infants housed together, but no cases of haemophilus infection emerged as a consequence. Yet another investigation had shown that high numbers of type b strains could be isolated from members of households in which there had been cases of haemophilus meningitis. Thus high carriage rates may sometimes be a consequence and not necessarily a primary cause of clinical infection; though it has been suggested that passage of the haemophilus through one or two partially immune subjects may be a necessary preliminary to meningeal infection.

The state of immunity of the patient is of importance in this respect, though the factors concerned are complex. It has been shown[30] that decline in influenzal meningitis coincided with appearance of antibodies; and a common species-specific (as opposed to strain-specific) antigen which is present in both capsulated and non-capsulated strains has been described.[68] Antibodies to these common antigens appear up to the age of about 5 years and may confer at least some protection against strains which possess type-specific polysaccharide capsular antigens. The picture is further complicated by the known cross-reactivity of Haemophilus capsular antibodies with capsular material from strains of pneumococci and vice versa; and Turk and May[69] have speculated that this may be the result of inter-*generic* exchange of genetic material, possibly even in the respiratory tracts of human hosts.

A more recent report[9] describes a number of different bacteria isolated from both humans and rabbits—including *Staphylococcus aureus*, *Staphylococcus epidermidis*, a β-haemolytic streptococcus, *Streptococcus viridans* and others—that developed precipitin lines due to polysaccharides cross-reactive with type b polysaccharides of *Haemophilus influenzae*. Thus "natural" immunity against a strain of Haemophilus may not necessarily be due to exposure to that strain itself. Conversely, lack of immunity to *H. influenzae* may be due to failure to encounter a bacterium of another species possessing the appropriate specific polysaccharide. These suggestions are speculative and require further investigation; they may prove to be important not only for elucidation of the role of natural immunity in providing protection against infection by *Haemophilus influenzae* but also as a basis for possible development of artificial immunization against this often fearsome organism.

Neisseria Meningitidis

This is a Gram-negative diplococcus which is the causative agent of meningococcal meningitis and which is frequently carried in the nose. The carrier rate varies, and there is no constant relationship between the number of carriers and incidence of meningeal infection. In normal persons, the carrier rate is taken to be about 5 per cent but can rise to about 50 per cent without producing any appreciable increase in the incidence of meningitis in the community.

Most surveys of meningococcal carriage rates have been carried out on communities of young adults, particularly people serving in armed services because epidemics were not uncommon in such communities. Little attention has been directed to colonization by meningococci in the newborn and in children, or to the carriage rate. However, it is known that when epidemics do occur, there is often a coincidental increase in the number of carriers[3] and it is thought that increased carriage is a reflection of increased infection rates rather than the converse.

The meningococcus is of importance as an upper respiratory tract colonizing bacterium because, when it is present, it is usually carried in the nose. Meningococcal meningitis is unusual during the first 3 months of life and extremely uncommon from birth to the age of 4 weeks. The most susceptible age group is 0–5 years and, thereafter, the incidence declines progressively with each succeeding quinquennium.

Neisseria meningitidis is divided serologically into four main groups, these being designated A, B, C and D.[10] Serological group B is regarded as the most virulent of the four groups and it is the one mainly responsible for epidemics of meningitis; it includes those strains that are most often sulphonamide-resistant. Furthermore, Group B is the least homogeneous of the three groups and includes a number of strains of differing antigenic properties. This variability has been studied[65,66] and it has been suggested that susceptibility to meningococcal meningitis may be a failure to develop immunity to all the types that may be encountered.

Diplococcus Pneumoniae

Diplococcus pneumoniae (the pneumococcus) is very commonly found in the nasopharynx of normal people at all ages and it is the commonest infective agent that causes lobar pneumonia. Since the advent of penicillin, that disease has declined considerably in importance; it is usually aborted early in its course by appropriate specific therapy so that classical progression through the well-known clinical and pathological stages is now seldom seen.

For this reason, little attention is now paid to the epidemiology of pneumococcal carriage. In former days, however, when outbreaks of pneumococcal sepsis did occur through lack of specific remedial agents, the typing of pneumococcal types was of some importance and over eighty different serotypes have been defined by antigenic analysis of capsular polysaccharides.[17]

Because of the diversity of types, children are more susceptible than adults because of their more limited experience of the possible range of pneumococci that may be encountered, and the incidence of pneumococcal meningitis is similar to that of the meningococcal form.

As the child becomes older, pneumococcal meningitis declines—especially after the age of 5—because subclinical infection can elicit immunity against further infection.[27] However, since there are so many different types it is unlikely that comprehensive immunity against all pneumococci can be achieved. Pneumococci can still, therefore, cause a variety of infections in children, especially in those that are particularly vulnerable to infection in general.

The Streptococci

Streptococci are frequently isolated from the throats of normal adults and children. The commonest and almost constant inhabitant of the throat is *Streptococcus viridans*—so called because of the green colour of the colonies on appropriate culture medium. It is α-haemolytic and generally behaves as a commensal organism. Its greatest pathological importance lies in its ability to cause subacute bacterial endocarditis in people with damaged hearts[15] and it is not infrequently isolated from dental abscesses. *Streptococcus viridans* is a ready secondary invader, particularly where there is pre-existing damage or infection, so that it may also be incriminated in middle ear, chest and wound infections.

The more virulent β-haemolytic *Streptococcus pyogenes* (known more commonly as the "haemolytic strep.") is not a normal member of the healthy nasopharynx, though symptomless carriers of this bacterium are often found. It was first described by Rosenbach in 1884[57] and has been consistently recognized as a cause of dangerous infection from that time.

The haemolytic streptococci are nowadays classified according to the serological typing method of Lancefield[45] and the most virulent human pathogen belongs to serological group A (this variety being implicit in the term "Haemolytic strep." when it is used in common parlance). *Streptococcus pyogenes* causes a variety of pyogenic and systemic infections ranging from cellulitis and otitis media to an overwhelming septicaemia. It can cause not only puerperal sepsis in the mother but can infect the umbilicus of the newborn.

Haemolytic streptococci of Lancefield Group A have remained consistently and without exception sensitive to penicillin. However, this is no cause for complacency since the very highly virulent nature of the bacterium still makes it a life-threatening organism that can cause severe illness with great rapidity.

At a further remove, *Streptococcus pyogenes* can cause

acute glomerulonephritis, acute rheumatic carditis, occasionally erythema nodosa and (though less frequently nowadays) scarlatina. For these reasons it cannot be regarded as a desirable inhabitant of the nasopharynx of a child, even when no immediate symptoms are produced.

Other Groups of Streptococci

A number of other haemolytic streptococci may be found in the throat of a child. *Streptococcus faecalis* is mentioned elsewhere in this discussion as a normally-occurring bacterium in the intestine; it is a member of Lancefield Group D and may frequently be found in the throat. It can also cause endocarditis.

Of the remaining Lancefield groups, Group B may be found as a commensal in the human throat and vagina (though it is primarily a parasite of cattle) and has been identified as a cause of neonatal meningitis[70] though it is generally of very low virulence in the human. Groups H and K—again strains of low virulence—have been found in the human throat and Group F, which can uncommonly cause abscesses associated with the intestine, has also been recovered from the nasopharynx.

In addition to the α- and β-haemolytic streptococci, a variety of non-haemolytic streptococci (typified by *Streptococcus salivarius*) may be present as commensals in the mouth and nasopharynx. Though not of great pathological significance, one member of this non-haemolytic group, *Streptococcus mutans*, is regarded as active in the production of dental caries. In this condition it may act in conjunction with *Lactobacillus odontolyticus* which is mentioned elsewhere in this discussion.

Other Micro-organisms of the Mouth and Nasopharynx

A spirochaete known as *Borrelia vincenti*, together with a variety of other spirochaetes, is a normal inhabitant of the mouth. It is usually associated with a fusiform bacillus called *Fusiformis fusiformis* which is an obligate anaerobe and often classified as a member of the group *Bacteroides*. These two organisms are of importance because, in conjunction, they cause the highly contagious Vincent's angina.

The remaining organism of importance in a child's mouth is the yeast *Candida albicans* which is described separately at the end of this chapter.

COLONIZATION OF THE FEMALE GENITAL TRACT

From the viewpoint of bacterial colonization of the genital tract, there are certain differences between vagina and vulva; these differences being based on the more exposed position of the vulva and the physiological conditions within the vagina.

Vagina

The vagina is sterile at birth, the first bacteria appearing during the 1st day of life. These bacteria consist essentially of faecal streptococci (Enterococci), staphylococci (including white varieties) and diphtheroid bacilli.

At the age of 2 or 3 days, these early colonizing bacteria are almost totally replaced by Döderlein's bacilli,[22] which are members of the Lactobacilli—acid-producing and acid-tolerant bacteria. The presence of Lactobacilli is dependent upon the glycogen content of the vaginal "mucosal" cells, glycogen deposition being dependent in turn on circulating oestrogens[21] derived from the maternal circulation.

Thus the vaginal secretions rapidly become acid through the fermentative action of the Lactobacilli on the vaginal glycogen, and conditions are produced which are less favourable for the existence of other vegetative (as opposed to spore-bearing) bacteria. However, the maternal oestrogens are soon excreted by the infant and the vagina reverts to the immature alkaline pre-pubertal state.

The vaginal flora now includes staphylococci (both *aureus* and *albus* varieties), faecal Gram-negative bacilli (*Escherichia*, *Klebsiella*, *Proteus* etc.), diphtheroids i.e. non-pathogenic *Corynebacteria*, and various streptococci.

With the onset of increased oestrogen secretion in adolescence, Döderlein's bacilli reappear, but the vaginal flora remains mixed and a pattern of colonization is established which persists until the menopause. The mature flora includes the bacteria already listed, and it should be noted that *Mycoplasmata* and fungi (including *Candida albicans*) may be isolated from vaginal material. The pattern of streptococcal colonization varies from one individual to another. *Streptococcus viridans* is frequently found, but streptococci of Lancefield Group A are found only infrequently. But streptococci belonging to other Lancefield groups, such as Groups F, G and B may be isolated fairly frequently. There is some controversy about the significance of anaerobic streptococci in vaginal secretions. These bacteria are relatively difficult to isolate and typify,[16] though it has been held that they comprise part of the normal vaginal flora.[74]

The flora of the lower female genital tract is extremely complex and, apart from the species already mentioned, various bacteria that are difficult to identify may be found, particularly by anaerobic methods. However, highly pathogenic varieties—either aerobic or anaerobic—are seldom found.

The pattern of colonization in both mature and immature female genital tracts is obviously a reflection of the bacteria found in the environment. In the newborn girl, the bacteria colonizing the vagina are samples of those already present in the mother, attendants, other children around and the place in which the baby is housed. In the older girl, the vaginal flora is derived largely from the bacteria resident in or on other parts of her body, the mature pattern being modified by the physiological condition obtaining at the time in the vagina (in particular, the degree of acid production).

Vulva

The vulva of the new-born child—like the vagina—is sterile at birth and remains so for a few hours. Thereafter, because of the exposed site, bacteria from the immediate environment begin to colonize and a complex flora soon becomes established. The bacteria found resemble those seen in the vagina at various stages of the girl's development (including any fungi that may be present) though large numbers of faecal bacteria predominate. At the same time, "skin bacteria" like Sarcinae (Gram-positive, packet-forming, non-pathogenic cocci) and *Staphylococcus albus* are present in appreciable numbers.

Bacteria of the Anterior Urethra

There is little of note in the bacterial population of the anterior urethra in either male or female normal children. The bacteria which may be isolated include diphtheroids, staphylococci or various micrococci, "coliforms" and other enteric bacteria. The *Mycoplasma* group is frequently represented.

In health, the higher reaches of the urinary tract are usually regarded as being sterile.

CANDIDA ALBICANS

Though this chapter is concerned with bacterial colonization of the developing child, any discussion of microbial flora would be incomplete without reference to the yeast-like fungus *Candida albicans*, otherwise known as *Monilia*.

A number of different members of the genus *Candida* are known, but *Candida albicans* is prominent as a cause of candidiasis.[61] The fungus is carried in the mouth, vagina and intestinal tract of some 40 per cent of normal people. It is usually acquired by the newborn baby from the mother and, thereafter, remains as a constituent of the infant's "normal" flora. When manifestations of candidiasis occur later, they are usually caused by overgrowth of the child's own *Candida*, that is to say, the infection is endogenous rather than the result of contagion or cross-infection.

In paediatric practice, the first and the commonest form of candidiasis is oral thrush, and this occurs particularly if the yeast is acquired during the first few days of the infant's life;[64] in this condition *Candida* acts as a primary infective agent. It can adopt a secondary role in childhood (and also in later life) in diabetes mellitus, when it may cause vulvo-vaginal candidiasis and, again, oral thrush.

Candida albicans overgrowth may also complicate antibiotic therapy.[54] In such a case, a variety of infections caused by the fungus may ensue; these range through recurrent oral thrush to intestinal and pulmonary infections, endocarditis, septicaemia and even meningitis. Candidiasis may complicate the use of corticosteroid drugs and may accompany a wide variety of malignant and debilitating conditions.

ACKNOWLEDGMENT

My thanks are due to Mrs. Lynda Burns for typing the manuscript.

FURTHER READING

Davies, P. A. (1971), "Bacterial Infection in the Fetus and Newborn," *Arch. Dis. Childh.*, **46,** 1–27.

Jawetz, E., Melnick, J. L. and Adelberg, E. A. (1970), *Review of Medical Microbiology*, (9th edition. Oxford and Edinburgh: Blackwell Scientific Publications.

Williams, R. E. O., Blowers, R., Garrod, L. P. and Shooter, R. A. (1966), *Hospital Infection. Causes and Prevention*, 2nd edition. London: Lloyd–Luke.

REFERENCES

1. Adinolfi, M., Glynn, A. A., Lindsay, M. and Miln, C. M. (1966), "Serological Properties of γA Antibodies to *E. coli* Present in Human Colostrum," *Immunology*, **10,** 517–526.
2. Alexander, M. B. (1948), "Infant Diarrhoea and Vomiting (A Review of 456 Infants Treated in a Hospital Unit for Enteritis)," *Brit. med. J.*, **ii,** 973–978.
3. Aycock, W. L. and Mueller, J. H. (1950), "Meningococcus Carrier Rates and Meningitis Incidence," *Bact. Rev.*, **14,** 115–160.
4. Baber, K. G., Corner, B., Duncan, E. H. L., Eades, S. M., Gillespie, W. A. and Walker, S. C. B. (1967), "A Prospective Study of Staphylococcal Infection and its Prevention Among Infants and Mothers After Childbirth in Hospital and at Home," *J. Hyg., Camb.*, **65,** 381–393.
5. Barrie, D. (1965), "Incubator-borne *Pseudomonas pyocyanea* Infection in a Newborn Nursery," *Arch. Dis. Childh.*, **40,** 555–558.
6. Barrie, D. (1966), "Staphylococcal Colonization of the Rectum in the Newborn," *Brit. med. J.*, **i,** 1574–1576.
7. Basch, R. S. (1965), "Inhibition of the Third Component of the Complement System by Deviations of Aromatic Amino Acids," *J. Immunol.*, **94,** 629–640.
8. Box, Q. T., Cleveland, R. T. and Willard, C. Y. (1961), "Bacterial Flora of the Upper Respiratory Tract. Comparative Evaluation of Anterior Nasal, Oropharyngeal and Nasopharyngeal swabs," *Amer. J. Dis. Child.*, **102,** 293–301.
9. Bradshaw, W., Schneerson, R., Parke, J. C. and Robbins, J. B. (1971), "Bacterial Antigens Cross-reactive with the Capsular Polysaccharide of *Haemophilus influenzae* Type b," *Lancet*, **i,** 1095–1097.
10. Branham, S. E. (1953), "Serological Relationships Among Meningococci," *Bact. Rev.*, **17,** 175–188.
11. Brimblecombe, F. S. W., Cruickshank, R., Masters, P. L., Reid, D. D. and Stewart, G. T. (1958), "Family Studies of Respiratory Infections," *Brit. med. J.*, **i,** 119–128.
12. Brumfitt, W., Willoughby, M. L. N. and Bromley, L. L. (1957), "An Evaluation of Sputum Examination in Chronic Bronchitis," *Lancet*, **ii,** 1306–1309.
13. Bullen, C. L. and Willis, A. T. (1971), "Resistance of the Breast-fed Infant to Gastro-enteritis," *Brit. med. J.*, **3,** 338–343.
14. Bullen, J. J., Rogers, H. J. and Leigh, L. (1972), "Iron-binding Proteins in Milk and Resistance to *Escherichia coli* Infection in Infants," *Brit. med. J.*, **i,** 69–75.
15. Cates, J. E. and Christie, R. V. (1951), "Subacute Bacterial Endocarditis. A Review of 472 Patients Treated in 14 Centres Appointed by the Penicillin Trials Committee of the Medical Research Council," *Quart. J. Med.*, **20,** 93–130.
16. Colebrook, L. and Hare, R. (1933), "Anaerobic Streptococci Associated with Puerperal Fever," *J. Obstet. Gynaec.*, **40,** 609–629.
17. Cooper, G. M. and Walter, A. W. (1935), "Application of the Neufeld Reaction to the Identification of Types of Pneumococci," *Amer. J. publ. Hlth.*, **25,** 469–474.
18. Cooper, M. L., Keller, H. M., Walters, E. W., Partin, J. C. and Boye, D. E. (1959), "Isolation of Enteropathogenic *Escherichia coli* from Mothers and Newborn Infants," *Amer. J. Dis. Child.*, **97,** 255–266.
19. Cottom, D. G. (1966), "Neonatal Sepsis," *Practitioner*, **197,** 338–344.

20. Cruickshank, R. (1925),' '*Bacillus bifidus:* Its Characters and Isolation from the Intestine of Infants," *J. Hyg., Camb.*, **24,** 241–255.

21. Cruickshank, R. and Sharman, A. (1934), "The Biology of the Vagina in the Human Subject," *J. Obstet. Gynaec.* **41,** 190–207.

22. Döderlein (1892), *Das Scheidensekret Und seine Bedeutung fur das Puerperalfieber*. Leipzig.

23. Eggerth, A. H. and Gagnon, B. H. (1933), "The Bacteroides of Human Feces," *J. Bact.*, **25,** 389–413.

24. Evans, C. A., Smith, W. M., Johnston, E. A. and Giblett, E. R. (1950), "Bacterial Flora of Normal Human Skin," *J. invest. Derm.*, **15,** 305–324.

25. Farmer, K. (1968), "The Influence of Hospital Environment and Antibiotics on the Bacterial Flora of the Upper Respiratory Tract of the Newborn," *N.Z. med. J.*, **67,** 541–544.

26. Finegold, S. M., Posnick, D. J., Miller, L. G. and Hewitt, W. L. (1965), "The Effects of Various Antibacterial Compounds on the Normal Human Fecal Flora. *Ernaehrungsforschung*, **10,** 316–341.

27. Finland, M., Brown, J. W. and Barnes, M. W. (1940), "Immune Reactions of Carriers and Non-carriers of Type-specific Pneumococci, a Bacteriological and Immunological Study of Hospital Contacts," *Amer. J. Hyg., Sect. B.*, **32,** 24–37.

28. Finland, M., Jones, W. F. and Barnes, M. W. (1959), "Occurrence of Serious Bacterial Infections Since the Introduction of Antibacterial Agents," *J. Amer. med. Ass.*, **170,** 2188–2197.

29. Forfar, J. O., Keay, A. J., Maccabe, A. F., Gould, J. C. and Bain, A. D. (1966), "Liberal Use of Antibiotics and its Effect on Neonatal Staphylococcal Infection, with Particular Reference to Erythromycin," *Lancet*, **ii,** 295–300.

30. Fothergill, L. D. and Wright, J. (1933), "Influenzal Meningitis. Relation of Age Incidence to the Bacteriocidal Power of Blood Against the Causative Organism," *J. Immunol.*, **24,** 273–284.

31. Gell, P. G. H. and Coombs, R. R. A. (1968), *Clinical Aspects of Immunology*. Oxford and Edinburgh: Blackwell Scientific Publications.

32. Gillespie, W. A., Simpson, K. and Tozer, R. C. (1958), "Staphylococcal Infection in a Maternity Hospital: Epidemiology and Control," *Lancet*, **ii,** 1075–1080.

33. Gindrat, J.-J., Gothefors, L., Hanson, L. Å. and Winberg, J. (1972), "Antibodies in Human Milk Against *E. coli* of the Serogroups Most Commonly Found in Neonatal Infections," *Acta Paediatr. Scand.*, **61,** 587–590.

34. Glover, J. A. (1948), "The Paediatric Approach to Tonsillectomy," *Arch. Dis. Childh.*, **23,** 1–6.

35. Glynn, A. A. (1968), "Lysozyme: Antigen, Enzyme and Antibacterial Agent," *Scientific Basis of Medicine Annual Reviews*, pp. 31–52.

36. Györgi, P., Norris, R. F. and Rose, C. S. (1954), "Bifidus Factor. I. A Variant of *Lactobacillus bifidus* Requiring a Special Growth Factor," *Arch. Biochem. Biophys.*, **48,** 193–201.

37. Hare, R. and Ridley, M. (1958), "Further Studies on the Transmission of *Staph. aureus*," *Brit. med. J.*, **i,** 69–73.

38. Hinton, N. A. and MacGregor, R. R. (1958), "A Study of Infections Due to Pathogenic Serogroups of *Escherichia Coli*," *Canad. Med. Ass. J.*, **79,** 359–364.

39. Hurst, V. (1960), "Transmission of Hospital Staphylococci Among Newborn Infants. Colonization of the Skin and Mucous Membranes of the Infants," *Paediatrics*, **25,** 204–213.

40. Iyengar, L. and Selvaraj, R. J. (1972), "Intestinal Absorption of Immunoglobulins by Newborn Infants," *Arch. Dis. Childh.*, **47,** 411–414.

41. Jacobs, S. I., Holzel, A., Wolman, B., Keen, J. H., Miller, V., Taylor, J. and Gross, R. J. (1970), "Outbreak of Infantile Gastro-enteritis Caused by *Escherichia coli* 0.114," *Arch. Dis. Childh.*, **45,** 656–663.

42. Jameson, J. E., Mann, T. P. and Rothfield, N. J. (1954), "Hospital Gastro-enteritis. An Epidemiological Survey of Infantile Diarrhoea and Vomiting Contracted in a Children's Hospital," *Lancet*, **ii,** 459–465.

43. Karzon, D. T. and Henderson, D. A. (1966), "Current Status of Live Attenuated Virus Vaccines," in *Advances in Paediatrics*, Vol. XIV (S. Z. Levine, Ed.). Year Book Medical Publishers, Inc.

44. Kneeland, Y. (1930), "Studies on the Common Cold. The Upper Respiratory Flora of Infants," *J. exp. Med.*, **51,** 617–624.

45. Lancefield, R. C. (1933), "A Serological Differentiation of Human and Other Groups of Haemolytic Streptococci," *J. exp. Med.*, **57,** 571–595.

46. Masters, P. L., Brumfitt, W., Mendez, R. L. and Likar, M. (1958), "Bacterial Flora of the Upper Respiratory Tract in Paddington Families, 1952–4," *Brit. med. J.*, **i,** 1200–1205.

47. Mata, L. J. and Urrutia, J. J. (1971), "Intestinal Colonization of Breast-fed Children in a Rural Area of Low Socioeconomic Level," *Ann. N.Y. Acad. Sci.*, **176,** 93–109.

48. Moro (1908), *Pfaundler–Schlausman*, American edition, **3,** 288 (*Cited by* Snyder, M. L., 1940), "The Normal Fecal Flora of Infants Between Two Weeks and One Year of Age," *J. infect. Dis.*, **66,** 1–16.

49. Nash, F. W., Mann, T. P. and Haydu, I. W. (1965), "An Outbreak of Streptococcal Infection in a Maternity Unit," *Postgrad. med. J.*, **41,** 182–184.

50. Perkins, F. T., Yetts, R. and Gaisford, W. (1958), "Serological Response of Infants to Poliomyelitis Vaccine," *Brit. med. J.*, **2,** 68–71.

51. Pittman, M. (1931), "Variation and Type Specificity in the Bacterial Species Haemophilus Influenzae. *J. exp. Med.*, **53,** 471–492.

52. Plueckhahn, V. D. (1961), "The Staphylococcus and the Newborn Child," *Brit. med. J.*, **ii,** 779–785.

53. Ridley, M. (1959), "Perineal Carriage of *Staph. aureus*," *Brit. med. J.*, **i,** 270–273.

54. Robinson, H. M. (1954), "Moniliasis Complicating Antibiotic Therapy," *Arch. Dermatol.*, **70,** 640–652.

55. Rogers, K. B. (1951), "The Spread of Infantile Gastro-enteritis in a Cubicled Ward," *J. Hyg. (Lond.)*, **49,** 140–151.

56. Rogers, K. B. and Koegler, S. J. (1951), "Inter-hospital Cross-infection of Epidemic Infantile Gastro-enteritis Associated with Type Strains of *Bacterium Coli*," *J. Hyg. (Lond.)*, **49,** 152–161.

57. Rosenbach, F. J. (1884), *Microorganismen bei den Wundinfektions Krankheiten des Menschen*. Wiesbaden.

58. Ross, C. A. C. and Dawes, E. A. (1954), "Resistance of the Breast-fed Infant to Gastro-enteritis," *Lancet*, **i,** 994–998.

59. Salton, M. R. J. (1957), "The Properties of Lysozyme and its Action on Micro-organisms," *Bact. Rev.*, **21,** 82–100.

60. Shallard, M. A. and Williams, A. L. (1966), "Studies on Gram-negative Bacilli in a Ward for New-born Babies," *Med. J. Aust.*, **2,** 455–459.

61. Skinner, C. E. (1947), "The Yeast-like Fungi: Candida and Brettanomyces," *Bact. Rev.*, **11,** 227–274.

62. Snyder, M. L. (1936), "The Bacterial Flora of Meconium Specimens Collected from Sixty-four Infants Within Four Hours After Delivery," *J. Paediat.*, **9,** 624–632.

63. South, M. A. (1971), "Enteropathogenic *Escherichia coli* Disease: New Developments and Perspectives," *J. Paediatr.*, **79,** 1–11.

64. Taschdjian, C. L. and Kozinn, P. J. (1957), "Laboratory and Clinical Studies on Candidiasis in the Newborn Infant," *J. Paediat.*, **50,** 426–433.

65. Thomas, L., Smith, H. W. and Dingle, J. H. (1943), "Investigations of Meningococcal Infection. II. Immunological Aspects," *J. clin. Invest.*, **22,** 361–373.

66. Thomas, L. and Dingle, J. H. (1943), "Investigations of Meningococcal Infection. III. Bactericidal Action of Normal and Immune Sera for the Meningococcus," *J. clin. Invest.*, **22,** 375–385.

67. Torrey, J. C. and Reese, M. K. (1945), "Initial Aerobic Flora of Newborn Infants. Selective Tolerance of the Upper Respiratory Tract for Bacteria," *Amer. J. Dis. Child.*, **69,** 208–214.

68. Tunevall, G. (1953), "Studies on *Haemophilus influenzae:* Haemophilus Influenzae Antigens Studied by the Gel Precipitation Method," *Acta path. microbiol. scand.*, **32,** 193–197.

69. Turk, D. C, and May, J. R. (1967), "*Haemophilus influenzae. Its Clinical Importance*. London: The English Universities Press.

70. Turner, E. K. (1959), "Neonatal Meningitis," *Med. J. Aust.*, **ii**, 806–808.
71. Wardlaw, A. C. (1962), "The Complement-dependent Bacteriolytic Activity of Normal Human Serum," *J. exp. Med.*, **115**, 1231–1249.
72. Warren, R. J., Lepow, M. L., Bartsch, G. E. and Robbins, F. C. (1964), "The Relationship of Maternal Antibody, Breast Feeding, and Age to the Susceptibility of Newborn Infants to Infection with Attenuated Polioviruses," *Paediatrics*, **34**, 4–13.
73. Weiss, J. E. and Rettger, L. F. (1937), "The Gram-negative *Bacteroides* of the Intestine," *J. Bact.*, **33**, 423–434.
74. White, E. (1933), "On the Source of Puerperal Infections with Anaerobic Streptococci," *J. Obstet. Gynaec.*, **40**, 630–632.
75. Williams, R. E. O. (1961), "Carriage of Staphylococci in the Newborn. A Comparison of Infants Born at Home with Those Born in Hospital," *Lancet*, **ii**, 173–175.
76. Williams, R. E. O. (1964), "Sex Distribution of Colonization and Infection with *Staphylococcus aureus* in the Newborn," *Lancet*, **i**, 274–275.

45. THE PHARMACOLOGY OF THE FETUS, BABY AND GROWING CHILD

SHELAGH GILL AND JOHN A. DAVIS

INTRODUCTION

"Most power to do most harm, least knowing ill;"

(*Shakespeare—Love's Labour's Lost.*)

The thalidomide tragedy, still unfolding after a decade, first brought home to us what is the theme of this chapter: that drugs acting on developing organisms may have effects different in both quality and magnitude from those predictable from experiment or experience in creatures which have reached maturity. Modern drugs are powerful agents, usually designed to influence metabolic processes in patients or in parasites which may share such processes with their hosts; and it is hardly surprising therefore that as such as they should sometimes cause untoward effects, particularly in tissues involved in cell division or maturation.[23] But quite apart from the question of increased vulnerability to side-effects, the absorption, distribution, break-down and elimination of drugs will, to a great extent, depend on the efficiency and capacity of the tissues and body compartments concerned, that is, on their functional maturity and relative size, and these in turn may be differently affected by disease processes in children as compared to adults. Thus dosage in children cannot be easily extrapolated from schedules appropriate for adults and it will be relatively easy to give too much or too little, too often or not enough, to achieve a desired result. The temperament of children has also to be taken into account in prescribing a drug to be given by a certain route over a specified period, bearing in mind that vehicles designed to make a drug palatable may themselves have effects locally or systemically. Knowledge in this field has, to date, been acquired largely through a process of haphazard trial and random error helped out by animal experiment.

The pages that follow are largely concerned with the observed effects of certain drugs or groups of drugs on fetuses and children. It is not possible at the time of writing to claim that more than a small proportion of such effects are understood in terms of general principles that are capable in turn of generating reasonable predictions about the possible effects of agents not yet tried; but enough is known for it to be mandatory that certain questions should be answered by every clinician before he causes a new drug to be administered to a pregnant woman or an infant: these being:

Are the properties of the drug, clinical and pharmacological, such that one might suspect their actions on growing tissues could be different in quality or magnitude from those described in adults—bearing in mind that many of the side-effects of drugs in adults are referable to effects on rapidly multiplying cells such as those of the bone marrow, gut lining and skin?

Will it be likely to cross the placenta from mother to fetus?

Is the drug likely to be absorbed more or less completely or rapidly by children than adults?

What is the distribution of the drug in adults and how will this vary in children according to the different sizes of their body compartments (total body water, extra-cellular fluid, fat—including myelin, plasma albumen as carrier, etc.); and is it likely to be concentrated in particular tissues as, for example, iodine is in the thyroid gland?

Is the effective plasma or tissue concentration the same as in the adult? For instance in the newborn infant adequate plasma levels of digitalis exceed the limits of tolerance in the adult.[106]

Are known or predictable side-effects in adults—such as vitamin deficiency or enzyme induction—likely to have more serious effects on children, and how far are these preventable.

How is the drug broken down in the adult and what is the nature and distribution of the products? Is the process one that requires enzyme induction in the first instance; and if it takes place in the liver, how will it be affected by the peculiarities of the hepatic circulation in the fetus and by the propensity of the fetus to swallow its own urine with recirculation of possibly toxic end products?

Are genetic factors involved and can the congenitally vulnerable be identified? Will it interact with other drugs as regards action or breakdown?

How is the drug eliminated in the adult and can the fetal or infantile kidneys be expected to achieve the same result in a given time bearing in mind their low glomerular filtration rate per nephron which may more than balance their smaller tubular reabortive capacity?

It is possible for drugs or their metabolites, or substances formed under their influence, to be incorporated in tissues being laid down once and for all—such as myelin or teeth.

Are there any actions of the drug likely to interfere with the organizers of tissue maturation or the organized induction of enzymes; as for instance, steroids in some species interfere with psychosomatic sexual differentiation, or with growth itself directly or indirectly?

Finally, how far should the age and condition of the child influence the taking of a known or possible risk (such as the administration of chloramphenicol to a newborn baby with meningitis)?

Taking into account all these factors, it will be apparent that the testing of drugs on growing animals will not yield more than superficial reassurance unless specific attention is given to choosing species likely to share the vulnerability of a human infant to a particular agent at a certain stage in development and bearing in mind its likely concentration and duration of action in the tissues at risk.

Clinical trials in normal pregnant women and children below the age of consent are ethically unjustified[40] and the requisite knowledge must be acquired by the slow accumulation of carefully observed and recorded clinical experience. It is therefore incumbent upon the paediatrician, when employing a new drug, to keep careful notes and to use all the resources available to monitor not only its actions but also the way in which it is handled by the body systems concerned with its absorption, distribution and excretion. Only in this way will paediatric pharmacology become more than a matter of random trial and error, bearing out Voltaire's well known taunt that the practice of medicine consists in giving drugs of which one knows little to patients of whom one knows less.

Almost every other section of this book contains information of relevance to paediatric pharmacology and should be referred to when questions arise relating to particular systems. What follows in this chapter is largely a catalogue of unwanted effects of drugs on the fetus and infant, taking for granted that their desirable effects are known and achieved by correct dosage. We hope that in some possible future edition the subject will have reached the "sure path of a science." At present it is very incomplete natural history and must be presented as such.

In discussing specific effects resulting from drug exposure in pregnancy and childhood, the term "drug" itself requires discussion. In the context of paediatrics any definition of the term must be a wide one, such as "a chemical agent affecting the metabolism of the mother or fetus or of the child."

To catalogue completely the possible actions and interactions of prescribed and self-administered drugs would be an almost impossible task. Once suspicion is voiced additional evidence is often forthcoming. Unfortunately the full effects and side-effects of maternally administered drugs on the fetus or child may not be immediately obvious and indeed may not be recognized for many years. Thus the carcinogenic potential of stilboestrol when used in pregnancy[47] has only recently been recognized in offspring reaching puberty. This gap between drug administration and the recognition of side-effects assumes greater importance in view of the fact that many of the drugs now on the market have only been introduced during the past twenty years.

Retrospective analysis of the effects of a drug is difficult even when the interval between drug administration and the investigation is short. In the case of thalidomide retrospective analysis showed that the available records were as often as not incomplete and that it is unreasonable to rely on the memories of doctors or patients for information on whether a drug has been prescribed, collected from the chemist and actually taken as instructed.[104] Records will also be incomplete because patients may not recognize that simple household remedies such as laxatives and analgesics that are obtainable without prescription are, in fact, drugs. The extent to which some drugs are used by pregnant women has been made clear by a number of studies which suggest that aspirin and antacids, for example, may be taken by up to 60 per cent of the pregnant population. Similarly, patients will not report spontaneously the use of alcohol or tobacco and will rarely admit to using addictive or abortificant drugs.

When considering the possible overall effects of drugs used in paediatric practice, either before they are prescribed or in a retrospective analysis, it is important to understand the many different factors that may influence their action. The general principles relating to the effects of physiological, environmental, genetic and pharmacological factors on drug action are fully discussed elsewhere.[54,96,113]

In summary, a drug's action (and potential toxicity) depends upon its

Method of administration	Nature Presentation Biological availability Absorption
Quantity taken	Dosage Duration of use
Tissue levels reached and duration of action	Distribution Metabolism Excretion
Interactions with other drugs given over the same period.[25,35]	

When the effects of drugs on the fetus are considered the timing of drug administration in relation to pregnancy is critical.

The administration of a drug and the quantity taken can with care be controlled by the physician; but the blood levels attained and the duration of action will be partly determined by the physiology of the individual patient, which in turn depends upon her genetic make up and previous exposure to drugs.

The rate of metabolism of many drugs is to some extent genetically determined; for example, the rate of acetylation varies considerably in individual patients who show different susceptibilities to drug action and toxicity.

UNTOWARD EFFECTS OF DRUGS ON THE DEVELOPING FETUS AND NEONATE

Agents Affecting the Fetus When Taken Before Conception

While direct evidence of damage to the human fetus is not always available, the following groups of drugs are suspected of possibly affecting the fetus if used before pregnancy.

Drugs Causing Chromosome Damage

Toxic effects on chromosomes are reported to occur with the use of perphenazine and, to a lesser degree, chlorpromazine. Chromosome abnormalities have also been reported in patients treated with lysergide (LSD) though this was possibly an artefact.

Cytotoxic Drugs

Some of the drugs now used in anti-cancer therapy are suspected of causing chromosome damage and inducing abnormal cell division. Drugs such as azothiaprine and cyclo-phosphamide are sometimes used in children for the treatment of nephritis and auto-immune disease; their possible effects on future reproduction and puberty are unknown. Present evidence suggests that reproductive capacity may not be affected when cyclophosphamide is used in boys.[9] When used in adult human males cyclophosphamide may cause sterility due to azoospermia which is probably permanent, while amenorrhoea (and possibly early menopause) is seen in women receiving this drug. Men previously treated with azothiaprine have later fathered normal children.[37] Animal experiments suggest that the use of these drugs in the female before conception may reduce fertility or litter size (resorptions) but teratogenic effects have not been reported.

Anaesthetic Gases

Evidence suggests that continuous exposure to operating theatre concentration of anaesthetic gases reduces fertility in the female and exposure during pregnancy leads to early spontaneous abortion, possibly due to an increased incidence in congenital malformation.[57] In the male exposure appears to affect the sex-ratio of the offspring.[12]

Drugs Used to Induce Ovulation

The use of these drugs may result in multiple pregnancies.

Drugs Used to Prevent Conception

These drugs may act by interfering with ovulation or implantation and it is now suggested that they may have long-term effects on maternal metabolism; for example, previous use of the "pill" may affect the fetus. In susceptible women Vitamin A levels are high for some months after cessation of treatment and such high levels may possibly be teratogenic.[42] The frequency and severity of respiratory distress syndrome in the newborn seem to be reduced after pre-pregnancy use of oral contraceptives and there is a possibility of an increased chance of subsequently delivered infants being female. It is also reported that neonatal jaundice in breast fed babies is associated with the taking of oral contraceptives prior to conception.[128]

Drugs Taken During Pregnancy

When discussing the possible adverse effects of drugs taken during pregnancy, it is important to bear in mind that some drugs, such as antibiotics used in the treatment of syphilis, have beneficial effects on the fetus.

The greatest problem in avoiding adverse effects of drugs on the fetus is that during the first three months of gestation, the period of greatest risk in pregnancy, the doctor and indeed the patient may be unaware that conception has occurred. Therefore in prescribing those drugs known to be contra-indicated in pregnancy,[116,123] it is important to check the date of the last period and to do a pregnancy test.

Drugs taken by the female after conception, but before implantation, have been shown in animal experiments to reach the pre-implantation blastocyst.[112] It is thus conceivable that drugs, particularly those which may accumulate in the uterine secretions, could harm the conceptus before implantation and this is relevant to the introduction of a "morning after" contraceptive pill.[124]

An important problem encountered with drug treatment during pregnancy is that of achieving complete records of maternal medication. This is difficult when information is distributed amongst the records of general practitioners, Local Authority clinics, gynaecologists and paediatricians and becomes even more complicated if other services are involved. For example, dentists may prescribe the use of trimethoprin and sulphamethoxazole, a combination of drugs which is suspected to be teratogenic, while psychiatrists may use mono-amine oxidase inhibitors (MAOI drugs), in which case the use of pethidine or general anaesthetics during labour is contra-indicated.

Drugs taken by the mother during pregnancy can affect the fetus in either or both of two ways; either directly after passage of the drug or its metabolites across the placenta, or indirectly by interfering with maternal or placental metabolism. The idea that the placenta is a selective barrier, protecting the fetus from harmful drugs, has had to be revised as an increasing number of drugs administered to mothers have been shown to damage the fetus.

Comparison of a review of ten years ago[81] with one published recently[45] shows that our knowledge of the basic mechanisms by which drugs pass the placenta has increased but little; however, our interpretation of the data available has improved and the application of new techniques may soon answer some of the outstanding questions.

In summary, the mechanisms of placental transfer are:

Simple diffusion	for example, oxygen	
Facilitated diffusion	for example, glucose	substances necessary for growth and development
Active transport	for example, Ca^{++}	
Special processes (for example, pinocytosis).	for example, antibodies	

Few of the substances necessary for the growth and development of the fetus cross the placenta by simple diffusion: that is, transfer along a concentration gradient; but other mechanisms ensure adequate supplies of nutrients to the fetus. Most drugs and drug metabolites, however, have been found to reach the fetus by simple diffusion, the exceptions being drugs with a structural similarity to amino acids, for example, methyl-dopa and the antimetabolites. This implies some selectivity on the part of the placenta, which has a very high metabolic activity. When the passage of drugs across the placenta is considered they have usually been classified into two groups, depending upon the ease with which they might be expected to cross from mother to fetus. Drugs which readily cross the placenta, such a thiopentone, are usually of small molecular weight, poorly ionized and highly lipid soluble, while drugs which cross only with difficulty, for example, d-tubocurarine, are of high molecular weight, highly ionized and of low solubility.

This distinction becomes less certain when we consider the factors influencing the diffusion of a drug across a semi-permeable membrane, such as the placenta, from an area of high concentration to one of low concentration. These factors are:

Surface area
Membrane thickness
Membrane pore size
Blood flow on each side
Perfusion pressure differences
Concentration gradient
Molecular configuration
Molecular size
Ionic dissociation
Lipid solubility
Differential solubility
Differential protein binding

The metabolites of a drug in the first group may have the characteristics of a drug in the second group and so cross the placenta more easily than expected. Moreover, it is thought that the surface area of the placenta increases towards the end of pregnancy, so that drugs given to the mother towards the end of pregnancy should reach the fetus in greater quantity than if given in the first or second trimesters. In abnormal pregnancies, in the course of which drugs are most likely to be prescribed, many of the factors listed above will operate; for example, during therapy the concentration gradient of a drug is in favour of transfer while therapeutic (high) maternal blood levels are maintained. Perfusion pressure is often increased in disease, such as toxaemia, and placental damage may increase the size of the placental "pores."

Drugs and drug metabolites do not need to cross the placenta to influence the fetus: they may also affect it indirectly by interfering with maternal or placental metabolism. This is difficult to predict as the placenta has a high metabolic rate and may itself be responsible for changes in drug metabolism in pregnancy. Ways in which drugs can affect the fetus indirectly include interference with:

(1) Placental blood flow—so reducing oxygen supply (this danger exists with migraine tablets and other vasospastic drugs);

(2) placental metabolism, which may be stimulated by previous drug exposure;

(3) facilitated diffusion—so reducing the supply of essential nutrients to the fetus;

(4) maternal enzyme systems;

(5) osmotic or electrolyte balance in the mother—the placenta does not act as a barrier to such changes which are reflected in the fetal blood;

(6) hormonal function of the placenta—this may be reflected in developing fetal systems such as those governing steroid hormone secretion;

(7) increased or decreased placental transfer of other drugs—animal experiments have shown that phenobarbitone reduces placental transfer of DDT, probably as a result of the increased rate of maternal metabolism, though altered blood flow and protein binding must also be considered. Similarly the effects of previous long-term drug therapy (or drug abuse) can increase the transfer of drugs across the placenta;

(8) interference with parturition—in animals this results from maternal administration of anti-inflammatory drugs and is possibly due to prostoglandin inhibition.

Transfer of drug from maternal to fetal circulation is related to the maternal plasma level of drug which, in turn, is dependent upon dose, formulation, bioavailability, route of administration, timing of administration, duration of dosage, rate of absorption, distribution, metabolism (which may be affected by the pregnant state) and excretion.

The amount of drug or metabolite reaching the placenta will be controlled by the maternal blood level and by the blood flow through the placenta from both mother and fetus.

Placental Metabolism of Drugs

The placental metabolism of most drugs has not been studied. Placental metabolism itself may be altered by drugs, such as steroids. Because of this the possible effects of drugs or their metabolites on the fetus are difficult to evaluate since it is often not known which compounds reach the fetus or in what concentration.[53,59]

While little is known of any differences in drug *distribution* in pregnancy, autoradiographic studies in animals suggest that some drugs may have a greater affinity for developing fetal tissues than for maternal tissues. If this is so, accumulation will occur and some studies of neonatal blood levels of drug compared with maternal levels have confirmed this possibility. Accumulation is also seen in the fetus with coumarin-type anti-coagulants as a result of another mechanism: the degree of ionic dissociation of maternal drug is related to blood pH and under normal conditions many drugs are only weakly ionized; the un-ionized molecules cross the placenta but as they do so the maternal equilibrium alters and more drug molecules become available to the fetus. Changes in ionization related to placental transfer can thus affect the relationship between fetal and maternal blood level of drug. The equilibrium will be altered still further in favour of drugs reaching the fetus if either redistribution, tissue binding or fetal metabolism reduce the fetal blood levels of drug.

It can be stated as a general rule that nearly all drugs given to a pregnant woman will reach the fetus or affect its well-being indirectly by effects on the mother or placenta.

Fetal Metabolism of Drugs

This is an almost unexplored field, but it is safe to say that metabolism will vary with the age of the fetus as enzyme and metabolic pathways develop.[36,92,96] Similarly excretory patterns change as the fetus develops. At first compounds are excreted through the skin and later by way of the developing kidneys. Excreted products reach the amniotic fluid and to some extent diffuse back to the mother. Other metabolites pass back to the mother across the placenta. But there is always the possibility that a drug that has been metabolized by the fetus may cross the placenta in reverse less easily than the parent drug, so reaching high concentrations in the fetus and amniotic fluid. Any drug accumulating in the amniotic fluid will again pass through the fetus as the fluid is swallowed.

The possible harmful effects of drugs taken after conception are reviewed elsewhere[3,26,95,116] and may be classified as follows:

Drugs Affecting Organogenesis

Teratogenic effects on the fetus will be seen with drugs administered while embryogenesis is proceeding; that is, before the twelth week of pregnancy. Drugs given to prevent or terminate conception are often given during this period. A few substances are known to be teratogenic from *clinical experience.* Those well-documented include thalidomide, aminopterin and ergometrine,[11,33,63] while maternal alcoholism has recently been reported to damage the fetus.[52]

Many common substances are implicated from *animal experiments,* for example, aspirin, caffeine, methaqualone and, predictably, anti-cancer drugs that act by inhibiting cell division or blocking biosynthetic pathways.

Some drugs have been implicated as a result of *retrospective human studies;* for example, anti-epileptic drugs in relation to cleft palate[39,66,67,86,89] while aspirin[103] barbiturates and antacids[87] are all associated, not necessarily causally, with a higher incidence of abnormalities than the 2–5 per cent which is average. Though cytotoxic drugs such as cyclophosphamide, which may have to be taken during pregnancy in the presence of malignant disease or to prevent rejection of an organ allograft, might be expected to be teratogenic, this is not substantiated by the reports on the outcome of pregnancies in which such drugs were administered during the first trimester. It is in fact difficult to correlate laboratory results and clinical experience particularly in retrospective studies, and more difficult still to interpret the possible effects and interactions of the many factors concerned. Animal work suggests the existence of "proteratogens," that is, non-teratogenic substances that can potentiate the teratogenic activity of other drugs which when used alone at the same dose level are non-teratogenic.[26]

The following classes of drug have been implicated by observation or animal experiment as potentially teratogenic.

Vitamins and Substances of Dietary Origin The presence or absence of specific substances in the diet may be teratogenic or the diet may influence the absorption or metabolism of teratogens. It has been suggested that compounds present in blighted potatoes may cause spina bifida.[102] Subnormal levels of folic acid and ascorbic acid are teratogenic in animals and may be so in humans. Vitamin D deficiency causes embryonic rickets while in animals excess Vitamin D causes bone changes, particularly in the skull.[93] Abnormal levels of trace elements can effect the fetus; thus both deficiency and excess of iodine can induce cretinism and also brain damage. There is evidence that iodine administered during pregnancy may induce goitre in the fetus while selenium and magnesium are implicated as teratogens from the results of animal experiments. Low maternal protein levels may affect free blood levels of drug and drug metabolism and therefore result in teratogenic effects in the fetus. Diet can also influence the gut flora and in certain circumstances this may result in the conversion of harmless compounds into carcinogens and teratogens.

Contaminants in Food, Water or Atmosphere. Substances in the environment may be proteratogens (*see above*), for example, DDT and other pesticides and possibly food additives or preservatives. These substances can also affect drug metabolism and placental drug transfer so that teratogenic levels of drugs or their metabolites may reach the fetus. Heavy metal poisoning can damage chromosomes and upset cell division. Lead and mercury are present in the atmosphere and possibly in the diet. Toxic levels of mercury have been found in fish[84] and lead accumulates in wine prepared at home in lead-glazed containers.

Fluoride content and the "hardness" of water supplies influence the incidence of congenital goitre and infant mortality.[29]

Abortifacients. Ergometrine used as an abortifacient is associated with the occurrence of Poland's anomaly (cutaneous syndactyly and absence of pectoralis major).[33]

Psychotropic Drugs. The subject has been reviewed by Kelsey.[55] Amphetamine has been implicated in the aetiology of biliary atresia but on the strength of one case report[64] while imipramine has been associated with congenital anomalies[15] as has chlordiazepoxide.[16] Lithium may induce goitre.[110]

Effects on Growth In Utero

Such effects are seen with drugs taken later in pregnancy and may often be caused by drugs that are teratogenic if taken earlier. They are due to interference by drugs or their metabolites with developing fetal systems, but at the lowest level may produce only a reduction in fetal size, possibly related to drug effects on the placenta and maternal metabolism. The effects of a specific drug on fetal growth and development may sometimes resemble the effects seen in the adult following overdosage or prolonged use of the same drug. While this may occasionally indicate which fetal system is at risk, such predictions cannot always be made since fetal drug metabolism, which changes as the fetus develops, may be different from that in the adult. At varying stages of fetal development different systems will be at risk. These include the following:

Fetal Growth. Smoking reduces fetal size and causes prematurity, possibly by causing chronic carboxyhaemoglobinaemia which affects the fetal more than the maternal blood and reduces oxygen delivery to the fetus.[13]

Chlorpropamide augments the effects on the fetus of the presence of maternal diabetes.[56]

Steroids in large doses over a period depress fetal growth resulting in the birth of a small for dates baby.[127]

Sexual Differentiation. Androgenic drugs and synthetic progestins such as norethisterone and progesterone can cause fetal masculinization, the degree of which depends upon the timing of maternal drug administration.[50] In animal experiments drug exposure during intra-uterine life has later prevented normal sexual maturation[55] and psycho-sexual orientation is disturbed through an action on the developing hypothalamus at a critical stage of maturation.[125]

Special Senses. The aminoglycoside antibiotics—streptomycin, kanamycin and gentamycin—are ototoxic, damaging the cochlea[130] as may nortriptiline.[114]

Chloroquine and the phenothiazines have been reported to damage the retina and quinine to cause deafness.[123]

Theoretically the Central Nervous System of the fetus is particularly vulnerable from 12–18 weeks. During this period the high blood phenylalanine levels or abnormal metabolism of phenylketonuric mothers may cause mental retardation in their normal offspring.[10]

Lung Maturation. Maternal heroin addiction appears to promote the neonatal surfactant producing mechanism[46,120] as does treatment with dexamethasone;[65] both however interfere with growth while promoting maturation.

Kidney. The kidney is at risk during the fetal life and after birth until maturation is complete at adolescence. Gentamycin, cephalosporin and the tetracyclines are known to be nephrotoxic.

Liver. Drugs which are enzyme inducers, for example, the barbituates, alcohol and DDT, will affect the maturation of enzyme systems in the fetal liver[28,71] as will some substances inhaled when smoking such as benzpyrene[129] and the diazapemes. This effect may be beneficial.

Calcified Tissues. Developing bones and teeth may be affected by chelating agents, for example, the effects of the tetracyclines are well documented.[83] Excess Vitamin D produces abnormal bone development[43,93] and excess fluoride may have a similar effect.

Soft Tissues. Defective collagen development has been reported after penicillamine[77] used for the treatment of Wilson's disease and rheumatoid arthritis[7], which prevents the cross linkage of elastin and collagen; however, this is so far a unique instance and the association may have been a chance one.

Skin. Rashes on fetal and neonatal skin are seen after maternal ingestion of many drugs including chloral, aspirin, barbiturates, sulphonamides and bromides. Occasionally more severe forms of dermatitis have been recorded. Diazoxide affects the growth of hair.[75]

Blood. Aspirin and anti-epileptic drugs can affect the fetal and neonatal clotting mechanisms[18,69,80] Agranulocytosis has been reported in babies of mothers taking amidopyrine. This subject has recently been reviewed by Pocheldy.[97]

Thyroid. Fetal goitre has been associated with maternal administration of lithium, codeine and antithyroid drugs such as thiouracil. Goitres may be big enough to obstruct labour or to cause respiratory obstruction. The subject has been reviewed by Shirkey.[110]

Emotional Development. No substantiated human examples exist, but evidence from animal work suggests that maternally administered drugs can influence the later emotional development of offspring (*see below*).

Drug Dependence. This can be induced in the fetus and neonate and is seen after chronic maternal medication with opiates.[99,124]

Some drug induced effects in the fetus are latent, a further stimulus being needed before they become manifest: for example, puberty appears to be the stimulus for the development of adeno-carcinoma of the vagina in daughters of mothers treated with stilboestrol for threatened abortion early in pregnancy.[47] The female offspring of stilboestrol treated animals were infertile. Some maternally administered drugs have been shown to induce tumours in fetal animals suggesting that the embryo is extra-sensitive to carcinogens, possibly due to differences in fetal as compared to adult metabolism or to an increased sensitivity of dividing cells. To date, maternally administered drugs have not been shown in the human situation to affect subsequent puberty in the offspring, but some authors have expressed concern over possible future effects of the steroidal contraceptive pills when these have been taken inadvertently during pregnancy. At least in theory latent behavioural effects in the offspring due to maternal drugs may be triggered by subsequent experiences.

Other developmental effects, including tissue destruction, may be seen after maternal administration of drugs that cause constriction of the uterine, placental or fetal blood vessels; for example, general anaesthetics and sympathomimetic drugs.

Drugs Given During Labour

Practically all drugs used in obstetrics have been shown to cross the placenta, for example, pethidine and chlorpromazine and their metabolites have been found in both amniotic fluid and neonatal urine. The passage of drugs across the placenta during labour follows the principles discussed above. Thus the highly soluble barbiturates reach the fetus within minutes of maternal administration, while skeletal muscle relaxants such as suxamethonium reach the fetus only if present maternally in very high concentrations.[109] However, the amount of drug reaching the fetus cannot be estimated from its chemical nature alone. The following factors must also be considered:

(1) Timing of administration prior to delivery.
(2) Dose of drug.
(3) Route of administration.
(4) Maternal drug redistribution—including protein binding and storage in maternal adipose tissue.
(5) Duration of drug action (dependent upon rates of metabolism and excretion).

These factors will affect the maternal blood level of drug and therefore levels of drugs or metabolites in the fetus. A drug given just prior to delivery will probably still reach the fetus if administered intravenously, while it may take over sixty minutes to reach mazimum fetal blood levels of maternal drugs administered subcutaneously or intramuscularly. Towards the end of labour placental blood flow and therefore drug passage may be difficult to estimate and will probably be irregular due to contractions.

The timing of drug administration before delivery may also affect fetal blood levels of drug due to:

(1) Drug metabolism by the fetus.
(2) Drug passage back across the placenta to maintain equilibrium as maternal drug is metabolized or redistributed.
(3) Possible drug redistribution in the fetus.

Residual Effects on the Newborn Infant

Pre-natally acquired drugs, often those administered to the mother during labour, will be detoxicated and excreted slowly by the fetus due to a combination of the following factors:

The immature kidney of the neonate.[49]

The poor development of the enzyme systems for drug conjugation and excretion, especially glucuronide formation.[61]

The frequency of acid-base disturbance in the neonatal period.

The poor control of blood glucose levels in the neonate.

The tendency of the neonate to hypothermia especially when narcotic drugs are present.

The poor protein binding capacity of the neonatal blood especially in premature infants with respiratory distress syndrome (RDS).

Elimination of maternally acquired drugs by the fetus is slow and drugs excreted as glucuronide may be present for 7–10 days after birth. Their effects are not usually observed after the first weeks of life, that is, they are not permanent. However, perinatal mortality may be increased due to the effects of maternally administered drugs.

The effects of maternal drugs commonly show in the neonate[82,116] as:

Depressed respiration, prolongation of primary apnoea or asphyxia—after morphine and barbiturates.[68,78]

Neonatal depression and inactivity—after reserpine, diazepam and pethidine. Diazepam is cleared very slowly by the baby.[116A]

Nasal congestion and snuffles which in the newborn may be life threatening—after reserpine.

Poor feeding—following maternal sedation in labour or at the end of pregnancy, especially with chlorpromazine.

Periodic breathing; poor temperature control—after diazepam.

Hypothermia—after pethidine.

Electrolyte imbalance—after diuretics.

Neonatal tremors—after diuretics.

Hypo/hyper/glycaemia—after insulin and oral hypoglycaemic drugs.

Haemorrhagic disease and neonatal purpura—after oral hypoglycaemic drugs.

Increased clotting times—after barbiturates, anti-epileptic drugs and aspirin.

Kernicterus at lower bilirubin levels; after Vitamin K, with protein bound drugs such as long acting sulphonamides and chlorpromazine.

Kernicterus with high bilirubin levels—neonatal thrombocytopaenia and haemolytic anaemia—after thiazides.

Circulatory collapse—after chloramphenicol.

Skin rashes—after many maternally administered drugs, for example, bromides and aspirin.

Apparently poor CNS development—after tranquillizers, sedatives.

Increased motor activity/sleeplessness—after MAOI drugs, imipramine.

Neonatal convulsions—as withdrawal effect if mother is a drug addict, seen with morphine and barbiturates.

Paralytic ileus—after ganglion blocking drugs, for example, hexamethonium.

Transient myasthenia—if mother has been treated for that condition with neostygmine.

Hypothyroidism—after iodides and thiouracil.

General Anaesthetics

All general anaesthetics cross the placenta very rapidly. The respiratory depression seen in a baby is always related to the depth and duration of maternal anaesthesia.

Nitrous oxide—depression of the neonate is unusual with maternal analgesic levels of the drug; babies are reported "sluggish" after prolonged use, but this may be due to the drug or to long delivery times.

Cyclopropane—fetal depression is minimal in the first 10 min. of maternal administration.

Tribromoethanol—should not be used as it gives prolonged depression of the neonate due to poor detoxication as the glucuronide.

Trilene—fetal concentrations are higher than maternal after 16 min. administration. After prolonged use neonatal depression is seen.

Barbiturates—ultra short acting barbiturates cross the placenta very rapidly but do not appear to cause undue neonatal depression.

Local Anaesthetics

Long acting local anaesthetics such as bupivacaine with adrenaline are used for epidural anaesthesia. This type of block results in lower maternal blood levels of drug than paracervical block and is therefore safer for the fetus.

High maternal and therefore fetal concentrations of local anaesthetics can cause fetal acidosis and bradycardia. This is to be expected if poor injection technique results in injection of local anaesthetic into fetal tissues and fetal death has been reported after paracervical and caudal anaesthesia. The breakdown by the neonate of local anaesthetics with an amide structure is only slow so prolonged neonatal depression is possible.

Mepivacaine; bupivacaine; propitocaine; lignocaine are all reported to cause fetal or neonatal depression and possibly also all can cause neonatal methaemoglobinaemia which has been reported after prilocaine and propitocaine.

Drugs Used to Induce or Delay Labour

Oxytocin—may predispose to neonatal jaundice.

Prostaglandins—no reference in literature to adverse effects.

β-agonists—no adverse effects reported over a decade.

Drugs Taken During Lactation

During lactation drugs can reach the baby from creams applied to the nipples and from nipple shields, formerly lead, now made from plastics, or by way of the milk. Little is known quantitatively about the passage of drugs into milk. It is an excretory mechanism so fat soluble drugs or drug metabolites might be expected to be present. Maternal antibodies reach the neonate in the milk and maternal infection can reach the child by the same route.[24,58,116B,121]

In principle the idea has been known for centuries; for example, the old midwives' tales relating maternal rhubarb and infantile diarrhoea. A more modern example in animal husbandry suggested that penicillin is found in cows' milk in sufficient concentration to prevent blue mould growing in Stilton cheese. Further analysis has shown that most antibiotics tested reach the infant in near therapeutic concentrations by way of the milk.

Most of the quantitative data available relates to drugs used for treatment of chronic maternal conditions like epilepsy and schizophrenia, but even where considerable information is available recommendations about breast feeding are very inconsistent and uncertain. As little is known about the long term effects of drugs or metabolites reaching the baby in this way, it may be best to avoid breast feeding unless it can be shown by analysis, preferably for the individual patient, that the amount of drug or metabolite reaching the child is insignificant. The possible effects of drugs reaching the child in this way will resemble those of drugs given to the neonate (*see below*), for example:

Drug or metabolite may be toxic to infant because of poor excretion.

Drug or metabolite may interfere with growth or development of the neonate.

Drug or metabolite may interfere with circadian rhythm development.[74]

Drug or metabolite may interfere with emotional development.

Drug or metabolite may cause sensitization of the baby, e.g. penicillin.

Other conditions where the maternal milk may be toxic to the infant include maternal beri-beri, where the reduction in the co-enzyme activity can lead to abnormal metabolism and accumulation of toxic products in the milk, and also inborn errors of metabolism and allergic conditions of the child. Breast feeding after maternal radioactive iodine is contra-indicated as it will result in destruction of the infant's thyroid gland. Occasionally unexpected or abnormal maternal metabolism of drugs can cause toxic symptoms in the baby.

In 1956 in Turkey hexachlorbenzene from treated grain in maternal diet was responsible for an epidemic of fatal fever, vomiting and skin lesions in babies.[31] Monosodium glutamate (MSG) has been reported to reach the milk and to cause CNS damage in baby animals. This compound is used in many "convenience" foods.

A further possibility known from animal experiments is that carcinogenic principles may be transferred from mother to offspring in the milk. This has lead to the suggestion that if breast cancer is viral in origin, then daughters of mothers who have had this disease should not be breast fed.

Some maternal drugs reduce the secretion of milk, for example, atropine, nicotine and the "pill," and secretion can be stopped by steroid treatment. Drugs commonly taken during lactation include both those prescribed and those taken by the mother, but not prescribed, such as laxatives.

The following have all been shown to cross in the milk and may exert an effect, long or short term, in the infant.

Laxatives—infant diarrhoea after senna, rhubarb.
Tranquillizers; sedatives; hypnotics—most drugs in these groups appear to cause some depression of the baby and consequently poor attention and feeding.
Tetracyclines—little staining of teeth occurs as the levels reaching the baby are low.
Penicillin (also from cows milk)—can cause sensitization and establishment of penicillin resistant organisms.
Salicylates—rashes in baby.
Sulphonamides—rashes in baby.

Unless the role of maternal drugs in the aetiology of the above conditions is appreciated neonatal mobidity will result. Many are self-perpetuating. For instance, the reduced ability of the infant in the presence of drugs to overcome hypothermia means that a greatly prolonged period of low temperature reduces still further the rate of drug metabolism and excretion which however is slow because of immaturity. The "vicious circle" that develops prolongs drug action still further and since the cold, depressed infant also feeds badly, enzyme development may also be slower than normal, again reducing the rate of drug detoxication and excretion. Drug effects will become more marked if poor feeding leads to dehydration and higher blood levels of drug. Adult therapeutic levels of maternal drugs are often recorded in the infant at least 4 days after birth and there is no way of knowing if these are harmful to the infant. Occasionally neonatal blood levels of maternally administered drugs are found to be higher than the corresponding maternal levels. This may be due to accumulation of the drug, for example, anti-coagulants by the fetus or to redistribution of fetally acquired drugs due to the changes in blood chemistry occurring at birth. When very high blood levels of drugs persist in the neonate, exchange transfusion may be the most logical way to reduce them. Stimulation of the infant's metabolism by enzyme inducing drugs, for example, phenobarbitone, takes a few days, is unreliable when the temperature is low, and may present the additional problem of possible drug inter-actions. Anticoagulants given to the mother are protein bound and the fetus or neonate may escape problems until another protein bound drug is administered and interaction occurs.[25]

PHARMACOLOGY OF THE BABY AND CHILD

Because the tissues and organ systems of the baby are in process of development, the toxic effects seen may be very different from those expected in the adult and different tissues may be at risk. As a general rule the toxicity of a drug may be expected to be greater in children than in adults; moreover, drug metabolism and excretion is often slower in the baby than in the adult and may not follow the same pathways. The formation of different metabolites may be responsible for unexpected toxic effects, often not looked for nor recorded because the patient cannot report them. The toxicity of a drug given to a baby is likely to be related to the following factors:

Genetic constitution, e.g. in congenital glucose-6-phosphate dehydrogenase deficiency, many drugs are capable of inducing haemolysis.[122]
Maturity of the kidneys—in immature kidneys there is poor renal clearance and accumulation can occur,[49] for example, with gentamycin.[76] Penicillin clearance is proportionate to that of creatinine.[72]
Enzyme development—this is incomplete in the neonate and therefore conjugation and detoxication may be slow leading to higher than expected blood levels of drugs. On the other hand, if enzyme induction has occurred because of exposure to drugs *in utero*, drug metabolism may be greater than expected and result in lower than expected blood levels of some drugs.
Protein binding—Protein binding of drugs in the newborn is unpredictable. If jaundice is present bilirubin may compete for binding sites (as will hydrogen ion in acidaemia) making the blood level of unbound and active drug achieved higher than might normally be expected. Alternatively, if the drug is more strongly bound to protein than bilirubin the latter will be dispersed and may cause kernicterus at relatively low bilirubin concentrations.
Organ sensitivity—some developing organs appear exceptionally sensitive to certain drugs. The neonatal retina is sensitive to high oxygen tension and exposure to excessive concentrations causes retrolental fibroplasia. Immature erythrocytes are sensitive to nitrites in water and to oxidizing drugs with the development of methaemoglobinaemia after limited exposure.
Distribution—body compartments in the baby are relatively as well as absolutely different in size from those in the adult. Babies have a higher total body water and a higher ratio of extra to intra-cellular fluid. Immature babies are relatively thinner, whereas most older infants are

fatter than most adults. The brain is relatively larger but contains a much smaller proportion of myelin than it does at maturity.

Central nervous system (CNS)—The central nervous system in babies is not fully developed and access of drugs to the CNS may also be different from that in adults. An example is the atropine sensitivity of young children.

Developing diurnal rhythms—These will affect the response to a drug such as steroids whose effect in supporting ACTH secretion depends upon the timing of administration.

In older children these factors will be of a diminishing importance as maturity is achieved. Other factors of importance include:

Plasma to tissue ratio—this decreases as a child develops and therefore plasma concentrations of drugs will vary with age.

Sex hormones—development of sex hormone production may affect response to drugs.

Effect on regulating mechanisms—propranolol appears to inhibit renin secretion.[22]

Diet—when body protein stores are low as in starvation, children cannot detoxicate drugs and certain substances may become carcinogenic.

Emotional experiences—These can affect hormone production, for example, adrenal steroid, and thus the metabolism of drugs such as the anti-convulsants.

The effect of the disease process on drug absorption—a fatality has been reported in a constipated child treated with a normal dose of neostygmine[21] due to enhanced absorption.

Thus it is difficult to predict either the toxic or therapeutic effects of a drug from available adult data. However, some reported drug effects may be related to adult data; for example, penicillin and carbenicillin are neurotoxic in babies because of poor renal clearance as they are in adults with reduced renal function.

Side Effects of Prescribed Drugs

Drugs used for long term treatment of children present additional problems to those encountered when drugs are prescribed for short term use. The dangers of unexpected side-effects and the problem of finding a suitable dosage and dosage form are still present but in addition dosage will have to be continually monitored as the child matures and increases in weight. Most important perhaps are the unknown effects of such therapy on the later development of the child or adult or on the offspring of parents subjected to long term therapy as children. This later consideration becomes increasingly important when drug therapy initiated during childhood is continued into adulthood; for instance, the use of penicillamine may become routine in the treatment of rheumatoid arthritis and its possible effects if given in pregnancy overlooked.

The ways in which drugs may affect the growth and development of babies, children and adolescents are essentially similar to those already described in the fetus after the completion of organogenesis, with the difference that ingress is via the gut rather than the placenta. The action may be "cidal" leading to the death of a proportion of cells or "static" by a slowing down or speeding up of cell multiplication. However, in certain tissues the capacity for cell division may be lost before conditions for multiplication are re-established in which case no catch-up is possible and a permanent deficit results. Some drugs act directly on cellular processes, others indirectly via regularizing mechanisms or by affecting nutrition. The developing science of paediatric pharmacology is concerned with the formulation of general principles whereby such actions will become understandable and predictable: the act of prescribing for children involves balancing the primary beneficial effects of drugs, including those which promote growth and development, against side-effects which may hinder or distort them. Drugs commonly prescribed for children fall into the following classes which will be considered within the light of available information on the mode of action and known side-effects. Groups of drugs used for long periods in children include:

Antibiotics and Antibacterial Agents

Some of these drugs act via processes that are shared between micro-organisms and their hosts—a relationship particularly close in the cases of viruses; an example is, cytosine arabinoside; others on processes exclusive to various classes of parasite. In the former case, the higher rate of multiplication of the parasite makes it more vulnerable to the drug than host cells but the balance may be precarious in the case of rapidly dividing cells in growing tissues. Clearly the second class of drugs, of which penicillin is the example, is fundamentally preferable for use in children in whom the use of certain drugs in the first class should be eschewed except in life-or-limb-threatening situations. The mode of action of the commonly used chemotherapeutic agents has been usefully reviewed.[23]

Some side-effects of this class of drug are listed below:

Chloramphenicol—tends to accumulate in young infants because it is only poorly detoxicated as the glucuronide. Toxicity shows as poor feeding and muscle tone—the "grey syndrome." Long term administration can produce optic atrophy and topical administration deafness.[27] Chloramphenicol has been shown to inhibit diphenylhydantoin metabolism and thus to potentiate its toxicity.[14]

Salazopyrine—is excreted after acetylation.[108] Prolonged administration has been associated with folate deficiency and anaemia.[118]

Penicillin—may induce allergy but probably less commonly than believed. In massive doses it causes haemolytic anaemia and is neurotoxic.[115] A dosage schedule for the newborn has been worked out by McCracken and colleagues.[72]

Ampicillin—caused development of a rash in patient with glandular fever.

Nitrofurantoin; tetracyclines— both affect growth of teeth and bone up to 7 years of age.[83] Tetracyclines are catabolic and may interfere with growth.[91]

Nalidixic acid—can induce serious acidosis in the newborn as well as rashes and raised intra-cranial pressure.[6]

Streptomycin; neomycin; gentamycin; kanamycin—All aminoglycoside antibiotics are ototoxic. Toxicity can be seen after these drugs have been used topically as they are easily absorbed through raw surfaces.

Long-acting sulphonomides; novobiocin—in immature babies their use can result in kernicterus due to central nervous system penetration of unconjugated bilirubin released from protein binding sites.

Izoniazid and PAS—INAH can cause fits and encephalopathy in slow acetylators.[2] Both can cause optic nerve damage and damage to the liver.

The intestinal antiseptic diodoquin (an oxyquinnoline) has been incriminated in the aetiology of subacute myelo-optic neuropathy.[70]

Anticonvulsants and Sedatives

It may turn out to be no accident that most teratogenic drugs so far described have an effect on central nervous system function, making this class of agents particularly suspect; moreover, they are often taken for long periods without a regular check on blood levels. A further consideration is that their very effects on nervous tissue make it likely that they may have subtle effects on the organization of nervous activity in the growing child and some have effects on behaviour which may distort personality development.

Barbiturates—excitation rather than sedation is often seen in children, especially in cases of temporal lobe epilepsy. Phenobarbitone suppresses cough in babies without depressing respiration.

Sulthiame (ospolot)—causes overbreathing and confusional state. This drug interferes with the breakdown of phenytoin.[48]

Phenytoin—toxicity (ataxia, said sometimes to be permanent) due to overdosage is often seen in epileptic children. The drug also interferes with folate absorption and may cause rickets and lymphomata.

Dichlorpenamide—this long-acting carbonic anhydrase inhibitor sometimes used as an anti-convulsant can cause hypercalcuria in some subjects and so predispose to stone formation.

Chloral hydrate—is only very slowly detoxicated and excreted by babies; accumulation is therefore possible.

Some anticonvulsants interfere with absorption of dietary folate and with Vitamin D metabolism with indirect effects on growth.[20]

Vitamins

Study of inborn metabolic error makes it clear that the provision of excess co-factor may act on the balance of a number of metabolic transformations, making it likely that maximum levels are not necessarily optimal. A number of these substances are known to be poisonous in excess; for instance, Vitamin D induces hypercalcaemia and Vitamin A is toxic in large doses.

Anti-inflammatory Agents

Indomethacin; chloroquine—may cause corneal opacities.[85]

Steroids—see below.

Salicylates—may cause acidosis when given freely and are known to interfere with carbohydrate metabolism and blood glucose levels. In genetically susceptible subjects urticuria is a side-effect. They have been incriminated in the causation of Reye's Syndrome.

Anti-hypertensives

Hydrallazine and practolol can induce a condition resembling disseminated lupus erythematosus.[1,107]

Hormones

It is obvious that the administration of hormones or their analogues especially over long periods and in pharmacological doses is likely to interfere with the normal regularizing processes by which hormones influence fundamental physiological processes including growth and development. One may cite the different effects of ACTH and of the steroid hormones on the growth and development of children treated by either agent for the same condition.[41] In the same context the action of certain growth promoting steroids in advancing bone age is of particular importance since their use may in fact permanently limit the ultimate height attained while causing a short-term growth spurt.

Anabolic steroids may be oncogenic[51] possibly by virtue of their action in stimulating microsome activity.

Appetite Suppressants

Amphetamine is an addictive drug.

Fenfluramine may suppress growth hormone secretion,[119] interact with other drugs, can cause bad dreams and induces depression on withdrawal.[5]

Antispasmodics

There is now convincing evidence that excessive administration of sympathomimetic drugs, especially by aerosol in uncontrolled dosage, can cause death in childhood asthma.[79,117]

Overdosage with aminophylline causes circulatory disturbance.

Anaesthetics

In genetically susceptible subjects anti-cholinesterases such as succinylcholine may cause prolonged apnoea.

Some inhalation anaesthetics are liable to precipitate malignant hyperpyrexia in genetically susceptible individuals with certain kinds of ill-defined muscular dystrophy.[62] Children and especially mongols are atropine sensitive. Children as a class seem more than normally liable to unexpected death during anaesthesia

Digitalis, Diuretics

Digitalis dosage in children has been worked out emprically and different departments used different schedules.[30]

Digitalis given by intra-muscular injection may not be well absorbed.[111] Children tend to tolerate higher blood levels than adults;[106] and side-effects are different. Deaths from overdosage have been distressingly frequent.

Most diuretics lead to potassium depletion which in turn affects growth—possibly as a result of depressing hormone activities.[98]

Medication by Mother

For example, drugs administered by mother as a result of pressure advertising or the advice of grandmother. This group of drugs include many which are packed with only poor instructions for use in children (many bear no indication of the amount which is an overdose, or the possible side-effects), and often a fatal dose is available in the pack, as with many baby aspirins. Over-dosage is easy if the baby is small or dehydrated or mother is over-enthusiastic.

Commonly used drugs include the following:

Vitamins—Vitamin A in excess causes manifestations resembling scurvy (toxicity described after ingestion of polar bear liver by Eskimo infants). Syrups containing Vitamin C damage the teeth if used in dummies. Excess Vitamin C as "cold cure" can possibly precipitate sickle cell crisis in thalassaemia. Excess Vitamin D causes calcification of the cornea and will affect bone development. It may precipitate infantile hypercalcaemia with resultant brain damage, aortic stenosis and renal insufficiency.

Aspirin—babies are easily overdosed with resulting acidosis.

Vermifuges—piperazine in excess dosage causes ataxia, dizziness, vomiting and convulsions. It is contra-indicated if there is any history of previous neurological problems, especially epilepsy.

Creams, ointments and powders—topical steroids may be absorbed and cause side-effects. Substances such as borax used to treat nappy rash may be absorbed through the skin with the danger of systemic poisoning and exfoliative dermatitis. Hexachlorophane applied in concentrations of 0·5 per cent can be toxic and CNS damage has been reported.[31]

Sedatives—a number of substances are administered to babies by their mothers just to keep them quiet, especially if father is on shift work or the family live in a small flat with neighbours who are censorious. Many of these substances can cause apparently unexplained CNS depression or coma in a baby unless the possibility of their use is remembered.

Types of drugs so used include:

Teething remedies—alcohol is often used and intoxication is sometimes seen. Hypoglycaemia may result from the concurrent administration of alcohol and fructose. Mercury poisoning is rare, but "pink disease" still occurs occasionally from the use of old powders or formulae.

Cough mixtures—used every half-hour rather than every four hours and often in adult dosage; overdosage with drugs like codeine is easily reached with resulting respiratory depression.

Travel sickness remedies—these are unsuitable under 3 years of age, but few of the available products state this on the pack. Hyoscine overdose in babies is common. Antihistamines cause sedation.

Addictive drugs—mothers who are addicts will sometimes give their drugs to their children.

Poisoning

Therapeutic

Examples of poisoning in children from accidental drug overdose have been given previously. The most common cause of poisoning in children is carelessness, including:

Prescribing the wrong medicament—usually names are confused.

Prescribing the wrong strength medicament: for instance, digitalis is often prescribed without sufficient care.

Misinterpretation of prescription—usually of decimal point or drug name.

Failure to read prescription correctly—decimal point or dosage errors.

Failure to read label before administering the drug.

Administration to the wrong patient.

Underdosage or overdosage resulting from failure to shake suspensions such as phenytoin.

Overdosage resulting from the use of old alcoholic solutions which have evaporated.

Corneal ulceration resulting from the use of "stale," concentrated solution of silver nitrate.

Poor injection technique may lead to too high a drug concentration in one area—toxicity shown as tissue damage.

Additions to an infusion may be toxic because of incompatibilities.

Domestic

In the House or Garden. The incidence of poisoning of children in the home is now very different from what it was fifty years ago. Lead poisoning from paint still occurs in children living in old property, but arsenic poisoning from wallpaper and sweet wrappers is no longer seen. It has been replaced by poisoning with household chemicals and medicaments prescribed for other members of the family (and often no longer used but kept "just in case needed"). The drugs involved are most commonly analgesics or sedatives which are rarely kept locked away and both drugs and household or garden chemicals are often found decanted into unexpected containers; bleach is regularly found in lemonade bottles. The containers used for dispensing are rarely child-proof and some, such as "bubble packs," are even attractive to children. The children at most risk from poisoning in the home appear to be those of young mothers who have more than two children under school age.

Common Sources of Poisoning in Children

Aspirin—junior aspirins taste like sweets; packs contain a fatal dose for a child.

Barbiturates—easily obtainable—represent 9 per cent of N.H.S. prescriptions.
Iron poisoning—iron tablets (especially ferromyn, ferrograd, ferrous sulphate) look like sweets. Latent period before their effects are seen.
Anti-depressants—circulatory collapse and coma with disturbance of cardiac rhythm.
Hyoscine—anti-sea sickness pills.
Atropine—eye ointments in tubes are fascinating to children.
Strychnine—Easton's tablets or syrup cause convulsions which are often fatal.
The "Pill"—easily obtainable and bubble packs attract children—apparently harmless.
Antihistamines—CNS over-stimulation followed by depression.
Paracetamol—combined renal and hepatic failure.
Digitalis—picked up in grandparents' homes.
Bleach and disinfectant—common—perhaps due to children copying father at whisky bottle, or use of wrongly identified containers.
Coal tar products—large number of liniments, embrocations and inhalants found in most homes. Some are corrosive; others poisonous.
Kerosene—lung damage.
Paraquat—almost always causes fatal lung fibrosis with denaturation of surfactant.
Alcohol—CNS depression.
Camphorated oils—convulsions.
Phenolic compounds—severe tissue destruction; CNS depression.
Toadstools—hepatotoxic.
Berries or leaves—laburnum, yew and daphne are all poisonous.
"Pica"—earth eating leads to iron deficiency anaemia. Lead poisoning may result from chewing paint.

Any "delayed-release" tablets are particularly dangerous to children as toxic quantities of drug may be absorbed before their ingestion is suspended.

Self-poisoning

This is becoming increasingly common in younger children (10–17 years) with barbiturates and amphetamines taken for "kicks." Solvent sniffing is also a cause of poisoning, often causing liver damage.

Smoking of substitutes for cannabis, for example, Cat-Nip (also available as aerosol for pets!) can also lead to bizarre effects.

Drug Dosage in Babies and Children

In view of the preceding examples of the possible effects of drug overdosage in children, it is obviously important to control drug administration in babies and children very carefully. Little is known about optimal or safe doses for children of many drugs and there are problems in obtaining data.

Clinical trials in children are difficult to carry out and it is not always possible to assess the applicability of the results of studies in immature animals to clinical paediatric practice.

Until more data is available all drugs must be used carefully in babies and children and all possible information relating to blood levels and toxic effects should be fully documented. Even when a drug is recommended by the manufacturer for paediatric use there are problems in assessing suitable dosages and administration schedules. There are a number of rules for calculating doses for children, mostly related to the child's weight; but other factors such as hepatic and renal capacity for conjugation and excretion need also to be taken into account together with age and build.

There have only been a few studies in humans relating drug effects to size and age.[60] Both the therapeutic and toxic doses of drugs have been shown to be related to body surface area, the square of the cube root of weight, to extracellular fluid volume or to metabolic rate which in turn are related to one another, a relationship which holds as regards most drugs for both children and adults (depending upon the distribution of the drug in body fluids). The percentage method of estimating doses for children is based upon this relationship of which the derivation is described in detail elsewhere.[36]

This method is preferable to some of the earlier systems of calculating doses for children which give variable answers. The dose of aspirin required by a 10 kg. infant (based on an adult dose of 600 mg./kg.) is quoted[36] as varying between 24 and 168 mg. However, this is based on the adult dose of the drug and there is some evidence to suggest that babies and children respond differently from adults to some drugs. Certainly this method is not applicable to premature infants where the detoxication and excretory mechanisms are very immature, and all drug doses for such babies must be evaluated individually. There is no method for calculating doses that takes into account genetic factors or the effect of disease processes such as dehydration.[36] The therapeutic dose of any drug is only that recommended for the "average" patient who varies from a 45 kg. female to a 100 kg. male.

Some drugs used for long term treatment are also monitored individually before dosage is stabilized, for example, insulin, anti-convulsants and L-Dopa. Increasingly it is becoming apparent that drug side-effects will be reduced if therapeutic drug levels are not exceeded and methods of estimating drug dosages for patients related to their serum level are being developed. These are based on the "occupancy" principle,[94] defined as "the time for which a unit quantity of a substance, administered in a specific way, occupies a part of the body before it is broken down or excreted."

$$\text{Total daily dosage} = \frac{\text{Desired Serum Level} \times 24}{\text{Occupancy (hr.)}}$$

The use of the "occupancy" principle to estimating doses for children would appear to be the ideal answer but there are problems in its application. Desired serum levels are based on "normal" data and this is not available for babies; moreover obtaining the figure for occupancy for the patient involves taking a number of blood samples which may not always be feasible in a tiny baby.

The problem of obtaining "normal" data in babies is considered below[60] and also discussed by other authors.[36]

Since bio-availability will affect drug absorption, chemically equivalent drugs may not always give the same blood levels in the baby; for example, of the tetracyclines and digoxin. Bio-availability has been shown to be related to such factors as the excipient used, particle size and tablet compression. The latter can vary with different batches of the same preparation.

The steady state blood levels of a drug are affected by different routes of administration. The rapid rate of absorption following intravenous injections in babies can have the effect of saturating metabolic processes and of giving unexpectedly high drug levels.

Routes of Administration

Intravenous Injections

All injections should be made very slowly to dilute the drug as the small size and blood volume of the baby increases the danger of a "bolus" of drug reaching the heart. Substances given inadvertently into the umbilical artery may cause some necrosis in the area of distribution.

Sub-cutaneous and Intra-muscular Injections

These are often difficult in babies because of the small size and the danger of nerve damage occurring. Often it is advisable to split the injection and give it in two sites. Repeated injections are a problem because of trauma, haematoma and continued bleeding as well as slow absorption and muscle necrosis. One alternative method of administration is intra-peritoneal injection.

Intra-peritoneal Injections

These are used in neonates as drug is rapldiy absorbed from the large surface area. They may also be useful if the child has poor peripheral circulation or is oedematous when drug absorption from sub-cutaneous or intra-muscular sites will be poor and erratic.

Rectal Administration

This can be useful but is undignified. Electrolytes and body fluids for replacement are well absorbed.

Topical Administration

Potent creams and ointments applied to the skin of babies and children should be covered to prevent their being ingested or transferred to the eyes, but occluding the area treated may increase drug absorption.

Topical application of drops to the eyes is of little use; constant irrigation with antibiotics has to be employed before therapeutic levels are reached.

SUMMARY—Use of Drugs in Babies and Children

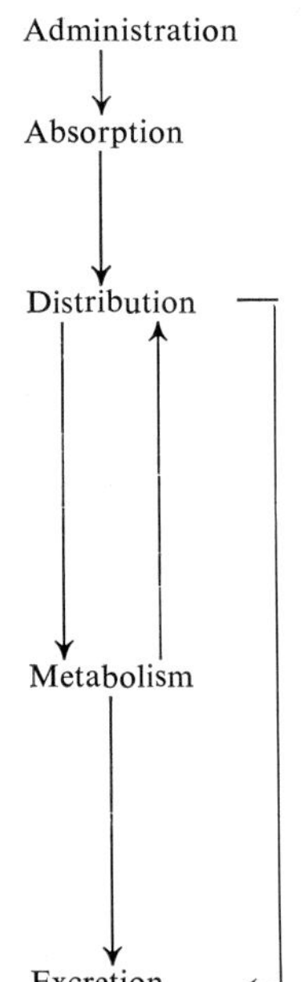

Formulation is important in relation to bio-availability. Not all routes are available in babies.

Absorption is very variable and timing in relation to feeds important. Diet, pH, intestinal flora and immaturity affect the bio-availability of drugs.

The baby has a large surface to volume ratio and the percentage of body water decreases with age; therefore in babies relatively high doses are required of drugs soluble in extracellular fluids. Toxic levels are easily reached if the baby is dehydrated.

Protein binding capacity is reduced in the presence of malnutrition, nephrosis and hepatic disease. Protein binding, fat storage and CNS transfer may alter with age.

In the newborn metabolism is slow if the temperature is low. Drug metabolizing enzymes develop as the baby matures, influenced by previous drug exposure. Metabolic rates in children may be different from those in adults giving different metabolic products and side-effects. Genetic differences in drug metabolism may be more important in babies than in adults.

Lung excretion may be important in neonate after maternal general anaesthesia.

The kidneys mature with age; if excretion is poor drug accumulation occurs. In the presence of dehydration some potentially nephrotoxic drugs can cause renal damage.

Finally, all these factors will be influenced by changes in acid/base balance.

Testing of Drugs Used in Pregnancy and Childhood

Some of the problems relating to the use of drugs in pregnancy and childhood have been considered previously. Before drugs can be used in either situation they must first be tested and as clinical trials are seldom justified in either situation, this can be very difficult. The main problems associated with testing drugs for use in these situations are as follows:

Species Differences in Pharmacological Activity

There are always difficulties in relating the results of animal tests to the human situation but these are intensified in pregnancy.

The placenta in different species varies in structure and function so that it is impossible to study placental passage of drugs in an animal model; also the metabolism of drugs and the placental passage of drugs or metabolites will be affected by placental metabolism which is often unknown in the human situation.

Animal models have been developed for testing for teratogenic agents but these can only give guide lines for drug usage. Individual differences in the rate of drug metabolism may still mean that teratogenic levels of a normally harmless drug can build up in some pregnancies.

Species differences in drug metabolism and detoxication mechanisms and in tissue distribution and protein binding make it very difficult to assess drug interactions and potentiation of teratogens in animal models.

Problems of Obtaining Information from the Fetus

Unfortunately most information about the effects of drugs on the fetus becomes available after the drug has been given "accidentaly" during a pregnancy. Usually, however, only information on the gross development of the fetus and later development of the baby is available.

In countries where therapeutic abortion is allowed, samples can be collected from the fetus to allow studies to be made of such facts as:

Blood levels of free drug in the fetus as related to absorption and distribution.

The presence and levels of drug metabolites in the fetus.

Enzyme levels in the fetus as a measure of possible enzyme induction by the drug.

Where the law allows experiments involving the fetus valuable information can be obtained by administering radio actively labelled drugs to the mother. This allows whole body auto-radiography studies of the fetus to be made, after abortion, which give an indication of the distribution of drug within the fetus. Further quantitative studies can also be made as drug assay is often easier when the isotopic marker is present.

Some information is, of course, available by analysis of the amniotic fluid during pregnancy; some drugs and metabolites being excreted into the sac. Also some information on the placental transfer of drugs has been obtained from studies carried out during or after labour when fetal blood samples have been obtained from the scalp and occasionally samples have been obtained *in utero* via the umbilical vessels, as when transfusions are carried out *in utero*.

At delivery further information on drug passage across the placenta can be obtained from the drug levels in the cord blood and in the first neonatal urine sample.

Problems of Obtaining Information from the Neonate

The small size of the neonate often means that only one or two small blood samples can be obtained. Unless there is a suitable micro assay for any drug suspected of being present then quantitative estimates are impossible. Suitable methods of assay may take a long time to develop as the metabolism in babies varies from that in adults and it may not be fully known. If a suitable method of assay is available small blood samples repeated every two to three days make it possible to follow the course of drug excretion by the baby. Urine samples though difficult to collect can also give information on drug metabolism and excretion.

Similarly when an assay is available drug dosage can be controlled using the "occupancy" principle referred to above. However, when repeated blood samples are required these can result in trauma to the baby and therefore they are probably best obtained via an umbilical catheter.

Testing Drugs in Children

When drugs are used in babies and children one big problem is often that their long term effects are not known (*see above*). Because of this, new drugs are used only where they appear to offer a decided advantage over established forms of therapy and their use would outweigh possible dangers. This means that it is not possible to obtain data relating to drug metabolism and blood levels in "normal" children; all data must come from patients. For maximum data to be available whenever a drug is used all clinical trials must be carefully planned.

Only occasionally have other studies been made on drug effects in children. Animal studies have shown that the effects of some drugs such as hypnotics and analgesics are age-dependent rather than dose dependent. A similar relationship has been shown for adults in geriatric practice. However, it is difficult to establish such drug effects in children, especially if they are too young to express themselves. One drug that has been investigated in humans is atropine, where the threshold dose supress salivation at different ages was studied. The data obtained for this drug suggests a linear relationship between age and dosage, but few similar studies have been carried out and the relationship between age, weight and surface area are complex.

These relationships are discussed further in refs.[36,60,90,105]

Reporting of Drug Effects

The problems of obtaining adequate data on the use of a drug in babies and children and in correlating clinical experience and the results of animal experiments make it tempting to draw inaccurate or unjustified conclusions. Examples have been "scares" over the use of hexachlorophane and cyclamates, both of which have later been followed by further, often contradictory, research and reports.

Ultimately data on drug dosage and effects in babies and children is dependent upon careful observation and recording of results and reporting of any apparent correlation between drugs and possible side-effects. If suitable records are available retrospective studies can often suggest the best therapeutic regimes for a drug and the side-effects to be expected.

Addiction

The medical profession cannot escape major responsibility for the assumption in our culture that there is a pharmacological way out of every human anxiety and emotional problem and it is only natural that independent adolescents should take to self-prescribed and self-administered drugs in this climate of opinion. This aspect of paediatric pharmacology has been usefully reviewed elsewhere; it cannot be adequately dealt with in this context.[131]

Acknowledgements

We should like to thank the staff of Manchester University Medical Library, Mrs. E. L. Crowther, Mrs. E. Robinson, Miss N. Burns and Mr. M. Hollingsworth for their great help in preparing the manuscript.

REFERENCES

1. Alarcon-Segovia, D. (1969), "Drug Induced Systemic Lupus Erythematosus," *Mayo Clin. Proc.*, **44,** 664–681.
2. Adams, P. and White, C. (1965), "Isoniazid-Induced Encephalopathy," *Lancet*, **i,** 680–682.
3. Adamsons, K. and Joelsson, I. (1966), "The Effects of Pharmacologic Agents upon the Fetus and Newborn," *Amer. J. Obstet. Gynec.*, **96,** 437–460.
4. Aiken, J. W. (1972), "Aspirin and Indomethacin Prolong Parturition in Rats; Evidence that Prostaglandins Contribute to Expulsion of Fetus," *Nature*, **240,** 21–25.

4a. Ajodhia, J. M. and Hope, G. M. (1973), "Anticonvulsant Drugs and Teratogenicity", *Pharm. J.*, **210,** 566–568.

5. Alvi, M. (1969), "Unusual Effects of Fenfluramine," *Brit. med. J.*, **4,** 237 (Letter).
6. Anderson, E. (1971), "Childhood Complications of Nalidixic Acid," *J. Amer. med. Ass.*, **216,** 1023–1024.
7. Andrews, F., Golding, D. N., Freeman, A. M., Golding, J. R., Day, A. T., Hill, A. G. S., Camp, A. V., Lewis-Faning, E. and Lyle, W. H. (1973), "Controlled Trial of D(–)Penicillamine in Severe Rheumatoid Arthritis," *Lancet*, **i,** 275–280.
8. Anon. (1967), "Drugs in Normal Labour," *Drug. Ther. Bull.*, **5,** 75–76.
9. Arneil, G. C. (1972), "Cyclophosphamide and the prepubertal testis," *Lancet*, **ii,** 1259–1260. (Letter).
10. Arthur, L. J. H. and Hulme, J. D. (1970), "Intelligent, Small for Dates Baby Born to Phenylketonuric Mother after Low Phenylalanine Diet During Pregnancy," *Pediatrics*, **46,** 235–239.
11. Ashton, H. (1971), "Drugs and the Fetus and Neonate," *Adv. Drug. React. Bull.*, No. **28,** 80–83.
12. Askrog, V. F. and Harvald, B. (1970), "Teratogen effeckt af inhalations anaesthetika," *Nord. Med.*, **83,** 498–500.
13. Astrup, P., Trolle, D., Olsen, H. M., and Kjeldren, K. (1972), "Effect of Moderate Carbon-monoxide Exposure on Fetal Development," *Lancet* **ii,** 1220–1222.
14. Ballek, R., Reidenberg, M. M. and Orr, L. (1973), "Inhibition of Diphenylhydantoin Metabolism by Chloramphenicol," *Lancet*, **i,** 150 (Letter).
15. Barson, A. J. (1972), "Malformed Infant", *Brit. med. J.*, **ii,** 45 (Letter).
16. Bitnum S. (1969), "Possible Effect of Chlordiazepoxide on the Fetus," *Canad. med. Ass. J.*, **100,** 351. (Letter).
17. Bleyer, W. A., Lange, W. A. and Raisz, L. G. (1970), "Fetal Exposure to Maternal Medication," *J. Amer. med. Ass.*, **213,** 2046–2048.
18. Bleyer, W. A. and Breckenridge, R. T. (1970), "The Effects of Pre-natal Aspirin on Newborn Hemostasis," *J. Amer. med. Ass.*, **213,** 2049–2053.
19. Bloom, A. (1972), "Induced Chromosomal Aberrations: Biological and Clinical Significance," *J. Pediat.*, **81,** 1–8.
20. Borgstedt, A. D., Bryson, M. F., Young, L. W. and Forbes, G. B. (1972), "Long term administration of antiepileptic drugs and the development of rickets," *J. Pediat.*, **81,** 9–15.
21. Briggs, J. C., Dobson, M., Smyth, W. E. and Livingston. A. (1969), "Death Due to Combination of Treatment (Neostigmine) and disease," *Brit. med. J.*, **ii,** 344.
22. Buhle, F., Laragh, J., Baer, L., Darracott, F. and Morehouse, D. (1972), "Propranolol Inhibition of Renin Secretion," *New Engl. J. Med.*, **287,** 1209–1215.
23. Carter, W. and McCarty, K. (1966), "Molecular Mechanisms of Antibiotic Action," *Ann. intern. Med.*, **64,** 1087–1113.
24. Catz, C. S. and Giacoia, G. P. (1972), "Drugs and Breast Milk," *Pediat. Clins. N. Am.*, **19,** 151–166.
25. Chudzik, G. M. and Yaffe, S. J. (1972), "Drug Interaction: an Important Consideration for Rational Pediatric Therapy," *Pediat. Clins. N. Am.*, **19,** 131–140.
26. Clegg, D. J. (1971), "Teratology," in *Advances in Pharmacology*, **6,** 409–424. (Eds. Costa, E. and Sandler, M.), London: Academic Press.
27. Coche, J., Browne, R., Geffert, L. and Preston, G. (1966), "Optic Atrophy with Prolonged Use of Chloramphenicol," *J. Pediat.*, **28,** 27–31.
28. Conway, A. H. (1967), "Pharmacological Complications of Microsomal Enzyme Induction," *Pharmacol. Rev.*, **19,** 317–366.
29. Crawford, M., Gardner, M. and Sedgwick, P. (1972), "Infant Mortality and Hardness of Local Water Supplies," *Lancet*, **i,** 988–992.
30. Cree, J. and Coltart, D. (1973), "Plasma Digoxin Concentration in Children with Heart Failure," *Brit. med. J.*, **i,** 443–444.
31. Curley, A., Hawk, R. E., Kimbrough, R. D., Nathensen, G. and Finberg, L. (1971), "Dermal Absorption of Hexachlorophane in Infants," *Lancet*, **ii,** 296–297.
32. Cutler, B. S., Forbes, A. P., Ingersoll, F. M. and Scully, R. E. (1972), "Endometrial Carcinoma after Stilboestrol Therapy in Gonadal Dysgenesis," *New Engl. J. Med.*, **287,** 628–631.
33. David, T. J. (1972), "Nature and etiology of the Poland anomaly." *New Engl. J. Med.*, **287,** 487–489.
34. Day, T. and Powell-Jackson, P. (1972), "Fluoride, Water Hardness and Endemic Goitre," *Lancet*, **i,** 1135–1138.
35. Dollery, C. T. (1971), "Drug Interactions," in *The Adverse Effects of Drugs*, pp. 7–11 (G. C. Hanson, Ed.). England: Beecham Research Laboratories.
36. Done, A. K. (1965), "Developmental Pharmacology," *Clin. Pharmac. Ther.*, **5,** 432–479.
37. Fairley, K. F., Barrie, J. and Johnson, W. (1972), "Sterility and Testicular Atrophy Related to Cyclophosphamide Therapy," *Lancet*, **i,** 568–569.
38. Farrell, P. and Zachan, R. (1972), "Immuno-assay of Lecithin Synthesis and Phosphoryl Choline Glyceride Transferase Activity in the Fetal Rabbit after Corticosteroid Administration," *Pediat. Res.*, **6,** 377 (Abstract).
39. Fedrick, J. (1973), "Epilepsy and Pregnancy—a Report from the Oxford Record Linkage Study," *Brit. med. J.*, **ii,** 443–448.
40. Franklin, A. W. Porter, A. M. W. and Raine, D. N. (1973), "Research Investigations in Children," *Brit. med. J.*, **i,** 403–407.
41. Friedman, M. and Strang, L. B. (1966), "Effects of Long-term Corticosteroid and Corticotrophin on the Growth of Children," *Lancet*, **ii,** 569–572.
42. Gal, I., Parkinson, C. and Craft, I. (1971), "Effects of Oral Contraceptives on Human Plasma Vitamin A Levels," *Brit. med. J.*, **ii,** 436–438.
43. Garcia, R. E., Friedman, W. F., Kalack, M. M. and Rowe, R. D. (1964), "Idiopathic Hypercalcaemia and Supravalvular Aortic Stenosis," *New Engl. J. Med.*, **271,** 117–120.
44. Ghosh, A. and Hudson, F. (1972), "Oxytoxic Agents and Neonatal Hyperbilirubinaemia," *Lancet*, **ii,** 823 (Letter).
45. Ginsburg, J. (1971), "Placental Drug Transfer," *Adv. Pharmacol. Chemother.*, **9,** 387–408.
46. Glass, I., Rajegorda, B. and Evans, H. (1971), "Absence of Respiratory Distress Syndrome in Premature Infants of Heroin Addicted Mothers," *Lancet*, **ii,** 685 (Letter).
47. Greenwald, P., Barlow, J. J., Nasca, P. C. and Burnett, W. S. (1971), "Vaginal Cancer after Maternal Treatment with Synthetic Estrogens," *New Engl. J. Med.*, **285,** 390–393.
48. Houghton, G. W. and Rickens, A. (1973), "Use of Sulthiame During Pregnancy," *Brit. med. J.*, **i,** 544.
49. Houston, I. Chapter 44 this volume.
50. Jacobson, B. D. (1962), "Hazards of Norethindrone Therapy During Pregnancy," *Amer. J. Obstet. Gynec.*, **84,** 962–968.
51. Johnson, F. L., Feagler, J., Lerner, K., Siegel, M., Hartman, J. and Thomas, E. (1972), "Androgen Anabolic Steroid Therapy and Hepato-cellular Carcinoma," *Lancet*, **ii,** 1273–1276.
52. Jones K. L. Smith, D., Uttland, C. and Streussg, T. H. (1973), "Pattern of Malformation of Chronic Alcoholic Mothers," *Lancet*, **i,** 1267–1271.
53. Juchea, M. R. and Dyer, D. C. (1972), "Pharmacology of the Placenta," *Pediat. Clins. N. Amer.*, **19,** 65–80.
54. Kalow, W. (1971), "Topics in Pharmaco-genetics," *Ann. N.Y. Acad. Sci.*, **179,** 654–659.
55. Kelsey, F. O. (1967), "Psychopharmaca in Pregnancy," in

Neuro-psycho-pharmacology; Proceedings of the Fifth International Congress of the Collegium Internationale Neuro-psycho-pharmacologicum, March, 1966, pp. 692–696 (H. Brill, Ed.) (International Congress Series, no. 129) Excerpta Medica, Amsterdam, 1967.

56. Kemball, M., McIver, C., Milner, R. D., Nourse, C., Schiff, D. and Tiernan, J. (1970), "Neonatal Hypoglycaemia in Infants of Diabetic Mothers Given Sulphonylurea Drugs in Pregnancy," *Arch. Dis. Childh.*, **45**, 696–701.
57. Knill-Jones, R. P., Rodriques, L. V., Moir, D. D. and Spence, A. A. (1972), "Anaesthetic Practice and Pregnancy. Controlled Survey of Women Anaesthetists in the United Kingdom," *Lancet*, **i**, 1326–1328.
58. Knowles, J. A. (1965), "Excretion of Drugs in Milk—A Review," *J. Pediat.*, **66**, 1068–1082.
59. Kyegombe, D., Franklin, C. and Turner, P. (1973), "Drug Metabolising Enzymes in the Human Placenta, Their Induction and Repression," *Lancet*, **i**, 405–406.
60. Lasagna, L. (1967), "Drug Evaluation in Minors,' in *Paediatric Pharmacology*, pp. 8–15. Proc. of 1967 Conference, U.S. Dept. of Health, Education and Welfare.
61. Lathe, Chapter 10 this volume.
62. Leading Article (1973), "Prevention of Malignant Hyperpyrexia," *Lancet*, **i**, 1225.
63. Lenz, W. (1966), "Malformations Caused by Drugs in Pregnancy," *Amer. J. Dis. Child.*, **112**, 99–106.
64. Levin, J. N. (1971), "Amphetamine Ingestion with Biliary Atresia," *J. Pediat.*, **79**, 130–131.
65. Liggins, G. C. and Howie, R. N. (1972), "A Controlled Trial of Antepartum Glucocorticoid Treatment for Prevention of the Respiratory Distress Syndrome in Premature Infants," *Pediatrics*, **50**, 515–525.
66. Loughran, P. M., Gold, H. and Vance, J. (1973), "Phenytoin Teratogenicity in Man," *Lancet*, **i**, 70–72.
67. Lowe, C. R. (1973), "Congenital Malformations Among Infants Born to Epileptic Women," *Lancet*, **i**, 9–10.
68. Lunel, J. (1970), "Drugs that Depress the Newborn Infant," *Pediat. Clin. N. Amer.*, **17**, 835–850.
69. MacDonald, M. and Robinson, D. (1968), "Clinical Observations of Possible Barbiturate Interference with Coagulation," *J. Amer. Med. Ass.*, **204**, 97–100.
70. Marsden, P. D. and Knight, R. (1971), "Halogenated Oxyquinoline Derivatives (SMON)," *Lancet*, **i**, 854 (Letter).
71. Maurer, H. M., Wolff, J. A., Finster, M., Poppers, P. J., Pantuck, E., Kuntzman, R. and Conney, A. H. (1968), "Reduction in Concentration of Total Serum Bilirubin in Offspring of Women Treated with Phenobarbitone During Pregnancy," *Lancet*, **ii**, 122–124.
72. McCracken, G., Ginberg, C., Chrane, D., Thomas, M. and Horton, L. (1973), "Clinical Pharmacology of Penicillin in Newborn Infants," *Pediatrics*, **82**, 692–698.
73. Mena, I., Lopez, G., Horiuchi, K. and Croxatto, H. (1972), "Susceptibility to Cold in Newborn of Levodopa-treated Rats," *Nature*, **239**, 285–287.
74. Mills, J. Chapter 42 this volume.
75. Milner, R. D. G. and Chouksey, S. K. (1972), "Effects of Fetal Exposure to Diazoxide in Man," *Arch. Dis. Childh.*, **47**, 537–549.
76. Milner, R. D. G., Ross, J., Froud, D. and Davis, J. A. (1972), "Clinical Pharmacology of Gentamycin in the Newborn Infant," *Arch. Dis. Child.*, **47**, 927–932.
77. Mjolnerod, O. K., Dommertrand, S., Rasmundsen, K. and Gjeroulsen, S. (1971), "Congenital Connective Tissue Defect Probably Due to D-penicillamine Treatment in Pregnancy," *Lancet*, **i**, 673–675.
78. Moore, M. and Davis, J. A. (1966), "Response of the Newborn Rabbit to Acute Anoxia and Variations Due to Narcotic Agents," *Brit. J. Anaesth.*, **38**, 787–793.
79. Morrison-Smith, J. (1966), "Death from Asthma," *Lancet*, **i**, 1042 (Letter).
80. Mountain, K. R., Hirsch, J. and Gallus, A. S. (1970), "Neonatal Coagulation Defect Due to Anticonvulsant Drug Treatment in Pregnancy," *Lancet*, **i**, 265–268.
81. Moya, F. and Thorndike, V. (1962), "Passage of Drugs Across the Placenta," *Amer. J. Obstet. Gynec.*, **84**, 1778–1798.
82. Moya, F. and Thorndike, V. (1964), "The Effects of Drugs Used in Labour on the Fetus and the Newborn," *Clin. Pharmac. Ther.*, **4**, 628–652.
83. Mull, M. M. (1966), "The Tetracyclines," *Amer. J. Dis. Child.*, **112**, 483–493.
84. Murikami, V. (1971), "The Effect of Organic Mercury on Intrauterine Life," in *Advances in Experimental Medicine and Biology*, **27**, 301–336 (M. A. Klinberg, A. Abramovich and J. Chemke, Eds.). New York: Plenum Press.
85. Mushin, A. S. (1972), "Ocular Damage by Drugs in Children," *Adv. Drug. React. Bull.*, No. **36**, 112–115.
86. Millar, J. and Nevin, N. (1973), "Congenital Malformations and Anticonvulsant Drugs," *Lancet*, **i**, 328 (Letter).
87. Nelson, M. M. and Forfar, J. O. (1971), "Associations Between Drugs Administered During Pregnancy and Congenital Abnormalities of the Fetus," *Brit. med. J.*, **i**, 523–527.
88. Nielson, J., Friedrich, U. and Tsuboi, T. (1969), "Chromosome Abnormalities in Patients Treated with Chlorpromazine, Perphenazine and Lysergide," *Brit. med. J.*, **iii**, 634–636.
89. Niswander, J. and Wentelecki, W. (1973), "Congenital Malformations Among Offspring of Epileptic Women," *Brit. med. J.*, **ii**, **1062** (Letter).
90. Nyhan, W. L. (1961), "Toxicity of Drugs in the Neonatal Period," *J. Pediat.*, **59**, 1–20.
91. Olson, C. and Riley, H. (1966), "Complications of Tetracycline Therapy," *Paed. pharm. therap.*, **68**, 783–793.
92. O'Malley, K., Cooke, J. and Drake, E. (1971), "Effect of Age and Sex on Human Drug Metabolism," *Brit. med. J.* **iii**, 607–609.
93. Ornoy, A., Horowitz, A., Kaspi, T., Michaeli, Y. and Nebel, L. (1971), "Anomalous Fetal and Neonatal Bone Development Induced by Administration of Cortisol and Vit. D.2. to pregnant Rats," in *Advances in Experimental Medicine and Biology*, **27**, 219–226 (M. A. Klingberg, A. Abramovici and J. Chemke, Eds.). New York: Plenum Press.
94. Orr, J. S., Spiers, C. S. and Shimmins, J. (1969) "Method for Estimating Individual Drug Dosage Regimens. An Application for the Occupancy Principle," *Lancet*, **ii**, 771–773.
95. Palmisano, P. A. and Polhill, R. B. (1972), "Fetal Pharmacology," *Pediat. Clins. N. Amer.*, **19**, 3–20.
96. Parke, D. V. (Ed.) (1968), "Factors which Affect the Metabolism of Drugs," in *Recent Advances in Pharmacology*, **4**, 75–98.
97. Pocheldy, C. (1972), "Adverse Haematologic Effects of Drugs," *Pediat. Clins. N. Amer.*, **19**, 1095–1011.
98. Podolsky, S., Simmerman, H. J., Burgess, B., Burrows, J., Cardarelli, J. R. and Pattavina, C. G. (1973), "Potassium Depletion in Cirrhosis: Impaired Growth-Hormone and Insulin Response," *New Engl. J. Med.*, **288**, 644–648.
99. Priestley, B. (1972), "Drug Addiction and the Newborn," *Proc. Roy. Soc. Med.*, **65**, 870.
100. Rane, A. and Sjoquist, F. (1972), "Drug Metabolism in the Human Fetus and Newborn Infant," *Pediat. Clins. N. Amer.*, **19**, 37–49.
101. Raftery, F. and Denman, A. (1973), "Systemic Lupus Erythematosis Syndrome Induced by Practolol," *Brit. med. J.*, **i**, 452–455.
102. Renick, J. H. (1972), "Potato Blight and Spina Bifida," *Brit. J. prev. soc. Med.*, **26**, 67–68.
103. Richards, I. D. G. (1972), "A Retrospective Enquiry into Possible Teratogenic Effects of Drugs in Pregnancy," in *Drugs and Fetal Development, Advances in Experimental Medicine and Biology 27* (M. A. Klingberg, A. Abramovici, and J. Chemke, Eds.), New York: Plenum Press.
104. Robinson, D. (1971), *The Process of Becoming Ill.* London: Routledge and Kegan Paul.
105. Robinson, G. C. and Williams, V. S. (1970), "Dosage and Methods of Administration of Drugs in Childhood," *Practitioner*, **204**, 5–13.
106. Rogers, M., Wierson, J., Goldblatt, A. and Smith, T. (1972), "Serum Digoxin Concentrations in the Human Fetus, Neonate and Infant," *New Engl. J. Med.*, **287**, 1010–1013.

107. Russell, K. P., quoted by Shirkey, H. C. (1972), in *Advances in Medicine and Biology*, *27*, *Drugs and Fetal Development*, *22* (M. A. Klingberg, A. Abramovici and J. Chemke, Eds.) New York: Plenum Press.
108. Schroder, H. and Price-Evans, D. A. (1972), "Acetylation Phenotype and Adverse Effects of Sulphasalazine in Healthy Subjects," *Gut*, **13**, 278–284.
109. Seeds, A. E. (1970), "Adverse Effects on the Fetus of Acute Events in Labour," *Pediat. Clins. N. Amer.*, **17**, 811–834.
110. Shirkey, H. (1971), "Human Experience Related to Adverse Drug Reactions of the Fetus or Neonate" in *Drugs and Fetal Development*, *Advances in Experimental Medicine and Biology*, **27**, 19–30 (M. A. Klingberg, A. Abramovici and J. Chemke, Eds.). New York: Plenum Press.
111. Sexton-Lewis, W. and Doherty, J. (1973), "Another Disadvantage of Intramuscular Digoxin," *New Engl. J. Med.*, **288**, 20, 1077 (Letter).
112. Sieber, S. M. and Fabro, S. (1971), "Identification of Drugs in the Pre-implantation Blastocyst and in the Plasma, Uterine Secretion and Urine of the Pregnant Rabbit," *J. Pharmacol. Exp. Therap.*, **176**, 65–75.
113. Smith, R. L. (1971), "A Biochemical Approach to the Problem of Adverse Drug Reactions in Man," in *The Adverse Effect of Drugs*, pp. 13–25 (G. C. Hanson, Ed.). England: Beecham Research Laboratories.
114. Smith, K. E., Reece, C. A. and Kauffman, R. (1972), "Ototoxic Reaction Associated with Use of Nortriptyline Hydrochloride: Case Report," *J. Pediat.*, **80**, 1046–1048.
115. Smith, H., Lerner, P. and Wentsen, L. (1967), "Neurotoxicity and Massive Intravenous Therapy with Penicillin," *Arch. intern. Med.*, **120**, 47–55.
116a. Smithells, R. W. and Levell, G. (1972), "Deleterious Aspects of the Placental Transfer of Drugs," in *The Therapeutic Choice in Paediatrics*, pp. 60–69 (W. L. Burland and B. M. Laurance, Eds.). Edinburgh and London: Churchill Livingstone.
116b. Smithells, R. W. and Morgan, D. M. (1970), "Transmission of Drugs by the Placenta and the Breasts," *Practitioner*, **204**, 14–19.
117. Speizer, F. E., Doll, R., Heaf, P. and Strang, L. B. (1968), "Investigation of the Use of Drugs Preceding Death from Asthma", *Brit. med. J.*, **i**, 339–343.
118. Spriggs, H., Smith, R., Griffith, H. and Trulove, S. (1958), "Heinz Body Anaemia Due to Salicylazosulphonamide," *Lancet*, **i**, 1039–1041.
119. Sulaiman, W. and Johnson, R. (1973), "Effect of Fenfluramine on Human Growth Hormone Release," *Brit. med. J.*, **ii**, 329–332.
120. Taeusch. N. W., Carson, S., Wang, N. S. and Avery, M. E. (1972), "The Effects of Heroin on Lung Maturation and Growth in Fetal Rabbits," *Pediat. Res.*, **6**, 335 (Abs.).
121. Takyi, B. E. (1970), "Excretion of Drugs in Human Milk," *J. Hosp. Pharm.*, **28**, 317–325.
122. Tarlov, A. R., Brewer, G. J., Carson, P. E. and Alving, A. S. (1962), "Primaquine Sensitivity. Glucose-6-Phosphate Dehydrogenase Deficiency: an Inborn Error of Med. and Biol. Sig.," *Arch. Intern. Med.*, **109**, 209–234.
123. Tesh, S. (1971), "Adverse Effects of Drugs on the Fetus," in *The Adverse Effects of Drugs*, pp. 57–68 (G. C. Hanson, Ed.). England: Beecham Research Lab.
124. Tylden, E. (1973), "The Effects of Maternal Drug Abuse on the Fetus and Infant," *Adv. Drug. React. Bull.*, **33**, 120–123.
125. Visser H. K. A., Chapter 26 this volume.
126. Wade, O. L. (1970), "Hazards of Drugs in Pregnancy, Lactation and the New-born," in *Adverse Reactions to Drugs*, 140–148. London: Heinemann.
127. Warrell, D. W. and Taylor, R. (1968), "Outcome for the Fetus of Mothers Receiving Prednisolone During Pregnancy," *Lancet*, **i**, 117–118.
128. Wong, Y. K. and Wood, B. S. B. (1971), "Breast Milk Jaundice and Oral Contraceptive," *Brit. med. J.*, **iv**, 403–404.
129. Welch, R. M., Harrison, F. and Gomme, B. (1969), "Stimulating Effect of Smoking on Enzymes in Human Placenta," *Clin. Pharmac. Ther.*, **10**, 100–109.
130. Wright, I. Chapter 39 this book.
131. Yancy, W., Nader, P. and Burnham, L. (1972), "Drug Use and Attitudes of High School Children," *Pediatrics*, **50**, 739–745.

FURTHER READING

1. Shirkey, H. D. (Ed.) (1972), *Pediatric Therapy*, 4th Edition. St. Louis: C. V. Mosby.
2. Klingberg, M. A., Abramovici, A., and Chemke J. (Eds.), (1972), "Drugs and Fetal Development," *Advances in Experimental Medicine and Biology*, **27**, New York: Plenum Press.
3. "Pediatric Pharmacology," (1972), *Ped. Clins. N. Amer.*, **19**, 1–259.
4. Burland, W. L. and Laurence, B. M. (Eds.), (1972), *The Therapeutic Choice in Paediatrics*, Edinburgh: Churchill Livingstone.
5. Bacq, Z. M., (Ed.), (1971), *Fundamentals of Biochemical Pharmacology*, Oxford: Pergamon Press.
6. Deichmann, W. B. and Gerarde, H. (1969), *Toxicology of Drugs and Chemicals*, New York: Academic Press.
7. Szoraky, I. (1973), *Pharmacogenetics; Principles and Paediatric Aspects*, Budapest: Akademiai Kiado.
8. Girdwood, R. H. (Ed.) (1973), "A Symposium on Adverse Drug Reactions," *Brit. J. Clin. Pract.*, **27**, 279–320.
9. "Symposium on Drugs and the unborn child." (1973) *Clin. Pharmat. Ther.*, **14**, 621–768.

INDEX

INDEX

Bold lettering indicates a complete chapter devoted to the topic.